Moe Is Best

by Richard Torrey

I Like to Read®

Holiday House / New York

To all of my brothers: Willie, Pete, Artie, Dave, Ty, Troy, Jack, Phil, and Mike

I LIKE TO READ is a registered trademark of Holiday House, Inc.

Copyright © 2014 by Richard Torrey
All Rights Reserved
HOLIDAY HOUSE is registered in the U.S. Patent and Trademark Office.
Printed and Bound in March 2014 at Tien Wah Press, Johor Bahru, Johor, Malaysia.
The artwork was created with pencil on illustration board,
which was then scanned and colored digitally.
www.holidayhouse.com
First Edition
1 3 5 7 9 10 8 6 4 2

Library of Congress Cataloging-in-Publication Data
Torrey, Rich.
Moe is best / by Richard Torrey. — First edition.
pages cm. — (I like to read)
Summary: Moe is still too little to accomplish certain tasks but he is best at trying.
ISBN 978-0-8234-2837-3 (hardcover)
[1. Size—Fiction. 2. Ability—Fiction. 3. Determination (Personality trait)—Fiction.] I. Title.
PZ7.T64573Mo 2014
[E]—dc23
2012033834

Moe is little.

But he is good at many things.

Moe can brush his teeth.

Moe can tie his shoes.

Moe can feed the cat.

Moe can drink all his milk.

Moe can read—almost.

And Moe can play basketball.

BATTLE OF THE BUGS

"INTO THE WILD BLUE YONDER"
Basil plants will repel mosquitoes and flies, just keep a plant or two around the house.

"KEEPING THE CRITTERS AT BAY"
Bay leaves should be placed in all kitchen drawers and in the flour and sugar containers to keep crawling insects away.

"Le Pew"
Mice can't stand the smell of fresh peppermint. Plant it around the outside of the house to keep them away. Oil of Peppermint placed on a piece of cloth and placed in their favorite location will also work.

"GETTING METHODICAL"
Ants - *Method 1:* To keep ants away, place whole cloves or sage around the windows and doors or anywhere else they appear. This works great!

Ants - *Method 2:* For a quick ant kill, mix two cups of borax with one cup of sugar in a quart jar. Punch holes in the lid and sprinkle around the outside of the house.

Ants - *Method 3:* To get rid of ants, pour Ivory Liquid Soap around. This is the only liquid soap that seems to work.

Ants - *Method 4:* To eliminate ants from your kitchen counters, try washing the counter with equal parts of water and white vinegar.

Ants - *Method 5:* If you have an area that ants travel most, just sprinkle a small amount of baby powder in that area. They will never cross the powder.

Ants - *Method 6:* Cucumber peelings will repel ants outside the house.

If all of the above fails to rid your premises of ants, try renting an Aardvark from the local zoo.

Roaches hate cucumber peels as well, just place a few in their favorite areas and you will never see them again.

A good roach killer can be made from 35% borax, 15% white flour, 10% powdered sugar and 40% cornmeal.

If you want to keep weevils and other crawling insects out of your grits and legumes, try placing a hot dried red pepper in with them.

A solution of weak tea, ammonia and dish soap placed in a spray bottle and sprayed on plants will keep most bugs away.

If you have a roach problem, fill a large bowl with cheap wine and place it under the sink. The roaches will drink the wine, get drunk, fall in and drown. Go ahead and laugh, but this is for real.

STAIN REMOVAL WITH FOODS, ETC.

Fruit berry stains can be removed by pouring hot water with salt added on the stain as soon as possible after the stain occurs, then wash the area with milk before placing it in a washing machine. Milk will provide a natural bleaching agent.

Cornstarch will remove blood stains. Use as a paste, then wash in warm soapy water.

If your dishwasher has stains in it, try filling your dispenser with powdered Gatorade and run it through a cycle.

Egg stains will respond to cold water only, hot water will only set the stain.

Water in which onions have been cooked will clean brass bottomed pots.

To make your porcelain sink look like new, place paper towels on the bottom and sides of the sink, then saturate with household bleach. Clean after an half-hour to one hour.

"RHUB-A-DUB-DUB"
Rust stains on clothing can be removed with rhubarb, Use the hot juice from 5-6 stalks.

Egg yolk mixed with warm water should remove most coffee or tea stains on fabrics.

"THE BUNDY SOLUTION"
If your shoes have an odor, treat them to a shot of baking soda. It does wonders.

Fruit juice can be removed from fabrics by pouring at least 3 quarts of boiling water slowly on the stain.

To remove most grease stains from cloth, try rubbing the stains with lard before washing with a detergent.

Carpet stains from oil or grease may be removed by rubbing cornmeal into the stain and allowing it to stand for 12 hours.

Keep an empty plastic soda bottle handy, in case you ever need a hot water bottle. Just fill it up with hot water and wrap it in a towel.

VINEGAR, THE ALL AROUND HELPER

"BE-WARE"
Never use a painted plate for serving with vinegar dressing. Vinegar will corrode the paint off the plate. This will not only ruin the plate, but may release harmful toxins into the foods.

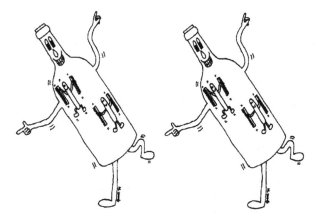

To de-crud a flower vase or wine bottle, try using a solution of 1 tablespoon of salt and 1 cup of white vinegar. If you still have some residue left, add some rice and shake.

White vinegar will remove coffee or tea stains.

Sour wines may be used in place of vinegar.

To remove water spots from stainless steel place alcohol or white vinegar on a cloth.

Lime deposits can be removed from teapots by filling the kettle with equal parts of vinegar and water, bringing to a boil and letting it stand overnight.

Use warm vinegar to remove old decals. Just allow the vinegar to soak in for a few minutes then sponge off the decal.

"DO THE TWIST"
Pour oil and vinegar into the remains on the bottom of a ketchup bottle, shake vigorously to make a great salad dressing.

To control the mold in your breadbox, try washing it occasionally with a mild solution of vinegar and water.

White vinegar will help eliminate the odor from a dog's accident on the carpet.

To make your hair shiny, try a teaspoon of vinegar in your final rinse.

CLEANING UP

"HI YO SILVER"
Wash silver or silverplate soon after it comes into contact with eggs, salad dressing, olives, vinegar and other foods that have been seasoned with salt. These will cause silver to tarnish faster.

To remove grease spots try using talcum powder.

Your oven can be cleaned easily with baking soda.

Corningware cookware can be cleaned by filling them with water and by dropping in two denture cleaning tablets. Let stand for 30-45 minutes.

"ANTI-FREEZE"
In winter, add denatured alcohol to your window cleaning solution to prevent freeze-ups.

Woodwork is easily cleaned with cold tea.

Silver polish will remove coffee stains from plastic cups.

To clean an oven spill, sprinkle the area with salt immediately; then when the oven has cooled, clean with a damp cloth.

Oven Guard used on a clean car bumper will make it easier to get the bugs off next time.

Left over cola drinks poured into your toilet, adds cleaning power to your cleaner as well as giving it a brilliant shine.

If you have problems cleaning a grater after grating cheese, rub raw potato over it before washing.

Use an old toothbrush to clean the grater.

A few drops of ammonia should be dropped into greasy pots before hot water is poured in. This will make them easier to clean.

An excellent way to clean butcher blocks is with a plastic window scraper.

Place a piece of chalk in a silver chest to absorb moisture and slow tarnishing.

"A LITTLE DIP WILL DO YA"
If you want your fingernails to be whiter, dip them in lemon juice. The acidic nature of the lemon juice will bleach them.

Always keep a clean small plastic baggie handy when you have both hands in any food you are mixing. If the phone rings, just slip your hands in the baggie.

To keep plant-eating pets out of your garden or from potential poisonings, place red or black pepper on the leaf tips of plants and especially African violets and other toxic houseplants.

"FOILED AGAIN"
To keep animals away from your plants, try placing tin foil around them. Most animals will stay clear.

The reason you can place your hand into a 500 degree oven and not into a pot of boiling water at 212 degrees is that air doesn't transfer heat well.

A FEW HELPFUL HEALING FACTS

Place an ice cube on a splinter a few seconds before removing it. This will deaden the area.

A slice of cold onion placed on a bee or insect bite should stop the pain and swelling.

To cure hiccups, try a cup of dill leaf tea sipped slowly.

Run a warm iron over contact paper and it should peel right off.

"SEASON YOUR CARPET"
Carpet colors will be more livelier if you sprinkle a small amount of salt on before vacuuming.

Empty ketchup or mustard containers are great for decorating cakes or cookies.

"KITCHEN KOPTER"
To get the last drop out of a ketchup bottle, grasp the bottom of the bottle firmly and swing it in a circular motion from your side. The remaining ketchup will go to the top.

"CRUMBY SECURITY"
Keep a jar handy for leftover crumbs from empty cereal boxes or cracker boxes. When you need bread crumbs they will be there for you.

Spray Pam on your snow shovel and the snow will slide right off.

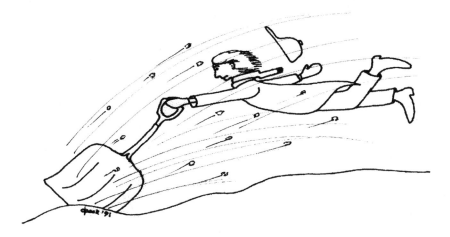

Milk cartons make excellent kindling. Fill with wood chips for a great fire starter.

A "SINKING" FEELING

To unclog a drain, try using a cup of salt mixed with a cup of baking soda (no liquid). Pour the dry solution into the drain followed by a pot of boiling water.

ODOR EATERS

To eliminate refrigerator odors, try a small amount of vanilla on a cotton ball.

If you boil several cloves in a cup of water, it will rid the house of unwanted food odors.

Cloves can also be combined with cinnamon, wrapped in a piece of cheesecloth and placed in boiling water. It will give off a pleasant fragrance.

Coffee grounds kept in an open jar will help absorb odors.

For an efficient refrigerator deodorizer, try using a few charcoal briquets on a small plate.

"AN UPLIFTING EXPERIENCE"

To raise the nap of carpeting after heavy furniture has matted it down, place one or two ice cubes on the area overnight. In the morning the carpet should be back up.

"A PERKER UPPER"

Dry eggshells in the oven them pulverize them in the blender and make a high calcium meal, which is excellent for plant fertilizer.

Club soda, that has lost its fizzle, has just the right chemicals left to add vigor and color to your plants.

To save washing extra cups and spoons, first measure all dry ingredients, place them on waxed paper, then use the same cup or spoon for measuring the liquids.

Save all microwave food containers, place leftovers in them and freeze them for later use.

"MICROWAVE SAVVY"

To check to see if a container is safe for use in the microwave, place the container next to a cup that is half-full of water. Use full power for one minute. If the container is hot to the touch, it cannot be used in the microwave, if its warm it may be used to reheat, and if its cool its OK.

To grease a pan easily, try using a soft bread crust spread with the butter or ?

FOR THE KIDS

'CHILD'S PLAY"

Formula for playdough: mix together ½ cup of salt, 2 tablespoons alum, 2 tablespoons cooking oil, then add the mixture to 2 cups of boiling water and knead.

Use natural food coloring for different colors.

"A BUBBLE TO BURST"

Formula for children's bubble solution: mix 1 tablespoon of glycerin with 2 tablespoons of a powdered detergent in 1 cup of water. Add food coloring if desired.

"GET A GRIP ON IT"

Wide rubber bands placed around drinking glasses give children a better grip.

"PLUG THE DIKE"

If you place a marshmallow on the bottom of an ice cream cone, the ice cream will not leak through.

When traveling with small children, carry a bottle of powdered milk instead of regular milk which spoils, all you have to do is add water and shake.

"REJUVENATION"

To bring ping pong balls back to life that have been dented, just place them in hot water for 15-20 minutes.

"COLD STORAGE"
Keep plastic wrap in the refrigerator to prevent it from sticking to itself when handled.

Hydrogen peroxide won't lose its fizzle if kept in the refrigerator.

Nail polish should be stored in the refrigerator. It will go on smoother and have a longer life.

"MIXER UPPER"
Keep a shaker of mixed salt and pepper near the stove. Use 3/4 part salt to 1/4 part pepper.

FOOD FIXER UPPERS

If food is scorched, place the pot immediately in cold water to stop the cooking action, which will eliminate the burnt taste from the food that was not scorched.

If you overdo the mayonnaise, add bread crumbs to absorb it.

"REVIVAL"
To bring the bounce back into tennis balls, place the can in the oven with the lid removed overnight. The heat from the pilot light will revive them.

If plastic has burned on an appliance, clean with lighter fluid.

To remove cigarette burns or coffee stains, rub the stain with a damp cloth dipped in baking soda.

To remove stains from enamel pots, mix bleach with water and boil in the pot until the stain is gone.

Stainless steel pots will remain shiny if you rub them with a piece of lemon rind, then wash in warm soapy water. If you have a problem, try adding a small amount of salt to the lemon.

BAKING SODA FACTS

Juice, coffee, and tea stains may be removed by scrubbing them vigorously with a paste made of baking soda and water.

Clean crayon marks off walls with baking soda on a damp cloth. Has just enough abrasive action to do the job without causing damage.

A thin layer of fresh baking soda should be placed on the bottom of a litter box before adding litter.

THE "NOSE" KNOWS
A small amount of baking soda applied to your armpits will replace your deodorant.

Baking soda works great in place of toothpaste.

To repair a nail hole on woodwork, just mix a small amount of instant coffee with spackling paste or starch and water and voila.

Mirrors can be brightened by rubbing them with a cloth dampened with alcohol.

"TROUBLE WAKING UP? TRY THIS ON"
Pantyhose will last longer if you freeze them before wearing. It strengthens the fibers.

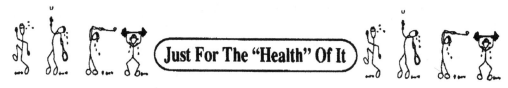

Water from boiled vegetables should be saved and mixed with your cat or dog's food to give them additional nutrients.

"TASTE BUD ALERT"
To check your salt intake, eat a piece of bacon, if it doesn't taste salty you're probably eating too much salt.

Aged wine and cheeses contain the substance tyramine, that in sensitive individuals can cause migraine headaches.

Tin coffee cans make excellent freezer containers for cookies.

Mayonnaise will remove dead skin on your elbows. Rub briskly.

"BRRRRRRRRRRR!!!"
To cool a hot dish more rapidly, place it in a pan of salted cold water. It will cool faster than if placed in cold water.

To keep milk from sticking to a pot, massage a little butter on the bottom of the pot.

Lightly grease gelatin molds before using. It will make it easier to remove the mold.

Add raw rice to the salt shaker to keep the salt free-flowing.

"SHOW STOPPERS"
To prevent carbonated beverages from fizzing over, try rinsing the ice-cubes with water first, before pouring the soda in. This will work for all sodas except root beer.

Place a hot dog in plastic wrap, then put it into a thermos of soup or coffee. When lunchtime arrives, put it into a bun for a real hot dog.

If you coat the bottom of pots used over an open fire with shaving cream before using, the black marks will come off easier.

Sugar bags can be used to store ice cubes. Much thicker than plastic ones.

Small marshmallows can be used for candle holders on cakes.

Sandwiches will not become limp and soggy as readily if you spread the butter or mayonnaise to the edge of the bread.

Many sandwiches can be frozen for up to two weeks. Best fillings are cold cuts, meat loaf, chicken, peanut butter (no jelly), tuna, and beef.

Floor tiles should be used instead of contact paper on kitchen shelves. They last longer and are easier to clean.

"SLICK IDEAS"
To prevent mildew from forming in the refrigerator, try spraying the insides of it with vegetable-oil spray after you defrost it. It will make the job much easier next time.

Blenders and egg beaters should be lubricated regularly. Use mineral oil instead of vegetable oil. Vegetable oil may cause corrosion.

If you use a small amount of oil on the threads of syrup bottles, it will stop the syrup from running down the sides of the bottle.

When you measure sticky liquids, try wiping the inside of the measuring cup with a small amount of oil. The liquids will flow freely.

To prevent ice-cube trays from sticking to the bottom of the shelf, place a piece of waxed paper underneath the tray.

A hair dryer will help defrost a freeze-up in the ice-maker.

When glasses are stuck together, just fill the top one with cold water and dip the bottom one in hot water.

The secret to keeping butcher blocks in good shape is to wash then dry, then cover with salt to draw the moisture out of the wood. Then treat with mineral oil for a smooth surface.

For clear ice cubes, just boil the water first.

When grating, chefs always grate the softest items first, then the firmer ones. This will keep the grater clean.

"STUCK UP"

When postage stamps have stuck together, try placing them into the freezer for 10 minutes, they should come apart without damaging the glue.

Any cloth material that has chewing gum stuck to it can be placed into the freezer. After about an hour the gum should break off easily.

WASHING DISHES

"A PENNY SAVED"

Save money by purchasing the least expensive dishwasher soap, then add a few teaspoons of vinegar to the dishwater. The vinegar cuts the grease and leaves the dishes spot-free and sparkling.

When washing greasy dishes, add a half-cup of baking soda to the water to cut the grease faster.

To clean an electric coffee pot, place one teaspoon of dish soap into the pot and boil.

Washing greasy dishes, add a half-cup of baking soda to the water to cut the grease faster.

When you want to fill a thermos bottle or small mouth container, try using a funnel.

To help a semi-solid soup slide right out of its can, try shaking the can first and them opening it from the bottom.

"NUKED"

Never lean on a microwave door. It may become misaligned and leak radiation.

Crisco can be used as a makeup remover.

Chapter 2

It's Party Time

ENTERTAINING FACTS

"FILLER UPPERS"
Use a large green pepper as a cup for dips. Cut off top, scrape pepper clean of ribs and seeds, then fill with dip.

Cucumbers make an excellent holder for dips. When cutting, leave a handle in the middle, like a basket.

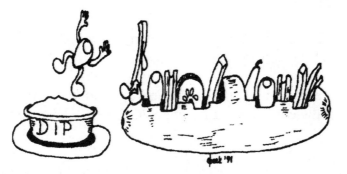

Use halved or hollowed-out melons, oranges or grapefruits as a cup to fill with cut-up fruit bits.

THE "NOSE" KNOWS"
Before your guests arrive, give your home that "something's bakin'" fragrance. Just sprinkle cinnamon and sugar in a tin pie pan and cook it on high heat slowly on the stove for a few minutes.

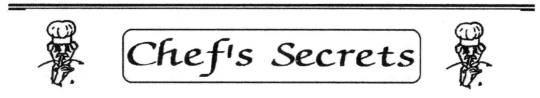

When making small finger sandwiches, use an electric knife to cut them and the filling won't run all over the counter.

To keep your pizza crust crispy, try placing the cheese before the tomato sauce.

To keep ice from melting, place a container of dry ice underneath the ice.

Champagne is best if not chilled for too long a period in the refrigerator.

To save leftover wines, freeze them in your ice cube trays. They can be used for any dish that you would season with wine or use in coolers.

"SPRINKLER HEAD ALERT"
For a flaming pudding, soak sugar cubes in orange or lemon extract. Place them on the pudding and light.

Cottage cheese can be used in place of sour cream when making dips. Just place it in the blender until it is creamed.

Cream cheese can be colored with powdered or liquid food coloring as a filler for dainty rolled sandwiches. Try a different color for each layer and slice as you would a jelly roll.

To stop hard candy from sticking together, just sift a little cornstarch on it.

"PARTY CUBES"
Freeze red and green maraschino cherries in ice cubes. Also, cocktail onions, mint leaves or green olives for martinis.

Freeze different colors of grapes to use in punches.

Freeze lemon peels in ice cubes for use in water glasses.

Use large ice cubes made from milk cartons for punches. The larger the ice cube the slower it melts.

"A CHILLING SUBJECT"
If you ever wondered how much ice you will need for a party, the rule of thumb is one pound per person.

"JOLLY GOOD SHOW"
Use crescent dinner rolls as a quick and easy pastry to prepare a Beef Wellington.

To make a quick and unusual dip or spread, try pureeing a can of well drained white beans and a package of herb flavored soft cheese together.

"FOILED AGAIN"
Place a piece of aluminum foil under your napkin or paper towel in a bread basket to keep the bread or rolls warm longer and protect the bread basket from stains.

Leftover sandwiches can be brushed with butter and cooked in a shallow pan.

"IT'S ZOO TIME"
When making sandwiches for the children, try using your animal shaped cookie cutters on them for a unique treat.

Place a damp paper towel over Hors d'oeuvres, meat or cheese platters to help retain the moistness and slow the drying out time.

"A REAL DE-CORKER"
To remove a cork from inside an empty wine bottle, pour some ammonia into the bottle, set it in a well ventilated location. In a few days the cork will be disintegrated.

Make your own Easter-egg dyes. Boil the eggs with grass for green, onion skins for yellow and beets for red.

For attractive individual butter servings, squeeze butter through a pastry bag or plastic bag onto a cookie sheet; set into refrigerator to harden.

"MEDICAL MIRACLE"
To preserve a Halloween pumpkin, just spray the inside and outside surfaces with an antiseptic spray to kill bacteria and keep the pumpkin in better shape.

"DOUBLE DECKER"

Salads and dips can be kept chilled by using two bowls. Place the salad or dip in the smaller bowl, partially fill the larger bowl with water and freeze. Then place the smaller bowl onto the larger one and serve.

When using a tray, place a damp napkin under the dishes to stop them from moving around.

"A LITTLE DAB WILL DO YA"

If red wine is spilled on a carpet, it may be cleaned with shaving cream, then sponged off with water. Club soda may also work.

After the holidays, purchase the large eggs and bunnies made from chocolate at half price or less. Use for any recipes to save dollars.

If vodka is kept in the refrigerator, it will be more flavorful.

Champagne should only be ice-chilled up to the neck of the bottle, any higher and the cork may be more difficult to remove.

Since most dips for chips contain a milk product that may spoil easily, it would be wise to place 1/2-1 inch of water in a bowl that is slightly larger than the dip bowl, then freeze the water and place the smaller bowl on top of the ice when serving. This will slow down the spoilage time.

"PEEK-A-BOO"

If a watermelon needs to be removed from the refrigerator and sit for a while before being cut, try placing it in a double brown bag to keep it cool longer.

To fancy up the top of a cake, cookies or pie, try placing a wide-patterned doily on top the sprinkle powdered sugar over it and remove.

"SMART MOVE"

If your table is set with candles, it would be wise to place a small amount of salt around the top to eliminate wax droppings on the tablecloth.

Chapter 3

Fruits of the Bloom

"The Words Out"

Sales of fruits and vegetables have increased significantly in 1994, while meat and cigarette sales have dropped.

"PEELING IT OFF"

To peel thin-skinned fruits and vegetables easily, place in a bowl and cover with boiling water, let stand for one-minute then peel with a sharp paring knife or spear the fruit with a fork and hold over a gas flame until the skin cracks.

To peel thick-skinned fruits, cut a small amount of peel from top and bottom, set fruit on a cutting board, cut off the peel in strips from top to bottom.

If the box is available that the fruit came in be sure to look for a government stamp such as "U.S. Grade No. 1" or that they have a USDA stamp.

For an easy dressing for fruit salad, try a grated orange rind and orange juice added to sour cream.

Just For The "Health" Of It

Canned pumpkin is one of the best sources of beta-carotene, it has approximately 27,000IU in a 40 calorie 8oz. serving.

Two of the most nutritious fruits are papaya and cantaloupe.

Wash all fruits and vegetables in cold water to remove any chemicals, but never soak or store them in water. Vitamins B and C are easily lost. Dry all fruits and vegetables After washing.

The more surface of a fruit or vegetable you expose, the more nutrients will be lost to oxidation.

Enzymes needed by the body will be completely destroyed by cooking.

Never allow your fruits and vegetables to be placed in the same bag with meats. Juices may leak and contaminate the fruit and vegetables.

"IT'S THE PITS"

Certain fruits such as apricots, apples, pears, cherries and peaches contain a small amount of the chemical "amygdalin" which tends to release cyanide, a deadly poison. Best advise is not to chew or ingest the pits, problems are rare and you would have to eat about 60 apricot pits to get a lethal dose.

Coconut water found inside a coconut is almost fat-free and high in vitamin K.

Coconut oil is made from the meat and is very high in saturated fat.

Maraschino cherries contain red dye #2, which, according to studies by the United Nations Food and Agriculture Report, may cause birth defects.

To preserve the nutritional value of fruits and vegetables, it is best to leave them in their original wrappings.

Excessive consumption of acidic fruit juices can wear away tooth enamel.

Order of nutritional quality of fruits - 1. Fresh, if grown properly, 2. Dehydrated Grade A, 3. Freeze Dried, 4. Frozen, 5. Canned.

Some of the best sources of pectin are figs, oranges, apples, bananas, pears and soybeans. Pectin is being studied as a significant factor in assisting the body to increase its good cholesterol (HDL) levels.

Dried fruits loses most of its vitamin C when dried, however, it does retain almost all of the minerals and is high in beta-carotene.

Dried fruits may contain sulfites as a preservative. Sulfites have been known to cause allergic reactions in susceptible individuals. It would be best to dehydrate your own.

Dentists are advising that dried fruits may stick to your teeth increasing your risk of tooth decay. Best to brush after eating dried fruits.

Toasting intensifies the flavor and adds crispness to nuts.

Raisins won't stick to a food chopper if they are soaked in cold water for a short period of time.

Cream won't curdle when poured over fruits if you add a pinch of baking soda with the cream before serving.

"BROWN-OUT"''
To reduce the amount of food discolorization, slice bananas, apples, pears, plums and peaches with a stainless steel knife, then either combine them with any citrus fruit or sprinkle them with lemon or pineapple juice. Refrigerate as soon as possible.

Keep the rinds of oranges and grapefruits. Grate them and store in a tightly sealed jar in the refrigerator. They will make excellent flavorings for cakes and frostings.

For the best flavor cook dried fruit in the same water it was thawed in.

If you add a small pat of butter when cooking fruit for jams and jellies and you won't have any foam to skim off the top.

If you have any problems with fruit jelly not setting up, place the jars in a shallow pan half-filled with cold water, then bake in a moderate oven for 30 minutes.
To make ripe olives taste better, soak them overnight in olive oil with a clove of garlic added.

When making fruit compote, try adding some herbs, such as sweet cicely, mint or basil to bring out a sweeter flavor.

To ripen fruit, place it in a brown paper bag in a dark place for a few days.

If whole citrus fruits are warmed in the microwave or oven for a few minutes, they will yield more juice.

Lemons, limes, and grapefruits will not wilt or shrink if stored in water in the refrigerator. Place a small saucer on top of the fruits if necessary, to keep them submerged.

Prunes are a natural laxative due to the ingredient diphenylisatin.

To make dry raisins plump again, wash them, place them in a shallow dish and bake them covered in a preheated 350° F oven for no more than 10 minutes.

THE "WILD" SIDE

The Aborigines' favorite fruit in Australia is the "green plum." A 3 ½ ounce portion contains 2,300 to 3,150 milligrams of vitamin C. Oranges, which we purchase fresh only contain 50-80mg. of vitamin C, if we are lucky enough to buy them freshly picked.

The Hadza hunters in Tarzania enjoy the "kongoroko fruit." A 3 ½ ounce serving contains 526 milligrams of calcium. The U.S. RDA is 1,000 milligrams per day for the average adult.

The South African cape buffalo contains 1.5% of its fat in the form of omega-3 fatty acids. One of the best sources we consume is usually from fish oil. Our beef contains hardly a trace. Cod liver oil which is considered one of the best sources contains only 5%.

To test fruit for ripeness, stick a toothpick in the fruit at the stem end. If it goes in and out clean and with ease the fruit is ripe and can be eaten.

Dried fruits are graded: Extra Fancy, Fancy, Extra Choice, Choice or Standard. These gradings are based solely on size, color, condition and water content, not nutrient content.

Dried fruits kept in an airtight container will keep up to 6 months in a cool dry place or up to 1 year if placed in the refrigerator.

To easily chop raisins, place a small amount of butter on both sides of the knife.

APPLES

Certain apples will taste different depending on the time of year purchased. If you are buying large quantities, it would be best to purchase a few and taste them. They should be firm, have no holes, be unbruised, and have a good even color. If the apple is not ripe, leave at room temperature for a day or two. Apples are capable of lasting 3-5 weeks in the refrigerator, and will still retain vitamin C content. Most apples are tart flavored. The best and sweetest eating apples are the Red and Golden Delicious varieties. There are many varieties of apples which make them available year round.

Apples will spoil 10 times faster at room temperature. After they are ripe, be sure to refrigerate them.

Apples will float because 25% of their volume is made up of air between the cells.

The soft texture of cooked apples is caused by the heat collapsing the air spaces between the cells.

Apple butter contains no fat if prepared properly with cinnamon and allspice.

Pare apples by pouring scalding water on them just before peeling them.

Cut apples into quarters before peeling, it will be easier.

To give applesauce a different flavor, add sliced unpeeled orange in the last few minutes of the cooking.

To avoid wrinkled skins on apples when baking, cut a few slits in the skin to allow for expansion.

Apples will store for a longer period if they do not touch one another.

For winter storage, wipe apples dry and pack in dry sand or sawdust. Keep in cool, dry place.

Fresh apple juice will only last for a few weeks, even if under refrigeration.

Most of an apple harvest ends up being made into pasteurized apple products or frozen in order to preserve it. When pasteurized at temperatures of 170° to 190°F. microorganisms are destroyed and the juice has a stable shelf life of up to one year.

If you purchase frozen apple concentrate, it will only last for a few weeks after it is thawed.

The tartness of an apple is derived from the balance of malic acid and the fruit's natural sugars.

Commercially prepared sweetened applesauce can contain as much as 77% more calories than unsweetened varieties.

Nutritionally there is no difference between "natural" and "regular" apple juice, even the fiber content is the same.

Apple juice is not high on the nutrient scale. It contains no vitamin C unless it has been added.

FDA testing can only detect 50% of the approved 110 pesticides that are used on apples. The worst ones are; Captan and Phosmet, both can be removed with washing or cooking.

Apple juice and cider should not be purchased unless you are sure that the whole apple was not used in their preparation. The pits contain a poison.

Americans eat approximately 22 pounds of apples per year per person. 33% of apples in one government study contained residues of pesticides. 43 different pesticides were detected in apples.

If you store apples along with green tomatoes, they will ripen at a faster pace.

There are 150 strains of Red and Golden Delicious apples.

APPLE VARIETIES

Akane - Do not store well. Have sweet-tart flavor. Skin is thin and usually tender. They retain their shape well when baked and have a tart flavor.

Braeburn - Store exceptionally well. Skin is tender, moderately tart. They keep shape well when baked and retain their tartness.

Cortland - Fragile and needs to be stored carefully. High in vitamin C and resists browning. Thin skinned with slight tart-sweet taste. Keeps shape well when baked.

Criterion - Yellow apples that are difficult to handle without bruising. High in vitamin C and resists browning. The skin is tender but flavor is bland when baked.

Elstar - Store well with their tart flavor mellowing when stored. They have tender skin and retain their flavor and shape well when baked.

Empire - Do not store well and tend to get mealy easily. High in vitamin C and will resist browning. Thick-skinned and bake well retaining flavor.

Fuji - Store well with tangy-sweet flavor. Will retain shape well when baked, but take longer to cook than most apples. Looks like an Asian pear.

Gala - Choose apples with pale-yellow background and light-reddish stripes. Sweet with slight tartness and have tender skin. Hold shape well when baked but does not retain flavor.

Golden Delicious - Stores well but spoils fast at room temperature. Should be light yellow not greenish. Skin is tender and flavor is sweet. High in vitamin C and resists browning. Retains shape well when baked.

Granny Smith - Best color is light green not intensely green and could even have a slight yellow tint. High in vitamin C and resists browning. Nicely balanced sweet-tart flavor. Cooks into excellent thick applesauce, but is not recommended for baking.

Gravenstein - Comes in both red and green. Excellent sweet-tart flavor and very juicy. Good for applesauce but not a good baking apple.

Idared - They keep exceptionally well and become sweeter during storage. Resembles Jonathans, skin is tender. When cooked they will retain full flavor.

Jonagold - Has good sweet-tart balance. A very juicy apple with tender skin. For best applesauce, cook with peel then strain.

Jonathan - Found in California around mid-August. They become soft and mealy quickly. Thin skinned, cook tender and make good applesauce. Retain shape well when baked.

McIntosh - Most come from British Columbia. Be careful when selecting, they get mushy and mealy easily. Skin is tough and will separate from flesh. Tend to fall apart when baked in pies.

Melrose - Normally found in the Northwest. Store very well and flavor actually improves after one or two months of storage. Well-balanced sweet and tart flavor. Retains shape well when cooked in pies.

Mutsu - (Crispin) Looks like Golden Delicious, but is greener and irregular in shape. Store very well. Has sweet but spicy taste with fairly coarse texture. For applesauce, cook with peels and strain.

Newton Pippin - Sometimes picked too green, wait until light green for sweetest flavor. Crisp, sweet-tart flavored apple. They keep shape when baked or used in pies. Makes a thick applesauce.

Northern Spy - A tart red/green apple, excellent for pies

Red Delicious - Ranges in color from red to red- striped. Store for up to 12 months. Will not last long at room temperature. Avoid any bruised ones. Normally are sweet and mellow with hint of tartness. When cooked they do not hold flavor well.

Rhode Island Greening - Best choice for pies, but not very available. Only available October and November on the East Coast.

Rome Beauty -If stored for long periods Rome Beauty apples will develop a bland flavor and get mealy. They are very mild and have a low acid level. The skin is thick, but tender. It is an excellent baking apple.

Spartan - Will not store for long periods and get mealy easily. Sweet flavor and very aromatic. Flavor is weak when cooked.

Stayman Winesap - Stores well. Spicy-tart flavor and good crisp apple. Have thick skins which separate easily. When cooked they will retain flavor well. Good for baking or pies.

APRICOTS

Usually the first fruit of the summer season. A relative of the peach and in one ounce they contain enough beta carotene to supply 20% of your daily vitamin A requirements. Astronauts ate apricots on the Apollo moon mission.

Apricots originally were grown in China over 4,000 years ago and were brought to California by the Spanish in the late 18th century.

California is the largest producer of apricots.

Over half the apricots grown are canned due to their short season.

3 ½ ounces of dried apricots can supply 4 million grams of beta carotene.

Dried apricots are over 40% sugar.

Try and purchase unsulphured dried apricots.

BANANAS

Available all year round. They should be plump. The skin should be free of bruises as well as black and brown spots. Bananas should be purchased green and allowed to ripen at home. They may be ripened at room temperature until they reach the desired stage, then refrigerated and used in a short period of time. Refrigeration may darken the outside of the bananas, but this will not effect the fruit on the inside. In fact, refrigeration allows for longer storage of bananas.

If you want to ripen bananas even more quickly, wrap them in a wet paper towel and place them into a brown paper sack.

The new size of miniature bananas now appearing in supermarkets has more taste than many of the larger ones.

Banana chips are usually fried in coconut oil and is not a good nutritious snack like a banana or air-dried banana chips. One ounce of fried chips can have as much as 150 calories and up to 10 grams of fat, much of which is saturated.

American consume 25 pounds of bananas per person annually.

Bananas contain less water than most other fruits.

Bananas are a type of berry from a tree classified as an herb tree which can grow up to 30 feet high.

They are the largest plant in the world without a woody stem.

VARIETIES INCLUDE:

Cavandish - This is the standard banana that we normally purchase and for the most part is grown in South America.

Manzano - Called finger bananas and turn black when they are ripe.

Plantains - Very large green bananas, high starch content and are usually cooked like a vegetable. Sometimes substituted for potatoes.

Red Bananas - Not usually curved, they turn a purplish color when ripe. Sweet tasting.

If a green banana is placed next to a ripe banana, it will ripen more quickly.

Unpeeled bananas will last longer if stored in the refrigerator in a sealed jar.

If you slice bananas with a sterling silver knife they will not darken as fast. Old wives tale??

BERRIES

Should be fairly firm. Color should be good and not faded. Berries should all be refrigerated and should not be allowed to dry out. Use within 2-3 days after purchase for best flavor and nutritional value. Berries do not ripen once picked. Choose only bright red strawberries and plump firm blueberries that are light to dark blue.

Always check the bottom of berry containers to be sure they are not stained from rotting berries or if they show any mold.

Mold on berries spreads quickly. Never leave a moldy berry next to a good one. This goes for all fruits.

Never hull strawberries until they have been washed or they will absorb too much water and become mushy.

Blueberries are higher in vitamin A then most berries.

By adding 1/4 teaspoon of baking soda to the cranberries when they are cooking, you will use less sweetener.

Fresh cranberries has 86% more vitamin C than canned cranberries.

One cup of strawberries contains only 55 calories and much more calcium, phosphorus, vitamin C, and potassium than blueberries, and raspberries.

Raspberries, strawberries, cranberries and loganberries contain "ellagic acid" a substance which is now being studied as a natural preventive for certain types of cancer.

Blueberries and blackberries are better if cooked since cooking will deactivate an enzyme that effects your absorption of vitamin B1.

Strawberries should be stored in the refrigerator in a plastic colander allowing the air to circulate around them.

A V-shaped can opener is ideal for hulling strawberries.

CANTALOUPES

Best June through September. They should be round, smooth, and have a depressed scar at the stem end. If the scar appears rough or the stem is still attached, the melon will not ripen well. Cantaloupes are best if the netting is an even yellow color with little or no green. Melons can be left at room temperature to ripen. The aroma will usually indicate if it is ripe and sweet. Refrigerate as soon as ripe. Whole melons will last for a week if kept cold. Cut melons, wrapped in plastic with seeds in and refrigerated, are best eaten in a few days.

If cantaloupe is ripe you should be able to hear the seeds rattling inside. It should also give off a sweet fragrance. The "belly button" should be somewhat soft, but if the melon is soft all over, it's probably overripe.

CHERRIES

Cherries are one of the most popular fruit and are grown in 20 countries worldwide. The United States grows approximately 150,000 tons of cherries annually.

The best known varieties are the Montmorency and the Bing. Available from May to August. Bings should be a dark purplish color and somewhat firm.

Europeans enjoy a chilled cherry soup as a summertime treat.

CRANBERRIES

A good cranberry will bounce. Buy berries that are hard, bright, light to dark-red. Sealed in plastic bags, they keep refrigerated for a month; frozen, they will keep up to one year.

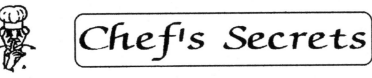

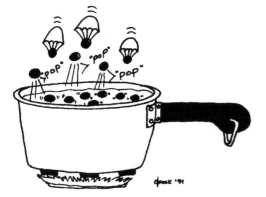

Cook cranberries only until they "pop". Further cooking makes them taste bitter. When cooking cranberries, always add one teaspoon of butter to each pound to eliminate over boiling and excess foam.

DATES

These are one of the sweetest fruits and may contain up to 70% sugar. California and Arizona are the major suppliers for the United States, however, Africa and the Middle East have been growing them for 4,000 years.

A date cluster can weigh up to 25 pounds. Supplies 250% more potassium than an orange and 64% more than a banana ounce for ounce.

FIGS

Figs are one of the oldest known fruits. 90% of all figs grown are dried. They were brought to California by the Spanish and most are still grown in California. The most popular fig is the Calimyrna. Size is not an indicator of the quality.

They are uniquely pollinated by small fig wasps.

GRAPEFRUIT

As with all citrus, the heavier the fruit, the juicier. Florida grapefruits are juicier than those from California and Arizona. However, Western fruit has a thicker skin which is easier to peel. If refrigerated, grapefruit will last for a few weeks. Grapefruit should be firm and not discolored. Fruit that is pointed at the end tend to be thicker skinned and have less meat and juice. White fruit has a stronger flavor than pink fruit. Available all year, but best January through May.

Grapefruits were developed from crossing an orange with a shaddock. Shaddock's are not usually found in the supermarkets since they have almost no juice, a thick skin, a sour taste and many seeds.

Just For The "Health" Of It

Recent studies show that grapefruit may be more effective in lowering cholesterol than any other pectin source.

Shredded grapefruit will be a great addition to any fish salad.

Chef's Secrets

If you allow a grapefruit to stand in boiling water for a few minutes it will be easier to peel.

"BELIEVE IT OR NOT"

Salt will make a grapefruit taste sweeter.

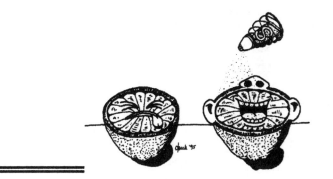

GRAPES

Should be plump and firmly attached to a green stem. Good color for type of grape, not faded. Grapes do not ripen off the vine, so be certain that they are ripe when chosen. Buy small quantity and taste. When refrigerated, grapes will last 5-7 days.

All grapes are really berries and are native to Asia Minor where they were cultivated for 6000 years.

Grapes are grown on 6 continents.

California produces 97% and Arizona produces 3% of all European varieties grown in the United States.

COMMON VARIETIES

Black Beauty - The only seedless black grape.

Calmeria - Large dark red grapes with a light gray finish. Has very few seeds.

Champagne - Used to make currents. Usually a gourmet product.

Concord - major variety of American grape. Blue/black with a sweet but somewhat tart flavor.

Delaware - Small pink-colored grape with a tender skin.

Emperor - One of the most popular small grape. Reddish/purple in color and seedless.

Exotic - Blue/black in color and have seeds.

Flame Seedless - Deep red and seedless, about the same size as the Emperor, but somewhat more tart.

Italia - Muscat, mainly for wine making. Green/gold grape with seeds.

Niagara - Large amber-colored grape, may be somewhat egg-shaped. Not as sweet as most other varieties.

Perlette Seedless - Green grape imported from Mexico.

Queen - Red, large grape that have a mild sweet flavor.

Red Globe - Very large grape with large seeds and a delicate flavor.

Red Malaga - Thick-skinned reddish somewhat sweet grape.

Ribier - Large blue/black grape with tender skins.

Ruby Seedless - Deep red grape, very sweet.

Steuben - A blue-black grape similar to the Concord.

Thompson Seedless - Everybodys favorite. The most common grape sold in the United States. Small green sweet grape. Common raisin grape.

Tokay - Sweeter version of the Flame Seedless.

HONEYDEW MELONS

The best are creamy white or pale yellow with a silky finish. They are best if purchased between June and October. A faint sweet smell indicates ripeness. Blossom end (the end opposite the stem) should be slightly soft. Like most melons, honeydews taste better if left unrefrigerated for a few days. Whole ones keep fresh for up to one week when refrigerated. Store cut melons with seeds in plastic bags. Eat within a few days.

KIWI

Firm kiwis, left at room temperature, soften and sweeten in 3-5 days. Ripe kiwis feel like ripe peaches. Refrigerated, they stay fresh for weeks. Average size 2-3 inches long. Has a furry brown skin which is peeled off before eating. The inside should be lime green. Kiwi may be used to tenderize meat. They are available June to March. When ripe, kiwi will give slightly to the touch. They are low in calories and are an excellent source of vitamin C.

Sometimes called a Chinese gooseberry, but is not related to the gooseberry.

2 kiwis = the fiber in 1 cup of bran flakes.

Peel with a vegetable peeler for less waste.

"RIPENS FASTER WITH FRIENDS"
To ripen faster, place them in a paper bag with an apple or a banana.

Excellent meat tenderizer when pureed and used in a marinade. Contains the chemical "actinidin" which also is the chemical in kiwi that causes the gelatin not to gel if you add kiwi to gelatin. Cooking the fruit even for a short period of time, however, deactivates the chemical.

LEMONS

If sprinkled with water and refrigerated in plastic bags, lemons (as well as limes) will last a month or more frozen, both their juices and grated peels last about 4 months. Look for lemons with the smoothest skin and the smallest points on each end. They have more juice and better flavor. Also, submerging a lemon in hot water for fifteen minutes before squeezing it will yield almost twice the amount of juice. Or, try warming lemons in your oven for a few minutes before squeezing them. If you need only a few drops of juice, prick one end with a fork and squeeze the desired amount. Return lemon to the refrigerator and it will be as good as new.

Lemons will keep longer in the refrigerator if you place them in a clean jar, cover them with cold water and seal the jar well.

After using one-half a lemon, store the other half in the freezer in a plastic baggie.

When lemon is used for a flavoring it tends to mask the craving for salt.

Lemon and lime peelings may cause skin irritation on susceptible persons. They contain the oil "limonene."

LIMES

Originated on the island of Tahiti. Key limes are a smaller variety with a higher acid content. The California variety is called "Bears" and is a seedless lime.

MANGOES

Available late December through August. Excellent source of Vitamin A & C. Should be eaten when soft, and will ripen at room temperature. Mangos are becoming a problem fruit. They are imported into this country with traces of a carcinogenic fumigant, ethylene dibromide (EDB). Purchase only mangos and papayas grown in Hawaii or Florida.

Mangos are one of the best sources of beta-carotene, they contain 20% more than cantaloupe and 50% more than apricots.

Mangos contain as much vitamin C as an orange.

Only 10% of all mangoes are grown in the United States.

NECTARINES

Their peak season is in July and August. They combine a peach and a plum characteristics. Color should be rich and bright. If too hard, allow to ripen at room temperature for a few days. Avoid very hard dull-looking nectarines.

There are 150 varieties of nectarines worldwide.

ORANGES

The color of an orange is no indication of its quality because oranges are usually dyed to improve their appearance. Brown spots on the skin indicate a good quality orange. Pick a sweet orange by examining the navel. Choose the ones with the biggest holes. If you put oranges in a hot oven before peeling them, no white fibers will be left on them.

Oranges that look green, have undergone a natural process called "regreening." This is due to a ripe orange pulling green chlorophyll pigment from the leaves. They are excellent eating and usually very sweet.

Chief food crop of the United States.

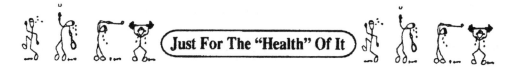

Orange juice is not necessarily high on the nutritional scale. While it may contain vitamin C and potassium, it provides little more than a source of carbohydrates in the form of a natural sugar.

Orange juice will lose more vitamin C content when stored in an open container or one with a plastic lid. Always store in a glass container with a screw cap.

Oranges that need to be peeled for dishes should be soaked in boiling water for at least 5-7 minutes before peeling. This will make it easier to peel and remove all the white pulp.

PAPAYAS

When ripe, they will be completely yellow. Papaya and kiwi both have tenderizing properties. They take 2-5 days to ripen at room temperature.

Papaya seeds are edible, wash them first. Similar flavor as that of pepper. Can be dried and ground for seasoning.

PEACHES

Peaches ripen quickly by placing them in a box covered with newspaper. Gases are sealed in. Skins come off smoothly if peach is peeled with a potato peeler. Remember when peaches had all that peach fuzz? Well, today peaches are defuzzed by a mechanical brushing process before shipment.

Peaches won't mature or get sweeter once picked.

PEARS

Ripen pears quickly by placing them in a brown paper bag along with a ripe apple. Place in a cool, shady spot and make certain a few holes are punched into the bag. The ripe apple will give off ethylene gas which will stimulate the other fruit to ripen. (This ripe-apple hint will also have the same effect on peaches and tomatoes).

Most of the vitamin C is located in the skin.

PERSIMMONS

Available October through January. They have a smooth, shiny, bright, orange skin, which is removed before eating or they will be sour. High in vitamins A, C, and potassium. May be ripened overnight by wrapping them in tin foil and placing into the freezer. Must be thawed at room temperature and eaten the next day.

PINEAPPLE

Available year round. Best March through June. Buy as large and heavy as available. Leaves at top should be deep green. Do not buy if they have soft spots. Refrigerate and use as soon as possible.

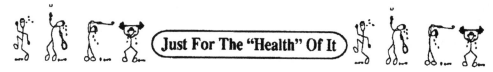

Just For The "Health" Of It

Fresh pineapple contains an enzyme that causes gelatin not to set-up. Canned is best.

Studies have shown that the chemical bromelin in pineapple may help keep arteries clean.

Chef's Secrets

To ripen a pineapple, cut off top, remove skin and slice. Place in pot and cover with water, sweeten to taste, boil for five minutes, cool and refrigerate.

Never use fresh pineapple in a gelatin mold or the protein will be broken down and the gelatin will not gel. This is caused by the chemical "bromelain" a potent protein tenderizer.

PLUMS

Available June through September. Buy only medium firm to slightly soft plums. Hard plums will not ripen well. To ripen, let stand at room temperature until fairly soft. May take 2-3 days. Refrigerate after ripe.

The traditional "English Plum Pudding" never contained plums, only currents and raisins.

California French is the most common plum variety used for prunes.

POMEGRANATES

Available September through December. Contain many seeds surrounded by red pulp, which are both edible. The sponge-like membrane is bitter and usually not eaten. Pomegranate juice is used to make grenadine syrup. Excellent source of potassium.

UGLI FRUIT

A close relative of oranges and grapefruit. Yellowish, pebbly skin with green blotches that turn orange when the fruit is ripe. Makes excellent eating and is high in vitamin C. Looks Ugli!

WATERMELON

The ground-based side of a perfect watermelon is yellow. The rest of the rind is smooth, waxy, green, with or without stripes. If cut, pick bright, crisp, even-colored flesh. Whole melons can stay unrefrigerated for a few days. Once they are cut, they must be kept covered and cold.

To test for ripeness in watermelon, snap thumb and third finger against the melon. If it says "pink" in a high, shrill tone, the melon isn't ripe. If you hear "punk" in a deep low tone, the melon is ready to eat.

The following is a list of salad bar items I encountered on a trip to a Palm Springs restaurant, it is the best I have ever seen:

Lettuce	Cabbage	Celery Carrots	Cauliflower
Broccoli	Radishes	Cucumbers	Raisins
Grapes	Cantaloupe	Honeydew	Cheeses
Tomatoes	Watermelon	Sprouts	Mushrooms
Peppers	Seeds	Avocado	Strawberries
Beans	Olives	Beets	Onions
Boiled Eggs	Anchovy	Pimentos	Nuts
Shrimp	Apple	Oranges	Cranberry
Jicama	String Beans	Snow Peas	Croutons
Coconut	Zucchini	Cottage Cheese	Lunch Meats
Macaroni Salad	Coleslaw	Caviar	Dates
Bacon Bits	Papaya	Kiwi	Spinach
Chestnuts	Ginger Root	Capers	Bananas
Breads	Tuna Salad	Seafood Salad	Pickles
Smoked Fish.			

Since nobody likes mushy fruit many recipes ask you to add sugar to the recipe. This strengthens the cell walls and brings the water back into the cells that the cooking has removed.

Fruit consumption in the United States has risen from 101 pounds per person in 1970 to 124 pounds in 1994.

Chapter 4

Vegetables, The Old and The New

Sea vegetables are becoming a new food experience. They may be called "wakame" or "kombu" and they are derived from seaweed which is high in minerals.

"BEST TO GET A 4.0"

There are three grades of canned, frozen and dried fruits and vegetables: U.S. Grade A (fancy), U.S. Grade B (choice or extra standard) and U.S. Grade C (standard). Grades B and C are just as nutritious but have more blemishes.

"FANCY THAT"

Most fresh fruits and vegetables have three grades: U.S. Fancy, U.S. Fancy No. 1 and U.S. Fancy No. 2. The grades are determined by the product's color, size, shape, maturity and the number of defects.

"SAY GOODBYE TO SOGGY SALADS"

To prevent soggy salads, place an inverted saucer in the bottom of the salad bowl. The excess liquid drains off under the saucer and the salad stays fresh and crisp.

Never salt any vegetable during cooking, the salt will draw the liquid out and they will not cook evenly.

Try freezing different fruits and vegetables for kids snacks, such as peas, blueberries, etc.

July is National Baked Bean Month.

A new category of foods is now known as the "fruit-vegetables" and includes eggplant, squash, peppers and tomatoes. These are all the seed-bearing bodies of the plants they grow on.

Just For The "Health" Of It

The chemical, solanine, has been associated with arthritis pain in a study by Rutgers University. Foods that contain high amounts of solanine are green potatoes, tomatoes, red and green peppers, eggplant and paprika.

Never eat home-canned vegetables before cooking them.

Cabbage, turnips, kale, rutabaga, watercress and rapeseed contain a harmful chemical called a thioglucoside, which may adversely affect the thyroid gland, but is destroyed by cooking.

Parsnips contain a chemical group called psoralens, which cause cancer readily in laboratory animals. They should be peeled and cooked to get rid of these toxins.

Vegetables high in beta carotene may interfere with menstruation. Women having problems should refrain from eating too many carrots, squash, broccoli and any vegetable high in carotene according to RN Magazine. It was also noted that their protein intake was increased.

Plants high in oxalic acid should be avoided as you approach middle age and beyond. These include; spinach, rhubarb and especially coco bean (chocolate). Studies have shown that they interfere with calcium absorption.

Parsley may make your skin sensitive to sunlight.

Wax coatings on fruits need to washed off or cut off. Check with your produce manager to find out which ones are waxed to increase their shelf life.

"SCRUB'EM OR PEEL'EM"
The FDA during a routine sampling of domestic and imported foods found pesticide residues in 31% of the 3,699 domestic vegetables. However, the FDA only tests 1% of all vegetables sold in the U.S.

It is best to save liquids from vegetables that you have cooked and use the liquids in soups, stews, etc.

Wash all fruits and vegetables in cold water, but never store them in water. If you do they will lose a large percentage of their nutrients.

Keep all produce wrapped loosely, especially if wrapped in plastic. Air must be allowed to circulate around them to reduce spoilage.

Order of nutritional quality (in most cases) (1) Fresh if grown properly, (2) Dehydrated Grade A, (3) Freeze Dried, (4) Frozen, (5) Canned.

Avoid baking soda around vegetables, many vitamins are acidic and turn into a salt.

Processing and storage times affect the nutrient content of both fruits and vegetables.

We have reduced our purchase of fresh vegetables 12% since the 1950's and have increased our use of canned and frozen vegetables by 50%.

If cut up greens need to be crisped up, place them in a the freezer in a metal bowl for 5-10 minutes. If they are wet, remember to place an inverted small saucer on the bottom to drain off the excess liquid.

"GREAT CAESARS SALAD"
Caesars Salad was named after a restaurant owner in Tijuana, Mexico. Caesar Cardini was in trouble and was running out of food, so he used the only ingredients left, and invented Caesars Salad.

Try placing a few unshelled pecans in your saucepan when cooking greens, kale or collards, it will help keep the odor down.

THE "NOSE" KNOWS
When cooking onions or cabbage, boil a small amount of vinegar in a pan to remove the odors.

The best method of cutting parsley is to use a scissors.

To place some life into your salads, try adding sorrel, cress or nasturtium to it.

If you sprinkle salt into the water when you are washing vegetables, it will draw out insects.

To caramelize vegetables and make the flavors and colors more intense, take carrots, celery, parsnips, onions or tomatoes and toss with olive oil then roast in a 500 degree F. oven for 30-40 minutes or until dark brown.

If you add a small amount of sugar to vegetables, it will bring out more flavor.

All leafy vegetables such as spinach, kale, greens and chard, should be cooked in water that clings to their leaves for the best flavor.

When boiling greens, add a pat of butter to the water. This will prevent them from boiling over without constant stirring.

"PERKER UPPER"
If you cook with a small amount of milk, it will help to retain the color of the vegetables.

Wilted vegetables can be freshened by soaking them for an hour in cold water with the juice of one lemon.

If you add salt to the water when washing vegetables, it will help remove any sand that is left.

Always line your refrigerator drawers with a double piece of paper towel to absorb the excess moisture.

Vegetable stains can be removed with a slice of wet potato or vinegar.

Tomatoes, cucumbers and carrots rank as the most popular salad fixings. The least popular are beans and peas.

Use a well-greased muffin tin to bake tomatoes, apples or bell peppers. They will keep their shape better.

"GETTING PICKLED"
When making pickles, cut off 1/4 inch from each end. The ends contain an enzyme that may cause the pickles to soften.

Pickle juice should be saved and used for making cole slaw, potato salad, etc.

If you will add a small piece of horseradish to the pickle jar, it will keep the vinegar active while keeping the pickles from becoming soft.

Choosing The Most Nutritious Greens:

1. Dandelion   - Use young leaves.
2. Arugula   - Slight mustard green flavor.
3. Kale   - Use young leaves.
4. Parsley   - Helps bring out the flavor of others.
5. Romaine   - Somewhat strong taste.
6. Spinach   - High in nutrients but contains oxalates.
7. Beet   - Best if you use young and small leaves.
8. Butter   - Lettuce.
9. Endive   - Contains oxalates. May affect calcium absorption.
10. Iceberg   - Most popular lettuce, least nutritious.

Never salt the water when cooking turnips, it will remove the sweetness.

The top 10 Fruits and vegetables in overall nutritional content:

1. Broccoli   6. Papaya
2. Cantaloupe   7. Pumpkin
3. Carrots   8. Red Bell Peppers
4. Kale   9. Spinach
5. Mango   10. Sweet Potato

Spinach should be washed quickly in warm water.

Chives need to be refrigerated and used within 3-4 days after purchase for the best flavor.

A new plastic wrap is being developed that will breathe and extend the life of wrapped vegetables. It is being developed by the U.S.D.A.

Vegetables are best steam cooked. The faster the better.

Coleslaw will taste better, if you use sweet pickle juice instead of vinegar.

Sour wines may be used in place of vinegar.

When taking salad greens on a picnic, wrap them in a damp towel and the dressing in a jar.

To crisp up salad greens, add 1 teaspoon of vinegar to a pan of water, then let the greens soak for 15 minutes.

If vegetables and salad are dry when served, the dressing will adhere better.

Parsley will cure bad breath.

CHOOSING THE "CREAM" OF THE CROP

ARTICHOKES

Best to purchase March through May. California is the main supplier. Choose from compact, tightly closed heads with green, clean-looking leaves. Their size is not related to quality. Avoid ones that have brown leaves or show signs of mold. Leaves that are separated, show that it is too old and will be tough and bitter.

There are 50 varieties of artichokes grown worldwide.

A single artichoke is an unopened flower bud from a thistle like plant.

Best to wear rubber gloves when working with artichokes.

Artichokes should never be cooked in aluminum pots. They tend to turn the pots a gray color.

Artichokes will burn unless kept completely covered with water while they are cooking. However, they are easy to overcook.

When cooking artichokes you can obtain a better flavor if you add a small amount of sugar and salt to the water. They will be sweeter and will retain their color better.

ASPARAGUS

Stalks should be green with compact, closed tips and tender. Avoid flat stalks or stalks that have a lot of white in them. Do not buy them if they are soaking in water. Asparagus toughen rapidly, and should be used soon after purchase. The best time of year to purchase is March to June. Refrigeration will help retain the B and C vitamins, but wrap the ends in moist paper towel, then seal in a plastic bag.

White asparagus is planted under mounds of soil, blocking sunlight and reducing the plants ability to produce chlorophyll.

If ridges form on stems, this is a sign of age and soaking in ice water will help revive it.

The water that vegetables are cooked in will be high in vitamins and minerals. Use for soups and stews.

To revive limp asparagus, try placing them in a tall pot with ice water in the refrigerator for thirty minutes.

"WHOOPS"

Always open asparagus cans from the bottom or you may break the tips. However, read the can carefully as they may be canned upside down.

To tenderize the asparagus stalks, try peeling the stalks with a potato peeler up to the bottom of the tips.

Asparagus contains a sulphur compound that may cause a strange odor in a persons urine. This happens in approximately 40% of the population and is harmless.

AVOCADOS

Available all year round. They should be fresh in appearance and the color should range from green to purple-black. They should feel heavy for their size and be slightly firm. Avoid ones with soft spots and discolorizations. Refrigerate and use within 5 days after ripening.

Avocados ripen quickly when placed in a brown paper bag and set in a warm place.

Avocados have a higher fat content than most other vegetables, but are still a good source of protein.

Avocados of the Florida (Trapp Type) is not recommended for persons watching their fat intake. They contain 22.1% palmitic acid. The California type (Fuerte Type) has only 9.1% palmitic acid.

California avocados that are picked in November to March have 1/3 less fat than those picked September and October. They are less mature and have only 2 grams of fat compared to 6 grams of fat.

Another method of ripening avocados is to place them in a plastic bag with a piece of banana peel.

Leaving the pit in a guacamole dip will not keep the dip from turning black. The only area that won't turn black is the area under the pit which protects the dip from oxygen and the color change.

Avocados will not ripen if placed in the refrigerator.

To ripen avocados quickly, place them into a wool sock, then set them in a dark place.

Ripe avocados should be stored in the refrigerator for longer life.

An avocado is ripe when it gives slightly to finger pressure.

The fat in avocados is mostly monounsaturated, which is one of the fats most preferred by the body.

BEANS, GARBANZO (chick peas)
Has a nut-like flavor and will puree easily to make dips.

BEANS (Edible Pods)
May be green, purple or yellow in color. They should have no scars or discolorizations. When broken, they should have a crisp snap. Available year round, but are best May through August. Store without slicing and refrigerate to retain vitamin content. Do not soak in water.

Varieties include:

| Chinese long beans | Snap Beans | Haricots verts |
| Italian | Purple wax beans | Scarlet runners |

Snap beans are found in green and yellow varieties.

Purple wax beans turn green when cooked.

Haricot verts are also called French Beans.

Chinese long beans may be up to 18 inches long.

Cooked beans will stay fresh in the refrigerator for approximately 5 days.

For a different taste, add celery soup to the green beans.

Boiling whole green beans instead of cut-up ones will retain 50% more of the nutrients.

BEANS (SHELL)
Higher in vitamin C than snap bean varieties. varieties include cranberry beans, fava beans and lima beans.
Shell beans should have a bulge and a tightly closed pod. If the pods are not opened they should last for 2-3 days.

BEANS, LIMA
Pods should be dark green and bright in color. Best May through October. When shelled, should appear green or greenish white. Very perishable and should be used as soon as purchased.

To help retain color, add a small amount of baking soda to the cooking water.

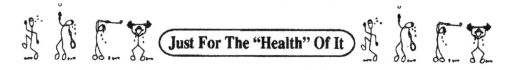

Just For The "Health" Of It

Gas-free lima beans are now being grown. They will contain less of the hard-to-digest sugars that cause the problem.

BEANS, SOY

The only natural food to contain all the essential amino acids that the body needs to synthesize all the other amino acids. Should be stored in their original package or in a covered container.

Soybeans and white beans are the highest in calcium of any bean.

Chickpeas have the most calories, however, beans for the most part are low in calories and contain hardly any fat. The only exception is soybeans which are high in polyunsaturated fat.

BEANS, PINTO

Should have a bright uniform color, fading is a sign of aging and long storage. Small beans cook faster and should not be mixed with large ones or they will be mush. Do not buy if they are cracked or if too much foreign material is found in the bin, especially small stones.

Beans can be stored in an airtight container and should last up to a year and still retaining a good nutrient level.

Beans contain 22% protein. Beef only 18% and eggs 13%.

To prevent beans from becoming mushy, try adding a small amount of baking soda to the water while they are cooking.

Cooked beans will store for up to six months in the freezer, but only 4-6 days in the refrigerator.

If beans get too salty, try using a small amount of brown sugar.

"OH, WHAT A RELIEF IT IS"
To eliminate gas in beans, try using "Beano". It can neutralize the sugar in the beans that causes gas production in the body.

Gas production from beans can also be eliminated by adding a teaspoon of fennel seed to the water the beans are soaking in.

"NUTRITIONALLY SPEAKING"
Beans are one of the best sources of protein. The following gives their quality of nutritional content on a scale of 1-10. 10 being the best.

Kidney beans.....10   Lentils.....7.0
Navy beans.......9.5   Chickpeas...6.5
Lima beans.......8.5   Split peas..5.5
Tofu........4.0

BEETS
Buy only small or medium-sized beets. Large beets are usually not very tender. Do not purchase if they look shriveled or flabby. Beets should be firm. They are high in vitamins and minerals. Greens should be used immediately and roots within 5-7 days.

Beets should be cooked whole to retain their red color.

Beets contain a chemical pigment called betacyanin which gives the beets their reddish color. Some people cannot metabolize this pigment and it may turn their feces and urine a red color for a few days after ingestion.

Sugar beets are approximately 20% sucrose by weight, twice the sugar content of standard beets. Approximately 100 pounds of sugar beets are needed to produce 5 pounds of sugar.

BROCCOLI

Available year round. Best from October to May. Stems should not be too thick. Wilted leaves may indicate old age. Do not buy if buds are open or yellowish. Bud clusters should be firm, closed and of good green color. Use as soon as purchased. Refrigeration will help retain the vitamin A and C content.

Broccoli (one cup chopped) contains 90% of RDA of vitamin A, 200% of vitamin C, 6% of niacin, 10% of calcium, 10% of thiamin, 10% of phosphorus and 8% of iron. It also provides 25% of your fiber needs and to top it off, five grams of protein.

The EPA has registered more than 50 pesticides that can be used on broccoli. 70% of these pesticides cannot be detected by the FDA. 13% of broccoli, in a study showed that pesticides residues remained. The worst one is Parathion and even after washing and boiling some reside may remain.

THE "NOSE" KNOWS
To eliminate the smell of broccoli, add a slice of bread to the pot.

Broccoli consumption has risen over 50% since 1983 to approximately 18 servings per person in 1994.

"EXTRA, EXTRA- BROCCOLI PARDONED"
Hillary Clinton places broccoli back on the White House menu after it was removed by President Bush.

Broccoli florets have about eight times as much beta-carotene as the stalks.

Broccoli that has been cooked still has 15% more vitamin C than an orange and as much calcium as milk.

To retain the nutrients in broccoli, either steam it, stir-fry it or boil it in a very small amount of water. Most other methods will cause a nutrient loss of about 25-35%.

Cruciferous vegetables such as broccoli tend to release strong-smelling chemical compounds when cooked. These ammonia and hydrogen sulfide compounds will smell up the kitchen. Steaming or cooking in a small amount of water and as fast as possible will reduce this problem.

BRUSSELS SPROUTS
When cooking Brussel sprouts, add a few pieces of white bread to the cooking water to reduce the odor.

Brussel sprouts are one of the better vegetable protein sources. Approximately 30% of their calories are from protein.

Best to refrigerate Brussel sprouts or the leaves will turn yellow quickly. Should be a bright green color.

CABBAGE
Available all year. There are three main varieties; red, green and savory which has crinkly leaves. Avoid cabbage with worm holes. Smell the core for sweetness. Green and red cabbage should have firm tight leaves with good color. Cabbage should be refrigerated in plastic bag and used within 7-14 days.

Present research shows that ½ head of cabbage a day may help to prevent certain types of cancer. The chemical indole may prove to prevent breast cancer.

THE "NOSE" KNOWS
Cabbage odors can be contained if you place a piece of bread on top of the cabbage when cooking in a covered pot.

When you need cabbage leaves for stuffed cabbage, try freezing the whole cabbage first, then let it thaw, and the leaves will come apart easier.

To keep red cabbage red, try adding a tablespoon of white vinegar to the cooking water.

CARROTS
Available all year. Should have smooth skins, good orange color and be well formed. Do not purchase if wilted, cracked or flabby or if tops are green. Keep refrigerated. High in vitamin A if not kept soaking in water.

To slip the skins off carrots, drop them in boiling water, let stand for 5 minutes, then drop them into cold water.

To curl carrots, peel slices with a potato peeler, then drop them in a bowl of ice water.

The tops of carrots should be removed before storing them in the refrigerator. Tops will drain the carrots of moisture, making them limp and dry.

For the best results when cooking frozen vegetables, cook them directly from the freezer (except, corn on the cob and spinach).

Keep carrots away from apples and tomatoes, these fruits give off higher amounts of ethylene gas and may make the carrots bitter.

When grating carrots, leave part of the green top on to use as a handle. Keeps your fingers intact.

"THE YOUNGER, THE BETTER"

If you wish to freeze vegetables, try to purchase "young" ones. They will be higher in nutrients and less starchy. Do not store for more than 10 hours before using for the best results.

"CARROT TOP"

Carrot greens are high in vitamin K which is lacking in the carrot itself.

Carrot skins contain 10% of all nutrients found in carrots.

Recently the USDA completed studies showing that 7 ounces of carrots consumed every day for 3 weeks lowered cholesterol levels by 11%. This was probably due to calcium pectate, a type of fiber found in carrots. A good percentage of which will be lost in juicing.

CAULIFLOWER

Best if purchased September through January, but available year round. Should have compact flower clusters(florets or curds) with green leaves. Do not purchase if flower clusters are open. If there is a speckled surface, this is a sign of insect injury, mold or rot. Store in the refrigerator.

To keep cauliflower white during cooking, add lemon to the water. Overcooking tends to darken cauliflower and make it tougher.

Due to certain chemicals in cauliflower it is best not to cook it in an aluminum or iron pot. Contact with these metals will turn the cauliflower yellow, brown or blue-green.

When you boil cauliflower, add a piece of white bread to eliminate the odor. Another method is to replace the water after it has cooked for 5-7 minutes.

Prior to cooking cauliflower, you should soak it head down for approximately 30 minutes in salted water to remove the grit and insects.

CELERY

Available year round. Stalks should have a very solid feel, since softness indicates pithiness. Do not purchase if there are any wilted stalks, even if all others are firm. Store in refrigerator. Lasts 7-10 days if not placed in water for prolonged period.

Don't discard celery leaves; dry them, then rub the leaves through a sieve turning them into powder that can be used to flavor soups, stews, salad dressings, etc. Also, can be made into celery salt.

Celery and lettuce will crisp up quickly, if you place them into a pan of cold water and then add a few slices of raw potatoes.

To prevent celery from turning brown, soak it in cold water with lemon juice before refrigerating.

 Chef's Secrets

Celery juice may be used as an effective stress reducer.

Celery may be bleached, using ethylene gas which will give it a clearer color. Also, it causes reduced vitamin potency.

CELERIAC

A root vegetable that looks like a turnip and is prepared like any other root vegetable.

CELTUCE

A combination of celery and lettuce which is prepared similar to cabbage.

CORN

Best May through September. Kernels should be a good yellow color. Do not buy if husks are straw colored, since they should be green. Straw colored husks and silks indicate decay or worm damage. Corn should be refrigerated. Yellow corn usually taste better than white corn and is higher in vitamin A content.

The best way to remove kernels from an ear of corn is to use a shoehorn or a spoon.

Corn contains 5-6% sugar by weight.

Americans eat about 25 pounds of corn per year.

There are more than 200 varieties of sweet corn.

When wrapping corn in tin foil for barbecuing, try adding a sprig of marjoram next to the corn.

Florida grows the most sweet corn and the best sweet corn is known as "Florida Sweet."

"PILED HIGHER AND DEEPER"

When storing corn, keep it cool. When corn gets warm the sugar tends to convert to starch. In fact, when corn is piled high in the markets and is allowed to stay for days, the bottom ones will be less sweet due to the heat generated by the weight of the ones on top.

The kernels at the tip of corn should be smaller. Larger kernels are a sign of over maturity.

If the kernels are shrunken away from the tip, the corn may be older and not as sweet.

Pop a kernel, the juice should be milky not a clear liquid.

Corn should not be stored more than a few hours after husking and should be refrigerated or cooked as soon as possible.

Never add salt to the cooking water, it toughens the corn.

Steaming corn for 6-10 minutes is one of the preferred cooking methods.

Yellow corn usually taste better than white corn and has a higher vitamin A content.

To store corn longer, cut a small piece off the stalk end, leave on the leaves, then store in a pot with about an inch of water, stems down.

 Chef's Secrets

To cook better tasting corn, add a little milk and sugar to the water.

A food brush will remove silk from corn.

To lighten the color of dark yellow corn, try adding a small amount of vinegar to the boiling water.

CUCUMBERS
Should be long and slender for best quality. Should be a good green color, either dark or light, but not yellow. Purchase only firm cucumbers and refrigerate. Available all year. Large ones are usually not the better ones and may be pithy.

Old cucumbers look shriveled and spongy.

Just For The "Health" Of It

Do not store cucumbers near fruits, many fruit surfaces may contain ethylene gas to enhance ripening and looks. This will cause the seeds to become hard.

Cucumbers have the highest water content of any vegetable and have only 13 calories per 3 1/2oz. serving.

"PICKLED CALORIES"
Dill or sour pickles contain about 3 calories per ounce, but sweet pickles have 30 calories per ounce.

EGGPLANT
Available all year. Best in August and September. Should have smooth, glossy, purple black skin, free of scars and must be firm. Soft eggplants are usually bitter. Keep cool and use in 2-4 days after purchase.

Never eat raw eggplant since it contains the toxin solamine. Solamine is destroyed by cooking.

Varieties of eggplant are Chinese purple, globular, Japanese and Italian Rosa Bianco.

"THE FAT SPONGE"
When eggplants are fried they tend to absorb four times more fat than an equal amount of potatoes. Studies have shown that eggplants will absorb 80 grams of fat in approximately 70 seconds which adds 700 calories to the eggplant. Best not to fry eggplant.

FENNEL
Has a rounded pale green bulb with a short stem and feathery green leaves. Looks like a "fat" bunch of celery. The bulbs should be firm and clean with fresh looking leaves. If any brown spots are seen avoid the fennel. Dries out quickly and should be wrapped and used within 3-4 days.

Fennel can be substituted for celery in all recipes or in salads.

JICAMA
A root vegetable similar to a potato. It has a slightly sweet flavor and is an excellent source of vitamin C. Only 45 calories in 3 ½ ounces.

LEEKS

Purchase between September through November. Tops should be green with white necks 2-3 inches from roots. Do not purchase if tops are wilted or if there appears to be signs of aging. Refrigerate and use within 5-7 days after purchase.

LETTUCE

Available year round. Should be heavy and solid with medium green outer leaves. Inspect for insects. Store in plastic bag in refrigerator. Remove all damaged leaves. Use within 4-6 days. The greener the leaves, the higher the vitamin and mineral content. Romaine is one of the best, while iceberg is the worst.

The outer lettuce leaves can be cooked like any type of green instead of throwing them away. Most are very nutritious except iceberg.

Varieties include:

butterhead	*iceberg*	*looseleaf*	*romaine*	*red oak leaf*
boston	*bibb*	*green leaf*	*stem*	

"OLD WIVES TALE"

Lettuce should always be torn, never cut or the edges will turn brown faster. Can't find out who started this rumor.

Never add salt to a lettuce salad until you are ready to serve it. The salt tends to wilt and toughen the lettuce.

Lettuce will not rust as quickly if you line the bottom of the refrigerator's vegetable compartment with paper towels or napkins. The paper absorbs the excess moisture.

To stop the lettuce from getting rusty, for a longer period of time hit the bottom of the lettuce hard against the counter and remove the core.

Americans eat approximately 11 pounds of lettuce per year, per person.

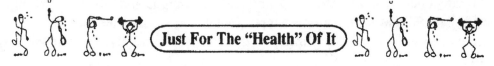

Romaine lettuce has six times as much vitamin C and eight times as much vitamin A as iceberg lettuce.

The greener leaves on the outside of lettuce contain more nutrients than the inner leaves. Try to save as much as possible.

Over 60 chemical agents can be applied to lettuce. Most can be removed by washing, but tests show that some cannot be removed by washing. The EPA can only detect 60% of these chemicals. However, the worst one is Permethrin, which can be reduced or removed totally by washing.

MUSHROOMS

Available year round. Best November through March. Caps should be closed around the stems. Avoid black or brown gills as this is a sign of old age. The tops are more tender than the stems. Refrigerate after purchase and use as soon as possible.

Never immerse mushrooms in a pan of cold water when cleaning, since they will absorb too much water. This will also make it more difficult to cook them, without losing flavor.

Mushrooms contain the same flavor enhancing substance found in MSG, glutamic acid.

Mushrooms are 90% water and do contain some natural toxins. Best not to eat too many raw ones, cooking tends to kill the toxins.

There are 38,000 varieties of mushrooms, some edible, some very poisonous.

"SNIFF, SNIFF, SNIFF"

Truffels grow underground, are an oak or hazel tree fungus and are found by pig or dog sniffing truffellors. There are two types, black and white. They have a distinctive taste and are prized by many chefs in France and Italy. They are very expensive.

A chemical compound extracted from shiitake mushrooms has been approved as an anticancer drug in Japan after it was proven to repress cancer cells in laboratory studies.

 Chef's Secrets

To keep mushrooms white and firm when sauteing them, add a teaspoon of lemon juice to each quarter pound of butter.

If you are not sure of the safety of a mushroom, don't eat it regardless of the following test. However, the experts use the method of sprinkling salt on the spongy part, or the gills. If they turn yellow, they are poisonous, if they turn black they are safe.

Store mushrooms unwashed and covered with a damp paper towel, then place inside a brown paper bag.

OKRA

The pods should be green and tender. Do not buy if the pods look dry or shriveled because they will lack flavor and be tough. Okra spoils quickly and should be refrigerated as soon as possible. Available May through October.

Okra has a flavor between eggplant and asparagus.

Never wash okra until your ready to use it or you will remove a protective coating that keeps the pods from becoming slimy.

ONIONS

Should be hard and dry. Avoid onions with wet necks, this indicates decay. Also, avoid onions that have sprouted. Onions can be stored at either room temperature or refrigerated.

To shed fewer tears when slicing onions, cut the root off last, refrigerate before slicing and peel them under cold water.

When cutting onions, place a piece of bread on the tip of the knife to absorb the fumes.

After slicing onions, wash your hands in cold water, then rub them with salt.

Salt or vinegar will remove onion smells from your hands.

If you chew gum while peeling onions you may not cry. Try it!

Varieties of onions include pearl, yellow globe, Spanish, white globe, boiling, large whites, red globe, shallots and large reds.

If you need only half of an onion, use the top half. The root will stay fresh longer in the refrigerator.

PARSNIPS
A root vegetable with a celerylike nutty flavor. Flavor is best in winter and will have a sweet taste after two weeks storage. Water hemlock is sometimes confused with parsnips since it looks similar but is a poisonous root.

Parsnips are best cooked as they tend to be very fibrous.

PEAS
Pods should be selected that are well-filled without bulging. Do not purchase flabby, spotted or yellow pods. Refrigerate and use within one week.

If you wish to avoid a hangover, remember to take your vitamin and mineral tablets during the period you are drinking. Your body tends to get depleted when you overindulge. The following are the supplements needed to metabolize alcohol: Vitamins B1, B2, niacin, pantothenic acid and biotin. Minerals; iron, zinc, copper, manganese, magnesium and potassium.

Both meats and sugar tend to cause a loss of calcium in the urine.

Remember to take a chewable vitamin C to counteract the effects of nitrites in bacon, lunch meats and hot dogs.

Mushrooms contain hydrazines, a substance that can affect vitamin B6 absorption.

Chocolate contains oxalates and theobromine which effects calcium metabolism and how the body utilizes protein.

Vitamins B and C are destroyed by boiling.
Many vitamins are acidic and are changed into a salt by contact with baking soda.

Chlorine reduces the effectiveness of vitamin C.

One years supply of folic acid (a B vitamin) would fit into 1/6th of a teaspoon.

Raw fish, shellfish, brussel sprouts and red cabbage contain thiaminase which may destroy the vitamin B's. Cooking, however, will inactivate them.

The FDA has taken isolated amino acids off the list of substances, generally regarded as safe (GRAS) saying that they may cause an imbalance of other amino acids and effect their absorption.

Tea and red wine contain tannins which interfere with the utilization of iron, thiamine and B12.

MINERAL INFORMATION, JUST THE FACTS

Iodine

Stimulates the thyroid
A deficiency may cause obesity, sluggish metabolism
needed to utilize fat

Zinc

A constituent of insulin
A constituent of male reproductive fluid
Combines with phosphorus to aid in respiration
Improves vitamin action
Helps food become absorbed through intestinal tract
Essential to nucleic acid metabolism
Used up fast in patients with major burns
Deficiency may be a factor in hardening of arteries

Magnesium

Acts as a starter for some chemical reactions
Sleep promoting material
Keeps you cool and calm
Relaxes your nerves

Manganese

Helps food in the digestive process
Aids in nerve health
Found to be deficient in alcoholism
Works with B vitamins to provide energy

Sodium

Helps maintain a normal water balance
Provides strength to your muscles
Deficiency may cause stomach gas
Helps process amino acids
Assists in the formation of stomach acids
Joins with chlorine to improve blood quality

Molybdenum

Possible role in iron metabolism
Is deficient in dental caries

Chromium

Necessary for normal glucose metabolism
Deficiency may be related to adult diabetes
Deficiency may be caused by excess of white sugar
Often deficient in pregnancies and malnutrition

Copper

Must be present to convert iron into hemoglobin
May prevent general weakness
Deficiencies occur in pregnancies
May prevent impaired respiration

Potassium

Works with sodium to regulate heartbeat
Joins with phosphorus to send oxygen to the brain
Stimulates the kidneys to dispose of body wastes
Deficiency may cause constipation and insomnia

Calcium
Needed for blood clotting
Needed to activate enzymes
Relaxes heart muscle
Prevents osteoporosis
Needed to help transport nerve impulses

Iron
Needed to prevent anemia
Carries oxygen to the brain
Deficiency may be implicated in a poor memory

Cooking not only destroys certain water soluble vitamins, but some of them will bind with other chemicals and then will not be absorbed by the body. Use very little liquid and cook for a short period of time.

A new soft drink that advertises that it contains 25% of your daily vitamin needs, only provides you with the more common vitamins that you could get in the most mediocre diet.

Coffee interferes with iron absorption and tends to leach magnesium out of the body.

Chocolate, cashews, collard greens, beet greens, Swiss chard, spinach, rhubarb and beets contain oxalates which interfere with the ability of the body to absorb calcium.

Vitamin C helps the iron in foods to be absorbed. We normally absorb only 15-30% of the iron in foods.

High doses of vitamin C may not be absorbed at the high level taken. Your body will only metabolize about 200-250mg per hour at the most.

PABA may retard graying hair and has even been known to bring back the original color.

Vitamin E is best absorbed in the intestines in the presence of fat. Best to take with meals containing some fat, even a glass of 2% milk would help.

Americans spend 3.4 billion on nutritional supplements annually.

A report in the Journal of the American Medical Society cited studies that revealed eating excessive amounts of foods high in vitamin A, such as; liver, carrots, etc. may cause headaches and vomiting.

Taking one teaspoon of pure crystalline vitamin C when you awake with 8oz. of water usually results in a bowel movement within 30 minutes.

For white males and black females calcium losses begin at a faster pace than the rest of the population after age 30. For white women, it begins at age 18. Black men seem to be exempt from this problem.

Calcium is best absorbed when taken with meals, since it is absorbed best in an acid environment.

Boron may assist bones to utilize calcium more efficiently. Best sources are prunes, raisins, almonds, peanuts, dates and honey.

Vitamins keep their potency longer if kept in the refrigerator.

Supplements have their highest absorption levels when taken with food.

New studies show that smoking one cigarette can destroy up to 100 milligrams of vitamin C.

Your body will lose vitamin C three times faster if you take aspirin.

Vitamin C helps the body absorb iron.

Calcium and vitamin C should be taken in small doses four times per day for the highest utilization rate.

If you lack vitamin A in your diet, it may lead to a weakened immune system and a loss of vitamin C. Also, adequate vitamin A is necessary to help your body absorb dietary zinc.

A small amount of sugar taken with a calcium supplement will increase the absorption rate.

If you drink soft water you should take a magnesium supplement.

If you are taking more than 500mg. of calcium daily, space out your dosage, it will absorb better and you shouldn't have a constipation problem.

"SOUNDS FISHY, BUT ISN'T"
Sardines are an excellent source of calcium. Three of those little fish supplies approximately 370mg. of calcium, more than 8oz. of milk.

Vitamins A,D,E and K should be taken with food, since they are fat soluble and will be absorbed more efficiently.

Vitamins B and C are water soluble and are absorbed easily in the intestinal tract.

"CHOP, CHOP, SLICE, SLICE, NO,NO"
Cutting or chopping any food high in vitamin C releases an enzyme that can destroy the vitamin. Leave all fruits and vegetables whole or in large pieces until ready to eat when possible.

PMS robs your body of vitamin C. Recommend 250mg. four times per day.

Breast cancer death rates are the highest in areas with the least amount of sunshine. Lack of vitamin D could be the problem.

Beta-carotene is only available from plants, Vitamin A comes from animal sources. Recommend a beta-carotene supplement every other day for antioxidant protection.

Vitamin Robbers

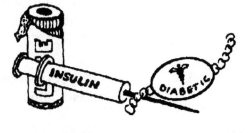

Vitamin A	- Mineral oil, air pollution, antacids, barbiturates, cholesterol lowering drugs.
Vitamin D	- Anti-convulsive drugs, mineral oil, antacids, sedatives, barbiturates, cortisone
Thiamine B1	- Antibiotics, excess heat/cooking, sugar consumption, alcohol, stress, antacids, coffee, raw shellfish.
Riboflavin B2	- Antibiotics, exposure to light, excess heat, alcohol, oral contraceptives, antacids, diuretics.
Niacin	- Antibiotics, sugar consumption, excess heat, alcohol, reduced during illness, diuretics, penicillin.
Pantothenic Acid B5	- Aspirin, methyl bromide.
Pyridoxine	- Aging (after 50), steroid hormones, B6 high blood pressure drugs, excess heat, food processing, antacids, aspirin, cortisone, diuretics, penicillin.

Folic Acid   - Oral contraceptives, stress, anti-convulsants, vitamin C deficiency, barbiturates, diuretics, antibiotics, antacids.

Vitamin B12   - Stress, oral contraceptives, menstruation, colchicine.

Biotin   - Excess heat, antibiotics, sulfa drugs, avidin (in raw egg whites).

Choline   - Sugar consumption, alcohol.

Vitamin C   - Smoking, stress, aspirin, carbon monoxide, alcohol, corticosteroids, diuretics, antihistamines.

Inositol   - Antibiotics.

Vitamin E   - Oral contraceptives, food processing, rancid fats and oils, chlorine.

Vitamin K   - Antibiotics, mineral oil, radiation, anticoagulants, alcohol, phenobarb, sulfonamides, tetracyclines.

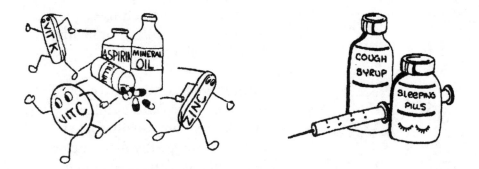

Vitamin C and aspirin should not be taken together, according to studies done at the University of Southern Illinois. The studies indicate that when combined, heavy doses produce excessive stomach irritation, which may lead to ulcers.

Studies by the USDA Human Nutrition Research Center suggests that vitamin C may prevent cataracts.

Processing Of Foods

Exposure To Heat:

Fried Foods - The longer the food is fried and the higher the temperature, the more vitamin and mineral potency is lost. Frying temperatures usually reach 375°F. Corn and safflower oils are best, due to their higher smoke points of 450° to 500°F.

Canned Foods - Nutrient losses occur from blanching and sterilization, which utilizes temperatures of 240°F. or higher for 25-40 minutes.

Frozen Foods - Many are cooked before they are frozen. Higher quality foods are usually sold as fresh. Lower quality foods are used in frozen foods due to their poor appearance.

Dehydrated Foods - Very dependent on the quality of the initial product. Some methods of commercial dehydration may use temperatures of 300°F.

Dairy Products - Many vitamins lose their potency or maybe totally destroyed by the pasteurization process. The homogenization process breaks down the normal-size fat particles, thus allowing the formation of the enzyme "Xanthene Oxidase." A Canadian study has shown that this enzyme may enter the bloodstream and destroy a vital body chemical that ordinarily provides protection for the coronary arteries.

NOTE:
Various nutrients have different degrees of stability under the conditions of processing and preparation. Vitamin A is easily destroyed by heat and light. Vitamin C is not only affected by heat, but also by contact with a variety of metals, such as bronze, brass, copper, cold rolled steel or black iron, found in some types of food processing equipment.

Studies conducted on the canning of foods found that peas and beans lose 75% of certain B vitamins, and tomatoes lose 80% of their naturally occurring zinc.

Exposure To Cold:

Frozen Foods - Freezing may have only minimal effects on vitamin and mineral potency, depending on the methods used and how soon they were frozen in relation to the time they were picked. Remember, the highest quality of foods are sold to restaurants or are sold fresh.

Fresh Fruits And Vegetables - Sometimes harvested before they are ripe, then allowed to ripen on their way to market, either naturally or with a bit of ethylene gas. This may cause a reduction of some of the trace minerals.

NOTE: There are four methods of commercially freezing foods:

(1) *Air Blast Freezing* - Products are frozen by high velocity cold air. This method is the most widely used on all kinds of products.

(2) *Plate Freezing* - The product is placed in contact with a cold metal surface.

(3) *Cryogenic Freezing* - Freezing at very low temperatures (below 100°F.) in direct contact with liquid nitrogen or carbon dioxide. Use for freezing meat patties and other meat products.

(4)   ***Freon Immersion Freezing*** - Utilizes freon to freeze the product instantaneously, thus allowing the product to retain its total weight. Presently, being used to freeze hard-boiled eggs, scrambled egg patties and shrimp. Some foods may retain more nutrients when they are frozen shortly after harvesting. A Stanford University study showed that frozen spinach had 212% more vitamin C than fresh. Frozen brussel sprouts had 27% more vitamin C than fresh.

Quality Of Food Processed:

Fruits And Vegetables - May be affected by genetic differences, climatic conditions, maturity at harvest, or soil variances.

Meat And Poultry - The lowest quality is used for canned goods, frozen foods and TV dinners.

Enrichment And Fortification:

Refining/Replacing Nutrients - Bread and milk are the two most abused products in this area.

Fortification - Vitamin D is added to milk, almost all breakfast cereals are fortified and vitamin C is added to hundreds of products.

NOTE: During processing more vitamin E is lost than any other vitamin. Wheat flour (except the 100% varieties) lose up to 90% of its vitamin E value. Rice cereal products may lose up to 70% of their vitamin E.

Nutrient Depleted Soil:

Soil Problems

Fertilizers - Farmers normally only replace the minerals that are crucial to crop growth, such as phosphorus, potassium and nitrates.

Trace Minerals - The selenium content in soils may vary by a factor of 200 in the United States. A kilogram of wheat may contain from 50mcg-800mcg of selenium depending on where it is grown.

Chromium and zinc are also critically deficient in the soil. This problem is presently under extensive study by the USDA.

NOTE:
Studies performed at Rutgers University by Dr. Firman E. Bear show that some carrots tested for nutrient potency were almost completely without nutrients. This reduction in nutrient potency occurred in carrots from different farms all over the United States.

Dr. William Albrecht at the University of Missouri has shown that over a 10 year period the protein content of grains in the Midwest has declined 11%.

The use of nitrogenous fertilizers is causing copper deficiencies and the overuse of potash fertilizers is creating magnesium deficiencies.

Smoking Effects On Vitamins:

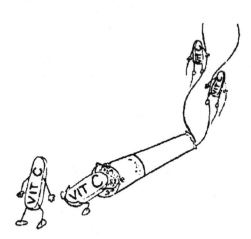

Vitamin C - Studies have shown that smokers require approximately 40% more vitamin C intake than non-smokers to achieve adequate blood levels. Every cigarette reduces bodily stores of vitamin C by about 30mg., which means a pack of cigarettes require at least a 600mg. increase in your vitamin C intake.

Vitamin B12 - Cigarette smoking reduces the blood levels of vitamin B12.

Storage of Foods:

Canned And Packaged Products - Supermarket foods may have an extended stay on the shelves as well as long warehouse times resulting in reduced potencies of vitamins and minerals.

Fruits And Vegetables - Usually are harvested before they are fully ripened then allowed to ripen in the markets. Fruits and vegetables are regularly cut into smaller sizes which expose their surfaces to the effects of light and air (oxidation) for long periods of time, thus reducing their nutrient potency.

Rotation Of Foods - Canned, frozen and packaged products in the home are rarely dated and rotated properly. Dehydrated foods as well, lose a percentage of nutrient potency over time and should be rotated.

Restaurants - Purchase in large quantities, possibly resulting in long storage times, especially if the restaurant is not too busy. Fast food chains avoid this problem due to faster food turnover.

NOTE:

Excess storage times may result in the purchase of foods thought to contain adequate amounts of certain nutrients only to end up with little or none. Oranges from supermarkets have been tested and found to contain no vitamin C content, while a fresh picked one contains approximately 180mg. Vitamin and mineral potency losses may occur before the product receives its expiration code date.

A potato in storage for a period of six months can lose approximately 50% of its vitamin C content. Most food charts will deduct 25% of the nutrient value of foods to allow for the effects of storage, packaging, transportation, processing, preservation and cooking. In some cases this is not enough.

Poorly Balanced Meals:

Meal Planning - Too few people plan their meals in advance. This results in poor combinations of foods, leading to inadequate vitamin and mineral intake.

Restaurants - The majority of these meals are lacking in fruits and vegetables.

Air Pollution:

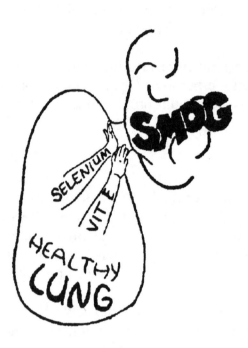

Smog - All major cities in the United States have some form of chemical air pollution. This pollution affect your lung capacity to deliver oxygen efficiently to the cells of the body. The anti-oxidants (vitamins C, A, E, selenium and beta-carotene) may prove to be effective in combating some of the effects of smog.

Smoke - Smoke from cigars, cigarettes and pipes all have a detrimental effect on the oxygen carrying capacity of the red blood cell. Smoke contains carbon monoxide may adhere to the site on the red blood cell that should be carrying oxygen.

Stress:

The Nervous System - The health of nerves and especially their protective sheath depend on an adequate supply of vitamin B.

Stress Tolerance - When under stress bodily needs for vitamin C may increase 100 times.

Dieting:

Endless Programs - Due to the multitude of diet programs available today, it is impossible to relate the nutritional inadequacies found in many of the programs. These programs do not take into consideration the individual life style differences in persons using their methods or products. Supplementation should be recommended in most programs.

Chapter 7

Egg Knowledge

Boil cracked eggs in aluminum foil twisted on the ends.

When making Easter eggs remove an egg that has cracked from boiling water and pour a generous amount of salt over the crack. This will seal the crack and contain the egg white.

There are three grades for eggs: U.S. Grade AA, U.S. Grade A and U.S. Grade B.

When using eggs and solid shortening, break the egg into the measuring cup before measuring the shortening, the shortening will come out easier.

"EGG-SCUSE ME"
In recent studies, egg yolks have less cholesterol than previously thought, and have been revised from 250mg to 200 mg per average yolk.

"BE SOMEWHAT GENTLE"
Egg whites should be beaten in a bowl with a small rounded bottom to reduce the work area and increase the volume.

Weight Of Eggs Per Dozen:

Jumbo..........................30 ounces
Extra Large.................27 ounces
Large..........................24 ounces
Medium.....................21 ounces
Small..........................18 ounces
Pewee.........................15 ounces

Calories:

1 Large Egg.....80 calories
1 Egg White....20 calories
1 Egg Yolk......60 calories

Refrigerator shelf life of an egg is approximately 10-14 days.

To store deviled eggs, place the halves together with the filling and wrap tightly with tin foil, then curl the ends.

Egg will clean off utensils better with cold water then using hot water.

Keep unbroken eggs in a covered bowl because the shells are porous and will absorb odors as well as lose moisture.

Never buy eggs in styrofoam containers, always buy them in paper cartons so that they will be recyclable.

Whole eggs cannot be frozen, the shells will crack as the liquid expands.

Yolks last longer when covered with water.

Egg whites should be kept in a tightly sealed container.

To remove eggs that are stuck to cartons, try wetting the carton.

To insure lasting freshness of eggs, rotate and mark them. If you place a small pencil mark on old eggs you will be certain to identify them and use them before recently purchased eggs.

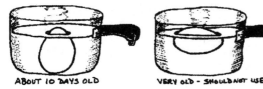

FRESH   3 - 4 DAYS OLD

ABOUT 10 DAYS OLD   VERY OLD - SHOULD NOT USE

To tell how old an egg is place the egg in a pan of cold water if it lies on its side, it's fresh; if it tilts on an angle, it's approximately 3-4 days old; if the egg stands upright, it's probably about 10 days old; if the egg floats to the top, it is old and should not be used.

"TOUGH GUY"

Hard cooked eggs should never be frozen because it changes the taste and texture of the egg.

Add salt to water when hard-cooking eggs, it makes them easier to peel.

"PEEK-A-BOO"

To easily separate egg yolks from whites, poke a small hole in the end of an egg and drain the white through the hole. After you've drained the egg white, just crack the egg open for the yolk.

To tell if an egg is hard boiled or raw, place the egg on it's side and spin it evenly on a level surface. If it wobbles it's raw.

To insure longer lasting freshness, rub oil, butter, or pure glycerin over the whole egg shell.

Never use aluminum bowls or cookware when beating egg whites, eggs tend to darken. Use glass, enamel or stainless-steel.

Dishes with caked on egg should be washed first in cold water which will release the egg protein better than hot water.

"NEW PRODUCT"

An excellent new product called "Just Whites" is a powdered egg white only product which reduces the fat in eggs and can be used in cakes, muffins, meringue and souffles.

"GETTING OLD FAST"

Eggs will age more during one day at room temperature than they will in one week under refrigeration. Eggs will only last 2-3 days without refrigeration.

Always thaw frozen eggs in the refrigerator.

Egg whites become firm at 145 degrees F., yolks at 155 degrees F.

Egg whites contain more than ½ the protein in an egg.

The twisted strands of egg white (chalazae) cords that hold the yolk in place are more prominent the fresher the egg.

The yolk color depends on the chicken's food source.

The yolk contains 3/4 of the eggs calories.

Never buy eggs that are shiney, they are probably old and of poor quality.

"QUACK, QUACK, QUACK"

Duck eggs develop harmful bacteria when they age. This can only be destroyed by boiling the eggs for 10-12 minutes.

For a good plant fertilizer, dry eggshells in the oven then pulverize them in a blender to make bonemeal.

 Chef's Secrets

When you poach eggs, try adding a little vinegar and salt to the water. This will set the eggs and keep them in shape.

When making scrambled eggs, use a small amount of water instead of milk. Milk makes the eggs watery and doesn't blend well. Water makes eggs fluffy.

When freezing eggs, you should always break the yolks. Whites can be frozen alone, yokes can be frozen alone or you can freeze them together. Yolks do not freeze well unless broken. This is also handy when you need just whites for angel food cake.

Remove eggs from the refrigerator at least ½ hour before beating. You will get more volume.

If you are going to whip eggs, they should be approximately three days old and at room temperature for the best results.

Always use fresh eggs for baking projects, the end results will always be better.

When poaching eggs, add a small amount of butter to the tin before placing the eggs in. It will prevent them from sticking and the yolks from breaking. Pan is easier to clean too!

To beat egg whites quicker and fluffier, add a small amount of salt, let them stand until they are room temperature, then beat.

When beating egg whites add a teaspoon of cold water and you will almost double the quantity.

Omelets won't collapse if you add a pinch of cornstarch and a pinch of confectioners sugar to the yolks before folding in the whites.

If you add one teaspoon of vinegar to water when boiling eggs they may not crack.

To guarantee a white film over the eggs when cooking, place a few drops of water in the pan just before the eggs are done and cover the pan.

When you fry eggs try dropping a small amount of flour into the pan to prevent splattering.

If you come up one egg short when baking a cake, substitute two tablespoons of mayonnaise. This will only work for one egg.

Add food coloring to the water before boiling eggs, then you can tell the hard-boiled ones from the raw ones.

To keep the yolks centered, stir the water while cooking hard-boiled eggs. Great for deviled eggs.

An easy way to separate eggs is to place a small funnel over a small measuring cup. Break the eggs into the funnel.

Eggs should always be cooked at low temperature to guarantee a tender white and smooth yolk.

Remove all traces of egg yolk with a Q-tip or edge of a paper towel, before trying to beat egg whites. The slightest trace of yolk will effect the results. Also, make sure your beater blades do not have any vegetable oil on them.

"A LITTLE DIP WILL DO YA"
If you are making a number of omelets or batches of scrambled eggs, try wiping the pan with a piece of paper towel dipped in table salt after three batches. Your results will be much better with less food sticking to the pan.

To make a better omelet or scrambled egg dish, try adding a small amount of water instead of milk when you are beating the eggs. Milk products tend to harden the yolk, while water tends to slow down the coagulation of the yolk.

"NOT SLIPPERY WHEN WET"
When handling eggs or removing them from the carton, try wetting your hands first and they won't slip away.

To remove an egg shell, crack the egg and roll it around in your hands with gentle pressure. You then insert a wet spoon between the shell and the egg white and rotate the egg.

You can substitute 2 egg yolks for 1 whole egg when making custards, cream pie fillings and salad dressings.

You can substitute 2 egg yolks plus 1 teaspoon of water for 1 whole egg in yeast dough or cookies.

Eggs yolks will keep better if you cover them with cold water and keep refrigerated.

Hard-boiled eggs will slice easier if you dip the knife in water before cutting.

There is no difference between white eggs and brown eggs in either nutritional quality or taste.

Measuring Eggs:

1 Large Egg (2 oz.)..................................1/4 cup
1 Medium Egg (1 3/4oz.)........................1/5 cup
1 Small Egg (1 1/2oz.)............................1/6 cup

The best egg shells should be dull not shiny or bright.

Egg sales have dropped 25% since 1984.

In a very fresh egg, the yolk will hardly be visible through the white.

The average hen produces about 200 eggs per year. The laying begins about 5 months after they are hatched.

Dried egg solids have 90% of the water removed.

"EGG KNOWLEDGE"

All egg cartons that are marked "A" or "AA" are not officially graded. Egg cartons must have the USDA grade shield to have been officially graded.

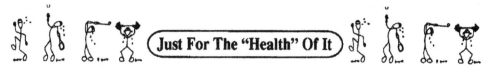

Just For The "Health" Of It

To reduce calories, fat and cholesterol in recipes, use more egg whites and fewer yolks. You won't know the difference.

If an egg has a crack of any kind it is best not to use it.

While eggs contain cholesterol, they also contain lecithin which may provide enough good cholesterol (HDL's) to counteract the bad cholesterol (LDL's).

The FDA regulations now say that eggs must be refrigerated at all times during shipping and when they are stacked in stores.

Because of recent Salmonella outbreaks on the East Coast, the internal temperature of eggs must be kept below 45 degrees Fahrenheit. Never buy eggs unless they are under refrigeration and ideally at a humidity level of 75%.

If eggs are dirty, do not wash before storing. You will remove a protective coating and they won't store as long.

A soft-boiled egg is safe to eat as long as its cooked for 3 ½ minutes. This should raise the temperature of the egg to approximately 140 degrees and will pasteurize it.

Some eggs have been found to contain "microcracks" that may allow harmful bacteria to enter. Cooking will kill these bacteria.

Basted eggs should be cooked for four minutes covered to be safe from bacteria.

The total digestive time for an egg is 4 hours.

The difference in the quality of eggs can be determined by the amount of spread when they are broken. U.S. Grade AA eggs will have a small spread, be thick, very white and have a firm high yolk. U.S. Grade A eggs will have more spread with a less thick white. U.S. Grade B eggs will have a wide spread, little thick white and probably a flat enlarged looking yolk. U.S. Grade C eggs have an even wider spread with a thin watery white.

HEALTH HINT:

After you make hard-boiled eggs, never place them in cool water after they are peeled. Eggs have a thin protective membrane that if removed or damaged and placed in water or a sealed container may allow for bacterial growth to begin.

To cool boiled eggs allow them to remain at room temperature and then refrigerate in an open bowl.

"TURNING GREEN?"
Don't overcook eggs or the yolk may turn a greenish color as a result of the leaching out of an iron compound. Happens more frequently in older eggs and is harmless.

Chapter 8

Cold and Freezing Facts

Do not buy frozen foods unless they are frozen solid and do not contain ice crystals which may be the result of thawing and refreezing..

Keep a frozen food inventory, foods tend to get lost in a large freezer.

Almost 97% of Americans eat ice cream regularly, however, the switch to low-fat yogurt is gaining momentum.

The average American consumes 15 quarts of ice cream annually.

To avoid "freezer burn" and ice crystals forming on foods, wrap the foods with plastic wrap or freezer paper and cover it with tin foil. If your storing foods for an extended period of time also place the packaged food in a sealed baggie.

A high quality ice cream has a butterfat content of 15%.

Frozen sandwiches will thaw by lunchtime, butter the bread and it won't absorb the filling.

Just For The "Health" Of It

Frozen foods are more nutritious than canned foods due to the method of processing.

Make your own frozen TV dinners from leftovers. They will be much higher in nutritional value than most store bought ones.

Date all frozen foods using a piece of tape or permanent marker pen.

"TO FREEZE OR REFREEZE, THAT IS THE QUESTION"

Refreezing foods will lower their quality. When foods are frozen the cellular fluid expands into crystals and causes a break in the cell membrane, disrupting other structures, thus changing the texture of the food. This may alter the taste of the food but does not affect the food safety factor regarding spoilage. Meats are an exception as well as dairy products since bacterial growth starts when they warmup and refreezing may just place the bacteria in a state of animation until the food is thawed out.

Remember the longer you freeze, the better the chances are to lose a percentage of the food quality.

Seal all freezer wrapped foods as well as possible so that freezer burn will not occur, double wrapping will help.

A good trick when you go away on vacation is to place a baggie with a few ice cubes in the freezer. If a power failure occurs while you are gone and the food thaws and then refreezes, you will know about it when you get home.

Baker's yeast will freeze for years without going bad.

If you freeze wild rice it will last for 3-4 months but only a week in the refrigerator.

A corned beef roast can be kept for up to one week in the refrigerator and up to two weeks if frozen.

Always remove meat from store packages and re-wrap using special freezer paper or aluminum foil if you are planning to freeze meats for more than 2-3 weeks.

Chops, cutlets and hamburgers should be freezer wrapped individually. This will assure maximum freshness and convenience.

Brown sugar won't harden if stored in the freezer.

Save the wrappings from sticks of butter or margarine. Keep them in the refrigerator in a plastic bag for future use in greasing baking utensils.

Unsalted butter can be stored in the freezer indefinitely if it is wrapped and sealed airtight. Salted butter can be stored for a shorter period of time in its original container with no wrapping.

Leftover whipped cream; drop dollops of whipped cream on a cookie sheet, then freeze before storing in plastic bags.

Freeze eggs whole or separated. Egg whites may get tough when frozen in a potato or macaroni salad.

Freeze fish in clean milk cartons full of water. When thawing the fish, use the water for fertilizer on household plants.

Flour can be frozen.

Honey can be frozen in ice cube trays. If the honey becomes granulated, simply place the cubes in a jar and place in very hot water.

If ice cream thaws it should not be re-frozen.

Fruits and vegetables should be frozen at their peak of flavor.

The freezer in your refrigerator is not the same as a food freezer. It is best used for storing foods for short periods only. Foods should be frozen as quickly as possible and temperatures should be 0 degrees Fahrenheit or below.

Jelly, salad dressing and mayonnaise do not freeze well on bread products.

When freezing casseroles, cook for a shorter period of time than normal, then cool quickly to stop cooking action. Make sure it is packed as solidly as possible, the fewer air spaces the better.

To prolong the freezer storage time for roasted meats, cover them with gravy.

Meat loaf may be frozen cooked or uncooked.

Freezer Temperature Changes And Their Effects On Foods:

Freezer Temperature	Quality Changes After
30°	5 Days
25°	10 Days
20°	3 Weeks
15°	6 Weeks
10°	4 Months
5°	6 Months
0°	1 Year

Potatoes will become mushy when frozen in stews or casseroles. Their cells are high in water content and break easily when frozen.

Any bakery item with a cream filling should not be frozen. They will become soggy.

Custard or meringue pies do not freeze well. The custard tends to separate and the meringue will become tough.

Mashed potatoes freeze well.

Waffles and pancakes may be frozen, then thawed and cooked in the toaster.

Freezer Storage Times At Zero Degrees Fahrenheit

MEATS

Food	Months
Beef, Lamb	6 - 12
Chops, Cutlets, Beef Hamburger	3 - 5
Ground Pork	1 - 3
Sausage	1 - 2

Bacon (unsliced)	3 - 5
Bacon (sliced)	< 1
Fish	3 - 6
Ham	3 - 4
Liver	3 - 4
Poultry	4 - 6
Giblets	3
Duck, Goose	5 - 6
Rabbit	9 - 12
Shrimp or shellfish (cooked)	2 - 3
Turkey	6 - 8
Hot Dogs	2 - 3
Luncheon Meats (ready to eat)	0

DAIRY PRODUCTS

Milk	< 2 weeks
Ice Cream	2 - 4 weeks
Cream (40%)	3 - 4
Eggs (not in shell)	7 - 10
Margarine	2 - 4
Butter	2 - 4
Cheddar Cheese	5 - 6
Frozen Milk Desserts (commercial)	1

FRUITS

Apples (sliced)	10 - 12
Apricots	10 - 12
Berries	11 - 12
Cherries (sour)	12

Chapter 9

Let's Not Chew The Fat

JUST THE NITTY GRITTY

Polyunsaturated Fats: This type remains liquid at room temperature. sunflower, safflower and corn are examples and tend to lower cholesterol levels in some studies.

Monounsaturated Fats: These are still liquid at room temperature but thicken when refrigerated. Examples are found in avocados, olive oil, rapeseed, and many nuts. Recent studies are showing that they may tend to lower cholesterol levels, especially olive oil and Canola oil.

Saturated Fats: These are either solid or semi-solid at room temperature. Examples are butter, hard margarine, lard and shortening. Exceptions to the rule are coconut and palm oils, which have very high saturated fat levels. They tend to raise the cholesterol levels in the body.

To make a creamy salad dressing, try pouring olive oil very slowly into a running blender containing the other ingredients.

An empty detergent or ketchup bottle will make it easier to add cooking oil to pans.

Olive oil needs no refrigeration and will keep longer than any other type of oil.

To remove the fat from drippings, just pour them into a tall narrow glass, leave it for 10 minutes, then remove the layer of fat.

The best quality oil is "Extra Virgin Oil." It is made from the finest plump olives, has the best flavor and is the least processed. Next is "Virgin Oil" then "Pure Olive Oil" which is a blend of both Extra Virgin and Virgin Oils.

Extra virgin olive oil contains less than 1% acidity, virgin olive oil contains 1 ½-3% acidity. The less acidity, the better the quality of the oil. Many oils must have neutralizing agents added to them to reduce their level of acidity.

Oil and vinegar will mix well together in solution if you add the contents of 1-2 lecithin capsules.

To eliminate the fat from soups, refrigerate the soup until the fat hardens on the top, then just remove.

If your recipe requires that you cream shortening with a sugary substance, try adding a few drops of water to the mixture to make it easier.

From preventing a cooking wine from going sour, try adding a tablespoon of vegetable oil to the bottle.

"THE FAT SPONGE"
When you are broiling meats, place a few pieces of dried bread in the broiler pan to soak up the dripping fat. This will eliminate the smoking fat and also reduces the risk of the fat catching fire.

When creaming butter, cut it up in small pieces to give the mixer a better chance to do the job right.

To test whether hot oil is still usable, drop a piece of white bread into the pan. If the bread develops dark specs, the oil is deteriorating.

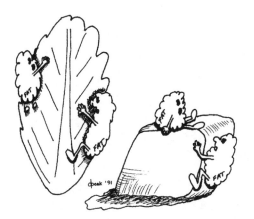

You could also wrap the ice cubes in a piece of cheesecloth or paper towel and just skim it over the top.

Another good way to remove fat is to use lettuce leaves. Place a few in the pot, the fat will cling to them, then just remove them. This is a very efficient method.

Never allow oil to heat to the smoke point, as it may ignite. It will also make food taste bitter and may irritate your eyes. The oils with the highest smoke points are Canola, safflower and corn oil.

The best butter is U.S. Grade AA which is made from fresh sweet cream. U.S. Grade A is close to AA but has a lower flavor rating. U.S. Grade B is usually made from sour cream. The milk-fat content of butter must be at least 80%.

A Fat Packed Meal

Total Calories		Calories From Fat
252	Hamburger	165
95	Bun	17
110	Cheese Slice	80
125	Special Sauce	100
115	Potato Chips	75

Olive oil is one of the best fats to use in salads or for low temperature cooking, for example in a Wok. It has a low smoke point and when used for higher temperature cooking, add a teaspoon of canola oil to it to raise the smoke point. This trick is also good to use with butter when your using it for cooking. Some studies have shown olive oil to lower cholesterol levels.

Most margarines contain over 90% fat. Diet margarines usually contain 80% fat, 16% water, 2% salt and 2% non-fat milk solids, and don't forget the colorings and additives. Margarines are naturally white. A liquid diet margarine, however, may contain as low as 40% fat.

Margarine has been found to contain a substance called trans-acids. If you use margarine, use the softest diet you can buy (more air and water) or my recommendation is whipped unsalted butter. Used in moderation the cholesterol content is not that high in 5-7 pats per week.

Do not save cooking oils or bacon drippings. The more these fats are re-cooked the higher the percentage of trans-acids. There are two forms of fats, cis and trans. When you first use an oil, the majority of the fat is of the good (cis) variety, but as it is heated a percentage changes to a potentially harmful substance, called a trans-acid.

"REMEMBER WHEN"
When grandmother fried foods she used to place a peeled potato into the oil to clean out the debris, swish it around remove it and throw it away. The oil was then placed into the freezer for use at a later date. After one using the oil was almost solid trans-fatty acids and the worst product we could put into our bodies.

Lard comes from the abdomen of pigs. Used in chewing gum bases, shaving creams, soaps and cosmetics. Future testing may implicate it in shortened life-spans and a factor in osteoporosis.

Most pork and trout contain approximately 40% fat calories.

Some of the highest fat crackers are Ritz, Town House and Goldfish which contains approximately 6 grams of fat per ounce.

Mayonnaise must contain at least 65% oil by weight. If it contains less, its called salad dressing.

"CAN'T WIN"
Most fat-free mayonnaise contains more sodium than the "real" mayonnaise.

A tablespoon of mayonnaise contains only about 5-10mg. of cholesterol. Very little egg yolk is really used in the product.

"PIG IN A BLANKET"
Pancakes wrapped around sausages on a stick delivers 60% of its calories from fat.

Leaf lard comes from the area of the kidneys in pigs. It is a higher quality than other types of lard.

Pates are bordered with pork fats from the flank of the pig.

The harder the margarine, the higher the percentage of saturated fat it contains. Saturated fat is still guilty of helping the body produce more cholesterol than you need.

From 1963 to 1985, the incidence of skin cancer has doubled to over 300,000 cases per year. Dietary fats are being implicated as one of the key factors.

Refined corn oil is a chemical extraction, a triglyceride with no relationship to the nutrients in a "real" ear of corn. The vitamins that would normally assist with the assimilation of the corn oil such as vitamin E, are absent.

Polyunsaturated fatty acids can cause premature wrinkling of the skin and can possibly be a factor in premature aging as well.

"AIN'T SCIENCE WONDERFUL"

If the list of ingredients lists an oil as "hydrogenated," the product is probably high in saturated fats. Hydrogenation is the process of adding water to the fat, the oil picks up the hydrogen atoms and it makes the fat more saturated and harder.

Always purchase oils in dark-colored or tin containers to avoid any rancidity problem.

Diets high in total fat have been related to cancer of the colon, the prostate and the breast.

High fat diets may reduce the efficiency of the immune system.

Young chickens and turkeys have less fat.

Every ounce of fat contains 250% more calories than an ounce of carbohydrate or protein.

Use buttermilk for baking, pancakes and especially mashed potatoes. Buttermilk is low-fat.

Fats should be included in all dietary plans, even those for weight control. Your body requires the "essential fatty acids."

A person can survive very nicely on only 5% fat in their diet, the right fats, of course.

Approximately 10 grams of fat is cleared from the stomach per hour. Two scrambled eggs, bread and butter, coffee and milk = 50 grams of fat. Assimilation time is 5-6 hours.

"AND AWAY IT GOES"

A high fat intake can cause calcium and vitamin C losses through the urine.

Butter will go farther and have fewer calories per serving if you beat it well. This increases the volume by adding air.

75% of the calories in bacon come from fat, the same amount that comes from cheddar cheese.

"OINK, OINK"
Americans spend $3 billion a year on bacon.

Most non-dairy creamers are made from coconut oil, which is very high in saturated fats. Mocha Mix is your best bet.

Rapeseed oil (Canola) for years has been grown as a forage crop for animals in the United States. Originally it was banned in the U.S. when imports from Canada showed high levels of erucic acid. However, new varieties have shown to contain lower acid levels and is now being produced and sold in large quantities. It is higher in monounsaturated fat and has a high smoke point, making it the preferred oil for frying.

Current studies show that if your body is higher in "brown fat" rather than "white fat," your fat is of the more active type and be able to control your weight better. These studies are now being conducted at Harvard Medical School.

Fats from beef should be from very lean cuts with all visible fat removed. Lean veal and lamb are permissible. Poultry should have all fat and skin removed, no duck or goose. Fish should be baked or broiled.

Most fats should be consumed either at breakfast or lunch, few, if any, for dinner. High fat meals during the evening hours may cause the digestive system to overwork while you are sleeping, causing restless sleep patterns.

Most butters and margarines contain about the same amount of saturated fats.

Doughnuts and cakes add a high amount of saturated fat to your diet. It is best to make these yourself and put lower fat ingredients in them.

"YOLKS AWAY"

To reduce fat when preparing omelets, discard every other yolk this will reduce the fat and cholesterol levels and you will never know the difference.

More soy oil is sold in the U.S. than any other kind of oil.

Cottonseed oil is 25% saturated fat and not the best to use.

Soy oil changes in flavor, the longer it is stored, due to the changes in the linolenic acid it contains.

64% of the calories in caviar are from fat.

Butter will absorb refrigerator odors and should be stored covered.

Butter stores in the refrigerator for only two weeks. If longer time is needed, freeze it.

One pound of butter = 2 cups.

If a recipe calls for butter, you may be able to replace it with a solid shortening, measure for measure. The water in the butter will balance off the air in the shortening.

Eight ounces of potato chips is the equivalent of eating 12-20 teaspoons of fat.

Try using water instead of fat in recipes. Fat does make dressings, etc. feel smooth to the taste, but if you thicken water with flour, cornstarch or potato starch it will save you calories.

Oils should be stored in opaque containers and placed in a dark, cool location to reduce the risk of rancidity.

"WHY CAROB?"
When carob is made into candy, fat is added for texture which brings the fat content closer to real chocolate. In fact, cocoa butter use in real chocolate is 60% saturated fat while the fat in carob candy is 85% saturated in most cases.

Using non-stick cookware and spraying with a vegetable spray will help lower fat intake.

Never eat a salad dressing or mayonnaise-based salad unless you are sure it has been refrigerated until just before you are ready to eat it. This causes thousands of cases of food poisoning yearly.

An 8oz. bag of potato chips contains approximately 6 tablespoons of fat.

The oils associated with fish are more beneficial than those associated with meats. Fish contain a high percentage of omega 3 fatty acids.

Any margarine containing coconut or palm oil will be very high in saturated fat. New labeling now calls them "tropical oils."

===

New fat substitutes are appearing in our foods, be aware that these are still synthetically produced and not a "natural" food. They should not be viewed as a panacea to replace the fats in our diet.

1. **Olestra** - *Procter & Gamble.* "This product has been approved by the FDA and is now available." No-cal fat substitute. Chemical name; *sucrose polyester.* It is a combination of sugar and soybean or other oil. The molecule is so large and dense that our enzymes that normally breakdown fat don't recognize it and it just passes through the body. The product will be sold in the following forms: 35% of a cooking oil or shortening, 75% of oils used in deep fat frying in restaurants and 75% of oils used in salted snacks.

2. Simplesse - As of January 1995 this fat substitute is being used in over 24 products. Originally it was made of egg whites and skim milk but is now being made from whey, a milk protein, and is a good quality product. Contains a few calories. Looks like mayonnaise and can be made as thick or thin as desired. Products seen on the market using Simplesse are for the most part salad dressings and frozen desserts.

3. Oatrim - (Trim Choice) made from oat flour is a carbohydrate now being used as a fat substitute. It was developed in 1993 by the USDA. It may also be called "hydrated oat flour." It adds a creamy fat-like texture to foods and is good for baking. Contains only 1 calorie per gram compared to fat at 9 calories per gram.

The best butter is made from U.S. Grade AA sweet cream.

One ounce of sunflower seeds contains 160 calories and is not a "diet" snack food.

A burrito topped with sour cream and guacamole may be as high as 1,000 calories and 59% fat.

Recent studies have shown that stearic acid one of the saturated fats has little effect on raising cholesterol levels. We are finding out more about which specific fats will raise cholesterol and which foods to avoid.

"AS THE COOKIE CRUMBLES"
Reduced fat oreo cookies contains 47 calories and 1.67 grams of fat. The original cookie has 53 calories and 2.33 grams of fat. Not a big savings.

"LET'S PULL THE WOOL OVER"
The new reduced-fat peanut butter has the same number of calories per serving as regular peanut butter, approximately 190 per serving, sweeteners were added in place of the fat.

When oils are refrigerated and become cloudy, it is due to the buildup of harmless crystals. Manufacturers will sometimes pre-chill the oils and remove the crystals in a process known as "winterizing." These oils will remain clear when refrigerated.

Salad and cooking oil use:

>
> 1909 - 1.5 pounds per person
> 1972 - 18 pounds per person
> 1990 - 29 pounds per person
> 1994 - 32 pounds per person

Margarine use:

> 1950 - 6 pounds per person
> 1972 - 11 pounds per person
> 1990 - 16 pounds per person
> 1994 - 18 pounds per person

Lard has large crystals and butter small ones. This has a lot to do with the texture of the fat and is controlled during the processing. Crystal sizes can be altered by agitating the oil when it is cooling.

Studies have shown that dieters miss fat more than sweets.

Persons who consume a high fat diet are more prone to colon cancer, prostate cancer and breast cancer. Studies in the future may show that there is also a detrimental effect on the immune system.

The average American diet is about 44% fat. Dietary guidelines suggest no more than 30% of total calories. My recommendation is no more than 25% or less. Your intake should lean more toward the polyunsaturates and monounsaturates with a maximum amount of fat from saturated fat at 10% or less of the 25%

Recent studies show that the percentage of fats vary in different foods that we associate with high fat content. The following are the results:

Potato Chips...................... 40%
Cheese Puffs...................... 39%
Corn Chips........................ 37%
Tortilla Chips.................... 24%
Doughnuts......................... 22%
Fried Chicken..................... 18%
French Fries...................... 14%
Fried Fish........................ 10%

Rating the oils by percentage of saturated fats from best to worst:

Canola........safflower.......sunflower.......corn......olive.......soybean.......peanut....... margarine........ palm oil........butter.........coconut oil.......

There are 312 fats and oils that can be used for frying.

"WHERE'S THE FAT?"....."HERE'S THE FAT"

Most of us never realize how much fat we really do eat. The following information will help you become more aware of the higher fat foods. We rarely think of fat in "teaspoons," but you may find it easier to comprehend when presented in this form.

<u>MEATS/FISH</u>

Hot Dog/All Beef	1 medium	2 ½ teaspoons
Bologna	1 slice	2 teaspoons
Big Mac	1	7-9 teaspoons
Turkey Pot Pie	12 oz	6 teaspoons
Sirloin TV Dinner	1 medium	7 teaspoons
Ham TV Dinner	1 medium	3 teaspoons
Chicken TV Dinner	1 medium	7 teaspoons
Lean Beef	3 oz	2 teaspoons
Medium-Fat Beef	3 oz	4 ½ teaspoons
Chicken Breast/No Skin	4 oz	1 teaspoon
Chicken Breast/Skin	4 oz	2 ½ teaspoons
Fried Oysters	1 serving	3 ½ teaspoons
Trout/Raw	3 ½ oz	3 teaspoons
Bacon	1 strip	1 1/4 teaspoons
Canadian Bacon	1 strip	1 teaspoon
Hamburger	1/4 pound	3 ½ teaspoons
Frog Legs	2 large	2 ½ teaspoons
Ham/Lean	2 slices	1 1/4 teaspoons
Pork Chop	3 ½ oz	6 ½ teaspoons
Veal Cutlet	3 ½ oz	4 teaspoons
Duck/Roasted	3 ½ oz	7 teaspoons
Goose	3 ½ oz	5 ½ teaspoons
Rabbit	3 ½ oz	1 ½ teaspoons
Squab	3 ½ oz	5 ½ teaspoons
Turkey	3 ½ oz	2 teaspoons
Lobster Newburg	3 ½ oz	2 ½ teaspoons
Salmon/Canned	3 ½ oz	3 ½ teaspoons

"EDUCATION STILL LACKING"

Americans consumed 53 pounds of fats and oils per person in 1970. In 1994 we consumed 65 pounds, this is not the direction we should be going.

Chapter 10

Cheese Facts

Cheese making is fast becoming the latest "yuppie" fad.

To keep cheese moist, wrap it in a soft cloth wrung out of vinegar and keep in an earthen jar with the cover slightly raised.

When too much fat is removed from cheese, it may have a rubbery texture. The fat in cheese gives it the smooth texture we prefer. Cheeses that are the exceptions, like ricotta, camembert and brie have a higher water content, and a low fat content.

Most cheese substitutes are produced from soybean vegetable fat.

The higher the water content of cheeses, such as cottage cheese, the faster they tend to go bad. Cottage cheese lasts for only three weeks after it is produced. Remember to store it upside down and mix the liquid (whey) back in.

Cheddar cheese is so low in moisture that it can last for years. However, it will get a stronger taste as it ages. Low-fat cheeses do not have a long shelf life due to their increased water content. Your just paying for more water.

Grate small bits of cheeses that are leftover to get variety. Makes a great topping for salads and casseroles.

100 grams of cheese = 25 grams of protein.

The average woman needs 46 grams of protein per day, the average man 56 grams.

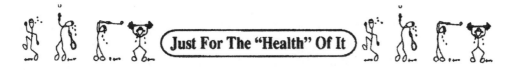

Just For The "Health" Of It

It takes 8 pounds of milk to make one pound of cheese. One ounce (average slice) of cheese = as much fat and protein as one cup of milk. Also, it is a concentrated source of cholesterol and saturated fat.

The cheese industry has developed numerous methods of changing a good quality product into a chemical smorgasbord. While most cheeses are naturally white (not yellow), the industry has resorted to a variety of artificial chemicals to make cheeses "more appealing" to us visually.

The following is just a partial list of these chemicals that are used to give cheese their sharp taste, to color them, to make them smell more appealing or to thicken them. They include: malic acid, tartaric acid, phosphoric acid, alginic acid, aluminum potassium phosphate, diacetyl, sodium carboxymethyl cellulose, benzyl peroxide and certain yellow dyes.

While all these chemicals have been approved by the appropriate federal agencies, we are told that in small quantities, they are harmless. However, if they are so harmless why are most of them still under further investigation?

These same chemicals that are used to alter cheeses are used for making cement, bleaching clothes, producing cosmetics and even rust-proofing metals.

 Cheese is an excellent food but you should be more aware of the kinds of cheeses to choose from. Try to purchase cheeses made from "part-skim milk," "low-fat milk" "non-fat milk" and are labeled "natural." Also, try to find one that says that it contains "no preservatives or additives."

An ounce of cream cheese may contain as much as 110 calories. True, it does have fewer calories than butter for a comparable weight, but we use more

Try to choose from low-sodium and reduced-fat cheeses. New varieties seem to be appearing weekly.

A recent dental study showed that a number of cheeses will actually help to prevent cavities. These include; Romano, Muenster, Gouda, Swiss, Edam, Monterey Jack, Tilsit, Port du Salut, processed American cheese singles and aged Cheddar.

Moldy cheese may contain a harmful toxin (aflatoxin), especially gorgonzola, blue cheese and roquefort.

If a cheese is "natural" the name of the cheese will be preceded by the word "natural" or will not have anything preceding the name of the cheese.

One cup of grated cheese is made from 1/4 pound of cheese.

The wax coating on cheeses will protect it. If there is an exposed edge try covering it with butter to keep the cheese moist and fresh.

Cottage cheese will remain fresher for a longer period of time if you store it upside down in the refrigerator. When this book was being researched we noticed that many chefs keep a number of different products upside down if they will move in the container. Slows the effects of oxidation.

To keep cheese longer without it forming mold, place a piece of paper towel that has been dampened with white vinegar in the bottom of a plastic container that has a good seal before adding the cheese.

Another way to prevent mold from forming on cheese is to store the cheese in a sealed container with two lumps of sugar.

Soft cheeses can be grated using a metal colander and a potato masher.

Dishes with cheese should be cooked slower to avoid curdling and stringiness.

A dull knife works better to cut cheese. Warm the knife and the cheese will cut like butter.

Yellow cheese: 71% of the calories are fat, 39% is saturated fat.

Dried out cheese (without mold) should be saved and grated, then used for cooking.

The U.S. is the leading producer of cheese in the world. Wisconsin is the leading state.

There are approximately 800 varieties of cheese in the world. The U.S. produces 200 of them.

Ripening Classifications

Unripened   These are consumed shortly after manufacture. One of the most common is cottage cheese, a high moisture soft cheese. Unripened low-moisture cheeses are Gjetost and Mysost.

Soft   Curing will progress from the outside or rind of the cheese, toward the center. Specific molds or cultures of bacteria which grow on the surface of the cheese assist in the specific characteristic flavors, body and texture. These cheeses contain a higher amount of moisture than semi-soft cheeses.

Semi-Soft   These cheeses ripen from the inside as well as from the surface. Curing will continue as long as the temperature is favorable. These are higher in moisture than firm-cheeses.

Firm   Ripen, utilizing a bacterial culture
                    throughout the whole cheese. Ripening occurs
                    as long as the temperature is favorable.
                    Lower in moisture than the softer varieties
                    and usually require a longer curing time.

Very Hard   Cured with the aid of a bacterial
                    culture with enzymes. Slow cured and
                    very low-moisture and contains a higher
                    salt content.

Blue-Vein   Curing is with the aid of mold bacteria and a
                    specific mold culture that will grow
                    throughout the inside of the cheese and produces
                    the familiar appearance and unique flavor.

Most Popular Cheeses

Blue (Bleu)   - Noted for its white and blue-streaked
                    markings, blue cheese has a soft and
                    often crumbly texture. Available in
                    various shapes. 1 ounce = 40 calories.

Brick   - A softer, yellow cheese available in
                    slightly soft-medium firm texture.
                    Commonly available in sliced, and brick
                    forms.

Brie   - Has an outer edible white coating, and
                    a mild-strong creamy inside. Originally
                    from France, brie is available in
                    wedge and round shapes.

Camembert   -Reputed to be the favorite cheese of
Napoleon, Camembert has a soft, yellow
inside. It's outer coating is also edible and is
usually a grayish-white color. This cheese takes
from 4-8 weeks to ripen.

Cheddar   -Normal color is white to medium-yellow.
Mild to very sharp taste. Firm smooth
texture. Comes in numerous shapes and
originated in England. 1 ounce =
105 calories. Artificial color is
usually added to make it more yellow.

Cheshire   -A semi-firm, mild creamy cheese, loosely
textured and crumbly. The flavor of red
and white are similar. The red is colored
with natural vegetable dye from the
seeds of the annatto tree and is the most
expensive. They ripen within a few weeks.
Ideal for Welch rarebit.

Colby   -A white to medium-yellow-orange cheese.
Has a mild to mellow flavor and has a
soft texture similar to cheddar. It is
available in cylindrical, pie-shaped
wedges. Originated in the U.S.

Coldpack   -Fresh and aged cheeses with whey
Cheese Food solids added. Mild flavor
and is very spreadable. Numerous
flavorings are added.

Cottage   -Made from cow's skimmed milk, plain
Cheese   cured or plain cured with cream. Soft
texture. Originated in the U.S. If you
see "curd by acidification" on the
label, don't buy it. Look for a more
natural one.

Cream Cheese   -Made with cream or concentrated milk. Very soft and spreadable. Never buy a cream cheese if it contains the chemical propylene glycol alginate.   Does not provide a good source of protein.

Edam   -Creamy yellow or medium yellow-orange cheese with a surface coating of red wax. Has a mellow nut-like flavor. Semi-soft to firm texture with small irregular shaped round holes. Milkfat content is lower than Gouda. Usually available in a cannonball shape. Imported cheeses will usually be free of additives, domestic varieties are not. Originated in the Netherlands.

Feta   -A curd cheese which is set in a very concentrated salt solution. Made from either goat's or sheep's milk. A sharp, salty cheese and usually found chemical-free.

Farmers Cheese   -Similar to cottage cheese and pot cheese but is pressed into a block form. Usually free of preservatives if bought in bulk from a Deli.

Gjetost   -Golden brown colored cheese with sweet caramel flavor. Made from whey or goat's milk. Has a firm buttery consistency. Available in cubes or rectangular pieces. Originated in Norway.

Gorgonzola   - Has a creamy white inside, mottled or streaked with blue-green ribbons of mold and a clay-colored surface. Has a tangy, peppery flavor and a semi-soft crumbly texture. Similar to Blue cheese. If made from goat's milk, it will be best.

Gouda   -A creamy yellow or medium yellow-orange cheese that usually has a red wax coating and a nutlike flavor. Semi-soft to firm texture. Higher fat content than Edam cheese. Contains small irregular shaped or round holes. Comes in a bell shape with flat top and bottom.

Gruyere   -A variation of Swiss cheese, but usually without the use of bleached milk making it higher in vitamin content. If mold inhibitors are added, the information will be on the label.

Limburger   -Has a creamy white interior and a reddish yellow surface. It is a highly pungent cheese with a very strong flavor. Ripens in 4-8 weeks and has a soft, smooth texture. Originated in Belgium.

Mozzarella   -A creamy white cheese made from whole or partly skimmed milk with a firm texture. Available in small round, shredded or in slices. Preservatives may be added in "low moisture" varieties. Originated in Italy.

Muenster

-Has a creamy white inside and a yellow tan surface. Mild to mellow flavor with a semi-soft texture. Contains more moisture than brick cheese. Available in wedges, blocks and circular cakes. Originated in Germany.

Mysost

-A light brown cheese with a sweet caramel flavor with a buttery consistency. Available in cubical, cylindrical and pie shaped wedges. Originated in Norway.

Neufchatel

-A white cheese with a mild acidic flavor. Has a smooth texture similar to cream cheese but lower in milkfat. Originated in France.

Parmesan

-Creamy white cheese with a hard granular texture and sharp piquant taste. It has less of a moisture content and a lower milkfat level than Romano. May be made from partially skimmed milk and may be bleached. Best to buy ungrated and grate yourself for a much better flavor. Originated in Italy.

Pasteurized Processed Cheese

-A blend of fresh and aged cheese which has a constant flavor after it has been processed. They melt easily and are used for cheeseburgers, etc.

Pasteurized Processed Cheese Food

-A blend of cheeses to which milk or whey have been added. Has a lower cheese and fat content. Soft texture and a milder flavor than regular processed cheeses due to a higher moisture content. 1 ounce = 90 calories.

Port du Salut -A creamy yellow cheese with a mellow to robust flavor. Has a buttery texture with small holes. Comes in wedges or wheels. Originated in France.

Pot Cheese -This is a similar cheese to cottage cheese, but is drier and never creamed. It is usually made without salt and additives.

Provolone -Has a light creamy interior with a light brown or golden yellow surface. The flavor is mellow and has a smooth texture. May have coloring added and is usually salted or smoked. It may also be produced from bleached milk which will reduce the vitamin potencies. Originated in Italy.

Ricotta -A normally white cheese with a somewhat sweet, nutlike flavor. Usually made from cow's milk, whole or partially skimmed with or without whey and resembles cottage cheese.

Romano -A yellow-white cheese with a greenish-black surface and a sharp flavor. It has a hard granular texture and is available in wedges or grated. Similar to Parmesan but made with whole milk giving it a higher fat content. May contain a number of preservatives. The best is made from sheep's milk. Originated in Italy.

Roquefort   -Has a white creamy interior and may be marbled or streaked with bluish veins of mold. Usually made of sheep's milk and has a peppery flavor with a semi-soft crumbly texture. It is available in wedges and is usually free of additives. Originated in France.

Stilton   -Has a creamy white inside with streaks of blue-green mold. Made with cow's milk and milder than Gorgonzola or Roquefort. The texture is semi-soft and is more crumbly than Blue cheese. Available in wedges and oblongs. Originated in England.

Swiss   -A light yellow cheese that has a sweet nut-like flavor and a smooth texture with a variety of different size holes. It has a good firm texture and is available in rectangular forms and slices. Originated in Switzerland. May use bleached milk to give it the yellow color. This will reduce the vitamin content. 1 ounce = 105 calories.

Tilsit   -Has ivory to yellow semi-soft interior. Made from raw milk and ripened for about five months. 30-50% fat. Originated in Germany.

Chapter 11

Meat Facts

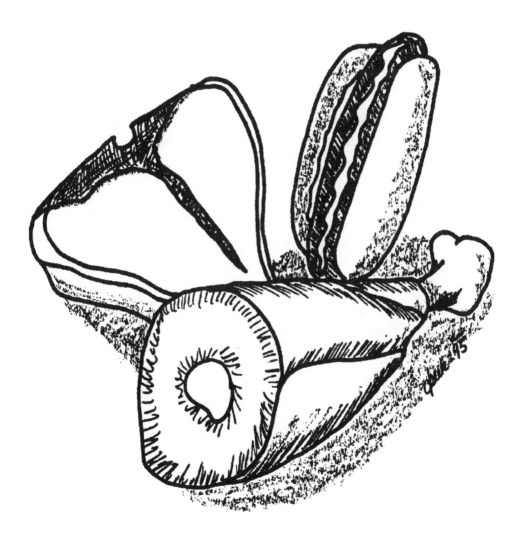

"DON'T BE THE EARLY BIRD WHO GETS THE WORM"

Only 1 in 1000 pigs are now found to contain the trichinosis parasite. However, I would still cook pork to an internal temperature of 160 degrees F. The parasite is killed at 137 degrees.

"EFFICIENCY EXPERT INFO"

Pigs are not an efficient source of protein. They require almost 8 pounds of grain and soy to produce 1 pound of meat. Cows require about 7 pounds and chickens less than 3 pounds.

"REAL BUMMER"

There are 1.3 billion head of cattle worldwide, which consume a third of the world's grain.

A BURGER BY ANY OTHER NAME

Argentina
Burgers are boiled and served with a fried egg on top of a piece of pumpernickel bread.

Germany
The ground beef is mixed with pieces of wet bread, onions, mustard and of course an egg has to be added.

Switzerland
Burgers are served American style but are always eaten with a knife and fork. Very civilized!

Korea
Add a unique touch of their own, kimchee, a mixture of pickled cabbage and very hot peppers.

Sweden
Burgers are called "pannbiff" which is beef mixed in a brown sauce with fried onions and of all things lingonberry preserves. Try it, you might like it!

A 4oz. serving of meat reduces to 3oz. after cooking, so plan accordingly.

Sweetbreads are a calf's thymus gland which helps the animal fight disease and disappears six months after they are born. Three ounces contain 21 grams of fat.

The latest 1994 statistics show that Americans love their beef. 91% eat beef regularly and the beef industry spends $42 million each year on advertising.

Americans consume approximately 11 ounces of meat per day, that calculates to approximately 250 pounds of beef annually, more than any other country in the world. The Japanese only eat 2 ounces of meat daily or approximately 46 pounds of beef annually.

Searing meat will not "lock in juices." It will, however, provide a crusty brown covering which is tasty.

Father's Day is the biggest beef eating day of the year, with over 80 million pounds consumed.

"WANTED, COW MASSEUR"
The Japanese are producing the world's most expensive beef. Kobe beef cattle are fed a diet of soybeans and beer and even given a daily massage. Kobe beef has 2-3 times the fat of prime U.S. beef.

Fall is the best time to find lower beef prices.

Meat grinders and cutting boards should be washed thoroughly after each use. Bacteria grows very quickly and may contaminate the next food.

"DON'T FENCE ME IN"
If you are troubled by meats turning grey when cooking, try cooking a smaller quantity the next time in the same size pot. Excess steam generated by overcrowding is the problem.

"RUDOLPHS IN TROUBLE"
Reindeer meat should be avoided if imported from Finland due to radiation contamination as a result of the 1986 Chernobyl nuclear disaster.

When buying meat, figure the cost per pound, a boneless cut usually cost less per serving.

To make a fatty roast look better, try refrigerating it after its cooked or until the fat solidifies, then remove the fat, baste and cook until re-heated.

Hamburgers will cook faster if you make a few punctures in them before cooking. This allows the heat to circulate more evenly.

Meat may sliced more thinly if it is partially frozen.

Tomatoes added to roasts will help tenderize them naturally. Tomatoes contain an acid that works well to break-down meats.

"FORE"
To eliminate bacon curling , try soaking the bacon in cold water for 2 minutes before frying. Dry well with paper towel. If they still curl, sprinkle with flour. If they still insist on curling poke some holes in them with your golf shoes or ?.

Meats should be stored in the refrigerator for no more than three days in the original wrapper.

Just For The "Health" Of It

"NOT A GOOD CURE"
In order to cure ham, a solution of brine salts, sugar and of course a good dose of nitrites are injected into the ham. If the total weight goes up 8%, the label may read "Ham, with Natural Juices". If it goes up over 8% it will read "Water Added".

Choose bacon with the most meat. The higher nitrite levels are found in the fat.

Bacon should be cooked on paper towels in a microwave oven to reduce the nitrosamine levels.

If you can find it use nitrite-free bacon. Most imitation bacon products still contain nitrites.

The fat content in some turkey bacon products may be close to equaling the real thing, read your labels carefully.

Never re-freeze meats. That includes luncheon meats and hot dogs. The salt content favors the development of rancidity.

Always completely cook meats, never leave them partially uncooked until another day.

The E. coli bacteria that may cause illness or even death normally resides only on the surface of meats, steaks or roasts grilled on both sides normally will kill any bacteria. Hamburger is another story since when it is ground the outside becomes the inside and a higher temperature is needed to cook the inside of the meat thoroughly.

Very Frank Furter Information

1937 Frankfurter	1990 Frankfurter	Grams Of Protein(3 1/2oz)
Fat..........19%	Fat.........28%	Frankfurter (2).......10
Protein......20%	Protein.....12%	Poultry..............26
No technology to	Technology was	Fish.................25
keep extra fat	developed which	Lean beef, pork, veal.24
and extra water	keeps added fat	Canned tuna...........17
from separating	and water from	
from ground meat.	separating from	
	ground meat.	

Most hot dogs contain large amounts of "edible offal" which may include animal skins, snouts, ears, esophagi, bone and etc., etc.

The best quality hot dog are Kosher, which contain only pure muscle meat. However, even though they don't contain edible offal they still have nitrites.

Bologna may contain up to 30% fat and 10% water.

Pork sausage and breakfast sausage may contain up to 50% fat.

If hot dogs are labeled "All Meat" or "All Beef" they must contain at least 85% meat or beef. The "All Meat" variety can contain a blend of beef, pork, chicken or turkey and of course, edible offal.

Smoked meats should be refrigerated.

Lean veal can have as little as one-tenth the fat as lean beef. Cholesterol content is the same.

Ground meats (hamburger and hot dogs) are prone to a process called "self-oxidation." The more surface of the meat you expose to oxygen, the faster the meat will deteriorate.

"HAVE A GOOD BREAKDOWN"

Meat that has been cooked, (the more well done the better) the more easily broken down and digested to a partial molecular breakdown. This only takes place the longer the meat is cooked, unless it is marinated or tenderized in a papaya-based product.

If meats are cooked only to medium-well (170°F.) it will increase the B1 availability by 15% over well done beef (185°F.).

Small cuts of beef will spoil faster and should not be kept in the refrigerator without freezing for more than 2-3 days. Liver, sweetbreads, cubed meats or marinated meats should be used within a day or frozen.

Amino acids, the building blocks of protein are best absorbed and utilized if they come from beef, approximately 90% absorption rate. Legumes are next with a rate of 80% with grains and vegetables at about 60-88%.

Remember when beef or hamburger is labeled "75% lean" it is still 25% fat content, which is a lot of fat. Since fat has twice as many calories as lean beef, a hamburger patty may be as high as 70% fat.

Beware of the words "lean" and "extra lean" on ground beef. When a steak is labeled "lean" it cannot have more than 10% fat, "extra lean" no more than 5% fat. However, ground beef has different standards and when labeled "lean" or "extra lean" can have as much as 22% fat.

Veal has less fat than any meat and usually comes from young milk-fed calves. It is more costly but has less hormones and is very tender.

Never eat raw meat of any type. Cooking destroys many toxins.

Three ounces of hamburger will supply you with twice the fat as lean beef (top sirloin).

Hormones are fed to almost all beef and fowl that are purchased from a supermarket. They are used to speed up the animal growth. Thus requiring less time from birth to marketable size. This means less food needed to raise them; it also means we are subjected to consuming meats that may contain hormones, the effect of which, on humans, are still under study.

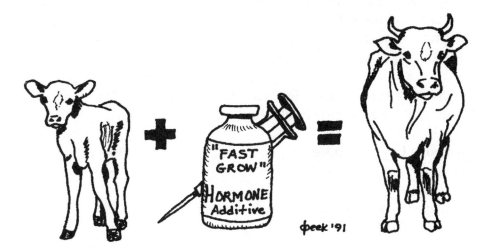

One pound of charcoal barbecued steak contains as much carcinogens (cancer forming agent) as the smoke in 15 cigarettes. The dripping fat on the charcoal causes a chemical substance called a benzopyrene to be released and is found in the black coating on the meat. Wrap the meat in foil for protection.

The best hamburger is made by choosing the leanest piece of round steak you can find, having the butcher cut off all visible fat and grind it through the grinder twice. Grinding twice will break the fat into smaller globules, allowing more to be lost in the cooking process.

"IN THE DOG HOUSE"
Hot dogs contain less protein in 3 ½ ounces than any other meat source. It also contains high quantities of edible offal and a good dose of nitrites.

Hot dogs may contain up to 56% water and up to 3% powdered bone, if listed on the ingredient list.

45% of all-meat hot dogs may consist of water, fat and additives.

Corn syrup is found in most hot dogs.

Pork sausage and breakfast sausage may contain up to 50% fat.

Lower grades of beef, such as standard and commercial are lower in fat, perfectly safe and just as nutritious as the more expensive choice and prime cuts. Their protein to fat ratio is much higher, due to the lower fat content. However, unless your buying hamburger, tenderization will probably be needed.

If meat is prepared several hours before cooking, it should be refrigerated and wrapped loosely, allowing air to circulate around it.

Meat consumed in large quantities can inhibit the absorption of the mineral manganese.

It takes 100 grams of beef to equal 20 grams of protein.

Hamburger will be found in a variety of grades and contains the highest percentage of saturated fat of any meat. Hamburger will be found graded "Lean," "Extra Lean," and even "Extra, Extra Lean." All of these will still have more fat than the ground round steak.

Bacon substitutes such as Sizzlean still contain sodium nitrite.

If you must eat luncheon meats, try to choose ones that are made from chicken or turkey and have the lowest percentage of fat content. Remember, they still contain nitrites.

Rotisserie-cooked meats and poultry will contain less fat than those that are fried or cooked in their own juices.

Ready-to-cook meat products will usually have more fat than the same meats in the meat cases. The market or manufacturer can get away with leaving more fat on the meat.

Ground pork products should be kept frozen for no longer than 2 months.

Meat tenderizers are usually made from extracts of papaya, pineapple or lemon.

Place leftover stews into individual baking dishes or small casserole dishes, cover with pie crust or dumpling mix and bake.

Herbs That Are Best Suited For Certain Meats

Beef..........Basil, thyme, sweet marjoram, summer
savory rosemary.

Veal.........Summer savory, rosemary, thyme, basil, tarragon.

Lamb.........Mint, summer savory, sweet marjoram,
dill, rosemary.

Pork.........Sweet marjoram, thyme, sage, chives,
basil.

Poultry.......Thyme, sage, tarragon, sweet marjoram,
chevil, summer savory.

Fish..........Chevil, fennel, sage, parsley, dill,
sweet marjoram, basil, chives.

"FIXER UPPER"
If you scorch meat, soak it in a towel in hot water and wring out as best as possible. Cover the meat and let it stand for five minutes before scraping off burned area with a knife.

To prevent the fat from splattering when frying sausage, try flouring them lightly.

Hamburger fried in catsup gives it a barbecue flavor and adds sugar.

If you place a small piece of ice inside your meatballs before browning, they will be moist.

"SAVE WEAR AND TEAR ON YOUR GOLF SHOES"
Flat beer and hard cider are excellent for tenderizing beef. Their fermentation qualities do the trick.

When making hamburger patties, chill them first and they will be easier to form.

To bread meats, shake them in a brown bag with flour and seasonings.

Always cut meats across the grain when possible, they will be easier to eat and have a better appearance.

To bring out the flavor in a ham loaf, add a small amount of rosemary.

To remove a ham rind easily, slit the rind lengthwise before it is placed in the pan. As it bakes, the rind will pull away and can be removed.

When cooking pork buttes, rub the meaty side with table salt an hour before cooking to draw any water in the pork to the surface. This will help tenderize and flavor the pork.

To avoid your meatloaf from cracking, try rubbing a small amount of cold water on the top and sides before placing it in the oven.

When frying meat, try sprinkling paprika over it and it will turn golden brown.

Place dry onion soup mix in the bottom of your roaster pan, when you remove the roast, add 1 can of mushroom soup and you will have a good brown gravy.

Another way to bread meats is to dip them into slightly beaten eggs with a little milk added, then into seasoned bread crumbs. Then place into the refrigerator for 40 minutes to allow the breading to adhere before cooking.

Liver will be more tender if soaked in milk or tomato juice and placed in the refrigerator for 1-2 hours before cooking.

When tenderizing your meat, try spreading a small amount of flour on the surface to help retain the juices.

To stop sausages from splitting open when they are fried, try making a few small punctures in the skins when they are cooking.

If you want cooked meat to remain tender, leave it in its own cooking juices when it is stored.

If venison is soaked in ginger ale overnight it will eliminate the gamey flavor.

Placing meats in white vinegar and water for 5 minutes will make it more tender.

To reduce the shrinkage in sausages, they should be boiled for 3-5 minutes before frying.

For a too-salty ham, partially bake it and drain all the juices. Pour a small bottle of ginger ale over it and let it bake until done.

To keep fat from splattering when frying bacon, sprinkle a small amount of salt in the frying pan.

"THE BOTTOM LINE"
When you figure the cost per meal of a meat portion, consider the weight of the fat and bone. It may account for as much as 30% of the cost.

When preparing meatloaf, place a slice or two of Sizzelean under the uncooked loaf, to keep it from sticking to the bottom of the pan.

Make meatloaf in muffin tins for individual servings that will be ready in only 15-20 minutes in a pre-heated 375 degree oven.

"TENDER BUNS"
When cooking hot dogs, try using the top of a double boiler to warm your buns.

To separate bacon slices, place the package in the microwave for a few seconds.

For a real treat, try mixing seasoned stuffing mix with hamburgers.

When re-heating meats, try placing the pieces in a casserole dish with lettuce leaves in between the slices. The slices will be tender and moist.

"STALKING THE PREY"
To keep lamb chops, pork chops or even poultry from sticking to the bottom of a pan, try placing a few stalks of celery in the bottom to act as a rack to hold them. This will also add flavor and moisture while they are cooking.

"HOW DRY I AM"
If the hamburger is too dry, due to a reduced fat content, try adding one stiffly beaten egg white for each pound of hamburger or adding one large grated onion for each 1 ½ pounds, or you could make the patties with a tablespoon of cottage cheese in the center. Instant potato flakes will also work well.

We get one pound of beef for every 16 pounds of grain.

In an average week, Americans eat 350 million hot dogs. This equates to a hot dog 60 feet thick and the length of a soccer field.

Government Meat Grading

U.S.D.A. Prime - Most tender cut, highest fat content.
U.S.D.A. Choice - Very tender cut, most common sold.
U.S.D.A. Good - Less fat, needs tenderizing.
U.S.D.A. Commercial - From older animals, tougher.
U.S.D.A. Utility, Cutter and Canner - Lowest grades.

Hamburger is the most popular meat purchased in the U.S. It contains more saturated fat per ounce than any other saleable meat.

"YUK, YUK"

Even though hamburger is sold as 100% pure beef, legally it can still contain "edible offal" which consists of beef lungs, hearts, lips, bone, ears, snouts and esophagi.

"DON'T GET BURNED"

A beef brisket is done when the fat starts to roll off, but will be overcooked if you can pull the fat off with your fingers.

The Skinniest Six Cuts Of Meat

Eye Of The Round	Top Round	Round Tip
143 Calories	153 Calories	157 Calories
4.2gr. of Fat	4.2gr. of Fat	5.9gr. of Fat
1.5gr. Sat. Fat	1.4gr. Sat Fat	2.1gr.Sat. Fat
59mg. Chol.	72mg. Chol	69mg. Chol

Top Sirloin	Top Loin	Tenderloin
165 Calories	176 Calories	179 Calories
6.1gr. of Fat	8.0gr. of Fat	8.5gr. of Fat
2.4gr. Sat. Fat	3.1gr. Sat. Fat	3.2gr. Sat. Fat
76mg. Chol.	65mg. Chol.	72mg. Chol

Americans average 75 pounds of beef, 44 pounds of pork and 40 pounds of chicken per year. This amounts to ½ pound of meat every day.

Gelatin comes from cattle skin and bones which are an excellent source of protein, but is missing two essential amino acids.

Beef should not be seasoned with any type of salt until it is 3/4 cooked. This will help retain the flavor and make it juicier.

When cooking (boiling) tough beef, add a small amount of vinegar to help tenderize it.

"A TENDER LITTLE MORSEL"
The most tender chuck steak is the first cut, which may also be called the blade cut. If you can see a small piece of white cartilage near the top of the steak, you have found the first cut.

"MORE TENDER LITTLE MORSELS"
The eye of the round steak is normally cut into two pieces. Best to buy the roast that has the same diameter ends. This will be the first cut and the most tender.

Always buy round steak in uneven "oyster-cut" shapes. These will be the first cuts and will be nearer the sirloin.

When buying lamb and you are only purchasing half a leg, make sure that it weighs at least 4 pounds. Any smaller and it will have a higher amount of bone and less meat.

To prevent sausages from shrinking, roll them in flour before frying.

An excellent substitute for bread crumbs is quick-rolled oats as a coating for meat loaf.

Place a few grapes in the pan when cooking venison for a special flavor treat.

15 billion pounds of beef were sold through retail outlets in 1990 compared to 19 billion pounds in 1976. Over the same period chicken sales increased from 43 pounds per person to 63 pounds per person.

To make beef easier to slice before cooking, freeze it for 45 minutes first.

SECRETS OF THE INNER COW

The 8 main cuts of beef are; shank, flank, brisket, chuck, round, rib, plate and loin.

The secondary name is the retail cut, such as sirloin, porterhouse, top round, etc. and explains the way the cow was cut up.

The tenderness of beef depends on how it was cut up.

The toughest cuts of beef are pot roasts and are cut from the cow's neck. These are also the least expensive.

Chuck Cuts
These usually need to be cooked for long periods of time in a liquid for tenderizing.

Rib Cuts
These include rib steaks, rib roasts or back ribs and should be cooked slowly in an oven or grilled for approximately 20-30 minutes per pound. Best to use a marinade or sauce.

Loin Cuts
These come from behind the ribs and are the most tender cuts, such as tenderloin roasts and the better steaks, such as porterhouse.

Round Cuts
These are top round, eye of the round, bottom round, etc. and should be braised and roasted similar to pot roasts.

Flank and Plate Cuts
These include flank steaks and skirt steaks. They are long and thin cuts and are best for stir-frying.

Brisket Cuts

Located in the area behind the cow's front leg or from the leg itself and are usually tough and need extensive cooking in a liquid for a considerable time.

For best results when cooking a roast, rotate it 1/4 turn every 20-25 minutes.

Wild game will be lower in fat and cholesterol. Best are venison, wild boar (not a party animal), pheasant, buffalo and elk. Prices are very high on some of these meats.

There are 1.6 million beef producers. They are for the most part on the "honor system" regarding hormonizing cattle to increase growth.

The USDA normally monitors only one to two percent of all beef carcasses for illegal drug residues, or in about 1.5 pounds out of the 74 pounds each person consumed in 1990. By the time a problem is found it is too late to recall the beef anyway, its been sold. The biggest problem is in the retired (older) cattle that are to be used in hamburger, soups, pot pies and of course our favorite TV dinners.

Thaw meats as quickly as possible, preferably under refrigeration, then cook immediately.

The approximate percentage of calories from fat in beef:

USDA Prime...................50%
USDA Choice.................39%
USDA Select/Good.........30%

The best lamb comes from New Zealand (spring lamb). Since it against the law to use hormones and tenderizers, the meat is safer than most countries.

There are five grades of lamb, Prime, Choice, Good, Utility and Cull. Prime never makes it to the markets and is only sold to restaurants. Choice and Good are usually available.

Fresh beef is cherry-red in color. The darker the beef the older the animal. Fat should be white not yellow.

Beef is the most readily available meat, but is usually the most tainted.

To cook ground meat for specialty dishes, try crumbling the meat into a microwave-safe colander and place it over a small bowl. The fat will drain out into the bowl.
A cow is more valuable for its milk, cheese, butter, yogurt, etc. than it is for its beef.

When cooking any type of meat always use a meat thermometer.

Thaw all meats in the refrigerator for maximum safety.

To keep your meatballs from falling apart when cooking, try placing them into the refrigerator for 20 minutes before cooking.

"WATCH FOR THESE"
Special words are used by supermarkets to make you believe you are getting better grades; "Premium," "Quality," "Select Cut," "Market Choice," "Prime Cut," etc.

High meat intake may cause excessive calcium losses through the urine.

Ratings of Non-Vegetable Proteins:

1. Fish
2. Turkey
3. Chicken
4. Bacon
5. Luncheon Meats
6. Deer
7. Lamb
8. Goat
9. Beef

Leftover cooked meat can be kept 4-5 days in the refrigerator.

Annual consumption of red meat in the United States has dropped from 132 pounds per person annually in 1970 to 112 pounds in 1994.

Chapter 12

Fowl Facts

The NAS (National Academy of Sciences) released a study in 1992 showing that toxic contamination of poultry poses a potential health risk . Most of the toxic chemicals and pathogens are largely undetected using the present poultry inspection procedures.

USDA food inspectors have increased their inspections of chicken slaughtering plants by over 50% in the last 10 years. We still have a long way to go, they have reduced the number of inspectors almost 30% in the last 10 years.

Americans consume over 6 billion chickens per year, of which possibly 2 billion are contaminated.

Chicken farming is a $14 billion dollar industry.

Studies by the National Academy of Science showed that 48% of food poisonings is caused by contaminated chicken. This affects approximately one in 50 persons in the U.S. annually.

THE SAFEST POULTRY IS KOSHER POULTRY:

Fact - During processing, defeathering takes place in cold water only, never in hot or warm water. Non-Kosher chickens and turkeys are always processed in water heated between 125° and 132° which is when bacterial growth is at its highest level. The hot water opens the pores and allows entry of every bit of undesirable matter that is floating in the hot bloody water of the communal bath.

Fact - Kosher poultry is soaked and submerged for 30 minutes in very cold water, then hand salted inside and out and allowed to hang for one hour to remove any remaining blood.

Fact - After salting the birds, they are rinsed 3 separate times to remove all the salt.

> ***Fact*** - The taste is clean and most people who eat chicken on a regular basis will immediately tell the difference.

> ***Fact*** - Many Kosher processed chickens never make it to the marketplace even when passed by government inspectors. The quality control differs from most other processors.

Compare nutrition labels when purchasing ground turkey. You may find that some brands have almost as much fat as lean beef.

A 3 pound chicken will yield about 2 1/2-3 cups of cut-up chicken.

A 5 ounce can of boned chicken will yield about 1/2 cup of cut-up chicken.

In a recent 1995 study 8 out of 10 people called the "stuff" inside a turkey "stuffing" and 20% called it "dressing." The 20% were all over age 65.

A lower to moderate cooking temperature will produce a juicier chicken, since more fat and moisture are retained.

To tenderize chicken and give it a unique flavor, try basting it with a small amount of white wine as it cooks.

Freeze leftover chicken broth in ice cube trays, then keep the cubes in a plastic bag in the freezer. When a recipe calls for chicken bouillon cubes, thaw out in the defrost cycle in the microwave.

Whether chicken is fresh or defrosted never leave in the refrigerator for more than 2 days. Same for hamburger.

To save dollars, purchase whole chickens and cut them up. Freeze the sections that you want together.

Ground poultry in supermarkets usually contain dark meat, skin and a high amount of fat.

Ground poultry should be labeled 98% fat free by weight.

A "Wellness Burger" still contains 30% fat by calories.

To thaw frozen chicken, place it in a pan of cold water with at least 1/4 cup of salt added. You will notice the improved flavor and have a cleaner chicken.

The average American ate 20 pounds of turkey in 1991 and 25 pounds in 1994. In 1930 it was only 2 pounds.

When stuffing your holiday turkey, try placing a piece of cheesecloth inside the cavity before adding the stuffing. When you remove the cloth, all the stuffing will come out at one time. Markets are now selling a "stuffing sac," one sac costs more than enough cheesecloth purchased in bulk to do 10 birds.

Turkey is eaten at dinner time over 50% of the time.

Turkey is usually a better buy than chicken, less bone and waste in proportion to its size.

When you buy large chickens they are older birds and will usually be tougher. Try slow cooking to make them more tender.

Dental floss makes an excellent truss for a fowl.

Turkeys should be left out of the oven 20-30 minutes covered with tin foil before carving. Hot birds are too difficult to cut properly. If you must, then use an electric knife or a very sharp bread knife.

Never buy a chicken on a Monday. It is likely you'll get one that wasn't purchased over the weekend.

Defrost a chicken by soaking in cold water, this will draw out any blood residues and will leave the breast very white.

After flouring a chicken, chill for one hour. The coating will adhere better during frying.

If you add a few slices of lemon to stewing chickens they will be more tender.

Try baking your "fried" chicken. Bread as you normally would then baste with orange juice to keep it moist and enhance your normal seasonings.

If you rub the skin of a turkey or other fowl with white vermouth it will make the skin a glossy brown color.

Have you ever wondered how the restaurants serve a very tender, moist chicken breast all the time? They submerge the breast in buttermilk for 3-4 hours under refrigeration before cooking.

If you must baste a chicken, never use butter. Just place a few bacon strips across the breast, works great, but also adds fat. Turkey bacon might be a good substitute.

Chickens should bear a shield shaped grade mark carrying the designation "U.S. Grade A", "U.S. Grade B", or "U.S. Grade C".

If the U.S. Grade stamp does not appear on the chicken, it is probably labeled by the supermarket as "Premium" or "Superior" and is in all actuality U.S. Grade B or C.

U.S. Grade A chickens are sold as fresh in supermarkets. U.S. Grades B & C are used for frozen dinners and canned products since they are more blemished.

One large chicken slaughtering plant may use up to 100 million gallons of water daily. This is equal to a city of 25,000 people.

Don't buy birds that are injected with a basting solution. You are just paying for extra fat.

A 3 pound chicken is raised on 6 pounds of feed, using hormones, of course.

Broilers and fryers come to market 7-10 weeks after they hatch.

A 3 pound chicken will provide approximately 1 pound 5 ounces of edible meat. It may be more expensive to buy a whole chicken than the parts.

If turkey salad is made, wait until fowl is fully cooked before adding any type of salad dressing.

Cook all poultry to a center temperature of 185°F.

A yellow chicken doesn't necessarily mean a healthier more nutritious chicken when compared to a pale one. Yellow skin results in the amount of yellow corn found in chicken feed. Some suppliers of feed also add substances which contain yellow pigment. Marigold petals are known to give chickens a healthy sheen.

Just For The "Health" Of It

The USDA reports that chickens today are getting fatter. In fact, today's poultry is bred to reach market weight in 6-8 weeks. This is half the time it previously took! This, however, has resulted in a disproportionate increase in body fat.

Dark meat turkey has a higher fat level, 4 grams of fat or more per 3 1/2 oz.

The poultry skin and the fat just under the skin have the highest percentage of total fat and cholesterol.

Remove all chicken-fat globules that are visible inside the chicken.

Americans are now eating 61 pounds of poultry annually compared to only 34 pounds in 1970.

Never stuff a turkey or other fowl with warm stuffing and leave overnight, even if refrigerated, always keep the stuffing separate and stuff before cooking.

Never leave gravy, stuffing or cooked fowl at room temperature for more than 30-45 minutes before refrigerating.

A 3 1/2 oz. serving of white meat turkey without the skin contains only 115 calories and one gram of fat which is approximately 10% less than white meat chicken.

Turkeys reach maturity in 14 to 22 weeks. They are more tender than chickens and have proportionally more breast meat.

"A FOWL SITUATION"
Most chickens in the U.S. are raised in giant coop farms holding more than 10,000 birds. Each bird is housed in a box and will have feed available with a light on so that they can eat 24 hours a day.

If you eat chicken in a foreign country you will probably notice the difference in the flavor. Most foreign countries do not allow fowls to be raised under the conditions that the U.S. fowls are raised under.

When stuffing a turkey, try sealing the opening with a small raw potato.

"VIEW FROM THE OTHER SIDE"
To keep white meat on a turkey from drying out, try cooking the turkey breast-side down, then turn it right-side up for the last hour. Juices will not buildup in this period of time and the bird will be easy to turn, especially if you use a "V" rack.

"GETTING BUFFALOED"

An order of chicken wings (buffalo wings) may supply as much as 30 grams of fat, more than half the fat you should be consuming in an 1800 calorie daily intake.

Chicken will keep longer if re-wrapped in wax paper instead of the plastic wrap used by the markets

A CHICKEN "YOLK" OR TWO

If the odor of a fresh chicken is offensive, try giving the bird a massage with the juice of 1/2 lemon and 1/4 teaspoon of salt. The bird will enjoy this and it will totally remove the odor.

Use poultry shears to de-bone a fowl, its better than hacking it to pieces.

A significant number of the poultry labeled "fresh" has been frozen and defrosted. This may affect the quality of the product.

After working with raw poultry, wash your hands, the utensils used and the surface before placing any other food on it. Poultry can be contaminated with a number of bacteria.

One of the easiest ways to singe a fowl is to saturate a wad of cotton with rubbing alcohol. Place it on the end of a short wire, and light it. This will never leave any black marks.

A quick way to stuff small poultry is to use salad tongs to insert the stuffing.

One of the biggest chicken farmers in the United States ships out approximately 23 million chickens weekly.

38 million chickens are processed in the United States in one day according to the National Broiler Council.

"GET A GRIP ON"
Use white cotton gloves to remove fat from inside chickens and turkeys, however, if you use your hands they are more easily washed for reuse.

Americans averaged 66 pounds of chicken annually in 1992.

A free-range chicken has approximately 11 - 24% fat compare to a standard supermarket bird at 15 - 18%.

Breast meat on migratory fowls is dark. The reason its white on the supermarket birds is that they don't fly and exercise.

"NEWS YOU CAN NEVER USE"
There are 426 chickens per person in Arkansas.

4.9 billion pounds of chicken are sold each year, deep fried by fast food outlets.

Almost 1/3 of the nations meat consumption is chicken.

95% of chickens sold in the U.S. are broilers or fryers, different name, same chicken.

In 1989 chicken farmers purchased almost $300 million worth of animal antibiotics.

"A REAL FOWL FACT"
Americans consume over 6 billion chickens per year, of which possibly 2 billion are contaminated.

Poultry Hotline - 1 (800)535-4555

Chapter 13

Fathoms of Fish

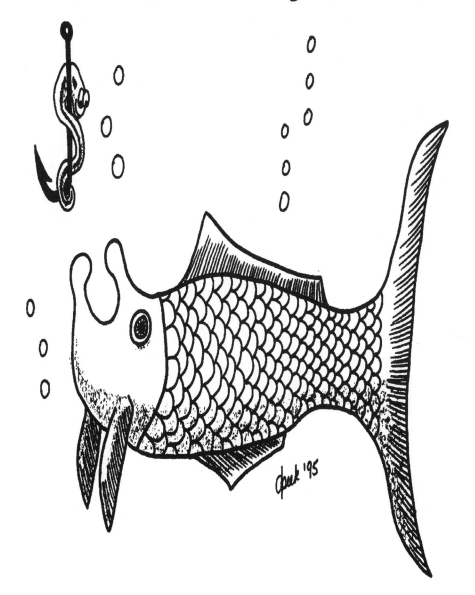

Try not to eat the skin or fat on fish. Most contaminants will be found in these areas.

If you marinate fish always do it in the refrigerator, never at room temperture, fish deteriorate very quickly at room temperture.

"BE SAFE NOT SORRY"
A "packed under federal inspection" (PUFI) label on the package means that the seafood has been processed and packaged in the presence of a federal inspector.

"SEAFOOD SAUNA"
To steam fish, place the fish in a microwave-safe (plain, no colored design) paper towel. Moisten under water and microwave for about 5 minutes.

"SKIP THE DETERGENT"
At the Montreal Expo '67 Eskimo women demonstrated how they cooked salmon in a dishwasher.

Fish should be labeled "Grade A."

"A WORD TO THE WISE"
If you see a seafood product with "USG Inspected" on the label it is not an authorized designation.

"A-10"
Petrale Sole is considered to be the highest quality fish for eating in the Pacific Ocean.

"EASY DOES IT"
Always cook fish at a low to moderate temperature to retain the moisture and preserve the tenderness. Never more than 350°F.

"AND AWAY SHE GOES"
If you doubt the freshness of a fish. place it in cold water, if it floats (or swims away) it has recently been caught.

"FISH SHAKE?"

Thaw frozen fish in milk. The milk draws out the frozen taste and provides a fresh caught flavor.

"NEW BAR DRINK"

If you soak oysters in club soda for about five minutes, they are usually more easily removed from the shells.

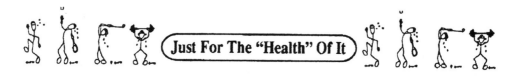

Just For The "Health" Of It

"PESKY LITTLE CRITTERS"

You should refrain from tasting meat, poultry or fish until the cooking has been completed. Parasites may not be dead and infestations have been known to occur from partially cooked fish especially.

Consumption of seafood in the United States has only risen from an annual consumption in 1970 of 12 pounds to 15 pounds in 1994. The contamination problem is a cause of concern to many.

Depending on the species 11-27% of the total fat in fish and shellfish is saturated. This can be compared to 37% in pork and 48% in most beef.

"THE FISHING LINE"

If you're going to the Caribbean, Florida or Hawaii and plan on eating tropical fish, it would be best to call the fish safety hotline to help you avoid "ciguatera" poisoning. They will tell you the current fish with problems.

FISH HOTLINE 1 (305)361-4619

Eating raw shellfish may cause viral and bacterial diseases. Most problems have been caused by shellfish caught in sewage polluted waters on the East Coast.

A regular course of fish 3-4 times per week will help keep you supplied with essential nucleic acids, DNA and RNA.

Due to contamination of fish in general, pregnant woman should not eat fish of any type more than twice per week.

A single 3 1/2 ounce serving of sardines is higher in calcium and phosphorus than a glass of milk. Sardines also contain vitamin D to assist the calcium in working properly.

A 100 gram serving of sardines provides up to 53% of your minimum requirement of protein. More than the same weight of T-Bone Steak.

New evidence shows that eating as little as one serving of fish per week can significantly reduce your risk of heart disease.

All shellfish are naturally high in sodium.

Bonita, a substitute for tuna and swordfish from the Pacific Ocean has been found to contain high levels of PCB's.

A high fish diet may aide in reducing the effects from increased salt intake.

"AH SO"
Sushi may contain larva of a parasite roundworm. Fish must be cooked to an internal temperature of 140° F or frozen for three days at -50° F to kill larva. Susceptible fish include; Mackerel, Herring, Squid, Sardines, Bonita, Salmon, Sea Trout and Porgy.

A frequent trip to the sushi bar may leave you short of vitamins thiamine and B1. Raw fish contains a substance that destroys these vitamins.

White Croakers are one of the most popular fish sold in markets on the west coast. They have been found to contain the highest levels of DDT and PCB's of any fish.

The safest fish to eat are halibut, sole, skipjack tuna, commercially raised trout and turbot.

Since most people do not eat large amounts of fish on a daily basis, the levels of contaminants that are consumed are negligible, and therefore you should not give up eating fish.

Mollusks, Clams and Oysters are "filter feeders" and may build up concentrations of any toxins present in water. Hepatitis has increased recently, resulting from shellfish caught in areas contaminated by human sewage. Cook all shellfish for protection against contaminants.

Shellfish live by filtering 15-20 gallons of water a day.

"BUYER BEWARE"
60% of all fish eaten in the United States comes from 116 foreign countries, many of which have poor sanitation conditions. Only 5% are actually inspected by U.S. Food & Drug.

"IT'S A BIRD, IT'S A PLANE, NO IT'S A FISH INSPECTOR"
The United States has approximately 2500 fish processing plants, 70,000 fishing ships and less than 200 inspectors who would have to be faster than a speeding bullet to do even an adequate job.

Fish that feed on the bottom of lakes, such as carp, and high-fat fish such as bluefish and bass have a higher incidence of contamination than others.

Cooking fish removes many of the contaminants which are usually found in the fat.

Clams and oysters are simple to open, if first washed with cold water, then placed into a plastic bag and kept in the freezer for 1/2 hour.

"CLAMMING UP"
Throw away any clams that do not open when steamed or boiled they are dead and probably contaminated.

"RELAXATION TECHNIQUE"

Clams may also be dropped into boiling water and let stand for a few minutes. This will relax their muscle and make them easier to open with a knife or beer can opener.

How To Choose Fresh Fish

Skin -   Should be firm and elastic. Skin should be shiny and color not faded. The skin should spring back when a finger pressure is exerted.

Eyes -   Bright, clear and somewhat bulging. Stale fish eyes are usually cloudy and sunken.

Scales -   Tight to skin, not falling off. Bright and shiny.

Gills -   No slime, reddish pink and clean looking. Not grayish.

Odor -   Not overly strong. Fish should never smell "fishy." The smell is from a chemical compound called "trimethylamine". It is produced from the deterioration and breakdown of the fish.

How To Choose A Frozen Fish

Odor -   Should have little or no odor. Don't buy if they have strong fish odor.

Skin -   Should be solidly frozen and have no discolorizations.

Wrappings   Moisture-proof with no air spaces between fish and wrapping.

The best seafood is the freshest seafood you can get, no more than 2-3 days out of water.

Total Fat In 3 1/2 Ounces Of Fish/Shellfish:

Bass	2.4 grams lean
Bluefish	6.5 grams lean
Butterfish	8.5 grams fat
Cod	4.6 grams lean
Flounder	3.9 grams lean
Grouper	2.8 grams lean
Haddock	4.9 grams lean
Hake	5.2 grams lean
Halibut	4.3 grams lean
Herring	9.0 grams fat
Mackerel	13.8 grams fat
Mullet	3.0 grams lean
Ocean Perch	2.8 grams lean
Pollack	4.2 grams lean
Pompano	9.5 grams fat
Porgie	10.4 grams fat
Red Snapper	4.5 grams lean
Salmon	8.6 grams fat

Shark	1.9 grams lean and mean
Sole	3.3 grams lean
Striped Bass	8.3 grams fat
Swordfish	2.2 grams lean
Tuna (bluefish)	6.5 grams lean
Crab	1.3 grams lean
Shrimp	1.1 grams lean
Oyster	2.4 grams lean

Supermarkets can offer up to 200 varieties of fish, some may be fresh.

Cooking fish should be more concerned with retaining flavor than tenderness as with meats. Fish is naturally tender.

Market Forms Of Fish

Whole Fish	- Marketed just as it is caught.
Drawn Fish	-Only entrails removed. Still needs cleaning.
Dressed Fish	- Scaled and entrails removed. Ready to cook.
Fish Steaks	- Slices cut crosswise.
Fish Fillets	- Boneless pieces cut from the sides.
Butterfly Fillets	- Two sides cut away from the backbone.
Cured Fish	- Cured by smoking, drying, salting or pickling.
Cold-Smoked	- Cured and partially dried. Won't keep long.
Hot-Smoked	- Partially or wholly cooked. Needs freezing.
Dried Fish	- Air or heat dried and salted. Lasts forever.
Salted Fish	- Dry-salted or brine-cured. Can be pickled.

"DO THE TWIST"

When purchasing live lobsters there should be movement in the legs.

Squid, shark and snails rate among the highest foods Americans hate the most.

The size of shrimp will not affect their quality. They should be tender and firm if cooked properly.

"PEEK-A-BOO"
Mussels, clams and oysters should be alive when purchased. Gaping shells should close when tapped. Discard dead ones.

"FISHERMAN'S FACT"
Minnows will stay alive longer if you add 6-8 drops of iodine to the water they are transported in.

THE "NOSE" KNOWS
If you wash your hands in cold water before handling fish your hands won't smell fishy.

To eliminate the fishy odor from a pan, try placing a small amount of vinegar in the pan before washing.

Cooked crab shells should be bright red in color (not orange) and have little or no odor. They should always be displayed on a bed of ice.

Frozen fish can be skinned easier than fresh ones.

Americans are eating more fish than ever, approximately 18 pounds per person in 1990. 21 pounds per person in 1994.

Aquaculture is fast becoming a major protein food industry in the United States.

The best eating fish and the safest are: Aquaculture raised Trout and Catfish, Halibut, Turbot, Skipjack, Sole and Pollack.

A small amount of grated onion added to the butter when cooking fish will add an excellent bit of flavor.

If you are planning on a fish barbecue, use the high-fat fish, they won't dry out as fast and will be juicer and more tasty.

Most fresh fish and shellfish are never inspected, make sure you are dealing with a quality fish market.

Never keep a shellfish in fresh water, it will kill them very quickly.

Try not to thaw frozen fish completely before cooking or it may make them very dry and mushy.

To eliminate the canned taste of shrimp, try soaking them for 10-15 minutes in a mixture of 2 tablespoons of vinegar and 1 teaspoon of sherry.

"CALL THE MASSEUR"
Lemon juice rubbed on fish before cooking will enhance the flavor and help maintain a good color.

The flavor of canned shrimp can be greatly improved if you soak the can in ice water for at least 1 hour before opening.

To de-vein shrimp, hold the shrimp under a slow stream of cold water and run the tip of an icepick down the back of the shrimp. This will clean the shrimp and leave it whole.

When frying fish sprinkle the bottom of the pan with a small amount of salt or use unsalted butter and the fish won't stick to the pan. Salted butter doesn't work well.

A small amount of grated onion added to the butter when cooking fish will add an excellent bit of flavor.

"A LITTLE TENDERNESS"
When making clam chowder, add the chopped clams during the last 15 minutes of cooking to avoid them from becoming mushy and tough.

When cooking fish wrapped in tin foil, add a sprig of dill and a lemon slice for a great taste treat.

When cooking shellfish, a heavily salted water will draw the sea salt out.

To make scaling a fish easier, try rubbing vinegar on the scales first.

When baking fish, try wrinkling up the tin foil before wrapping the fish. This will cause the fish to brown better and it won't stick to the foil.

Avoid making tough shrimp by first cooling the shrimp under very cold water for 1-2 minutes, then place them in a deep pot (not over the heat) with a small amount of salt, then cover them with rapidly boiling water, tightly covered. Large shrimp take approximately 5-7 minutes, average size are done in about 4 minutes.

Shark is an excellent eating fish, young ones are best.

The best tuna is labeled "white" and is albacore. Three other types are sold, namely "light", "dark", and "blended". The darker the tuna, the stronger the flavor and usually the oilier. These are mostly Skipjack and Bluefin.

SHELLFISH

Abalone- The edible portion is the foot, which is very tough and needs to be pounded into tenderness. Has been so overfished that they are becoming rare. The price is very high and they are considered the delicacy of shellfish.

Clams - Hard-shell are the most sought after. Soft-shell clams cannot close its shell because its neck sticks out too far. The largest soft-shell is the geoduck, which may weigh up to 3 pounds. Sea clams are usually used for canning or in packaged soups.

If you dig your own clams, you must purge them of sand and debris before eating. Allow the clams to stand 20-25 minutes in clear sea water. The water should be changed at least 3-4 times to be sure they are free of residues.

Crab - Blue crab is from the Atlantic and Gulf areas. Dungeness is caught in the Pacific Ocean. King and snow crab are caught in the north off the coast of Canada and Alaska. Stone crab comes from Florida.

Soft-shell crab comes in 4 sizes; "spiders" which are the bare legal size of 3 1/2 inches across, "hotel prime" at 4-4 1/2 inches, "prime" at 5-5 1/2 inches and "jumbo" at 6-7 inches across.

Crayfish - Small freshwater crustaceans. Louisiana produces about 20 million pounds a year. Similar to shrimp, all the meat is in the tail. Also called "crawdads."

Langostinos - A crustacean, sometimes sold as rock shrimp. Usually sold frozen and used mainly in soups and salads.

Lobster - Two main lobsters are sold in the United States they are: Maine and Spiney. The most prized Maine lobster is excellent tasting and more sought after. The Spiney lobster has most of the meat in the tail and has smaller claws.

The "Newburg" in lobster means that the recipe contains a cream and sherry mixture. Newburg pertains to an old Scottish fishing village.

Mussels - Mussel farming is becoming a popular business. They are raised on ropes, which keep them from the silty bottom, thus making them more cleaner and more salable. When grown in this manner they are also twice the size of ordinary mussels.

Oyster - Over 90 million pounds are consumed worldwide. About 50% are now aquafarmed. The flavor and texture will vary depending on where they are harvested.

Scallops - A mollusk that dies very quickly when removed from the water. They should not be overcooked or will become tough. They are usually shucked at the time they are caught and placed on ice. There are over 400 varieties of sea scallops.

Shrimp - There are over 250 varieties of shrimp. They are classified as number of shrimp per pound. The jumbo shrimp should average 16 to 25 per pound, large shrimp average 20 to 32 per pound, medium shrimp average 28 to 40 per pound, while tiny ocean shrimp can average over 70 per pound. One pound of raw shrimp will yield 1/2 to 3/4 pound after cooking. Large shrimp are called "prawns."

White shrimp are milder in flavor and more expensive than brown. Brown feed more on algae and have a stronger iodine taste.

If shrimp has a slight ammonia smell, it is deteriorating.

The FDA has taken action against some firms that overbread shrimp to raise the weight and price.

Shrimp may have more cholesterol than any other shellfish but are very low in saturated fat.

"OFF WITH THEIR HEADS"
Shrimp with heads are more perishable than those without their heads.

"TALK ABOUT THINGS IN A SMALL PACKAGE"
A shrimp head contains almost all its organs including most of the digestive system.

The dark colored intestinal tube running down a shrimp's back is OK to eat as long as its cooked. However it may be a little gritty due to the bacteria and other residues of digestion. The bacteria is killed by cooking the shrimp.

Shrimp deteriorates very quickly and should be used the same day you purchase it, or at least no later then the next day. Never refreeze thawed shrimp, most of the shrimp you buy has been frozen. If you wish to keep it longer, buy it frozen solid.

Squid - Usually not thought of as shellfish. Normally called "calamari." To keep it tender, don't cook it for more than 3 minutes. If stewing it, cook it for at least 15-20 minutes. The whole body and tentacles are edible. Squid has more cholesterol than shrimp.

SALTWATER FISH

Anchovy - The majority of anchovies gathered in Southern California waters (250 million pounds) are ground up and sold as poultry feed. The average market size is 4-6 inches. Commercially, they are sold rolled or flat and are cured in olive oil and canned.

If anchovies are too salty, try soaking them in tap water for 10-15 minutes, then store in the refrigerator for 30 minutes before using.

Angler - This category includes the Monkfish, Sea Devil, Bellyfish, Lotte and Goosefish. They are for the most part all low-fat with a firm texture. They can weigh from 2-25 pounds and only the tapered tail section is edible. Tastes similar to a lobster.

Barracuda - A moderate-fat fish that runs from 4-8 pounds. The only variety that is best for eating is the Pacific Barracuda which has an excellent taste. Great Barracudas are known for their toxicity.

Blue Fish - Usually weighs in at 3-6 pounds. Does not freeze well. When using, be sure to remove the dark strip of flesh running down its center. This may give the fish a strong undesirable flavor.

Butterfish - Also, known as Pacific Pompano or Dollar fish. It is a high-fat fish that usually weighs in at 1/4 to 1 pound. These are small fish that are usually cooked whole or smoked. A very fine textured fish.

Cod - The three main types are: Atlantic Cod, Pacific Cod and Scrod. They are a low-fat fish with a firm texture. The Atlantic is the largest variety and the Scrod is the smallest (a young cod). Available in many cuts; fillets, steaks, whole or dressed.

Croaker - Varieties include; Atlantic Croaker, Redfish, Spot, Kingfish, Corvina and Black Drum. All are low-fat except Corvina. Size varies from 1/4 pound for the Spot to 30 pounds for the large Redfish, a popular chowder fish.

Cusk - A fish gaining popularity with a taste similar to cod. Low-fat and excellent for stews and soups. Weights in at 1 1/2 to 5 pounds. Sold as fillets or whole.

Eel - A firm-textured fish that may run up to 3 feet long and has a tough skin that is removed prior to cooking. More popular in Europe and Japan.

Flounder - Also, called Sole. The most popular fish in the United States. The varieties seem endless and all are low-fat with a fine texture. Most are found 1/2 to 3 pounds with some varieties weighing in at up to 10 pounds. One of the best eating fishes.

Grouper - Can weigh in from 3-25 pounds and may be called "Sea Bass." The skin is tough and should be removed. It has a firm texture and may be cooked in almost any manner.

Haddock - A close relation to the Cod and usually weighs in at 3-5 pounds. Smoked Haddock is known as "Finnan Haddie."

Hake - Usually caught in the Atlantic during summer and early fall. It is a low-fat, firm textured fish. Usually weighs in at 1-8 pounds and is very mild flavored.

Halibut - A flatfish that usually weighs in from 5-20 pounds. A low-fat very popular fish with a firm texture.

Herring - A small 1/4 to 1 pound fish with a fine soft texture and is high-fat. Usually used for appetizers and sold pickled or smoked.

Mackerel - Sold under a number of names, such as: Wahoo, Atlantic Mackerel, Pacific Jack, King Mackerel and Spanish Mackerel. A high-fat fish with a firm texture. A commonly canned fish.

Mahi Mahi - Also, known as the "Dolphin Fish" or "Dorodo." However, it is no relation to the Dolphin nor does it look like a Dolphin. May weigh up to 40 pounds. Excellent eating fish.

Mullet - The fat content will vary, but is usually a moderate to high fat fish with a firm texture. Has a mild nut-like flavor.

Ocean - Perch A low-fat fish with a firm texture. Most is Perch imported from Iceland. Usually weighs in at 1/2 to 2 pounds and available fresh or frozen.

Orange - Roughy One of the most popular fish sold. Imported from New Zealand and is low-fat with a firm texture. Available in 2-5 pound weights. Very similar to Sole but at a better price.

Pollack - A close relative to Cod with a firm texture. Fresh usually weighs in at 4-12 pounds. Best when sold as fillets.

Pompano - Rated as one of the best eating fishes. It has a moderate fat level and a firm texture. One of the more expensive fishes.

Porgy - A firm textured, low-fat fish that usually weighs in at 1/2 to 2 pounds. Primarily caught in New England waters.

Red -
Snapper Has a very rose-colored skin and red eyes. It is low-fat with a firm texture. Excellent for soups and stews.

Rockfish - Available in more than 50 varieties. Often sold under the name of Pacific Snapper. They have a firm texture and are low-fat.

Sablefish - Also, known as Alaskan Cod or Butterfish. A very high-fat fish with a soft texture due to its fat content. Makes an excellent smoking fish and is usually sold as smoked.

Salmon - (Blueback) Red salmon is the highest in fat, is the most expensive and the highest grade. The lower grades are red or sockeye, chinook or king, and pink salmon is the lowest grade.

Three ounces of salmon contains 120 calories. 1/2 cup of salmon contains more grams of protein than two lamb chops.

"GOOD NEWS FOR BAGELS AND CREAM CHEESE"
Smoked salmon (Lox) is heavily salted unless you purchase the "Nova" variety. Salmon used for smoking is usually raised on aquaculture farms and has never had a reported incidence of parasite contamination.

Salmon used for sushi gives you a 1 in 10 chance of consuming a roundworm from the "anisakis family" of parasites, according to the FDA in samples from 32 restaurants.

If you see a label on canned salmon that says "Norwegian Salmon" be aware that there is no such species.

Sardines - These are actually soft-boned herring. They are descaled before being canned and the scales used to make artificial pearls and cosmetics. The Norwegian bristling sardine is the finest. Maine sardines are almost as good and cost considerably less. They are high-fat and best used for appetizers.

Sea Bass - A moderate fat fish with a firm texture. It has a mild flavor and is a popular seller.

Sea Trout - A moderate fat fish with a fine texture, excellent baked or broiled. Usually caught in the Southeastern United States.

Shad - A high-fat fish with a fine texture. A difficult fish to bone and almost always sold as fillet. The eggs (roe) are considered a delicacy.

Shark - Shark steaks are one of the most vitamin-rich foods in the sea. It is low-fat and has a firm, dense texture, occasionally sold in chunks. Is fast becoming a popular eating fish.

There are 350 species of Shark. In Asia, dried Shark Fins sell for $53 per pound and are used to make Shark soup. In Hong Kong, a bowl of Shark soup sells for $50 per bowl.

Shark cont.	The 60 foot Whale Shark is the world's largest fish. In 1990 over 100 million Sharks were caught.
Skate -	The wings are the only part that is edible. They have a flavor similar to scallops and are low-fat with a firm texture.
Swordfish -	The flavor is not as strong as Shark and is best served as steaks. It is somewhat higher in fat than Shark but has a similar texture.
Tuna -	White Tuna is from Albacore tuna and is the best grade of tuna. Light Tuna comes from the other five species of tuna. It is nutritious and usually tastes just as good.

The average American eats more than 3.7 pounds of tuna per year.

Tuna packed in oil has 50% more calories as water packed tuna.

Recent studies show that mercury contamination in tuna is too low to be concerned about.

Solid pack tuna is tuna that is composed of the loins of the tuna with a few flakes.

Chunk tuna will include pieces that will have a part of the muscle structure attached.

Flake tuna has the muscle structure and a high percentage of the pieces are under 1/2 inch.

Grated tuna is just above a paste.

When tuna is packed in olive oil it is sometimes called "tonno tuna."

Bluefin tuna may weigh up to 1000 pounds.

If you are making tuna salad for sandwiches, it may not matter which tuna you choose. It is more a matter of taste.

If you have noticed that tuna in cans is darker than it used to be, your right, the reason being is that smaller nets are being used so that the porpoises won't be netted. This means that the larger tuna won't be netted either. The smaller tuna has darker meat.

"SOUNDS LIKE A HORSE RACE"

Tuna still ranks as the number one consumed fish in the U.S. in 1994. Shrimp came in second with cod coming in third. Alaska pollack finished fourth due to its popularity in imitation crabmeat.

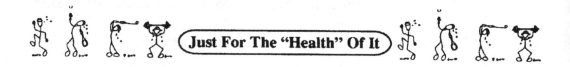

Just For The "Health" Of It

Watch the tuna label for the chemical pyrophosphate, a preservative that you should not eat.

Turbot -	A low-fat fish with a firm texture. Similar to flounder, a flatfish. Usually sold only as fillets.
Whiting -	A relative of Hake. Low-fat with a firm texture. Best broiled or steamed.

FRESHWATER FISH

Buffalo - **Fish**	A moderate fat fish with a firm texture. Usually caught in the Mississippi and the Great Lakes. Weighs in fresh at 2-8 pounds.

Carp -   The first fish to be aquacultured hundreds of years ago in China. A scavenger fish which is only recommended for fishing if aquacultured. Usually a moderate fat fish.

Catfish -   Approximately 70% of all catfish sold are from aquacultured farms. There are over 20 varieties of catfish. They are low-fat with a firm texture. Another scavenger fish which is healthier and only purchased from the farms.

Perch -   A small fish which is usually pan-fried whole. A low-fat, firm textured fish that is excellent eating.

Pike -   Has been fished out of existence. An excellent eating low-fat fish. The most popular being the Walleyed Pike.

Smelt -   A very small fish that is usually pan-fried and eaten whole (head and all). Larger ones are usually cleaned and gutted in the usual manner. They are high-fat with a firm texture.

Sturgeon -   The largest freshwater fish in the world. They can weigh up to 1000 pounds. They are high-fat with a very dense texture. Their eggs (roe) is a favorite for caviar.

Trout -   There are three main varieties: Lake Trout, Rainbow Trout and Steelhead. All contain moderate to high levels of fat with a firm texture. One of the best eating fishes with a delicate flavor. All Rainbow Trout are presently from aquacultured farms.

Whitefish -   Ranks as the best freshwater eating fish. It is high-fat with a firm texture and is best when broiled or baked.

Biologic Value Of Protein Foods

When amino acids are broken down, a percentage of the protein is lost in the process. Therefore, the quality and quantity of that protein that will remain useful to the body is called the "biologic value" of that protein. The following is a classification of the more common proteins we consume:

Protein Foods	*Biologic Value %*
Egg Yolk	95
Egg, Whole	94
Milk, Whole	90
Milk, Evaporated	88
Milk, Skim	84
Egg White	83
Pork Tenderloin	79
Corn, Germ	78
Beef Liver	77
Beef Muscle	76
Wheat Germ	75
Rice	75
Soybean Flour	75
Ham	74
Swiss cheese	73
Watermelon Seed	73
Red Salmon	72
Cashew	72
Sweet Potato	72
Coconut	71
Sesame Seed	71
Limburger Cheese	69
Potato	67
Whole Wheat	67
Brewer's Yeast	63
Pumpkin Seed	63
Pecan	60

Corn, Whole	60
Soybeans, Raw	59
Rye	58
Peanut, Roasted	56
Walnut	56
White Flour	52
Almond	51
Peas, Raw	48
Cocoa	37

Chapter 14

Beverage Facts

The average person consumes about 129 gallons of fluid per year. This includes water, milk, colas, beer, wine, etc.

More beer than milk is consumed in the United States. We average 34 gallons of beer per person opposed to 26 gallons of milk.

Americans spend an average of $297 per person on alcoholic beverages annually.

Just For The "Health" Of It

If your nerves are on edge, try a glass of celery juice or tonic.

Food slows down the absorption rate of alcohol and you won't feel the effects as fast.

Alcohol consumption has been linked to breast cancer in recent studies by Harvard University.

The liver must handle 90% of the alcohol, the other 10% is excreted in the urine or expired in air.

"THE DELICATE BALANCE"
The body uses 8 ounces of water to metabolize (break down) just 1 ounce of alcohol. Effects of dehydration may include dry mouth, hangovers, headaches and queasy stomachs.

Fatty foods will slow down the rate at which alcohol is absorbed into the general circulation. Any food will actually slow the rate down to some degree, fatty foods break down slower than the other foods.

Canned juices are usually an enriched product since the heat used in the processing destroys most of the vitamins.

If the fruit juice is labeled "cold-pressed" it is a higher quality product with most of its vitamin content intact.

Scotch has been found to contain small amounts of nitrosamines (a carcinogen) as a result of the way malt barley is dried.

Studies show that 3 beers a day may control your cholesterol levels. It seems to cause an increase in the good cholesterol (HDL), however, so does moderate exercise in the same study. The two together do not work beneficially.

Those who drink one or two alcoholic beverages per day are less likely to die of coronary heart disease than those who abstain. Helps to reduce stress levels.

Some of the hangover problems are caused by cogeners (toxic substances caused by fermentation). Alcoholic beverages with the lowest levels of cogeners are vodka and gin. Some of the worst are bourbon, blended scotch, and brandy.

An ounce and a half of 80 proof whiskey, a 5 ounce glass of wine and a 12 ounce can of beer all have the same amount of alcohol.

Food sensitivities may increase if you consume alcohol at the same time.

Red wine, in recent studies has been associated with stomach cancer. It was not determined in the study, however, whether the problem is from the grapes and the chemical quercetin, or as a result of the processing.

To improve the taste of tomato juice, pour it into a glass bottle and add one green onion and one stalk of celery cut into small pieces.

Hot drinks do not raise body temperture.

Watered down juices go under a variety of names: "orange juice drink", "orange drink", "orange-flavored drink" and "orange juice blend."
Canned beer tends to start deteriorating in approximately 3 months, however, it takes 5 months when bottled.

A "juice-drink" may contain up to 50% juice. An "ade-drink" may contain up to 25% juice and a "drink" can have as little as 10% juice.

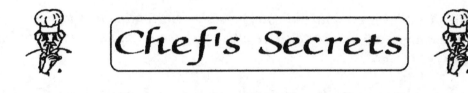

Chef's Secrets

When making lemonade, put the lemons through a meat grinder. You will get more juice and it will have a richer flavor.

As a rule of thumb for almost all sauces or soups containing wine, use 1 tablespoon of wine per cup of sauce or soup.

To keep juice cold without watering it down, place a tightly sealed plastic bag of ice into the juice.

A "lite" beer may not refer to the fact that the beer is lower in calories, but may pertain to the color of the beer.

When serving fruit juices, lemonade or punch, try making ice cubes from the drinks. These will keep the drinks from becoming watered down.

ALCOHOL OVERUSE:

Vitamins and Minerals - To be broken down by the body alcohol requires numerous B vitamins and minerals. The following is a list of nutrients that need to be available.

B Vitamins	Minerals
Thiamin	*Iron*
Riboflavin	*Zinc*
Niacin	*Manganese*
Pantothenic	*Phosphorus*
Acid	*Copper*
Biotin	*Magnesium*

NOTE: Alcohol causes excretion of zinc, possibly contributing to prostate problems as a man ages. It also causes excretion of magnesium, which may lead to extreme nervousness.

Two glasses of white wine per day can supply you with half your daily supply of chromium. Plain grape juice will work just as well.

Wine is composed of water, alcohol, various pigments, esters, some vitamins and minerals, acids and tannins. It does not remain in a constant state and is continually changing.

Traditional Wine/Food Combinations

Meats	- Rose or Cabernet Sauvignon
Seafoods	- Chablis, Chardonney, Pinot Blanc, Sauterne
Pasta	- Chianti
Cheese/Fruit	- Port, Muscatel, Cream Sherry, Tokay
Dessert	- Sweet Sauterne

Fruit juices help to maintain a proper acid-base balance in the stomach.

Ulcers may be irritated by fruit juices.

Bourbon is too sweet to be used in most recipes.

Wines should not be used in tart or heavily seasoned foods.

Wine should be counted as part of the total liquid in any recipe,

To avoid curdling in recipes containing dairy products in which wine is added, try adding the wine before adding the dairy product, then keep the dish warm until served.

Brandy, sherry and whiskey will reduce the "fishiness" of a seafood recipe.

When heating wine, remember that wine will reduce from 1 cup to 1/4 cup in approximately 10 minutes of cooking.

"DON'T WHINE ABOUT YOUR WINE"
If you wish to taste the wine in your recipe, don't add the wine until you are near completion, the alcohol content will be lost to the cooking.

Keep smaller bottles to store leftover wine. The less space between the wine and the cork, the longer it will retain it freshness.

Wine should be used in cooking with the utmost discretion, since it should not dominate the taste. Just use it to improve the flavor of the ingredients.

WHAT WINES TO USE WHERE

SHERRY

Best when used in soups and sauces. The most popular dishes are those with seafood, chicken and in desserts.

WHITE WINE

Usually used in fish and chicken dishes.

RED WINE

Usually used in meat dishes, stews, gravies and sauces. Also, used to marinate meats.

DESSERT WINES

These are the sweet wines and are used in fruit compotes and sweet sauces.

BRANDY

Used in meat and chicken dishes as well as puddings and custards. Very popular in fruit compotes.

RUM

Usually used in desserts containing pineapple or in sweet sauces.

Chapter 15

Grain and Nut Facts

"DO THE TWIST"
Pretzels are the fastest growing snack food in the United States, most products are almost fat-free.

"THE FIRST REAL POPPERS"
The Aztecs were the first to pop corn and use it as a decoration.

"REAL CORNEY"
Every man, woman and child in the United States eat approximately 47 quarts of popcorn each year. After the fat content was released in 1994, consumption decreased approximately 15%.

"A SLIPPERY SUBJECT"
Movie theaters that were offering popcorn popped in both coconut oil and canola, dropped the coconut oil popcorn completely after sales dropped below 10% of all sales.

"GOOD FAT, BAD FAT"
Canola is now used in almost all movie theaters. At least we now get an oil that is high in monounsaturated fat instead of saturated fat.

"BRING YOUR OWN"
Use herbs to replace salt on popcorn. Garlic powder, chili powder, basil and oregano work well.

There is no nutritional difference between regular popcorn and gourmet popcorn. There is only a variation in size.

"BETTCHA CAN'T EAT JUST ONE"
Two quarts of plain popcorn = the calories in 15 potato chips.

"WEAR YOUR GOGGLES"
Corn used for popcorn needs to contain enough moisture to puff up the starches when it is heated. The hull is thick enough to contain steam, yet is easily able to explode.

"CAN'T WIN"
Air poppers make the popcorn pop into larger blossoms, but they are usually tougher and less crisp.

Jasmine rice has an aroma and flavor similar to popcorn or roasted nuts. Makes a great side dish.

"BUTTERY ROULETTE"
Buttered flavored popcorn may be real butter, margarine, butter flavored oil or a soy-based artificial concoction. Ask the theater, they may know!

"TOO POOPED TO POP"
To restore moisture to "old maids" (stubborn kernels that refuse to pop): Fill a one-quart jar three quarters full of unpopped kernels, add one tablespoon of water, cover the jar and shake for 2-3 minutes or until all the water is absorbed. Store the container in a cool place (not the refrigerator) for 2-3 days before popping.

When brown rice is cooked it looks similar to white rice but retains a higher amount of nutrients.

To Crunch Or Not To Crunch

Wheat berries (cracked wheat) is made from toasted grain keeping the bran and germ intact. It is usually prepared by grinding it into coarse, medium or fine granulations for faster cooking. Cracked wheat can replace rice in most recipes but it is a little more crunchier.

To make an exceptional dessert from leftover rice , try folding stiffly beaten whipped cream, then add fresh fruit.

Many hot cereal products are "degerminated" reducing their nutritional quality to make them more palatable. These include Cream Of Wheat and Farina.

"A.K.A.'S"
Cereals are now changing their names so that you won't see the "sugar." Post's Super Sugar Crisp is now Super Golden Crisp and Kellogg's Sugar Frosted Flakes has been changed to Frosted Flakes.

A peanut butter sandwich without jelly will last for 2-3 days without refrigeration.

One of the best cereals on the market is Cherrios. It has an excellent nutrient content and is low in sugar.

"VISA VERSA"
If you run out of chopped nuts, try using a coarse bran, you'll hardly notice the difference. If you run out of coarse bran, use chopped nuts.

To shell nuts more easily, store them in the freezer.

Brown rice is only available in small boxes because the bran portion is higher in fat which may cause the rice to go rancid if not used in a short period of time.

Corn chips in all colors have the same amount of fat and calories, unless they are labeled fat-free or baked.

"TOOK A WHILE TO FIGURE THIS ONE OUT"
Blue corn chips are made from blue corn instead of yellow corn.

Remember one-half cup of rice is only equivalent to 2-3 heaping tablespoons.

Twice as much of our protein was coming from grains and cereals in the early 1900's compared to 1995.

Natural peanut butter will remain fresh longer if you store the bottle upside down in the refrigerator.

Just For The "Health" Of It

Enriched rice has a few of the vitamins that were lost in the milling process added back. As the rice is washed and cooked it will be lost again, for the most part.

6 tortillas plus 1/4 cup of beans = 14 grams of top quality protein, contains good fiber and is high in vitamins and minerals. Corn tortillas has less fat then flour ones.

"THE PERFECT PROTEIN"
1 ½ cups of beans plus 4 cups of rice = the protein in a 19 ounce steak.

½ cup of peanut butter plus 100% whole wheat bread, made with 3 cups of whole wheat flour and 1/4 cup of skimmed milk = the protein equivalent of a 16 ounce steak.

Wheat flour is not as good as whole wheat flour, and that is not as good as 100% whole wheat flour or whole grain flour.

Wheat bran contains 86% of the niacin, 73% of the pyridoxine, 50% of the pantothenic acid, 42% of the riboflavin, 33% of the thiamin and 20% of the protein. This is what is thrown away when we process bread.

Whole wheat flour is more difficult to digest than white flour. It may also cause gas and intestinal upsets in susceptible persons.

Consumption of grains in 1970 was 135 pounds per person annually. In 1994 it was 189 pounds.

A good test for the nutritive quality of grains: pour a quantity of the grain into a pot of water, if the majority of the grain sinks to the bottom, they still contain most of their nutrients.

The higher the percentage of sugar in cereals the less room for nutrients. Some cereals can have as much as 56% sugar.

Spaghetti products that are advertised as "lite" are lower in calories due to their ability to absorb more water.

Nuts, beans, whole grain, corn and peanut butter should be thrown out if there is the slightest signs of mold or unusual odor. They may contain dangerous aflatoxins.

Triticale is a man-made hybrid grain. It is a cross between rye and wheat and has a higher protein biologic value than even soy beans which contains all the essential amino acids.

GRAINY INFORMATION:

Couscous
Finely cracked wheat granules with a soft buttery flavor. makes an excellent bed for salad dishes or stews.

Bulgur
Granules of crushed wheat with a nutty flavor. Best used in a broth, bean dishes or mixed with rice for an unusual pilaf.

Roasted Buckwheat Groats
Also known as kasha. They are not really grains, but resemble grains and have a brown pyramid shape. Best used in broths and stir-fried eggs.

Barley
Grains look like smooth small pearls. Excellent source of soluble fiber and in some studies has been shown to lower cholesterol. Best used in salads or with tuna.

Amaranth
Resembles golden poppy seeds. When cooked it has a consistency of a crunchy porridge. Has a corn-like flavor and best used as a breakfast cereal.

Quinoa (keen-wa)
A mild-flavored grain that will substitute for rice. Has a bitter coating and should be rinsed under cold running water several times before cooking.

Millet
A popular grain used for numerous vegetarian dishes or in tomato sauce.

If you eat pasta without a protein dish you may feel sluggish 1-2 hours later. This is related to a blood sugar level changes in some individuals.

Oriental noodle soups and many of your popular soups usually contain MSG.

Oats have the highest fat content of any grain.

Corn is one of the least nutritionally complete grains.

Long grain rice contains more protein, but has fewer minerals than most standard rice.

"FLUFFIER BEATS MUSHIER"
Converted rice is actually parboiled rice, rice which has been soaked, steamed and dried in such a way as to make it fluffier instead of mushier.

Granola bars when they first arrived on the scene contained 50-60% sweeteners and fat. The present bar averages 70-80% sweeteners and fat and only have a slight edge over a candy bar.

"CAN'T CHOOSE YOUR RELATIVES"
Eating poppy seeds may cause you to have a positive urine test for drugs. Poppy seeds are a relative of morphine and codeine.

"NATURAL HIGH?"
Sunflower seeds produce a similar action on the body as smoking a cigarette. It causes the body to produce adrenalin, which will go to the brain, resulting in a pleasant feeling. The seeds must, however, be raw, not roasted.

Millet is one of the highest nutritional quality grains.

Amaranth, originally an Aztec grain, unlike other grains is not deficient in the amino acid lysine. When this grain is eaten with rice, wheat or barley it can provide a complete protein containing all amino acids.

There are 70,000 seeds in 1 pound of amaranth.

Amaranth can be popped like popcorn.

"HIC"
The majority of barley grown in the United States is used to produce alcoholic beverages. The malt is made by soaking whole barley seeds until they convert to sugar.

"STRANGE FAMILY TREE"
Buckwheat is not related to the wheat or grain family, but is actually a fruit and a relative of rhubarb.

Minute and instant rice have the lowest nutritional content of any rice.

"UP, UP AND AWAY"
Quinona (keen-wa) is a grainlike product, related to Swiss chard and spinach. Often referred to as a "supergrain" because of its high levels of iron.

"DOWN THE DRAIN"
Never rinse packaged domestic rice before cooking, it's not necessary and may wash away some of the nutrients that were added as an enrichment. The cooking removes enough anyway.

"USE YOUR PASTA-MAKER"
Pasta products can be considered a low-fat food, homemade is best.

Avoid any pasta product that lists "disodium phosphate" on the label. It is a chemical softening agent that helps the pasta cook faster.

"NATURAL RELAXER"
Serotonin, a chemical produced by the body that helps you relax, can be increased by a complex carbohydrate (pasta) meal.

"USE IT, OR LOSE IT"
Whole wheat flour should be used within 2 months of purchase to avoid rancidity. Refrigeration, however, will delay the rancidity for up to 4 months.

Pasta products are easily digested due to their low fiber content. This makes them an ideal food for young children, infants and the elderly.

Most pasta is made with very little or no salt. Good for low sodium diet.

Uncooked pasta has a protein content of approximately 12%. 3.4 grams per 3/4 cup serving.

Triticale is made from wheat and rye and is more nutritious than wheat. One of the highest nutrient flours. Highly recommended.

"A LITTLE OF THIS AND A LITTLE OF THAT"
Be aware that your favorite brand of grain cereal may contain so many additives that it may not be as healthy a product as you are made to believe.

The best quality pasta is made from amber durum wheat which comes from Russia.

"DEFINITELY, NOT SQUARE"
90% of all durum wheat grown in the U.S. is grown in Northeastern North Dakota. This area is known as the "durum triangle."

When durum wheat is cooked it is always tender and does not become mushy or pasty.

If you use durum wheat pasta it is not necessary to rinse it before using.

"AN ALL AROUND WINNER"

Chestnuts are the only nut that contains vitamin C and has a low fat and calorie content.

Before cooking chestnuts, cut an "X" on the pointed end. This will keep them from exploding when roasting and also will make them easier to peel.

Dry-roasted nuts and regular roasted nuts have about the same number of calories.

A Nut By Any Other Name

Roasted Nuts
Usually fried in oil, and not always a good oil. many are roasted in coconut oil which is high in saturated fat.

Dry-Roasted
Not cooked in oil, but still contain a high fat content and is usually high in salt, sweeteners and preservatives may be added.

Raw Nuts
Usually sold in vacuum packed cans to retain the freshness. May go bad and become rancid rather quickly. Try and keep them refrigerated, this will slow down the process and they will last longer.

Defatted (lite) Peanuts
Some of the oils have been removed through processing, but this doesn't change their fat content appreciably.

"BONE FOOD"
One ounce of almonds have as much calcium as 1/4 cup of milk.

"NUT, NOT RELATED TO THE NUT FAMILY TREE"
Peanuts are really not in the nut family, but are legumes, a type of bean.

"MODERN-AGE NUT CRACKER"

Black walnuts are very difficult to crack open. One of the best ways if you have a trash compactor or have a friend who has one, is to place a wood platform on the bottom raising it up a few inches, make sure you have a clean bag and crush away.

To remove the burnt taste from rice, try placing a piece of very fresh white bread on top of the rice, then cover the pot. It should only take a few minutes for the burnt taste to disappear.

Never add salt to rice until fully cooked, it will toughen the rice.
When making lasagna, use a small amount of olive oil in the water to prevent the sections from sticking together.

"I WONDER WHERE THE YELLOW WENT"

To keep rice white while cooking, add a few drops of lemon juice to the water.

A few minutes before your rice is done, place a double paper towel just under the lid and finish cooking. The rice will come out more fluffy and dry.

"RICE SCIENCE 101"

To obtain the right amount of water to cook rice without measuring, place a quantity of rice in a pot, shake the pot to smooth out and settle the rice, then place your index finger lightly on top of the rice - don't make a dent - add water until your first knuckle is covered (about 1" above the surface of the rice).

If you are chopping nuts in a blender, add a small amount of sugar and they won't clump together.

One cup uncooked pasta = Two cups cooked pasta.

PASTA SAUCES:

Genovese - A thick meat sauce, flavored with garlic, tomato and herbs.

Marinara - A zesty tomato sauce flavored with garlic, and herbs.

Neopolitan - A blend of tomato sauce, herbs, garlic, mushrooms and bell pepper.

Alfredo - Made with fresh cream, garlic and parmesan cheese.

Alla Panna - Combines fresh cream, garlic, marsala wine, parmesan cheese, mushrooms and smoked ham.

Formaggi - Made with fresh cream, garlic, parmesan, romano and Swiss cheeses.

Pesto - Made from extra virgin olive oil, fresh basil, garlic, pine nuts and fresh cream.

Clam Sauce - Made with clam broth, tomatoes, crushed red pepper. Red is spicy, green is mild.

"MAKING A RAINBOW"

Pasta made from durum flour and whole eggs is naturally a golden-yellow color. When spinach is added, you will get green, blending tomato paste into the dough and will result in a salmon-toned pasta.

Kasha (buckwheat groats) is the fruit of the buckwheat plant. Prepare the same as rice. Very healthy.

PASTA SHAPES:

Cresti-di-gali	- Looks like a roosters comb.
Cannelloni	- Hollow tubes up to 2 inches long.
Ditalini	- Small thimble shapes.
Farfalle	- Shaped like a bowtie. The word means butterfly in Italian.
Funghini	- These pasta are related to the mushroom family and used in soups and stews.
Fusilli bucati	- Corkscrew-shaped pasta.
Lumache	- Pasta shaped like a snails shell.
Macaroni	- Curved pasta, comes in many sizes with a hollow center.
Occhi-di-lupo	- Very large tubes of pasta sometimes referred to as "wolf's eyes."
Orcchiette	- Pasta shaped like ears.
Pulcini	- Used mainly in soups and called "little chickens."
Ravioli	- Small squares of pasta stuffed with different ingredients.

Riccini	- Pasta shaped like ringlet curls.
Ruoti	- Round pasta with spokes, looks like a wagon wheel.
Tortellini	- Pasta that is supposed to resemble the Roman Goddess Venus' navel.
Vermicelli	- Italian word for worms, which they resemble. Also known as spaghetti.
Ziti	- Very short tubular shaped pasta.

Arkansas is the largest rice producer in the United States.

Pasta should be cooked firm and slightly chewy. Excess cooking decreases the nutrient content.

"PASTY PASTA"
Pasta will not get sticky if you place it in a warm colander then into a warm dish. The cold colander causes the starch to get sticky.

There are over 300 types of pasta.

When cooking pasta, cover the pot after you place the pasta into the boiling water. The water should be kept boiling and not cool down to any great degree for the best results.

Pasta consumption in the United States in 1994 was approximately 20 pounds per person and going up every year.

"THE PASTA WINNERS"
Italians, however, consume an average of 60 pounds of pasta annually.

Any pasta that is packaged in clear plastic containers are subject to nutrient loss from the lights in the market. Purchase pasta in boxes whenever possible.

Noodles must contain 5-6% egg solids by law.

Do not purchase any grains that are not whole. If you see numerous broken pieces, don't buy the grains.

Cooked wild rice will only keep in the refrigerator for 1 week.

Bulgar wheat is not a good quality nutritious whole wheat product unless their granules still have their dark brown coating.

Bulgar should be steamed, then dried and cracked into three different granulations. The coarsest is used for pilaf; the medium is used for cereals; and the finest for tabbouleh.

Bulgar requires less cooking time than cracked wheat.

Tabbouleh is a Middle Eastern dish made from cracked wheat or bulgar, lemon juice,, olive oil, parsley, dill or mint, plum tomatoes, scallions, minced garlic, salt, pepper and other cold vegetables if desired.

Use your frying basket or a large metal strainer when cooking pasta. This will save you the trouble of draining.

After opening pasta, save the unused portion in a glass jar.

Rice was first cultivated in Thailand in 3500 B.C.

Asia produces over 90% of the world's rice.

Rice is the staple grain of over 60% of the people of the world.

Brown rice is rice with only the husk removed.

Converted rice has been parboiled to remove the surface starch.

Unopened packages of rice should be stored at a cool room temperature.

To tenderize brown rice, allow rice to soak for an hour or two before cooking.

To cook rice, bring to a boil, cover and simmer on low heat 35 minutes, turn off heat and let stand covered for 10 minutes.

To make an exceptional dessert from leftover rice, try folding in stiffly beaten whipped cream, then add fresh fruit.

Always wash rice before using, this cleans out the hulls and other debris.

Whole grain products should be stored in solid tightly covered containers.

Glass dishes will bake bread faster than metal pans.

Macadamia nuts have more fat and calories than any other nut.

Before measuring a whole grain flour, sift it with a coarse sifter. Avoid the squeeze handle types. Sifting will make a difference of up to two tablespoons per cup.

Chapter 16

Bread and Muffin Facts

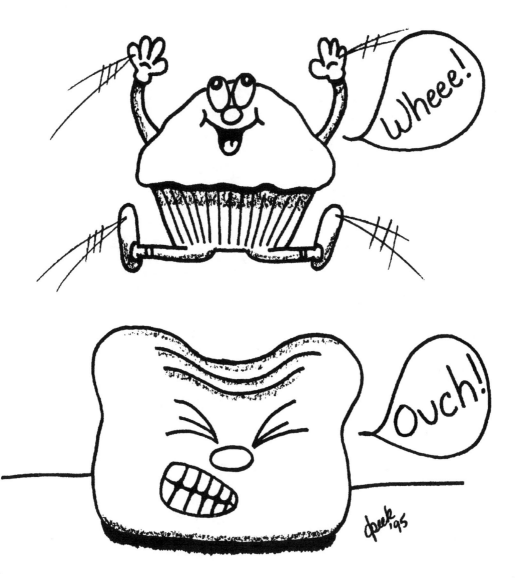

"DON'T CHILL IT, BOX IT"

Storing bread is best in a breadbox at room temperature, it will stay fresh for days if wrapped. Bread goes stale up to 6 times faster at room temperature.

Bread labeled "cracked wheat," "sprouted wheat" or "wheat bread" usually contain white flour.

"HEAVVVY"

Never expect whole wheat bread to raise as high as white bread or be as airy, there is more volume to it.

"CALL THE WARDEN"

If your using a bread mixer, try spraying a liquid oil on the dough hook to keep the dough from climbing up and escaping.

Bread holds water well and will last for weeks in the freezer.

"BAGELLA CRAZE"

Bagel sales have increased 169% in 1994 and now ranks as one of the most popular breakfast foods.

When thawing a frozen bread, it should be consumed shortly after, otherwise it will dry out.

If you make french toast and pancakes ahead of time and freeze them you can pop them into the toaster anytime you want.

Rye bread usually contains white flour. Make sure the label says "whole-rye flour."

Whole wheat bread will rise faster if you add 1 tablespoon of lemon juice to the dough when you are mixing it.

After you boil potatoes, try using the water in your bread recipe and the bread will stay fresher longer at room temperature. The water will have a high starch content.

If you run out of yeast and need it to make biscuits, try using a teaspoon of baking soda and an equal amount of vitamin C. The results will be the same, since a similar chemical reaction occurs.

"DON'T SETTLE FOR LESS"
When making pancakes or waffles, be sure and mix the batter between batches to avoid settling. You will be surprised at the difference in the quality of the dish.

100% whole wheat bread will be more moist if you add as little flour as possible to the dough. Whole grain tends to absorb water more slowly than standard refined flour and becomes dry as the dough rises.

"IT'S A KILLER"
Add yeast to water, never water to yeast. Be gentle to the little yeasties.

"WHAT A LITTLE SWEETNESS WILL DO"
Remember, yeast is a living organism, there are approximately 3000 billion cells in one pound. Their food supple is sugar and they produce alcohol and carbon dioxide (the riser we want). Enzymes in the wheat starch produce the sugar for the reaction to begin.

"SUSPENDED ANIMATION"
Dry yeast will last longer if refrigerated.

When reheating biscuits, place them in a well dampened paper bag, seal up tightly and heat in oven on low temperature reading.

"MAY NEED SEAT BELTS"
Always bake biscuits on pans without sides, the heat circulates more evenly.

Biscuits will brown to a rich golden color if you add a teaspoon of granulated sugar to the dry ingredients.

To reduce rising time approximately 1 hour, try adding 1 extra packet or cube of yeast. This will not change the taste.

Use the ice cube divider to cut biscuits into small squares.

"TIRE PUMP MAY WORK"
The secret to light dumplings is to puncture them when they are finished cooking, allowing the air to circulate within.

"BE GENTLE"
Remember that salt and cold retard yeast growth, sweetness and warmth (up to a point) increases it. Oven temperatures will kill it.

To place moisture into a stale loaf of bread, wrap it in a damp cloth or towel for about 1-2 minutes then place it in a preheated 350°F. oven for about 20 minutes.

"A COLD SHOWER"
To replace moisture into French or Italian bread or hard rolls, sprinkle the crust with cold water and place into a 350°F. oven for about 10 minutes.

To remove rolls or muffins more easily, try placing the pan directly from the oven on a wet towel for 20-30 seconds.

For a hard to knead doughs, try oiling your hands before working it.

To avoid fresh baked bread from getting moldy, try wrapping the bread in waxed paper and storing in the refrigerator.

Kneading dough is easier if you place the dough in a plastic bag.

"RIP VAN WINKLE"
If you store yeast or a flour product containing yeast in the refrigerator make sure you allow it to warm to room temperature before using it to wake up the yeast. Cold inactivates yeast.

"ANCIENT YEAST TRAPPERS"
Sourdough bread is produced from a living bacterial culture called a "starter." The starter consists of water and flour which ferment and as it does traps wild yeasts from the air giving it its distinctive "sour" taste.

"SAUNA?"

Place a pan of water in the oven when baking breads to keep the crusts from becoming too hard. The moisture and steam works great.

Try placing a piece of tin foil under your towel in the bread basket when serving rolls. It will keep them warm longer.

"CIRCULATE"

Freshly baked breads should be cooled on a rack so that air can circulate around it as it cools. Keeps the bread from becoming soggy.

"LEVITATION"

Use a heating pad on medium to help your dough rise perfectly. Place the dough in a pan then place it on the pad.

Bread sticks may contain up to 42% fat.

Pita bread pockets usually contain no sugar or added fat.

A quality brown bread should contain 100% whole wheat flour or whole grain flour.

Pita bread has almost no fat and contains only 75 calories per ounce.

A 7 inch pita pocket weighs only 2 ounces and has 120-150 calories.

Avoid any baked product made with most shortenings, hydrogenated oils or lard. It will be high in saturated fat.

Moldy bread should be disposed of. Throw out the whole bread even if only one piece has the mold. Mold sends feelers out that are invisible to the naked eye.

Quick breads are leavened with the use of baking powder or baking soda in place of yeast. No rising time is needed. The baking powder or soda react with water and acid in the dough at the oven temperatures and forms carbon dioxide which causes the rise.

"JOLLY POOR SHOW"
English muffins have no nutritional advantage over white bread.

Bagels have a low-fat content and have more protein than 2 slices of white bread. However they are getting so large that they are no longer considered a low-calorie food.

Toasting bread reduces the protein efficiency ratio from 0.90 out of a possible 2.5, to approximately 0.32.

If you must buy white bread, make sure it says "enriched," many do not!

To increase the protein value of bread, remove 1-2 tablespoons of whole wheat flour and replace it with an equal amount of soy flour.

Enriched white flour - The milling and bleaching process destroys 86% of the niacin, 73% of the vitamin B6, 33% of the thiamin, 50% of the pantothenic acid, 42% of the vitamin B2 and 19% of the protein.

To make cutouts from bread slices, try freezing the bread first. This will give your cutouts clean, sharp edges.

Pumpernickel is usually made from white or rye flour and colored with caramel.

To cut pizza easily, just use a scissors.

Bagels are made from a high protein flour and little or no shortening.

Bread pans should never be scoured to a shiny glean. Bread bakes better in a dull pan.

To keep bread fresh when freezing, tuck a paper towel into the bag with the bread or rolls. The paper towel will absorb the moisture that usually makes breads mushy when thawed.

Buy the thinnest sliced white bread you can. It will reduce the calories about 50%.

Your best white breads are Italian, French or sour dough, if they say "enriched."

White bread should be made from "unbleached flour" instead of "white flour" or just "flour" on the list of ingredients.

Chapter 17

A Cup of Joe, A Spot of Tea

Tea was originated in China and then was introduced to Japan.

Iced tea and coffee can be greatly improved if the ice cubes are made of coffee or tea instead of water.

You can avoid cloudiness in iced tea by letting freshly brewed tea cool to room temperature before refrigerating it. If the tea does become cloudy, pour a little boiling water into it until it becomes clear.

For a new taste in tea, add a small bit of dried orange peel to the teapot.

The Island of Ceylon is the world's leading producer of tea.

"HOW MANY LEAVES CAN A PICKER PLUCK?"
An experienced picker can pluck about 40 pounds of tea leaves a day.

Classifications of Tea

Black Tea - Turns black due to oxidation. This is the best quality tea. Includes; Assam, Ceylon, Darjeeling, English Breakfast, Keemun, Lapsang and Souchong.

Green Tea - Oxidation is omitted. The natural color is green. Two main types; Basket Fired and Gunpowder.

Oolong Tea - Semi-processed, makes the leaves partly green and brown. Two types; Formosa Oolong and Jasmine.

Just For The "Health" Of It

Salada and Bigelow English Teatime are two of the highest caffeine content teas. They average about 60mg. of caffeine per 8oz. cup.

When drinking tea, never use polystyrene cups with lemon. The combination of the hot tea and the lemon will corrode the cup away releasing carcinogens into your drink. It will actually eat right through the cup.

Tannin, found in tea and red wine may interfere with the body's use of iron, thiamin and vitamin B12.

At present there is no risk factor related to drinking tea and heart disease.

"TEA TIME"
Black teas are the most popular in the U.S. We Import 130 million pounds per year. The yearly consumption is 35 billion servings.

"TEA TRIVIA"
Iced tea was first created at the 1904 Louisiana Purchase Exposition in St Louis, MO.

One pound of tea will brew approximately 200 cups (200 teabags).

The U.S. imports approximately 72% of its tea from India.

Toxic Teas

Buckthorn	May cause diarrhea.
Burdock	Blocks nerve impulses to organs.
Comfrey	Can cause liver problems.
Foxglove	May cause heart arrythmias.
Groundsel	May cause liver problems.
Hops	Can destroy red blood cells.
Jimsonweed	Blurred vision problems, hallucinations.
Kava-Kava	May cause deafness, lack of coordination.
Lobelia	May cause liver problems.
Mandrake	May block nerve impulses to organs.
Meliot	Can cause tendency to hemorrhage.
Nutmeg	Can cause hallucinations.
Oleander	Can cause heart stoppage.
Pokeweed	May cause breathing difficulties.
Sassafras	May cause liver cancer.
Senna	May cause diarrhea.
Thorn Apple	Blocks nerve impulses.
Tonka Bean	Causes tendency to hemorrhage.
Woodruff	Causes tendency to hemorrhage.

Decaffeinated Coffee

1973 - Trichloroethylene used - Found in 1975 to cause liver cancer in mice.

1975 - Methylene Chloride - Found in 1981 to cause cancer in lab animals. FDA said that the tests were not conclusive. Residues are low in coffee and may not be harmful in humans.

1981 -   Ethyl Acetate - A number of coffee
               companies switch to ethyl acetate which is
               also found in bananas and pineapple. In
               concentrated form, its vapors have been
               known to cause damage to lungs, heart and
               livers in lab test animals. It is also
               used as a cleaner and solvent for leather
               and plastics. Still in use.

1984 -   Water Process - Was developed by Swiss and
               Belgium companies. A harmless method, but
               may cause some loss of flavor. Now being
               used by a number of U.S. companies.

Coffee manufacturers do not have to disclose their method of decaffeination.

Brazil has experienced two major frosts in 1994 that destroyed over 1 billion pounds of coffee, approximately 10% of the world's coffee supply, raising prices worldwide.

Consumption of decaf coffee is up 13% and general coffee consumption is down 23% according to the NPD group, inc.

The United States consumes about 1/3 of all coffee worldwide, approximately 400 million cups per day.

The only coffee grown in the United States is Kona, which is grown on the island of Hawaii. The coffee is grown in volcanic soil and has the richest coffee flavor in the world.

"BUMMER"
If you give up coffee and are drinking two cups a day or more you will probably have withdrawal symptoms, such as headaches, nausea and possibly depression.

"BROWN FILTERS ARE BEST"
The safest way to prepare coffee is to boil it in water instead of filtering it. This is the way it is prepared in the Scandinavian countries.

Fresh roasted coffee beans are usually packed in non-airtight bags to allow the carbon monoxide formed during the roasting process to escape. If the carbon monoxide doesn't escape, the coffee may have a poor taste.

The "Swiss Water" decaffeinated process is the best. Check the label. Other "water processed" methods are not as good.

"CHUG-A-LUG"

The freshness of a cup of coffee only survives 10-30 minutes in a coffee warmer.

Coffee will taste better if you start with a quality cold water, not hot tap water.

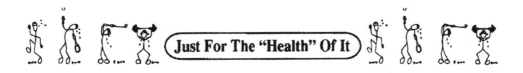

There is a 60% greater risk of heart disease if you consume 2-5 regular cups of coffee per day, and 120% greater risk for over 6 cups per day.

Purchase only "unbleached" brown coffee filters. The chemical digoxin is used to bleach filters white and may leave a residue.

Dripped coffee has almost twice the caffeine as instants.

Beverages that contain caffeine may cause your skin to become dehydrated and promotes premature aging.

The polyphenols in coffee and the tannins in tea may reduce the amount of iron available for the body to use. One cup of coffee consumed with a hamburger reduces the amount of iron absorbed by approximately 40%, tea by 90%.

Caffeine takes approximately 30 minutes to affect your brain and lasts for 2-6 hours.

Two cups of coffee will cause an increase in hydrochloric acid in the stomach for at least an hour.

Coffee reduces the healing time of stomach ulcers.

One cup of coffee or one cigarette will cause a rise in blood pressure.

Studies also show that caffeine may be related to fibrocystic breast disease.

"A REAL BUMMER"

Caffeine may affect zinc absorption which may adversely affect the prostate gland and possibly reduce sexual urges in some people.

Withdrawal symptoms will appear if caffeine is discontinued. These usually start with headaches but only last for 3-5 days. The cells become dependent on the drug.

If you consume more than 300mg. of caffeine a day it will overstimulate the Central Nervous System and may cause insomnia, nervousness, diarrhea and increase your heart rate.

Coffee drinkers have a higher incidence of heart disease.

Caffeine causes chemical changes in cells that cause excess triglycerides to be released into the blood stream.

Caffeine reduces the body's ability to handle stress.

In pregnant woman caffeine will enter the fetal circulation in the same concentrations as it enters the mother's with a possible relation to birth defects.

A dash of salt added to coffee that has been overcooked or reheated will freshen the taste.

Coffee trees originally came from Africa.

The first people known to actually drink the beverage known as "coffee" were the Arabs who would not allow the beans to be exported. They were finally smuggled to Holland in 1660 and then to Brazil in 1727.

Opened coffee cans should be stored in the refrigerator upside down. The coffee will retain its' freshness and flavor longer.

Leftover coffee and tea can be frozen in ice cube trays then used to cool hot coffee or tea or in other beverages.

"COOL IT"
For a fast cup of coffee, have a cup of fresh coffee in a sealed container in the refrigerator. Coffee will warm up and have an excellent taste.

Hills Brothers Coffee was the first commercial company to sell vacuum packed coffee in 1900.

Coffee trees require 70 inches of rainfall per year.

Ground coffee oxidizes very fast and coffee is best purchased in vacuum cans.

Americans consume 4,848 cups per second, 24 hours a day.

A coffee tree produces approximately one to twelve pounds of coffee cherries" from a six-year old tree.

"BELIEVE IT OR NOT"
Approximately 2000 coffee cherries are required to produce one pound of coffee, the crop of one tree.

The U.S. is the largest consumer of coffee. About three billion pounds are used annually.

When reheating coffee, never boil it, as this will cause an undesirable flavor.

Espresso Beverages

Espresso-   A dark roasted coffee, prepared by a rapid infusion of very hot water through the coffee grounds. The coffee is served in petit cups. Sometimes served with a twist of lemon. The strength of the coffee is controlled by the darkness of the beans after roasting, how dense they are packed and the amount of water that is forced through them.

Cappuccino-   A combination of one shot of espresso, hot steamed milk, topped with a frothy head of milk, and to top it off a shake of cinnamon or cocoa. It will vary depending on the strength of the espresso.

Caffe Mocha-   One shot of espresso, topped with the froth from hot chocolate.

Caffe Latte-   One shot of espresso with a goodly amount of steamed milk. Some are served with a slightly higher amount of milk than espresso. Latte's are usually topped with a large amount of foam, while others have no foam at all.

Macchiato-	One shot of espresso with a dollop of foam on top. Served in a petit cup.
Latte-	Served in a large glass containing mostly steamed milk with a small amount of espresso on top. The espresso should remain on top but colors the milk a coffee color.
Cafe Au Lait-	A mixture of strong coffee (not espresso) and steamed milk. Usually served in bowls.
Caffe Borgia-	A frothy caffe mocha with orange and lemon peels.
Cafe L'Amore-	A petit cup of espresso with a topping of gelato.

Caffeine In Foods

<u>Coffee</u>	<u>Per 8 oz. Serving</u>
Perc...	190 - 270 mg.
Drip...	178 - 200 mg.
Instant...	90 - 112 mg.
Decaf..	3 - 7 mg.
Instant Decaf...	3 mg.

Tea   Per 8 oz. Serving

Black 5 Minute Brew..............................32 - 78 mg.
Iced..34 - 65 mg.
Oolong 5 Minute Brew.............................45 mg.
Instant..20 - 34 mg.
Decaf.. 8 - 16 mg.

Chocolate

Cocoa (8 oz.)................................... 6 - 8 mg.
Milk Chocolate (1 oz.)......................... 5 - 6 mg.
Semi-Sweet Chocolate (1 oz.)..................20 - 35 mg.

Soft Drinks   Per 12 oz. Serving

Jolt Cola.......................................68 mg.
Diet Dr. Pepper.................................65 mg.
Mountain Dew....................................49 mg.
Coke..45 mg.
Diet Coke.......................................44 mg.
Dr. Pepper......................................44 mg.
Pepsi...35 mg.
Diet Pepsi......................................34 mg.
RC Cola...34 mg.
Mr. Pibb..33 mg.
7 Up... 0 mg.

There is more sodium in a thick shake than in an order of french fries, due to the additives.

The chocolate coating on soft ice creams is a blend of oils that have a low melting point. It is a high-fat treat.

Chicken coatings contain a higher fat content than most hamburgers.

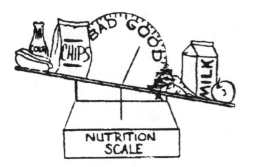

The pure vegetable oils used by many fast food restaurants for frying may contain high levels of coconut and palm oils. Both are very high in saturated fat content.

A triple cheeseburger contains 983 calories, 576 of those calories come from fat, and contains over 1200mg. of sodium.

When fish is coated and fried it ends up 50% fat in most cases, equal or higher in fat than some burgers.

Baked fish is available at Long John Silver's, a reduction of over 200 calories over fried fish. Even the sodium content is in an acceptable range of 361mg. instead of the usual 1200mg.

A shrimp salad at Jack In The Box has only 115 calories and less than 8% fat, providing you use "lite" dressing.

Arby's now has a roasted chicken sandwich.

Multi-grain buns are showing up everywhere and are an excellent source of fiber.

When fast food restaurants advertise 100% pure beef and you find a large assortment of gristle material in your burger, you might ask them what grade of beef they are using, or what percentage of edible offal they allow in the beef. It's all 100% beef!

A questionable food coloring FD&C Yellow Dye #5 can be found in McDonald's shakes, soft ice cream, Chicken McNuggets, hot cakes and their sundae toppings. MSG can be found in their bacon bits.

Roy Rogers uses MSG as a flavor enhancer in their chicken and roast beef seasonings.

Burger king's chicken sandwich contains 42 grams of fat, equal to a pint and a half of ice cream.

McDonald's has now introduced the "Lite Mac."

Salads and salad bars are now more than ever at fast food restaurants.

Carl's Jr has a BBQ Chicken Sandwich that has been approved by the American Heart Association.

Rating The Fast Foods:

FOOD	BEST RESTAURANT
1. Pizza (vegetarian)	Godfathers
2. Rotisserie Chicken	Kenny Rogers
3. Roast Beef Sandwich	Roy Rogers
4. Hamburger (McLean)	McDonald's
5. Fish Sandwich	None

Since most fast foods contain many additives, large amount of fats and calories galore, you may be interested in writing your favorite one for further information:

Arby's
Ten Piedmont Ctr.
3495 Piedmont Rd. NE
Atlanta, GA 30305

Burger King
P.O. Box 520783
General Mail Facility
Miami, FL 33152

Burger Chef
College Park Pyramids
P.O. Box 927
Indianapolis, IN 46206

Church's Fried Chicken
P.O. Box BH001
San Antonio, TX 78284

Hardee's
1233 N. Church St.
Rocky Mount, NC 27801

Jack In The Box
Foodmaker, Inc.
9330 Balboa Ave
San Diego, CA 92123

Kentucky Fried Chicken
P.O. Box 32070
Louisville, KY 40232

Long John Silver's
P.O. Box 11988
Lexington, KY 40579

McDonald's
McDonald Plaza
Oak Brook, IL 60521

Pizza Hut
P.O. Box 428
Wichita, KS 67201

Roy Rogers
Marriott Corp.
Marriott Dr.
Washington, D.C. 20058

Wendy's
4288 W. Dublin Granville
Dublin, OH 43017

HEALTH HINT:
Milk Shakes "Alias Thick Shake"

The word "milk" in milk shakes use to mean that you were actually purchasing a healthy product that contained "real milk." But, those days are over. Now when you order what you think is a shake, you receive a chemical concoction composed of fat-free milk solids, sweeteners, chemical thickeners, colorings and flavoring agents and a good dose of saturated fat.

These "shakes" are not called milk shakes anymore because they are not even a relative of a "milk shake." New names for these concoctions are: "thick shakes," "super shakes," "vanilla shake," or "chocolate shake." Be aware, however, that some companies are using a small amount of "real milk products" in these shakes so that they can use the word "milk" in their advertisements.

A milk shake is made with "real milk," "real ice cream"and natural syrup or fruit to flavor. These can be made with 1% low-fat milk, a good "natural" low-fat ice cream and "real fruit."

Chapter 20

Food Safety Facts

In a 1994 national survey 44% of the population, results were that the government was only doing a fair job of adequately inspecting fruits and vegetables regarding pesticide and fertilizer residues.

It was determined in a 1994 study that wooden cutting boards may be a source of contamination and cleaning them with hot soapy water doesn't make a significant difference in the bacteria levels. Bleach will do the trick in most instances, make sure you dilute it and rinse thoroughly. Acrylic cutting boards are the best according to the latest studies.

E. coli bacteria may be responsible for 20,000+ cases of food poisoning each year. For your protection cook all meat and poultry to an internal temperature of 160 degrees, wash all fruits and vegetables grown in manure and drink only pasteurized milk and cider.

Many bacteria are found on the surfaces of fruits and vegetables, even melons. Wash all surfaces before slicing any type of food, otherwise the knife may carry the bacteria to the inside.

It takes 4 hours for bacteria on melons to start multiplying. Try to eat it within this period, Refrigeration halts the growth or retards it significantly.

Harmful bacteria do not stop multiplying unless they are refrigerated below 40 degrees. Most refrigerators rarely hold this temperature.

Freezing does not kill bacteria it only stops their growth. The only thing that kills the bacteria is cooking.

Foodborne illness strikes 80 million Americans yearly. Most are mild cases, however, 9,000 are fatal. Most caused from meat and poultry.

Never store wine or spirits in a lead crystal decanter for a long period. They may leach out the lead. Vinegar dressing may also do the same due to its acidic nature.

Reported salmonella food poisoning cases have increased over 40% during the last ten years. A good percentage of these cases have been associated with fast food restaurants.

Boil all kitchen sponges at least once per week to be sure they are contaminant-free.

Never re-heat or save infant formula after a child has drunken from it. Bacteria will still remain alive, should be discarded.

Never slow cook a turkey overnight at 200 degrees. This gives the bacteria too long a period to multiply.

A cooked or raw turkey should never be kept unrefrigerated for more than 45 minutes.

MEAT AND POULTRY SAFETY LINE- 1 (800)535-4555

If the contents of a can or jar have a funny smell, are moldy or have an off color look, don't eat it!

Never eat foods directly from a jar or can, saliva may contaminate the contents.

THE "NOSE" KNOWS
Never smell a moldy food, it may cause an allergic reaction.

Meats should be kept hot. Use a thermometer to keep the temperature of meats, poultry and pork at 140°F.

Always keep eggs under refrigeration.

Refrigerate foods as soon as possible. Bacterial growth starts very quickly at between 45 °F. and 120 °F.

Anyone with an infection or cold should be kept away from the kitchen.

Small areas of mold on solid fruits or vegetables can usually be removed leaving the food still edible. Cut away an extra inch in case the mold has already sent feelers out.

Antibiotics should not be taken with food, it slows its absorption and possibly its potency levels.

Mayonnaise and salad dressing under normal conditions would not have to be refrigerated after opening. The reason it is recommended is that when you are making a salad, you tend to keep dipping the spoon in for more mayonnaise and leave residues of the salad in the jar.

Never eat food if it has been prepared by someone who is smoking at the time of preparation. Saliva from their hands, from continuously touching the cigarette may contaminate the food.

Never cover refrigerator shelves with tin foil. Air should be able to circulate around the foods.

Peanut butter should be stored in the refrigerator after opening to keep the fats from becoming rancid.

Leftovers that have remained in the refrigerator more than 36 hours should be recooked.

Never place cooked foods on the same surface that has fresh food on it.

Thaw frozen foods in the refrigerator, not at room temperature.

Your can opener should be washed after each use. Food left behind may be contaminated after a few days and cause food poisoning. This is one of the most common sources of food poisoning.

Consuming a large quantity of natural licorice may cause hypertension, heart enlargement and sodium retention due to the chemicals glycynhizic acid and menthol. 3 1/2oz. per day over a prolonged period can be harmful.

Always strain soups that may contain pieces of bone through a strainer. Place a coarse strainer inside a fine one for the best results.

To avoid the fat from catching fire when broiling meats, place a few pieces of dried bread in the broiler pan to soak up the dripping fat.

Never stuff a turkey or other fowl with warm stuffing and leave overnight, even if refrigerated.

Do not leave gravy, stuffing or cooked fowl at room temperature for more than 30-45 minutes before refrigerating.

If turkey or chicken salad is made, wait until the meat is fully cooled before adding any type of salad dressing or mayonnaise.

There are 1800 strains of salmonella, most of which will cause food poisoning. Millions of Americans annually suffer from food poisoning episodes. Most problems occur as a result of human error.

A large majority of food poisonings are related to the "pot luck" type of event. These usually are from poor temperature controls of foods containing egg or meat products.

Either keep foods cold or hot and you will reduce the risk of a problem. It is the mid-ranges that cause the most bacteria growth.

If mold is seen in jams and jellies (a small spot), scoop it out with a clean spoon, then scoop out a little more with a another clean spoon. If the balance tastes fermented, throw it out.

Throw out moldy vegetables, especially tomatoes, cucumbers and lettuce.

A good rule of thumb is just to throw out any food item that contains mold. Cheese may be the only exception, but be sure to cut away at least ½ to 1 inch away from the moldy area.

Foods cooked in aluminum pans that are damaged may absorb the metal, if there are any corroded areas marked by pitting and surrounded by white areas and if the pot is used frequently it may result in high risk of impaired kidney function and behavioral anomalies.

When you marinate any meat or poultry, make sure you leave it in the refrigerator while it is marinating.

Never place barbecued meats of any type on the same plate that held the raw meat after it has been cooked. This is one of the most common causes of food poisoning when barbecuing. Also, never continue to use the same utensils that touched the raw meat.

Use a fresh dish towel after you clean up from handling meats or poultry, then throw it in the wash and don't leave it sit out for further use.

A new study completed in 1995 by the federal government Center For Food Safety and Applied Nutrition showed that only one out of four people wash their cutting boards after cutting or preparing raw meats and poultry.

Chapter 21

Food, Not For Eating

Hot white vinegar will remove the non-slip decals from the bathtub as well as stickers on dishes.

"BLACK-OUT"
Margarine will remove tar off vinyl surfaces.

"SQUEAKY CLEAN"
A good cleaner that won't leave a film on tile is a mixture of white vinegar and water. Use approximately one quarter cup of vinegar to 1 gallon of warm water.

Peanut butter will remove gum from a person's hair.

"I WONDER WHERE THE YELLOW WENT"
Stale milk or leftover milk makes an excellent cleaner for plant leaves.

Mayonnaise can be used to oil wood.

Salt is handy for sopping up wine spills. Pour the salt on the spill, wait until it dries, then vacuum it up.

After boiling potatoes, use the water to polish silver. Just place the silver in the warm water. Place a washcloth on the bottom of the pot before placing silver in.

A paste of baking soda will remove black heel marks from a vinyl floor.

Top clean stains from aluminum pots, try boiling rhubarb in the pan until the stain disappears.

Meat tenderizer can be used to relieve the pain and itching from insect bites. Dissolve 1/4 to ½ teaspoon in a small amount of water.

Tomato juice will remove ink spots on clothing. Allow to soak for 20 minutes before washing.

Orange juice can be used to clean chrome.

Banana skins will provide an excellent source of plant nutrients if buried just below the surface. Especially good for flowers.

Egg-white sponged on leather will revive its luster.

Half a lemon dipped in salt will clean copper or brass, then rinse in warm water and polish with soft cloth.

Brewer's yeast rubbed on a dog or cat's fur will repel fleas. Giving them a vitamin B supplement approved by your vet will also help.

THE "NOSE" KNOWS
A few drops of vanilla extract placed in a bottle top in the refrigerator, will remove odors.

If your white socks are getting dingy, just boil a pot of water, add 2 slices of lemon or ½ teaspoon of lemon juice and soak for ten minutes. Then wash as you normally would.

Dry mustard will remove onion odors from your hands or cutting board. Rub in then rinse off.

Ink stains can usually be removed by placing a slice of tomato on the stain. It should soak up the stain. Hair spray may also work on an old stain.

Don't buy dustcloths treated to attract dust, just dip a piece of cheesecloth in a solution of 2 cups of water and 1/4 cup of lemon oil, then allow it to dry before using it.

Leftover tea will clean varnished furniture.

After you polish your wood furniture, sprinkle a small amount of cornstarch on and rub until you get a high gloss. The cornstarch will absorb oil and leave a great shine.

Sheer curtains will come out of the washer "wrinkle-free" if you dissolve a package of unflavored gelatin in a cup of boiling water and then add it to the final rinse.

For a brighter shoe shine, place a few drops of lemon juice on your shoes when you are polishing them.

Lemon juice and salt will remove mold and mildew.

Glue on containers can be removed by using vegetable oil.

Diamonds and gold can be cleaned with a solution of vinegar and water. Never place opals, emeralds and pearls in the solution or any other soft stone or costume jewelry.

Costume jewelry can be cleaned with a weak solution of baking soda and water. Then scrub lightly with a toothbrush.

If you burn your tongue, try sprinkling a few grains of sugar on it for instant relief.

To polish brass, use a small amount of Worcestershire sauce, clean off, then polish with olive oil.

Baking soda makes an excellent fire extinguisher. It smothers the flames by cutting off the oxygen supply.

If you have a problem removing a nut and bolt, just pour some carbonated soda on it and let it sit for 15 minutes.

Battery posts can be cleaned with a thick solution of baking soda and water. Allow it to soak for 10-15 minutes before washing it off. Baking soda is a base and will neutralize a weak acid.

To remove unwanted grass from between sidewalk and driveway cracks, try using vinegar or salt.

An inexpensive method of cleaning dentures is to soak them overnight in white vinegar.

Vinegar can be used to clean pipes.

White rings on furniture may be removed using a paste of salad oil and salt. Let the solution stand for a few hours then wipe it off.

Baking soda added to furniture oil may remove stains from woodwork. Adds just the right amount of mild abrasive.

To remove grease stains on your carpet, try placing corn starch on the area, leave overnight, then vacuum up.

Corn starch and water made into a paste may remove grease stains on some wallpapers. Try an area that doesn't show first, to be sure that the wallpaper won't be damaged.

A minor burn can be relieved by rubbing a slice of raw potato on the burn gently.

To stop a bad sunburn from blistering, try using a small amount of white vinegar.

Vanilla extract will relieve the pain of a grease burn.

"SMOKERS BEWARE"
To remove cigarette smoke from a room, try soaking a towel in a solution of vinegar and water, ring out completely, then wave it in a circular motion around the room.

Accidently hitting the smoker also helps.

To tenderize meats when barbecuing, add green papaya to the barbecue sauce. Don't leave the meat in too long or it will become mushy.

Buttermilk can be used to soften dry cheese.

Pecans, walnuts or peanuts can be used to mask scratches on furniture. Use a broken edge of the nut.

"SPOT OFF TEA"
Cold tea is a good cleaning agent for woodwork of any kind.

A slice of bread will often remove makeup smudges from dark clothes. It's not necessary to use the nutritious ones.

Along with your detergent, add a bottle of cola to a load of greasy work clothes. It will help loosen the serious dirt.

Instead of throwing leftover cola down the kitchen drain, dump it down the toilet bowl and watch what happens. After it has soaked for awhile the toilet bowl should be sparkling clean.

Lemon extract will remove black scuff marks from luggage.

Stains from ball-point pens can be removed by sponging the area with milk until it disappears.

"ELIMINATING A CRACK-UP"
A simple way to remove cracks in china cups is to simmer the cup in milk for 30-45 minutes, depending on the size of the crack. If the crack is not too wide, the protein in the milk will seal it.

After grating cheese, clean the grater with a raw potato.

Ball point pen stains can be removed with 70% alcohol or hair spray.

Chapter 22

Packaging and Food Nutrient Facts

IS FRESH FOOD REALLY FRESH?

The freshness and quality depends on many factors such as:

Transportation times
Storage conditions
Methods of packaging
Type of fertilizer used
Time of harvesting
Number of washings in supermarket
Exposure to air and light
Soil nutrient content

Fresh foods are usually the best choice, regardless of these factors. Some supermarket chains have become more aware of pesticide and fertilizer contamination and the percentage of filth on fruits and vegetables and are doing more than ever to correct this problem. One of the best examples of this is the Raley's Supermarket chain in Northern California.

CANNED FOODS:

The majority of canned foods are flavor poor with a "canned taste." Shelf life, however, is excellent and is usually between 2-4 years, depending on the food item.

Many of the vitamins and minerals tend to wash out over time from the liquid, usually resulting in a chemical breakdown of the nutrient. Enzymes are non-existent.

The cost of canned foods are generally twice the cost of dehydrated foods, since the consumer pays for the water weight as well as the food. Up to ½ the weight of a canned product may be water.

Nutritionally the products are generally low in nutrient quality due the intense heat processing they undergo. If you consume most of your fruits and vegetables from canned goods, it is recommended that you take a vitamin/mineral supplement.

FROZEN FOODS:

The flavor varies from excellent to poor depending on the product. If the foods are frozen at the time they are picked, the nutritional quality may be equal to, or even better than fresh, at the time of purchase.

Shelf life and quality is very dependent on the maintenance of proper freezer chest temperature levels.
Also, they should not be relied upon for long term storage or emergency use.

The cost is higher than dehydrated or canned but nutritional quality drops, the longer the freezer time.

DRIED FOODS:

Flavor varied depending on the age. These foods should not be stored for a long period of time, since the moisture content is only 25-30% water.

FREEZE DRIED FOODS:

Excellent flavor, but they yield considerably less servings per can, due to retention of their cellular structure, and have less shrinkage than dehydrated foods.

Shelf life is generally considered to be 4-7 years, if properly packed. Once opened they will spoil within 5-7 days.

The cost is considerably more than dehydrated foods, and has a moisture content of approximately 25-30%.

DEHYDRATED FOODS:

Many are vine-ripened with excellent flavor. In some instances it was found that dehydration actually enhanced the flavor of the foods.

The following is an example of dehydration reduction:

> 12 pounds of fresh beans = 1 pound of dehydrated
> 14 pounds of carrots = 1 pound of dehydrated
> 6 pounds of cheese = 1 pound of dehydrated

Most dehydrated foods are nitrogen vacuum packaged and if unopened may last indefinitely. They would be capable of sustaining life even after many years of storage. However, the nutritive life span is probably only 5-7 years.

For best results, foods should be rotated and used allowing a shelf life of 2-3 years maximum. Once the cans are opened they should be kept covered with a good sealing lid. The nitrogen in the can will leak out if the can is tipped over after opening and the product should then be used up soon after.

Storage locations should be located in a cool place.

Dehydrated foods are processed under a very high vacuum and very low drying temperature, making it possible to remove all but 2-3% of the moisture in the food. These foods also retain their nutritional value since they are not cooked to death in a canning process.

Purchasing and using dehydrated foods may reduce your grocery bill by as much as 40%, if incorporated into the diet properly and frequently.

Generally, as a rule of thumb, dehydrated foods will reconstitute two or three times their weight. This will call for conservative measures when using these foods.

Chapter 23

Soft Drink Facts

The Coca Cola Company purchases more sugar than any other company in the world.

According to an article in the Pennsylvania Medical Journal, a study showed that the increase in carbonic acid use may lead to an increase in nearsightedness.

Due to quantity of refined sugar in soft drinks, they tend to cause a rise in blood sugar levels for a short period of time. The levels then may plummet down causing a severe drop in physical strength and mental alertness.

Excess dietary phosphorus is fast becoming a medical concern. The ideal calcium to phosphorus ratio is approximately 50/50 in adults. The concern is that soft drinks supply an excess amount of phosphorus, upsetting this ratio. This may lead to a calcium deficiency, which should be of special concern to women entering their "osteoporosis years."

The average intake of phosphorus in the U.S. is now about 1500-1600mg per day. The recommended daily allowance is 800mg. The following is the phosphorus content of a few soft drinks:

Soft Drinks	Milligrams of Phosphorus/oz.
Coke	69.9
Pepsi-Cola	57.2
Diet Cherry Coke	55.7
Diet Pepsi	49.3
Dr. Pepper	44.7
Tab	44.4
Kool-Aide (lemonade flavor)	31.6
Hires Root Beer	22.4
Hawaiian Punch (lemonade flavor)	16.7
7-Up	3.0
Canada Dry Ginger Ale	3.0
A&W Root Beer	3.0

The "fizz" in soft drinks in most cases is produced by reacting chalk, limestone or bicarbonate of soda with sulfuric acid.

If the drink does not say "natural sources" it probably contains a color or flavoring that is made from "coal tars."

Coca-Cola is consumed 190 million times every 24 hours in more than 80 languages and in over 35 countries.

The soft drink industry is a $40 billion dollar a year business.

Soft-drinks account for one-quarter of all sugar consumed by Americans.

A child who consumes 4 colas per day takes in the equivalent caffeine of two cups of coffee. The carbonic acid and phosphorus content can affect the potency of a number of vitamins.

Colas that contain Nutrasweet may go stale after only 3 months, look for the expiration dates. Drinks may get a bitter taste as the sweetener breaks down.

A study in Florida showed that people who drank a large number of Dr. Pepper or Diet Coke had problems with recurrent kidney stones probably from the phosphoric acid used in the carbonation process. Persons with stone problems should avoid these drinks. Read the list of ingredients, many sodas use the same carbonating agent.

"BOTTOMS UP"
Soda pop is the beverage of choice over milk and juice in children across the United States, mainly due to baby bottles being produced that look like 7-Up. Pepsi and Coke containers.

"SOMETHINGS GONE WRONG"
Americans in 1990 spent three times the dollars on soft drinks than they did on milk, six times more on alcohol.

"LACK OF NUTRITION EDUCATION IN SCHOOLS"

Americans consumed 24 gallons of soft drinks per person in 1970. In 1994 we outdid ourselves and consumed 46 gallons per person.

Diet sodas may still be high in sodium.

Soft drinks may react with certain antacids, leading to constipation, headaches and even vomiting.

We have increased our soft drink consumption 200% over the 1950's.

The efficiency of the certain antibiotics can be reduced by consuming soft drinks.

We consume 500 bottles or cans of soft drinks per person per year.

Millions of American are now being called "colaholics" due to their addiction to the cola beverages.

Withdrawal symptoms usually occur from "caffeine highs" when cola drinks are given up. These include headaches, nervousness, diarrhea and constipation.

Colas have a higher physiological dependence than smoking and alcohol and is harder to give up.

Sugar supplies 99% of the 144 calories in a 12 ounce Coke.

40% of the nation's 1-2 year olds drink an average of 9 ounces of soft drinks per day.

Teenagers now prefer soft-drinks over milk. 10% of these soft-drinks are consumed at breakfast.

Calcium levels are marginal in teenagers due to their soft-drink consumption.

The acid in soft-drinks can erode tooth enamel.

The average adult consumes about 182.5 gallons of liquid annually. The following is the breakdown:

44.5 gallons of soft drinks
44.3 gallons of water
26.3 gallons of coffee
23.8 gallons of beer
20.1 gallons of milk
23.5 gallons of tea, juice, and other
alcoholic drinks

The average level of caffeine in colas is 26.5mg per cola.

Chapter 24

Supermarket Facts

Be sure that all foods that should be under refrigeration are under refrigeration and not stacked up over the cold line. Supermarkets are known to stack whole poultry higher than they should. This causes bacterial growth to begin.

Make sure the store is clean, if not don't shop there!

Are the employees neat and clean looking?

"BRRRRRRRRRRR"
Check the thermometer in the meat cases. They should be between 28° and 38°F. The dairy products should be between 35° and 45°F. Ice cream should be approximately -12°F.

Don't buy frozen foods if there are large ice crystals on the packages, foods may have been thawed and re-frozen.

Processed hams should be under refrigeration, frequently they are not. Canned ones as well.

Never buy a jar if it is sticky, somethings gone wrong somewhere.

"WHAT'S IN A NAME"
Many markets have their own names to make you think that the product is of a higher grade than it really is.

These names are similar to ones used by the USDA in most cases. They include: "Premium", "Quality", "Select Cut", "Market Choice", "Prime Cut", etc.

Shop when the store is not crowded so that you can see the specials.

Most weekend specials start midweek.

Foods on the lowest shelves are usually the least expensive.

Tumble displays are more common than the old pyramid type, since shoppers hate to disturb a neat display.

Buy by the case whenever possible, if the market has a sale.

Check the weights of fruits and vegetables, the heaviest not the biggest is usually the best value.

Don't be afraid to return poor quality products.

The most commonly purchased items are usually found in the center of an aisle.

Highest profit items are found at eye level.

Items found in bins at greatly reduced prices near the checkout register are usually products that have been difficult to sell.

Avoid bruised fruits and vegetables.

Label Terminology:

- All food ingredients must be on the label.
- All additives must be listed.
- Many food products still do not require nutrition information.
- Symbols:

"R" means that the trademark used on the label is registered with the U.S. Patent Office.

"C" indicates that any literary and artistic content on the label is protected by copyright.

"K" indicates that the food is Kosher.

Chapter 25

Restaurant Facts

Restaurants are becoming more willing to serve salad dressings and mayonnaise on the side than ever before. Don't trade with one that doesn't.

Most restaurants will now prepare your food broiled or baked instead of fried when you request them to do so, especially the better restaurants.

If you have a question regarding substitutions, talk to the manager directly and don't deal with the waitress.

Return any meat or poultry that is not fully cooked, this is one of the most common causes of food poisoning, the most common problems are usually in chicken and hamburger.

If you are going to eat a salad or other food from a buffet or salad bar, make sure that they are not browned or dried out before being seated.

Be sure custard, whipped cream and cream-filled desserts are refrigerated. In many of the largest buffets these are just placed out on a tray with the rest of the dessert items.

Are the dishes and silverware clean.

Does the server touch the top of the glasses where you drink from?

Ask for a straw for all beverages served in a glass.

Is the cream for the tea or coffee kept at room temperature instead of being refrigerated.

Are the servers in clean uniforms?

Are the dishes chipped or discolored, restaurants that do not care about the little things are not too careful about cleanliness.

Are the bathrooms clean?

Look at the window sills for insect residues and dirt.

Are the curtains or blinds clean and dust-free?

If the menus are stained with food or have actual food residues, it is best to leave while you have a chance.

The condiment containers should be clean and not caked with the product.

Cream containers should be kept under refrigeration and brought to the table when requested.

Do the employees have their long hair tied back properly.

Chapter 26

Consumer Awareness Facts

If you see a label on an individual food stating that it is "low-cholesterol" it cannot contain more than 20mg. of cholesterol per serving and 2 grams of fat.

The government allows 350 pesticide ingredients to be used on crops. Approximately 70 of these have been classified as possible carcinogens.

If a food is labeled "low-fat" it cannot contain more than 3 grams of fat per individual serving. This may still be high since most companies figure 30% of your calories can come from fat. Still need to calculate and multiply 9 calories per gram times the total amount of fat you are actually eating. I prefer no more than 20% fat in a diet.

The only "low-fat" milks are 1% which is 16% fat after you remove the water, skim and buttermilk.

If the label reads "low in saturated fat" the food cannot have more than 1 gram of fat per serving. Make sure, however, that you count up the total in the full amount your eating, it may be higher than you think.

Filth in food guidelines in foods are controlled by the FDA. The following levels of contamination (insects, etc.) if found in food would be cause for the FDA to take legal action to remove the food from the supermarket. This is just a small example:

Apricots -	Canned, average of 2% insect infested or damaged.
Coffee Beans -	If 10% by count are insect infested or insect damaged or show evidence of mold.
Citrus Juice -	Canned, microscopic mold count average of 10%. Drosophila and other fly eggs: 5 per 250ml. Drosophila larva: 1 per 250ml. If average of 5% by count contain larvae.

Peaches -   Canned, Average of 5% wormy or moldy fruit or 4% if a whole larva or equivalent is found in 20% of the cans.

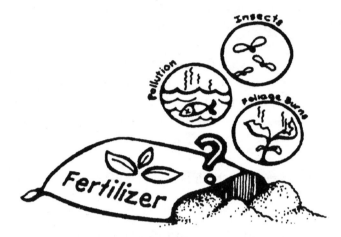

Popcorn -   One rodent pellet in one or more sub-samples upon examination of ten 225gm. sub-samples or six 10 ounce consumer-size packages, and 1 rodent hair in other subsamples; or 2 rodent hairs per pound and any rodent hairs in 50% of the sub-samples; or 20 gnawed grains per pound and rodent hairs in 50% of the sub-samples.

Asparagus -   Canned. 15% of spears by count infested with 6 attached asparagus beetle eggs or egg sacs.

Broccoli -   Frozen, average of 80 aphids or thrips per 100 grams.

Tomato Juice -   10 fly eggs per 3 ½ oz. or 5 fly eggs and 1 larva per 3 ½ oz. or 2 larva per 3 ½ oz.

Raisins -   Average of 40mm. of sand and grit per
                         3 ½ oz. or 10 insects and 35 fly eggs
                         per 8 oz. of golden bleached raisins.

Wheat -   One rodent pellet per pint. 1% by weight
                         of insect-damaged kernels.

**Brussel
Sprouts** -   Average of 40 aphids per 3 ½ oz.

Flour -   The FDA allows wheat flour to contain
                         approximately 50 insect parts per 2
                         ounces of flour. These are harmless and
                         won't affect your health.

Sorbital, used as a sweetener in diabetic candies can cause diarrhea.

Pineapple juice may help keep arteries clear with the chemical bromelin.

Label Terminology

Low-Calorie -   Allowed to contain only 40 calories
                         per serving or a maximum of .4
                         calories per gram.

Reduced Calorie -   Must have at least 1/3 fewer
                         calories than the original product and
                         should include a comparison of both
                         versions.

Diet or Dietetic -   The product may be lower in calories,
                         sodium or sugar.

Lite or Light -   This term can have any meaning the
manufacturer wants to use it for, such
as a relation to taste, texture,
color, or may have a lowered calorie,
fat or sodium content.

No Cholesterol -   Means that the item has no cholesterol
but may still be high in saturated
fats which may assist the body to
produce cholesterol.

Low-Fat -   When pertaining to dairy products,
they must only contain between 0.45
and 2% fat by weight.

Extra Lean -   Usually pertains to meat and poultry.
They must have no more than 5% fat by
weight.

*If a food is labeled "extra lean" it may contain more saturated fat than a "low in
saturated fat" food.*

Lean -   Usually pertains to meat and poultry.
They must have no more than 10% fat by
weight.

Leaner -   Usually pertains to meat and poultry.
Must have at least 25% less fat than
the standard.

Sugar-Free -
or
Sugarless
Should contain no table sugar, but
still may contain some of the
following; honey, corn syrup,
sorbital or fructose. Most of which
are just other forms of sugar and
still high in calories.

Sodium-Free -   Should contain less than 5mg per serving.

Very Low Sodium -   Contains 35mg or less per serving.

Low Sodium -   Contains 140mg or less per serving.

Reduced Sodium -   The normal level of sodium in the product has been reduced by at least 75%.

No Salt Added -   Salt has not been added during the unsalted processing. The food may still have other ingredients that contain sodium.

Imitation -   A food which is a substitute for another food and is usually nutritionally inferior. May still contain the same number of calories and fat.

Organic -   May pertain to almost anything. Usually means a food that is grown without the use of artificial fertilizers.

Natural -   May mean anything, no regulations apply and may be seen on foods that have additives and preservatives.

Enriched -   A degraded, processed product that or Fortified has nutrients added back in.

97% of people who purchased processed foods never read the labels according to a 1988 survey. In 1994 the same survey showed that 84% still don't read the labels. We are making progress but have a long way to go.

RECOMMENDED SHELF LIFE FOR SOME NESTLE PRODUCTS

The Nestle Company was kind enough to release data regarding the shelf life of some of their products and their dating code system. What may surprise you is the length of time that a product is considered safe to sell. There was no mention, however, how much of the nutritional quality was left after 1-2 years in a package.

SHELF LIFE - CONFECTIONS

7 Months:	Baby Ruth- bars, nuggets
10 Months:	Butterfingers, Goobers, Oh Henry
12 Months:	Crunch, 100 Grand, Raisinets, Chunky, After Eight, DeMet's Turtles
15 Months:	Milk Chocolate Bar
18 Months:	Caramel, Licorice, Butter Rum, Chocolate Mint
24 Months:	Sno Caps

SHELF LIFE - BAKING CHOCOLATE

12 Months:	Premier White Morsels
15 Months:	White Baking Bars
18 Months:	Butterscotch Morsels
24 Months:	Semi-sweet and Unsweetened Baking Bars, Choco-Bake, Nestle Cocoa, Milk Chocolate, Mint, Rainbow Morsels

SHELF LIFE - BAKING PRODUCTS

9 Months:	Carnation Lite Skimmed Evaporated Milk
12 Months:	Carnation Low-Fat Evaporated, Non-Fat Dry Milk
15 Months:	Carnation Evaporated Milk
24 Months:	Libby's Solid Pack Pumpkin, Libby's Pumpkin Pie Mix

SHELF LIFE - CULINARY

18 Months: Libby's Dinner, Contadina Pizza Squeeze
24 Months: Contadina Canned Products, Contadina Bread
               Crumbs, Libby's/Broadcast canned meats,
               Libby's canned salmon, Libby's tomato sauce

SHELF LIFE - NUTRITIONAL PRODUCTS

9 Months: Sweet Success: Snack Bars, Chocolate Oatmeal
               Raisin, Chocolate Peanut Butter and Chocolate
               Raspberry
12 Months: Carnation Breakfast Bars, Carnation Instant
               Breakfast, Sweet Success: ready-to-drink cans
24 Months: Sweet Success: powder

PRODUCTION CODES

Nestle products display one of two production code formats. This will assist you in determining the age of their products.

1.   *First example: "KA201."*

The part of this code you will need is the part that tells you the month and the year. The second letter in the code "A" stands for the month. "A" = January, "B" = February and so on, omitting "I." The first number "2" stands for the year. "2" = 1992, "1" = 1991, "0" =1990, "9" = 1989 and so on.

2.   *Second example: "3029WW 1823"*

The part of the code that you need is the part that tells the year and day of the year. The first number of the code stands for the last digit of the year (in this example, 1993). The next three numbers, 029, stand for the twenty-ninth day (month of January) of 1993. A code of 2259WW1579 would mean that the product was produced on the 259th day (month of September) of 1992.

Chapter 27

Cooking Facts

Microwave ovens that do not have a movable turntable may be guilty of leaving cold spots that result in undercooked areas of the food. This may result in bacteria not being killed in that area.

Measurement Facts:

60 drops = 1 teaspoon	3 teaspoons = 1 tablespoon
2 tablespoons = 1 fl. oz.	8 tablespoons = ½ cup
Juice of 1 orange = 5-6 tsp.	5 large eggs = 1 cup
2 tablespoons butter = 1 oz.	

"ANY PAN WON'T DO"
The type of pan you use to cook in may make a difference in the quality of the finished product. Best to bake in a dull finish aluminum pan. A dark pan may cool too quickly and a shinny pan reflects heat to such a degree that you may not get even cooking.

"CURDLING UP"
Always cook recipes that contain eggs, sour cream or cream at a lower setting to avoid curdling.

"GETTING DIRECTIONS RIGHT"
When cooking in a microwave, be sure to place the thicker tougher areas of foods toward the outer edges of the cooking pan.

"PAN ALERT, PAN ALERT"
Non-stick pans, including all of the best brands may be dangerous if you allow them to boil dry. At 400 degrees F. the pans may release toxic fumes after about 20 minutes, enough to make a person sick. This could be even more serious for birds and other small pets.

To avoid damage to your microwave oven, keep a cup of water in it when its not in use. If it is turned on accidently by a child, damage may occur.

If food has a higher water content it will cook better in a microwave.

"KA-BOOM, KA-BOOM"
Never microwave any food in a sealed container, it will probably explode.

"GIVE THE DOG THE BONE"
When microwaving meats with bones, remember the bone attracts more microwave energy than the meat and the meat may not cook evenly.

"USELESS FACT"
Microwave ovens are used most by people age 44 or younger.

It is just as safe to cook foods in a microwave as it is on a range or in an oven.

Never place a whole egg in the shell in the microwave, it might explode and make a mess.

"A FINE MESS YOU GOT INTO"
When cooking an egg that is out of the shell in a microwave, prick the yolk with a fine pin or it may pop and you've got another mess.

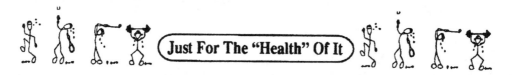

Just For The "Health" Of It

When deep fat frying, use a pure vegetable oil, preferably one with a high smoke point such as corn or safflower. A new oil Canola is also excellent.

Butter, margarine or lard will burn before reaching the temperature desired for frying.

Fat should only be heated to 400°F. Any higher will cause the fat to deteriorate.

Cook all vegetables at the highest power setting in a microwave. The faster they cook the more nutrients will be retained.

Baking soda should never be added to foods that are cooking, since it may destroy certain B vitamins.

Unless you fry or cook an oil, cooking lowers the fat content of any meat.

If fat is too hot, the food is apt to be too brown and dry on the outside and uncooked on the inside.

After you cook in a Wok, wipe the inner surface with vegetable oil to retard any rust forming.

When foods are cut they should be of uniform sizes to assure that they will cook and be done at the same time.

Foods that are to be fried, should be dried thoroughly before frying to avoid splattering.

If you use glass or Corning Ware dishes in the oven, you can reduce the heat by 25°F.

If you add 1 ½ teaspoons of butter to a cooking pasta or soup it will not boil over.

Always use a shallow pot for cooking a roast, they will allow air to circulate better than deep ones.

Try not to fry too much food at once to avoid a fat overflow. Recommended is only a half-full fryer basket.

To avoid food from sticking together, try lifting the basket out of the fat several times before allowing it to stay in the fat.

All fried foods should be placed on paper towels and allowed to drain for a few minutes before serving.

Cooking Vegetables

Baking Vegetables -   Their skins will preserve most of their nutrient value. When baking, the vegetable must have a high enough water content not to dry out. Root vegetables are the best to bake as well as any potato, winter squash or onion.

Steaming -   Probably the best for all types of vegetables. It retains the nutrients and cooks in a short period of time.

Pressure Cooking -   Will shorten cooking times thus saving the nutrients. The problem here is if you overcook even for a short period of time the vegetables turn to mush. Since vegetables all have a different consistency this is a problem.

Pan Frying -   Using a small amount of oil is another fast method of cooking. A Wok is fine too. Remember, however, that when cooking vegetables in oils, the fat soluble vitamins may end up in the oil. You may want to keep the oil for the sauce.

Waterless Cooking -   Works well for green leafy vegetables using only the water that adheres to their leaves after washing. This usually takes only 3-5 minutes.

Boiling-   Not recommended, due to the high loss of nutrients. If you must use this method, add the vegetables only after the water starts boiling and cook for the shortest period of time possible.

Crock Pot - Should only be used for vegetables if they are precooked then added to the stew, etc. just before you serve the dish.

Microwave - Cooking is fast and will retain the nutrient levels very well. Cooking times will vary depending on the wattage of your unit.

NOTE:
Refrigerate all foods as soon as possible, this will help you retain the potencies of the nutrients. Whole boiled carrots will retain 90% of their vitamin C and most of their minerals, but if you slice it up before cooking you will lose almost all of the vitamin C and niacin content.

HEALTH HINT:

When boiling vegetables there are a few good rules to follow:

(1)   Allow the water to boil for at least 2 minutes since the water will lose a high percentage of its oxygen. It is this high oxygen content of the water that causes the vitamin C potency to be reduced.

(2)   Cook the vegetables in as large a piece as possible, then cut them up after they cook.

(3)   Never place vegetables in cold water and then bring it to a boil. If this is done some vegetables can lose up to 10-12 times their vitamin C content.

When cooking potatoes it is best to pierce the skin with a fork to allow the steam to escape.

Salt should be added after cooking so that it won't draw the liquids out of the foods.

"Cookware - Just The Current 1995 Facts"

Aluminum

50% of all cookware sold in the United States is aluminum. Recent 1994 evidence shows that aluminum cookware does not pose any health risks. Especially increasing the risk of Alzheimers Disease.

Iron

Can supply a small amount of iron to your diet. Acidic foods such as tomatoes and applesauce when cooked for prolonged periods will absorb the most iron. After 25 minutes spaghetti sauce will have about 6mg. of iron per 3 1/2oz. serving.

Stainless Steel

Not the best heat conductor unless they have a copper or aluminum bottom. When acidic foods are cooked in stainless steel it may leach a number of metals into the food, some such as chlorine and iron are useful, but others such as nickel are not as healthful.

Non-Stick Coated

Such as Teflon and Silver Stone, are made of a type of fluorocarbon resin that will not react with foods. If a small portion does flake off and get into the food it would pass harmlessly through your body.

Glass, Copper Pots and Enamalized Cookware

These do not react with foods and are safe to cook in. Copper conducts heat well and is preferred by many chef's. Copper pans should have a liner of tin or stainless steel to be safe.

When cooking a complicated dish that takes a long time to cook, try partially cooking it in the microwave first.

Microwave food packages may now pollute your food. Popcorn and pizza are the two that are under investigation, and may leak hazardous chemicals into the foods.

When cooking custard, place a piece of waxed paper over it while it is still hot to avoid a skin from forming.

Preparation Of Foods:

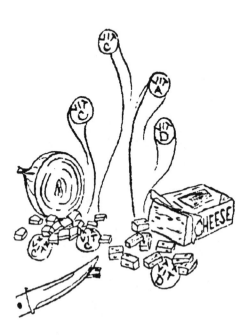

Washing/Soaking - Many vitamins are water soluble and will be lost through washing, scrubbing or long periods of soaking. Soaking carrots causes the loss of the natural sugar, all the B vitamins, vitamin C and D and all the minerals except calcium.

Dice/Slice/Peel/Shred - The smaller you cut fruits and vegetables, the more surface is exposed to temperature, the air (oxidation) and light. Prepare as close to serving time as possible. Shredding for salads cause a 20% loss of vitamin C and an additional 20% loss if the salad stands for an hour before eating.

NOTE:
The skin of fruits and vegetables contain at least 10% of the nutritional content of that food.

HEALTH HINT:
The worst pots to use, due to metals leaching into the foods or reactions of acidic or alkaline foods are unlined copper, aluminum or stainless steel pots. Non-stick pots are okay as long as the coating is unbroken.

BARBECUING FOOD FACTS:

Pour enough briquets into a grocery bag for one barbecue and fold it down. When you have a quantity of bags filled, pile one on top of another until you are ready to barbecue. Just light the bag and the charcoal will catch very quickly.

When barbecuing place herbs on the coals to enhance the flavors of meat and poultry. Try using stalks of savory, rosemary or dried basil seed pods.

For a smaller fire, fill egg or milk cartons with briquettes, then light them as needed.

When flare-ups from fat drippings start to burn the meat, place lettuce leaves over the hot coals to eliminate the problem.

Coat your grill with oil before cooking, then clean it shortly after the barbecue.

Window cleaner sprayed on a warm grill will make it easier to clean.

HEALTH HINT:
> Charcoal cooking may release a chemical benzopyrene
> into the foods, a known carcinogen. Also, there may be
> a relationship between this type of cooking and the
> effectiveness of some antiasthmatic medications.

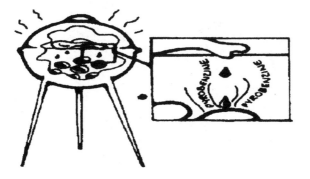

Chapter 28

Herb & Spicy Facts

"SALT OF THE EARTH"
The average person consumes about 4500mg of salt per day, about 2 teaspoons. The body only requires about 200mg.

"SCIENCE AT ITS BEST"
Flavoring extracts come in two forms: pure extracts and imitation flavorings. The pure is derived from natural sources and diluted with ethyl alcohol. Imitations are man-made chemicals concocted in a laboratory.

"USE IT, OR LOSE IT"
Spices should never be stored near a microwave exhaust fan or range top. The heat tends to cause a loss of flavor, potency and even color. All spices should be stored in a cool dried location or in the refrigerator.

If your spices seem to have lost their potency, try rubbing them between your fingers for a few seconds to rejuvenate them.

Hot or spicy foods do not irritate your stomach or aggravate ulcers in most people.

Place a toothpick in a garlic clove before placing it into a stew and it will be easy to retrieve.

Sour wines may be used in place of vinegar.

When you are doubling a recipe, don't double the seasonings until you taste the dish.

ALLSPICE:

Has the aroma of a blend of cinnamon, cloves and nutmeg. Grown in Jamaica, Central and South America. Sold both whole and ground. Whole is mainly used in pickling, meats, fish and gravies. Ground is used in baked goods, relishes, puddings and fruit preserves. It can also be found in a number of ready-to-serve foods such as; hot dogs, soups and baked beans.

ANISE:

Used in licorice. Imported from Mexico and Spain. Marketed as anise seed. Also, used in candies, cookies, pickles and as a flavoring for beverages. Gives the liquor anisette its aroma.

BASIL:

Comes from a plant belonging to the mint family, native to India and Iran. Also, known as "sweet basil" and is grown in the United States. Sold in the form of basil leaves. Used in tomato paste and tomato and squash dishes and, of course, turtle soup. Commonly found in ready-to-serve products such as pizza sauce, soups and dressings.

Try adding a small amount of basil to your tuna salad for a great taste.

BAY LEAF:

Oblong green leaves, sold as leaves and used in stews, sauces, soups and pickling. Used in numerous ready-to-serve foods such as soups, French dressing, dill pickles, etc.

CARAWAY SEEDS:

Ripe caraway seeds are usually harvested at night before the dew evaporates. Most seeds come from the Netherlands. Used in rye bread, cabbage, sauerkraut, soft cheese spreads, sweet pickles and French dressing.

CARDAMON SEED:

Spicy, sweet seeds belonging to the ginger family. They are native to India. They are sold whole or ground. Widely used in Scandinavian dishes. Used in pickling, as a demitasse flavoring, grape jellies, marmalade and frankfurters. These seeds are also used as an excellent cover-up for liquor breath.

CAYENNE PEPPER:

Also, known as red pepper and is available in crushed, ground or whole form. Used in relishes, salsas, chili products, Italian foods, sausages, and dressings.

CELERY SEED:

Celery seed and celery salt are used in salad dressings, fish dishes, salads, pickling and many vegetable dishes. The supply comes mainly from India and France.

CELERY FLAKES:

Made from dehydrated leaves and stalks of celery. Made in the United States. Used in stews, stuffings, soups and sauces.

CHERVIL:

A French herb excellent for flavoring salad dressings. used similar to parsley.

CHILI PEPPERS:

To prepare them you must toast them with a long handled fork on top of the stove making sure that they blister on all sides. As soon as the skin is evenly blistered and puffed up away from the pulp, lay the pods on a cloth, sprinkle them with water and cover them with another cloth so that they steam. The skins will then pull away easily and the seeds and veins can be removed. All of the pulp can be used, but only use a few of the seeds.

Chili peppers and paprika are high in vitamin A. One teaspoon can supply up to 25% of your daily requirement.

CHILI POWDER:

The major ingredients are cumin seed, chili peppers, oregano, salt, cayenne pepper, garlic and allspice.

CHIVES:

Chives are a member of the onion family, but much milder. Used to flavor dips, sauces, spreads and ,of course, baked potatoes.

CINNAMON:

Obtained from the bark of the laurel tree, native to China and Indonesia. The cassia variety is used in the United States. In the whole form, it is used in preserving, flavoring puddings, pickling and hot wine drinks. Ground is used in sweet pickles, ketchup, vegetables, apple butter, mustards, and spiced peaches.

CLOVE

Comes from a tree which a member of the Myrtle family. First discovered in Indonesia. Whole cloves are used for pickling, ham roasts and spiced syrups. Ground cloves are used for making baked goods, puddings, mustards, soups, hot dogs, sausage, and barbecue sauces.

CORIANDER SEED:

Come from a small plant of the carrot family. They have a sweet musky flavor and are native to the Mediterranean area. Sold in seed and ground forms. Normally used in gingerbread, cookies, cakes, biscuits, poultry stuffing and is excellent if rubbed on fresh pork before roasting.

CUMIN SEED:

The flavor resembles caraway seed and it is native to Egypt. Sold in both seed and ground form. It is an essential ingredient in curry, chili powder, soups, stuffed eggs and chili con carne.

CURRY POWDER:

Curry powder is a blend of 20 spices, herbs and even some seeds. Some of the ingredients are chilies, cloves, coriander, fennel seed, nutmeg, mace, cayenne, black pepper, sesame seeds, saffron, turmeric, etc. The turmeric gives many of the dishes its yellow color.

DILL:

Used for pickling, soups, sauerkraut, salads, fish and meat sauces, green apple pie and spiced vinegar.

When making egg salad, try adding a small amount of dill to liven it up.

FENNEL:

Has a sweet anise-like flavor and is available in seed form. It is used in Italian sausage, sweet pickles, fish dishes, candies, pastries, oxtail soup and pizza sauce. Can be brewed as a tea and served hot.

FENUGREEK:

Has a similar aroma to curry powder and are bitter in flavor. It's main use is in imitation maple flavor.

GARLIC:

Grown in the United States and is a member of the Lily family. It is sold as garlic salt and garlic powder. Used in hundreds of dishes from pizza sauce to chicken pot pies.
Garlic has been used for centuries as a blood cleanser and in recent times to help lower blood pressure.

To peel garlic more easily, place it in very hot water for 2-3 minutes. Garlic cloves should be stored in a small amount of vegetable oil. They won't dry out and the oil can be used with a garlic flavor.

When peeling garlic, try rinsing the garlic in hot water first. The skin will come off easier.

To preserve garlic cloves after they have been peeled, try placing them in a sealed jar and cover them with olive oil. They will stay fresh for 3-4 months.

Before adding your salad ingredients to a bowl, rub a clove of crushed garlic on the sides of the bowl.

Garlic is more nutritious than onions.

Americans consume 250 million pounds of garlic annually.

Garlic salt may contain over 900mg. of sodium per teaspoon. Our average daily consumption should be no more than about 1500mg.

There are 300 varieties of garlic grown worldwide.

Elephant garlic has very large cloves, but is actually a form of leek and has a milder flavor.

Garlic will keep for up to 3 months if stored properly in a cool, dark, dry location. If the cloves sprout, the garlic is still usable and the sprouts can be used for salads.

If you nick a clove of garlic, it must be used or it will get moldy very quickly.

To make garlic vinegar, place 2-3 fresh cloves in each pint and let stand for two weeks before using. Works great for your oils too.

Never freeze garlic, it will destroy the flavor.

Garlic oil products should contain an antibacterial or acidifying agent such as phosphoric acid or citric acid or at least be kept under refrigeration.

Garlic butter should only be stored in the refrigerator for no more than 10-14 days for maximum safety.

Once garlic has been processed it is more perishable than most people realize.

"WITH TONGUE IN CHEEK"
Historically, garlic has been known to repel vampires providing it is no more than 1 month old, made into a circle, worn around the neck and each whole garlic separated by no more than 2 inches.

GINGER:

Has a pungent spicy flavor and is grown in India and West Africa. Sold in whole or ground form and is used in pickling, conserves, dried fruits and of course, gingerbread and pumpkin pies.

MACE:

Mace is a fleshy growth between the nutmeg shell and the outer husk. It is sold in ground form and used in pound cake and chocolate dishes. In it's whole form it is used in pickling, ketchup, baked beans, soups, deviled chicken and ham spreads and French dressing.

MARJORAM:

Has a sweet minty flavor and is an herb of the mint family. It is available in leaves and is imported from France, Chile and Peru. Usually combined with other herbs and used in soups, stews, poultry seasonings, sauces and fish dishes.

MINT FLAKES:

They are dehydrated flakes of peppermint and spearmint plants and have a strong sweet flavor. Grown in the United States and Europe. Used to flavor stews, soups, fish dishes, sauces, desserts and jellies. For an instant breath freshener, try chewing a few mint leaves.

MSG:

Monosodium glutamate has no taste of its own but helps to bring out the natural food flavors as well as helping foods blend better with one another. MSG has been implicated in enough adverse physical problems that it is recommended not to use it.

MUSTARD:

The yellow or white seeds produce a mild mustard, while the brown seeds produce the more spicy variety. Powdered mustard has hardly any aroma until mixed with a liquid. Has hundreds of uses and is one of the most popular spices worldwide.

NUTMEG:

Available in ground form and is imported from the East and West Indies. Used in sauces, puddings, as a topping for custards, eggnogs and whipped creams. Also, used in sausages, frankfurters, and ravioli. Best used in ground form only.

OREGANO:

A member of the mint family and also known as origanum and Mexican sage. Available in leaf or ground forms. Used mostly in Italian specialties such as pizza and a variety of spaghetti sauces.

 Chef's Secrets

Some oregano on a grilled cheese sandwich will really perk it up and you will probably never eat another one without it.

PAPRIKA:

Ground pods of sweet pepper. The red sweet mild type is widely used and grown in the United States. Used in a variety of dishes such as vegetables, mustards, dressings, ketchup, sausages and fish dishes and, of course, as a garnish.

PARSLEY:

Grown in the United States and Southern Europe. Used as a flavor in salads, soups, vegetable dishes, chicken pot pies, herb dressings and even peppermint soup. A favorite garnish and high in nutrients. makes your breath fresh since it is high in chlorophyll. When storing it should be kept in a plastic bag in the freezer.

Parsley can be dried in the microwave and frozen.

PEPPER:

Pepper is the most popular spice in the world. Sold in both black and white varieties and for the most part is imported from India, Indonesia and Borneo. Sold in whole or ground varieties. Used in almost every dish imaginable at one time or another.

POPPY SEED:

Have a nut-like flavor and are used in salads, cookies, pastry fillings and as toppings for numerous baked products.

POULTRY SEASONING:

The major ingredients are; sage, thyme, marjoram and savoy.

ROSEMARY:

A sweet fragrant spicy herb, imported from Spain and Portugal, used in stews, meat dishes, dressings and Italian foods. Great in gin drinks.

SAFFRON:

One of the most expensive of all herbs. It is derived from the stigma of a flowering crocus. It is imported from Spain and is used primarily in baked goods and rice dishes.

SAGE:

A member of the mint family and is available in leaf or ground form. Used in pork products, stuffings, salads, fish dishes and pizza sauces.

SALT:

In the purifying process of salt, the native minerals are stripped away and it is then enriched with iodine and dextrose to stabilize it, sodium bicarbonate to keep it white and anti-caking agents to keep it "free flowing." Morton's Special Salt is the only salt, to my knowledge that has no additives. Salt is used in almost every food in the food processing industry.

A simple barometer of your salt intake is to eat a slice of bacon–if it doesn't taste excessively salty, you are probably eating too much salt.

Your daily sodium intake per day should be no more than 230mg. per day, about 1/10 teaspoon. We consume about 25 times that amount.

Buy "Lite Salt" or a salt-free seasoning.

Mother's milk contains 16 mg. of sodium per 100 gr.

Canned baby food may contain 300 mg. of sodium per 100 gr.

Canned peas have 100 times the sodium of raw peas.

Sodium in Public Water Supplies:

Milligrams of Sodium In Public Water Supplies

Aberdeen, SD........48.0	Bismark, ND........14.4
Biloxi, Miss........55.2	Crandall,TX.......408
Galveston, TX.......81.6	Kansas City, MO....23.6
Los Angeles, CA.....40.1	Oklahoma City, OK..23.6
Phoenix, AZ.........25.9	San Diego, CA......12.0
New York, NY.........0.7	Reno, NV............1.1

40% of table salt is sodium.

Lite salt which is 50% table salt (nacl) is 20% sodium.

Excess amounts of dietary sodium places a burden on your kidneys, causing a possible malfunction, thus allowing extra amounts of sodium to build up in the bloodstream where it retains extra water, causing an increase in blood volume. This causes the heart to work harder, thus leading to an increase in blood pressure. Fast foods may use large quantities of salt to mask the offensive flavors of low quality foods.

Ground kelp can be used in place of salt. It contains only about 4% sodium. Try a kelp shaker at your table.

HIGH SODIUM FOODS

Food Item	Serving Size	Sodium mg.
Onion Soup (dry)	1 ½ oz.	3288
Pretzel Twists	3 ½ oz.	2370
Deviled Crab (frozen)	1 cup	2085
Dill Pickle	1 large	1935
Turkey Dinner (frozen)	1 large	1830
Saltines	3 ½ oz.	1794
Cream of Asparagus Soup	8 oz. can	1662
Dill Pickle	1 medium	1426
Lobster	1 pound	1359
Soy Sauce	1 Tbsp.	1320
Toasted Corn	3 ½ oz.	1307
Spaghetti & Meat Sauce	1 cup canned	1220
Puff Balls	3 ½ oz.	1190
Macaroni & Cheese (frzn)	1 cup	1090
Onion Soup	1 cup	1051
Chop Suey with Meat	1 cup	1050
Chicken Noodle Soup	1 cup	979
Pretzels	1 oz.	890
Sauerkraut (canned)	½ cup	880

Cinnamon Roll	1 reg.	805
Corned Beef (cooked)	3 oz.	800
Tuna Oil (packed)	3 ½ oz.	800
Corn Chips	3 ½ oz.	741
Sunflower Seeds	3 ½ oz.	721
Potato Salad (canned)	½ cup	660
Chicken Noodle Soup	5 oz.	655
Peanuts (roasted in oil)	1 cup	662
Creamed Corn (canned)	1 cup	671
Italian Dressing	2 Tbsp.	624
Salted Peanuts	3 ½ oz.	595
Pork & Beans (canned)	½ cup	590
Wheat Crackers	3 ½ oz.	566
Scalloped Potatoes	½ cup	540
Oyster Stew	5 oz.	510
Beef Hot Dogs	1 reg.	495
Chocolate Pudding	½ cup	490
Apple Pie	1/6 pie	486
Tomato Soup	5 oz.	475
Tortilla Chips	3 ½ oz.	468
Bologna	2 slices	450

MEDIUM SODIUM FOODS

American Cheese (slices)	1 oz.	447
Hash Browns (frozen)	1 cup	446
Mustard	2 Tbsp.	444
Pancakes (mix)	3 - 4" cakes	435
White Pudding Cake (mix)	1/8 cake	410
Cheese Cake (no bake)	1/8 cake	380
Mashed Potatoes(instant)	½ cup	375
Cheese Pizza (frozen)	1 med. slice	370
Wheat Crackers	16 small	370
Carrots (canned)	1 cup	366
Bran Flakes	3/4 cup	340
Cheese Crackers	10 small	325
Tomato Juice	½ cup	320

Cottage Cheese (creamed)	½ cup	320
Baking Soda	1 Tsp.	315
Italian Salad Dressing	1 Tbsp.	315
Worcestershire Sauce	1 Tbsp.	315
Ketchup	2 Tbsp.	308
Corn Flakes	3/4 cup	305
Corn Bread	2 inch square	283
Granola Snack Bar	One Bar	273
Buttermilk	1 cup	225
French Salad Dressing	1 Tbsp.	220
Muenster Cheese	1 oz.	220
Swiss Cheese	1 oz.	220
Doughnut	1 med.	210
Parmesan Cheese	1 oz.	210
Beets (canned)	½ cup	195
Cheddar Cheese	1 oz.	190
Bleu Cheese Dressing	1 Tbsp.	180
Oatmeal (cooked)	3 oz.	175
Tomato Ketchup	1 Tbsp.	155
Green Olive	1 Lg.	155
Celery (raw)	1 cup	151
Rye Bread	1 slice	140
Angel Food Cake	1/12 cake	130
Whole Wheat Bread	1 slice	130
Chocolate Candy Bar	3/4 oz.	115

LOW SODIUM FOODS

Graham Cracker	1 lg.	95
Brownie	1 reg.	90
Oysters (raw)	½ cup	90
Lima Beans (frozen)	½ cup	90
Mayonnaise	1 med.	70
Egg	1 med.	70
Turkey	3 oz.	70
Coffee (black)	1 cup	59
Margarine (salted)	1 tsp.	50

Cottage Cheese	½ cup	30
Oatmeal Cookie	1 med.	20
Fruit Cocktail	½ cup	7
Orange Juice	½ cup	2
Macaroni	1 cup	1

SAVORY:

Another member of the mint family that has a sweet flavor. Available in leaf and ground forms and primarily used to flavor meats, poultry and fish.

SESAME:

Has a nut-like flavor with a high oil content. Primary use is as a topping on baked goods and in halavah.

TARRAGON:

An anise flavored leaf that is a native of Siberia and imported from Spain and France. Used in sauces, meat dishes, salads, herb dressings and tomato casseroles.

THYME:

Belongs to the mint family and is available in leaf or ground form. Used in soups, stews, sauces, chipped beef (old army favorite), sausages, clam chowder, herb dressings and mock turtle soup.

TURMERIC:

A member of the ginger family and imported from India and Peru. Used in meats, dressings, curry powder, spanish rice, relishes and mustards.

VANILLA:

Beans:
Long, thin dark brown beans are expensive and not as easy to use as the extract. To use the bean, split it and scrape out the powder-fine seeds. The seeds from a single vanilla bean is. equal to 2-3 teaspoons of extract. Beans should be stored in a sealed plastic bag and refrigerated.

Pure Extract:
Comes from the vanilla bean, but the taste is less intense. Has excellent flavor, similar to the real bean.

Imitation Extract:
Made from artificial flavorings, tastes stronger and is harsher than pure vanilla. Should only be used in recipes where the vanilla flavor does not predominate the taste.

Mexican Extract:
A possible dangerous extract. This poor quality inexpensive product may contain coumarin, a blood thinning drug and banned in the U.S. due to possible toxic effects.

VINEGAR:

Produced from ethyl alcohol. A bacteria, acetobacter feeds on the alcohol, converting into acetic acid (vinegar). Vinegar can, however, be made from a number of other foods, such as; apples or grains. Distilled vinegar is best used for cleaning purposes and not for foods.

Balsamic vinegar produced in Italy is made from sugars that are converted to alcohol with the addition of boiled down grape juice are the best. They can be used for salad dressing and bring out the flavors in many vegetables.

Chapter 29

Food Additive Facts

"YUM, YUM"
Americans eat approximately 6-9 pounds of chemical food additives per year.

Today's foods contain over $500 million worth of additives.

"YOUR POOR LIVER"
Over 1 billion pounds of chemical additives are consumed every year. Your liver is in charge of detoxifying this garbage. The liver is the major organ that has the job of breaking down and disposing of all this material. In most cases it requires a number of nutrients to break them down, hopefully, they will be available.

The outside leaves of lettuce should be discarded. They may contain sulfites. Celery may also be guilty.

White bread may have as many as 16 chemical additives just to keep it fresh. Some of these may be in the wrapper.

BETA-CAROTENE: (pre-curser to vitamin A)

A natural substance found in all plants and animals. Has a yellowish-orange color and is especially prevalent in carrots and squash. Used as a food coloring agent in foods and cosmetics. Recent studies have shown beta-carotene to be an effective anti-oxidant. Best to take instead of vitamin A, has almost no toxicity.

BROMELIN:

Extracted from pineapple and used in meat tenderizers. A very effective protein-digesting enzyme. If a piece of meat is allowed to set in bromelin for a prolonged period, you will be able to drink your steak.

CITRATE SALTS:

Used in cheese spreads and pasteurized process cheeses. May tend to mask the results of laboratory tests for pancreatic and liver function and blood acid-base balances.

CITRUS RED #2:

Had been used for coloring Florida oranges, but in recent years has been discontinued. The dye remained in the peel and did not enter the pulp. However, if the dye is ingested in quantity, it could cause numerous serious visual, circulatory and urinary system problems.

COLORINGS:

The majority of the colorings presently being used are derived from coal-tars (carcinogens). As the years go on more and more of these colorings are being further tested and banned.

GELATIN:

Derived from boiling skin, muscle and hoofs of animals. Mainly used as a thickener and stabilizer for fruit gelatins. Also, helps strengthen fingernails.

METHYLENE CHLORIDE:

A gas used in the decaffeination of coffee. Residues may remain and coffee companies do not have to tell you their method of decaffeination on the label. Only drink decaf if you know the method used by the manufacturer. Water is the best method.

MSG:

Monosodium glutamate has no taste of its own but helps to bring out the natural flavors as well as helping foods blend better with one another. MSG has been implicated in enough adverse physical problems that it is recommended not to use it. When eating Chinese food always inquire whether MSG has been used in the food. If you find out that it has, refuse to eat it.

NITRITES:

One of the most dangerous additives used in our foods are the nitrites and nitrates. They are found in almost all processed meats,such as; luncheon meats, bacon, sausage, hot dogs, smoked fish and canned meats.

The chemical is mainly used for cosmetic purposes, to stabilize the color of the product. The industry also claims it is needed to retard bacterial growth and also reduce the possibility of botulism. Because of the risks involved with this chemical, the general consensus among scientists, is that companies should be researching a new and safer chemical compound instead of taking the easier and less expensive way out.

Nitrite studies have shown that in laboratory animals malignant tumors have developed in over 90% within 6 months, and death approximately afterwards. Other incidents have been reported and documented where high levels of nitrites in food have caused "cardiovascular collapse" in humans and even death from eating "hot dogs" and "blood sausage" that were produced by local processors in different areas of the U.S.

In Israel, studies on animals discovered problems related to brain damage when they were fed an equivalent amount of nitrites to heavy eaters of processed luncheon meats and hot dogs.

The biochemical changes that occur in the food take the following course: Nitrites are broken down into nitrous acid which combines with the hemoglobin of the meat or fish, forming a permanent red color.

In humans, there are two pathways that the ingested nitrites may take that could be harmful: (1) Nitrite is eaten and may react with the hemoglobin of the blood to produce a pigment called meth-hemoglobin which may seriously depress the oxygen carrying capacity of the red blood cell. (2) The possible cancer connection is when nitrites are biochemically altered to a substance called "nitrosamine."

This reaction usually occurs in the stomach and requires the presence of "amines" and "gastric juices." Amines are usually in adequate supply, since they are a product of protein metabolism, and protein foods often carry the nitrites. The end results are the formation of the "nitrosamines" which are classified as carcinogenic(cancer forming agents).

It is necessary, however, to clarify two points: (1) Just because you may eat meat containing nitrites does not mean that you will automatically produce nitrosamines. (2) If the nitrosamine is produced, your immune system may destroy it as soon as it is produced.

Vitamin C has been found to neutralize the reaction that takes place in the stomach, by interfering with the amine combining with the nitrite. Due to recent studies, relating to these neutralizing effects of vitamin C (ascorbic acid), some manufacturers are adding ascorbic acid to their products.

As a measure of protection it would be wise to chew a vitamin C tablet or drink a small amount of orange juice before consuming foods that contain nitrites.

NOTE:
Many countries have already banned nitrites from foods.
However, the USDA and the FDA will not prohibit its use
until a good substitute is found.

SORBITOL:

Extracted mainly from berries and some fruits. It is an alcohol that produces a sweet taste and is used in dietetic products as a replacement for sugar. Also, has numerous other uses as a food binder, thickener, texturing agent, humectant and food stabilizer.

SULFITES:

Three types may be used as an anti-browning agent, sodium, potassium and ammonium can be used on any food except meats or a high vitamin B content food. Used on salad bars to prevent fruits and lettuce from browning, also, to enhance their crispness. Physiologic reaction to sulfites are numerous with the most common taking the form of acute asthmatic attacks. My recommendation is to avoid any food that has been treated with sulfites.

SULPHUR DIOXIDE:

A chemical formed from the burning of sulphur. A food bleach, preservative, anti-oxidant and anti-browning agent. Its most common visibility is in golden raisins. Tends to destroy vitamin A and should not be used on meats or high vitamin A content vegetables.

Types Of Additives:

Flavorings - There are approximately 1,100 to 1,400 natural and synthetic flavorings available to food processors. Scientists are most concerned regarding the toxicity of a number of the ones that are commonly used. Flavorings give foods a more acceptable taste, restore lost flavors due to processing and in some cases will improve natural flavors.

Stabilizers/Gelling Agents/Thickeners -
These are used to keep products in a "set-state" such as jellies, jams and baby foods. They are also used to keep ice cream creamy. They generally improve consistency and will affect the appearance and texture of foods. The more common ones are modified food starch and vegetable gum.

Colorings - *Ninety percent are artificial and do not contain any nutritional value. Some foods have a tendency to lose their natural color when processed and must be dyed back to make them more appealing to the consumer. An example of this is banana ice cream which is dyed yellow and marachino cherries which are dyed red and green.*

Sweeteners -   The United States consumption of artificial sweeteners is estimated at approximately 6-9 pounds per person, per year. These are designed to make the foods more palatable.

Aroma Enhancers -   An example, is yellowish-green liquid diacetyl which is used in some cottage cheeses to produce an artificial butter aroma.

Preservatives - *Helps maintain freshness and prevents spoilage that is caused by fungi, yeast, molds and bacteria. Extends shelf life and protects the natural colors or flavors.*

Acids/Bases -   Provides a tart flavor for many fruits and is used in pickling as well as putting the "fizz" in soft drinks (phosphoric acid).

Antioxidants -   Reduces the possibility of rancidity in fats and oils. Natural ones are vitamins C, E, A, selinium and beta-carotene. Artificial ones are BHA and BHT.

Taste Enhancers -   Brings out the flavors of certain foods. MSG is a good example but is not recommended.

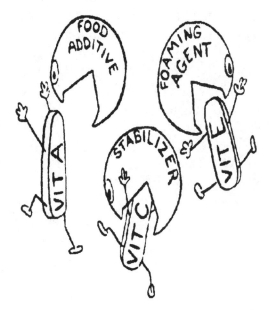

Improving Agents - Examples
include:

(1) Humectants - Controls the
humidity of a food.

(2) Anti-Caking Agents - Keeps
salt and powders free-
flowing.

(3) Firming/Crisping Agents -
Used for processed fruits
and vegetables.

(4) Foaming Agents - Used for
whipped creams.

(5) Anti-Foaming Agents -
Keeps pineapple juice from
bubbling over a filled
container.

Emulsifiers - These help evenly mix small particles of one liquid with another, such as water and oil. Lecithin is a good example of a natural emulsifier.

NOTE:
Keep in mind that you are rarely aware of the quantity of additives you consume.
Almost all these additives require vitamins and minerals to assist with their
breakdown, so that they can be properly disposed of, usually by the liver. These
additional nutrients must come from somewhere in the body that could probably
use them more.

HEALTH HINTS: Processed meats (hot dogs, bacon, lunch meats, etc.) are so high in additives, artificial colorings and preservatives that they can deplete the body of many nutrients needed to break them down, especially our anti-stress fighting vitamin B's.

Pharmacies are now selling a "sulfite test strip" that can be used to test produce just   by touching the strip to it. If the strip turns red, don't buy the produce.

"SHOE LEATHER, AU JUS"
When making stew, never add boiling water to the stew, if more water is needed, always use cold water. The boiling water may toughen the meat.

"JEWISH PENICILLIN"
When making chicken soup, use a quart of water to each pound of chicken.

Soups and stews when cooking should only simmer, never boil.

"TV DINNERS"
Place leftover stews into individual baking dishes or small casserole dishes, cover with pie crust or dumpling, mix and bake.

Store the liquids from canned mushrooms or vegetables, freeze it, then use it in soups or stews.

Just For The "Health" Of It

Refrigerate cooked or canned stews and soups overnight before serving. The fat will rise to the top, then you can just skim it off before heating and serving.

Read the label when buying soups. MSG and disodium inosinate and guanylate are favorite flavor enhancers.

Many vitamins are lost to the liquid when cooking vegetables. The liquid should be saved and frozen to be used when your making soups, etc.

One of the best commercial canned foods is Progresso. However, still watch out for the ones that have MSG.

Dry soup mixes are usually additive-free and only contain a few dried vegetables and seasonings.

Soup will go farther if you add pasta, rice or barley.

For an easy treat when making stews, take a stack of tortillas and cut into long thin pieces and add to the stew during the last 15 minutes of cooking. Corn tortillas are lower in fat than flour tortillas.

A good trick to avoid burning the peas in split-pea soup is to add a slice of white bread when you are cooking the peas and liquid together. Peas are an excellent source of protein.

When making stews, try adding a tablespoon of molasses for flavor.

If you add ½ cup of strong tea to the stew, it will help tenderize the meat and reduce the cooking time.

Leftover soups can be frozen in an ice cube tray and used in soups or stews at another time.

To thicken stews use a small amount of quick-cooking oats or a grated potato.

If your making vegetable soup, pour enough water into the pot to cover the vegetables by only 2 inches.

To reduce the saltiness of soups, add a can of peeled tomatoes, if feasible.

Another method of hiding the salty taste in soups, is to use a small quantity of brown sugar.

Oversalting soups and stews can be repaired by adding a piece of sliced apple or potato to the mixture for a short period of time, then remove and discard.

If you would like a sweeter taste in your soups or stews, try adding a small amount of pureed carrots.

Never use dark-colored bones in soups, they are too old and have deteriorated.

The best way to make stew or soup stock is to use a metal pasta cooker basket. Place it into your pot and cook all your ingredients, including any food containing bones. Remove the basket and it will have all the veggies or bones you don't want.

If you obtain too heavy a garlic flavor when cooking, place a few parsley flakes in a tea ball to soak up all the excess garlic.

To make soups or stews thicker, try adding a tablespoon or more of instant potatoes or ½ cup of rolled oats or wheat flakes.

When preparing tomato soup, always pour the tomato soup into the milk, this will prevent curdling. Low-fat milk works just as well.

To make a clear noodle soup, cook the noodles, then drain them before adding them to the soup.

When making a cream soup, try adding a little flour to the milk, it will make it smoother and will work with a low-fat milk.

Chapter 35

Food Canning Facts

When processing foods using the "open kettle" method, jars should still be sterilized.

When you cook the foods in the jars, the jars do not need sterilization, but should be thoroughly washed.

"EASY DOES IT"

Peas, corn, lima beans and most meats should be packed loosely, since heat penetration of these foods is slow. Fruits and berries should be packed solidly due to shrinkage and the fact that their texture does not retard the heat penetration.

Never use preservatives or any other type of artificial chemical substance in the product being canned.

"THE HIDEAWAY"

Canned products should always be stored in cool or cold dark locations. The excessive heat of a hot summer may cause a location to develop enough heat. Dormant bacteria will start growing.

When canned goods are frozen, then thawed, the texture may change but the food is still safe to eat. Be sure the seal is intact.

Canned foods will keep for an indefinite period of time as long as the seal is intact and they have been properly processed.

"MUSIC TO YOUR EARS"

After canning the food, tap the top, you should hear a clear "ringing note." If food is touching the top, this may not occur, but as long as the top does not move up and down, the food does not have to be reprocessed.

Black deposits that are occasionally found on the underneath side of the lid, are usually nothing to worry about (as long as the jar is still sealed) and are probably caused by tannins in the food or by hydrogen sulfide released by the foods during their processing.

Corn, lima beans and peas or any very starchy food needs to be packed loosely due to their expansion when processed.

Cloudy liquid in the jar probably means that the food is spoiled. Be very cautious, it probably should not be eaten or even opened.

When canning jellies or jams, it makes no difference whether you use cane or beet sugar, they are both the same.

The best vinegar to use when pickling is pure apple cider with 4-5% acidity

The outside of jars should be wiped with vinegar before storing to reduce the risk of mold forming on any food that wasn't cleaned off well.

Pickles will become soft if you use a brine or not enough vinegar or if the vinegar acidity is too weak.

To avoid hard water deposits on sealers, add vinegar to the water bath when canning.

Jars of frozen fruits should be thawed in the refrigerator. This will allow the fruit to absorb the sugar as it thaws.

Jelly jars should have a small piece of string placed on top of the wax before sealing the jar. This will make it easier to remove the wax.

Chapter 36

Substitution Facts

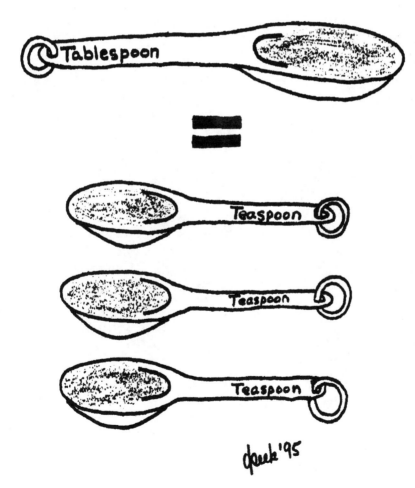

You can substitute ½ cup plain non-fat yogurt for the equal amount of mayonnaise. You will save approximately 90 grams of fat and almost 800 calories in a recipe.

2 teaspoons of baking soda to 1 cup of sour milk = ½ teaspoon of baking powder to 1 cup of sweet milk.

If Short This Item	You Can Substitute This
1 Teaspoon Lemon Juice	½ Teaspoon Vinegar
1 Tablespoon Cornstarch	2 Tablespoons of Flour
1 Cup Pre-sifted Flour Sifted Cake Flour	1 Cup & 2 Tablespoons
1 Cup Sour Milk / Buttermilk 1 Tablespoon Vinegar	1 Cup Sweet Milk plus
2/3 Cup of Honey	1 Cup sugar plus 1/3 Cup of Water
1 ½ Cup Corn Syrup	1 Cup Sugar plus ½ Cup Of Water
1 Whole Egg	2 Egg Yolks plus 1 Tablespoon of Water
1 Teaspoon of Oregano	1 Teaspoon of Marjoram
1 Teaspoon Allspice	½ Teaspoon Cinnamon plus 1/8 Teaspoon of Ground Cloves
Few Drops of Tabasco	Dash of Cayenne or Red Pepper

Chapter 37

Statistical Facts

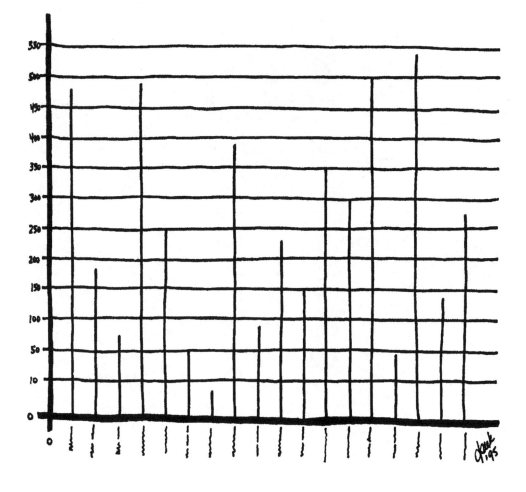

82% of the American public feel that a poor diet can increase their risk of cancer. Of these 82%, however, only 17% are willing to change their diet to reduce that risk.

A person consumes approximately 1600-2000 calories and 60-70 grams of fat in the average holiday dinner.

Almost 3 times the amount of synthetic pesticides are being used now than were used in 1965, over 800 million pounds annually.

"THE HIGH COST OF FOOD, AND WHY!"
By the time your food is picked, moved to a storage facility, then transported for processing and finally ends up in the supermarket, the food has traveled almost 1200 miles on the average.

According to the National Cancer Institute, diet is to blame for 30-35% of all cancer deaths.

Americans consume approximately 100 tablespoons of peanut butter annually.

The average American consumed 7.4 pounds of carrots, 4 pounds of green peppers, 3 pounds of cauliflower and 3 pounds of broccoli in 1993.

It takes up to 17 times as much acreage to produce 20 pounds of beef protein as it takes to produce 356 pounds of soybean protein.

Sales of "natural foods" exceeded 6 billion dollars in 1993, up 18% over 1992 according to the Natural Food Merchandiser.

"UP, UP AND AWAY"
A normal airline meal can cost the airline as much as $40 to produce and deliver to your seat.

The high-fat breakfast meal served on an airline of a cheese omelet and sausage is ordered over the healthier breakfast 70% of the time.

The average household in Honolulu spends $5,634 on food per year, Atlanta is only $4,187.

A supermarket has over 30,000 items.

The average amount of dollars spent in a supermarket in 1994 was $18.11 according to the Food Marketing Institute.

Top Grossing Restaurants

Tavern On The Green, New York City.............27 million
Rainbow Room, New York City....................25 million
Windows On The World, New York City.............24 million
Smith & Wollensky, New York City................18 million
Bob Chinn's Crabhouse, Wheeling, IL.............16 million
Gladstone's For Fish, Pacific Palisades, CA.....13 million

Only 9% of all Americans eat enough fruit and vegetables according to the National Cancer Society.

23% of Americans don't even eat 1 serving of fruits and vegetables per day.

Each year Americans consume approximately 5 gallons of frozen desserts, most of which is ice cream.

Four out of five Americans own a microwave oven.

We spend 8.5 cents out of every dollar for food packaging.

Animal fat versus vegetable fat used in restaurants:

> **1989**.....................62% used vegetable fat
> **1990.**....................89% used vegetable fat
> **1994**.....................93% used vegetable fat

In one year the average American consumes the following:

> 100 Pounds of Refined Sugar
> 55 Pounds of Fats and Oils
> 300 cans of Soft Drinks
> 200 Sticks of Gum
> 18 Pounds of Candy
> 5 Pounds of Potato Chips
> 7 pounds of Corn Chips, Popcorn & Pretzels
> 63 Dozen Doughnuts
> 50 Pounds of Cakes & Cookies
> 20 Gallons of Ice Cream

During the last ten years, over 10,000 new "convenience processed foods" have been introduced in the United States.

Approximately $50 million worth of Twinkies were sold in the U.S. in 1990.

More than 8,000 people in the U.S. die from food poisonings each year.

Americans drink 4,848 cups of coffee every second of every day.

It takes 10-14 ears of corn to produce 1 tablespoon of corn oil.

Food manufacturers spend $4 billion for advertising per year.
The average American teenager consumes approximately 1,800 pounds of food per year.

In a 24 hour period in the U.S., the following are consumed:

55 Tons of Caffeine (coffee, tea, soda)
985 Tons of Alcoholic Beverages

The average American consumes approximately 209 pounds of vegetables and 149 pounds of fruit per year.

The most favorite treat in the U.S. is ice cream. It is chosen first by 41% of women and 24% of men. In second place was cake/brownies, then chocolate and cookies.

Athletes prefer fresh fruit before a sporting event 25% of the time. In second place was fruit juice at 22% with water third.

More adults over 35 drink coffee than those under 35.

The most popular business lunch is now a salad by 43% over a meat dish 26%.

The choice meal of intimate dinners is lobster, 35% of the time.

Chapter 38

Dairy Facts

"LAST BUT WILL PROBABLY NOT BE LEAST"
Milk processed at high temperatures that has been sold in Europe for years will be available soon in the United States. UHT or ultra-high temperture milk is a process whereby the milk is sterilized while preserving its nutritional qualities. The process allows milk to be stored unopened without refrigeration for as much as 6 months.

"SLOWPOKES"
UHT milk has been sold in Europe for 30 years, we're not too far behind the times.

"OUI, OUI, SI, SI"
In France and Spain UHT milk accounts for 80-90% of all milk sold. Should be great for picnics or company trips.

California produces the most milk, 3 billion gallons per year.

"GOOD ALL-AROUND ADVISE"
When milking your cows, keep them calm and relaxed, they will "let down" and allow the milk to flow better. Talk to them in a low voice and play soothing music.

Wisconsin produces the most cheese, over 2 billion pounds per year.

Overall milk consumption in the United States is down 17% in the 1990's. One reason is the number of meals we eat out substituting soda and other beverages for the milk.

MILK FACTS:

When milk is discussed, the mineral calcium always seems to enter the conversation. While milk is a good source of calcium, so is cheese and dark green leafy vegetables. In fact, to obtain the same amount of calcium from 5 ½ pints of milk you need only to eat 2 ounces of cheese. This information is not being provided to discourage people from drinking milk, milk is an excellent source of vitamins, minerals and protein.

If milk is getting close to the curdling stage, try adding a teaspoon or two of baking soda to the milk. It will give you a few more good days.

While milk has been described in numerous nutrition publications as a "near-perfect food," there are two facts that should be taken into consideration:

> - Milk quality is dependent on the feeding habits of the cows. Poor feeding habits with insufficient green feed produces a lower nutrient milk.

> - Many cows will receive large doses of antibiotics, traces of which have shown up in milk.

 # Chef's Secrets

Thin cream can be whipped by adding 1 tablespoon of unflavored gelatin that is dissolved in 1 tablespoon of hot water. If you add this to 2 cups of cream, it will whip up as good as heavy cream and will keep in the refrigerator for 3-4 hours.

Heavy cream will whip faster if you add 6-8 drops of lemon juice per pint, which will make 2 cups of cream.

"WHIPPET"
Cream whips and milk doesn't! The reason being the higher fat content, whole milk is only 3.3% fat while heavy cream is 38% fat. During the whipping process the fat globules break open causing them to stick together in clumps. Also, air is trapped between the fat globules.

Milk that has been pasteurized and homogenized may be frozen for up to 2 weeks, but be sure to pour off a small amount to allow for expansion.

Fresh milk will stay fresher longer, if you add a pinch of salt to each quart.

After you open a can of evaporated milk, place a wad of wax paper in the holes to keep it fresh longer and to stop the milk from crusting in the holes.

"WELL I'LL BE"
Cottage cheese will last longer if you store it upside down.
Spores get into the cottage cheese and live on the oxygen layer when closed up. When you turn it upside down, you eliminate a percentage of the available oxygen and the spores can't grow as fast.

Cottage cheese only retains 25-50% of the calcium from the milk it's made out of.

"BE AWARE"
There are no federal regulations regarding frozen yogurt, many are closer to ice milk in nutrient content than real yogurt, especially where calcium is concerned. While this may not be bad, watch out for the sugar content.

Yogurt consumption in the United States has risen from 1 pound per person annually in 1970 to 4 pounds per person in 1994.

When boiling milk, you can prevent it from sticking to the pot if you rinse the pot in cold water before starting.

Sour cream can be homemade by adding 3-4 drops of pure lemon juice to every 3/4 cup of whipping cream. Let sit at room temperature for 30-40 minutes.

Sour cream contains about 18% milk fat; light sour cream has 10-12% milk fat.

Many brands of frozen yogurt have as many calories as ice cream. All they do is substitute sugar for fat.

Commercial ice cream must contain at least 10% milk fat.

Powdered milk should always be kept on hand, especially if you run out of milk.

If skim milk is too thin and watery for you, try adding a tablespoon or two of non-fat dried milk to it. It will become thicker and richer as well as having a higher calcium and protein content, with no added fat.

To avoid freezer burn on ice cream, cover the top of the container with a plastic bag.

Lower price ice creams are usually lower in fat and calories due to their higher levels of air and water.

When whipping cream, place the bowl in the sink for less mess.

"I AIN'T GOT NO BODY"
Whipped cream will not hold its shape well unless the label says "heavy." The cream will have a butterfat content of 40% which gives it the body.

"KEEPING IT UP"
If you have trouble keeping your whipped cream up, try adding a small amount of gelatin when whipping it.

To avoid milk from boiling over, rinse the pot in cold water first.

Buttermilk was named for the product left over after cream was churned.

Buttermilk today comes from skim milk which has been cultured. This milk has a rich flavor and almost no fat.

A cow is more valuable for its milk, cheese, butter and yogurt than for its beef.

Evaporated milk can be used in place of whipping cream if you first place the can in the freezer until almost frozen, then pour it into a pre-cooled bowl and add 1 tablespoon of lemon juice and 2/3 cup of milk. Should whip up nicely.

When you are whipping cream, the bowl and the beaters should be placed in the refrigerator for 30 minutes before they are used. When whipping, place the bowl into a larger bowl filled with ice cubes, with a light layer of salt on top to make it even colder.

Imitation milk contains no real milk. It is made from water, sugar and vegetable fat. Usually contains only 1% protein compared to 3.5% in whole milk.

Filled milk is a combination of skim milk using vegetable oil to replace the milk fat. Sometimes contains coconut oil.

Milk will not burn if you sprinkle a teaspoon of sugar on top of the milk, before starting to cook. However, if you stir it, it may still burn.

Cottage Cheese

Creamed   - Contains 4.2% fat or 9.5 grams per cup. Not recommended for dieters.

Low-Fat   - Contains 1% or 2% low-fat milk.

Uncreamed   - Similar to low-fat and is often sold salt-free and can be used in recipes calling for cottage cheese. Usually, it will need more seasoning than standard cottage cheese.

Milk can retain its freshness for up to 1 week after the expiration date on the carton.

Buttermilk contains only 1% milk fat.

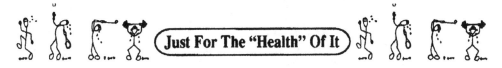

Just For The "Health" Of It

The pasteurization process has been related to the following:
* Milk allergies in children.
* The loss of calcium/phosphorus supplies, which may affect the metabolism of calcium, phosphorus and nitrogen.
* Destroys 50% of the vitamin C content.
* Destroys 25% of the vitamin B1.
* Destroys 9-15% of the vitamin B2.

Whole milk is the highest source of saturated fatty acids in the American diet.

"GOING UP"
Americans are now drinking 16 gallons of low-fat milk per person annually. In 1970 they were drinking only 6 gallons per person.

"GOING DOWN"
Americans were drinking 26 gallons of whole milk per person annually in 1970. In 1994 the annual consumption is only 9 gallons.

"NOSY SUBJECT"
New studies from Australia have shown that the milk-mucous controversy has proven to a degree that milk products did not produce an increase in mucous production.

"ZZZZZZZZZZZZZZZZZ"
A glass of warm milk before bedtime can be a very soothing drink containing the amino acid trytophan, which can reduce anxiety and stressful feelings.

Chocolate milk may interfere with calcium from the milk. The chocolate contains the chemical oxalate, a calcium neutralizer which affect the absorption.

Throw out any milk product that has mold on it.

Warm milk can cause insomnia in persons who have a milk lactose intolerance.

Calcium in milk stimulates the secretion of stomach acids that may irritate ulcers. Antacids with high buffering qualities are better. Food will also act as a buffer.

MILK ALERT
Milk is better purchased in paper cartons which block 98% of the harmful effect of the light. The plastic containers in just four hours of store light, can destroy 44% of the vitamin A in low-fat and skim milk containers. Some markets have installed light shields to avoid the problem.

Cream cheese has a higher percentage of saturated fat than any other cheese. Two tablespoons contain approximately 10.6 grams of fat and only 0.3 grams of polyunsaturated fat. 90% of its calories are fat.

The homogenization process, may allow an enzyme xanthane oxidase to be released into the bloodstream and reduce the effectiveness of important body chemicals that protect the small coronary arteries.

The pasteurization process has also related to a number of potential health problems:

> Milk allergies in children and adults destroys 50% of the vitamin C content.
> Destroys 25% of the vitamin B1 content.
> Destroys 9-15% of vitamin B2 content.
>
> Whole milk contains 3.5% fat.
> Low-fat milk contains 2% fat.
> Skim milk contains no fat.

Certified raw milk is the best milk, but you need to be sure the product is pure.

Whole milk contains 65% saturated fatty acids.

Many people do not have the proper enzyme (lactase) to break milk down, thus causing digestive problems and diarrhea.

BGH (Bovine growth hormone) is used to help cows increase milk production, it is not banned by the FDA and according to the latest studies and tests, traces have not been found in milk.

CALCIUM RICH FOODS

FOOD	SERVING SIZE	MG. CALCIUM
Milk Products		
Chocolate Milk	12 fl. ozs.	506
Low-Fat Milk	1 cup	298
Whole Milk	1 cup	288
Yogurt	½ cup	146
Condensed Milk	½ cup	393
Ice Cream	½ cup	131
Instant Breakfast	1 cup	407
Egg Nog	1 cup	330
Sour Cream	1 oz.	31
Evaporated Milk	½ cup	252
Non-Fat Milk Powder	½ cup	388
Ice Milk	½ cup	140

FOOD	SERVING SIZE	MG. CALCIUM
Cheese		
Cheddar Cheese	1 oz.	209
Swiss Cheese	1 oz.	255
Cottage Cheese	½ cup	105
Mozzarella	1 oz.	145
Ricotta	½ cup	337
American Cheese	1 oz.	195
Seafood		
Shrimp	1/4 cup	68
Lobster	3 ½ oz.	29
Sardines	3 ½ oz.	449
Salmon (canned)	½ cup	196

Beans, Nuts, Seeds

Sesame Seeds	½ cup	808
Soy Beans	½ cup	226
Garbanzo Beans	½ cup	150
Sunflower Seeds	3 ½ oz.	120
Peanuts	½ cup	88
Beans, Pinto	½ cup	70

Vegetables/Fruits

Prunes	8 lg.	90
Greens (all types)	1 cup	340
Kale	1 cup	170
Spinach	1 cup	180
Figs (dried)	5 med.	126
Watercress	1 cup	120
Broccoli	1 cup	115
Orange	1 med.	96
Dates	10 med.	59
Cranberries	1 cup	100

Grain Products

Oatmeal	3/4 cup	151
Cream Of Wheat	3/4 cup	142
Farina	3/4 cup	125
Wheat Germ	3 ½ oz.	72
Cornbread	3 ½ oz.	28

Combination Foods

Omelet/Cheese 2 oz.	1 serving	470
Macaroni & Cheese	½ cup	204
Pizza	1med. slice	140
Tostada	1 reg.	190
Cheeseburger	1 small	158
Vegetable Bean Soup	8 oz.	95

Desserts

Banana Split	1 reg.	350
Bread/Raisin Pudding	3/4 cup	210
Coconut Custard Pie	1/6 pie	145
Vanilla Pudding	½ cup	146
Rice Pudding	3/4 cup	142
Cake/Made With Milk	3 ½ oz.	130
Blackstrap Molasses	1 tbl.	116
Custard	½ cup	163

Chapter 39

Vegetarian Facts

jpeek '95

GENERAL OVERVIEW

An ever-increasing segment of the American public is choosing not to eat meat. Approximately 12 million Americans consider themselves vegetarians, or at least ovo-lacto vegetarian (one who eats milk and eggs). This food trend is pursued for a variety of reasons, such as considering it wrong to kill animals, a waste of natural resources by using large quantities of grain to feed beef and hogs, to religious beliefs and just the belief that it is healthier.

While vegetarianism is way of achieving a healthier diet for most of the public, it is a radical change and one that is not easily adhered to. There are sufficient studies and evidence that do provide us with the proof, that even a modified vegetarian diet is beneficial and results in a healthier longer life.

One of the major concerns among non-vegetarians who wish to consider changing to vegetarianism is that they will lack protein. There are of course, many excellent vegetable sources that are capable of supplying all your amino acid (protein) needs.

One of the best plant sources of protein is soybean, which contains 30-40% protein and is closer to meat protein than vegetable when examined under amino acid pattern analysis.

The question also arises regarding the lack of B12 in a vegetarian diet, but most vegetarians do eat some form of dairy products eliminating that problem.

If you are planning to change your dietary patterns to vegetarianism, it would be wise to purchase a book on vegetarianism and learn to do extensive meal planning, especially for the first 6 months.

Types Of Vegans

True Vegetarians
Eats nothing from an animal, fresh or processed.

Lacto-Vegetarian
Includes dairy products in their diet.

Ovo-Vegetarian
The only animal product is eggs.

Pesco-Vegetarian
Includes fish, chicken, eggs and dairy products, no red meat.

Meat is not necessary for a healthy diet.

B12 is usually taken as a supplement, since it is found only in sufficient quantities in animal products.

Most vegetarians have lower cholesterol levels than meat eaters.

Vegetarians have fewer cases of colon cancer and digestive problems.

They have a lower overall incidence of cancer.

Soy products contain high levels of phytoestrogens which scientists now think will reduce the risks of breast and prostate cancer.

Tofu products may vary significantly regarding nutritional content, best to read the labels.

Tempeh is a chunky, chewy soybean product that has been mixed with rice or millet.

Miso is a combination of soybeans and a grain. Has very little fat and usually used as a seasoning for soups, dips and stews.

Iron and zinc are not as easily absorbed by true vegetarians and may have to be supplemented.

Beans and rice are one of the best combinations to acquire all the essential amino acids.

A good source of calcium is dark green leafy vegetables.

Vegetarian products made from soybeans have a lower fat content and still provide an excellent source of protein.

Most vegetarian foods contain too much sodium. When preparing vegetarian foods, try to omit the soy sauce which seems to be the high sodium source.

Chapter 40

Water Facts

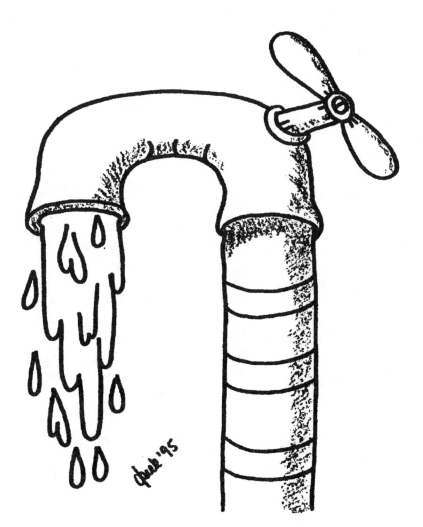

Approximately 75% of Americans are concerned about the quality of their drinking water according to a 1994 survey.

Approximately 97% of the Earth's water is in the oceans as salt water. Desalinization is becoming more popular and cost effective.

2/3 of all rural households are drinking water that is in violation of EPA standards.

Just For The "Health" Of It

Water, the most abundant and most important nutrient in the body is as essential to life as the air we breathe. Since all body functions are dependent on water, it is evident that water is important for general physical fitness. Thus, the quality of the water we consume becomes of more than just academic interest to us all.

Alcohol, tea, coffee, and colas are not ideal as a water source, because they tend to have a diuretic effect on the body.

Medical experts agree that a water with a good mineral balance is the best bet for you. A good quality still water or a sparkling water labelled from a "natural" source would be the healthiest choice.

Copper excesses have been found in tissues of schizophrenic patients and have been traced to soft water eroding away copper pipes.

Water filters are only good if they remove the particular problem in your area and are serviced properly, this includes changing the filters on a regular basis.

According to the National Cancer Institute, nine recent studies correlated water quality and cancer with the drinking water in Pittsburgh, New Orleans, and various cities in Ohio, New York, and New Jersey.

Private wells, as a result of using soft water for drinking may be the cause of mental illnesses in one out of every 10 families.

Ice water may be harmful to persons with cardiovascular disease. Sudden drops in tissue temperatures are a shock to the system and cause a strain on the heart.

The colder the water we do drink with meals, the slower the digestive process works.

Drinking water with meals is not beneficial, since we have the tendency to wash foods down instead of adequately chewing them up.

Hot water is more dangerous than using cold water and heating it. Hot water is more corrosive and can contain larger amounts of dangerous debris.

If you consume 15-23 eight ounce glasses of water in a one hour period, it could be dangerous to your health.

Homes with copper plumbing that have no soldered joints may be hazardous to your health.

If it were not for the water secreted by the salivary gland in the mouth, we would be unable to swallow and then digest the foods we eat.

Water in our bodies dissolves the foods, carries nutrients to various parts of the body, leaves the body as perspiration, helps maintain the normal body temperature, cleanses our systems of wastes, and is then eliminated through the kidneys at the rate of 3-8 pints per day.

Americans are spending over $2.4 billion dollars on bottled water annually and are purchasing almost that dollar amount in home purifying equipment.

A family consisting of five people, uses approximately 326,000 gallons of water a year.

There are over 50,000 water contaminants and only 100 are subject to regulation. These include organic compounds, biological, heavy metal salts, inorganic compounds, gases and suspended solid particles.

In the United States each year about 30 outbreaks of diseases are traced to bacterial or chemical contamination of water supplies.

Most all filter systems only remove large particles. They still leave the small ones, such as viruses, etc.

There are 55,000 chemical dump-holes across the United States according to the EPA that can leak contaminants into the water supplies in those areas.

All water is mineral water except distilled. Even rain water contains many impurities.

A study of 969 water systems in the United States showed that 41% had impure water that was being delivered to 2.5 million people.

Rinsing vegetables in a sink filled with water will save approximately 200 gallons of water per month.

Waiting for water to get hot wastes 200 gallons per month. Try saving the water for the plants or a refrigerator bottle.

To grow one pound of meat, it requires 2,500 to 6,000 pounds of water.

You will use one gallon of water to just brush your teeth.

If you weigh 150 pounds, your body contains approximately 90 pounds of water.

Humans are 60-70% water by weight.

Brain	-75%	Kidney	-83%
Heart	-75%	Bone	-22%
Muscle	-75%	Blood	-83%
Lungs	-86%	Saliva	-95%
Liver	-85%	Perspiration	-95%

An earthworm is 80% water.

A carrot is 90% water.

Salt used to give you better traction on roads in the winter can raise the sodium content of your tap water.

Mineral water from famous name spas have no particular health benefits.

When water is called for in a recipe it should between 60-80 degrees for the best reasons.

Soft water is the best for most cooking if available. Real soft water, not artificially softened.

Let your water run in the morning before using it, there may be lead from pipes in the first water that comes out.

If the recipe calls for water by weight, remember 1 tablespoon = 1/2 oz., 2 cups = 1 pound.

Sugar lowers the boiling point of water.

The average person requires about six pints of water per day to replace losses.

A runner may lose 7-9 pints of fluid during a marathon.

The body absorbs cold water more quickly.

It takes 100,000 gallons of water to produce 1 auto.

To print 1 copy of the Sunday paper it takes 280 gallons of water.

It takes 5 gallons of water to produce 1 gallon of milk.

1 out of 12 household in the United States use bottled water as their main source of drinking water.

A laundromat with 10 washing machines, uses 1,800 gallons of water per day.

A carwash, handling 24 cars per hour, uses 8,000 gallons of water per day.

47% of our nation's water supply goes for food production.

To feed one person in the United States for a year, it requires approximately 1,726,000 gallons of water.

> 1 average baked potato requires 12 gallons of water to grow.
> 1 pat of butter takes 100 gallons of water to produce.
> 2 dinner rolls require 26 gallons of water before they
> make it to your table.

If you are on a well, have your water tested every six months.

It takes 325 gallons of water to make one gallon of alcohol.

It takes 375 gallons of water to produce a one pound sack of flour.

Every person drinks approximately 16,000 gallons of water in their lifetime.

WATER QUALITY:

The quality of water we consume is as diversified as the sources from which it is derived. Most tap water comes from streams, rivers, and lakes. If the water has flowed down a mountainside, for example, it may very likely come in contact with, and carry a variety of impurities in suspension.

Surface water may contain pollutants and agricultural wastes. Fertilizers and insecticide residues are frequently found when water is tested. Air pollutants and lead from automobiles and industrial exhausts may all end up in our drinking water supply.

Other chemicals, such as chlorine, fluorine, phosphates, alum, sodium aluminate, and others are frequently added to drinking water for purification. Fluoridation is considered by some to be the most dangerous of all methods of treating water. Sodium fluoride, one of the most poisonous of all chemical compounds, is the active ingredient in rat poisons and moth control preparations.

Water should not be relied upon as a healthy source of minerals. Frequently, it may contain inorganic minerals which cannot be assimilated by the body, but rather are deposited in various parts of the body, with the end result of arthritis, calcium-hardened arteries and stones.

It cannot be taken for granted that the water we drink is beneficial to our health. A home filtering device or purchasing a quality bottled water may be the best bet.

Water Treatment Methods

Filtration: Units that contain carbon usually in the from of activated charcoal. Very effective in removing odor, chlorine, pesticides, and organic compounds. Not as effective for bacterial removal or heavy metals and hard minerals. Attracts particles from the water until it reaches the saturation point.

Chlorination: Designed to kill bacteria with chlorine. Has a tendency to leave an objectionable taste and odor. It also may form a potentially dangerous element.

Microstrainers: Capable of removing bacteria and some chemicals from water, but cannot remove nitrates.

Reverse Osmosis Systems:
                        Contains a sediment filter and an activated filter. Effective in removing 60-90% of most minerals and inorganic compounds. Does not produce a large amount of water in a 24 hour period.

Distillation: Boils water to produce steam, which is then cooled to produce a relatively clean water. However, this method will usually not clean the water of gases.

Aeration: The best method to remove radon gas which is one of the worst environmental hazards to man. The EPA estimates that over 8 million people may be at risk in the United States from high radon levels in their water.

Sediment Filters: Screen that filter out suspended particles such as detergents.

**Ultraviolet
Radiation Purifiers**:
                        Effective for the removal of bacteria. Usually installed on wells with other types of filters.

**Electrohydrolysis
Units:**   Demineralizes the water by passing a current of electricity through it to remove inorganic minerals. This method is not very effective in removing organic substances or bacteria.

Ozonators: Utilizes a highly activated form of oxygen to burn up bacteria.

Water Softeners: Removes hard minerals such as calcium or magnesium and replaces them with sodium through a process of ion-exchange. The addition of the sodium softens the water and makes it more effective for washing clothes, bathing, and doing dishes. The high salt content does not make it recommended for drinking.

Ultra Filters: Uses membranes similar to those used in reverse osmosis units, but utilizing a different method of operation. The membrane is designed to collect relatively large organic molecules as they remove dissolved inorganic solids or bacteria.

Types Of Water

Sparkling Water: Carbonated water obtained either through natural underground springs or made by dissolving CO_2 gas in water. Carbonation lasts longer in naturally carbonated waters.

Mineral Water: Contains dissolved minerals. Various brands will contain different levels of minerals. Some mineral waters are made from tap water, then minerals are added or removed as desired.

Club Soda: Usually tap water that has been filtered and carbonated. Minerals and mineral salts are added. Club soda will also take tomato juice stains out of your carpet.

Seltzer: Usually tap water, filtered and carbonated. No mineral or mineral salts are added.

Soft Water: Low mineral content water. Usually comes from deep in the earth with its principal mineral being sodium. Will dissolve soap better, and won't leave a ring around the bathtub. Will dissolve minerals such as lead from pipes.

Hard Water: High mineral content water. Usually comes from shallow ground that has high concentrations of calcium and magnesium. Hard water leaves a residue of rock-like crystals

Spring Water: Water without gas bubbles, usually tap water or natural spring water. Bottled "bulk" water falls into this category. When purchasing bottled water, try buying it in glass bottles labeled "natural."

There are more than 64 rare and different formulas for water utilizing hydrogen and oxygen isotopes. We still have a lot to learn about water.

97% of all water on earth is in the ocean. Only 3% is fresh water, which concerns all of us. 3/4 of the fresh water is frozen in glaciers.

The average person uses 75 gallons of water each day in their home, and another 100 gallons outside of their home.

43% of our water is used commercially.

Safe drinking hotline 1-(800) 426-4791

FOOD TERMINOLOGY
From A to Z

"A"

A la mode   Means the addition of a food item to another food item. Pie a la mode is pie which includes the ice cream.

Allemande   A thick sauce made from meat stock with egg yolks and lemon juice.

Angelica   Refers to a candied leafstalk, part of a European herb. Used for cake and dessert decorating.

Anglaise   A typical English dish that is boiled or roasted.

Antipasto   An Italian word for an assortment of appetizers, such as cold cuts, olives, pickles, peppers, and vegetables.

Aspic   Gelatin made from concentrated vegetables and meat stocks. Usually contains tomato juice.

A buerre   Either "with" or "cooked in butter."

Au gratin   Usually refers to a dish that has a browned covering of bread crumbs, usually mixed with cheese or butter.

"B"

Baba   A rum or fruit juice flavored French cake made with yeast dough.

Bake   To use dry heat, such as in a oven when cooking.

Barbecue   Using hot coals to cook meats on a grill while basting it with a seasoned sauce.

Barquette   A pastry in a boat shape.

Bar-le-duc   A French jam made with currants and honey. The French variety is best with the seeds removed. The American version leaves the seeds in.

Baste   A process of moistening foods while they are cooking, usually by spooning liquid over them.

Batter   A combination of a liquid and flour or other ingredient and thin enough to pour. Mainly used to coat other foods.

Bavaroise   A creamy custard that is set with gelatin.

Beat   To vigorously mix in order to have the food become smooth or increase the air in the food.

Beignets   Any food that has been dipped in batter, then deep fried in fat.

Beurre noir   A butter sauce that is browned.

Bigarade   Foods cooked in orange juice.

Bisque   A rich creamy soup made from fish or game or a frozen ice cream dessert.

Blanch   Plunging a food into boiling water usually to remove the skin off of fruit and vegetables.

Blend   Mixing thoroughly.

Bombe	A dessert made using a melon-shaped mold and filling one layer of ice cream with another.
Bordelaise	A brown sauce made using Bordeaux wine as one of its main components.
Borscht	A soup made from beets and sour cream.
Bouillabaisse	A soup made from a variety of fish, usually containing many fish parts such as the heads.
Bouillon	A clear soup made from meat broth.
Bouquet garni	Combines herbs in a cheesecloth and then used to season soups and stews.
Braise	Lightly browning the exterior of meats.
Bread	Applying a coating of bread crumbs, flour and eggs.
Brioche	A sweet French breakfast yeast bun.
Broil	Placing the food directly under a heating element.
Brunoise	A generic term referring to a food that contains finely diced vegetables.
Brush	To apply a coating thinly over a food surface.

"C"

Cafe au lait	Coffee with hot milk added.
Canape	A small piece of toasted bread topped with a variety of foodstuffs.

Capers	The unopened flower buds of the caper plant usually preserved in a vinegar solution.
Capon	An emasculated male chicken.
Carmelize	Melting granulated sugar over a medium heat forming a brown syrup.
Caviar	Fish eggs (roe). May be red, black, or gold. Caviar is obtained from a variety of fish such as the sturgeon. The finest is called Beluga Caviar.
Chantilly	A name derived from a castle near Paris which refers to a dish that contains whipped cream.
Chapon	A small crust of bread that has been flavored with garlic.
Charlotte	A dessert made from whipped cream lined with lady fingers or sponge cake, and served in a gelatin mold.
Charlotte Russe	Sponge cake in a small cardboard cup with a whipped cream topping and a cherry.
Chill	Allowing food to become thoroughly cool.
Chop	To cut foods into pieces, large or small.
Chorizio	A heavily seasoned Mexican pork sausage.
Chowder	A very thick creamy soup usually made from fish, clams, vegetables, potatoes, and onions then cooked in milk.

Chutney A sweet relish made from a combination of fruits and vegetables.

Coat To cover the food with a thin film of sugar, bread crumbs, icing, crushed nuts, etc.

Coddle A gentle simmering in liquid for a short period.

Compote Usually refers to a stew of mixed fruits cooked at a slow temperature in a syrup allowing the fruits to remain in their natural from.

Condiment A substance to make a food more appetizing such as; ketchup, mustard, chutney.

Consomme A clear broth usually made from chicken or veal.

Cool To allow a dish to set at room temperature until it is no longer hot.

Coquille A dish cooked in a scallop shell.

Cracklings The crisp remains of fat after lard has been cooked out of food.

Cream To blend shortening and sugar against the sides of a bowl or with a beater until creamy.

Creole A heavily seasoned food containing a blend of pepper, onions, bell peppers, and tomatoes.

Crepe A very thin pancake of French origin.

Croquette A crisply fried, chopped meat patty made with a white sauce and coated with crumbs and egg.

Croutons	Very small pieces or cubes of bread that have been toasted until they are crisp. Usually served with soups and salads.
Cube	Cutting foods into pieces with six equal sides.
Curry	A dish that is cooked and flavored with curry. Usually a stew.
Cutin	The process of adding fat into a flour mixture with a pastry blender or other utensil.
Cutlet	A piece of meat cut from the leg or ribs and usually fried or broiled. Most popular is the veal cutlet

"D"

Daube	A piece of braised meat.
Demitasse	A small cup of after dinner coffee.
Devil	A preparation made with spicy seasoning or sauce.
Dice	Cutting into very small cubes of food.
Dough	A combination of flour, liquid and other ingredients used to prepare pastries and breads.
Dredge	To place a thick coating of a flour mixture on a food.
Drippings	Meat juices or fat that collects in the bottom of cooking pans.

"E"

Eclair
An oblong shaped pastry, filled with whipped cream or custard and usually topped with a chocolate icing.

En Brochette
To be cooked on a skewer.

Entree
A dish that is served between heavy dishes at a formal meal.

"F"

Fillet mignon
A small round-cut piece of meat from the beef tenderloin.

Fillet
A thin boneless strip of lean meat or fish. Usually a choice piece.

Flake
To break up a food into small pieces.

Flambe
Setting a food aflame.

Fold In
The process of cutting into the center of a batter with a wooden spoon or spatula and adding ingredients then stirring them in gently and slowly.

Fondant
A sugary syrup that is cooked to a soft ball stage (234°F.) then cooked and kneaded to a creaminess.

Fondue
A Swiss Cheese dip for small pieces of bread.

Frappe
Frozen, diluted, sweet fruit juice that has been made into a "mushy" consistency.

French Fry	Cooking foods in a deep fat until they are able to float.
Fricassee	To cook a meat by braising, and chicken by stewing.
Frizzle	The process of pan frying until the edges curl.
Fromage	French for cheese.
Frost	The process of covering a food with icing.
Fry	Cooking a food in a pan with a small amount of fat.

"G"

Garnish	To use colorful foods to decorate with.
Glace	Coating a food with a sugar syrup then cooking it to "crack" stage.
Glaze	Coating a food with a sugar syrup or jelly to add luster. The food can then be heated or chilled.
Gnocci	A very light dumpling made from flour, or potatoes and eggs.
Goulash	A thick, beefy stew flavored with paprika, and vegetables.
Grate	Shredding food either manually or with a machine.
Grind	To crush foods through a grinder.
Grits	Coarsely ground corn that has been hulled.

Gumbo	A thick soup usually made with okra and a combination of other vegetables and seasonings. A Creole dish.

"H"

Hache	Hashed or minced foods.
Haricot	A term used to describe a thick meat stew.
Herbs	Plants used for seasoning, garnish, and also used for medicinal purposes.
Hollaindaise	A sauce made from egg yolk, butter and seasonings. Usually served hot over vegetables and fish.
Hors d'oeuvres	A selection of different canapes and appetizers.

"I"

Ice	Usually referred to as a frozen dessert made of fruit juice, sugar and water.

"J"

Julienne	Foods are cut into long, thin strips.
Junket	A sweet milk dessert coagulated by rennet and flavored.

"K"

King, a la	A food served in a rich, creamy sauce.
Kisses	Very small dollops of meringue.
Knead	Working dough with a downward pressing motion with occasional folding and stretching.

"L"

Lard	The fat made from swine.
Leavening	Placed in baked foods to make them light and porous by releasing gas during baking.
Leek	A pungent onion-like vegetable.
Legumes	Beans, peas, lentils.
Lyonnaise	Usually means a dish that has been seasoned with onions and parsley.

"M"

Macaroons	Cookie-like pastry made from egg whites, sugar, almond paste and coconut.
Macedoine	A mixture of vegetables and fruits.
Maigre, Au	A dish prepared without meat.
Marguerites	A baked salty cracker covered with frosting and nuts.
Marinade	Usually referred to as a meat tenderizer or flavor enhancer. An oil acid mixture sometimes utilizing pineapple or papaya.
Marinate	The actual process of allowing a meat to stand in the marinade mixture for a period of time.
Marzipan	A candy made with the paste of almonds and sugar and usually shaped into miniature fruits and vegetables.

Meringue	A stiffly beaten mixture of egg whites and sugar that is used for pies, or made into small kisses.
Mignon	The most tender cut of meat.
Mince	The process of cutting foods into very small pieces.
Minestrone	A very thick Italian vegetable soup.
Mix	Combining ingredients by stirring.
Mocha	A coffee flavoring.
Mornay	A rich, cheesy sauce.
Mousse	A frozen dessert usually made from whipped egg white or cream.

"N"

Navarin	A lamb stew.

"P"

Panada	A thick sauce containing bread or flour.
Pan-Broil	Cooking in an uncovered, lightly greased pan and removing excess fat as it accumulates.
Pan- Fry	Also called "saute". Cooking in a small amount of fat.
Parboil	Partial cooking of food in boiling water and then completing the cooking by another method.
Parch	Browning with dry heat.
Pare	Removing the outer skin from apples or potatoes.

Parfait	Either an ice cream sundae or a frozen dessert made from whipped cream and eggs then cooked with syrup and flavored.
Patty	Puffed pastry shell filled with a creamed chicken, meat or fish dish.
Peel	The process of removing the outer covering of a fruit or vegetable.
Petits fours	Small fancy cakes made by cutting a square sheet cake into different shapes then decorating each differently.
Pilaf	A rice that has been specially seasoned and used as a bed under meat, chicken or fish dishes.
Piquant	Having a sharp flavor.
Poach	Cooking foods by surrounding them with boiling water to retain their form.
Poivrade	A strongly peppered flavored dish.
Polenta	A corn meal or farina mush , to which Italians usually add cheese.
Potage	A thick Soup.
Puree	To press fruits or vegetables through a small sieve to reduce them to almost liquid form.

"Q"

Quenelles	Meat that is finely ground, mixed with eggs and shaped into ovals then poached.

"R"

Ragout	A very thick meat stew heavily seasoned.
Ramekin	Individual baking dishes.
Ravioli	Small square pasta shapes filled with cheese or meats.
Relish	A flavored blend of spices and sweet pickles.
Render	The process of removing fat from meat usually over a low heat.
Rissole	A mixture of meats encased in a pastry shell and deeply fried.
Roast	Meat cooked in the oven or over a dry heat.
Roe	Fish eggs.
Roux	A special cooked mixture of flour and butter usually used to thicken sauces and stews.

"S"

Saute	Browning or cooking in a pan using a small amount of fat.
Scald	Heating a semi-liquid until a skin forms on the top. Usually to a point just before the boiling point.
Scallop	A sea food baked in a sauce.
Score	Cutting narrow gashes partially through the outer surface of a fruit or vegetable to prevent curling.
Sear	A quick browning of the surface of a food.

Shortening	A fat used for baking or frying.
Shred	The process of tearing or cutting foods into small, narrow pieces.
Sift	To pass through a sieve to remove lumps.
Simmer	Cooking just below the boiling point.
Skewer	A long metal stick to which food items are attached for cooking.
Soubise	A food that is strongly flavored with an onion puree.
Souffle	A custard that is delicately baked and contains cheeses, meats, vegetables or fruits.
Sponge	A light cake with air and steam.
Steam'bake	A dish baked in the oven in a "dish set" in a larger dish of boiling water.
Steep	Allowing a food to cook just below the boiling point in order to extract flavor.
Sterilize	Using boiling water to kill microorganisms.
Stew	Cooking a combination of meats and vegetables in a small amount of liquid for a long time.
Stir	Mixing, using a fast rotary motion.
Stock	A liquid in which meats and poultry have been cooked.

"T"

Tartare	A sauce made from mayonnaise, capers, pickles and mustard.
Timbale	A custard or white sauce, unsweetened, with vegetables, meats, fish or poultry baked in individual dishes.
Torte	A cake made from crumbs, nuts and eggs.
Tortilla	A thin round Mexican flat bread either corn or flour.
Toss	To mix a number of ingredients without squashing them.
Truss	To tie a poultry or roast for cooking so that it won't fall apart.
Tutti-frutti	A combination of fruits.

"U"

Until set	The time it takes to set a liquid such as gelatin or custard.

"V"

Veloute	A rich sauce that is made with cream and a fish or chicken stock.
Vinaigrette	A dressing made from vinegar, oil, salt, pepper and herbs.

"W"

Whip	Beating a food to increase its volume by aeration.

"Z"

Zest	The oil found in the outer yellow or orange rind of a citrus fruit.

Zwieback   A variety of toasted bread.

REFERENCES

American Medical Association, Department of Drugs
American Heart Journal
American Journal of Clinical Nutrition
American Journal of Public Health
Archives of Biochemistry
Archives of Environmental Health
British Heart Journal
International Journal of Vitamin and Nutrition Research
Journal of Agriculture and Food Chemistry
JAMA
Journal of the Dietetic Association
Journal of Nutrition
Journal of Occupational Medicine
National Institute of Health
New England Journal of Medicine
United States Center for Health Statistics

Index

"A"

"B"

"C"

"G"

"H"

"I"

"J"

"K"

"L"

"M"

"N"

"O"

"P"

"R"

"S"

"T"

(Mex) Mexican—mejicano
mf masculine or feminine noun according to sex—nombre masculino o nombre femenino según el sexo
(mil) military—militar
(min) mining—minería
(mineral) mineralogy—mineralogía
(mountaineering) alpinismo
(mov) moving pictures—cine
mpl masculine noun plural—nombre masculino plural
msg masculine noun singular—nombre masculino singular
(mus) music—música
(myth) mythology—mitología
m & f masculine and feminine noun without regard to sex—nombre masculino y femenino sin tener en cuenta el sexo
(naut) nautical—náutico
(nav) naval—naval militar
neut neuter—neutro
(obs) obsolete—desusado
(obstet) obstetrics—obstetricia
(opt) optics—óptica
(orn) ornithology—ornitología
(paint) painting—pintura
(Pan) Panamanian—panameño
(Para) Paraguayan—paraguayo
(pathol) pathology—patología
pers personal—personal
(Peru) Peruvian—peruano
(pharm) pharmacy—farmacia
(philol) philology—filología
(philos) philosophy—filosofía
(phonet) phonetics—fonética
(phot) photography—fotografía
(phys) physics—física
(physiol) physiology—fisiología
pl plural—plural
(poet) poetical—poético
(pol) politics—política
poss possessive—posesivo
pp past participle—participio pasado
(P-R) Puerto Rican—puertorriqueño
prep preposition—preposición
pres present—presente

pret preterit—pretérito
pron pronoun—pronombre
(psychoanalysis) sicoanálisis
(psychol) psychology—sicología
(rad) radio—radio
ref reflexive verb—verbo reflexivo
reflex reflexive—reflexivo
rel relative—relativo
(rhet) rhetoric—retórica
(rr) railway—ferrocarril
s substantive—substantivo
(SAm) South American—sudamericano
(scornful) despreciativo
(sculp) sculpture—escultura
(S-D) Santo Domingo—República Dominicana
(sew) sewing—costura
sg singular—singular
(slang) jerga
spl substantive plural—substantivo plural
(sport) deporte
ssg substantive singular—substantivo singular
subj subjunctive—subjuntivo
super superlative—superlativo
(surg) surgery—cirugía
(surv) surveying—agrimensura
(taur) bullfighting—tauromaquia
(telg) telegraphy—telegrafía
(telp) telephony—telefonía
(telv) television—televisión
(tennis) tenis
(theat) theater—teatro
(theol) theology—teología
tr transitive verb—verbo transitivo
(typ) printing—imprenta
(Urug) Uruguayan—uruguayo
v verb—verbo
var variant—variante
v aux auxiliary verb—verbo auxiliar
(Ven) Venezuelan—venezolano
(vet) veterinary medicine—veterinaria
(vulg) vulgar—grosero
(W-I) West Indian—antillano
(zool) zoology—zoología

SPANISH-
ENGLISH

ESPAÑOL-
INGLÉS

A, a (a) *f* first letter of the Spanish alphabet
a *prep* at; for, to; on, upon; in, into; by; from; **a decir verdad** to tell the truth; **a la española** in the Spanish manner; **a lo que parece** as it seems; **a no ser por** if it weren't for; **a saberlo yo** if I had known it; **oler a** to smell of
abacería *f* grocery store
abace•ro -ra *mf* grocer
abad *m* abbot
abadejo *m* codfish; (orn) kinglet; (ent) Spanish fly
abadesa *f* abbess
abadía *f* abbacy; abbey
abajar *ref* to lower oneself
abaje•ño -ña *adj* (Mex) coastal, lowland ‖ *mf* (Mex) lowlander
abaje•ro -ra *adj* (Arg) lower, under ‖ *f* (Arg) bellyband, bellystrap; (Arg) saddlecloth
abají•no -na *adj* (Col, Chile) northern ‖ *mf* (Col, Chile) northerner
abajo *adv* down, underneath; downwards; downstairs; **abajo de** down; **más abajo** lower down; **río abajo** downstream ‖ *interj* down with. . . !
abalanzar §60 *tr* to hurl ‖ *ref* to rush; venture; (*un caballo*) rear
abalear *tr* (SAm) to shoot
abalizar §60 *tr* to mark with buoys ‖ *ref* (naut) to take bearings
abalorio *m* glass bead
abaluartar *tr* to bulwark
abanar *tr* to fan
abanderado *m* colorbearer
abanderar *tr* (*un buque*) to register
abanderizar §60 *tr* to organize into bands ‖ *ref* to band together; (Chile, Peru) to join up
abandona•do -da *adj* lonely
abandonar *tr* to abandon, forsake ‖ *intr* to give up ‖ *ref* to abandon oneself; give up
abandonismo *m* defeatism
abandonista *adj & mf* defeatist
abandono *m* abandon, abandonment; neglect; forlornness; yielding
abanicar §73 *tr* to fan
abanico *m* fan; fanlight; sword; **abanico de chimenea** fire screen
abaniquear *tr* to fan
abaniqueo *m* fanning; gesticulations
abanto *adj* skittish (*bull*)
abaratamiento *m* cheapening

abaratar *tr* to cheapen; (*precios*) lower ‖ *intr & ref* to get cheap
abarca *f* sandal
abarcar §73 *tr* to embrace; encompass; surround; corner, monopolize
abarloar *tr* (naut) to bring alongside ‖ *ref* to snuggle up
abarquillar *tr & ref* to curl up
abarraganamiento *m* illicit cohabitation
abarrancar *ref* to get into a difficult situation
abarrota•do -da *adj* overcrowded
abarrotar *tr* to bar; bind, fasten; jam, pack, stuff; overstock ‖ *ref* to become a glut on the market
abarrote *m* (naut) packing; **abarrotes** groceries; hardware
abarrotería *f* (Guat) grocery store; (CAm) hardware store
abarrote•ro -ra *mf* grocer
abastecer §22 *tr* to supply, provide
abastecimiento *m* supplying; supplies, provisions
abasto *m* supply; abundance; **dar abasto** to be sufficient
abatanar *tr* to full
abatí *m* (Arg, Para) corn; corn whiskey
abatible *adj* collapsible, folding
abati•do -da *adj* downcast; abject, contemptible ‖ *f* abatis
abatimiento *m* discouragement; descent
abatir *tr* to lower; knock down; shoot down; take apart; humble; discourage ‖ *intr* (aer) to drift; (naut) to have leeway ‖ *ref* to be discouraged; be humbled; drop, fall; swoop down
abdicar §73 *tr & intr* to abdicate
abdomen *m* abdomen
abecé *m* A B C
abecedario *m* A B C's
abedul *m* birch
abeja *f* bee; **abeja maestra** or **abeja reina** queen bee
abejar *m* apiary, beehive
abejarrón *m* bumblebee
abeje•ro -ra *mf* beekeeper
abejorro *m* bumblebee
aberración *f* aberration; deviation
abertura *f* aperture; opening, crack, slit; cove; openness, frankness
abeto *m* fir tree; hemlock; **abeto del Norte, abeto falso** spruce tree
abier•to -ta *adj* open; frank
abigarra•do -da *adj* motley, variegated

abigeo *m* horse thief, cattle thief
abijar *tr* (Col) to sic
abiselar *tr* to bevel
abisma•do -da *adj* absorbed, lost in thought; mysterious
abismar *tr* to cast down; humble; spoil, ruin ‖ *ref* to sink; cave in; be humbled; give in; lose oneself; be surprised
abismo *m* abyss, chasm
abjurar *tr* to abjure; renounce
ablandabre•vas *m* (*pl* -vas) or **ablandahi•gos** *m* (*pl* -gos) good-for-nothing
ablandar *tr* to soften; soften up; soothe; loosen ‖ *intr* (*el tiempo*) to moderate ‖ *ref* to soften; relent; (*el tiempo*) moderate
ablativo *m* ablative
abnegación *f* abnegation; self-denial
abnega•do -da *adj* self-denying
abnegar *ref* to deny oneself; sacrifice oneself
aboba•do -da *adj* stupid, stupid-looking
abobar *tr* to make stupid ‖ *ref* to grow stupid
aboca•do -da *adj* (*vino*) mild, smooth; vulnerable; **abocado a** verging on
abocar §73 *tr* to bite; pour; bring near ‖ *intr* to enter ‖ *ref* to approach; have an interview
abocinar *tr* to give a flare to ‖ *intr* to fall on the face ‖ *ref* to flare
abochornar *tr* to overheat; make blush ‖ *ref* to blush; wilt
abofa•do -da *adj* (Cuba, Mex) swollen
abofetear *tr* to slap in the face
abogacía *f* law, legal profession
abogaderas *fpl* (CAm) specious arguments
abogado *m* lawyer; **abogado criminalista** criminal lawyer; **abogado de secano** quack lawyer; **abogado firmón** lawyer who will sign anything; **abogado trampista** shyster
abogar §44 *intr* to plead; **abogar por** to advocate, back
abolengo *m* ancestry, descent; inheritance
abolición *f* abolition
abolir §1 *tr* to revoke, repeal
abolorio *m* ancestry
abolladura *f* dent; bump, bruise; embossing
abollar *tr* to bump, bruise; dent; stun; emboss ‖ *ref* to get bumped, get bruised; dent, be dented
abollonar *tr* to emboss
abombar *tr* to make convex; stun, confound ‖ *ref* to rot, decompose
abominable *adj* abominable, very bad
abominación *f* abomination
abominar *tr* to detest, abominate ‖ *intr* — **abominar de** to abominate
abona•do -da *adj* trustworthy; apt, likely ‖ *mf* subscriber; (*al gas, electricidad, etc.*) consumer; (*a una localidad en el teatro*) season-ticket holder; (*al ferrocarril*) commuter
abonanzar §60 *intr* (*el tiempo*) to clear up; (*el viento*) abate
abonar *tr* to vouch for; certify; improve; fertilize; **abonar en cuenta a** to credit to the account of ‖ *intr* (*el tiempo*) to clear up ‖ *ref* to subscribe
abonaré *m* promissory note

abono *m* subscription; credit; installment; voucher; fertilizer, manure
abordar *tr* to approach; accost; undertake, plan; (naut) to board; (naut) to run afoul of; (naut) to dock ‖ *intr* to run afoul; (naut) to put into port
aborigen *adj invar* aboriginal, native; **aborígenes** *mpl* aborigines, natives
aborrascar §73 *ref* to get stormy
aborrecer §22 *tr* to abhor, detest, hate; bore ‖ *ref* to get bored
aborrecible *adj* abhorrent, hateful
aborrega•do -da *adj* (*nubes*) fleecy; (*cielo*) mackerel
aborregar *ref* (SAm) to become stupid
abortar *tr & intr* to abort
abortista *mf* abortionist
aborto *m* abortion; miscarriage; **aborto despenalizado** legalized abortion
abotagar §44 *ref* to become bloated, swell up
abotonador *m* buttonhook
abotonar *tr* to button ‖ *intr* to bud
abovedar *tr* to arch, vault
abozalar *tr* to muzzle
abra *f* cove; vale; fissure; (Mex) clearing
abrasa•do -dora *adj* burning, hot
abrasar *tr* to set fire to, burn; parch; nip; squander; shame ‖ *intr* to burn ‖ *ref* to burn; become parched; (fig) to be burning up
abrasi•vo -va *adj & m* abrasive
abrazadera *f* clasp, clip, clamp; (typ) bracket
abrazar §60 *tr* to embrace, clasp; include; take in ‖ *ref* (*dos personas*) to embrace
abrazo *m* embrace, hug
abrebo•cas *m* (*pl* -cas) mouth prop, mouth gag
abrebote•llas *m* (*pl* -llas) bottle opener
abrecar•tas *m* (*pl* -tas) knife, letter opener
abreco•ches *m* (*pl* -ches) doorman
abrela•tas *m* (*pl* -tas) can opener
abreos•tras *m* (*pl* -tras) oyster knife
abrevadero *m* watering place, drinking trough
abrevar *tr* to water; wet, soak; irrigate; size ‖ *ref* to drink
abreviación *f* abridgment, abbreviation, shortening; hastening
abreviar *tr* to abridge; abbreviate; shorten; hasten ‖ *intr* to be quick; **abreviar con** to make short work of
abreviatura *f* abbreviation; **en abreviatura** in a hurry
abridero *m* (Mex, P-R) dive, joint
abridor *m* opener; grafting knife; **abridor de guantes** glove stretcher
abridura *f* (act of) opening
abrigadero *m* windbreak
abrigar §44 *tr* to shelter; protect; (*esperanzas, sospechas*) harbor ‖ *ref* to take shelter; wrap oneself up
abrigo *m* shelter; aid, support; cover, wrap; overcoat; (naut) harbor; **abrigo antiaéreo** air-raid shelter; **abrigo de entretiempo** topcoat, spring-and-fall coat; **al abrigo de** sheltered from, protected from; sheltered

by, protected by; (*ropa*) **de mucho abrigo** heavy

abril *m* April

abrillantar *tr* to polish; glaze

abrir *m* opening; **en un abrir y cerrar de ojos** in the twinkling of an eye ‖ §83 *tr* to open; unlock, unfasten; (*el apetito*) whet; (*el bosque*) clear ‖ *intr* to open ‖ *ref* to open; **abrirse a** or **con** to unbosom oneself to

abrochador *m* buttonhook

abrochar *tr* to button, hook, fasten

abrogación *f* repeal; abrogation

abrogar *tr* to repeal; abrogate; annul

abrojo *m* thistle, thorn; **abrojos** reef, hidden rocks

abrótano *m* southernwood

abruma•do -da *adj* hazy; foggy

abruma•dor -dora *adj* crushing, oppressing; overwhelming

abrumar *tr* to crush, oppress; overwhelm; annoy ‖ *ref* to become foggy

abrup•to -ta *adj* abrupt, steep; rough, rugged

absceso *m* abscess

absenta *f* absinth

ábsida *f* or **ábside** *m* apse

absolución *f* absolution; acquittal

absoluta *f* dogmatic statement; (mil) discharge

absolutamente *adv* absolutely; by no means

absolu•to -ta *adj* absolute; arbitrary ‖ *m* absolute; **en absoluto** absolutely not ‖ *f* see **absoluta**

absolvederas *fpl* — **tener buenas absolvederas** to be an indulgent confessor

absolver §47 & §83 *tr* to absolve; to solve, to answer

absorbente *adj* absorbent; (*interesante*) absorbing

absorber *tr* to absorb; use up; attract

absorción *f* absorption

absor•to -ta *adj* absorbed; entranced

abste•mio -mia *adj* abstemious

abstener §71 *ref* to abstain

abstensionismo *m* nonparticipation

abstinente *adj* abstinent

abstracción *f* abstraction; absorption, deep thought; **hacer abstracción de** to leave out, disregard

abstrac•to -ta *adj* abstract

abstraer §75 *tr* to abstract ‖ *intr* — **abstraer de** to do without, leave aside ‖ *ref* to be abstracted or absorbed; **abstraerse de** to do without, leave aside

abstraí•do -da *adj* absorbed in thought; withdrawn

abstru•so -sa *adj* abstruse

absurdidad *f* absurdity

absur•do -da *adj* absurd ‖ *m* absurdity

abuchear *tr* & *intr* to boo, hoot

abuela *f* grandmother; **cuénteselo a su abuela** tell that to the marines

abuelo *m* grandparent; grandfather; **abuelos** grandparents; ancestors

abulta•do -da *adj* bulky, massive

abultar *tr* to enlarge; exaggerate ‖ *intr* to be bulky

abundamiento *m* abundance; **a mayor abundamiento** with greater reason

abundancia *f* abundance, plenty

abundante *adj* abundant

abundar *intr* to abound

abur *interj* good-bye!, so long!

aburguesa•do -da *adj* middle-class, bourgeois

aburguesar *ref* to become middle-class, become bourgeois

aburri•do -da *adj* bored; tiresome

aburrimiento *m* weariness, fatigue; dullness

aburrir *tr* to bore, tire ‖ *ref* to become bored

abusar *intr* to go too far; **abusar de** to abuse; impose on; overindulge in

abusión *f* superstition

abusi•vo -va *adj* abusive

abuso *m* abuse; imposition

abyec•to -ta *adj* abject

A.C. *abbr* **año de Cristo**

acá *adv* here, around here; **acá y allá** here and there; **de ayer acá** since yesterday; **¿de cuándo acá?** since when?; **desde entonces acá** since then; **más acá** here closer; **muy acá** right here

acaba•do -da *adj* complete, perfect; worn-out, exhausted ‖ *m* finish

acabamiento *m* end; completion; death; decline

acabar *tr* to end, finish, complete ‖ *intr* to end; die; **acabar con** to put an end to; end in; **acabar de** to finish; have just, e.g., **acaba de salir** he has just left; **acababa de salir** he had just left; **acabar por** to end in; end by; **no acabar de decidirse** to be unable to make up one's mind ‖ *ref* to end; be exhausted; be all over; run out of, e.g., **se me acabó el café** I have run out of coffee

acabóse *m* limit, last straw

acacia *f* acacia; **acacia falsa** locust tree

academia *f* academy

académi•co -ca *adj* academic ‖ *mf* academician

acaecer §22 *intr* to happen, occur

acaecimiento *m* happening, occurrence

acalenturar *ref* to get a fever

acalora•do -da *adj* heated; warm; fiery, excited

acaloramiento *m* ardor; passion

acalorar *tr* to heat, warm; incite, encourage; stir up ‖ *ref* to become heated; warm up

acallar *tr* to quiet, silence; pacify

acampada *f* camp

acamar *tr* (*las mieses la lluvia o el viento*) to beat down, blow over

acampamento *m* camp, encampment

acampana•do -da *adj* bell-shaped

acampar *tr*, *intr* & *ref* to encamp

acanalar *tr* to groove; flute; channel; corrugate

acantila•do -da *adj* rocky; steep; precipitous ‖ *m* cliff, bluff

acantonamiento *m* cantonment

acantonar *tr* to canton, quarter ‖ *ref* to be quartered; **acantonarse en** to limit one's activities to

acaparar *tr* to corner; monopolize; hoard
acaramela•do -da *adj* candied; smooth, honey-tongued
acarar *tr* to bring face to face
acarear *tr* to bring face to face; face, brave
acariciar *tr* to caress; (*una ilusión*) cherish
acarraladura *f* (Chile, Peru) run (*in stockings*)
acarreadi•zo -za *adj* transportable
acarrear *tr* to cart, transport, carry along; cause, occasion || *ref* to incur, bring upon oneself
acarreo *m* cartage, drayage; conveyance
acartonar *ref* to shrivel up, become wizened
acasera•do -da *adj* (Chile, Peru) home-loving; (*parroquiano*) (Chile, Peru) regular || *mf* (Chile, Peru) stay-at-home, home-body; (Chile, Peru) regular customer
acaso *m* chance, accident; **al acaso** at random || *adv* maybe, perhaps; **por si acaso** in case of need, just in case
acatamiento *m* homage; respect
acatar *tr* to respect, hold in awe; observe
acatarrar *tr* to chill, give a cold to; (Chile, Mex) to bother, annoy || *ref* to catch cold; get tipsy
acaudala•do -da *adj* rich, well-to-do
acaudalar *tr* to acquire, accumulate
acaudillar *tr* to lead, command; direct
acceder *intr* to accede; agree
accesible *adj* accessible
accesión *f* accession; acquiescence; access, entry
accésit *m* second prize, honorable mention
acceso *m* access, approach; attack, fit, spell; **acceso prohibido** no admittance
acceso•rio -ria *adj* accessory || *m* accessory, fixture, attachment; **accesorios** (theat) properties
accidenta•do -da *adj* agitated; restless; rough, uneven || *mf* victim, casualty
accidental *adj* accidental; acting, pro-tempore, temporary
accidentar *tr* to injure, hurt || *ref* to faint
accidente *m* accident; (*del terreno*) roughness, unevenness; fainting spell
acción *f* action; gesture; (*parte del capital de una sociedad*) share; stock certificate; **acción crecedera** growth stock; **acción de gracias** thanksgiving; **acción liberada** stock dividend; **poner en acción** to set in motion
accionar *tr* to drive || *intr* to gesticulate
accionista *mf* shareholder, stockholder
acebo *m* holly tree
acebuche *m* wild olive
acecinar *tr* to dry-cure, dry-salt; (*el salmón o el arenque*) kipper || *ref* to shrivel up
acechar *tr* to watch, to spy on
acecho *m* watching, spying; **al acecho** or **en acecho** on the watch, spying
acedar *tr* to turn sour; embitter || *ref* to turn sour; wither
acedía *f* sourness; crabbedness; heartburn
ace•do -da *adj* sour, tart; crabbed
aceitar *tr* to oil; grease
aceite *m* oil; olive oil; **aceite de hígado de**

bacalao cod-liver oil; **aceite de linaza** linseed oil; **aceite de pie de buey** neat's-foot oil; **aceite de ricino** castor oil; **aceite mineral** coal oil
aceite•ro -ra *adj* oil || *mf* oiler; oil dealer || *f* oilcan; oil cup; **aceiteras** cruet stand
aceito•so -sa *adj* oily, greasy
aceituna *f* olive
aceituno *m* olive tree
aceleración *f* acceleration
acelerador *m* accelerator
acelerar *tr & ref* to accelerate; hasten, hurry
acelga *f* Swiss chard
acémila *f* beast of burden, pack animal; dolt; drudge
acendra•do -da *adj* refined; stainless, spotless
acendrar *tr* to refine; purify, make stainless
acento *m* accent; **acento de altura** pitch accent; **acento ortográfico** written accent, accent mark; **acento prosódico** stress accent, tonic accent
acentuar §21 *tr* to accent; accentuate, emphasize
aceña *f* water-driven flour mill
acepción *f* meaning
acepillar *tr* to plane; brush; smooth
aceptable *adj* acceptable
aceptación *f* acceptance; **aceptación de personas** discrimination; partiality
aceptar *tr* to accept
acequia *f* irrigation ditch; (Bol, Col, Peru) stream, rivulet
acera *f* sidewalk
acera•do -da *adj* steel, steely; (fig) cutting, biting, sharp
acerar *tr* to steel, harden; line with a sidewalk || *ref* to harden; steel oneself
acer•bo -ba *adj* sour, bitter; harsh
acerca *adv* — **acerca de** about, with regard to
acercamiento *m* approach, rapprochement
acercar §73 *tr* to bring near or nearer || *ref* to approach, come near or nearer
acería *f* steel mill
acerico *m* small cushion; pincushion
acero *m* steel; sword; courage, spirit
acérri•mo -ma *adj* all-out; (*enemigo*) bitter
acerrojar *tr* to bolt
acerta•do -da *adj* fit, right; skillful, sure; well-aimed
acertante *mf* winner
acertar §2 *tr* to hit; hit upon; figure out correctly; find; do right || *intr* to be right; succeed; guess right; **acertar a** to happen to; succeed in; **acertar con** to come upon; find
acertijo *m* conundrum, riddle
acervo *m* heap; assets, estate; shoal; store, fund, hoard
acetato *m* acetate
acéti•co -ca *adj* acetic
acetificar §73 *tr & ref* to acetify
acetileno *m* acetylene
acetona *f* acetone
acia•go -ga *adj* unlucky, ill-fated, evil
acial *m* (CAm, Ecuad) whip

acíbar *m* aloes; bitterness, sorrow

acicalar *tr* to polish, burnish; dress, dress up ‖ *ref* to get all dressed up

acicate *m* long-pointed spur; incentive, stimulus

acicatear *tr* to spur, urge

acidez *f* acidity

acidificar §73 *tr & ref* to acidify

áci•do -da *adj* acid, tart, sour ‖ *m* acid

acierto *m* lucky hit, good shot; good guess; tact, prudence; ability, skill; accuracy; success

aci•mut *m* (*pl* -**muts**) azimut

aclamación *f* acclaim, applause

aclamar *tr & intr* to acclaim, to hail, to cheer

aclarar *tr* to brighten, clear; rinse; explain ‖ *intr* to get bright; clear up; dawn

aclarato•rio -ria *adj* explanatory

aclimatar *tr & ref* to acclimate

acne *f* acne

acobardar *tr* to cow, intimidate ‖ *ref* to be frightened

acocear *tr* to kick; trample upon, ill-treat

acocil *m* Mexican crayfish; **estar como un acocil** (Mex) to blush, be abashed

acoda•do -da *adj* elbow-shaped

acodar *tr* (*el brazo*) to lean; prop; (hort) to layer ‖ *ref* to lean

acodillar *tr* to bend at an angle ‖ *ref* to double up; to bend, to crumple

acogencia *f* (CAm) acceptance; reception

acoger §17 *tr* to receive, welcome; accept ‖ *ref* to take refuge; resort

acogida *f* reception, welcome; meeting place, confluence; refuge, shelter; **dar acogida a** (com) to honor

acolada *f* accolade

acolchar *tr* to quilt, pad

acolchí *m* (Mex) red-winged blackbird

acólito *m* acolyte; altar boy

acollador *m* (naut) lanyard

acomedi•do -da *adj* obliging

acometer *tr* to attack; undertake; (*el sueño, la enfermedad, el deseo a una persona*) overcome

acometida *f* attack; (*p.ej., de una línea eléctrica*) house connection

acomodación *f* accommodation

acomodadi•zo -za *adj* accommodating, obliging

acomoda•do -da *adj* convenient, suitable; comfort-loving; well-to-do

acomoda•dor -dora *adj* accommodating, obliging ‖ *mf* usher

acomodar *tr* to accommodate; usher; reconcile; suit; furnish, supply ‖ *intr* to be suitable, be convenient ‖ *ref* to comply; come to terms; hire out; make oneself comfortable

acomodo *m* arrangement, adjustment; lodgings; job, position; (Chile) neatness, tidiness

acompañador *m* companion; accompanist

acompañamiento *m* accompaniment; escort, retinue; (theat) extras, supernumeraries

acompañanta *f* female companion or escort; accompanist

acompañante *m* companion; accompanist

acompañar *tr* to accompany; escort; enclose; sympathize with

acompaño *m* (CAm) meeting; encounter

acompasa•do -da *adj* rhythmic; slow; easy-going; cautious

acompleja•do -da *adj* full of complexes

aconchar *tr* to push to safety; (naut) to beach, run aground ‖ *ref* to take shelter; (naut) to run aground; (Chile) to form a deposit

acondiciona•do -da *adj* conditioned; **bien acondicionado** well-disposed; in good condition; **mal acondicionado** ill-disposed; in bad condition

acondicionador *m* conditioner; **acondicionador de aire** air conditioner

acondicionamiento *m* conditioning; **acondicionamiento del aire** air conditioning

acondicionar *tr* to condition; put in condition; repair; season ‖ *ref* to qualify; find a job

acongojar *tr* to grieve, afflict ‖ *ref* to grieve

aconsejable *adj* advisable

aconsejar *tr* to advise, counsel, warn ‖ *ref* to seek advice, get advice

acontecer §22 *intr* to happen, occur

acontecimiento *m* happening, event

acopiar *tr* to gather together

acopio *m* gathering; stock; abundance

acoplado *m* (Arg, Chile, Urug) trailer trolley car

acoplamiento *m* coupling; joint; connection; linkup (in space)

acoplar *tr* to couple; join; connect; hitch; reconcile ‖ *ref* to be reconciled; mate; be intimate

acoquinar *tr* to intimidate

acoraza•do -da *adj* armored, armor-plated; contrary ‖ *m* battleship

acorazar §60 *tr* to armor-plate

acorchar *tr* to line with cork; turn into cork ‖ *ref* to get spongy; wither, shrivel; become corky or pithy; get numb

acorchetar *tr* to bracket

acordar §61 *tr* to agree upon; authorize; reconcile; make level or flush; remind of; tune ‖ *intr* to agree; blend ‖ *ref* to be agreed, come to an agreement; remember; **acordarse de** to remember

acorde *adj* agreed, in accord; in tune ‖ *m* accord; (mus) chord

acordeón *m* accordion

acordonar *tr* to cord, lace; (*monedas*) knurl, mill; rope off

acornar §61 *tr* gore; butt

acornear *tr* to gore; butt

acorralar *tr* to corral, corner; intimidate

acortar *tr* to shorten; reduce; slow down; check, stop ‖ *ref* to become shorter; hold back; be timid; slow down; shrink

acosar *tr* to harass; pester

acosijar *tr* (Mex) to pursue, press, track down

acostar §61 *tr* to lay down; put to bed; (naut) to bring alongside ‖ *ref* to lie down; go to bed; (CAm, Mex) to give birth

acostumbra•do -da *adj* accustomed; customary, usual

acostumbrar *tr* to accustom ‖ *intr* to be accustomed ‖ *ref* to accustom oneself; become accustomed

acotación *f* boundary mark; marginal note; elevation mark

acotamiento *m* boundary mark; marginal note; elevation mark; stage direction

acotar *tr* to mark off, map; annotate; admit, accept; check; vouch for; select; mark elevations on

acotillo *m* sledge hammer

acre *adj* acrid; austere; biting, mordant

acrecentamiento *m* increase, growth; promotion

acrecentar §2 *tr* to increase; promote ‖ *ref* to increase; bud, blossom

acreditar *tr* to accredit; credit; get a reputation for ‖ *ref* to get a reputation, prove oneself

acree•dor -dora *adj* accrediting; deserving ‖ *mf* creditor; **acreedor hipotecario** mortgagee

acribar *tr* to sift; riddle

acribillar *tr* to riddle; harass, plague, pester

acriminar *tr* to incriminate; exaggerate

acrimonio•so -sa *adj* acrid; acrimonious

acriollar *ref* to acquire Spanish American ways

acrisolar *tr* to purify, refine; reveal, bring out

acrobacia *f* acrobatics

acróbata *mf* acrobat

acrobatismo *m* acrobatics

acrónimo *m* acronym

acrópo•lis *adj* (*pl* **-lis**) acropolis

acróstico *m* acrostic

acta *f* minutes; certificate; **acta notarial** affidavit; **actas** proceedings, transactions; **levantar acta** to write up the minutes

actitud *f* attitude; **en actitud de** getting ready to

activar *tr* to activate; hasten, expedite

actividad *f* activity

activista *mf* activist

acti•vo -va *adj* active ‖ *m* (com) assets; (com) credit side

acto *m* act; ceremony, function; commencement; thesis; **acto carnal** sexual intercourse; **acto continuo** right afterward; **acto seguido** right afterward; **acto seguido de** right after; **en acto de servicio** in the line of duty; **hacer acto de presencia** to honor with one's presence

actor *m* actor; agent; **primer actor** leading man

ac•triz *f* (*pl* **-trices**) actress; **primera actriz** leading lady

actuación *f* acting, performance; action; operation; behavior; **actuación en directo** live performance; **actuaciones** legal proceedings

actual *adj* present, present-day; up-to-date ‖ *m* current month

actualidad *f* present time; timeliness; **actualidades** current events; newsreel; **actuali-**

dad escénica theater news; **actualidad gráfica** news in pictures

actualizar §60 *tr* to bring up to date

actualmente *adv* at present, at the present time

actuante *mf* participant

actuar §21 *tr* to actuate ‖ *intr* to act; perform

actua•rio -ria *mf* actuary

acuaplano *m* aquaplane

acuarela *f* water color

acuario *m* aquarium; **Acuario** *m* (astr) Aquarius

acuartelar *tr* to billet, quarter

acuáti•co -ca *adj* aquatic

acuatizaje *m* (aer) alighting on water; (*de nave espacial*) splashdown

acuatizar §60 *intr* (aer) to alight on water

acucia *f* zeal, diligence; yearning

acuciar *tr* to goad, prod; harass; yearn for

acuclillar *ref* to squat, crouch

acuchilla•do -da *adj* knife-shaped; schooled by experience; (*vestido*) slashed

acuchillar *tr* to stab; stab to death; slash

acudir *intr* to come up, respond; apply; hang around; come to the rescue; **acudir a las urnas** to vote

acueducto *m* aqueduct

acuerdo *m* accord; agreement; memory; **de acuerdo con** in accord with; **de común acuerdo** with one accord; **estar en su acuerdo** to be in one's right mind; **ponerse de acuerdo** to come to an agreement; **recobrar su acuerdo** to come to; **tomar un acuerdo** to make a decision; **volver en su acuerdo** to come to; to change one's mind

acuitar *tr* & *ref* to grieve

acullá *adv* yonder, over there

acumulador *m* storage battery

acumular *tr* to accumulate, gather; store up ‖ *intr* & *ref* to accumulate, gather

acunar *tr* to rock; cradle

acuñación *f* coining, minting; wedging

acuñar *tr* to coin, mint; wedge; key, lock; (typ) to quoin

acuo•so -sa *adj* watery; juicy

acupuntura *f* acupuncture

acurrucar §73 *ref* to squat, crouch; huddle

acusación *f* accusation

acusa•do -da marked ‖ *mf* accused

acusar *tr* to accuse; show; (*recibo de una carta*) acknowledge ‖ *ref* to confess

acusati•vo -va *adj* & *m* accusative

acuse *m* acknowledgment

acústi•co -ca *adj* acoustic ‖ *f* acoustics

achacar §73 *tr* to impute, attribute

achaco•so -sa *adj* ailing, sickly

achaparra•do -da *adj* stocky; stubby; chubby

achaparrar *ref* to become stunted

achaque *m* sickliness, indisposition; excuse, pretext; matter, subject; weakness; (coll) monthlies

achatar *tr* to flatten ‖ *ref* (Mex) to become frightened, afraid

achica•do -da *adj* childish; abashed, disconcerted

achicador *m* scoop

achicar §73 *tr* to make smaller; humble; bail, to bail out

achicoria *f* chicory

achicharrar *tr* to scorch; bedevil ‖ *ref* to get scorched

achicharronar *tr* to squash

achín *m* (CAm) peddler; door-to-door salesman

achiquitar *ref* to lose heart, cower

achispa•do -da *adj* tipsy

achispar *tr* to make tipsy ‖ *ref* to get tipsy

achuchar *tr* to incite; crumple, crush; jostle ‖ *ref* (Arg, Urug) to shiver, have a chill

adagio *m* adage

adalid *m* chief; guide, leader; champion

adama•do -da *adj* womanish; chic, stylish

adamar *ref* to become effeminate

adán *m* dirty, ragged fellow; lazy, careless fellow ‖ **Adán** *m* Adam

adaptación *f* adaptation

adaptar *tr* to adapt

adarga *f* oval or heart-shaped leather shield

adarvar *tr* to bewilder, stun

A. de C. *abbr* **año de Cristo**

adecentar *tr* to clean up, tidy up ‖ *ref* to put on a clean shirt, dress up

adecua•do -da *adj* fitting, suitable

adecuar *tr* to fit, adapt

adefesio *m* nonsense; outlandish outfit; queer-looking fellow

adehala *f* gratuity, extra

adehesar *tr* to convert into pasture

adelanta•do -da *adj* precocious; bold, forward; (*reloj*) fast; **por adelantado** in advance ‖ *m* provincial governor

adelantamiento *m* anticipation; advancement, promotion, progress

adelantar *tr* to move forward; outstrip, get ahead of; advance; promote; improve ‖ *intr* to advance; improve; be fast ‖ *ref* to move forward; gain, be fast

adelante *adv* ahead; forward; **más adelante** farther on; later ‖ *interj* go ahead!; come in!

adelanto *m* advance, progress, improvement; advancement; payment in advance

adelfa *f* oleander

adelgazar §60 *tr* to make thin; taper; purify; argue subtly about; weaken, lessen ‖ *intr* & *ref* to get thin; taper

ademán *m* attitude; gesture; **ademanes** manners; **en ademán de** getting ready to; **hacer ademán de** to make a move to

además *adv* moreover, besides; **además de** in addition to, besides

adentellar *tr* to sink one's teeth into

adentrar *intr* & *ref* to go in; **adentrarse en el mar** to go farther out to sea

adentro *adv* inside; **mar adentro** out at sea; **ser muy de adentro** to be like a member of the family; **tierra adentro** inland ‖ **adentros** *mpl* inmost being, inmost thoughts; **en** or **para sus adentros** to oneself, to himself, etc.

adep•to -ta *adj* initiated ‖ *mf* follower

aderezar §60 *tr* to dress, adorn; cook; (*una tela*) starch; season; repair; lead; (*bebidas*) mix; (*vinos*) blend ‖ *ref* to dress, get ready

aderezo *m* dressing; seasoning, condiment; starch; finery; equipment; set of jewelry

adestrar §2 *tr* & *ref* var of **adiestrar**

adeuda•do -da *adj* indebted, in debt

adeudar *tr* to owe; to be liable for; charge ‖ *intr* to become related by marriage ‖ *ref* to run into debt

adeudo *m* debt, indebtedness; customs duty; charge, debit

adherencia *f* adhesion; **tener adherencias** to have connections

adherente *adj* adherent ‖ *m* adherent; **adherentes** accessories

adherir §68 *intr* & *ref* to adhere; stick

adhesión *f* adherence, adhesion

adhesi•vo -va *adj* adhesive

adición *f* addition; (*en un café o restaurante*) check

adicionar *tr* to add; add to

adic•to -ta *adj* devoted; supporting ‖ *mf* supporter, follower

adiestramiento *m* training; breaking in

adiestrar *tr* to train; teach; lead, guide ‖ *ref* to train, practice

adietar *tr* to put on a diet

adinera•do -da *adj* wealthy, well-to-do

adiós *m* adieu, good-bye ‖ *interj* adieu!, good-bye!

aditamento *m* addition; accessory

aditi•vo -va *adj* & *m* additive

adivinación *f* prophecy; guessing, divination; **adivinación del pensamiento** mind reading

adivina•dor -dora *mf* guesser; good guesser; **adivinador del pensamiento** mind reader

adivinaja *f* riddle, puzzle

adivinanza *f* riddle; guess

adivinar *tr* to prophesy; guess, divine; (*un enigma*) solve; (*el pensamiento ajeno*) read

adivi•no -na *mf* fortuneteller; guesser

adjetivo *m* adjective

adjudicar §73 *tr* to adjudge, award ‖ *ref* to appropriate

adjuntar *tr* to join, connect; add; enclose

adjun•to -ta *adj* added, attached; enclosed ‖ *mf* associate ‖ *m* adjunct; adjective

adminículo *m* aid, auxiliary; gadget; meddler; **adminículos** emergency equipment

administración *f* administration, management; headquarters

administra•dor -dora *mf* administrator, manager; **administrador de correos** postmaster

administrar *tr* to administer, manage

admiración *f* admiration; wonder; exclamation mark

admira•dor -dora *mf* admirer

admirar *tr* to admire; surprise ‖ *ref* to wonder; **admirarse de** to wonder at

admisible *adj* admissible

admisión *f* admission; (mach) intake

admitir *tr* to admit; allow; accept, recognize; agree to

adobar *tr* to repair, restore; dress, prepare; cook, stew; (*carne, pescado*) pickle; (*pieles*) tan

adobe *m* adobe

adobera *f* (SAm) brick-shaped cheese; mold for brick-shaped cheese

adobo *m* repairing; dressing; cooking; pickling; tanning; pickled meat or fish

adocena•do -da common, ordinary

adoctrinar *tr* to indoctrinate, teach, instruct

adolecer §22 *intr* to fall sick; **adolecer de** to suffer from ‖ *ref* — **adolecerse de** (archaic) to sympathize with, feel sorry for

adolescencia *f* adolescence

adolescente *adj & mf* adolescent

adonde *conj* where, whither

adónde *adv* where, whither

adopción *f* adoption

adoptar *tr* to adopt

adoquín *m* paving stone, paving block; (coll) blockhead

adoquina•do -da *adj* paved with cobblestones ‖ *m* cobblestone paving

adorable *adj* adorable

adoración *f* adoration, worship; **Adoración de los Reyes** Epiphany

adora•dor -dora *mf* adorer, worshiper ‖ *m* suitor

adorar *tr & intr* to adore, worship

adormecer §22 *tr* to put to sleep ‖ *ref* to go to sleep; get sleepy

adormeci•do -da *adj* sleepy, drowsy; numb; calm

adormidera *f* opium poppy

adormilar *ref* to doze, drowse

adornar *tr* to adorn; (*un cuento*) embroider

adornista *mf* decorator

adorno *m* adornment, decoration; **adorno de escaparate** window dressing

adosar *tr* to lean; push close

adquirir §40 *tr* to acquire; **adquirir en propiedad** to buy, purchase

adquisición *f* acquisition

adrede *adv* on purpose

Adriáti•co -ca *adj & m* Adriatic

adscribir §83 *tr* to attribute; assign

adscripción *f* attribution; assignment

aduana *f* customhouse; **aduana seca** inland customhouse; **exento de aduana** duty-free; **sujeto de aduana** dutiable

aduane•ro -ra *adj* customhouse; customs ‖ *m* customhouse officer, customs inspector

aduar *m* Arab settlement; gipsy camp; Indian ranch

adueñar *ref* to take possession

adujar *tr* (naut) to coil ‖ *ref* (naut) to curl up

adular *tr* to flatter, fawn on

adu•lón -lona *adj* fawning, groveling ‖ *mf* fawner

adúltera *f* adulteress

adulterar *tr* to adulterate ‖ *intr* to commit adultery ‖ *ref* to become adulterated, to spoil

adulterio *m* adultery

adúlte•ro -ra *adj* adulterous ‖ *m* adulterer ‖ *f* see **adúltera**

adultez *f* adulthood

adul•to -ta *adj & mf* adult

adulzar §60 *tr* to sweeten; (*metales*) soften

adunar *tr* to join, bring together

adundar *ref* (CAm) to become stupid

adus•to -ta *adj* grim, stern, gloomy; scorching hot

advenedi•zo -za *adj* strange; foreign ‖ *mf* stranger; foreigner; outsider; parvenu, upstart; nouveau riche

advenimiento *m* advent, coming; accession; **esperar el santo advenimiento** to wait in vain

advenir §79 *intr* to come, arrive; happen

adverbio *m* adverb

adversa•rio -ria *mf* adversary

adversidad *f* adversity

advertencia *f* observation; notice, remark; warning; preface

adverti•do -da *adj* capable, clever, wide-awake

advertir §68 *tr* to notice, observe; notify, warn; point out ‖ *ref* to become aware

Adviento *m* (eccl) Advent

adyacente *adj* adjacent

aeración *f* aeration; ventilation; air conditioning

aére•o -a *adj* air, aerial; overhead, elevated; airy, light, fanciful

aerodinámi•co -ca *adj* aerodynamic ‖ *f* aerodynamics

aeródromo *m* aerodrome, airdrome; **aeródromo de urgencia** emergency-landing field

aerofluyente *adj* streamlined

aeroespacial *adj* aerospace

aerofumigación *f* crop dusting

aeromedicina *f* aviation medicine

aeromodelismo *m* model-airplane building

aeromodelista *mf* model-airplane builder

aeromodelo *m* model airplane

aeromotor *m* windmill; airplane motor

aeromoza *f* air hostess, stewardess

aeronáuti•co -ca *adj* aeronautic ‖ *f* aeronautics

aeronave *f* airship; **aeronave cohete** rocket ship

aeropista *f* landing strip

aeroplano *m* aeroplane

aeroposta *f* air mail

aeropostal *adj* air-mail

aeropropulsor *m* airplane engine; **aeropropulsor por reacción** jet engine

aeropuerto *m* airport

aeroscala *f* transit point

aerosol *m* aerosol

aeroste•ro -ra *adj* aviation ‖ *m* flyer; airman

aerotaxi *m* air taxi

aeroterrestre *adj* air-ground

aerovía *f* airway

afable *adj* affable, friendly, agreeable

afama•do -da *adj* noted, famous

afamar *tr* to make famous ‖ *ref* to become famous

afán *m* hard work; eagerness, zeal; task; worry

afanar *tr* to press, hurry ‖ *intr* to strive, toil ‖ *ref* to strive, toil; busy oneself

afano•so -sa *adj* hard, laborious; hard-working

afarolar *ref* to make a fuss, get excited

afear tr to deface, disfigure; blame
afeblecer §22 intr to grow feeble, get thin
afección f affection, fondness; (med) affection
afectación f affectation
afecta·do -da adj affected; **estar afectado de** (p.ej., los riñones) to have (e.g., kidney) trouble
afectar tr to affect; hurt, injure ‖ ref to be moved, be stirred
afecti·vo -va adj emotional
afec·to -ta adj fond; kind; affected; **afecto a** fond of; (un empleo, un servicio, etc.) attached to; **afecto de** suffering from ‖ m affection, fondness; emotion
afectuo·so -sa adj affectionate; kind
afeitado m shave; **afeitado a ras** close shave
afeitar tr to shave; adorn; ‖ ref to shave; paint
afeite m cosmetics, rouge, make-up
afeminación f effeminacy
afemina·do -da adj effeminate
afeminar tr to effeminate ‖ ref to become effeminate
aferra·do -da adj stubborn, obstinate
aferrar tr to seize; catch; hook; (naut) to moor; (naut) to furl ‖ ref to interlock, hook together; cling; insist
Afganistán, el Afghanistan
afga·no -na adj & mf Afghan
afianzar §60 tr to guarantee, vouch for; bail; fasten; prop up; grasp; support ‖ ref to hold fast, steady oneself
afición f fondness, liking, taste; ardor, zeal; fans, public
aficiona·do -da adj fond; amateur; **aficionado a** fond of ‖ mf amateur; fan, follower
aficionar tr to win, win the attachment of ‖ ref — **aficionarse a** or **de** to become fond of; become a follower of, become a fan of
afiebra·do -da adj feverish
afiebrar ref (SAm) to get a fever
afi·jo -ja adj affixed ‖ m affix
afila·do -da adj sharp; tapering; pointed; peaked
afilador m grinder, sharpener; razor strop
afilalápi·ces m (pl -ces) pencil sharpener
afilar tr to grind, sharpen; (una navaja de afeitar) strop; (Arg & Urug) to flirt with ‖ ref to sharpen, get sharp; taper, get thin
afiliar §77 & regular tr to affiliate, take in ‖ ref — **afiliarse a** to join
afiligranar tr to filigree; adorn, embellish
afilón m knife sharpener; razor strop
afín adj near, bordering; like, similar; related ‖ mf relative by marriage
afinador m tuner; tuning hammer, tuning key
afinar tr to purify, refine, perfect; trim; tune
afincar §73 intr & ref to buy up real estate
afinidad f affinity; **por afinidad** by marriage
afirmar tr to strengthen, secure, fasten; assert ‖ ref to hold fast; steady oneself
afirmati·vo -va adj & f affirmative
aflicción f affliction; sorrow, grief
afligir §27 tr to afflict, grieve; (Mex) to beat, whip ‖ ref to grieve
aflojar tr to slacken, let go; loosen ‖ intr to

slacken, slow up; abate, lessen ‖ ref to come loose; slacken
aflora·do -da adj flour; fine, elegant
aflorar tr to sift ‖ intr to crop out
afluencia f flowing; affluence, abundance; crowd, jam, rush; fluency; **horas de afluencia** rush hour
afluente adj flowing; abundant; fluent ‖ m tributary
afluir §20 intr to flow; pour, flock
afmo. abbr. **afectísimo**
afofar tr to make fluffy, make spongy
afonizar §60 tr & ref to unvoice
aforar tr to gauge, measure; appraise
aforismo m aphorism
afortuna·do -da adj fortunate; happy
afrancesa·do -da adj & mf Francophile
afrecho m bran
afrenta f affront
afrentar tr to affront ‖ ref to be ashamed
afrento·so -sa adj outrageous, disgraceful
Africa f Africa
africa·no -na adj & mf African
afrodisía·co -ca adj & m aphrodisiac
afrontamiento m confrontation
afrontar tr to bring face to face; defy ‖ ref — **afrontarse con** to confront, meet face to face
afuera adv outside ‖ interj clear the way!, look out! ‖ **afueras** fpl outskirts, environs
afuetada f or **afuetadura** f (SAm) beating
agachadiza f snipe; **hacer la agachadiza** to duck
agachar tr to lower, bend down ‖ ref to crouch, squat; cower; (SAm) to give in, yield
agalla f gallnut; (de pez) gill; (de ave) ear lobe; **agallas** courage, guts
ágape m banquet, love feast
agarradera f hold, grip; handle; **tener agarraderas** to have connections
agarrada f brawl, fight, scrap
agarra·do -da adj stingy, tight ‖ f see **agarrada**
agarrar tr to grab, grasp; take hold of; get, obtain ‖ intr to take hold; take root; stick ‖ ref to grapple; have a good hold; worry; **agarrarse a** to take hold of, cling to
agarro m clench, clutch, grip
agarrochar tr to jab with a goad
agarrón m brawl, fight; grip, tug
agarrotar tr to garrote; bind, tie up ‖ ref to become numb
agasajar tr to regale, lionize, make a fuss over
agasajo m kindness, attention; lionization; favor, gift; treat; party
agavillar tr to bind or tie in sheaves ‖ ref to band together
agazapar tr to grab, to nab ‖ ref to crouch; to hide
agencia f agency; bureau; (Chile) pawn shop; **agencia de noticias** news agency; **agencia matrimonial** marriage broker
agenciar tr to manage to bring about; promote ‖ ref to manage
agenda f notebook

agente *m* agent; policeman; **agente de policía** policeman; **agente viajero** traveling salesman, commercial traveler

agigantar *tr* to make huge ‖ *ref* to become huge

ágil *adj* agile; flexible, light

agilitar *tr* & *ref* to limber up

agita•do -da *adj* agitated, excited, exalted; (*mar*) rough

agitar *tr* to agitate; shake; wave; stir ‖ *intr* to agitate ‖ *ref* to be agitated; shake; wave; get excited; (*el mar*) get rough

aglomeración *f* agglomeration; crowd; built-up area

aglomerado *m* briquet, coal briquet

aglutinar *tr* to stick together ‖ *ref* to cake

agnósti•co -ca *adj* & *mf* agnostic

agobiar *tr* to overburden; exhaust, oppress

agolpar *ref* to flock, throng

agonía *f* agony, throes of death; agony, anguish; yearning; craving

agonizar §60 *tr* (*al moribundo*) to assist, attend; harass ‖ *intr* to be in the throes of death

agorar §3 *tr* to augur, foretell

agore•ro -ra *adj* fortunetelling; ill-omened; superstitious ‖ *mf* fortuneteller

agostar *tr* to burn up, to parch ‖ *ref* to dry up; (*la esperanza, la felicidad*) fade away

agostero *m* harvest helper

agosto *m* August; harvest; harvest time; **hacer su agosto** to make hay while the sun shines

agota•do -da *adj* exhausted; sold out; out of print

agotar *tr* to exhaust, wear out, use up ‖ *ref* to become exhausted, be used up; go out of print; run out

agracia•do -da *adj* charming, graceful; nice, pretty ‖ *mf* winner

agradable *adj* agreeable; pleasant

agradar *tr* to please ‖ *intr* to be pleasing ‖ *ref* to be pleased

agradecer §22 *tr* to thank; **agradecerle a uno una cosa** to thank someone for something

agradeci•do -da *adj* thankful, grateful; rewarding

agradecimiento *m* thanks, gratitude

agrado *m* agreeableness, graciousness; pleasure, liking

agrandar *tr* to enlarge ‖ *ref* to grow larger

agranelar *tr* (*cuero*) to grain, pebble

agrapar *tr* to clamp

agrariense *adj* & *mf* agrarian

agra•rio -ria *adj* agrarian

agravar *tr* to weigh down; aggravate; exaggerate; oppress ‖ *ref* to get worse

agraviar *tr* to wrong, offend ‖ *ref* to take offense

agravio *m* wrong, offense; **agravios de hecho** assault and battery

agravio•so -sa *adj* offensive, insulting

agraz *m* (*pl* **agraces**) sour grape; sour-grape juice; bitterness, displeasure; **en agraz** prematurely

agredir §1 *tr* to attack, assault

agregado *m* aggregate; concrete block; attaché; (Arg) tenant farmer

agregar §44 *tr* to add; attach; appoint ‖ *ref* to join

agremiado *m* union member

agremiar *tr* to unionize

agresión *f* aggression

agresi•vo -va *adj* aggressive

agre•sor -sora *adj* aggressive ‖ *mf* aggressor

agreste *adj* country, rustic; wild, rough; uncouth

agriar §77 & **regular** *tr* to make sour; exasperate ‖ *ref* to turn sour; become exasperated

agrícola *adj* agricultural ‖ *mf* farmer

agricultura *f* agriculture

agridulce *adj* bittersweet

agriera *f* (Chile) heartburn; **agrieras** (Col) cruet stand

agrietar *tr* & *ref* to crack

agrimensor *m* surveyor

agrimensura *f* surveying

agringar §44 *ref* to act like a gringo

a•grio -gria *adj* sour, acrid; uneven, rough; brittle ‖ **agrios** *mpl* citrus fruit

agronomía *f* agronomy

agropecua•rio -ria *adj* land-and-cattle, farm

agrumar *tr* & *ref* to curd, clot

agrupar *tr* & *ref* to group, cluster

agrura *f* sourness; unpleasantness; **agruras** citrus fruit

agua *f* water; (*de un tejado*) slope; **agua abajo** downstream; **agua arriba** upstream; **agua bendita** holy water; **agua corriente** running water; **agua de Colonia** eau de Cologne; **agua de marea** tidewater; **agua gaseosa** carbonated water; **agua oxigenada** hydrogen peroxide; **aguas** mineral springs; (*de sedas; de piedras preciosas*) water, sparkle; **aguas mayores** equinoctial tide; feces; **aguas menores** ordinary tide; urination; **cubrir aguas** to have under roof; **entre dos aguas** under water, under the surface of the water; (coll) undecided

aguacate *m* avocado, alligator pear; pear-shaped emerald

aguacero *m* shower

aguada *f* source of water; water color; watering station

aguade•ro -ra *adj* water ‖ *m* watering place

agua•do -da *adj* watery; thin, watered; weak, washed out, limp; dull, insipid ‖ *f* see **aguada**

agua•dor -dora *mf* water carrier ‖ *m* paddle, bucket

aguafies•tas *mf* (*pl* **-tas**) kill-joy, wet blanket, crapehanger

aguafortista *mf* etcher

aguafuerte *f* etching; **grabar al aguafuerte** to etch

aguaitar *intr* to spy, watch ‖ *tr* to watch, wait for

aguaje *m* watering place; tidal wave; strong current; (*de buque*) wake

aguamala *f* jellyfish

aguamanil *m* ewer, wash pitcher; washstand

aguama•nos *m* (*pl* **-nos**) water for washing hands; washstand
aguamarina *f* aquamarine
aguanie•ves *f* (*pl* **-ves**) wagtail
aguano•so -sa *adj* watery, soaked
aguantada *f* patience, forbearance
aguantar *tr* to hold up, sustain; bear, endure, tolerate; hold back, control ‖ *intr* to last, hold out ‖ *ref* to restrain oneself; keep quiet; **aguantarse las lágrimas** to swallow one's tears
aguante *m* patience, endurance; strength, vigor
aguar §10 *tr* to water; spoil, mar ‖ *ref* to become watery; fill up with water; be spoiled
aguardar *tr* to await, wait for; grant time to ‖ *intr* to wait; **aguardar a que** to wait until
aguardentera *f* liquor bottle, brandy flask
aguardentería *f* liquor store
aguardento•so -sa *adj* brandy; (*voz*) whiskey
aguardiente *m* brandy; spirituous liquor; **aguardiente de caña** rum; **aguardiente de manzana** applejack
aguardo *m* hunter's blind
aguarrás *m* turpentine, oil of turpentine
aguasar *ref* (Arg & Chile) to become countrified
aguazal *m* swamp, pool
agudeza *f* acuteness, acuity; sharpness; witticism; **agudeza visual** visual acuity
agu•do -da *adj* acute; sharp; keen; witty
agüero *m* augury; omen; forecast
aguerri•do -da *adj* inured, hardened
aguijada *f* goad, spur; prod
aguijar *tr* to goad, spur, prod ‖ *intr* to hurry along
aguijón *m* goad, spur; sting; thorn; stimulus; **dar coces contra el aguijón** to kick against the pricks
aguijonear to goad, incite; sting
águila *f* eagle; **¿águila o sol?** (Mex) heads or tails?; **ser un águila** to be wide-awake, be a wizard
aguile•ño -ña *adj* aquiline; sharp-featured
aguilón *m* (*de grúa*) boom, jib; (*del tejado*) gable
aguinaldo *m* Christmas gift, Epiphany gift; Christmas carol
aguja *f* needle; hatpin; steeple, spire; (*del reloj*) hand; **aguja de gancho** crochet needle; **aguja de hacer media** knitting needle; **aguja de zurcir** darning needle; **agujas** (rr) switch; **buscar una aguja en un pajar** to look for a needle in a haystack
agujerear *tr* to make a hole in, pierce, perforate
agujero *m* hole; pincushion; **agujero negro** black hole
agujeta *f* (*de la jeringa*) needle; shoestring; **agujetas** stitches, twinges
agusanar *ref* to get wormy; become wormeaten
aguzanie•ves *f* (*pl* **-ves**) wagtail
aguzar §60 *tr* to sharpen; incite, stir up; stare at; (*las orejas*) prick up
ah-chís *interj* kerchoo!

aherrojar *tr* to fetter, shackle; oppress
aherrumbrar *tr* & *ref* to rust
ahí *adv* there; **de ahí que** hence; **por ahí** that way
ahija•do -da *mf* godchild; protégé ‖ *m* godson ‖ *f* goddaughter
ahilar *ref* to faint from hunger; waste away; grow poorly; turn sour
ahincar §73 *tr* to urge, press; importune ‖ *ref* to hasten
ahinco *m* earnestness, zeal, eagerness
ahitar *tr* to cloy, surfeit, stuff
ahi•to -ta *adj* surfeited, stuffed; fed up, disgusted ‖ *m* surfeit; indigestion
ahoga•do -da *adj* drowned; smothered; sunk; close, unventilated; **mate ahogado** stalemate; **perecer ahogado** to drown; **verse ahogado** to be swamped
ahogar §44 *tr* to drown; suffocate, smother; (*cal*) slake; (*plantas*) soak; oppress; extinguish; stalemate ‖ *ref* to drown; suffocate; drown oneself
ahogo *m* shortness of breath; great sorrow; stringency
ahondar *tr* to make deeper; go deep into ‖ *intr* to go deep, go deeper
ahora *adv* now; presently; **ahora bien** now then, so then; **ahora mismo** right now; **por ahora** for the present
ahorcajar *ref* to sit astride
ahorcar §73 *tr* to hang ‖ *ref* to hang, be hanged; hang oneself
ahorra•do -da *adj* saving, thrifty
ahorrar *tr* to save; spare ‖ *ref* to save or spare oneself
ahorrati•vo -va *adj* saving, thrifty; stingy ‖ *f* economy
ahorro *m* economy; **ahorros** savings
ahuchar *tr* to hoard
ahuecar §73 *tr* to hollow, hollow out; loosen, fluff up; **ahuecar la voz** to speak in deep and solemn tones ‖ *ref* to be puffed up
ahula•do -da *adj* waterproof, impermeable *m* overshoe
ahumar *tr* to smoke ‖ *intr* to be smoky ‖ *ref* to get smoked up; look or taste smoky; get drunk
ahusar *tr* & *ref* to taper
ahuyentar *tr* to put to flight; scare away ‖ *ref* to flee, run away
aira•do -da *adj* angry; wild; depraved
airar §4 *tr* to anger ‖ *ref* to get angry
aire *m* air; **al aire libre** in the open air; **darse aires** to put on airs
airear *tr* to air, aerate, ventilate ‖ *ref* to get aired; catch cold
airón *m* aigrette, panache; gray heron
airo•so -sa *adj* airy; drafty; graceful, light; resplendent; successful
aislación *f* insulation
aislacionista *adj* & *mf* isolationist
aislador *m* insulator
aislamiento *m* isolation; (elec) insulation
aislar §4 *tr* to isolate; detach, separate; (elec) to insulate ‖ *ref* to live in seclusion

ajar *m* garlic field ‖ *tr* to crumple, muss; (*marchitar*) wither; tamper with; abuse, ill-treat ‖ *ref* to get mussed; wither

ajedrea *f* (bot) savory

ajedrecista *mf* chess player

ajedrez *m* chess; chess set

ajenjo *m* (*Artemisia*) wormwood; (*licor*) absinthe; (*sinsabores y penas*) (fig) wormwood, bitterness; **ajenjo del campo** or **ajenjo mayor** (*Artemisia absinthium*) wormwood

aje•no -na *adj* another's; extraneous, foreign; different; contrary; free; insane; uninformed; **lo ajeno** what belongs to someone else

ajetrear *tr* to drive, harass ‖ *ref* to bustle about; fidget

ajetreo *m* bustle, fuss

ají *m* (*pl* **ajíes**) chili; chili sauce; **ponerse como un ají** (Chile) to turn red as a tomato

aji•mez *m* (*pl* **-meces**) mullioned window

ajo *m* garlic; garlic clove; garlic sauce

ajorca *f* bracelet, anklet

ajornalar *tr* to hire by the day ‖ *ref* to hire out by the day

ajuar *m* housefurnishings; trousseau

ajuiciar *tr* to bring to one's senses ‖ *ref* to come to one's senses

ajustable *adj* adjustable

ajusta•do -da *adj* just, right; tight, close-fitting

ajustar *tr* to adapt, fit, adjust; hire; arrange; reconcile; fasten; settle ‖ *intr* to fit ‖ *ref* to fit; hire out; be hired; come to an agreement

ajuste *m* fit; fitting, adjustment; hiring; arrangement; reconciliation; settlement; agreement

ajusticiar *tr* to execute, put to death

ala *f* wing; (*del sombrero*) brim; (*de puerta, mesa, etc.*) leaf; (*de pez*) fin; (*de hélice*) blade; (football) end; **ahuecar el ala** to beat it; **ala en flecha** (aer) sweptback wing; **alas** boldness, courage; **volar con sus propias alas** to stand on one's own feet

Alá *m* Allah

alabanza *f* praise

alabar *tr* to praise ‖ *ref* to boast

alabarda *f* halberd

alabardero *m* halberdier; hired applauder, claqueur

alabastro *m* alabaster

álabe *m* drooping branch; bucket, paddle; cog

alabear *tr* & *ref* to warp

alacena *f* cupboard, wall closet; (naut) locker; (Mex) booth, stall

alacrán *m* scorpion

ala•do -da *adj* winged

alamar *m* frog (*button and loop on a garment*)

alambica•do -da *adj* precious, oversubtle, fine-spun; begrudged

alambicar §73 *tr* to distill; refine to excess

alambique *m* still, alembic; (*de laboratorio*) retort; **por alambique** sparingly

alambrada *f* chicken wire; wire mesh; (mil) barbed wire; (elec) wiring

alambrado *m* chicken wire; wire mesh; wire fence; (elec) wiring; (mil) wire entanglement

alambraje *m* (elec) wiring

alambrar *tr* to fence with wire; string with wire; wire

alambre *m* wire; **alambre cargado** live wire; **alambre de púas** barbed wire; **alambre sin aislar** bare wire

alambrera *f* wire screen; wire cover

alameda *f* poplar grove; mall, shaded walk

álamo *m* poplar; **álamo de Italia** Lombardy poplar; **álamo negro** black poplar; **álamo temblón** aspen

alampar *ref* to have a craving

alancear *tr* to lance, spear

alano *m* mastiff, great Dane

alarde *m* display, ostentation; (mil) review; **hacer alarde de** to make a show of; boast of

alardear *intr* to boast, brag, show off

alardo•so -sa *adj* showy, ostentatious

alargar §44 *tr* to extend, lengthen, stretch; hand; to increase; let out ‖ *ref* to go away, withdraw; grow longer; be long-winded

alarido *m* howl, shout, yell, whoop

alarma *f* alarm; (aer) alert; **alarma aérea** air-raid warning; **alarma de incendios** fire alarm; **alarma de ladrones** burglar alarm

alarmar *tr* to alarm; alert ‖ *ref* to become alarmed

alarmista *mf* alarmist

alastrar *tr* (*las orejas*) to throw back; (naut) to ballast ‖ *ref* to lie flat, cower

ala•zán -zana *adj* sorrel, reddish-brown ‖ *mf* sorrel horse

alba *f* dawn, daybreak

albacea *m* executor ‖ *f* executrix

albahaquero *m* flowerpot

alba•nés -nesa *adj* & *mf* Albanian

albañal *m* sewer, drain

albañil *m* mason, bricklayer

albañilería *f* masonry

albarán *m* rent sign; bulletin; (com) check list

albarca *f* sandal

albarda *f* packsaddle

albardilla *f* (*tejadillo sobre los muros*) coping; shoulder pad

albaricoque *m* apricot

albaricoquero *m* apricot tree

alba•tros *m* (*pl* **-tros**) albatross

albayalde *m* white lead

albear *intr* to turn white; (Arg) to get up at dawn

albedrío *m* free will; fancy, caprice, pleasure; **libre albedrío** free will

albéitar *m* veterinarian

alberca *f* pond, pool; tank, reservoir; **en alberca** roofless

albérchigo *m* clingstone peach

albergar §44 *tr* to shelter, harbor; house ‖ *intr* & *ref* to take shelter; take lodgings

albergue *m* shelter, refuge; lodging; den, lair

albero *m* dishcloth, dishrag; white earth

al•bo -ba *adj* (poet) white ‖ *f* see **alba**
albóndiga *f* meat ball, fish ball
albor *m* whiteness; dawn
alborada *f* dawn; morning serenade; reveille
alborear *intr* to dawn
albor•noz *m* (*pl* **-noces**) terry cloth; burnoose; cardigan; beach robe
alborota•do -da *adj* hasty, rash; noisy; rough
alborota•dor -dora *mf* agitator, rioter
alborotapue•blos *mf* (*pl* **-blos**) (coll) rabble rouser
alborotar *tr* to agitate, arouse, stir up ‖ *intr* to make a racket ‖ *ref* to get excited; riot; (*la mar*) get rough
alboroto *m* agitation, disturbance; noise, riot; **alborotos** (CAm) candied popcorn; **armar un alboroto** to raise a racket
alborozar §60 *tr* to gladden, cheer, overjoy, elate
alborozo *m* joy, merriment, elation
albricias *fpl* reward for good news; reward given on the occasion of some happy event; **en albricias de** as a token of ‖ *interj* good news!, congratulations!
albufera *f* saltwater lagoon
ál•bum *m* (*pl* **-bumes**) album; **álbum de recortes** scrapbook
albumen *m* albumen
albúmina *f* albumin
albuminar *tr* (phot) to emulsify
albur *m* risk, chance
alcachofa *f* artichoke
alcahue•te -ta *mf* bawd, procurer, go-between; screen, fence; schemer; gossip
alcahuetear *tr* to procure; harbor ‖ *intr* to pander
alcaide *m* governor, warden, jailer
alcalde *m* mayor, chief burgess; **alcalde de monterilla** small-town mayor; **tener el padre alcalde** to have a friend at court
alcaldesa *f* mayoress
álcali *m* alkali
alcali•no -na *adj* alkaline
alcallería *f* pottery
alcana *f* henna
alcance *m* reach, scope, extent; range; pursuit; capacity; late news; import; coverage; brains, intelligence; **al alcance de** within reach of, within range of; **alcance de la vista** eyesight, eyeshot; **alcance del oído** earshot; **dar alcance a** to catch up with
alcancía *f* child's bank; bin, hopper
alcanfor *m* camphor
alcantarilla *f* sewer; culvert
alcantarillar *tr* to sewer
alcanza•do -da *adj* needy, hard up
alcanzar §60 *tr* to reach; overtake, catch up to; grasp; obtain; understand; live through ‖ *intr* to succeed; (*un arma de fuego*) carry; manage; suffice
alcaparrosa *f* vitriol
alcaravea *f* caraway
alcatraz *m* gannet, pelican
alcázar *m* fortress; castle, royal palace; quarterdeck
alce *m* elk, moose
alcista *adj* bullish ‖ *mf* (fig) bull

alcoba *f* bedroom; **alcoba de respeto** master bedroom
alcohol *m* alcohol
alcohóli•co -ca *adj & mf* alcoholic
alconafta *f* gasohol
alcor *m* hill, elevation, eminence
alcornoque *m* cork oak; blockhead
alcorque *m* cork-soled shoe; trench for water around a tree
alcorza *f* sugar paste, sugar icing; **ser una alcorza** (Arg) to be highly emotional
alcurnia *f* ancestry, lineage
alcuza *f* olive-oil can
aldaba *f* knocker, door knocker; bolt, crossbar; latch; hitching ring; **aldaba dormida** deadlatch; **tener buenas aldabas** to have pull
aldabonazo *m* knock on the door
aldea *f* village, hamlet
aldea•no -na *adj* village; rustic ‖ *mf* villager
aleación *f* alloy
alear *tr* to alloy ‖ *intr* to flap the wings; to flap one's arms; to convalesce
aleccionar *tr* to teach, instruct; to train, to coach
aleda•ño -ña *adj* bordering ‖ *m* border, boundary
alega•dor -dora *adj* quarrelsome; litigious
alegar §44 *tr* to allege; to declare, assert ‖ *intr.* (Col, Hond) to quarrel
alegoría *f* allegory
alegóri•co -ca *adj* allegoric(al)
alegrar *tr* to cheer, gladden; (*un fuego*) to stir ‖ *ref* to be glad, to rejoice; to get tipsy
alegre *adj* glad; bright; cheerful, light-hearted; careless; fast, spicy; **alegre de cascos** scatterbrained
alegría *f* cheer, joy, gladness; brightness, gaiety
aleja•do -da *adj* distant, remote
alejandri•no -na *adj & mf* Alexandrine
alejar *tr & ref* to move aside, move away
alelar *tr* to make stupid ‖ *ref* to grow stupid
aleluya *m & f* hallelujah ‖ *m* Easter time ‖ *f* doggerel; daub; **aleluya navideña** Christmas card ‖ *interj* hallelujah!
ale•mán -mana *adj & mf* German
Alemania *f* Germany
alenta•do -da *adj* brave, spirited; proud, haughty; well, healthy ‖ *f* deep breath
alentar §2 *tr* to encourage, cheer up ‖ *intr* to breathe ‖ *ref* to take heart; get well, recover
alerce *m* larch
alergia *f* allergy
alero *m* eaves
alerón *m* aileron
alerta *adv* on the alert ‖ *interj* watch out!, look out! ‖ *m* (mil) alert; (mil) watchword
alertar *tr* to alert
aler•to -ta *adj* alert, watchful, vigilant
alesaje *m* bore
alesna *f* awl
aleta *f* small wing; (*de pez*) fin; (*de hélice*) blade; **aletas** (*natación*) flippers
aletargar §44 *tr* to benumb; put to sleep ‖ *ref* to get drowsy, fall asleep

aletear *intr* to flap the wings; flap, flip, flutter
aleve *adj* treacherous, perfidious
alevosía *f* treachery, perfidy
alevo•so -sa *adj* treacherous, perfidious
alfabetizar §60 *tr* to alphabetize; teach reading and writing to
alfabeto *m* alphabet
alfaneque *m* buzzard
alfanje *m* cutlass
alfarería *f* pottery
alfarero *m* potter
alféizar *m* splay; embrasure
alfeñicar §73 *tr* to candy, ice ‖ *ref* to grow thin; be affected, finical
alfeñique *m* almond-flavored sugar paste; affectation, prudery; thin, delicate person; weakling
alfé•rez *m* (*pl* **-reces**) (mil) second lieutenant; (mil) subaltern (Brit); **alférez de fragata** (nav) ensign; **alférez de navío** (nav) lieutenant (j.g.)
alfil *m* bishop
alfiler *m* pin; **alfiler de corbata** stickpin, scarfpin; **alfiler de madera** clothespin; **alfiler de seguridad** safety pin; **alfileres** pin money
alfilerar *tr* to pin, pin up
alfiletero *m* pincase, needlecase
alfombra *f* carpet; rug
alfombrar *tr* to carpet
alforfón *m* buckwheat
alforja *f* shoulder bag; traveling supplies; **pasarse a la otra alforja** to go too far, take too much liberty
alforza *f* pleat, tuck
al•foz *m* (*pl* **-foces**) outskirts; dependence; mountain pass
alga *f* alga; **alga marina** seaweed; **algas** algae
algaida *f* brush, thicket; sandbank
algalia *f* civet; catheter
algarabía *f* Arabic; (coll) gibberish, jabber; (coll) hubbub, uproar
algarada *f* outcry; uproar
algarroba *f* carob bean
algarrobo *m* carob
algazara *f* Moorish battle cry; din, uproar
álgebra *f* algebra
algebrai•co -ca *adj* algebraic
álgi•do -da *adj* cold, icy, frigid
algo *pron indef* something; anything; **algo por el estilo** something of the sort ‖ *adv* somewhat, a little, rather
algodón *m* cotton; **algodón pólvora** guncotton; **estar criado entre algodones** to be brought up in comfort
algodoncillo *m* milkweed
algodono•so -sa *adj* cottony
alguacil *m* bailiff; mounted police officer at the head of the processional entrance of the bullfighters
alguien *pron indef* somebody, someone
algún *adj indef* apocopated form of **alguno**, used only before masculine singular nouns and adjectives

algu•no -na *adj indef* some, any; not any; **alguna vez** sometimes; ever ‖ *pron indef* someone; **algunos** some
alhaja *f* jewel, gem; **buena alhaja** a bad egg, a sly fellow
alhajera *f* or **alhajero** *m* jewelry box
alharaca *f* fuss, ado, ballyhoo; **hacer alharacas** to make a fuss
alharaquien•to -ta *adj* fussy, noisy
alhe•lí *m* (*pl* **-líes**) gillyflower (*Matthiola incana*); wallflower (*Cheiranthus*)
alheña *f* henna; blight, mildew
alheñar *tr* to henna; blight, mildew ‖ *ref* (*el pelo*) to henna
alhucema *f* lavender
alhumajo *m* pine needles
alia•do -da *adj* allied ‖ *mf* ally
aliaga *f* furze, gorse
alianza *f* alliance; wedding ring; (Bib) covenant
aliar §77 *tr* to ally ‖ *ref* to ally, become allied; form an alliance
alias *adj* & *m* alias
alicaí•do -da *adj* failing, weak; crestfallen, discouraged
alicates *mpl* pliers
aliciente *m* inducement, incentive
alienar *tr* to alienate; enrapture
aliento *m* breath, breathing; courage, spirit; **dar aliento a** to encourage; **de mucho aliento** arduous, difficult, endless; **nuevo aliento** second wind; **sin aliento** out of breath
alifafe *m* complaint, indisposition
aligerar *tr* to lighten; alleviate, ease; hasten; shorten
aligustre *m* privet
alijador *m* lighter; lighterman; sander
alijar *tr* to unload, lighten; sandpaper
aligeramiento *m* easing; alleviation; **aligeramiento de impuestos** tax relief
alimaña *f* varmint, small predacious animal
alimentante *mf* person obliged to provide child support
alimentar *tr* to feed, nourish; (*p.ej., esperanzas*) to cherish, foster ‖ *ref* to feed, nourish oneself
alimenti•cio -cia *adj* alimentary, nourishing
alimento *m* food, nourishment; encouragement; **alimentos** foodstuffs; allowance; alimony
alindar *tr* to mark off; embellish, prettify ‖ *intr* to border, be contiguous
alinea•do -da *adj* lined up, aligned; **no alineado** nonaligned, Third World
alinear *tr* & *ref* to align, line up
aliñar *tr* to dress, season
aliño *m* dressing, seasoning
aliquebra•do -da *adj* crestfallen
alisar *tr* to smooth; polish, sleek; iron lightly
aliso *m* alder tree
alistar *tr* to list; enlist, enroll; stripe ‖ *ref* to enlist, enroll; get ready
aliteración *f* alliteration
aliviar *tr* to alleviate, relieve, soothe; remedy; lighten; hasten ‖ *ref* to get better, recover

alivio *m* alleviation, relief; remedy

aljaba *f* quiver

aljama *f* mosque; synagogue; Moorish quarter; ghetto

aljamía *f* Spanish of Moors and Jews; Spanish written in Arabic characters

aljez *m* gypsum

aljibe *m* water tender, tank barge; oil tanker; cistern

aljófar *m* imperfect pearl; (fig) dewdrops

aljofifa *f* floor mop

aljofifar *tr* to mop

alma *f* soul, heart, spirit; (*persona*) living soul; crux, heart; sweetheart; (*de carril*) web; (*de cañón*) bore; (*de escalera*) newel; **dar el alma, entregar el alma, rendir el alma** to give up the ghost

almacén *m* warehouse; store, department store; storehouse; (phot) magazine

almacenaje *m* storage; **almacenaje de datos** (*ordenador*) data storage, memory

almacenamiento *m* storage; (*ordenador*) data storage, memory

almacenar *tr* to store; store up, hoard; to store (electronic) data

almacenista *mf* storekeeper ‖ *m* warehouseman

almáciga *f* seedbed, tree nursery

almádana *f* spalling hammer

almagre *m* red ocher

almajara *f* (hort) hotbed

almanaque *m* almanac; calendar

almeja *f* clam

almena *f* merlon

almenaje *m* battlement

almendra *f* almond; (*de cualquier fruto drupáceo*) kernel; **almendra amarga** bitter almond; **almendra de Málaga** Jordan almond; **almendra tostada** burnt almond

almendrado *m* macaroon

almendro *m* almond tree

almiar *m* haystack, hayrick

almíbar *m* simple syrup; fruit juice; **estar hecho un almíbar** to be as sweet as pie

almibarar *tr* to preserve in syrup; (*sus palabras*) honey ‖ *intr* to candy

almidón *m* starch; paste; **almidón de maíz** cornstarch

almidona•do -da *adj* starched; spruce, dapper; stiff, prim

almidonar *tr* to starch

alminar *m* minaret

almiranta *f* admiral's wife; flagship

almirante *m* admiral

almi•rez *m* (*pl* **-reces**) brass mortar

almizcle *m* musk

almizclera *f* muskrat

almizclero *m* musk deer

almohada *f* pillow; **consultar con la almohada** to sleep it over

almohadilla *f* cushion; pad; (Chile) pincushion

almohaza *f* currycomb

almohazar §60 *tr* to currycomb

almoneda *f* auction; clearance sale

almonedar *tr* to auction

almorranas *fpl* piles, hemorrhoids

almorta *f* grass pea

almorzada *f* double handful, heavy breakfast

almorzar §35 *tr* to lunch on ‖ *intr* to lunch, have lunch

almuecín *m* or **almuédano** *m* muezzin

almuerzo *m* lunch

alna•do -da *mf* stepchild

aloca•do -da *adj* mad, wild, reckless ‖ *mf* madcap

alocar §73 *tr* to drive crazy

alocución *f* address, speech

áloe *m* or **aloe** *m* aloe; aloes

alojar *tr* to lodge; quarter, billet ‖ *intr* & *ref* to lodge; be quartered or billeted

alojo *m* accommodations, lodging

alondra *f* lark

aloquecer §22 *ref* to go crazy, lose one's mind

alosa *f* shad

alpaca *f* alpaca; alpaca wool; alpaca cloth; German silver

alpargata *f* hemp sandal, espadrille

alpende *m* tool shed; lean-to, penthouse

Alpes *mpl* Alps

alpestre *adj* alpine

alpinismo *m* mountain climbing

alpi•no -na *adj* alpine

alpiste *m* canary seed, birdseed; **quedarse alpiste** to be disappointed

alquería *f* farmhouse

alquibla *f* kiblah

alquiladi•zo -za *adj* & *mf* hireling

alquilar *tr* to rent, let, hire ‖ *ref* to hire out; be for rent

alquiler *m* rent, rental, hire; **alquiler de coches** car-rental service; **alquiler sin chófer** drive-yourself service; **de alquiler** for rent, for hire

alquilona *f* cleaning woman, charwoman

alquimia *f* alchemy

alquitarar *tr* to distill

alquitrán *m* tar; **alquitrán de hulla** coal tar

alquitranado *m* tarpaulin

alquitranar *tr* to tar

alrededor *adv* around; **alrededor de** around; about, approximately ‖ **alrededores** *mpl* environs, surroundings, outskirts

Alsacia *f* Alsace

alsacia•no -na *adj* & *mf* Alsatian

alta *f* discharge from hospital; (mil) certificate of induction into active service; **dar de alta** to discharge from the hospital; **darse de alta** to join, be admitted; (mil) to report for duty

altane•ro -ra *adj* towering; arrogant, haughty

altar *m* altar; **altar mayor** high altar; **conducir al altar** to lead to the altar

alta•voz *m* (*pl* **-voces**) loudspeaker

altea *f* (bot) marshmallow

alteración *f* alteration; disturbance; uneven pulse; altercation, quarrel

alterar *tr* to alter; disturb; agitate, upset; falsify; lessen ‖ *ref* to alter; be disturbed; be agitated; lessen; (*el pulso*) flutter

altercación *f* or **altercado** *m* argument, wrangle, bickering

altercar §73 *intr* to argue, bicker, wrangle

alternar *tr* & *intr* to alternate; **alternar con** to go around with

alternati•vo -va *adj* alternating, alternative; *f* choice, option; admission as a matador; **no tener alternativa** to have no choice

alter•no -na *adj* alternate

alteza *f* sublimity ‖ **Alteza** *f* (*tratamiento*) Highness

altibajo *m* downward thrust; **altibajos** uneven ground; ups and downs

altillo *m* hillock; (*oficina en una tienda o taller*) balcony; (Arg, Ecuad) attic, garret

altimetría *f* altimetry

altiplanicie *f* tableland

altitud *f* altitude; height

altivez *f* or **altiveza** *f* arrogance, haughtiness, pride

alti•vo -va *adj* haughty, proud; high, lofty

al•to -ta *adj* high; upper; top; loud; (*horas*) late; **ponerse tan alto** to take offense, be hoity-toity ‖ *m* height, altitude; story, floor; stop, halt; **de alto a bajo** from top to bottom; **hacer alto** to stop; **pasar por alto** to overlook, disregard ‖ *f* see **alta** ‖ **alto** *adv* high up; loud; aloud ‖ **alto** *interj* halt!

altoparlante *m* loudspeaker

altozanero *m* (Col) public errand boy

altozano *m* hill, knoll; upper part of town; (CAm, Col, Ven) parvis

altruísta *adj* altruistic ‖ *mf* altruist

altura *f* height, altitude; high seas; juncture, point, stage; (mus) pitch; (naut) latitude; **a estas alturas** at this juncture; **a la altura de** (naut) off; **estar a la altura de** to be up to, be equal to; be abreast of; **por estas alturas** around here

alucinación *f* hallucination

alucinante *adj* hallucinogenic

alud *m* avalanche

aludi•do -da *adj* above-mentioned

aludir *intr* to allude

alumbra•do -da *adj* lighted; enlightened; tipsy ‖ *m* lighting; lighting system

alumbramiento *m* lighting; childbirth, accouchement

alumbrar *tr* to light, illuminate; (*a los ciegos*) give sight to; enlighten; (*aguas subterráneas*) discover and bring to the surface ‖ *intr* to have a child ‖ *ref* to get tipsy

alumbre *m* alum

aluminio *m* aluminum

alumnado *m* student body

alum•no -na *mf* (*niño criado como si fuera hijo*) foster child; (*discípulo*) pupil, student; **alumno mimado** teacher's pet

alunizaje *m* lunar landing

alunizar §60 *intr* to land on the moon

alusión *f* allusion

álveo *m* bed of a stream, river bed

alvéolo *m* alveolus; (*de diente*) socket; (*de rueda de agua*) bucket

alza *f* rise, advance, increase; **jugar al alza** to bull the market

alzada *f* height (*e.g., of a horse*)

alza•do -da *adj* (SAm) insolent; rebellious; *m* lump sum, cash settlement; front elevation; (bb) quire, gathering

alzapaño *m* curtain holder; tieback

alzapié *m* snare, trap

alzaprima *f* crowbar, lever; (*de instrumento de arco*) (mus) bridge

alzaprimar *tr* to pry, pry up; arouse, stir up

alzapuer•tas *m* (*pl* -tas) (archaic) dumb player, supernumerary

alzar §60 *tr* to raise, lift, hoist; pick up; (*la hostia*) elevate; hide, lock up; (*naipes*) cut; (bb) to gather ‖ *ref* to rise, get up; revolt; **alzarse con** to abscond with

alzaválvu•las *m* (*pl* -las) tappet

alzo *m* (CAm) theft

allá *adv* there, over there; back there; **allá en** over in; back in; **el más allá** the beyond; **más allá** farther on, farther away; **más allá de** beyond; **por allá** thereabouts; that way

allanar *tr* to level, smooth, flatten; (*una dificultad*) iron out, overcome, get around; (*una casa*) break into; to subdue ‖ *intr* to level off ‖ *ref* to tumble down; yield, submit; humble oneself

allega•do -da *adj* near, close; related; partisan ‖ *mf* relative; partisan

allegar §44 *tr* to collect, gather; reap ‖ *intr* to approach ‖ *ref* to approach; be attached, be a follower, agree

allende *adv* beyond; **allende de** besides, in addition to ‖ *prep* beyond

allí *adv* there; **allí dentro** in there; **por allí** that way; around there

ama *f* housekeeper; housewife, lady of the house; landlady, proprietress; **ama de casa** housewife; **ama de cría** or **de leche** wet nurse; **ama de llaves** housekeeper; **ama seca** dry nurse

amable *adj* amiable, kind, obliging; (*digno de ser amado*) lovable

amachinar *ref* to cohabit; get intimate

ama•do -da *adj* & *mf* beloved

ama•dor -dora *adj* fond, loving ‖ *mf* lover

amadrigar §44 *tr* to welcome, receive with open arms ‖ *ref* to burrow; go into seclusion

amaestrar *tr* to teach, coach; (*a los animales*) train

amagar §44 *tr* to show signs of, threaten; feint ‖ *intr* to look threatening

amago *m* threat, menace; sign, indication; feint

amainar *tr* to lessen; (naut) to lower, shorten ‖ *intr* to subside, die down; lessen; yield ‖ *ref* to lessen; yield

amalgama *f* amalgam

amalgamar *tr* & *ref* to amalgamate

amamantar *tr* to nurse, to suckle

amancebamiento *m* cohabitation, concubinage, liaison

amancebar *ref* to cohabit, live in concubinage

amancillar *tr* to stain, spot; sully, tarnish

amanecer *m* dawn, daybreak ‖ *v* §22 *intr* to dawn, begin to get light; begin to appear; get awake, start the day

amanecida f dawn, daybreak

amanera•do -da adj mannered, affected

amansar tr (animal) to tame; (caballo) break; soothe, appease

amante adj fond, loving ǁ mf lover

amaño m skill, cleverness, dexterity; trick; **amaños** tools, implements

amapola f poppy

amar tr to love

amaraje m alighting on water

amarar intr to alight on water

amargar §44 tr to make bitter; embitter; (una tertulia, una velada) spoil ǁ intr & ref to become bitter; become embittered

amar•go -ga adj bitter; sour; distressing ǁ **amargos** mpl bitters

amargura f bitterness; sorrow, grief

amarillear intr to turn yellow, show yellow

amarillecer §22 intr to become yellow

amarillen•to -ta adj yellowish

amarillez f yellowness

amari•llo -lla adj & m yellow

amarra f mooring cable; **amarras** support, protection; **soltar las amarras** (naut) to cast off

amarrar tr to moor; lash, tie up; (las cartas) stack

amartelar tr to make love to; make jealous ǁ ref to fall in love; become jealous

amartillar tr to hammer; (un arma de fuego) to cock

amasar tr to knead; mix; massage; (dinero) amass; concoct

amatista f amethyst

Amazonas m Amazon

ambages mpl ambiguity, quibbling; **sin ambages** straight to the point

ámbar m amber

Amberes f Antwerp

ambición f ambition

ambicionar tr to strive for, be eager for

ambicio•so -sa adj ambitious; eager; **ambicioso de figurar** social climber

ambiental adj environmental

ambiente m atmosphere; **medio ambiente** environment; situation

ambi•gú m (pl -gúes) buffet supper; bar, refreshment bar

ambigüedad f ambiguity

ambi•guo -gua adj ambiguous; (género) (gram) common

ámbito m boundary, limit; compass, scope

ambladura f amble

amblar intr to amble

am•bos -bas adj & pron indef both; **ambos a dos** both, both together

ambrosía f ragweed

ambulancia f ambulance; **ambulancia de correos** mail car, railway post office

ambulante adj itinerant, traveling ǁ m railway mail clerk

ambulato•rio -ria adj ambulatory ǁ m welfare center, public clinic; ambulance

amedrentar tr to frighten, scare

amelona•do -da adj melon-shaped; mentally retarded; lovesick

amén interj amen! ǁ m amen ǁ adv — **amén de** aside from; in addition to

amenaza f threat, menace

amenazar §60 tr to threaten, menace

amenguar §10 tr to lessen, diminish; belittle; dishonor

amenidad f amenity

amenizar §60 tr to make pleasant, brighten, cheer

ame•no -na adj agreeable, pleasant

amento m catkin

América f America; **la América Central** Central America; **la América del Norte** North America; **la América del Sur** South America; **la América Latina** Latin America

americana f sack coat, jacket

americanizar §60 tr to Americanize

america•no -na adj & mf American; Spanish American ǁ f see **americana**

amerizar §60 intr to alight on water

ametralladora f machine gun

ametrallar tr to machine-gun

amiba f amoeba

amiga f friend; mistress; schoolmistress; girls' school

amigable adj amicable, friendly

amigacho m chum, crony, pal

amígdala f tonsil

amigdalitis f tonsillitis

ami•go -ga adj friendly; fond ǁ mf friend; sweetheart; **amigo del alma** bosom friend ǁ f see **amiga**

amigote m chum, crony, pal

amilanar tr to terrify, intimidate

aminorar tr to lessen, diminish

amistad f friendship; liaison; **hacer las amistades** to make up; **romper las amistades** to fall out, become enemies

amistar tr to bring together ǁ ref to become friends

amisto•so -sa adj friendly

amniocentesis f amniocentesis

amnistía f amnesty

amnistiar §77 tr to amnesty, grant amnesty to

amo m head of family; landlord, proprietor; boss; **ser el amo del cotarro** to rule the roost

amoblar §61 tr to furnish

amodorrar ref to get drowsy; fall asleep; grow numb

amohinar tr to annoy, irritate, vex

amojonar tr to mark off with landmarks

amoladera f grindstone, whetstone

amolar §61 tr to grind, sharpen; bore, annoy

amoldar tr to mold; model, pattern, fashion; adjust, adapt

amonestación f admonition; marriage banns

amonestar tr to admonish, warn; publish the banns of

amoníaco m ammonia

amontonar tr to heap, pile; accumulate; hoard ǁ ref to collect, gather; crowd; get angry; (Mex) to gang up

amor m love; **al amor del agua** with the current; obligingly; **al amor de la lumbre**

by the fire, in the warmth of the fire; **amores** love affair; **amor propio** amour-propre; conceit; **por amor de** for the sake of

amorata•do -da *adj* livid, black-and-blue

amordazar §60 *tr* to muzzle; gag

amorío *m* love-making; love affair

amoro•so -sa *adj* loving, affectionate, amorous

amortajar *tr* to shroud; (carp) to mortise

amortecer §22 *tr* to deaden, muffle ‖ *ref* to die away, become faint

amortiguador *m* shock absorber; door check; (*de automóvil*) bumper; **amortiguador de luz** dimmer; **amortiguador de ruido** muffler

amortiguar §10 *tr* to deaden, muffle; soften, tone down; dim; damp; (*un golpe*) cushion; (*ondas electromagnéticas*) damp

amortizar §60 *tr* to amortize; (*una deuda*) pay off

amoscar §73 *ref* to get peeved; (Mex) to blush, be embarrassed

amotina•do -da *adj* mutinous, rebellious ‖ *mf* mutineer, rebel, rioter

amotinar *tr* to stir up; incite to mutiny ‖ *ref* to rise up, mutiny, rebel

amover §47 *tr* to discharge, dismiss

amovible *adj* removable, detachable

amparar *tr* to shelter, protect ‖ *ref* to seek shelter; protect oneself

amparo *m* shelter, protection, refuge; stall; aid, favor

amperio *m* ampere

amperio-hora *m* (*pl* **amperios-hora**) ampere-hour

ampliación *f* amplification; (phot) enlargement

ampliar §77 *tr* to amplify, enlarge; widen; (phot) to enlarge

amplificador *m* amplifier

amplificar §73 *tr* to amplify; expand, enlarge; magnify

am•plio -plia *adj* ample; spacious, roomy

amplitud *f* amplitude; roominess

ampo *m* dazzling white; snowflake

ampolla *f* blister; bubble; cruet; bulb, light bulb

ampollar *tr* & *ref* to blister

ampolleta *f* vial; sandglass, hourglass; bulb, light bulb; cruet

ampulosidad *f* bombast, pomposity

ampulo•so -sa *adj* bombastic, pompous

amputar *tr* to amputate

amueblar *tr* to furnish

amujera•do -da *adj* effeminate

amuleto *m* amulet, charm

amurallar *tr* to wall, wall in

amurcar §73 *tr* to gore

amusgar §44 *tr* (*las orejas el toro, el caballo*) to throw back

anacardo *m* cashew; cashew nut

anacróni•co -ca *adj* anachronistic

anacronismo *m* anachronism

ánade *mf* duck

anadear *intr* to waddle

anadeo *m* waddle, waddling

anales *mpl* annals

analfabetismo *m* illiteracy

analfabe•to -ta *adj* & *mf* illiterate

analgési•co -ca *adj* analgesic ‖ *m* painkiller, analgesic

análi•sis *m* & *f* (*pl* **-sis**) analysis; **análisis costobeneficio** cost-benefit analysis; **análisis de sistemas** systems analysis; **análisis gramatical** parsing; **análisis ocupacional** job analysis

analista *mf* analyst; annalist

analíti•co -ca *adj* analytic(al)

analizar §60 *tr* to analyze; **analizar gramaticalmente** to parse

analogía *f* analogy; similarity

análo•go -ga *adj* analogous; similar

ana•ná *m* (*pl* **-naes**) pineapple

ananás *m* pineapple

anaquel *m* shelf

anaranja•do -da *adj* & *m* (*color*) orange

anarquía *f* anarchy

anárqui•co -ca *adj* anarchic(al)

anarquista *mf* anarch, anarchist

anatema *m* & *f* anathema; curse

anatomía *f* anatomy

anatómi•co -ca *adj* anatomic(al) ‖ *mf* anatomist

anatomista *mf* anatomist

anca *f* croup, haunch; buttock, rump; **a ancas** or **a las ancas** mounted behind another person; **anca de rana** frog's leg; **dar ancas vueltas** (Mex) to give odds

ancianidad *f* old age

ancia•no -na *adj* old, aged ‖ *m* old man; (eccl) elder ‖ *f* old woman

ancla *f* anchor; **echar anclas** to cast anchor; **levar anclas** to weigh anchor

anclar *intr* to anchor

anclote *m* kedge, kedge anchor

ancón *m* bay, cove

áncora *f* anchor

ancorar *intr* to anchor

ancheta *f* (Arg) foolishness; ridiculous act

an•cho -cha *adj* wide, broad; full, ample; loose, loose-fitting ‖ *m* width, breadth

anchoa *f* anchovy

anchura *f* width, breadth; fullness, ampleness; looseness; comfort, ease

anchuro•so -sa *adj* wide, broad; spacious, roomy

andada *f* thin, hard-baked cracker; **andadas** (*de conejos y otros animales*) tracks; **volver a las andadas** to revert to one's old tricks

andaderas *fpl* gocart, walker

anda•do -da *adj* gone by, elapsed; frequented, trodden; worn, used; ordinary ‖ *m* gait ‖ *f* see **andada**

andadores *mpl* leading strings

andadura *f* pace, gait; amble; (Mex) mount

Andalucía *f* Andalusia

anda•luz -luza *adj* & *mf* Andalusian

andaluzada *f* tall story, exaggeration, fish story

andamiaje *m* scaffolding

andamio *m* scaffold; platform

andanada f (naut) broadside; (taur) covered upper section; (coll) scolding; (fig) fusillade

andante adj walking; errant, wandering

andanza f wandering, rambling; fate, fortune

andar m gait, pace, walk ‖ §5 tr (p.ej., dos millas) to go; (un camino) go down or up ‖ intr to go, walk; run; travel; act, behave; (p.ej., un reloj) go, run, work; be, feel; go by, pass, elapse; go (to bear up, to last), e.g., **anduve diez horas sin comer** I went ten hours without eating ‖ ref to go by, to pass, to elapse; to go away; **andarse sin** to go without

andarie·go -ga adj wandering, roving; swift, fleet

andas fpl litter; stretcher; bier

andén m railway platform; quay; footpath

Andes mpl Andes

andinismo m mountain climbing in the Andes

andi·no -na adj Andean

andraje·ro -ra mf ragpicker

andrajo m rag, tatter; ragamuffin, scalawag

andrajo·so -sa adj ragged, raggedy, in tatters

andurriales mpl byways, out-of-the-way place

anea f cattail, bulrush

aneblar §2 tr to cloud; becloud ‖ ref to become clouded; get dark

anécdota f anecdote

anegar §44 tr to flood; drown ‖ ref to become flooded; drown

ane·jo -ja adj annexed; accessory ‖ m annex; dependency; supplement

anemia f anaemia

anémi·co -ca adj anaemic

anestesia f anaesthesia

anestesiar tr anaesthetize

anestési·co -ca adj & m anaesthetic

aneurisma m & f aneurysm

anexar tr to annex

ane·xo -xa adj annexed; accessory ‖ m annex; dependency

anfi·bio -bia adj amphibious

anfiteatro m amphitheater

anfitrión m host

anfitriona f hostess

ánfora f voting urn, ballot box

anfractuo·so -sa adj winding, tortuous

angarillas fpl handbarrow; panniers; cruet stand

ángel m angel; **ángel custodio** or **de la guarda** guardian angel; **ángel patudo** wolf in sheep's clothing; **tener ángel** to have great charm

angelical or **angéli·co -ca** adj angelic(al)

angina f angina; **angina de pecho** angina pectoris

angloparlante adj English-speaking ‖ mf speaker of English

anglosa·jón -jona adj & mf Anglo-Saxon

angos·to -ta adj narrow

anguila f eel; **anguilas** (para botar un barco al agua) ways; **escurrirse como una anguila** to be as slippery as an eel

angular adj angular

ángulo m angle; corner

angulo·so -sa adj (facciones) angular

angurria f (SAm) raging hunger; greed

angustia f anguish, distress, grief

angustia·do -da adj distressed, grieved

angustiar tr to distress, afflict, grieve

angustio·so -sa adj distressed, grieved; worrisome

anhelar tr to crave, want badly ‖ intr to pant; yearn; **anhelar por** to long for

anhélito m hard breathing

anhelo m craving; yearning, longing

anhelo·so -sa adj eager, yearning; breathless, panting

anhi·dro -dra adj anhydrous

Aníbal m Hannibal

anidar tr to harbor, shelter ‖ intr & ref to nestle, make a nest; live

anilina f aniline

anilla f curtain ring; (en la gimnasia) ring; hoop

anillo m ring; cigar band; **anillo de compromiso** or **de pedida** engagement ring; **anillo sigilar** signet ring

ánima f soul; (de arma de fuego) bore

animación f animation; liveliness; bustle, movement

anima·do -da adj animated, lively

animador m (de un café-cantante) master of ceremonies

animal adj & m animal

animar tr to enliven; encourage; strengthen; drive ‖ ref to take heart, feel encouraged

ánimo m mind, spirit; courage, valor, energy; attention, thought

animosidad f animosity, ill will

animo·so -sa adj brave, courageous; spirited; ready, disposed

aniña·do -da adj babyish, childish

anión m anion

aniquilar tr to annihilate, destroy ‖ ref to be annihilated; decline, waste away; be humbled

anís m anise; anise-flavored brandy

aniversa·rio -ria adj & m anniversary

anoche adv last night

anochecer m nightfall, dusk ‖ v §22 intr to grow dark; arrive or happen at nightfall; end the day; go to sleep ‖ ref to get dark; get cloudy; slip away

anochecida f nightfall, dusk

anodi·no -na adj innocuous, ineffective, harmless

ánodo m anode

anomalía f anomaly

anóma·lo -la adj anomalous

anonadar tr to annihilate, destroy; overwhelm; humble

anóni·mo -ma adj anonymous ‖ m anonymity; **guardar** or **conservar el anónimo** to preserve one's anonymity

anorexia f anorexia

anormal adj abnormal

anotar tr to annotate; note, jot down; point out

anquilosa·do -da adj stiff-jointed; old-fashioned

ánsar m goose; wild goose

ansia *f* anxiety, anguish; eagerness; **ansias** (Ven) nausea

ansiar §77 & regular *tr* to long for, yearn for ‖ *intr* to be madly in love

ansiedad *f* anxiety, worry; pain

ansio•so -sa *adj* anxious; anguished; longing; covetous

ant. *abbr* **anticuado**

anta *f* elk

antagonismo *m* antagonism

antaño *adv* last year; of yore, long ago

antárti•co -ca *adj* antarctic

ante *prep* before, in the presence of; in front of; at, with ‖ *m* elk; buff

antea•do -da *adj* buff; (Mex) damaged, shopworn

anteanoche *adv* the night before last

anteayer *adv* the day before yesterday

antebrazo *m* forearm

antecámara *f* antechamber, anteroom

antecedente *adj* antecedent ‖ *m* antecedent; **antecedentes** antecedents

anteceder *tr* to precede, go before

antece•sor -sora *mf* predecessor; ancestor

antedatar *tr* to antedate

antedi•cho -cha *adj* aforesaid, abovementioned

antelación *f* previousness, anticipation

antemano — **de antemano** in advance, beforehand

antena *f* (ent) antenna; (rad) antenna, aerial; **antena de conejo** rabbit ears; **en antena** on the air; **antena interior incorporada** built-in antenna; **llevar a las antenas** to put on the air

antenombre *m* title, honorific

anteojera *f* spectacle case; blinker, blinder

anteojo *m* eyeglass; spyglass; **anteojos** eyeglasses, spectacles; binoculars; blinkers

antepasa•do -da *adj* before last ‖ **antepasados** *mpl* ancestors

antepecho *m* railing, guardrail; parapet; window sill

antepenúltima *f* antepenult

anteponer §54 *tr* to place in front; prefer

anteportada *f* half title, bastard title

anteportal *m* porch, vestibule

antepuer!a *f* portière

antepuerto *m* entrance to a mountain pass; (naut) outer harbor

anterior *adj* front; previous; earlier

antes *adv* before; sooner, soonest; rather; previously; **antes bien** rather; on the contrary; **antes de** before; **antes (de) que** before; **cuanto, antes** as soon as possible

antesala *f* antechamber; (*p.ej., de médico*) waiting room; **hacer antesala** to dance attendance

antiaére•o -a *adj* antiaircraft

antiartísti•co -ca *adj* inartistic

antibéli•co -ca *adj* antiwar

anticartel *adj* antitrust

anticientífi•co -ca *adj* unscientific

anticipación *f* preparation, anticipation; **con anticipación** in advance

anticipa•do -da *adj* future; advance; **por anticipado** in advance

anticipar *tr* to anticipate, hasten; to move ahead ‖ *ref* to happen early; **anticiparse a** to anticipate, to get ahead of

anticipo *m* anticipation; advance payment, down payment; retaining fee

anticoncepti•vo -va *adj* & *m* contraceptive

anticongelante *m* antifreeze

anticonstitucional *adj* unconstitutional

anticua•do -da *adj* antiquated; old-fashioned; obsolete

anticua•rio -ria *adj* antiquarian ‖ *mf* antiquarian, antiquary; antique dealer

anticuerpo *m* antibody

antideporti•vo -va *adj* unsportsmanlike

antiderrapante or **antideslizante** *adj* nonskid

antideslumbrante *adj* antiglare

antidetonante *adj* & *m* antiknock

antídoto *m* antidote

antieconómi•co -ca *adj* uneconomic(al)

antier *adv* the day before yesterday

antiesclavista *adj* antislavery ‖ *mf* abolitionist

anti•faz *m* (*pl* **-faces**) veil, mask

antífona *f* anthem

antigás *adj invar* gas (*e.g., mask, shelter*)

antigramatical *adj* ungrammatical

antigravedad *f* weightlessness

antigualla *f* antique; relic, antique; has-been

antiguar §10 *intr* & *ref* to attain seniority

antigüedad *f* antiquity; seniority; (*mueble u otro objeto de arte antiguos*) antique; **antigüedades** antiquities; antiques

anti•guo -gua *adj* old; ancient; antique; former ‖ *mf* veteran; senior

antihigiéni•co -ca *adj* unsanitary

antílope *m* antelope

antilla•no -na *adj* & *mf* West Indian

Antillas *fpl* Antilles

antimateria *f* antimatter

antimonio *m* antimony

antiobre•ro -ra *adj* antilabor

antiparras *spl* spectacles

antipatía *f* dislike, antipathy

antipáti•co -ca *adj* disagreeable, uncongenial

antipatrióti•co -ca *adj* unpatriotic

antiproyectil *adj* antimissile

antirreflejo *adj invar* nonreflecting

antirresbaladi•zo -za *adj* nonskid

antirrobo *adj invar* theft-proof, burglar-proof

antisemíti•co -ca *adj* anti-Semitic

antisépti•co -ca *adj* & *m* antiseptic

antisono•ro -ra *adj* soundproof

antisoviéti•co -ca *adj* anti-Soviet

antitanque *adj* antitank

antiterrorista *adj invar* & *mf* antiterrorist

antíte•sis *f* (*pl* **-sis**) antithesis

antitóxi•co -ca *adj* antitoxic

antitoxina *f* antitoxin

antojadi•zo -za *adj* capricious, whimsical

antojar *ref* to seem; fancy; seem likely; have a notion to + *inf*; take a fancy to + *inf*

antojo *m* caprice, fancy, whim; snap judgment; birthmark; **antojos** moles, warts; **a su antojo** as one pleases

antología *f* anthology

antónimo *m* antonym

antorcha f torch; **antorcha a soplete** blowtorch

antracita f anthracite

ántrax m anthrax

antro m cave, cavern; (fig) den

antropología f anthropology

antruejo m carnival

anual adj annual

anualidad f annuity; year's pay; annual occurrence

anuario m yearbook; directory; bulletin, catalogue; **anuario telefónico** telephone directory

anublar tr to cloud; dim, darken; blight, wither || ref to become cloudy; be withered; (las esperanzas de uno) fade away

anudar tr to tie, fasten, knot; unite; resume || ref to get knotted; be united; fade away, wilt, fail

anuente adj consenting

anular tr to annul; nullify; remove, discharge || ref to be passed over

anunciar tr to announce; advertise || intr to advertise

anunciante mf advertiser

anuncio m announcement; advertisement

anverso m obverse

anzuelo m fishhook; **picar en el anzuelo** or **tragar el anzuelo** to swallow the bait, swallow the hook

añadi•do -da adj additional || m false hair, switch

añadidura f addition; extra weight, extra measure; **de añadidura** extra, in the bargain; **por añadidura** besides

añadir tr to add; increase

añafil m straight Moorish trumpet

añagaza f bird call; decoy, lure; trap, trick

añe•jo -ja adj aged; stale; musty, rancid

añicos mpl bits, pieces; **hacer añicos** to tear to pieces, break to pieces; **hacerse añicos** to wear oneself out

añil m indigo; bluing

añilar tr to dye with indigo; (la ropa blanca) to blue

año m year; **año bisiesto** leap year; **año económico** fiscal year; **año lectivo** school year; **año luz** (pl años luz) light-year; **años** birthday; **cumplir . . . años** to be . . . years old

añoranza f longing, sorrow

añorar tr to long for, sorrow for; grieve over || intr to yearn; sorrow, grieve

año•so -sa adj aged, old

aojada f (Col) skylight; (Col) transom

aojar tr to cast the evil eye on, jinx

aojo m evil eye, jinx

aovar intr to lay eggs

ap. abbr **aparte, apóstol**

apabilar tr to trim

apabullar tr to mash, crush; squelch

apacentar §2 tr & ref to pasture, graze; feed

apacible adj gentle, mild; calm

apaciguamiento m pacification, appeasement

apaciguar §10 tr to pacify, appease || ref to calm down

apachurrar tr to crush, squash, mash

apadrinar tr to sponsor; act as godfather for; back, support; second

apagabron•cas m (pl -cas) bouncer

apagador m extinguisher; (de piano) damper

apagaincen•dios m (pl -dios) fire extinguisher

apagar §44 tr to extinguish, put out; (la luz, la radio) turn off; (la cal) slake; (el sonido) damp, muffle; (el fuego del enemigo) silence; (la sed) quench; (el dolor) deaden || ref to go out; subside, calm down, fade away

apagón m blackout

apalabrar tr to bespeak; consider || ref to agree

apalabrear intr (SAm) to make an appointment

apalancar §73 tr to raise with a lever or crowbar

apalear tr to shovel; beat; pile up

apandar tr to steal

apantallar tr to dazzle, amaze; (elec) to shield, screen

apañar tr to grasp; pick up; steal; repair, mend; wrap up || ref to be handy

apañuscar §73 tr to crumple, rumple; steal; (CAm, Col, Ven) to jam, crowd

aparador m sideboard, buffet; showcase; workshop; (Mex) show window, store window

aparar tr to prepare; adorn; block; (las manos, la falda, el pañuelo, la capa) hold out

aparato m apparatus; ostentation, show; exaggeration; radio set; television set; telephone; airplane; camera; bandage, application; (theat) scenery, properties; **aparato auditivo** hearing aid; **aparato de relojería** clockwork; **aparatos sanitarios** bathroom fixtures; **ponerse al aparato** to go or to come to the phone

aparato•so -sa adj showy, pompous, ostentatious

aparcamiento m parking; parking space; **aparcamiento subterraneo** underground garage

aparcar §44 tr & intr to park

aparcería f partnership, sharecropping

aparce•ro -ra mf partner, sharecropper; (Arg) customer

aparear tr to pair, match; mate || ref to pair; mate

aparecer §22 intr & ref to appear; show up

aparecido m ghost, specter

aparejador m builder

aparejar tr to prepare; prime, size; harness

aparejo m preparation; harness; set, kit; priming, sizing; (mas) bond; **aparejos** tools, implements, equipment

aparentar tr to feign, pretend; look, look to be

aparente adj apparent, seeming; evident; right, proper

aparición f apparition

apariencia f appearance, aspect; sign, indication; **salvar las apariencias** to save face

aparqueamiento m parking

aparquear *tr* & *intr* to park

aparqueo *m* parking

aparragar §44 *ref* to crouch, squat; (CAm) to loll, sprawl

apartadero *m* siding, side track; turnout

aparta•do -da *adj* distant, remote; aloof; (*camino*) side, back; different ‖ *m* side room; post-office box; vocabulary entry; section

apartamento *m* apartment, apartment house

apartar *tr* to take aside; separate; push away; shunt; (*el ganado*) sort ‖ *ref* to separate; move away, keep away, stand aside; withdraw; get divorced; give up

aparte *adv* apart, aside; **aparte de** apart from ‖ *prep* apart from ‖ *m* (theat) aside

apasiona•do -da *adj* passionate; devoted, tender, loving; sore

apasionar *tr* to impassion, appeal deeply to; afflict ‖ *ref* to become impassioned; be stirred up; fall madly in love

apatía *f* apathy

apáti•co -ca *adj* apathetic

apatusco *m* ornament, finery

apdo. *abbr* **apartado**

apeadero *m* horse block; flag stop, wayside station; platform; temporary quarters

apear *tr* to help dismount, help down; bring down; remove; overcome; prop up ‖ *ref* to dismount, get off; back down; stop, put up

apechugar §44 *intr* to push with the chest; **apechugar con** to make the best of

apedazar §60 *tr* to mend, patch; cut or tear to pieces

apedrear *tr* to stone; stone to death; pit; speckle ‖ *intr* to hail ‖ *ref* to be damaged by hail; be pitted

apegar §44 *ref* to become attached, grow fond

apego *m* attachment, fondness

apelación *f* medical consultation; remedy, help; (law) appeal

apelante *adj* appellate

apelar *intr* to appeal, make an appeal; have recourse; refer

apelativo *m* (CAm) surname, family name

apeldar *tr* — **apeldarlas** (coll) to flee, run away

apelmazar §60 *tr* to squeeze, compress ‖ *ref* to cake

apelotonar *tr* to form into a ball ‖ *ref* to form a ball; curl up

apellidar *tr* to call, name; proclaim

apellido *m* name; surname, last name, family name; **apellido de soltera** maiden name

apenar *tr* & *ref* to grieve

apenas *adv* hardly, scarcely; **apenas si** hardly, scarcely ‖ *conj* no sooner, as soon as

apéndice *m* appendage; (anat) appendix

apendicitis *f* appendicitis

apercancar §73 *ref* (Chile) to get moldy, mildew

apercibir *tr* to prepare; provide; warn; perceive; collect ‖ *ref* to get ready; be provided; **apercibirse de** to notice

apergaminar *ref* to dry up, become yellow and wrinkled

aperitivo *m* appetizer

aperla•do -da *adj* pearly

apero *m* tools, equipment, outfit; riding gear

aperrear *tr* to set the dogs on; harass, plague, pester

apersogar §44 *tr* to tether

apersona•do -da *adj* — **bien apersonado** presentable; **mal apersonado** unpresentable

apersonar *ref* to appear in person; have an interview

apertura *f* opening

apesadumbrar or **apesarar** *tr* & *ref* to grieve

apestar *tr* to infect with the plague; corrupt; sicken, nauseate; infest ‖ *intr* to stink ‖ *ref* to be infected with the plague

apesto•so -sa *adj* stinking, foul-smelling; pestilent; sickening

apetecer §22 *tr* to hunger for, thirst for, crave

apetecible *adj* desirable, tempting

apetencia *f* hunger, appetite, craving

apetito *m* appetite

apetito•so -sa *adj* tasty; tempting; gourmand

ápex *m* apex

apiadar *tr* to move to pity; take pity on ‖ *ref* to have pity

ápice *m* apex; bit, whit; crux; **estar en los ápices de** to be up in

apilar *tr* & *ref* to pile, pile up

apimpollar *ref* to sprout, put forth shoots

apiñar *tr* & *ref* to crowd, jam

apio *m* celery

apisonadora *f* road roller

apisonar *tr* to tamp; roll

aplacar §73 *tr* to placate, appease, pacify; (*la sed*) to quench

aplanacalles *m* (SAm) idler; lazy person

aplanar *tr* to smooth, make even; to astonish; **aplanar las calles** to loaf, bum around ‖ *ref* to collapse; become discouraged

aplanchar *tr* to iron

aplanetizar §60 *intr* to land on another planet

aplastar *tr* to flatten, crush, smash; dumbfound

aplaudida *f* applause

aplaudir *tr* & *intr* to applaud

aplauso *m* applause; **aplausos** applause

aplazada *f* or **aplazamiento** *m* delay; procrastination

aplazar §60 *tr* to postpone; convene; summon

aplicación *f* appliance, application; diligence

aplica•do -da *adj* industrious, studious; applied

aplicar §73 *tr* to apply; attribute ‖ *ref* to apply; apply oneself

aplomar *tr* to plumb; make straight or vertical ‖ *intr* to be vertical ‖ *ref* to collapse; (Chile) to be embarrassed; (Mex) to be slow, be backward

aplomo *m* aplomb, poise, self-possession; gravity

apoca•do -da *adj* diffident, timid, irresolute; humble, lowly

apocar §73 *tr* to cramp, contract; narrow; humble, belittle

apodar *tr* to nickname; make fun of

apoders•do -da *adj* empowered, authorized || *m* proxy; attorney

apoderamiento *m* authorization; power of attorney

apoderar *tr* to empower, authorize || *ref*— **apoderarse de** to seize, grasp; take possession of

apodo *m* nickname

apofanía *f* ablaut

apogeo *m* apogee; (fig) height, apogee

apolilla•do -da *adj* moth-eaten, mothy

apolilladura *f* moth hole

apolillar *tr* (*la polilla, p.ej., las ropas*) to eat || *ref* to become moth-eaten

apoliti•co -ca *adj* apolitical, nonpolitical

apología *f* eulogy

apoltronar *ref* to loaf around; loll, sprawl

apontizaje *m* deck-landing

apontizar §60 *intr* to deck-land

apoplejía *f* apoplexy

apopléti•co -ca *adj & mf* apoplectic

aporcar §73 *tr* (*las hortalizas*) to hill

aporrear *tr* to beat, club, cudgel; annoy || *ref* to drudge, slave

aportación *f* contribution; dowry

aportar *tr* to contribute; bring; lead; (*como dote*) bring || *intr* to show up; reach port

aporte *m* contribution

aposentar *tr* to put up, lodge || *ref* to take lodging

aposento *m* lodging; room; inn

apostadero *m* stand, post; naval station

apostar *tr* to post, station || §61 *tr* to bet, wager || *intr* to bet; compete

apostilla *f* note, comment

apóstol *m* apostle

apóstrofe *m & f* apostrophe (*words addressed to absent person*)

apóstrofo *m* apostrophe (*written sign*)

apostura *f* neatness, spruceness; bearing, carriage

apoyabra•zos *m* (*pl* **-zos**) armrest

apoyali•bros *m* (*pl* **-bros**) book end

apoyar *tr* to support, hold up; lean, rest; abet, back || *intr & ref* to lean, rest, be supported

apoyatura *f* (mus) grace note

apoyo *m* support, prop; backing, approval

apreciable *adj* appreciable; estimable

apreciación *f* appraisal

apreciar *tr* to appreciate; appraise; esteem

aprecio *m* appreciation, esteem

aprehender *tr* to apprehend, catch; think, conceive

aprehensión *f* apprehension

aprehensi•vo -va *adj* apprehensive

aprehensor *m* captor

apremiar *tr* to press, urge; compel; force; hurry; harass; (*a un deudor*) dun || *intr* to be urgent

apremio *m* pressure; urgency; compulsion; oppression; surtax for late payment; (*demanda de pago*) dun

aprender *tr & intr* to learn; **aprender haciendo** to learn by doing

apren•diz -diza *mf* apprentice; **aprendiz de imprenta** printer's devil

aprendizaje *m* apprenticeship; **pagar el aprendizaje** to pay for one's inexperience

aprensar *tr* to press; oppress

aprensión *f* apprehension; misgiving, prejudice

aprensi•vo -va *adj* apprehensive

apresar *tr* to grasp, seize; capture

aprestador *m* primer

aprestar *tr* to prepare; (*tejidos*) process; prime; size || *ref* to get ready

apresto *m* preparation; equipment; priming; sizing

apresurar *tr & ref* to hurry, hasten

apretadera *f* strap, rope; **apretaderas** pressure

apreta•do -da *adj* compact, tight; close, intimate; dense, thick; difficult, dangerous; mean, stingy; **estar muy apretado** to be in a bad way

apretar §2 *tr* to tighten; squeeze; pinch; hug; harass, importune; afflict, beset; (*un botón*) press; (*los puños*) clench; (*los dientes*) grit; (*la mano*) shake || *intr* to pinch; insist; get worse; push hard, press forward; **apretar a correr** to start running; **apretar con** to close in on || *ref* to grieve, be distressed; crowd

apretón *m* pressure, squeeze; struggle; dash, run; **apretón de manos** handshake

apretura *f* crush, jam; tightness; fix, trouble; need, want

aprietarropa *m* clothespin

¡aprieta! *interj* (coll) baloney!

aprieto *m* crush, jam; fix

aprisa *adv* fast, quickly

aprisco *m* sheepfold

aprisionar *tr* to imprison; bind, tie; shackle

aprobación *f* approbation, approval; pass, passing grade

aproba•do -da *adj* excellent || *m* pass

aprobar §61 *tr & intr* to approve; pass

aprontar *tr* to hand over without delay; expedite

apropia•do -da *adj* appropriate, fitting, proper

apropiar *tr* to hand over; fit, adapt || *ref* to appropriate; preëmpt

aprovechable *adj* available, usable

aprovecha•do -da *adj* thrifty; stingy; diligent; well-spent || *mf* opportunist

aprovechar *tr* to make good use of, take advantage of; (*una caída de agua*) harness || *intr* to be useful; progress, improve || *ref*— **aprovecharse de** to avail oneself of, take advantage of

aprovisionar *tr* to provision, supply, furnish

aproxima•do -da *adj* approximate, rough

aproximar *tr* to bring near; approximate || *ref* to come near; approximate

aptitud *f* aptitude; suitability

ap•to -ta *adj* apt; suitable

apuesta *f* bet, wager

apues•to -ta *adj* neat, spruce, elegant || *f* see **apuesta**

apulgarar *ref* to become mildewed

apuntador *m* (theat) prompter

apuntalar *tr* to prop up, underpin

apuntar *tr* to point; point at; aim; aim at; take note of; sharpen; stitch, darn, patch; correct; prompt; stake, to put up; (theat) to prompt ‖ *intr* to begin to appear; dawn ‖ *ref* (*el vino*) to begin to turn sour; register; get tipsy

apunte *m* note; rough sketch; stake; rogue, rascal; (theat) cue

apuñalar *tr & intr* to stab

apuñear *tr* to punch

apura•do -da *adj* needy, hard up; difficult, dangerous; hurried, rushed

apurar *tr* to purify, refine; clear up, verify; finish; drain, use up, exhaust; hurry, press; annoy ‖ *ref* to worry, grieve; exert oneself, strive

apuro *m* need, want; grief, sorrow; haste, urgency; **apuros** financial embarrassment

aquejar *tr* to grieve, afflict

aquel, aquella *adj dem* (*pl* **aquellos, aquellas**) that, that . . . yonder

aquél, aquélla *pron dem* (*pl* **aquéllos, aquéllas**) that; that one, that one yonder; the one; the former ‖ *m* charm, appeal

aquelarre *m* witches' Sabbath

aquello *pron dem* that; that thing, that matter

aquende *adv* on this side ‖ *prep* on this side of

aquerenciar *ref* to become fond or attached

aquí *adv* here; **aquí dentro** in here; **de aquí en adelante** from now on; **por aquí** this way

aquiescencia *f* acquiescence

aquietar *tr* to quiet, calm

aquilatar *tr* to assay; check; refine

Aquiles *m* Achilles

aquilón *m* north wind

ara *f* altar; altar slab; **en aras de** for the sake of

árabe *adj* Arab, Arabian; (archit) Moresque ‖ *mf* Arab, Arabian ‖ *m* (*idioma*) Arabic

Arabia, la Arabia

arábi•go -ga *adj* Arabian, Arabic ‖ *m* (*idioma*) Arabic; **estar en arábigo** (coll) to be Greek

arabismo *m* (*estudio, voz, rasgo*) Arabism

aracanga *f* macaw

arado *m* plow

Aragón *m* Aragon

arago•nés -nesa *adj & mf* Aragonese

arancel *m* tariff

arancelar *tr* (CAm) to pay

arancela•rio -ria *adj* tariff, customs

arándano *m* whortleberry; **arándano agrio** cranberry

arandela *f* bobèche; (mach) washer

araña *f* spider; chandelier

arañar *tr* to scratch; scrape; scrape together

arañazo *m* scratch

araño *m* scratching

aráquida *f* peanut

arar *tr* to plow

arbitraje *m* arbitration

arbitrar *tr & intr* to arbitrate; referee; umpire

arbitra•rio -ria *adj* arbitrary

arbitrio *m* free will; means, ways; **arbitrios** excise taxes

arbitrista *mf* wild-eyed dreamer

árbi•tro -tra *mf* arbiter; referee ‖ *m* umpire

árbol *m* tree; axle, shaft; **árbol del caucho** rubber plant; **árbol de levas** camshaft; **árbol de mando** drive shaft; **árbol de Navidad** Christmas tree; **árbol motor** drive shaft

arbola•do -da *adj* wooded; (mar) high ‖ *m* woodland

arboleda *f* grove

arbollón *m* sewer, drain

arbotante *m* flying buttress

arbusto *m* shrub

arca *f* chest, coffer; tank; ark; **arca de agua** water tower; **arca de la alianza** ark of the covenant; **arca de Noé** ark, Noah's ark

arcada *f* arcade; archway; stroke of bow; **arcadas** retching

arcai•co -ca *adj* archaic

arcaísmo *m* archaism

arcaizante *adj* obsolescent

arcángel *m* archangel

arca•no -na *adj & m* secret

arcar §73 *tr* to arch

arce *m* maple tree

arcilla *f* clay; **arcilla figulina** potter's clay

arco *m* arch; (*de cuna o mecedor*) rocker; (elec, geom) arc; (mus) bow; **arco iris** rainbow; **arco triunfal** triumphal arch; memorial arch

arcón *m* large chest; bin, bunker

archiduque *m* archduke

archienemigo *m* archenemy

archipiélago *m* archipelago; (coll) maze, entanglement ‖ **Archipiélago** *m* Aegean Sea

archiva•dor -dora *mf* file clerk ‖ *m* filing cabinet; letter file

archivar *tr* to file; file away; hide away

archivero *m* city clerk

archivo *m* archives; files; filing; (Col) office

ardentía *f* heartburn; (*en las olas de la mar*) phosphorescence

arder *tr* to burn ‖ *intr* to burn; blaze; **estar que arde** to be coming to a head ‖ *ref* to burn up

ardid *m* artifice, trick, wile

ardi•do -da *adj* burnt-up; bold, intrepid; angry

ardiendo *adj invar* burning

ardiente *adj* ardent; fiery, passionate; burning, hot

ardilla *f* squirrel; **ardilla de tierra** gopher; **ardilla ladradora** prairie dog; **ardilla listada** chipmunk

ardillón *m* gopher

ardite *m* old Spanish coin of little value; **no me importa un ardite** (coll) I don't care a hang; **no valer un ardite** to be not worth a straw

ardor *m* ardor; eagerness, fervor, zeal; vehemence; courage, dash

ardoro•so -sa *adj* fiery, enthusiastic; balky, restive

ar•duo -dua *adj* arduous, difficult

área f area; small plot; **área de descansar** rest area; **área de servicio** service area

arena f sand; grit; arena; **arena movediza** quicksand; **arenas** arena; (pathol) stones

arenal m sandy place; quicksand

arenga f harangue

arengar tr & intr to harangue

arenis•co -ca adj sandy, gritty; sand ‖ f sandstone

areno•so -sa adj sandy

arenque m herring

areómetro m hydrometer

arepa f corn griddle cake

arete m eardrop, earring

arfada f (naut) pitching

arfar intr (naut) to pitch

argadijo m or **argadillo** m bobbin, reel; restless fellow

argado m prank, trick, artifice

argamasa f mortar

argamasar tr to mortar, plaster; (los materiales de construcción) mix

árgana f (mach) crane; **árganas** panniers

Argel f Algiers

Argelia f Algeria

argeli•no -na adj & mf Algerian

argentar tr to silver

argenti•no -na adj & mf Argentine, Argentinean ‖ **la Argentina** Argentina, the Argentine

argolla f large iron ring; (que se pone en la nariz a un animal) ring; engagement ring

argonauta m Argonaut

argucia f subtlety; trick

argüir §6 tr to argue, argue for; prove; accuse ‖ ref to argue, dispute

argumenta•dor -dora adj argumentative ‖ mf arguer

argumentar tr to argue for; prove ‖ intr & ref to argue, dispute

argumento m argument

aria f (mus) aria

aridez f aridity, dryness

ári•do -da adj arid; (aburrido, falto de interés) dry

Aries m Aries

ariete m battering ram; **ariete hidráulico** hydraulic ram

arimez m projection

a•rio -ria adj & mf Aryan ‖ f see **aria**

aris•co -ca adj churlish, surly, evasive; (caballo) vicious

arista f edge; (intersección de dos planos) ridge; (del grano de trigo) beard; **arista de encuentro** (archit) groin

aristocracia f aristocracy

aristócrata mf aristocrat

aristocráti•co -ca adj aristocratic

Aristóteles m Aristotle

aristotéli•co -ca adj & mf Aristotelian

aritméti•co -ca adj arithmetical ‖ mf arithmetician ‖ f arithmetic

arlequín m harlequin

arma f arm, weapon; **alzarse en armas** to rise up, rebel; **arma blanca** steel blade; **arma corta** pistol; **arma de fuego** firearm;

jugar a las armas to fence; **sobre las armas** under arms

armada f fleet, armada; navy

armadía f raft, float

armadijo m trap, snare

arma•do -da adj armed; (hormigón) reinforced ‖ f see **armada**

arma•dor -dora mf assembler ‖ m recruiter of fishermen and whalers

armadura f armor; framework; skeleton; (elec) armature; (de imán) keeper

armamentismo m military preparedness

armamentis•to -ta adj militarist, arms ‖ mf arms dealer

armamento m armament

armar tr to arm; (un arma) load; (una bayoneta) fix; mount, assemble; build; equip; (el hormigón) reinforce; (una nave) fit out; (caballero) dub; start, stir up; **armarla** to start a row ‖ ref to arm oneself; get ready; balk

armario m closet, wardrobe; **armario botiquín** medicine cabinet; **armario de luna** wardrobe with mirror; **armario frigorífico** refrigerator

armatoste m hulk

armazón f frame; assemblage; skeleton

armella f screw eye, eyebolt

arme•nio -nia adj & mf Armenian ‖ **Armenia** f Armenia

armería f arms shop; arms museum; arms

armero m gunsmith; (para las armas) rack

armiño m ermine

armisticio m armistice

armonía f harmony

armóni•co -ca adj & m harmonic ‖ f harmonica; **armónica de boca** mouth organ

armonio•so -sa adj harmonious

armonizar §60 tr & intr to harmonize

arnés m armor, coat of mail; harness; **arneses** harness, trappings; outfit, equipment; accessories

aro m hoop; rim; **aro de émbolo** piston ring

aroma m aroma, fragrance

aromáti•co -ca adj aromatic

arpa f harp

arpar tr to claw, scratch; tear, rend

arpegio m arpeggio

arpeo m grappling iron

arpía f harpy; shrew, jade

arpillera f burlap, sackcloth

arpista mf harpist

arpón m harpoon

arponear tr & intr to harpoon

arqueada f (mus) bow

arquear tr to arch; (la lana) beat; (una nave) gauge; to audit ‖ intr to retch ‖ ref to bow

arqueología f archeology

arquería f arcade

arquero m archer, bowman; goalkeeper, goalie

arquitecto m architect

arquitectóni•co -ca adj architectural

arquitectura f architecture

arrabal m suburb; **arrabales** outskirts

arracada f earring with pendant

arracimar ref to cluster, bunch

arraiga•do -da *adj* deep-rooted; property-owning, landed

arraigar §44 *tr* to establish, strengthen ‖ *intr* to take root ‖ *ref* to take root; become settled

arraigo *m* taking root; stability; property, real estate

arramblar *tr* to cover with sand or gravel; sweep away

arrancadero *m* starting point

arrancar §73 *tr* to root up, pull out, pull up; snatch, wrest; (*lágrimas*) draw forth ‖ *intr* to start; set sail; leave; originate

arranque *m* pull; fit, impulse; jerk, sudden start; sally, outburst; (aut) start, starter; **arranque a mano** (aut) hand cranking; **arranque automático** (aut) self-starter

arrapiezo *m* rag, tatter; whippersnapper

arras *fpl* earnest money, pledge; dowry

arrasar *tr* to level; wreck, demolish; fill to the brim ‖ *intr* to clear up ‖ *ref* to clear up; fill up

arrastra•do -da *adj* mean, crooked ‖ *mf* wretch, crook

arrastrar *tr* to drag, drag along; drag down; impel ‖ *intr* to drag, trail; crawl, creep ‖ *ref* to drag, trail; crawl, creep; drag on; cringe

arrastre *m* drag; crawl; washout; influence; haulage; (*influencia política y social*) (Cuba, Mex) drag

arrayán *m* myrtle

arre *interj* gee!, get up!

arreador *m* muleteer; (SAm) whip

arrear *tr* to drive ‖ *intr* to hurry ‖ *ref* to lose all one's money

arrebata•do -da *adj* rash, reckless; (*color del rostro*) flushed, ruddy

arrebatar *tr* to snatch; carry away; attract; move, stir ‖ *ref* to be carried away, be overcome

arrebatiña *f* scuffle, scramble; **andar a la arrebatiña** to scramble

arrebato *m* rage, fury; ecstasy, rapture

arrebol *m* (*de las nubes*) red; (*de las mejillas*) rosiness; (*afeite*) rouge; **arreboles** red clouds

arrebozar §60 *tr* to muffle ‖ *ref* to muffle one's face

arrebujar *tr* to jumble together; wrap ‖ *ref* to wrap oneself up

arreciar *intr* & *ref* to grow worse; become more violent; grow stronger

arrecife *m* stone-paved road; dike; reef; **arrecife de coral** coral reef

arredrar *tr* to drive back; frighten ‖ *ref* to draw back; shrink; be frightened

arregazar §60 *tr* to tuck up

arreglar *tr* to adjust, regulate, settle; arrange; fix, repair ‖ *ref* to adjust, settle; arrange; conform; **arreglárselas** to manage, make out

arreglo *m* adjustment, regulation; settlement; arrangement; order, rule; agreement; **con arreglo a** in accordance with

arregostar *ref* to take a liking

arregosto *m* liking, taste

arrellanar *ref* to loll, sprawl; like one's work

arremangar §44 *tr* (*las mangas*) to turn up; (*la ropa*) to tuck up ‖ *ref* to turn up one's sleeves; tuck up one's dress; take a firm stand

arremeter *tr* to attack, assail; (*un caballo*) to spur ‖ *intr* to attack; be offensive to look at; **arremeter contra** to light into, sail into

arremetida *f* attack; (*de un caballo*) sudden start; push; short, wild run

arremolinar *ref* to crowd, mill around; whirl

arrendajo *m* (orn) jay; mimic

arrendar §2 *tr* to rent; (*una caballería*) tie ‖ *ref* to rent, be rented

arreo *m* adornment; (SAm) drove; **arreos** harness, trappings

arrepenti•do -da *adj* repentant ‖ *mf* penitent

arrepentimiento *m* repentance

arrepentir §68 *ref* to repent, be repentant; **arrepentirse de** (*p.ej., un pecado*) to repent

arrequives *mpl* finery; attendant circumstances

arresta•do -da *adj* bold, daring

arrestar *tr* to arrest ‖ *ref* to rush boldly

arresto *m* arrest; boldness, daring; **bajo arresto** under arrest

arrezagar §44 *tr* to tuck up

arriada *f* flood

arriar §77 *tr* to flood; (naut) to lower, strike; slacken ‖ *ref* to be flooded

arriba *adv* up, upward; above; upstairs; uptown; on top; **arriba de** up; **de arriba abajo** from top to bottom; from beginning to end; superciliously; **más arriba** farther up; **río arriba** upstream ‖ *interj* up with . . . !

arribada *f* arrival (*by sea*); **de arribada** (naut) emergency

arribar *intr* to put into port; arrive; to recover, make a comeback; (naut) to fall off to leeward

arribista *adj* & *mf* parvenu, upstart

arribo *m* arrival

arricete *m* shoal, bar

arriendo *m* rent, rental; lease

arriero *m* muleteer

arriesga•do -da *adj* dangerous, risky; bold, daring

arriesgar §44 *tr* to risk, jeopardize ‖ *ref* to take a risk

arriesgo *m* (SAm) risk; hazard

arrimadillo *m* wainscot

arrimar *tr* to bring close, move up; (*un golpe*) give; abandon, neglect; give up; get rid of ‖ *ref* to come close, move up; snuggle up; lean; depend

arrinconar *tr* to corner; put aside; abandon, neglect; get rid of ‖ *ref* to live in seclusion

arrisca•do -da *adj* enterprising; brisk, spirited; craggy

arriscar §73 *tr* to risk ‖ *ref* to take a risk; (*las reses*) plunge over a cliff

arrisco *m* risk

arritmia *f* arrhythmia

arrivista *adj* & *mf* parvenu, upstart

arrizar §60 *tr* to reef

arroba *f* Spanish weight of about 25 pounds
arrobar *tr* to entrance, enrapture ‖ *ref* to be enraptured
arrobo *m* ecstasy, rapture
arroce•ro -ra *adj* rice ‖ *mf* rice grower; rice merchant
arrocinar *tr* to bestialize ‖ *ref* to become bestialized; fall madly in love
arrodajar *ref* (CAm) to squat down with one's legs crossed
arrodillar *ref* to kneel, kneel down
arrogancia *f* arrogance
arrogante *adj* arrogant
arrogar §44 *tr* to adopt ‖ *ref* to arrogate to oneself
arrojadi•zo -za *adj* for throwing, projectile
arroja•do -da *adj* bold, fearless, rash
arrojalla•mas *m* (*pl* -**mas**) flame thrower
arrojar *tr* to throw, hurl; emit; bring forth; yield ‖ *ref* to rush, rush forward
arrojo *m* boldness, fearlessness, rashness
arrollado *m* (elec) coil
arrolla•dor -dora *adj* sweeping, devastating
arrollamiento *m* winding
arrollar *tr* to roll; roll up; wind, coil; (*al enemigo*) rout; dumbfound; knock down, run over
arropar *tr* to wrap, wrap up ‖ *ref* to bundle up
arrope *m* grape syrup; honey syrup
arropía *f* taffy
arrostrar *tr* to face; to like ‖ *intr* —**arrostrar con** or **por** to face, resist ‖ *ref* to rush into the fight
arroyada *f* gully; flood, freshet
arroyo *m* stream, brook; gutter; street; (*de lágrimas, sangre, etc.*) stream
arroz *m* rice
arrufar *tr* to sic, incite
arruga *f* wrinkle; crease, rumple
arrugar §44 *tr* to wrinkle; crease, rumple; (*la frente*) to knit; (Cuba, Mex) to bother, annoy ‖ *ref* to wrinkle; crease, rumple; shrink, shrivel; (Cuba, Mex) to lose courage, lose heart
arruinar *tr* to ruin ‖ *ref* to go to ruin
arrullar *tr* to sing to sleep, lull to sleep; to court, woo ‖ *intr* to coo ‖ *ref* to coo; (*las palomas*) to bill
arrullo *m* billing and cooing; lullaby
arrumaje *m* stowage; ballast
arrumar *tr* to stow ‖ *ref* to become overcast
arrumbar *tr* to cast aside, neglect; silence; (*una costa*) determine the lay of ‖ *intr* (naut) to take bearings ‖ *ref* to get seasick; (naut) to take bearings
arsenal *m* arsenal, armory; dockyard, shipyard
arsénico *m* arsenic
art. *abbr* **artículo**
arte *m* & *f* art; trick; knack; fishing gear; **artes y oficios** arts and crafts; **bellas artes** fine arts; **no tener arte ni parte en** to have nothing to do with
artefacto *m* artifact; appliance, device, contrivance; **artefactos de alumbrado** lighting fixtures; **artefactos sanitarios** bathroom fixtures
artemisa *f* sagebrush
arteria *f* artery
artería *f* craftiness, cunning
arte•ro -ra *adj* crafty, cunning, sly
artesa *f* trough; Indian canoe
artesanía *f* craftsmanship
artesa•no -na *mf* artisan, craftsman ‖ *f* craftswoman
artesón *m* kitchen tub; coffer, caisson (*in ceiling*)
árti•co -ca *adj* arctic
articulación *f* articulation; (*de huesos*) joint; **articulación universal** universal joint
articular *tr* to articulate
articulista *mf* feature writer
artículo *m* article; item; joint; (*en un diccionario*) entry; **artículo de fondo** leader, editorial; **artículos de consumo** consumers' goods; **artículos de deporte** sporting goods; **artículos de primera necesidad** basic commodities; **artículos para caballeros** men's furnishings
artífice *mf* artificer; craftsman
artificial *adj* artificial
artificio *m* artifice; workmanship; appliance, device; cunning; trick, ruse
artificio•so -sa *adj* ingenious, skillful; cunning, scheming, deceptive
artilugio *m* contraption, jigger
artillería *f* artillery
artillero *m* artilleryman, gunner
artimaña *f* trap; trick, cunning
artista *mf* artist
artísti•co -ca *adj* artistic
artolas *fpl* mule chair, cacolet
artríti•co -ca *adj* & *mf* arthritic
artritis *f* arthritis
arúspice *m* diviner, soothsayer
arveja *f* vetch, tare; (Chile) pea
arzobispo *m* archbishop
arzón *m* saddletree; **arzón delantero** saddlebow; **arzón trasero** cantle
as *m* ace; **as de fútbol** football star; **as de la pantalla** movie star; **as del volante** speed king
asa *f* handle; juice; **en asas** with arms akimbo
asa•do -da *adj* roasted; **bien asado** well done; **poco asado** rare ‖ *m* roast
asador *m* spit
asadura *f* entrails
asalaria•do -da *mf* wage earner
asaltar *tr* to assail, assault, storm; overtake, overcome
asalto *m* assault, attack; (box) round; (mil) storm; **tomar por asalto** to take by storm
asamblea *f* assembly
asar *tr* to roast ‖ *ref* to be burning up
asbesto *m* asbestos
ascendencia *f* ancestry
ascendente *adj* ascending; up
ascender §51 *tr* to promote ‖ *intr* to ascend, go up; be promoted; **ascender a** to amount to
ascendiente *adj* ascending; up ‖ *mf* ancestor ‖ *m* ascendancy, upper hand

ascensión f ascension, ascent
ascenso m ascent; promotion
ascensor m elevator; freight elevator
ascensorista mf elevator operator
asceta mf ascetic
ascéti•co -ca adj ascetic
asco m disgust, nausea, loathing; **dar asco** to turn the stomach; **estar hecho un asco** to be filthy; **hacer ascos de** to turn one's nose up at; **ser un asco** to be contemptible; be worthless
ascua f ember, live coal; **estar sobre ascuas** to be on needles and pins ‖ **ascuas** interj ouch!
asea•do -da adj clean, neat, tidy
asear tr & ref to clean up, tidy up; make one's toilet
asechamiento m or **asechanza** f snare, trap
asechar tr to set a trap for
asediar tr to besiege; harass
asedio m siege
asegundar tr to repeat right away
asegurable adj insurable
aseguración f insurance policy
asegura•dor -dora mf insurer, underwriter
asegurar tr to fasten, secure; assure; assert; seize; imprison; (garantizar por un precio contra determinado accidente o pérdida) insure ‖ ref to make sure; take out insurance
asemejar tr to make like; compare; resemble ‖ ref to be similar
asenso m assent; **dar asenso a** to believe
asentada f sitting; **de una asentada** at one sitting
asentaderas fpl (coll) buttocks
asentadillas — a asentadillas sidesaddle
asenta•do -da adj sedate; stable ‖ f see asentada
asentador m strap, razor strop
asentar §2 tr to seat; place; establish; tamp down, level; hone, sharpen; note down; (un golpe) impart; (en la mente de uno) impress; affirm; suppose ‖ intr to be becoming ‖ ref to sit down; be established, establish oneself; settle
asentimiento m assent
asentir §68 intr to assent
aseo m cleanliness, neatness, tidiness; care; toilet
asépti•co -ca adj aseptic
aseptizar §60 tr to purify, make aseptic
asequible adj accessible, obtainable
aserción f assertion
aserradero m sawmill
aserra•dor -dora mf sawyer; (coll) fiddler ‖ f power saw
aserraduras fpl sawdust
aserrar §2 tr to saw
aserrín m sawdust
aserruchar tr (SAm) to saw
aserto m assertion
asesinar tr to assassinate, murder
asesinato m assassination, murder
asesi•no -na adj murderous ‖ mf assassin, murderer

asesorar tr to advise ‖ ref to seek advice; get advice
asestar tr to aim; shoot; (un golpe) deal
aseveración f assertion, declaration
aseverar tr to assert, declare
asfaltar tr to asphalt
asfalto m asphalt
asfixia f asphyxiation
asfixiar tr to asphyxiate
así adv so, thus; **así . . . como** both . . . and; **así como** as soon as; as well as; **así que** as soon as; with the result that; **así y todo** even so, anyhow; **por decirlo así** so to speak; **y así sucesivamente** and so on
Asia f Asia; **el Asia Menor** Asia Minor
asiáti•co -ca adj & mf Asian, Asiatic
asidero m handle; occasion, pretext
así•duo -dua adj assiduous; frequent, persistent
asiento m seat; site; (de un edificio) settling; (de una botella, una silla, etc.) bottom; sediment; list, roll; wisdom, maturity; **asiento abatible** reclining seat; **asiento de rejilla** cane seat; **asiento lanzable** (aer) ejection seat; **asientos** buttocks; **planchar el asiento** to be a wallflower; **tome Vd. asiento** have a seat
asignación f assignment; salary; allowance
asignar tr to assign
asignatorio m heir, inheritor
asignatura f course, subject
asila•do -da mf inmate
asilar tr to shelter; place in an asylum; silo ‖ ref to take refuge; be placed in an asylum
asilo m asylum; shelter, refuge; (para menesterosos) home; **asilo de huérfanos** orphan asylum; **asilo de locos** insane asylum; **asilo de pobres** poorhouse
asilla f fastener; collarbone; **asillas** shoulder pole
asimetría f asymmetry
asimilar tr to compare; take in ‖ intr to be alike ‖ ref to assimilate; **asimilarse a** to resemble
asimismo adv also, likewise
asir §7 tr to grasp, seize ‖ intr to take root ‖ ref to take hold; fight, grapple; **asirse a** or **de** to cling to
Asiria f Assyria
asi•rio -ria adj & mf Assyrian
asistencia f attendance; assistance; reward; audience, persons present; welfare, social work; (Mex) sitting room, parlor; **asistencias** allowance, support
asistenta f charwoman, cleaning woman
asistente adj attendant; present ‖ m assistant, helper; bystander, spectator, person present; (mil) orderly
asistir tr to assist, help; attend; serve, wait on ‖ intr to be present; **asistir a** to be present at, attend
asma f asthma
asna f she-ass, jenny ass; **asnas** rafters
asnal adj donkey; brutish
asno m ass, donkey, jackass
asociación f association

asocia•do -da *adj* associated; associate ‖ *mf* associate, partner

asociar *tr* to associate; take as partner ‖ *ref* to become associated; become a partner; become partners

asolamiento *m* razing, destruction

asolar *tr* to parch, burn ‖ *ref* to become parched ‖ §61 *tr* to raze, destroy

asoleada *f* or **asoleadura** *f* (SAm) sunstroke

asolear *tr* to sun ‖ *ref* to bask; get sunburned

asomar *tr* (*p.ej.*, *la cabeza*) to show, stick out ‖ *intr* to begin to show or appear; show ‖ *ref* to show, appear; stick out; get tipsy

asombradi•zo -za *adj* timid, shy

asombrar *tr* to shade; (*un color*) darken; frighten; astonish, amaze ‖ *ref* to be frightened; be astonished, amazed

asombro *m* fright; astonishment

asombro•so -sa *adj* astonishing, amazing

asomo *m* mark, token, sign; appearance; **ni por asomo** nothing of the kind, not by a long shot

asordar *tr* to deafen

aspa *f* X-shaped figure; reel; (*de molino de viento*) wheel, vane; propeller blade

aspar *tr* to reel; crucify; annoy, harass ‖ *ref* to writhe; take great pains

aspaviento *m* fuss, excitement

aspecto *m* aspect

aspereza *f* harshness; roughness; bitterness, sourness; gruffness

asperjar *tr* to sprinkle; sprinkle with holy water

áspe•ro -ra *adj* harsh; rough; bitter; gruff

áspid *m* asp

aspirador *m* vacuum cleaner; **aspirador de gasolina** (aut) vacuum tank

aspirante *m* applicant, candidate; **aspirante a cabo** private first class; **aspirante de marina** midshipman

aspirar *tr* to suck in, draw in; inhale ‖ *intr* to aspire; inhale, breathe in

aspirina *f* aspirin

asquear *tr* to loathe ‖ *ref* to be nauseated

asquero•so -sa *adj* disgusting, loathsome; nauseating; squeamish

asta *f* spear; shaft; flagpole, staff, mast; antler; (*de toro*) horn; **a media asta** at half-mast; **dejar en las astas del toro** to leave high and dry

asta•do -da *adj* horned ‖ *m* bull

ástato *m* astatine

aster *m* aster

asterisco *m* asterisk

astil *m* handle; shaft

astilla *f* chip, splinter

astillar *tr* & *ref* to chip, splinter

Astillejos *mpl* (astr) Castor and Pollux

astillero *m* dockyard, shipyard

astro *m* star, heavenly body; (fig) star, leading light

astrofísica *f* astrophysics

astrología *f* astrology

astronauta *m* astronaut

astronáuti•co -ca *adj* astronautic ‖ *f* astronautics

astronave *f* spaceship; **astronave tripulada** manned spaceship

astronavegación *f* space travel

astronomía *f* astronomy

astronómi•co -ca *adj* astronomic(al)

astróno•mo -ma *mf* astronomer

astro•so -sa *adj* ill-fated; vile, contemptible; ragged, shabby

astucia *f* cunning, craftiness; trick

asturia•no -na *adj* & *mf* Asturian

astu•to -ta *adj* astute, cunning; tricky

asueto *m* day off; leisure

asumir *tr* to assume, take on

asunción *f* assumption

asunto *m* subject, matter; affair, business; theme; **asuntos internacionales** world affairs

asurar *tr* to burn; parch; harass, worry

asurcar §73 *tr* to furrow, plow

asustadi•zo -za *adj* scary, skittish

asustar *tr* to scare, frighten

atabal *m* kettledrum; timbrel

ataca•do -da *adj* irresolute, undecided; mean, stingy

atacar §73 *tr* to attack; attach, fasten; pack, jam; (*un barreno*) tamp; corner, contradict ‖ *intr* to attack

ata•do -da *adj* timid, shy; weak, irresolute; insignificant; cramped ‖ *m* pack, bundle, roll

ataguía *f* cofferdam

atajar *tr* to stop, intercept, interrupt; to partition off ‖ *intr* to take a short cut ‖ *ref* to be abashed

atajo *m* short cut; (*en un escrito*) cut

atalaya *m* guard, lookout ‖ *f* watchtower; elevation

atalayar *tr* to watch from a watchtower; spy on

atanquía *f* depilatory ointment

atañer §70 *tr* to concern

ataque *m* attack; **ataque por sorpresa** surprise attack

atar *tr* to tie, fasten

ataracea *f* marquetry, inlaid work

atarantar *tr* to stun, daze

atardecer *m* late afternoon ‖ *v* §22 *intr* to draw toward evening; happen in the late afternoon

atarea•do -da *adj* busy

atarear *tr* to give an assignment to; overload with work ‖ *ref* to toil, work hard, keep busy

atarjea *f* sewer

atarugar §44 *tr* to peg, wedge; plug; stuff, fill; silence, shut up ‖ *ref* to become confused

atasajar *tr* to slash, hack; (*carne*) jerk

atascadero *m* mudhole; (fig) pitfall

atascar §73 *tr* to stop, stop up, clog, obstruct ‖ *ref* to get stuck; stuff oneself; clog, get clogged

atasco *m* sticking, clogging; obstruction

ataúd *m* casket, coffin

ataujía *f* damascene work

ataujiar §77 *tr* to damascene

ataviar §77 *tr* to dress, adorn, deck out

atávi•co -ca *adj* atavistic
atavío *m* dress, adornment; **atavíos** finery, frippery, chiffons
atediar *tr* to tire, bore
ateísmo *m* atheism
ateísta *mf* atheist
atelaje *m* harness
atemorizar §60 *tr* to frighten
atemperar *tr* to soften, moderate, temper; adjust, adapt
Atenas *f* Athens
atención *f* attention; **en atención a** in view of
atender §51 *tr* to attend to; heed, pay attention to; take care of; (*a los parroquianos*) wait on
atener §71 *ref* — **atenerse a** to abide by, rely on
ateniense *adj* & *mf* Athenian
atenta•do -da *adj* moderate, prudent; cautious ‖ *m* attempt, assault
atentar *tr* to attempt, try to commit ‖ *intr* — **atentar a** or **contra** (*p.ej.*, *la vida de una persona*) to attempt ‖ §2 *ref* to grope
aten•to -ta *adj* attentive; courteous, polite ‖ *f* favor (*letter*)
atenuar §21 *tr* to extenuate
ate•o -a *adj* & *mf* atheist
aterciopela•do -da *adj* velvety
ateri•do -da *adj* stiff, numb with cold
aterrada *f* landfall
aterrajar *tr* to thread, tap
aterraje *m* landing
aterrar *tr* to terrify ‖ §2 *tr* to destroy, demolish; cover with earth ‖ *intr* to land ‖ *ref* to stand inshore
aterrizaje *m* landing; **aterrizaje a ciegas** blind landing; **aterrizaje aplastado** or **en desplome** pancake landing; **aterrizaje forzoso** emergency landing; **aterrizaje sin choque** soft landing
aterrizar §60 *intr* to land
aterronar *tr* to make lumpy ‖ *ref* to cake, lump
aterrorizar §60 *tr* to terrify
atesorar *tr* to treasure; hoard; (*virtudes, perfecciones*) possess
atesta•do -da *adj* stuffed, jammed; obstinate, stubborn ‖ *m* certificate
atestar *tr* (law) to attest ‖ §2 & **regular** *tr* to jam, pack, stuff, cram; stuff
atestiguar §10 *tr* to attest, testify, depose
atezar §60 *tr* to tan; blacken ‖ *ref* to become tanned, become sunburned
atiborrar *tr* to stuff ‖ *ref* to stuff, stuff oneself
atiesar *tr* to stiffen; tighten ‖ *ref* to become stiff; become tight
atildar *tr* to mark with a tilde, dash, or accent mark; point out; find fault with; tidy up, trim, adorn
atina•do -da *adj* careful, keen, wise
atinar *tr* to find, come upon ‖ *intr* to guess, guess right; be right; manage
atirantar *tr* (Mex) to make taut; brace ‖ *ref* (Mex) to die, pass away
atisbadero *m* peephole
atisbar *tr* to watch, spy on

atisbo *m* glimpse, look, peek
atizar §60 *tr* to stir, poke; snuff; rouse; (*p.ej.*, *un puntapié*) let go
Atlánti•co -ca *adj* & *m* Atlantic
at•las *m* (*pl* **-las**) atlas
atleta *mf* athlete
atleticismo *m* athletics
atléti•co -ca *adj* athletic ‖ *f* athletics
atmósfera *f* atmosphere
atmosféri•co -ca *adj* atmospheric
atoar *tr* (naut) to tow
atocinar *tr* (*un cerdo*) to cut up; make into bacon; (coll) to murder ‖ *ref* to get angry; fall madly in love
atocha *f* esparto
atolondra•do -da *adj* confused; scatterbrained
atolondrar *tr* to confuse, bewilder
atolladero *m* mudhole; obstacle, difficulty
atollar *intr* & *ref* to get stuck, get stuck in the mud
atómi•co -ca *adj* atomic
átomo *m* atom
atóni•to -ta *adj* astounded, aghast
atontar *tr* to stun; to confuse, bewilder
atorar *tr* to clog, obstruct ‖ *intr* & *ref* to stick, get stuck; choke
atormentar *tr* to torment; torture
atornillar *tr* to screw; screw on
atortillar *tr* (SAm) to squash, flatten
atortolar *tr* to rattle, scare, intimidate
atosigar §44 *tr* to poison; harass ‖ *ref* to be in a hurry
atrabanca•do -da *adj* overworked; (Mex) hasty, rash; (Ven) deep in debt
atrabancar §73 *tr* & *intr* to rush through
atrabilia•rio -ria *adj* irascible, grouchy
atracada *f* quarrel, row
atracador *m* hold-up man
atracar §73 *tr* to hold up; bring up; stuff; (naut) to bring alongside, dock ‖ *intr* (naut) to come alongside, dock ‖ *ref* to stuff; quarrel
atracción *f* attraction; amusement
atraco *m* holdup
atracón *m* stuffing, gluttony; fight; push, shove
atracti•vo -va *adj* attractive ‖ *m* attraction; attractiveness
atraer §75 *tr* to attract
atragantar *tr* to choke down ‖ *ref* to choke; **atragantarse con** to choke on
atraillar §4 *tr* to leash; master, subdue
atrampar *ref* to fall into a trap; be stopped up; stick; get stuck
atrancar §73 *tr* to bar; obstruct ‖ *intr* to stride; read falteringly ‖ *ref* to get stuck; (*una ventana*) stick; (Mex) to stick to one's opinion
atrapamos•cas *m* (*pl* **-cas**) flytrap; (bot) Venus's-flytrap
atrapar *tr* to trap, catch; get, land, net
atrás *adv* back, backward; behind; before; previously; **atrás de** back of, behind; **hacerse atrás** to back up, move back; **hacia atrás** backwards; the other way

atrasa•do -da *adj* late; (*reloj*) slow; needy; back; retarded; in arrears; **atrasado de medios** short of funds; **atrasado de noticias** behind the times

atrasar *tr* to slow down; retard; set back, turn back; delay; leave behind; postdate ‖ *intr* to be slow ‖ *ref* to be slow; lose time; lag, stay behind; be late; be in debt

atraso *m* delay, slowness; backwardness; lag; **atrasos** arrears, delinquency

atravesada *f* (SAm) crossing

atravesar §2 *tr* to cross, go across; pierce; pass through, go through; put crosswise; stake, wager ‖ *ref* to butt in; fight, wrangle; get stuck

atrayente *adj* attractive

atreguar §10 *tr* to give a truce to; grant an extension to ‖ *ref* to agree to a truce

atrever *ref* to dare; **atreverse con** or **contra** to be impudent toward

atrevi•do -da *adj* bold, daring; impudent

atrevimiento *m* boldness, daring; impudence

atribuir §20 *tr* to attribute, ascribe ‖ *ref* to assume

atribular *tr & ref* to grieve

atributo *m* attribute

atril *m* lectern; music stand

atrincherar *tr* to entrench ‖ *ref* to dig in

atrio *m* hall, vestibule; court, courtyard; parvis

atri•to -ta *adj* contrite

atrocidad *f* atrocity; enormity

atrofia *f* atrophy

atrofiar *tr & ref* to atrophy

atrojar *tr* (*granos*) to garner; (Mex) to befuddle

atrona•do -da *adj* reckless, thoughtless

atronar §61 *tr* to deafen; stun ‖ *intr* to thunder

atropella•do -da *adj* brusk, violent; hasty; tumultuous

atropellar *tr* to trample; knock down; run over; disregard; do hurriedly ‖ *intr & ref* to act hastily or recklessly

atropello *m* trampling; knocking down; running over; abuse, insult; outrage

a•troz *adj* (*pl* **-troces**) atrocious; huge, enormous

atto. *abbr* **atento**

atufar *tr* to anger, irritate ‖ *ref* to get angry; (*el vino*) turn sour

atún *m* tuna

aturdi•do -da *adj* reckless, harebrained

aturdir *tr* to stun; perplex, bewilder

atusar *tr* to trim; smooth ‖ *ref* to dress fancily; (*el bigote*) twist

audacia *f* audacity

au•daz *adj* (*pl* **-daces**) audacious

audición *f* audition; hearing; concert; listening

audiencia *f* audience, hearing; audience chamber; royal tribunal; provincial high court

audífono *m* hearing aid; earphone

audiofrecuencia *f* audio frequency

audiómetro *m* audiometer

auditor *m* judge advocate; **auditor de guerra** judge advocate (*in army*); **auditor de marina** judge advocate (*in navy*)

auditorio *m* (*concurso de oyentes*) audience; (*local*) auditorium

auge *m* height, acme; boom; vogue; **estar en auge** to be booming

augur *m* augur

augurar *tr* to augur; wish ‖ *intr* to augur

augurio *m* augury; wish

augus•to -ta *adj* august

aula *f* classroom, lecture room; **aula magna** assembly hall

aulaga *f* gorse, furze

aullar §8 *intr* to howl

aullido *m* howl, howling

aúllo *m* howl

aumentar *tr* to augment, increase, enlarge; promote; exaggerate ‖ *intr & ref* to augment, increase

aumento *m* augmentation, increase, enlargement; promotion; (Guat, Mex) postscript, addition; **ir en aumento** to be on the increase

aun *adv* even; **aun cuando** although

aún *adv* still, yet

aunar §8 *tr & ref* to join, unite; combine, mix

aunque *conj* although, though

aúpa *interj* up!; **de aúpa** swanky; **los de aúpa** (taur) the picadors

aupar §8 *tr* to help up; extol

aura *f* gentle breeze; breath; popularity; turkey vulture

áure•o -a *adj* gold, golden

aureola *f* halo, aureole

auricular *m* earpiece, receiver; **auricular de casco** headpiece

auriga *m* (poet) coachman, charioteer

aurora *f* aurora, dawn; roseate hue

ausencia *f* absence

ausentar *tr* to send away ‖ *ref* to absent oneself

ausente *adj* absent; absent-minded ‖ *mf* absentee

auspiciar *tr* to sponsor, foster, back

auspicio *m* auspice; **bajo los auspicios de** under the auspices of

auste•ro -ra *adj* austere; harsh; honest; penitent

Australia *f* Australia

australia•no -na *adj & mf* Australian

Austria *f* Austria

austría•co -ca *adj & mf* Austrian

austro *m* south wind

auténtica *f* certificate; certification

autenticar §73 *tr* to authenticate

auténti•co -ca *adj* authentic; real ‖ *f* see **auténtica**

autillo *m* tawny owl

autísti•co -ca *adj* autistic

auto *m* edict; short Biblical play; miracle play; auto; **auto de prisión** commitment, warrant for arrest; **auto sacramental** play in honor of the Sacrament

autoabastecimiento *m* self-sufficiency

autoadhesi•vo -va *adj* self-adhesive

autoamortizable *adj* self-liquidating
autobanco *m* drive-in bank
autobiografía *f* autobiography
autobombo *m* self-glorification
autobús *m* autobus, bus
autocamión *m* motor truck
autocasa *f* motor home; mobile home; trailer
autocine *m* (Chile, Cuba) drive-in theater
autocinema *f* (Mex) drive-in theater
autocráti•co -ca *adj* autocratic(al)
autócto•no -na *adj* native, indigenous
autodefensa *f* self-defense
autodestrucción *f* self-destruction
autodeterminación *f* self-determination
autodidac•to -ta *adj* self-taught
autodisciplina *f* self-discipline
autodominio *m* self-control
autódromo *m* automobile race track
auto-escuela *f* driving school
autógena *f* welding
autogestión *f* self-administration; independence
autogobierno *m* self-government
autografiar §77 *tr* to autograph
autógra•fo -fa *adj & m* autograph
autoguia•do -da *adj* self-guided, homing
autolimpiador or **autolimpiante** *adj invar* self-cleaning
automación *f* automation
autómata *m* automaton
automáti•co -ca *adj* automatic
automatización *f* automation
automóvil *m* automobile
automovilista *mf* motorist
autonomía *f* autonomy; cruising radius
autóno•mo -ma *adj* autonomous, independent
autopega•do -da *adj* self-sealing
autopiano *m* player piano
autopista *f* turnpike, automobile road
autopsia *f* autopsy
au•tor -tora *mf* author; (*de un crimen*) perpetrator ‖ *f* authoress
autoreactor *m* ramjet (engine)
autoridad *f* authority; pomp, display
autorita•rio -ria *adj & mf* authoritarian
autoriza•do -da *adj* authoritative
autorizar §60 *tr* to authorize; legalize; exalt
autorretrato *m* self-portrait
autoservicio *m* self-service
autostop *m* hitchhiking; **viajar en autostop** to hitchhike
autostopista *mf* hitchhiker
auto-teatro *m* drive-in movie theater
autovía *m* railway motor coach ‖ *f* turnpike, automobile road
auxiliar *adj* auxiliary ‖ *mf* auxiliary; aid, helper; substitute teacher ‖ *v* §77 **& regular** *tr* to aid, help, assist; (*a un moribundo*) attend
auxilio *m* aid, help, assistance; **acudir en auxilio a** or **de** to come to the aid of; **auxilio en carretera** road service; **primeros auxilios** first aid
avahar *tr* to steam; breathe warmth on ‖ *intr* to steam, give off vapor ‖ *ref* to steam,

give off vapor; warm one's hands with one's breath
aval *m* indorsement; countersignature
avalancha *f* avalanche
avalorar *tr* to estimate; encourage
avaluación *f* appraisal, valuation
avaluar §21 *tr* to appraise, estimate
avalúo *m* appraisal, valuation
avance *m* advance; advance payment; (com) balance; (com) estimate; (mov) preview; **avance rápido** (mach, mov) fast forward
avante *adv* (naut) fore
avanza•do -da *adj* advanced; **avanzado de edad** advanced in years ‖ *f* outpost, advance guard
avanzar §60 *tr* to advance, extend; propose ‖ *intr & ref* to advance; approach
avanzo *m* balance sheet; estimate
avaricia *f* avarice
avaricio•so -sa *adj* avaricious
avarien•to -ta *adj* avaricious ‖ *mf* miser
ava•ro -ra *adj* miserly ‖ *mf* miser
avasallar *tr* to subject, subjugate, enslave ‖ *ref* to submit
ave *f* bird; fowl; **ave canora** songbird; **ave de corral** barnyard fowl; **ave de mal agüero** Jonah, jinx; **ave de paso** bird of passage; **ave de rapiña** bird of prey; **ave fría** lapwing; **ave zancuda** wading bird
avecinar *tr* to bring near ‖ *ref* to approach; take up residence
avecindar *tr* to domicile ‖ *ref* to become a resident
avejentar *tr & ref* to age prematurely
avejigar §44 *tr, intr & ref* to blister
avellana *f* hazelnut
avellanar *tr* to countersink ‖ *ref* to shrivel, shrivel up
avellano *m* hazel, hazel tree
avemaría *f* Hail Mary, Ave Maria; **al avemaría** at sunset; **en un avemaría** in a jiffy; **saber como el avemaría** to have a thorough knowledge of
avena *f* oats
avenar *tr* to drain
avenate *m* gruel, oatmeal gruel
avenencia *f* agreement; deal, bargain
avenida *f* avenue; allée; flood, freshet; gathering, assemblage
aveni•do -da *adj* — **bien avenido** in agreement; **mal avenido** in disagreement ‖ *f* see **avenida**
avenimiento *m* agreement; reconciliation
avenir §79 *tr* to reconcile, bring together ‖ *ref* to be reconciled, agree; compromise; correspond
aventa•dor -dora *mf* winnower ‖ *m* fan
aventaja•do -da *adj* excellent, outstanding; advantageous
aventajar *tr* to advance; put ahead; excel ‖ *ref* to advance, win an advantage; excel
aventar §2 *tr* to fan; winnow; scatter to the winds; blow; drive away ‖ *ref* to swell up; flee, run away
aventón *m* (Guat, Mex, Peru) push, shove; (*llevada gratuita*) (Mex) free ride; **pedir aventón** (Mex) to hitchhike

aventura f adventure; danger, risk
aventura•do -da adj hazardous, venturesome
aventurar tr to adventure, venture, hazard ‖ ref to adventure, take a risk; venture, to risk
aventure•ro -ra adj adventuresome, adventurous ‖ m adventurer, soldier of fortune ‖ f adventuress
avergonzar §9 tr to shame; embarrass ‖ ref to be ashamed; be embarrassed
avería f aviary; breakdown, failure; (com) damage; (naut) average
averiar §77 tr to damage ‖ ref to suffer damage; break down
averiguable adj ascertainable
averiguar §10 tr to ascertain, find out
aversión f aversion, dislike; **cobrar aversión a** to take a dislike for
aves•truz m (pl **-truces**) ostrich
avezar §60 tr to accustom ‖ ref to become accustomed
aviación f aviation
avia•dor -dora m/f aviator, flyer ‖ m aviator, airman; (mil) airman; **aviador postal** airmail pilot ‖ f aviatrix, airwoman
aviar §77 tr to make ready, prepare; equip, provide; **estar, encontrarse** or **quedar aviado** to be in a mess, be in a jam ‖ ref to hurry; (aer) to take off
avia•triz (pl **-trices**) aviatrix
avidez f avidity, greediness
ávi•do -da adj avid, greedy, eager
aviejar tr & ref to age prematurely
aviento m winnowing fork, pitchfork
avie•so -sa adj crooked, distorted; evil-minded, perverse
avilantar ref to be insolent
avilantez f insolence; meanness
avillana•do -da adj rustic, boorish
avillanar tr to debase, make boorish ‖ ref to become boorish
avinagra•do -da adj vinegarish, sour, crabbed
avinagrar tr to sour ‖ ref to become sour; turn into vinegar
avío m provision; arrangement; load; **¡al avío!** let's go!; **avíos** equipment, tools, outfit; **avíos de pescar** fishing tackle
avión m airplane; (orn) martin; **avión birreactor** twin-jet plane; **avión de caza** pursuit plane; **avión a chorro, avión de propulsión a chorro** or **a reacción** jet plane; **avión de travesía** airliner; **avión supersónico** supersonic aircraft
avión-correo m mailplane
avioneta f small plane; **avioneta de alquiler** taxiplane
avisaco•ches m (pl **-ches**) car caller
avisa•do -da adj prudent, wise; **mal avisado** rash, thoughtless
avisa•dor -dora adj warning ‖ m/f informer; adviser ‖ m electric bell; **avisador de incendio** fire alarm
avisar tr to advise, inform; warn; report on
aviso m advice, information; warning; care, prudence; dispatch boat; advertisement; **sobre aviso** on the lookout

avispa f wasp
avispa•do -da adj brisk, wide-awake; (SAm) startled, scared
avispar tr to spur; to stir up ‖ ref to fret, worry
avispón m hornet
avistar tr to descry ‖ ref to meet, have an interview
avitaminosis f vitamin deficiency
avituallar tr to supply, provision ‖ ref to take in supplies
avivar tr to brighten, enlive, revive ‖ intr & ref to brighten, revive
avizor adj watchful, alert ‖ m watcher; **avizores** (slang) eyes
avizorar tr to watch, spy on ‖ ref to hide and watch, spy
ax interj ouch!, ow!
axioma m axiom
axiomáti•co -ca adj axiomatic
ay interj ay!, alas! **¡ay de mí!** woe is me! ‖ m sigh
aya f nurse, governess
ayer adj & m yesterday
ayo m tutor
ayuda m valet; **ayuda de cámera** valet de chambre ‖ f help, aid; enema
ayudanta f assistant; **ayudanta de cocina** kitchenmaid
ayudante m aid, assistant; adjutant; **ayudante de campo** aide-de-camp
ayudantía f (universidad) assistantship
ayudar tr to aid, help, assist
ayunar intr to fast
ayu•no -na adj fasting; uninformed; **en ayunas** or **en ayuno** fasting; before breakfast; uninformed; missing the point ‖ m fast, fasting
ayuntamiento m town or city council; town or city hall; sexual intercourse
azabacha•do -da adj jet, jet-black
azabache m jet; **azabaches** jet trinkets
aza•cán -cana adj menial ‖ m/f drudge ‖ m water carrier
azada f hoe
azadón m hoe; grub hoe; **azadón de peto** or **de pico** mattock
azadonar tr to hoe
azafata f air hostess, stewardess; lady of the queen's wardrobe
azafate m wicker tray
azafrán m saffron
azafrana•do -da adj saffron
azafranar tr to saffron
azahar m orange or lemon blossom
azar m chance, hazard; accident, misfortune; fate, destiny; losing card; losing throw; (persona o cosa que traen mala suerte) Jonah
azarar ref to go awry; get rattled
azaro•so -sa adj hazardous, risky; unlucky
ázi•mo -ma adj unleavened
azófar m brass
azoga•do da adj fidgety, restless ‖ m quicksilver foil; **temblar como un azogado** to shake like a leaf

au
az

azogar §44 *tr* (*un espejo*) to silver ‖ *ref* to have mercury poisoning; shake, become agitated
azogue *m* quicksilver; market place; (coll) mirror
azonza•do -da *adj* stupid, dumb
azor *m* goshawk
azorar *tr* to abash; excite, stir up
Azores *fpl* Azores
azotar *tr* to whip, scourge; beat; flail; beat down upon
azote *m* whip; lash; (fig) scourge; **azotes y galeras** tiresome fare
azotea *f* flat roof, roof terrace
azteca *adj* & *mf* Aztec

azúcar *m* sugar; **azúcar de caña** cane sugar; **azúcar de remolacha** beet sugar
azucarar *tr* to sugar, sugarcoat; sugar over
azucare•ro -ra *adj* sugar ‖ *m* sugar bowl
azucena *f* Madonna lily, white lily
azufrar *tr* to sulfur
azufre *m* sulfur; brimstone
azul *adj* & *m* blue; **azul marino** navy blue
azular *tr* to color blue, dye blue
azulear *intr* to turn blue
azulejar *tr* to tile, cover with tiles
azulejo *m* glazed colored tile (orn) roller; (orn) indigo bunting; (orn) bee eater
azulones *mpl* blue jeans
azuzar §60 *tr* to sic; tease, incite

B

B, b (be) *f* second letter of the Spanish alphabet
B. *abbr* **Beato, Bueno**
baba *f* drivel, spittle, slobber; (*de culebras, peces, etc.*) slime
babear *intr* to slobber; froth
babel *m* & *f* (coll) bedlam, confusion; **estar en babel** to be daydreaming
babero *m* bib
Babia *f*— **estar en Babia** to be daydreaming
babieca *adj* silly, simple ‖ *mf* simpleton
Babilonia *f* (*imperio*) Babylonia; (*ciudad*) Babylon
babilóni•co -ca *adj* Babylonian
babilo•nio -nia *adj* & *mf* Babylonian ‖ *f* see **Babilonia**
bable *m* Asturian dialect; patois
babor *m* (naut) port
babosa *f* slug
babosada *f* (CAm, Mex) stupidity; foolish act
babosear *tr* to slobber over ‖ *intr* to slobber
babo•so -sa *adj* slobbery; (*con las damas*) (coll) mushy ‖ *m* (CAm) scoundrel ‖ *f* see **babosa**
babucha *f* slipper, mule
babuino *m* baboon
bacalao or **bacallao** *m* codfish
baceta *f* (cards) widow
bacía *f* basin, vessel; shaving dish
bacilo *m* bacillus
bacín *m* chamber pot
Baco *m* Bacchus
bacteria *f* bacterium
bacteria•no -na *adj* bacterial
bacteriología *f* bacteriology
bacteriólo•go -ga *mf* bacteriologist
báculo *m* staff; crook; (fig) staff, comfort; **báculo pastoral** crozier
bacha *f* (Mex) (cigarette) butt
bache *m* hole, rut; blip; **bache aéreo** air pocket

bachi•ller -llera *adj* garrulous ‖ *mf* garrulous person ‖ **bachiller** *mf* bachelor
bachillerar *tr* to confer the bachelor's degree on ‖ *ref* to receive the bachelor's degree
bachillerato *m* baccalaureate, bachelor's degree
bachillerear *intr* to babble, prattle
bachillería *f* babble, prattle; gossip
badajo *m* clapper
badana *f* (dressed) sheepskin; **zurrarle a uno la badana** to tan someone's hide
badén *m* gully, gutter
badil *m* fire shovel
badulaque *m* nincompoop
bagaje *m* beast of burden; (mil) baggage
bagatela *f* trinket; triviality; (Chile, Peru) pinball
bagazo *m* waste pulp, bagasse
bagre *adj* (Bol, Col) showy, gaudy; (CAm) sly, slick; (SAm) coarse, ill-bred; (Mex) stupid ‖ *m* catfish
bahareque *m* (CAm, Col, Ven) small hut
bahía *f* bay
bahorrina *f* slop; riffraff
bailable *adj* for dancing ‖ *m* ballet
bailadero *m* dance floor, dance hall
baila•dor -dora *mf* dancer
bailar *tr* (*p.ej., un vals*) to dance; (*un trompo*) spin ‖ *intr* to dance; spin; wobble
baila•rín -rina *mf* dancer ‖ *f* ballerina; **bailarina ombliguista** belly dancer
baile *m* dance; ball; ballet; **baile de etiqueta** dress ball, formal dance; **baile de los globos** bubble dance; **baile de máscaras** masked ball, masquerade ball; **baile de San Vito** (pathol) Saint Vitus's dance; **baile de trajes** costume ball, fancy-dress ball
baja *f* (*de los precios*) fall, drop; (*en la guerra*) casualty; **dar baja** to go down, decline; **dar de baja** to drop; (mil) to mark absent; **darse de baja** to drop out; **jugar a la baja** to bear the market

bajaca f (Ecuad) hair ribbon

bajada f descent; slope; downspout; (rad) lead-in wire

bajagua f (Mex) cheap tobacco

bajamar f low tide

bajar tr to lower, take down; bring down; (la escalera) go down, descend; humble ‖ intr to come down, go down; get off ‖ ref to bend down; get off; humble oneself

bajel m ship, vessel

bajeza f humbleness, lowliness; meanness, baseness

bajío m shoal, sandbank; pitfall; lowland

bajista adj bearish ‖ mf (fig) bear

ba•jo -ja adj low, under, lower; short; mean, base; lowly, humble; (mus) bass ‖ m shoal, sandbank; (mus) bass ‖ f see **baja** ‖ **bajo** adv down; low, in a low voice ‖ **bajo** prep under

bajón m bassoon; (en el caudal, la salud, etc.) decline, loss

bajonista mf bassoon player

bajorrelieve m bas-relief

bala f bullet; bale; **bala fría** spent bullet; **bala perdida** stray bullet; **ni a bala** (SAm) under no circumstances

balaca f boasting, show

balaceo m or **balacera** f (SAm) shooting; shootout

balada f ballad; (mus) ballade

bala•dí adj (pl -díes) trivial, paltry, cheap

baladro m scream, shout, outcry

baladronada f boast, boasting

baladronear intr to boast, brag

bálago m chaff

balance m balance, balance sheet; rocking, swinging; hesitation, doubt; (de una nave) rolling

balancear tr to balance ‖ intr & ref to rock, swing; hesitate, waver; (la nave) roll

balancín m balance beam; singletree; rocker arm; seesaw

balandra f sloop

balandrán m cassock

balanza f scales, balance; comparison, judgment; **balanza de pagos** balance of payments

balar intr to bleat; (coll) to pine

balastar tr to ballast

balasto m ballast

balaustre m baluster, banister

balay m wicker basket

balazo m shot; bullet wound

balbucear tr to stammer ‖ intr to stammer, stutter; to babble, to prattle

balbucir §1 tr & intr var of **balbucear**

Balcanes, los the Balkans

balcarrotas fpl (SAm) sideburns; (Mex) locks falling over sides of face

balcón m balcony

baldar tr to cripple; incapacitate; inconvenience; trump

balde m bucket, pail; **de balde** free, gratis; over, in excess; **en balde** in vain

baldear tr to wash with pails of water; (una excavación) bail out

baldí•o -a adj uncultivated; idle, lazy; careless; useless, vain; unfounded ‖ m untilled land

baldón m insult; blot, disgrace

baldonar tr to insult; stain, disgrace

baldosa f floor tile, paving tile; flagstone

baldra•gas m (pl -gas) jellyfish

balduque s red tape, wrapping tape

balear tr to shoot at, shoot, shoot to death

baleo m (SAm) shooting

balido m bleat, bleating

balísti•co -ca adj ballistic

baliza f buoy, beacon; danger signal

balizaje m (aer) airway lighting; (naut) buoys

balizar §60 tr to mark with buoys; mark off

balnea•rio -ria adj bathing ‖ m watering place, spa

balompié m football, soccer

balón m football; bale; balloon

baloncesto m basketball

balota f ballot

balotar intr to ballot

balsa f pool, puddle; raft; float; corkwood; **balsa salvavidas** life float

bálsamo m balsam, balm

balsear tr to cross by raft; ferry across

balsero m ferryman

bálti•co -ca adj Baltic

baluarte m bulwark

balumba f confusion; row

ballena f whale; whalebone; (de corsé) stay

ballesta f crossbow; spring, auto spring

ba•llet m (pl -llets) ballet

bambalinas fpl (theat) flies, borders

bambolear intr to sway, reel, wobble

bambolla f hulk; show, sham; show-off

bam•bú m (pl -búes) bamboo

banana f banana; (rad) plug

banane•ro -ra adj banana ‖ m banana tree

banano m banana tree

banas fpl (Mex) banns

banasta f hamper, large basket

banca f bench; banking; stand, fruit stand; (en el juego) bank; **banca de hielo** iceberg; **hacer saltar la banca** to break the bank

banca•rio -ria adj banking, bank

bancarrota f bankruptcy; **hacer bancarrota** to go bankrupt

bancarrote•ro -ra adj & mf bankrupt

banco m bench; bank; (de peces) school; **banco de ahorros** savings bank; **banco de datos** (ordenador) data bank; memory; **banco de hielo** iceberg; **banco de liquidación** clearing house

banda f band; ribbon; faction, party; flock; border, edge; bank, shore; (de la mesa de billar) cushion; **banda ciudadana** citizens band, CB; **banda de rodamiento** (aut) tread; **banda de tambores** drum corps; **irse a la banda** (naut) to list

bandada f flock, covey; (de gente) (coll) flock

bandaje m tire

bandazo m swerving; (naut) lurch

bandear tr to go through, pierce; to pursue; to make love to ‖ ref to manage

bandeja f tray; dish, platter

bandera *f* flag, banner; **con banderas desplegadas** with flying colors

banderilla *f* (taur) banderilla; **poner una banderilla a** to taunt; hit for a loan

banderín *m* (mil) color corporal; recruiting post

banderola *f* streamer, pennant; transom

bandido *m* bandit

bando *m* proclamation; faction, side

bandolera *f* bandoleer; female bandit; **en bandolera** across the shoulders

bandolero *m* highwayman, brigand

bandurria *f* Spanish lute

banquero *m* banker

banqueta stool, footstool; (Guat, Mex) sidewalk

banquete *m* banquet

banquetear *tr, intr & ref* to banquet

banquisa *f* floe, iceberg

bañadera *f* bathtub

bañado *m* chamber pot; marshland

baña·dor -dora *adj* bathing || *mf* bather || *m* bathing suit

bañar *tr* to bathe; dip; coat by dipping || *ref* to bathe

bañera *f* bathtub

bañista *mf* bather; frequenter of a spa or seaside resort

baño *m* bath; bathing; bathroom; bathtub; **baño de asiento** sitz bath; **baño de ducha** shower bath; **baños** bathing place; spa

bao *m* (naut) beam

baptista *adj & mf* Baptist

baptisterio *m* baptistery

baque *m* thud, thump; bump, bruise

baquelita *f* bakelite

ba·quet *m* (*pl* **-quets**) bucket seat

baqueta *f* ramrod; drumstick; **correr baquetas** or **pasar por baquetas** to run the gauntlet

baquía *f* knowledge of the road, paths, rivers, etc. of a region; manual skill

baquia·no -na *adj* skillful, expert || *mf* scout, pathfinder, guide

báqui·co -ca *adj* Bacchic

bar *m* bar; cocktail bar

barahunda *f* uproar, tumult

baraja *f* (*de naipes*) deck, pack; gang, mob; confusion, mix-up

barajadura *f* shuffling; dispute, quarrel

barajar *tr* (*naipes*) to shuffle; jumble, to mix || *intr* to shuffle; fight, quarrel || *ref* to get jumbled or mixed

baranda *f* railing; (*de la mesa de billar*) cushion

barandilla *f* balustrade, railing

barata *f* cheapness; barter; (Mex) bargain sale; (Chile, Peru) cockroach; (Col, Mex) junk store

baratero *m* shopkeeper

baratía *f* (SAm) cheapness

baratija *f* trinket

baratillo *m* second-hand goods; second-hand shop; bargain counter

baratío *m* (CAm) junk store

bara·to -ta *adj* cheap || *m* bargain sale; **dar de barato** to admit for the sake of argu-

ment; **de barato** gratis, free || *f* see **barata** || **barato** *adv* cheap

báratro *m* (poet) hell

baratura *f* cheapness

baraúnda *f* uproar, tumult

barba *f* (*parte de la cara*) chin; (*pelo en ella*) beard; (*del papel*) deckle edge; (*de ave*) gill, wattle; **barba española** Spanish moss; **barbas** whiskers; **hacer la barba a** to shave; to bore, annoy; (Mex) to fawn on; **llevar por la barba** to lead by the nose; **mentir por la barba** (coll) to tell fish stories || *m* (theat) old man

barbacoa *f* barbecue; (Col) kitchen cupboard; (Peru) attic

barbada *f* lower jaw of horse; bridle curb || **la Barbada** Barbados

barbar *intr* to grow a beard; strike root

barbaridad *f* barbarism; outrage; piece of folly; large amount; **¡qué barbaridad!** how awful!, what nonsense!

barbarie *f* barbarity, barbarism

barbarismo *m* illiteracy; outrage; (gram) barbarism

bárba·ro -ra *adj* barbaric; barbarous || *mf* barbarian

barbear *tr* to reach with the chin; be as high as || *intr* to reach the same height; **barbear con** to be as high as

barbechar *tr* to plow for seeding; fallow

barbecho *m* fallow; **firmar como en un barbecho** to sign with one's eyes closed

barbería *f* barber shop

barberil *adj* barber

barbe·ro -ra *mf* barber; (Mex) flatterer

barbilampi·ño -ña *adj* smooth-faced, beardless; beginning, green

barbilla *f* tip of chin; (*de pluma*) barb; (*de pez*) wattle

bar·bón -bona *adj* bearded || *m* graybeard; solemn old fellow; billy goat

barboquejo *m* chin strap

barbotar *tr & intr* to mutter, mumble

barbuchas *adj* beardless

barbu·do -da *adj* bearded, long-bearded, heavy-bearded || *m* shoot, sucker

barbullar *tr & intr* to blabber

barca *f* small boat; bark; **barca perforador** offshore (oil) rig

barcia *f* chaff

barco *m* boat, ship; **barco cisternas** or **barco tanque** tanker; **barco de carga** cargo boat; **barco náufrago** shipwreck

barchi·lón -lona *mf* (Ecuad, Peru) nurse, orderly; (Arg, Bol, Peru) quack

barda *f* thatch; bard, horse armor

bardana *f* burdock

bardar *tr* to thatch; (*caballo*) bard

bardo *m* bard

baremo *m* (*escala*) scale; rate table

bargueño *m* carved inlaid secretary

bario *m* barium

barjuleta *f* haversack

barloventear *intr* to wander around; turn to windward

barlovento *m* windward

barman *m* bartender

bar·niz *m* (*pl* **-nices**) varnish; (*de la loza, la porcelana, etc.*) glaze; gloss, polish; (*conocimientos superficiales*) smattering; (aer) dope

barnizar §60 *tr* to varnish

barómetro *m* barometer; **barómetro aneroide** aneroid barometer

barón *m* baron

baronesa *f* baroness

barquero *m* boatman

barquilla *f* (naut) log; (naut) log chip; (aer) nacelle

barquillero *m* waffle iron; harbor boatman

barquillo *m* cone; waffle

barquín *m* bellows

barra *f* bar; (*de dinamita*) stick; (*en el tribunal*) bar, railing; **barra colectora** (elec) bus bar; **barra de labios** or **para los labios** lipstick; **barra imantada** bar magnet; **barras paralelas** (sport) parallel bars

barrabasada *f* fiendish prank, mean trick

barraca *f* cabin, hut; cottage; storage shed

barracón *m* barracks; fair booth

barragana *f* concubine

barranca *f* gorge, ravine, gully

barranco *m* gorge, ravine, gully; difficulty, obstruction; cliff, precipice

barrar *tr* to daub, smear

barrear *tr* to barricade; bar shut

barredera *f* street sweeper

barre·dor -dora *mf* sweeper; **barredora de alfombras** carpet sweeper; **barredora de nieve** snowplow

barredura *f* sweeping; **barreduras** sweepings

barremi·nas *m* (*pl* **-nas**) mine sweeper

barrena *f* auger, drill, gimlet; (*espiga para taladrar*) bit; (aer) spin; **barrena picada** (aer) tail spin; **entrar en barrena** (aer) to go into a spin

barrenar *tr* to drill; (*un buque*) to scuttle; blast; upset, frustrate; violate

barrende·ro -ra *mf* sweeper

barreno *m* large drill; drill hole; blast hole; pride, vanity; (Chile) mania, pet idea; **dar barreno a** (*un buque*) to scuttle

barreño *m* earthen dishpan

barrer *tr* to sweep, sweep away; graze ‖ *intr* to sweep; **barrer hacia dentro** to look out for oneself

barrera *f* barrier; barricade; (mil) barrage; crockery cupboard; tollgate; (rr) crossing gate; (taur) fence around inside of ring; (taur) first row of seats; **barrera de arrecifes** barrier reef; **barrera de paso a nivel** (rr) crossing gate; **barrera de sonido** or **barrera sónica** sound barrier

barriada *f* district, quarter

barrial *m* (SAm) mudhole; muddy ground

barrica *f* cask, barrel

barriga *f* belly; (*de una vasija, una pared, etc.*) bulge

barri·gón -gona or **barrigu·do -da** *adj* big-bellied

barril *m* barrel

barrilero *m* cooper, barrel maker

barrio *m* ward, quarter; suburb; **barrio bajo** slums; **barrio comercial** shopping district, business district; **el otro barrio** the other world; **estar vestido de barrio** to be dressed in house clothes

barro *m* mud; clay; earthenware; pimple; (coll) money; (Arg, Urug) blunder

barro·co -ca *adj & m* baroque

barro·so -sa *adj* muddy; pimply

barrote *m* heavy bar; bolt; cross brace

barruntar *tr* to guess; to sense

barrunto *m* guess, conjecture; sign, token, foreboding

bartola *f* belly; **a la bartola** lazily

bartolina *f* (CAm, W-I) jail, dungeon

bártulos *mpl* household tools; **liar los bártulos** to pack up one's belongings

barullo *m* confusion, tumult

basar *tr* to base; build ‖ *ref* — **basarse en** to base one's judgment on, rely on

basca *f* nausea, squeamishness; fit of temper, tantrum

basco·so -sa *adj* nauseated, squeamish

báscula *f* scales; platform scale

base *f* base; basis; **a base de** on the basis of

bási·co -ca *adj* basic

Basilea *f* Basle, Basel

basílica *f* basilica

basilisco *m* basilisk; **estar hecho un basilisco** to be in a rage

basquear *intr* to be nauseated

basquetbol *m* basketball

bastante *adj* enough ‖ *adv* enough; fairly, rather ‖ *m* enough

bastar *intr* to be enough, suffice; abound, be more than enough ‖ *ref* to be self-sufficient

bastardilla *f* italics

bastar·do -da *adj & mf* bastard

bastedad *f* coarseness; roughness; (CAm) abundance; excess

bastidor *m* frame; stretcher; (theat) wing; **entre bastidores** behind the scenes

bastilla *f* hem

bastillar *tr* to hem

bas·to -ta *adj* coarse, rough; uncouth ‖ *m* packsaddle; (*naipe*) club; **el basto** the ace of clubs

bastón *m* stick, staff; cane, walking stick; baton; **bastón de esquiar** ski pole or stick

bastoncillo *m* small stick; (*de la retina*) rod

bastonear *tr* to cane, beat

basura *f* sweepings, rubbish, litter, refuse; horse manure

basural *m* (SAm) dump; trash pile

basurero *m* trash can; rubbish dump; rubbish collector

basurita *f* trifle

bata *f* smock; dressing gown, wrapper; **bata de baño** bathrobe

batacazo *m* thud, bump

bataclán *m* (Cuba) burlesque show

bataclana *f* (Cuba) showgirl, stripteaser

batahola *f* racket, hubbub

batalla *f* battle; (*de un vehículo*) wheel base; (*de la silla de montar*) seat; (paint) battle piece; **batalla campal** pitched battle; **librar batalla** to do battle

batallar *intr* to battle, fight; hesitate, waver

bata·llón -llona adj (cuestión) controversial, moot ‖ m battalion

batata f sweet potato; (Arg) timidity

bate m baseball bat

batea f tray; flat-bottomed boat; (rr) flatcar

bateador m batter

batear tr & intr to bat

batel m small boat

batelero m boatman

batería f battery; footlights; **batería de cocina** kitchen utensils

baterista mf drummer

batiboleo m (Cuba, Mex) noise; confusion

bati·do -da adj (camino) beaten; (tejido) moiré ‖ m batter; milk shake; (rad) beat ‖ f battue; combing, search

batidor m beater; scout, ranger; **batidor de huevos** egg beater; **batidor de oro** goldbeater

batidora • beater, mixer

batiente m jamb; (hoja de puerta) leaf, door; (de piano) damper; wash, place where surf breaks

batihoja m goldbeater; sheet-metal worker

batimiento m beating; (phys) beat

batín m smoking jacket

batintín m Chinese gong

batir tr to beat; batter, beat down; (las alas) flap; (manos) clap; (las olas) ply; **batir tiendas** (mil) to strike camp

batiscafo m bathyscaphe

bato m simpleton, rustic

batuque m (Arg) uproar, rumpus, jamboree; **armar un batuque** (Arg) to raise a rumpus

baturrillo m hodgepodge

batuta f (mus) baton; **llevar la batuta** to boss the show

baúl m trunk; **baúl mundo** large trunk; **baúl ropero** wardrobe trunk

bauprés m bowsprit

bautismo m baptism; **bautismo de aire** first flight

bautista adj Baptist ‖ mf Baptist; baptizer; **el Bautista** John the Baptist

bautisterio m baptistery

bautizar §60 tr to baptize; (el vino) water

bautizo m baptism; christening party

báva·ro -ra adj & mf Bavarian

Baviera f Bavaria

baya f berry

bayeta f baize

ba·yo -ya adj bay ‖ m bay horse ‖ f see **baya**

bayoneta f bayonet

bayonetear tr to bayonet

bayunca f or **bayuna** f (CAm) bar; tavern

baza f trick; **meter baza en** to butt into

bazar m bazaar

ba·zo -za adj yellowish-brown ‖ m yellowish brown; spleen ‖ f see **baza**

bazofia f refuse, offal, garbage

bazuca f bazooka

bazucar §73 tr to stir, shake; tamper with

be m baa

beata f lay sister

beatería f cant, hypocrisy

beatificar §73 tr to beatify

beatísi·mo -ma adj most holy

bea·to -ta adj blessed; pious, devout; bigoted, prudish ‖ mf beatified person; devout person; bigot; churchgoer ‖ f see **beata**

bebé m baby; doll

bebede·ro -ra adj (archaic) drinkable ‖ m watering place; (Col, Ecuad, Mex) watering trough

bebedi·zo -za adj drinkable ‖ m potion, philter

bebe·dor -dora adj drinking ‖ mf drinker; hard drinker

beber m drink, drinking ‖ tr & intr to drink; **beber de** or **en** to drink out of ‖ ref to drink, drink up; (p.ej., un libro) to drink in

bebestible adj drinkable ‖ m drink

bebezón f (Col) drunk, spree

bebible adj drinkable

bebi·do -da adj tipsy, unsteady ‖ f drink

bebistrajo m dose, mixture

beborrotear intr to tipple

beca f scholarship, fellowship; (de los colegiales) sash

becacín m snipe, whole snipe

becacina f snipe, great snipe

becada f woodcock

beca·rio -ria mf scholar, fellow

becerra f snapdragon

becerrillo m calfskin

bece·rro -rra mf yearling calf ‖ m calfskin ‖ f see **becerra**

becuadro m (mus) natural sign

bedel m beadle

befa f jeer, flout, scoff

befar tr to jeer at, to scoff at ‖ intr (un caballo) to move the lips

be·fo -fa adj blobber-lipped; knock-kneed ‖ m (de animal) lip ‖ f see **befa**

beisbol m baseball

beisbolero m or **beisbolista** m baseball player

bejuco m cane, liana

beldad f beauty

beldar §2 tr to winnow

belén m crèche; bedlam, confusion; madhouse; gossip ‖ **Belén** Bethlehem

bel·fo -fa adj (labio) blobber; blobber-lipped ‖ m (de animal) lip; blobber lip

belga adj & mf Belgian

Bélgica f Belgium

bélgi·co -ca adj Belgian ‖ f see **Bélgica**

belicista mf warmonger

béli·co -ca adj warlike

belico·so -sa adj bellicose

beligerante adj & mf belligerent

belitre adj low, mean ‖ m scoundrel

bella·co -ca adj cunning, sly; wicked ‖ mf scoundrel

bellaquear intr to cheat, be crooked; (SAm) to be stubborn; rear

bellaquería f cunning, slyness; wickedness

belleza f beauty; **belleza exótica** glamour girl

be·llo -lla adj beautiful, fair

bellota f acorn; carnation bud

bem·bo -ba adj thick-lipped; (Mex) simple, silly ‖ mf (persona) thicklips

bemol adj & m (mus) flat; **tener bemoles** to be a tough job

bencedrina *f* benzedrine
bencina *f* benzine
bendecir §11 *tr* to bless; consecrate; **bendecir la mesa** to say grace
bendición *f* benediction, blessing; godsend; (*en la mesa*) grace; **bendiciones** wedding ceremony; **echar la bendicióna** to have nothing more to do with
bendi•to -ta *adj* blessed, saintly; simple, silly; happy; (*agua*) holy; **como el pan bendito** as easy as pie ‖ *m* simple-minded soul
benedícite *m* grace; **rezar el benedícite** to say grace
benedicti•no -na *adj* & *mf* Benedictine ‖ *m* benedictine
beneficencia *f* beneficience; charity, welfare; social service
beneficia•do -da *mf* person or charity receiving the proceeds of a benefit performance
beneficiar *tr* to benefit; (*la tierra*) cultivate; (*una mina*) work, exploit; (*minerales*) process, reduce; (*una región del país*) serve; season; slaughter ‖ *ref* — **beneficiarse de** to take advantage of
beneficia•rio -ria *mf* beneficiary
beneficio *m* benefit; profit, gain, yield; (*de una mina*) exploitation; smelting, ore reduction; benefit performance; **a beneficio de** for the benefit of; on the strength of; **beneficios sociales** fringe benefits
beneficio•so -sa *adj* beneficial, profitable
benéfi•co -ca *adj* charitable, benevolent
beneméri•to -ta *adj* & *mf* worthy; **benemérito de la patria** national hero
beneplácito *m* approval, consent
benevolencia *f* benevolence
benévo•lo -la *adj* benevolent, kind-hearted
bengala *f* Bengal light; (aer) flare
benignidad *f* benignity, mildness, kindness; (*del tiempo*) mildness
benig•no -na *adj* benign, mild, kind; (*tiempo*) clement, mild
benjamín *m* baby (*the youngest child*)
beodez *f* drunkenness
beo•do -da *adj* & *mf* drunk
bequista *mf* (CAm, Cuba) scholarship holder; grant winner
berbi•quí *m* (*pl* -**quíes**) brace; **berbiquí y barrena** brace and bit
berenjena *f* eggplant
berenjenal *m* eggplant patch; (coll) predicament, jam, fix
bergante *m* scoundrel, rascal
bergantín *m* (naut) brig; **bergantín goleta** (naut) brigantine
berilio *m* beryllium
berkelio *m* berkelium
berli•nés -nesa *adj* Berlin ‖ *mf* Berliner
bermejear *intr* to turn bright red; look bright red
berme•jo -ja *adj* vermilion, bright-red
berme•jón -jona *adj* red, reddish
bermellón *m* vermilion
berrear *intr* to bellow, low; bawl, yowl
berrenchín *m* rage, tantrum
berrido *m* bellow; scream, yowl

berrín *m* touchy person, cross child
berrinche *m* tantrum, conniption
berro *m* water cress
berza *f* cabbage
berzal *m* cabbage patch
berzas *m* or **berzotas** *m* dunderhead, flop
besalamano *m* (obs) announcement, written in the third person and marked B.L.M. (*kisses your hand*)
besamanos *m* levee, reception at court; throwing kisses
besar *tr* to kiss; to graze ‖ *ref* to bump heads together
beso *m* kiss; **beso sonado** buss
bestia *adj* stupid ‖ *mf* dunce ‖ *f* beast; **bestia de carga** beast of burden
bestial *adj* beastly; (coll) terrific
besucar §73 *tr* & *intr* to keep on kissing
besu•cón -cona *adj* kissing ‖ *mf* kisser
besuquear *tr* & *intr* to keep on kissing
betabel *m* (Mex) beet
betún *m* bitumen, pitch; shoe polish
bezo *m* blubber lip; proud flesh
bezu•do -da *adj* thick-lipped
biberón *m* nursing bottle
Biblia *f* Bible
bíbli•co -ca *adj* Biblical
bibliófi•lo -la *mf* bibliophile
bibliografía *f* bibliography
bibliógra•fo -fa *mf* bibliographer
biblioteca *f* library; **biblioteca de consulta** reference library; **biblioteca de préstamo** lending library
biblioteca•rio -ria *mf* librarian
bibliotecnia *f* bookmaking; library science
biblioteconomía *f* library science
bicameral *adj* bicameral
bicarbonato *m* bicarbonate
bicicleta *f* bicycle
bicherío *m* (SAm) vermin
bichero *m* boat hook
bicho *m* bug, insect; vermin; animal; fighting bull; simpleton; brat; **bicho viviente** living soul; **mal bicho** scoundrel; ferocious bull
bidón *m* (*bote, lata*) can; (*tonel de metal*) drum
biela *f* connecting rod
bielda *f* winnowing rack; winnowing
bieldar *tr* to winnow
bieldo *m* winnowing pitch rake
bien *adv* well; readily; very; indeed; **ahora bien** now then; **bien como** just as; **bien que** although; **más bien** rather; somewhat; **no bien** as soon as; scarcely ‖ *s* welfare; property; darling; **bienes** wealth, riches, possessions; **bienes de fortuna** worldly possessions; **bienes dotales** dower; **bienes inmuebles** real estate; **bienes muebles** personal property; **bienes raíces** real estate; **bienes relictos** estate; **bienes semovientes** livestock; **bien público** commonweal; **en bien de** for the sake of
bienal *adj* biennial
bienama•do -da *adj* dearly beloved
bienandanza *f* happiness, prosperity
bienaventura•do -da *adj* happy, blissful; blessed; simple

bienaventuranza *f* happiness, bliss; blessedness

bienestar *m* well-being, welfare

bienhabla•do -da *adj* well-spoken

bienhada•do -da *adj* fortunate, lucky

bienhe•chor -chora *adj* beneficent ‖ *m* benefactor ‖ *f* benefactress

bienintenciona•do -da *adj* well-meaning

bienio *m* biennium

bienquerencia *f* affection, fondness

bienquistar *tr* to bring together, reconcile

bienvenida *f* safe arrival; welcome; **dar la bienvenida a** to welcome

bienveni•do -da *adj* welcome ‖ *f* see **bienvenida**

bienvivir *intr* to live in comfort; live decently, properly

bif•tec *m* (*pl* **-tecs**) beefsteak

bifurcar §73 *ref* to branch, fork

bigamia *f* bigamy

bíga•mo -ma *adj* bigamous ‖ *mf* bigamist

bigornia *f* two-horn anvil

bigote *m* mustache; **bigotes** (*del gato*) whiskers; **tener bigotes** to have a mind of one's own

bigudí *m* hair curler

bikini *m* bikini (swimsuit)

bilingüe *adj* bilingual

bilis *f* bile; **descargar la bilis** to vent one's spleen

bilma *f* (med) compress

billar *m* billiards; billiard table; billiard room; **billar romano** pinball

billete *m* ticket; note, bill; **billete de abono** season ticket; commutation ticket; **billete de banco** bank note; **billete de ida y vuelta** round-trip ticket; **billete kilométrico** mileage ticket; **medio billete** half fare

billetero *m* billfold; ticket agent

billón *m* (U.S.A.) trillion; (Brit) billion

bimba *f* top hat; (Mex) drinking spree

bimotor *adj* twin-motor ‖ *m* twin-motor plane

biodegradable *adj* biodegradable

biofísi•co -ca *adj* biophysical ‖ *f* biophysics

biografía *f* biography

biógra•fo -fa *mf* biographer

biología *f* biology

biólo•go -ga *mf* biologist

biombo *m* folding screen

bioplasma *f* bioplasm

biopsia *f* biopsy

bióxido *m* dioxide

bioquími•co -ca *adj* biochemical ‖ *mf* biochemist ‖ *f* biochemistry

bipartición *f* fission, splitting

bípe•do -da *adj & mf* biped; human

biplano *m* biplane

biplaza *m* (aer) two-seater

birimbao *m* jews'-harp

birlar *tr* to knock down, shoot down; outwit; **birlar algo a alguien** to snitch something from someone

birlocha *f* kite

Birmania *f* Burma

birma•no -na *adj & mf* Burmese

biro *m* or **birome** *f* (Arg) ball-point pen

birreta *f* biretta, red biretta

birrete *m* mortarboard, academic cap

bis *interj* encore! ‖ *m* encore

bisabue•lo -la *mf* great-grandparent ‖ *m* great-grandfather ‖ *f* great-grandmother

bisagra *f* hinge

bisar *tr* to repeat

bisbisar *tr* to mutter, mumble

bisecar §73 *tr* to bisect

bisel *m* bevel edge

biselar *tr* to bevel

bisies•to -ta *adj* leap

bismuto *m* bismuth

bisnie•to -ta *mf* great-grandchild ‖ *m* great-grandson ‖ *f* great-granddaughter

biso•jo -ja *adj* squint-eyed, cross-eyed

bisonte *m* bison; buffalo

biso•ño -ña *adj* green, inexperienced ‖ *mf* greenhorn, rookie

bisté *m* or **bistec** *m* beefsteak

bisun•to -ta *adj* dirty, greasy

bisutería *f* costume jewelry

bitácora *f* binnacle

bitoque *m* bung; (CAm) sewer; (Mex) spigot

Bizancio Byzantium

bizanti•no -na *adj & mf* Byzantine

bizarría *f* gallantry, bravery; magnanimity

biza•rro -rra *adj* gallant, brave; magnanimous

bizcar §73 *tr* to wink ‖ *intr* to squint

biz•co -ca *adj* squint-eyed, cross-eyed

bizcocho *m* biscuit; cake, sponge cake; hardtack; bisque

bizma *f* poultice

bizmar *tr* to poultice

biznie•to -ta *mf* var of **bisnieto**

bizquear *intr* to squint

bizquera *f* squint

blanca *f* steel blade; **sin blanca** penniless

blanca•zo -za *adj* whitish

blan•co -ca *adj* white; (*tez*) fair; (*fuerza*) water; (*arma*) steel; (*cobarde*) yellow; blank ‖ *mf* (*persona*) white; coward ‖ *m* (*color*) white; blank; target; aim, object; interval; white heat; blank form; **dar en el blanco** to hit the mark; **en blanco** (*hoja*) blank; **hacer blanco** to hit the mark; **quedarse en blanco** to not get the point; to be disappointed ‖ *f* see **blanca**

blancor *m* whiteness

blancura *f* whiteness; purity

blancuz•co -ca *adj* whitish; dirty-white

blandear *tr* to persuade; brandish ‖ *intr & ref* to yield, give in

blandengue *adj* soft, colorless

blandir §1 *tr, intr & ref* to brandish

blan•do -da *adj* bland, soft; indulgent; flabby; sensual; cowardly; (*ojos*) tender

blandón *m* wax candle; candlestick

blandura *f* blandness, softness; tolerance; flabbiness; sensuality; flattery; mild weather; cowardice

blanqueadura *f* whitening; bleaching; whitewash

blanquear *tr* to whiten, bleach; blanch; whitewash; tin ‖ *intr* to turn white

blanqueci•no -na *adj* whitish

blanqui•llo -lla *adj* white, whitish ‖ *m* (Guat, Mex) egg; (Chile, Peru) white peach
blasfemar *tr* to blaspheme, curse
blasfemia *f* blasphemy
blasfe•mo -ma *adj* blasphemous ‖ *mf* blasphemer
blasón *m* (*ciencia de los escudos de armas; escudo de armas*) heraldry; (heral) charge; (fig) glory, honor
blasonar *tr* to emblazon; (fig) to emblazon, extol ‖ *intr* to boast; **blasonar de** to boast of being
bledo *m* straw; **no me importa un bledo** or **no se me da un bledo de ello** that doesn't matter a rap to me
blindaje *m* armor; (elec) shield
blindar *tr* to armor, armor-plate; (elec) to shield
B.L.M. *abbr* **besalamano**
bloc *m* (*pl* **bloques**) pad
blof *m* bluff
blofear *intr* to bluff
blon•do -da *adj* blond, fair, flaxen, light; (Arg) curly ‖ *f* blond lace
bloque *m* block; (*de papel*) pad; **bloque de hormigón** concrete block
bloquear *tr* to blockade; (*un coche, un tren*) brake; (*créditos*) freeze
bloqueo *m* blockade; (*de crédito*) freezing; **bloqueo vertical** (telv) vertical hold
b.l.p. *abbr* **besa los pies**
blujins *mpl* blue jeans
blusa *f* blouse, smock; (*de mujer*) shirtwaist; (Col) jacket
boardilla *f* dormer window; garret
boato *m* show, pomp
bobada *f* folly, piece of folly
bobalías *mf* simpleton, dunce
bobali•cón -cona *adj* simple, silly ‖ *mf* simpleton, nitwit
bobear *intr* to talk nonsense; to dawdle, loiter around
bobería *f* folly, nonsense
bóbilis—de bóbilis free, for nothing; without effort
bobina *f* bobbin; (elec) coil; **bobina de chispas** spark coil; **bobina de encendido** ignition coil, spark coil; **bobina de sintonía** tuning coil
bobinar *tr* to wind
bo•bo -ba *adj* simple, foolish, stupid ‖ *mf* simpleton, fool ‖ *m* (archaic) clown, jester
boca *f* mouth; speech; taste, flavor; (*del estómago*) pit; **a boca de jarro** immoderately; at close range; **boca de agua** hydrant; **boca de dragón** (bot) snapdragon; **boca de riego** hydrant; **buscarle a uno la boca** to draw someone out; **decir con la boca chica** to offer as a mere formality; **no decir esta boca es mía** to not say a word
bocacalle *f* street entrance; intersection
boca•caz *m* (*pl* **-caces**) spillway
bocadillo *m* tape, ribbon; snack, bite; farmer's snack in the field; sandwich
bocadito *m* little bit; (Cuba) cigarillo (*cigaret wrapped in tobacco*)

bocado *m* bite, morsel; bit; **bocado de Adán** Adam's apple; **no tener para un bocado** to not have a cent
bocal *m* narrow-mouthed pitcher; (*de un puerto*) narrows
bocallave *f* keyhole
bocamanga *f* cuff, wristband
bocanada *f* (*de líquido*) swallow; (*de humo*) puff; (*de viento*) gust; boasting
bocartear *tr* to crush, stamp
bocaza *f* loudmouth; gossip
bocera *f* smear on lips
boceto *m* sketch, outline; wax model, clay model
bocina *f* horn, trumpet; auto horn; phonograph horn; ear trumpet
bocio *m* goiter
bocoy *m* large barrel
bocha *f* bowling ball
bochar *tr* (Mex, Ven) to turn down; (Mex, Ven) insult
boche *m* small hole in ground for boys' game; (Ven) slight, snub
bochinche *m* uproar, tumult, row
bochorno *m* sultry weather; blush, embarrassment, shame
bochorno•so -sa *adj* sultry, stuffy; embarrassing, shameful
boda *f* marriage, wedding; **bodas de Camacho** banquet, lavish feast
bodega *f* wine cellar; dock warehouse; granary; grocery store; (*de nave*) hold; cellar; (*hombre que bebe mucho*) tank
bodegón *m* hash house, beanery; saloon; still life
bodegue•ro -ra *mf* cellarer; grocer
bodijo *m* unequal match; simple wedding
bodoque *m* lump; dunce, dolt; (Mex) bump, lump
bodoquera *f* peashooter
bóer *mf* Boer
bofe *adj invar* (CAm) unpleasant, disgusting ‖ *m* (coll) lung; (P-R) cinch, snap; **echar el bofe** or **los bofes** to drudge, to grind; **bofes** lights (*of sheep, etc.*)
bofetada *f* slap in the face
boga *mf* rower ‖ *f* vogue, fashion; rowing
bogar §44 *intr* to row
bogavante *m* lobster
bohardilla *f* dormer window; garret
bohe•mio -mia *adj* & *mf* Bohemian
bohío *m* hut, shack
boicotear *tr* to boycott
boicoteo *m* boycott, boycotting
boina *f* beret
boj *m* boxwood
boja *f* southernwood
bojar *tr* to measure the perimeter of; (*el cuero*) scrape clean ‖ *intr* to measure
bola *f* ball; marble; bowling; shoe polish; shoeshine; (cards) slam; lie, deceit; (Mex) brawl, riot; **bola de alcanfor** moth ball; **bola de cristal** crystal ball; **bola de nieve** snowball; **bola rompedora** wrecking ball; **bolas** Gaucho lasso tipped with balls; **dejar que ruede la bola** to let things take

their course; **raspar la bola** (Chile) to clear out, beat it

bolada f (*de una bola*) throw; luck, opportunity; (Arg) billiard stroke; (Chile) dainty, tidbit; (Guat, Mex) lie, fib

bolado m (CAm) rumor

bolazo m hit with a ball; **de bolazo** (coll) hurriedly, right away; (Mex) at random

bolchevique adj & mf Bolshevik

bolchevismo m Bolshevism

boleada f (Arg) hunting with bolas; (Mex) shoeshine; (Peru) flunking

bolear tr to throw; (Arg) to catch with bolas; (*zapatos*) (Mex) to shine; (SAm) to kick out, flunk ‖ intr to play for fun; lie; boast ‖ ref (Arg, Urug) to rear and fall backwards; upset; blush

bole•ro -ra mf bolero dancer ‖ m bolero (*dance; music; jacket*); (Mex) bootblack ‖ f bowling alley; **bolera encespada** bowling green

boleta f pass, permit, admission ticket; (mil) billet; ballot

boletería f ticket office

boletín m bulletin; ticket; form; press release

boleto m ticket

boliche m bowling; bowling alley; (SAm) hash house

bólido m fireball, bolide

bolígrafo m ball-point pen

bolilápiz m (Mex) ball-point pen

bolillo m bobbin for making lace; frame for stiffening lace cuffs

Bolivia f Bolivia

bolivia•no -na adj & mf Bolivian

bo•lo -la adj (CAm, Mex) drunk; m ninepin, tenpin; dunce, blockhead; (*de escalera*) newel; (cards) slam; **bolos** bowling, ninepins, tenpins; **jugar a los bolos** to bowl

Bolonia f Bologna

bolsa f purse, pocketbook; pouch; stock exchange, stock market; (*en el vestido*) bag, pucker; grant, award; **bolsa de agua caliente** hotwater bottle; **bolsa de aire** (aut) air bag; **bolsa de hielo** ice bag; **bolsa de trabajo** employment bureau; **bolsa isotérmica** Thermos bottle; **hacer bolsa** (*un vestido*) to bag; **jugar a la bolsa** to play the market

bolsear tr to pick the pocket of; (Arg, Bol, Urug) to jilt; (Chile) to sponge on

bolsero m (SAm) sponger; (Mex) pickpocket

bolsicalculadora f pocket calculator

bolsillo m pocket; purse, pocketbook

bolsista m broker, stockbroker; (CAm, Mex) pickpocket

bolso m purse, pocketbook; **bolso de mano** handbag

bollo m bun, roll; bump, lump; dent; (*en un vestido*) puff; (*en adorno de tapicería*) tuft; **bollo de crema** cream puff

bomba f pump; bomb; fire engine; lamp globe; high hat; firecracker; soap bubble; bombshell; **a prueba de bombas** bombproof; **bomba atómica** atomic bomb; **bomba coche** car bomb; **bomba cohete** rocket bomb; **bomba de engrase** grease

gun; **bomba de hidrógeno** hydrogen bomb; **bomba de incendios** fire engine; **bomba de profundidad** depth bomb; **bomba de sentina** bilge pump; **bomba estomacal** stomach pump; **bomba neutrónica** neutron bomb; **bomba rompedora** blockbuster; **bomba volante** buzz bomb; **caer como una bomba** to fall like a bombshell; to burst in unexpectedly

bombachas fpl loose-fitting baggy trousers

bombardear tr & intr to bomb; bombard; **bombardear en picado** to dive-bomb

bombardeo m bombing; bombarding; **bombardeo en picado** dive bombing

bombardero m bomber; bombardier

bomba-reloj f time bomb

bombazo m bomb explosion; bomb hit; bomb damage

bombear tr to bomb; ballyhoo, puff up; pump; (SAm) to reconnoiter; (Col) to fire, dismiss ‖ ref to camber, bulge

bombero m fireman; pumpman

bombilla f bulb, light bulb; lamp chimney; tube for sucking up maté; **bombilla de destello** flash bulb

bombillo m trap, stench trap; (naut) pump

bombista m lamp maker; (*el que da bombos*) booster

bom•bo -ba adj astounded, stunned; (W-I) lukewarm ‖ m bass drum; ballyhoo; (naut) barge, lighter; **dar bombo a** to ballyhoo, puff up; **irse al bombo** (Arg) to fail ‖ f see **bomba**

bombón m bonbon, candy

bombona f carboy

bombonera f candy box

bona•chón -chona adj goodnatured, kind, simple

bonancible adj (*tiempo*) fair; (*mar*) calm; (*viento*) moderate

bonanza f fair weather, calm seas; prosperity, boom; rich ore pocket

bona•zo -za adj kind-hearted

bondad f kindness; favor; **tener la bondad de** to have the kindness to

bondado•so -sa adj kind, generous

bonete m cap, hat; candy bowl

bonetería f hat shop; notion store

bongo m (SAm) barge; canoe

boniato m sweet potato

bonificar §73 tr to improve; give a discount on

boni•to -ta adj pretty, nice; pretty good

bono m bond; food voucher

boñiga f manure, cow dung

boom m (*mercado, bolsa*) boom

boqueada f gasp of death

boquear tr to pronounce, utter ‖ intr to gasp

boquerel m nozzle

boquete m gap, breach, opening

boquiabier•to -ta adj open-mouthed

boquian•cho -cha adj wide-mouthed

boquiangos•to -ta adj narrow-mouthed

boquihundi•do -da adj hollow-mouthed

boquilla f (*de instrumento de viento*) mouthpiece; (*de pipa*) stem; (*de cigarro*) tip; (*de aparato de alumbrado*) burner; cigar holder, cigarette holder; (*de manguera*) nozzle; opening in irrigation canal; opening at bottom of trouser leg

boquirro•to -ta *adj* garrulous

boquiverde *adj* obscene, smutty

bórax *m* borax

borbollar or **borbollear** *intr* to bubble up

borbollón *m* bubbling; **a borbollones** impetuously

borborigmos *mpl* rumbling of the bowels

borbotar *intr* to bubble up, bubble over

borce•guí *m* (*pl* **-guíes**) high shoe

borda *f* hut; (naut) gunwale; **arrojar, echar** or **tirar por la borda** to throw overboard

bordada *f* (naut) tack; **dar bordadas** (naut) to tack; pace to and fro

bordado *m* embroidery

bordadura *f* embroidery

bordar *tr* to embroider

borde *m* border, edge; fringe; rim; **borde de la acera** curb; **borde del mar** seaside

bordear *tr* to border ‖ *intr* to go on the edge; (naut) to tack

bordo *m* (naut) board; (naut) side; (naut) tack; (Guat, Mex) dam, dike; **a bordo** (naut) on board; **al bordo** (naut) alongside; **de alto bordo** seagoing; distinguished, important

bordón *m* (*de tambor*) snare; pilgrim's staff; pet word; burden, refrain

bordonear *intr* to grope along with a stick; to go around begging

borgoña *m* Burgundy (*wine*) ‖ **la Borgoña** Burgundy

borgo•ñón -ñona *adj & mf* Burgundian

boricua or **borinque•ño -ña** *adj & mf* Puerto Rican

borla *f* tassel; powder puff; **tomar la borla** to take a higher degree, take the doctor's degree

borne *m* binding post; (*de la lanza*) tip

bornear *tr* to bend, twist; (*sillares pesados*) set in place ‖ *intr* to swing at anchor ‖ *ref* to warp

borra *f* fuzz, nap, lint

borrachera *f* drunkenness; spree; binge; great exaltation; (coll) piece of folly; **pegarse una borrachera** to go on a binge

borrachería *f* (Mex) bar, tavern

borrachín *m* drunkard

borra•cho -cha *adj* drunk; (*habitualmente*) drinking ‖ *mf* drunkard

borrador *m* blotter, day book; rough draft; eraser

borradura *f* striking out, scratching out

borraj *m* borax

borrajear *tr & intr* to scribble; doodle

borrar *tr* to scratch out, cross out; erase, rub out; darken, obscure; blot, smear

borrasca *f* storm, tempest; upset, setback

borrasco•so -sa *adj* stormy

borregos *mpl* fleecy clouds

borrica *f* she-ass; stupid woman

borrico *m* ass, donkey; sawhorse; stupid fellow, ass

borricón *m* or **borricote** *m* drudge

borrón *m* blot; rough draft; blemish; (fig) blot, stain

borronear *tr* to scribble

borro•so -sa *adj* blurred, smudgy, fuzzy; muddy, thick

boruca *f* noise, clamor, uproar

borujo *m* lump, clump

boscaje *m* woodland; (paint) woodland scene

bosque *m* forest, woodland; **bosque maderable** timberland

bosquejar *tr* to sketch, outline; make a rough model of

bosquejo *m* sketch, outline; rough model

bostezar §60 *intr* to yawn, gape

bostezo *m* yawn, yawning

bota *f* shoe, boot; leather wine bag; liquid measure (*125 gallons or 516 liters*); **bota de agua** gum boot; **bota de montar** riding boot; **ponerse las botas** (coll) to hit the jack pot, come out on top

botador *m* boat pole; punch, nailset

botadura *f* launching

botafuego *m* hothead, firebrand

botalón *m* (naut) boom; **botalón de foque** (naut) jib boom

botáni•co -ca *adj* botanical ‖ *mf* botanist ‖ *f* botany

botanista *mf* botanist

botar *tr* to throw, hurl; throw away, throw out; (*un buque*) launch; (*el timón*) shift; fire, dismiss; squander ‖ *intr* to jump; bounce ‖ *ref* (*un caballo*) to buck

botarate *m* madcap, wild man; spendthrift

bote *m* boat, small boat; can, jar, pot; bounce; blow, thrust; (Mex) jug, jail; **bote de paso** ferryboat; **bote de porcelana** apothecary's jar; **bote de remos** rowboat; **bote de salvamento** or **bote salvavidas** lifeboat; **bote en bote** crowded, jammed; **de bote y voleo** thoughtlessly

botella *f* bottle

botica *f* drug store; medicine

botica•rio -ria *mf* druggist, apothecary

botija *f* earthenware jug with short narrow neck; (CAm, Ven) hidden treasure; (SAm) belly; **decirle a uno botija verde** (Cuba) to let someone have it, tell someone off; **estar hecho una botija** (*un niño*) to be cross and scream; (*una persona*) be fat, be pudgy

botijo *m* earthenware jar with spout and handle

botín *m* booty, plunder, spoils; spat, legging; (Chile) sock

botina *f* shoe, high shoe

botiquín *m* medicine kit, first-aid kit; medicine chest; first-aid station; (Ven) saloon

bo•to -ta *adj* (*sin filo o punta*) blunt, dull; (fig) dull, slow ‖ *m* leather bag ‖ *f* see **bota**

botón *m* button; (*de mueble o puerta*) knob; (*de reloj de bolsillo*) stem; (bot) bud; (elec) push button; **botón de oro** buttercup; **botón de puerta** doorknob; **botones** *msg* bellboy, bellhop

bou *m* fishing with a dragnet between two boats

bóveda f dome, vault; crypt; (aut) cowl; **bóveda celeste** canopy of heaven
boxeador m boxer; (Mex) brass knuckles
boxear intr to box
boxeo m boxing
bóxer m brass knuckles
boxibalón m punching bag
boya f buoy; **boya salvavidas** life buoy
boyante adj buoyant; lucky, successful; (que no cala lo que debe calar) (naut) light
boyera f or **boyeriza** f ox stable
boyerizo m or **boyero** m ox driver
bozal adj simple, stupid ‖ m muzzle; head-harness bells; headstall
bozo m down on upper lip; lips, mouth; headstall
B.p. abbr **Bendición papal**
Br. abbr **bachiller**
bracear intr to swing the arms; swim with overhead strokes; struggle
brace•ro -ra adj arm, hand; thrown with the hand ‖ m man who offers his arm to a lady; day laborer; migrant worker; **de bracero** arm in arm
bra•co -ca adj pug-nosed
braga f diaper, clout; hoisting rope; **bragas** panties, step-ins; breeches; **calzarse las bragas** to wear the pants
bragadura f crotch
braga•zas m (pl **-zas**) easy mark, henpecked fellow
braguero m (para hernias) truss; (entre-piernas) crotch
bragueta f fly
bragui•llas m (pl **-llas**) brat
brama f rut, mating, mating time
bramante adj bellowing, roaring ‖ m pack-thread, twine
bramar intr to bellow, roar; (el viento) howl; rage, storm
bramido m bellow, roar; howling; raging
brasa f live coal, red-hot coal
brasero m brazier; (Col) bonfire; (Mex) hearth, fireplace
Brasil, el Brazil
brasile•ño -ña adj & mf Brazilian
bravata f bravado, bragging; **echar bravatas** to talk big
bravatear intr to brag, boast
bravear intr to talk big, four-flush
braveza f bravery; ferocity; (de los elementos) fury, violence
bravío -a adj ferocious; wild, untamed, un-cultivated; crude, unpolished; (mar) rough, wild; (terreno) rough, rugged
bra•vo -va adj (valiente) brave; fine, excel-lent; fierce, savage, wild; (mar) rough; magnificent; angry, mad; (perro) vicious; (toro) game; boasting; (chili) strong ‖ interj bravo!
bravu•cón -cona adj four-flushing ‖ mf four-flusher
bravura f bravery, fierceness; gameness; bra-vado, boasting
braza f fathom
brazada f stroke, pull (with the arm); **bra-zada de pecho** breast stroke

brazado m armful, armload
brazal m arm band; **brazal de luto** mourning band
brazalete m bracelet
brazo m arm; (de animal) foreleg; **a brazo partido** hand to hand (i.e., without weap-ons); **asidos del brazo** arm in arm; **brazo derecho** right-hand man; **brazos** hands, workmen; backers; **hecho un brazo de mar** dressed to kill
brea f tar, wood tar; calking substance; pack-ing canvas; **brea seca** rosin
brear tr to annoy, mistreat, beat; tar
brebaje m beverage, drink
brécol m or **brécoles** mpl broccoli
brecha f opening; (en un muro) breach; breakthrough
brega f fight, struggle, quarrel; trickery; drudgery
bregar §44 intr to strive, struggle, toil
breña f or **breñal** m or **breñar** m rocky thicket
breque m brake
brequear tr & intr to brake
bresca f honeycomb
Bretaña f Brittany; **la Gran Bretaña** Great Britain
brete m fetters, shackles; tight squeeze, fix
bretones mpl Brussels sprouts
breva f early fig; cinch, snap
breval m early-fig tree
breve adj brief, short; **en breve** shortly, soon
brevedad f brevity, shortness; **a la mayor brevedad** as soon as possible
brevete m note, mark
brezal m heath, moor
brezo m heath, heather
briba f loafing; **andar a la briba** to loaf around
bri•bón -bona adj loafing, crooked ‖ mf loafer, crook
bribonada f loafing, crookedness
bribonear intr to loaf around, be crooked
brida f bridle
brigada f brigade; gang, squad; warrant of-ficer
brillante adj bright, brilliant, shining ‖ m diamond, gem
brillantez f brilliance
brillantina f brilliantine; metal polish
brillar intr to shine; sparkle
brillazón f (Arg, Bol, Urug) pampa mirage
brillo m brightness, brilliance; sparkle; **sacar brillo a** to shine
brillo•so -sa adj (que brilla por el mucho uso) shiny; shining, brilliant
brin m canvas
brincar §73 tr to bounce up and down; skip; skip over ‖ intr to jump, leap; be touchy, get angry easily
brinco m bounce; jump, leap; **en dos brincos** or **en un brinco** in an instant
brindador m toaster
brindar tr to invite; offer; **brindar a uno con una cosa** to offer someone something ‖ intr — **brindar a** or **por** to drink to, toast ‖ ref — **brindarse a** to offer to

brin•dis *m* (*pl* **-dis**) invitation, treat; toast
brío *m* spirit, enterprise; elegance; **cortar los bríos a** to cut the wings of
brio•so -sa *adj* spirited, lively, enterprising; elegant
brisa *f* breeze; residue of pressed grapes
brisera *f* or **brisero** *m* glass lamp shade (*for candles*)
británi•co -ca *adj* British, Britannic
brita•no -na *adj* British ‖ *mf* Briton, Britisher
brizna *f* chip, particle; (Ven) drizzle
brl. *abbr* **barril**
broca *f* reel, spindle; drill, bit
brocado *m* brocade
brocal *m* (*de pozo*) curbstone; (*de bota*) mouthpiece; (*de banqueta*) (Mex) curb
brocamantón *m* diamond brooch
bróculi *m* broccoli
brocha *f* brush; loaded dice; **de brocha gorda** house (*painter*); (coll) crude, heavy-handed
brochada *f* stroke with a brush; rough sketch
brochazo *m* stroke with a brush
broche *m* clasp, clip, fastener; (*conjunto de dos piezas*) hook and eye; (Chile) paper clip; **broche de oro** punch line; **broche de presión** snap, catch; **broches** (Ecuad) cuff buttons
brocheta *f* skewer
broma *f* joke, jest; fun; shipworm; **bromas aparte** joking aside; **en broma** in fun, jokingly; **gastar una broma a** to play a joke on
bromear *intr & ref* to joke, jest; have a good time
bromhídri•co -ca *adj* hydrobromic
bromista *adj* joking ‖ *mf* joker
bromo *m* bromine
bromuro *m* bromide
bronca *f* row, quarrel; rough joke, poor joke; **armar una bronca** to start a row
bronce *m* bronze; **bronce de cañón** gun metal
broncea•do -da *adj* bronze; tanned, sunburned ‖ *m* bronzing; bronze finish; tan, sunburn
bronceador *m* suntan lotion
broncear *tr, intr & ref* to bronze; tan, sunburn
bron•co -ca *adj* coarse, rough; gruff, crude; (*voz*) harsh, hoarse ‖ *f* see **bronca**
bronquitis *f* bronchitis
broquel *m* buckler, shield; (fig) shield
broqueta *f* skewer
brota *f* bud, shoot
brotadura *f* budding, sprouting; gushing; (*de la piel*) eruption, rash
brotar *tr* to bring forth, produce ‖ *intr* to bud, sprout; gush; (*la piel*) break out
brote *m* bud, shoot; outbreak; (*de petróleo*) gush, spurt
broza *f* (*maleza*) underbrush; (*hojas, ramas, cortezas*) brushwood; (*desperdicio*) trash, rubbish; printer's brush
bruces — **dar** or **caer de bruces** to fall on one's face

bruja *f* witch, sorceress; barn owl; (*mujer fea*) hag; (*mujer de mala vida*) prostitute; (W-I) spook
brujear *tr* (*bestias salvajes*) (Ven) to hunt ‖ *intr* to practice witchcraft
brujería *f* witchcraft, sorcery, magic
brujo *m* sorcerer, wizard
brújula *f* (*flechilla*) magnetic needle; (*instrumento*) compass; (*agujero para la puntería*) sight; **perder la brújula** to lose one's touch
brujulear *tr* (*las cartas*) to uncover gradually; suspect
brulote *m* fire ship; (Arg, Chile, Bol) vulgarity, insult
bruma *f* fog, mist
brumo•so -sa *adj* foggy, misty
bruñido *m* burnish, polish; burnishing
bruñir §12 *tr* to burnish, polish; put rouge on; (CAm) to annoy
brus•co -ca *adj* brusque, gruff; sudden; (*curva*) sharp
bruselas *fpl* tweezers ‖ **Bruselas** Brussels
brusquedad *f* brusqueness, gruffness; suddenness; (*de una curva*) sharpness
brutal *adj* brutal; sudden; huge, terrific; stunning
brutalidad *f* brutality; stupidity; tremendous amount
bruteza *f* brutality; (archaic) roughness
bru•to -ta *adj* brute; rough, coarse; stupid; gross ‖ *mf* (*persona*) brute; blockhead ‖ *m* (*animal*) brute
bu *m* (*pl* **búes**) bugaboo; **hacer el bu a** to scare, frighten
buceador *m* or **buceadora** *f* diver
bucear *intr* to dive, be a diver; delve, search
buceo *m* diving
bucle *m* curl, lock
buche *m* (*de ave*) craw, crop, maw; (*de líquido*) mouthful; (*del vestido*) bag, pucker; (*para secretos*) bosom; belly; (Ecuad) high hat; (Guat, Mex) goiter; **sacar el buche a** to make (*someone*) open up
budín *m* pudding
buen *adj* var of **bueno,** used before masculine singular nouns
buenamente *adv* with ease; gladly, willingly; conveniently
buenaventura *f* fortune, good luck; (*adivinación*) fortune; **decirle a uno la buenaventura** to tell someone his fortune
bue•no -na *adj* good; kind; (*sano*) well; (*tiempo*) good, fine; **a buenas** willingly; **¡buena es ésa** (or **ésta)!** that's a good one; **de buenas a primeras** all of a sudden; from the start; **¿de dónde bueno?** where have you been?, what's new?
buey *m* ox, bullock, steer
búfa•lo -la *mf* buffalo
bufanda *f* muffler, scarf
bufar *intr* to snort
bufete *m* writing desk; law office; (*de un abogado*) clients; law practice; refreshment; (Col) bedpan; **abrir bufete** to open a law office
bufido *m* snort

bu•fo -fa *adj* comic; (Ven) spongy ‖ *mf* buffoon
bu•fón -fona *adj* clownish ‖ *m* clown, buffoon; jester; peddler
bufonada *f* buffoonery; sarcasm
bufonería *f* buffoonery; peddling
bufones•co -ca *adj* clownish; coarse, crude
bugui-bugui *m* boogie-woogie
buharda *f* dormer; dormer window; garret
buhardilla *f* dormer window; garret
buho *m* eagle owl; shy fellow
buhonería *f* peddler's kit; peddler's wares
buhonero *m* peddler, hawker
buitre *m* vulture
buje *m* axle box, bushing
bujería *f* gewgaw, trinket
bujía *f* candle; candlestick; candle power; (*de motor de explosión*) spark plug
bulbo *m* bulb
bulevar *m* boulevard
bulevardero *m* boulevardier, man about town
Bulgaria *f* Bulgaria
búlga•ro -ra *adj* & *mf* Bulgarian
bulimia *f* bulimia
bulto *m* bulk, volume; bust, statue; parcel, piece of baggage; bump, swelling; pillowcase; form, mass; **a bulto** broadly, by guess; **buscar el bulto a** to keep after; **de bulto** evident; **escurrir** or **huir el bulto** to duck
bulla *f* noise; crowd; loud argument
bullaje *m* crush, mob (*of people*)
bullanga *f* racket, disturbance
bullebulle *mf* busybody, bustler
bulle•ro -ra *adj* noisy; inflammatory
bullicio *m* brawl, riot, uprising; (*rumor que hace mucha gente*) rumble
bullicio•so -sa *adj* brawling, riotous; rumbling ‖ *mf* rioter
bullir §13 *tr* to move ‖ *intr* to boil; abound; bustle, hustle; swarm; move, stir; be restless ‖ *ref* to move, stir
buniato *m* sweet potato
buñuelo *m* cruller, fritter, bun; botch, bungle
buque *m* ship, vessel; (*de una nave*) hull; (*de cualquier cosa*) capacity; (C-R) doorframe; **buque almirante**; **buque cisterna** tanker; **buque de guerra** warship; **buque de vapor** steamer, steamship; **buque de vela** sailboat; **buque escucha** vedette; **buque escuela** training ship; **buque fanal** or **buque faro** lightship; **buque mercante** merchantman, merchant vessel; **buque portaminas** mine layer; **buque tanque** tanker; **buque velero** sailing vessel
burbuja *f* bubble
burbujear *intr* to bubble
burdégano *m* hinny
burdel *m* brothel, disorderly house
Burdeos Bordeaux
bur•do -da *adj* coarse, rough
burear *tr* (Col) to fool ‖ *intr* to have fun
burga *f* hot springs
bur•gués -guesa *adj* middle-class, bourgeois; (*antiartístico*) bourgeois ‖ *m* middle-class man ‖ *f* middle-class woman

burguesía *f* middle class, bourgeoisie; **alta burguesía** upper middle class; **pequeña burguesía** lower middle class
burla *f* hoax, trick; joke; ridicule; **burlas aparte** joking aside; **de burlas** in fun, for fun
burladero *m* safety island, safety zone; (*en las plazas de toros*) covert; (*en los túneles*) safety niche; hiding place
burla•dor -dora *adj* joking; deceptive ‖ *mf* wag, prankster, practical joker ‖ *m* seducer, libertine
burlar *tr* to make fun of; deceive; disappoint; outwit, frustrate; (*a una mujer*) seduce ‖ *intr* to scoff ‖ *ref* to joke; **burlarse de** to make fun of
burlería *f* derision, mockery; deception, trick; scorn, derision; fish story
burles•co -ca *adj* funny, comic, burlesque
burlete *m* weather stripping
bur•lón -lona *adj* joking ‖ *mf* joker ‖ *m* mockingbird
bu•ró *m* (*pl* **-rós**) writing desk; (Mex) night table
burócrata *mf* jobholder, bureaucrat
burra *f* she-ass; stupid woman; drudge (*woman*)
burrajear *tr* & *intr* to scribble; doodle
burra•jo -ja *adj* (Mex) coarse, stupid ‖ *m* dung (*used as fuel*)
bu•rro -rra *adj* stupid, asinine ‖ *m* donkey, jackass; sawbuck, sawhorse; (Mex) stepladder; **burro cargado de letras** learned jackass; **burro de carga** drudge ‖ *f* see **burra**
bursátil *adj* stock-market
busca *f* search; **en busca de** in search of
buscani•guas *m* (*pl* **-guas**) (Col) snake
buscapié *m* (*para dar a entender algo*) hint; (*para averiguar algo*) feeler ‖ **busca•piés** *m* (*pl* **-piés**) snake
buscaplei•tos *mf* (*pl* **-tos**) troublemaker
buscar §73 *tr* to seek, hunt, look for; (Mex) to provoke; **buscar tres pies al gato** to be looking for trouble ‖ *ref* to take care of oneself; **buscársela** to manage to get along; to ask for it
buscareta *f* wren
buscarrui•dos *mf* (*pl* **-dos**) troublemaker
buscavi•das *mf* (*pl* **-das**) snoop, busybody; go-getter
bus•cón -cona *adj* searching; cheating ‖ *mf* seeker; thief, cheat; (min) prospector ‖ *f* loose woman
busi•lis *m* (*pl* **-lis**) trouble; **ahí está el busilis** that's the trouble; **dar en el busilis** to hit the nail on the head
búsqueda *f* search, hunt
busto *m* bust
butaca *f* armchair, easy chair; orchestra seat
butifarra *f* Catalonian sausage; loose sock, loose stocking; (Peru) ham and salad sandwich
bution•do -da *adj* lewd, lustful
buz *m* (*pl* **buces**) kiss of gratitude and reverence; lip; **hacer el buz** (archaic) to bow and scrape

buzo *m* diver
buzón *m* plug, stopper; mailbox, letter box; (*agujero para echar las cartas*) slot, letter

drop; **buzón de alcance** special-delivery box; late-collection slot

C

C, c (ce) *f* third letter of the Spanish alphabet
c. *abbr* **capítulo, compañía, corriente, cuenta**
c *abbr* **caja, cargo, contra, corriente**
cabal *adj* exact; full, complete, perfect; **no estar en sus cabales** to be not in one's right mind ‖ *adv* exactly; completely ‖ *interj* right!
cábala *f* intrigue; divination
cabalgada *f* raid on horseback; gathering of riders
cabalgador *m* rider, horseman
cabalgadura *f* mount, horse; beast of burden
cabalgar §44 *intr* to go horseback riding
cabalgata *f* cavalcade
caballa *f* mackerel
caballada *f* drove of horses; nonsense, stupidity
caballaje *m* stud service
caballazo *m* collision of two horses, trampling by a horse; (Chile, Peru) bitter attack
caballerango *m* (Mex) stableman
caballeres•co -ca *adj* chivalric, knightly; gentlemanly
caballerete *m* (coll) dude
caballería *f* mount, horse, mule; cavalry; chivalry, knighthood; **andarse en caballerías** to fall all over oneself in compliments; **caballería andante** knight-errantry; **caballería mayor** horse, mule; **cabellería menor** ass, donkey
caballeriza *f* stable; stable hands
caballerizo *m* groom, stableman
caballe•ro -ra *adj* riding, mounted; stubborn ‖ *m* knight, nobleman; gentleman; mister; horseman, cavalier, rider; **armar caballero** to knight; **caballero andante** knight errant; **caballero de industria** crook, adventurer, sharper; **Caballero de la triste figura** Knight of the Rueful Countenance (*Don Quijote*); **ir caballero en** to ride
caballerosidad *f* chivalry, gentlemanliness
caballerote *m* boorish fellow, cad
caballete *m* (*bastidor para sostener un cuadro o pizarra*) easel; (*de tejado*) ridge, hip; (*lomo de tierra*) ridge; (*artificio usado como soporte*) trestle, sawbuck, horse; (*de la nariz*) bridge; chimney cap; (*del ave*) breastbone; little horse
caballista *m* horseman; mounted smuggler ‖ *f* horsewoman
caballito *m* little horse; merry-go-round; **caballito del diablo** dragonfly
caballo *m* horse; (*en ajedrez*) knight; playing card (*figure on horseback equivalent to*

queen); (slang) heroin; **a caballo** on horseback; **a caballo de** astride; **a caballo regalado no se le mira el diente** never look a gift horse in the mouth; **caballo blanco** (*persona que da dinero para una empresa dudosa*) angel; **caballo de batalla** battle horse; (*de una controversia*) gist, main point; (*aquello en que uno sobresale*) forte, strong point; **caballo de carreras** race horse; **caballo de fuerza** French horsepower, metric horsepower; **caballo de tiro** draft horse; **caballo de Troya** Trojan horse; **caballo de vapor** French horsepower, metric horsepower; **caballo de vapor inglés** horsepower; **caballo mecedor** rocking horse, hobbyhorse; **caballo padre** stallion; **caballo semental** stallion
caballu•no -na *adj* horse, horselike
cabaña *f* cabin, hut; drove, flock; livestock; pastoral scene; (Arg) cattlebreeding ranch
cabañuelas *fpl* (Arg, Bol) first summer rains; (Mex) winter rains
caba•ret *m* (*pl* **-rets**) cabaret
cabecear *tr* (*un libro*) to put a headband on; (*el vino*) head; (*una media*) put a new foot on ‖ *intr* to nod; bob the head; (*en señal de negación*) shake the head; (*los caballos*) toss the head; (*la caja de un carruaje*) lurch; (*un buque*) pitch
cabeceo *m* (*de la cabeza*) nod, bob, shake; (*de la caja del carruaje*) lurching; (*del buque*) pitch, pitching
cabecera *f* (*de cama, mesa, etc.*) head; bedside; headboard; headwaters; (*de una casa, un campo*) end; (*del capítulo de un libro*) heading; (*de periódico*) headline; capital, county seat; bolster, pillow; (typ) headpiece, vignette; **cabecera de cartel** top billing; **cabecera de puente** (mil) bridgehead
cabecilla *mf* scalawag ‖ *m* ringleader ‖ *f* **cabecilla de alfiler** pinhead
cabellar *intr* to grow hair; to put on false hair ‖ *ref* to put on false hair
cabellera *f* head of hair; foliage; (*del cometa*) coma; (bot) mistletoe
cabello *m* hair; **cabello de Venus** maidenhair; **cabellos de ángel** cotton candy; **en cabello** with the hair down; **en cabellos** bareheaded; **traído por los cabellos** farfetched
cabellu•do -da *adj* hairy
caber §14 *intr* to fit, go; have enough room; be possible; happen, befall; **no cabe duda** there is no doubt; **no cabe más** that's the

limit; **no caber de** to be bursting with; **no caber en sí** to be beside oneself; be puffed up with pride; **todo cabe en** anything can be expected of

cabestrar *tr* to put a halter on

cabestrillo *m* sling

cabestro *m* halter; **llevar** or **traer del cabestro** to lead by the halter; (fig) to lead by the nose

cabeza *f* head; chief city, capital; **cabeza de chorlito** scatterbrains; (Arg) forgetful person; **cabeza de motín** ringleader; **cabeza de playa** beachhead; **cabeza de puente** bridgehead; **cabeza de turco** butt, scapegoat; **cabeza mayor** head of cattle; **cabeza menor** head of sheep, goats, etc.; **de cabeza** headfirst; on end; on one's own; by heart; **ir cabeza abajo** to go downhill; **irse de la cabeza** to go out of one's mind; **mala cabeza** headstrong person; **por su cabeza** on one's own; **romperse la cabeza** to rack one's brains

cabezada *f* butt with the head; blow on the head; (*de buque*) pitch, pitching; (*de bota*) instep; (*de libro*) headband; **dar cabezadas** to nod; (*un buque*) to pitch

cabezal *m* pillow, cushion; bolster

cabezo *m* hillock; summit, peak; reef

cabe•zón -zona *adj* big-headed; stubborn; (*licor*) (Chile) strong ‖ *m* (*en la ropa*) hole for the head; tax register

cabezonada *f* stubbornness

cabezu•do -da *adj* big-headed; headstrong; (*vino*) heady

cabezuela *f* little head; (*harina gruesa del trigo*) middling; cornflower

cabida *f* room, space, capacity; influence, pull; **tener cabida en** to be included in

cabildear *intr* to lobby

cabildeo *m* lobbying

cabildero *m* lobbyist

cabildo *m* chapter (*of a cathedral*); chapter meeting; town hall

cabina *f* cabin; (*locutorio del teléfono*) booth; bathhouse, dressing room

cabio *m* rafter; joist

cabizba•jo -ja *adj* crestfallen, downcast

cable *m* cable; rope, hawser; **cable de remolque** towline; **cable de retén** guy wire

cablegrafiar §77 *tr & intr* to cable

cablegráfi•co -ca *adj* cable

cablegrama *m* cablegram

cabo *m* end, tip; (*punta de tierra que penetra en el mar*) cape; (*mango*) handle; small bundle; small piece; boss, foreman; cord, rope, cable; (mil) corporal; **al cabo** finally, at last; **al cabo de** at the end of; **atar cabos** (coll) to put two and two together; **Cabo de Buena Esperanza** Cape of Good Hope; **Cabo de Hornos** Cape Horn; **cabos** (*de caballo*) paws, nose, and mane; eyes, eyebrows, and hair; clothing; **cabo suelto** loose end; **estar al cabo de** to be well informed about; **llevar a cabo** to carry out, to accomplish

cabotaje *m* coasting trade

cabra *f* goat; nanny goat; (Chile) light two-wheel carriage; (Chile) sawbuck; (Col, Cuba, Ven) trick, gyp, loaded dice; **cabras** light clouds

cabrahigo wild fig

cabrería *f* goat stable; goat-milk dairy

cabre•ro -ra *mf* goatherd

cabrestante *m* capstan

cabrilla *f* sawbuck, sawhorse; (ichth) grouper; **cabrillas** skipping stones; (*olas blancas en el mar*) whitecaps

cabrillear *intr* (*el mar*) to be covered with whitecaps; shimmer

cabrio *m* rafter; joist

cabrí•o -a *adj* goat; goatish ‖ *m* herd of goats

cabriola *f* caper; somersault; **dar cabriolas** to cut capers

cabriolear *intr* to caper, frisk, prance

cabritilla *f* kid, kidskin

cabrito *m* kid; **cabritos** (Chile) popcorn

cabrón *m* buck, billy goat; complaisant cuckold; (Chile) pimp

cabronada *f* shamelessness; shameless forbearance

cabru•no -na *adj* goat

cacahuate *adj* (Mex) pocked ‖ *m* peanut

cacahuete *m* peanut

cacahuete•ro -ra *mf* peanut vendor

cacalote *m* (Mex) raven; (CAm, Mex) candied popcorn; (Cuba) break, blunder

cacao *m* chocolate tree; cocoa, chocolate; **pedir cacao** to call quits; **tener mucho cacao** (Guat) to have a lot of pep

cacaraña *f* pit, pock

cacarear *tr* to crow over, boast of ‖ *intr* (*la gallina*) to cackle; (*el gallo*) crow

cacareo *m* (*de la gallina*) cackling; (*del gallo*) crowing; (*de una persona*) (coll) crowing, boasting

cacatúa *f* cockatoo

cacea *f* trolling; **pescar a la cacea** to troll

cacear *tr* to stir with a dipper or ladle ‖ *intr* to troll

cacería *f* hunting; hunting party; (*animales cobrados en la caza*) bag; hunting scene

cacerola *f* casserole, saucepan

cacique *m* Indian chief; bossy fellow; (*en asuntos políticos*) (coll) boss; (Chile) lazy lummox; **cacique veranero** Baltimore oriole, hangbird

caciquismo *m* bossism

cacle *m* (Mex) sandal

caco *m* thief, pickpocket; coward

cacto *m* cactus

cacumen *m* summit; acumen, keen insight

cacha•co -ca *adj* (SAm) sporty ‖ *m* (SAm) sport, dude

cachada *f* thrust or wound made with the horns

cachalote *m* sperm whale

cachar *tr* to break to pieces; (*la madera*) slit, split; to butt with the horns; (Arg, Ecuad, Urug) to make fun of; (Chile) to grasp, understand

cacharpari *m* (Arg, Bol, Peru) send-off party

cacharro *m* crock, earthen pot; piece of crockery; piece of junk; (CAm, W-I) jail; (Col) trinket

cachaza *f* sloth, phlegm; rum; first froth on cane juice when boiled

cachazu•do -da *adj* slothful, phlegmatic ‖ *mf* sluggard

cachear *tr* to frisk

cacheo *m* frisking

cachetada *f* box on the ear

cachete *m* slap in the face; cheek, swollen cheek; dagger

cachetear *tr* to box on the ear

cachetero *m* dagger; dagger man

cachetina *f* brawl, fistfight

cachicuer•no -na *adj* horn-handled

cachillada *f* brood, litter

cachimba *f* (*para fumar*) pipe; (Arg, Urug) well, spring; (Chile) revolver

cachimbo *m* (*para fumar*) pipe; (Cuba) sugar mill; **chupar cachimbo** (Ven) to smoke a pipe; (*un niño*) (Ven) to suck its finger

cachiporra *f* billy, bludgeon

cachivache *m* good-for-nothing; **cachivaches** broken pottery; pots and pans; junk, trash

cacho *m* slice, piece; (*mercadería que no se vende*) (Chile) drug on the market

cachón *m* (*ola de agua*) breaker; splash of water; **cachones** surf

cachon•do -da *adj* (*perra*) in rut; sexy

cacho•rro -rra *mf* cub, whelp, pup ‖ *m* little pistol

cachucha *f* rowboat; cap; Andalusian dance

cachuela *f* gizzard; fricassee of pork

cachu•pín -pina *mf* (CAm, Mex) Spanish settler in Latin America

cada *adj* each; every; **cada vez más** more and more; **cada vez que** whenever

cadalso *m* stand, platform; (*para la ejecución de un reo*) scaffold

cadarzo *m* floss, floss silk

cadáver *m* corpse, cadaver

cadavéri•co -ca *adj* cadaverous

cadena *f* chain; (telv) network; **cadena antirresbaladiza** (aut) skid chain; **cadena de presidiarios** chain gang; **cadena perpetua** life imprisonment

cadencia *f* cadence, rhythm

cadencio•so -sa *adj* rhythmical

cadenero *m* (surv) lineman

cadera *f* hip

cadete *m* (mil) cadet; (Arg, Bol) apprentice (*without pay*), errand boy

cadillo *m* burdock

cadmio *m* cadmium

caducar §73 *intr* to be in one's dotage; be worn out; lapse, expire

caducidad *f* feebleness; expiration

caedi•zo -za *adj* tottery, ready to fall over ‖ *m* lean-to

caer §15 *intr* to fall; droop; fall due; be, be found; fade; (*el sol, el día, el viento*) decline; happen; **caer a** to face, overlook; **caer bien** to fit; be becoming; make a hit; **caer de plano** to fall flat; **caer en** (*cierto día*) to come on, fall on, happen on; (*cierta página*) be found on; **caer en cama** to fall

ill; **caer en favor** to be in favor; **caer en la cuenta** to catch on, get the point; **caer en que** to realize that; **caer mal** to fit badly; be unbecoming; fall flat; **no caigo** (coll) I don't get it ‖ *ref* to fall, fall down; be, be found; **caerse de su peso, caerse de suyo** to be self-evident; **caerse muerto de** (*p.ej., alegría, miedo, risa*) to be overcome with

café *adj* tan ‖ *m* coffee; coffee tree; coffee house; café; (Arg) reprimand; (Mex) tantrum; **café cantante** night club; **café de maquinilla** drip coffee; **café solo** black coffee

cafetal *m* coffee plantation

cafetalero *m* (SAm) coffee planter; coffee dealer

cafetear *intr* to drink coffee

cafetera *f* coffee pot; (Arg) jalopy; **cafetera eléctrica** electric percolator

cafetería *f* cafeteria

cafete•ro -ra *adj* coffee ‖ *mf* coffee dealer; coffee-bean picker ‖ *f* see **cafetera**

cafeto *m* coffee tree

cagar §44 *tr* to spot, stain, spoil ‖ *intr* to defecate ‖ *ref* to defecate; be scared

cagatin•ta *m* or **cagatin•tas** *m* (*pl* -tas) office drudge, penpusher

ca•gón -gona *adj* cowardly ‖ *mf* coward

caída *f* fall; spill, tumble; drop; failure; blunder, slip; (*de una cortina*) hang; **a la caída de la noche** at nightfall; **a la caída del sol** at sunset; **caída de agua** waterfall; **caída radiactiva** fallout; **caídas** coarse wool; witticisms

caí•do -da *adj* fallen; (*cuello*) turndown; (*párpado, hombro*) drooping; dejected; crestfallen; **caído en desuso** obsolete ‖ **caídos** *mpl* interest due; **los caídos** (*en la guerra*) the fallen ‖ *f* see **caída**

caimán *m* alligator; schemer

Caín *m* Cain; **pasar las de Caín** (coll) to have a frightful time

Cairo, El Cairo

caja *f* box; case, chest, coffer; (*de caudales*) safe, strongbox; (*para dinero contante*) cashbox; (*dinero contante*) cash; (*ataúd*) casket, coffin; (*de reloj de bolsillo*) case; (*donde se pagan las cuentas en los hoteles*) desk; cashier's desk; (*del aparato de radio o televisión*) cabinet; (*de coche*) body; (*tambor*) drum; (*de fusil*) stock; (*de ascensor, de escalera*) shaft, well; (mach) housing; (typ) case; **caja alta** upper case; **caja baja** lower case; **caja clara** snare drum; **caja de ahorros** savings bank; **caja de cambio de marchas** transmission-gear box; **caja de caudales** safe; **caja de cigüeñal** crankcase; **caja de colores** paintbox; **caja de embalaje** packing box or case; **caja de enchufe** (elec) outlet; **caja de engranajes** gear case; **caja de fuego** firebox; **caja de fusibles** fuse box; **caja de ingletes** miter box; **caja de menores** petty cash; **caja de registro** manhole; **caja de reloj** watchcase; **caja de seguridad** safe; safe-deposit box; **caja de sorpresa** jack-in-the-box; **caja de velocidades** transmission-gear box; **caja fuerte** safe, bank vault; **caja postal de ahorros** postal savings bank; **caja registradora** cash register; **despedir** or **echar con cajas destempladas** to send packing, give the gate

caje•ro -ra *mf* boxmaker; (*en un banco*) cashier, teller; (*en un hotel*) desk clerk

cajeta *f* little box; tobacco box; **de cajeta** (CAm, Mex) fine

cajetilla *f* pack (*of cigarettes*)

cajetín *m* rubber stamp; (typ) box

cajista *mf* compositor

cajón *m* large box, bin; (*caja movible de un mueble*) drawer; (*que se cierra con llave*) locker; (*que sirve de tienda*) booth, stall; (Chile) long gully; (Mex) dry-goods store; (SAm) coffin; **cajón de aire comprimido** caisson; **cajón de sastre** (coll) odds and ends; muddlehead; **ser de cajón** to be in vogue, be the thing

cal *f* lime; **cal apagada** slaked lime; **cal viva** quicklime; **de cal y canto** strong, tough

cala *f* calla lily; cove, inlet; (*de fruta*) sample slice; (*de buque*) hold; suppository

calabacear *tr* (*a un alumno*) to flunk; (*una mujer a un pretendiente*) to jilt

calabacera *f* calabash, pumpkin, squash

calabaza *f* calabash, gourd, pumpkin, squash; dolt; **dar calabaza** a (*un alumno*) to flunk; (*un pretendiente*) to jilt

calabo•bos *m* (*pl* **-bos**) steady drizzle

calabocero *m* jailer, warden

calabozo *m* dungeon; cell, prison cell

calada *f* soaking; (*del ave de rapiña*) swoop; scolding

calado *m* openwork, drawn work; fretwork; (*del agua*) depth; (naut) draught

calafatear *tr* to calk

calafateo *m* calking

calamar *m* squid

calambre *m* cramp

calamidad *f* calamity

calamita *f* magnetic needle

calamito•so -sa *adj* calamitous

cálamo *m* reed, stalk; (poet) pen; (poet) flute, reed

calamoca•no -na *adj* (*algo embriagado*) tipsy; (*chocho*) doddering

calaña *f* nature, kind; pattern; fan

calar *tr* to pierce; soak; wedge; cut open work in; (*un melón*) cut a plug in; (*la bayoneta*) fix; (*un puente levadizo*) lower; (*las redes de pesca*) lower in the water; (*un buque cierta profundidad*) draw; (*a una persona o las intenciones de una persona*) size up, see through; (Arg) to stare at ‖ *ref* to get soaked, get drenched; (*introducirse*) slip in; (*el ave de rapiña*) swoop down; miss fire; (*el sombrero*) pull down tight; (*las gafas*) stick on; **calarse hasta los huesos** to get soaked to the skin

cala•to -ta *adj* (Peru) naked; (Peru) penniless

calavera *m* daredevil; libertine ‖ *f* skull; (*imitación de la calavera*) death's-head; (Mex) tail light

calaverada *f* recklessness, daredeviltry; escapade

calaverear *tr* to spoil, make ugly ‖ *intr* to act recklessly; go on a spree

calcado *m* tracing

calcañal *m* or **calcañar** *m* heel

calcar §73 *tr* to trace; copy, imitate; tread on

calce *m* wedge; iron tire; iron tip; (*de un documento*) (CAm, Mex, P-R) bottom, foot

calceta *f* stocking; fetter, shackle; **hacer calceta** to knit

calcetería *f* hosiery; hosiery shop

calcete•ro -ra *mf* hosier; stocking mender

calcetín *m* sock

calcificar §73 *tr* & *ref* to calcify

calcio *m* calcium

calco *m* tracing; copy, imitation

calcula•dor -dora *adj* calculating; (*egoísta, interesado*) (fig) calculating ‖ *mf* calculator ‖ *f* calculating machine; **calculadora de bolsillo** pocket calculator

calcular *tr* & *intr* to calculate; (*suponer*) (fig) calculate

cálculo *m* calculation; (math, pathol) calculus; **cálculo biliar** gallstone; **cálculo renal** kidney stone

calchona *f* (Chile) goblin, bogey; (Chile) witch, old hag

calda *f* heating, warming; **caldas** hot springs

caldeamiento *m* heating

caldear *tr* to heat; weld ‖ *ref* to get hot; get overheated

caldeo *m* heating; welding

caldera *f* boiler; pot, kettle; (Arg) coffee pot, teapot

calderero *m* boilermaker

calderilla *f* holy-water vessel; copper coin; small change; mountain currant

caldero *m* kettle, pot; (*reloj de bolsillo*) (Arg) turnip

calderón *m* caldron; (*signo*) (mus) pause, hold

caldillo *m* light broth; sauce for fricassee; (Mex) meat bits in broth

caldo *m* broth; sauce, gravy, dressing; salad dressing; (Mex) syrup; (Mex) sugar-cane juice; **caldo de la reina** eggnog; **caldos** wet goods

calefacción *f* heating; **calefacción por agua caliente** hot-water heat; **calefacción por aire caliente** hot-air heat

calefactor *m* heater man; (electron) heater, heater element

calefón *m* (Arg) hot-water heater

calendar *tr* to date

calendario *m* calendar; **hacer calendarios** to meditate; to make wild predictions

calenta•dor -dora *adj* heating ‖ *m* heater; warming pan; (*reloj de bolsillo*) turnip; **calentador a gas** gas heater; **calentador de agua** water heater

calentamiento *m* heating

calentar §2 *tr* to heat; warm; beat; (Chile) to bore, annoy; **calentar la silla** (*detenerse demasiado*) to warm a chair ‖ *ref* to heat up, run hot; warm oneself; warm up; (*estar en celo las bestias*) be in heat; (Chile, Ven) to become annoyed, get angry

calentón *m* warm-up; **darse un calentón** to stop and warm up

calentura *f* fever, temperature

calenturien•to -ta *adj* feverish; exalted; (Chile) consumptive

calenturón *m* high fever

calenturo•so -sa *adj* feverish

calera *f* limekiln; limestone quarry

calesa *f* chaise

caleta *f* cove, inlet

caletre *m* judgment, acumen

calibrador *m* calipers; **calibrador de alambre** wire gauge

calibrar *tr* to calibrate; to gauge

calibre *m* caliber; gauge; bore, diameter

calicanto *m* rubble masonry

cali•có *m* (*pl* **-cós**) calico

calidad *f* quality; condition, term; rank, nobility; importance; **a calidad de que** provided that; **calidad de vida** quality of life; **en calidad de** in the capacity of

cáli•do -da *adj* warm, hot

calidoscopio *m* kaleidoscope

calientaca•mas *m* (*pl* **-mas**) bed warmer

calienta•piés *m* (*pl* **-piés**) foot warmer

caliente *adj* hot; fiery, vehement; (*en celo*) hot; **caliente de cascos** hotheaded; **en caliente** while hot; at once

califa *m* caliph

califato *m* caliphate

calificación *f* qualification; (*nota en un examen*) grade, mark; rating, standing

calificar §73 *tr* to qualify; certify; ennoble; (*un examen*) mark; (*en los registros electorales*) (Chile) to register ‖ *ref* (archaic) to prove one's noble birth; (*en los registros electorales*) (Chile) to register

calificati•vo -va *adj* qualifying ‖ *m* (*nota en la escuela*) grade, mark; (*en un diccionario*) usage label

California *f* California; **la Baja California** Lower California

caligrafía *f* penmanship

calina *f* haze

calino•so -sa *adj* hazy

Calíope *f* Calliope

calipso *m* calypso ‖ **Calipso** *f* Calypso

calistenia *f* calisthenics

calisténi•co -ca *adj* calisthenic

cá•liz *m* (*pl* **-lices**) chalice; **cáliz de dolor** cup of sorrow

cali•zo -za *adj* lime, limestone ‖ *f* limestone

calma *f* calm; calm weather; quiet, tranquillity; slowness; (*cesación*) letup, suspension; **calma chicha** dead calm; **calmas ecuatoriales** doldrums; **en calma** in suspension; (*mercado*) steady; (*mar*) calm, smooth

calmante *adj* soothing; pain-relieving ‖ *m* sedative

calmar *tr* to calm, soothe ‖ *intr* to grow calm; abate ‖ *ref* to calm down

calmazo *m* dead calm

cal•mo -ma *adj* barren, treeless; fallow, uncultivated ‖ *f* see **calma**

calmo•so -sa *adj* calm; slow, lazy

calmu•do -da *adj* calm; (*viento*) (naut) light; (*tiempo*) (naut) mild

caló *m* gypsy slang, underworld slang

calofriar §77 *ref* to become chilled

calofrío *m* chill

calor *m* heat; warmth; (fig) warmth, enthusiasm; **hace calor** it is hot, it is warm; **tener calor** (*una persona*) to be hot, be warm

calorífe•ro -ra *adj* heat ‖ *m* heater, furnace; heating system; foot warmer

calorífu•go -ga *adj* heatproof; fireproof

caloro•so -sa *adj* warm, hot; (fig) warm, enthusiastic, hearty

calotear *tr* (Arg) to gyp, cheat

calpul *m* (Guat) gathering, meeting; (Hond) Indian mound

caluma *f* (Peru) gorge in the Andes; (Peru) Indian hamlet

calumnia *f* calumny, slander

calumniar *tr* to slander

calumnio•so -sa *adj* slanderous

caluro•so -sa *adj* warm, hot; (fig) warm, enthusiastic, hearty

calva *f* bald spot; bare spot, clearing; (*en un tejido*) worn spot

calvario *m* (*sufrimiento moral*) cross; series of misfortunes; string of debts ‖ **Calvario** *m* Calvary; Stations of the Cross

calvero *m* clearing; clay pit

calvez *f* or **calvicie** *f* baldness

cal•vo -va *adj* bald; barren, bare ‖ *f* see **calva**

calza *f* wedge; stocking; **calzas** hose, breeches, tights; **en calzas prietas** in a tight fix

calzada *f* highway, causeway; (S-D) sidewalk

calzado *m* footwear, shoes

calzador *m* shoehorn

calzar §60 *tr* to shoe, put shoes on; provide with shoes; (*cierto tamaño de zapatos, guantes, etc.*) wear, take; (*un zapato a una persona*) fit; wedge; (*una rueda*) block, scotch; (*la pata de una mesa*) block up; tip or trim with iron; (*plantas*) (hort) to hill ‖ *intr* (Arg) to get the place sought; **calzar bien** to wear good footwear; **calzar mal** to wear poor footwear ‖ *ref* to get; (*zapatos, guantes*) put on, wear; put one's shoes on; (*a una persona*) dominate, manage

calzo *m* wedge; chock, skid

calzón *m* trousers, pants; **calzones** trousers, breeches; **calzarse los calzones** to wear the pants

calzonarias *fpl* (Col) suspenders

calzona•zos *m* (*pl* **-zos**) jellyfish; henpecked husband

calzoncillos *mpl* underdrawers

callada *f* (naut) abatement, lull; **a las calladas** or **de callada** on the quiet; **dar la callada por respuesta** to give no answer

calla•do -da *adj* silent; mysterious, secret ‖ *f* see **callada**

callampa *f* (Chile) felt hat; (Chile) large ear; (Chile) mushroom

callana *f* (SAm) Indian baking bowl; (*reloj de bolsillo*) (Chile) turnip; (Chile) behind; (Chile, Peru) flowerpot

callao *m* pebble

ca
ca

callar _tr_ to silence; not mention; (_un secreto_) keep; calm, quiet ‖ _intr & ref_ to become silent, keep silent; keep quiet, keep still; **callarse la boca** (coll) to shut up, clam up
calle _f_ street; **calle de travesía** cross street; **calle mayor** main street; **dejar en la calle** to deprive of one's livelihood
calleja _f_ side street, alley; subterfuge, pretext
callejear _intr_ to walk around the streets, to ramble around
calleje•ro -ra _adj_ street; gadabout ‖ _m_ street guide; list of addresses of newspaper subscribers
callejón _m_ alley, lane; **callejón sin salida** blind alley
callejuela _f_ side street, alley; subterfuge, pretext
callicida _m_ corn cure
callo _m_ callus; (_en el pie_) corn; **callos** tripe
callo•so -sa _adj_ callous
cama _f_ bed; (_para las bestias_) bedding, litter; **cama imperial** four-poster; **cama turca** day bed; **guardar cama** to be sick in bed
camachuelo _m_ (orn) bullfinch
camada _f_ brood, litter; layer, stratum; (_de ladrones_) den
camafeo _m_ cameo
camaleón _m_ chameleon
cámara _f_ chamber; hall; (_cuerpo legislador_) house, chamber; (_aparato fotográfico_) camera; (_tubo de goma del neumático_) inner tube; (_del arma de fuego_) chamber, breech; (_para cartuchos_) magazine; board, council; (_mueble donde se conservan los alimentos_) icebox; (_evacuación_) bowels; (aer) cockpit; **cámara agrícola** grange; **cámara ardiente** funeral chamber; **cámara cinematografica** movie camera; **cámara de combustión** (aut) combustion chamber; **cámara de compensación** clearing house; **cámara de fuelle** folding camera; **cámara de las máquinas** (naut) engine room; **Cámara de los Comunes** House of Commons; **Cámara de los Lores** House of Lords; **cámara de oxígeno** oxygen tent; **Cámara de Representantes** House of Representatives; **cámara frigorífica** cold-storage room; **cámara indiscreta** candid camera; **cámaras** loose bowels
camarada _m_ comrade
camarera _f_ waitress; chambermaid, maid; (_en los barcos_) stewardess; (_que sirve a una reina o princesa_) lady in waiting
camarero _m_ waiter; valet; (_en un barco o avión_) steward
camarilla _f_ clique, coterie, cabal; palace coterie
camarín _m_ boudoir; (theat) dressing room
cámaro _m_ var of **camarón**
camarógrafo _m_ cameraman
camarón _m_ shrimp, prawn; (CAm, Col) tip, gratuity; (Ven) nap; **ponerse como un camarón** to blush
camarote _m_ stateroom, cabin
camasquin•ce _mf_ (_pl_ **-ce**) meddlesome person, kibitzer
cambalachar _tr & intr_ var of **cambalachear**

cambalache _m_ exchange, swap; (Arg) second-hand shop
cambalachear _tr_ to swap, exchange, trade off ‖ _intr_ to swap, exchange
cambiadis•cos _m_ (_pl_ **-cos**) record changer
cambiante _adj_ changing; fickle; iridescent ‖ **cambiantes** _mpl_ iridescence
cambiar _tr_ to change; exchange ‖ _intr_ to change; **cambiar de** (_p.ej., sombreros, ropa, trenes_) change; **cambiar de marcha** to shift gears ‖ _ref_ to change
cambiavía _m_ switch; switchman
cambio _m_ change; exchange; rate of exchange; (aut) shift; (rr) switch; **cambio de marchas, cambio de velocidades** gearshift; **en cambio** on the other hand
cambista _mf_ moneychanger; banker ‖ _m_ (Arg) switchman
cambullón _m_ (Mex, Col, Ven) barter, exchange; (Chile) subversion; (Peru) scheming, trickery
camelar _tr_ to flirt with; cajole, tease
camelo _m_ flirtation; joke; false rumor
camellero _m_ camel driver
camello _m_ camel
camellón _m_ drinking trough; flower bed
came•ro -ra _adj_ bed ‖ _mf_ maker of bedding ‖ _m_ (Col) highway
camilla _f_ stretcher; couch; round table with heater underneath; (Mex) clothing store
camillero _m_ stretcher-bearer
caminante _mf_ walker; traveler on foot ‖ _m_ groom attending his master's horse
caminar _tr_ (_cierta distancia_) to walk ‖ _intr_ to walk; go; travel, journey; behave
caminata _f_ long walk, hike; outing, jaunt
camine•ro -ra _adj_ road, highway
camino _m_ road, way; (_viaje_) journey; (_tira larga que se pone en mesas o pisos_) (SAm) runner; **a medio camino (entre)** halfway (between); **camino de** on the way to; **camino de herradura** bridle path; **camino de hierro** railway; **camino de ruedas** wagon road; **Camino de Santiago** Way of St. James (_Milky Way_); **camino de sirga** towpath; **camino de tierra** dirt road; **camino real** highroad; **camino trillado** beaten path; **echar camino adelante** to strike out
camión _m_ truck, motor truck; (Mex) bus; **camión volquete** dump truck
camionaje _m_ trucking
camione•ro -ra _adj_ truck ‖ _m_ trucker, teamster
camioneta _f_ light truck; station wagon
camionetilla _f_ (Guat) station wagon
camión-grua _m_ tow truck
camionista _m_ trucker, teamster
camisa _f_ (_de hombre_) shirt; (_de mujer_) chemise; (_de la culebra_) slough; (_de un libro_) jacket; (_para papeles_) folder; (_de una pieza mecánica_) jacket, casing; (_de un horno de fundición_) lining; **camisa de agua** water jacket; **camisa de dormir** nightshirt; **camisa de fuerza** strait jacket; **cambiarse la camisa** to become a turncoat
camisería _f_ haberdashery; shirt factory

camise•ro -ra *mf* haberdasher; shirt maker
camiseta *f* undershirt; (*de traje de baño*) top
camisola *f* stiff shirt
camisolín *m* dickey, shirt front
camón *m* bay window; **camón de vidrios** glass partition
camorra *f* quarrel, row; **armar camorra** to raise Cain, raise a row; **buscar camorra** to be looking for trouble
camorrista *adj* quarrelsome ‖ *mf* quarrelsome person
camote *m* onion; (Mex) sweet potato; (Chile) lie, fib; (Chile, Peru) sweetheart; (Arg, Ecuad) blockhead; (Mex) churl; (El Salv) black-and-blue mark; **tomar un camote** to become infatuated
camotear *tr* (Arg) to filch, snitch; (Guat) to bother ‖ *intr* (Mex) to wander around aimlessly
campal *adj* pitched (*battle*)
campamento *m* camp; encampment
campana *f* bell; (*para la protección de plantas*) bell glass, bell jar; (*de las guarniciones de alumbrado eléctrico*) canopy; **campana de buzo** diving bell; **por campana de vacante** (Mex) rarely, seldom
campanada *f* stroke of a bell, ring of a bell; scandal
campanario *m* belfry, steeple
campanear *tr* (*las campanas*) to ring ‖ *intr* to ring the bells ‖ *ref* to strut
campanero *m* bell ringer; bell founder
campanil *adj* bell ‖ *m* belfry, bell tower
campanilla *f* hand bell; door bell; bubble; (anat) uvula; **de (muchas) campanillas** of great importance
campano *m* cowbell
campante *adj* proud, satisfied; outstanding
campanu•do -da *adj* bell-shaped; pompous, high-sounding
campaña *f* campaign; cruise; countryside
campar *intr* to camp; to excel, stand out
campear *intr* to go to pasture; (*las sementeras*) turn green; stand out, excel; reconnoiter; ride through the fields to check the cattle
campecha•no -na *adj* frank, good-natured, cheerful ‖ *f* (Mex) mixed drink; (Ven) hammock
campeche *m* logwood
campeón *m* champion; **campeón de venta** best seller
campeona *f* championess
campeonato *m* championship
campe•ro -ra *adj* unsheltered, in the open
campesi•no -na *adj* country, rural, peasant ‖ *mf* peasant, farmer ‖ *m* countryman ‖ *f* countrywoman
campestre *adj* country, rural
campiña *f* countryside, open country
campo *m* (*terreno sembradío; sitio o foco de varias actividades*) field; (*en oposición a la ciudad*) country; ground, background; (*campamento*) (mil) camp; **a campo traviesa** across country; **campo de batalla** battlefield; **campo de ensayos** proving ground; **campo de juego** playground;

campo de pruebas testing ground; **campo de tiro** range, shooting range; **campo magnético** magnetic field; **campo santo** cemetery; **levantar el campo** (mil) to break camp; **quedar en el campo** to fall in battle
camposanto *m* cemetery
camuesa *f* pippin (*apple*)
camueso *m* pippin (*tree*)
camuflaje *m* camouflage
camuflar *tr* to camouflage
can *m* dog; (*de arma de fuego*) trigger
cana *f* gray hair; **echar una cana al aire** to cut loose, step out; **peinar canas** to be getting old
Canadá, el Canada
canadiense *adj & mf* Canadian
canal *m* (*cauce artificial*) canal; (*estrecho en el mar*) channel; (anat) duct, canal; (telv) channel; **Canal de la Mancha** English Channel; **Canal de Panamá** Panama Canal; **Canal de Suez** Suez Canal; **canal alimenticio** alimentary canal ‖ *f* channel; (*conducto del tejado*) gutter; (*estría*) flute, groove; pipe; (*de un libro*) fore edge
canalización *f* (*de agua o gas*) mains, pipes; ductwork; (elec) wiring; **canalización de consumo** (elec) house current
canalizar §60 to channel; pipe; (elec) to wire
canalizo *m* (naut) waterway, fairway
canalón *m* rain-water spout; shovel hat; **canalones** ravioli
canalla *m* churl, scoundrel ‖ *f* riffraff, canaille
canallada *f* dirty trick, meanness
canana *f* cartridge belt
canapé *m* sofa, couch
Canarias *fpl* Canaries
cana•rio -ria *adj & mf* Canarian ‖ *m* canary, canary bird ‖ *fpl* see **Canarias**
canasta *f* basket, hamper
canastilla *f* basket; (*ropa para el niño que ha de nacer*) layette; (*equipo de novia*) (dial) trousseau
canastillo *m* basket-weave tray
canasto *m* hamper ‖ **canastos** *interj* confound it!
cáncamo *m* eyebolt; **cáncamo de argolla** ringbolt
cancanear *intr* to loaf around; stammer
cancel *m* storm door; folding screen
cancela *f* door of ironwork
cancelar *tr* to cancel; (*una deuda*) pay off
cáncer *m* cancer; **Cáncer** (astr) Cancer; **cáncer pulmonar** lung cancer
cancerología *f* cancer research; oncology
cance•ro•so -sa *adj* cancerous
cancilla *f* lattice gate
canciller *m* chancellor
cancillería *f* chancellery
canción *f* song; poem, lyric poem; **canción de amor** love song; **canción de cuna** cradlesong, lullaby; **canción típica** folk song; **volver a la misma canción** to sing the same old song
cancionero *m* songbook; anthology
cancionista *mf* popular singer

ca
ca

canco *m* (Chile) flowerpot; (Chile) earthen jug; (Chile) chamber pot; (Bol) buttock; **cancos** (Chile) woman's broad hips

cancón *m* bugaboo; **hacer un cancón a** (Mex) to try to bluff

cancha *f* field, ground; race track; golf links; tennis court; cockpit; (Urug) path, way; **estar en su cancha** (Arg, Chile, Urug) to be in one's element; **tener cancha** (Arg) to have pull ‖ *interj* gangway!

canche *adj* (Col) tasteless, poorly seasoned; (CAm) blond

candado *m* padlock

candar *tr* to lock, padlock

candela *f* candle; candlestick; fire, light; **con la candela en la mano** at death's door

candelabro *m* candelabrum

candelecho *m* elevated hut for watching the vineyard

candelero *m* candlestick; brass olive-oil lamp; fishing torch

candelilla *f* catkin; (Arg, Chile) will-o'-the-wisp; glowworm

candida•to -ta *mf* candidate

candidatura *f* candidacy; list of candidates; voting paper

candidez *f* whiteness; innocence

cándi•do -da white; simple, innocent

candil *m* open olive-oil lamp

candilejas *fpl* footlights

candon•go -ga *adj* fawning, slick; loafing, shirking ‖ *mf* fawner, flatterer; loafer, shirker ‖ *f* fawning; teasing

candonguear *tr* to kid, tease ‖ *intr* to scheme to get out of work

candor *m* innocence, ingenuousness

caneca *f* glazed earthen bottle

cane•co -ca *adj* (Arg, Bol) tipsy ‖ *f* see **caneca**

canela *f* cinnamon; (*cosa fina*) (coll) peach

canela•do -da *adj* cinnamon-colored

cane•lo -la *adj* cinnamon ‖ *m* (*árbol*) cinnamon ‖ *f* see **canela**

canelón *m* rain-water spout; large icicle; cinnamon candy

cane•sú *m* (*pl* -**súes**) (*prenda*) guimpe; (*pieza de una prenda*) yoke

cangilón *m* jug, jar, bucket; (*de draga*) bucket, scoop; rut, track

cangrejo *m* crab

cangrena *f* gangrene

cangrenar *ref* to have gangrene

canguro *m* kangaroo

caníbal *adj* & *mf* cannibal

canica *f* (*bolita*) marble; (*juego*) marbles

canicie *f* whiteness (*of hair*)

canícula *f* dog days ‖ **Canícula** *f* Dog Star

caniculares *mpl* dog days

cani•jo -ja *adj* (coll) weak, sickly ‖ *mf* (coll) weakling

canilla *f* shank (*of leg*); (*espita, grifo*) tap; bobbin, spool; (Mex) strength

cani•no -na *adj* canine ‖ *m* canine, canine tooth ‖ *f* excrement of dogs

canje *m* exchange

canjear *tr* to exchange

ca•no -na *adj* gray; gray-haired; hoary, old ‖ *f* see **cana**

canoa *f* canoe; launch

canoe•ro -ra *mf* canoeist

canon *m* canon

canóni•co -ca *adj* canonical ‖ *f* rules of canonical life

canóniga *f* nap before eating; drunk

canónigo *m* canon

canonizar §60 *tr* to canonize; approve

canonjía *f* sinecure

cano•ro -ra *adj* (*voz*) melodious; (*ave*) song, sweet-singing

cano•so -sa *adj* gray-haired

canotié *m* straw hat, skimmer

cansa•do -da *adj* tired, weary; exhausted, worn-out; tiresome

cansancio *m* tiredness, fatigue

cansar *tr* to tire, weary; bore ‖ *intr* be tiresome ‖ *ref* to tire, get tired

cantable *adj* tuneful, singable ‖ *m* (*del libreto de una zarzuela*) lyric; (*de una zarzuela*) musical passage

canta•dor -dora *mf* singer of popular songs

cantaletear *tr* to say over and over again; make fun of

cantalupo *m* cantaloupe

cantante *adj* singing ‖ *mf* singer

cantar *m* song, singing; chant; **Cantar de los Cantares** Song of Songs ‖ *tr* to sing; chant; sing of; **cantarlas claras** to speak out ‖ *intr* to sing; chant; creak, squeak; squeal, peach; **cantar de plano** to make a full confession

cántara *f* jug, pitcher

cantárida *f* Spanish fly

canta•rín -rina *adj* (*voz*) melodious; fond of singing ‖ *mf* singer ‖ *m* professional singer

cántaro *m* jug, pitcher; jugful; ballot box; **llover a cántaros** to rain pitchforks

canta•triz *f* (*pl* -**trices**) singer

cantautor *m* song writer

cantera *f* quarry; talent, genius

cántico *m* canticle

cantidad *f* quantity; amount; sum; **cantidad de movimiento** (mech) momentum

cantiga *f* poem of the troubadours

cantilena *f* ballad, song; **salir con la misma cantilena** to sing the same old song

cantimplora *f* siphon; carafe, decanter; (*frasco para llevar bebida*) canteen; (Col) powder flask; (Guat) mumps

cantina *f* cantine; lunchroom, station restaurant; barroom

cantinera *f* camp follower

cantinero *m* bartender

canto *m* song; singing; (*división del poema épico*) canto; (*de notas iguales y uniformes*) chant; (*extremidad*) edge; (*esquina*) corner; (*de cuchillo*) back; (*de pan*) crust; stone, pebble; **canto de corte** cutting edge; **canto del cisne** swan song

cantonera *f* corner reinforcement; corner table, corner shelf; streetwalker

cantonero *m* corner loafer

can•tor -tora *adj* singing; (*pájaro*) song ‖ *mf* singer ‖ *m* chanter; minstrel; poet, bard

canto•so -sa *adj* rocky, stony
canturrear *tr* & *intr* to hum
canturreo *m* hum, humming
canzonetista *mf* popular singer
caña *f* cane; reed; stalk, stem; (*del brazo o la pierna*) long bone; (*de bota o media*) leg; wineglass; **caña de azúcar** sugar cane; **caña de pescar** fishing rod
cañada *f* glen, ravine, gully; cattle path; brook
cañamazo *m* canvas, burlap; embroidered canvas
cañamiel *f* sugar cane
cáñamo *m* hemp
cañamones *mpl* birdseed
cañaveral *m* canebrake; sugar-cane plantation
cañería *f* pipe; pipe line; piping; **cañería maestra** gas main, water main
cañero *m* pipe fitter, plumber; sugar-cane dealer; (SAm) cheat; (SAm) bluffer
cañista *m* pipe fitter, plumber
caño *m* pipe, tube; gutter, sewer; ditch; (*chorro*) spurt, jet; (*canal angosto*) channel; organ pipe; (*río pequeño*) (Col) stream
cañón *m* (*pieza de artillería*) cannon; (*valle estrecho*) canyon; (*de arma de fuego; de pluma*) barrel; (*pluma de ave*) quill; (*de escalera*) well; (*de columna; de ascensor*) shaft; organ pipe; (Col) trunk of tree; **cañón de campaña** fieldpiece; **cañón de chimenea** flue, chimney flue; **cañón obús** howitzer
cañonear *tr* to cannonade, to shell
cañutazo *m* gossip
caoba *f* mahogany
caos *m* chaos
caóti•co -ca *adj* chaotic
cap. *abbr* **capitán, capítulo**
capa *f* cloak, cape, mantle; (*de pintura*) coat; (*lo que cubre*) bed, layer; (*apariencia, pretexto*) (fig) cloak, mask; **capa del cielo** canopy of heaven; **capa de ozono** ozone layer; **andar de capa caída** to be on the decline, be in a bad way; (*comedia*) **de capa y espada** cloak-and-sword; (*intriga, espionaje*) **de capa y espada** cloak-and-dagger; **so capa de** under the guise of
capacidad *f* capacity; **capacidad competitiva** competitiveness
capacitar *tr* to enable, qualify; to empower ‖ *ref* to become qualified
capacha *f* fruit basket; (SAm) jail
capacho *m* fruit basket; hamper; (*de albañil*) hod
capar *tr* to geld, castrate; curtail
caparazón *m* caparison; horse blanket; nose bag; (*de crustáceo*) shell
caparrosa *f* vitriol
capa•taz *m* (*pl* **-taces**) overseer, foreman, boss
ca•paz *adj* (*pl* **-paces**) (*grande*) capacious, spacious; (*que tiene cierta aptitud; diestro, instruído*) capable; **capaz de** capable of; with a capacity of; **capaz para** competent in; qualified for; with room for
capcio•so -sa *adj* crafty, deceptive

capea *f* amateur free-for-all bullfight
capear *tr* (*al toro*) to challenge; (*el mal tiempo*) weather; deceive, take in ‖ *intr* (naut) to lay to; (Guat) to play hooky
capellán *m* chaplain
capeo *m* capework (*of bullfighter*)
caperucita *f* little pointed hood; **Caperucita Roja** Little Red Ridinghood
caperuza *f* pointed hood; chimney cap
capilla *f* (*parte de una iglesia con altar*) chapel; (*de los reos de muerte*) death house; (*pliego suelto*) proof sheet; cowl, hood, cape; **estar en capilla** to be in the death house; to be on pins and needles; **estar expuesto en capilla ardiente** to be on view, to lie in state
capiller *m* churchwarden, sexton
capillo *m* baby cap; baptismal cap; hood; cocoon; (*del cigarro*) filler
capirotazo *m* fillip
capirote *m* hood; doctor's cap and hood; cardboard or paper cone (*worn on head*); fillip
capitación *f* poll tax
capital *adj* capital; main, principal; paramount; (*enemigo*) mortal ‖ *m* (*dinero que produce renta*) capital; (*dinero que se presta para producir renta*) principal; **capital de inversión** investment capital ‖ *f* capital
capitalismo *m* capitalism
capitalista *adj* capitalistic ‖ *mf* capitalist; shareholder, investor
capitalizar §60 *tr* to capitalize; (*los intereses devengados*) compound
capitán *m* captain; leader; **capitán de bandera** flag captain; **capitán de corbeta** (nav) lieutenant commander; **capitán del puerto** harbor master
capitana *f* flagship
capitanear *tr* to captain; lead, command
capitanía *f* captaincy; (mil) company
capitel *m* (*de una iglesia*) spire; (*de una columna*) capital
capitolio *m* capitol
capitoste *m* big shot
capítula *f* chapter (*of Scriptures*)
capitular *tr* to accuse; agree on ‖ *intr* to capitulate
capitulear *intr* (Arg, Chile, Peru) to lobby
capituleo *m* (Arg, Chile, Peru) lobbying
capitulero *m* (Arg, Chile, Peru) political henchman, lobbyist
capítulo *m* chapter; chapter house; subject, matter; errand; main point; **ganar capítulo** (coll) to win one's point; **llamar a capítulo** to take to task, call to account; **perder capítulo** to lose one's point
ca•pó *m* (*pl* **-pós**) hood (*of auto*)
capolar *tr* to cut to pieces, chop up
ca•pón -pona *adj* castrated ‖ *m* eunuch; (*pollo*) capon; bundle of firewood; (*golpe*) fillip ‖ *f* shoulder strap
caponera *f* coop for fattening capons; place of welcome; (*cárcel*) coop, jail
caporal *m* chief, leader; foreman (*on cattle ranch*)

capota _f_ bonnet; (aer) cowling; (aut) top
capotaje _m_ (aer) nosing over
capotar _intr_ to upset; (aer) to nose over
capote _m_ cape, cloak; (coll) frown, scowl; (Chile, Mex) beating; **capote de monte** poncho; **de capote** (Mex) on the sly; **dar capote a** to flabbergast; (_un rezagado_) to leave hungry; **decir para su capote** to say to oneself; **echar un capote** to turn the conversation
capotear _tr_ (_al toro_) to challenge; (_dificultades_) evade, duck; beguile, take in; (_una obra teatral_) cut, make cuts in
Capricornio _m_ Capricorn
capricho _m_ caprice, whim, fancy
caprichoso -sa _adj_ capricious, whimsical; willful
caprichudo -da _adj_ capricious, whimsical
cápsula _f_ capsule; (_de botella_) cap
capsular _tr_ to cap
captación _f_ capture; (_de las aguas de un río_) harnessing; (rad) tuning in, picking up
captar _tr_ to catch; (_la confianza de una persona_) win; (_las aguas de un río_) harness; (_las ondas radiofónicas_) tune in, pick up; (_lo que uno dice_) get, grasp ‖ _ref_ to attract, win
captura _f_ capture, catch
capturar _tr_ to capture, catch
capucha _f_ cowl, hood; circumflex accent
capuchina _f_ garden nasturtium, Indian cress; Capuchin nun; confection of egg yolks
capucho _m_ cowl, hood
capuchón _m_ lady's cloak and hood; (_de una plumafuente_) cap; (aut) valve cap
capullo _m_ cocoon; coarse spun silk; bud; **capullo de rosa** rosebud
capuzar §60 _tr_ to throw in headfirst; (_un buque_) overload at the bow
caqui _adj_ khaki ‖ _m_ khaki; Japanese persimmon
caquinos _mpl_ (Mex) guffaw, outburst of laughter
cara _f_ face; look, countenance; façade; front; (_de disco de fonógrafo_) side; **a cara descubierta** openly; **a cara o cruz** heads or tails; **cara a** facing; **cara al público** with an audience; **cara de acelga** sallow face; **cara de ajo** vinegar face; **cara de hereje** (_persona de feo aspecto_) fright, baboon; **cara de vinagre** vinegar face; **dar la cara** to take the consequences; **de cara** in the face; facing; **echar a cara o cruz** to flip a coin; **hacer cara a** to stand up to; **tener buena cara** to look well, to look good; **tener mala cara** to look ill, to look bad
cárabe _m_ amber
carabina _f_ carbine; chaperon
caracol _m_ snail; snail shell; (_de pelo_) curl; (_trazado en espiral_) spiral; (_del oído_) cochlea
carácter _m_ (_pl_ **caracteres**) character; (_marca que se pone a las reses_) brand
característi·co -ca _adj_ characteristic ‖ _m_ (theat) old man ‖ _f_ characteristic; (theat) old woman
caracteriza·do -da _adj_ distinguished

caracterizar §60 _tr_ to characterize; to confer a distinction on; (_un personaje en la escena_) to interpret ‖ _ref_ to dress and make up for a role
caradu·ro -ra _adj_ brazen; shameless ‖ _f_ scoundrel
caramba _interj_ confound it!; upon my word!
carámbano _m_ icicle
carambola _f_ carom; double shot; trick, cheating
carambolear _intr_ to carom ‖ _ref_ to get tipsy
caramelo _m_ caramel; drop, lozenge
carantamaula _f_ ugly false face; (_persona_) ugly mug
carantoña _f_ ugly false face; **carantoñas** adulation, fawning
carátula _f_ mask; (_profesión de actor_) stage, theater; title page; (_de reloj_) (Mex, Guat) face
caravana _f_ caravan; (_casa rodante_) trailer
caravanera _f_ caravansary
caray _m_ var of **carey**
carbohielo _m_ dry ice
carbóli·co -ca _adj_ carbolic
carbón _m_ (_de leña_) charcoal; (_de piedra_) coal; (_electrodo de carbono de la lámpara de arco o la pila_) carbon; black crayon; (_honguillo parásito_) smut; **carbón de bujía** cannel coal, jet coal; **carbón tal como sale** run-of-mine coal
carboncillo _m_ charcoal, charcoal pencil
carbonera _f_ bunker, coal bunker; coalbin; (Col) coal mine
carbonería _f_ coalyard
carbone·ro -ra _adj_ coal, charcoal; coaling ‖ _mf_ coaldealer; charcoal burner ‖ _f_ see **carbonera**
carbonilla _f_ fine coal; (_en los cilindros_) carbon
carbonizar §60 _tr_ to char
carbono _m_ carbon
carbunclo _m_ (_piedra_) carbuncle; (pathol) carbuncle
carbunco _m_ (pathol) carbuncle
carbúnculo _m_ (_piedra_) carbuncle
carburador _m_ carburetor
carburo _m_ carbide
carcacha _f_ (Mex) jalopy
carcaj _m_ quiver
carcajada _f_ outburst of laughter
cárcel _f_ jail, prison; (_para oprimir dos piezas de madera encoladas_) clamp
carcele·ro -ra _adj_ jail ‖ _m_ jailer, warden
carcinóge·no -na _adj_ carcinogenic; cancer-causing ‖ _m_ carcinogen
carcinoma _f_ carcinoma
carcoma _f_ woodworm, borer; anxiety, worry; spendthrift
carcomer _tr_ to bore, gnaw away at; undermine, harass ‖ _ref_ to become worm-eaten
cardán _m_ universal joint
cardenal _m_ cardinal; cardinal bird; black-and-blue mark
cardenillo _m_ verdigris
cárde·no -na _adj_ purple; dapple-gray; (_agua_) opaline

cardía‑co -ca *adj* cardiac ‖ *mf (persona que padece del corazón)* cardiac ‖ *m (remedio)* cardiac

cardinal *adj* cardinal

cardo *m* thistle

cardume *m* school *(of fish)*

carear *tr* to bring face to face; compare ‖ *intr* — **carear a** to overlook ‖ *ref* to meet face to face

carecer §22 *intr* — **carecer de** to lack, need, be in want of

carecimiento *m* lack, need, want

carencia *f* lack, need, want

carente *adj* — **carente de** lacking

careo *m* meeting; confrontation

care‑ro -ra *adj* dear, expensive

carestía *f* scarcity, want, dearth; high prices; **carestía de la vida** high cost of living

careta *f* mask; **careta antigás** gas mask

carey *m* hawksbill turtle; tortoise shell

carga *f* load, loading; *(mercancías que se transportan)* freight, cargo; *(peso u obligación que pesan sobre una persona)* burden; *(de substancia explosiva, de electricidad, de soldados contra el enemigo)* charge; charge, responsibility, obligation; **carga de familia** dependent; **carga de punta** (elec) peak load; **carga por eje** axle load; **carga útil** pay load; **echar la carga a** to put the blame on; **volver a la carga** to keep at it

cargaderas *fpl* (Col) suspenders

cargadero *m* loading platform; freight station

carga‑do -da *adj (cielo)* overcast, cloudy; *(atmósfera, tiempo)* close, sultry; *(alambre eléctrico)* hot, charged; *(café, té)* strong; *(rato, hora)* busy; **cargado de años** along in years; **cargado de espaldas** round-shouldered, stoop-shouldered

cargador *m* loader, stevedore; carrier, porter; *(de acumulador)* charger

cargamento *m* load; (naut) loading; (naut) cargo, shipment

cargante *adj* boring, annoying, tiresome

cargar §44 *tr (un peso, mercancías; un carro, un mulo, un barco; un horno; un arma de fuego; a una persona)* to load; *(a una persona con un peso u obligación)* burden; *(un acumulador; al enemigo)* charge; *(a una persona)* charge with; entrust with; annoy, bore, weary; **cargar en cuenta a** *(una persona)* to charge to the account of; **cargar** *(a una persona)* **de** to charge with; burden with ‖ *intr* to load; *(el viento)* turn; crowd, incline, tip; *(el acento)* fall; eat too much, drink too much; **cargar con** to pick up; walk away with; *(un fusil)* shoulder; take on; **cargar sobre** to rest on; bother, pester; devolve on ‖ *ref (el cielo)* to become overcast; *(el viento)* turn; become annoyed, be bored; **cargarse de** to have a lot of; *(lágrimas)* be bathed in

cargaréme *m* receipt, voucher

cargazón *f* loading; *(en el estómago, la cabeza, etc.)* heaviness; mass of heavy clouds; (Arg) clumsy job; (Chile) good

crop; **cargazón alta** (coll) high office; high official

cargo *m* job, position; duty, responsibility; burden, weight; management; *(falta que se atribuye a uno; cantidad que uno debe y la acción de anotarla)* charge; **a cargo de** in charge of; **cargo de conciencia** sense of guilt; **girar a cargo de** to draw on; **hacerse cargo de** to take charge of; to realize, become aware of; to look into; **librar a cargo de** to draw on; **vestir el cargo** to look the part

cargosear *tr* (Arg, Chile) to pester

cargo‑so -sa *adj* annoying, bothersome; onerous, costly

carguero *m* (naut) freighter; (Arg, Urug) beast of burden

cariaconteci‑do -da *adj* downcast, woebegone

cariar §77 *tr & intr* to decay

cariátide *f* caryatid

Caribdis *f* Charybdis

caribe *adj* Caribbean ‖ *m* savage, brute

caricatura *f (descripción o figura grotescas; retrato festivo)* caricature; *(retrato festivo)* cartoon

caricaturista *mf* caricaturist; cartoonist

caricaturizar §60 *tr* to caricature; cartoon

caricia *f* caress; endearment

caridad *f* charity; **la caridad bien ordenada empieza por uno mismo** charity begins at home

caries *f* decay, tooth decay; caries

carilla *f (de colmenero)* mask; *(de libro)* page

carille‑no -na *adj* full-faced

carillón *m* carillon

carine‑gro -gra *adj* swarthy

cariño *m* love, affection; loved one; (Chile) gift, present; **cariños** caresses, endearments; (Arg) greetings

cariño‑so -sa *adj* loving, affectionate

caripare‑jo -ja *adj* stone-faced, impassive

carirraí‑do -da *adj* brazen-faced, shameless

carisma *f* charisma

carismáti‑co -ca *adj* charismatic

carita *f* little face; **dar** or **hacer carita** *(una mujer coqueta)* (Mex) to smile back

caritati‑vo -va *adj* charitable

cariz *m (de la atmósfera, el tiempo)* appearance, look; *(de un asunto)* look, outlook; *(de la cara de uno)* look; **mal cariz** angry look, scowl

carlinga *f* (aer) cockpit

Carlomagno *m* Charlemagne

Carlos *m* Charles

carlota *f* pudding; **carlota rusa** charlotte russe ‖ **Carlota** *f* Charlotte

carmelita *f* (Hond) station wagon

carmen *m* song, poem; house and garden *(in Granada)*

carmesí *(pl -síes) adj & m* crimson

carnada *f* bait; (coll) bait, trap

carnal; *adj* carnal; *(hermano)* full; *(primo)* first

carnaval *m* carnival

carne *f (parte blanda del cuerpo humano y del animal)* flesh; *(la comestible del ani-*

mal) meat; **carne de cañón** cannon fodder; **carne de cerdo asada** roast pork; **carne de cordero** lamb; **carne de gallina** goose flesh; **carne de horca** gallows bird; **carne de res** beef; **carne de ternera** veal; **carne de vaca asada** roast of beef; **carne de venado** venison; **carne fiambre** cold meat; **carne sin hueso** cinch, snap; **carne y sangre** flesh and blood; **cobrar carnes** to put on flesh; **echar carnes** (Mex) to swear, curse; **en carnes** naked; **en vivas carnes** stark-naked

carnear *tr* (Arg, Chile, Urug) to butcher, slaughter; (Arg, Urug) to stab; (Chile) to take in, swindle

carnero *m* sheep; (*carne de este animal*) mutton; (*osario*) charnel house; family vault; (*persona que no tiene voluntad propia*) (Arg, Chile) sheep; **cantar para el carnero** (Arg, Bol, Urug) to die; **no hay tales carneros** there's no truth to it

car•net *m* (*pl* **-nets**) notebook; membership card; (Arg) dance card; **carnet de chófer** driver's license; **carnet de identidad** identification card

carnicería *f* butcher shop, meat market; (fig) carnage, massacre

carnice•ro -ra *adj* carnivorous; bloodthirsty ‖ *mf* butcher

carnosidad *f* fleshiness, corpulence; (*excrecencia carnosa anormal*) proud flesh

carno•so -sa *adj* fleshy; meaty, fat

ca•ro -ra *adj* (*de subido precio; amado, querido*) dear ‖ *f* see **cara** ‖ **caro** *adv* dear

carpa *f* carp; awning, tent; stand at a fair; **carpa dorada** goldfish

carpanta *f* raging hunger

carpeta *f* (*cubierta para mesas*) table cover; (*par de cubiertas para documentos*) letter file, portfolio; (*factura*) invoice; (Col) accounting department; (Peru) writing desk

carpintería *f* carpentry; carpenter shop; **carpintería de taller** millwork

carpintero *m* carpenter; woodpecker; **carpintero de carreta** wheelwright

carra•co -ca *adj* old, decrepit ‖ *f* (*barco viejo*) tub, hulk; (*instrumento de madera para producir un ruido desapacible*) rattle; (*berbiquí*) ratchet drill ‖ **la Carraca** Cádiz navy yard

carraspear *intr* to be hoarse

carraspera *f* hoarseness

carrera *f* (*paso del que corre*) run; (*lucha de velocidad*) race; (*sitio para correr*) race track; (*espacio recorrido corriendo*) course, stretch; (*curso de la vida, profesión*) career; (*calle*) avenue, boulevard; (*raya, crencha*) part (*in hair*); (*en las medias*) run; (*hilera*) row, line; (*viga*) rafter, girder; (*movimiento del émbolo del motor*) stroke; **a carrera abierta** at full speed; **carrera a pie** foot race; **carrera armamentista** or **de armamentos** arms race; **carrera ascendente** upstroke; **carrera de baquetas** gauntlet; **carrera de caballos** horse race; **carrera de campanario** steeplechase; **carrera de obstáculos** obstacle

race; steeplechase; **carrera de relevos** relay race; **carrera descendente** downstroke; **carrera de vallas** hurdle race; **carreras** horse racing, turf

carrerista *adj* horsy ‖ *mf* racegoer; auto racer; bicycle racer ‖ *m* outrider ‖ *f* (slang) streetwalker

carreta *f* cart; **carreta de bueyes** oxcart

carrete *m* reel, spool; fishing reel; (elec) coil

carretear *tr* to cart, haul; (*un carro, una carreta*) drive; (aer) to taxi ‖ *intr* (aer) to taxi

carretera *f* highway, road; **carretera de peaje** turnpike; **carretera de vía libre** expressway, limited-access highway

carretería *f* carts; wagon work; carting business; wagon shop

carrete•ro -ra *adj* wagon, carriage ‖ *m* wheelwright; teamster; charioteer; **jurar como un carretero** to swear like a trooper ‖ *f* see **carretera**

carretilla *f* wheelbarrow; baggage truck; (*para enseñar a los niños a andar*) gocart; (*buscapiés*) snake, serpent; (Arg, Chile, Urug) jaw; **carretilla de mano** handcart; **carretilla elevadora** lift truck; **de carretilla** offhand

carretón *m* cart, wagon, dray; gocart; (rr) truck; covered wagon

carricoche *m* covered wagon

carricuba *f* street sprinkler

carril *m* (*barra de acero en el ferrocarril*) rail, track; (*huella*) track, rut; (*hecho por el arado*) furrow; lane, path; (Chile) train; (Chile, P-R) railroad; **carril de toma** third rail

carrilera *f* track, rut

carrilero *m* (Peru) railroader

carrillera *f* jaw; chin strap

carrillo *m* cheek, jowl; pulley; **comer a dos carrillos** to eat like a glutton; have two sources of income; play both sides

carrizo *m* ditch reed

carro *m* cart, wagon; car, auto; (mach) carriage; **carro alegórico** float; **carro blindado** armored car; **carro correo** mail car; **carro de asalto** tank; **carro de combate** combat car, tank; **carro de equipajes** baggage car; **carro de mudanza** moving van; **carro de riego** street sprinkler; **carro frigorífero** refrigerator car; **carro fúnebre** hearse; **Carro mayor** Big Dipper; **Carro menor** Little Dipper; **carro romano** chariot; **pare Vd. el carro** hold your horses

ca•rró *m* (*pl* **-rrós**) diamond

carrocería *f* (*de automóvil*) body

carrocha *f* eggs (*of insect*)

carromato *m* covered wagon

carro•ño -ña *adj & f* carrion

carro-patrulla *f* (SAm) patrol car; police car

carroza *f* coach, carriage; **carroza alegórica** float; **carroza fúnebre** hearse

carruaje *m* carriage

carta *f* (*comunicación escrita*) letter; (*constitución escrita de un país*) charter; (*naipe*) card, playing card; map; **carta aérea** airmail letter; **carta blanca** carte blanche;

carta calumniosa poison-pen letter; **carta certificada** registered letter; **carta de marear** (naut) chart; **carta de naturaleza** naturalization papers; **carta general** form letter; **carta por avión** air-mail letter; **poner las cartas boca arriba** to put one's cards on the table

cartabón m carpenter's square

cartagi•nés -nesa adj & mf Carthaginian

Cartago f Carthage

cartapacio m notebook; schoolboy's satchel; writing book; (*papeles contenidos en una carpeta*) file, dossier

cartear intr to play low cards (*in order to see how the game stands*) ‖ ref to write to each other

cartel m show bill, poster, placard; cartel, trust; (*pasquín*) lampoon; (*de toreros*) bill, line-up; (*del torero*) fame, reputation; **cartel de teatro** bill, show bill; **dar cartel a** to headline; **se prohibe fijar carteles** post no bills; **tener cartel** to be the rage

cartela f card; bracket

cartelera f billboard; (*en los periódicos*) amusement page, theater section

cartelero m billposter

cartelón m show bill

carteo m finessing; exchange of letters

cárter m (mach) housing; **cárter de engranajes** gearcase; **cárter del cigüeñal** crankcase

cartera f portfolio; pocket flap; **cartera de bolsillo** billfold, wallet

cartería f sorting room

carterista m pickpocket, purse snatcher

cartero m letter carrier, postman

cartilagino•so -sa adj gristly

cartílago m gristle

cartilla f primer, speller, reader; notebook; (*de la caja de ahorros*) deposit book; **cartilla de racionamiento** ration book

cartivana f (bb) hinge, joint

cartón m cardboard, pasteboard; cardboard box; **cartón de yeso y fieltro** plasterboard; **cartón picado** stencil; **cartón tabla** wallboard

cartoné — **en cartoné** (bb) in boards, bound in boards

cartucho m cartridge

cartulina f fine cardboard

casa f (*edificio para habitar*) house; (*hogar, domicilio*) home; (*establecimiento comercial o industrial*) firm, concern; (*familia*) household; (*escaque*) square; **a casa** home, homeward; **casa consistorial** town hall, city hall; **casa de azotea** penthouse; **casa de campo** country house; **casa de caridad** poorhouse; **casa de citas** house of assignation; **casa de correos** post office; **casa de empeños** pawnshop; **casa de expósitos** foundling home; **casa de fieras** menagerie; **casa de huéspedes** boarding house; **casa de juego** gambling house; **casa de locos** madhouse; **casa de modas** dress shop; **casa de moneda** mint; **casa de préstamos** pawnshop; **casa de salud** private hospital; **casa de socorro** first-aid station; **casa de**

vecindad or **de vecinos** apartment house, tenement house; **casa editorial** publishing house; **casa matriz** main office; **casa pública** brothel; **casa real** royal palace; royal family; **casas baratas** low-cost housing; **casa solar** or **solariega** ancestral mansion, manor house; **casa y comida** board and lodging; **¡convida la casa!** the drinks are on the house!; **en casa** home, at home; **ir a buscar casa** to go house hunting; **poner casa** to set up housekeeping

casabe m var of **cazabe**

casaca f dress coat; marriage contract; (Guat, Hond) lively whispered conversation; **volver la casaca** to become a turncoat

casade•ro -ra adj marriageable

casa•do -da adj married ‖ mf married person; **(los) no casados** (coll) singles

casal m country place; (Arg) pair, couple

casamente•ro -ra adj matchmaking ‖ mf matchmaker

casamiento m marriage; wedding

casapuerta f entrance hall, vestibule

casaquilla f jacket

casar tr to marry; marry off; match; harmonize; (law) to annul, repeal ‖ intr to marry, get married ‖ ref to marry, get married; **no casarse con nadie** to get tied up with nobody

casatienda f store and home combined

cascabel m sleigh bell, jingle bell; rattlesnake; **ponerle cascabel al gato** to bell the cat

cascabelear intr to jingle; to act tactlessly

cascabeleo m jingle

cascabele•ro -ra adj tactless, thoughtless ‖ mf featherbrain ‖ m baby's rattle

cascabillo m jingle bell; chaff, husk; cup of acorn

cascada f cascade, waterfall

cascajo m pebble; gravel, rubble; broken jar; piece of junk; **estar hecho un cascajo** to be old and worn-out, be a wreck

cascanue•ces m (pl -ces) nutcracker

cascar §73 tr to crack, break, split; beat, strike, hit ‖ ref to crack, break, split

cáscara f hull, peel, rind, shell; bark, crust; **cáscara rueda** (Arg) ring-around-a-rosy; **ser de la cáscara amarga** to be wild and flighty; hold advanced views; (Mex) to be determined

cascarón m eggshell

cascarra•bias mf (pl -bias) crab, grouch

casco m (*pieza que sirve para proteger la cabeza del soldado, el bombero, etc.*) helmet; (*uña de las caballerías*) hoof; (*pedazo de vasija rota*) potsherd; (*capa de la cebolla*) coat, shell; (*del sombrero*) crown; (*cuerpo de la nave*) hull; (*de un barco inservible*) hulk; (*barril, pipa*) barrel, tank, cask, vat; (*pieza del teléfono*) headset, headpiece; bottle; (mach) shell, casing; (*gajo de la naranja*) (Arg, Col, Chile) slice; (Peru) chest, breast; **casco de población** or **casco urbano** city limits; **romperse los cascos** to rack one's brain

casera f landlady; housekeeper

casería f country place; customers

caserío *m* country house; small settlement, hamlet

case•ro -ra *adj* homemade; homeloving; (*remedio*) household; house, home; (*sencillo*) homely ‖ *mf* owner, proprietor; renter; caretaker; janitor; huckster; vendor ‖ *m* landlord ‖ *f* see **casera**

caseta *f* (*casa sin piso alto*) cottage; (*de una feria*) stall, booth; bathhouse

casete *m* cassette

casi *adv* almost, nearly; **casi nada** next to nothing; **casi nunca** hardly ever

casilla *f* hut, shack, shed; cabin, lodge; stall, booth; (*escaque*) square; (*compartimiento en un mueble*) pigeonhole; (*división del papel rayado*) column, square; (*taquilla*) ticket office; (*de locomotora o camión*) cab; (Bol, Chile, Peru, Urug) post-office box; (Ecuad) water closet; (Cuba) bird trap; **sacarle a uno de sus casillas** to jolt someone out of his old habits; drive someone crazy

casille•ro -ra *mf* (rr) crossing guard ‖ *m* filing cabinet, set of pigeonholes

casino *m* casino; club; clubhouse

caso *m* case; chance; event; **caso de conformidad** in case you agree; **caso que** in case; **de caso pensado** deliberately, on purpose; **en todo caso** at all events; **hacer al caso** to be to the purpose; **hacer caso de** to take into account, pay attention to; **hacer caso omiso de** to pass over in silence, not mention; **no venir al caso** to be beside the point; **poner por caso** to take as an example; **venir al caso** to be just the thing

casorio *m* hasty marriage, unwise marriage

caspa *f* dandruff, scurf

cáspita *interj* well well!, upon my word!

caspo•so -sa *adj* full of dandruff

casquete *m* (*cubierta que se ajusta al casco de la cabeza*) skullcap; skull, cranium; (*pieza de la armadura que cubre el casco de la cabeza*) helmet; (*pieza del teléfono*) headset

casquillo *m* butt, cap, tip; bushing, sleeve; ferrule; horseshoe

casquiva•no -na *adj* scatterbrained

casta *f* caste; kind, quality; breed, race

castaña *f* chestnut; (*moño*) knot, chignon; demijohn; **castaña de Indias** horse chestnut; **castaña de Pará** Brazil nut

castañeta *f* castanet; snapping of the fingers

castañetear *tr* (*los dedos*) to snap, click; (*p.ej., una seguidilla*) click off with the castanets ‖ *intr* to click; (*los dientes*) chatter

casta•ño -ña *adj* chestnut, chestnut-colored; (*p.ej., pelo*) brown; (*p.ej., ojos*) hazel ‖ *m* chestnut tree; **castaño de Indias** horse chestnut ‖ *f* see **castaña**

castañuela *f* castanet; **estar como unas castañuelas** to be bubbling over with joy

castella•no -na *adj* & *mf* Castilian ‖ *m* Castilian, Spanish (*language*) ‖ *f* chatelaine

casticidad *f* purity, correctness (*in language*)

casticismo *m* purism

castidad *f* chastity

castiga•dor -dora *mf* punisher ‖ *m* seducer, Don Juan

castigar §44 *tr* to punish, chastise; (*la carne*) mortify; (*los gastos*) cut down, curtail; (*obras, escritos*) correct, emend; (*un tornillo*) (Mex) tighten

castigo *m* punishment, chastisement

Castilla *f* Castile; **Castilla la Nueva** New Castile; **Castilla la Vieja** Old Castile

castillete *m* (min) derrick; tower

castillo *m* castle; (*montura sobre un elefante*) howdah; **castillo en el aire** castle in Spain, castle in the air; **castillo de naipes** house of cards; **castillo de proa** forecastle

casti•zo -za *adj* chaste, pure, correct; pure-blooded; real, regular

cas•to -ta *adj* chaste, pure ‖ *f* see **casta**

castor *m* beaver

castrar *tr* to castrate; (*una planta*) prune, cut back; weaken

casual *adj* casual, accidental, chance

casualidad *f* accident, chance; chance event; **por casualidad** by chance

casuca or **casucha** *f* shack, shanty

casulla *f* chasuble

cata *f* tasting; taste, sample

catacal•dos *mf* (*pl* -**dos**) rolling stone; busybody

catacumba *f* catacomb

catafoto *m* (rear) reflector

cata•lán -lana *adj* & *mf* Catalan, Catalonian

catalejo *m* spyglass

catalogar §44 *tr* to catalogue

catálogo *m* catalogue

Cataluña *f* Catalonia

cataplasma *f* poultice; **cataplasma de mostaza** mustard plaster

catapulta *f* catapult

catapultar *tr* to catapult

catar *tr* to taste, sample; check, examine; be on the lookout for

catarata *f* cataract, waterfall; (pathol) cataract

catarro *m* (*inflamación de las membranas mucosas*) catarrh; (*resfriado*) head cold

catástrofe *f* catastrophe

catavino *m* cup for tasting wine

catavi•nos *m* (*pl* -**nos**) winetaster; (*borracho*) rounder

catear *tr* to hunt, look for; (*a un alumno*) to flunk; to explore; (*una casa*) to search

catecismo *m* catechism

cátedra *f* chair, professorship; academic subject; teacher's desk; classroom; **poner cátedra** to hold forth

catedral *f* cathedral

catedrático *m* university professor

categoría *f* category; status, standing; class, kind; condition, quality; **de categoría** prominent

caterva *f* throng, crowd

catéter *m* catheter

cateterizar §60 *tr* to catheterize

cátodo *m* cathode

católi•co -ca *adj* catholic; Catholic; **no estar muy católico** to be under the weather ‖ *mf*

Catholic; **católico romano** Roman Catholic

catorce *adj & pron* fourteen ‖ *m* fourteen; *(en las fechas)* fourteenth

catorcea•vo -va *adj & m* fourteenth

catorza•vo -va *adj & m* fourteenth

catre *m* cot; **catre de tijera** folding cot

catrecillo *m* campstool, folding canvas chair

ca•trín -trina *adj* (CAm, Mex) sporty, swell ‖ *mf* (CAm, Mex) sport, dude

caucasia•no -na or **caucási•co -ca** *adj & mf* Caucasian

Cáucaso *m* Caucasus

cauce *m* river bed; channel, ditch, trench

caución *f* precaution; (law) bail, security

caucionar *tr* to guard against; (law) to give bail for

cauchal *m* rubber plantation

caucho *m* rubber; rubber plant; (Col) rubber raincoat; **caucho esponjoso** foam rubber; **cauchos** *(chanclos)* rubbers

caudal *adj* of great volume ‖ *m (de agua)* volume; abundance; wealth

caudalo•so -sa *adj* of great volume; abundant; rich, wealthy

caudillo *m* chief, leader; military leader; caudillo, head of state

causa *f* cause; (law) suit, trial; (Chile) bite, snack; (Peru) potato salad; **a** or **por causa de** on account of, because of

causa•dor -dora *adj* causing ‖ *mf (persona)* cause

causante *mf (persona)* cause; (law) principal, constituent; (Mex) taxpayer

causar *tr* to cause

causear *tr* (Chile) to get the best of ‖ *intr* (Chile) to have a bite

causeo *m* (Chile) bite, snack

cáusti•co -ca *adj* caustic

cautela *f* caution

cautelo•so -sa *adj* cautious, guarded

cauterizar §60 *tr* to cauterize

cautín *m* soldering iron

cautivar *tr* to take prisoner; attract, win over; *(encantar)* captivate

cautiverio *m* or **cautividad** *f* captivity

cauti•vo -va *adj & mf* captive

cau•to -ta *adj* cautious

cavar *tr* to dig, dig up ‖ *intr (una herida)* to go deep; *(el caballo)* to paw; **cavar en** to study thoroughly, to delve into

caverna *f* cavern, cave

cavidad *f* cavity

cavilar *tr* to brood over ‖ *intr* to worry, fret

cavilo•so -sa *adj* suspicious, mistrustful; (CAm) gossipy; (Col) touchy

cayado *m (de pastor)* crook; *(de obispo)* crozier

cayo *m* key, reef; **Cayo Hueso** Key West; **Cayos de la Florida** Florida Keys

caz *m (pl* **caces)** flume, millrace

caza *m* pursuit plane, fighter; **caza de reacción** jet fighter ‖ *f* chase, hunt; hunting; *(animales que se cazan)* game; **a caza de** on the hunt for; **caza al hombre** man hunt; **caza de grillos** fool's errand, wild-goose chase; **ir de caza** to go hunting

cazaautógra•fos *mf (pl* **-fos)** autograph seeker

cazabe *m* cassava, manioc; cassava bread

caza•dor -dora *adj* hunting ‖ *m* hunter; huntsman; **cazador de alforja** trapper; **cazador de cabezas** head-hunter; **cazador de dotes** fortune hunter; **cazador furtivo** poacher ‖ *f* huntress; hunting jacket; jacket

cazanoti•cias *(pl* **-cias)** *m* newshawk ‖ *f* newshen

cazasubmarinos *m* sub(marine) chaser

cazar §60 *tr* to chase; hunt; catch; *(en un descuido o error)* catch up; *(un descuido o error)* catch; *(adquirir con maña)* wangle; *(con halagos o engaños)* take in ‖ *intr* to hunt

cazarreactor *m* jet fighter

cazcalear *intr* to buzz around

cazo *m* dipper, ladle; glue pot; *(de cuchillo)* back

cazuela *f* earthen casserole; stew; (archaic) gallery for women; (SAm) chicken stew

cazu•rro -rra *adj* sullen, surly

cazuz *m* ivy

C. de J. *abbr* **Compañía de Jesús**

cebada *f* barley

cebadera *f* nose bag

cebador *m* (mach) primer

cebar *tr (a un animal)* to fatten; *(un horno)* feed; *(un arma de fuego, una bomba, un carburador)* prime; *(una pasión, la esperanza)* nourish; *(atraer)* lure; *(un clavo, un tornillo)* make catch, make take hold; *(un anzuelo)* bait ‖ *intr (un clavo, un tornillo)* to catch, take hold ‖ *ref (una enfermedad, una epidemia)* to rage; **cebarse en** to be absorbed in; vent one's fury on

cebo *m* fattening; feed; bait; lure; *(carga de un arma de fuego)* primer; priming

cebolla *f* onion; bulb; *(del velón)* oil receptacle

cebra *f* zebra

ce•bú *m (pl* **-búes)** zebu

ceca *f* mint; **de Ceca en Meca** or **de la Ceca a la Meca** hither and thither, from pillar to post

cecear *intr* to lisp

ceceo *m* lisp, lisping

cecina *f* dried beef

cedazo *m* sieve

ceder *tr* to yield, cede, give up ‖ *intr* to yield, give way, give in; slacken, relax; go down, decline

cedro *m* cedar; **cedro de Virginia** juniper, red cedar

cédula *f (de papel)* slip; form, blank; rent sign; certificate, document; **cédula de vecindad** or **cédula personal** identification papers

cedulón *m* proclamation, public notice; *(pasquín)* lampoon

céfiro *m* zephyr

cegar §66 *tr* to blind; *(un agujero)* plug, stop up; *(una puerta, una ventana)* wall up ‖ *intr* to go blind; be blinded ‖ *ref* to be blinded

cega•to -ta *adj* dim-sighted, weak-eyed

ceguedad *f* blindness

ca
ce

ceguera f blindness; blackout
Ceilán Ceylon
ceila·nés -nesa adj & mf Ceylonese
ceja f (pelo sobre la cuenca del ojo) eyebrow; edge, rim; cloud cap; clearing for a road; **arquear las cejas** to raise one's eyebrows; **fruncir las cejas** to knit one's brow; **quemarse las cejas** to burn the midnight oil
cejar intr to back up; turn back; slacken
cejijun·to -ta or **ceju·do -da** adj beetle-browed; scowling
celada f ambush; trap, trick
celador m guard (e.g., in a museum); (elec) lineman; (Urug) policeman
celaje m cloud effect; skylight, transom; ghost
celar tr to see to; watch over, keep an eye on; hide; carve
celda f cell; **celda de castigo** solitary confinement
celdilla f cell; niche
celebración f celebration; applause; (de una reunión) holding
celebrante m (sacerdote) celebrant
celebrar tr to celebrate; (una reunión) hold; (aprobar) welcome; (un matrimonio) perform; (misa) say ‖ intr (decir misa) to celebrate; be glad ‖ ref to take place, be held; be celebrated
célebre adj celebrated, famous; funny, witty; pretty
celebridad f (fama; persona) celebrity
celeridad f speed, swiftness
celeste adj celestial; sky-blue
celestial adj celestial, heavenly; stupid, silly
celestina f procuress, bawd
celestinaje m procuring, pandering
celibato m celibacy; bachelor
célibe adj celibate, single, unmarried ‖ mf celibate, single person ‖ m bachelor ‖ f unmarried woman
celinda f mock orange
celo m zeal; envy; (impulso reproductivo en las bestias) heat, rut; **celos** jealousy
celofán m or **celofana** f cellophane
celosía f (celotipia) jealousy; (enrejado de listoncillos) lattice window, jalousie
celo·so -sa adj (que tiene celo) zealous; (que tiene celos) jealous; fearful, distrustful; (naut) unsteady
celotipia f jealousy
celta adj Celtic ‖ mf Celt ‖ m (idioma) Celtic
célti·co -ca adj Celtic
célula f cell
celuloide m celluloid; **llevar al celuloide** to put on the screen
cellisca f sleet, sleet storm
cellisquear intr to sleet
cementerio m cemetery
cemento m cement; concrete; **cemento armado** reinforced concrete
cena f supper; dinner ‖ **la Cena** the Last Supper
cena·dor -dora mf diner-out ‖ m arbor, bower, summerhouse
cenaduría f (Mex) supper club
cenagal m quagmire
cenago·so -sa adj muddy, miry

cenaoscu·ras mf (pl -ras) recluse; skinflint
cenar tr to have for supper, have for dinner ‖ intr to have supper, have dinner
cencerrada f tin-pan serenade
cencerrear intr to keep jingling; rattle, jangle; play out of tune
cencerro m cowbell; **a cencerros tapados** cautiously
cendal m gauze, sendal
cenefa f edging, trimming, border
cenicero m ash tray
cenicien·to -ta adj ashen, ash-gray ‖ **la Cenicienta** Cinderella
cenit m zenith
ceniza f ash; ashes; **cenizas** ashes; **huir de las cenizas y caer en las brasas** to jump from the frying pan into the fire
ceni·zo -za adj ashen, ash-gray ‖ f see **ceniza**
cenojil m garter
cenote m (Mex) deep underground water reservoir
censo m census; **levantar el censo** to take the census
censor m censor; **censor jurado de cuentas** certified public accountant
censura f censure; censoring; gossip; **censura de cuentas** auditing
censurar tr (criticar, reprobar) to censure; (formar juicio de) censor
centauro m centaur
centa·vo -va adj hundredth ‖ m hundredth; cent
centella f flash of lightning; flash of light; spark; (de ingenio, de ira) (fig) spark, flash
centellar or **centellear** intr to flash, spark; glimmer, gleam, twinkle
centenar m hundred; **a centenares** by the hundreds
centena·rio -ria adj centennial ‖ mf centenarian ‖ m centennial
cente·no -na adj hundredth ‖ m rye
centési·mo -ma adj & m hundredth
centígra·do -da adj centigrade
centímetro m centimeter
cénti·mo -ma adj hundredth ‖ m hundredth; centime
centinela mf (persona) watch, guard ‖ m & f (soldado) sentinel, sentry; **hacer de centinela** to stand sentinel
centípedo m centipede
central adj central ‖ m sugar mill, sugar refinery ‖ f headquarters, main office; powerhouse; (telp) exchange, central; **central de correos** main post office; **central de teléfonos** telephone exchange
centralista mf telephone operator
centralizar §60 tr & ref to centralize
centrar tr to center; hit the center ‖ ref to concentrate; stress
céntri·co -ca adj center, central; (próximo al centro de la ciudad) downtown
centrifugadora f centrifuge; spin-dryer
centro m center; middle; business district, downtown; club; object, goal, purpose; **centro de mesa** centerpiece; **centro docente** educational institution; **pegar centro** (CAm) to hit the bull's-eye

Centro América f Central America
centroamerica•no -na adj & mf Central American
cénts. abbr **céntimos**
ceñi•do -da adj tight, tight-fitting; lithe, svelte; thrifty
ceñidor m belt, girdle, sash
ceñir §72 tr to gird; girdle; fasten around the waist; fasten, tie; abridge, shorten; surround; (la espada) gird on; (mil) to besiege ‖ ref (reducirse en los gastos) to tighten one's belt; (a pocas palabras) restrict oneself; adapt oneself; **ceñirse a** (p.ej., un muro) to hug, keep close to
ceño m frown; (del cielo, las nubes, el mar) threatening look; (cerco, aro) hoop, ring, band; **arrugar el ceño** to knit one's brow; **mirar con ceño** to frown at
ceño•so -sa or **ceñu•do -da** adj beetlebrowed; frowning, grim, gruff
cepa f (de árbol) stump; (de la cola del animal) stub; (de la vid) vinestalk; (de una famila o linaje) strain; **de buena cepa** of well-known quality
cepillar tr to plane; brush; smooth; (SAm) to flatter
cepillo m (instrumento para alisar la madera) plane; (utensilio para limpieza) brush; (cepo para limosnas) charity box, poor box; (CAm, Mex) flatterer; **cepillo de cabeza** hairbrush; **cepillo de dientes** toothbrush; **cepillo de ropa** clothesbrush; **cepillo de uñas** nail brush
cepo m (de limosnas) poor box; (rama de árbol) bough, branch; (trampa) snare, trap; (del yunque) stock; (para devanar la seda) reel; clamp, vise; (para asegurar a un reo) stocks, pillory; **¡cepos quedos!** quiet!, stop it!
cera f wax; **cera de abejas** beeswax; **cera de los oídos** earwax; **cera de lustrar** polishing wax; **cera de pisos** floor wax; **ceras** honeycomb; **ser como una cera** to be wax in one's hands
cerámi•co -ca adj ceramic
cerbatana f peashooter; ear trumpet; spokesperson, go-between
cerca m close-up; **tener buen cerca** to look good at close quarters ‖ f fence, wall; **cerca viva** hedge ‖ adv near; **cerca de** near, close to; about; to, at the court of; **de cerca** closely; at close range
cercado m fence, wall; walled-in garden or field
cercanía f nearness, proximity; **cercanías** neighborhood, vicinity
cerca•no -na adj close, near; adjoining, neighboring; (que debe acontecer en breve) early
cercar §73 tr to fence in, wall in; encircle, surround; crowd around; (mil) to besiege
cercenar tr to clip, trim; curtail; cut out
cerciorar tr to inform, assure ‖ ref to find out; **cerciorarse de** to ascertain, find out about
cerco m (aro, anillo) hoop, ring; (marco de puerta o ventana) casing, frame; (círculo

que aparece alrededor del sol o la luna) halo; (reunión de personas) circle, group; fence, wall; (mil) siege; **poner cerco a** (mil) to lay siege to
cerda f bristle, horsehair; (hembra del cerdo) sow
cerdear intr to be weak in the forelegs; (las cuerdas de un instrumento) rasp, grate; hold back, look for excuses
Cerdeña f Sardinia
cerdo m hog; (persona sucia) pig, swine; (hombre sin cortesía) cad, ill-bred fellow; **cerdo de muerte** pig to be slaughtered; **cerdo de vida** pig not old enough to be slaughtered; **cerdo marino** porpoise
cerdo•so -sa adj bristly
cereal adj & m cereal
cerebro m brain; (seso, inteligencia) brain, brains
ceremonia f ceremony; formality; **de ceremonia** formal; **hacer ceremonias** to stand on ceremony; **por ceremonia** as a matter of form
ceremonio•so -sa adj ceremonious, punctilious; (que gusta de ceremonias) formal
cereza f cherry
cerezo m cherry tree
cerilla f wax taper; wax match
cerillera f or **cerillero** m match box
cerneja f fetlock
cerner §51 tr to sift; (el horizonte) scan ‖ intr to bud, blossom; drizzle ‖ ref to waddle; (el ave) soar, hover; (un mal) threaten; **cernerse sobre** (amenazar) to hang over
cernícalo m (orn) sparrow hawk; ignoramus; jag, drunk
cernir §28 tr to sift
cero m zero; **empezar de cero** to start from scratch; **ser un cero a la izquierda** to not count, be a nobody
cerote m shoemaker's wax; fear
cerotear tr (el hilo) to wax ‖ intr (Chile) to drip
cerra•do -da adj closed; close; incomprehensible; (cielo) cloudy, overcast; (barba) thick; (curva) sharp; quiet, reserved, secretive; dense, stupid
cerradura f lock; closing, locking; **cerradura embutida** mortise lock
cerrajería f locksmith business; hardware; hardware store
cerrajero m locksmith; hardware dealer; (el que trabaja el hierro frío) ironworker
cerrar §2 tr to close, shut; lock; bolt; (el puño) clench; enclose; (la radio) turn off; **cerrar con llave** to lock ‖ intr to close, shut; (la noche) fall; **cerrar con** (el enemigo) to close in on; **cerrar en falso** (una puerta, cerradura, etc.) to not catch ‖ ref to close, to shut; lock; **cerrarse en falso** to not heal right
cerrazón f gathering storm clouds; (Arg) heavy fog
cerre•ro -ra adj free, loose; untamed; haughty; (Mex) rough, unpolished; (café) (Ven) bitter

cerril *adj* rough, uneven; wild, untamed; boorish, rough

cerrillar *tr* to knurl, mill

cerro *m* hill, hillock; (*entre dos surcos*) ridge; (*espinazo*) backbone; (*del animal*) neck; **en cerro** bareback; **echar por los cerros de Úbeda** to talk nonsense; **por los cerros de Úbeda** off the beaten path

cerrojo *m* bolt; **cerrojo dormido** dead bolt

certamen *m* literary competition; contest, match

certe·ro -ra *adj* certain, sure, accurate; well-informed; (*tiro*) well-aimed; (*tirador*) good, crack

certeza *f* certainty

certidumbre *f* certainty; sureness

certificación *f* certification; certificate

certifica·do -da *adj* registered ‖ *m* registered letter, registered package; certificate; **certificado de estudios** transcript

certificar §73 *tr* to certify; (*una carta*) register

certitud *f* certainty

cerval *adj* deer; (*miedo*) intense

cervato *m* fawn

cervecería *f* brewery; beer saloon

cervece·ro -ra *adj* beer ‖ *mf* brewer

cerveza *f* beer; **cerveza a presión** draught beer; **cerveza de marzo** bock beer

cer·viz *f* (*pl* **-vices**) cervix; nape of the neck; **bajar** or **doblar la cerviz** to humble oneself; **levantar la cerviz** to raise one's head, become proud; **ser de dura cerviz** to be ungovernable

cesación *f* cessation, suspension

cesante *adj* retired, out of office ‖ *mf* pensioner

cesantía *f* retirement; dismissal (*of a public official*)

cesar *intr* to stop, cease

César *m* Caesar

cese *m* ceasing; notice of retirement; **cese de alarma** all-clear; **cese de fuego** ceasefire

césped *m* lawn, sward; sod, turf

cesta *f* basket; (*para jugar a la pelota*) wicker scoop; **cesta de costura** sewing basket; **cesta para compras** market basket

cesto *m* basket; washbasket; **cesto de la colada** clothesbasket, washbasket; **estar hecho un cesto** to be overcome with sleep; **ser un cesto** to be crude and ignorant

cetrería *f* falconry

cetrero *m* falconer

cetri·no -na *adj* (*tez*) sallow; jaundiced, melancholy

cetro *m* scepter; (*para aves*) perch, roost; (*eccl*) verge; **cetro de bufón** bauble; **cetro de locura** fool's scepter; **empuñar el cetro** to ascend the throne

cf. *abbr* **confesor**

cg. *abbr* **centigramo**

C.I. *abbr* **cociente intelectual**

cía. *abbr* **compañía**

cía *f* hipbone

cianamida *f* cyanamide

cianuro *m* cyanide

ciar §77 *intr* to back up; back water; ease up

cibernética *f* cybernetics

ciborio *m* ciborium

cicatear *intr* to be stingy

cicate·ro -ra *adj* stingy ‖ *mf* miser, niggard

cica·triz *f* (*pl* **-trices**) scar

cicatrizar §60 *tr* to heal; (*una impresión dolorosa*) (Arg) to heal ‖ *ref* to heal; to scar

Cicerón *m* Cicero

ciclamor *m* Judas tree; **ciclamor del Canadá** redbud

cícli·co -ca *adj* cyclic(al)

ciclismo *m* bicycle racing

ciclista *mf* bicyclist; bicycle racer

ciclo *m* cycle; series (of lectures); (*en las escuelas*) (Arg, Urug) term

ciclón *m* cyclone

cicuta *f* hemlock

cidra *f* citron (*fruit*)

cidrada *f* citron (*candied rind*)

cidro *m* citron (*tree or shrub*)

cie·go -ga *adj* blind; blocked, stopped up; **más ciego que un topo** blind as a bat ‖ *mf* blind person ‖ *m* blind man ‖ *f* blind woman; **a ciegas** blindly; thoughtlessly; without looking

cielo *m* sky, heavens; (*clima, tiempo*) skies, climate, weather; (*de una cama*) canopy; (*mansión de los bienaventurados*) Heaven; **a cielo abierto** in the open air, outdoors; **a cielo descubierto** openly; **a cielo raso** in the open air, outdoors; in the country; **cielo de la boca** roof of the mouth; **cielo máximo** (aer) ceiling; **cielo raso** ceiling; **llovido del cielo** heaven-sent, manna from heaven

cielorraso *m* ceiling

ciem·piés *m* (*pl* **-piés**) centipede

cien *adj* hundred, a hundred, one hundred

ciénaga *f* swamp, marsh, mudhole

ciencia *f* science; knowledge; learning; **a ciencia cierta** with certainty

ciencia-ficción *f* science fiction

cieno *m* mud, mire, silt

cieno·so -sa *adj* muddy, miry, silty

ciento *adj* & *m* hundred, a hundred, one hundred; **por ciento** per cent

cierne *m* budding, blossoming; **en cierne** in blossom; only beginning

cierrarrenglón *m* marginal stop

cierre *m* closing; shutting; snap, clasp, fastener; latch, lock; (*de una tienda, de la Bolsa*) close; (*paro de trabajo*) shutdown; **cierre cremallera** zipper; **cierre de portada** metal shutter (*of store front*); **cierre de puerta** door check; **cierre hermético** weather stripping; **cierre relámpago** zipper

cierro *m* closing; shutting; (Chile) fence, wall; (Chile) envelope

cier·to -ta *adj* certain; a certain; (*acertado, verdadero*) true; (*seguro*) sure; **por cierto** for sure ‖ *cierto adv* surely, certainly

cierva *f* hind

ciervo *m* deer, stag, hart

cierzo *m* cold north wind

cifra f (*número*) cipher; (*escritura secreta*) code; (*enlace de dos o más letras empleado en sellos*) device, monogram, emblem; abbreviation; amount, sum; **en cifra** in code; in brief; mysteriously

cifrar tr to cipher, code; abridge; calculate; **cifrar la dicha en** to base one's happiness in; **cifrar la esperanza en** to place one's hope in ‖ ref to be abridged; **cifrarse en** to be based on

cifrario m (com) code

cigarra f harvest fly, locust

cigarrera f cigar case; cigar girl

cigarrería f cigar store, tobacco store

cigarre•ro -ra mf cigar maker; cigar dealer ‖ f see **cigarrera**

cigarrillo m cigarette; **cigarrillo con filtro** filter cigarette

cigarro m cigar; **cigarro de papel** cigarette; **cigarro puro** cigar

cigoñal m well sweep; (*del motor de explosión*) crankshaft

cigüeña f stork; crank, winch

cigüeñal m var of **cigoñal**

cilampa f (CAm) drizzle

cilicio m haircloth, hair shirt

cilindrada f piston displacement

cilindrar tr to roll

cilíndri•co -ca adj cylindrical

cilindro m cylinder; roll, roller; (Mex) barrel organ, hand organ

cima f (*de árbol*) top; (*de montaña*) top, summit; **dar cima a** to complete, to carry out; **por cima** (coll) at the very top

cimarra f — **hacer cimarra** (Arg, Chile) to play hooky

cima•rrón -rrona adj (*animal*) wild, untamed; (*planta*) wild; (*esclavo*) fugitive; (*marinero*) lazy; (*maté*) (Arg, Urug) black, bitter

cimarronear intr (Arg, Urug) to drink black maté ‖ ref (*el esclavo*) to flee, run away

címbalo m cymbal

cimbel m decoy pigeon, stool pigeon

cimborio or **cimborrio** m dome

cimbrar or **cimbrear** tr to brandish; swing, sway; bend; thrash, beat ‖ ref to swing, sway; shake

cimbre•ño -ña adj flexible, pliant; lithe, willowy

cimentar §2 tr to found, establish; lay the foundations of

cime•ro -ra adj top, uppermost

cimiento m foundation, groundwork; basis, source

cimitarra f scimitar

cinabrio m cinnabar

cinanquia f quinsy

cinc m (pl **cinces**) zinc

cincel m chisel, graver

cincelar tr to chisel, engrave

cinco adj & pron five; **las cinco** five o'clock ‖ m five; (*en las fechas*) fifth; **¡choque Vd. esos cinco!** or **¡vengan esos cinco!** put it here!, shake!; **decirle a uno cuántas son cinco** to tell someone what's what

cincograbado m zinc etching

cincuenta adj, pron & m fifty

cincuenta•vo -va adj & m fiftieth

cincha f cinch; **a revienta cinchas** at breakneck speed; reluctantly

cinchar tr to cinch; band, hoop

cincho m girdle, sash; iron hoop; iron tire

cine m movie; **cine en colores** color movies; **cine hablado** talkie; **cine mudo** silent movie; **cine parlante** talkie; **cine sonoro** sound movie

cineasta mf motion-picture producer; movie fan ‖ m movie actor ‖ f movie actress

cinedrama m screenplay

cinelandia f (coll) movieland

cinema m var of **cine**

cinemateca f film library

cinematografiar §77 tr & intr to cinematograph, film

cinematógrafo m cinematograph; motion picture; motion-picture projector; motion-picture theater

cinematurgo m scriptwriter

cinescopio (telv) m kinescope

cineteatro m movie house

cinéti•co -ca adj kinetic ‖ f kinetics

cínga•ro -ra adj & mf gypsy

cíni•co -ca adj cynical; impudent; slovenly, untidy ‖ mf cynic ‖ m Cynic

cinismo m cynicism; impudence

cinta f ribbon; (*tira de papel, celuloide, etc.*) tape; film; measuring tape; (*borde de la acera*) curb; fillet, scroll; **cinta aislante** electric tape, friction tape; **cinta de medir** tape measure; **cinta de teleimpresor** ticker tape; **cinta grabada de televisión** video tape; **cinta perforada** punched tape

cintillo m hatband; fancy hat cord; ring set with a gem; (*borde de la acera*) (P-R) curb; hair ribbon

cinto m belt, girdle; waist

cintura f (*parte estrecha del cuerpo humano sobre las caderas*) waist; waistline; (*de una chimenea*) throat; **meter en cintura** to bring to reason

cinturón m belt, sash; sword belt; **cinturón de asiento** seat belt; **cinturón de seguridad** safety belt; **cinturón retráctil** retractable safety belt; **cinturón salvavidas** safety belt

cíper m (Mex) zipper

cipo m milestone; signpost; memorial pillar

cipote adj (Col, Ven) stupid; (Guat) chubby ‖ mf (Hond, El Salv, Ven) brat

ciprés m cypress

circo m circus

circón m zircon

circonio m zirconium

circuito m circuit; (*de carreteras, ferrocarriles, etc.*) network; race track; **corto circuito** (elec) short circuit

circulación f circulation; traffic; **circulación rodada** vehicular traffic

circular adj circular ‖ f circular, circular letter; **circular noticiera** newsletter ‖ tr & intr to circulate

círculo m circle; club; clubhouse

circuncidar tr to circumcise; clip, curtail

ce
ci

circundante *adj* surrounding
circundar *tr* to surround, go around
circunferencia *f* circumference
circunfle•jo -ja *adj* circumflex
circunlocución *f* or **circunloquio** *m* circumlocution
circunnavegación *f* circumnavigation
circunnavegar §44 *tr* to circumnavigate
circunscribir §83 *tr* to circumscribe ‖ *ref* to hold oneself down; be held down
circunscripción *f* circumscription; district, subdivision
circunspec•to -ta *adj* circumspect
circunstancia *f* circumstance
circunstancia•do -da *adj* circumstantial, detailed
circunstancial *adj* circumstantial
circunstanciar *tr* to circumstantiate, to describe in detail
circunstante *adj* surrounding; present ‖ *mf* bystander, onlooker
circunveci•no -na *adj* neighboring
circunvolar §61 *tr* to fly around
cirial *m* (eccl) processional candlestick
ciriga•llo -lla *mf* gadabout
ciríli•co -ca *adj* Cyrillic
cirio *m* wax candle
Ciro *m* Cyrus
ciruela *f* plum; **ciruela claudia** greengage; **ciruela pasa** prune
ciruelo *m* plum, plum tree; stupid fellow
cirugía *f* surgery; **cirugía cosmética, decorativa** or **estética** face lifting
ciruja•no -na *mf* surgeon
ciscar §73 *tr* to soil, dirty; (Cuba, Mex) to shame; annoy ‖ *ref* to soil one's clothes, have an accident
cisco *m* culm; row, disturbance
cisma *m* schism; discord, disagreement; (Arg) worry, concern; (Col) gossip; (Col) fastidiousness
cismáti•co -ca *adj* schismatic; dissident; (Col) gossipy; (Col) fastidious ‖ *mf* schismatic; dissident
cisne *m* swan; (Arg) powder puff
cisterna *f* cistern; reservoir; toilet tank
cita *f* date, appointment, engagement; (*mención, pasaje textual*) citation, quotation; **cita a ciegas** blind date; **cita previa** by appointment; **darse cita** to make a date
citación *f* citation, quotation; (*ante un juez*) citation, summons
citar *tr* to make a date with, have an appointment with; cite, quote; (*ante un juez*) cite, summon; (*al toro*) incite, provoke ‖ *ref* to make a date, have an appointment
cítara *f* (mus) zither
ciudad *f* city; city council; **la ciudad Condal** Barcelona; **la ciudad del Apóstol** Santiago de Compostela; **la ciudad del Betis** Seville; **la ciudad del Cabo** Capetown or Cape Town; **la ciudad de los Califas** Cordova; **la ciudad de los Reyes** Lima, Peru; **la ciudad de María Santísima** Seville; **la ciudad Imperial** or **Imperial ciudad** Toledo

ciudadanía *f* citizenship
ciudada•no -na *adj* city; citizen; civic ‖ *mf* citizen; urbanite
ciudadela *f* citadel; (Cuba) tenement house
cívi•co -ca *adj* civic; city; domestic; public-spirited
civil *adj* civil; civilian ‖ *mf* civilian ‖ *m* guard, policeman
civilidad *f* civility
civilista *adj* civil-law ‖ *mf* authority on civil law; (Chile) antimilitarist
civilización *f* civilization
civilizar §60 *tr* to civilize
civismo *m* good citizenship
cizalla *f* shears; metal shaving, metal clipping; **cizalla de guillotina** gate shears, guillotine shears; **cizallas** shears
cizallar *tr* to shear
cizaña *f* darnel; contamination, corruption; discord; **sembrar cizaña** to sow discord
clac *m* (*pl* **claques**) opera hat, claque, crush hat; (*sombrero de tres picos*) cocked hat
clamar *tr* to cry out for ‖ *intr* to cry out; **clamar contra** to cry out against; **clamar por** to cry out for
clamor *m* clamor, outcry; (*toque de difuntos*) knell, toll; fame
clamorear *tr* to clamor for ‖ *intr* to clamor; (*tocar a muerto*) toll
clamoreo *m* clamoring; tolling
clamoro•so -sa *adj* clamorous; loud, noisy
clan *m* clan
clandestinista *mf* (Guat) bootlegger
clandesti•no -na *adj* clandestine
claque *f* claque, hired clappers
clara *f* white of egg; bald spot; (*de un trozo de tela*) thin spot; (*en el tiempo lluvioso*) break, let-up
claraboya *f* (*ventana en el techo*) skylight; (*en la parte alta de la pared*) transom; (*esp. en las iglesias la parte superior de la nave que tiene una serie de ventanas*) clerestory
clarear *tr* to brighten, light up ‖ *intr* (*empezar a amanecer*) to get light, dawn; (*el mal tiempo*) clear up ‖ *ref* (*una tela*) to show through; show one's hand
clarecer §22 *ref* to dawn
clarete *m* claret
claridad *f* clarity; clearness; brightness; fame, glory; blunt remark; **claridades** plain language
clarido•so -sa *adj* (CAm, Mex) blunt, rude, plain-spoken
clarificar §73 *tr* to clarify; brighten, light up; (*lo que estaba turbio*) clear
clarín *m* clarion; fine cambric; (Chile) sweet pea
clarinada *f* clarion call; uncalled-for remark
clarinete *m* clarinet
clarión *m* chalk
clarividencia *f* clairvoyance; clear-sightedness
clarividente *adj* clairvoyant; clear-sighted ‖ *mf* clairvoyant

cla·ro -ra *adj* clear; (*de color*) light; (*pelo*) thin, sparse; (*té*) weak; famous, illustrious; (*cerveza*) light; **a las claras** publicly, openly, frankly ‖ *m* gap; (*en el bosque*) glade, clearing; space, interval; (*ventana u otra abertura*) light; (*claraboya*) skylight; (*en las nubes*) break; **claro de luna** brief moonlight; **de claro en claro** evidently; from one end to the other; **pasar la noche de claro en claro** to not sleep all night; **poner** or **sacar en claro** to explain, clear up; (*un borrador*) to copy ‖ *f* see **clara** ‖ **claro** *adv* clearly ‖ **claro** *interj* sure!, of course!; **¡claro está!**, **¡claro que sí!** sure!, of course!

claror *m* brightness; **claror de luna** moonlight, moonglow

claru·cho -cha *adj* watery, thin

clase *f* class; classroom; **clase alta** upper class; **clase baja** lower class; **clase media** middle class; **clase obrera** working class; **clases** noncommissioned officers, warrant officers; **clases pasivas** pensioners

clasicista *mf* classicist

clási·co -ca *adj* classical ‖ *mf* classicist ‖ *m* classic

clasificador *m* filing cabinet

clasificar §73 *tr* to classify; class; sort; file ‖ *ref* to class

clasismo *m* segregation

clasista *mf* segregationist

claudicar §73 *intr* (*cojear*) to limp; (*obrar defectuosamente*) bungle; back down

claustral *adj* cloistral

claustro *m* cloister; (*junta de la universidad*) faculty

cláusula *f* (*de un contrato u otro documento*) clause; (gram) sentence

clausula·do -da *adj* (*estilo*) choppy ‖ *m* series of clauses

clausular *tr* to close, finish, conclude

clausura *f* confinement; seclusion; enclosure; adjournment

clausurar *tr* (*una asamblea, un tribunal, etc.*) to close, adjourn; (*un comercio por orden gubernativa*) suspend, close up

clava *f* club

clavadista *mf* (Mex) diver

clava·do -da *adj* studded with nails; exact, precise; (*reloj*) stopped; sharp, e.g., **a las siete clavadas** at seven o'clock sharp ‖ *m* (Mex) dive

clavar *tr* to nail; (*un clavo*) drive; (*una daga, un punzón*) stick; (*una piedra preciosa*) set; (*los ojos, la atención*) fix; (*a un caballo al herrarlo*) prick; cheat ‖ *ref* to prick oneself; get cheated; (Mex) to dive; **clavárselas** (CAm) to get drunk

clave *m* harpsichord ‖ *f* (*de un enigma, código, etc.*) key; (*piedra con que se cierra el arco*) (archit) keystone; (mus) clef

clavel *m* carnation, pink; **clavel de ramillete** sweet william; **clavel reventón** double-flowered carnation

clavelón *m* marigold

clavellina *f* carnation, pink

clave·ro -ra *mf* keeper of the keys ‖ *m* clove tree ‖ *f* nail hole

claveta *f* peg, wooden peg

clavetear *tr* to stud; tip, put a tip on; wind up, settle

clavicordio *m* clavichord

clavícula *f* clavicle, collarbone

clavija *f* pin, peg, dowel; (elec) plug; (mus) peg; **apretarle a uno las clavijas** to put the screws on someone

clavillo *m* or **clavito** *m* brad, tack; (*que sujeta las hojas de unas tijeras*) pin, rivet; clove

clavo *m* nail; (*capullo seco de la flor del clavero*) clove; migraine; keen sorrow; (*artículo que no se vende*) (Arg, Bol, Chile) drug on the market; (Col) bad deal; (Hond, Mex) rich vein of ore; (Ven) heartburn; **clavo de alambre** wire nail; **clavo de especia** (*flor*) clove; **clavo de herrar** horseshoe nail; **dar en el clavo** to hit the nail on the head

clemátide *f* clematis

clemencia *f* clemency

clemente *adj* clement, merciful

cleptóma·no -na *mf* kleptomaniac

clerecía *f* clergy

clerical *adj* & *m* clerical

clericato *m* or **clericatura** *f* priesthood

clerigalla *f* (contemptuous) priests

clérigo *m* cleric, priest; **clérigo de misa y olla** priestlet

clerizonte *m* shabby-looking priest; fake priest

clero *m* clergy

clerófo·bo -ba *adj* priest-hating ‖ *mf* priest hater

cliché *m* (*lugar común*) cliché

cliente *mf* (*parroquiano de una tienda*) customer; (*de un abogado*) client; (*de un médico*) patient; (*de un hotel*) guest

clientela *f* customers; clientele; patronage, protection; practice

clima *m* climate; country, region; **clima artificial** air conditioning

climatización *f* air conditioning

climatizar §60 *tr* to air-condition

clíni·co -ca *adj* clinical ‖ *mf* clinician ‖ *f* clinic; private hospital; **clínica de reposo** nursing home, convalescent home

clip *m* paper clip

cliqueteo *m* clicking

clisar *tr* (typ) to plate

clisé *m* (*plancha clisada*) cliché, plate; (phot) plate; (*lugar común*) cliché

clo *m* cluck; **decir clo** (Chile) to kick the bucket; **hacer clo clo** (*la gallina clueca*) to cluck

cloaca *f* sewer

clocar §81 *intr* to cluck

cloquear *intr* to cluck

cloqueo *m* cluck, clucking

clorhídri·co -ca *adj* hydrochloric

cloro *m* chlorine

clorofila *f* chlorophyll

cloroformizar §60 *tr* to chloroform

cloroformo *m* chloroform

cloruro *m* chloride

ci
cl

clóset *m* (SAm) (wall) closet
club *m* (*pl* **clubs**) club; **club náutico** yacht club
clubista *mf* club member
clue•co -ca *adj* broody; decrepit
c.m.b., C.M.B. *abbr* **cuyas manos beso**
coa *f* (Mex) hoe; (Chile) thieves' jargon
coacción *f* coercion, compulsion
coaccionar *tr* to coerce, compel
coacervar *tr* to pile up
coactar *tr* to coerce, compel
coadunar *tr & ref* to mix together
coadyuvar *tr & intr* to help, aid, assist
coagular *tr & ref* (*la sangre*) to coagulate; (*la leche*) curdle
coágulo *m* clot
coalición *f* coalition
coalla *f* woodcock
coartada *f* alibi
coartar *tr* to limit, restrict
coba *f* hoax; flattery
cobalto *m* cobalt
cobarde *adj* cowardly; timid; (*vista*) dim, weak ‖ *mf* coward
cobardear *intr* to act cowardly; be timid
cobardía *f* cowardice; timidity
cobayo *m* guinea pig
cobertera *f* lid; bawd, procuress
cobertizo *m* shed; (*tejado saledizo*) covered balcony, penthouse
cobertor *m* bedcover, bedspread; lid
cobertura *f* cover; covering; (*garantía metálica*) coverage
cobija *f* curved tile; top, lid; short mantilla; (W-I) guano roof; **cobijas** bedclothes
cobijar *tr* to cover; shelter, protect
cobijo *m* covering; shelter, protection; (*hospedaje sin manutención*) lodging
cobra *f* team of mares used in threshing; (hunt) retrieval
cobra•dor -dora *adj* (*perro*) retrieving ‖ *mf* collector; trolley conductor
cobranza *f* collecting; (hunt) retrieval
cobrar *tr* (*lo perdido*) to recover; (*lo que otro le debe*) collect; (*un cheque*) cash; (*cierto precio*) charge; acquire, get; (*una cuerda*) pull in; (*pedir, reclamar*) dun; (hunt) to retrieve; **cobrar afición a** to take a liking for; **cobrar al número llamado** (telp) to reverse the charges; **cobrar ánimo** to take courage; **cobrar carnes** to put on flesh; **cobrar fuerzas** to gain strength ‖ *intr* to get hit ‖ *ref* to recover, come to
cobre *m* copper; copper or brass kitchen utensils; **batir el cobre** to hustle, work with a will; **cobres** (mus) brasses
cobre•ño -ña *adj* copper
cobrero *m* coppersmith
cobri•zo -za *adj* coppery
cobro *m* collection; recovery; **cobro contra entrega** collect on delivery; **en cobro** in a safe place
coca *f* (*en una cuerda*) kink; (coll) head; (slang) cocaine; **de coca** (Mex) free; (Mex) in vain
cocaína *f* cocaine

cocción *f* cooking, baking; (*de objetos cerámicos*) baking, burning
cocear *intr* to kick; (*resistir*) balk, rebel
cocer §16 *tr* to cook; boil; (*pan; ladrillos*) bake; digest ‖ *intr* to cook; boil; ferment ‖ *ref* to suffer a long time
coci•do -da *adj* cooked ‖ *m* Spanish stew
cociente *m* quotient; **cociente intelectual** intelligence quotient
cocina *f* (*pieza*) kitchen; (*arte*) cooking, cuisine; (*aparato*) stove; **cocina de presión** pressure cooker; **cocina económica** kitchen range
cocinar *tr* to cook ‖ *intr* to meddle
cocine•ro -ra *mf* cook
cocinilla *m* meddler ‖ *f* kitchenette; chafing dish; **cocinilla sin fuego** fireless cooker
coco *m* cocoanut; (*moño*) topknot, chignon; (*duende*) bogeyman; (*gesto, mueca*) face, grimace; (*sombrero hongo*) (Col, Ecuad) derby hat; **hacer cocos** to make a face; (*los enamorados*) to make eyes
cocodrilo *m* crocodile
cócora *adj* boring, tiresome ‖ *mf* bore, pest
coco•so -sa *adj* worm-eaten
cocotero *m* cocoanut palm or tree
coctel *m* or **cóctel** *m* cocktail; cocktail party
coctelera *f* cocktail shaker
cocuma *f* (Peru) roast corn on the cob
cochambre *m* dirty, stinking thing, pigsty
cochambro•so -sa *adj* dirty, stinking
coche *m* carriage; coach; car; taxi; (*puerco*) hog; **caminar en el coche de San Francisco** to go or to ride on shank's mare; **coche bar** (rr) club car; **coche bomba** fire engine; (coll) car bomb; **coche celular** Black Maria, prison van; **coche de alquiler** cab, hack; **coche de carreras** racing car; **coche de correos** mail car; **coche de plaza** or **de punto** cab, hack; **coche de reparto** (delivery) van; **coche de serie** (aut) stock car; **coche fúnebre** hearse; **coche rural** station wagon
coche-cama *m* (*pl* **coches-camas**) sleeping car
cochecillo *m* baby carriage; **cochecillo para inválidos** wheelchair; **cochecillo para niños** baby carriage
coche-comedor *m* (*pl* **coches-comedores**) (rr) diner, dining car
coche-correo *m* (*pl* **coches-correo**) (rr) mail car
coche-fumador *m* (*pl* **coches-fumadores**) (rr) smoker, smoking car
coche-habitación *m* (*pl* **coches-habitación**) trailer
cochera *f* coach house; livery stable; carbarn; garage
cochería *f* (Arg, Chile) livery stable
coche•ro -ra *adj* easy to cook ‖ *m* coachman, driver; **cochero de punto** cabby, hackman ‖ *f* see **cochera**
cocherón *m* coach house; (*depósito de locomotoras*) roundhouse
coche-salón *m* (*pl* **coches-salón**) (rr) parlor car
cochevira *f* lard

cochina f sow; (*mujer sucia y desaliñada*) trollop
cochinada f piggishness, filthiness; dirty trick
cochinillo m sucking pig
cochi•no -na adj piggish, filthy; (*tacaño*) stingy; (Ven) cowardly ‖ mf hog; (*persona muy sucia*) (coll) pig, dirty person ‖ f see **cochina**
cochite hervite adj, adv & m helter-skelter
cochitril m pigsty; den, hovel
cochura f batch of dough
codadura f (hort) layer
codal adj elbow ‖ m prop, shoring
codazo m poke, nudge; **dar codazo a** (Mex) to tip off
codear tr (SAm) to sponge on ‖ intr to elbow, elbow one's way ‖ ref to hobnob, rub elbows
codelincuencia f complicity
codelincuente mf accomplice
codera f elbow patch; elbow itch
códice m codex
codicia f covetousness, greed, cupidity
codiciar tr to covet
codicilo m codicil
codicio•so -sa adj covetous, greedy; (*laborioso*) hard-working
codificar §73 tr to codify
código m code; **código penal** criminal code; **código universal de producto** universal product code (UPC)
codillo m (*de animal*) knee; (*estribo*) stirrup; (*de un tubo*) elbow; (*de la rama cortada*) stump
codo m elbow; (Guat, Mex) miser, tightwad; **dar de codo a** to nudge; to spurn; **empinar el codo** to crook the elbow; **hablar por los codos** to talk too much
codor•niz f (pl **-nices**) quail
coeducación f coeducation
coeficiente adj & m coefficient
coetáne•o -a adj & mf contemporary
coexistencia f coexistence
coexistir intr to coexist
cofa f (naut) top; **cofa de vigía** (naut) crow's-nest
cofrade mf member, fellow member ‖ m brother ‖ f sister
cofradía f brotherhood, sisterhood; association, fraternity
cofre m coffer, chest, trunk
cogedor m dustpan; coal shovel, ash shovel
coger §17 tr to catch, seize, take hold of: collect, gather, pick; overtake; surprise; hold ‖ intr to be, be located; fit ‖ ref to get caught; cling; get involved
cogida f collecting, gathering, picking; (taur) hook
cogollo m (*de la lechuga*) heart; (*de la berza*) head; (*de una planta*) shoot; (*del árbol*) top; (*lo mejor*) cream, pick
cogote m back of the neck
cogotera f havelock
cogotu•do -da adj thick-necked; (coll) proud, stiff-necked; (SAm) moneyed
cogulla f cowl, frock; **cogulla de fraile** (bot) monkshood

cohabitar intr to live together; (*el hombre y la mujer*) cohabit
cohechar tr to bribe; plow just before sowing ‖ intr to take a bribe
cohecho m bribe
coherede•ro -ra mf coheir ‖ f coheiress
coherente adj coherent
cohesión f cohesion
cohete m (*fuego artificial*) rocket, skyrocket; (*motor a reacción*) rocket; (coll) fidgety person; **cohete de señales** (aer) flare; **cohete intermedio** or **cohete de alcance medio** intermediate-range missile; **cohete lanzador** booster rocket
cohetería f missilery
cohibente adj (elec) nonconducting
cohibi•do -da adj timid, self-conscious
cohibir tr to check, restrain, inhibit; (Mex) to oblige
cohombro m cucumber
cohonestar tr to gloss over, rationalize
coima f rake-off paid to operator of a gambling table; concubine; (SAm) bribe
coincidencia f coincidence
coincidir intr to coincide; happen at the same time; be at the same time (*at a given place*); agree
coito m coition, coitus
coja f lame woman; lewd woman
cojear intr to limp; (*una mesa, una silla*) wobble; (*adolecer de algún vicio*) slip, lapse, have a weakness
cojera f (*anormalidad del que cojea*) lameness; (*movimiento del que cojea*) limp
cojijo m bug, insect; peeve
cojijo•so -sa adj peevish
cojín m cushion
cojincillo m pad
cojinete m cushion; sewing cushion; (mach) bearing; **cojinete de bolas** ball bearing; **cojinete de rodillos** roller bearing
co•jo -ja adj lame, crippled; (*mesa, silla*) wobbly; (*pierna*) game ‖ mf lame person, cripple ‖ f see **coja**
cojón m testicle
cok m var of **coque**
col. abbr **colonia, columna**
col f cabbage; **col de Bruselas** Brussels sprouts
cola f (*de animal, de ave, de cometa*) tail; (*de un vestido*) train, trail; (*de personas que esperan turno*) queue; (*extremidad posterior*) tail end, rear end; (*de una clase de alumnos*) bottom; (*pasta fuerte*) glue; **cola del pan** bread line; **cola de milano** or **cola de pato** dovetail; **cola de pescado** isinglass; **cola de retazo** size, sizing; **hacer cola** to queue, to stand in line
colaboración f collaboration; (*en un periódico, coloquio, etc.*) contribution
colaboracionista mf collaborationist
colabora•dor -dora adj collaborating ‖ mf collaborator; contributor
colaborar intr to collaborate; (*en un periódico, coloquio, etc.*) contribute
colación f (*cotejo; refacción ligera*) collation; (*de un grado de universidad*) conferring;

parish land; **sacar a colación** to mention, bring up; **traer a colación** to bring up; adduce as proof; bring up irrelevantly

colacionar *tr* to collate; compare; (*un beneficio*) confer

colactánea *f* foster sister

colactáneo *m* foster brother

colada *f* washing powder; wash; (*garganta entre montañas*) gulch; cattle run; **todo saldrá en la colada** it will all come out in the wash; the day of reckoning will come

coladera *f* strainer; (Mex) sewer

coladero *m* strainer; cattle run; narrow pass

colador *m* strainer, colander

colapez *f* or **colapiscis** *f* isinglass

colapso *m* breakdown, collapse; **colapso nervioso** nervous breakdown

colar *tr* (*un grado universitario*) to confer ‖ §61 *tr* (*un líquido*) to strain; bleach in hot lye, buck; (*metales*) cast; (*una moneda falsa*) pass off; **colar el hueso por** (coll) to squeeze through ‖ *intr* to run, ooze; squeeze through; come in, slip in; drink wine; **colar a fondo** to sink; **no colar** (*una cosa*) to not be believed ‖ *ref* to seep, seep through; slip in, slip through; make a slip; lie; **colarse de gorra** to crash the gate

colateral *adj* collateral ‖ *mf* (*pariente*) collateral ‖ *m* (com) collateral

colcrén *m* cold cream

colcha *f* quilt, counterpane, bedspread

colchón *m* mattress; **colchón de aire** air mattress; **colchón de muelles** bedspring, spring mattress; **colchón de plumas** feather bed

coleada *f* wag (*of the tail*); (Mex, Ven) throwing the bull by twisting its tail

colear *tr* (taur) to grab by the tail; (*la res*) (Mex, Ven) to throw by twisting the tail; (Col, Ven) to nag, harass; (Guat) to trail after; (*reprobar en un examen*) (Chile) to flunk ‖ *intr* to wag the tail; stay alive, keep going; (*los últimos vagones de un tren*) sway; (aer) to fishtail; **colear en** (*cierta edad*) (CAm, W-I) to border on, be close to; **todavía colea** it's not over yet

colección *f* collection

coleccionar *tr* to collect

coleccionista *mf* collector

colecta *f* collection for charity; (eccl) collect

colectar *tr* to collect; (*obras antes sueltas*) collect in one volume

colecticio -cia *adj* new, untrained, green; (*tomo*) omnibus

colectivo -va *adj* collective

colector *m* collector; catch basin; (elec) commutator; (aut) manifold

colega *mf* colleague ‖ *m* confrere

colegial *m* schoolboy; (Mex) greenhorn, beginner

colegiala *f* schoolgirl

colegiatura *f* scholarship; (Mex) tuition

colegio *m* school, academy; (*sociedad de hombres de una misma profesión*) college (*e.g., of cardinals, electors*)

colegir §57 *tr* to gather, collect; conclude, infer

cólera *m* cholera‖ *f* anger, wrath; (*bilis*) bile; **montar en cólera** to fly into a rage

colérico -ca *adj* choleric, irascible

colesterol *m* cholesterol

coleta *f* pigtail; (*del torero*) cue, queue; (coll) postscript; **cortarse la coleta** to quit the bull ring; to quit, retire; **tener** or **traer coleta** to have serious consequences

coletero *m* wren

coleto *m* buff jacket; (coll) body, one's body, oneself; **decir para su coleto** (coll) to say to oneself; **echarse al coleto** to eat up, drink up; read from cover to cover

colgadero *m* hanger, hook; clothes rack

colgadizo *m* lean-to, penthouse; projection over a door, canopy

colgado -da *adj* pending, unsettled; **dejar colgado** to disappoint, frustrate; **quedarse colgado** to be disappointed, frustrated

colgador *m* clothes hanger, coat hanger

colgajo *m* rag, tatter

colgante *adj* hanging, dangling; (*puente*) suspension ‖ *m* drop, pendant; (archit) festoon; (P-R) watch fob

colgar §63 *tr* to hang; impute, attribute; (*a un alumno*) flunk; (*a un reo*) hang ‖ *intr* to hang, hang down, dangle; droop; (telp) to hang up; **colgar de** to hang from, hang on; depend on

colibrí *m* (*pl* -**bríes**) humming bird

cólico -ca *adj* & *m* colic ‖ *f* upset stomach

coliche *m* (coll) at-home, open house

coliflor *f* cauliflower

coligar §44 *ref* to join forces, make common cause

colilla *f* butt, stump, stub

colín -lina *adj* (*caballo o yegua*) bobtailed ‖ *m* bobwhite; **colín de Virginia** bobwhite ‖ *f* see **colina**

colina *f* hill, knoll

colindante *adj* adjacent, contiguous

colindar *intr* to be adjacent

colinoso -sa *adj* hilly

colirio *m* eyewash

coliseo *m* coliseum

colisión *f* collision; bruise, bump

colista *mf* person standing in line

colitis *f* colitis

colmado -da *adj* abundant, plentiful ‖ *m* food store, grocery store; seafood restaurant

colmar *tr* to fill up; (*las esperanzas de uno*) fulfill; overwhelm; **colmar de** to shower with, overwhelm with

colmena *f* beehive

colmenar *m* apiary

colmenero -ra *mf* beekeeper

colmillo *m* eyetooth, canine tooth; (*del elefante*) tusk; **tener el colmillo retorcido** to cut one's eyeteeth

colmo -ma *adj* brimful, overflowing ‖ *m* overflow; thatch, thatch roof; (*de un sorbete*) topping; **eso es el colmo** (coll) that's the limit; **para colmo de** to top off

colocación *f* (*acción de poner una persona o cosa en un lugar*) location; (*disposición de una cosa respecto del lugar que ocupa*) placement; (*inversión de dinero*) invest-ment; (*empleo*) position, employment, job

colocar §73 *tr* to place, put; (*una trampa*) set ‖ *ref* to get placed, find a job; (*venderse*) sell

colodra *f* milk bucket; drinking horn; (*bebe-dor de vino*) (coll) toper

colofón *m* colophon

colofonia *f* rosin

coloide *adj* & *m* colloid

colon *m* colon; (gram) main clause

Colón *m* Columbus

colonia *f* colony; cologne; silk ribbon; hous-ing development; (W-I) sugar plantation ‖ **Colonia** *f* Cologne; **la Colonia del Cabo** Cape Colony

colonial *adj* colonial; overseas ‖ **coloniales** *mpl* imported foods

colonizar §60 *tr* & *intr* to colonize

colono *m* colonist, settler; tenant farmer; (W-I) owner of sugar plantation

coloquial *adj* colloquial

coloquialismo *m* colloquialism

coloquio *m* colloquy, talk, conference

color *m* color; (*substancia para pintar*) paint; (*para pintarse el rostro*) rouge; **colores** (*bandera*) colors; (*persona*) **de color** of color, colored; (*zapatos*) tan; **sacar los colores a** to make blush; **so color de** under color of, under pretext of; **verlo todo de color de rosa** to see everything through rose-colored glasses

colora•do -da *adj* red, reddish; (*libre, ob-sceno*) off-color; (*aparentemente justo y razonable*) specious; **ponerse colorado** to blush

colorado•te -ta *adj* ruddy, sanguine

colorante *adj* & *m* coloring

colorar *tr* to color; dye; stain

colorear *tr* to color; (fig) to color, excuse, palliate ‖ *ref* (*la cereza, el tomate, etc.*) to redden, turn red

colorete *m* rouge; **ponerse colorete** to put on rouge

colorir §1 *tr* to color; (fig) to color, palliate ‖ *intr* to take on color

colosal *adj* colossal

coloso *m* colossus

columbrar *tr* to discern, descry, glimpse; to guess

columna *f* column; **columna de dirección** steering column; **quinta columna** fifth col-umn

columnata *f* colonnade

columnista *mf* columnist

columpiar *tr* to swing ‖ *ref* to swing; to seesaw; (coll) to swing, swagger

columpio *m* swing; **columpio de tabla** see-saw

colusión *f* collusion

collada *f* mountain pass; (naut) steady blow

collado *m* hill, height

collar *m* necklace; dog collar, horse collar; (*aro de hierro asegurado al cuello del malhechor*) collar, band; (*plumas del cuello de ciertas aves*) frill, ring; (*cadena que rodea el cuello como insignia*) cord, chain; (mach) collar

collera *f* horse collar; chain gang; **colleras** (Arg, Chile) cuff links

co•llón -llona *adj* cowardly ‖ *mf* coward

coma *m* (pathol) coma ‖ *f* comma; (*en inglés se emplea el punto en aritmética para separar los enteros de las fracciones deci-males*) decimal point

comadre *f* mother or godmother (*with respect to each other*); gossip (*woman*); friend, neighbor (*woman*)

comadrear *intr* to gossip, go around gossip-ing

comadreja *f* weasel

comadrería *f* gossip, idle gossip

comadre•ro -ra *adj* gossipy ‖ *mf* gossip

comadrón *m* accoucheur

comadrona *f* midwife

comandancia *f* command; commander's headquarters; (mil) majority

comandante *m* commander, commandant; (mil) major

comandar *tr* (mil, nav) to command

comando *m* (mil) command; **comando a distancia** remote control

comarca *f* district, region, country

comarcar §73 *tr* to plant in a line at regular intervals ‖ *intr* to border, be contiguous

comato•so -sa *adj* comatose

comba *f* bend, curve; warp, bulge; skipping rope; **saltar a la comba** to jump rope, skip rope

combar *tr* to bend, curve ‖ *ref* to bend, curve; warp, bulge; sag

combate *m* combat, fight; **combate revan-cha** (box) return bout; **fuera de combate** hors de combat; (box) knockout

combatiente *adj* & *m* combatant

combatir *tr* to combat, fight; beat, beat upon ‖ *intr* & *ref* to combat, fight, struggle

combinación *f* combination; (*de trenes*) con-nection

combinar *tr* & *ref* to combine

com•bo -ba *adj* bent, curved, crooked; warped ‖ *m* trunk or rock to stand wine casks on ‖ *f* see **comba**

combustible *adj* combustible ‖ *m* (*substancia que arde con facilidad*) combustible; (*sub-stancia que sirve para calentar, cocinar, etc.*) fuel; **combustible alternativo** alter-nate fuel

combustión *f* combustion

comede•ro -ra *adj* eatable ‖ *m* manger, feed trough; (Mex) haunt, hangout; **limpiarle a uno el comedero** to deprive someone of his bread and butter

comedia *f* drama, play; theater; comedy; (fig) farce; **comedia cómica** (*drama de desen-lace festivo*) comedy; **hacer la comedia** to pretend, make believe

comedian•te -ta *mf* hypocrite ‖ *m* actor, comedian ‖ *f* actress, comedienne

comedi•do -da *adj* courteous, polite; moder-ate; obliging, accommodating

comedimiento *m* courtesy, politeness; mod-eration

comediógra•fo -fa *mf* playwright

comedir §50 *ref* to be courteous; restrain oneself, be moderate; be obliging; **comedirse a** to offer to, volunteer to

comedón *m* blackhead

come•dor -dora *adj* heavy-eating ‖ *m* dining room; restaurant, eating place; dining-room suite; **comedor de beneficencia** soup kitchen

comején *m* termite

comendador *m* prelate, prior; knight commander; (*de una orden militar*) commander

comensal *mf* dependent, servant; table companion

comentar *tr* to comment on ‖ *intr* to comment; to gossip

comentario *m* comment, commentary; **comentarios** talk, gossip

comentarista *mf* commentator

comento *m* comment, commentary; deceit, falsehood

comenzar §18 *tr & intr* to commence, begin, start

comer *m* eating, food ‖ *tr* to eat; to feed on; to gnaw away; to consume; (*alguna renta*) to enjoy; to itch; (*una pieza en el juego de damas*) to take; **comer vivo** to have it in for; **sin comerlo ni beberlo** (coll) without having anything to do with it; **tener qué comer** to have enough to live on ‖ *intr* to eat; to dine, to have dinner; to itch ‖ *ref* to eat up; (*las uñas*) to bite; (*el dinero*) (coll) to consume, eat up; (*omitir*) to skip, skip over; **comerse unos a otros** to be at loggerheads

comerciable *adj* marketable; sociable

comercial *adj* commercial, business

comerciante *mf* merchant,. trader, dealer; **comerciante al por mayor** wholesaler; **comerciante al por menor** retailer

comerciar *intr* to trade, deal

comercio *m* commerce, trade, business; store, shop; business center; commerce, intercourse; **comercio de artículos de regalo** gift shop; **comercio exterior** foreign trade

comestible *adj* eatable ‖ *m* food, foodstuff

cometa *m* comet ‖ *f* kite

cometer *tr* (*un crimen, una falta*) to commit; (*un negocio a una persona*) commit, entrust; (*figuras retóricas*) employ

cometido *m* assignment, duty; commitment

comezón *f* itch

comicastro *m* ham, ham actor

comicios *mpl* polls; **acudir a los comicios** to go to the polls

cómi•co -ca *adj* comic, comical; dramatic ‖ *mf* actor; comedian; **cómico de la legua** strolling player, barnstormer ‖ *f* actress; comedienne

comida *f* (*alimento*) food; (*el que se toma a horas señaladas*) meal; (*el principal de cada día*) dinner; **comida corrida** (Mex) table d'hôte

comidilla *f* hobby; **la comidilla del pueblo** the talk of the town

comienzo *m* beginning, start; **a comienzos de** around the beginning of

comilitona *f* spread, feast

comi•lón -lona *adj* heavy-eating ‖ *mf* hearty eater ‖ *f* hearty meal, spread

comillas *fpl* quotation marks

cominear *intr* (*el hombre*) to fuss around like a woman

comiquear *intr* to put on amateur plays

comiquillo *m* ham, ham actor

comisar *tr* to seize, confiscate

comisario *m* commissary; commissioner; **comisario de a bordo** purser

comisión *f* commission; committee; (*recado*) errand

comisiona•do -da *mf* commissioner ‖ *m* committeeman

comisionar *tr* to commission

comiso *m* seizure, confiscation; confiscated goods

comisura *f* corner (*e.g., of lips*)

comité *m* committee; **comité planeador** steering committee

comitente *mf* constituent

comitiva *f* retinue, suite; procession

como *adv* as, like; so to speak, as it were ‖ *conj* as; when; if; so that; as soon as; as long as; inasmuch as; **así como** as well as; **como no** unless; **como que** because, inasmuch as; **como quien dice** so to speak; **tan luego como** as soon as

cómo *adv* how; why; what; **¿a cómo es. . . ?** how much is. . . ?; **¿cómo no?** why not?

cómoda *f* bureau, commode, chest

comodidad *f* comfort; convenience; advantage, interest

comodín *m* joker, wild card; gadget, jigger; excuse, alibi

cómo•do -da *adj* handy, convenient; comfortable ‖ *f* see **cómoda**

como•dón -dona *adj* comfort-loving, self-indulgent, easy-going

compac•to -ta *adj* compact

compadecer §22 *tr* to pity, feel sorry for ‖ *ref* to harmonize; **compadecerse con** to harmonize with; **compadecerse de** to pity, feel sorry for

compadraje *m* clique, cabal

compadrar *intr* to become a godfather; become friends

compadre *m* father or godfather (*with respect to each other*); friend, companion

compadrear *intr* to be close friends; (Arg, Urug) to brag, show off

compadrería *f* close companionship

compadrito *m* (Arg) bully

compaginar *tr* to arrange, put in order ‖ *ref* to fit, agree; blend

companage *m* snacks, cold cuts

compañerismo *m* companionship

compañe•ro -ra *mf* companion; partner; mate; **compañero de cama** bedfellow; **compañero de candidatura** (pol) running mate; **compañero de cuarto** roommate; **compañero de juego** playmate; **compañero de viaje** fellow traveler ‖ *f* (*esposa*) helpmeet

compañía *f* company; society; **compañía de desembarco** (nav) landing force; **compañía matriz** parent company; **hacerle compañía a una persona** to keep someone company

compañón *m* testicle; **compañón de perro** orchid

comparación *f* comparison

comparar *tr* to compare

comparati•vo -va *adj* comparative

comparecencia *f* (law) appearance

comparecer §22 *intr* (law) to appear

comparendo *m* (law) summons

comparsa *mf* (theat) supernumerary, extra ‖ *f* supernumeraries, extras

compartimiento *m* distribution, division, compartment; **compartimiento estanco** watertight compartment

compartir *tr* to distribute, divide; share

compás *m* (*brújula*) compass; (*instrumento para trazar curvas*) compass or compasses; rule, measure; (mus) time, measure; (mus) bar, measure; (mus) beat; **a compás** (mus) in time; **compás de calibres** calipers; **compás de división** dividers; **llevar el compás** (mus) to keep time

compasible *adj* compassionate; pitiful

compasión *f* compassion; **¡por compasión!** for pity's sake!

compasi•vo -va *adj* compassionate

compatri•cio -cia *mf* or **compatriota** *mf* fellow countryman, compatriot

compeler *tr* to compel

compendiar *tr* to condense, summarize

compendio *m* compendium; **en compendio** in a word

compendio•so -sa *adj* compendious

compensación *f* compensation; (com) clearing, clearance

compensar *tr* to compensate; compensate for ‖ *intr* to compensate ‖ *ref* to be compensated for

competencia *f* (*aptitud*) competence; (*rivalidad*) competition; dispute; area, field; **de la competencia de** in the domain of; **sin competencia** unmatched (*prices*)

competente *adj* competent; reliable

competer *intr* to be incumbent

competición *f* competition

competi•dor -dora *adj* competing ‖ *mf* competitor

competir §50 *intr* to compete; **poder competir** to be competitive

compilación *f* compilation

compilar *tr* to compile

compinche *mf* chum, crony, pal

complacencia *f* complacency

complacer §22 *tr* to please, humor ‖ *ref* to be pleased, take pleasure

complaciente *adj* obliging; indulgent

comple•jo -ja *adj* & *m* complex; **complejo de inferioridad** inferiority complex

complementar *tr* to complement

complemento *m* complement; completion; perfection; accessory; **complemento directo** (gram) direct object

completar *tr* to complete; perfect

comple•to -ta *adj* complete; (*autobús, tranvía*) full

complexión *f* constitution

complexiona•do -da *adj* — **bien complexionado** strong, robust; **mal complexionado** weak, frail

comple•xo -xa *adj* complex

complica•do -da *adj* complicated, complex

complicar §73 *tr* to complicate; involve ‖ *ref* to become complicated; become involved

cómplice *mf* accomplice, accessory

complicidad *f* complicity

com•plot *m* (*pl* **-plots**) plot, intrigue

compone•dor -dora *mf* composer, compositor; typesetter; arbitrator; repairer ‖ *m* stick, composing stick; **amigable componedor** mediator, umpire

componenda *f* compromise, settlement, reconciliation

componente *adj* component, constituent ‖ *m* component, constituent; member ‖ *f* (mech) component

componer §54 *tr* to compose; compound; mend, repair; pacify, reconcile; arrange, put in order; restore, strengthen; (*huesos dislocados*) (Am) to set; (Col) to bewitch ‖ *ref* to compose oneself; get dressed; make up, become friends again; (*pintarse el rostro*) make up; **componérselas** to make out, manage

comportable *adj* bearable, tolerable

comportamentismo *m* behaviorism

comportamiento *m* behavior, conduct

comportar *tr* to support; bring about, entail ‖ *ref* to act, behave

comporte *m* behavior; carriage, bearing

composición *f* composition; agreement; (*circunspección*) composure, restraint; **hacer una composición de lugar** to lay one's plans carefully

compositi•vo -va *adj* (gram) combining

composi•tor -tora *mf* composer ‖ *m* (Arg, Urug) horse trainer, trainer of fighting cocks

compostura *f* composition; agreement; (*circunspección*) composure, restraint; repair, repairing, mending; (*aseo*) neatness; adulteration; (Arg, Urug) training

compota *f* compote, preserves; **compota de frutas** stewed fruit; **compota de manzanas** applesauce

compotera *f* (*vasija*) compote

compra *f* purchase, buy; shopping; **compra al contado** cash purchase; **compra a plazos** installment buying; **hacer compras, ir de compras** to go shopping

compra•dor -dora *mf* purchaser, buyer; shopper

comprar *tr* to purchase, buy; (*sobornar*) buy off ‖ *intr* to shop

compraventa *f* dealing, business, bargain, trading; resale

comprender *tr* (*entender*) to understand; (*entender; abrazar*) comprehend; (*contener, incluir*) comprise

comprensible *adj* comprehensible, understandable

comprensión *f* understanding, comprehension; inclusion

comprensi•vo -va *adj* understanding; comprehensive; **comprensivo de** inclusive of

compresa *f* (med) compress; **compresa higiénica** sanitary napkin

compresión *f* compression

comprimido *m* tablet

comprimir *tr* to compress; restrain, repress; flatten

comprobación *f* checking, verification; proof

comprobante *adj* proving ‖ *m* certificate, voucher, warrant; proof; claim check

comprobar §61 *tr* to check, verify; prove

comprometer *tr* to compromise, endanger, jeopardize; force, oblige; (*un negocio a un tercero*) entrust ‖ *ref* to promise; commit oneself; become engaged

comprometi•do -da *adj* awkward, embarrassing; engaged to be married

comprometimiento *m* commitment, promise; predicament, awkward situation; compromise

compromiso *m* commitment, promise; appointment, engagement; predicament, awkward situation; betrothal

compuerta *f* hatch, half door; floodgate, sluice

compues•to -ta *adj & m* composite, compound

compulsar *tr* to collate; make an authentic copy of

compungi•do -da *adj* remorseful

compungir §27 *tr* to make remorseful ‖ *ref* to feel remorse

compurgar §44 *tr* (*el reo la pena*) (Mex) to finish serving

computar *tr & intr* to compute

cómputo *m* computation, calculation

comulgante *mf* (eccl) communicant

comulgar §44 *tr* to administer communion to ‖ *intr* to take communion

comulgatorio *m* communion rail, altar rail

común *adj* common ‖ *m* community; water closet; toilet; **el común de las gentes** the general run of people; **por lo común** commonly

comunal *adj* common; community ‖ *m* community

comune•ro -ra *adj* popular ‖ *m* shareholder

comunicación *f* communication; connection

comunicado *m* communiqué; letter to the editor, official announcement

comunica•dor -dora *adj* communicating

comunicante *mf* communicant, informant

comunicar §73 *tr* to communicate; notify, inform; connect, put into communication ‖ *intr* to communicate ‖ *ref* to communicate; communicate with each other

comunicati•vo -va *adj* communicative

comunidad *f* community

comunión *f* communion; political party; sect

comunismo *m* communism

comunista *mf* communist

comunistizar §60 *tr* to convert to communism ‖ *ref* to become communistic

comunizar §60 *tr* to communize

con *prep* with; to, towards; in spite of; **con que** and so; whereupon; **con tal (de) que** provided that; **con todo** however, nevertheless

conato *m* effort, endeavor; (*delito que no llegó a consumarse*) attempt

cónca•vo -va *adj* concave

concebible *adj* conceivable

concebir §50 *tr & intr* to conceive

conceder *tr* to concede, admit; grant

concejal *m* alderman, councilman; **concejales** city fathers

concejo *m* town council; town hall; council meeting; (*expósito*) foundling

concentrar *tr & ref* to concentrate

concéntri•co -ca *adj* concentric

concepción *f* conception

concepto *m* concept; opinion, judgment; (*dicho ingenioso*) conceit, witticism; point of view; **en concepto de** under the head of; **tener buen concepto de** or **tener en buen concepto** to have a high opinion of, to hold in high esteem

conceptuar §21 *tr* to deem, judge, regard

conceptuo•so -sa *adj* witty, epigrammatic

concerniente *adj* relative

concernir §28 *tr* to concern

concertar §2 *tr* to concert; mend, repair; (*un casamiento; la paz*) arrange; (*huesos dislocados*) set; (*poner de acuerdo*) reconcile; (*un pacto*) conclude; harmonize ‖ *intr* to concert; agree ‖ *ref* to come to terms, become reconciled; agree

concertino *m* concertmaster

concertista *mf* (mus) manager; (mus) performer, soloist

concesión *f* concession, admission; grant

concesionario *m* licensee; (*comerciante*) dealer

concesi•vo -va *adj* concessive

conciencia *f* (*conocimiento que uno tiene de su propia existencia*) consciousness; (*sentimiento del bien y del mal*) conscience; (*conocimiento*) awareness; **cobrar conciencia de** to become aware of; **en conciencia** in all conscience

concienciación *f* consciousness raising

concienzu•do -da *adj* conscientious; thorough

concierto *m* concert, harmony; (*función de música*) concert; (*composición de música*) concerto

concilia•dor -dora *adj* conciliatory

conciliar *tr* to conciliate, reconcile ‖ *ref* (*el respeto, la estima, etc.*) to conciliate, win

concilio *m* (eccl) council

conci•so -sa *adj* concise

concitar *tr* to stir up, incite, agitate

conciudada•no -na *mf* fellow citizen

concluir §20 *tr* to conclude; convince ‖ *intr & ref* to conclude, end

conclusión *f* conclusion

concluyente *adj* conclusive, convincing

concomitar *tr* to accompany, go with

concordancia *f* concordance; (gram, mus) concord

concordar §61 *tr* to harmonize; reconcile; make agree ‖ *intr* to agree

concordia *f* concord; **de concordia** by common consent

concre•to -ta *adj* concrete

concubina *f* concubine

concubio *m* (archaic) bedtime

concuñada *f* sister-in-law

concuñado *m* brother-in-law

concurrencia *f* (*acaecimiento de varios sucesos en un mismo tiempo*) concurrence; (*competencia comercial*) competition; (*ayuda*) assistance, crowd, gathering, attendance

concurrente *adj* concurrent; competing ‖ *mf* competitor, contender, entrant

concurri•do -da *adj* crowded, full of people; well-attended

concurrir *intr* to concur; gather, meet, come together; compete, contend; coincide; **concurrir con** (*p.ej., dinero*) to contribute

concursante *mf* contender

concursar *tr* to declare insolvent ‖ *intr* to contend, compete

concurso *m* contest, competition; (*de gente*) concourse, crowd, throng; backing, coöperation; show, exhibition; **concurso de acreedores** meeting of creditors; **concurso de belleza** beauty contest; **concurso hípico** horse show

concusión *f* concussion; extortion, shakedown

concha *f* (*de molusco o crustáceo*) shell; (*cada una de las dos partes del caparazón de los moluscos bivalvos*) half shell; (*en que se sirve el pescado*) scallop; (*carey*) tortoise shell; oyster; shellfish; horseshoe bay; (theat) prompter's box; **concha de peregrino** scallop shell; (zool) scallop; (*ostras*) **en su concha** on the half shell; **tener muchas conchas** to be sly, cunning

conchabanza *f* comfort; collusion, cabal

conchabar *tr* to join, unite; hire ‖ *ref* to gang up; hire out

conchabero *m* (Col) pieceworker

condado *m* county; earldom

conde *m* count, earl; gypsy chief

condecoración *f* decoration

condecorar *tr* to decorate

condena *f* sentence; penalty, jail term; **condena judicial** conviction

condenación *f* condemnation; (*la eterna*) damnation

condena•do -da *adj* condemned; damned; (Chile) shrewd, clever ‖ *mf* sentenced person; **los condenados** the damned

condenar *tr* to condemn; convict; (*a la pena eterna*) damn; (*p.ej., una ventana*) shut off, block up; (*una habitación*) padlock ‖ *ref* to condemn oneself, confess one's guilt; (*a la pena eterna*) be damned

condensar *tr* to condense ‖ *ref* to condense, be condensed

condesa *f* countess

condescendencia *f* acquiescence, compliance

condescender §51 *intr* to acquiesce, comply; **condescender a** to accede to

condescendiente *adj* acquiescent, obliging

condición *f* condition, state; position, situation; standing; nature, character, temperament; **a condición (de) que** on condition that; **en buenas condiciones** in good condition, in good shape; **tener condición** to have a bad temper

condicional *adj* conditional

condimentar *tr* to season

condimento *m* condiment, seasoning

condiscípulo *m* fellow student

condolencia *f* condolence

condoler §47 *ref* to condole; **condolerse de** to sympathize with, feel sorry for, commiserate with

condominio *m* condominium

condonar *tr* to condone, overlook

cóndor *m* condor; (Chile, Ecuad) gold coin

conducción *f* conveyance, transportation; guiding, leading; (aut) drive, driving; **conducción a la derecha** right-hand drive; **conducción a la izquierda** left-hand drive; **conducción interior** closed car

conducente *adj* conducive

conducir §19 *tr* to conduct; manage, direct; guide, lead; convey, transport; drive; employ, hire ‖ *intr* to lead; conduce ‖ *ref* to conduct oneself, behave

conducta *f* conduct; management, direction; guidance; conveyance; conduct, behavior

conducto *m* pipe; conduit; (anat) duct, canal; agency, intermediary, channel; **por conducto de** through

conduc•tor -tora *adj* conducting ‖ *mf* driver, motorist; (*cobrador en un vehículo público*) conductor ‖ *m & f* (elec & phys) conductor; **buen conductor, buena conductora** good conductor; **mal conductor, mala conductora** bad or poor conductor ‖ *m* (rr) engineman, engine driver

conectar *tr* to connect

conecti•vo -va *adj* connective

conejera *f* burrow, warren; (coll) joint, dive

conejillo *m* young rabbit; **conejillo de Indias** guinea pig

conejo *m* rabbit

conexión *f* connection

conexionar *tr* to connect; put in touch ‖ *ref* to connect; make contacts

confabulación *f* collusion, connivance

confabular *ref* to connive, scheme, plot

confección *f* making, preparation, confection; tailoring; ready-made suit; **confección a medida** suit made to order; **de confección** ready-made

confeccionar *tr* (*ropa*) to make; (*una receta*) make up, concoct

confeccionista *mf* ready-made clothier

confederación *f* confederacy; alliance

confedera•do -da *adj & mf* confederate

confederar *tr & ref* to confederate

conferencia *f* (*reunión para tratar asuntos internacionales, etc.*) conference; (*plática para tratar de algún negocio*) interview; (*disertación en público o en la universidad*) lecture; **conferencia telefónica** (telp) long-distance call

conferenciante *mf* conferee; lecturer
conferenciar *intr* to confer, hold an interview
conferencista *mf* (Arg) lecturer
conferir §68 *tr* to confer, award, bestow; discuss; compare ‖ *intr* to confer
confesante *mf* confessor
confesar §2 *tr*, *intr* & *ref* to confess
confesión *f* confession; denomination, faith, religion
confe•so -sa *adj* confessed; (*judío*) converted ‖ *mf* converted Jew ‖ *m* lay brother
confesonario *m* confessional
confesor *m* confessor
confiable *adj* reliable, dependable
confia•do -da *adj* unsuspecting; haughty, self-confident
confianza *f* confidence; self-confidence, self-assurance; familiarity; secret deal; **de confianza** reliable
confianzu•do -da *adj* overconfident; overfamiliar
confiar §77 *tr* to confide, entrust; strengthen the confidence of ‖ *intr* & *ref* to confide, trust; **confiar** or **confiarse de** or **en** to confide in, trust in; rely on
confidencia *f* confidence; secret; **de mayor confidencia** top secret
confidencial *adj* confidential
confiden•te -ta *adj* trustworthy, faithful ‖ *mf* confident ‖ *m* spy; informer; secret agent; love seat
configurar *tr* to shape, form
confín *m* confine, border, boundary; **los confines** the confines
confina•do -da *adj* exiled ‖ *m* prisoner
confinamiento *m* confinement; abutment
confinar *tr* to exile; confine ‖ *intr* to border
confirmar *tr* to confirm
confiscar §73 *tr* to confiscate
confita•do -da *adj* hopeful, confident; (*bañado de azúcar*) candied
confitar *tr* (*frutas*) to candy; (*en almíbar*) preserve; (*endulzar*) sweeten
confite *m* candy, bonbon, confection; **confites** confectionery
confitera *f* candy box; candy jar
confitería *f* confectionery; confectionery store
confite•ro -ra *mf* confectioner ‖ *f* see **confitera**
confitura *f* preserves, confiture; **confituras** confectionery
conflagración *f* conflagration
conflagrar *tr* to set fire to
conflicti•vo -va *adj* conflicting; anguished
conflicto *m* conflict; (*apuro*) fix, jam
confluencia *f* confluence
confluir §20 *intr* to flow together; crowd, gather
conformador *m* hat block
conformar *tr* to shape; (*un sombrero*) to block ‖ *intr* & *ref* to conform, comply, yield, agree
conforme *adj* in agreement ‖ *adv* depending on circumstances; fine, O.K.; **conforme a** according to ‖ *conj* as, in proportion as; as soon as ‖ *m* approval

conformidad *f* conformance, conformity; resignation
confort *m* comfort
confortable *adj* comfortable; comforting
confortante *adj* comforting; tonic ‖ *mf* comforter ‖ *m* tonic
confr. *abbr* **confesor**
confricar §73 *tr* to rub
confrontar *tr* (*poner en presencia; cotejar*) to confront ‖ *intr* to border; to agree ‖ *ref* to get along, agree; **confrontarse con** (*hacer frente a*) to confront
confundir *tr* to confuse; (*turbar, dejar desarmado*) confound ‖ *ref* to become confused; (*en la muchedumbre*) get lost
confusión *f* confusion
confutar *tr* to confute
congal *m* (Mex) brothel, whorehouse
congelador *m* freezer
congelar *tr* to congeal, freeze; (*créditos*) (fig) to freeze ‖ *ref* to congeal, freeze
congenial *adj* congenial (*having the same nature*)
congeniar *intr* to be congenial, get along well
congéni•to -ta *adj* congenital
congestión *f* congestion
congestionar *tr* to congest ‖ *ref* to congest, become congested
conglobar *tr* to lump together
congoja *f* anguish, grief
congojo•so -sa *adj* distressing; distressed
congosto *m* narrow mountain pass
congraciar *tr* to win over ‖ *ref* to ingratiate oneself; **congraciarse con** to get into the good graces of
congratulación *f* congratulation
congratular *tr* to congratulate ‖ *ref* to congratulate oneself, rejoice
congregación *f* congregation; **la Congregación de los fieles** the Roman Catholic Church
congregar §44 *tr* to bring together ‖ *ref* to congregate, come together
congresal *m* (Arg, Chile) congressman
congresista *mf* delegate; member of congress ‖ *m* congressman ‖ *f* congresswoman
congreso *m* (*asamblea legislativa*) congress; (*reunión para deliberar sobre intereses comunes*) meeting, convention
congrio *m* conger eel
cóni•co -ca *adj* conical
conjetura *f* conjecture, guess
conjeturar *tr* & *intr* to conjecture, guess
conjugación *f* conjugation
conjugar §44 *tr* to conjugate; combine
conjunción *f* conjunction; combination
conjuntamente *adv* together
conjuntista *m* chorus man ‖ *f* chorus girl
conjunti•vo -va *adj* conjunctive; subjunctive
conjun•to -ta *adj* joined, combined, united ‖ *m* whole, entirety, ensemble; unit; group; (theat) chorus; **de conjunto** general; **en conjunto** as a whole; **en su conjunto** in its entirety
conjura or **conjuración** *f* conspiracy, plot

conjuramentar *tr* to swear in ‖ *ref* to take an oath

conjurar *tr* to swear in; conjure, entreat; conjure away, exorcise ‖ *intr* to conspire, plot ‖ *ref* to conspire, join in a conspiracy

conjuro *m* (*invocación supersticiosa*) conjuration; adjuration, entreaty

conllevar *tr* (*los trabajos*) to share in bearing; (*a una persona*) tolerate, stand for; (*las adversidades*) suffer

conmemorar *tr* to commemorate, memorialize

conmigo *pron* with me, with myself

conmilitón *m* fellow soldier

conminar *tr* to threaten

conmoción *f* commotion; concussion, shock

conmove•dor -dora *adj* touching, moving, stirring

conmover §47 *tr* to touch, move, affect; stir, stir up; shake, upset ‖ *ref* to be touched, be moved

conmutación *f* commutation

conmutador *m* (elec) change-over switch; (SAm) telephone exchange

conmutar *tr* to commute

connivencia *f* connivance; **estar en connivencia** to connive

cono *m* cone; **cono de proa** nose cone; **cono de viento** (aer) wind cone, wind sock

conoce•dor -dora *adj* knowledgeable ‖ *mf* expert, connoisseur

conocer §22 *tr* to know; meet, get to know; tell, distinguish; (law) to try ‖ *intr* to know; **conocer de** or **en** to know, have knowledge of ‖ *ref* to know oneself; know each other; meet, meet each other

conoci•do -da *adj* known, well-known, familiar; distinguished, prominent ‖ *mf* acquaintance

conocimiento *m* knowledge; understanding; acquaintance; consciousness; (com) bill of lading; **con conocimiento de causa** knowingly, with full knowledge; **conocimiento de embarque** (com) bill of lading; **conocimientos** knowledge; **hablar con pleno conocimiento de causa** to know what one is talking about; **perder el conocimiento** to lose consciousness; **por su real conocimiento** (Arg) for real money; **recobrar el conocimiento** to regain consciousness; **venir en conocimiento de** to come to know

conque *adv* and so ‖ *m* condition, terms

conquista *f* conquest

conquista•dor -dora *adj* conquering ‖ *m* conqueror; (*ladrón de corazones*) ladykiller

conquistar *tr* to conquer; (*ganar la voluntad de*) win over

consabi•do -da *adj* well-known; above-mentioned

consagrar *tr* to consecrate; devote; dedicate; (*una nueva palabra*) authorize ‖ *ref* to devote oneself; make a name for oneself

consciente *adj* conscious

conscripción *f* conscription

conscripto *m* conscript, draftee

consecución *f* obtaining, getting

consecuencia *f* (*correspondencia lógica entre sus elementos*) consistency; (*acontecimiento que resulta necesariamente de otro*) consequence; **en consecuencia** accordingly; **guardar consecuencia** to remain consistent; **traer a consecuencia** to bring in

consecuente *adj* (*que tiene proporción consigo mismo*) consistent; (*que sigue en orden a otra cosa*) consecutive

consecuti•vo -va *adj* consecutive

conseguir §67 *tr* to get, obtain; **conseguir + inf** to succeed in + ger

conseja *f* story, fairy tale; cabal

conseje•ro -ra *adj* advisory ‖ *mf* advisor, counselor; councilor

consejo *m* advice, counsel; board; council; **consejos** advice; **un consejo** a piece of advice

consenso *m* consensus

consenti•do -da *adj* spoiled, pampered; (*marido*) indulgent

consenti•dor -dora *adj* acquiescent; pampering ‖ *mf* acquiescent person; (*de niños*) pamperer ‖ *m* cuckold

consentimiento *m* consent

consentir §68 *tr* to allow; admit; pamper, spoil ‖ *intr* to consent; come loose; **consentir + inf** to think that + ind; **consentir con** to be indulgent toward; **consentir en** to consent to ‖ *ref* to begin to crack up; (Arg) to be proud

conserje *m* janitor, concierge

conserva *f* preserves; preserved food; pickles; (naut) convoy; **conservas alimenticias** canned goods; **llevar en su conserva** (naut) to convoy; **navegar en (la) conserva** (naut) to sail in a convoy

conservación *f* conservation; preservation; self-preservation; maintenance, upkeep

conserva•dor -dora *adj* preservative; (pol) conservative ‖ *mf* conservative ‖ *m* curator

conservar *tr* to conserve, keep, maintain; preserve ‖ *ref* to take good care of oneself; keep

conservati•vo -va *adj* conservative, preservative

conservatorio *m* (*p.ej., de música*) conservatory; (Arg) private school; (Chile) hothouse, greenhouse

conservera *f* cannery; (Mex) preserve dish

conservería *f* canning

conserve•ro -ra *adj* canning ‖ *mf* canner ‖ *f* see **conservera**

considerable *adj* considerable; large, great, important

consideración *f* consideration; **ser de consideración** to be of importance, be of concern; **someter a consideración** to take under advisement

considera•do -da *adj* (*que guarda consideración a los demás*) considerate; (*digno de respeto*) respected, esteemed; (*que obra con reflexión*) cautious, prudent

considerando *conj* & *m* whereas

considerar *tr* to consider; treat with consideration

consigna f slogan; watchword; (mil) orders; (rr) checkroom
consignación f consignment
consignar tr to consign; assign; state in writing, set forth
consignatario m consignee
consigo pron with him, with her, with them, with you; with himself, with herself, with themselves, with yourself or yourselves
consiguiente adj consequential; **ir** or **proceder consiguiente** to act consistently ‖ m consequence; **por consiguiente** consequently, therefore
consilia•rio -ria mf advisor, counselor
consistencia f consistence, consistency
consistente adj consistent
consistir intr to consist; **consistir en** (estar compuesto de) to consist of; (residir en) consist in
consistorio m consistory; town council; town hall
conso•cio -cia mf copartner; companion, fellow member
consola f console, console table; bracket
consolación f consolation
consolar §61 tr to console
consolidar tr to fund, refund; strengthen; repair
consommé m consommé
consonancia f consonance; rhyme
consonante adj consonantal; rhyming ‖ m rhyme ‖ f consonant
consonar §61 intr to be in harmony; rhyme
cónsone adj harmonious ‖ m (mus) chord
consorcio m consortium; partnership; fellowship
consorte mf consort, mate, spouse; partner, companion; **consortes** (law) colitigants; (law) accomplices
conspi•cuo -cua adj outstanding, prominent
conspiración f conspiracy
conspirar intr to conspire
constancia f constancy; certainty, proof
constante adj constant; steady, regular; sure, certain ‖ f constant
constar intr to be clear, be certain; be on record; have the right rhythm; **constar de** to consist of; **hacer constar** to state, make known; **y para que conste** in witness whereof
constatación f proof
constatar tr to prove, establish, show
constelación f constellation; climate, weather; epidemic
consternar tr to depress, dismay
constipación f or **constipado** m cold, cold in the head
constipar tr (los poros) to stop up ‖ ref to catch cold
constitución f constitution
constituir §20 tr to constitute; establish, found; **constituir en** to force into ‖ ref — **constituirse en** to set oneself up as
constituti•vo -va adj & m constituent
constituyente adj (para dictar o reformar la constitución) constituent

constreñir §72 tr to constrain, force, compel; constrict, compress
construcción f construction; building, structure; **construcción de buques** shipbuilding
construc•tor -tora adj construction ‖ mf builder, constructor; **constructor de buques** shipbuilder
construir §20 tr to build, construct
consuegro m fellow father-in-law (with respect to the father of one's son-in-law or daughter-in-law), father-in-law of one's child
consuelda f comfrey; **consuelda real** field larkspur; **consuelda sarracena** goldenrod
consuelo m consolation; joy, delight; **sin consuelo** inconsolably; to excess
consueta m (theat) prompter
consuetudina•rio -ria adj customary, usual
cónsul m consul
consulado m consulate, consulship; (casa u oficina) consulate
consular adj consular
consulta f consultation; opinion; reference
consultación f consultation
consultar tr to consult; take up, discuss; advise ‖ intr to consult, confer
consulti•vo -va adj advisory
consul•tor -tora mf consultant
consultorio m dispensary
consuma•do -da adj consummate ‖ m consommé
consumar tr to consummate; fulfill, carry out
consumerismo m consumerism
consumición f consumption; drink (in bar or restaurant)
consumi•do -da adj thin, weak, emaciated; fretful
consumi•dor -dora mf consumer; customer (in bar or restaurant)
consumir tr to consume; exhaust; harass, wear down ‖ ref to consume, waste away; long, yearn
consumo m consumption; drink (in bar or restaurant); customers; **consumos** octroi
consunción f consumption; (pathol) consumption
consuno adv — **de consuno** together, in accord
consunti•vo -va adj consumptive; (crédito) consumer
contabilidad f accounting, bookkeeping
contabilista mf accountant, bookkeeper
contabilizadora f computer
contabilizar §60 tr to enter in the ledger
contable adj countable ‖ mf accountant, bookkeeper
contactar intr to contact, be in contact
contacto m contact; **ponerse en contacto con** to get in touch with
conta•do -da adj scarce, rare; **al contado** cash, for cash; **contados** a few; **de contado** right away; **por de contado** of course
contador m counter; accountant; (que mide el agua, gas, electricidad) meter; (law) receiver; **contador de abonado** house meter; **contador de Geiger** Geiger counter; **contador kilométrico** speedometer; **contador**

público titulado certified public accountant

contaduría f accountancy; accountant's office; box office for advanced sales

contagiar tr to infect; corrupt

contagio m contagion

contagio•so -sa adj contagious

contaminación f contamination; **contaminación ambiental** environmental pollution

contaminante m pollutant

contaminar tr to contaminate; (un texto) corrupt; (la ley de Dios) break

contante adj (dinero) ready

contar §61 tr to count; regard, consider; tell, relate; **contar . . . años** to be . . . years old; **dejarse contar diez** (box) to take the count; **tiene sus horas contadas** his days are numbered ‖ intr to count; **a contar desde** beginning with; **contar con** to count on, rely on; reckon with; expect to

contemplación f contemplation; leniency, condescension

contemplar tr to contemplate; be lenient to ‖ intr to contemplate

contemporáne•o -a adj contemporaneous, contemporary ‖ mf contemporary

contemporizar §60 intr to temporize

contención f containment; contention, strife; (law) suit, litigation

contencio•so -sa adj contentious

contender §51 intr to contend

contendiente mf contender, contestant

contenedor m container

contener §71 tr to contain ‖ ref to contain oneself

conteni•do -da adj moderate, restrained ‖ m content, contents

contenta f gift or treat; indorsement; (mil) certificate of good conduct; (law) release

contentadi•zo -za adj easy to please

contentamiento m contentment

contentar tr to content; reconcile; (com) to indorse

conten•to -ta adj content, contented, glad ‖ m content, contentment; **a contento** to one's satisfaction; **no caber de contento** (coll) to be beside oneself with joy ‖ f see **contenta**

conteo m calculation, estimate, count

contera f tip, metal tip

contesta f answer; (Mex) chat

contestación f answer; argument, debate; **mala contestación** back talk

contestar tr to answer ‖ intr to answer; agree

contesto m (Mex) reply

contexto m interweaving; context

conticinio m dead of night

contienda f contest, dispute, fight

contigo pron with thee, with you

conti•guo -gua adj contiguous, adjoining

continencia f continence

continental adj continental

continente adj continent ‖ m (cosa que contiene en sí a otra) container; (aire del semblante, compostura del cuerpo) mien, bearing; (gran extensión de tierra rodeada por los océanos) continent

contingencia f contingency

contingente adj contingent ‖ m contingent; share, quota

continuar §21 tr & intr to continue; **continuará** to be continued

continuidad f continuity

conti•nuo -nua adj continuous, continual; (mach) endless ‖ **continuo** adv continuously

contonear ref to strut, swagger

contoneo m strut, swagger

contorcer §74 ref to writhe

contorno m contour, outline; **contornos** environs, neighborhood

contorsión f contortion

contra prep against; toward, facing ‖ m (concepto opuesto) con ‖ f trouble, inconvenience; (al comprador) (Cuba) gift, extra; (Chile) antidote; **llevar la contra a** to disagree with

contraalmirante m rear admiral

contraatacar §73 tr & intr to counterattack

contraataque m counterattack

contrabajo m contrabass, double bass

contrabajón m double bassoon

contrabalancear tr to counterbalance

contrabalanza f counterbalance

contrabandear intr to smuggle

contrabandista adj smuggling; contraband ‖ mf smuggler, contrabandist

contrabando m smuggling, contraband; **meter de contrabando** to smuggle, smuggle in

contrabarrera f second row of seats (in bull ring)

contracalle f parallel side street

contracarril m (rr) guardrail

contracción f contraction; (reducción del ritmo normal de los negocios) recession; (al estudio) (Chile, Peru) concentration

contracepti•vo -va adj & m contraceptive

contracorriente f countercurrent, crosscurrent; (entre aguas) undertow

contracultura f counterculture

contrachapado m plywood

contradecir §24 (impv sg -dice) tr to contradict

contradicción f contradiction

contradic•tor -tora adj contradictory ‖ mf contradicter

contradicto•rio -ria adj contradictory

contraer §75 tr to contract; (deudas) incur; (el discurso o idea) condense ‖ ref to contract; shrink; (Chile, Peru) to concentrate, apply oneself

contraescalón m riser (of stairway)

contraespía mf counterspy

contraespionaje m counterespionage

contrafallar tr & intr to overtrump

contrafallo m overtrump

contrafigura f counterpart

contrafuero m infringement, violation

contrafuerte m abutment, buttress

contragolpe m counterstroke; kickback; (box) counter

contrahace•dor -dora adj counterfeiting; fake ‖ mf counterfeiter; fake; impersonator

contrahacer §39 *tr* to counterfeit, copy, imitate; fake; impersonate; (*un libro*) pirate ‖ *ref* to pretend to be

contra·haz *f* (*pl* -**haces**) wrong side

contrahe·cho -**cha** *adj* counterfeit, fake; deformed

contrahechura *f* counterfeit, fake

contrahuella *f* riser (*of stairway*)

contralor *m* comptroller

contralto *mf* contralto (*person*) ‖ *m* contralto (*voice*)

contraluz *f* view against the light; **a contraluz** against the light

contramaestre *m* foreman; (*naut*) boatswain; **segundo contramaestre** boatswain's mate

contramandar *tr* to countermand

contramandato *m* countermand

contramano *adv* — **a contramano** in the wrong direction, the wrong way

contramarcha *f* countermarch; reverse

contramarchar *intr* to countermarch; to go in reverse

contraofensiva *f* counteroffensive

contraorden *f* cancellation

contraparte *f* counterpart

contrapasar *intr* to go over to the other side

contrapelo *adv* — **a contrapelo** against the hair, against the grain; the wrong way; **a contrapelo de** against, counter to

contrapesar *tr* to offset, counterbalance

contrapeso *m* counterweight; counterbalance; (*para completar el peso de carne, etc.*) makeweight

contraponer §54 *tr* to set opposite; oppose; compare

contraportada *f* (*del disco*) flip side

contraprestación *f* return favor

contraproducente *adj* self-defeating, unproductive

contraprueba *f* second proof

contrapuerta *f* storm door; vestibule door

contrapuntear *tr* to sing in counterpoint; taunt, be sarcastic to ‖ *ref* to taunt each other

contrapunto *m* counterpoint

contrapunzón *m* nailset, punch

contrariar §77 *tr* to counteract, oppose; annoy, provoke

contrariedad *f* opposition; interference; annoyance, bother

contra·rio -**ria** *adj* opposite, contrary; harmful ‖ *mf* enemy, opponent, rival ‖ *m* opposite, contrary; **al contrario** on the contrary; **de lo contrario** otherwise

contrarreferencia *f* cross reference

Contrarreforma *f* Counter Reformation

contrarregistro *m* (*para comprobar si algún género ha pasado por la frontera*) double check; (*de una experiencia científica*) control

contrarréplica *f* (law) rejoinder

contrarrestar *tr* to resist, counteract; (*la pelota*) return

contrarrevolución *f* counterrevolution

contrasentido *m* misinterpretation; mistranslation; nonsense

contraseña *f* countersign; baggage check; **contraseña de salida** (mov, theat) check

contrastar *tr* to resist; (*las pesas y medidas*) check ‖ *intr* to resist; contrast

contraste *m* resistance; contrast; assayer; assayer's office; (naut) sudden shift in the wind

contratar *tr* to contract for; hire, engage

contratiempo *m* misfortune, disappointment, setback

contratista *mf* contractor

contrato *m* contract

contratreta *f* counterplot

contratuerca *f* lock nut, jam nut

contravalidación *f* (*documento*) validation

contravalidar *tr* to validate; confirm

contraveneno *m* counterpoison, antidote

contravenir §79 *intr* to act contrary; **contravenir a** to contravene, act counter to

contraventana *f* window shutter

contravidriera *f* storm sash

contrayente *mf* contracting party (*to a marriage*)

contribución *f* contribution; tax; **contribución de sangre** military service; **contribución industrial** excise tax; **contribución territorial** land tax

contribui·dor -**dora** *mf* contributor; taxpayer

contribuir §20 *tr* & *intr* to contribute

contribuyente *mf* contributor; taxpayer

contrición *f* contrition

contrincante *m* competitor, rival; fellow candidate

contristar *tr* to sadden

contri·to -**ta** *adj* contrite

control *m* control, check; **control de la natalidad** or **de los nacimientos** birth control; **control remoto** remote control

controlador *m* controller; **controlador aéreo** air-traffic controller

controlar *tr* to control, check

controversia *f* controversy

controvertible *adj* controversial, controvertible

controvertir §68 *tr* to controvert

contubernio *m* cohabitation; evil alliance

contumacia *f* contumacy; (law) contempt

contu·maz *adj* (*pl* -**maces**) contumacious; germ-bearing; (law) guilty of contempt of court

contumelia *f* contumely

contundente *adj* bruising; impressive, convincing

contundir *tr* to bruise

conturbar *tr* to trouble, worry, upset

contusión *f* contusion

contusionar *tr* (Chile) to bruise

convalecencia *f* convalescence

convalecer §22 *intr* to convalesce, recover

convaleciente *adj* & *mf* convalescent

convalidar *tr* to confirm

conveci·no -**na** *adj* neighboring ‖ *mf* neighbor

convencer §78 *tr* to convince

convencimiento *m* conviction

convención *f* (*acuerdo; conformidad; asamblea*) convention; political convention

convencional *adj* conventional

convenible *adj* docile, compliant; (*precio*) fair, reasonable

conveniencia *f* (*comodidad*) convenience; (*acuerdo, convenio*) agreement; fitness, suitability; (*formas sociales*) propriety; domestic employment; **conveniencias** income, property

convenienciе•ro -ra *adj* comfort-loving

conveniente *adj* (*cómodo*) convenient; fit, suitable; advantageous; proper

convenio *m* pact, covenant, treaty

convenir §79 *intr* to agree; (*concurrir, juntarse*) convene; be. suitable, be becoming; be important, be necessary; **conviene a saber** to wit, namely ‖ *ref* to agree, come to an agreement

conventiilo *m* (SAm) tenement house

convento *m* convent, monastery; **convento de religiosas** convent

converger §17 or **convergir** §27 *intr* to converge; concur

conversa *f* chat, conversation

conversación *f* conversation

conversacional *adj* conversational

conversar *intr* to converse; live, dwell

conversión *f* conversion

conver•so -sa *adj* converted ‖ *mf* convert ‖ *m* lay brother ‖ *f* see **conversa**

convertible *adj* convertible ‖ *m* (aut) convertible

convertir §68 *tr* to convert; turn ‖ *ref* to convert; be converted; **convertirse en** to turn into, become

conve•xo -xa *adj* convex

convic•to -ta *adj* convicted, found guilty

convida•do -da *mf* guest ‖ *f* treat

convidar *tr* to invite; treat; move, incite; **convidarle a uno con alguna cosa** to treat someone to something ‖ *ref* to offer one's services

convincente *adj* convincing

convite *m* invitation; treat, banquet, party; **convite a escote** Dutch treat

convivir *intr* to live together

convocar §73 *tr* to convoke, call together; (*p.ej., una huelga*) call; acclaim

convoy *m* convoy; escort; cruet stand; (rr) train

convoyar *tr* to convoy

convulsionar *tr* to convulse

conyugal *adj* conjugal

cónyuge *mf* spouse, consort ‖ **cónyuges** *mpl* couple, husband and wife

co•ñac *m* (*pl* **-ñacs** or **-ñaques**) cognac

cooperación *f* coöperation

cooperar *intr* to coöperate

cooperati•vo -va *adj* coöperative

cooptar *tr* to coöpt

coordena•do -da *adj* coördinate ‖ *f* (math) coördinate

coordinante *adj* (gram) coördinating

coordinar *tr* & *intr* to coördinate

copa *f* goblet, wineglass; (*del sombrero*) crown; brazier; vase; drink; sundae; playing card, representing a bowl, equivalent to heart; (*del dolor*) (fig) cup; (sport) cup

copar *tr* (*la puesta equivalente a todo el dinero de la banca*) to cover; (*todos los puestos en una elección*) sweep; (mil) to cut off and capture

copartícipe *mf* copartner, joint partner

copear *intr* to sell wine or liquor by the glass; (coll) to tipple

copero *m* cabinet for wineglasses

copete *m* (*cabello levantado sobre la frente*) pompadour; (*de plumas; de una montaña*) crest; (*de un caballo*) forelock; (*de lana, cabello, plumas, etc.*) tuft; (*de un mueble*) top, finial; (*de un sorbete*) topping; **de alto copete** aristocratic, important; **tener mucho copete** to be high-hat

copetu•do -da *adj* tufted; high, lofty; high-hat

copia *f* plenty, abundance; copy; **copia al carbón** carbon copy; **copia fiel** true copy

copiador *m* or **copiadora** *f* copy(ing) machine; duplicator

copiante *mf* copier, copyist

copiar *tr* to copy, copy down

copiloto *m* copilot

copio•so -sa *adj* copious, abundant

copista *mf* copier, copyist

copla *f* couplet; ballad, popular song; **coplas** verse, poetry; **coplas de ciego** doggerel

cople•ro -ra *mf* vendor of ballads; poetaster

coplista *mf* poetaster

copo *m* bundle of cotton, flax, hemp, etc. to be spun; **copo de nieve** snowflake; **copos de jabón** soap flakes

copón *m* ciborium, pyx

copo•so -sa *adj* bushy; flaky, woolly

copu•do -da *adj* bushy, thick

copular *ref* to copulate

coque *m* coke

coqueluche *f* whooping cough

coqueta *adj* coquettish ‖ *f* coquette, flirt; (W-I) dressing table

coquetear *intr* to coquette, flirt; try to please everybody

coquetería *f* coquetry, flirting; affectation

coque•tón -tona *adj* coquettish, kittenish ‖ *m* flirt, lady-killer

coracha *f* leather bag

coraje *m* anger; mettle, spirit

coraju•do -da *adj* ill-tempered; (Arg) brave, courageous

coral *adj* (mus) choral ‖ *m* (mus) chorale; (*zoófito; esqueleto calizo del zoófito; color*) coral; **corales** coral beads

corambre *f* hides, skins

Corán *m* Koran

coranvo•bis *m* (*pl* **-bis**) fat solemn look

coraza *f* armor; cuirass; (sport) guard

corazón *m* heart; (*centro de una cosa*) core; **de corazón** heartily; **hacer de tripas corazón** to pluck up courage

corazonada *f* impulsiveness; hunch, presentiment; entrails

corbata *f* necktie, cravat; scarf; **corbata de mariposa, corbata de lazo** bow tie; **corbata de nudo corredizo** four-in-hand tie

corbatín *m* bow tie

corbeta *f* corvette

Córcega f Corsica
corcel m steed, charger
corcova f hump, hunch
corcova•do -da adj humpbacked, hunch-backed ‖ mf humpback, hunchback
corcovar tr to bend
corcovear intr to buck; grumble; (Mex) to be afraid
corcha f cork bark; cork bucket (for cooling wine)
corchea f (mus) quaver, eighth note
corche•ro -ra adj cork ‖ f cork bucket (for cooling wine)
corcheta f eye (of hook and eye)
corchete m snap; hook and eye; hook (of hook and eye); (signo) bracket; corchete de presión snap fastener
corcho m cork; cork, cork stopper; cork wine cooler; cork box; cork mat; corcho bornizo, corcho virgen virgin cork
cordada f (mountaineering) party of two or three men roped together
cordaje m cordage; (naut) rigging
cordal adj wisdom (tooth) ‖ m (mus) tail-piece
cordel m cord, string; (distance of) five steps; cattle run; a cordel in a straight line
cordelejo m string; dar cordelejo a to make fun of; (Mex) to keep putting off
cordera f ewe lamb; (mujer dócil y humilde) (fig) lamb
cordería f cordage
corderillo m lambskin
corderi•no -na adj lamb ‖ f lambskin
cordero m lamb; lambskin; (hombre dócil y humilde) (fig) lamb
corderuna f lambskin
cordial adj cordial; (dedo) middle ‖ m cordial
cordialidad f cordiality
cordillera f chain of mountains
cordobana f — andar a la cordobana to go naked
cordón m lace; (de cuerda o alambre) strand; cordon; milled edge of coin; (de monje) rope belt; cordón umbilical umbilical cord
cordoncillo m rib, ridge; braid; (de monedas) milling
cordura f prudence, wisdom
Corea f Korea; la Corea del Norte North Korea; la Corea del Sur South Korea
corea•no -na adj & mf Korean
corear tr to compose for a chorus; accompany with a chorus; join in singing; agree obsequiously with
coreografía f choreography
coriáce•o -a adj leathery
Corinto f Corinth
corista m choir priest; (theat) chorus man ‖ f chorus girl, chorine
cori•to -ta adj naked; bashful, timid
cormorán m cormorant
cor•nac m (pl -nacs) or cornaca m mahout
cornada f hook with horns; goring; (en la esgrima) upward thrust
cornadura f or cornamenta f (del toro, la vaca, etc.) horns; (del ciervo) antlers

cornamusa f bagpipe
córnea f cornea
cornear tr to butt; to gore
corneja f daw, crow
cornejo m dogwood
córne•o -a adj horn, horny ‖ f see córnea
corneta f bugle; swineherd's horn; corneta acústica ear trumpet; corneta de llaves cornet, cornet-à-pistons; corneta de monte hunting-horn
cornisa f cornice
cornisamento m (archit) entablature
corno m horn; dogwood; corno inglés (mus) English horn
Cornualles Cornwall
cornucopia f cornucopia; sconce with mirror
cornu•do -da adj horned, antlered; cuckold ‖ m cuckold
coro m chorus; choir; choir loft; a coros alternately; de coro by heart; hacer coro a to echo
corolario m corollary
corona f (cerco de metal; moneda; dignidad real; parte visible de una muela) crown; (cerco de flores) garland, wreath; (aureola) halo; (de eclesiástico) tonsure; (la que corresponde a un título nobiliario) coronet; corona nupcial bridal wreath
coronación f coronation
coronamento m or coronamiento m coronation; completion, termination; (archit) coping; (naut) taffrail
coronar tr to crown; complete, finish; top; surmount; (checkers) to crown
coronel m colonel
coronelía f colonelcy
coronilla f (de la cabeza) crown; andar or bailar de coronilla to be hard at it; estar hasta la coronilla to be fed up
corotos mpl belongings; utensils
corpiño m bodice, waist; (Arg) brassiere
corporación f corporation
corporal adj corporal, bodily
corpu•do -da adj corpulent
corpulen•to -ta adj corpulent
corpúsculo m corpuscle; particle
corral m corral, stockyard; barnyard; fishpond; theater; corral de madera lumberyard; corral de vacas pigpen; hacer corrales to play hooky
correa f strap, thong; (aer, mach) belt; besar la correa to eat humble pie; correa de seguridad (aer, aut) safety belt
corrección f (acción de corregir; reprensión) correction; (calidad de correcto) correctness
correcti•vo -va adj & m corrective
correc•to -ta adj correct
correc•tor -tora mf corrector; corrector de pruebas proofreader
corredera f track, slide; slide valve; (del trombón) slide; (naut) log; (naut) log line; (puerta) de corredera sliding
corredi•zo -za adj slide; sliding; (nudo) slip
corre•dor -dora adj running ‖ mf runner ‖ m corridor; porch, gallery; (el que interviene en compras y ventas de efectos comer-

ciales, etc.) broker; (mil) scout; **corredor de apuestas** bookmaker

corregidor *m* Spanish magistrate; chief magistrate of Spanish town

corregir §57 *tr* to correct; temper, moderate ‖ *intr* (W-I) to have a bowel movement ‖ *ref* to mend one's ways

correlación *f* correlation

correlacionar *tr & intr* to correlate

correlati•vo -va *adj & m* correlative

corre•lón -lona *adj* (SAm) fast, swift; (Col, Mex) cowardly

correncia *f* bashfulness; looseness of the bowels

correntí•o -a *adj* running; free, easy ‖ *f* looseness of the bowels

corren•tón -tona *adj* jolly, full of fun

corrento•so -sa *adj* swift, rapid

correo *m* mail; post office; mail train; postman; courier; **correo aéreo** air mail; **correo urgente** special delivery; **echar al correo** to mail, to post

correo•so -sa *adj* leathery, tough

correr *tr* (*un caballo*) to run, race; (*un riesgo*) run; travel over; overrun; (*una cortina*) draw; (*un toro*) fight; chase, pursue; auction; confuse; throw out; **correrla** to run around all night ‖ *intr* to run; race; pass, elapse; circulate, be common talk; be current; **a todo correr** at full speed; **correr a** to sell for; **correr a cargo de** or **por cuenta de** to be the business of; **correr con** to be on good terms with; be in charge of; (*mes*) **que corre** current ‖ *ref* (*a derecha o a izquierda*) to turn; be confused; be embarrassed, be ashamed; slide, glide; (*una bujía, un color*) run; go too far

correría *f* short trip, excursion; foray, raid

correspondencia *f* correspondence; contact, communication; agreement, harmony; (*en el metro*) connection; (*en una carretera*) interchange

corresponder *intr* to correspond; (*dos habitaciones*) communicate; **corresponder a** (*un beneficio, el afecto de una persona*) to return, reciprocate; concern; be up to ‖ *ref* (*comunicarse por escrito*) to correspond; (*dos cosas*) correspond with each other; be in agreement; be attached to each other

correspondiente *adj* corresponding; correspondent; respective ‖ *mf* correspondent

corresponsal *mf* correspondent

corretaje *m* brokerage

corretear *tr* to harass, pursue; (CAm) to drive away; (Chile) to speed up ‖ *intr* to race around

correveidi•le *mf* (*pl* **-le**) gossip; go-between

corrida *f* run; bullfight; (*carrera de entrenamiento de un caballo*) trial run; **corrida de banco** run on the bank; **corrida de toros** bullfight

corri•do -da *adj* (*peso, medida*) in excess; (*letra*) cursive; continued, unbroken; abashed, ashamed; wordly-wise, sophisticated ‖ *m* overhang; street ballad ‖ *f* see **corrida**

corriente *adj* (*agua*) running; (*actual*) current; common, ordinary; regular; well-known; fluent ‖ *adv* all right, O.K. ‖ *m* current month; **al corriente** on time; informed, aware, posted ‖ *f* current, stream; (elec) current; **corriente de aire** draft; **Corriente del Golfo** Gulf Stream; **ir contra la corriente** to go against the tide

corrillo *m* circle, clique

corrimiento *m* running; sliding; watery discharge; embarrassment, shyness; landslide; rheumatism

corro *m* (*cerco de gente; espacio circular*) ring; (*juego de niñas*) ring-around-a-rosy; **corro de brujas** fairy ring; **hacer corro** to make room

corroborar *tr* to corroborate; strengthen

corroer §62 *tr & ref* to corrode

corromper *tr* to corrupt; spoil; rot; seduce; bribe; annoy ‖ *intr* to smell bad ‖ *ref* to become corrupted; spoil; rot

corrosión *f* corrosion

corrosi•vo -va *adj & m* corrosive

corrugar §44 *tr* to shrink; wrinkle

corrupción *f* corruption; seduction; bribery; stench

corruptela *f* corruption

corruptible *adj* corruptible; (*p.ej., frutas*) perishable

corrusco *m* crust of bread

corsa *f* (naut) day's run

corsario *m* corsair

corsé *m* corset

cor•so -sa *adj & mf* Corsican ‖ *m* (naut) privateering; (SAm) drive, promenade ‖ *f* see **corsa**

corta *f* clearing, cutting, felling

cortaalam•bres *m* (*pl* **-bres**) wire cutter

cortabol•sas *m* (*pl* **-sas**) pick-pocket

cortacésped *m* lawn mower

cortaciga•rros *m* (*pl* **-rros**) cigar cutter

cortacircui•tos *m* (*pl* **-tos**) (elec) fuse

cortacorriente *m* (elec) change-over switch

cortada *f* cut, cutting

cortadillo *m* drinking cup

corta•do -da *adj* (*estilo*) choppy; (SAm) hard up ‖ *f* see **cortada**

corta•dor -dora *adj* cutting ‖ *mf* cutter ‖ *m* butcher ‖ *f* cutting machine

cortafrío *m* cold chisel

cortafuego *s* fire wall

cortahie•los *m* (*pl* **-los**) icebreaker

cortalápi•ces *m* (*pl* **-ces**) pencil sharpener

cortante *adj* cutting, sharp ‖ *m* butcher; butcher knife

cortapape•les *m* (*pl* **-les**) paper cutter

cortapi•cos *m* (*pl* **-cos**) (ent) earwig; **cortapicos y callares** little children should be seen and not heard

cortaplu•mas *m* (*pl* **-mas**) penknife

cortapu•ros *m* (*pl* **-ros**) cigar cutter

cortar *tr* to cut; trim; chop; cut off; cut out, omit; cut short; cut up; carve; (*la corriente; la ignición*) cut off ‖ *intr* to cut; (*el viento, el frío*) be cutting; **cortar de vestir** to cut cloth; gossip ‖ *ref* to become speechless;

(*la leche*) curdle, turn sour; (*la piel*) chap, crack
cortarrenglón *m* marginal stop
cortaú•ñas *m* (*pl* **-ñas**) nail clipper
cortavi•drios *m* (*pl* **-drios**) glass cutter
cortaviento *m* windshield
corte *m* cut; cutting; (*filo de un arma, cuchillo, etc.; borde de un libro*) edge; cross section; (*de un vestido*) cut, fit; piece of material; harvest; **corte de pelo** haircut; **corte de pelo a cepillo** crew cut; **corte de traje** suiting ‖ *f* (*de un rey*) court; (*corral*) yard; stable, fold; (*tribunal de justicia*) court; **Cortes** Parliament; **darse cortes** (SAm) to put on airs; **hacer la corte a** to pay court to; **la Corte** the Capital (*Madrid*)
cortedad *f* shortness; smallness; lack; bashfulness
cortejar *tr* to escort, attend, court; court, woo
cortejo *m* courting; courtship; (*séquito*) cortege; gift, treat; (coll) beau
cortera *f* (Chile) streetwalker
cortero *m* (Chile) day laborer
cortés *adj* courteous, polite, courtly
cortesana *f* courtesan
cortesana•zo -za *adj* overpolite, obsequious
cortesanía *f* courtliness
cortesa•no -na *adj* courtly, courteous ‖ *m* courtier ‖ *f* see **cortesana**
cortesía *f* courtesy, politeness, courtliness; gift, favor; (*inclinación de la cabeza o el cuerpo en señal de respeto*) curtsy; (*de una carta*) conclusion; **hecer una cortesía** to make a bow; curtsy
corteza *f* bark; peel, rind, skin; (*de pan*) crust; coarseness; (*envoltura exterior de un órgano*) cortex; **corteza cerebral** cortex
cortijo *m* farm, farmhouse
cortil *m* barnyard
cortina *f* curtain; **correr la cortina** to pull the curtain aside; **cortina de hierro** iron curtain; **cortina de humo** smoke screen
cortinal *m* fenced-in field
cortinilla *f* shade, window shade
cortisona *f* cortisone
cor•to -ta *adj* short; dull; bashful, shy; speechless; **a la corta o a la larga** sooner or later; **desde muy corta edad** from earliest childhood ‖ *f* see **corta**
cortocircuitar *tr* & *ref* (elec) to short-circuit
cortocircuito *m* (elec) short circuit
cortometraje *m* (mov) short
corva *f* ham, back of knee; (vet) curb
corvejón *m* gambrel, hock; (orn) cormorant
cor•vo -va *adj* arched, bent, curved ‖ *m* hook ‖ *f* see **corva**
cor•zo -za *mf* roe deer
cosa *f* thing; **cosa de** a matter of; **cosa de cajón** a matter of course; **cosa de mieles** something fine; **cosa de nunca acabar** endless bore; **cosa de oír** something worth hearing; **cosa de risa** something to laugh at; **cosa de ver** something worth seeing; **cosa nunca vista** something unheard-of; **cosa que** so that; **cosa rara** strange to say; **como si tal cosa** as if nothing had hap-

pened; **en cosa de** in a matter of; **no . . . gran cosa** not much; **no haber tal cosa** to be not so; **otra cosa** something else; **¿qué cosa?** what's new?
cosa•co -ca *adj* & *mf* Cossack ‖ *m* Cossack (*horseman*)
coscolina *f* (Mex) loose woman
cos•cón -cona *adj* sly, crafty
cosecha *f* crop, harvest; harvest time; **cosecha de vino** vintage; **de su cosecha** (coll) out of one's own head
cosechar *tr* to harvest, reap ‖ *intr* to harvest
coseche•ro -ra *mf* harvester, reaper; vintner
cose-pape•les *m* (*pl* **-les**) stapler
coser *tr* to sew; join, unite closely; **coser a preguntas** to riddle with questions; **coser a puñaladas** to cut to pieces ‖ *intr* to sew; **ser coser y cantar** to be a cinch ‖ *ref* — **coserse con** or **contra** to be closely attached to
cosméti•co -ca *adj* & *m* cosmetic
cósmi•co -ca *adj* cosmic
cosmonauta *mf* cosmonaut
cosmonave *f* spacecraft
cosmonavegación *f* space travel
cosmopolita *adj* & *mf* cosmopolitan
cosmos *m* cosmos; (bot) cosmos
coso *m* enclosure for bullfighting
cosquillas *fpl* tickling, ticklishness; **buscarle a uno las cosquillas** to try to irritate a person; **no sufrir cosquillas** or **tener malas cosquillas** to be touchy
cosquillear *tr* to tickle; tease, taunt; stir up the curiosity of; scare ‖ *intr* to tickle ‖ *ref* to be curious; enjoy oneself
cosquilleo *m* tickling, tickling sensation
cosquillo•so -sa *adj* ticklish; (*que se ofende fácilmente*) touchy
costa *f* coast, shore; cost, price; **a toda costa** at all costs; **Costa Brava** Mediterranean coast in province of Gerona, Spain; **Costa Firme** Spanish Main; **costa marítima** seacoast; **costas** (law) costs
costado *m* side; (*del ejército*) flank; (Mex) station platform; **costados** ancestors, stock
costal *m* bag, sack; **costal de los pecados** human body (*full of sin*); **estar hecho un costal de huesos** to be nothing but skin and bones
costanera *f* slope; **costaneras** rafters
costane•ro -ra *adj* sloping; coastal ‖ *f* see **costanera**
costanilla *f* short steep street
costar §61 *intr* to cost; **cueste lo que cueste** cost what it may
costarricense or **costarrique•ño -ña** *adj* & *mf* Costa Rican
coste *m* cost; **a coste y costas** at cost
costear *tr* to pay for, defray the cost of; sail along the coast of ‖ *intr* to sail along the coast ‖ *ref* to pay; pay one's way
coste•ño -ña *adj* sloping; coastal
coste•ro -ra *adj* coastal
costilla *f* rib; wealth; **costillas** back, shoulders
costillu•do -da *adj* heavy-set, broadshouldered

costo *m* cost; **costo de la vida** cost of living; **costo, seguro y flete** cost, insurance, and freight

costo•so -sa *adj* costly, expensive; grievous

costra *f* scab, scale; (*moco de una vela*) snuff

costro•so -sa *adj* scabby, scaly

costumbre *f* custom, habit; **de costumbre** usual; usually; **tener por costumbre** to be in the habit of

costumbrista *mf* critic of manners and customs

costura *f* sewing, needlework; dressmaking; (*unión de dos piezas cosidas*) seam; **alta costura** fashion designing, haute couture

costurar or **costurear** *tr* (CAm, Mex) to sew

costurera *f* seamstress, dressmaker

costurero *m* sewing table

cota *f* coat of arms; coat of mail

cotarrera *f* gossipy woman

cotarro *m* night shelter (*for beggars and tramps*); **alborotar el cotarro** to raise a row

cotejar *tr* to compare, collate

cotejo *m* comparison, collation

cotidia•no -na *adj* daily, everyday

cotilla *f* gossip, tattletale

cotín *m* (sport) backstroke

cotización *f* quotation; dues

cotizante *adj* dues-paying

cotizar §60 *tr* to quote; prorate ‖ *intr* to collect dues; pay dues

coto *m* price; fixed price; term, limit

cotón *m* printed cotton

cotona *f* work shirt

cotonía *f* dimity

cotorra *f* parrot; parakeet; magpie; chatterbox; (Mex) night shelter

cotorrear *intr* to gossip, gabble

cotufa *f* Jerusalem artichoke; delicacy, tidbit; **hacer cotufas** (Bol) to be fastidious; **pedir cotufas en el golfo** to ask for the moon

coturno *m* buskin

covacha *f* cave; cubbyhole; shanty; doghouse

covachuelista *m* clerk, government clerk

coxcojita *f* hopscotch; **a coxcojita** hippety-hop

coy *m* (naut) hammock

coyunda *f* strap for yoking oxen; sandal string; marriage; tyranny

coyuntura *f* joint, articulation; (*sazón, oportunidad*) juncture

coz *f* (*pl* **coces**) kick; big end; ebb; (coll) insult; **dar coces contra el aguijón** to kick against the pricks

c.p.b., C.P.B. *abbr* **cuyos pies beso**

cps. *abbr* **compañeros**

crabrón *m* hornet

crac *m* (*ruido seco*) crack; crash; **hacer crac** to crash, fail

cráneo *m* cranium, skull

crápula *f* drunkenness, debauchery; riffraff

crapulo•so -sa *adj* drunken; vicious, evil

crascitar *intr* to crow, croak

cra•so -sa *adj* fat, greasy, thick; (*ignorancia*) crass, gross

cráter *m* crater

creación *f* creation

crea•dor -dora *adj* creative ‖ *mf* creator

crear *tr* to create; appoint; found ‖ *ref* to make for oneself, build up; trump up

creati•vo -va *adj* creative

crecede•ro -ra *adj* growth; large enough to allow for growth

crecepelo *m* hair restorer

crecer §22 *intr* to grow; increase; (*el río*) rise, swell; (*la luna*) wax ‖ *ref* to grow; take on more authority; get bolder

creces *fpl* growth, increase; excess, extra; **con creces** amply, in abundance

crecida *f* freshet, flood

creciente *adj* growing, increasing ‖ *f* —**creciente de la luna** waxing of the moon, crescent; **creciente del mar** high tide, flood tide

crecimiento *m* growth, increase; **crecimiento cero** zero growth

credenciales *fpl* credentials

crédito *m* credit

credo *m* creed; credo; **con el credo en la boca** with one's heart in one's mouth; **en un credo** in a trice

crédu•lo -la *adj* credulous

creederas *fpl* — **tener buenas creederas** to be gullible

creencia *f* belief; (*crédito que se presta a un hecho*) credence; (*secta*) creed

creer §43 *tr & intr* to believe; **¡ya lo creo!** I should say so! ‖ *ref* to believe; believe oneself to be

creíble *adj* believable, credible

creí•do -da *adj* credulous; gullible

crema *f* cream; cold cream; shoe polish; (gram) diaeresis; **crema de menta** creme de menthe; **crema dental** or **crema dentífrica** toothpaste; **crema desvanecedora** vanishing cream

cremación *f* cremation

cremallera *f* rack; zipper

cremato•rio -ria *adj & m* crematory

crémor *m* cream of tartar

cremo•so -sa *adj* creamy

crencha *f* part (*in hair*); hair on each side of part

crepitar *intr* to crackle

crepuscular *adj* twilight

crepúsculo *m* twilight

cresa *f* maggot

crespar *tr & ref* to curl

cres•po -pa *adj* curly; curled; angry, irritated; stylish, conceited; (*estilo*) turgid ‖ *m* curl

crespón *m* crape; **crespón fúnebre** crape; mourning band

cresta *f* crest; **cresta de gallo** cockscomb; (bot) cockscomb

creta *f* chalk ‖ **Creta** *f* Crete

cretense *adj & mf* Cretan

cretona *f* cretonne

creyente *adj* believing ‖ *mf* believer

creyón *m* crayon

cría *f* brood, litter; breeding; raising, rearing; nursing

criada *f* female servant, maid; **criada de casa, criada de servir** housemaid

co
cr

criadero *m* nursery, tree nursery; fish hatchery; oyster bed

criadilla *f* testicle; potato

cria•do -da *adj* — **bien criado** well-bred; **mal criado** ill-bred ‖ *mf* servant ‖ *f* see **criada**

cria•dor -dora *mf* breeder ‖ *f* wet nurse

criamiento *m* care, upkeep

crianza *f* raising, rearing; nursing; (*urbanidad*) breeding, manners; **buena crianza** good breeding; **mala crianza** bad breeding

criar §77 *tr* to raise, rear, bring up; breed; grow; nurse, nourish; fatten; create; foster

criatura *f* (*toda cosa creada; persona que debe su cargo o situación a otra*) creature; little child, little creature

criba *f* screen, sieve

cribar *tr* to screen, sieve

cribo *m* screen, sieve

cric *m* (*pl* **crics**) jack

crimen *m* crime; **crimen de lesa majestad** lese majesty; **crímenes de oficinistas** white-collar crime

criminal *adj* & *mf* criminal

criminar *tr* to accuse, incriminate

criminología *f* criminology

crimino•so -sa *adj* & *mf* criminal

crines *fpl* mane

crío *m* (coll) baby, infant

crio•llo -lla *adj* & *mf* Creole

cripta *f* crypt

crisálida *f* chrysalis

crisantemo *m* chrysanthemum

cri•sis *f* (*pl* **-sis**) crisis; (*pánico económico*) depression, slump; mature judgment; **crisis del servicio doméstico** servant problem; **crisis de llanto** crying fit; **crisis de vivienda** housing shortage; **crisis energética** energy crisis; **crisis ministerial** cabinet crisis; **crisis nerviosa** fit of nerves

crisma *f* (coll) head, bean

crisol *m* crucible

crispar *tr* to cause to twitch ‖ *ref* to twitch

crispatura *f* twitch, twitching

crispir *tr* to grain, to marble

cristal *m* crystal; glass; pane of glass; mirror, looking glass; **cristal cilindrado** plate glass; **cristal de reloj** watch crystal; **cristal de roca** rock crystal; **cristal hilado** glass wool, spun glass; **cristal laminado** laminated glass, safety glass; **cristal tallado** cut glass

cristalera *f* China closet; sideboard; glass door

cristalería *f* glassworks, glass store; glassware; glass cabinet

cristali•no -na *adj* crystalline ‖ *m* lens, crystalline lens

cristalizar §60 *tr* & *ref* to crystallize

cristianar *tr* to baptize, christen

cristiandad *f* Christendom

cristianismo *m* Christianity

cristianizar §60 *tr* to Christianize

cristia•no -na *adj* & *mf* Christian ‖ *m* soul, person; Spanish; watered wine

Cristo *m* Christ; crucifix; **donde Cristo dió las tres voces** in the middle of nowhere

Cristóbal *m* Christopher

criterio *m* criterion

crítica *f* (*juicio sobre una obra literaria, etc.; censura de la conducta de alguno*) criticism; (*arte de juzgar una obra literaria, etc.*) critique; gossip

criticar §73 *tr* & *intr* to criticize

críti•co -ca *adj* critical; (*criticón*) critical (*faultfinding*) ‖ *mf* critic ‖ *f* see **crítica**

criti•cón -cona *adj* critical, faultfinding ‖ *mf* critic, faultfinder

critiquizar §60 *tr* to overcriticize

crizneja *f* braid of hair

croar *intr* to croak

croata *adj* & *mf* Croatian

crocante *m* almond brittle, peanut brittle

crocitar *intr* to crow, croak

croco *m* crocus

croché *m* crochet

crochet *m* (box) hook

croma•do -da *adj* chrome ‖ *m* chromium plating

cromar *tr* to chrome

cromo *m* chromium

cromosoma *m* chromosome

crónica *f* chronicle; news chronicle, feature story

cróni•co -ca *adj* chronic; longstanding; (*vicio*) inveterate ‖ *f* see **crónica**

cronista *mf* chronicler; reporter, feature writer; **cronista de radio** newscaster

cronología *f* chronology

cronometra•dor -dora *mf* (sport) timekeeper

cronometraje *m* (sport) clocking, timing

cronómetro *m* chronometer; stop watch

croqueta *f* croquette

cro•quis *m* (*pl* **-quis**) sketch

croscitar *intr* to crow, croak

crótalo *m* rattlesnake; castanet

cruce *m* crossing; crossroads, intersection; exchange (*e.g., of letters*); (*avería*) (elec) crossed wires, short circuit; **cruce a nivel** grade crossing; **cruce en trébol** cloverleaf intersection

crucero *m* crossroads; railroad crossing; (archit) transept; (aer, naut) cruise, cruising; (nav) cruiser; **crucero a nivel** grade crossing

crucial *adj* crucial

crucificar §73 *tr* to crucify

crucifijo *m* crucifix

crucifixión *f* crucifixion

crucigrama *m* crossword puzzle

cruda *f* (Mex) hangover

crudeza *f* crudeness, rawness; (*del agua*) hardness; harshness, roughness; blustering; **crudezas** undigested food

cru•do -da *adj* crude, raw; (*agua*) hard; harsh, rough; (*tiempo*) raw; (*lienzo*) unbleached; (P-R) to be rusty; (Mex) to have a hangover ‖ *f* see **cruda**

cruel *adj* cruel

crueldad *f* cruelty

cruen•to -ta *adj* bloody

crujía *f* corridor, hall; hospital ward; block of houses; (naut) midship gangway; **crujía de**

piezas suite of rooms; **sufrir una crujía** (coll) to have a hard time of it

crujido *m* creak; crackle; clatter; chatter; rustle

crujir *intr* to creak; crackle; clatter; chatter; rustle; crunch

crup *m* croup

crustáce•o -a *adj* crustaceous ‖ *m* crustacean

cruz *f* (*pl* **cruces**) cross; (*de una moneda*) tails; (typ) dagger; **Cruz del Sur** Southern Cross; **¡cruz y raya!** (coll) that's enough!; **de la cruz a la fecha** from beginning to end

cruza *f* (SAm) intersection; crossbreeding

cruzada *f* (*expedición contra los infieles; propaganda contra un vicio*) crusade; crossroads, intersection

cruza•do -da *adj* crossed; (*de raza mixta*) cross; double-breasted ‖ *m* (*el que toma parte en una cruzada*) crusader; (*caballero de una orden militar*) knight; twill ‖ *f* see **cruzada**

cruzar §60 *tr* to cross; (*la tela*) twill; (*cartas*) exchange; crossbreed; (naut) to cruise, cruise over ‖ *intr* to cross; cruise ‖ *ref* to cross each other, cross one another's path; (*alistarse para una cruzada*) take the cross; **cruzarse con** (*otro automóvil*) to pass; **cruzarse de brazos** (*estar ocioso*) to cross one's arms

cs. *abbr* **céntimos, cuartos**

cte. *abbr* **corriente**

c/u *abbr* **cada uno**

cuad. *abbr* **cuadrado**

cuaderna *f* (naut) frame

cuaderno *m* notebook; folder; **cuaderno de bitácora** (naut) logbook; **cuaderno de hojas cambiables** or **sueltas** loose-leaf notebook

cuadra *f* hall, large room; stable; dormitory, ward; croup, rump; block

cuadra•do -da *adj* square; square-shouldered; perfect ‖ *m* square; (*regla*) ruler; (*en las medias*) clock; **de cuadrado** perfectly; (*que se mira frente a frente*) full-faced

cuadragési•mo -ma *adj & m* fortieth

cuadrangular *adj* quadrangular ‖ *m* home run

cuadrángu•lo -la *adj* quadrangular ‖ *m* quadrangle

cuadrante *m* quadrant; (*de reloj*) face, dial; **cuadrante solar** sundial

cuadrar *tr* to square; please; (*al toro*) (taur) to square off, line up ‖ *ref* to square; stand at attention; take on a serious air

cuadrilla *f* group, party; crew, gang

cuadrillazo *m* (SAm) surprise attack

cuadrillo *m* (*saeta*) bolt (*arrow*)

cuadrimotor *m* four-motor plane

cua•dro -dra *adj* square ‖ *m* square; (*lienzo, pintura*) painting, picture; (*marco de pintura, ventana, etc.*) frame; (*de jardín*) patch, flower bed; staff, personnel; (mil) cadre; (sport) team; (theat) scene; (coll) sight, mess; **a cuadros** checked; **cuadro de costumbres** sketch of manners and customs; **cuadro de distribución** switchboard;

cuadro de mando instrument panel; (aut) dashboard; **cuadro indicador** score board; **cuadro vivo** tableau; **en cuadro** square, e.g., **ocho pulgadas en cuadro** eight inches square; topsy-turvy; **quedarse en cuadro** to be all alone in the world; (mil) to be skeletonized ‖ *f* see **cuadra**

cuadrúpe•do -da *adj & m* quadruped

cuádruple *adj & m* quadruple

cuadruplicar §73 *tr & ref* to quadruple

cuajada *f* curd

cuajado *m* mincemeat

cuajar *tr* to curd, curdle, thicken, jelly; please, suit ‖ *intr* to take hold, catch on, jell, take shape; (Mex) to chatter, prattle ‖ *ref* to curd, curdle, thicken, jelly; sleep sound; become crowded

cuajo *m* curd; (Mex) chatter, prattle; (*en la escuela*) (Mex) recess

cual *adj rel & pron rel* such as; **el cual** which; who; **lo cual** which; **por lo cual** for which reason ‖ *adv* as ‖ *prep* like

cuál *adj interr & pron interr* which, what; which one

cualidad *f* quality, characteristic, trait

cualquier *adj indef* (*pl* **cualesquier**) apocopated form of **cualquiera**, used only before masculine nouns and adjectives

cualquiera (*pl* **cualesquiera**) *pron indef* anyone; **cualquiera que** whichever; whoever ‖ *adj indef* any ‖ *adj rel* whichever ‖ *m* (*persona poco importante*) nobody

cuan *adv* as

cuán *adv* how, how much

cuando *conj* when; although; in case; since; **aun cuando** even if, even though; **cuando más** at most; **cuando menos** at least; **cuando mucho** at most; **cuando quiera** whenever; **de cuando en cuando** from time to time ‖ *prep* (coll) at the time of

cuándo *adv* when; **cuándo . . . cuándo** sometimes . . . sometimes; **¿de cuándo acá?** since when?; how come?

cuantía *f* quantity; importance; **delito de mayor cuantía** felony; **delito de menor cuantía** misdemeanor; **de mayor cuantía** first-rate; **de menor cuantía** second-rate, of little importance

cuantiar §77 *tr* to estimate, appraise

cuánti•co -ca *adj* quantum

cuantio•so -sa *adj* large, substantial

cuan•to -ta *adj rel & pron rel* as much as, whatever, all that which; **cuantos** as many as, all those who, everybody who; **unos cuantos** some few ‖ **cuanto** *adv* as soon as; as long as; **cuanto antes** as soon as possible; **cuanto más . . . tanto más** the more . . . the more; **cuanto más que** all the more because; **en cuanto** as soon as; while; insofar as; **en cuanto a** as to, as for; **por cuanto** inasmuch as; **por cuanto . . .** **por tanto** inasmuch as . . . therefore ‖ **cuan•to** *m* (*pl* **-ta**) quantum

cuán•to -ta *adj interr & pron interr* how much; **cuántos** how many ‖ **cuánto** *adv* how, how much; how long; how long ago; **cada cuánto** how often

cr
cu

cuáque•ro -ra adj & mf Quaker
cuarenta adj, pron & m forty
cuarenta•vo -va adj & m fortieth
cuarentena f forty; quarantine; forty days, forty months, forty years; **poner en cuarentena** to quarantine; withhold one's credence in
cuaresma f Lent
cuaresmal adj Lenten
cuarta f fourth, fourth part; (de la mano) span; (CAm, W-I) horse whip
cuartago m nag, pony
cuartear tr to divide in four parts; divide; (la aguja) (naut) to box; (CAm, W-I) to whip ‖ ref to crack, split; (taur) to step aside, dodge
cuartel m quarter; (de una ciudad) section, ward; (terreno) lot; flower bed; (mil) barracks; (buen trato) (mil) quarter; (armazón de tablas para cerrar la escotilla) (naut) hatch; (coll) house, home; **cuartel de bomberos** engine house, firehouse; **cuarteles** (mil) quarters; **cuartel general** (mil) headquarters
cuartelada f mutiny, military uprising
cuartelazo m (mil) coup, putsch; (mil) takeover
cuarte•rón -rona mf quadroon ‖ m quarter; (de puerta) panel; (de ventana) shutter
cuarteto m quartet
cuartilla f sheet of paper
cuar•to -ta adj fourth; quarter ‖ m fourth; quarter; room, bedroom; quarter-hour; **cuarto creciente** (de la luna) first quarter; **cuarto de aseo** lavatory; **cuarto de baño** bathroom; **cuarto de dormir** bedroom; **cuarto de estar** living room; **cuarto delantero** (de la res) forequarter; **cuarto de los niños** nursery; **cuarto de luna** quarter; **cuarto menguante** (de la luna) last quarter; **cuarto obscuro** (phot) darkroom; **cuartos** money, cash; **cuarto trasero** (p.ej., de vaca) rump ‖ f see **cuarta**
cuarzo m quartz
cuate adj (Mex) twin; (Mex) like ‖ mf (Mex) twin; (Mex) pal
cuatrilli•zo -za mf quadruplet
cuatrinca f foursome
cuatro adj & pron four; (Mex) deceit, swindle; **las cuatro** four o'clock ‖ m four; (en las fechas) fourth; (de voces) quartet; **más de cuatro** (coll) quite a number
cuatrocien•tos -tas adj & pron four hundred ‖ **cuatrocientos** m four hundred
cuba f cask, barrel; tub, vat; (persona de mucho vientre) (coll) tub; (persona que bebe mucho) (coll) toper; **cuba de riego** street sprinkler
cuba•no -na adj & mf Cuban
cubertería f silverware, cutlery
cubeta f keg, cask; pail; bowl, toilet bowl; (del termómetro) cup; (chem, phot) tray; (Mex) high hat
cubicaje m piston displacement, cylinder capacity

cubicar tr (elevar al cubo) to cube; measure the volume of; have a piston displacement of
cúbi•co -ca adj cubic; (raíz) cube
cubierta f cover; envelope; roof; (de un libro) paper cover; (de un neumático) casing, shoe; (del motor de un coche) hood; (naut) deck; **bajo cubierta separada** under separate cover; **cubierta de aterrizaje** (nav) flight deck; **cubierta de cama** bedcover; **cubierta de mesa** table cover; **cubierta de paseo** (naut) promenade deck; **cubierta de vuelo** (nav) flight deck; **cubierta principal** (naut) main deck; **entre cubiertas** (naut) between decks
cubiertamente adv secretly
cubier•to -ta adj covered; (cielo) overcast ‖ m cover, roof, shelter; (servicio de mesa para una persona) cover; knife, fork, and spoon; table d'hôte, prix fixe; **a cubierto de** under cover of; protected from; **bajo cubierto** under cover, indoors ‖ f see **cubierta**
cubil m (de fieras) lair, den; (de arroyo) bed
cubilete m (de cocinero) copper mold; dice-box; mince pie; high hat; (SAm) scheming, wirepulling
cubo m bucket; (de rueda) hub; (de un candelero; de una llave de caja) socket; cube; (mach) barrel, drum; (math) cube; (Arg) finger bowl
cubreasiento m seat cover
cubrecama f counterpane, bedcover
cubrecorsé m corset cover
cubrefuego m curfew
cubrelibro m jacket
cubrenuca f havelock
cubrerrueda f mudguard
cubresexo m G-string
cubretablero m (aut) cowl
cubretetera f cozy, tea cozy
cubrir §83 tr to cover, cover over, cover up ‖ ref to cover oneself; be covered; put one's hat on; (el cielo) become overcast; (satisfacer una deuda) cover
cucaña f greased pole to be climbed as a game; (coll) cinch
cucañe•ro -ra mf loafer, parasite
cucar §73 tr to wink; to make fun of; (la caza) to sight; to incite, stir up ‖ intr (el ganado) to go off on a run (when bitten by flies)
cucaracha f roach, cockroach
cucarache•ro -ra adj (W-I) sly, tricky; (W-I) amorous, lecherous
cucarda f cockade
cuclillas — **en cuclillas** squatting, crouching
cuclillo m cuckoo; (coll) cuckold
cu•co -ca adj sly, tricky; cute ‖ mf sly person ‖ m bogeyman; cuckoo; **hacer cuco a** to poke fun at
cu•cú m (pl **-cúes**) cuckoo (call)
cuculla f cowl, hood
cucurucho m paper cone, ice-cream cone; **hacer cucurucho a** (Chile) to deceive, take in

cuchara f spoon; (*cazo*) dipper, ladle; (*para áridos; para achicar el agua en los botes*) scoop; (*de albañil*) trowel; (Mex) pickpocket; **cuchara de sopa** tablespoon; **media cuchara** (Mex) mason's helper; ordinary fellow; fellow with heavy accent; **meter su cuchara** to butt in

cucharada f spoonful; ladleful; scoop

cucharear tr to spoon, ladle out

cucharetear intr to stir the pot, stir with a spoon; to meddle

cucharilla f teaspoon; (*de soldador*) ladle

cucharón m large spoon; soup ladle, dipper; scoop; **despacharse con el cucharón** to look out for number one

cuchichear intr to whisper

cuchilla f knife; (*hoja de arma blanca de corte*) blade; (*de patín de hielo*) runner; (*cerro escarpado*) hogback; (*de interruptor*) (elec) blade; (poet) sword; **cuchilla de carnicero** butcher knife, cleaver

cuchillada f slash, gash, hack; **cuchilladas** fight, quarrel; **dar cuchillada** (*un actor o un teatro*) to be the hit of the town

cuchillería f cutlery; cutler's shop

cuchillero m cutler

cuchillo m knife; (*en un vestido*) gore; (naut) triangular sail; **cuchillo de trinchar** carving knife; **cuchillo de vidriero** putty knife; **pasar a cuchillo** to put to the sword

cuchitril m hovel, den

cuchufleta f joke, fun, wisecrack

cuchufletear intr to joke, make fun, wisecrack

cuelga f fruit hung up for keeping; birthday present

cuelgaca•pas m (*pl* -**pas**) cloak hanger

cuello m (*del cuerpo*) neck; (*de una prenda*) collar; shirt collar; **cuello almidonado** stiff collar; **cuello de camisa** shirtband; **cuello de cisne** gooseneck; **cuello de pajarita** or **doblado** wing collar; **levantar el cuello** to get back on one's feet again

cuenca f wooden bowl; (*del ojo*) socket; basin, river basin; **cuenca de polvo** dust bowl

cuenco m earthen bowl; hollow

cuenta f count, calculation; account; (*factura*) bill; (*en un restaurante*) check; (*del rosario*) bead; **abonar en cuenta a** to credit to the account of; **a cuenta** or **a buena cuenta** on account; **adeudar en cuenta a** to charge to the account of; **a fin de cuentas** after all; **caer en la cuenta** to get the point; **cargar en cuenta a** to charge to the account of; **correr por cuenta de** to be the responsibility of; to be under the administration of; **cuenta atrás** countdown; **cuenta corriente** current account; **cuenta de gastos** expense account; **cuenta de la vieja** counting on one's fingers; **cuentas del gran capitán** overdrawn account; **cuentas galanas** illusions; **darse cuenta de** to realize, become aware of; **de cuenta** of importance; **más de la cuenta** too long; too much; **pedir cuentas a** to bring to account; **por la cuenta** apparently;

por mi cuenta to my way of thinking; **tomar por su cuenta** to take upon oneself; **vamos a cuentas** (coll) let's settle this

cuentacorrentista mf depositor

cuentago•tas m (*pl* -**tas**) dropper, medicine dropper

cuentakilóme•tros m (*pl* -**tros**) odometer

cuente•ro -ra adj (coll) gossipy ‖ mf (coll) gossip

cuentista adj (coll) gossipy ‖ mf story teller; short-story writer; (coll) gossip

cuento m story, tale; short story; prop, support; tip, point; (*cómputo*) count; (coll) gossip, evil talk; (coll) disagreement; **cuento de hadas** fairy tale; **cuento del tío** (SAm) gyp, swindle; **cuento de nunca acabar** (coll) endless affair; **cuento de penas** (coll) hard-luck story; **cuento de viejas** old wives' tale; **Cuentos de Calleja** collection of nursery stories; **dejarse de cuentos** (coll) to come to the point; **estar en el cuento** to be well-informed; **¡puro cuento!** pure fiction!; **sin cuento** countless; **traer a cuento** to bring up; **venir a cuento** (coll) to be opportune; **vivir del cuento** to live by one's wits

cuerda f cord, rope; watch spring; winding a watch or clock; (*acción de ahorcar*) hanging; fishing line; (aer, anat, geom) chord; (mus) string; **acabarse la cuerda** to run down, e.g., **se acabó la cuerda** the watch ran down; **bajo cuerda** secretly, underhandedly; **cuerda de presos** chain gang; **cuerda de remolcar** tow rope; **cuerda de tripa** (mus) catgut; **cuerda tirante** tight rope; **dar cuerda a** to give free rein to; (*un reloj*) to wind; **estar en su cuerda** to be in one's element; **sin cuerda** unwound, rundown

cuer•do -da adj wise, prudent; sane ‖ f see **cuerda**

cuerna f antler; horns

cuerno m horn; (mus) horn; **cuerno de caza** huntinghorn; **cuerno inglés** (mus) English horn

cuero m (*pellejo de buey*) hide; (*después de curtido*) leather; wineskin; **cuero cabelludo** scalp; **cuero en verde** rawhide; **en cueros** stark-naked

cuerpear intr (Arg) to duck, dodge

cuerpo m body; (*parte del vestido hasta la cintura*) waist; (*talle, aspecto*) build; (*de escritos, leyes, etc.*) corpus; corps, staff; (mil) corps; **cuerpo a cuerpo** hand to hand; **cuerpo celeste** heavenly body; **cuerpo compuesto** (chem) compound; **cuerpo de aviación** air corps; **cuerpo de baile** corps de ballet; **cuerpo de bomberos** fire brigade, fire company; **cuerpo de ejército** army corps; **Cuerpo de Paz** Peace Corps; **cuerpo de redacción** editorial staff; **cuerpo simple** (chem) simple substance; **dar con el cuerpo en tierra** (coll) to fall flat on the ground; **de cuerpo entero** full-length; **de medio cuerpo** half-length; **descubrir el cuerpo** to drop one's guard; **en cuerpo** or **en cuerpo de camisa** in shirt sleeves; **estar de cuerpo presente** to be on view, to lie in state; **hacer del cuerpo** (coll) to have a movement of the bowels

cueru·do -da *adj* thick-skinned; annoying, boring; bold, shameless

cuervo *m* raven; **cuervo marino** cormorant; **cuervo merendero** rook

cuesco *m* (*de la fruta*) stone; (*del molino de aceite*) millstone; windiness

cuesta *f* hill, slope, grade; charity drive; **cuesta abajo** downhill; **cuesta arriba** uphill; **llevar a cuestas** to be burdened with

cuestión *f* question; dispute, quarrel; matter; **cuestión batallona** much-debated question; **cuestión palpitante** burning question; **en cuestión de** in a matter of

cuestionable *adj* questionable

cuestionar *tr* to question || *intr* (Arg) to argue

cuestionario *m* questionnaire

cuestua·rio -ria or **cuestuo·so -sa** *adj* profitable, lucrative

cuetear *ref* (Col) to blow up, explode; (Col) to die, kick the bucket; (Mex) to get drunk

cueva *f* cave; cellar; (*de ladrones, fieras, etc.*) den

cufi·fo -fa *adj* (Chile) tipsy

cugulla *f* cowl

cui·co -ca *adj* foreign, outside || *m* (Mex) cop, policeman

cuidado *m* care, concern, worry; **¡cuidado con . . .!** beware of . . .!, look out for!; **de cuidado** dangerously; **estar de cuidado** to be dangerously ill; **pierda Vd. cuidado** don't worry; **salir de su cuidado** (*una mujer*) to be delivered; **tener cuidado** to beware, be careful

cuidadora *f* (Mex) governess, chaperon

cuidado·so -sa *adj* careful, concerned, worried; watchful

cuidar *tr* to take care of, watch over || *intr* — **cuidar de** to take care of, care for; care to || *ref* to take care of oneself; **cuidarse de** to care about; be careful to

cuita *f* trouble, worry; longing, yearning

cuja *f* bedstead

culata *f* buttock, haunch; (*de la escopeta*) butt; (*de imán*) keeper, yoke; **culata de cilindro** cylinder head

culatazo *m* kick, recoil

culebra *f* snake; (*del alambique*) coil; **culebra de anteojos** cobra; **culebra de cascabel** rattlesnake; **saber más que las culebras** to be crafty

culebrear *intr* to wriggle; wind, meander; zigzag

culebrón *m* foxy fellow; (Mex) poor farce

cule·co -ca *adj* self-satisfied; madly in love

cu·lí *m* (*pl* **-líes**) coolie

culina·rio -ria *adj* culinary

culipandear *intr* & *ref* (CAm, W-I) to welsh, be evasive

culminar *intr* to culminate

culo *m* seat, behind, backside; (*de animal*) buttocks; (*de un vaso*) bottom; **culo de mal asiento** fidgety person; **volver el culo to** run away

culote *m* base

culpa *f* blame, guilt, fault; **echar la culpa a** to put the blame on; **tener la culpa** to be wrong, be to blame

culpable *adj* blamable, guilty, culpable

culpa·do -da *adj* guilty || *mf* culprit

culpar *tr* to blame, censure, accuse || *ref* to take the blame

cultedad *f* fustian, affectation

culteranismo *m* euphuism, Gongorism

cultiparlar *intr* to speak in a euphuistic manner

cultismo *m* learned word; cultism, Gongorism

cultivar *tr* to cultivate; till

cultivo *m* cultivation; **cultivo de secano** dry farming

cul·to -ta *adj* cultivated, cultured; (*vocablo*) learned || *m* worship; cult; **culto a la personalidad** personality cult

cultura *f* culture, cultivation

culturar *tr* to cultivate, till

cumbre *adj* top, greatest || *f* summit; acme, pinnacle; **conferencia en la cumbre** summit meeting

cúmel *m* kümmel

cumiche *m* (CAm) baby (*youngest member of family*)

cumpa *m* (SAm) pal, buddy; comrade

cúmplase *m* approval, O.K.

cumplea·ños *m* (*pl* **-ños**) birthday

cumpli·do -da *adj* full; perfect; (*en muestras de urbanidad*) correct || *m* correctness; courtesy; present

cumplimentar *tr* to compliment; to pay a complimentary visit to; to carry out, execute; (*un cuestionario*) to fill out

cumplimente·ro -ra *adj* effusive, obsequious

cumplimiento *m* (*muestra de urbanidad*) compliment; (*conducta decorosa*) correctness; fulfillment; perfection; **por cumplimiento** as a matter of pure formality

cumplir *tr* to fulfill, perform, execute; **cumplir años** to have a birthday; **cumplir . . . años** to be . . . years old || *intr* to fall due; to expire; to keep one's promise; to finish one's service in the army; **cumplir con** to fulfill; to fulfill one's obligation to; **cumplir por** to act on behalf of; to pay the respects of || *ref* to be fulfilled, to come true; to fall due; **cúmplase** approved

cumquibus *m* wherewithal

cúmulo *m* heap, pile, lot

cuna *f* cradle

cundido *m* olive, vinegar, and salt for shepherds; olive oil, cheese, and honey to make children eat

cundir *intr* to spread; swell, puff up; increase

cunear *tr* to cradle, rock in a cradle || *intr* to rock, swing, sway

cune·co -ca *mf* (Ven) baby (*youngest member of family*)

cuneta *f* gutter, ditch

cuña *f* wedge; (typ) quoin; **ser buena cuña to** take up a lot of room

cuñada *f* sister-in-law

cuñado *m* brother-in-law

cuñete *m* keg

cuño *m* die; stamp; mark
cuota *f* quota, share; fee, dues; tuition fee
cupé *m* coupé
cupo *m* quota, share; (Mex) capacity
cupón *m* coupon; **cupón de racionamiento** ration coupon
cúpula *f* cupola; dome
cuquillo *m* cuckoo
cura *m* curate; (coll) priest; **este cura** (*yo*) (coll) yours truly (*I*) ‖ *f* cure; care, treatment; **cura de aguas** water cure; **cura de almas** care of souls; **cura de hambre** starvation diet; **cura de reposo** rest cure; **cura de urgencia** first aid; **no tener cura** to be hopeless, be incorrigible
curaca *m* (SAm) boss, chief ‖ *f* (Bol, Peru) priest's housekeeper
curación *f* cure, treatment
curade•ro -ra *mf* caretaker ‖ *m* (law) guardian
curande•ro -ra *mf* quack, healer
curar *tr* (*a un enfermo*) to treat; (*sanar*) cure, heal; (*curtir*) cure; (*la madera*) season; (*una herida*) dress ‖ *intr* to cure; recover; **curar de** to take care of; recover from; mind, pay attention to ‖ *ref* to cure; cure oneself; get well, recover; get drunk; **curarse de** to recover from, get over; **curarse en salud** to be forewarned
curati•vo -va *adj & f* curative
curda *f* jag, drunk
cureña *f* gun carriage
curia *f* (hist) curia; (*de rey*) court; (*conjunto de abogados*) bar
curiales•co -ca *adj* hairsplitting, legalistic
curiosear *tr* to pry into ‖ *intr* to snoop; browse around
curiosidad *f* curiosity; (*objeto de arte raro y curioso*) curio; neatness, tidiness; care, carefulness
curio•so -sa *adj* curious; neat, tidy; careful ‖ *mf* busybody ‖ *m* (Ven) healer, medical man
currinche *m* cub reporter; hit playwright
cu•rro -rra *adj* flashy, sporty ‖ *m* sport, dandy
curruca *f* (orn) whitethroat; **curruca de cabeza negra** blackcap, warbler
curruta•co -ca *adj* dudish, sporty; chubby ‖ *m* dude, sport ‖‖ *f* chic dame

cursa•do -da *adj* skilled, experienced; (*asignatura*) taken
cursante *mf* student
cursar *tr* (*una materia, estudios*) to take, study; (*conferencias*) attend; (*una carta*) forward; (*un paraje*) frequent, to haunt ‖ *intr* to study; be current
cursear *intr* to have diarrhea
cursería *f* cheapness, flashiness, vulgarity; flashy lot of people
cursi *adj* cheap, flashy, vulgar, loud ‖ *m* sporty guy ‖ *f* flashy dame
cursien•to -ta *adj* diarrheic
cursilería *f* cheapness, flashiness, vulgarity; flashy lot of people
cursillo *m* refresher course; short course of lectures
cursi•vo -va *adj* cursive; italic ‖ *f* cursive; italics
curso *m* course; academic year, school year; price, quotation, current rate; **curso académico** academic year; **curso legal** legal tender; **cursos** loose bowels; **dar curso a** to give way to; to forward
cursor *m* slide; sliding contact; **cursor de procesiones** marshal
curtiduría *f* tannery
curtiembre *f* tannery
curtir *tr* (*las pieles*) to tan; (*el cutis de una persona*) tan, sunburn; harden, inure; **estar curtido en** to be skilled in, be expert in ‖ *ref* to become tanned, sunburned; become hardened; be weather-beaten
curva *f* curve; bend
curvadura *f* painful exhaustion
cur•vo -va *adj* curved, bent ‖ *f* see **curva**
cusca *f* (Col) jag, drunk; (Mex) prostitute, slut
cúspide *f* (*de montaña*) peak; (*de diente*) cusp; apex, tip, top
custodia *f* custody, care; (*de un preso*) guard; (eccl) monstrance
custodiar *tr* to guard, watch over
custodio *m* custodian; guard
cususa *f* (CAm) rum
cu•tí *m* (*pl* -**tíes**) bedtick, ticking
cutícula *f* cuticle
cutio *m* work, labor
cu•tis *m* (*& f*) (*pl* -**tis**) skin, complexion; **cutis anserina** goose flesh
cu•yo -ya *adj rel* whose
c/v *abbr* **cuenta de venta**

cu
ch

Ch

Ch, ch (che) *f* fourth letter of the Spanish alphabet
chabacanada or **chabacanería** *f* crudeness, coarseness, vulgarity
chabaca•no -na *adj* crude, coarse, vulgar ‖ *m* (Mex) apricot tree
chabola *f* shack, shanty; (mil) foxhole
chacal *m* jackal

chacanear *tr* (Chile) to spur, goad on; (Chile) to annoy, bother
chacare•ro -ra *mf* (SAm) farm laborer, field worker; (Col) quack doctor; (Urug) gossip
chacarrachaca *f* row, racket
chacolotear *intr* to clatter
chacota *f* laughter, racket; **hacer chacota de** to make fun of

chacotear *intr* to laugh and make a racket

chacra *f* farm house; small farm; sown field

chacua•co -ca *adj* ugly, crude, boorish ‖ *m* (CAm) cigar butt; (CAm) cheap cigar

cháchara *f* chatter, idle talk; **chácharas** trinkets, junk

chacharear *intr* to chatter

chafallar *tr* to botch

chafandín *m* conceited ass

chafar *tr* to rumple, muss; flatten; cut short; (Chile) to dismiss, send off

chafarrinar *tr* to blot, stain

chafarrinón *m* blot, stain; **echar un chafarrinón a** to insult, throw mud at

chaflán *m* chamfer

chaflanar *tr* to chamfer

chal *m* shawl

cha•lán -lana *adj* horse-dealing ‖ *mf* horse dealer; horse trader ‖ *m* broncobuster, horsebreaker ‖ *f* scow, flatboat

chalanear *tr* (*un negocio*) to pull off shrewdly; (*un caballo*) break; (Arg) to take advantage of ‖ *intr* to horse-trade

chalanería *f* horse trading

chalanes•co -ca *adj* horse-trading

chaleco *m* vest, waistcoat; **al chaleco** (Mex) by force; (Mex) for nothing; **chaleco salvavidas** life jacket

chalecón *m* (Mex) crook

chalupa *f* small two-master; launch, lifeboat; (Mex) corncake

chama•co -ca *mf* (Mex) youngster, urchin

chamago•so -sa *adj* (Mex) dirty, filthy; (Mex) botched

chamarasca *f* brushwood; brush fire

chamarille•ro -ra *mf* junk dealer, secondhand dealer ‖ *m* gambler

chamari•llón -llona *mf* poor card player

chamarra *f* sheepskin jacket

chamarreta *f* loose jacket; square poncho

chamba *f* fluke, scratch; (Mex) work

chambelán *m* chamberlain; (Mex) atomizer, spray

chambergo *m* (orn) bobolink; (Arg) soft hat

chambe•rí *adj* (*pl* **-ríes**) (Peru) showy, flashy

cham•bón -bona *adj* awkward, clumsy; lucky

chambonada *f* awkwardness, clumsiness; stroke of luck

chambonear *intr* to foozle

chambra *f* blouse; (Ven) din, uproar

chambrana *f* trim (*around a door*)

chamburgo *m* (Col) stagnant water, puddle

chamico *m* jimson weed; **dar chamico a** (SAm) to bewitch

chamorrar *tr* to shear

champán *m* sampan; (coll) champagne

champaña *m* champagne

cham•pú *m* (*pl* **-púes**) shampoo

chamuchina *f* rabble; populace

chamuscar §73 *tr* to singe, scorch; (Mex) to undersell

chamusco *m* singe, scorch

chamusquina *f* singeing; fight, row, quarrel; **oler a chamusquina** to look like a fight; smack of heresy

chancar §73 *tr* to crush; beat, beat up; botch

chance *m* (SAm) opportunity, chance

chancear *intr* & *ref* to joke, jest

chance•ro -ra *adj* joking, jesting

chanciller *m* chancellor

chancla *f* old shoe; house slipper

chancleta *mf* good-for-nothing ‖ *f* slipper; (Ven) accelerator

chanclo *m* overshoe, rubber

chancha *f* cheat, lie; (Chile) slut; **hacer la chancha** (Bol, Col, Chile) to play hooky

chanche•ro -ra *mf* (Arg, Chile) pork butcher

chan•cho -cha *adj* dirty, filthy ‖ *m* pig ‖ *f* see **chancha**

chanchulle•ro -ra *mf* crook

chandal *m* or **chándal** *m* jump suit, gym suit

changador *m* (SAm) errand boy

changarro *m* (Mex) small shop

chan•go -ga *adj* (Chile) dull, stupid; (Mex) sly, crafty ‖ *mf* (Mex) monkey ‖ *m* (Arg) house boy

chan•guí *m* (*pl* **-guíes**) trick, deception

chantaje *m* blackmail

chantajista *mf* blackmailer

chantar *tr* to put on; (SAm) to throw hard; (Urug) to keep waiting ‖ *ref* (*p.ej., el sombrero*) to clap on

chantre *m* cantor, precentor

chanza *f* joke, jest

chao *interj* (coll) good-by

chapa *f* sheet, plate; (*hoja fina de madera*) veneer; (*en las mejillas*) flush; (coll) good sense, judgment; (Chile) lock, bolt; **chapa de circulación** (aut) license plate; **chapas** flipping coins

chapa•do -da *adj* plated; veneered; **chapado a la antigua** old-fashioned

chapalear *intr* (*el agua; las manos y los pies en el agua*) to splash; (*la herradura floja*) clatter

chapar *tr* to cover or line with sheets of metal; veneer

chaparrear *intr* to pour

chapa•rro -rra *mf* (Mex) child, little one; (Mex) runt ‖ *m* scrub oak

chaparrón *m* downpour

chapea•do -da *adj* lined with sheets of metal; veneered ‖ *m* plywood; veneer

chapear *tr* to cover or line with sheets of metal; veneer

chapista *m* tinsmith, tinman

chapitel *m* (*remate de torre*) spire; (*capitel de columna*) capital

chapodar *tr* to trim, clear of branches; to curtail

chapotear *tr* to sponge, moisten ‖ *intr* to splash

chapucear *tr* & *intr* to botch, bungle

chapuce•ro -ra *adj* crude, rough; clumsy, bungling ‖ *mf* bungler; amateur ‖ *m* blacksmith; junk dealer

chapurrar *tr* & *intr* to jabber

chapurreo *m* jabber

cha•puz *m* (*pl* **-puces**) duck, ducking

chapuzar §60 *tr*, *intr* & *ref* to duck

chaqué *m* cutaway coat, morning coat

chaqueta *f* jacket

chaquetilla *f* short jacket; (Ecuad) lady's vest

chaquetón *m* reefer, pea jacket

charamusca *f* brushwood, firewood; (Mex) candy twist

charanga *f* (mil) brass band

charangue•ro -ra *adj* crude, rough; bungling, clumsy ‖ *mf* bungler

charca *f* pool

charco *m* puddle

charla *f* talk, chat; talk, lecture; chatter, prattle

charla•dor -dora *adj* garrulous; gossipy ‖ *mf* chatterbox; gossip

charlar *intr* to talk, chat; chatter, prattle

charla•tán -tana *adj* garrulous; gossipy ‖ *mf* chatterbox; gossip; charlatan

charlatanería *f* garrulity, loquacity

charlatanismo *m* charlatanism; garrulity, loquacity

charnela *f* (*de puerta; de molusco*) hinge; (mach) knuckle

charol *m* varnish; patent leather; lacquered tray; **calzarse las de charol** (Arg, Urug) to hit the jackpot; **darse charol** to blow one's own horn

charola•do -da *adj* shiny

charolar *tr* to varnish, lacquer

charpa *f* pistol belt; (*cabestrillo*) sling

charquear *tr* (*carne de vaca*) to jerk; slash, cut to pieces

charqui *m* jerked beef

charrada *f* country dance; boorishness; tawdry ornamentation

charretera *f* epaulet; garter; (*del aguador*) shoulder pad

charriada *f* (Mex) rodeo

cha•rro -rra *adj* coarse, ill-bred; flashy, loud, showy; Salamanca ‖ *mf* peasant; Salamanca peasant ‖ *m* broad-brimmed hat; Mexican cowboy

chasca *f* brushwood

chascar §73 *tr* (*la lengua*) to click; (*algún manjar*) crunch; (*engullir*) swallow ‖ *intr* to crack, crackle

chascarrillo *m* funny story

chas•co -ca *adj* (Arg, Bol) crinkly, crinkly-haired ‖ *m* joke, trick; disappointment; **dar un chasco a** to play a trick on; **llevar** or **llevarse (un) chasco** to be disappointed

chas•cón -cona *adj* (Bol, Chile) disheveled; (Bol, Chile) bushy-haired; (Bol, Chile) clumsy, unskilled

cha•sis *m* (*pl* **-sis**) chassis

chasquear *tr* (*un látigo*) to crack; play a trick on; disappoint ‖ *intr* to crack ‖ *ref* to be disappointed

chasqui *m* (SAm) messenger, courier

chasquido *m* crack; crackle

chata *f* barge, scow; flatcar; bedpan; (Mex) dear, darling

chatarra *f* iron slag; junk, scrap iron

chatarrería *f* junk yard

chatarre•ro -ra *mf* junk dealer, scrapiron dealer

cha•to -ta *adj* flat; flat-nosed; blunt; commonplace; disappointed ‖ *m* wineglass ‖ *f* see **chata**

chatre *adj* (Chile, Ecuad) all dressed up

chauvinismo *m* chauvinism

cha•val -vala *adj* (coll) young ‖ *m* lad ‖ *f* lass

chaveta *f* cotter pin; **perder la chaveta** to go out of one's head

chayote *m* chayote, vegetable pear; dunce, fool

chazar §60 *tr* (*la pelota*) to stop; (*el sitio donde paró la pelota*) to mark

che *interj* (SAm) say!, hey!

checar *tr* (Mex) to check

che•co -ca *adj & mf* Czech

checoeslova•co -ca *adj & mf* Czecho-Slovak

Checoeslovaquia *f* Czecho-Slovakia

checoslova•co -ca *adj & mf* Czecho-Slovak

Checoslovaquia *f* Czecho-Slovakia

chechén *m* (Mex) poison ivy

chécheres *mpl* trinkets, junk

chelín *m* shilling

cheque *m* check; **cheque de viajeros** traveler's check

chequear *tr* (CAm, W-I) to check

chequeo *m* control; checkup

chequera *f* checkbook

chévere *adj invar* terrific, fabulous; **¡que chévere!** terrific!

chica *f* lass, little girl; girl; my dear; **chica de cita** call girl; **chica de la vida alegre** party girl

chicalote *m* Mexican poppy

chicle *m* chewing gum

chiclear *intr* (Mex) to chew gum

chi•co -ca *adj* small, little; young ‖ *mf* child, youngster ‖ *m* lad, little boy; young fellow; old man; hand, turn ‖ *f* see **chica**

chicolear *intr* to pay compliments, to flirt ‖ *ref* (Arg, Peru) to enjoy oneself

chico•te -ta *mf* husky youngster ‖ *m* cigar; cigar stub; whip

chicotear *tr* to beat up; kill

chicue•lo -la *adj* small, little ‖ *m* little boy ‖ *f* little girl

chicha *f* corn liquor; **no ser ni chicha ni limonada** to be good for nothing

chícharo *m* pea; (Col) poor cigar; (Mex) apprentice

chicharra *f* harvest fly; chatterbox; **cantar la chicharra** (coll) to be hot and sultry

chicharrón *m* residue of hog's fat; burnt meat; sunburned person; wrinkled person

chiche *adj invar* nice, pretty

chichear *tr & intr* to hiss

chi•chón -chona *adj* (CAm) easy; (SAm) joking; (Guat) large-breasted ‖ *m* lump, bump on the head

chifla *f* hissing, whistling; paring knife; **estar de chifla** (Mex) to be in a bad humor

chifla•do -da *adj* (coll) daffy, nutty ‖ *mf* crackbrain, nut

chifladura *f* daffiness, nuttiness; whim, wild idea

chiflar *tr* (*a un actor*) to hiss; (*vino o licor*) to gulp down; (*el cuero*) to pare ‖ *intr* to whistle; (*las aves*) (Guat, Mex) to sing ‖ *ref* to go crazy

chifle *m* whistle; (*para cazar aves*) bird call; powder flask

chiflido *m* whistle, hiss

ch
ch

chiflón m (SAm) cold blast of air; rapids; slide of loose stone

chilaba f jelab, jellaba

Chile m Chile

chile•no -na adj & mf Chilean

chilote m (CAm) ear of corn

chilla f fox call, hare call; clapboard; (Chile) small fox; (Mex) top gallery

chillar intr to shriek; to squeak; to hiss, sizzle; (los colores) to scream || ref to take offense

chillido m shriek, scream

chi•llón -llona adj shrill, high-pitched; screaming; (color) loud

chimenea f chimney, smokestack; fireplace, hearth; stovepipe hat; (naut) funnel

chimpancé m chimpanzee

china f Chinese woman; china, porcelain; pebble; nursemaid; (Col) spinning top || **China** f China

chinche mf bore, tiresome person || m (clavito de cabeza chata) thumbtack || f (insecto) bedbug; **caer** or **morir como chinches** to die like flies

chinchorre•ro -ra adj gossipy, mischievous

chincho•so -sa adj boring, tiresome

chinero m china closet

chines•co -ca adj Chinese || **chinescos** mpl (mus) bell tree

chingar §44 tr to tipple; (CAm) to bob, dock; (CAm, Mex) to bother, annoy || ref to tipple; fail

chin•go -ga adj (CAm) short; (CAm) dull, blunt; (CAm) naked

chinguirito m cheap rum; swig of liquor

chi•no -na adj & mf Chinese || m (idioma) Chinese; (Col) boy, newsboy; (Mex) curl || f see **china**

chipichipi m drizzle, mist

Chipre f Cyprus

chiquero m pigsty; bull pen

chiquillada f childish prank

chiqui•to -ta adj small, little || mf little one || m (de vino) snifter; (Arg) moment, instant || f five cents; **no andarse con** or **en chiquitas** to talk right off the shoulder

chiquitura f trifle, small matter

chiribita f spark; daisy; **chiribitas** spots before the eyes

chiribitil m garret; cubbyhole

chirimbolos mpl utensils, vessels

chirimía f hornpipe

chiripa f (billiards) fluke, scratch; stroke of luck

chirivía f parsnip

chirle adj insipid, tasteless

chirlo m slash or scar on the face

chirlota f (Mex) meadow lark

chirona f jail, jug

chirriar §77 intr to creak, squeak; shriek; hiss, sizzle; sing or play out of tune || ref (Col) to go on a spree; (Col) to shiver

chirrido m creak, squeak; shriek; hiss, sizzle

chirrión m squeaky cart; (SAm) whip

chis interj sh-sh!; ¡chis, chis! pst!

chischás m clash of swords

chisguete m swig of wine; squirt

chisme m piece of gossip; trinket; **chisme de vecindad** idle talker; **chismes** gossip; articles; **chismes de aseo** toilet articles

chismear intr to gossip

chismo•so -sa adj gossipy, catty || mf gossip

chispa f spark; (pequeña cantidad) lightning; (fig) sparkle, wit; (coll) drunk, spree; (Col) rumor; **coger una chispa** to go on a drunk; **chispa de entrehierro** (elec) jump spark; **chispas** sprinkle (of rain); **dar chispa** (Guat, Mex) to work, to click; **echar chispas** to blow up, hit the ceiling

chispeante adj sparkling

chispar tr to throw (someone) out

chispear intr to spark; sparkle; drizzle, sprinkle

chis•po -pa adj tipsy || m swallow, drink || f see **chispa**

chisporrotear intr to spark, sputter

chispo•so -sa adj sputtering, sparking

chisquero m pocket lighter

chistar intr to speak, say something; **no chistar** to not say a word

chiste m joke; witticism; **caer en el chiste** to get the point; **dar en el chiste** to hit the nail on the head

chistera f fish basket; (coll) top hat

chisto•so -sa adj funny; witty || mf funny person; wit

chita f anklebone; quoits; **a la chita callando** quietly, secretly; **dar en la chita** to hit the nail on the head

chiticalla mf (persona que no revela lo que sabe) (coll) clam || f (coll) secret

chito interj hush!, sh-sh!

chivato m kid, young goat; (soplón) squealer; (Bol) apprentice, helper; (Chile) cheap rum

chi•vo -va mf kid || m billy goat; (Mex) day's wage; (Col, Ecuad, Ven) fit of rage || f nanny goat

chocante adj shocking; coarse, crude; (Col) annoying; (Mex) disagreeable

chocar §73 tr to shock, annoy, irritate; surprise; (vasos) clink; please; ¡choque Vd. esos cinco! shake! || intr to shock; collide; clash, fight

chocarre•ro -ra adj coarse, crude || mf crude joker

choclo m wooden overshoe; (Mex) low shoe; (SAm) tender ear of corn

chocolate m chocolate

chocha f woodcock

chochear intr to be in one's dotage; dote, be infatuated

chochera f dotage; (Arg, Peru) favorite

cho•chez f (pl -checes) dotage; doting act or remark

cho•cho -cha adj doting; doddering || m stick of cinnamon candy; **chochos** candy to quiet a child || f see **chocha**

chófer m chauffeur

chofeta f fire pan (for lighting cigars)

cho•lo -la adj half-breed (Indian and white) || mf Indian; half-breed; (Chile) coward; (SAm) darling

cholla f (coll) noodle, head; (coll) ability, brains

chomite *m* (Mex) coarse wool; (Mex) woolen skirt

chontal *m* uneducated person

chopo *m* black poplar; gun, rifle; **chopo de Italia** Lombardy poplar; **chopo del Canadá** or **de Virginia** cottonwood; **chopo lombardo** Lombardy poplar

choque *m* shock; collision, impact; clash, conflict, skirmish; (elec) choke, choke coil; **choque en cadena** (aut) pileup, mass collision

choricería *f* sausage shop

chorizo *m* smoked pork sausage

chorlito *m* plover, golden plover; scatterbrains

chorrea•do -da *adj* dirty; spotty

chorrear *intr* to gush, spurt, spout; drip; trickle

chorrera spout, channel; cut, gulley; rapids; lace front, jabot; (Arg) string, stream

chorrillo *m* constant stream; **irse por el chorrillo** to follow the current; **tomar el chorrillo de** to get the habit of

chorro *m* jet, spurt; stream, flow; **a chorros** in abundance; **chorro de arena** sandblast

chotaca•bras *m* (*pl* **-bras**) goatsucker

chotear *tr* to make fun of; (Guat) to keep an eye on

choteo *m* jeering, mocking

choza *f* hut, cabin, lodge

chubasco *m* squall, shower; (fig) temporary setback; **chubasco de agua** rainstorm; **chubasco de nieve** blizzard

chubasco•so -sa *adj* stormy, threatening

chucruta *f* sauerkraut

chucha *f* female dog, bitch; drunk, jag; (Col) opossum; (Col) body odor

chuchaque *m* (Ecuad) hangover

chuchear *tr* (*caza menor*) to trap ‖ *intr* to whisper

chuchería *f* knickknack, trinket; delicacy, tidbit

chu•cho -cha *adj* (CAm) mean, stingy; (*fruto*) (Col) watery; (Col) wrinkled ‖ *m* (coll) dog ‖ *f* see **chucha**

chue•co -ca *adj* (Mex) twisted, bent; (SAm) bow-legged; (Mex) crippled ‖ *m* (Mex) dealing in stolen goods ‖ *f* stump; hockey; hockey ball

chufa *f* groundnut

chufletear *intr* to joke, jest

chula *f* flashy dame (*in lower classes of Madrid*)

chulada *f* light-hearted remark; vulgarity

chul•co -ca *mf* (Bol) baby (*youngest child*)

chulear *tr* to tease; (Mex) to flirt with

chuleta *f* chop, cutlet; slap, smack; (*de los estudiantes*) (coll) crib, pony; **chuleta de cerdo** pork chop; **chuleta de ternera** veal chop; **chuletas** sideburns, side whiskers

chu•lo -la *adj* flashy, sporty; foxy, slick; (Guat, Mex) pretty, cute ‖ *m* sporty fellow (*in lower classes of Madrid*); pimp, procurer; gigolo; butcher's helper; (taur) attendant on foot ‖ *f* see **chula**

chumbera *f* prickly pear

chume•ro -ra *mf* (CAm) apprentice

chunches *mpl* (CAm) junk, stuff

chunga *f* jest, fun

chunguear *ref* to jest, joke

chupa *f* frock, coat; (Arg) drunk, jag; (Arg) tobacco pouch

chupa•do -da *adj* thin, skinny; drunk; (*falda*) tight ‖ *f* suck; pull (*on a cigar*)

chupador *m* teething ring, pacifier

chupaflor *m* (Mex, Ven) hummingbird

chupalla *f* straw hat

chupamirto *m* (Mex) hummingbird

chupar *tr* to suck; (*la hacienda ajena*) milk, sap; absorb ‖ *intr* to suck ‖ *ref* to get thin, lose strength; (*los labios*) smack

chupatin•tas *mf* (*pl* **-tas**) (coll) office drudge

chupete *m* (*para un niño*) pacifier; lollipop; **de chupete** fine, splendid

chu•pón -pona *mf* swindler ‖ *m* (bot) sucker, shoot; (mach) plunger; baby bottle; pacifier

chupópte•ro -ra *mf* sponger

chuquisa *f* (Chile, Peru) prostitute

churrasco *m* barbecue

churrasquear *tr* to barbecue

churre *m* filth, dirt, grease

churrete *m* dirty spot (*on hands or face*)

churrigueres•co -ca *adj* churrigueresque; loud, flashy, tawdry

chu•rro -rra *adj* (*lana*) coarse; (*carnero*) coarse-wooled ‖ *m* coarse-wooled sheep; fritter; botch

churrulle•ro -ra *adj* gossipy, loquacious ‖ *mf* gossip, chatterbox

churrusco *m* burnt piece of bread

churumbela *f* hornpipe, flageolet; maté cup; (Col) worry, anxiety; (Col, Ecuad) pipe

churumo *m* (coll) substance (*money, brains, etc.*)

chus *interj* here! (*to call a dog*); **no decir chus ni mus** to not say boo

chus•co -ca *adj* droll, funny; (Peru) ill-mannered; (*perro*) (Peru) mongrel

chusma *f* galley slaves; mob, rabble

chuza *f* (Mex) strike (*in bowling*)

D

D, d (de) *f* fifth letter of the Spanish alphabet

D. *abbr* **don**

D.ª *abbr* **doña**

daca give me, hand over; **andar al daca y toma** to be at cross purposes

dactilógra•fo -fa *mf* typist ‖ *m* typewriter

dactilograma *m* fingerprint

dádiva *f* gift, present

dadivo•so -sa *adj* liberal, generous

da•do -da *adj* given; **dado que** provided, as

long as ‖ *m* die; **cargar los dados** to load the dice; **dados** dice; **el dado está tirado** the die is cast

daga *f* dagger

dalia *f* dahlia

dama *f* lady, dame; maid-in-waiting; (*en el juego de damas*) king; (*en el ajedrez y los naipes*) queen; (*theat*) leading lady; concubine, mistress; **dama joven** (*theat*) young lead; **damas** checkers; **señalar dama** (*en el juego de damas*) to crown a man

damajuana *f* demijohn

damasquina•do -da *adj & m* damascene

damasquinar *tr* to damascene

damasqui•no -na *adj* damascene

damero *m* checkerboard

damisela *f* young lady; courtesan

damnación *f* damnation

damnificar §73 *tr* to damage, hurt

da•nés -nesa *adj* Danish ‖ *mf* Dane ‖ *m* (*idioma*) Danish

dáni•co -ca *adj* Danish

Danubio *m* Danube

danza *f* dance; dancing; dance team; **danza de cintas** Maypole dance; **danza de figuras** square dance; **meter en la danza** to drag in, involve

danza•dor -dora *mf* dancer

danzar §60 *tr* to dance ‖ *intr* to dance; butt in

danza•rín -rina *mf* dancer; meddler, scatterbrain

dañable *adj* harmful; reprehensible

daña•do -da *adj* bad, wicked; spoiled

dañar *tr* to hurt, damage, injure; spoil ‖ *ref* to be damaged; spoil

dañi•no -na *adj* harmful, destructive, noxious; wicked

daño *m* damage, harm; (Arg) witchcraft; **a daño de** on the responsibility of; **daños y perjuicios** (law) damages; **en daño de** to the detriment of; **hacer daño** to be harmful; **hacer daño a** to hurt; **hacerse daño** to hurt oneself; to get hurt

daño•so -sa *adj* harmful, injurious

dar §23 *tr* to give; cause; hit, strike; (*el reloj la hora*) strike; (*cartas*) deal; (*un paseo*) take; (*los buenos días*) wish; (*un film*) show; (*una capa de pintura*) put on, apply; **dar a conocer** to make known; **dar a luz** to bring out, publish; **dar cuerda a** (*un reloj*) to wind; **dar curso a** to circulate; **dar de beber a** to give something to drink to; **dar de comer a** to give something to eat to; **dar la razón a** to admit that (*someone*) is right; **dar prestado** to lend; **dar palmadas** to clap the hands; **dar por** to consider as; **dar que hablar** to cause talk; to stir up criticism; **dar que hacer** to cause annoyance or trouble; **dar que pensar** to give food for thought; to give rise to suspicion ‖ *intr* to take place; to hit, strike; (*el reloj; dos, tres, etc. horas*) to strike; to tell, intimate; **dar a** to overlook; **dar con** to run into; **dar contra** to run against, strike against; **dar de sí** to stretch, to give; **dar en** to overlook; to hit; to run into; to fall into; to be bent on; (*un chiste*)

to catch on to; **dar sobre** to overlook; **dar tras** to pursue hotly ‖ *ref* to give oneself up; to give in, yield; to occur, be found; **darse a** to devote oneself to; **darse a conocer** to make a name for oneself, make oneself known; to get to know each other; **darse cuenta de** to realize, become aware of; **darse la mano** to shake hands; **dárselas de** to pose as; **darse por aludido** to take the hint; **darse por entendido** to show an understanding; to show appreciation; **darse por ofendido** to take offense; **darse por vencido** to give up, to acknowledge defeat

dardo *m* dart; cutting remark

dares y tomares *mpl* quarrels, disputes

dársena *f* basin, marina, inner harbor

darvinia•no -na *adj & mf* Darwinian, Darwinist

darvinismo *m* Darwinism

data *f* date; (*en una cuenta*) item; **de larga data** of long standing; **estar de mala data** to be in a bad humor

datar *tr & intr* to date; **datar de** to date from

dátil *m* date

datilera *f* date, date palm

dati•vo -va *adj & m* dative

dato *m* datum; basis, foundation

de *prep* of; from; about; **acompañado de** accompanied by; **cubierto de** covered with; **de noche** in the nighttime; **de no llegar nosotros a la hora** if we do not arrive on time; **más de** more than; **tratar de** to try to

deán *m* (eccl) dean

deanato *m* or **deanazgo** *m* deanship

debajo *adv* below, underneath; **debajo de** below, under

debate *m* debate; altercation, argument

debatir *tr & intr* to debate; fight, argue ‖ *ref* to struggle

debe *m* debit

debelar *tr* to conquer, vanquish

deber *m* duty; (*deuda*) debt; homework, school work; **últimos deberes** last rites ‖ *tr* to owe ‖ *v aux* to have to, ought to, must, should; **deber de** must, most likely ‖ *ref* to be committed; **deberse a** to be due to

debidamente *adv* duly

debi•do -da *adj* due, owed; proper, right; **debido a** due to

débil *adj* weak

debilidad *f* weakness, debility

debilitar *tr & ref* to weaken

débito *m* debt, debit; responsibility

debutante *mf* debutant(e), beginner

debutar *intr* to make one's start, appear for the first time

década *f* decade

decadencia *f* decadence

decadente *adj & mf* decadent

decaer §15 *intr* to decay, decline, fail, weaken; (naut) to drift from the course

decampar *intr* (mil) to decamp

decanato *m* deanship

decano *m* dean

decanta•do -da *adj* puffed-up, overrated

decapitar *tr* to decapitate

decelerar *tr, intr, & ref* to decelerate
decencia *f* decency
decenio *m* decade
dece•no -na *adj & m* tenth
decentar §2 *tr* to cut the first slice of; begin to damage ‖ *ref* to get bedsores
decente *adj* decent, proper; decent-looking
decepción *f* disappointment
decepcionar *tr* to disappoint
decidi•do -da *adj* decided, determined
decidir *tr* to decide; persuade ‖ *intr & ref* to decide
deci•dor -dora *adj* facile, fluent, witty
decimal *adj & m* decimal
déci•mo -ma *adj & m* tenth
decimocta•vo -va *adj* eighteenth
decimocuar•to -ta *adj* fourteenth
decimono•no -na *adj* nineteenth
decimonove•no -na *adj* nineteenth
decimoquin•to -ta *adj* fifteenth
decimosépti•mo -ma *adj* seventeenth
decimosex•to -ta *adj* sixteenth
decimoterce•ro -ra *adj* thirteenth
decimoter•cio -cia *adj* thirteenth
decir *m* say-so; **al decir de** according to ‖ §24 *tr* to say; tell; (*disparates*) talk; **como si dijéramos** so to speak, in a manner of speaking; **decir entre sí** to say to oneself; **decirle a uno cuántas son cinco** to tell a person what's what; **decir para sí** to say to oneself; **decir por decir** to talk for talk's sake; **decir que no** to say no; **decir que sí** to say yes; **decírselo a una persona deletreado** to spell it out to a person; **es decir** that is to say; **mejor dicho** rather; **¡por algo te lo dije!** I told you so!; **por decirlo así** so to speak ‖ *intr* to suit, fit; **¡diga!** (*al contestar el teléfono*) hello! ‖ *ref* to be said; be called; **se dice** it is said, they say
decisión *f* decision
decisi•vo -va *adj* decisive
declamar *tr & intr* to declaim
declaración *f* declaration; (*en bridge*) bid; **declaración de renta** tax return
declarante *mf* declarant, deponent; (*en el juego de bridge*) bidder
declarar *tr* to declare; (*en bridge*) bid; (law) to depose ‖ *ref* to declare oneself; break out, take place
declarati•vo -va *adj* declarative
declinación *f* declination; fall, drop; decline; (gram) declension
declinar *tr & intr* to decline
declive *m* descent, declivity, slope
declividad *f* declivity
decodificador *m* (telv) decoder
decollaje *m* (aer) take-off
decollar *intr* (aer) to take off
decomisar *tr* to seize, confiscate
decomiso *m* seizure, confiscation
decoración *f* decoration; memorizing; (theat) set, scenery; **decoraciones** (theat) scenery; **decoración interior** interior decoration
decorado *m* decoration; (theat) décor, scenery; memorizing
decora•dor -dora *mf* decorator
decorar *tr* to decorate; memorize

decoro *m* decorum; honor, respect; decency, propriety
decoro•so -sa *adj* decorous; respectful; decent
decrecer §22 *intr* to decrease, grow smaller, grow shorter
decrepitar *intr* to crackle
decrépi•to -ta *adj* decrepit
decretar *tr* to decree
decreto *m* decree
decurso *m* course; **en el decurso de** in the course of
dechado *m* sample, model, example: (*labor de las niñas*) sampler
dedada *f* touch, spot; **dar una dedada de miel a** to feed the hopes of
dedal *m* thimble
dedalera *f* foxglove
dedeo *m* (mus) finger dexterity
dedicación *f* dedication; (*aplicación*) diligence
dedicar §73 *tr* to dedicate; devote; autograph ‖ *ref* to devote oneself
dedicatoria *f* dedication
dedil *m* fingerstall
dedillo *m* little finger; **saber** or **tener al dedillo** to have at one's finger tips, have a thorough knowledge of
dedo *m* finger; toe; bit; **alzar el dedo** (*en señal de dar palabra*) to raise one's hand; **cogerse los dedos** to burn one's fingers; **dedo auricular** little finger; **dedo cordial, de en medio,** or **del corazón** middle finger; **dedo gordo** thumb; big toe; **dedo índice** index finger, forefinger; **dedo meñique** little finger; **dedo mostrador** forefinger; **dedo pulgar** thumb; big toe; **estar a dos dedos de** to be within an ace of; **irse de entre los dedos** (coll) to slip between the fingers; **tener en la punta de los dedos** to have at one's fingertips
deducción *f* deduction; drawing off
deducir §19 *tr* (*concluir*) to deduce; (*rebajar*) deduct; (law) to allege
defecar §73 *intr* to defecate
defección *f* defection
defeccionar *intr & ref* (Chile) to defect
defecti•vo -va *adj* defective
defecto *m* defect; shortage, lack; **en defecto de** for lack of
defectuo•so -sa *adj* defective; lacking
defender §51 *tr* to defend; protect; delay, interfere with
defensa *f* defense; fender, guard; (*del toro*) horn; (*del elefante*) tusk; (*del automóvil*) bumper; **defensa marítima** (Arg) sea wall; **defensa propia** self-defense
defensi•vo -va *adj & f* defensive
defen•sor -sora *adj* defending ‖ *mf* defender; (law) counsel for the defense
deferencia *f* deference
deferente *adj* deferential
deferir §68 *tr* to delegate ‖ *intr* to defer
deficiencia *f* deficiency
deficiente *adj* deficient
défi•cit *m* (pl **-cits**) deficit
deficita•rio -ria *adj* deficit

da
de

definición *f* definition; decision, verdict
defini•do -da *adj* definite; sharp, defined
definir *tr* to define; settle, determine
definiti•vo -va *adj* definitive; **en definitiva** after all, in short
deflación *f* deflation
deflector *m* baffle
deformación *f* deformation; (rad) distortion
deformar *tr* to deform; disfigure; distort
deforme *adj* deformed
deformidad *f* deformity; gross error
defraudar *tr* to defraud, cheat; *(las esperanzas de una persona)* defeat; *(la claridad del día)* cut off
defuera *adv* outside; **por defuera** on the outside
defunción *f* decease, demise
degeneración *f* *(acción y efecto de degenerar)* degeneration; *(estado de degenerado; depravación)* degeneracy
degenera•do -da *adj & mf* degenerate
degenerar *intr* to degenerate
deglutir *tr & intr* to swallow
degollar §3 *tr* to cut the throat of; kill, massacre; *(un vestido)* cut low in the neck; *(el actor una obra dramática)* butcher, murder; become obnoxious to
degradante *adj* degrading
degradar *tr* to degrade; (mil) to break
degüello *m* throat-cutting; massacre; *(de un arma)* neck; **tirar a degüello** to try to harm
degustar *tr* *(probar)* to taste; *(percibir con deleite el sabor de)* to savor
dehesa *f* pasture land, meadow; (taur) range
deidad *f* deity
deificar §73 *tr* to deify
dejación *f* abandonment; (CAm, Chile, Col) negligence
dejadez *f* laziness; negligence; slovenliness; low spirits
deja•do -da *adj* lazy; negligent; slovenly; dejected
dejamiento *m* laziness; negligence; indolence, languor, indifference
dejar *tr* to leave; abandon; let, allow, permit; **dejar caer** to drop, let fall; **dejar feo** to slight; **dejar fresco** to leave in the lurch; **dejar por** + *inf* or **que** + *inf* to leave *(something)* to be + *pp*, e.g., **hemos dejado dos manuscritos por corregir** or **que corregir** we left two manuscripts to be corrected || *intr* to stop; **dejar de** to stop, cease; fail to || *ref* to be slovenly, neglect oneself; *(una barba)* grow; **dejarse de** *(disparates)* to cut out; *(preguntas)* stop asking; *(dudas)* put aside; **dejarse ver** to show up; be evident
dejillo *m* *(gusto que deja alguna comida)* aftertaste; *(acento regional)* local accent
dejo *m* *(gusto que deja alguna comida)* aftertaste; abandonment; slovenliness, neglect; local accent; *(placer o disgusto que queda después de hecha una cosa)* (fig) aftertaste
delación *f* accusation, denunciation
delantal *m* apron

delante *adv* before, ahead, in front; **delante de** before, ahead of, in front of
delantera *f* front; front row; advantage, lead; cowcatcher; **coger** or **tomar la delantera a** to get ahead of; get a start on; **delanteras** overalls
delante•ro -ra *adj* front, foremost, first || *m* — **delantero centro** *(fútbol)* center forward || *f* see **delantera**
delatar *tr* to accuse, denounce
delega•do -da *mf* delegate
delegar §44 *tr* to delegate
deleitable *adj* delectable, enjoyable
deleitar *tr & ref* to delight
deleite *m* delight
deleito•so -sa *adj* delightful
deletrear *tr & intr* to spell; decipher
deletreo *m* spelling
deleznable *adj* *(poco durable)* perishable; *(que se rompe fácilmente)* crumbly, fragile; *(que se desliza con facilidad)* slippery
delfín *m* *(primogénito del rey de Francia)* dauphin; *(mamífero cetáceo)* dolphin
delgadez *f* thinness, leanness; delicateness, lightness; perspicacity
delga•do -da *adj* thin, lean; delicate, light; sharp, perspicacious; *(terreno)* poor, exhausted || *adv* — **hilar delgado** to hew close to the line; split hairs
delgadu•cho -cha *adj* skinny; slight
deliberar *tr & intr* to deliberate
delicadeza *f* delicacy, delicateness; scrupulousness
delica•do -da *adj* delicate; scrupulous
delicia *f* delight
delicio•so -sa *adj* delicious, delightful
delicti•vo -va *adj* punishable; criminal
delincuencia *f* guilt, criminality
delincuente *adj* guilty, criminal || *mf* criminal
delineante *mf* designer || *m* draughtsman
delinquir §25 *intr* to transgress, be guilty
deliquio *m* faint, swoon; weakening
delirante *adj* delirious
delirar *intr* to be delirious, rant, rave; talk nonsense
delirio *m* delirium; nonsense
delito *m* crime; **delito de incendio** arson; **delito de lesa majestad** lese majesty; **delito de mayor cuantía** (law) felony; **delito de menor cuantía** (law) misdemeanor
deludir *tr* to delude
demacra•do -da *adj* emaciated, wasted, thin
demago•go -ga *mf* demagogue
demanda *f* demand, petition; charity box; lawsuit; undertaking; *(del Santo Grial)* quest; **demanda maxima** (elec) peak load; **en demanda de** in search of; **tener demanda** to be in demand
demanda•do -da *mf* (law) defendant
demandante *mf* (law) complainant, plaintiff
demandar *tr* to ask for, request; (law) to sue || *intr* (law) to sue, bring suit
demarcar §73 *tr* to demarcate
demás *adj* — **el demás** . . . the other. . . , the rest of the . . . ; **estar demás** to be useless, to be in the way; **lo demás** the

rest; **por lo demás** furthermore, besides ‖ *pron* others; **los demás** the others, the rest ‖ *adv* besides; **por demás** in vain; too, too much

demasía *f* excess, surplus; daring, boldness; evil, guilt, wrong; insolence; **en demasía** excessively, too much

demasia•do -da *adj & pron* too much; **demasia•dos -das** too many ‖ **demasiado** *adv* too, too much, too hard

demasiar §77 *intr* to go too far

demediar *tr* to divide in half; use up half of; reach the middle of ‖ *intr* to be divided in half

dementa•do -da *adj* insane; demented

demente *adj* insane ‖ *mf* lunatic

democracia *f* democracy

demócrata *mf* democrat

democráti•co -ca *adj* democratic

demoler §47 *tr* to demolish

demolición *f* demolition

demonía•co -ca *adj* demoniacal

demonio *m* demon, devil; **estudiar con el demonio** to be full of devilishness

demora *f* delay

demorar *tr & ref* to delay

demostración *f* demonstration

demostra•dor -dora *mf* demonstrator ‖ *m* hand (*of clock*)

demostrar §61 *tr* to demonstrate

demostrati•vo -va *adj* demonstrative

demudar *tr* to change, alter; disguise, cloak ‖ *ref* to change countenance, color

denegación *f* denial, refusal

denegar §66 *tr* to deny, refuse

denegrecer §22 *tr* to blacken ‖ *ref* to turn black

dengo•so -sa *adj* affected, finicky, overnice; (Col) strutting

dengue *m* affectation, finickiness, overniceness; (Col) strut, swagger

denguear *ref* (Col) to strut, swagger

denigrar *tr* to defame, revile; insult

denominación *f* denomination

denoda•do -da *adj* bold, daring

denostar §61 *tr* to abuse, insult, mistreat

denotar *tr* to denote

densidad *f* density; darkness, confusion

den•so -sa *adj* dense; dark, confused; crowded, thick, close

denta•do -da *adj* toothed; (*sello de correo*) perforated ‖ *m* gear; teeth

dentadura *f* set of teeth; **dentadura artificial** or **postiza** denture

dental *adj & f* dental

dentellada *f* bite; tooth mark

dentellar *intr* (*los dientes*) to chatter

dentellear *tr* to nibble, nibble at

dentera *f* envy; eagerness; **dar dentera** to set the teeth on edge; make the mouth water

dentición *f* teething

dentífri•co -ca *adj* (*pasta, polvos*) tooth ‖ *m* dentifrice

dentista *mf* dentist

dentistería *f* dentistry

dentística *f* (Chile) dentistry

dentro *adv* inside, within; **dentro de** inside,

within; **dentro de poco** shortly; **por dentro** on the inside

denuedo *m* bravery, courage, daring

denuesto *m* abuse, insult, mistreatment

denuncia *f* denunciation; report; proclamation

denunciar *tr* to denounce; report; (*la guerra*) proclaim

deparar *tr* to furnish, provide; offer, present

departamento *m* department; (rr) compartment; (*piso*) apartment; naval district (*in Spain*)

departir *intr* to chat, converse

depauperación *f* impoverishment; exhaustion, weakening

depauperar *tr* to impoverish; exhaust, weaken

dependencia *f* dependence, dependency; branch, branch office; relationship, friendship; accessory; personnel

depender *intr* to depend; **depender de** to depend on; be attached to, belong to

dependienta *f* female employee, clerk

dependiente *adj* dependent; branch ‖ *mf* employee, clerk

deplorable *adj* deplorable

deplorar *tr* to deplore

deponer §54 *tr* to depose; set aside, remove; (*las armas*) lay down ‖ *intr* to depose; (*evacuar el vientre*) have a movement; (CAm, Mex) to vomit

deportación *f* deportation

deporta•do -da *mf* deportee

deportar *tr* to deport

deporte *m* sport; outdoor recreation

deportista *mf* sport fan ‖ *m* sportsman ‖ *f* sportswoman

deporti•vo -va *adj* sport, sports

depositante *mf* depositor

depositar *tr* to deposit; (*la esperanza, la confianza*) put, place; (*el equipaje*) check; (*a una persona en seguro*) commit; store ‖ *ref* to deposit, settle

deposita•rio -ria *mf* trustee; (*de un secreto*) repository ‖ *m* public treasurer

depósito *m* deposit; depot, warehouse; tank, reservoir; (*de libros en una biblioteca*) stack; (mil) depot; **depósito comercial** bonded warehouse; **depósito de agua** reservoir; **depósito de cadáveres** morgue; **depósito de cereales** grain elevator; **depósito de equipajes** (rr) checkroom; **depósito de gasolina** (aut) gas tank; **depósito de locomotoras** roundhouse; **depósito de municiones** munition dump

depravación *f* depravity, depravation

deprava•do -da *adj* depraved

depravar *tr* to deprave ‖ *ref* to become depraved

deprecar §73 *tr* to entreat, implore

depreciación *f* depreciation

depreciar *tr & ref* to depreciate

depresión *f* depression; drop, dip; (*en un muro*) recess

deprimir *tr* to depress; press down; push in; belittle; humiliate ‖ *ref* to be depressed; (*la frente de una persona*) recede

de
de

depurar *tr* to purify, cleanse; purge

derecha *f* right hand; right-hand side; (pol) right; **a la derecha** on the right, to the right

derechamente *adv* rightly; straight, direct; properly; wisely

derechazo *m* blow with the right; (box) right

derecheᐧro -ra *adj* right, just

derechista *adj* rightist ‖ *mf* rightist, right-winger

dereᐧcho -cha *adj* right; right-hand; right-handed; straight; upright, standing; (CAm) lucky ‖ *m* right; law; exemption, privilege; road, path; (*de tela, papel, tabla*) right side; **derecho consuetudinario** common law; **derecho de gentes** law of nations, international law; **derecho de subscripción** (*a una nueva emisión de acciones*) (com) right; **derecho de tránsito** or **paso** right of way; **derecho internacional** international law; **derecho penal** criminal law; **derechos** dues, fees, taxes; (*de aduana*) duties; **derechos de almacenaje** storage, cost of storage; **derechos de autor** royalty; **derechos del hombre** rights of man; **derechos de propiedad literaria** or **derechos reservados** copyright; **derechos humanos** human rights; **según derecho** by right, by rights ‖ *f* see **derecha** ‖ **derecho** *adv* straight, direct; rightly

deriva (aer, naut) drift; **ir a la deriva** (naut) to drift, be adrift

derivado *m* by-product

derivar *tr* to derive ‖ *intr & ref* to derive, be derived; (aer, naut) to drift

dermatitis *f* dermatitis

derogar §44 *tr* to abolish, destroy, repeal

derrabar *tr* to dock, cut off the tail of

derramaᐧdo -da *adj* extravagant, lavish

derramamiento *m* pouring, spilling; shedding; spreading; lavishing, wasting

derramar *tr* to pour, spill; (*sangre*) shed; spread, publish abroad; (*dinero*) lavish, waste ‖ *ref* to run over, overflow; spread, scatter; (*una corriente, un río*) open, empty; (*la plumafuente*) leak

derrame *m* pouring, spilling; (*de sangre*) shed, shedding; spread, scattering; lavishing, wasting; overflow; leakage; slope; chamfering; (pathol) discharge, effusion

derrapada *f* or **derrapaje** *f* (aut) skidding

derredor *m* circumference; **al** or **en derredor** around, round about

derrelícto *m* (naut) derelict

derrelínquir §25 *tr* to abandon, forsake

derrengaᐧdo -da *adj* crooked, out of shape; crippled, lame

derrengar §44 or §66 *tr* to bend, make crooked; cripple

derreniego *m* curse

derretiᐧdo -da *adj* madly in love; (*mantequilla*) drawn ‖ *m* concrete

derretimiento *m* thawing, melting; intense love, passion

derretir §50 *tr* to thaw, melt; (*la mantequilla*) draw; (*la hacienda*) squander ‖ *ref* to thaw, melt; fall madly in love; be quite susceptible; be worried, be impatient

derribar *tr* to destroy, tear down, knock down; wreck; (*un árbol*) fell; bring down, shoot down; overthrow; humiliate ‖ *ref* to fall down, tumble down; throw oneself on the ground

derribo *m* demolition, wrecking; (*de un árbol*) felling; overthrow; (*de un avión enemigo*) bringing down; **derribos** debris, rubble

derrocadero *m* rocky precipice

derrocar §73 or §81 *tr* to throw or hurl from a height; ruin, wreck, tear down; bring down, humble, overthrow

derrochaᐧdor -dora *mf* wastrel, squanderer

derrochar *tr* to waste, squander

derroche *m* wasting, squandering, extravagance

derrota *f* defeat, rout; road, route, way; (*de embarcación*) course

derrotadamente *adv* shabbily, poorly

derrotar *tr* to rout, put to flight; wear out; ruin ‖ *ref* (naut) to drift from the course

derrotero *m* course, route; ship's course

derrotismo *m* defeatism

derrotista *adj & mf* defeatist

derrubiar *tr & ref* to wash away, wear away

derrubio *m* washout

derruir §20 *tr* to tear down, demolish

derrumbadero *m* crag, precipice; hazard, risky business

derrumbamiento *m* headlong plunge; cave-in, collapse; **derrumbamiento de tierra** landslide

derrumbar *tr* to throw headlong ‖ *ref* to plunge headlong; collapse, cave in, crumble

derrumbe *m* precipice; landslide; cave-in

derviche *m* dervish

desabonar *ref* to drop one's subscription

desabono *m* cancellation of subscription; discredit, disparagement

desabor *m* insipidity, tastelessness

desabotonar *tr* to unbutton ‖ *intr* to blossom, bloom

desabriᐧdo -da *adj* insipid, tasteless; gruff, surly; (*tiempo*) unsettled

desabrigar §44 *tr* to uncover, bare ‖ *ref* to bare oneself; undress

desabrir *tr* to give a bad taste to; displease, embitter

desabrochar *tr* to unclasp, unbutton, unfasten ‖ *ref* to unbosom oneself

desacalorar *ref* to cool off

desacatamiento *m* incivility, disrespect

desacatar *tr* to treat disrespectfully

desacato *m* incivility, disrespect, contempt; (*para con las cosas sagradas*) profanation

desacelerar *tr & ref* to decelerate

desacertaᐧdo -da *adj* mistaken, wrong

desacertar §2 *intr* to be mistaken, be wrong

desacierto *m* error, mistake, blunder

desacomodaᐧdo -da *adj* inconvenient; out of work; in straightened circumstances

desacomodar *tr* to inconvenience; discharge, dismiss

desacomodiᐧdo -da *adj* (SAm) rude; impolite

desacomodo *m* discharge, dismissal

desaconseja•do -da *adj* ill-advised
desaconsejar *tr* to dissuade
desacordar §61 *tr* to put out of tune ‖ *ref* to get out of tune; become forgetful
desacorde *adj* out of tune; incongruous
desacostumbra•do -da *adj* unusual
desacostumbrar *tr* to break of a habit
desacreditar *tr* to discredit; disparage
desacuerdo *m* discord, disagreement; error, mistake; unconsciousness; forgetfulness
desadaptación *f* maladjustment
desadeudar *tr* to free of debt ‖ *ref* to get out of debt
desadormecer §22 *tr* to awaken; free of numbness ‖ *ref* to get awake; shake off the numbness
desadorna•do -da *adj* unadorned, plain; bare, uncovered
desadverti•do -da *adj* unnoticed; inattentive
desadvertimiento *m* inadvertence
desafección *f* dislike
desafec•to -ta *adj* adverse, hostile; opposed ‖ *m* dislike
desaferrar *tr* to unfasten, loosen; make (*a person*) change his mind; (*las áncoras*) weigh
desafiar §77 *tr* to challenge, defy, dare; rival, compete with
desafición *f* dislike
desaficionar *tr* to cause to dislike
desafilar *tr* to make dull ‖ *ref* to become dull
desafina•do -da *adj* flat, out of tune
desafío *m* challenge, dare; rivalry, competition
desafora•do -da *adj* colossal, huge; disorderly, outrageous
desafortuna•do -da *adj* unfortunate
desafuero *m* excess, outrage
desagracia•do -da *adj* ungraceful, graceless
desagradable *adj* disagreeable
desagradar *tr & intr* to displease ‖ *ref* to be displeased
desagradeci•do -da *adj* ungrateful
desagradecimiento *m* ungratefulness
desagrado *m* displeasure
desagraviar *tr* to make amends to, indemnify
desagravio *m* amends, indemnification
desagregación *f* disintegration
desagregar §44 *tr* to disintegrate
desaguadero *m* drain, outlet; (*ocasión de continuo gasto*) (fig) drain
desaguar §10 *tr* to drain, empty; squander, waste ‖ *intr* to flow, empty ‖ *ref* to drain, be drained
desagüe *m* drainage, sewerage; drain, outlet
desaguisa•do -da *adj* illegal ‖ *m* offense, outrage, wrong
desahijar *tr* (*las crías del ganado*) to wean ‖ *ref* (*las abejas*) to swarm
desahogadamente *adv* freely; comfortably, easily; impudently
desahoga•do -da *adj* brazen, forward; roomy; in comfortable circumstances
desahogar §44 *tr* to relieve, comfort; (*deseos, pasiones*) give free rein to ‖ *ref* to take it easy, get comfortable; unbosom oneself, open up one's heart; get out of

debt; **desahogarse en** (*denuestos*) to burst forth in
desahogo *m* brazenness; ample room; comfort; outlet, relief; comfortable circumstances
desahuciar *tr* to deprive of hope; evict, oust, dispossess ‖ *ref* to lose all hope
desahucio *m* eviction, ousting, dispossession
desaira•do -da *adj* unattractive, unprepossessing; unsuccessful
desairar *tr* to slight, snub, disregard
desaire *m* slight, snub, disregard; unattractiveness, lack of charm
desajustar *tr* to put out of order ‖ *ref* to get out of order; disagree
desalabanza *f* belittling, disparagement
desalabar *tr* to belittle, disparage
desala•do -da *adj* eager, in a hurry
desalar *tr* to desalt; clip the wings of ‖ *ref* to hasten, rush; **desalarse por** to be eager to
desalentar §2 *tr* to put out of breath; discourage ‖ *ref* to become discouraged
desalforjar *ref* to loosen one's clothing
desaliento *m* discouragement
desalinización *f* desalinization
desaliña•do -da *adj* slovenly, untidy; careless, slipshod
desaliño *m* slovenliness, untidiness; carelessness, neglect
desalma•do -da *adj* cruel, inhuman
desalojar *tr* to oust, evict; (*al enemigo*) to dislodge; (*el camino*) to clear ‖ *intr* to leave, move away, move out
desalquila•do -da *adj* vacant, unrented
desalterar *tr* to calm, quiet
desalumbra•do -da *adj* dazzled, blinded, confused, unsure of oneself
desamable *adj* unlikeable, unlovable
desamar *tr* to dislike, hate, detest
desamarrar *tr* to untie, unfasten; (naut) to unmoor
desamistar *ref* to fall out, become estranged
desamor *m* dislike, coldness; hatred
desamorrar *tr* to make (*a person*) talk
desamparar *tr* to abandon, forsake; give up
desamparo *m* abandonment, desertion; helplessness
desamuebla•do -da *adj* unfurnished
desandar §5 *tr* to retrace, go back over
desandraja•do -da *adj* ragged, in tatters
desangrar *tr* to bleed; drain; (fig) to bleed, impoverish ‖ *ref* to lose a lot of blood
desanimación *f* discouragement, downheartedness
desanima•do -da *adj* discouraged, downhearted; (*reunión*) lifeless, dull
desanimar *tr* to discourage, dishearten ‖ *ref* to become discouraged
desánimo *m* discouragement
desanublar *tr & ref* to clear up, brighten up
desanudar *tr* to untie; disentangle
desapacible *adj* unpleasant, disagreeable
desapadrinar *tr* to disavow; disapprove
desaparecer §22 *intr & ref* to disappear
desapareci•do -da *adj* missing; extinct ‖ **desaparecidos** *mpl* missing persons
desaparecimiento *m* disappearance

desaparejar *tr* to unharness, unhitch; (naut) to unrig

desaparición *f* disappearance; (Ven) death

desapasiona•do -da *adj* dispassionate, impartial

desapego *m* dislike, coolness, indifference

desapercibi•do -da *adj* unprepared; wanting; unnoticed

desapiada•do -da *adj* merciless, pitiless

desaplica•do -da *adj* idle, lazy

desapodera•do -da *adj* headlong, impetuous; violent, wild; excessive

desapoderar *tr* to dispossess; deprive of power ‖ *ref* — **desapoderarse de** to lose possession of, give up possession of

desapolillar *tr* to free of moths ‖ *ref* to expose oneself to the weather

desapreciar *tr* to depreciate

desaprecio *m* depreciation

desaprender *tr* to unlearn

desaprensión *f* composure, nonchalance

desapretar §2 *tr* to slacken, loosen; (typ) to unlock

desaprobación *f* disapproval

desaprobar §61 *tr & intr* to disapprove

desapropiar *tr* to divest ‖ *ref* — **desapropiarse de** to divest oneself of

desaprovecha•do -da *adj* unproductive; indifferent, lackadaisical

desaprovechar *tr* to not take advantage of ‖ *intr* to slip back

desarmable *adj* dismountable

desarmador *m* hammer (*of gun*); (Mex) screwdriver

desarmamiento *m* disarmament; arms reduction

desarmar *tr* to disarm; dismount, dismantle, take apart; (*la cólera*) temper, calm ‖ *intr & ref* to disarm

desarme *m* disarmament; dismantling, dismounting

desarraigar §44 *tr* to uproot, dig up; expel, drive out

desarregla•do -da *adj* out of order; slovenly, disorderly; intemperate

desarrimo *m* lack of support; stand-offishness

desarrollar *tr & intr* to develop; unroll, unfold ‖ *ref* to develop; unroll, unfold; take place

desarrollo *m* development; unrolling, unfolding; **ayuda al desarrollo** developmental aid

desarropar *tr & ref* to undress

desarrugar §44 *tr & ref* to unwrinkle

desarzonar *tr* to unsaddle, unhorse

desasea•do -da *adj* dirty, unclean, slovenly

desasentar §2 *tr* to remove; displease ‖ *ref* to stand up

desaseo *m* dirtiness, uncleanliness, slovenliness

desasir §7 *tr* to let go, let go of ‖ *ref* to come loose; let go; **desasirse de** to let go of; give up, get free of

desasosegar §66 *tr* to disquiet, worry, disturb

desasosiego *m* disquiet, worry

desastra•do -da *adj* disastrous; unfortunate, wretched; ragged, shabby

desastre *m* disaster; **ir al desastre** to go to rack and ruin

desastro•so -sa *adj* disastrous

desatacar §73 *tr* to unbuckle, untie

desatar *tr* to untie, undo, unfasten; solve, unravel ‖ *ref* to come loose; free oneself; (*la tempestad*) break loose; forget oneself, go too far; **desatarse en** (*denuestos*) to burst forth in

desatascar §73 *tr* to pull out of the mud; (*un conducto obstruído*) unclog; (*a una persona de un apuro*) extricate

desataviar §77 *tr* to disarray, undress

desatavío *m* disarray, undress, slovenliness

desate *m* (*de palabras*) flood; **desate del vientre** loose bowels

desatención *f* inattention; discourtesy, disrespect

desatender §51 *tr* to slight, disregard, pay no attention to

desatenta•do -da *adj* wild, disorderly, extreme

desaten•to -ta *adj* inattentive; discourteous, disrespectful

desatina•do -da *adj* wild, disorderly; foolish, nonsensical ‖ *mf* fool

desatinar *tr* to bewilder, confuse ‖ *intr* to talk nonsense, act foolishly; lose one's bearings

desatino *m* folly, nonsense; awkwardness, loss of touch

desatolondrar *tr* to bring to ‖ *ref* to come to one's senses

desatollar *tr* to pull out of the mud

desatornillador *m* screwdriver

desatornillar *tr* to unscrew

desatraillar §4 *tr* to unleash

desatrampar *tr* to unclog

desatrancar §73 *tr* to unbar, unbolt; unclog

desatufar *ref* to get out of the close air; cool off, quiet down

desautoriza•do -da *adj* unauthorized

desavenencia *f* disagreement, discord

desavenir §79 *tr* to cause disagreement among ‖ *ref* to disagree; **desavenirse con** to differ with, disagree with

desaventura *f* misfortune

desaviar §77 *tr* to mislead, lead astray

desavisa•do -da *adj* unadvised; ill-advised; thoughtless, careless

desayuna•do -da *adj* — **estar desayunado** to have had breakfast

desayunar *intr* to breakfast ‖ *ref* to breakfast; **desayunarse con** to have breakfast on; **desayunarse de** to get the first news of

desayuno *m* breakfast

desazón *f* insipidity, tastelessness; annoyance, displeasure; discomfort

desazonar *tr* to make tasteless; annoy, displease ‖ *ref* to feel ill

desbancar §73 *tr* to win the bank from; cut out, to supplant

desbandada *f* — **a la desbandada** helter-skelter, in confusion

desbandar *ref* to run away; disband; desert

desbarajustar *tr* to put out of order ‖ *ref* to get out of order, break down

desbarata•do -da *adj* debauched, corrupt ‖ *mf* libertine

desbaratar *tr* to destroy, spoil, ruin; squander, waste; (mil) to rout, throw into confusion ‖ *intr* to talk nonsense ‖ *ref* to be unbalanced

desbarrancadero *m* precipice

desbastar *tr* to smooth off; waste, weaken; (*a una persona inculta*) polish ‖ *ref* to become polished

desbautizar §60 *ref* to lose one's temper

desbeber *intr* (coll) to urinate

desbloquear *tr* to relieve the blockade of; (*crédito*) to unfreeze

desboca•do -da *adj* (*pieza de artillería*) wide-mouthed; (*herramienta*) nicked; (*caballo*) runaway; (*persona*) foul-mouthed

desbocar §73 *tr* to break the mouth of, break the spout of ‖ *intr* (*un río*) to empty; (*una calle*) run, open, end ‖ *ref* (*un caballo*) to run away, break loose; curse, swear

desbordamiento *m* overflow

desbordar *tr* to overwhelm ‖ *intr* & *ref* to overflow

desbozalar *tr* to unmuzzle

desbravar *tr* to tame, break in ‖ *intr* & *ref* to abate, moderate; cool off, calm down

desbrozar §60 *tr* to clear of underbrush, clear of rubbish

desbulla *f* oyster shell

desbulla•dor -dora *mf* oyster opener ‖ *m* oyster fork

desbullar *tr* (*la ostra*) to open

descabal *adj* incomplete, imperfect

descabalgar §44 *intr* to dismount, alight from a horse

descabella•do -da *adj* disheveled; rash, wild

descabellar *tr* to muss, dishevel

descabeza•do -da *adj* crazy, rash, wild

descabezar §60 *tr* to behead; (*un árbol*) top; (*una dificultad*) get the best off; **descabezar el sueño** to doze, snooze ‖ *intr* to border ‖ *ref* to rack one's brains

descabullir §13 *ref* to sneak out, slip away; refuse to face the facts

descachalandra•do -da *adj* untidy; tattered

descacharra•do -da *adj* (CAm) dirty, slovenly, ragged

descaecer §22 *intr* to decline, lose ground

descaecimiento *m* weakness; depression, despondency

descalabazar §60 *ref* to rack one's brain

descalabra•do -da *adj* banged on the head; **salir descalabrado** to come out the loser, be worsted

descalabrar *tr* to bang on the head; knock down ‖ *ref* to bang one's head

descalabro *m* misfortune, setback, loss

descalcificar §73 *tr* to decalcify

descalificar §73 *tr* to disqualify

descalzar §60 *tr* (*las botas, los guantes*) to take off; (*a una persona*) take the shoes or stockings off; undermine ‖ *ref* to take one's shoes or stockings off; take one's gloves

off; (*las botas, los guantes*) take off; (*el caballo*) lose a shoe

descal•zo -za *adj* barefooted; seedy, down at the heel

descamar *ref* to scale, scale off

descaminadamente *adv* off the road, on the wrong track

descaminar *tr* to mislead, lead astray ‖ *ref* to get lost; run off the road

descamino *m* going astray; leading astray; nonsense; contraband, smuggled goods

descamisa•do -da *adj* shirtless, ragged ‖ *m* wretch, ragamuffin

descampa•do -da *adj* free, open ‖ *m* open country

descansadero *m* resting place, stopping place

descansa•do -da *adj* rested, refreshed; calm, restful

descansar *tr* to rest, relieve; (*la cabeza, el brazo*) rest, lean ‖ *intr* to rest; lean; not worry; (*yacer en el sepulcro*) rest; **descansar en** to trust in

descanso *m* rest; peace, quiet; (*de la escalera*) landing; (theat) intermission; (Chile) toilet

descantillar *tr* to chip off; deduct

descañonar *tr* to pluck; shave against the grain; gyp

descapiruzar §60 *tr* (Col) to muss, rumple, crumple

descapotable *adj* & *m* (aut) convertible

descara•do -da *adj* barefaced, brazen, saucy

descarar *ref* to be impudent; **descararse a** to have the nerve to

descarga *f* unloading; (*de un arma de fuego*) discharge; (com) discount; (elec) discharge; **descarga de aduana** customhouse clearance

descargar §44 *tr* to unload; (*de una deuda u obligación*) free; (*un arma de fuego*) discharge; (*un golpe*) strike, deal; (elec) to discharge ‖ *intr* to unload; (*un río*) empty; (*una calle, paseo*) open; (*una nube en lluvia*) burst ‖ *ref* to unburden oneself; resign; **descargarse con** or **en uno de algo** to unload something on someone; **descargarse de** to get rid of; resign from; (*una imputación, un cargo*) clear oneself of

descargo *m* unloading; (*de una obligación*) discharge; (*del cargo que se hace a uno*) release, acquittal; receipt

descargue *m* unloading

descariño *m* coolness, indifference

descarnadamente *adv* right off the shoulder, bluntly

descarnar *tr* to remove the flesh from; chip; wear away; detach from earthly matters ‖ *ref* to lose flesh

descaro *m* brazenness, effrontery

descarriar §77 *tr* to mislead, lead astray ‖ *ref* to go wrong, go astray

descarrilamiento *m* derailment

descarrilar *intr* to jump the track; wander from the point ‖ *ref* to jump the track

descartable *adj* disposable

de
de

descartar *tr* to cast aside, reject; discard || *ref* to shirk, evade; **descartarse de** (*un compromiso*) to shirk, evade

descarte *m* casting aside, rejection; discarding; (*cartas desechadas*) discard; shirking, evasion

descasar *tr* to divorce; disturb, disarrange

descascar §73 *tr* to husk, shell, peel || *ref* to break to pieces; jabber, talk too much

descascarar *tr* to shell, peel || *ref* to shell off, peel off

descascarillar *tr* & *ref* to shell, peel

descasta•do -da *adj* ungrateful, ungrateful to one's family

descaudala•do -da *adj* ruined, penniless

descendencia *f* descent

descendente *adj* descendent, descending; (*tren*) down

descender §51 *tr* to bring down, lower; (*la escalera*) descend, go down || *intr* to descend, go down; flow, run; decline

descendiente *mf* descendant

descenso *m* descent; (*de temperatura*) drop; decline

descentralizar §60 *tr* to decentralize

desceñi•do -da *adj* loose-fitting, loose

descepar *tr* to pull up by the roots; extirpate, exterminate

descerebrar *tr* to brain

descerraja•do -da *adj* corrupt, evil, wicked

desciframiento *m* deciphering, decoding; resolving

descifrar *tr* to decipher, decode, figure out

desclasificar §73 *tr* to disqualify

descocer §16 *tr* to digest

descoco *m* impudence, insolence

descocholla•do -da *adj* (Chile) ragged

descolar *tr* to dock, crop; (*a un empleado*) (CAm) to discharge, fire; (Mex) to slight, snub

descolgar §63 *tr* to unhook; take down, lower; (*el auricular*) pick up || *ref* to come down, come off; to show up suddenly; **descolgarse con** to blurt out

descolón *m* (Mex) slight, snub

descolorar *tr* & *ref* to discolor, fade

descolori•do -da *adj* faded, off color

descollante *adj* prominent, outstanding; chief, main

descollar §61 *intr* to tower, stand out; (fig) to excel, stand out

descomedi•do -da *adj* immoderate, excessive; rude, discourteous

descomedir §50 *ref* to be rude, be discourteous

descomer *intr* to have a bowel movement

descómo•do -da *adj* inconvenient

descompasa•do -da *adj* extreme, excessive

descompletar *tr* to break (*a set or series*)

descomponer §54 *tr* to decompose; disturb, disorganize; put out of order; set at odds || *ref* to decompose; (*una persona, la salud de una persona*) fall to pieces; (*el tiempo*) change for the worse; (*el rostro*) become distorted; (*un aparato*) get out of order; to lose one's temper; **descomponerse con** get angry with

descomposición *f* decomposition; disorder, disorganization; discord

descompostura *f* decomposition; disorder, untidiness; brazenness

descompresión *f* decompression

descompues•to -ta *adj* out of order; brazen, discourteous; irritated; drunk

descomulgar §44 *tr* to excommunicate

descomunal *adj* huge, colossal, enormous, extraordinary; (coll) humongous

desconcerta•do -da *adj* out of order; disconcerted, baffled, bewildered; slovenly; unbridled

desconcertar §2 *tr* to put out of order; disturb, upset; (*un hueso*) dislocate; disconcert, bewilder

desconcierto *m* disrepair; disorder; mismanagement; confusion; discomfiture; disagreement; lack of restraint; loose bowels

desconchabar *tr* to dislocate || *ref* to become dislocated; disagree, fall out

desconchado *m* scaly part of wall; (*en la porcelana*) chip

desconchar *tr* & *ref* to chip, chip off; scale off

desconectar *tr* to detach; disconnect

desconfia•do -da *adj* distrustful, suspicious

desconfianza *f* distrust

desconfiar §77 *intr* to lose confidence; **desconfiar de** to lose confidence in, to distrust

desconformar *intr* to dissent, disagree || *ref* to not go well together

descongelación *f* thaw, thawing out

descongelador *m* defroster

descongelar *tr* to melt; defrost; (com) to unfreeze

descongestión *f* decongestion; freeing up

descongestionar *tr* to decongest; free up

desconocer §22 *tr* to not know; disavow, disown; not recognize; slight, ignore; not see || *ref* to be unknown; be quite changed, be unrecognizable

desconocidamente *adv* unknowingly

desconoci•do -da *adj* unknown; strange, unfamiliar; ungrateful || *mf* unknown, unknown person

desconsentir §68 *tr* to not consent to

desconsidera•do -da *adj* ill-considered; inconsiderate

desconsola•do -da *adj* disconsolate, downhearted; (*estómago*) weak

desconsuelo *m* disconsolateness, grief; upset stomach

descontaminación *f* decontamination; **descontaminación de radiactividad** radioactive decontamination

descontar §61 *tr* to discount; deduct; take for granted; **dar por descontado que** to take for granted that

descontentadi•zo -za *adj* hard to please

desconten•to -ta *adj* & *m* discontent

descontinuar §21 *tr* to discontinue

descontrola•do -da *adj* uncontrolled; deregulated

descontrolar *tr* (com) deregulate; decontrol

desconvenar *tr* to call off

desconvenir §79 *intr* to disagree; not go together, not match; not be suitable ‖ *ref* to disagree

desconvidar *tr* to cancel an invitation to; (*lo prometido*) take back

descopar *tr* to top (*a tree*)

descorazonar *tr* to discourage

descorchar *tr* to remove the bark from; (*una botella*) uncork; break into

descornar §61 *tr* to dehorn ‖ *ref* to rack one's brains

descorrer *tr* to run back over; (*una cortina, un cerrojo*) draw ‖ *intr* & *ref* to flow, run off

descortés *adj* discourteous, impolite

descortesía *f* discourtesy, impoliteness

descortezar §60 *tr* to strip the bark from; take the crust off; polish ‖ *ref* to become polished

descoser *tr* to unstitch, rip ‖ *ref* to loose one's tongue; (coll) to break wind

descosi•do -da *adj* disorderly, wild; indiscreet; desultory ‖ *m* wild man; rip, open seam

descote *m* low neck

descoyuntar *tr* to dislocate; bore, annoy ‖ *ref* (*p.ej., el brazo*) to throw out of joint

descrédito *m* discredit

descreer §43 *tr* to disbelieve; discredit ‖ *intr* to disbelieve

descreí•do -da *adj* disbelieving, unbelieving ‖ *mf* disbeliever, unbeliever

descriar §77 *ref* to spoil; waste away

describir §83 to describe

descripción *f* description

descripti•vo -va *adj* descriptive

descto. *abbr* **descuento**

descuadrar *intr* to disagree; **descuadrar con** (Mex) to displease

descuajar *tr* to liquefy, dissolve; uproot; discourage ‖ *ref* to liquefy; drudge

descuartizar §60 *tr* to tear to pieces; quarter

descubierta *f* open pie; inspection; reconnoitering; (naut) scanning the horizon; **a la descubierta** openly; in the open; reconnoitering

descubiertamente *adv* clearly, openly

descubier•to -ta *adj* bareheaded; (*campo*) bare, barren; (*expuesto a reconvenciones*) under fire ‖ *m* deficiency, shortage; exposition of the Holy Sacrament; **al descubierto** in the open; unprotected; (*sin tener disponibles las acciones que se venden*) short, e.g., **vender al descubierto** to sell short ‖ *f* see **descubierta**

descubri•dor -dora *mf* discoverer ‖ *m* (mil) scout

descubrimiento *m* discovery

descubrir §83 *tr* to discover; uncover, lay open, reveal; invent; (*p.ej., una estatua*) unveil ‖ *ref* to take off one's hat, uncover; be discovered; open one's heart

descuello *m* excellence, superiority; great height; haughtiness

descuento *m* discount; deduction, rebate

descuerar *tr* (Chile) to skin, flay; (Chile) to discredit, flay

descuerno *m* slight, snub

descuida•do -da *adj* careless, negligent; slovenly, dirty; off guard

descuidar *tr* to overlook, neglect; divert, distract, relieve ‖ *ref* to be careless, not bother; be diverted

descuide•ro -ra *mf* sneak thief

descuido *m* carelessness, negligence, neglect; slip, mistake, blunder; oversight; **al descuido** with studied carelessness; **en un descuido** when least expected

descuita•do -da *adj* carefree

deschavetar *intr* to get rattled; go mad; flip one's lid

desde *prep* since, from; after; **desde ahora** from now on; **desde entonces** since then, ever since; **desde hace** for, e.g., **estoy aquí desde hace cinco días** I've been here for five days; **desde luego** at once; of course; **desde que** since

desdecir §24 (*impv sg* **-dice**) *intr* to slip back; be out of harmony ‖ *ref* — **desdecirse de** to take back, retract

desdén *m* scorn, disdain; **al desdén** with studied neglect

desdenta•do -da *adj* toothless

desdeñar *tr* to scorn, disdain ‖ *ref* to be disdainful; **desdeñarse de** to loathe, despise; not deign to

desdeño•so -sa *adj* scornful, disdainful

desdicha *f* misfortune; indigence

desdicha•do -da *adj* unfortunate, unlucky; poor, wretched; backward, timid

desdinerar *tr* to impoverish

desdoblar *tr* & *intr* to unfold, spread open; split, divide

desdorar *tr* to remove the gold or gilt from; tarnish, sully; disparage

desdoro *m* tarnish, blemish, blot; disparagement

deseable *adj* desirable

desear *tr* to desire, wish

desecar §73 *tr* & *ref* to dry; drain

desechable *adj* disposable

desechar *tr* to discard, throw out, cast aside; underrate; blame, censure; (*la llave de una puerta*) turn

desecho *m* remainder; offal, rubbish; castoff; scorn, contempt; short cut; **desecho de hierro** scrap iron

desegregación *f* desegregation

desellar *tr* to unseal

desembalaje *m* unpacking

desembalar *tr* to unpack

desembarazar §60 *tr* to free, clear, empty, open ‖ *ref* to free oneself; be emptied; **desembarazarse de** to get rid of

desembarazo *m* naturalness, lack of restraint; delivery, childbirth; **con desembarazo** naturally, readily

desembaracadero *m* wharf, pier, landing

desembarcar §73 *tr* to unload, debark, disembark ‖ *intr* to land, debark, disembark; (*de un carruaje*) get out, alight; (*la escalera al plano bajo*) end ‖ *ref* to land, debark, disembark

desembarco *m* landing, debarkation, disembarkation; *(de la escalera)* landing

desembarque *m* unloading, debarkation, disembarkation

desembocadura *f (de una calle)* opening, outlet; *(de un río)* mouth

desembocar §73 *intr (una calle)* open, to end; *(un río)* flow, empty

desembolsar *tr* to disburse, pay out

desembolso *m* disbursement, payment

desembragar §44 *tr (el motor)* to disengage || *intr* to throw the clutch out

desembrague *m* disengagement, clutch release

desembravecer §22 *tr* to tame; calm, quiet, pacify

desembriagar §44 *tr & ref* to sober up

desembrollar *tr* to untangle, unravel

desemejante *adj* — **desemejante de** dissimilar from or to, unlike; **desemejantes** dissimilar, unlike

desemejar *tr* to change, disfigure || *intr* to be different, not look alike

desempacar §73 *tr* to unpack, unwrap || *ref* to cool off, calm down

desempalagar §44 *tr* to rid of nausea || *ref* to get rid of nausea

desempañar *tr (el vidrio)* to wipe the steam or smear from; take the diaper off

desempapelar *tr* to unwrap; *(una pared, una habitación)* scrape the wallpaper from

desempaquetar *tr* to unpack; unwrap

desempatar *tr* to break the tie between; *(los votos)* break the tie in

desempate *m* breaking a tie

desempedrar §2 *tr* to remove the paving stones from; *(un sitio empedrado)* pound; **ir desempedrando la calle** to dash down the street

desempeñar *tr (un papel)* to play *(a rôle)*; *(un cargo)* fill, perform; *(a uno de un empeño)* disengage; *(un deber)* discharge; free of debt; take out of hock || *ref* to get out of a jam; get out of debt

desempeño *m* acting, performance; disengagement; *(de un deber)* discharge; payment of a debt; taking out of hock

desempernar *tr* to unbolt

desemplea·do -da *adj & mf* unemployed

desempleo *m* unemployment; **desempleo en masa** mass unemployment

desempolvar *tr* to dust; renew, take up again || *ref* to brush up

desempolvorar *tr* to dust, dust off

desenamorar *tr* to alienate; *ref* to grow apart; **desenamorarse de** to get fed up with

desencadenar *tr* to unchain, unleash || *ref* to break loose

desencajar *tr* to dislocate; disconnect || *ref* to get out of joint; *(el rostro)* be contorted

desencaminar *tr* to lead astray, mislead

desencantamiento *m* disenchantment, disillusion

desencantar *tr* to disenchant, disillusion

desencantarar *tr (nombres o números)* to draw; *(un nombre o nombres)* exclude from balloting

desencanto *m* disenchantment, disillusion

desencarecer §22 *tr* to lower the price of || *intr & ref* to come down in price

desencerrar §2 *tr* to release, set free; disclose, reveal

desencoger §17 *tr* to unfold, spread out || *ref* to relax, shake off one's timidity

desencolar *tr* to unglue || *ref* to become unglued

desenconar *tr* to take the soreness out of; calm down

desenchufar *tr* to unplug, disconnect

desendiosar *tr* to bring down a peg

desenfadaderas *fpl* — **tener buenas desenfadaderas** to be resourceful

desenfada·do -da *adj* free, easy, unconstrained

desenfado *m* ease, naturalness; relaxation, calmness

desenfoca·do -da *adj* out of focus

desenfrena·do -da *adj* unbridled, wanton, licentious

desenfrenar *tr* to unbridle || *ref* to yield to temptation; fly into a passion; *(la tempestad, el viento)* break loose

desenfreno *m* unruliness, wantonness, licentiousness

desenfundar *tr* to take out of its sheath, bag, pillowcase, etc.

desenganchar *tr* to unhook, uncouple, unfasten, disengage; to unhitch

desenganche *m* unhooking, disengaging; unhitching

desengañar *tr* to disabuse, undeceive; disillusion; disappoint

desengaño *m* disabusing; disillusionment; disappointment; plain fact, plain truth

desengrana·do -da *adj* out of gear

desengranar *tr* to unmesh; disengage, throw out of gear

desengraso *m* (Chile) dessert

desenlace *m* outcome, result; *(de un drama, novela, etc.)* dénouement

desenlazar §60 *tr* to untie; solve; *(el nudo de un drama)* unravel

desenmarañar *tr* to disentangle; *(una cosa obscura)* unravel

desenmascarar *tr* to unmask || *ref* to take one's mask off

desenojar *tr* to appease, free of anger || *ref* to calm down; be amused

desenredar *tr* to disentangle; clear up || *ref* to extricate oneself

desenredo *m* disentanglement; *(de un drama, novela, etc.)* dénouement

desenrollar *tr* to unroll, unwind, unreel

desensartar *tr* to unstring, unthread

desensillar *tr* to unsaddle *(a horse)*

desentablar *tr* to disrupt; break off *(a bargain, friendship, etc.)*

desentender §51 *ref* — **desentenderse de** to take no part in, not participate in; affect ignorance of, pretend to be unaware of

desenterrar §2 *tr* to dig up; disinter; (fig) to unearth, dig up; (fig) to recall to mind

desentona·do -da *adj* out of tune, flat

desentonar _tr_ to humble, bring down a peg ‖ _intr_ to be out of tune; be out of harmony ‖ _ref_ to talk loud and disrespectfully

desentono _m_ dissonance, false note; loud tone of voice

desentornillar _tr_ to unscrew

desentrampar _ref_ to get out of debt

desentrañar _tr_ to disembowel; figure out, unravel ‖ _ref_ to give away all that one has

desentrena•do -da _adj_ out of training

desentronizar §60 _tr_ to dethrone; strip of influence

desentumecer §22 _tr_ to relieve of numbness ‖ _ref_ to be relieved of numbness

desenvainar _tr_ to unsheathe; (_las uñas el animal_) show, stretch out; bare, uncover

desenvoltura _f_ naturalness, ease of manner, offhandedness; fluency; lewdness, boldness (_chiefly in women_)

desenvolver §47 & §83 _tr_ to unfold, unroll, unwrap; unwind; unravel, clear up; develop ‖ _ref_ to unroll; unwind; develop, evolve; extricate oneself; be forward

desenvuel•to -ta _adj_ free and easy, offhand; fluent; brazen, bold, lewd

deseo _m_ desire, wish

deseo•so -sa _adj_ desirous, anxious

desequilibra•do -da _adj_ unbalanced

desequilibrar _tr_ to unbalance ‖ _ref_ to become unbalanced

desequilibrio _m_ disequilibrium, imbalance; derangement, mental instability

deserción _f_ desertion

desertar _tr_ & _intr_ to desert

desertor _m_ deserter

deservicio _m_ disservice

desesperación _f_ despair; **ser una desesperación** to be unbearable

desespera•do -da _adj_ despairing, desperate ‖ _mf_ desperate person

desesperanza _f_ hopelessness

desesperanza•do -da _adj_ hopeless

desesperanzar §60 _tr_ to discourage ‖ _ref_ to lose hope

desesperar _tr_ to drive to despair; exasperate ‖ _intr_ to lose hope; be exasperated ‖ _ref_ to be desperate, lose all hope

desestancar §73 _tr_ to open up, unclog; make free of duty; open the market to

desestimar _tr_ to hold in low regard; refuse, reject

deséxito _m_ failure

desfachata•do -da _adj_ brazen, impudent

desfachatez _f_ brazenness, impudence

desfalcar §73 _tr_ & _intr_ to embezzle

desfalco _m_ embezzlement

desfallecer §22 _tr_ to weaken ‖ _intr_ to grow weak; faint, faint away; lose courage

desfalleci•do -da _adj_ weak; faint

desfallecimiento _m_ weakness; fainting; discouragement

desfavorable _adj_ unfavorable

desfigurar _tr_ to disfigure; distort, misrepresent; disguise; change, alter ‖ _ref_ to look different

desfiladero _m_ defile, pass

desfilar _intr_ to defile, parade, file by

desfile _m_ review, parade

desflorar _tr_ to deflower; mention in passing

desfogar §44 _tr_ (_un horno_) to vent; (_la cal_) slake; (_una pasión_) give free rein to ‖ _intr_ (_una tempestad_) to break into rain and wind ‖ _ref_ to give vent to one's anger

desfondar _tr_ to stave in; (_una nave_) bilge; (agr) to trench-plow

desforestar _tr_ to deforest

desgaire _m_ slovenliness; disdain, scorn; **al desgaire** scornfully; carelessly, with affected carelessness

desgajar _tr_ to tear off; split off ‖ _ref_ to come off, come loose; arise, originate; separate, break away

desgana _f_ lack of appetite; indifference; boredom; **a desgana** unwillingly, reluctantly

desgarba•do -da _adj_ ungainly, uncouth

desgarrar _tr_ to tear, rend; (_la flema_) cough up ‖ _ref_ to tear oneself away

desgarro _m_ tear, rent; brazenness, effrontery; boasting, bragging; (Chile, Col) phlegm, mucus

desgasta•do -da _adj_ worn (out); eroded; (_llanta_) treadless; (_tela_) threadbare

desgastar _tr_ to wear away, wear down; to weaken, spoil ‖ _ref_ to wear away; grow weak, decline

desgaste _m_ wear, wearing away

desgoberna•do -da _adj_ ungovernable, uncontrollable

desgobernar §2 _tr_ to misgovern; (_un hueso_) dislocate ‖ _intr_ (naut) to steer poorly ‖ _ref_ to twist and turn in dancing

desgobierno _m_ misgovernment; dislocation

desgonzar §60 _tr_ to unhinge; disconnect

desgracia _f_ misfortune; (_acontecimiento adverso_) mishap; (_pérdida de favor_) disfavor, disgrace; (_aspereza en el trato_) gruffness; (_falta de gracia_) lack of charm; **correr con desgracia** to have no luck; **por desgracia** unfortunately

desgracia•do -da _adj_ unfortunate; unattractive, unpleasant; disagreeable ‖ _mf_ wretch, unfortunate

desgraciar _tr_ to displease; spoil ‖ _ref_ to spoil; fail; fall out, disagree

desgranar _tr_ (_el maíz_) to shell; (_un racimo_) to pick the grapes from ‖ _ref_ (_piezas ensartadas_) to come loose

desgreñar _tr_ to dishevel ‖ _ref_ to get disheveled; pull each other's hair

deshabita•do -da _adj_ unoccupied

deshabituar §21 _tr_ to break of a habit

deshacer §39 _tr_ to undo; untie; take apart; wear away, consume, destroy; melt; put to flight, rout; (_un tratado o negocio_) violate ‖ _ref_ to get out of order; vanish, disappear; **deshacerse de** to get rid of; **deshacerse en** (_cumplidos_) to lavish; (_lágrimas_) burst into; **deshacerse por** to strive hard to

desharrapa•do -da _adj_ ragged, in rags

deshebillar _tr_ to unbuckle

deshebrar _tr_ to unravel, unthread

deshecha _f_ sham, pretense; dismissal; **hacer la deshecha** to feign, pretend; (Mex) to pretend lack of interest

de
de

deshelar §2 *tr* to thaw, melt; defrost; (aer) to deice ‖ *intr* to thaw, melt

deshereda•do -da *adj* disinherited; underprivileged

desheredar *tr* to disinherit ‖ *ref* to be a disgrace to one's family

desherrar §2 *tr* to unchain, unshackle; (*a una caballería*) unshoe

desherrumbrar *tr* to remove the rust from

deshidratar *tr* to dehydrate

deshielo *m* thaw; defrosting; détente

deshilachar *ref* to fray

deshila•do -da *adj* in a file; **a la deshilada** in single file; secretly ‖ *m* openwork, drawn work

deshilar *tr* to unweave; (*reducir a hilos*) shred ‖ *ref* to fray; get thin

deshilvana•do -da *adj* disconnected, desultory

deshincar §73 *tr* to pull up, pull out

deshinchar *tr* to deflate; (*la cólera*) give vent to ‖ *ref* (*un tumor*) to go down; (*una persona orgullosa*) become deflated

deshojar *tr* to strip of leaves; tear the pages out of ‖ *ref* to lose the leaves

deshollejar *tr* (*la uva*) to peel, skin; (*las habichuelas*) shell

deshollina•dor -dora *mf* chimney sweep; curious observer ‖ *m* long-handled brush or broom

deshones•to -ta *adj* immodest, indecent; improper

deshonor *m* dishonor; disgrace

deshonorar *tr* to dishonor; degrade; disfigure

deshonra *f* dishonor; disrespect; **tener a deshonra** to consider improper

deshonrabue•nos *mf* (*pl* -**nos**) slanderer; (coll) black sheep

deshonrar *tr* to disgrace; (*a una mujer*) seduce; insult

deshonro•so -sa *adj* disgraceful, improper, discreditable

deshora *f* wrong time; **a deshora** at the wrong time, inopportunely; suddenly, unexpectedly

deshuesar *tr* (*la carne de un animal*) to bone; (*la fruta*) stone, take the pits out of

deshumedecer §22 *tr* to dehumidify

desidia *f* laziness, indolence

desidio•so -sa *adj* lazy, indolent ‖ *mf* lazy person

desier•to -ta *adj* desert; deserted ‖ *m* desert; wilderness

designar *tr* to designate; (*un trabajo*) plan

designio *m* design, plan, scheme

desigual *adj* unequal; unlike; rough, uneven; difficult; inconstant

desigualar *tr* to make unequal ‖ *ref* to become unequal; (*aventajarse*) get ahead

desigualdad *f* inequality; roughness, unevenness

desilusión *f* disillusionment; disappointment

desilusionar *tr* to disillusion; disappoint ‖ *ref* to become disillusioned; be disappointed

desimanar or **desimantar** *tr* to demagnetize

desimpresionar *tr* to undeceive

desinclina•do -da *adj* disinclined

desinencia *f* (gram) termination, ending

desinfectante *adj* & *m* disinfectant

desinfectar or **desinficionar** *tr* to disinfect

desinflación *f* deflation

desinflamar *tr* to take the soreness out of

desinflar *tr* to deflate; let the air out of; (*a una persona*) deflate

desinhibición *f* loss of inhibitions

desinsectación *f* insect control

desinsectar *intr* to exterminate insects

desintegración *f* disintegration

desintegrar *tr* & *ref* to disintegrate

desinterés *m* disinterestedness

desinteresa•do -da *adj* (*imparcial*) disinterested; (*poco interesado*) uninterested

desinteresar *ref* to lose interest

desintonizar §60 *tr* (rad) to tune out; (rad) to put out of tune

desintoxicación *f* detoxification; sobering (up)

desintoxicar *tr* to detoxify; sober up

desistir *intr* to desist

desjarretar *tr* to hamstring; bleed to excess

desjuicia•do -da *adj* lacking judgment, senseless

desjuntar *tr* to disjoin, separate

deslabonar *tr* to unlink; disconnect ‖ *ref* to come loose; withdraw

deslastrar *tr* to unballast

deslava•do -da *adj* faded, colorless; barefaced ‖ *mf* barefaced person

deslavar *tr* to wash superficially; fade, take the life out of

desleal *adj* disloyal; unfair

deslealtad *f* disloyalty

deslechar *tr* (Col) to milk

desleír §58 *tr* to dissolve; dilute; (*los colores, la pintura*) thin; (*sus pensamientos*) express too diffusely ‖ *ref* to dissolve; become diluted

deslengua•do -da *adj* foul-mouthed, shameless

desliar §77 *tr* to untie, undo; unravel ‖ *ref* to come untied

desligar §44 *tr* to untie, unbind; disentangle; excuse ‖ *ref* to come untied, come loose

deslindar *tr* to mark the boundaries of; distinguish; define, explain

des•liz *m* (*pl* -**lices**) sliding; (*superficie lisa*) slide; slip, blunder; peccadillo, indiscretion

deslizade•ro -ra *adj* slippery ‖ *m* slippery place; launching way

deslizadi•zo -za *adj* slippery

deslizador *m* (aer) glider

deslizar §60 *tr* to slide; (*decir por descuido*) let slip ‖ *intr* to slide; slip; glide ‖ *ref* to slide; slip; glide; slip away, sneak away; (*un reparo*) slip out; (*caer en una flaqueza*) slide back, backslide

deslomar *tr* to break or strain the back of ‖ *ref* to break or strain one's back; **no deslomarse** to not strain oneself

desluci•do -da *adj* quiet, lackluster; dull, undistinguished

deslucir §45 *tr* to tarnish; deprive of charm, deprive of distinction; discredit

deslumbramiento *m* dazzle, glare; bewilderment, confusion

deslumbrante *adj* dazzling; bewildering, confusing

deslumbrar *tr* to dazzle; bewilder, confuse

deslustra•do -da *adj* dull, flat, dingy; (*vidrio*) ground, frosted

deslustrar *tr* to tarnish; dull, dim; (*el vidrio*) frost; discredit ‖ *ref* to tarnish

deslustre *m* tarnishing; dulling, dimming; discredit; (*del vidrio*) frosting

deslustro•so -sa *adj* ugly, unbecoming

desmadejar *tr* to enervate, weaken

desmagnetizar §60 *tr* to demagnetize

desmán *m* excess, misconduct; misfortune, mishap

desmanchar *tr* (Chile) to clean of spots

desmanda•do -da *adj* disobedient, unruly

desmandar *tr* to cancel, countermand ‖ *ref* to misbehave; go away, keep apart; get out of control

desmanear *tr* to unfetter, unshackle

desmantela•do -da *adj* dilapidated

desmantelar *tr* to dismantle; (naut) to unmast; (naut) to unrig

desmaña *f* awkwardness, clumsiness

desmaña•do -da *adj* awkward, clumsy

desmaquillar *tr* & *ref* to take makeup off

desmaya•do -da *adj* faint, languid, weak; unconscious; (*color*) dull

desmayar *tr* to depress, discourage ‖ *intr* to lose heart, be discouraged; falter ‖ *ref* to faint

desmayo *m* depression, discouragement; faint, fainting fit; weeping willow

desmedi•do -da *adj* excessive; boundless, limitless

desmedir §50 *ref* to go too far, be impudent

desmedra•do -da *adj* weak, run-down

desmedrar *tr* to impair ‖ *intr* & *ref* to decline, deteriorate

desmejorar *tr* to impair, spoil ‖ *intr* & *ref* to decline, go into a decline

desmelenar *tr* to muss, dishevel, rumple

desmembrar §2 *tr* to dismember

desmemoria *f* forgetfulness

desmemoria•do -da *adj* forgetful

desmemoriar *ref* to become forgetful

desmentida *f* contradiction; **dar una desmentida a** to give the lie to

desmentir §68 *tr* to belie, give the lie to; conceal ‖ *intr* to be out of line ‖ *ref* to contradict oneself

desmenudear *tr* & *intr* (Col) to sell at retail

desmenuzar §60 *tr* to crumble; chop up; examine in detail; criticize harshly ‖ *ref* to crumb, crumble

desmerece•dor -dora *adj* unworthy

desmerecer §22 *tr* to be unworthy of ‖ *intr* to decline in value; **desmerecer de** to compare unfavorably with

desmesura *f* excess, lack of restraint

desmesura•do -da *adj* excessive, disproportionate; insolent ‖ *mf* insolent person

desmigajar *tr* & *ref* to crumble, break up

desmigar §44 *tr* & *ref* to crumble, crumb

desmilitarizar §60 *tr* to demilitarize; **zona desmilitarizada** demilitarized zone

desmirria•do -da *adj* exhausted, emaciated, run-down

desmochar *tr* (*un árbol*) to top; (*al toro*) dehorn; (*una obra artística*) cut

desmodular *tr* to demodulate

desmola•do -da *adj* toothless

desmontable *adj* demountable

desmontar *tr* (*un terreno*) to level; (*un bosque*) clear; dismantle, dismount, take apart, knock down; (*las piezas de artillería del enemigo*) knock out; (*al jinete el caballo*) unhorse, to throw; (*un arma de fuego*) uncock ‖ *ref* to dismount, alight

desmoralizar §60 *tr* to demoralize

desmoronadi•zo -za *adj* crumbly

desmoronar *tr* to wear away ‖ *ref* to wear away; crumble, decline

desmotadera *f* burler; **desmotadera de algodón** cotton gin

desmotar *tr* (*la lana*) to burl; (*el algodón*) gin

desmovilizar §60 *tr* to demobilize

desmurador *m* mouser

desnatadora *f* cream separator

desnatar *tr* to skim; remove the slag from; take the choicest part of

desnaturalizar §60 *tr* to denaturalize; (*el alcohol*) denature; alter, pervert

desnivel *m* unevenness; difference of level

desnivelar *tr* to make uneven ‖ *ref* to become uneven

desnudar *tr* to undress; strip, lay bare; (*la espada*) draw ‖ *ref* to undress, get undressed; become evident; **desnudarse de** to get rid of

desnudez *f* nakedness; bareness

desnu•do -da *adj* naked, nude; bare; destitute, penniless ‖ **el desnudo** the nude

desnutrición *f* undernourishment, malnutrition

desnutri•do -da *adj* undernourished

desobedecer *tr* & *intr* to disobey

desobediencia *f* disobedience

desobediente *adj* disobedient

desocupación *f* unemployment; idleness, leisure

desocupa•do -da *adj* unemployed; idle; free, unoccupied, vacant, empty ‖ *mf* unemployed person

desocupar *tr* to empty, vacate ‖ *intr* (*una mujer*) to be delivered ‖ *ref* to become empty, vacated; become unemployed, become idle

desodorante *adj* & *m* deodorant

desodorizar §60 *tr* to deodorize

desoír §48 *tr* to not hear, pretend not to hear

desolación *f* desolation

desola•do -da *adj* desolate, disconsolate

desolar §61 *tr* to desolate, lay waste ‖ *ref* to be desolate, be disconsolate

desoldar §61 *tr* to unsolder ‖ *ref* to come unsoldered

desolla•do -da *adj* brazen, impudent

desollar §61 *tr* to skin, flay; harm, hurt; **desollar vivo** (*hacer pagar mucho más de*

lo justo) fleece, skin alive; (*murmurar acerbamente de*) (coll) to flay
desopilar *ref* to roar with laughter
desopinar *tr* to defame, discredit
desorbita•do -da *adj* popeyed; crazy
desorbitar *tr* to pop wide-open
desorden *m* disorder
desordena•do -da *adj* disorderly, unruly
desordenar *tr* to put out of order ‖ *ref* to get out of order; be unruly; go too far
desoreja•do -da *adj* infamous, degraded; (*que canta mal*) (Peru) off tune; (Cuba) shameless; (Cuba) spendthrift, prodigal; (Guat) stupid; (Chile) without handles
desorganizar §60 *tr* to disorganize
desorientación *f* disorientation; confusedness; going astray
desorientar *tr* to lead astray; confuse
desovar *intr* to spawn
desove *m* spawning; spawning season
desovillar *tr* to unravel, disentangle; encourage
desoxidar *tr* to deoxidize; clean of rust
despabiladeras *fpl* snuffers
despabila•do -da *adj* wide-awake
despabilar *tr* (*una candela*) to snuff, trim; (*la hacienda*) dissipate; (*una comida*) dispatch; (*robar*) snitch; (*matar*) dispatch ‖ *ref* to brighten up; wake up; leave, disappear
despacio *adv* slow, slowly; at leisure; (Arg, Chile) in a low voice
despacio•so -sa *adj* slow, easy-going
despachaderas *fpl* surly reply; resourcefulness
despacha•do -da *adj* brazen, impudent; quick, resourceful
despachante *m* (Arg) clerk; **despachante te de aduana** (Arg) customhouse broker
despachar *tr* to send, ship; dispatch, expedite; discharge, dismiss; decide, settle; sell; (*a los parroquianos*) wait on; (*la correspondencia*) attend to; hurry; (*matar*) dispatch, kill ‖ *intr* to hurry; make up one's mind; work, be employed ‖ *ref* to hurry; (*una mujer*) be delivered; speak out
despacho *m* shipping; dispatch, expedition; discharge, dismissal; (*tienda*) store, shop; (*aposento para el estudio*) study; (*aposento para los negocios*) office; (*comunicación por telégrafo o teléfono*) dispatch; (Chile) attic; **despacho de billetes** ticket office; **despacho de localidades** box office; **estar al despacho** to be pending; **tener buen despacho** to be expeditious
despachurrar *tr* to crush, smash, squash; (*dejar sin tener que replicar*) squelch; (*lo que uno trata de decir*) butcher, murder
despampanante *adj* stunning, terrific
despampanar *tr* (*las vides*) to prune, trim; astound ‖ *intr* to give vent to one's feelings ‖ *ref* to fall and hurt oneself
despancar §73 *tr* to husk (*corn*)
desparejar *tr* (*dos cosas que forman pareja*) to break, separate (*a pair*)
desparpajar *tr* to tear apart ‖ *intr* to rant, rave ‖ *ref* to rant, rave; (CAm, Mex, W-I) to wake up

desparramar *tr* to scatter, spread; (*el agua*) to spill; (*la hacienda*) squander ‖ *ref* to scatter, spread; make merry
despartir *tr* to divide, part, separate; to reconcile
despatarrada *f* split (*in dancing*); **hacer la despatarrada** to stretch out on the floor pretending to be ill or injured
despatarrar *tr* to dumbfound ‖ *ref* to open one's legs wide, fall down with legs outspread; lie motionless; be dumbfounded
despavori•do -da *adj* terrified
despea•do -da *adj* footsore
despear *ref* to get sore feet
despecti•vo -va *adj* contemptuous; (gram) pejorative
despecha•do -da *adj* spiteful, enraged
despechar *tr* to spite, enrage; (*destetar*) to wean ‖ *ref* to be enraged; despair, lose hope
despecho *m* spite; despair; weaning; **a despecho de** despite, in spite of; **por despecho** out of spite
despechugar §44 *tr* to carve the breast of ‖ *ref* (coll) to go with bare breast, bare one's breast
despedazar §60 *tr* to break to pieces; (*la honra de uno*) to ruin; (*el alma de una persona*) break ‖ *ref* to break to pieces; **despedazarse de risa** to split one's sides laughing
despedida *f* farewell, leave-taking; (*de una carta*) close, conclusion; (*copla final*) envoi
despedir §50 *tr* to throw; emit, send forth; discharge, dismiss; (*al que sale de la casa*) see off; (*un mal pensamiento*) banish; **despedir en la puerta** to see to the door ‖ *ref* to take leave, say good-by; give up one's job; **despedirse a la francesa** to take French leave; **despedirse de** to take leave of, say good-by to
despega•do -da *adj* gruff, surly
despegar §44 *tr* to loosen, unglue, unseal; open; separate, detach ‖ *intr* (aer) to take off ‖ *ref* to come off; **despegarse con** to be unbecoming to
despego *m* dislike, indifference
despegue *m* (aer) take-off; **despegue vertical** vertical take-off
despeina•do -da *adj* unkempt
despeja•do -da *adj* (*frente*) wide; (*día, cielo*) clear, cloudless; bright, sprightly; (*en el trato*) unconstrained
despejar *tr* to clarify, explain; free; (*una incógnita*) (math) to find ‖ *ref* to brighten up, cheer up; (*el cielo, el tiempo; una situación dificultosa*) clear up; (*un borracho*) sober up
despejo *m* ease, naturalness; talent, intelligence, understanding
despelotar *ref* to disrobe
despeluzar §60 *tr* to muss the hair of; make the hair of (*a person*) stand on end ‖ *ref* (*el pelo*) to stand on end
despeluznante *adj* hair-raising, horrifying
despellejar *tr* to skin, flay; slander, malign

despenalización *f* legalization
despenalizar §**60** *tr* to legalize; condone
despenar *tr* to console; (coll) to kill; (Chile) to deprive of hope
despender *tr* to spend, squander; (*el tiempo*) to waste
despensa *f* pantry; food supplies; day's marketing; stewardship; (naut) storeroom
despensero *m* butler, steward; (naut) storekeeper
despeñadamente *adv* hastily; boldly
despeñade•ro -ra *adj* precipitous ‖ *m* precipice; danger, risk
despeñadi•zo -za *adj* precipitous
despeñar *tr* to hurl, throw, push ‖ *ref* to hurl oneself, jump; fall headlong; (*en vicios, pecados, pasiones*) plunge downward
despeño *m* plunge; headlong fall; ruin, failure, collapse; (coll) loose bowels
despepitar *tr* to seed, remove the seeds from ‖ *ref* to rush around madly, go around screaming; **despepitarse por** to be mad about
desperdicia•do -da *adj* wasteful, prodigal ‖ *mf* spendthrift, prodigal
desperdiciar *tr* to waste, squander; (*la ocasión de aprovechar una cosa*) miss, lose
desperdicio *m* waste, squandering; **desperdicios** waste; waste products; by-products; rubbish; **no tener desperdicio** to be excellent, be useful
desperdigar §**44** *tr* to separate, scatter
desperecer §**22** *ref* to long eagerly
desperezar §**60** *ref* to stretch, stretch one's arms and legs
desperfecto *m* blemish, flaw, imperfection
desperna•do -da *adj* footsore, weary
desperta•dor -dora *mf* awakener ‖ *m* alarm clock; warning
despertar §**2** *tr* to awaken; arouse, stir ‖ *intr & ref* to awaken, wake up
despestañar *tr* to pluck the eyelashes of ‖ *ref* to look hard, strain one's eyes
despiada•do -da *adj* cruel, pitiless
despichar *tr* to squeeze dry; (Col, Chile) to crush, flatten ‖ *intr* (coll) to croak, die
despidiente *m* stick placed between a hanging scaffold and wall; **despidiente de agua** flashing
despido *m* layoff, discharge
despier•to -ta *adj* wide-awake, alert; **soñar despierto** to daydream
despilfarra•do -da *adj* wasteful; ragged ‖ *mf* prodigal; raggedy person
despilfarrar *tr* to squander, waste ‖ *ref* to spend recklessly
despilfarro *m* squandering, waste, extravagance; slovenliness
despintar *tr* to remove the paint from; disfigure, distort, spoil; **no despintarle a uno los ojos** to not take one's eyes from a person ‖ *intr* to decline, slip back; **despintar de** to be unworthy of ‖ *ref* to fade, wash off; **no despintársele a uno** to not fade from one's memory
despiojar *tr* to delouse; (coll) to free from poverty

despique *m* revenge
despistar *tr* to outwit, throw off the track ‖ *ref* to run off the track, run off the road
desplacer *m* displeasure ‖ §**22** *tr* to displease
desplantar *tr* to uproot; throw out of plumb ‖ *ref* to get out of plumb; lose one's upright posture
desplaya•do -da *adj* broad, open, wide ‖ *m* (Arg) wide sandy beach
desplayar *tr* to widen, spread out ‖ *ref* (*el mar*) to recede from the beach
desplaza•do -da *adj* displaced ‖ *mf* displaced person
desplazar §**60** *tr* (*cierto peso de agua*) to displace; move, transport ‖ *ref* to move
desplegar §**66** *tr* to unfold, spread; display; explain; (mil) to deploy ‖ *ref* to unfold, spread out; (mil) to deploy
despliegue *m* unfolding, spreading out; display; (mil) deployment
desplomar *tr* to throw out of plumb ‖ *ref* to get out of plumb; collapse, tumble; fall down in a faint; (*un trono*) crumble; (aer) to pancake
desplome *m* leaning; collapse, tumbling; falling in a faint; downfall; (aer) pancaking
desplumar *tr* to pluck; (*dejar sin dinero*) fleece ‖ *ref* to molt
despoblado *m* wilderness, deserted spot
despoblar §**61** *tr* to depopulate; lay waste; clear, lay bare
despojar *tr* to strip, despoil, divest; dispossess ‖ *ref* to undress; **despojarse de** to divest oneself of; (*ropa*) take off
despojo *m* dispoilment; dispossession; booty, plunder, spoils; prey, victim; **despojos** scraps, leavings; .mortal remains; secondhand building materials
despolarizar §**60** *tr* to depolarize
despolvar *tr* to dust
despolvorear *tr* to dust, dust off; scatter
desportillar *tr* to chip, nick ‖ *ref* to chip, chip off
desposa•do -da *adj* handcuffed; newly married ‖ *mf* newlywed
desposar *tr* to marry ‖ *ref* to be betrothed, get engaged; get married
desposeer §**43** *tr* to dispossess ‖ *ref* —**desposeerse de** to divest oneself of
desposorios *mpl* betrothal, engagement; marriage, nuptials
despostar *tr* to cut up, carve; butcher
déspota *m* despot
despóti•co -ca *adj* despotic
despotismo *m* despotism
despotricar §**73** *intr & ref* to rave, rant
despreciable *adj* contemptible, despicable
despreciar *tr* to scorn, despise; slight, snub; overlook, forgive; reject ‖ *ref* —**despreciarse de** to not deign to
despreciati•vo -va *adj* contemptuous, scornful
desprecio *m* scorn, contempt; slight, snub
desprender *tr* to loosen, unfasten, detach; emit, give off; (chem) to liberate ‖ *ref* to come loose, come off; issue, come forth;

desprenderse de to give up, part with; be deduced from

desprendi·do -da *adj* generous, disinterested

desprendimiento *m* loosening, detachment; emission, liberation; generosity, disinterestedness; landslide; (chem) liberation

despreocupación *f* relaxation; impartiality; indifference

despreocupa·do -do *adj* relaxed, unconcerned; impartial; indifferent

despreocupante *adj* relaxing

despreocupar *ref* to relax; **despreocuparse de** to forget about, be unconcerned about

desprestigiar *tr* to disparage, run down ‖ *ref* to lose caste, lose one's standing, lose face

desprestigio *m* disparagement; loss of standing, discredit

despreveni·do -da *adj* off one's guard; **coger a uno desprevenido** to catch someone unawares

desproporciona·do -da *adj* disproportionate

despropósito *m* absurdity, nonsense; malapropism

desproveer §43 & §83 *tr* to deprive

desprovis·to -ta *adj* destitute; **desprovisto de** lacking, devoid of

después *adv* after, afterwards; **después de** after; **después (de) que** after

despuli·do -da *adj* ground (*glass*)

despumar *tr* to skim

despuntar *tr* to dull, blunt; (*un cabo o punta*) (naut) to double, round ‖ *intr* to begin to sprout; (*empezar a amanecer*) dawn; stand out ‖ *ref* to get dull

desquiciar *tr* to unhinge; shake loose, upset; unsettle, perturb; overthrow, undermine

desquitar *tr* to recover, retrieve; compensate ‖ *ref* to retrieve a loss; get revenge, get even

desquite *m* recovery, retrieval; retaliation, revenge; (sport) return match

desrazonable *adj* unreasonable

desrielar *intr* to jump the track

destaca·do -da *adj* outstanding, distinguished

destacamento *m* (mil) detachment; (mil) detail

destacar §73 *tr* to highlight, point up; emphasize; make stand out; (mil) to detach; (mil) to detail ‖ *intr* to stand out, be conspicuous ‖ *ref* to stand out, project; (fig) to stand out

destajar *tr* to arrange for, establish the terms for; (*la baraja*) cut; carve up

destaje·ro -ra or **destajista** *mf* pieceworker, jobber; free lance

destajo *m* piecework; job; contract; **a destajo** by the piece, by the job; freelancing; **hablar a destajo** to talk too much

destapar *tr* to open, uncover, take the lid off; uncock, unplug; reveal ‖ *ref* to get uncovered; throw off the covers; unbosom oneself

destaponar *tr* to uncock, unplug; (*una botella; las fosas nasales*) unstop

destartala·do -da *adj* tumble-down, ramshackle

destazar §60 *tr* to carve up

destechar *tr* to unroof

destejar *tr* to remove the tiles from; leave unprotected

destejer *tr* to unbraid, unknit, unweave; upset, disturb

destellar *tr* & *intr* to flash

destello *m* flash, beam, sparkle

destempla·do -da *adj* disagreeable, unpleasant; inharmonious, out of tune; indisposed; (*clima; pulso*) irregular

destemplanza *f* unpleasantness; discord; indisposition; (*del pulso*) irregularity; (*del tiempo*) inclemency; excess

destemple *m* dissonance; indisposition; disorder, disturbance

desteñir §72 *tr* to discolor ‖ *intr* & *ref* to fade

desternillante *adj* sidesplitting

desternillar *ref* — **desternillarse de risa** to split one's sides with laughter

desterra·do -da *adj* exiled ‖ *mf* exile

desterrar §2 *tr* to exile, banish; (fig) to banish

destetar *tr* to wean ‖ *ref* — **destetarse con** to have known since childhood

destete *m* weaning

destiempo *m* — **a destiempo** untimely

destiento *m* surprise, shock

destierro *m* exile; backwoods

destilación *f* distillation

destiladera *f* still; scheme, stratagem

destilar *tr* to distill; filter; exude ‖ *intr* to drip

destilatorio *m* distillery; (*alambique*) still

destilería *f* distillery

destinación *f* destination

destinar *tr* to destine; assign, designate

destinata·rio -ria *mf* addressee; consignee; (*de homenaje, aplausos*) recipient

destino *m* (*lugar a donde va una persona o una remesa*) destination; (*suerte, encadenamiento fatal de los sucesos*) fate, destiny; employment; place of employment; **con destino a** bound for

destituir §20 *tr* to deprive; dismiss, discharge

destorcer §74 *tr* to untwist, straighten ‖ *ref* to become untwisted; (naut) to drift

destornilla·do -da *adj* rash, reckless, out of one's head

destornillador *m* screwdriver

destornillar *tr* to unscrew ‖ *ref* to lose one's head, go berserk

destoser *ref* to cough (*artificially, to attract attention*)

destrabar *tr* to loosen, untie, detach

destraillar §4 *tr* unleash

destral *m* hatchet

destreza *f* skill, dexterity

destripacuen·tos *m* (*pl* -tos) (coll) butter-in

destripar *tr* to disembowel, gut; crush, mangle; spoil (*a story by telling its outcome*)

destripaterro·nes *m* (*pl* -nes) (coll) clodhopper

destriunfar *tr* to force to play trump

destrocar §81 *tr* to swap back again

destronar *tr* to dethrone; overthrow

destroncar §73 *tr* to chop down; chop off; ruin; exhaust, wear out

destrozar §60 *tr* to shatter, break to pieces; destroy; squander; (*al ejército enemigo*) wipe out

destrozo *m* havoc, destruction; rout, annihilation, defeat

destrucción *f* destruction

destructi•vo -va *adj* destructive

destructor *m* (nav) destroyer

destruir §20 *tr* to destroy ‖ *ref* (alg) to cancel each other

desuellaca•ras *m* (*pl* -ras) sloppy barber; scoundrel

desuello *m* skinning, flaying; shamelessness; (*precio excesivo*) (coll) highway robbery

desuncir §36 *tr* to unyoke

desunir *tr* to disunite; take apart ‖ *ref* to disunite; come apart

desusa•do -da *adj* obsolete, out of use; uncommon, unusual; **estar desusado** (*perder la práctica*) to be rusty

desuso *m* disuse; **caído en desuso** obsolete

desvaí•do -da *adj* lank, ungainly; (*color*) dull

desvainar *tr* to shell

desvali•do -da *adj* helpless, destitute

desvalijar *tr* (*una valija, baúl, etc.*) to rifle; rob, wipe out

desvalorar *tr* to devalue

desvalorizar §60 *tr* to devalue

desván *m* garret, loft

desvanecedor *m* (phot) mask

desvanecer §22 *tr* to dispel, dissipate; (*una conspiración*) break up; (*la sospecha*) banish; (phot) to mask ‖ *ref* to disappear, vanish, evanesce; evaporate; faint, faint away, swoon; (rad) to fade

desvanecimiento *m* disappearance, evanescence; dissipation; pride, vanity; faintness, fainting spell; (phot) masking; (rad) fading, fadeout

desvaria•do -da *adj* delirious, raving

desvariar §77 *intr* to be delirious, rave, rant

desvarío *m* delirium, raving; absurdity, nonsense, extravagance; whim, caprice; inconstancy

desvela•do -da *adj* wakeful, sleepless; watchful, vigilant; anxious, worried

desvelar *tr* to keep awake, not let sleep ‖ *ref* to keep awake, go without sleep; be watchful, be vigilant; **desvelarse por** to be anxious about, be worried about

desvelo *m* wakefulness, sleeplessness; watchfulness, vigilance; anxiety, worry, concern

desvenar *tr* to strip (*tobacco*)

desvencija•do -da *adj* rickety, ramshackle

desvencijar *tr* to break, tear apart ‖ *ref* to go to rack and ruin

desvendar *tr* to unbandage, undress

desventaja *f* disadvantage

desventaja•do -da *adj* disadvantaged; deprived

desventajo•so -sa *adj* disadvantageous

desventura *f* misfortune

desventura•do -da *adj* unfortunate; fainthearted; stingy

desvergonza•do -da *adj* shameless, impudent

desvergüenza *f* shamelessness, impudence

desvestir §50 *tr & ref* to undress

desviación *f* deviation, deflection; detour; (rad, telv) drift

desviacionismo *m* deviationism

desviacionista *mf* deviationist

desviadero *m* (rr) siding, turnout

desvia•do -da *adj* devious; (gone) astray; off track; lost

desviar §77 *tr* to deviate, deflect; turn aside; dissuade; parry, ward off; (rr) to switch ‖ *ref* to deviate, deflect; turn aside; branch off; be dissuaded

desvío *m* deviation, deflection; coldness, indifference; detour; (rr) siding, sidetrack

desvirgar §44 *tr* to deflower, ravish

desvirtuar §21 *tr* to weaken, spoil, impair

desvivir *ref* — **desvivirse por** to be crazy about; **desvivirse por** + *inf* to be eager to + *inf*, to do one's best to + *inf*

desvolvedor *m* wrench

desvolver §47 & §83 *tr* to alter, change; (*la tierra*) turn up; (*una tuerca o tornillo*) loosen, unscrew

detall *m* — **al detall** at retail

detalladamente *adv* in detail

detallar *tr* to detail, tell in detail; retail, sell at retail

detalle *m* detail; retail; **ahí está el detalle** that's the point

detallista *mf* retailer; person fond of details

detección *f* detection

detectar *tr* to detect

detective *m* detective

detector *m* detector; **detector de mentiras** lie detector

detención *f* detention, detainment; delay; care, thoroughness

detener §71 *tr* to detain; stop; arrest; keep, retain; (*el aliento*) hold ‖ *ref* to stop; linger, tarry

detenidamente *adv* carefully, thoroughly

deteni•do -da *adj* careful, thorough; hesitant, timid; stingy, mean ‖ *mf* person held in custody

detenimiento *m* var of **detención**

detergente *adj & m* detergent

deteriorar *tr & ref* to deteriorate

deterioro *m* deterioration

determinación *f* determination; decision

determina•do -da *adj* determined, resolute; (*artículo*) (gram) definite

determinar *tr* to determine; cause, bring about ‖ *ref* to decide

detestar *tr* to detest; curse; **detestar** + *inf* to hate to + *inf*

detonar *intr* to detonate

detraer §75 *tr* to withdraw, take away, detract; defame, vilify

detrás *adv* behind; **detrás de** behind, back of; **por detrás** behind; behind one's back; **por detrás de** behind the back of

detrimento *m* harm, detriment

deuda *f* debt; indebtedness

deu•do -da *mf* relative ‖ *m* kinship ‖ *f* see **deuda**

deu•dor -dora *adj* indebted ‖ *mf* debtor; **deudor hipotecario** mortgagor; **deudor moroso** delinquent (*in payment*)

de
de

devalar *intr* (naut) to drift from the course
devaluación *f* devaluation
devanar *tr* to wind, roll; (*un cuento*) to unfold ‖ *ref* (CAm, Mex, W-I) to roll with laughter; (CAm, Mex, W-I) to writhe in pain
devanear *intr* to talk nonsense; loaf around
devaneo *m* nonsense; loafing; flirtation
devastación *f* devastation
devastar *tr* to devastate
develar *tr* to reveal; (*p.ej., una estatua*) unveil
devengar §44 *tr* (*salarios*) to earn; (*intereses*) draw, earn
devoción *f* devotion
devolución *f* return, restitution
devolver §47 & §83 *tr* to return, give back, send back; pay back; (coll) to vomit ‖ *ref* to return, come back
devorar *tr* to devour
devo•to -ta *adj* devout; devoted; devotional ‖ *mf* devotee; devout person; **devoto del volante** car enthusiast ‖ *m* object of worship
D.F. *abbr* **Distrito Federal**
d/f *abbr* **días fecha**
dho. *abbr* **dicho**
día *m* day; daytime; daylight; **al día** per day; up to date; **al otro día** on the following day; **buenos días** good morning; **dar los días a** to wish (*someone*) many happy returns of the day; **de día** in the daytime, in the daylight; **día de años** birthday; **día de ayuno** fast day; **día de carne** meat day; **día de engañabobos** December 28th, day when practical jokes are played on unsuspecting people; **día de inauguración** (fa) private view; **día de la raza** Columbus Day; **día del juicio** judgment day; **día de los caídos** Memorial Day; **día de los difuntos** All Souls' Day; **día de ramos** Palm Sunday; **día de Reyes** Epiphany; **día de todos los santos** All Saints' Day; **día de trabajo** workday; weekday; **día de vigilia** fast day; **día festivo** holiday; **día inhábil** day off; holiday; **día laborable** workday, weekday; **día lectivo** school day; **día puente** day off between two holidays; **el día de Año Nuevo** New Year's Day; **el día menos pensado** when least expected; **el mejor día** some fine day; **en cuatro días** in a few days; **en pleno día** in broad daylight; **en su día** in due time; **ocho días** a week; **poner al día** to bring up to date; **quince días** two weeks, a fortnight; **tener sus días** to be up in years; **un día sí y otro no** every other day; **vivir al día** to live from hand to mouth
diabetes *f* diabetes
diabéti•co -ca *adj* & *mf* diabetic
diablillo *m* imp
diablo *m* devil; (Chile) ox-drawn log drag; **ahí será el diablo** (coll) there will be the devil to pay; **diablo cojuelo** tricky devil; **diablos azules** delirium tremens
diablura *f* devilment, deviltry, mischief
diabóli•co -ca *adj* devilish, diabolical

diaconisa *f* deaconess
diácono *m* deacon
diacríti•co -ca *adj* diacritical
diadema *f* diadem; (*adorno femenino*) tiara
diáfa•no -na *adj* diaphanous
diafragma *m* diaphragm
diagno•sis *f* (*pl* **-sis**) diagnosis
diagnosticar §73 *tr* to diagnose
diagonal *adj* diagonal ‖ *f* diagonal, bias
diagrama *m* diagram
dialecto *m* dialect
dialogar *intr* to talk
diálogo *m* dialogue
diamante *m* diamond
diametral or **diamétri•co -ca** *adj* diametrical
diámetro *m* diameter
diana *f* bull's-eye; (mil) reveille; **hacer diana** to hit the bull's-eye
diantre *m* devil ‖ *interj* the devil!, the deuce!
diapasón *m* tuning fork; pitch pipe; (*p.ej., del violín*) finger board; **bajar el diapasón** to lower one's voice, to change one's tune
diapositiva *f* slide, lantern slide
dia•rio -ria *adj* daily ‖ *m* diary; daily, daily paper; **diario hablado** newscast
diarismo *m* journalism
diarrea *f* diarrhea
diástole *f* diastole
diatermia *f* diathermy
dibujante *mf* sketcher, illustrator ‖ *m* draftsman
dibujar *tr* to draw, sketch, design; outline ‖ *ref* to be outlined; appear, show
dibujo *m* drawing, sketch, design; outline; **dibujo al carbón** charcoal drawing; **dibujo animado** animated cartoon; **no meterse en dibujos** to attend to one's business
di•caz *adj* (*pl* **-caces**) sarcastic, witty
dicción *f* diction; word
diccionario *m* dictionary
díceres *mpl* sayings; rumor(s)
diciembre *m* December
dicloruro *m* dichloride
dicotomía *f* dichotomy; (*entre médicos*) split fee
dictado *m* dictation; **escribir al dictado** to take dictation; (*lo que otro dicta*) to take down
dictador *m* dictator
dictadura *f* dictatorship
dictáfono *m* dictaphone
dictamen *m* dictum, judgment, opinion
dictar *tr* to dictate; (*una ley*) promulgate; inspire, suggest; (*una conferencia*) give, deliver (*a lecture*)
dicterio *m* taunt, insult
dicha *f* happiness; luck; **por dicha** by chance
dicharache•ro -ra *adj* obscene, vulgar
dicharacho *m* obscenity, vulgarity; wisecrack
di•cho -cha *adj* said; **dicho y hecho** no sooner said than done; **mejor dicho** rather; **tener por dicho** to consider settled ‖ *m* saying; promise of marriage, one's word; witticism; insult; **dicho de las gentes** talk, hearsay, gossip ‖ *f* see **dicha**

dicho•so -sa *adj* happy; lucky, fortunate; annoying, tiresome

didácti•co -ca *adj* didactic

diecinueve *adj & pron* nineteen ‖ *m* nineteen; (*en las fechas*) nineteenth

diecinuevea•vo -va *adj & m* nineteenth

dieciocha•vo -va *adj m* eighteenth

dieciocho *adj & pron* eighteen ‖ *m* eighteen; (*en las fechas*) eighteenth

dieciséis *adj & pron* sixteen ‖ *m* sixteen; (*en las fechas*) sixteenth

dieciseisa•vo -va *adj & m* sixteenth

diecisiete *adj & pron* seventeen ‖ *m* seventeen; (*en las fechas*) seventeenth

diecisietea•vo -va *adj & m* seventeenth

diente *m* tooth; (*de elefante y otros animales*) tusk, fang; (*de peine, sierra, rastrillo*) tooth; (*de rueda dentada*) cog; **dar diente con diente** to shake all over; **decir entre dientes** to mutter, to mumble; **diente canino** eyetooth, canine tooth; **diente de león** dandelion; **estar a diente** to be famished; **tener buen diente** to be a hearty eater; **traer entre dientes** to have a grudge against; to talk about

diére•sis *f* (*pl* **-sis**) diaeresis; (*señal que indica la metafonía*) umlaut

diesel *m* diesel motor

dieseléctri•co -ca *adj* diesel-electric

dies•tro -tra *adj* right; handy, skillful; shrewd, sly; favorable; **a diestro y siniestro** wildly, right and left ‖ *m* expert fencer; bullfighter on foot; matador; halter, bridle ‖ *f* right hand; **juntar diestra con diestra** to join forces

dieta *f* diet; **dietas** per diem; **estar a dieta** to diet, be on a diet

dietario *m* family budget

dietista *mf* dietitian

diez *adj & pron* ten; **las diez** ten o'clock ‖ *m* ten; (*en las fechas*) tenth

diezmar *tr* (*causar gran mortandad en*) to decimate; (*pagar el diezmo de*) tithe

diezmo *m* tithe

difamación *f* defamation, vilification

difamar *tr* to defame, vilify

diferencia *f* difference; **a diferencia de** unlike; **partir la diferencia** to split the difference

diferenciar *tr* to differentiate ‖ *intr* (*discordar*) to differ, dissent ‖ *ref* (*distinguirse una cosa de otra*) to differ, be different

diferente *adj* different

diferir §68 *tr* to defer, postpone, put off ‖ *intr* to differ, be different

difícil *adj* difficult, hard; hard to please

difícilmente *adv* with difficulty

dificultad *f* difficulty; (*reparo que se opone a una opinión*) objection

dificultar *tr* to make difficult; consider difficult ‖ *intr* to raise objections ‖ *ref* to become difficult

dificulto•so -sa *adj* difficult, troublesome; objecting; (coll) ugly, homely

difidencia *f* distrust

difidente *adj* distrustful

difteria *f* diphtheria

difundir *tr* to diffuse; spread, disseminate; divulge, publish; broadcast ‖ *ref* to diffuse; spread

difun•to -ta *adj & mf* deceased; **difunto de taberna** dead-drunk ‖ *m* corpse

difu•so -sa *adj* diffuse; extended; wordy

digerible *adj* digestible

digerir §68 *tr* to digest; **no digerir** to not bear, not stand ‖ *intr* to digest

digestible *adj* digestible

digestión *f* digestion

digesti•vo -va *adj & m* digestive

digesto *m* (law) digest

dígito *m* digit

dignación *f* condescension

dignar *ref* to deign, condescend

dignatario *m* dignitary, official

dignidad *f* dignity; bishop, archbishop

dignificar §73 *tr* to dignify

dig•no -na *adj* worthy; fitting, suitable; (*grave, decoroso*) dignified

digresión *f* digression

dije *m* amulet, charm, trinket; (*persona de excelentes cualidades*) jewel; person all dressed-up; handy person

dilacerar *tr* to tear to pieces; (*la honra, el orgullo*) damage

dilación *f* delay

dilapidación *f* waste; squandering

dilapidar *tr* to squander

dilatación *f* expansion; serenity

dilatar *tr* to dilate, expand; defer, postpone; (*p.ej., la fama*) spread ‖ *ref* to dilate, expand; spread; be wordy; delay

dilección *f* true love

dilec•to -ta *adj* dearly beloved

dilema *m* dilemma

diletante *adj & mf* dilettante

diletantismo *m* dilettantism

diligencia *f* diligence; step, démarche; errand; dispatch, speed; stagecoach; **hacer una diligencia** to do an errand; to have a bowel movement

diligente *adj* diligent; quick, ready

dilucidación *f* explanation; enlightenment

dilucidar *tr* to elucidate, explain

dilución *f* dilution

diluí•do -da *adj* dilute

diluir §20 *tr* to dilute; thin ‖ *ref* to dilute; melt; dissolve

diluviar *intr* to rain hard, pour

diluvio *m* deluge

dimanar *intr* to spring up; **dimanar de** to spring from, originate in

dimensión *f* dimension

dimes *mpl* — **andar en dimes y diretes con** to bicker with

diminuti•vo -va *adj & m* (gram) diminutive

diminu•to -ta *adj* tiny, diminutive; defective

dimisión *f* resignation

dimisorias *fpl* — **dar dimisorias a** to discharge, fire

dimitir *tr* to resign, resign from ‖ *intr* to resign

din *m* (coll) dough, money

Dinamarca *f* Denmark

de
di

dinamar·qués -quesa *adj* Danish ‖ *mf* Dane ‖ *m* Danish (*language*)
dinámi·co -ca *adj* dynamic
dinamita *f* dynamite
dinamitar *tr* to dynamite
dínamo *f* dynamo
dinasta *m* dynast
dinastía *f* dynasty
dindán *m* ding-dong
dinerada *f* or **dineral** *m* large sum of money
dinero *m* money; currency; wealth; **dinero contante** cash; **dinero contante y sonante** ready cash, spot cash; **dinero de bolsillo** pocket money
dinero·so -sa *adj* moneyed, wealthy
dintel *m* lintel, doorhead
dióce·si *f* or **dióce·sis** *f* (*pl* **-sis**) diocese
diodo *m* diode
dios *m* god; **Dios mediante** God willing; **¡por Dios!** goodness!, for heaven's sake; **¡válgame Dios!** bless me!; **¡vaya con Dios!** off with you!
diosa *f* goddess
diploma *m* diploma
diplomacia *f* diplomacy
diploma·do -da *adj* & *mf* graduate
diplomar *tr* & *ref* to graduate
diplomáti·co -ca *adj* diplomatic ‖ *mf* diplomat
diptongar §44 *tr* & *ref* to diphthongize
diptongo *m* diphthong
diputación *f* congress; commission
diputa·do -da *mf* deputy, representative
diputar *tr* to commission, delegate; designate
dique *m* dike, jetty; dry dock; check, stop; **dique seco** dry dock
dirección *f* direction; (*señas en una carta*) address; administration, management; directorship; (*aut*) steering; **de dirección única** one-way; **dirección a la derecha** right-hand drive; **dirección a la izquierda** left-hand drive; **perder la dirección** to lose control of the car
directi·vo -va *adj* managing ‖ *mf* director, manager ‖ *f* management
direc·to -ta *adj* direct; straight
direc·tor -tora *adj* directing, guiding; managing, governing ‖ *mf* director, manager; (*de un periódico*) editor; (*de una escuela*) principal; (*de una orquesta*) conductor; **director de escena** stage manager; **director de funeraria** funeral director; **director gerente** managing director
directorio *m* directorship; directory
dirigente *mf* leader, head, executive
dirigible *adj* & *m* dirigible
dirigir §27 *tr* to direct; manage; (*un automóvil*) steer; (*una carta; la palabra*) address; (*una obra*) dedicate ‖ *ref* to go, betake oneself; turn; **dirigirse a** to address; apply to
dirimir *tr* to dissolve, annul; (*una dificultad*) solve; (*una controversia*) settle, mediate
discar §73 *tr* & *intr* to dial
disceptar *intr* to discuss, debate
discerniente *adj* discerning
discernir §28 *tr* to discern; distinguish

disciplina *f* discipline; **disiplinas** scourge, whip
disciplina·do -da *adj* disciplined; (*flores*) many-colored
disciplinar *tr* to discipline; teach; scourge, whip
disciplinazo *m* lash
discípu·lo -la *mf* disciple; pupil
disco *m* disk; (*del gramófono*) record, disk; (*sport*) discus; **disco de cola** (rr) taillight; **disco de goma** (*para un grifo*) washer (*for a spigot*); **disco de identificación** identification tag; **disco de larga duración** long-playing record; **disco de señales** (rr) semaphore; **disco selector** (telp) dial; **disco vertebral** spinal disk; **siempre el mismo disco** the same old song
discóbolo *m* discus thrower
discófi·lo -la *mf* record lover, discophile
dísco·lo -la *adj* ungovernable, wayward
disconforme *adj* disagreeing
discontinuar §21 *tr* to discontinue
discordancia *f* discordance
discordar §61 *intr* to be out of tune; disagree
discorde *adj* discordant, disagreeing; (*mus*) discordant, out of tune
discordia *f* discord
discoteca *f* discothèque, disco; record cabinet; record library
discreción *f* discretion; wit; witticism; **a discreción** at discretion; (mil) unconditionally
discrepancia *f* discrepancy; dissent
discrepar *intr* to differ, disagree
discretear *intr* to try to be clever, try to sparkle
discre·to -ta *adj* (*juicioso*) discreet; (*discontinuo*) discrete; witty
discrimen *m* risk, hazard; difference
discriminación *f* discrimination
discriminar *tr* to discriminate against ‖ *intr* to discriminate
discriminato·rio -ria *adj* discriminatory
disculpa *f* excuse, apology
disculpar *tr* to excuse; pardon, overlook ‖ *ref* to apologize; **disculparse con** to apologize to; **disculparse de** to apologize for
discurrir *tr* to contrive, invent; guess, conjecture ‖ *intr* to ramble, roam; occur, take place; discourse; reason; pass, elapse
discursis·to -ta *adj* long-winded; (coll) windy; *mf* windbag; big talker
discursi·vo -va *adj* meditative
discurso *m* discourse, speech; (*paso del tiempo*) course; **discurso de sobremesa** after-dinner speech
discusión *f* discussion
discutible *adj* debatable
discutir *tr* to discuss ‖ *intr* to discuss; argue
disecar §73 *tr* to dissect; (*un animal muerto*) stuff; (*una planta*) mount
diseminar *tr* to disseminate; scatter ‖ *ref* to scatter
disensión *f* (*oposición*) dissent; (*contienda*) dissension
disentería *f* dysentery
disentir §68 *intr* to dissent
diseñar *tr* to draw, sketch; design, outline

diseño *m* drawing, sketch; design, outline
disertar *intr* to discourse, discuss
diser•to -ta *adj* fluent, eloquent
disfavor *m* disfavor
disforme *adj* formless; monstrous, ugly
disforzar §35 *ref* (Peru) to be prudish, be finical
dis•fraz *m* (*pl* **-fraces**) disguise; (*traje de máscara*) costume, fancy dress
disfrazar §60 *tr* to disguise ‖ *ref* to disguise oneself; wear fancy dress, masquerade, dress in costume
disfrutar *tr* to enjoy, to use ‖ *intr* —**disfrutar de** to enjoy, use; **disfrutar con** to enjoy, take enjoyment in
disfrute *m* enjoyment, use
disfunción *f* dysfunction
disgregar §44 *tr* & *intr* to disintegrate, break up
disgusta•do -da *adj* tasteless, insipid; sad, sorrowful; disagreeable; (Mex) hard to please
disgustar *tr* to displease ‖ *ref* to be displeased; fall out, become estranged
disgusto *m* displeasure; annoyance, unpleasantness; grief, sorrow; difference, quarrel; **a disgusto** against one's will
disidencia *f* dissidence; (*de una doctrina*) dissent
disidente *adj* dissident ‖ *mf* dissident, dissenter
disidir *intr* to dissent
disíla•bo -ba *adj* dissyllabic ‖ *m* dissyllable
disímil *adj* dissimilar
disimilar *tr* & *ref* to dissimilate
disimula•do -da *adj* sly, underhanded; **a lo disimulado** or **a la disimulada** underhandedly; **hacer la disimulada** to feign ignorance
disimular *tr* to dissemble, dissimulate, hide, conceal; overlook, pardon ‖ *intr* to dissemble, dissimulate
disimulo *m* dissembling, dissimulation; indulgence
disipación *f* dissipation
disipa•do -da *adj* dissipated; spendthrift ‖ *mf* debauchee; spendthrift
disipar *tr* to dissipate ‖ *ref* to be dissipated; disappear, evanesce
dislate *m* nonsense
dislocar §73 *tr* to dislocate ‖ *ref* to dislocate; be dislocated
disloque *m* tops, top notch
disminución *f* diminution; decrease; **disminución física** handicap, disability
disminuir §20 *tr, intr* & *ref* to diminish
disociar *tr* to dissociate
disolución *f* dissolution; disbandment; (*relajación de costumbres*) dissoluteness, dissipation
disolu•to -ta *adj* dissolute ‖ *mf* debauchee
disolver §47 & §83 *tr* to dissolve; disband; destroy, ruin ‖ *intr* & *ref* to dissolve
disonancia *f* dissonance
disonar §61 *intr* to be dissonant, lack harmony, disagree; cause surprise; sound bad

dispar *adj* unlike, different; (*que no hace juego*) odd
disparada *f* sudden flight; **a la disparada** like a shot, in mad haste; **de una disparada** (Arg) right away; **tomar la disparada** (Arg) to take to one's heels
disparadero *m* trigger
disparador *m* trigger; (*de reloj*) escapement; **poner en el disparador** to drive mad
disparar *tr* to throw, hurl; shoot, fire ‖ *intr* to rant, talk nonsense ‖ *ref* to dash away, rush away; (*un caballo*) run away; (*una escopeta*) to go off; be beside oneself
disparata•do -da *adj* absurd, nonsensical; frightful
disparatar *intr* to talk nonsense; act foolishly
disparate *m* folly, nonsense; blunder, mistake; outrage
dispare•jo -ja *adj* unequal, different, uneven, disparate; rough, broken
disparidad *f* disparity
disparo *m* shot, discharge; nonsense; (mach) release, trip; **cambiar disparos** to exchange shots
dispendio *m* waste, extravagance
dispendio•so -sa *adj* expensive
dispensar *tr* to excuse, pardon; exempt; dispense; dispense with
dispensario *m* dispensary; **dispensario de alimentos** soup kitchen
dispepsia *f* dyspepsia
dispersar *tr* & *ref* to disperse
displicente *adj* disagreeable; cross, fretful, peevish
disponer §54 *tr* to dispose, arrange; direct, order ‖ *intr* to dispose; **disponer de** to dispose of, have at one's disposal ‖ *ref* to prepare, get ready; get ready to die, make one's will
disponible *adj* available, disposable
disposición *f* disposition, arrangement, layout; inclination; preparation; disposal; predisposition; state of health; elegance; **estar a la disposición de** to be at the disposal of, be at the service of; **última disposición** last will and testament
dispositivo *m* appliance, device
dispues•to -ta *adj* ready, prepared; comely, graceful; clever, skillful; **bien dispuesto** well-disposed; well, in good health; **mal dispuesto** ill-disposed, unfavorable; ill, indisposed
disputa *f* dispute; fight, struggle; **sin disputa** beyond dispute
disputar *tr* to dispute, question; argue over; fight for ‖ *intr* to dispute; debate, argue; fight
disquería *f* record shop
disque•ro -ra *mf* record dealer
distancia *f* distance; **a distancia** at a distance; **a larga distancia** long-distance; **tomar distancia** to stand aside, stand off
distante *adj* distant
distar *intr* to be distant, be far; be different
distender §51 *tr* to distend; (*p.ej., las piernas*) stretch ‖ *ref* to distend; relax; (*un reloj*) run down

di
di

distensión _f_ distension; relaxation of tension

distinción _f_ (_honor, prerrogativa_) distinction; (_diferencia_) distinctness; **a distinción de** unlike

distingui•do -da _adj_ distinguished; refined, urbane, smooth

distinguir §29 _tr_ to distinguish; give distinction to; make out

distinti•vo -va _adj_ distinctive ‖ _m_ badge, insignia; distinction; distinctive mark

distin•to -ta _adj_ distinct; different; **distintos** various, several

distorsión _f_ distortion

distorsionar _tr_ to distort, twist, bend

distracción _f_ distraction; (_licencia en las costumbres_) dissipation; (_substracción de fondos_) embezzlement

distraer §75 _tr_ to distract; amuse, divert, entertain; seduce; embezzle

distraí•do -da _adj_ absent-minded, distracted; licentious, dissolute; (Chile, Mex) untidy, careless

distribución _f_ distribution; electric supply system; timing gears, valve gears

distribui•dor -dora _adj_ distributing ‖ _mf_ distributor ‖ _m_ (aut) distributor; slide valve; **distribuidor automático** vending machine

distribuir §20 _tr_ to distribute

distrito _m_ district; (rr) section; **distrito electoral** precinct; **distrito postal** zone, postal zone

disturbar _tr_ to disturb

disturbio _m_ disturbance

disuadir _tr_ to dissuade

disyunti•vo -va _adj_ disjunctive ‖ _f_ dilemma

disyuntor _m_ circuit breaker

dita _f_ bond, surety

diuca _m_ (Arg, Chile) teacher's pet ‖ _f_ (Arg, Chile) finch (_Fringilla diuca_)

diuréti•co -ca _adj_ & _m_ diuretic

diur•no -na _adj_ day, daytime

diva _f_ goddess; (mus) diva

divagación _f_ digression; wandering

divagar §44 _intr_ to digress; ramble, wander

diván _m_ divan; **diván cama** day bed

divergir §27 _intr_ to diverge

diversidad _f_ diversity; abundance

diversificación _f_ diversification

diversificar §73 _tr_ & _ref_ to diversify

diversión _f_ diversion

diver•so -sa _adj_ diverse, different; **diversos** several, various, divers

diverti•do -da _adj_ amusing, funny; (Am) tipsy

divertimiento _m_ diversion, amusement

divertir §68 _tr_ to divert; amuse ‖ _ref_ to enjoy oneself, have a good time

dividendo _m_ dividend

dividir _tr_ to divide ‖ _ref_ to divide, be divided; separate

divieso _m_ boil

divinidad _f_ divinity; (_persona dotada de gran belleza_) beauty

divinizar §60 _tr_ to deify; exalt, extol

divi•no -na _adj_ divine

divisa _f_ badge; emblem; motto; goal, ideal; currency, foreign exchange

divisar _tr_ to descry, espy

división _f_ division; (_deportes_) class, category; league

divisor _m_ (math) divisor; **máximo común divisor** greatest common divisor; **divisor de voltaje** (rad) voltage divider

divisoria _f_ dividing line; (geog) divide

di•vo -va _adj_ godlike, divine ‖ _m_ god; (mus) opera star ‖ _f_ see **diva**

divorciar _tr_ to divorce ‖ _ref_ to divorce, get divorced

divorcio _m_ divorce; divergency (_in opinion_); (Col) jail for women

divulgación _f_ divulging, disclosure; popularization

divulgar §44 _tr_ to divulge, disclose; popularize

D.ⁿ _abbr_ **don**

dobladillar _tr_ to hem

dobladillo _m_ hem

dobla•do -da _adj_ rough, uneven; stocky, thickset; double-dealing ‖ _m_ (mov) dubbing

doblaje _m_ (mov) dubbing

doblar _tr_ to double; fold, crease; bend; (_una esquina_) turn, round; (_un promontorio_) double; (_una película, generalmente en otro idioma_) dub; (bridge) to double; (Mex) to shoot down ‖ _intr_ to turn; (_tocar a muerto_) toll; (mov, theat) to double, stand in; (bridge) to double ‖ _ref_ to double; fold, crease; bend; bow, stoop; give in, yield

doble _adj_ double; heavy, thick; stocky, thickset; deceitful, two-faced ‖ _adv_ double, doubly ‖ _mf_ (mov, theat) double, stand-in ‖ _m_ double; fold, crease; (_toque de difuntos_) toll, knell; (_suma que se paga por la prórroga de una operación a plazos en la bolsa_) margin; **al doble** doubly

doblegar §44 _tr_ to fold; bend; (_una espada_) brandish, flourish; sway, dominate ‖ _ref_ to fold; bend; give in, yield

doblete _adj_ medium ‖ _m_ (_piedra falsa; cada una de dos palabras que poseen un mismo origen_) doublet; (bridge) doubleton

do•blez _m_ (_pl_ **-bleces**) fold, crease; (_del pantalón_) cuff; duplicity, double-dealing

doce _adj_ & _pron_ twelve; **las doce** twelve o'clock ‖ _m_ twelve; (_en las fechas_) twelfth

docea•vo -va _adj_ & _m_ twelfth

docena _f_ dozen; **docena del fraile** baker's dozen

docencia _f_ (Arg) teaching; (Arg) teaching staff

docente _adj_ educational, teaching

dócil _adj_ docile; soft, ductile

doc•to -ta _adj_ learned ‖ _mf_ scholar

doc•tor -tora _mf_ doctor ‖ _f_ (coll) bluestocking

doctorado _m_ doctorate

doctoran•do -da _mf_ candidate for the doctor's degree

doctorar _tr_ to grant the doctor's degree to ‖ _ref_ to get the doctor's degree

doctrina _f_ doctrine; teaching, instruction; learning; catechism; preaching the Gospel

doctrinar _tr_ to teach, instruct

doctrino *m* orphan (*in orphanage*); **parecer un doctrino** to look scared
documentación *f* documentation; **documentación del buque** ship's papers
documental *adj* documentary ‖ *m* (mov) documentary
documentar *tr* to document
documento *m* document; **documento de prueba** (law) exhibit
dogal *m* (*para atar las caballerías*) halter; (*para ahorcar a un reo*) noose, halter, hangman's rope; **estar con el dogal a la garganta** or **al cuello** to be in a tight spot
dogmáti•co -ca *adj* dogmatic
do•go -ga *mf* bulldog
dolamas *fpl* or **dolames** *mpl* hidden defects of a horse; complaints, aches and pains
dolar §61 *tr* to hew
dólar *m* dollar
dolencia *f* ailment, complaint
doler §47 *tr* to pain; grieve, distress; **dolerle a uno el dinero** to hate to spend money ‖ *intr* to ache, hurt, pain ‖ *ref* to complain; feel sorry; repent
doliente *adj* sick, ill; aching, suffering; sad, sorrowful ‖ *mf* sufferer, patient ‖ *m* mourner
dolo *m* deceit, fraud, guile
dolor *m* ache, pain; grief, sorrow; regret, repentance; **dolor de cabeza** headache; **dolor de muelas** toothache; **dolor de oído** earache; **dolor de yegua** (CAm) lumbago; **estar con dolores** to be in labor
dolori•do -da *adj* sore, painful; grieving, disconsolate
doloro•so -sa *adj* painful; sorrowful, sad
dolo•so -sa *adj* deceitful, guileful
domador *m* horsebreaker; animal tamer
domar *tr* to tame, break; master
domeñar *tr* to master, subdue
domesticar §73 *tr* to domesticate; tame
domésti•co -ca *adj* domestic, household ‖ *mf* domestic, servant
domiciliar *tr* to domicile, settle; (*una carta*) (Mex) to address ‖ *ref* to be domiciled, take up one's residence
domicilio *m* domicile, home; dwelling, house; **domicilio social** home office, company office
dominación *f* domination; (mil) eminence, high ground
dominante *adj* dominant; (*mandón*) domineering ‖ *f* (mus) dominant
dominar *tr* to dominate; check, restrain, subdue; (*una ciencia, un idioma*) master ‖ *intr* to dominate; (*mandar imperiosamente*) domineer ‖ *ref* to restrain oneself
dómine *m* schoolmaster, Latin teacher; pedant
domingo *m* Sunday; **domingo de ramos** Palm Sunday; **domingo de resurrección** Easter Sunday; **guardar el domingo** to keep the Sabbath
dominguillo *m* tumbler
dominica•no -na *adj & mf* Dominican

dominio *m* dominion; domain; (*de una ciencia, de un idioma*) mastery; (*del aire*) supremacy
domi•nó *m* (*pl* **-nós**) (*traje*) domino; (*juego*) dominoes; (*fichas*) set of dominoes
dom.° *abbr* **domingo**
domo *m* dome
dompedro *m* four-o'clock
don *m* gift, present; talent, natural gift; Don (*Spanish title used before masculine Christian names*); **don de acierto** knack for doing the right thing; **don de errar** knack for doing the wrong thing; **don de gentes** charm, social grace; **don de lenguas** linguistic facility; **don de mando** ability to lead, generalship
dona *f* gift, present; **donas** wedding presents from the bridegroom to the bride
donación *f* gift, bequest; endowment
donada *f* lay sister
donado *m* lay brother
dona•dor -dora *mf* donor
donaire *m* charm, grace; witticism; cleverness
donairo•so -sa *adj* charming, graceful; witty, clever
donar *tr* to donate, give
doncel *adj* mild, mellow ‖ *m* (*joven noble aun no armado caballero*) bachelor; (*hombre virgen*) virgin
doncella *f* maiden, virgin; housemaid; lady's maid; maid of honor; (Col, Ven) felon, whitlow
doncellez *f* maidenhood, virginity
doncellona *f* or **doncellueca** *f* unmarried woman, maiden lady
donde *conj* where; wherever; in which; **donde no** otherwise; **por donde quiera** anywhere, everywhere ‖ *prep* at or to the house, office, or store of
dónde *adv* where; **a dónde** where, whither; **de dónde** from where, whence; **por dónde** which way; for what cause, for what reason
dondequiera *adv* anywhere; **dondequiera que** wherever
dondiego *m* four-o'clock; **dondiego de día** morning-glory; **dondiego de noche** four-o'clock
donillero *m* sharper, smoothy
donjuán *m* four-o'clock
donosidad *f* charm, grace, wit
dono•so -sa *adj* charming, graceful, witty
donostiarra *adj* San Sebastian ‖ *mf* native or inhabitant of San Sebastian
donosura *f* charm, grace, wit
doña *f* Doña (*Spanish title used before feminine Christian names*)
doñear *intr* (coll) to hang around women
doquier or **doquiera** *conj* wherever; **por doquier** everywhere
dorada *f* (ichth) gilthead
doradillo *m* fine brass wire
dora•do -da *adj* golden; gilt ‖ *m* gilt, gilding; **dorados** bronze trimmings (*on furniture*) ‖ *f* see **dorada**

di
do

dorar *tr* to gold-plate; gild; (*tostar ligeramente*) brown; (*paliar*) sugar-coat ‖ *ref* to turn golden; turn brown

dormi•lón -lona *adj* sleepy ‖ *mf* sleepyhead ‖ *f* reclining armchair; mimosa; (Mex) headrest; (Ven) sleeping gown; **dormilonas** pearl earrings

dormir §30 *tr* to put to sleep; (*p.ej., una borrachera*) sleep off ‖ *intr* to sleep; spend the night ‖ *ref* to sleep; fall asleep; (*entorpecerse, p.ej., el pie*) go to sleep

dormirlas *m* hide-and-seek

dormitar *intr* to doze, nap

dormitorio *m* bedroom; (*muebles propios de esta habitación*) bedroom suit

dorsal *m* (sport) number (*worn on shirt*)

dorso *m* back

dos *adj & pron* two; **las dos** two o'clock ‖ *m* two; (*en las fechas*) second

dosal•bo -ba *adj* (*horse*) with two white feet

doscien•tos -tas *adj & pron* two hundred ‖ **doscientos** *m* two hundred

dosel *m* canopy, dais

doselera *f* valance, drapery

dosificación *f* dosage

dosificar §73 *tr* (*un medicamento*) to dose, give in doses

do•sis *f* (*pl* **-sis**) dose

dos-pie•zas *m* (*pl* **-zas**) two-piece bathing suit

dotación *f* (*de una mujer; de una fundación*) endowment; (nav) complement; (aer) crew; (*de remeros*) (sport) crew; staff, personnel

dotar *tr* to give a dowry to; endow; (*un buque*) staff, man; (*una oficina*) staff; equip; fix the wages for

dote *m & f* dowry, marriage portion ‖ *m* (*en el juego de naipes*) stack of chips ‖ *f* endowment, talent, gift; **dotes de mando** leadership

dovela *f* voussoir

doza•vo -va *adj & m* twelfth

d/p *abbr* **días plazo**

dracma *f* (*moneda griega*) drachma; (*peso farmacéutico*) dram

draga *f* dredge; (*barco*) dredger

dragado *m* dredging

dragami•nas *m* (*pl* **-nas**) mine sweeper

dragar §44 *tr* to dredge

dragón *m* dragon; (*planta*) snapdragon; (*soldado*) dragoon

dragonear *intr* to flirt; boast; **dragonear de** to boast of being; pretend to be, pass oneself off as

drama *m* drama

dramáti•co -ca *adj* dramatic ‖ *mf* (*autor*) dramatist; actor ‖ *f* (*arte y género*) drama

dramatizar §60 *tr* to dramatize

dramaturgo *m* dramatist

drásti•co -ca *adj* drastic

dren *m* drain

drenaje *m* drainage

drenar *tr* to drain

driblar *tr & intr* to dribble

dril *m* drill; duck; **dril de algodón** denim

driza *f* (naut) halyard

dro. *abbr* **derecho**

droga *f* drug; annoyance, bother; deceit, trick; (Chile, Mex, Peru) bad debt; (Cuba) drug on the market; **drogas milagrosas** wonder drugs

drogadic•to -ta *adj* drug-addicted ‖ *mf* drug addict

drogado *m* doping

drogar §44 *tr* to dope

droguería *f* drug store; drug business; (*comercio de substancias usadas en química, industria, medicina, bellas artes*) drysaltery (Brit)

drogue•ro -ra *mf* druggist; drysalter (Brit)

droguista *mf* druggist; (coll) crook, cheat; (Arg) toper, drunk

drolátí•co -ca *adj* droll, snappy

dromedario *m* dromedary; big heavy animal; brute (*person*)

druida *m* druid

dúa *f* (min) gang of workmen

dual *adj & m* dual

dualidad *f* duality; (Chile) tie vote

ducado *m* duchy, dukedom; (*moneda antigua*) ducat; **gran ducado** grand duchy

dúctil *adj* ductile; easy to handle

ducha *f* (*chorro de agua en una cavidad del cuerpo*) douche; (*chorro de agua sobre el cuerpo entero*) shower bath; (*lista en los tejidos*) stripe; **ducha en alfileres** needle bath

duchar *tr* to douche; give a shower bath to ‖ *ref* to douche; take a shower bath

du•cho -cha *adj* experienced, expert, skillful ‖ *f* see **ducha**

duda *f* doubt; **sin duda** doubtless, no doubt, without doubt

dudable *adj* doubtful

dudar *tr* to doubt; question ‖ *intr* to hesitate; **dudar de** to doubt

dudo•so -sa *adj* doubtful; dubious

duela *f* stave (*of barrel*)

duelista *m* duelist

duelo *m* (*combate entre dos*) duel; grief, sorrow; bereavement, mourning; (*los que asisten a los funerales*) mourners; **batirse en duelo** to duel, to fight a duel; **duelos** hardships; **sin duelo** in abundance

duende *m* elf, goblin; gold cloth, silver cloth; (coll) restless daemon; **tener duende** to be burning within

due•ño -ña *mf* owner, proprietor; **dueño de sí mismo** one's own master; **ser dueño de** to be master of; be at liberty to, be free to ‖ *m* master, landlord ‖ *f* mistress, landlady, housekeeper; duenna; matron; **dueña de casa** housewife

duermevela *f* doze, light sleep; (*sueño fatigoso e interrumpido*) fitful sleep

dula *f* common pasture land; land irrigated from common ditch

dulce *adj* sweet; (*agua*) fresh; (*metal*) soft, ductile; gentle, mild, pleasant; (*manjar*) tasteless, insipid ‖ *m* candy; piece of candy; preserves; **dulce de almíbar** preserved fruit; **dulces** candy

dulcera *f* candy dish, preserve dish

dulcería *f* candy store, confectionery store

dulce•ro -ra *adj* sweet-toothed ‖ *mf* confectioner ‖ *f* see **dulcera**
dulcificar §73 *tr* to sweeten; appease, mollify ‖ *ref* to sweeten, turn sweet
dulcinea *f* sweetheart; ideal
dulzaina *f* flageolet
dulza•rrón -rrona *adj* cloying, sickening
dulzo•so -sa *adj* sweetish
dulzura *f* sweetness; pleasantness, kindliness; (*del clima*) mildness; endearment, sweet word
duna *f* dune
dun•do -da *adj* (CAm, Col) simple, stupid ‖ *mf* (CAm, Col) simpleton
dúo *m* duet, duo
duodéci•mo -ma *adj & m* twelfth
duodeno *m* duodenum
duplica•do -da *adj & m* duplicate; **por duplicado** in duplicate
duplicar §73 *tr* to duplicate; double; repeat
duplicata *f* duplicate
duplicidad *f* (*falsedad*) duplicity; (*calidad de doble*) doubleness
du•plo -pla *adj & m* double
duque *m* duke; **gran duque** grand duke
duquesa *f* duchess; **gran duquesa** grand duchess
dura *f* durability; **de dura** or **de mucha dura** strong, durable

durable *adj* durable, lasting
duración *f* duration, endurance; (*espacio de tiempo del uso de una cosa*) life
durade•ro -ra *adj* durable, lasting
durante *prep* during, for
durar *intr* to last; remain; (*la ropa*) last, wear, wear well
durazno *m* peach; peach tree
dureza *f* hardness; harshness, roughness; **dureza de corazón** hardheartedness; **dureza de oído** hardness of hearing; **dureza de vientre** constipation
durmiente *adj* sleeping; **la Bella Durmiente** Sleeping Beauty ‖ *mf* sleeper ‖ *m* girder, sleeper, stringer; tie, railroad tie; (Ven) steel bar
du•ro -ra *adj* hard; (*huevo*) hard-boiled; harsh, rough; cruel; stubborn, obstinate; unbearable; strong, tough; stingy; (*tiempo*) stormy; **duro de corazón** hard-hearted; **duro de oído** hard of hearing; **duro de película** movie hero; **estar muy duro con** to be hard on; **ser duro de pelar** to be hard to put across; be hard to deal with ‖ *m* dollar (*Spanish coin worth five pesetas*) ‖ *f* see **dura** ‖ **duro** *adv* hard
dux *m* (*pl* **dux**) doge
d/v *abbr* **días vista**

do
ec

E

E, e (e) *f* sixth letter of the Spanish alphabet
e *conj* (used before words beginning with *i* or *hi* not followed by a vowel) and
ea *interj* hey!
ebanista *m* cabinetmaker, woodworker
ebanistería *f* cabinetmaking, woodwork; cabinetmaker's shop
ébano *m* ebony
ebriedad *f* drunkenness
e•brio -bria *adj* drunk; (*p.ej., de ira*) blind ‖ *mf* drunk
ebrio•so -sa *adj* drinking ‖ *mf* drinker
ebullición *f* boiling
ecléctl•co -ca *adj & mf* eclectic
eclesiásti•co -ca *adj & m* ecclesiastic
eclipsar *tr* to eclipse; (fig) to outshine ‖ *ref* to be in eclipse; (fig) to disappear
eclipse *m* eclipse
eclip•sis *f* (*pl* **-sis**) var of **elipsis**
eclisa *f* (rr) fishplate
eco *m* echo; (*del tambor*) rumbling; **hacer eco** to echo; attract attention; **tener eco** to be well received, catch on
ecología *f* ecology
ecológi•co -ca *adj* ecologic(al)
ecologista *mf* or **ecólogo** *m* ecologist
economato *m* stewardship; commissary, company store, coöperative store

economía *f* economy; want, poverty; **economía política** economics; **economías** savings
económi•co -ca *adj* economic; (*que gasta poco; poco costoso*) economical; cheap; miserly, niggardly
economista *mf* economist
economizar §60 *tr* to economize, save; avoid ‖ *intr* to economize, save; skimp
ecónomo *m* steward, trustee; supply priest
ecuación *f* equation
ecuador *m* equator ‖ **el Ecuador** Ecuador
ecuánime *adj* calm, composed; impartial
ecuanimidad *f* equanimity; impartiality
ecuatoria•no -na *adj & mf* Ecuadoran, Ecuadorian
ecuestre *adj* equestrian
eculcorante *adj* sweetening ‖ *m* sweetener
ecuméni•co -ca *adj* ecumenic(al)
eczema *m & f* eczema
echacan•tos *m* (*pl* **-tos**) good-for-nothing
echacuer•vos *m* (*pl* **-vos**) pimp, procurer; cheat
echada *f* cast, throw; man's length; (Arg, Mex) boast, hoax
echadero *m* place to stretch out
echadi•zo -za *adj* discarded, waste; spying ‖ *mf* foundling ‖ *m* spy

echa•do -da *adj* stretched out; (C-R) lazy, indolent; **estar echado** (CAm, Mex, P-R) to have an easy job (or easy life) ‖ *f* see **echada**

echar *tr* to throw, throw away, throw out; issue, emit; publish; discharge, dismiss; swallow; (*p.ej., agua*) pour; (*p.ej., un cigarrillo*) smoke; (*la baraja*) deal; (*una partida de cartas*) play; (*una llave*) turn; (*un discurso*) deliver; (*un drama*) put on; (*maldiciones*) utter; (*pelo, dientes, renuevos*) grow, put forth; (*impuestos*) impose, levy; (*la buenaventura*) tell; (*precio, distancia, edad, etc.*) ascribe, attribute; (*una mirada*) cast; (*sangre*) shed; (*la culpa*) lay; (*una mano*) lend; **echar abajo** to demolish, destroy; overthrow; **echar a pasear** to dismiss unceremoniously; **echar a perder** to spoil, ruin; **echar a pique** to sink; **echar de menos** to miss; **echarla de** to claim to be, boast of being; **echarlo todo a rodar** to upset everything; hit the ceiling ‖ *intr* — **echar a** to begin to; burst out (*e.g., crying*); **echar a perder** to spoil, ruin; **echar de ver** to notice, happen to see; **echar por** (*un empleo, un oficio*) to go into, take up; (*la derecha, la izquierda*) turn toward; (*un camino*) go down ‖ *ref* to throw oneself; lie down, stretch out; (*el viento*) fall; (*un abrigo*) throw on; (*una gallina*) set; **echarse a** to begin to; **echarse a morir** to give up in despair; **echarse a perder** to spoil, be ruined; **echarse atrás** to back out; **echarse de ver** to be easy to see; **echárselas de** to claim to be, boast of being; **echarse sobre** to rush at, fall upon

echazón *f* jettison, jetsam

echiquier *m* Exchequer

edad *f* age; **edad crítica** change of life; **edad de quintas** draft age; **edad escolar** school age; **Edad Media** Middle Ages; **edad viril** prime of life; **mayor edad** majority; **menor edad** minority

edecán *m* aide-de-camp

edema *f* edema

edición *f* edition; publication; **la segunda edición de** the spit and image of

edicto *m* edict

edificación *f* construction, building; buildings; (*inspiración con el buen ejemplo*) edification, uplift

edificante *adj* edifying

edificar §73 *tr* to construct, build; (*dar buen ejemplo a*) edify, uplift

edificio *m* edifice, building

editar *tr* to publish

edi•tor -tora *adj* publishing ‖ *mf* publisher

editorial *adj* publishing; editorial ‖ *m* editorial ‖ *f* publishing house

editorialista *mf* editorial writer

editorializar §60 *intr* (Urug) to editorialize

edredón *m* eider down

educación *f* education

educacional *adj* educational

educa•dor -dora *mf* educator

educan•do -da *mf* pupil, student

educar §73 *tr* to educate; (*los sentidos*) train; (*al niño o el adolescente*) rear, bring up

educati•vo -va *adj* educational

EE.UU. *abbr* **Estados Unidos**

efectismo *m* sensationalism

efectista *adj* sensational, theatrical ‖ *mf* sensationalist

efectivamente *adv* actually, really; as a matter of fact

efecti•vo -va *adj* actual, real; (*empleo, cargo*) regular, permanent; (*vigente*) effective; **hacer efectivo** to carry out; (*un cheque*) to cash; **hacerse efectivo** to become effective ‖ *m* cash; **efectivo en caja** cash on hand

efecto *m* effect; end, purpose; article; (*en el juego de billar*) English; **a ese efecto** for that purpose; **al efecto** for the purpose; **con efecto** or **en efecto** indeed, as a matter of fact; **efecto útil** efficiency, output; **llevar a efecto** or **poner en efecto** to put into effect, carry out; **surtir efecto** to work, have the desired effect

efectuar §21 *tr* to carry out, effect, effectuate ‖ *ref* to take place

efervescencia *f* effervescence

efervescente *adj* effervescent

eficacia *f* efficacy

efi•caz *adj* (*pl* **-caces**) efficacious, effectual; efficient

eficiencia *f* efficiency

eficiente *adj* efficient

efigie *f* effigy

efíme•ro -ra *adj* ephemeral

efugio *m* evasion, subterfuge

efusión *f* effusion; (*manifestación de afectos muy viva*) warmth, effusiveness; **efusión de sangre** bloodshed

efusi•vo -va *adj* effusive

égida *f* aegis

egip•cio -cia *adj* & *mf* Egyptian

Egipto *m* Egypt

eglantina *f* sweetbriar

eglefino *m* haddock

égloga *f* eclogue

egoísmo *m* egoism

egoísta *adj* egoistic ‖ *mf* egoist

egolatría *f* self-worship, self-glorification

egotismo *m* egotism

egotista *adj* egotistic(al) ‖ *mf* egotist

egre•gio -gia *adj* distinguished, eminent

egresar *intr* to graduate

egreso *m* departure; graduation

eje *m* (*pieza alrededor de la cual gira un cuerpo*) axle, shaft; (*línea que divide en dos mitades; línea recta alrededor de la cual se supone que gira un cuerpo*) axis; (fig) core, crux; **eje de balancín** rocker, rockershaft; **eje de carretón** axletree; **eje motor** drive shaft; **eje tándem** dual axle; dual rear

ejecución *f* execution

ejecutante *mf* performer

ejecutar *tr* to execute; perform

ejecutivamente *adv* expeditiously

ejecuti•vo -va *adj* urgent, pressing; insistent; executive ‖ *m* executive

ejecu•tor -tora *adj* executive ‖ *mf* executor;

ejecutor de la justicia executioner; **ejecutor testamentario** executor (*of a will*) ‖ *f —* **ejecutora testamentaria** executrix

ejemplar *adj* exemplary ‖ *m* pattern, model; (*de una obra impresa*) copy; precedent; (*caso que sirve de escarmiento*) example; **ejemplar de cortesía** complimentary copy; **ejemplar muestra** sample copy; **sin ejemplar** unprecedented; as a special case

ejemplarizar §60 *tr* to set an example to; exemplify

ejemplificar §73 *tr* to exemplify

ejemplo *m* example, instance; **por ejemplo** for example, for instance; **sin ejemplo** unexampled

ejercer §78 *tr* (*la medicina*) to practice; (*la caridad*) show, exercise; (*una fuerza*) exert ‖ *intr* to practice; **ejercer de** to practice as, work as

ejercicio *m* exercise; drill, practice; (*de un cargo u oficio*) tenure; (*uso constante*) exertion; (*año económico*) fiscal year; **hacer ejercicio** to take exercise; (mil) to drill

ejercitar *tr* to exercise; practice; drill, train ‖ *ref* to exercise; practice

ejército *m* army; **ejército permanente** standing army; **los tres ejércitos** the three arms of the service

ejido *m* commons

ejote *m* (CAm, Mex) string bean

el, la (*pl* **los, las**) *art def* the ‖ *pron dem* that, the one; **el que** who, which, that; he who, the one that

él *pron pers masc* he, it; him, it

elabora•do -da *adj* elaborate; finished

elaborar *tr* to elaborate; (*una teoría*) work out; (*el metal, la madera*) fashion, to work

elación *f* magnanimity, nobility; (*de estilo y lenguaje*) pomposity

elástica *f* knit undershirt; **elásticas** (Ven) suspenders

elasticidad *f* elasticity

elásti•co -ca *adj* elastic ‖ *m* elastic; bedspring ‖ *f see* **elástica**

eléboro *m* hellebore

elección *f* election; choice

electi•vo -va *adj* elective

elec•to -ta *adj* elect

electorado *m* electorate

electorero *m* henchman, heeler

electricidad *f* electricity

electricista *mf* electrician

eléctrico -ca *adj* electric(al)

electrificar §73 *tr* to electrify

electrizar §60 *tr* to electrify

electro *m* electromagnet

electroafeitadora *f* electric shaver

electrocutar *tr* to electrocute

electrodo *m* electrode

electrodomésti•co -ca *adj* electric-appliance ‖ *m* electric appliance

electróge•no -na *adj* generating electricity ‖ *m* electric generator

electroimán *m* electromagnet

electrólisis *f* electrolysis

electrólito *m* electrolyte

electromagnéti•co -ca *adj* electromagnetic

electromo•tor -tora or **-triz** *adj* (*pl* **-tores -toras -trices**) electromotive

electrón *m* electron

electróni•co -ca *adj* electronic ‖ *f* electronics

electrostáti•co -ca *adj* electrostatic

electrotecnia *f* electrical engineering

electrotipar *tr* to electrotype

electrotipo *m* electrotype

elefante *m* elephant; **elefante blanco** (fig) (SAm) white elephant

elegancia *f* elegance; style, stylishness

elegante *adj* elegant; stylish ‖ *mf* fashion plate

eleganto•so -sa *adj* elegant

elegía *f* elegy

elegía•co -ca *adj* elegiac

elegible *adj* eligible

elegir §57 *tr* to elect; choose, select

elemental *adj* (*primordial; simple, no compuesto*) elemental; (*que se refiere a los principios de una ciencia o arte; de fácil comprensión*) elementary

elemento *m* element; (*de una pila o batería*) cell; **elemento de compuestos** (gram) combining form; **elemento en rastro** trace element; **estar en su elemento** to be in one's element

elenco *m* catalogue, list, table; (theat) cast

elepé *adj* (*disco*) long-playing; LP ‖ *m* long-playing record

elevación *f* elevation; **elevación a potencias** (math) involution

eleva•do -da *adj* elevated, high; lofty, sublime

elevador *m* elevator; **elevador de granos** grain elevator

elevar *tr* to elevate, lift; (math) to raise ‖ *ref* to ascend, rise; be exalted; become conceited

elfo *m* elf

elidir *tr* to eliminate; (*una vocal*) elide

eliminar *tr* to eliminate; strike out ‖ *ref* (Mex) to go away, leave

elipse *f* (geom) ellipse

elip•sis *f* (*pl* **-sis**) (gram) ellipsis

elípti•co -ca *adj* (geom & gram) elliptic(al)

elisión *f* elision

elitista *adj* & *mf* elitist

elocución *f* public speaking, elocution

elocuencia *f* eloquence

elocuente *adj* eloquent

elogiable *adj* praiseworthy

elogiar *tr* to praise, eulogize

elogio *m* praise, eulogy

elogio•so -sa *adj* laudatory, glowing

elote *m* (Mex, Guat) ear of corn; **coger asando elotes** (CAm) to catch in the act; **pagar los elotes** (CAm) to be the goat

elucidar *tr* to elucidate

eludir *tr* to elude, evade, avoid

elusi•vo -va *adj* evasive; elusive

ella *pron pers fem* she, it; her, it; (coll) the trouble

ello *pron pers neut* it; (coll) the trouble; **ello es que** the fact is that ‖ *m* (psychoanalysis) id

ec
el

E.M. *abbr* **Estado Mayor**
emancipar *tr* to emancipate
embadurnamiento *m* daub, daubing
embadurnar *tr* to daub
embaír §1 *tr* to deceive, take in, hoax
embajada *f* embassy; ambassadorship; (iron) fine proposition
embajador *m* ambassador; **embajadores** ambassador and wife
embajadora *f* ambassadress
embalaje *m* packing; package; (sport) sprint
embalar *tr* to pack ‖ *intr* (sport) to sprint ‖ *ref* (*el motor*) to race; (sport) to sprint
embaldosado *m* tile paving
embaldosar *tr* to pave with tile
embalsamar *tr* to embalm; perfume
embalsar *tr* to dam, dam up
embalse *m* dam; damming; backwater
embanastar *tr* to put in a basket; pack, jam, overcrowd
embanquetar *tr* (Mex) to line with sidewalks
embarazada *adj fem* pregnant ‖ *f* pregnant woman
embarazar §60 *tr* (*estorbar*) to embarrass; obstruct; make pregnant ‖ *ref* to be embarrassed, be encumbered; become pregnant
embarazo *m* embarrassment; obstruction; awkwardness; pregnancy
embarazo•so -sa *adj* embarrassing, troublesome
embarbillar *tr* to rabbet
embarcación *f* boat, ship; embarkation (*of passengers*)
embarcadero *m* pier, wharf; (rr) platform; **embarcadero de ganado** (Arg) loading chute; **embarcadero flotante** landing stage
embarcador *m* shipper
embarcar §73 *tr* to ship ‖ *intr* to entrain ‖ *ref* to embark, ship; get involved
embarco *m* embarkation (*of passengers*)
embargar §44 *tr* to embargo; paralyze; (law) to seize, attach
embargo *m* embargo; indigestion; (law) seizure, attachment; **sin embargo** however, nevertheless
embarnizar §60 *tr* to varnish
embarque *m* shipment, embarkation (*of freight*)
embarrada *f* blunder
embarrancar §73 *tr, intr & ref* to run into a ditch; (*una nave*) run aground
embarrar *tr* to splash with mud; smear, stain; (CAm, Mex) to involve in a shady deal; **embarrarla** (Arg) to spoil the whole thing
embarrilar *tr* to barrel, put in barrels
embarullar *tr* to muddle, make a mess of; bungle, botch
embastar *tr* to baste, stitch
embate *m* blow, attack; (*del mar*) beating, dashing; (*de viento*) gust; **embates de la fortuna** hard knocks
embauca•dor -dora *mf* trickster; impostor; con man
embaucar §73 *tr* to trick, bamboozle, swindle

embaula•do -da *adj* crowded, packed, jammed
embaular §8 *tr* to put in a trunk; jam, pack in
embayar *ref* (Ecuad) to fly into a rage
embazar §60 *tr* to dye brown; hinder, obstruct; astound, dumbfound ‖ *ref* to get bored; be upset, get sick at the stomach
embebecer §22 *tr* to entertain, amuse, fascinate, enchant
embeber *tr* to absorb, soak up; soak; contain, include; embed; contract, shrink ‖ *intr* to contract, shrink ‖ *ref* to be enchanted, be enraptured; become absorbed or immersed; become well versed
embebi•do -da *adj* (*vocal*) elided; (*columna*) engaged
embelecar §73 *tr* to cheat, dupe, bamboozle
embeleco *m* cheating, fraud; bore; **embelecos** cuteness
embeleñar *tr* to dope, stupefy; enchant, bewitch
embelequería *f* (Col, Mex, W-I) fraud, swindle
embelesar *tr* to charm, enrapture, fascinate
embeleso *m* charm, fascination, delight
embellece•dor -dora *adj* embellishing, beautifying ‖ *m* (aut) hubcap ‖ *f* beautician
embellecer §22 *tr* to embellish, beautify
embellecimiento *m* embellishment, beautification
embermejecer §22 *tr* to dye red; make blush ‖ *ref* to blush
emberrinchar *ref* to fly into a rage
embestida *f* attack, assault; (*detención intempestiva*) buttonholing
embesti•dor -dora *mf* beat, sponger
embestir §50 *tr* to attack, assail; to strike; buttonhole, waylay ‖ *intr* to attack, charge, rush
embetunar *tr* to blacken; cover with tar
embicar §73 *tr* (Mex) to turn upside down, tilt ‖ *intr* (Arg, Chile) to run aground
emblandecer §22 *tr* to soften; placate, mollify ‖ *ref* to soften, yield
emblanquecer §22 *tr* to whiten; bleach ‖ *ref* to turn white
emblema *m* emblem
emblemáti•co -ca *adj* emblematic(al)
embobar *tr* to amaze, fascinate ‖ *ref* to stand gaping
embocadero *m* mouth, outlet
embocadura *f* nozzle; (*de río*) mouth; (*del freno; de instrumento de viento*) mouthpiece; (*de cigarrillo*) tip; (*del vino*) taste; stage entrance
embocar §73 *tr* to catch in the mouth; put in the mouth; take on, undertake; gulp down; try to put over ‖ *intr & ref* to enter, pass
embolada *f* stroke
embolado *m* bull with wooden balls on horns; (theat) minor role; (coll) trick, hoax
embolar *tr* (*los cuernos del toro*) to put wooden balls on; (*ei calzado*) to shine ‖ *ref* (CAm, Mex) to get drunk
embolia *f* embolism
émbolo *m* (mach) piston; **émbolo buzo** (mach) plunger

embolsar *tr* to pocket, take in

embonar *tr* to fertilize; suit, be becoming to

emboquillar *tr* (*los cigarrillos*) to put tips on; (*una galería o túnel*) cut an entrance in; (*las junturas entre los ladrillos*) (Chile) to point, chink

emborrachar *tr* to intoxicate ‖ *ref* to get drunk; (*los colores de una tela*) run

emborrar *tr* to stuff, pad, wad; gulp down

emborrascar §73 *tr* to stir up, irritate ‖ *ref* to get stormy; (*un negocio*) fail; (*la veta de una mina*) (Arg, CAm, Mex) to peter out

emborronar *tr* to blot; scribble

emboscada *f* ambush, ambuscade

emboscado *m* draft dodger

emboscar §73 *tr* (*tropas para sorprender al enemigo*) to ambush ‖ *ref* to ambush, lie in ambush; shirk, take an easy way out

embota•do -da *adj* blunt, dull; (Chile) black-pawed

embotadura *f* bluntness, dullness

embotar *tr* to blunt, dull; dull, weaken; (*el tabaco*) put in a jar

embotella•do -da *adj* (*discurso*) prepared ‖ *m* bottling; (*del tráfico*) bottleneck

embotellamiento *m* bottling; traffic jam

embotellar *tr* to bottle; (*un negocio*) tie up; (nav) to bottle up

embotijar *tr* (*un suelo*) to underlay with jugs ‖ *ref* to swell up with anger

embovedar *tr* to vault, vault over; put in a vault

emboza•do -da *adj* muffled up ‖ *mf* person muffled up to eyes

embozar §60 *tr* to muffle up to the eyes; (*p.ej., a un perro*) muzzle; disguise ‖ *ref* to muffle oneself up to the eyes

embozo *m* muffler, cloak held over the face; fold back (*of bed sheet*); cunning, dissimulation; **quitarse el embozo** to drop one's mask

embragar §44 *tr* (*el motor*) to engage ‖ *intr* to throw the clutch in

embrague *m* clutch; engagement

embravecer §22 *tr* to enrage, make angry ‖ *ref* to get angry; (*el mar*) get rough

embraveci•do -da *adj* angry; rough, wild

embrear *tr* to tar, cover with tar; calk with tar

embregar §44 *ref* to wrangle

embriagar §44 *tr* to intoxicate, make drunk; enrapture ‖ *ref* to get drunk

embriaguez *f* drunkenness; rapture

embridar *tr* to bridle; check, restrain

embriología *f* embryology

embrión *m* embryo

embroca *f* poultice

embrocar §73 *tr* to empty; (*el toro al torero*) to catch between the horns ‖ *ref* (C-R) to fall on one's face; (Mex) to put on over the head

embrollar *tr* to tangle, muddle, embroil

embrollo *m* entanglement, muddle, embroilment; deception, trick

embromar *tr* to joke with, play jokes on; bore, annoy ‖ *ref* to be bored, be annoyed

embrujar *tr* to bewitch

embrutecer §22 *tr* to brutify, stupefy

embrutecimiento *m* brutalization; coarsening

embuchado *m* pork sausage; subterfuge; (*de la urna electoral*) stuffing (of ballot box)

embudar *tr* to put a funnel in; trick, trap

embudista *adj* tricky, scheming ‖ *mf* schemer

embudo *m* funnel; trick; (mil) shell hole; **embudo de bomba** (mil) bomb crater

embullar *tr* to stir up, excite, key up ‖ *ref* to become excited, keyed up

emburujar *tr* to jumble, pile up ‖ *ref* to wrap oneself up

embuste *m* lie, falsehood, trick; **embustes** baubles, trinkets; (*del niño*) cuteness

embuste•ro -ra *adj* lying, false, tricky ‖ *mf* liar, cheat

embuti•do -da *adj* inlaid, flush ‖ *m* inlay, marquetry; pork sausage; lace insertion

embutir *tr* to stuff, pack tight; insert; inlay; set flush; (*una hoja de metal*) fashion, hammer into shape ‖ *ref* to squeeze in; stuff oneself

emergencia *f* emergence; incident

emerger §17 *intr* to emerge; (*un submarino*) surface

emersión *f* emersion; (*de un submarino*) surfacing

eméti•co -ca *adj & m* emetic

emigración *f* emigration; migration

emigra•do -da *mf* émigré

emigrante *adj & mf* emigrant

emigrar *intr* to emigrate; migrate

eminencia *f* eminence

eminente *adj* eminent

emisa•rio -ria *mf* emissary ‖ *m* outlet

emisión *f* (*acción de exhalar; acción de lanzar ondas luminosas, etc.*) emission; (*títulos creados de una vez*) (com) issue; (*acción de emitir títulos nuevos*) (com) issuance; (rad) broadcast; **emisión seriada** (rad) serial

emi•sor -sora *adj* emitting; broadcasting ‖ *m* (rad) transmitter ‖ *f* broadcasting station

emitir *tr* to emit, send forth; issue, give out; (*p.ej., opiniones*) utter, express; (com) to issue; (rad) to broadcast

emoción *f* emotion

emocional *adj* emotional

emocionante *adj* moving, touching; thrilling, exciting

emocionar *tr* to move, stir; thrill

emoti•vo -va *adj* emotional

empacadi•zo -za *adj* (Arg) touchy

empaca•do -da *adj* (Arg) gruff, grim

empacar §73 *tr* to pack, crate ‖ *ref* to be stubborn; (*un animal*) balk, get balky

empa•cón -cona *adj* stubborn; balky

empacha•do -da *adj* backward, fumbling

empachar *tr* to hinder, embarrass; disguise; surfeit, upset the stomach of ‖ *ref* blush, be embarrassed; be upset, have indigestion

empacho *m* hindrance; embarrassment, bashfulness; indigestion

empacho•so -sa *adj* sickening; shameful

empadronar *tr* to register, take the census of ‖ *ref* to register, be registered in the census

em
em

empalagar §44 *tr* to cloy, pall, surfeit; bore, weary

empalago•so -sa *adj* cloying, sickening, mawkish; boring, annoying; fawning

empalar *tr* impale

empalizada *f* palisade, stockade, fence

empalizar §60 *tr* to fence in

empalmar *tr* to splice, connect, join, couple; combine ‖ *intr* to connect, make connections; **empalmar con** to connect with; follow, succeed

empalme *m* splice, connection, joint, coupling; combination; (elec) joint; (rr) connection, junction

empanada *f* pie; fraud

empanadilla *f* pie

empana•do -da *adj* unlighted, unventilated ‖ *f* see **empanada**

empanar *tr* to crumb, bread; (*las tierras*) sow with wheat

empantanar *tr* to flood; obstruct

empaña•do -da *adj* dim, misty; blurred, fogged; (*voz*) flat

empañar *tr* (*a las criaturas*) to swaddle; blur, fog, dim, dull; tarnish, sully ‖ *ref* to blur, fog, dim, dull

empañetar *tr* to plaster

empapar *tr* to soak; soak up, absorb; drench ‖ *ref* to soak; be soaked; to become imbued; be surfeited

empapelado *m* papering, paper hanging; wallpaper; paper lining

empapela•dor -dora *mf* paper hanger

empapelar *tr* to wrap in paper; paper, line with paper; wallpaper; bring a criminal charge against

empaque *m* packing; look, appearance, mien; stiffness, stuffiness; brazenness

empaquetadura *f* gasket

empaquetar *tr* to pack; jam, stuff ‖ *ref* to pack; pack in; dress up

empareda•do -da *mf* recluse ‖ *m* sandwich

emparedar *tr* to wall in, confine

emparejar *tr* to pair, match; smooth, make level; even, make even; (*una puerta*) close flush ‖ *intr* to come up, come abreast; **emparejar con** to catch up with ‖ *ref* to pair, match

emparentar §2 *intr* to become related by marriage; **emparentar con** (*buena gente*) to marry into the family of; (*una familia rica*) marry into

emparrado *m* arbor, bower

emparrillar *tr* to grill

empasta•dor -dora *mf* bookbinder

empastadura *f* binding

empastar *tr* (*un diente*) to fill; (*un libro*) bind with stiff covers; convert into pasture land ‖ *ref* (Chile) to be overgrown with weeds

empaste *m* (*de diente*) filling; stiff binding

empastelar *tr* (typ) to pie

empatar *tr* (*en la votación y los juegos*) to tie; join, connect; tie, fasten ‖ *intr* to tie ‖ *ref* to tie; **empatársela a una persona** to be a match for someone; **empatárselo a una persona** (Guat, Hond) to put it over on someone

empate *m* tie, draw; (Col) penholder; (Ven) waste of time

empatía *f* empathy

empavar *tr* (Ecuad) to annoy; (Peru) to kid, razz

empavesado *m* (naut) dressing, bunting

empavesar *tr* to bedeck with flags and bunting; (*un buque*) dress; (*un monumento*) veil ‖ *ref* to become overcast

empavonar *tr* to blue; grease, spread grease over ‖ *ref* (CAm) to dress up

empecina•do -da *adj* stubborn

empecinamiento *m* stubbornness; determination

empecinar *tr* to tar; dip in pitch ‖ *ref* to be stubborn; persist

empederni•do -da *adj* hardened, inveterate; hard-hearted

empedra•do -da *adj* cloud-flecked; pockmarked; (*caballo*) dark-spotted ‖ *m* stone paving

empedrar §2 *tr* to pave with stones; bespatter

empegado *m* tarpaulin

empegar §44 *tr* to coat with pitch, dip in pitch; (*el ganado lanar*) mark with pitch

empeine *m* instep; (*de la bota*) vamp; (*enfermedad cutánea*) tetter; (*región central del hipogastrio*) pubes

empelotar *ref* to get all tangled up; get into a row; take all one's clothes off; (Mex, W-I) to fall madly in love

empella *f* vamp

empellar *tr* to push, shove

empeller §31 *tr* to push, shove

empellón *m* push, shove; **a empellones** pushing, roughly

empenachar *tr* to adorn with plumes

empeña•do -da *adj* (*disputa*) bitter, heated; **no empeñado** noncommitted

empeñar *tr* (*dar en prenda*) to pawn; (*una lucha*) launch, begin; (*prendar, hipotecar*) pledge; (*la palabra*) pledge; force, compel ‖ *ref* to commit oneself, bind oneself; go into debt; (*una lucha, una disputa*) begin, start; **empeñarse en** to engage in; persist in, insist on

empeñe•ro -ra *mf* (Mex) pawnbroker

empeño *m* pledge, engagement, commitment; (*prenda*) pawn; pawnshop; persistence, insistence; eagerness, perseverance; effort, endeavor; pledge, backer, patron; favor, protection; **con empeño** eagerly

empeño•so -sa *adj* eager, persistent

empeorar *tr* to impair, make worse ‖ *intr* & *ref* to get worse, deteriorate

empequeñecer §22 *tr* (*hacer más pequeño*) to make smaller, dwarf; (*amenguar la importancia de*) belittle ‖ *ref* to get smaller, dwarf

emperador *m* emperor; **los emperadores** the emperor and empress

empera•triz *f* (*pl* **-trices**) empress

emperchar *tr* to hang on a clothes rack

emperejilar *tr* & *ref* to dress up, spruce up

emperezar §60 *tr* to delay, put off ‖ *intr* & *ref* to get lazy

empericar §73 *ref* (Col, Ecuad) to get drunk; (Mex) to blush

emperifollar *tr & ref* to dress up gaudily

empernar *tr* to bolt

empero *conj* but, however, yet

emperrar *ref* to get stubborn

empezar §18 *tr & intr* to begin

empicar §73 *ref* to become infatuated

empicotar *tr* to pillory

empiema *m* empyema

empina·do -da *adj* high, lofty; steep; stiff, stuck-up ‖ *f* (aer) zoom, zooming; **irse a la empinada** (*un caballo*) to rear

empinar *tr* to raise, lift; tip over; (*el codo*) crook; (aer) to zoom ‖ *intr* to be a toper ‖ *ref* to stand on tiptoe; (*un caballo*) rear; tower, rise high; (aer) to zoom

empingorota·do -da *adj* influential; proud, haughty

empingorotar *tr* to put on top ‖ *ref* to climb up, get up; be stuck-up

empíre·o -a *adj & m* empyrean

empíri·co -ca *adj* empiric(al) ‖ *mf* empiricist

empizarrado *m* slate roof

empizarrar *tr* to roof with slate

emplastar *tr* to put a plaster on; put make-up on; (*un negocio*) tie up, obstruct ‖ *ref* to put make-up on; smear oneself up

emplásti·co -ca *adj* sticky

emplasto *m* plaster, poultice

emplazamiento *m* emplacement, location; (law) summons

emplazar §60 *tr* to place, locate; summon, summons

emplea·do -da *mf* employee; (*de oficina, de tienda*) clerk; **empleado público** civil servant

emplear *tr* to employ; use; (*el dinero*) invest; **estarle a uno bien empleado** to serve someone right ‖ *ref* to be employed; busy oneself; **empleárselo mal** to act up, misbehave

empleo *m* employ, employment; use; job, position, occupation

empleomanía *f* eagerness to hold public office

empleóma·no -na *mf* public officeholder, bureaucrat

emplomar *tr* to lead; line with lead; (*un techo*) cover with lead; put a lead seal on; (*un diente*) (Arg) to fill

emplumar *tr* to put a feather on; adorn with feathers; tar and feather; (Hond) to thrash; **emplumarlas** (Col) to beat it ‖ *intr* to fledge, grow feathers

emplumecer §22 *intr* to fledge, grow feathers

empobrecer §22 *tr* to impoverish ‖ *intr & ref* to become poor

empodrecer §22 *intr & ref* to rot

empolva·do -da *adj* (Mex) rusty

empolvar *tr* to cover with dust; (*el rostro*) powder ‖ *ref* to get dusty; (*el rostro*) powder; (Mex) to get rusty

empolla·do -da *adj* primed for an examination

empollar *tr* (*huevos*) to brood, hatch; (*estudiar con mucha detención*) bone up on ‖ *intr* to grind, be a grind; **empollar sobre** to bone up on ‖ *ref* to hatch; bone up on

empo·llón -llona *mf* (coll) grind

emponcha·do -da *adj* (SAm) poncho-wearing; (SAm) crafty, hypocritical; (SAm) suspicious-looking

emponzoñar *tr* to poison; corrupt

emporcar §81 *tr* to soil, dirty

emporra·do -da *adj* (*drogas*) high

empotra·do -da *adj* built-in; recessed

empotrar *tr* to embed, recess, fasten in a wall ‖ *intr & ref* to fit, interlock

emprende·dor -dora *adj* enterprising

emprender *tr* to undertake; **emprenderla con** to squabble with, have it out with; **emprenderla para** to set out for

empreñar *tr* to make pregnant ‖ *ref* to become pregnant

empresa *f* enterprise, undertaking; company, concern, firm; device, motto; (*la parte patronal*) management; **empresa anunciadora** advertising agency; **empresa de tranvías** traction company; **pequeña empresa** small business

empresarial *adj* managerial

empresa·rio -ria *mf* contractor; business leader, industrialist; manager; promoter; theatrical manager; **empresario de circo** showman; **empresario de pompas fúnebres** undertaker; **empresario de publicidad** advertising man; **empresario de teatro** impresario, theater manager

emprestar *tr* to borrow

empréstito *m* loan, government loan

empujar *tr* to push, shove; replace ‖ *intr* to push, shove

empujatierra *f* bulldozer

empuje *m* push; (*fuerza o presión ejercidas por una cosa sobre otra*) thrust; (*espíritu emprendedor*) enterprise, push

empujón *m* hard push, shove; **tratar a empujones** to push around

empuñadura *f* (*de la espada*) hilt; first words of a story; (*de bastón o paraguas*) handle

empuñar *tr* to seize, grasp, clutch; (*un empleo o puesto*) obtain; (*la mano*) (Chile) to clench; (Bol) to punch; **empuñar el bastón** (fig) to seize the reins

emular *tr & intr* to emulate; **emular con** to emulate, vie with

ému·lo -la *adj* emulous ‖ *mf* rival

emulsión *f* emulsion

emulsionar *tr* to emulsify

en *prep* at; in; into; by; on; of, e.g., **pensar en** to think of

enaceitar *tr* to oil ‖ *ref* to get oily, get rancid

enagua *f* petticoat; skirt; **enaguas** petticoat

enagüillas *fpl* kilt; short skirt

enajenación *f* alienation; estrangement; rapture; (*distracción*) absent-mindedness; **enajenación mental** mental derangement

enajenar *tr* (*la propiedad, el dominio; a un amigo*) to alienate, estrange; enrapture, transport ‖ *ref* to be enraptured, be transported; **enajenarse de** to dispossess one-

self of; (*un amigo*) become alienated from
enaltecer §22 *tr* to exalt, extol
enamoradi•zo -za *adj* susceptible
enamora•do -da *adj* lovesick; (*propenso a enamorarse*) susceptible ‖ *mf* sweetheart ‖ *m* lover
enamorar *tr* to make love to; enamor, captivate ‖ *ref* to fall in love
enamoricar §73 *ref* to trifle in love
enangostar *tr* & *ref* to narrow
ena•no -na *adj* dwarfish ‖ *mf* dwarf
enarbolar *tr* to hoist, hang out; (*una espada*) brandish ‖ *ref* to get angry; (*el caballo*) rear
enarcar §73 *tr* to arch; (*los toneles*) hoop ‖ *ref* to become confused, be bashful; (*el caballo*) (Mex) to rear
enardecer §22 *tr* to inflame, excite ‖ *ref* to get excited; (*una parte del cuerpo*) become inflamed, get sore
enarenar *tr* to throw sand on ‖ *ref* (naut) to run aground
enastar *tr* (*una herramienta*) to put a handle on; (*una bandera*) put a shaft on
encabalgamiento *m* gun carriage; trestlework; (*en el verso*) enjambment
encabalgar §44 *tr* to provide with horses ‖ *intr* to lean, rest
encaballar *tr* to overlap; (typ) to pie
encabezamiento *m* heading; (*fórmula con que comienza un documento*) opening words; tax list; tax rate; **encabezamiento de factura** billhead
encabezar §60 *tr* (*un escrito*) to put a heading or title on; head; register; (*vinos*) fortify
encabritar *ref* (*un caballo*) to rear; (*un buque*) shoot up, pitch up; (*un avión*) nose up
encadenar *tr* to chain, put in chains; brace, buttress; bind, tie together; tie down
encajar *tr* to fit, fit in, make fit; insert, put in; (*un golpe*) give, let go; (*dinero*) put away; (*un chiste*) tell at the wrong time; to palm off; throw, hurl; **encajar una cosa a uno** to foist something on someone, palm something off on someone ‖ *intr* to fit; (*una puerta*) close right ‖ *ref* to squeeze one's way; (*una prenda de vestir*) put on; butt in, intrude
encaje *m* (*tejido de mallas*) lace; (*labor de taracea*) inlay, mosaic; recess, groove; fitting, matching; insertion; appearance, look
encaje•ro -ra *mf* lacemaker; lace dealer
encajonado *m* cofferdam
encajonar *tr* to box, crate, case; squeeze in ‖ *ref* (*un río*) to narrow, narrow down; squeeze in, squeeze through
encalambrar *ref* to get cramps
encalar *tr* (*espolvorear con cal*) to lime, sprinkle with lime; (*blanquear con cal*) whitewash
encalma•do -da *adj* (*mercado de valores*) dull, quiet; (*mar, viento*) becalmed
encalvecer §22 *intr* to get bald
encalladero *m* sand bank, shoal
encallar *intr* to run aground; fail, get stuck

encallecer §22 *intr* (*la piel*) to become callous ‖ *ref* to become callous; (fig) to become callous, become hardened
encamar *tr* to spread out on the ground ‖ *ref* to take to bed; (*el grano*) droop, bend over
encaminar *tr* to direct, show the way to; (*sus esfuerzos, su atención*) direct ‖ *ref* to set out
encanalar *tr* to channel, pipe
encandecer §22 *tr* to make white-hot
encandila•do -da *adj* (*sombrero*) cocked; stiff, erect
encandilar *tr* to daze, befuddle; (*un fuego*) to stir ‖ *ref* (*los ojos*) to flash
encanecer §22 *intr* & *ref* to turn gray; get old; become moldy
encanta•do -da *adj* absent-minded, distracted; (*casa*) rambling
encanta•dor -dora *adj* charming, enchanting ‖ *mf* charmer ‖ *f* enchantress
encantamiento *m* charm, enchantment
encantar *tr* to charm, enchant, bewitch
encante *m* auction sale; auction house
encanto *m* charm, enchantment, spell
encantusar *tr* to coax, wheedle
encañada *f* gorge, ravine
encañar *tr* (*el agua*) to pipe; (*las tierras*) drain; (*las plantas*) prop up; wind on a spool
encañizada *f* reed fence; weir
encañonar *tr* to pipe; wind on a spool; (*un pliego*) (typ) to tip in
encaperuzar §60 *tr* to put a hood on ‖ *ref* to put on one's hood
encapotar *tr* to cloak ‖ *ref* to frown; cloud over, become overcast
encaprichar *ref* to insist on getting one's way; become infatuated
encaracolado *m* spiral ornament, spiral work
encara•do -da *adj* — **bien encarado** well-featured; **mal encarado** ill-featured
encaramar *tr* to raise up, lift up; praise, extol; elevate, exalt ‖ *ref* to climb, get on top; rise, tower; blush
encarar *tr* to aim, point; (*una dificultad*) face ‖ *intr* & *ref* to come face to face
encarcelar *tr* to incarcerate, imprison, jail; (*piezas de madera recién encoladas*) clamp; plaster in ‖ *ref* to stay indoors
encarecer §22 *tr* (*el precio*) to raise; raise the price of; extol; urge; overrate ‖ *intr* & *ref* to rise, rise in price
encarecidamente *adv* earnestly, insistently, eagerly
encarga•do -da *mf* agent, representative; **encargado de negocios** chargé d'affaires
encargamiento *m* duty; obligation; charge
encargar §44 *tr* (*mercancías*) to order; (*confiar*) entrust; urge; warn ‖ *ref* to take charge, be in charge
encargo *m* assignment, job, charge; (*pedido*) order; warning; **como de encargo** or **ni de encargo** just the thing, as if made to order
encariñamiento *m* endearment
encariñar *tr* to awaken love in ‖ *ref* — **encariñarse con** to become fond of, become attached to

encarnación *f* incarnation, embodiment

encarna•do -da *adj* red; Caucasian-skin-("flesh")-colored; (*de forma humana*) incarnate

encarnar *tr* to incarnate, embody; (*el anzuelo*) bait ‖ *intr* to become incarnate; (*una herida*) heal over

encarnecer §22 *intr* to put on flesh

encarniza•do -da *adj* bloodshot; bloody, fierce, bitter, hard-fought

encarnizar §60 *tr* to anger, provoke ‖ *ref* to get angry; become fierce; **encarnizarse con** or **en** to be merciless to

encaro *m* aim; stare; blunderbuss

encarrilar *tr* to put back on the rails; set right, put on the right track; guide, direct

encarruja•do -da *adj* wrinkled; (*pelo*) kinky; (*terreno*) (Mex) rough

encartar *tr* to enroll, register; outlaw; (*un naipe*) slip in ‖ *ref* to be unable to discard

encartonar *tr* to cover with cardboard; (*libros*) bind in boards

encasar *tr* (*un hueso dislocado*) to set (*a broken bone*)

encasillado *m* set of pigeonholes; (*lista de candidatos apoyados por el gobierno*) government slate; (SAm) checkerwork

encasillar *tr* to pigeonhole; sort out, classify; (*el gobierno a un candidato*) slate

encasquetar *tr* (*un sombrero*) to stick on the head; (*una idea*) drive in; force on

encasquillar *tr* to put a tip on; (*un caballo*) shoe ‖ *ref* to stick, get stuck

encastilla•do -da *adj* haughty, proud

encastillar *tr* to fortify with castles; pile up ‖ *ref* to stick, get stuck; take to the hills; stick to one's opinion

encastrar *tr* to engage, mesh

encastre *m* engaging, meshing; groove, socket; insert

encauchar *tr* to cover with rubber, line with rubber

encausar *tr* to prosecute, sue, bring to trial

encausticar §73 *tr* to wax

encáustico *m* floor wax, furniture polish

encauzar §60 *tr* (*una corriente*) to channel; guide, direct

encavar *ref* to hide, burrow

encebollado *m* beef stew with onions

encelar *tr* to make jealous ‖ *ref* to get jealous; be in rut

encella *f* cheese mold

encenagar §44 *ref* to get covered with mud; wallow in vice

encencerrar *tr* (*al ganado*) to put a bell on

encendajas *fpl* kindling, brush

encendedor *m* lighter; **encendedor de bolsillo** pocket lighter

encender §51 *tr* to light, kindle; ignite, fire to; (*la luz, la radio*) turn on; (*la lengua*) burn; stir up, excite ‖ *ref* to catch fire, ignite; become excited; blush

encendi•do -da *adj* bright, high-colored; red, flushed; keen, enthusiastic ‖ *m* ignition

encenizar §60 *tr* to cover with ashes ‖ *ref* to get covered with ashes

encepar *tr* to put in the stocks ‖ *intr* & *ref* to take deep root

encera•do -da *adj* wax, wax-colored; (*huevo*) boiled ‖ *m* oilcloth; tarpaulin; (*pizarra*) blackboard

encerar *tr* to wax ‖ *intr* & *ref* (*el grano*) to ripen, turn yellow

encerotar *tr* (*el hilo*) to wax

encerradero *m* sheepfold; (taur) bull pen

encerrar §2 *tr* to shut in; lock in, lock up; contain, include; encircle; imply ‖ *ref* to lock oneself in; go into seclusion; **encerrarse con** to be closeted with

encerrona *f* dilemma; tight spot; (coll) fix

encespedar *tr* to sod

encestar *tr* to put in a basket; (coll) to sink (*a basketball*)

encía *f* gum

encíclica *f* encyclical

enciclopedia *f* encyclopedia

enciclopédi•co -ca *adj* encyclopedic

encierro *m* locking up, confinement; inclusion; encirclement; lockup, prison; solitary confinement; retirement, retreat; (taur) bull pen

encima *adv* above, overhead, on top; at hand, here now; besides, in addition; **de encima** (Chile) in the bargain; **echarse encima** to take upon oneself; **encima de** on, upon; above, over; **por encima** hastily, superficially; **por encima de** above, over; in spite of; **quitarse de encima** to get rid of, shake off

encina *f* holm oak, evergreen oak

encinta *adj* pregnant; **dejar encinta** to make pregnant

encintado *m* curb

encintar *tr* to trim with ribbons; provide with curbs

enclaustrar *tr* to cloister; hide away

enclavar *tr* to nail; pierce, transfix; (*el pie del caballo*) prick; cheat

enclave *m* enclave

enclavijar *tr* to dowel; (*un instrumento*) to peg

enclenque *adj* sickly, feeble

enclíti•co -ca *adj* & *m* enclitic

enclocar §81 *intr* & *ref* to brood

encofrado *m* planking, timbering; (*para el hormigón*) form

encoger §17 *tr* to shrink, shrivel; discourage; draw in ‖ *intr* to shrink, shrivel ‖ *ref* to shrink, shrivel; be discouraged; be bashful; (*humillarse*) cringe; (*en la cama*) curl up; **encogerse de hombros** to shrug one's shoulders

encogi•do -da *adj* bashful, timid

encogimiento *m* shrinkage; crouch; bashfulness, timidity; **encogimiento de hombros** shrug

encojar *tr* to cripple, lame ‖ *ref* to become lame; feign illness

encolar *tr* to glue; (*la superficie que ha de pintarse*) size; (*el vino*) clarify; (*p.ej., una pelota*) throw out of reach

encolerizar §60 *tr* to anger ‖ *ref* to get angry

encomendar §2 *tr* to commend, entrust, commit; knight ‖ *ref* to commend oneself; send regards

encomiar *tr* to praise, extol

encomienda *f* charge, commission; commendation, praise; favor, protection; knight's cross; royal land grant (*with Indian inhabitants*); parcel post; (Mex) fruit stand

encomio *m* encomium

enconamiento *m* soreness; rancor, ill will

enconar *tr* to make sore, inflame; aggravate, irritate ‖ *ref* to get sore, become inflamed; (*una herida; el ánimo de uno*) rankle, fester

enconchar *ref* to draw back into one's shell, keep aloof

encono *m* rancor, ill will; (Col, Chile, Mex, W-I) soreness

encono•so -sa *adj* sore, sensitive; harmful; rancorous

encontra•do -da *adj* opposite, facing; contrary; hostile; **estar encontrados** to be at odds

encontrar *tr* to encounter, meet; (*hallar*) find ‖ *intr* to meet; collide ‖ *ref* to meet, meet each other; be, be situated; find oneself; **encontrarse con** to meet, run into

encontrón *m* bump, jolt, collision

encopeta•do -da *adj* aristocratic, of noble descent; conceited, boastful

encorajar *tr* to encourage ‖ *ref* to fly into a rage

encorajinar *ref* to fly into a rage; (Chile) to break up, go to ruin

encorchar *tr* (*botellas*) to cork; (*abejas*) to hive

encordar §61 *tr* (*un violín, una raqueta*) to string; wrap, wind up with rope

encordelar *tr* to string; tie with strings

encornudar *tr* to cuckold, make a cuckold of ‖ *intr* to grow horns

encorralar *tr* to corral

encortinar *tr* to curtain

encorvada *f* stoop, bending over; **hacer la encorvada** to malinger

encorvar *tr* to bend over ‖ *ref* to stoop, bend over; be partial, be biased

encovar §61 *tr* & *ref* to hide away

encrespar *tr* to curl; (*el pelo*) make stand on end; (*plumas*) ruffle; (*las olas*) stir up; irritate, anger ‖ *ref* to curl; bristle, stand on end; (*el mar, las olas*) get rough; get involved; bristle, get angry

encresta•do -da *adj* proud, haughty

encrucijada *f* crossroads, street intersection; ambush, snare, trap

encrudecer §22 *tr* to make raw; aggravate

encuadernación *f* bookbinding; (*taller*) bindery; **encuadernación a la holandesa** half binding

encuaderna•dor -dora *mf* bookbinder

encuadernar *tr* to bind; **sin encuadernar** unbound

encuadrar *tr* (*encerrar en un marco o cuadro*) to frame; (*incluir dentro de sí*) encompass; (*encajar*) insert, fit in; (Arg) to summarize

encuadre *m* film adaptation; (mov & telv) frame

encubar *tr* to put in a cask or vat; (min) to shore up

encubierta *f* fraud, deception

encubrimiento *m* concealment; (law) complicity

encubrir §83 *tr* to hide, conceal ‖ *ref* to hide; disguise oneself

encuentro *m* encounter, meeting; clash, collision; (*hallazgo*) find; (sport) game, match; **encuentro fronterizo** border clash; **llevarse de encuentro** (CAm, Mex, W-I) to knock down, run over; (CAm, Mex, W-I) to drag down to ruin; **mal encuentro** foul play; **salir al encuentro a** to go to meet; get ahead of; take a stand against

encuerar *tr* to strip of clothes; fleece ‖ *ref* to strip, get undressed

encuesta *f* inquiry; **encuesta demoscópica** opinion poll; survey

encuestador *m* pollster

encuitar *ref* to grieve

encumbra•do -da *adj* high, lofty; sublime; influential

encumbramiento *m* height, elevation; exaltation

encumbrar *tr* to raise, elevate; exalt ‖ *ref* to rise; be exalted; be proud; be flowery, use flowery speech; (*subir una cosa a mucha altura*) tower

encunar *tr* to cradle; catch between the horns

encurtido *m* pickle

encurtir *tr* to pickle

enchapado *m* veneer

enchapar *tr* to veneer

encharcar §73 *tr* to make a puddle of; (*el estómago*) upset ‖ *ref* to turn into a puddle; wallow in vice

enchavetar *tr* to key

enchichar *ref* (SAm) to get drunk; (CAm) to get angry

enchilada *f* (Guat, Mex) corn cake with tomato sauce seasoned with chili

enchilado *m* (Cuba, Mex) shellfish stew with chili sauce

enchilo•so -sa *adj* (CAm, Mex) spicy, hot

enchinar *tr* to pave with pebbles; (Mex) to curl ‖ *ref* (Mex) to get goose flesh

enchispar *tr* to make drunk ‖ *ref* to get drunk

enchivar *ref* (Col, Ecuad, CAm) to fly into a rage

enchufar *tr* (*un tubo o caño*) to fit; (*dos tubos o caños*) connect, connect together; (*dos negocios*) merge; (elec) to connect, plug in ‖ *intr* to fit ‖ *ref* to merge

enchufe *m* fitting; (*de tubo o caño*) male end; (*de dos*) joint; (elec) connector; (elec) plug; (elec) receptacle; sinecure, easy job; **tener enchufe** to have pull, have a drag

enchufismo *m* spoils system; wire pulling

enchufista *m* spoilsman

ende *adv* — **por ende** therefore

endeble *adj* feeble, weak; worthless

endecha *f* dirge

endechadera *f* hired mourner

endemia *f* endemic

endémi·co -ca *adj* endemic

endemonia·do -da *adj* possessed of the devil; furious, wild; (coll) devilish

endenantes *adv* recently

endentar §2 *tr & intr* to mesh

endentecer §22 *intr* to teethe

enderezar §60 *tr* to stand up; straighten; direct; put in order; regulate ‖ *intr* to go straight ‖ *ref* to stand up, straighten up; head, make one's way; go straight; (aer) to flatten out, level off

endeuda·do -da *adj* indebted

endeudamiento *m* indebtedness

endeudar *ref* to run into debt; acknowledge one's indebtedness

endevota·do -da *adj* pious, devout; fond, devoted

endiabla·do -da *adj* devilish; deformed, ugly; mean, wicked; (Arg) difficult, complicated

endilgar §44 *tr* to send, direct; to spring, unload

endiosar *tr* to deify ‖ *ref* to get stuck-up; get absorbed

endominga·do -da *adj* Sunday; all dressed up

endomingar §44 *ref* to get dressed in one's Sunday best

endosante *mf* endorser

endosar *tr* (*un documento de crédito*) to endorse; (*una cosa poco grata*) unload

endosata·rio -ria *mf* endorsee

endoso *m* endorsement

endriago *m* fabulous monster

endri·no -na *adj* sloe-colored ‖ *m* (*arbusto*) sloe, blackthron ‖ *f* (*fruto*) sloe

endrogar §44 *ref* to run into debt

endulzar §60 *tr* to sweeten; make bearable

endura·dor -dora *adj* saving, stingy

endurar *tr* to harden; delay, put off; (*tolerar*) endure; save, spare ‖ *ref* to get hard

endurecer §22 *tr* to harden; (*robustecer*, *acostumbrar*) inure

endureci·do -da *adj* hard, strong; inured; hard-hearted; tenacious, obstinate

enebrina *f* juniper berry

enebro *m* juniper

enecha·do -da *adj & mf* foundling

eneldo *m* dill

enema *f* enema

enemiga *f* enmity, hatred

enemi·go -ga *adj* enemy; hostile ‖ *mf* enemy, foe; **el enemigo malo** the Evil One ‖ *f* see **enemiga**

enemistad *f* enmity

enemistar *tr* to make an enemy of; make enemies of ‖ *ref* to become enemies

energéti·co -ca *adj* energy; power

energía *f* energy; power; **energía atómica** atomic power (or energy); **energías alternas** alternate energy sources; **energía solar** solar energy

enérgi·co -ca *adj* energetic

energúme·no -na *adj* fiendish ‖ *mf* crazy person, wild person

enero *m* January

enervar *tr* to enervate; weaken

enési·mo -ma *adj* nth

enfadadi·zo -za *adj* peevish, irritable

enfadar *tr* to annoy, bother; anger

enfado *m* annoyance, bother; anger

enfado·so -sa *adj* annoying, disagreeable

enfaldar *ref* to tuck up one's skirt

enfardar *tr* to bale, pack

énfa·sis *m* (*pl* -**sis**) emphasis; bombast, affected speech

enfasizar §60 *tr* to emphasize

enfáti·co -ca *adj* emphatic; affected

enfermar *tr* to make sick ‖ *intr* to get sick

enfermedad *f* sickness, illness, disease

enfermera *f* nurse; **enfermera ambulante** visiting nurse

enfermería *f* infirmary

enfermero *m* male nurse

enfermi·zo -za *adj* sickly; (*clima*) unhealthy

enfer·mo -ma *adj* sick, ill; (*enfermizo*) sickly; **enfermo de amor** lovesick ‖ *mf* patient

enfermo·so -sa *adj* sickly

enfiestar *ref* to have a good time

enfilar *tr* to line up; (*p.ej., perlas*) string; aim; go down, go up; (mil) to enfilade ‖ *intr* to bear

enfisema *m* emphysema

enflaquecer §22 *tr* to make thin; weaken ‖ *intr* to get thin; flag, slacken ‖ *ref* to get thin, lose weight

enflauta·do -da *adj* pompous, inflated

enflautar *tr* to blow up, inflate; cheat

enfocar §73 *tr* to focus; (fig) to size up

enfoque *m* focus, focusing; (fig) approach (*to a problem*)

enfoscar §73 *tr* to trim with mortar; patch with mortar; darken, make dark ‖ *ref* to become sullen, become grouchy; become absorbed in business; become overcast

enfrailar *tr* to make a friar or monk of ‖ *ref* to become a friar or monk

enfranque *m* shank

enfrascar §73 *tr* to bottle ‖ *ref* to become involved, intangled; be sunk in work; have a good time

enfrenar *tr* (*un caballo*) to bridle; (*un tren*) brake; check

enfrentamiento *m* (*policía, masas*) confrontation

enfrentar *tr* to put face to face; (*p.ej., al enemigo*) face ‖ *intr* to be facing ‖ *ref* to meet face to face; **enfrentarse con** to stand up to; cope with

enfrente *adv* opposite, in front; **enfrente de** opposite, in front of; opposed to

enfriadera *f* bottle cooler, ice pail

enfriar §77 *tr* to cool, chill; kill ‖ *intr & ref* to cool off

enfundar *tr* to sheathe, put in a case; stuff; (*un tambor*) muffle

enfurecer §22 *tr* to infuriate, anger ‖ *ref* to rage

enfurruñar *ref* to sulk

engalanar *tr* to adorn, deck out, dress

engalla·do -da *adj* straight, erect; haughty

engallador *m* checkrein

enganchar *tr* to hook; (*un caballo*) hitch; (*un coche de ferrocarril*) couple; recruit; inveigle ‖ *intr* to get caught ‖ *ref* to get caught; (mil) to enlist

en en

enganche *m* hook; hooking; hitching; coupling; inveigling; recruiting; enlisting; (rr) coupler

engañabo•bos *mf* (*pl* -**bos**) bamboozler

engaña•dor -**dora** *adj* deceptive; (*simpático*) winsome

engañar *tr* to deceive, cheat, fool; (*el tiempo*) while away; (*el sueño, el hambre*) ward off; wheedle ‖ *ref* to be mistaken

engañifa *f* deception, trick

engaño *m* deception, deceit, fraud; mistake; falsehood; **llamarse a engaño** to back out because of fraud

engaño•so -**sa** *adj* deceptive

engargantar *tr* (*un ave*) to stuff the throat of ‖ *intr & ref* to mesh, engage

engarzar §60 *tr* to link, string, wire; curl; enchase; (Col) to hook

engastar *tr* to enchase, mount, set

engaste *m* enchasing, mounting, setting

engatusar *tr* to coax, wheedle; inveigle

engendrar *tr* to beget, engender; (geom) to generate

engendro *m* foetus; botch, bungle; (*criatura informe*) runt, stunt; **mal engendro** (coll) young tough

engolfar *intr* to go far out in the ocean ‖ *ref* to go far out in the ocean; become deeply involved; be lost in thought

engoma•do -**da** *adj* (Chile) all dressed up ‖ *m* (CAm) hangover

engomar *tr* to gum ‖ *ref* to have a hangover

engorda *f* fattening; animals being fattened

engordar *tr* to fatten ‖ *intr* to get fat; (coll) to get fat, get rich

engorro *m* bother, nuisance, obstacle

engorro•so -**sa** *adj* annoying

engoznar *tr* to hinge, to hang on a hinge

engranaje *m* gear, gears, teeth; (fig) link, connection; **engranaje de distribución** (aut) timing gears; **engranaje de tornillo sin fin** worm gear

engranar *tr* to gear, mesh; throw into gear ‖ *intr* to gear, mesh

engrandecer §22 *tr* to amplify, enlarge, magnify; exalt, extol; enhance

engrane *m* gear; mesh

engranerar *tr* (*el grano*) to store

engrapa•dor -**dora** *mf* stapler

engrapar *tr* to clamp, cramp

engrasador *m* grease cup; **engrasador de pistón** grease gun

engrasar *tr* to grease; smear with grease

engrase *m* greasing; grease

engravar *tr* to spread gravel over

engredar *tr* to chalk, to clay

engreí•do -**da** *adj* conceited, vain

engreimiento *m* conceit, vanity

engreír §58 *tr* to make conceited; spoil, pamper ‖ *ref* to become conceited

engreña•do -**da** *adj* disheveled

engrescar §73 *tr* to incite to fight; incite to merriment ‖ *ref* to pick a fight; join in the fun

engrifar *tr* to curl, crisp ‖ *ref* to curl up; stand on end; (*un caballo*) rear

engrillar *tr* to shackle, fetter ‖ *ref* (*las patatas*) to sprout

engringar §44 *ref* to act like a foreigner

engrosar §61 *tr* to broaden; enlarge ‖ *intr* to get fat ‖ *ref* to broaden; swell, get bigger

engrudar *tr* to paste

engrudo *m* paste

engualdrapar *tr* to caparison

enguapear *ref* (Mex) to get drunk

enguirnaldar *tr* to garland, wreathe; trim, bedeck

engullir §13 *tr* to gulp down

engurrio *m* sadness, melancholy

enhebrar *tr* (*una aguja*) to thread; (*perlas*) string; (*mentiras*) rattle off

enhestar §2 *tr* to stand upright, erect; hoist, lift up

enhies•to -**ta** *adj* upright, straight, erect

enhilar *tr* to thread; direct; line up; (*ideas*) marshal ‖ *intr* to set out

enhorabuena *adv* safely, luckily; **enhorabuena que** thank heavens that ‖ *f* congratulations; **dar la enhorabuena a** to congratulate

enhoramala *adv* unluckily, under an unlucky star; **nacer enhoramala** to be born under an unlucky star; **vete enhoramala** go to the devil

enhornar *tr* to put into the oven

enigma *m* enigma, riddle, puzzle

enigmáti•co -**ca** *adj* enigmatic(al)

enjabonar *tr* to soap, lather; (*adular*) (coll) to soft-soap; (*reprender*) (coll) to upbraid

enjaezar §60 *tr* to harness, put trappings on

enjalbegado *m* whitewashing

enjalbegar §44 *tr* to whitewash; (*el rostro*) paint ‖ *ref* to paint the face

enjambrar *intr* (*las abejas*) to swarm; to multiply in great numbers

enjambre *m* swarm

enjaretado *m* grating, lattice work

enjarrar *ref* (C-R, Mex) to stand with arms akimbo

enjaular *tr* to cage; jail, lock up

enjergar §44 *tr* to launch, get started, start on a shoestring

enjoyar *tr* to adorn with jewels; set with precious stones; adorn

enjuagadien•tes *m* (*pl* -**tes**) mouthwash

enjuagar §44 *tr* to rinse, rinse out

enjuague *m* rinse; rinsing water; mouthwash; rinsing cup; (coll) plot

enjugador *m* drier; clotheshorse

enjuga•nos *m* (*pl* -**nos**) towel, hand towel

enjugaparabri•sas *m* (*pl* -**sas**) windshield wiper

enjugar §44 *tr* (*secar*) to dry; (*el sudor*) wipe, wipe off; (*lágrimas*) wipe away; (*deudas, un déficit*) wipe out ‖ *ref* to lose weight

enjuiciamiento *m* procedure; prosecution, suit; trial; judgment, sentence

enjuiciar *tr* to prosecute, sue; try; judge

enjundio•so -**sa** *adj* fatty, greasy; solid, substantial

enju•to -**ta** *adj* (*tiempo, clima; ojos*) dry; lean, skinny; quiet, stolid ‖ **enjutos** *mpl* brushwood; (*para excitar la gana de beber*) tidbits

enlabiar *tr* to entice, take in; press one's lips against

enlace *m* connection, linking; relationship; betrothal, engagement; marriage; (mil, phonet) liaison; (rr) connection, junction

enlaciar *tr, intr & ref* to wither, wilt, shrivel; rumple

enladrillado *m* brickwork; bricklaying; brick paving

enladrillar *tr* to pave with bricks

enlajado *m* (Ven) flagstone

enlajar *tr* (Ven) to pave with flagstones

enlardar *tr* to baste

enlatado *m* canning

enlatar *tr* to can; roof with tin, line with tin

enlazar §60 *tr* to connect, link; lace; (*un animal con el lazo*) lasso ‖ *intr* (p.ej., *dos trenes*) to connect ‖ *ref* to be connected, be linked; connect; get married; become related by marriage

enlechar *tr* to grout

enlistonado *m* lathing, lath

enlistonar *tr* to lath

enlodar *tr* to muddy, smear with mud; plaster with mud; seal with mud; (fig) to sling mud at

enloquecer §22 *tr* to drive crazy ‖ *intr* to go crazy

enloquecimiento *m* insanity, madness

enlosado *m* flagstone paving

enlosar *tr* to pave with flagstone

enlozar §60 *tr* to enamel

enlozado *m* enamelware

enlucido *m* plaster, coat (*of plaster*)

enlucir §45 *tr* (*una pared*) to plaster; (*la plata*) polish

enlutar *tr* to put in mourning, hang with crape; darken, sadden ‖ *ref* to dress in mourning

enmaderar *tr* to cover with boards; build the framework for

enmagrecer §22 *tr* to make thin ‖ *intr & ref* to get thin

enmalecer §22 *tr* to spoil ‖ *ref* to get full of weeds, be overgrown with weeds

enmarañar *tr* to entangle; confuse ‖ *ref* to become entangled; become overcast, get cloudy

enmarcar §73 *tr* to frame

enmarchitar *tr & ref* to wither

enmaridar *intr & ref* to take a husband

enmarillecer §22 *ref* to turn yellow, turn pale

enmasar *tr* (*tropas*) to mass

enmascarar *tr* to mask; camouflage ‖ *ref* to put on a mask; masquerade

enmasillar *tr* to putty

enmendación *f* emendation

enmendar §2 *tr* (*corregir*) to emend; (*reformar*) amend; (*resarcir*) make amends for ‖ *ref* to amend, mend one's ways, go straight

enmienda *f* (*corrección*) emendation; (*propuesta de variante*) amendment; (*satisfacción del daño hecho*) amends

enmohecer §22 *tr* to make moldy; rust; neglect ‖ *ref* to get moldy; rust; (*la memoria*) get rusty; fade away

enmontar *ref* (CAm, Mex, Col, Ven) to become overgrown with brush

enmudecer §22 *tr* to hush, silence ‖ *intr* to hush up, keep quiet; become dumb, lose one's voice

enmuescar §73 *tr* to notch; (carp) to mortise

ennegrecer §22 *tr* to blacken, dye black ‖ *ref* to turn black; (*el porvenir*) be black

ennoblecer §22 *tr* to ennoble; glorify, enhance

ennoblecimiento *m* ennoblement; glory, splendor; (*grandeza de alma*) nobility

enodio *m* fawn, young deer

enojada *f* (Mex) fit of anger

enojadi•zo -za *adj* irritable, ill-tempered

enojar *tr* to anger; annoy, vex ‖ *ref* to get angry; **enojarse con** or **contra** to get angry with (*a person*); **enojarse de** to get angry at (*a thing*)

enojo *m* anger; annoyance, bother

eno•jón -jona *adj* (Chile, Ecuad, Mex) irritable, ill-tempered

enojo•so -sa *adj* annoying, bothersome

enorgullecer §22 *tr* to fill with pride, make proud ‖ *ref* to be proud; **enorgullecerse de** to pride oneself on

enorme *adj* enormous, huge

enotecnia *f* wine making; oenology

enquiciar *tr* (*una puerta, una ventana*) to hang; fasten, make firm

enrabiar *tr* to enrage ‖ *intr* to have rabies ‖ *ref* to become enraged

enramar *tr* (*ramos*) to intertwine; adorn with branches ‖ *intr* to sprout branches ‖ *ref* to hide in the branches

enranciar *tr* to make rancid ‖ *ref* to get rancid

enrarecer §22 *tr* to rarefy; make scarce ‖ *intr* to become scarce ‖ *ref* to rarefy; become scarce

enrarecimiento *m* (p.ej., *del aire*) thinness; scarceness, scarcity

enrasar *tr* to make flush; grade, level ‖ *intr* to be flush

enratonar *ref* to get sick from eating mice; (Ven) to have a hangover

enredadera *adj* (*planta*) climbing ‖ *f* climbing plant, vine

enreda•dor -dora *mf* gossip, busybody

enredar *tr* to catch in a net; (*redes, una trampa*) set; tangle up; involve, entangle; (*una pelea*) start; intertwine, interweave; endanger, compromise ‖ *intr* to romp around, be frisky ‖ *ref* to get tangled up; get involved, become entangled; (coll) to have an affair

enredijo *m* entanglement

enredo *m* tangle; involvement, entanglement, complication; restlessness; friskiness; mischievous lie; (*de una novela, un drama*) plot; (*trato ilícito de hombre y mujer*) liaison

enre•dón -dona *adj* scheming ‖ *mf* schemer

enredo•so -sa *adj* entangled, complicated, difficult

enrejado *m* grating, trellis, latticework; iron railing; grill; openwork embroidery

enrejar *tr* to grate, lattice; (*una ventana*) put a grate on; fence with an iron grating; (*ladrillos, tablas*) pile alternately crosswise; (Mex) to darn

enrielar *tr* to make into ingots; lay rails on; put on the tracks; put on the right track

enriquecer §22 *tr* to enrich ‖ *intr* & *ref* to get rich

enrisca•do -da *adj* craggy, full of cliffs

enrizar §60 *tr* & *ref* to curl

enrocar §73 *tr* & *intr* (chess) to castle

enrodrigar §44 *tr* to prop, prop up

enrojar *tr* to redden, make red; (*el horno*) to heat up ‖ *ref* to redden, turn red

enrojecer §22 *tr* to make red; make red-hot; make blush ‖ *intr* to blush ‖ *ref* to turn red; get red-hot; flush; get sore, get inflamed

enromar *tr* to make dull, make blunt

enronquecer §22 *tr* to make hoarse ‖ *intr* & *ref* to get hoarse

enronquecimiento *m* hoarseness

enroque *m* (chess) castling

enroscar §73 *tr* to coil, twist, screw in ‖ *ref* to coil, twist

enrubiar *tr* to bleach, make blond ‖ *ref* to turn blond

enrubio *m* bleaching; bleaching lotion

enrular *tr* & *ref* (Arg) to curl

ensacar §73 *tr* to bag, put in a bag

ensaimada *f* twisted coffee cake

ensalada *f* salad; hodgepodge; fiasco, flop

ensaladera *f* salad bowl

ensalmar *tr* (*un hueso*) to set; treat or heal by incantation

ensalmo *m* incantation, spell; **como por ensalmo** as if by magic

ensalzar §60 *tr* to exalt, elevate, extol

ensamblar *tr* to assemble, join, fit together; **ensamblar a cola de milano** or **a cola de pato** to dovetail

ensanchador *m* glove stretcher

ensanchar *tr* to widen, enlarge; (*una prenda ajustada*) ease, let out; (*el corazón*) unburden ‖ *intr* & *ref* to be proud and haughty

ensanche *m* widening, extension; (*de una calle*) extension; suburban development; allowance (*for enlargement of garment*)

ensandecer §22 *intr* to go crazy

ensangrenta•do -da *adj* bloody, gory

ensangrentar §2 *tr* to bathe in blood; stain with blood ‖ *ref* to rage, go wild; (*p.ej., las manos*) bloody, make bloody

ensañar *tr* to anger, enrage ‖ *ref* to be cruel, be merciless; (*una enfermedad*) rage

ensartar *tr* (*una aguja*) to thread; (*cuentas*) string; stick; rattle off ‖ *ref* to squeeze in

ensayar *tr* to try, try on, try out; (*un espectáculo*) rehearse; (*minerales*) assay; teach, train; test ‖ *ref* to practice

ensaye *m* assay

ensayista *mf* essayist; (Chile) assayer

ensayo *m* trying, trial; testing, test; (*género literario*) essay; (*de minerales*) assay; exer-

cise, practice; (theat) rehearsal; **ensayo de choque** (aut) crash test; **ensayo general** dress rehearsal

ensenada *f* inlet, cove

enseña *f* standard, ensign

enseña•do -da *adj* trained, informed; (*perro de caza*) trained

enseñanza *f* teaching; education, instruction; (*ejemplo que sirve de experiencia*) lesson; **enseñanza superior** higher education

enseñar *tr* to teach; train; show, point out ‖ *intr* to teach

enseñorear *ref* to control oneself; **enseñorearse de** to take possession of

enseres *mpl* utensils, equipment, household goods

enseriar *ref* to become serious

ensillar *tr* to saddle

ensimismamiento *m* absorption in thought, deep thought

ensimismar *ref* to become absorbed in thought; (Chile, Ecuad, Peru) to be proud, be boastful

ensoberbecer §22 to make proud ‖ *ref* to become proud; (*el mar, las olas*) swell, get rough

ensoberbecimiento *m* haughtiness

ensombrecer §22 *tr* to darken ‖ *ref* to get dark; become sad and gloomy

ensoña•dor -dora *adj* dreamy ‖ *mf* dreamer

ensopar *tr* to dip, dunk; soak, drench

ensordece•dor -dora *adj* deafening

ensordecer §22 *tr* to deafen; (*una consonante sonora*) unvoice ‖ *intr* to become deaf; play deaf, not answer ‖ *ref* to unvoice

ensortijar *tr* to curl, make curly; (*la nariz de un animal*) ring, put a ring in ‖ *ref* to curl

ensuciar *tr* to dirty, soil; stain, smear; defile, sully ‖ *ref* to soil oneself; take bribes

ensueño *m* dream; daydream

entablado *m* flooring; wooden framework

entablar *tr* to board, board up; (*un hueso roto*) splint; (*una conversación*) start; (*p.ej., una batalla*) launch; (*un pleito*) bring; (*las piezas del ajedrez y de las damas*) set up ‖ *ref* (*el viento*) to settle

entable *m* boarding; (*en los juegos de ajedrez y damas*) position of men; (Col) business, undertaking

entablillar *tr* (*un hueso roto*) to splint

enta•blón -blona *adj* (Peru) blustering, bragging ‖ *mf* (Peru) bully

entalegar §44 *tr* to bag, put in a bag; (*dinero*) hoard

entalladura *f* carving, sculpture; engraving; slot, groove, mortise; cut, incision (*in a tree*)

entallar *tr* to carve, sculpture; engrave; notch; groove, mortise; (*un traje*) fit, tailor ‖ *intr* to take shape; (*el vestido*) fit; go well, be fitting

entallecer §22 *intr* & *ref* to shoot, sprout

entapizar §60 *tr* to tapestry, hang with tapestry; cover with a fabric; overgrow, spread over

entarimado *m* parquet, inlaid floor, hardwood floor

entarimar *tr* to parquet, to put an inlaid floor on ‖ *ref* to put on airs

entarugar §44 *tr* to pave with wooden blocks ‖ *ref* (*el sombrero*) (Ven) to stick on

ente *m* being; (coll) guy, odd fellow

enteca•do -da or **ente•co -ca** *adj* sickly, frail

enteleri•do -da *adj* shaking with cold, shaking with fright; sickly, frail

entena *f* lateen yard

entena•do -da *mf* stepchild ‖ *m* stepson ‖ *f* stepdaughter

entendederas *fpl* (coll) brains; **tener malas entendederas** (coll) to have no brains

entende•dor -dora *adj* understanding, intelligent ‖ *mf* understanding person; **al buen entendedor, pocas palabras** a word to the wise is enough

entender *m* understanding, opinion ‖ §51 *tr* to understand; intend, mean ‖ *intr* —**entender de** to be a judge of; be experienced as; **entender de razón** to listen to reason; **entender en** to be familiar with, deal with ‖ *ref* to be understood; be meant; have a secret understanding; **entenderse con** to get along with; concern; (*una mujer*) have an affair with

entendi•do -da *adj* expert, skilled; informed; **no darse por entendido** to take no notice, pretend not to understand; **los entendidos** informed sources; **un entendido en** a well-informed person in

entendimiento *m* understanding

entenebrecer §22 *tr* to darken; confuse ‖ *ref* to get dark; become confused

entera•do -da *adj* informed, posted; (Chile) conceited; (Chile) intrusive, meddlesome ‖ *mf* insider

enterar *tr* to inform, acquaint; to pay; (Arg, Chile) to complete ‖ *intr* (Chile) to get better; (Chile) to drift along ‖ *ref* to find out; to recover; **enterarse de** to find out about, become aware of

entereza *f* entirety, completeness; wholeness; perfection; fairness; constancy, fortitude; strictness

enteri•zo -za *adj* in one piece

enternece•dor -dora *adj* moving, touching

enternecer §22 *tr* to move, touch ‖ *ref* to be moved to pity

enternecimiento *m* pity, compassion

ente•ro -ra *adj* entire, whole, complete; honest, upright; firm, energetic; sound, vigorous; (*tela*) strong, heavy ‖ *m* (arith) integer; payment; (Chile) balance; **por entero** entirely, wholly, completely

enterrador *m* gravedigger

enterramiento *m* burial, interment; (*hoyo*) grave; (*monumento*) tomb

enterrar §2 *tr* to bury, inter; outlive, survive ‖ *ref* to hide away

entesar §2 *tr* to stretch, make taut

entibar *tr* to prop up, shore up ‖ *intr* to rest, lean

entibiar *tr* to cool off; temper, moderate ‖ *ref* to cool off, cool down

entidad *f* entity; importance, consequence, moment; body, organization

entierramuer•tos *m* (*pl* **-tos**) gravedigger

entierro *m* burial, interment; (*hoyo*) grave; (*monumento*) tomb; funeral; funeral cortege; buried treasure

entintar *tr* to ink; ink in; stain with ink; dye

entoldar *tr* to cover with awnings; adorn with hangings ‖ *ref* to get cloudy, become overcast; swell with pride

entomología *f* entomology

entonación *f* intonation; blowing of bellows

entona•do -da *adj* arrogant; haughty; harmonious, in tune

entonar *tr* to intone; sing in tune; (*el órgano*) blow; (*colores*) harmonize; tone, tone up; (*alabanzas*) sound ‖ *intr* to sing in tune ‖ *ref* to be puffed up with pride

entonces *adv* then ‖ *m* — **por aquel entonces** at that time

entonelar *tr* to put in barrels, put in casks

entongar §44 *tr* (Mex, W-I) to pile up, pile in rows; (Col) to drive crazy

entono *m* intoning; arrogance, haughtiness

entontecer §22 *tr* to make foolish, make stupid ‖ *intr* & *ref* to become foolish, become stupid

entorchado *m* bullion; **ganar los entorchados** to win one's stripes

entorna•do -da *adj* ajar, half-closed

entornar *tr* to half-close; (*los ojos*) squint; (*una puerta*) leave ajar; (*volcar*) upset ‖ *ref* to upset

entornillar *tr* to twist, screw up

entorno *m* environment

entorpecer §22 *tr* to stupefy; obstruct, delay; benumb; (*una cerradura, una ventana*) make stick ‖ *ref* to stick, get stuck

entortar §61 *tr* to bend, make crooked; knock out the eye of ‖ *ref* to bend, get crooked

entrada *f* entrance, entry; admission; arrival; income, receipts; admission ticket; entrance hall; (*número de personas que asisten a un espectáculo*) house; (*producto de cada función*) gate; (*amistad en alguna casa*) entree; (*naipes que guarda un jugador*) hand; (*de una comida*) entree; (*visita breve*) short call; (Col) down payment; (Mex) attack, onslaught; (elec) input; **dar entrada a** to admit; to give an opening to; (*un buque*) to give the right of entry to; **entrada de taquilla** gate; **entrada general** top gallery; **entrada llena** full house; **mucha entrada** good house, good turnout; **se prohíbe la entrada** no admittance

entra•do -da *adj* (Chile) officious, self-assertive; **entrado en años** advanced in years ‖ *f* see **entrada**

entra•dor -dora *adj* (*enamoradizo*) susceptible; (Mex) lively, energetic; (Chile) officious, self-assertive

entrama•do -da *adj* half-timbered ‖ *m* timber framework

entram•bos -bas *adj* & *pron indef* both; **entrambos a dos** both

entrampar *tr* to ensnare, trap; trick, deceive; overload with debt ‖ *ref* to get trapped; be tricked; run into debt

entrante *adj* entering; (*p.ej.*, *tren*) inbound, incoming; (*próximo, que viene*) next ‖ *mf* entrant; **entrantes y salientes** (coll) hangers-on

entraña *f* internal organ; (fig) heart, center; **entrañas** entrails; (fig) heart, feeling; (fig) disposition, temper

entrañable *adj* close, intimate

entrañar *tr* to put away deep, bury deep; involve; (*malos pensamientos*) harbor ‖ *ref* to go deep into; be buried deep; be close, be intimate

entrapajar *tr* to wrap up, bandage

entrar *tr* to bring in; overrun, invade; influence ‖ *intr* to enter, go in, come in; (*un río*) empty; (*el viento, la marea*) rise; attack; begin; **entrar a matar** (taur) to go in for the kill; **entrar en** to enter, enter into, go into; fit into; adopt, take up; **que entra** next

entre *prep* (*en medio de*) between; (*en el número de*) among; (*en el intervalo de*) in the course of; **entre manos** at hand; **entre mí** to myself; **entre que** while; **entre tanto** meanwhile; **entre Vd. y yo** between you and me

entreabier•to -ta *adj* half-open; (*puerta*) ajar

entreabrir §83 *tr* to half-open; leave ajar

entreacto *m* entr'acte

entreca•no -na *adj* graying, grayish

entrecarril *m* (Ven) gauge

entrecejo *m* space between the eyebrows; frown; **fruncir el entrecejo** to frown; **mirar con entrecejo** to frown at

entrecoger §17 *tr* to catch, seize; press hard, hold down

entrecoro *m* chancel

entrecorta•do -da *adj* broken, intermittent

entrecortar *tr* to break in on, keep interrupting

entre•cruz *m* (*pl* **-cruces**) interweaving

entrecruzar §60 *tr* & *ref* to intercross; interweave, interlace; to interbreed

entrecubiertas *fpl* between-decks

entrechocar §73 *ref* to collide, clash

entredicho *m* interdiction, prohibition; (law) injunction; (Bol) alarm bell; **poner en entredicho** to cast doubt upon

entredós *m* (*tira de encaje*) insertion; (typ) long primer

entrefilete *m* short feature, special item

entrefi•no -na *adj* medium

entrega *f* delivery; (*p.ej.*, *de una plaza fuerte*) surrender; (*cuaderno de un libro que se vende suelto*) fascicle; (*de una revista*) issue, number; **por entregas** in instalments

entregar §44 *tr* to deliver; hand over, surrender; fit in, insert; **entregarla** to die ‖ *ref* to give in, surrender; abandon oneself; to devote oneself; **entregarse de** to take possession of, take charge of

entrehierro *m* (elec) spark gap; (phys) air gap

entrelazar §60 *tr* to interlace, interweave

entremediar *tr* to put between

entremedias *adv* in between; in the meantime; **entremedias de** between; among

entremés *m* hors d'œuvre, side dish; short farce (*inserted in an auto or performed between two acts of a comedia*)

entremesear *tr* (*una conversación*) to enliven

entremeter *tr* to put in, insert ‖ *ref* to meddle, intrude, butt in

entremeti•do -da *adj* meddling, meddlesome ‖ *mf* meddler, intruder, busybody

entremezclar *tr* & *ref* to intermingle, intermix

entremorir §30 & §83 *intr* to flicker, die out

entrenador *m* (sport) coach, trainer, handler

entrenamiento *m* (sport) coaching, training

entrenar *tr* & *ref* (sport) to coach, train

entrepaño *m* (*de una puerta*) panel; (*espacio entre dos columnas, etc.*) pier; shelf

entreparecer §60 *ref* to show through

entrepiernas *fpl* crotch; patches in the crotch of trousers; (Chile) bathing trunks

entrepuentes *mpl* between-decks; (naut) steerage

entrerrenglón *m* interline; space between the lines

entrerrenglonar *tr* to write between the lines

entrerriel *m* gauge

entrerrisa *f* giggle

entrerrosca *f* (mach) nipple

entresacar §73 *tr* to pick, pick out, select; cull, sift; (*árboles; el pelo*) thin out

entresemana *adv* (SAm) weekdays; workdays

entresijo *m* secret; mystery; **tener muchos entresijos** to be mysterious, be hard to figure out

entresuelo *m* mezzanine, entresol

entretallar *tr* to carve, engrave; carve in bas-relief; do openwork in; intercept

entretanto *adv* meantime, meanwhile ‖ *m* meanwhile; **en el entretanto** in the meantime

entretecho *m* (Arg, Chile, Urug) attic, garret

entretejer *tr* to interweave

entretela *f* interlining

entretelar *tr* to interline

entretención *f* amusement, entertainment

entretener §71 *tr* to amuse, entertain; (*el tiempo*) while away; maintain, keep up; put off, delay; (*el dolor*) allay; (*el hambre*) stave off (*by taking a bite before mealtime*); try to get one's mind off ‖ *ref* to amuse oneself, be amused

entreteni•do -da *adj* amusing, entertaining; (rad) continuous, undamped ‖ *f* kept woman; **dar la entretenida a** or **dar con la entretenida a** to stall off by constant talk

entretenimiento *m* amusement, entertainment; upkeep, maintenance

entretiempo *m* in-between season; **de entretiempo** spring-and-fall (*coat*)

entreventana *f* pier

entrever §80 *tr* to glimpse, descry, catch a glimpse of; guess, suspect

entreverar *tr* to mix ‖ *ref* (Arg) to get all mixed together; (*dos grupos de caballería*) (Arg) to clash in hand-to-hand combat

entrevía *f* gauge

entrevista *f* interview

entrevistar *ref* to have an interview
entristecer §22 *tr* to sadden, make sad ‖ *ref* to sadden, become sad
entrojar *tr* to store in a granary
entrometer *tr* & *ref* var of **entremeter**
entrometi•do -da *adj* & *mf* var of **entremetido**
entronar *tr* to enthrone
entroncamiento *m* connection, relationship; (*de caminos, ferrocarriles*) junction
entroncar §73 *tr* to prove relationship between ‖ *intr* to be related; (*dos caminos, ferrocarriles, etc.*) connect
entronerar *tr* (*una bola de biliar*) to pocket
entronizar §60 *tr* to enthrone; exalt; popularize ‖ *ref* to be puffed up with pride
entronque *m* connection, relationship; (*de caminos, ferrocarriles*) junction
entruchar *tr* to decoy, trick
entru•chón -chona *adj* tricky ‖ *mf* trickster
entuerto *m* wrong, harm, injustice
entumecer §22 *tr* to make numb ‖ *ref* (*un miembro*) to get numb, go to sleep; (*el mar*) swell, get rough
entupir *tr* to stop up, clog; pack tight ‖ *ref* to get stopped up, get clogged
enturbiar *tr* to stir up, make muddy; confuse, upset
entusiasmar *tr* to enthuse, make enthusiastic ‖ *ref* to enthuse, become enthusiastic
entusiasmo *m* enthusiasm; inspiration
entusiasta *adj* enthusiastic ‖ *mf* enthusiast
entusiásti•co -ca *adj* enthusiastic
enumerar *tr* to enumerate
enunciar *tr* to enunciate, enounce
enunciati•vo -va *adj* (gram) declarative
envainar *tr* to sheathe
envalentonar *tr* to embolden, make bold ‖ *ref* to pluck up, take courage
envanecer §22 *tr* to make vain ‖ *ref* to become vain, get conceited
envanecimiento *m* vanity, conceit
envaramiento *m* stiffness
envarar *tr* to make numb, to stiffen ‖ *ref* to get stiff; get numb
envasar *tr* (*p.ej., trigo*) to pack, sack; (*p.ej., vino*) bottle; (*p.ej., pescado*) can; (*una espada*) thrust, poke; (*mucho vino*) put away ‖ *intr* to tipple
envase *m* container; bottle, jar; can; packing; bottling; canning; **envase de hojalata** tin can
envedijar *ref* to get tangled; come to blows
envejecer §22 *tr* to age, make old ‖ *intr* & *ref* to age, grow old; get out of date
envejeci•do -da *adj* old, aged; experienced, tried
envenenar *tr* to poison; (*llenar de amargura*) envenom, embitter; (*las palabras o conducta de una persona*) put an evil interpretation on ‖ *ref* to take poison
enverdecer §22 *intr* to turn green
envergadura *f* (*de las alas abiertas del ave*) spread; (*ancho de una vela*) breadth; (aer) span, wingspread; (fig) compass, spread, reach

envés *m* wrong side; (*del cuerpo humano*) back
enviado *m* envoy
enviar §77 *tr* to send; (*mercancías*) ship; **enviar a buscar** to send for; **enviar a paseo** to send on his way, dismiss without ceremony; **enviar por** to send for
enviciar *tr* to corrupt, vitiate; (*mimar*) spoil ‖ *intr* to have many leaves and little fruit ‖ *ref* to become addicted; **enviciarse con** or **en** to addict oneself to, become addicted to
envidar *tr* to bid against, bet against ‖ *intr* to bid, bet
envidia *f* envy; desire
envidiable *adj* enviable
envidiar *tr* to envy, begrudge; desire, want
envidio•so -sa *adj* envious; greedy, covetous ‖ *mf* envious person
envilecer §22 *tr* to debase, vilify, revile ‖ *ref* to degrade oneself
envío *m* sending; (*de mercancías*) shipment; (*de dinero*) remittance; (*en una obra*) autograph, inscription
envirota•do -da *adj* stiff, stuck-up
envite *m* bet; bid, offer, invitation; push, shove; (*apuesta adicional a un lance o suerte*) side bet; **al primer envite** right off, at the start
enviudar *intr* (*una mujer*) to become a widow; (*un hombre*) become a widower
envoltorio *m* bundle; (*defecto en el paño*) knot
envoltura *f* cover, wrapper, envelope; swaddling clothes
envolver §47 & §83 *tr* to wrap, wrap up; (*hilo, cinta*) wind, roll up; (*al niño*) swaddle; imply, mean; involve; envelop; (*dejar cortado y sin salida en la disputa*) floor; (mil) to encircle ‖ *ref* to become involved; have an affair
enyerbar *tr* (Col, Chile, Mex) to bewitch ‖ *ref* to be covered with grass; (Mex) to fall madly in love; (Mex) to take poison
enyesar *tr* to plaster; put in a plaster cast; (*la tierra, el vino*) gypsum
enyugar §44 *tr* to yoke
enzima *f* enzyme
enzolvar *tr* (Mex) to clog, stop up
epazote *m* (CAm, Mex) Mexican tea
E.P.D. *abbr* **en paz descanse**
epénte•sis *f* (*pl* **-sis**) epenthesis
eperlano *m* smelt
épica *f* epic poetry
epice•no -na *adj* (gram) epicene, common
épi•co -ca *adj* epic ‖ *m* epic poet ‖ *f* see **épica**
epicúre•o -a *adj* epicurean ‖ *mf* epicurean, epicure
epidemia *f* epidemic
epidémi•co -ca *adj* epidemic
epidemiología *f* epidemiology
epidermis *f* epidermis; **tener la epidermis fina** or **sensible** to be touchy
Epifanía *f* Epiphany, Twelfth-day
epígrafe *m* epigraph; inscription; headline, title; device, motto
epigrama *m* epigram
epilepsia *f* epilepsy

en
ep

epilépti•co -ca *adj & mf* epileptic
epilogar §44 *tr* to sum up, summarize
episcopalista *adj & mf* Episcopalian
episodio *m* episode
epistemología *f* epistemology
epístola *f* epistle
epitafio *m* epitaph
epíteto *m* epithet
epitomar *tr* to epitomize
epítome *m* epitome
E.P.M. *abbr* **en propia mano**
época *f* epoch; **hacer época** to be epoch-making
epopeya *f* epic, epic poem
equidad *f* equity; (*templanza habitual*) equableness; (*moderación en el precio*) reasonableness
equiláte•ro -ra *adj* equilateral
equilibra•do -da *adj* balanced; (fig) sensible, even-tempered
equilibrar *tr* to balance, equilibrate; (*el presupuesto*) balance ‖ *ref* to balance, equilibrate
equilibrio *m* equilibrium, balance, equipoise; (*del presupuesto*) balancing; **equilibrio político** balance of power
equilibrista *mf* balancer, ropedancer
equinoccial *adj* equinoctial
equinoccio *m* equinox
equipaje *m* baggage; piece of baggage; equipment; (naut) crew; **equipaje de mano** hand baggage
equipar *tr* to equip
equiparar *tr* to compare
equi•pier *m* (*pl* **-piers**) teammate
equipo *m* equipment, outfit; crew, gang; (sport) team; **equipo de alta fidelidad** stereo system; hi-fi set; **equipo de novia** trousseau; **equipo de urgencia** first-aid kit
equitación *f* horsemanship, riding
equitati•vo -va *adj* fair, equitable; (*tranquilo*) equable
equivalente *adj & m* equivalent
equivaler §76 *intr* to be equal, be equivalent
equivocación *f* mistake; mistakenness
equivoca•do -da *adj* mistaken, wrong
equivocar §73 *tr* (*una cosa por otra*) to mistake, mix ‖ *ref* to be mistaken, make a mistake; **equivocarse con** to be wrong in, take the wrong . . .
equívo•co -ca *adj* equivocal, ambiguous ‖ *m* equivocation, ambiguity; pun
equivoquista *mf* equivocator; punster
era *f* era, age; threshing floor; vegetable patch, garden bed
eral *m* two-year-old bull
erario *m* state treasury
erección *f* erection; foundation, establishment
eremita *m* hermit
ergástulo *m* dungeon, slave prison
ergio *m* erg
ergotismo *m* argumentativeness; (pathol) ergotism
ergotista *adj invar* argumentative; dogmatic; *mf* dogmatist; know-it-all

erguir §33 *tr* to raise; straighten up ‖ *ref* to straighten up; swell with pride
erial *adj* unplowed, uncultivated ‖ *m* unplowed land, uncultivated land
erigir §27 *tr* to erect, build; found, establish; (*a nueva condición*) elevate ‖ *ref*—**erigirse en** to be elevated to; set oneself up as
eriza•do -da *adj* bristling, bristly, spiny
erizar §60 *tr* to make stand on end, cause to bristle ‖ *ref* to stand on end, to bristle
erizo *m* (*mamífero*) hedgehog; (*zurrón espinoso de la castaña*) bur, thistle; (*púas de hierro que coronan lo alto de una muralla*) cheval-de-frise; (*persona de carácter áspero*) curmudgeon; **erizo de mar** (zool) sea urchin
ermita *f* hermitage
ermita•ño -ña *mf* hermit
erogación *f* (*de bienes o caudales*) distribution; expenditure; (Peru, Ven) gift, charity; (Mex) outlay
erogar §44 *tr* to distribute; (Ecuad) to contribute; (Mex) to cause
erosión *f* erosion
erosionar *tr & ref* to erode
erradicar §73 *tr* to eradicate
erra•do -da *adj* mistaken, wrong
errar §34 *tr* to miss ‖ *intr* to err, be mistaken, be wrong; wander ‖ *ref* to be mistaken, be wrong
errata *f* erratum; printer's error
erróne•o -a *adj* erroneous
error *m* error, mistake; **error de pluma** clerical error; **salvo error u omisión** barring error or omission
eructar *intr* to belch; (coll) to brag
eructo *m* belch, belching
erudición *f* erudition, learning
erudi•to -ta *adj* erudite, learned ‖ *mf* scholar, savant; **erudito a la violeta** egghead, highbrow
erugino•so -sa *adj* rusty
erumpir *intr* (*un volcán*) to erupt
erupción *f* eruption
esbel•to -ta *adj* slender, lithe, willowy
esbirro *m* bailiff, constable; (*el que ejecuta órdenes injustas*) myrmidon, henchman
esbozar §60 *tr* to sketch, outline
esbozo *m* sketch, outline
escabechar *tr* to pickle; (*el pelo, la barba*) dye; (*reprobar en un examen*) flunk; stab to death ‖ *ref* to dye one's hair; (*el pelo, la barba*) dye
escabeche *m* pickle; pickled fish; hair dye
escabel *m* stool; footstool; (*para medrar*) stepping stone
escabio•so -sa *adj* mangy
escabro•so -sa *adj* scabrous, risqué; scabrous, uneven, rough, harsh
escabuche *m* weeding hoe
escabullir §13 *ref* to slip away, sneak away; slip out, wiggle out
escafandra *f* diving suit; **escafandra espacial** space suit
escafandrista *mf* diver

escala *f* (*escalera de mano*) ladder, stepladder; (*línea graduada de instrumento*) scale; (*de buque*) call; (*de avión*) stop; (*puerto donde toca una embarcación*) port of call; (*serie de las notas musicales*) scale; **en escala de** on a scale of; **en grande escala** on a large scale; **escala móvil** (*de salarios*) sliding scale; **hacer escala** (naut) to call

escalada *f* scaling, climbing; breaking in; escalation

escalador *m* climber; (*ladrón*) burglar, housebreaker

escalación *f* escalation

escalafón *m* roster, roll, register

escalar *tr* (*subir, trepar*) to scale; break in, burglarize; (*la compuerta de la acequia*) open ‖ *intr* to climb; (naut) to call ‖ *ref* to escalate

escalato•rres *m* (*pl* **-rres**) steeplejack, human fly

escalda•do -da *adj* cautious, scared, wary; (*mujer*) lewd, loose

escaldar *tr* to scald; make red hot ‖ *ref* to get scalded; chafe

escalera *f* stairs, stairway; (*la portátil*) ladder; (*de naipes*) sequence; (*en el póker*) straight; **de escalera abajo** from below stairs, from the servants; **escalera de caracol** winding stairway; **escalera de escape** fire escape; **escalera de husillo** winding stairway; **escalera de incendios** fire escape; **escalera de mano** ladder; **escalera de salvamento** fire escape; **escalera de tijera** or **escalera doble** ladder; **escalera excusada** or **falsa** private stairs; **escalera extensible** extension ladder; **escalera hurtada** secret stairway; **escalera mecánica, móvil** or **rodante** escalator, moving stairway

escalerilla *f* low step; car step; (*en las medias*) runner; (*de naipes*) sequence; thumb index

escalfar *tr* (*huevos*) to poach; (*el pan*) bake brown

escalinata *f* stone steps, front steps

escalo *m* burglary, breaking in

escalofria•do -da *adj* chilly

escalofrío *m* chill

escalón *m* step, rung; (*grada de la escalera*) tread; (fig) step, echelon, grade; (*paso con que uno adelanta sus pretensiones*) (fig) stepping stone; (mil) echelon; (rad) stage

escalonamiento *m* ranking; gradation

escalonar *tr* to space out, spread out; (*las horas de trabajo*) stagger; (mil) to echelon

escalope *m* (*loncha delgada de carne*) scallop (*thin slice of meat*)

escalpar *tr* to scalp

escalpelo *m* scalpel

escama *f* scale; fear, suspicion

escamar *tr* (*los peces*) to scale; (coll) to frighten ‖ *ref* to be frightened

escamondar *tr* to trim, prune

escamo•so -sa *adj* scaly

escamotea•dor -dora *mf* prestidigitator; swindler

escamotear *tr* to whisk out of sight, cause to vanish; (*una carta*) palm; swipe, snitch

escampada *f* clear spell, break in rain

escampar *tr* to clear out ‖ *intr* to stop raining; ease up; **¡ya escampa!** there you go again! ‖ *ref* — **escamparse del agua** to get in out of the rain

escampavía *f* (naut) cutter, revenue cutter

escamujar *tr* (*un árbol, esp. un olivo*) to prune; (*ramas*) clear out

escanciar *tr* (*vino*) to pour, serve, drink ‖ *intr* to drink wine

escandalizar §60 *tr* to scandalize ‖ *ref* to be scandalized; be outraged, be exasperated

escándalo *m* scandal; **causar escándalo** to make a scene

escandalo•so -sa *adj* scandalous; noisy, riotous; loud, flashy

escandallo *m* (naut) sounding lead; (*del contenido de varios envases*) testing, sampling; cost accounting

escandina•vo -va *adj* & *mf* Scandinavian

escandir *tr* (*versos*) to scan

escansión *f* scansion; (telv) scanning

escaño *m* settle, bench with a back; (*en las Cortes*) seat; park bench; (Guat) nag

escañuelo *m* footstool

escapada *f* escape, flight; short trip, quick trip

escapar *tr* to free, save; (*un caballo*) drive hard ‖ *intr* to escape; flee, run away; **escapar en una tabla** to have a narrow escape ‖ *ref* to escape; flee, run away; (*el gas, el agua*) leak; **escapársele a uno** to let slip; not notice

escaparate *m* show window; (*armario con cristales*) cabinet; wardrobe, clothes closet; **escaparete de tienda** shop window

escaparatista *mf* window dresser

escapatoria *f* escape, getaway; (*de atenciones, deberes, etc.*) (fig) escape; (*efugio, pretexto*) (coll) evasion, subterfuge

escape *m* escape; flight; (*de gas, agua*) leak; (*de reloj*) escapement; (aut) exhaust valve; (aut) exhaust, exhaust pipe; **a escape** at full speed, on the run; **escape de rejilla** (rad) grid leak; **escape libre** (aut) cutout

escápula *f* shoulder blade, scapula

escaque *m* square; **escaques** chess

escarabajear *tr* to bother, worry, harass ‖ *intr* to swarm, crawl; scrawl, scribble

escarabajo *m* black beetle; (*imperfección en los tejidos*) flaw; (*persona pequeña*) runt

escaramuza *f* skirmish

escaramuzar §60 *intr* to skirmish

escarapela *f* (*divisa en forma de lazo*) cockade; dispute ending in hair pulling

escarapelar *intr* & *ref* to quarrel, wrangle

escarbadien•tes *m* (*pl* **-tes**) toothpick

escarbar *tr* (*el suelo*) to scratch, scratch up; (*la lumbre*) poke; (*los dientes, los oídos*) pick; pry into

escarcha *f* frost, hoarfrost

escarchar *tr* (*confituras*) to frost, put frosting on; (*la tierra del alfarero*) dilute with water; spangle ‖ *intr* — **escarcha** there is frost

ep
es

escardar or **escardillar** *tr* to weed, weed out
escardillo *m* weeding hoe
escariar *tr* to ream
escarlata *adj* scarlet || *f* scarlet fever
escarlatina *f* scarlet fever
escarmentar §2 *tr* to make an example of || *intr* to learn one's lesson
escarmiento *m* example, lesson, warning; caution, wisdom; punishment
escarnecer §22 *tr* to scoff at, make fun of
escarnio *m* scoff, scoffing
escarola *f* endive
escarpa *f* scarp, escarpment; (Mex) sidewalk
escarpa•do -da *adj* steep; abrupt, craggy
escarpia *f* hooked spike
escarpín *m* pump
escasamente *adv* barely; hardly
escasear *tr* to give sparingly; cut down on, avoid; bevel || *intr* to be scarce
escase•ro -ra *adj* sparing; saving, frugal; stingy || *mf* skinflint
escasez *f* (*falta de una cosa*) scarcity; (*pobreza*) need, want; (*mezquindad*) stinginess
esca•so -sa *adj* (*poco abundante*) scarce; (*no cabal*) scant; (*muy económico*) parsimonious, frugal; (*tacaño*) stingy; (*oportunidad*) dim, slim, slight; **estar escaso de** to be short of
escatimar *tr & intr* to scrimp
escena *f* (*parte del teatro donde se representan las obras*) stage; (*subdivisión de un acto*) scene; incident, episode; **poner en escena** to stage
escenario *m* stage; (*disposición de la representación*) setting; (*guión de un cine*) scenario; (*antecedentes de una persona o cosa*) background
escenarista *mf* scenarist
escéni•co -ca *adj* scenic
escenificar §73 *tr* to adapt for the stage
escépti•co -ca *adj* sceptic(al) || *mf* sceptic
Escila *f* Scylla; **entre Escila y Caribdis** between Scylla and Charybdis
Escipión *m* Scipio
escisión *f* (biol) fission; (surg) excision
esclarecer §22 *tr* to light up, brighten; explain, elucidate; ennoble || *intr* to dawn
esclareci•do -da *adj* noble, illustrious
esclavitud *f* slavery
esclavización *f* enslavement
esclavizar §60 *tr* to enslave
escla•vo -va *adj & mf* slave
escla•vón -vona *adj & mf* Slav
esclerosis múltiple *f* multiple sclerosis
esclusa *f* lock; floodgate; **esclusa de aire** caisson
esclusero *m* lock tender
escoba *f* broom
escobada *f* sweep; sweeping
escobar *tr* to sweep with a broom
escobazar §60 *tr* to sprinkle with a wet broom
escobén *m* (naut) hawse
escobilla *f* brush, whisk; gold and silver sweepings; (elec) brush
escocer §16 *intr* to smart, sting || *ref* to hurt; chafe, become chafed

esco•cés -cesa *adj* Scotch, Scottish || *mf* Scot || *m* Scotchman; (*whisky; dialecto*) Scotch; **los escoceces** the Scotch, the Scottish
Escocia *f* Scotland; **la Nueva Escocia** Nova Scotia
escofina *f* rasp
escofinar *tr* to rasp
escoger §17 *tr* to choose, pick out
escogi•do -da *adj* choice, select
escolar *adj* school || *m* pupil
escolaridad *f* schooling, school attendance; curriculum
escolimo•so -sa *adj* impatient, gruff, restless
escolta *f* escort
escoltar *tr* to escort
escollar *intr* (Arg) to run aground on a reef; (Arg, Chile) to fail
escollera *f* jetty, breakwater
escollo *m* (*peñasco a flor de agua*) reef, rock; (*peligro*) pitfall; (*obstáculo*) stumbling block
escombrar *tr* to clear out
escombro *m* (pez) mackerel; **escombros** debris, rubble, rubbish
esconder *tr* to hide, conceal; harbor, contain || *ref* to hide; lurk
escondi•do -da *adj* hidden; **a escondidas** secretly; **a escondidas de** without the knowledge of
escondite *m* hiding place; (*juego de muchachos*) hide-and-seek; **jugar al escondite** to play hide-and-seek
escondrijo *m* hiding place
escopeta *f* shotgun; **escopeta blanca** gentleman hunter; **escopeta de caza** fowling piece; **escopeta de dos cañones** double-barreled shotgun; **escopeta de viento** air rifle; **escopeta negra** professional hunter
escopetazo *m* gunshot; gunshot wound; bad news, blow; (SAm) sarcasm; insult
escoplear *tr* to chisel
escoplo *m* chisel
escorbuto *m* scurvy
escoria *f* dross, scoria, slag; (fig) dross, dregs
escorial *m* cinder bank, slag dump
escorpión *m* scorpion; **Escorpión** *m* (astr) Scorpio
escorzar §60 *tr* to foreshorten
escorzo *m* foreshortening
escota *f* (naut) sheet
escota•do -da *adj* low-neck || *m* low neck
escotadura *f* low neck, low cut in neck
escotar *tr* to cut to fit; draw water from, drain; cut low in the neck || *intr* to go Dutch
escote *m* low neck; (*encajes en el cuello de una vestidura*) tucker; **ir a escote** or **pagar a escote** to go Dutch
escotilla *f* (naut) hatchway, scuttle
escotillón *m* hatch, trap door, scuttle; (theat) trap door
escozor *m* burning, smarting, stinging; grief, sorrow
escriba *m* scribe
escribanía *f* court clerkship; desk; writing materials
escribano *m* court clerk; lawyer's clerk

escribiente *mf* clerk, office clerk; **escribiente a máquina** typist

escribir §83 *tr & intr* to write ‖ *ref* to enroll, enlist; write to each other; **no escribirse** to be impossible to describe

escriño *m* casket, jewel case; straw basket

escri•to -ta *adj* streaked ‖ *m* writing; (law) brief, writ; **poner por escrito** to write down, put in writing

escri•tor -tora *mf* writer

escritorio *m* writing desk; office; **escritorio ministro** kneehole desk, office desk; **escritorio norteamericano** rolltop desk

escritura *f* writing; script, handwriting, longhand; (law) deed, indenture; (law) sworn statement; **escritura al tacto** touch typewriting ‖ **Escritura** *f* Scripture; **Sagrada Escritura** Holy Scripture, Holy Writ

escriturar *tr* to notarize; (*p.ej., a un actor*) book ‖ *ref* (taur) to sign up for a fight

escrnía. *abbr* **escribanía**

escrno. *abbr* **escribano**

escrófula *f* scrofula

escrúpulo *m* scruple

escrupulo•so -sa *adj* scrupulous; exact

escrutar *tr* to scrutinize; (*los votos*) count

escrutinio *m* scrutiny; counting of votes

escuadra *f* (*pequeño número de personas o de soldados*) squad; (*pieza de metal para asegurar las ensambladuras*) angle iron; (*de carpintero*) square; (*de dibujante*) triangle; (nav) squadron

escuadrar *tr* (carp) to square

escuadrilla *f* (aer) squadron

escuadrón *m* (mil) squadron

escualidez *f* squalor

escuáli•do -da *adj* squalid

escualor *m* squalor

escucha *mf* listener ‖ *m* (mil) scout, vedette ‖ *f* listening; (*en un convento*) chaperon; **escuchas telefónicas** listening in on telephone conversations; wiretapping; **estar de escucha** (coll) to eavesdrop

escuchar *tr* to listen to; (*atender a*) heed; (*radiotransmisiones*) monitor ‖ *intr* to listen ‖ *ref* to like the sound of one's own voice

escudar *tr* to shield

escudero *m* esquire; nobleman; lady's page

escudete *m* escutcheon; (*refuerzo en la ropa*) gusset; (*planchuela delante de la cerradura*) escutcheon, escutcheon plate

escudilla *f* bowl

escudo *m* shield; buckler; (*delante de la cerradura*) escutcheon plate; **escudo de armas** coat of arms; **escudo térmico** (*de una cápsula espacial*) heat shield

escudriñar *tr* to scrutinize

escuela *f* school; **escuela de artes y oficios** trade school; **escuela de párvulos** kindergarten; **escuela de verano** summer school; **escuela dominical** Sunday school; **Escuela Naval Militar** Naval Academy; **escuela preparatoria** prep school; **hacer escuela** to be the leader of a school (*of thought*)

escuelante *mf* (Mex) schoolteacher ‖ *m* (Mex) schoolboy ‖ *f* (Mex) schoolgirl

escuerzo *m* toad

escue•to -ta *adj* free, unencumbered; bare, unadorned

escuintle *adj* (Mex) sickly ‖ *m* (*perro*) (Mex) mutt; (Mex) brat

esculcar §73 *tr* to frisk

esculpir *tr & intr* to sculpture, carve; engrave

escultismo *m* outdoor activities

escultista *m* outdoorsman

escultor *m* sculptor

escultora *f* sculptress

escultura *f* sculpture

escultural *adj* sculptural; statuesque

escupidera *f* cuspidor; chamber pot

escupidura *f* spit; fever blister

escupir *tr & intr* to spit

escurrepla•tos *m* (*pl* **-tos**) dish rack

escurridero *m* drainpipe; drainboard; slippery spot

escurridi•zo -za *adj* slippery

escurri•do -da *adj* narrow-hipped; abashed, confused

escurridor *m* colander

escurriduras *fpl* dregs, lees

escurrir *tr* (*una vasija; un líquido; la vajilla*) to drain; to wring, wring out; **escurrir el bulto** to duck ‖ *intr* to drip, ooze, trickle; slide, slip ‖ *ref* to drip, ooze, trickle; slide, slip; slip away; (*un reparo*) slip out

esdrúju•lo -la *adj* accented on the antepenult ‖ *m* word or verse accented on the antepenult

ese, esa *adj dem* (*pl* **esos, esas**) that (*near you*) ‖ **ese** *f* sound hole (*of violin*); **hacer eses** to reel, stagger

ése, ésa *pron dem* (*pl* **ésos, ésas**) that (*near you*); **ésa** your city

esencia *f* essence; **esencia de pera** banana oil; **quinta esencia** quintessence

esencial *adj & m* essential

esfera *f* sphere; (*del reloj*) dial

esféri•co -ca *adj* spherical ‖ *m* football

esfero *m* or **esferográfica** *f* (Col) ball-point pen

esfinge *f* sphinx; spiteful woman

esforza•do -da *adj* brave, vigorous, enterprising

esforzar §35 *tr* to strengthen, invigorate; encourage ‖ *ref* to exert oneself; strive

esfuerzo *m* effort, exertion, endeavor; courage, vigor, spirit

esfumar *tr* to stump ‖ *ref* to disappear, fade away

esgarrar *tr* (*la flema*) to try to cough up ‖ *intr* to clear the throat

esgrima *f* fencing

esgrimidura *f* fencing

esgrimir *tr* to wield, brandish; (*un argumento*) swing ‖ *intr* to fence

esgrimista *mf* (Arg, Chile, Peru) fencer; (Chile) swindler, panhandler

esguazar §60 *tr* to ford

esguazo *m* fording; ford

esguince *m* dodge, duck; (*gesto de disgusto*) frown; twist, sprain, wrench

es
es

eslabón m (*de cadena*) link; (*hierro acerado para sacar fuego de un pedernal; cilindro de acero para afilar cuchillos*) steel
eslabonar tr to link; link together, string together ‖ intr to link
eslálom m slalom
esla•vo -va adj Slav, Slavic ‖ mf Slav ‖ m (*idioma*) Slavic
esla•vón -vona adj & mf Slav
eslogan m (*consigna usada en fórmulas publicitarias*) slogan
eslora f (naut) length
eslova•co -ca adj & mf Slovak
esmaltar tr to enamel; embellish
esmalte m enamel; **esmalte para las uñas** nail polish
esmera•do -da adj careful, painstaking
esmeralda f emerald
esmerar tr to polish, shine; examine, check ‖ ref to take pains, do one's best
esmeril m emery
esmeriladora f emery wheel
esmerilar tr to grind or polish with emery
esmero m care, neatness
esmoladera f grindstone
esmoquin m tuxedo, dinner coat
esnifar tr & intr (*heroína*) to sniff
esnob adj snobbish ‖ mf (pl **esnobs**) snob
esnobismo m snobbery, snobbishness
esnobista adj snobbish
eso pron dem that; **a eso de** about; **eso es** that's it; that is; **por eso** for that reason; therefore
esófago m esophagus
espabila•do -da adj intelligent; bright
espabilar ref to know the ropes; be well informed
espaciador m space bar
espacial adj space, spatial
espaciar §77 (Arg, Chile) & regular tr to space; spread, scatter ‖ ref to expatiate; amuse oneself, relax
espacio m space; **espacio de chispa** spark gap; **espacio exterior** outer space; **espacio libre** (*entre dos cosas*) clearance; **espacio muerto** (*en el cilindro de un motor*) clearance; **por espacio de** in the space of
espacio•so -sa adj spacious, roomy; slow, deliberate
espada m swordsman; (taur) matador ‖ f sword; playing card (*representing a sword*) equivalent to spade; **entre la espada y la pared** between the devil and the deep blue sea
espadachín m swordsman; (*amigo de pendencias*) bully
espadaña f cattail, bulrush, reed mace; (*campanario*) bell gable
espadilla f (*remo que se usa como timón*) scull; (*aguja para sujetar el pelo*) bodkin; red insignia of Order of Santiago
espadín m rapier
espadón m (coll) brass hat
espagueti m spaghetti
espalar tr to shovel
espalda f back; **a espaldas de uno** behind one's back; **de espaldas a** with one's back

to; **tener buenas espaldas** to have broad shoulders; **volver las espaldas a** to turn a cold shoulder to
espaldar m (*de silla*) back; (*enrejado para plantas*) trellis, espalier
espaldarazo m slap on the back; (*ceremonia para armar caballero*) accolade; **dar el espaldarazo a** to accept, approve
espalera f trellis, espalier
espantada f (*de un animal*) sudden flight; (*desistimiento ocasionado por el miedo*) cold feet
espantadi•zo -za adj shy, skittish, scary
espantajo m scarecrow; (*persona fea*) fright
espantamos•cas m (pl -**cas**) (*para poner a los caballos*) fly net; (*aparato para asustar y alejar las moscas*) fly chaser
espantapája•ros m (pl -**ros**) scarecrow
espantar tr to scare, frighten; scare away ‖ ref to get scared; be surprised, marvel
espanto m fright, terror; (*amenaza*) threat; ghost
espantosidad f fright; frightfulness; awfulness
espanto•so -sa adj frightening, terrifying
España f Spain; **la Nueva España** New Spain (*Mexico in the early days*)
espa•ñol -ñola adj Spanish; **a la española** in the Spanish manner ‖ mf Spaniard ‖ m (*idioma*) Spanish; **los españoles** the Spanish ‖ f Spanish woman
españolería f Spanishness; hispanophilia
españolada f Spanish mannerism; Spanish remark
españolizar §60 tr to make Spanish, Hispanicize; translate into Spanish ‖ ref to become Spanish
esparadrapo m sticking plaster
esparaván m spavin
esparavel m mortarboard
esparcimiento m spreading, scattering, dissemination; diversion, relaxation; frankness, openness
esparcir §36 tr to spread, scatter; divert, relax ‖ ref to spread, scatter; disperse; take it easy, relax
espárrago m asparagus; (*perno*) stud bolt; awning pole
esparrancar §73 ref to spread one's legs wide apart
esparta•no -na adj & mf Spartan
esparto m esparto grass
espasmo m spasm
espasmódi•co -ca adj spasmodic
espásti•co -ca adj spastic
espato m spar; **espato flúor** fluor spar
espátula f spatula; putty knife
especia f spice
especia•do -da adj spicy
especial adj especial, special
especialidad f speciality; (*ramo a que se consagra una persona o negocio*) specialty
especialista mf specialist
especializar §60 tr, intr & ref to specialize
especiar tr to spice
especie f (*categoría de la clasificación biológica*) species; (*clase, género*) sort, kind;

(*caso, asunto*) matter; (*chisme, cuento*) news, rumor; appearance, pretext, show; remark; **en especie** in kind; **soltar una especie** to try to draw someone out
especie·ro -ra *mf* spice dealer ‖ *m* spice box
especificar §73 *tr* to specify; itemize
especí·co -ca *adj* specific ‖ *m* specific; patent medicine
espécimen *m* (*pl* **especímenes**) specimen
especio·so -sa *adj* (*engañoso*) specious; nice, neat, perfect
especiota *f* hoax, wild idea
espectáculo *m* spectacle; **dar un espectáculo** to make a scene; **espectáculo de atracciones** side show
especta·dor -dora *mf* witness; spectator
espectral *adj* ghostly
espectro *m* specter, phantom, ghost; (phys) spectrum
especular *tr* to check, examine; contemplate ‖ *intr* to speculate
espejear *intr* to sparkle
espejismo *m* mirage
espejo *m* mirror, looking glass; model; **espejo de cuerpo entero** full-length mirror, pier glass; **espejo de retrovisión** rear-view mirror; **espejo de vestir** full-length mirror, pier glass; **espejo retrovisor** rear-view mirror
espelunca *f* cave, cavern
espeluznante *adj* hair-raising
espera *f* wait, waiting; (*puesto para cazar*) blind, hunter's blind; composure, patience, respite; delay; (law) stay; **no tener espera** to be of the greatest urgency
esperanza *f* hope; **tener puesta su esperanza en** to pin one's faith on
esperanza·do -da *adj* hopeful (*having hope*)
esperanza·dor -dora *adj* hopeful (*giving hope*)
esperanzar §60 *tr* to give hope to
esperanzo·so -sa *adj* hopeful, full of hope
esperar *tr* (*aguardar*) to wait for, await; (*tener esperanza de conseguir*) expect, hope for; **ir a esperar** to go to meet ‖ *intr* to wait; hope; **esperar** + *inf* to hope to + *inf;* **esperar a que** to wait until; **esperar desesperando** to hope against hope; **esperar en** to put one's hope in; **esperar que** to hope that; **esperar sentado** to have a good wait
esperinque *m* smelt
esperma *f* sperm
esperpento *m* monstrosity; freak; nonsense
espesar *m* depth, thickness (*of woods*) ‖ *tr* to thicken; (*un tejido*) weave tighter ‖ *ref* to thicken, get thick or thicker
espe·so -sa *adj* thick, dirty, greasy
espesor *m* thickness; (*de un flúido, gas, masa*) density
espesura *f* thickness; (*matorral*) thicket; (*cabellera muy espesa*) shock of hair; dirtiness, greasiness
espetar *tr* to skewer; pierce, pierce through; **espetar algo a** to spring something on ‖ *ref* to be solemn, be pompous; settle down

espetón *m* (*hurgón*) poker; (*asador*) skewer, spit; jab, poke
espía *mf* spy; squealer ‖ *f* (naut) warping; (*cuerda*) (naut) warp
espiar §77 *tr* to spy on ‖ *intr* to spy; (naut) to warp
espichar *tr* to prick; (*dinero*) (Chile) to cough up; (Chile, Peru) to tap ‖ *intr* (coll) to die ‖ *ref* (Mex, W-I) to get thin
espiche *m* (*arma o instrumento puntiagudo*) prick; (naut) peg, bung
espichón *m* stab, prick
espiga *f* (bot) ear, spike; peg, pin, tenon; (*clavo sin cabeza*) brad; (*badajo*) clapper; (*de una llave*) stem
espigar §44 *tr* to glean; tenon, dowel ‖ *intr* (*los cereales*) to form ears ‖ *ref* to grow tall, shoot up
espigón *m* sharp point, spur; (*mazorca*) ear of corn; (*cerro puntiagudo*) peak; breakwater
espina *f* thorn, spine; (*de los peces*) fishbone; doubt, uncertainty; sorrow; (anat) spine; **dar mala espina a** to worry; **espina de pescado** herringbone; **espina de pez** fishbone; **espina dorsal** spinal column; **estar en espinas** to be on pins and needles
espinaca *f* spinach; **espinacas** spinach
espinal *adj* spinal
espinapez *m* herringbone; thorny matter, difficulty
espinar *m* thorny spot; (fig) thorny matter ‖ *tr* to prick; (*árboles*) protect with thornbushes; hurt, offend
espinazo *m* backbone; (*de un arco*) keystone
espinel *m* trawl, trawl line
espineta *f* spinet
espinilla *f* (*de la pierna*) shin, shinbone; (*granillo en la piel*) blackhead
espino *m* hawthorn; **espino artificial** barbed wire; **espino negro** blackthorn
espinochar *tr* (*el maíz*) to husk
espino·so -sa or **espinu·do -da** *adj* thorny; (*pez*) bony; (*difícil*) (fig) thorny, knotty
espiocha *f* pickaxe
espión *m* spy
espionaje *m* spying, espionage
espira *f* turn
espiración *f* breathing; exhalation
espiral *adj* spiral ‖ *f* (*línea curva que da vueltas alrededor de un punto*) spiral; (*del reloj*) hairspring; (*de humo*) curl, wreath
espirar *tr* to breath; encourage ‖ *intr* to breathe; exhale, expire; (*el viento*) (poet) to blow gently
espiritismo *m* spiritualism
espirito·so -sa *adj* spirited, lively; (*licor*) spirituous
espíritu *m* spirit; (*mente*) mind; (*aparecido, fantasma*) ghost, spirit; **espíritu de equipo** teamwork; **Espíritu Santo** Holy Ghost, Holy Spirit; **dar, despedir, exhalar** or **rendir el espíritu** to give up the ghost
espiritual *adj* spiritual; sharp, witty
espiritualismo *m* spiritualism
espita *f* tap, cock; (coll) tippler
espitar *tr* to tap
esplendidez *f* splendor, magnificence

es
es

espléndi·do -da *adj* splendid, magnificent; generous, open-handed; (poet) brilliant, radiant

esplendor *m* splendor

esplendoro·so -sa *adj* resplendent

espliego *m* lavender

esplín *m* melancholy

espolada *f* prick with spur; **espolada de vino** shot of wine

espolear *tr* to spur, spur on

espoleta *f* fuse; (*hueso*) wishbone

espolón *m* (*del gallo, una montaña, un buque de guerra*) spur; dike, jetty, mole, cutwater; (*prominencia córnea de las caballerías*) fetlock; (*sabañón*) chilblain

espolvorear *tr* (*quitar el polvo de; esparcir el polvo sobre*) dust; (*el azúcar*) sprinkle

esponja *f* sponge; (*sablista*) sponge, sponger; **beber como una esponja** to drink like a fish; **tirar la esponja** to throw in (or up) the sponge

esponja·do -da *adj* proud, puffed-up; fresh, healthy

esponjar *tr* to puff up, make fluffy ‖ *ref* to puff up, become fluffy; be puffed up, be conceited; look fresh and healthy

esponjo·so -sa *adj* spongy

esponsales *mpl* betrothal, engagement

espontanear *ref* to make a clean breast of it, open one's heart

espontáne·o -a *adj* spontaneous ‖ *m* (taur) spectator who jumps into the ring to take on the bull

espora *f* spore

esporádi·co -ca *adj* sporadic

esposa *f* wife; **esposas** handcuffs, manacles

esposar *tr* to handcuff, manacle

espo·so -sa *mf* spouse ‖ *m* husband ‖ *f* see **esposa**

espuela *f* spur; **echar la espuela** (coll) to take a nightcap; **espuela de caballero** delphinium, rocket larkspur; **espuela de galán** nasturtium

espuelar *tr* (SAm) to spur, goad

espuerta *f* two-handled esparto basket

espulgar §44 *tr* to delouse; scrutinize

espuma *f* foam; (*en un vaso de cerveza; saliva parecida a la espuma*) froth; (*película de impurezas en la superficie de un líquido*) scum; **crecer como espuma** to grow like weeds; to have a meteoric rise; **espuma de caucho** foam rubber; **espuma de jabón** lather; **espuma de mar** meerschaum

espumadera *f* skimmer

espumajear *intr* to froth at the mouth

espumajo·so -sa *adj* foamy, frothy

espumante *adj* foaming; (*vino*) sparkling

espumar *tr* to skim ‖ *intr* to foam, froth; (*el jabón*) lather; (*el vino*) sparkle; increase rapidly

espumarajo *m* froth, frothing at the mouth

espumilla *f* voile; (CAm, Ecuad) meringue

espumo·so -sa *adj* foamy, frothy; (*cubierto de una película*) scummy; (*jabonoso*) lathery; (*vino*) sparkling

espu·rio -ria *adj* spurious

espurrear or **espurriar** *tr* to squirt with water from the mouth

esputar *tr* & *intr* to spit

esputo *m* spit, saliva

esq. *abbr* **esquina**

esqueje *m* cutting, slip

esquela *f* note; announcement; death notice; **esquela amorosa** billet-doux

esquelétι·co -ca *adj* skeleton; skeletal, thin, wasted

esqueleto *m* skeleton; (CAm, Mex) blank form; (Chile) sketch, outline

esquema *m* scheme, diagram

es·quí *m* (*pl* **-quís**) ski; skiing; **esquí acuático** water ski; water skiing; **esquí remolcado** ski-joring

esquia·dor -dora *adj* ski ‖ *mf* skier

esquiar §77 *intr* to ski

esquiciar *tr* to sketch

esquicio *m* sketch

esquifar *tr* (naut) to fit out, staff, man

esquife *m* skiff

esquiismo *m* skiing

esquila *f* sheepshearing; hand bell

esquilar *tr* to shear, fleece

esquilimo·so -sa *adj* fastidious, squeamish

esquilmar *tr* to harvest; (*las plantas el jugo de la tierra*) drain, exhaust; (*una fuente de riqueza*) drain, squander, use up; carry away, steal

esquilmo *m* harvest, farm produce; (Mex) farm scrapings

esquilmo·so -sa *adj* fastidious

esquimal *adj* & *mf* Eskimo

esquina *f* corner; (SAm) corner store; **a la vuelta de la esquina** around the corner; **doblar la esquina** to turn the corner; **hacer esquina** (*un edificio*) to be on the corner; **las cuatro esquinas** puss in the corner

esquina·do -da *adj* sharp-cornered; difficult, unsociable

esquinar *tr* to be on the corner of; put in the corner; alienate ‖ *intr* — **esquinar con** to be on the corner of ‖ *ref* — **esquinarse con** to fall out with

esquinazo *m* corner; (Arg, Chile) serenade; **dar esquinazo a** to give the slip to, to shake off

esquinencia *f* quinsy

esquinera *f* corner piece (*of furniture*)

esquirla *f* splinter

esquirol *m* scab, strikebreaker

esquisto *m* schist

esquite *m* (CAm, Mex) popcorn

esquivar *tr* to avoid, evade, shun; dodge ‖ *ref* to withdraw; dodge

esquivez *f* aloofness, gruffness

esqui·vo -va *adj* aloof, gruff

estable *adj* stable, permanent; full-time ‖ *mf* regular guest, permanent guest

establecer §22 *tr* to establish, institute ‖ *ref* to settle, take up residence; start a business, open an office

establecimiento *m* establishment; place of business; decree, ordinance, statute

establo *m* stable

estaca *f* stake, picket, pale; cudgel, club; (*clavo largo*) spike; (hort) cutting

estacada *f* stockade, palisade; dueling ground; **dejar en la estacada** to leave in the lurch; **quedarse en la estacada** to succumb on the field of battle, fall in a duel; fail; lose out

estacar §73 *tr* to stake, stake off; tie to a stake ‖ *ref* to stand stiff

estación *f* (*cada una de las cuatro divisiones del año*) season; (*sitio en que paran los trenes; radioemisora*) station; (*lugar en que se hace alto en un paseo, etc.*) stop; **estación balnearia** bathing resort; **estación de cabeza** (rr) terminal; **estación de carga** freight station; **estación de empalme** junction; **estación de gasolina** gas station, filling station; **estación de la seca** dry season; **estación de paso** (rr) way station; **estación depuradora** sewage-disposal plant; **estación de radiodifusión** broadcasting station; **estación de seguimiento** tracking station; **estación de servicio** service station; **estación difusora** or **emisora** broadcasting station; **estación espacial** space station; **estación gasolinera** gas station, filling station; **estación meteorológica** weather station; **estación telefónica** telephone exchange

estacional *adj* seasonal

estacionamiento *m* stationing; parking; parking lot

estacionar *tr* to station; stand, park ‖ *intr* to stand, park ‖ *ref* to station oneself; be stationary; stand, park; **se prohibe estacionarse** no standing, no parking

estaciona•rio -ria *adj* stationary

estada *f* stay, stop

estadía *f* (*ante un pintor*) sitting; stop, stay; (com) demurrage

estadio *m* stadium; phase, stage; (*longitud*) furlong

estadista *mf* (*perito en estadística*) statistician ‖ *m* statesman

estadística *f* statistics

estadísti•co -ca *adj* statistical ‖ *m* statistician ‖ *f* see **estadística**

estadiunense *adj* American, United States ‖ *mf* American

estadi•zo -za *adj* (*aire*) heavy, stifling; (*agua*) stagnant

estado *m* state; state, condition, status; statement, report; **en estado de buena esperanza** or **en estado interesante** in the family way; **estado asistencial** welfare state; **estado civil** marital status; **estado de ánimo** state of mind; **estado de cuentas** (com) statement; **estado libre asociado** commonwealth; **estado llano** commons, common people; **estado mayor** (mil) staff; **estado mayor conjunto** joint chiefs of staff; **estado mayor general** general staff; **Estados Unidos** *msg* the United States; **estado tapón** buffer state; **estar en estado de guerra** to be under martial law; **los Estados Unidos** *mpl* the United States;

tomar estado to take a wife; to go into the church

estado-policía *m* (*pl* **estados-policías**) police state

estadounidense or **estadunidense** *adj* American, United States ‖ *mf* American

estafa *f* swindle, trick; (*estribo*) stirrup

estafar *tr* to swindle, trick; overcharge

estafeta *f* post, courier; post office; diplomatic mail

estallar *intr* to burst; explode; (*un incendio, una revolución; la guerra*) break out; (*la ira*) break forth

estallido *m* report, crash, explosion; crack; (*p.ej., de la guerra*) outbreak; **dar un estallido** to crash, explode

estambre *m* (*hebras de lana e hilo formado de ellas*) worsted; (bot) stamen; **estambre de la vida** course or thread of life

estampa *f* stamp, print, engraving; press, printing; footstep, track; aspect, appearance; **dar a la estampa** to publish, bring out; **parecer la estampa de la herejía** to be a sight, be a mess; **la propia estampa de** the very image of

estampado *m* printing, stamping; printed fabric, cotton print

estampar *tr* to stamp, print, engrave; (*en al ánimo*) fix, engrave; (*p.ej., el pie*) leave a mark of; (bb) to tool; (*arrojar con fuerza*) (coll) to dash, slam

estampida *f* report, crash, explosion; stampede

estampido *m* report, crash, explosion; **estampido sónico** (aer) sonic boom

estampilla *f* (*sello con letrero para estampar*) stamp; (*sello con una firma en facsímile*) rubber stamp; (*sello de correos o fiscal*) stamp

estampillar *tr* to stamp; rubber-stamp

estanca•do -da *adj* stagnant; (fig) stagnant, dead

estancar §73 *tr* to stanch; stem, check; (*un negocio*) suspend, hold up; corner; monopolize ‖ *ref* to become stagnant, become choked up

estancia *f* stay, sojourn; (*aposento*) living room; day in hospital; cost of day in hospital; (*estrofa*) stanza; (mil) bivouac; (Arg, Urug, Chile) cattle ranch; (Col) small country place; (Ven) truck farm

estanciero *m* rancher, cattle raiser

estan•co -ca *adj* stanch, watertight ‖ *m* government monopoly; cigar store, government store (*for sale of tobacco, matches, postage stamps, etc.*); archives; (Ecuad) liquor store

estándar *m* standard

estandardizar §60 or **estandarizar** §60 *tr* to standardize

estandarte *m* banner, standard

estandartizar §60 *tr* to standardize

estanque *m* basin, reservoir; pond, pool

estanque•ro -ra *mf* storekeeper, tobacconist; (Ecuad) saloonkeeper ‖ *m* reservoir tender

es
es

estanquillo *m* cigar store, government store (*for sale of tobacco, matches, postage stamps, etc.*); (Col, Ecuad) bar, saloon; (Mex) booth, stand

estante *adj* located, being; settled, permanent ‖ *m* shelf; shelving; bookcase, open bookcase

estantería *f* shelves, shelving; book stack

estañar *tr* to tin; tin-plate; solder; (Ven) to hurt, injure; (Ven) to fire

estaño *m* tin

estaquilla *f* peg, dowel, pin; (*clavo pequeño sin cabeza*) brad; (*clavo largo*) spike

estaquillar *tr* to peg, dowel; nail

estar §37 *v aux* (*to form progressive form*) to be, e.g., **están aprendiendo el español** they are learning Spanish ‖ *intr* to be; be in, be home; be ready; **¿a cuántos estamos?** what day of the month is it?; **¡está bien!** O.K.!, all right!; **estar a** to cost, sell at; **estar bien** to be well; **estar bien con** to be on good terms with; **estar de** to be (*on a temporary basis*); **estar de más** to be in the way; be unnecessary; be idle; **estar de viaje** to be on a trip; **estar mal** to be sick, be ill; **estar mal con** to be on bad terms with; **estar para** to be about to; **estar por** to be for, in favor of; to be about to; to have a mind to; to remain to be + *pp*; **estar sobre sí** to be wary, be on one's guard ‖ *ref* (*p.ej., en casa*) to stay; (*p.ej., quieto*) to keep

estarcido *m* stencil

estarcir §36 *tr* to stencil

estatal *adj* state

estáti•co **-ca** *adj* static; dumbfounded, speechless

estatificar §73 *tr* to nationalize

estatizar §60 *tr* to nationalize

estatorreactor *m* ramjet (engine)

estatua *f* statue; **quedarse hecho una estatua** to stand aghast

estatuir §20 *tr* to order, decree; establish, prove

estatura *f* stature

estatuta•rio **-ria** *adj* statutory

estatuto *m* statute

estay *m* (naut) stay; **estay mayor** (naut) mainstay

este, esta *adj dem* (*pl* **estos, estas**) this ‖ *m* east; east wind

éste, ésta *pron dem* (*pl* **éstos, éstas**) this one, this one here; the latter; **ésta** this city

estela *f* (*de un buque*) wake; (*de cohete, humo, cuerpo celeste, etc.*) trail

estenógrafo *m* (Cuba) ball-point pen

estenotipia *f* stenotypy; machine stenography

estepa *f* steppe

estera *f* mat; matting; **cargado de esteras** out of patience

esterar *tr* to cover with matting ‖ *intr* to bundle up for the cold

estercolar *m* dunghill ‖ §61 *tr* to dung, to manure

estercolero *m* manure pile, dunghill; manure collector

estereofóni•co **-ca** *adj* stereophonic, stereo

estereoscópi•co **-ca** *adj* stereoscopic, stereo

estereotipa•do **-da** *adj* stereotyped

estéril *adj* (*que no produce nada*) sterile; (*inútil, vano*) futile

esterilización *f* sterilization

esterilizar §60 *tr* to sterilize ‖ *ref* to become sterile

esterlina *adj fem* (*libra*) sterling (*pound*)

esternón *m* breastbone

estero *m* tideland; estuary; (Arg) swamp, marsh; (Chile) stream; (Col, Ven) pool, puddle

esterto *m* death rattle; (*ruido en ciertas enfermedades, perceptible por la auscultación*) stertor, râle; **estertor agónico** death rattle

esteta *mf* aesthete ‖ *f* beautician

estéti•co **-ca** *adj* aesthetic ‖ *f* aesthetics

estetoscopio *m* stethoscope

estiaje *m* low water

estiba *f* (naut) stowage

estibador *m* stevedore, longshoreman

estibar *tr* to pack, stuff; (naut) to stow

estiércol *m* dung, manure

esti•gio **-gia** *adj* Stygian ‖ **Estigia** *f* Styx

estigma *m* stigma

estigmatizar §60 *tr* to stigmatize

estilar *tr* (*una escritura*) to draw up in proper form; be given to ‖ *intr & ref* to be in fashion

estilete *m* (*puñal*) stiletto

estilo *m* style; **por el estilo** like that, of the kind; **por el estilo de** like; **estilo directo** (gram) direct discourse; **estilo indirecto** (gram) indirect discourse

estilográfica *f* fountain pen

estima *f* esteem; (naut) dead reckoning

estimable *adj* estimable; considerable; appreciable, computable; esteemed

estimación *f* esteem, estimation; estimate, evaluation

estimar *tr* (*tener en buen concepto*) to esteem; (*apreciar, valuar*) estimate; think, believe; appreciate, thank; be fond of, like; **estimar en poco** to hold in low esteem

estimativa *f* judgment; instinct

estimulante *adj & m* stimulant

estimular *tr* to stimulate

estímulo *m* stimulus

estío *m* summer

estipendio *m* stipend; wages

estípti•co **-ca** *adj* styptic; constipated; mean, stingy

estipular *tr* to stipulate

estiradamente *adv* scarcely, hardly; violently

estira•do **-da** *adj* conceited, stuck-up; prim, neat; tight, closefisted

estirar *tr* to stretch; (*alambre, metal*) draw; (*planchar ligeramente*) iron lightly; (*un escrito, discurso, cargo, etc.*) (fig) to stretch out; (*el dinero*) (fig) to stretch ‖ *ref* to stretch; put on airs

estirón *m* jerk, tug; **dar un estirón** to grow up in no time

estirpe *f* race, stock, lineage; (*linaje*) strain, pedigree

estitiquez *f* constipation

estival *adj* summer

esto *pron dem* that; **en esto** at this point; **por esto** for this reason

estocada *f* thrust, stab, lunge; (*herida*) stab, stab wound; (*cosa que ocasiona dolor*) blow

Estocolmo *f* Stockholm

estofa *f* brocade; quality, kind

estofado *m* stew

estoi•co -ca *adj & mf* stoic

estóli•do -da *adj* stupid, imbecile

estómago *m* stomach; **estómago de avestruz** iron digestion; **tener buen estómago** or **mucho estómago** to be thick-skinned; have an easy conscience

estopa *f* (*de lino o cáñamo*) tow; (*de calafatear*) (naut) oakum; **estopa de acero** steel wool; **estopa de algodón** cotton waste

estopilla *f* (*tela muy sutil*) lawn; (*tela ordinaria de algodón*) cheesecloth

estoque *m* rapier; sword lily, gladiola

estoquear *tr* to stab with a rapier

estor *m* blind, shade, window shade

estorbar *tr* to hinder, obstruct; inconvenience, bother, annoy ‖ *intr* to be in the way

estorbo *m* hindrance, obstruction; inconvenience, bother, annoyance

estorbo•so -sa *adj* hindering; bothersome, annoying

estornino *m* starling; **estornino de los pastores** grackle, myna

estornudar *intr* to sneeze

estornudo *m* sneeze, sneezing

estrado *m* (*tarima del trono*) dais; lecture platform; (archaic) lady's drawing room; **estrados** courtrooms, law courts; **citar para estrados** to subpoena

estrafala•rio -ria *adj* odd, eccentric; sloppy, sloppily dressed ‖ *mf* screwball

estragar §44 *tr* to spoil, damage, vitiate

estrago *m* damage, ruin, havoc

estrambote *m* tail (*of sonnet*)

estrambóti•co -ca *adj* odd, weird

estrangul *m* (mus) reed, mouthpiece

estrangular *tr & ref* to strangle, choke

estraperlear *intr* to deal in the black market

estraperlista *adj* black-market ‖ *mf* black-market dealer

estraperlo *m* black market

estrapontín *m* folding seat, jump seat

estratagema *f* stratagem; craftiness

estratega *m* strategist

estrategia *f* strategy; **alta estrategia** grand strategy

estratégi•co -ca *adj* strategic(al) ‖ *m* strategist

estratificar §73 *tr & ref* to stratify

estrato *m* stratum, layer

estratosfera *f* stratosphere

estraza *f* rag; brown paper

estrechar *tr* (*reducir a menor ancho*) narrow; (*apretar*) tighten; press, pursue; force, compel; hug, embrace; squeeze; **estrechar la mano a** to shake hands with ‖ *ref* to narrow down; contract; hug, embrace; (*reducir los gastos*) retrench; **estrecharse en**

to squeeze in; **estrecharse la mano** (*dos personas*) to shake hands

estrechez *f* narrowness; rightness; (*amistad íntima*) closeness, intimacy; austerity, strictness; poverty, want, need; trouble, jam; **estrechez de miras** narrow outlook, narrow-mindedness; **hallarse en gran estrechez** to be in dire straits

estre•cho -cha *adj* narrow; tight; close, intimate; austere, strict; stingy, tight; poor, needy; mean ‖ *m* (*paso angosto en el mar*) strait; fix, predicament

estrechura *f* narrowness; tightness; closeness, intimacy; austerity, strictness; trouble, predicament

estregar §66 *tr* to rub hard; scour

estregón *m* hard rub

estrella *f* star; (typ) asterisk, star; (mov & theat) star; (*hado, destino*) (fig) star; **estrella de los Alpes** edelweiss; **estrella de mar** starfish; **estrella de rabo** comet; **estrella filante** or **fugaz** shooting star; **estrella fulgurante** (astr) flare star; **estrella polar** pole-star; **estrella vespertina** evening star; **ver las estrellas** (fig) to see stars

estrella•do -da *adj* (*cielo*) starry; star-spangled; star-shaped; (*huevos*) fried

estrellamar *m* starfish

estrellar *adj* star ‖ *tr* to star, spangle with stars; (*huevos*) fry; shatter, dash to pieces ‖ *ref* to be spangled with stars; crash; **estrellarse con** to clash with

estrellón *m* large star; (*fuego artificial*) star; smash-up

estremecer §22 *tr* to shake; (*el aire*) rend; (fig) to shake, upset ‖ *ref* to shake, tremble, shiver, shudder

estrena *f* (*regalo que se da en señal de agradecimiento*) handsel; first use

estrenar *tr* to use for the first time, wear for the first time; (*un drama*) perform for the first time; (*un cine*) show for the first time; try out for the first time ‖ *ref* to make the day's first transaction; appear for the first time; (*un drama, un cine*) open

estrenista *mf* first-nighter

estreno *m* beginning, debut; première, first performance; first use

estre•nuo -nua *adj* strenuous, vigorous, enterprising

estreñimiento *m* constipation

estreñir §72 *tr* to constipate

estrépito *m* racket, crash; fuss, show

estrepito•so -sa *adj* loud, noisy, boisterous; notorious; shocking

estría *f* flute, groove

estriar §77 *tr* to flute, groove

estribar *intr* to lean, rest; be based, depend

estriberón *m* stepping stone

estribillo *m* (*de un poema*) burden, refrain; pet word, pet phrase

estribo *m* (*de coche*) step; (*de automóvil*) running board; (*apoyo para el pie*) footboard; (*para el pie del jinete*) stirrup; abutment, buttress; (fig) foundation, support;

perder los estribos to fly off the handle; lose one's head
estribor *m* starboard
estricnina *f* strychnine
estricote *m* (Ven) riotous living; **al estricote** hither and thither
estric•to -ta *adj* strict, severe, rigorous; proper, punctual; (*sentido de una palabra*) narrow
estrictura *f* (pathol) stricture
estrige *f* barn owl; (*Athene noctua*) little owl
estro *m* poetic inspiration; (*de animal*) rut, heat
estrofa *f* strophe
estroncio *m* strontium
estropajo *m* mop; dishcloth; **servir de estropajo** to be forced to do the dirty work; be treated with indifference
estropajo•so -sa *adj* raggedy, slovenly; (*carne*) tough, leathery; spluttering
estropear *tr* to spoil, ruin, damage; abuse, mistreat; cripple, maim ‖ *ref* to spoil, go to ruin; fail
estropicio *m* breakage; havoc, ruin; fracas, rumpus
estructura *f* structure
estruendo *m* noise, crash, boom; confusion, uproar; pomp, show; fame
estruendo•so -sa *adj* noisy, booming
estrujar *tr* to squeeze; press, crush, mash; bruise; rumple; drain, exhaust
estuante *adj* hot, burning
estuario *m* estuary; tideland
estucar §73 *tr* to stucco
estuco *m* stucco; **estuco de París** plaster of Paris
estuche *m* case, box; (*caja y utensilios que se guardan en ella*) kit; casket, jewel case; (*para tijeras*) sheath; **estuche de afeites** compact, vanity case; **ser un estuche** to be a handy fellow
estudia•do -da *adj* affected, studied
estudiantado *m* student body
estudiante *mf* student
estudiantil *adj* student
estudiar *tr* to study; (*la lección a una persona*) to hear (*someone's lesson*) ‖ *intr* to study; **estudiar para . . .** to study to become . . .
estudio *m* study; (*aposento*) studio; (mus) étude; **altos estudios** advanced studies
estudio•so -sa *adj* studious ‖ *m* student, scholar
estufa *f* stove; steam cabinet, steam room; foot stove; (*invernáculo*) hothouse
estul•to -ta *adj* stupid, silly, foolish
estupefac•to -ta *adj* stupefied, dumbfounded
estupen•do -da *adj* stupendous; famous, distinguished
estúpi•do -da *adj* stupid ‖ *mf* dolt
estupor *m* stupor; surprise, amazement
estuprar *tr* to rape, violate
estupro *m* rape, violation
estuque *m* stucco
esturión *m* sturgeon
etapa *f* stage; **a etapas pequeñas** by easy stages

éter *m* ether
etére•o -a *adj* ethereal
eternidad *f* eternity
eternizar §60 *tr* to prolong endlessly ‖ *ref* to be endless, be interminable
eter•no -na *adj* eternal
éti•co -ca *adj* ethical ‖ *f* ethics
etileno *m* ethylene
etilo *m* ethyl
étimo *m* etymon
etimología *f* etymology; **etimología popular** folk etymology
etíope *adj & mf* Ethiopian
etiópi•co -ca *adj & m* Ethiopic
etiqueta *f* (*marbete*) tag, label; (*ceremonial que se debe observar*) etiquette; (*ceremonia en la manera de tratarse*) formality; **de etiqueta** formal, full-dress; **de etiqueta menor** semiformal; **estar de etiqueta** to have become cool toward each other
etiquetar *tr* to tag, label
etiquete•ro -ra *adj* formal, ceremonious; full of compliments
etiquez *f* (pathol) consumption
étni•co -ca *adj* ethnic(al); (gram) gentilic
etnografía *f* ethnography
etnología *f* ethnology
E.U.A. *abbr* **Estados Unidos de América**
eucalipto *m* eucalyptus
Eucaristía *f* Eucharist
eufemismo *m* euphemism
eufemísti•co -ca *adj* euphemistic
eufonía *f* euphony
eufóni•co -ca *adj* euphonic, euphonious
euforia *f* euphoria; endurance, fortitude
eufuísmo *m* euphuism
eufuísti•co -ca *adj* euphuistic
eugenesia *f* eugenics
eunuco *m* eunuch
euritmia *f* regular pulse
euro *m* east wind
Europa *f* Europe
europe•o -a *adj & mf* European
eutanasia *f* euthanasia
eutrapelia *f* moderation; lightheartedness; simple pastime
evacuación *f* evacuation; **evacuación de basuras** garbage disposal
evacuar §21 **& regular** *tr* to evacuate; (*un trámite*) transact; (*una visita*) pay; (*un encargo, un asunto*) do, carry out; **evacuar el vientre** to have a bowel movement ‖ *intr* to evacuate; have a bowel movement
evadi•do -da *adj* escaped ‖ *mf* escapee
evadir *tr* to avoid, evade, elude ‖ *ref* to evade; escape, flee
evaluar §21 *tr* to evaluate; value
evangéli•co -ca *adj* evangelic(al)
evangelio *m* gospel, gospel truth ‖ **Evangelio** *m* Gospel, Evangel
evangelista *m* Gospel singer or chanter; (Mex) public writer, penman ‖ **Evangelista** *m* Evangelist
evaporar *tr & ref* to evaporate
evaporizar §60 *tr, intr & ref* to vaporize
evasión *f* (*efugio, evasiva*) evasion; (*fuga*) escape

evasi•vo -va *adj* evasive ‖ *f* loophole, pretext, excuse

evento *m* chance, happening, contingency; (Col) sports event; **a todo evento** in any event

eventual *adj* contingent; (*emolumentos; gastos*) incidental

eventualidad *f* eventuality, contingency; uncertainty

evidencia *f* evidence, obviousness; (*prueba judicial*) evidence; **evidencia moral** moral certainty

evidenciar *tr* to show, make evident

evidente *adj* evident, obvious

evitable *adj* avoidable

evitación *f* avoidance; prevention

evitar *tr* to avoid, shun; (*p.ej., el polvo*) keep off; prevent; **evitar + inf** to avoid + ger; save from + ger, e.g., **la luz de la luna nos evitó tener que encender los faroles** the light of the moon saved us from having to light the lights

evo *m* (poet) age, aeon; (theol) eternity

evocar §73 *tr* to evoke; (*p.ej., los demonios*) invoke

evolución *f* evolution; change, development (*of one's point of view, plans, conduct, etc.*)

evolucionar *intr* to evolve; change, develop; (mil & nav) to maneuver

evolucionista *adj & mf* evolutionist; evolutionary

ex *adj* ex- (*former*), e.g., **el ex presidente** the ex-president

ex abrupto *adv* brashly ‖ *m* brash remark

exacción *f* (*de impuestos, deudas, multas, etc.*) exaction, levy; (*cobro injusto*) extortion

exacerbar *tr* to exacerbate, aggravate

exactitud *f* exactness; punctuality

exac•to -ta *adj* exact; punctual, faithful ‖ **exacto** *interj* right!

exactor *m* tax collector

exagerar *tr* to exaggerate

exalta•do -da *adj* exalted; extreme, hotheaded; wrought-up; radical

exaltar *tr* to exalt; extol ‖ *ref* to be wrought-up, get excited

examen *m* examination; **examen de ingreso** entrance examination; **sufrir un examen** to take an examination

examinar *tr* to examine; inspect ‖ *ref* to take an examination; **examinarse de ingreso** to take entrance examinations

exangüe *adj* bloodless; weak, exhausted; dead

exánime *adj* (*sin vida*) lifeless; (*desmayado*) faint, in a faint, lifeless

exasperar *tr* to exasperate

Exc.ª *abbr* **Excelencia**

excandecer §22 *tr* to incense, enrage

excarcelación *f* release

excarcelar *tr* (*a un preso*) to release

excavadora *f* power shovel

excavar *tr* to excavate; loosen soil around

excedente *adj* excess; excessive; on leave ‖ *m* excess, surplus; **excedente de ganancia** profit margin

exceder *tr* (*ser mayor que*) to exceed; (*aventajar*) excel ‖ *ref* to go too far, go to extremes; **excederse a sí mismo** to outdo oneself

excelencia *f* excellence, excellency; **por excelencia** par excellence; **Su Excelencia** Your Excellency

excelente *adj* excellent

excel•so -sa *adj* lofty, sublime ‖ **el Excelso** the Most High

excéntrica *f* eccentric

excentricidad *f* eccentricity

excéntri•co -ca *adj* eccentric; (*barrio*) outlying ‖ *mf* eccentric ‖ *f* see **excéntrica**

excepción *f* exception; **a excepción de** with the exception of

excepcional *adj* exceptional

excepto *prep* except

exceptuar §21 *tr* to except; (*eximir*) exempt

excerpta or **excerta** *adj* excerpt

excesi•vo -va *adj* excessive; excess

exceso *m* excess; **exceso de equipaje** excess baggage; **exceso de peso** excess weight; **exceso de velocidad** speeding

excitable *adj* excitable

excitación *f* excitement; excitation

excitante *adj & m* stimulant

excitar *tr* to excite, stir up, stimulate ‖ *ref* to become excited

exclamación *f* exclamation

exclamar *tr & intr* to exclaim

exclaustrar *tr* (*a un religioso*) to secularize

excluir §20 *tr* to exclude

exclusión *f* exclusion; **con exclusión de** to the exclusion of; **exclusión de contribución** tax deduction

exclusiva *f* rejection, turndown; sole right, monopoly; (*anticipación de una noticia por un periódico*) news beat

exclusive *adv* exclusively ‖ *prep* exclusive of, not counting

exclusivista *adj* exclusive, clannish ‖ *mf* snob

exclusi•vo -va *adj* exclusive ‖ *f* see **exclusiva**

Exc.mo *abbr* **Excelentísimo**

ex combatiente *m* ex-serviceman

excomulgar §44 *tr* to excommunicate; ostracize, banish

excomunión *f* excommunication

excoriar *tr* to skin ‖ *ref* to skin oneself; (*p.ej., el codo*) skin

excrementar *intr* to have a bowel movement

excremento *m* excrement

exculpar *tr* to exculpate, exonerate

excursión *f* excursion, outing

excursionista *mf* excursionist, tourist

excusa *f* excuse; **a excusa** secretly; **excusa es decir** it is unnecessary to say

excusabaraja *f* basket with lid

excusable *adj* excusable; avoidable

excusadamente *adv* unnecessarily

excusa•do -da *adj* exempt; unnecessary; private, set apart; (*puerta*) side ‖ *m* toilet

excusa•lí *m* (*pl* **-líes**) small apron

es
ex

excusar *tr* to excuse; exempt; avoid; prevent; make unnecessary; **excusar** + *inf* to not have to + *inf* ‖ *ref* to excuse oneself; apologize; **excusarse de** + *inf* to decline to + *inf*

exención *f* exemption

exencionar *tr* to exempt

exentamente *adv* freely; frankly, simply

exentar *tr* to exempt

exen•to -ta *adj* exempt; open, unobstructed; free, disengaged

exequias *fpl* obsequies

exfolia•dor -dora *adj* tear-off

exhalación *f* exhalation; flash of lightning; shooting star; fume, vapor; **como una exhalación** like a flash of lightning

exhalar *tr* to exhale, emit; (*suspiros, quejas*) breathe forth; **exhalar el último suspiro** to breathe one's last ‖ *ref* to exhale; (*con el ejercicio violento del cuerpo*) breathe hard; hurry; crave

exhausti•vo -va *adj* exhaustive

exhaus•to -ta *adj* exhausted; wasted away

exheredar *tr* to disinherit

exhibición *f* exhibition; exhibit; **exhibición repetida** (telv) rerun

exhibición-venta *f* sales exhibit

exhibir *tr* to exhibit; (Mex) to pay ‖ *ref* to make oneself evident

exhilarante *adj* exhilarating; (*gas*) laughing

exhortar *tr* to exhort

exhumar *tr* to exhume

exigencia *f* exigency, requirement

exigente *adj* exigent, demanding

exigir §27 *tr* to exact, require, demand

exi•guo -gua *adj* meager, scanty

exila•do -da *adj* & *mf* exile

exi•mio -mia *adj* choice, select, superior; distinguished

eximir *tr* to exempt

existencia *f* existence; **en existencia** in stock; **existencias** (com) stock

existente *adj* existing, extant; in stock

existir *intr* to exist

exitazo *m* smash hit

exitista *adj* (Arg) me-too ‖ *mf* (Arg) me-tooer

éxito *m* (*resultado feliz*) success; (*canción, cine, etc. que ha tenido mucho éxito*) hit; (*resultado de un negocio*) outcome, result; **éxito de librería** best seller; **éxito de taquilla** box-office hit, good box office; **éxito de venta** best seller; **éxito rotundo** smash hit

exito•so -sa *adj* (Arg) successful

ex li•bris *m* (*pl* **-bris**) bookplate

exobiología *f* exobiology

éxodo *m* exodus; **éxodo de técnicos** brain drain

exonerar *tr* to exonerate, relieve; discharge, dismiss; **exonerar el vientre** to have a bowel movement

exorar *tr* to beg, entreat

exorbitante *adj* exorbitant

exorcizar §60 *tr* to exorcise

exornar *tr* to adorn, embellish

exóti•co -ca *adj* exotic; striking, stunning, glamorous

expandir *tr* & *ref* (Arg, Chile) to expand, extend, spread

expansión *f* expansion; (*manifestación efusiva*) expansiveness; (*difusión de una opinión*) spread; rest, recreation

expansionar *ref* to expand; open one's heart; relax, take it easy

expansi•vo -va *adj* expansive

expatria•do -da *adj* & *mf* expatriate

expectación *f* expectancy; **expectación de vida** life expectancy

expectativa *f* expectation; **estar en la expectativa de** to be expecting, be on the lookout for

expectorar *tr* & *intr* to expectorate

expediar *tr* to expedite; handle without delay; rush, speed

expedición *f* (*excursión para realizar una empresa*) expedition; (*remesa*) shipment; (*de un certificado, títulos, etc.*) issuance; (*agilidad, facilidad*) expedition

expedi•dor -dora *mf* sender, shipper

expediente *m* expedient; makeshift, apology; (*agilidad, facilidad*) expedition; (*todos los papeles correspondientes a un asunto*) dossier; (law) action, proceedings; **expediente académico** (educ) record

expedienteo *m* red tape

expedir §50 *tr* to send, ship, remit; (*títulos*) issue; (*despachar, cursar*) expedite

expediti *tr* to expedite

expediti•vo -va *adj* expeditious

expedi•to -ta *adj* ready; clear, open, unencumbered

expeler *tr* to expel, eject

expende•dor -dora *mf* dealer, retailer; ticket agent; **expendedor de moneda falsa** distributor of counterfeit money

expendeduría *f* cigar store (*for sale of state-monopolized articles*)

expender *tr* to spend; dispense; sell at retail; (*moneda falsa*) circulate

expendio *m* shop, store; retail; (Mex) cigar store

expensar *tr* (Chile, Guat, Mex) to pay the cost of

expensas *fpl* expenses

experiencia *f* (*enseñanza que se adquiere con la práctica o con el vivir; suceso en que uno ha participado, cosa que uno ha experimentado*) experience; (*ensayo, experimento*) experiment

experimenta•do -da *adj* experienced

experimentar *tr* to experience, undergo, feel; test, try, try out ‖ *intr* to experiment

experimento *m* experiment; **experimento piloto** pilot test, pilot run

exper•to -ta *adj* & *m* expert

expiación *f* expiation, atonement; purification

expiar §77 *tr* to expiate, atone for; purify

expirar *intr* to expire

explanación *f* grading, leveling; explanation

explanada *f* esplanade

explanar *tr* to grade, level; explain

explayar *tr* to enlarge, extend ‖ *ref* to spread out, extend; go for an outing; expatiate, talk at length; **explayarse con** to unbosom oneself to

explicación f explanation

explicar §73 tr to explain; (exponer) expound; (exculpar) explain away; (una clase) teach ‖ intr to explain ‖ ref to explain oneself; understand, make out

explicati•vo -va adj explanatory

explíci•to -ta adj explicit

exploración f exploration; (mil) scouting; (telv) scanning

explora•dor -dora mf explorer ‖ m boy scout; (mil) scout

explorar tr to explore; (mil) to scout; (telv) to scan

explosión f explosion; (de gases en un motor) combustion

explosi•vo -va adj & m explosive ‖ ‖ f (phonet) explosive

explotación f operation, running; exploitation; **explotación abusiva** (geol) overexploitation (of resources)

explotar tr to operate, run; (una mina) work; exploit ‖ intr to explode

exponente m exponent; (fig) interpreter, apologist

exponer §54 tr to expose; (explicar) expound; (a un niño recién nacido) abandon ‖ intr to display, show, exhibit; (eccl) to expose the Host ‖ ref to expose oneself; be on view

exportación f exportation, export; (mercaderías que se exportan) exports

exporta•dor -dora mf exporter

exportar tr & intr to export

exposición f exposition; (a un peligro; con relación a los puntos cardinales) exposure; (phot) exposure; (rhet) exposition; **exposición universal** world's fair

exposición-venta f sales exhibit

exposímetro m light meter

expósi•to -ta mf foundling

exposi•tor -tora mf exhibitor

exprés m express train; (Mex) express company

expresa•do -da adj above-mentioned

expresamente adv express, expressly

expresar tr to express ‖ ref to express oneself

expresión f expression; (acción de exprimir) squeezing; (zumo exprimido) juice; **expresiones** regards

expresi•vo -va adj expressive; kind, affectionate

expre•so -sa adj express ‖ m (tren muy rápido; correo extraordinario) express; express company

exprimidera f squeezer; **exprimidera de naranjas** orange squeezer

exprimi•do -da adj lean, skinny; stiff, stuck-up; affected, prim, prudish

exprimidor m wringer; squeezer; **exprimidor de ropa** clothes wringer

exprimir tr to squeeze, press; (p.ej., la ropa blanca) wring, wring out; (extraer apretando) express

ex profeso adv on purpose

expropiar tr to expropriate

expues•to -ta adj dangerous, hazardous

expugnar tr to take by storm

expulsanie•ves m (pl -ves) snowplow

expulsar tr to expel

expulsión f expulsion

expurgar §44 tr to expurgate

exquisi•to -ta adj exquisite

extasiar §77 & **regular** ref to go into ecstasy

éxta•sis m (pl -sis) ecstasy

extáti•co -ca adj ecstatic

extemporal adj unseasonable

extemporáne•o -a adj unseasonable; untimely, inopportune

extender §51 tr to extend, stretch out, spread out; spread; (un documento) draw up ‖ ref to extend, stretch out; spread; **extenderse a** or **hasta** to amount to

extendidamente adv at length, in detail

extensión f extension; (vasta superficie, p.ej., del océano) expanse; (alcance, importancia) extent; extending

extensi•vo -va adj extensive; **hacer extensivos a** to extend (e.g., good wishes) to

exten•so -sa adj extensive, extended, vast; **por extenso** at length, in detail

extenuar §21 tr to weaken, emaciate

exterior adj exterior, outer, outside; foreign ‖ m exterior, outside; appearance, bearing; **al exterior** or **a lo exterior** on the outside; outwardly; **del exterior** from abroad; **en el exterior** on the outside; abroad; **en exteriores** (mov) on location

exterioridad f externals, outward appearance; **exterioridades** pomp, show

exteriorista adj outgoing, outgiving ‖ mf extrovert

exteriorizar §60 tr to reveal ‖ ref to unbosom one's heart

exterminar tr to exterminate

exterminio m extermination

exter•no -na adj external ‖ mf day pupil

extinción f extinction; cancellation, elimination

extinguidor m (SAm) (incendios) fire extinguisher

extinguir §29 tr to extinguish, put out; wipe out, put an end to; fulfil, carry out; (un plazo, un tiempo) spend, serve ‖ ref to be extinguished, go out; come to an end

extin•to -ta adj (volcán) extinct; deceased ‖ mf deceased

extintor m fire extinguisher; **extintor de espuma** foam extinguisher; **extintor de granada** fire grenade

extirpar tr to extirpate, eradicate

extorno m premium adjustment (based on change in policy)

extorsión f extortion; harm, damage

extorsionar tr to harm, damage; extort

extra adj extra; **extra de** in addition to, besides ‖ mf (theat) extra ‖ m (de un periódico) extra; extra, bonus

extracción f extraction; (en la lotería) drawing numbers; **extracción de raíces** (math) evolution

extractar tr (un escrito) to abstract

extracto *m* (*de un escrito*) abstract; (pharm) extract

extractor *m* extractor; remover; **extractor de aire** ventilator; **extractor de humos** smoke evacuator

extracurricular *adj* extracurricular

extradición *f* extradition

extraer §75 *tr* to extract; pull; (*la raíz*) (math) to extract

extrafuerte *adj* heavy-duty

extragalácti•co -ca *adj* extragalactic

extralimitar *ref* to go too far

extramural *adj* extramural

extanjerismo *m* borrowing

extranje•ro -ra *adj* foreign, alien ‖ *mf* foreigner, alien; **extranjero enemigo** enemy alien ‖ *m* foreign country; **al extranjero** abroad; **del extranjero** from abroad; **en el extranjero** abroad

extrañar *tr* to banish, expatriate; surprise; find strange; miss ‖ *ref* to be surprised; refuse

extrañeza *f* strangeness, peculiarity; (*desavenencia*) estrangement; wonder, surprise

extra•ño -ña *adj* foreign; (*raro, singular*) strange; extraneous; **extraño a** unconnected with ‖ *mf* foreigner

extraoficial *adj* unofficial

extraordina•rio -ria *adj* extraordinary; extra, special ‖ *m* extra dish; special mail; (*de un periódico*) extra

extrapla•no -na *adj* extra-flat

extrapolar *tr & intr* to extrapolate

extrarradio *m* outer edge of town

extrasensorial *adj* extrasensory

extraterrestre *adj* extraterrestrial; otherworldly

extravagancia *f* (*singularidad, ridiculez*) extravagance, wildness, folly

extravagante *adj* (*singular, ridículo*) extravagant, wild, foolish; (*correspondencia en la casa de correos*) in transit

extravia•do -da *adj* lost, misplaced; astray, gone astray; (*lugar*) out-of-the-way

extraviar §77 *tr* to lead astray, mislead; mislay, misplace ‖ *ref* to get lost, go astray; go wrong; get out of line

extravío *m* going astray; loss; misleading; misconduct; misplacement

extrema *f* (*escasez grande*) extremity; (*de la vida*) end, last moment

extremar *tr* to carry far, carry to the limit ‖ *ref* to strive hard

extremaunción *f* extreme unction; last rites (*Roman Catholic*)

extreme•ño -ña *adj* frontier

extremidad *f* extremity; end, tip; **extremidades** (*pies y manos*) extremities; **la última extremidad** one's last moment

extremismo *m* extremism

extremista *mf* extremist

extre•mo -ma *adj* extreme; utmost; critical, desperate ‖ *m* extremity; (*de la calle*) end; (*del dedo*) tip; (*punto último*) extreme; great care; (*de una conversación, una carta*) point; winter pasture; **al extremo de** to the point of; **de extremo a extremo** from one end to the other; **hacer extremos** to be demonstrative, gush ‖ *f* see **extrema**

extremo•so -sa *adj* extreme, forthright; effusive, gushy, demonstrative

extrínse•co -ca *adj* extrinsic

extroversión *f* extroversion

extroverti•do -da *mf* extrovert

exuberante *adj* exuberant; luxuriant

exudar *tr & intr* to exude

exultante *adj* exultant

exultar *intr* to exult

exvoto *m* votive offering

eyacular *tr & intr* to ejaculate

F

F, f (efe) *f* seventh letter of the Spanish alphabet

f.a.b. *abbr* **franco a bordo**

fabada *f* pork-and-bean stew (*in Asturias*)

fábrica *f* factory, plant; building, masonry; (eccl) vestry

fabricación *f* manufacture; **fabricación en serie** mass production

fabricante *mf* manufacturer

fabricar §73 *tr* to manufacture; devise, invent; fabricate

fabril *adj* factory

fabriquero *m* manufacturer; charcoal burner; churchwarden

fábula *f* fable; (*p.ej., de un drama*) plot, story; rumor, gossip; (*mentira*) story, lie; (*objeto de murmuración*) talk of the town

fabulario *m* book of fables

fabulo•so -sa *adj* fabulous

facción *f* faction; feature; battle; **estar de facción** (mil) to be on duty; **facciones** features

facciona•rio -ria *adj* factional

faceta *f* facet

facetada *f* (Mex) flat joke

face•to -ta *adj* (Mex) affected; (Mex) finicky ‖ *f* see **faceta**

facial *adj* facial

fácil *adj* easy; pliant, yielding; likely; loose, wanton

facilidad *f* facility, ease, easiness; **facilidades de pago** easy payments

facilitar *tr* to facilitate, expedite; furnish, supply

facili·tón -tona *adj* bumbling, brash ‖ *mf* bumbler

facinero·so -sa *adj* wicked ‖ *mf* villain

facistol *m* choir desk

facón *m* (Arg, Urug) gaucho knife

facsimilar *tr* to facsimile; copy

facsímile *m* facsimile

factible *adj* feasible

factor *m* factor; commission merchant; baggageman; freight agent

factoría *f* trading post; (Ecuad, Peru) foundry; (Mex) factory

factura *f* invoice, bill; workmanship; **factura simulada** pro forma invoice; **según factura** as per invoice

facturación *f* invoicing, billing (*del equipaje*) checking

facturar *tr* to invoice, bill; (*el equipaje*) check

facultad *f* faculty; (*de la universidad*) school; knowledge, skill; power; **facultad de altos estudios** graduate school

facultar *tr* to empower, authorize

facultati·vo -va *adj* faculty; optional ‖ *m* doctor, physician

facundia *f* eloquence, fluency

facun·do -da *adj* eloquent, fluent

facha *mf* (*adefesio*) sight ‖ *f* look, appearance; **facha a facha** face to face

fachada *f* façade; (*de un libro*) title page; look, build, bearing; **hacer fachada con** to overlook, to look out on

facha·do -da *adj* — **bien fachado** good-looking ‖ *f* see *fachada*

fachenda *m* boaster, show-off ‖ *f* boasting

fachendear *intr* to boast, show off

fachendista or **fachen·dón -dona** or **fachendo·so -sa** *adj* boastful ‖ *mf* boaster, show-off

fachinal *m* (Arg) marshland

fada *f* fairy, witch

faena *f* work; toil; chore, task, job; (taur) windup; (taur) stunt, trick; (mil) fatigue, fatigue duty; (Guat, Mex, W-I) extra work, overtime; (Ecuad) morning work in the field; (Chile) gang of farm hands

faenero *m* (Chile) farm hand

Faetón *m* Phaëthon

fagot *m* bassoon

faisán *m* pheasant

faja *f* sash, girdle; bandage; band, strip; newspaper wrapper; (*de carretera*) lane; (*de tierra*) strip; **faja central** or **divisoria** median strip; **faja medical** supporter

fajar *tr* to wrap; bandage; swaddle; (*un periódico o revista*) put a wrapper on; beat, thrash; to attack ‖ *ref* to put on a sash

fajardo *m* meat pie

fajín *m* sash

fajina *f* bundle of sticks; fire wood; (mil) call to quarters

fajo *m* bundle; (*de papel moneda*) roll; swig; (Mex) blow; (Mex) leather belt; **fajos** swaddling clothes

falacia *f* deception; deceitfulness

falange *f* phalanx

falangia *f* daddy-longlegs

fa·laz *adj* (*pl* **-laces**) deceitful; deceptive

falba·lá *m* (*pl* **-aes**) gore; flounce, ruffle

falce *m* sickle; falchion

falda *f* skirt, dress; (*regazo*) lap; flap; fold; (*del sombrero*) brim; foothill; (*mujer*) skirt; **cosido a las faldas de** tied to the apron strings of

falde·ro -ra *adj* skirt; (*perro*) lap; lady-loving ‖ *m* lap dog

faldillas *fpl* skirts, coattails

faldón *m* coattail; shirttail; saddle flap

falible *adj* fallible

fáli·co -ca *adj* phallic

falo *m* penis, phallus

falsada *f* swoop (*of bird of prey*)

falsa·rio -ria *adj* lying ‖ *mf* falsifier, crook; liar

falsear *tr* to falsify; counterfeit; forge; (*la verdad*) distort; (*una cerradura*) pick; bevel ‖ *intr* to sag, buckle; give, give way

falsedad *f* falsity; (*mentira*) falsehood

falsete *m* falsetto; plug, tap; door (*between rooms*)

falsetista *f* falsetto

falsía *f* falsity, treachery; unsteadiness

falsificación *f* falsification; fake; counterfeit; forgery

falsificar §73 *tr* to falsify; fake; counterfeit; forge

falsilla *f* guide lines

fal·so -sa *adj* false; counterfeit; (*caballo*) vicious ‖ *m* patch; **coger en falso** (Mex) to catch in a lie; **envidar en falso** to bluff

falta *f* fault; lack, want; misdeed; absence; (*ausencia de la clase*) cut; (sport) fault; **a falta de** for want of; **echar en falta** to miss; **falta de ortografía** misspelling; **hacer falta** to be needed; be lacking; **hacerle falta a uno** to need, e.g., **le hacen falta a Juan estos libros** John needs these books; to miss, e.g., **Vd. me hace mucha falta** I miss you very much; **sin falta** without fail

faltar *intr* to be missing, be lacking, be wanting; fall short; run out; be absent; fail; die; lack, need, e.g., **me falta dinero** I lack money, I need money; **faltar a la clase** to cut class; **faltar a la verdad** to fail to tell the truth; **faltar a una cita** to fail to keep an appointment; **faltar . . . para** to be . . . to, e.g., **faltan cinco minutos para las dos** it is five minutes to two; **faltar poco para** to come near; **faltar por** to remain to be, e.g., **faltan por escribir dos cartas** two letters remain to be written

fal·to -ta *adj* short, lacking; (*peso o medida*) short; (Arg) dull, stupid; (Col) proud, vain; **falto de** short of ‖ *f* see **falta**

fal·tón -tona *adj* dilatory, remiss; (Arg) simple-minded

falto·so -sa *adj* addlebrained; (Col) quarrelsome; (CAm, Mex) disrespectful

faltriquera *f* pocket; handbag; **faltriquera de reloj** watch fob; **rascarse la faltriquera** to cough up

falúa *f* barge, tender

falucho *m* felucca

ex
fa

falla *f* failure, breakdown; defect; (geol) fault; (Mex) baby's bonnet

fallar *tr* to trump; judge, pass judgment on ‖ *intr* to fail, miss; misfire; sag, weaken; break down; judge, pass judgment

falleba *f* espagnolette

fallecer §22 *intr* to die; fail, expire

falleci•do -da *adj* deceased, late

falli•do -da *adj* unsuccessful; bankrupt; (*deuda*) uncollectible

fallir §13 *intr* to fail; (Ven) to go bankrupt

fa•llo -lla *adj* (Chile) silly, simple; **estar fallo a** to be out of (*cards of a suit*) ‖ *m* short suit; decision; judgment; verdict; **fallo humano** human error; **tener fallo a** or **de** to be out of ‖ *f* see **falla**

fama *f* fame; reputation; rumor; (Chile) bull's-eye; **correr fama** to be rumored; **es fama** it is said, it is rumored

faméli•co -ca *adj* famished, starving

familia *f* family

familiar *adj* familiar; family; (*sin ceremonia*) informal; (*lenguaje, estilo*) colloquial ‖ *m* member of the family; member of the household; acquaintance; **familiar dependiente** dependent

familiaridad *f* familiarity

familiarizar §60 *tr* to familiarize ‖ *ref* to become familiar; become too familiar; familiarize oneself

famo•so -sa *adj* famous; (*excelente*) famous; (*formidable*) some, e.g., **famoso sujeto** some guy

fámu•lo -la *mf* servant

fanal *m* beacon, lighthouse; lantern; bell glass, bell jar; lamp shade

fanáti•co -ca *adj* fanatic(al) ‖ *mf* fanatic; (sport) fan

fanatismo *m* fanaticism

fanega *f* 1.58 bu.; **fanega de tierra** 1.59 acres

fanfarria *f* fanfare; blustering

fanfa•rrón -rrona *adj* blustering, bragging; flashy ‖ *mf* blusterer, braggart

fanfarronada *f* bluster, bravado

fanfarronnear *intr* to bluster, brag

fanfarronería *f* blustering, bragging, sword rattling

fanfurriña *f* pet, peeve

fango *m* mud, mire; **llenar de fango** (fig) to sling mud at

fango•so -sa *adj* muddy; sticky, gooey

fanguero *m* (Cuba, Mex, P-R) mud, quagmire

fantasear *tr* to dream of ‖ *intr* to fancy, to daydream; **fantasear de** to boast of being

fantasía *f* fantasy; fancy, conceit, vanity; imagery; **con fantasía** (Arg) hard; **de fantasía** fancy, imitation; **tocar por fantasía** (Ven) to play by ear

fantasio•so -sa *adj* vain, conceited

fantasma *m* phantom, ghost; stuffed shirt; (telv) ghost; **fantasma magnético** magnetic curves ‖ *f* scarecrow, hobgoblin

fantas•món -mona *adj* (coll) conceited ‖ *mf* conceited person ‖ *m* stuffed shirt; (coll) scarecrow

fantásti•co -ca *adj* fantastic; fancy; conceited

fantoche *m* puppet, marionette; nincompoop, whippersnapper

faquín *m* street porter, errand boy

fara•lá *m* (*pl* -laes) ruffle, flounce; frill

faramalla *mf* cheat, swindler ‖ *f* jabber, claptrap; bluff, fake; (Chile) bragging

faramalle•ro -ra or **farama•llón -llona** *adj* scheming, swindling ‖ *mf* schemer, swindler

farándula *f* (*baile*) farandole; gossip, scheming; theater people; (*de gente*) (Arg) crush, milling

farandulear *intr* to boast, to show off

Faraón *m* Pharaoh

faraute *m* herald, messenger; interpreter; (*actor*) prologue; busybody

fardel *m* bag, bundle; sloppy person

fardo *m* bundle, package

farero *m* lighthouse keeper

farfa•lá *m* (*pl* -laes) ruffle, flounce

farfullar *tr* (*p.ej., una lección*) to sputter through; (*p.ej., una tarea*) stumble through ‖ *intr* to sputter

faringe *f* pharynx

fariseo *m* pharisee; Pharisee; lanky good-for-nothing

farmacéuti•co -ca *adj* pharmaceutical ‖ *mf* pharmacist

farmacia *f* pharmacy, drug store; **farmacia de guardia** drug store open all night

fármaco *m* drug, medicine

faro *m* lighthouse, beacon; floodlight; (aut) headlight; (fig) beacon; **faro piloto** (aut) spotlight; **faros de carretera** (aut) bright lights; **faros de cruce** (aut) dimmers; **faros de población** or **de situación** (aut) parking lights

farol *m* lamp, light; lantern; street light; (rr) headlight; (coll) conceited fellow; (Bol) bay window; **farol de tope** (naut) headlight

farola *f* lighthouse; street lamp, lamppost

farolear *intr* to boast, brag

farole•ro -ra *adj* boasting ‖ *mf* boaster ‖ *m* lamplighter

farolillo *m* heartseed; Canterbury bell; **farolillo veneciano** Chinese lantern, Japanese lantern

farota *f* minx, vixen

farotear *intr* (Col) to romp around, make a racket

faro•tón -tona *adj* brazen, cheeky ‖ *mf* cheeky person

farra *f* salmon trout; (SAm) revelry

fárrago *m* hodgepodge

farraquista *m* scatterbrain; muddlehead

farrear *intr* to celebrate; (coll) to goof off

farro *m* grits

farru•co -ca *adj* bold, fearless; ill-humored ‖ *mf* Galician abroad, Asturian abroad

farru•to -ta *adj* (Arg, Bol, Chile) sickly

farsa *f* farce; humbug

farsante *adj* & *mf* fake, fraud, humbug

fas — por fas o por nefas rightly or wrongly, in any event

fascinante *adj* fascinating

fascinar *tr* to fascinate, bewitch; cast a spell on, cast the evil eye on

fascismo *m* fascism

fascista *adj* & *mf* fascist

fase *f* phase

fastidiar *tr* to bore, annoy; cloy, sicken; disappoint ‖ *ref* to get bored; suffer, be a victim

fastidio *m* boredom, annoyance; distaste, nausea

fastidio•so -sa *adj* boring, annoying; cloying, sickening; annoyed, displeased

fas•to -ta *adj* happy, blessed ‖ *m* pomp, show

fastuo•so -sa *adj* vain, pompous; magnificent

fatal *adj* fatal; bad, evil; (law) unextendible

fatalidad *f* fatality; misfortune

fatalismo *m* fatalism

fatalista *mf* fatalist

fatalmente *adv* fatally; inevitably; unfortunately; badly, poorly

fatídi•co -ca *adj* ominous, fateful

fatiga *f* fatigue; hard breathing; **fatigas** hardship

fatigante *adj* tiresome; fatiguing

fatigar §44 *tr* to fatigue, tire, weary; annoy, bother ‖ *ref* to get tired

fatigo•so -sa *adj* fatiguing, tiring; trying, tedious

fa•tuo -tua *adj* fatuous; conceited ‖ *mf* simpleton

fauces *fpl* (anat) fauces; (fig) jaws, mouth

fauna *f* fauna

fauno *m* faun

faus•to -ta *adj* happy, fortunate ‖ *m* pomp, magnificence

fausto•so -sa *adj* magnificent

fau•tor -tora *mf* abettor, accomplice

favor *m* favor; **a favor de** under cover of; by means of; in favor of; **hágame Vd. el favor de** do me the favor to; **por favor** please; **vender favores** to peddle influence

favorable *adj* favorable

favorecer §22 *tr* to favor; flatter

favoritismo *m* favoritism

favori•to -ta *adj* & *mf* favorite

fayanca *f* unstable posture

faz *f* (*pl* **faces**) face; aspect, look; (*de monedas o medallas*) obverse; **faces** cheeks; **faz a faz** face to face

F.C. *abbr* **ferrocarril**

fe *f* faith; testimony, witness; certificate; **¡a fe mía!** upon my faith!; **dar fe de** to certify; **en fe de lo cual** in witness whereof; **fe de erratas** list of errata; **hacer fe** to be valid; **la fe del carbonero** simple faith

fealdad *f* ugliness

Febe *f* Phoebe

feble *adj* weak, sickly; (*moneda, aleación*) lacking in weight or fineness

Febo *m* Phoebus

febrero *m* February

febril *adj* feverish

fécula *f* starch

feculen•to -ta *adj* starchy; fecal

fecundar *tr* to fecundate, to fertilize

fecun•do -da *adj* fecund, fertile

fecha *f* date; **con fecha de** under date of; **de**

larga fecha of long standing; **hasta la fecha** to date

fechador *m* (Chile, Mex) canceler, postmark

fechar *tr* to date

fechoría *f* misdeed, villainy

federación *f* federation

federal *adj* & *mf* federal

federar *tr* & *ref* to federate

feéri•co -ca *adj* fairy

fehaciente *adj* authentic

feldespato *m* feldspar

felicidad *f* felicity, happiness; luck

felicitar *tr* to felicitate, congratulate, wish happiness to

feli•grés -gresa *mf* parishioner, church member

feligresía *f* parish; congregation

Felipe *m* Philip

fe•liz *adj* (*pl* **-lices**) happy; lucky; (*oportuno*) felicitous

fe•lón -lona *adj* perfidious, treacherous ‖ *mf* wicked person

felonía *f* perfidy, treachery

felpa *f* plush; drubbing; severe reprimand

felpu•do -da *adj* plushy, downy ‖ *m* mat, door mat

femenil *adj* feminine, womanly

femeni•no -na *adj* feminine; (*sexo*) female ‖ *m* feminine

fementi•do -da *adj* false, treacherous

feminismo *m* feminism

fenecer §22 *tr* to finish, close ‖ *intr* to come to an end; die

Fenicia *f* Phoenicia

feni•cio -cia *adj* & *mf* Phoenician ‖ *f* see Fenicia

fé•nix *m* (*pl* **-nix** or **-nices**) phoenix

fenobarbital *m* phenobarbital

fenomenal *adj* phenomenal

fenómeno *m* phenomenon; monster, freak

fe•o -a *adj* ugly ‖ *m* slight; **hacer un feo a** to slight ‖ **feo** *adv* (Arg, Col, Mex) bad, e.g., **oler feo** to smell bad

feo•te -ta *adj* ugly, hideous

feral *adj* cruel, bloody

fe•raz *adj* (*pl* **-races**) fertile

féretro *m* bier

feria *f* weekday; market; fair; day off; (Mex) small change; (Mex) con man; (CAm, Mex) extra, tip, gratuity; **revolver la feria** to upset the applecart

ferial *adj* week (*day*); market (*day*) ‖ *m* market; fair

feriante *adj* fair-going ‖ *mf* fairgoer

feriar *tr* to buy, sell; give, present; (Mex) to give change for

feri•no -na *adj* wild, savage; (*tos*) whooping (*cough*)

fermentación *f* ferment; fermentation

fermentar *tr* & *intr* to ferment

fermento *m* ferment

ferocidad *f* ferocity, fierceness

ferósti•co -ca *adj* irritable; hideous

fe•roz *adj* (*pl* **-roces**) ferocious, fierce

férre•o -a *adj* iron

ferrería *f* ironworks, foundry

ferretear *tr* to trim with iron; work in iron

fa
fe

ferretería *f* ironworks; hardware; hardware store

ferrete•ro -ra *mf* hardware dealer

ferrocarril *m* railroad, railway; **ferrocarril de cremallera** rack railway, mountain railroad

ferrocarrile•ro -ra *adj* railroad, rail ‖ *m* railroader

ferrotipo *m* tintype

ferrovia•rio -ria *adj* railroad, rail ‖ *m* railroader

fértil *adj* fertile

fertilizar §60 *tr* to fertilize

férula *f* flexible splint; ferule; **estar bajo la férula de** to be under the thumb of

férvi•do -da *adj* fervid; (*fiebre; sed*) burning

ferviente *adj* fervent

fervor *m* fervor, zeal

fervoro•so -sa *adj* ardent, zealous

festejar *tr* to fete, honor, entertain; celebrate; court, woo; (Mex) to beat, thrash

festejo *m* feast, entertainment; celebration; courting, wooing; (Peru) revelry; **festejos** public festivities

festín *m* feast, banquet

festinar *tr* to hurry through; (CAm) to entertain

festival *m* festival, music festival

festividad *f* festivity; feast day; witticism

festi•vo -va *adj* festive, gay; witty; (*digno no de celebrarse*) solemn

festón *m* festoon

festonear *tr* to festoon

fetiche *m* fetish

féti•do -da *adj* fetid, foul

feto *m* fetus

feú•co -ca or **feú•cho -cha** *adj* hideous, repulsive

feudal *adj* feudal

feudalismo *m* feudalism

feudo *m* fief; **feudo franco** freehold

fiable *adj* trustworthy

fiado *m* — **al fiado** on credit; **en fiado** on bail

fia•dor -dora *mf* bail; **salir fiador por** to go bail for ‖ *m* fastener; catch, pawl; (Chile, Ecuad) chin strap

fiambre *adj* cold, cold-served; (*noticias*) old, stale ‖ *m* cold lunch, cold food; stale news; (Arg) dull party; **fiambres** cold cuts

fiambrera *f* dinner pail, lunch basket

fiambrería *f* (Arg) delicatessen store

fianza *f* guarantee, surety; bond; bail; **fianza carcelera** bail

fiar §77 *tr* to entrust, confide; guarantee; give credit to; sell on credit ‖ *intr & ref* to trust

fiasco *m* fiasco

fibra *f* fiber; (fig) fiber, strength, vigor; **fibras del corazón** heartstrings

fibro•so -sa *adj* fibrous

ficción *f* fiction

ficciona•rio -ria *adj* fictional

fice *m* (ichth) hake

ficti•cio -cia *adj* fictitious

ficha *f* chip; counter; domino; filing card; police record; (elec) plug; **ficha catalográfica** index card; **ficha perforada** punch card; **llevar ficha** to have a police record; **ser una buena ficha** to be a sly fox

ficha•dor -dora *mf* file clerk

fichar *tr* to file; play, move; black-list; (Cuba) to cheat ‖ *intr* (Col) to die

fichero *m* card index, filing cabinet

fidedig•no -na *adj* reliable, trustworthy

fideicomisa•rio -ria *mf* trustee

fideicomiso *m* trusteeship

fidelería *f* (Arg, Ecuad, Peru) vermicelli factory, noodle factory

fidelidad *f* fidelity; punctiliousness; **alta fidelidad** (rad) high fidelity

fideo *m* skinny person; (Arg) joke; (Arg) confusion, disorder; **fideos** vermicelli

Fidias *m* Phidias

fiducia•rio -ria *adj & mf* fiduciary

fiebre *f* fever; **fiebre del heno** hay fever; **fibre tifoidea** typhoid fever

fiel *adj* faithful; exact; punctilious; honest, trustworthy ‖ *m* inspector of weights and measures; (*en las balanzas*) pointer; (*de las tijeras*) pin; **fiel de romana** inspector of weights in a slaughterhouse; **los fieles** the faithful

fielato *m* inspector's office; octroi

fieltro *m* felt; felt hat; felt rug

fiera *f* wild animal; (*persona*) fiend; (taur) bull; **ser una fiera para** to be a fiend for

fierabrás *m* spitfire, little terror

fierecilla *f* shrew

fiereza *f* fierceness; cruelty; deformity

fie•ro -ra *adj* fierce, wild; cruel; deformed, ugly; huge, tremendous; **echar** or **hacer fieros** to bluster ‖ *f* see **fiera**

fierro *m* (SAm) branding iron

fierros *mpl* (Ecuad, Mex) tools

fiesta *f* feast, holy day; holiday; celebration, festivity; **estar de fiesta** (coll) to be in a holiday mood; **fiesta de la hispanidad** or **fiesta de la raza** Columbus Day; **fiesta de todos los santos** All Saints' Day; **fiesta onomástica** saint's day, birthday; **fiestas** holiday, vacation; **hacer fiesta** to take off (*from work*); **hacer fiestas a** to act up to, to fawn on; **la fiesta brava** bullfighting; **no estar para fiestas** to be in no mood for joking; **por fin de fiestas** to top it off; **se acabó la fiesta** let's drop it

fieste•ro -ra *adj* merry, cheerful ‖ *mf* merrymaker, party-goer

figón *m* cheap restaurant

figura *f* figure; face, countenance; (*naipe*) face card; (mus) note; (theat) character; **figura retórica** figure of speech; **hacer figura** to cut a figure

figuración *f* representation; (Arg) status, social standing

figura•do -da *adj* figurative

figurar *tr* to depict, trace, represent; feign ‖ *intr* to figure, be in the limelight ‖ *ref* to figure, imagine

figurati•vo -va *adj* figurative, representative

figurería *f* face, grimace

figurilla *mf* silly little runt ‖ *f* figurine

figurín *m* dummy, model; fashion plate

figurina *f* figurine

figurita *mf* silly little runt

figurón *m* stuffed shirt; **figurón de proa** (naut) figurehead

fija *f* hinge; trowel; (*caballo*) (Peru) sure bet; **la fija** sure thing

fijacarte•les *m* (*pl* **-les**) billposter

fijación *f* fixing, fastening; posting; **fijación de precios** price fixing

fijado *m* (phot) fixing

fija•dor -dora *adj* fixing ‖ *m* carpenter who installs doors and windows; fixing bath; sprayer; (mas) pointer; hair set, hair spray

fijamárge•nes *m* (*pl* **-nes**) margin stop

fijapeína•dos *m* (*pl* **-dos**) hair set, hair spray

fijar *tr* to fix; fasten; (*carteles*) post; (*una fecha; los cabellos; una imagen fotográfica; los precios; la atención; una hora, una cita*) fix; (*residencia*) establish; paste, glue ‖ *ref* to settle; notice; **fijarse en** to notice; pay attention to; be intent on

fijeza *f* firmness, stability; steadfastness; **mirar con fijeza** to stare at

fi•jo -ja *adj* fixed; firm, solid, secure, fast; sure, determined; **de fijo** surely ‖ *f* see **fija**

fil *m* — **estar en fil** or **en un fil** to be alike; **fil derecho** leapfrog

fila *f* row, line; file; (*línea que los soldados forman de frente*) rank; dislike, hatred; **cerrar las filas** (mil) to close ranks; **en fila** in single file; **en filas** (mil) in active service; **fila india** single file, Indian file; **llamar a filas** (mil) to call to the colors; **pasarse a las filas de** to go over to; **romper filas** (mil) to break ranks

filamento *m* filament

filantropía *f* philanthropy

filántrop•po -pa *mf* philanthropist

filar *tr* (naut) to pay out slowly

filarmónica *f* (Mex) accordion

filarmóni•co -ca *adj* philharmonic

filatelia *f* philately

filatelista *mf* philatelist

filatería *f* fast talking; wordiness

filate•ro -ra *adj* fast-talking; wordy ‖ *mf* fast talker; great talker

file•no -na *adj* cute, tiny

filete *m* (*de carne o pescado*) filet or fillet; (*asador*) spit; edge, rim; narrow hem; (*de tornillo*) thread; snaffle bit; (archit, bb) fillet; (typ) rule, fancy rule

filetear *tr* to fillet; (*un tornillo*) thread; (bb) to tool

filiación *f* filiation; description, characteristics; (mil) regimental register

filial *adj* filial ‖ *f* affiliate, branch

filiar §77 *tr* to register ‖ *ref* to enroll

filibustero *m* filibuster, buccaneer

filigrana *f* filigree; (*en el papel*) watermark

filipi•no -na *adj* Filipine, Filipino ‖ *mf* Filipino ‖ **Filipinas** *fpl* Philippines

Filipo *m* Philip (*of Macedonia*)

Filis *f* Phyllis

filiste•o -a *adj* & *mf* Philistine ‖ *m* tall, fat fellow

film *m* (*pl* **-films** or **filmes**) film

filmadora *f* movie camera

filmar *tr* to film, shoot

filo *m* edge; ridge; dividing line; (CAm, Mex) hunger; **al filo de** at, at about; **dar filo a** to sharpen; **filo del viento** direction of the wind; **pasar al filo de la espada** to put to the sword; **por filo** exactly

filobús *m* trolley bus, trackless trolley

filocommunista *adj* & *mf* procommunist

filología philology

filólo•go -ga *mf* philologist

filón *m* seam, vein; (fig) gold mine

filo•so -sa *adj* sharp

filosofía *f* philosophy

filosófi•co -ca *adj* philosophic(al)

filóso•fo -fa *mf* philosopher

filote *m* (Col) corn silk; (Col) ear of green corn

filtración *f* filtering; leak; (fig) leak, loss

filtrado *m* filtrate

filtrar *tr* to filter ‖ *intr* to leak; ooze ‖ *ref* to filter; (*el dinero*) leak away, disappear

filtro *m* filter; (*brebaje para conciliar el amor*) philter, love potion

filu•do -da *adj* (SAm) sharp-edged

filván *m* featheredge

fimo *m* dung, manure

fin *m* end; aim, purpose, end; **a fin de** to, in order to; **a fin de que** in order that, so that; **a fines de** toward the end of, late in; **al fin** finally; **al fin del mundo** far, far away; **al fin y a la postre** or **al fin y al cabo** after all, in the end; **dar fin a** to put an end to; **fin de semana** weekend; **por fin** finally, in short; **sin fin** endless; endlessly; **un sin fin de** no end of

fina•do -da *adj* deceased, late ‖ *mf* deceased

final *adj* final ‖ *m* end; (mus) finale; **por final** finally ‖ *f* (sport) finals; **final de partido** windup

finalidad *f* end, purpose

finalista *mf* finalist

finalizar §60 *tr* to end, terminate; (*una escritura*) (law) to execute ‖ *intr* to end, terminate

financiación *f* financing

financiamiento *m* (SAm) financial backing

financiar *tr* to finance

financie•ro -ra *adj* financial ‖ *mf* financier

finanzas *fpl* finances

finar *intr* to die ‖ *ref* to yearn

finca *f* property, piece of real estate; farm, ranch; **buena finca** sly fellow

fincar §73 *tr* (P-R) to cultivate, farm ‖ *intr* to buy up real estate; (Col) to reside, rest, be based ‖ *ref* to buy up real estate

fincha•do -da *adj* vain, conceited

fi•nés -nesa *adj* Finnic; Finnish ‖ *mf* Finn ‖ *m* (*idioma uraliano*) Finnic; (*idioma de Finlandia*) Finnish

fineza *f* fineness; kindness, courtesy; token of affection, favor

fingi•do -da *adj* fake, sham; false, deceitful

fingir §27 *tr* & *intr* to feign, pretend, fake ‖ *ref* to pretend to be

finiquitar *tr* (*una cuenta*) to settle, to close; finish, wind up

finiquito *m* settlement, closing; **dar finiquito a** to settle, close; finish, wind up

fe
fi

finíti•mo -ma *adj* bordering, neighboring

fini•to -ta *adj* finite

finlan•dés -desa *adj* Finnish ‖ *mf* Finn, Finlander ‖ *m* Finnish

Finlandia *f* Finland

fi•no -na *adj* fine; (*ligero, casi transparente*) sheer; (*esbelto*) thin, slender; (*paño, papel, etc.*) thin; (*agua*) pure; polite, courteous; shrewd, cunning

finta *f* feint

finura *f* fineness, excellence; politeness, courtesy

finústi•co -ca *adj* overobsequious

firma *f* signature; signing; firm; firm name; mail to be signed; **con mi firma** under my hand; **firma en blanco** blank check

firmamento *m* firmament

firmante *adj* signatory ‖ *mf* signer, signatory

firmar *tr & intr* to sign

firme *adj* firm, steady; solid, hard; staunch, unswerving ‖ *adv* firmly, steadily ‖ *m* roadbed; **de firme** hard, e.g., **llover de firme** to rain hard

firmeza *f* firmness, constancy, fortitude

firmón *m* shyster who signs anything

fiscal *adj* fiscal, treasury ‖ *m* treasurer; district attorney; busybody

fiscalizar §60 *tr* to control, inspect; prosecute; pry into

fisco *m* state treasury, exchequer

fisga *f* fish spear; prying, snooping; banter, raillery

fisgar §44 *tr* to harpoon, fish with a spear; pry into ‖ *intr* to pry, snoop; mock, jeer ‖ *ref* to mock, jeer

fis•gón -gona *mf* (coll) mocker, jester; (coll) snooper, busybody

físi•co -ca *adj* physical; (Mex, W-I) finicky, prudish ‖ *mf* physicist ‖ *m* physique ‖ *f* physics; **física de las partículas** particle physics; **física del estado sólido** solid state physics; **física molecular** molecular physics

fisil *adj* fissionable

fisiología *f* physiology

fisiológi•co -ca *adj* physiological

fisión *f* fission

fisionable *adj* fissionable

fisonomía *f* physiognomy

fistol *m* sly fellow; (Mex) necktie pin

fisura *f* (anat, min) fissure; **fisura del paladar** cleft palate

fla•co -ca *adj* thin, skinny; feeble, weak, frail; insecure, unstable ‖ *m* weak spot

flacu•cho -cha *adj* skinny

flagrante *adj* occurring, actual; **en flagrante** in the act

flamante *adj* bright, flaming; brand-new, spick-and-span

flameante *adj* flamboyant

flamear *intr* to flame; flare up (*with anger*); flutter, wave

flamen•co -ca *adj* Flemish; buxom; Andalusian gypsy; flashy, snappy, gypsyish ‖ *mf* Fleming ‖ *m* (*idioma*) Flemish; Andalusian gypsy dance, song, or music; (orn) flamingo

fláme•o -a *adj* flamelike

flamíge•ro -ra *adj* (poet) flaming; (archit) flamboyant

flan *m* custard

flanco *m* side, flank; **coger por el flanco** to catch off guard

Flandes *f* Flanders

flanquear *tr* to flank

flaquear *intr* to weaken, flag; become faint; become discouraged

flaqueza *f* thinness, skinniness; weakness; instability

flashback *m* (*retrospectiva*) flashback

flato *m* gas; gloominess, melancholy

flato•so -sa *adj* flatulent, windy; gloomy, melancholy

flauta *f* flute

flautín *m* piccolo

flautista *mf* flautist, flutist

flebitis *f* phlebitis

fleco *m* fringe; ragged edge; **flecos** bangs

flecha *f* arrow; (aer) sweepback

flechar *tr* (*el arco*) to draw; (*a una persona*) wound with an arrow, kill with an arrow; infatuate

flechero *m* archer, bowman

fleje *m* iron strap, iron hoop

flema *f* phlegm

flemáti•co -ca *adj* phlegmatic(al); (coll) cool

flemón *m* gumboil

flequillo *m* bangs

Flesinga *f* Flushing

fletante *m* shipowner; (Arg, Chile, Ecuad) conveyancer

fletar *tr* (*una nave*) to charter; (*ganado*) load; (*bestias de carga, carros, etc.*) to hire ‖ *ref* (Arg) to sneak in, slip in; (Cuba, Mex) to beat it, clear out

flete *m* (naut) freight, cargo; (Arg, Bol, Col, Urug) race horse; **salir sin flete** (Col, Ven) to beat it

flexible *adj* flexible; (*sombrero*) soft ‖ *m* soft hat; (elec) flexible cord

flexo *m* gooseneck lamp

flinflanear *intr* to tinkle

flirt *m* or **flirtación** *f* flirting

flirtear *intr* to flirt

flojear *intr* to ease up, idle; flag, weaken

flojedad *f* slackness; looseness; limpness; laziness; weakness

flojel *m* fluff, nap; down, soft feathers

flo•jo -ja *adj* slack, loose; limp; languid; lazy; weak; (*precios*) sagging; (*viento*) light; lax, careless

flor *f* flower; (*de árbol frutal*) blossom; (*del cuero*) grain; (fig) compliment, bouquet; **a flor de** even with, flush with; **a flor de agua** at water level; **decir flores a** to flatter; to flirt with; **flor de la edad** bloom of youth; **flor de la vida** prime of life; **flor del campo** wild flower; **flor de lis** (*escudo de armas de Francia*) lily, fleur-de-lis; **flor de mano** paper flower, artificial flower; **la flor de la canela** the tops; **la flor y nata de** the cream of

flora *f* flora

floral *adj* floral

florcita *f* little flower; **andar de florcita** (Arg, Bol, Chile, Urug) to stroll around with a flower in one's buttonhole, take it easy

florear *tr* to flower, decorate with flowers; (*los naipes*) stack; (*harina*) bolt ‖ *intr* (*la punta de la espada*) to quiver; twang away on a guitar; throw bouquets

florecer §22 *intr* to flower, blossom, bloom; (*prosperar*) flourish ‖ *ref* to become moldy

floreciente *adj* flowering, florescent; flourishing

florenti•no -na *adj & mf* Florentine

floreo *m* idle talk; bright remark; (*de la punta de la espada*) quivering; (*de la guitarra*) twanging; (mus) flourish; **andarse con floreos** to beat about the bush

florera *f* flower girl

florería *f* flower shop

flore•ro -ra *adj* flattering, jesting ‖ *mf* flatterer, jester; florist ‖ *m* (*vaso para flores*) vase; (*maceta con flores*) flowerpot; flower stand, jardiniere; (*cuadro, pintura*) flower piece ‖ *f* see **florera**

florescencia *f* florescence

floresta *f* woods, woodland; grove; rural setting; anthology

florete *m* (*esgrima*) fencing; (*espadín*) foil

floretear *tr* to decorate with flowers ‖ *intr* to fence

flori•do -da *adj* flowery, full of flowers; choice, select

florilegio *m* anthology

floripondio *m* (SAm) angel's-trumpet

florista *mf* florist

floristería *f* flower shop

florón *m* large flower; finial; rosette; (typ) tailpiece, vignette

flota *f* fleet; **flota petrolera** tanker fleet

flotación *f* buoyancy

flotador *m* float

flotaje *m* log driving

flotante *adj* floating; (*barba*) flowing ‖ *m* (Col) braggart

flotar *intr* to float; (*una bandera*) wave

flote *m* floating; **a flote** afloat

fluctuar §21 *intr* to fluctuate; bob up and down; wave; waver; be in danger

fluente *adj* fluent, flowing; (*hemorroides*) bleeding

fluidez *f* fluidity

fluí•do -da *adj* fluid; (*estilo, lenguaje*) fluent ‖ *m* fluid

fluir §20 *intr* to flow

flujo *m* flow, flux; (*acceso de la marea*) floodtide; **flujo de risa** fit of noisy laughter; **flujo de vientre** loose bowels; **flujo y reflujo** ebb and flow

flúor *m* fluorine

fluorescencia *f* fluorescence

fluorescente *adj* fluorescent

fluorhídri•co -ca *adj* hydrofluoric

fluorización *f* fluoridation

fluorizar §60 *tr* to fluoridate

fluoroscopio *m* fluoroscope

fluoruro *m* fluoride

flux *m* (*en el póker*) flush; suit of clothes; **estar en flux** to be penniless; **hacer flux** to blow in everything without settling accounts; **tener flux** to be lucky

fluxión *f* (*acumulación morbosa de humores*) congestion; (*enrojecimiento de la cara y el cuello*) flush; (*constipado de narices*) cold in the head; **fluxión de muelas** swollen cheek; **fluxión de pecho** pneumonia

foca *f* seal

focal *adj* focal

foco *m* focus; (*de vicios*) center; (*de un absceso*) core; electric light

fodo•lí *adj* (*pl* **-líes**) meddlesome

fodon•go -ga *adj* (Mex) dirty, slovenly

fo•fo -fa *adj* soft, fluffy, spongy

fogaje *m* (*contribución*) hearth money; blush, flush; (Arg) fire, blaze; (Arg, Mex) rash, eruption

fogata *f* blaze, bonfire

fogón *m* cooking stove; (*de máquina de vapor*) firebox

fogonazo *m* powder flash

fogonero *m* fireman, stoker

fogosidad *f* fire, spirit, dash

fogo•so -sa *adj* fiery, spirited

fol. *abbr* folio

folgo *m* foot muff

foliar *tr* to folio

folio *m* folio; **al primer folio** right off; **de a folio** enormous; **en folio** folio

folklore *m* folklore

follaje *m* foliage; gaudy ornament; (*palabrería*) fustian

follar *tr* to shape like a leaf ‖ §61 *tr* to blow with bellows

folletín *m* newspaper serial (*printed at bottom of page*); pamphlet

folleto *m* brochure, pamphlet, tract

fo•llón -llona *adj* careless, indolent, lazy; arrogant, cowardly ‖ *mf* lazy loafer, knave ‖ *m* noiseless rocket

fomentar *tr* to foment; foster, encourage, promote; warm

fonda *f* inn, restaurant; (Chile) refreshment stand

fondeadero *m* anchorage

fondea•do -da *adj* well-heeled

fondear *tr* (*un buque*) to search; scrutinize, examine closely ‖ *intr* to cast anchor ‖ *ref* to save up for a rainy day

fondillos *mpl* seat (*of trousers*)

fondista *mf* innkeeper

fondo *m* bottom; (*de un cuarto, una tienda*) back, rear; (*del mar, de una piscina, etc.*) floor; (*de un cilindro, barril, etc.*) head; background; (*de una casa*) depth; (*de un paño*) ground; (*caudal*) fund; (*lo esencial*) bottom; **a fondo** thoroughly; **bajos fondos sociales** underworld, scum of the earth; **colar a fondo** to sink; **dar fondo** to cast anchor; **echar a fondo** to sink; **en el fondo** at bottom; **estar en fondos** to have funds available; **fondo de amortización** sinking fund; **fondos** (*caudales, dinero*) funds; **irse a fondo** to go to the bottom; (*un negocio*)

to fail; **tener buen fondo** to be good-natured
fonducho *m* cheap eating house
fonéti·co -ca *adj* phonetic
foniatría *f* speech correction
fónica *f* phonics
fono *m* (Chile) earphone
fonoabsorbente *adj* sound-absorbent; sound-deadening
fonocaptor *m* pickup
fonógrafo *m* phonograph; record player
fonología *f* phonology
fontanería *f* plumbing; water-supply system
fontane·ro -ra *adj* fountain ‖ *m* plumber, tinsmith
foque *m* (naut) jib; (coll) piccadilly collar
foraji·do -da *adj* fugitive ‖ *mf* fugitive, outlaw, bandit
foráne·o -a *adj* foreign, strange; offshore
foraste·ro -ra *adj* outside, strange; foreign ‖ *mf* outsider, stranger
forbante *m* freebooter
forcejar or **forcejear** *intr* to struggle, resist, contend
forceju·do -da *adj* strong, husky, robust
fór·ceps *m* (*pl* **-ceps**) forceps
forestal *adj* forest
forja *f* forge; forging; silversmith's forge; foundry, ironworks; mortar
forjar *tr* to forge; build with stone and mortar; roughcast; (*mentiras*) forge ‖ *ref* to forge; hatch, think up
forma *f* form, shape; way; (*de un libro*) format; **de forma que** so that, with the result that; **tener buenas formas** to have a good figure
formación *f* formation; **formación de palabras** word formation
formal *adj* formal, ceremonious; express, definite; reliable; sedate; serious
formalidad *f* formality; reliability; seriousness
formar *tr* to form; to shape, fashion; train, educate ‖ *intr* to form; form a line, stand in line ‖ *ref* to form; form a line, stand in line; take form, grow, develop
formato *m* format
formidable *adj* formidable
formidolo·so -sa *adj* scared, frightened; frightful, horrible
fórmula *f* formula; prescription; **por fórmula** as a matter of form
formular *tr* to formulate
formulario *m* form, blank; **formulario de pedido** order blank
fornicación *f* fornication
fornicar *intr* to fornicate; to have sex
forni·do -da *adj* husky, sturdy, robust
foro *m* forum; (*abogacía*) bar; (*del escenario*) back, rear
forrado *m* lining; padding
forraje *m* forage, fodder
forrajear *tr & intr* to forage
forrar *tr* to line; (*un vestido*) face; (*un libro, un paraguas*) cover; (*un lienzo*) stretch ‖ *ref* (Guat, Mex) to stuff oneself
forro *m* lining; cover, covering; (naut)

sheathing, planking; **forro de freno** brake lining; **ni por el forro** not by a long shot
fortalecer §22 *tr* to fortify, strengthen
fortaleza *f* fortitude; strength, vigor; fortress, stronghold
fortificación *f* fortification
fortificante *m* tonic
fortificar §73 *tr* to fortify
fortín *m* small fort; bunker
fortui·to -ta *adj* fortuitous
fortuna *f* fortune; **correr fortuna** (naut) to ride the storm; **de fortuna** makeshift; **por fortuna** fortunately; **probar fortuna** to try one's luck
fortunón *m* windfall
forza·do -da *adj* forced; (*p.ej., entrada*) forcible; (*sonrisa*) (fig) forced; (*trabajos*) hard ‖ *m* galley slave
forzar §35 *tr* to force
forzo·so -sa *adj* unavoidable; strong, husky; (*trabajos*) hard; (*aterrizaje; marcha*) forced ‖ *f* — **hacer la forzosa a** to put the squeeze on
forzu·do -da *adj* strong, husky, robust
fosa *f* grave; (aut) pit; **fosa de los leones** (Bib) lions' den
fosar *tr* to dig a ditch around
fos·co -ca *adj* dark; cross, sullen; (*tiempo*) threatening
fosfato *m* phosphate
fosforera *f* matchbox
fosforescente *adj* phosphorescent
fósforo *m* (*cuerpo simple*) phosphorus; match; **fósforo de seguridad** safety match
fósil *adj & m* fossil
foso *m* hole, pit; (*que rodea un castillo o fortaleza*) moat; (theat & aut) pit
fotingo *m* jalopy, jitney
foto *f* photo; **foto fija** still
fotocopia *f* photocopy
fotocopiador *m* or **fotocopiadora** *f* photocopier
fotocopiar *tr* to photocopy
fotodrama *m* photoplay
fotofija *m* photo-finish camera
fotogéni·co -ca *adj* photogenic
fotograbado *m* photoengraving
fotografía *f* (*arte*) photography; (*imagen, retrato*) photograph; photograph gallery; **fotografía aérea** aerial photograph(y)
fotografiar §77 *tr & intr* to photograph
fotógra·fo -fa *mf* photographer
fotómetro *m* light meter
fotoperiodismo *m* photojournalism
fotopila *f* solar battery
fotostatar *tr & intr* to photostat
fotostato *m* photostat
fototubo *m* phototube
fra. *abbr* **factura**
frac *m* (*pl* **-fraques**) full-dress coat, tails, swallow-tailed coat
fracasar *intr* to fail; break to pieces
fracaso *m* failure; breakdown, crash
fracción *f* fraction
fraccionar *tr* to divide up; break up
fracciona·rio -ria *adj* fractional

fractura *f* fracture; breaking open, breaking in

fracturar *tr* to fracture; break open, break in ‖ *ref* (*p.ej., un brazo*) to fracture

fragancia *f* fragrance; good reputation

fragante *adj* fragrant; **en fragante** (archaic) in the act

fragata *f* frigate; **fragata ligera** corvette

frágil *adj* fragile; (*quebradizo; que cae fácilmente en el pecado*) frail; (Mex) poor, needy

fragmento *m* fragment

fragor *m* crash, roar, thunder

fragoro•so -sa *adj* noisy, thundering

fragosidad *f* roughness, unevenness; (*de un bosque*) thickness, denseness; rough road

frago•so -sa *adj* rough, uneven; thick, dense; noisy, thundering

fragua *f* forge

fraguar §10 *tr* to forge; hatch, scheme; (*mentiras*) forge ‖ *intr* to forge; (*la cal, el cemento*) set

fraile *m* friar, monk; **fraile de misa y olla** friarling; **fraile rezador** praying mantis

frambesia *f* (pathol) yaws

frambuesa *f* raspberry

frambueso *m* raspberry bush

francachela *f* feast, spread; carousal, high time; (Arg) excessive familiarity

francalete *m* strap with buckle

fran•cés -cesa *adj* French; **despedirse a la francesa** to take French leave ‖ *m* Frenchman; (*idioma*) French ‖ *f* Frenchwoman

francesada *f* French remark; French invasion of Spain in 1808

francesilla *f* French roll; (bot) turban buttercup

Francia *f* France

francisca•no -na *adj & mf* Franciscan

francmasón *m* Freemason

francmasonería *f* Freemasonry

fran•co -ca *adj* generous, liberal; outspoken, candid, frank; (*camino*) free, open; (*suelo*) loamy; free, gratis; Frankish; **franco a bordo** free on board; **franco de porte** postpaid ‖ *mf* Frank ‖ *m* franc; (*idioma*) Frankish

francolín *m* black partridge

franco•te -ta *adj* frank, wholehearted

francotirador *m* sniper

franela *f* flannel

frangente *m* accident, mishap

frangir §27 *tr* to break up, break to pieces

frangollar *tr* to bungle, to botch

frangollo *m* porridge; mash for cattle; bungle, botch

franja *f* fringe; strip, band; (opt) fringe

franjar *tr* to fringe

franquear *tr* to exempt; cross, go over; grant; free, enfranchise; (*un camino*) open, clear; (*una carta*) frank, pay the postage for; **a franquear en destino** postage will be paid by addressee ‖ *ref* to yield; **franquearse con** to open one's heart to

franqueo *m* freeing, liberation; postage; **franqueo concertado** postage permit

franqueza *f* generosity; candidness, frankness; freedom

franquía *f* (naut) sea room; **en franquía** (naut & fig) in the open

franquicia *f* franchise; exemption, tax exemption; **franquicia postal** franking privilege

franquista *mf* Francoist

frasca *f* leaves, twigs, brush; (Guat, Mex) high jinks

frasco *m* flask; (*p.ej., de aceitunas*) jar

frase *f* phrase; (*oración cabal*) sentence; idiom; **frase hecha** saying, proverb; cliché; **gastar frases** to talk all around the subject

frasear *tr* to phrase ‖ *intr* to talk all around the subject

frasquera *f* bottle frame, liquor case

fratás *m* plastering trowel

fraternal *adj* brotherly, fraternal

fraternidad *f* fraternity, brotherhood

fraternizar §60 *intr* to fraternize

frater•no -na *adj* brotherly, fraternal

fraude *m* fraud; **fraude fiscal** tax evasion

fraudulen•to -ta *adj* fraudulent

fray *m* Fra

frecuencia *f* frequency; **alta frecuencia** high frequency; **baja frecuencia** low frequency; **con frecuencia** frequently

frecuentar *tr* (*ir con frecuencia a*) to frequent; keep up, repeat

frecuente *adj* frequent; (*usual*) common

fregadero *m* sink, kitchen sink

frega•do -da *adj* annoying, bothersome; cunning; (SAm) stubborn; (P-R) brazen ‖ *m* scrubbing; mopping; mess

frega•dor -dora *mf* dishwasher

fregar §66 *tr* (*restregar*) to rub; (*restregar para limpiar*) scrub, scour; (*el pavimento*) mop; (*los platos*) wash; annoy, bother

fregasue•los *m* (*pl* -los) mop, floor mop

frega•triz *f* (*pl* -trices) var of **fregona**

fre•gón -gona *adj* annoying, bothersome; brazen ‖ *f* (*criada que friega el pavimento*) scrub woman; (*criada que lava la vajilla*) dishwasher, scullery maid

freiduría *f* fried-fish shop

freír §58 & §83 *tr* to fry; bore to death ‖ *intr* to fry; **dejarle a uno freír en su aceite** to let someone stew in his own juice ‖ *ref* to fry; be bored to death; **freírsele a** to try to fool, scheme to deceive

fréjol *m* kidney bean

frenar *tr* to bridle, check, hold back; (*un automóvil, tren*) brake

frene•sí *m* (*pl* -síes) frenzy

frenéti•co -ca *adj* frantic; mad, furious; wild

frenillo *m* muzzle; **no tener frenillo en la lengua** to not mince one's words

freno *m* (*parte de la brida*) bit; (*aparato para parar el movimiento de los vehículos*) brake; (fig) brake, check, curb; **freno de contrapedal** coaster brake; **freno de disco** disk brake; **freno de tambor** drum brake; **morder el freno** to champ the bit

frenología *f* phrenology

frentazo *m* (Mex) rebuff

frente *m & f* (*de un edificio*) front ‖ *m* (mil)

front, front line; **al frente de** at the head of, in charge of ‖ *f* brow, forehead; face, front; head; **a frente** straight ahead; **arrugar la frente** to knit the brow; **de frente** straight ahead; abreast; **en frente de** in front of; against, opposed to; **frente a** in front of; compared with

freo *m* channel, strait

fresa *f* strawberry; (*de fresadora*) cutter

fresado *m* milling, millwork

fresadora *f* milling machine

fresal *m* strawberry patch

fresar *tr* to mill

fresca *f* fresh air; cool part of the day; blunt remark, piece of one's mind

fresca•chón -chona *adj* bouncing, buxom; (*viento*) brisk

fresca•les *mf* (*pl* **-les**) forward sort of person

frescamente *adv* recently; cheekily, brazenly

fres•co -ca *adj* (*acabado de hacer o suceder*) fresh; (*moderadamente frío*) cool; (*pintura*) fresh, wet; (*tela, vestido*) light; calm, unruffled; buxom, ruddy, cheeky, fresh; **estar fresco** to be in a fine pinch; **quedarse tan fresco** to show no offense, be indifferent or unconcerned ‖ *m* coolness; fresh air; fresh bacon; (fa) fresco; cool drink; **al fresco** in the open air; in the night air; **hace fresco** it is cool; **tomar el fresco** to go out for some fresh air ‖ *f* see **fresca**

frescor *m* freshness; cool, coolness

fresco•te -ta *adj* plump and rosy

frescura *f* freshness; cool, coolness; unconcern, offhand manner; sharp reply; cheek, impudence

fresno *m* ash tree; (*madera*) ash

fresquera *f* meat closet, food cabinet, icebox

fresquería *f* ice-cream parlor, soft-drink store

fresque•ro -ra *mf* fish dealer; (Peru) soft-drink vendor ‖ *f* see **fresquera**

freudismo *m* Freudianism

freza *f* dung; spawning; hole made by game

frialdad *f* coldness; carelessness, laxity; stupidity; (pathol) frigidity; (pathol) impotence; (fig) coolness, coldness

friáti•co -ca *adj* chilly; awkward, stupid; (*ropa*) cold

fricar §73 *tr* to rub

fricasé *m* fricassee

fricción *f* rubbing; massage; (pharm) rubbing liniment; (phys) friction

friccionar *tr* to rub; massage

friega *f* rubbing, massage; annoyance, bother; flogging, whipping

frigidez *f* frigidity; coldness

frígi•do -da *adj* frigid; cold

frigorífero *m* freezing chamber

frigorífi•co -ca *adj* refrigerating; cold-storage ‖ *m* refrigerator; (Arg, Urug) packing house, cold-storage plant

frijol *m* bean, kidney bean; **frijol de media luna** Lima bean; **¡frijoles!** (W-I) absolutely no!

frijolear *tr* (Guat) to annoy, molest

frijolizar §60 *tr* (Peru) to bewitch

frí•o -a *adj* cold; dull, weak, colorless; (fig) cold, cool ‖ *m* cold; **fríos** chills and fever;

coger frío to catch cold; **hace frío** it is cold; **tener frío** (*una persona*) to be cold; **tomar frío** to catch cold

friole•ro -ra *adj* chilly ‖ *f* trifle, trinket; snack, bite

frisar *tr* to rub; to fit, fasten; (naut) to calk ‖ *intr* to agree, get along; **frisar con** or **en** to border on

friso *m* dado, wainscot; (archit) frieze

fri•són -sona *adj & mf* Frisian

fritada *f* fry

fri•to -ta *adj* fried; bored to death ‖ *m* fry; (Ven) daily bread

fritura *f* fry

frívo•lo -la *adj* frivolous; trifling

fronda *f* leaf; (*de helecho*) frond; sling-shaped bandage; **frondas** frondage, foliage

frondo•so -sa *adj* leafy; woodsy

frontalera *f* yoke pad

frontera *f* frontier, border; front, façade

fronteri•zo -za *adj* frontier, border; facing, opposite

fronte•ro -ra *adj* frontier, border; facing, opposite; front ‖ *f* see **frontera**

frontín *m* (Mex) flip, fillip

fron•tis *m* (*pl* **-tis**) front, façade

frontispicio *m* frontispiece; (coll) face

frontón *m* (*encima de puertas o ventanas*) gable, pediment; pelota court; pelota wall; handball court

frotamiento *m* rubbing; (phys) friction

frotar *tr* to rub; to chafe ‖ *ref* to rub

fro•tis *m* (*pl* **-tis**) (bact) smear

fructuo•so -sa *adj* fruitful

frugal *adj* (*en comer y beber*) temperate; (*no muy abundante*) frugal

fruición *f* enjoyment, satisfaction; (*del mal ajeno*) evil satisfaction

fruiti•vo -va *adj* enjoyable

frunce *m* shirr, shirring, gathering

frunci•do -da *adj* grim, gruff, stern; (Chile) temperate; (Chile) sad, gloomy ‖ *m* shirr, shirring, gathering

fruncir §36 *tr* to wrinkle, pucker, pleat; (*la frente*) knit; (*los labios*) curl, purse; (*la verdad*) twist, disguise; shirr, gather ‖ *ref* to affect modesty, be shocked

fruslería *f* trifle, trinket; (coll) futility, triviality

frusle•ro -ra *adj* futile, trivial, trifling ‖ *m* rolling pin

frustrar *tr* to frustrate, thwart

fruta *f* fruit; **fruta del tiempo** fruit in season; **fruta de sartén** fritter, pancake; **frutas** fruit; **frutas agrias** citrus fruit

frutal *adj* fruit ‖ *m* fruit tree

frutería *f* fruit store

frute•ro -ra *adj* fruit ‖ *mf* fruit dealer ‖ *m* fruit dish; tray of imitation fruit

frutilla *f* (*del rosario*) bead; Chilean strawberry; gumdrop

fruto *m* (bot & fig) fruit; **fruto de bendición** legitimate offspring; **frutos** produce; **sacar fruto de** to derive benefit from

fu *interj* faugh! fie!; (*del gato*) spit!; **ni fu ni fa** neither this nor that

fucilazo *m* heat lightning, sheet lightning

fuego *m* fire; (*para encender un cigarrillo*) light; (*de arma de fuego*) firing; lighthouse, beacon; hearth, home; rash, eruption; sore, fever blister; **abrir fuego** to open fire; **echar fuego** to blow up, hit the ceiling; **¡fuego!** fire!; **fuego fatuo** will-o'-the-wisp; **fuego graneado** or **nutrido** drumfire; **fuegos artificiales** fireworks; **hacer fuego** to fire, shoot; **marcar a fuego** to brand; **pegar fuego a** to set fire to, set on fire; **poner a fuego y sangre** to lay waste; **prenderse fuego** to catch on fire; **romper fuego** to open fire; stir up a row; **tocar a fuego** to sound the fire alarm

fuelle *m* fold, pucker, wrinkle; (*instrumento para soplar*) bellows; (*cubierta de coche*) folding carriage top; wind clouds; (*persona soplona*) gossip, talebearer

fuente *f* fountain, spring; public hydrant; font, baptismal font; platter, tray; (fig) source; **beber en buenas fuentes** to have good sources of information; **fuente de gasolina** gasoline pump; **fuente de sodas** soda fountain; **fuente para beber** drinking fountain; **fuentes termales** hot springs

fuer *m* — **a fuer de** as a, by way of

fuera *adv* out, outside; away, out of town; **desde fuera** from the outside; **fuera de** outside of; away from; out of; aside from; in addition to; **fuera de que** aside from the fact that; **fuera de sí** beside oneself; **por fuera** on the outside

fuera-bordo *m* outboard motor

fuere•ño -ña *mf* (Mex) hick, stranger

fuero *m* law, statute; code of laws; jurisdiction; exemption, privilege; **fuero interior** conscience, inmost heart; **fueros** pride, arrogance

fuerte *adj* strong; hard; loud; heavy; **hacerse fuerte** to stick to one's guns; (mil) to hole up, to dig in ‖ *adv* hard; loud ‖ *m* fort, fortress; forte, strong point

fuerza *f* force, strength, power; (*de un ejército*) main body; literal meaning; (phys) force; **a fuerza de** by dint of, by force of; **a la fuerza** forcibly, by force; **a viva fuerza** by main strength; **fuerza aérea** air force; **fuerza de agua** water power; **fuerza de sangre** animal power; **fuerza mayor** (law) force majeure, act of God; **fuerza motriz** motive power; **fuerza pública** police; **fuerza viva** kinetic energy; **hacer fuerza** to strain, struggle; to carry weight; **por fuerza** perforce, necessarily; **ser fuerza +** *inf* to be necessary to + *inf*

fuete *m* whip

fufar *intr* (*el gato*) to spit

fuga *f* flight; (*salida de un gas o líquido*) leak; ardor, vigor; (mus) fugue; **darse a la fuga** to take flight, run away; **fuga de capitales** capital flight; **poner en fuga** to put to flight

fugar §44 *ref* to flee, escape, run away

fu•gaz *adj* (*pl* **-gaces**) fleeting, passing; (*estrella*) shooting

fugiti•vo -va *adj & mf* fugitive

fugui•llas *m* (*pl* **-llas**) (coll) hustler

fula•no -na *mf* so-and-so

fulcro *m* fulcrum

fulgor *m* brilliance, radiance

fulgurar *intr* to flash

fulmicotón *m* guncotton

fulminar *tr* to strike with lightning; strike dead; (*censuras, amenazas, etc.*) thunder; (*balas o bombas*) hurl

fullería *f* trickery, cheating

fulle•ro -ra *adj* crooked, cheating ‖ *mf* crook, cheat; **fullero de naipes** cardsharp

fumada *f* puff, whiff

fumadero *m* smoking room; **fumadero de opio** opium den

fuma•dor -dora *adj* smoking ‖ *mf* smoker

fumar *tr* to smoke ‖ *intr* to smoke; **fumar en pipa** to smoke a pipe; **se prohibe fumar** no smoking ‖ *ref* to squander; stay away from; (*la clase*) cut

fumarada *f* (*de humo*) puff; (*de tabaco*) pipeful

fumigación *f* fumigation; **fumigación aérea** crop dusting

fumigar §44 *tr* to fumigate

fumista *m* stove or heater repairman; stove or heater dealer

fumistería *f* stove or heater shop

fumo•so -sa *adj* smoky

funámbu•lo -la *mf* ropewalker

función *f* function; duty, office, function; (*espectáculo teatral*) show, performance; **entrar en funciones** to take office, take up one's duties; **función benéfica** charitable performance; **función de aficionados** amateur performance; **función de títeres** puppet show; **función secundaria** side show

funcional *adj* functional

funcionariado *m* bureaucracy

funcionario *m* functionary, public official, civil servant

funcione•ro -ra *adj* officious, fussy

fund. *abbr* **fundador**

funda *f* case, sheath, envelope, slip; (*para una espada*) scabbard; (*para proteger los muebles*) slip cover; **funda de almohada** pillowcase; **funda de asientos** seat cover; **funda de gafas** spectacle case

fundación *f* foundation

fundadamente *adv* with good reason; on good authority

funda•dor -dora *adj* founding ‖ *mf* founder

fundamental *adj* fundamental

fundamentar *tr* to lay the foundations of

fundamento *m* foundation; (*razón, motivo*) grounds, reason; basis; reliability, sense; (Col) skirt

fundar *tr* to found, base ‖ *ref* — **fundarse en** to be based on; base one's opinion on

fundente *adj* molten ‖ *m* flux

fundería *f* foundry

fundible *adj* fusible

fundición *f* (*acción de fundir*) founding; (*fábrica*) foundry; (*herrería*) forge; (*hierro colado*) cast iron; (typ) font

fundi•do -da *adj* melted; (*individuo*) ruined; (elec) shorted, blown out

fundidor *m* founder, foundryman

fundillo m (Cuba, Mex) behind, buttocks
fundir tr (p.ej., metales) to found; (campanas, estatuas) cast; (derretir para purificar) smelt; (colores) mix; (un filamento eléctrico) burn out ‖ intr to smelt ‖ ref to melt; fuse; (un filamento eléctrico) burn out; fail, founder; (fig) to fuse, merge
fúnebre adj (marcha, procesión) funeral; (triste) funereal
funeral adj funeral; (triste, lúgubre) funereal ‖ m funeral; **funerales** funeral
funerala — a la funerala (mil) with arms inverted (as a token of mourning)
funera·rio -ria adj funeral ‖ m mortician, funeral director ‖ f (empresa) undertaking establishment; (local) funeral home, funeral parlor
funes·to -ta adj ill-fated; sad, sorrowful; (p.ej., influencia) baneful
fungir §27 intr (CAm, Mex) to act, function
fungo m (pathol) fungus
fungo·so -sa adj fungous
funicular adj & m funicular
fuñique adj awkward; dull, tiresome
furgón m wagon, truck; (rr) freight car, boxcar; (rr) caboose
furgoneta f light truck, delivery truck
furia f fury
furibun·do -da adj furious, frenzied

furio·so -sa adj furious; (muy grande) terrific, tremendous
furor m rage, furor; **causar furor** to make a splash, cause a stir; **hacer furor** to be all the rage
furti·vo -va adj furtive; sneaky, poaching
furúnculo m boil
fusa f (mus) demisemiquaver
fus·co -ca adj dark
fusela·do -da adj streamlined
fuselaje m fuselage
fusible adj fusible ‖ m (elec) fuse
fusil m gun, rifle
fusilar tr to shoot, execute; plagiarize
fusilazo m (tiro de fusil) gunshot, rifle shot; (relámpago sin ruido) heat lightning, sheet lightning
fusilería f rifle corps; rifles, guns; (descarga) fusillade
fusión f fusion; melting; **fusión de empresas** (com) merger
fusionar tr & ref to fuse, merge
fusta f brushwood, twigs; teamster's whip
fustán m fustian; cotton petticoat; (Ven) skirt
fuste m wood, timber; shaft, stem; (fig) importance, substance
fustigar §44 tr to whip, lash; rebuke harshly
fútbol m football; soccer, **fútbol asociación** soccer
fútil adj futile, trifling, inconsequential
futilidad f futility
futre m (SAm) dandy, dude
futu·ro -ra adj future ‖ m future; (gram) future; fiancé; **futuros** (com) futures ‖ f fiancée

G

G, g (ge) f eighth letter of the Spanish alphabet
G. abbr gracia
gaba·cho -cha adj & mf Pyrenean; (coll) Frenchy ‖ m (coll) Frenchified Spanish (language)
gabán m overcoat
gabardina f gabardine; raincoat with belt
gabarra f barge, lighter
gabarro m (en una piedra) nodule; (en un tejido) flaw, defect; mistake
gabinete m cabinet; (de médico, abogado, etc.) office; studio, study; laboratory; (Col) glassed-in balcony; **de gabinete** armchair, theoretical; **gabinete de aseo** washroom; **gabinete de lectura** reading room
gablete m gable
gacela f gazelle
gaceta f government journal; newspaper; **mentir más que la gaceta** to lie like a trooper
gacetilla f town talk, gossip column; short item
gacetillero m gossip columnist
gacetista mf newspaper reader; newsmonger
gacilla f (CAm) safety pin

gacha f watery mass; (Col, Ven) earthenware bowl; **gachas** mush, pap; porridge; mud; **gachas de avena** oatmeal; **hacerse unas gachas** to be mushy
ga·cho -cha adj turned down; flopping; (sombrero) slouch; **a gachas** on all fours ‖ f see **gacha**
gachumbo m (SAm) hard fruit shell
gachu·pín -pina mf (CAm, Mex) Spanish settler in Latin America
gaéli·co -ca adj Gaelic ‖ mf Gael ‖ m Gaelic (language)
gafa f clamp; (enganche de los anteojos) temple; **gafas** glasses; **gafas de sol** or **gafas para sol** sunglasses
gafe m jinx, hoodoo
ga·fo -fa adj claw-handed; foot-sore ‖ f see **gafa**
gaguear intr to stutter
gaita f hornpipe; hurdy-gurdy; chore, hard task; neck; **gaita gallega** bagpipe
gaite·ro -ra adj flashy, gaudy ‖ m piper, bagpipe player
gajes mpl wages, salary; **gajes del oficio** cares of office, occupational annoyances

gajo *m* broken branch; (*de un racimo de uvas*) small stem; (*división interior de ciertas frutas*) slice; (*de horca*) tine, prong; (*ramal de montes*) spur; curl

gala *f* fine clothes; (*lo más selecto*) choice, cream; tip, fee; **de gala** full-dress; **hacer gala de** to glory in; **llevarse la gala** to win approval

galafate *m* slick thief

galai·co -ca *adj* Galician

galán *m* good-looking fellow; lover, gallant, ladies' man; (*el que sirve de escolta a una dama*) escort, cavalier; (theat) leading man; **galán joven** (theat) juvenile; **primer galán** (theat) leading man

galancete *m* (theat) juvenile

gala·no -na *adj* elegant, graceful; spruce, smartly dressed; rich, tasteful

galante *adj* (*con las damas*) gallant; (*con los caballeros*) flirtatious; (*mujer*) wanton, loose

galantear *tr* to court, woo, make love to; sue, entreat

galantería *f* gallantry; charm, elegance; generosity

galanura *f* charm, elegance

galápago *m* pond tortoise; (*del arado*) moldboard; light saddle; ingot

galardón *m* reward, recompense

galardonar *tr* to reward, recompense

galaxia *f* galaxy

galbana *f* laziness; shiftlessness

galbano·so -sa *adj* lazy; phlegmatic

gale·no -na *adj* gentle; mild ‖ *m* (coll) physician, doctor

galeón *m* (naut) galleon

galeote *m* galley slave

galera *f* covered wagon; women's jail; (*de hospital*) ward; (naut & typ) galley

galerada *f* wagonload; (typ) galley; (typ) galley proof

galería *f* gallery; **galería de tiro** shooting gallery; **galerías** department store; **hablar para la galería** to play to the gallery

galerna *f* stormy wind from the northwest (*on the northern coast of Spain*)

Gales *f* Wales; **el país de Gales** Wales; **la Nueva Gales del Sur** New South Wales

ga·lés -lesa *adj* Welsh ‖ *m* Welshman; Welsh (*language*) ‖ *f* Welsh woman

galguear *intr* (CAm, Mex, Arg) to be hungry

gal·go -ga *adj* (Col) sweet-toothed ‖ *m* greyhound ‖ *f* greyhound bitch; rolling stone; mange, rash

Galia, la Gaul

gálibo *m* template, pattern; (rr) gabarit

galicismo *m* Gallicism

gáli·co -ca *adj* Gallic ‖ *m* syphilis; syphilitic

galillo *m* uvula; gullet

galimatí·as *m* (*pl* **-as**) gibberish, nonsense; confusion

galiparia *f* Frenchified Spanish

ga·lo -la *adj* Gaulish ‖ *mf* Gaul ‖ *m* Gaulish (*language*)

galocha *f* clog, wooden shoe

galón *m* braid, galloon; (*medida para líquidos*) gallon; (mil) chevron, stripe

galopar *intr* to gallop

galope *m* gallop; **a galope** at a gallop; in great haste; **a galope tendido** on the run

galopea·do -da *adj* hasty, sketchy ‖ *m* beating, punching

galopear *intr* to gallop

galopillo *m* scullion, kitchen boy

galopín *m* ragamuffin; (*hombre taimado*) wise guy; (naut) cabin boy

galpón *m* (SAm) iron shed; (Col) tile works

galvanizar §60 *tr* to electroplate; galvanize

galvanoplastia *f* electroplating

galladura *f* tread (*of egg*)

gallardete *m* streamer, pennant

gallardía *f* gallantry; elegance; nobility; generosity

gallar·do -da *adj* gallant; elegant; noble; generous; (*temporal*) fierce

gallear *intr* to stand out, excel; shout, yell, threaten

galle·go -ga *adj* & *mf* Galician

gallera *f* cockpit

galleta *f* hardtack, ship biscuit; cracker; little pitcher; slap

gallina *adj* chicken-hearted ‖ *mf* chicken-hearted person ‖ *f* hen; **estar como gallina en corral ajeno** to be like a fish out of water; **gallina ciega** blindman's buff; **gallina de Guinea** guinea fowl

gallinería *f* poultry shop; cowardice

galline·ro -ra *mf* poultry dealer ‖ *m* hencoop, henhouse; poultry basket; top gallery; babel, madhouse

gallipavo *m* turkey; sour note

gallito *m* (*el que figura sobre los demás*) somebody; **gallito del lugar** cock of the walk

gallo *m* cock, rooster; false note, sour note; boss; frog in the throat; (box) bantamweight; (Col, C-R, Mex) strong man; **gallo de bosque** wood grouse; **gallo de pelea** gamecock; **tener mucho gallo** to be cocky

gallofa *f* vegetables; French roll; talk, gossip

gallofear *intr* to beg, bum, loaf around

gallofe·ro -ra *adj* begging, loafing ‖ *mf* beggar, loafer

gama *f* doe, female fallow deer; (mus & fig) gamut

gamberrismo *m* gangsterism, rowdyism

gambe·rro -rra *adj* & *mf* libertine ‖ *m* hoodlum, tough, rowdy

gambeta *f* crosscaper; caper, prance

gambito *m* gambit

gamo *m* buck, male fallow deer

gamón *m* asphodel

gamonal *m* field of asphodel; boss

gamuza *f* chamois

gana *f* desire; will; **darle a uno la gana de** to feel like, e.g., **le da la gana de trabajar** he feels like working; **de buena gana** willingly; **de gana** in earnest; willingly; **de mala gana** unwillingly; **tener ganas de** to feel like, to have a mind to

ganadería *f* cattle, livestock; brand, stock; cattle raising; cattle ranch

ganade·ro -ra *adj* cattle, livestock ‖ *mf* cattle breeder; cattle dealer ‖ *m* cattleman

fu
ga

ganado *m* cattle, livestock; **ganado caballar** horses; **ganado cabrío** goats; **ganado lanar** sheep; **ganado mayor** large farm animals (*cows, bulls, horses, and mules*); **ganado menor** small farm animals (*sheep, goats, pigs*); **ganado menudo** young cattle; **ganado moreno** swine; **ganado ovejuno** sheep; **ganado porcino** swine; **ganado vacuno** cattle

gana•dor -dora *adj* winning; earning; hardworking ‖ *mf* winner; earner

ganancia *f* gain, profit; (Guat, Mex) extra, bonus; **ganancias y pérdidas** profit and loss

ganancial *adj* profit

ganancio•so -sa *adj* gainful, profitable; earning ‖ *mf* earner

ganapán *m* errand boy; boor

ganapierde *m & f* giveaway

ganar *tr* (*dinero trabajando*) to earn; (*la victoria luchando*) win; (*beneficios en los negocios*) gain; (*a una persona en una contienda*) beat, defeat; (*aventajar*) excel; (*la voluntad de una persona*) win over; (*alcanzar*) reach; **ganar algo a alguien** to win something from someone; **ganar de comer** to earn a living ‖ *intr* to earn; (*mejorar*) improve ‖ *ref* to win over; **ganarse la vida** to earn a livelihood

ganchero *m* log driver; (Chile) odd-jobber; (Ecuad) gentle mount

ganchillo *m* crochet needle; crochet, crochet work; **hacer ganchillo** to crochet

gancho *m* hook;. shepherd's crook; coaxer; procurer, pimp; hairpin; (Col, Ecuad) lady's saddle; **gancho de botalones** (naut) gooseneck; **echar el gancho a** to hook in, to land; **tener gancho** (*una mujer*) to have a way with the men

gandaya *f* (coll) bumming, loafing

gandujar *tr* to pleat, shirr

gan•dul -dula *adj* loafing, idling ‖ *mf* loafer, idler

gandulear *intr* to loaf, idle

ganfo•rro -rra *mf* scoundrel

ganga *f* bargain

ganglio *m* ganglion

gangocho *m* burlap

gango•so -sa *adj* snuffling, nasal

gangrena *f* gangrene

gangrenar *tr & ref* to gangrene

gángster *m* gunman, gangster

gangsteril *adj* gangster(like)

gangsterismo *m* gangsterism; mobsterism

ganguear *intr* to snuffle, talk through the nose

gangue•ro -ra *adj* bargain-hunting; self-seeking ‖ *mf* bargain hunter

gano•so -sa *adj* desirous; (*caballo*) (Chile) spirited, fiery

gan•so -sa *mf* dope, dullard ‖ *m* goose; gander; **ganso bravo** wild goose ‖ *f* female goose

Gante Ghent

ganzúa *f* (*garfio*) picklock, lock pick; (*persona*) picklock; pumper (*of secrets*)

gañán *m* farm hand; rough, husky fellow

gañido *m* yelp; croak

gañir §12 *intr* (*el perro*) to yelp; (*p.ej., el cuervo*) croak

garabatear *tr* to scribble ‖ *intr* to hook; beat about the bush; scribble

garabato *m* hook; pothook; scribbling; weeding hoe; (*bozal*) muzzle; (*de una mujer*) winsomeness; **garabato de carnicero** meathook; **garabatos** wiggling of hands and fingers

garabato•so -sa *adj* full of scrawls; winsome

garage *m* or **garaje** *m* garage

garagista *m* garbage man

garambaina *f* gaudy trimming; **garambainas** simpering, smirking; (coll) scribble

garante *adj* responsible ‖ *mf* guarantor, voucher

garantía *f* guarantee, guaranty; warranty; **garantía anticorrosión** antirust warranty

garantir §1 *tr* to guarantee

garantizar §60 *tr* to guarantee

garañón *m* stud jackass; stud camel; stallion

garapiña *f* icing, sugar-coating; iced pineapple drink

garapiñar *tr* to ice, sugar-coat; candy

garapiñera *f* ice-cream freezer

garbanzo *m* chickpea; **garbanzo negro** (fig) black sheep

garbeo *m* walk; promenade

garbillar *tr* to sieve, screen riddle

garbillo *s* sieve, screen; riddled ore

garbo *m* jauntiness, grace, fine bearing; generosity

garbo•so -sa *adj* jaunty, graceful, spruce, sprightly; generous

gardu•ño -ña *mf* (archaic) sneak thief ‖ *f* stone marten, beech marten

garete *m* — **al garete** (naut) adrift

garfa *f* claw

garfio *m* hook, gaff

gargajear *intr* to cough up phlegm, hawk

gargajo *m* phlegm

garganta *f* throat; (*de un río, una vasija, etc.*) neck, throat; (*del pie*) instep; (*entre montañas*) ravine, gorge; (*del arado*) sheath; (*de una polea*) groove; (archit) shaft; **tener buena garganta** to have a good voice

gargantear *intr* to warble

gargantilla *f* necklace

gárgara *f* gargling; **gárgaras** (*líquido*) gargle; **hacer gárgaras** to gargle

gargarear *intr* to gargle

gargarismo *m* gargling; (*líquido*) gargle

gargarizar §60 *intr* to gargle

gárgola *f* gargoyle

garguero *m* gullet; (*caña del pulmón*) windpipe

garita *f* sentry box; porter's lodge; (*de una fortificación*) watchtower; railroad-crossing box; privy (*with one seat*); **garita de centinela** sentry box; **garita de señales** (rr) signal tower

garito *m* gambling den

garlito *m* fish trap; trap, snare

garlopa *f* jack plane, trying plane

garnar *intr* to drizzle

garra f claw, talon; catch, hook; **caer en las garras de** to fall into the clutches of
garrafa f carafe, decanter; **garrafa corchera** demijohn
garrafal adj awful, terrible
garrafiñar tr to snatch
garrafón m carboy, demijohn
garramar tr to snitch
garranchuelo m crab grass
garrapata f cattle tick, sheep tick; (mil) disabled horse; (Chile) little runt; (Mex) slut
garrapatear intr to scrawl, scribble
garrapato m pothook, scrawl; **garrapatos** scrawl
garri·do -da adj handsome, elegant
garroba f carob bean
garrocha f goad; (sport) pole
garrotazo m blow with a club
garrote m club, cudgel; garrote (method of execution; iron collar used for such execution); (Mex) brake; **dar garrote a** to garrote
garrote·ro -ra adj (Chile) stingy ‖ m (Mex) brakeman
garrotillo m croup
garrucha f pulley, sheave
gárru·lo -la adj chirping; (hablador) garrulous; (arroyo) babbling; (viento) rustling
garúa drizzle
garuar §21 intr to drizzle
garulla f mob, rabble
garza f heron; **garza real** gray heron
gar·zo -za adj blue ‖ f see garza
garzón m boy, youth; suitor; woman chaser
gas m gas; **gas de alumbrado** illuminating gas; **gas exhilarante** or **hilarante** laughing gas; **gas lacrimógeno** tear gas; **gas mostaza** mustard gas
gasa f gauze, chiffon; (tira de gasa negra con que se rodea el sombrero en señal de luto) hatband
Gascuña f Gascony
gasear tr to gas
gaseo·so -sa adj gaseous ‖ f soda water, carbonated water
gasificar §73 tr to gasify; exalt, elate ‖ ref to gasify
gasista m gas fitter; (Chile) gasworker
gasoducto m gas pipe line
gasógeno m gas generator, gas producer; mixture of benzine and alcohol used for lighting and cleaning
gas-oil m diesel oil
gasolina f gasoline
gasolinera f motor boat; gas station, filling station
gasómetro m gasholder, gas tank
gastadero m waste
gasta·do -da adj worn-out; used up; spent; (chiste) crummy, corny
gasta·dor -dora adj & mf spendthrift ‖ m convict; (mil) sapper, pioneer
gastadura f worn spot
gastar tr (dinero, tiempo) to spend; (en cosas inútiles) waste; (echar a perder con el uso) wear out; (consumir) use up; (p.ej., una

barba) wear; (un coche) keep; **gastarlas** to act, behave ‖ intr to spend ‖ ref to wear; wear out; become used up; waste away
gasto m cost, expense; wear; **gastos de conservación** or **de entretenimiento** upkeep; **gastos de explotación** operating expenses; **gastos menudos** petty expenses; **hacer el gasto** to do most of the talking; to be the subject of conversation; **hacer frente a los gastos** to meet expenses; **meterse en gastos con** to go to the expense of
gasto·so -sa adj wasteful, extravagant
gástri·co -ca adj gastric
gastronomía f gastronomy
gastróno·mo -ma mf gourmet
gata f she-cat; low-hanging cloud; Madrid woman; (Mex) maid, servant girl; **a gatas** on all fours, on hands and knees
gatada f catty act
gatatumba f faked attention, fake emotion, faked pain
gatazo m gyp
gatea·do -da adj catlike; grained, striped ‖ m crawling, climbing; scratching, clawing
gatear tr to scratch, claw; snitch ‖ intr to crawl, climb
gatera f cathole; (naut) hawsehole
gatería f cats; gang of toughs; fake humility
gate·ro -ra adj full of cats ‖ mf cat lover ‖ f see gatera
gates·co -ca adj catlike, feline
gatillo m (de arma de fuego) trigger; little pickpocket
gato m cat; tomcat; (instrumento para levantar pesos) jack, lifting jack; sneak thief; native of Madrid; **gato montés** wildcat; **gato rodante** dolly; **vender gato por liebre** to gyp, cheat
gatopardo m cheetah
gauchada f (SAm) sly trick; (SAm) good turn
gauchaje m (SAm) gathering of Gauchos
gauches·co -ca adj Gaucho
gau·cho -cha adj (SAm) Gaucho; (Arg, Chile) sly, crafty ‖ m (SAm) Gaucho; (SAm) good horseman ‖ m (Arg) mannish woman; (Arg) loose woman
gaultería f wintergreen
gaveta f drawer, till
gavia f ditch, drain; (ave) gull; (min) gang of basket passers; (naut) topsail
gavilán m sparrow hawk; (de la pluma) nib; (en la escritura) hair stroke; ingrowing nail
gavilla f sheaf, bundle; gang
gaviota f sea gull
gavota f gavotte
gaya f colored stripe; (ave) magpie
gayar tr to trim with colored stripes
ga·yo -ya adj cheerful, bright, showy ‖ m (orn) jay ‖ f see gaya
gayola f cage; jail
gayomba f Spanish broom
gazapa f lie
gazapatón m blunder, slip
gazapera f rabbit warren; gang, gang of thugs; brawl, row

ga
ga

gazapo *m* young rabbit; sly fellow; slip, boner, blunder; (*de actor*) fluff

gazmiar *tr* (*oliendo*) to sniff; (*comiendo*) nibble ‖ *ref* to complain

gazmoñada *f* or **gazmoñería** *f* prudishness, priggishness

gazmoñe•ro -ra or **gazmo•ño -ña** *adj* prudish, priggish, strait-laced, demure ‖ *mf* prude, prig

gaznápiro *m* gawk, boob, bumpkin

gaznate *m* gullet; (Mex) fritter

gazpacho *m* cold vegetable soup; (Hond) leftovers

gazuza *f* hunger

Gedeón *m* Gideon

gehena *m* Gehenna

géiser *m* geyser

gel *m* gel

gelatina *f* gelatine

gema *f* gem; (bot) bud

geme•lo -la *adj & mf* twin; **gemelos** twins; binoculars; cuff links; **gemelos de campo** field glasses; **gemelos de teatro** opera glasses ‖ **Gemelos** *mpl* (astr) Gemini

gemido *m* moan, groan; wail, whine; howl, roar

Géminis *m* (astr) Gemini

gemiquear *intr* (Chile) to whine

gemir §50 *intr* to moan, groan; wail, whine; howl, roar

gen *m* gene

genciana *f* gentian

gendarme *m* policeman

genealogía *f* genealogy

generación *f* generation

genera•dor -dora *adj* generating ‖ *m* generator

general *adj* general; common, usual; **en general** or **por lo general** in general ‖ *m* general; **capitán general de ejército** fivestar general; **general de brigada** brigadier, brigadier general; **general de división** major general ‖ **generales** *fpl* general information, personal data

generala *f* general's wife; call to arms

generalato *m* generalship

generalidad *f* generality; majority; **la generalidad de** the general run of

generalísimo *m* generalissimo

generalizar §60 *tr & intr* to generalize ‖ *ref* to become generalized

generar *tr* to generate

genéri•co -ca *adj* generic; (*artículo*) indefinite; (*nombre*) common; showing gender

género *m* kind, sort; way, manner; cloth, material; (biol, log) genus; (gram) gender; **de género** genre; **género chico** one-act play, one-act operetta; **género de punto** knit goods, knitwear; **género humano** humankind; **género ínfimo** light vaudeville; **género novelístico** fiction; **género picaresco** burlesque; **géneros** goods, merchandise, material; **géneros de pieza** yard goods; **géneros para vestidos** dress goods

genero•so -sa *adj* generous; highborn; noble, magnanimous; (*vino*) rich, full

géne•sis *f* (*pl* -sis) genesis ‖ **el Génesis** (Bib) Genesis

genéti•co -ca *adj* genetic ‖ *f* genetics

genial *adj* inspired, geniuslike; pleasant, agreeable; temperamental

geniazo *m* fiery temper

genio *m* (*índole, carácter*) temperament, disposition; (*don altísimo de invención; persona que lo posee; espíritu tutelar, deidad pagana*) genius; fire, spirit

genital *adj* genital ‖ **genitales** *mpl* genitals

geniti•vo -va *adj* genitive

genitourina•rio -ria *adj* genitourinary

genocida *adj* genocidal ‖ *mf* genocide

genocidio *m* genocide

Génova *f* Genoa

geno•vés -vesa *adj & mf* Genoese

gente *f* people; (*parentela, familia*) folks; race, nation; troops; **gente baja** lower classes, rabble; **gente bien** nice people; **gente de bien** decent people; **gente de capa parda** country people; **gente de coleta** bullfighters; **gente de color** colored people; **gente de la cuchilla** butchers; **genta de la vida airada** bullies; underworld; **gente del bronce** bright, lively people; **gente del rey** convicts; **gente de mal vivir** toughs, underworld; **gente de mar** seafaring people; **gente de paz** (*palabras con las cuales se contesta al que pregunta ¿quién?*) friend; **gente de pluma** (coll) clerks; **gente de su majestad** convicts; **gente de trato** tradespeople; **gente forzada** convicts; **gente menuda** small fry; common people

gentecilla *f* mob, rabble

gentil *adj* heathen, gentile; elegant, genteel; noble ‖ *mf* heathen, pagan

gentileza *f* elegance, gentility, courtesy; gallantry; show, splendor; (*hidalguía*) nobility

gentilhombre *m* (*pl* **gentileshombres**) gentleman; messenger to the king; my good man; **gentilhombre de cámara** gentleman in waiting

gentili•cio -cia *adj* national; family; (gram) gentile

gentilidad *f* heathendom

gentío *m* crowd, mob

gentualla or **gentuza** *f* rabble, riffraff

genui•no -na *adj* genuine

geofísi•co -ca *adj* geophysical ‖ *mf* geophysicist ‖ *f* geophysics

geografía *f* geography

geográfi•co -ca *adj* geographic(al)

geógra•fo -fa *mf* geographer

geología *f* geology

geológi•co -ca *adj* geologic(al)

geólo•go -ga *mf* geologist

geómetra *mf* geometrician

geometría *f* geometry; **geometría del espacio** solid geometry

geométri•co -ca *adj* geometric(al)

geopolíti•co -ca *adj* geopolitical ‖ *f* geopolitics

geranio *m* geranium

gerencia *f* management; manager's office

gerente *m* manager, director; **gerente de**

publicidad advertising manager; **gerente de ventas** sales manager

geriatría f geriatry

geriatra adj geriatrical ‖ mf geriatrician

geriátri·co -ca adj geriatrical

germanía f gypsy slang, cant of thieves

germanizar §60 tr to Germanize

germen m germ; **germen plasma** germ plasm

germicida adj germicidal ‖ m germicide

germinal adj germ; germinal

germinar intr to germinate

gerontología f gerontology

gerundio m gerund; present participle; bombastic writer or speaker

gestación f gestation

gestear intr to make faces

gesticular intr to make a face, to make faces; (hacer ademanes) to gesticulate

gestión f step, measure; management; action, proceeding, negotiation

gestionar tr to promote, pursue; manage; negotiate

gesto m face; wry face, grimace; look, appearance; (movimiento, ademán) gesture

ges·tor -tora adj managing ‖ m manager

gestu·do -da adj cross-looking

ghetto m ghetto

giba f hump; annoyance

giga f jig

giganta f giantess

gigante adj giant ‖ m giant; (en las procesiones) giant figure

gigantes·co -ca adj gigantic

gigantez f giant size

gigantilla f large-headed masked figure; little fat woman

gigan·tón -tona mf huge giant ‖ m giant figure

gigote m chopped-meat stew; **hacer gigote** to chop up

gilí adj foolish, stupid

gimnasia f gymnastics; **gimnasia sueca** Swedish movements, setting-up exercises

gimnasio m gymnasium; secondary school, academy

gimnasta mf gymnast

gimnásti·co -ca adj gymnastic ‖ f gymnastics

gimotear intr to whine

gimoteo m whining

ginebra f gin; (de voces) buzz, din; confusion, disorder ‖ **Ginebra** f Geneva

ginebri·no -na adj & mf Genevan

ginecología f gynecology

ginecológi·co -ca adj gynecologic(al)

ginecólo·go -ga mf gynecologist

ginesta f Spanish broom

gira f var of **jira**

gira·do -da mf drawee

gira·dor -dora mf drawer

giralda f weathercock (in the form of person or animal)

girándula f girandole

girar tr (una visita) to pay; (com) to draw ‖ intr to turn; rotate, gyrate; trade; (com) to draw

girasol m sunflower, sycophant

girato·rio -ria adj revolving ‖ f revolving bookcase

gi·ro -ra adj (Guat) drunk; (Mex) cocky ‖ m turn; rotation; revolution; course, trend, turn; turn of phrase; boast, threat; gash, slash; line of business; trade; (com) draft; **giro a la vista** sight draft; **giro postal** money order ‖ f see **gira**

giroflé m clove

giroscopio m gyroscope

gis m (Col) slate pencil

gitana f gypsy woman, gypsy girl

gitanada f gypsy trick; fawning, flattery

gitanería f band of gypsies; gypsy life; fawning, flattery

gitanes·co -ca adj gypsyish

gita·no -na adj gypsy; flattering; sly, tricky ‖ mf gypsy ‖ m Gypsy (language) ‖ f see **gitana**

glaciación f freezing

glacial adj glacial; (zona) frigid; (fig) cold, indifferent

glaciar m glacier

glándula f gland; **glándula cerrada** ductless gland

glasé m glacé silk

glasea·do -da adj glossy, shiny

glicerina f glycerin

global adj total; global, world-wide

globo m globe; (aparato que, lleno de un gas, se eleva en el aire) balloon; (bomba de lámpara) globe, lamp shade; **globo de aire** (aut) air bag; **globo del ojo** eyeball; **globo sonda** trial balloon; **lanzar un globo sonda** (fig) to send up a trial balloon

glóbulo m globule; (physiol) corpuscle; **glóbulo rojo** red cell

gloria f glory; **ganar la gloria** to go to glory; **oler a gloria** to smell heavenly; **saber a gloria** to taste heavenly

gloriar §77 tr to glorify ‖ intr to recite the rosary ‖ ref to glory

glorieta f arbor, bower, summerhouse; public square; traffic circle

glorificar §73 tr to glorify ‖ ref to glory

glorio·so -sa adj glorious; boastful

glosa f gloss

glosa·dor -dora adj commenting ‖ mf commentator

glosar tr to gloss; audit; (Col) to scold ‖ intr to find fault

glosario m glossary

glóti·co -ca adj glottal

glo·tón -tona adj gluttonous ‖ mf glutton

glotonería f gluttony

glucosa f glucose

gluglú m (del agua) gurgle, glug; (del pavo) gobble; **hacer gluglú** to gurgle, to glug

gluglutear intr to gobble

gnomo m gnome

gob. abbr **gobierno**

gobernación f governing; government; department of the interior; (Arg) territory

gobernad·dor -dora adj governing ‖ m governor

gobernalle m rudder, helm

ga
go

gobernante *adj* governing ‖ *mf* ruler ‖ *m* self-appointed head

gobernar §2 *tr* to govern; guide, direct; control, rule; (*un buque*) steer ‖ *intr* to govern; steer

goberno•so -sa *adj* orderly

gobierno *m* government; governor's office; governorship; management; control, rule; guidance; (*de un buque*) navigability; **de buen gobierno** (*buque*) navigable; **gobierno de monigotes** puppet government; **gobierno doméstico** housekeeping; **gobierno exilado** government in exile; **para su gobierno** for your guidance; **servir de gobierno** to serve as a guide

goce *m* enjoyment

go•do -da *adj* Gothic ‖ *mf* Goth; Spanish noble; (Arg, Chile) Spaniard

gofio *m* roasted corn meal

gol *m* goal

gola *f* gullet

goldre *m* quiver

goleta *f* schooner

golf *m* golf

golfán *m* white water lily

golfista *mf* golfer

gol•fo -fa *mf* ragamuffin ‖ *m* gulf; open sea; **golfo de Méjico** Gulf of Mexico; **golfo de Vizcaya** Bay of Biscay

Gólgota, el (Bib) Golgotha

golilla *f* gorget, ruff; magistrate's collar; pipe flange; (*de los caños de barro*) collar, sleeve; (*del gallo*) erectile bristles

golondrina *f* swallow; **empresa golondrina** fly-by-night outfit

golosina *f* delicacy, tidbit; eagerness, appetite; trifle

golosinear *intr* to go around eating candy

golo•so -sa *adj* sweet-toothed; (*glotón*) gluttonous; (*apetitoso*) tasty

golpe *m* blow, stroke, hit; bump, bruise; heartbeat; crowd, throng, flock; (*del bolsillo*) flap; (*pestillo*) bolt, latch; (*de licor*) shot; surprise, wonder; (*infortunio*) blow; witticism; **dar golpe** to make a hit; **de golpe** all at once, suddenly; **de golpe y porrazo** slambang; **de un golpe** at one stroke; **golpe de ariete** water hammer; **golpe de calor** heatstroke; **golpe de estado** coup d'état; **golpe de fortuna** stroke of fortune; **golpe de gracia** coup de grâce; **golpe de mano** surprise attack; **golpe de mar** surge; **golpe de ojo** glance; **golpe de teatro** dramatic turn of events; **golpe de tos** fit of coughing; **golpe de vista** glance, look; view; **golpe en vago** miss, flop; **golpe mortal** deathblow; **no dar golpe** to not raise a hand, not do a stroke of work

golpear *tr* to strike, hit, beat; bump, bruise ‖ *intr* to beat, strike; (*el reloj*) tick; (*el motor de combustión interna*) knock

golpete *m* door catch, window catch

golpetear *tr & intr* to beat; rattle

golpismo *m* government by coup d'état

gollería *f* delicacy, dainty; **pedir gollerías** to ask for too much

gollete *m* throat, neck; (*de botella*) neck

goma *f* gum, rubber; (*tira de goma elástica*) rubber band; (*neumático*) tire; **goma arábiga** gum arabic; **goma de borrar** eraser, rubber; **goma de mascar** chewing gum; **goma espumosa** foam rubber; **goma laca** shellac

gomecillo *m* blind man's guide

gomia *f* bugaboo; waster; glutton

gomo•so -sa *adj* gum; gummy ‖ *m* dude, dandy

góndola *f* gondola

gondolero *m* gondolier

gongo *m* gong

gonorrea *f* gonorrhea

gordal *adj* large-size

gordia•no -na *adj* Gordian

gordi•flón -flona or **gordin•flón -flona** *adj* chubby, pudgy, fatty ‖ *mf* fatty

gor•do -da *adj* fat, plump; fatty, greasy; coarse; big, large; whopping big; (*agua*) hard ‖ *m* fat, suet; first prize (*in lottery*) ‖ **gordo** *adv* — **hablar gordo** to talk big

gordura *f* fatness, plumpness, stoutness, corpulence; fat, grease

gorgojo *m* grub, weevil; dwarf, runt; **gorgojo del algodón** boll weevil

gorgojo•so -sa *adj* grubby

gorgón *m* (Col) concrete

gorgonear *intr* (*el pavo*) to gobble

gorgoritear *intr* to trill

gorgorito *m* trill

gorgotear *intr* to burble, gurgle

gorgotero *m* peddler, hawker

gorigori *m* lugubrious funeral chant

gorila *f* gorilla; (coll) thug; strong-arm man

gorjear *intr* to warble, trill ‖ *ref* (*el niño*) to gurgle

gorra *f* cap; bumming, sponging; **andar de gorra** to sponge; **colarse de gorra** (coll) to crash the gate; **gorra de visera** cap; **vivir de gorra** to live on other people

gorrada *f* tipping the hat

gorrear *intr* (Ecuad) to sponge

gorretada *f* tipping the hat

gorrión *m* sparrow; **gorrión triguero** bunting

gorrista *adj* sponging ‖ *mf* sponger

gorro *m* cap, bonnet; baby's bonnet; **gorro de dormir** nightcap

go•rrón -rrona *adj* sponging ‖ *mf* sponger ‖ *m* pivot; journal, gudgeon

gota *f* drop; (pathol) gout; **gotas** touch of rum or brandy in coffee; **sudar la gota gorda** to work one's head off

gotear *intr* to drip, dribble; (*llover a gotas espaciadas*) sprinkle

gotera *f* drip, dripping; mark left by dripping; (*en el techo*) leak; (*adorno de una cama*) valance; **estar lleno de goteras** to be full of aches and pains; **es una gotera** it's a constant drain; **goteras** aches, pains; (Col) environs, outskirts

góti•co -ca *adj* Gothic; noble, illustrious ‖ *m* Gothic

goto•so -sa *adj* gouty ‖ *mf* gout sufferer

gozar §60 *tr* (*poseer*) to enjoy ‖ *intr* to enjoy oneself; **gozar de** (*poseer*) to enjoy ‖ *ref* to enjoy oneself; rejoice

gozne *m* hinge

gozo *m* joy, enjoyment; **no caber en sí de gozo** to be beside oneself with joy; **saltar de gozo** to leap with joy

gozo•so -sa *adj* joyful; **gozoso con** or **de** joyful over

gozque *m* or **gozquejo** *m* little yapping dog

grabación *f* (*de disco*) recording; **grabación sobre cinta** tape recording

grabado *m* engraving; print, cut, picture; (*de disco*) recording; **grabado en madera** wood engraving, woodcut; **grabado fuera de texto** inset, insert

graba•dor -dora *adj* recording ‖ *mf* engraver ‖ *f* recorder; **grabadora de cinta** tape recorder

grabador-reproductor *m* cassette recorder

grabadura *f* engraving

grabar *tr* to engrave; (*un sonido, una canción, un disco, etc.*) record; **grabar en** or **sobre cinta** to tape-record ‖ *ref* to become engraved

gracejada *f* (CAm, Mex) cheap comedy, clownishness

gracejar *intr* to be engaging, witty; joke

gracejo *m* lightness, winsome manner, charm; (CAm, Mex) clown

gracia *f* witticism, witty remark, joke; grace; gracefulness; favor; pardon; (*de un chiste*) point; name; **caer en gracia a** to be pleasing to; **de gracia** gratis; **decir dos gracias a** to tell someone a thing or two; **en gracia a** because of; **gracia de Dios** daily bread; air and sunshine; **gracias** thanks; **¡gracias!** thanks!; **gracias a** thanks to; **¡gracias a Dios!** thank heavens!; **hacer gracia** to be pleasing; **hacer gracia de algo a uno** to exempt or free someone from something; **hacerle a uno gracia** to strike someone as funny; **¡linda gracia!** nonsense!; **tener gracia** to be funny, be surprising

graciable *adj* kind, gracious; easy to grant

grácil *adj* thin, small, slender

gracio•so -sa *adj* (*que tiene donaire, gracia*) graceful; (*afable, fino*) gracious; (*agudo, chistoso*) funny, witty; (*que se da de balde*) free, gratis ‖ *mf* comic ‖ *m* gracioso (*gay, comic character in Spanish comedy*)

grada *f* step, stair; row of seats; grandstand; altar step; (agr) harrow; (*plano inclinado sobre el cual se construyen los barcos*) slip; **gradas** stone steps; (Chile, Peru) atrium; **gradas al aire libre** bleachers

gradar *tr* (agr) to harrow

gradería *f* stone steps; row of seats; bleachers; **gradería cubierta** grandstand

gradiente *m* (phys) gradient ‖ *f* slope, gradient

grado *m* step; grade; degree; (*título que se da en las universidades*) degree; (*sección en las escuelas*) grade, form, class; (mil) rank; **de buen grado** willingly; **de grado en grado** by degrees; **de grado o por fuerza** willy-nilly; **de mal grado** unwillingly; **en sumo grado** to a great extent; **mal de mi grado** unwillingly, against my wishes

graduación *f* graduation; (*de las bebidas espirituosas*) strength; (mil) rank

gradual *adj* gradual

graduan•do -da *mf* (*persona próxima a graduarse en la universidad*) graduate (*candidate for a degree*)

graduar §21 *tr* to graduate, grade; (*un grifo, una válvula, etc.*) regulate; appraise, estimate ‖ *ref* to graduate

grafía *f* graph

gráfi•co -ca *adj* graphic(al); printing; illustrated; picture, camera ‖ *m* diagram ‖ *f* graph

grafito *m* graphite

grafospasmo *m* writer's cramp

gragea *f* colored candy; sugar-coated pill

grajear *intr* (*los cuervos*) to caw; (*los niños*) gurgle

grajien•to -ta *adj* foul-smelling

gra•jo -ja *mf* rook, crow; chatterbox ‖ *m* body odor

gral. *abbr* **general**

gramática *f* grammar; **gramática parda** shrewdness, mother wit

gramatical *adj* grammatical

gramáti•co -ca *adj* grammatical ‖ *mf* grammarian ‖ *f* see **gramática**

gramil *m* marking gauge, gauge

gramo *m* gram

gramófono *m* gramophone

gramola *f* console phonograph; portable phonograph

gran *adj* apocopated form of **grande,** used only before nouns of both genders in the singular

grana *f* seed; seeding; seeding time; red; **dar en grana** to go to seed

granada *f* pomegranate; (*proyectil explosivo*) grenade; **granada de mano** hand grenade; **granada de metralla** shrapnel; **granada extintora** fire extinguisher, fire grenade

granadero *m* grenadier

granadilla *f* passionflower

granadina *f* grenadine

grana•do -da *adj* choice, select; mature, expert ‖ *m* pomegranate; **granado blanco** rose of Sharon ‖ *f* see **granada**

granalla *f* filings

granangular *adj* wide-angle

granate *m* adj invar & *m* garnet

Gran Bretaña, la Great Britain

grande *adj* big, large; great ‖ *m* grandee

grandeza *f* bigness, largeness; greatness; (*tamaño*) size; (*magnificencia*) grandeur; grandees; grandeeship

grandi•llón -llona *adj* oversize, overgrown

grandio•so -sa *adj* grandiose, grand

grandor *m* size

granea•do -da *adj* spattered; (*fuego*) heavy and continuous

granear *tr* to sow; (*la pólvora; una piedra litográfica*) grain; stipple

granel — a granel in bulk, loose; at random; lavishly

granelar *tr* (*el cuero*) to grain

granero *m* granary

granete *m* center punch

go
gr

granífu•go -ga *adj* hail-dispersing
granito *m* granite
granizada *f* hailstorm; (Arg, Chile) iced drink
granizar §60 *tr* (*p.ej., golpes*) to hail; sprinkle || *intr* to hail
granizo *m* hail
granja *f* farm, grange; dairy; country place
granjear *tr* to earn, gain; win, win over || *ref* to win, win over
granjería *f* husbandry; gain, profit
granje•ro -ra *mf* farmer; merchant, trader
grano *m* grain; (*baya*) berry; (*baya de la uva*) grape; (*tumorcillo en la piel*) pimple; (*peso*) grain; grano de belleza beauty spot; grano de café coffee bean; granos (*fruto de los cereales*) grain; ir al grano to come to the point
granuja *m* scoundrel; (*muchacho vagabundo*) waif || *f* loose grape; grapeseed
granujo *m* pimple
granular *adj* granular; pimply || *tr* & *ref* to granulate
gránulo *m* granule
grapa *f* clamp, clip, staple
grasa *f* fat, grease; (*polvo*) pounce; (Mex) shoe polish; grasa de ballena blubber; grasas slag
grasien•to -ta *adj* greasy
grasilla *f* pounce
gra•so -sa *adj* fatty, greasy || *m* fattiness, greasiness || *f* see grasa
grasones *mpl* wheat porridge
graso•so -sa *adj* greasy; (pathol) fatty
grata *f* wire brush; (*carta*) favor
gratificar §73 *tr* to gratify; reward, recompense; tip, fee
gratín *m* — al gratín au gratin
gratis *adv* gratis
gratisda•to -ta *adj* free, gratis
gratitud *f* gratitude
gra•to -ta *adj* pleasing; free; (Bol, Chile) grateful || *f* see grata
gratuidad *f* cost exemption; exemption from fees
gratui•to -ta *adj* gratuitous; free, gratis
grava *f* gravel; crushed stone
gravamen *m* burden, obligation; encumbrance, lien; assessment
gravar *tr* to burden, encumber; assess || *ref* to get worse
grave *adj* grave, serious, solemn; hard, difficult; (*que pesa*) heavy; (*sonido*) grave, deep, low; (*música*) majestic, noble; (*negocio*) important; (*enfermedad*) serious; (*acento*) grave; paroxytone
gravedad *f* gravity; seriousness; de gravedad seriously; gravely; gravedad nula weightlessness, zero gravity
gravedo•so -sa *adj* heavy, pompous
gravidez *f* pregnancy
grávi•do -da *adj* pregnant
gravitación *f* gravitation
gravitar *intr* to gravitate; gravitar sobre to weigh down on
gravo•so -sa *adj* burdensome, onerous, costly; boring, tiresome

graznar *intr* to caw, croak; cackle; (*al cantar*) (fig) cackle
graznido *m* caw, croak; cackle; (*canto que disuena mucho*) (fig) cackle
Grecia *f* Greece
grecia•no -na *adj* Grecian
gre•co -ca *adj* & *mf* Greek
greda *f* clay, fuller's earth
grega•rio -ria *adj* (*que vive confundido con otros*) gregarious; slavish, servile
gregoria•no -na *adj* Gregorian
gremial *adj* guild; trade-union, union || *m* guildsman; union member
gremio *m* guild, corporation; trade union, union; association, society
greña *f* confusion, entanglement; (*de cabello*) shock, tangled mop; andar a la greña to get into a hot argument; (*dos mujeres*) to pull each other's hair
greñu•do -da *adj* bushy-headed, shock-headed
gres *m* sandstone; stoneware
gresca *f* tumult, uproar; row, quarrel
grey *f* (*de ganado menor*) flock; group, party; nation, people; (*de fieles*) flock, congregation
grie•go -ga *adj* Greek || *mf* Greek || *m* (*idioma*) Greek; hablar en griego to not make sense
grieta *f* crack, crevice, chink; (*en la piel*) chap
grieta•do -da *adj* crackled || *m* crackleware
grietar *ref* to crack, split; (*la piel*) become chapped
gri•fo -fa *adj* (*pelo*) kinky, tangled; (*letra*) script; (W-I) colored; (Mex) drunk; (Col) conceited || *mf* (W-I) person of color; (Mex) drunk || *m* faucet, spigot, tap, cock; (myth) griffin; (Peru) gas station, (Mex) marijuana || *f* (Mex) marijuana
grilla *f* female cricket; (rad) grid; (Col) fight, quarrel; (SAm) annoyance, bother; ¡ésa es grilla! (coll) you expect me to believe that!
grillar *intr* (*el grillo*) to chirp || *ref* (*las semillas, bulbos, etc.*) to sprout
grillete *m* fetter, shackle
grillo *m* (*insecto*) cricket; (*brote tierno*) sprout, shoot; grillos fetters, shackles
grima *f* fright, horror; dar grima to grate on the nerves
grin•go -ga *mf* (disparaging) foreigner; (*anglosajón*) gringo || *m* gibberish; hablar en gringo to talk nonsense
griñón *m* (*toca de monja*) wimple; (*melocotón*) nectarine
gripe *f* grippe
gris *adj* gray; dull, gloomy || *m* gray; hacer gris (*el tiempo*) to be sharp, be brisk
grisáce•o -a *adj* grayish
gri•sú *m* (*pl* -súes) firedamp
grita *f* shouting; hubbub, uproar; dar grita a to hoot at
gritar *intr* to shout, cry out
gritería *f* shouting, outcry, uproar
grito *m* cry, shout; scream, shriek; el último grito the latest thing, all the rage; poner el

grito en el cielo to raise the roof, scream wildly

gro. *abbr* **género**

Groenlandia *f* Greenland

grosella *f* currant; **grosella silvestre** gooseberry

grosellero *m* currant bush; **grosellero silvestre** gooseberry bush

grosería *f* grossness, coarseness; churlishness, rudeness; stupidity; vulgarity

grose·ro -ra *adj* gross, coarse; churlish, rude; stupid; vulgar ‖ *mf* churl, boor

grosor *m* thickness, bulk

grosura *f* fat, suet, tallow; meat diet; coarseness, vulgarity

grotes·co -ca *adj* grotesque

grúa *f* crane, derrick; **grúa de bote** (naut) davit; **grúa de auxilio** wrecking crane; **grúa de caballete** gantry crane

grúa-remolque *m* tow truck

grue·so -sa *adj* big, thick, bulky, heavy; coarse, ordinary; stout, fat; (*mar*) rough, heavy; **en grueso** in gross, in bulk ‖ *f* (*doce docenas*) gross

grulla *f* (orn) crane

grumete *m* ship's boy, cabin boy

grumo *m* clot, curd; bunch, cluster

grumo·so -sa *adj* clotty, curdly

gruñido *m* (*de cerdo*) grunt; (*de perro cuando amenaza*) growl; (*de persona*) grumble; (*de puerta*) creak; grumble, scolding

gruñir §12 *intr* (*el cerdo*) to grunt; (*el perro*) growl; (*una persona*) grumble; (*una puerta*) creak

gru·ñón -ñona *adj* grumpy, grumbly ‖ *mf* crosspatch

grupa *f* croup, rump

grupada *f* squall

grupal *adj* group

grupo *m* group; (mach & elec) unit

grupúsculo *m* splinter group

gruta *f* grotto

grutes·co -ca *adj* & *m* (fa) grotesque

Gruyère *m* Swiss cheese

gte. *abbr* **gerente**

guaca *f* (Bol, Peru) Indian tomb; hidden treasure

guacal *m* crate

guacama·yo -ya *adj* (P-R) flashy, sporty ‖ *m* macaw

guachapear *tr* to splash with the feet; bungle, botch ‖ *intr* to clank, clatter

guachinan·go -ga *adj* flattering, sly ‖ *mf* (disparaging term used by Cubans) Mexican

gua·cho -cha *adj* (SAm) homeless, orphan; (SAm) odd, unmatched

guadal *m* bog, swamp; sand hill, dune

Guadalupe *f* Gaudeloupe

guadama·cí *m* (*pl* -cíes) embossed leather

guadaña *f* scythe

guadañadora *f* mowing machine

guadañar *tr* to cut with a scythe

guadarnés *m* harness room; harness man

guagua *f* trifle; (SAm) baby; (W-I) bus; (Col) paca

guagüita *f* (Cuba, P-R) station wagon

guajada *f* (Mex) nonsense, folly

guaje *adj* (Hond, Mex) foolish, stupid ‖ *m* (Hond, Mex) calabash, gourd; (CAm) piece of junk

guaji·ro -ra *mf* (W-I) peasant, yokel

guajolote *m* turkey; (Mex) simpleton

gualda *f* (bot) weld, dyer's rocket

gual·do -da *adj* yellow ‖ *f* see **gualda**

gualdrapa *f* housing, trappings; dirty rag hanging from clothes

gualdrapear *tr* to line up head to tail ‖ *intr* (*las velas*) to flap

Gualterio *m* Walter

guanaco *m* (SAm) dope, simpleton; (SAm) tall lanky fellow; (zool) guanaco

guanajo *m* turkey; (W-I) boob, dunce

guano *m* palm tree; bird manure

guante *m* glove; **arrojar el guante** to throw down the gauntlet; **echar un guante** to pass the hat; **guantes** tip, fee; **recoger el guante** to take up the gauntlet; **salvo el guante** excuse my glove

guantelete *m* gauntlet

guantería *f* glove shop

guantón *m* box on the ear

guapear *intr* to bluster, swagger; dress to kill

guape·tón -tona *adj* handsome; flashy, sporty; bold, fearless ‖ *m* bully, tough

guapeza *f* good looks; flashiness, sportiness; (coll) boldness, daring; bravado

gua·po -pa *adj* handsome, good-looking; flashy, sporty; bold, daring ‖ *m* (*hombre pendenciero*) bully; gallant, lady's man

guapura *f* good looks

guarache *m* (Mex) leather sandal; (Mex) tire patch

guarapo *m* sugar-cane juice; fermented juice of sugar cane

guarda *mf* guard, custodian ‖ *m* (Arg) trolley-car conductor; **guarda de la aduana** customhouse officer; **guarda forestal** forest ranger ‖ *f* guard, custody; (*de la ley*) observance; (*de la espada*) guard; (*de la cerradura*) ward; (bb) flyleaf

guardabarrera *mf* (rr) gatekeeper

guardaba·rros *m* (*pl* -rros) fender, mudguard, dashboard

guardabosque *m* gamekeeper; forest ranger; shortstop

guardabrisa *m* windshield; (naut) glass candle shade

guardacantón *m* spur stone

guardacarril *m* (rr) railguard

guardacar·tas *m* (*pl* -tas) letter file

guardaco·ches *m* (*pl* -ches) car watcher

guardacos·tas *m* (*pl* -tas) revenue cutter, coast guard cutter; **guardacostas** *mpl* (*servicio*) coast guard

guarda·dor -dora *adj* guarding, protecting; mindful, observant; stingy ‖ *m* guardian, keeper; observer

guardaespal·das *m* (*pl* -das) bodyguard

guardafango *m* fender, mudguard

guardafre·nos *m* (*pl* -nos) (rr) brakeman, flagman

guardafuego *m* fender, fireguard

guardagu·jas *m* (*pl* -jas) (rr) switchman

guardajo•yas *m* (*pl* -**yas**) jewel case
guardalado *m* railing, parapet
guardalmacén *m* warehouseman; (Cuba) country station master
guardamalleta *f* valance
guardameta *m* goalkeeper
guardamue•bles *m* (*pl* -**bles**) warehouse, furniture warehouse
guardanieve *m* snowshed
guardapelo *m* locket
guardapolvo *m* (*sobretodo ligero*) duster; (*resguardo para preservar del polvo*) cover, cloth; (*del reloj*) inner lid; (*sobre una puerta o ventana*) hood
guardapuerta *f* storm door
guardar *tr* to guard; watch over; protect; put away; show, observe; save, e.g., **¡Dios guarde a la Reina!** God save the Queen ǁ *intr* to keep, save; **¡guarda!** look out!, watch out! ǁ *ref* to be on one's guard; **guardarse de** to look out for, watch out for, guard against
guardarraya *f* (CAm, W-I) boundary line, property line
guardarropa *mf* keeper of the wardrobe ǁ *m* (*armario donde se guarda la ropa*) wardrobe; (*local destinado a la custodia de ropa en establecimientos públicos*) checkroom, cloakroom; check boy ǁ *f* check girl, hat girl
guardarropía *f* (theat) wardrobe
guardasilla *f* chair rail
guardaventana *f* storm window
guardavía *m* (rr) trackwalker, lineman
guardavida *m* lifeguard
guardavien•tos *m* (*pl* -**tos**) (*abrigo contra los vientos*) windbreak; (*mitra de chimenea*) chimney pot
guardavivo *m* bead, corner bead
guardería *f* guard, guardship; **guardería infantil** day nursery
guardesa *f* woman guard
guardia *m* guard, guardsman; **guardia civil** rural policeman; **guardia marina** midshipman, middy; **guardia urbano** policeman ǁ *f* (*cuerpo de hombres armados; manera de defenderse en la esgrima*) guard; (naut) watch; **de guardia** on duty; on guard; **guardia civil** rural police; **guardia de asalto** shock troops; **guardia de corps** (mil) bodyguard; **guardia de cuartillo** (naut) dogwatch; **guardia suiza** Swiss Guards
guar•dián -**diana** *mf* guardian ǁ *m* watchman
guardilla *f* attic; attic room
guardo•so -**sa** *adj* careful, neat, tidy; (*que ahorra mucho*) thrifty; (*mezquino*) stingy
guarecer §22 *tr* to take in, give shelter to; keep, preserve; (*a un enfermo*) treat ǁ *ref* to take refuge, take shelter
guarida *f* den, lair; shelter; haunt, hangout, hide-out
guarismo *m* cipher, figure

guarnecer §22 *tr* to trim, adorn; equip, provide; bind, edge; (*joyas*) set; stucco, plaster; (*frenos*) line; (*un cojinete*) bush; (*una plaza fuerte*) man, garrison; (culin) garnish
guarnición *f* trimming; equipping; binding, edging; (*de joyas*) setting; stuccoing, plastering; (*de la espada*) guard; (*de frenos*) lining; (*del émbolo*) packing; (*tropa que guarnece un lugar*) garrison; (culin) garnish; **guarniciones** fixtures, fittings; (*de la caballería*) harness
guarnicionar *tr* to garrison
guarnicionero *m* harness maker
guaro *m* (CAm) sugar-cane liquor
gua•rro -**rra** *mf* hog
guasa *f* heaviness, churlishness; joking, kidding
guasca *f* rawhide; whip; **dar guasca a** to whip, thrash
guasería *f* (SAm) coarseness, crudity; (Chile) timidity
gua•so -**sa** *adj* (SAm) coarse, crude, uncouth ǁ *mf* (Chile) peasant ǁ *f* see **guasa**
gua•són -**sona** *adj* heavy, churlish; funny, comical ǁ *mf* dullard, churl; joker, kidder
guata *f* wadding, padding; (Arg, Chile, Peru) belly, paunch; (*de una pared*) (Chile) bulging, warping; (Ecuad) boon companion; **echar guata** (Chile) to prosper
guatemalte•co -**ca** *adj* & *mf* Guatemalan
guáter *m* toilet, water closet
guau *m* (*ladrido del perro*) bowwow; (bot) woodbine, Virginia creeper; **guau guau** (*perro*) bowwow ǁ *interj* bowwow!
guay *interj* — **¡guay de mí!** (poet) woe is me!
guayaba *f* guava, guava apple
guayabo *m* guava tree; lie, trick
guayaco *m* lignum vitae
Guayana *f* Guyana
gubernamental *adj* governmental; (*defensor*) strong-government
gubernati•vo -**va** *adj* governmental
gubia *f* gouge
guedeja *f* shock of hair; lion's mane
guerra *f* war, warfare; billiards; **Gran guerra** Great War; **guerra a muerte** war to the death; **guerra bacteriana** or **bacteriológica** germ warfare; **guerra de guerrillas** guerrilla warfare; **guerra de las dos Rosas** War of the Roses; **guerra de los Cien Años** Hundred Years' War; **guerra del Transvaal** Boer War; **guerra de ondas** radio jamming; **guerra de Troya** Trojan War; **guerra fría** cold war; **Guerra Mundial** World War; **guerra nuclear** nuclear war; **guerra relámpago** blitzkrieg; **hacer la guerra** to wage war
guerrea•dor -**dora** *adj* warring ǁ *mf* warrior
guerrear *intr* to war, wage war, fight; struggle, resist
guerre•ro -**ra** *adj* war, warlike; warring; mischievous ǁ *mf* fighter ǁ *m* warrior, soldier, fighting man ǁ *f* tight-fitting military jacket

guerrilla *f* band of skirmishers; guerrilla band; guerrilla warfare

guerrillear *intr* to skirmish; wage guerrilla warfare

guerrillero *m* guerrilla

guía *mf* guide, leader; adviser ‖ *m* (mil) guide ‖ *f* guide; guidance; directory; (*del viajero*) guidebook; (*caballo*) leader; (*de la bicicleta*) handle bar; (*del bigote*) turned-up end; (*de la sierra*) fence; marker; shoot, sprout; (mach) guide; (rr) timetable; **guías** reins; **guía sonora** sound track; **guía telefónica** telephone directory; **guía turística** tourist guide

guiadera *f* (mach) guide

guiar §77 *tr* to guide, lead; (*un automóvil*) steer, drive; pilot; (*una planta, una vid*) train ‖ *intr* to shoot, sprout ‖ *ref* — **guiarse por** to be guided by, go by

guija *f* pebble; grass pea

guijarro *m* cobble, cobblestone

guije·ño -ña *adj* pebbly; hard-hearted

guijo *m* gravel

guijo·so -sa *adj* gravelly; pebbly

güila *f* (Mex) prostitute

guillame *m* rabbet plane

Guillermo *m* William

guillotina *f* guillotine; paper cutter

guillotinar *tr* to guillotine

guimbalete *m* pump handle

guinche *m* or **güinche** *m* (mach) crane

guinda *f* sour cherry

guindal *m* sour cherry tree

guindaleza *f* (naut) hawser

guindar *tr* to hoist, raise; win; (*ahorcar*) hang, string up

guindilla *m* policeman, cop; Guinea pepper

guindo *m* sour cherry tree

guindola *f* (naut) boatswain's chair; (naut) life buoy

guinea *f* (*moneda*) guinea

guineo *m* small banana

guinga *f* gingham

guiña *f* (Col, Ven) bad luck

guiñada *f* wink; (naut) yaw

guiñapo *m* rag, tatter; ragamuffin

guiñar *tr* (*el ojo*) to wink ‖ *intr* to wink; (naut) to yaw ‖ *ref* to wink at each other

guiño *m* wink; **hacer guiños a** to make eyes at; **hacerse guiños a** to make faces at each other

guión *m* banner, standard; cross (*carried before prelate in procession*); (*signo ortográfico*) hyphen; (*signo ortográfico largo*) dash; (mil) guidon; (mov & theat) scenario; (rad & telv) script; (mus) repeat sign; **guión de montaje** (mov) cutter's script; **guión de rodaje** (mov) shooting script

guionista *mf* (mov) scenarist; (mov) scriptwriter; (mov) subtitle writer

guirigay *m* gibberish; confusion, hubbub

guirindola *f* frill, jabot

guirlache *m* almond brittle, peanut brittle

guirnalda *f* garland, wreath

guisa *f* way, manner, wise; **a guisa de** in the manner of, like

guisado *m* stew, meat stew

guisante *m* pea; **guisante de olor** sweet pea

guisar *tr* to cook; stew; arrange, prepare ‖ *intr* to cook

guiso *m* dish

guisote *m* hash

guita *f* twine; (coll) dough, money

guitarra *f* guitar

guitarrista *mf* guitarist

gui·tón -tona *mf* tramp, bum

gula *f* gluttony; gorging, guzzling

gulo·so -sa *adj* gluttonous; guzzling

gumía *f* Moorish poniard

gurrumi·no -na *adj* weak, puny ‖ *m* henpecked husband ‖ *f* uxoriousness

gusanear *intr* to swarm

gusanera *f* nest of worms; ruling passion

gusanien·to -ta *adj* wormy, grubby

gusanillo *m* small worm; twist stitch; (*de la barrena*) spur; **matar el gusanillo** to take a shot of liquor before breakfast

gusano *m* worm; **gusano de luz** glowworm; **gusano de seda** silk worm; **gusano de tierra** earthworm

gusano·so -sa *adj* wormy, grubby

gusarapo *m* waterworm, vinegar worm

gustación *f* tasting; taste

gustar *tr* to taste; try, sample; please, be pleasing to; like, e.g., **me gustan estas peras** I like these pears ‖ *intr* to like e.g., **como Vd. guste** as you like; **gustar de** to like; like to

gustillo *m* slight taste, touch

gusto *m* taste; flavor; liking; caprice, whim; pleasure; **a gusto** as you like it; **con mucho gusto** with pleasure, gladly; **encontrarse a gusto** or **estar a gusto** to like it (*e.g., in the country*); **tanto gusto** so glad to meet you

gusto·so -sa *adj* tasty; agreeable, pleasant; ready, willing, glad

gutapercha *f* gutta-percha

gutural *adj* guttural

gu
ha

H

H, h (hache) *f* ninth letter of the Spanish alphabet

haba *f* bean, broad bean; (*simiente del café y el cacao*) bean; **ser habas contadas** to be a sure thing

Habana, La Havana

haber *m* salary, wages; credit, credit side; **haberes** property, wealth ‖ *v* §38 *tr* to have; get, get hold of ‖ *v aux* to have, e.g., **lo he visto a menudo** I have seen it often; **haber de** + *inf* to be to + *inf*, e.g., **ha de llegar a mediodía** he is to arrive at noon ‖ *v impers* there to be, e.g., **ha habido tres personas allí** there were three people there; **haber que** + *inf* to be necessary to + *inf;* **no hay de qué** you're welcome, don't mention it ‖ *ref* to behave oneself; **habérselas con** to deal with; to have it out with

habichuela *f* kidney bean; **habichuela verde** string bean

hábil *adj* skillful, capable; (*día*) work

habilidad *f* skill, ability, capability; (*lo que se ejecuta con gracia*) feat; (*enredo, embuste*) scheme, trick

habilido•so -sa *adj* skillful

habilitación *f* qualification; backing, financing; equipping, outfitting; **habilitaciones** fixtures

habilitar *tr* to qualify; back, finance; equip, fit out; (*en un examen*) pass

habitabilidad *f* habitability; (aut) interior (space)

habitable *adj* inhabitable

habitación *f* habitation; (*edificio donde se habita*) house, home, dwelling; (*aposento de la casa o el hotel*) room; (*donde vive una especie vegetal o animal*) habitat

habitante *mf* (*de una casa*) dweller, occupant; (*de una población*) inhabitant

habitar *tr* to inhabit, live in; (*una casa, un piso*) occupy ‖ *intr* to live

hábito *m* garment, dress; habit, custom; **ahorcar los hábitos** to doff the cassock, to leave the priesthood; to change jobs; **el hábito no hace al monje** clothes don't make the man

habitua•do -da *mf* habitué

habitual *adj* habitual; regular, usual

habituar §21 *tr* to accustom ‖ *ref* to become accustomed

habitud *f* relationship, connection; custom, habit

habla *f* speech; **al habla** speaking

hablada *f* talk, talking

habla•dor -dora *adj* talkative; gossipy ‖ *mf* talker, chatterbox; gossip

habladuría *f* cut, sarcasm; **andar con habladurías** to go around gossiping

hablante *adj* speaking ‖ *mf* speaker

hablar *tr* (*una lengua*) to speak, talk; (*disparates*) talk ‖ *intr* to speak, talk; **es hablar por demás** it's wasted talk; **estar hablando** (*una pintura, una estatua*) to be almost alive; **hablar claro** to talk straight from the shoulder

hablilla *f* story, piece of gossip

hablista *mf* speaker, good speaker

hacede•ro -ra *adj* feasible, practicable

hacenda•do -da *adj* landed, property-owning ‖ *mf* landholder, property owner; cattle rancher; plantation owner

hacendar §2 *tr* (*el dominio de bienes raíces*) to pass on ‖ *ref* to buy property in order to settle down

hacende•ro -ra *adj* thrifty

hacendista *m* economist, fiscal expert; man of independent means

hacendo•so -sa *adj* hard-working, thrifty

hacer §39 *tr* (*crear, producir, formar*) to make; (*ejecutar, llevar a cabo*) do; (*un baúl*) pack; (*un papel*) play; (*un mandato*) give; (*un drama*) act, perform; pretend to be; (*una pregunta*) ask; **hace** ago, e.g., **hace un mes** a month ago; **hacer** + *inf* to have + *inf*, e.g., **le hice tomar un libro en la biblioteca** I had him get a book at the library; to make + *inf*, e.g., **el médico me hizo guardar cama** the doctor made me stay in bed; to have + *pp*, e.g., **hará construir una casa** he will have a house built; **hacer . . . que** to be . . . since, e.g., **hace un año que yo estuve aquí** it is a year since I was here; to be for. . . , e.g., **hace un año que estoy aquí** I have been here for a year; for expressions like **hacer frío** to be cold, see the noun ‖ *intr* to act; **hacer a** to fit; **hacer al caso** (coll) to be to the purpose; **hacer como que** + *ind* to pretend to + *inf;* **hacer de** to act as, work as; **hacer por** to try to ‖ *ref* to become, get to be, grow; **hacerse a** to become accustomed to; **hacerse a un lado** to step aside; **hacerse con** to make off with; **hacerse chiquito** to sing small; **hacérsele a uno difícil** to strike one as difficult; **hacerse viejo** to grow old; kill time

hacia *prep* toward; (*cierta hora o época*) about, near; **hacia abajo** downward; **hacia adelante** forward; **hacia arriba** upward; **hacia atrás** backward; the wrong way; **hacia dentro** inward; **hacia fuera** outward

hacienda *f* farmstead, landed estate, country property; property, possessions; ranch; (Arg) cattle, livestock; **hacienda pública** public finance, federal income; **haciendas** household chores

hacina *f* pile, heap; shock, stack

hacinar *tr* to pile, heap, stack

hacha *f* axe; (*hacha pequeña*) hatchet; torch; firebrand; four-wick wax candle; **hacha de armas** battleaxe

hachazo *m* blow with an axe

hachear *tr* & *intr* to hew, hack, or chop with an axe

hachero *m* torchbearer; (*candelero*) torch stand; (*leñador*) woodcutter

hachich *m* or **hachís** *m* hashish

hacho *m* torch; (*sitio elevado cerca de la costa*) beacon, beacon hill

hada *f* fairy; (*mujer que encanta por su belleza, gracia, etc.*) charmer; **hada madrina** fairy godmother

hadar *tr* (*determinar el hado*) to predestine, foreordain; (*pronosticar*) to foretell; (*encantar*) to charm, cast a spell on

hado *m* fate, destiny

haiga *m* (slang) flashy auto; (slang) sport

halagar §44 *tr* (*lisonjear*) to flatter; (*demostrar cariño a*) cajole, fawn on; (*agradar*) gratify, please

halago *m* flattery; cajolery; gratification; **halagos** flattery, blandishments

halagüe•ño -ña *adj* flattering; fawning; gratifying, pleasing; bright, rosy, promising

halar *tr* (naut) to haul, pull

halcón *m* falcon

halconear *intr* (*la mujer*) to chase after men

halconería *f* falconry

halconero *m* falconer

halda *f* skirt; **poner haldas en cinta** to pull up one's skirts to run; roll up one's sleeves

halieto *m* fish hawk, osprey

hálito *m* breath; vapor; (poet) gentle breeze

halitosis *f* halitosis

halo *m* halo

haló *interj* (*teléfono*) hello!

halógeno *m* halogen

halterio *m* dumbbell

halterofilia *f* weight lifting

halterofilista *mf* weight lifter

haluro *m* halide

hallar *tr* to find; (*averiguar*) find out, discover ‖ *ref* to find oneself; to be; **hallarse bien con** to be satisfied with; **hallárselo todo hecho** to never have to turn a hand; **no hallarse** to feel uncomfortable, not like it

hallazgo *m* (*cosa hallada*) find; (*acción de hallar*) finding, discovery; (*premio al que ha hallado una cosa perdida*) reward, finder's reward, e.g., **diez dólares de hallazgo** ten dollars reward

hallulla *f* bread baked on embers or hot stones; (Chile) fine bread

hamaca *f* hammock

hamamelina *f* witch hazel

hambre *f* hunger; (*escasez general de comestibles*) famine; **matar de hambre** to starve to death; **morir de hambre** to starve to death, die of starvation; **pasar hambre** to go hungry; **tener hambre** to be hungry

hambrear *tr & intr* to starve, famish

hambrien•to -ta *adj* hungry, starving

hambruna *f* (SAm) mad hunger; (Ecuad) starvation

hamburguesa *f* hamburger sandwich

hamo *m* fishhook

hampa *f* underworld life; denizens of the underworld

hampes•co -ca *adj* underworld

hampón *m* bully, tough

hangar *m* (aer) hangar

hara•gán -gana *adj* idling, loafing, lazy ‖ *mf* idler, loafer

haraganear *intr* to idle, loaf, hang around

harapien•to -ta *adj* ragged, tattered

harapo *m* rag, tatter; **andar** or **estar hecho un harapo** (coll) to go around in rags

harapo•so -sa *adj* ragged, tattered

harén *m* harem

harina *f* (*especialmente del trigo*) flour; (*de cualquier grano*) meal; **estar metido en harina** to be deeply absorbed; to be fat and heavy; **harina de avena** oatmeal; **harina de maíz** corn meal; **ser harina de otro costal** to be a horse of another color

harine•ro -ra *adj* flour ‖ *m* flour dealer; flour bin

harino•so -sa *adj* floury, mealy

harnear *tr* (Col, Chile) to sift

harnero *m* sieve

ha•rón -rona *adj* lazy ‖ *mf* lazy loafer

harpillera *f* burlap, sackcloth

hartar *tr* to stuff, cram; satisfy, satiate; tire, bore; overwhelm, deluge ‖ *intr* to have one's fill ‖ *ref* to stuff; be satiated; tire, be bored

hartazgo *m* or **hartazón** *m* fill, bellyful; **darse un hartazgo** to eat one's fill; **darse un hartazgo de** to have or to get one's fill of

har•to -ta *adj* full, fed up; very much; **harto de** full of, fed up with, sick of ‖ **harto** *adv* enough; very, quite

hartura *f* fill, satiety; full satisfaction; abundance

hasta *adv* even ‖ *prep* until, till; to, as far as; down to, up to; as much as; **hasta ahora** up till now; **hasta aquí** so far; **hasta después** so long, good-by; **hasta la vista** or **hasta luego** so long, good-by; **hasta mañana** see you tomorrow; **hasta más no poder** to the utmost; **hasta no más** to the utmost; **hasta que** until, till

hastial *m* gable end; (*hombrón rústico*) bumpkin

hastiar §77 *tr* to surfeit, sicken, cloy; (*fastidiar*) bother, annoy, bore

hastío *m* surfeit, loathing, disgust; bother, annoyance, boredom

hataca *f* large wooden ladle; (*cilindro para extender la masa*) rolling pin

hatajo *m* small herd, small flock; (*p.ej., de disparates*) lot, flock

hato *m* (*de ganado vacuno*) herd; (*de ovejas*) flock; (*de ropa*) pack, bundle; (*de gente*) clique, ring; (*de gente malvada*) gang; everyday outfit; (*de disparates*) flock, lot; cattle ranch; **liar el hato** to pack up, pack one's baggage; **revolver el hato** to stir up trouble

haya *f* beech tree; (*madera*) beech ‖ **La Haya** The Hague

hayaca *f* (Ven) mince pie

hayo *m* (Col) coca; (Col) coca leaves (*mixed for chewing*)

hayuco *m* beechnut, mast

haz *m* (*pl* **haces**) bunch, bundle; (*de leña*) fagot; (*de mieses*) sheaf; (*de rayos*) beam, pencil; (*de soldados*) file ‖ *f* (*pl* **haces**) face; (*de la tierra*) surface; (*de paño o tela*) right side; (*de un edificio*) façade, front; **a sobre haz** on the surface; **ser de dos haces** to be two-faced

hazaña *f* feat, exploit, deed

hazañería *f* fuss

hazañe•ro -ra *adj* fussy

hazaño•so -sa *adj* gallant, courageous

hazmerreír *m* laughingstock, butt

he *adv* behold, lo and behold; **he aquí** here is, here are; **he allí** there is, there are

hebilla f buckle

hebra f thread; fiber; (*en la madera*) grain; (*del discurso*) (fig) thread; **de una hebra** (Chile) all at once; **pegar la hebra** to strike up a conversation; to keep on talking

hebre•o -a adj & mf Hebrew || m (*idioma*) Hebrew

hebro•so -sa adj fibrous, stringy

hecatombe f hecatomb

hechicera f witch, sorceress; (*mujer que por su belleza cautiva*) enchantress

hechicería f witchcraft, sorcery, wizardry; (fig) fascination, charm

hechice•ro -ra adj bewitching, charming, enchanting; magic || mf sorcerer, magician; charmer, enchanter || m wizard, sorcerer || f see **hechicera**

hechizar §60 tr to bewitch, cast a spell on; (fig) to bewitch, charm, enchant || intr to practice sorcery; (fig) to be charming, enchant

hechi•zo -za adj fake, artificial; (*de quita y pon*) detachable; made, manufactured; (*producto*) local, home || m spell, charm; magic, sorcery; (fig) magic, sorcery, glamour; (fig) charmer; **hechizos** (*de una mujer*) charms

he•cho -cha adj accustomed; finished; turned into; (*traje*) ready-made; (*llegado a la edad adulta*) full-grown || m act, deed; fact; event; (*hazaña*) feat; **de hecho** in fact; **en hecho de verdad** as a matter of fact; **estar en el hecho de** to catch on to; **hecho consumado** fait accompli || **hecho** interj all right!, OK!

hechura f form, shape, cut, build; creation, creature; workmanship; (Chile) drink, treat; **hechuras** cost of making; **no tener hechura** to be impracticable

heder §51 tr to bore, annoy, tire || intr to stink, reek

hediondez f stench, stink

hedion•do -da adj stinking, smelly; annoying, boring; obscene, filthy, dirty || m bean trefoil; skunk

hedor m stench, stink

helada f freezing; (*escarcha*) frost; **helada blanca** hoarfrost

heladera f refrigerator; (Chile) ice-cream tray

heladería f ice-cream parlor

hela•do -da adj cold, icy; (*pasmado por el miedo, la sorpresa, etc.*) frozen; (*esquivo, indiferente*) cold, chilly; (*cubierto de azúcar*) (Ven) iced || m cold drink; (*manjar*) water ice; (*sorbete*) ice cream; **helado al corte** brick ice cream || f see **helada**

hela•dor -dora adj freezing || f ice-cream freezer

helar §2 tr to freeze; harden, congeal; dumbfound; discourage || intr to freeze || ref to freeze; harden, congeal, set; (*cubrirse de hielo*) to ice

helecho m fern

heléni•co -ca adj Hellenic

hele•no -na adj Hellenic || mf Hellene

helero m glacier

hélice f helix; (*de un buque*) screw, propeller; (*de un avión*) propeller

helicóptero m helicopter

helio m helium

heliotropo m heliotrope

helipuerto m heliport

hematíe m red cell

hembra adj invar (*animal, planta, herramienta*) female; weak, thin, delicate || f female; (*del corchete*) eye; (*tuerca*) nut; **hembra de terraja** (mach) die

hembraje m (SAm) females of a flock or herd

hembrilla f (mach) female part or piece; (*armella*) eyebolt

hemeroteca f periodical library

hemiciclo m (*semicírculo*) hemicycle; (*gradería semicircular*) amphitheater; (*espacio central del salón de sesiones de las Cortes*) floor

hemisferio m hemisphere

hemistiquio m hemistich

hemofilia f hemophilia

hemoglobina f hemoglobin

hemorragia f hemorrhage

hemorroides fpl hemorrhoids

hemóstato m hemostat

henal m hayloft

henar m hayfield

henchir §50 tr to fill; (*un colchón*) stuff; (*a una persona, p.ej., de favores*) heap, shower || ref to be filled; stuff, stuff oneself

hendedura f crack, split, cleft

hender §51 tr to crack, split, cleave; (*el aire, las ondas*) cleave; make one's way through || ref to crack, split

hendidura f crack, split, cleft

henil m hayloft, haymow

henna f henna

heno m hay

heñir §72 tr to knead; **hay mucho que heñir** there's still a lot of work to do

heraldía f heraldry

heráldi•co -ca adj heraldic || f heraldry

heraldo m herald

herbáce•o -a adj herbaceous

herbajar tr & intr to graze

herbaje m herbage

herba•rio -ria adj herbal || m (*libro*) herbal; (*colección*) herbarium

herbicida m weed killer

herbo•so -sa adj grassy

hercúle•o -a adj herculean

heredad f country estate

heredar tr & intr to inherit; **heredar a** to inherit from

herede•ro -ra mf heir, inheritor; owner of an estate; **heredero forzoso** heir apparent || m heir || f heiress

heredita•rio -ria adj hereditary

hereje mf heretic

herejía f heresy; insult, outrage; outrageous price

herencia f heritage, inheritance; (*transmisión de caracteres biológicos*) heredity; (*patrimonio de un difunto*) estate

heréti•co -ca adj heretic(al)

herida f injury, wound; insult, outrage; **renovar la herida** to open an old sore; **tocar en la herida** to sting to the quick

heri•do -da adj hurt, wounded; (*ofendido*) hurt ‖ mf injured person, wounded person; **los heridos** the injured, the wounded ‖ f see **herida**

herir §68 tr to injure, hurt, wound; (*ofender*) hurt; (*golpear*) strike; (*el sol sobre*) beat down upon; (*un instrumento de cuerda*) play; (*la cuerda de un instrumento*) pluck; touch, move

hermana f sister; **hermana de leche** foster sister; **hermana política** sister-in-law; **media hermana** half sister

hermanar tr to match, mate; combine, join; harmonize ‖ ref to match; become attached as brothers or sisters or brother and sister

hermanastra f stepsister

hermanastro m stepbrother

hermandad f brotherhood; sisterhood; close friendship; close relationship

herma•no -na adj (*p.ej., idioma*) sister ‖ mf companion, mate ‖ m brother; **hermano de leche** foster brother; **hermano político** brother-in-law; **hermanos** brother and sister; brothers and sisters; **hermanos siameses** Siamese twins; **medio hermano** half brother; **primo hermano** first cousin ‖ f see **hermana**

herméti•co -ca adj hermetic(al); air-tight; impenetrable; tight-lipped

hermosear tr to beautify, embellish

hermo•so -sa adj beautiful; (*caballero*) handsome

hermosura f beauty; (*mujer hermosa*) belle, beauty

hernia f hernia

héroe m hero

heroi•co -ca adj heroic; (*remedio*) desperate

heroína f heroine; (pharm) heroin

heroinómano m heroin addict

heroísmo m heroism

herrada f wooden bucket

herrador m horseshoer

herradura f horseshoe; **mostrar las herraduras** (*un caballo*) to kick, be vicious; (coll) to show one's heels

herraje m hardware, ironwork

herramental adj tool ‖ m toolbox, tool bag

herramienta f tool; set of tools; (coll) teeth; (coll) horns

herrar §2 tr (*guarnecer con hierro*) to fit with hardware; (*un caballo*) to shoe; (*marcar con hierro candente*) to brand; (*un barril*) to hoop

herrería f forge, blacksmith shop; blacksmithing; ironworks; rumpus

herrero m blacksmith; **herrero de grueso** ironworker; **herrero de obra** steelworker

herrete m tip, metal tip

herretear tr to tip, put a metal tip on

herrín m rust

herón m (*tejo de hierro horadado*) quoit; (*arandela*) washer

herrumbre f rust; (*honguillo parásito*) rust, plant rot

herrumbro•so -sa adj rusty

herventar §2 tr to boil

hervidero m boiling; bubbling spring; (*en el pecho*) rattle; (*de gente*) swarm

hervidor m boiler, cooker

hervir §68 intr to boil; (*el mar; una persona encolerizada*) boil, seethe; swarm, teem

hervor m boil, boiling; (*de la juventud*) fire, restlessness; **alzar el hervor** to begin to boil

hervoro•so -sa adj ardent, fiery, impetuous

heterócli•to -ta adj irregular; unconventional

heterodinar tr to heterodyne

heterodi•no -na adj heterodyne

heterodo•xo -xa adj heterodox

heterogeneidad f heterogeneity

heterogéne•o -a adj heterogeneous

hexámetro m hexameter

hez f (pl **heces**) (fig) scum, dregs; **heces** lees, dregs; feces, excrement

hiato m hiatus

hibisco m hibiscus

hibridación f hybridization

hibridar tr & intr to hybridize

híbri•do -da adj & m hybrid

hidal•go -ga adj noble, illustrious ‖ m nobleman ‖ f noblewoman

hidalguez f or **hidalguía** f nobility

hidra f hydra

hidratar tr & ref to hydrate

hidrato m hydrate

hidráuli•co -ca adj hydraulic ‖ f hydraulics

hidroala m (*vehículo mixto de buque y avión*) hydrofoil

hidroaleta f (*miembro alar del hidroala*) hydrofoil

hidroavión m hydroplane

hidrocarburo m hydrocarbon

hidroeléctri•co -ca adj hydroelectric

hidrófi•lo -la adj (*algodón*) absorbent (*cotton*)

hidrofobia f hydrophobia

hidrófu•go -ga adj waterproof

hidrógeno m hydrogen

hidropesía f dropsy

hidróxido m hydroxide

hiedra f ivy

hiel f bile, gall; (fig) gall, bitterness, sorrow; **echar la hiel** to strain, overwork

hielo m ice; (fig) coldness, coolness; **hielo flotante** drift ice, ice pack; **hielo seco** dry ice; **romper el hielo** (*quebrantar la reserva*) to break the ice

hiena f hyena

hienda f dung

hierba f grass; (*especialmente la que tiene propiedades medicinales*) herb; **hierba de la plata** honesty; **hierba del asno** evening primrose; **hierba de París** truelove; **hierba gatera** catnip; **hierba pastel** woad; **hierbas** grass, pasture; herb poison; years of age (*said of animals*); **mala hierba** weed; wayward young fellow

hierbabuena *f* mint
hierro *m* iron; (*marca candente que se pone a los ganados*) brand; **hierro colado** cast iron; **hierro colado en barras** pig iron; **hierro de desecho** scrap iron; **hierro de marcar** branding iron; **hierro dulce** wrought iron; **hierro fundido** cast iron; **hierro galvanizado** galvanized iron; **hierro ondulado** corrugated iron; **hierros** irons, fetters; **llevar hierro a Vizcaya** to carry coals to Newcastle
higa *f* baby's fist-shaped amulet; scorn, contempt; **dar higa** to misfire; **no dar dos higas por** to not give a rap for
hígado *m* liver; **echar los hígados** to strain, to overwork; **hígados** guts, courage; **malos hígados** hatred, grudge; **ser un hígado** to be a nuisance
higiene *f* hygiene
higiéni•co -ca *adj* hygienic
higo *m* fig; **higo chumbo** prickly pear; **higo paso** dried fig; **no valer un higo** to be not worth a continental
higuera *f* fig tree; **higuera chumba** prickly pear
hija *f* daughter; **hija política** daughter-in-law
hijas•tro -tra *mf* stepchild ‖ *m* stepson ‖ *f* stepdaughter
hi•jo -ja *mf* child; (*de un animal*) young; **hijo de bendición** legitimate child; good child; **hijo de la cuna** foundling; **hijo del amor** love child; **hijo de leche** foster child ‖ *m* son; **cada hijo de vecino** every man Jack, every mother's son; **hijo del agua** good sailor; good swimmer; **hijo de su padre** chip of the old block; **hijo de sus propias obras** self-made man; **hijo político** son-in-law; **hijos** children; descendants ‖ *f* see **hija**
hijodalgo *m* (*pl* **hijosdalgo**) nobleman
hijuela *f* little girl, little daughter; (*tira de tela*) gore; branch drain; side path
hijuelero *m* rural postman
hijuelo *m* shoot, sucker
hila *f* row, line; (*acción de hilar*) spinning; **a la hila** in single file; **hilas** (*hebras para curar heridas*) lint
hilacha *f* shred, fraying; **hilacha de acero** steel wool; **hilacha de algodón** cotton waste; **hilacha de vidrio** spun glass; **hilachas** lint; **mostrar la hilacha** (Arg) to show one's worst side
hilachen•to -ta *adj* tattered; in rags
hilachos *mpl* (Mex) rags, tatters
hilacho•so -sa *adj* frayed, raggedy
hilada *f* row, line; (mas) course
hilado *m* spinning; (*hilo*) yarn, thread
hila•dor -dora *adj* spinning ‖ *mf* spinner ‖ *f* spinning machine
hilandería *f* spinning; spinning mill
hilande•ro -ra *adj* spinning ‖ *m* spinning mill
hilar *tr & intr* to spin; **hilar delgado** to hew close to the line; **hilar largo** to drag on
hilarante *adj* laughable; (*gas*) laughing
hilaza *f* yarn, thread; lint; **descubrir la hilaza** to show one's true nature

hilera *f* row, line; fine thread, fine yarn; (*parhilera*) ridgepole; (mil) file
hilo *m* thread; (*hebras retorcidas*) yarn; (*alambre*) wire; (*de perlas*) string; (*de agua*) thin stream; (*de luz*) beam; linen, linen fabric; (*de un discurso, de la vida*) (fig) thread; **hilo bramante** twine; **hilo de la muerte** end of life; **hilo de masa** (aut) ground wire; **hilo de medianoche** midnight sharp; **hilo dental** dental floss; **hilo de tierra** (elec) ground wire; **irse al hilo** or **tras el hilo de la gente** to follow the crowd; **manejar los hilos** to pull strings; **perder el hilo de** to lose the thread of
hilván *m* basting, tacking; basting stitch; (Chile) basting thread; (Ven) hem; **hablar de hilván** to jabber along
hilvanar *tr* to baste, tack; sketch, outline; (*hacer con precipitación*) hurry; (Ven) to hem ‖ *intr* to baste, tack
himnario *m* hymnal, hymn book
himno *m* hymn; **himno nacional** national anthem
hin *m* neigh, whinny
hincadura *f* driving, thrusting, sticking
hincapié *m* stamping the foot; **hacer hincapié en** to lay great stress on, to emphasize
hincar §73 *tr* to drive, thrust, stick, sink; (*la rodilla*) go down on, fall on ‖ *ref* to kneel, kneel down; **hincarse de rodillas** to go down on one's knees
hincha *mf* (sport) fan, rooter ‖ *f* grudge, ill will
hinchable *adj* inflatable; (*goma de mascar*) bubble
hincha•do -da *adj* swollen; swollen with pride; (*estilo, lenguaje*) pompous, highflown ‖ *m* (*de un neumático*) inflation ‖ *f* (sport) fans, rooters
hinchar *tr* to swell; inflate; (*un neumático*) pump up; exaggerate, embroider ‖ *ref* to swell; swell up, become puffed up (*with pride*)
hinchazón *f* swelling; vanity, conceit; (*del estilo, lenguaje*) bombast
hinchismo *m* (sport) fans, rooters
hin•dú -dúa (*pl* **-dúes -dúas**) *adj & mf* Hindoo, Hindu
hiniesta *f* Spanish broom
hinojo *m* fennel; **de hinojos** on one's knees
hipar *intr* to hiccup; (*los perros cuando siguen la caza*) pant, snuffle; (*gimotear*) whimper; be worn out; **hipar por** to long for; long to
hiperacidez *f* hyperacidity
hipérbola *f* (geom) hyperbola
hipérbole *f* (rhet) hyperbole
hiperbóli•co -ca *adj* (geom & rhet) hyperbolic
hipersensible *adj* (*alérgico*) hypersensitive
hipertensión *f* hypertension, high blood pressure
hípica *f* (horseback) riding; equestrianism
hípi•co -ca *adj* horse, equine
hipnosis *f* hypnosis

hipnóti•co -ca *adj* hypnotic ‖ *mf* hypnotic ‖ *m* (*medicamento que provoca el sueño*) hypnotic

hipnotismo *m* hypnotism

hipnotista *mf* hypnotist

hipnotizar §60 *tr* to hypnotize

hipo *m* hiccup; longing, desire; **tener hipo contra** to have a grudge against; **tener hipo por** to desire eagerly

hipocondría•co -ca *adj* & *mf* hypochondriac

hipocresía *f* hypocrisy

hipócrita *adj* hypocritical ‖ *mf* hypocrite

hipodérmi•co -ca *adj* hypodermic

hipódromo *m* hippodrome, race track

hipopótamo *m* hippopotamus

hiposulfito *m* hyposulfite

hipoteca *f* mortgage; **¡buena hipoteca!** you may believe it, if you want to!

hipotecar §73 *tr* to mortgage

hipoteca•rio -ria *adj* mortgage

hipotenusa *f* hypotenuse

hipóte•sis *f* (*pl* -sis) hypothesis; **hipótesis de guía** working hypothesis

hipotéti•co -ca *adj* hypothetic(al)

hiriente *adj* cutting, stinging

hirsu•to -ta *adj* hairy, bristly; (fig) brusque, gruff

hirviente *adj* boiling

hisopear *tr* to sprinkle with holy water

hisopo *m* (bot) hyssop; aspergillum, sprinkler of holy water; paint brush, shaving brush

hispalense *adj* & *mf* Sevillian

hispáni•co -ca *adj* & *mf* Hispanic

hispanista *mf* Hispanist

hispa•no -na *adj* Spanish; Spanish American ‖ *mf* Spaniard; Spanish American

hispanohablante or **hispanoparlante** *adj* Spanish-speaking ‖ *mf* speaker of Spanish

híspi•do -da *adj* bristly, spiny

histéri•co -ca *adj* hysterical

histerismo *m* hysteria

histología *f* histology

historia *f* history; story, tale; **de historia** notorious, infamous; **dejarse de historias** to come to the point; **historia de lagrimitas** (coll) sob story; **historias** gossip, meddling; **pasar a la historia** to become a thing of the past; **picar en historia** to turn out to be serious

historia•do -da *adj* richly adorned; overadorned; (*cuadro, dibujo*) storied

historial *adj* historical ‖ *m* record, dossier

historiar §77 & **regular** *tr* to tell the history of; tell the story of; (*un suceso histórico*) (fa) to depict

histori•co -ca *adj* historic(al)

historieta *f* anecdote, brief story; **historieta gráfica** comic strip

histrión *m* actor; juggler, buffoon

histrióni•co -ca *adj* histrionic

hita *f* brad; landmark, milestone

hi•to -ta *adj* fixed, firm; (*casa, calle*) next; (*caballo*) black ‖ *m* (*clavo fijado en la tierra*) peg, hob; (*juego*) quoits; (*blanco*) target; (*mojón*) landmark, milestone; **dar en el hito** to hit the nail on the head; **mirar**

de hito en hito to eye up and down ‖ *f* see **hita**

Hno. *abbr* **Hermano**

hoba•chón -chona *adj* lumpish

hocicar §73 *tr* to nuzzle, root; keep on kissing ‖ *intr* to nuzzle, root; run into a snag; (*la proa*) (naut) to dip

hocico *m* snout; (*de una persona*) snout; sour face; **caer de hocicos** to fall on one's face; **meter el hocico en todo** to poke one's nose into everything; **poner hocico** to make a face

hogaño *adv* this year; at the present time

hogar *m* fireplace, hearth; furnace; home; family life; (*hoguera*) bonfire

hogare•ño -ña *adj* home-loving ‖ *mf* homebody, stay-at-home

hogaza *f* large loaf of bread

hoguera *f* bonfire

hoja *f* (*de planta, libro, mesa, muelle, puerta plegadiza, etc.; pétalo de flor*) leaf; (*de planta acuática*) pad; (*de papel*) sheet; blank sheet; (*de cuchillo, sierra, espada, etc.*) blade; (*hojuela de metal*) foil; (*de persiana*) slat; (*del patín*) runner; **doblar la hoja** to change the subject; **hoja clínica** clinical chart; **hoja de afeitar** razor blade; **hoja de embalaje** packing slip; **hoja de encuadernador** (bb) end paper; **hoja de estaño** tin foil; **hoja de estudios** transcript; **hoja de guarda** (bb) flyleaf; **hoja del anunciante** tear sheet; **hoja de lata** tin, tin plate; **hoja de nenúfar** lily pad; **hoja de paga** pay roll; **hoja de parra** fig leaf; **hoja de pedidos** order blank; **hoja de rodaje** (mov) shooting record; **hoja de ruta** waybill; **hoja de servicios** service record; **hoja de trébol** cloverleaf (*intersection*); **hoja maestra** master blade (*of spring*); **hojas del autor** (typ) advance sheets; **hoja suelta** leaflet, handbill; (bb) flyleaf; **hoja volante** leaflet, handbill

hojalata *f* tin, tin plate

hojalatería *f* tinsmith's shop; tinwork

hojalatero *m* tinsmith, tinner

hojaldre *m* & *f* puff paste

hojarasca *f* dead leaves; trash, rubbish; bluff, vain show

hojear *tr* to leaf through ‖ *intr* to scale off; (*las hojas de los árboles*) flutter

hojita *f* leaflet; **hojita de afeitar** razor blade

hojo•so -sa *adj* leafy

hojuela *f* (*hoja de otra compuesta*) leaflet; (*fruta de sartén*) pancake; (*hoja muy delgada de metal*) foil; **hojuela de estaño** tin foil

hola *interj* hey!, hello!

Holanda *f* Holland

holan•dés -desa *adj* Dutch; **a la holandesa** (bb) half-bound ‖ *mf* Hollander ‖ *m* Dutchman; (*idioma*) Dutch ‖ *f* Dutch woman

holga•chón -chona *adj* lazy, idle ‖ *mf* loafer, idler

holgadero *m* hangout

holga•do -da *adj* idle, unoccupied; (*vestido*) loose, full, roomy; (*que vive con bienestar*) fairly well-off

hi
ho

holganza *f* idleness, leisure; pleasure, enjoyment

holgar §63 *intr* to idle, be idle; take it easy, rest up; not fit, be too loose; be unnecessary, be of no use; be glad ‖ *ref* to be glad; be amused

holga‧zán -zana *adj* idle, lazy ‖ *mf* idler, loafer

holgazanear *intr* to idle, loaf, bum around

hol‧gón -gona *adj* pleasure-loving ‖ *mf* loafer, lizard

holgorio *m* fun, merriment

holgura *f* looseness, fulness; enjoyment, merriment; comfort, easy circumstances; (mach) play

holocausto *m* holocaust

hollar §61 *tr* to tread on, to trample on

hollejo *m* hull, peel, skin

hollín *m* soot

hollinar *tr* (Chile) to cover with soot

hollinien‧to -ta *adj* sooty

hombracho *m* big husky fellow

hombrada *f* manly act

hombradía *f* manliness, courage

hombre *m* man; husband, man; my boy, old chap; **buen hombre** good-natured fellow; **¡hombre al agua!** or **¡hombre a la mar!** man overboard!; **hombre bueno** arbiter, referee; **hombre de bien** honorable man; **hombre de buenas prendas** man of parts; **hombre de ciencia** scientist; **hombre de dinero** man of means; **hombre de estado** statesman; **hombre de letras** man of letters; **hombre de mundo** man of the world; **hombre de suposición** man of straw; **hombre hecho** grown man ‖ *interj* man alive!, upon my word!

hombre-anuncio *m* sandwich man

hombrear *tr* (Arg) to carry on the shoulders; (Mex) to aid, back ‖ *intr* to try to be somebody; (*una mujer*) to be mannish; **hombrear con** to try to be equal

hombrecillo *m* little man; (*lúpulo*) hop

hombrera *f* (*del vestido*) shoulder; shoulder pad; epaulet

hombre-rana *m* (*pl* **hombres-ranas**) frogman

hombría *f* manliness; **hombría de bien** honor, probity

hombrillo *m* (*de la camisa*) yoke; shoulder piece

hombro *m* shoulder; **arrimar el hombro** to lend a hand, put one's shoulder to the wheel; **encoger los hombros** to let one's shoulders droop; **encogerse de hombros** to shrug one's shoulders; to crouch, to shrink with fear; to not answer; **mirar por encima del hombro** to look down upon; **salir en hombros** to be carried off on the shoulders of the crowd

hombru‧no -na *adj* mannish

homenaje *m* homage; (feud) homage; (Chile) gift, favor; **homenaje de boca** lip service; **rendir homenaje a** to swear allegiance to

homeópata *mf* homeopath

homeopatía *f* homeopathy

homicida *adj* homicidal ‖ *mf* homicide

homicidio *m* homicide

homilía *f* homily

homogeneidad *f* homogeneity

homogeneizar §60 *tr* to homogenize

homogéne‧o -a *adj* homogeneous

homologación *f* confirmation, ratification; (sport) validation

homologar §44 *tr* to confirm, ratify; (*un récord*) (sport) to validate

homólo‧go -ga *adj* homologous ‖ *m* colleague

homóni‧mo -ma *adj* homonymous; of the same name ‖ *mf* namesake ‖ *m* homonym

homosexual *adj* & *mf* homosexual; gay

homúnculo *m* guy, little runt

honda *f* sling

hondazo *m* blow with a sling

hondear *tr* (naut) to sound

hondillos *mpl* patches in the crotch of pants

hon‧do -da *adj* deep; (*terreno*) low ‖ *m* bottom ‖ *f* see **honda** ‖ **hondo** *adv* deep

hondón *m* (*de la aguja*) eye; (*de un vaso*) bottom; lowland

hondonada *f* lowland, ravine

hondura *f* depth, profundity; **meterse en honduras** to go beyond one's depth

hondure‧ño -ña *adj* & *mf* Honduran

honestidad *f* decency; chastity; modesty; honesty, probity; fairness, reasonableness

hones‧to -ta *adj* decent; chaste, pure; modest; honest, upright; (*precio*) fair, reasonable

hongo *m* fungus, mushroom; (*sombrero*) bowler, derby

honor *m* honor; **en honor a la verdad** as a matter of fact, to tell the truth; **hacer honor a** to do honor to; (*la firma*) to honor

honorable *adj* honorable

honora‧rio -ria *adj* honorary ‖ *s* fee, honorarium

honorífi‧co -ca *adj* honorific

honra *f* honor; **tener a mucha honra** to be proud of

honradez *f* honesty, integrity

honra‧do -da *adj* honorable

honrar *tr* to honor ‖ *ref* to feel honored

honrilla *f* — **por la negra honrilla** out of concern for what people will say

honro‧so -sa *adj* honorable

hopo *m* tuft, shock (*of hair*); bushy tail; **seguir el hopo a** (coll) to keep right after

hora *f* hour; (*momento determinado para algo*) time; **a la hora** on time; **a la hora de ahora** right now; **a la hora en punto** on the hour; **a las pocas horas** within a few hours; **dar hora** to fix a time; **dar la hora** (*el reloj*) to strike; **de última hora** up-to-date; most up-to-date; (*noticias*) late; **en buen hora** or **en hora buena** safely, luckily; all right; **en mal hora** or **en hora mala** unluckily, in an evil hour; **fuera de horas** after hours; **hasta altas horas** until late into the night; **hora de acostarse** bedtime; **hora de aglomeración** rush hour; **hora de cierre** closing time; curfew; **hora de comer** mealtime; **hora deshorada** fatal hour; **hora de verano** daylight-saving time; **hora de verdad** (taur) kill; **hora legal** or

oficial standard time; **hora punta** peak hour; rush hour; **horas de afluencia** rush hour; **horas extra** overtime; **horas de consulta** office hours (*of a doctor*); **horas de ocio** leisure hours; **horas de punta** rush hour; **horas extraordinarias de trabajo** overtime

horadar *tr* to drill, bore, pierce

hora•rio -ria *adj* hour ‖ *m* hour hand; clock; (*de ferrocarriles*) timetable; **horario escolar** roster

horca *f* (*para levantar la paja*) pitchfork; (*para ahorcar a un condenado*) gallows, gibbet; (*de ajos, cebollas, etc.*) string

horcajadas — a horcajadas astride, astraddle

horcajadillas — a horcajadillas astride, astraddle

horcajadura *f* crotch

horcajo *m* (*confluencia de dos ríos*) fork; (*para mulas*) yoke

horcón *m* pitchfork; forked prop (*for fruit trees*); upright, prop

horchata *f* orgeat

horda *f* horde

horero *m* (*reloj*) hour hand

horizontal *adj & f* horizontal

horizonte *m* horizon

horma *f* form, mold; shoe tree; hat block; **hallar la horma de su zapato** to meet one's match

hormiga *f* ant; (*enfermedad que causa comezón*) itch

hormigón *m* concrete; **hormigón armado** reinforced concrete

hormigonera *f* concrete mixer

hormigo•so -sa *adj* antlike; full of ants; ant-eaten; (*picante*) itchy

hormiguear *intr* (*ponerse en movimiento gente o animales*) to swarm; (*experimentar una sensación de hormigas corriendo por el cuerpo*) crawl, creep; abound, teem

hormiguero *m* anthill; (*de gente*) swarm, mob

hormillón *m* hat block

hormón *m* or **hormona** *f* hormone

hornacina *f* niche

hornada *f* (*cantidad que se cuece de una vez en un horno*) batch, bake; (*conjunto de individuos de una misma promoción*) crop

hornazo *m* Easter cake filled with hard-boiled eggs; Easter gift to Lenten preacher

horne•ro -ra *mf* baker

hornilla *f* kitchen grate; pigeonhole

hornillo *m* kitchen stove; hot plate; (*de la pipa de fumar*) bowl

horno *m* oven, furnace; (*para cocer ladrillos*) kiln; **alto horno** blast furnace; **horno de cal** limekiln; **horno de fundición** smelting furnace; **horno de ladrillero** brickkiln

horóscopo *m* horoscope; **sacar un horóscopo** to cast a horoscope

horqueta *f* pitchfork; fork, prop; (*ángulo agudo en un río*) (Arg) bend

horquilla *f* pitchfork; (*de bicicleta*) fork; (*de microteléfono*) cradle; (*alfiler para sujetar el pelo*) hairpin

horrar *tr* to save

hórreo *m* granary; (in Asturias and Galicia) crib or granary raised on pillars (*to protect grain from mice and dampness*)

horrible *adj* horrible

horripilante *adj* hair-raising, blood-curdling

horror *m* horror; **tener horror a** to have a horror of

horrorizar §60 *tr* to horrify

horroro•so -sa *adj* horrid; hideous, ugly

hortaliza *f* vegetable

hortela•no -na *adj* garden ‖ *mf* gardener

hortera *m* clerk, helper ‖ *f* wooden bowl

hortícola *adj* horticultural

horticul•tor -tora *mf* horticulturist

horticultura *f* horticulture

hos•co -ca *adj* dark, dark-skinned; sullen, grim, gloomy

hospedaje *m* lodging

hospedar *tr* to lodge ‖ *ref* to lodge, stop, put up

hospedería *f* hospice; inn, hostelry

hospede•ro -ra *mf* innkeeper

hospicio *m* hospice; poorhouse; orphan asylum

hospital *m* hospital; **estar hecho un hospital** (*una persona*) to be full of aches and pains; (*una casa*) to be turned into a hospital; **hospital de la sangre** poor relations; **hospital de primera sangre** (mil) field hospital; **hospital robado** bare house

hospitala•rio -ria *adj* hospitable

hospitalidad *f* hospitality; (*estancia del enfermo en el hospital*) hospitalization

hospitalizar §60 *tr* to hospitalize

hosquedad *f* darkness; sullenness, grimness, gloominess

hostelería *f* restaurant and hotel business

hostería *f* inn, hostelry

hostia *f* sacrificial victim; wafer; (eccl) wafer, Host

hostigar §44 *tr* to scourge; harass; to pester; cloy, surfeit

hostigo•so -sa *adj* cloying, sickening

hostil *adj* hostile

hostilidad *f* hostility

hostilizar §60 *tr* to antagonize; (*al enemigo*) harry, harass

hotel *m* (*establecimiento donde se da comida y alojamiento por dinero*) hotel; (*casa particular lujosa*) mansion

hotele•ro -ra *adj* hotel ‖ *mf* hotelkeeper

hoy *adv & s* today; **de hoy a mañana** any time now; **de hoy en adelante** from now on; **hoy día** nowadays

hoya *f* hole, pit, ditch; (*sepultura*) grave; valley; (*almáciga*) seedbed; river basin

hoyanca *f* potter's field

hoyo *m* hole; grave; pockmark

hoyo•so -sa *adj* full of holes

hoyuelo *m* dimple; (*juego de muchachos*) pitching pennies

hoz *f* (*pl* **hoces**) sickle; narrow pass, defile; **de hoz y de coz** headlong, recklessly

hozar §60 *tr & intr* to nuzzle, root
hta. *abbr* **hasta**
huacal *m* var of **guacal**
huachinango *m* (Mex) red snapper
hucha *f* workingman's chest; (*alcancía*) toy bank; (*dinero ahorrado*) savings, nest egg
huchear *intr* to cry, shout
hue·co -ca *adj* hollow; (*mullido*) soft, fluffy, spongy; (*voz*) deep, resounding; vain, conceited; (*estilo, lenguaje*) affected, pompous ‖ *m* hollow; interval; (*en un muro, una hilera de coches, etc.*) opening; (*empleo sin proveer*) opening; **hueco de la axila** armpit; **hueco de escalera** stair well
huélfago *m* (vet) heaves
huelga *f* (*ocio*) rest, leisure, idleness; recreation; pleasant spot; (*cesación del trabajo en señal de protesta*) strike; (mach) play; **huelga de brazos caídos** sit-down strike; **huelga de hambre** hunger strike; **huelga general** general strike; **huelga patronal** lockout; **huelga por solidaridad** sympathy strike; **huelga sentada** sit-down strike; **ir a la huelga** or **ponerse en huelga** to go on strike
huelguista *mf* striker
huella *f* track, footprint; trace, mark; rut; (*acción de hollar*) tread, treading; (*peldaño en que se asienta el pie*) tread; **huella dactilar** or **digital** fingerprint; **huella de sonido** sound track; **seguir las huellas de** to follow in the footsteps of
huérfa·no -na *adj* orphan; orphaned; alone, deserted ‖ *mf* orphan; (Chile, Peru) foundling
hue·ro -ra *adj* rotten; (fig) empty, hollow; (Guat, Mex) blond; **salir huero** (coll) to flop, turn out bad ‖ *mf* (Guat, Mex) blond
huerta *f* vegetable garden; fruit garden; irrigated region
huerte·ro -ra *mf* (Arg, Peru) gardener
huerto *m* (*de árboles frutales*) orchard; (*de verduras*) kitchen garden
huesa *f* grave
huesear *intr* to beg (alms)
huesillo *m* (Chile, Peru) sun-dried peach
hueso *m* bone; (*de ciertas frutas*) stone, pit; drudgery; **a otro perro con ese hueso** tell that to the marines; **calarse hasta los huesos** to get soaked to the skin; **hueso de la alegría** crazy bone, funny bone; **hueso de la suerte** wishbone; **hueso duro de roer** a hard nut to crack; **la sin hueso** the tongue; **no dejarle a uno un hueso sano** to beat someone up; to pick someone to pieces; **no poder con sus huesos** to be all in; **soltar la sin hueso** to talk too much; to pour forth insults; **tener los huesos molidos** to be all fagged out
hueso·so -sa *adj* bony
hués·ped -peda *mf* (*persona alojada en casa ajena*) guest; (*persona que hospeda a otra en su casa*) host; (*mesonero*) innkeeper, host
hueste *f* followers; (*ejército*) army, host
huesu·do -da *adj* bony, big-boned
hueva *f* roe, fish roe

hueve·ro -ra *mf* egg dealer ‖ *f* eggcup; oviduct
huevo *m* egg; **huevo a la plancha** fried egg; **huevo al plato** shirred egg; **huevo del té** tea ball; **huevo de zurcir** darning egg or gourd; **huevo duro** hard-boiled egg; **huevo escalfado** poached egg; **huevo estrellado** or **frito** fried egg; **huevo pasado por agua** soft-boiled egg; **huevos revueltos** scrambled eggs
huída *f* flight; (*de un líquido*) leak; (*ensanche en un agujero*) flare, splay; (*de caballo*) shying
huidi·zo -za *adj* fugitive; evasive
huincha *f* (SAm) tape; (SAm) tape measure
huipil *m* (Mex) colorful poncho worn by Indian women
huir §20 *tr* to flee, avoid, shun; (*el cuerpo*) duck ‖ *intr* to flee; (*el tiempo*) fly; (*de la memoria*) to slip ‖ *ref* to flee
hule *m* (*tela impermeable*) oilcloth; rubber; (taur) blood, goring
hulear *intr* (CAm) to gather rubber
hulla *f* coal; **hulla azul** tide power; wind power; **hulla blanca** white power; water power
hullera *f* colliery, coal mine
humanidad *f* humanity; fatness
humanista *adj & mf* humanist
humanita·rio -ria *adj & mf* humanitarian
huma·no -na *adj* (*perteneciente al hombre*) human; (*compasivo, misericordioso; civilizador*) humane
humareda *f* cloud of smoke
humeante *adj* smoking, smoky; steamy, reeking
humear *tr* (SAm) to fumigate ‖ *intr* to smoke; steam, reek; put on airs; (*reliquias de un alboroto, enemistad, etc.*) last, persist
humectador *m* humidifier
humedad *f* humidity, dampness, moisture
humedecer §22 *tr* to humidify, dampen, moisten, wet
húme·do -da *adj* humid, damp, moist
humero *m* smokestack, chimney
húmero *m* humerus
humidificador *m* air humidifier
humildad *f* humility
humilde *adj* humble
humilladero *m* calvary, road shrine; priedieu
humillante *adj* humiliating
humillar *tr* (*abatir el orgullo de*) to humble; (*avergonzar*) humiliate, (*la cabeza*) bow; (*el cuerpo, las rodillas*) bend ‖ *ref* to humble oneself; cringe, grovel
humo *m* smoke; steam, fume; **a humo de pajas** lightly, thoughtlessly; **bajar los humos** (coll) to humble, take down a peg; **echar más humo que una chimenea** to smoke like a chimney; **humos** airs, conceit; hearths, homes; **irse todo en humo** to go up in smoke; **tragar el humo** to inhale; **vender humos** to peddle influence

humor *m* humor; **de mal humor** out of humor; **estar de humor para** to be in the humor for; **seguir el humor a** to humor
humorismo *m* humor, humorousness
humorista *mf* humorist
humorísti•co -ca *adj* humorous
humo•so -sa *adj* smoky
hundible *adj* sinkable
hundir *tr* to sink; plunge; (*abrumar*) overwhelm; confound, confute; destroy, ruin ‖ *ref* to sink; collapse; settle, cave in; come to ruin; disappear, vanish
húnga•ro -ra *adj & mf* Hungarian ‖ *m* (*idioma*) Hungarian
Hungría *f* Hungary
hupe *m* punk
huracán *m* hurricane
huraña *f* shyness, unsociability
hura•ño -ña *adj* shy, unsociable
hurgar §44 *tr* to poke; (fig) to stir up, incite; **peor es hurgallo** (i.e., **hurgarlo**) better keep hands off ‖ *intr* to poke ‖ *ref* (*la nariz*) to pick
hurgón *m* poker; thrust, stab
hurgonazo *m* (*con hurgón*) poke; jab, stab, thrust
hurgonear *tr* to poke; to jab, to stab at
hurgonero *m* poker

hu•rón -rona *adj* shy, diffident ‖ *mf* prier, snooper; shy person, diffident person ‖ *m* ferret
huronear *tr* to ferret, hunt with a ferret; to ferret out
huronera *f* ferret hole; lair, hiding place
hurtadillas — a hurtadillas by stealth, on the sly; **a hurtadillas de** unbeknown to
hurtar *tr* to steal; (*en pesos y medidas*) cheat; (*el suelo*) wear away; plagiarize; **hurtar el cuerpo** to dodge, duck ‖ *ref* to withdraw, hide
hurto *m* thieving; theft; **a hurto** stealthily, on the sly; **coger con el hurto en las manos** to catch with the goods; **hurto mayor** grand larceny
husma *f* snooping; **andar a la husma** to go around snooping
husmear *tr* to scent, smell out; pry into ‖ *intr* (*la carne*) to smell bad, become gamy
husmo *m* gaminess, high odor; **estar al husmo** to wait for a chance
huso *m* (*para hilar*) spindle; (*para devanar*) bobbin; (*cilindro del torno*) drum; **huso horario** time zone; **ser más derecho que un huso** to be as straight as a ramrod
huta *f* hunter's blind
huy *interj* ouch!
huyente *adj* (*frente*) receding; (*ojeada*) shifty

I

I, i (i) *f* tenth letter of the Spanish alphabet
ib. *abbr* **ibídem**
ibéri•co -ca *adj* Iberian
ibe•ro -ra *adj & mf* Iberian
íbice *m* ibex
ice•berg *m* (*pl* **-bergs**) iceberg
iconoclasia *f* or **iconoclasmo** *m* iconoclasm
iconoclasta *mf* iconoclast
iconoscopio *m* (telv) iconoscope
ictericia *f* jaundice
ictericia•do -da *adj* jaundiced
ictiología *f* ichthyology
ida *f* going; departure; rashness; sally; trail; **de ida y vuelta** round-trip; **idas y venidas** comings and goings
idea *f* idea; **mudar de idea** to change one's mind
ideal *adj & m* ideal
idealista *adj & mf* idealist
idealizar §60 *tr* to idealize
idear *tr* to think up, devise
idemista *adj* yes-saying ‖ *mf* yes sayer
idénti•co -ca *adj* identic(al); (*muy parecido*) very similar
identidad *f* identity, sameness
identificación *f* identification
identificar §73 *tr* to identify
ideología *f* ideology
idíli•co -ca *adj* idyllic

idilio *m* idyll
idioma *m* language; (*modo particular de hablar*) idiom, speech
idiomáti•co -ca *adj* idiomatic; language, linguistic
idiosincrasia *f* idiosyncrasy
idiota *adj* idiotic ‖ *mf* idiot
idiotez *f* idiocy
idiotismo *m* ignorance; (*idiotez*) idiocy; (gram) idiom
i•do -da *adj* wild, scatterbrained; drunk ‖ **los idos** the dead ‖ *f* see **ida**
idolatrar *tr* to idolize
idolatría *f* idolatry; (*amor excesivo a una persona*) idolization
ídolo *m* idol
idoneidad *f* fitness, suitability
idóne•o -a *adj* fit, suitable
idus *mpl* ides
iglesia *f* church; **entrar en la iglesia** to go into the church; **llevar a la iglesia** to lead to the altar
iglesie•ro -ra *adj* (Arg) church-going ‖ *mf* (Arg) church goer
igna•ro -ra *adj* ignorant
ignominio•so -sa *adj* ignominious
ignorancia *f* ignorance
ignorante *adj* ignorant ‖ *mf* ignoramus
ignorar *tr* to not know, be ignorant of

igno•to -ta *adj* unknown

igual *adj* equal; (*liso, llano*) smooth, even, level; (*no variable*) firm, constant, equable; indifferent; **me es igual** it makes no difference to me ‖ *m* equal; equal sign; **al igual de** like, after the fashion of; **al igual que** as; while, whereas; **en igual de** instead of

iguala *f* equalization; agreement

igualización *f* equalization; agreement

igualar *tr* to equal; (*alisar, allanar*) smooth, even, level; make equal, match; deem equal ‖ *intr & ref* to be equal

igualdad *f* equality; smoothness, evenness; **igualdad de ánimo** equanimity; **igualdad de oportunidades** equal opportunity

igualmente *adv* likewise; **igualmente que** the same as

ijada *f* (*de animal*) flank; (*del cuerpo humano*) loin; (*dolor en estas partes*) stitch; **tener su ijada** to have its weak side or point

ijadear *intr* to pant

ijar *m* flank; loin

ilegal *adj* illegal

ilegible *adj* illegible

ilegíti•mo -ma *adj* illegitimate

ile•so -sa *adj* unscathed, unharmed

iletra•do -da *adj* unlettered, uncultured

ilíci•to -ta *adj* illicit, unlawful

ilimita•do -da *adj* limitless

ilitera•to -ta *adj* illiterate

ilógi•co -ca *adj* illogical

ilote *m* ear of corn

iludir *tr* to elude, evade

iluminación *f* illumination

iluminador *m* lighting engineer

iluminar *tr* to illuminate, light, light up ‖ *ref* to light up, brighten

ilusión *f* illusion; (*esperanza infundada*) delusion; enthusiasm, zeal; dream; **forjarse** or **hacerse ilusiones** to kid oneself, indulge in wishful thinking

ilusionar *tr* to delude ‖ *ref* to have illusions, indulge in wishful thinking; be enraptured, be beguiled

ilusionista *mf* prestidigitator, magician

ilusi•vo -va *adj* illusive

ilu•so -sa *adj* deluded, misguided; (*propenso a ilusionarse*) visionary

iluso•rio -ria *adj* illusory

ilustración *f* illustration; enlightenment; illustrated magazine

ilustra•do -da *adj* illustrated; learned, informed; enlightened

ilustrar *tr* (*adornar con grabados alusivos al texto*) to illustrate; make illustrious, make famous; explain, elucidate; enlighten ‖ *ref* to become famous; be enlightened

ilustre *adj* illustrious

imagen *f* image; picture

imaginación *f* imagination

imaginar *tr, intr & ref* to imagine

imagina•rio -ria *adj* imaginary

imaginati•vo -va *adj* imaginative ‖ *f* imagination; understanding

imaginería *f* fancy colored embroidery; carving or painting of religious images

imán *m* magnet; (fig) lodestone; **imán de herradura** horseshoe magnet; **imán inductor** (elec) field magnet

imanar or **imantar** *tr* to magnetize

imbatible *adj* unbeatable

imbécil *adj & mf* imbecile

imbecilidad *f* imbecility

imberbe *adj* beardless

imbíbi•to -ta *adj* including; included

imbornal *m* drain hole

imborrable *adj* indelible; unforgettable

imbuir §20 *tr* to imbue

imitación *adj invar* imitation ‖ *f* imitation; **a imitación de** in imitation of; **de imitación** imitation, fake

imita•do -da *adj* imitated; mock, sham; imitation

imitar *tr* to imitate

impaciencia *f* impatience

impacientar *tr* to make impatient ‖ *ref* to get impatient

impaciente *adj* impatient

impacto *m* impact, hit; (*señal que deja el proyectil*) mark; **impacto directo** direct hit

impar *adj* odd, uneven; (*que no tiene igual*) unmatched ‖ *m* odd number

imparcial *adj* impartial; (*que no entra en ningún partido*) nonpartisan

impartir *tr* to distribute, impart; (*lecciones*) to give

impás *m* finesse

impasible *adj* impassible, impassive

impávi•do -da *adj* dauntless, fearless, intrepid

impecable *adj* impeccable

impedancia *f* impedance

impedi•do -da *adj* disabled, crippled

impedimento *m* impediment, obstacle, hindrance

impedir §50 *tr* to hinder, prevent

impeler *tr* to impel; spur, incite

impenetrable *adj* impenetrable

impenitente *adj & mf* impenitent

impensable *adj* unthinkable

impensa•do -da *adj* unexpected

imperar *intr* to rule, reign, command

imperati•vo -va *adj & m* imperative

imperceptible *adj* imperceptible

imperdible *m* safety pin

imperdonable *adj* unpardonable, unforgivable

imperece•ro -ra *adj* imperishable, undying

imperfección *f* imperfection

imperfec•to -ta *adj & m* imperfect

imperial *adj* imperial ‖ *f* imperial, roof (*of a coach or bus*)

imperialista *adj & mf* imperialist

impericia *f* unskillfulness, inexpertness

imperio *m* empire; dominion, sway

imperio•so -sa *adj* (*que manda con imperio*) imperious; (*indispensable*) imperative

imperi•to -ta *adj* unskilled, inexpert

impermeable *adj* impermeable; water-proof ‖ *m* raincoat

impersonal *adj* impersonal

impertérri•to -ta *adj* dauntless, intrepid
impertinencia *f* impertinence; irrelevance; fussiness
impertinente *adj* impertinent; (*que no viene al caso*) irrelevant; (*nimiamente susceptible*) fussy ‖ **impertinentes** *mpl* lorgnette
impetrar *tr* to beg (for); obtain by entreaty
ímpetu *m* impetus; force; haste
impetuo•so -sa *adj* impetuous
impiedad *f* (*falta de religión*) impiety; (*falta de compasión*) pitilessness
impí•o -a *adj* (*irreligioso*) impious; (*falto de compasión*) pitiless
impla *f* wimple
implacable *adj* relentless
implantar *tr* to implant; introduce
implementos *mpl* implements; tools
implicar §73 *tr* (*envolver*) to implicate; (*incluir en esencia*) imply ‖ *intr* to stand in the way
implíci•to -ta *adj* implicit, implied
implorar *tr* to implore
implume *adj* featherless
imponente *adj* imposing ‖ *mf* depositor, investor
imponer §54 *tr* (*la voluntad de uno, silencio, tributos*) to impose; (*dinero a rédito*) invest; (*dinero en depósito*) deposit; instruct; impute falsely ‖ *intr* to dominate, command respect ‖ *ref* (*responsabilidades*) to assume; command attention, command respect; **imponerse a** to dominate, command the respect of; **imponerse de** to learn, to find out
imponible *adj* taxable
impopular *adj* unpopular
impopularidad *f* unpopularity
importación *f* importation; import; imports
importa•dor -dora *mf* importer
importancia *f* importance; (*extensión, tamaño*) size; **ser de la importancia de** to be the concern of
importante *adj* important; large
importar *tr* (*introducir en un país*) to import; amount to; involve, imply; concern ‖ *intr* to import; be important; matter
importe *m* amount
importunar *tr* to importune
importu•no -na *adj* (*molesto*) importunate; (*fuera de sazón*) inopportune
imposibilita•do -da *adj* paralyzed, disabled
imposibilitar *tr* to make impossible ‖ *ref* to become paralyzed, become disabled
imposible *adj* impossible
imposición *f* (*de la voluntad de uno*) imposition; burden; imposture; (*de dinero*) deposit; (typ) make-up
impos•tor -tora *mf* impostor; slanderer
impostura *f* imposture
impotable *adj* undrinkable
impotencia *f* impotence
impotente *adj* impotent
impracticable *adj* impracticable, impassable; impractical
impreci•so -sa *adj* imprecise; vague
impregnar *tr* to impregnate, saturate
impremedita•do -da *adj* unpremeditated

imprenta *f* printing; printing shop; (*lo que se publica impreso*) printed matter; (*máquina para imprimir o prensar; conjunto de periódicos o periodistas*) press
imprentar *tr* (*la ropa*) (Chile) to press, iron; (Ecuad) to mark
imprescindible *adj* indispensable, essential
impresentable *adj* unpresentable
impresión *f* (*efecto producido en el ánimo; señal que una cosa deja en otra por presión*) impression; (*acción de imprimir*) printing; (*los ejemplares de una edición*) edition, issue; (phot) print; **impresión dactilar** or **digital** fingerprint
impresionable *adj* impressionable
impresionante *adj* impressive
impresionar *tr* to impress; (*un disco fonográfico*) record; (phot) to expose ‖ *intr* to make an impression ‖ *ref* to be impressed
impreso *m* printed paper or book; **impreso derivado** (*ordenador*) printout; **impresos** printed matter
impre•sor -sora *mf* printer
imprevisible *adj* unforeseeable
imprevisión *f* improvidence, lack of foresight
imprevi•sor -sora *adj* improvident
imprevis•to -ta *adj* unforeseen, unexpected ‖ **imprevistos** *mpl* emergencies, unforeseen expenses
imprimar *tr* to prime
imprimir *tr* (*respeto, miedo; movimiento*) to impart ‖ §83 *tr* to stamp, imprint, impress; (*un disco fonográfico*) press; (typ) to print
improbable *adj* improbable
improbar §61 *tr* to disapprove
improbidad *f* dishonesty; hardness, arduousness
ímpro•bo -ba *adj* dishonest; (*trabajo*) arduous
improcedente *adj* wrong; unfit, untimely
improducti•vo -va *adj* unproductive; unemployed
impronunciable *adj* unpronounceable
improperar *tr* to insult, revile
improperio *m* insult, affront
impropi•cio -cia *adj* unpropitious
impro•pio -pia *adj* improper; (*ajeno*) foreign
impróspe•ro -ra *adj* unsuccessful
impróvi•do -da *adj* unprepared
improvisación *f* improvisation; meteoric rise; (mus) impromptu
improvisadamente *adv* suddenly, unexpectedly; extempore
improvisar *tr* & *intr* to improvise
improvi•so -sa *adj* unforeseen, unexpected
imprudencia *f* imprudence; **imprudencia temeraria** criminal negligence
imprudente *adj* imprudent
impudicia *f* immodesty
impúdi•co -ca *adj* immodest
impues•to -ta *adj* informed ‖ *m* tax; **impuesto sobre el valor añadido** or **impuesto al valor agregado** value-added tax; **impuesto sobre la renta** income tax
impugnar *tr* to impugn, contest
impulsar *tr* to impel; drive

ig
im

impulsión f impulse, drive
impulsi•vo -va adj impulsive
impulso m impulse
impune adj unpunished
impunidad f impunity
impureza f impurity
impu•ro -ra adj impure
imputar tr to impute; credit on account
inabordable adj unapproachable
inacabable adj endless, interminable
inaccesible adj inaccessible
inacción f inaction
inacentua•do -da adj unaccented
inactividad f inactivity
inacti•vo -va adj inactive
inadecua•do -da adj inadequate; unsuited
inadvertencia f inadvertence, oversight
inadverti•do -da adj inadvertent, unwitting;
  careless, thoughtless; unseen, unnoticed
inagotable adj inexhaustible
inaguantable adj unbearable
inalámbri•co -ca adj wireless
inalcanzable adj unattainable
inamisto•so -sa adj unfriendly
inamovible adj irremovable; undetachable;
  (incorporado) built-in
inamovilidad f irremovability; tenure, permanent tenure
inane adj inane
inanición f starvation
inanima•do -da adj inanimate, lifeless
inapelable adj unappealable; unavoidable
inapetencia f loss of appetite
inapreciable adj inappreciable; imperceptible
inarmóni•co -ca adj unharmonious
inarrugable adj wrinkle-free
inarticula•do -da adj inarticulate
inartísti•co -ca adj inartistic
inasequible adj unattainable; unobtainable
inastillable adj nonshatterable, shatter-proof
inatacable adj unattackable; **inatacable por**
  resistant to
inaudi•to -ta adj unheard-of; outrageous
inauguración f inauguration; (de una estatua) unveiling
inaugural adj inaugural
inaugurar tr to inaugurate; (p.ej., una estatua) unveil
inaveriguable adj unascertainable
inca mf Inca
incai•co -ca adj Inca, Incan
incalificable adj unqualifiable; (infame,
  atroz) unspeakable
incambiable adj unchangeable
incandescente adj incandescent
incansable adj untiring, indefatigable
incapacitar tr to incapacitate; (law) to declare incompetent
inca•paz adj (pl **-paces**) incapable, unable;
  not large enough; stupid; (law) incompetent; frightful, unbearable
incasable adj unmarriageable; opposed to
  marriage; (por su fealdad) unable to find a
  husband
incautar ref — **incautarse de** to hold until
  claimed; (law) to seize, attach

incau•to -ta adj unwary, heedless
incendajas fpl kindling
incendiar tr to set on fire ‖ ref to catch fire
incendia•rio -ria adj incendiary ‖ mf incendiary, firebug
incendio m fire; (fig) fire, passion
incensar §2 tr to incense, burn incense before; (fig) to flatter
incensario m censer, incense burner
incenti•vo -va adj & m incentive
inceremonio•so -sa adj unceremonious
incertidumbre f uncertainty, incertitude
incesante adj unceasing
incesto m incest
incestuo•so -sa adj incestuous
incidencia f incidence; **por incidencia** by
  chance
incidente adj incident; incidental ‖ m incident
incidir tr to make an incision in ‖ intr —
  incidir en culpa to fall into guilt; **incidir
  en** or **sobre** to strike, impinge on
incienso m incense; (olíbano) frankincense
incier•to -ta adj uncertain
incineración f incineration; (de cadáveres)
  cremation
incinerar tr to incinerate; (cadáveres) cremate
incipiente adj incipient
incisión f incision; (mordacidad en el
  lenguaje) incisiveness, sarcasm
incisi•vo -va adj incisive; biting, sarcastic
inci•so -sa adj (estilo del escritor) choppy ‖
  m comma; clause; sentence
incitar tr to incite
incivil adj rude, impolite
inciviliza•do -da adj uncivilized
inclemencia f inclemency; **a la inclemencia**
  in the open, without shelter
inclemente adj inclement
inclinación f inclination; bent, leaning, propensity; nod, bow
inclinar tr, intr & ref to incline; bend, bow
íncli•to -ta adj illustrious, renowned
incluir §20 tr to include; (en una carta)
  inclose
inclusa f foundling home
incluse•ro -ra mf foundling
inclusión f inclusion; friendship
inclusive adv inclusive, inclusively ‖ prep
  including
inclusi•vo -va adj inclusive
inclu•so -sa adj inclosed ‖ f see **inclusa** ‖
  incluso adv inclusively; (hasta, aun) even
  ‖ **incluso** prep including
incobrable adj uncollectible; irrecoverable
incógni•to -ta adj (no conocido) unknown;
  (que no se da a conocer) incognito ‖ mf
  (persona) incognito ‖ m (condición de no
  ser conocido) incognito; **de incógnito** (sin
  ser conocido) incognito ‖ f (math & fig)
  unknown quantity
incoherente adj incoherent
íncola m inhabitant
incolo•ro -ra adj colorless
incólume adj unharmed, safe

incombustible *adj* incombustible, fireproof; cold, indifferent

incomerciable *adj* unmarketable

incomible *adj* uneatable, inedible

incomodar *tr* to inconvenience, disturb

incomodidad *f* inconvenience; annoyance, discomfort

incómo•do -da *adj* inconvenient; annoying, uncomfortable ‖ *m* inconvenience; discomfort

incomparable *adj* incomparable

incompartible *adj* unsharable

incompasi•vo -va *adj* pitiless, unsympathetic

incompatible *adj* incompatible; (*acontecimientos, citas, horas de clase, etc.*) conflicting

incompetente *adj* incompetent

incompetible *adj* unmatchable

incomple•to -ta *adj* incomplete

incomponible *adj* unmendable, beyond repair

incomprable *adj* unpurchasable

incomprensible *adj* incomprehensible

incomprensión *f* incomprehension

incomunicación *f* isolation, solitary confinement

incomunica•do -da *adj* incommunicado; in solitary confinement

inconcebible *adj* inconceivable

inconclu•so -sa *adj* unfinished

inconcluyente *adj* inconclusive

inconcu•so -sa *adj* undeniable

incondicional *adj* unconditional

incone•xo -xa *adj* unconnected; (*inaplicable*) irrelevant

inconfidente *adj* distrustful

inconformidad *f* nonconformity; disagreement

inconformista *mf* nonconformist

inconfundible *adj* unmistakable

incon•gruo -grua *adj* incongruous

inconocible *adj* unknowable

inconquistable *adj* unconquerable; (*que no se deja vencer con ruegos y dádivas*) unbending, unyielding

inconsciencia *f* unconsciousness; unawareness

inconsciente *adj* unconscious; unaware; **lo inconsciente** the unconscious

inconsecuencia *f* (*falta de consecuencia o correspondencia en dichos y hechos*) inconsistency

inconsecuente *adj* inconsistent; (*que no se deduce de otra cosa*) inconsequential

inconsidera•do -da *adj* inconsiderate

inconsiguiente *adj* inconsequential, illogical

inconsistencia *f* (*falta de cohesión*) inconsistency

inconsistente *adj* inconsistent

inconsolable *adj* inconsolable

inconstante *adj* inconstant

inconstitucional *adj* unconstitutional

inconsútil *adj* seamless

incontable *adj* countless, innumerable

incontenible *adj* irrepressible

incontestable *adj* incontestable

incontinente *adj* incontinent ‖ *adv* at once, instantly

incontrastable *adj* invincible; inconvincible; (*argumento*) unanswerable

incontrovertible *adj* incontrovertible

inconveniencia *f* inconvenience; unsuitability; impoliteness; impropriety

inconveniente *adj* inconvenient; unsuitable; impolite; improper ‖ *m* drawback; disadvantage; objection

incordio *m* bore, nuisance

incorporación *f* incorporation, embodiment

incorpora•do -da *adj* (*el que estaba echado*) sitting up; (*montado en la construcción*) built-in

incorporar *tr* to incorporate, embody ‖ *ref* to incorporate; (*el que estaba echado*) sit up; **incorporarse a** to join

incorrec•to -ta *adj* incorrect

incrédu•lo -la *adj* incredulous ‖ *mf* disbeliever, doubter

increíble *adj* incredible

incremento *m* increment, increase

increpar *tr* to chide, rebuke

incriminar *tr* to incriminate; (*un delito, falta, defecto*) exaggerate the gravity of

incruen•to -ta *adj* bloodless

incrustar *tr* to incrust; (*embutir por adorno*) inlay

incubadora *f* incubator

incubar *tr* & *intr* to incubate ‖ *ref* (fig) to be brewing

incuestionable *adj* unquestionable

inculcar §73 *tr* to inculcate‖ *ref* to become obstinate

inculpable *adj* blameless, guiltless

inculpar *tr* to accuse, blame

incultivable *adj* untillable

incul•to -ta *adj* uncultivated, untilled; uncultured; (*estilo*) coarse, sloppy

incumbencia *f* incumbency, duty, obligation, province

incumbir *intr* — **incumbir a** to be incumbent on

incumplimiento *m* nonfulfillment

incunable *m* incunabulum

incurable *adj* & *mf* incurable

incuria *f* carelessness, negligence

incurio•so -sa *adj* careless, negligent

incurrir *intr* — **incurrir en** to incur

incursión *f* incursion, inroad, raid

indagación *f* investigation, research

indagatorio *m* deposition of the accused

indagar §44 *tr* to investigate

indebidamente *adv* unduly

indebi•do -da *adj* undue; wrong

indecencia *f* indecency

indecente *adj* indecent

indecible *adj* unspeakable, unutterable

indeci•so -sa *adj* undecided, indecisive; (*contorno, forma*) vague, obscure

indeclinable *adj* unavoidable; (gram) indeclinable

indecoro•so -sa *adj* improper

indefectible *adj* unfailing

indefendible *adj* indefensible

indefen•so -sa *adj* defenseless, undefended

im
in

indefinible *adj* indefinable
indefini•do -da *adj* indefinite; limitless; vague
indeleble *adj* indelible
indelibera•do -da *adj* unpremeditated
indelica•do -da *adj* indelicate
indemne *adj* unharmed, undamaged
indemnidad *f* (*seguridad contra un daño*) indemnity
indemnización *f* (*compensación*) indemnity, indemnification; **indemnización por despido** severance pay
indemnizar §60 *tr* to indemnify
independencia *f* independence
independiente *adj & mf* independent
independizar §60 *tr* to free, emancipate ‖ *ref* to become independent
indescriptible *adj* indescribable
indeseable *adj & mf* undesirable
indesea•do -da *adj* unwanted
indesmallable *adj* runproof
indestructible *adj* indestructible
indetermina•do -da *adj* indeterminate; (*gram*) indefinite
indevo•to -ta *adj* impious; not fond, not devoted
india *f* wealth, riches; **Indias Occidentales** West Indies; **la India** India
indiana *f* printed calico
india•no -na *adj & mf* Spanish American; East Indian; West Indian ‖ *m* man back from America with great wealth; **indiano de hilo negro** (*coll*) skinflint ‖ *f* see **indiana**
indicación *f* indication; **por indicación de** at the direction of
indica•do -da *adj* appropriate, advisable; **muy indicado** just the thing, just the person
indica•dor -dora *adj* indicating, pointing ‖ *m* indicator; gauge; (*de tránsito*) traffic signal
indicar §73 *tr* to indicate
indicati•vo -va *adj & m* indicative
índice *m* index; **índice de libros prohibidos** (*eccl*) Index; **índice de materias** table of contents; **índice en el corte** thumb index
indiciar *tr* to betoken, indicate; surmise, suspect
indicio *m* sign, token, indication; **indicios vehementes** circumstantial evidence
indiferente *adj* indifferent; (*que no importa*) immaterial
indígena *adj* indigenous ‖ *mf* native
indigente *adj* indigent
indigestar *ref* to be indigestible; be disliked, be unbearable
indigestible *adj* indigestible
indigestión *f* indigestion
indignación *f* indignation
indigna•do -da *adj* indignant
indignar *tr* to anger, provoke ‖ *ref* to become indignant
indignidad *f* (*falta de mérito*) unworthiness; (*acción reprobable*) indignity
indig•no -na *adj* unworthy
índigo *m* indigo
in•dio -dia *adj & mf* Indian ‖ *f* see **india**

indirec•to -ta *adj* indirect ‖ *f* hint, innuendo; **indirecta del padre Cobos** broad hint
indiscernible *adj* indiscernible
indiscre•to -ta *adj* indiscreet
indiscrimina•do -da *adj* indiscriminate; non-discriminating
indisculpable *adj* inexcusable
indiscutible *adj* undeniable
indisoluble *adj* indissoluble
indispensable *adj* unpardonable; indispensable
indisponer §54 *tr* (*alterar la salud de*) to indispose, upset; disturb, upset; **indisponer a uno con** to set someone against, prejudice someone against ‖ *ref* to become indisposed; **indisponerse con** to fall out with
indisponible *adj* unavailable
indispues•to -ta *adj* indisposed
indistintamente *adv* indistinctly; indiscriminately, without distinction
indistin•to -ta *adj* indistinct
individual *adj* individual; (*habitación en un hotel; partido de tenis*) single
individualidad *f* individuality
indivi•duo -dua *adj* individual; indivisible ‖ *mf* (*persona indeterminada*) (*coll*) individual ‖ *m* (*cada persona*) individual; (*miembro de una corporación*) member, fellow
indócil *adj* unteachable; headstrong, unruly
indocumenta•do -da *adj* unidentified; unqualified ‖ *mf* nobody (*person of no account*)
indochi•no -na *adj & mf* Indo-Chinese ‖ **la Indochina** Indochina
indoeurope•o -a *adj & m* Indo-European
índole *f* kind, class; nature, disposition, temper
indolente *adj* stolid, impassive; (*perezoso*) indolent
indolo•ro -ra *adj* painless
indoma•do -da *adj* untamed
indone•sio -sia *adj & mf* Indonesian ‖ **la Indonesia** Indonesia
inducción *f* induction
inducido *m* (*de dínamo o motor*) (*elec*) armature
inducir §19 *tr* to induce
inductor *m* (*de dínamo o motor*) (*elec*) field
indudable *adj* doubtless
indulgente *adj* indulgent
indultar *tr* to pardon; free, exempt
indulto *m* pardon; exemption
indumentaria *f* clothing, dress; historical study of clothing
indumento *m* clothing, dress
industria *f* industry; **de industria** on purpose
industrial *adj* industrial ‖ *m* industrialist
industrializar §60 *tr* to industrialize
industriar *tr* to teach, instruct, train ‖ *ref* to get along, manage
industrio•so -sa *adj* industrious
inédi•to -ta *adj* unpublished; new, novel, unknown
inefable *adj* ineffable
ineficacia *f* inefficacy

inefi•caz adj (pl **-caces**) inefficacious, ineffectual
inelegible adj ineligible
ineludible adj inescapable
inenarrable adj indescribable
inencogible adj unshrinkable
inencontrable adj unobtainable
inequidad f inequity
inequívo•co -ca adj unmistakable
inercia f inertia
inerme adj unarmed
inerte adj inert; slow, sluggish
inescrupulo•so -sa adj unscrupulous
inescrutable or **inescudriñable** adj inscrutable
inespera•do -da adj unexpected, unforeseen; unhoped for
inestable adj unstable
inevitable adj unavoidable, inevitable
inexactitud f inaccuracy, inexactness
inexac•to -ta adj inaccurate, inexact
inexcusable adj inexcusable, unpardonable; unavoidable; indispensable
inexistencia f nonexistence
inexorable adj inexorable
inexperiencia f inexperience
inexplicable adj inexplicable, unexplainable
inexplica•do -da adj unexplained, unaccounted for
inexplora•do -da adj unexplored; (mar) uncharted
inexpresable adj inexpressible
inexpues•to -ta adj (phot) unexposed
inexpugnable adj impregnable; firm, unshakable
inextinguible adj unextinguishable; perpetual, lasting; (sed) unquenchable; (risa) uncontrollable
inextirpable adj ineradicable
infalible adj infallible
infamación f defamation
infamar tr to defame, discredit
infame adj infamous; vile, frightful ‖ mf scoundrel
infamia f infamy
infancia f infancy
infan•do -da adj odious, unmentionable
infanta f female child; infanta (any daughter of a king of Spain; wife of an infante)
infante m male child; infante (any son of a king of Spain who is not heir to the throne); (mil) infantryman; **infante de coro** choirboy
infantería f infantry; **infantería de marina** marines, marine corps
infantil adj infant, infantile, childlike; innocent
infarto m (heart) infarct
infatigable adj indefatigable
infatuar §21 tr to make vain ‖ ref to become vain
infaus•to -ta adj fatal, unlucky
infección f infection
infeccionar tr to infect
infeccio•so -sa adj infectious
infectar tr to infect
infec•to -ta adj foul, corrupt; infected; fetid

infecun•do -da adj sterile, barren
infe•liz (pl **-lices**) adj unhappy; simple, good-hearted ‖ m wretch, poor soul
inferior adj inferior; lower; **inferior a** inferior to; lower than; less than; smaller than ‖ m inferior
inferioridad f inferiority
inferir §68 tr to infer; lead to, entail; (una herida) inflict; (una ofensa) cause, offer
infernáculo m hopscotch
infernal adj infernal
infernar §2 tr to damn; irritate, annoy
infernillo m chafing dish
infestar tr to infest ‖ ref to become infested
inficionar tr to infect ‖ ref to become infected
infidelidad f infidelity; (conjunto de infieles) unbelievers
infidente adj faithless, disloyal
infiel adj (falto de fidelidad) unfaithful; (no exacto) inaccurate, inexact; (no cristiano) infidel ‖ mf infidel
infierno m hell; **en el quinto infierno** or **en los quintos infiernos** far, far away
infijo m (gram) infix
infiltrar tr & ref to infiltrate
ínfi•mo -ma adj lowest; humblest, most abject; meanest, vilest
infinidad f infinity
infiniti•vo -va adj & m infinitive
infini•to -ta adj infinite ‖ m infinite; (math) infinity ‖ **infinito** adv greatly, very much
infirme adj infirm
inflación f inflation; (vanidad) conceit
inflaciona•rio -ria adj inflationary
inflado m inflation (of a tire)
inflamable adj inflammable, flammable
inflamación f ignition, inflammation; ardor, enthusiasm; (pathol) inflammation
inflamar tr to set on fire; inflame ‖ ref to catch fire; become inflamed
inflar tr to inflate; exaggerate; puff up with pride ‖ ref to inflate; be puffed up with pride
inflexible adj inflexible; unyielding, unbending
inflexión f inflection; **inflexión vocálica** (metafonía) umlaut
inflexionar tr to umlaut
infligir §27 tr to inflict
influencia f influence
influenciar tr to influence
influenza f influenza
influir §20 intr to have influence; have great weight; **influir en** or **sobre** to influence
influjo m influence; rising tide
influyente adj influential
información f information; (law) judicial inquiry, investigation; **informaciones** testimonial
informal adj (que no se ajusta a las reglas debidas) informal; unreliable
informar tr & intr to inform ‖ ref to inquire, find out
informática f computer science
informati•vo -va adj informational; (sección de un periódico) news

in
in

informe *adj* shapeless, formless; misshapen ‖ *m* piece of information; report; **informes** information; **informes confidenciales** inside information

infortuna•do -da *adj* unfortunate, unlucky

infortunio *m* misfortune; (*acaecimiento desgraciado*) mishap

infracción *f* infraction, infringement

infraconsumo *m* underconsumption

infrac•to -ta *adj* unperturbable

infraestructura *f* substructure; (rr) roadbed

inframundo *m* underworld

infrarro•jo -ja *adj & m* infrared

infrascri•to -ta *adj* undersigned; hereinafter mentioned

infrecuente *adj* infrequent

infringir §27 *tr* to infringe, break, violate

infructuo•so -sa *adj* fruitless, unfruitful

ínfulas *fpl* conceit, airs; **darse ínfulas** to put on airs

infunda•do -da *adj* unfounded, groundless, baseless

infundio *m* lie, fib

infundir *tr* to infuse, instill

infusión *f* infusion; (*acción de echar agua sobre el que se bautiza*) sprinkling; **estar en infusión para** to be all set for

ingeniar *tr* to think up ‖ *ref* to manage; **ingeniarse a** or **para** to manage to; **ingeniarse para ir viviendo** to manage to get along

ingeniería *f* engineering; **ingeniería genética** genetic engineering

ingeniero *m* engineer; **ingeniero de caminos, canales y puertos** government civil engineer

ingenio *m* talent, creative faculty; talented person; cleverness, skill, wit; (*artificio mecánico*) apparatus, device; (*del encuadernador*) paper cutter; engine of war; **afilar** or **aguzar el ingenio** to sharpen one's wits; **ingenio de azúcar** sugar refinery

ingeniosidad *f* ingenuity; wittiness

ingenio•so -sa *adj* (*dotado de ingenio; hecho con ingenio*) ingenious; (*agudo, sutil*) witty

ingéni•to -ta *adj* innate, inborn

ingente *adj* huge, enormous

ingenuidad *f* ingenuousness

inge•nuo -nua *adj* ingenuous

ingerir §68 *tr & ref* var of **injerir**

ingestión *f* (food) consumption; ingestion

Inglaterra *f* England

ingle *f* groin

in•glés -glesa *adj* English; **a la inglesa** in the English manner ‖ *m* Englishman; (*idioma*) English; **el inglés medio** Middle English; **los ingleses** the English ‖ *f* Englishwoman

ingramatical *adj* ungrammatical

ingratitud *f* ingratitude, ungratefulness

ingra•to -ta *adj* (*desagradecido*) ungrateful; (*desagradecido; desagradable, áspero; improductivo*) thankless ‖ *mf* ingrate

ingravidez *f* lightness, tenuousness; (*gravedad nula*) weightlessness

ingrávi•do -da *adj* light, tenuous; weightless

ingrediente *m* ingredient

ingresa•do -da *mf* new student

ingresar *tr* to deposit ‖ *intr* to enter, become a member; (*beneficios*) come in ‖ *ref* (Mex) to enlist

ingreso *m* entrance; admission; **ingresos** income, revenue

íngri•mo -ma *adj* solitary, alone

inhábil *adj* unable; unskillful; unfit, unqualified

inhabilidad *f* inability; unskillfulness; unfitness

inhabilitar *tr* to disable, to disqualify, to incapacitate

inhabita•do -da *adj* uninhabited

inhabitua•do -da *adj* unaccustomed

inherente *adj* inherent

inhibir *tr* to inhibit

inhospitala•rio -ria *adj* inhospitable

inhóspi•to -ta *adj* inhospitable

inhumanidad *f* inhumanity

inhuma•no -na *adj* inhuman, inhumane; (Chile) filthy

iniciación *f* initiation

inicial *adj & f* initial

iniciar *tr* to initiate ‖ *ref* to be initiated

iniciativa *f* initiative

ini•cuo -cua *adj* wicked, iniquitous

inigualable *adj* incomparable

iniguala•do -da *adj* unequaled

ininteligente *adj* unintelligent

ininteligible *adj* unintelligible

ininterrumpi•do -da *adj* uninterrupted

iniquidad *f* iniquity

injerencia *f* interference, meddling

injerir §68 *tr* to insert, introduce; (*alimentos*) take in; (hort) to graft ‖ *ref* to interfere, meddle, intrude

injertar *tr* (hort & surg) to graft

injerto *m* (hort & surg) graft; transplant

injuria *f* offense, insult; abuse, wrong; damage, harm

injuriar *tr* to offend, insult; abuse, wrong; harm, damage

injurio•so -sa *adj* offensive, insulting; abusive; harmful; (*lenguaje*) profane

injusticia *f* injustice

injustifica•do -da *adj* unjustified

injus•to -ta *adj* unjust

inmacula•do -da *adj* immaculate

inmanejable *adj* unmanageable; unhandy

inmarcesible *adj* unfading

inmaterial *adj* immaterial

inmaturo -ra *adj* immature

inmediación *f* immediacy; proximity, nearness; **inmediaciones** neighborhood, outskirts

inmediatamente *adv* immediately; **inmediatamente que** as soon as

inmedia•to -ta *adj* immediate; close, adjoining, next; next above; next below; (*pago*) prompt; **venir a las inmediatas** to get into the thick of the fight

inmejorable *adj* superb, unsurpassable

inmemorial *adj* immemorial

inmen•so -sa *adj* immense

inmensurable *adj* immeasurable

inmereci•do -da *adj* undeserved

inmergir §27 *tr* to immerse

inmersión f immersion
inmigración f immigration
inmigrante mf immigrant
inmigrar intr to immigrate
inminente adj imminent
inmiscuir §20 & **regular** tr to mix ‖ ref to meddle, interfere
inmobilia•rio -ria adj real-estate
inmoble adj motionless; firm, constant
inmodera•do -da adj immoderate
inmodes•to -ta adj immodest
inmódi•co -ca adj excessive
inmoral adj immoral
inmortal adj immortal, deathless ‖ mf immortal
inmortalizar §60 tr to immortalize
inmotiva•do -da adj groundless; unmotivated
inmovilizar §60 tr to immobilize; (un caudal) tie up
inmueble m property, piece of real estate; **inmuebles** real estate
inmun•do -da adj dirty, filthy
inmune adj immune
inmunizar §60 tr to immunize
inmutar tr to change, alter; disturb, upset ‖ ref to change, alter; change countenance; **sin inmutarse** without batting an eye
inna•to -ta adj innate, inborn; natural
innatural adj unnatural
innavegable adj (río) unnavigable; (embarcación) unseaworthy
innecesa•rio -ria adj unnecessary
innegable adj undeniable
innoble adj ignoble
innocuidad f harmlessness
inno•cuo -cua adj harmless
innovación f innovation
innovar tr to innovate
innumerable adj innumerable
inocencia f innocence
inocentada f simpleness; blunder; (Ecuad) April Fools' joke
inocente adj & mf innocent; **coger por inocente** to make an April fool of
inocen•tón -tona adj simple, gullible ‖ mf gull, dupe
inoculación f inoculation
inocular tr to inoculate; contaminate, pervert
inodo•ro -ra adj odorless ‖ m deodorizer; (excusado que funciona con agua corriente) toilet
inofensi•vo -va adj inoffensive
inolvidable adj unforgettable
inope adj impecunious
inopia f indigence
inoportu•no -na adj inopportune, untimely
inorgáni•co -ca adj inorganic
inortodo•xo -xa adj unorthodox
inoxidable adj (acero) stainless; inoxidizable
inquietante adj disquieting, upsetting
inquietar tr to disquiet, worry; stir up, excite
inquie•to -ta adj anxious, worried
inquietud f disquiet, worry, concern
inquili•no -na mf tenant, renter
inquina f aversion, dislike, ill will
inquirir §40 tr to inquire, inquire into
inquisición f inquiry; inquisition

insabible adj unknowable
insaciable adj insatiable
insania f insanity
insa•no -na adj insane; imprudent
insatisfacción f dissatisfaction
insatisfe•cho -cha adj unsatisfied
inscribir §83 tr to inscribe; (law) to record ‖ ref to enroll, register
inscripción f inscription; enrollment, registration
insecticida adj & m insecticide
insecto m insect
insegu•ro -ra adj insecure, unsafe; uncertain
insensa•to -ta adj foolish, stupid
insensible adj callous, hard-hearted, unfeeling; imperceptible
inseparable adj inseparable; undetachable ‖ mf inseparable ‖ m lovebird
insepul•to -ta adj unburied
inserción f insertion
inserir §68 tr to insert; (injertar) graft, engraft
insertar tr to insert
inservible adj useless
insidia f snare, ambush; plotting
insidiar tr to ambush, waylay; trap, trick
insidio•so -sa adj insidious
insigne adj noted, famous, renowned
insignia f badge, decoration, insignia; banner, standard
insignificante adj insignificant
insince•ro -ra adj insincere
insinuación f insinuation, hint
insinuante adj engaging, slick, crafty
insinuar §21 tr to insinuate; suggest, hint at ‖ ref to creep in, slip in; ingratiate oneself; flow, run; **insinuarse en** to work one's way in
insípi•do -da adj insipid, vapid
insistir intr to insist
ínsi•to -ta adj inbred, innate
insociable adj unsociable
insolencia f insolence
insolentar tr to make insolent ‖ ref to become insolent
insolente adj insolent
insóli•to -ta adj unusual
insoluble adj insoluble
insolvencia f insolvency
insomne adj sleepless
insomnio m insomnia
insondable adj fathomless; inscrutable
insonorización f soundproofing
insonoriza•do -da adj soundproof
insonorizar §60 tr to soundproof
insono•ro -ra adj soundproof
insospecha•do -da adj unsuspected
insostenible adj untenable
inspección f inspection; inspectorship; **inspección técnica de vehículos (I.T.V.)** car inspection
inspeccionar tr to inspect
inspiración f inspiration; inhalation
inspirante adj inspiring
inspirar tr & intr to inspire; (atraer a los pulmones) inhale, breathe in ‖ ref to be inspired

in
in

instalación *f* plant, factory; outfit, equipment; arrangements, fittings; installment; **instalación sanitaria** plumbing
instalar *tr* to install ‖ *ref* to settle
instantáne•o -a *adj* instantaneous ‖ *f* snapshot
instante *m* instant, moment; **al instante** right away, immediately; **por instantes** uninterruptedly; any time
instar *tr* to press, urge ‖ *intr* to be pressing, be urgent
instaurar *tr* to restore; reestablish
instigar §44 *tr* to instigate
instilar *tr* to instill
instinti•vo -va *adj* instinctive
instinto *m* instinct
institución *f* institution; **instituciones** (*de un Estado*) constitution; (*de una ciencia, arte, etc.*) principles
instituir §20 *tr* to institute, found
instituto *m* institute; (*de una orden religiosa*) rule, constitution; **instituto de segunda enseñanza** or **de enseñanza media** high school
institu•triz *f* (*pl* **-trices**) governess
instrucción *f* instruction; education
instructi•vo -va *adj* instructive
instruc•tor -tora *mf* teacher, instructor ‖ *m* (mil) drillmaster ‖ *f* instructress
instruí•do -da *adj* well-educated; well-posted
instruir §20 *tr* to instruct; (*un proceso o expediente*) draw up
instrumentar *tr* to instrument
instrumentista *mf* instrumentalist
instrumento *m* instrument; (*persona que se emplea para alcanzar un resultado*) tool; **instrumento de cuerda** (mus) stringed instrument; **instrumento de viento** (mus) wind instrument
insubordina•do -da *adj* insubordinate
insubstituíble *adj* irreplaceable
insudar *intr* to drudge
insuficiente *adj* insufficient
insufrible *adj* insufferable
ínsula *f* island; one-horse town
insular *adj* insular ‖ *mf* islander
insulina *f* insulin
insulsez *f* tastelessness; dullness, heaviness
insul•so -sa *adj* tasteless; dull, heavy
insultada *f* insult
insultar *tr* to insult ‖ *ref* to faint, swoon
insulto *m* insult; fainting spell
insume *adj* expensive
insumergible *adj* unsinkable
insuperable *adj* insurmountable
insurgente *adj* & *mf* insurgent
insurrección *f* insurrection
intac•to -ta *adj* intact, untouched
intachable *adj* blameless, irreproachable
integración *f* integration
integridad *f* integrity; virginity
ínte•gro -gra *adj* integral, whole; honest
intelecto *m* intellect
intelectual *adj* & *mf* intellectual

intelectualidad *f* intellectuality; (*conjunto de los intelectuales de un país o región*) intelligentsia
inteligencia *f* intelligence; **estar en inteligencia con** to be in collusion with
inteligente *adj* intelligent; trained, skilled
inteligible *adj* intelligible
intemperancia *f* intemperance
intemperante *adj* intemperate
intemperie *f* inclement weather; **a la intemperie** in the open, unsheltered
intempesti•vo -va *adj* unseasonable, inopportune, untimely
intención *f* intention; (*cautelosa advertencia*) caution; (*instinto dañino de un animal*) viciousness; **con intención** deliberately, knowingly; **de intención** on purpose
intendencia *f* intendance; (SAm) mayoralty
intendente *m* intendant; quartermaster general; (SAm) mayor
intensar *tr* & *ref* to intensify
intensidad *f* intensity
intensificar §73 *tr* & *ref* to intensify
intensión *f* intensity
intensi•vo -va *adj* intensive
inten•so -sa *adj* intense
intentar *tr* to try, to attempt; intend; try out
intento *m* intent, purpose; **de intento** on purpose
intentona *f* rash attempt (*to rob, escape, etc.*)
interacción *f* interaction
interamerica•no -na *adj* inter-American
intercalar *tr* to intercalate, insert
intercambiar *tr* & *ref* to interchange
intercambio *m* interchange, exchange
interceder *intr* to intercede
interceptar *tr* to intercept
intercep•tor -tora *mf* interceptor ‖ *m* trap; separator; (aer) interceptor
interdecir §24 *tr* to interdict, forbid
interés *m* interest; **intereses creados** vested interests; **poner a interés** to put out at interest
interesa•do -da *adj* interested ‖ *mf* interested party
interesante *adj* interesting
interesar *tr* to interest; involve ‖ *intr* to be interesting ‖ *ref* — **interesarse en** or **por** to be interested in, take an interest in
interescolar *adj* interscholastic, intercollegiate
interfec•to -ta *adj* murdered ‖ *mf* victim of murder
interferencia *f* interference
interferir §68 *tr* to interfere with ‖ *intr* to interfere
interfono *m* intercom
ínterin *adv* meanwhile ‖ *conj* while, as long as ‖ *m* (*pl* **ínterines**) temporary incumbency
interinar *tr* to fill temporarily, fill in an acting capacity
interi•no -na *adj* temporary, acting, interim
interior *adj* interior, inner, inside; home, domestic ‖ *m* interior, inside; mind, soul; **interiores** entrails, insides

interioridad _f_ inside; **interioridades** inside story, private matters
interjección _f_ interjection
interlinear _tr_ to interline; (typ) to space, lead
interlocu•tor -tora _mf_ speaker, party; interviewer
intermedia•rio -ria _adj & mf_ intermediary ‖ _m_ (com) middleman
interme•dio -dia _adj_ intermediate ‖ _m_ interval, interim; (mus) intermezzo; (theat) intermission, entr'acte
intermitente _adj_ intermittent ‖ _m_ (aut) direction light, turning light
internacional _adj_ international
internacionalizar §60 _tr_ to internationalize
interna•do -da _mf_ (mil) internee ‖ _m_ boarding school
internamiento _m_ internment
internar _tr_ to send inland; intern ‖ _intr_ to move inland ‖ _ref_ to move inland; take refuge, hide; insinuate oneself; **internarse en** to go deeply into
internista _mf_ internist
inter•no -na _adj_ internal; inside ‖ _mf_ boarding-school student; **interno de hospital** intern
interpelar _tr_ to seek the protection or aid of; interrogate; interpellate
interpolar _tr_ to interpolate; interpose; interrupt briefly
interponer §54 _tr_ to interpose; appoint as mediator ‖ _ref_ to intervene, intercede
interprender _tr_ to take by surprise
interpresa _f_ surprise action; surprise seizure
interpretar _tr_ to interpret
intérprete _mf_ interpreter
interrogación _f_ interrogation; question mark
interrogar §44 _tr & intr_ to question, interrogate
interrumpir _tr_ to interrupt
interruptor _m_ (elec) switch; **interruptor automático** (elec) circuit breaker; **interruptor del encendido** (aut) ignition switch; **interruptor de resorte** (elec) snap switch
intersección _f_ (geom) intersection
intersticio _m_ interstice; interval
intervalo _m_ interval
intervención _f_ intervention; inspection; (_de cuentas_) audit, auditing; (surg) operation; **intervención de los precios** price control; **no intervención** nonintervention
intervenir §79 _tr_ to take up, work on; inspect, supervise; (_cuentas_) audit; (_un teléfono_) tap; (surg) operate on ‖ _intr_ to mediate, intervene, intercede; participate; happen
interventor _m_ election supervisor; (com) auditor
inter•viev _m_ (_pl_ **-vievs**) interview
intervievar _tr_ to interview
intesta•do -da _adj & mf_ intestate
intesti•no -na _adj_ internal; domestic ‖ _m_ intestine; **intestino delgado** small intestine; **intestino grueso** large intestine
intimación _f_ announcement, notification
intimar _tr_ to announce ‖ _intr & ref_ to become well-acquainted, to become intimate

intimidad _f_ intimacy; (_parte íntima o personal_) privacy
intimidar _tr_ to intimidate
inti•mo -ma _adj_ intimate; (_más interno_) innermost
intitular _tr_ to entitle ‖ _ref_ to use a title; be called
intocable _mf_ untouchable
intolerante _adj & mf_ intolerant
inton•so -sa _adj_ unshorn; ignorant; (_libro o revista_) uncut ‖ _mf_ ignoramus
intoxicación _f_ intoxication; poisoning
intoxicar §73 _tr_ to poison, intoxicate
intracruzamiento _m_ inbreeding
intranquilidad _f_ uneasiness, worry
intranquilizar §60 _tr_ to make uneasy, worry
intranqui•lo -la _adj_ uneasy, worried
intransigente _adj & mf_ intransigent, die-hard
intransiti•vo -va _adj_ intransitive
intrascendente _adj_ unimportant; nonessential
intratable _adj_ unmanageable; impassable; unsociable
intrepidez _f_ intrepidity
intrépi•do -da _adj_ intrepid
intriga _f_ intrigue
intrigar §44 _tr_ (_excitar la curiosidad de_) to intrigue ‖ _intr_ to intrigue ‖ _ref_ to be intrigued
intrinca•do -da _adj_ intricate
intrincar §73 _tr_ to complicate; confuse, bewilder
intríngu•lis _m_ (_pl_ **-lis**) hidden motive, mystery
intrínse•co -ca _adj_ intrinsic(al)
introducción _f_ introduction
introducir §19 _tr_ to introduce; insert, put in ‖ _ref_ to gain access; meddle, interfere, intrude
introito _m_ (_de un escrito o una oración_) introduction; (_de un poema dramático_) prologue; (eccl) introit
introspecti•vo -va _adj_ introspective
introverti•do -da _mf_ introvert
intru•so -sa _adj_ intrusive ‖ _mf_ intruder, interloper
intuición _f_ intuition
intuir §20 _tr_ to guess, sense
intuito _m_ view, glance, look; **por intuito de** in view of
inundación _f_ flood, inundation
inundar _tr_ to flood, inundate
inurba•no -na _adj_ discourteous, unmannerly
inusita•do -da _adj_ (_no ordinario_) unusual; obsolete, out of use
inusual _adj_ unusual
inútil _adj_ useless
invadir _tr_ to invade
invalidar _tr_ to invalidate
invalidez _f_ invalidity
inváli•do -da _adj & mf_ invalid
invariable _adj_ invariable
invasión _f_ invasion
inva•sor -sora _mf_ invader
invectiva _f_ invective
invectivar _tr_ to inveigh against
invencible _adj_ invincible

invención *f* invention; finding, discovery; deception

invendible *adj* unsalable

inventar *tr* to invent

inventariar §77 & **regular** *tr* to inventory

inventario *m* inventory

inventi•vo -va *adj* inventive ‖ *f* inventiveness

invento *m* invention

inven•tor -tora *adj* inventive ‖ *mf* inventor

inverecun•do -da *adj* shameless, brazen

inverisímil *adj* improbable, unlikely

invernáculo *m* greenhouse, hothouse, conservatory

invernada *f* wintertime; (SAm) pasture land; (Ven) torrential rain

invernadero *m* greenhouse, hothouse; winter resort; winter pasture

invernal *adj* winter ‖ *m* cattle shed (*in winter-pasture land*)

invernar §2 *intr* to winter; be winter

inverni•zo -za *adj* winter; wintery

inverosímil *adj* improbable, unlikely

inversión *f* inversion; (*de dinero*) investment; (gram) inverted order

inversionista *adj* investment ‖ *mf* investor

inver•so -sa *adj* inverse, opposite; **a** or **por la inversa** on the contrary

inversor *m* investor

invertebra•do -da *adj* & *m* invertebrate

inverti•do -da *adj* inverted ‖ *mf* invert

invertir §68 *tr* to invert; (*dinero*) invest; (*tiempo*) spend; reverse

investidura *f* investment, investiture; station, standing

investigación *f* investigation, research; **investigación mercológica** market research

investigar §44 *tr* to investigate ‖ *intr* to research

investir §50 *tr* — **investir con** or **de** (*poner en posesión de*) to invest with

invetera•do -da *adj* inveterate, confirmed

invic•to -ta *adj* unconquered

invidencia *f* blindness

invidente *adj* blind ‖ *mf* blind person

invierno *m* winter; rainy season

inviolabilidad *f* inviolability; undamageability

invisible *adj* invisible ‖ *m* (Mex) hair net; **en un invisible** in an instant

invitación *f* invitation

invita•do -da *mf* guest

invitar *tr* to invite

invocar §73 *tr* to invoke

involunta•rio -ria *adj* involuntary

invulnerable *adj* invulnerable

inyección *f* injection; **inyección secundaria** booster shot

inyectable *adj* injectable ‖ *m* ampule, phial

inyecta•do -da *adj* bloodshot, inflamed

inyectar *tr* to inject ‖ *ref* to become congested; become inflamed

ionizar §60 *tr* to ionize ‖ *ref* to be ionized

ionosfera *f* ionosphere

ir §41 *intr* to go; be becoming, fit, suit; be at stake; **ir a** + *inf* to be going to + *inf* (*to express futurity*); **ir a buscar** to go get, go for; **ir a parar en** to end up in; **ir con**

cuidado to be careful; **ir con miedo** to be afraid; **ir con tiento** to watch one's step; **ir de caza** to go hunting; **ir de pesca** to go fishing; **lo que va de** so far (as); **¡qué va!** of course not!; **¡vaya!** the deuce!; what a. . . ! ‖ *ref* to go away; leak; wear away; get old; break to pieces

ira *f* anger, wrath, ire

iracun•do -da *adj* angry, wrathful, irate

Irak, el Iraq

Irán, el Iran

ira•nés -nesa or **ira•nio -nia** *adj* & *mf* Iranian

ira•qués -quesa or **iraquiano -na** *adj* & *mf* Iraqi

iris *m* (*pl* **iris**) (*del ojo*) iris; rainbow

Irlanda *f* Ireland

irlan•dés -desa *adj* Irish ‖ *m* Irishman; (*idioma*) Irish; **los irlandeses** the Irish ‖ *f* Irishwoman

ironía *f* irony

iróni•co -ca *adj* ironic(al)

ironizar §60 *tr* to ridicule

irracional *adj* irrational

irradiar *tr* to radiate, irradiate; (*difundir*) broadcast ‖ *intr* to radiate

irrazonable *adj* unreasonable

irreal *adj* unreal

irrealidad *f* unreality

irrebatible *adj* irrefutable

irreconocible *adj* unrecognizable

irrecuperable *adj* irretrievable

irrecusable *adj* unimpeachable

irredimible *adj* irredeemable

irreemplazable *adj* irreplaceable

irreflexión *f* rashness, thoughtlessness

irreflexi•vo -va *adj* rash, thoughtless

irregular *adj* irregular ‖ *m* (mil) irregular

irregularidad *f* irregularity; embezzlement

irrelevante *adj* irrelevant

irreligio•so -sa *adj* irreligious

irrellenable *adj* nonrefillable

irremediable *adj* irremediable

irremisible *adj* unpardonable

irreparable *adj* irreparable

irreprimible *adj* irrepressible

irreprochable *adj* irreproachable

irresistible *adj* irresistible

irresoluble *adj* unworkable, unsolvable

irrespetuo•so -sa *adj* disrespectful

irresponsable *adj* irresponsible

irresuel•to -ta *adj* hesitant, wavering

irreverente *adj* irreverent

irrigación *f* irrigation

irrigar §44 *tr* to irrigate

irrisible *adj* laughable, absurd

irrisión *f* derision, ridicule; laughingstock

irritante *adj* & *m* irritant

irritar *tr* to irritate ‖ *ref* to become exasperated

irrompible *adj* unbreakable

irrumpir *intr* to burst in; **irrumpir en** to burst into

irrupción *f* sudden attack; invasion

isi•dro -dra *mf* hick, jake, yokel

isla *f* island; (*manzana de casas*) block; **isla de peatones** or **isla de seguridad** safety zone (for pedestrians); **islas Baleares** Balearic Islands; **islas Canarias** Canary Islands; **islas de Barlovento** Windward Islands; **islas de Sotavento** Leeward Islands; **islas Filipinas** Philippine Islands

Islam, el Islam

islan‧dés -desa adj Icelandic ‖ mf Icelander ‖ m (idioma) Icelandic

Islandia f Iceland

isle‧ño -ña adj island ‖ mf islander; (Cuba) Canarian

isleta f isle

isométri‧co -ca adj isometric

isométrica f isometrics

isósce‧les adj (pl -les) isosceles

isótopo m isotope

israe‧lí (pl -líes) adj & mf Israeli

israelita adj & mf Israelite

istmo m isthmus

Italia f Italy

italia‧no -na adj & mf Italian

itáli‧co -ca adj Italic; (typ) italic ‖ f (typ) italics

itinera‧rio -ria adj & m itinerary

izar §60 tr (naut) to hoist, haul up

izquierda f left hand; left-hand side; (pol) left; **a la izquierda** left, on the left, to the left

izquierdear intr to go wild, go astray, go awry

izquierdista adj leftist ‖ mf leftist, leftwinger

izquierdizante adj leftish

izquier‧do -da adj left; left-hand; left-handed; crooked; **levantarse del izquierdo** to get out of bed on the wrong side ‖ f see **izquierda**

J

J, j (jota) f eleventh letter of the Spanish alphabet

jabalcón m strut, brace

jaba‧lí m (pl -líes) wild boar

jabalina f javelin; wild sow

jabardillo m (de insectos) noisy swarm; noisy throng

jabeque m (naut) xebec; gash in the face

jabón m soap; cake of soap; **dar jabón a** to softsoap; **dar un jabón a** (coll) to upbraid, to reprimand; **jabón de afeitar** shaving soap; **jabón de Castilla** Castile soap; **jabón de tocador** or **de olor** toilet soap; **jabón de sastre** soapstone, French chalk; **jabón en polvo** soap powder

jabonado m soaping; (ropa lavada o por lavar) wash

jabonadura f soaping; **dar una jabonadura a** to lambaste, upbraid; **jabonaduras** soapy water; soapsuds

jabonar tr to soap; reprimand

jaboncillo m cake of toilet soap; **jaboncillo de sastre** soapstone, French chalk

jabone‧ro -ra adj soap; (toro) yellowish, dirty-white ‖ mf soapmaker; soap dealer ‖ f soap dish

jabonete m cake of toilet soap

jabono‧so -sa adj soapy, lathery

jaca f pony, jennet

jacal m (Guat, Mex, Ven) hut, shack

jácara f merry ballad; cheerful song and dance; night revelers; story, argument; fake, hoax, lie; annoyance, bother

jacarear intr to go serenading, go singing in the street; be disagreeable

jáca‧ro -ra adj & m braggart ‖ f see **jácara**

jacinto m hyacinth

jaco m nag, jade; gray parrot

jactancia f boasting, bragging

jactancio‧so -sa adj boastful, bragging

jactar ref to boast, brag; **jactarse de** to boast of

jade m jade

jadeante adj panting

jadear intr to pant

jadeo m panting

ja‧ez m (pl -eces) harness, piece of harness; ilk, stripe, kind; **jaeces** trappings

jaguar m jaguar

jagüel m (Arg) reservoir

jaharrar tr to plaster

jalar tr to pull; flirt with ‖ intr to get out, beat it ‖ ref to get drunk

jalbegar §44 tr to whitewash; (el rostro) to paint ‖ ref to paint the face

jalbegue m whitewash; whitewashing; paint, make-up

jalda‧do -da adj bright-yellow

jalea f jelly; **hacerse una jalea** to be madly in love

jalear tr (a los que bailan y cantan) to animate with clapping and shouting; (a los perros) to incite, urge on; (Chile) to tease, pester ‖ intr to dance the jaleo ‖ ref to have a noisy time; swing and sway

jaleo m cheering, shouting; jamboree; jaleo (vivacious Spanish solo dance)

jalis‧co -ca adj (Guat, Mex) drunk ‖ m (Mex) straw hat

jalma f small packsaddle

jalón m surveying rod, range pole; (Guat, Mex) swig of liquor; (CAm) beau; **jalón de mira** leveling rod

jalonar tr to stake out, mark out

jalonear tr (Mex) to pull, jerk

jalonero m (surv) rodman

jamaica m Jamaica rum ‖ f (Mex) charity fair

jamaica‧no -na or **jamaiqui‧no -na** adj & mf Jamaican

jamar tr to eat

jamás adv never; ever

in
ja

jamba f jamb
jambaje m doorframe, window frame
jamelgo m jade, nag
jamete m samite
jamón m ham
jamona f fat middle-aged woman
jamugas fpl mule chair
jánda•lo -la adj & mf Andalusian
Jantipa f or **Jantipe** f Xanthippe
Japón, el Japan
japo•nés -nesa adj & mf Japanese ‖ m
(idioma) Japanese
jaque m (lance del ajedrez) check; bully; **dar
jaque a** to check; **dar jaque mate a** to
checkmate; **en jaque** in check; **estar muy
jaque** to be full of pep; **jaque mate** checkmate; **tener en jaque** to hold a threat over
the head of ‖ interj check!
jaquear tr to check; (al enemigo) harass
jaqueca f sick headache; **dar una jaqueca a**
to bore to death
jacqueco•so -sa adj boring, tiresome
jaquemar m jack (figure that strikes a clock
bell)
jarabe m syrup; sweet drink; **jarabe de pico**
lip service, idle promise
jarana f merrymaking; rumpus; carousal,
spree; trick, deceit; jest, joke; small guitar;
ir de jarana to go on a spree
jaranear tr (CAm, Col) to swindle, cheat ‖
intr to go on a spree; raise a rumpus; joke
jarane•ro -ra adj merrymaking; cheerful,
merry ‖ mf merrymaker, reveler
jarano m sombrero
jarcia f fishing tackle; jumble, mess; **jarcias**
tackle, rigging; **jarcia trozada** junk (old
cable)
jardín m garden, flower garden; (baseball)
field, outfield; (naut) privy, latrine; **jardín
central** (baseball) center field; **jardín de la
infancia** kindergarten; **jardín derecho**
(baseball) right field; **jardín izquierdo**
(baseball) left field
jardinera f jardiniere, flower stand; basket
carriage; summer trolley car, open trolley
car
jardinería f gardening
jardine•ro -ra mf gardener; **jardinero adornista** landscape gardener ‖ m (baseball)
fielder, outfielder ‖ f see **jardinera**
jardinista mf landscape gardener
jarea f (Mex) hunger
jarear intr (Bol) to stop for a rest ‖ ref (Mex)
to flee, run away; (Mex) to swing, sway;
(Mex) to die of starvation
jareta f (sew) casing
jari•fo -fa adj showy, spruce, natty
jaro•cho -cha adj brusk, bluff ‖ m insulting
fellow; Veracruz peasant
jarope m syrup; nasty potion
jarra f jug, jar, water pitcher; **de jarras** or **en
jarras** with arms akimbo
jarrete m hock, gambrel
jarretera f garter
jarro m pitcher; **echar un jarro de agua
(fría) a** to pour cold water on
jarrón m (vaso para adornar chimeneas,

consolas, etc.) vase; (sobre un pedestal)
urn
jaspe m jasper
jaspea•do -da adj marbled, speckled ‖ m
marbling, speckling
jaspear tr to marble, speckle
jateo m foxhound
ja•to -ta mf calf
Jauja f Cockaigne; **¿estamos aquí o en
Jauja?** where do you think you are?; **vivir
en Jauja** to live in the lap of luxury
jaula m cage; (embalaje de listones de madera) crate; (Mex) open freight car; (Cuba,
P-R) police wagon; **jaula de locos** insane
asylum, madhouse
jauría f pack (of hounds)
java•nés -nesa adj & mf Javanese ‖ m
(idioma) Javanese
jazmín m jasmine; **jazmín de la India** gardenia
jazz m jazz
J.C. abbr Jesucristo
jebe m alum; (SAm) rubber
jedive m khedive
jefa f female head or leader; **jefa de ruta**
hostess (on a bus)
jefatura f headship, leadership; (de policía)
headquarters
jefe m chief, boss, head, leader; (de una
tribu) chieftain; **jefe de cocina** chef; **jefe
do coro** choirmaster; **jefe de equipajes** (rr)
baggage master; **jefe de estación** station-
master; **jefe del estado** chief of state; **jefe
del gobierno** chief executive; **jefe de redacción** editor in chief; **jefe de ruta** guide;
jefe de tren (rr) conductor; **jefe de tribu**
chieftain; **quedar jefe** (Chile) to gamble
away everything
jején m gnat, sandfly
jenabe m or **jenable** m mustard
jengibre m ginger
Jenofonte m Xenophon
jeque m sheik
jerarca m hierarch, head
jerarquía f hierarchy; **de jerarquía** important
jeremiada f jeremiad
jeremiquear intr to moan; pour out one's
troubles
jerez m sherry
jerga f coarse cloth; straw mattress; (lenguaje
especial de ciertos oficios; lenguaje difícil
de entender) jargon
jergón m straw mattress; ill-fitting clothes;
(persona torpe y estúpida) lummox
Jericó Jericho
jerife m shereef
jerigonza f (lenguaje especial de ciertos oficios; lenguaje difícil de entender) jargon;
(lenguaje vulgar, caló) slang; piece of folly
jeringa f syringe; (para inyectar materias
blandas en una máquina) gun; annoyance,
plague; **jeringa de engrase** or **grasa** grease
gun
jeringar §44 tr to syringe; inject; give an
enema to; plague
jeringazo m injection, shot; squirt

jeringuilla f (*jeringa pequeña*) syringe; (bot) mock orange

Jerjes m Xerxes

jeroglífi•co -ca adj & m hieroglyphic

Jerónimo m Jerome

jer•sey m (*pl* **-seis**) jersey, sweater

Jerusalén Jerusalem

Jesucristo m Jesus Christ

jesuíta adj & m Jesuit

jesuíti•co -ca adj Jesuitic(al)

Jesús m Jesus; (*imagen del niño Jesús*) bambino; **en un decir Jesús** in an instant; **¡Jesús, María y José!** my gracious!

jeta f hog's snout, pig face; (*rostro de una persona*) phiz, mug; **estar con tanta jeta** to make a long face; **poner jeta** to pucker one's lips

jetu•do -da adj thick-lipped; grim, gruff

Jhs. abbr **Jesús**

jíba•ro -ra mf (W-I) white peasant

jibia f cuttlefish

jícara f chocolate cup; (CAm, Mex, W-I) calabash cup

jícaro m calabash (tree)

jifia f swordfish

jilguero m linnet, goldfinch

jilote m (Mex) green ear of corn

jineta f (zool) genet

jinete m rider, horseman

jinetear tr (*caballos cerriles*) to break in ‖ intr to show off one's horsemanship

jinglar intr to swing, to rock

jingoísmo m jingoism

jingoísta adj & mf jingo

jipa•to -ta adj pale, wan; insipid, tasteless; (Guat) drunk

jipijapa m Panama hat ‖ f jipijapa; strip of jipijapa straw

jira f strip of cloth; outing, picnic; trip, tour; swing, political trip

jirón m rag, tatter, shred; (*de una falda*) facing; pennant; bit, drop, shred; **hacer jirones** to tear to shreds

jitomate m (Mex) tomato

joco•so -sa adj jocose, jocular

jocotal m (CAm, Mex) Spanish plum (*tree*)

jocote m (CAm, Mex) Spanish plum (*fruit*)

jocoyote m (Mex) baby (*youngest child*)

jofaina f washbowl, basin

jolgorio m fun, merriment

jonrón m (baseball) home run

Jordán m Jordan (*river*); **ir al Jordán** to be born again

Jordania f Jordan (*country*)

jorda•no -na adj & mf Jordanian

jorguín m sorcerer, wizard

jorguina f sorceress, witch

jorguinería f sorcery, witchcraft

jornada f journey, trip, stage; day's journey; (*horas del trabajo diario del obrero*) workday; (*tiempo que dura la vida de un hombre*) lifetime; battle; (*muerte*) passing; summer residence of diplomat or diplomatic corps; event, occasion; undertaking; (mil) expedition; (*de un drama*) (archaic) act; **a grandes** or **largas jornadas** by forced marches; **al fin de la jornada** in the

end; **caminar por sus jornadas** to proceed with circumspection; **hacer mala jornada** to get nowhere; **jornada ordinaria** full time; **jornada reducida** reduced working hours

jornal m day's work; day's pay; **a jornal** by the day; **jornal mínimo** minimum wage

jornalero m day laborer

joroba f hump; annoyance, bother

joroba•do -da adj humpbacked, hunchbacked; annoyed, bothered ‖ mf humpback, hunchback

jorobar tr to annoy, pester

jorongo m (Mex) poncho; (Mex) woolen blanket

jota f (*letra del alfabeto*) J; jota (*Spanish folk dance and music*); jot, iota, tittle; vegetable soup; **sin faltar una jota** with not a whit left out

joven adj young; **ser joven de esperanzas** to have a bright future ‖ mf youth, young person; **de joven** as a youth, as a young man, as a young woman

jovial adj jovial

joya f jewel; (*brocamantón*) diamond brooch; (*agasajo*) gift, present; (*persona o cosa de mucha valía*) (fig) jewel, gem; **joya de familia** heirloom; **joyas** jewelry; trousseau; **joyas de fantasía** costume jewelry

joyante adj glossy

joyelero m jewel case, casket

joyería f (*conjunto de joyas*) jewelry; jewelry shop; jewelry trade

joye•ro -ra mf jeweler ‖ m jewel case, casket

Juan m John; **Buen Juan** sap, easy mark; **Juan Español** the Spanish people, the typical Spaniard; **San Juan Bautista** John the Baptist

Juana f Jane, Jean, Joan; **Juana de Arco** Joan of Arc, Jeanne d'Arc; **juanas** glove stretcher

juanete m bunion; high cheekbone

jubilación f retirement; (*renta de la persona jubilada*) pension, retirement annuity

jubila•do -da adj retired ‖ mf retired person, pensioner

jubilar tr to retire, pension; throw out ‖ intr to rejoice; retire, be pensioned ‖ ref to rejoice; retire, be pensioned; (Col) to decline, go to pieces; (CAm, Ven) to play hooky; (Cuba, Mex) to become a past master

jubileo m much coming and going, great doings; (eccl) jubilee; **por jubileo** once in a long time

júbilo m jubilation

jubilo•so •sa adj jubilant, joyful

jubón m jerkin

judaísmo m Judaism

judería f (*raza judaica*) Jewry; (*barrio de los judíos*) ghetto

judía f Jewess; kidney bean, string bean; **judía de careta** black-eyed bean; **judía de la peladilla** Lima bean

judicatura f judicature; (*cargo de juez*) judgeship

judicial adj judicial, judiciary

ja
ju

judí•o -a adj Jewish ‖ mf Jew ‖ f see **judía**
juego m (acción de jugar) play, playing; (ejercicio recreativo en el cual se gana o se pierde) game; (vicio de jugar) gambling; (lugar donde se ejecutan ciertos juegos): (bowling) alley; (tennis) court; (baseball) field; (tantos necesarios para ganar la partida) game;·(de muebles) suit, suite; (de café) service; (de vajilla) set; (de luces, colores, aguas) play; (mach) play; (p.ej., de diplomacia) (fig) game; **a juego** to match, e.g., **una silla a juego** a chair to match; **conocer el juego de** to see through, to have the number of; **en juego** at hand; **hacer juego** to match; **hacer juego con** to match, to go with; **juego de alcoba** bedroom suit; **juego de azar** game of chance; **juego de bolas** (mach) ball bearing; **juego de campanas** chimes; **juego de comedor** dining-room suit; **juego de envite** gambling game, game played for money; **juego de escritorio** desk set; **juego de la cuna** cat's cradle; **juego de la pulga** tiddlywinks; **juego del corro** ring-around-a-rosy; **juego del salto** leapfrog; **juego del tres en raya** tick-tack-toe played with movable counters or pebbles; **juego de manos** legerdemain, sleight of hand; roughhousing; **juego de niños** (cosa muy fácil) child's play; **juego de palabras** play on words, pun; **juego de pelota** ball game; pelota; **juego de piernas** footwork; **juego de por ver** (Chile) game played for fun; **juego de prendas** game of forfeits, forfeits; **juego de suerte** game of chance; **juego de tejo** shuffleboard; **juego de timbres** glockenspiel; **juego de vocablos** or **voces** play on words, pun; **juego limpio** fair play; **juego público** gambling house; **juegos de sociedad** parlor games; **juegos malabares** juggling; flimflam; **juego sucio** foul play; **no ser cosa de juego** to be no laughing matter; **por juego** in fun, for fun; **verle a uno el juego** to be on to someone
juerga f carousal, spree; **juerga de borrachera** drinking bout, binge; **ir de juerga** (coll) to go on a spree
juerguista mf carouser, reveler
jue•ves m (pl -ves) Thursday; **Jueves Santo** Maundy Thursday
juez m (pl **jueces**) judge; **juez de alzadas** appellate judge; **juez de guardia** coroner; **juez de instrucción** examining magistrate; **juez de paz** justice of the peace; **juez de salida** (sport) starter; **juez de tiempo** (sport) timekeeper
jugada f (lance) play, throw, stroke, move; **mala jugada** dirty trick
juga•dor -dora mf player; gambler; **jugador de manos** prestidigitator; **jugador de ventaja** sharper
jugar §42 tr (p.ej., un naipe, una partida de juego) to play; (una espada) wield; (arriesgar) stake, risk; (las manos, los dedos) move; **jugarle a uno las bebidas** to match someone for the drinks ‖ intr to play; to gamble; (hacer juego dos cosas) match;

(intervenir) figure, participate; **jugar a** (p.ej., los naipes, el tenis) to play; **jugar con** (un contrario) to play; (una persona; los sentimientos de una persona) toy with; match; **jugar en** to have a hand in ‖ ref (p.ej., la vida) to risk; to be at stake; **jugarse el todo por el todo** to stake all, shoot the works
jugarreta f bad play, poor play; mean trick, dirty trick
juglar m minstrel, jongleur; (bufón) (archaic) juggler
juglaría f minstrelsy
jugo m (p.ej., de la naranja) juice; (de la carne) gravy; (líquido orgánico) juice; (fig) gist, essence, substance; **en su jugo** (culin) au jus; **jugo de muñeca** elbow grease
jugo•so -sa adj juicy; substantial, important
juguete m toy, plaything; (burla) joke, jest; (theat) skit; **de juguete** toy, e.g., **soldado de juguete** toy soldier; **juguete de movimiento** mechanical toy; **por juguete** for fun, in fun
juguetear intr to frolic, romp, sport
juguete•ro -ra adj toy ‖ mf toy dealer ‖ m whatnot, étagère
juguete-sorpresa m (pl **juguetes-sorpresa**) jack-in-the-box
jugue•tón -tona adj playful, frisky
juicio m judgment; (law) trial; **estar en su cabal juicio** to be in one's right mind; **estar fuera de juicio** to be out of one's mind; **juicio de Dios** (hist) ordeal; **pedir en juicio** (law) to sue
juicio•so -sa adj judicious, wise
julepe m julep; scolding; scare, fright
julepear tr to scold; whip; (SAm) to scare, frighten; (Mex) to weary, tire out
julio m July
julo m lead cow, lead mule
jumen•to -ta mf ass, donkey
juncal adj willowy, rushy; (fig) willowy, lissome
juncia f sedge; **vender juncia** to boast, brag
junco m (embarcación china) junk; (bot) rush, bulrush; **junco de Indias** (bot) rattan; **junco de laguna** (bot) rush, bulrush
junco•so -sa adj rushy, full of rushes
jungla f jungle
junio m June
junípero m juniper
junquera f rush, bulrush
junquillo m jonquil
junta f meeting, conference; board, council; junction, union; joint, seam; (empaquetadura) gasket; (arandela) washer; **junta de comercio** board of trade; **junta de charnela** (mach) knuckle; **junta de sanidad** board of health; **junta universal** (mach) universal joint
juntamente adv together; at the same time
juntar tr to join, unite; gather, gather together; (una puerta) half-close ‖ ref to gather together; go along; copulate
jun•to -ta adj joined, united; **jun•tos -tas** together ‖ f see **junta** ‖ **junto** adv together;

at the same time; **junto a** near, close to; **junto con** along with, together with; **todo junto** at the same time, all at once

juntura f junction; (*p.ej., de una cañería; de un hueso*) joint; connection, coupling

jura f oath

jura•do -da adj (*enemigo*) sworn ‖ m (*conjunto de cuidadanos encargados de determinar la culpabilidad del acusado; conjunto de examinadores de un certamen*) jury; (*cada uno de los expresados individuous*) juror; juryman

juramentar tr to swear in ‖ ref to take an oath, be sworn in

juramento m oath; (*voto, reniego*) curse, swearword; **prestar juramento a** to swear to; **tomar juramento a** to swear in

jurar tr to swear; (*la verdad de una cosa*) swear to; swear allegiance to ‖ intr (*pronunciar un juramento*) to swear, take an oath; (*echar votos o reniegos*) swear, curse; **jurar** + *inf* to swear to + *inf* ‖ ref to swear; **jurársela** or **jurárselas a uno** to have it in for someone, swear to get even with someone

jure•ro -ra mf (SAm) false witness

jurídi•co -ca adj juridical

jurisconsulto m (*el que escribe sobre el derecho*) jurist; (*jurisperito*) legal expert

jurisdicción f jurisdiction

jurisperito m jurist, legal expert

jurisprudencia f jurisprudence

jurista mf jurist

juro m right of perpetual ownership; **de juro** inevitably, for sure

justa f joust, tournament

justamente adv just, just at that time; justly; (*ajustadamente*) tightly

justar intr to joust, to tilt

justicia f justice; (*castigo de muerte*) execution; **de justicia** justly, deservedly; **hacer justicia a** to do justice to; **ir por justicia** to go to court, to bring suit

justicie•ro -ra adj just, fair; stern, righteous

justificable adj justifiable

justifica•do -da adj (*hecho*) just, right; (*persona*) just, upright

justificante m voucher, proof

justificar §73 tr to justify; (typ) to justify

justillo m jerkin, waist

justipreciar tr to estimate, appraise

jus•to -ta adj just; right, exact; (*apretado*) tight ‖ mf just person ‖ f see **justa** ‖ **justo** adv just; right, in tune; tight; (*con estrechez*) in straitened circumstances

Jutlandia f Jutland

ju•to -ta mf Jute

juvenil adj juvenile, youthful

juventud f youth; young people

juzgado m court of law; courtroom; court of one judge

juzgar §44 tr & intr to judge; **a juzgar por** judging by; **juzgar de** to judge, pass judgment on

K

K, k (ka) f twelfth letter of the Spanish alphabet

karate m or **karaté** m karate

karateka m karate expert

kermesse f var of **quermés**

keroseno m kerosene, coal oil

kg. abbr **kilogramo**

kilate m var of **quilate**

kilo m kilo, kilogram

kilociclo m kilocycle

kilogramo m kilogram

kilometraje m kilometrage, distance in kilometers

kilométri•co -ca adj kilometric; (coll) interminable, long-drawn-out

kilómetro m kilometer

kilovatio m kilowatt

kilovatio-hora m (pl **kilovatios-hora**) kilowatt-hour

kimono m var of **quimono**

kinescopio m (telv) kinescope

kiosco m var of **quiosco**

kirieleisón m dirge; **cantar el kirieleisón** to beg mercy

km. abbr **kilómetro**

kph. abbr **kilómetros por hora**

kv. abbr **kilovatio**

kv-h abbr **kilovatio-hora**

L

L, l (ele) thirteenth letter of the Spanish alphabet

la art def fem of **el** ‖ pron pers fem her, it; you ‖ pron dem that, the one; **la que** who, which, that; she who, the one that

laberinto m labyrinth, maze

labia f fluency, smoothness

labial adj & f labial

labio m lip; (fig) edge, lip; **chuparse los labios** to smack one's lips; **labio leporino** harelip; **leer en los labios** to lip read

labiolectura f lip reading

labio•so -sa *adj* fluent, smooth

labor *f* labor, work; (*cultivo de los campos*) farming, tilling; (*obra de coser, bordar, etc.*) needlework, fancywork, embroidery; **hacer labor** to match; **labor blanca** linen work, linen embroidery; **labor de ganchillo** crocheting

laborable *adj* workable; arable, tillable; (*dia*) work

laborante *m* journeyman; political henchman

laborar *tr* to work ‖ *intr* to scheme

laboratorio *m* laboratory; **laboratorio de idiomas** language laboratory; **laboratorio espacial** space laboratory; Skylab

laborio•so -sa *adj* (*trabajador*) laborious, industrious; (*trabajoso*) laborious, arduous

laborismo *m* British Labour Party

laborista *adj* Labour ‖ *mf* Labourite

laborterapia *f* work therapy

labra *f* carving

labrada *f* fallow ground (*to be sown the following year*)

labrade•ro -ra *adj* arable, tillable

labra•do -da *adj* wrought, fashioned; carved; figured, embroidered ‖ *m* carving; **labrado de madera** wood carving ‖ *f* see **labrada**

labra•dor -dora *adj* work; farm ‖ *mf* farmer; (*campesino*) peasant ‖ *m* plowman; **el Labrador** Labrador

labrantí•o -a *adj* farm ‖ *m* farmland

labranza *f* farming; farm, farmland

labrar *tr* to work, fashion; (*la piedra, la madera*) carve; (*arar*) plow; (*construir o mandar construir*) build; till, cultivate; cause, bring about ‖ *intr* to make a lasting impression

labrie•go -ga *mf* peasant

laca *f* lacquer; shellac; **laca de uñas** nail polish; **lacas** lacquer ware

lacayo *m* lackey, footman

lacear *tr* to tie with a bow; adorn with bows; (*la caza*) drive within shot; (*la caza menor*) trap, snare

laceria *f* poverty, want; trouble, bother; leprosy

lacerio•so -sa *adj* poor, needy

lacero *m* lassoer; poacher; dogcatcher

la•cio -cia *adj* faded, withered; languid; (*cabello*) lank, straight

lacóni•co -ca *adj* laconic

lacra *f* fault, defect; (*señal dejada por una enfermedad*) mark, remains; sore; scab, scar

lacrimóge•no -na *adj* tear, tear-producing

lacrimo•so -sa *adj* lachrymose, tearful

lactar *tr* to suckle

lácte•o -a *adj* milky

lacustre *adj* lake

ladear *tr* to tip, tilt; bend, lean; (*un avión*) bank ‖ *intr* to tip, tilt; bend, lean; turn away, turn off; (*la aguja de brújula*) deviate ‖ *ref* to tip, tilt; bend, lean; be equal, be even; (Chile) to fall in love; **ladearse a** (*un dictamen, un partido*) to lean to or toward

ladeo *m* tipping, tilting; bending, leaning; inclination, bent

lade•ro -ra *adj* side, lateral ‖ *f* hillside

ladilla *f* crab louse; **pegarse como ladilla** to stick like a leech

ladi•no -na *adj* crafty, sly, cunning; polyglot

lado *m* side; direction; (*del hilo telefónico*) end; **al lado** nearby; **dejar a un lado** to leave aside; **de lado** square, e.g., **diez centímetros de lado** ten centimeters square; **de otro lado** on the other hand; **de un lado** on the one hand; **echar a un lado** to cast aside; to finish up; **hacer lado** to make room; **hacerse a un lado** to step aside; **lados** backers, advisers; **mirar de lado** or **de medio lado** to look askance at; to sneak a look at; **ponerse al lado de** to take sides with; **por el lado de** in the direction of; **tirar por su lado** to pull for oneself

ladrar *tr* (*p.ej., injurias*) to bark ‖ *intr* to bark

ladrido *m* bark, barking; slander, blame

ladrillador *m* bricklayer

ladrillal *m* brickyard

ladrillo *m* brick; (*azulejo*) tile; (*p.ej., de chocolate*) cake; **ladrillo de fuego** or **ladrillo refractario** firebrick

la•drón -drona *adj* thievish, thieving ‖ *mf* thief ‖ *m* sluice gate; **ladrón de corazones** heartbreaker, lady-killer

ladronera *f* den of thieves; thievery; (*alcancía*) child's bank

ladronerío *m* (Arg) gang of thieves; (Arg) wave of thieving

ladronzue•lo -la *mf* petty thief

lagaña *f* var of **legaña**

lagar *m* wine press; olive press; (*establecimiento*) winery

lagarta *f* female lizard; sly woman; (ent) gypsy moth

lagartija *f* green lizard; wall lizard

lagarto *m* lizard; sly fellow; (Mex) fop, dandy; **lagarto de Indias** alligator

lago *m* lake

lagotear *tr* & *intr* to flatter, wheedle

lágrima *f* tear; (*de cualquier licor*) drop; **beberse las lágrimas** to hold back one's tears; **deshacerse en lágrimas** to weep one's eyes out; **lágrimas de cocodrilo** crocodile tears; **llorar a lágrima viva** to shed bitter tears

lagrimear *intr* to weep easily, be tearful; (*los ojos*) fill

lagrimo•so -sa *adj* tearful; (*ojos*) watery

laguna *f* (*lago pequeño*) lagoon; (*hueco, omisión*) lacuna, gap

laical *adj* lay

laicismo *m* secularism

laja *f* slab, flagstone

lama *f* mud, ooze, slim; pond scum

lambrija *f* earthworm; skinny person

lamedero *m* salt lick

lame•dor -dora *adj* licking ‖ *mf* licker ‖ *m* syrup; **dar lamedor** to lose at first in order to take in one's opponent

lamedura *f* lick, licking

lamentable *adj* lamentable

lamentación *f* lamentation

lamentar *tr, intr* & *ref* to lament, mourn

lamento *m* lament
lamento‧so **-sa** *adj* lamentable; plaintive
lamer *tr* to lick; lap, lap against; (*las llamas un tejado*) to lick ‖ *ref* (*p.ej.*, *los dedos*) to lick
lame‧rón **-rona** *adj* (coll) sweet-toothed
lametada *f* lap, lick
lámina *f* sheet, plate, strip; (*plancha grabada*) engraving; (*pintura en cobre*) copper plate; (*figura estampada*) cut, picture, illustration
laminador *m* rolling mill
laminar *tr* to laminate; (*el hierro, el acero*) roll
lampadario *m* floor lamp
lámpara *f* lamp, light; (*mancha en la ropa*) grease spot, oil spot; (rad) vacuum tube; **atizar la lámpara** to fill up the glasses again; **lámpara de alcohol** spirit lamp; **lámpara de arco** arc lamp, arc light; **lámpara de bolsillo** flashlight; **lámpara de carretera** (aut) bright light; **lámpara de cruce** (aut) dimmer; **lámpara de pie** floor lamp; **lámpara de sobremesa** table lamp; **lámpara de socorro** trouble light; **lámpara de soldar** blowtorch; **lámpara de techo** ceiling light; (aut) dome light; **lámpara inundante** floodlight; **lámpara testigo** pilot light
lamparilla *f* rushlight; aspen
lampi‧ño **-ña** *adj* beardless; hairless
lampista *mf* lamplighter ‖ *m* tinsmith, plumber, glazier, electrician
lana *f* wool; (CAm) common person; (CAm) swindler; **lana de acero** steel wool; **lana de ceiba** kapoc; **lana de escorias** mineral wool, rock wool; **lana de vidrio** glass wool
lance *m* cast, throw; (*en la red*) catch, haul; (*accidente en el juego*) play, move, stroke; (*ocasión crítica*) chance, pass, juncture; incident, event; (*riña*) row, quarrel; (taur) capework; **de lance** cheap; secondhand; **echar buen lance** to have a break; **lance de honor** affair of honor, duel; **tener pocos lances** to be dull and uninteresting
lancero *m* lancer, spearman, pikeman
lanceta *f* (surg) lancet; (Mex, SAm) sting
lancinante *adj* piercing
lancha *f* barge, lighter; flagstone, slab; (naut) longboat; (nav) launch; (Ecuad) mist, fog; (Ecuad) frost; **lancha automóvil** launch, motor launch; **lancha de auxilio** lifeboat (*stationed on shore*); **lancha de carreras** speedboat; **lancha de desembarco** (nav) landing craft; **lancha salvavidas** lifeboat (*on shipboard*)
lanchar *intr* (Ecuad) to get foggy; (Ecuad) to freeze
lan‧dó *m* (*pl* **-dós**) landau
landre *f* swollen gland; hidden pocket
lanería *f* wool shop; **lanerías** woolens, woolen goods
langosta *f* (*insecto*) locust; (*crustáceo*) lobster, spiny lobster
langostera *f* lobster pot
langostín *m* or **langostino** *m* prawn (*Peneus*)
langostón *m* green grasshopper
languidecer §22 *intr* to languish

languidez *f* languor
lángui‧do **-da** *adj* languid, languorous
lano‧so **-sa** *adj* woolly
lanu‧do **da** *adj* woolly; (Ecuad, Ven) coarse, ill-bred
lanza *f* lance, pike; (*de la manguera*) nozzle; (*palo de coche*) wagon pole
lanzabom‧bas *m* (*pl* **-bas**) (aer) bomb release; (mil) trench mortar
lanzacohe‧tes *m* (*pl* **-tes**) rocket launcher
lanzadera *f* shuttle; **parecer una lanzadera** to buzz around
lanza‧do **-da** *adj* sloping; (*salida de una carrera*) (sport) running (*start*)
lanza‧dor **-dora** *mf* thrower; **lanzador de lodo** (fig) mudslinger ‖ *m* launcher; (aer) jettison gear; (baseball) pitcher
lanzaespu‧mas *m* (*pl* **-mas**) foam extinguisher
lanzalla‧mas *m* (*pl* **-mas**) flame thrower
lanzamiento *m* throw, hurl, fling, launch; (*de un buque*) launching; (*de un cohete*) shot, launch; (*p.ej.*, *de víveres*) (aer) airdrop; (*de bombas*) (aer) release; (*de paracaidistas*) (aer) jump; (law) dispossession; (naut) steeve
lanzami‧nas *m* (*pl* **-nas**) (nav) mine layer
lanzapla‧tos *m* (*pl* **-tos**) trap
lanzar §60 *tr* to throw, hurl, fling; (*un proyecto, un cohete, maldiciones, una ofensiva, un producto nuevo, un buque*) launch; (*una mirada*) cast; vomit, throw up; (*flores, hojas una planta*) put forth; (*una advertencia*) toss, toss out; (aer) to airdrop; (*bombas*) (aer) to release; (law) to dispossess ‖ *ref* to launch, launch forth; throw oneself; dash, rush; (aer) to jump; (sport) to sprint
lanzatorpe‧dos *m* (*pl* **-dos**) (nav) torpedo tube
laña *f* clamp; rivet
lañar *tr* to clamp; (*objetos de porcelana*) rivet
lapicero *m* pencil holder; mechanical pencil; ball-point pen; **lapicero fuente** fountain pen
lápida *f* tablet, stone; **lápida supulcral** gravestone
lapidar *tr* to stone to death
lá‧piz *m* (*pl* **-pices**) (*grafito*) black lead; (*barrita que sirve para escribir*) pencil, lead pencil; **lápiz de bolilla** (Para) ball-point pen; **lápiz de labios** lipstick; **lápiz de pizarra** slate pencil; **lápiz de pasta** (Chile) ball-point pen; **lápiz de plomo** graphite; **lápiz estíptico** styptic pencil; **lápiz labial** lipstick
lapizar §60 *tr* to mark or line with a pencil
la‧pón **-pona** *adj* Lapp ‖ *mf* Lapp, Laplander ‖ *m* (*idioma*) Lapp
Laponia *f* Lapland
lapso *m* lapse
laquear *tr* to lacquer
lardo‧so **-sa** *adj* greasy, fatty
larga *f* long billiard cue; **dar largas a** to postpone, put off
largamente *adv* at length, extensively; in comfort; generously; long, for a long time
largar §44 *tr* to let go, release; ease, slack; utter; (*un golpe*) deal, strike, give; (naut) to

unfurl; (Col) to give ‖ *ref* to move away; get away, sneak away, beat it; take to sea; (*el ancla*) to come loose

lar‧go -ga *adj* long; abundant; liberal, generous; quick, ready; shrewd, cunning; (naut) loose, slack; **a la larga** in the long run, in the end; **a lo largo** lengthwise; at great length; far away; **a lo largo de** along; along with; throughout; in the course of; (*el mar*) far out in; **a lo más largo** at most; **hacerse a lo largo** to get out in the open sea; **largo de lengua** loose-tongued; **largo de uñas** light-fingered; **pasar de largo** to pass without stopping; take a quick look; miss; **ponerse de largo** to come out, make one's debut; **vestir de largo** to wear long clothes ‖ *m* length ‖ *f* see **larga** ‖ **largo** *adv* at length, at great length; abundantly ‖ **largo** *interj* get out of here!

largometraje *m* full-featured film, full-length movie

largor *m* length

larguero *m* (*palo, madero*) stringer; (*almohada larga*) bolster; (aer) longeron

largueza *f* length; liberality, generosity

larguiru‧cho -cha *adj* gangling, lanky

largura *f* length

lárice *m* larch tree

laringe *f* larynx

larínge‧o -a *adj* laryngeal

laringitis *f* laryngitis

laringoscopio *m* laryngoscope

larva *f* larva; mask; (*duende*) hobgoblin

lasca *f* advantage, benefit

lascar §73 *tr* (naut) to pay out, slacken; (Mex) to scratch, bruise; (*un objeto de porcelana*) (Mex) to chip

lascivia *f* lasciviousness

lasci‧vo -va *adj* lascivious; playful

láser *m* laser

la‧so -sa *adj* tired, exhausted; weak, wan

lástima *f* pity; (*quejido*) complaint; **contar lástimas** to tell a hard-luck story; **dar lástima** to be pitiful; **es lástima (que)** it is a pity (that); **estar hecho una lástima** to be a sorry sight; **hacer lástima** to be pitiful; **llorar lástimas** to put on a show of tears; **poner lástima** to be pitiful; **¡qué lástima!** what a pity!, what a shame!; **¡qué lástima de saliva!** what a waste of breath!

lastimar *tr* to hurt, injure; hurt, offend; bruise ‖ *ref* to hurt oneself; bruise oneself; complain

lastime‧ro -ra *adj* hurtful, injurious; pitiful, sad, doleful

lastimo‧so -sa *adj* pitiful

lastra *f* slab, flagstone

lastrar *tr* (aer & naut) to ballast

lastre *m* (aer & naut) ballast; (fig) wisdom, maturity; (coll) food; (rr) (Chile) ballast

lat. *abbr* **latín, latitud**

lata *f* (*hojalata*) tin, tin plate; (*envase*) tin, tin can; (*madero sin pulir*) log; (*tabla delgada*) lath; annoyance, bore; **dar la lata a** (coll) to pester; **es una lata** that's terribly boring; **estar en la lata** (Col) to be penni-

less; **¡que lata!** what a nuisance! what a curse!

latebra *f* hiding place

latebro‧so -sa *adj* furtive, secretive

latente *adj* latent

lateral *adj* lateral

latido *m* (*del perro*) yelp; (*del corazón*) beat, throb; (*dolor*) pang, twinge

latifundio *m* large neglected landed estate

latigazo *m* lash; crack of whip; (*reprensión áspera*) lashing

látigo *m* whip, horsewhip; cinch strap

latiguear *tr* to lash, whip ‖ *intr* crack a whip

latiguillo *m* small whip; (*del actor u orador*) claptrap

latín *m* Latin; **latín de cocina** dog Latin, hog Latin; **latín rústico** or **vulgar** Vulgar Latin; **saber latín** or **mucho latín** to be very shrewd

latinajo *m* dog Latin, hog Latin; Latin word or phrase (*slipped into the vernacular*)

latinar or **latinear** *intr* to use Latin

lati‧no -na *adj* Latin; (naut) lateen ‖ *mf* Latin

Latinoamérica *f* Latin America

latinoamerica‧no -na *adj* Latin-American ‖ *mf* Latin American

latir *tr* (Ven) to annoy, bore, molest ‖ *intr* (*el perro*) to bark, yelp; (*el corazón*) beat, throb; **me late que** (Mex) I have a hunch that

latitud *f* latitude

la‧to -ta *adj* broad ‖ *f* see **lata**

latón *m* brass; (Cuba) garbage pail

lato‧so -sa *adj* annoying, boring ‖ *mf* bore

latrocinio *m* thievery; thievishness

laucha *f* (Arg, Chile) mouse

laúd *m* (mus) lute; (zool) leatherback turtle

laudable *adj* laudable

láudano *m* laudanum

laudato‧rio -ria *adj* laudatory

laudo *m* (law) finding, decision

láurea *f* laurel wreath

laurea‧do -da *adj* & *mf* laureate

laurean‧do -da *mf* graduate, candidate for a degree

laurear *tr* to trim or adorn with laurel; crown with laurel; decorate, honor, reward

laurel *m* laurel; (*de la victoria*) laurels; **dormirse sobre sus laureles** to rest or sleep on one's laurels

láure‧o -a *adj* laurel ‖ *f* see **láurea**

lauréola *f* crown of laurel, laurel wreath; (*aureola*) halo

lava *f* lava; (min) washing

lavable *adj* washable

lavabo *m* washstand; washroom, lavatory

lavaca‧ras *mf* (*pl* -ras) fawner, flatterer, bootlicker

lavaco‧ches *m* (*pl* -ches) car washer

lavada *f* wash(ing)

lavade‧dos *m* (*pl* -dos) finger bowl

lavadero *m* laundry; (*tabla de lavar*) washboard; (*a orillas de un río*) washing place; (Guat, Mex, SAm) placer

lava‧do -da *adj* brazen, fresh, impudent ‖ *m* wash, washing; **lavado a seco** dry cleaning; **lavado cerebral** or **de cerebro** brainwashing; **lavado químico** dry cleaning

lava•dor -dora *mf* washer ‖ *m* (phot) washer ‖ *f* washing machine; **lavadora de platos** or **de vajilla** dishwasher

lavadura *f* washing; (*agua sucia; rozadura de una cuerda*) washings

lavafru•tas *m* (*pl* **-tas**) fruit bowl, finger bowl

lavama•nos *m* (*pl* **-nos**) (*pila con caño y llave*) washstand; (*jofaina*) washbowl

lavanda *f* lavender

lavandera *f* laundress, laundrywoman, washerwoman; (orn) sandpiper

lavandero *m* launderer, laundryman

lavándula *f* lavender

lavao•jos *m* (*pl* **-jos**) eyecup

lavaparabri•sas *m* (*pl* **-sas**) windshield washer

lavapla•tos (*pl* **-tos**) *mf* (*persona*) dishwasher ‖ *m* (*aparato*) dishwasher; (Chile) kitchen sink

lavar *tr* & *ref* to wash

lavativa *f* enema; annoyance, bore

lavatorio *m* washing; washstand; toilet; washroom; (*ceremonia de lavar los pies*) maundy; (med) wash, lotion

lavavajillas *m* dishwasher

lavazas *fpl* dirty water, wash water

laxante *adj* & *m* laxative

laxar *tr* to ease, slack; (*el vientre*) loosen

la•xo -xa *adj* lax, slack; (fig) lax, loose

laya *f* spade; kind, quality

layar *tr* to spade, dig with a spade

lazada *f* bowknot

lazar §60 *tr* to lasso

lazarillo *m* blind man's guide

lazari•no -na *adj* leprous ‖ *mf* leper

lázaro *m* raggedy beggar; **estar hecho un lázaro** to be full of sores

lazo *m* bow, knot, tie; lasso, lariat; snare, trap; bond, tie; **armar lazo a** to set a trap for; **caer en el lazo** to fall into the trap; **lazo de amor** truelove knot; **lazo de unión** (fig) tie, bond

Ldo. *abbr* **Licenciado**

le *pron pers* to him, to her, to it; to you; him; you

leal *adj* loyal, faithful; reliable, trustworthy ‖ *m* loyalist

lealtad *f* loyalty; reliability, trustworthiness

le•brel -brela *mf* whippet, small greyhound

lebrillo *m* earthen washtub

lebrón *m* large hare; coward; (Mex) slicker

lección *f* lesson; (*interpretación de un pasaje*) reading; **dar la lección** to recite one's lesson; **echar** or **señalar lección** to assign the lesson; **tomar una lección a** to hear the lesson of

leccionista *mf* private tutor

lecti•vo -va *adj* school (*e.g., day*)

lec•tor -tora *adj* reading ‖ *mf* reader ‖ *m* foreign-language teacher; (*empleado que anota el consumo registrado por el contador de agua, gas o electricidad*) meter reader; **lector mental** mind reader

lectura *f* reading; broad culture; public lecture; college subject; (*interpretación de un*

pasaje) reading; (elec) playback; (typ) pica; **lectura de la mente** mind reading

lechada *f* grout; whitewash; (*para hacer papel*) pulp; (CAm, Mex, W-I) whitewash

lechar *tr* to milk; (CAm, Mex, W-I) to whitewash

leche *f* milk; (coll) sperm; **estar con la leche en los labios** to lack experience, to be young and inexperienced; **leche de manteca** buttermilk; **leche desnatada** skim milk; **leche en polvo** milk powder; **tener mala leche** to behave like a cad

lechecillas *fpl* sweetbread

lechera *f* milkmaid, dairymaid; (*vasija para guardar la leche*) milk can; (*vasija para servir la leche*) milk pitcher

lechería *f* dairy, creamery

leche•ro -ra *adj* (*que da leche*) milch; (*perteneciente a la leche*) milk; (*cicatero*) (coll) stingy ‖ *m* milkman, dairyman; (coll) lucky dog ‖ *f* see **lechera**

lecho *m* bed; (*especie de sofá*) couch; (*cauce de río*) bed; layer, stratum; **abandonar el lecho** to get up (*from illness*); **lecho de plumas** (fig) feather bed

le•chón -chona *adj* filthy, sloppy ‖ *mf* suckling pig; (*persona sucia, desaseada*) pig ‖ *m* pig ‖ *f* sow

lecho•so -sa *adj* milky ‖ *m* papaya (*tree*) ‖ *f* papaya (*fruit*)

lechuga *f* lettuce; head of lettuce; (*fuelle formado en la tela*) frill; **lechuga romana** romaine lettuce

lechugui•no -na *adj* stylish, sporty ‖ *m* dandy ‖ *f* stylish young lady

lechuza *f* barn owl, screech owl; owllike woman

lechu•zo -za *adj* owlish; (*muleto*) yearling ‖ *m* bill collector; summons server; owllike fellow ‖ *f* see **lechuza**

leer §43 *tr* to read ‖ *intr* to read; lecture; **leer en** to read (*someone's thoughts*) ‖ *ref* to read, e.g., **este libro se lee con facilidad** this book reads easily

leg. *abbr* **legal, legislatura**

lega *f* lay sister

legación *f* legation

legado *m* (*don que se hace por testamento*) legacy; (*enviado diplomático*) legate

legajo *m* file, docket, dossier

legal *adj* legal; faithful, prompt, right

legalidad *f* legality; faithfulness, promptness

legalizar §60 *tr* to legalize; authenticate

légamo *m* slime, ooze

legamo•so -sa *adj.* slimy, oozy

legaña *f* gum (*on edge of eyelids*)

legaño•so -sa *adj* gummy

legar §44 *tr* to bequeath, will

legata•rio -ria *mf* legatee

legenda•rio -ria *adj* legendary

legible *adj* legible

legión *f* legion

legislación *f* legislation

legisla•dor -dora *adj* legislating ‖ *mf* legislator

legislar *intr* to legislate

legislati•vo -va *adj* legislative

la
le

legislatura *f* (session of a) legislature
legista *m* law professor; law student
legitimar *tr* to legitimate; legitimize
legitimidad *f* legitimacy
legíti•mo -ma *adj* legitimate
le•go -ga *adj* lay; uninformed ‖ *m* layman; lay brother ‖ *f* see **lega**
legua *f* league; **a leguas** far, far away
leguleyo *m* pettifogger
legumbre *f* (*hortaliza*) vegetable; (bot) legume; (Chile) vegetable stew
leíble *adj* legible, readable
leída *f* reading
leí•do -da *adj* well-read; **leído y escribido** (coll) posing as learned ‖ *f* see **leída**
lejanía *f* distance, remoteness
leja•no -na *adj* distant, remote; (*pariente*) distant
lejía *f* lye; wash water; severe rebuke
lejiadora *f* washing machine
lejos *adv* far; **a lo lejos** in the distance; **de lejos** or **desde lejos** from a distance ‖ *m* glimpse; look from afar; **tener buen lejos** to look good at a distance
le•lo -la *adj* stupid, inane
lema *m* motto, slogan; theme
len *adj* soft, flossy
lena *f* spirit, vigor; breathing
lencería *f* linen goods, dry goods; linen closet; dry-goods store
lence•ro -ra *mf* linen dealer, dry-goods dealer
lendrera *f* fine-toothed comb
lendro•so -sa *adj* nitty, lousy
lene *adj* (*suave al tacto*) soft; (*ligero*) light; kind, agreeable
lengua *f* (anat) tongue; (*idioma*) language, tongue; (*de tierra, de fuego, de zapato; badajo de campana; lengua de un animal usada como alimento*) tongue; **buscar la lengua a** to pick a fight with; **dar la lengua** to chew the rag; **hacerse lenguas de** to rave about; **írsele a** (*uno*) **la lengua** to blab; **lengua madre** or **matriz** mother tongue (*language from which another is derived*); **lengua materna** mother tongue (*language acquired by reason of nationality*); **morderse la lengua** to hold one's tongue; **tener en la lengua** to have on the tip of one's tongue; **tener la lengua gorda** to talk thick; to be drunk; **tener mala lengua** to be blasphemous; to have an evil tongue; **tener mucha lengua** to be a great talker; **tirar de la lengua a** to draw out; **tomar en lenguas** to gossip about; **tomar lengua** or **lenguas** to pick up news
lenguado *m* sole
lenguaje *m* language
lengua•raz (*pl* **-races**) *adj* foul-mouthed, scurrilous; polyglot ‖ *mf* linguist
len•guaz *adj* (*pl* **-guaces**) garrulous
lengüeta *f* (*de la balanza*) pointer, needle; (*del zapato*) tongue; (anat) epiglottis; (carp) tongue; (*de un instrumento de viento*) (mus) reed; (Chile) paper cutter; (Mex) petticoat fringe; (SAm) chatterbox
lengüetada *f* licking, lapping

lengüetear *intr* to stick the tongue out; flicker, flutter; jabber, rant; lick
lengüilar•go -ga *adj* foul-mouthed, scurrilous
lengüisu•cio -cia *adj* (Mex, P-R) foul-mouthed, scurrilous
lenidad *f* lenience
lenocinio *m* pandering, procuring
lente *m* & *f* lens; **lente de aumento** magnifying glass; **lente de contacto** or **lente invisible** contact lens; **lentes** *mpl* nose glasses; **lentes de nariz** or **de pinzas** pince-nez; **lente telefotográfica** tele(photo)lens
lenteja *f* lentil; (*del reloj*) bob, pendulum bob
lentejuela *f* sequin, spangle
lentillas *fpl* contact lenses
lentitud *f* slowness
len•to -ta *adj* slow; sticky; (*fuego*) low
leña *f* firewood, kindling wood; **cargar de leña** to give a drubbing to; **llevar leña al monte** to carry coals to Newcastle
leña•dor -dora *mf* woodcutter ‖ *m* woodsman
leñame *m* lumber, timber; stock of firewood
leñero *m* wood merchant; wood purchaser; (*sitio donde se guarda la leña*) woodshed
leño *m* (*madera*) wood; (*tronco de árbol, limpio de ramas*) log; sap, blockhead; (poet) ship, vessel; **dormir como un leño** to sleep like a log
leño•so -sa *adj* woody
Leo *m* (astr) Leo
león *m* lion
leona *f* lioness
leona•do -da *adj* tawny, fulvous
leonera *f* lion cage, den of lions; dive, gambling joint; junk room, lumber room
leonero *m* lion keeper; keeper of a gambling joint
leontina *f* watch chain
leopardo *m* leopard
leopoldina *f* watch fob; (mil) Spanish shako
leotardo *m* leotard
lépa•ro -ra *adj* (CAm, Mex) indecent, improper
lepe *m* (Ven) flip in the ear; **saber más que Lepe** to be wide-awake
leperada *f* (CAm, Mex) coarseness, vulgarity
lepisma *f* (ent) silver fish, fish moth
lepori•no -na *adj* hare, harelike
lepra *f* leprosy
leprosería *f* leper house
lepro•so -sa *adj* leprous ‖ *mf* leper
lerdera *f* (CAm) laziness, apathy; (CAm) slowness
ler•do -da *adj* slow, dull; coarse, crude
lesbianismo *m* lesbianism
les•bio -bia *adj* & *mf* Lesbian ‖ *f* (*mujer homosexual*) Lesbian, lesbian
lesión *f* harm, hurt; (pathol) lesion
lesionar *tr* to harm, hurt, injure
lesi•vo -va *adj* harmful, injurious
lesna *f* awl
le•so -sa *adj* hurt, harmed, injured; wounded; offended; perverted; (SAm) simple, foolish
leste *m* (naut) east
letal *adj* lethal, deadly
letame *m* manure
letanía *f* litany; (*enumeración seguida*) litany

letárgi•co -ca *adj* lethargic
letargo *m* lethargy
letargo•so -sa *adj* lethargic
le•tón -tona *adj* Lettish ‖ *mf* Lett ‖ *m (idioma)* Lettish, Lett
Letonia *f* Latvia
letra *f (del alfabeto)* letter; *(modo de escribir propio de una persona)* hand, handwriting; *(de una canción)* words, lyric; (com) draft; (typ) type; *(sentido material)* (fig) letter; **a la letra** *(al pie de la letra)* to the letter; **a letra vista** (com) at sight; **bellas letras** belles lettres; **cuatro letras** or **dos letras** *(esquela, cartita)* a line; **en letras de molde** in print; **escribir en letra de molde** to print; **las letras y las armas** the pen and the sword; **letra a la vista** (com) sight draft; **letra de cambio** (com) bill of exchange; **letra de imprenta** (typ) type; **letra de mano** handwriting; **letra de molde** printed letter; **letra menuda** fine print; (fig) cunning; **letra muerta** dead letter; **letra negrilla** (typ) boldface; **letra redonda** or **redondilla** (typ) roman; **letras** *(literatura)* letters; (coll) a few words, a line; **primeras letras** elementary education, three R's
letra•do -da *adj* learned, lettered; pedantic ‖ *m* lawyer
letrero *m* sign, notice; *(p.ej., en una botella)* label
letrina *f* privy, latrine; *(cloaca)* sewer; *(cosa sucia)* (fig) cesspool
letrista *mf* lyricist, writer of lyrics *(for songs)*; calligrapher, engrosser
leucemia *f* leukemia
leucorrea *f* leucorrhea
leudar *tr* to leaven, ferment with yeast ‖ *ref (la masa con la levadura)* to rise
leu•do -da *adj* leavened, fermented
leva *f* weighing anchor; (mach) cam; (mil) levy; (CAm, Col) trick; (CAm, Col) swindle
levada *f (de la espada, el florete, etc.)* flourish; *(de los astros)* rise; *(del émbolo)* stroke
levadi•zo -za *adj (puente)* lift
levadura *f* leaven; leavening; yeast; *(tabla)* board; **levadura comprimida** yeast cake; **levadura de cerveza** brewer's yeast; **levadura en polvo** baking powder
levantaco•ches *m (pl* **-ches)** auto jack
levantada *f* rising, getting up *(from bed or from sickbed)*
levantamiento *m* rise, elevation; insurrection, revolt, uprising; **levantamiento del cadáver** inquest; **levantamiento del censo** census taking; **levantamiento de planos** surveying
levantar *tr* to raise, lift, elevate; agitate, rouse, stir up; *(una sesión)* adjourn; *(la mesa)* clear; *(la voz)* raise; *(el campo)* break; *(gente para el ejército; un sitio; fondos)* raise; *(el ancla)* weigh; straighten up; build, construct, erect; establish, found; **levantar casa** to break up housekeeping; **levantar planos** to make a survey ‖ *ref* to rise; *(de la cama)* get up; *(de una silla)*

stand up; straighten up; *(sublevarse)* rise up, rebel
levantaválvu•las *m (pl* **-las)** valve lifter
levantaventana *m* sash lift
levante *m* east; *(viento)* levanter; (CAm, P-R) slander, libel ‖ **Levante** *m (países de la parte oriental del Mediterráneo)* Levant; northeastern Mediterranean shores of Spain, especially around Valencia, Alicante, and Murcia
levanti•no -na *adj* Levantine; of the northeastern Mediterranean shores of Spain ‖ *mf* Levantine; native or inhabitant of the northeastern Mediterranean shores of Spain
levar *tr (el ancla)* to weigh ‖ *ref* to set sail
leve *adj (de poco peso)* light; slight, trivial, trifling
levedad *f* lightness; trivialness
leviatán *m* (Bib & fig) leviathan
levita *m* deacon ‖ *f* coat, frock coat
levitón *m* heavy frock coat
léxi•co -ca *adj* lexical ‖ *m* lexicon; *(caudal de voces de un autor)* vocabulary; *(conjunto de vocablos de una lengua o dialecto)* wordstock
lexicografía *f* lexicography
lexicográfi•co -ca *adj* lexicographic(al)
lexicógra•fo -fa *mf* lexicographer
lexicología *f* lexicology
lexicón *m* lexicon
ley *f* law; loyalty, devotion; norm, standard; *(de un metal)* fineness; **a ley de caballero** on the word of a gentleman; **de buena ley** sterling, genuine; **ley de la selva** law of the jungle; **ley del menor esfuerzo** line of least resistance; **ley marcial** martial law; **ley seca** dry law; **tener** or **tomar ley a** to become devoted to; **venir contra una ley** to break a law
leyenda *f* legend
leyente *adj* reading ‖ *mf* reader
lezna *f* awl
lía *f* plaited esparto rope; **lías** lees, dregs
lianza *f* (Chile) account, credit *(in a store)*
liar §77 *tr* to tie, bind; tie up, wrap up; *(un cigarillo)* roll; embroil, involve; **liarias** to beat it; kick the bucket ‖ *ref* to join together, be associated; have a liaison; become embroiled, become involved; **liárselos** to roll one's own *(i.e., cigarettes)*
libación *f* libation; *(acción de beber vino u otro licor)* libation
liba•nés -nesa *adj & mf* Lebanese
Libano, el Lebanon
libar *tr* to suck; taste, sip ‖ *intr* to pour out a libation; imbibe
libelo *m* lampoon, libel; (law) petition
libélula *f* dragonfly
liberación *f* liberation; *(cancelación de la carga que grava un inmueble)* redemption; *(de una cuenta)* settlement, closing; quittance
liberal *adj* liberal; *(expedito)* quick, ready; (pol) liberal; *(de amplias miras)* (Arg) liberal-minded ‖ *mf* (pol) liberal
liberalidad *f* liberality
liberar *tr* to free

le
li

libertad *f* liberty, freedom; **libertad de cáte-dra** academic freedom; **libertad de cultos** freedom of worship; **libertad de empresa** free enterprise; **libertad de enseñanza** academic freedom; **libertad de imprenta** freedom of the press; **libertad de los mares** freedom of the seas; **libertad de palabra** freedom of speech, free speech; **libertad de reunión** freedom of assembly; **libertad vigilada** probation; **plena libertad** free hand; **tomarse la libertad de** to take the liberty to

liberta•do -da *adj* bold, daring; free, brash, unrestrained

liberta•dor -dora *mf* liberator

libertar *tr* to liberate, set free; *(de un peligro, la muerte, etc.)* save

liberta•rio -ria *adj* anarchistic

libertinaje *m* licentiousness, profligacy; impiety, ungodliness

liberti•no -na *adj & mf* libertine

liber•to -ta *mf* (law) probationer ‖ *m* freedman ‖ *f* freedwoman

libídine *f* lewdness, lust; *(impulso a las actividades sexuales)* libido

libidino•so -sa *adj* libidinous

libido *f* libido

libra *f* pound; **Libra** *f* (astr) Libra; **libra esterlina** pound sterling

libraco *m* or **libracho** *m* trashy book

libra•do -da *mf* (com) drawee

libra•dor -dora *mf* (com) drawer

libranza *f* (com) draft; **libranza postal** money order

librar *tr* to free; save, spare; *(la esperanza)* place; *(batalla)* give, join; (com) to draw ‖ *intr* to be delivered, give birth; *(una religiosa)* receive a visitor in the locutory; (com) to draw; **librar bien** to come off well, succeed; **librar mal** to come off badly, fail ‖ *ref* to free oneself; escape

libre *adj* free; free, brash, outspoken; free, unmarried; free, loose, licentious; innocent, guiltless; **libre de culpa** *(seguro, divorcio)* no-fault; **libre de porte** postage prepaid

librea *f* livery

librecambio *m* free trade

librecambista *mf* freetrader

librepensa•dor -dora *adj* freethinking ‖ *mf* freethinker

librería *f* bookstore, bookshop; book business; *(mueble)* bookshelf; **librería de viejo** second-hand bookshop

libreril *adj* book

librero *m* bookseller; *(encuadernador)* bookbinder; (Cuba, Mex) bookshelf

libres•co -ca *adj* bookish

libreta *f* notebook; **libreta de banco** bankbook

libreto *m* (mus) libretto

librillo *m* earthen washtub; *(de papel de fumar, de sellos, etc.)* book

libro *m* book; **ahorcar los libros** to become a dropout; **a libro abierto** at sight; **hacer libro nuevo** to turn over a new leaf; **libro a la rústica** paperbound book; **libro de caballerías** romance of chivalry; **libro de cocina** cookbook; **libro de cheques** checkbook; **libro de chistes** joke book; **libro de lance** second-hand book; **libro de mayor venta** best seller; **libro de memoria** memo book; **libro de oro** guest book; **libro de recuerdos** scrapbook; **libro de teléfonos** telephone book; **libro de texto** textbook; **libro diario** day book; **libro en imágenes** picture book; **libro en rústica** paperbound book; **libro mayor** (com) ledger; **libro talonario** checkbook, stub book

libro-registro *m* (com) book

licencia *f* license; leave of absence; (mil) furlough; **licencia absoluta** (mil) discharge; **licencia por enfermedad** sick leave

licencia•do -da *adj* pedantic ‖ *mf* licenciate ‖ *m* lawyer; (mil) discharged soldier; university student *(wearing the long student gown)*

licenciar *tr* to license; allow, permit; confer the degree of licenciate or master on; (mil) to discharge ‖ *ref* to receive the degree of licenciate or master; become dissolute; (mil) to be discharged

licenciatura *f* licenciate, master's degree; graduation with a licenciate or master's degree; work leading to a licenciate or master's degree

licencio•so -sa *adj* licentious

liceo *m (sociedad literaria, establecimiento de enseñanza popular)* lyceum; *(instituto de segunda enseñanza)* (Chile) lycée; (Mex) primary school

licitación *f* bidding

licita•dor -dora *mf* bidder

licitar *tr* to bid on; (Arg) to buy at auction, to sell at auction ‖ *intr* to bid

líci•to -ta *adj* fair, just; licit, legal

licor *m (bebida espiritosa; cuerpo líquido)* liquor; *(bebida espiritosa preparada por mezcla de azúcar y substancias aromáticas)* liqueur

licorera *f* cellaret

licorista *mf* distiller; liquor dealer

licoro•so -sa *adj* spirituous, alcoholic; *(vino)* rich, generous

licuar §21 & regular *tr* to liquefy

lid *f* fight, combat; dispute, argument; **en buena lid** by fair means

líder *adj* leading ‖ *m* leader

liderar *tr & intr* to lead, be the leader

lidia *f* fight; bullfight

lidiadera *f* (Ecuad) quarreling, bickering

lidia•dor -dora *mf* fighter ‖ *ref* bullfighter

lidiar *tr (un toro)* to fight ‖ *intr* to fight; **lidiar con** to fight with; have to put up with

liebre *f* hare; *(hombre cobarde)* coward

liendre *f* nit

lien•to -ta *adj* damp, dank

lienza *f* strip of cloth

lienzo *m* linen (cloth); linen handkerchief; *(de edificio o pared)* face, front; *(pintura sobre lienzo)* canvas

liga *f* (*cinta elástica para asegurar las medias*) garter; (*aleación*) alloy; (*materia pegajosa para cazar pájaros*) birdlime; (*confederación, alianza*) league; (*muérdago*) mistletoe; band; **liga de goma** rubber band

ligado *m* (mus & typ) ligature

ligadura *f* tie, bond; (mus) ligature, glide; (surg) ligature

ligamento *m* ligament

ligar §44 *tr* to tie, bind; join, combine; alloy; (*bebidas*) mix; (surg) to ligate ‖ *ref* to league together; be committed; be bound or attached (*e.g., in friendship*)

ligereza *f* lightness; speed, rapidity; fickleness, inconstancy; tactlessness

lige•ro -ra *adj* light; (*té*) weak; (*tejido*) light, thin; quick; slight; **a la ligera** lightly; quickly; unceremoniously; **de ligero** thoughtlessly, rashly; **ligero de cascos** light-headed, scatter-brained; **ligero de lengua** loose-tongued; **ligero de pies** light-footed; **ligero de ropa** scantily clad ‖ **ligero** *adv* fast, rapidly

lignito *m* lignite

ligustro *m* privet

lija *f* (*pez*) dogfish; (*papel que sirve para pulir*) sandpaper; **darse lija** (W-I) to boast, brag, pat oneself on the back

lijar *tr* to sand, sandpaper

lila *adj* silly, simple ‖ *m* lilac (*color*) ‖ *f* lilac (*plant and flower*)

li•lac *f* (*pl* **-laques**) lilac

liliputiense *adj & mf* Lilliputian

lima *f* (*herramienta*) file; sweet lime; sweet-lime tree; (*del tejado*) hip; hip rafter; correcting, polishing; **lima de uñas** nail file; **lima hoya** valley (*of roof*)

limadura *f* filing; (*partecillas*) filings

limalla *f* filings

limar *tr* to file; file down; polish, touch up; smooth, smooth over; (*cercenar*) curtail

limaza *f* (*babosa*) slug; (Ven) large file

limazo *m* slime, sliminess

limbo *m* (*borde*) edge; (theol) limbo; **estar en el limbo** to be quite distraught

limen *m* (physiol, psychol & fig) threshold

limenso *m* (Chile) honeydew melon

lime•ño -ña *adj & mf* Limean

limero *m* sweet-lime tree

limita•do -da *adj* limited; dull-witted

limitador *m* — **limitador de corriente** clock meter; slot meter

limitar *tr* to limit; cut down, reduce ‖ *intr* — **limitar con** to border on

límite *m* limit; boundary, border

limítrofe *adj* bordering

limo *m* slime, mud

limón *m* lemon; lemon tree; (*de un coche o carro*) shaft

limonada *f* lemonade

limoncillo *m* citronella

limonera *f* shaft

limonero *m* lemon tree

limosna *f* alms

limosnear *intr* to beg

limosne•ro -ra *adj* almsgiving, charitable ‖ *mf* almsgiver; beggar ‖ *m* alms box

limo•so -sa *adj* slimy, muddy

limpia *f* cleaning

limpiaba•rros *m* (*pl* **-rros**) scraper, foot scraper

limpiabo•tas *m* (*pl* **-tas**) shoeshiner, bootblack; (fig) flatterer

limpiacrista•les *m* (*pl* **-les**) windshield washer

limpiachimene•as *m* (*pl* **-as**) chimney sweep

limpiadien•tes *m* (*pl* **-tes**) toothpick

limpia•dor -dora *adj* cleaning ‖ *mf* cleaner

limpiadura *f* cleaning; **limpiaduras** cleanings, dirt

limpiama•nos *m* (*pl* **-nos**) (Guat, Hond) towel

limpiamente *adv* in a clean manner; with ease, skillfully; simply, sincerely; unselfishly

limpiameta•les *m* (*pl* **-les**) metal polish

limpianieve *m* snowplow

limpiaparabri•sas *m* (*pl* **-sas**) windshield wiper

limpia•piés *m* (*pl* **-piés**) (Mex) door mat

limpiapi•pas *m* (*pl* **-pas**) pipe cleaner

limpiaplu•mas *m* (*pl* **-mas**) penwiper

limpiar *tr* to clean; (*purificar*) cleanse; (*de culpas*) exonerate; (*un árbol*) clean out, prune; (*zapatos*) shine; (*hurtar*) snitch; (*a una persona en el juego*) clean out; (*dinero en el juego*) clean up; (mil) to mop up; **limpiarle a uno de** to clean someone out of ‖ *ref* to clean, clean oneself

limpiau•ñas *m* (*pl* **-ñas**) nail cleaner, orange stick

limpiaví•as *m* (*pl* **-as**) track cleaner

limpieza *f* (*acción de limpiar*) cleaning; (*calidad de limpio*) cleanness; (*hábito del aseo*) cleanliness; neatness, tidiness; honesty; chastity; ease, skill; (*observancia de las reglas en los juegos*) fair play; **limpieza de bolsa** emptiness of the pocketbook; **limpieza de la casa** house cleaning; **limpieza en seco** dry cleaning

lim•pio -pia *adj* clean; (*que tiene el hábito del aseo*) cleanly; neat, tidy; honest; chaste; clear, free; **dejar limpio** to clean out; **en limpio** (com) net; **estar limpio** to have no (criminal) record; be clean; **limpio de polvo y paja** free, for nothing; net, after deducting expenses; **poner en limpio** to make a clear or fair copy of; **quedar limpio** to be cleaned out; **sacar en limpio** to make a clear or clean copy of; deduce, understand ‖ *f* see **limpia** ‖ **limpio** *adv* fair; cleanly; **jugar limpio** to play fair

limpión *m* (*limpiadura ligera*) lick; (coll) cleaner; (Col) scolding; (Col, Ven) dustcloth; (Ecuad) dishcloth

limusina *f* limousine

lín. *abbr* **línea**

lina *f* (Chile) coarse wool

linaje *m* lineage; class, description; **linaje humano** mankind

linaju•do -da *adj* highborn ‖ *mf* highborn person

linaza *f* flaxseed, linseed

lince *adj* keen, shrewd, discerning; (*ojos*) keen ‖ *m* lynx; (fig) keen person

lincear *tr* to see into

linchamiento *m* lynching
linchar *tr* to lynch
lindante *adj* bordering, adjoining
lindar *intr* to border, be contiguous; **lindar con** to border on
linde *m & f* limit, boundary
linde•ro -ra *adj* bordering, adjoining ‖ *m* edge; boundary stone, landmark ‖ *f* limit, boundary; (bot) spicebush
lindeza *f* prettiness, niceness; elegance; witticism, funny remark; flirting; **lindezas** insults
lin•do -da *adj* pretty, nice, fine, perfect; **de lo lindo** a lot, a great deal; wonderfully ‖ *m* dude, sissy
lindura *f* prettiness, niceness
línea *f* line; (*contorno de una figura, un vestido*) lines; figure, waistline; **conservar la línea** to keep one's figure; **leer entre líneas** to read between the lines; **línea de agua** water line; **línea de batalla** line of battle; **línea de empalme** (rr) branch line; **línea de flotación** water line; **línea de fuego** firing line; **línea de fuerza** (elec) power line; (phys) line of force; **línea del partido** party line; **línea de mira** line of sight; **línea de montaje** assembly line; **línea de puntos** dotted line; **línea de tiro** (mil) line of fire; **línea férrea** railway; **línea internacional de cambio de fecha** international date line; **línea suplementaria** (mus) added line, ledger line
lineal *adj* linear
lineamentos *mpl* lineaments
linfa *f* lymph; (poet) water
linfáti•co -ca *adj* lymphatic
lingote *m* ingot, slug; (naut) ballast bar
lingual *adj & f* lingual
lingüista *mf* linguist
lingüísti•co -ca *adj* linguistic ‖ *f* linguistics
linimento *m* liniment
lino *m* flax; (*tela*) linen; (poet) sail
linóleo *m* linoleum
linón *m* lawn
linotipia *f* linotype
linotípi•co -ca *adj* linotype
linotipista *mf* linotype operator
linotipo *m* linotype
linterna *f* lantern; **linterna eléctrica** flashlight
lío *m* bundle; (*de papeles*) batch; muddle, mess; liaison, affair; **armar un lío** to raise a row; **hacerse un lío** to get into a jam
liofilización *f* freeze-drying
liofilizar §60 *tr* to freeze-dry
lionesa — **a la lionesa** (culin) lyonnaise
liorna *f* hubbub, uproar ‖ **Liorna** *f* Leghorn
lio•so -sa *adj* trouble-making, knotty, troublesome
liq.ⁿ *abbr* **liquidación**
líq.° *abbr* **líquido**
liquen *m* lichen
liquidación *f* (*de una cuenta*) sale
liquidar *tr* to liquefy; (com) to liquidate ‖ *intr* (com) to liquidate ‖ *ref* to liquefy
liquidez *f* liquidity

líqui•do -da *adj & m* liquid; (com) net ‖ *f* (phonet) liquid
lira *f* (mus) lyre; (*numen de un poeta*) inspiration; poems, poetry
lírica *f* lyric poetry
líri•co -ca *adj* lyric(al); (*músico, operístico*) lyric; fantastic, utopian ‖ *m* lyric poet; (Arg, Ven) visionary ‖ *f* see **lírica**
lirio *m* (bot) iris; **lirio blanco** (*azucena*) Madonna lily; **lirio de agua** (bot) calla, calla lily; **lirio de los valles** (bot) lily of the valley
lirismo *m* lyricism; spellbinding; fancy, illusion
lirón *m* (bot) water plantain; (zool) dormouse; (coll) sleepyhead
lis *m* (bot) lily ‖ *f* (bot) iris; (heral) fleur-de-lis
Lisboa *f* Lisbon
lisia•do -da *adj* hurt, injured; crippled; (*muy deseoso*) eager ‖ *mf* cripple
lisiar *tr* to hurt, injure; cripple ‖ *ref* to become crippled
lisimaquia *f* loosestrife
li•so -sa *adj* even, smooth; (*vestido*) plain, unadorned; (*franco, sincero*) simple, plain-dealing; brash, insolent; **liso y llano** simple, easy
lisonja *f* flattery
lisonjear *tr* to flatter; please ‖ *intr* to flatter
lisonje•ro -ra *adj* flattering; pleasing ‖ *mf* flatterer
lista *f* list; (*tira*) strip; (*en un tejido*) colored stripe; (*recuento en alta voz de las personas que deben estar en un lugar*) roll call; **lista de bajas** casualty list; **lista de comidas** bill of fare; **lista de correos** general delivery; **lista de espera** waiting list; **lista de frecuencia** frequency list; **lista de pagos** pay roll; **pasar lista** to call the roll
listar *tr* to list
listero *m* roll keeper, timekeeper
listín *m* telephone directory; (S-D) newspaper
lis•to -ta *adj* ready; quick, prompt; alert, wide-awake; **estar listo** to be ready; to be finished; **listo de manos** light-fingered; **pasarse de listo** to be shrewd, be clever ‖ *f* see **lista**
listón *m* (*cinta*) ribbon, tape; (*pedazo de tabla angosta*) lath, strip of wood
listonado *m* lath, lathing
lisura *f* evenness, smoothness; plainness; candor; brashness, insolence
lit. *abbr* **literalmente**
lite *f* lawsuit
litera *f* (*vehículo llevado por hombres o por animales*) litter; (*cama fija en los camarotes*) berth; **litera alta** upper berth; **litera baja** lower berth
literal *adj* literal
litera•rio -ria *adj* literary
litera•to -ta *adj* literary ‖ *mf* literary person; **literatos** literati
literatura *f* literature; **literatura de escape** or **de evasión** escape literature
litigación *s* litigation
litigante *adj & mf* litigant

litigar §44 *tr* & *intr* to litigate
litigio *m* litigation, lawsuit; dispute
litigio•so -sa *adj* litigious
litina *s* (chem) lithia
litio *m* (chem) lithium
litisexpensas *fpl* (law) costs
litografía *f* (*arte de grabar en piedra para la reproducción en estampa*) lithography; (*estampa*) lithograph
litografiar §77 *tr* to lithograph
litógra•fo -fa *mf* lithographer
litoral *adj* coastal, littoral ‖ *m* coast, shore
litro *m* liter
liturgia *f* liturgy
litúrgi•co -ca *adj* liturgic(al)
liviandad *f* lightness; inconstancy, fickleness; lewdness
livia•no -na *adj* light; inconstant, fickle; lewd ‖ *m* leading donkey; **livianos** lights, lungs
lívi•do -da *adj* livid
liza *f* combat, fight; (*campo para lidiar*) lists; **entrar en liza** to enter the lists
lo *art def neut* (used with *masc sg* form of *adj*) the, e.g., **lo bueno** the good; what is, e.g., **lo útil** what is useful; **lo mío** what is mine; (used with *adv* or inflected *adj*) the + noun, e.g., **lo aprisa que habla** the speed with which he speaks; **lo tacaños que son** the stinginess of them; how, e.g., **Vd., no sabe lo felices que son** you do not know how happy they are; **lo más** as . . . as, e.g., **lo más temprano posible** as early as possible ‖ *pron pers masc* him, it; you; (with **estar, ser, parecer,** and the like, it stands for an adjective or noun understood and is either not translated or is translated by ''so''), e.g., **Vd. está preparado pero ella no lo está** you are ready but she is not ‖ *pron dem* that; **de lo que** + *verb* than + *verb*, e.g., **ese libro ha costado más dinero de lo que vale** that book cost more money than it is worth; **lo de** the matter of, the question of, e.g., **lo de sus deudas** the matter of your debts; **lo de que** the fact that, the statement that; **lo de siempre** the same old story; **lo que** what, that which; **todo lo que** all (that), e.g., **me dió todo lo que tenía** he gave me all he had
loa *f* praise; (*del teatro antiguo*) prologue; short dramatic poem
loable *adj* laudable, praiseworthy
loar *tr* to praise
loba *f* she-wolf; ridge
lobagante *m* lobster (*Homarus*)
lobanillo *m* wen, cyst
lobato *m* wolf cub
lo•bo -ba *adj* & *mf* (Mex) half-breed ‖ *m* wolf; **coger** or **pillar un lobo** (coll) to go on a jag; **desollar** or **dormir un lobo** to sleep off a drunk; **lobo de mar** (ichth) sea wolf; (coll) old salt, sea dog; **lobo solitario** (fig) lone wolf ‖ *f* see **loba**
lóbre•go -ga *adj* dark, dismal; gloomy
lobreguez *f* darkness; gloominess
lobu•no -na *adj* wolf, wolfish
locación *f* lease
local *adj* local ‖ *m* quarters, place

localidad *f* (*lugar, sitio*) location, locality; (*plaza en un tren*) accommodations; (theat) seat
localización *f* localization; location; **localización de averías** trouble shooting
localizar §60 *tr* (*limitar a un punto determinado*) to localize; (*determinar el lugar de*) locate
locería *f* pottery
loción *f* wash; (pharm) lotion; **loción facial** after-shave lotion
lo•co -ca *adj* crazy, insane, mad; terrific, wonderful; **estar loco por** to be crazy about, to be mad about; **loco de amor** madly in love; **loco de atar** raving mad; **loco perenne** insane, demented; full of fun; **loco rematado** stark-mad; **volver loco** to drive crazy ‖ *mf* crazy person, lunatic ‖ *m* (*bufón*) fool
locomotora *f* engine, locomotive; **locomotora de maniobras** shifting engine
locro *m* (SAm) meat and vegetable stew
lo•cuaz *adj* (*pl* **-cuaces**) loquacious
locución *f* expression, locution; idiomatic phrase, idiom
locuela *f* speech, way of speaking
locue•lo -la *adj* wild, frisky ‖ *f* see **locuela**
locura *f* insanity, madness; folly, madness
locu•tor -tora *mf* announcer, commentator
locutorio *m* (*en un convento de monjas*) parlor, locutory; telephone booth
lodazal *m* mudhole
lodo *m* mud, mire; (*substancia que sirve para cerrar junturas, tapar grietas, etc.*) (chem) lute
lodo•so -sa *adj* muddy
logaritmo *m* logarithm
logia *f* (*p.ej., de francmasones*) lodge; (archit) loggia
lógi•co -ca *adj* logical ‖ *mf* logician ‖ *f* logic
logísti•co -ca *adj* logistic(al) ‖ *f* logistics
logopedía *f* speech correction
logrado -da *adj* successful
lograr *tr* to get, obtain; achieve, attain; **lograr** + *inf* to succeed in + *ger* ‖ *ref* to be successful
logrear *intr* to be a moneylender; profiteer
logre•ro -ra *adj* moneylending; profiteering ‖ *mf* moneylender; profiteer; (Chile) sponger
logro *m* attainment, success; gain, profit; usury; **dar** or **prestar a logro** to lend at usurious rates
loma *f* low hill, elevation
Lombardía *f* Lombardy
lombar•do -da *adj* & *mf* Lombard
lombriguera *f* wormhole in the ground; (bot) tansy
lom•briz *f* (*pl* **-brices**) worm, earthworm; (pathol) worm; (*persona muy alta y delgada*) beanpole; **lombriz de tierra** earthworm; **lombriz solitaria** tapeworm
lomera *f* (*de la guarnición*) backstrap; (*del tejado*) ridgepole; (bb) backing
lominhies•to -ta *adj* high-backed; conceited
lomo *m* (*de animal, libro, cuchillo*) back; (*tierra que levanta el arado*) ridge; (*carne*

li
lo

de lomo del animal) loin; (*pliegue del tejido*) crease; (bb) spine; **lomos** ribs
lona *f* canvas; sailcloth; (Mex) burlap
loncha *f* slab, flagstone; slice, strip
lonchería *f* snack bar
londinense *adj* London ‖ *mf* Londoner
Londres *m* London; **el Gran Londres** Greater London
longáni•mo -ma *adj* long-suffering
longaniza *f* pork sausage
longevidad *f* longevity
longe•vo -va *adj* long-lived
longitud *f* length; (astr & geog) longitud
lonja *f* exchange, commodity exchange; grocery store; wool warehouse; (*de carne*) slice; (*de cuero*) strip; (*a la entrada de un edificio*) elevated parvis; (Arg) rawhide
lonjeta *f* bower, summerhouse
lonjista *mf* grocer
lontananza *f* (*de una pintura*) background; **en lontananza** in the distance, on the horizon
loor *m* praise
loquear *intr* to talk nonsense, play the fool; carry on, have a high time
loquera *f* insanity
loquería *f* (Chile) madhouse, insane asylum
loque•ro -ra *mf* guard in a mental hospital ‖ *m* (Arg) confusion, pandemonium; (Arg) insane asylum
loques•co -ca *adj* crazy; funny, jolly
lorán *m* (naut) loran
lord *m* (*pl* **lores**) lord
lo•ro -ra *adj* dark-brown ‖ *m* parrot; cherry laurel; (Chile) spy; (Chile) glass bedpan; (Chile) third degree
losa *f* slab, flagstone; tomb
losange *m* lozenge; (baseball) diamond
lote *m* lot, share, portion; lottery prize; (Cuba, Mex) remnant; (Arg) dunce, simpleton; (Col) swallow, swig; (*de terreno*) (Cuba, Mex) lot
lotear *tr* (Chile) to divide up, divide into lots
lotería *f* lottery; (*juego casero*) lotto; (*cosa insegura, riesgo*) gamble
lote•ro -ra *mf* vendor of lottery tickets
lotizar §60 *tr* (Peru) to divide into lots
loto *m* lotus
loza *f* (*barro cocido y barnizado*) porcelain; crockery, earthenware; **loza fina** china, chinaware
lozanear *intr* to be luxuriant; be full of life ‖ *ref* (*deleitarse*) to luxuriate
lozanía *f* luxuriance, verdure; exuberance, vigor; pride, haughtiness
loza•no -na *adj* luxuriant, verdant; exuberant, vigorous, proud, haughty
lubricante *adj* & *m* lubricant
lubricar §73 *tr* to lubricate
lúbri•co -ca *adj* (*resbaladizo; lascivo*) lubricous (*slippery; lewd*)
lubrificar §73 to lubricate
lucera *f* skylight
lucerna *f* large chandelier; (*abertura, tronera*) loophole
lucero *m* bright star; (*planeta*) Venus; (*ventanillo en un muro*) light; **lucero del alba** or

de la mañana morning star; **lucero de la tarde** evening star; **luceros** (poet) eyes
luci•do -da *adj* generous, magnificent; brilliant, successful; sumptuous; (Arg) striking, dashing
lúci•do -da *adj* lucid
luciente *adj* bright, shining
luciérnaga *f* glowworm, firefly
lucifer *m* overbearing fellow ‖ **Lucifer** *m* Lucifer
lucífe•ro -ra *adj* (poet) bright, dazzling ‖ *m* morning star; (Col) match
lucimiento *m* brilliance, luster; show, dash; success; **quedar** or **salir con lucimiento** to come off with flying colors
lu•cio -cia *adj* shiny ‖ *m* salt pool; (*pez*) pike, luce
lucir §45 *tr* to light, light up; show, display; (*p.ej., un traje nuevo*) sport; help; plaster ‖ *intr* to shine ‖ *ref* to dress up; come off with great success; (*sobresalir, distinguirse*) shine; flop, e.g., **lucido me quedé** I was a flop
lucrar *tr* to get, obtain ‖ *intr* & *ref* to profit, make money
lucrati•vo -va *adj* lucrative
lucro *m* gain, profit; **lucros y daños** profit and loss
lucro•so -sa *adj* lucrative
luctuo•so -sa *adj* sad, mournful, gloomy
lucha *f* fight; (*disputa*) quarrel; (*actividad forzada*) struggle; (*combate cuerpo a cuerpo*) wrestling; **lucha antipolución** antipollution movement (or campaign); **lucha de la cuerda** (sport) tug of war; **lucha por la vida** struggle for existence
lucha•dor -dora *mf* fighter, wrestler
luchar *intr* (*combatir*) to fight; (*disputar*) quarrel; (*esforzarse*) struggle; (*pelear cuerpo a cuerpo*) wrestle
ludibrio *m* derision, mockery, scorn
ludir *tr*, *intr* & *ref* to rub, rub together
luego *adv* next, then; therefore; soon; once in a while; **desde luego** right away; of course; **hasta luego** good-bye, so long; **luego como** as soon as; **luego de** after, right after; **luego que** as soon as
luen•go -ga *adj* long
lúes *f* pestilence; **lúes canina** distemper; **lúes venérea** syphilis
lugano *m* (orn) siskin
lugar *m* place; site, spot; job, position; (*espacio*) room, space; (*asiento*) seat; village, hamlet; (geom) locus; **dar lugar** to make room; **dar lugar a** to give cause for; give rise to; **en lugar de** instead of, in place of; **hacer lugar** to make room; **lugar común** (*expresión trivial*) commonplace; (*retrete*) toilet, water closet; **lugar de cita** tryst; **lugares estrechos** close quarters; **lugar geométrico** locus; **lugar religioso** place of burial
lugarejo *m* hamlet
lugare•ño -ña *adj* village ‖ *mf* villager
lugarteniente *m* lieutenant
luge *m* sled
lúgubre *adj* dismal, gloomy, lugubrious

luir §20 *tr* (naut) to gall, wear; (Chile) to muss, rumple; (*vasijas de barro*) (Chile) to polish ‖ *ref* (Chile) to rub, wear away

luisa *f* (bot) lemon verbena

lujo *m* luxury; **de lujo** de luxe; **gastar mucho lujo** to live in high style; **lujo de** abundance of, excess of

lujo‧so -sa *adj* luxurious

lujuria *f* lust, lechery

lujuriante *adj* (*lozano*) luxuriant, lush; (*libidinoso*) lustful

lujuriar *intr* to lust, be lustful; (*los animales*) copulate

lujurio‧so -sa *adj* lustful, lecherous ‖ *mf* lecher

lu‧lo -la *adj* (Chile) lank, slender ‖ *m* (Chile) bundle

lu‧lú *m* (*pl* **-lúes**) spitz dog

lumbago *m* lumbago

lumbre *f* light; fire; (*para encender el cigarrillo*) light; (*hueco en un muro por donde entra la luz*) light; brightness, brilliance; knowledge, learning; **echar lumbre** to blow one's top; **lumbre del agua** surface of the water; **lumbres** tinderbox; **ni por lumbre** not for love or money; **ser la lumbre de los ojos de** to be the light of the eyes of

lumbrera *f* light, source of light; light, lamp; (*abertura por donde entran el aire y la luz*) louver; skylight; dormer window; air duct, ventilating shaft; (*persona insigne*) light, luminary; (mach) port; **lumbreras** eyes

luminar *m* luminary

luminiscente *adj* luminescent

lumino‧so -sa *adj* luminous; (*idea*) bright

luminotecnia *f* lighting engineering

lun. *abbr* **lunes**

luna *f* moon; moonlight; (*tabla de cristal*) plate glass; (*espejo*) mirror; (*de los anteojos*) lens, glass; whim; **estar de buena luna** to be in a good mood; **estar de mala luna** to be in a bad mood; **luna de miel** honeymoon; **luna llena** full moon; **luna menguante** waning moon; **luna nueva** new moon; **media luna** half moon; (*figura de cuarto de luna creciente o menguante*) crescent; **quedarse a la luna de Valencia** to be disappointed

lunar *adj* lunar ‖ *m* (*mancha de la piel*) mole; (*punto en un diseño de puntos*) polka dot; (fig) stain, blot, stigma; **lunar postizo** beauty spot

lunáti‧co -ca *adj* & *mf* lunatic

lu‧nes *m* (*pl* **-nes**) Monday; **hacer San Lunes** to knock off on Monday

luneta *f* (*de los anteojos*) lens, glass; orchestra seat; (aut) rear window

lunfardo *m* (Arg) thief; underworld slang

lupa *m* magnifying glass

lupanar *m* brothel, bawdyhouse

lupia *mf* (Hond) quack, healer ‖ *f* wen, cyst; **lupias** (Col) small amount of money, small change

lúpulo *m* (*vid*) hop; (*flores desecadas de la vid*) hops

luquete *m* slice of orange or lemon used to flavor wine; (Chile) bald spot; (*en la ropa*) (Chile) spot, hole

lu‧rio -ria *adj* (Mex) mad, crazy

lusitanismo *m* Lusitanism

lusita‧no -na *adj* & *mf* Lusitanian, Portuguese

lustrabo‧tas *m* (*pl* **-tas**) shoeshiner

lustrar *tr* to shine, polish ‖ *intr* to wander, roam

lustre *m* shine, polish; luster, gloss; (*fama, gloria*) (fig) luster

lustrina *f* (Chile) shoe polish

lustro *m* five years; chandelier

lustro‧so -sa *adj* shining, bright, lustrous

lutera‧no -na *adj* & *mf* Lutheran

luto *m* (*señal exterior de duelo*) mourning; (*duelo, aflicción*) sorrow, bereavement; **estar de luto** to be in mourning; **lutos** crape; **luto riguroso** deep mourning

lutocar *m* (Chile) trash cart

luz *f* (*pl* **luces**) light; window, light; electricity; (*dinero*) money; cash; **a primera luz** at dawn; **a toda luz** or **a todas luces** everywhere; by all means; **dar a luz** to have a child; to give birth to; to bring out; to publish; **entre dos luces** at twilight; half-seas over; **luces de carretera** (aut) bright lights; **luces de cruce** (aut) dimmers; **luz de balizaje** (aer) marker light; **luz de magnesio** magnesium light; flash bulb, flashlight; **luz de matrícula** license-plate light; **luz de parada** stop light; **luz trasera** taillight; **sacar a luz** to bring to light; **salir a luz** to come to light; come out, be published; take place; **ver la luz** to see the light, see the light of day

Luzbel *m* Lucifer

lo
ll

Ll

Ll, ll (elle) *f* fourteenth letter of the Spanish alphabet

llaga *f* sore, ulcer; sorrow, grief; (*entre dos ladrillos*) (mas) seam, joint; (fig) ulcer

llagar §44 *tr* to make sore; hurt

llama *f* flame, blaze; marsh, swamp; (zool) llama; (fig) fire, passion; **saltar de las**

llamas y caer en las brasas to jump out of the frying pan into the fire

llamada *f* call; (*movimiento con que se llama la atención de uno*) sign, signal; knock, ring; reference, reference mark; (mil) call, call to arms; (Mex) cowardice; **batir** or **tocar a llamada** (mil) to sound the call to arms; **llamada a filas** (mil) call to the colors; **llamada a quintas** draft call; **llamada por cobrar** collect call

llamadera *f* goad

llama•do -da *adj* so-called ‖ *f* see **llamada**

llama•dor -dora *mf* caller ‖ *m* messenger; door knocker; push button

llamamiento *m* call; calling, vocation

llamar *tr* to call; (*dar nombre a*) name, call; summon; invoke, call upon; (*la atención*) attract ‖ *intr* to call; (*golpear en la puerta*) knock; (*hacer sonar la campanilla*) ring; (*el viento*) (naut) to veer ‖ *ref* to be called, be named; **se llama Juan** his name is John

llamarada *f* blaze, flare-up; (*encendimiento repentino del rostro*) flush; (fig) flare-up, outburst

llamarón *m* flare-up

llamati•vo -va *adj* showy, loud, flashy, gaudy; (*manjar*) thirst-raising

llamazar *m* swamp, marsh

llame *m* (Chile) bird net, bird trap

llamear *intr* to blaze, flame, flash

lla•món -mona *adj* (Mex) cowardly

llampo *m* (Chile) ore

llana *f* trowel, float; plain; **dar de llana** to smooth with the trowel

llanada *f* plain

llanero *m* ranger, plainsman

llaneza *f* plainness, simplicity; familiarity; sincerity

lla•no -na *adj* even, level, smooth; (*parecido a un plano geométrico*) plane; (*sencillo*) plain, simple; clear, evident; (*palabras*) frank; accented on the next to last syllable ‖ *m* plain; (*de la escalera*) landing ‖ *f* see **llana**

llanque *m* (Peru) rawhide sandal

llanta *f* (*cerco exterior de la rueda*) tire (*of iron or rubber*); (*borde exterior de la rueda*) rim; (*pieza de hierro más ancha que gruesa*) iron flat; **llanta de goma** rubber tire; **llanta de invierno** snow tire; **llanta de oruga** (*de un tractor de oruga*) track

llanto *m* weeping, crying; **en llanto** in tears

llanura *f* evenness, level, smoothness; (*terreno extenso y llano*) plain

llapan•go -ga *adj* (Ecuad) barefooted

llares *m* pothanger

llave *adj* key ‖ *f* (*pieza para abrir y cerrar las cerraduras*) key; (*herramienta*) wrench; (*grifo*) faucet, spigot, cock; (*de arma de fuego*) cock; (elec) switch; (*de un instrumento de viento*) (mus) key; (*de un enigma, secreto, traducción, cifra; lugar estratégico más propicio*) key; **bajo llave** under lock and key; **echar la llave a** to lock; **llave de caja** socket wrench; **llave de caño** pipe wrench; **llave de cubo** socket wrench; **llave de chispa** flintlock; **llave de estufa** damper; **llave de mandíbulas dentadas** alligator wrench; **llave de paso** stopcock; passkey; **llave de purga** drain cock; **llave espacial** space key; **llave inglesa** monkey wrench; **llave maestra** master key, skeleton key; **llave para tubos** pipe wrench

llave•ro -ra *mf* keeper of the keys; (*carcelero*) turnkey ‖ *m* key ring

llavín *m* latchkey

llegada *f* arrival

llegar §44 *tr* to bring up, bring close ‖ *intr* to arrive; happen; **llegar a** to arrive at; reach; amount to; be equal to; **llegar a** + *inf* to come to + *inf;* succeed in + *ger;* **llegar a ser** to become ‖ *ref* to come close

llena *f* flood

llenado *m* filling

llena•dor -dora *adj* (*alimento*) (Chile) filling

llenar *tr* to fill; (*un formulario*) fill out; (*ciertas condiciones*) fulfill; satisfy; (*colmar*) overwhelm ‖ *intr* (*la luna*) to be full ‖ *ref* to fill, fill up; stuff oneself; **llenarse a rebosar** to be filled to overflowing

llene *m* filling; full tank

lle•no -na *adj* full; **lleno a rebosar** full to overflowing; **lleno de goteras** full of aches and pains ‖ *m* fill, plenty; fulness, full enjoyment; completeness; full moon; (*en el teatro*) full house ‖ *f* see **llena**

lleva or **llevada** *f* carrying, conveying; ride; **lleva gratuita** free ride

llevade•ro -ra *adj* bearable, tolerable

llevar *tr* (*transportar*) to carry; (*traer consigo*) take; (*conducir*) lead; carry away, take away; (*cuentas, libros; la anotación en los naipes*) keep; (*la correspondencia con una persona*) carry on; (*un drama a la pantalla*) put on; (*buena o mala vida*) lead; (*aguantar*) bear, stand for; (*castigo*) suffer; get, obtain; win; (*cierto precio*) charge; (*traje, vestido*) wear; (*armas*) bear; (*cierto tiempo*) have been, e.g., **llevo ocho días en cama** I have been in bed for a week; (*ropa*) **a todo llevar** for all kinds of wear; **llevar** (*cierto tiempo*) **a** (*uno*) to be older than (*someone*) by (*a certain age*); (*cierta distancia*) **a** (*uno*) to be ahead of (*someone*) by (*a certain distance*); (*cierto peso*) **a** (*uno*) to be heavier than (*someone*) by (*a certain weight*); **llevar a las antenas** to put on the air; **llevarla hecha** to have it all figured out; **llevar puesto** to wear, to have on; **llevar** + *pp* to have + *pp*, e.g., **lleva conseguidas muchas victorias** he has won many victories ‖ *ref* to carry away; take, take away; carry off; win; get along; **llevarse algo a alguien** to take something away from someone

lloradue•los *mf* (*pl* -**los**) crybaby, sniveler

lloralásti•mas *mf* (*pl* -**mas**) poverty-crying skinflint

llorar *tr* to weep over; mourn, lament ‖ *intr* to weep, cry; (*los ojos*) water, run

llorera *f* crying; sobbing

lloriquear *intr* to whine, to whimper

lloriqueo *m* whining, whimpering

lloro *m* weeping, crying; tears

llo•rón -rona *adj* weeping, crying ‖ *mf* weeper, crybaby ‖ *m* weeping willow; pendulous plume ‖ *f* hired mourner

lloro•so -sa *adj* weepy; sad, tearful

llovedi•zo -za *adj* (*agua*) rain; (*techo*) leaky

llover §47 *tr* (*enviar como lluvia*) to rain ‖

intr to rain; **como llovido** unexpectedly; **llueva o no** rain or shine; **llueve** it is raining ‖ *ref* (*el techo*) to leak
llovido *m* stowaway
llovizna *f* drizzle
lloviznar *intr* to drizzle

llovizno•so -sa *adj* moist, damp (*from drizzle*); drizzly
lluvia *f* rain; rain water; (*copia, muchedumbre*) (fig) shower, downpour; **lluvia ácida** acid rain; **lluvia radiactiva** fallout, radioactive fallout
lluvio•so -sa *adj* rainy

M

M, m (eme) *f* fifteenth letter of the Spanish alphabet
m. *abbr* **mañana, masculino, meridiano, metro, minuto, muerto**
maca *f* flaw, blemish; bruise (*on fruit*); spot, stain; hammock
maca•co -ca *adj* ugly, misshapen ‖ *m* — **macaco de la India** rhesus
macadamizar §60 *tr* to macadamize
macadán *m* macadam
macana *f* cudgel, club; drug on the market; nonsense; (Arg) botch; (Arg) lie, trick
macanear *intr* to fib, lay it on; (Col, Ven) to manage (well)
macanu•do -da *adj* terrific, swell, grand; (Col, Ecuad) strong, husky
macarrón *m* macaroon; **macarrones** macaroni
macear *tr* to mace, hammer ‖ *intr* to pester, bore
macelo *m* slaughterhouse
macero *m* macebearer
maceta *f* stone hammer; flowerpot; flower vase; (*de herramienta*) handle; (*de cantero*) hammer; (Mex) head
macfarlán *m* inverness cape
macilen•to -ta *adj* pale, wan, gaunt
macillo *m* hammer (*of piano*)
macis *m* mace (*spice*)
macizar §60 *tr* to fill in, fill up
maci•zo -za *adj* solid; massive ‖ *m* solid; flower bed; bulk, mass; massif; wall space
macu•co -ca *adj* (Chile) sly, cunning; (Arg, Chile, Ven) important, notable; (Ecuad) old, worthless; (Arg, Chile, Peru) strong, husky ‖ *m* (Arg, Bol, Col) overgrown boy
mácula *f* spot; stain; blemish; trick, deception
macha *f* (Bol) drunkenness; (Arg) joke; (Bol) mannish woman
machaca *mf* pest, bore ‖ *f* crusher
machacar §73 *tr* to crush, mash, pound ‖ *intr* to pester, bore
macha•cón -cona *adj* boring, tiresome, importunate ‖ *mf* bore
machada *f* flock of billy goats; stupidity
machado *m* hatchet
machamartillo — **a machamartillo** solidly, firmly, lastingly
machaque•ro -ra *adj* tiresome, boring ‖ *mf* bore

machar *tr* to crush, grind, pound ‖ *ref* (Bol, Ecuad) to get drunk
machete *m* machete, cane knife
machi *mf* (Chile) quack, healer
machihembrar *tr* (*ensamblar a ranura y lengüeta*) to feather; (*ensamblar a caja y espiga*) mortise
machina *f* derrick, crane; pile driver; (P-R) merry-go-round
machismo *m* machismo; male chauvinism
machista *m* male chauvinist
macho *adj invar* (*animal, planta, herramienta*) male; strong, robust; dull, stupid ‖ *m* sledge hammer; abutment, pillar; male; he-mule; dullard; (*del corchete*) hook; (mach) male piece; (coll) he-man; (C-R) blond foreigner; **macho cabrío** he-goat, billy goat; **macho de aterrajar** or **macho de terraja** (mach) tap, screw tap
machona *f* (Arg, Bol, Ecuad, Guat) mannish woman
macho•rro -rra *adj* barren, sterile ‖ *f* barren woman; (Mex) mannish woman
machucar §73 *tr* to beat, pound, bruise
machu•cho -cha *adj* sedate, judicious; elderly
madamita *m* (coll) sissy
madeja *f* hank, skein; tangle of hair; (*hombre flojo*) jellyfish; **madeja sin cuenda** hopeless tangle
madera *m* Madeira wine ‖ *f* wood; piece of wood; knack, flair; makings; **madera aserradiza** lumber; **madera contrachapada** plywood; **madera de sierra** lumber; **madera laminada** plywood; **tener madera de** to have what it takes to
maderada *f* raft, float
maderaje *m* or **maderamen** *m* woodwork
maderería *f* lumberyard
madere•ro -ra *adj* lumber ‖ *m* lumberman; carpenter; log driver
madero *m* log, beam; ship, vessel; blockhead
madrastra *f* stepmother; bother
madraza *f* doting mother
madre *adj* mother ‖ *f* mother; matron; womb; main sewer; river bed; dregs; sediment; **madre adoptiva** foster mother; **madre de leche** wet nurse; **madre patria** mother country, old country; **madre política** mother-in-law; stepmother; **sacar de madre** to annoy, to upset

‖
ma

madreperla f (*molusco*) pearl oyster; (*nácar*) mother-of-pearl

madreselva f honeysuckle

madriga•do -da adj twice-married; (*toro*) that has sired; worldly-wise

madriguera f burrow, lair, den

madrile•ño -ña adj Madrid || mf native or inhabitant of Madrid

madrina f godmother; patroness, protectress; prop, shore, brace; joke; leading mare; **madrina de boda** bridesmaid; **madrina de guerra** war mother

madrugada f early morning, dawn; early rising

madruga•dor -dora adj early-rising || mf early riser

madrugar §44 intr to get up early; be out in front

madurar tr to ripen; mature; think out || intr to ripen; mature

madurez f ripeness; maturity

madu•ro -ra ripe; mature

maestra f teacher; elementary girls' school; **maestra de escuela** schoolmistress

maestranza f arsenal, armory; navy yard; order of equestrian knights

maestría f mastery; mastership

maes•tro -tra adj master; masterly; chief; main; (*perro*) trained || m master; teacher; (*en la música y la pintura*) maestro; **maestro de capilla** choirmaster; **maestro de ceremonias** master of ceremonies; **maestro de equitación** riding master; **maestro de escuela** elementary schoolteacher; **maestro de esgrima** fencing master; **maestro de obras** master builder || f see **maestra**

Magallanes m Magellan

magancear intr (Col, Chile) to loaf around

magan•to -ta adj dull, spiritless

magia f magic

magiar adj & mf Magyar; Hungarian

mági•co -ca adj magic || mf magician, wizard || f magic

magín m fancy, imagination

magisterio m teaching; teachers

magistrado m magistrate

magistral adj masterly

magnáni•mo -ma adj magnanimous

magnesio m magnesium; (phot) flashlight

magnéti•co -ca adj magnetic

magnetismo m magnetism

magnetizar §60 tr magnetize

magneto m & f magneto

magnetofón m or **magnetófono** m tape recorder

magnetoscopia f video recorder

magnificar §73 tr to magnify; exalt

magnífi•co -ca adj magnificent

magnitud f magnitude

mag•no -na adj great, e.g., **Alejandro Magno** Alexander the Great

mago m magician; soothsayer; (fig) wizard, expert; **Magos de Oriente** Wise Men of the East

ma•gro -gra adj lean, thin || m loin of pork || f slice of ham

maguar §10 ref (Ven, W-I) to be disappointed

magüeta f heifer

magüeto m young bull

maguey m century plant

magullar tr to bruise || ref to get bruised

magullón m bruise; contusion

mahometa•no -na adj & mf Mohammedan

mahometismo m Mohammedanism

mahones mpl (P-R, S-D) blue jeans

mahonesa f mayonnaise

maído m meow

maitines mpl matins

maíz m maize, Indian corn; **comer maíz** to accept bribes; **maíz en la mazorca** corn on the cob

maizal m cornfield

maja f flashy dame

majada f sheepfold; dung, manure

majaderear tr to bother, annoy

majadería f nonsensical remark; bother, nuisance

majade•ro -ra adj pestiferous, stupid || mf bore, dunce || m pestle

majar tr to crush, mash, grind, pound; annoy, bother

majestad f majesty

majestuo•so -sa adj majestic

ma•jo -ja adj sporty; handsome, dashing; pretty, nice; all dressed up || mf sport || m bully || f see **maja**

mal adj apocopated form of **malo,** used only before nouns in masculine singular || adv badly, poorly; wrong; hardly, scarcely; **mal de** short of; **mal que le pese** in spite of him || m evil; damage, harm; wrong; sickness; misfortune; **mal de altura** mountain sickness; **mal de la tierra** homesickness; **mal de mar** seasickness; **mal de piedra** (pathol) stone; **mal de rayos** radiation sickness; **mal de vuelo** airsickness; **por mal de mis pecados** to my sorrow; **tener a mal** to object to; **¡mal haya . . . !** curses on . . . !

mala f mail; mailbag; mailboat

malabarista mf juggler; sneak thief

malacate m whim; (*hoisting machine*) (Mex, Hond) spindle

malaconseja•do -da adj ill-advised

malacrianza f var of **malcriadez**

malagradeci•do -da adj ungrateful

malandante adj unlucky, unfortunate

malandanza f bad luck, misfortune

malan•drín -drina adj evil, wicked || mf scoundrel, rascal

malaria f malaria

malaventura f misfortune

mala•yo -ya adj & mf Malay

mala•zo -za adj perverse; evil; wicked

malbaratar tr to undersell; squander

malcasa•do -da adj mismated; undutiful

malcasar tr to mismate || intr & ref to be mismated

malcaso m treachery

malconten•to -ta adj & mf malcontent

malcriadez f rudeness; bad manners

malcria•do -da adj ill-bred

malcriar §77 tr to spoil, pamper

maldad *f* evil, wickedness

maldecir §11 *tr* to curse || *intr* to curse, damn; **maldecir de** to slander, vilify

maldición *f* malediction, curse; oath, curse

maldispues•to -ta *adj* ill, indisposed; unwilling, ill-disposed

maldi•to -ta *adj* damned, accursed; wicked; (Mex) coarse, crude, indecent; **no saber maldita la cosa de** to not know a single thing about || **el Maldito** the Evil One || *f* (coll) tongue; **soltar la maldita** to talk too much

maleante *adj* wicked, evil || *mf* crook, hoodlum, rowdy

malear *tr* to spoil; corrupt || *ref* to spoil, get spoiled; be corrupted

malecón *m* levee, dike, mole, jetty

maledicencia *f* calumny, slander

maleficiar *tr* to damage, harm; to curse, bewitch, cast a spell on

maleficio *m* curse, spell; witchcraft

maléfi•co -ca *adj* evil; harmful

malentender §51 *tr* to misunderstand

malentendido *m* misunderstanding, misapprehension

malestar *m* malaise, indisposition

maleta *m* bungler; ham bullfighter || *f* valise; **hacer la maleta** to pack up

maletín *m* satchel

malevolencia *f* malice, malevolence

malévo•lo -la *adj* malevolent

maleza *f* thicket, underbrush; weeds

malfuncionamiento *m* malfunction

malgasta•do -da *adj* ill-spent

malgastar *tr* to waste, squander

malgenio•so -sa *adj* ill-tempered, irritable

malhabla•do -da *adj* foul-mouthed

malhada•do -da *adj* ill-starred

malhe•cho -cha *adj* deformed || *m* misdeed

malhe•chor -chora *mf* malefactor || *f* malefactress

malherir §68 *tr* to injure badly

malhumora•do -da *adj* ill-humored

malicia *f* (*maldad*) evil; (*bellaquería, malevolencia*) malice; insidiousness, trickiness; suspicion

malicio•so -sa *adj* evil; malicious; insidious, tricky

malignar *tr* to corrupt, vitiate; spoil

malignidad *f* malignity

malig•no -na *adj* (*malévolo; pernicioso*) malign; (*malicioso; perjudicial*) malignant; (pathol) malignant

malintenciona•do -da *adj* ill-disposed, evil-minded

malmaridada *f* faithless wife

malmeter *tr* to lead astray, misguide; alienate, estrange

ma•lo -la *adj* bad, poor, evil; (*travieso*) naughty, mischievous; (*enfermo*) sick, ill; (*que no es como debiera ser*) wrong; (*inflamado, dolorido*) sore; **a la mala** (Cuba, P-R) by force; (Mex) insincere; (Mex) mean; **estar de malas** to be out of luck; **lo malo es que** the trouble is that; **malo con** or **para con** mean to; **por malas o por buenas** willingly or unwillingly; **ser malo**

de engañar to be hard to trick || **el Malo** the Evil One || *f* see **mala**

malogra•do -da *adj* late, ill-fated

malograr *tr* to miss || *ref* to fail; come to an untimely end

malogro *m* failure, disappointment

maloliente *adj* malodorous, foul-smelling

malón *m* mean trick; (SAm) Indian incursion; (Chile) surprise party

malpara•do -da *adj* hurt; **salir malparado (de)** to fail (in), come out worsted (in)

malparar *tr* to mistreat

malparir *intr* to miscarry, have a miscarriage

malparto *m* miscarriage

malquerencia *f* dislike

malquerer §55 *tr* to dislike

malquistar *tr* to alienate, estrange || *ref* to become alienated

malquis•to -ta *adj* disliked, unpopular

malrotar *tr* to squander

malsa•no -na *adj* unhealthy

malsín *m* mischief-maker

malsonante *adj* obnoxious, odious

malsufri•do -da *adj* impatient

malta *m* malt || *f* asphalt, tar; dark beer; (Chile) premium beer

maltraer §75 *tr* to abuse, ill-treat; call down, scold

maltratar *tr* to abuse, ill-treat, maltreat; damage, spoil

maltre•cho -cha *adj* battered, damaged

malu•co -ca or **malu•cho -cha** *adj* sickish, upset

malva *f* mallow; **malva arbórea** hollyhock, rose mallow; **ser como una malva** to be meek and mild

malva•do -da *adj* evil, wicked || *mf* evildoer

malvarrosa *f* hollyhock, rose mallow

malvavisco *m* marsh mallow

malvender *tr* to sell at a loss

malversación *f* graft, embezzlement, misappropriation

malversar *tr* & *intr* to graft, embezzle

malvezar §60 *tr* to give bad habits to || *ref* to acquire bad habits

malla *f* mesh, meshing; (*de la armadura*) mail; (*traje*) tights; bathing suit

mallete *m* mallet

Mallorca *f* Majorca

mallor•quín -quina *adj* & *mf* Majorcan

mama *f* mamma

ma•má *f* (*pl* **-más**) mamma

mamada *f* suck; sucking; cinch; advantageous deal; easy profit

mama•lón -lona *adj* (Ven, W-I) loafing || *mf* (Cuba) sponger

mamama *f* (Hond) granny

mamamama *f* (Peru) granny

mamar *tr* to suck; learn as a child; swallow; wangle; **mamóla** he was taken in || *intr* to suck || *ref* to swallow; (*obtener sin mérito*) wangle; (SAm) to get drunk; **mamarse a uno** to get the best of someone; take someone in; (Col, Chile, Peru) to do away with someone

mamarracho *m* mess, sight; (*hombre ridículo*) milksop

mamelón m knoll, mound

mamífe•ro -ra adj mammalian ‖ m mammal, mammalian

mamola f chuck (under the chin); **hacer la mamola a** to chuck under the chin; take in, make a fool of

ma•món -mona adj sucking; fond of sucking ‖ mf suckling ‖ m shoot, sucker; (Guat, Hond) club; (Mex) soft cake ‖ f chuck (under chin)

mamonear tr (Guat, Hond) to beat, cudgel; (S-D) to put off, delay; (el tiempo) (S-D) to waste

mamotreto m memo book; batch of papers; hulk, bulk

mampara f screen; folding screen; (Peru) glass door

mamparo m bulkhead

mampostería f rubble, rubblework; masonry, stone masonry

ma•mut m (pl **-muts**) mammoth

manada f (de ganado vacuno) herd, drove; (de ganado lanar) flock; (de lobos) pack; (de gente) gang, troop; (de hierba, trigo, etc.) handful

manade•ro -ra adj flowing ‖ m spring, source; shepherd

manantial adj flowing, running ‖ m spring, source; (fig) source

manar tr to run with ‖ intr to pour forth, run; abound

manaza f big hand

mancar §73 tr to maim, cripple ‖ intr (el viento) (naut) to abate, subside

manca•rrón -rrona adj (caballería) skinny, worn-out; (Chile) tired out, exhausted ‖ m old nag; (Chile, Peru) dam, dike

manceba f mistress, concubine

mancebía f bawdyhouse, brothel; wild oats; youth

mance•bo -ba adj youthful ‖ m youngster; youth, young man; (en una farmacia, barbería, etc.) helper ‖ f see **manceba**

mancerina f saucer with hook to hold chocolate cup

mancilla f spot, blemish

mancillar tr to spot, blemish

man•co -ca adj armless, one-armed; one-handed; defective, faulty ‖ mf cripple ‖ m (Chile) old nag

mancomún — **de mancomún** jointly, in common

mancomunar tr to unite, combine; (fuerzas, caudales, etc.) pool ‖ ref to unite, combine

mancomunidad f association, union; (asociación de provincias) commonwealth

mancornar §61 tr (un novillo) to throw and hold on the ground; (una res vacuna) tie a horn and front leg of; (dos reses) tie together by the horns; (coll) to join, bring together

mancornas or **mancuernas** fpl (Mex) cuff links

mancuernillas fpl (Guat, Hond) cuff links

mancha f spot, stain; (de vegetación) patch; speckle; (fig) stain, blot; **mancha solar** sunspot

manchar tr to spot, stain; speckle; (fig) to stain, disgrace ‖ intr to spot; ¡**mancha!** wet paint!

manda f gift, offer; bequest, legacy

mandade•ro -ra mf messenger ‖ m errand boy

mandado m order, command; errand; **hacer un mandado** to run an errand

manda•más m (pl **-mases**) (slang) big shot; (jefe político) (slang) boss

mandamiento m order, command; (Bib) commandment; (law) writ; **los cinco mandamientos** the five fingers of the hand

mandar tr to order, command; (legar) bequeath; (enviar) send; **mandar a distancia** to operate by remote control; **mandar +** inf to have + inf, e.g., **la mandé leer en voz alta** I had her read aloud ‖ intr to be in command, be the boss; **mandar llamar** to send for; **mandar por** to send for; **mande Vd.** I beg your pardon ‖ ref (un enfermo) to manage to get around; (dos piezas) be communicating; **mandarse con** (otra pieza) to communicate with; be rude to

mandarina f tangerine

mandatario m agent, proxy; chief executive

mandato m mandate; term (of office)

mandíbula f jaw, jawbone; **reír a mandíbula batiente** to roar with laughter

mandil m apron

mando m command; control, drive; **alto mando** (mil) high command; **mando a distancia** remote control; **mando a punta de dedo** finger-tip control; **mando de las válvulas** timing gears; **mando por botón** push-button control; **tener el mando y el palo** to be the boss, rule the roost

mandolina f mandolin

man•dón -dona adj bossy ‖ mf domineering person ‖ m (en las minas) boss, foreman; (en las carreras de caballos) (Chile) starter

mandrágora f mandrake

mandril m (mach) chuck

mandrilar tr to bore

manea f hobble

manear tr to hobble

manecilla f (de reloj) hand; clasp, book clasp; (bot) tendril; (typ) fist, index

manejable adj manageable

manejar tr to manage; handle, wield; (un automóvil) drive ‖ ref to behave; get around, move about

manejo m management; handling; intrigue, scheming; horsemanship; driving; **manejo a distancia** remote control; **manejo doméstico** housekeeping

manera f manner, way; **a la manera de** in the manner of; like; **de manera que** so that; **en gran manera** to a great extent; extremely; **sobre manera** exceedingly

manga f (parte del vestido) sleeve; (tubo de caucho) hose; waterspout; (bridge) game; **en mangas de camisa** in shirt-sleeves; **ir de manga** to be in cahoots; **manga de**

agua waterspout; cloudburst; **manga de camisa** shirt-sleeve; **manga de riego** watering hose; **manga de viento** whirlwind; **manga marina** waterspout; **mangas extras,** profits

mangana f lasso

manganear tr to lasso; (Peru) to annoy, bother

manganeso m manganese

mango m handle; **mango de escoba** broomstick; (aer) stick, control stick

mangonear tr to plunder || intr to loaf around; meddle; dabble

mangosta f mongoose

mangote m sleeve protector

manguera f hose; (tubo de ventilación) funnel

mangueta f fountain syringe; door jamb

manguitero m furrier

manguito m muff; sleeve guard; coffee cake; (mach) sleeve

ma•ní m (pl -níes or -nises) peanut

manía f mania; craze, whim; grudge; **tener manía a** to dislike

maniabier•to -ta adj open-handed

manía•co -ca adj maniac(al) || mf maniac

maníaco-depresi•vo -va adj manic-depressive

maniatar tr to tie the hands of

maniáti•co -ca adj stubborn; queer, eccentric; (entusiasta) crazy || mf crank, eccentric

manicero m peanut vendor

manicomio m madhouse, insane asylum

manicor•to -ta adj closefisted, tight

manicu•ro -ra mf manicure, manicurist || f manicure, manicuring

mani•do -da adj shabby, worn; hackneyed; (culin) high || f haunt, hangout

manifestación f manifestation; (reunión pública para dar a conocer un sentimiento u opinión) demonstration

manifestante mf demonstrator

manifestar §2 tr to manifest; (el Santísimo Sacramento) expose || intr to demonstrate || ref to become manifest

manifies•to -ta adj manifest || m manifesto; (eccl) exposition of the Host; (naut) manifest

manigua f (Mex, W-I) thicket, jungle; **irse a la manigua** (W-I) to revolt

manija f handle; clamp; crank

manilar•go -ga adj ready-fisted; generous

manilla f bracelet; handcuff; manacle

manillar m handle bar

maniobra f handling; lever; maneuver; (naut) gear, tackle

maniobrar intr to work with the hands; maneuver; (rr) to shift

maniota f hobble

manipula•dor -dora mf manipulator || m (telg) key

manipular tr to manipulate

mani•quí m (pl -quíes) manikin, mannequin; (para exponer prendas de ropa) dress form; (de pintores y escultores) lay figure; (fig) puppet; **ir hecho un maniquí** to be a

fashion plate || f (mujer joven que luce los trajes de última moda) mannequin, model

manirro•to -ta adj lavish, prodigal

manivací•o -a adj empty-handed

manivela f crank; **manivela de arranque** starting crank

manjar m dish, food, tidbit, delicacy; lift, recreation

mano m first to play, e.g., **soy mano** I'm first || f hand; (de cuadrúpedo) forefoot; (de pintura) coat; (de papel) quire; (saetilla de reloj u otro instrumento) hand; (lance en un juego) round, hand; (del elefante) trunk; pestle, masher; **a la mano** at hand, on hand; within reach; understandable; **a mano airada** violently; **asidos de la mano** hand in hand; **bajo mano** underhandedly; **caer en manos de** to fall into the hands of; **¡dame esa mano!** put it here!; **dar la mano** to lend a hand; **darse las manos** to join hands; to shake hands; **de las manos** hand in hand; **de primera mano** at first hand; first-hand; **de segunda mano** second-hand; **echar mano de** to resort to; **echar una mano** to lend a hand; to play a game; **en buena mano está** after you, you drink first; **escribir a mano** to take dictation; **escribir a manos de** to write in care of; **estrecharse la mano** to shake hands; **ganarle a uno por la mano** to steal a march on someone; **lavarse las manos de** to wash one's hands of; **llegar a las manos** to come to blows; **malas manos** awkwardness; **mano de gato** cat's-paw; master hand, master touch; **mano de obra** labor; **mano derecha** right-hand man; **mano de santo** sure cure; **¡manos a la obra!** let's get to work!; **manos libres** outside work; **manos limpias** extras, perquisites; clean hands; **manos puercas** graft; **probar la mano** to try one's hand; **tener mano con** to have a pull with; **tener mano izquierda** to be on one's toes; **untar la mano a** to grease the palm of; **venir a las manos** to come to blows; **vivir de la mano a la boca** to live from hand to mouth

manojo m bunch, bundle, handful; **a manojos** in abundance

manopla f gauntlet; postilion's whip; (Chile) knuckles, brass knuckles

manosear tr to finger, paw; muss, rumple; fiddle with; pet || ref to spoon, neck

manotada f slap

manotear tr to slap, smack; (Arg, Mex) to steal, snitch; || intr to gesticulate

manquedad f lack of one or both hands or arms; disability; deficiency

mansalva — a mansalva without risk; without warning; **a mansalva de** safe from

mansarda f mansard, mansard roof

mansedumbre f gentleness, mildness, meekness; tameness

mansión f stay, sojourn; abode, dwelling; **hacer mansión** to stop, stay

man•so -sa adj gentle, mild, meek; tame || m bellwether; farm

manta *f* blanket; heavy shawl; (coll) beating, thrashing; (Chile, Ecuad) poncho; (Col, Mex, Ven) coarse cotton cloth; **a manta de Dios** copiously; **dar una manta a** to toss in a blanket; **manta de coche** lap robe; **manta de viaje** steamer rug; **tirar de la manta** to let the cat out of the bag

mantear *tr* to toss in a blanket; abuse, mistreat

manteca *f* (*grasa de los animales, esp. la del cerdo*) lard; butter; pomade; (*dinero*) (slang) dough; **como manteca** smooth as butter; **manteca de puerco** lard; **manteca de vaca** butter

mantecado *m* custard ice cream, French ice cream

mantecón *m* mollycoddle, milksop

mantel *m* tablecloth; altar cloth

mantelería *f* table linen

mantelillo *m* embroidered centerpiece

mantelito *m* lunch cloth

mantener §71 *tr* to maintain; keep; keep up; sustain, defend ‖ *ref* to keep, remain, continue

mantenida *f* kept woman

mantenido *m* (*hombre que vive a expensas de su mujer*) (Guat, Mex, W-I) gigolo; (Guat, Mex, W-I) sponger

mantenimiento *m* maintenance; food, support, living

manteo *m* mantle, cloak

mantequera *f* churn, butter churn; butter dish

mantequería *f* creamery; delicatessen

mantequilla *f* butter; **mantequilla azucarada** hard sauce; **mantequilla derretida** drawn butter

mantilla *f* mantilla (*silk or lace head scarf*); **mantillas** swaddling clothes

mantillo *m* humus, mold

manto *m* mantle, cloak; (*de chimenea*) mantel; (*ropa talar de algunos religiosos, catedráticos, alumnos*) robe, gown; (fig) cloak

mantón *m* shawl, kerchief

manuable *adj* handy

manual *adj* (*que se hace con las manos*) hand; (*fácil de manejar*) handy; easy; easy to understand; easy-going; manual ‖ *m* manual, handbook; notebook

manubrio *m* handle; crank, winch

manuela *f* open hack (*in Madrid*)

manufactura *f* (*fábrica*) factory; (*obra fabricada*) manufacture

manufacturar *tr* to manufacture

manuscribir §83 *tr* to write by hand

manuscri•to -ta *adj & m* manuscript

manutención *f* maintenance; care, upkeep; shelter, protection

manutener §71 *tr* (law) to maintain, support

manzana *f* apple; (*conjunto aislado de varias casas contiguas*) block, city block; (*remate en un mueble*) knob, finial; **manzana de Adán** (Chile) Adam's apple

manzanar *m* apple orchard

manzanilla *f* camomile; (*aceituna pequeña; vino blanco*) manzanilla (*small olive; white wine*); (*remate en un mueble*) knob, finial

manzano *m* apple tree

maña *f* skill, dexterity; cunning, craftiness; bad habit, vice; (*de lino, cáñamo, etc.*) bunch; sister; **darse maña** to manage, contrive; **hacer maña** (Col) to fool around

mañana *adv* tomorrow; ¡hasta mañana! see you tomorrow!; **pasado mañana** the day after tomorrow ‖ *m* tomorrow; (*tiempo venidero*) morrow ‖ *f* morning; **de mañana** in the morning; **muy de mañana** very early in the morning; **por la mañana** in the morning; **tomar la mañana** to get up early; have a shot of liquor before breakfast

mañanear *intr* to be in the habit of getting up early

mañane•ro -ra *adj* morning; early-rising

mañanica *f* early morning, break of day

mañanita *f* woman's bed jacket

mañear *tr* to manage craftily ‖ *intr* to act with cunning

mañerear *intr* (Arg) to dawdle, dilly-dally

mañería *f* sterility

mañe•ro -ra *adj* clever, shrewd; simple, easy; skittish

ma•ño -ña *mf* (coll) Aragonese ‖ *m* brother ‖ *f* see **maña**

maño•so -sa *adj* skillful, clever; crafty, tricky; vicious

mañuela *f* craftiness, trickiness

mañue•las *mf* (*pl* **-las**) tricky person

mapa *m* map; **mapa itinerario** road map ‖ *f* — **llevarse la mapa** to take the prize

mapache *m* coon, raccoon

mapamundi *m* map of the world; (coll) buttocks, behind

mapurite *m* (CAm) skunk

maque *m* lacquer

maquear *tr* to lacquer; (Mex) to varnish

maqueta *f* (*en tamaño reducido*) maquette; (*en tamaño natural*) mock-up; (*de un libro*) dummy

maquillador *m* (theat) make-up man

maquillaje *m* (theat) make-up

maquillar *tr & ref* to make up

máquina *f* machine; (*motor*) engine; locomotive; plan, project; (fig) machinery; (coll) heap, pile, lot; (Cuba) auto; (Chile) ganging up; **escribir a máquina** to typewrite; **máquina de afeitar** safety razor; **máquina de apostar** gambling machine; **máquina de componer** typesetter; **máquina de coser** sewing machine; **máquina de escribir** typewriter; **máquina de lavar** washing machine; **máquina de sumar** adding machine; **máquina de volar** flying machine; **máquina fotográfica** camera; **máquina sacaperras** slot machine

maquinación *f* machination, scheming

máquina-herramienta *f* (*pl* **máquinas-herramientas**) machine tool

maquinal *adj* mechanical

maquinar *tr* to plot, scheme

maquinaria *f* machinery; applied mechanics

maquinilla *f* windlass, winch; clippers; **maquinilla cortapelos** clippers, hair clippers; **maquinilla de afeitar** safety razor; **maquinilla de rizar** curling iron

maquinista *mf* (*persona que fabrica máquinas*) machinist; (*persona que dirige una máquina o locomotora*) engineer; **segundo maquinista** (naut) machinist

mar *m & f* sea; tide, flood; **alta mar** high seas; **a mares** abundantly, copiously; **arrojarse a la mar** to plunge, take great risks; **baja mar** low tide; **correr los mares** to follow the sea; **hablar de la mar** to talk wildly, talk on and on; **hacerse a la mar** to put to sea; **la mar de** (fig) oceans of, large numbers of; **mar alta** rough sea; **mar ancha** high seas; **mar bonanza** calm sea; **mar Caribe** Caribbean Sea, Caribbean; **mar de las Antillas** Caribbean Sea; **mar de las Indias** Indian Ocean; **mar de nubes** cloud bank; **mar Latino** Mediterranean Sea; **mar llena** high tide; **meter la mar en un pozo** to attempt the impossible; **meterse mar adentro** (fig) to go beyond one's depth

maraña *f* undergrowth, thicket; silk waste; (*de hilo, pelo, etc.*) tangle; trick, scheme; puzzle

marañón *m* cashew

maraño•so -sa *adj* scheming ‖ *mf* schemer

maravilla *f* wonder, marvel; (bot) marigold, calendula; **a las maravillas** or **a las mil maravillas** magnificently; **a maravilla** wonderfully well; **por maravilla** rarely, occasionally

maravillar *tr* to astonish ‖ *ref* to wonder, marvel; **maravillarse con** or **de** to marvel at, wonder at

maravillo•so -sa *adj* wonderful, marvelous

marbete *m* label, tag; baggage check; edge, border; **marbete engomado** sticker

marca *f* mark; (*tipo de producto*) make, brand; (*de tamaño*) standard; score; record; height-measuring device; **de marca** outstanding; **marca de agua** watermark; **marca de fábrica** trademark; **marca de reconocimiento** (naut) landmark, seamark; **marca de taquilla** box-office record; **marca registrada** registered trademark

marca•do -da *adj* marked, pronounced

marcaje *m* (sport) scoring; (sport) interfering; (telp) dialing

marcapaso *m* or **marcapasos** *m* (heart) pacemaker

marcar §73 *tr* to mark; brand; embroider; (*p.ej., un pañuelo*) initial; (*la hora un reloj*) show; (*un tanto*) make, score; (*el número telefónico*) dial ‖ *ref* (*un buque*) to take bearings

marcear *tr* to shear ‖ *ref* to be Marchlike

marcial *adj* martial; gallant, noble

marcia•no -na *adj & mf* Martian

marco *m* frame; framework; (*de pesas y medidas*) standard

marcha *f* march; (*funcionamiento*) running, operation; (*p.ej., de los astros*) course, path; (*desenvolvimiento de un asunto*) course, march, progress; (*grado de velocidad*) rate of speed; (*de los engranajes*) (aut) speed; **cambiar de marcha** to shift gears; **en marcha** on the march; underway;

in motion; **marcha atrás** reverse; **marcha del hambre** hunger march; **marcha directa** high gear; **marcha forzada** (mil) forced march

marchamo *m* customhouse mark; (Arg, Bol) tax on slaughtered cattle

marchante *adj* commercial ‖ *m* dealer, merchant; customer

marchapié *m* running board

marchar *intr* to march; run, work, go; leave, go away; come along, proceed; **marchar en vacío** to idle ‖ *ref* to leave, go away

marchitar *tr* to wilt, wither ‖ *ref* to wilt, wither; languish

marchi•to -ta *adj* withered, faded; (fig) languid

marea *f* tide; tideland; gentle sea breeze; dew; drizzle; **marea alta** high tide; **marea baja** low tide; **marea creciente** or **entrante** flood tide; **marea menguante** ebb tide; **marea muerta** neap tide; **marea viva** spring tide; **rendir la marea** to stem the tide

marea•do -da *adj* nauseated, sick, lightheaded; seasick

mareaje *m* navigation, seamanship; (*de un buque*) course

marear *tr* to sail; annoy, pester ‖ *intr* to be annoying ‖ *ref* to get sick, get giddy; get seasick; be damaged at sea; fade

marejada *f* heavy sea; (*de desorden*) stirring, undercurrent; **marejada de fondo** ground swell

maremagno *m* or **maremágnum** *m* big mess

mareo *m* nausea, dizziness, sickness; seasickness; annoyance

marfil *m* ivory

marfile•ño -ña *adj* ivory

mar•fuz -fuza *adj* (*pl* **-fuces -fuzas**) cast aside, rejected; deceptive

marga *f* marl

margar §44 *tr* to marl

margarita *f* pearl; (bot) daisy; **margarita de los prados** English daisy; **margarita** (*impresora*) (*ordenador*) daisy wheel

margen *m & f* margin; border, edge; marginal note; **al margen de** aloof from; outside of; independent of; aside from; **dar margen para** to give occasion for; **dejar al margen** to leave out; **quedar al margen** to be left out of

marginal *adj* marginal

mariache *m* Mexican band and singers

marica *m* sissy, milksop ‖ *f* magpie

maricón *m* sissy

maridable *adj* marital

maridaje *m* married life; (fig) union

maridar *tr* to combine, unit ‖ *intr* to get married; to live as man and wife

marido *m* husband

mariguana *f* marihuana

mariguanza *f* (Chile) hocus-pocus; (Chile) pirouette; **mariguanzas** (Chile) clowning; (Chile) powwowing

marimacho *m* mannish woman

marimandona *f* queen bee, bossy woman

marimarica *m* sissy

ma
ma

marimorena f fight, row

marina f navy; (*conjunto de buques*) marine, fleet; (*cuadro o pintura*) seascape; shore, seaside; sailing, navigation; **marina de guerra** navy; **marina mercante** merchant marine

marinar tr to marinate, salt; (*un buque*) staff, man ‖ intr to be a sailor

marinera f sailor blouse; (*blusa de niño*) middy, middy blouse

marinería f sailoring; sailors

marine•ro -ra adj sea, marine; seaworthy; seafaring ‖ m mariner, seaman, sailor; **marinero de agua dulce** (*el que ha navegado poco*) landlubber (*person unacquainted with the sea*); **marinero matalote** (*hombre de mar, rudo y torpe*) landlubber (*awkward and unskilled seaman*) ‖ f see **marinera**

marines•co -ca adj sailor; sailorly

mari•no -na adj marine, sea ‖ m mariner, seaman, sailor ‖ f see **marina**

marioneta f marionette

mariposa f butterfly; butterfly valve; wing nut; rushlight; (Col) blindman's buff; **mariposa nocturna** moth

mariposear intr to flit about; be fickle

mariposón m (Cuba, Guat, Mex) fickle flirt

mariquita m sissy, milksop, popinjay ‖ f (ent) ladybird

marisabidilla f bluestocking

mariscal m blacksmith; (mil) marshal; **mariscal de campo** (mil) field marshal

marisco m shellfish; **mariscos** seafood

marisma f swamp, marsh, salt marsh

marisquería f seafood store, seafood restaurant

maríti•mo -ma adj maritime; marine, sea

maritor•nes f (pl -nes) mannish maidservant, wench

marmita f pot, boiler, kettle

marmitón m kitchen scullion

mármol m marble

marmóre•o -a adj marble

marmosete m vignette

marmota f marmot; sleepyhead; worsted cap; **marmota de Alemania** hamster; **marmota de América** ground hog, woodchuck

maroma f hemp rope, esparto rope; acrobatic stunt

maromear intr to perform acrobatic stunts, walk the tight rope; wobble, sway from side to side (*e.g., in politics*); hesitate

marome•ro -ra mf acrobat, tightrope walker; weaseler; opportunist

marqués m marquis; **los marqueses** the marquis and marchioness

marquesa f marchioness, marquise; (*sobre la puerta de un hotel*) marquee

marquesina f cover over field tent; (*sobre la puerta de un hotel*) marquee; locomotive cab

marquetería f cabinetwork, woodwork; (*taracea*) marquetry

marra•jo -ja adj sly, tricky; (*toro*) vicious

marrana f sow; slattern, slut

marranada f piggishness, filth

marranalla f rabble, riffraff

marra•no -na adj base, vile; dirty, sloppy ‖ mf hog ‖ m male hog, boar; filthy person, hog; cad, cur ‖ f see **marrana**

marrar intr to miss, fail; go astray

marras adv long ago; **hacer marras que** (Bol, Ecuad) to be a long time since

marro m game resembling quoits and played with a stone; (*juego de muchachos*) tag; (*ladeo*) dodge, duck; slip, miss

marrón adj invar maroon (*dark-red*); tan (*shoes*) ‖ m maroon; candied chestnut; stone (*used as a sort of quoit*)

marro•quí (pl **-quíes**) adj & mf Moroccan ‖ m morocco, morocco leather

marro•quín -quina adj & mf var of **marroquí**

marrubio m horehound

marrue•co -ca adj & mf Moroccan

Marruecos m Morocco

marrulle•ro -ra adj cajoling, wheedling ‖ mf cajoler, wheedler

Marsella f Marseille

marsopa f or **marsopla** f porpoise

mart. abbr **martes**

marta f pine marten; **marta cebellina** sable, Siberian sable; **marta del Canadá** fisher

Marte m Mars

mar•tes m (pl **-tes**) Tuesday; **martes de carnaval** or **carnestolendas** Shrove Tuesday

martillar tr to hammer; pester, worry ‖ intr to hammer

martillazo m blow with a hammer

martillear tr & intr var of **martillar**

martillero m (Chile) auctioneer

martillo m hammer; auction house; (*persona*) scourge; (mus) tuning hammer; (*de arma de fuego*) cock

martín m — **martín pescador** (pl **martín pescadores**) kingfisher

martinete m drop hammer; pile driver; (*del piano*) hammer

martínico m ghost, goblin

mártir mf martyr

martirio m martyrdom

márts. abbr **mártires**

marullo m surge, swell

marxista adj & mf Marxist or Marxian

marzo m March

mas conj but

más adv more; most; **a lo más** at most, at the most; **a más de** besides, in addition to; **como el que más** as the next one, as well as anybody; **cuando más** at the most; **de más** extra; too much, too many; **estar de más** to be in the way; be unnecessary; be superfluous; **los más de** most of, the majority of; **más bien** rather; **más de** + *número* more than; **más de lo que** + *verbo* more than; **más que** more than; better than; **no . . . más** no longer; **no . . . más nada** nothing more; **no . . . más que** only ‖ prep plus ‖ m more; (*signo de adición*) plus

masa f mass; (*pasta que se forma con agua y harina*) dough; (*masa aplastada*) mash;

nature, disposition; (Chile, Ecuad) puff paste; (*p.ej., de un automóvil*) (elec) ground; **las masas** the masses

masada *f* farm

masadero *m* farmer

masaje *m* massage; **masaje facial** facial

masajear *tr* to massage

masajista *m* masseur ‖ *f* masseuse

masar *tr* to knead; massage

mascar §73 *tr* to chew; mumble, mutter ‖ *ref* (*un cabo*) (naut) to gall

máscara *mf* (*persona*) mask, mummer ‖ *f* mask; (*traje, disfraz*) masquerade; **máscara antigás** gas mask

mascarada *f* masquerade

mascarilla *f* half mask; false face; death mask

mascarón *m* false face; (*persona fea*) fright; (archit) mask; **mascarón de proa** (naut) figurehead

mascota *f* mascot

mascujar *tr* & *intr* to chew with difficulty; mumble

masculi•no -na *adj* masculine; (*sexo*) male; (*traje*) men's ‖ *m* masculine

mascullar *tr* & *intr* to mumble, mutter; to chew with difficulty

masera *f* kneading trough

masilla *f* putty

masita *f* (mil) money withheld for clothing; (Arg, Bol) cake

masón *m* Mason

masonería *f* Masonry

masoquis•to -ta *adj* masochistic ‖ *mf* masochist

mastelero *m* (naut) topmast

masticar §73 *tr* to chew, masticate; meditate on; mumble

mástil *m* (*de una embarcación*) mast; (*de un violín o guitarra*) neck; stalk; (*de pluma*) shaft, stem; upright

mas•tín -tina *mf* mastiff; **mastín danés** Great Dane

mastodonte *m* mastodon

mastuerzo *m* (bot) cress; dolt

masturbación *f* masturbation

masturbar *tr* & *ref* to masturbate

mat. *abbr* **matemática**

mata *f* bush, shrub; blade, sprig; brush, underbrush; **mata de pelo** crop of hair, head of hair; **mata parda** chaparro (*oak*); **saltar de la mata** to come out of hiding

mataca•bras *m* (*pl* -bras) cold blast from the north

matacán *m* dog poison

matacande•las *m* (*pl* -las) candle snuffer

matadero *m* abattoir, slaughterhouse; drudgery

mata•dor -dora *mf* killer ‖ *m* matador; **matador de mujeres** lady-killer

matadura *f* sore, gall

matafue•gos *m* (*pl* -gos) fire extinguisher; (*oficial*) fireman

matalo•bos *m* (*pl* -bos) wolf's-bane

mata•lón -lona *mf* skinny old nag

matalotaje *m* (naut) ship stores; mess, hodgepodge

matamale•zas *m* (*pl* -zas) weed killer

matamari•dos *f* (*pl* -dos) many times a widow

matamo•ros *m* (*pl* -ros) bully

matamos•cas *m* (*pl* -cas) fly swatter; flypaper

matanza *f* slaughter, massacre; butchering; pork products; (CAm) butcher shop; (Ven) slaughterhouse

matape•rros *m* (*pl* -rros) harum-scarum, street urchin

matar *tr* to kill; butcher; (*el fuego, la luz*) put out; (*la cal*) slack; (*el metal*) mat; (*un color*) tone down; (*un naipe*) spot; play a card higher than; (*a un caballo*) gall; bore to death; (*el tiempo, el hambre, etc.*) (fig) to kill ‖ *intr* to kill ‖ *ref* to kill oneself; drudge, overwork; be disappointed; **matarse con** to quarrel with; **matarse por** to struggle for; struggle to

matarratas *m* rat poison; (*aguardiente de mala calidad*) rotgut

matarro•tos *m* (*pl* -tos) (Chile) pawnshop

matasa•nos *m* (*pl* -nos) quack doctor

matasellar *tr* to cancel, postmark

matase•llos *m* (*pl* -llos) postmark

matasie•te *m* (*pl* -te) bully, swashbuckler

matatí•as *m* (*pl* -as) moneylender, pawnbroker

matazar•zas *m* (*pl* -zas) weed killer

mate *adj* dull, flat ‖ *m* checkmate; (SAm) maté; (SAm) maté gourd; **dar mate a** to checkmate; make fun of; **dar mate ahogado a** to stalemate; **mate ahogado** stalemate

matear *tr* to plant at regular intervals; make dull; (Chile) to checkmate ‖ *ref* (*el trigo*) to sprout; (*un perro de caza*) hunt through the bushes

matemáti•co -ca *adj* mathematical ‖ *mf* mathematician ‖ *f* mathematics; **matemáticas** mathematics

materia *f* matter; material, stuff; **materia colorante** dyestuff; **materia de guerra** matériel; **materia prima** or **primera materia** raw material

material *adj* material; (*grosero*) crude ‖ *m* material; (*conjunto de objetos necesario para un servicio*) matériel; (typ) matter, copy; **material de guerra** matériel; **material fijo** (rr) permanent way; **material móvil** or **rodante** (rr) rolling stock; **ser material** to be immaterial

materialismo *m* materialism

materialista *mf* materialist; (Mex) truck driver

materializar §60 *tr* (*beneficios*) to realize

maternal *adj* maternal, mother; (*afectos, cuidados, etc.*) motherly

maternidad *f* maternity; motherhood

mater•no -na *adj* maternal, mother

matinal *adj* morning

matinée *f* matinée; dressing gown, wrapper

ma•tiz *m* (*pl* -tices) shade, hue, nuance

matizar §60 *tr* (*diversos colores*) to blend; (*un color, un sonido*) shade; (*en cuanto al color*) match

matón *m* bully, browbeater

matorral *m* thicket, underbrush

matraca *f* rattle, noisemaker; taunting, bantering; bore, pest; **dar matraca a** to taunt, to tease

matraquear *intr* to make a racket; to taunt, tease

ma·traz *m* (*pl* **-traces**) flask

matre·ro -ra *adj* cunning, shrewd ‖ *m* (SAm) cheat, swindler

matriarca *f* matriarch

matricida *adj* matricidal ‖ *mf* matricide

matricidio *m* matricide

matrícula *f* register, roster, roll; license; registry

matricular *tr & ref* to matriculate

matrimonialmente *adv* as husband and wife

matrimoniar *intr* to marry, get married

matrimonio *m* marriage, matrimony; (*marido y mujer*) married couple; **matrimonio consensual** common-law marriage

ma·triz *adj* (*pl* **-trices**) main, first, mother ‖ *f* matrix; (*de libro talonario*) stub; screw nut; first draft

matrona *f* matron; matronly lady

matronal *adj* matronly

matun·go -ga *adj* skinny, full of sores ‖ *m* old nag

maturran·go -ga *adj* (SAm) poor, clumsy ‖ *m* (SAm) stranger; (SAm) old nag ‖ *f* trickery

Matusalén *m* Methuselah; **vivir más años que Matusalén** to be as old as Methuselah

matute *m* smuggling; smuggled goods; gambling den

matutear *intr* to smuggle

matute·ro -ra *mf* smuggler

matutinal or **matuti·no -na** *adj* morning

maula *mf* lazy loafer; poor pay; tricky person, cheat ‖ *f* junk, trash; remnant; trickery

maulería *f* remnant shop; trickiness

maullar §8 *intr* to meow

maullido *m* or **maúllo** *m* meow

mausoleo *m* mausoleum

máxima *f* maxim; principle

máxime *adv* chiefly, mainly, especially

máxi·mo -ma *adj* maximum; top; superlative ‖ *m* maximum ‖ *f* see **máxima**

may. *abbr* **mayúscula**

maya *f* May queen; English daisy

mayal *m* flail

mayear *intr* to be Maylike

mayestáti·co -ca *adj* royal

mayido *m* meow

mayo *m* May; Maypole

mayonesa *f* mayonnaise

mayor *adj* greater; larger; older, elder; greatest; largest; oldest, eldest; major; elderly; (*calle*) main; (*altar; misa*) high; **hacerse mayor de edad** to come of age; **ser mayor de edad** to be of age ‖ *m* chief, head, superior; **al por mayor** wholesale; **mayor de edad** (*persona de edad legal*) major; **mayores** elders; ancestors, forefathers; **mayor general** staff officer

mayoral *m* boss, foreman; head shepherd; stagecoach driver; (Arg) streetcar conductor

mayorazgo *m* primogeniture; entailed estate descending by primogeniture; first-born son

mayordoma *f* stewardess, housekeeper

mayordomo *m* steward, butler, majordomo

mayoreo *m* wholesale

mayoría *f* (*mayor edad; el mayor número, la mayor parte*) majority; superiority; **alcanzar su mayoría de edad** to come of age; **mayoría cómoda** solid majority; **mayoría de edad** majority

mayoridad *f* majority

mayorista *adj* (Arg, Chile) wholesale ‖ *mf* (Arg, Chile) wholesaler

mayorita·rio -ria *adj* majority

mayormente *adv* chiefly, mainly, mostly

mayúscu·lo -la *adj* (*letra*) capital; awful, tremendous ‖ *f* capital, capital letter

maza *f* mace; heavy drumstick; bore, pedant; **la maza y la mona** constant companions; **maza de gimnasia** Indian club

mazacote *m* barilla; concrete, cement; botched job; tough, doughy food; (coll) bore

mazar §60 *tr* to churn

mazmorra *f* dungeon

mazo *m* mallet, maul; bunch; (*de la campana*) clapper; (*hombre fastidioso*) bore, pest

mazonería *f* stone masonry; (*obra de relieve*) relief; gold or silver embroidery

mazorca *f* ear of corn; cocoa bean; (*husada*) spindleful; (*de un balustre*) spindle; **comer maíz de** or **en la mazorca** to eat corn on the cob

mazorral *adj* coarse, crude

m/c *abbr* **mi cargo, mi cuenta, moneda corriente**

m/cta *abbr* **mi cuenta**

m/cte *abbr* **moneda corriente**

me (used as object of verb) *pron pers* me, to me ‖ *pron reflex* myself; to myself

meada *f* urination, water; urine stain

meadero *m* urinal

meados *mpl* urine

meaja *f* crumb; **meaja de huevo** tread

meandro *m* meander; wandering speech, wandering writing

mear *tr* to urinate on ‖ *intr & ref* to urinate

Meca, La Mecca

¡mecachis! *interj* wow!, geez!

mecáni·co -ca *adj* mechanical; low, mean ‖ *m* (*obrero perito en el arreglo de las máquinas*) mechanic; (*obrero que fabrica y compone máquinas*) machinist; workman, repairman; driver, chauffeur; **mecánicos** (CAm, Cuba, S-D) blue jeans ‖ *f* mechanics; (*aparato que da movimiento a un artefacto*) machinery, works; meanness; **mecánicas** household chores

mecánico-dentista *m* dental technician

mecanismo *m* mechanism, machinery

mecanizar §60 *tr* to mechanize; motorize

mecanógrafa *f* typist

mecanografía *f* typewriting; **mecanografía al tacto** touch typewriting

mecanografiar §77 *tr & intr* to typewrite

mecanógra•fo -fa *mf* typist, typewriter
mecapale•ro -ra *m* (Mex) messenger, porter
mece•dor -dora *adj* swinging, rocking ‖ *m* stirrer; (*columpio*) swing ‖ *f* rocker, rocking chair
mecer §46 *tr* (*un líquido*) to stir; (*la cuna*) rock ‖ *ref* to rock, swing
mecha *f* (*de vela o bujía*) wick; (*tubo de pólvora*) fuse; lock of hair; (*para mechar carne*) slice of bacon; bundle of thread; (Col, Ecuad, Ven) joke
mechar *tr* (*la carne*) to lard, interlard
mechera *f* shoplifter
mechero *m* (*p.ej., de cigarrillos*) lighter, pocket lighter; (*de aparato de alumbrado*) burner; (*de candelero*) socket; shoplifter; **mechero encendedor** pilot, pilot light
mechón *m* cowlick; (Guat) torch
medalla *f* medal; medallion
medallón *m* medallion; (*joya en que se colocan retratos, etc.*) locket
médano *m* dune, sandbank
media *f* stocking; (math) mean; **media corta** (Arg) sock; **media media** (Arg, Ecuad, Ven) sock; **y media** half past, e.g., **las dos y media** half past two
mediación *f* mediation
media•do -da *adj* half over; half-full; **a mediados de** about the middle of; **mediada la tarde** in the middle of the afternoon
media•dor -dora *mf* mediator
mediana *f* long billiard cue
medianería *f* party wall; party fence
mediane•ro -ra *adj* middle; mediating ‖ *mf* mediator; partner; owner of a row house
medianía *f* average; (*persona que carece de dotes relevantes*) mediocrity
media•no -na *adj* middling, medium; average, fair; mediocre ‖ *f* see **mediana**
medianoche *f* midnight; small meat pie
mediante *adj* interceding ‖ *prep* by means of, by virtue of
mediar *intr* to be half over; be in the middle; intercede, mediate; elapse; take place
mediatinta *f* half-tone
medible *adj* measurable
medical *adj* medical
medicamento *m* medicine
medicamento•so -sa *adj* medicinal
medicastro *m* quack
medicina *f* medicine; **medicina general** general medicine
medicinar *tr* to treat ‖ *ref* to take medicine
medición *f* measurement; metering
médi•co -ca *adj* medical ‖ *mf* doctor, physician; **médico de cabecera** family physician; **médico de urgencia** emergency doctor; **médico general** general practitioner
medida *f* measurement; measure; caution, moderation; **a medida de** in proportion to; according to; **a medida que** in proportion as; **en la medida que** to the extent that; **hecho a la medida** custom-made; **medida para áridos** dry measure; **medida para líquidos** liquid measure; **tomarle a uno las medidas** to take someone's measure, size up someone

medidamente *adv* with moderation
medidor *m* measurer; (Mex, SAm) meter
medie•ro -ra *mf* hosier; partner
medieval *adj* medieval
medievalista *mf* medievalist
medievo *m* Middle Ages
me•dio -dia *adj* middle; medium; medieval; half; a half, e.g., **media libra** a half pound; half a, e.g., **media naranja** half an orange; average, mean; mid, in the middle of, e.g., **a media tarde** in mid afternoon, in the middle of the afternoon; **a medias** half; half-and-half; **ir a medias** (con) to go halves (with), go fifty-fifty (with) ‖ *m* middle; medium, environment; step, measure; means; (*en el espiritismo*) medium; (baseball) shortstop; (arith) half; (*del ruedo*) (taur) center; **a medio** half; **en medio de** in the middle of; in the midst of; **justo medio** happy medium, golden mean; **medio ambiente** environment; situation; **medio centro** (*deporte*) center half; **medios de comunicación** mass media; **por medio de** by means of; **quitarse de en medio** to get out of the way ‖ *f* see **media** ‖ **medio** *adv* half
mediocre *adj* mediocre
mediocridad *f* mediocrity
mediodía *m* noon, midday; south; **en pleno mediodía** at high noon; **hacer mediodía** to stop for the noon meal
mediquillo *m* quack
medir §50 *tr* to measure ‖ *intr* to measure ‖ *ref* to act with moderation
meditabun•do -da *adj* meditative
meditar *tr* to meditate; plan, contemplate ‖ *intr* to meditate
mediterráne•o -a *adj* inland ‖ **Mediterráne•o -na** *adj* & *m* Mediterranean
mé•dium *m* (*pl* **-dium** or **diums**) medium
medra *f* growth, prosperity
medrana *f* fear
medrar *intr* to thrive, prosper, improve
medro *m* growth, prosperity; **medros** progress
medro•so -sa *adj* fearful, scared; frightful, terrible
médula *f* or **medula** *f* marrow, medulla; (bot) pith; (fig) pith, gist, essence; **médula espinal** spinal cord
medular *adj* pithy
medusa *f* jellyfish
mefistoféli•co -ca *adj* Mephistophelian
megaciclo *m* megacycle
megáfono *m* megaphone
me•go -ga *adj* meek, gentle, mild
megohmio *m* megohm
Méj. *abbr* **Méjico**
mejica•no -na *adj* & *mf* Mexican
Méjico *m* Mexico; **Nuevo Méjico** New Mexico
meji•do -da *adj* beaten with sugar and milk
mejilla *f* cheek
mejor *adj* better; best; (*licitador*) highest; **a lo mejor** unexpectedly; worse luck; perhaps, maybe; **el mejor día** some fine day ‖ *adv* better; best; **mejor dicho** rather

ma
me

mejora f growth, improvement; higher bid; alteration

mejoramiento m improvement

mejorana f sweet marjoram

mejorar tr to improve; (los licitadores el precio de una cosa) raise; **mejorando lo presente** present company excepted ‖ intr & ref to improve, get better, recover; make progress; (el tiempo) to clear up; **¡que se mejore!** get well!

mejoría f improvement; (en una enfermedad) betterment, recovery

mejunje m brew, potion, mixture

mela•do -da adj honey-colored ‖ m thick cane syrup

melancolía f (tristeza vaga) melancholy; (depresión moral) melancholia

melancóli•co -ca adj melancholy

melaza f molasses

melcocha f taffy, molasses candy

melchor m German silver

melena f hair falling over the eyes; long hair, loose hair; (del león) mane; (del caballo) forelock; **andar a la melena** to pull each other's hair; to get into a fight; **estar en melena** (coll) to have one's hair down

melga f ridge made by plow; (Col, Chile) plot of ground to be sown; (Hond) small piece of work to be finished

melindre m honey fritter; (dulce de pasta de mazapán) ladyfinger; narrow ribbon; prudery, finickiness

melindrear intr to be prudish, be finicky

melindro•so -sa adj prudish, finicky

melocotón m peach tree; peach

melocotonero m peach tree

melodía f melody

melodio•so -sa adj melodious

melodramáti•co -ca adj melodramatic

melón m melon; (Cucumis melo) muskmelon; blockhead; bald head; **melón de agua** watermelon

melo•so -sa adj sweet, honeyed; gentle, mild, mellow

mella f dent, nick, notch; gap, hollow; harm, injury; **hacer mella a** to have an effect on; **hacer mella en** to harm

mellar tr to dent, nick, notch; harm

melli•zo -za adj & mf twin

membrana f membrane; (del teléfono, micrófono) diaphragm

membrete m note, memo; letterhead; heading; written invitation

membrillero m quince tree

membrillo m quince; quince tree

membru•do -da adj brawny, burly

memeches — **a memeches** (CAm) on horseback

memela f (CAm, Mex) cornmeal pancake

me•mo -ma adj foolish, simple ‖ mf fool, simpleton

memorán•dum m (pl -dum) memorandum book, notebook; (sección en los periódicos) professional services; (papel con membrete) letterhead

memorar tr & ref to remember

memoria f memory; (exposición de ciertos hechos) memoir; account, record; (ordenador) data storage, memory; **de memoria** by heart; **encomendar a la memoria** to commit to memory; **hablar de memoria** (coll) to say the first thing that comes to one's mind; **hacer memoria de** to bring up; **memorias** memoirs; regards

memorial m memorandum book; memorial, petition; (law) brief

memorizar §60 tr to memorize

mena f ore

menaje m household furniture; school supplies

mención f mention

mencionar tr to mention

men•daz adj (pl -daces) mendacious ‖ mf liar

mendicante adj & mf mendicant

mendigante adj begging, mendicant ‖ mf beggar, mendicant

mendigar §44 tr to beg for ‖ intr to beg, go begging

mendi•go -ga mf beggar

mendiguez f begging

mendo•so -sa adj false, wrong

mendrugo m crumb, crust

menear tr to stir, shake, wiggle; (la cola) wag; (un negocio) manage; **peor es meneallo** (i.e., **menearlo**) better keep hands off ‖ ref to shake; wiggle; wag; hustle, bestir oneself

meneo m stirring, shaking; wagging; hustling; drubbing, thrashing

menester m need; want, lack; job, occupation; **haber menester** to be necessary, to be need for; **menesteres** bodily needs; property; implements, tools; **ser menester** to be necessary

menestero•so -sa adj needy ‖ mf needy person

menestra f vegetable soup

menes•tral -trala mf mechanic

meng. abbr **menguante**

mengua f want, lack; poverty; decline; decrease, diminution; **en mengua de** to the discredit of

mengua•do -da adj timid, cowardly; simple, silly; mean, stingy; wretched, miserable; poor, needy; fatal

menguante adj decreasing; declining; waning ‖ f decrease; decline; low water; ebb tide; **menguante de la luna** wane, waning of the moon

menguar §10 tr to diminish, lessen; discredit ‖ intr to diminish, lessen; decline; decrease; (la luna) wane; (la marea) fall

mengue m (coll) devil

menina f young lady in waiting

menino m noble page of the royal family

menor adj less, lesser; smaller; younger; least; smallest; youngest; slightest; minor ‖ m minor; **al por menor** retail; **menor de edad** minor; **por menor** retail; in detail, minutely ‖ f minor premise

Menorca f Minorca

menoría f inferiority, subordination; (tiempo de menor edad) minority

menorista *adj* (Arg, Chile) retail ‖ *mf* (Arg, Chile) retailer

menor•quín -quina *adj & mf* Minorcan

menos *adv* less; fewer; least; fewest; **al menos** at least; **a lo menos** at least; **a menos que** unless; **echar de menos** to miss; **¡menos mal!** lucky break!; **menos mal que** it is a good thing that; **no poder menos de** + *inf* to not be able to help + *ger*; **por lo menos** at least; **tener en menos** to think little of; **venir a menos** to decline; become poor ‖ *prep* less, minus; (*al decir la hora*) of, to, e.g., **las tres menos diez** ten minutes of (or to) three ‖ *m* less; (*signo de resta o sustracción*) minus, minus sign

menoscabar *tr* to lessen, diminish, reduce; damage; discredit

menoscabo *m* lessening, reduction; damage; discredit; **con menoscabo de** to the detriment of

menoscuenta *f* part payment

menospreciable *adj* despicable, contemptible

menospreciar *tr* to underestimate, underrate; scorn, despise

menosprecio *m* underestimation; scorn

mensaje *m* message

mensajería *f* public conveyance; **mensajerías** transportation company; shipping line

mensaje•ro -ra *mf* messenger ‖ *m* harbinger

men•so -sa *adj* (Mex) foolish, stupid

menstruar §21 *intr* to menstruate

menstruo *m* menses

mensual *adj* monthly

mensualidad *f* monthly pay, monthly installment

ménsula *f* bracket; elbow rest

mensurar *tr* to measure

menta *f* mint; **menta piperita** peppermint; **menta romana** or **verde** spearmint

menta•do -da *adj* famous, renowned

mentar §2 *tr* to mention

mente *f* mind

mentecatería or **mentecatez** *f* simpleness, folly

menteca•to -ta *adj* simple, foolish ‖ *mf* simpleton, fool

mentidero *m* hangout; gossip column

mentir §68 *tr* to disappoint ‖ *intr* to lie; be misleading; (*un color*) clash; **¡miento!** my mistake!

mentira *f* lie; error, mistake; **mentira inocente** or **oficiosa** white lie; **parece mentira** it's hard to believe

mentirilla *f* fib, white lie; **de mentirillas** for fun

mentirón *m* whopper

mentiro•so -sa *adj* lying; false, deceptive; full of errors ‖ *mf* liar

men•tís *m* (*pl* **-tís**) insulting contradiction; **dar un mentís a** to give the lie to

mentón *m* chin

me•nú *m* (*pl* **-nús**) menu

menudamente *adv* in detail; at retail

menudear *tr* to make frequently; tell in detail; (Col) to sell at retail ‖ *intr* to happen

frequently, be frequent; go into detail; (Arg) to grow, increase

menudencia *f* smallness; trifle; meticulousness; **menudencias** pork products; (Col, Mex) giblets

menudeo *m* constant repetition; detailed accounting; **al menudeo** at retail

menudillos *mpl* giblets

menu•do -da *adj* small, slight, minute; futile, worthless; meticulous; common, vulgar; petty ‖ *m* innards (*of fowl and other animals*); rice coal; **al menudo** at retail; **a menudo** often; **menudos** small change; **por menudo** in detail; at retail

meñique *adj* little, tiny; (*dedo*) little ‖ *m* little finger

meollo *m* marrow; pith; (*seso*) brain; brains, intelligence; gist, marrow, essence

me•ón -ona *adj* (*niño*) piddling; (*niebla*) dripping

mequetrefe *m* whippersnapper

mercachifle *m* peddler; small dealer

mercadear *intr* to deal, trade

merca•der -dera *mf* merchant; **mercader de grueso** wholesale merchant

mercadería *f* merchandise, commodity; **mercaderías** goods, merchandise

mercado *m* market; **lanzar al mercado** to put on the market; **mercado de valores** stock market; **mercado negro** black market

mercaduría *f* commodity

mercancía *f* trade, commerce; merchandise; piece of merchandise; **mercancías** goods, merchandise ‖ **mercancías** *msg* (*pl* **-as**) freight train

mercante *adj & m* merchant

mercantil *adj* mercantile

mercar §73 *tr* to buy ‖ *intr* to trade

merced *f* pay, wages; favor, grace; **a merced de** at the mercy of; **merced a** thanks to; **merced de agua** distribution of irrigating water; **vuestra merced** your grace

mercena•rio -ria *adj* mercenary ‖ *m* mercenary; day laborer, hireling

mercería *f* haberdashery, notions store; dry-goods store; hardware store

mercología *f* marketing

mercurio *m* mercury

merecer §22 *tr* to deserve, merit; (*lo que se desea*) attain; (*alabanza*) win; (*cierta suma*) be worth; **merecer la pena** to be worthwhile ‖ *intr* to be deserving; **merecer bien de** to deserve the gratitude of

mereci•do -da *adj* deserved ‖ *m* just deserts; **llevar su merecido** to get what's coming to one

mereciente *adj* deserving

merecimiento *m* desert, merit

merendar §2 *tr* to lunch on, have for lunch; keep an eye on, peep at ‖ *intr* to lunch ‖ *ref* to manage to get; (*en el juego*) (Chile) to clean out

merendero *m* lunchroom; picnic grounds

merendona *f* fine spread

merengar §44 *tr* to whip (*cream*)

merengue *m* meringue

mere•triz *f* (*pl* **-trices**) harlot

meridiana *f* lounge, couch; afternoon nap; meridian line; **a la meridiana** at noon

meridia•no -na *adj* meridian; bright, dazzling ‖ *m* meridian ‖ *f* see **meridiana**

meridional *adj* southern ‖ *mf* southerner

merienda *f* lunch, snack; hunchback

meri•no -na *adj* merino; (*cabello*) thick and curly ‖ *mf* merino ‖ *m* merino shepherd; merino wool

mérito *m* merit, desert; value, worth; **hacer mérito de** to make mention of; **hacer méritos** to try to please, put one's best foot forward

merito•rio -ria *adj* meritorious ‖ *m* volunteer worker; unpaid learner, apprentice

merluza *f* (*pez*) hake; drunk, spree

merma *f* decrease, reduction; leakage, shrinkage

mermar *tr* to decrease, reduce ‖ *intr* to decrease, shrink, dwindle

mermelada *f* marmalade

me•ro -ra *adj* mere, pure; (Col, Ven) alone ‖ *m* grouper, jewfish ‖ **mero** *adv* (CAm) almost, soon

merodea•dor -dora *adj* marauding ‖ *m* marauder

merodear *intr* to maraud

mes *m* month; monthly pay; menses; **caer en el mes del obispo** to come at the right time

mesa *f* table; (*mostrador*) counter; (*escritorio*) desk; (*de arma blanca o herramienta*) flat side; (*de escalera*) landing; (*comida*) fare, food; (*conjunto de dirigentes*) board; **alzar la mesa** to clear the table; **hacer mesa limpia** to clean up (*in gambling*); **levantar la mesa** to clear the table; **mesa de batalla** sorting table; **mesa de extensión** extension table; **mesa de juego** gambling table; **mesa de milanos** scanty fare; **mesa de trucos** pool table; **mesa perezosa** drop table; **poner la mesa** to set or lay the table; **tener a mesa y mantel** to feed, support; **tener mesa** to keep open house

mesana *f* (naut) mizzen

mesar *tr* (*los cabellos*) to tear, pull out ‖ *ref* — **mesarse los cabellos** to pull out one's hair; pull out each other's hair

mescolanza *f* jumble, hodgepodge, medley

meseguería *f* harvest watch

mesera *f* waitress

mesero *m* journeyman on monthly pay; waiter

meseta *f* plateau, tableland; (*de escalera*) landing

Mesías *m* Messiah

mesilla *f* mantel, mantelpiece; (*de escalera*) landing; window sill

mesita *f* stand, small table; **mesita portate-léfono** telephone table

mesnada *f* armed retinue; band, company

mesón *m* inn, tavern; (Chile) bar; (Chile) counter

mesone•ro -ra *adj* inn, tavern ‖ *mf* innkeeper, tavern keeper

mester *m* (archaic) craft, trade; (archaic) literary genre; **mester de clerecía** clerical verse of the Middle Ages; **mester de ju-**

glaría popular minstrelsy of the Middle Ages

mesti•zo -za *adj* & *mf* half-breed; (*perro*) mongrel

mesura *f* dignity, gravity; calm, restraint; courtesy, civility

mesura•do -da *adj* dignified, sedate; calm, restrained; polite; moderate, temperate

mesurar *tr* to temper, moderate ‖ *ref* to act with restraint

meta *f* goal

metafonía *f* umlaut

metáfora *f* metaphor

metafóri•co -ca *adj* metaphorical

metal *m* metal; money; (*de la voz*) timbre; condition, quality; (mus) brass; **el vil metal** filthy lucre; **metal blanco** nickel silver; **metal de imprenta** type metal

metale•ro -ra *adj* (Bol, Chile, Peru) metal ‖ *m* (Bol, Chile, Peru) metalworker

metáli•co -ca *adj* metallic ‖ *m* metalworker; cash, coin

metalistería *f* metalwork

metalizar §60 *tr* to make metallic; put a metal coating on; turn into cash ‖ *ref* to become mercenary

metaloide *m* nonmetal

metalurgia *f* metallurgy

metamorfo•sis *f* (*pl* **-sis**) metamorphosis

metano *m* methane

metástasis *f* metastasis

metate *m* (CAm, Mex) flat stone on which corn is ground

metáte•sis *f* (*pl* **-sis**) metathesis

mete•dor -dora *mf* smuggler

metedura *f* disgrace, shame

meteduría *f* smuggling

metemuer•tos *m* (*pl* **-tos**) stagehand; busybody, meddler

meteo *f* weather bureau, weather report

meteóri•co -ca *adj* meteoric

meteoro *m* or **metéoro** *m* meteor; atmospheric phenomenon

meteorología *f* meteorology

meter *tr* to put, place; insert; (*un ruido*) make; (*miedo*) cause; (*mentiras*) tell; (*chismes, enredos*) start; (*dinero en el juego*) stake; to smuggle; (*un golpe*) strike ‖ *ref* to project; meddle, butt in; **meterse a** to set oneself up as; take it upon oneself to; **meterse con** to pick a quarrel with; **meterse en** to get into; to plunge into; empty into

meticulo•so -sa *adj* meticulous; shy, timid

meti•do -da *adj* close, tight; rich, abundant; meddlesome; **muy metido con** on close terms with; **muy metido en** deeply involved in ‖ *m* push; punch; strong lye; loose leaf; (*tela*) seam

metódi•co -ca *adj* methodic(al)

metodista *adj* & *mf* Methodist

método *m* method

metraje *m* distance or length in meters; (*cine*) **de corto metraje** short; (*cine*) **de largo metraje** full-length

metralla *f* scrap iron; grapeshot; shrapnel

métri•co -ca *adj* metric(al) ‖ *f* prosody

metro *m* meter; ruler; tape measure; subway; **metro plegadizo** folding rule

metrónomo *m* metronome

metrópoli *f* metropolis; mother country

metropolita•no -na *adj* metropolitan ‖ *m* subway; (eccl) metropolitan

Méx. *abbr* **México**

mexcal *m* agave liquor

mexica•no -na *adj & mf* Mexican

México *m* Mexico; **Nuevo México** New Mexico

mezcal *m* var of **mexcal**

mezcla *f* mixture; (*argamasa*) mortar; (*tejido*) tweed

mezclar *tr* to mix; blend ‖ *ref* to mix; (*introducirse uno entre otros*) mingle; intermarry; meddle

mezclilla *f* light tweed

mezcolanza *f* jumble, hodgepodge, medley

mezquinar *tr* to be stingy with ‖ *intr* to be stingy

mezquindad *f* meanness, stinginess; need, poverty; smallness, tininess; wretchedness

mezqui•no -na *adj* mean, stingy; needy, poor; small, tiny; wretched

mezquita *f* mosque

mi *adj poss* my

mí (used as object of a preposition) *pron pers* me ‖ *pron reflex* myself

miar §77 *intr* to meow

miau *m* meow

mica *f* mica; (Guat) flirt; **ponerse una mica** (CAm) to go on a jag

mico *m* long-tailed monkey; libertine; hoodlum; **dar mico** to not keep a date

microbio *m* microbe

microbiología *f* microbiology

microbús *m* (Chile) jitney

microfaradio *m* microfarad

microficha *f* microcard

micro•film *m* (*pl* **-films** or **-filmes**) microfilm

microfilmar *tr* to microfilm

micrófono *m* microphone

microonda *f* microwave

microordenador *m* microcomputer

micropelícula *f* microfilm

microprocesador *m* chip, microprocessor

microscópi•co -ca *adj* microscopic

microscopio *m* microscope

microsurco *adj invar* microgroove ‖ *m* microgroove

microteléfono *m* handset, French telephone

mi•cho -cha *mf* pussy cat

miedo *m* fear, dread; **miedo cerval** great fear; **por miedo de** for fear of; **por miedo (de) que** for fear that; **tener miedo (a)** to be afraid (of); **tener miedo de** to be in fear of, be afraid of; be afraid to

miedo•so -sa *adj* fearful, afraid

miel *f* honey; (*jarabe saturado*) molasses; **dejar con la miel en los labios** to spoil the fun for; **hacerse de miel** to be peaches and cream

mielga *f* lucerne

miembro *m* member; (*extremidad del hombre y los animales*) member, limb

mientes *fpl* mind, thought; wish, desire; **caer en las mientes** or **en mientes** to come to mind; **parar** or **poner mientes en** to reflect on; **venírsele a uno a las mientes** to come to one's mind

mientras *conj* while; whereas; **mientras que** while; whereas; **mientras tanto** meanwhile

miérco•les *m* (*pl* **-les**) Wednesday; **miércoles de ceniza** Ash Wednesday

mies *f* cereal, grain; harvest time; **mieses** grain fields

miga *f* (*porción pequeña*) bit; (*parte más blanda del pan*) crumb; (fig) substance; **hacer buenas migas con** to get along well with; **migas** fried crumbs

migaja *f* bit, piece; (*de inteligencia*) smattering; **migajas** crumbs; leavings

migajón *m* crumb; substance

migar §44 *tr* (*el pan*) to crumb; (*p.ej., la leche*) put crumbs in

migrato•rio -ria *adj* migratory

miguelear *tr* (CAm) to make love to

miguele•ño -ña *adj* (Hond) impolite, discourteous

mijo *m* millet

mil *adj & m* thousand, a thousand, one thousand; **a las mil quinientas** at an unearthly hour

milagre•ro -ra *adj* superstitious; miracle-working

milagro *m* (*hecho sobrenatural*) miracle; (*cosa rara*) wonder; votive offering; **colgar el milagro a** to put the blame on; **vivir de milagro** to have a hard time getting along; have had a narrow escape

milagrón *m* fuss, excitement

milagro•so -sa *adj* miraculous; marvelous, wonderful

milano *m* burr, down; (orn) kite

mil•deu *m* (*pl* **-deues**) mildew

milena•rio -ria *adj* millennial ‖ *m* millennium

milenio *m* millennium

milenrama *f* yarrow

milési•mo -ma *adj & m* thousandth

miliamperio *m* milliampere

milicia *f* militia; soldiery; warfare; military service

milicia•no -na *adj* military ‖ *m* militiaman

miligramo *m* milligram

milímetro *m* millimeter

militante *adj* militant

militar *adj* military; army ‖ *m* soldier, military man ‖ *intr* to fight, go to war; struggle; serve in the army; (*surtir efecto*) militate

militarismo *m* militarism

militarista *adj & mf* militarist

militarizar §60 *tr* to militarize

mílite *m* soldier

milpa *f* (CAm, Mex) cornfield

milla *f* mile

millar *m* thousand

millarada *f* about a thousand; **echar millaradas** to boast about one's wealth

millo *m* millet

millón *m* million

millona•rio -ria *adj* of a million or more inhabitants ‖ *mf* millionaire
mimar *tr* to fondle, pet; pamper, indulge, spoil
mimbre *m & f* (bot) osier; wicker, withe
mimbrear *intr & ref* to sway
mimbre•ño -ña *adj* willowy
mimbrera *f* (bot) osier, osier willow
mimbro•so -sa *adj* osier; (*hecho de mimbre*) wicker
mimeografiar §77 *tr* to mimeograph
mimeógrafo *m* mimeograph
mímica *f* mimicry; sign language
mimo *m* (*entre los griegos y romanos*) mime; fondling, petting; pampering
mimo•so -sa *adj* delicate, tender; finicky, fussy
mina *f* mine; (*de lápiz*) lead; (fig) mine, gold mine, storehouse; underground passage; (SAm) moll; **beneficiar una mina** to work a mine; **mina de carbón** or **mina hullera** coal mine; **voló la mina** the truth is out
minado *m* mine work; (nav) mining
mina•dor -dora *adj* (nav) mine-laying ‖ *m* (mil) miner; (nav) mine layer
minar *tr* to mine; undermine; consume; plug away at ‖ *intr* to mine
minarete *m* minaret
mineraje *m* mining; **mineraje a tajo abierto** strip mining
mineral *adj & m* mineral
mineralogía *f* mineralogy
minería *f* mining; mine operators
mine•ro -ra *adj* mining ‖ *m* miner; mine operator; (fig) source, origin
mingitorio *m* street urinal
min•gón -gona *adj* (Ven) spoiled, pampered
miniar *tr* to paint in miniature; (*un manuscrito*) illuminate
miniatura *f* miniature
miniaturización *f* miniaturization
minifalda *f* miniskirt
míni•mo -ma *adj* minimum; tiny, small, minute; least, smallest ‖ *m* minimum ‖ *f* tiny bit
mini•no -na *mf* kitty, pussy
miniordenador *m* minicomputer
ministerial *adj* ministerial
ministerio *m* ministry, cabinet, government; **formar ministerio** to form a government; **ministerio de Hacienda** Treasury Department (U.S.A.); Treasury (Brit); **ministerio de la Gobernación** Department of the Interior (U.S.A.); Home Office (Brit); **ministerio del Ejército** Department of the Army (U.S.A.); War Office (Brit); **ministerio de Marina** Department of the Navy (U.S.A.); Board of Admiralty (Brit); **Ministerio de Relaciones Exteriores** State Department; Foreign Ministry; **ministerio radiofónico** (theol) radio ministry
ministrar *tr* to administer; furnish
ministro *m* minister; bailiff, constable; **ministro de asuntos exteriores** foreign minister; **ministro de Gobernación** Home Secretary (Brit); **ministro de Hacienda** Secretary of the Treasury (U.S.A.); Chan-cellor of the Exchequer (Brit); **ministro de Justicia** Attorney General (U.S.A.); **primer ministro** prime minister, premier
minorar *tr* to diminish, reduce; weaken
minorati•vo -va *adj & m* laxative
minoría *f* minority
minoridad *f* minority
minorista *m* retailer
minorita•rio -ria *adj* minority
minucia *f* trifle; **minucias** minutiae
minucio•so -sa *adj* minute, meticulous
minué *m* or **minuete** *m* minuet
minúscu•lo -la *adj* (*letra*) small; small, tiny ‖ *f* small letter
minusvalía *f* (physical) handicap
minuta *f* first draft, rough draft; memorandum; menu, bill of fare; roll, list
minutero *m* minute hand
minu•to -ta *adj* minute ‖ *m* minute ‖ *f* see **minuta**
mí•o -a *adj poss* mine; of mine, e.g., **un amigo mío** a friend of mine ‖ *pron poss* mine
miope *adj* near-sighted ‖ *mf* near-sighted person
miopía *f* near-sightedness
mira *f* (*de arma de fuego, telescopio, etc.*) sight; aim, object, purpose; target; watchtower; **estar a la mira** to be on the lookout; **poner la mira en** to have designs on
mirada *f* glance, look; **apuñalar con la mirada** to look daggers at; **mirada de soslayo** side glance
miradero *m* (*lugar desde donde se mira*) lookout; (*persona o cosa que es objeto de la atención pública*) cynosure
mira•do -da *adj* cautious, circumspect; **bien mirado** highly regarded ‖ *f* see **mirada**
mirador *m* belvedere; bay window, oriel
miramiento *m* considerateness, courtesy, regard; look; **miramientos** fuss, bother
miranda *f* eminence, vantage point
mirar *tr* to look at, watch; consider, contemplate; **mirar bien** to look with favor on; **mirar por encima** to glance at ‖ *intr* to look, glance; ¡**mira!** look out!; **mirar a** to look at, glance at; face, overlook; aim at; aim to; **mirar por** to look after ‖ *ref* to look at oneself; look at each other; **mirarse en ello** to watch one's step; **mirarse en una persona** to be all wrapped up in a person
mirasol *m* sunflower
miríada *f* myriad
mirilla *f* peephole; (*para dirigir visuales*) target; (phot) finder
miriñaque *m* hoop skirt, crinoline; bauble; trinket; (Arg) cowcatcher
mirística *f* nutmeg tree
mirlar *ref* to try to look important
mirlo *m* blackbird; solemn look; **mirlo blanco** rare bird; **soltar el mirlo** to start to jabber
mirmidón *m* tiny fellow, nincompoop
mi•rón -rona *adj* onlooking; nosy ‖ *mf* onlooker; (*de una partida de juego*) kibitzer; busybody

mirra f myrrh
mirto m myrtle
misa f mass; **cantar misa** to say mass; **como en misa** in dead silence; **misa cantada** High Mass; **misa de prima** early mass; **misa mayor** High Mass; **misa rezada** Low Mass
misal m missal
misantropía f misanthropy
misántropo m misanthrope
misar intr to say mass; to hear mass
misario m acolyte
misceláne·o -a adj miscellaneous ‖ f miscellany
miserable adj miserable, wretched; mean, stingy; despicable, vile ‖ mf cur, cad; wretch; miser
miseran·do -da adj pitiful
miserear intr to be stingy
miseria f misery, wretchedness; poverty; stinginess; trifle, pittance; **comerse de miseria** to live in great poverty
misericordia f compassion, mercy, pity
misericordio·so -sa adj merciful
míse·ro -ra adj miserable, wretched ‖ mf wretch
mísil m missile; **mísil crucero** cruise missile; **mísil dirigible** guided missile
misión f mission; ration for harvesters; **ir a misiones** to go away as a missionary
misional adj missionary
misionario m missionary; envoy, messenger
misionero m missionary
misi·vo -va adj & f missive
mismísi·mo -ma adj very same, self-same
mis·mo -ma adj & pron indef same; own, very; -self, e.g., **ella misma** herself; myself, e.g., **yo mismo** I myself; yourself, himself, herself, itself; **así mismo** likewise, also; **casi lo mismo** much the same; **lo mismo** just the same; **lo mismo me da** it's all the same to me; **mismo . . . que** same . . . as; **por lo mismo** for that very reason ‖ mismo adv right, e.g., **ahora mismo** right now; **aquí mismo** right here
mistela f flavored brandy; needled must, spiked must
misterio m mystery; **hablar de misterio** to talk mysteriously
misterio·so -sa adj mysterious
misticismo m mysticism
místi·co -ca adj mystic(al) ‖ mf mystic
mistificación f hoax, mystification
mistificar §73 tr to hoax, mystify
mistifori m hodgepodge
misturera f (Peru) flower girl
mita f mite, cheese mite; (SAm) Indian slave labor; (turno en el trabajo) (Arg, Chile) shift, turn
mitad f half; middle; **a (la) mitad de** halfway through; **cara mitad** better half; **en la mitad de** in the middle of; **la mitad de** half the; **mitad y mitad** half-and-half; **por la mitad** in half, in the middle
míti·co -ca adj mythical
mitigar §44 tr to mitigate, appease, allay
mitin m (pl **mitins** or **mítines**) meeting, rally

mito m myth
mitología f mythology
mitológi·co -ca adj mythological
mitón m mitten
mitra f chimney pot; (eccl) miter
mixtificación f hoax, mystification
mixtificar §73 tr to hoax, mystify
mixtifori m hodgepodge
mixtión f mixture
mix·to -ta adj mixed ‖ m compound number; sulphur match; explosive compound
mixtura f mixture
mixturar tr to mix
mixturera f (Peru) flower girl
miz interj here, pussy!, here, kitty!
mízcalo m edible milk mushroom
m/l abbr **mi letra**
m/n abbr **moneda nacional**
mobilia·rio -ria adj personal (property) ‖ m furniture, suite of furniture
moblaje m furniture, suite of furniture
moblar §61 tr to furnish
moca m Mocha coffee ‖ f (Ecuad) mudhole; (Mex) wineglass
mocador m handkerchief
mocar §73 tr to blow the nose of ‖ ref to blow one's nose
mocarro m snot
mocasín m moccasin
mocear intr to act young; sow one's wild oats
mocedad f youth; wild oats
mocerío m young people
mocero adj masc woman-crazy
mocetón m strapping young fellow
mocetona f buxom young woman
mocil adj youthful
moción f motion, movement; (en junta deliberante) motion; **hacer** or **presentar una moción** to make a motion
mocionante mf mover
mocionar tr & intr to move
moci·to -ta adj young ‖ mf youngster
moco m (humor segregado por una membrana mucosa) mucus; (mocarro) snot; (extremo del pabilo de una vela) snuff; **a moco de candil** by candle light; **llorar a moco tendido** to cry like a baby; **moco de pavo** crest of a turkey; trifle; (bot) cockscomb
moco·so -sa adj snotty, snively; rude, ill-bred; flip, saucy; mean, worthless ‖ mf brat
mochar tr to butt; chop off; (Arg) to rob; (Col) to fire
mochil m errand boy for farmers in the field
mochila f knapsack, haversack; tool bag; (mil) ration
mochín m (slang) executioner
mo·cho -cha adj blunt, stub, flat; (árbol) topped; stub-horned; mutilated; (Mex) reactionary ‖ m butt end
mochuelo m (orn) little owl; (de una o más palabras) omission; **cargar con el mochuelo** or **tocarle a** (uno) **el mochuelo** to get the worst of a deal
moda f fashion, mode, style; **a la moda de** after the fashion of, in the style of; **alta**

mi
mo

moda haute couture; **de moda** in fashion; **fuera de moda** out of fashion; **pasar de moda** to go out of fashion

modales *mpl* manners

modalidad *f* manner, way, nature, kind

modelar *tr* to model; to form, shape; to mold ‖ *ref* to model; **modelarse sobre** to pattern oneself after

modelo *adj invar* model, e.g., **ciudad modelo** model city ‖ *mf* model, mannequin, fashion model ‖ *m* model, pattern; form, blank; equal, peer; style; **modelo estrella** (aut) crest-line model

modera•do -da *adj* moderate

moderador *m* regulator; (*para retardar el efecto de los neutrones*) moderator

moderar *tr* to moderate, control, restrain ‖ *ref* to moderate, control oneself, restrain oneself

modernizar §60 *tr* to modernize

moder•no -na *adj* modern

modestia *f* modesty

modes•to -ta *adj* modest

modicidad *f* moderateness, reasonableness

módi•co -ca *adj* moderate, reasonable

modificante *adj* modifying ‖ *m* (gram) modifier

modificar §73 *tr* to modify

modismo *m* idiom

modista *f* dressmaker; **modista de sombreros** milliner

modistería *f* dressmaking; ladies' dress shop

modistilla *f* dressmaker's helper; unskilled dressmaker

modisto *m* ladies' tailor

modo *m* manner, mode, way; (gram) mood, mode; **al** or **a modo de** like, on the order of; **de buen modo** politely; **de ese modo** at that rate; **de tal modo que** with the result that; **de modo que** so that; and so; **de ningún modo** by no means; **de todos modos** anyhow, at any rate; **en cierto modo** after a fashion; **modo de empleo** usage; instructions for use; **modo de ser** nature, disposition; **por modo de** as, by way of; **sobre modo** extremely; **uno a modo de** a sort of, a kind of

modorra *f* drowsiness, heaviness

modorrar *tr* to make drowsy ‖ *ref* to get drowsy, fall asleep; (*la fruta*) get squashy

modo•rro -rra *adj* drowsy, heavy; dull, stupid; (*fruta*) squashy ‖ *f* see **modorra**

modo•so -sa *adj* quiet, well-behaved

modrego *m* boor, awkward fellow

modulación *f* modulation; **modulación de altura** or **de amplitud** amplitude modulation; **modulación de frecuencia** frequency modulation

modular *tr* & *intr* to modulate

módulo *m* module; **módulo lunar** lunar lander, lunar module

modulo•so -sa *adj* harmonious

mofa *f* jeering, scoffing, mockery

mofeta *f* skunk; (*gas pernicioso que se desprende de las minas*) blackdamp, firedamp

moflete *m* fat cheek, jowl

mofletu•do -da *adj* fat-cheeked

mo•gol -gola *adj* & *mf* Mongol, Mongolian

mogollón *m* — **comer de mogollón** (coll) to sponge

mo•gón -gona *adj* one-horned, broken-horned

mogote *m* knoll, hillock; stack of sheaves; budding antler

mohatra *f* fake sale; cheating

mohien•to -ta *adj* moldy, musty; (*hierro*) rusty

mohín *m* face, grimace

mohina *f* annoyance, displeasure

mohi•no -na *adj* sad, melancholy, moody; (*caballo, buey, vaca*) black, black-nosed ‖ *mf* hinny ‖ *m* blue magpie ‖ *f* see **mohina**

moho *m* mold, must; (*del hierro*) rust; laziness; **no dejar criar moho** to keep in constant use, to use up quickly

moho•so -sa *adj* moldy, rusty; (*hierro*) rusty; (*chiste*) stale

Moisés *m* Moses

moja•do -da *adj* wet; (*p.ej., por la lluvia*) drenched, soaked; (*húmedo*) moist; (phonet) liquid ‖ *m* (Mex) wetback

mojar *tr* to wet; (*la lluvia a una persona*) drench, soak; (*humedecer*) dampen, moisten; (*ensopar*) dunk; stab ‖ *intr* — **mojar en** to get mixed up in ‖ *ref* to get wet; get drenched, get soaked

mojarrilla *mf* jolly person

moje *m* or **mojete** *m* sauce, gravy

mojicón *m* muffin, bun; slap in the face

mojiganga *f* masquerade, mummery; clowning

mojigatería or **mojigatez** *f* hypocrisy; prudery, sanctimoniousness

mojiga•to -ta *adj* hypocritical; prudish, sanctimonious ‖ *mf* hypocrite; prude, sanctimonious person

mojinete *m* (*de un muro*) coping; (*de un tejado*) ridge; (Arg) gable; (Chile) gable end

mojón *m* boundary stone, landmark; (*montón sin orden*) pile, heap; (*guía en desplobado*) road mark; (*porción de excremento humano*) turd

moldar *tr* to mold; put molding on

molde *m* mold; pattern; cast, stamp, matrix; (*persona*) model, ideal; (*letra*) **de molde** printed; **venir de molde** to be just right

moldear *tr* to mold; (*vaciar*) cast; put molding on

moldura *f* molding

moldurar *tr* to put molding on

mole *adj* soft ‖ *m* (Mex) stew seasoned with chili sauce ‖ *f* bulk, mass

molécula *f* molecule

molende•ro -ra *mf* miller, grinder ‖ *m* chocolate grinder; (CAm) grinding table

moler §47 *tr* (*granos*) to grind, mill; annoy, harass, weary; tire out, fatigue; chew; **moler a palos** to beat up

molesquina *f* moleskin

molestar *tr* to disturb, molest; bother, annoy; tire, weary ‖ *ref* to bother; be annoyed; **molestarse en** to take the trouble to

molestia _f_ disturbance, discomfort; annoyance, bother, nuisance

moles•to -ta _adj_ bothersome, troublesome; boring, tedious; bored, tired

molesto•so -sa _adj_ bothersome

moleteado _m_ knurl

moletear _tr_ to knurl

molibdeno _m_ molybdenum

molicie _f_ softness; effeminacy; voluptuous living

moli•do -da _adj_ ground; exhausted, worn out

molienda _f_ grinding, milling; (_cantidad que se muele de una vez_) grist; (_molino_) mill; bore, annoyance; fatigue, weariness

molimiento _m_ grinding; weariness

moline•ro -ra _adj_ mill ‖ _m_ miller ‖ _f_ miller's wife

molinete _m_ little mill; ventilating fan; (_juguete de papel_) windmill; (_movimiento que se hace con el bastón_) twirl; (_con la espada_) flourish; (naut) windlass; (_rueda de cohetes_) (Mex) pinwheel

molinillo _m_ hand mill; **molinillo de café** coffee grinder

molino _m_ mill; **luchar con los molinos de viento** to tilt at windmills; **molino de sangre** animal-driven mill; **molino de viento** windmill; **molino harinero** gristmill, flour mill

moloc _m_ (Ecuad) mashed potatoes

molondrón _m_ lazy bum; (Ven) large inheritance, much money

molusco _m_ mollusk

mollar _adj_ soft, tender; mushy, squashy; (_carne_) lean; profitable; gullible, easily taken in

mollear _intr_ to give, yield; bend

molleja _f_ gizzard; **criar molleja** to get lazy; **mollejas** sweetbread

mollejón _m_ grindstone; big fat loafer; good-natured fellow

mollera _f_ crown (_of the head_); brains, sense; **cerrado de mollera** stupid; **duro de mollera** stubborn

mollete _m_ muffin

molli•no -na _adj_ drizzly ‖ _f_ drizzle

mollizna _f_ drizzle

momentáne•o -a _adj_ momentary

momento _m_ moment; **a cada momento** constantly, all the time; **al momento** at once; **de un momento a otro** at any moment

momería _f_ clowning

mome•ro -ra _adj_ clowning ‖ _mf_ clown

momia _f_ mummy

momificar §73 _tr_ to mummify

mo•mio -mia _adj_ lean, skinny ‖ _m_ extra; (_ganga_) bargain; sinecure ‖ _f_ see **momia**

momo _m_ face, grimace; (coll) caress

mona _f_ female monkey; Barbary ape; ape, copycat; drunkenness; (_persona_) drunk; (taur) guard for right leg; **dormir la mona** to sleep off a drunk; **pillar una mona** to go on a jag; **pintar la mona** to put on airs

monacal _adj_ monachal

monacato _m_ monkhood

monacillo _m_ altar boy, acolyte

monada _f_ monkeyshine; (_gesto_) face, grimace, monkey face; darling; cuteness; flattery; folly, childishness

monaguillo _m_ altar boy, acolyte

monaquismo _m_ monasticism

monarca _m_ monarch

monarquía _f_ monarchy

monárqui•co -ca _adj_ monarchic(al) ‖ _mf_ monarchist

monasterio _m_ monastery

monásti•co -ca _adj_ monastic

monda _f_ pruning, trimming; parings, peelings; beating, whipping

mondadien•tes _m_ (_pl_ -tes) toothpick

mondadura _f_ pruning, trimming; **mondaduras** peelings

mondar _tr_ to clean; prune, trim; peel, pare, hull, husk; (_quitar con engaño los bienes a_) fleece; beat, whip

mon•do -da _adj_ clean; pure; **mondo y lirondo** pure, unadulterated ‖ _f_ see **monda**

mondonga _f_ kitchen wench

mondongo _m_ intestines, insides; (_del hombre_) guts

monear _intr_ to act like a monkey; boast ‖ _ref_ (Hond) to plug away; (Hond) to punch each other

moneda _f_ coin; money; **la Moneda** the government of Chile; **moneda corriente** currency; common knowledge; **moneda falsa** counterfeit; **moneda menuda** change; **moneda metálica** or **sonante** specie; **moneda suelta** change; **pagar en la misma moneda** to pay back in one's own coin

monedar _tr_ to coin, mint

monedero _m_ moneybag; **monedero falso** counterfeiter

monería _f_ monkeyshine; cuteness; childishness

mones•co -ca _adj_ apish

moneta•rio -ria _adj_ monetary

mon•gol -gola _adj_ & _mf_ Mongol, Mongolian

monigote _m_ lay brother; rag figure, stuffed form; botched painting, botched statue; sap, boob

monipodio _m_ collusion, deal, plot

monís _m_ trinket; **monises** money, dough

mónita _f_ cunning, smoothness, slickness

monitor _m_ monitor

monja _f_ nun; **monjas** lingering sparks in burning paper

monje _m_ monk

monjía _f_ monkhood

monjil _adj_ nunnish ‖ _m_ nun's dress

mono -na _adj_ cute, nice; blond; (_cabello_) red ‖ _m_ monkey, ape; (_traje de faena_) coveralls; whippersnapper, squirt; (_drogas_) withdrawal symptom; (coll) clown; (taur) attendant of picador; (Chile) pyramid of fruit or vegetables; **estar de monos** to be on the outs; **mono de Gibraltar** Barbary ape ‖ _f_ see **mona**

monóculo _m_ monocle

monogamia _f_ monogamy

monografía _f_ monograph

monograma _m_ monogram

monolíti•co -ca _adj_ monolithic

mo
mo

monologar §44 *intr* to soliloquize
monólogo *m* monologue
monomanía *f* monomania
monomio *m* monomial
mono•no -na *adj* cute, sweet
monopatín *m* scooter
monoplano *m* monoplane
monopolio *m* monopoly
monopolizar §60 *tr* to monopolize
monorriel *m* monorail
monosabio *m* (taur) attendant of picador
monosílabo *m* monosyllable
monoteísta *adj* monotheistic || *mf* monotheist
monotipia *f* or monotipo *m* monotype
monotonía *f* monotony
monóto•no -na *adj* monotonous
monóxido *m* monoxide
monseñor *m* monseigneur; (eccl) monsignor
monserga *f* gibberish
monstruo *m* monster
monstruosidad *f* monstrosity
monstruo•so -sa *adj* monstrous
monta *f* sum, total; de poca monta of little account
montacar•gas *m* (*pl* -gas) hoist, freight elevator
montadero *m* horse block
montadura *f* mounting; (*de una caballería de silla*) harness; (*engaste*) setting, mount
montaje *m* montage; setting up; (mach) assembly; (rad) hookup
montanero *m* forest ranger
montante *m* post, upright; (*suma*) amount; (*hueco cuadrilongo sobre una puerta*) transom; (*espadón*) broadsword || *f* flood tide
montaña *f* mountain; mountain country; la Montaña the Province of Santander, Spain; montaña de hielo iceberg; montaña rusa roller coaster
monta•ñés -ñesa *adj* mountain || *mf* mountaineer, highlander
montaño•so -sa *adj* mountainous
montapla•tos *m* (*pl* -tos) dumbwaiter
montar *tr* to mount, get on; (*un caballo, una bicicleta, los hombros de una persona*) ride; (*un servicio*) set up, establish; (*un fusil*) cock; (*una piedra preciosa*) set, mount; (*el caballo a la yegua*) cover; (*un reloj*) wind; (elec) to hook up; (mach) to assemble, to mount; (*la guardia*) (mil) to mount; (*un cabo*) (naut) to round; (*un buque*) (naut) to command; (*importar*) amount to || *intr* to mount; get on top; weigh, be important; tanto monta it's all the same || *ref* to mount; get on top; montarse en cólera to fly into a rage
monta•raz *adj* (*pl* -races) backwoods; wild, untamed || *m* forester, warden
monte *m* mountain, mount; woods, woodland; obstruction, interference; backwoods, wilds; bank, kitty; dirty head of hair; andar al monte to take to the woods; monte alto forest; monte bajo thicket, brushwood; monte de piedad pawnshop; monte pío pension fund for widows and orphans; mutual benefit society; monte tallar tree farm

montear *tr* to hunt, track down; make a working drawing of; arch, vault
montecillo *m* mound, hillock
montepío *m* pension fund for widows and orphans; mutual benefit society
montera *f* cloth cap; glass roof; wife of hunter; bullfighter's black bicorne; (Hond) drunk, jag
montería *f* hunting, big-game hunting; hunting party; (Bol, Ecuad) canoe to shoot the rapids; (Mex) lumberman's camp
monterilla *f* (naut) moonsail
montero *m* hunter, huntsman; (Mex) sawmill
montés or montesi•no -na *adj* wild (*e.g., goat*)
montículo *m* mound, hillock
montilla *f* montilla (*a pale dry sherry*)
monto *m* sum, total
montón *m* pile, heap; (*de gente*) crowd; lot, great deal, great many; a, de, or en montón taken together; a montones in abundance; ser del montón to be quite ordinary
montonera *f* heap, pile; band of mounted rebels
montonero *m* guerrilla
montu•no -na *adj* wooded; wild, untamed, rustic
montuo•so -sa *adj* wooded, woody; rugged, hilly
montura *f* (*cabalgadura*) mount; (*de una cabalgadura*) harness; seat, saddle; (*de una piedra preciosa, de un instrumento astronómico*) mounting; (*de gafas*) frame
monumento *m* monument
monzón *m* monsoon
moña *f* doll; mannequin; ribbon, hair ribbon; drunk, jag
moño *m* topknot; crest, top; (Col) caprice, whim; (*de caballo*) (Chile) forelock; moños frippery
moquear *intr* to snivel
moqueo *m* snivel, sniveling
moquero *m* handkerchief
moquete *m* punch in the nose
moquillo *m* runny nose; (vet) distemper
moquita *f* mucus, snivel
mor *m* — por mor de for love of; because of
mora *f* black mulberry; blackberry; brambleberry; white mulberry
morada *f* dwelling; stay, sojourn
mora•do -da *adj* purple, mulberry || *f* see morada
moral *adj* moral || *m* black mulberry tree || *f* (*ciencia de la conducta; conducta*) morals; (*espíritu, confianza*) morale; (*p.ej., de una fábula*) moral
moraleja *f* moral
moralidad *f* morality; (*de una fábula*) moral
morar *intr* to live, dwell
moratoria *f* moratorium
mórbi•do -da *adj* (*perteneciente a la enfermedad*) morbid; soft, delicate, mellow
morbo *m* sickness, illness; morbo gálico syphilis; morbo regio jaundice
morbo•so -sa *adj* morbid, diseased

morcilla *f* blood pudding, black pudding; (*añadidura que mete un actor en su papel*) gag

mor•daz *adj* (*pl* **-daces**) mordant, mordacious, sharp, caustic

mordaza *f* (*pañuelo o instrumento que se pone en la boca para impedir el hablar*) gag; (*aparato que sirve para apretar*) clamp, jaw; pipe vise; **poner la mordaza a** to gag

mordedura *f* bite

morder §47 *tr* to bite; nibble at; wear away; gossip about, ridicule; (Mex, Ven, W-I) to cheat ‖ *intr* to bite; take hold

mordicar §73 *tr & intr* to bite, sting

mordida *f* bite; (*para eludir una multa*) (Mex) payoff

mordiente *m* mordant

mordiscar §73 *tr* to nibble at ‖ *intr* to nibble, gnaw away; champ

mordisco *m* nibble, bite; champ

more•no -na *adj* brown, dark-brown; dark, dark-complexioned; (*de la raza negra*) black; mulato ‖ *mf* black person; mulato ‖ *m* brunet ‖ *f* brunette; loaf of brown bread; rick of new-mown hay

morería *f* Moorish quarter; Moorish land

moretón *m* black-and-blue mark

morfina *f* morphine

morfinomanía *f* morphine habit, drug habit

morfinóma•no -na *adj* addicted to morphine, addicted to drugs ‖ *mf* morphine addict, drug addict

morfología *f* morphology

moribun•do -da *adj* moribund, dying ‖ *mf* dying person

morillo *m* andiron, firedog

morir §30 & §83 *intr* to die; (*el fuego, la luz, etc.*) die away; **morir ahogado** to drown; **morir de risa** to die laughing; **morir de viejo** to die of old age; **morir helado** to freeze to death; **morir quemado** to burn to death; **morir vestido** to die a violent death ‖ *ref* to die; be dying; die away, die out; (*una pierna, un brazo*) go to sleep; **morirse por** to be crazy about; be dying to

moris•co -ca *adj* Morisco, Moorish ‖ *mf* Moor converted to Christianity (*after the Reconquest*); (*descendiente de mulato y española o de mulata y español*) (Mex) Morisco

mo•ro -ra *adj* Moorish; (*vino*) unwatered ‖ *mf* Moor; **hay moros en la costa** there's trouble brewing; **moro de paz** man of peace ‖ *f* see **mora**

moro•cho -cha *adj* strong, robust; (SAm) dark

morón *m* mound, knoll; moron

moron•do -da *adj* bare, stripped

moronga *f* (CAm, Mex) sausage

moro•so -sa *adj* slow, tardy; (*retrasado en el pago de deudas*) delinquent

morra *f* (*de la cabeza*) top, crown; (*de gato*) purr; **andar a la morra** to come to blows

morrada *f* slap, punch; (*golpe dado con la cabeza*) butt

morral *m* nose bag; (*saco de cazador*) game bag; (*de soldado, viandante, etc.*) knapsack; boor, lout

morralla *f* small fish; (*gente de escaso valor*) rabble, trash; (*mezcla de cosas inútiles*) junk, trash; (Mex) change, small change

morriña *f* blues, melancholy; **morriña de la tierra** homesickness

morriño•so -sa *adj* sickly; (coll) blue, melancholy

morrión *m* helmet; (mil) bearskin

morro *m* (*cosa redonda*) knob; (*monte redondo*) knoll; (*guijarro*) pebble; (*saliente que forman los labios*) snout; **beber a morro** (slang) to drink out of the bottle; **estar de morro** or **de morros** to be on the outs; **poner morro** to make a snout; **por el morro** just like that, simply so

morrocotu•do -da *adj* strong, thick, heavy; (*asunto, negocio*) weighty; big, enormous; (Col) rich, wealthy; (Chile) graceless, monotonous

morsa *f* walrus

mortaja *f* shroud, winding sheet; cigarette paper; (carp) mortise

mortal *adj* mortal; deadly; mortally ill; deathly pale; sure, conclusive ‖ *m* mortal

mortalidad *f* mortality; death rate

mortandad *f* massacre, mortality, butchery

morteci•no -na *adj* dead; dying; failing, weak; **hacer la mortecina** to play dead, to play possum

mortero *m* (*vaso que sirve para machacar; argamasa*) mortar; (*en los molinos de aceite*) nether stone; (arti) mortar

mortífe•ro -ra *adj* deadly

mortificar §73 *tr* to vex, annoy, bother; mortify ‖ *ref* (Mex) to be mortified, be embarrassed

mortual *m* (CAm, Mex) inheritance

mortuo•rio -ria *adj* mortuary, funeral; (*casa*) of the deceased ‖ *m* (archaic) funeral

morueco *m* ram

moru•no -na *adj* Moorish

mosai•co -ca *adj* Mosaic ‖ *m* tile, paving tile; mosaic; **mosaico de madera** marquetry

mosca *f* fly; (*barba*) imperial; cash, dough; disappointment; bore, nuisance; **aflojar la mosca** to shell out, to fork out; **mosca borriquera** horsefly; **mosca de las frutas** fruit fly; **mosca del vinagre** fruit fly; **mosca muerta** hypocrite; **moscas** sparks; **moscas volantes** spots before the eyes; **papar moscas** to gape, gawk

moscareta *f* (orn) flycatcher

moscona *f* hussy, brazen woman

Moscú Moscow

mosquear *tr* (*moscas*) to shoo; beat, whip; answer sharply ‖ *intr* (Mex) to sneak a ride ‖ *ref* to shake off annoyances; take offense

mosquero *m* flytrap; fly swatter

mosquete *m* musket

mosquetear *intr* (Arg, Bol) to snoop

mosquete•ro -ra *adj* idle ‖ *mf* (Arg, Bol) bystander, snooper ‖ *m* musketeer ‖ *f* wallflower

mosquetón *m* snap hook

mosquitera *f* or **mosquitero** *m* mosquito net; fly net

mosquito *m* (*Culex pungens*) mosquito; (*insecto parecido al anterior*) gnat; (coll) tippler

mostacera *f* mustard jar

mostacho *m* mustache; spot on the face

mostachón *m* macaroon

mostaza *f* mustard; (*semilla; munición*) mustard seed; **subírsele a** (*uno*) **la mostaza a las narices** to fly into a rage

mosto *m* must; **mosto de cerveza** wort

mostrador *m* (*en las tiendas*) counter; (*en las tabernas*) bar; (*de reloj*) dial

mostrar §61 *tr* to show ‖ *ref* to show; show oneself to be

mostrear *tr* to spot, splash

mostren•co -ca *adj* ownerless, unclaimed; (*que no tiene casa ni hogar*) homeless; (*animal*) stray; slow, dull; fat, heavy ‖ *mf* dolt, dullard

mota *f* mote, speck; (*en el paño*) burl, knot; hill, rise; defect, fault; (Mex, W-I) powder puff

mote *m* device, emblem, riddle; (*apodo*) nickname; (Chile) mistake; (SAm) stewed corn

motear *tr* to speck, speckle; dapple, mottle ‖ *intr* (Peru) to eat stewed corn

motejar *tr* to call names; scoff at, make fun of; **motejar de** to brand as

motín *m* mutiny, riot

motinista *m* (Peru) rioter

motivar *tr* to explain, account for; rationalize

moti•vo -va *adj* motive ‖ *m* motive, reason; (mus) motif; **con motivo de** because of; on the occasion of; **de su motivo propio** on his own accord; **motivo conductor** (mus) leitmotif; **motivos** grounds, reasons; (Chile) finickiness, prudery

moto *m* guidepost, landmark ‖ *f* motorcycle

motobomba *f* fire truck, fire engine

motocarro *m* three-wheel delivery truck

motocicleta *f* motorcycle

motocine *m* drive-in theater

motogrúa *f* truck crane

motoli•to -ta *adj* simple, stupid; **vivir de motolito** to be a sponger, live on other people ‖ *f* (orn) wagtail; (Ven) decent woman

motón *m* (naut) block, pulley

motonáuti•co -ca *adj* motorboat ‖ *f* motorboating

motonaustismo *m* (sport) motorboating

motonave *f* motor launch; motor ship

motoneta *f* motor scooter; moped; light three-wheel delivery truck

mo•tor -tora *adj* motor, motive ‖ *m* motor, engine; **motor a chorro** jet engine; **motor de arranque** (aut) starter, starting motor; **motor de cuatro tiempos** four-cycle engine; **motor de dos tiempos** two-cycle engine; **motor de explosión** internal-combustion engine; **motor de reacción** jet engine; **motor fuera de borda** outboard motor; **motor térmico** heat engine ‖ *f* small motor boat

motorista *mf* motorist; motorcyclist; motorcycle racer ‖ *m* motorcycle policeman; motorman

motorización *f* motorization

motorizar §60 *tr* to motorize

motosegadora *f* power mower

motovelero *m* (naut) motor sailer

motriz *adj fem* (*fuerza*) motive

movedi•zo -za *adj* shaky, unsteady; fickle, inconstant; (*arena*) quick, shifting

mover §47 *tr* to move; (*la cola el perro*) wag; (*discordia*) stir up ‖ *intr* to move; abort, miscarry; bud, sprout ‖ *ref* to move; be moved

movible *adj* movable; fickle, inconstant, changeable

móvil *adj* movable, mobile; fickle, changeable; moving ‖ *m* moving body; cause, motive

movilizar §60 *tr* to mobilize

movimiento *m* movement, motion; **movimiento feminista** women's liberation (movement)

moza *f* girl, lass; mistress, concubine; maid; kitchen maid; (*en algunos juegos de naipes*) last hand; wash bat; **buena moza** or **real moza** good-looking woman; **moza de fortuna** or **del partido** prostitute; **moza de taberna** barmaid

mozalbete *m* lad, young fellow

mozárabe *adj* Mozarabic ‖ *mf* Mozarab

mo•zo -za *adj* young, youthful; single, unmarried ‖ *m* youth, lad; (*camarero*) waiter; (*criado*) servant; porter; (*cuelgacapas*) cloak hanger; **buen mozo** or **real mozo** handsome fellow; **mozo de caballerías** hostler, stable boy; **mozo de café** waiter; **mozo de cámara** (naut) cabin boy; **mozo de ciego** blind man's guide; **mozo de cordel** street porter, public errand boy; **mozo de cuadra** stable boy; **mozo de cuerda** public errand boy; **mozo de espuelas** groom who walks in front of master's horse; **mozo de esquina** street porter, public errand boy; **mozo de estación** station porter; **mozo de estoques** (taur) sword handler; **mozo de hotel** porter, bellhop; **mozo de paja y cebada** hostler (*at an inn*); **mozo de restaurante** waiter ‖ *f see* **moza**

mozue•lo -la *mf* youngster ‖ *m* lad, young fellow ‖ *f* lass, young woman

m/p *abbr* **mi pagaré**

m/r *abbr* **mi remesa**

Mro. *abbr* **Maestro**

M.S. *abbr* **manuscrito**

mtd. *abbr* **mitad**

mu *m* moo ‖ *f* bye-bye; **ir a la mu** to go bye-bye

muaré *adj invar* & *m* moiré

muca•mo -ma *mf* (Arg, Urug) house servant ‖ *f* (Arg, Chile, Urug) servant girl

muceta *f* (*de los doctores en los actos universitarios*) hood; (eccl) mozzetta

muco•so -sa *adj* mucous ‖ *f* mucous membrane

múcura *f* (Bol, Col, Ven, W-I) water pitcher; (Col) thickhead

muchacha *f* girl; young woman; servant girl

muchachada *f* youthful prank

muchachez *f* boyishness, girlishness

mucha•cho -cha *adj* young, youthful ‖ *mf* youth, young person; servant ‖ *m* boy ‖ *f* see **muchacha**

muchedumbre *f* crowd, multitude, flock

mu•cho -cha *adj* much, a lot of, a great deal of; (*tiempo*) a long ‖ *pron* much, a lot, a great deal ‖ **mu•chos -chas** *adj & pron* many ‖ **mucho** *adv* much; (*más de lo regular*) hard; often; a long time; **con mucho** by far; **ni con mucho** or **ni mucho menos** not by a long shot; **por mucho que** however much; **sentir mucho** to be very sorry; **tener mucho de** to take after

muda *f* change; change of voice; change of clothes; (*cambio de plumas o de piel*) molt, molting; molting season; **estar de muda** to be changing one's voice; **estar en muda** (coll) to keep too quiet; **hacer la muda** to molt; **muda de ropa** change of clothing

mudable *adj* fickle, inconstant

mudada *f* change of clothing; move, change of residence

mudadi•zo -za *adj* fickle, inconstant

mudanza *f* change; (*cambio de domicilio*) moving; fickleness, inconstancy; (*en el baile*) figure

mudar *tr* to change ‖ *intr* to change; **mudar de** to change ‖ *ref* to change; change clothing; move; move away; have a bowel movement; **mudarse de** to change

mudez *f* muteness, dumbness; continued silence

mu•do -da *adj* dumb, mute; (phonet) voiceless, surd ‖ *mf* mute ‖ *f* see **muda**

mueblaje *m* furniture, suite of furniture

mueble *adj* movable ‖ *m* piece of furniture; (*p.ej., de un aparato de radio*) cabinet; **muebles** furniture

mueblería *f* furniture shop

mueblista *mf* furniture dealer

mueca *f* face, grimace

muela *f* grindstone; knoll, mound; back tooth; grinder; **muela cordal** wisdom tooth; **muela de esmeril** emery wheel; **muela del juicio** wisdom tooth; **muela de molino** millstone

muellaje *m* dockage, wharfage

muelle *adj* soft; voluptuous ‖ *m* (*pieza elástica de metal*) spring; (*obra en la orilla del mar o de un río*) dock, wharf, pier; (rr) freight platform; **muelle real** mainspring

muérdago *m* mistletoe

muérgano *m* (Col, Ven) piece of junk, drug on the market; (Col, Ecuad, Ven) boor, nobody

muermo *m* (vet) glanders

muerte *f* death; **cada muerte de obispo** once in a blue moon; **dar la muerte a** to put to death; **de mala muerte** crummy, not much of a; **estar a la muerte** to be at death's door; **muerte chiquita** nervous shudder

muer•to -ta *adj* dead; (*apagado, marchito*) flat, dull; (*cal, yeso*) slaked; **muerto de** dying of; **muerto por** crazy about ‖ *mf*

corpse, dead person ‖ *m* (*en los naipes*) dummy; **hacerse el muerto** to play possum; play deaf; **tocar a muerto** to toll

muesca *f* nick, notch; (carp) mortise

muestra *f* (*porción de un producto que sirve para conocer su calidad*) sample; model, specimen; (*rótulo sobre una tienda u hotel*) sign; show, exhibition, indication; (*esfera de reloj*) dial, face; (*parada del perro para levantar la caza*) set; (*ademán, porte*) bearing; **dar muestras de** to show signs of

mugido *m* moo, low; bellow, roar

mugir §27 *intr* (*la res vacuna*) to moo, low; (*con ira*) bellow; (*el viento, el mar*) roar

mugre *f* dirt, filth, grime

mugrien•to -ta *adj* dirty, filthy, grimy

muguete *m* lily of the valley

mujer *f* woman; (*esposa*) wife; **mujer de gobierno** housekeeper; **mujer de su casa** good manager; **mujer fatal** vamp; **ser mujer** to be a grown woman

mujeren•go -ga *adj* (Arg, Urug, CAm) effeminate

mujerie•go -ga *adj* feminine, womanly; effeminate, womanish; fond of women; **a mujeriegas** sidesaddle ‖ *m* flock of women

mujeril *adj* womanly; womanish

mújol *m* mullet, striped mullet

mula *f* mule, she-mule; junk, trash; (Arg) ingrate, traitor; (Arg) hoax; (C-R) jag, drunk; (Guat, Hond) anger, rage; (Mex) drug on the market; (Ven) flask; **devolver la mula** (CAm) to pay back in one's own coin; **echar la mula a** (Mex) to rake over the coals; **en mula de San Francisco** on shank's mare

mulada *f* drove of mules

muladar *m* dungheap, dunghill; dump, trash heap; filth

mula•to -ta *adj & mf* mulatto

muleta *f* (*palo para apoyarse al andar*) crutch; muleta (*cloth attached to a stick, used by matador*); support, prop; snack

muletilla *f* cross-handle cane; pet word, pet phrase; (taur) muleta

mulo *m* mule

multa *f* fine

multar *tr* to fine

multicopista *m* copying machine

multigrafiar §77 *tr* to multigraph

multígrafo *m* multigraph

multilateral *adj* multilateral

multiláte•ro -ra *adj* multilateral

multinacionales *mpl* multinational corporations

múltiple *adj* multiple, manifold ‖ *m* manifold; **múltiple de admisión** intake manifold; **múltiple de escape** exhaust manifold; **múltiple de uso** multipurpose

multiplicar §73 *tr, intr & ref* to multiply

multiplicidad *f* multiplicity

múlti•plo -pla *adj* multiple, manifold ‖ *m* (math) multiple

multitud *f* multitude

mulli•do -da *adj* soft, fluffy ‖ *m* stuffing (*for cushions, pillows, etc.*) ‖ *f* bedding, litter (*for animals*)

mo
mu

mullir §13 *tr* to soften, fluff up; (*la cama*) beat up, shake up; (*la tierra*) loosen around a stalk ‖ *ref* to get fluffy

munda•no -na *adj* mundane, worldly; (*mujer*) loose

mundial *adj* world-wide, world

mundillo *m* arched clotheshorse; cushion for making lace; warming pan; guelder-rose, cranberry tree; world (*of artists, scholars, etc.*)

mundo *m* world; **así va el mundo** so it goes; **desde que el mundo es mundo** since the world began; **echar al mundo** to bring into the world; to bring forth; **el otro mundo** the other world; **gran mundo** high society; **medio mundo** (*mucha gente*) half the world; **nada del otro mundo** nothing special, no great thing; **tener mucho mundo** to know one's way around; **todo el mundo** everybody; **ver mundo** to see the world, to travel

mundonuevo *m* peep show

munición *f* munition, ammunition; **de munición** (mil) government issue; (coll) done hurriedly

municionar *tr* to supply with munition

municipal *adj* municipal ‖ *m* policeman

munícipe *m* citizen

municipio *m* municipality; town council

munidad *f* susceptibility to infection

munífi•co -ca *adj* munificent

muñeca *f* (*figurilla infantil con que juegan las niñas*) doll; (*parte del cuerpo humano en donde se articula la mano con el brazo*) wrist; manikin, dress form; tea bag; (*mujer linda; mozuela frívola*) doll; **muñeca de trapo** rag doll, rag baby; **muñeca parlante** talking doll

muñeco *m* doll (*representing a male child or animal*); dummy, manikin; fop, effeminate fellow; (fig) puppet; (coll) lad, little fellow

muñequera *f* strap for wrist watch

muñequilla *f* (mach) chuck; (Arg, Chile) young ear of corn

muñidor *m* heeler, henchman

muñir §12 *tr* to convoke, summon; (pol) to fix, rig

muñón *m* (*p.ej., de un brazo cortado*) stump; (mach) journal, gudgeon; **muñón de cola** dock

mural *adj* mural

muralla *f* wall, rampart

murar *tr* to surround with a wall

murciélago *m* bat

murga *f* tin-pan band; trouble, bother; torment

muriente *adj* dying, faint

murmujear *tr* & *intr* to mumble

murmullar *intr* to murmur

murmullo *m* murmur; whisper; (*de aguas corrientes*) ripple; (*del viento*) rustle

murmurar *tr* to murmur, mutter; murmur at ‖ *intr* to murmur, mutter; whisper; (*las aguas corrientes*) ripple, purl; (*el viento*) rustle; gossip

muro *m* wall; **muro del sonido** sound barrier

murria *f* (coll) blues, dejection

musa *f* muse; **las Musas** the Muses; **soplarle a uno la musa** to be inspired to write poetry; be lucky at games of chance

musaraña *f* shrew, shrewmouse; bug, worm; **mirar a las musarañas** to stare vacantly

músculo *m* muscle

musculo•so -sa *adj* muscular

muselina *f* muslin

museo *m* museum; **museo de cera** waxworks

muserola *f* noseband

mus•go -ga *adj* dark-brown ‖ *m* moss

musgo•so -sa *adj* mossy, moss-covered

música *f* music; (*músicos que tocan juntos*) band; noise, racket; **con la música a otra parte** don't bother me, get out; **música celestial** nonsense; **música de fondo** background music; **poner en música** to set to music

musical *adj* musical

musicalidad *f* musicianship

music-hall *s* vaudeville theater, burlesque show

músi•co -ca *adj* musical ‖ *mf* musician; **músico mayor** bandmaster ‖ *f* see **música**

musicología *f* musicology

musicólo•go -ga *mf* musicologist

musiquero *m* music cabinet

musitar *tr* & *intr* to mutter, mumble

muslime *adj* & *mf* Muslim

muslo *m* thigh; (*de ave cocida*) leg, drumstick

mustiar *ref* to wither

mus•tio -tia *adj* sad, gloomy; (*marchito*) withered; (Mex) hypocritical; (Mex) standoffish

musul•mán -mana *adj* & *mf* Muslim

mutación *f* mutation; unsettled weather, change of weather; (biol) mutation, sport; (theat) change of scene

mutila•do -da *adj* crippled ‖ *mf* cripple

mutilar *tr* to mutilate; cripple

múti•lo -la *adj* mutilated; crippled

mutis *m* (theat) exit; **hacer mutis** (theat) to exit; keep quiet

mutual *adj* mutual

mutualidad *f* mutuality; mutual benefit; mutual benefit association

mutualista *mf* member of a mutual benefit association

mu•tuo -tua *adj* mutual, reciprocal

muy *adv* very; very much; too, e.g., **es muy tarde para dar un paseo tan largo** it is too late to take such a long walk; **muy de noche** late at night; **Muy señor mío** Dear Sir

N, n (ene) *f* sixteenth letter of the Spanish alphabet

n/ *abbr* **nuestro**

N. *abbr* **Norte**

nabo *m* turnip; (naut) mast

Nabucodonosor *m* Nebuchadnezzar

nácar *m* mother-of-pearl

nacara•do -da *adj* mother-of-pearl

nacatamal *m* (CAm, Mex) meat-filled tamale

nacela *f* nacelle

nacencia *f* birth; growth, tumor

nacer §22 *intr* to be born; bud, take rise, originate, appear; dawn ‖ *ref* bud, shoot, sprout; (*abrirse la ropa por las costuras*) split

naci•do -da *adj* natural, innate; apt, proper, fit; **nacida** née or nee ‖ *m* human being; growth, boil

naciente *adj* incipient; resurgent; (*sol*) rising ‖ *m* east

nacimiento *m* birth; origin, beginning, fountainhead; descent, lineage; (*de agua*) spring, fountainhead; crèche

nación *f* nation

nacional *adj* national; domestic ‖ *mf* national ‖ *m* militiaman

nacionalidad *f* nationality

nacionalismo *m* nationalism

nacionalista *adj & mf* nationalist

nacionalizar §60 *tr* to nationalize ‖ *ref* to be naturalized; become a citizen

nacista *adj & mf* Nazi

naco *m* (Arg, Bol, Urug) black rolled leaf of chewing tobacco; (Arg) fear, scare; (Col) stewed corn; (Col) mashed potatoes

nada *pron indef* nothing, not . . . anything; **de nada** don't mention it, you're welcome ‖ *adv* not at all

nadaderas *fpl* water wings

nada•dor -dora *adj* swimming, floating ‖ *mf* swimmer ‖ *m* (Chile) fishnet float

nadar *intr* to swim; float; fit loosely or too loosely; **nadar en** (*riqueza*) to be rolling in; (*suspiros*) be full of; (*sangre*) be bathed in

nadear *tr* to destroy, wipe out

nadería *f* trifle

nadie *pron indef* nobody, not . . . anybody; **nadie más** nobody else; **nadie más que** nobody but ‖ *m* nobody; **un don nadie** a nonentity

nado — **a nado** swimming, floating; **echarse a nado** to dive in; **pasar a nado** to swim across

nafta *f* naphtha

nagual *m* (Guat, Hond) (*dícese de un animal*) inseparable companion; (Mex) sorcerer, wizard; (Mex) lie

nagualear *intr* (Mex) to lie; (Mex) to be out looking for trouble all night

naguas *fpl* petticoat

naipe *m* playing card; deck of cards; **naipe de figura** face card; **tener buen naipe** to be lucky

naire *m* mahout

nalgada *f* shoulder, ham; blow on or with the buttocks

nalgas *fpl* buttocks, rump

nana *f* grandma; lullaby, cradlesong; (CAm, Mex, W-I) child's nurse; (Arg, Chile, Urug) child's complaint

nao *f* ship, vessel

napoleóni•co -ca *adj* Napoleonic

Nápoles *f* Naples

napolita•no -na *adj & mf* Neapolitan

naranja *f* orange; **media naranja** (coll) sidekick, better half; **naranja cajel** Seville orange, sour orange; **¡naranjas!** nonsense!

naranjada *f* orangeade; orange juice; orange marmalade

naranjal *m* orange grove

naranjo *m* orange tree; boob, simpleton

narciso *m* narcissus; fop, dandy; **narciso trompón** daffodil ‖ **Narciso** *m* Narcissus

narcóti•co -ca *adj & m* narcotic

narcotizar §60 *tr* to dope, drug

narcotraficante *mf* drug dealer

narguile *m* hookah

narigada *f* (SAm) pinch of snuff

nari•gón -gona *adj* big-nosed ‖ *m* big nose

narigu•do -da *adj* big-nosed; nose-shaped

nariguera *f* nose ring

na•riz *f* (*pl* **-rices**) nose; nostril; sense of smell; (*del vino*) bouquet; **nariz de pico de loro** hooknose; **sonarse las narices** to blow one's nose; **tabicarse las narices** to hold one's nose; **tener agarrado por las narices** to lead by the nose

narración *f* narration

narra•dor -dora *adj* narrating ‖ *mf* narrator

narrar *tr* to narrate

narrati•vo -va *adj* narrative ‖ *f* (*relato; habilidad en narrar*) narrative

narria *f* sled, sledge, drag

nasal *adj & f* nasal

nasalizar §60 *tr* to nasalize

nata *f* cream; whipped cream; élite, choice; skim, scum

natación *f* swimming

natal *adj* natal; native ‖ *m* birth; birthday

natali•cio -cia *adj* birth ‖ *m* birthday

natalidad *f* birth rate

naterón *m* cottage cheese

natillas *fpl* custard

natividad *f* birth; Christmas; (*día; festividad; pintura*) Nativity

nati•vo -va *adj* native; natural; natural-born; innate

na•to -ta *adj* born, e.g., **criminal nato** born criminal ‖ *f* see **nata**

natural *adj* natural; native; (mus) natural ‖ *mf* native ‖ *m* temper, disposition, nature; **al natural** au naturel; rough, unfinished; live; **del natural** from life, from nature

naturaleza *f* nature; disposition, temperament; nationality; **naturaleza muerta** still life

naturalidad *f* naturalness; nationality

naturalismo *m* naturalism

naturalista *mf* naturalist

mu
na

naturalización *f* naturalization
naturalizar §60 *tr* to naturalize; acclimatize ‖ *ref* to become·naturalized; go native
naturalmente *adv* naturally; easily, readily
naturismo *m* nudism
naufragar §44 *intr* to be shipwrecked; fail
naufragio *m* shipwreck; failure, ruin
náufra·go -ga *adj* shipwrecked ‖ *mf* shipwrecked person ‖ *m* shark
náusea *f* nausea; **dar náuseas a** to nauseate; sicken, disgust; **tener náuseas** to be nauseated, be sick at one's stomach
nauseabun·do -da *adj* nauseating, nauseous, loathsome, sickening
nauta *m* mariner, sailor
náuti·co -ca *adj* nautical ‖ *f* sailing, navigation
nava *f* hollow plain between mountains
navaja *f* folding knife; razor; penknife; tusk of wild boar; razor clam; evil tongue; **navaja barbera** straight razor
navajada *f* or **navajazo** *m* slash, gash
navajero *m* razor case; razor cloth
naval *adj* naval; nautical; **naval militar** naval
nava·rro -rra *adj* & *mf* Navarrese ‖ **Navarra** *f* Navarre
navazo *m* garden in sandy marshland
nave *f* ship, vessel; (*de un taller, fábrica, tienda, iglesia, etc.*) aisle; commercial ground floor; hall, shed, bay, building; **nave central** or **principal** (archit) nave; **nave lateral** (archit) aisle
navegable *adj* navigable
navegación *f* navigation; sailing; sea voyage; **navegación a vela** sailing
navega·dor -dora or **navegante** *adj* navigating ‖ *mf* navigator
navegar §44 *tr* to sail ‖ *intr* to navigate, sail; move around; (Mex) to suffer, bear
navel *f* (*pl* **-vels**) navel orange
Navidad *f* Christmas; Christmas time; **¡Felices Navidades!** Merry Christmas!; **contar** or **tener muchas Navidades** to be pretty old
navidal *m* Christmas card
navide·ño -ña *adj* Christmas
navie·ro -ra *adj* ship, shipping ‖ *m* shipowner; outfitter
navío *m* ship, vessel; **navío de guerra** warship
náyade *f* naiad
nazare·no -na *adj* & *mf* Nazarene ‖ *m* penitent in Passion Week procession ‖ **nazarenas** *fpl* (SAm) large gaucho spurs
nazi *adj* & *mf* Nazi
N.B. *abbr* **nota bene** (Lat) note well
nébeda *f* catnip
neblina *f* fog, mist
neblino·so -sa *adj* foggy, misty
nebulo·so -sa *adj* nebulous, cloudy, misty, hazy, vague; gloomy, sullen ‖ *f* nebula
necedad *f* foolishness, stupidity, nonsense
necesa·rio -ria *adj* necessary ‖ *f* water closet, privy
neceser *m* toilet case; sewing kit; **neceser de belleza** vanity case; **neceser de costura** workbasket

necesidad *f* necessity; need, want; starvation; **de necesidad** from weakness; of necessity; **necesidad mayor** bowel movement; **necesidad menor** urination
necesita·do -da *adj* necessitous, poor, needy; **estar necesitado de** to be in need of ‖ *mf* needy person
necesitar *tr* to necessitate; need; **necesitar + inf** to have to, need to + *inf* ‖ *intr* to be in need; **necesitar de** to be in need of, need ‖ *ref* to be needed, be necessary
ne·cio -cia *adj* foolish, stupid; imprudent; stubborn; touchy ‖ *mf* fool
necrología *f* necrology
necromancia *f* necromancy
néctar *m* nectar
neerlan·dés -desa *adj* Netherlandish, Dutch ‖ *mf* Netherlander ‖ *m* Dutchman; (*idiom₋,* Netherlandish or Dutch ‖ *f* Dutchwoman
nefalista *mf* teetotaler
nefan·do -da *adj* base, infamous
nefas·to -ta *adj* ominous, fatal, tragic
negable *adj* deniable
negación *f* negation; denial; refusal
nega·do -da *adj* unfit, incompetent; dull, indifferent
negar §66 *tr* to deny; refuse; prohibit; disown; conceal ‖ *intr* to deny ‖ *ref* to avoid; refuse; deny oneself to callers; **negarse a** to refuse; **negarse a + inf** to refuse to + *inf*
negati·vo -va *adj* negative ‖ *f* negative; denial; refusal
negligencia *f* negligence
negligente *adj* negligent
negociable *adj* negotiable
negociación *f* negotiation; deal, matter
negociado *m* department, bureau; affair, business; (SAm) illegal dealing; (Chile) store
negociante *m* dealer, trader
negociar *tr* to negotiate ‖ *intr* to negotiate; deal, trade
negocio *m* business; affair, deal, transaction; profit; (SAm) store
negocio·so -sa *adj* businesslike
negrear *intr* to turn black; look black
negre·ro -ra *adj* slave-trading; (fig) slave-driving ‖ *mf* slave trader; (fig) slave driver
negrilla *f* (typ) boldface
ne·gro -gra *adj* black, dark; gloomy; fatal, wicked; (coll) broke ‖ *mf* black (person); dear, darling ‖ *m* black; **negro de humo** lampblack
negror *m* or **negrura** *f* blackness
negruz·co -ca *adj* blackish
néme·sis *f* (*pl* **-sis**) (*justo castigo; castigador*) nemesis ‖ **Némesis** Nemesis
nemoro·so -sa *adj* (poet) woody, sylvan
ne·ne -na *mf* baby; dear, darling ‖ *m* rascal, villain
nenúfar *m* white water lily
neo *m* neon
neocelan·dés -desa *adj* New Zealand ‖ *mf* New Zealander
neoesco·cés -cesa *adj* & *mf* Nova Scotian
neófi·to -ta *mf* neophyte

neologismo *m* neologism
neomejica•no -na *adj* & *mf* New Mexican
neomicina *f* neomycin
neón *m* neon
neoyorki•no -na *adj* New York ‖ *mf* New
   York
Nepal, el Nepal
nepa•lés -lesa *adj* & *mf* Nepalese
nepente *m* nepenthe
nepote *m* relative and favorite of the Pope ‖
   Nepote Nepos
neptunio *m* neptunium
Neptuno *m* Neptune
nereida *f* Nereid
Nerón *m* Nero
nervio *m* nerve; (*del ala del insecto*) rib;
   strength, vigor
nerviosidad *f* nervousness
nervio•so -sa *adj* nervous; energetic, vigorous, sinewy; (*célula; centro; tónico*) nerve;
   (*sistema; enfermedad; postración, colapso*)
   nervous
nervosidad *f* nervosity; ductility, flexibility;
   (*de un argumento*) force, cogency
nervo•so -sa *adj* var of **nervioso**
nervu•do -da *adj* vigorous, sinewy
nervura *f* backbone (*of book*)
nesga *f* gore
nesgar §44 *tr* to gore
ne•to -ta *adj* net
neumáti•co -ca *adj* pneumatic; air ‖ *m* tire
neumonía *f* pneumonia
neuralgia *f* neuralgia
neurología *f* neurology
neurona *f* neuron
neuro•sis *f* (*pl* **-sis**) neurosis; **neurosis de**
   guerra shell shock
neuróti•co -ca *adj* & *mf* neurotic
neutral *adj* & *mf* neutral
neutralidad *f* neutrality
neutralismo *m* neutralism
neutralista *adj* & *mf* neutralist
neutralizar §60 *tr* to neutralize
neu•tro -tra *adj* neuter; (*que no es de un*
   color ni de otro) neutral; (bot, chem, elec,
   phonet, zool) neutral; (*verbo*) intransitive
neutrón *m* neutron
neva•do -da *adj* snow-covered; snow-white ‖
   f snowfall
nevar §2 *tr* to make snow-white ‖ *intr* to
   snow
nevasca *f* snowfall; snowstorm, blizzard
nevazón *f* (SAm) snowfall
nevera *f* icebox, refrigerator; icehouse; (P-R)
   jail
nevería *f* ice-cream parlor
neve•ro -ra *mf* ice-cream dealer ‖ *m* place of
   perpetual snow; perpetual snow ‖ *f* see
   nevera
nevisca *f* snow flurry
neviscar §73 *intr* to snow lightly
nevo *m* mole; **nevo materno** birth mark
nevo•so -sa *adj* snowy
ni *conj* neither, nor; **ni . . . ni** neither . . .
   nor; **ni . . . siquiera** not even
niacina *f* niacin

nicaragüense or **nicaragüe•ño -ña** *adj* & *mf*
   Nicaraguan
Nicolás *m* Nicholas
nicotina *f* nicotine
nicho *m* niche
nidada *f* (*huevos en el nido*) nestful of eggs;
   (*pajarillos en el nido*) nest, brood, hatch
nidal *m* (*donde la gallina pone sus huevos*)
   nest; nest egg; haunt; source; basis, foundation
nido *m* nest; haunt; home; source; (*de la-*
   drones) nest, den
niebla *f* fog, mist, haze; mildew; fog, confusion; **hay niebla** it is foggy; **niebla artifi-**
   cial smoke screen
nie•to -ta *mf* grandchild ‖ *m* grandson; **nietos**
   grandchildren ‖ *f* granddaughter
nieve *f* snow; water ice
nigromancia *f* necromancy
nihilismo *m* nihilism
nihilista *mf* nihilist
Nilo *m* Nile; **Nilo Azul** Blue Nile
nilón *m* nylon
nimbo *m* nimbus; halo
nimiedad *f* excess; fussiness, fastidiousness;
   timidity
ni•mio -mia *adj* excessive; fussy, fastidious;
   tiny
ninfa *f* nymph; **ninfa marina** mermaid
ninfea *f* white water lily
ningún *adj indef* apocopated form of
   ninguno, used only before masculine singular nouns and adjectives
ningu•no -na *adj indef* no, not any ‖ *pron*
   indef none, not any; neither, neither one;
   ninguno de los dos neither one ‖ **ninguno**
   pron indef nobody, no one
niña *f* child, girl; (*del ojo*) pupil; **niña del ojo**
   apple of one's eye; **niña exploradora** girl
   scout
niñada *f* childishness
niñera *f* nursemaid
niñería *f* childishness; trifle
niñe•ro -ra *adj* fond of children ‖ *f* see **niñera**
niñez *f* childhood; childishness; (fig) infancy
ni•ño -ña *adj* childlike, childish; young, inexperienced ‖ *mf* child; (*persona joven e*
   inexperta) babe; **desde niño** from childhood; **niño expósito** foundling; **niño tra-**
   vieso imp ‖ *m* child, boy; **niño bonito**
   playboy; **niño de coro** choirboy; **niño de**
   la bola child Jesus; lucky fellow; **niño**
   explorador boy scout; **niño gótico** playboy ‖ *f* see **niña**
niño-probeta *m* test-tube baby
ni•pón -pona *adj* & *mf* Nipponese
níquel *m* nickel
niquelar *tr* to nickel-plate
nirvana, el nirvana
níspero *m* medlar (*tree and fruit*)
níspola *f* medlar (*fruit*)
nitidez *f* brightness, clearness; sharpness
níti•do -da *adj* bright, clear; sharp
nitrato *m* nitrate
nítri•co -ca *adj* nitric
nitro *m* niter; **nitro de Chile** saltpeter
nitrógeno *m* nitrogen

nitroglicerina f nitroglycerine
nitro•so -sa adj nitrous
nitruro m nitride
nivel m level; **nivel de burbuja** spirit level; **nivel de vida** standard of living; **nivel sonoro** noise level
nivelar tr to level; even, make even, grade; survey
no adv not; no; **¿cómo no?** why not?; of course, certainly; **creer que no** to think not, believe not; **¿no?** is it not so?; **no bien** no sooner; **no más que** not more than; only; **no sea que** lest; **no . . . sino** only; **ya no** no longer
nobabia f (aer) dope
noble adj noble ‖ m noble, nobleman
nobleza f nobility
noción f notion, idea; rudiment
nocividad f harmfulness
noci•vo -va adj noxious, harmful
noctur•no -na adj nocturnal; lonely, sad, melancholy; night, nighttime
noche f night, nighttime; darkness; **buenas noches** good evening; good night; **de la noche a la mañana** overnight; unexpectedly, suddenly; **de noche** at night, in the nighttime; **esta noche** tonight; **hacer noche en** to spend the night in; **hacerse de noche** to grow dark; **muy de noche** late at night; **por la noche** at night, in the nighttime; **noche buena** Christmas Eve; **noche de estreno** (theat) first night; **noche de uvas** New Year's Eve; **noche vieja** New Year's Eve; watch night
nochebuena f Christmas Eve
nochebueno f Christmas cake; Yule log
nochero m sleepwalker
nodo m (astr, med, phys) node
No-Do m (acronym for **Noticiario y Documentales**) newsreel; newsreel theater
nodriza f wet nurse; vacuum tank
Noé m Noah
nogal m walnut; **nogal de la brujería** witch hazel
nómada or **nómade** adj & mf nomad
nomádi•co -ca adj nomadic
nombradía f fame, renown, reputation
nombra•do -da adj famous
nombramiento m naming; appointment
nombrar tr to name; appoint
nombre m name; fame, reputation; nickname; watchword; noun; **del mismo nombre** (elec) like; **de nombres contrarios** (elec) unlike; **nombre com. :cial** firm name; **nombre de lugar** place name; **nombre de pila** first name, Christian name; **nombre de soltera** maiden name; **nombre substantivo** noun; **nombre supuesto** alias
nomeolvi•des f (pl **-des**) forget-me-not
nómina f list, roll; payroll
nominal adj nominal; noun
nominar tr to name; appoint
nominati•vo -va adj & m nominative
non adj odd, uneven ‖ m odd number
nonada f trifle, nothing

no•no -na adj & m ninth
nopal m prickly pear
norcorea•no -na adj & mf North Korean
nordestada f or **nordeste** m (viento) northeaster (wind)
noria f chain pump; (pozo) draw well; Ferris wheel; treadmill, drudgery
norma f norm, standard; rule, method; (carp) square
normal adj normal; standard; perpendicular
Normandía f Normandy
norman•do -da adj & mf Norman ‖ m Norseman
norte m north; north wind; (guía) (fig) polestar, lodestar
Norteamérica f North America; America, the United States
norteamerica•no -na adj & mf North American; (estadunidense) American
norte•ño -ña adj northern
norue•go -ga adj & mf Norwegian ‖ **Noruega** f Norway
nos (used as object of verb) pron pers us; to us ‖ pron reflex ourselves, to ourselves; each other, to each other
noso•tros -tras pron pers we; us; ourselves
nostalgia f nostalgia
nota f note; (en la escuela) mark, grade; (en el restaurante) check; (mus) note; **nota de adorno** grace note; **nota tónica** keynote
notables mpl notables; prominent persons; (coll) VIPs
notar tr to note; dictate; annotate; criticize; discredit
notario m notary, notary public
noticia f news; notice, information; notion, rudiment; knowledge; **noticias de actualidad** news of the day; **noticias de última hora** late news; **una noticia** a piece of news, a news item
noticiar tr to notify; give notice of
noticia•rio -ria adj news ‖ m up-to-the-minute news; newsreel; newscast; **noticiario gráfico** picture page; **noticiario teatral** theater page
noticie•ro -ra adj news ‖ m newsman, reporter; late news
notici•o•so -sa adj informed; learned; well-informed; newsy ‖ m news item
notificar §73 tr to notify; report on
no•to -ta adj known, well-known ‖ m south wind ‖ f see **nota**
notoriedad f general knowledge; fame
noto•rio -ria adj manifest, well-known
nov. abbr **noviembre**
novatada f hazing; beginner's blunder
nova•to -ta adj beginning ‖ mf beginner; freshman
novecien•tos -tas adj & pron nine hundred ‖ **novecientos** m nine hundred
novedad f newness, novelty; news; fashion; happening; change; failing health; **sin novedad** as usual; safe; well; without anything happening
novel adj new, inexperienced, beginning ‖ m beginner

novela *f* novel; story, lie; **novela caballista** novel of western life; **novela policíaca** or **policial** detective story; **novela por entregas** serial

novele·ro -ra *adj* fond of novelty; fond of fiction; gossipy; fickle

noveles·co -ca *adj* novelistic, fictional; romantic, fantastic

novelista *mf* novelist

novelísti·co -ca *adj* fictional ‖ *f* fiction

novelizar §60 *tr* to fictionalize

nove·no -na *adj & m* ninth

noventa *adj, pron & m* ninety

noventa·vo -va *adj & m* ninetieth

novia *f* fiancée; bride; **novia de guerra** war bride

noviazgo *m* engagement, courtship

novi·cio -cia *adj & mf* novice

noviembre *m* November

novilunio *m* new moon

novilla *f* heifer

novillada *f* drove of young bulls; (taur) fight with young bulls by aspiring bullfighters

novillero *m* herdsman of young cattle; (taur) aspiring fighter, untrained fighter; truant

novillo *m* young bull; (coll) cuckold; (Mex, P-R) fiancé; **hacer novillos** to play truant

novio *m* suitor; fiancé; bridegroom; **novios** engaged couple; bride and groom, newlyweds

novocaína *f* novocaine

nro. *abbr* **nuestro**

N.S. *abbr* **Nuestro Señor**

ntro. *abbr* **nuestro**

nubada *f* local shower; abundance

nubarrón *m* storm cloud

nube *f* cloud; **andar** *(los precios)* **por las nubes** to be sky-high; **bajar de las nubes** to come back to or down to earth; **poner en or sobre las nubes** to praise to the skies

nube-hongo *f* mushroom cloud

nubla·do -da *adj* cloudy ‖ *m* storm cloud; impending danger; abundance; **aguantar el nublado** to suffer resignedly

nublar *tr* to cloud, cloud over ‖ *ref* to become cloudy

nu·blo -bla *adj* cloudy ‖ *m* storm cloud

nublo·so -sa *adj* cloudy; adverse, unfortunate

nubosidad *f* clouding, clouds

nubo·so -sa *adj* cloudy

nuca *f* nape

nuclear *adj* nuclear

núcleo *m* nucleus; core; *(de nuez)* kernel; *(de la fruta)* stone; *(de un electroimán)* core

nudillo *m* knuckle; stocking stitch; plug (in wall)

nudo *m* knot; bond, tie, union; crux; tangle; plot; difficulty; *(en el drama)* crisis; center, juncture; (bot) node; (naut) knot; **cortar el**

nudo gordiano to cut the Gordian knot; **hacérsele a** *(uno)* **un nudo en la garganta** to get a lump in one's throat

nudo·so -sa *adj* knotted, knotty

nuera *f* daughter-in-law

nues·tro -tra *adj poss* our ‖ *pron poss* ours

nueva *f* news; piece of news; **nuevas** *fpl* news

Nueva York *m & f* New York; **el Gran Nueva York** Greater New York

Nueva Zelandia New Zealand

nueve *adj & pron* nine; **las nueve** nine o'clock ‖ *m* nine; *(en las fechas)* ninth

nue·vo -va *adj* new; **de nuevo** again, anew; **nuevo flamante** brand-new; **¿qué hay de nuevo?** what's new? ‖ *mf* novice; freshman ‖ *f* see **nueva**

nuevomejica·no -na *adj & mf* New Mexican

Nuevo Méjico *m* New Mexico

nuez *f* *(pl* **nueces)** nut; walnut; Adam's apple; **nuez dura** *(árbol)* hickory; hickory nut; **nuez moscada** nutmeg

nulidad *f* nullity; incapacity; nobody

nu·lo -la *adj* null, void, worthless

núm. *abbr* **número**

numen *m* deity; inspiration

numeral *adj* numeral

numerar *tr* to number; count; numerate

numerario *m* cash, coin, specie

numéri·co -ca *adj* numerical

número *m* number; *(de un periódico)* copy, issue; *(de zapatos)* size; lottery ticket; **cargar** or **cobrar al número llamado** (telp) to reverse the charges; **de número** *(dícese de los individuos de una sociedad)* regular; **mirar por el número uno** to look out for number one; **número de serie** series number; **número equivocado** (telp) wrong number

numero·so -sa *adj* numerous

nunca *adv* never; **no . . . nunca** not . . . ever, never; **nunca jamás** nevermore

nupcial *adj* nuptial

nupcialidad *f* marriage rate

nupcias *fpl* nuptials, marriage; **casarse en segundas nupcias** to marry the second time

nutria *f* otter

nutrición *f* nutrition

nutri·do -da *adj* great, intense, robust, vigorous, steady; full, abounding, rich, heavy; *(carácter, letra)* thick; *(cañoneo)* heavy, sustained

nutrimento *m* or **nutrimiento** *m* nourishment, nutriment

nutrir *tr* to nourish, feed; supply, stock; support, back up; fill to overflowing

nu·triz *f* *(pl* **-trices)** wet nurse

Ñ

Ñ, ñ (eñe) *f* seventeenth letter of the Spanish alphabet

ñadi *m* (Chile) broad, shallow swamp

ñajú *m* okra, gumbo

ñámbar *m* Jamaica rosewood

ñame *m* yam; (W-I) blockhead, dunce

ñan•dú *m* (*pl* -dúes) nandu, American ostrich

ñaño -ña *adj* close, intimate; spoiled, overindulged ‖ *m* elder brother ‖ *f* elder sister; nursemaid; dear

ñapa *f* something thrown in, lagniappe; **de ñapa** in the bargain

ñaque *m* junk, pile of junk

ña•to -ta *adj* pug-nosed; (Arg) ugly, deformed

ñeque *adj* (Am) strong, vigorous; (*dícese de los ojos*) drooping ‖ *m* slap, blow; pep

ñiqueñaque *m* (coll) trash

ñisca *f* bit, fragment; excrement

ñoclo *m* macaroon

ñolombre *m* old peasant; **¡viene ñolombre!** here comes the bogeyman

ñon•go -ga *adj* slow, lazy; foolish, stupid; tricky; suspicious

ñoñería *f* or **ñoñez** *f* timidity; inanity; dotage

ño•ño -ña *adj* timid; inane; doting

O

O, o (o) eighteenth letter of the Spanish alphabet

o *conj* or; **o . . . o** either . . . or

oa•sis *m* (*pl* -sis) oasis

ob. *abbr* obispo

obduración *f* obduracy

obedecer §22 *tr* (with personal **a**) to obey ‖ *intr* to obey; **obedecer a** to yield to, be due to, be in keeping with, arise from

obediencia *f* obedience

obediente *adj* obedient

obelisco *m* obelisk; (typ) dagger

obertura *f* (mus) overture

obesidad *f* obesity

obe•so -sa *adj* obese

obispo *m* bishop

óbito *m* decease, demise

obituario *m* obituary

objeción *f* objection

objetable *adj* objectionable (*open to objection*)

objetar *tr* to object; (*dudas*) raise; (*una razón contraria*) set up, offer, present; object to

objeti•vo -va *adj* & *m* objective

objeto *m* object; subject matter; **objetos de cotillión** favors; **objeto volante no identificado** (ovni) unidentified flying object (UFO)

oblea *f* wafer; pill, tablet; **hecho una oblea** nothing but skin and bones

obli•cuo -cua *adj* oblique

obligación *f* obligation, duty; bond, debenture; **obligaciones** family responsibilities

obligacionista *mf* bondholder

obliga•do -da *adj* obliged, grateful; submissive; (mus) obbligato ‖ *m* (mus) obbligato

obligar §44 *tr* to obligate; oblige

obliterar *tr* to cancel

oblon•go -ga *adj* oblong

oboe *m* oboe; oboist

oboísta *mf* oboist

óbolo *m* mite

obra *f* work; **obra de** a matter of; **obra de consulta** reference work; **obra maestra** masterpiece; **obra pía** charity; useful effort; **obra prima** shoemaking; **obras** construction, repairs, alterations; **obra segunda** shoe repairing; **poner por obra** to undertake, set to work on

obra•dor -dora *mf* worker ‖ *m* workman; shop, workshop ‖ *f* workingwoman

obraje *m* manufacture; processing

obrajero *m* foreman; (Arg) lumberman; (Bol) artisan

obrar *tr* to build; perform; work ‖ *intr* to work; act, operate, proceed; have a movement of the bowels; **obra en mi poder** I have at hand, I have in my possession

obrera *f* workingwoman

obrerismo *m* labor; labor movement

obre•ro -ra *adj* working; labor ‖ *m* workman; **los obreros** labor ‖ *f* see **obrera**

obrero-patronal *adj* labor management

obscenidad *f* obscenity

obsce•no -na *adj* obscene

obscurecer §22 *tr* to darken; dim; discredit; cloud, confuse ‖ *intr* to grow dark ‖ *ref* to cloud over; become dimmed; fade away

obscuridad *f* obscurity; darkness

obscu•ro -ra *adj* obscure; dark; gloomy; uncertain, dangerous; **a obscuras** in the dark ‖ *m* dark; (paint) shading

obsequia•do -da *mf* recipient; guest of honor

obsequiar *tr* to fawn over, flatter; present, give; court, woo

obsequio *m* flattery; gift; attention, courtesy; **en obsequio de** in honor of

obsequio•so -sa *adj* obsequious; obliging, courteous

observación *f* observation

observa•dor -dora *adj* observant ‖ *mf* observer

observancia *f* observance; deference, respectfulness

observar *tr* to observe

observatorio *m* observatory

obsesión *f* obsession

obsesionar *tr* to obsess

obsole•to -ta *adj* obsolete
obstaculizar §60 *tr* to prevent; obstruct
obstáculo *m* obstacle
obstante *adj* standing in the way; **no obs-tante** however, nevertheless; in spite of
obstar *intr* to stand in the way; **obstar a** or **para** to hinder, check, oppose
obstetricia *f* obstetrics
obstétri•co -ca *adj* obstetrical ‖ *mf* obstetrician
obstinación *f* obstinacy
obstina•do -da *adj* obstinate
obstinar *ref* to be obstinate
obstrucción *f* obstruction
obstruccionar *tr* to hinder, obstruct
obstruir §20 *tr* to obstruct; block; stop up
obtención *f* obtaining
obtener §71 *tr* to obtain; keep
obtenible *adj* obtainable
obturación *f* plugging up, sealing off
obturador *m* stopper, plug; (aut) choke; (aut) throttle; (phot) shutter; **obturador de gui-llotina** drop shutter
obtu•so -sa *adj* obtúse
obús *m* howitzer; shell; (*de válvula de neu-mático*) plunger
obvención *f* extra, bonus, incidental
obvencional *adj* incidental
obviar §77 **& regular** *tr* to obviate, prevent ‖ *intr* to stand in the way
ob•vio -via *adj* obvious; unnecessary
oca *f* goose
ocasión *f* occasion; opportunity, chance; danger, risk; **aprovechar la ocasión** to improve the occasion; **aprovechar la ocasión de** to avail oneself of the opportunity to; **asir la ocasión por la melena** to take time by the forelock; **de ocasión** secondhand
ocasiona•do -da *adj* dangerous, risky; exposed, subject, liable; annoying
ocasionar *tr* to occasion, cause; stir up; endanger
ocasional *adj* occasional; causal; causing; (*causa*) responsible; accidental
ocaso *m* west; (*de un cuerpo celeste*) setting; sunset; decline; end, death
occidental *adj* western; occidental
occidente *m* occident
oceáni•co -ca *adj* oceanic
océano *m* ocean
ocio *m* idleness, leisure; distraction, pastime; spare time
ocio•so -sa *adj* idle; useless, needless
oclusión *f* occlusion
oclusi•vo -va *adj* & *f* occlusive
ocote *m* (Mex) torch pine
octava *f* octave
octavilla *f* handbill; eight-syllable verse
octavín *m* piccolo
octa•vo -va *adj* eighth ‖ *mf* octoroon ‖ *m* eighth ‖ *f* see **octava**
oct. *abbr* octubre
octogési•mo -ma *adj* & *m* eightieth
octubre *m* October
ocular *adj* ocular, eye ‖ *m* eyepiece, eyeglass, ocular
oculista *mf* oculist; fawner, flatterer

ocultar *tr* & *ref* to hide
ocul•to -ta *adj* hidden, concealed; (*misterioso, sobrenatural*) occult
ocupación *f* occupation; occupancy; employment
ocupa•do -da *adj* busy; occupied; **ocupada** pregnant
ocupante *adj* occupying ‖ *mf* occupant ‖ **ocupantes** *mpl* occupying forces
ocupar *tr* to occupy; busy, keep busy; employ; bother, annoy; attract the attention of ‖ *ref* to be occupied; be busy; be preoccupied; bother
ocurrencia *f* occurrence; witticism; bright idea
ocurrente *adj* witty
ocurrir *intr* to occur, happen; come; (*venir a la mente*) occur
ocha•vo -va *adj* eighth; octagonal ‖ *m* eighth; octagon
ochenta *adj*, *pron* & *m* eighty
ochenta•vo -va *adj* & *m* eightieth
ocho *adj* & *pron* eight; **las ocho** eight o'clock ‖ *m* eight; (*en las fechas*) eighth
ochocien•tos -tas *adj* & *pron* eight hundred ‖ **ochocientos** *m* eight hundred
oda *f* ode
odiar *tr* to hate
odio *m* hate, hatred
odio-amor *m* love-hate
odio•so -sa *adj* odious, hateful
Odisea *f* Odyssey
Odiseo *m* Odysseus
odontología *f* odontology, dentistry
odontólo•go -ga *mf* odontologist, dentist
odre *m* goatskin wine bag; (coll) toper
OEA *f* OAS
oeste *m* west; west wind
ofender *tr* & *intr* to offend ‖ *ref* to take offense
ofensa *f* offense
ofensi•vo -va *adj* & *f* offensive
ofen•sor -sora *adj* offending ‖ *mf* offender
oferta *f* offer; gift, present; **oferta y de-manda** supply and demand
oficial *adj* official ‖ *m* official, officer; skilled workman; clerk, office worker; journeyman; commissioned officer; **oficial de de-rrota** navigator
oficiar *tr* to announce officially in writing; (*la misa*) celebrate; officiate at ‖ *intr* to officiate; **oficiar de** to act as
oficina *f* office; shop; pharmacist's laboratory; **oficina de objetos perdidos** lost-and-found department
oficines•co -ca *adj* office, clerical; bureaucratic
oficinista *mf* clerk, office worker
oficio *m* office, occupation; function, rôle; craft, trade; memo, official note; (eccl) office, service; **de oficio** officially; professionally; **hacer oficios de** to function as; **tomar por oficio** to take to, keep at
oficio•so -sa *adj* diligent; obliging; officious, meddlesome; profitable; unofficial
ofrecer *tr* & *intr* to offer; (*una recepción*) give ‖ *ref* to offer; offer oneself; happen

ñ
of

ofrecimiento *m* offer, offering; **ofrecimiento de presentación** introductory offer

ofrenda *f* offering; gift

ofrendar *tr* to make offerings of; contribute

oftalmología *f* ophthalmology

oftalmólo•go -ga *mf* ophthalmologist

ofuscación *f* obfuscation; (mental) derangement

ofuscar §73 *tr* to obfuscate; dazzle

ogro *m* ogre

Oh *interj* O!, Oh!

ohmio *m* ohm

oíble *adj* audible

oída *f* hearing; **de** or **por oídas** by hearsay

oído *m* hearing; ear; **abrir tanto oído** to be all ears; **al oído** by listening; confidentially; **decir al oído** to whisper; **hacer** or **tener oídos de mercader** to turn a deaf ear

oír §48 *tr* to hear; listen to; (*una conferencia*) attend; **oír** + *inf* to hear + *inf*, e.g., **oí entrar a mi hermano** I heard my brother come in; hear + *ger*, e.g., **oí cantar a la muchacha** I heard the girl singing; hear + *pp*, e.g., **oí tocar la campana** I heard the bell rung; **oír decir que** to hear that; **oír hablar de** to hear about ‖ *intr* to hear; listen; **¡oíga!** say!, listen!; the idea!, the very idea!

ojada *f* (Col) skylight

ojal *m* buttonhole; eyelet; grommet

ojalá *interj* God grant . . . !, would to God . . . !; **¡ojalá que** would that . . . !, I hope that . . . !

ojeada *f* glimpse, glance; **buena ojeada** eyeful

ojear *tr* to eye, stare at; cast the evil eye on; (*la caza*) start, rouse; frighten, startle

ojera *f* eyecup, eyeglass; **ojeras** (*bajo los párpados inferiores*) rings, circles

ojeriza *f* grudge, ill will

ojero•so -sa *adj* with rings or circles under the eyes

ojete *m* eyelet, eyehole

ojienju•to -ta *adj* dry-eyed, tearless

ojituer•to -ta *adj* cross-eyed

ojiva *f* ogive, pointed arch

ojo *m* eye; (*de la escalera*) opening, well; (*del puente*) bay, span; (*de agua*) spring; **a ojos vistas** visibly, openly; **costar un ojo de la cara** to cost a mint, cost a fortune; **dar los ojos de la cara por** to give one's eyeteeth for; **hasta los ojos** up to one's ears; **mirar con ojos de carnero degollado** to make sheep's eyes at; **no pegar el ojo** to not sleep a wink; **ojo de buey** (archit, meteor, naut) bull's-eye; (bot) oxeye; **ojo de la cerradura** keyhole; **poner los ojos en blanco** to roll one's eyes; **saltar a los ojos** to be self-evident; **valer un ojo de la cara** to be worth a mint ‖ *interj* beware!; look out!; attention!; **¡mucho ojo!** be careful!, watch out!; **¡ojo con . . . !** look out for . . . !; **¡ojo, mancha!** fresh paint!

ojota *f* (SAm) sandal; (SAm) tanned llama hide

ola *f* wave; (*de gente apiñada*) surge

ole *m* or **olé** *m* bravo ‖ *interj* bravo!

oleada *f* big wave; (*de gente apiñada*) surge, swell

oleaje *m* surge, rush of waves

óleo *m* oil; holy oil; oil painting; **los santos óleos** extreme unction

oleoducto *m* pipe line

oler §49 *tr* to smell; pry into; sniff out ‖ *intr* to smell, smell fragrant, smell bad; **no oler bien** to look suspicious; **oler a** to smell of, smell like; smack of

olfatear *tr* to smell, scent, sniff; (*p.ej., un buen negocio*) scent, sniff out

olfato *m* smell, sense of smell; scent; keen insight

olíbano *m* frankincense

oliente *adj* smelling, odorous

oligarquía *f* oligarchy

Olimpíada *f* Olympiad

olímpi•co -ca *adj* Olympian; Olympic; haughty

oliscar §73 *tr* to smell, scent, sniff; investigate ‖ *intr* to smell bad

oliva *f* olive; olive tree; barn owl; olive branch, peace

olivar *m* olive grove

olivillo *m* mock privet

olivo *m* olive tree; **tomar el olivo** (taur) to duck behind the barrier; beat it

olmeda *f* or **olmedo** *m* elm grove

olmo *m* elm tree

olor *m* odor; promise, hope; trace, suspicion; **olores** (Chile, Mex) spice, condiment

oloro•so -sa *adj* odorous, fragrant

olote *m* (CAm & Mex) cob, corncob

olvidadi•zo -za *adj* forgetful; ungrateful

olvida•do -da *adj* forgetful; ungrateful

olvidar *tr & intr* to forget; **olvidar** + *inf* to forget to + *inf* ‖ *ref* to forget oneself; **olvidarse de** to forget; **olvidarse de** + *inf* to forget to + *inf*; **olvidársele a uno** to forget, e.g., **se me olvidó mi pasaporte** I forgot my passport; **olvidársele a uno** + *inf* to forget to + *inf*, e.g., **se me olvidó cerrar la ventana** I forgot to close the window

olvido *m* forgetfulness; oblivion

olla *f* pot, kettle; stew; eddy, whirlpool; **olla a** or **de presión** pressure cooker

ollería *f* potter's shop

ollero *m* potter

ombligo *m* navel; (*centro, punto medio*) (fig) navel

omino•so -sa *adj* ominous

omisión *f* omission; oversight, neglect

omi•so -sa *adj* neglectful, remiss

omitir *tr* to omit; overlook, neglect

ómni•bus *adj* (*tren*) accommodation ‖ *m* (*pl* -bus) bus, omnibus; **ómnibus de dos pisos** double-decker

omnímo•do -da *adj* all-inclusive

omnipotente *adj* omnipotent

omnisciente *adj* or **omnis•cio -cia** *adj* omniscient

omnívo•ro -ra *adj* omnivorous

omóplato *m* shoulder blade

once *adj & pron* eleven; **las once** eleven o'clock ‖ *m* eleven; (*en las fechas*) eleventh

oncea•vo -va *adj & m* eleventh

once•no -na *adj & mf* eleventh

oncología *f* oncology

onda *f* wave; flicker; (*en el pelo*) wave; **onda portadora** (rad) carrier wave; **ondas entretenidas** (rad) continuous waves

ondear *tr* (*en el pelo*) to wave ‖ *intr* to wave; ripple; flow; flicker; be wavy ‖ *ref* to wave, sway, swing

ondo•so -sa *adj* wavy

ondulación *f* undulation; wave; wave motion

ondula•do -da *adj* wavy, ripply; rolling; corrugated ‖ *m* (*en el pelo*) wave

ondular *tr* (*el pelo*) to wave ‖ *intr* to undulate; (*una bandera*) wave, flutter; (*las ondas del mar*) billow; (*una culebra*) wriggle

onero•so -sa *adj* onerous, burdensome

ónice *m* or **ónique** *m* or **ónix** *m* onyx

onomásti•co -ca *adj* of proper names ‖ *m* name day ‖ *f* study of proper names

onomatopéyi•co -ca *adj* onomatopoeic

ONU *f* UN

onza *f* ounce; (zool) snow leopard

onza•vo -va *adj & m* eleventh

opa•co -ca *adj* opaque; sad, gloomy

ópalo *m* opal

opción *f* option, choice; **opción nula** or **opción cero** zero option

ópera *f* opera; **ópera semiseria** light opera; **ópera seria** grand opera

operación *f* operation; transaction; **operaciones** (*ordenador*) software

operar *tr* to operate on ‖ *intr* to operate; work ‖ *ref* to occur, come about; be operated on

opera•rio -ria *mf* worker ‖ *m* workman ‖ *f* working woman

opereta *f* operetta

operista *mf* opera singer

operísti•co -ca *adj* operatic

opia•to -ta *adj m & f* opiate

opinable *adj* moot

opinar *intr* to opine; think; pass judgment

opinión *f* opinion, view; reputation, public image

opio *m* opium

opípa•ro -ra *adj* sumptuous, lavish

oponer §54 *tr* to oppose; (*resistencia*) to offer, put up ‖ *ref* to oppose each other; face each other; **oponerse a** to oppose, be opposed to; be against, resist; compete for

oporto *m* port, port wine

oportunidad *f* opportunity; opportuneness; **oportunidades** *fpl* witticisms

oportunista *adj* opportunistic ‖ *mf* opportunist

oportu•no -na *adj* opportune, timely; proper; witty

oposición *f* opposition; competitive examination

oposi•tor -tora *adj* rivaling, competing ‖ *mf* opponent; competitor

opresión *f* oppression

opresi•vo -va *adj* oppressive

opre•sor -sora *adj* oppressive ‖ *mf* oppressor

oprimir *tr* to oppress; squeeze, press

oprobiar *tr* to defame, revile

oprobio *m* opprobrium

oprobio•so -sa *adj* opprobrious

optar *tr* to enter; assume ‖ *intr* — **optar entre** to choose between; **optar por** to choose to

ópti•co -ca *adj* optical ‖ *mf* optician ‖ *f* optics

óptimamente *adv* to perfection

optimismo *m* optimism

optimista *adj* optimistic ‖ *mf* optimist

ópti•mo -ma *adj* fine, excellent

optometrista *mf* optometrist

opues•to -ta *adj* opposite, contrary

opugnar *tr* to attack; lay siege to; contradict

opulen•to -ta *adj* opulent

opúsculo *m* short work, opuscule

oquedad *f* hollow; hollowness

ora *conj* — **ora . . . ora** now . . . now, now . . . then

oración *f* oration, speech; prayer; sentence; **oración dominical** Lord's prayer; **ponerse en oración** to get down on one's knees

oráculo *m* oracle

ora•dor -dora *mf* orator, speaker; **orador de plazuela** soapbox orator; **orador de sobremesa** after-dinner speaker

oraje *m* rough weather, storm

oral *adj* oral

orangután *m* orang-outang

orar *intr* to pray; make a speech

orato•rio -ria *adj* oratorical ‖ *m* oratorio; (*capilla privada*) oratory ‖ *f* (*arte de la elocuencia*) oratory

orbe *m* orb; world

órbita *f* orbit

orca *f* killer whale

Órcadas *fpl* Orkney Islands

órdago — **de órdago** (coll) swell, real

orden *m & f* order; **hasta nueva orden** until further notice; **orden** *f* **de allanamiento** search warrant; **orden** *m* **de colocación** word order; **orden de pago** money order

ordenador *m* computer; **ordenador de viaje** on-board computer

ordenancista *adj* strict, severe ‖ *mf* taskmaster, disciplinarian, martinet

ordenanza *m* errand boy; (mil) orderly ‖ *f* ordinance; order, system; command; **ser de ordenanza** to be the rule

ordenar *tr* to order; put in order; ordain ‖ *ref* to be ordained, take orders

ordeñadero *m* milk pail

ordeñar *tr* to milk

ordeño *m* milking

ordinal *adj* orderly; ordinal ‖ *m* ordinal

ordinariez *f* coarseness, crudeness

ordina•rio -ria *adj* ordinary ‖ *m* daily household expenses; delivery man

orear *tr* to air ‖ *ref* to be aired; dry in the air; take an airing

orégano *m* pot or wild marjoram, winter sweet

oreja f ear; (*del zapato*) flap; (*de martillo*) claw; lug, flange, **aguzar las orejas** to prick up one's ears; **con las orejas caídas** crestfallen; **con las orejas tan largas** all ears; **descubrir** or **enseñar las orejas** to give oneself away

oreja•no -na adj (*res*) unbranded; (*animal*) skittish; shy; cautious

orejera f earflap, earmuff

orejeta f lug

ore•jón -jona adj coarse, uncouth; (Mex) skinny ‖ m strip of dried peach; pull on the ear; (*de la hoja de un libro*) dog's-ear

oreju•do -da adj big-eared

oreo m breeze

orfanato m orphanage

orfandad f orphanage, orphanhood

orfebre m goldsmith; silversmith

orfelinato m (SAm) orphanage

Orfeo m Orpheus

orfeón m glee club, choral society

organ•dí m (pl **-díes**) organdy

orgáni•co -ca adj organic

organillero -ra mf organ-grinder

organillo m barrel organ, hand organ, hurdy-gurdy

organismo m organism; organization

organista mf organist

organización f organization; **Organización de las Naciones Unidas (ONU)** United Nations (UN); **Organización de los Estados Americanos (OEA)** Organization of American States (OAS); **Organización del Tratado del Sudeste Asiático (O.T.A.S.E.)** Southwest Asia Treaty Organization (SEATO); **Organización para el Tratado del Atlántico Norte (O.T.A.N.)** North Atlantic Treaty Organization (NATO)

organizar §60 tr to organize

órgano m organ; (*de una máquina*) part; (*medio, conducto*) organ; (mus) organ

orgasmo m orgasm

orgía f orgy

orgiásti•co -ca adj orgiastic

orgullo m haughtiness; pride

orgullo•so -sa adj haughty; proud

oriental adj eastern; oriental

orientar tr to orient; guide, direct; (*una vela*) trim ‖ ref to orient oneself; find one's bearings

oriente m east; source, origin; east wind; youth ‖ **Oriente** m Orient; **el Cercano Oriente** the Near East; **el Extremo Oriente** the Far East; **el Lejano Oriente** the Far East; **el Oriente Medio** the Middle East; **el Próximo Oriente** the Near East; **gran oriente** (*logia masónica central*) grand lodge

orificar §73 tr to fill with gold

orífice m goldsmith

orificio m orifice, aperture, hole

origen m origin; source

original adj original; strange, odd, quaint ‖ m original; character; **de buen original** on good authority; **original de imprenta** copy

originar tr & ref to originate, start

orilla f border, edge; margin; bank, shore; sidewalk; breeze; **orillas** (Arg, Mex) outskirts; **salir a la orilla** to manage to get through

orillar tr to put a border or edge on; trim ‖ intr to come up to the shore

orillo m selvage, list

orín m rust; **orines** urine; **tomarse de orines** to get rusty

orina f urine

orinal m chamber pot

orinar tr to pass, urinate ‖ intr & ref to urinate

oriun•do -da adj & mf native; **ser oriundo de** to come from, hail from

orla f border, edge; trimming, fringe

orlar tr to border, put an edge on; trim, trim with a fringe

orn. abbr **orden**

ornamentar tr to ornament, adorn

ornamento m ornament, adornment

ornar tr to adorn

ornato m adornment, show

oro m gold; playing card (*representing a gold coin*) equivalent to diamond; **de oro y azul** all dressed up; **oro batido** gold leaf; **oro de ley** standard gold; **poner de oro y azul** to rake over the coals; **ponerle colores al oro** to gild the lily

oron•do -da adj big-bellied; hollow, spongy, puffed up; pompous, self-satisfied

oropel m tinsel; **gastar mucho oropel** to put up a big front

oropéndola f golden oriole

orozuz m licorice

orquesta f orchestra; **orquesta típica** regional orchestra

orquestar tr to orchestrate

órquide f or **orquídea** f orchid

ortiga f nettle; **ser como unas ortigas** to be a grouch

orto m rise (*of sun or star*)

ortodoncia f orthodontics; **aparato de orto-doncia** orthodontic appliance, braces

ortodo•xo -xa adj orthodox

ortografía f orthography; spelling

ortografiar §77 tr & intr to spell

oruga f caterpillar

orujo m bagasse of grapes or olives

orzuelo m sty

os pron pers & reflex (used as object of verb and corresponding to **vos** and **vosotros**) you, to you; yourself, to yourself; yourselves, to yourselves; each other, to each other

osa f she-bear; **Osa mayor** Great Bear; **Osa menor** Little Bear

osadía f boldness, daring

osa•do -da adj bold, daring

osamenta f skeleton; bones

osar intr to dare

osario m ossuary, charnel house

oscilar intr to oscillate; fluctuate; waver, hesitate

ósculo m kiss

oscurecer §22 tr, intr & ref var of **obscu-recer**

oscuridad f var of **obscuridad**
oscu•ro -ra adj & m var of **obscuro**
osera f bear's den
osificar §73 tr & ref to ossify
oso m bear; **hacer el oso** to make a fool of oneself; to make love in the open; **oso blanco** polar bear; **oso hormiguero** ant bear; anteater; **oso lavador** raccoon
ostensorio m (eccl) monstrance
ostentar tr to show; make a show of ‖ ref to show off; boast
ostentati•vo -va adj ostentatious
ostento m portent, prodigy
ostento•so -sa adj magnificent, showy
osteópata mf osteopath
osteopatía f osteopathy
ostión m large oyster
ostra f oyster; **ostras en su concha** oyster cocktail, oysters on the half shell
ostracismo m ostracism
ostral m oyster bed, oyster farm
ostrería f oysterhouse
ostre•ro -ra adj oyster ‖ m oysterman; oyster bed, oyster farm
osu•do -da adj bony
osu•no -na adj bearish, bearlike
O.T.A.N., la NATO
O.T.A.S.E., la SEATO
otate m Mexican giant grass (Guadua amplexifolia); otate stick
otero m hillock, knoll
otomán m ottoman
otoma•no -na adj & mf Ottoman ‖ f ottoman
otoñal adj autumnal
otoño m autumn, fall
otorgar §44 tr to agree to; grant, confer; (law) to execute

o•tro -tra adj indef other, another ‖ pron indef other one, another one; **como dijo el otro** as someone said
ovación f ovation
ovacionar tr to give an ovation to
oval adj oval
óvalo m oval
ovante adj victorious, triumphant
ovario m ovary
oveja f ewe, female sheep; **oveja negra** (fig) black sheep; **oveja perdida** (fig) lost sheep
oveje•ro -ra adj sheep ‖ mf sheep raiser
oveju•no -na adj sheep, of sheep
ove•ro -ra adj blossom-colored; egg-colored
overol m overall
Ovidio m Ovid
ovillar tr to wind up; sum up ‖ intr to form into a ball ‖ ref to curl up into a ball
ovillo m ball of yarn; ball, heap; tangled ball; **hacerse un ovillo** to cower, recoil; (hablando) get all tangled up
ovni m UFO
óvulo m ovule; ovum
oxear tr & intr to shoo
oxiacanta f hawthorn
oxidación f oxidation
oxidar tr to oxidize ‖ ref to oxidize; get rusty
óxido m oxide; **óxido de carbono** carbon monoxide; **óxido de mercurio** mercuric oxide
oxígeno m oxygen
oxíto•no -na adj oxytone
oxte interj get out!, beat it!, **sin decir oxte ni moxte** without opening one's mouth
oyente mf hearer; (a la radio) listener; (en la escuela) auditor
ozono m ozone

P

P, p (pe) f nineteenth letter of the Spanish alphabet
P. abbr **Padre, Papa, Pregunta**
pabellón m pavilion; bell tent; flag, banner; (de fusiles) stack; canopy; summerhouse; (de instrumento de viento) bell
pabilo or **pábilo** m wick
Pablo m Paul
pábulo m food; support, encouragement, fuel
pacana f pecan
paca•to -ta adj mild, gentle
pacer §22 tr to pasture, graze; gnaw, eat away ‖ intr to pasture, graze
paciencia f patience
paciente adj & mf patient
pacienzu•do -da adj long-suffering
pacificar §73 tr to pacify ‖ intr to sue for peace ‖ ref to calm down
pacífi•co -ca adj pacific
pacifismo m pacifism
pacifista adj & mf pacifist

pa•co -ca adj (Chile) bay, reddish ‖ m paco, alpaca; Moorish sniper; sniper ‖ **Paco** m Frank
pacotilla f trash, junk; (Chile) rabble, mob; **hacer su pacotilla** to make a cleanup; **ser de pacotilla** to be shoddy, be poorly made
pacotille•ro -ra mf (Chile, Ven) peddler
pactar tr to agree upon ‖ intr to come to an agreement
pacto m pact, covenant
pacha•cho -cha adj (Chile) short-legged; (Chile) lax, lazy; (Chile) chubby
pa•chón -chona adj (CAm) shaggy, hairy, wooly ‖ m (perro) pointer; (hombre flemático) sluggard
pachorra f sluggishness, indolence
pachotada f silliness
padecer §22 tr to suffer; be victim of ‖ intr to suffer
padrastro m stepfather; hangnail

padre *adj* huge; (Peru) terrific ‖ *m* father; stallion, sire; **padres** parents; ancestors; **tener el padre alcalde** to have pull, have a friend at court

padrina *f* godmother

padrinazgo *m* godfathership; sponsorship, patronage

padrino *m* godfather; sponsor; (*en un desafío*) second; **padrino de boda** best man; **padrinos** godparents

padrón *m* poll, census; pattern, model; memorial column; indulgent father; stallion; (Col) stock bull

padrote *m* stock animal; (Mex) pimp, procurer

paella *f* saffron-flavored stew of chicken, seafood, and rice with vegetables

paf *interj* bang!

pág. *abbr* **página**

paga *f* pay, payment; wages; fine; **como paga y señal** on account; as down payment

paga-alquiler *f* rent, rent money

pagadero -ra *adj* payable

paga•do -da *adj* pleased, cheerful; **estamos pagados** we are quits; **pagado de sí mismo** self-satisfied, conceited

paga•dor -dora *adj* paying ‖ *mf* payer ‖ *m* paymaster

paganismo *m* paganism

paga•no -na *adj* & *mf* pagan ‖ *m* easy mark

pagar §44 *tr* to pay; pay for; (*una bondad, una visita*) return ‖ *intr* to pay ‖ *ref* to become fond; be flattered; boast; be satisfied

pagaré *m* promissory note, I.O.U.

página *f* page

paginar *tr* to page

pago *m* payment; (*de viñas u olivares*) district, region

pagote *m* easy mark

paila *f* large pan

pairar *intr* (naut) to lie to

país *m* country, land; landscape; **el país de Gales** Wales; **los Países Bajos** (*Bélgica, Holanda y Luxemburgo*) the Low Countries; (*Holanda*) The Netherlands; **países no alineados** nonaligned nations; Third World countries

paisaje *m* landscape

paisajista *mf* landscape painter

paisa•no -na *adj* of the same country ‖ *mf* peasant; civilian; (Mex) Spaniard ‖ *m* fellow countryman; **de paisano** in civies

paja *f* straw; chaff; trash, rubbish; **no dormirse en las pajas** to not let the grass grow under one's feet; **no levantar paja del suelo** to not lift a hand, not do a stroke of work

pájara *f* paper kite; paper rooster; bird; crafty female

pajarera *f* aviary; large bird cage

pajarería *f* flock of birds; bird store; pet shop

pajare•ro -ra *adj* bright, cheerful; bright-colored, gaudy ‖ *m* bird dealer; bird fancier ‖ *f* see **pajarera**

pajarita *f* paper kite; bow tie; wing collar; piccadilly

pájaro *m* bird; crafty fellow; expert; **pájaro bobo** penguin; motmot; **pájaro carpintero** woodpecker; **pájaro de cuenta** big shot; **pájaro mosca** hummingbird

pajarota *f* or **pajarotada** *f* hoax, canard

paje *m* page; valet; dressing table; (naut) cabin boy

pajilla *f* cornhusk cigarette; **pajilla de madera** excelsior

paji•zo -za *adj* straw; straw-colored; straw-thatched

pajuela *f* short straw; sulfur match or fuse; toothpick; (Bol) match

Pakistán, el var of **Paquistán**

pakista•ní (*pl* **-níes**) *adj* & *mf* var of **paquistaní**

pala *f* shovel; (*de remo, de la azada, etc.*) blade; (*del panadero*) peel; scoop; racket; (*del calzado*) upper; (*de excavadora*) bucket; shoulder strap; (coll) cunning, craftiness

palabra *f* word; speech; (*de una canción*) words; (*derecho para hablar en asambleas*) floor; **palabras mayores** words, angry words; **remojar la palabra** to wet one's whistle; **usar de la palabra** to speak, make a speech

palabre•ro -ra *adj* wordy, windy ‖ *mf* windbag

palabrota *f* vulgarity, obscenity

palabru•do -da *adj* talkative; chattering

palacie•go -ga *adj* palace, court ‖ *m* courtier

palacio *m* palace; mansion; **palacio municipal** city hall

palada *f* shovelful; (*de remo*) stroke

paladar *m* palate; taste; gourmet

paladear *tr* to taste, relish

paladín *m* champion, hero

palafrén *m* palfrey

palanca *f* lever; pole; crowbar; **palanca de mando** (aer) control stick; **palanca de mayúsculas** shift key

palancada *f* leverage

palangana *f* washbowl, basin

palanganear *intr* to brag, give oneself airs

palanganero *m* washstand

palangre *m* trawl, trawl line

palanqueta *f* jimmy; **palanquetas** (Arg) dumbbell

palatal *adj* & *f* palatal

palco *m* (theat) box

palear *tr* to beat, pound; shovel

palenque *m* paling, palisade; (SAm) hitching post; (C-R) Indian ranch; (Chile) pandemonium

paleta *f* palette; small shovel; trowel; (*de una rueda*) paddle; blade, bucket, vane; shoulder blade; (*dulce con un palito que sirve de mango*) lollipop

paletilla *f* shoulder blade

paleto *m* fallow deer; rustic, yokel

palia *f* altar cloth; (eccl) pall

paliacate *m* (Mex) bandanna

paliar §77 & **regular** *tr* to palliate

palidecer §22 *intr* to pale, to turn pale

palidez *f* paleness, pallor

páli•do -da *adj* pale, pallid

palillo _m_ toothpick; drumstick; bobbin; **palillos** chopsticks; castanets; rudiments; trifles

palinodia _f_ backdown; **cantar la palinodia** to eat crow, eat humble pie

palique _m_ chit-chat, small talk

paliquear _intr_ to chat, to gossip

paliza _f_ beating, thrashing

palizada _f_ fenced-in enclosure; stockade; embankment

palma _f_ (_de la mano_) palm; (_árbol y hoja_) palm; **batir palmas** to clap, to applaud; **llevarse la palma** to carry off the palm

palmada _f_ slap; hand, applause, clapping; **dar palmadas** to clap hands

palma·rio -ria _adj_ clear, evident

palmatoria _f_ candlestick

palmera _f_ date palm

palmito _m_ palmetto; woman's face; slender figure

palmo _m_ span, palm; **dejar con un palmo de narices** to disappoint

palmotear _tr_ to pat; clap, applaud ‖ _intr_ to clap, applaud

palo _m_ stick; pole; staff; handle; tree; (_golpe_) whack; (_madera_) wood; (_grupo de naipes de la baraja_) suit; (_naut_) mast; **dar palos de ciego** to lay about, swing wildly; **de tal palo tal astilla** like father like son; **palo de escoba** broomstick; **palo en alto** (fig) big stick; **palo mayor** (naut) mainmast; **servir del palo** to follow suit

paloma _f_ pigeon, dove; prostitute; (fig) dove, meek person; **paloma mensajera** carrier pigeon; **palomas** whitecaps

palomar _m_ pigeon house, dovecot

palomilla _f_ doveling; small butterfly; white horse; (_del caballo_) back; pillow block, journal bearing; (CAm, Mex) rabble, scum; **palomillas** whitecaps

palomita _f_ doveling; (baseball) fly; **palomitas** popcorn

palpable _adj_ palpable

palpar _tr_ to touch, feel; grope through ‖ _intr_ to grope

palpitante _adj_ throbbing; thrilling; (_cuestión_) burning

palpitar _intr_ to palpitate, throb; (_un afecto_) flash, break forth

pálpito _m_ (SAm) hunch

palta _f_ (SAm) alligator pear, avocado (_fruit_)

palto _m_ (SAm) alligator pear, avocado (_tree_)

palúdi·co -ca _adj_ marshy; malarial

paludismo _m_ malaria

palur·do -da _adj_ rustic, boorish ‖ _mf_ rustic, boor

pallador _m_ (SAm) Gaucho minstrel

pampa _f_ pampa; **La Pampa** the Pampas

pámpana _f_ vine leaf

pámpano _m_ tendril; vine leaf

pan _m_ bread; loaf; loaf of bread; wheat; food; livelihood; pie dough; (_de jabón, cera, etc._) cake; gold foil or leaf; silver foil or leaf; **como el pan bendito** as easy as pie; **de pan llevar** arable, tillable; **llamar al pan pan y al vino vino** to call a spade a spade; **panes** grain, breadstuff; **venderse**

como pan bendito to sell like hot cakes ‖ **Pan** _m_ Pan

pana _f_ corduroy; (aut) breakdown

panacea _f_ panacea

panadería _f_ bakery; baking business

panade·ro -ra _mf_ baker; (Chile) flatterer

panadizo _m_ felon; sickly person

panal _m_ honeycomb

pana·má _m_ (_pl_ -**maes**) Panama hat

paname·ño -ña _adj & mf_ Panamanian

panamerica·no -na _adj_ Pan-American

pancarta _f_ placard, poster

pancista _adj_ weaseling ‖ _mf_ weaseler

páncre·as _m_ (_pl_ -**as**) pancreas

pancho _m_ paunch, belly

pandear _intr & ref_ to warp, bulge, buckle, sag, bend

pandereta _f_ tambourine

pandilla _f_ party, faction; gang, band; picnic, excursion

pan·do -da _adj_ bulging; slow-moving; slow, deliberate

pandorga _f_ kite; fat, lazy woman

panecillo _m_ roll, crescent

panfleto _m_ pamphlet

paniaguado _m_ servant, minion; protégé, favorite

páni·co -ca _adj_ panic, panicky ‖ _m_ panic

panizo _m_ Italian millet; (Chile) gangue; (Chile) abundance

panocha _f_ ear of grain; ear of corn; pancake made of corn and cheese; (Mex) panocha (_brown sugar_)

panoja _f_ ear of grain; ear of corn

panorama _m_ panorama

pano·so -sa _adj_ mealy

panqué _m_ or **panqueque** _m_ pancake

pantalán _m_ pier, wooden pier

pantalón _m_ trousers; **calzarse los pantalones** to wear the pants; **pantalones** trousers, pants; **pantalones azules** (CAm) blue jeans; **pantalones de mezclilla** (C-R, Mex) blue jeans

pantalla _f_ lamp shade; fire screen; motion-picture screen; television screen; (_persona que encubre a otra_) blind; (_cine, arte del cine_) screen; fan; **llevar a la pantalla** to put on the screen; **pantalla acústica** loudspeaker; **pantalla de plata** silver screen; **pequeña pantalla** television screen; **servir de pantalla a** to be a blind for

pantano _m_ bog, marsh, swamp; dam, reservoir; trouble, obstacle

pantano·so -sa _adj_ marshy, swampy; muddy; knotty, difficult

panteísmo _m_ pantheism

panteón _m_ pantheon; cemetery

pantera _f_ panther

pantomima _f_ pantomime

pantoque _m_ (naut) bilge

pantorrilla _f_ calf (_of leg_)

pantufla _f_ or **pantuflo** _m_ house slipper

panty _m_ panty hose

panza _f_ paunch, belly

panzu·do -da _adj_ paunchy, big-bellied

pañal _m_ diaper; shirttail; **pañales** swaddling clothes; infancy; early stages

pañe•ro -ra *adj* dry-goods, cloth ‖ *mf* dry-goods dealer, clothier

paño *m* cloth; rag; (*de agujas*) paper; (*ancho de la tela*) breadth; (*mancha en el rostro*) spot; (*en, p.ej., un espejo*) blur; sailcloth, canvas; **al paño** off-stage; **conocer el paño** to know one's business, to know the ropes; **paño de adorno** doily; **paño de cocina** washrag, dishcloth; **paño de lágrimas** helping hand, stand-by; **paño de mesa** tablecloth; **paño de tumba** crape; **paño mortuorio** pall; **paños menores** under-clothing; **paños tibios** appeasement attempts

pañuelo *m* handkerchief; shawl; **pañuelo de hierbas** bandanna

papa *m* pope ‖ *f* potato; fake, hoax; food, grub; snap, cinch; **ni papa** nothing

pa•pá *m* (*pl* **-pás**) papa, daddy

papada *f* double chin; (*de animal*) dewlap; (Guat) stupidity

papado *m* papacy

papagayo *m* parrot

papalina *f* sunbonnet; drunk

papana•tas *m* (*pl* **-tas**) simpleton, gawk

paparrucha *f* hoax; trifle

papel *m* paper; piece of paper; rôle, part; character, figure; **desempeñar** or **hacer un papel** to play a rôle; **papel alquitranado** tar paper; **papel cebolla** onionskin; **papel de empapelar** wallpaper; **papel de esmeril** emery paper; **papel de estaño** tin foil; **papel de excusado** toilet paper; **papel de fumar** cigarette paper; **papel de lija** sandpaper; **papel de oficio** foolscap; **papel de seda** tissue paper; **papel de segundón** (fig) second fiddle; **papel de tornasol** litmus paper; **papel filtrante** filter paper; **papel higiénico** toilet paper; **papel moneda** paper money; **papel pintado** wallpaper; **papel secante** blotting paper; **papel viejo** waste paper; **papel volante** handbill, printed leaflet

papelada *f* farce; ridiculous act

papeleo *m* red tape

papelera *f* paper case; writing desk; waste-basket; paper factory

papelería *f* stationery store; mess of papers, litter

papelerío *m* paper work

papele•ro -ra *adj* paper; boastful, showy ‖ *mf* stationer; paper manufacturer; (Mex) paperboy ‖ *f* see **papelera**

papeleta *f* slip of paper; card, file card; ticket; **papeleta de empeño** pawn ticket

papelista *m* paper maker, paper manufacturer; stationer; paper hanger

pape•lón -lona *adj* bluffing, four-flushing ‖ *mf* bluffer, four-flusher ‖ *m* thin cardboard

papelonear *intr* to bluff, to four-flush

papelote *m* worthless piece of paper; paper kite

papel-prensa *m* newsprint

papera *f* goiter; mumps

papilla *f* pap; guile, deceit

papiro *m* papyrus

papirote *m* fillip, flick; nincompoop

paq. *abbr* **paquete**

paquear *tr* to snipe at ‖ *intr* to snipe

paque•te -ta *adj* self-important, pompous; (Arg) chic, dolled-up ‖ *m* package, parcel, bundle, bale; sport, dandy; **darse paquete** (Guat, Mex) to put on airs; **en paquete aparte** under separate cover, in a separate package; **paquetes postales** parcel post

Paquistán, el Pakistan

paquista•ní (*pl* **-níes**) or **paquistano -na** *adj* & *mf* Pakistani

Paquita *f* Fanny

par *adj* like, similar, equal; (math) even ‖ *m* pair, couple; peer; (elec, mech) couple; (math) even number; **a pares** in twos; **de par en par** wide-open; completely; overtly; **¿pares o nones?** odd or even? ‖ *f* par; **a la par** equally; jointly; at the same time; at par; **bajo la par** below par, under par; **sobre la par** above par

para *prep* to, for; towards; compared to; (*antes de*) by; **para + inf** in order to + *inf;* **para con** towards; **para que** in order that, so that

parabién *m* congratulation

parábola *f* parable

parabri•sa *m* or **parabri•sas** *m* (*pl* **-sas**) windshield

paracaí•das *m* (*pl* **-das**) parachute; **lanzarse en paracaídas** to parachute; **salvarse en paracaídas** to parachute to safety

paracaidismo *m* parachute jumping; (sport) sky diving

paracaidista *mf* parachutist ‖ *m* paratrooper

parachis•pas *m* (*pl* **-pas**) spark arrester

paracho•ques *m* (*pl* **-ques**) bumper

parachutar *intr* to parachute

parada *f* stop; end; stay; shutdown; (*en el juego*) stake; dam; (*para el ganado*) stall; stud farm; (*en la esgrima*) parry; (*tiro de caballerías de reemplazo*) relay; (mil) parade, dress parade, review; **parada de taxi** taxi stand

paradero *m* end; whereabouts; stopping place; wayside station

para•do -da *adj* slow, spiritless, witless; idle, unemployed; closed; proud, stiff; **quedar bien parado** to be lucky; **quedar mal parado** to be unlucky ‖ *f* see **parada**

paradoja *f* paradox

paradóji•co -ca *adj* paradoxical

parador *m* inn, wayside inn; motel; **parador de carretera** drive-in restaurant

parafina *f* paraffin

paragol•pes *m* (*pl* **-pes**) buffer, bumper

para•guas *m* (*pl* **-guas**) umbrella

Paraguay, el Paraguay

paraguaya•no -na or **paragua•yo -ya** *adj* & *mf* Paraguayan

paragüero *m* umbrella man; umbrella stand

paraíso *m* paradise

paraje *m* place, spot; state, condition

paralela *f* parallel, parallel line; **paralelas** parallel bars

paralelizar §60 *tr* to parallel, compare

parale•lo -la *adj* parallel ‖ *m* (geog) parallel ‖ *f* see **paralela**

paráli•sis *f* (*pl* **-sis**) paralysis
paralíti•co -ca *adj* & *mf* paralytic
paralizar §60 *tr* to paralyze ‖ *ref* to become paralyzed
parámetro *m* parameter; established boundary
páramo *m* high barren plain; bleak windy spot; (Bol, Col, Ecuad) cold drizzle
paranie•ves *m* (*pl* **-ves**) snow fence
paraninfo *m* assembly hall, auditorium
paranoi•co -ca *adj* & *mf* paranoiac
parapeto *m* parapet
paraplegia *f* paraplegia
parar *tr* to stop; check; change; prepare; put up, stake; parry; order; get, acquire; (*la atención*) fix; (*la caza*) point; (*typ*) to set ‖ *intr* to stop; (*en un hotel*) put up; **parar en** to become; run to, run as far as ‖ *ref* to stop; stop work; stand; turn, become; (*el perro de muestra*) point; (*el pelo*) stand on end; **pararse en** to pay attention to
pararra•yo *m* or **pararra•yos** *m* (*pl* **-yos**) (*barra metálica que sirve para preservar los edificios del rayo*) lightning rod; (*dispositivo que sirve para preservar una instalación eléctrica de la electricidad atmosférica o de las chispas que produce*) lightning arrester
parasíti•co -ca *adj* parasitic
parási•to -ta *adj* parasitic; (elec) stray ‖ *m* parasite; **parásitos atmosféricos** atmospherics, static
parasol *m* parasol
parato•pes *m* (*pl* **-pes**) bumper
Parcas *fpl* Fates
parcela *f* particle; plot of ground
parcelar *tr* to parcel, divide into lots
parcial *adj* partial; partisan ‖ *mf* partisan
par•co -ca *adj* frugal, sparing; moderate
parcómetro *m* parking meter
parchar *tr* to mend, patch
parche *m* plaster, sticking plaster; patch; drum; drumhead; daub, botch, splotch; **parche poroso** porous plaster
pardal *m* linnet; sly fellow
pardiez *interj* by Jove!
pardillo *m* linnet
par•do -da *adj* brown, drab; dark; cloudy; (*voz*) dull, flat; (*cerveza*) dark; mulatto ‖ *mf* mulatto ‖ *m* brown, drab; leopard
pardus•co -ca *adj* dark-brown, drabbish
parea•do -da *adj* rhymed ‖ *m* couplet
parear *tr* to pair; match ‖ *ref* to pair off
parecer *m* opinion; look, mien, countenance ‖ *v* §22 *intr* to appear; show up; look, seem; **me parece que. . . .** I think that. . . . ‖ *ref* to look alike, resemble each other; **parecerse a** to look like
pareci•do -da *adj* like, similar; **bien parecido** good-looking; **parecido a** like, e.g., **esta casa es parecida a la otra** this house is like the other one; **parecidos** alike, e.g., **estas casas son parecidas** these houses are alike ‖ *m* similarity, resemblance, likeness; **tener un gran parecido** to be a good likeness

pared *f* wall; **dejar pegado a la pared** to nonplus; **paredes** house
pareja *f* pair, couple; dancing partner; **correr parejas** or **a las parejas** to be abreast, arrive together; go together, match, be equal; **correr parejas con** to keep up with, keep abreast of; **parejas** (*de naipes*) pair
pareje•ro -ra *adj* even, equal; servile, fawning; forward, overfamiliar ‖ *m* race horse
pare•jo -ja *adj* equal, like; even, smooth ‖ *m* (CAm) dancing partner ‖ *f* see **pareja**
parentela *f* kinsfolk, relations
parentesco *m* relationship; bond, tie
parénte•sis *m* (*pl* **-sis**) parenthesis; break, interval
parhilera *f* ridgepole
paria *mf* pariah, outcast
paridad *f* par, parity; comparison
parien•te -ta *adj* related ‖ *mf* relative; (coll) spouse
parihuela *f* handbarrow; (*camilla*) stretcher
parir *tr* to bear, give birth to, bring forth ‖ *intr* to give birth; come forth, come to light; talk well
parisiense *adj* & *mf* Parisian
parking *m* parking (space)
parlamentar *intr* to talk, chat; parley
parlamento *m* parliament; parley; speech; (theat) speech
parlan•chín -china *adj* jabbering ‖ *mf* chatterbox
parlante *m* loudspeaker
parlar *intr* to speak with facility; chatter, talk too much; (*el loro*) talk
parle•ro -ra *adj* loquacious, garrulous; gossipy; (*ave*) singing, song; (*ojos*) expressive; (*arroyo, fuente*) babbling
parlotear *intr* to prattle, jabber, chin
parloteo *m* jabber, prattle
parnaso *m* (*colección de poesías*) Parnassus; **el Parnaso** Parnassus, Mount Parnassus
paro *m* shutdown, work stoppage; lockout; titmouse; (*de dados*) (SAm) throw; **paro forzoso** layoff
parodia *f* parody, travesty
parodiar *tr* to parody, travesty, burlesque
parón *m* stop; delay
paroxíto•no -na *adj* & *m* paroxytone
parpadear *intr* to blink, wink; flicker
parpadeo *m* blinking, winking; flicker
párpado *m* eyelid
parque *m* park; parking; parking lot; **parque de atracciones** amusement park
parqué *m* floor, inlaid floor
parqueadero *m* (Col) parking lot
parquear *tr* to park
parquímetro *m* parking meter
parra *f* grapevine; earthen jug
párrafo *m* paragraph; chat
parral *m* grape arbor
parranda *f* spree, party; (Col) large number; **andar de parranda** to go out on a spree, go out to celebrate
parricida *mf* patricide, parricide
parricidio *m* patricide, parricide

pa
pa

parrilla *f* grill, gridiron, broiler; grate, grating; grillroom, grill; **asar a la parrilla** to broil

párroco *m* parish priest

parroquia *f* parish; parish church; customers, clientele

parroquial *adj* parochial

parroquia•no -na *mf* parishioner; customer

parte *m* dispatch, communiqué; **parte meteorológico** weather report ‖ *f* part; share; party; side; direction; (*papel de un actor*) role; (law) party; **de un mes a esta parte** for about a month past; **en ninguna otra parte** nowhere else; **en ninguna parte** nowhere; **ir a la parte** to go shares; **la mayor parte** most, the majority; **parte del león** lion's share; **parte de por medio** (theat) bit part, walk-on; **partes** parts, gifts, talent; faction; parts, genitals; **por otra parte** in another direction; elsewhere; on the other hand; **por todas partes** everywhere; **salva sea la parte** excuse me for not mentioning where

partea•guas *m* (*pl* **-guas**) divide, ridge

partear *tr* to deliver

parte•luz *m* (*pl* **-luces**) mullion, sash bar

Partenón *m* Parthenon

partera *f* midwife

partición *f* partition, division

participar *tr* to notify, inform; give notice of ‖ *intr* to participate; partake

participio *m* participle

partícula *f* particle

particular *adj* particular; peculiar; private, personal ‖ *m* particular; matter, subject; individual; **particular a particular** (telp) person-to-person

particulizar §60 *tr* to itemize ‖ *ref* to stand out; specialize

partida *f* departure; entry, item; certificate; party, group, band; band of guerrillas; game; (*de cartas*) hand; (*de tenis*) set; lot, shipment; behavior; **mala partida** mean trick; **partida de campo** picnic; **partida doble** (com) double entry; **partida sencilla** (com) single entry

partida•rio -ria or **partidista** *adj & mf* partisan

parti•do -da *adj* generous, open-handed ‖ *m* (pol) party; decision; profit; advantage; step, measure; deal, agreement; protection; support; (*casamiento que elegir*) match; district, county; (sport) team; (sport) game, match; **partido de desempate** play-off; **tomar partido** to take a stand, take sides ‖ *f* see **partida**

partir *tr* to divide; distribute; share; split, split open; break, crack; upset, disconcert ‖ *intr* to start, depart, leave, set out; **a partir de** beginning with ‖ *ref* to become divided; crack, split

partisa•no -na *mf* (mil) partisan

partitura *f* (mus) score

parto *m* childbirth, confinement; newborn child; offspring; **estar de parto** to be in labor, be confined; **parto del ingenio** brain child

parva *f* light breakfast (*on fast days*); heap of unthreshed grain; heap, pile

parvulario *m* nursery school; kindergarten

parvulista *mf* kindergarten teacher

párvu•lo -la *adj* small, tiny; simple, innocent; humble ‖ *mf* child, tot; (*niño*) kindergartner

pasa *f* raisin; (*del pelo de los negros*) kink; **pasa de Corinto** currant

pasada *f* passage; passing; **de pasada** in passing, hastily; **mala pasada** mean trick

pasade•ro -ra *adj* passable ‖ *f* stepping stone; walkway, catwalk

pasadizo *m* passage, corridor, hallway, alley; catwalk

pasa•do -da *adj* past; gone by; overripe; spoiled; overdone; stale; burned out; antiquated; faded ‖ *m* past; **pasados** ancestors ‖ *f* see **pasada**

pasa•dor -dora *mf* smuggler ‖ *m* door bolt; bolt, pin; hatpin; brooch; stickpin; safety pin; strainer

pasaje *m* passage; fare; fares; passengers; **cobrar el pasaje** to collect fares

pasaje•ro -ra *adj* passing, fleeting; (*camino, calle*) common, traveled ‖ *mf* passenger; hotel guest; **pasajero colgado** straphanger; **pasajero no presentado** no-show

pasamano *m* lace trimming; (*baranda*) handrail; (naut) gangway

pasamonta•ña *m* or **pasamonta•ñas** *m* (*pl* **-ñas**) ski mask, storm hood

pasaporte *m* passport

pasapuré *m* potato masher

pasar *m* livelihood ‖ *tr* to pass; cross; take across; send, transfer, transm:t; (*contrabando*) slip in; spend; swallow; excel; overlook, stand for; undergo, suffer; (*un libro*) go through; (*una película*) show; dry in the sun; tutor; study with or under; **pasarlo** to get along; live; (*dícese de la salud*) be; **pasar por alto** to disregard; omit, leave out; skip ‖ *intr* to pass; go; pass away; pass over; happen; last; spread; get along; yield; come in, e.g., **pase Vd.** come in; **pasar de** to go beyond, exceed; to go above; be more than; **pasar por** to pass by, down, through, over, etc.; pass as, pass for; stop or call at; **pasar sin** to do without ‖ *ref* to pass; go; excel; pass over; get along; pass away; take an examination; leak; go too far; become overripe, become overcooked; rot; melt; burn out; (*una llave, un tornillo*) not fit, be loose; forget; **pasarse por** to stop or call at; **pasarse sin** to do without

pasarela *f* footbridge; catwalk, gangplank

pasatiempo *m* pastime

pascua *f* Passover; Easter; Twelfth-night; Pentecost; Christmas; **dar las pascuas** to wish a Happy New Year; **estar como una pascua** or **unas pascuas** (coll) to be bubbling over with joy; **¡Felices Pascuas!** Merry Christmas!; **Pascua de flores** Easter; **Pascua del Espíritu Santo** Pentecost; **Pascua de Navidad** Christmas; **Pascua de Resurrección** or **Pascua florida** Easter; **Pascuas navideñas** Christmas

pase *m* (*permiso; billete gratuito; movimiento de las manos del mesmerista, el torero*) pass; (*en la esgrima*) feint; **pase de cortesía** complimentary ticket
paseante *adj* strolling ‖ *mf* stroller
pasear *tr* to walk; promenade, show off ‖ *intr* to take a walk; go for a ride ‖ *ref* to take a walk; go for a ride; wander, ramble; take it easy
paseíllo *m* processional entrance of bullfighters
paseo *m* walk, stroll, promenade; ride; drive; avenue; **dar un paseo** to take a walk; take a ride; **enviar a paseo** to send on his way, dismiss without ceremony; **paseo de caballos** bridle path; **paseo de la cuadrilla** processional entrance of the bullfighters
pasillo *m* short step; passage, corridor; (theat) short piece, sketch
pasión *f* passion
pasi•vo -va *adj* passive; (*pensión*) retirement ‖ *m* liabilities; debit side
pasmar *tr* to chill; frostbite; stun, benumb; dumbfound, astound ‖ *ref* to chill; become frostbitten; be astounded; get lockjaw; (*los colores*) become dull or flat
pasmo *m* cold; lockjaw, tetanus; astonishment; wonder, prodigy
pasmo•so -sa *adj* astounding; awesome
paso *m* step, pace; (*de la escalera*) step; gait; walk; passing; passage; step, measure, démarche; pass, permit; strait; footstep, footprint; incident, happening; (*de hélice, tornillo*) pitch; (elec) pitch; (rad) stage; (theat) short piece, sketch, skit; **al paso** in passing, on the way; **al paso que** at the rate that; (*a la vez que, mientras*) while, whereas; **ceder el paso** to make way; to keep clear; **de paso** in passing; at the same time; **paso a nivel** grade crossing; **paso de ganado** cattle crossing; **paso de ganso** goose step
paspa *f* (SAm) crack in the lips
pasquín *m* lampoon
pasquinar *tr* to lampoon
pasta *f* paste, dough, pie crust, soup paste; mash; (*para hacer papel*) pulp; cardboard; board binding; (*de un diente*) filling; (*dinero*) (coll) dough; **pasta dentrífica** toothpaste; **pasta española** marbled leather binding, tree calf; **pastas** noodles, macaroni, spaghetti, etc.; **pasta seca** cookie
pastar *tr & intr* to graze
pastel *m* pie; pastry roll; pastel; settlement, pacification; cheat, trick; (typ) pi; (typ) smear; (coll) plot, deal; **pastel de cumpleaños** birthday cake
pastelería *f* pastry; pastry shop
pastele•ro -ra *mf* pastry cook
pastelillo *m* tart, cake; (*de mantequilla*) pat
pasterizar §60 *tr* to pasteurize
pastilla *f* tablet, lozenge, drop; (*pequeña masa pastosa*) dab; (*de jabón, chocolate, etc.*) cake
pasto *m* pasture; grass; food, nourishment; **a pasto** to excess; in abundance; **a todo**

pasto freely, without restriction; **de pasto** ordinary, everyday
pastor *m* shepherd; pastor
pastora *f* shepherdess
pastoral *adj & f* pastoral
pastorear *tr* (*a las ovejas o los fieles*) to shepherd; lie in ambush for; spoil, pamper; (Arg, Urug) to court
pasto•so -sa *adj* pasty, doughy; (*voz*) mellow; (Arg, Chile) grassy
pastura *f* pasture; fodder
pasu•do -da *adj* kinky
pata *f* paw, foot, leg; (*de un mueble*) leg; duck; **a cuatro patas** on all fours; **estirar la pata** to kick the bucket; **meter la pata** to butt in, to put one's foot in it; **pata de gallo** crow's-foot; blunder; piece of nonsense; **pata de palo** peg leg, wooden leg; **pata galana** game leg; lame person; **patas arriba** on one's back, upside down; topsyturvy
patada *f* kick; stamp, stamping; step; footstep, track; **en dos patadas** in a jiffy
patalear *intr* to kick; stamp the feet
pataleta *f* fit; feigned fit or convulsion; (dial) tantrum
patán *m* churl, boor, lout; peasant
pataplún *interj* kerplunk!
patata *f* potato
patear *tr* to kick; trample on ‖ *intr* to stamp one's foot; bustle around; kick
patentar *tr* to patent
patente *adj* patent, clear, evident ‖ *f* grant, privilege, warrant; patent; **de patente** (Chile) excellent, first-class; **patente de circulación** owner's license; **patente de invención** patent; **patente de sanidad** bill of health
paternal *adj* paternal, fatherly
paternidad *f* paternity, fatherhood; **paternidad literaria** authorship
pater•no -na *adj* paternal
pateta *m* (coll) the devil; cripple
patéti•co -ca *adj* pathetic
patetismo *m* pathos
patibula•rio -ria *adj* hair-raising
patíbulo *m* scaffold
patiesteva•do -da *adj* bowlegged
patilla *f* small paw or foot; pocket flap; watermelon; (naut) compass; **patillas** sideburns, side whiskers
patín *m* small patio; skate; skid, slide, runner; (*ave marina*) petrel; **patín de cuchilla** or **de hielo** ice skate; **patín de ruedas** roller skate
patinada *f* (SAm) (aut) skidding
patinadero *m* skating rink
patina•dor -dora *mf* skater
patinaje *m* skating; skidding; **patinaje artístico** figure skating; **patinaje de fantasía** fancy skating; **patinaje de figura** figure skating
patinar *intr* to skate; skid; slip
patinazo *m* skid; slip; slip, blunder
patinete *m* scooter
patio *m* patio, court, yard; campus; (rr) yard, switchyard; **patio de recreo** playground

patituer•to -ta *adj* crooked-legged; crooked, lopsided
patizam•bo -ba *adj* knock-kneed
pato *m* duck, drake; **pagar el pato** to be the goat; **pato de flojel** eider duck
patochada *f* blunder, stupidity
patojo *m* (CAm) street urchin
patología *f* pathology
patota *f* (Arg, Urug) teen-age gang
patraña *f* fake, humbug, hoax
patria *f* country; mother country, fatherland, native land; birthplace; (*p.ej., de las artes*) home; **patria chica** native heath
patriarca *m* patriarch
patri•cio -cia *adj* & *mf* patrician
patrimonio *m* patrimony
pa•trio -tria *adj* native, home; paternal ‖ *f* see **patria**
patriota *mf* patriot
patrióti•co -ca *adj* patriotic
patriotismo *m* patriotism
patrocinar *tr* to sponsor, patronize
patrocinio *m* sponsorship
patrón *m* sponsor, protector; patron saint; patron; landlord; owner, master; boss, foreman; host; (*de un barco*) skipper; pattern; standard; **patrón oro** gold standard; **patrón picado** stencil
patrona *f* patroness; landlady; owner, mistress; hostess
patronal *adj* management, employers
patronato *m* employers' association; foundation; board of trustees; patronage
patronear *tr* to skipper
patro•no -na *mf* sponsor, protector; employer ‖ *m* patron; landlord; boss, foreman; lord of the manor; **los patronos** the management ‖ *f* see **patrona**
patrulla *f* patrol; gang, band
patrullar *tr* & *intr* to patrol
paulati•no -na *adj* slow, gradual
pausa *f* pause; slowness, delay; (mus) rest
pausa•do -da *adj* slow, calm, deliberate ‖ **pausado** *adv* slowly, calmly
pausar *tr* & *intr* to slow down
pauta *f* ruler; guide lines; guideline, rule, guide, standard, model
pava *f* turkey hen; **pelar la pava** to make love at a window
pavesa *f* ember, cinder, spark
pavimentar *tr* to pave
pavimento *m* pavement
pa•vo -va *adj* (coll) silly, stupid ‖ *m* turkey; turkey cock; **comer pavo** to be a wallflower; **pavo real** peacock
pavón *m* bluing; peacock
pavonar *tr* to blue
pavonear *intr* & *ref* to strut, swagger
pavor *m* fear, terror, dread
pavoro•so -sa *adj* frightful, dreadful
payador *m* (SAm) gaucho minstrel
payasada *f* clownishness, clownish remark
payaso *m* clown; laughingstock
paz *f* (*pl* **paces**) peace; peacefulness; **dejar en paz** to leave alone, stop pestering; **estar en paz** to be even; to be quits; **hacer las paces con** to make peace with, to come to terms with; **salir en paz** to break even
pazgua•to -ta *adj* simple, doltish ‖ *mf* simpleton, dolt
pazpuerca *f* slut, slattern
P.D. *abbr* **posdata**
peaje *m* toll
peatón *m* pedestrian; rural postman
pebete *m* punk, joss stick; fuse; (*cosa hedionda*) (coll) stinker
peca *f* freckle
pecado *m* sin
peca•dor -dora *adj* sinning, sinful ‖ *mf* sinner
pecamino•so -sa *adj* sinful
pecar §73 *intr* to sin; **pecar de** to be too, e.g., **pecar de confiado** to be too trusting
pecera *f* fish globe, fish bowl
pecino•so -sa *adj* slimy
pecio *m* flotsam
pecíolo *m* leafstalk
pécora *f* head of sheep; **buena pécora** or **mala pécora** schemer, scheming woman
peco•so -sa *adj* freckly, freckle-faced
peculado *m* embezzlement, peculation
peculiar *adj* peculiar
pecunia•rio -ria *adj* pecuniary
pechada *f* bump or push with the chest; tossing an animal (*with a bump of horse's chest*); bumping contest between two horsemen
pechar *tr* to pay as a tax; fulfill; take on; drive one's horse against; bump with the chest; strike for a loan ‖ *ref* (*dos jinetes*) to vie in a bumping contest
pechera *f* shirt front, shirt bosom; chest protector; (*del delantal*) bib; breast strap; (coll) bosom; **pechera postiza** dickey
pecho *m* chest; breast, bosom; heart; courage; **dar el pecho** to nurse, suckle; face it out; **de dos pechos** double-breasted; **de un solo pecho** single-breasted; **echar el pecho al agua** to put one's shoulder to the wheel; (coll) to speak out; **en pechos de camisa** in shirt sleeves; **tomar a pecho** to take to heart; **¡pecho al agua!** take heart!, put your shoulder to the wheel!
pechuga *f* (*del ave*) breast; slope, hill; brass, cheek; treachery, perfidy; (coll) bosom, breast
pechu•gón -gona *adj* big-chested; brazen ‖ *mf* sponger ‖ *m* slap or blow on the chest; fall on the chest
pedagogía *f* pedagogy
pedal *mf* pedal, treadle
pedalear *intr* to pedal
pedante *adj* pedantic ‖ *mf* pedant
pedantería *f* pedantry
pedantes•co -ca *adj* pedantic
pedantismo *m* pedantry
pedazo *m* piece; **hacer pedazos** to break to pieces; **hacerse pedazos** (coll) to fall to pieces; to strain, to wear oneself out; **pedazo de alcornoque, de animal** or **de bruto** dolt, imbecile, good-for-nothing; **pedazo del alma, de las entrañas** or **del corazón** (*niño*) darling, apple of one's eye; **pedazo de pan** (*pequeña cantidad*) crumb; (*precio bajo*) song

pederastia *f* pederasty
pedernal *m* flint; flintiness; flint-hearted person
pedestal *m* pedestal
pedestre *adj* pedestrian
pedestrismo *m* pedestrianism; walking; foot racing; cross-country racing
pediatra *mf* pediatrician
pediatría *f* pediatrics
pedido *m* request; (*encargo de mercancías*) order
pedigüe•ño -ña *adj* insistent, demanding, bothersome
pedir §50 *tr* to ask, ask for; request; demand, require; need; ask for the hand of; (*mercancías*) order; (gram) to govern; **pedir prestado a** to borrow from ‖ *intr* to ask; beg; bring suit; **a pedir de boca** opportunely; as desired
pedorre•ro -ra *adj* flatulent ‖ *f* flatulence; (orn) tody; **pedorreras** tights
pedrada *f* stoning; hit or blow with a stone; hint, taunt
pedregal *m* rocky ground; pile of rocks
pedrego•so -sa *adj* stony, rocky; suffering from gallstones ‖ *mf* sufferer from gallstones
pedrejón *m* boulder
pedrera *f* quarry, stone quarry
pedrería *f* precious stones, jewelry
pedrusco *m* boulder
pedúnculo *m* stem, stalk
peer §43 *intr & ref* to break wind
pega *f* sticking; pitch varnish; drubbing; (*en un examen*) catch question; trick, joke; (W-I) work, jobs; **de pega** (coll) fake
pegadi•zo -za *adj* sticky; catching, contagious; sponging; fake, imitation
pegajo•so -sa *adj* sticky; contagious; tempting; soft, gentle; mushy
pegapega *f* glue
pegar §44 *tr* to stick, paste; fasten, attach, tie; (*carteles*) post; (*fuego*) set; (*una enfermedad*) transmit; (*un botón*) sew on; (*un grito*) let out; (*un salto*) take; (*un golpe, una bofetada*) let go; beat; **no pegar el ojo** to not sleep a wink ‖ *intr* to stick, catch; take root, take hold; cling; join; fit, match; be fitting; pass, be accepted; beat; knock ‖ *ref* to stick, catch; take root, take hold; hang on, stick around; (*una enfermedad*) be catching; **pegársela a uno** to make a fool of someone
pegatina *f* sticker (or tag)
pegotear *intr* to hang around, sponge
peina•do -da *adj* groomed; effeminate ‖ *m* hairdo, coiffure; (*manera de componer el pelo*) hairstyle; (*policía, soldados*) search; **peinado al agua** finger wave
peina•dor -dora *mf* hairdresser ‖ *m* wrapper, dressing gown; dressing table
peinar *tr* to comb; (*policía, soldados*) search ‖ *ref* to comb oneself, comb one's hair
peine *m* comb; sly fellow
peineta *f* back comb
pelada *f* pelt, sheepskin
peladero *m* wasteland

peladilla *f* sugar almond; small pebble
peladillo *m* clingstone peach
pela•do -da *adj* bare; bald; barren; penniless; (*decena, centena, etc.*) even ‖ *m* raggedy fellow; (W-I) haircut ‖ *f* see **pelada**
pelafus•tán -tana *mf* derelict, good-for-nothing
pelaga•tos *m* (*pl* -tos) wretch, ragamuffin
pelaje *m* coat, fur; (*especie, calidad*) sort, stripe
pelar *tr* (*pelo*) to cut; (*pelo, plumas*) pluck, pull out; peel, skin, husk, hull, shell; (*los dientes*) show; (*en el juego*) clean out; beat, thrash ‖ *ref* to peel off; lose one's hair; get a haircut; clear out, make a getaway; **pelárselas por** to crave; crave to
pelazón *f* poverty; misery
peldaño *m* step
pelea *f* fight; quarrel; struggle; **pelea de gallos** cockfight
pelear *intr* to fight; quarrel; struggle ‖ *ref* to fight, fight each other
pele•ón -ona *adj* pugnacious, quarrelsome; (*vino*) cheap, ordinary ‖ *mf* quarrelsome person ‖ *m* cheap wine ‖ *f* row, scuffle, fracas
peletería *f* furriery; fur shop; (Cuba) shoe store
pelete•ro -ra *mf* furrier; (Cuba) shoe dealer
peliagu•do -da *adj* furry, long-haired; arduous, ticklish
película *f* film; motion picture; **película de dibujos** animated cartoon; **película del Oeste** western; **película de terror** or **película horripilante** horror movie; **película sonora** sound film
pelicule•ro -ra *adj* moving-picture ‖ *mf* scenario writer ‖ *m* movie actor ‖ *f* movie actress
peligrar *intr* to be in danger
peligro *m* danger, peril, risk; **ponerse en peligro de paz** to be alerted for war
peligro•so -sa *adj* dangerous
pelillo *m* trifle; **echar pelillos a la mar** to bury the hatchet; **no pararse en pelillos** to not bother about trifles, pay no attention to small matters; **no tener pelillos en la lengua** to speak right out
pelirro•jo -ja *adj* red-haired, redheaded ‖ *mf* redhead
pelo *m* hair; (*en las frutas y el cuerpo humano*) down; (*del paño*) nap; (*de la madera*) grain; (*de un animal*) coat; (*en las piedras preciosas*) flaw; (*del caballo*) color; (*en el billar*) kiss; (*del reloj*) hairspring; hair trigger; fiber, filament; raw silk; **al pelo** with the hair, with the nap; perfectly, to the point; **con todos sus pelos y señales** chapter and verse; **en pelo** bareback; **escapar por un pelo** to escape by a hairbreadth, have a narrow escape; **no tener pelos en la lengua** to be outspoken, not mince words; **ponerle a uno los pelos de punta** to make one's hair stand on end; **tomar el pelo a** to make fun of, make a fool of; **venir a pelo** to come in handy

pa
pe

pe•lón -lona *adj* bald, hairless; dull, stupid; penniless

Pélope *m* Pelops

peloponense *adj & mf* Peloponnesian

Peloponeso *m* Peloponnesus

pelo•so -sa *adj* hairy

pelota *f* ball; ball game; handball; **en pelota** stripped; stark-naked; **pelota acuática** water polo; **pelota rodada** (baseball) grounder; **pelota vasca** pelota, jai alai

pelotari *mf* pelota player

pelotear *intr* to knock a ball around; wrangle, argue

pelotera *f* row, brawl

pelotón *m* large ball; gang, crowd; platoon; **pelotón de fusilamiento** firing squad; **pelotón de los torpes** awkward squad

peltre *m* pewter

peluca *f* wig

peluche *m* plush, pile

pelu•do -da *adj* hairy, furry; bushy

peluquear *tr* (Col, Ven) to cut the hair of ‖ *intr* (Col, Ven) to get a haircut

peluquería *f* hairdresser's, barbershop

peluque•ro -ra *mf* hairdresser; barber; wigmaker

peluquín *m* hairpiece; toupee

pelusa *f* down; lint, fuzz; nap; ʲealousy, envy

pellejo *m* skin; pelt, rawhide; peel, rind; wineskin; (*la vida de uno*) (coll) hide, skin; (coll) sot, drunkard; **dar, dejar** or **perder el pellejo** to die

pellizcar §73 to pinch; nip; take a pinch of ‖ *ref* to long, pine

pellizco *m* pinch; nip; bit, pinch

pena *f* punishment; penalty; pain, hardship; toil; sorrow, grief; effort, trouble; **a duras penas** hardly, with great difficulty; **de pena** of a broken heart; **pena privativa de libertad** imprisonment; **¡qué pena!** what a pity!; **so pena de** on pain of, under penalty of; **valer la pena** to be worthwhile (to)

penacho *m* crest; tuft, plume; arrogance; (bot) tassel

pena•do -da *adj* afflicted, grieved; difficult ‖ *mf* convict

penalidad *f* trouble, hardship; (law) penalty

penalizar §60 *tr* to punish; penalize

penar *tr* to penalize; punish ‖ *intr* to suffer; linger; **penar por** to pine for, long for ‖ *ref* to grieve

penca *f* pulpy leaf; cowhide; **coger una penca** to get a jag on

penco *m* nag, jade; boor

pendejo *m* pubes; pubic hair; (coll) coward

pendencia *f* dispute, quarrel, fight; pending litigation

pendencie•ro -ra *adj* quarrelsome ‖ *mf* wrangler

pender *intr* to hang, dangle; depend; be pending

pendiente *adj* pendent, hanging, dangling; pending; under way; expecting; **estar pendiente de** (*las palabras de una persona*) to hang on; depend on; be in the process of ‖ *m* earring, pendant; watch chain ‖ *f* slope, grade; dip; pitch

péndola *f* feather; pendulum; clock; pen, quill; queen post

pendolón *m* king post

pendón *m* banner, standard, pennon

péndulo *m* pendulum; clock

pene *m* penis

penetrar *tr* to penetrate; pierce; grasp, fathom ‖ *intr* to penetrate ‖ *ref* to grasp, fathom; realize; become convinced

penicilina *f* penicillin

península *f* peninsula

peninsular *adj & mf* peninsular; (*ibero*) Peninsular

penique *m* penny

penitencia *f* penitence; penance; **hacer penitencia** to do penance; eat sparingly; take potluck

penitente *adj & mf* penitent

penol *m* (naut) yardarm

peno•so -sa *adj* arduous, difficult; suffering; conceited; shy

pensa•dor -dora *adj* thinking ‖ *mf* thinker

pensamiento *m* thought; (*planta y flor*) pansy

pensar §2 *tr* to think; think over; (*un naipe, un número, etc.*) think of; intend to; **pensar de** to think of, e.g., **¿qué piensa Vd. de este libro?** what do you think of this book? ‖ *intr* to think; **pensar en** (*dirigir sus pensamientos a*) to think of (*to turn one's thoughts to*)

pensati•vo -va *adj* pensive, thoughtful

pensión *f* pension; annuity; allowance; boardinghouse; (*para ampliar estudios*) fellowship; **pensión completa** board and lodging

pensionar *tr* to pension

pensionista *mf* pensioner; boarder; boarding-school pupil; **medio pensionista** day boarder

pentagrama *m* staff, musical staff

Pentecostés, el Pentecost

penúlti•mo -ma *adj* penultimate; next to last ‖ *f* penult

penumbra *f* penumbra; semidarkness, half-light

penuria *f* shortage

peña *f* rock, boulder; cliff; club, group, circle

peñasco *m* pinnacle; crag

peñasco•so -sa *adj* rocky, craggy

peñón *m* rock, spire; **peñón de Gibraltar** rock of Gibraltar

peón *m* laborer; pedestrian; foot soldier; farm hand; (*en el ajedrez*) pawn; (*en las damas*) man; top, peg top; spindle, axle; (taur) attendant; **peón de albañil** or **de mano** hod carrier

peor *adj & adv* worse; worst

pepa *f* (*de la manzana*) (Col) seed; (*del durazno*) (Arg) stone; (*canica*) (Arg) marble; (Col) lie, cheat, trick

pepe *mf* foundling ‖ *m* bib; **Pepe** *m* Joe

pepinillo *m* gherkin

pepino *m* cucumber; **me importa un pepino** I couldn't care less

pepita *f* seed, pip; nugget; (vet) pip

peque *m* tot

pequén *m* (Chile) burrowing owl

peque•ñez f (pl **-ñeces**) smallness; infancy; trifle

peque•ño -ña adj little, small; young; low, humble

pequeño-burgués adj petit bourgeois

Pequín m Peking

pequi•nés -nesa adj & mf Pekinese

pera f pear; goatee; cinch, sinecure; pear-shaped bulb; pear-shaped switch

peral m pear tree

perca f (ichth) perch

percance m mischance, misfortune; **percances** perquisites

percatar ref — **percatarse de** to be aware of; beware of, guard against

percebe m barnacle; fool, sap

percepción f perception; collection

percibir tr to perceive; collect

percudir tr to tarnish, dull; spread through

percha f perch, pole, roost; clothes tree; coat hanger; coat hook; barber pole

perchero m rack, clothes rack, clothes hanger

perde•dor -dora losing ‖ mf loser

perder §51 tr to lose; waste, squander; (un tren, una ocasión) miss; (una asignatura) flunk; ruin; spoil ‖ intr to lose; fade ‖ ref to get lost; miscarry; sink; become ruined; spoil; go to the dogs

perdición f perdition; loss; outrage; ruination

pérdida f loss; waste; ruination; **no tener pérdida** to be easy to find; **pérdida de reclamable** tax loss

perdi•do -da adj (bala) stray, wild; (manga) wide, loose; fruitless; (horas) off, spare, idle; distracted; inveterate; madly in love ‖ m profligate, rake

perdido•so -sa adj unlucky; easily lost

perdigón m young partridge; profligate; heavy loser; (alumno) failure; **perdigones** (granos de plomo) shot; **perdigón zorrero** buckshot

per•diz f (pl **-dices**) partridge

perdón m pardon, forgiveness; **con perdón** by your leave

perdonable adj pardonable

perdonar tr to pardon, forgive, excuse; **no perdonar** to not miss, not omit

perdula•rio -ria adj careless, sloppy; incorrigible, vicious ‖ mf good-for-nothing, profligate

perdurable adj long-lasting; everlasting

perdurar intr to last, last a long time, survive

perecede•ro -ra adj perishable; mortal ‖ m extreme want

perecer §22 intr to perish; suffer; be in great want ‖ ref to pine; **perecerse por** to be dying for; (una mujer) be mad about

peregrinación f peregrination; pilgrimage

peregri•no -na adj wandering, traveling; foreign; rare, strange; beautiful; mortal; (ave) migratory ‖ mf pilgrim

perejil m parsley; (coll) frippery

perenne adj perennial

pereza f laziness; slowness

perezo•so -sa adj lazy; slow, dull, heavy ‖ mf lazybones; sleepyhead ‖ m (zool) sloth

perfección f perfection

perfeccionar tr to perfect, improve

perfec•to -ta adj & m perfect

perfidia f perfidy

pérfi•do -da adj perfidious

perfil m profile; side view; cross section; thin stroke; outline, sketch; **perfil aerodinámico** streamlining; **perfiles** finishing touches; courtesies

perfila•do -da adj (cara) long and thin; (nariz) well-formed; (facciones) delicate; streamlined

perfilar tr to profile, outline; perfect, polish, finish ‖ ref to be outlined; show one's profile, stand sidewise; stand out; dress up

perforación f perforation; drilling; puncture; keypunching

perfora•dor -dora adj perforating; drilling ‖ f pneumatic drill, rock drill

perforar tr to perforate; drill, bore; puncture; (una tarjeta) punch

perforista mf keypuncher

perfumar tr to perfume

perfume m perfume

pergamino m parchment

pergenio m rascal

pericia f skill, expertness

periclitar intr to be in jeopardy, be shaky

perico m (pelo postizo) periwig; parakeet; (slang) chamber pot; (CAm) compliment; **perico entre ellas** lady's man

periferia f periphery; surroundings

perifollos mpl finery, frippery, chiffons

perilla f pear-shaped ornament; goatee; knob, doorknob; (del arzón) pommel; (de la oreja) lobe; **de perilla** apropos, to the point

periodísti•co -ca adj newspaper, journalistic

periódi•co -ca adj periodic ‖ m newspaper; periodical

periodismo m journalism

periodista mf journalist ‖ m newspaperman ‖ f newspaperwoman

período m period; compound sentence; (phys) cycle; **período lectivo** (en la escuela) term

peripues•to -ta adj dudish, all spruced up, sporty

periquete m jiffy; **en un periquete** in a jiffy

periquito m parakeet; **periquito de Australia** budgerigar

periscopio m periscope

peri•to -ta adj skilled, skillful; expert ‖ m expert

perjudicar §73 tr to damage, impair, hurt, prejudice

perjudicial adj harmful, injurious, detrimental, prejudicial

perjuicio m harm, injury, damage, prejudice; **en perjuicio de** to the detriment of

perjurar intr to commit perjury; swear, be profane ‖ ref to commit perjury; perjure oneself

perjurio m perjury

perla f pearl; **de perlas** perfectly

perlesía f palsy

permanecer §22 intr to stay, remain

permanencia f permanence; stay, sojourn

pe
pe

permanente *adj* permanent ‖ *f* permanent wave

permiso *m* permission; permit; time off; (*en el monedaje*) tolerance; leave; **con permiso** excuse me; **permiso de circulación** owner's license; **permiso de conducir** driver's license

permitir *tr* to permit, allow ‖ *ref* to be permitted; **no se permite fumar** no smoking

permutar *tr* to interchange; barter; to permute

pernear *intr* to kick; hustle; fuss, fret

pernera *f* trouser leg

pernicio•so -sa *adj* pernicious

pernil *m* trouser leg; (*anca y muslo*) ham

perno *m* bolt; **perno con anillo** ringbolt; **perno roscado** screw bolt

pernoctar *intr* to spend the night

pero *conj* but, yet ‖ *m* but; fault, defect; **poner pero a** to find fault with

perogrullada *f* platitude, inanity

peroración *f* peroration; harangue

perorar *intr* to perorate; orate

peróxido *m* peroxide; **peróxido de hidrógeno** hydrogen peroxide

perpendicular *adj & f* perpendicular

perpetrar *tr* to perpetrate

perpetuar §21 *tr* to perpetuate

perpe•tuo -tua *adj* perpetual; life

perplejidad *f* perplexity; worry, anxiety

perple•jo -ja *adj* perplexed; worried, anxious; baffling, perplexing

perra *f* bitch; tantrum; drunkenness

perrada *f* pack of dogs; dirty trick

perrera *f* kennel, doghouse; tantrum; toil, drudgery

perro *m* dog; **el perro del hortelano** dog in the manger; **perro caliente** (slang) hot dog; **perro cobrador** retriever; **perro de aguas** spaniel; **perro de lanas** poodle; **perro de muestra** pointer; **perro faldero** lap dog; **perro marino** dogfish, shark; **perro raposero** foxhound; **perro viejo** (coll) wise old owl

perro-lazarillo *m* (*pl* **perros-lazarillos**) Seeing Eye dog

persa *adj & mf* Persian

persecución *f* persecution; pursuit; annoyance, harassment

perseguir §67 *tr* to persecute; pursue; annoy, harass

perseverar *intr* to persevere

persiana *f* slatted shutter; flowered silk; louver; Venetian blind; **persiana del radiador** (aut) louver

persistir *intr* to persist

persona *f* person; personage; **persona desplazada** displaced person; **personas** people; **por persona** per capita

personaje *m* personage; (theat) character; person of importance

personal *adj* personal ‖ *m* personnel, staff, force

personalidad *f* personality

personificar §73 *tr* to personify

perspectiva *f* perspective; outlook, prospect; appearance

perspi•caz *adj* (*pl* **-caces**) perspicacious, discerning; keen-sighted

persuadir *tr* to persuade

persuasión *f* persuasion

pertenecer §22 *intr* to belong; pertain ‖ *ref* to be independent, be free

perteneciente *adj* pertaining

pértiga *f* pole, rod, staff

perti•naz *adj* (*pl* **-naces**) pertinacious; (*dolor de cabeza*) persistent

pertinente *adj* pertinent, relevant

pertrechos *mpl* supplies, provisions, equipment; tools; **pertrechos de guerra** ordnance

perturbar *tr* to perturb; disturb; upset, disconcert; confuse, interrupt

Perú, el Peru

perua•no -na *adj & mf* Peruvian

perversidad *f* perversity

perversión *f* perversion

perver•so -sa *adj* perverse; wicked, depraved ‖ *mf* profligate

perverti•do -da *mf* pervert

pervertir §68 *tr* to pervert ‖ *ref* to become perverted; go to the bad

pesa *f* weight; (CAm, Col, Ven) butcher shop

pesacar•tas *m* (*pl* **-tas**) letter scales

pesadez *f* heaviness; slowness; tiresomeness; harshness; (phys) gravity

pesadilla *f* nightmare

pesa•do -da *adj* heavy; slow; tiresome; harsh; boring

pesadumbre *f* sorrow, grief; trouble; weight, heaviness

pesaje *m* weighing; (sport) weigh-in

pésame *m* condolence; **dar el pésame a** to extend one's sympathy to

pesantez *f* (phys) gravity

pesar *m* sorrow, regret; **a pesar de** in spite of ‖ *tr* to weigh; make sorry ‖ *intr* to weigh; be heavy; cause regret, cause sorrow

pesaro•so -sa *adj* sorrowful, regretful

pesca *f* fishing; catch; **ir de pesca** to go fishing; **pesca de bajura** off-shore fishing; **pesca de gran altura** deep-sea fishing

pescadería *f* fish market; fish store; fish stand

pescade•ro -ra *mf* fish dealer, fishmonger

pescado *m* fish (*that has been caught*)

pesca•dor -dora *adj* fishing ‖ *m* fisherman ‖ *f* fisherwoman, fishwife

pescante *m* coach box; (*de una grúa*) jib; (aut) front seat; (naut) davit; (theat) trap door

pescar §73 *tr* to fish; fish for; fish out; (*peces*) catch; (coll) to manage to get ‖ *intr* to fish

pescozón *m* slap on the neck or head

pescuezo *m* neck

pesebre *m* crib, rack, manger; crèche

pesero *m* (CAm, Col, Ven) butcher; (Mex) shared taxi

pesimismo *m* pessimism

pesimista *adj* pessimistic ‖ *mf* pessimist

pési•mo -ma *adj* very bad, abominable

peso *m* weight; scale, balance; burden, load; judgment, good sense; (*unidad monetaria*) peso; **caerse de su peso** to be self-evident; **llevar el peso de la batalla** to bear the brunt of the battle; **peso atómico** atomic weight; **peso molecular** molecular weight
pespuntar *tr & intr* to backstitch
pespunte *m* backstitch
pesquera *f* fishery; fishing grounds; (*presa para detener los peces*) weir
pesquería *f* fishing; fishery
pesque•ro -ra *adj* fishing ‖ *m* fishing boat ‖ *f* see **pesquera**
pesquis *m* acumen, keenness
pesquisa *m* (Arg) detective ‖ *f* inquiry, investigation
pesquisar *tr* to investigate, inquire into
pestaña *f* eyelash; flange; fringe, edging; index tab
pestañear *intr* to wink, blink; **sin pestañear** without batting an eye
peste *f* pest, plague; epidemic; stink, stench; abundance; (Col, Peru) head cold; (Chile) smallpox; **pestes** insults
pesticida *m* pesticide
pestífe•ro -ra *adj* pestiferous; stinking
pestilencia *f* pestilence
pestillo *m* bolt; doorlatch
petaca *f* cigar case; cigarette case; tobacco pouch; leather-covered hamper
pétalo *m* petal
petardear *tr* to swindle ‖ *intr* (aut) to backfire
petardeo *m* swindling; (aut) backfire
petardo *m* petard; bomb; swindle, cheat
petate *m* sleeping bag; bedding; luggage; cheat; poor soul; **liar el petate** to pack up and get out; to kick the bucket
petición *f* petition; request; plea; (law) claim, bill; **a petición de** at the request of; **petición de mano** formal betrothal
petimetre *m* dude, sport, dandy
petirrojo *m* redbreast, robin
Petrarca *m* Petrarch
petrificar §73 *tr & ref* to petrify
petróleo *m* petroleum; **petróleo combustible** fuel oil
petrole•ro -ra *adj* oil, petroleum ‖ *mf* oil dealer ‖ *m* oil tanker
petroquími•co -ca *adj* petrochemical
petulancia *f* flippancy, pertness
petulante *adj* flippant, pert
pez *m* (*pl* **peces**) fish; reward, just desert; **como un pez en el agua** snug as a bug in a rug; **pez de plata** (ent) silverfish; **salga pez o salga rana** blindly, hit or miss ‖ *f* pitch, tar
pezón *m* stem; nipple, teat
pezonera *f* linchpin
pezuña *f* hoof
piado•so -sa *adj* merciful; pitiful; pious
piafar *intr* (*el caballo*) to paw, to stamp
piano *m* piano; **piano de cola** grand piano; **piano de media cola** baby grand
piar §77 *intr* to peep, chirp
pica *f* pike; pikeman; picador's goad; (Col) pique, resentment

picada *f* peck; bite; (Bol) knock at the door; (Arg, Bol, Urug) narrow ford; (SAm) path, trail
picadillo *m* (*carne, verduras, ajos, etc. reducidos a pequeños trozos*) hash; (*carne picada*) mincemeat
pica•do -da *adj* perforated; pitted; (*tabaco*) cut; (*hielo*) cracked; (*mar*) choppy; piqued ‖ *m* mincemeat; (aer) dive; **picado con motor** (aer) power dive ‖ *f* see **picada**
picador *m* horsebreaker; (*torero de a caballo*) picador (*mounted bullfighter*); chopping block; meat grinder
picadura *f* bite, prick, sting; nick; puncture; cut tobacco; (*en un diente*) cavity
picaflor *m* hummingbird
picahie•los *m* (*pl* **-los**) ice pick
picamade•ros *m* (*pl* **-ros**) green woodpecker
picante *adj* biting, pricking, stinging; piquant, juicy, racy; (SAm) highly seasoned ‖ *m* mordancy; piquancy
pícap *m* (Bol, Chile, Col) var of **pick-up**
picapedrero *m* stonecutter
picaplei•tos *m* (*pl* **-tos**) troublemaker; shyster, pettifogger
picaporte *m* latch; latchkey; door knocker
picar §73 *tr* to prick, pierce, puncture; sting; bite; burn; peck; nibble; pit, pock; mince, chop up, cut up; stick, poke; spur; goad; perforate; (*hielo*) crack; harass, pursue; tame; pique, annoy ‖ *intr* to itch; (*el sol*) burn; nibble; have a smattering; be catching; (*los negocios*) pick up; (aer) to dive; (*caer en el lazo*) (coll) to bite; **picar en** to nibble at; dabble in; **picar muy alto** aim high, expect too much ‖ *ref* to rot; (*la ropa*) be moth-eaten; (*el vino*) turn sour; (*un diente*) be decayed; (*el mar*) get rough; be offended; get drunk; (*drogas*) get a fix, shoot up; **picarse de** to boast of being
picardía *f* roguishness, knavery; crudeness, coarseness; mischief
picares•co -ca *adj* roguish, rascally; picaresque; rough, coarse, crude; witty, humorous
píca•ro -ra *adj* roguish; scheming, tricky; low, vile; mischievous ‖ *mf* rogue; schemer
picaza *f* magpie
picazón *f* itch, itching; annoyance
pícea *f* spruce tree
pick-up *m* pickup; phonograph
pico *m* beak, bill; (*de jarra*) spout; (*del yunque*) beak; (*del pañuelo*) corner; nib, tip; (*de la pluma de escribir*) point; peak; (*herramienta*) pick; (*de dinero*) pile, lot; talkativeness; (elec) peak; (naut) bow, prow; **callar el pico** to shut up; **darse el pico** (*las palomas*) to bill; **pico de oro** silver-tongue; **tener mucho pico** to talk too much; **y pico** odd, e.g., **trescientos y pico** three hundred odd; a little after, e.g., **a las tres y pico** a little after three o'clock
picor *m* (*del paladar*) smarting; itch, itching, burning
pico•so -sa *adj* pock-marked
picota *f* pillory; peak, point, spire
picotazo *m* peck

picotear *tr* to peck ‖ *intr* (*el caballo*) to toss the head; chatter, jabber, gab; (*las mujeres*) wrangle

pichel *m* pewter tankard

pichón -chona *mf* darling ‖ *m* young pigeon; **pichón de barro** clay pigeon

pie *m* foot; footing; foothold; base, stand; (*de copa*) stem; (*de la cama*) footboard; cause, origin, reason; (*de la página*) foot, bottom; (theat) cue; (Chile) down payment; **a cuatro pies** on all fours; **al pie de fábrica** at the factory; **al pie de la letra** literally; **al pie de la obra** (com) delivered; **a pie** on foot, walking; **buscar cinco** (or **tres**) **pies al gato** to be looking for trouble; **de pie** standing; up and about; firm, steady; firmly, steadily; **en pie de guerra** on a war footing; **ir a pie** to go on foot, to walk; **morir al pie del cañon** to die in the harness, to die with one's boots on; **nacer de pie** or **de pies** to be born with a silver spoon in one's mouth; **pie de atleta** athlete's foot; **pie de cabra** crowbar; **pie de imprenta** imprint, printer's mark; **pie derecho** upright, stanchion; **pie marino** sea legs; **pie plano** flatfoot; **pie quebrado** (*de verso*) short line; **vestirse por los pies** to be a man

piedad *f* (*devoción a las cosas santas*) piety; (*misericordia*) pity, mercy

piedra *f* stone; rock; (*pedernal*) flint; heavy hailstone; (pathol) stone; **piedra angular** cornerstone; (fig) cornerstone, keystone; **piedra arenisca** sandstone; **piedra azul** (chem) bluestone; **piedra de albardilla** copestone; **piedra de amolar** grindstone; **piedra de chispa** flint; **piedra de pipas** meerschaum; **piedra imán** loadstone; **piedra miliar** or **miliaria** milestone; **piedra movediza** rolling stone; **piedra pómez** pumice, pumice stone

piel *f* skin; hide, pelt; fur; leather; (*de las frutas*) peel, skin; **piel de cabra** goatskin; **piel de foca** sealskin; **piel de gallina** goose flesh ‖ *m* — **piel roja** (*pl* **pieles rojas**) (*indio norteamericano*) redskin

pienso *m* feed, feeding; **ni por pienso** by no means, don't think of it

pierna *f* leg; post, upright; **dormir a pierna suelta** or **tendida** to sleep like a log; **estirar la pierna** to lie down on the job; kick the bucket; **estirar** or **extender las piernas** to stretch one's legs, go for a walk; **ser buena pierna** (Arg, Urug) to be a good-natured fellow

pieza *f* (*órgano de una máquina o artefacto; obra dramática; composición suelta de múscia; cañón; figura que sirve para jugar a las damas, al ajedrez, etc.; moneda*) piece; (*objeto; mueble; porción de tela*) piece or article; (*habitación, cuarto*) room; **buena pieza** hussy; sly fox; **pieza de recambio** or **de repuesto** spare part; **quedarse en una pieza** or **hecho una pieza** to be dumbfounded, stand motionless

pífano *m* fife; fifer

pifia *f* (billiards) miscue; (coll) miscue, slip

pifiar *intr* to miscue

pigmentar *tr* & *ref* to pigment

pigmento *m* pigment

pigme•o -a *adj* & *mf* pygmy

pijama *f* pajamas

pila *f* basin; trough; sink; font; pile, heap; (elec) battery, cell; (elec & phys) pile; **pila de linterna** flashlight battery

pilar *m* (*de una fuente*) basin, bowl; pillar; stone post, milestone; (*persona*) (fig) pillar ‖ *tr* (*el grano*) to crush, pound

Pilatos *m* Pilate

píldora *f* pill; bad news; **píldora para dormir** sleeping pill

pileta *f* sink; basin, bowl; font; swimming pool

pilón *m* pylon; drinking trough; loaf of sugar; counterpoise; drop hammer; (Mex, Ven) tip, gratuity; **de pilón** in addition, on top of it

pilotar *tr* to pilot

pilote *m* pile

piloto *m* pilot; first mate; (Chile) hail fellow well met

pillar *tr* to pillage, plunder; catch

pi•llo -lla *adj* roguish, rascally; sly, crafty ‖ *m* rogue, rascal; crafty fellow

pilluelo *m* scamp, little scamp

pimentero *m* pepper, black pepper; pepperbox

pimentón *m* cayenne pepper, red pepper; (*condimento preparado moliendo pimientos encarnados secos*) paprika

pimienta *f* pepper, black pepper; allspice, pimento; allspice tree

pimiento *m* (*planta*) pepper, black pepper; Guinea pepper

pimpante *adj* smart, spruce

pimpollo *m* sucker, shoot, sprout; rosebud; (*árbol nuevo*) sapling; handsome child; handsome young person

pina *f* fellow

pinacoteca *f* picture gallery

pináculo *m* pinnacle

pincel *m* brush; painter; painting; (*de luz*) pencil, beam

pincelada *f* brush stroke; touch, finish, flourish

pincelar *tr* to paint; picture; (med) to pencil

pincia•no -na *adj* Valladolid ‖ *mf* native or inhabitant of Valladolid

pincha *f* kitchenmaid

pinchar *tr* to prick, jab, pierce, puncture; stir up, prod, provoke ‖ *intr* to have a puncture; **no pinchar ni cortar** to have no say ‖ *ref* (*drogas*) to get a fix, shoot up

pinchazo *m* prick, jab, puncture; provocation; **a prueba de pinchazos** punctureproof

pinche *m* scullion, kitchen boy; helper

pincho *m* thorn, prick; snack; spike

Píndaro *m* Pindar

pingajo *m* rag, tatter

pingo *m* rag, tatter; ragamuffin; horse; **andar** or **ir de pingo** (*una mujer*) to gad about

pingüe *adj* oily, greasy, fat; abundant, rich; fertile; profitable

pingüino *m* penguin
pinito *m* first step, little step; **hacer pinitos** to begin to walk; (fig) to take the first steps
pino *m* pine tree; first step; **hacer pinos** to begin to walk; (fig) to take the first steps
pinocha *f* pine needle
pinta *m* scoundrel ‖ *f* spot, mark, sign; dot; pint
pintacilgo *m* goldfinch
pintada *f* Guinea hen
pinta•do -da *adj* spotted, mottled; tipsy; accented; **el más pintado** the aptest one; the shrewdest one; the best one; **venir como pintado** to be just the thing ‖ *m* (*acto de pintar*) painting ‖ *f* see **pintada**
pintar *tr* to paint; (*una letra, un acento, etc.*) draw; picture, depict; put an accent mark on; **pintarla** to put it on, put on airs ‖ *intr* to paint; begin to turn red, begin to ripen; show, turn out ‖ *ref* to paint, put on make-up; begin to turn red, begin to ripen
pintarrajear *tr* to daub, smear
pin•to -ta *adj* speckled, spotted ‖ *f* see **pinta**
pin•tor -tora *mf* painter; **pintor de brocha gorda** painter, house painter; dauber
pintores•co -ca *adj* picturesque
pintura *f* (*color preparado para pintar*) paint; (*arte; obra pintada*) painting; **hacer pinturas** to prance; **no poder ver ni en pintura** to not be able to stand the sight of
pinture•ro -ra *adj* showy, conceited ‖ *mf* show-off
pinza *f* clothespin; (*de langosta, cangrejo, etc.*) claw; **pinzas** pliers; pincers; tweezers; forceps
pinzón *m* pump handle; (orn) finch
piña *f* fir cone, pine cone; knob; plug; cluster, knot; pineapple
piñonear *intr* (*un arma de fuego*) to click; reach the age of puberty; (coll) to be an old goat
piñoneo *m* click (*of a firearm*)
pí•o -a *adj* pious; merciful, compassionate; (*caballo*) pied, dappled ‖ *m* peeping, chirping; keen desire
piocha *f* jeweled head adornment; artificial flower made of feathers; pick
piojo *m* louse
piojo•so -sa *adj* lousy; mean, stingy
piola *f* string, cord
pione•ro -ra *adj* & *mf* pioneer
pipa *f* (*para fumar tabaco*) pipe; (*medida para vinos*) butt; wine cask; (*simiente*) pip; (mus) pipe, reed; (coll) handgun; **pipa de espuma de mar** meerschaum pipe; **pipa de riego** watering cart; **pipa de tierra** clay pipe
pipí *m* (coll) pee, urine; **hacer pipí** to pee, urinate
pipiolo *m* (CAm, Mex) child
pique *m* pique, resentment; eagerness; (*insecto*) chigger; (*naipe*) spade; **a pique** steep; **a pique de** in danger of; on the verge of; **echar a pique** to sink; ruin; **irse a pique** to sink; go to ruin, be ruined
piquera *f* bung, bunghole; (Mex) dive, joint

piquete *m* sharp jab; small hole; stake, picket; (*de soldados, de huelguistas*) picket; **piquete de ejecución** firing squad; **piquete de salvas** firing squad
pira *f* pyre
piragua *f* pirogue; (sport) single shell
piragüismo *m* canoeing
piragüista *m* (sport) crewman
pirámide *f* pyramid
pirata *m* pirate; **pirata aéreo** hijacker
piratear *intr* to pirate, be a pirate
piratería *f* piracy; **piratería aérea** hijacking, skyjacking, air piracy
pirca *f* (SAm) dry stone wall
pirco *m* (Chile) succotash
Pireo, el Piraeus
pirine•o -a *adj* Pyrenean ‖ **Pirineos** *mpl* Pyrenees
pirita *f* pyrites
pirófa•go -ga *adj* fire-eating ‖ *mf* fire-eater
piropear *tr* to flatter, flirt with
piropo *m* garnet, carbuncle; flattery, compliment, flirtatious remark
piróscafo *m* steamship
pirotecnia *f* pyrotechnics
pirotécni•co -ca *adj* pyrotechnical ‖ *m* powder maker, fireworks manufacturer
pirueta *f* pirouette; somersault; caper
piruetear *intr* to pirouette
pisada *f* tread; footstep; footprint; trampling
pisapape•les *m* (*pl* -les) paperweight
pisar *tr* to trample, tread on, step on; tamp, pack down; (*p.ej., uvas*) tread; cover part of; ram; (*una tecla*) strike; (mus) to pluck; (coll) to abuse, tread all over; **pisar algo a alguien** to snitch something from someone ‖ *intr* to be right above; step ‖ *ref* (Arg) to guess wrong, come out wrong
pisaverde *m* fop, dandy
piscina *f* swimming pool; fishpond
Piscis *m* (astr) Pisces
pisco *m* Peruvian brandy
pisicorre *f* (W-I) station wagon
piso *m* tread; floor; flooring; (*de una carretera*) surface; flat, apartment; **buscar piso** to be looking for a place to live; **piso alto** top floor; **piso bajo** street floor, ground floor; **piso principal** main floor, second floor
pisón *m* ram, tamper
pisotear *tr* to trample, tread on, tread under foot; abuse, tread all over
pistón *m* stamp, tread
pista *f* track; trace, trail; clew; race track; (*de bolera*) alley; (*de cabaret*) floor; (aer) runway; **pista de esquí** ski run; **pista de patinar** skating rink
pisto *m* (*para los enfermos*) chicken broth; vegetable cutlet; jumbled speech or writing; mess; (CAm, Mex) money
pistola *f* pistol; sprayer; rock drill; **pistola de arzón** horse pistol; **pistola engrasadora** grease gun
pistolera *f* holster
pistolerismo *m* gangsterism
pistolero *m* gangster, gunman
pistón *m* piston

pistonear *intr* to knock
pistoneo *m* knock
pistonu•do -da *adj* stunning, swank
pita *f* century plant; hiss, hissing; glass marble; string, thread
pitar *tr* to pay, pay off; (*a un torero*) whistle disapproval of ‖ *intr* to blow a whistle, whistle; blow the horn, honk; talk nonsense; **no pitar** to not be popular; **salir pitando** to run away, dash away
pitazo *m* blast, toot, honk, whistle (sound)
pitear *intr* to whistle
pitillera *f* cigarette maker; cigarette case
pitillo *m* cigarette
pito *m* whistle; horn; fife; fifer; cigarette; jackstone; (*insecto*) tick; woodpecker; (coll) continental, straw, tinker's damn
pitón *m* lump, sprig; tenderling; (*del cuerno*) tip; nozzle, spout; python
pitonisa *f* witch, siren; pythoness
pitu•so -sa *adj* tiny, cute ‖ *mf* tot
piular *intr* to peep, chirp
pivotar *intr* to pivot
pivote *m* pivot; **pivote de dirección** (aut) kingpin
píxide *f* pyx
pizarra *f* slate; blackboard
pizarrero *m* roofer, slater
pizarrín *m* slate pencil
pizca *f* mite, whit, jot
placa *f* plaque, tablet; badge; plate; slab, sheet; scab; (anat, elec, electron, phot, zool) plate; **placa de matrícula** license plate; **placa giratoria** (*de ferrocarril; de gramófono*) turntable
placaminero *m* persimmon
placebo *m* placebo
pláceme *m* congratulation
placente•ro -ra *adj* pleasant, agreeable
placer *m* pleasure; sandbank, reef; **a placer** at one's convenience ‖ *v* §52 *tr* to please
place•ro -ra *adj* public ‖ *mf* market vendor; loafer, town gossip
pláci•do -da *adj* placid; pleasing
plaga *f* plague; pest; scourge; abundance; sore; clime, region
plagar §44 *tr* to plague, infest; (*de minas*) sow
plagiar *tr* to plagiarize
plagio *m* plagiarism; abduction, kidnaping
plan *m* plan; level, height; **plan de estudios** or **plan escolar** curriculum
plana *f* plain, flat country; trowel; cooper's plane; page
plancha *f* plate, sheet; iron, flatiron; gangplank; (coll) blunder; **a la plancha** grilled; (*huevo*) fried; **plancha de blindaje** armor plate
planchado *m* ironing; pressing
planchar *tr* (*la ropa interior blanca*) to iron; (*un traje de hombre*) to press ‖ *intr* to be a wallflower
planchear *tr* to plate
planear *tr* to plan, outline; (*una tabla*) plane ‖ *intr* to hover; (aer) to volplane, glide
planeta *m* planet
planicie *f* plain

planificar §73 *tr* to plan
planilla *f* list, roll, schedule; (*de candidatos para un puesto público*) (Mex) panel; (Mex) ballot; (Mex) commutation ticket
pla•no -na *adj* plane; level, smooth, even; flat ‖ *m* plan; map; (*superficie*) plane; (aer) plane; **de plano** clearly, plainly, flatly; flat; **levantar un plano** to make a survey; **primer plano** foreground ‖ *f* see **plana**
planta *f* (*del pie*) sole; foot; plan; project; floor plan; (*del personal de una oficina*) roster; plant, factory; (bot) plant; (sport) stance; **de planta** from the ground up; **echar plantas** to swagger, bully; **planta baja** ground floor; **planta del sortilegio** (bot) witch hazel; **tener buena planta** to make a fine appearance
plantar *tr* to plant; establish, found; (*un golpe*) plant; jilt; (*en la calle, en la cárcel*) throw ‖ *ref* to take a stand; gang together; (*un animal*) balk; land, arrive
plantear *tr* to plan, outline; establish, execute, carry out; state, set up, expound, pose
plantel *m* nursery garden; educational establishment
plantificar §73 *tr* to plan, outline; (*un golpe*) plant; (*en la calle, la cárcel*) throw ‖ *ref* to land, arrive
plantilla *f* plantlet, young plant; insole; reinforced sole; model, pattern, template; (*de empleados*) staff; (*del personal de una oficina*) roster; plan, design; (*bizcocho*) ladyfinger
plantío *m* planting; garden patch; tree nursery
plantón *m* (*que ha de ser transplantado*) shoot; graft; guard, watchman; waiting, standing around
plañide•ro -ra *adj* mournful, plaintive ‖ *f* hired mourner
plañir §12 *tr* to lament, grieve over ‖ *intr* to lament, grieve, bewail
plasma *m* plasma
plasmar *tr* to mold, shape
plasta *f* paste, soft mass; flattened object; poor job, bungle
plástica *f* (*arte de plasmar*) plastic; plastic arts
plásti•co -ca *adj* plastic ‖ *m* (*substancia*) plastic ‖ *f* see **plástica**
plata *f* silver; (*moneda o monedas*) silver; wealth; money; **en plata** briefly, to the point, plainly; **plata de ley** sterling silver
plataforma *f* platform; platform car; (*del ferrocarril*) roadbed; (*programa político*) platform; (*de lanzamiento de cohete*) pad; **plataforma giratoria** (rr) turntable
platal *m* piles of money, fortune
platanal *m* or **platanar** *m* banana plantation
plátano *m* banana; banana tree; plane tree; **plátano de occidente** buttonwood tree
platea *f* (theat) orchestra, parquet
platea•do -da *adj* silvered; silver-plated; (coll) well-to-do
platear *tr* to silver, coat or plate with silver
platero *m* silversmith; jeweler

plática f talk, chat; talk, informal lecture; sermon

platicar §73 *tr* to talk over, discuss ‖ *intr* to talk, chat; discuss; preach

platillo *m* plate; saucer; (*de la balanza*) pan; (mus) cymbal; **platillo volador** or **volante** flying saucer

platino *m* platinum

plato *m* dish; plate; (*de una comida*) course; daily fare; **plato fuerte** main course; **plato giratorio** (*del gramófono*) turntable

pla•tó *m* (*pl* -**tós**) (mov) set

Platón *m* Plato

platu•do -da *adj* rich

plausible *adj* praiseworthy; acceptable

playa f beach, shore, strand; **playa infantil** sand pile

playera f fishwoman; beach shoe

plaza f plaza, square; market place; town, city; fortified town; space, room; yard; office, employment; character, reputation; seat; **sentar plaza** to enlist; **plaza de armas** parade ground; public square; **plaza de gallos** cockpit; **plaza de toros** bullring; **plaza mayor** main square

plazo *m* term; time; time limit; date of payment; instalment; **a plazo** on credit, on time; **en plazos** in installments

pleamar f high tide, high water

plebe f common people

plebe•yo -ya *adj* & *mf* plebeian

plegadi•zo -za *adj* folding; pliable

plegar §66 *tr* to fold; crease; pleat ‖ *ref* to yield, give in

plegaria f prayer; noon call to prayer

pleito *m* litigation, lawsuit; dispute, quarrel; fight; **pleito de acreedores** bankruptcy proceedings; **pleito homenaje** (feud) homage; **pleito viciado** mistrial

plenilunio *m* full moon

plenitud f fullness, abundance

ple•no -na *adj* full; **en plena marcha** in full swing; **en pleno rostro** right in the face

pleuresía f pleurisy

pliego *m* (*de papel*) sheet; folder; cover, envelope; bid, specification; sealed letter; printer's proof

pliegue *m* fold, crease, pleat; **pliegue de tabla** box pleat

plisar *tr* to pleat

plomada f carpenter's lead pencil; plummet; plumb bob; sinker, sinkers; scourge tipped with lead balls

plomar *tr* to seal with lead

plomazo *m* (Guat, Mex, W-I) gunshot

plomería f lead roofing; leadwork, plumbing

plomero *m* lead worker; plumber

plomi•zo -za *adj* lead, leaden

plomo *m* lead; (*pedazo de plomo; bala*) lead; (elec) fuse; (coll) bore; **a plomo** plumb, perpendicularly; straight down; just right

pluma f feather; quill; plume; pen; faucet; (CAm) hoax; (Chile) crane, derrick; **pluma esferográfica** ball-point pen; **pluma estilográfica** or **pluma fuente** fountain pen

plumaje *m* plumage

plúmbe•o -a *adj* lead

plumero *m* (*caja o vaso para las plumas*) penholder; feather duster

plumífe•ro -ra *adj* (*escritor*) hack, second-rate; (poet) feathered ‖ *m* padded or quilted jacket, ski jacket; hack writer; newshound

plumilla f small feather; (*de la pluma fuente*) point, tip; (Ven) ball-point pen

plumón *m* down; feather bed; (Mex) felt-tipped pen

plumo•so -sa *adj* downy, feathery

plural *adj* & *m* plural

pluriempleo *m* moonlighting

plus *m* extra, bonus

plusmarca f (sport) record

plusmarquista *mf* (sport) record breaker

plusvalía f appreciation (*in value*)

Plutarco *m* Plutarch

plutonio *m* plutonium

población f population; village, town, city

poblada f (SAm) riot, mob

pobla•do -da *adj* thick, bushy ‖ *m* town, community ‖ f see **poblada**

poblar §61 *tr* to people, populate; found, settle, colonize; (*un estanque, una colmena*) stock; (*con árboles*) plant ‖ *intr* to settle, colonize; multiply, be prolific ‖ *ref* to become full, covered, or crowded

pobre *adj* poor ‖ *mf* pauper; beggar

pobreza f poverty, want; poorness

pocilga f pigpen

poción f potion, dose

po•co -ca *adj* & *pron* (*comp* & *super* **menos**) little; few, e.g., **poca gente** few people; **pocos** few; **unos pocos** a few ‖ **poco** *adv* little; **a poco** shortly afterwards; **a poco de** shortly after; **dentro de poco** shortly; **por poco** almost, nearly; **tener en poco** to hold in low esteem, think little of; **un poco (de)** a little

po•cho -cha *adj* faded, discolored; overripe; rotten; (Chile) chubby

podar *tr* to prune, to trim

podenco *m* hound

poder *m* power; power of attorney, proxy; **el cuarto poder** the fourth estate; **obra en mi poder** I have at hand, I have in my possession; **poder adquisitivo** purchasing power ‖ *v* §53 *intr* to be possible; be able, have power or strength; **a más no poder** as hard as possible; **no poder con** to not be able to stand, not be able to manage; **no poder más** to be exhausted, be all in; **no poder menos de** to not be able to keep from, not be able to help ‖ *v aux* to be able to, may, can, might, could; **no poder ver** to not be able to stand

poderhabiente *mf* attorney, proxy

poderío *m* power, might; wealth, riches; sway, dominion

podero•so -sa *adj* powerful, mighty; wealthy, rich

podio *m* podium

podre f pus

podredumbre f corruption, putrefaction; pus; deep grief

poema *m* poem

poesía *f* poetry; poem; **bella poesía** (fig) fairy tale

poeta *m* poet

poéti•co -ca *adj* poetic(al) ‖ *f* poetics

poetisa *f* poetess

pola•co -ca *adj* Polish ‖ *mf* Pole ‖ *m* (*idioma*) Polish

polaina *f* legging

polar *adj* pole; polar ‖ *f* polestar

polarizar §60 *tr* to polarize

polea *f* pulley

poleame *m* (naut) tackle

polen *m* pollen

policía *m* policeman ‖ *f* police; policing; politeness; cleanliness; neatness; **policía urbana** street cleaning

policía•co -ca or policial *adj* police; (*novela*) detective

polifacéti•co -ca *adj* many-sided

políga•mo -ma *adj* polygamous ‖ *mf* polygamist

poliglo•to -ta *adj* polyglot ‖ *mf* polyglot, linguist

polígono *m* polygon

polígrafo *m* prolific writer; copying machine; ball-point pen; lie detector

polilla *f* moth

Polimnia *f* Polyhymnia

polinizar §60 *tr* to pollinate

polinomio *m* polynomial

polio *f* (path) polio

pólipo *m* polyp

polisón *m* bustle

polista *mf* poloist, polo player

politeísta *adj* polytheistic ‖ *mf* polytheist

política *f* politics; policy; manners, politeness, courtesy; **política de café** parlor politics; **política del buen vecino** Good Neighbor Policy

políti•co -ca *adj* political; politic, tactful; polite, courteous; -in-law; e.g., **padre político** father-in-law ‖ *mf* politician ‖ *f* see **política**

polivalente *adj* manifold; (chem, bact) polyvalent

póliza *f* policy, contract; draft, check; customhouse permit; **póliza de seguro** insurance policy

polizón *m* bum, tramp; stowaway

polizonte *m* cop, policeman

polo *m* pole; popsicle; (*juego*) polo; **polo de agua** water polo; **polo de atracción popular** drawing card

pololear *tr* to bother, annoy; (Chile) to flirt with

polo•lo -la *adj* (Chile) youngster ‖ *m* (Chile) flirt; side job

Polonia *f* Poland

pol•trón -trona *adj* idle, lazy, comfort-loving ‖ *f* easy chair

polución *f* (*del ambiente*) pollution

polvareda *f* cloud of dust; rumpus

polvera *f* compact, powder case

polvo *m* dust; powder; pinch of snuff; **polvo dentífrico** tooth powder; **polvos** dust; powder; **polvos de la madre Celestina**

hocus-pocus; **polvos de talco** talcum powder

pólvora *f* powder, gunpowder; fireworks; (*persona avispada*) live wire; **correr como pólvera en reguero** to spread like wildfire

polvorear *tr* to dust, sprinkle with dust or powder

polvorien•to -ta *adj* dusty; powdery

polvorín *m* powder magazine; powder flask; (*insecto*) tick; (Chile) spitfire

polvoro•so -sa *adj* dusty; **poner pies en polvorosa** to take to one's heels

polla *f* pullet; (*puesta en juegos de naipes*) stake, kitty; (coll) lassie

pollera *f* poultry woman; chicken coop; poultry yard; go-cart; (Arg, Chile) skirt

pollero *m* poulterer; poultry yard

polli•no -na *mf* donkey, ass

polli•to -ta *mf* chick; (*persona joven*) chick, chicken

pollo *m* chicken; (*persona joven*) chicken

pomada *f* pomade

pómez *f* pumice stone

pomo *m* pome; (*de la guarnición de la espada*) pommel; (*bola aromática*) pomander; (*frasco para perfume*) flacon; **pomo de puerta** doorknob

pompa *f* pomp; soap bubble; swell, bulge; (*de la ropa*) billowing, ballooning; (*de las alas del pavo real*) spread; (naut) pump; **pompa fúnebre** funeral

pompis *m* behind, butt, rear end

pompo•so -sa *adj* pompous; high-flown; highfalutin

pómulo *m* cheekbone

ponche *m* (*bebida*) punch; **ponche de huevo** eggnog

ponchera *f* punch bowl

pon•cho -cha *adj* lazy, careless, easy-going; (Col) chubby ‖ *m* poncho; greatcoat

ponderar *tr* to weigh; ponder, ponder over; exaggerate; praise to the skies; balance; weight

ponencia *f* paper, report

poner §54 *tr* to put, place, lay, set; arrange, dispose; (*una observación*) put in; (*una pieza dramática*) put on; (*la mesa*) set; assume, suppose; (*una ley, un impuesto*) impose; wager, stake; (*huevos*) lay; (*por escrito*) set down, put down; (*tiempo*) take; (*p.ej., miedo*) cause; make, turn; (*la luz, la radio*) turn on; (*marcha directa*) (aut) to go in; **poner en acción** to set in motion; **poner en limpio** to make a clean copy of; **poner por encima** to prefer, put ahead ‖ *ref* to put or place oneself; become, get, turn; (*el sol, los astros*) set; (*sombrero, saco, etc.*) put on; dress, dress up; get spotted; get, reach, arrive; **ponerse a** to set out to, begin to; **ponerse tan alto** to take offense, become hoity-toity

poniente *m* west; west wind

ponqué *m* poundcake

pontífice *m* pontiff

pontón *m* pontoon; pontoon bridge; (*buque viejo*) hulk

ponzoña *f* poison

ponzoño•so -sa *adj* poisonous
popa *f* poop, stern
popote *m* (Mex) straw for brooms; (*para tomar refrescos*) (Mex) straw
populache•ro -ra *adj* popular; cheap, vulgar; rabble-rousing ‖ *mf* rabble-rouser
populacho *m* populace, mob, rabble
popular *adj* popular
popularizar §60 *tr* to popularize
populo•so -sa *adj* populous
popu•rrí *m* (*pl* **-rríes**) medley
poquedad *f* paucity, scantiness; scarcity; timidity; trifle
poqui•to -ta *adj* very little; timid, shy, backward
por *prep* by; through, over; via, by way of; in, e.g., **por la mañana** in the morning; for; because of; for the sake of; on account of; in exchange for; in order to; as; about, e.g., **por Navidad** about Christmastime; out of, e.g., **por ignorancia** out of ignorance; times, e.g., **tres por cuatro** four times three; **estar por** to be on the point of, be ready to; be still to be, e.g., **la carta está por escribir** the letter is still to be written; **ir por** to go for, to go after; to follow; **por ciento** per cent; **por entre** among, between; **por que** because; in order that; **por qué** why; **por + *adj* or *adv* + que** however
porcelana *f* porcelain, chinaware; (*usado por los plateros*) enamel; (Mex) washbowl
porcentaje *m* percentage
porción *f* portion
porche *m* porch, portico
pordiosear *intr* to beg, go begging
pordiose•ro -ra *mf* beggar
porfía *f* persistence, stubbornness, obstinacy; **a porfía** in emulation; insistently
porfia•do -da *adj* persistent, stubborn, obstinate; opinionated
porfiar §77 *intr* to persist; argue stubbornly
pórfido *m* porphyry
pormenor *m* detail, particular
pormenorizar §60 *tr* to detail, tell in detail; to itemize
poro *m* pore
poro•so -sa *adj* porous
poroto *m* (SAm) bean, string bean; (Chile) little runt
porque *conj* because; in order that
porqué *m* why; quantity, share; wherewithal, money
porquería *f* dirt, filth; trifle; crudity; (*alimento dañoso a la salud*) junk
porra *f* club, bludgeon; bore, nuisance; boasting; (*pelos enredados*) (Arg, Bol) knot, tangle; (Mex) claque
porrazo *m* clubbing; blow, bump, thump
porro *m* (*mariguana*) joint
porta *f* porthole
portaavio•nes *m* (*pl* **-nes**) aircraft carrier, flattop
portacandado *m* hasp
portada *f* front, façade; portal; title page; (*de una revista*) cover; **falsa portada** half title

portadis•cos *m* (*pl* **-cos**) turntable
porta•dor -dora *adj* (*onda*) (rad) carrier ‖ *mf* bearer; carrier ‖ *m* waiter's tray
portaequipaje *m* (aut) trunk
portaequipa•jes *m* (*pl* **-jes**) baggage rack
portaguan•tes *m* (*pl* **-tes**) (aut) glove compartment
portal *m* vestibule, entrance hall; porch, portico; arcade; city gate; (*de un túnel*) portal *m;* crèche
portalámpa•ras *m* (*pl* **-ras**) (elec) socket
portalón *m* gate, portal; (*en el costado del buque*) gangway
portamira *m* (surv) rodman
portamone•das *m* (*pl* **-das**) pocketbook
portanue•vas *mf* (*pl* **-vas**) newsmonger
portañuela *f* (*de los pantalones*) fly; (Col, Mex) carriage door
portapape•les *m* (*pl* **-les**) brief case
portaplu•mas *m* (*pl* **-mas**) penholder
portar *tr* to carry, bear; (hunt) to retrieve ‖ *ref* to behave, conduct oneself
portase•nos *m* (*pl* **-nos**) brassiere
portátil *adj* portable
portatinte•ro *m* inkstand
portavian•das *m* (*pl* **-das**) dinner pail
porta•voz *m* (*pl* **-voces**) megaphone; mouthpiece, spokesperson
portazgo *m* toll, road toll
portazo *m* bang, slam
porte *m* portage; carrying charge; freight; postage; behavior, conduct; dress, bearing; size, capacity; (Chile) birthday present; **porte concertado** mailing permit; **porte pagado** postage prepaid, freight prepaid
portear *tr* to carry, transport ‖ *intr* to slam ‖ *ref* (*las aves*) to migrate
portento *m* prodigy, wonder
portento•so -sa *adj* portentous, extraordinary
porte•ño -ña *adj* Buenos Aires; Valparaiso; pertaining to any large South American city with a port ‖ *mf* native or inhabitant of Buenos Aires, Valparaiso or any large South American city with a port
porte•ro -ra *mf* doorkeeper; gatekeeper; (sport) goalkeeper ‖ *m* porter, janitor; doorman; **portero electrónico** automatic door opener ‖ *f* portress, janitress
portezuela *f* small door; (*de un coche o automóvil*) door; pocket flap
pórtico *m* portico, porch; little gate
portilla *f* porthole; private cart road, private cattle pass
portillo *m* gap, opening; nick, notch; (*puerta chica en otra mayor*) wicket; gate; narrow pass; side entrance
portorrique•ño -ña *adj & mf* Puerto Rican
portua•rio -ria *adj* port, harbor, dock ‖ *m* dock hand, dock worker
Portugal *m* Portugal
portu•gués -guesa *adj & mf* Portuguese
porvenir *m* future
pos — **en pos de** after, behind; in pursuit of
posa *f* knell, toll
posada *f* inn, wayside inn; lodging; boardinghouse; home, dwelling; camp; **posadas** (Mex) pre-Christmas celebration

po
po

posade•ro -ra *mf* innkeeper; **posaderas** buttocks

posar *tr* to put down ‖ *intr* to put up, lodge; alight, perch; pose ‖ *ref* to alight, perch; settle; rest

posbéli•co -ca *adj* postwar

posdata *f* postscript

pose *f* pose; (phot) exposure

poseer §43 *tr* to own, possess, hold; have a mastery of ‖ *ref* to control oneself

posesión *f* possession; **tomar posesión** (*un cargo*) to take up

posesionar *tr* to give possession to ‖ *ref* to take possession

posesor *m* owner

poseta *f* (Ven) toilet, washroom

posfecha *f* postdate

posguerra *f* postwar period

posible *adj* possible; **hacer todo lo posible** to do one's best ‖ **posibles** *mpl* means, income, property

posición *f* position; standing

positi•vo -va *adj* positive ‖ *f* (phot) print, positive

poso *m* sediment, dregs; grounds; rest, quiet; **poso del café** coffee grounds

posponer §54 *tr* to subordinate; think less of

posta *f* (*de caballos*) relay; posthouse; stage; stake, wager; slice; **a posta** on purpose; **por la posta** posthaste; **postas** buckshot

postal *adj* postal ‖ *f* post card; **postal ilustrada** picture post card

poste *m* post, pillar, pole; **poste de alumbrado** or **de farol** lamppost; **poste de telégrafo** telegraph pole; (*persona muy alta y delgada*) beanpole; **poste indicador** road sign

póster *m* poster

postergar §44 *tr* to delay, postpone; pass over

posteridad *f* posterity; posthumous fame

posterior *adj* back, rear; later, subsequent

postigo *m* (*puerta chica en otra mayor*) wicket; (*puertecilla en una ventana*) peep window; (*puerta excusada*) postern; shutter

posti•zo -za *adj* false, artificial; (*cuello*) detachable ‖ *m* switch, false hair, rat

postóni•co -ca *adj* posttonic

postor *m* bidder; **el mejor postor** the highest bidder

postración *f* prostration

postrar *tr* to prostrate; weaken, exhaust ‖ *ref* to collapse, be prostrated; prostrate oneself

postre *adj* last, final; **a la postre** at last; afterwards ‖ *m* dessert; **postres** dessert

postulación *f* postulation; nomination

postulante *mf* applicant, candidate

póstu•mo -ma *adj* posthumous

postura *f* posture; attitude, stand; stake, wager; agreement, pact; egg, eggs; (*de huevos*) laying; **postura del sol** sunset

potabilizar §60 *tr* to make drinkable

potable *adj* drinkable

potaje *m* pottage; jumble; (*bebida*) mixture; scheme; **potajes** vegetables

potasa *f* potash

potasio *m* potassium

pote *m* pot, jug; flowerpot; **a pote** in abundance

potencia *f* potency; power; **potencia de choque** striking power

potenciación *f* (math) involution

potencial *adj* & *m* potential

potenciar *tr* (*las aguas de un río; el entusiasmo de una persona*) to harness; (*elevar a una potencia*) (math) to raise

potentado *m* potentate

potente *adj* powerful; big, huge

potestad *f* power

potista *mf* toper, soak

potosí *m* great wealth, gold mine

potra *f* filly; hernia, rupture

potranca *f* young mare

potro *m* colt; pest, annoyance

pozal *m* bucket, pail

pozo *m* well; pit; whirlpool; (min) shaft; (naut) hold; (Chile, Col) pool, puddle; (Ecuad) spring, fountain; **pozo de ciencia** fountain of knowledge; **pozo de lanzamiento** launching silo; **pozo de lobo** (mil) foxhole; **pozo negro** cesspool

P.P. *abbr* **porte pagado, por poder**

p.p.^do *abbr* **próximo pasado**

práctica *f* practice; method; skill; **prácticas** studies, training

prácticamente *adv* through practice, by experience

practicar §73 *tr* to practice; bring about; (*un agujero*) make, cut

prácti•co -ca *adj* practical; skillful, practiced; practicing ‖ *m* medical practitioner; (naut) pilot ‖ *f* see **práctica**

pradera *f* meadowland; prairie

prado *m* meadow, pasture; promenade

Praga *f* Prague

pral. *abbr* **principal**

pralte. *abbr* **principalmente**

prángana — **estar en la prángana** (Mex, W-I) to be broke; (P-R) to be naked

preámbulo *m* preamble; evasion; **no andarse en preámbulos** to come to the point

prebéli•co -ca *adj* prewar

prebenda *f* prebend; sinecure

preca•rio -ria *adj* precarious

precaución *f* precaution

precaver *tr* to stave off, head off ‖ *intr* & *ref* to be on one's guard; **precaverse contra** or **de** to guard against

precavido -da *adj* cautious

precedente *adj* preceding ‖ *m* precedent

preceder *tr* & *intr* to precede

precepto *m* precept; order, injunction; **los preceptos** the Ten Commandments

preces *fpl* devotions; supplications

precia•do -da *adj* esteemed, valued; precious, valuable; boastful, proud

preciar *tr* to appraise, estimate ‖ *ref* to boast

precintar *tr* to bind, strap; seal

precio *m* price; value, worth; esteem, credit; **a precio de quemazón** at a giveaway price; **precios de cierre** closing prices; **precio tope** ceiling price

preciosidad *f* preciousness; beauty, gem, jewel

precio•so -sa *adj* precious; valuable; witty; beautiful
preciosura *f* beauty; pretty woman
precipicio *m* precipice; destruction
precipitación *f* precipitation; **precipitación acuosa** rainfall; **precipitación radiactiva** fallout
precipitar *tr* to precipitate; rush, hurl, throw headlong ‖ *ref* to rush, throw oneself headlong
precipito•so -sa *adj* precipitous, rash, reckless; risky, dangerous
precisar *tr* to state precisely, specify; fix; need; oblige, force; determine ‖ *intr* to be necessary; be important; be urgent; **precisar de** to need
precisión *f* precision; necessity, obligation; (Chile) haste; **precisiones** data
preci•so -sa *adj* necessary; precise; (Ven) haughty
precita•do -da *adj* above-mentioned
precla•ro -ra *adj* illustrious, famous
preconizar §60 *tr* to proclaim, commend publicly
pre•coz *adj* (*pl* **-coces**) precocious
predato•rio -ria *adj* predatory
predecir §24 *tr* to predict, foretell
prédica *f* Protestant sermon; harangue
predicar §73 *tr* to preach; praise to the skies; scold, preach to
predicción *f* prediction; **predicción del tiempo** weather forecasting
predilec•to -ta *adj* favorite, preferred
predio *m* property, estate
predisponer §54 *tr* to predispose
predominante *adj* predominant
preeminente *adj* preëminent
preestreno *m* (mov) preview
prefabricar §73 *tr* to prefabricate
prefacio *m* preface
preferencia *f* preference; **de preferencia** preferably
preferente *adj* preferable; favored; (*acciones*) preferred
preferible *adj* preferable
preferir §68 *tr* to prefer
prefigurar *tr* to foreshadow
prefijar *tr* to prefix; prearrange
prefijo *m* prefix
pregón *m* proclamation, public announcement (*by town crier*)
pregonar *tr* to proclaim, announce publicly; hawk; reveal; outlaw; praise openly
pregonero *m* auctioneer; town crier
preguerra *f* prewar period
pregunta *f* question; **hacer una pregunta** to ask a question
preguntar *tr* to ask; to question ‖ *intr* to ask, inquire; **preguntar por** to ask after or for ‖ *ref* to ask oneself; wonder
pregun•tón -tona *adj* inquisitive ‖ *mf* inquisitive person
prejudicio *m* or **prejuicio** *m* prejudgment; prejudice
prelado *m* prelate
preliminar *adj & m* preliminary; **preliminares** (*de un libro*) front matter

preludio *m* prelude
premeditar *tr* to premeditate
premiar *tr* to reward; give an award to
premio *m* reward, prize; premium; **a premio** at a premium; **premio de enganche** (mil) bounty; **premio gordo** first prize
premio•so -sa *adj* tight, close; bothersome; strict, rigid; slow, dull
premisa *f* premise; mark, token, clue
premura *f* pressure, haste, urgency
premuro•so -sa *adj* pressing, urgent
prenda *f* pledge; security; pawn; jewel, household article; garment, article of clothing; gift, talent, darling, loved one; **en prenda** in pawn; **en prenda de** as a pledge of; **prenda perdida** forfeit; **prendas** (*juego*) forfeits; **prendas interiores** underwear
prendar *tr* to pawn; pledge; charm, captivate ‖ *ref* — **prendarse de** to take a liking for, fall in love with
prendedero *m* or **prendedor** *m* fillet, brooch; stickpin
prender *tr* to seize, grasp; catch; imprison; dress up; pin; fasten ‖ *intr* to catch; catch fire; take root; turn out well ‖ *ref* to dress up; be fastened; catch hold
prendería *f* second-hand shop
prende•ro -ra *mf* second-hand dealer
prenombra•do -da *adj* above-mentioned; foregoing
prensa *f* press; printing press; vise; press, newspapers; press, frame; **entrar en prensa** to go to press; **meter en prensa** to put the squeeze on; **prensa amarilla** yellow press; **prensa taladradora** drill press
prensado *m* pressing; (*lustre de los tejidos prensados*) sheen
prensador *m* (CAm) paper clip
prensar *tr* to press; squeeze
preña•do -da *adj* pregnant; sagging, bulging; full, charged
preñez *f* pregnancy; fullness; impending danger; inherent confusion
preocupación *f* (*posesión anticipada; cuidado, desvelo*) preoccupation; (*posesión anticipada*) preoccupancy; bias, prejudice
preocupar *tr* to preoccupy, worry ‖ *ref* to become preoccupied, be worried
preparación *f* preparation
prepara•do -da *adj* ready, prepared ‖ *m* (pharm) preparation
preparar *tr* to prepare ‖ *ref* to prepare, get ready
preparati•vo -va *adj* preparatory ‖ *m* preparation, readiness
preponderante *adj* preponderant
preposición *f* preposition
prepóste•ro -ra *adj* reversed, upset, out of order, inopportune
prerrogativa *f* prerogative
presa *f* capture, seizure; catch, prey; booty; spoils; dam; trench, ditch, flume; bit, morsel; fang, tusk, claw; fishweir; (sport) hold; **hacer presa** to seize; **ser presa de** to be a victim of; be prey to
presagiar *tr* to presage, forebode

po
pr

presagio *m* presage, omen, token
présbita or **présbite** *adj* far-sighted ‖ *mf* far-sighted person
presbiteria•no -na *adj* & *mf* Presbyterian
prescindir *intr* — **prescindir de** to leave aside, leave out, disregard; do without, dispense with; avoid
prescribir §83 *tr* & *intr* to prescribe
presencia *f* presence; show, display; **presencia de ánimo** presence of mind
presenciar *tr* to witness, be present at
presentación *f* presentation; (*de una persona en el trato de otra u otras*) introduction; (*de un nuevo automóvil, libro, etc.*) appearance
presentador *m* or **presentadora** *f* (telv) moderator
presentar *tr* to present; introduce ‖ *ref* to present oneself; appear, show up; introduce oneself
presente *adj* present; **hacer presente** to notify of, remind of; **tener presente** to bear or keep in mind ‖ *interj* here!, present! ‖ *m* present, gift; person present
presentimiento *m* presentiment, premonition
presentir §68 *tr* to have a presentiment of
preservar *tr* to preserve, protect
preservati•vo -va *adj* & *m* preventive; preservative
presidencia *f* presidency; chairmanship
presidente *m* president; chairman; presiding judge
presidiario *m* convict
presidio *m* garrison; fortress; citadel; penitentiary; imprisonment; hard labor; aid, help
presidir *tr* to preside over; dominate ‖ *intr* to preside
presilla *f* loop, fastener; clip; paper clip; shoulder strap
presión *f* pressure; (*cerveza*) **a presión** on draught; **presión de inflado** tire pressure
presionar *tr* to press; put pressure on ‖ *intr* to press; **presionar sobre** to put pressure on
pre•so -sa *adj* seized; imprisoned ‖ *mf* prisoner; convict; **preso preventivo** pretrial prisoner; *f* see **presa**
presta•do -da *adj* lent, loaned; **dar prestado** to lend; **pedir** or **tomar prestado** to borrow
prestamista *mf* moneylender; pawnbroker
préstamo *m* loan; **préstamo lingüístico** loan word, borrowing
prestar *tr* to lend, loan; (*oído; ayuda; noticias*) give; (*atención*) pay; (*un favor*) do; (*un servicio*) render; (*juramento*) take; (*silencio*) keep; (*paciencia*) show ‖ *intr* (*un paño, la ropa*) give, yield; be useful ‖ *ref* to lend oneself, lend itself
prestata•rio -ria *mf* borrower
presteza *f* speed, promptness, readiness
prestidigitación *f* sleight of hand
prestidigita•dor -dora *adj* captivating ‖ *mf* magician; faker, impostor
prestigio *m* prestige; good standing; spell; illusion
prestigio•so -sa *adj* captivating, spellbinding; famous, renowned; illusory

pres•to -ta *adj* quick, prompt, ready; nimble ‖ **presto** *adv* right away
presumi•do -da *adj* conceited, vain ‖ *mf* would-be
presumir *tr* to presume ‖ *intr* to boast, be conceited
presunción *f* presumption; conceit
presuntuo•so -sa *adj* conceited, vain
presuponer §54 *tr* to presuppose; budget
presupuestar *tr* to budget; (*el coste de una obra*) estimate
presupuesto *m* budget; reason, motive; supposition; estimate
presuro•so -sa *adj* speedy, quick, hasty; zealous, persistent
pretencio•so -sa *adj* pretentious, showy; conceited, vain
pretender *tr* to claim, pretend to; try for, try to do; be a suitor for ‖ *intr* to insist; **pretender** + *inf* to try to + *inf*
pretendiente *mf* pretender, claimant; office seeker ‖ *m* suitor
pretensión *f* pretension; claim; pretense; presumption; effort, pursuit
pretéri•to -ta *adj* & *m* past
pretil *m* parapet, railing; walk along a parapet
pretina *f* girdle, belt; waistband
pretóni•co -ca *adj* pretonic
prevalecer §22 *intr* to prevail; take root; thrive
prevaler §76 *ref* — **prevalerse de** to avail oneself of, take advantage of
prevaricar §73 *intr* to collude, connive; play false; transgress; rave, be delirious
prevención *f* preparation; prevention; foresight; warning; prejudice; stock, supply; jail, lockup; guardhouse; **a** or **de prevención** spare, emergency
preveni•do -da *adj* prepared, ready; foresighted, forewarned; stocked, full
prevenir §79 *tr* to prepare, make ready; forestall, prevent, anticipate; overcome; warn; prejudice ‖ *intr* (*una tempestad*) to come up ‖ *ref* to get ready; come to mind
prever §80 *tr* to foresee
pre•vio -via *adj* previous; preliminary; after, with previous, subject to, e.g., **previo acuerdo** subject to agreement; **cita previa** by appointment
previsión *f* prevision, foresight; foresightedness; forecast; **previsión del tiempo** weather forecasting
prie•to -ta *adj* dark, blackish; stingy, mean; tight, compact; dark-complexioned ‖ *mf* (W-I) darling
prima *f* early morning; bonus, bounty; (ins) premium; (mil) first quarter of the night; (*cuerda*) (mus) treble
pri•mal -mala *adj* & *mf* yearling
prima•rio -ria *adj* primary ‖ *m* (elec) primary
primavera *f* spring, springtime; cowslip, primrose; robin
primer *adj* apocopated form of **primero**, used only before masculine singular nouns and adjectives

prime•ro -ra *adj* first; former; early; primary; prime; *(materia)* raw ‖ *m* first; **a primeros de** around the beginning of ‖ **primero** *adv* first

primicia *f* first fruits

primige•nio -nia *adj* original, primitive

primiti•vo -va *adj* primitive

pri•mo -ma *adj* first; prime, excellent; skillful; *(materia)* raw ‖ *mf* cousin; sucker, dupe; **primo carnal** or **primo hermano** first cousin, cousin-german ‖ *f* see **prima** ‖ **primo** *adv* in the first place

primogéni•to -ta *adj & mf* first-born

primor *m* care, skill, elegance; beauty

primoro•so -sa *adj* careful, skillful, elegant; fine, exquisite

princesa *f* princess; **princesa viuda** dowager princess

principal *adj* principal, main, chief; first, foremost; essential, important; famous, illustrious; *(piso)* second ‖ *m* principal, head, chief

príncipe *m* prince; **portarse como un príncipe** to live like a prince; **príncipe de Asturias** heir apparent of the King of Spain; **príncipe de Gales** prince of Wales; **príncipes** prince and princess

principiante *adj* beginning ‖ *mf* beginner, apprentice, novice

principiar *tr, intr & ref* to begin

principio *m* start, beginning; principle; origin, source; *(culin)* entree; **a principios de** around the beginning of; **en un principio** at the beginning; **principio de admiración** inverted exclamation point; **principio de interrogación** inverted question mark

pringar §44 *tr* to dip or soak in grease or fat; spot or stain with grease; make bleed; slander, run down; splash ‖ *intr* to meddle; (CAm, Mex) to drizzle ‖ *ref* to peculate

pringo•so -sa *adj* greasy, fatty

prioridad *f* priority; **de máxima prioridad** of the highest priority

prisa *f* hurry, haste; urgency; crush, crowd; **darse prisa** to hurry, make haste; **estar de prisa** or **tener prisa** to be in a hurry

prisión *f* seizure, capture; imprisonment; prison; **prisión celular** cell house; **prisiones** shackles, fetters

prisione•ro -ra *mf* prisoner; *(cautivo de una pasión o afecto)* captive ‖ *m* setscrew; studbolt

prisma *m* prism

prismáticos *mpl* binoculars

priva•do -da *adj* private ‖ *m (de un alto personaje)* favorite ‖ *f* cesspool

privar *tr* to deprive; forbid, prohibit ‖ *intr* to be in vogue; prevail; be in favor ‖ *ref* to deprive oneself; **privarse de** to give up

privilegiar *tr* to grant a privilege to

privilegio *m* privilege

pro *m & f* profit, advantage; **¡buena pro!** good appetite!; **de pro** of note, of worth; **el pro y el contra** the pros and the cons; **en pro de** on behalf of

proa *f* (aer) nose; (naut) prow

probable *adj* probable, likely

probador *m* fitting room

probar §61 *tr* to prove; test; try; *(clothing)* try on; try out; sample; fit; suit; *(vino)* touch ‖ *intr* to taste; **probar de** to take a taste of ‖ *ref* to try on

probidad *f* probity, integrity, honesty

problema *m* problem

pro•caz *adj* (*pl* **-caces**) impudent, insolent, bold

procedencia *f* origin, source; point of departure

procedente *adj* coming, originating; proper

proceder *m* conduct, behavior ‖ *intr* to proceed; originate; behave; be proper

procedimiento *m* procedure; proceeding; process

procelo•so -sa *adj* tempestuous, stormy

prócer *adj* high, lofty ‖ *m* hero, leader

procesamiento *m* (data) processing

procesar *tr* to sue, prosecute; indict; try; *(ordenador)* to process, data-process

procesión *f* procession; origin, emergence

proceso *m* process; progress; suit, lawsuit; **proceso verbal** minutes

proclama *f* proclamation; marriage banns

proclamar *tr* to proclaim; acclaim

proclíti•co -ca *adj & m* proclitic

procurador *m* attorney, solicitor; proxy

procurar *tr* to strive for; manage as attorney; yield, produce; try to

prodigar §44 *tr* to lavish; squander; waste ‖ *ref* to be a show-off

prodigio *m* prodigy

prodigio•so -sa *adj* prodigious, marvelous; fine, excellent

pródi•go -ga *adj* prodigal; lavish ‖ *mf* prodigal

producción *f* production; crop, yield, produce; **producción en masa** or **en serie** mass production

producir §19 *tr* to produce; yield, bear; cause, bring about ‖ *ref* to explain oneself; come about; take place

producto *m* product; produce; proceeds

proeza *f* prowess; feat, stunt

prof. *abbr* **profeta**

profanar *tr* to profane

profa•no -na *adj* profane; indecent, immodest; worldly; lay ‖ *mf* profane; worldly person; layman

profecía *f* prophecy ‖ **las Profecías** (Bib) the Prophets

proferir §68 *tr* to utter

profesar *tr & intr* to profess

profesión *f* profession; **profesión de fe** confession of faith

profe•sor -sora *mf* teacher; professor

profeta *m* prophet

profetisa *f* prophetess

profetizar §60 *tr* to prophesy

profilácti•co -ca *adj & m* prophylactic; preventive ‖ *f* hygiene

prófu•go -ga *adj & mf* fugitive ‖ *m* slacker, draft dodger

profundidad *f* profundity; depth

profundizar §60 *tr* to deepen; fathom, get to the bottom of

pr
pr

profun•do -da *adj* profound; deep
progenie *f* descent, lineage, parentage
progno•sis *f* (*pl* **-sis**) prognosis; (*del tiempo*) forecast
programa *m* program; **programa continuo** (mov) continuous showing; **programa de estudios** curriculum; **programa (para ordenador)** program(me), software
programación *f* (*ordenador*) program(m)ing; (telv) scheduling
programador *m* or **programadora** *f* (*ordenador*) program(m)er
programar *tr* to program; (*ordenador*) program(me)
progresar *intr* to progress
progresista *adj* & *mf* (pol) progressive
progreso *m* progress; **hacer progresos** to make progress
prohibir *tr* to prohibit, forbid ‖ *ref* **se prohíbe fijar carteles** post no bills
prohijar *tr* to adopt
prohombre *m* (*en los gremios de los artesanos*) master; leader, head; (coll) big shot
prójimo *m* fellow man, fellow creature, neighbor; fellow
pról. *abbr* **prólogo**
prole *f* progeny, offspring
proletariado *m* proletariat
proleta•rio -ria *adj* & *m* proletarian
proliferar *intr* to proliferate
prolífi•co -ca *adj* prolific
proli•jo -ja *adj* tedious, too long; fussy, fastidious; long-winded; tiresome
prologar §44 *tr* to preface, write a preface for
prólogo *m* prologue; preface
prolongar §44 *tr* to prolong, extend; (geom) to produce
promediar *tr* to divide into two equal parts; average ‖ *intr* to mediate; be half over
promedio *m* average, mean; middle
promesa *f* promise
promete•dor -dora *adj* promising
prometer *tr* & *intr* to promise ‖ *ref* to become engaged
prometi•do -da *adj* engaged, betrothed ‖ *m* promise; fiancé ‖ *f* fiancée
prominente *adj* prominent
promiso•rio -ria *adj* promissory
promoción *f* promotion; advancement; (*conjunto de individuos que obtienen un grado en un mismo año*) class, year, crop
promontorio *m* promontory, headland; unwieldy thing
promover §47 *tr* to promote; advance, further
promulgar §44 *tr* to promulgate
pronombre *m* pronoun
pronosticar §73 *tr* to prognosticate, foretell
pronóstico *m* prognostic, forecast; almanac; (med) prognosis
pron•to -ta *adj* quick, speedy; prompt; ready ‖ *m* jerk; sudden impulse, fit of anger ‖ **pronto** *adv* right away, soon; early; promptly; **lo más pronto posible** as soon as possible; **tan pronto como** as soon as
pronunciación *f* pronunciation

pronuncia•do -da *adj* marked; (*curva*) sharp; (*pendiente*) steep; bulky
pronunciamiento *m* insurrection, uprising; (*golpe de estado militar*) pronunciamiento; (law) decree
pronunciar *tr* to pronounce; utter; (*un discurso*) make, deliver; decide on ‖ *ref* to rebel; declare oneself
propaganda *f* propaganda; advertising
propagar §44 *tr* to propagate; spread; broadcast
propalar *tr* to divulge, spread
proparoxíto•no -na *adj* & *m* proparoxytone
propasar *ref* to go too far, take undue liberty
propender *intr* to tend, incline, be inclined
propensión *f* propensity; predisposition
propen•so -sa *adj* inclined, disposed, prone
propiciar *tr* to propitiate; support, favor, sponsor
propi•cio -cia *adj* propitious, favorable
propiedad *f* property; ownership; naturalness, likeness; **es propiedad** copyrighted; **propiedad horizontal** one-floor ownership in an apartment house; **propiedad literaria** copyright
propieta•rio -ria *mf* owner ‖ *m* proprietor ‖ *f* proprietress
propina *f* tip, fee, gratuity
propinar *tr* (*algo a beber*) to offer; (*medicamentos*) prescribe or administer; (*palos, golpes, etc.*) give ‖ *ref* (*una bebida*) to treat oneself to
propin•cuo -cua *adj* near, close at hand
pro•pio -pia *adj* proper, suitable; peculiar, characteristic; natural; same; himself, herself, etc.; own ‖ *m* messenger; native; **propios** public lands
proponer §54 *tr* to propose; propound; (*a una persona para un empleo*) name, present ‖ *ref* to plan; propose
proporción *f* proportion; opportunity
proporciona•do -da *adj* proportionate; fit, suitable
proporcionar *tr* to furnish, provide, supply; give; proportion; adapt, adjust
proposición *f* proposition; **proposición dominante** main clause
propósito *m* aim, purpose, intention; subject matter; **a propósito** by the way; apropos, fitting; in place; **a propósito de** apropos of; **de propósito** on purpose; **fuera de propósito** irrelevant, beside the point
propuesta *f* proposal, proposition
propulsar *tr* to propel, drive
propulsión *f* propulsion; **propulsión a chorro** jet propulsion; **propulsión a cohete** rocket propulsion
pror. *abbr* **procurador**
prorratear *tr* to prorate
prórroga *f* extension, renewal
prorrogar §44 *tr* to defer, postpone, extend
prorrumpir *intr* to spurt, shoot forth; break forth, burst out
prosa *f* prose; chatter, idle talk
prosai•co -ca *adj* prose; prosaic, dull
proscribir §83 *tr* to outlaw, proscribe
proscrip•to -ta *mf* exile, outlaw

prosecución f continuation, prosecution; pursuit

proseguir §67 tr to continue, carry on ‖ intr to continue

prosélito m proselyte

prosista mf prose writer; chatterbox

prosódi•co -ca adj (acento) stress

prospectar tr & intr to prospect

prosperar tr to make prosper ‖ intr to prosper, thrive

prosperidad prosperity

próspe•ro -ra adj prosperous, thriving, successful

prosternar ref to prostrate oneself

prostituir §20 tr to prostitute ‖ ref to prostitute oneself; become a prostitute

prostituta f prostitute

prosu•do -da adj (Chile, Ecuad, Peru) pompous, solemn

protagonista mf protagonist

protagonizar §60 tr to play the leading rôle of

protección f protection; **protección aduanera** protective tariff; **protección a la infancia** child welfare

proteger §17 tr to protect

protegida f protégée

protegido m protégé

proteína f protein

proter•vo -va adj perverse

protesta f protest; pledge, promise

protestante adj & mf protestant; Protestant

protestar tr to protest, asseverate; (la fe) profess ‖ intr to protest; **protestar de** (aseverar con ahinco) to protest (to state positively); **protestar contra** (negar la validez de) to protest (to deny forcibly)

protocolo m protocol

protoplasma m protoplasm

prototipo m prototype

protozoario m or **protozoo** m protozoön

provec•to -ta adj old, ripe

provecho m advantage, benefit; profit, gain; advance, progress; **¡buen provecho!** good luck!; good appetite!; **de provecho** useful; **provechos** perquisites

provecho•so -sa adj advantageous, beneficial; profitable; useful

proveedor -dora mf supplier, provider, purveyor; steward

proveer §43 & §83 tr to provide, furnish; supply; resolve, settle ‖ intr to provide; **proveer a** to provide for ‖ ref to supply oneself; have a bowel movement

provenir §79 intr to come, arise

Provenza, la Provence

provenzal adj & mf Provençal

proverbio m proverb

providencia f providence, foresight; step, measure

providencial adj providential

provincia f province

provisión f provision; supply, stock; **provisiones de boca** foodstuffs

proviso•rio -ria adj provisory, provisional

provocar §73 tr to provoke; promote, bring about; incite, tempt, move ‖ intr to provoke; vomit

proxeneta mf go-between

proximidad f proximity; **proximidades** neighborhood

próxi•mo -ma adj next; near; neighboring, close; early; **próximo pasado** last

proyección f projection; influence

proyectar tr to project; cast; design ‖ ref to project, stick out; (una sombra) be projected, fall

proyectil m projectile; **proyectil buscador del blanco** homing missile; **proyectil dirigido** or **teleguiado** guided missile

proyecto m project; **proyecto de ley** bill

proyector m projector, searchlight; projection machine

prudencia f prudence

prudente adj prudent

prueba f proof; trial, test; examination; (de un traje) fitting; (de un alimento o una bebida) sample, sampling; evidence; acrobatics; sleight of hand; (sport) event; **a prueba** on approval, on trial; **a prueba de** proof against, -proof, e.g., **a prueba de escaladores** burglarproof; **a prueba de incendio** fireproof; **prueba de alcohol** alcohol-level test; **pruebas de planas** page proof; **pruebas de primeras** first proof (for proofreader); **pruebas de segundas** galley proof (for author)

pruebista mf acrobat

prurito m itching; eagerness, itch

psicoanálisis m psychoanalysis

psicoanalizar §60 tr to psychoanalyze

psicodéli•co -ca adj psychedelic

psicología f psychology

psicológi•co -ca adj psychologic(al)

psicólo•go -ga mf psychologist

psicópata mf psychopath

psico•sis f (pl -sis) psychosis; **psicosis de guerra** war psychosis, war scare

psicoterapia f psychotherapy; **psicoterapia de grupo** group therapy

psicóti•co -ca adj & mf psychotic

psique f cheval glass ‖ **Psique** f Psyche

psiquiatra mf psychiatrist

psiquiatría f psychiatry

psíqui•co -ca adj psychic

P.S.M. abbr **por su mandato**

pte. abbr **parte, presente**

púa f point; prick, barb; tine, prong; (del fonógrafo) needle; (del peine) tooth; thorn; (del puerco espín) spine, quill; sting; graft; plectrum; tricky person

pubertad f puberty

publicación f publication

publicar §73 tr to publish; publicize

publicidad f publicity; advertising; **publicidad de lanzamiento** advance publicity

publicita•rio -ria adj publicity; advertising

públi•co -ca adj & m public

pucha f (W-I) small bouquet; (Mex) crescent roll

púcher m (drogas) pusher

puchero *m* pot, kettle; stew; daily bread; pouting; **hacer pucheros** to pout, screw up one's face

pucho *m* fag end, remnant; (*de cigarro*) stump; trifle, trinket; (*el hijo menor*) baby

puden•do -da *adj* ugly, shameful; obscene; (*partes*) private

pudiente *adj* powerful; well-off, well-to-do

pudín *m* pudding

pudor *m* modesty, shyness; chastity

pudoro•so -sa *adj* modest, shy; chaste

pudrición *f* rot, rotting

pudrir §83 *tr* to rot; worry ‖ *intr* to be dead and buried ‖ *ref* to rot; be worried; (*en la cárcel*) languish

pueblo *m* people; common people; town, village; **puebla de Dios** or **de Israel** children of Israel

puente *m* bridge; (dent, mus) bridge; (aut) axle, rear axle; **hacer puente** to take the intervening day off; **puente aéreo** airlift, air bridge; **puente colgante** suspension bridge; **puente de engrase** grease lift; **puente levadizo** drawbridge, lift bridge

puer•co -ca *adj* piggish, hoggish; dirty, filthy; slovenly; coarse, mean; lewd ‖ *m* hog; **puerco espín** or **espino** porcupine ‖ *f* sow; slattern, slut

puericia *f* childhood

puericultura *f* child rearing, infant care

pueril *adj* puerile, childish

puerilidad *f* puerility, childishness

puerro *m* leek; (*mariguana, hachich*) joint

puerta *f* door, doorway; gate, gateway; **a puerta cerrada** or **a puertas cerradas** behind closed doors

puerto *m* harbor, port; haven; mountain pass; **puerto aéreo** airport; **puerto brigantino** Corunna; **puerto de arribada** port of call; **puerto de mar** seaport; **puerto franco** free port; **puerto marítimo** dock, port; **puerto seco** frontier customhouse

puertorrique•ño -ña *adj & mf* Puerto Rican

pues *adv* then, well; yes, certainly; why; anyhow; **pues bien** well then; **pues que** since ‖ *conj* for, since, because, inasmuch as ‖ *interj* well!, then!

puesta *f* setting; laying; putting; (*dinero apostado*) stake; **a puesta del sol** or **a puestas del sol** at sunset; **puesta a punto** adjustment; carrying out, completion; **puesta a tierra** (elec) grounding; **puesta de largo** coming out, social debut

pues•to -ta *adj* dressed; **puesto que** since, inasmuch as ‖ *m* place; booth, stand; office; station; barracks; (*para cazadores*) blind; **puesto a punto** (aut) tuning; **puesto de socorros** first-aid station ‖ *f* see **puesta**

púgil *m* pugilist

pugilato *m* boxing; fist fight

pugilismo *m* pugilism

pugna *f* fight, battle; struggle, conflict; **en pugna con** at issue; **en pugna con** at odds with

pugnar *intr* to fight, struggle; strive, persist

pug•naz *adj* (*pl* -naces) pugnacious

pujante *adj* powerful, mighty, vigorous

pujar *tr* (*un proyecto*) to push; (*un precio*) raise, bid up ‖ *intr* to struggle, strain; falter; (*por decir una cosa*) grope; snivel; **pujar para adentro** (CAm, W-I) to keep silent, say nothing

pul•cro -cra *adj* neat, tidy, trim; circumspect

pulga *f* flea; **de malas pulgas** peppery, hot-tempered; **hacer de una pulga un camello** or **un elefante** to make a mountain out of a molehill; **no aguantar pulgas** to stand for no nonsense

pulgada *f* inch

pulgar *m* thumb

puli•do -da *adj* pretty; neat; polished; clean, spotless

pulimentar *tr* to polish

pulimento *m* polish

pulir *tr* to polish; finish; give a polish to

pulmón *m* lung; **pulmón de acero** or **de hierro** iron lung

pulmonía *f* pneumonia

púlpito *m* pulpit

pulpo *m* octopus

pulque *m* (Mex) agave brandy

pulsación *f* pulsation, throb, beat; strike, striking; (*del pianista, el mecanógrafo*) touch

pulsar *tr* (*un botón*) to push; (*un piano, arpa, guitarra*) play; (*una tecla*) strike; feel or take the pulse of; sound out, examine ‖ *intr* to pulsate, throb, beat

pulsear *intr* to hand-wrestle

pulsera *f* bracelet; wristlet, watch strap; **pulsera de pedida** engagement bracelet

pulso *m* pulse; steadiness, steady hand; tact, care, caution; bracelet; wrist watch; **a pulso** with hand and wrist; by main strength; (*dibujo*) freehand; **sacar a pulso** to carry out against odds; **tomar el pulso a** to take the pulse of

pulular *intr* to swarm; bud, sprout

pulverizar §60 *tr* to pulverize; atomize; spray

pulla *f* dig, cutting remark; filthy remark; witticism

pum *interj* bang!

puma *m* cougar

puna *f* (SAm) bleak tableland in the Andes; (SAm) mountain sickness

pundonor *m* point of honor; face

pundonoro•so sa *adj* punctilious, scrupulous; haughty, dignified

pungir §27 *tr* to prick; sting

punta *f* (*extremo agudo*) point; tip, end; (*del cigarro*) butt; nail; point, cape, headland; (*del toro*) horn; (*del asta del ciervo*) tine, prong; style, graver; touch, tinge, trace; (*del vino*) souring; (elec) point; **de punta** on end; on tiptoe; **de punta en blanco** in full armor; in full regalia; **estar de punta** (con) to be at odds (with); **punta de combate** (*del torpedo*) warhead; **punta de lanza** spearhead; **punta de París** wire nail; **sacar punta a** to put a point on, to sharpen; **tener en la punta de la lengua** to have on the tip of one's tongue

puntabola *f* (Bol) ball-point pen

puntada *f* hint; (sew) stitch; (*dolor agudo*) stitch, sharp pain

puntal *m* prop, support; stay, stanchion; backing, support; bite, snack; (naut) depth of hold

puntapié *m* kick; **echar a puntapiés** to kick out

puntear *tr* to dot, mark with dots; (*guitarra*) pluck; stipple; stitch ‖ *intr* (naut) to tack

puntera *f* toe, toe patch; leather tip; (coll) kick

puntería *f* aim, aiming; marksmanship

puntero *m* pointer; (*del reloj*) hand; stonecutter's chisel; punch; leading animal

puntiagu·do -da *adj* sharp-pointed

puntilla *f* brad; narrow lace edging; (*de la pluma fuente*) point; (carp) tracing point; dagger; **de puntillas** on tiptoe; **puntilla francesa** finishing nail

puntillero *m* bullfighter who delivers coup de grace with dagger

puntillo·so -sa *adj* punctilious

punto *m* (*señal de dimensiones poco perceptibles*) point, dot; stitch, loop; mesh; (*rotura en un tejido de punto*) break; jot; cabstand, hackstand; (gram) period; (math, typ, sport, fig) point; **a buen punto** opportunely; **al punto** at once; **a punto de** on the point of; **a punto fijo** for certain; **de punto** knitted; **dos puntos** (gram) colon; **en punto** sharp, on the dot; **poner punto final a** to wind up, to bring to an end; **punto de admiración** exclamation mark or point; **punto de aguja** knitting; **punto de Hungría** herringbone; **punto de media** knitwork; **punto de mira** aim; center of attraction; **¡punto en boca!** mum's the word!; **punto interrogante** question mark; **punto menos** almost; **punto muerto** dead center; (aut) neuter; **puntos y rayas** dots and dashes; **punto y coma** *msg* semicolon

puntuación *f* punctuation; mark, grade; scoring

puntual *adj* punctual; certain, sure; exact, accurate

puntualizar §60 *tr* to fix in the memory; give a detailed account of; finish; draw up

puntuar §21 *tr & intr* to punctuate; score

puntura *f* puncture, prick

punzada *f* prick; shooting pain; (*del remordimiento*) pang

punzante *adj* sharp, pricking; barbed, biting, caustic

punzar §60 *tr* to prick, puncture, punch; to sting; to grieve ‖ *intr* to sting

punzón *m* punch; pick; burin, graver; budding horn, tenderling; **punzón de marcar** center punch

puñada *f* punch

puñado *m* handful, bunch

puñal *m* dagger, poniard

puñalada *f* stab; blow, sudden sorrow; **puñalada de misericordia** coup de grâce; **puñalada trapera** stab in the back

puñetazo *m* punch; bang with the fist

puño *m* fist; cuff; wristband; grasp; fistful, handful; hilt; (*p.ej., del paraguas*) handle; (*del bastón*) head; punch; **como un puño** whopping big; tiny, microscopic; closefisted; **de su propio puño** or **de su puño y letra** in his own hand, in his own writing; **puño de herro** brass knuckles

pupa *f* pimple; fever blister

pupila *f* (*del ojo*) pupil

pupi·lo -la *mf* boarder; orphan, ward; pupil ‖ *f* see **pupila**

pupitre *m* writing desk

puquio *m* (SAm) spring or pool of fresh, clear water

puré *m* purée; **puré de patatas** mashed potatoes; **puré de tomates** stewed tomatoes

purera *f* cigar case

pureza *f* purity

purga *f* purge; purgative; drain valve

purgante *adj & m* purgative

purgar §44 *tr* to purge; physic; drain; purify; refine; expiate; (*pasiones*) control, check; (*sospechas*) clear away ‖ *ref* to take a physic; unburden oneself

puridad *f* purity

purificar §73 *tr* to purify

purita·no -na *adj & mf* puritan; Puritan

pu·ro -ra *adj* pure; sheer; (*cielo*) clear; out-and-out, outright; **de puro** completely, totally; because of being ‖ *m* cigar

púrpura *f* purple

purpura·do -da *adj* purple ‖ *m* (eccl) cardinal

purpúre·o -a *adj* purple

pusilánime *adj* pusillanimous

pústula *f* pustule

puta *f* whore

putañear or **putear** *intr* to whore around, chase after lewd women

putati·vo -va *adj* spurious

putrefac·to -ta *adj* rotten, putrid

pútri·do -da *adj* putrid, rotten

puya *f* steel point; (*del gallo*) spur

Q

Q, q (cu) *f* twentieth letter of the Spanish alphabet

q.b.s.m. *abbr* **que besa su mano**

q.e.p.d. *abbr* **que en paz descanse**

q.e.s.m. *abbr* **que estrecha su mano**

quántum *m* (*pl* **quanta**) quantum

que *pron rel* that, which; who, whom; **el que** he who; which, the one which; who, the one who ‖ *adv* than ‖ *conj* that; for, because; let, e.g., **que entre** let him come in; **a que** I'll bet that

qué *adj & pron interr* what, which; **¿qué tal?**

how?; hello, how's everything? ‖ *interj* what!; what a!; how!

quebrada *f* gorge, ravine, gap; brook; failure, bankruptcy

quebradi•zo -za *adj* brittle, fragile; frail

quebra•do -da *adj* weakened; bankrupt; ruptured; rough; winding ‖ *m* (math) fraction ‖ *f* see **quebrada**

quebrantable *adj* breakable

quebrantar *tr* to break; break open; break out of; grind, crush; soften, mollify; (*un contrato; la ley; un hábito; un testamento; el corazón de una persona*) break ‖ *ref* to break; become broken

quebrantaterro•nes *m* (*pl* **-nes**) clodhopper

quebranto *m* break, breaking; heavy loss; great sorrow; discouragement

quebrar §2 *tr* to break; bend, twist; crush; overcome; temper, soften ‖ *intr* to break; fail; weaken, give in ‖ *ref* to break; weaken; become ruptured

queda *f* curfew

quedar *intr* to remain; stay; be left; be left over; stop, leave off; turn out; be; be found, be located; **quedar en** to agree on; agree to; **quedar por** + *inf* or **sin** + *inf* to remain to be + *pp* ‖ *ref* to remain; stay; stop; be; be left; put up; **quedarse con** to keep, to take; **quedarse tan fresco** to show no offense

que•do -da *adj* quiet, still; gentle ‖ *f* see **queda** ‖ **quedo** *adv* softly, in a low voice; gropingly

quehacer *m* work, task, chore

queja *f* complaint, lament; whine, moan

quejar *ref* to complain, lament; whine, moan

quejido *m* complaint, whine, moan

quejumbre *f* complaining, whine, moan

quejumbro•so -sa *adj* complaining; whining, whiny

quema *f* fire; burning; **a quema ropa** point-blank; **de quema** distilled; **hacer quema** (Arg, Bol) to hit the mark

quemada *f* burnt brush; (Mex) fire

quemadero *m* incinerator; (*poste destinado para quemar a los condenados a la pena de fuego*) stake

quema•do -da *adj* burned; burnt out; angry ‖ *m* burnt brush; **oler a quemado** to smell of fire; **saber a quemado** to taste burned ‖ *f* see **quemada**

quema•dor -dora *adj* burning; incendiary ‖ *m* burner

quemadura *f* burn; (agr) smut

quemar *tr* to burn; scald; set on fire; scorch; frostbite; sell too cheap; (CAm, Mex) to betray, inform against ‖ *intr* to burn, be hot ‖ *ref* to burn; be burning up; fret; (*estar cercano a lo que se busca*) be warm, be hot; **quemarse las cejas** to burn the midnight oil

quemarropa — **a quemarropa** point-blank

quemazón *f* burn; burning; intense heat; (*de un fusible*) blowout; itch; cutting remark; pique, anger; (hum) bargain sale; (Arg, Bol, Chile) mirage on the pampas

que•pis *m* (*pl* **-pis**) kepi

queque *m* cake

querella *f* complaint; dispute, quarrel

querellar *ref* to complain; whine

querencia *f* liking, affection; attraction; love of home; (*de animales*) haunt; favorite spot

querencio•so -sa *adj* homing; (*sitio*) favorite

querer *m* love, affection; liking, fondness ‖ *v* §55 *tr* to wish, want, desire; like; love; **como quiera** anyhow; anyway; **como quiera que** whereas; inasmuch as; no matter how; **cuando quiera** any time; **donde quiera** anywhere; **querer bien** to love; **sin querer** unwillingly; unintentionally ‖ *v aux* to wish to, want to, desire to; will; be about to, be trying to, e.g., **quiere llover** it is trying to rain; **querer decir** to mean; **querer más** to prefer to, would rather

queri•do -da *adj* dear ‖ *mf* lover; paramour; dearie ‖ *f* mistress

quermés *f* or **quermese** *f* bazaar; village or country fair

queroseno *m* var of **keroseno**

querubín *m* cherub

quesadilla *f* cheesecake; sweet pastry

quese•ro -ra *adj* cheesy ‖ *mf* cheesemonger; cheesemaker ‖ *f* cheese board; cheese mold; cheese dish

queso *m* cheese; **queso de cerdo** headcheese; **queso helado** brick ice cream; **queso para extender** cheese spread

quevedos *mpl* nose glasses

quiá *interj* oh, no!

quicio *m* pivot hole (*of hinge*); **fuera de quicio** out of order; **sacar de quicio** to put out of order; unhinge

quiebra *f* crack; damage, loss; bankruptcy

quien *pron rel* who, whom; he who, she who; someone who, anyone who

quién *pron interr* who, whom

quienquiera *pron indef* anyone, anybody; **quienquiera que** whoever; **a quienquiera que** whomever

quie•to -ta *adj* quiet, calm; virtuous

quietud *f* quiet, calm, stillness

quijada *f* jaw, jawbone

quijotes•co -ca *adj* quixotic

quilate *m* carat

quilo *m* kilogram; **sudar el quilo** to slave, be a drudge

quilla *f* keel; (*de ave*) breastbone; **dar de quilla** (naut) to keel over

quimera *f* chimera; dispute, quarrel

química *f* chemistry

quími•co -ca *adj* chemical ‖ *mf* chemist ‖ *f* see **química**

quimicultura *f* tank farming

quimono *m* kimono

quimioterapia *f* chemotherapy

quina *f* cinchona, Peruvian bark

quincalla *f* hardware

quincallería *f* hardware store; hardware business; hardware factory

quincalle•ro -ra *mf* hardware merchant

quince *adj & pron* fifteen ‖ *m* fifteen; (*en las fechas*) fifteenth

quincea•vo -va *adj & m* fifteenth

quince•no -na *adj & m* fifteenth ‖ *f* fortnight, two weeks; two weeks' pay
quincuagési•mo -ma *adj & m* fiftieth
quiniela *f* pelota game of five; soccer lottery; daily double; (Arg, Urug) numbers game
quinien•tos -tas *adj & pron* five hundred ‖ **quinientos** *m* five hundred
quinina *f* quinine
quinqué *m* student lamp, oil lamp
quinquenal *adj* five-year
quinta *f* villa, country house; draft, induction; **ir a quintas** to be drafted; **redimirse de las quintas** to be exempted from the draft
quintacolumnista *mf* fifth columnist
quintal *m* quintal, hundredweight
quintar *tr* to draft
quinteto *m* quintet
quintilla *f* five-line stanza of eight syllables and two rhymes; any five-line stanza with two rhymes
quintilli•zo -za *mf* quint, quintuplet
Quintín — **armar la de San Quintín** to raise a rumpus, raise a row
quin•to -ta *adj* fifth ‖ *m* fifth; lot; pasture; draftee ‖ *f* see **quinta**
quinza•vo -va *adj & m* fifteenth
quiosco *m* kiosk, summerhouse; stand; **quiosco de música** bandstand; **quiosco de necesidad** comfort station; **quiosco de periódicos** newsstand
quiquiri•quí *m* (*pl* **-quíes**) cock-a-doodle-doo; cock of the walk
quirófano *m* operating room
quiromancia *f* or **quiromancía** *f* palmistry
quiropodista *mf* chiropodist
quiroprácti•co -ca *adj* chiropractic ‖ *mf* chiropractor
quirúrgi•co -ca *adj* surgical
quirurgo *m* surgeon
quiscal *m* grackle

quisicosa *f* puzzler
quisqui•do -da *adj* (Arg) constipated
quisquilla *f* trifle, triviality; **pararse en quisquillas** to bicker, make a fuss over trifles; **quisquillas** hairsplitting, quibbling
quisquillo•so -sa *adj* trifling; touchy; fastidious; hairsplitting
quiste *m* cyst
quis•to -ta *adj* — **bien quisto** well-liked, welcome; **mal quisto** disliked, unwelcome
quitaesmalte *m* nail-polish remover
quitaman•chas *mf* (*pl* **-chas**) (*persona*) clothes cleaner, spot remover ‖ *m* (*substancia*) clothes cleaner, spot remover
quitamo•tas *mf* (*pl* **-tas**) bootlicker, apple polisher
quitanie•ve *m* or **quitanie•ves** *m* (*pl* **-ves**) snowplow
quitapie•dras *m* (*pl* **-dras**) cowcatcher
quitapintura *m* paint remover
quitapón *m* pompon for draft mules; **de quitapón** detachable, removable
quitar *tr* to remove; take away; (*la mesa*) clear; (*esfuerzo, trabajo*) save; (*tiempo*) take; free; parry; **quitar algo a algo** to take something off something, remove something from something; **quitar algo a uno** to remove something from someone; take something away from someone ‖ *intr* — **de quita y pon** detachable, removable ‖ *ref* (*el sombrero, una prenda de vestir*) to take off; (*el sombrero en señal de cortesía*) tip; (*una mancha*) come out, come off; (*un vicio*) give up; withdraw
quitasol *m* parasol
quite *m* removal; hindrance; dodge; (*en la esgrima*) parry; (taur) passes made with the cape to draw the bull away from the man in danger
quizá or **quizás** *adv* maybe, perhaps
quó•rum *m* (*pl* **-rum**) quorum

R

R, r (ere) *f* twenty-first letter of the Spanish alphabet
R. *abbr* respuesta, Reverencia, Reverendo
rabada *f* hind quarter, rump
rabadilla *f* base of the spine
rábano *m* radish; **rábano picante** or **rusticano** horseradish; **tomar el rábano por las hojas** to be on the wrong track
ra•bí *m* (*pl* **-bíes**) rabbi
rabia *f* anger, rage; (*hidrofobia*) rabies; **tener rabia a** to have a grudge against
rabiar *intr* to rage, rave; get mad; go mad, have rabies; **que rabia** like the deuce; **rabiar por** to be dying for; be dying to
rabieta *f* tantrum
rabillo *m* leafstalk; flower stalk; (*en los cereales*) mildew spot; (*del ojo*) corner

rabio•so -sa *adj* mad, rabid
rabo *m* tail; (*del ojo*) corner; (fig) tail, train; **rabo verde** (CAm) old rake
ra•bón -bona *adj* bobtail; (Chile) bare, naked; (Mex) mean, wretched ‖ *f* camp follower; **hacer rabona** to play hooky
rabotada *f* swish of the tail; coarse remark
rabu•do -da *adj* long-tailed
racial *adj* racial
racimar *ref* to cluster, gather together
racimo *m* bunch; cluster; (*de perlas*) string
raciocinio *m* reasoning
ración *f* ration; allowance; **ración de hambre** starvation wages
racional *adj* rational
racionar *tr* to ration
racismo *m* racism

racista *adj & mf* racist

racha *f* split, crack; chip; squall, gust of wind; streak of luck

rada *f* (naut) road, roadstead

radar *m* radar

radiación *f* radiation

radiacti•vo -va *adj* radioactive

radia•dor -dora *adj* radiating ‖ *m* radiator

radiante *adj* radiant; (*alegre, sonriente*) radiant

radiar *tr* to radiate; radio; broadcast; cross out, erase ‖ *intr* to radiate

radicación *f* taking root; (math) evolution

radical *adj & m* radical

radicar §73 *intr* to take root; be located ‖ *ref* to take root; settle; (*un negocio*) be based

radio *m* edge, outskirts; (*de una rueda*) spoke, rung; (*de acción*) radius; (chem) radium; (math) radius ‖ *m & f* radio

radioaficiona•do -da *mf* radio amateur, radio fan

radiodifundir *tr & intr* to broadcast

radiodifusión *f* broadcasting

radioemisora *f* broadcasting station

radioescucha *mf* radio listener; radio monitor

radiofrecuencia *f* radio frequency

radiografiar §77 *tr* to X-ray; radio

radiograma *m* X-ray (*photograph*)

radiola *f* record player

radioperturbación *f* jamming

radioteléfono *m* radio(tele)phone

radioterapia *f* radiotherapy

radioyente *mf* radio listener

raer §56 *tr* to scrape, scrape off; smooth, level; wipe ‖ *ref* to become frayed, wear away

ráfaga *f* gust, puff; gust of wind; flash of light; (*de ametralladora*) burst; **ráfaga violenta** (aer) wind shear

raí•do -da *adj* threadbare; barefaced

ra•íz *f* (*pl* **-íces**) root; **a raíz de** close to the root of; even with; right after, hard upon; **de raíz** by the root; completely; **echar raíces** to take root

raja *f* crack, split; splinter, chip; slice

rajar *tr* to crack, split; splinter, chip; slice ‖ *intr* to boast; chatter ‖ *ref* to crack, split; splinter, chip; (Mex, CAm, W-I) to back down, break one's promise

rajatabla — **a rajatabla** desperately, ruthlessly

ralea *f* kind, quality; breed, ilk

ralear *intr* to thin out; be true to form

ralentí *m* slow motion

ra•lo -la *adj* sparse, thin

rallador *m* grater

rallar *tr* to grate; grate on, annoy

rallo *m* grater; scraper; rasp; (*de la regadera*) spout, nozzle; unglazed porous jug (*for cooling water by evaporation*)

rama *f* branch, bough; **andarse por las ramas** to beat about the bush; **en rama** raw; unbound, in sheets; in the grain

ramaje *m* branches, foliage

ramal *m* (*de una cuerda*) strand; halter; branch; (rr) branch line

ramalazo *m* lash; (*señal en el cutis por un golpe o enfermedad*) spot, pock; sharp pain; blow, sudden sorrow

rambla *f* dry ravine; avenue, boulevard

ramera *f* whore, harlot

ramificar §73 *tr & ref* to ramify

ramillete *m* bouquet; centerpiece, epergne; (bot) cluster

ramo *m* branch, limb; bouquet, cluster; (*de géneros, negocios, etc.*) line; (*p.ej., de una ciencia*) branch; (*de una enfermedad*) touch, slight attack

ramojo *m* brushwood, dead wood

ramonear *intr* to trim twigs; browse

rampa *f* ramp; cramp; (aer) apron; (Bol) litter, stretcher; **rampa de lanzamiento** launching pad

ram•plón -plona *adj* (*zapato*) heavy, coarse; common, vulgar

ramplonería *f* coarseness, vulgarity

rana *f* frog; **no ser rana** to be a past master; **rana toro** bullfrog

ran•cio -cia *adj* rank, rancid, stale; (*vino*) old; old, ancient; old, old-fashioned

ranchar *ref* (Col, Ven) to balk

ranchear *tr* to sack, pillage ‖ *intr & ref* to build huts, form a settlement

ranchera *f* (Ven) station wagon

ranchero *m* messman; rancher, ranchman

rancho *m* mess; meeting, gathering; camp; thatched hut; ranch; (naut) stock of provisions; (Arg) straw hat; **hacer rancho** to make room; **hacer rancho aparte** to be a lone wolf, go one's own way

randa *mf* pickpocket ‖ *f* lace trimming

rango *m* rank; class, nature; pomp, splendor; (*elevada condición social*) status, standing

ranura *f* groove; slot

rapagón *m* stripling

rapar *tr* to shave; crop; scrape; snatch, filch ‖ *ref* to shave; (*una vida regalada*) lead

ra•paz (*pl* **-paces**) *adj* thievish; rapacious ‖ *m* young boy, lad

rapaza *f* young woman, lass

rapé *m* snuff

rápi•do -da *adj* rapid ‖ *m* (rr) express; **rápidos** (*de un río*) rapids

raposa *f* fox; female fox; (*persona*) (coll) fox

raposo *m* male fox; foxy fellow; slipshod fellow

raptar *tr* to abduct; kidnap

rapto *m* abduction; kidnaping; rapture; faint, swoon

raque *m* beachcombing; **andar al raque** to go beachcombing

raquear *intr* to beachcomb

raquero *m* priate; beachcomber

raqueta *f* racket; battledore; badminton; snowshoe; **raqueta y volante** battledore and shuttlecock

raquíti•co -ca *adj* (*que padece raquitis*) rickety; flimsy, weak, miserable

raquitis *f* rickets

raramente *adv* rarely, seldom; oddly

rareza *f* rareness; rarity; oddness, strangeness; peculiarity

ra•ro -ra *adj* rare; odd, strange; thin, sparse

ras *m* evenness; **a ras** close, even, flush; **a ras de** even with, flush with; **ras con ras** flush, at the same level; grazing

rasar *tr* to graze, skim ‖ *ref* to clear up

rascacie•los *m* (*pl* **-los**) skyscraper

rascamoño *m* fancy hairpin; (bot) zinnia

rascar §73 *tr* to scrape; scuff; scratch; scrape clean ‖ *ref* (*una cicatriz, un grano*) to pick; get drunk

rasete *m* satinet

rasga•do -da *adj* (*boca; ventana*) wide-open; (*ojos*) large; outspoken; (Col) generous ‖ *m* tear, rip, rent

rasgar §44 *tr* to tear, rip ‖ *ref* to become torn

rasgo *m* (*de una pluma de escribir*) flourish, stroke; trait, characteristic; feat, deed; flash of wit, bright remark; **a grandes rasgos** in bold strokes; **rasgos** (*de la cara*) features

rasguear *tr* to thrum on ‖ *intr* to make a flourish

rasgón *m* tear, rip, rent

rasguñar *tr* to scratch; sketch, outline

rasguño *m* scratch; sketch, outline

ra•so -sa *adj* smooth, flat, level, even; common, plain; clear, cloudless; (coll) brazen, shameless ‖ *m* flat country; satin; **al raso** in the open

raspa *f* stalk, stem; (*de mazorca de maíz*) beard; (*de pez*) spine, backbone; shell, rind; (CAm, Mex) dirty trick, nasty joke

raspadura *f* scraping; erasure; pan sugar

raspar *tr* to scrape, scrape off; scratch, scratch out; graze; (*el vino*) bite; take, steal; (W-I) to dismiss, fire; (W-I) to scold ‖ *intr* (Ven) to go away; (Ven) to die

raspear *tr* (SAm) to scold ‖ *intr* (*una pluma*) to scratch

rastra *f* rake; harrow; drag; track, trail; (*p.ej., de cebollas*) string; (naut) drag; **pescar a la rastra** to trawl

rastracuero *m* show-off; upstart; sharper, adventurer

rastreador *m* dredge; (nav) mine sweeper

rastrear *tr* to trail, track, trace; drag; dredge; check into ‖ *intr* to rake; skim the ground, fly low

rastre•ro -ra *adj* dragging, trailing; creeping; low-flying; groveling, cringing; low, vile

rastrillar *tr* to rake; (*cáñamo, lino*) hatchel, comb; (Arg, Col) to shoot, to fire; (*un fósforo*) (Arg, Col) to strike (*a match*)

rastrillo *m* rake; hackle, hatchel, flax comb; (*de cerradura o llave*) ward; grating, iron grate; (rr) cowcatcher

rastro *m* rake; harrow; track, trail; scent; trace, vestige; slaughterhouse; wholesale meat market; rag fair; **rastro de condensación** (aer) contrail

rastrojo *m* stubble

rasura *f* shaving; scraping

rasurar *tr* & *ref* to shave

rata *f* rat; female rat; **rata del trigo** hamster

ratear *tr* to apportion; snitch

ratería *f* baseness, meanness, vileness; petty thievery; petty theft

rate•ro -ra *adj* thievish; trailing, dragging; base, vile ‖ *mf* sneak thief

raticida *f* rat poison

ratificar §73 *tr* to ratify

rato *m* time, while, little while; **a ratos** from time to time; **a ratos perdidos** in spare time, in one's leisure hours; **buen rato** pleasant time; large amount; **pasar el rato** to waste one's time; **un rato** awhile

ratón *m* mouse; (Ven) hangover; **ratón de biblioteca** bookworm

ratonera *f* (*trampa*) mousetrap; (*agujero*) mousehole; nest of mice; hut, shop

raudal *m* stream, torrent; abundance

rau•do -da *adj* rapid, swift, impetuous

raya *f* stripe; (*línea fina; pez*) ray; (*en la imprenta, la escritura y la telegrafía*) dash; (*de los pantalones*) crease; (*en los cabellos*) part; boundary line, limit; (*para impedir la comunicación del incendio en los campos*) firebreak; (*del espectro*) (phys) line; (Mex) pay, wages; **a rayas** striped; **hacerse la raya** to part one's hair; **pasar de la raya** to go too far; **tener a raya** to keep within bounds

raya•no -na *adj* bordering; borderline

rayar *tr* (*papel*) to rule, line; stripe; scratch, score, mark; cross out; underscore ‖ *intr* to border; stand out; (*el alba, el día, la luz, el sol*) begin, arise, come forth; **rayar en** to verge on, border on ‖ *ref* (Col) to get rich

rayo *m* (*de luz*) ray; (*de rueda*) spoke; lightning, flash of lightning, stroke of lightning, thunderbolt; (*persona*) (fig) live wire; **echar rayos** to blow up, hit the ceiling; **rayo mortífero** death ray; **rayos X** X rays

rayón *m* rayon

raza *f* race; breed, stock; crack, slit; quality; ray of light (*coming through a crack*)

razón *f* reason; right, justice; account, story; (*cantidad o grado medidos por otra cosa tomada como unidad*) rate; (math) ratio; **a razón de** at the rate of; **con razón o sin ella** right or wrong; **hacer la razón** to return a toast; join at table; **meterse en razón** to listen to reason; **no tener razón** to be wrong; **razón social** firm name, trade name; **tener razón** to be right; be in the right

razonable *adj* reasonable

razonar *tr* to reason, reason out; itemize ‖ *intr* to reason

reabrir §83 *tr* & *ref* to reopen

reacción *f* reaction; **reacción en cadena** chain reaction

reaccionar *intr* to react

reacciona•rio -ria *adj* & *mf* reactionary

rea•cio -cia *adj* stubborn, obstinate

reactivo *m* reagent

real *adj* real; royal; fine, splendid ‖ *m* army camp; fairground; real (*old Spanish coin; Spanish money of account equal to a quarter of a peseta*)

realce *m* embossment, raised work; enhancement, lustre; emphasis; **bordar de realce** to embroider in relief; (fig) to embroider, to exaggerate

ra
re

realeza *f* royalty

realidad *f* reality; truth; **hecho realidad** come true, e.g., **un sueño hecho realidad** a dream come true

realismo *m* realism

realista *mf* (*persona que tiende a ver las cosas como son*) realist; (*partidario de la monarquía*) royalist

realización *f* realization, fulfillment; achievement; sale; **realización de beneficios** profit taking

realizar §60 *tr* to fulfill; carry out; turn into cash || *ref* to become fulfilled; be carried out

realquilar *tr* to sublet

realzar §60 *tr* to raise, elevate; emboss; enhance, set off; emphasize

reanimar *tr* to revive, restore; cheer, encourage || *ref* to revive, recover one's spirits

reanudar *tr* to renew, resume

reaparecer §22 *intr* to reappear

reata *f* rope to keep animals in single file; single file; **de reata** in single file; in blind submission; next, following

rebaba *f* burr, fin

rebaja *f* rebate; diminution

rebajar *tr* to lower; diminish, reduce; rebate; (*precios*) mark down; (*a una persona*) deflate; (carp) to rabbet || *ref* to stoop; humble oneself

rebajo *m* rabbet, groove; offset, recess

rebalsar *tr* to dam || *ref* to become dammed up; be checked; pile up, accumulate

rebanada *f* slice

rebanar *tr* to slice; cut through

rebañadera *f* grapnel

rebaño *m* flock

rebarbati•vo -va *adj* crabbed, surly

rebasar *tr* to exceed; overflow; sail past

rebatiña *f* grabbing, scramble; **andar a la rebatiña** to scramble

rebatir *tr* to repel, drive back; check; resist; strengthen; rebut, refute; deduct, rebate; beat hard

rebato *m* alarm, call to arms; alarm, excitement; (mil) surprise attack

rebeca *f* cardigan

rebelar *ref* to revolt, rebel; resist; break away

rebelde *adj* rebellious; stubborn || *mf* rebel

rebeldía *f* rebelliousness; defiance, stubbornness

rebelión *f* rebellion, revolt

rebe•lón -lona *adj* balky, restive

rebobinar *tr* to rewind; unwind

reborde *m* flange, rim, collar

rebosar *tr* to cause overflow || *intr* to overflow, run over; be in abundance; **rebosar de** or **en** to overflow with, burst with; be rich in; have an abundance of || *ref* to overflow, run over

rebotar *tr* to bend back; repel; annoy, worry || *intr* to bounce; bounce back, rebound || *ref* to become annoyed, become worried

rebote *m* bounce; rebound

rebozar §60 *tr* (*la cara*) to muffle up; cover with batter || *ref* to muffle up, muffle oneself up

rebozo *m* muffling; muffler; shawl; **de rebozo** secretly; **sin rebozo** frankly, openly

rebulta•do -da *adj* bulky, massive

rebullicio *m* hubbub, loud uproar

rebullir §13 *intr* to stir, begin to move; give signs of life || *ref* to stir, begin to move

rebusca *f* seeking, searching; gleaning; leavings, refuse

rebusca•do -da *adj* affected, unnatural, recherché

rebuscar §73 *tr* to seek after; search into; to glean

rebuznar *intr* to bray; talk nonsense

rebuzno *m* braying; nonsense

recade•ro -ra *mf* messenger || *m* errand boy

recado *m* errand; message; gift, present; daily marketing; compliments, regards; safety, security; equipment, outfit; **mandar recado** to send word; **recado de escribir** writing materials

recaer §15 *intr* to fall again; fall back; relapse; backslide; **recaer en** to fall to; **recaer sobre** to fall upon, devolve upon

recaída *f* relapse; backsliding

recalar *tr* to soak, saturate || *intr* to sight land

recalcar §73 *tr* to press, squeeze; cram, pack, stuff; (*sus palabras*) stress || *intr* (naut) to list, heel; **recalcar en** to lay stress on || *ref* to harp on the same string; sprawl; (*p.ej., la muñeca*) sprain

recalentar §2 *tr* to overheat; (*la comida*) to warm over

recalmón *m* (naut) lull

recamado *m* embroidery

recamar *tr* to embroider

recámara *f* dressing room; (*de un arma de fuego*) breech, chamber; reserve, caution; (Mex) bedroom

recamarera *f* (Mex) chambermaid

recambio *m* spare part; (*parte, rueda, etc.*) **de recambio** spare

recapacitar *tr* to run over in one's mind || *intr* to refresh one's memory; reflect

recargable *adj* rechargeable

recargar §44 *tr* to reload; overload; recharge; overcharge; overadorn; (*una cuota de impuesto*) increase; (elec) to recharge || *ref* to become more feverish

recargo *m* new burden; extra charge; new charge; (*que paga el contribuyente moroso*) penalty; (pathol) rise in temperature; **recargo de tarifa** extra fare

recata•do -da *adj* cautious, circumspect; modest; shy

recatar *tr* to hide, conceal || *ref* to hide; be afraid to take a stand

recato *m* caution, reserve; modesty

recauchutaje *m* recapping, retreading

recauchutar *tr* to recap, retread

recaudar *tr* (*impuestos, tributos*) to gather, collect; guard, watch over

recaudo *m* tax collecting; care, precaution; bail, surety; **a buen recaudo** under guard, in safety

recelar *tr* to fear, distrust || *intr & ref* to fear, be afraid

recelo *m* fear, distrust

recelo•so -sa *adj* fearful, distrustful
recensión *f* review, book review
recepción *f* reception; reception desk
recepcionista *m* room clerk ‖ *f* receptionist
receptáculo *m* receptacle; shelter, refuge
receptador *m* (coll) fence, holder of stolen goods
receptar *tr* to receive, welcome; (*delincuentes*) hide, conceal; (*cosas robadas*) receive
recepti•vo -va *adj* receptive; susceptible
receptor *m* receiver; **receptor de cabeza** headpiece; **receptor telefónico** receiver
receta *f* recipe; (pharm) prescription
recetar *tr* (*un medicamento*) to prescribe; request
recibí *m* receipt; received payment
recibida *f* reception, admission
recibi•dor -dora *mf* receiver; receiving teller; ticket collector ‖ *m* reception room
recibimiento *m* reception; welcome; reception room; (*visita en que una persona recibe a sus amistades*) at-home
recibir *tr* to receive; (*visitas*) entertain ‖ *intr* to receive; entertain ‖ *ref* to be received, be admitted; **recibirse de** to be admitted to practice as; be graduated as
recibo *m* reception; receipt; hall; parlor; at-home; **acusar recibo de** to acknowledge receipt of; **estar de recibo** to be at home; **ser de recibo** to be acceptable
reciclable *adj* recyclable
reciclado *m* or **reciclaje** *m* recycling
reciclar *tr* to recycle
recién *adv* (used before past participles) recently, just, newly, e.g., **recién llegado** newly arrived; just now, recently
reciente *adv* recently
recinto *m* area, inclosure, place
re•cio -cia *adj* strong; thick, coarse, heavy; harsh; hard, bitter, arduous; (*tiempo*) severe; swift, impetuous ‖ **recio** *adv* strongly; swiftly; hard; loud
reciprocidad *f* reciprocity
recípro•co -ca *adj* reciprocal
recital *m* (*de música o poesía*) recital
recitar *tr* to recite; (*un discurso*) deliver
reclamación *f* claim, demand; objection; protest, complaint
reclamar *tr* to claim, demand; (*un ave*) decoy, lure ‖ *intr* to cry out, protest, complain
réclame *m* & *f* advertising
reclamo *m* bird call; decoy bird; (*para aves*) lure; allurement, attraction; advertisement; blurb, puff; reference; (typ) catchword; (SAm) complaint
reclinar *tr* (*p.ej., la cabeza*) to lean, bend ‖ *ref* to recline
reclinatorio *m* prie-dieu; couch, lounge
recluir §20 *tr* to seclude, shut in; imprison ‖ *ref* to go into seclusion
reclusión *f* seclusion; imprisonment
reclu•so -sa *adj* secluded; imprisoned ‖ *mf* prisoner; inmate
recluta *m* recruit ‖ *f* recruiting; (*del ganado disperso*) (Arg) roundup

reclutar *tr* to recruit; (Arg) to round up
recobrar *tr* to recover ‖ *ref* to recover; come to
recobro *m* recovery; (*de un motor*) pickup
recodar *intr* to lean; bend, twist, turn, wind
recodo *m* bend, twist, turn
recoger §17 *tr* to pick up; gather, collect; harvest; shorten, draw in; keep; welcome; lock up ‖ *ref* to take shelter, take refuge; withdraw; (*echarse en la cama*) retire; go home; cut down expenses
recogida *f* collection; withdrawal; suspension; **recogida de basuras** garbage collection
recogimiento *m* gathering, collecting; harvesting; seclusion, retreat; concentration; self-communion
recolectar *tr* to gather, gather in; (*el algodón*) pick
recombina•do -da *adj* (genética) recombinant
recomendable *adj* commendable
recomendar §2 *tr* to recommend; commend
recompensa *f* recompense, reward
recompensar *tr* to recompense, reward
recompostura *f* repair
recomprar *tr* to buy back, repurchase
reconcentrar *tr* to bring together; (*un sentimiento o afecto*) conceal, disguise ‖ *ref* to come together; be absorbed in thought
reconciliar *tr* to reconcile ‖ *ref* to become reconciled
recóndi•to -ta *adj* hidden, concealed
reconfortar *tr* to comfort, cheer
reconocer §22 *tr* to recognize; admit, acknowledge; examine; (mil) to reconnoiter ‖ *intr* (mil) to reconnoiter ‖ *ref* to be clear
reconoci•do -da *adj* grateful
reconocimiento *m* recognition; admission; acknowledgment; gratitude; reconnaissance; **reconocimiento médico** inquest
reconquista *f* reconquest
reconsiderar *tr* to reconsider
reconstruir §20 *tr* to reconstruct, rebuild, recast
recontar §61 *tr* (*volver a contar; narrar*) to recount (*to count again; narrate*)
reconvenir §79 *tr* to expostulate with, to remonstrate with
reconversión *f* reconversion
recopilar *tr* to compile
record *m* (pl **records**) (sport) record; **batir un record** to break a record; **establecer un récord** to make a record
recordar §61 *tr* to remember; remind ‖ *intr* to remember; get awake; come to; **si mal no recuerdo** if I remember correctly
recordati•vo -va *adj* reminding, reminiscent ‖ *m* reminder
recordatorio *m* reminder; memento
record•man (pl **-men**) record holder
recorrer *tr* to go over, go through; look over, look through; (*un libro*) run through; overhaul
recorrido *m* trip, run, route; (*del émbolo*) stroke; repair
recortado *m* cutout

recortar *tr* to trim, cut off; *(figuras en una tela, en un papel)* cut out; outline ‖ *ref* to stand out

recorte *m* cutting; *(de un periódico)* clipping; dodge, duck; **recortes** cuttings, trimmings

recostar §61 *tr* to lean ‖ *ref* to lean, lean back, sit back

recova *f* poultry business; poultry stand; (Arg) portico; (SAm) food market

recoveco *m* bend, turn, twist; subterfuge, trick

recreación *f* recreation

recreo *m* recreation; place of amusement

recrudecer §22 *intr & ref* to flare up, get worse

rectángu•lo -la *adj* right-angled ‖ *m* rectangle

rectificar §73 *tr* to rectify; *(un cilindro de motor)* rebore

rec•to -ta *adj* straight; *(ángulo)* right; right, just, righteous ‖ *m* rectum

rec•tor -tora *adj* governing, managing ‖ *mf* principal, superior ‖ *m* rector; *(de una universidad)* rector, president

recua *f* drove; *(de personas o cosas)* string, line

recuadro *m* panel, square; *(sección de un impreso encerrada dentro de un marco)* box

recubrir §83 *tr* to cover, cap, coat

recuento *m* count; recount; inventory

recuerdo *m* memory, remembrance; keepsake, souvenir

recuero *m* muleteer

recular *intr* to back up; *(un arma de fuego)* recoil; back down

reculón *m* backing; **a reculones** backing away, recoiling

recuperar *tr & ref* to recuperate, recover

recurrir *intr* to resort, have recourse; revert

recurso *m* recourse; resource; resort; appeal, petition

recusar *tr* to refuse, reject; (law) to challenge

rechazar §60 *tr* to refuse, reject; repel, drive back

rechazo *m* rejection; rebound, recoil

rechifla *f* catcall

rechiflar *tr & intr* to catcall, hiss ‖ *ref* to make fun

rechinar *intr* to creak, grate, squeak; act with bad grace; (Mex) to rage

rechistar *intr* to stir, say a word; **sin rechistar** without protest

rechon•cho -cha *adj* chubby, tubby, plump

rechupete — de rechupete fine, wonderful

red *f* net; netting; network, system; baggage netting; (fig) net, snare, trap; **a red barredera** with a clean sweep; **red barredera** dragnet

redacción *f* writing; editing; editorial staff; newspaper office, city room

redactar *tr* to write up; edit

redac•tor -tora *mf* writer; editor, newspaper editor; **redactor publicitario** copy writer

redada *f* *(de peces)* catch, netful; *(p.ej., de criminales)* haul, roundup

redecilla *f* hair net

rededor *m* surroundings; **al rededor (de)** around

redención *f* redemption; help, recourse

reden•tor -tora *mf* redeemer

redición *f* constant repetition

redi•cho -cha *adj* overprecise

redil *m* sheepfold

redimir *tr* to redeem; ransom; buy back

rédito *m* income, revenue, yield

redituar §21 *tr* to yield, produce

redobla•do -da *adj* stocky, heavy-built; heavy, strong; (mil) double-quick

redoblar *tr* to double; clinch; repeat ‖ *intr* *(un tambor)* to roll

redoble *m* doubling; clinching; repeating; roll of a drum

redoma *f* phial, flask

redoma•do -da *adj* sly, crafty

redonda *f* district, neighborhood; (mus) semibreve; **a la redonda** around, roundabout

redondear *tr* to round, make round; round off; round out ‖ *ref* to be well-off; be out of debt

redondel *m* circle; round cloak; *(espacio destinado a la lidia)* (taur) ring

redondilla *f* eight-syllable quatrain with rhyme abba or abab

redon•do -da *adj* round; straightforward; *(terreno)* pasture; honest; stupid ‖ *m* ring, circle; cash ‖ *f* see **redonda**

redopelo *m* row, scuffle; **al redopelo** against the grain, the wrong way; roughly, violently

reducir §19 *tr & ref* to reduce; **reducirse a** to come to, amount to; be obliged to

reducto *m* (fort) redoubt

redundante *adj* redundant

redundar *intr* to redound; overflow; **redundar en** to redound to

reduplicación *f* doubling

reelección *f* reëlection

reembarcar §73 *tr, intr & ref* to reship, reëmbark

reembarco *m* reshipment *(of persons)*, reëmbarkation

reembarque *m* reshipment *(of goods)*

reembolsar *tr* to reimburse; refund ‖ *ref* to collect a debt, be reimbursed

reembolso *m* reimbursement; refund; **contra reembolso** collect on delivery; cash on delivery

reemplazar §60 *tr* to replace

reemplazo *m* replacement; (mil) replacements; *(hombre que sirve en lugar de otro)* (mil) replacement

reencuadernar *tr* (bb) to rebind

reencuentro *m* collision; *(de tropas)* clash

reenganchar *tr & ref* to reënlist

reentrada *f* reëntry

reestrenar *tr* (theat) to revive

reestreno *m* (theat) revival

reexamen *m* or **reexaminación** *f* reëxamination

reexpedición *f* forwarding, reshipment

reexpedir §50 *tr* to forward, reship

refacción *f* refreshment; allowance; repair, repairs; extra, bonus; spare part

refaccionar *tr* to finance; (SAm) to repair, renovate

refajo *m* underskirt, slip

referencia *f* reference; account, report

referi•do -da *adj* above-mentioned

referir §68 *tr* to refer; tell, report ‖ *ref* to refer

refinamiento *m* refinement

refinar *tr* to refine; polish, perfect

refinería *f* refinery

reflejar *tr* to reflect; reflect on; show, reveal ‖ *intr* to reflect

reflejo *m* glare; reflection; reflex; **reflejo acondicionado** conditioned reflex; **reflejo patelar** or **rotuliano** knee jerk

reflexión *f* reflection

reflexionar *tr* to reflect on or upon ‖ *intr* to reflect

reflugo *m* ebb

refocilar *tr* to cheer; strengthen ‖ *intr* (Arg, Urug) to lighten ‖ *ref* to be cheered; take it easy

reforma *f* reform; reformation; alteration, renovation ‖ **la Reforma** the Reformation

reformación *f* reformation

reformar *tr* to reform; mend, repair; alter, renovate; revise; reorganize ‖ *ref* to reform; hold oneself in check

reforzar §35 *tr* to reinforce; strengthen; encourage

refracción *f* refraction

refracta•rio -ria *adj* rebellious, unruly, stubborn

refrán *m* proverb, saying

refregar §66 *tr* to rub; upbraid

refrenar *tr* to curb, rein; check, restrain

refrendar *tr* to countersign; authenticate; visé; repeat

refrescar §73 *tr* to refresh; cool, refrigerate ‖ *intr & ref* to refresh; refresh oneself; cool off; go out for fresh air; (*el viento*) (naut) to blow up

refresco *m* refreshment; cold drink, soft drink

refriega *f* fray, scuffle

refrigerador *m* refrigerator; ice bucket

refrigerio *m* coolness; relief; pick-me-up, light lunch

refuerzo *m* reinforcement

refugia•do -da *mf* refugee

refugiar *tr* to shelter ‖ *ref* to take refuge

refugio *m* refuge; hospice; shelter; haunt; (*para peatones en medio de la calle*) safety zone; **refugio antiaéreo** air-raid shelter; **refugio antiatómico** fallout shelter

refundición *f* recast; revision; (*de una pieza dramática*) adaptation

refundir *tr* to recast; revise; (*una pieza dramática*) adapt ‖ *intr* to redound

refunfuñar *intr* to grumble, growl

refutar *tr* to refute

regadera *f* watering can; street sprinkler

regadí•o -a or **regadi•zo -za** *adj* irrigable ‖ *m* irrigated land

regala *f* gunwale

regala•do -da *adj* dainty, delicate; pleasing, pleasant; (*vida*) of ease

regalar *tr* to give; regale, entertain; treat; caress, fondle; indulge

regalía *f* privilege, perquisite; bonus; royalty; (Arg, Chile) muff

regaliz *m* licorice

regalo *m* gift, present; treat; joy, pleasure; **regalos de fiesta** favors

rega•lón -lona *adj* comfort-loving, pampered; (*vida*) soft, easy

regañar *tr* to scold ‖ *intr* to growl, snarl; grumble; quarrel; scold

regaño *m* scolding; growl, snarl; grumble

regar §66 *tr* to water, sprinkle; irrigate; spread, sprinkle, strew

regate *m* dodge, duck; (fig) dodge, subterfuge

regatear *tr* to haggle over; sell at retail; avoid, shun ‖ *intr* to haggle, bargain; duck, dodge; (naut) to race

regazo *m* lap

regenerar *tr & ref* to regenerate

regente *m* director, manager; registered pharmacist; (typ) foreman

regicida *mf* regicide

regicidio *m* regicide

regi•dor -dora *adj* ruling, governing ‖ *m* alderman, councilman

régimen *m* (*pl* **regímenes**) regime; diet; rate; management; (gram) government; **régimen de hambre** starvation diet; **régimen de justicia** rule of law

regimental *adj* regimental

regimentar §2 *tr* to regiment

regimiento *m* regiment; rule, government; city council

re•gio -gia *adj* regal, royal; magnificent

región *f* region

regir §57 *tr* to rule, govern; control, manage; guide, steer; (gram) to govern ‖ *intr* to prevail, be in force

registra•dor -dora *adj* registering; recording ‖ *m* registrar, recorder; inspector ‖ *f* cash register

registrar *tr* to register; record; examine, inspect ‖ *ref* to register; be recorded; take place

registro *m* registration, registry; recording; examination, inspection; entry, record; bookmark; manhole; (*de chimenea*) damper; (*de reloj*) regulator; (*de órgano*) (mus) stop; (*de piano*) (mus) pedal

regla *f* rule; (*para trazar líneas*) ruler; measure, moderation; order; menstruation; **regla de cálculo** slide rule; **reglas** monthlies, menses

reglamenta•rio -ria *adj* prescribed, statutory

reglamento *m* rules, regulations

reglar *tr* to regulate; (*papel*) rule ‖ *ref* to guide oneself, be guided

regleta *f* (typ) lead

regletear *tr* (typ) to lead, space

regocijar *tr* to cheer, delight ‖ *ref* to rejoice

regocijo *m* cheer, delight, rejoicing

regoldar §3 *intr* to belch

regolfar *intr & ref* to surge back, flow back, back up

regorde•te -ta *adj* dumpy, plump

re
re

regresar *intr* to return
regreso *m* return; **estar de regreso** to be back
regüeldo *m* belch, belching
reguero *m* drip, trickle; (*señal que deja una cosa que se va vertiendo*) track; irrigating ditch; **ser un reguero de pólvora** to spread like wildfire
regulador *m* regulator; (*de locomotora*) throttle; (mach) governor
regular *adj* regular; fair, moderate, medium; **por lo regular** as a rule ‖ *tr* to regulate; put in order; throttle
rehabilitación *f* rehabilitation
rehacer §39 *tr* to remake, make over, do over; mend, repair, renovate ‖ *ref* to recover, rally
rehén *m* hostage; **llevarse en rehenes** to carry off as a hostage; **toma de rehenes** hostage taking
rehilandera *f* pinwheel
rehilar *intr* to quiver; whiz by
rehilete *m* shuttlecock; (*que se lanza por diversión*) dart; dig, cutting remark; (taur) banderilla
rehuir §20 *tr* to avoid, shun; shrink from; refuse; dislike ‖ *intr* & *ref* to flee
rehusar *tr* to refuse, turn down
reimpresión *f* reprint
reimprimir §83 *tr* to reprint
reina *f* queen; **reina Margarita** aster, China aster; **reina viuda** queen dowager
reinado *m* reign
reinar *intr* to reign; prevail
reincidir *intr* to backslide; repeat an offense
reingreso *m* reëntry
reino *m* kingdom; **Reino Unido** United Kingdom
reinstalar *tr* to reinstate, reinstall
reintegrar *tr* to refund, pay back
reintegro *m* refund, payment
reír §58 *tr* to laugh at ‖ *intr* & *ref* to laugh; **reír de** or **reírse de** to laugh at
reja *f* grate, grating, grille; plowshare, colter; **entre rejas** behind bars
rejilla *f* screen; grating; lattice, latticework; cane, cane upholstery; foot brasier; fire grate; (electron) grid; (*de acumulador*) (elec) grid; (rr) baggage rack
rejón *m* spear; dagger; (taur) lance
rejonear *tr* (*el jinete al toro*) (taur) to jab with a lance made to break off in the bull's neck
rejuvenecimiento *m* rejuvenation
relación *f* relation; account, list; (*en un drama*) speech; **relación de ciego** blind man's ballad; **relaciones** betrothal, engagement; **relaciones públicas** public relations
relacionar *tr* to relate ‖ *ref* to be related
relai *m* or **relais** *m* (elec) relay
relajación *f* or **relajamiento** *m* relaxation; slackening; laxity; rupture, hernia
relajar *tr* to relax; slacken; debauch ‖ *intr* to relax ‖ *ref* to relax, become relaxed; become debauched; be ruptured
relamer *ref* to lick one's lips; gloat; to relish; boast; slick oneself up
relami•do -da *adj* prim, overnice

relámpago *m* flash of lightning; flash of wit; **relámpago fotogénico** flash bulb, flashlight; **relámpagos** lightning
relampaguear *intr* to lighten; flash
relatar *tr* to relate, report
relati•vo -va *adj* relative
relato *m* story; statement, report
relé *m* (elec) relay; **relé de televisión** television relay system
releer §43 *tr* to reread
relegar §44 *tr* to relegate; banish, exile; shelve, lay aside
relente *m* night dew, light drizzle
relevador *m* (elec) relay
relevancia *f* relevance; significance
relevante *adj* outstanding
relevar *tr* to emboss; make stand out; relieve; release; absolve; replace ‖ *intr* to stand out in relief
relevo *m* (elec) relay; (mil) relief; **relevos** (sport) relay race
relicario *m* shrine; (*medallón*) locket
relieve *m* relief; merit, distinction; **en relieve** in relief; **poner de relieve** to point out; to make stand out; **relieves** scraps, leftovers
religión *f* religion
religio•so -sa *adj* religious
relinchar *intr* to neigh
relincho *m* neigh, neighing; cry of joy
reliquia *f* relic; trace, vestige; **reliquia de familia** heirloom
reloj *m* watch; clock; meter; **como un reloj** like clockwork; **conocer el reloj** to know how to tell time; **reloj de caja** grandfather's clock; **reloj de carillón** chime clock; **reloj de cuarzo** quartz watch; **reloj de cuclillo** cuckoo clock; **reloj de ocho días cuerda** eight-day clock; **reloj de pulsera** wrist watch; **reloj de sol** sundial; **reloj despertador** alarm clock; **reloj registrador** time clock; **reloj registrador de tarjetas** punch clock
relojera *f* watch case; watch pocket
relojería *f* watchmaking, clockmaking; watchmaker's shop
reloje•ro -ra *mf* watchmaker, clockmaker ‖ *f* see **relojera**
reluciente *adj* shining, brilliant, flashing
relucir §45 *intr* to shine
relumbrar *intr* to shine, dazzle, glare
relumbre *m* beam, sparkle; flash; dazzle, glare
relumbrón *m* flash, glare; tinsel; **de relumbrón** showy, tawdry
rellano *m* (*en la pendiente de un terreno*) level stretch; (*de escalera*) landing
rellenar *tr* to refill; fill up; stuff; pad; fill out; cram, stuff ‖ *ref* to fill up; cram, stuff oneself
relle•no -na *adj* full, packed; stuffed ‖ *m* refill; filling, stuffing; padding, wadding; (*en un escrito*) filler
remachar *tr* (*un clavo ya clavado*) to clinch; (*un roblón*) rivet; stress, emphasize ‖ *ref* (Col) to maintain strict silence
remache *m* clinching; riveting; rivet
remanso *m* dead water, backwater

remar *intr* to row; toil, struggle

remata·do -da *adj* hopeless; **loco rematado** raving mad

rematador *m* auctioneer

rematar *tr* to finish, put an end to; finish off, kill off; (*en una subasta*) knock down ‖ *intr* to end ‖ *ref* to come to ruin

remate *m* end; crest, top, finial; closing; highest bid; (*en una subasta*) sale; **de remate** hopelessly

rembolsar *tr* to reimburse; repay; redeem

rembolso *m* reimbursement; **contra rembolso** C.O.D. (cash on delivery)

remecer §46 *tr & ref* to shake, swing, rock

remedar *tr* to copy, imitate; ape, mimic; mock

remediar *tr* to remedy; help; prevent; (*del peligro*) free, save

remediava·gos *m* (*pl* -gos) short cut

remedio *m* remedy; help; recourse; **no hay remedio** or **no hay más remedio** it can't be helped; **no tener remedio** to be unavoidable

remedión *m* (theat) substitute performance

remedo *m* copy, imitation; poor imitation

remendar §2 *tr* to patch, mend, repair; darn; emend, correct; touch up

remen·dón -dona *mf* mender, repairer; shoe mender; tailor (*who does mending*)

reme·ro -ra *mf* rower ‖ *m* oarsman

remesa *f* remittance; shipment

remesar *tr* to remit; ship

remezón *m* hard shake; tremor

remiendo *m* patch; mending, repair; retouching; emendation, correction; job printing, job work; **a remiendos** piecemeal

remilga·do -da *adj* prim and finicky; affected, smirking

remilgar §44 *intr* to be prim and finicky; smirk

remilgo *m* primness, affectation

remira·do -da *adj* circumspect, discreet

remisión *f* remission; reference

remitente *mf* sender, shipper

remitido *m* (*noticia de un particular a un periódico*) personal; letter to the editor

remitir *tr* to remit; forward, send, ship; refer; defer, postpone; pardon, forgive ‖ *intr* to remit, let up; refer ‖ *ref* to remit, let up; defer, yield

remo *m* oar; leg, arm, wing; toil, labor; (sport) rowing; **aguantar los remos** to lie or rest on one's oars

remoción *f* discharge, dismissal; removal

remodelación *f* remodeling

remodelar *tr* to remodel

remojar *tr* to soak, steep, dip; celebrate with a drink; **remojar la palabra** to wet one's whistle

remojo *m* soaking, steeping; **poner en remojo** to put off to a more suitable time

remolacha *f* beet; **remolacha azucarera** sugar beet

remolcador *m* tug, tugboat; towboat; tow car

remolcar §73 *tr* to tow; take in tow

remoler §47 *tr* to grind up; bore

remolinear *tr, intr & ref* to eddy, whirl about

remolino *m* eddy, whirlpool; swirl, whirl; disturbance, commotion; throng, crowd; cowlick

remo·lón -lona *adj* lazy, indolent ‖ *mf* shirker, quitter

remolonear *intr* to refuse to budge

remolque *m* tow; towing; trailer; **a remolque** in tow

remontar *tr* to mend, repair; frighten away; elevate, raise up; (*p.ej., un río*) go up ‖ *intr* (*en el tiempo*) go back ‖ *ref* to rise, rise up; soar; (*en el tiempo*) go back

remontuar *m* stem-winder

remoquete *m* punch; nickname; sarcasm; flirting

rémora *f* hindrance, obstacle

remordimiento *m* remorse

remo·to -ta *adj* remote; unlikely; **estar remoto** to be rusty

remover §47 *tr* to remove; shake; stir; disturb, upset; dismiss, discharge ‖ *ref* to move away

remozar §60 *tr* to rejuvenate ‖ *ref* to become rejuvenated

rempujar *tr* to push, jostle

rempujón *m* push, jostle

remuda *f* change, replacement; change of clothes

remudar *tr* to change, replace; move around

remuneración *f* remuneration; **remuneración por rendimiento** piece wage

renacer §22 *intr* to be reborn, be born again; recover

renacimiento *m* rebirth; renaissance

renacuajo *m* tadpole; (coll) shrimp, little squirt

Renania *f* Rhineland

ren·co -ca *adj* lame

rencor *m* rancor; **guardar rencor** to bear malice

rendición *f* surrender; submission; fatigue, exhaustion; yield

rendi·do -da *adj* tired, worn-out; submissive

rendija *f* crack, split, slit

rendimiento *m* submission; exhaustion; yield; output; (mech) efficiency

rendir §50 *tr* to conquer; subdue; surrender; exhaust, wear out; return, give back; yield, produce; (*gracias, obsequios, homenaje*) render ‖ *intr* to yield ‖ *ref* to surrender; yield, give in; be exhausted, be worn out

renegar §66 *tr* to deny vigorously; abhor, detest ‖ *intr* to curse; be insulting; **renegar de** to deny; curse; abhor, detest

renegociación *f* renegotiation

Renfe, la acronym for **la Red Nacional de los Ferrocarriles Españoles** the Spanish National Railroad System

renglón *m* line; **a renglón seguido** right below; **leer entre renglones** to read between the lines

reniego *m* curse

reno *m* reindeer

renombra·do -da *adj* renowned, famous

renombre *m* renown, fame

renovar §61 *tr* to renew; renovate; transform, restore; remodel

re
re

renquear *intr* to limp

renta *f* income; private income; annuity; public debt; rent; **renta nacional** gross national product

rentar *tr* to produce, yield

rentista *mf* bondholder; financier; person of independent means

renuente *adj* reluctant, unwilling

renuevo *m* sprout, shoot; renewal

renuncia *f* renunciation; resignation; (law) waiver

renunciar *tr* to renounce; resign ‖ *intr* to renounce; (*no servir al palo que se juega*) renege; **renunciar a** to give up, renounce, waive

renuncio *m* slip, mistake; (*en juegos de naipes*) renege; lie

reñi•do -da *adj* on bad terms; bitter, hard-fought

reñir §72 *tr* (*regañar*) to scold; (*una batalla, un desafío*) fight ‖ *intr* to fight; be at odds, fall out

re•o -a *adj* guilty, criminal ‖ **reo** *mf* offender, criminal; (law) defendant

reojo — **de reojo** askance, out of the corner of one's eye; hostilely

reorganizar §60 *tr & ref* to reorganize

reorientación *f* reorientation

reóstato *m* rheostat

repanchigar or **repantigar** §44 *ref* to sprawl, loll

reparar *tr* to repair, mend; make amends for; notice, observe; (*un golpe*) parry ‖ *intr* to stop; **reparar en** to notice, pay attention to ‖ *ref* to stop; refrain

reparo *m* repairing, repairs; notice, observation; doubt, objection; shelter; bashfulness

repa•rón -rona *adj* faultfinding ‖ *mf* faultfinder

repartida *f* distribution; issuing

repartir *tr* to distribute; (*naipes*) deal

reparto *m* distribution; (*de naipes*) deal; (theat) cast; **reparto de acciones gratis** stock dividend

repasar *tr* to repass; retrace; review; revise; (*la ropa*) mend

repasata *f* scolding, reprimand

repaso *m* revision; (*de una lección*) review; mending; reprimand

repatriar §77 *tr* to repatriate; send home ‖ *intr & ref* to be repatriated; go or come home

repeler *tr* to repel, repulse

repente *m* start, sudden movement; **de repente** suddenly

repenti•no -na *adj* sudden, unexpected

repentista *mf* (mus) improviser; (mus) sight reader

repentizar §60 *intr* to improvise; (mus) to sight-read, perform at sight

repercutir *intr* to rebound; reëcho, reverberate

repertorio *m* repertory

repetición *f* repetition; (mus) repeat

repetir §50 *tr & intr* to repeat

repicar §73 *tr* to mince, chop up; ring, sound; sting again ‖ *intr* peal, ring out, resound ‖ *ref* to boast, be conceited

repique *m* chopping, mincing; peal, ringing; squabble, quarrel

repiqueteo *m* pealing, ringing; beating, rapping

repisa *f* shelf, ledge; bracket; **repisa de chimenea** mantelpiece; **repisa de ventana** window sill

replantear *tr* to lay out again; reaffirm, reimplement

replegar §66 *tr* to fold over and over ‖ *ref* to fold, fold up; (mil) to fall back

reple•to -ta *adj* replete, full, loaded; fat, chubby

réplica *f* answer, retort; replica

replicar §73 *tr* to argue against ‖ *intr* to answer back, retort

repli•cón -cona *adj* saucy, flip

repliegue *m* fold, crease; (mil) falling back

repollo *m* cabbage; (*p.ej., de lechuga, col*) head

reponer §54 *tr* to replace, put back; restore; (*una pieza dramática*) revive; **repuso** he replied ‖ *ref* to recover; calm down

reportaje *m* reporting; news coverage; report

reportar *tr* to check, restrain; get, obtain; bring, carry; report ‖ *ref* to restrain or control oneself

reporte *m* report, news report; gossip

repórter *m* reporter

reporte•ro -ra *mf* reporter

reposa cabezas *f* (aut) head rest

reposar *intr & ref* to rest, repose; take a nap; (*en la sepultura*) lie, be at rest; (*poso, sedimento*) settle

reposición *f* replacement; (*de la salud*) recovery; (theat) revival

reposo *m* rest, repose

repostar *tr, intr & ref* to stock up; refuel

repostería *f* pastry shop, confectionery; pantry

reposte•ro -ra *mf* pastry cook, confectioner

repregunta *f* (law) cross-examination

repreguntar *tr* (law) to cross-examine

reprender *tr* to reprehend, scold

represa *f* dam; damming; repression, check; (*de un buque*) recapture

represalia *f* reprisal; retaliation

represar *tr* to dam; repress, check; (*de un buque*) to recapture

representación *f* representation; dignity, standing; performance; **en representación de** representing; **representación exclusiva** sole dealership

representante *adj* representing ‖ *mf* representative; actor, player; (com) agent, representative

representar *tr* to represent; show, express; state, declare; act, perform, play; (*determinada edad*) appear to be ‖ *ref* to imagine

representati•vo -va *adj* representative

reprimenda *f* reprimand

reprimir *tr* to repress

reprobación *f* reproof; flunk, failure

reprobar §61 *tr* to reprove; flunk, fail

reprochar *tr* to reproach

reproche *m* reproach
reproducción *f* reproduction; breeding
reproducir §19 *tr & ref* to reproduce
repro•pio -pia *adj* balky
reptar *intr* to crawl; to cringe
reptil *m* reptile
república *f* republic
republica•no -na *adj & mf* republican ‖ *m* patriot
repudiar *tr* to repudiate, disown, disavow
repues•to -ta *adj* secluded; spare, extra ‖ *m* stock, supply; serving table; pantry; **de repuesto** spare, extra
repugnante *adj* repugnant, disgusting
repugnar *tr* to conflict with; contradict; object to, avoid; revolt, be repugnant to ‖ *intr* to be repugnant
repujar *tr* to emboss
repulgar §44 *tr* to hem, border
repulgo *m* hem, border
repuli•do -da *adj* highly polished; all dolled up
repulsar *tr* to reject, refuse
repulsi•vo -va *adj* repulsive
repuntar *tr* (*animales dispersos*) (Arg, Chile, Urug) to round up ‖ *intr* to begin to appear; (naut) to begin to rise; (naut) to begin to ebb ‖ *ref* to begin to turn sour; fall out
repuso see **reponer**
reputación *f* reputation, repute
reputar *tr* to repute; esteem
requebra•dor -dora *adj* flirtatious ‖ *mf* flirt
requebrar §2 *tr* to break into smaller pieces; flatter, flirt with
requemar *tr* to burn again; parch; overcook; inflame; bite, sting ‖ *ref* to become tanned or sunburned; smolder, burn within
requerir §68 *tr* to notify; summon; request; urge; check, examine; require; seek, look for; reach for; court, make love to
requesón *m* cottage cheese
requiebro *m* fine crushing; flattery, flattering remarks, flirtation
requisi•to -ta *adj* requisite ‖ *m* requisite, requirement; accomplishment; **requisito previo** prerequisite
res *f* head of cattle; beast; **reses** cattle
resabio *m* unpleasant aftertaste; bad habit, vice
resabio•so -sa *adj* sly, crafty; (*caballo*) vicious
resaca *f* surge, surf; undertow; (com) redraft; (slang) hangover
resalir §65 *intr* to jut out, project
resaltar *tr* to emphasize ‖ *intr* to bounce, rebound; jut out, project; stand out
resanar *tr* to retouch, patch, repair
resarcir §36 *tr* to indemnify, make amends to; (*un daño, un agravio*) repay; (*una pérdida*) make good; to mend, repair ‖ *ref* — **resarcirse de** to make up for
resbaladi•zo -za *adj* slippery; skiddy; risky; (*memoria*) shaky
resbalar *intr* to slide; skid; slip ‖ *ref* to slide; slip; (fig) to slip, to misstep

rescatar *tr* to ransom, redeem; rescue; (*el tiempo perdido*) make up for; relieve; atone for; (Mex) to resell
rescate *m* ransom, redemption; rescue; salvage; ransom money
rescindir *tr* to rescind
rescoldera *f* heartburn
rescoldo *m* embers; smoldering; doubt, scruple; **arder en rescoldo** to smolder
resenti•do -da *adj* resentful
resentimiento *m* resentment; sorrow, disappointment
resentir §68 *ref* to be resentful; **resentirse de** to feel the bad effects of; resent; suffer from
reseña *f* outline; book review; newspaper account; (mil) review
reseñador *m* reviewer; critic
reseñar *tr* to outline; (*un libro*) review; (mil) to review
reserva *f* reserve; reservation; **con** or **bajo la mayor reserva** in strictest confidence; **reserva de caza** game preserve
reservar *tr* to reserve; put aside; postpone; exempt; keep secret ‖ *ref* to save oneself, bide one's time; beware, be distrustful
resfriado *m* cold
resfriar §77 *tr* to cool, chill ‖ *intr* to turn cold ‖ *ref* to catch cold; cool off, grow cold
resguardar *tr* to defend; protect, shield ‖ *ref* to take shelter; protect oneself
resguardo *m* defense; protection; check, voucher; collateral; (naut) wide berth, sea room
residencia *f* residence; impeachment; **residencia de ancianos** nursing home; home for the aged
residenciar *tr* to call to account; impeach
residir *intr* to reside
residuo *m* residue, remains; remainder; **residuos radiactivos** radioactive waste
resignación *f* resignation
resignar *tr* to resign ‖ *ref* to resign, become resigned; **resignarse con** (*p.ej., su suerte*) to be resigned to
resina *f* resin
resistencia *f* resistance; strength; **resistencia de rejilla** (electron) grid leak
resistente *adj* resistant; strong; (hort) hardy; **resistente al rayado** scratch-resistant
resistir *tr* to bear, stand; (*la tentación*) resist ‖ *intr* to resist; hold out; **resistir a** (*la violencia; la risa*) resist; refuse to ‖ *ref* to resist; struggle; **resistirse a** to refuse to
resma *f* ream
resobrina *f* grandniece, greatniece
resobrino *m* grandnephew, greatnephew
resolución *f* resolution; **en resolución** in brief, in a word
resolver §47 & §83 *tr* to resolve; solve; decide on; dissolve ‖ *ref* to resolve; make up one's mind
resollar §61 *intr* to breathe; breathe hard, pant; stop for a rest
resonar §61 *intr* to resound, echo
resoplar *intr* to puff; snort
resoplido *m* puffing; snort

resorte *m* spring; springiness; means; province, scope; rubber band; **resorte espiral** coil spring; **tocar resortes** to pull wires, pull strings

respailar *intr* — **ir respailando** to scurry along

respaldar *m* back; ‖ *tr* to back; indorse ‖ *ref* to lean back; sprawl

respaldo *m* back; backing; indorsement

respectar *tr* (with personal **a**) to concern; **por lo que respecta a . . .** as far as . . . is concerned

respecti•vo -va *adj* respective

respecto *m* respect, reference, relation; **al respecto** in the matter; **respecto a** or **de** with respect to, in or with regard to

respetable *adj* respectable

respetar *tr* to respect

respeto *m* respect; consideration; **campar por sus respetos** to be inconsiderate, go one's (his, her, etc.) own way; **de respeto** spare, extra

respetuo•so -sa *adj* respectful; awesome, impressive; humble, obedient

respigón *m* hangnail

respingar §44 *intr* to balk, shy; (*elevarse el borde, p.ej., de la falda*) curl up; give in unwillingly

respin•gón -gona *adj* (*nariz*) snubby, upturned; surly, churlish

respirar *tr* to breathe ‖ *intr* to breathe; breathe freely; breathe a sigh of relief; catch one's breath, stop for a rest; **no respirar** to not breathe a word; **sin respirar** without respite, without letup

respiro *m* breathing; respite, breather, breathing spell; (*para el pago de una deuda*) extension of time

resplandecer §22 *intr* to shine; flash, glitter

resplandeciente *adj* brilliant; resplendent

resplandor *m* brilliance, radiance; resplendence; glare

responder *tr* to answer ‖ *intr* to answer, respond; correspond; answer back; **responder de** (*una cosa*) to answer for; **responder por** (*una persona*) to answer for

respon•dón -dona *adj* (coll) saucy

responsable *adj* responsible; **responsable de** responsible for

responsabilizar *tr* to put in charge; hold responsible ‖ *ref* to assume responsibility

respuesta *f* answer, response

resquebrajar *tr* & *ref* to crack, split

resquemar *tr* & *intr* to bite, sting ‖ *ref* to be parched; (*resentirse sin manifestarlo*) smolder

resquemo *m* bite, sting

resquicio *m* crack, chink; chance, opportunity

restablecer §22 *tr* to reëstablish, restore ‖ *ref* to recover

restañar *tr* to retin; (*sangre*) stanch, stop the flow of

restar *tr* to deduct; reduce; take away; (*una pelota*) return; subtract ‖ *intr* to remain, be left

restaurante *m* restaurant; **restaurante automático** automat

restaurar *tr* to restore; to recover

restitución *f* restitution, return

restituir §20 *tr* to return, give back; restore ‖ *ref* to return, come back

resto *m* rest, remainder, residue; (*en juegos de naipes*) stakes; (*de una pelota*) return; **a resto abierto** without limit; **echar el resto** to stake all, shoot the works; **restos** remains, mortal remains; **restos de serie** remnants

restregar §66 *tr* to rub hard; scrub hard

restringir §27 *tr* to restrict; constrict, to contract

resucitar *tr* & *intr* to resuscitate; resurrect; revive

resuel•to -ta *adj* resolute, resolved, determined; prompt, quick

resuello *m* breathing; hard breathing, panting

resulta *f* result; outcome; vacancy; **de resultas de** as a result of

resultado *m* result

resultar *intr* to result; prove to be, turn out to be; be, become

resumen *m* summary, résumé; **en resumen** in brief, in a word

resumir *tr* to summarize, sum up ‖ *ref* to be reduced, be transformed

resurrección *f* resurrection

retaguardia *f* rearguard

retal *m* piece, remnant

retama *f* Spanish broom; **retama de escoba** furze

retar *tr* to challenge, dare; blame, find fault with

retardación *f* retardation

retardar *tr* to retard, slow down

retardo *m* retard, delay

retazo *m* piece, remnant; scrap, fragment

retén *m* store, stock, reserve; catch, pawl; (mil) reserve

retener §71 *tr* to retain, keep, withhold; detain, arrest; (*el pago de un haber*) stop

retentiva *f* memory; recall

reticente *adj* deceptive, misleading; noncommital

retintín *m* jingle, tinkling; (*en el oído*) ringing; tone of reproach, sarcasm, mockery

retiñir §12 *intr* to jingle, tinkle (*los oídos*) ring

retirada *f* retirement, withdrawal; place of refuge; (mil) retreat, retirement; (*toque*) (mil) retreat; **batirse en retirada** to beat a retreat

retirar *tr* to retire, withdraw; take away; pull back ‖ *ref* to retire, withdraw; (mil) to retire

reto *m* challenge, dare; threat

retocar §73 *tr* to retouch; touch up; (*un disco de fonógrafo*) play back

retoño *m* sprout, shoot, sucker

retorcer §74 *tr* to twist; twist together; (*las manos*) wring; (fig) to twist, misconstrue ‖ *ref* to twist; writhe

retóri•co -ca *adj* rhetorical ‖ *f* rhetoric

retornar *tr* to return, give back; back, back up ‖ *intr* & *ref* to return, go back

retorno *m* return; barter, exchange; reward, requital; **retorno terrestre** (elec) ground

retorta *f* (chem) retort

retozar §60 *intr* to frolic, gambol, romp

retozo *m* frolic, gambol, romping; **retozo de la risa** giggle, titter

reto•zón -zona *adj* frolicsome, frisky

retracción *f* retraction; (pathol) atrophy

retractar *tr* & *ref* to retract

retráctil *adj* retractable

retraer §75 *tr* to bring again, bring back; dissuade ‖ *ref* to withdraw, retire; take refuge

retraí•do -da *adj* solitary; reserved, shy

retransmisión *f* rebroadcasting

retransmitir *tr* to rebroadcast

retrasa•do -da *adj* (mentally) retarded

retrasar *tr* to delay, retard; put off; (*un reloj*) set or turn back ‖ *intr* to be too slow; (*en los estudios*) be or fall behind ‖ *ref* to delay, be late, be slow, be behind time; (*un reloj*) go or be slow

retraso *m* delay; **tener retraso** to be late

retratar *tr* to portray; photograph; imitate ‖ *ref* to sit for a portrait; have one's picture taken

retrato *m* portrait; photograph; copy, imitation; description; **el vivo retrato de** the living image of

retrepar *ref* to lean back, lean back in the chair

retreta *f* (mil) retreat, tattoo; outdoor band concert

retrete *m* toilet, lavatory

retribuir §20 *tr* to repay, pay back

retroacti•vo -va *adj* retroactive

retroalimentación *f* feedback

retroceder *intr* to retrogress; back away; back down, back out

retroceso *m* retrogression; (*de un arma de fuego*) recoil; (*de una enfermedad*) flare-up; (mach, mov) rewind(ing)

retrocohete *m* retrorocket

retrodisparo *m* retrofiring

retropropulsión *f* (aer) jet propulsion

retrospecti•vo -va *adj* retrospective ‖ *f* (mov) flashback

retrovisor *m* rear-view mirror

retrucar §73 *intr* to answer, reply; (billiards) kiss

retruco *m* (billiards) kiss

retruécano *m* pun

retumbar *intr* to resound, rumble

retumbo *m* resounding, rumble, echo

reumáti•co -ca *adj* & *mf* rheumatic

reumatismo *m* rheumatism

reunificación *f* reunification

reunión *f* reunion, gathering, meeting; assemblage

reunir §59 *tr* to join, unite; assemble, gather together, bring together; reunite; (*dinero*) raise ‖ *ref* to unite; assemble, gather together, come together, meet; reunite

reválida *f* final examination (*for a higher degree*)

revalorar *tr* to revaluate

revalorizar §60 *tr* to revaluate

revejecer §22 *intr* & *ref* to grow old before one's time

revelación *f* revelation

revelado *m* (phot) development

revelador *m* (phot) developer

revelar *tr* to reveal; (phot) to develop

revender *tr* to resell; retail

reventa *f* resale

reventar §2 *tr* to smash, crush; burst, blow out, explode; ruin; annoy, bore; (*a una persona*) work to death; (*a un caballo*) run to death ‖ *intr* to burst, blow out, explode; (*las olas*) break; (*morir*) croak; (*de ira*) blow up, hit the ceiling; **reventar por** to be dying to ‖ *ref* to burst, blow out, explode; be worked to death; (*un caballo*) be run to death

reventón *m* burst; (aut) blowout

rever §80 *tr* to revise, review; (*un caso legal*) retry

reverberar *intr* to reverberate

reverbero *m* reflector; street lamp; chafing dish

reverencia *f* reverence; bow, curtsy

reverenciar *tr* to revere, reverence ‖ *intr* to bow, curtsy

reveren•do -da *adj* & *m* reverend

reverso *m* back; wrong side; reverse

revertir §68 *intr* to revert

revés *m* back, reverse; wrong side; backhand; (*desgracia, contratiempo*) reverse, setback; **al revés** wrong side out; inside out; upside down; backwards

revestir §50 *tr* to put on, don; cover, coat, face, line, surface; assume, take on; disguise; (*un cuento*) adorn; invest ‖ *ref* to put on vestments; be haughty; gird oneself

revirar *tr* to turn, twist; turn over

revisada *f* examination; revision

revisar *tr* to revise, review, check; audit

revisión *f* revision, review, check

revisionismo *m* revisionism

revisionista *adj* & *mf* revisionist

revisor *m* inspector, examiner; (rr) conductor, ticket collector

revista *f* review; (mil) review; (theat) review, revue; (law) new trial

revistar *tr* (mil) to review

revivir *tr* & *intr* to revive

revocar §73 *tr* to revoke; dissuade; drive back, drive away; plaster, stucco

revocatoria *f* (SAm) recall; repeal; cancellation

revolar §61 *intr* & *ref* to flutter, flutter around

revolcar §81 *tr* to knock down; (*a un adversario*) floor; (*a un alumno en un examen*) flunk, fail ‖ *ref* to wallow, roll around; be stubborn

revolotear *tr* to fling up ‖ *intr* to flutter, flutter around, flit

revoltijo *m* or **revoltillo** *m* mess, jumble; stew

re
re

revolto•so -sa *adj* rebellious, riotous; *(niño)* unruly, mischievous; complicated; winding ‖ *mf* troublemaker, rioter

revolución *f* revolution

revoluciona•rio -ria *adj* & *mf* revolutionary

revolver §47 & §83 *tr* to shake; stir; turn around; turn upside down; wrap up; mess up; disturb; *(sus pasos)* retrace; alienate, estrange ‖ *intr* to retrace one's steps ‖ *ref* to retrace one's steps; turn around; toss and turn; *(un astro en su órbita)* revolve; *(el mar)* get rough

revólver *m* revolver

revuelco *m* upset, tumble; wallowing

revuelo *m* whirl, flying around; stir, commotion

revuelta *f* revolution, revolt; disturbance; turning point; fight, row

rey *m* king; swineherd; **los Reyes Católicos** Ferdinand and Isabella; **los Reyes Magos** the Three Wise Men; **ni rey ni roque** nobody; **rey de zarza** wren; **reyes** king and queen; **Reyes** Twelfth-night

reyerta *f* quarrel, wrangle

reyezuelo *m* (orn) kinglet; **reyezuelo moñudo** goldcrest

rezaga•do -da *mf* straggler, laggard

rezagar §44 *tr* to outstrip, leave behind; postpone ‖ *ref* to fall behind

rezar §60 *tr (una oración)* to pray; *(una oración; la misa)* say; (coll) to say, to read; *(anunciar)* (coll) to call for ‖ *intr* to pray; grumble; (coll) to say, to read; **rezar con** to concern

rezo *m* prayer; devotions

rezón *m* grapnel

rezongar §44 *tr* (CAm) to scold ‖ *intr* to grumble, growl

rezumar *intr* to ooze, seep ‖ *ref* to ooze, seep; to leak; *(una especie)* leak out

ría *f* estuary, fiord

riachuelo *m* rivulet, streamlet

riada *f* flood, freshet

ribazo *m* slope, embarkment

ribera *f* bank, shore; riverside

ribere•ño -ña *adj* riverside

ribero *m* levee, dike

ribete *m* edge, trimming, border; *(a un cuento)* embellishment

ribetear *tr* to edge, trim, border, bind

ri•co -ca *adj* rich; dear, darling

ridiculizar §60 *tr* to ridicule

ridícu•lo -la *adj* ridiculous; touchy ‖ *m* ridiculous situation; **poner en ridículo** to ridicule, expose to ridicule

riego *m* irrigation; watering

riel *m* ingot; curtain rod; rail

rielar *intr* to shimmer, gleam; (poet) to twinkle

rienda *f* rein; **a rienda suelta** swiftly, violently; with free rein

riente *adj* laughing; bright, cheerful

riesgo *m* risk, danger; **correr riesgo** to run or take a risk

riesgo•so -sa *adj* risky; dangerous

rifa *f* raffle; fight, quarrel

rifar *tr* to raffle, raffle off ‖ *intr* to raffle; fight, quarrel

rígi•do -da *adj* rigid, stiff; strict, severe

riguro•so -sa *adj* rigorous; severe

rima *f* rhyme; **rimas** poems, poetry

rimar *tr* & *ref* to rhyme

rimbombante *adj* resounding; flashy

rímel *m* mascara

rimero *m* heap, pile

Rin *m* Rhine

rincón *m* corner; nook; piece of land; (coll) home

rinconera *f* corner piece of furniture; corner table; corner cupboard

ringla *f*, **ringle** *m* or **ringlera** *f* row, tier

ringorrango *m* curlicue; frill, frippery

rinoceronte *m* rhinoceros

riña *f* fight, scuffle

riñón *m* kidney; (fig) heart, center, interior; **tener bien cubierto el riñón** to be well-heeled

río *m* river; **pescar en río revuelto** to fish in troubled waters

riostra *f* brace, stay; guy wire

riostrar *tr* to brace, stay

ripia *f* shingle

ripio *m* debris; rubble; *(palabras inútiles empleadas para completar el verso)* padding; **no perder ripio** to not miss a trick

riqueza *f* riches, wealth; richness; **riquezas del subsuelo** mineral resources

risa *f* laugh, laughter

risco *m* cliff, crag; honey fritter

risible *adj* laughable

risotada *f* guffaw, horse laugh

ristra *f* string of onions, string of garlic; (coll) string, row, file

ristre *m* lance rest

risue•ño -ña *adj* smiling

rítmi•co -ca *adj* rhythmic(al)

ritmo *m* rhythm; **a gran ritmo** at great speed

rito *m* rite

rival *mf* rival

rivalidad *f* rivalry; enmity

rivalizar §60 *intr* to vie, compete; **rivalizar con** to rival

riza•do -da *adj* curly; ripply ‖ *m* curl, curling; rippling

rizador *m* curling iron, hair curler

rizar §60 *tr* & *ref* to curl; *(la superficie del agua)* ripple

ri•zo -za *adj* curly ‖ *m* curl, ringlet; ripple; (aer) loop; **rizar el rizo** (aer) to loop the loop

ro *interj* — **¡ro ro!** hushaby!, bye-bye!

roba•dor -dora *mf* robber, thief

róbalo or **robalo** *m* (*Labrax lupus*) bass; (*Centropomus undecimalis*) snook

robar *tr* to rob, steal; *(un naipe o ficha de dominó)* draw ‖ *intr* & *ref* to steal

robinete *m* faucet, spigot, cock

roblar *tr* to clinch, rivet

roble *m* oak; (*Quercus robur*) British oak tree; husky fellow

roblón *m* rivet

robo *m* robbery, theft; (*naipe tomado del monte*) draw; **robo con escalamiento** burglary

ro•bot *m* (*pl* -**bots**) robot

robótica *f* robotics

robotización *f* use of robots; robotization

robus•to -ta *adj* robust

roca *f* rock

rocalla *f* pebbles; stone chips; large glass bead

rocallo•so -sa *adj* stony, pebbly

roce *m* rubbing; close contact

rociada *f* sprinkling; dew; (*de balas, piedras, etc.*) shower; (*de invectivas*) volley

rociadera *f* sprinkling can

rociar §77 *tr* to sprinkle; spray; bedew; scatter ‖ *intr* to drizzle; **rocía** there is dew

rocín *m* hack, nag; work horse; draft horse; riding horse; rough guy

rocío *m* dew; drizzle; sprinkling

rocke•ro -ra *mf* rock singer

roco•so -sa *adj* rocky

rodada *f* rut, track

roda•do -da *adj* (*fácil, flúido*) rounded, fluent; (*tránsito*) vehicular ‖ *f* see **rodada**

rodadura *f* rolling; rut; (*de neumático*) tread

rodaja *f* disk, caster; round slice

rodaje *m* wheels; (*de una película cinematográfica*) shooting, filming; **en rodaje** (aut) being run in; (mov) being filmed

rodamiento *m* bearing; (*de un neumático*) tread; **rodamientos** running gear

Ródano *m* Rhone

rodante *adj* rolling; on wheels; (Chile) wandering

rodapié *m* baseboard, washboard

rodar §61 *tr* to roll; (*una película cinematográfica*) shoot, film, take; screen, project; drag along; (*una llave*) turn; (*la escalera*) roll down; (*un nuevo coche*) run in; (*válvulas de un motor*) grind ‖ *intr* to roll, roll along; roll down; rotate, revolve; tumble; roam, wander about; (*por medio de ruedas*) run; prowl

Rodas *f* Rhodes

rodear *tr* to surround; round up ‖ *intr* to go around; go by a roundabout way; beat about the bush ‖ *ref* to turn, twist, toss about

rodela *f* buckler, target; padded ring

rodeo *m* detour, roundabout way; dodge, duck; rodeo, roundup; **andar con rodeos** to beat about the bush; **dar un rodeo** to go a roundabout way

rodilla *f* knee; floor rag, mop; padded ring; **de rodillas** kneeling, on one's knees

rodillera *f* kneepad; baggy knee; (*de prenda de vestir*) knee; (*del órgano*) (mus) knee swell

rodillo *m* roller; rolling pin; road roller; inking roller; (*de la máquina de escribir*) platen

rodrigar §44 *tr* to prop, prop up, stake

rodrigón *m* prop, stake

roer §62 *tr* to gnaw, gnaw away at; (*un hueso*) pick; wear down

rogar §63 *tr* & *intr* to beg; pray; **hacerse de rogar** to like to be coaxed

roí•do -da *adj* miserly, stingy

ro•jo -ja *adj* red; ruddy; red-haired; Red ‖ *mf* (*comunista*) Red ‖ *m* red; **al rojo** to a red heat

rollar *tr* to roll, roll up

rolli•zo -za *adj* round, cylindrical; plump, stocky ‖ *m* round log

rollo *m* roll, coil; roller, rolling pin; round log; yoke pad; rôle; (*de tela*) bolt

romadizo *m* cold in the head

romance *adj* (*neolatino*) Romance ‖ *m* Romance language; Spanish language; romance of chivalry; octosyllabic verse with alternate lines in assonance; narrative poem in octosyllabic verse; ballad; **romance heroico** hendecasyllabic verse with alternate lines in assonance

romancero *m* collection of Old Spanish romances

romancillo *m* verse of less than eight syllables with alternate lines in assonance

románi•co -ca *adj* (*neolatino*) Romance, Romanic; (*arquitectura*) Romanesque ‖ *m* Romanesque

roma•no -na *adj* & *mf* Roman

romanticismo *m* romanticism

romántì•co -ca *adj* romantic

romanza *f* (mus) romance, romanza

romería *f* pilgrimage; crowd, gathering

rome•ro -ra *mf* pilgrim ‖ *m* rosemary

ro•mo -ma *adj* blunt, dull; flat-nosed

rompeáto•mos *m* (*pl* -**mos**) atom smasher

rompecabe•zas *m* (*pl* -**zas**) riddle, puzzle; (*figura que ha sido cortada en trozos menudos y que hay que recomponer*) jigsaw puzzle

rompehie•los *m* (*pl* -**los**) iceboat, icebreaker

rompehuel•gas *m* (*pl* -**gas**) strikebreaker

rompeo•las *m* (*pl* -**las**) mole, breakwater

romper §83 *tr* to break; break through; break up; tear ‖ *intr* to break; (*las flores*) break open, burst open; break down; **romper a** to start to, burst out

rompiente *m* reef, shoal; (*oleaje que choca contra las rocas*) breaker

rompope *m* eggnog

ron *m* rum; **ron de laurel** or **de malagueta** bay rum

ronca *f* (*época del celo*) rut; cry of buck in rutting season; bullying

roncar §73 *intr* to snore; (*el viento, el mar*) roar; cry in rutting season; bully

ronce•ro -ra *adj* slow, poky ‖ grouchy

ron•co -ca *adj* hoarse; harsh ‖ *f* see **ronca**

roncha *f* weal, welt; black-and-blue mark

ronchar *tr* to crunch

ronda *f* (*de un policía; de visitas; de cigarros o bebidas*) round; (*juego del corro*) (Chile) ring-around-a-rosy; **ronda negociadora** round of negotiations

rondar *tr* to go around; fly around; patrol; hang around; court ‖ *intr* to patrol by night; gad about at nighttime; go serenading; prowl; (mil) to make the rounds

ronquedad *f* hoarseness; harshness

re
ro

ronquera *f* hoarseness
ronquido *m* snore; rasping sound
ronronear *intr* to purr
ronroneo *m* purr, purring
ronzal *m* halter
ronzar §60 *tr* to crunch, munch
roña *f* scab, mange; sticky dirt; pine bark; stinginess; spite, ill will; (Col) malingering; **jugar a roña** (Peru) to play for fun
roño•so -sa *adj* scabby, mangy; dirty, filthy; stingy; spiteful
ropa *f* clothing, clothes; dry goods; **a quema ropa** point-blank; **ropa blanca** linen; **ropa de cama** bed linen; bed-clothes; **ropa dominguera** Sunday best; **ropa hecha** ready-made clothes; **ropa interior** underwear; **ropa sucia** laundry
ropaje *m* clothes, clothing; gown, robe; drapery
ropaveje•ro -ra *mf* old-clothes dealer
rope•ro -ra *mf* ready-made clothier; wardrobe keeper ‖ *m* wardrobe, clothes closet
roque *m* rook, castle
roque•ño -ña *adj* rocky; hard, flinty
rorro *m* baby; (Mex) doll
rosa *f* rose; **rosa de los vientos** or **rosa náutica** (naut) compass card; **rosas** popcorn; **verlo todo de color de rosa** to see everything through rose-colored glasses
rosa•do -da *adj* rose-colored, rosy; pink; flushed ‖ *f* frost
rosaleda or **rosalera** *f* rose garden
rosario *m* rosary; (*de sucesos*) string; chain pump
ros•bif *m* (*pl* **-bifs**) roast beef
rosca *f* coil, spiral; (*de una espiral*) turn; twisted roll; (*de un tornillo*) thread; (Chile) padded ring
roscar §73 *tr* to thread
roseta *f* sprinkling spout or nozzle; red spot on cheek; **rosetas** popcorn
rosetón *m* rose window
rosita *f* little rose; (Chile) earring; **rositas** popcorn
rosquilla *f* coffeecake, doughnut, cruller
rostro *m* face; snout; beak; (*retrato*) **de rostro entero** full-faced
rostropáli•do -da *mf* paleface
rota *f* rout, defeat; (naut) route, course
rotisería *f* fast-food restaurant; delicatessen
rotograbado *m* rotogravure
rótula *f* lozenge; kneecap; knuckle
rotulador *m* felt pen
rotular *tr* to label, title, letter
rótulo *m* label, title; poster, show bill
rotun•do -da *adj* round; rotund, sonorous, full; peremptory
rotura *f* break, breaking; breach, opening; tear, tearing
roturación *f* (agr) reclamation
roya *f* (agr) blight, rust
rozamiento *m* rubbing; friction; (*desavenencia*) (fig) friction
rozar §60 *tr* to graze; scrape; border on; grub, stub; (*las tierras*) clear; (*la hierba*) nibble; (*leña menuda*) cut and gather ‖ *intr*

to graze by ‖ *ref* to be on close terms, rub elbows, hobnob; falter, stammer; be alike
roznar *tr* to crunch ‖ *intr* to bray
roznido *m* crunch, crunching noise; bray, braying
Rte. *abbr* **Remite**
ru•bí *m* (*pl* **-bíes**) ruby; (*de un reloj*) ruby, jewel
rubia *f* blonde; station wagon; peseta; **rubia oxigenada** peroxide blonde; **rubia platino** platinum blonde
rubia•les *mf* (*pl* **-les**) goldilocks
ru•bio -bia *adj* blond, fair; golden ‖ *m* blond ‖ *f* see **rubia**
rublo *m* ruble
rubor *m* bright red; blush, flush; bashfulness
ruborizar §60 *tr* to make blush ‖ *ref* to blush
rúbrica *f* title, heading; (*rasgo después de la firma de uno*) flourish
rubricación *f* listing; itemization
ru•bro -bra *adj* red ‖ *m* title, heading; (Chile) (com) entry
rudimento *m* rudiment
ru•do -da *adj* coarse, rough; rude, crude; dull, stupid; hard, severe
rueca *f* distaff
rueda *f* wheel; caster, roller; (*de gente*) ring, circle; round slice; pinwheel; (*de la cola del pavo*) spread; sunfish; **hacer la rueda** (*el pavo*) to spread its tail; **hacer la rueda a** to play up to; **rueda de andar** treadmill; **rueda de cadena** sprocket, sprocket wheel; **rueda de escape** escapement wheel; **rueda de fuego** pinwheel; **rueda dentada** gearwheel; **rueda de paletas** paddle wheel; **rueda de prensa** press conference; **rueda de presos** line-up; **rueda de recambio** spare wheel; **rueda de tornillo sin fin** worm wheel; **rueda motriz** drive wheel
ruedo *m* turn, rotation; round mat; selvage; hemline; (taur) ring; **a todo ruedo** at all events
ruego *m* request, entreaty; prayer
ru•fián -fiana *mf* bawd, go-between ‖ *m* cur, cad
ru•fo -fa *adj* sandy, sandy-haired; curly-haired
rugido *m* roar; (*de las tripas*) rumble
rugir §27 *intr* to roar; rumble
rugo•so -sa *adj* rugged, wrinkled
ruibarbo *m* rhubarb
ruido *m* noise; rumor; row, rumpus
ruido•so -sa *adj* noisy; loud; sensational
ruin *adj* base, mean, vile; stingy; (*animal*) vicious
ruina *f* ruin
ruindad *f* baseness, meanness, vileness; stinginess; viciousness
ruino•so -sa *adj* tottery, run-down
ruiseñor *m* nightingale
ruleta *f* roulette; (CAm, Arg) tape measure
ruletero *m* (Mex) cruising taxi driver (*in search of fares*)
rulo *m* roll; rolling pin; (hair) curler
ruma•no -na *adj* & *mf* Rumanian

rumbo *m* bearing, course, direction; pomp, show; generosity; (CAm) noisy celebration; **por aquellos rumbos** in those parts; **rumbo a** bound for

rumbo•so -sa *adj* pompous, magnificent; generous

rumiar *tr & intr* to ruminate

rumor *m* rumor; (*de voces*) murmur, buzz; rumble

rumorear *tr* to rumor, circulate by a rumor ‖ *intr* to murmur, buzz, rumble ‖ *ref* to be rumored; **se rumorea que** it is rumored that

rumoro•so -sa *adj* noisy, loud, rumbling

runfla *f* or **runflada** *f* string, row; (*en los naipes*) sequence

ruptor *m* (elec) contact breaker

ruptura *f* rupture, break; crack, split; (*cesación de relaciones*) rupture

Rusia *f* Russia; **la Rusia Soviética** Soviet Russia

ru•so -sa *adj & mf* Russian

rúst. *abbr* **rústica**

rústi•co -ca *adj* rustic; coarse, crude, clumsy; (*latín*) Vulgar; **en rústica** paper-bound ‖ *m* rustic, peasant

ruta *f* route; **ruta aérea** air lane

rutilante *adj* shining, sparkling

rutina *f* routine

rutina•rio -ria *adj* routine

S

S, s (ese) *f* twenty-second letter of the Spanish alphabet

S. *abbr* **San, Santo, sobresaliente, sur**

sábado *m* (*de los cristianos*) Saturday; (*de los judíos*) Sabbath

sábalo *m* shad

sabana *f* savanna, pampa; **ponerse en la sabana** (Ven) to get rich overnight

sábana *f* sheet; altar cloth

sabandija *f* insect, bug, worm; (*persona*) vermin; **sabandijas** (*animales o personas*) vermin

sabanilla *f* kerchief; altar cloth

sabañón *m* chilblain

sabe•dor -dora *adj* aware, informed

sabelotodo *m* (*pl* **sabelotodo**) know-it-all, wise guy

saber *m* knowledge, learning ‖ *v* §64 *tr & intr* to know; to find out; to taste; **a saber** namely, to wit; **me sabe mal** I'm sorry, I regret; **no saber dónde meterse** to not know which way to turn; **que yo sepa** as far as I know; **saber a** to taste of; smack of; **saber a poco** to be just a taste, taste like more; **saber de** to be aware of; hear from ‖ *ref* to know; be or become known

sabidi•llo -lla *adj & mf* know-it-all

sabi•do -da *adj* well-informed; learned; **de sabido** certainly, surely

sabiduría *f* wisdom; knowledge, learning

sabiendas — **a sabiendas** knowingly, consciously; **a sabiendas de que** knowing that, aware that

sabihon•do -da *adj & mf* know-it-all

sa•bio -bia *adj* wise; learned; (*animal*) trained ‖ *mf* wise person, scholar, scientist ‖ *m* wise man, sage

sablazo *m* stroke with a saber, wound made by a saber; sponging; **dar un sablazo a** to hit for a loan

sable *m* saber, cutlass; (coll) sponging

sablear *tr* to hit for a loan, sponge on ‖ *intr* to go around sponging

sablista *mf* sponger

sabor *m* taste, flavor

saborcillo *m* slight taste, touch

saborear *tr* to flavor; taste; savor; entice; ‖ *ref* to smack one's lips; **saborearse de** to taste; to savor

sabotaje *m* sabotage

sabotear *tr & intr* to sabotage

sabro•so -sa *adj* tasty, savory, delicious

sabueso *m* bloodhound; sleuth

saburro•so -sa *adj* (*boca*) foul; (*lengua*) coated

sacaboca•do *m* or **sacaboca•dos** *m* (*pl* **-dos**) ticket punch; sure thing

sacabotas *m* (*pl* **-tas**) bootjack

sacacor•chos *m* (*pl* **-chos**) corkscrew

sacaman•chas *mf* (*pl* **-chas**) clothes cleaner, spot remover; dry cleaner; dyer

sacamue•las *m* (*pl* **-las**) tooth puller; quack, cheat

sacamuer•tos *m* (*pl* **-tos**) stagehand

sacapintura *m* paint remover

sacapun•tas *m* (*pl* **-tas**) pencil sharpener

sacar §73 *tr* (*un clavo, una espada, agua, una conclusión*) to draw; pull out; pull up; take out; extract, remove; show; bring out, publish; find out, solve; (*un secreto*) elicit, draw out; copy; (*una fotografía*) take; except, exclude; get, obtain; produce, invent, imitate; (*un premio*) win; (*una pelota*) serve; (*el pecho*) stick out; **sacar a bailar** to drag in; **sacar a relucir** to bring up unexpectedly; **sacar en claro** or **en limpio** to recopy clearly; deduce, clear up ‖ *ref* (Mex) to make off

sacarina *f* saccharin

sacasi•llas *m* (*pl* **-llas**) stagehand

sacerdocio *m* priesthood

sacerdote *m* priest

saciar *tr* to satiate

ro
sa

saco *m* bag, sack; coat, jacket; sack, plunder, pillage; (*de mentiras*) pack; **saco de dormir** sleeping bag; **saco de noche** overnight bag

sacramento *m* sacrament

sacrificar §73 *tr* to sacrifice; slaughter ‖ *intr* to sacrifice ‖ *ref* to sacrifice; sacrifice oneself

sacrificio *m* sacrifice; **sacrificio del altar** Sacrifice of the Mass

sacrilegio *m* sacrilege

sacríle•go -ga *adj* sacrilegious

sacristán *m* sacristan; sexton; **sacristán de amén** yes man

sacristía *f* sacristy, vestry

sa•cro -cra *adj* sacred

sacudida *f* shake, jar, jolt, jerk, bump; (elec) shock

sacudi•do -da *adj* intractable; determined ‖ *f* see **sacudida**

sacudir *tr* to shake; beat; jar, jolt, rock; shake off ‖ *ref* to shake, to shake oneself; rock; **sacudirse bien** to wangle one's way out

sádi•co -ca *adj* sadistic ‖ *mf* sadist

saeta *f* arrow, dart; (*del reloj*) hand; magnetic needle

saetilla *f* small arrow; (*del reloj*) hand; magnetic needle; (bot) arrowhead

saetín *m* flume, millrace

sa•gaz *adj* (*pl* **-gaces**) sagacious; keen-scented

Sagitario *m* (astr) Sagittarius

sagra•do -da *adj* sacred ‖ *m* asylum, haven, sanctuary; **acogerse a sagrado** to take sanctuary

sagrario *m* sanctuary, shrine; ciborium

sahariana *f* tight-fitting military jacket

sahornar *ref* to skin oneself

sahumar *tr* to perfume with smoke or incense; (Chile) to gold-plate, silver-plate

sainete *m* one-act farce; flavor, relish, spice, zest; sauce, seasoning; tidbit

sa•jón -jona *adj* & *mf* Saxon

sal *f* salt; grace, charm; wit; (CAm) misfortune; **sal de sosa** washing soda; **sales aromáticas** smelling salts; **sal gema** rock salt

sala *f* hall; drawing room, living room, sitting room; **sala de batalla** sorting room; **sala de calderas** boiler room; **sala de enfermos** infirmary; **sala de espera** waiting room; **sala de estar** living room, sitting room; **sala de fiestas** night club; **sala del cine** moving-picture house; **sala de máquinas** engine room

saladillo *m* salted peanut

Salamina *f* Salamis

salar *tr* to salt; spoil, ruin; bring bad luck to

salario *m* wages, pay; **salario de hambre** starvation wages

salcochar *tr* to boil in salt water

salcocho *m* food boiled in salt water

salchicha *f* sausage

salchiche•ro -ra *mf* pork butcher

saldar *tr* to settle, liquidate; sell out

saldo *m* settlement; balance; remnant; bargain; **saldo de mercancías** job lot; **saldo deudor** debit balance

salero *m* saltshaker, saltcellar; salt lick; grace, charm, wit

salero•so -sa *adj* charming, winsome, lively; salty, witty

salgar §44 *tr* (*el ganado*) to salt

salida *f* start; departure; exit; outcome, result; subterfuge; pretext; outlay, expenditure; projection; outlying fields; (elec) output; (sport) start; (mil) sally, sortie; (coll) witticism, sally; **salida de baño** bathrobe; **salida del sol** sunrise; **salida de teatro** evening wrap; **salida de teatros** after-theater party; **salida de tono** irrelevancy, impropriety; **salida lanzada** (sport) running start; **tener salida** to sell well; (*una muchacha*) to be popular with the boys

saliente *adj* projecting; (*p.ej., tren*) outbound; (*sol*) rising ‖ *m* east ‖ *f* projection; (*de la carretera*) shoulder

salir §65 *intr* to go out, come out; leave, go away, depart; sail; run out, come to an end; appear, show up; (*una mancha*) come out, come off; (*p.ej., el sol*) rise; shoot, spring, come up; project, stick out; make the first move; result, turn out; be elected; **salga lo que saliere** come what may; **salir a** to amount to; open into; resemble, look like; **salir al, encuentro a** to go to meet; take a stand against; get ahead of; **salir bien en un examen** to pass an examination; **salir con bien** to be successful; **salir de** to depart from; cease being; get rid of; (*p.ej., su juicio, sentido*) lose; **salir disparado** to start like a shot; **salir pitando** to start off on a mad run; blow up, hit the ceiling; **salir reprobado** (*en un examen*) to fail ‖ *ref* to slip out, escape; slip off, run off; leak; boil over; **salirse con la suya** to have one's own way; carry one's point

salitre *m* saltpeter

saliva *f* saliva; **gastar saliva** to rattle along; to waste one's breath

salmo *m* psalm

salmón *m* salmon

salmuera *f* brine, pickle; salty food or drink

salobre *adj* brackish, saltish

salón *m* salon, drawing room; (*de un buque*) saloon; meeting room; **salón de actos** auditorium; **salón de baile** ballroom; **salón de belleza** beauty parlor; **salón del automóvil** automobile show; **salón de refrescos** ice-cream parlor; **salón de tertulia** or **salón social** lounge

saloncillo *m* (*p.ej., de un teatro*) rest room

salpicadero *m* control panel; (aut) dashboard

salpicar §73 *tr* to splash; sprinkle

salpimentar §2 *tr* to salt and pepper, season with salt and pepper; (fig) to sweeten

salpullido *m* rash, eruption

salpullir §13 *tr* to cause a rash on; splotch ‖ *ref* to break out

salsa *f* sauce, dressing, gravy; **salsa de ají** chili sauce; **salsa de tomate** catsup, ketchup; **salsa inglesa** Worcestershire sauce

salsera *f* gravy dish; small saucer (*to mix paints*)

saltaban•co *m* or **saltaban•cos** *m* (*pl* -**cos**) quack, mountebank; prestidigitator; nuisance

saltamon•tes *m* (*pl* -**tes**) grasshopper

saltar *tr* to jump, jump over; skip, skip over ‖ *intr* to jump, leap, hop, skip; bounce; shoot up, spurt; come loose, come off; crack, break, burst; chip; project, stick out; **saltar a la vista** or **los ojos** to be self-evident; **saltar por** to jump over, jump out of ‖ *ref* to skip; come off

saltatum•bas *m* (*pl* -**bas**) burying parson

salteador *m* highwayman, holdup man

saltear *tr* to attack, hold up, waylay; take by surprise

saltimbanco *m* var of **saltabanco**

salto *m* jump, leap, bound; skip; dive; fall, waterfall; leapfrog; **salto de altura** high jump; **salto de ángel** swan dive; **salto de cama** morning wrap, dressing gown; **salto de carpa** jackknife; **salto de esquí** ski jump; **salto de viento** (naut) sudden shift in the wind; **salto mortal** somersault; **salto ornamental** fancy dive

salubre *adj* healthful, salubrious

salud *f* health; welfare; salvation; greeting; **gastar, vender** or **verter salud** to radiate health ‖ *interj* greetings!; **¡salud y pesetas!** health and wealth!

saludar *tr* to greet, salute, hail, bow to; give regards to ‖ *intr* to salute; bow

saludo *m* greeting, salute, bow; salutation; **saludo final** conclusion

salutación *f* salutation, greeting, bow

salva *f* greeting, welcome; salvo; oath; tray; (*de aplausos; de una batería de artillería*) round

salvado *m* bran

salva•dor -dora *mf* savior, saver, rescuer ‖ **el Salvador** the Saviour; (*país de la América Central*) El Salvador

salvadore•ño -ña *adj & mf* Salvadoran

salvaguardar *tr* to safeguard

salvaguardia *m* bodyguard, escort ‖ *f* safeguard, safe-conduct; protection, shelter

salvaje *adj* wild, uncultivated; savage; stupid ‖ *mf* savage; dolt

salvaji•no -na *adj* wild; (*de la carne de los animales monteses*) gamy ‖ *f* wild animal; wild animals

salvamante•les *m* (*pl* -**les**) coaster

salvamento *m* salvation; lifesaving; rescue; salvage; place of safety

salvar *tr* to save, rescue; to salvage; (*una dificultad*) avoid, overcome; (*un obstáculo*) clear, get around; (*una distancia*) cover, get over; rise above; jump over; make an exception of; **salvar apariencias** to save face ‖ *ref* to save oneself, escape danger; be saved; **sálvese el que pueda** every man for himself

salvavi•das *m* (*pl* -**das**) life preserver; lifeboat; (*empleado de una estación de salvamento*) lifeguard

salvedad *f* reservation, exception

salvia *f* (bot) sage

sal•vo -va *adj* safe; omitted; **a salvo** safe, out

of danger; **a salvo de** safe from ‖ **salvo** *prep* save, except for; **salvo error u omisión (s.e.u.o.)** barring error or omission; **salvo que** unless ‖ *f* see **salva**

salvoconducto *m* safe-conduct

sámara *f* (bot) key, key fruit

san *adj* apocopated and unstressed form of **santo**

sanaloto•do *m* (*pl* -**do**) cure-all

sanar *tr* to cure, heal ‖ *intr* to heal; recover

sanción *f* (*aprobación*) sanction; (*castigo, pena*) penalty

sancionar *tr* (*aprobar*) to sanction; (*imponer pena a*) penalize

sancochar *tr* to parboil

sandalia *f* sandal

sándalo *m* (yellow) sandalwood

san•dez *f* (*pl* -**deces**) folly, nonsense; piece of folly

sandía *f* watermelon

san•dio -dia *adj* foolish, nonsensical

saneamiento *m* sanitation, drainage; guarantee

sanear *tr* to guarantee; indemnify; make sanitary, drain, dry up

sangrar *tr* to bleed; drain; tap; (typ) to indent; (coll) to rob ‖ *intr* to bleed; **estar sangrando** to be new or recent; be plain or obvious ‖ *ref* to have oneself bled; (*los colores*) run

sangre *f* blood; **a sangre** by horsepower; **a sangre fría** in cold blood; **pura sangre** *m* thoroughbred; **sangre torera** bullfighting in the blood

sangría *f* bleeding; outlet, draining; ditch, trench; (*bebida*) sangaree; tap; tapping; (typ) indentation

sangrien•to -ta *adj* bloody; bleeding; cruel, sanguinary

sangrigor•do -da *adj* unpleasant

sangrilige•ro -ra *adj* nice, pleasant

sangripesa•do -da *adj* unpleasant

sangüesa *f* raspberry

sangüeso *m* raspberry bush

sanguijuela *f* leech

sanguina•rio -ria *adj* sanguinary, blood-thirsty

sanidad *f* healthiness; healthfulness; health; sanitation; **sanidad pública** health department

sanita•rio -ria *adj* sanitary

sa•no -na *adj* hale, healthy; healthful; sound; sane; earnest, sincere; safe, sure; whole, untouched, unharmed; **sano y salvo** safe and sound

santiague•ro -ra *adj* Santiago de Cuba ‖ *mf* native or inhabitant of Santiago de Cuba

santia•gués -guesa *adj* Santiago de Compostela ‖ *mf* native or inhabitant of Santiago de Compostela

santiagui•no -na *adj* Santiago de Chile ‖ *mf* native or inhabitant of Santiago de Chile

santiamén *m* jiffy; **en un santiamén** in the twinkling of an eye

santidad *f* holiness, sanctity, saintliness; **su Santidad** his Holiness

santificar §73 *tr* to sanctify, hallow, consecrate; (*las fiestas*) keep; excuse, justify

santiguar §10 *tr* to bless, make the sign of the cross over; punish, slap, abuse ‖ *ref* to cross oneself, make the sign of the cross

san•to -ta *adj* holy, saintly, blessed; (*día*) live-long; artless, simple; **santo y bueno** well and good ‖ *mf* saint ‖ *m* name day; image of a saint; **a santo de** because of; **desnudar a un santo para vestir a otro** to rob Peter to pay Paul; **írsele a uno el santo al cielo** to forget what one was up to; **santo y seña** password, watchword

Santo Domingo Hispaniola

santuario *m* sanctuary, shrine; (Col) buried treasure; (Col, Ven) Indian idol

santu•rrón -rrona *adj* sanctimonious ‖ *mf* sanctimonious person

saña *f* fury, rage; cruelty

sañu•do -da *adj* furious, enraged; cruel

sapiente *adj* wise, intelligent

sapo *m* toad; (coll) stuffed shirt; (Chile) little runt

saque *m* (*en el tenis*) serve, service; server; service line; (Col) distillery; **tener buen saque** to be a heavy eater and drinker

saquear *tr* to sack, plunder, pillage, loot

sarampión *m* measles

sarao *m* soirée, evening party

sarape *m* (Guat, Mex) bright-colored woolen poncho

sarcasmo *m* sarcasm

sarcásti•co -ca *adj* sarcastic

sardina *f* sardine; **como sardinas en banasta** or **en lata** packed in like sardines

sar•do -da *adj* & *mf* Sardinian

sarga *f* serge

sargento *m* sergeant

sarmiento *m* vine shoot, running stem

sarna *f* itch, mange

sarno•so -sa *adj* itchy, mangy

sarrace•no -na *adj* & *mf* Saracen

sarracina *f* scuffle, free fight; bloody brawl

sarro *m* crust; (*p.ej., en la lengua*) fur; (*en los dientes*) tartar

sarta *f* string; line, fine, series

sartén *f* frying pan; **saltar de la sartén y dar en las brasas** to jump from the frying pan into the fire

sastre *m* tailor

satélite *m* satellite; **satélite de comunicaciones** communications satellite; **satélite espía** spy satellite

satelizar §60 *tr* to put into orbit; (pol) to make a satellite of ‖ *ref* to go into orbit

satén *m* sateen

satíri•co -ca *adj* satiric(al) ‖ *mf* satirist

satirizar §60 *tr* & *intr* to satirize

satisfacción *f* satisfaction

satisfacer §39 *tr* & *intr* to satisfy ‖ *ref* to satisfy oneself, be satisfied, take satisfaction

satisfacto•rio -ria *adj* satisfactory

saturar *tr* to saturate; satiate

sauce *m* willow tree; **sauce de Babilonia** or **sauce llorón** weeping willow

saúco *m* elder, elderberry

savia *f* sap

saxofón *m* or **saxófono** *m* saxophone

saya *f* skirt; petticoat

sayo *m* smock frock, tunic; garment

sazón *f* ripeness; season; time, occasion; taste, seasoning; **a la sazón** at that time; **en sazón** in season, ripe; on time, opportunely

sazonar *tr* to ripen; season ‖ *ref* to ripen, mature

s/c *abbr* **su cuenta**

S.E. *abbr* **Su Excelencia**

se *pron reflex* himself, to himself; herself, to herself; itself, to itself; themselves, to themselves; yourself, to yourself; yourselves, to yourselves; oneself, to oneself; each other, to each other ‖ *pron pers* (used before the pronouns **lo, la, le,** etc.) to him, to her, to it, to them, to you

sebo *m* tallow; fat, suet

seca *f* drought; dry season

secador *m* drier, hair drier

secadora *f* clothes drier

secafir•mas *m* (*pl* **-mas**) blotter

secano *m* dry land, unwatered land

secansa *f* sequence

secante *m* blotting paper

secar §73 *tr* to dry, wipe dry; annoy, bore ‖ *ref* to dry, get dry; dry oneself; wither; be dry, be thirsty; (*un pozo*) run dry

secarropa *f* clothes dryer; **secarropa de travesaños** clotheshorse

sección *f* section; cross section; **sección de fondo** editorial section

secesión *f* secession

se•co -ca *adj* dry; dried up, withered; lank, lean; harsh, sharp; (*bebida*) straight, indifferent; plain, unadorned ‖ *f* see **seca**

secreta•rio -ria *adj* confidential, trusted ‖ *mf* secretary

secreter *m* secretary (*writing desk*)

secre•to -ta *adj* secret ‖ *m* secret; secrecy; hiding place, secret drawer; (*mecanismo oculto para abrir una cerradura*) key; **en el secreto de las cosas** on the inside

secta *f* sect

secta•rio -ria *adj* & *mf* sectarian

sector *m* sector; **sector de distribución** house current, power line

se•cuaz *adj* (*pl* **-cuaces**) partisan ‖ *mf* partisan, follower

secuela *f* sequel, result

secuencia *f* sequence

secuestrar *tr* to kidnap; (*un avión*) to hijack; (law) to sequester

secular *adj* secular

secundar *tr* to second, back

secunda•rio -ria *adj* secondary ‖ *m* (elec) secondary

sed *f* thirst; drought; **tener sed** to be thirsty

seda *f* silk; **como una seda** smooth as silk; easy as pie; sweet-natured; **seda encerada** dental floss

sedal *m* fish line

sedán *m* sedan; **sedán de reparto** delivery truck

sede *f* (*p.ej., del gobierno*) seat; (eccl) see; **Santa Sede** Holy See

sedenta·rio -ria _adj_ sedentary
sede·ño -ña _adj_ silk, silken
sedición _f_ sedition
sedicio·so -sa _adj_ seditious
sedien·to -ta _adj_ thirsty; (_terreno_) dry; anxious, eager
sedimento _m_ sediment
sedo·so -sa _adj_ silky
seducción _f_ seduction; charm, captivation
seducir §19 _tr_ to seduce; tempt, lead astray; charm, captivate
seducti·vo -va _adj_ seductive; tempting; charming, captivating
seduc·tor -tora _adj_ seductive; tempting; charming || _mf_ seducer; tempter; charmer
sefar·dí (_pl_ **-díes**) _adj_ Sephardic || _mf_ Sephardi
sega·dor -dora _adj_ harvesting || _m_ harvestman || _f_ harvester; mowing machine; **segadora de césped** lawn mower; **segadora trilladora** combine
segar §66 _tr_ to reap, harvest, mow; mow down || _intr_ to reap, harvest, mow
segazón _f_ harvest; harvest time
seglar _adj_ secular, lay || _m_ layman || _f_ laywoman
segmento _m_ segment; **segmento de émbolo** piston ring
segregacionista _mf_ segregationist
segregar §44 _tr_ to segregate
seguida _f_ series, succession; **de seguida** without interruption, continuously; at once; in a row; **en seguida** at once, immediately
seguidilla _f_ Spanish stanza made up of a quatrain and a tercet; **seguidillas** seguidilla (_Spanish dance and music_)
segui·do -da _adj_ continued, successive; straight, direct; running, in a row; **todo seguido** straight ahead || _f_ see **seguida**
seguimiento _m_ chase, hunt, pursuit; continuation; (_de vehículos espaciales_) tracking
seguir §67 _tr_ to follow; pursue; continue; dog, hound || _intr_ to go on, continue; still be, be now; keep + _ger_ || _ref_ to follow, ensue; issue, spring
según _prep_ according to, as per; **según que** according as || _conj_ as, according as
segunda _f_ double meaning; (aut & mus) second
segundero _m_ second hand; **segundero central** sweep-second, center-second
segun·do -da _adj_ second || _m_ second; **ser sin segundo** to be second to none || _f_ see **segunda**
segur _f_ axe; sickle
segurador _s_ security, bondsman
seguridad _f_ security; safety; surety; certainty; assurance; confidence
segu·ro -ra _adj_ sure, certain; secure, safe; reliable; constant; steady, unfailing || _m_ assurance, certainty; safety; confidence; insurance; **a buen seguro** surely, truly; **seguro contra accidentes** accident insurance; **seguro de desempleo** or **desocupación** unemployment insurance; **seguro de enfermedad** health insurance; **seguro de incendios** fire insurance; **seguro**

sobre la vida life insurance; **sobre seguro** without risk || **seguro** _adv_ surely
seis _adj_ & _pron_ six; **las seis** six o'clock || _m_ six; (_en las fechas_) sixth
seiscien·tos -tas _adj_ & _pron_ six hundred || **seiscientos** _m_ six hundred
selección _f_ selection
seleccionar _tr_ to select, choose
selec·to -ta _adj_ select, choice
selva _f_ forest, woods; jungle
selváti·co -ca _adj_ woodsy; rustic, wild
sellar _tr_ to seal; stamp; close; finish up
sello _m_ seal; stamp; signet; wafer; **sello aéreo** air-mail stamp; **sello de correo** postage stamp; **sello de urgencia** special-delivery stamp; **sello fiscal** revenue stamp
semáforo _m_ semaphore; traffic light
semana _f_ week; week's pay; **semana inglesa** working week of five and a half days
semanal _adj_ weekly
semanalmente _adv_ weekly
semana·rio -ria _adj_ & _m_ weekly
semánti·co -ca _adj_ semantic || _f_ semantics
semblante _m_ face, mien, countenance; appearance, expression, look
semblanza _f_ biographical sketch, portrait
sembrado _m_ sown ground, grain field
sembrar §2 _tr_ to seed, sow; scatter, spread; sprinkle
semejante _adj_ like, similar; such; **semejante a** like; **semejantes** alike, e.g., **estas sillas son semejantes** these chairs are alike || _m_ resemblance, likeness; fellow, fellow man
semejanza _f_ similarity, resemblance; simile; **a semejanza de** like
semejar _tr_ to resemble, be like || _intr_ & _ref_ to be alike; **semejar a** or **semejarse a** to resemble, be like
semen _m_ semen
semental _adj_ (_animal_) stud, breeding || _m_ sire; stallion; stock bull
semestral _adj_ semester
semestre _m_ semester
semibola _f_ little slam
semibreve _f_ (mus) whole note
semiconductor _m_ semiconductor
semiconsciente _adj_ semiconscious
semicul·to -ta _adj_ semilearned
semidifun·to -ta _adj_ half-dead
semidormi·do -da _adj_ half-asleep
semifinal _adj_ & _f_ (sport) semifinal
semilla _f_ seed; **semilla de césped** grass seed
semillero _m_ seedbed
seminario _m_ seminary; seminar; nursery
semi-remolque _m_ semitrailer
semita _mf_ Semite || _m_ (_idioma_) Semitic
semíti·co -ca _adj_ Semitic
semivi·vo -va _adj_ half-alive
semovientes _mpl_ stock, livestock
sempiter·no -na _adj_ everlasting
Sena _m_ Seine
senado _m_ senate
senador _m_ senator
senaduría _f_ senatorship
sencillez _f_ simplicity, plainness, candor
senci·llo -lla _adj_ simple, plain, candid; single || _m_ change, loose change

sa
se

senda f path, footpath

sendero m path, footpath, byway

sen•dos -das adj pl one each, one to each, e.g., **les dio sendos libros** he gave one book to each of them, he gave each of them a book

senectud f age, old age

senil adj senile

senilidad f senility

senilismo m (pathol) senility

seno m bosom, breast; lap; heart; womb; bay, gulf; cavity, hollow, recess; asylum, refuge

sensación f sensation

sensatez f good sense

sensa•to -ta adj sensible

sensibilizar §60 tr to sensitize

sensible adj appreciable, perceptible, noticeable, sensible; considerable; sensitive; deplorable, regrettable

sensiblería f mawkishness

sensible•ro -ra adj mawkish

sensiti•vo -va (de los sentidos) sense, sensitive; sentient; stimulating

senso•rio -ria adj sensory

sensual adj sensual, sensuous

sentada f sitting; **de una sentada** at one sitting

senta•do -da adj seated; settled; stable, permanent; sedate; **dar por sentado** to take for granted || f see **sentada**

sentar §2 tr to seat; settle; fit, suit; agree with || ref to sit, sit down; settle, settle down

sentencia f maxim; (law) sentence

sentenciar tr to sentence; (una cuestión) to decide; (p.ej., un libro a la hoguera) to consign

senti•do -da adj felt; deep-felt; sensitive; eloquent; **darse por sentido** to take offense || m sense, meaning; direction; consciousness; **sentido común** common sense

sentimiento m sentiment; feeling; sorrow, regret

sentir m feeling; opinion; judgment || §68 tr to feel; hear; be or feel sorry for; sense || intr to feel; be sorry, feel sorry || ref to feel; feel oneself to be; be resentful; crack, be cracked; **sentirse de** to feel; have a pain in; resent

seña f sign, mark, token; password, watchword; **por las señas** to all appearances; **por más señas** or **por señas** as a greater proof; **seña de tráfico** traffic sign; **señas** address; description

señal f sign, mark, token; landmark; bookmark; trace, vestige; scar; signal; traffic light; representation; reminder; pledge; brand; down payment; **señal de ocupado** (telp) busy signal; **señal de tramo** (rr) block signal; **señal de vídeo** video signal; **señal digital** fingerprint; **señal para marcar** (telp) dial tone

señala f (Chile) earmark (on livestock)

señala•do -da adj noted, distinguished

señalar tr to mark; show, indicate; point at, point out; signal; brand; determine, fix; appoint; sign and seal; scar; threaten || ref to distinguish oneself, excel

señalizar §60 tr to signal

señor m sir, mister; lord, master, owner; **muy señor mío** Dear Sir; **señores** Mr. and Mrs.; ladies and gentlemen

señora f madam, missus; mistress, owner; wife; **muy señora mía** Dear Madam; **Nuestra Señora** our Lady; **señora de compañía** chaperon

señorear tr to dominate, rule; master, control; seize, take control of; tower over; excel || intr to strut, swagger || ref to strut, swagger; control oneself; **señorearse de** to seize, take control of

señoría f lordship; ladyship; rule, sway

señoril adj lordly; haughty; majestic

señorío m dominion, sway, rule; mastery; arrogance, lordliness, majesty; gentry, nobility

señorita f young lady; miss

señorito m master; young gentleman; playboy

señuelo m decoy, lure; bait; enticement

separación f separation; **separación de poderes** (pol) separation of powers

separa•do -da adj separate; separated; apart; **por separado** separately; under separate cover

separar tr to separate; dismiss, discharge || ref to separate; resign

separata f reprint, offprint

sept.ᵉ abbr **septiembre**

septeto m septet

sépti•co -ca adj septic

septiembre m September

sépti•mo -ma adj & m seventh

sepulcro m sepulcher, tomb, grave; **santo sepulcro** Holy Sepulcher

sepultar tr to bury; hide away

sepultura f burial; grave; **estar con un pie en la sepultura** to have one foot in the grave

sepulturero m gravedigger

sequedad f dryness, drought; gruffness, surliness

sequía f drought

séquito m retinue, suite; following, popularity

ser m being; essence; life || v §69 v aux (to form passive voice) to be, e.g., **el discurso fue aplaudido por todos** the speech was applauded by everybody || intr to be; **a no ser por** if it were not for; **a no ser que** unless; **érase que se era** once upon a time there was; **es decir** that is to say; **sea lo que fuere** be that as it may; **ser de** to belong to; become of; be, e.g., **el reloj es de oro** the watch is gold; **ser de ver** to be worth seeing; **soy yo** it is me, it is I

serafín m seraph; great beauty (person)

serena f night love song; night dew, night air

serenar tr to calm; pacify; cool; settle

serenata f serenade

serenidad f serenity; **serenidad del espíritu** peace of mind

sere•no -na *adj* serene, calm; clear, cloudless ‖ *m* night watchman; night dew, night air ‖ *f* see **serena**

serial *adj* serial ‖ *m* (telv) serial; **serial lacrimógeno** soap opera; **serial radiado** (rad) serial

serie *f* series; **de serie** serial; stock, e.g., **coche de serie** stock car; **en serie** mass; **fuera de serie** custom-built, special; outsize

seriedad *f* seriousness; reliability; sternness, severity; solemnity

se•rio -ria *adj* serious; reliable; stern; solemn

sermón *m* sermon

sermonear *tr & intr* to sermonize

serpear or **serpentear** *intr* to wind, meander; wriggle, squirm

serpentín *m* coil

serpiente *f* serpent, snake; **serpiente de cascabel** rattlesnake

serranía *f* range of mountains, mountainous country

serra•no -na *adj* highland, mountain ‖ *mf* highlander, mountaineer

serrar §2 *tr* to saw

serrería *f* sawmill

serrín *m* sawdust

serrucho *m* handsaw

Servia *f* Serbia

servicial *adj* accommodating, obliging

servicio *m* service; (tennis) service, serve; (Am) toilet; **en acto de servicio** in the line of duty; **fuera de servicio** out of service; inoperative; (coll) down; **libre servicio** self-service; **servicio de grúa** (aut) towing service; **servicio postventa** customer service; **servicio telegráfico y telefónico** wire service

servi•dor -dora *mf* servant; humble servant; (tennis) server; **servidor de Vd.** your servant, at your service ‖ *m* waiter; suitor ‖ *f* waitress

servidumbre *f* servitude; servants, help; compulsion; (law) easement; **servidumbre de la gleba** serfdom; **servidumbre de paso** (law) right of way; **servidumbre de vía** (rr) right of way

servil *adj* servile

servilleta *f* napkin

servilletero *m* napkin ring

ser•vio -via *adj & mf* Serbian ‖ *f* see **Servia**

servir §50 *tr* to serve; help, wait on; (*un pedido*) fill; (tennis) serve; **para servir a Vd.** at your service ‖ *intr* to serve; (*en los naipes*) follow suit; **servir de** to serve as; be used as; **servir para** to be good for, be used for ‖ *ref* to help oneself, serve oneself; have the kindness to, deign to; **servirse de** to use, make use of; **sírvase** please

serv.° *abbr* **servicio**

servocroata *adj & mf* Serbo-Croatian

servodirección *f* (aut) power steering

servoembrague *m* (aut) automatic clutch

servofreno *m* power brake

sésamo *m* sesame; **sésamo ábrete** open sesame

sesenta *adj, pron & m* sixty

sesenta•vo -va *adj & m* sixtieth

sesgar §44 *tr* (*el paño*) to cut on the bias; bevel, slant, slope

ses•go -ga *adj* beveled, slanting, sloped; oblique; stern; calm ‖ *m* bevel; bias; slant, slope; turn; compromise; **al sesgo** obliquely; on the bias

sesión *f* session; sitting; meeting; (*cada representación de un drama o película*) show; **sesión continua** (mov) continuous showing; **sesión de espiritistas** séance, spiritualistic séance

sesionar *intr* to be in session

seso *m* brain; brains, intelligence; **calentarse** or **devanarse los sesos** to rack one's brain

sestear *intr* to take a siesta; (*el ganado*) rest in the shade

sesu•do -da *adj* brainy; (Chile) stubborn

seta *f* bristle; toadstool

setecien•tos -tas *adj & m* seven hundred ‖ **setecientos** *m* seven hundred

setenta *adj, pron & m* seventy

setenta•vo -va *adj & m* seventieth

seto *m* fence; **seto vivo** hedge, quickset

seudónimo *m* pseudonym, pen name

s.e.u.o. *abbr* **salvo error u omisión**

seve•ro -ra *adj* severe; stern; strict

sevicia *f* ferocity, cruelty

sexo *m* sex; **el bello sexo** the fair sex; **el sexo feo** the sterner sex

sextante *m* sextant

sex•to -ta *adj & m* sixth

sexual *adj* sexual, sex

si *conj* if; whether; I wonder if; **por si acaso** just in case; **si acaso** if by chance; **si no** otherwise

sí *adv* yes; indeed; (gives emphasis to verb and is often equivalent to English auxiliary verb) **él sí habla español** he does speak Spanish ‖ *pron reflex* himself, herself, itself, themselves; yourself, yourselves; oneself; each other ‖ *m* (*pl* **-síes**) yes; **dar el sí** to say yes

sia•més -mesa *adj & mf* Siamese

siberia•no -na *adj & mf* Siberian

sibila *f* sibyl

sicalipsis *f* spiciness, suggestiveness

sicalípti•co -ca *adj* spicy, suggestive, sexy

Sicilia *f* Sicily

sicilia•no -na *adj & mf* Sicilian

sico. . . var of **psico. . .**

sicofanta *m* or **sicofante** *m* informer, spy; slanderer

sico•sis *f* (*pl* **-sis**) psychosis; (*afección de la piel*) sycosis

SIDA *abbr* **síndrome de inmunidad deficiente adquirida**

sideral or **sidére•o -a** *adj* sidereal

siderurgia *f* iron and steel industry

sidra *f* cider; **sidra achampañada** hard cider

siega *f* reaping, mowing; harvest; crop

siembra *f* sowing; seeding; seedtime; sown field

siempre *adv* always; **de siempre** usual; **para siempre** or **por siempre** forever; **por siempre jamás** forever and ever; **siempre que** whenever; provided

siempreviva *f* everlasting flower

sien *f* temple (*of head*)

sierpe *f* serpent, snake

sierra *f* saw; sierra, mountain range; **sierra circular** buzz saw; **sierra continua** band saw; **sierra de armero** hacksaw; **sierra de bastidor** bucksaw; **sierra de hilar** ripsaw; **sierra de vaivén** jig saw; **sierra sin fin** band saw

sier•vo -va *mf* slave; servant; **siervo de la gleba** serf

sieso *m* anus

siesta *f* siesta; hot time of day; **siesta del carnero** nap before lunch

siete *adj & pron* seven; **las siete** seven o'clock ‖ *m* seven; (*en las fechas*) seventh; (coll) V-shaped tear or rip

sífilis *f* syphilis

sifón *m* siphon; siphon bottle; (*tubo doblemente acodado*) trap

sig.ᵉ *abbr* siguiente

sigilar *tr* to seal, stamp; conceal, keep silent

sigilo *m* seal; concealment, reserve; **sigilo sacramental** inviolable secrecy of the confessional

sigilo•so -sa *adj* tight-lipped; reserved

sigla *f* initial; abbreviation, symbol

siglo *m* (*cien años*) century; (*comercio de los hombres*) world; (*largo tiempo*) age; **siglo de la ilustración** or **de las luces** Age of Enlightenment

signar *tr* to mark; sign; make the sign of the cross over

signatura *f* library number; (mus & typ) signature

significado *m* meaning

significar §73 *tr* to signify, mean; point out, make known ‖ *intr* to be important

signo *m* sign; mark; sign of the cross; fate, destiny; **signo de admiración** exclamation mark; **signo de interrogación** question mark; **signo externo** status symbol

siguiente *adj* following; next

sílaba *f* syllable; **última sílaba** ultima

silbar *tr* (*p.ej., una canción*) to whistle; (*un silbato*) blow; (*a un actor*) hiss ‖ *intr* to whistle; (*ir zumbando por el aire*) whiz, whiz by

silbato *m* whistle

silbido *m* whistle, whistling, hiss; (rad) howling, squealing; **silbido de oídos** ringing in the ears

silbo *m* whistle, hiss

silenciador *m* silencer; (aut) muffler

silencio *m* silence; (*toque que manda que cada cual se acueste*) (mil) taps; (mus) rest

silencio•so -sa *adj* silent, noiseless; quiet, still ‖ *m* (aut) muffler

sílfide *f* sylph

silo *m* silo; cave, dark place

silogismo *m* syllogism

silueta *f* silhouette

silva *f* (*materias escritas sin orden*) miscellany; verse of iambic hendecasyllables intermingled with seven-syllable lines

silvestre *adj* wild; rustic, uncultivated

silvicultura *f* forestry

silla *f* chair; **silla alta** high chair; **silla de balanza** rocking chair; **silla de cubierta** deck chair; **silla de junco** rush-bottomed chair; **silla de manos** sedan chair; **silla de montar** saddle, riding saddle; **silla de ruedas** wheel chair; **silla de tijera** folding chair; **silla giratoria** swivel chair; **silla hamaca** (Arg) rocking chair; **silla plegadiza** folding chair; **silla poltrona** armchair, easy chair; **sillas apilables** chairs that can be stacked or nested

sillar *m* ashlar

silleta *f* bedpan

sillico *m* chamber pot, commode

sillín *m* saddle (*of bicycle*)

sillón *m* armchair, easy chair; **sillón de orejas** wing chair

sima *f* chasm, abyss

simbióti•co -ca *adj* symbiotic

simbóli•co -ca *adj* symbolic(al)

simbolizar §60 *tr* to symbolize

símbolo *m* symbol; **Símbolo de la fe** or **de los Apóstoles** Apostles' Creed

simetría *f* symmetry

simétri•co -ca *adj* symmetric(al)

simiente *f* seed, sperm

símil *adj* like, similar ‖ *m* similarity; (rhet) simile

similar *adj* similar

similigrabado *m* (typ) half-tone

similor *m* ormolu, similor; **de similor** fake, sham

simio *m* monkey

simpatía *f* affection, attachment, liking; friendliness; congeniality; **tomar simpatía a** to take a liking for

simpáti•co -ca *adj* agreeable, pleasant, likeable, congenial

simpatizar §60 *intr* to be congenial, get on well together; **simpatizar con** to get on well with

simple *adj* simple; single ‖ *mf* simpleton ‖ *m* (*planta medicinal*) simple

simpleza *f* simpleness; stupidity

simplificar §73 *tr* to simplify

simulacro *m* phantom, vision; idol, image; semblance, show; pretense; sham battle; **simulacro de ataque aéreo** air-raid drill; **simulacro de combate** sham battle

simula•do -da *adj* fake; (com) pro forma

simular *tr* to simulate, feign, fake ‖ *intr* to malinger; pretend

simultanear *tr* to do simultaneously ‖ *intr* to work simultaneously

simultáne•o -a *adj* simultaneous

sin *prep* without; **sin embargo** nevertheless, however; **sin que** + *subj* without + *ger*

sinagoga *f* synagogue

sinapismo *m* mustard plaster; bore, nuisance

sincerar *tr* to vindicate, justify

sinceridad *f* sincerity

since•ro -ra *adj* sincere

síncopa f (phonet) syncope
síncope m fainting spell
sincróni•co -ca adj synchronous
sincronizar §60 tr & intr to synchronize
sindicar §73 tr & ref to syndicate
sindicato m syndicate; labor union
síndico m trustee; (en una quiebra) receiver
sin•diós (pl -diós) adj godless || mf atheist
síndrome m syndrome; **síndrome de choque tóxico** toxic-shock syndrome; **síndrome de inmunidad deficiente adquirida (SIDA)** acquired immune-deficiency syndrome (AIDS)
sinecura f sinecure
sinfín m endless amount, number
sinfonía f symphony
sinfóni•co -ca adj symphonic
singladura f (naut) day's run
singular adj singular; special; single || m singular; **en singular** in particular
singularizar §60 tr to distinguish, single out || ref to distinguish oneself, stand out
sinhueso f (coll) tongue
sinies•tro -tra adj evil, perverse; calamitous, disastrous || m calamity, disaster || f left hand, left-hand side
sinnúmero m great amount, great number
sino conj but, except; **no . . . sino** only; **no . . . sino que** only; **no solo . . . sino que** not only . . . but also || m fate, destiny
sinóni•mo -ma adj synonymous || m synonym
sinop•sis f (pl -sis) synopsis
sinrazón f wrong, injustice
sinsabor m displeasure; anxiety, trouble, worry
sinsonte m mockingbird
sinsostenismo m (coll) bra-less fashion
sintaxis f syntax
sínte•sis f (pl -sis) synthesis
sintéti•co -ca adj synthetic(al)
sintetizar §60 tr to synthesize
síntoma m symptom; sign; **síntoma de abstinencia** withdrawal symptom
sintonía f (rad) tuning; (rad) theme song
sintonizar §60 tr (el aparato receptor) to tune; (la estación emisora) tune in
sinuo•so -sa adj sinuous, winding; wavy; evasive
sinvergüenza adj brazen, shameless || mf scoundrel, rascal
sionismo m Zionism
siqui. . . var of **psiqui. . .**
siquiera adv even; at least || conj although, even though
sirena f siren; mermaid; **sirena de la playa** bathing beauty; **sirena de niebla** foghorn
sirga f towrope, towline
sirgar §44 tr to tow
Siria f Syria
si•rio -ria adj & mf Syrian || **Sirio** m (astr) Sirius || f see **Siria**
sirvienta f maid, servant girl
sirviente m servant; waiter
sisa f petty theft; (para fijar los panes de oro) sizing
sisal m sisal, sisal hemp

sisar tr to filch, snitch; (lo que se ha de dorar) size
sisear tr to hiss || intr to hiss; sizzle
siseo m hiss, hissing; sizzle, sizzling
Sísifo m Sisyphus
sismógrafo m seismograph
sismología f seismology
sistema m system; **el Sistema** the Establishment, established order
sistematizar §60 tr to systematize
sístole f systole
sitial m place of honor
sitiar tr to surround, hem in; siege, besiege
sitio m place, spot, room; location, site; country place; seat; cattle ranch; taxi stand; (mil) siege
si•to -ta adj situated, located
situación f situation, position; **pedir situación** (aer) to ask for bearings
situar §21 tr to situate, locate, place; (dinero) place, invest; (un pedido) place || ref to take a position; settle; take place; (aer) to get one's bearings
s.l. abbr **sin lugar**
S.M. abbr **Su majestad**
smo•king m (pl -kings) tuxedo, dinner coat
so prep under, e.g., **so pena de** under penalty of || interj whoa!; you. . . !, e.g., **¡so animal!** you beast!
sobaco m armpit
sobajar tr to crush, to rumple; to humiliate
sobaquera f (en el vestido) armhole; (para resguardar del sudor la parte del vestido correspondiente al sobaco) shield
sobaquina f underarm odor
sobar tr to knead; massage; beat, slap; paw, pet, feel; annoy, be fresh to; flatter; (un hueso dislocado) (CAm) to set; (la cabalgadura) (Arg) to tire out; (Col) to flay, skin; (P-R) to bribe
soberanía f sovereignty
sobera•no -na adj sovereign; superb || mf sovereign || m (moneda) sovereign
sober•bio -bia adj proud, haughty; arrogant; magnificent, superb || f pride, haughtiness; arrogance; magnificence
so•bón -bona adj malingering; fresh, mushy, spoony
soborna•do -da adj twisted; out of shape
sobornar tr to bribe
soborno m bribery; (SAm) extra load; **de soborno** (Bol) in addition; **soborno de testigo** (law) subornation of perjury
sobra f extra, surplus; **sobras** leftovers, leavings; trash
sobradillo m penthouse
sobra•do -da adj excessive, superfluous; bold, daring; rich, wealthy || m attic, garret || **sobrado** adv too
sobrante adj remaining, leftover, surplus || m leftover, surplus
sobrar tr to exceed, surpass || intr to be more than enough; be in the way; be left, remain
sobre prep on, upon; over; above; about; near; after; in addition to; out of, e.g., **en nueve casos sobre diez** in nine out of ten

cases ‖ *m* envelope; **sobre de ventanilla** window envelope

sobrealimentar *tr* to overfeed; supercharge

sobrecama *f* bedspread

sobrecarga *f* overload, extra load; overcharge; surcharge

sobrecargar §44 *tr* to overload, overburden; overcharge; surcharge; (aer) to pressurize

sobrecargo *m* (naut) supercargo; purser ‖ *f* flight attendant, stewardess

sobrecejo *m* frown

sobreceño *m* frown

sobrecoger §17 *tr* to surprise, catch; scare, terrify ‖ *ref* to be surprised; be scared; **sobrecogerse de** to be seized with

sobrecubierta *f* extra cover; (*de un libro*) jacket, dust jacket

sobredi•cho -cha *adj* above-mentioned

sobredosis *f* overdose

sobreestimar *tr* to overestimate

sobreexcitar *tr* to overexcite ‖ *ref* to become overexcited

sobreexponer §54 *tr* to overexpose

sobreexposición *f* overexposure

sobregirar *tr* & *intr* to overdraw

sobregiro *m* overdraft

sobreherido *adj* slightly wounded

sobrehombre *m* superman

sobrehuma•no -na *adj* superhuman

sobrellevar *tr* to bear, carry; (*la carga de otra persona*) ease; (*los trabajos o molestias de la vida*) share; (*molestias*) suffer with patience

sobremanera *adv* exceedingly, beyond measure

sobremesa *f* tablecloth, table cover; **de sobremesa** desk, e.g., **reloj de sobremesa** desk clock; after-dinner, e.g., **discurso de sobremesa** after-dinner speech

sobremodo *adv* var of **sobremanera**

sobrenadar *intr* to float

sobrenatural *adj* supernatural

sobrenombrar *tr* to surname; nickname

sobrenombre *m* surname; nickname

sobrentender §51 *tr* to understand ‖ *ref* to be understood, be implied

sobrepasar *tr* to excel, surpass, outdo; exceed; overtake ‖ *ref* to outdo each other; go too far

sobrepeine *adv* slightly, briefly ‖ *m* hair trimming

sobrepe•lliz *f* (*pl* **-llices**) surplice

sobreponer §54 *tr* to superpose, put on top; superimpose ‖ *ref* to control oneself; triumph over adversity; **sobreponerse a** to overcome

sobreprecio *m* extra charge, surcharge

sobreproducción *f* overproduction

sobrepujar *tr* to excel, surpass

sobresaliente *adj* projecting; conspicuous, outstanding; (*en un examen*) distinguished ‖ *mf* substitute; understudy

sobresalir §65 *intr* to project, jut out; stand out, excel

sobresaltar *tr* to assail, rush upon; startle, frighten ‖ *intr* to stand out clearly ‖ *ref* to be startled, be frightened; start, wince

sobresalto *m* fright, scare; start, shock, wince; **de sobresalto** suddenly, unexpectedly

sobrescribir §83 *tr* to address

sobrescrito *m* address

sobrestante *m* boss, foreman

sobresueldo *m* extra wages, extra pay

sobretiro *m* offprint

sobretodo *adv* especially ‖ *m* overcoat, topcoat

sobrevenir §79 *intr* to happen, take place; supervene, set in; **sobrevenir a** to overtake

sobrevidriera *f* window screen; window grill; storm window

sobrevivencia *f* (Ecuad) survival

sobreviviente *adj* surviving ‖ *mf* survivor

sobrevivir *intr* to survive; **sobrevivir a** to survive, outlive

sobrevolar §61 *tr* to overfly

sobriedad *f* sobriety, moderation

sobrina *f* niece

sobrino *m* nephew

so•brio -bria *adj* sober, moderate, temperate

socaire *m* (naut) lee; **al socaire de** (naut) under the lee of; (coll) under the shelter of; **estar al socaire** to shirk

socapa *f* subterfuge; **a socapa** clandestinely

socarrén *m* eaves

socarrar *tr* to singe, scorch

soca•rrón -rrona *adj* crafty, cunning, sly; sneering; roguish

socavar *tr* to undermine, dig under

socavón *m* cave-in; cave; (min) gallery

sociable *adj* sociable

social *adj* social; company, e.g., **edificio social** company building

socialismo *m* socialism

socialista *mf* socialist

sociedad *f* society; company, firm; **buena sociedad** (*mundo elegante*) society; **sociedad anónima** stock company; **sociedad de control** holding company; **Sociedad de las Naciones** League of Nations; **sociedad distribuidora** (wholesale) distributor

so•cio -cia *mf* partner; companion; member ‖ *m* fellow; (scornful) guy

sociología *f* sociology

socorrer *tr* to aid, help, succor

socorri•do -da *adj* ready; handy, useful; hackneyed, trite, worn; well stocked

socorrismo *m* first aid

socorro *m* aid, help, succor

socoyote *m* (Mex) baby, youngest son

soda *f* soda; soda water

sodio *m* sodium

so•ez *adj* (*pl* **-eces**) base, mean, vile

so•fá *m* (*pl* **-fás**) sofa; **sofá cama** day bed

soflama *f* glow, flicker; blush; deceit, cheating

soflamar *tr* to flimflam; make blush ‖ *ref* to become scorched

sofocar §73 *tr* to choke, suffocate, stifle, smother; quench, extinguish; make blush; bother, harass ‖ *ref* to choke, suffocate; blush; get excited; get out of breath

sofoco *m* blush, embarrassment

sofrenar *tr* (*un caballo*) to check suddenly; (*una pasión*) control; chide, reprimand

soga *m* sly fellow ‖ *f* rope, cord; **dar soga a** to make fun of; **hacer soga** to lag behind

soja *f* soy, soy bean

sojuzgar §44 *tr* to subjugate, subdue

sol *m* sun; sunlight; sunny side; **de sol a sol** from sunrise to sunset; **hacer sol** to be sunny; **soles** (poet) eyes

solamente *adv* only

solana *f* sunny spot; sun porch

solanera *f* sunburn; sunny spot

solapa *f* lapel; pretext, pretense; flap

solapa•do -da *adj* overlapping; cunning, underhanded, sneaky

solapar *tr* to put lapels on; overlap; conceal, cover up ‖ *intr* to overlap

solapo *m* lapel; flap; chuck under chin

solar *adj* solar; ancestral ‖ *m* ground, plot; backyard; manor house, ancestral mansion; noble lineage; (Cuba) tenement ‖ *v* §61 *tr* to pave, floor; (*zapatos*) sole

solarie•go -ga *adj* ancestral; manorial

solario *m* sun porch

so•laz *m* (*pl* -laces) solace, consolation; recreation; **a solaz** with pleasure

soldada *f* wages, pay

soldadera *f* (Mex) camp follower

soldadesca *f* soldiery; undisciplined troops

soldado *m* soldier; **soldado de a pie** foot soldier; **soldado de juguete** toy soldier; **soldado de marina** marine; **soldado de plomo** tin soldier; **soldado de primera** private first class; **soldado raso** buck private

soldadura *f* solder; soldering; weld; welding; **soldadura al arco** arc welding; **soldadura autógena** welding; **soldadura a tope** butt welding; **soldadura por puntos** spot welding

soldar §61 *tr* to solder; (*sin materia extraña*) weld ‖ *ref* (*los huesos*) to knit

solear *tr* to sun ‖ *ref* to sun, sun oneself

soledad *f* solitude, loneliness; longing, grieving; lonely spot

soledo•so -sa *adj* solitary, lonely; longing, grieving

solemne *adj* solemn; (*error, mentira, etc.*) downright

soler §47 *intr* to be accustomed to

solera *f* crossbeam; lumber; timber; mother liquor, mother of the wine; blend of sherry; old vintage sherry; tradition, standing; (Chile) curb; (Mex) brick, tile, stone; **de solera** or **de rancia solera** of the good old school, of the good old times

solevantar *tr* to raise up; rouse, stir up, incite ‖ *ref* to rise up; revolt

solevar *tr* to raise up; incite to rebellion ‖ *ref* to rise up; revolt

solicitante *mf* petitioner; applicant

solicitar *tr* to solicit, ask for; apply for; woo, court; drive, pull; (*la atención*) attract; (phys) to attract

solíci•to -ta *adj* solicitous; careful, diligent; obliging; fond, affectionate

solicitud *f* solicitude; petition, request; application

solidar *tr* to harden; establish, prove

solida•rio -ria *adj* jointly liable; jointly binding; **solidario con** or **de** integral with

solidarizar §60 *ref* to declare one's solidarity (with); identify (with)

solidez *f* solidity; strength, soundness; constancy

sóli•do -da *adj* solid; strong, sound ‖ *m* solid

soliloquio *m* soliloquy

solista *adj* (*p.ej., instrumento*) (mus) solo ‖ *mf* (mus) soloist

solita•rio -ria *adj* solitary; lonely ‖ *mf* hermit, recluse, solitary ‖ **en solitario** alone, solo ‖ *m* (*juego y diamante*) solitaire ‖ *f* tapeworm

sóli•to -ta *adj* accustomed, customary

soliviantar *tr* to rouse, stir up, incite

soliviar *tr* to lift, lift up

so•lo -la *adj* only, sole; alone; lonely; (*p.ej., whisky*) straight; (*café*) black; **a mis solas** alone, all by myself; **a solas** alone, unaided ‖ *pron* only one ‖ *m* (mus) solo

sólo *adv* only, solely

solomillo *m* sirloin

solomo *m* sirloin; loin of pork

solsticio *m* solstice

soltador *m* release; **soltador del margen** margin release

soltar §61 *tr* to untie, unfasten, loosen; let go; let go of; (*una observación*) drop, let slip; (*el agua*) turn on ‖ *ref* to get loose or free; come loose, come off; loosen up; burst out; thaw out, let oneself go

solte•ro -ra *adj* single, unmarried ‖ *m* bachelor ‖ *f* unmarried woman

solterona *f* older unmarried woman

soltura *f* looseness; agility, ease, freedom; fluency; dissoluteness; release

solución *f* solution

solucionar *tr* to solve, resolve

solventar *tr* (*lo que uno debe*) to settle, pay up; (*una dificultad*) solve

solvente *adj* solvent; (*fuente*) believable; reliable ‖ *m* solvent

sollastre *m* scullion

sollozar §60 *intr* to sob

sollozo *m* sob

sombra *f* (*falta de luz brillante*) shade; (*imagen obscura que proyecta un cuerpo opaco*) shadow; shady side; darkness; parasol; ignorance; ghost, spirit; grace, charm, wit; favor, protection; luck; **a la sombra** in the shade; in jail; **a sombra de tejado** stealthily, sneakingly; **ni por sombra** by no means; without any notice; **no ser su sombra** to be but a shadow of one's former self; **sombra (de ojos)** eye shadow; **tener buena sombra** to be likeable; to bring good luck

sombrear *tr* to shade; (*un dibujo*) hatch

sombrerera *f* bandbox, hatbox

sombrerería *f* hat store, hat factory; millinery shop

sombrere•ro -ra *mf* hatter, hat maker ‖ *f* see **sombrerera**

sombrero *m* hat; **sombrero de copa** high hat, top hat; **sombrero de muelles** opera hat; **sombrero de paja** straw hat; **sombrero de pelo** high hat; **sombrero de tres picos** three-cornered hat; **sombrero gacho** slouch hat; **sombrero hongo** derby; **sombrero jarano** sombrero

sombrilla *f* parasol, sunshade; **sombrilla de playa** beach umbrella; **sombrilla protectora** (mil) umbrella

sombrí•o -a *adj* shady; somber; gloomy

sombro•so -sa *adj* shadowy, full of shadows; shady

some•ro -ra *adj* brief, summary; slight; superficial, shallow

someter *tr* to subdue, subject; (*razones, reflexiones; un negocio*) submit ‖ *ref* to yield, submit, surrender

someti•do -da *adj* humble, submissive

sometimiento *m* subjection

somier *m* bedspring, spring mattress

somnolencia *f* sleepiness, drowsiness

somorgujar *tr* to plunge, submerge ‖ *intr* to dive, ‖ *ref* to plunge

son *m* sound; news, rumor; pretext, motive; manner, mode; **en son de** in the manner of, by way of; as

sona•do -da *adj* talked-about; famous, noted

sonaja *f* jingle

sonajero *m* rattle, child's rattle

sonámbu•lo -la *mf* sleepwalker, somnambulist

sonar §61 *tr* to sound, ring; (*un instrumento de viento, un silbato*) blow; (*un instrumento de viento*) play ‖ *intr* to sound, ring; (*un reloj*) strike; seem; sound familiar; **sonar a** to sound like, have the appearance of ‖ *ref* to be rumored; (*las narices*) blow

sonda *f* sounding; plummet, lead; drill; (surg) probe, sound

sondar or **sondear** *tr & intr* to sound, probe

sonetizar §60 *intr* to sonneteer

soneto *m* sonnet

sóni•co -ca *adj* sonic

sonido *m* sound; report, rumor

sonido silencioso ultrasound

sonoridad *f* sonority

sonorizar §60 *intr* (*una película cinematográfica*) to record sound effects on; (*una consonante sorda*) voice ‖ *ref* to voice

sono•ro -ra *adj* sound; clear, loud, resounding

sonreír §58 *intr & ref* to smile

sonriente *adj* smiling

sonrisa *f* smile

sonrojar or **sonrojear** *tr* to make one blush ‖ *ref* to blush

sonrojo *m* blush; word that causes blushing

sonrosar or **sonrosear** *tr* to rose-color; make blush ‖ *ref* to become rose-colored; blush

sonsacar §73 *tr* to pilfer; entice away; elicit, draw out

son•so -sa *adj* stupid

sonsonete *m* rhythmical tapping; sing-song

soña•dor -dora *adj* dreamy ‖ *mf* dreamer

soñar §61 *tr* to dream; **ni soñarlo** not even in a dream, by no means ‖ *intr* to dream;

soñar con to dream of; **soñar despierto** to daydream

soñolien•to -ta *adj* sleepy, dozy, drowsy, somnolent; lazy

sopa *f* (*pan u otra cosa empapada en un líquido*) sop; soup; **hecho una sopa** soaked to the skin, sopping wet; **sopa de pastas** noodle soup

sopapo *m* chuck under the chin; blow, slap

sopetear *tr* to dip, dunk; abuse

sopetón *m* slap, box; **de sopetón** suddenly

sopista *mf* beggar

soplar *tr* to blow; blow away; blow up, inflate; snitch, swipe; inspire; prompt; tip off; (*la dama a un rival*) cut out; squeal on ‖ *intr* to blow; squeal ‖ *ref* to be puffed up, be conceited; swill, gulp, gobble

soplete *m* blowpipe

soplillo *m* blower, fan; chiffon, silk gauze; light sponge cake

soplo *m* blowing, blast; breath; gust of wind; instant, moment; (*informe dado en secreto*) tip; squealing; squealer

so•plón -plona *adj* tattletale ‖ *mf* tattletale, squealer

sopor *m* sleepiness, drowsiness; stupor

soporífico *m* soporific; nightcap

soportal *m* porch, portico, arcade

soportar *tr* to support, hold up, bear; endure, suffer

soporte *m* support, bearing, rest, standard; base, stand

soprano *mf* (*persona*) soprano ‖ *m* (*voz*) soprano

sor *f* (used before names of nuns) Sister

sorber *tr* to sip; absorb, soak up

sorbete *m* sherbet, water ice

sorbetera *f* ice-cream freezer; high hat

sorbo *m* sip; gulp

sordera or **sordez** *f* deafness

sórdi•do -da *adj* sordid

sordina *f* silencer; (mus) mute; (mus) damper; **a la sordina** silently, on the quiet

sor•do -da *adj* deaf; silent, mute; muffled, dull; (*dolor, ruido*) dull ‖ *mf* deaf person; **hacerse el sordo** to pretend to be deaf; turn a deaf ear

sordomu•do -da *adj* deaf and dumb ‖ *mf* deaf-mute

sorgo *m* sorghum, broomcorn

sorna *f* slowness; sluggishness; cunning

sorochar *ref* to blush; (SAm) to become mountain-sick

soroche *m* flush, blush; (SAm) mountain sickness; (Bol, Chile) silver-bearing galena

sorprendente *adj* surprising·

sorprender *tr* to surprise; catch; (*un secreto*) discover ‖ *ref* to be surprised

sorpresa *f* surprise; surprise package

sorpresi•vo -va *adj* surprising

sortear *tr* to draw or cast lots for; choose by lot; dodge; duck through ‖ *intr* to draw or cast lots

sorteo *m* drawing, casting of lots; choosing by lot; dodging; (taur) workout, performance

sortija _f_ ring; curl; hoop; **sortija de sello** signet ring

sortilegio _m_ sorcery, witchery

sortíle•go -ga _mf_ fortuneteller ‖ _m_ sorcerer ‖ _f_ sorceress

sosa _f_ soda

sosega•do -da _adj_ calm, quiet, peaceful

sosegar §66 _tr_ to calm, quiet, allay ‖ _intr_ to become calm, rest ‖ _ref_ to calm down, quiet down

sosiega _f_ nightcap

sosiego _m_ calm, quiet, serenity

sosla•yo -ya _adj_ slanting, oblique; **al soslayo** or **de soslayo** slantingly; askance

so•so -sa _adj_ insipid; tasteless; dull, inane ‖ _f_ see **sosa**

sospecha _f_ suspicion

sospechar _tr_ to suspect

sospecho•so -sa _adj_ suspicious; suspect ‖ _m_ suspect

sostén _m_ support; (_de un buque_) steadiness; brassiere

sostener §71 _tr_ to support, hold up; sustain; maintain; bear, stand ‖ _ref_ to remain

sosteni•do -da _adj_ & _m_ (mus) sharp

sota _m_ (Chile) boss, foreman ‖ _f_ (_en los naipes_) jack; jade, hussy

sotana _f_ soutane, cassock

sótano _m_ basement, cellar

sotavento _m_ (naut) leeward

soterrar §2 _tr_ to bury; hide away

soto _m_ grove; brush, thicket, copse

so•viet _m_ (_pl_ **-viets**) soviet

soviéti•co -ca _adj_ soviet, sovietic

sovoz — **a sovoz** sotto voce, in a low tone

soya _f_ soybean

Sr. _abbr_ **Señor**

Sra. _abbr_ **Señora**

Srta. _abbr_ **Señorita**

S.S.S. _abbr_ **su seguro servidor**

ss.ss. _abbr_ **seguros servidores**

stock _m_ stock; inventory; **tener en stock** to carry; have in stock

su _adj poss_ his, her, its, their, your, one's

suave _adj_ suave, smooth, soft; gentle, mild, meek

suavizador _m_ razor strop

suavizar §60 _tr_ to smooth, ease, sweeten, soften, mollify; (_una navaja de afeitar_) strop

subalter•no -na _adj_ & _mf_ subaltern, subordinate

subasta _f_ auction, auction sale; **sacar a pública subasta** to sell at auction

subastar _tr_ to auction, sell at auction

subcampe•ón -ona _mf_ (sport) runner-up

subcentral _f_ (elec) substation

subconsciencia _f_ subconscious, subconsciousness

subconsciente _adj_ subconscious

subdesarrolla•do -da _adj_ underdeveloped

súbdi•to -ta _adj_ & _mf_ subject

subentender §51 _tr_ to understand ‖ _ref_ to be understood, be implied

subestimar _tr_ to underestimate

subfusil _m_ submachine gun

subi•do -da _adj_ high, fine, superior; strong, intense; (_color_) bright; high, high-priced ‖ _f_ rise; ascent; (_p.ej., al trono_) accession

subir _tr_ to raise; lift; carry up; (_p.ej., una escalera_) go up; (mus) to raise the pitch of ‖ _intr_ to go up, come up; rise; get worse; spread; **subir a** to climb; climb on; get in or into; get on, mount ‖ _ref_ to rise

súbi•to -ta _adj_ sudden, unexpected; hurried; hasty, impetuous ‖ **súbito** _adv_ suddenly

subjeti•vo -va _adj_ subjective

subjunti•vo -va _adj_ & _m_ subjunctive

sublevación _f_ uprising, revolt

sublevado _m_ rebel, insurrectionist

sublevar _tr_ to incite to rebellion ‖ _ref_ to revolt

submarinista _mf_ (sport) scuba diver; skin diver ‖ _m_ (nav) submariner

submari•no -na _adj_ underwater, submarine ‖ _m_ submarine

subnormal _adj_ (mentally) retarded

suboficial _m_ sergeant major; noncommissioned officer

subordina•do -da _adj_ & _mf_ subordinate

subordinar _tr_ to subordinate

subproducto _m_ by-product

subrayar _tr_ to underline; emphasize

subrepti•cio -cia _adj_ surreptitious

subsanar _tr_ to excuse, overlook; correct, repair

subscribir §83 _tr_ to subscribe; subscribe to, endorse; subscribe to or for; sign; sign up ‖ _ref_ to subscribe

subseguir §67 _intr_ & _ref_ to follow next

subsidiar _tr_ to subsidize

subsidiarias _fpl_ feeder industries

subsidiario _m_ subsidiary

subsidio _m_ subsidy; aid, help

subsiguiente _adj_ subsequent

subsistencia _f_ subsistence, sustenance

subsistir _intr_ to subsist

subsóni•co -ca _adj_ subsonic

substancia _f_ substance

substanciar _tr_ to abstract, abridge

substanti•vo -va _adj_ & _m_ substantive

substitución _f_ replacement; (chem, law, math) substitution

substitui•dor -dora _adj_ & _mf_ substitute

substituir §20 _tr_ to replace; substitute for, take the place of ‖ _intr_ to take someone's place ‖ _ref_ to be replaced; relieve each other

substituti•vo -va _adj_ & _m_ substitute

substitu•to -ta _mf_ substitute

substraer §75 _tr_ to remove; deduct; rob, steal; subtract ‖ _ref_ to withdraw; **substraerse a** to evade, avoid, slip away from

subte _m_ (Arg, Urug) subway

subteniente _m_ second lieutenant

subterráne•o -a _adj_ subterranean, underground ‖ _m_ subterranean; (Arg) subway

subtitular _tr_ to subtitle

subtítulo _m_ subtitle, subheading

suburbio _m_ suburb; outlying slum

subvención _f_ subvention, subsidy

subvencionar _tr_ to subvention, subsidize

so
su

subvenir §79 *intr* to provide; **subvenir a** to provide for; (*gastos*) defray

subvertir §68 *tr* to subvert

subyugar §44 *tr* to subjugate, subdue

sucedàne•o -a *adj & m* substitute

suceder *tr* to succeed, follow ‖ *intr* to happen; **suceder a** (*p.ej., el trono*) to succeed to ‖ *ref* to follow one another

sucesi•vo -va *adj* successive; **en lo sucesivo** in the future

suceso *m* event, happening; issue, outcome; **sucesos de actualidad** current events

suciedad *f* dirt, filth; dirtiness, filthiness

su•cio -cia *adj* dirty, filthy; base, low; tainted; blurred; (sport) foul ‖ **sucio** *adv* (sport) foully, unfairly

sucumbir *intr* to succumb

sucursal *f* branch, branch office

Sudamérica *f* South America

sudamerica•no -na *adj & mf* South American

sudar *tr* to sweat; cough up ‖ *intr* to sweat; (*trabajar mucho*) sweat

sudario *m* shroud, winding sheet

sudcorea•no -na *adj & mf* South Korean

sudor *m* sweat; (fig) sweat, toil; **chorrear de sudor** to swelter

sudoro•so -sa *adj* sweaty

Suecia *f* Sweden

sue•co -ca *adj* Swedish ‖ *mf* Swede ‖ *m* (*idioma*) Swedish

suegra *f* mother-in-law

suegro *m* father-in-law

suela *f* sole; sole leather; (*fish*) sole

sueldacostilla *f* grape hyacinth

sueldo *m* salary, pay; **a sueldo** (*gángster*) on a contract, hired (to kill)

suelo *m* ground, soil, land; floor, flooring; pavement; (*p.ej., de una botella*) bottom; **no pisar en el suelo** to walk on air; **suelo franco** loam; **suelo natal** home country

suel•to -ta *adj* loose; free; easy; swift, agile, nimble; fluent; bold, daring; (*ejemplar*) single; (*verso*) blank; odd, separate; spare; bulk; **suelto de lengua** loose-tongued ‖ *m* small change; news item

sueñecillo *m* nap; **descabezar un sueñecillo** to take a nap

sueño *m* sleep; dream; (*cosa de gran belleza*) (fig) dream; **conciliar el sueño** to manage to go to sleep; **ni por sueños** by no means; **no dormir sueño** to not sleep a wink; **tener sueño** to be sleepy; **último sueño** (*muerte*) last sleep; **sueño hecho realidad** dream come true; **sueños dorados** daydreams

suero *m* serum

suerte *f* fortune, luck; piece of luck; fate, lot; kind, sort; way, manner; feat, trick; (taur) play, suerte; (Peru) lottery ticket; **de esta suerte** in this way; **de suerte que** so that, with the result that; **la suerte está echada** the die is cast; **suerte de capa** (taur) capework

suerte•ro -ra *adj* fortunate, lucky ‖ *m* (coll) lucky dog

sué•ter *m* (*pl* **-ters**) sweater

suficiente *adj* sufficient; adequate; fit, competent

sufijo *m* suffix

sufragar §44 *tr* to help, support, favor; defray ‖ *intr* (SAm) to vote

sufragio *m* help, succor; benefit; (*voto*) suffrage

sufragismo *m* woman suffrage

sufragista *mf* woman-suffragist ‖ *f* suffragette

sufri•do -da *adj* long-suffering; (*color*) serviceable; (*marido*) complaisant

sufrir *tr* to suffer; undergo, experience; support, hold up; tolerate; (*un examen*) take ‖ *intr* to suffer

sugerencia *f* suggestion

sugerir §68 *tr* to suggest

sugestión suggestion

sugestionar *tr* to influence by suggestion

sugesti•vo -va *adj* suggestive; stimulating, striking, conspicuous

suicida *adj* suicidal ‖ *mf* suicide

suicidar *ref* to commit suicide

suicidio *m* suicide

Suiza *f* Switzerland

sui•zo -za *adj & mf* Swiss ‖ *f* see **Suiza**

sujeción *f* subjection; surrender; fastening; fastener

sujetador *m* bra(ssiere)

sujetahilo *m* (elec) binding post

sujetapape•les *m* (*pl* **-les**) paper clip

sujetar *tr* to subject; subdue; fasten, tighten ‖ *ref* to subject oneself, submit; stick, adhere

suje•to -ta *adj* subject, liable; able, capable ‖ *m* subject; fellow, individual; **buen sujeto** good egg

sulfato *m* sulfate

sulfito *m* sulfite

sulfúri•co -ca *adj* sulfuric

sulfuro *m* sulfide; **sulfuro de hidrógeno** hydrogen sulfide

sulfuro•so -sa *adj* sulfurous

sultán *m* sultan; (*galanteador*) sheik

suma *f* sum, addition; summary; sum and substance; **en suma** in short, in a word

sumadora *f* adding machine

sumamente *adv* extremely, exceedingly

sumar *tr* to add; sum up; amount to ‖ *intr* to add; amount; **suma y sigue** add and carry ‖ *ref* to add up; adhere

suma•rio -ria *adj & m* summary

sumergir §27 *tr* to submerge ‖ *ref* to submerge; (*un submarino*) dive

sumersión *f* submersion; (*de un submarino*) dive

sumidad *f* top, apex, summit

sumidero *m* drain, sewer; sink

suministrar *tr* to provide, supply

suministro *m* provision, supply; **suministros** supplies

sumir *tr* to sink; press down; overwhelm ‖ *ref* to sink; (*p.ej., los carrillos, el pecho*) be sunken; shrink, shrivel; cower; (*p.ej., el sombrero*) pull down

sumisión *f* submission (*sometimiento*) subjection

sumi•so -sa *adj* submissive

su•mo -ma *adj* high, great, extreme; supreme; **a lo sumo** at most, at the most ‖ *f* see **suma**

suncho *m* hoop

suntuo•so -sa *adj* sumptuous

supeditar *tr* to hold down, oppress

superar *tr* to surpass, excel; conquer

superávit *m* (com) surplus

supercarburante *m* high-test fuel

superchería *f* fraud, deceit

superficial *adj* superficial; surface

superficie *f* surface; exterior, outside; area; **superficie de sustentación** (aer) airfoil

super•fluo -flua *adj* superfluous

superhombre *m* superman

superintendente *mf* superintendent, supervisor; **superintendente de patio** (rr) yardmaster

superior *adj* superior; upper; higher; **superior a** superior to; higher than; more than; larger than ‖ *m* superior

superiora *f* mother superior

superiordad *f* superiority; authorities

superlati•vo -va *adj* & *m* superlative

supermercado *m* supermarket

super•no -na *adj* highest, supreme

superpetrolero *m* supertanker

superpoblar §61 *tr* to overpopulate

superponer §54 *tr* to superpose

superproduction *f* overproduction

supersóni•co -ca *adj* supersonic ‖ *f* supersonics

superstición *f* superstition

supersticio•so -sa *adj* superstitious

supertanquero *m* (SAm) supertanker

supervisar *tr* to supervise

supervivencia *f* survival; (law) survivorship

súpi•to -ta *adj* sudden; impatient; (Col) dumbfounded

suplantar *tr* to supplant by treachery; (*un documento*) to alter fraudulently

suplefal•tas *mf* (*pl* **-tas**) substitute, fill-in

suplemento *m* supplement; excess fare; **suplemento dominical** (*periódico*) Sunday supplement

súplica *f* entreaty, supplication; request

suplicante *adj* & *mf* suppliant

suplicar §73 *tr* & *intr* to entreat, implore; (law) to petition

suplicio *m* torture; punishment, execution; anguish

suplir *tr* to supplement, make up for; replace, take the place of; (*un defecto de otra persona*) cover up; (gram) to understand

suponer §54 *tr* to suppose; presuppose, imply; entail ‖ *intr* to have weight, have authority

suposición *f* supposition; distinction; falsehood, imposture

supositorio *m* suppository

supradi•cho -cha *adj* above-mentioned

supre•mo -ma *adj* supreme

supresión *f* suppression, elimination, omission; cancellation; deletion

suprimir *tr* to suppress, eliminate, do away with; cancel; delete

supues•to -ta *adj* supposed, assumed, hypothetical; **supuesto que** since, inasmuch as ‖ *m* assumption, hypothesis; **dar por supuesto** to take for granted; **por supuesto** of course, naturally

supurar *intr* suppurate, discharge pus

sur *m* south; south wind

Suramérica *f* South America

surcar §73 *tr* to furrow; plough; cut through; streak through

surco *m* furrow; wrinkle, rut, cut; (*del disco gramofónico*) groove; **echarse en el surco** to lie down on the job

surcorea•no -na *adj* & *mf* South Korean

sure•ño -ña *adj* southern ‖ *mf* southerner

surestada *f* (Arg) southeaster

surgir §27 *intr* to spout, spurt; come forth, spring up; arise, appear

suripanta *f* (hum) chorus girl; (scornful) slut, jade

surti•do -da *adj* assorted ‖ *m.* assortment; supply, stock

surtidor *m* jet, spout, fountain; **surtidor de gasolina** gasoline pump

surtir *tr* to furnish, provide, supply ‖ *intr* to spout, spurt, shoot up

susceptible *adj* susceptible; touchy

suscitar *tr* to stir up, provoke; (*dudas, una cuestión*) to raise

susodi•cho -cha *adj* above-mentioned

suspender *tr* to hang; suspend; astonish; postpone; fail, flunk ‖ *ref* to be suspended

suspensión *f* suspension; astonishment; **suspensión de fuegos** cease fire

suspen•so -sa *adj* suspended, hanging; baffled, bewildered; (theat) closed ‖ *m* flunk, condition

suspensores *mpl* suspenders

suspensorio *m* jockstrap, supporter

suspi•caz *adj* (*pl* **-caces**) suspicious, distrustful

suspirar *intr* to sigh

suspiro *m* sigh; ladyfinger; (mus) quarter rest

sustentación *f* support, prop; (aer) lift

sustentar *tr* to sustain, support, feed; maintain; (*una tesis*) defend

sustento *m* sustenance, support, food; maintenance

susto *m* scare, fright

susurrar *tr* to whisper ‖ *intr* to whisper; murmur, rustle, purl, hum; be bruited about ‖ *ref* to be bruited about

susurro *m* whisper; murmur, rustle, purling, hum

susu•rrón -rrona *adj* whispering ‖ *mf* whisperer

sutil *adj* subtle; keen, observant; thin, delicate

su•yo -ya *adj poss* of his, of hers, of yours, of theirs, e.g., **un amigo suyo** a friend of his; *pron poss* his, hers, yours, theirs, its, one's; **hacer de las suyas** to be up to one's old tricks; **salirse con la suya** to have one's way; to carry one's point

su
su

T

T, t (te) *f* twenty-third letter of the Spanish alphabet

t. *abbr* **tarde**

taba *f* anklebone; (*del carnero*) knucklebone; (*juego*) knucklebones

tabaco *m* tobacco; cigar; snuff; (Cuba, CAm, Mex) punch; **tabaco en rama** leaf tobacco; **tabaco sin humo** smokeless tobacco

tabalada *f* bump, thump, heavy fall; slap

tabalear *tr* to rock, sway ‖ *intr* to drum with the fingers

tabanazo *m* slap; slap in the face

tabanco *m* stand, stall, booth

tábano *m* horsefly, gadfly

tabanque *m* treadle wheel

tabaola *f* noise, hubbub

tabaquera *f* snuffbox; (*de la pipa de fumar*) bowl; (Arg, Chile) tobacco pouch

tabaquería *f* tobacco store, cigar store

tabaque•ro -ra *adj* tobacco ‖ *mf* tobacconist; cigar maker ‖ *m* (Bol) pocket handkerchief ‖ *f* see **tabaquera**

tabardete *m* or **tabardillo** *m* sunstroke; harum-scarum

tabarra *f* bore, tiresome talk

taberna *f* tavern, saloon, barroom, pub

tabernáculo *m* tabernacle

tabernera *f* barmaid

tabernero *m* tavern keeper; bartender

tabica *f* (*para cubrir un hueco*) board; (*del frente de un escalón*) riser

tabicar §73 *tr* to close up, shut up; wall up

tabique *m* thin wall; partition wall, partition

tabla *f* (*de madera*) board; (*de metal*) sheet; (*de piedra*) slab; (*de tierra*) strip; (*cuadro pintado en una tabla*) panel; (*lista, catálogo; índice de materias*) table; **escapar** or **salvarse en una tabla** to have a narrow escape; **tabla de lavar** washboard; **tabla de planchar** ironing board; **tabla de salvación** lifesaver, helping hand; **tablas** draw, tie; (*escenario del teatro*) stage; (*de la plaza de toros*) barrier; **tener tablas** to have stage presence

tablado *m* flooring; scaffold; (*escenario del teatro*) stage

tablear *tr* to cut into boards; divide into plots or patches; level, grade

tablero *m* boarding; timber; table top; gambling table; cutting board; checkerboard, chessboard; counter; blackboard; **poner al tablero** to risk; **tablero de instrumentos** (aer) control panel; (aut) dashboard

tableta *f* small board; (*taco de papel; comprimido, pastilla*) tablet

tabletear *intr* to rattle

tabilla *f* tablet; splint; bulletin board

tablón *m* plank; beam

tabloncillo *m* (taur) seat in last row

ta•bú *m* (*pl* **-búes**) taboo

tabuco *m* hovel

tabulador *m* tabulator

tabular *tr* to tabulate

taburete *m* stool

tac *m* tick

tacada *f* stroke (*of a billiard cue*)

taca•ño -ña *adj* stingy

táci•to -ta *adj* tacit; silent

tacitur•no -na *adj* taciturn; melancholy

taco *m* bung, plug; wad, wadding; billiard cue; pad, tablet; drumstick; snack, bite; drink; oath, curse; heel; muddle, mess; (Mex) rolled-up tortilla with fillings, taco

tacón *m* heel

taconear *tr* (Chile) to fill, stuff ‖ *intr* to click the heels; strut

taconeo *m* click, clicking (*of heels*)

tácti•co -ca *adj* tactical ‖ *m* tactician ‖ *f* tactics

tacto *m* (sense of) touch; (*del dactiló-grafo, el pianista, el instrumento*) touch; skill; tact

tacha *f* defect, fault, flaw

tachar *tr* to erase; strike out; blame, find fault with

tacho *m* tin sheet; (Arg) garbage can; (Arg) watch; (Arg, Chile) boiler; (Cuba) sugar pan

tachón *m* scratch, erasure; ornamental tack or nail; trimming

tachonar *tr* to adorn with ornamental tacks; trim with ribbon; spangle, stud

tachuela *f* tack; hobnail; (Chile, Mex) runt, half pint; (SAm) drinking cup

Tadeo *m* Thaddeus

tafetán *m* taffeta; **tafetanes** flags, colors; finery; **tafetán inglés** court plaster

tafilete *m* morocco leather; sweatband

tagarote *m* sparrow hawk; scrivener; lout; gentleman sponger

tagua *f* (Chile) mud hen; (*arbusto*) (SAm) ivory palm; (*fruto*) (SAm) ivory nut

taha•lí *m* (*pl* **-líes**) baldric

tahona *f* horse-driven flour mill; bakery

ta•hur -hura *adj* gambling; cheating ‖ *mf* gambler; cheat; cardsharp

tailan•dés -desa *adj* & *mf* Thai

Tailandia *f* Thailand

taima•do -da *adj* sly, crafty; (Arg, Ecuad) lazy; (Chile) gruff, sullen

tajada *f* cut; slice; hoarseness; drunk

tajadero *m* chopping block

tajalá•piz *m* (*pl* **-pices**) pencil sharpener

tajamar *m* cutwater; dike, dam

tajar *tr* to cut; slice; (*un lápiz*) sharpen

tajo *m* cut; cutting edge; chopping block; execution block; steep cliff ‖ **Tajo** *m* Tagus

tal *adj indef* such; such a ‖ *pron indef* so-and-so; such a thing; someone ‖ *adv* so; in such a way; **con tal (de) que** provided (that); **¿qué tal?** how?; hello!, how's everything?

talabarte *m* sword belt

talabartero *m* saddler, harness maker

talache *m* or **talacho** *m* (Mex) mattock

taladrar *tr* to bore, drill, pierce, perforate; (*un billete*) punch; (*un problema*) get to the bottom of

taladro *m* drill; auger; drill hole; drill press

tálamo *m* bridal bed

talán *m* ding-dong

talante *m* countenance, mien; desire, will, pleasure; way, manner

talar *adj* (*traje, vestidura*) long ‖ *tr* (*árboles*) to fell; destroy, lay waste

talco *m* tinsel; talc; **talco en polvo** talcum powder

talega *f* bag, sack; **talegas** money, wealth

talego *m* big bag, sack; slob; **tener talego** to have money tucked away

taleguilla *f* small bag; bullfighter's breeches

talento *m* talent

talento•so -sa *adj* talented

Tales *m* Thales

Talía *f* Thalia

talismán *m* talisman

talón *m* heel; (aut) lug, flange; check, voucher, coupon; (*de un cheque*) stub

talona•rio -ria *adj* stub ‖ *m* stub book, checkbook

talonear *intr* to dash along

talud *m* slope

talla *f* cut; carving; height, stature; size; ransom; reward; (*diamante*) cut, polish; (Arg) chatting, prattle; (CAm) fraud, lie; (Col) beating, thrashing

tallar *tr* to carve; (*una piedra preciosa*) cut; (*naipes*) deal; appraise; engrave; grind; size up; (Col) beat, thrash ‖ *intr* (Arg) to chat, converse; (Chile) to make love

tallarín *m* noodle

talle *m* shape, figure, stature; waist; fit; appearance, outline; bodice

taller *m* shop, workshop; factory, mill; atelier, studio; laboratory; **taller agremiado** closed shop; **taller carrocero** (aut) body shop; **taller franco** open shop; **taller penitenciario** workhouse

tallo *m* stem, stalk; shoot, sprout; (Col) cabbage

tamal *m* (CAm, Mex) tamale; (Chile) bundle; (coll) intrigue

tamañi•to -ta *adj* so small; very small; confused, disconcerted

tama•ño -ña *adj* so big; such a big; very big, very large; so small; **abrir tamaños ojos** to open one's eyes wide ‖ *m* size

tambaleante *adj* staggering

tambalear *intr* & *ref* to stagger, reel, totter

también *adv* also, too

tambo *m* (Arg, Chile) brothel; (SAm) roadside inn; (Arg, Urug) dairy

tambor *m* drum; (*persona que toca el tambor*) drummer; sieve, screen; eardrum, coffee roaster; **a tambor batiente** with drums beating; in triumph; **tambor mayor** drum major

tamborilear *tr* to praise to the skies ‖ *intr* to drum

Támesis *m* Thames

ta•miz *m* (*pl* -**mices**) sieve

tamizar §60 *tr* to sift, sieve

tamo *m* fuzz, fluff

tampoco *adv* neither, not either; **ni yo tampoco** nor I either

tampón *m* stamp pad

tan *adv* so; **tan . . . como** or **cuan** as . . . as;

tan siquiera at least; **un tan** +*adj* such a +*adj* ‖ *m* boom (*of a drum*)

tanatología *f* thanatology

tanda *f* turn; shift, relay; task; coat, layer; game, match; flock, lot, pack; show; habit, bad habit

tangente *adj* & *f* tangent; **escaparse, irse** or **salir por la tangente** to evade the issue

Tánger *f* Tangier

tanguista *f* hostess (*in a night club*)

ta•no -na *adj* & *mf* (Arg) Neapolitan, Italian

tanque *m* tank; (dial) dipper, drinking cup

tantán *m* tom-tom; clanging; boom

tantear *tr* to compare; size up; probe, test, feel out; sketch, outline; keep the score of ‖ *intr* to keep score; to grope; **¡tantee Vd.!** just imagine!, fancy that!

tanteo *m* comparison; careful consideration; test, probe, trial; trial and error; score

tan•to -ta *adj* & *pron indef* so much; as much; **tanto . . . como** as much . . . as; both . . . and; **tan•tos -tas** so many; as many; **tantos . . . como** as many . . . as; **y tantos** odd, or more, e.g., **veinte y tantos** twenty odd, twenty or more ‖ *m* copy; counter, chip; point; portion, part; **apuntar los tantos** to keep score; **entre tanto** in the meantime; **estar al tanto de** to be aware of, to be or keep informed about; **poner al tanto de** to make aware of, to keep informed of; **por lo tanto** or **por tanto** therefore ‖ **tanto** *adv* so much; so hard; so often; so long; as much

tañer §70 *tr* (*un instrumento músico*) to play; (*una campana*) to ring ‖ *intr* to drum with the fingers

tañido *m* sound, tone; twang; ring, tang

tapa *f* lid, cover, top, cap; (*de un cilindro, un barril*) head; (*de una compuerta*) gate; (*de un libro*) board cover; shirt front; (aut) valve cap; **levantarse** or **saltarse la tapa de los sesos** to blow one's brains out; **tapas** appetizer, free lunch

tapabalazo *m* fly (*of trousers*)

tapabarro *m* (Chile) mudguard

tapaboca *f* slap in the mouth; muffler; squelch, squelcher

tapacu•bo *m* or **tapacu•bos** *m* (*pl* -**bos**) (aut) hubcap

tapadera *f* lid, cover, cap

tapagote•ras *m* (*pl* -**ras**) (Arg) roofing cement; (Col) roofer

tapaguje•ros *m* (*pl* -**ros**) (coll) bungling mason; substitute, replacement

tapar *tr* to cover; cover up, hide; plug, stop, stop up; conceal; obstruct; wrap up; (*un diente*) (Chile) to fill

tapara *f* (Ven) gourd; **vaciarse como una tapara** (Ven) to spill all one knows

taparrabo *m* loincloth; bathing trunks

tapera *f* (SAm) ruins; (SAm) shack

tapete *m* rug; runner; table scarf; **estar sobre el tapete** to be on the carpet, be under discussion; **tapete verde** card table, gambling table

tapia *f* mud wall, adobe wall

tapiar *tr* to wall up, wall in; close up

t
ta

tapicería _f_ tapestries; upholstery; tapestry shop; upholstery shop

tapicero _m_ tapestry maker; upholsterer; carpet maker; carpet layer

ta•piz _m_ (_pl_ **-pices**) tapestry

tapizar §60 _tr_ to tapestry; upholster; carpet; cover

tapon _m_ stopper, cork; cap; bottle cap; bung, plug; (elec) fuse; (surg) tampon; **tapón de algodón** (surg) swab; **tapón de cubo** (aut) hubcap; **tapón de desagüe** drain plug; **tapón de tráfico** traffic jam; **tapón de vaciado** (aut) drain plug

taponar _tr_ to plug, stop up; (surg) to tampon

taponazo _m_ pop

taque _m_ click; knock, rap

taqué _m_ (aut) tappet

taquigrafía _f_ shorthand, stenography

taquigrafiar §77 _tr_ to take down in shorthand ‖ _intr_ to take shorthand

taquígra•fo -fa _mf_ stenographer

taquilla _f_ ticket rack; ticket window; ticket office; box office; gate, take; file; (C-R) inn, tavern

taquille•ro -ra _adj_ box-office ‖ _mf_ ticket agent

taquimeca _mf_ shorthand-typist

taquimecanógra•fo -fa _mf_ shorthand-typist

tarabilla _f_ millclapper; catch; turnbuckle; (_de la hebilla de la correa_) tongue; chatterbox; jabber; **soltar la tarabilla** to talk a blue streak

tarabita _f_ (_clavillo de la hebilla_) tongue; (SAm) rope of rope bridge

taracea _f_ marquetry, inlaid work

tarambana _adj & mf_ (coll) crackpot

tararear _tr & intr_ to hum

tarasca _f_ dragon (_in Corpus Christi procession_); (_mujer fea_) hag

tarascada _f_ bite; tart reply

tardanza _f_ slowness, delay, tardiness

tardar _intr_ to be long, be slow; be late; **a más tardar** at the latest; **tardar en** + _inf_ to be late in + _ger_ ‖ _ref_ to be long, be slow; be late

tarde _adv_ late; too late; **hacerse tarde** to grow late; **tarde o temprano** sooner or later ‖ _f_ afternoon; evening; **de la tarde a la mañana** overnight; suddenly, in no time; unexpectedly

tardecer §22 _intr_ to grow dark, grow late

tardí•do -a _adj_ late, delayed; dilatory, tardy; slow

tar•do -da _adj_ slow; late; slow, dull, dense

tar•dón -dona _mf_ poke, slow poke

tarea _f_ task, job; care, worry

tarifa _f_ tariff; price list; rate; fare; (telp) toll; **tarifa recargada** extra fare

tarima _f_ platform; stand; stool; low bench; (_entablado para dormir_) bunk

tarjeta _f_ card; **tarjeta de buen deseo** or **de felicitación** greeting card; **tarjeta de crédito** credit card; **tarjeta de visita** calling card, visiting card; **tarjeta navideña** Christmas card; **tarjeta perforada** punch card; **tarjeta postal** post card, postal card

tarjetero _m_ card case; card index

tarquín _m_ mire, slime, mud

tarro _m_ jar; milk pail; horn; (SAm) top hat

tarta _f_ tart, cake; pan

tartajear _intr_ to stutter

tartalear _intr_ to stagger, sway; be speechless

tartamudear _intr_ to stutter, stammer

tartamudeo _m_ stuttering, stammering

tartamu•do -da _mf_ stutterer, stammerer

tartán _m_ Scotch plaid

tarugo _m_ wooden plug; wooden paving block; (Guat, Mex) dolt, blockhead

tasa _f_ appraisal; measure, standard; rate; ceiling price

tasación _f_ appraisal; regulation

tasajo _m_ jerked beef

tasar _tr_ to appraise; regulate; hold down, keep within bounds; grudge

tasca _f_ dive, joint; tavern; (Peru) surf, breakers

tata _m_ daddy ‖ _f_ nursemaid; little sister

tate _m_ hashish; hashish user

tato _m_ little brother

tatuaje _m_ tattoo, tattooing

tatuar §21 _tr & ref_ to tattoo

tauri•no -na _adj_ bullfighting

Tauro _m_ (astr) Taurus

taurófi•lo -la _mf_ bullfight fan

tauromaquia _f_ bullfighting

taxear _intr_ (aer) to taxi

taxi _m_ taxi, taxicab ‖ _f_ taxi dancer

taxista _mf_ taxi driver

taza _f_ cup; (_de la fuente_) basin; (_del inodoro_) bowl

te _pron pers & reflex_ thee, to thee; you, to you; thyself, to thyself; yourself, to yourself

té _m_ tea; **té bailable** tea dance

tea _f_ torch, firebrand

teatral _adj_ theatrical

teatre•ro -ra _mf_ theater-goer

teatro _m_ theater; **dar teatro a** to bally-hoo; **teatro de estreno** first-run house; **teatro de repetorio** stock company

teatrólo•go -ga _mf_ theater critic ‖ _m_ actor ‖ _f_ actress

Tebas _f_ Thebes

tebe•o -a _adj & mf_ Theban ‖ _m_ comic book, funny paper

teca _f_ teak

tecla _f_ (_de piano, máquina de escribir, etc._) key; touchy subject; **dar en la tecla** to get the knack of it; **tecla de cambio** shift key; **tecla de escape** margin release; **tecla de espacios** space bar; **tecla de retroceso** backspacer

teclado _m_ keyboard; **teclado manual** (mus) manual

teclear _tr_ to feel out ‖ _intr_ to run over the keys; drum, thrum; (Chile) to be at death's door; (_un jugador_) (Chile) to be losing one's last cent

tecleo _m_ fingering; touch; (_de la máquina de escribir_) click

técni•co -ca _adj_ technical ‖ _m_ technician; expert ‖ _f_ technique; technics

tecolote _m_ eagle owl (_of Central America_); (Mex) night policeman

techado *m* roof; **bajo techado** indoors
techar *tr* to roof
techo *m* ceiling; roof; (*sombrero*) hat; **techo de paja** thatched roof
techumbre *f* ceiling; roof
tedio *m* ennui, boredom
tedio•so -sa *adj* tedious, boresome
teja *f* roofing tile; shovel hat; yew tree; linden tree; **a toca teja** (coll) for cash; **teja de madera** shingle
tejadillo *m* cover, top; (*de coche*) roof
tejado *m* tile roof; roof; **tejado de vidrio** (fig) glass house
tejama•ní *m* (*pl* -níes) shake (*long shingle*)
tejar *m* tile works ‖ *tr* to tile, roof with tiles
teja•roz *m* (*pl* -roces) eaves
teje•dor -dora *adj* weaving; scheming ‖ *mf* weaver; schemer
tejer *tr* & *intr* to weave
tejido *m* weave, texture; web; fabric, textile; tissue; (biol & fig) tissue; **tejido adhesivo** friction tape; **tejido conjunctivo** (anat) connective tissue; **tejido de saco** (Mex) burlap; **tejido de punto** knitted fabric, jersey
tejo *m* disk; quoit; yew tree
tejón *m* badger
tela *f* cloth, fabric; (*de cebolla*) skin; (*del insecto*) web; film; (bb) cloth; (paint) canvas; (*dinero*) (slang) dough; **poner en tela de juicio** to question, doubt; **tela de alambre** wire screen; **tela de araña** spider web, cobweb; **tela emplástica** court plaster; **tela metálica** chicken wire; wire screen
telar *m* loom; frame; embroidery frame; (bb) sewing press
telaraña *f* spider web, cobweb
telecomedia serial *f* sitcom
telecontrol *m* remote control
telediario *m* daytime television news
teledifundir *tr* & *intr* to telecast
teledifusión *f* telecasting; telecast
telefonar *tr* & *intr* to telephone
telefonazo *m* telephone call
telefonear *tr* & *intr* to telephone
telefonema *m* telephone message
telefonista *mf* telephone operator
teléfono *m* telephone; **teléfono automático** dial telephone; **teléfono público** pay phone
teleg. *abbr* **telégrafo, telegrama**
telegrafiar §77 *tr* & *intr* to telegraph
telegrafista *mf* telegrapher
telégrafo *m* telegraph; **telégrafo de banderas** wigwagging; **telégrafo de máquinas** (naut) engine-room telegraph; **telégrafo sin hilos** wireless telegraph
telegrama *m* telegram
teleimpresor *m* teletype, teleprinter
Telémaco *m* Telemachus
telemando *m* remote control
telemetrar *tr* to telemeter
telemetría *f* telemetry
telémetro *m* telemeter; (mil) range finder
telen•do -da *adj* sprightly, lively
telerreceptor *m* television set
telescopar *tr* & *ref* to telescope

telescopio *m* telescope
telesilla *f* chair lift
telespecta•dor -dora *mf* viewer, televiewer; **telespectadores** television audience
telesquí *m* ski lift, ski tow
teleta *f* blotter, blotting paper
teletipo *m* teletype
teletubo *m* (telv) picture tube
televidente *mf* viewer, televiewer
televisar *tr* to televise
televisión *f* television; **televisión en circuito cerrado** closed-circuit television; **televisión en colores** color television; **televisión por cable** cable television
televi•sor -sora *adj* televising; television ‖ *m* television set ‖ *f* television transmitter
telón *m* drop curtain; **telón de acero** (fig) iron curtain; **telón de boca** (theat) front curtain; **telón de fondo** or **foro** (theat) backdrop
tema *m* theme, subject; exercise; (gram) stem; (mus) theme ‖ *f* fixed idea; persistence; grudge; **a tema** in emulation
temario *m* agenda
temblar §2 *intr* to tremble, shake, quiver, shiver; **estar temblando** to teeter
tem•blón -blona *adj* shaking, tremulous ‖ *m* aspen tree
temblor *m* temor, shaking, trembling; **temblor de tierra** earthquake
tembloro•so -sa *adj* trembling, shaking, tremulous
tem•bo -ba *adj* (Col) silly, stupid
temer *tr* & *intr* to fear
temera•rio -ria *adj* rash, reckless, foolhardy
temeridad *f* rashness, recklessness, foolhardiness, temerity
temero•so -sa *adj* frightful, dread; timid; fearful
temible *adj* dreadful, terrible, fearful
temor *m* fear, dread
témpano *m* small drum; drumhead; (*de barril*) head; (*de tocino*) flitch; (*de hielo*) iceberg, floe; (archit) tympan; (mus) kettledrum
temperamental *adj* temperamental
temperamento *m* temperament; conciliation, compromise; weather
temperar *tr* to temper, soften, moderate, calm; tune ‖ *intr* to go to a warmer climate
temperatura *f* temperature; weather
temperie *f* weather, state of the weather
tempestad *f* storm, tempest; **tempestad de arena** sandstorm; **tempestades de risas** gales of laughter
tempesti•vo -va *adj* opportune, timely
tempestuo•so -sa *adj* stormy, tempestuous
templa•do -da *adj* temperate; moderate; lukewarm, medium; brave, courageous; drunk, tipsy; (SAm) in love; (CAm, Mex) clever
templanza *f* temperence; mildness
templar *tr* to temper; soften; ease, dilute; (*colores*) blend; (*velas*) trim ‖ *intr* (*el tiempo*) to warm up ‖ *ref* to temper; moderate; fall in love; die

ta
te

temple *m* weather, state of the weather; temper, disposition; humor; average; dash, boldness; (*del acero, el vidrio, etc.*) temper

templo *m* temple

témpora *f* Ember days

temporada *f* season; period; (*p.ej., de buen tiempo*) spell; **de temporada** temporarily; vacationing

temporal *adj* temporal; temporary ‖ *m* weather; storm, tempest; spell of rainy weather

temporáne•o -a or **tempora•rio -ria** *adj* temporary

temporizar §60 *intr* to temporize; putter around

temprane•ro -ra *adj* early

tempra•no -na *adj* early ‖ **temprano** *adv* early

tenacidad *f* tenacity; persistence

tenacillas *fpl* sugar tongs; hair curler; tweezers; snuffers

te•naz *adj* (*pl* **-naces**) tenacious; persistent

tenazas *fpl* pincers, pliers; tongs

tenazón — a or **de tenazón** without taking aim; offhand

tenazuelas *fpl* tweezers

tendedera *f* clothesline; litter

tendedero *m* drier, frame for drying clothes; drying ground

tendencia *f* tendency

tender §51 *tr* to spread; stretch out; extend; reach out; offer, tender; (*la ropa*) hang out; (*con una capa de cal o yeso*) coat; (*un puente*) throw, build; (*una trampa*) set; (*conductores eléctricos, vías de ferrocarril, cañerías*) lay; (*la cama*) make; (*un cadáver*) lay out ‖ *intr* to tend ‖ *ref* to stretch out; throw one's cards on the table; run at full gallop

ténder *m* tender

tenderete *m* stand, booth

tende•ro -ra *mf* shopkeeper, storekeeper ‖ *m* tent maker

tendido *m* (*p.ej., de un cable*) laying; (*de una cortina de humo*) spreading; (*de alambres*) hanging, stretching; wires; (*trecho de ferrocarril*) stretch; (*ropa que tiende la lavandera*) wash; (*de cal o yeso*) coat; (*del tejado*) slope; (*de panes*) batch; (taur) uncovered stand; (Col) bedclothes

tendón *m* tendon

tenducha *f* or **tenducho** *m* miserable old store

tenebro•so -sa *adj* dark, gloomy; (*negocio*) dark, shady; (*estilo*) obscure

tenedor *m* holder, bearer; fork, table fork; **tenedor de acciones** stockholder; **tenedor de bonos** bondholder; **tenedor de libros** bookkeeper

teneduría *f* bookkeeping

tenencia *f* tenure, tenancy; (mil & nav) lieutenancy

tener §71 *tr* to have; hold; keep; own, possess; consider; (*recibir*) get; esteem; stop; **no tenerlas todas consigo** to be alarmed, dismayed; **no tener nada que ver con** to have nothing to do with; **no tener sobre qué caerse muerto** to not have a cent to one's name; **tener que** to have to; for expressions like **tener hambre** to be hungry, see the noun ‖ *ref* to stop; catch oneself, keep from falling; consider oneself; fit, go

tenería *f* tannery

tenida *f* meeting, session

teniente *adj* holding, owning; unripe; mean, miserly; hard of hearing ‖ *m* lieutenant; **teniente coronel** lieutenant colonel; **teniente de navío** (nav) lieutenant

tenis *m* tennis

tenista *mf* tennis player

tenor *m* tenor, character, import, drift; (mus) tenor; **a tenor de** in accordance with

tenorio *m* lady-killer

tensión *f* tension, stress; (elec) tension, voltage; (mech) stress; **tensión arterial** or **sanguínea** blood pressure

ten•so -sa *adj* tense, tight, taut

tentación *f* temptation

tentáculo *m* tentacle, feeler

tenta•dor -dora *adj* tempting ‖ *m* tempter

tentar §2 *tr* to touch; (*el camino*) feel; try, attempt; examine; try out, test; tempt; probe

tentati•vo -va *adj* tentative ‖ *f* attempt; trial, feeler

tentempié *m* snack, bite, pick-me-up; (*juguete*) tumbler

tenue *adj* tenuous; light, soft; faint, subdued; (*estilo*) simple

teñir §72 *tr* to dye; stain; tinge, shade, color

teología *f* theology; **no meterse en teologías** to keep out of deep water; *teología liberacionista* liberation theology

teorema *m* theorem

teoría *f* theory; *teoría ondulatoria* wave theory

tepe *m* turf, sod

tequila *m* (Mex) tequila (*distilled liquor*)

terapéuti•co -ca *adj* therapeutic(al) ‖ *f* therapeutics

terapia *f* therapy; *terapia vocacional* occupational therapy

tercena *f* government tobacco warehouse; (Ecuad) butcher shop

tercermundista *adj* Third World

terce•ro -ra *adj* third ‖ *mf* third; mediator; go-between ‖ *m* procurer, bawd; referee, umpire

Tercero Mundo *m* Third World; nonaligned nations

terceto *m* tercet; trio

terciar *tr* to place diagonally; divide into three parts; (*p.ej., la capa, el fusil*) to swing over one's shoulder; (*licor*) water ‖ *intr* to intercede, mediate ‖ *ref* to happen; be opportune

tercia•rio -ria *adj* tertiary

ter•cio -cia *adj* third ‖ *m* third; (mil) corps; **hacer buen tercio a** to do a good turn

terciopelo *m* velvet

ter•co -ca *adj* stubborn; hard, resistant

Teresa *f* Theresa

tergiversar *tr* to slant, twist, distort
terliz *m* ticking
termal *adj* thermal; steam
termas *fpl* hot baths
térmi•co -ca *adj* temperature; steam; steam-generated
terminación *f* termination
terminal *adj* terminal ‖ *m* (elec) terminal
terminante *adj* final, definitive, peremptory
terminar *tr* to end, terminate; finish ‖ *intr* to end, terminate
término *m* end, limit; boundary; bearing, manner; term; **medio término** subterfuge, evasion; compromise; **primer término** foreground; (mov) close-up; **segundo término** middle distance; **término medio** average; **último término** background
termistor *m* (elec) thermistor
termite *m* termite
termoaislante *adj* heaᵗ-insulated
termodinámi•co -ca *adj* thermodynamic ‖ *f* thermodynamics
termómetro *m* thermometer; **termómetro clínico** clinical thermometer
termonuclear *adj* thermonuclear
termopar *m* (elec) thermocouple
Termópilas, las Thermopylae
ter•mos *m* (*pl* **-mos**) thermos bottle; hot-water heater; **termos de acumulación** (elec) off-peak heater
termosifón *m* hot-water boiler
termóstato *m* thermostat
terna *f* trio
terne•jo -ja *adj* (Ecuad, Peru) peppy, energetic
ternera *f* calf; (*carne*) veal
terneza *f* tenderness; fondness; love; **ternezas** flirting, flirtation
ternilla *f* gristle
terno *m* suit of clothes; oath, curse; trio; piece of luck; (Col) cup and saucer; (W-I) set of jewelry
ternura *f* tenderness; fondness, love
terquedad *f* stubbornness; hardness, resistance
terraja *f* diestock
terral *adj* (*viento*) land ‖ *m* land breeze
Terranova *m* (*perro*) Newfoundland (*dog*) ‖ *f* (*isla y provincia*) Newfoundland (*island and province*)
terraplén *m* fill; embankment; terrace, platform; earthwork, rampart
terrateniente *mf* landholder, landowner
terraza *f* terrace; veranda; flat roof; (*de jardín*) border; edge; sidewalk cafe; glazed jar with two handles
terremoto *m* earthquake
terrenal *adj* earthly, mundane, worldly
terre•no -na *adj* terrestrial; mundane, worldly ‖ *m* land, ground, terrain; lot, plot; (sport) field; (fig) field, sphere; **sobre el terreno** on the spot; with data in hand; **terreno echadizo** refuse dump
terre•ro -ra *adj* earthly; of earth; humble ‖ *m* pile, heap; mark, target; terrace; public square; (min) dump
terrestre *adj* terrestrial; ground, land

terrible *adj* terrible; gruff, surly, ill-tempered
territorio *m* territory
terromontero *m* hill, butte
terrón *m* clod; lump, cake
terror *m* terror
terrorismo *m* terrorism, frightfulness
terrorista *adj* & *mf* terrorist
terro•so -sa *adj* earthly, dirty
terruño *m* piece of ground; soil; country, native soil
ter•so -sa *adj* smooth, glossy, polished; smooth, limpid, flowing
tertulia *f* party, social gathering; literary gathering; game room; **estar de tertulia** to sit around and talk
tertulia•no -na *mf* party-goer; regular member
Tesalia, la Thessaly
te•sis *f* (*pl* **-sis**) thesis
te•so -sa *adj* taut, tight, tense ‖ *m* top of hill; (*en superficie lisa*) rough spot
tesón *m* grit, pluck, tenacity
tesone•ro -ra *adj* obstinate, stubborn, tenacious
tesorería *f* treasury
tesore•ro -ra *mf* treasurer
tesoro *m* treasure; treasury; treasure house; thesaurus
Tespis *m* Thespis
testa *f* head; front; head, brains; **testa coronada** crowned head
testaferro *m* dummy, figurehead, straw man
testamento *m* testament, will; **Antiguo Testamento** Old Testament; **Nuevo Testamento** New Testament; **Viejo Testamento** Old Testament
testar *tr* (Ecuad) to cross out ‖ *intr* to make a will
testaru•do -da *adj* stubborn, pig-headed
testera *f* front; (*de animal*) forehead; (*de coche*) back seat
testículo *m* testicle
testificar §73 *tr* & *intr* to testify
testigo *mf* witness; **testigo de vista, testigo ocular,** or **testigo presencial** eyewitness ‖ *m* (*evidencia*) witness; (*en un experimento*) control
testimoniar *tr* to attest, testify to, bear witness to
testimonio *m* testimony; affidavit; false witness
tes•tuz *m* (*pl* **-tuces**) (*p.ej., de caballo*) face; nape
teta *f* teat; breast
tetera *f* teapot; teakettle
tetilla *f* nipple
tétri•co -ca *adj* dark gloomy; sad, sullen, gloomy
textil *adj* & *m* textile
texto *m* text; **fuera de texto** tipped-in
textura *f* texture
tez *f* complexion
ti *pron pers* thee; you
tía *f* aunt; old lady, old woman; bawd; **no hay tu tía** there's no chance; **tía abuela** grandaunt
tiara *f* tiara

tibante adj (Col) haughty, proud
tibia f shinbone; pipe, flute
ti•bio -bia adj tepid, lukewarm; (SAm) angry ‖ f see **tibia**
tibor m large porcelain vase; chamber pot
tiburón m shark
Ticiano, El Titian
tictac m tick-tock
tiempo m time; weather; (gram) tense; (de un motor de combustión interna) cycle; (de una sinfonía) (mus) movement; (mus) tempo; **darse buen tiempo** to have a good time; **de cuatro tiempos** (mach) four-cycle; **de dos tiempos** (mach) two-cycle; **de un tiempo a esta parte** for some time now; **el Tiempo** Father Time; **fuera de tiempo** untimely, at the wrong time; **hacer buen tiempo** to be clear; **mucho tiempo** a long time; **tomarse tiempo** to bide one's time
tienda f store, shop; tent; **ir de tiendas** to go shopping; **tienda de campaña** army tent; camping tent; **tienda de modas** ladies' dress shop; **tienda de objetos de regalo** gift shop; **tienda de raya** (Mex) company store
tienta f cleverness; probe; (taur) testing the mettle of a young bull; **andar a tientas** to grope in the dark; feel one's way
tiento m touch; blind man's stick; ropewalker's pole; steady hand; care, caution; mahlstick; blow, hit; swig; **andarse con tiento** to watch one's step; **perder el tiento** to lose one's touch
tier•no -na adj tender; loving; tearful; soft
tierra f earth; ground; land; dirt; (elec) ground; **dar en tierra con** to upset, overthrow, ruin; **echar tierra a** to hush up; **en tierra, mar y aire** on land, on sea, and in the air; **irse a tierra** to topple, to collapse; **la tierra de nadie** (mil) no man's island; **tierra adentro** inland; **tierra de pan llevar** wheat land, cereal-growing land; **tierra firme** mainland; land, terra firma; **Tierra Firme** Spanish Main; **Tierra Santa** Holy Land; **tierra y escombros** landfill; **tomar tierra** to land; to fine one's way around; **venir** or **venirse a tierra** to topple, to collapse; **ver tierras** to see the world, to go traveling
tierral m cloud of dust
tie•so -sa adj stiff; tight, taut, tense; stubborn; bold, enterprising; strong, well; stiff, stuck-up; **tenérselas tiesas a** or **con** to stand up to ‖ **tieso** adv hard
ties•to -ta adj stiff; tight, taut, tense; stubborn ‖ m flowerpot; (pedazo roto) postherd ‖ **tiesto** adv hard
tiesura f stiffness
ti•fo -fa adj full, satiated ‖ m typhus; **tifo de América** yellow fever; **tifo de Oriente** bubonic plague
tifón m waterspout; typhoon
tigra f tigress; (female) jaguar
tigre m tiger; (male) jaguar
tijera f scissors, shears; sawbuck; **buena tijera** good cutter; good eater; gossip; **tijeras** scissors, shears

tijeretear tr to snip, clip, cut; meddle with ‖ intr to gossip
tila f linden tree; linden-blossom tea
tildar tr to put a tilde or dash over; erase, strike out; **tildar de** to brand as
tilde m & f tilde; accent mark; superior dash; blemish, flaw; censure ‖ f jot, tittle
tiliche m (CAm, Mex) trinket
tiliche•ro -ra mf (CAm) peddler
tilín m ting-a-ling
tilo m linden tree; linden-blossom tea
tilo•so -sa adj (CAm) dirty, filthy
timar tr to snitch; swindle ‖ ref to make eyes at each other
timba f game of chance; gambling den; (CAm, Mex) belly
timbal m kettledrum; (pastel relleno) casserole
timbrar tr to stamp
timbre m stamp, seal; tax stamp; stamp tax; deed of glory; (phonet & phys) timbre; **timbre nasal** twang; **timbres** glockenspiel
tími•do -da adj timid, bashful
timo m theft, swindle; lie; catch phrase
timón m (del arado) beam; rudder; (fig) helm; **timón de dirección** (aer) vertical rudder; **timón de profundidad** (aer) elevator
timonel m helmsman, steersman
timonera f (naut) pilot house, wheelhouse
timora•to -ta adj God-fearing; chickenhearted
tímpano m eardrum; kettledrum
tina f large earthen jar; wooden vat; bathtub
tinaja f large earthen jar
tincazo m (Arg, Ecuad) fillip
tinglado m shed; intrigue, trick; (zool) leatherback
tinieblas fpl darkness
tino m feel (for things); good aim; knack; insight, wisdom; **coger el tino** to get the knack of it
tinta f ink; tint, hue; dyeing; **de buena tinta** on good authority; **tinta china** India ink; **tinta simpática** invisible ink
tinte m dye; dyeing; dyer's shop; (fig) coloring, false appearance
tinterillo m clerk, lawyer's clerk; pettifogger
tintero m inkstand, inkwell
tintín m clink; jingle
tintinear intr to clink; jingle
tin•to -ta adj red ‖ m red table wine ‖ f see **tinta**
tintorería f dyeing; dyeing establishment; dry-cleaning establishment
tintore•ro -ra mf dyer; dry cleaner
tintura f dye; dyeing; rouge; tincture; (fig) smattering; **tintura de tornasol** litmus, litmus solution; **tintura de yodo** iodine
tiña f ringworm; stinginess
tiño•so -sa adj scabby, mangy; stingy
tío m uncle; old man; guy, fellow; **tío abuelo** granduncle; **tíos** uncle and aunt
tiovivo m merry-go-round, carrousel
tipiadora f (máquina) typewriter; (mujer) typist
tipiar tr & intr to type, typewrite

tipicista *adj* regional, local

típi•co -ca *adj* typical; regional; quaint

tipismo *m* quaintness

tipista *mf* typist, typewriter

tiple *mf* soprano (*person*); treble-guitar player ‖ *m* soprano (*voice*); treble guitar

tipo *m* type; (*de descuento, de interés, de cambio*) rate; shape, figure, build; fellow, guy, specimen; **tener buen tipo** to have a good figure; **tipo de ensayo** or **prueba** eye-test chart; **tipo de impuesto** tax rate; **tipo de letra** typeface; **tipo menudo** small print

tipografía *f* typography

típula *f* (ent) daddy-longlegs

tira *m* (Arg, Chile, Col) detective ‖ *f* strip; **hecho tiras** (Chile) in rags; **tira emplástica** (Arg) court plaster; **tira proyectable** film strip; **tiras cómicas** comics, funnies

tirabala *f* popgun

tirabuzón *m* corkscrew; corkscrew curl

tirada *f* throw; distance, stretch; time, period; printing; edition, issue; shooting party; hunting party; tirade; **de** or **en una tirada** at one stroke; **tirada aparte** reprint

tira•do -da *adj* dirt-cheap; (*letra*) cursive ‖ *f* see **tirada**

tira•dor -dora *mf* shot, good shot ‖ *m* knob; doorknob; pull chain; **tirador certero** sharpshooter; **tirador emboscado** sniper

tirafondo *m* wood screw

tiraje *m* draft; printing, edition

tiramira *f* long, narrow mountain range; (*de personas o cosas*) string; distance, stretch

tiranía *f* tyranny

tiráni•co -ca *adj* tyrannic(al)

tira•no -na *adj* tyrannous ‖ *mf* tyrant

tirante *adj* tense, taut, tight; (fig) tense, strained ‖ *m* (*de los arreos de una caballería*) trace; **tirantes** suspenders

tirantez *f* tenseness, tautness, tightness; strain

tirar *tr* to throw, cast, fling; throw away; shoot, fire; (*alambre*) draw, pull, stretch; (*una línea*) draw; (*una coz, un pellizco*) give; print; attract; tear down, knock down; (phot) to print ‖ *intr* to pull; last; appeal, have an appeal; (*una chimenea*) draw; (*a la derecha, a la izquierda*) bear, turn; **ir tirando** to get along; **tirar a** to shoot at; (*la espada*) handle; shade into; tend to; aspire to; **tirar de** to pull, pull on; (*una espada*) draw; attract; boast of being; **tira y afloja** give and take; hot and cold ‖ *ref* to rush, throw oneself; give oneself over; lie down; serve time (in prison)

tirilla *f* neckband; **tirilla de bota** bootstrap; **tirilla de camisa** collarband

tiritar *intr* to shiver

tiro *m* throw; shot; charge, load; (*estampido*) report; rifle range; (*p.ej., de chimenea*) draft; (*de caballos*) team; (*de escalera*) flight; (*de las guarniciones*) trace; (*de un paño*) length; pull cord, pull chain; reach; hurt, damage; trick; theft; (min) shaft; (sport) drive, shot; (*alusión desfavorable*) shot; (fig) shot, marksman; **a tiro de fusil** within gunshot; **a tiro de piedra** within a

stone's throw; **matar a tiros** to shoot to death; **ni a tiros** not for love nor money; **poner el tiro muy alto** to hitch one's wagon to a star; **tiro al blanco** target practice; **tiro al vuelo** trapshooting; **tiro de la pesa** (sport) shot-put

tirón *m* tyro, novice; jerk; tug, pull; **de un tirón** all at once; at a stretch

tirotear *tr* to snipe at, blaze away at ‖ *ref* to fire at each other; bicker

tirria *f* dislike, grudge; **tener tirria a** to have it in for

tisana *f* tea, infusion

tísi•co -ca *adj* tubercular ‖ *mf* tubercular person, tubercular

tisis *f* consumption, tuberculosis

titanio *m* titanium

tít. *abbr* **título**

títere *m* marionette, puppet; fixed idea; whipper-snapper, nincompoop; **no dejar títere con cabeza** or **cara** to upset the applecart; **títeres** puppet show

titilar *tr* to titillate ‖ *intr* to flutter, quiver; twinkle

titubear *intr* to stagger, totter; stammer, stutter; waver, hesitate

titular *m* bearer, holder; incumbent; headline ‖ *f* capital letter ‖ *tr* to title, entitle ‖ *intr* to receive a title ‖ *ref* to be called; call oneself

titulillo *m* running head

título *m* title; titled person; regulation; bond; certificate; degree; diploma; headline; **a título de** as a, by way of, on the score of; **títulos** credentials

tiza *f* chalk

tiznar *tr* to soil with soot; spot, stain; to defame ‖ *ref* to become soiled; get spotted or stained; (Arg, Chile, CAm) to get drunk

tizne *m* & *f* soot ‖ *m* firebrand

tiznón *m* smudge, spot of soot

tizón *m* brand, firebrand; wheat smut; brand, dishonor

tizonear *intr* to stir up the fire

tlapalería *f* (Mex) paint store

toalla *f* towel; **toalla rusa** Turkish towel; **toalla sin fin** roller towel

toallero *m* towel rack

toar *tr* (naut) to tow

tobar *tr* (Col) to tow

tobillera *f* anklet; (sport) ankle support; (coll) subdeb; (coll) flapper

tobillo *m* ankle

tobo *m* (Ven) bucket

tobogán *m* toboggan; chute, slide

toca *f* toque; headdress

tocadis•cos *m* (*pl* -cos) record player; **toca-discos automático** record changer

toca•do -da *adj* (*echado a perder; medio loco*) touched; **tocado de la cabeza** touched in the head ‖ *m* hairdo, coiffure; headdress

toca•dor -dora *mf* performer; player ‖ *m* boudoir; dressing table; dressing case, toilet case

tocante *adj* touching; **tocante a** concerning, with reference to

tocar §73 *tr* to touch; touch on; feel; ring; toll; strike; come to know, suffer, feel; (*el cabello*) do; (*un tambor*) beat; (mus) to play; (paint) to touch up ‖ *intr* to touch; **tocar a** to knock at; pertain to, concern; fall to the lot of; be the turn of; (*el fin*) approach; **tocar en** (*un puerto*) to touch at; (*tierra*) touch; touch on; approach, border on ‖ *ref* to put one's hat on, cover one's head; touch each other; be related; make one's toilet; become mentally unbalanced; (*el sombrero*) tip; **tocárselas** to beat it

toca•yo -ya *mf* namesake

tocino *m* bacon; salt pork

tocón *m* stump

tocuyo *m* (SAm) coarse cotton cloth

tochimbo *m* (Peru) smelting furnace

to•cho -cha *adj* rough, coarse, crude

todavía *adv* still, yet; **todavía no** not yet

to•do -da *adj* all, whole, every; any ‖ *m* whole; everything; **con todo** still, however; **del todo** wholly, entirely; **jugar el todo por el todo** to stake everything, shoot the works; **sobre todo** above all, especially; **todo el que** everybody who; **todo lo que** all that; **todos** all, everybody; **todos cuantos** all those who

todopodero•so -sa *adj* all-powerful, almighty

toga *f* (academic) gown

toldilla *f* poop, poop deck

toldería *f* (SAm) Indian camp, Indian village

toldo *m* awning; pride, haughtiness; (SAm) Indian hut

tole *m* hubbub, uproar; **tole tole** gossip, talk; **tomar el tole** to run away

tolerancia *f* tolerance; **por tolerancia** on sufferance

tolerar *tr* to tolerate

tolete *m* club, cudgel; raft; (Cuba) dunce

toletole *m* (Col) persistence, obstinacy; (Ven) merry life of a wanderer

tolon•dro -dra *adj* scatterbrained ‖ *mf* scatterbrain ‖ *m* bump, lump

tolva *f* hopper; chute

tolvanera *f* dust storm

tolla *f* quagmire; (Cuba) watering trough

tom. *abbr* **tomo**

toma *f* taking; seizure, capture; tap; intake; inlet; (elec) tap, outlet; (elec) plug; (elec) terminal; (*de rapé*) pinch; **toma de posesión** installation, induction; inauguration; **toma de tierra** (aer) landing; (rad) ground connection; **toma directa** high gear

toma-corrien•te *m* or **toma-corrien•tes** *m* (*pl* **-tes**) (elec) current collector; (elec) tap, outlet; (elec) plug

tomadero *m* handle; intake, inlet

toma•dor -dora *mf* (com) drawee; thief; drinker, toper

tomar *tr* to take; get; seize; take on; (*un resfriado*) catch; (*p.ej., el desayuno*) have, eat; (*el café, un trago*) take, drink; **tomar a bien** to take in the right spirit; **tomar a mal** to take offense at; **tomarla con** to pick a quarrel with; have a grudge against; **tomar prestado** to borrow; **tomar sobre sí** to take upon oneself ‖ *intr* to take, turn ‖

ref to take; (*p.ej., el desayuno*) have, eat; (*el café*) take, drink; get rusty

tomate *m* tomato; (*en medias, calcetines, etc.*) tear, run

tomavis•tas *m* (*pl* **-tas**) movie camera; cameraman

tómbola *f* raffle, charity raffle

tomillo *m* thyme

tomo *m* volume; bulk, importance, consequence; **de tomo y lomo** of consequence; bulky and heavy

ton. *abbr* **tonelada**

ton *m* — **sin ton ni son** without rhyme or reason

tonada *f* air, melody, song; singsong; (Cuba) hoax; (*pronunciación particular*) (Arg, Chile) accent

tonel *m* cask, barrel

tonelada *f* (*unidad de peso; unidad de volumen; unidad de desplazamiento*) ton; (*medida de capacidad para el vino*) tun

tonelaje *m* tonnage

tonele•ro -ra *mf* barrelmaker, cooper

tonga *f* coat, layer; (Arg, Col) task; (Col) sleep; (Cuba) heap, pile

tongonear *ref* to strut, swagger

tóni•co -ca *adj* & *m* tonic ‖ *f* (mus) keynote

tonillo *m* singsong; (*pronunciación particular*) accent

tono *m* tone; tune; (mus) pitch; (mus) key; (*de un instrumento de bronce*) (mus) slide; **dar el tono** to set the standard; **darse tono** to put on airs; **de buen tono** stylish, elegant; **estar a tono** to be in style; **poner a tono** (*un motor de automóvil*) to tune up; **tono mayor** (mus) major key; **tono menor** (mus) minor key

tonsila *f* tonsil

tonsilitis *f* tonsilitis

tonsurar *tr* to shear, clip

tontear *intr* to talk nonsense, act foolishly

tontería *f* foolishness, nonsense

ton•to -ta *adj* foolish, stupid, silly; **a tontas y a locas** wildly, recklessly; in disorder, haphazardly ‖ *mf* fool, dolt; **tonto de capirote** blatant fool

tonu•do -da *adj* (Arg) magnificent, showy, conceited

topacio *m* topaz

topar *tr* to butt; bump; run into, encounter ‖ *intr* to butt; succeed; lie, be found; **topar con** or **en** to run into, encounter

tope *adj* (*precio*) top; (*fecha*) last ‖ *m* butt; bumper; bump, collision; rub, difficulty; scuffle; masthead; **al tope** or **a tope** end to end; flush; **estar hasta el tope** or **los topes** to be loaded to the gunwales; be fed up; **tope de puerta** doorstop

topera *f* molehill

topetada *f* butt

topetar *tr* to butt ‖ *intr* to butt; **topetar con** to bump, bump into; to run across

topetón *m* butt; bump, collision

tópi•co -ca *adj* local ‖ *m* topic; (med) external application

topinera *f* molehill; **beber como una topinera** to drink like a fish

topo *m* mole; blunderer; stumbler, awkward person
topografía *f* topography
toque *m* touch; (*de una campana*) ringing; (*del tambor*) beat; sound; knock; stroke; check, test; (*punto esencial*) gist; (paint) touch; (coll) blow; **dar un toque a** to put to the test; feel out, sound out; **toque a muerto** knell, toll; **toque de diana** reveille; **toque de queda** curfew; **toque de retreta** (mil) tattoo; **toque de tambor** drumbeat
torada *f* drove of bulls
tó•rax *m* (*pl* **-rax**) thorax
torbellino *m* whirlwind; (*persona bulliciosa*) harum-scarum
torcecuello *m* (orn) wryneck
torcedura *f* twist; sprain; dislocation
torcer §74 *tr* to twist; bend; turn; sprain; (*la cara*) screw up; (*el tobillo*) wrench; turn; (*interpretar mal*) distort, misconstrue ‖ *intr* to turn ‖ *ref* to twist; bend; sprain, dislocate; turn sour; go crooked; fail
torci•do -da *adj* twisted; crooked; bent; (*ojos*) cross; (*persona o conducta*) crooked; (Guat) unlucky ‖ *f* wick, lampwick; curl-paper
tor•do -da *adj* dapple-gray ‖ *mf* dapple-gray horse ‖ *m* thrush; starling
torear *tr* (*toros*) to fight; banter, tease, string along ‖ *intr* to fight bulls, be a bullfighter
toreo *m* bullfighting; (taur) performance
tore•ro -ra *adj* bullfighting ‖ *mf* bullfighter
toril *m* (taur) bull pen
tormenta *f* storm; adversity, misfortune
tormento *m* torment, torture; anguish
tormento•so -sa *adj* stormy; (*barco*) storm-ridden
torna *f* return; dam; tap; **se han vuelto las tornas** the luck has changed; **volver las tornas** to give tit for tat
tornar *tr* to return, give back; turn, make ‖ *intr* to return; turn; **tornar a** + *inf* verb + again, e.g., **tornó a abrir la puerta** he opened the door again ‖ *ref* to turn, become
tornasol *m* sunflower; litmus; iridescence
tornasola•do -da *adj* changeable, iridescent
tornavía *m* (rr) turntable
torna•voz *m* (*pl* **-voces**) sounding board; **hacer tornavoz** to cup one's hands to one's mouth
tornear *tr* to turn, turn up ‖ *intr* to go around; tourney; muse, meditate
torneo *m* tourney; match, tournament; **torneo radiofónico** quiz program
tornillo *m* (*cilindro que entra en la tuerca*) screw; (*clavo con resalto helicoidal*) bolt; (*instrumento con dos mandíbulas*) vise; (mil) desertion; (CAm, Ven) screw tree; **apretar los tornillos a** to put the screws on; **tener flojos los tornillos** to have a screw loose; **tornillo de mariposa** or **de orejas** thumbscrew; **tornillo de presión** setscrew; **tornillo para metales** machine screw
torniquete *m* (*para contener hemorragias*)

tourniquet; (*torno para cerrar un paso*) turnstile; **dar torniquete a** to twist the meaning of
torno *m* turn, revolution; (*máquina simple que consiste en un cilindro que gira sobre su eje*) winch, windlass; (*de alfarero*) potter's wheel; (*instrumento con dos mandíbulas*) vise; (*máquina herramienta que sirve para labrar metal o madera*) lathe; (*de coche*) brake; (*de un río*) bend, turn; revolving server; **en torno a** or **de** around; **torno de alfarero** potter's wheel; **torno de banco** bench vise; **torno de hilar** spinning wheel
toro *m* bull; **toro corrido** smart fellow; **toros** bullfight
torón *m* strand
toronja *f* grapefruit
toronjo *m* grapefruit (*tree*)
torpe *adj* slow, heavy; clumsy, awkward; stupid; lewd; crude, ugly
torpedear *tr* to torpedo
torpedo *m* torpedo; touring car
torpeza *f* torpidity, slowness; clumsiness, awkwardness; stupidity; lewdness; turpitude; crudeness, ugliness
torrar *tr* to toast
torre *f* tower; watchtower; (*en el ajedrez*) castle, rook; **torre del homenaje** donjon, keep; **torre de lanzamiento** launching tower; **torre de marfil** (fig) ivory tower; **torre de vigía** (naut) crow's-nest; **torre maestra** donjon, keep; **torre reloj** clock tower
torreja *f* (dial, Am) French toast
torrentada *f* flash flood
torrente *m* torrent
torreón *m* (archit) turret
torreta *f* (nav) turret
tórri•do -da *adj* torrid
torrija *f* French toast
torta *f* cake; (typ) font; slap; **ser tortas y pan pintado** to be a cinch; **torta a la plancha** hot cake, griddle cake
torticolis *m* or **tortícolis** *m* wryneck, stiff neck
tortilla *f* omelet; (CAm, Mex) tortilla (*cornmeal cake*); **tortilla a la española** potato omelet; **tortilla a la francesa** plain omelet; **tortilla de tomate** Spanish omelet
tórtola *f* turtledove
tortuga *f* tortoise, turtle
tortuo•so -sa *adj* winding; (fig) devious
tortura *f* torture
torturar *tr* to torture
tor•vo -va *adj* grim, stern
tos *f* cough; **tos ferina** whooping cough
tosca•no -na *adj* Tuscan ‖ **la Toscana** Tuscany
tos•co -ca *adj* coarse, rough; uncouth
toser *intr* to cough
tósigo *m* poison; sorrow
tosiguero *m* poison ivy
tosquedad *f* coarseness, roughness; uncouthness

tostada *f* piece of toast; toast; **dar** or **pegar la tostada** or **una tostada a** to cheat, trick; **tostadas** toast

tosta•do -da *adj* brown; tan, sunburned ‖ *m* toasting; roasting ‖ *f* see **tostada**

tostador *m* toaster, roaster

tostar §61 *tr & ref* to toast; roast; tan, burn

tostón *m* roasted chickpea; toast dipped in olive oil; roast pig; scorched food

total *adj & m* total ‖ *adv* in a word

totalidad *f* totality; entirety; **en su totalidad** in its entirety

tóxi•co -ca *adj & m* toxic

toxicomanía *f* drug addiction

toxicóma•no -na *adj* drug-addicted ‖ *mf* drug addict

tozu•do -da *adj* stubborn

tpo. *abbr* **tiempo**

traba *f* bond, tie; clasp, lock; hobble, clog; obstacle, hindrance

traba•do -da *adj* tied, fastened; joined, connected; robust, sinewy; (*sílaba*) checked; tongue-tied; (*ojos*) (Col) cross

trabaja•do -da *adj* overworked, worn-out; strained, forced, labored; busy

trabaja•dor -dora *adj* working; industrious, hard-working ‖ *mf* worker, toiler ‖ *m* workman, workingman ‖ *f* workingwoman

trabajar *tr* to work; till; bother, disturb; (*a una persona*) work, drive ‖ *intr* to work; strain; warp; **trabajar en** or **por** to strive to ‖ *ref* to strive, exert oneself

trabajo *m* work; trouble; (*en contraposición de capital*) labor; **costar trabajo** + *inf* to be hard to + *inf;* **trabajo a destajo** piecework; **trabajo a domicilio** homework; **trabajo a jornal** timework; **trabajo de menores** child labor; **trabajo de oficina** clerical work; **trabajo de taller** shopwork; **trabajos** hardships, tribulations; **trabajos forzados** or **forzosos** hard labor, penal labor

trabajo•so -sa *adj* arduous, laborious; (*magr•anto*) wan, languid; (*falto de espontaneidad*) labored; unpleasant, annoying

trabalen•guas *m* (*pl* -guas) tongue twister, jawbreaker

trabar *tr* to join, unite; catch, seize; fasten; fetter; lock; begin; (*una batalla*) join; (*una conversación, amistad*) strike up ‖ *intr* to take hold ‖ *ref* to become entangled; jam; to foul; **trabársele a uno la lengua** to become tongue-tied

trabe *f* beam

trabilla *f* gaiter strap; belt loop; end stitch, loose stitch

trabuco *m* blunderbuss; popgun

trac *m* stage fright

tracale•ro -ra *adj* (CAm, Mex, W-I) cheating, tricky ‖ *mf* (CAm, Mex, W-I) cheat, trickster

tracción *f* traction; **tracción delantera** front drive; **tracción trasera** rear drive

tractor *m* tractor; **tractor de oruga** caterpillar tractor

tradición *f* tradition

tradicionista *mf* folklorist

traducción *f* translation; **traducción automática** machine translation

traducir §19 *tr* to translate; change

traduc•tor -tora *mf* translator

traer §75 *tr* to bring; bring on; draw, pull; make, keep; wear; have, carry; **traer a mal traer** to abuse, mistreat ‖ *intr* — **traer y llevar** to gossip ‖ *ref* to dress; behave; **traérselas** to get worse and worse, cause a lot of trouble

tráfago *m* traffic, trade; toil, drudgery

trafa•gón -gona *adj* hustling, lively; slick, tricky ‖ *mf* hustler, live wire

traficante *mf* dealer, merchant

traficar §73 *intr* to deal, trade, traffic; travel about

tráfico *m* trade; traffic

tragaderas *fpl* gullibility; tolerance; **tener buenas tragaderas** to be too gullible

tragalda•bas *mf* (*pl* -bas) glutton; easy mark

tragale•guas *mf* (*pl* -guas) (coll) great walker

traga•luz *m* (*pl* -luces) skylight, bull's-eye; cellar window

tragamone•das *m* (*pl* -das) or **tragape•rras** *m* (*pl-* -rras) slot machine

tragar §44 *tr* to swallow; swallow up; gulp down; (*creer fácilmente*) swallow; overlook; **no poder tragar** to not be able to stomach ‖ *intr & ref* to swallow

tragasable *m* sword swallower

tragavenado *f* (SAm) anaconda

tragaviro•tes *m* (*pl* -tes) stuffed shirt

tragedia *f* tragedy

trági•co -ca *adj* tragic(al) ‖ *m* tragedian

trago *m* swallow; swig; misfortune; **a tragos** slowly

tra•gón -gona *adj* gluttonous ‖ *mf* glutton

traición *f* treachery, betrayal; (*delito contra la patria*) treason; treacherous act; **alta traición** high treason; **a traición** treacherously; **hacer traición a** to betray

traicionar *tr* to betray

traicione•ro -ra *adj* treacherous; treasonable ‖ *mf* traitor

traída *f* conveyance, transfer; (Guat) sweetheart; **traída de aguas** water supply

traí•do -da *adj* worn, threadbare ‖ *f* see **traída**

trai•dor -dora *adj* treacherous; treasonable ‖ *mf* traitor; betrayer ‖ *m* villain ‖ *f* traitoress

traílla *f* leash; road scraper

traje *m* suit; clothes; dress; gown; **cortar un traje a** to gossip about; **traje a la medida** suit made to order; **traje de baño** bathing suit; **traje de calle** street clothes; **traje de ceremonia** or **de etiqueta** dress suit; full dress; evening clothes; **traje de faena** (mil) fatigue clothes; **traje de luces** bullfighter's costume; **traje de malla** tights; **traje de montar** riding habit; **traje de paisano** civilian clothes; **traje hecho** ready-made suit; **traje sastre** lady's tailor-made suit; **traje serio** formal dress; **vestir su primer traje largo** to come out, make one's debut

trajear *tr* to dress, clothe

trajín *m* carrying, transfer, conveyance; going and coming; bustle, commotion

trajinar *tr* to carry, convey; (Arg, Chile) to poke into; (Arg, Chile) to deceive; (Pan) to annoy ‖ *intr* to bustle around

tralla *f* lash, whiplash, whipcord

trama *f* weft, woof; plot, scheme, machination; (*de un drama o novela*) plot

tramar *tr* to weave; plot, scheme; (*un enredo*) hatch (*a plot*)

trambucar §73 *intr* (Col, Ven) to be shipwrecked; (Col, Ven) to go out of one's mind

tramitación *f* transaction, negotiation; procedure, steps; **tramitación automática de datos** data processing

tramitar *tr* to transact, negotiate

trámite *m* step, procedure; proceeding; transaction

tramo *m* tract; stretch; (*de una escalera*) flight; (*de un puente*) span; (*de un canal entre dos esclusas*) level

tramontana *f* north; north wind; pride, haughtiness

tramoya *f* stage machinery; scheme

tramoyista *adj* scheming, tricky ‖ *mf* schemer, impostor ‖ *m* stagehand

trampa *f* trap; trap door; (*de un mostrador*) flap; (*de los pantalones*) fly; **armar una trampa a** to lay a trap for; **trampa explosiva** (mil) booby trap

trampear *tr* to trick, swindle ‖ *intr* to cheat; manage to get along

trampilla *f* peephole in the floor; (*de los pantalones*) fly; (*de un secreter*) top, lid; (*de una mesa*) leaf, hinged leaf

trampolín *m* diving board; springboard; ski jump

trampo•so -sa *adj* tricky, crooked ‖ *mf* cheat, swindler

tranca *f* beam, pole; crossbar; (Arg, Chile) drunk, spree; (P-R) dollar; **a trancas y barrancas** through fire and water

trancar §73 *tr* to bar ‖ *intr* to stride along

trance *m* crisis; peril; trance; **a todo trance** at any cost; **último trance** (*de la vida*) last stage, end

tranco *m* long stride; threshold

tranquera *f* palisade, fence

tranquilidad *f* tranquillity

tranquilizante *m* tranquilizer

tranquilizar §60 *tr, intr & ref* to tranquilize, calm down

tranqui•lo -la *adj* tranquil, calm

tranquilla *f* feeler

tranquillo *m* knack

transacción *f* settlement, compromise; transaction

transaéreo *m* airliner

transar *tr* to settle ‖ *intr* to yield, give in, compromise

transatlánti•co -ca *adj & m* transatlantic

transbordador *m* ferry; **transbordador espacial** space shuttle

transbordar *tr* to transship; transfer ‖ *intr* to transfer, change trains

transbordo *m* transshipment; transfer

transcribir §83 *tr* to transcribe

transcripción *f* transcription

transcurrir *intr* to pass, elapse

transcurso *m* course (*of time*)

transepto *m* transept

transeúnte *adj* transient ‖ *mf* transient; passer-by

transferencia *f* transfer

transferir §68 *tr* to transfer; postpone

transformador *m* transformer

transformar *tr* to transform ‖ *ref* to transform, be transformed

tránsfuga *mf* turncoat; fugitive

transfusión *f* transfusion; **transfusión de sangre** transfusion, blood transfusion

transgredir §1 *tr* to transgress

transgresión *f* transgression

transi•do -da *adj* overcome, paralyzed; mean, cheap, stingy

transigencia *f* compromise; compromising

transigente *adj* compromising

transigir §27 *tr* to settle, compromise ‖ *intr* to settle, compromise; agree

transistor *m* transistor

transistorizar §60 *tr* transistorize

transitable *adj* passable, practicable

transitar *intr* to go, walk; to travel

transiti•vo -va *adj* transitive

tránsito *m* transit; traffic; stop; passage; transfer

transito•rio -ria *adj* transitory

translúci•do -da *adj* translucent

tránsmisión *f* transmission; **transmisión del pensamiento** thought transference

transmisor *m* transmitter; **transmisor de órdenes** (naut) engine-room telegraph

transmitir *tr & intr* to transmit

transmudar *tr* to transfer; persuade, convince

transmutar *tr, intr & ref* to transmute

transparecer §22 *intr* to show through

transparencia *f* transparency; slide

transparentar *ref* to show through

transparente *adj* transparent ‖ *m* curtain, window curtain; **transparente de resorte** window blind or shade

transpirar *intr* to transpire; (*dejarse conocer una cosa secreta*) transpire

transplantar *tr* to transplant

transponer §54 *tr* to transpose; disappear behind ‖ *ref* (*ocultarse detrás del horizonte*) to set; get sleepy

transportar *tr* to transport; (mus) to transpose

transporte *m* transport; transportation; (aer & naut) transport; **transporte colectivo** public transportation

transportista *mf* transport worker

transvesti•do -da *adj & mf* transvestite

tranvestismo *m* transvestism

tranvía *m* trolley, trolley car; streetcar; **tranvía de sangre** horsecar

tranzar §60 *tr* to cut off, rip off; plait, braid

trapacear *tr* to chear, swindle

trapacería *f* cheating, swindling

trapace•ro -ra *adj* cheating, swindling ‖ *mf* cheat, swindler

trapajo *m* rag, tatter

to

tr

trápala *adj* chattering; cheating ‖ *mf* chatterbox; cheat ‖ *m* loquacity ‖ *f* noise, uproar; (*del trote de un caballo*) clatter; cheating

trapear *tr* to mop

trapecio *m* (geom) trapezoid; (sport) trapeze

trapecista *mf* trapeze performer

trape•ro -ra *mf* ragpicker; junk dealer

trapiche *m* sugar mill; olive press; ore crusher

trapien•to -ta *adj* raggedy, in rags

trapío *m* flipness, pertness; (*del toro de lidia*) spirit

trapisonda *f* brawl, row; scheming

trapisondista *mf* schemer

trapo *m* rag; (naut) canvas, sails; bullfighter's bright-colored cape; (*de la muleta*) cloth; **a todo trapo** full sail; **poner como un trapo** to rake over the coals; **sacar los trapos a la colada, a relucir** or **al sol** to wash one's dirty linen in public; **soltar el trapo** to burst out crying, to burst out laughing; **trapos** rags, duds; **trapos de cristianar** Sunday best

trapo•so -sa *adj* raggedy, in rags

tráquea *f* trachea, windpipe

traquea•do -da *adj* (*sendero*) (Arg) beaten

traquear *tr* to shake, rattle; fool with ‖ *intr* to crackle; rattle, chatter

traqueo *m* shake, rattle, chatter

traquetear *tr* & *intr* to rattle, jerk

tras *prep* after; behind; **tras de** behind; in addition to

trasatlánti•co -ca *adj* & *m* var of **transatlántico**

trasbordador *m* var of **transbordador**

trasbordar *tr* & *intr* var of **trasbordar**

trasbordo *m* var of **transbordo**

trascendencia *f* penetration, keenness; importance

trascendente *adj* penetrating; important

trascender §51 *tr* to go into, dig up ‖ *intr* to smell; come to be known, leak out

trascendi•do -da *adj* keen, perspicacious

trascocina *f* scullery

trascorral *m* back yard; backside

trascribir §83 *tr* var of **transcribir**

trascripción *f* var of **transcripción**

trascuarto *m* back room

trascurrir *intr* var of **transcurrir**

trascurso *m* var of **transcurso**

trasegar §66 *tr* to upset, turn topsy-turvy; decant, draw off

trase•ro -ra *adj* back, rear ‖ *m* buttock, rump

trasferir §68 *tr* var of **transferir**

trasformador *m* var of **transformador**

trasformar *tr* & *intr* var of **transformar**

trásfuga *mf* var of **tránsfuga**

trasfusión *f* var of **transfusión**

trasgo *m* goblin, hobgoblin; imp

trashojar *tr* to leaf through

trashumante *adj* nomadic, migrating

trasiego *m* upset, disorder; decantation

trasladar *tr* to transfer; postpone; copy, transcribe; transmit; move ‖ *intr* to go; move

traslado *m* transfer; copy, transcript; moving

traslapar *tr, intr* & *ref* to overlap

traslapo *m* lap, overlap

traslúci•do -da *adj* var of **translúcido**

traslucir §45 *tr* to guess ‖ *intr* to leak out ‖ *ref* to be translucent; leak out

traslumbrar *tr* to dazzle ‖ *ref* to be dazzled; vanish

trasluz *m* diffused light; glint, gleam; **al trasluz** against the light

trasmisión *f* var of **transmisión**

trasmisor *m* var of **transmisor**

trasmitir *tr* & *intr* var of **transmitir**

trasmóvil *m* (Col) mobile unit, radio pickup

trasmudar *tr* var of **transmudar**

trasmundo *m* afterlife, future life

trasmutar *tr, intr* & *ref* var of **transmutar**

trasnocha•do -da *adj* stale; haggard, run-down; hackneyed ‖ *f* last night; sleepless night; (mil) night attack

trasnocha•dor -dora *mf* night owl

trasnochar *tr* (*un problema*) to sleep over ‖ *intr* to spend the night; spend a sleepless night; stay up late

trasoír §48 *tr* to hear wrong

traspapelar *tr* to mislay ‖ *ref* to become mislaid

trasparecer §22 *intr* var of **transparecer**

trasparencia *f* var of **transparencia**

trasparente *adj* & *m* var of **transparente**

traspasar *tr* to cross, cross over; send; transfer; move; pierce, transfix; pain, grieve ‖ *ref* to go too far

traspié *m* slip, stumble; trip

traspirar *intr* var of **transpirar**

trasplantar *tr* var of **transplantar**

trasponer §54 *tr* & *ref* var of **transponer**

trasportar *tr* var of **transportar**

trasporte *m* var of **transporte**

trasportista *mf* var of **transportista**

traspunte *m* (theat) callboy

traspuntín *m* flap seat, folding seat, jump seat

trasquilar *tr* to crop, lop; (*las ovejas*) shear; curtail

trastazo *m* whack, blow

traste *m* fret; **dar al traste con** to throw away, ruin, spoil

trastera *f* attic, junk room

trastienda *f* back room

trasto *m* piece of furniture; piece of junk; good-for-nothing; **trastos** tools, implements, utensils; arms, weapons; junk; muleta and sword

trastornar *tr* to upset; overturn; disturb; perplex; daze, make dizzy; persuade

trastorno *m* upset; disturbance

trastrocar §81 *tr* to turn around, reverse, change

trasudor *m* cold sweat

trasueño *m* blurred dream, vague recollection

trasuntar *tr* to copy; abstract, sum up

trasunto *m* copy; record; likeness

trasverter §51 *intr* to run over, overflow

trasvolar §61 *tr* to fly over

trata *f* traffic, trade, slave trade; **trata de blancas** white slavery; **trata de esclavos** slave trade

tratado *m* (*escrito, libro*) treatise; (*convenio entre gobiernos*) treaty; agreement

tratamiento *m* treatment; title; **apear el tratamiento** to leave off the title

tratante *mf* dealer, retailer

tratar *tr* to handle; deal with; treat; **tratar a uno de** to address someone as; charge someone with being ‖ *intr* to deal; treat; try; **tratar de** to deal with; treat of; come in contact with; try to ‖ *ref* to deal; behave; (*bien o mal*) live; **tratarse de** to deal with; be a question of

trate•ro -ra *mf* (Chile) pieceworker

trato *m* treatment; deal, agreement; manner; business; title; friendly relations; **tener buen trato** to be very nice, be very pleasant; **trato colectivo** collective bargaining; **trato doble** double-dealing; **¡trato hecho!** it's a deal!

través *m* bend, bias, turn; reverse, misfortune; (naut) beam; **al** or **a través de** through, across; **dar al través con** to do away with; **mirar de través** to squint; look at out of the corner of one's eye

travesaño *m* crosspiece; (*de cama*) bolster; (*p.ej., de una sila*) rung

travesear *intr* to romp, carry on; sparkle, be witty; lead a wild life

travesía *f* crossing, voyage; crossroad; distance, passage; cross wind; (Arg, Bol) wasteland; (Chile) west wind

travesura *f* prank, antic, caper; mischief; sparkle, wit; slick trick

traviesa *f* crossing, voyage; rafter; side bet; (rr) tie

travie•so -sa *adj* cross; keen, shrewd; restless, fidgety; naughty, mischievous; debauched ‖ *f* see **traviesa**

trayecto *m* journey, passage, course; stretch, run

trayectoria *f* trajectory; path

traza *f* plan, design; scheme; means; appearance; mark, trace; footprint; streak, trait; **tener trazas de** to show signs of; look like

trazar §60 *tr* to plan, design; outline; trace; (*una línea*) draw; lay out, plot

trazo *m* line, stroke; trace; outline

trebejo *m* implement; chessman

trébol *m* clover; (*naipe que corresponde al basto*) club

trece *adj & pron* thirteen ‖ *m* thirteen; (*en las fechas*) thirteenth; **estarse, mantenerse** or **seguir en sus trece** to stand firm

trecea•vo -va *adj & m* thirteenth

trecho *m* stretch; while; **a trechos** at intervals

tregua *f* truce; respite, letup

treinta *adj & pron* thirty ‖ *m* thirty; (*en las fechas*) thirtieth

treinta•vo -va *adj & m* thirtieth

tremar *intr* to tremble, shake

tremen•do -da *adj* frightful, terrible, tremendous; (*muy grande*) tremendous

trementina *f* turpentine

tremer *intr* to tremble, shake

tremolar *tr & intr* to wave

tren *m* (*de coches o vagones; de ondas*) train; outfit, equipment; following, retinue; show, pomp; (*de la vida*) way; **tren aerodinámico de lujo** (rr) streamliner; **tren**

ascendente (rr) up train; **tren correo** (rr) mail train; **tren de aterrizaje** (aer) landing gear; **tren de laminadores** rolling mill; **tren de lavado** laundry; **tren de mercancías** freight train; **tren de mudadas** moving company; **tren descendente** (rr) down train; **tren de viajeros** passenger train; **tren ómnibus** (rr) accomodation train; **tren rápido** (rr) flyer

treno *m* dirge

trenza *f* braid, plait; tress; (*p.ej., de ajos*) string; **en trenzas** with her hair down

trenzar §60 *tr* to braid, plait ‖ *intr* to caper; prance

trepa•dor -dora *adj* climbing ‖ *mf* climber ‖ *f* (bot) climber

trepar *tr* to climb; drill, bore ‖ *intr* to climb; **trepar por** to climb up ‖ *ref* to lean back

trepidar *intr* to shake, vibrate; (Chile) to hesitate, waver

tres *adj & pron* three; **las tres** three o'clock ‖ *m* three; (*en las fechas*) third

trescien•tos -tas *adj & pron* three hundred ‖ **trescientos** *m* three hundred

tresillo *m* ombre; three-piece living-room suite; (mus) triplet

tresnal *m* (agr) shock

treta *f* trick, scheme; (*del esgrimidor*) feint

treza•vo -va *adj & m* thirteenth

triángulo *m* triangle

triar §77 *tr* to sort

tribu *f* tribe

tribuna *f* tribune, rostrum, platform; grandstand; (*en la iglesia*) gallery; **tribuna de la prensa** press box; **tribuna del órgano** (mus) organ loft; **tribuna de los acusados** (law) dock

tribunal *m* tribunal, court; **tribunal de apelación** appellate court; **tribunal tutelar de menores** juvenile court

tributar *tr* (*contribuciones, impuestos, etc.*) to pay; (*admiración, gratitud, etc.*) render

tributario -ria *adj* tributary; tax; **ser tributario de** to be indebted to ‖ *m* tributary

tributo *m* tribute; tax

tricornio *m* tricorn, three-cornered hat

trifocal *adj* trifocal

trifulca *f* wrangle, squabble

trigési•mo -ma *adj & m* thirtieth

trigo *m* wheat; (slang) dough, money; **trigo entero** whole wheat; **trigo sarraceno** buckwheat

trigonometría *f* trigonometry

trigue•ño -ña *adj* swarthy, olive-skinned

trilogía *f* trilogy

trilla *f* threshing

trilla•do -da *adj* (*sendero*) beaten; trite, commonplace

trilladora *f* threshing machine

trillar *tr* to thresh; mistreat; frequent

trilli•zo -za *mf* triplet

trillón *m* British trillion; quintillion (*in U.S.A.*)

trimestral *adj* quarterly

trimestre *m* quarter

trinado *m* trill, warble

tr
tr

trinar *intr* to trill, warble, quaver; get angry
trinca *f* trinity
trincar §73 *tr* to bind, lash, tie fast; crush; (slang) to kill ‖ *intr* to take a drink
trinchar *tr* to carve, slice
trinchera *f* cut; trench; trench coat
trineo *m* sleigh, sled
Trinidad *f* Trinity
trino *m* trill
trinquete *m* pawl, ratchet; (naut) foresail
trin·quis *m* (*pl* -**quis**) drink, swig
trío *m* sorting; trio; (mus) trio
tripa *f* gut, intestine; belly; (*del cigarro*) filler; **hacer de tripas corazón** to pluck up courage
triple *adj & m* triple
triplica·do -da *adj & m* triplicate; **por triplicado** in triplicate
triplicar §73 *tr* to triplicate ‖ *intr* to treble
trípode *m* tripod
tríptico *m* triptych
tripu·do -da *adj* big-bellied, potbellied
tripulación *f* crew
tripulante *m* crew member
tripular *tr* to man; fit out, equip
trique *m* crack, swish; **a cada trique** at every turn; **triques** (Mex) tools, implements
triquiñuela *f* chicanery, subterfuge
triquitraque *m* clatter; firecracker
tris *m* crackle; shave, inch; trice
trisar *tr* (Chile) to crack, chip ‖ *intr* to chirp
triscar §73 *tr* to mix; (*una sierra*) set ‖ *intr* to stamp the feet; romp, frisk around; (Col) to gossip
trismo *m* lockjaw
triste *adj* sad; dismal, gloomy; (*despreciable, ridículo*) sorry
tristeza *f* sadness; gloominess
tris·tón -tona *adj* wistful, melancholy
tritón *m* eft, newt, triton; (*hombre experto en la natación*) merman
trituradora *f* crushing machine
triturar *tr* to grind, crush; abuse
triunfal *adj* triumphal
triunfante *adj* triumphant
triunfar *intr* to triumph; trump; **triunfar de** to triumph over; trump
triunfo *m* triumph; trump; **sin triunfo** no trump
trivial *adj* trivial; trite, commonplace; (*sendero*) beaten
trivialidad *f* triviality; triteness
triza *f* shred; **hacer trizas** to tear to pieces
trizar §60 *tr* to tear to pieces
trocar §81 *tr* to exchange, swap; barter; confuse, twist, distort ‖ *intr* to swap ‖ *ref* to change; change seats
trocha *f* trail, narrow path; gauge
trofeo *m* trophy; victory
troj *f* or **troje** *f* granary; olive bin
trole *m* trolley pole
trolebús *m* trolley bus, trackless trolley
tromba *f* (*de polvo, agua, etc.*) whirl, column; **tromba marina** waterspout; **tromba terrestre** tornado
trombón *m* trombone
trompa *f* (*del elefante*) trunk; waterspout;

top; nozzle; (anat) duct, tube; (mus) horn; (Col, Chile) cowcatcher; **trompa de armonía** French horn; **trompa de Eustaquio** Eustachian tube
trompada *f* bump, collision; punch
trompar *intr* to spin a top
trompeta *f* trumpet; bugle, clarion; good-for-nothing; drunkenness
trompetear *intr* to trumpet, sound the trumpet
trompetilla *f* ear trumpet; Bronx cheer
trompicar §44 *tr* to trip, make stumble ‖ *intr* to stumble
trompicón *m* stumble
trompiza *f* fist fight
trompo *m* (*juguete*) top; (*en el ajedrez*) man; (*buque malo y pesado*) tub
tronada *f* thunderstorm
tronar §61 *tr* (Mex) to shoot ‖ *intr* to thunder; fail, collapse; **por lo que pueda tronar** just in case
troncar §44 *tr* to cut off the head of; (*un escrito*) cut, shorten
tronco *m* (*del cuerpo, del árbol, de una familia, del ferrocarril*) trunk; (*leño*) log; (*de caballerías*) team; sap, fathead; **estar hecho un tronco** to be knocked out; be sound asleep
troncha *f* slice; cinch
tronchar *tr* to smash, split; chop off
tronera *m* madcap, roisterer ‖ *f* embrasure, loophole; louver; (*de la mesa de billar*) pocket
tronido *m* thunderclap
trono *m* throne
tronquista *m* driver, teamster
tronzar §60 *tr* to shatter, break to pieces; pleat; wear out
tropa *f* troop; herd, drove; **en tropa** straggling, without formation; **tropas de asalto** shock troops, storm troops
tropel *m* crowd, throng; rush, hurry; jumble; **de** or **en tropel** in a mad rush
tropelía *f* mad rush; outrage
tropero *m* (Arg) cowboy
tropezar §18 *tr* to strike ‖ *intr* to stumble; slip, blunder; **tropezar con** or **en** to stumble over, trip over; run into; come upon
trope·zón -zona *adj* stumbly ‖ *m* stumble; stumbling place; **a tropezones** by fits and starts; falteringly; **dar un tropezón** to stumble, trip
tropical *adj* tropic(al)
trópico *m* tropic
tropiezo *m* stumble; stumbling block; slip, blunder, fault; obstacle; quarrel
tropilla *f* (Arg, Urug) drove of horses following a leading mare
troposfera *f* troposphere
troquel *m* die
trotaconven·tos *f* (*pl* -**tos**) procuress, bawd
trotamun·dos *m* (*pl* -**dos**) globetrotter
trotar *intr* to trot; to hustle
trote *m* trot; chore; **al trote** right away; **para todo trote** for everyday wear; **trote de perro** jog trot
trotona *f* chaperone

trovador *m* troubadour
trovadores•co -ca *adj* troubadour
trovero *m* trouvère
Troya *f* Troy; **ahí fué Troya** it's a shambles; **¡arda Troya!** come what may!
troya•no -na *adj & mf* Trojan
troza *f* log
trozar §60 *tr* to break to pieces; (*un tronco*) cut into logs
trozo *m* piece, fragment; block; excerpt, selection
truco *m* contrivance, device; trick; pocketing of ball; **truco de naipes** card trick; **trucos** pool
truculen•to -ta *adj* truculent
trucha *f* trout
trueno *m* thunder, thunderclap; shot, report; rake, roué; **trueno gordo** finale (*of fireworks*); big scandal; **truenos** (Ven) heavy shoes
trueque *m* barter; exchange, swap; trade-in; **a trueque de** in exchange for; **trueques** (Col) change
trufa *f* truffle; fib, lie
tru•hán -hana *adj* crooked; clownish ‖ *mf* crook; clown
trujal *m* wine press; oil press
trulla *f* noise, bustle; crowd; trowel
truncar §73 *tr* to cut off the head of; (*palabras o frases*) cut, slash; cut off, interrupt
trusas *fpl* trunk hose; trunks
tu *adj poss* thy, your
tú *pron pers* thou, you
tubérculo *m* (*rizoma engrosado, p.ej., de la patata*) tuber; (*protuberancia*) tubercle
tuberculosis *f* tuberculosis
tubería *f* tubing; piping
tubo *m* tube; pipe; **tubo de desagüe** drainpipe; **tubo de ensayo** test tube; **tubo de humo** flue; **tubo de imagen** picture tube; **tubo de vacío** vacuum tube; **tubo digestivo** alimentary canal; **tubo sonoro** chime
tuerca *f* nut; **tuerca de aletas** wing nut
tuer•to -ta *adj* crooked, bent; one-eyed; **a tuertas** upside down; crosswise; **a tuertas o a derechas** rightly or wrongly; thoughtlessly ‖ *mf* one-eyed person ‖ *m* wrong, harm, injustice; **tuertos** afterpains
tuétano *m* marrow; pith; **hasta los tuétanos** through and through; head over heels
tufi•llas *mf* (*pl* -**llas**) touchy person
tufillo *m* whiff, smell
tufo *m* fume, vapor; sidelock; foul odor, foul breath; **tufos** airs, conceit
tugurio *m* shepherd's hut; hovel
tuición *f* protection, custody
tulipán *m* tulip
tullecer §22 *tr* to abuse, mistreat ‖ *intr* to be crippled
tulli•do -da *adj* paralyzed, crippled ‖ *mf* paralytic, cripple
tullir §13 *tr* to cripple, paralyze; abuse, mistreat ‖ *ref* to become crippled or paralyzed
tumba *f* grave, tomb; tombstone; arched top; felling of trees

tumbacuarti•llos *mf* (*pl* -**llos**) old toper, rounder
tumbar *tr* to knock down; catch, trick; stun ‖ *intr* to tumble; capsize ‖ *ref* to lie down
tumbo *m* fall, tumble; boom, rumble; crisis; rise and fall of sea; rough surf
tumbona *f* hammock
tumor *m* tumor
túmulo *m* catafalque
tumulto *m* tumult
tuna *f* loafing, bumming; (bot) prickly pear
tunante *adj* bumming, loafing; crooked, tricky ‖ *mf* bum, loafer; crook
tundidora *f* lawn mower
tuneci•no -na *adj & mf* Tunisian
túnel *m* tunnel; **túnel de lavado** automatic car wash
tunes *mpl* (Col) little steps, first steps
Túnez (*ciudad*) Tunis; (*país*) Tunisia
tungsteno *m* tungsten
túnica *f* tunic
tu•no -na *adj* crooked, tricky ‖ *mf* crook ‖ *f* see **tuna**
tupé *m* toupee; nerve, cheek, brass
tupi•do -da *adj* thick, dense, compact; dull, stupid; clogged up
tupir *tr* to pack tight ‖ *ref* to stuff, stuff oneself
turba *f* crowd, mob; peat
turbamulta *f* job, rabble
turbar *tr* to disturb, trouble; stir up ‖ *ref* to be confused
turbiedad *f* muddiness; confusion
turbina *f* turbine
tur•bio -bia *adj* turbid, muddy, cloudy; confused; obscure
turbión *m* squall, thunderstorm; (*p.ej., de balas*) (fig) hail
turbocompresor *m* turbocompressor
turbohélice *m* turboprop
turbopropulsor *m* turboprop (*engine*)
turborreactor *m* turbojet (*engine*)
turbosupercargador *m* turbosupercharger
turbulen•to -ta *adj* turbulent
tur•co -ca *adj* Turkish ‖ *mf* Turk ‖ *m* (*idioma*) Turkish ‖ *f* (coll) binge; boozing; **coger una turca** to get drunk
turfista *adj* horsy ‖ *m* turfman
turismo *m* touring; touring car
turista *mf* tourist
turísti•co -ca *adj* tourist; touring
turnar *intr* to alternate, take turns
tur•nio -nia *adj* (*ojos*) cross; cross-eyed; (*que mira con ceño*) cross-looking
turno *m* turn, shift; **aguardar turno** to wait one's turn; **por turno** in turn; **turno diurno** day shift
turón *m* polecat
turquesa *s* turquoise
Turquía *s* Turkey
turrón *m* nougat; plum
tusa *f* corncob; corn silk; (Chile) mane; (Col) pockmark; (CAm, W-I) trollop
tusar *tr* to shear, clip, cut
tutear *tr* to thou, address familiarly ‖ *ref* to thou each other, address each other familiarly

tutela *f* guardianship; protection
tutelar *adj* guardian; protecting ‖ *tr* to protect, shelter, guide
tu•tor -tora or **-triz** *mf* (*pl* **-trices**) guardian, tutor

tu•yo -ya *adj poss* of thee ‖ *pron poss* thine, yours
tuza *f* gopher

U

U, u (u) *f* twenty-fourth letter of the Spanish alphabet
u *conj* (used before words beginning with *o* or *ho*) or
U. *abbr* **usted**
ubicar §73 *tr* to locate, place ‖ *intr* & *ref* to be situated
ubi•cuo -cua *adj* ubiquitous
ubre *f* udder
Ucrania *f* Ukraine
ucrania•no -na *adj* & *mf* Ukrainian
ucra•nio -nia *adj* & *mf* Ukrainian ‖ *f* see **Ucrania**
Ud. *abbr* **usted**
Uds. *abbr* **ustedes**
ufanar *ref* — **ufanarse con** or **de** to boast of, be proud of
ufanía *f* pride, conceit; cheer, satisfaction; ease, smoothness
ufa•no -na *adj* proud, conceited; cheerful, satisfied; easy, smooth
ujier *m* doorman, usher
úlcera *f* ulcer, fester, sore; **úlcera de decúbito** bedsore
ulcerar *tr* & *ref* to ulcerate, fester
ulterior *adj* ulterior; subsequent
ulteriormente *adv* subsequently, later
últimamente *adv* finally; lately, recently
ultimar *tr* to finish, end, conclude, wind up; kill, finish off
ultimátum *m* (*pl* **-tums**) ultimatum; definite decision
últi•mo -ma *adj* last, latest; final; excellent, superior; (*precio*) lowest, final; most remote; (*piso*) top; (*hora*) late; **a la última** in the latest fashion; **a última hora** at the eleventh hour; **a últimos de** toward the end of, in the latter part of; **de última hora** last-minute; **estar a lo último** or **en las últimas** to be up to date, be well-informed; be on one's last-legs; **por último** at last, finally; **último suplicio** capital punishment
ultraatmosféri•co -ca *adj* outer (*space*)
ultraeleva•do -da *adj* (rad) ultrahigh
ultrajar *tr* to outrage, offend
ultraje *m* outrage, offense
ultrajo•so -sa *adj* outrageous, offensive
ultramar *m* country overseas
ultramari•no -na *adj* overseas ‖ **ultramarinos** *mpl* groceries, delicatessen
ultranza — **a ultranza** to the death; unflinchingly
ultrarro•jo -ja *adj* & *m* infrared
ultratumba *adv* beyond the grave

ultraviola•do -da or **ultravioleta** *adj* & *m* ultraviolet
ululación *f* howl; whoop; (*del buho*) hoot; (*del disco del fonógrafo*) wow
ulular *intr* to howl; whoop; (*el buho*) hoot
ululato *m* howl; (*del buho*) hoot
umbilical *adj* umbilical
umbral *m* threshold, doorsill; (*madero que sostiene el muro encima de un vano*) lintel; (physiol, psychol & fig) threshold; **atravesar** or **pisar los umbrales** to cross the threshold; **estar en los umbrales de** to be on the threshold of
umbralada *f* (Col) threshold
umbrí•o -a *adj* shady ‖ *f* shady side
umbro•so -sa *adj* shady
un, una (the apocopated form **un** is used before masculine singular nouns and adjectives and before feminine singular nouns beginning with stressed *a* or *ha*) *art indef* a ‖ *adj* one
unánime *adj* unanimous
unanimidad *f* unanimity
unción *f* unction
uncir §36 *tr* (*bueyes*) to yoke, hitch
undéci•mo -ma *adj* & *m* eleventh
undo•so -sa *adj* wavy
ungir §27 *tr* to smear with ointment or with oil; anoint
ungüento *m* unguent, ointment, salve
únicamente *adv* only, solely
úni•co -ca *adj* only, sole; (*sin otro de su especie*) unique; one, e.g., **precio único** one price
unicornio *m* unicorn
unidad *f* (*concepto de una sola cosa o persona; cantidad que se toma como medida común de todas las demás de su clase; el número entero más pequeño*) unit; (*indivisión; armonía de conjunto; el número uno*) unity
uni•do -da *adj* united; smooth, even; close-knit
unifamiliar *adj casa* one-family
unificar §73 *tr* to unify
uniformar *tr* to make uniform; provide with a uniform
uniforme *adj* uniform ‖ *m* uniform; **uniforme de gala** (mil) full dress
uniformidad *f* uniformity
unilateral *adj* unilateral
unión *f* union; double ring; **Unión Soviética** Soviet Union
unir *tr* & *ref* to unite

unisonancia f (mus) unison; (de un orador) monotony

unísono — **al unísono** in unison; unanimously; **al unísono de** in unison with

unita•rio -ria adj unit

universal adj universal; all-purpose; (teclado de máquina de escribir) standard

universidad f university

universita•rio -ria adj university ‖ mf university student, college student ‖ m university professor

universo m universe

u•no -na pron one, someone; **a una** of one accord; **la una** one o'clock; **somos uno** we are one; **uno a otro, unos a otros** each other, one another; **uno que otro** one or more, a few; **u•nos -nas** some; pair of, e.g., **unas gafas** a pair of glasses; **unas tijeras** a pair of scissors; **unos cuantos** some; **uno y otro** both ‖ pron indef one, e.g., **uno no sabe qué hacer aquí** one does not know what to do here ‖ m (unidad y signo que la representa) one

untar tr to smear, grease; anoint; bribe ‖ ref to get smeared; grease oneself; embezzle

unto m grease; (gordura del cuerpo del animal) fat; (Chile) shoe polish; **unto de Méjico** or **de rana** bribe money

untuo•so -sa adj unctuous, greasy, sticky

uña f nail, fingernail, toenail; (pezuña) hoof; (del ancla) fluke, bill; (mach) claw, gripper; **enseñar** or **mostrar las uñas** to show one's teeth; **ser largo de uñas** to have long fingers; **ser uña y carne** to be hand in glove; **tener en la uña** to have on the tip of one's fingers

uñada f scratch, nail scratch; (impulso dado con la uña) flip

uñero m ingrowing nail; (inflamación del dedo en la raíz de la uña) whitlow

ural adj Ural ‖ **Urales** mpl Urals

uranio m uranium

urbanidad f urbanity

urbanismo m city planning

urbanista mf city planner

urbanísti•co -ca adj city-planning ‖ f city planning

urbanizar §60 tr (convertir en poblado) to urbanize; refine; polish

urba•no -na adj urban, city; (atento, cortés) urbane ‖ m policeman

urbe f metropolis

urdema•las mf (pl -las) schemer

urdimbre f warp; scheme, scheming; **estar en la urdimbre** (Chile) to be thin, be emaciated

urdir tr (los hilos) to beam; (una conspiración) hatch

urente adj burning, smarting

uretra f urethra

urgencia f urgency; **de urgencia** special-delivery

urgente adj urgent; (correo) special-delivery

urgir §27 intr to be urgent

urina•rio -ria adj urinary ‖ m urinal

urna f glass case; ballot box; (para guardar las cenizas de los cadáveres) urn; **acudir** or **ir a las urnas** to go to the polls

urología f urology

urraca f magpie

U.R.S.S. abbr **Unión de Repúblicas Socialistas Soviéticas**

urticaria f hives

Uruguay, el Uruguay

urugua•yo -ya adj & mf Uruguayan

usa•do -da adj (empleado; gastado por el uso; acostumbrado) used; skilled, experienced; (vocablo) **poco usado** rare

usanza f use, usage, custom

usar tr to use, make use of; (un cargo, un oficio) follow ‖ intr — **usar + inf** to be accustomed to + inf; **usar de** to use, have recourse to; **usar de la palabra** to speak, make a speech ‖ ref to be the custom

usina f factory, plant; powerhouse; (estación de tranvía) (Arg) carbarn

uso m use; custom, usage; wear, wear and tear; habit, practice; **al uso** according to custom; **en buen uso** in good condition; **hacer uso de la palabra** to speak, make a speech

usted pron pers you

usual adj (de uso común) usual; (que se usa con facilidad) usable; sociable

usualmente adv usually

usua•rio -ria mf user

usufructo m use, enjoyment

usufructuar §21 tr to enjoy the use of

usura f usury; profit; **pagar con usura** to pay back a thousandfold

usurero m loan shark; profiteer

usurpar tr to usurp

utensilio m utensil

útero m uterus, womb

útil adj useful ‖ **útiles** mpl utensils, tools, equipment

utilería f (Arg) properties, stage equipment

utilero m (Arg) property man

utilidad f utility, usefulness; profit, earnings

utilita•rio -ra adj utilitarian

utilizable adj usable

utilizar §60 tr to utilize, use ‖ ref — **utilizarse con, de** or **en** to make use of; **utilizarse para** to be good for

utopía f utopia

utopista adj & mf utopian

UU. abbr **ustedes**

uva f grape; wart on eyelid; (baya) berry; **estar hecho una uva** to have a load on; **uva crespa** gooseberry; **uva de Corinto** currant; **uva de raposa** nightshade; **uva espín** or **espina** gooseberry; **uva pasa** raisin; **uvas verdes** (de la fábula de Esopo) sour grapes

uve f (letra del alfabeto) V

uxoricida m uxoricide (husband)

uxoricidio m uxoricide (act)

uxo•rio -ria adj uxorious

V, v (ve *or* uve) *f* twenty-fifth letter of the Spanish alphabet

V. *abbr* **usted, vease, venerable**

V.A. *abbr* **Vuestra Alteza**

vaca *f* cow; (*cuero*) cowhide; (*carne de vaca o de buey*) beef; gambling pool; **hacer vaca** (Peru) to play truant; **vaca de la boda** (coll) goat, laughingstock; friend in need; **vaca de leche** milch cow; **vaca de San Antón** (ent) ladybird

vacación *f* (*cargo que está sin proveer*) vacancy; **de vacaciones** on vacation; **vacaciones** vacation; **vacaiones retribuídas** vacation with pay

vacacionista *mf* vacationist

vacancia *f* vacancy

vacante *adj* vacant ‖ *f* vacancy

vacar §73 *intr* (*un empleo, un cargo*) to be vacant, be unfilled; take off, take a vacation; **vacar a** to attend to; **vacar de** to lack, be devoid of

vacia•do -da *adj* hollow-ground ‖ *m* cast, casting; plaster cast

vaciante *f* ebb tide

vaciar §77 **& regular** *tr* to empty, drain; cast, mold; (*formar un hueco en*) hollow out; sharpen on a grindstone; copy, transcribe; explain in detail ‖ *intr* to empty; flow; (*el agua en el río*) fall, go down ‖ *ref* to blab

vacilación *f* vacillation; flickering; hesitancy, hesitation

vacilada *f* (Mex) spree, high time; (Mex) drunk

vacilante *adj* vacillating; (*luz*) flickering; (*irresoluto*) hesitant

vacilar *intr* to vacillate; (*la luz*) flicker; shake, wobble; (*estar irresoluto*) hesitate, waver

vací•o -a *adj* empty; (*hueco*) hollow; idle; useless, unsuccessful; (*vaca*) barren; presumptuous ‖ *m* emptiness; (*laguna, abertura; vacante*) vacancy; (*espacio que no contiene ninguna materia*) void; (*espacio de que se ha extraído el aire*) vacuum; (*ijada*) side, flank; **de vacío** light, unloaded; **hacer el vacío a** to isolate

vacuidad *f* vacuity, emptiness

vacuna *f* (*enfermedad de las vacas*) cowpox; (*virus cuya inoculación preserva de una enfermedad determinada*) vaccine

vacunación *f* vaccination

vacunar *tr* to vaccinate

vacu•no -na *adj* bovine; cowhide ‖ *f* see **vacuna**

va•cuo -cua *adj* vacant ‖ *m* cavity, hollow

vadear *tr* (*un río*) to ford; wade through; overcome; sound out ‖ *ref* to behave; manage

vado *m* ford; expedient, resource; **al vado o a la puente** one way or another; **no hallar vado** to see no way out; **tentar el vado** to feel one's way

vagabundaje *m* vagrancy

vagabundear *intr* to wander, roam; loaf around

vagabun•do -da *adj* vagabond ‖ *mf* vagabond, tramp; wanderer

vagancia *f* loafing, vagrancy

vagar *m* leisure; **con vagar** slowly; **estar de vagar** to have nothing to do ‖ §44 *intr* to wander, roam; be idle; have plenty of leisure; (*una cosa*) lie around; (*p.ej., una sonrisa por los labios*) play

vagido *m* cry of a newborn baby

vagina *f* vagina

vagneria•no -na *adj* & *mf* Wagnerian

va•go -ga *adj* wandering, roaming; idle, loafing; lax, loose; hesitating, wavering; (*indefinido, indeciso*) vague; (*mirada*) blank ‖ *m* vagabond; idler, loafer; **en vago** shakily; in vain; in the air; **poner en vago** to tilt

vagón *m* car, railroad car; **vagón cama** sleeping car; **vagón carbonero** coal car; **vagón cerrado** boxcar; **vagón cisterna** tank car; **vagón de carga** freight car; **vagón de cola** caboose; **vagón de mercancías** freight car; **vagón de plataforma** flatcar; **vagón frigorífico** refrigerator car; **vagón salón** chair car; **vagón tolva** hopper-bottom car; **vagón volquete** dump car

vagoneta *f* tip car; station wagon

vaguear *intr* to wander around

vaguedad *f* vagueness; vague remark

vaguido *m* faintness, fainting spell

vaharada *f* breath, exhalation

vahear *intr* to emit odors, give forth an aroma

vahído *f* faintness, fainting spell

vaho *m* odor, aroma, vapor, fume

vaina *f* sheath; scabbard; knife case; (*de ciertas semillas*) pod, husk; annoyance, bother; (Col) luck, stroke of luck

vainica *f* hemstitch

vainilla *f* vanilla

vainita *f* (Ven) string bean

vaivén *m* swing, seesaw, backward and forward motion; unsteadiness, inconstancy; risk, chance

vajilla *f* dishes, set of dishes; **lavar la vajilla** to wash the dishes; **vajilla de oro** gold plate; **vajilla de plata** silver plate, silverware; **vajilla de porcelana** chinaware

vale *m* promissory note; voucher; farewell; (Ven) chum, pal; **vale respuesta** reply coupon

valede•ro -ra *adj* valid, effective

vale•dor -dora *mf* defender, protector; (Mex) friend, companion

valedura *f* (Mex) favor, protection

valencia *f* (chem) valence

valentía *f* bravery, valor; feat, exploit; dash, boldness; boast; **pisar de valentía** to strut, swagger

valen•tón -tona *adj* arrogant, boastful ‖ *mf* braggart, boaster ‖ *f* bragging

valer *m* worth, merit, value ‖ §76 *tr* to defend, protect; favor, patronize; avail; yield; be worth, be valued at; be equal to; suit; **valer la pena** to be worthwhile (to);

valerle a uno + *inf* to help someone to + *inf*, to get someone to + *inf*; **valor lo que pesa** to be worth its (his, her, etc.) weight in gold; **valga lo que valiere** come what may; **¡válgame Dios!** bless my soul!, so help me God! ‖ *intr* to have worth; be worthy; be valuable; be valid; prevail; hold, count; have influence; **hacer valer** (*sus derechos*) to assert; make felt; make good; turn to account; **más vale** it is better (to); **vale** O.K.; **valer para** to be useful for; **valer por** to be equal to ‖ *ref* to help oneself, defend oneself; **valerse de** to make use of, avail oneself of

valero•so -sa *adj* valorous, brave; strong, active, effective

va•let *m* (*pl* **-lets**) (cards) jack

valía *f* value, worth; favor, influence; **mayor valía** or **plus valía** appreciation, increased value; unearned increment

validación *f* validation

validar *tr* to validate

validez *f* validity; strength, vigor

vali•do -da *adj* highly esteemed, influential ‖ *m* court favorite; prime minister

váli•do -da *adj* valid; strong, robust

valiente *adj* valiant; strong, robust; fine, excellent; (*grande y excesivo*) terrific ‖ *m* brave fellow; bully

valija *f* satchel, brief case; mailbag, mailpouch; mail; **valija diplomática** diplomatic pouch

valimiento *m* favor, protection; favor at court, favoritism

valio•so -sa *adj* valuable; influential; wealthy

va•lón -lona *adj & mf* Walloon

valor *m* value, worth; valor, courage; meaning, import; efficacy; equivalence; (*rédito*) income, return; effrontery; (*persona, cosa o cualidad dignas de ser poseídas*) (fig) asset; **¿cómo va ese valor?** how are you?; **valor de rescate** (ins) surrender value; **valores** securities

valoración *f* valuation, appraisal

valorar or **valorear** *tr* (*poner precio a*) to value, appraise; enhance the value of

valorizar §60 *tr* to value; enhance the value of; sell of (*for quick realization*)

vals *m* waltz

valsar *intr* to waltz

valuación *f* valuation, appraisal

valuar §21 *tr* to estimate

válvula *f* valve; **válvula corredize** slide valve; **válvula de admisión** intake valve; **válvula de escape** exhaust valve; **válvula de escape libre** cutout; **válvula de seguridad** safety valve; **válvula en cabeza** valve in the head, overhead valve

valla *f* fence, railing; barricade; hindrance, obstacle; (sport) hurdle; (W-I) cockpit; **valla paranieves** snow fence

vallado *m* barricade, stockade

valle *m* valley; river bed; valley dwellings; **valle de lágrimas** vale of tears

vampiresa *f* vampire

vampíri•co -ca *adj* vampire; ghoulish

vampiro *m* vampire; (*persona que se deleita con cosas horribles*) ghoul

vanadio *m* vanadium

vanagloriar §77 & regular *ref* to boast

vanaglorio•so -sa *adj* vainglorious, conceited, boastful

vanamente *adv* vainly

vandalismo *m* vandalism

vánda•lo -la *adj & mf* Vandal; (fig) vandal

vanguardia *f* (mil & fig) vanguard, van; **a vanguardia** in the vanguard

vanguardismo *m* avant-garde

vanguardista *adj* avant-garde ‖ *mf* avant-gardist

vanidad *f* vanity; (*fausto*) pomp, show; **ajar la vanidad de** to take down a peg; **hacer vanidad de** to boast of

vanido•so -sa *adj* vain, conceited

va•no -na *adj* vain; hollow, empty; **en vano** in vain ‖ *m* opening in a wall

vapor *m* steam; (*el visible: exhalación, vaho, niebla, etc.*) vapor; steamer, steamboat; **al vapor** at full speed; **vapores** gas (*belched*); blues; **vapor volandero** tramp steamer

vaporar *tr & ref* to evaporate

vaporizador *m* atomizer, sprayer

vaporizar §60 *tr* to vaporize; spray ‖ *ref* to vaporize

vaporo•so -sa *adj* vaporous

vapular or **vapulear** *tr* whip, flog

vaquería *f* drove of cattle; dairy; (Mex) party

vaqueri•zo -za *adj* cattle ‖ *f* winter stable for cattle

vaque•ro -ra *adj* cattle ‖ *mf* cattle tender; (Peru) truant ‖ *m* cow hand; cowboy; **vaqueros** blue jeans

vaqueta *f* leather; (P-R) strop; **zurrarle a uno la vaqueta** to tan someone's hide

vaquillona *f* (Arg, Chile) heifer

vara *f* pole, rod, staff; (*de carruaje*) shaft; (*bastón de mando*) wand; measuring stick; (taur) thrust with goad; **tener vara alta** to have the upper hand; **vara alcándara** shaft; **vara alta** upper hand; **vara buscadora** divining rod (*ostensibly to discover water or metals*); **vara de adivinar** divining rod; **vara de oro** goldenrod; **vara de pescar** fishing rod; **vara de San José** goldenrod

vara-alta *m* boss

varada *f* beaching; running aground

varadero *m* repair dock

varapalo *m* long pole; setback, disappointment, reverse

varar *tr* (*una embarcación*) to beach ‖ *intr* to run aground; (*un negocio*) come to a standstill

varear *tr* (*los frutos de los árboles*) to beat down, knock down; beat, strike; (taur) to goad; (*los caballos de carreras*) (SAm) to exercise, train ‖ *ref* to lose weight, get thin

varec *m* (bot) wrack

varenga *f* (naut) floor, floor timber

vareta *f* twig, stick; lime twig for catching birds; colored stripe; cutting remark; hint; **irse de vareta** to have diarrhea

variable *adj & f* variable

variación *f* variation

v
va

varia•do -da *adj* varied; variegated
variante *adj & f* variant
variar §77 to vary, change ‖ *intr* to vary, change; be different; **variar de** or **en opinión** to change one's mind
varice *f* or **várice** *f* varicose veins
varicela *f* chicken pox
varico•so -sa *adj* varicose
variedad *f* variety; **variedades** variety show, vaudeville
varilla *f* rod, stem, twig; (*bastón de mando*) wand; (*de paraguas, abanico, etc.*) rib; (*del corsé*) stay; (*de rueda*) wire spoke; jawbone; (Mex) peddler's wares; **varilla de nivel** dipstick; **varilla de virtudes** wand, magician's wand
varillaje *m* ribs, ribbing; (*de máquina de escribir*) type bars
varille•ro -ra *adj* (*caballo*) (Ven) race ‖ *m* (Mex) peddler
va•rio -ria *adj* (*de diversos colores; que tiene variedad*) various, varied; fickle, inconstant; **varios** various; several
varón *adj* male, e.g., **hijo varón** male child ‖ *m* man, male; grown man, adult male; man of standing; **santo varón** plain artless fellow
varonía *f* male issue
varonil *adj* manly, virile; courageous
Varsovia *f* Warsaw
vasa•llo -lla *adj & mf* vassal
vas•co -ca *adj & mf* Basque (*of Spain and France*) ‖ *m* Basque (*language*)
vas•cón -cona *adj & mf* Basque (*of old Spain*)
vasconga•do -da *adj & mf* Basque (*of Spain*) ‖ *m* Basque (*language*) ‖ **las Vascongadas** the Basque Provinces
vascuence *adj & m* Basque (*language*) ‖ *m* gibberish
vaselina *f* Vaseline
vasera *f* kitchen shelf; bottle rack, tumbler rack
vasija *f* container, vessel
vaso *m* tumbler, glass; vase, flower jar; (anat) duct, vessel; **vaso de engrase** (mach) grease cup; **vaso de noche** pot, chamber pot; **vaso graduado** measuring glass; **vaso sanguíneo** blood vessel
vástago *m* shoot, sapling; scion, offspring; rod, stem; **vástago de émbolo** piston rod; **vástago de válvula** valve stem
vastedad *f* vastness
vas•to -ta *adj* vast
vate *m* bard, seer, poet
váter *m* toilet, water closet
vataije *m* wattage
vaticinar *tr* to prophesy, predict
vaticinio *m* prophecy, prediction
vatídi•co -ca *adj* prophetical ‖ *mf* prophet
vatímetro *m* wattmeter
vatio *m* watt
vatio-hora *m* (*pl* **vatios-hora**) watt-hour
vaya *f* jest, jeer
Vd. *abbr* **usted**
Vds. *abbr* **ustedes**
V.E. *abbr* **Vuestra Excelencia**

vece•ro -ra *adj* alternating; yielding in alternate years ‖ *mf* person waiting his turn
vecinamente *adv* nearby
vecindad *f* neighborhood, vicinity; residency; residents; **hacer mala vecindad** to be a bad neighbor
vecindario *m* neighborhood, community; people, population
veci•no -na *adj* neighboring; like, similar ‖ *mf* neighbor; resident, citizen
veda *f* prohibition; (*de la caza y la pesca*) closed season
vedado *m* game preserve
vedar *tr* to forbid, prohibit; hinder, stop; veto
vedija *f* fleece, tuft of wool; mat of hair; matted hair
vee•dor -dora *adj* curious, spying ‖ *mf* busybody ‖ *m* supervisor, overseer
vega *f* fertile plain; (Cuba) tobacco plantation
vegetación *f* vegetation; **vegetaciones adenoideas** adenoids
vegetal *adj & m* vegetable
vegetaria•no -na *adj & mf* vegetarian
vego•so -sa *adj* (Chile) damp, wet
vehemencia *f* vehemence
vehemente *adj* vehement
vehículo *m* vehicle; **vehículo espacial** space vehicle
veinta•vo -va *adj & m* twentieth
veinte *adj & pron* twenty; **a las veinte** late, untimely ‖ *m* twenty; (*en las fechas*) twentieth
vientena *f* score, twenty
veintiún *adj* this apocopated form of **veintiuno** is used before masculine singular nouns and adjectives
veintiu•no -na *adj & pron* twenty-one ‖ *m* twenty-one; (*en las fechas*) twenty-first ‖ *f* (*juego de naipes*) twenty-one
vejación *f* vexation, annoyance
vejamen *m* vexation, annoyance; bantering, taunting
vejar *tr* to vex, annoy; taunt
vejestorio *m* old dodo
vejete *m* little old fellow
vejez *f* old age; oldness; dotage; platitude, old story; **a la vejez, viruelas** there's no fool like an old fool
vejiga *f* (*órgano que recibe la orina de los riñones*) bladder; (*ampolla*) blister; (*saco hecho de piel, goma, etc.*) bag, pouch, bladder; **vejiga de la bilis** or **de la hiel** gall bladder
vela *f* wakefulness; pilgrimage; evening; work in the evening; sail; sailboat; (*cilindro con una torcida que sirve para alumbrar*) candle; vigil (*before Eucharist*) awning; (Mex) scolding; **a toda vela** full sail; **a vela** under sail; **a vela llena** under full sail; **en vela** awake; **estar entre dos velas** to be half-seas over, have a sheet in the wind; **hacerse a la vela** to set sail; **vela latina** lateen sail; **vela mayor** mainsail; **vela romana** Roman candle
velada *f* evening party, soirée; vigil, watch
vela•do -da *adj* veiled, hidden; (phot) light-struck ‖ *f* see **velada**

velador *m* pedestal table, gueridon; wooden candlestick; watchman; (SAm) night table; (Mex) lamp globe

velaje *m* or **velamen** *m* (naut) canvas, sails

velar *adj* & *f* velar ‖ *tr* to watch over; guard; (*la guardia*) keep; hold a wake over; (*cubrir con un velo*) veil; (phot) to fog; (fig) to veil, hide, conceal ‖ *intr* to stay awake; stay awake working; keep vigil; (*el viento*) keep up all night; (*un escollo, un peñasco*) stick up out of the water; **velar por** or **sobre** to watch over ‖ *ref* (phot) to fog, be light-struck

velatorio *m* wake

veleidad *f* whim, caprice; fickleness, flightiness

veleido•so -**sa** *adj* whimsical, capricious; fickle, flighty

vele•ro -**ra** *adj* swift-sailing ‖ *m* sailboat

veleta *mf* (*persona inconstante*) weathercock ‖ *f* vane, weathervane, weathercock; (*de un molino*) rudder vane; (*de la caña de pescar*) bob; streamer, pennant; **veleta de manga** (aer) air sleeve, air sock

velís *m* (Mex) valise

velita *f* little candle

velo *m* veil; taking the veil; confusion, perplexity; (*disfraz*) veil; (*de lágrimas*) mist; (phot) fog; **correr el velo** to pull aside the curtain, to dispel the mystery; **tomar el velo** to take the veil; **velo del paladar** soft palate

velocidad *f* (*rapidez*) speed, velocity; (mech) velocity; **en gran velocidad** (rr) by express; **en pequeña velocidad** (rr) by freight; **primera velocidad** (aut) low gear; **segunda velocidad** (aut) second; **tercera velocidad** (aut) high gear; **velocidad con respecto al suelo** (aer) ground speed; **velocidad de crucero** cruising speed; **velocidad permitida** speed limit

velocímetro *m* speedometer

velón *m* brass olive-oil lamp

velorio *m* evening party or bee; wake; wake for a dead child; dull party; come-on

ve•loz *adj* (*pl* -**loces**) swift, speedy; agile, quick

vello *m* down, fuzz

vellocino *m* fleece; **vellocino de oro** Golden Fleece

vellón *m* fleece; unsheared sheepskin; lock of wool; copper coin; copper-silver alloy

vello•so -**sa** *adj* downy, hairy, fuzzy

velludillo *m* velveteen

vellu•do -**da** *adj* shaggy, hairy, fuzzy ‖ *m* (*felpa*) plush; (*terciopelo*) velvet

vena *f* vein; (*en piedras*) grain; (fig) poetical inspiration; **estar en vena** to be all set, be inspired; sparkle with wit; **vena de loco** fickle disposition

venablo *m* dart, javelin; **echar venablos** to burst forth in anger

venado *m* deer, stag; **pintar el venado** (Mex) to play hooky

venáti•co -**ca** *adj* fickle, unsteady; daffy, nutty

vence•dor -**dora** *adj* conquering, victorious ‖ *mf* conqueror, victor

vencejo *m* band, string; (orn) European swift, black martin

vencer §78 *tr* to vanquish, conquer; excel, outdo; overcome, surmount ‖ *intr* to conquer, be victorious; (*un plazo*) be up; (*un contrato*) expire; (*una letra*) mature, fall due ‖ *ref* to control oneself; (*un camino*) bend, turn; (Chile) to wear out, become useless

vencetósigo *m* milkweed, tame poison

venci•do -**da** *adj* conquered; (com) due, mature, payable

vencimiento *m* (*acción de vencer*) victory; (*hecho de ser vencido*) defeat; (com) expiration, maturity

venda *f* (*para ligar un miembro herido*) bandage; (*para tapar los ojos*) blindfold

vendaje *m* bandage, dressing; **vendaje enyesado** plaster cast

vendar *tr* (*un miembro, una herida*) to bandage; (*los ojos*) blindfold; (*cegar*) (fig) to blind; (*engañar*) (fig) to hoodwink

vendaval *m* strong southeasterly wind from the sea; strong wind, gale

vendedera *f* saleswoman, saleslady

vende•dor -**dora** *adj* selling ‖ *m* salesman ‖ *f* saleslady, sales girl

vendehu•mos *mf* (*pl* -**mos**) influence peddler

vendeja *f* public sale

vender *tr* to sell; betray, sell out; **vender salud** to be the picture of health ‖ *intr* to sell; **¡vendo, vendo, vendí!** going, going, gone! ‖ *ref* to sell oneself; sell, be for sale; betray oneself, give oneself away; **venderse caro** to be hard to see; be quite a stranger; **venderse en** (*p.ej., cien pesetas*) to sell for; **venderse por** to pass oneself off as

ven•dí *m* (*pl* -**díes**) certificate of sale

vendible *adj* salable, marketable

vendimia *f* vintage; (fig) big profit

vendimia•dor -**dora** *mf* vintager

vendimiar *tr* (*la uva*) to gather, harvest; (*las viñas*) gather the grapes of; make off with; kill

venduta *f* public sale; (W-I) greengrocery

Venecia *f* (*ciudad*) Venice; (*provincia*) Venetia

venecia•no -**na** *adj* & *mf* Venetian

veneno *m* poison, venom

veneno•so -**sa** *adj* poisonous, venomous

venera *f* scallop shell; (*manantial de agua*) spring; **empeñar la venera** to go all out, spare no expense

venerable *adj* venerable

venerar *tr* to venerate, revere; worship

venére•o -**a** *adj* venereal ‖ *m* venereal disease

venero *m* (*de agua*) spring; (*filón de mineral*) lode, vein; (fig) source

venezola•no -**na** *adj* & *mf* Venezuelan

Venezuela *f* Venezuela

venga•dor -**dora** *adj* avenging ‖ *mf* avenger

venganza *f* vengeance, revenge

vengar §44 *tr* to avenge ‖ *ref* to take revenge; **vengarse de** to take revenge on

vengati•vo -va *adj* vengeful, vindictive

venia *f* forgiveness, pardon; leave, permission; bow, greeting

venida *f* coming; return; flood, freshet

venide•ro -ra *adj* coming, future ‖ **venideros** *mpl* successors, posterity

venir §79 *intr* to come; **que viene** coming, next; **venga lo que viniere** come what may; **venir** + *ger* to be + *ger;* **venir a** + *inf* to come to + *inf;* to amount to + *ger;* to happen to + *inf;* to finally + *inf,* e.g., **después de una larga enfermedad, vino a morir** after a long illness he finally died; **venir a ser** to turn out to be ‖ *ref* to ferment; **venirse abajo** to collapse

veno•so -sa *adj* venous

venta *f* sale; roadside inn; (Chile) refreshment stand; (S-D) grocery store; **de venta** or **en venta** on sale, for sale; **ser una venta** to be an expensive place; **venta al descubierto** short sale

ventaja *f* advantage; (*en juegos o apuestas*) odds; extra pay

ventajo•so -sa *adj* advantageous

ventalla *f* valve

ventana *f* window; (*de la nariz*) nostril; **echar la casa por la ventana** to go to a lot of expense; **ventana batiente** casement; **ventana de guillotina** sash window; **ventana salediza** bay window

ventanal *m* church window; picture window

ventanear *intr* to be at the window all the time

ventanilla *f* (*de coche, de banco, de sobre*) window; ticket window; (*de la nariz*) nostril

ventanillo *m* (*postigo de puerta o ventana*) wicket; (*mirilla*) peephole

ventar §2 *tr* to sniff ‖ *impers* — **vienta** it is windy

ventarrón *m* gale, windstorm

ventear *tr* to sniff; dry in the wind; snoop into ‖ *intr* to snoop, pry around ‖ *impers* — **ventea** it is windy ‖ *ref* (*henderse*) to split; break wind; spend a lot of time in the open

vente•ro -ra *mf* innkeeper

ventilador *m* ventilator; fan; (naut) funnel; **ventilador aspirador** exhaust fan

ventilar *tr* to ventilate; (fig) to air, ventilate

ventisca *f* drift, snowdrift; (*borrasca*) blizzard

ventiscar §73 *intr* to snow and blow; (*la nieve*) drift

ventisquero *m* snowdrift; blizzard; snow-capped mountain; glacier

ventolera *f* blast of wind; (*molinete*) pinwheel; vanity, pride; wild idea; (Mex) wind

ventosa *f* vent, air hole; **pegar una ventosa a** to swindle

ventosear *intr* to break wind

vento•so -sa *adj* windy ‖ *f* see **ventosa**

ventregada *f* brood, litter; outpouring, abundance

ventrículo *m* ventricle

ventrílo•cuo -cua *mf* ventriloquist

ventriloquia *f* or **ventriloquismo** *m* ventriloquism

ventura *f* happiness; luck, chance; danger; risk; **a la ventura** at random; at a risk; **por ventura** perhaps, perchance; **probar ventura** to try one's luck

venture•ro -ra *adj* adventurous; fortunate, lucky ‖ *mf* adventurer

ventu•ro -ra *adj* future, coming ‖ *f* see **ventura**

venturón *m* stroke of luck

venturo•so -sa *adj* fortunate, lucky

Venus *m* (astr) Venus ‖ *f* (myth) Venus; (*mujer de belleza*) Venus

venus•to -ta *adj* beautiful, graceful

venza *f* goldbeater's skin

ver *m* (*vista*) sight; (*apariencia*) appearance; opinion; **a mi ver** in my opinion ‖ §80 *tr* to see; look at; (law) to hear, try; **no poder ver** to not be able to bear; **no tener nada que ver con** to have nothing to do with; **ver** + *inf* to see + *inf,* e.g., **ví entrar a mi hermano** I saw my brother come in; to see + *ger,* e.g., **ví bailar a la muchacha** I saw the girl dancing; to see + *pp.* e.g., **ví ahorcar al criminal** I saw the criminal hanged; **ver venir a uno** to see what someone is up to ‖ *intr* to see; **a más ver** so long; **a ver** let's see; **hasta más ver** good-bye, so long; **ver de** to try to; **ver y creer** seeing is believing ‖ *ref* to be seen; be obvious; see oneself; see each other; meet; (*encontrarse*) be, find oneself; **verse con** to see, have a talk with; **ya se ve** of course, certainly

vera *f* edge, border; **a la vera de** near, beside; **de veras** in truth; **jugar de veras** to play for keeps; **veras** truth, reality; earnestness

veracidad *f* veracity, truthfulness

veranda *f* verandah; bay window, closed porch

veraneante *mf* summer vacationist, summer resident

veranear *intr* to summer

veranie•go -ga *adj* summer; unimportant, insignificant

veranillo *m* Indian summer; **veranillo de San Martín** Indian summer

ve•raz *adj* (*pl* **-races**) veracious, truthful

verbena *f* fair, country fair, night festival; (bot) verbena

verbigracia *adv* for example

verbo *m* verb ‖ **Verbo** *m* (theol) Word

verbo•so -sa *adj* verbose, wordy

verdacho *m* green earth

verdad *f* truth; **a la verdad** in truth, as a matter of fact; **de verdad** really; **la verdad desnuda** the plain truth; **¿no es verdad?** or **¿verdad?** isn't that so? La traducción al inglés de esta pregunta depende generalmente de la aseveración que la precede. Si la aseveración es afirmativa, la pregunta es negativa, p.ej., **Vd. vivió aquí. ¿No es verdad?** You lived here. Did you not?; Si la aseveración es negativa, la pregunta es afirmativa, p.ej., **Vd. no vivió aquí. ¿No**

es verdad? You did not live here? Did you? Si el sujeto de la aseveración es un nombre sustantivo, va representado en la pregunta con un pronombre personal, p.ej., **Juan no estuvo aquí anoche. ¿No es verdad?** John was not here last evening. Was he?; **ser verdad** to be true; **verdad trillada** truism

verdade•ro -ra *adj* true; real; (*que dice siempre la verdad*) truthful

verde *adj* green; young, youthful; (*viuda*) merry; (*cuento*) shady, off-color; **están verdes** they're hard to reach ‖ *m* green; foliage, verdure

verdear *intr* to turn green, look green

verdecer §22 *intr* to turn green, grow green again

verdecillo *m* (orn) greenfinch

verdemar *m* sea green

verdete *m* verdigris

verdín *m* fresh green; (*capa verde de aguas estancadas*) mold, pond scum; (*cardenillo*) verdigris

verdise•co -ca *adj* half-dry

verdor *m* verdure; youth

verdo•so -sa *adj* greenish

verdugado *m* hoop skirt

verdugo *m* shoot, sucker; (*estoque*) rapier; (*azote*) scourge; (*roncha*) welt; executioner, hangman; torment; butcher bird, shrike

verdugón *m* wale, weal

verdulería *f* greengrocery

verdule•ro -ra *mf* greengrocer ‖ *f* fishwife

verdura *f* greenness; (*color verde de las plantas*) verdure; (*obscenidad*) smuttiness; **verduras** vegetables, greens

verecundia *f* bashfulness, shyness

verecun•do -da *adj* bashful, shy

vereda *f* path, lane; sidewalk

veredicto *m* verdict

verga *f* (naut) yard

vergel *m* flower and fruit garden

vergonzo•so -sa *adj* (*que causa vergüenza*) shameful; (*que tiene vergüenza*) ashamed; (*que se avergüenza con facilidad*) bashful, shy; (*que causa humillación*) embarrassing; shabby, wretched ‖ *mf* bashful person ‖ *m* armadillo

vergüenza *f* (*arrepentimiento*) shame; (*oprobio*) shamefulness; (*pudor, timidez*) bashfulness, shyness; (*desconcierto, humillación*) embarrassment; (*pundonor*) dignity, face; public punishment; **¡qué vergüenza!** shame on you!; **tener vergüenza** to be ashamed; **vergüenzas** privates, genitals

vericueto *m* rough, rocky ground

verídi•co -ca *adj* truthful

verificación *f* verification; checking, testing, inspection; **verificación a la ventura** spot check

verifica•dor -dora *adj* verifying ‖ *m* meter inspector

verificar §73 *tr* to verify, check; (*llevar a cabo*) carry out; (*los contadores de agua, gas y electricidad*) inspect ‖ *ref* to prove true; take place

verja *f* iron gate, iron fence, grating

ver•mú *m* (*pl* **-mús**) vermouth; matinée

vernácu•lo -la *adj* vernacular

verónica *f* (bot) veronica; (taur) veronica (*graceful pass in which the bullfighter waits for the bull with open cape*)

veroniquear *intr* (taur) to perform veronicas

verosímil *adj* likely, probable

verraco *m* male hog, boar

verraquear *intr* to grunt, grumble; cry hard

verruga *f* wart; bore, nuisance

verrugo *m* miser

versal *adj* & *f* capital

versalilla or **versalita** *f* small capital

Versalles Versailles

versar *intr* — **versar acerca de** or **sobre** to deal with, treat of ‖ *ref* — **versarse en** to be or become versed in

versátil *adj* fickle; versatile; (*arma*) multipurpose

versículo *m* verse (*in the Bible*)

versificación *f* versification

versificar §73 *tr* & *intr* to versify

versión *f* version; translation

verso *m* verse; (typ) verso; **versos pareados** rhymed couplet

vertebra•do -da *adj* & *m* vertebrate

vertedero *m* dump; weir, spillway

verter §51 *tr* (*un líquido, un polvo*) to pour; (*un recipiente*) empty; (*lágrimas; luz; sangre*) shed; (*descargar*) dump; translate ‖ *intr* to flow ‖ *ref* to run, empty

vertical *adj* & *f* vertical

vértice *m* vertex

vertiente *m* & *f* (*declive*) slope; (*colina por donde corre el agua*) shed ‖ *f* (Arg, Col, Chile) spring, fountain

vertigino•so -sa *adj* dizzy

vértigo *m* vertigo, dizziness; fit of insanity

vesícula *f* vesicle; **vesícula biliar** gall bladder

veso *m* polecat

Véspero *m* Vesper

vesperti•no -na *adj* evening ‖ *m* evening sermon

vestíbulo *m* vestibule; (theat) foyer, lobby

vestido *m* clothing, dress; (*de mujer*) gown, dress; (*de hombre*) suit; costume; **vestido de ceremonia** dress suit; **vestido de etiqueta** evening clothes; **vestido de etiqueta de mujer** or **vestido de noche** evening gown; **vestido de gala** (mil) full dress; **vestido de serio** evening clothes; **vestido de tarde-noche** cocktail dress

vestidura *f* clothing; (*del sacerdote*) vestment

vestigio *m* vestige, trace; track, footprint

vestir §50 *tr* to dress, clothe; adorn; cover up; disguise; (*tal o cual vestido*) put on; **vestir el cargo** to look the part ‖ *intr* to dress; (*una prenda o la materia*) be dressy; **vestir de** (*p.ej., blanco*) to dress in; **vestir de etiqueta** to dress in evening clothes; **vestir de paisano** to dress in civilian clothes ‖ *ref* to dress, get dressed; dress oneself; (*de una enfermedad*) be up, be about; **vestirse de** (*nubes, flores, hierba, etc.*) to be covered with; (*importancia, humildad, etc.*) assume

vestuario *m* (*las prendas de uno*) wardrobe;

ve
ve

dressing room; bathhouse; checkroom; cloakroom; (mil) uniform; (theat) dressing room
Vesubio, el Vesuvius
veta *f* vein; streak, stripe; **descubrir la veta de** to be on to
vetar *tr* to veto
vetea•do -da *adj* veined, striped ‖ *m* graining ‖ *f* (Ecuad) whipping
vetear *tr* to grain, stripe; (Eucad) to whip, flog
veteranía *f* experience, know-how
vetera•no -na *adj* & *mf* veteran
veterina•rio -ria *adj* veterinary ‖ *mf* veterinarian ‖ *f* veterinary medicine
vetus•to -ta *adj* old, ancient
vez *f* (*pl* **veces**) time; (*tiempo de hacer una cosa por turno*) turn; **a la vez** at the same time; **a la vez que** while; **alguna vez** sometimes; ever; **a su vez** in turn; on his part; **a veces** at times, sometimes; **cada vez** every time; **cada vez más** more and more; **cuántas veces** how often; **de una vez** at one time; once and for all; **de vez en cuando** once in a while; **dos veces** twice; **en vez de** instead of; **esperar vez** to wait one's turn; **hacer las veces de** to take the place of; **las más veces** most of the time; **muchas veces** often; **otra vez** again; **raras veces** or **rara vez** seldom, rarely; **repetidas veces** over and over again; **tal vez** perhaps; **tomar la vez a** to get ahead of; **una que otra vez** once in a while; **una vez** once
veza *f* vetch, spring vetch
v.g. or **v.gr.** *abbr* **verbigracia**
vía *f* road, route, way; (*par de rieles y el suelo en que se asientan*) (rr) track; (*el mismo carril*) (rr) rail, track; (anat) passage, tract; (fig) way; **por la vía de** via; **por vía aérea** by air; **por vía bucal** by mouth; **vía aérea** airway; **vía ancha** (rr) broad gauge; **vía de agua** waterway; (naut) leak; **vía estrecha** (rr) narrow gauge; **vía férrea** railway; **vía fluvial** waterway; **Vía Láctea** Milky Way; **vía muerta** (rr) siding; **vía normal** (rr) standard gauge; **vía pública** thoroughfare; **vías de hecho** (law) assault and battery ‖ *prep* via
viable *adj* feasible
viaducto *m* viaduct
viajante *adj* traveling ‖ *mf* traveler ‖ *m* drummer, traveling salesman
viajar *tr* to sell on the road; (*ciertas comarcas*) cover as salesman ‖ *intr* to travel, journey
viaje *m* trip, journey; travel book; water supply; (*drogas*) trip; **¡buen viaje!** bon voyage!; **viaje de ida y vuelta** or **viaje redondo** round trip; **viaje de pruebas** shakedown cruise, trial cruise
viaje•ro -ra *adj* traveling ‖ *mf* traveler; passenger
vial *adj* road, highway ‖ *m* tree-lined road
vianda *f* food, viand; meal
viandante *mf* traveler; itinerant
vitático *m* travel allowance; (eccl) viaticum

víbora *f* viper
vibración *f* vibration
vibrar *tr* to vibrate; (*la voz; la r*) roll; (*una lanza*) hurl ‖ *intr* to vibrate ‖ *ref* to be thrilled
vicaría *f* vicarage
vicario *m* vicar
vicealmirante *m* vice-admiral
vicepresiden•te -ta *mf* vice-president
viceversa *adv* vice versa
viciar *tr* to vitiate; (*una proposición*) to slant ‖ *ref* to become vitiated; give oneself up to vice; become addicted; (*una tabla*) warp
vicio *m* vice; pampering, spoiling; luxuriance, overgrowth; **hablar de vicio** to talk all the time, talk too much; **quejarse de vicio** to be a chronic complainer
vicio•so -sa *adj* vicious; faulty, defective; strong, robust; luxuriant, overgrown; dissolute; (*niño*) spoiled
víctima *f* victim, **víctima propiciatoria** scapegoat
victimar *tr* to kill, murder
victoria *f* victory
victorio•so -sa *adj* victorious
vid *f* vine, grapevine
vida *f* life; living, livelihood; **darse buena vida** to live high; live in comfort; **de por vida** for life; **en mi vida** never; **escapar con vida** to have a narrow escape; **ganar** or **ganarse la vida** to earn one's livelihood, make a living; **hacer por la vida** to get a bite to eat; **mudar de vida** to mend one's ways; **¡por vida mía!** upon my soul!; **vida airada** licentious living; **vida ancha** loose living; **vida de familia** or **de hogar** home life; **vida mía** my darling
vidalita *f* (Arg, Chile, Urug) mournful love song
vidente *mf* clairvoyant ‖ *m* prophet, see ‖ *f* seeress
videocasete *m* video cassette
videodisco *m* video disk
videograbación *f* video-tape recording
video-juego *m* video game
videoseñal *f* picture signal
videotocadiscos *m* video-disk player
vidria•do -da *adj* glazed; brittle ‖ *m* glaze, glazing; glazed pottery; dishes
vidriar §77 & regular *tr* to glaze ‖ *ref* (*los ojos*) to become glassy
vidriera *f* glass window, glass door; shop-window, store window; **vidriera de colores** or **vidriera pintada** stained-glass window
vidriería *f* glassworks; glass store
vidriero *m* glass blower, glassworker; glazier; glass dealer
vidrio *m* glass; piece of glass; windowpane; **pagar los vidrios rotos** to take the blame, to be the goat; **vidrio cilindrado** plate glass; **vidrio de aumento** magnifying glass; **vidrio de color** stained glass; **vidrio deslustrado** ground glass; **vidrio tallado** cut glass
vidrio•so -sa *adj* glassy, vitreous; (*quebradizo*) brittle; (*resbaladizo*) slippery; (*que se*

resiente fácilmente) touchy; (*mirada, ojos*) (fig) glassy

vie•jo -ja *adj* old ‖ *m* old man; **viejo verde** old goat, old rake ‖ *f* old woman

vie•nés -nesa *adj & mf* Viennese

viento *m* wind; course, direction; (*cuerda que mantiene una cosa derecha*) guy; (*gases intestinales*) wind; **ceñir el viento** (naut) to sail close to the wind; **viento de cola** (aer) tail wind; **viento en popa** (naut) tail wind; **vientos alisios** trade winds

vientre *m* belly; (*parte de la ondulación entre dos nodos*) (phys) loop; **evacuar** or **exonerar el vientre** to have a bowel movement; **vientre flojo** loose bowels

vier•nes *m* (*pl* **-nes**) Friday; **Viernes santo** Good Friday

viertea•guas *m* (*pl* **-guas**) *m* flashing

vietna•més -mesa *adj & mf* Vietnamese

viga *f* beam, girder, rafter; **estar contando las vigas** to gaze blankly at the ceiling; **viga de celosía** lattice girder

vigencia *f* force, operation; (*de una póliza de seguro*) life; **en vigencia** in force, in effect

vigente *adj* effective, in force

vigési•mo -ma *adj & m* twentieth

vigía *m* lookout, watch; **vigía de incendios** firewarden ‖ *f* watch; watchtower; (naut) rock, reef

vigiar §77 *tr* to watch over

vigilancia *f* vigilance, watchfulness; **bajo vigilancia médica** under the care of a physician

vigilante *adj* vigilant, watchful ‖ *m* guard, watchman; **vigilante nocturno** night watchman

vigilar *tr* to watch over; look out for ‖ *intr* to watch, keep guard

vigilia *f* vigil; wakefulness; night work, night study; (*víspera*) eve; (mil) guard, watch; **comer de vigilia** to fast, abstain from meat

vigor *m* vigor; **en vigor** in force; into effect

vigoriza•dor -dora *adj* invigorating ‖ *m* tonic; **vigorizador del cabello** hair tonic

vigorizante *adj* invigorating

vigorizar §60 *tr* to invigorate; encourage

vigoro•so -sa *adj* vigorous

vigueta *f* small beam, small girder

vihuela *f* Spanish lute

vil *adj* vile, base, mean ‖ *mf* scoundrel

vilano *m* bur, down

vileza *f* vileness, baseness

vilipendiar *tr* to scorn, despise

vilipendio•so -sa *adj* contemptible

vilo — **en vilo** in the air; (fig) up in the air

vilorta *f* reed hoop; (*arandela*) washer

villa *f* town; (*casa de recreo en el campo*) villa; **la Villa** the city (Madrid)

villancico *m* carol, Christmas carol

villanes•co -ca *adj* boorish, crude, rustic

villanía *f* humbleness, humble birth; vileness, meanness; foul remark

villa•no -na *adj* base, vile; rude, impolite ‖ *mf* peasant; knave, scoundrel

villorrio *m* small country town

vinagre *m* vinegar; (*persona de genio áspero*) grouch

vinagrera *f* vinaigrette; (bot) sorrel; (SAm) heartburn; **vinagreras** cruet stand

vinagreta *f* French dressing, vinaigrette sauce

vinagro•so -sa *adj* vinegary

vinariego *m* vineyardist

vinatería *f* wine business; wine shop

vinate•ro -ra *adj* wine ‖ *m* wine dealer, vintner

vincular *tr* to bind, tie, unite; continue, perpetuate; (*esperanzas*) found, base; (law) entail

vínculo *m* bond, tie; (law) entail

vindicar §73 *tr* (*vengar*) to avenge; (*exculpar*) vindicate

vindicta *f* revenge

vinicul•tor -tora *mf* winegrower

vinicultura *f* winegrowing

vinilo *m* vinyl

vino *m* wine; sherry reception, wine party; **tener mal vino** to be a quarrelsome drunk; **vino cubierto** dark-red wine; **vino de Jerez** sherry; **vino del terruño** local wine; **vino de mesa** table wine; **vino de Oporto** port wine; **vino de pasto** table wine; **vino de postre** after-dinner wine; **vino de segunda** second-run wine; **vino de solera** solera sherry; **vino tinto** red table wine

vinolen•to -ta *adj* too fond of wine

viña *f* vineyard; **ser una viña** to be a mine; **tener una viña** to have a sinecure

viña•dor -dora *mf* vineyardist, vinedresser ‖ *m* guard of a vineyard

viñedo *m* vineyard

viñeta *f* vignette, headpiece

viola•do -da *adj & m* violet (*color*)

violar *m* bed of violets ‖ *tr* to violate; ravish, rape; profane, desecrate; tamper with

violencia *f* violence

violentar *tr* to do violence to; (*p.ej., una casa*) break into ‖ *ref* to force oneself

violen•to -ta *adj* violent

violeta *m* (*color; colorante*) violet ‖ *f* (bot) violet

violín *m* violin; (billiards) bridge, cue rest; **embolsar el violín** (Arg, Ven) to cower, to slink away

violinista *mf* violinist

violón *m* (mus) bass viol; **tocar el violón** to talk nonsense

violoncelista *mf* cellist, violoncellist

violoncelo *m* (mus) cello, violoncello

violonchelista *mf* cellist, violoncellist

violonchelo *m* (mus) cello, violoncello

vira *f* welt; (*saetilla*) dart

virada *f* turn, change of direction; (naut) tack

virago *f* mannish woman

viraje *m* turn, swerve; (phot) toning

virar *tr* (naut) to wind; (naut) to tack, veer; (phot) to tone ‖ *intr* to turn, swerve; (naut) to tack, veer

virgen *adj* virgin ‖ *f* virgin, maiden

virginidad *f* virginity

Virgo *m* (astr) Virgo

vírgula *f* rod; thin line, light dash

virgulilla *f* fine line; diacritic mark

virilidad *f* virility

virin•go -ga *adj* (Col) naked

ve
vi

virolen•to -ta *adj* pock-marked; having small-pox
virología *f* virology
virote *m* (*saeta*) bolt; sporty young fellow; (coll) stuffed shirt
virrey *m* viceroy
virtual *adj* virtual
virtud *f* virtue
virtuosismo *m* virtuosity
virtuo•so -sa *adj* virtuous ‖ *m* virtuoso
viruela *f* smallpox; pock mark; **viruelas lo-cas** chicken pox
virulencia *f* virulence
virulen•to -ta *adj* virulent
vi•rus *m* (*pl* **-rus**) virus
viruta *f* shaving
virutilla *f* thin shaving; **virutillas de acero** steel wool
visado *m* visa
visaje *m* face, grimace
visar *tr* to visa; to O.K.; (arti & surv) to sight
vísceras *fpl* viscera
visco *m* birdlime
viscosa *f* viscose
viscosilla *f* rayon thread
visco•so -sa *adj* viscous ‖ *f* see **viscosa**
visera *f* (*del yelmo, de las gorras, del para-brisas del automóvil, etc.*) visor; (*pequeña pantalla que se pone en la frente para resguardar la vista*) eyeshade; (W-I) blink-er, blinker
visible *adj* visible; (*manifiesto*) evident; (*que llama la antención*) conspicuous
visigo•do -da *adj* Visigothic ‖ *mf* Visigoth
visillo *m* window curtain, window shade
visión *f* vision; view; (*persona fea y ridícula*) sight, scarecrow; **ver visiones** to be seeing things; **visión negra** (*del aviador*) blackout
visionar *tr* to contemplate, look at
visiona•rio -ria *adj* & *mf* visionary
visir *m* vizier; **gran visir** grand vizier
visita *f* visit; visitor, caller; inspection; **ir de visitas** to go calling; **pagar la visita a** to return the call of; **tener visita** to have callers; **visita de cumplido** formal call; **visita de médico** short call
visita•dor -dora *mf* frequent caller ‖ *m* in-spector ‖ *f* (Hond, Ven) enema
visitante *adj* visiting ‖ *mf* visitor
visitar *tr* to visit; inspect
visite•ro -ra *adj* visiting; (*médico*) fond of making calls ‖ *mf* visitor
vislumbrar *tr* to descry, glimpse; surmise, suspect ‖ *ref* (*verse confusamente por la distancia*) glimmer; (*aparecer en la distan-cia*) loom
vislumbre *f* glimpse, glimmer; **vislumbres** inkling, notion
viso *m* sheen, gleam; (*de ciertas telas*) luster; streak, strain; appearance, thin veneer; el-evation, height; colored material worn un-der transparent outer garment; **a dos visos** with a double purpose; **de viso** conspicu-ous; **hacer visos** to be iridescent
visón *m* mink
visor *m* (aer) bombsight; (phot) finder
víspera *f* eve, day before; **en vísperas de** on

the eve of; **víspera de año nuevo** New Year's Eve; **víspera de Navidad** Christ-mas Eve; **vísperas** (eccl) vespers, even-song
vista *m* custom-house inspector ‖ *f* (*sentido del ver*) vision, sight; (*paisaje que se ve desde un punto; estampa que representa un lugar*) view; (*panorama, perspectiva*) vis-ta; comparison; purpose, design; (*ojeada*) glance, look; interview; eye; eyes; (law) hearing, trial; **a la vista** (com) at sight; **a vista de** in view of; compared with; **con vistas a** with a view to; **de vista** by sight; **doble vista** second sight; **hacer la vista gorda ante** to shut one's eyes to; **hasta la vista** good-bye, so long; **medir con la vista** to size up; **saltar a la vista** to be self-evident; **tener a la vista** to keep one's eyes on; (*p.ej., una carta*) to have at hand; **torcer la vista** to squint; **vista a ojo de pájaro** bird's-eye view; **vistas** (*aberturas de un edificio*) lights, openings; view, out-look; visible parts, parts that show
vistazo *m* look, glance
vistillas *fpl* eminence, height; **irse a las vistillas** to try to get a look at one's opponent's cards
vis•to -ta *adj* evident, obvious; in view of; **bien visto** looked upon with approval; **mal visto** looked upon with disapproval; **no visto** or **nunca visto** unheard-of; **por lo visto** apparently, judging from the facts; **visto bueno** approved, O.K.; **visto que** whereas, inasmuch as ‖ *m* whereas ‖ *f* see **vista**
visto•so -sa *adj* showy, flashy, loud
visual *adj* visual ‖ *f* line of sight
vital *adj* vital
vitali•cio -cia *adj* life, lifetime ‖ *m* life-insurance policy; life annuity
vitalidad *f* vitality
vitalizar §60 *tr* to vitalize
vitamina *f* vitamin
vitan•do -da *adj* hateful, odious; being shunned
vitela *f* vellum
viticul•tor -tora *mf* grape grower, vineyardist
viticultura *f* grape growing
vitola *f* cigar size; mien, appearance; (Cuba) cigar band
vítor *interj* hurray! ‖ *m* panegyric tablet; triumphal pageant
vitorear *tr* to cheer, acclaim
vitral *m* stained-glass window
vítre•o -a *adj* vitreous, glassy
vitrina *f* showcase, glass cabinet; shopwin-dow
vitrióli•co -ca *adj* (chem) vitriolic
vitrola *f* record player
vituallas *fpl* victuals
vituperable *adj* vituperable
vituperar *tr* to vituperate
viuda *f* widow; **viuda de marido vivo** or **viuda de paja** grass widow
viudedad *f* widowhood; dower; widow's pension

viudez *f* (*estado de viuda*) widowhood; (*estado de viudo*) widowerhood

viu•do -da *adj* left a widow; left a widower || *m* widower || *f* see **viuda**

viva *interj* viva!, long live! || *m* viva

vivacidad *f* longevity; vivacity, liveliness; brightness, brilliance

vivande•ro -ra *mf* (mil) sutler, camp follower

vivaque *m* bivouac; guardhouse; police headquarters; **estar al vivaque** to bivouac

vivaquear *intr* to bivouac

vivar *m* warren, burrow; aquarium || *tr* to cheer, acclaim

vivara•cho -cha *adj* vivacious, lively

vi•vaz *adj* (*pl* -**vaces**) long-lived; vivacious, lively; keen, perceptive; (bot) perennial

víveres *mpl* food, provisions, victuals

vivero *m* tree nursery; fishpond; (*origen de cosas perjudiciales*) (fig) hotbed

viveza *f* agility, briskness; ardor, vehemence; sharpness, keenness; perception; brightness, brilliance; witticism; (*de los ojos*) sparkle; (*acción o palabra poco consideradas*) thoughtlessness

vivide•ro -ra *adj* livable

vívi•do -da *adj* quick, perceptive; lively

vivienda *f* dwelling; life, way of life; **vivienda unifamiliar** one-family house

viviente *adj* living, alive

vivificar §73 *tr* to vivify, enliven

vivir *m* life, living || *tr* (*una experiencia o ventura*) to live; (*toda la vida; la vejez*) live out; (*habitar*) live in || *intr* to live; **¿quién vive?** (mil) who goes there?; **vivir de** (*p.ej., carne*) to live on; **vivir para ver** to live and learn; **vivir y dejar vivir** to live and let live

vivisección *f* vivisection

vi•vo -va *adj* living, alive, live; (*lleno de vida; intenso*) live; (*sutil, agudo*) sharp, keen; (*dolor*) acute; (*carne*) raw; active, effective; (*luz*) bright, intense; (*pronto y ágil*) quick; (*idioma*) living, modern; **de viva voz** viva voce, by word of mouth; **herir en lo vivo** to cut or to sting to the quick || *mf* living person; **los vivos y los muertos** the quick and the dead || *m* edging, border; (vet) mange

Vizcaya *f* Biscay; **llevar hierro a Vizcaya** to carry coals to Newcastle

vizconde *m* viscount

vizcondesa *f* viscountess

V.M. *abbr* **Vuestra Majestad**

V.°B.° *abbr* **visto bueno**

vocablista *mf* punster

vocablo *m* word; **jugar del vocablo** to pun

vocabulario *m* vocabulary

vocación *f* vocation, calling

vocal *adj* vocal || *mf* director || *f* vowel

vocalista *mf* singer, vocalist

vocativo *m* vocative

voceador *m* town crier; (Col, Ecuad) paper boy

vocear *tr* to cry, shout; cheer, acclaim; call, page; boast about publicly || *intr* to shout

vocería *f* shouting, outcry; spokesmanship

vocerío *m* shouting, outcry

vocero *m* spokesman, mouthpiece

vociferar *tr* (*injurias*) to shout; boast loudly about || *intr* to vociferate, shout

vocingle•ro -ra *adj* loudmouthed; loud, talkative

vo•dú *m* (*pl* -**dúes**) voodoo

voduísta *adj* & *mf* voodoo

vol. *abbr* **volumen, voluntad**

volada *f* short flight; (*del jugador de billar*) (Arg) stroke; (Col, Ecuad) trick; (*noticia inventada*) (Mex) hoax

voladi•zo -za *adj* projecting || *m* projection

vola•do -da *adj* (typ) superior || *f* see **volada**

vola•dor -dora *adj* flying; hanging, dangling; swift, fast || *m* rocket; flying fish

voladura *f* blast, explosion

volandas — en volandas in the air; fast

volante *adj* flying; unsettled || *m* shuttlecock; battledore and shuttlecock; (*rueda que regula el movimiento de una máquina*) flywheel; (*rueda de mano para la dirección del automóvil*) steering wheel; (*pieza del reloj movida por la espiral*) balance wheel; flunkey, lackey; (*criado que iba a pie delante del coche o caballo*) outrunner; (*de papel*) slip, leaflet; (sew) flounce, ruffle; **un buen volante** a good driver

volan•tín -tina *adj* unsettled || *m* fish line; kite

volantista *m* driver, man at the wheel

volan•tón -tona *mf* fledgling || *f* (Ven) loose woman

volapié *m* (taur) stroke in which the matador moves in for the kill; **a volapié** half running, half flying; half walking, half swimming

volar §61 *tr* (*llevar en un aparato de aviación*) to fly; blow up, explode; irritate; (*una letra, tipo o signo*) (typ) to raise || *intr* to fly; fly away; disappear; jut out, project; (*una especie*) spread rapidly; (*p.ej., una torre*) rise in the air; **volar sin motor** (aer) to glide || *ref* to fly away; fly off the handle

volatería *f* fowling with decoys; **de volatería** offhand

volátil *adj* volatile

volatilizar *tr* & *ref* to volatilize

volatín *m* ropewalker, acrobat, tumbler

volatine•ro -ra *mf* ropewalker, acrobat, tumbler

volcán *m* volcano

volcar §81 *tr* to upset, overturn, dump; tip, tilt; (*a una persona un olor fuerte*) to make dizzy; change the mind of; irritate, tease || *intr* to upset || *ref* to turn upside down

volear *tr* (tennis) to volley

voleo *m* (tennis) volley; reeling punch; **del primer voleo** or **de un voleo** with a smash, all at once; **sembrar al voleo** to sow, broadcast

volframio *m* wolfram

volibol *m* volleyball

volquete *m* dumpcart, dump truck

voltai•co -ca *adj* voltaic

voltaje *m* voltage

volta•rio -ria *adj* fickle, inconstant; (Chile) willful; (Chile) sporty

voltea•do -da *mf* (Col) turncoat, deserter

voltear *tr* to upset, turn over; turn around; move, transform ‖ *intr* to roll over, tumble

volteo *m* upset, overturning; tumbling; (P-R) scolding

voltereta *f* tumble; turning up card to determine trump

voltímetro *m* voltmeter

voltio *m* volt

volti•zo -za *adj* curled, twisted; fickle

voluble *adj* easily turned; fickle, inconstant

volumen *m* volume; **volumen sonoro** volume; (geom) volume

volumino•so -sa *adj* voluminous

voluntad *f* will; (*amor, cariño*) fondness, love; **a voluntad** at will; **buena voluntad** willingness; **de buena voluntad** willingly; **de mala voluntad** unwillingly; **de su propia voluntad** of one's own volition; **última voluntad** last will and testament; last wish; **voluntad de hierro** iron will

voluntariedad *f* willfulness

volunta•rio -ria *adj* (*que se hace por espontánea voluntad*) voluntary; (*que tiene voluntad obstinada*) willful; (*que se presta voluntariamente a hacer algo*) volunteer ‖ *mfr* volunteer

voluntario•so -sa *adj* willful

voluptuo•so -sa *adj* (*que inspira complacencia en los placeres sensuales*) voluptuous; (*dado a los placeres sensuales*) voluptuary ‖ *mf* voluptuary

voluta *f* (archit) scroll, volute; (*p.ej., de humo*) ring

volvedor *m* screwdriver; (Col) extra, something thrown in; **volvedor de machos** tap wrench

volver §47 & §83 *tr* to turn; turn upside down; turn inside out; return, send back, give back; (*una puerta*) push to, pull to; translate; vomit ‖ *intr* to turn; return, come back; **volver a** + *inf* verb + again, e.g., **volvió a abrir la puerta** he opened the door again; **volver en sí** to come to; **volver por** to defend, stand up for ‖ *ref* to become; turn around; return, come back; change one's mind; turn, turn sour; **volverse atrás** to back out; **volverse contra** to turn on

vomitar *tr* to vomit, throw up; (*fuego los cañones*) belch forth; (*maldiciones*) utter; (*un secreto*) let out; (*lo que uno retiene indebidamente*) cough up ‖ *intr* to vomit, throw up; come across, disgorge

vómito *m* vomit, vomiting; **provocar a vómito** to nauseate; **vómitos del embarazo** morning sickness

voracidad *f* voracity

vorágine *f* whirlpool, vortex

vo•raz *adj* (*pl* **-races**) voracious

vormela *f* polecat

vórtice *m* vortex

vos *pron pers* (subject of verb and object of preposition; takes plural form of verb but is singular in meaning; used in addressing the Deity, the Virgin, etc., and distinguished persons; in Spanish America is much used instead of **tú**) you

voso•tros -tras *pron pers* (plural of **tú**) you

votación *f* vote, voting; **votación de desempate** runoff election

votante *adj* voting ‖ *mf* voter

votar *tr* to vote for; (*sí, no*) vote; (*p.ej., un cirio a la Virgen*) vow ‖ *intr* to vote; vow; swear, curse

voti•vo -va *adj* votive

voto *m* (*sufragio; derecho de votar; persona que da su voto*) vote; (*promesa solemne*) vow; (*exvoto*) votive offering; (*blasfemia*) oath, curse; wish, desire; **echar votos** to swear, to curse; **regular los votos** to tally the votes; **voto de amén** vote of a yes man; yes man; **voto de calidad** casting vote; **voto informativo** straw vote; **votos** good wishes; **¡voto va!** come now!

voz *f* (*pl* **voces**) voice; (*vocablo*) word; **aclarar la voz** to clear one's throat; **a una voz** with one voice; **a voces** shouting; **a voz en cuello** or **en grito** at the top of one's voice; **correr la voz que** to be rumored that; **dar voces** to shout, cry out; **de viva voz** viva voce, by word of mouth; **en alta voz** aloud, in a loud voice; **en voz baja** in a low voice; **llevar la voz cantante** to have the say, be the boss; **voces** outcry

voz-guía *f* (*diccionario*) entry word

vro. *abbr* **vuestro**

V.S. *abbr* **Vueseñoría**

vuelco *m* upset, overturn; **darle a uno un vuelco el corazón** to have a presentiment

vuelo *m* flight; flying; (*de una falda*) flare, fullness; projection; lace cuff trimming; **al vuelo** at once; on the wing; scattered at random; (chess) en passant; **alzar el vuelo** to take flight; to dash away; **echar a vuelo las campanas** to ring a full peal; **tirar al vuelo** to shoot on the wing; **tocar a vuelo las campanas** to ring a full peal; **vuelo a ciegas** (aer) blind flying; **vuelo de distancia** (aer) long-distance flight; **vuelo de enlace** connecting flight; **vuelo de ensayo** or **de prueba** (aer) test flight; **vuelo espacial tripulado** manned space flight; **vuelo planeado** (aer) volplane; **vuelo rasante** (aer) hedgehopping; **vuelo sin escala** (aer) nonstop flight; **vuelo sin motor** (aer) glide, gliding

vuelta *f* turn; (*regreso; devolución*) return; (*dinero sobrante de un pago*) change; (*de un camino*) bend, turn; (*del pantalón*) cuff; cuff trimming; (*paseo corto*) stroll; (*revés*) other side; (*paliza*) beating, whipping; (*en un cabo*) loop; (*en la media*) clock; (*mudanza*) change; **a la vuelta** on returning; please turn the page; **a la vuelta de** at the end of; at the turn of; (*la esquina*) around; **a vuelta de** about; **a vuelta de correo** by return mail; **dar cien vueltas a** to run rings around, be way ahead of; **dar la vuelta de campana** to turn somersault; **darse una vuelta a la redonda** to tend to one's own business; **dar una vuelta** to take a stroll; take a walk; take a look; change one's ways; **dar vuelta** to turn around; (*el vino*) turn sour; **dar vuelta a** to reverse, turn around; **estar de vuelta** to be back; **quedarse con la vuelta** to keep the change; **vuelta de campana** somersault; **vuelta del mundo** trip around the world

vuelto *m* change

vues•tro -tra (corresponds to **vos** and **vosotros**) *adj poss* your ‖ *pron poss* yours

vulcanizar §60 *tr* to vulcanize

vulgacho *m* populace, mob

vulgar *adj* vulgar, popular, common, vernacular

vulgarismo *m* popular expression; (philol) popular word, popular form

vulgarizar §60 *tr* to popularize; translate into the vernacular ‖ *ref* to associate with the people

Vulgata *f* Vulgate

vulgo *adv* commonly ‖ *m* common people; (*personas que en una materia sólo conocen la parte superficial*) laity

vulnerable *adj* vulnerable

vulnerar *tr* to hurt, injure; (*la reputación de una persona*) damage; (*una ley, un precepto*) break

vulpeja *f* she-fox, vixen

V.V. or **VV** *abbr* **ustedes**

X

X, x (equis) *f* twenty-sixth letter of the Spanish alphabet

xenia *f* xenia

xenofobia *f* xenophobia

xenófo•bo -ba *mf* xenophobe

xenón *m* xenon

xerografía *f* xerography

xerografiar §77 *tr* to xerograph ‖ *intr* to make xerograph copies

xilófono *m* (mus) xylophone

xilografía *f* (*arte*) xylography; (*grabado*) xylograph

xpiano *abbr* **cristiano**

Xpo *abbr* **Cristo**

xptiano *abbr* **cristiano**

Xpto *abbr* **Cristo**

xunde *m* (Mex) reed basket, palm basket

Y

Y, y (ye) *f* twenty-seventh letter of the Spanish alphabet

y *conj* and

ya *adv* already; right away; now; **no ya** not only; **ya no** no longer; **ya que** since, inasmuch as

yac *m* (*bandera de proa*) (naut) jack; (*bóvido del Tibet*) yak

yacer §82 *intr* to lie

yacija *f* bed, couch; (*sepultura*) grave

yacimiento *m* bed, field, deposit; **yacimiento de petróleo** oil field

yámbi•co -ca *adj* iambic

yambo *m* iamb, iambus

yanqui *adj & mf* Yankee

Yanquilandia *f* Yankeedom

yapa *f* bonus, extra, allowance; **de yapa** in the bargain, extra

yarda *f* yard, yardstick

yate *m* yacht

yedra *f* ivy

yegua *f* mare; (CAm) cigar butt

yeguada *f* stud

yelmo *m* helmet

yema *f* (*de huevo*) yolk; candied yolk; (*del invierno*) dead; (*renuevo*) bud; (fig) cream; **dar en la yema** to put one's finger on the

spot; **yema del dedo** finger tip; **yema mejida** eggnog

yente — **yentes y vinientes** *mpl* habitués, frequenters

yerba *f* var of **hierba**

yer•mo -ma *adj* deserted, uninhabited; (*suelo*) unsown; (*mujer*) not pregnant ‖ *m* desert, wilderness

yerno *m* son-in-law

yerro *m* error, mistake; **yerro de cuenta** miscalculation; **yerro de imprenta** printer's error

yer•to -ta *adj* stiff, rigid

yesca *f* punk, tinder; (*cosa que excita una pasión*) fuel; **echar una yesca** to strike a light

yeso *m* gypsum; plaster cast

yo *pron pers* **I; soy yo** it's me, it is I

yodhídri•co -ca *adj* hydriodic

yodo *m* iodine

yoduro *m* iodide

yoga *f* yoga

yogui *m* yogi

yogurt *m* yogurt

yola *f* shell (*boat*)

yonquí *m* (*drogas*) junkie, drug addict

yugo *m* yoke; **sacudir el yugo** to throw off the yoke

vo
yu

Yugoeslavia f Yugoslavia
yugoesla•vo -va adj & mf Yugoslav
yugular adj & f jugular ‖ tr to cut off, nip in the bud
yunque m anvil; drudge, work horse

yunta f yoke, team
yute m jute
yuxtaponer §54 tr to juxtapose
yuyo m (Arg, Chile) weed; **yuyos** (Col, Ecuad, Peru) greens

Z

Z, z (zeda or zeta) f twenty-eighth letter of the Spanish alphabet
zabordar intr (naut) to run aground
zabullir §13 tr (p.ej., a un perro) to duck, give a ducking to; throw, hurl ‖ ref (meterse debajo del agua con ímpetu) to dive; (esconderse rápidamente) duck
zacapela f or **zacapella** f row, rumpus
zacate m (CAm, Mex) hay, fodder; **zacate de empaque** excelsior
zacateca m (Cuba) undertaker, gravedigger
zacatín m old-clothes market
zacear tr (al perro) to chase away ‖ intr to lisp
zafaduría f (Arg) brazenness, effrontery
zafar tr to adorn, bedeck; loosen, untie; clear, free; (un buque) lighten ‖ ref to slip away; slip off, come off; **zafarse de** to get out of
zafarrancho m (naut) clearing the decks; (coll) havoc, ravage; (coll) scuffle, row; **zafarrancho de combate** (naut) clearing the deck for action
za•fio -fia adj rough, uncouth, boorish
zafiro m sapphire
za•fo -fa adj unhurt, intact; (naut) free, clear ‖ **zafo** prep (Col) except
zafra f olive-oil can; drip jar; sugar crop; sugar making; sugar-making season; (min) rubbish, muck
zaga f rear; load carried in the rear; (mil) rearguard; **a la zaga, a zaga** or **en zaga** behind, in the rear; **no ir en zaga a** to not be behind, be as good as
zagal m young fellow; strapping young fellow; shepherd boy; footboy
zagala f lass, maiden; young shepherdess
zaguán m vestibule, hall, entry
zague•ro -ra adj back, rear ‖ m (sport) back, backstop
zaherir §68 tr to upbraid, reproach; scold shamefully
zahones mpl chaps, hunting breeches
zaho•rí m (pl **-ríes**) keen observer; seer, clairvoyant
zahurda f pigpen
zai•no -na adj treacherous, false; (caballo) vicious; (caballo) dark-chestnut; **mirar a lo zaino** or **de zaino** to look askance at
za•lá f (pl **-laes**) Muslim prayer; **hacer la zalá a** to fawn on

zalagarda f ambush; skirmish; (trampa para cazar animales) trap; trick; row, rumpus; mock fight
zalamería f flattery, cajolery
zalame•ro -ra adj flattering, fawning ‖ mf flatterer, fawner
zalea f unsheared sheepskin
zalear tr to drag around, shake; (al perro) chase away
zalema f salaam
zamacuco m blockhead; sullen fellow; drunkenness
zamacueca f cueca (Chilean courtship dance)
zamarra f undressed sheepskin; sheepskin jacket
zam•bo -ba adj knock-kneed
zambra f merrymaking, celebration; Moorish boat
zambucar §73 tr to slip away, hide away
zambullida f dive, plunge; (fencing) thrust to the breast
zambulli•dor -dora adj diving, plunging ‖ mf diver, plunger ‖ m (orn) diver, loon
zambullir §13 tr (p.ej., a un perro) to duck, give a ducking to; throw, hurl ‖ ref (meterse debajo del agua con ímpetu) to dive; (esconderse rápidamente) duck
zampa f pile, bearing pile
zampacuarti•llos mf (pl **-llos**) toper, soak
zampalimos•nas mf (pl **-nas**) bum, ordinary bum
zampar tr to slip away, hide away; gobble down ‖ ref to slip away, hide away
zampator•tas mf (pl **-tas**) glutton; boor
zampear tr (el terreno) to strengthen with piles and rubble
zampoña f shepherd's pipe, rustic flute; nonsense, folly
zampuzar §60 tr to duck, give a ducking to; slip away, hide away
zanahoria f carrot
zanca f long leg; (de la escalera) horse
zancada f long stride; **en dos zancadas** in a flash, in a jiffy
zancadilla f booby trap; **echar la zancadilla a** to stick out one's foot and trip
zancajo m heel; **no llegar a los zancajos a** to not come up to, not be equal to
zancajo•so -sa adj duck-toed; down-at-the-heel
zancarrón m dirty old fellow
zanco m stilt; **en zancos** from a vantage point

zancu•do -da adj long-legged; (orn) wading || m mosquito || f wading bird

zanfonía f hurdy-gurdy

zangala f buckram

zangamanga f trick

zanganada f impertinence, impudence

zanganear intr to loaf around

zángano m (ent) drone; (fig) drone, loafer; (CAm) scoundrel

zangarrear intr to thrum a guitar

zangolotear tr to jiggle || intr to fuss around || ref to jiggle, flop around, rattle

zangoloteo m jiggle, jiggling, rattle; fuss, bother

zanguanga f malingering; flattery; **hacer la zanguanga** to malinger

zanguan•go -ga adj slow, lazy || mf loafer || f see **zanguanga**

zanja f ditch, trench; (SAm) gully; **abrir las zanjas** to lay the foundations

zanquear intr to waddle; to rush around

zanquilar•go -ga adj leggy, long-legged

zanquituer•to -ta adj bandy-legged

zapa f spade; sharkskin, (mil) sap

zapapico m mattock, pickax

zapar tr (mil) to sap, mine, excavate

zaparrastrar intr — **ir zaparrastrando** to go along trailing one's clothes on the ground

zapateado m clog dance, tap dance

zapatear tr to hit with the shoe; tap with the feet; abuse, ill-treat || intr to tap-dance; (las velas) flap || ref — **zapatearse con** to hold out against

zapatería f shoemaking; shoemaker's shop; (tienda) shoe store

zapate•ro -ra adj poorly cooked || mf shoemaker; shoe dealer; **quedarse zapatero** to not take a trick; **¡zapatero, a tus zapatos!** stick to your last!; **zapatero de viejo** or **zapatero remendón** cobbler, shoemaker

zapatilla f slipper; (escarpín) pump; (del grifo) washer; (del florete) leather tip or button; cloven hoof

zapato m shoe, low shoe; **andar con zapatos de fieltro** to gumshoe; **como tres en un zapato** hard up; like sardines; **zapato de goma** overshoe; **zapato inglés** low shoe

zapatón m (Guat, SAm) overshoe

zapear tr (al gato) to scare away, chase away

zaque m wineskin; tippler, drunk

zaquiza•mí m (pl -míes) attic, garret; hovel, pigpen

zar m czar

zarabanda f (mus) saraband; noise, confusion, uproar; (Mex) beating, thrashing

zaragata f scuffle, row; **zaragatas** (W-I) flattery

Zaragoza f Saragossa

zaranda f sieve, screen; colander; (Ven) horn; (Ven) top

zarandajas fpl odds and ends, trinkets

zarandar tr to sift, screen; winnow, pick out, select; jiggle || ref to jiggle; swagger, strut

zaraza f chintz, printed cotton

zarcillo m eardrop; (bot) tendril

zarigüeya f opossum

zarina f czarina

zarpa f claw, paw; (naut) weighing anchor

zarpar tr (el ancla) (naut) to weigh (anchor) || intr (naut) to weigh anchor, set sail

zarpo•so -sa adj mud-splashed

zarracatería f cajolery, insincere flattery

zarracatín m sharp trader

zarramplín m botcher, bungler

zarrien•to -ta adj mud-splashed

zarza f blackberry, bramble (bush)

zarzamora f blackberry (fruit)

zarzaparrilla f sarsaparilla

zarzo m hurdle, wattle

zarzo•so -sa adj brambly

zarzuela f small bramble; (theat) zarzuela (Spanish musical comedy); **zarzuela grande** three-act zarzuela

zas interj bang!; **¡zas, zas!** bing, bang!

zascandilear intr to meddle, scheme

zepelín m zeppelin

Zeus m Zeus

zigzag m zigzag

zigzaguear intr to zigzag

zinc m (pl **zinces**) zinc

zipizape m scuffle, row, rumpus

ziszás m zigzag

zoca f public square

zócalo m (archit) socle; (de una pared) dado; (rad) socket; (Mex) public square, center square

zoca•to -ta adj (fruto) corky, pithy; left; left-handed || mf left-handed person

zoclo m clog, wooden shoe

zo•co -ca adj left; left-handed || mf left-handed person || m clog, wooden shoe; Moroccan market place; (archit) socle; **andar de zocos en colodros** to jump from the frying pan into the fire || f see **zoca**

zodíaco m zodiac

zofra f Moorish carpet, Moorish rug

zolo•cho -cha adj stupid, simple || mf simpleton

zollipar intr to sob

zollipo m sob

zona m (pathol) shingles || f zone; (banda, faja) belt, girdle; **zona a batir** target area; **zona desmilitarizada** demilitarized zone; **zona siniestrada** disaster area

zon•zo -za adj tasteless, insipid; dull, inane || mf dolt, dimwit

zoófito m zoöphyte

zoología f zoölogy

zoológi•co -ca adj zoölogic(al)

zoólo•go -ga mf zoölogist

zopen•co -ca adj dull, stupid || mf dullard, blockhead

zopilote m (Mex, CAm) turkey buzzard, turkey vulture

zo•po -pa adj crippled; awkward, gauche || mf cripple

zoquete m (de madera) block, chunk, end; (de pan) bit, crust; chump, lout

zoquetu•do -da adj coarse, crude

zorra f fox; female fox; cunning person; prostitute; drunkenness; dray, truck; **pillar una zorra** to get drunk

yu

zo

zorrera f (*cueva de zorros*) foxhole; smoke-filled room; worry, confusion

zorrería f foxiness, craftiness

zorre•ro -ra adj sly, foxy; slow, heavy, tardy ‖ f see **zorrera**

zorrillo m skunk

zorro m male fox; (*piel*) fox; (*hombre taimado*) fox; **estar hecho un zorro** to be overwhelmed with sleep; be dull and sullen; **zorros** duster

zorral m (orn) fieldfare; sly fellow; (Chile) simpleton

zozobra f capsizing, sinking; anxiety

zozobrar tr (*un buque*) to sink; (*un negocio*) wreck ‖ intr to capsize, sink; (*la embarcación en la tempestad*) wallow; (*un negocio*) be in great danger; be greatly worried ‖ ref to capsize, sink

zueco m clog, wooden shoe, sabot

zulacar §73 tr to waterproof

zulaque m waterproofing

zulú adj & mf (pl **-lús** o **-lúes**) Zulu

zullar ref to have a bowel movement; break wind

zullen•co -ca adj windy, flatulent

zumaque m sumach; wine

zumaya f (*autillo*) tawny owl; (*chotacabras*) goatsucker

zumba f bell worn by leading mule; (Mex) drunkenness; **hacer zumba a** to make fun of; **sin zumba** (Mex) in a rush, in a hurry

zumbador m buzzer; (Mex) pauraque; (Mex, CAm, W-I) hummingbird

zumbar tr to make fun of; (*un golpe, una bofetada*) let have ‖ intr to buzz; zoom; (*los oídos*) ring; **zumbar a** (*frisar con*) to be close to, border on ‖ ref (Cuba) to go too far, forget oneself; (P-R) to rush ahead; **zumbarse de** to make fun of

zumbido m buzz; zoom; blow, smack; **zumbido de ocupación** (telp) busy signal; **zumbido de oídos** ringing in the ears

zum•bón -bona adj waggish, playful ‖ mf wag, jester

zumien•to -ta adj juicy

zumo m juice; advantage, profit; **zumo de cepas** or **de parras** fruit of the vine

zumo•so -sa adj juicy

zunchar tr to band, hoop

zuncho m band, hoop

zupia f (*del vino*) dregs; slop, wine full of dregs; (fig) junk, trash

zurcido m darning; darn; invisible mending

zurcir §36 tr to darn; (*una mentira*) hatch, concoct; (*unas mentiras*) weave (*a tissue of lies*)

zurdazo m (box) left, blow with the left

zur•do -da adj left; left-handed; **a zurdas** with the left hand; the wrong way ‖ mf left-handed person

zurear intr to coo

zuro m stripped corncob

zurra f dressing, currying; scuffle, quarrel; drubbing, thrashing; (*trabajo o estudio continuados*) grind

zurrapa f thread, filament; trash, rubbish; **con zurrapas** in a sloppy manner

zurrar tr (*el cuero*) to dress, curry; get the best of; (*censurar con dureza*) dress down; (*castigar con azotes*) drub, thrash ‖ ref (*hacer sus necesidades involuntariamente*) to have an accident; be scared to death; (Arg) to break wind noiselessly

zurriagar §44 tr to whip, horsewhip

zurriago m whip, lash

zurribanda f rain of blows; rumpus, scuffle

zurrir intr to buzz, grate

zurrón m shepherd's leather bag; leather bag; (*cáscara*) husk

zurrona f loose, evil woman

zurullo m soft roll; turd

zurupeto m unregistered broker; shyster notary

zuta•no -na mf so-and-so

Spanish Irregular Verbs

All simple tenses are shown in these tables if they contain one irregular form or more, except the conditional (which can always be derived from the stem of the future indicative) and the imperfect and future subjunctive (which can always be derived from the third plural preterit indicative minus the last syllable -ron).

The numbers are those that accompany the respective verbs and verbs of identical patterns where they are listed in their alphabetical places in this Dictionary. The letters (a) to (h) identify the tenses as follows:

(a)	gerund	(e)	present subjunctive
(b)	past participle	(f)	imperfect indicative
(c)	imperative	(g)	future indicative
(d)	present indicative	(h)	preterit indicative

§1 **abolir:** defective verb used only in forms whose endings contain the vowel **i**

§2 **acertar**
(c) **acierta**, acertad
(d) **acierto, aciertas, acierta**, acertamos. acertáis, **aciertan**
(e) **acierte, aciertes, acierte**, acertemos, acertéis, **acierten**

§3 **agorar:** like §61 but with diaeresis on the **u** of **ue**
(c) **agüera**, agorad
(d) **agüero, agüeras, agüera**, agoramos, agoráis, **agüeran**
(e) **agüere, agüeres, agüere**, agoremos, agoréis, **agüeren**

§4 **airar**
(c) **aíra**, airad
(d) **aíro, aíras, aíra**, airamos, airáis, **aíran**
(e) **aíre, aíres, aíre**, airemos, airéis, **aíren**

§5 **andar**
(h) **anduve, anduviste, anduvo, anduvimos, anduvisteis, anduvieron**

§6 **argüir:** like §20 but with diaeresis on **u** in forms with accented **i** in the ending
(a) **arguyendo**
(b) **argüido**
(c) **arguye**, argüid
(d) **arguyo, arguyes, arguye**, argüimos, argüís, **arguyen**
(e) **arguya, arguyas, arguya, arguyamos, arguyáis, arguyan**
(h) **argüí, argüiste, arguyó**, argüimos. argüisteis, **arguyeron**

§7 **asir**
(d) **asgo**, ases, ase. asimos. asís, asen
(e) **asga, asgas, asga, asgamos, asgáis, asgan**

§8 **aunar**
(c) **aúna**, aunad
(d) **aúno, aúnas, aúna**, aunamos. aunáis, **aúnan**
(e) **aúne, aúnes, aúne**, aunemos, aunéis, **aúnen**

§9 **avergonzar:** combination of §3 and §60
(c) **avergüenza**, avergonzad
(d) **avergüenzo, avergüenzas, avergüenza**, avergonzamos, avergonzáis, **avergüenzan**
(e) **avergüence, avergüences, avergüence, avergoncemos, avergoncéis, avergüencen**
(h) **avergoncé**, avergonzaste, avergonzó, avergonzamos, avergonzasteis, avergonzaron

§10 **averiguar**
(e) **averigüe, averigües, averigüe, averigüemos, averigüéis, averigüen**
(h) **averigüé**, averiguaste, averiguó. averiguamos, averiguasteis, averiguaron

§11 bendecir
   (a) **bendiciendo**
   (c) **bendice,** bendecid
   (d) **bendigo, bendices, bendice,** bendecimos, bendecís, **bendicen**
   (e) **bendiga, bendigas, bendiga, bendigamos, bendigáis, bendigan**
   (h) **bendije, bendijiste, bendijo, bendijimos, bendijisteis, bendijeron**

§12 bruñir
   (a) **bruñendo**
   (h) **bruñí, bruñiste, bruñó,** bruñimos, bruñisteis, **bruñeron**

§13 bullir
   (a) **bullendo**
   (h) **bullí, bulliste, bulló,** bullimos, bullisteis, **bulleron**

§14 caber
   (d) **quepo,** cabes, cabe, cabemos, cabéis, caben
   (e) **quepa, quepas, quepa, quepamos, quepáis, quepan**
   (g) **cabré, cabrás, cabrá, cabremos, cabréis, cabrán**
   (h) **cupe, cupiste, cupo, cupimos, cupisteis, cupieron**

§15 caer
   (a) **cayendo**
   (b) **caído**
   (d) **caigo,** caes, cae, caemos, caéis, caen
   (e) **caiga, caigas, caiga, caigamos, caigáis, caigan**
   (h) caí, **caíste, cayó, caímos, caísteis, cayeron**

§16 cocer: combination of §47 and §78
   (c) **cuece,** coced
   (d) **cuezo, cueces, cuece,** cocemos, cocéis, **cuecen**
   (e) **cueza, cuezas, cueza, cozamos, cozáis, cuezan**

§17 coger
   (d) **cojo,** coges, coge, cogemos, cogéis, cogen
   (e) **coja, cojas, coja, cojamos, cojáis, cojan**

§18 comenzar: combination of §2 and §60
   (c) **comienza,** comenzad
   (d) **comienzo, comienzas, comienza,** comenzamos, comenzáis, **comienzan**
   (e) **comience, comiences, comience, comencemos, comencéis, comiencen**
   (h) **comencé,** comenzaste, comenzó, comenzamos, comenzasteis, comenzaron

§19 conducir
   (d) **conduzco,** conduces, conduce, conducimos, conducís, conducen
   (e) **conduzca, conduzcas, conduzca, conduzcamos, conduzcáis, conduzcan**
   (h) **conduje, condujiste, condujo, condujimos, condujisteis, condujeron**

§20 construir
   (a) **construyendo**
   (b) **construído**
   (c) **construye,** construid
   (d) **construyo, construyes, construye,** construimos, construís, **construyen**
   (e) **construya, construyas, construya, construyamos, construyáis, construyan**
   (h) construí, construiste, **construyó,** construimos, construisteis, **construyeron**

§21 continuar
   (c) **continúa,** continuad
   (d) **continúo, continúas, continúa,** continuamos, continuáis, **continúan**
   (e) **continúe, continúes, continúe,** continuemos, continuéis, **continúen**

§22 crecer
   (d) **crezco,** creces, crece, crecemos, crecéis, crecen
   (e) **crezca, crezcas, crezca, crezcamos, crezcáis, crezcan**

§23 **dar**
   (d) **doy**, das, da, damos, dais, dan
   (e) **dé**, des, **dé**, demos, deis, den
   (h) **dí**, **diste**, **dio**, **dimos**, **disteis**, **dieron**

§24 **decir**
   (a) **diciendo**
   (b) **dicho**
   (c) **di**, decid
   (d) **digo**, **dices**, **dice**, decimos, decís, **dicen**
   (e) **diga**, **digas**, **diga**, **digamos**, **digáis**, **digan**
   (g) **diré**, **dirás**, **dirá**, **diremos**, **diréis**, **dirán**
   (h) **dije**, **dijiste**, **dijo**, **dijimos**, **dijisteis**, **dijeron**

§25 **delinquir**
   (d) **delinco**, delinques, delinque, delinquimos, delinquís, delinquen
   (e) **delinca**, **delincas**, **delinca**, **delincamos**, **delincáis**, **delincan**

§26 **desosar**: like §61 but with **h** before **ue**
   (c) **deshuesa**, desosad
   (d) **deshueso**, **deshuesas**, **deshuesa**, desosamos, desosáis, **deshuesan**
   (e) **deshuese**, **deshueses**, **deshuese**, desosemos, desoséis, **deshuesen**

§27 **dirigir**
   (d) **dirijo**, diriges, dirige, dirigimos, dirigís, dirigen
   (e) **dirija**, **dirijas**, **dirija**, **dirijamos**, **dirijáis**, **dirijan**

§28 **discernir**
   (c) **discierne**, discernid
   (d) **discierno**, **disciernes**, **discierne**, discernimos, discernís, **disciernen**
   (e) **discierna**, **disciernas**, **discierna**, discernamos, discernáis, **disciernan**

§29 **distinguir**
   (d) **distingo**, distingues, distingue, distinguimos, distinguís, distinguen
   (e) **distinga**, **distingas**, **distinga**, **distingamos**, **distingáis**, **distingan**

§30 **dormir**
   (a) **durmiendo**
   (c) **duerme**, dormid
   (d) **duermo**, **duermes**, **duerme**, dormimos, dormís, **duermen**
   (e) **duerma**, **duermas**, **duerma**, **durmamos**, **durmáis**, **duerman**
   (h) dormí, dormiste, **durmió**, dormimos, dormisteis, **durmieron**

§31 **empeller**
   (a) **empellendo**
   (h) empellí, empelliste, **empelló**, empellimos, empellisteis, **empelleron**

§32 **enraizar**: combination of §4 and §60
   (c) **enraíza**, enraizad
   (d) **enraízo**, **enraízas**, **enraíza**, enraizamos, enraizáis, **enraízan**
   (e) **enraíce**, **enraíces**, **enraíce**, enraicemos, enraicéis, **enraícen**
   (h) **enraicé**, enraizaste, enraizó, enraizamos, enraizasteis, enraizaron

§33 **erguir**: combination of §29 and §50 or §68
   (a) **irguiendo**
   (c) **irgue** or **yergue**, erguid
   (d) **irgo**, **irgues**, **irgue**, ⎫ erguimos, erguís, ⎧ **irguen**
          yergo, **yergues**, **yergue**, ⎭   ⎩ **yerguen**
   (e) **irga**, **irgas**, **irga**, ⎫ irgamos, irgáis, ⎧ **irgan**
          yerga, **yergas**, **yerga**, ⎭   ⎩ **yergan**
   (h) erguí, erguiste, **irguió**, erguimos, erguisteis, **irguieron**

§34 **errar**: like §2 but with initial **ye** for **ie**
   (c) **yerra**, errad
   (d) **yerro**, **yerras**, **yerra**, erramos, erráis, **yerran**
   (e) **yerre**, **yerres**, **yerre**, erremos, erréis, **yerren**

§35 **esforzar:** combination of §60 and §61
    (c) **esfuerza,** esforzad
    (d) **esfuerzo, esfuerzas, esfuerza,** esforzamos, esforzáis, **esfuerzan**
    (e) **esfuerce, esfuerces, esfuerce, esforcemos, esforcéis, esfuercen**
    (h) **esforcé,** esforzaste, esforzó, esforzamos, esforzasteis, esforzaron

§36 **esparcir**
    (d) **esparzo,** esparces, esparce, esparcimos, esparcís, esparcen
    (e) **esparza, esparzas, esparza, esparzamos, esparzáis, esparzan**

§37 **estar**
    (c) **está,** estad
    (d) **estoy, estás, está,** estamos, estáis, **están**
    (e) **esté, estés, esté,** estemos, estéis, **estén**
    (h) **estuve, estuviste, estuvo, estuvimos, estuvisteis, estuvieron**

§38 **haber**
    (c) **hé,** habed
    (d) **he, has, ha, hemos,** habéis, **han** (*v impers*) **hay**
    (e) **haya, hayas, haya, hayamos, hayáis, hayan**
    (g) **habré, habrás, habrá, habremos, habréis, habrán**
    (h) **hube, hubiste, hubo, hubimos, hubisteis, hubieron**

§39 **hacer**
    (b) **hecho**
    (c) **haz,** haced
    (d) **hago,** haces, hace, hacemos, hacéis, hacen
    (e) **haga, hagas, haga, hagamos, hagáis, hagan**
    (g) **haré, harás, hará, haremos, haréis, harán**
    (h) **hice, hiciste, hizo, hicimos, hicisteis, hicieron**

§40 **inquirir**
    (c) **inquiere,** inquirid
    (d) **inquiero, inquieres, inquiere,** inquirimos, inquirís, **inquieren**
    (e) **inquiera, inquieras, inquiera,** inquiramos, inquiráis, **inquieran**

§41 **ir**
    (a) **yendo**
    (c) **vé, vamos,** id
    (d) **voy, vas, va, vamos, vais, van**
    (e) **vaya, vayas, vaya, vayamos, vayáis, vayan**
    (f) **iba, ibas, iba, íbamos, ibais, iban**
    (h) **fui, fuiste, fue, fuimos, fuisteis, fueron**

§42 **jugar:** like §63 but with radical **u**
    (c) **juega,** jugad
    (d) **juego, juegas, juega,** jugamos, jugáis, **juegan**
    (e) **juegue, juegues, juegue, juguemos, juguéis, jueguen**
    (h) **jugué,** jugaste, jugó, jugamos, jugasteis, jugaron

§43 **leer**
    (a) **leyendo**
    (b) **leído**
    (h) **leí, leíste, leyó, leímos, leísteis, leyeron**

§44 **ligar**
    (e) **ligue, ligues, ligue, liguemos, liguéis, liguen**
    (h) **ligué,** ligaste, ligó, ligamos, ligasteis, ligaron

§45 **lucir**
    (d) **luzco,** luces, luce, lucimos, lucís, lucen
    (e) **luzca, luzcas, luzca, luzcamos, luzcáis, luzcan**

§46 **mecer**
    (d) **mezo,** meces, mece, mecemos, mecéis, mecen
    (e) **meza, mezas, meza, mezamos, mezáis, mezan**

§47 mover
(c) **mueve,** moved
(d) **muevo, mueves, mueve,** movemos, movéis, **mueven**
(e) **mueva, muevas, mueva,** movamos, mováis, **muevan**

§48 oír
(a) **oyendo**
(b) **oído**
(c) **oye, oíd**
(d) **oigo, oyes, oye, oímos,** oís, **oyen**
(e) **oiga, oigas, oiga, oigamos, oigáis, oigan**
(h) **oí,** oíste, **oyó, oímos,** oísteis, **oyeron**

§49 oler: like §47 but with **h** before **ue**
(c) **huele,** oled
(d) **huelo, hueles, huele,** olemos, oléis, **huelen**
(e) **huela, huelas, huela,** olamos, oláis, **huelan**

§50 pedir
(a) **pidiendo**
(c) **pide,** pedid
(d) **pido, pides, pide,** pedimos, pedís, **piden**
(e) **pida, pidas, pida, pidamos, pidáis, pidan**
(h) pedí, pediste, **pidió,** pedimos, pedisteis, **pidieron**

§51 perder
(c) **pierde,** perded
(d) **pierdo, pierdes, pierde,** perdemos, perdéis, **pierden**
(e) **pierda, pierdas, pierda,** perdamos, perdáis, **pierdan**

§52 placer
(d) **plazco,** places, place, placemos, placéis, placen
(e) **plazca, plazcas, plazca, plazcamos, plazcáis, plazcan**
(h) plací, placiste, plació (or **plugo**), placimos, placisteis, placieron

§53 poder
(a) **pudiendo**
(c) (**puede,** poded)
(d) **puedo, puedes, puede,** podemos, podéis, **pueden**
(e) **pueda, puedas, pueda,** podamos, podáis, **puedan**
(g) **podré, podrás, podrá, podremos, podréis, podrán**
(h) **pude, pudiste, pudo, pudimos, pudisteis, pudieron**

§54 poner
(b) **puesto**
(c) **pon,** poned
(d) **pongo,** pones, pone, ponemos, ponéis, ponen
(e) **ponga, pongas, ponga, pongamos, pongáis, pongan**
(g) **pondré, pondrás, pondrá, pondremos, pondréis, pondrán**
(h) **puse, pusiste, puso, pusimos, pusisteis, pusieron**

§55 querer
(c) **quiere,** quered
(d) **quiero, quieres, quiere,** queremos, queréis, **quieren**
(e) **quiera, quieras, quiera,** queramos, queráis, **quieran**
(g) **querré, querrás, querrá, querremos, querréis, querrán**
(h) **quise, quisiste, quiso, quisimos, quisisteis, quisieron**

§56 raer
(a) **rayendo**
(b) **raído**
(d) **raigo** (or **rayo**), raes, rae, raemos, raéis, raen
(e) **raiga** (or **raya**), **raigas, raiga, raigamos, raigáis, raigan**
(h) **raí, raíste, rayó, raímos, raísteis, rayeron**

§57 **regir:** combination of §27 and §50
   (a) **rigiendo**
   (c) **rige,** regid
   (d) **rijo, riges, rige,** regimos, regís, **rigen**
   (e) **rija, rijas, rija, rijamos, rijáis, rijan**
   (h) regí, registe, **rigió,** regimos, registeis, **rigieron**

§58 **reír**
   (a) **riendo**
   (b) **reído**
   (c) **ríe, reíd**
   (d) **río, ríes, ríe, reímos,** reís, **ríen**
   (e) **ría, rías, ría, riamos, riáis, rían**
   (h) reí, **reíste, rió, reímos, reísteis, rieron**

§59 **reunir**
   (c) **reúne,** reunid
   (d) **reúno, reúnes, reúne,** reunimos, reunís, **reúnen**
   (e) **reúna, reúnas, reúna,** reunamos, reunáis, **reúnan**

§60 **rezar**
   (e) **rece, reces, rece, recemos, recéis, recen**
   (h) **recé,** rezaste, rezó, rezamos, rezasteis, rezaron

§61 **rodar**
   (c) **rueda,** rodad
   (d) **ruedo, ruedas, rueda,** rodamos, rodáis, **ruedan**
   (e) **ruede, ruedes, ruede,** rodemos, rodéis, **rueden**

§62 **roer**
   (a) **royendo**
   (b) **roído**
   (d) **roo (roigo,** or **royo),** roes, roe, roemos, roéis, roen
   (e) **roa (roiga,** or **roya),** roas, roa, roamos, roáis, roan
   (h) roí, **roíste, royó, roímos, roísteis, royeron**

§63 **rogar:** combination of §44 and §61
   (c) **ruega,** rogad
   (d) **ruego, ruegas, ruega,** rogamos, rogáis, **ruegan**
   (e) **ruegue, ruegues, ruegue, roguemos, roguéis, rueguen**
   (h) **rogué,** rogaste, rogó, rogamos, rogasteis, rogaron

§64 **saber**
   (d) **sé,** sabes, sabe, sabemos, sabéis, saben
   (e) **sepa, sepas, sepa, sepamos, sepáis, sepan**
   (g) **sabré, sabrás, sabrá, sabremos, sabréis, sabrán**
   (h) **supe, supiste, supo, supimos, supisteis, supieron**

§65 **salir**
   (c) **sal,** salid
   (d) **salgo,** sales, sale, salimos, salís, salen
   (e) **salga, salgas, salga, salgamos, salgáis, salgan**
   (g) **saldré, saldrás, saldrá, saldremos, saldréis, saldrán**

§66 **segar:** combination of §2 and §44
   (c) **siega,** segad
   (d) **siego, siegas, siega,** segamos, segáis, **siegan**
   (e) **siegue, siegues, siegue, seguemos, seguéis, sieguen**
   (h) **segué,** segaste, segó, segamos, segasteis, segaron

§67 **seguir:** combination of §29 and §50
   (a) **siguiendo**
   (c) **sigue,** seguid
   (d) **sigo, siegues, sigue,** seguimos, seguís, **siguen**
   (e) **siga, sigas, siga, sigamos, sigáis, sigan**
   (h) seguí, seguiste, **siguió,** seguimos, seguisteis, **siguieron**

§68 sentir
  (a) **sintiendo**
  (c) **siente,** śentid
  (d) **siento, sientes, siente,** sentimos, sentís, **sienten**
  (e) **sienta, sientas, sienta, sintamos, sintáis, sientan**
  (h) sentí, sentiste, **sintió,** sentimos, sentisteis, **sintieron**

§69 ser
  (c) **sé,** sed
  (d) **soy, eres, es, somos, sois, son**
  (e) **sea, seas, sea, seamos, seáis, sean**
  (f) **era, eras, era, éramos, erais, eran**
  (h) **fui, fuiste, fue, fuimos, fuisteis, fueron**

§70 tañer
  (a) **tañendo**
  (h) tañí, tañiste, **tañó,** tañimos, tañisteis, **tañeron**

§71 tener
  (c) **ten,** tened
  (d) **tengo, tienes, tiene,** tenemos, tenéis, **tienen**
  (e) **tenga, tengas, tenga, tengamos, tengáis, tengan**
  (g) **tendré, tendrás, tendrá, tendremos, tendréis, tendrán**
  (h) **tuve, tuviste, tuvo, tuvimos, tuvisteis, tuvieron**

§72 teñir: combination of §12 and §50
  (a) **tiñendo**
  (c) **tiñe,** teñid
  (d) **tiño, tiñes, tiñe,** teñimos, teñis, **tiñen**
  (e) **tiña, tiñas, tiña, tiñamos, tiñáis, tiñan**
  (h) teñi, teñiste, **tiñó,** teñimos, teñisteis, **tiñeron**

§73 tocar
  (e) **toque, toques, toque, toquemos, toquéis, toquen**
  (h) **toqué,** tocaste, tocó, tocamos, tocasteis, tocaron

§74 torcer: combination of §47 and §78
  (c) **tuerce,** torced
  (d) **tuerzo, tuerces, tuerce,** torcemos, torcéis, **tuercen**
  (e) **tuerza, tuerzas, tuerza, torzamos, torzáis, tuerzan**

§75 traer
  (a) **trayendo**
  (b) **traído**
  (d) **traigo,** traes, trae, traemos, traéis, traen
  (e) **traiga, traigas, traiga, traigamos, traigáis, traigan**
  (h) **traje, trajiste, trajo, trajimos, trajisteis, trajeron**

§76 valer
  (d) **valgo,** vales, vale, valemos, valéis, valen
  (e) **valga, valgas, valga, valgamos, valgáis, valgan**
  (g) **valdré, valdrás, valdrá, valdremos, valdréis, valdrán**

§77 variar
  (c) **varía,** variad
  (d) **varío, varías, varía,** variamos, variáis, **varían**
  (e) **varíe, varíes, varíe,** variemos, variéis, **varíen**

§78 vencer
  (d) **venzo,** vences, vence, vencemos, vencéis, vencen
  (e) **venza, venzas, venza, venzamos, venzáis, venzan**

§79 venir
  (a) **viniendo**
  (c) **ven,** venid
  (d) **vengo, vienes, viene,** venimos, venís, **vienen**
  (e) **venga, vengas, venga, vengamos, vengáis, vengan**

(g) vendré, vendrás, vendrá, vendremos, vendréis, vendrán
(h) vine, viniste, vino, vinimos, vinisteis, vinieron

§80 ver
(b) visto
(d) veo, ves, ve, vemos, veis, ven
(e) vea, veas, vea, veamos, veáis, vean
(f) veía, veías, veía, veíamos, veíais, veían

§81 volcar: combination of §61 and §73
(c) vuelca, volcad
(d) vuelco, vuelcas, vuelca, volcamos, volcáis, vuelcan
(e) vuelque, vuelques, vuelque, volquemos, volquéis, vuelquen
(h) volqué, volcaste, volcó, volcamos, volcasteis, volcaron

§82 yacer
(c) yaz (or yace), yaced
(d) yazco (yazgo, or yago), yaces, yace, yacemos, yacéis, yacen
(e) yazca (yazga, or yaga), yazcas, yazca, yazcamos, yazcáis, yazcan

§83 The following verbs, some of which are included in the foregoing table, and their compounds have irregular past participles:

abrir	hacer	escrito	poner	ver	podrido
cubrir	imprimir	frito	proveer	volver	roto
decir	abierto	hecho	pudrir	muerto	suelto
escribir	cubierto	impreso	romper	puesto	visto
freír	dicho	morir	solver	provisto	vuelto

350

ENGLISH-
SPANISH

INGLÉS-
ESPAÑOL

A, a [e] primera letra del alfabeto inglés

a [e] *art indef* un

aback [ə'bæk] *adv* atrás; **to be taken aback** quedar desconcertado; **to take aback** desconcertar

abaft [ə'bæft] *adv* a popa, en popa; *prep* detrás de

abandon [ə'bændən] *s* abandono ‖ *tr* abandonar

abandonment [ə'bændənmənt] *s* abandono, abandonamiento; desembarazo

abase [ə'bes] *tr* degradar, humillar

abash [ə'bæʃ] *tr* avergonzar

abashed [ə'bæʃt] *adj* avergonzado; humillado

abate [ə'bet] *tr* disminuir, reducir; deducir ‖ *intr* disminuir, moderarse

aba-tis ['æbətɪs] *s* (*pl* **-tis**) abatida

abattoir ['æbə,twar] *s* matadero

abba-cy ['æbəsi] *s* (*pl* **-cies**) abadía

abbess ['æbɪs] *s* abadesa

abbey ['æbi] *s* abadía

abbot ['æbət] *s* abad *m*

abbreviate [ə'brivɪ,et] *tr* abreviar

abbreviation [ə,brivɪ'eʃən] *s* (*shortening*) abreviación; (*shortened form*) abreviatura

A B C [,e,bi'si] *s* abecé *m*; **A B C's** abecedario

abdicate ['æbdɪ,ket] *tr* & *intr* abdicar

abdomen ['æbdəmən] o [æb'domən] *s* abdomen *m*

abduct [æb'dʌkt] *tr* raptar, secuestrar

abduction [æb'dʌkʃən] *s* rapto; secuestro

abed [ə'bɛd] *adv* en cama, acostado

aberration [,æbɛ'reʃən] *s* aberración; (*mind*) extravío

abet [ə'bɛt] *v* (*pret* & *pp* **abetted**; *ger* **abetting**) *tr* incitar (*a una persona, esp. al mal*); fomentar (*el crimen*)

abeyance [ə'be-əns] *s* suspensión; **in abeyance** en suspenso

ab-hor [æb'hɔr] *v* (*pret* & *pp* **-horred**; *ger* **-horring**) *tr* aborrecer, detestar

abhorrence [əb'hɔrəns] *s* aversión; aborrecimiento

abhorrent [æb'hɔrənt] *adj* aborrecible, detestable

abide [ə'baɪd] *v* (*pret* & *pp* **abode** o **abided**) *tr* esperar; tolerar ‖ *intr* permanecer; **to abide by** cumplir con; atenerse a

abili-ty [ə'bɪlɪti] *s* (*pl* **-ties**) habilidad, capacidad; talento

abject [æb'dʒɛkt] *adj* abyecto, servil

abjure [æb'dʒur] *tr* abjurar

ablative ['æblətɪv] *s* ablativo

ablaut ['æblaut] *s* apofonía

ablaze [ə'blez] *adj* brillante; ardiente; encolerizado ‖ *adv* en llamas, ardiendo

able ['ebəl] *adj* hábil, capaz; **to be able to** poder

able-bodied ['ebəl'badid] *adj* sano; fornido; experto

abloom [ə'blum] *adj* floreciente ‖ *adv* en flor

abnormal [æb'nɔrməl] *adj* anormal

aboard [ə'bord] *adv* a bordo; al bordo; **all aboard!** ¡señores viajeros al tren!; **to go aboard** ir a bordo; **to take aboard** embarcar ‖ *prep* a bordo de; (*a train*) en

abode [ə'bod] *s* domicilio, residencia

abolish [ə'balɪʃ] *tr* eliminar, suprimir

abolition [,æbə'lɪʃən] *s* abolición

A-bomb ['e,bam] *s* bomba atómica

abominable [ə'bamɪnəbəl] *adj* abominable

abomination [ə',bamɪ'neʃən] *s* abominación

aborigines [,æbə'rɪdʒɪ,niz] *spl* aborígenes *mf*

abort [ə'bɔrt] *tr* & *intr* abortar

abortion [ə'bɔrʃən] *s* aborto

abortionist [ə'bɔrʃənɪst] *s* abortista *mf*

abound [ə'baund] *intr* abundar

about [ə'baut] *adv* casi; aquí; **to be about to** estar a punto de, estar para ‖ *prep* acerca de; con respecto a; cerca de; hacia, a eso de; **to be about** tratar de

above [ə'bʌv] *adj* antedicho ‖ *adv* arriba, encima ‖ *prep* sobre, encima de, más alto que; superior a; **above all** sobre todo

above-mentioned [ə'bʌv'mɛnʃənd] *adj* sobredicho, antedicho, susodicho, prenombrado

abrasive [ə'bresɪv] o [ə'breziv] *adj* & *s* abrasivo

abreast [ə'brɛst] *adj* & *adv* de frente; **to be abreast of** correr parejas con; estar al corriente de

abridge [ə'brɪdʒ] *tr* abreviar; disminuir; condensar, resumir

abroad [ə'brɔd] *adv* al extranjero; en el extranjero; fuera de casa

abrupt [ə'brʌpt] *adj* brusco; repentino; áspero; abrupto, escarpado

abscess ['æbsɛs] *s* absceso

abscond [æb'skand] *intr* irse a hurtadillas; **to abscond with** alzarse con

absence ['æbsəns] *s* ausencia

absent ['æbsənt] *adj* ausente ‖ [æb'sɛnt] *tr*— **to absent oneself** ausentarse

absentee [‚æbsən'ti] *s* ausente *mf*
absent-minded ['æbsənt'maɪndɪd] *adj* distraído, absorto
absinth ['æbsɪnθ] *s* (*plant*) absintio, ajenjo; (*drink*) absenta, ajenjo
absolute ['æbsə,lut] *adj & s* absoluto
absolutely 'æbsə,lutli] *adv* absolutamente ‖ [‚æbsə'lutli] *adv* (coll) positivamente
absolution ['æbsə'luʃən] *s* absolución
absolve [æb'sɑlv] *tr* absolver
absorb [æb'sɔrb] *tr* absorber; **to be** or **become absorbed** ensimismarse
absorbent [æb'sɔrbənt] *adj* absorbente; (*cotton*) hidrófilo
absorbing [æb'sɔrbɪŋ] *adj* absorbente
absorption [æb'sɔrpʃən] *s* abstracción; embebecimiento; absorción
abstain [æb'sten] *intr* abstenerse
abstemious [æb'stimɪ‑əs] *adj* abstemio, sobrio
abstinent ['æbstɪnənt] *adj* abstinente
abstract ['æbstrækt] *adj* abstracto ‖ *s* resumen *m*, sumario, extracto ‖ *tr* resumir, compendiar, extractar ‖ [æb'strækt] *tr* abstraer; quitar
abstruse [æb'strus] *adj* abstruso
absurd [æb'sʌrd] o [æb'zʌrd] *adj* absurdo
absurdi‑ty [æb'sʌrdɪti] o [æb'zʌrdɪti] *s* (*pl* -ties) absurdidad, absurdo
abundance [ə'bʌndəns] *s* abundancia, copia; (CAm) bastedad
abundant [ə'bʌndənt] *adj* abundante
abuse [ə'bjus] *s* maltrato; injuria, insulto; (*bad practice; injustice*) abuso ‖ [ə'bjuz] *tr* maltratar; injuriar, insultar; (*to misapply, take unfair advantage of*) abusar de
abusive [ə'bjusɪv] *adj* injurioso, insultante; abusivo
abut [ə'bʌt] *v* (*pret & pp* **abutted**; *ger* **abutting**) *intr*—**to abut on** confinar con, terminar en
abutment [ə'bʌtmənt] *s* confinamiento; estribo, contrafuerte *m*
abyss [ə'bɪs] *s* abismo
academic [‚ækə'dɛmɪk] *adj* académico
academic costume *s* toga, traje *m* de catedrático
academic freedom *s* libertad de cátedra, libertad de enseñanza
academician [ə,kædə'mɪʃən] *s* académico
academic subjects *spl* materias no profesionales
academic year *s* año escolar
acade‑my [ə'kædəmi] *s* (*pl* -mies) academia
accede [æk'sid] *intr* acceder; **to accede to** acceder a, condescender a; (*e.g., the throne*) ascender a, subir a
accelerate [æk'sɛlə,ret] *tr* acelerar ‖ *intr* acelerarse
accelerator [æk'sɛlə,retər] *s* acelerador *m*
accent ['æksɛnt] *s* acento ‖ ['æksɛnt] o [æk'sɛnt] *tr* acentuar
accent mark *s* acento ortográfico
accentuate [æk'sɛntʃu,et] *tr* acentuar
accept [æk'sɛpt] *tr* aceptar
acceptable [æk'sɛptəbəl] *adj* aceptable
acceptance [æk'sɛptəns] *s* aceptación

access ['æksɛs] *s* acceso
accessible [æk'sɛsɪbəl] *adj* accesible
accession [æk'sɛʃən] *s* accesión; (*to a dignity*) ascenso; (*of books in a library*) adquisición
accesso‑ry [æk'sɛsəri] *adj* accesorio ‖ *s* (*pl* -ries) accesorio; (*to a crime*) cómplice *mf*
accident ['æksɪdənt] *s* accidente *m*; **by accident** por casualidad
accidental [‚æksɪ'dɛntəl] *adj* accidental
acclaim [ə'klem] *s* aclamación ‖ *tr & intr* aclamar
acclimate ['æklɪ,met] *tr* aclimatar ‖ *intr* aclimatarse
accolade [‚ækə'led] *s* acolada; elogio, premio
accommodate [ə'kamə,det] *tr* acomodar; alojar
accommodating [ə'kamə,detɪŋ] *adj* acomodadizo, servicial
accommodation [ə,kamə'deʃən] *s* acomodación; **accommodations** facilidades, comodidades; (*in a train*) localidad; (*in a hotel*) alojamiento
accommodation train *s* tren *m* omnibus
accompaniment [ə'kʌmpənɪmənt] *s* acompañamiento
accompanist [ə'kʌmpənɪst] *s* acompañante *m*
accompa‑ny [ə'kʌmpəni] *v* (*pret & pp* -nied) *tr* acompañar
accomplice [ə'kamplɪs] *s* cómplice *mf*, codelincuente *mf*
accomplish [ə'kamplɪʃ] *tr* realizar, llevar a cabo
accomplished [ə'kamplɪʃt] *adj* realizado; culto, talentoso; (*fact*) consumado
accomplishment [ə'kamplɪʃmənt] *s* realización; **accomplishments** prendas, talentos
accord [ə'kɔrd] *s* acuerdo; **in accord with** de acuerdo con: **of one's own accord** de buen grado, voluntariamente; **with one accord** de común acuerdo ‖ *tr* conceder, otorgar ‖ *intr* concordar, avenirse
accordance [ə'kɔrdəns] *s* conformidad; **in accordance with** de acuerdo con
according [ə'kɔrdɪŋ] *adj* — **according as** según que; **according to** según
accordingly [ə'kɔrdɪŋli] *adv* en conformidad; por consiguiente
accordion [ə'kɔrdɪ‑ən] *s* acordeón *m*; filarmónica (Mex)
accost [ə'kɔst] o [ə'kast] *tr* abordar, acercarse a
accouchement [ə'kuʃmənt] *s* alumbramiento, parto
accoucheur [‚æku'ʃʌr] *s* comadrón *m*
accoucheuse [‚æku'ʃuz] *s* comadrona
account [ə'kaʊnt] *s* informe *m*, relato; cuenta; estado de cuenta; importancia; **by all accounts** según el decir general; **of no account** de poca importancia; **on account** como paga y señal; **on account of** a causa de; **to bring to account** pedir cuentas a; **to buy on account** comprar a plazos; **to turn to account** sacar provecho de, hacer valer

‖ *intr*—**to account for** explicar; responder
de
accountable [ə'kaʊntəbəl] *adj* responsable;
explicable
accountant [ə'kaʊntənt] *s* contador *m*, contable *m*
accounting [ə'kaʊntɪŋ] *s* arreglo de cuentas;
contabilidad
accouterments [ə'kutərmənts] *spl* equipo,
avíos
accredit [ə'krɛdɪt] *tr* acreditar
accrue [ə'kru] *intr* acumularse; resultar
acct. *abbr* **account**
accumulate [ə'kjumjə,let] *tr* acumular ‖ *intr*
acumularse
accuracy ['ækjərəsi] *s* exactitud, precisión
accurate ['ækjərɪt] *adj* exacto
accusation [,ækjə'zeʃən] *s* acusación
accusative [ə'kjuzətɪv] *adj & s* acusativo
accuse [ə'kjuz] *tr* acusar
accustom [ə'kʌstəm] *tr* acostumbrar
ace [es] *s* as *m*; **to be within an ace of** estar
a dos dedos de
acetate ['æsɪ,tet] *s* acetato
acetic acid [ə'sitɪk] *s* ácido acético
aceti·fy [ə'sɛtɪ,faɪ] *v* (*pret & pp* **-fied**) *tr*
acetificar ‖ *intr* acetificarse
acetone ['æsɪ,ton] *s* acetona
acetylene [ə'sɛtɪ,lin] *s* acetileno
acetylene torch *s* soplete oxiacetilénico
ache [ek] *s* achaque *m*, dolor *m* ‖ *int* doler
achieve [ə'tʃiv] *tr* llevar a cabo; alcanzar,
ganar, lograr
achievement [ə'tʃivmənt] *s* realización; (*feat*)
hazaña
Achilles' heel [ə'kɪliz] *s* talón *m* de Aquiles
acid ['æsɪd] *adj* ácido; agrio, mordaz ‖ *s*
ácido
acidi·fy [ə'sɪdɪ,faɪ] *v* (*pret & pp* **-fied**) *tr*
acidificar ‖ *intr* acidificarse
acidi·ty [ə'sɪdɪti] *s* (*pl* **-ties**) acidez *f*
acid rain *s* lluvia ácida
acid test *s* prueba decisiva
ack·ack ['æk'æk] *s* (slang) artillería antiaérea; (slang) fuego antiaéreo
acknowledge [æk'nɑlɪdʒ] *tr* reconocer; acusar (*recibo de una carta*); agradecer (*p.ej.,
un favor*)
acknowledgment [æk'nɑlɪdʒmənt] *s* reconocimiento; (*of receipt of a letter*) acuse *m*;
(*of a favor*) agradecimiento
acme ['ækmi] *s* auge *m*, colmo
acne ['ækni] *s* acne *f*
acolyte ['ækə,laɪt] *s* acólito
acorn ['ekɔrn] o ['ekərn] *s* bellota
acoustic [ə'kustɪk] *adj* acústico ‖ **acoustics**
ssg acústica
acquaint [ə'kwent] *tr* informar, poner al corriente; **to be acquainted** conocerse; **to be
acquainted with** conocer; estar al corriente
de
acquaintance [ə'kwentəns] *s* conocimiento;
(*person*) conocido
acquiesce [,ækwɪ'ɛs] *intr* consentir, condescender, asentir
acquiescence [,ækwɪ'ɛsəns] *s* consentimiento, condescendencia, aquiescencia

acquire [ə'kwaɪr] *tr* adquirir
**acquired im·mune'-de·fi'cien·cy syndrome
(AIDS)** *s* síndrome *m* de inmunidad deficiente adquirida (SIDA)
acquired taste *s* gusto adquirido
acquisition [,ækwɪ'zɪʃən] *s* adquisición
acquit [ə'kwɪt] *v* (*pret & pp* **acquitted;** *ger*
acquitting) *tr* absolver, exculpar; **to acquit oneself** conducirse, portarse
acquittal [ə'kwɪtəl] *s* absolución, exculpación
acrid ['ækrɪd] *adj* acre, acrimonioso
acrobat ['ækrə,bæt] *s* acróbata *mf*
acrobatic [,ækrə'bætɪk] *adj* acrobático ‖ **acrobatics** *ssg* (*profession*) acrobatismo; *spl*
(*stunts*) acrobacia
acronym ['ækrənɪm] *s* acrónimo
acropolis [ə'krɑpəlɪs] *s* acrópolis *f*
across [ə'krɔs] o [ə'krɑs] *prep* al través de; al
otro lado de; **to come across** encontrarse
con; **to go across** atravesar
across'-the-board' *adj* comprensivo, general
acrostic [ə'krɔstɪk] o [ə'krɑstɪk] *s* acróstico
act [ækt] *s* acto; (law) decreto; **in the act** en
flagrante ‖ *tr* representar; desempeñar (*un
papel*); **to act the fool** hacer el bufón; **to
act the part of** hacer o desempeñar el
papel de ‖ *intr* actuar; funcionar, obrar;
conducirse; **to act as if** hacer como que; **to
act for** representar; **to act up** travesear; **to
act up to** hacer fiestas a
acting ['æktɪŋ] *adj* interino ‖ *s* actuación
action ['ækʃən] *s* acción; **to take action**
tomar medidas
activate ['æktɪ,vet] *tr* activar
active ['æktɪv] *adj* activo
activi·ty [æk'tɪvɪti] *s* (*pl* **-ties**) actividad
act of God *s* fuerza mayor
actor ['æktər] *s* actor *m*
actress ['æktrɪs] *s* actriz *f*
actual ['æktʃʊ·əl] *adj* real, efectivo
actually ['æktʃʊ·əli] *adv* en realidad
actuar·y ['æktʃʊ,ɛri] *s* (*pl* **-ies**) actuario (de
seguros)
actuate ['æktʃʊ,et] *tr* actuar; estimular,
mover
acuity [ə'kju·ɪti] *s* agudeza
acumen [ə'kjumən] *s* cacumen *m*, perspicacia
acupuncture ['ækjə,pʌŋktʃər] *s* acupuntura
acute [ə'kjut] *adj* agudo
A.D. *abbr* **anno Domini** (Lat) **in the year of
our Lord**
ad [æd] *s* (coll) anuncio
adage ['ædɪdʒ] *s* adagio, refrán *m*
Adam ['ædəm] *s* Adán *m;* **the old Adam** la
inclinación al pecado
adamant ['ædəmənt] *adj* firme, inexorable
Adam's apple *s* nuez *f*
adapt [ə'dæpt] *tr* adaptar; refundir (*un
drama*)
adaptation [,ædæp'teʃən] *s* adaptación; (*of a
play*) refundición
add [æd] *tr* agregar, añadir; sumar ‖ *intr*
sumar; **to add up to** subir a; (coll) querer
decir
added line *s* (mus) línea suplementaria

adder ['ædər] s víbora; serpiente f
addict ['ædɪkt] s enviciado; adicto, partidario ‖ [ə'dɪkt] tr enviciar; entregar; **to addict oneself to** enviciarse con o en; entregarse a
addiction [ə'dɪkʃən] s enviciamiento; adhesividad
adding machine s sumadora, máquina de sumar
addition [ə'dɪʃən] s adición; **in addition** de pilón; **in addition to** además de
additive ['ædɪtɪv] adj & s aditivo
address [ə'drɛs] o ['ædrɛs] s dirección; consignación ‖ [ə'drɛs] s alocución, discurso; **to deliver an address** hacer uso de la palabra ‖ tr dirigirse a; dirigir (p.ej., una alocución, una carta); consignar
addressee [,ædrɛ'si] s destinatario; (com) consignatario
addressing machine s máquina para dirigir sobres
adduce [ə'djus] o [ə'dus] tr aducir
adenoids ['ædə,nɔɪdz] spl vegetaciones adenoides
adept [ə'dɛpt] adj & s experto, perito
adequate ['ædɪkwɪt] adj suficiente
adhere [æd'hɪr] intr adherir, adherirse; conformarse
adherence [æd'hɪrəns] s adhesión
adherent [æd'hɪrənt] adj & s adherente m
adhesion [æd'hiʒən] s (sticking) adherencia; (support, loyalty) adhesión; (pathol) adherencia; (phys) adherencia o adhesión
adhesive [æd'hisɪv] adj adhesivo
adhesive tape s tafetán adhesivo
adieu [ə'dju] o [ə'du] interj ¡adiós! ‖ s (pl adieus o adieux) adiós m; **to bid adieu to** desperdirse de
adjacent [ə'dʒesənt] adj adyacente
adjective ['ædʒɪktɪv] adj & s adjetivo
adjoin [ə'dʒɔɪn] tr lindar con ‖ intr colindar
adjoining [ə'dʒɔɪnɪŋ] adj colindante, contiguo
adjourn [ə'dʒʌrn] tr prorrogar, suspender ‖ intr prorrogarse, suspenderse; (coll) ir
adjournment [ə'dʒʌrnmənt] s prorrogación, suspensión
adjust [ə'dʒʌst] tr ajustar, arreglar; corregir, verificar; (ins) liquidar
adjustable [ə'dʒʌstəbəl] adj ajustable, arreglable
adjustment [ə'dʒʌstmənt] s ajuste m, arreglo; (ins) liquidación de la avería
adjutant ['ædʒətənt] s ayudante m
ad-lib [,æd'lɪb] v (pret & pp -libbed; ger -libbing) tr & intr improvisar
Adm. abbr **Admiral**
administer [æd'mɪnɪstər] tr administrar; **to administer an oath** tomar juramento ‖ intr **— to administer to** cuidar de
administrator [æd'mɪnɪs,tretər] s administrador m
admiral ['ædmɪrəl] s almirante m; buque m almirante
admiral·ty ['ædmɪrəlti] s (pl -ties) almirantazgo
admire [æd'maɪr] tr admirar

admirer [æd'maɪrər] s admirador m; enamorado
admissible [æd'mɪsɪbəl] adj admisible
admission [æd'mɪʃən] s admisión; (in a school) ingreso; (reception) recibida; precio de entrada; **to gain admission** lograr entrar
ad·mit [æd'mɪt] v (pret & pp -mitted; ger -mitting) tr admitir ‖ intr dar entrada; **to admit of** admitir, permitir
admittance [æd'mɪtəns] s admisión; derecho de entrar; **no admittance** acceso prohibido, se prohibe la entrada
admonish [æd'mɑnɪʃ] tr amonestar
ado [ə'du] s bulla, excitación
adobe [ə'dobi] s adobe m; casa de adobe
adolescence [,ædə'lɛsəns] s adolescencia
adolescent [,ædə'lɛsənt] adj & s adolescente mf
adopt [ə'dɑpt] tr adoptar
adoption [ə'dɑpʃən] s adopción
adorable [ə'dorəbəl] adj adorable
adore [ə'dor] tr adorar
adorn [ə'dɔrn] tr adornar
adornment [ə'dɔrnmənt] s adorno
adrenal gland [æd'rinəl] s glándula suprarrenal
Adriatic [,edri'ætɪk] adj & s Adriático
adrift [ə'drɪft] adj & adv al garete, a la deriva
adroit [ə'drɔɪt] adj diestro
adult [ə'dʌlt] o ['ædʌlt] adj & s adulto
adulterate [ə'dʌltə,ret] tr adulterar
adulterer [ə'dʌltərər] s adúltero
adulteress [ə'dʌltərɪs] s adúltera
adulter·y [ə'dʌltəri] s (pl -ies) adulterio
adulthood [ə'dʌlt,hʊd] s adultez f
advance [æd'væns] adj adelantado; anticipado ‖ s adelanto, avance m; aumento, subida; **advances** propuestas; requerimiento amoroso; propuesta indecente; préstamo; **in advance** de antemano, por anticipado ‖ tr adelantar ‖ intr adelantar; adelantarse
advanced [æd'vænst] adj avanzado; **advanced in years** avanzado de edad, entrado en años
advanced standing s traspaso de matrículas, traspaso de crédito académico
advanced studies spl altos estudios
advancement [æd'vænsmənt] s adelanto, avance m; subida; promoción
advance publicity s publicidad de lanzamiento
advantage [æd'væntɪdʒ] s ventaja; lasca; **to take advantage of** aprovecharse de; abusar de, engañar
advantageous [,ædvən'tedʒəs] adj ventajoso
advent ['ædvɛnt] s advenimiento ‖ **Advent** s (eccl) Adviento
adventure [æd'vɛntʃər] s aventura ‖ tr aventurar ‖ intr aventurarse
adventurer [æd'vɛntʃərər] s aventurero
adventuresome [æd'vɛntʃərsəm] adj aventurero
adventuress [æd'vɛntʃərɪs] s aventurera
adventurous [æd'vɛntʃərəs] adj aventurero

adverb ['ædvʌrb] *s* adverbio
adversar·y ['ædvər,sɛri] *s (pl -ies)* adversario
adversi·ty [æd'vʌrsiti] *s (pl -ties)* adversidad
advertise ['ædvər,taiz] *tr & intr* anunciar
advertisement [,ædvər'taizmənt] o [æd-'vʌrtizmənt] *s* anuncio
advertiser ['ædvər,taizər] *s* anunciante *mf*
advertising ['ædvər,taiziŋ] *s* propaganda, publicidad, anuncios; reclame *m & f*
advertising agency *s* empresa anunciadora
advertising campaign *s* campaña de publicidad
advertising man *s* empresario de publicidad
advertising manager *s* gerente *m* de publicidad
advice [æd'vais] *s* consejo; aviso, noticia; **a piece of advice** un consejo
advisable [æd'vaizəbəl] *adj* aconsejable
advise [æd'vaiz] *tr* aconsejar, asesorar; advertir, avisar
advisement [æd'vaizmənt] *s* consideración; **to take under advisement** someter a consideración
advisory [æd'vaizəri] *adj* consultivo
advocate ['ædvə,ket] *s* defensor *m;* abogado ‖ *tr* abogar por
Aegean Sea [i'dʒiən] *s* Archipiélago; *(of the ancients)* mar Egeo
aegis ['idʒis] *s* égida
aerate ['eret] o ['e·ə,ret] *tr* airear
aerial ['ɛriəl] *adj* aéreo ‖ *s* antena
aerialist ['ɛri·əlist] *s* volatinero
aerial photograph *s* fotografía aérea
aerodrome ['ɛrə,drom] *s* aeródomo
aerodynamic [,ɛrodai'næmik] *adj* aerodinámico ‖ **aerodynamics** *ssg* aerodinámica
aeronaut ['ɛrə,nɔt] *s* aeronauta *mf*
aeronautic [,ɛrə'nɔtik] *adj* aeronáutico ‖ **aeronautics** *ssg* aeronáutica
aerosol ['ɛrə,sol] *s* aerosol *m*
aerospace ['ɛro,spes] *adj* aeroespacial
aesthete ['ɛsθit] *s* esteta *mf*
aesthetic [ɛs'θɛtik] *adj* estético ‖ **aesthetics** *ssg* estética
afar [ə'far] *adv* lejos
affable ['æfəbəl] *adj* afable
affair [ə'fɛr] *s* asunto, negocio; lance *m;* amorío; encuentro, combate *m;* **affairs** negocios
affect [ə'fɛkt] *tr* influir en; impresionar, enternecer; *(to assume; to pretend)* afectar; aficionarse a
affectation [,æfɛk'teʃən] *s* afectación
affected [ə'fɛktid] *adj* afectado
affection [ə'fɛkʃən] *s* afecto, cariño, afección; *(pathol)* afección
affectionate [ə'fɛkʃənit] *adj* afectuoso, cariñoso
affidavit [,æfi'devit] *s* declaración jurada, acta notarial
affiliate [ə'fili,et] *adj* afiliado ‖ *s* afiliado; filial *f* ‖ *tr* afiliar ‖ *intr* afiliarse
affini·ty [ə'finiti] *s (pl -ties)* afinidad
affirm [ə'fʌrm] *tr & intr* afirmar
affirmative [ə'fʌrmətiv] *adj* afirmativo ‖ *s* afirmativa

affix ['æfiks] *s* añadidura; *(gram)* afijo ‖ [ə'fiks] *tr* añadir; atribuir *(p.ej., culpa);* poner *(una firma, sello, etc.)*
afflict [ə'flikt] *tr* afligir; **to be afflicted with** sufrir de, adolecer de
affliction [ə'flikʃən] *s* aflicción, desgracia; achaque *m*
affluence ['æflu·əns] *s (abundance)* afluencia; *(wealth)* opulencia
afford [ə'ford] *tr* proporcionar; **to be able to afford (to)** poder darse el lujo de, poder permitirse
affray [ə'fre] *s* pendencia, riña
affront [ə'frʌnt] *s* afrenta ‖ *tr* afrentar
Afghan ['æfgæn] *adj & s* afgano
Afghanistan [æf'gæni,stæn] *s* el Afganistán
afire [ə'fair] *adj & adv* ardiendo
aflame [ə'flem] *adj & adv* en llamas
afloat [ə'flot] *adj & adv* a flote; a bordo; inundado; sin rumbo; *(rumor)* en circulación
afoot [ə'fut] *adj & adv* a pie; en marcha
afoul [ə'faul] *adj & adv* enredado; en colisión; **to run afoul of** enredarse con
afraid [ə'fred] *adj* asustado; **to be afraid** tener miedo
Africa ['æfrikə] *s* Africa
African ['æfrikən] *adj & s* africano
aft [æft] *adj & adv* en popa
after ['æftər] *adj* siguiente ‖ *adv* después ‖ *prep* después de; según; **after all** al fin y al cabo ‖ *conj* después de que
af'ter-din'ner speaker *s* orador *m* de sobremesa
after-dinner speech *s* discurso de sobremesa
af'ter-hours' *adv* después del trabajo
af'ter-life' *s* vida venidera; resto de la vida
aftermath ['æftər,mæθ] *s* segunda siega; consecuencias, consecuencias desastrosas
af'ter-noon' *s* tarde *f*
af'ter-shave' lotion *s* loción facial
af'ter-taste' *s* dejo, gustillo, resabio
af'ter-thought' *s* idea tardía, expediente tardío
afterward ['æftəwərd] *adv* después, luego
af'ter-while' *adv* dentro de poco
again [ə'gɛn] *adv* otra vez, de nuevo; además; **to + inf + again** volver a + *inf,* p.ej., **he will come again** volverá a venir
against [ə'gɛnst] *prep* contra; cerca de; en contraste con; por; para
agape [ə'gep] *adj* abierto de par en par ‖ *adv* con la boca abierta
agave [ə'gavi] *s* agave *f*
agave brandy *s* pulque *m* (Mex)
agave liquor *s* mexcal *m,* mezcal *m*
age [edʒ] *s* edad; *(old age)* vejez *f; (one hundred years; a long time)* siglo; edad mental; **of age** mayor de edad; **to come of age** alcanzar su mayoría de edad, llegar a mayor edad; **under age** menor de edad ‖ *tr* envejecer ‖ *intr* envejecer, envejecerse
age bracket *s* grupo de personas de la misma edad
aged [edʒd] *adj* de la edad de ‖ ['edʒid] *adj* anciano, viejo

ad
ag

ageism ['edʒɪzəm] *s* discriminación contra los ancianos

ageless ['edʒlɪs] *adj* eternamente joven

agen‧cy ['edʒənsi] *s* (*pl* **-cies**) agencia; mediación

agenda [ə'dʒɛndə] *s* agenda, temario

agent ['edʒənt] *s* agente *m*

Age of Enlightenment *s* siglo de las luces

agglomeration [ə,glɑmə'reʃən] *s* aglomeración

aggrandizement [ə'grændɪzmənt] *s* engrandecimiento

aggravate ['ægrə,vet] *tr* agravar; (coll) exasperar, irritar

aggregate ['ægrɪ,get] *adj* & *s* agregado ‖ *tr* agregar, juntar; ascender a

aggression [ə'grɛʃən] *s* agresión

aggressive [ə'grɛsɪv] *adj* agresivo

aggressor [ə'grɛsər] *s* agresor *m*

aghast [ə'gæst] *adj* horrorizado

agile ['ædʒɪl] *adj* ágil

agitate ['ædʒɪ,tet] *tr* & *intr* agitar

aglow [ə'glo] *adj* & *adv* fulgurante

agnostic [æg'nɑstɪk] *adj* & *s* agnóstico

ago [ə'go] *adv* hace, p.ej., **two days ago** hace dos días

ago‧ny ['ægəni] *s* (*pl* **-nies**) angustia, congoja; (*anguish; death struggle*) agonía

agrarian [ə'grɛrɪ‧ən] *adj* agrario ‖ *s* agrariense *mf*

agree [ə'gri] *intr* estar de acuerdo, ponerse de acuerdo; sentar bien; (gram) concordar

agreeable [ə'gri‧əbəl] *adj* (*to one's liking*) agradable; (*willing to consent*) acorde, conforme

agreement [ə'grimənt] *s* acuerdo, convenio; concordancia; **in agreement** de acuerdo

agric. *abbr* **agriculture**

agriculture ['ægrɪ,kʌltʃər] *s* agricultura

agronomy [ə'grɑnəmi] *s* agronomía

aground [ə'graund] *adv* encallado, varado; **to run aground** encallar, varar

agt. *abbr* **agent**

ague ['egju] *s* escalofrío; fiebre *f* intermitente

ahead [ə'hɛd] *adj* & *adv* delante, al frente; **ahead of** antes de; delante de; al frente de; **to get ahead (of)** adelantarse (a)

ahoy [ə'hɔɪ] *interj* — **ship ahoy!** ¡ah del barco!

aid [ed] *s* ayuda, auxilio; (mil) ayudante *m* ‖ *tr* ayudar, auxiliar; **to aid and abet** auxiliar e incitar, ser cómplice de ‖ *intr* ayudar

aide [ed] *s* ayudante *m;* (mil) edecán *m*

aide-de-camp ['eddə'kæmp] *s* (*pl* **aides-de-camp**) ayudante *m* de campo, edecán *m*

AIDS [edz] *abbr* **acquired immune-deficiency syndrome**

ail [el] *tr* inquietar; **what ails you?** ¿qué tiene Vd.? ‖ *intr* sufrir, estar enfermo

aileron ['elə,rɑn] *s* alerón *m*

ailing ['elɪŋ] *adj* enfermo, achacoso

ailment ['elmənt] *s* enfermedad, achaque *m*

aim [em] *s* puntería; intento; punto de mira ‖ *tr* apuntar, encarar; dirigir (*p.ej., una observación*) ‖ *intr* apuntar

air [ɛr] *s* aire *m*; **by air** por vía aérea; **in the open air** al aire libre; **on the air** en antena, en la radio; **to let the air out of** desinflar; **to put on airs** darse aires; **to put on the air** llevar a las antenas; **to walk on air** no pisar en el suelo ‖ *tr* airear, ventilar; radiodifundir; (fig) ventilar

air'-a‧tom'ic *adj* aeroatómico

air bag *s* (aut) globo de aire, bolsa de aire

air'borne' *adj* aerotransportado

air brake *s* freno de aire comprimido

air castle *s* castillo en el aire

air'-condi'tion *tr* climatizar

air conditioner *s* acondicionador *m* de aire

air conditioning *s* acondicionamiento del aire, clima *m* artificial, climatización

air corps *s* cuerpo de aviación

air'craft' *ssg* máquina de volar; *spl* máquinas de volar

aircraft carrier *s* portaaviones *m*

airdrome ['ɛr,drom] *s* aeródromo

air'drop' *s* lanzamiento ‖ *tr* lanzar

air field *s* campo de aviación

air'foil' *s* superficie *f* de sustentación

air force *s* fuerza aérea, ejército del aire

air gap *s* (phys) entrehierro

air'-ground' *adj* aeroterrestre

air hostess *s* aeromoza, azafata

air humidifier *s* humidificador *m*

air lane *s* ruta aérea

air'lift' *s* puente aéreo

air liner *s* transaéreo, avión *m* de travesía

air mail *s* correo aéreo, aeroposta

air'-mail' letter *s* carta aérea, carta por avión

air-mail pilot *s* aviador *m* postal

air-mail stamp *s* sello aéreo

air‧man ['ɛrmən] *s* (*pl* **-men** [mən]) aviador *m*

air'plane' *s* avión *m*, aparato

airplane carrier *s* portaaviones *m*

air pocket *s* bache aéreo

air pollution *s* contaminación atmosférica

air'port' *s* aeropuerto

air raid *s* ataque aéreo

air'-raid' drill *s* simulacro de ataque aéreo

air-raid shelter *s* abrigo antiaéreo

air-raid warning *s* alarma aérea

air rifle *s* escopeta de viento, escopeta de aire comprimido

air'ship' *s* aeronave *f*

air'sick' *adj* mareado en el aire

air'sick'ness *s* mal *m* de vuelo

air sleeve o **sock** *s* veleta de manga

air'strip' *s* pista de despegue, pista de aterrizaje

air taxi *s* aerotaxi *m*

air'tight' *adj* herméticamente cerrado, estanco al aire

air'-traff'ic controller *s* controlador aéreo

air'waves' *spl* ondas de radio

air'way' *s* aerovía, vía aérea

airway lighting *s* balizaje *m*

air‧y ['ɛri] *adj* (*comp* **-ier;** *super* **-iest**) airoso; aireado; alegre; impertinente; (coll) afectado

aisle [aɪl] *s* (*in theater, movie, etc.*) pasillo; (*in a store, factory, etc.*) nave *f*; (archit) nave *f* lateral; (*any of the long passageways of a church*) (archit) nave *f*

ajar [ə'dʒɑr] *adj* entreabierto, entornado
akimbo [ə'kɪmbo] *adj & adv* — **with arms akimbo** en jarras
akin [ə'kɪn] *adj* emparentado; semejante
alabaster ['ælə,bæstər] *s* alabastro
alarm [ə'lɑrm] *s* alarma ‖ *tr* alarmar
alarm clock *s* reloj *m* despertador
alarmist [ə'lɑrmɪst] *s* alarmista *mf*
alas [ə'læs] o [ə'lɑs] *interj* ¡ay!, ¡ay de mí!
Albanian [æl'benɪ•ən] *adj & s* albanés *m*
albatross ['ælbə,trɔs] o ['ælbə,trɑs] *s* albatros *m*
album ['ælbəm] *s* álbum *m*
albumen [æl'bjumən] *s* albumen *m;* albúmina
alchemy ['ælkɪmi] *s* alquimia
alcohol ['ælkə,hɔl] o ['ælkə,hɑl] *s* alcohol *m*
alcoholic [,ælkə'hɔlɪk] o [,ælkə'hɑlɪk] *adj & s* alcohólico
al'co•hol-lev'el test *s* prueba de alcohol
alcove ['ælkov] *s* gabinete *m*, rincón *m;* (*in a bedroom*) trasalcoba; (*in a garden*) cenador *m*
alder ['ɔldər] *s* aliso
alder•man ['ɔldərmən] *s* (*pl* -**men** [mən]) concejal *m*
ale [el] *s* ale *f* (*cerveza inglesa, obscura, espesa y amarga*)
alembic [ə'lɛmbɪk] *s* alambique *m*
alert [ə'lʌrt] *adj* listo, vivo; vigilante ‖ *s* (aer) alarma; (mil) alerta *m;* **to be on the alert** estar sobre aviso, estar alerta ‖ *tr* alertar
Aleutian Islands [ə'luʃən] *spl* islas Aleutas, islas Aleutianas
Alexandrine [,ælɪg'zændrɪn] *adj & s* alejandrino
alg. *abbr* algebra
algae ['ældʒi] *spl* algas
algebra ['ældʒɪbrə] *s* álgebra
algebraic [,ældʒɪ'bre•ɪk] *adj* algebraico
Algeria [æl'dʒɪrɪ•ə] *s* Argelia
Algerian [æl'dʒɪrɪ•ən] *adj & s* argelino
Algiers [æl'dʒɪrz] *s* Argel *f*
alias ['elɪ•əs] *adv* alias ‖ *s* alias *m*, nombre supuesto
ali•bi ['ælɪ,baɪ] *s* (*pl* -**bis**) coartada; (coll) excusa
alien ['elɪ•ən] *adj & s* extranjero
alienate ['eljə,net] o ['elɪ•ə,net] *tr* enajenar, alienar; desenamorar
alight [ə'laɪt] *v* (*pret & pp* **alighted** o **alit** [ə'lɪt]) *intr* bajar, apearse; posarse (*un ave*)
align [ə'laɪn] *tr* alinear ‖ *intr* alinearse
alike [ə'laɪk] *adj* semejantes; **to look alike** parecerse ‖ *adv* igualmente
alimentary canal [,ælɪ'mɛntəri] *s* canal alimenticio, tubo digestivo
alimony ['ælɪ,moni] *s* alimentos
alive [ə'laɪv] *adj* vivo, viviente; animado; **alive to** despierto para, sensible a; **alive with** hormigueante en
alka•li ['ælkə,laɪ] *s* (*pl* -**lis** o -**lies**) álcali *m*
alkaline ['ælkə,laɪn] *adj* alcalino
all [ɔl] *adj indef* todo, todos; todo el, todos los ‖ *pron indef* todo; todos, todo el mundo; **after all** sin embargo; **all of** todo el, todos

los; **all that** todo lo que, todos los que; **for all I know** que yo sepa; a lo mejor; **not at all** nada; no hay de qué ‖ *adv* enteramente; **all along** desde el principio; a lo largo de; **all at once** de golpe; **all right** bueno, corriente; **all too** excesivamente
Allah ['ælə] *s* Alá *m*
allay [ə'le] *tr* aliviar, calmar
all-clear [ɔl'klɪr] *s* cese *m* de alarma
allege [ə'lɛdʒ] *tr* alegar
allegiance [ə'lidʒəns] *s* fidelidad, lealtad; homenaje *m;* **to swear allegiance to** jurar fidelidad a; rendir homenaje a
allegoric(al) [,ælɪ'gɑrɪk(əl)] o [,ælɪ'gɔrɪk(əl)] *adj* alegórico
allego•ry ['ælɪ,gori] *s* (*pl* -**ries**) alegoría
aller•gy ['ælərdʒi] *s* (*pl* -**gies**) alergia
alleviate [ə'livɪ,et] *tr* aliviar
alleviation [ə,livɪ'eʃən] *s* aligeramiento
alley ['æli] *s* callejuela; paseo arbolado, paseo de jardín; (bowling) pista; (tennis) espacio lateral
All Fools' Day *s var of* **April Fools' Day**
Allhallows [,ɔl'hæloz] *s* día *m* de todos los santos
alliance [ə'laɪ•əns] *s* alianza
alligator ['ælɪ,getər] *s* caimán *m*
alligator pear *s* aguacate *m*
alligator wrench *s* llave *f* de mandíbulas dentadas
alliteration [ə,lɪtə'reʃən] *s* aliteración
all-knowing ['ɔl'no•ɪŋ] *adj* omnisciente
allocate ['ælə,ket] *tr* asignar, distribuir
allot [ə'lɑt] *v* (*pret & pp* **allotted;** *ger* **allotting**) *tr* asignar, distribuir
all'-out' *adj* acérrimo
allow [ə'lau] *tr* dejar, permitir; admitir; conceder ‖ *intr* — **to allow for** tener en cuenta; **to allow of** permitir; admitir
allowance [ə'lau•əns] *s* permiso; concesión; ración; descuento, rebaja; tolerancia; **to make allowance for** tener en cuenta
alloy ['ælɔɪ] o [ə'lɔɪ] *s* aleación, liga ‖ [ə'lɔɪ] *tr* alear, ligar
all'-pow'er•ful *adj* todopoderoso
all'-pur'pose *adj* universal, para todo uso
All Saints' Day *s* día *m* de todos los santos
All Souls' Day *s* día *m* de los difuntos
allspice ['ɔl,spaɪs] *s* pimienta inglesa
all'-star' game *s* (sport) juego de estrellas
allude [ə'lud] *intr* aludir
allure [ə'lur] *s* tentación, encanto, fascinación ‖ *tr* tentar, encantar
alluring [ə'lurɪŋ] *adj* tentador, encantador, fascinante
allusion [ə'luʒən] *s* alusión
all'-weath'er *adj* para todo tiempo
al•ly ['ælaɪ] o [ə'laɪ] *s* (*pl* -**lies**) aliado ‖ [ə'laɪ] *v* (*pret & pp* -**lied**) *tr* aliar ‖ *intr* aliarse
almanac ['ɔlmə,næk] *s* almanaque *m*
almighty [ɔl'maɪti] *adj* todopoderoso, omnipotente
almond ['amənd] o ['æmənd] *s* almendra
almond brittle *s* crocante *m*
almond tree *s* almendro
almost ['ɔlmost] o [ɔl'most] *adv* casi

alms [amz] *s* limosna
alms'house' *s* casa de beneficencia
aloe ['ælo] *s* áloe *m*
aloft [ə'lɔft] o [ə'lɑft] *adv* arriba; (aer) en vuelo; (naut) en la arboladura
alone [ə'lon] *adj* solo; **let alone** sin mencionar; y mucho menos; **to let alone** no molestar; no mezclarse en ‖ *adv* solamente
along [ə'lɔŋ] o [ə'lɑŋ] *adv* conmigo, consigo, etc.; **all along** desde el principio; **along with** junto con ‖ *prep* a lo largo de
along'side' *adv* a lo largo; (naut) al costado; **to bring alongside** acostar ‖ *prep* a lo largo de; (naut) al costado de
aloof [ə'luf] *adj* apartado; reservado ‖ *adv* lejos, a distancia
aloud [ə'laud] *adv* alto, en voz alta
alphabet ['ælfə,bɛt] *s* alfabeto
alpine ['ælpaɪn] *adj* alpestre, alpino
Alps [ælps] *spl* Alpes *mpl*
already [ɔl'rɛdi] *adv* ya
Alsace [æl'ses] o ['ælsæs] *s* Alsacia
Alsatian [æl'seʃən] *adj & s* alsaciano
also ['ɔlso] *adv* también
alt. *abbr* **alternate, altitude**
altar ['ɔltər] *s* altar *m;* **to lead to the altar** conducir al altar
altar boy *s* acólito, monaguillo
altar cloth *s* sabanilla, palia
al'tar-piece' *s* retablo
altar rail *s* comulgatorio
alter ['ɔltər] *tr* alterar ‖ *intr* alterarse
alteration [,ɔltə'reʃən] *s* alteración; (*in a building*) reforma; (*in clothing*) arreglo
alternate ['ɔltərnɪt] o ['ɛltərnɪt] *adj* alterno ‖ ['ɔltər,net] o ['æltər,net] *tr & intr* alternar
alternating current *s* corriente alterna o alternativa
although [ɔl'ðo] *conj* aunque
altimetry [æl'tɪmɪtri] *s* altimetría
altitude ['æltɪ,tjud] *s* altitud, altura
al•to ['ælto] *s* (*pl* **-tos**) contralto
altogether [,ɔltə'gɛðər] *adv* enteramente; en conjunto
altruist ['æltru•ɪst] *s* altruísta *mf*
altruistic [,æltru'ɪstɪk] *adj* altruísta
alum ['æləm] *s* alumbre *m*
aluminum [ə'lumɪnəm] *s* aluminio
alum•na [ə'lʌmnə] *s* (*pl* **-nae** [ni]) graduada
alum•nus [ə'lʌmnəs] *s* (*pl* **-ni** [naɪ]) graduado
alveo•lus [æl'vi•ələs] *s* (*pl* **-li** [,laɪ]) **alvéolo**
always ['ɔlwɪz] o ['ɔlwez] *adv* siempre
A.M. *abbr* **ante meridiem,** i.e., **before noon; amplitude modulation**
Am. *abbr* **America, American**
amalgam [ə'mælgəm] *s* amalgama *f*
amalgamate [ə'mælgə,met] *tr* amalgamar ‖ *intr* amalgamarse
amass [ə'mæs] *tr* amontonar; amasar (*dinero*)
amateur ['æmətʃər] *adj & s* chapucero, principiante *mf;* aficionado
amateur performance *s* función de aficionados
amaze [ə'mez] *tr* asombrar, maravillar

amazing [ə'mezɪŋ] *adj* asombroso, maravilloso
Amazon ['æmə,zɑn] *s* Amazonas *m*
ambassador [æm'bæsədər] *s* embajador *m*
ambassadress [æm'bæsədrɪs] *s* embajadora
amber ['æmbər] *adj* ambarino ‖ *s* ámbar *m*
ambigui•ty [,æmbɪ'gju•ɪti] *s* (*pl* **-ties**) ambigüedad
ambiguous [æm'bɪgju•əs] *adj* ambiguo
ambition [æm'bɪʃən] *s* ambición
ambitious [æm'bɪʃəs] *adj* ambicioso
amble ['æmbəl] *s* ambladura ‖ *intr* amblar
ambulance ['æmbjələns] *s* ambulancia
ambush ['æmbuʃ] *s* emboscada; **to lie in ambush** estar emboscado ‖ *tr* (*to station in ambush*) emboscar; (*to lie in wait for and attack*) insidiar ‖ *intr* emboscarse
ame•ba [ə'mibə] *s* (*pl* **-bas** o **-bae** [bi]) amiba
amelioration [ə,miljə'reʃən] *s* mejoramiento
amen ['e'mɛn] o ['a'mɛn] *interj* ¡amén! ‖ *s* amén *m*
amenable [ə'minəbəl] o [ə'mɛnəbəl] *adj* dócil; responsable
amend [ə'mɛnd] *tr* enmendar ‖ *intr* enmendarse ‖ **amends** *spl* enmienda; **to make amends for** enmendar
amendment [ə'mɛndmənt] *s* enmienda
ameni•ty [ə'minɪti] o [ə'mɛnɪti] *s* (*pl* **-ties**) amenidad
America [ə'mɛrɪkə] *s* América
American [ə'mɛrɪkən] *adj & s* americano; norteamericano, estadounidense
Americanize [ə'mɛrɪkə,naɪz] *tr* americanizar
amethyst ['æmɪθɪst] *s* amatista
amiable ['emɪ•əbəl] *adj* amable, bonachón
amicable ['æmɪkəbəl] *adj* amigable
amid [ə'mɪd] *prep* en medio de
amidship [ə'mɪdʃɪp] *adv* en medio del navío
amiss [ə'mɪs] *adj* inoportuno; malo ‖ *adv* inoportunamente; mal; **to take amiss** llevar a mal, tomar en mala parte
ami•ty ['æmɪti] *s* (*pl* **-ties**) amistad
ammeter ['æm,mitər] *s* anmetro, amperímetro
ammonia [ə'monɪ•ə] *s* amoníaco; agua amoníacal
ammunition [,æmjə'nɪʃən] *s* munición
amnes•ty ['æmnɪsti] *s* (*pl* **-ties**) amnistía ‖ *v* (*pret & pp* **-tied**) *tr* amnistiar
amniocentesis [,æmnɪ•osen'tisɪs] *s* amniocentesis *f*
amoeba [ə'mibə] *s* var of **ameba**
among [ə'mʌŋ] *prep* entre, en medio de, en el número de
amorous ['æmərəs] *adj* amoroso; erótico, sensual, voluptuoso
amortize ['æmər,taɪz] *tr* amortizar
amount [ə'maunt] *s* cantidad, importe *m* ‖ *intr* — **to amount to** ascender a; significar
amp. *abbr* **ampere, amperage**
ampere ['æmpɪr] *s* amperio
am'pere-hour' *s* amperio-hora *m*
amphibious [æm'fɪbɪ•əs] *adj* anfibio
amphitheater ['æmfɪ,θi•ətər] *s* anfiteatro
ample ['æmpəl] *adj* amplio; bastante, suficiente; abundante
amplifier ['æmplɪ,faɪ•ər] *s* amplificador *m*

ampli•fy [ˈæmplɪˌfaɪ] v (pret & pp **-fied**) tr amplificar ‖ intr espaciarse

amplitude [ˈæmplɪˌtjud] s amplitud

amplitude modulation s modulación de amplitud

ampule [ˈæmpjul] s inyectable m

amputate [ˈæmpjəˌtet] tr amputar

amt. abbr **amount**

amuck [əˈmʌk] adv frenéticamente; **to run amuck** atacar a ciegas

amulet [ˈæmjəlɪt] s amuleto

amuse [əˈmjuz] tr divertir, entretener

amusement [əˈmjuzmənt] s diversión, entretenimiento; pasatiempo, recreación; (in a park or circus) atracción

amusement park s parque m de atracciones

amusing [əˈmjuzɪŋ] adj divertido, gracioso

an [æn] o [ən] art indef (antes de sonido vocal) un

anachronism [əˈnækrəˌnɪzəm] s anacronismo

anachronistic [əˌnækrəˈnɪstɪk] adj anacrónico

anaemia [əˈnimɪ•ə] s anemia

anaemic [əˈnimɪk] adj anémico

anaesthesia [ˌænɪsˈθiʒə] s anestesia

anaesthetic [ˌænɪsˈθɛtɪk] adj & s anestésico

anaesthetize [æˈnɛsθɪˌtaɪz] tr anestesiar

analogous [əˈnæləgəs] adj análogo

analo•gy [əˈnælədʒi] s (pl **-gies**) analogía

analyse [ˈænəˌlaɪz] tr analizar

analy•sis [əˈnælɪsɪs] s (pl **-ses** [ˌsiz]) análisis m & f

analyst [ˈænəlɪst] s analista mf

analytic(al) [ˌænəˈlɪtɪk(əl)] adj analítico

analyze [ˈænəˌlaɪz] tr analizar

anarchist [ˈænərkɪst] s anarquista mf

anarchy [ˈænərki] s anarquía

anathema [əˈnæθɪmə] s anatema m & f

anatomic(al) [ˌænəˈtɑmɪk(əl)] adj anatómico

anato•my [əˈnætəmi] s (pl **-mies**) anatomía

ancestor [ˈænsɛstər] s antecesor m, antepasado

ances•try [ˈænsɛstri] s (pl **-tries**) abolengo, alcurnia

anchor [ˈæŋkər] s ancla, áncora; (fig) áncora; **to cast anchor** echar anclas; **to weigh anchor** levar anclas ‖ tr sujetar con el ancla ‖ intr anclar, ancorar

ancho•vy [ˈæntʃovi] s (pl **-vies**) anchoa

ancient [ˈenʃənt] adj antiguo

and [ænd] o [ənd] conj y; **and so forth** y así sucesivamente

Andalusia [ˌændəˈluʒə] s Andalucía

Andalusian [ˌændəˈluʒən] adj & s andaluz m

Andean [ænˈdi•ən] adj & s andino

Andes [ˈændiz] spl Andes mpl

andirons [ˈændˌaɪ•ərnz] spl morillos

anecdote [ˈænɪkˌdot] s anécdota

anemia [əˈnimɪ•ə] s anemia

anemic [əˈnimɪk] adj anémico

aneroid barometer [ˈænəˌrɔɪd] s barómetro aneroide

anesthesia [ˌænɪsˈθiʒə] s anestesia

anesthetic [ˌænɪsˈθɛtɪk] adj & s anestésico

anesthetize [æˈnɛsθɪˌtaɪz] tr anestesiar

aneurysm [ˈænjəˌrɪzəm] s aneurisma m

anew [əˈnju] o [əˈnu] adv de nuevo, nuevamente

angel [ˈendʒəl] s ángel m; (financial backer) caballo blanco

angelic(al) [ænˈdʒɛlɪk(əl)] adj angélico, angelical

anger [ˈæŋgər] s cólera, ira ‖ tr encolerizar, airar

angina pectoris [æñˈdʒainə ˈpɛktərɪs] s angina de pecho

angle [ˈæŋgəl] s ángulo; punto de vista ‖ intr pescar con caña; intrigar

angle iron s ángulo de hierro, hierro angular

angler [ˈæŋglər] s pescador m de caña; intrigante mf

Anglo-Saxon [ˌæŋgloˈsæksən] adj & s anglosajón m

an•gry [ˈæŋgri] adj (comp **-grier**; super **-griest**) encolerizado, airado; (pathol) inflamado, irritado; **to become angry at** enojarse de; **to become angry with** enojarse con o contra

anguish [ˈæŋgwɪʃ] s angustia, congoja

angular [ˈæŋgjələr] adj angular; (features) anguloso

anhydrous [ænˈhaɪdrəs] adj anhidro

aniline dyes [ˈænɪlɪn] o [ˈænɪˌlaɪn] s colores mpl de anilina

animal [ˈænɪməl] adj & s animal m

animal spirits spl ardor m, vigor m, vivacidad

animated cartoon [ˈænɪˌmetɪd] s película de dibujos, dibujo animado

animation [ˌænɪˈmeʃən] s animación

animosi•ty [ˌænɪˈmɑsɪti] s (pl **-ties**) animosidad

anion [ˈænˌaɪ•ən] s anión m

anise [ˈænɪs] s anís m

aniseed [ˈænɪˌsid] s grano de anís

anisette [ˌænɪˈzɛt] s anisete m

ankle [ˈæŋkəl] s tobillo

an'kle•bone' s hueso del tobillo

ankle support s tobillera

anklet [ˈæŋklɪt] s ajorca; (sock) tobillera

annals [ˈænəlz] spl anales mpl

anneal [əˈnil] tr recocer

annex [ˈænɛks] s anexo; (of a building) pabellón m ‖ [əˈnɛks] tr anexar

annihilate [əˈnaɪ•ɪˌlet] tr aniquilar

anniversa•ry [ˌænɪˈvʌrsəri] adj aniversario ‖ s (pl **-ries**) aniversario

annotate [ˈænəˌtet] tr anotar

announce [əˈnauns] tr anunciar

announcement [əˈnaunsmənt] s anuncio

announcer [əˈnaunsər] s anunciador m; (rad) locutor m

annoy [əˈnɔɪ] tr fastidiar, molestar; majaderear; pololear; (Cuba, Mex) ciscar

annoyance [əˈnɔɪ•əns] s fastidio, molestia

annoying [əˈnɔɪ•ɪŋ] adj fastidioso, molesto

annual [ˈænjuˌəl] adj anual ‖ s publicación anual; planta anual

annui•ty [əˈnjuˌɪti] o [əˈnuˌɪti] s (pl **-ties**) anualidad; renta vitalicia

an•nul [əˈnʌl] v (pret & pp **-nulled**; ger **-nulling**) tr anular, invalidar

anode [ˈænod] s ánodo

al
an

anoint [ə'nɔɪnt] *tr* ungir, untar
anomalous [ə'nɑmələs] *adj* anómalo
anoma•ly [ə'nɑməli] *s* (*pl* **-lies**) anomalía
anon. *abbr* **anonymous**
anonymity [,ænə'nɪmɪti] *s* anónimo; **to preserve one's anonymity** guardar o conservar el anónimo
anonymous [ə'nɑnɪməs] *adj* anónimo
another [ə'nʌðər] *adj & pron indef* otro
ans. *abbr* **answer**
answer ['ænsər] *s* contestación, respuesta; solución ‖ *tr* contestar, responder; resolver (*un problema o un enigma*) ‖ *intr* contestar, responder; **to answer for** responder de (*una cosa*); responder por (*una persona*)
ant [ænt] *s* hormiga
antagonism [æn'tægə,nɪzəm] *s* antagonismo
antagonize [æn'tægə,naɪz] *tr* oponerse a; enemistar, enajenar
antarctic [ænt'ɑrktɪk] *adj* antártico ‖ **the Antarctic** las Tierras Antárticas
antecedent [,æntɪ'sidənt] *adj* antecedente ‖ *s* antecedente *m*; **antecedents** antecedentes *mpl*; antepasados
antechamber ['æntɪ,tʃembər] *s* antecámara
antedate ['æntɪ,det] *tr* antedatar; preceder
antelope ['æntɪ,lop] *s* antílope *m*
anten•na [æn'tɛnə] *s* (*pl* **-nae** [ni]) (ent) antena ‖ *s* (*pl* **-nas**) (rad) antena
autepenult [,æntɪ'pinʌlt] *s* antepenúltima
anteroom ['æntɪ,rum] *s* antecámara
anthem ['ænθəm] *s* himno; antífona
ant'hill' *s* hormiguero
antholo•gy [æn'θɑlədʒi] *s* (*pl* **-gies**) antología
anthracite ['ænθrə,saɪt] *s* antracita
anthrax ['ænθræks] *s* ántrax *m*
anthropology [,ænθrə'pɑlədʒi] *s* antropología
anti-aircraft [,æntɪ'ɛr,kræft] *adj* antiaéreo
antibiotic [,æntɪbaɪ'ɑtɪk] *adj & s* antibiótico
antibod•y ['æntɪ,bɑdi] *s* (*pl* **-ies**) anticuerpo
anticipate [æn'tɪsɪ,pet] *tr* esperar, prever; anticipar; (*to get ahead of*) anticiparse a; impedir; prometerse (*p.ej., un placer*); temerse (*algo desagradable*)
antics ['æntɪks] *spl* cabriolas, gracias, travesuras
antidote ['æntɪ,dot] *s* antídoto
antifreeze [,æntɪ'friz] *s* anticongelante *m*
antiglare [,æntɪ'glɛr] *adj* antideslumbrante
antiknock [,æntɪ'nɑk] *adj & s* antidetonante *m*
antilabor [,æntɪ'lebər] *adj* antiobrero
Antilles [æn'tɪliz] *spl* Antillas
antimatter ['æntɪ,mætər] *s* antimateria
antimissile [,æntɪ'mɪsɪl] *adj* antiproyectil
antimony ['æntɪ,moni] *s* antimonio
antipas•to [,ɑntɪ'pɑsto] *s* (*pl* **-tos**) aperitivo, entremés *m*
antipa•thy [æn'tɪpəθi] *s* (*pl* **-thies**) antipatía
antipollution movement [,æntɪpə'luʃən] *s* lucha antipolución
antiquar•y ['æntɪ,kwɛri] *s* (*pl* **-ies**) anticuario
antiquated ['æntɪ,kwetɪd] *adj* anticuado
antique [æn'tik] *adj* antiguo ‖ *s* antigüedad
antique dealer *s* anticuario

antique store *s* tienda de antigüedades
antiqui•ty [æn'tɪkwɪti] *s* (*pl* **-ties**) antigüedad
anti-Semitic [,æntɪsɪ'mɪtɪk] *adj* antisemítico
antiseptic [,æntɪ'sɛptɪk] *adj & s* antiséptico
antislavery [,æntɪ'slevəri] *adj* antiesclavista
anti-Soviet [,æntɪ'sovɪ,ɛt] *adj* antisoviético
antitank [,æntɪ'tæŋk] *adj* antitanque
antiterrorist [,æntɪ'tɛrərɪst] *adj & s* antiterrorista *mf*
antithe•sis [æn'tɪθɪsɪs] *s* (*pl* **-ses** [,siz]) antítesis *f*
antitoxin [,æntɪ'tɑksɪn] *s* antitoxina
antitrust [,æntɪ'trʌst] *adj* anticartel
antiwar [,æntɪ'wɔr] *adj* antibélico
antler ['æntlər] *s* cuerna
antonym ['æntənɪm] *s* antónimo
Antwerp ['æntwərp] *s* Amberes *f*
anvil ['ænvɪl] *s* yunque *m*
anxie•ty [æŋ'zaɪ•əti] *s* (*pl* **-ties**) ansiedad, inquietud; ansia, anhelo
anxious ['æŋkʃəs] *adj* ansioso, inquieto; anhelante; **to be anxious to** tener ganas de
any ['ɛni] *adj indef* algún, cualquier; todo; **any place** dondequiera; **any time** cuando quiera; alguna vez ‖ *pron indef* alguno, cualquiera ‖ *adv* algo
an'y•bod'y *pron indef* alguno, alguien, cualquiera, quienquiera; todo el mundo; **not anybody** nadie
an'y•how' *adv* de cualquier modo; de todos modos; sin embargo
an'y•one' *pron indef* alguno, alguien, cualquiera
an'y•thing' *pron indef* algo, alguna cosa; cualquier cosa; todo cuanto; **anything at all** cualquier cosa que sea; **anything else** cualquier otra cosa; **anything else?** ¿algo más?; **not anything** nada
an'y•way' *adv* de cualquier modo; de todos modos; sin embargo; sin esmero, sin orden ni concierto
an'y•where' *adv* dondequiera; adondequiera; **not anywhere** en ninguna parte
apace [ə'pes] *adv* aprisa
apart [ə'pɑrt] *adv* aparte; en pedazos; **to fall apart** caerse a pedazos; desunirse; ir al desastre; **to live apart** vivir separados; vivir aislado; **to stand apart** mantenerse apartado; **to take apart** descomponer, desarmar, desmontar; **to tell apart** distinguir
apartment [ə'pɑrtmənt] *s* apartamento
apartment house *s* casa de pisos
apathetic [,æpə'θɛtɪk] *adj* apático
apa•thy ['æpəθi] *s* (*pl* **-ties**) apatía; lerdera
ape [ep] *s* mono ‖ *tr* imitar, remedar
aperture ['æpərtʃər] *s* abertura, orificio
apex ['epɛks] *s* (*pl* **apexes** o **apices** ['æpɪ,siz]) ápex *m*, ápice *m*
aphorism ['æfə,rɪzəm] *s* aforismo
aphrodisiac [,æfrə'dɪzɪ,æk] *adj & s* afrodisíaco
apiar•y ['epɪ,ɛri] *s* (*pl* **-ies**) abejar *m*, colmenar *m*
apiece [ə'pis] *adv* cada uno; por persona
apish ['epɪʃ] *adj* monesco; tonto
aplomb [ə'plɑm] *s* aplomo, sangre fría
apogee ['æpə,dʒi] *s* apogeo

apologetic [ə‚palə'dʒɛtɪk] *adj* lleno de excusas

apologist [ə'palədʒɪst] *s* defensor *m*; exponente *m*

apologize [ə'palə‚dʒaɪz] *intr* excusarse, disculparse; **to apologize for** disculparse de; **to apologize to** disculparse con

apology [ə'palədʒi] *s* (*pl* **-gies**) excusa; (*makeshift*) expediente *m*

apoplectic [‚æpə'plɛktɪk] *adj & s* apoplético

apoplexy ['æpə‚plɛksi] *s* apoplejía

apostle [ə'pasəl] *s* apóstol *m*

apostrophe [ə'pastrəfi] *s* (*written sign*) apóstrofo; (*words addressed to absent person*) apóstrofe *m & f*

apothecar·y [ə'paθɪ‚kɛri] *s* (*pl* **-ies**) boticario

apothecary's jar *s* bote *m* de porcelana

apothecary's shop *s* botica

appall [ə'pɔl] *tr* espantar, pasmar

appalling [ə'pɔlɪŋ] *adj* aterrador, espantoso, pasmoso

appara·tus [‚æpə'retəs] o [‚æpə'rætəs] *s* (*pl* **-tus** o **-tuses**) aparato

apparel [ə'pærəl] *s* indumentaria, vestido

apparent [ə'pærənt] *adj* aparente

apparition [‚æpə'rɪʃən] *s* aparición

appeal [ə'pil] *s* súplica, instancia, solicitud; atracción, interés *m*; (law) apelación ‖ *intr* ser atrayente; **to appeal to** (*to make an entreaty to*) suplicar; (*to be attractive to*) atraer, interesar; (law) apelar a

appear [ə'pɪr] *intr* (*to come into sight; to be in sight; to be published*) aparecer; (*to come into sight; to be in sight; to look; to seem*) parecer; (*to come before the public*) presentarse; (*to come before a court*) comparecer

appearance [ə'pɪrəns] *s* (*act of appearing*) aparición; (*outward look*) apariencia, aspecto; (law) comparecencia

appease [ə'piz] *tr* apaciguar

appeasement [ə'pizmənt] *s* apaciguamiento

appeasement attempts *spl* (coll) paños tibios *mpl*

appellate [ə'pɛlɪt] *adj* apelante

appellate court *s* tribunal *m* de apelación

appellate judge *s* juez *m* de alzadas

appendage [ə'pɛndɪdʒ] *s* apéndice *m*

appendicitis [ə‚pɛndɪ'saɪtɪs] *s* apendicitis *f*

appen·dix [ə'pɛndɪks] *s* (*pl* **-dixes** o **-dices** [dɪ‚siz]) apéndice *m*

appertain [‚æpər'ten] *intr* relacionarse

appetite ['æpɪ‚taɪt] *s* apetito

appetizer ['æpɪ‚taɪzər] *s* aperitivo, apetite *m*

appetizing ['æpɪ‚taɪzɪŋ] *adj* apetitoso

applaud [ə'plɔd] *tr & intr* aplaudir

applause [ə'plɔz] *s* aplauso, aplausos

apple ['æpəl] *s* manzana

ap'ple·jack *s* aguardiente *m* de manzana

·apple of the eye *s* niña del ojo

apple pie *s* pastel *m* de manzana

apple polisher *s* (slang) quitamotas *mf*

ap'ple·sauce *s* compota de manzanas; (slang) música celestial

apple tree *s* manzano

appliance [ə'plaɪ·əns] *s* artificio, dispositivo, aparato; aplicación

applicant ['æplɪkənt] *s* aspirante *mf*, pretendiente *mf*, solicitante *mf*

ap·ply [ə'plaɪ] *v* (*pret & pp* **-plied**) *tr* aplicar ‖ *intr* aplicarse; dirigirse; **to apply for** pedir, solicitar

appoint [ə'pɔɪnt] *tr* designar, nombrar; señalar; amueblar

appointment [ə'pɔɪntmənt] *s* designación, nombramiento; empleo, puesto; cita; **appointments** instalación, accesorios, adornos; **by appointment** cita previa

apportion [ə'pɔrʃən] *tr* prorratear

appraisal [ə'prezəl] *s* tasación, valoración, apreciación

appraise [ə'prez] *tr* tasar, valorar, apreciar

appreciable [ə'priʃɪ·əbəl] *adj* apreciable; sensible

appreciate [ə'priʃɪ‚et] *tr* apreciar; aprobar; comprender; estar agradecido por ‖ *intr* subir de valor

appreciation [ə‚priʃɪ'eʃən] *s* aprecio; agradecimiento, plusvalía, aumento de valor

appreciative [ə'priʃɪ‚etɪv] *adj* apreciador; agradecido

apprehend [‚æprɪ'hɛnd] *tr* aprehender, prender; comprender; temer

apprehension [‚æprɪ'hɛnʃən] *s* aprehensión; (*fear, worry*) aprensión; comprensión

apprehensive [‚æprɪ'hɛnsɪv] *adj* (*fearful, worried*) aprehensivo, aprensivo

apprentice [ə'prɛntɪs] *s* aprendiz *m*, meritorio; chumero, chumera (CAm) ‖ *tr* poner de aprendiz

apprenticeship [ə'prɛntɪsʃ‚ɪp] *s* aprendizaje *m*

apprise o **apprize** [ə'praɪz] *tr* informar; apreciar, tasar

approach [ə'protʃ] *s* acercamiento; vía de entrada; proposición; (*to a problem*) enfoque *m* ‖ *tr* abordar, acercarse a; (*to bring closer*) acercar ‖ *intr* acercarse, aproximarse

approbation [‚æprə'beʃən] *s* aprobación

appropriate [ə'propri·ɪt] *adj* apropiado, a propósito ‖ [ə'propri‚et] *tr* apropiarse; asignar, destinar (*el parlamento determinada suma a un determinado fin*)

approval [ə'pruvəl] *s* aprobación; **on approval** a prueba

approve [ə'pruv] *tr & intr* aprobar

approximate [ə'praksɪmɪt] *adj* aproximado ‖ [ə'praksɪ‚met] *tr* aproximar ‖ *intr* aproximarse

apricot ['epri‚kat] o ['æpri‚kat] *s* albaricoque *m*

apricot tree *s* albaricoquero

April ['eprɪl] *s* abril *m*

April fool *s* — **to make an April fool of** coger por inocente

April Fools' Day *s* día *m* de engañabobos, primer día de abril, en que se coge por inocente a la gente

apron ['eprən] *s* delantal *m*; (*of a workman*) mandil *m*; **tied to the apron strings of** cosido a las faldas de

apropos [‚æprə'po] adj oportuno ‖ adv a propósito; **apropos of** a propósito de
apse [æps] s ábside m
apt [æpt] adj apto; a propósito; dispuesto; inclinado
aptitude ['æptɪ‚tjud] s aptitud
aquamarine [‚ækwəmə'rin] s aguamarina
aquaplane ['ækwə‚plen] s acuaplano ‖ intr correr en acuaplano
aquari•um [ə'kwɛrɪ•əm] s (pl -ums o -a [ə]) acuario
Aquarius [ə'kwɛrɪ•əs] s (astr) Acuario
aquatic [ə'kwætɪk] o [ə'kwɑtɪk] adj acuático ‖ **aquatics** spl deportes acuáticos
aqueduct ['ækwə‚dʌkt] s acueducto
aquiline nose ['ækwɪ‚laɪn] s nariz aguileña
Arab ['ærəb] adj árabe ‖ s árabe mf; caballo árabe
Arabia [ə'rebɪ•ə] s la Arabia
Arabian [ə'rebɪ•ən] adj árabe; arábigo ‖ s árabe mf
Arabic ['ærəbɪk] adj arábigo ‖ s árabe m. arábigo
Aragon ['ærə‚gɑn] s Aragón m
Arago•nese [‚ærəgə'niz] adj aragonés ‖ s (pl -nese) aragonés m
arbiter ['ɑrbɪtər] s árbitro
arbitrary ['ɑrbɪ‚trɛri] adj arbitrario
arbitrate ['ɑrbɪ‚tret] tr & intr arbitrar
arbitration [‚ɑrbɪ'treʃən] s arbitraje m
arbor ['ɑrbər] s emparrado, glorieta
arbore•tum [‚ɑrbə'ritəm] s (pl -tums o -ta [tə]) jardín botánico de árboles
arbor vitae ['ɑrbər 'vaɪti] s árbol m de la vida
arbutus [ɑr'bjutəs] s madroño
arc [ɑrk] s arco
arcade [ɑr'ked] s arcada, galería
arch. abbr archaic, archaism, archipelago, architect
arch [ɑrtʃ] adj astuto; travieso; principal ‖ s arco ‖ tr arquear, enarcar; atravesar
archaeology [‚ɑrkɪ'ɑlədʒi] s arqueología
archaic [ɑr'ke•ɪk] adj arcaico
archaism ['ɑrke‚ɪzəm] s arcaísmo
archangel ['ɑrk‚endʒəl] s arcángel m
archbishop ['ɑrtʃ'bɪʃəp] s arzobispo
archduke ['ɑrtʃ'djuk] s archiduque m
archene•my ['ɑrtʃ‚ɛnimi] s (pl -mies) archienemigo
archeology [‚ɑrkɪ'ɑlədʒi] s arqueología
archer ['ɑrtʃər] s arquero, flechero
archery ['ɑrtʃəri] s tiro de flechas
archipela•go [‚ɑrkɪ'pɛləgo] s (pl -gos o -goes) archipiélago
architect ['ɑrkɪ‚tɛkt] s arquitecto
architectural [‚ɑrkɪ'tɛktʃərəl] adj arquitectónico, arquitectural
architecture ['ɑrkɪ‚tɛktʃər] s arquitectura
archives ['ɑrkaɪvz] spl archivo
arch'way' s arcada
arc lamp s lámpara de arco
arctic ['ɑrktɪk] adj ártico ‖ **the Arctic** las Tierras Articas
arc welding s soldadura de arco
ardent ['ɑrdənt] adj ardiente
ardor ['ɑrdər] s ardor m

arduous ['ɑrdju•əs] adj arduo, difícil; enérgico; (steep) escarpado
area ['ɛrɪ•ə] s área, superficie f; comarca, región; zona; patio
ar'ea•way' s entrada baja de un sótano
Argentina [‚ɑrdʒən'tinə] s la Argentina
Argentine ['ɑrdʒən‚tin] o ['ɑrdʒən‚taɪn] adj & s argentino ‖ **the Argentine** la Argentina
Argentinean [‚ɑrdʒən'tɪnɪ•ən] adj & s argentino
Argonaut ['ɑrgə‚nɔt] s argonauta m
argue ['ɑrgju] tr argüir; **to argue into** persuadir a + inf; **to argue out of** disuadir de + inf ‖ intr argüir
argument ['ɑrgjəmənt] s argumento; disputa
argumentative [‚ɑrgjə'mɛntətɪv] adj argumentador; ergotista masc
argumentativeness [‚ɑrgjə'mɛntətɪvnɪs] s ergotismo
aria ['ɑrɪ•ə] o ['ɛrɪ•ə] s (mus) aria
arid ['ærɪd] adj árido
aridity [ə'rɪdɪti] s aridez f
Aries ['ɛriz] s (astr) Aries m
aright [ə'raɪt] adv acertadamente; **to set aright** rectificar
arise [ə'raɪz] v (pret arose [ə'roz]; pp arisen [ə'rɪzən]) intr levantarse; subir; aparecer; **to arise from** provenir de
aristocra•cy [‚ærɪs'tɑkrəsi] s (pl -cies) aristocracia
aristocrat [ə'rɪstə‚kræt] s aristócrata mf
aristocratic [ə‚rɪstə'krætɪk] adj aristocrático
Aristotelian [‚ærɪstə'tilɪ•ən] adj & s aristotélico
Aristotle ['ærɪs‚tɑtəl] s Aristóteles m
arith. abbr arithmetic
arithmetic [ə'rɪθmətɪk] s aritmética
arithmetical [‚ærɪθ'mɛtɪkəl] adj aritmético
arithmetician [ə‚rɪθmə'tɪʃən] s aritmético
ark [ɑrk] s arca de Noé
ark of the covenant s arca de la alianza
arm [ɑrm] s brazo; (weapon) arma; **arm in arm** de bracero, asidos del brazo; **in arms** de pecho, de teta; **the three arms of the service** los tres ejércitos; **to be up in arms** estar en armas; **to keep at arm's length** mantener a distancia; mantenerse a distancia; **to lay down one's arms** rendir las armas; **to rise up in arms** alzarse en armas; **under arms** sobre las armas ‖ tr armar ‖ intr armarse
armament ['ɑrməmənt] s armamento
armature ['ɑrmə‚tʃər] s armadura; (of a dynamo or motor) (elec) inducido
arm'chair' adj de gabinete ‖ s butaca, sillón m. silla de brazos
Armenian [ɑr'minɪ•ən] adj & s armenio
armful ['ɑrm‚fʊl] s brazado
arm'hole' s (in clothing) sobaquera
armistice ['ɑrmɪstɪs] s armisticio
armor ['ɑrmər] s armadura; coraza, blindaje m ‖ tr acorazar, blindar
armored car s carro blindado
armorial bearings [ɑr'morɪ•əl] spl blasón m. escudo de armas
armor plate s plancha de blindaje

ar'mor-plate' *tr* acorazar, blindar

armor•y [`armǝri] *s* (*pl* -**ies**) arsenal *m;* (*arms factory*) armería

arm'pit' *s* sobaco, hueco de la axila

arm'rest' *s* apoyabrazos *m*

arms race *s* carrera armamentista

arms reduction *s* desarmamiento

ar•my [`armi] *adj* militar, castrense ‖ *s* (*pl* -**mies**) ejército

army corps *s* cuerpo de ejército

aroma [ǝ`romǝ] *s* aroma *m*, fragancia

aromatic [,ærǝ`mætık] *adj* aromático

around [ǝ`raund] *adv* alrededor, a la redonda; en la dirección opuesta ‖ *prep* alrededor de, en torno a o de; cerca de; (*the corner*) a la vuelta de

arouse [ǝ`rauz] *tr* despertar; excitar, incitar

arpeg•gio [ar`pɛdʒo] *s* (*pl* -**gios**) arpegio

arraign [ǝ`ren] *tr* acusar; presentar al tribunal

arrange [ǝ`rendʒ] *tr* arreglar, disponer; (mus) adaptar, refundir

array [ǝ`re] *s* orden *m;* orden *m* de batalla; adorno, atavío ‖ *tr* poner en orden; poner en orden de batalla; adornar, ataviar

arrears [ǝ`rırz] *spl* atrasos; **in arrears** atrasado en pagos

arrest [ǝ`rɛst] *s* arresto, prisión; detención; **under arrest** bajo arresto ‖ *tr* arrestar; detener; atraer (*la atención*)

arresting [ǝ`rɛstıŋ] *adj* impresionante

arrhythmia [ǝ`rıθmi•ǝ] *s* arritmia

arrival [ǝ`raıvǝl] *s* llegada; (*person*) llegado

arrive [ǝ`raıv] *intr* llegar; tener éxito

arrogance [`ærǝgǝns] *s* arrogancia

arrogant [`ærǝgǝnt] *adj* arrogante

arrogate [`ærǝ,get] *tr* — **to arrogate to oneself** arrogarse

arrow [`æro] *s* flecha

ar'row-head' *s* punta de flecha; (bot) saetilla

arsenal [`arsǝnǝl] *s* arsenal *m*

arsenic [`arsınık] *s* arsénico

arson [`arsǝn] *s* incendio premeditado, delito de incendio

art [art] *s* arte *m & f*

arter•y [`artǝri] *s* (*pl* -**ies**) arteria

artful [`artfǝl] *adj* astuto, mañoso; diestro, ingenioso

arthritic [ar`θrıtık] *adj & s* artrítico

arthritis [ar`θraıtıs] *s* artritis *f*

artichoke [`artı,tʃok] *s* alcachofa

article [`artıkǝl] *s* artículo; **an article of clothing** una prenda de vestir

articulate [ar`tıkjǝlıt] *adj* claro, distinto; capaz de hablar ‖ [ar`tıkjǝ,let] *tr* articular

artifact [`artı,fækt] *s* artefacto

artifice [`artıfıs] *s* artificio

artificial [,artı`fıʃǝl] *adj* artificial

artillery [ar`tılǝri] *s* artillería

artillery•man [ar`tılǝrimǝn] *s* (*pl* -**men** [mǝn]) artillero

artisan [`artızǝn] *s* artesano

artist [`artıst] *s* artista *mf*

artistic [ar`tıstık] *adj* artístico

artistry [`artıstri] *s* habilidad artística

artless [`artlıs] *adj* sencillo, natural; ingenuo, inocente; (*crude, clumsy*) chabacano

arts and crafts *spl* artes y oficios

art•y [`arti] *adj* (*comp* -**ier;** *super* -**iest**) (coll) ostentoso artístico

Aryan [`ɛrı•ǝn] o [`arjǝn] *adj & s* ario

as [æz] o [ǝz] *pron rel* que; **the same as** el mismo que ‖ *adv* tan; **as . . . as** tan . . . como; **as for** en cuanto a; **as long as** mientras que; ya que; **as many as** tantos como; **as much as** tanto como; **as regards** en cuanto a; **as soon as** tan pronto como; **as soon as possible** cuanto antes, los más pronto posible; **as though** como si; **as to** en cuanto a; **as well** también; **as yet** hasta ahora ‖ *conf* como; que; ya que; a medida que; **as it seems** por lo visto, según parece ‖ *prep* por, como; **as a rule** por regla general

asbestos [æs`bɛstǝs] *s* asbesto, amianto

ascend [ǝ`sɛnd] *tr* subir a (*p.ej., el trono*) ‖ *intr* ascender

ascendancy [ǝ`sɛndǝnsi] *s* ascendiente *m*

ascension [ǝ`sɛnʃǝn] *s* ascensión

Ascension Day *s* fiesta de la Ascensión

ascent [ǝ`sɛnt] *s* ascensión, subida; ascenso, promoción

ascertain [,æsǝr`ten] *tr* averiguar

ascertainable [,æsǝr`tenǝbǝl] *adj* averiguable

ascetic [ǝ`sɛtık] *adj* ascético ‖ *s* asceta *mf*

ascorbic acid [ǝ`skɔrbık] *s* ácido ascórbico

ascribe [ǝ`skraıb] *tr* atribuir

aseptic [ǝ`sɛptık] o [e`sɛptık] *adj* aséptico

ash [æʃ] *s* ceniza; (*tree; wood*) fresno; **ashes** ceniza, cenizas; (*mortal remains*) cenizas

ashamed [ǝ`ʃemd] *adj* avergonzado; **to be ashamed** tener vergüenza

ashlar [`æʃlǝr] *s* sillar *m*

ashore [ǝ`ʃor] *adv* en tierra, a tierra

ash tray *s* cenicero

Ash Wednesday *s* miércoles *m* de ceniza

Asia [`eʒǝ] o [`eʃǝ] *s* Asia

Asia Minor *s* el Asia Menor

Asian [`eʒǝn] o [`eʃǝn] o **Asiatic** [,eʒı`ætık] o [,eʃı`ætık] *adj & s* asiático

aside [ǝ`saıd] *adv* aparte; **aside from** además de; **to step aside** hacerse a un lado ‖ *s* (theat) aparte *m*

asinine [`æsı,naın] *adj* tonto, necio

ask [æsk] o [ask] *tr* (*to request*) pedir; (*to inquire of*) preguntar; hacer (*una pregunta*); invitar; **to ask in** invitar a entrar ‖ *intr*—**to ask about, after,** or **for;** preguntar por; **to ask for** pedir

askance [ǝ`skæns] *adv* al sesgo, de soslayo; con desdén, sospechosamente

asleep [ǝ`slip] *adj* dormido; **to fall asleep** dormirse

asp [æsp] *s* áspid *m*

asparagus [ǝ`spærǝgǝs] *s* espárrago

aspect [`æspɛkt] *s* aspecto

aspen [`æspǝn] *s* tiemblo, álamo temblón

aspersion [ǝ`spʌrʒǝn] o [ǝ`spʌrʃǝn] *s* calumnia, difamación

asphalt [`æsfɔlt] *s* asfalto ‖ *tr* asfaltar

asphyxiate [æs`fıksı,et] *tr* asfixiar

aspirant [ǝ`spaırǝnt] o [`æspırǝnt] *s* pretendiente *mf*, candidato

aspire [ǝ`spaır] *intr* aspirar

aspirin [`æspırın] *s* aspirina

ass [æs] *s* asno
assail [ə'sel] *tr* asaltar, acometer
assassin [e'sæsɪn] *s* asesino
assassinate [ə'sæsɪ,net] *tr* asesinar
assassination [ə,sæsɪ'neʃən] *s* asesinato
assault [ə'sɔlt] *s* asalto ‖ *tr* asaltar
assault and battery *s* vías de hecho, violencias
assay [ə'se] o ['æse] *s* ensaye *m;* muestra de ensaye ‖ [ə'se] *tr* ensayar; apreciar
assemble [ə'sɛmbəl] *tr* reunir; (mach) armar, montar ‖ *intr* reunirse
assem•bly [ə'sɛmbli] *s* (*pl* -**blies**) asamblea; reunión; (mach) armadura, montaje *m*
assembly hall *s* aula magna, paraninfo; salón *m* de sesiones
assembly line *s* línea de montaje
assembly plant *s* fábrica de montaje
assembly room *s* sala de reunión; (mach) taller *m* de montaje
assent [ə'sɛnt] *s* asentimiento, asenso ‖ *intr* asentir
assert [ə'sʌrt] *tr* afirmar, aseverar, declarar; **to assert oneself** imponerse, hacer valer sus derechos
assertion [ə'sʌrʃən] *s* aserción, aseveración
assess [ə'sɛs] *tr* amillarar, gravar; fijar (*daños y perjuicios*); apreciar, estimar
assessment [ə'sɛsmənt] *s* amillaramiento, gravamen *m;* fijación; apreciación, estimación
asset ['æsɛt] *s* posesión, ventaja; (*person, thing, or quality worth having*) (fig) valor *m;* **assets** (com) activo
assiduous [ə'sɪdju•əs] *adj* asiduo
assign [ə'saɪn] *tr* asignar
assignment [ə'saɪnmənt] *s* asignación, cometido; lección
assimilate [ə'sɪmɪ,let] *tr* asimilarse (*los alimentos, el conocimiento*) ‖ *intr* asimilarse
assist [ə'sɪst] *tr* ayudar, asistir, auxiliar
assistant [ə'sɪstənt] *adj & s* auxiliar *mf,* ayudante *mf*
assistantship [ə'sɪstənt,ʃɪp] *s* ayudantía
assn. *abbr* **association**
associate [ə'soʃɪ•ɪt] *adj* asociado ‖ *s* asociado, socio ‖ [ə'soʃɪ,et] *tr* asociar ‖ *intr* asociarse
association [ə,soʃɪ'eʃən] *s* asociación
assort [ə'sɔrt] *tr* clasificar, ordenar
assortment [ə'sɔrtmənt] *s* surtido; clase *f,* grupo
asst. *abbr* **assistant**
assume [ə'sum] o [ə'sjum] *tr* asumir (*p.ej., responsabilidades*); arrogarse; suponer, dar por sentado
assumption [ə'sʌmpʃən] *s* asunción; suposición
assurance [ə'ʃurəns] *s* aseguramiento; seguridad, confianza; (com) seguro
assure [ə'ʃur] *tr* asegurar; (com) asegurar
Assyria [ə'sɪrɪ•ə] *s* Asiria
Assyrian [ə'sɪrɪ•ən] *adj & s* asirio
astatine ['æstə,tin] *s* ástato
aster ['æstər] *s* (bot) aster *m;* (*China aster*) reina Margarita
asterisk ['æstə,rɪsk] *s* asterisco

astern [ə'stʌrn] *adv* por la popa
asthma ['æzmə] o ['æsmə] *s* asma *f*
astonish [ə'stanɪʃ] *tr* asombrar
astonishing [ə'stanɪʃɪŋ] *adj* asombroso
astound [ə'staund] *tr* pasmar
astounding [ə'staundɪŋ] *adj* pasmoso
astraddle [ə'strædəl] *adv* a horcajadas
astray [ə'stre] *adv* por mal camino; **to go astray** extraviarse; **gone astray** desviado; **to lead astray** extraviar
astride [ə'straɪd] *adv* a horcajadas ‖ *prep* a horcajadas de
astrology [ə'stralədʒi] *s* astrología
astronaut ['æstrə,nɔt] *s* astronauta *m*
astronautic [,æstrə'nɔtɪk] *adj* astronáutico ‖ **astronautics** *s* astronáutica
astronavigation [,æstro,nævɪ'geʃən] *s* astronavigación
astronomer [ə'stranəmər] *s* astrónomo
astronomic(al) [,æstrə'namɪk(əl)] *adj* astronómico
astronomy [ə'stranəmi] *s* astronomía
astrophysics [,æstro'fɪzɪks] *s* astrofísica
Asturian [ə'stʊrɪ•ən] *adj & s* asturiano
astute [ə'stjut] *adj* astuto, sagaz
asunder [ə'sʌndər] *adv* a pedazos, en dos
asylum [ə'saɪləm] *s* asilo
asymmetry [ə'sɪmɪtri] *s* asimetría
at [æt] o [ət] *prep* en, p.ej., **I saw her at the library** la vi en la biblioteca; a, p.ej., **at five o'clock** a las cinco; de, p.ej., **to be surprised at** estar sorprendido de; **to laugh at** reírse de; en casa de, p.ej., **at John's** en casa de Juan
atavistic [,ætə'vɪstɪk] *adj* atávico
atheism ['eθi,ɪzəm] *s* ateísmo
atheist ['eθi•ɪst] *s* ateísta *mf,* ateo
Athenian [ə'θini•ən] *adj & s* ateniense *mf*
Athens ['æθɪnz] *s* Atenas *f*
athirst [ə'θʌrst] *adj* sediento
athlete ['æθlit] *s* atleta *mf*
athlete's foot *s* pie *m* de atleta
athletic [æθ'lɛtɪk] *adj* atlético ‖ **athletics** *s* atletismo
Atlantic [æt'læntɪk] *adj & s* Atlántico
atlas ['ætləs] *s* atlas *m*
atmosphere ['ætməs,fɪr] *s* atmósfera
atmospheric [,ætməs'fɛrɪk] *adj* atmosférico ‖ **atmospherics** *spl* parásitos atmosféricos
atom ['ætəm] *s* átomo
atom bomb *s* bomba atómica
atomic [ə'tamɪk] *adj* atómico
atomic bomb *s* bomba atómica
atomic weight *s* peso atómico
atomize ['ætə,maɪz] *tr* atomizar
atomizer ['ætə,ɹaɪzər] *s* pulverizador *m,* vaporizador *m*
atom smasher *s* rompeátomos *m*
atone [ə'ton] *intr* dar reparación; **to atone for** dar reparación por, expiar
atonement [ə'tonmənt] *s* reparación, expiación
atop [ə'tap] *adv* encima ‖ *prep* encima de
atrocious [ə'troʃəs] *adj* atroz; (coll) abomina-. ble, muy malo
atroci•ty [ə'trasɪti] *s* (*pl* -**ties**) atrocidad

atro•phy ['ætrəfi] *s* (pathol) atrofia, retracción ‖ *v* (*pret & pp* **-phied**) *tr* atrofiar ‖ *intr* atrofiarse

attach [ə'tætʃ] *tr* atar, ligar; atribuir (*p.ej.*, *importancia*); (law) embargar; **to be attached to** aficionarse a; (*to be officially associated with*) depender de

attaché [,ætə'ʃe] *s* agregado

attachment [ə'tætʃmənt] *s* atadura, enlace *m*; atribución; apego, cariño; accesorio; (law) embargo

attack [ə'tæk] *s* ataque *m* ‖ *tr & intr* atacar

attain [ə'ten] *tr* alcanzar, lograr

attainment [ə'tenmənt] *s* consecución, logro; **attainments** dotes *fpl*, prendas

attempt [ə'tɛmpt] *s* tentativa; (*assault*) atentado, conato ‖ *tr* procurar, intentar; (*e.g.*, *the life of a person*) atentar a o contra

attend [ə'tɛnd] *tr* atender, asistir; asistir a (*p.ej.*, *la escuela*); auxiliar (*a un moribundo*) ‖ *intr* atender; **to attend to** atender a

attendance [ə'tɛndəns] *s* asistencia, concurrencia; **to dance attendance** hacer antesala

attendant [ə'tɛndənt] *adj & s* asistente *mf*; concomitante *m*

attention [ə'tɛnʃən] *s* atención; **to attract attention** llamar la atención; **to call attention to** hacer presente; **to pay attention to** hacer caso de

attentive [ə'tɛntɪv] *adj* atento

attenuate [ə'tɛnjʊ,et] *tr* adelgazar; debilitar ‖ *intr* debilitarse; desaparecer

attest [ə'tɛst] *tr* atestiguar; juramentar ‖ *intr* dar fe; **to attest to** dar fe de

attic ['ætɪk] *s* buharda, guardilla, desván *m*

attire [ə'taɪr] *s* atavío, traje *m* ‖ *tr* ataviar, vestir

attitude ['ætɪ,tjud] o ['ætɪ,tud] *s* actitud, ademán *m*

attorney [ə'tʌrni] *s* abogado; procurador *m*

attract [ə'trækt] *tr* atraer; llamar (*la atención*)

attraction [ə'trækʃən] *s* atracción; (*personal charm*) atractivo

attractive [ə'træktɪv] *adj* atractivo; (*agreeable, interesting*) atrayente

attribute ['ætrɪ,bjut] *s* atributo ‖ [ə'trɪbjut] *tr* atribuir

atty. *abbr* **attorney**

auburn ['ɔbərn] *adj & s* castaño rojizo

auction ['ɔkʃən] *s* almoneda, remate *m*, subasta ‖ *tr* rematar, subastar

auctioneer [,ɔkʃən'ɪr] *s* subastador *m*, rematador *m* ‖ *tr & intr* rematar, subastar

auction house *s* martillo

audacious [ɔ'deʃəs] *adj* audaz

audaci•ty [ɔ'dæsɪti] *s* (*pl* **-ties**) audacia

audience ['ɔdɪəns] *s* (*hearing; formal interview*) audiencia; público, auditorio

audio frenquency ['ɔdɪ,o] *s* audiofrecuencia

audiometer [,ɔdɪ'amɪtər] *s* audiómetro

audit ['ɔdɪt] *s* intervención ‖ *tr* intervenir

audition [ɔ'dɪʃən] *s* audición ‖ *tr* dar audición a

auditor ['ɔdɪtər] *s* oyente *mf*; (com) interventor *m*

---

auditorium [,ɔdɪ'torɪ•əm] *s* auditorio, anfiteatro, paraninfo

auger ['ɔgər] *s* barrena

augment [ɔg'mɛnt] *tr & intr* aumentar

augur ['ɔgər] *s* augur *m* ‖ *tr & intr* augurar; **to augur well** ser de buen agüero

augu•ry ['ɔgəri] *s* (*pl* **-ries**) augurio

august [ɔ'gʌst] *adj* augusto ‖ **August** ['ɔgəst] *s* agosto

aunt [ænt] o [ant] *s* tía

aurora [e'rorə] *s* aurora

auspice ['ɔspɪs] *s* auspicio; **under the auspices of** bajo los auspicios de

austere [ɔs'tɪr] *adj* austero

Australia [ɔ'streljə] *s* Australia

Australian [ɔ'streljən] *adj & s* australiano

Austria ['ɔstrɪ•ə] *s* Austria

Austrian ['ɔstrɪ•ən] *adj & s* austríaco

authentic [ɔ'θɛntɪk] *adj* auténtico

authenticate [ɔ'θɛntɪ,ket] *tr* autenticar

author ['ɔθər] *s* autor *m*

authoress ['ɔθərɪs] *s* autora

authoritarian [ɔ,θɔrɪ'tɛrɪ•ən] *adj & s* autoritario

authoritative [ɔ'θɔrɪ,tetɪv] *adj* autorizado; (*dictatorial*) autoritario

authori•ty [ɔ'θɔrɪti] *s* (*pl* **-ties**) autoridad; **on good authority** de buena tinta, de fuente fidedigna

authorize ['ɔθə,raɪz] *tr* autorizar

authorship ['ɔθər,ʃɪp] *s* paternidad literaria

autistic [ɔ'tɪstɪk] *s* autístico

au•to ['ɔto] *s* (*pl* **-tos**) (coll) auto, coche *m*

autobiogra•phy [,ɔtobaɪ'agrəfi] *s* (*pl* **-phies**) autobiografía

autobus ['ɔto,bʌs] *s* autobús *m*

autocratic(al) [,ɔtə'krætɪk(əl)] *adj* autocrático

autograph ['ɔtə,græf] *adj & s* autógrafo ‖ *tr* autografiar

autograph seeker *s* cazaautógrafos *m*

automat ['ɔtə,mæt] *s* restaurante automático

automatic [,ɔtə'mætɪk] *adj* automático

automatic car wash *s* túnel *m* de lavado

automatic clutch *s* servoembrague *m*

automation [,ɔtə'meʃən] *s* automación, automatización

automa•ton [ɔ'tamə,tan] *s* (*pl* **-tons** o **-ta** [tə]) autómata

automobile [,ɔtəmo'bil] u [,ɔtə'mobil] *s* automóvil *m*

automobile show *s* salón *m* del automóvil

autonomous [ɔ'tanəməs] *adj* autónomo

autonomy [ɔ'tanəmi] *s* autonomía

autop•sy ['ɔtapsi] *s* (*pl* **-sies**) autopsia

autumn ['ɔtəm] *s* otoño

autumnal [ə'tʌmnəl] *adj* otoñal

auxilia•ry [ɔg'zɪljəri] *adj* auxiliar ‖ *s* (*pl* **-ries**) auxiliar *mf*; **auxiliaries** tropas auxiliares

av. *abbr* **avenue, average, avoirdupois**

avail [ə'vel] *s* provecho, utilidad ‖ *tr* beneficiar; **to avail oneself of** aprovecharse de, valerse de ‖ *intr* aprovechar

available [ə'veləbəl] *adj* disponible; **to make available to** poner a la disposición de

avalanche ['ævə,læntʃ] *s* alud *m*, avalancha

---

as

av

avant-garde [ə,vɑnt'gɑrd] *adj* vanguardista ‖ *s* vanguardismo
avant-guardist [ə,vɑnt'gɑrdist] *s* vanguardista *mf*
avarice ['ævərɪs] *s* avaricia
avaricious [,ævə'rɪʃəs] *adj* avaricioso, avariento
Ave. *abbr* **Avenue**
avenge [ə'vɛndʒ] *tr* vengar; **to avenge oneself on** vengarse en
avenue ['ævə,nju] o ['ævə,nu] *s* avenida
aver [ə'vʌr] *v* (*pret & pp* **averred**; *ger* **averring**) *tr* afirmar, declarar
average ['ævərɪdʒ] *adj* común, mediano, ordinario ‖ *s* promedio, término medio; (naut) avería ‖ *tr* calcular el término medio de; prorratear; ser de un promedio de
averse [ə'vʌrs] *adj* renuente, contrario
aversion [ə'vʌrʒen] *s* aversión, antipatía; cosa aborrecida
avert [ə'vʌrt] *tr* apartar, desviar; impedir
aviar·y ['evɪ,ɛri] *s* (*pl* **-ies**) avería, pajarera
aviation [,evɪ'eʃən] *s* aviación
aviation medicine *s* aeromedicina
aviator ['evɪ,etər] *s* aviador *m*
avid ['ævɪd] *adj* ávido
avidity [ə'vɪdɪti] *s* avidez *f*
avocado [,ævə'kɑdo] *s* aguacate *m*
avocation [,ævə'keʃən] *s* distracción, diversión
avoid [ə'vɔɪd] *tr* evitar
avoidable [ə'vɔɪdəbəl] *adj* evitable
avoidance [ə'vɔɪdəns] *s* evitación
avow [ə'vau] *tr* admitir, confesar
avowal [ə'vau·əl] *s* admisión, confesión
await [ə'wet] *tr* aguardar, esperar
awake [ə'wek] *adj* despierto ‖ *v* (*pret & pp* **awoke** [ə'wok] o **awaked**) *tr & intr* despertar
awaken [ə'wekən] *tr & intr* despertar
awakening [ə'wekəniŋ] *s* despertamiento; desilusión

award [ə'wɔrd] *s* premio; condecoración; adjudicación ‖ *tr* conceder; adjudicar
aware [ə'wɛr] *adj* enterado; **to become aware of** enterarse de, darse cuenta de
awareness [ə'wɛrnɪs] *s* conciencia
away [ə'we] *adj* ausente; distante ‖ *adv* lejos; a lo lejos; **away from** lejos de; **to do away with** deshacerse de; **to get away** escapar; **to go away** irse; **to make away with** robar, hurtar; **to run away** fugarse; **send away** enviar; despedir; **to take away** llevarse; quitar
awe [ɔ] *s* temor *m* reverencial ‖ *tr* infundir temor reverencial a
awesome ['ɔsəm] *adj* imponente
awestruck ['ɔ,strʌk] *adj* espantado
awful ['ɔfəl] *adj* atroz, horrible; impresionante; (coll) muy malo, muy feo, enorme
awfully ['ɔfəli] *adv* atrozmente, horriblemente; (coll) muy, excesivamente
awfulness ['ɔfəlnɪs] *s* espantosidad (SAm)
awhile [ə'hwaɪl] *adv* un rato, algún tiempo
awkward ['ɔkwərd] *adj* desmañado, torpe, lerdo; embarazoso, delicado
awkward squad *s* pelotón *m* de los torpes
awl [ɔl] *s* alesna, lezna
awning ['ɔniŋ] *s* toldo
ax [æks] *s* hacha
axiom ['æksɪ·əm] *s* axioma *m*
axiomatic [,æksɪ·ə'mætɪk] *adj* axiomático
axis ['æksɪs] *s* (*pl* **axes** ['æksiz]) *s* eje *m*
axle ['æksəl] *s* eje *m*, árbol *m*
axle load *s* carga por eje
ax'le·tree *s* eje *m* de carretón
ay [aɪ] *adv & s* sí ‖ [e] *adv* siempre; **for ay** por siempre ‖ [e] *interj* ¡ay!
aye [aɪ] *adv & s* sí ‖ [e] *adv* siempre; **for aye** por siempre
azimuth ['æzɪməθ] *s* acimut *m*
Azores [ə'zorz] o ['ezorz] *spl* Azores *fpl*
Aztec ['æztɛk] *adj & s* azteca *mf*
azure ['æʒər] o ['eʒər] *adj & s* azul *m*

B

B, b [bi] segunda letra del alfabeto inglés
b. *abbr* **bass, bay, born, brother**
baa [bɑ] *s* be *m*, balido ‖ *intr* balar
babble ['bæbəl] *s* barboteo; charla; (*of a brook*) murmullo ‖ *tr* barbotar; decir indiscretamente ‖ *intr* barbotar; murmurar (*un arroyo*)
babe [beb] *s* rorro, criatura; (*innocent, gullible person*) niño; (slang) chica, chica hermosa
baboon [bæ'bun] *s* babuíno
ba·by ['bebi] *s* (*pl* **-bies**) rorro, criatura, bebé *m*; (*the youngest child*) benjamín *m* ‖ *v* (*pret & pp* **-bied**) *tr* mimar; tratar como niño
baby carriage *s* cochecillo para niños

baby grand *s* piano de media cola
babyhood ['bebi,hud] *s* primera infancia, niñez *f*
babyish ['bebi·ɪʃ] *adj* aniñado, infantil
Babylon ['bæbɪlən] o ['bæbɪ,lɑn] *s* Babilonia (*ciudad*)
Babylonia [,bæbɪ'loni·ə] *s* Babilonia (*imperio*)
Babylonian [,bæbɪ'loni·ən] *adj & s* babilonio
baby sitter *s* niñera tomada por horas
baccalaureate [,bækə'lɔri·ɪt] *s* bachillerato
bachelor ['bætʃələr] *s* (*unmarried man*) soltero; (*holder of bachelor's degree*) bachiller *mf*; (*apprentice knight*) doncel *m*
bachelorhood ['bætʃələr,hud] *s* celibato, soltería (*del hombre*)

bacil·lus [bə'sɪləs] s (pl **-li** [laɪ]) bacilo

back [bæk] adj trasero, posterior; atrasado || adv atrás, detrás; de vuelta; (ago) hace; **back of** detrás de; **to go back to** remontarse a; **to send back** devolver || s espalda; dorso; (of a coin) reverso; (of a chair) espaldar m, respaldo; (of an animal, of a book) lomo; (of a hall, a room) fondo; (of a writing, a book) final m; **behind one's back** a espaldas de uno; **on one's back** postrado, en cama; a cuestas || tr mover hacia atrás; apoyar, respaldar || intr moverse hacia atrás; **to back down** u **out** volverse atrás, echarse atrás; **to back up** retroceder; regolfar (el agua)

back'ache' s dolor m de espalda

back'bone' s espinazo; (of a book) nervura; firmeza, resistencia

back'break'ing adj deslomador

back'down' s palinodia, retractación

back'drop' s telón m de fondo o de foro

backer ['bækər] s sostenedor m, defensor m; (of a business venture) impulsador m

back'fire' s (aut) petardeo || intr (aut) petardear

back'ground' s fondo; antecedentes mpl; conocimientos, educación; (of a painting) lontananza

background music s música de fondo

backing ['bækɪŋ] s apoyo, sostén m; garantía, respaldo; financiamiento; (bb) lomera

back'lash' s (mach) contragolpe m; (mach) juego; (fig) reacción violenta

back'log' s (com) reserva de pedidos pendientes; (e.g., of work) acumulación

back number s número atrasado; (coll) persona anticuada

back pay s sueldo retrasado

back seat s puesto secundario; **to take a back seat** perder influencia

back'side' s espalda; trasero

back'slide' v (pret & pp **-slid** [,slɪd]) intr reincidir

backspacer ['bæk,spesər] s tecla de retroceso

back'stage' adv detrás del telón; entre bastidores

back'stairs' adj indirecto, secreto

back stairs spl escalera trasera; medios indirectos

back'stitch' s pespunte m || tr & intr pespuntar

back'stop' s reja o red f para detener la pelota

back'swept' wing s (aer) ala en flecha

back talk s respuesta insolente

backward ['bækwərd] adj atrasado, tardío; tímido || adv de atrás; de espaldas; al revés; cada vez peor; para atrás, hacia atrás

back'wa'ter s remanso; (fig) atraso, yermo

back'woods' spl monte m, región alejada de los centros de población

back yard s patio trasero, corral trasero

bacon ['bekən] s tocino

bacteria [bæk'tɪrɪə] pl de **bacterium**

bacterial [bæk'tɪrɪəl] adj bacteriano

bacteriologist [bæk,tɪrɪ'alədʒɪst] s bacteriólogo

bacteriology [bæk,tɪrɪ'alədʒɪ] s bacteriología

bacteri·um [bæk'tɪrɪ·əm] s (pl **-a** [ə]) bacteria

bad [bæd] adj (comp **worse** [wʌrs]; super **worst** [wʌrst] malo; (money) falso; (debt) incobrable; **from bad to worse** de mal en peor; **to be in bad** (coll) caer en desgracia; **to be too bad** ser lástima; **to go to the bad** (coll) ir por mal camino; (coll) arruinarse; **to look bad** tener mala cara

bad breath s mal aliento

badge [bædʒ] s divisa, insignia

badger ['bædʒər] s tejón m

badly ['bædli] adv mal; con urgencia; gravemente

badly off adj malparado; muy enfermo

badminton ['bædmɪntən] s juego del volante

baffle ['bæfəl] s deflector m; (rad) pantalla acústica || tr confundir; burlar, frustrar

baffling ['bæflɪŋ] adj perplejo, desconcertador

bag [bæg] s saco; saquito de mano; (in clothing) bolsa; (purse) bolso; (take of game) caza; **to be in the bag** (slang) ser cosa segura || v (pret & pp **bagged**; ger **bagging**) tr ensacar; coger, cazar || intr hacer bolsa (un vestido)

baggage ['bægɪdʒ] s equipaje m; (mil) bagaje m

baggage car s furgón m de equipajes

baggage check s contraseña de equipajes

baggage rack s red f de equipajes

baggage room s sala de equipajes

bag'pipe' s gaita, cornamusa

bag'pi'per s gaitero

bail [bel] s caución, fianza; **to go bail for** salir fiador por || tr caucionar, afianzar; achicar (la embarcación; el agua); **to bail out** salir fiador por; achicar || intr achicar; **to bail out** lanzarse en paracaídas

bailiff ['belɪf] s alguacil m, corchete m

bailiwick ['belɪwɪk] s alguacilazgo; **to be in the bailiwick of** ser de la pertenencia de

bait [bet] s carnada, cebo; señuelo; **to swallow the bait** tragar el anzuelo || tr cebar, encarnar (el anzuelo); tentar, seducir; (to pester) hostigar

baize [bez] s bayeta

bake [bek] tr cocer al horno; cocer (loza, gres, etc.)

bakelite ['bekə,laɪt] s baquelita

baker ['bekər] s panadero, hornero

baker's dozen s docena del fraile

baker·y ['bekəri] s (pl **-ies**) panadería

baking powder ['bekɪŋ] s levadura en polvo

baking soda s bicarbonato de sosa

bal. abbr **balance**

balance ['bæləns] s (instrument for weighing) balanza; (state of equilibrium) equilibrio; (amount left over) resto; (amount still owed) saldo; (statement of debits and credits) balance m; **to lose one's balance** perder el equilibrio; **to strike a balance** hacer o pasar balance || tr balancear; equilibrar; equilibrar, nivelar (el presupuesto) || intr equilibrarse; (to waver) balancear

balanced ['bælənst] *adj* equilibrado
balance of payments *s* balanza de pagos
balance of power *s* equilibrio político
balance sheet *s* balance *m*, avanzo
balco•ny ['bælkəni] *s* (*pl* -nies) balcón *m;* (*in a theater*) galería, paraíso
bald [bold] *adj* calvo; franco, directo
baldness ['boldnɪs] *s* calvicie *f*
baldric ['boldrɪk] *s* tahalí *m*
bale [bel] *s* bala || *tr* embalar
Balearic [,bælɪ'ærɪk] *adj* balear
Balearic Islands *spl* islas Baleares
baleful ['belfəl] *adj* funesto, maligno
balk [bɔk] *tr* burlar, frustrar || *intr* emperrarse, resistirse
Balkan ['bolkən] *adj* balcánico || **the Balkans** los Balcanes
balk•y ['boki] *adj* (*comp* -ier; *super* -iest) rebelón, repropio
ball [bol] *s* bola, pelota; esfera, globo; (*of wool, yarn*) ovillo; (*of finger*) yema; (*projectile*) bala; (*dance*) baile *m*
ballad ['bæləd] *s* balada
ballade [bə'lad] *s* (mus) balada
ballast ['bæləst] *s* (aer, naut) lastre *m;* (rr) balasto || *tr* lastrar; balastar
ball bearing *s* cojinete *m* de bolas
ballerina [,bælə'rinə] *s* bailarina
ballet ['bæle] *s* ballet *m*, baile *m*
ballistic [bə'lɪstɪk] *adj* balístico
balloon [bə'lun] *s* globo
ballot ['bælət] *s* balota; sufragio || *intr* balotar
ballot box *s* urna electoral
ball'play'er *s* pelotari *m;* beisbolero
ball'-point' pen *s* bolígrafo, pluma estilográfica; biro (Arg); birome *f* (Arg, Urug); puntabola, punto bola (Bol); lapicero (CAm, Col); lápiz *m* de pasta (Chile); esferográfica, esfero (Col); estenógrafo (Cuba); lápiz *n:* de bolilla (Peru); plumilla (Ven)
ball'room' *s* salón *m* de baile
ballyhoo ['bælɪ,hu] *s* alharaca, bombo || *tr* dar teatro a, dar bombo a
balm [bam] *s* bálsamo
balm•y ['bami] *adj* (*comp* -ier; *super* -iest) bonancible, suave
baloney [bə'loni] *interj* (coll) ¡aprieta!
balsam ['bolsəm] *s* bálsamo
Baltic ['boltɪk] *adj* báltico
Baltimore oriole ['boltɪ,mor] *s* cacique veranero
baluster ['bæləstər] *s* balaustre *m*
bamboo [bæm'bu] *s* bambú *m*
bamboozle [bæm'buzəl] *tr* (coll) embaucar, engañar
bamboozler [bæm'buzlər] *s* (coll) embaucador *m*, engañabobos *mf*
ban [bæn] *s* prohibición; excomunión, entredicho; (*of marriage*) amonestación || *v* (*pret* & *pp* **banned;** *ger* **banning**) *tr* prohibir; excomulgar
banana [bə'nænə] *s* banana, plátano; (*tree*) banano, bananero, plátano
banana oil *s* esencia de pera

band [bænd] *s* banda; (*of people*) cuadrilla; (*of a hat*) cintillo; (*of a cigar*) anillo; liga de goma; (mus) banda, música, charanga || *intr* abanderizarse
bandage ['bændɪdʒ] *s* venda || *tr* vendar
bandanna [bæn'dænə] *s* pañuelo de hierbas
band'box' *s* sombrerera
bandit ['bændɪt] *s* bandido
band'mas'ter *s* músico mayor
bandoleer [,bændə'lɪr] *s* bandolera
band saw *s* sierra continua, sierra sin fin
band'stand' *s* quiosco de música
baneful ['benfəl] *adj* nocivo, venenoso; (*e.g., influence*) funesto
bang [bæŋ] *adv* de golpe || *interj* ¡pum! || *s* golpazo; (*of a door*) portazo; **bangs** flequillo || *tr* golpear con ruido; cerrar (*p.ej., una puerta*) de golpe || *intr* hacer estrépito
banish ['bænɪʃ] *tr* desterrar; despedir (*p.ej., miedo*)
banishment ['bænɪʃmənt] *s* destierro
banister ['bænɪstər] *s* balaustre *m*
bank [bæŋk] *s* banco; (*in certain games*) banca; (*small container for coins*) alcancía; (*of a river*) ribera, orilla; (*of earth, snow, clouds*) montón *m* || *tr* depositar o guardar (*dinero*) en un banco; amontonar; cubrir (*un fuego*) con cenizas || *intr* depositar dinero; **to bank on** (coll) contar con
bank account *s* cuenta de banco
bank'book' *s* libreta de banco
banker ['bæŋkər] *s* banquero
banking ['bæŋkɪŋ] *adj* bancario || *s* banca
bank note *s* billete *m* de banco
bank roll *s* lío de papel moneda
bankrupt ['bæŋkrʌpt] *adj* & *s* bancarrotero; **to go bankrupt** hacer bancarrota || *tr* hacer quebrar; arruinar
bankrupt•cy ['bæŋkrʌptsi] *s* (*pl* -cies) bancarrota
banner ['bænər] *s* bandera, estandarte *m*
banner cry *s* grito de combate
banquet ['bæŋkwɪt] *s* banquete *m* || *tr* & *intr* banquetear
bantamweight ['bæntəm,wet] *s* (box) gallo
banter ['bæntər] *s* burla, chanza || *intr* burlar, chancear
baptism ['bæptɪzəm] *s* bautismo, bautizo; (fig) bautismo
Baptist ['bæptɪst] *adj* & *s* baptista *mf*, bautista *mf*
baptister•y ['bæptɪstəri] *s* (*pl* -ies) baptisterio, bautisterio
baptize ['bæptaɪz] *tr* bautizar
bar. *abbr* **barometer, barrel, barrister**
bar [bar] *s* barra; (*of door or window*) tranca; (*of jail*) reja; barrera; (*legal profession*) abogacía; (*members of legal profession*) curia; (*of public opinion*) tribunal *m;* (mus) barra; (*unit between two bars*) (mus) compás *m;* **behind bars** entre rejas || *prep* salvo; **bar none** sin excepción || *v* (*pret* & *pp* **barred;** *ger* **barring**) *tr* barrear, atrancar; impedir; prohibir; excluir
bar association *s* colegio de abogados
barb [barb] *s* púa, lengüeta; (*of a pen*) barbilla

Barbados [bɑr'bedoz] *s* la Barbada
barbarian [bɑr'bɛrɪ•ən] *s* bárbaro
barbaric [bɑr'bærɪk] *adj* bárbaro
barbarism ['bɑrbə,rɪzəm] *s* barbaridad *f;* (*gram*) barbarismo
barbari•ty [bɑr'bærɪti] *s* (*pl* **-ties**) barbarie *f*
barbarous ['bɑrbərəs] *adj* bárbaro
Barbary ape ['bɑrbəri] *s* mono de Gibraltar
barbed [bɑrbd] *adj* armado de púas; mordaz, punzante
barbed wire *s* alambre *m* de espino, alambre de púas
barber ['bɑrbər] *adj* barberil ‖ *s* barbero, peluquero
barber pole *s* percha de barbero
bar'ber•shop' *s* barbería, peluquería
bard [bɑrd] *s* bardo; (*horse armor*) barda ‖ *tr* bardar
bare [bɛr] *adj* desnudo; (*head*) descubierto; (*unfurnished*) desamueblado; (*wire*) sin aislar; mero, sencillo, puro ‖ *tr* desnudar; descubrir
bare'back' *adj & adv* en pelo, sin silla
barefaced ['bɛr,fest] *adj* desvergonzado
bare'foot' *adj* descalzo ‖ *adv* con los pies desnudos
bareheaded ['bɛr,hɛdɪd] *adj* descubierto ‖ *adv* con la cabeza descubierta
barelegged ['bɛr,lɛgɪd] o ['bɛr,lɛgd] *adj* con las piernas desnudas
barely ['bɛrli] *adv* aspenas; escasamente
bargain ['bɑrgɪn] *s* (*deal*) convenio, trato; (*cheap purchase*) ganga; **in the bargain** de añadidura ‖ *tr* — **to bargain away** vender regalado ‖ *intr* negociar; (*to haggle*) regatear
bargain counter *s* baratillo
bargain sale *s* venta de saldos
barge [bɑrdʒ] *s* gabarra, lanchón *m;* bongo (SAm) ‖ *intr* moverse pesadamente; **to barge in** entrar sin pedir permiso, entrar sin llamar a la puerta
barium ['bɛrɪ•əm] *s* bario
bark [bɑrk] *s* (*of tree*) corteza; (*of dog*) ladrido; (*boat*) barca ‖ *tr* ladrar (*p.ej., injurias*) ‖ *intr* ladrar
barley ['bɑrli] *s* cebada
barley water *s* hordiate *m*
bar magnet *s* barra imantada
bar'maid' *s* moza de taberna
barn [bɑrn] *s* granero, troje *m;* caballeriza, establo; cochera
barnacle ['bɑrnəkəl] *s* cirrópodo
barn owl *s* lechuza, oliva
barn'yard' *s* corral *m*
barnyard fowl *spl* aves *fpl* de corral
barometer [bə'rɑmɪtər] *s* barómetro
baron ['bærən] *s* barón *m*
baroness ['bærənɪs] *s* baronesa
baroque [bə'rok] *adj & s* barroco
barracks ['bærəks] *spl* cuartel *m*
barrage [bə'rɑʒ] *s* (*dam*) presa; (*mil*) barrera de fuego
barrel ['bærəl] *s* barril *m*, tonel *m;* (*of a gun, pen, etc.*) cañón *m*
barrel organ *s* organillo
barren ['bærən] *adj* árido, estéril

barricade [,bærɪ'ked] *s* barrera ‖ *tr* barrear
barrier ['bærɪ•ər] *s* barrera
barrier reef *s* barrera de arrecifes
barrister ['bærɪstər] *s* (Brit) abogado
bar'room' *s* bar *m*, cantina
bar'tend'er *s* cantinero, tabernero, barman *m*
barter ['bɑrtər] *s* trueque *m* ‖ *tr* trocar
base [bes] *adj* bajo, humilde; infame, vil; (*metal*) bajo de ley ‖ *s* base *f;* (*of electric light or vacuum tube; of projectile*) culote *m;* (*mus*) bajo ‖ *tr* basar
base'ball' *s* beisbol *m;* pelota de beisbol
baseball player *s* beisbolero, beisbolista *m*
base'board' *s* rodapié *m*
Basel ['bɑzəl] *s* Basilea
baseless ['beslɪs] *adj* infundado
basement ['besmənt] *s* sótano
bashful ['bæʃfəl] *adj* encogido, tímido
basic ['besɪk] *adj* básico
basic commodities *spl* artículos de primera necesidad
basilica [bə'sɪlɪkə] *s* basílica
basin ['besɪn] *s* jofaina, palangana; (*of a fountain*) tazón *m;* (*of a river*) cuenca; (*of a harbor*) dársena
ba•sis ['besɪs] *s* (*pl* **-ses** [siz]) base *f;* **on the basis of** a base de
bask [bæsk] o [bɑsk] *intr* asolearse, calentarse
basket ['bæskɪt] *s* cesta; (*large basket*) cesto; (*with two handles*) canasta; (*with lid*) excusabaraja; (*sport*) cesto, red *f*
bas'ket•ball' *s* baloncesto, basquetbol *m*
Basle [bɑl] *s* Basilea
Basque [bæsk] *adj & s* (*of Spain*) vascongado; (*of Spain and France*) vasco; (*of old Spain*) vascón *m*
bas-relief [,bɑrɪ'lif] *s* bajo relieve
bass [bes] *adj & s* (mus) bajo ‖ [bæs] *s* (ichth) róbalo; (ichth) micróptero
bass drum *s* bombo
bass horn *s* tuba
bas•so ['bæso] *s* (*pl* **-sos** o **-si** [si]) (mus) bajo
bassoon [bə'sun] *s* bajón *m*
bass viol ['vaɪ•əl] *s* violón *m*, contrabajo
bastard ['bæstərd] *adj & s* bastardo
bastard title *s* anteportada
baste [best] *tr* (*to sew slightly*) hilvanar; (*to moisten with drippings while roasting*) enlardar; (*to thrash*) azotar; (*to scold*) regañar
bat. *abbr* **battalion, battery**
bat [bæt] *s* palo; (coll) golpe *m;* (zool) murciélago ‖ *v* (*pret & pp* **batted;** *ger* **batting**) *tr* golpear; batear (*una pelota*); **without batting an eye** sin inmutarse, sin pestañear ‖ *intr* golpear
batch [bætʃ] *s* (*of bread*) hornada; (*of papers*) lío
bath [bæθ] *s* baño
bathe [beð] *tr* bañar ‖ *intr* bañarse; **to go bathing** ir a bañarse
bather ['beðər] *s* bañista *mf*
bath'house' *s* casa de baños; caseta de baños
bathing beach *s* playa de baños
bathing beauty *s* sirena de la playa
bathing resort *s* estación balnearia
bathing suit *s* traje *m* de baño, bañador *m*

bathing trunks *spl* taparrabo
bath′robe′ *s* albornoz *m*, bata de baño; bata, peinador *m*
bath′room′ *s* baño, cuarto de baño
bathroom fixtures *spl* aparatos sanitarios
bath′tub′ *s* bañera, baño
bathyscaphe [ˈbæθəˌskæf] *s* batiscafo
baton [bæˈtɑn] *s* bastón *m*; (mus) batuta
battalion [bəˈtæljən] *s* batallón *m*
batter [ˈbætər] *s* pasta, batido; (*baseball*) bateador *m* ‖ *tr* magullar, estropear
battering ram *s* ariete *m*
batter·y [ˈbætəri] *s* (*pl* -ies) batería; (*primary*) (elec) pila; (*secondary*) (elec) acumulador *m*; (law) violencia
battle [ˈbætəl] *s* batalla; **to do battle** librar batalla ‖ *tr* batallar
battle array *s* orden *m* de batalla
battle cry *s* grito de combate
battledore [ˈbætəlˌdor] *s* raqueta; **battledore and shuttlecock** raqueta y volante
bat′tlefield′ *s* campo de batalla
battle front *s* frente *m* de combate
battlement [ˈbætəlmənt] *s* almenaje *m*
battle piece *s* (paint) batalla
bat′tle·ship′ *s* acorazado
battue [bæˈtu] o [bæˈtju] *s* batida
bauble [ˈbɔbəl] *s* chuchería; cetro de bufón
Bavaria [bəˈvɛrɪ·ə] *s* Baviera
Bavarian [bəˈvɛrɪ·ən] *adj & mf* bávaro
bawd [bɔd] *s* alcahuete *m*, alcahueta
bawd·y [ˈbɔdi] *adj* (*comp* -ier; *super* -iest) indecente, obsceno
bawd′y·house′ *s* mancebía, lupanar *m*
bawl [bɔl] *s* voces *fpl*, gritos ‖ *tr* — **to bawl out** (slang) regañar ‖ *intr* vocear, gritar; llorar ruidosamente
bay [be] *adj* bayo ‖ *s* bahía; aullido, ladrido; caballo bayo; (bot) laurel *m*; **to keep at bay** tener a raya ‖ *intr* aullar, ladrar
Bay of Biscay *s* golfo de Vizcaya
bayonet [ˈbe·ənɪt] *s* bayoneta ‖ *tr* herir o matar con bayoneta
bay rum *s* ron *m* de laurel, ron de malagueta
bay window *s* ventana salediza, mirador *m*
bazooka [bəˈzukə] *s* bazuca
bbl. *abbr* **barrel, barrels**
B.C. *abbr* **before Christ**
bd. *abbr* **board**
be [bi] *v* (*pres* **am** [æm], **is** [ɪz] **are** [ɑr]; *pret* **was** [wɑz] o [wʌz], **were** [wʌr]; *pp* **been** [bɪn]) *intr* estar; ser; tener, p.ej., **to be cold** tener frío; **to be wrong** no tener razón; tener la culpa; **here is** o **here are** aquí tiene Vd.; **there is** o **there are** hay ‖ *v aux* estar, p.ej., **he is studying** está estudiando; ser, p.ej., **she was hit by a car** fué atropellada por un coche: deber, p.ej., **what am I to do?** ¿qué debo hacer? ‖ *v impers* ser, p.ej., **it is necessary to get up early** es necesario levantarse temprano; haber, p.ej., **it is sunny** hay sol; hacer, p.ej., **it is cold** hace frío
beach [bitʃ] *s* playa
beach′comb′ *intr* raquear; **to go beachcombing** andar al raque
beach′comb′er *s* raquero; vago de playa

beach′head′ *s* cabeza de playa
beach robe *s* albornoz *m*
beach shoe *s* playera
beach umbrella *s* sombrilla de playa
beach wagon *s* rubia, coche *m* rural
beacon [ˈbikən] *s* señal luminosa; (*lighthouse*) faro; (*hill overlooking sea*) hacho; radiofaro; (*guide*) faro ‖ *tr* iluminar, guiar ‖ *intr* brillar
bead [bid] *s* cuenta; (*of glass*) abalorio; (*of sweat*) gota; (*moulding on corner of wall*) guardavivo; **to say** o **tell one's beads** rezar el rosario
beadle [ˈbidəl] *s* bedel *m*
beagle [ˈbigəl] *s* sabueso
beak [bik] *s* pico; cabo, promontorio
beam [bim] *s* (*of wood*) viga; (*of light, heat, etc.*) rayo; (naut) bao; (*direction perpendicular to the keel*) (naut) través *m*; (*of hope*) (fig) rayo; **on the beam** siguiendo el haz del radiofaro; (coll) siguiendo el buen camino ‖ *tr* emitir (*luz, ondas*) ‖ *intr* brillar; sonreír alegremente
bean [bin] *s* haba (*Vicia faba*); alubia, judía (*Phaseolus vulgaris*); (*of coffee, cocoa*) haba; (slang) cabeza
bean′pole′ *s* rodrigón *m* para frijoles; (*tall, skinny person*) (coll) poste *m* de telégrafo
bear [bɛr] *s* oso; (*in stock market*) bajista *mf* ‖ *v* (*pret* **bore** [bor]; *pp* **borne** [born]) *tr* cargar; traer; llevar (*armas*); apoyar; aguantar; sentir, experimentar; producir, rendir (*frutos; interés*); (*to give birth to*) parir; tener (*amor, odio*); **to bear out** confirmar ‖ *intr* dirigirse, volver; **to bear on** referirse a; **to bear up** no perder la esperanza; **to bear with** ser indulgente para con
beard [bɪrd] *s* barba; (*of wheat*) arista
beardless [ˈbɪrdlɪs] *adj* imberbe
bearer [ˈbɛrər] *s* portador *m*
bearing [ˈbɛrɪŋ] *s* porte *m*, presencia; referencia, relación; (mach) cojinete *m*; **bearings** orientación; **to lose one's bearings** desorientarse
bearish [ˈbɛrɪʃ] *adj* bajista
bear′skin′ *s* piel *f* de oso; (*military cap*) morrión *m*
beast [bist] *s* bestia
beast·ly [ˈbistli] *adj* (*comp* -lier; *super* -liest) bestial; (coll) muy malo ‖ *adv* (coll) muy mal
beast of burden *s* bestia de carga, acémila
beat [bit] *s* golpe *m*; (*of heart*) latido; (*of rhythm*) compás *m*; marca del compás; (mus) tiempo; (phys) batimiento; (rad) batido; (*of a policeman*) ronda; (*sponger*) (slang) embestidor *m* ‖ *v* (*pret* **beat**; *pp* **beat** o **beaten**) *tr* azotar, pegar; batir; sacudir (*una alfombra*); aventajar; llevar (*el compás*); tocar (*un tambor*); (*a una persona en una contienda*) ganar; **to beat it** (slang) largarse; **to beat up** batir (*p.ej., huevos*); (slang) aporrear ‖ *intr* batir; latir (*el corazón*); **to beat against** azotar
beaten path [ˈbitən] *s* camino trillado
beater [ˈbitər] *s* batidor *m*; (*mixer*) batidora

beati•fy [bɪ'ætɪ,faɪ] v (pret & pp **-fied**) tr beatificar

beating ['bitɪŋ] s golpeo; (of wings) aleteo; (with a whip) paliza; (defeat) derrota

beau [bo] s (pl **beaus** o **beaux** [boz]) galán m, cortejo; novio; elegante m

beautician [bju'tɪʃən] s embellecedora, esteta mf, esteticista mf

beautiful ['bjutɪfəl] adj bello, hermoso

beauti•fy ['bjutɪ,faɪ] v (pret & pp **-fied**) tr hermosear, embellecer

beau•ty ['bjuti] s (pl **-ties**) beldad f, belleza; (person) preciosura

beauty contest s concurso de belleza

beauty parlor s salón m de belleza

beauty queen s reina de la belleza

beauty sleep s primer sueño (antes de medianoche)

beauty spot s lunar postizo; sitio pintoresco

beaver ['bivər] s castor m; piel f de castor

becalm [bɪ'kɑm] tr calmar, serenar

because [bɪ'kɔz] conj porque; **because of** por, por causa de

beck [bɛk] s seña (con la cabeza o la mano); **at the beck and call of** a la disposición de

beckon ['bɛkən] s seña (con la cabeza o la mano) ‖ tr llamar por señas; atraer, tentar ‖ intr hacer señas

be•come [bɪ'kʌm] v (pret **-came;** pp **-come**) tr convenir, sentar bien ‖ intr hacerse; llegar a ser; ponerse, volverse; convertirse en; **to become of** ser de, p.ej., **what will become of the soldier?** ¿qué será del soldado? hacerse, p.ej., **what became of his pencil?** ¿qué se ha hecho su lápiz?

becoming [bɪ'kʌmɪŋ] adj conveniente, decente; que sienta bien

bed [bɛd] s cama; (of a river) cauce m; (of flower garden) macizo; **to go to bed** acostarse; **to take to bed** encamarse

bed and board s pensión completa, casa y comida

bed'bug' s chinche f

bed'cham'ber s alcoba, cuarto de dormir

bed'clothes' spl ropa de cama

bed'cov'er s cubrecama, cobertor m

bedding ['bɛdɪŋ] s ropa de cama; (for animals) cama

bedev•il [bɪ'dɛvəl] v (pret & pp **-iled** o **-illed;** ger **-iling** o **-illing**) tr atormentar, confundir

bed'fast' adj postrado en cama

bed'fel'low s compañero o compañera de cama

bedlam ['bɛdləm] s confusión, desorden m, tumulto

bed linen s ropa de cama

bed'pan' s silleta

bed'post' s pilar m de cama

bedridden ['bɛd,rɪdən] adj postrado en cama

bed'room' s alcoba, cuarto de dormir

bed'side' s cabecera

bed'sore' s úlcera de decúbito; **to get bedsores** decentarse

bed'spread' s sobrecama, cobertor m

bed'spring' s colchón m de muelles, somier m

bed'stead' s cuja

bed'straw' s paja de jergón

bed'tick' s cutí m

bed'time' s hora de acostarse

bed warmer s calientacamas m

bee [bi] s abeja

beech [bitʃ] s haya

beech'nut' s hayuco

beef [bif] s carne f de vaca; ganado vacuno de engorde; (coll) fuerza muscular; (slang) queja ‖ tr — **to beef up** (coll) reforzar ‖ intr (slang) quejarse; (slang) soplar

beef cattle s ganado vacuno de engorde

beef'steak' s biftec m

bee'hive' s colmena

bee'line' s — **to make a beeline for** ir en línea recta hacia, ir derecho a

beer [bɪr] s cerveza; **dark beer** cerveza parda, cerveza negra; **light beer** cerveza clara

beeswax ['biz,wæks] s cera de abejas ‖ tr encerar

beet [bit] s remolacha

beetle ['bitəl] s escarabajo

beetle-browed ['bitəl,braʊd] adj cejijunto; (sullen) ceñudo

beet sugar s azúcar m de remolacha

be•fall [bɪ'fɔl] v (pret **-fell** ['fɛl]; pp **-fallen** ['fɔlən]) tr acontecer a ‖ intr acontecer

befitting [bɪ'fɪtɪŋ] adj conveniente; decoroso

before [bɪ'for] adv antes; delante, enfrente ‖ prep (in time) antes de; (in place) delante de; (in the presence of) ante ‖ conj antes (de) que

before'hand' adv de antemano, con anticipación

befriend [bɪ'frɛnd] tr ofrecer amistad a, amparar, proteger

befuddle [bɪ'fʌdəl] tr aturdir, confundir

beg [bɛg] v (pret & pp **begged;** ger **begging**) tr pedir, rogar, solicitar; mendigar; huesar ‖ intr mendigar; **to beg off** excusarse

be•get [bɪ'gɛt] v (pret **-got** ['gɑt]; pp **-gotten** o **-got;** ger **-getting**) tr engendrar

beggar ['bɛgər] s mendigo; pobre mf; pícaro, bribón m; sujeto, tipo

be•gin [bɪ'gɪn] v (pret **-gan** ['gæn]; pp **-gun** ['gʌn]; ger **-ginning**) tr & intr comenzar, empezar; **beginning with** a partir de

beginner [bɪ'gɪnər] s principiante mf; iniciador m

beginning [bɪ'gɪnɪŋ] s comienzo, principio

begrudge [bɪ'grʌdʒ] tr dar de mala gana; envidiar

beguile [bɪ'gaɪl] tr engañar; divertir, entretener; engañar (el tiempo)

behalf [bɪ'hæf] — **on behalf of** en nombre de; a favor de

behave [bɪ'hev] intr conducirse, comportarse; portarse bien; funcionar

behavior [bɪ'hevjər] s conducta, comportamiento; funcionamiento

behaviorism [bɪ'hevjə,rɪzəm] s comportamentismo

behead [bɪ'hɛd] tr decapitar, descabezar

behind [bɪ'haɪnd] adv detrás; hacia atrás; con retraso; **to stay behind** quedarse atrás ‖

prep detrás de; **behind the back of** a espaldas de; **behind the times** astrasado de noticias; **behind time** tarde ‖ *s* (slang) trasero, pompis *m*

behold [bɪˈhold] *v* (*pret & pp* **-held** [ˈhɛld]) *tr* contemplar ‖ *interj* ¡he aquí!

behoove [bɪˈhuv] *tr* convenir, tocar

being [ˈbiɪŋ] *adj* existente; **for the time being** por ahora, por el momento ‖ *s* ser, ente *m*

belch [bɛltʃ] *s* eructo, regüeldo ‖ *tr* vomitar (*p.ej., llamas, injurias*) ‖ *intr* eructar, regoldar

beleaguer [bɪˈligər] *tr* sitiar, cercar

bel·fry [ˈbɛlfri] *s* (*pl* **-fries**) campanario

Belgian [ˈbɛldʒən] *adj & s* belga *mf*

Belgium [ˈbɛldʒəm] *s* Bélgica

be·lie [bɪˈlaɪ] *v* (*pret & pp* **-lied** [ˈlaɪd]; *ger* **-lying** [ˈlaɪɪŋ]) *tr* desmentir

belief [bɪˈlif] *s* creencia

believable [bɪˈlivəbəl] *adj* creíble; (*source*) solvente

believe [bɪˈliv] *tr & intr* creer

believer [bɪˈlivər] *s* creyente *mf*

belittle [bɪˈlɪtəl] *tr* empequeñecer, despreciar

bell [bɛl] *s* campana; (*electric bell*) timbre *m*, campanilla; (*ring of bell*) campanada ‖ *intr* bramar, berrear

bell′boy′ *s* botones *m*

belle [bɛl] *s* beldad *f*, belleza

belles-lettres [ˌbɛlˈlɛtrə] *spl* bellas letras

bell gable *s* espadaña

bell glass *s* fanal *m*

bell′hop′ *s* (slang) botones *m*

bellicose [ˈbɛlɪˌkos] *adj* belicoso

belligerent [bəˈlɪdʒərənt] *adj & s* beligerante *mf*

bellow [ˈbɛlo] *s* bramido; **bellows** fuelle *m*, barquín *m* ‖ *tr* gritar ‖ *intr* bramar

bell ringer *s* campanero

bellwether [ˈbɛlˌwɛðər] *s* manso

bel·ly [ˈbɛli] *s* (*pl* **-lies**) barriga, vientre *m*; estómago ‖ *v* (*pret & pp* **-lied**) *intr* hacer barriga; hacer bolso (*las velas*)

bel′ly·ache′ *s* (slang) dolor *m* de barriga ‖ *intr* (slang) quejarse

belly button *s* (coll) ombligo

belly dance *s* (coll) danza del vientre

bellyful [ˈbɛlɪˌful] *s* (slang) panzada

bel′ly-land′ *intr* (aer) aterrizar de panza

belong [bɪˈlɔŋ] *intr* pertenecer; deber estar

belongings [bɪˈlɔŋɪŋz] *spl* pertenencias, efectos; corotos

beloved [bɪˈlʌvɪd] o [bɪˈlʌvd] *adj & s* querido, amado

below [bɪˈlo] *adv* abajo; (*in a text*) más abajo; bajo cero, p.ej., **ten below** diez grados bajo cero ‖ *prep* debajo de; inferior a

belt [bɛlt] *s* cinturón *m*; (aer, mach) correa; (geog) faja, zona; **to tighten one's belt** ceñirse

bemoan [bɪˈmon] *tr* deplorar, lamentar

bench [bɛntʃ] *s* banco; (law) tribunal *m*

bend [bɛnd] *s* curva; (*in a road, river, etc.*) recodo, vuelta ‖ *v* (*pret & pp* **bent** [bɛnt]) *tr* encorvar; doblar (*un tubo; la rodilla*);

inclinar (*la cabeza*); dirigir (*sus esfuerzos*) ‖ *intr* encorvarse; doblarse; inclinarse

beneath [bɪˈniθ] *adv* abajo ‖ *prep* debajo de; inferior a

benediction [ˌbɛnɪˈdɪkʃən] *s* bendición *f*

benefaction [ˌbɛnɪˈfækʃən] *s* beneficio

benefactor [ˈbɛnɪˌfæktər] o [ˌbɛnɪˈfæktər] *s* bienhechor *m*

benefactress [ˈbɛnɪˌfæktrɪs] o [ˌbɛnɪˈfæktrɪs] *s* bienhechora

beneficence [bɪˈnɛfɪsəns] *s* beneficencia

beneficent [bɪˈnɛfɪsənt] *adj* bienhechor

beneficial [ˌbɛnɪˈfɪʃəl] *adj* beneficioso

beneficiar·y [ˌbɛnɪˈfɪʃɪˌɛri] *s* (*pl* **-ies**) beneficiario

benefit [ˈbɛnɪfɪt] *s* beneficio; lasca; **for the benefit of** a beneficio de ‖ *tr* beneficiar

benefit performance *s* beneficio

benevolence [bɪˈnɛvələns] *s* benevolencia

benevolent [bɪˈnɛvələnt] *adj* benévolo; (*e.g., institution*) benéfico

benign [bɪˈnaɪn] *adj* benigno

benigni·ty [bɪˈnɪgnɪti] *s* (*pl* **-ties**) benignidad *f*

bent [bɛnt] *adj* encorvado, doblado, torcido; **bent on** resuelto a, empeñado en; **bent over** cargado de espaldas ‖ *s* encorvadura; inclinación *f*, propensión *f*

benzedrine [ˈbɛnzəˌdrin] *s* bencedrina

benzine [ˈbɛnzin] *s* bencina

bequeath [bɪˈkwið] o [bɪˈkwiθ] *tr* legar

bequest [bɪˈkwɛst] *s* manda, legado

berate [bɪˈret] *tr* regañar, reñir

be·reave [bɪˈriv] *v* (*pret & pp* **-reaved** o **-reft** [ˈrɛft]) *tr* despojar, privar; desconsolar

bereavement [bɪˈrivmənt] *s* despojo, privación *f*; desconsuelo

berkelium [bərˈkilɪəm] *s* berkelio

Berliner [bərˈlɪnər] *s* berlinés *m*

ber·ry [ˈbɛri] *s* (*pl* **-ries**) baya; (*of coffee plant*) grano, haba

berserk [ˈbʌrsʌrk] *adj* frenético ‖ *adv* frenéticamente

berth [bʌrθ] *s* (*bed*) litera; (*room*) camarote *m*; (*for a ship*) amarradero; (coll) empleo, puesto

beryllium [bəˈrɪlɪəm] *s* berilio

be·seech [bɪˈsitʃ] *v* (*pret & pp* **-sought** [ˈsɔt] o **-seeched**) *tr* suplicar

be·set [bɪˈsɛt] *v* (*pret & pp* **-set**; *ger* **-setting**) *tr* acometer, acosar; cercar, sitiar

beside [bɪˈsaɪd] *adv* además, también ‖ *prep* cerca de, junto a; en comparación de; excepto; **beside oneself** fuera de sí; **beside the point** incongruente

besiege [bɪˈsidʒ] *tr* asediar, sitiar

besmirch [bɪˈsmʌrtʃ] *tr* ensuciar, manchar

bespatter [bɪˈspætər] *tr* salpicar

be·speak [bɪˈspik] *v* (*pret* **-spoke** [ˈspok]; *pp* **-spoken**) *tr* apalabrar, pedir de antemano

best [bɛst] *adj* *super* mejor; óptimo ‖ *adv* *super* mejor; **had best** debería ‖ *s* (lo) mejor; (lo) más; **at best** a lo más; **to do one's best** hacer lo mejor posible; **to get the best of** aventajar, sobresalir; **to make the best of** sacar el mejor partido de

best girl *s* (coll) amiga preferida, novia

be•stir [bɪ'stʌr] v (pret & pp **-stirred;** ger **-stirring**) tr excitar, incitar; **to bestir one-self** esforzarse, afanarse

best man s padrino de boda

bestow [bɪ'sto] tr otorgar, conferir; dedicar

best seller s éxito de venta, campeón m de venta; éxito de librería

bet. abbr **between**

bet [bɛt] s apuesta ‖ v (pret & pp **bet** o **betted;** ger **betting**) tr & intr apostar; **I bet a que,** apuesto a que; **to bet on** apostar por; **you bet** (slang) ya lo creo

be•take [bɪ'tek] v (pret **-took** ['tʊk]; pp **-taken**) tr — **to betake oneself** dirigirse; darse, entregarse

be•think [bɪ'θɪŋk] v (pret & pp **-thought** ['θɔt]) tr — **to bethink oneself of** considerar, acordarse de

Bethlehem ['bɛθlɪ,hɛm] s Belén m

betide [bɪ'taɪd] tr presagiar; acontecer a ‖ intr acontecer

betoken [bɪ'tokən] tr anunciar, indicar, presagiar

betray [bɪ'tre] tr traicionar; descubrir, revelar

betrayal [bɪ'tre•əl] s traición; descubrimiento, revelación

betroth [bɪ'troð] o [bɪ'troθ] tr prometer en matrimonio; **to become betrothed** desposarse

betrothal [bɪ'troðəl] o [bɪ'troθəl] s desposorios, esponsales mpl

betrothed [bɪ'troðd] o [bɪ'troθt] s prometido, novio

better ['bɛtər] adj comp mejor; **it is better to** más vale; **to grow better** mejorarse; **to make better** mejorar ‖ adv comp mejor; más; **had better** debería; **to like better** preferir ‖ s superior; ventaja; **to get the better of** llevar la ventaja a ‖ tr aventajar; mejorar; **to better oneself** mejorar su posición

better half s (coll) cara mitad

betterment ['bɛtərmənt] s mejoramiento; (in an illness) mejoría

between [bɪ'twin] adv en medio, entremedias ‖ prep entre; **between you and me** entre Vd. y yo; acá para los dos

be•tween'-decks' s entrecubiertas, entrepuentes mpl

between decks adv entrecubiertas

bev•el ['bɛvəl] adj biselado ‖ s (instrument) cartabón m; (sloping part) bisel m ‖ v (pret & pp **-eled** o **-elled;** ger **-eling** o **-elling**) tr biselar

beverage ['bɛvərɪdʒ] s bebida

bev•y ['bɛvi] s (pl **-ies**) (of birds) bandada; (of girls) grupo

bewail [bɪ'wel] tr & intr lamentar

beware [bɪ'wɛr] tr guardarse de ‖ intr tener cuidado; **beware of . . . !** ¡ojo con . . . !, ¡cuidado con . . . !; **to beware of** guardarse de

bewilder [bɪ'wɪldər] tr aturdir, dejar perplejo, desatinar

bewilderment [bɪ'wɪldərmənt] s aturdimiento, perplejidad

beyond [bɪ'jɑnd] adv más allá, más lejos ‖ prep más allá de; además de; no capaz de; **beyond a doubt** fuera de duda; **beyond the reach of** fuera del alcance de ‖ s — **the great beyond** el más allá, el otro mundo

bg. abbr **bag**

bias ['baɪ•əs] s sesgo, diagonal f; prejuicio; (electron) polarización de rejilla ‖ tr predisponer, prevenir

Bib. abbr **Bible, Biblical**

bib [bɪb] s babero; pepe m; (of apron) pechera

Bible ['baɪbəl] s Biblia

Biblical ['bɪblɪkəl] adj bíblico

bibliographer [,bɪblɪ'ɑgrəfər] s bibliógrafo

bibliogra•phy [,bɪblɪ'ɑgrəfi] s (pl **-phies**) bibliografía

bibliophile ['bɪblɪ•ə,faɪl] s bibliófilo

bicameral [baɪ'kæmərəl] adj bicameral

bicarbonate [baɪ'kɑrbə,net] s bicarbonato

bicker ['bɪkər] s discusión ociosa ‖ intr discutir ociosamente

bicycle ['baɪsɪkəl] s bicicleta

bid [bɪd] s oferta, postura; (in bridge) declaración ‖ v (pret **bade** [bæd] o **bid;** ger **bidden** ['bɪdən]) tr & intr ofrecer, pujar, licitar; (in bridge) declarar

bidder ['bɪdər] s postor m; (in bridge) declarante mf; **the highest bidder** el mejor postor

bidding ['bɪdɪŋ] s mandato, orden f; postura; (in bridge) declaración

bide [baɪd] tr — **to bide one's time** esperar la hora propicia

biennial [baɪ'ɛnɪ•əl] adj bienal

bier [bɪr] s féretro, andas

bifocal [baɪ'fokəl] adj bifocal ‖ **bifocals** spl anteojos bifocales

big [bɪg] adj (comp **bigger;** super **biggest**) grande; (considerable) importante; (grown-up) adulto; **big with child** preñada ‖ adv (coll) con jactancia; **to talk big** (coll) hablar gordo

bigamist ['bɪgəmɪst] s bígamo

bigamous ['bɪgəməs] adj bígamo

bigamy ['bɪgəmi] s bigamia

big-bellied ['bɪg,bɛlɪd] adj panzudo

Big Dipper s Carro mayor

big game s caza mayor

big-hearted ['bɪg,hɑrtɪd] adj magnánimo, generoso

bigot ['bɪgət] s intolerante mf, fanático

bigoted ['bɪgətɪd] adj intolerante, fanático

bigot•ry ['bɪgətri] s (pl **-ries**) intolerancia, fanatismo

big shot s (slang) pájaro de cuenta, señorón m, capitoste m

big stick s palo en alto

big toe s dedo gordo o grande (del pie)

bikini [bɪ'kini] s bikini m

bile [baɪl] s bilis f

bilge [bɪldʒ] s pantoque m ‖ tr desfondar

bilge pump s bomba de sentina

bilge water s agua de pantoque

bilge ways spl anguilas

bilingual [baɪ'lɪŋgwəl] adj bilingüe

be
bi

bilious [ˈbɪljəs] *adj* bilioso
bilk [bɪlk] *tr* estafar, trampear
bill [bɪl] *s* (*statement of charges for goods or service*) cuenta, factura; (*paper money*) billete *m;* (*poster*) cartel *m,* aviso; cartel de teatro; (*draft of law*) proyecto de ley; (*handbill*) hoja suelta; (*of bird*) pico; (*com*) giro, letra de cambio ‖ *tr* facturar; cargar en cuenta a; anunciar por carteles ‖ *intr* darse el pico (*las palomas*); acariciarse (*los enamorados*); **to bill and coo** acariciarse y arrullarse
bill'board' *s* cartelera
billet [ˈbɪlɪt] *s* (mil) boleta; (mil) alojamiento ‖ *tr* alojar
billet-doux [ˈbɪleˈdu] *s* (*pl* **billets-doux** [ˈbɪleˈduz]) esquela amorosa
bill'fold' *s* cartera de bolsillo, billetero
bill'head' *s* encabezamiento de factura
billiards [ˈbɪljərdz] *s* billar *m*
billion [ˈbɪljən] *s* (U.S.A.) mil millones; (Brit) billón *m*
bill of exchange *s* letra de cambio
bill of fare *s* lista de comidas, menú *m*
bill of lading [ˈledɪŋ] *s* conocimiento de embarque
bill of sale *s* escritura de venta
billow [ˈbɪlo] *s* oleada, ondulación ‖ *intr* ondular, hincharse
bill'post'er *s* fijacarteles *m,* fijador *m* de carteles
bil•ly [ˈbɪli] *s* (*pl* **-lies**) cachiporra
billy goat *s* macho cabrío
bin [bɪn] *s* arcón *m,* hucha
bind [baɪnd] *v* (*pret & pp* **bound** [baʊnd]) *tr* ligar, atar; juntar, unir; (*with a garland*) enguirlandar; ribetear (*la orilla del vestido*); agavillar (*las mieses*); vendar (*una herida*); encuadernar (*un libro*); estreñir (*el vientre*)
binder•y [ˈbaɪndəri] *s* (*pl* **-ies**) taller *m* de encuadernación
binding [ˈbaɪndɪŋ] *s* atadura; (*of a book*) encuadernación
binding post *s* borne *m,* sujetahilo
binge [bɪndʒ] *s* (slang) borrachera; turca; **to go on a binge** (slang) pegarse una mona, coger una turca
binnacle [ˈbɪnəkəl] *s* bitácora
binoculars [bɪˈnɑkjələrz] o [baɪˈnɑkjələrz] *spl* gemelos, prismáticos
biochemical [ˌbaɪ•əˈkɛmɪkəl] *adj* bioquímico
biochemist [ˌbaɪ•əˈkɛmɪst] *s* bioquímico
biochemistry [ˌbaɪ•əˈkɛmɪstri] *s* bioquímica
biodegradable [ˌbaɪ•ədɪˈgredəbəl] *adj* biodegradable
biog. *abbr* **biographical, biography**
biographer [baɪˈɑgrəfər] *s* biógrafo
biographic(al) [ˌbaɪ•əˈgræfɪk(əl)] *adj* biográfico
biogra•phy [baɪˈɑgrəfi] *s* (*pl* **-phies**) biografía
biologist [baɪˈɑlədʒɪst] *s* biólogo
biology [baɪˈɑlədʒi] *s* biología
biophysical [ˌbaɪ•əˈfɪzɪkəl] *adj* biofísico
biophysics [ˌbaɪ•əˈfɪzɪks] *s* biofísica
bioplasm [ˈbaɪ•əˌplæzəm] *s* bioplasma

biopsy [ˈbaɪ•ɑpsi] *s* biopsia
biped [ˈbaɪpɛd] *adj & s* bípedo
birch [bʌrtʃ] *s* abedul *m* ‖ *tr* azotar, varear
bird [bʌrd] *s* ave *f,* pájaro
bird cage *s* jaula
bird call *s* reclamo
bird'lime' *s* liga
bird of passage *s* ave *f* de paso
bird of prey *s* ave *f* de rapiña
bird'seed' *s* alpiste *m,* cañamones *mpl*
bird's'-eye' view *s* vista a ojo de pájaro
bird shot *s* perdigones *mpl*
birth [bʌrθ] *s* nacimiento; (*childbirth*) parto; origen *m*
birth certificate *s* partida de nacimiento
birth control *s* limitación de la natalidad, control de la natalidad, control de los nacimientos
birth'day' *s* cumpleaños *m,* natal *m;* (*of any event*) aniversario; **to have a birthday** cumplir años
birthday cake *s* pastel *m* de cumpleaños
birthday present *s* regalo de cumpleaños
birth'mark' *s* antojo, nevo materno
birth'place' *s* suelo natal, patria, lugar *m* de nacimiento
birth rate *s* natalidad
birth'right' *s* derechos de nacimiento; primogenitura
Biscay [ˈbɪske] *s* Vizcaya
biscuit [ˈbɪskɪt] *s* panecillo redondo; bizcocho
bisect [baɪˈsɛkt] *tr* bisecar ‖ *intr* empalmar (*dos caminos*)
bishop [ˈbɪʃəp] *s* obispo; (*in chess*) alfil *m*
bismuth [ˈbɪzməθ] *s* bismuto
bison [ˈbaɪsən] *s* bisonte *m*
bit [bɪt] *s* poquito, pedacito; (*of food*) bocado; (*of time*) ratito; (*part of bridle*) bocado, freno; (*for drilling*) barrena; **a good bit** una buena cantidad
bitch [bɪtʃ] *s* (*dog*) perra; (*fox*) zorra; (*wolf*) loba; (*vulg*) mujer *f* de mal genio
bite [baɪt] *s* mordedura; (*of bird or insect*) picadura; (*burning sensation on tongue*) resquemo; (*of food*) bocado; (*snack*) (coll) tentempié *m,* refrigerio ‖ *v* (*pret* **bit** [bɪt]; *pp* **bit** o **bitten** [ˈbɪtən]) *tr* morder; picar (*los peces, los insectos*); resquemar (*la lengua los alimentos*); comerse (*las uñas*) ‖ *intr* morder; picar; resquemar; (*to be caught by a trick*) (slang) picar
biting [ˈbaɪtɪŋ] *adj* penetrante; mordaz, picante
bitter [ˈbɪtər] *adj* amargo; (*e.g., struggle*) encarnizado; **to the bitter end** hasta el extremo; hasta la muerte
bitter almond *s* almendra amarga
bitterness [ˈbɪtərnɪs] *s* amargura
bitumen [bɪˈtjumən] *s* betún *m*
bivou•ac [ˈbɪvuˌæk] *s* vivaque *m* ‖ *v* (*pret & pp* **-acked;** *ger* **-acking**) *intr* vivaquear
bizarre [bɪˈzɑr] *adj* original, raro
bk. *abbr* **bank, block, book**
bkg. *abbr* **banking**
bl. *abbr* **barrel**
b.l. *abbr* **bill of lading**

blabber [ˈblæbər] *tr* & *intr* barbullar
black [blæk] *adj* negro ‖ *s* negro; luto; **to wear black** ir de luto
black'-and-blue' *adj* encardenalado, amoratado
black'-and-white' *adj* en blanco y negro
black'ber'ry *s* (*pl* **-ries**) (*bush*) zarza; (*fruit*) zarzamora
black'bird' *s* mirlo
black'board' *s* encerado, pizarra
black box *s* registrador *m* de vuelo
black'damp' *s* mofeta
blacken [ˈblækən] *tr* ennegrecer; (*to defame*) desacreditar, denigrar
blackguard [ˈblægard] *s* bribón *m*, canalla *m* ‖ *tr* injuriar, vilipendiar
black'head' *s* espinilla, comedón *m*
black hole *s* (astr) agujero negro
blackish [ˈblækɪʃ] *adj* negruzco
black'jack' *s* (*club*) cachiporra; (*flag*) bandera negra (*de pirata*) ‖ *tr* aporrear
black'mail' *s* chantaje *m* ‖ *tr* amenazar con chantaje
blackmailer [ˈblæk,melər] *s* chantajista *mf*
Black Maria [məˈraɪ•ə] *s* (coll) coche *m* celular
black market *s* estraperlo, mercado negro
blackness [ˈblæknɪs] *s* negror *m*, negrura
black'out' *s* (*in wartime*) apagón *m;* (*in theater*) apagamiento de luces; (*of aviators*) visión negra; pérdida de la memoria; cegura
black sheep *s* (fig) oveja negra, garbanzo negro
black'smith' *s* (*man who works with iron*) herrero; (*man who shoes horses*) herrador *m*
black'thorn' *s* espino negro, endrino
black tie corbata de smoking; smoking *m*
bladder [ˈblædər] *s* vejiga
blade [bled] *s* (*of a knife, sword*) hoja; (*of a propeller*) aleta; (*of a fan*) paleta; (*of an oar*) pala; (*of an electric switch*) cuchilla; (*sword*) espada; tallo de hierba; (coll) gallardo joven
blame [blem] *s* culpa ‖ *tr* culpar
blameless [ˈblemlɪs] *adj* inculpable, irreprochable
blanch [blænʧ] *tr* blanquear ‖ *intr* palidecer
bland [blænd] *adj* apacible; suave; (*character; weather*) blando
blandish [ˈblændɪʃ] *tr* engatusar, lisonjear
blank [blæŋk] *adj* en blanco; blanco, vacío; (*stare, look*) vago ‖ *s* blanco; papel blanco; formulario
blank check *s* firma en blanco; (fig) carta blanca
blanket [ˈblæŋkɪt] *adj* general, comprensivo ‖ *s* manta, frazada; (fig) capa, manto ‖ *tr* cubrir con manta; cubrir, obscurecer
blasé [blɑˈze] *adj* hastiado
blaspheme [blæsˈfim] *tr* blasfemar contra ‖ *intr* blasfemar
blasphemous [ˈblæsfɪməs] *adj* blasfemo
blasphe•my [ˈblæsfɪmi] *s* (*pl* **-mies**) blasfemia

blast [blæst] *s* (*of wind*) ráfaga; (*of air, sand, water*) chorro; (*of bellows*) soplo; (*of a horn*) toque *m;* carga de pólvora; voladura, explosión; **full blast** en plena marcha ‖ *tr* (*to blow up*) volar; arruinar; infamar, maldecir
blast furnace *s* alto horno
blast'off' *s* lanzamiento de cohete
blatant [ˈbletənt] *adj* ruidoso; vocinglero; intruso; chillón, cursi
blaze [blez] *s* llamarada; (*fire*) incendio; (*bonfire*) hoguera; luz *f* brillante ‖ *tr* encender, inflamar; **to blaze a trail** abrir una senda ‖ *intr* encenderse; resplandecer
bldg. *abbr* **building**
bleach [bliʧ] *s* blanqueo ‖ *tr* blanquear; colar (*la ropa*)
bleachers [ˈbliʧərz] *spl* gradas al aire libre
bleak [blik] *adj* desierto, yermo, frío, triste
bleat [blit] *s* balido ‖ *intr* balar
bleed [blid] *v* (*pret* & *pep* **bled** [blɛd]) *tr* & *intr* sangrar
blemish [ˈblɛmɪʃ] *s* mancha ‖ *tr* manchar
blend [blɛnd] *s* mezcla; armonía ‖ *v* (*pret* & *pp* **blended** o **blent** [blɛnt]) *tr* mezclar; armonizar; fusionar ‖ *intr* mezclarse; armonizar; fusionarse
bless [blɛs] *tr* bendecir; **to be blessed with** estar dotado de
blessed [ˈblɛsɪd] *adj* bendito, santo
blessedness [ˈblɛsɪdnɪs] *s* bienaventuranza
blessing [ˈblɛsɪŋ] *s* bendición
blight [blaɪt] *s* niebla, roya; ruina ‖ *tr* anublar; arruinar
blimp [blɪmp] *s* dirigible pequeño
blind [blaɪnd] *adj* ciego ‖ *s* (*window shade*) estor *m*, transparente *m* de resorte; (*Venetian blind*) persiana; pretexto, subterfugio ‖ *tr* cegar; (*to dazzle*) deslumbrar; (*to deceive*) cegar, vendar
blind alley *s* callejón *m* sin salida
blind date *s* cita a ciegas
blinder [ˈblaɪndər] *s* anteojera
blind flying *s* (aer) vuelo a ciegas
blind'fold' *adj* vendado de ojos ‖ *s* venda ‖ *tr* vendar los ojos a
blind landing *s* aterrizaje *m* a ciegas
blind man *s* ciego
blind'man's' buff *s* gallina ciega
blindness [ˈblaɪndnɪs] *s* ceguedad
blink [blɪŋk] *s* guiñada, parpadeo ‖ *tr* guiñar (*el ojo*) ‖ *intr* guiñar, parpadear, pestañear; oscilar (*la luz*)
blip [blɪp] *s* bache *m*
bliss [blɪs] *s* bienaventuranza, felicidad
blissful [ˈblɪsfəl] *adj* bienaventurado, feliz
blister [ˈblɪstər] *s* ampolla, vejiga ‖ *tr* ampollar ‖ *intr* ampollarse
blithe [blaɪð] *adj* alegre, animado
blitzkrieg [ˈblɪts,krig] *s* guerra relámpago
blizzard [ˈblɪzərd] *s* ventisca, chubasco de nieve
bloat [blot] *tr* hinchar ‖ *intr* hincharse, abotagarse
block [blɑk] *s* bloque *m;* (*of hatter*) horma; (*of houses*) manzana; (*for chopping meat*)

tajo; estorbo, obstáculo ‖ *tr* cerrar, obstruir; conformar (*un sombrero*)
blockade [blɑ'ked] *s* bloqueo ‖ *tr* bloquear
blockade runner *s* forzador *m* de bloqueo
block and tackle *s* aparejo de poleas
block'bust'er *s* (coll) bomba rompedora
block'head' *s* tonto, zoquete *m*
block signal *s* (rr) señal *f* de tramo
blond [blɑnd] *adj* rubio, blondo ‖ *s* rubio (*hombre rubio*)
blonde [blɑnd] *s* rubia (*mujer rubia*)
blood [blʌd] *s* sangre *f;* **in cold blood** a sangre fría
bloodcurdling ['blʌd,kʌrdlɪŋ] *adj* horripilante
blood'hound' *s* sabueso
blood poisoning *s* envenenamiento de la sangre
blood pressure *s* presión arterial
blood pudding *s* morcilla
blood relation *s* pariente consanguíneo
blood'shed' *s* efusión de sangre
blood'shot' *adj* inyectado en sangre, encarnizado
blood'stream' *s* corriente *f* sanguínea
blood test *s* análisis *m* de sangre
blood'thirst'y *adj* sanguinario
blood transfusion *s* transfusión de sangre
blood vessel *s* vaso sanguíneo
blood•y ['blʌdi] *adj* (*comp* -**ier;** *super* -**iest**) sangriento ‖ *v* (*pret* & *pp* -**ied**) *tr* ensangrentar
bloom [blum] *s* florecimiento; flor *f* ‖ *intr* florecer
blossom ['blɑsəm] *s* brote *m,* flor *f;* **in blossom** en cierne ‖ *intr* cerner, florecer
blot [blɑt] *s* borrón *m* ‖ *v* (*pret* & *pp* **blotted;** *ger* **blotting**) *tr* (*to smear*) borrar; secar con papel secante; **to blot out** borrar ‖ *intr* borrarse; echar borrones (*una pluma*)
blotch [blɑʧ] *s* manchón *m; (in the skin)* erupción
blotter ['blɑtər] *s* teleta, secafirmas *m*
blotting paper *s* papel *m* secante
blouse [blaus] *s* blusa
blow [blo] *s* (*hit, stroke*) golpe; (*blast of air*) soplo, soplido; (*blast of wind*) ventarrón *m; (of horn*) toque *m,* trompetazo; (*sudden sorrow*) estocada, ramalazo; (*boaster*) (slang) fanfarrón *m;* **to come to blows** venir a las manos ‖ *v* (*pret* **blew** [blu]; *pp* **blown**) ‖ *tr* soplar; sonar, tocar (*un instrumento de viento*); silbar (*un silbato*); sonarse (*las narices*); quemar (*un fusible*); (slang) malgastar (*dinero*); **to blow out** apagar soplando; quemar (*un fusible*); **to blow up** (*with air*) inflar; (*e.g., with dynamite*) volar, hacer saltar; ampliar (*una foto*) ‖ *intr* soplar; (*to pant*) jadear, resoplar; fundirse (*un fusible*); (slang) fanfarronear; **to blow out** apagarse con el aire; quemarse, fundirse (*un fusible*); reventar (*un neumático*); **to blow up** volarse; (*to fail*) fracasar; (*with anger*) (slang) estallar, reventar

blow'out' *s* (aut) reventón *m; (of a fuse)* quemazón *f;* (slang) tertulia concurrida, festín *m*
blowout patch *s* parche *m* para neumático
blow'pipe' *s* (*torch*) soplete *m; (peashooter*) cerbatana
blow'torch' *s* antorcha a soplete, lámpara de soldar
blubber ['blʌbər] *s* grasa de ballena; lloro ruidoso ‖ *intr* llorar ruidosamente
bludgeon ['blʌdʒən] *s* cachiporra ‖ *tr* aporrear; intimidar
blue [blu] *adj* azul; abatido, triste ‖ *s* azul *m;* **the blues** la murria, la morriña ‖ *tr* azular; añilar (*la ropa blanca*) ‖ *intr* azularse
blue'ber'ry *s* (*pl* -**ries**) mirtilo
blue chip *s* valor *m* de primera fila
blue'jay' *s* cianocita
blue jeans *spl* blujins *mpl,* vaqueros; pantalones de mezclilla (C-R, Mex); mecánicos (CAm, Cuba, S-D); pantalones azules (CAm); azulones (El Salv); mahones (P-R, S-D)
blue moon *s* cosa muy rara; **once in a blue moon** cada muerte de obispo, de Pascuas a Ramos
Blue Nile *s* Nilo Azul
blue'-pen'cil *tr* marcar o corregir con lápiz azul
blue'print' *s* cianotipo ‖ *tr* copiar a la cianotipia
blue'stock'ing *s* (coll) marisabidilla
blue streak *s* (coll) rayo; **to talk a blue streak** (coll) soltar la tarabilla
bluff [blʌf] *adj* escarpado ‖ *s* risco, peñasco escarpado; (*deception*) farol *m,* blof *m;* **to call someone's bluff** cogerle la palabra a uno ‖ *intr* farolear, papelonear
blunder ['blʌndər] *s* disparate *m,* desatino ‖ *intr* disparatar, desatinar
blunt [blʌnt] *adj* despuntado, embotado; brusco, franco, directo ‖ *tr* despuntar, embotar
bluntness ['blʌntnɪs] *s* embotadura; brusquedad, franqueza
blur [blʌr] *s* borrón *m,* mancha ‖ *v* (*pret* & *pp* **blurred;** *ger* **blurring**) *tr* empañar; obscurecer (*la vista*) ‖ *intr* empañarse
blurb [blʌrb] *s* anuncio efusivo
blurt [blʌrt] *tr* — **to blurt out** soltar abrupta e impulsivamente
blush [blʌʃ] *s* rubor *m,* sonrojo ‖ *intr* ruborizarse, sonrojarse
bluster ['blʌstər] *s* tumulto, gritos; jactancia ‖ *intr* soplar con furia (*el viento*); bravear, fanfarronear
blustery ['blʌstəri] *adj* tempestuoso; (*wind*) violento; (*swaggering*) fanfarrón
blvd. *abbr* **boulevard**
boar [bor] *s* (*male swine*) verraco; (*wild hog*) jabalí *m*
board [bord] *s* tabla; (*to post announcements*) tablillo; (*table with meal*) mesa; (*daily meals*) pensión; (*organized group*) junta, consejo; (naut) bordo; **in boards** (bb) en cartoné; **on board** en el tren; (naut) a bordo ‖ *tr* entablar; subir a (*un tren*);

embarcarse en (un buque) ‖ intr hospedarse; estar de pupilo

board and lodging s mesa y habitación, pensión completa

boarder ['bordər] s pensionista mf, pupilo

boarding house s pensión, casa de huéspedes

boarding school s escuela de internos

board of health s junta de sanidad

board of trade s junta de comercio

board of trustees s consejo de administración

board'walk' s paseo entablado a la orilla del mar

boast [bost] s jactancia, baladronada ‖ intr jactarse, baladronear, bravatear

boastful ['bostfəl] adj jactancioso

boat [bot] s barco, buque m, nave f; (small boat) bote m; **to be in the same boat** correr el mismo riesgo

boat hook s bichero

boat'house' s casilla para botes

boating ['botɪŋ] s paseo en barco

boat•man ['botmən] s (pl -men [mən]) barquero, lanchero

boat race s regata

boatswain s ['bosən] s contramaestre m

boatswain's chair s guindola

boatswain's mate s segundo contramaestre

bob [bab] s (of pendulum of clock) lenteja; (of plumb line) plomo; (of a fishing line) corcho; (of a horse) cola cortada; (of a girl) pelo cortado corto; (jerky motion) sacudida ‖ v (pret & pp **bobbed; ger bobbing**) tr cortar corto ‖ intr agitarse, menearse; **to bob up and down** subir y bajar con sacudidas cortas

bobbin ['babɪn] s broca, canilla, bobina

bobby pin ['babi] s horquillita para el pelo

bob'by•socks' spl (coll) tobilleras (de jovencita)

bobbysoxer ['babɪ,saksər] s (coll) tobillera

bobolink ['babə,lɪŋk] s chambergo

bob'sled' s doble trineo articulado

bob'tail' s animal m rabón; cola corta; cola cortada

bob'white' s colín m de Virginia

bock beer [bak] s cerveza de marzo

bode [bod] tr & intr anunciar, presagiar; **to bode ill** ser un mal presagio; **to bode well** ser un buen presagio

bodice ['badɪs] s jubón m, corpiño

bodily ['badɪli] adj corporal, corpóreo ‖ adv en persona; en conjunto

bodkin ['badkɪn] s (needle) aguja roma; (for lady's hair) espadilla; (to make holes in cloth) punzón m

bod•y ['badi] s (pl **-ies**) cuerpo; (of a carriage or auto) caja, carrocería

bod'y•guard' s (mil) guardia de corps; guardaespaldas m

body shop s taller m carrocero

Boer [bor] o [bʊr] s bóer mf

Boer War s guerra del Transvaal

bog [bag] s pantano ‖ v (pret & pp **bogged; ger bogging**) intr — **to bog down** atascarse, hundirse

bogey ['bogi] s duende m, coco

bo'gey•man' s (pl **-men** [,mɛn]) duende m, espantajo

bogus ['bogəs] adj (coll) fingido, falso

bo•gy ['bogi] s (pl **-gies**) duende m, demonio, coco

Bohemian [bo'himɪ•ən] adj & s bohemio

boil [bɔɪl] s hervor m, ebullición; (pathol) divieso, furúnculo ‖ tr hacer hervir, herventar ‖ intr hervir, bullir; **to boil over** salirse (un líquido) al hervir

boiler ['bɔɪlər] s caldera; (for cooking) marmita, olla

boil'er•mak'er s calderero

boiler room s sala de calderas

boiling ['bɔɪlɪŋ] adj hirviente, hirviendo ‖ s hervor m, ebullición

boiling point s punto de ebullición

boisterous ['bɔɪstərəs] adj bullicioso, ruidoso, estrepitoso

bold [bold] adj audaz, arrojado, osado; descarado, impudente; temerario

bold'face' s negrilla

boldness ['boldnɪs] s audacia, arrojo, osadía; descaro, impudencia; temeridad

Bolivia [bo'lɪvɪ•ə] s Bolivia

Bolivian [bo'lɪvɪ•ən] adj & s boliviano

boll weevil [bol] s gorgojo del algodón

Bologna [bə'lonjə] s Bolonia

Bolshevik ['balʃəvɪk] o ['bolʃəvɪk] adj & s bolchevique mf

Bolshevism ['balʃə,vɪzəm] o ['bolʃə,vɪzəm] s bolchevismo

bolster ['bolstər] s (of bed) larguero, travesaño; refuerzo, soporte m ‖ tr apoyar, sostener; animar, alentar

bolt [bolt] s perno; (to fasten a door) cerrojo, pasador m; (arrow) cuadrillo; (of lightning) rayo; (of cloth or paper) rollo ‖ tr empernar; acerrojar; deglutir de una vez; cribar, tamizar; disidir de (un partido político) ‖ intr salir de repente; disidir; desbocarse (un caballo)

bolter ['boltər] s disidente mf; (sieve) criba, tamiz m

bolt from the blue s rayo en cielo sin nubes; suceso inesperado

bomb [bam] s bomba ‖ tr bombear, bombardear

bombard [bam'bard] tr bombardear; (e.g., with questions) asediar

bombardment [bam'bardmənt] s bombardeo

bombast ['bambæst] s ampulosidad

bombastic [bam'bæstɪk] adj ampuloso

bomb crater s (mil) embudo de bomba

bomber ['bamər] s bombardero

bomb'proof' adj a prueba de bombas

bomb release s lanzabombas m

bomb'shell' s bomba; **to fall like a bombshell** caer como una bomba

bomb shelter s refugio antiaéreo

bomb'sight' s mira de bombardeo, visor m

bona fide ['bonə,faɪdə] adj & adv de buena fe

bonbon ['ban,ban] s bombón m, confite m

bond [band] s (tie, union) enlace m, vínculo, lazo de unión; (interest-bearing certificate) bono, obligación; (*surety*) fianza; (mas) aparejo; **bonds** cadenas, grillos; **in bond** en depósito bajo fianza

bondage ['bɑndɪdʒ] *s* cautiverio, servidumbre

bonded warehouse *s* depósito comercial

bond'hold'er *s* obligacionista *mf*, tenedor *m* de bonos

bonds•man ['bɑndzmən] *s* (*pl* **-men** [mən]) fiador *m*

bone [bon] *s* hueso; (*of fish*) espina; **bones** esqueleto; (*mortal remains*) huesos; castañuelas; (*dice*) (coll) dados; **to have a bone to pick with** tener una queja con; **to make no bones about** no andarse con rodeos en ‖ *tr* desosar; quitar la espina a; emballenar (*un corsé*) ‖ *intr* — **to bone up on** (coll) empollar, estudiar con ahinco

bone'head' *s* (coll) mentecato, zopenco

boneless ['bonlɪs] *adj* mollar, desosado; (*fish*) sin espinas

boner ['bonər] *s* (coll) patochada, plancha, gazapo

bonfire ['bɑn,faɪr] *s* hoguera

bonnet ['bɑnɪt] *s* gorra; (*sunbonnet*) papalina; (*of auto*) cubierta, capó *m*

bonus ['bonəs] *s* prima, plus *m;* dividendo extraordinario

bon•y ['boni] *adj* (*comp* **-ier;** *super* **-iest**) osudo; descarnado; (*fish*) espinoso

boo [bu] *s* rechifla; **not to say boo** no decir ni chus ni mus ‖ *tr & intr* abuchear, rechiflar

boo•by ['bubi] *s* (*pl* **-bies**) bobalicón *m*, zopenco; el peor jugador

booby prize *s* premio al peor jugador

booby trap *s* (*mine*) trampa explosiva; (*trick*) zancadilla

boogie-woogie ['bugi'wugi] *s* bugui-bugui *m*

book [buk] *s* libro; (*bankbook*) libreta; (*book containing records of business transactions*) libro-registro; (*of cigaret paper, stamps, etc.*) librillo; **to keep books** llevar libros ‖ *tr* reservar (*un pasaje*); escriturar (*a un actor*)

bookbinder ['buk,baɪndər] *s* encuadernador *m*

book'bind'er•y *s* (*pl* **-ies**) encuadernación (*taller*)

book'bind'ing *s* encuadernación (*acción, arte*)

book'case' *s* armario para libros, estante *m* para libros

book end *s* apoyalibros *m*

bookie ['buki] *s* (coll) corredor *m* de apuestas

booking ['bukɪŋ] *s* (*of passage*) reservación; (*of an actor*) escritura

booking clerk *s* taquillero (*que despacha pasajes o localidades*)

bookish ['bukɪʃ] *adj* libresco

book'keep'er *s* tenedor *m* de libros

book'keep'ing *s* teneduría de libros, contabilidad

book'mak'er *s* corredor *m* de apuestas

book'mark' *s* registro

book'plate' *s* ex libris *m*

book review *s* reseña

book'sell'er *s* librero

book'shelf' *s* (*pl* **-shelves** [, ʃɛlvz] estante *m* para libros

book'stand' *s* (*rack*) atril *m;* mostrador *m* para libros; puesto de venta para libros

book'store' *s* librería

book'worm' *s* polilla que roe los libros; (fig) ratón *m* de biblioteca

boom [bum] *s* (*sudden prosperity*) auge *m*, boom *m;* (*noise*) estampido, trueno; (*of a crane*) aguilón *m;* (naut) botalón *m* ‖ *intr* hacer estampido, tronar; estar en auge

boomerang ['bumə,ræŋ] *s* bumerán *m*

boom town *s* pueblo en bonanza

boon [bun] *s* bendición, dicha

boon companion *s* buen compañero

boor [bur] *s* patán *m*, rústico

boorish ['burɪʃ] *adj* rústico, zafio

boost [bust] *s* empujón *m* hacia arriba; (*in price*) alza; alabanza; ayuda ‖ *tr* empujar hacia arriba; alzar (*el precio*); alabar; ayudar

booster ['bustər] *s* cohete *m* lanzador; primera etapa de un cohete lanzador; (*enthusiastic backer*) bombista *mf*

booster shot *s* inyección secundaria

boot [but] *s* bota; **to boot** de añadidura, además; **to die with one's boots on** morir al pie del cañón ‖ *tr* dar un puntapié a; **to boot out** (slang) poner en la calle

boot'black' *s* limpiabotas *m*

booth [buθ] *s* casilla, quiosco; (*to telephone, to vote, etc.*) cabina; (*at a fair or market*) puesto

boot'jack' *s* sacabotas *m*

boot'leg' *adj* contrabandista; de contrabando ‖ *s* contrabando de licores ‖ *v* (*pret & pp* **-legged;** *ger* **-legging**) *tr* pasar de contrabando ‖ *intr* contrabandear en bebidas alcohólicas

bootlegger ['but,lɛgər] *s* destilador *m* clandestino, contrabandista *m*

boot'leg'ging *s* contrabando en bebidas alcohólicas

bootlicker ['but,lɪkər] *s* (slang) quitamotas *mf*, lavacaras *mf*

boot'strap' *s* tirilla de bota

boo•ty ['buti] *s* (*pl* **-ties**) botín *m*, presa

booze [buz] *s* (coll) bebida alcohólica ‖ *intr* borrachear

bor. *abbr* **borough**

borax ['boræks] *s* bórax *m*

Bordeaux [bɔr'do] *s* Burdeos

border ['bɔrdər] *adj* frontero, fronterizo ‖ *s* borde *m*, margen *m & f;* frontera; **borders** bambalinas ‖ *tr* bordear; deslindar ‖ *intr* confinar

border clash *s* encuentro fronterizo

bor'der•line' *adj* incierto, indefinido ‖ *s* frontera

bore [bor] *s* (*drill hole*) barreno; (*size of hole*) calibre *m;* (*of firearm*) alma, ánima; (*of cylinder*) alesaje *m;* (*wearisome person*) latoso, machaca *mf;* fastidio ‖ *tr* aburrir, fastidiar; barrenar, hacer (*un agujero*)

boredom ['bordəm] *s* aburrimiento, fastidio

boring ['borɪŋ] *adj* aburrido, pesado; **that's terribly boring** es una lata

born [bɔrn] *adj* nacido; (*natural, by birth*) nato, innato; **to be born** nacer

borough [ˈbʌro] *s* (*town*) villa; distrito electoral de municipio

borrow [ˈbaro] o [ˈbɔro] *tr* pedir o tomar prestado; apropiarse (*p.ej., una idea*); incorporar (*un elemento lingüístico extranjero*); **to borrow trouble** tomarse una molestia sin motivo alguno

borrower [ˈbaro•ər] o [ˈbɔro•ər] *s* prestatario

borrowing [ˈbaro•ɪŋ] o [ˈbɔro•ɪŋ] *s* préstamo; préstamo lingüístico, extranjerismo

bosom [ˈbʊzəm] *s* seno; (*of shirt*) pechera; corazón *m*, pecho

bosom friend *s* amigo de la mayor confianza

Bosporus [ˈbaspərəs] *s* Bósforo

boss [bɔs] o [bas] *s* (coll) amo, capataz *m*, mandamás *m*, jefe *m*; (*in politics*) (coll) cacique *m*; protuberancia ‖ *tr* (coll) mandar, dominar

bossism [ˈbɔsɪzəm] *s* caciquismo

boss•y [ˈbɔsi] *adj* (*comp* **-ier**; *super* **-iest**) mandón

botanical [bəˈtænɪkəl] *adj* botánico

botanist [ˈbatənɪst] *s* botánico

botany [ˈbatəni] *s* botánica

botch [batʃ] *s* remiendo chapucero ‖ *tr* remendar chapuceramente

both [boθ] *adj* & *pron* ambos ‖ *adv* igualmente ‖ *conj* a la vez; **both . . . and** tanto . . . como, así . . . como

bother [ˈbaðər] *s* incomodidad, molestia, majadería, murga ‖ *tr* incomodar, molestar, majaderear, pololear ‖ *intr* molestarse

bothersome [ˈbaðərsəm] *adj* incómodo, molesto, fastidioso

bottle [ˈbatəl] *s* botella, frasco ‖ *tr* embotellar; **to bottle up** (nav) embotellar

bot'tle•neck' *s* gollete *m*; (*in traffic*) embotellado

bottle opener [ˈopənər] *s* abrebotellas *m*

bottom [ˈbatəm] *adj* (*price*) (el) más bajo; (*e.g., dollar*) último ‖ *s* fondo; (*of a chair*) asiento; (*of jar*) culo; (coll) trasero *m*; **at bottom** en el fondo; **to go to the bottom** irse a pique

bottomless [ˈbatəmlɪs] *adj* sin fondo, insondable

boudoir [buˈdwar] *s* tocador *m*

bough [baʊ] *s* rama

bouillon [ˈbʊljan] *s* caldo

boulder [ˈboldər] *s* pedrejón *m*

boulevard [ˈbʊlə,vard] *s* bulevar *m*

bounce [baʊns] *s* rebote *m* ‖ *tr* hacer botar; (slang) despedir ‖ *intr* botar, rebotar; saltar; **to bounce along** dar saltos al andar

bouncer [ˈbaʊnsər] *s* cosa grande; (slang) apagabroncas *m*

bouncing [ˈbaʊnsɪŋ] *adj* frescachón, vigoroso; (*baby*) gordinflón

bound [baʊnd] *adj* atado, ligado; (*book*) encuadernado; dispuesto, propenso; puesto en aprendizaje; **bound for** con destino a, con rumbo a; **bound in boards** (bb) encartonado, en cartoné; **bound up in** entregado

a, muy adicto a; absorto en ‖ *s* salto; (*of a ball*) bote *m*; límite *m*, confín *m*; **bounds** región, comarca; **out of bounds** fuera de los límites; **within bounds** a raya

bounda•ry [ˈbaʊndəri] *s* (*pl* **-ries**) límite *m*, frontera; (*established*) parámetro

boundary mark *s* (*annotation*) acotamiento

boundary stone *s* mojón *m*

bounder [ˈbaʊndər] *s* persona vulgar y malcriada

boundless [ˈbaʊndlɪs] *adj* ilimitado, inmenso, infinito

bountiful [ˈbaʊntɪfəl] *adj* generoso, liberal; abundante

boun•ty [ˈbaʊnti] *s* (*pl* **-ties**) generosidad, liberalidad; don *m*, favor *m*; galardón *m*, premio; (*bonus*) prima; (mil) premio de enganche

bouquet [buˈke] *s* ramillete *m*; (*aroma of a wine*) nariz *f*

bourgeois [ˈbʊrʒwa] *adj* & *s* burgués *m*

bourgeoisie [,bʊrʒwaˈzi] *s* burguesía

bout [baʊt] *s* encuentro; rato; (*of an illness*) ataque *m*

bow [baʊ] *s* inclinación, reverencia; (*of a ship*) proa ‖ *tr* inclinar (*la cabeza*) ‖ *intr* inclinarse; **to bow and scrape** hacer reverencias obsequiosas; **to bow to** saludar, inclinarse delante ‖ [bo] *s* (*for shooting an arrow*) arco; lazo, nudo; (mus) arco; (*stroke of bow*) (mus) arqueada ‖ *tr* (mus) tocar con arco ‖ *intr* arquearse

bowdlerize [ˈbaʊdlə,raɪz] *tr* expurgar

bowel [ˈbaʊ•əl] *s* intestino; **bowels** intestinos; (*inner part*) entrañas

bowel movement *s* evacuación del vientre; **to have a bowel movement** evacuar el vientre

bower [ˈbaʊ•ər] *s* emparrado, glorieta

bower•y [ˈbaʊ•əri] *adj* frondoso, sombreado ‖ *s* (*pl* **-ies**) finca, granja

bowknot [ˈbo,nat] *s* lazada

bowl [bol] *s* (*for soup or broth*) escudilla, cuenco; (*for washing hands*) jofaina, palangana; (*of toilet*) cubeta, taza; (*of fountain*) tazón *m*; (*of spoon*) paleta; (*of pipe*) hornillo; (*hollow place*) concavidad, cuenco ‖ *tr* — **to bowl over** tumbar ‖ *intr* jugar a los bolos; **to bowl along** rodar

bowlegged [ˈbo,lɛgd] o [ˈbo,lɛgɪd] *adj* patiestevado

bowler [ˈbolər] *s* jugador *m* de bolos; (Brit) sombrero hongo

bowling [ˈbolɪŋ] *s* juego de bolos, boliche *m*

bowling alley *s* bolera, boliche *m*

bowling green *s* bolera encespada

bowshot [ˈbo,ʃat] *s* tiro de flecha

bowsprit [ˈbaʊsprɪt] o [ˈbosprɪt] *s* bauprés *m*

bow tie [bo] *s* corbata de mariposa, pajarita

bowwow [ˈbaʊ,waʊ] *interj* ¡guau! ‖ *s* guau guau *m*

box [baks] *s* caja; (*slap*) bofetada; (*plant*) boj *m*; (*in newspaper*) recuadro; (theat) palco ‖ *tr* encajonar; (*to slap*) abofetear; (naut) cuartear (*la aguja*) ‖ *intr* boxear

box'car' *s* vagón *m* de carga cerrado

bo
bo

boxer [ˈbɑksər] s embalador m; (sport) boxeador m

boxing [ˈbɑksɪŋ] s embalaje m; (sport) boxeo

boxing gloves spl guantes mpl de boxeo

box office s taquilla, despacho de localidades; boletería

box'-of'fice hit s éxito de taquilla

box-office record s marca de taquilla

box-office sale s venta de localidades en taquilla

box pleat s pliegue m de tabla

box seat s asiento de palco

box'wood' s boj m

boy [bɔɪ] s muchacho; (servant) mozo; (coll) compadre m

boycott [ˈbɔɪkɑt] s boicoteo ‖ tr boicotear

boyhood [ˈbɔɪhʊd] s muchachez f; muchachería

boyish [ˈbɔɪɪʃ] adj amuchachado, muchachil

boy scout s niño explorador

Bp. abbr **bishop**

b.p. abbr **bills payable, boiling point**

br. abbr **brand, brother**

b.r. abbr **bills receivable**

bra [brɑ] s (coll) portasenos m, sostén m, sujetador m

brace [bres] s riostra; berbiquí m; **braces** (Brit) tirantes mpl; (on teeth) aparato de ortodoncia ‖ tr arriostrar; asegurar, vigorizar; **to brace oneself** (coll) cobrar ánimo ‖ intr — **to brace up** (coll) cobrar ánimo

brace and bit s berbiquí y barrena

bracelet [ˈbreslɪt] s brazalete m, pulsera

bracer [ˈbresər] s (coll) trago de licor

bracing [ˈbresɪŋ] adj fortificante, tónico

bracket [ˈbrækɪt] s puntal m, soporte m; ménsula, repisa; (mark used in printing) corchete m; clase f, categoría ‖ tr acorchetar; agrupar

brackish [ˈbrækɪʃ] adj salobre

brad [bræd] s clavito, estaquilla

brag [bræg] s jactancia ‖ v (pret & pp **bragged**; ger **bragging**) intr jactarse, bravatear, palanganear

braggart [ˈbrægərt] s fanfarrón m

braid [bred] s (flat strip of cotton, silk, etc.) cinta, galón m; (something braided) trenza ‖ tr encintar, galonear; trenzar

brain [bren] s cerebro; **brains** cerebro, inteligencia; **to rack one's brains** devanarse los sesos ‖ tr descerebrar

brain child s parto del ingenio

brain drain s (coll) éxodo de técnicos

brainless [ˈbrenlɪs] adj tonto, sin seso

brain power s capacidad mental

brain'storm' s acceso de locura; confusión mental; buena idea, hallazgo

brain trust s grupo de peritos

brain'wash'ing s lavado cerebral

brain wave s onda encefálica; (coll) buena idea, hallazgo

brain'work' s trabajo intelectual

brain·y [ˈbreni] adj (comp **-ier**; super **-iest**) (coll) inteligente, sesudo

braise [brez] tr soasar y cocer (la carne) a fuego lento en vasija bien tapada

brake [brek] s freno; breque m; (for dressing flax) agramadera; (thicket) matorral m; (fern) helecho común ‖ tr frenar; brequear; agramar (el lino o el cañamo)

brake band s cinta de freno

brake drum s tambor m de freno

brake lining s forro o cinta de freno

brake·man [ˈbrekmən] s (pl **-men** [mən]) guardafrenos m

brake shoe s zapata de freno

bramble [ˈbræmbəl] s frambueso, zarza

bram·bly [ˈbræmbli] adj (comp **-blier**; super **-bliest**) zarzoso

bran [bræn] s afrecho, salvado

branch [bræntʃ] s (of tree) rama; (smaller branch; branch cut from tree; of a science, etc.) ramo; (of vine) sarmiento; (of road, railroad) ramal m; (of candlestick, river, etc.) brazo; (of a store, bank) sucursal f ‖ intr ramificarse; **to branch out** extender sus actividades

branch line s ramal m, línea de empalme

branch office s sucursal f

brand [brænd] s (kind, make) marca; (trademark) marca de fábrica; (branding iron) hierro de marcar; (mark stamped with hot iron) hierro; (dishonor) tizón m ‖ tr poner marca de fábrica en; herrar con hierro candente; tiznar (la reputación de una persona); **to brand as** tildar de

brandied [ˈbrændid] adj macerado en aguardiente

branding iron s hierro de marcar; fierro

brandish [ˈbrændɪʃ] tr blandear

brand'-new' adj nuevecito, flamante

bran·dy [ˈbrændi] s (pl **-dies**) aguardiente m

brash [bræʃ] adj atrevido, impetuoso; descarado, respondón; s acceso, ataque m

brass [bræs] s latón m; (in army and navy) (slang) los mandamases; (coll) descaro; **brasses** (mus) cobres mpl

brass band s banda, charanga

brass hat s (slang) espadón m, mandamás m

brassiere [brəˈzɪr] s portasenos m, sostén m, sujetador m

brass knuckles spl llave inglesa, bóxer m

brass tack s clavito dorado de tapicería; **to get down to brass tacks** (coll) entrar en materia

brass winds spl (mus) cobres mpl, instrumentos músicos de metal

brass·y [ˈbræsi] adj (comp **-ier**; super **-iest**) hecho de latón; metálico; descarado

brat [bræt] s rapaz m, mocoso, braguillas m

brava·do [brəˈvado] s (pl **-does** o **-dos**) bravata

brave [brev] adj bravo, valiente ‖ s valiente m; guerrero indio norteamericano ‖ tr hacer frente a, arrostrar; desafiar, retar

bravery [ˈbrevəri] s bravura, valor m

bra·vo [ˈbravo] interj ¡bravo! ‖ s (pl **-vos**) bravo

brawl [brɔl] s pendencia, reyerta; alboroto ‖ intr armar pendencia; alborotar

brawler [ˈbrɔlər] s pendenciero; alborotador m

brawn [brɔn] s fuerza musculosa

brawn·y ['brɔni] *adj* (*comp* **-ier;** *super* **-iest**) fornido, musculoso

bray [bre] *s* rebuzno ‖ *intr* rebuznar

braze [brez] *s* soldadura de latón ‖ *tr* soldar con latón; cubrir de latón; adornar con latón

brazen ['brezən] *adj* de latón; descarado ‖ *tr* — **to brazen through** llevar a cabo descaradamente

brazier ['breʒər] *s* brasero

Brazil [brə'zɪl] *s* el Brasil

Brazilian [brə'zɪljən] *adj & s* brasileño

Brazil nut *s* castaña de Pará

breach [britʃ] *s* (*opening*) abertura; (*in a wall*) brecha; abuso, violación ‖ *tr* abrir brecha en

breach of faith *s* falta de fidelidad

breach of peace *s* perturbación del orden público

breach of promise *s* incumplimiento de la palabra de matrimonio

breach of trust *s* abuso de confianza

bread [brɛd] *s* pan *m* ‖ *tr* empanar

bread and butter *s* pan *m* con mantequilla; (coll) pan de cada día

bread crumbs *spl* pan rallado

breaded ['brɛdɪd] *adj* empanado

bread line *s* cola del pan

breadth [brɛdθ] *s* anchura; alcance *m*, extensión; (*e.g., of judgment*) amplitud *f*

bread'win'ner *s* sostén *m* de la familia

break [brek] *s* rompimiento; interrupción; intervalo, pausa; (*split*) hendidura, grieta; (*in prices*) baja; (*in clouds*) claro; (*from jail*) evasión, huída; (*among friends*) ruptura; (*luck, good or bad*) (slang) suerte *f*; (slang) disparate *m*; **to give someone a break** abrirle a uno la puerta ‖ *v* (*pret* **broke** [brok]; *pp* **broken**) *tr* romper, quebrar; cambiar (*un billete*); comunicar (*una mala noticia*); suspender (*relaciones*); faltar a (*la palabra*); batir (*un récord*); cortar (*un circuito*); quebrantar (*un testamento; un hábito*); romper (*una ley*); levantar (*el campo*); (mil) degradar; **to break in** forzar (*una puerta*); **to break open** abrir por la fuerza ‖ *intr* romperse, quebrarse; reventar; aclarar (*el tiempo*); bajar (*los precios*); quebrantarse (*la salud*); **to break down** perder la salud; prorrumpir en llanto; **to break even** salir sin ganar ni perder; **to break in** entrar por fuerza; irrumpir en; **to break loose** desprenderse; escaparse; desbocarse (*un caballo*); desencadenarse (*una tempestad*); **to break out** estallar, declararse; (*in laughter, weeping*) romper; (*on the skin*) brotar granos; **to break through** abrirse paso; abrir paso por entre; **to break up** desmenuzarse; levantarse (*una reunión*); **to break with** romper con

breakable ['brekəbəl] *adj* rompible

breakage ['brekɪdʒ] *s* estropicio; indemnización por objetos rotos

break'down' *s* mal éxito; avería, pana; (*in health*) colapso; (*in negotiations*) ruptura; análisis *m*

breaker ['brekər] *s* cachón *m*, rompiente *m*

breakfast ['brɛkfəst] *s* desayuno ‖ *intr* desayunar

breakfast food *s* cereal *m* para el desayuno

break'neck' *adj* vertiginoso; **at breakneck speed** a mata caballo

break of day *s* alba, amanecer *m*

break'through' *s* (mil) brecha, ruptura; (fig) descubrimiento sensacional

break'up' *s* disolución, dispersión; desplome *m*; (*in health*) postración

break'wa'ter *s* rompeolas *m*, escollera

breast [brɛst] *s* pecho, seno; (*of fowl*) pechuga; (*of garment*) pechera; **to make a clean breast of it** confesarlo todo

breast'bone' *s* esternón *m*; (*of fowl*) quilla

breast drill *s* berbiquí *m* de pecho

breast'pin' *s* alfiler *m* de pecho

breast stroke *s* brazada de pecho

breath [brɛθ] *s* aliento, respiración; **out of breath** sin aliento; **short of breath** corto de resuello; **to gasp for breath** respirar anhelosamente; **under one's breath** por lo bajo, en voz baja

breathe [brið] *tr* respirar; **to breathe one's last** dar el último suspiro ‖ *intr* respirar; **to breathe freely** cobrar aliento; **to breathe in** aspirar; **to breathe out** espirar

breathing spell *s* respiro, rato de descanso

breathless ['brɛθlɪs] *adj* falto de aliento, jadeante; intenso, vivo; sin aliento

breath'tak'ing *adj* conmovedor, imponente

breech [britʃ] *s* culata, recámara; **breeches** ['brɪtʃɪz] calzones *mpl*; (coll) pantalones *mpl*; **to wear the breeches** (coll) calzarse los pantalones

breed [brid] *s* casta, raza; clase *f*, especie *f* ‖ *v* (*pret & pp* **bred** [brɛd]) *tr* criar ‖ *intr* criar; criarse

breeder ['bridər] *s* (*of animals*) criador *m*; (*animal*) reproductor *m*

breeding ['bridɪŋ] *s* cría; crianza, modales *mpl*; **bad breeding** mala crianza; **good breeding** buena crianza

breeze [briz] *s* brisa

breez·y ['brizi] *adj* (*comp* **-ier;** *super* **-iest**) airoso; animado, vivo; (coll) desenvuelto, vivaracho

brevi·ty ['brɛvɪti] *s* (*pl* **-ties**) brevedad

brew [bru] *s* calderada de cerveza; mezcla ‖ *tr* fabricar (*cerveza*); preparar (*té*); (fig) tramar, urdir ‖ *intr* amenazar (*una tormenta*)

brewer ['bruər] *s* cervecero

brewer's yeast *s* levadura de cerveza

brewer·y ['bruəri] *s* (*pl* **-ies**) cervecería, fábrica de cerveza

bribe [braɪb] *s* soborno; **to take bribes** comer maíz ‖ *tr* sobornar

briber·y ['braɪbəri] *s* (*pl* **-ies**) soborno

bric-a-brac ['brɪkə,bræk] *s* chucherías, curiosidades *fpl*

brick [brɪk] *s* ladrillo; (coll) buen sujeto ‖ *tr* enladrillar

brick'bat' *s* pedazo de ladrillo; (coll) palabra hiriente

brick ice cream s queso helado, helado al corte
brickkiln ['brɪk,kɪln] s horno de ladrillero
bricklayer ['brɪk,le•ər] s ladrillador m
brick'yard' s ladrillal m
bridal ['braɪdəl] adj nupcial; de novia
bridal wreath s corona nupcial
bride [braɪd] s desposada, novia
bride'groom' s desposado, novio
bridesmaid ['braɪdz,med] s madrina de boda
bridge [brɪdʒ] s puente m; (of nose) caballete m; (card game) bridge m ‖ tr tender un puente sobre; salvar (un obstáculo); colmar, llenar (un vacío)
bridge'head' s (mil) cabeza de puente
bridle ['braɪdəl] s brida ‖ tr embridar ‖ intr engallarse, erguirse
bridle path s camino de herradura
brief [brif] adj breve, corto, conciso ‖ s resumen m; (law) escrito; **in brief** en resumen ‖ tr resumir; dar consejos anticipados a; dar informes a
brief case s cartera
briefing ['brifɪŋ] s órdenes fpl; (of the press) informe m
brier ['braɪ•ər] s zarza; brezo blanco
brig [brɪg] s (naut) bergantín m; prisión en buque de guerra
brigade [brɪ'ged] s brigada
brigadier [,brɪgə'dɪr] s general m de brigada
brigand ['brɪgənd] s bandolero
brigantine ['brɪgən,tin] s (naut) bergantín m goleta
bright [braɪt] adj brillante; (e.g., day) claro; (color) subido, listo, inteligente, despierto; (idea, thought) luminoso; (disposition) alegre, vivo
brighten ['braɪtən] tr abrillantar; alegrar, avivar ‖ intr avivarse; alegrarse; despejarse (el cielo)
bright lights spl luces fpl brillantes; (aut) faros o luces de carretera
brilliance ['brɪljəns] o **brilliancy** ['brɪljənsi] s brillantez f, brillo
brilliant ['brɪljənt] adj brillante
brillantine ['brɪljəntin] s brillantina
brim [brɪm] s borde m; (of hat) ala
brim'stone' s azufre m
brine [braɪn] s salmuera, agua salobre
bring [brɪŋ] v (pret & pp **brought** [brɔt]) tr traer; llevar; **to bring about** efectuar; **to bring back** devolver; **to bring down** abatir; **to bring forth** dar a luz; **to bring in** traer a colación; servir (una comida); introducir, presentar; **to bring into play** poner en juego; **to bring on** causar, producir; **to bring out** sacar; presentar al público; **to bring suit** poner pleito; **to bring to** sacar de un desmayo; **to bring together** reunir; confrontar; reconciliar; **to bring to pass** efectuar, llevar a cabo; **to bring up** arrimar (p.ej., una silla); educar, criar; traer a colación; **to bring upon oneself** atraerse (un infortunio)
bringing-up ['brɪŋɪŋ'ʌp] s educación, crianza

brink [brɪŋk] s borde m, margen m; **on the brink of** al borde de
brisk [brɪsk] adj animado, vivo, vivaz
bristle ['brɪsəl] s cerda ‖ intr erizarse, encresparse; (to be visibly annoyed) encresparse
bris•tly ['brɪsli] adj (comp **-tlier;** super **-tliest**) cerdoso, erizado
Britannic [brɪ'tænɪk] adj británico
British ['brɪtɪʃ] adj británico ‖ **the British** los britanos
Britisher ['brɪtɪʃər] s britano
Briton ['brɪtən] s britano
Brittany ['brɪtəni] s Bretaña
brittle ['brɪtəl] adj quebradizo, frágil
bro. abbr **brother**
broach [brotʃ] s (skewer) asador m, espetón m; (ornamental pin) broche m, prendedero ‖ tr sacar a colación
broad [brɔd] adj ancho; liberal, tolerante; (day, noon, etc.) pleno
broad'cast' s radiodifusión; audición, programa radiotelefónico ‖ v (pret & pp **-cast**) tr difundir, esparcir ‖ (pret & pp **-cast** o **-casted**) tr radiodifundir, radiar, emitir
broadcasting station s emisora, estación de radiodifusión
broad'cloth' s paño fino
broaden ['brɔdən] tr ensanchar ‖ intr ensancharse
broad'loom' adj tejido en telar ancho y en color sólido
broad-minded ['brɔd'maɪndɪd] adj tolerante, de amplias miras
broad-shouldered ['brɔd'ʃoldərd] adj ancho de espaldas
broad'side' s (naut) costado m; (naut) andanada; (coll) torrente m de injurias
broad'sword' s espada ancha
brocade [bro'ked] s brocado
broccoli ['brakəli] s brécol m, brécoles mpl
brochure [bro'ʃur] s folleto
brogue [brog] s acento irlandés
broil [brɔɪl] tr asar a la parrilla ‖ intr asarse
broiler ['brɔɪlər] s parrilla; pollo para asar a la parrilla
broken ['brokən] adj roto, quebrado; agotado; amansado; (accent) chapurrado; suelto
bro'ken-down' adj abatido; descompuesto; destartalado
broken-hearted ['brokən'hartɪd] adj abrumado por el dolor
broker ['brokər] s corredor m
brokerage ['brokərɪdʒ] s corretaje m
bromide ['bromaɪd] s bromuro; (slang) trivialidad
bromine ['bromin] s bromo
bronchitis [braŋ'kaɪtɪs] s bronquitis f
bron•co ['braŋko] s (pl **-cos**) potro cerril
bron'co•bust'er s domador m de potros; vaquero
bronze [branz] adj bronceado ‖ s bronce m ‖ tr broncear ‖ intr broncearse
brooch [brotʃ] o [brutʃ] s alfiler m de pecho, prendedero, pasador m

brood [brud] *s* cría; nidada; casta, raza ‖ *tr* empollar ‖ *intr* enclocar; **to brood on** meditar con preocupación

brook [bruk] *s* arroyo ‖ *tr* — **to brook no** no tolerar, no aguantar

broom [brum] o [brʊm] *s* escoba; (bot) hiniesta

broom'corn' *s* sorgo

broom'stick' *s* palo de escoba

bros. *abbr* **brothers**

broth [brɔθ] o [braθ] *s* caldo

brothel ['brɑθəl] o ['braðəl] *s* burdel *m;* (Mex) congal *m*

brother ['brʌðər] *s* hermano

brotherhood ['brʌðər,hʊd] *s* hermandad

broth'er-in-law' *s* (*pl* **brothers-in-law**) cuñado, hermano político; (*husband of one's wife's or husband's sister*) concuñado

brotherly ['brʌðərli] *adj* fraternal

brow [braʊ] *s* (*forehead*) frente *f;* (*eyebrow*) ceja; **to knit one's brow** fruncir las cejas

brow'beat' *v* (*pret* **-beat;** *pp* **beaten**) *tr* intimidar con mirada ceñuda

brown [braʊn] *adj* pardo, castaño, moreno; (*race*) cobrizo; tostado del sol ‖ *s* castaño, moreno ‖ *tr* poner moreno; tostar, quemar, broncear; (culin) dorar

brownish ['braʊnɪʃ] *adj* que tira a moreno

brown study *s* absorción, pensamiento profundo, ensimismamlento

brown sugar *s* azúcar terciado

browse [braʊz] *s* *intr* (*to nibble at twigs*) ramonear; (*to graze*) pacer; hojear un libro ociosamente; **to browse about** o **around** curiosear

bruise [bruz] *s* contusión, magulladura, magullón *m* ‖ *tr* contundir, magullar ‖ *intr* contundirse, magullarse

brunet [bru'nɛt] *adj* moreno ‖ *s* moreno (*hombre moreno*)

brunette [bru'nɛt] *s* morena (*mujer morena*)

brunt [brʌnt] *s* fuerza, choque *m,* empuje *m;* (*e.g., of a battle*) peso, (lo) más reñido

brush [brʌʃ] *s* brocha, cepillo, escobilla; (*stroke*) brochada; (*light touch*) roce *m;* (*brief encounter*) encuentro, escaramuza; (*growth of bushes*) maleza; (elec) escobilla ‖ *tr* acepillar; (*to graze*) rozar; **to brush aside** echar a un lado ‖ *intr* pasar ligeramente; **to brush up on** repasar

brush'-off' *s* (slang) desaire *m;* **to give the brush-off to** (slang) despedir noramala

brush'wood' *s* broza, ramojo

brusque [brʌsk] *adj* brusco, rudo

brusqueness ['brʌsknɪs] *s* brusquedad

Brussels ['brʌsəlz] *s* Bruselas

Brussels sprouts *spl* bretones *mpl,* col *f* de Bruselas

brutal ['brutəl] *adj* brutal, bestial

brutali·ty [bru'tælɪti] *s* (*pl* **-ties**) brutalidad, crueldad

brutalization [,brutələ'zeʃən] *s* embrutecimiento

brute [brut] *adj* bruto; (*force*) inconsciente, ciego ‖ *s* bruto

brutish ['brutɪʃ] *adj* abrutado, estúpido

bu. *abbr* **bushel**

bubble ['bʌbəl] *s* burbuja; ampolla; ilusión, quimera ‖ *intr* burbujear; **to bubble over** desbordar, rebosar

buck [bʌk] *s* (*goat*) cabrón *m;* (*deer*) gamo; (*rabbit*) conejo; (*of a horse*) corveta, encorvada; (*youth*) pisaverde *m;* (slang) dólar *m;* **to pass the buck** (coll) echar la carga a otro ‖ *tr* hacer frente a, resistir a; (*to butt*) acornear, topetar; colar (*la ropa*); **to buck up** (coll) alentar, animar ‖ *intr* botarse, encorvarse; **to buck against** embestir contra

bucket ['bʌkɪt] *s* balde *m,* cubo; (*of a well*) pozal *m;* **to kick the bucket** (slang) estirar la pata, liar el petate

bucket seat *s* baquet *m*

buckle ['bʌkəl] *s* hebilla; (*bend, bulge*) alabeo, pandeo ‖ *tr* abrochar con hebilla ‖ *intr* (*to bend, bulge*) alabearse, pandear; **to buckle down to** (coll) dedicarse con empeño a

buck private *s* (slang) soldado raso

buckram ['bʌkrəm] *s* zangala; (bb) bocací *m,* bucarán *m*

buck'saw' *s* sierra de bastidor

buck'shot' *s* postas

buck'tooth' *s* (*pl* **-teeth**) diente *m* saliente

buck'wheat' *s* alforfón *m,* trigo sarraceno

bud [bʌd] *s* botón *m,* brote *m;* **to nip in the bud** cortar de raíz ‖ *v* (*pret & pp* **budded;** *ger* **budding**) *intr* abotonar, brotar

bud·dy ['bʌdi] *s* (*pl* **-dies**) (coll) camarada *m,* cumpa *m* (coll) muchachito

budge [bʌdʒ] *tr* mover ‖ *intr* moverse

budget ['bʌdʒɪt] *s* presupuesto ‖ *tr* presuponer, presupuestar

budgetary ['bʌdʒɪ,tɛri] *adj* presupuestario

buff [bʌf] *adj* de ante ‖ *s* (*leather*) ante *m;* color *m* de ante; chaqueta de ante; rueda pulidora; (coll) piel desnuda; aficionado ‖ *tr* dar color de ante a; pulimentar

buffa·lo ['bʌfə,lo] *s* (*pl* **-loes** o **-los**) búfalo ‖ *tr* (slang) intimidar

buffer ['bʌfər] *s* amortiguador *m* de choques; tope *m,* paragolpes *m;* pulidor *m*

buffer state *s* estado tapón

buffet [bu'fe] *s* (*piece of furniture*) aparador *m;* restaurante *m* de estación ‖ ['bʌfɪt] *tr* abofetear, golpear, pegar

buffet car *s* coche *m* bar

buffet lunch *s* servicio de bufet

buffet supper *s* ambigú *m,* bufet *m*

buffoon [bə'fun] *s* bufón *m,* payaso

buffooner·y [bə'funəri] *s* (*pl* **-ies**) bufonada, chocarrería

bug [bʌg] *s* insecto, bicho, sabandija; microbio; (*bedbug*) (Brit) chinche *f;* (coll) defecto; (slang) micrófono escondido; (slang) loco; (slang) entusiasta *mf* ‖ *v* (*pret & pp* **bugged;** *ger* **bugging**) *tr* (slang) esconder un micrófono en

bug'bear' *s* espantajo; aversión

bug·gy ['bʌgi] *adj* (*comp* **-gier;** *super* **-giest**) infestado de bichos; (slang) loco ‖ *s* (*pl* **-gies**) calesa

bug'house' *adj* (slang) loco ‖ *s* (slang) manicomio, casa de locos

bugle [ˈbjugəl] *s* corneta
bugle call *s* toque *m* de corneta
bugler [ˈbjuglər] *s* corneta *m*
build [bɪld] *s* forma, hechura, figura; (*of human being*) talle *m* ‖ *v* (*pret & pp* **built** [bɪlt]) *tr* construir, edificar; componer; establecer, fundar; crearse (*p.ej.*, *una clientela*)
builder [ˈbɪldər] *s* constructor *m;* aparejador *m*, maestro de obras
building [ˈbɪldɪŋ] *s* construcción; edificio; (*one of several in a group*) pabellón *m*
building and loan association *s* sociedad *f* de crédito para la construcción
building lot *s* solar *m*
building site *s* terreno para construir
building trades *spl* oficios de edificación
build′-up′ *s* acumulación, formación; (coll) propaganda anticipada
built′in′ *adj* integrante, incorporado, empotrado
built′-up′ *adj* armado, montado; (*land*) aglomerado
bulb [bʌlb] *s* (*of plant*) bulbo; (*of thermometer*) bola, cubeta; (*of syringe*) pera; (*of electric light*) ampolla, bombilla
Bulgaria [bʌlˈgɛrɪ•ə] *s* Bulgaria
Bulgarian [bʌlˈgɛrɪ•ən] *adj & s* búlgaro
bulge [bʌldʒ] *s* protuberancia, bulto, bombeo; **to get the bulge on** (coll) llevar la ventaja a ‖ *intr* hacer bulto, bombearse
bulimia [bjuˈlimi•ə] *s* bulimia
bulk [bʌlk] *s* bulto, volumen *m;* (*main mass*) grueso; **in bulk** a granel ‖ *intr* abultar, hacer bulto; tener importancia
bulk′head′ *s* mamparo; tabique hermético
bulk•y [ˈbʌlki] *adj* (*comp* -**ier;** *super* -**iest**) abultado, voluminoso, grueso
bull [bʊl] *s* toro; (*in stockmarket*) alcista *m;* (*papal document*) bula; disparate *m;* **to take the bull by the horns** asir al toro por las astas ‖ *tr* — **to bull the market** jugar al alza
bull′dog′ *s* dogo
bulldoze [ˈbʊl,doz] *tr* coaccionar, intimidar con amenazas
bulldozer [ˈbʊl,dozər] *s* explanadora de empuje, empujatierra
bullet [ˈbʊlɪt] *s* bala
bulletin [ˈbʊlətɪn] *s* boletín *m;* comunicado; (*of a school*) anuario
bulletin board *s* tablilla
bul′let•proof′ *adj* a prueba de balas, blindado
bull′fight′ *s* corrida de toros
bull′fight′er *s* torero
bull′fight′ing *adj* torero ‖ *s* toreo
bull′finch′ *s* (orn) camachuelo
bull′frog′ *s* rana toro
bull-headed [ˈbʊl,hɛdɪd] *adj* obstinado, terco
bullion [ˈbʊljən] *s* oro en barras, plata en barras; (*twisted fringe*) entorchado
bullish [ˈbʊlɪʃ] *adj* obstinado; (*market*) en alza; (*speculator*) alcista; optimista
bullock [ˈbʊlək] *s* buey *m*
bull′pen′ *s* (taur) toril *m;* (*jail*) (coll) prevención

bull′ring′ *s* plaza de toros
bull′s-eye [ˈbʊlz,aɪ] *s* (*of a target*) diana; (archit, meteor, naut) ojo de buey; **to hit the bull's-eye** hacer diana
bul•ly [ˈbʊli] *adj* (coll) excelente, magnífico ‖ *s* (*pl* -**lies**) matón *m*, valentón *m* ‖ *v* (*pret & pp* -**lied**) *tr* intimidar, maltratar
bulrush [ˈbʊl,rʌʃ] *s* junco; junco de laguna; (*Typha*) anea, espadaña; (Bib) papiro
bulwark [ˈbʊlwərk] *s* baluarte *m* ‖ *tr* abaluartar; defender, proteger
bum [bʌm] *s* (slang) holgazán *m;* (slang) vagabundo; (slang) mendigo ‖ *v* (*pret & pp* **bummed;** *ger* **bumming**) *tr* (slang) mendigar ‖ *intr* holgazanear; (slang) vagabundear; (slang) mendigar
bumblebee [ˈbʌmbəl,bi] *s* abejorro
bump [bʌmp] *s* (*collision*) topetón *m;* (*shake*) sacudida; (*on falling*) batacazo; (*of plane in rough air*) rebote *m;* (*swelling*) hinchazón *f*, chichón *m;* protuberancia ‖ *tr* dar contra, topar; (*to bruise*) abollar ‖ *intr* chocar; dar sacudidas; **to bump into** tropezar con; encontrarse con
bumper [ˈbʌmpər] *adj* (coll) abundante, grande ‖ *s* tope *m*, paratopes *m;* (aut) amortiguador *m*, parachoques *m;* vaso lleno
bumpkin [ˈbʌmpkɪn] *s* patán *m*, palurdo
bumptious [ˈbʌmpʃəs] *adj* engreído, presuntuoso
bump•y [ˈbʌmpi] *adj* (*comp* -**ier;** *super* -**iest**) (*ground*) desigual, áspero; (*air*) agitado
bun [bʌn] *s* buñuelo, bollo; (*of hair*) castaña
bunch [bʌntʃ] *s* manojo, puñado; (*of grapes, bananas, etc.*) racimo; (*of flowers*) ramillete *m;* (*of people*) grupo ‖ *tr* agrupar, juntar ‖ *intr* agruparse; arracimarse
bundle [ˈbʌndəl] *s* atado, bulto, lío, paquete *m;* (*of papers*) legajo; (*of wood*) haz *m* ‖ *tr* atar, liar, empaquetar, envolver; **to bundle off** despedir precipitadamente; **to bundle up** arropar ‖ *intr* — **to bundle up** arroparse
bung [bʌŋ] *s* bitoque *m*, tapón *m*
bungalow [ˈbʌŋgə,lo] *s* bungalow *m*, casa de una sola planta
bung′hole′ *s* piquera, boca de tonel
bungle [ˈbʌŋgəl] *s* chapucería ‖ *tr & intr* chapucear
bungler [ˈbʌŋglər] *s* chapucero
bungling [ˈbʌŋglɪŋ] *adj* chapucero ‖ *s* chapucería
bunion [ˈbʌnjən] *s* juanete *m*
bunk [bʌŋk] *s* tarima; (slang) palabrería vana, música celestial
bunker [ˈbʌŋkər] *s* carbonera; (mil) fortín *m*
bun•ny [ˈbʌni] *s* (*pl* -**nies**) conejito
bunting [ˈbʌntɪŋ] *s* banderas colgadas como adorno; (*of a ship*) empavesado; (orn) gorrión triguero
buoy [bɔɪ] o [ˈbu•i] *s* boya; boya salvavidas, guindola ‖ *tr* — **to buoy up** mantener a flote; animar, alentar
buoyancy [ˈbɔɪ•ənsi] o [ˈbujənsi] *s* flotación; alegría, animación
buoyant [ˈbɔɪ•ənt] o [ˈbujənt] *adj* boyante; alegre, animado

bur [bʌr] s erizo, vilano

burble ['bʌrbəl] s burbujeo ‖ intr burbujear

burden ['bʌrdən] s carga; (of a speech) tema m; (of a poem) estribillo ‖ tr cargar; agobiar, gravar

burden of proof s peso de la prueba

burdensome ['bʌrdənsəm] adj gravoso, oneroso

burdock ['bʌrdak] s bardana, cadillo

bureau ['bjuro] s cómoda; despacho, oficina; departamento, negociado

bureaucra•cy [bju'rakrəsi] s (pl -cies) burocracia; funcionariado

bureaucrat ['bjurə,kræt] s burócrata mf

bureaucratic [,bjurə'krætɪk] adj burocrático

burgess ['bʌrdʒɪs] s burgués m, ciudadano; alcalde m de un pueblo o villa

burglar ['bʌrglər] s escalador m

burglar alarm s alarma de ladrones

bur'glar•proof' adj a prueba de escaladores; antirrobo

burglar•y ['bʌrgləri] s (pl -ies) robo con escalamiento

Burgundian [bər'gʌndɪ•ən] adj & s borgoñón m

Burgundy ['bʌrgəndi] s la Borgoña; (wine) borgoña m

burial ['bɛrɪ•əl] s entierro

burial ground s cementerio

burlap ['bʌrlæp] s arpillera

burlesque [bər'lɛsk] adj burlesco, festivo ‖ s parodia ‖ tr parodiar

burlesque show s espectáculo de bailes y cantos groseros, music-hall m; bataclán m (SAm)

bur•ly ['bʌrli] adj (comp -lier; super -liest) fornido, corpulento, membrudo

Burma ['bʌrmə] s Birmania

Bur•mese [bər'miz] adj birmano ‖ s (pl -mese) birmano

burn [bʌrn] s quemadura, quemazón f ‖ v (pret & pp **burned** o **burnt** [bʌrnt]) tr quemar ‖ intr quemar, quemarse; estar encendido (p.ej., un faro); **to burn out** quemarse (un fusible); fundirse (una bombilla); **to burn within** requemarse

burner ['bʌrnər] s (of furnace) quemador m; (of gas fixture or lamp) mechero

burning ['bʌrnɪŋ] adj ardiente ‖ s quema, incendio

burning question s cuestión palpitante

burnish ['bʌrnɪʃ] s bruñido ‖ tr bruñir ‖ intr bruñirse

burnoose [bər'nus] s albornoz m

burnt almond [bʌrnt] s almendra tostada

burr [bʌr] s (of plant) erizo; (of cut in metal) rebaba

burrow ['bʌro] s madriguera, conejera ‖ tr hacer madrigueras en; socavar ‖ intr amadrigarse; esconderse

bursar ['bʌrsər] s tesorero universitario

burst [bʌrst] s explosión, reventón m, estallido; (of machine gun) ráfaga; salida brusca ‖ v (pret & pp **burst**) tr reventar ‖ intr reventar, reventarse; partirse (el corazón); **to burst into** irrumpir en (un cuarto); desatarse en (amenazas); prorrumpir en

(lágrimas); **to burst out crying** deshacerse en lágrimas; **to burst with laughter** reventar de risa

bur•y ['bɛri] v (pret & pp -ied) tr enterrar; **to be buried in thought** estar absorto en meditación; **to bury the hatchet** hacer la paz, echar pelillos a la mar

burying ground s cementerio

bus. abbr business

bus [bʌs] s (pl **busses** o **buses**) autobús m ‖ tr llevar en un autobús

bus boy s ayudante m de camarero

bus•by ['bʌzbi] s (pl -bies) morrión m de húsar, colbac m

bush [buʃ] s arbusto; (scrubby growth) matorral m, monte m; **to beat about the bush** andar con rodeos

bushel ['buʃəl] s medida para áridos (35,23 litros en E.U.A. y 36,35 litros en Inglaterra)

bushing ['buʃɪŋ] s buje m, forro

bush•y ['buʃi] adj (comp -ier; super -iest) arbustivo; peludo, lanudo; espeso

business ['bɪznɪs] adj comercial, de negocios ‖ s negocio, comercio; (company, concern) empresa; (job, employment) empleo, oficio; (matter) asunto, cuestión; (duty) obligación; (right) derecho; **on business** por negocios; **to have no business to** no tener derecho a; **to make it one's business to** proponerse; **to mean business** (coll) obrar en serio, hablar en serio; **to mind one's own business** no meterse en lo que no le importa a uno; **to send about one's business** mandar a paseo

business district s barrio comercial

businesslike ['bɪznɪs,laɪk] adj práctico, sistemático, serio

business•man ['bɪznɪs,mæn] s (pl -men [,mɛn]) comerciante m, hombre m de negocios

business suit s traje m de calle

bus•man ['bʌsmən] s (pl -men [mən]) conductor m de autobús

buss [bʌs] s (coll) beso sonado ‖ tr dar besos sonados a ‖ intr dar besos sonados; darse besos sonados

bust [bʌst] s busto; (of woman) pecho; (slang) fracaso, borrachera ‖ tr (slang) reventar, romper; (slang) arruinar; (slang) golpear, pegar ‖ intr (slang) reventar, fracasar

buster ['bʌstər] s muchachito

bustle ['bʌsəl] s (of woman's dress) polisón m; alboroto, bullicio ‖ intr ajetrearse, menearse

bus•y ['bɪzi] adj (comp -ier; super -iest) ocupado; (e.g., street) concurrido; (meddling) intruso, entremetido ‖ v (pret & pp -ied) tr ocupar; **to busy oneself with** ocuparse de

busybod•y ['bɪzɪ,badi] s (pl -ies) entremetido, fisgón m

busy signal s (telp) señal f de ocupado

but [bʌt] adv sólo, solamente, no . . . más que; **but for** a no ser por; **but little** muy poco ‖ prep excepto, salvo; **all but** casi ‖

conj pero; sino, p.ej., **nobody came but John** no vino sino Juan

butcher [ˈbʊtʃər] *s* carnicero; pesero (CAm, Col, Ven) ‖ *tr* matar (*reses para el consumo*); dar muerte a; (*to bungle*) chapucear

butcher knife *s* cuchilla de carnicero

butcher shop *s* carnicería; pesa (CAm, Col, Ven)

butcher·y [ˈbʊtʃəri] *s* (*pl* **-ies**) (*slaughterhouse*) matadero; (*wanton slaughter*) matanza, carnicería

butler [ˈbʌtlər] *s* despensero, mayordomo

butt [bʌt] *s* (*of gun*) culata; (*of cigaret*) colilla, punta; (*of horned animal*) cabezada, topetada, topetón *m*; (*target*) blanco; hazmerreír *m*; (*large cask*) pipa; (*rear end*) pompis *m* ‖ *tr* topar, topetar; acornear ‖ *intr* dar cabezadas; **to butt against** confinar con; **to butt in** (slang) entremeterse

butter [ˈbʌtər] *s* mantequilla ‖ *tr* untar con mantequilla; **to butter up** (coll) adular, lisonjear

but'ter·cup' *s* botón *m* de oro

butter dish *s* mantequillera

but'ter·fly' *s* (*pl* **-flies**) mariposa

butter knife *s* cuchillo mantequillero

but'ter·milk' *s* leche *f* de manteca

butter sauce *s* mantequilla fundida

but'ter·scotch' *s* bombón *m* escocés, bombón hecho con azúcar terciado y mantequilla

buttocks [ˈbʌtəks] *spl* nalgas; fundillo (Cuba, Mex)

button [ˈbʌtən] *s* botón *m* ‖ *tr* abotonar, abrocharse

but'ton·hole' *s* ojal *m* ‖ *tr* detener con conversación

but'ton·hook *s* abotonador *m*

but'ton·wood' **tree** *s* plátano de occidente

buttress [ˈbʌtrɪs] *s* contrafuerte *m*; (fig) apoyo, sostén *m* ‖ *tr* estribar; (fig) apoyar, sostener

butt weld *s* soldadura a tope

buxom [ˈbʌksəm] *adj* rolliza, frescachona

buy [baɪ] *s* (coll) compra; (*bargain*) (coll) ganga ‖ *v* (*pret* & *pp* **bought** [bɔt]) *tr* comprar; **to buy back** recomprar; **to buy off** comprar, sobornar; **to buy out** comprar la parte de (*un socio*); **to buy up** acaparar

buyer [ˈbaɪər] *s* comprador *m*

buzz [bʌz] *s* zumbido ‖ *intr* zumbar; **to buzz about** ajetrearse, cazcalear

buzzard [ˈbʌzərd] *s* alfaneque *m*

buzz bomb *s* bomba volante

buzzer [ˈbʌzər] *s* zumbador *m*

buzz saw *s* sierra circular

bx. *abbr* box

by [baɪ] *adv* cerca; a un lado; **by and by** luego ‖ *prep* por; cerca de, al lado de; (*not later than*) para; **by far** con mucho; **by the way** de paso; a propósito

by-and-by [ˈbaɪ·ənd·ˈbaɪ] *s* porvenir *m*

bye-bye [ˈbaɪ·ˈbaɪ] *s* mu *f*; **to go bye-bye** ir a la mu ‖ *interj* (coll) ¡adiosito!; (*to a child*) ¡ro ro!

bygone [ˈbaɪˌgɔn] o [ˈbaɪˌgɑn] *adj* pasado ‖ *s* pasado; **let bygones be bygones** olvidemos lo pasado

bylaw [ˈbaɪˌlɔ] *s* reglamento, estatuto

bypass [ˈbaɪˌpæs] *s* desviación; tubo de paso ‖ *tr* desviar; eludir

by'-prod'uct *s* subproducto, derivado

bystander [ˈbaɪˌstændər] *s* asistente *mf*, circunstante *mf*

byway [ˈbaɪˌwe] *s* camino apartado

byword [ˈbaɪˌwʌrd] *s* objeto de oprobio; refrán *m*, muletilla; apodo

Byzantine [ˈbɪzənˌtin] o [bɪˈzæntin] *adj* & *s* bizantino

Byzantium [bɪˈzænʃɪ·əm] o [bɪˈzæntɪ·əm] *s* Bizancio

C

C, c [si] tercera letra del alfabeto inglés

c. *abbr* **cent, center, centimeter**

C. *abbr* **centigrade, Congress, Court**

cab [kæb] *s* coche *m* de plaza o de punto; taxi *m*; (*of a truck*) casilla

cabaret [ˌkæbəˈre] *s* cabaret *m*

cabbage [ˈkæbɪdʒ] *s* col *f*, berza

cab driver *s* cochero de plaza; taxista *mf*

cabin [ˈkæbɪn] *s* (*hut, cottage*) cabaña; (aer) cabina; (naut) camarote *m*

cabin boy *s* mozo de cámara

cabinet [ˈkæbɪnɪt] *s* (*piece of furniture for displaying objects*) escaparate *m*, vitrina; (*for a radio*) caja, mueble *m*; (*closet*) armario; (*private room; ministry of a government*) gabinete *m*

cab'inet·ma'ker *s* ebanista *m*

cab'inet·ma'king *s* ebanistería

cable [ˈkebəl] *adj* cablegráfico ‖ *s* cable *m*; cablegrama *m* ‖ *tr* & *intr* cablegrafiar

cable address *s* dirección cablegráfica

cable car *s* tranvía *m* de tracción por cable

cablegram [ˈkebəlˌgræm] *s* cablegrama *m*

cable television *s* televisión por cable

caboose [kəˈbus] *s* (rr) furgón de cola

cab'stand' *s* punto de coches, punto de taxis

cache [kæʃ] *s* escondrijo; víveres escondidos ‖ *tr* depositar en un escondrijo; ocultar

cachet [kæˈʃe] *s* sello

cackle [ˈkækəl] *s* (*of a hen*) cacareo; (*idle talk*) charla ‖ *intr* cacarear; charlar

cac·tus [ˈkæktəs] *s* (*pl* **-tuses** o **-ti** [taɪ]) cacto

cad [kæd] *s* sinvergüenza *mf*; **to behave like a cad** tener mala leche

cadaver [kə'dævər] s cadáver m
cadaverous [kə'dævərəs] adj cadavérico
caddie ['kædi] s caddie m (muchacho que lleva los utensilios en el juego de golf) ‖ intr servir de caddie
cadence ['kedəns] s cadencia
cadet [kə'dɛt] s hermano menor, hijo menor; (student at military school) cadete m
cadmium ['kædmɪ•əm] s cadmio
cadre ['kædri] s (mil) cuadro
Caesar ['sizər] s César m
café [kæ'fe] s bar m, cabaret m; restaurante m
café society s gente f del mundo elegante que frecuenta los cabarets de moda
cafeteria [,kæfə'tɪrɪ•ə] s cafetería
cage [kedʒ] s jaula ‖ tr enjaular
cageling ['kedʒlɪŋ] s pájaro enjaulado
ca•gey ['kedʒi] adj (comp -gier; super -giest) (coll) astuto
cahoots [kə'huts] s — **to be in cahoots** (slang) confabularse (dos o más personas); **to go cahoots** (slang) entrar por partes iguales
Cain [ken] s Caín m; **to raise Cain** (slang) armar camorra
Cairo ['kaɪro] s El Cairo
caisson ['kesən] s cajón m de aire comprimido, esclusa de aire
cajole [kə'dʒol] tr adular, lisonjear, halagar
cajoler•y [kə'dʒoləri] s (pl -ies) adulación, lisonja, halago
cake [kek] s pastel m, bollo, queque m; (small cake) pastelillo; (sponge cake) bizcocho; (of fish) fritada; (of earth) terrón m; (of soap) pan m, pastilla; (of ice) témpano; **to take the cake** (coll) ser el colmo ‖ intr apelmazarse, aterronarse
calabash ['kælə,bæʃ] s calabacera; jícaro, (fruit) calabaza
calamitous [kə'læmɪtəs] adj calamitoso
calami•ty [kə'læmɪti] s (pl -ties) calamidad
calci•fy ['kælsɪ,faɪ] v (pret & pp -fied) calcificar ‖ intr calcificarse
calcium ['kælsɪ•əm] s calcio
calculate ['kælkjə,let] tr calcular; (to reckon) (coll) calcular ‖ intr calcular; **to calculate on** contar con
calculating ['kælkjə,letɪŋ] adj de calcular; astuto, intrigante
calculating machine s calculadora, máquina de calcular
calcu•lus ['kælkjələs] s (pl -luses o -li [,laɪ]) (math, pathol) cálculo
caldron ['kɔldrən] s calderón m
calendar ['kæləndər] s calendario, almanaque m
calf [kæf] o [kɑf] s (pl calves [kævz] o [kɑvz]) ternero; (of the leg) pantorrilla
calf'skin' s becerro, becerrillo
caliber ['kælɪbər] s calibre m
calibrate ['kælɪ,bret] tr calibrar
cali•co ['kælɪ,ko] s (pl -coes o -cos) calicó m, indiana
California [,kælɪ'fɔrnɪ•ə] s California
calipers ['kælɪpərz] spl calibrador m, compás m de calibres
caliph ['kelɪf] o ['kælɪf] s califa m

caliphate ['kælɪ,fet] s califato
calisthenic [,kælɪs'θɛnɪk] adj calisténico ‖ **calisthenics** spl calistenia
calk [kɔk] tr calafatear
calking ['kɔkɪŋ] s calafateo
call [kɔl] s llamada; visita; (of a boat or airplane) escala; vocación; (within call al alcance de la voz ‖ tr llamar; convocar (p.ej., una huelga); **to call back** mandar volver; **to call down** (coll) reprender, regañar; **to call in** hacer entrar; (from circulation) retirar; **to call off** aplazar, suspender; desconvocar; **to call out** llamar (a uno) que salga; **to call together** convocar, reunir; **to call up** llamar por teléfono; evocar, recordar ‖ intr llamar, gritar; hacer una visita; (naut) hacer escala; **to call on** acudir a; visitar; **to call out** gritar; **to go calling** ir de visitas
calla lily ['kælə] s cala, lirio de agua
call bell s timbre m de llamada
call'boy' s (in a hotel) botones m; (theat) traspunte m
caller ['kɔlər] s visitante mf
call girl s chica de cita
calling ['kɔlɪŋ] s profesión, vocación
calling card s tarjeta de visita
calliope [kə'laɪ•əpi] o ['kælɪ•op] s (mus) órgano de vapor ‖ **Calliope** [kə'laɪ•əpi] s Calíope f
call number s número de teléfono; (of a book) número de clasificación
callous ['kæləs] adj calloso; (fig) duro, insensible
call to arms s — **to sound the call to arms** (mil) batir o tocar a llamada
call to the colors s (mil) llamada a filas
callus ['kæləs] s callo
calm [kɑm] adj tranquilo, quieto; (sea) bonancible ‖ s tranquilidad, calma ‖ tr tranquilizar, calmar ‖ intr — **to calm down** tranquilizarse, calmarse; abonanzar, calmar (el viento, el tiempo)
calmness ['kɑmnɪs] s tranquilidad, calma
calorie ['kæləri] s caloría
calum•ny ['kæləmni] s (pl -nies) calumnia
calva•ry ['kælvəri] s (pl -ries) (at the entrance to a town) humilladero ‖ **Calvary** s Calvario
calyp•so [kə'lɪpso] s (pl -sos) calipso ‖ **Calypso** s Calipso f
cam [kæm] s leva
cambric ['kembrɪk] s batista
camel ['kæməl] s camello
came•o ['kæmɪ•o] s (pl -os) camafeo
camera ['kæmərə] s cámara fotográfica, máquina fotográfica
camera•man ['kæmərə,mæn] s (pl -men [,mɛn]) camarógrafo, tomavistas m
camomile ['kæmə,maɪl] s manzanilla
camouflage ['kæmə,flɑʒ] s camuflaje m ‖ tr camuflar
camp [kæmp] s campamento ‖ intr acampar
campaign [kæm'pen] s campaña ‖ intr hacer campaña
campaigner [kæm'penər] s propagandista mf; veterano

bu
ca

camp'fire' s hoguera de campamento

camphor ['kæmfər] s alcanfor m

camp'stool' s silla de tijera, catrecillo

campus ['kæmpəs] s terrenos, recinto (de la universidad)

cam'shaft' s árbol m de levas

can [kæn] s bote m, envase m, lata ‖ v (pret & pp canned; ger canning) tr envasar, enlatar ‖ v (pret & cond could) v aux he can come tomorrow puede venir mañana; can you swim? ¿sabe Vd. nadar?

Canada ['kænədə] s el Canadá

Canadian [kə'nedɪ•ən] adj & s canadiense

canal [kə'næl] s canal m

canar•y [kə'nɛri] s (pl -ies) canario ‖ Canaries spl Canarias

can•cel ['kænsəl] v (pret & pp -celed o -celled; ger -celing o -celling) tr cancelar, eliminar, suprimir; matasellar, obliterar (sellos de correo)

canceler ['kænsələr] s matasellos m

cancellation [,kænsə'leʃən] s cancelación, eliminación, supresión; revocatoria; (of stamps) obliteración

cancer ['kænsər] s cáncer m; Cancer s (astr) Cáncer m

cancerous ['kænsərəs] adj canceroso

candela•brum [,kændə'lebrəm] s (pl -bra [brə] o -brums) candelabro

candid ['kændɪd] adj franco, sincero; imparcial

candida•cy ['kændɪdəsi] s (pl -cies) candidatura

candidate ['kændɪ,det] s candidato; (for a degree) graduando

candid camera s cámara indiscreta

candle ['kændəl] s bujía, candela, vela

can'dle•hold'er s candelero

can'dle•light' s luz f de vela; crepúsculo

candle power s bujía

can'dle•stick' s palmatoria

candor ['kændər] s franqueza, sinceridad; imparcialidad

can•dy ['kændi] s (pl -dies) bombón m, confite m, dulce m; dulces mpl ‖ v (pret & pp -died) tr almibarar, confitar, garapiñar ‖ intr almibararse

candy box s bombonera, confitera

candy store s confitería, dulcería

cane [ken] s (plant; stem) caña; (walking stick) bastón m; (for chair seats) junco, mimbre m, rejilla

cane seat s asiento de rejilla

cane sugar s azúcar m de caña

canine ['kenaɪn] adj canino ‖ s (tooth) canino; perro

canned goods spl conservas alimenticias

canner•y ['kænəri] s (pl -ies) conservera, fábrica de conservas

cannibal ['kænɪbəl] adj & s caníbal mf

canning ['kænɪŋ] adj conservero ‖ s conservería

cannon ['kænən] s cañón m; cañones

cannonade [,kænə'ned] s cañoneo ‖ tr cañonear

cannon ball s bala de cañón

cannon fodder s carne f de cañón

can•ny ['kæni] adj (comp -nier; super -niest) cauteloso, cuerdo; astuto

canoe [kə'nu] s canoa; bongo (SAm)

canoeing [kə'nu•ɪŋ] s piraguismo

canoeist [kə'nu•ɪst] s canoero

canon ['kænən] s canon m; (priest) canónigo

canonical [kə'nɑnɪkəl] adj canónico; aceptado, auténtico, establecido ‖ canonicals spl vestiduras sacerdotales

canonize ['kænə,naɪz] tr canonizar

canon law s cánones mpl, derecho canónico

canon•ry ['kænənri] s (pl -ries) canonjía

can opener ['opənər] s abrelatas m

cano•py ['kænəpi] s (pl -pies) dosel m, pabellón m; (over an entrance) marquesina; (for electrical fixtures) campana

canopy of heaven s bóveda celeste

cant [kænt] s hipocresía; jerga, jerigonza

cantaloupe ['kæntə,lop] s cantalupo

cantankerous [kæn'tæŋkərəs] adj de mal genio, pendenciero

canteen [kæn'tin] s (shop) cantina; (water flask) cantimplora; (mil) centro de recreo

canter ['kæntər] s medio galope ‖ intr ir a medio galope

canticle ['kæntɪkəl] s cántico

cantilever ['kæntɪ,livər] adj voladizo ‖ s viga voladiza

cantle ['kæntəl] s arzón trasero

canton [kæn'tɑn] tr acantonar

cantonment [kæn'tɑnmənt] s acantonamiento

cantor ['kæntər] s chantre m; (in a synagogue) cantor m principal

canvas ['kænvəs] s cañamazo, lona; (naut) vela, lona; (painting) lienzo; under canvas (mil) en tiendas; (naut) con las velas izadas

canvass ['kænvəs] s pesquisa, escrutinio; (of votes) solicitación ‖ tr escrutar, solicitar; discutir detenidamente

canyon ['kænjən] s cañón m

cap. abbr capital, capitalize

cap [kæp] s gorra, gorra de visera; (of academic costume) birrete m; (of bottle) cápsula; (e.g., of a fountain pen) capuchón m ‖ v (pret & pp capped; ger capping) tr cubrir con gorra; capsular (una botella); to cap the climax ser el colmo

capabili•ty [,kepə'bɪlɪti] s (pl -ties) habilidad, capacidad

capable ['kepəbəl] adj hábil, capaz

capacious [kə'peʃəs] adj espacioso, capaz

capaci•ty [kə'pæsɪti] s (pl -ties) (room, space; ability, aptitude) capacidad; (status, function) calidad; in the capacity of en calidad de

cap and bells spl caperuza de bufón; cetro de la locura

cap and gown s birrete y toga

caparison [kə'pærɪsən] s caparazón m ‖ tr engualdrapar

cape [kep] s cabo, promontorio; (garment) capa, esclavina

Cape Colony s la Colonia del Cabo

Cape Horn s el Cabo de Hornos

Cape of Good Hope s Cabo de Buena Esperanza

caper [ˈkepər] s (*gay jump*) cabriola; (*prank*) travesura; **to cut capers** dar cabriolas; hacer travesuras ‖ *intr* cabriolear; retozar

Capeˈtownˈ o **Cape Town** s El Cabo, la Ciudad del Cabo

capeˈworkˈ s (taur) suerte *f* de capa, lance *m*

capital [ˈkæpɪtəl] *adj* capital ‖ s (*money*) capital *m*; (*city*) capital *f*; (*top of a column*) capitel *m*; **to make capital out of** sacar beneficio de

capital flight s fuga de capitales

capitalism [[ˈkæpɪtə,lɪzəm] s capitalismo

capitalize [ˈkæpɪtə,laɪz] *tr* escribir con mayúscula; capitalizar ‖ *intr* — **to capitalize on** aprovecharse de

capital letter s letra mayúscula

capital punishment s pena capital, último suplicio

capitol [ˈkæpɪtəl] s capitolio

capitulate [kəˈpɪtʃə,let] *intr* capitular

capon [ˈkepɑn] s capón *m*

caprice [kəˈpris] s capricho, antojo; veleidad

capricious [kəˈprɪʃəs] *adj* caprichoso, antojadizo

Capricorn [ˈkæprɪ,kɔrn] s (astr) Capricornio

capsize [ˈkæpsaɪz] *tr* volcar ‖ *intr* volcar; tumbar, zozobrar (*un barco*)

capstan [ˈkæpstən] s cabrestante *m*

capˈstoneˈ s coronamiento

capsule [ˈkæpsəl] s cápsula

Capt. *abbr* **Captain**

captain [ˈkæptən] s capitán *m* ‖ *tr* capitanear

captain·cy [ˈkæptənsi] s (*pl* **-cies**) capitanía

caption [ˈkæpʃən] s título; (*in a movie*) subtítulo

captivate [ˈkæptɪ,vet] *tr* cautivar, encantar

captive [ˈkæptɪv] *adj* & s cautivo

captivi·ty [kæpˈtɪvɪti] s (*pl* **-ties**) cautividad, cautiverio

captor [ˈkæptər] s aprenhensor *m*

capture [ˈkæptʃər] s apresamiento, captura; (*of a stronghold*) toma ‖ *tr* apresar, capturar; tomar (*una plaza*); captar (*p.ej., la atención de una persona*)

Capuchin nun [ˈkæpjutʃɪn] o [ˈkæpjuʃɪn] s capuchina

car [kɑr] s coche *m*; (*of an elevator*) caja, carro

carafe [kəˈræf] s garrafa

caramel [ˈkærəməl] o [ˈkɑrməl] s (*burnt sugar*) caramelo; bombón *m* de caramelo

carat [ˈkærət] s quilate *m*

caravan [ˈkærə,væn] s caravana

caravansa·ry [,kærəˈvænsəri] s (*pl* **-ries**) caravanera

caraway [ˈkærə,we] s alcaravea

carˈbarnˈ s cochera de tranvías

carbide [ˈkɑrbaɪd] s carburo

carbine [ˈkɑrbaɪn] s carabina

carbolic acid [kɑrˈbɑlɪk] s ácido carbólico

car bomb s coche bomba

carbon [ˈkɑrbən] s (*chemical element*) carbono; (*pole of arc light or battery*) carbón *m*; papel *m* carbón; (*in auto cylinders*) carbonilla

carbon copy s copia al carbón

carbon dioxide s dióxido de carbono

carbon monoxide s óxido de carbono, monóxido de carbono

carbon paper s papel *m* carbón

carˈboyˈ s bombona, garrafón *m*

carbuncle [ˈkɑrbʌŋkəl] s (*stone*) carbunclo, carbúnculo; (*pathol*) carbunclo, carbunco

carburetor [ˈkɑrbə,retər] s carburador *m*

car caller s avisacoches *m*

carcass [ˈkɑrkəs] s res muerta, cadáver *m*

carcinogen [kɑrˈsɪnəjən] s carcinógeno

carcinoma [,kɑrsəˈnomə] s carcinoma

card [kɑrd] s tarjeta; (*for playing games*) naipe *m*, carta; (*for filing*) ficha; (*person*) (coll) sujeto, tipo

cardˈboardˈ s cartón *m*

cardboard binding s encuadernación en pasta

card case s tarjetero

card catalogue s catálogo de fichas

cardiac [ˈkɑrdɪ,æk] *adj* cardíaco ‖ s (*medicine; sufferer*) cardíaco

cardigan [ˈkɑrdɪgən] s albornoz *m*, rebeca

cardinal [ˈkɑrdɪnəl] *adj* cardinal; purpurado ‖ s (*prelate; bird*) cardenal *m*; número cardinal

card index s fichero, tarjetero

card party s tertulia de baraja

cardˈsharpˈ s fullero, tahur *m*

card trick s truco de naipes

care [kɛr] s (*worry*) inquietud, ansiedad; (*watchful attention*) esmero; (*charge*) cargo, custodia; **care of** suplicada en casa de; **to take care of oneself** cuidarse ‖ *intr* inquietarse, preocuparse; **to care for** cuidar de; amar, querer; **to care to** tener ganas de; **I couldn't care less** me importe un pepino

careen [kəˈrin] *intr* inclinarse; mecerse precipitadamente

career [kəˈrɪr] *adj* de carrera ‖ s carrera

careˈfreeˈ *adj* despreocupado, libre de cuidados

careful [ˈkɛrfəl] *adj* (*acting with care*) cuidadoso; (*done with care*) esmerado; **to be careful to** cuidarse de

careless [ˈkɛrlɪs] *adj* descuidado, negligente

carelessness [ˈkɛrlɪsnɪs] s descuido, negligencia

car enthusiast s devoto del volante

caress [kəˈrɛs] s caricia ‖ *tr* acariciar ‖ *intr* acariciarse

caretaker [ˈkɛr,tekər] s curador *m*, guardián *m*, custodio

careˈwornˈ *adj* fatigado, rendido

carˈfareˈ s pasaje *m* de tranvía o autobús

car·go [ˈkɑrgo] s (*pl* **-goes** o **-gos**) carga, cargamento

cargo boat s barco de carga

Caribbean [,kærɪˈbiən] o [kəˈrɪbi·ən] *adj* caribe ‖ s mar *m* Caribe

caricature [ˈkærɪkətʃər] s caricatura ‖ *tr* caricaturizar

caricaturist [ˈkærɪkətʃərɪst] s caricaturista *mf*

carillon [ˈkærɪ,lɑn] o [kəˈrɪljən] s carillón *m*

carˈloadˈ s furgonada, vagonada

ca
ca

carnage ['karnɪdʒ] s carnicería, matanza

carnation [kar'neʃən] adj encarnado ‖ s clavel m, clavel reventón

carnival ['karnɪvəl] adj carnavalesco ‖ s (period before Lent) carnaval m; verbena, espectáculo de atracciones

car•ol ['kærəl] s canción alegre, villancico ‖ v (pret & pp -oled o -olled; ger -oling o -olling); tr celebrar con villancicos ‖ intr cantar con alegría

carom ['kærəm] s carambola ‖ intr carambolear

carousal [kə'rauzəl] s juerga, borrachera, jarana

carouse [kə'rauz] intr emborracharse, jaranear

carp [karp] s (pez) carpa ‖ intr quejarse

carpenter ['karpəntər] s carpintero

carpentry ['karpəntri] s carpintería

carpet ['karpɪt] s alfombra; **to be on the carpet** estar sobre el tapete ‖ tr alfombrar

carpet sweeper s barredora de alfombras

car'-rent'al service s alquiler m de coches

carriage ['kærɪdʒ] s carruaje m; (cost of carrying) porte m, transporte m; (bearing) porte m, continente m; (mach) carro

carrier ['kærɪ•ər] s portador m, transportador m; portador de gérmenes; empresa de transportes; (mailman) cartero; vendedor m de periódicos; portaaviones m; (rad) onda portadora

carrier pigeon s paloma mensajera

carrier wave s (rad) onda portadora

carrion ['kærɪ•ən] adj carroño; inmundo ‖ s carroña; inmundicia

carrot ['kærət] s zanahoria

carrousel [,kærə'zɛl] s caballitos, tiovivo

car•ry ['kæri] v (pret & pp -ried) tr llevar, portar, traer; transportar; sostener (una carga); **to carry away** llevarse; encantar, entusiasmar; **to carry into effect** llevar a cabo; **to carry one's point** salirse con la suya; **to carry out** llevar a cabo; **to carry the day** quedar victorioso, ganar la palma; **to carry weight** ser de peso ‖ intr tener alcance; **to carry on** continuar, perseverar; (coll) travesear; (coll) comportarse de un modo escandaloso; (coll) hacer locuras

cart [kart] s carreta, carro ‖ tr carretear

carte blanche ['kart'blanʃ] s carta blanca

cartel [kar'tɛl] s cartel m

Carthage ['karθɪdʒ] s Cartago

Carthaginian [,karθə'dʒɪnɪ•ən] adj & s cartaginés m

cart horse s caballo de tiro

cartilage ['kartɪlɪdʒ] s cartílago

cartoon [kar'tun] s caricatura; (comic strip) tira cómica; (film) película de dibujos ‖ tr caricaturizar

cartoonist [kar'tunɪst] s caricaturista mf

cartridge ['kartrɪdʒ] s cartucho

cartridge belt s canana

carve [karv] tr trinchar (carne); esculpir, tallar

carving knife ['karvɪŋ] s cuchillo de trinchar

car washer s lavacoches m

caryatid [,kærɪ'ætɪd] s cariátide f

cascade [kæs'ked] s cascada

case [kes] s (instance; form of a word) caso; (box) caja; (small container) estuche m; (for cigarettes) pitillera; (sheath) vaina, funda; (law) causa, pleito; **in case** caso que; **in no case** de ninguna manera ‖ tr encajonar, enfundar

casement ['kesmənt] s ventana batiente; bastidor m (de la ventana)

cash [kæʃ] s dinero contante; pago al contado; **cash on delivery** contra reembolso, pago contra entrega; **to pay cash** pagar al contado ‖ tr cobrar (un cheque el portador); abonar, pagar (un cheque el banco) ‖ intr — **to cash in on** (coll) sacar provecho de

cash and carry s pago al contado con transporte a cargo del comprador

cash'box' s caja

cashew ['kæʃu] s anacardo, marañón m

cashew nut s anacardo, nuez f de marañón

cashier [kæ'ʃɪr] s cajero ‖ tr destruir; (in the army) degradar

cashier's check s cheque m de caja

cashier's desk s caja

cashmere ['kæʃmɪr] s casimir m, cachemir m

cash on hand s efectivo en caja

cash payment s pago al contado

cash purchase s compra al contado

cash register s caja registradora

casing ['kesɪŋ] s caja, cubierta, envoltura; (of door or window) marco, cerco; (of tire) cubierta; (sew) jareta

cask [kæsk] s casco, pipa, tonel m

casket ['kæskɪt] s (box for valuables) cajita, joyero; (coffin) caja, ataúd m

cassava [kə'savə] s cazabe m, casabe m

casserole ['kæsə,rol] s cacerola; (dish cooked in a casserole) timbal m

cassette [kæ'sɛt] s casete m

cassette player s grabador-reproductor m

cassock ['kæsək] s balandrán m, sotana

cast [kæst] s echada, tiro; forma, molde m; aire m, semblante m; matiz m, tinte m; (of actors) reparto ‖ v (pret & pp cast) tr echar, tirar; volver (los ojos); proyectar (una sombra); colar, fundir (metales); depositar (votos); echar (suertes); (theat) repartir (papeles); **to cast aside** desechar; **to cast loose** soltar; **to cast out** arrojar, echar fuera; despedir, desterrar ‖ intr echar los dados; arrojar el sedal o el anzuelo; **to cast about** revolver proyectos; **to cast off** (naut) soltar las amarras

castanet [,kæstə'nɛt] s castañuela, castañeta

cast'a•way' adj & s proscrito, réprobo; náufrago

caste [kæst] s casta; **to lose caste** desprestigiarse

caster ['kæstər] s ruedecilla de mueble; (cruet stand) angarillas, vinagreras; frasco

Castile [kæs'til] s Castilla

Castile soap s jabón m de Castilla

Castilian [kæs'tɪljən] adj & s castellano

casting ['kæstɪŋ] s fundición, pieza fundida; (theat) reparto

casting vote s voto de calidad

cast iron _s_ hierro colado, hierro fundido
cast'-i'ron _adj_ de hierro colado; fuerte, endurecido; duro, inflexible
castle ['kæsəl] _s_ castillo; (chess) roque _m_, torre _f_ ‖ _tr & intr_ (chess) enrocar
castle in Spain o **castle in the air** _s_ castillo en el aire
cast'off' _adj_ abandonado, desechado; (_clothing_) de desecho ‖ _s_ desecho
castor oil ['kæstər] _s_ aceite _m_ de ricino
castrate ['kæstret] _tr_ capar, castrar
casual ['kæʒu•əl] _adj_ casual, fortuito; descuidado, indiferente
casual•ty ['kæʒu•əlti] _s_ (_pl_ **-ties**) desgracia, accidente _m;_ accidentado, víctima; (_in war_) baja
casualty list _s_ lista de bajas
cat. _abbr_ **catalogue, catechism**
cat [kæt] _s_ gato; mujer maligna; **to bell the cat** ponerle cascabel al gato; **to let the cat out of the bag** revelar el secreto
catacomb ['kætə,kom] _s_ catacumba
Catalan ['kætə,læn] _adj & s_ catalán _m_
catalogue ['kætə,lɔg] o ['kætə,lag] _s_ catálogo ‖ _tr_ catalogar
Catalonia [,kætə'loni•ə] _s_ Cataluña
Catalonian [,kætə'loni•ən] _adj & s_ catalán _m_
catapult ['kætə,pʌlt] _s_ catapulta ‖ _tr_ catapultar
cataract ['kætə,rækt] _s_ catarata; (pathol) catarata
catarrh [kə'tɑr] _s_ catarro
catastrophe [kə'tæstrəfi] _s_ catástrofe _f_
cat'call' _s_ rechifla ‖ _tr & intr_ rechiflar
catch [kætʃ] _s_ (_of a ball_) cogida; (_of fish_) pesca; (_of a lock_) cerradera, pestillo; (_booty_) botín _m_, presa; (_fastener_) broche _m;_ (_good match_) buen partido ‖ _v_ (_pret & pp_ **caught** [kɔt]) _tr_ asir, coger, atrapar; llegar a oír; coger (_un resfriado_); (_to come upon suddenly_) sorprender; comprender; capturar (_al delincuente_); **to catch fire** encenderse; **to catch hold of** agarrar, coger, apoderarse de; **to catch it** (coll) merecerse un regaño; **to catch oneself** contenerse; recobrar el equilibrio; **to catch sight of** alcanzar a ver; **to catch up** arrebatar; coger al vuelo; (_in a mistake_) cazar ‖ _intr_ pegarse (_una enfermedad_); enredarse; encenderse; **to catch at** agarrarse a, tratar de asir; **to catch on** prender en (_p.ej., un gancho_); comprender, coger el tino; **to catch up** salir del atraso; (_in one's debts_) ponerse al día; **to catch up with** emparejar con
catcher ['kætʃər] _s_ (baseball) receptor, parador _m_
catching ['kætʃɪŋ] _adj_ pegajoso, contagioso; atrayente, cautivador
catch question _s_ pega
catchup ['kætʃəp] _s_ salsa de tomate condimentada
catch'word' _s_ lema _m_, palabra de efecto; (_actor's cue_) pie _m;_ (typ) reclamo
catch•y ['kætʃi] _adj_ (_comp_ **-ier;** _super_ **-iest**) (_tune_) animado, vivo; (_title of a book_) impresionante, llamativo; (_question_) intrincado; (_breathing_) espasmódico

catechism ['kætɪ,kɪzəm] _s_ catecismo
catego•ry ['kætɪ,gori] _s_ (_pl_ **-ries**) categoría; (_sports_) division
cater ['ketər] _tr & intr_ abastecer, proveer; **to cater to** proveer a
cater-cornered ['kætər,kɔrnərd] _adj_ diagonal ‖ _adv_ diagonalmente
caterer ['ketərər] _s_ abastecedor _m_, proveedor _m_ de alimentos (_esp. para fiestas caseras_)
caterpillar ['kætər,pɪlər] _s_ oruga
caterpillar tractor _s_ tractor _m_ de oruga
cat'fish' _s_ bagre _m_
cat'gut' _s_ (mus) cuerda de tripa; (surg) catgut _m_
Cath. _abbr_ **Catholic**
cathartic [kə'θɑrtɪk] _adj & s_ catártico
cathedral [kə'θidrəl] _s_ catedral _f_
catheter ['kæθɪtər] _s_ catéter _m_
catheterize ['kæθɪtə,raɪz] _tr_ cateterizar
cathode ['kæθod] _s_ cátodo
catholic ['kæθəlɪk] _adj_ católico ‖ **Catholic** _adj & s_ católico
catkin ['kætkɪn] _s_ candelilla, amento
cat nap _s_ sueñecito
catnip ['kætnɪp] _s_ hierba gatera, nébeda
cat-o'-nine-tails [,kætə'naɪn,telz] _s_ azote _m_ con nueve ramales
cat's cradle _s_ juego de la cuna
cat's-paw o **catspaw** ['kæts,pɔ] _s_ mano _f_ de gato, instrumento
catsup ['kætsəp] o [kɛtʃəp] _s_ salsa de tomate condimentada
cat'tail' _s_ anea, espadaña; amento
cattle ['kætəl] _s_ ganado vacuno
cattle crossing _s_ paso de ganado
cattle•man ['kætəlmən] _s_ (_pl_ **-men** [mən]) _s_ ganadero
cattle raising _s_ ganadería
cattle ranch _s_ hacienda de ganado
cat•ty ['kæti] _adj_ (_comp_ **-tier;** _super_ **-tiest**) (_like a cat_) felino, gatuno; (_spiteful_) malicioso; (_gossipy_) chismoso
cat'walk' _s_ pasadero, pasarela
Caucasian [kɔ'keʒən] _adj & s_ caucasiano, caucásico
Caucasus ['kɔkəsəs] _s_ Cáucaso
caucus ['kɔkəs] _s_ junta de políticos
cauliflower ['kɔlɪ,flau•ər] _s_ coliflor _f_
cause [kɔz] _s_ causa; (_person_) causante _mf_ ‖ _tr_ causar
cause'way' _s_ (_highway_) calzada; calzada elevada
caustic ['kɔstɪk] _adj_ cáustico
cauterize ['kɔtə,raɪz] _tr_ cauterizar
caution ['kɔʃən] _s_ (_carefulness_) cautela; (_warning_) advertencia, amonestación ‖ _tr_ advertir, amonestar
cautious ['kɔʃəs] _adj_ cauteloso, cauto
Cav. _abbr_ **Cavalry**
cavalcade [,kævəl'ked] o ['kævəl,ked] _s_ cabalgata
cavalier [,kævə'lɪr] _adj_ (_haughty_) altivo, desdeñoso; (_offhand_) alegre, desenvuelto, inceremonioso ‖ _s_ (_horseman_) caballero; (_lady's escort_) galán _m_
caval•ry ['kævəlri] _s_ (_pl_ **-ries**) caballería

ca
ca

cavalry•man ['kævəlrimən] s (pl -men [mən]) soldado de caballería

cave [kev] s cueva, caverna ‖ intr — to cave in hundirse; (to give in, yield) (coll) ceder, rendirse

cave'-in' s hundimiento, derrumbe m, socavón m

cave man s hombre grosero

cavern ['kævərn] s caverna

cav•il ['kævɪl] v (pret & pp -iled o -illed; ger -iling o -illing) intr buscar quisquillas

cavi•ty ['kævɪti] s (pl -ties) cavidad; (in a tooth) picadura

cavort [kə'gɔrt] intr (coll) cabriolar

caw [kɔ] s graznido ‖ intr graznar

CB abbr **citizens band**

cc. abbr **cubic centimeter**

CD abbr **compact disk**

cease [sis] tr parar, suspender ‖ intr cesar; cesar de, dejar de + inf

cease'fire' s cese m de fuego ‖ intr suspender hostilidades

ceaseless ['sislɪs] adj incesante, continuo

cedar ['sidər] s ced. o

cede [sid] tr ceder, traspasar

ceiling ['silɪŋ] s techo, cielo raso; (aer) techo, cielo máximo

ceiling price s precio tope

celebrant ['sɛlɪbrənt] s celebrante m

celebrate ['sɛlɪ,bret] tr celebrar ‖ intr (to say mass) celebrar; divertirse, festejarse; farrear

celebrated ['sɛlɪ,bretɪd] adj célebre, renombrado

celebration [,sɛlɪ'breʃən] s celebración; diversión, festividad

celebri•ty [sɪ'lɛbrɪti] s (pl -ties) (fame; famous person) celebridad

celery ['sɛləri] s apio

celestial [sɪ'lɛstʃəl] adj celeste, celestial

celiba•cy ['sɛlɪbəsi] s (pl -cies) celibato

celibate ['sɛlɪbɪt] adj & s célibe mf

cell [sɛl] s (of convent or jail) celda; (of honeycomb) celdilla; (of electric battery) elemento; (of plant or animal; of photo-electric device; of political group) célula

cellar ['sɛlər] s sótano; (for wine) bodega

cellaret [,sɛlə'rɛt] s licorera

cell house s prisión celular

cellist o **'cellist** ['tʃɛlɪst] s violoncelista mf

cel•lo o **'cel•lo** ['tʃɛlo] s (pl -los) violoncelo

cellophane ['sɛlə,fen] s celofán m

celluloid ['sɛljə,lɔɪd] s celuloide m

Celt [sɛlt] o [kɛlt] s celta mf

Celtic ['sɛltɪk] o ['kɛltɪk] adj céltico ‖ s (language) celta m

cement [sɪ'mɛnt] s cemento ‖ tr revestir con cemento; (la amistad) consolidar

cemeter•y ['sɛmɪ,tɛri] s (pl -ies) cementerio

cen. abbr **central**

censer ['sɛnsər] s incensario

censor ['sɛnsər] s censor m ‖ tr censurar

censure ['sɛnʃər] s censura ‖ tr censurar

census ['sɛnsəs] s censo; **to take the census** levantar el censo

cent. abbr **centigrade, central, century**

cent [sɛnt] s centavo

centaur ['sɛntɔr] s centauro

centennial [sɛn'tɛnɪ•əl] adj & s centenario

center ['sɛntər] adj centrista ‖ s centro ‖ tr centrar

center half s (ball games) medio centro

cen'ter•piece' s centro de mesa

center punch s granete m, punzón m de marcar

centigrade ['sɛntɪ,gred] adj centígrado

centimeter ['sɛntɪ,mitər] s centímetro

centipede ['sɛntɪ,pid] s ciempiés m

central ['sɛntrəl] adj central ‖ s (telp) central f, central de teléfonos; (operator) telefonista mf

Central America s Centro América, la América Central

Central American adj & mf centroamericano

centralize ['sɛntrə,laɪz] tr centralizar ‖ intr centralizarse

centrifuge ['sɛntrəfjudʒ] s centrifugadora

centu•ry ['sɛntʃəri] s (pl -ries) siglo

century plant s pita, maguey m

ceramic [sɪ'ræmɪk] adj cerámico

cereal ['sɪrɪ•əl] adj & s cereal m

ceremonious [,sɛrɪ'monɪ•əs] adj ceremonioso, etiquetero

ceremo•ny ['sɛrɪ,moni] s (pl -nies) ceremonia; **to stand on ceremony** hacer ceremonias, ser etiquetero

certain ['sʌrtən] adj cierto; **a certain** cierto; **for certain** por cierto

certainly ['sʌrtənli] adv ciertamente; (gladly) con mucho gusto

certain•ty ['sʌrtənti] s (pl -ties) certeza; **with certainty** a ciencia cierta

certificate [sər'tɪfɪkɪt] s certificación, certificado; (of birth, death, etc.) partida, fe f; (document representing financial assets) título ‖ [sər'tɪfɪ,ket] tr certificar

certified public accountant ['sʌrtɪ,faɪd] s contador público, censor jurado de cuentas

certi•fy ['sʌrtɪ,faɪ] v (pret & pp -fied) tr certificar

cervix ['sʌrvɪks] s (pl cervices [sər'vaɪsiz]) cerviz f

cessation [sɛ'seʃən] s cesación

cessation of hostilities s suspensión de hostilidades

cesspool ['sɛs,pul] s pozo negro; (fig) sitio inmundo

Ceylon [sɪ'lɑn] s Ceilán m

Ceylo•nese [,silə'niz] adj ceilanés ‖ s (pl -nese) ceilanés m

cf. abbr **confer,** i.e., **compare**

C.F.I., c.f.i. abbr **cost, freight, and insurance**

cg. abbr **centigram**

ch. abbr **chapter, church**

chafe [tʃef] s fricción, roce m; desgaste m; irritación ‖ tr (to rub) frotar; (to rub and make sore) escocer; (to wear) desgastar; irritar ‖ intr escocerse; desgastarse; irritarse

chaff [tʃæf] s barcia; paja menuda; broza, desperdicio

chafing dish ['tʃefɪŋ] s cocinilla, infernillo

ca
ch

chagrin [ʃə'grɪn] *s* desazón *f*, disgusto ‖ *tr* desazonar, disgustar
chain [tʃen] *s* cadena ‖ *tr* encadenar
chain gang *s* cadena de presidiarios, collera, cuerda de presos
chain reaction *s* reacción en cadena
chain′smoke′ *intr* fumar un pitillo tras otro
chain store *s* empresa con una cadena de tiendas; tienda de una cadena de tiendas
chair [tʃɛr] *s* silla; *(de catedrático)* cátedra; presidencia; **to take the chair** presidir la reunión; abrir la sesión ‖ *tr* presidir *(una reunión)*
chair lift *s* telesilla
chair·man ['tʃɛrmən] *s* *(pl* -**men** [mən]) presidente *m*
chairmanship ['tʃɛrmən,ʃɪp] *s* presidencia
chair rail *s* guardasilla
chalice ['tʃælɪs] *s* cáliz *m*
chalk [tʃɔk] *s* *(soft white limestone)* creta; *(piece used for writing)* tiza ‖ *tr* marcar o escribir con tiza; **to chalk up** apuntar; marcar *(un tanto)*
challenge ['tʃælɪndʒ] *s* desafío; *(law)* recusación ‖ *tr* desafiar; *(law)* recusar
chamber ['tʃembər] *s* cámara; *(of a gun)* recámara; dormitorio; **chambers** oficina de juez
chamberlain ['tʃembərlɪn] *s* chambelán *m*
cham′ber·maid′ *s* camarera
chamber pot *s* orinal *m*
chameleon [kə'milɪ·ən] *s* camaleón *m*
chamfer ['tʃæmfər] *s* chaflán *m* ‖ *tr* chaflanar
cham·ois ['ʃæmi] *s* *(pl* -**ois**) gamuza
champ [tʃæmp] *s* mordisco; *(slang)* campeón *m* ‖ *tr & intr* mordiscar; *(el freno)* morder
champagne [ʃæm'pen] *s* champaña *m*
champion ['tʃæmpɪ·ən] *s* campeón *m* ‖ *tr* defender
championess ['tʃæmpɪ·ənɪs] *s* campeona
championship ['tʃæmpɪ·ən,ʃɪp] *s* campeonato
chance [tʃæns] o [tʃɑns] *adj* casual, imprevisto ‖ *s* oportunidad, ocasión; casualidad, suerte *f*; probabilidad; peligro, riesgo; chance *m* (SAm); **by chance** por casualidad; **to not stand a chance** no tener probabilidad de éxito; **to take a chance** probar fortuna; comprar un billete de lotería; **to take chances** probar fortuna; **to wait for, a chance** esperar la oportunidad ‖ *intr* acontecer; **to chance on** o **upon** tropezar con; **to chance to** acertar a
chancel ['tʃænsəl] o ['tʃɑnsəl] *s* entrecoro
chanceller·y ['tʃænsələri] o ['tʃɑnsələri] *s* *(pl* -**ies**) cancillería
chancellor ['tʃænsələr] *s* canciller *m*
chandelier [,ʃændə'lɪr] *s* araña de luces
change [tʃendʒ] *s* cambio, mudanza; suelto, moneda suelta; *(surplus money returned with a purchase)* vuelta; *(of clothing)* muda; **for a change** por variedad; **to keep the change** quedarse con la vuelta; ‖ *tr* cambiar, mudar; cambiar de, mudar de; reemplazar; **to change clothes** cambiar de ropa; **to change gears** cambiar de velocidades; **to change hands** cambiar de dueño;

to change money cambiar moneda; **to change one's mind** cambiar de parecer; **to change trains** cambiar de tren, transbordar ‖ *intr* cambiar, mudar; corregirse
changeable ['tʃendʒəbəl] *adj* cambiable; inconstante, cambiante, mudable
change of clothing *s* muda de ropa
change of heart *s* arrepentimiento, conversión
change of life *s* cesación natural de las reglas
change of voice *s* muda
chan·nel ['tʃænəl] *s* *(body of water joining two others)* canal *m*; *(bed of river)* álveo, cauce *m*; *(means of communication)* vía; *(passage)* conducto; *(groove)* ranura, surco; *(telv)* canal *m*; **the Channel** el Canal de la Mancha ‖ *v* *(pret & pp* -**neled** o -**nelled**; *ger* -**neling** o -**nelling**) *tr* acanalar; canalizar *(esfuerzos, dinero, etc.)*
chant [tʃænt] *s* *(song)* canción; *(song sung in a monotone)* canto ‖ *tr & intr* cantar
chanter ['tʃæntər] *s* cantor *m*; *(priest)* chantre *m*
chanticleer ['tʃæntɪ,klɪr] *s* el gallo
chaos ['ke·ɑs] *s* caos *m*
chaotic [ke'ɑtɪk] *adj* caótico
chap. *abbr* **chaplain, chapter**
chap [tʃæp] *s* *(jaw)* mandíbula; *(cheek)* mejilla; *(crack in the skin)* grieta; chico, tipo; **chaps** zahones *mpl* ‖ *v* *(pret & pp* **chapped;** *ger* **chapping)** *tr* agrietar, rajar ‖ *intr* agrietarse, rajarse
chapel ['tʃæpəl] *s* capilla
chaperon o **chaperone** ['ʃæpə,ron] *s* carabina, señora de compañía ‖ *tr* acompañar *(una señora a una o más señoritas)*
chaplain ['tʃæplɪn] *s* capellán *m*
chaplet ['tʃæplɪt] *s* *(wreath for head)* guirnalda; rosario
chapter ['tʃæptər] *s* capítulo; *(of the Scriptures)* capítula; *(of a cathedral)* cabildo
chapter and verse *adv* con todos sus pelos y señales
char [tʃɑr] *v* *(pret & pp* **charred;** *ger* **charring)** *tr* carbonizar; *(to scorch)* socarrar
character ['kærɪktər] *s* carácter *m*; *(conspicuous person; person in a play or novel)* personaje *m*; *(part or role in a play)* papel *m*; *(fellow)* (coll) tipo, sujeto
character assassination *s* asesinato de carácter
characteristic [,kærɪktə'rɪstɪk] *adj* característico ‖ *s* característica
characterize ['kærɪktə,raɪz] *tr* caracterizar
char′coal′ *s* carbón *m* de leña; *(for sketching)* carboncillo; *(sketch)* dibujo al carbón
charcoal burner *s* *(person)* carbonero; horno para hacer carbón de leña
charge [tʃɑrdʒ] *s* *(of an explosive, of electricity, of soldiers against the enemy; responsibility)* carga; *(accusation; amount owed; recording of amount owed)* cargo; encargamiento; *(heral)* blasón *m*; *(attack)* embestida; **in charge of** a cargo de; **to put in charge** responsabilizar; **to reverse the charges** (telp) cargar al número llamado; **to take charge of** hacerse cargo de ‖ *tr*

cargar; cobrar (*cierto precio*); (*to order*) encargar, mandar; cargar (*un acumulador;* **al** *enemigo*); **to charge to the account of someone** cargarle a uno en cuenta; **to charge with** cargar de || *intr* embestir

charge account *s* cuenta corriente

chargé d'affaires [ʃɑrˈʒe dəˈfɛr] *s* (*pl* **chargés d'affaires**) encargado de negocios

charger [ˈtʃɑrdʒər] *s* caballo de guerra; (*of a battery*) cargador *m*

chariot [ˈtʃæriət] *s* carro romano

charioteer [ˌtʃæriəˈtɪr] *s* carretero, auriga *m*

charisma [kəˈrɪzmə] *s* carisma

charismatic [ˌkɑrɪzˈmætɪk] *adj* carismático

charitable [ˈtʃærɪtəbəl] *adj* caritativo

chari•ty [ˈtʃærɪti] *s* (*pl* **-ties**) caridad; asociación de beneficencia, obra pía; **charity begins at home** la caridad bien ordenada empieza por uno mismo

charity performance *s* función benéfica

charlatan [ˈʃɑrlətən] *s* charlatán *m*

charlatanism [ˈʃɑrlətənˌɪzəm] *s* charlatanismo

Charlemagne [ˈʃɑrləˌmen] *s* Carlomagno

Charles [tʃɑrlz] *s* Carlos *m*

charlotte [ˈʃɑrlət] *s* carlota || **Charlotte** *s* Carlota

charlotte russe [ˈʃɑrlət ˈrus] *s* carlota rusa

charm [tʃɑrm] *s* encanto, hechizo; (*trinket*) amuleto, dije *m* || *tr* encantar, hechizar

charming [ˈtʃɑrmɪŋ] *adj* encantador

charnel [ˈtʃɑrnəl] *adj* cadavérico, horrible || *s* carnero, osario

charnel house *s* carnero, osario

chart [tʃɑrt] *s* mapa geográfico; (naut) carta de marear; cuadro, diagrama *m* || *tr* bosquejar; **to chart a course** trazar una ruta

charter [ˈtʃɑrtər] *s* carta (de privilegio) || *tr* alquilar (*un autobús*); fletar (*un barco*)

charter member *s* socio fundador

char•woman [ˈtʃɑrˌwumən] *s* (*pl* **-women** [ˌwɪmɪn]) alquilona, asistenta

Charybdis [kəˈrɪbdɪs] *s* Caribdis *f*

chase [tʃes] *s* caza, persecución || *tr* cazar, perseguir; **to chase away** ahuyentar

chasm [ˈkæzəm] *s* abismo

chas•sis [ˈtʃæsi] *s* (*pl* **-sis** [siz]) chasis *m*

chaste [tʃest] *adj* casto; (*style*) castizo

chasten [ˈtʃesən] *tr* castigar, corregir

chastise [tʃæsˈtaɪz] *tr* castigar

chastity [ˈtʃæstɪti] *s* castidad

chasuble [ˈtʃæzjəbəl] *s* casulla

chat [tʃæt] *s* charla, plática || *v* (*pret & pp* **chatted**; *ger* **chatting**) *intr* charlar, platicar

chatelaine [ˈʃætəˌlen] *s* castellana

chattels [ˈtʃætəlz] *spl* bienes *mpl* muebles, enseres *mpl*

chatter [ˈtʃætər] *s* (*talk*) cháchara; (*rattling*) traqueo; (*of teeth*) castañeteo; (*of birds*) chirrido || *intr* chacharear; traquear; castañetear, dentellar (*los dientes*)

chat'ter•box' *s* charlador *m*, tarabilla

chattering [ˈtʃætərɪŋ] *adj* palabrudo

chauffeur [ˈʃofər] o [ʃoˈfʌr] *s* chófer *m*

chauvinism [ˈʃovɪnɪzəm] *s* chauvinismo

cheap [tʃip] *adj* barato; (*charging low prices*) no carero, baratero; (*flashy*) cursi; baladí;

to feel cheap sentirse avergonzado || *adv* barato

cheapen [ˈtʃipən] *tr* abaratar

cheapness [ˈtʃipnɪs] *s* baratura; baratía; (*flashiness*) cursilería

cheat [tʃit] *s* trampa, fraude *m;* (*person*) trampista *mf*, defraudador *m* || *tr* trampear, defraudar

check [tʃɛk] *s* (*of bank*) cheque *m;* (*for baggage*) talón *m*, contraseña; (*in a restaurant*) cuenta; (*in theater or movie*) contraseña, billete *m* de salida; (*restraint*) freno; (*to hold a door*) amortiguador *m;* (*in chess*) jaque *m;* inspección; comprobación, verificación; (*cloth*) paño a cuadros; **in check** en jaque; **to hold in check** contener, refrenar || *interj* ¡jaque! || *tr* parar súbitamente; contener, refrenar; amortiguar; facturar (*equipajes*); inspeccionar; comprobar, verificar; marcar, señalar; chequear; (*in chess*) jaquear, dar jaque a; **to check up** comprobar, verificar || *intr* pararse súbitamente; corresponder punto por punto; **to check in** (*at a hotel*) llegar e inscribirse; **to check out** pagar la cuenta y despedirse; (slang) morir

check'book' *s* talonario (de cheques), chequera

checker [ˈtʃɛkər] *s* inspector *m;* cuadro; dibujo a cuadros; (*in game of checkers*) ficha, pieza; **checkers** damas, juego de damas || *tr* marcar con cuadros; diversificar, variar

check'er•board' *s* damero, tablero

check girl *s* moza de guardarropa

checking account *s* cuenta corriente

check'mate' *s* mate *m*, jaque *m* mate || *tr* dar mate a, dar jaque mate a; (fig) derrotar completamente

check'out' *s* (*from a hotel*) salida; hora de salida; (*in a self-service retail store*) revisión y pago

checkout counter *s* mostrador *m* de revisión

check'point' *s* punto de inspección

check'rein' *s* engallador *m*

check'room' *s* guardarropa *m;* (rr) consigna, depósito de equipajes

check'up' *s* verificación rigurosa; chequeo; (*of an automobile*) revisión; (med) reconocimiento general

cheek [tʃik] *s* mejilla, carrillo; (coll) descaro, frescura

cheek'bone' *s* pómulo

cheek by jowl *adv* cara a cara, en estrecha intimidad

cheek•y [ˈtʃiki] *adj* (*comp* **-ier;** *super* **-iest**) (coll) descarado, fresco

cheer [tʃir] *s* alegría, regocijo; (*shout*) viva *m*, aplauso; **what cheer?** ¿qué tal? || *tr* alegrar, animar; aplaudir, vitorear; dar la bienvenida a, con vivas y aplausos || *intr* alegrarse, animarse; **cheer up!** ¡ánimo!

cheerful [ˈtʃɪrfəl] *adj* alegre

cheerio [ˈtʃɪriˌo] *interj* (coll) ¡hola! ¡qué tal!; (coll) ¡adiós! ¡hasta la vista!

cheerless [ˈtʃɪrlɪs] *adj* sombrío, triste

cheese [tʃiz] *s* queso

cheese'cloth' *s* estopilla
cheese spread *s* queso para extender
cheetah ['ʧitə] *s* gatopardo; leopardo indio
chef [ʃɛf] *s* primer cocinero, jefe *m* de cocina
chem. *abbr* **chemical, chemist, chemistry**
chemical ['kɛmɪkəl] *adj* químico ‖ *s* producto químico, substancia química
chemise [ʃə'miz] *s* camisa (de mujer)
chemist ['kɛmɪst] *s* químico
chemistry ['kɛmɪstri] *s* química
chemotherapy [ˌkimo'θɛrəpi] *s* quimioterapia
cherish ['ʧɛriʃ] *tr* acariciar; (*a hope*) abrigar, acariciar
cher·ry ['ʧɛri] *s* (*pl* **-ries**) (*fruit; color*) cereza; (*tree*) cerezo
cher·ub ['ʧɛrəb] *s* (*pl* **-ubim** [əbɪm]) querubín *m* ‖ *s* (*pl* **-ubs**) niño angelical
chess [ʧɛs] *s* ajedrez *m*
chess'board' *s* tablero de ajedrez
chess·man ['ʧɛs,mæn] *s* (*pl* **-men** [ˌmɛn]) pieza de ajedrez, trebejo
chess player *s* ajedrecista *mf*
chess set *s* ajedrez *m*
chest [ʧɛst] *s* (*part of body*) pecho; (*receptacle*) cajón *m*, cofre *m*; (*piece of furniture*) cómoda
chestnut ['ʧɛsnət] *s* (*tree, wood, color*) castaño; (*fruit*) castaña
chest of drawers *s* cómoda
cheval glass [ʃə'væl] *s* psique *f*
chevalier [ˌʃɛvə'lɪr] *s* caballero
chevron ['ʃɛvrən] *s* galón *m* en forma de V invertida
chew [ʧu] *s* mascadura ‖ *tr* mascar; **to chew gum** chiclear; **to chew the rag** (slang) dar la lengua ‖ *intr* mascar
chewing gum *s* goma de mascar, chicle *m*
chg. *abbr* **charge**
chic [ʃik] *adj & s* chic *m*
chicaner·y [ʃɪ'kenəri] *s* (*pl* **-ies**) triquiñuela
chick [ʧik] *s* pollito; (slang) polla
chicken ['ʧikən] *s* pollo; (*young person*) pollo; (*young girl*) polla
chicken coop *s* pollera
chicken feed *s* (coll) calderilla
chickenhearted ['ʧikən,hartɪd, varicela] *adj* gallina
chicken pox *s* viruelas locas, varicela
chicken wire *s* alambrada, tela metálica
chick'pea' *s* garbanzo
chico·ry ['ʧikəri] *s* (*pl* **-ries**) achicoria
chide [ʧaɪd] *v* (*pret* **chided** o **chid** [ʧɪd]; *pp* **chided, chid** o **chidden** ['ʧɪdən]) *tr* reprender, regañar
chief [ʧif] *adj* principal ‖ *s* jefe *m*; (*of American Indians*) cacique *m*
chief executive *s* jefe *m* del gobierno
chief justice *s* presidente *m* de sala; presidente del tribunal supremo
chiefly ['ʧifli] *adv* principalmente, mayormente
chief of staff *s* jefe *m* de estado mayor
chief of state *s* jefe *m* del estado
chieftain ['ʧiftən] *s* (*of a clan or tribe*) jefe *m*; adalid *m*, caudillo

chiffon [ʃɪ'fan] *s* gasa, soplillo; **chiffons** atavíos, perifollos
chiffonier [ˌʃɪfə'nɪr] *s* cómoda alta
chignon ['ʃinjan] *s* castaña, moño
chilblain ['ʧɪl,blen] *s* sabañón *m*
child [ʧaɪld] *s* (*pl* **children** ['ʧɪldrən]) *s* (*infant, youngster*) niño; pipiolo (CAm, Mex); (*one's offspring*) hijo; descendiente *mf*; **with child** encinta, embarazada
child'birth' *s* alumbramiento, parto
childhood ['ʧaɪldhʊd] *s* niñez *f*, puericia; **from childhood** desde niño
childish ['ʧaɪldɪʃ] *adj* aniñado, pueril
childishness ['ʧaɪldɪʃnɪs] *s* puerilidad
child labor *s* trabajo de menores
childless ['ʧaɪldlɪs] *adj* sin hijos
child'like' *adj* aniñado
child'-rear'ing *s* puericultura
child's play *s* juego de niños
child welfare *s* protección a la infancia
Chile ['ʧili] *s* Chile *m*
Chilean ['ʧili·ən] *adj & s* chileno
chili sauce ['ʧili] *s* ají *m*, salsa de ají
chill [ʧɪl] *adj* frío ‖ *s* frío desapacible; (*sensation of cold*) escalofrío; (*lack of cordiality*) frialdad ‖ *tr* enfriar ‖ *intr* calofriarse
chill·y ['ʧili] *adj* (*comp* **-ier**; *super* **-iest**) (*causing shivering*) frío; (*sensitive to cold*) escalofriado, friolero; (*indifferent*) (fig) frío
chime [ʧaɪm] *s* campaneo, repique *m*; tubo sonoro; **chimes** juego de campanas ‖ *tr & intr* campanear, repicar
chime clock *s* reloj *m* de carillón
chimera [kaɪ'mɪrə] o [kɪ'mɪrə] *s* quimera
chimney ['ʧɪmni] *s* chimenea; (*for a lamp*) tubo
chimney cap *s* caperuza
chimney flue *s* cañón *m* de chimenea
chimney pot *s* mitra, guardavientos *m*
chimney sweep *s* limpiachimeneas *m*, deshollinador *m*
chimpanzee [ʧɪm'pænzi] o [ˌʧɪmpæn'zi] *s* chimpancé *m*
chin [ʧɪn] *s* barba, mentón *m*; **to keep one's chin up** (coll) no desanimarse ‖ *v* (*pret & pp* **chinned**; *ger* **chinning**) *intr* (coll) charlar
china ['ʧaɪnə] *s* china, porcelana ‖ **China** *s* China
china closet *s* chinero
China·man ['ʧaɪnəmən] *s* (*pl* **-men** [mən]) (offensive) chino
chi'na·ware' *s* porcelana, vajilla de porcelana
Chi·nese [ʧaɪ'niz] *adj* chino ‖ *s* (*pl* **-nese**) chino
Chinese gong *s* batintín *m*
Chinese lantern *s* farolillo veneciano
Chinese puzzle *s* problema embrollado
chink [ʧɪŋk] *s* grieta, hendidura; sonido metálico
chin strap *s* barboquejo, carrillera
chintz [ʧɪnts] *s* zaraza
chip [ʧɪp] *s* astilla, brizna; (*in china*) deschado; (*in poker*) ficha; **chip off the old block** hijo de su padre ‖ *v* (*pret & pp* **chipped**; *ger* **chipping**) *tr* astillar (*la ma-*

dera); desconchar (*la porcelana*); **to chip in** contribuir con su cuota ‖ *intr* astillarse; desconcharse

chipmunk [ˈtʃɪpˌmʌŋk] *s* ardilla listada

chipper [ˈtʃɪpər] *adj* (coll) alegre, jovial, vivo

chiropodist [kaɪˈrɑpədɪst] o [kɪˈrɑpədɪst] *s* quiropodista *mf*

chiropractor [ˈkaɪrəˌpræktər] *s* quiropráctico

chirp [tʃʌrp] *s* chirrido, gorjeo ‖ *intr* chirriar, gorjear; hablar alegremente

chisel [ˈtʃɪzəl] *s* (*for wood*) escoplo, formón *m*; (*for stone and metal*) cincel *m* ‖ *v* (*pret & pp* -eled o -elled; *ger* -eling o -elling) *tr* escoplear; cincelar; (slang) estafar

chit-chat [ˈtʃɪtˌtʃæt] *s* charla, palique *m*; hablilla, chismes *mpl*

chivalric [ˈʃɪvəlrɪk] o [ʃɪˈvælrɪk] *adj* caballeresco

chivalrous [ˈʃɪvəlrəs] *adj* caballeroso

chivalry [ˈʃɪvəlri] *s* (*knighthood*) caballería; (*gallantry, gentlemanliness*) caballerosidad

chloride [ˈklɔraɪd] *s* cloruro

chlorine [ˈklorin] *s* cloro

chloroform [ˈklɔrəˌfɔrm] *s* cloroformo ‖ *tr* cloroformizar

chlorophyll [ˈklɔrəfɪl] *s* clorofila

chock-full [ˈtʃɑkˈfʊl] *adj* de bote en bote, colmado

chocolate [ˈtʃɑkəlɪt] *s* chocolate *m*

choice [tʃɔɪs] *adj* escogido, selecto, superior ‖ *s* elección, selección; lo más escogido; **to have no choice** no tener alternativa

choir [kwaɪr] *s* coro

choir'boy' *s* niño de coro, infante *m* de coro

choir desk *s* facistol *m*

choir loft *s* coro

choir'mas'ter *s* jefe *m* de coro, maestro de capilla

choke [tʃok] *s* estrangulación; (*of carburetor*) cierre *m*, obturador *m*; (elec) choque *m* ‖ *tr* ahogar, sofocar, estrangular; obstruir, tapar; (aut) obturar; **to choke down** atragantar ‖ *intr* sofocarse; atragantarse; **to choke on** atragantarse con

choke coil *s* (elec) bobina de reacción, choque *m*

cholera [ˈkɑlərə] *s* cólera *m*

choleric [ˈkɑlərɪk] *adj* colérico

cholesterol [kəˈlɛstəˌrol] *s* colesterol *m*

choose [tʃuz] *v* (*pret* chose [tʃoz]; *pp* chosen [ˈtʃozən]) *tr* escoger, elegir ‖ *intr* — **to choose between** optar entre; **to choose to** optar por

chop [tʃɑp] *s* golpe *m* cortante; (*of meat*) chuleta; **chops** boca, labios ‖ *v* (*pret & pp* chopped; *ger* chopping) *tr* cortar, tajar; picar (*la carne*); **to chop off** tronchar; **to chop up** desmenuzar

chop'house' *s* restaurante *m*, figón *m*, colmado

chopper [ˈtʃɑpər] *s* (*person*) tajador *m*; (*tool*) hacha; (*of butcher*) cortante *m*; (slang) helicóptero

chopping block *s* tajo

chop•py [ˈtʃɑpi] *adj* (*comp* -pier; *super* -piest) (*sea*) agitado, picado; (*wind*) variable; (*style*) cortado, inciso

chop'sticks' *spl* palillos

choral [ˈkorəl] *adj* coral

chorale [koˈral] *s* coral *m*

choral society *s* orfeón *m*

chord [kɔrd] *s* (*harmonious combination of tones*) (mus) acorde *m*; (aer, anat, geom) cuerda

chore [tʃor] *s* tarea, quehacer *m*

choreography [ˌkoriˈɑgrəfi] *s* coreografía

chorine [koˈrin] *s* (slang) corista, suripanta

chorus [ˈkorəs] *s* coro; (*refrain of a song*) estribillo

chorus girl *s* corista, conjuntista

chorus man *s* corista *m*, conjuntista *m*

chowder [ˈtʃaʊdər] *s* estofado de almejas o pescado

Chr. *abbr* **Christian**

Christ [kraɪst] *s* Cristo

christen [ˈkrɪsən] *tr* bautizar

Christendom [ˈkrɪsəndəm] *s* cristiandad

christening [ˈkrɪsənɪŋ] *s* bautismo, bautizo

Christian [ˈkrɪstʃən] *adj & s* cristiano

Christianity [ˌkrɪstʃiˈæniti] *s* cristianismo

Christianize [ˈkrɪstʃəˌnaɪz] *tr* cristianizar

Christian name *s* nombre *m* de pila

Christmas [ˈkrɪsməs] *adj* navideño ‖ *s* Navidad, Pascua de Navidad

Christmas card *s* aleluya navideña

Christmas carol *s* villancico

Christmas Eve *s* nochebuena

Christmas gift *s* aguinaldo, regalo de Navidad

Christmas tree *s* árbol *m* de Navidad

Christopher [ˈkrɪstəfər] *s* Cristóbal *m*

chrome [krom] *adj* cromado ‖ *s* cromo ‖ *tr* cromar

chromium [ˈkromɪ•əm] *s* cromo

chro•mo [ˈkromo] *s* (*pl* -mos) (*colored picture*) cromo; (*piece of junk*) (slang) trasto

chromosome [ˈkroməˌsom] *s* cromosoma *m*

chron. *abbr* **chronological, chronology**

chronic [ˈkrɑnɪk] *adj* crónico

chronicle [ˈkrɑnɪkəl] *s* crónica ‖ *tr* narrar en una crónica; narrar, contar

chronicler [ˈkrɑnɪklər] *s* cronista *mf*

chronolo•gy [krəˈnɑlədʒi] *s* (*pl* -gies) cronología

chronometer [krəˈnɑmɪtər] *s* cronómetro

chrysanthemum [krɪˈsænθɪməm] *s* crisantemo

chub•by [ˈtʃʌbi] *adj* (*comp* -bier; *super* -biest) rechoncho, regordete

chuck [tʃʌk] *s* (*throw*) echada, tirada; (*under the chin*) mamola; (*of a lathe*) mandril *m* ‖ *tr* arrojar; **to chuck under the chin** hacer la mamola a

chuckle [ˈtʃʌkəl] *s* risa ahogada ‖ *intr* reírse con risa ahogada

chug [tʃʌg] *s* ruido explosivo sordo; (*of a locomotive*) resoplido ‖ *v* (*pret & pp* chugged; *ger* chugging) *intr* hacer ruidos explosivos sordos, moverse con ruidos explosivos sordos

ch
ci

chum [tʃʌm] s (coll) compinche *mf;* compañero de cuarto ‖ *v* (*pret & pp* **chummed;** *ger* **chumming**) *intr* (coll) ser compinche, ser compinches; (coll) compartir un cuarto

chum·my [ˈtʃʌmi] *adj* (*comp* **-mier;** *super* **-miest**) muy amigable, íntimo

chump [tʃʌmp] s tarugo, zoquete *m;* (coll) estúpido, tonto

chunk [tʃʌnk] s trozo, pedazo grueso

church [tʃʌrt] s iglesia

churchgoer [ˈtʃʌrtʃˌgoˑər] s persona que frecuenta la iglesia

church·man [ˈtʃʌrtʃmən] s (*pl* **-men** [mən]) sacerdote *m,* eclesiástico; feligrés *m*

church member s feligrés *m*

Church of England s Iglesia Anglicana

church'ward'en s capiller *m*

church'yard' s patio de iglesia; cementerio

churl [tʃʌrl] s palurdo, patán *m*

churlish [ˈtʃʌrlɪʃ] *adj* palurdo, insolente

churn [tʃʌrn] s mantequera ‖ *tr* mazar (*leche*); hacer (*mantequilla*) en una mantequera; agitar, revolver ‖ *intr* revolverse

chute [ʃut] s cascada, salto de agua; rápidos; conducto inclinado; (*e.g., into a swimming pool*) tobogán *m;* (*e.g., for grain*) tolva; paracaídas *m*

cibori·um [sɪˈborɪˑəm] s (*pl* **-a** [ə]) (*canopy*) ciborio, baldaquín *m;* (*cup*) copón *m*

Cicero [ˈsɪsəˌro] s Cicerón *m*

cider [ˈsaɪdər] s sidra

C.I.F., c.i.f. *abbr* **cost, insurance, and freight**

cigar [sɪˈgɑr] s cigarro, puro

cigar band s anillo de cigarro

cigar case s cigarrera, petaca

cigar cutter s cortacigarros *m*

cigaret o **cigarette** [ˌsɪgəˈrɛt] s cigarrillo, pitillo

cigarette case s pitillera

cigarette holder s boquilla

cigarette lighter s mechero, encendedor *m* de bolsillo

cigarette paper s papel *m* de fumar

cigar holder s boquilla

cigar store s estanco, tabaquería

cinch [sɪntʃ] s (*of saddle*) cincha; (*sure grip*) (coll) agarro; (*something easy*) (slang) breva ‖ *tr* cinchar; (coll) agarrar

cinder [ˈsɪndər] s ceniza; (*coal burning without flame*) pavesa

cinder bank s escorial *m*

Cinderella [ˌsɪndəˈrɛlə] s la Cenicienta

cinder track s pista de cenizas

cinema [ˈsɪnəmə] s cine *m*

cinematograph [ˌsɪnəˈmætəˌgræf] o [ˌsɪnəˈmætəˌgrɑf] s cinematógrafo ‖ *tr & intr* cinematografiar

cinnabar [ˈsɪnəˌbɑr] s cinabrio

cinnamon [ˈsɪnəmən] s canela

cipher [ˈsaɪfər] s cifra; cero; (*nonentity*) cero a la izquierda; (*key to a cipher*) clave *f* ‖ *tr* cifrar; calcular

circle [ˈsʌrkəl] s círculo ‖ *tr* circundar; dar la vuelta a; girar alrededor de

circuit [ˈsʌrkɪt] s circuito

circuit breaker s disyuntor *m*

circuitous [sərˈkjuˑɪtəs] *adj* indirecto, tortuoso

circular [ˈsʌrkjələr] *adj* tortuoso ‖ s circular *f,* carta circular

circularize [ˈsʌrkjələˌraɪz] *tr* anunciar por circular; enviar circulares a

circulate [ˈsʌrkjəˌlet] *tr & intr* circular

circumcise [ˈsʌrkəmˌsaɪz] *tr* circuncidar

circumference [sərˈkʌmfərəns] s circunferencia

circumflex [ˈsʌrkəmˌflɛks] *adj* circunflejo

circumlocution [ˌsʌrkəmloˈkjuʃən] s circunlocución, circunloquio

circumnavigate [ˌsʌrkəmˈnævɪˌget] *tr* circunnavegar

circumnavigation [ˌsʌrkəmˌnævɪˈgeʃən] s circunnavegación

circumscribe [ˌsʌrkəmˈskraɪb] *tr* circunscribir

circumspect [ˈsʌrkəmˌspɛkt] *adj* circunspecto

circumstance [ˈsʌrkəmˌstæns] s circunstancia; ceremonia, ostentación; **in easy circumstances** acomodado; **under no circumstances** de ninguna manera, ni a bala

circumstantial [ˌsʌrkəmˈstænʃəl] *adj* (*derived from circumstances*) circunstancial; (*detailed*) circunstanciado

circumstantial evidence s (law) indicios vehementes

circumstantiate [ˌsʌrkəmˈstænʃɪˌet] *tr* apoyar con pruebas y detalles; (*to describe in detail*) circunstanciar

circumvent [ˌsʌrkəmˈvɛnt] *tr* (*to catch by a trick*) entrampar, embaucar; (*to outwit*) burlar; (*to keep away from, get around*) evitar

circus [ˈsʌrkəs] s circo

cistern [ˈsɪstərn] s cisterna, aljibe *m*

citadel [ˈsɪtədəl] s ciudadela

citation [saɪˈteʃən] s (*of a text*) cita; (*before a court of law*) citación; (*for gallantry*) mención

cite [saɪt] *tr* (*to quote; to summon*) citar; (*for gallantry*) mencionar

citizen [ˈsɪtɪzən] s ciudadano; (*civilian*) paisano

citizen·ry [ˈsɪtɪzənri] s (*pl* **-ries**) conjunto de ciudadanos

citizens band s banda ciudadana

citizenship [ˈsɪtɪzənˌʃɪp] s ciudadanía

citron [ˈsɪtrən] s (*fruit*) cidra; (*tree*) cidro; (*candied rind*) cidrada

citronella [ˌsɪtrəˈnɛlə] s limoncillo (*Andropogon nardus*); aceite *m* de limoncillo

citrus fruit [ˈsɪtrəs] s agrios, frutas cítricas

cit·y [ˈsɪti] s (*pl* **-ies**) ciudad

city clerk s archivero

city council s ayuntamiento

city editor s redactor de periódico encargado de noticias locales

city fathers spl concejales *mpl*

city hall s casa consistorial

city plan s plano de la ciudad

city planner s urbanista *mf*

city planning s urbanismo

city room s redacción

cit′y-state′ s ciudad-estado f
civic [ˈsɪvɪk] adj cívico ‖ **civics** s estudio de los deberes y derechos del ciudadano
civic-mindedness [ˈmaɪndɪdnɪs] s civismo
civies [ˈsɪviz] spl (coll) traje m de paisano; **in civies** (coll) de paisano
civil [ˈsɪvɪl] adj civil
civilian [sɪˈvɪljən] adj civil ‖ s civil mf, paisano
civilian clothes spl traje m de paisano
civili•ty [sɪˈvɪlɪti] s (pl **-ties**) civilidad
civilization [ˌsɪvɪlɪˈzeʃən] s civilización
civilize [ˈsɪvɪˌlaɪz] tr civilizar
civil servant s funcionario del estado
claim [klem] s demanda, pretensión, reclamación ‖ tr demandar, pretender, reclamar; afirmar, declarar; **to claim to + inf** pretender + inf
claim check s comprobante m
clairvoyance [klɛrˈvɔɪ•əns] s clarividencia
clairvoyant [klɛrˈvɔɪ•ənt] adj & s clarividente mf
clam [klæm] s almeja; (tight-lipped person) (coll) chiticalla m ‖ intr — **to clam up** (coll) callarse la boca
clamber [ˈklæmər] intr — **to clamber up** subir gateando
clamor [ˈklæmər] s clamor m, clamoreo ‖ intr clamorear
clamorous [ˈklæmərəs] adj clamoroso
clamp [klæmp] s abrazadera, grapa; (vise-like device) mordaza ‖ tr agrapar, afianzar con abrazadera; sujetar en una mordaza ‖ intr — **to clamp down on** (coll) apretar los tornillos a
clan [klæn] s clan m
clandestine [klænˈdɛstɪn] adj clandestino
clang [klæŋ] s tantán m, sonido metálico resonante ‖ tr hacer sonar fuertemente ‖ intr sonar fuertemente
clank [klæŋk] s sonido metálico seco ‖ tr hacer sonar secamente ‖ intr sonar secamente
clannish [ˈklænɪʃ] adj exclusivista
clap [klæp] s golpe seco; (of the hands) palmada; (of thunder) estampido ‖ v (pret & pp **clapped**; ger **clapping**) tr batir (palmas); palmotear, aplaudir; **to clap shut** cerrar de golpe ‖ intr palmotear, dar palmadas
clap of thunder s estampido de trueno
clapper [ˈklæpər] s palmoteador m; (of a bell) badajo; (to cause grain to slide) tarabilla
clap′trap′ s faramalla; (of an actor) latiguillo
claque [klæk] s (paid clappers) claque f; (crush hat) clac m
claret [ˈklærɪt] s clarete m
clari•fy [ˈklærɪˌfaɪ] v (pret & pp **-fied**) tr clarificar; encolar (el vino)
clarinet [ˈklærɪˈnɛt] s clarinete m
clarion [ˈklærɪ•ən] adj claro, brillante ‖ s clarín m
clarity [ˈklærɪti] s claridad
clash [klæʃ] s choque m, encontrón m; estruendo, ruido ‖ intr chocar, entrechocarse

clasp [klæsp] s (fastener) abrazadera, cierre m; (for, e.g., a necktie) broche m; (buckle) hebilla; (embrace) abrazo; (grip) agarro ‖ tr abrochar; abrazar; agarrar, apretar (la mano); apretarse (la mano)
class. abbr **classical**
class [klæs] s clase f; ó (slang) elegancia, buen tono; (sports) división ‖ tr clasificar ‖ intr clasificarse
class consciousness s sentimiento de clase
classic [ˈklæsɪk] adj & s clásico; **the classics** las obras clásicas
classical [ˈklæsɪkəl] adj clásico
classical scholar s erudito en las lenguas clásicas
classicist [ˈklæsɪsɪst] s clasicista mf
classified [ˈklæsɪˌfaɪd] adj clasificado; clasificado como secreto
classified ads spl anuncios clasificados en secciones
classi•fy [ˈklæsɪˌfaɪ] v (pret & pp **-fied**) tr clasificar
class′mate′ s compañero de clase
class′room′ s aula, sala de clase
class struggle s lucha de clases
class•y [ˈklæsi] adj (comp **-ier**; super **-iest**) (slang) elegante
clatter [ˈklætər] s estruendo confuso; algazara, gresca; (of hoofs) trápala ‖ intr caer o moverse con estruendo confuso; hablar rápida y ruidosamente; **to clatter down the stairs** bajar la escalera ruidosamente
clause [klɔz] s (article in a legal document) cláusula; (gram) oración dependiente
clavichord [ˈklævɪˌkɔrd] s clavicordio
clavicle [ˈklævɪkəl] s clavícula
clavier [ˈklævɪ•ər] o [kləˈvɪr] s teclado [kləˈvɪr] s instrumento musical con teclado
claw [klɔ] s garra, uña; (of lobster, crab, etc.) pinza; (of hammer, wrench, etc.) oreja; (coll) dedos, mano f ‖ tr (to clutch) agarrar; (to scratch) arañar; (to tear) desgarrar
clay [kle] adj arcilloso ‖ s arcilla
clay pigeon s pichón m de barro
clay pipe s pipa de tierra
clean [klin] adj limpio; distinto, neto, nítido; completo ‖ adv completamente; **to come clean** (slang) confesarlo todo ‖ tr limpiar; (to tidy up) asear; **to be cleaned out** (of money) (slang) quedar limpio; **to clean out** limpiar; (slang) dejar limpio ‖ intr limpiarse; asearse; **to clean up** limpiarse; (coll) llevárselo todo; (in gambling) (slang) hacer mesa limpia; **to clean up after someone** limpiar lo que alguno ha ensuciado
clean bill of health s patente limpia de sanidad
cleaner [ˈklinər] s limpiador m; (dry cleaner) tintorero; (preparation) quitamanchas m; **to send to the cleaners** (slang) dejar limpio
cleaning [ˈklinɪŋ] s limpieza
cleaning fluid s quitamanchas m
cleaning woman s criada que hace la limpieza, alquilona

cleanliness ['klɛnlɪnɪs] *s* limpieza

clean•ly ['klɛnli] *adj* (*comp* **-lier;** *super* **-liest**) limpio (*que tiene el hábito del aseo*)

cleanse [klɛnz] *tr* limpiar, lavar, depurar

clean-shaven ['klin'ʃevən] *adj* lisamente afeitado

clean'up' *s* limpieza general; **to make a cleanup** (slang) hacer su pacotilla

clear [klɪr] *adj* claro; (*cloudless*) despejado; (*of debts, etc.*) libre || *adv* claro, claramente; **clear through** de parte a parte || *tr* despejar (*un bosque*); clarificar (*lo que estaba turbio*); (*to make less dark*) aclarar; saltar por encima de; (*to prove the innocence of*) absolver; sacar (*una ganancia neta*); abonar, acreditar; liquidar (*una cuenta*); (*in the customhouse*) despachar; salvar (*un obstáculo*); levantar (*la mesa*); desmontar (*un terreno*); **to clear the way** abrir camino || *intr* clarificarse; aclararse; **to clear away** irse, desaparecer; **to clear up** abonanzarse (*el tiempo*); despejarse (*el cielo, el tiempo*)

clearance ['klɪrəns] *s* aclaración; abono, acreditación; espacio libre; (*in a cylinder*) espacio muerto; (com) compensación

clearance sale *s* venta de liquidación

clearing ['klɪrɪŋ] *s* (*in a woods*) claro; (com) compensación

clearing house *s* cámara de compensación

clear-sighted ['klɪr'saɪtɪd] *adj* clarividente, perspicaz

clear'sto'ry *s* (*pl* **-ries**) var of **clerestory**

cleat [klit] *s* abrazadera, listón *m*

cleavage ['klivɪdʒ] *s* división, hendidura; (fig) desunión

cleave [kliv] *v* (*pret & pp* **cleft** [klɛft] o **cleaved**) *tr* rajar, partir; hender (*las aguas un buque, los aires una flecha*) || *intr* adherirse, pegarse; apegarse, ser fiel

cleaver ['klivər] *s* cortante *m*, cuchilla de carnicero

clef [klɛf] *s* (mus) clave *f*

cleft palate [klɛft] *s* fisura del paladar

clematis ['klɛmətɪs] *s* clemátide *f*

clemen•cy ['klɛmənsi] *s* (*pl* **-cies**) clemencia; (*of the weather*) benignidad

clement ['klɛmənt] *adj* clemente; (*weather*) benigno

clench [klɛntʃ] *s* agarro || *tr* agarrar; apretar, cerrar (*el puño, los dientes*)

cleresto•ry ['klɪr,stori] *s* (*pl* **-ries**) claraboya

cler•gy ['klɛrdʒi] *s* (*pl* **-gies**) clerecía, clero

clergy•man ['klɛrdʒimən] *s* (*pl* **-men** [mən]) clérigo, pastor *m*

cleric ['klɛrɪk] *s* clérigo

clerical ['klɛrɪkəl] *adj* (*of clergy*) clerical; (*of office work*) oficinesco || *s* clérigo, eclesiástico; (*supporter of power of clergy*) clerical *m;* **clericals** (coll) hábitos clericales

clerical error *s* error *m* de pluma

clerical work *s* trabajo de oficina

clerk [klʌrk] *s* (*in a store*) dependiente *mf;* (*in an office*) oficinista *mf;* (*in a city hall*) archivero; (*in a church*) lego, seglar *m;* (*in law office, in court*) escribano

clever ['klɛvər] *adj* hábil, diestro, mañoso; inteligente

cleverness ['klɛvərnɪs] *s* habilidad, destreza, maña; inteligencia

clew [klu] *s* indicio, pista

cliché [kli'ʃe] *s* (*printing plate*) clisé *m;* (*trite expression*) cliché *m*

click [klɪk] *s* golpecito; (*of typewriter*) tecleo; (*of firearm*) piñoneo; (*of heels*) taconeo; (*of tongue*) claqueo, chasquido || *tr* hacer sonar con un golpecito seco; chascar (*la lengua*); **to click the heels** taconear; cuadrarse (*un soldado*) || *intr* sonar con un golpecito seco; piñonear (*el gatillo de un arma de fuego*); claquear (*la lengua*)

client ['klaɪ•ənt] *s* cliente *mf;* cliente de abogado

clientele [,klaɪ•ən'tɛl] *s* clientela

cliff [klɪf] *s* acantilado, escarpa, risco

climate ['klaɪmɪt] *s* clima *m*

climax ['klaɪmæks] *s* colmo; orgasmo; **to cap the climax** ser el colmo

climb [klaɪm] *s* subida, trepa || *tr & intr* escalar, subir, trepar

climber ['klaɪmər] *s* trepador *m;* ambicioso de figurar; (bot) enredadera, trepadora

clinch [klɪntʃ] *s* agarro, abrazo; (*of a nail*) remache *m* || *tr* afianzar, sujetar; agarrar, abrazar; apretar (*el puño*); remachar (*un clavo ya clavado*); resolver decisivamente

cling [klɪŋ] *v* (*pret & pp* **clung** [klʌŋ]) *intr* adherirse, pegarse; **to cling to** agarrarse a, asirse de

cling'stone' peach *s* albérchigo, peladillo

clinic ['klɪnɪk] *s* clínica

clinical ['klɪnɪkəl] *adj* clínico

clinical chart *s* hoja clínica

clinician [klɪ'nɪʃən] *s* clínico

clink [klɪŋk] *s* tintín *m* || *tr* hacer tintinear; chocar (*vasos, copas*) || *intr* tintinear

clinker ['klɪŋkər] *s* escoria de hulla

clip [klɪp] *s* tijereteo, esquileo; grapa, pinza; (*to fasten papers*) sujetapapeles *m*, presilla de alambre; **at a good clip** a buen paso || *v* (*pret & pp* **clipped;** *ger* **clipping**) *tr* tijeretear, esquilar; (*to fasten with a clip*) afianzar, sujetar; recortar (*p.ej., un cupón*) || *intr* moverse con rapidez

clipper ['klɪpər] *s* tijera, cizalla; **clippers** maquinilla cortapelos; tijeras podadoras

clipping ['klɪpɪŋ] *s* tijereteo, esquileo; (*from a newspaper*) recorte *m*

clique [klik] *s* pandilla, corrillo || *intr* — **to clique together** apandillarse

cliquish ['klikɪʃ] *adj* exclusivista

clk. *abbr* **clerk, clock**

cloak [klok] *s* capote *m;* (*disguise, excuse*) capa || *tr* encapotar; disimular, encubrir

cloak-and-dagger ['klokən'dægər] *adj* de capa y espada (*dícese de duelos, espionaje, etc.*)

cloak-and-sword ['klokən'sord] *adj* de capa y espada (*dícese, p.ej., de las costumbres caballerescas*)

cloak hanger *s* cuelgacapas *m*

cloak'room' *s* guardarropa *m;* (Brit) excusado

ci
cl

clock [klɑk] *s* reloj *m* (de pared o de mesa); (*in a stocking*) cuadrado ‖ *tr* registrar; (sport) cronometrar

clock'mak'er *s* relojero

clock tower *s* torre *f* reloj

clock'wise' *adj & adv* en el sentido de las agujas del reloj

clock'work' *s* mecanismo de relojería; **like clockwork** como un reloj

clod [klɑd] *s* terrón *m*

clod'hop'per *s* destripaterrones *m*, quebrantaterrones *m*; **clodhoppers** zapatos fuertes de trabajo

clog [klɑg] *s* estorbo, obstáculo; (*wooden shoe*) zueco; (*dance*) zapateado; (*hobble on animal*) traba ‖ *v* (*pret & pp* **clogged;** *ger* **clogging**) *tr* atascar ‖ *intr* atascarse; bailar el zapateado

clog dance *s* zapateado

cloister ['klɔɪstər] *s* claustro ‖ *tr* enclaustrar

cloistral ['klɔɪstrəl] *adj* claustral

close [klos] *adj* cercano, próximo; casi igual; (*translation*) fiel, exacto; (*fabric*) compacto; (*weather, atmosphere*) pesado, sofocante; (*stingy*) tacaño; (*battle, race, election*) reñido; (*friend*) íntimo; (*shut in, enclosed*) cerrado; (*narrow*) estrecho ‖ *adv* cerca; **close to** cerca de ‖ [kloz] *s* fin *m*, terminación; (*of business, of stock market*) cierre *m*; **at the close of day** a la caída de la tarde; **to bring to a close** poner término a; **to come to a close** tocar a su fin ‖ *tr* cerrar; (*to cover*) tapar; (*to finish*) concluir; saldar (*una cuenta*); cerrar (*un trato*); **to close in** cerrar, encerrar; **to close ranks** cerrar las filas ‖ *intr* cerrar, cerrarse; **to close in on** cerrar con (*el enemigo*)

close call [klos] *s* (coll) escape *m* por un pelo

closed car [klozd] *s* coche cerrado, conducción interior

closed chapter *s* asunto concluído

closed season *s* veda

closed shop *s* taller agremiado

closefisted ['klos'fɪstɪd] *adj* cicatero, tacaño, manicorto

close-fitting ['klos'fɪtɪŋ] *adj* ajustado, ceñido al cuerpo

close-lipped ['klos'lɪpt] *adj* callado, reservado

closely ['klosli] *adv* de cerca; estrechamente; fielmente; atentamente

close quarters [klos] *spl* lugar muy estrecho, lugares estrechos

close shave [klos] *s* afeitado a ras; (coll) escape *m* por un pelo

closet ['klɑzɪt] *s* (*wall*) alacena, closet *m*; (*wardrobe*) armario; (*small private room*) aposento, gabinete *m*; (*for keeping clothing*) guardarropa *m*; (*toilet*) retrete *m* ‖ *tr* — **to be closeted with** encerrarse con

close-up ['klos͵ʌp] *s* (*moving picture*) vista de cerca; fotografía de cerca

closing ['klozɪŋ] *s* cerradura, cierre *m*

closing prices *spl* precios de cierre

closing time *s* hora de cierre

clot [klɑt] *s* grumo, coágulo ‖ *v* (*pret & pp* **clotted;** *ger* **clotting**) *intr* engrumecerse, coagularse

cloth [klɔθ] o [klɑθ] *s* paño, tela; ropa clerical; (*canvas, sails*) lona, trapo, vela; (*for binding books*) tela; **the cloth** la clerecía

clothe [kloð] *v* (*pret & pp* **clothed** o **clad** [klæd]) *tr* trajear, vestir; cubrir; (*e.g., with authority*) investir

clothes [kloz] o [kloðz] *spl* ropa, vestidos; ropa de cama

clothes'bas'ket *s* cesto de la ropa, cesto de la colada

clothes'brush' *s* cepillo de ropa

clothes closet *s* ropero

clothes dryer *s* secadora de ropa, secarropa

clothes hanger *s* colgador *m*, perchero

clothes'horse' *s* enjugador *m*, secarropa de travesaños

clothes'line' *s* cordel *m* para tender la ropa, tendedera

clothes'pin' *s* pinza, alfiler *m* de madera

clothes tree *s* percha

clothes wringer *s* exprimidor *m* de ropa

clothier ['kloojər] *s* (*person who sells ready-made clothes*) ropero; (*dealer in cloth*) pañero

clothing ['kloðɪŋ] *s* ropa, vestidos, ropaje *m*

cloud [klaud] *s* nube *f* ‖ *tr* anublar ‖ *intr* — **to cloud over** anublarse

cloud bank *s* mar *m* de nubes

cloud'burst' *s* aguacero, chaparrón *m*

cloud-capped ['klaud͵kæpt] *adj* coronado de nubes

cloudless ['klaudlɪs] *adj* despejado, sin nubes

cloud of dust *s* polvareda, nube *f* de polvo

cloud•y ['klaudi] *adj* (*comp* **-ier;** *super* **-iest**) nuboso, nublado; (*muddy, turbid*) turbio; confuso, obscuro; melancólico, sombrío

clove [klov] *s* (*flower*) clavo de especia; (*spice*) clavo

clover ['klovər] *s* trébol *m*; **to be in clover** vivir en el lujo

clo'ver-leaf' *s* (*pl* **-leaves** [͵livz]) *s* cruce *m* en trébol

clove tree *s* clavero

clown [klaun] *s* bufón *m*, payaso; (*rustic*) patán *m* ‖ *intr* hacer el payaso

clownish ['klaunɪʃ] *adj* bufonesco; rústico

cloy [klɔɪ] *tr* hastiar, empalagar

club [klʌb] *s* porra, clava; (*playing card*) basto, trébol *m*; club *m*, casino ‖ *v* (*pret & pp* **clubbed;** *ger* **clubbing**) *tr* aporrear ‖ *intr* — **to club together** unirse; formar club

club car *s* coche *m* club, coche bar

club'house' *s* casino, club *m*

club•man ['klʌbmən] *s* (*pl* **-men** [mən]) clubista *m*

club•woman ['klʌb͵wumən] *s* (*pl* **-women** [͵wɪmɪn]) clubista *f*

cluck [klʌk] *s* cloqueo, clo clo ‖ *intr* cloquear, hacer clo clo

clue [klu] *s* indicio, pista

clump [klʌmp] *s* (*of earth*) terrón *m*; (*of trees or shrubs*) grupo; pisada fuerte ‖ *intr* — **to clump along** andar pesadamente

clum·sy ['klʌmzi] *adj* (*comp* **-sier;** *super* **-siest**) (*worker*) chapucero, desmañado, torpe; (*work*) chapucero, tosco, grosero

cluster ['klʌstər] *s* grupo; (*of grapes or other things growing or joined together*) racimo ‖ *intr* arracimarse; **to cluster around** reunirse en torno a; **to cluster together** agruparse

clutch [klʌtʃ] *s* (*grasp, grip*) agarro, apretón *m* fuerte; (aut) embrague *m;* (aut) pedal *m* de embrague; **to fall into the clutches of** caer en las garras de; **to throw the clutch in** embragar; **to throw the clutch out** desembragar ‖ *tr* agarrar, empuñar

clutter ['klʌtər] *tr* — **to clutter up** cubrir o llenar desordenadamente

cm. *abbr* **centimeter**

cml. *abbr* **commercial**

Co. *abbr* **Company, County**

coach [kotʃ] *s* coche *m,* diligencia; (aut) coche cerrado; (rr) coche de viajeros, coche ordinario *m;* (sport) entrenador *m* ‖ *tr* aleccionar; (sport) entrenar ‖ *intr* entrenarse

coach house *s* cochera

coaching ['kotʃɪŋ] *s* lecciones *fpl* particulares; (sport) entrenamiento

coach·man ['kotʃmən] *s* (*pl* **-men** [mən]) *s* cochero

coagulate [ko'ægjə,let] *tr* coagular ‖ *intr* coagularse

coal [kol] *s* carbón *m,* hulla ‖ *tr* proveer de carbón ‖ *intr* proveerse de carbón

coal'bin' *s* carbonera

coal bunker *s* carbonera

coal car *s* vagón carbonero

coal'deal'er *s* carbonero

coaling ['kolɪŋ] *adj* carbonero ‖ *s* toma de carbón

coalition [,ko·ə'lɪʃən] *s* unión; (*alliance between states or factions*) coalición

coal mine *s* mina de carbón

coal oil *s* aceite *m* mineral

coal scuttle *s* cubo para carbón

coal tar *s* alquitrán *m* de hulla

coal'yard' *s* carbonería

coarse [kors] *adj* (*of inferior quality*) basto, burdo; (*composed of large particles*) grueso; (*crude in manners*) grosero, rudo, vulgar

coarseness ['korsnɪs] *s* bastedad

coast [kost] *s* costa; **the coast is clear** ya no hay peligro ‖ *tr* costear ‖ *intr* deslizarse cuesta abajo; **to coast along** avanzar sin esfuerzo

coastal ['kostəl] *adj* costero

coaster ['kostər] *s* salvamanteles *m*

coaster brake *s* freno de contrapedal

coast guard *s* guardacostas *mpl;* guardia *m* de los guardacostas

coast guard cutter *s* escampavía de los guardacostas

coasting trade *s* cabotaje *m*

coast'land' *s* litoral *m*

coast'line' *s* línea de la costa

coast'wise' *adj* costanero ‖ *adv* a lo largo de la costa

coat [kot] *s* (*jacket*) americana, saco; (*topcoat*) abrigo, sobretodo; (*of an animal*) lana, pelo; (*of paint*) capa, mano *f* ‖ *tr* cubrir, revestir; dar una capa de pintura a

coated ['kotɪd] *adj* revestido; (*tongue*) saburroso

coat hanger *s* colgador *m*

coating ['kotɪŋ] *s* revestimiento; (*of paint*) capa; (*of plaster*) enlucido

coat of arms *s* escudo de armas

coat'room' *s* guardarropa *m*

coat'tail' *s* faldón *m*

coax [koks] *tr* engatusar

cob [kab] *s* zuro; **to eat corn on the cob** comer maíz en la mazorca

cobalt ['kobɔlt] *s* cobalto

cobbler ['kablər] *s* remendón *m,* zapatero de viejo

cob'ble·stone' *s* guijarro

cob'web' *s* telaraña

cocaine [ko'ken] *s* cocaína; (slang) coca

cock [kak] *s* (*rooster*) gallo; (*faucet, valve*) espita, grifo; (*of firearm*) martillo; (*weathervane*) veleta; caudillo, jefe *m* ‖ *tr* amartillar (*un arma de fuego*); ladear (*la cabeza*); enderezar, levantar

cockade [ka'ked] *s* cucarda, escarapela

cock-a-doodle-doo ['kakə,dudəl'du] *s* quiquiriquí *m*

cock-and-bull story ['kakənd'bul] *s* cuento absurdo, cuento increíble

cocked hat [kakt] *s* sombrero de candil, sombrero de tres picos; **to knock into a cocked hat** (slang) apaballar

cockeyed ['kak,aɪd] *adj* bisojo, bizco; (coll) encorvado, torcido; (slang) disparatado, extravagante

cock'fight' *s* pelea de gallos

cockney ['kakni] *s* londinense *mf* de la clase pobre que habla un dialecto característico; dialecto de la clase pobre de Londres

cock of the walk *s* quiquiriquí *m,* gallito del lugar

cock'pit' *s* gallera; (aer) carlinga

cock'roach' *s* cucaracha

cockscomb ['kaks,kom] *s* cresta de gallo; gorro de bufón; (bot) cresta de gallo, moco de pavo

cock'sure' *adj* muy seguro de sí mismo

cock'tail' *s* coctel *m;* (*of fruit, oysters, etc.*) aperitivo

cocktail party *s* coctel *m*

cocktail shaker ['ʃekər] *s* coctelera

cock·y ['kaki] *adj* (*comp* **-ier;** *super* **-iest**) (coll) arrogante, hinchado; **to be cocky** (coll) tener mucho gallo

cocoa ['koko] *s* cacao; (*drink*) chocolate *m*

cocoanut o **coconut** ['kokə,nʌt] *s* coco

cocoanut palm o **tree** *s* cocotero

cocoon [kə'kun] *s* capullo

C.O.D., c.o.d. *abbr* **collect on delivery;** (Brit) **cash on delivery**

cod [kad] *s* abadejo, bacalao

coddle ['kadəl] *tr* consentir, mimar

code [kod] *s* (*of laws; of manners; of signals*) código; (*of telegraphy*) alfabeto; (*secret system of writing*) cifra, clave *f;* (com)

cl
co

cifrario; **in code** en cifra ‖ *tr (to put in code)* cifrar

code word *s* clave telegráfica

codex ['kodɛks] *s (pl* **codices** ['kodɪ,siz] o ['kadɪ,siz]) *s* códice *m*

cod'fish' *s* abadejo, bacalao

codger ['kadʒər] *s* — **old codger** (coll) anciano, tío

codicil ['kadɪsɪl] *s* codicilo; apéndice *m*

codi•fy ['kadɪ,faɪ] o ['kodɪ,faɪ] *v (pret & pp* **-fied)** *tr* codificar

cod'-liv'er oil *s* aceite *m* de hígado de bacalao

coed o **co-ed** ['ko,ɛd] *s* alumna de una escuela coeducativa

coeducation [,ko,ɛdʒə'keʃən] *s* coeducación

coefficient [,ko•ɪ'fɪʃənt] *adj & s* coeficiente *m*

coerce [ko'ʌrs] *tr* forzar, coactar

coercion [ko'ʌrʃən] *s* compulsión, coacción

coeval [ko'ivəl] *adj & s* coetáneo

coexist [,ko•ɪg'zɪst] *intr* coexistir

coexistence [,ko•ɪg'zɪstəns] *s* coexistencia

coffee ['kɔfi] o ['kafi] *s* café *m; (plant)* cafeto; **black coffee** café solo; **to drink coffee** cafetear

coffee bean *s* grano de café

cof'fee•cake' *s* rosquilla (que se come con el café)

coffee dealer *s* cafetalero

coffee grinder *s* molinillo de café

coffee grounds *spl* poso del café

coffee mill *s* molinillo de café

coffee plantation *s* cafetal *m*

coffee planter *s* cafetalero

coffee pot *s* cafetera

coffee tree *s* cafeto

coffer ['kɔfər] o ['kafər] *s* arca, cofre *m;* **coffers** tesoro, fondos

cof'fer•dam' *s* ataguía, encajonado

coffin ['kɔfɪn] o ['kafɪn] *s* ataúd *m*

C. of S. *abbr* **Chief of Staff**

cog [kag] *s* diente *m (de rueda dentada);* rueda dentada; **to slip a cog** equivocarse

cogency ['kodʒənsi] *s* fuerza *(de un argumento)*

cogent ['kodʒənt] *adj* fuerte, convincente

cogitate ['kadʒɪ,tet] *tr & intr* cogitar, meditar

cognac ['kanjæk] *s* coñac *m*

cognizance ['kagnɪzəns] o ['kanɪzəns] *s* conocimiento; **to take cognizance of** enterarse de

cognizant ['kagnɪzənt] o ['kanɪzənt] *adj* sabedor, enterado

cog'wheel' *s* rueda dentada

cohabit [ko'hæbɪt] *intr* cohabitar

coheir [ko'ɛr] *s* coheredero

cohere [ko'hɪr] *intr* adherirse, pegarse; conformarse, corresponder

coherent [ko'hɪrənt] *adj* coherente

cohesion [ko'hiʒən] *s* cohesión

coiffeur [kwa'fʌr] *s* peluquero

coiffure [kwa'fjur] *s* peinado, tocado

coil [kɔɪl] *s (something wound in a spiral)* rollo; *(single turn of spiral)* vuelta; *(of a still)* serpentín *m; (of hair)* rizo; *(of a spring)* espiral *f;* (elec) carrete *m* ‖ *tr*

arrollar, enrollar; (naut) adujar ‖ *intr* arrollarse, enrollarse; *(like a snake)* serpentear

coil spring *s* resorte *m* espiral

coin [kɔɪn] *s* moneda; *(wedge)* cuña; **to pay back in one's own coin** pagar en la misma moneda; **to toss a coin** echar a cara o cruz ‖ *tr* acuñar; forjar, inventar *(palabras o frases);* **to coin money** (coll) ganar mucho dinero

coincide [,ko•ɪn'saɪd] *intr* coincidir

coincidence [ko'ɪnsɪdəns] *s* coincidencia

coition [ko'ɪʃən] o **coitus** ['ko•ɪtəs] *s* coito

coke [kok] *s* coque *m,* cok *m*

col. *abbr* **colored, colony, column**

colander ['kʌləndər] o ['kaləndər] *s* colador *m,* escurridor *m*

cold [kold] *adj* frío; **to be cold** *(said of a person)* tener frío; *(said of the weather)* hacer frío ‖ *s* frío; *(indisposition)* resfriado; **to catch cold** resfriarse, coger un resfriado

cold blood *s* — **in cold blood** a sangre fría

cold chisel *s* cortafrío

cold comfort *s* poca consolación

cold cream *s* colcrén *m*

cold cuts *spl* fiambres *mpl*

cold feet *spl* (coll) desánimo, miedo

cold'heart'ed *adj* duro, insensible

cold meat *s* carne *f* fiambre

coldness ['koldnɪs] *s* frialdad

cold shoulder *s* — **to turn a cold shoulder on** (coll) tratar con suma frialdad

cold snap *s* corto rato de frío agudo

cold storage *s* conservación en cámara frigorífica

cold war *s* guerra fría

coleslaw ['kol,slɔ] *s* ensalada de col

colic ['kalɪk] *adj & s* cólico

coliseum [,kalɪ'si•əm] *s* coliseo

colitis [kə'laɪtɪs] *s* colitis *f*

coll. *abbr* **colleague, collection, college, colloquial**

collaborate [kə'læbə,ret] *intr* colaborar

collaborationist [kə,læbə'reʃənɪst] *s* colaboracionista *mf*

collaborator [kə'læbə,retər] *s* colaborador *m*

collapse [kə'læps] *s* desplome *m; (in business)* fracaso; (pathol) colapso ‖ *intr* desplomarse; fracasar; postrarse, sufrir colapso

collapsible [kə'læpsɪbəl] *adj* abatible, plegable, desmontable

collar ['kalər] *s* cuello; *(of dog, horse)* collar *m;* (mach) collar

col'lar•band' *s* tirilla de camisa

col'lar•bone' *s* clavícula

collate [kə'let] o ['kalet] *tr* colacionar, cotejar

collateral [kə'lætərəl] *adj* colateral ‖ *s (relative)* colateral *mf;* (com) colateral *m*

collation [kə'leʃən] *s (act of comparing; light meal)* colación

colleague ['kalig] *s* colega *mf;* homólogo

collect ['kalɛkt] *s* (eccl) colecta ‖ [kə'lɛkt] *tr* acumular, reunir; colectar, recaudar *(impuestos);* coleccionar *(sellos de correo, antiguallas);* recolectar *(cosechas);* cobrar *(pasajes;* recoger *(billetes; el correo);* **to**

collect oneself reponerse ‖ *intr* acumularse; **collect on delivery** contra reembolso, cobro contra entrega

collect call *s* llamada por cobrar

collected [kə'lɛktɪd] *adj* sosegado, dueño de sí mismo

collection [kə'lɛkʃən] *s* colección; (*of taxes*) recaudación; (*of mail*) recogida

collection agency *s* agencia de cobros de cuentas

collective [kə'lɛktɪv] *adj* colectivo

collector [kə'lɛktər] *s* (*of stamps, antiques*) coleccionista *mf*; (*of taxes*) recaudador *m*; (*of tickets*) cobrador *m*

college ['kɑlɪdʒ] *s* colegio universitario; (*of cardinals, electors, etc.*) colegio

collide [kə'laɪd] *intr* chocar; **to collide with** chocar con

collie ['kɑli] *s* perro pastoril escocés

collier ['kɑljər] *s* barco carbonero; minero de carbón

collier•y ['kɑljəri] *s* (*pl* **-ies**) mina de carbón

collision [kə'lɪʒən] *s* colisión

colloid ['kɑlɔɪd] *adj & s* coloide *m*

colloquial [kə'lokwɪ•əl] *adj* coloquial, familiar

colloquialism [kə'lokwɪ•ə,lɪzəm] *s* coloquialismo

collo•quy ['kɑləkwi] *s* (*pl* **-quies**) coloquio

collusion [kə'luʒən] *s* colusión, confabulación; **to be in collusion with** estar en inteligencia con

cologne [kə'lon] *s* agua de colonia, colonia ‖ **Cologne** *s* Colonia

colon ['kolən] *s* (anat) colon *m*; (gram) dos puntos

colonel ['kʌrnəl] *s* coronel *m*

colonel•cy ['kʌrnəlsi] *s* (*pl* **-cies**) coronelía

colonial [kə'lonɪ•əl] *adj* colonial ‖ *s* colono

coloniẑe ['kɑlə,naɪz] *tr & intr* colonizar

colonnade [,kɑlə'ned] *s* columnata

colo•ny ['kɑləni] *s* (*pl* **-nies**) colonia

colophon ['kɑlə,fɑn] *s* colofón *m*

color ['kʌlər] *s* color; **the colors** los colores, la bandera; **to call to the colors** llamar a filas; **to give** o **to lend color to** dar visos de probabilidad a; **under color of** so color de, bajo pretexto de; **with flying colors** con banderas desplegadas ‖ *tr* colorar, colorear; (*to excuse, palliate*) colorear; (*to dye*) teñir ‖ *intr* sonrojarse, ponerse colorado, demudarse

col'or-blind' *adj* ciego para los colores

colored ['kʌlərd] *adj* de color; (*specious*) colorado

colorful ['kʌlərfəl] *adj* colorido; pintoresco

coloring ['kʌlərɪŋ] *adj & s* colorante *m*

colorless ['kʌlərlɪs] *adj* incoloro; (fig) insulso

color photography *s* fotografía en colores

color salute *s* (mil) saludo con la bandera

color sergeant *s* sargento abanderado

color screen *s* (phot) pantalla de color

color television *s* televisión en colores

colossal [kə'lɑsəl] *adj* colosal

colossus [kə'lɑsəs] *s* coloso

colt [kolt] *s* potro

Columbus [kə'lʌmbəs] *s* Colón *m*

Columbus Day *s* día *m* de la raza, fiesta de la hispanidad

column ['kɑləm] *s* columna

columnist ['kɑləmɪst] *s* columnista *mf*

com. *abbr* **comedy, commerce, common**

Com. *abbr* **Commander, Commissioner, Committee**

coma ['komə] *s* (pathol) coma *m*

comb [kom] *s* peine *m*; (*currycomb*) almohaza; (*of rooster*) cresta; cresta de ola ‖ *tr* peinar; explorar con minuciosidad

com•bat ['kɑmbæt] *s* combate *m* ‖ ['kɑmbæt] o [kəm'bæt] *v* (*pret & pp* **-bated** o **-batted**; *ger* **-bating** o **-batting**) *tr & intr* combatir

combatant ['kɑmbətənt] *adj & s* combatiente *m*

combat duty *s* servicio de frente

combination [,kɑmbɪ'neʃən] *s* combinación

combine ['kɑmbaɪn] *s* monopolio; segadora trilladora; (coll) combinación ‖ [kəm'baɪn] *tr* combinar ‖ *intr* combinarse

combining form *s* (gram) elemento de compuestos

combustible [kəm'bʌstɪbəl] *adj* combustible; (fig) ardiente, impetuoso ‖ *s* combustible *m*

combustion [kəm'bʌstʃən] *s* combustión

combustion chamber *s* cámara de combustión

come [kʌm] *v* (*pret* **came** [kem]; *pp* **come**) *intr* venir; **to come about** suceder; **to come across** encontrarse con; **to come after** venir detrás de; venir después de; venir por, venir en busca de; **to come again** volver; **to come apart** desunirse, desprenderse; **to come around** restablecerse; volver en sí; rendirse; ponerse de acuerdo; cambiar de dirección; **to come at** alcanzar; **to come back** volver; rehabilitarse; **to come before** anteponerse; **to come between** interponerse; desunir, separar; **to come by** conseguir; **to come down** bajar; (*in social position, etc.*) descender; (*from one person to another*) ser transmitido; **to come downstairs** bajar (*de un piso a otro*); **to come down with** enfermarse de; **to come for** venir por, venir en busca de; **to come forth** salir; aparecer; **to come forward** avanzar; presentarse; **to come from** venir de; provenir de; **to come in** entrar; entrar en; empezar; ponerse en uso; **to come in for** conseguir, recibir; **to come into one's own** ser reconocido; **to come off** desprenderse; acontecer; **to come out** salir; salir a luz; ponerse de largo (*una joven*); divulgarse (*una noticia*); **to come out for** anunciar su apoyo de; **to come out with** descolgarse con; **to come over** dejarse persuadir; pasar, p.ej., **what's come over him?** ¿qué le ha pasado?; **to come through** salir bien, tener éxito; ganar; **to come to** volver en sí; **to come together** juntarse, reunirse; **to come true** hacerse realidad; **to come up** subir; presentarse; **to come upstairs** subir (*de un piso a otro*); **to come up to** acercarse a;

subir a; estar a la altura de; **to come up
with** proponer
come'back' s rehabilitación; (slang) respuesta aguda; **to stage a comeback** rehabilitarse
comedian [kəˈmidɪ•ən] s cómico, comediante
m; autor m de comedias
comedienne [kə,midɪˈɛn] s cómica, come-
dianta
come'down' s humillación, revés m
come•dy [ˈkɑmədi] s (pl **-dies**) comedia cómica; (comicalness) comicidad
come•ly [ˈkʌmli] adj (comp **-lier;** super
-liest) (attractive) donairoso, gracioso;
(decorous) conveniente, decente
comet [ˈkɑmɪt] s cometa m
comfort [ˈkʌmfərt] s comodidad, confort m;
(encouragement, consolation) conforta-
ción; (person) confortador m; (bed cover)
colcha, cobertor m || tr confortar
comfortable [ˈkʌmfərtəbəl] adj cómodo,
confortable; (fairly well off) holgado;
(salary) (coll) suficiente || s colcha, cober-
tor m
comforter [ˈkʌmfərtər] s confortador m,
consolador m; colcha, cobertor m; bufanda
de lana
comforting [ˈkʌmfərtɪŋ] adj confortante
comfort station s quiosco de necesidad
comfrey [ˈkʌmfri] s consuelda
comic [ˈkɑmɪk] adj cómico || s cómico; pe-
riódico cómico; **comics** tiras cómicas
comical [ˈkɑmɪkəl] adj cómico
comic book s tebeo
comic opera s ópera cómica
comic strip s tira cómica
coming [ˈkʌmɪŋ] adj que viene, venidero;
prometedor || s venida
coming out s (of stocks, bonds, etc.) emisión; (of a young girl) puesta de largo,
entrada en sociedad
comma [ˈkɑmə] s coma
command [kəˈmænd] s (commanding) dominio, mando; (order, direction) mandato,
orden f; (e.g., of a foreign language) dominio; (mil) comando; **to be in command
of** estar al mando de; **to take command**
tomar el mando || tr mandar, ordenar;
dominar (un idioma extranjero); merecer
(p.ej., respeto); (mil) comandar || intr
mandar
commandant [,kɑmənˈdænt] o [,kɑmən-
ˈdɑnt] s comandante m
commandeer [,kɑmənˈdɪr] tr reclutar forzosamente; expropiar; (coll) apoderarse de
commander [kəˈmændər] s comandante m;
(of a military order) comendador m
commandment [,kəˈmændmənt] s (Bib)
mandamiento
commemorate [kəˈmɛmə,ret] tr conmemorar
commence [kəˈmɛns] tr & intr comenzar,
empezar
commencement [kəˈmɛnsmənt] s comienzo,
principio; día m de graduación; ceremonia
de graduación

commend [kəˈmɛnd] tr (to entrust) encargar,
encomendar; (to recommend) recomendar;
(to praise) alabar, elogiar
commendable [kəˈmɛndəbəl] adj recomendable
commendation [,kɑmənˈdeʃən] s encargo,
encomienda; recomendación; alabanza,
elogio
comment [ˈkɑmɛnt] s comentario, comento ||
intr comentar; **to comment on** comentar
commentar•y [ˈkɑmən,tɛri] s (pl **-ies**) comentario
commentator [ˈkɑmən,tetər] s comentarista
mf
commerce [ˈkɑmərs] s comercio
commercial [kəˈmʌrʃəl] adj comercial || s
anuncio publicitario radiofónico o televi-
sivo; (rad & telv) programa publicitario
commercial traveler s agente viajero
commiserate [kəˈmɪzə,ret] intr — **to commiserate with** condolerse de
commiseration [kə,mɪzəˈreʃən] s conmiseración
commissar [,kɑmɪˈsɑr] s comisario (en Rusia)
commissar•y [ˈkɑmɪ,sɛri] s (pl **-ies**) (deputy)
comisario; (store) economato
commission [kəˈmɪʃən] s comisión; (mil)
nombramiento; **to put in commission**
poner en uso; poner (un buque) en servicio
activo; **to put out of commission** inutili-
zar, descomponer; retirar (un buque) del
servicio activo || tr comisionar; poner en
uso; poner (un buque) en servicio activo;
(mil) nombrar
commissioned officer s oficial m
commissioner [kəˈmɪʃənər] s comisario;
(person authorized by a commission) co-
misionado
com•mit [kəˈmɪt] v (pret & pp **-mitted;** ger
-mitting) tr cometer (un crimen, una falta;
un negocio a una persona); (to hand over)
confiar, entregar; dar, empeñar (la palabra); (to bind, pledge) comprometer; internar (a un demente); (to memory) encomendar; **to commit oneself** comprometerse,
empeñarse; **to commit to writing** poner
por escrito
commitment [kəˈmɪtmənt] s (act of commit-
ting) comisión; (to an asylum) internación;
(written, order) auto de prisión; compromiso, cometido, empeño
committee [kəˈmɪti] s comité m, comisión
commode [kəˈmod] s (chest of drawers)
cómoda; (washstand) lavabo; (chamber
pot) sillico
commodious [kəˈmodɪ•əs] adj espacioso,
holgado
commodi•ty [kəˈmɑdɪti] s (pl **-ties**) artículo
de consumo, mercancía
commodity exchange s lonja, bolsa mercantil
common [ˈkɑmən] adj común || s campo
común, ejido; **commons** estado llano; (of a
school) refectorio; **the Commons** (Brit) los
Comunes
common carrier s empresa de transportes
públicos
commoner [ˈkɑmənər] s plebeyo; (Brit)
miembro de la Cámara de los Comunes

common law _s_ derecho consuetudinario

com'mon-law' marriage _s_ matrimonio consensual

com'mon•place' _adj_ común, trivial, ordinario ‖ _s_ lugar _m_ común, trivialidad

common sense _s_ sentido común

com'mon-sense' _adj_ cuerdo, razonable

common stock _s_ acción ordinaria; acciones ordinarias

commonweal ['kamən,wil] _s_ bien público

com'mon•wealth' _s_ estado, nación; república; (_state of U.S.A._) estado; (_self-governing associated country_) estado libre asociado; (_association of states_) mancomunidad

commotion [kə'moʃən] _s_ conmoción

commune [kə'mjun] _intr_ conversar; (eccl) comulgar

communicant [kə'mjunıkənt] _s_ comunicante _mf;_ (eccl) comulgante _mf_

communicate [kə'mjunı,ket] _tr_ comunicar ‖ _intr_ comunicarse

communicating [kə'mjunı,ketıŋ] _adj_ comunicador

communication [kə,mjunə'keʃən] _s_ comunicación

communications satellite _s_ satélite _m_ de comunicaciones

communicative [kə'mjunı,ketıv] _adj_ comunicativo

communion [kə'mjunjən] _s_ comunión; **to take communion** comulgar

communion rail _s_ comulgatorio

communiqué [kə,mjunı'ke] o [kə'mjunı,ke] _s_ comunicado, parte _m_

communism ['kamjə,nızəm] _s_ comunismo

communist ['kamjənıst] _s_ comunista _mf_

communi•ty [kə'mjunıti] _s_ (_pl_ **-ties**) vecindario; (_group of people living together_) comunidad

communize ['kamjə,naız] _tr_ comunizar

commutation ticket [,kamjə'teʃən] _s_ billete _m_ de abono

commutator ['kamjə,tetər] _s_ (elec) colector _m_

commute [kə'mjut] _tr_ conmutar ‖ _intr_ viajar con billete de abono

commuter [kə'mjutər] _s_ abonado al ferrocarril

comp. _abbr_ **compare, comparative, composer, composition, compound**

compact [kəm'pækt] _adj_ compacto; breve, preciso ‖ ['kampækt] _s_ convenio, pacto; estuche _m_ de afeites

compact disk _s_ disco compacto

companion [kəm'pænjən] _s_ compañero

companionable [kəm'pænjənəbəl] _adj_ afable, sociable, simpático

companionship [kəm'pænjən,ʃıp] _s_ compañerismo

companionway [kəm'pænjən,we] _s_ (naut) escalera de cámara

compa•ny ['kampəni] _s_ (_pl_ **-nies**) compañía; visita, visitas, invitado, invitados; (naut) tripulación; **to be good company** ser compañero alegre; **to keep company** ir juntos (_un hombre y una mujer_); **to keep some-**

one company hacerle compañía a una persona; **to part company** separarse; enemistarse

company building _s_ edificio social

company office _s_ domicilio social

comparative [kəm'pærətıv] _adj_ & _s_ comparativo

compare [kəm'pɛr] _s_ — **beyond compare** sin comparación, sin par ‖ _tr_ comparar

comparison [kəm'pærısən] _s_ comparación

compartment [kəm'partmənt] _s_ compartimiento; (rr) departamento

compass ['kʌmpəs] _s_ brújula, compás _m;_ ámbito, recinto; alcance _m,_ extensión; **compass** o **compasses** (_for drawing circles_) compás _m_

compass card _s_ (naut) rosa náutica, rosa de los vientos

compassion [kəm'pæʃən] _s_ compasión

compassionate [kəm'pæʃənıt] _adj_ compasivo

com•pel [kəm'pɛl] _v_ (_pret & pp_ **-pelled;** _ger_ **-pelling**) _tr_ forzar, obligar, compeler; imponer (_respeto, silencio_)

compendious [kəm'pɛndı•əs] _adj_ compendioso

compendi•um [kəm'pɛndı•əm] _s_ (_pl_ **-ums** o **-a** [ə]) compendio

compensate ['kampən,set] _tr & intr_ compensar; **to compensate for** compensar

compensation [,kampən'seʃən] _s_ compensación

compete [kəm'pit] _intr_ competir

competence ['kampıtəns] o **competency** ['kampıtənsi] _s_ (_aptitude; legal capacity_) competencia; (_sufficient means to live comfortably_) buen pasar _m_

competent ['kampıtənt] _adj_ competente

competition [,kampı'tıʃən] _s_ (_rivalry_) competencia; (_in a match, examination, etc._) certamen _m_, concurso; (_in business_) concurrencia

competitive [kəm'pɛtıtıv] _adj_ — **to be competitive** poder competir

competitive examination _s_ oposición

competitiveness [kəm'pɛtıtıvnıs] _s_ capacidad competiva

competitive prices _spl_ precios de competencia

competitor [kəm'pɛtıtər] _s_ competidor _m_

compilation [,kampı'leʃən] _s_ compilación, recopilación

compile [kəm'paıl] _tr_ compilar, recopilar

complacence [kəm'plesəns] o **complacency** [kəm'plesənsi] _s_ (_quiet satisfaction_) complacencia; satisfacción de sí mismo

complacent [kəm'plesənt] _adj_ (_willing to please_) complaciente; satisfecho de sí mismo

complain [kəm'plen] _intr_ quejarse

complainant [kəm'plenənt] _s_ (law) demandante _mf_

complaint [kəm'plent] _s_ queja; reclamo; (_grievance_) agravio; (_illness_) enfermedad, mal _m;_ (law) demanda, querella

complaisance [kəm'plezəns] o ['kamplı,zæns] _s_ amabilidad, cortesía

complaisant [kəm'plezənt] o ['kamplı,zænt] _adj_ amable, cortés

complement ['kɑmplɪmənt] s complemento; (nav) dotación ‖ tr complementar
complete [kəm'plit] adj completo ‖ tr completar, terminar, realizar
completion [kəm'pliʃən] s terminación, realización
complex [kəm'plɛks] o ['kɑmplɛks] adj (not simple) complexo; (composite) complejo; (intricate) complicado ‖ ['kɑmplɛks] s complejo; (psychol) complejo; (coll) obsesión
complexion [kəm'plɛkʃən] s (constitution) complexión; (texture of skin, esp. of face) tez f; aspecto general, índole f
compliance [kəm'plaɪəns] s condescendencia; sumisión, rendimiento; **in compliance with** de acuerdo con, en conformidad con
complicate ['kɑmplɪ,ket] tr complicar
complicated ['kɑmplɪ,ketɪd] adj complicado
complication ['kɑmplɪ,keʃən] s complicación
complici·ty [kəm'plɪsɪti] s (pl **-ties**) complicidad, codelincuencia
compliment ['kɑmplɪmənt] s (show of courtesy) cumplimiento; (praise) alabanza, halago; perico (CAm); **compliments** saludos, recuerdos ‖ ['kɑmplɪ,mɛnt] tr cumplimentar; alabar, halagar
complimentary copy [,kɑmplɪ'mɛntəri] s ejemplar m de cortesía
complimentary ticket s billete m de regalo, pase m de cortesía
com·ply [kəm'plaɪ] v (pret & pp **-plied**) intr conformarse; **to comply with** conformarse con, obrar de acuerdo con
component [kəm'ponənt] adj componente ‖ m componente m
compose [kəm'poz] tr componer; **to be composed of** estar compuesto de
composed [kəm'pozd] adj sosegado, tranquilo
composer [kəm'pozer] s componedor m; (mus) compositor m; autor m
composing stick s componedor m
composite [kəm'pɑzɪt] adj & s compuesto
composition [,kɑmpə'zɪʃən] s composición
compositor [kəm'pɑzɪtər] s cajista mf, componedor m
composure [kəm'poʒər] s serenidad, sosiego
compote ['kɑmpot] s (stewed fruit) compota; (dish) compotera
compound ['kɑmpaʊnd] adj compuesto ‖ s compuesto; (gram) vocablo compuesto ‖ [kɑm'paʊnd] tr componer, combinar; (interest) capitalizar
comprehend [,kɑmprɪ'hɛnd] tr comprender
comprehensible [,kɑmprɪ'hɛnsɪbəl] adj comprensible
comprehension [,kɑmprɪ'hɛnʃən] s comprensión
comprehensive [,kɑmprɪ'hɛnsɪv] adj comprensivo, inclusivo, completo
compress ['kɑmprɛs] s (med) compresa, bilma ‖ [kəm'prɛs] tr comprimir
compression [kəm'prɛʃən] s compresión
comprise o **comprize** [kəm'praɪz] tr abarcar, comprender, incluir

compromise ['kɑmprə,maɪz] s (adjustment) componenda, transigencia, transacción; (endangering) comprometimiento ‖ tr (by mutual concessions) componer, transigir; (to endanger) comprometer, exponer ‖ intr transigir, avenirse
comptroller [kən'trolər] s contralor m, interventor m
compulsory [kəm'pʌlsəri] adj obligatorio
computable [kəm'pjutəbəl] adj calculable
computation [,kɑmpju'teʃən] s cálculo, cómputo
compute [kəm'pjut] tr & intr computar, calcular
computer [kəm'pjutər] s ordenador m, computador m; (person) computador m, calculador m
computer dating s citas computerizadas
computer science s informática
comrade ['kɑmræd] o ['kɑmrɪd] s camarada m; cumpa m (SAm)
con. abbr **conclusion, consolidated, contra**
con [kɑn] s (opposite opinion) contra m; (slang) engaño ‖ v (pret & pp **conned**); ger **conning** tr leer con atención, aprender de memoria; (slang) engañar
concave ['kɑnkev] o [kɑn'kev] adj cóncavo
conceal [kən'sil] tr encubrir, ocultar
concealment [kən'silmənt] s encubrimiento, ocultación; (place) escondite m
concede [kən'sid] tr conceder
conceit [kən'sit] s (vanity) orgullo, engreimiento; (witty expression) concepto, dicho ingenioso
conceited [kən'sitɪd] adj orgulloso, engreído
conceivable [kən'sivəbəl] adj concebible
conceive [kən'siv] tr & intr concebir
concentrate ['kɑnsən,tret] tr concentrar ‖ intr concentrarse; **to concentrate on** o **upon** reconcentrarse en
concentric [kən'sɛntrɪk] adj concéntrico
concept ['kɑnsɛpt] s concepto
conception [kən'sɛpʃən] s concepción
concern [kən'sʌrn] s (business establishment) empresa, casa comercial, razón f social; (worry) inquietud, preocupación; (relation, reference) concernencia; (matter) asunto, negocio ‖ tr atañer, concernir; interesar; **as concerns** respecto de; **to whom it may concern** a quien pueda interesar, a quien corresponda
concerning [kən'sʌrnɪŋ] prep respecto de, tocante a
concert ['kɑnsərt] s concierto ‖ [kən'sʌrt] tr & intr concertar
con·cert·mas·ter s concertino
concer·to [kən'ʧɛrto] s (pl **-tos** o **-ti** [ti]) concierto
concession [kən'sɛʃən] s concesión
concessive [kən'sɛsɪv] adj concesivo
concierge [,kɑnsɪ'ʌrʒ] s conserje m
conciliate [kən'sɪli,et] tr conciliar; conciliarse (el respeto, la estima)
conciliatory [kən'sɪli·ə,tori] adj conciliador
concise [kən'saɪs] adj conciso
conclude [kən'klud] tr & intr concluir
concluding [kən'kludɪŋ] adj final

conclusion [kən'kluʒən] s conclusión; (of a letter) despedida
conclusive [kən'klusɪv] adj concluyente
concoct [kən'kɑkt] tr confeccionar; (a story) forjar, inventar
concomitant [kən'kɑmɪtənt] adj & s concomitante m
concord ['kɑŋkɔrd] s concordia; (gram, mus) concordancia
concordance [kən'kɔrdəns] s concordancia
concourse ['kɑŋkors] s (of people) concurso; (of streams) confluencia; bulevar m, gran vía; (of railroad station) gran salón m
concrete ['kɑnkrit] o [kɑn'krit] adj concreto; de hormigón ‖ s hormigón m
concrete block s bloque m de hormigón
concrete mixer s hormigonera, mezcladora de hormigón
concubine ['kɑŋkjə,baɪn] s concubina
con·cur [kən'kʌr] v (pret & pp -curred; ger -curring) intr concurrir
concurrence [kən'kʌrəns] s (happening together) concurrencia; (agreement) acuerdo
concussion [kən'kʌʃən] s concusión
condemn [kən'dɛm] tr condenar
condemnation [,kɑndɛm'neʃən] s condenación
condense [kən'dɛns] tr condensar ‖ intr condensarse
condescend [,kɑndɪ'sɛnd] intr dignarse
condescending [,kɑndɪ'sɛndɪŋ] adj condescendiente con inferiores
condescension [,kɑndɪ'sɛnʃən] s dignación, aire m protector
condiment ['kɑndɪmənt] s condimento
condition [kən'dɪʃən] s condición; on condition that a condición (de) que ‖ tr acondicionar
conditional [kən'dɪʃənəl] adj condicional
conditioned reflex [kən'dɪʃənd] s reflejo acondicionado
condole [kən'dol] intr condolerse
condolence [kən'doləns] s condolencia
condominium [,kɑndə'mɪnɪ·əm] s condominio
condone [kən'don] tr condonar; (legally) despenalizar
condor ['kɑndər] s cóndor m
conduce [kən'djus] intr conducir
conducive [kən'djusɪv] adj conducente, contribuyente
conduct ['kɑndʌkt] s conducta ‖ [kən'dʌkt] tr conducir; to conduct oneself conducirse, comportarse
conductor [kən'dʌktər] s conductor m, guía mf; (elec & phys) conductor m, conductora f; (rr) revisor m; (on trolley or bus) cobrador m
conduit ['kɑndɪt] o ['kɑndu·ɪt] s canal f para alambres o cables
cone [kon] s cono; (of pastry) barquillo; (of paper) cucurucho
confectioner·y [kən'fɛkʃə,nɛri] s (pl -ies) (shop) confitería; (sweetmeats) dulces mpl, confites mpl, confituras

confedera·cy [kən'fɛdərəsi] s (pl -cies) confederación; (for unlawful purpose) conjuración
confederate [kən'fɛdərɪt] s confederado; cómplice mf ‖ [kən'fɛdə,ret] tr confederar ‖ intr confederarse
con·fer [kən'fʌr] v (pret & pp -ferred; ger -ferring) tr conferir ‖ intr conferenciar, consultar
conference ['kɑnfərəns] s conferencia, coloquio
confess [kən'fɛs] tr confesar ‖ intr confesarse
confession [kən'fɛʃən] s confesión
confessional [kən'fɛʃənəl] s confesonario
confession of faith s profesión de fe
confessor [kən'fɛsər] s (person who confesses) confesante mf; (Christian, esp. in spite of persecution; priest) confesor m
confide [kən'faɪd] tr confiar ‖ intr confiar, confiarse; to confide in confiarse en
confidence ['kɑnfɪdəns] s confianza; (secret) confidencia; in strictest confidence bajo la mayor reserva
confident ['kɑnfɪdənt] adj seguro ‖ s confidente m, confidenta
confidential [,kɑnfɪ'dɛnʃəl] adj confidencial
confine ['kɑnfaɪn] s confín m; the confines los confines ‖ [kən'faɪn] tr (to keep within limits) limitar, restringir; (to keep shut in) encerrar; to be confined estar de parto; to be confined to bed tener que guardar cama
confinement [kən'faɪnmənt] s limitación; encierro; parto, sobreparto
confirm [kən'fʌrm] tr confirmar
confirmed [kən'fʌrmd] adj confirmado; empedernido, inveterado
confiscate ['kɑnfɪs,ket] tr confiscar
conflagration [,kɑnflə'greʃən] s conflagración
conflict ['kɑnflɪkt] s conflicto; (of interests, class hours, etc.) incompatibilidad ‖ [kən'flɪkt] intr chocar, desavenirse
conflicting [kən'flɪktɪŋ] adj contradictorio; (events, appointments, class hours, etc.) incompatible, conflictivo
confluence ['kɑnflu·əns] s confluencia
conform [kən'fɔrm] intr conformar, conformarse
conformance [kən'fɔrməns] s conformidad
conformi·ty [kən'fɔrmɪti] s (pl -ties) conformidad
confound [kɑn'faund] tr confundir ‖ ['kɑn'faund] tr maldecir; confound it! ¡maldito sea!
confounded [kɑn'faundɪd] adj confundido; aborrecible; maldito
confrere ['kɑnfrɛr] s colega m
confront [kən'frʌnt] tr (to face boldly) confrontarse con, hacer frente a; (to meet face to face) encontrar cara a cara; (to bring face to face; to compare) confrontar
confrontation [,kɑnfrʌn'teʃən] s enfrentamiento
confuse [kən'fjuz] tr confundir
confusedness [kən'fjuzɪdnɪs] s desorientación

confusion [kən'fjuʒən] s confusión
confute [kən'fjut] tr confutar
Cong. abbr **Congregation, Congressional**
congeal [kən'dʒil] tr congelar ‖ intr congelarse
congenial [kən'dʒinjəl] adj simpático; agradable; compatible; (having the same nature) congenial
congenital [kən'dʒɛnɪtəl] adj congénito
conger eel ['kɑŋgər] s congrio
congest [kən'dʒɛst] tr congestionar ‖ intr congestionarse
congestion [kən'dʒɛstʃən] s congestión
congratulate [kən'grætʃə,let] tr congratular, felicitar
congratulation [kən,grætʃə'leʃən] s congratulación, felicitación
congregate ['kɑŋgrɪ,get] intr congregarse
congregation [,kɑŋgrɪ'geʃən] s congregación; feligresía, fieles mf (de una iglesia)
congress ['kɑŋgrɪs] s congreso
congress·man ['kɑŋgrɪsmən] s (pl -men [mən]) congresista m
conical ['kɑnɪkəl] adj cónico
conj. abbr **conjugation, conjunction**
conjecture [kən'dʒɛktʃər] s conjetura ‖ tr & intr conjeturar
conjugal ['kɑndʒəgəl] adj conyugal
conjugate ['kɑndʒə,get] tr conjugar
conjugation [,kɑndʒə'geʃən] s conjugación
conjunction [kən'dʒʌŋkʃən] s conjunción
conjuration [,kɑndʒə'reʃən] s (superstitious invocation) conjuro; (magic spell) hechizo
conjure [kən'dʒʊr] tr (to appeal to solemnly) conjurar ‖ ['kʌndʒər] o ['kɑndʒər] tr (to exorcise, drive away) conjurar; **to conjure away** conjurar; **to conjure up** evocar; crear, suscitar (dificultades)
con man [kɑn] s (coll) embaucador m, embaucadora
connect [kə'nɛkt] tr conectar; asociar, relacionar ‖ intr enlazarse; asociarse, relacionarse; empalmar, enlazar (dos trenes)
connecting flight s vuelo de enlace
connecting rod s biela
connection [kə'nɛkʃən] s conexión; (relative) pariente mf; (of trains) combinación, enlace m, empalme m; (in subway) correspondencia; **in connection with** con respecto a; juntamente con
connective tissue [kə'nɛktɪv] s (anat) tejido conjuntivo
conning tower ['kɑnɪŋ] s torreta de mando
conniption [kə'nɪpʃən] s pataleta, berrinche m
connive [kə'naɪv] intr confabularse, estar en connivencia
conquer ['kɑŋkər] tr vencer; (by force of arms) conquistar ‖ intr triunfar
conqueror ['kɑŋkərər] s conquistador m, vencedor m
conquest ['kɑŋkwɛst] s conquista
conscience ['kɑnʃəns] s conciencia; **in all conscience** en conciencia
conscientious [,kɑnʃɪ'ɛnʃəs] adj concienzudo
conscientious objector [ab'dʒɛktər] s objetante m de conciencia

conscious ['kɑnʃəs] adj (aware of one's own existence) consciente; (deliberate) intencional; (self-conscious) encogido, tímido; **to become conscious** volver en sí
consciousness ['kɑnʃəsnɪs] s conciencia, conocimiento
consciousness raising s concienciación
conscript ['kɑnskrɪpt] s conscripto, quinto ‖ [kən'skrɪpt] tr reclutar
conscription [kən'skrɪpʃən] s conscripción, quinta
consecrate ['kɑnsɪ,kret] tr consagrar
consecutive [kən'sɛkjətɪv] adj (successive) consecutivo; (continuous) consecuente
consensus [kən'sɛnsəs] s consenso; **the consensus of opinion** la opinión general
consent [kən'sɛnt] s consentimiento; **by common consent** de común acuerdo ‖ intr consentir; **to consent to** consentir en
consequence ['kɑnsɪ,kwɛns] s consecuencia; aires mpl de importancia
consequential [,kɑnsɪ'kwɛnʃəl] adj consiguiente; importante; altivo, pomposo
consequently ['kɑnsɪ,kwɛntli] adv por consiguiente
conservation [,kɑnsər'veʃən] s conservación
conservatism [kən'sʌrvə,tɪzəm] s conservadurismo
conservative [kən'sʌrvətɪv] adj (preservative) conservativo; (disposed to maintain existing views and institutions) conservador; cauteloso, moderado ‖ s preservativo; conservador m
conservato·ry [kən'sʌrvə,tori] s (pl -ries) (school of music) conservatorio; (greenhouse) invernadero
consider [kən'sɪdər] tr considerar
considerable [kən'sɪdərəbəl] adj considerable
considerate [kən'sɪdərɪt] adj considerado
consideration [kən,sɪdə'reʃən] s consideración; **for a consideration** por un precio; **in consideration of** en consideración de; en cambio de; **on no consideration** bajo ningún concepto; **out of consideration for** por respeto a; **without due consideration** sin reflexión
considering [kən'sɪdərɪŋ] adv (coll) teniendo en cuenta las circunstancias ‖ prep en vista de, en razón de ‖ conj en vista de que
consign [kən'saɪn] tr consignar
consignee [,kɑnsaɪ'ni] s consignatario
consignment [kən'saɪnmənt] s consignación
consist [kən'sɪst] intr — **to consist in** consistir en; **to consist of** consistir en, constar de
consisten·cy [kən'sɪstənsi] s (pl -cies) (firmness, amount of firmness) consistencia; (logical connection) consecuencia
consistent [kən'sɪstənt] adj (holding firmly together) consistente; (agreeing with itself or oneself) consecuente; **consistent with** (in accord with) compatible con
consisto·ry [kən'sɪstəri] s (pl -ries) consistorio
consolation [,kɑnsə'leʃən] s consolación, consuelo

console ['kansol] *s* consola; mesa de consola ‖ [kən'sol] *tr* consolar
consommé [,kansə'me] *s* consumado, consommé *m*
consonant ['kansənənt] *adj & s* consonante *f*
consort ['kansort] *s* consorte *mf;* embarcación que acompaña a otra ‖ [kən'sort] *tr* asociar ‖ *intr* asociarse; armonizar, concordar
consorti•um [kən'sorʃɪ•əm] *s* (*pl* -a [ə]) consorcio
conspicuous [kən'spɪkjυ•əs] *adj* manifiesto, claro, evidente; llamativo, vistoso, sugestivo; conspicuo, notable
conspira•cy [kən'spɪrəsi] *s* (*pl* -cies) conspiración, conjuración
conspire [kən'spaɪr] *intr* conspirar, conjurar
constable ['kanstəbəl] o ['kʌnstəbəl] *s* policía *m,* guardia *m,* alguacil *m*
constancy ['kanstənsi] *s* constancia; fidelidad
constant ['kanstənt] *adj* constante; incesante; fiel ‖ *s* constante *f*
constellation [,kanstə'leʃən] *s* constelación
constipate ['kanstɪ,pet] *tr* estreñir
constipation [,kanstɪ'peʃən] *s* estreñimiento, estiquez *f*
constituen•cy [kən'stɪtʃυ•ənsi] *s* (*pl* -cies) votantes *mpl;* clientela; comitentes *mpl;* distrito electoral
constituent [kən'stɪtʃυ•ənt] *adj* constitutivo, componente; (*having power to create or revise a constitution*) constituyente ‖ *s* constitutivo, componente *m;* (*person who appoints another to act for him*) comitente *m*
constitute ['kanstɪ,tjut] *tr* constituir
constitution [,kanstɪ'tju•ʃən] *s* constitución
constrain [kən'stren] *tr* constreñir; detener, encerrar; restringir
construct [kən'strʌkt] *tr* construir
construction [kən'strʌkʃən] *s* construcción; interpretación
construe [kən'stru] *tr* interpretar; deducir, inferir; traducir; (*to combine syntactically*) construir; (*to explain the syntax of*) analizar
consul ['kansəl] *s* cónsul *m*
consular ['kansələr] *adj* consular
consulate ['kansəlɪt] *s* consulado
consulship ['kansəl,ʃɪp] *s* consulado
consult [kən'sʌlt] *tr & intr* consultar
consultant [kən'sʌltənt] *s* consultor *m*
consultation [,kansəl'teʃən] *s* (*consulting*) consulta; (*meeting*) consulta, consultación
consume [kən'sum] o [kən'sjum] *tr* consumir; (*to absorb the interest of*) preocupar; ‖ *intr* consumirse
consumer [kən'sumər] *s* consumidor *m;* (*gas, electricity, etc.*) abonado
consumer credit *s* crédito consuntivo
consumer goods *spl* bienes *mpl* de consumo
consumerism [kən'sumə,rɪzəm] *s* consumerismo
consummate [kən'sʌmɪt] *adj* consumado ‖ ['kansə,met] *tr* consumar
consumption [kən'sʌmpʃən] *s* consunción, consumo; (*pathol*) consunción, tisis *f*

consumptive [kən'sʌmptɪv] *adj* consuntivo; (*path*) tísico ‖ *s* tísico
cont. *abbr* **contents, continental, continued**
contact ['kantækt] *s* contacto; (*elec*) contacto; (*elec*) toma de corriente ‖ *tr* (*coll*) ponerse en contacto con ‖ *intr* contactar
contact breaker *s* (*elec*) ruptor *m*
contact lens *s* lente *m* de contacto, lente invisible, lentilla
contagion [kən'tedʒən] *s* contagio
contagious [kən'tedʒəs] *adj* contagioso
contain [kən'ten] *tr* contener; **to contain oneself** contenerse, refrenarse
container [kən'tenər] *s.* continente *m,* recipiente *m,* vaso, caja, envase *m,* contenedor *m*
containment [kən'tenmənt] *s* contención, refrenamiento
contaminate [kən'tæmɪ,net] *tr* contaminar
contamination [kən,tæmɪ'neʃən] *s* contaminación
contd. *abbr* **continued**
contemplate ['kantəm,plet] *tr & intr* contemplar; pensar, proyectar
contemplation [,kantəm'pleʃən] *s* contemplación; intención, propósito
contemporaneous [kən,tɛmpə'renɪ•əs] *adj* contemporáneo
contemporar•y [kən'tɛmpə,rɛri] *adj* contemporáneo, coetáneo ‖ *s* (*pl* -ies) contemporáneo, coetáneo
contempt [kən'tɛmpt] *s* desprecio; (*law*) contumacia
contemptible [kən'tɛmptɪbəl] *adj* despreciable
contemptuous [kən'tɛmptʃυ•əs] *adj* despreciativo, desdeñoso
contend [kən'tɛnd] *tr* sostener, mantener ‖ *intr* contender
contender [kən'tɛndər] *s* contendiente *mf,* concurrente *mf*
content [kən'tɛnt] *adj & s* contento ‖ ['kantɛnt] *s* contenido; **contents** contenido ‖ [kən'tɛnt] *tr* contentar
contented [kən'tɛntɪd] *adj* contento, satisfecho
contentedness [kən'tɛntɪdnɪs] *s* contentamiento, satisfacción
contention [kən'tɛnʃən] *s* (*strife; dispute*) contención; (*point argued for*) argumento
contentious [kən'tɛnʃəs] *adj* contencioso
contentment [kən'tɛntmənt] *s* contentamiento, contento
contest ['kantɛst] *s* (*struggle, fight*) contienda; (*competition*) competencia, concurso ‖ [kən'tɛst] *tr* disputar; tratar de conseguir ‖ *intr* contender
contestant [kən'tɛstənt] *s* contendiente *mf*
context ['kantɛkst] *s* contexto
contiguous [kən'tɪgjυ•əs] *adj* contiguo
continence [kən'tɪnəns] *s* continencia
continent ['kantɪnənt] *adj & s* continente *m;* **the Continent** la Europa continental
continental [,kantɪ'nɛntəl] *adj* continental ‖ **Continental** *s* habitante *mf* del continente europeo

CO
CO

contingen•cy [kən'tɪndʒənsi] *s* (*pl* -cies) contingencia

contingent [kən'tɪndʒənt] *adj* & *s* contingente *m*

continual [kən'tɪnjʊ•əl] *adj* continuo

continue [kən'tɪnjʊ] *tr* & *intr* continuar; **to be continued** continuará

continui•ty [,kantɪ'nju•ɪti] o [,kantɪ'nu•ɪti] *s* (*pl* -ties) continuidad; (mov, rad, telv) guión *m*; (rad, telv) comentarios o anuncios entre las partes de un programa

continuous [kən'tɪnjʊ•əs] *adj* continuo

continuous showing *s* (mov) sesión continua

continuous waves *spl* (rad) ondas entretenidas

contortion [kən'tɔrʃən] *s* contorsión

contour ['kantʊr] *s* contorno

contr. *abbr* **contracted, contraction**

contraband ['kantrə,bænd] *adj* contrabandista ‖ *s* contrabando

contrabass ['kantrə,bes] *s* contrabajo

contraceptive [,kantrə'sɛptɪv] *adj* & *s* anticonceptivo, contraceptivo

contract ['kantrækt] *s* contrato; **on a contract (to kill)** a sueldo ‖ ['kantrækt] o [kən'trækt] *tr* contraer (*p.ej., matrimonio* ‖ *intr* (*to shrink*) contraerse; (*to enter into an agreement*) comprometerse; **to contract for** contratar

contraction [kən'trækʃən] *s* contracción

contractor [kən'træktər] *s* contratista *mf*

contradict [,kantrə'dɪkt] *tr* contradecir

contradiction [,kantrə'dɪkʃən] *s* contradicción

contradictory [,kantrə'dɪktəri] *adj* (*involving contradiction*) contradictorio; (*inclined to contradict*) contradictor

contrail ['kan,trel] *s* (aer) estela de vapor, rastro de condensación

contral•to [kən'trælto] *s* (*pl* -tos) (*person*) contralto *mf*; (*voice*) contralto *m*

contraption [kən'træpʃən] *s* (coll) artilugio, dispositivo

contra•ry ['kantrɛri] *adv* contrariamente ‖ *adj* contrario ‖ [kən'trɛri] *adj* obstinado, terco ‖ ['kantrɛri] *s* (*pl* -ries) contrario; **on the contrary** al contrario

contrast ['kantræst] *s* contraste *m* ‖ [kən'træst] *tr* comparar; poner en contraste ‖ *intr* contrastar

contravene [,kantrə'vin] *tr* contradecir; contravenir a (*una ley*)

contribute [kən'trɪbjʊt] *tr* contribuir ‖ *intr* contribuir; (*to a newspaper, conference, etc.*) colaborar

contribution [,kantrɪ'bjuʃən] *s* contribución; (*to a newspaper, conference, etc.*) colaboración

contributor [kən'trɪbjʊtər] *s* contribuidor *m*, contribuyente *mf*; colaborador *m*

contrite [kən'traɪt] *adj* contrito

contrition [kən'trɪʃən] *s* contrición

contrivance [kən'traɪvəns] *s* aparato, dispositivio; idea, plan *m*, designio

contrive [kən'traɪv] *tr* (*to devise*) idear, inventar; (*to scheme up*) maquinar, tramar;

(*to bring about*) efectuar; **to contrive to** + *inf* ingeniarse a + *inf* ‖ *intr* maquinar

con•trol [kən'trol] *s* gobierno, mando; chequeo; (*of a scientific experiment*) contrarregistro, control *m*; **controls** mandos; **to get under control** conseguir dominar (*un incendio*) ‖ *v* (*pret* & *pp* -trolled; *ger* -trolling) *tr* gobernar, mandar; comprobar, controlar; **to control oneself** dominarse

controlling interest *s* (el) mayor porcentaje de acciones

control panel *s* (aer) tablero de instrumentos

control stick *s* (aer) mango de escoba, palanca de mando

controversial [,kantrə'vʌrʃəl] *adj* controvertible, disputable; disputador

controver•sy ['kantrə,vʌrsi] *s* (*pl* -sies) controversia, polémica

controvert ['kantrə,vʌrt] o [,kantrə'vʌrt] *tr* (*to argue against*) contradecir; (*to argue about*) controvertir

contumacious [,kantju'meʃəs] *adj* contumaz

contuma•cy ['kantjuməsi] *s* (*pl* -cies) contumacia

contume•ly ['kantjumɪli] *s* (*pl* -lies) contumelia

contusion [kən'tjuʒən] *s* contusión; magullón *m*

conundrum [kə'nʌndrəm] *s* acertijo, adivinanza; problema complicado

convalesce [,kanvə'lɛs] *intr* convalecer

convalescence [,kanvə'lɛsəns] *s* convalecencia

convalescent [,kanvə'lɛsənt] *adj* & *s* convaleciente *mf*

convalescent home *s* clínica de reposo

convene [kən'vin] *tr* convocar ‖ *intr* convenir, reunirse

convenience [kən'vinjəns] *s* comodidad, conveniencia; **at your earliest convenience** a la primera oportunidad que Vd. tenga

convenient [kən'vinjənt] *adj* cómodo, conveniente; próximo

convent ['kanvɛnt] *s* convento; convento de religiosas

convention [kən'vɛnʃən] *s* (*agreement*) convención, conveniencia; (*accepted usage*) costumbre *f*, conveniencia social, convención; (*meeting*) congreso, convención

conventional [kən'vɛnʃənəl] *adj* convencional

conventionali•ty [kən,vɛnʃə'nælɪti] *s* (*pl* -ties) precedente *m* convencional

converge [kən'vʌrʒ] *intr* convergir

conversant [kən'vʌrsənt] *adj* familiarizado, versado

conversation [,kanvər'seʃən] *s* conversación

conversational [,kanvər'seʃənəl] *adj* conversacional

converse ['kanvʌrs] *adj* & *s* contrario ‖ [kən'vʌrs] *intr* conversar

conversion [kən'vʌrʒən] *s* conversión; (*unlawful appropriation*) malversación

convert ['kanvʌrt] *s* convertido, converso ‖ [kən'vʌrt] *tr* convertir ‖ *intr* convertirse

convertible [kən'vʌrtɪbəl] *adj* convertible ‖ *s* (aut) convertible *m*, descapotable *m*

convex [ˈkɑnvɛks] o [kɑnˈvɛks] *adj* convexo
convey [kənˈve] *tr* llevar, transportar; comunicar, participar (*informes*); transferir, traspasar (*bienes de una persona a otra*)
conveyance [kənˈve•əns] *s* transporte *m;* comunicación, participación; vehículo; (*transfer of property*) traspaso; escritura de traspaso
convict [ˈkɑnvɪkt] *s* reo convicto, presidiario ‖ [kənˈvɪkt] *tr* probar la culpabilidad de; declarar convicto (*a un acusado*)
conviction [kənˈvɪkʃən] *s* convencimiento; condena, fallo de culpabilidad
convince [kənˈvɪns] *tr* convencer
convincing [kənˈvɪnsɪŋ] *adj* convincente
convivial [kənˈvɪvɪ•əl] *adj* jovial
convocation [ˌkɑnvəˈkeʃən] *s* asamblea
convoke [kənˈvok] *tr* convocar
convoy [ˈkɑnvɔɪ] *s* convoy *m,* conserva ‖ *tr* convoyar
convulse [kənˈvʌls] *tr* convulsionar; agitar; **to convulse with laughter** mover a risas convulsivas
coo [ku] *intr* arrullar
cook [kʊk] *s* cocinero ‖ *tr* cocer, cocinar, guisar; **to cook up** (coll) falsificar; (coll) maquinar, tramar ‖ *intr* cocer, cocinar
cook′book′ *s* libro de cocina
cookie [ˈkʊki] *s* var de **cooky**
cooking [ˈkʊkɪŋ] *s* cocina, arte *m* de cocinar
cook′stove′ *s* cocina económica
cook•y [ˈkʊki] *s* (*pl* -ies) pasta seca, pastelito dulce
cool [kul] *adj* fresco; frío, indiferente ‖ *s* fresco ‖ *tr* refrescar; moderar ‖ *intr* refrescarse; moderarse; **to cool off** refrescarse; serenarse
cooler [ˈkulər] *s* heladera, refrigerador *m;* refrigerante *m;* cárcel *f*
cool′-head′ed *adj* sereno, tranquilo, juicioso
coolie [ˈkuli] *s* culí *m*
coolish [ˈkulɪʃ] *adj* fresquito
coolness [ˈkulnɪs] *s* fresco, frescura; (fig) frialdad
coon [kun] *s* mapache *m,* oso lavandero
coop [kup] *s* gallinero; (*for fattening capons*) caponera; jaula, redil *m;* (*jail*) (slang) caponera; **to fly the coop** (slang) escabullirse ‖ *tr* encerrar en un gallinero; enjaular; **to coop up** emparedar
coöp. *abbr* **cooperative**
cooper [ˈkupər] *s* barrilero, tonelero
coöperate [koˈɑpə,ret] *intr* cooperar
coöperation [ko,ɑpəˈreʃən] *s* cooperación
coöperative [koˈɑpə,retɪv] *adj* cooperativo
coöpt [koˈɑpt] *tr* cooptar
coördinate [koˈɔrdɪnɪt] *adj* coordenado; (gram) coordinante ‖ *s* (math) coordenada ‖ [koˈɔrdɪ,net] *tr & intr* coordinar
cootie [ˈkuti] *s* (slang) piojo
cop [kɑp] *s* (slang) polizonte *m* ‖ *v* (*pret & pp* **copped;** *ger* **copping**) *tr* (slang) hurtar
copartner [koˈpɑrtnər] *s* consocio, copartícipe *mf*
cope [kop] *intr* — **to cope with** hacer frente a, enfrentarse con
cope′stone′ *s* piedra de albardilla

copier [ˈkɑpɪ•ər] *s* (*person who copies*) copiante *mf,* copista *mf,* imitador *m;* (*apparatus*) copiador *m,* copiadora
copilot [ˈko,paɪlət] *s* copiloto
coping [ˈkopɪŋ] *s* albardilla
copious [ˈkopɪ•əs] *adj* copioso
copper [ˈkɑpər] *adj* cobreño; (*in color*) cobrizo ‖ *s* cobre *m;* (*coin*) calderilla, vellón *m;* (slang) polizonte *m*
cop′per•head′ *s* víbora de cabeza de cobre
cop′per•smith′ *s* cobrero
coppery [ˈkɑpərɪ] *adj* cobreño; (*in color*) cobrizo
coppice [ˈkɑpɪs] o **copse** [kɑps] *s* soto, monte bajo
copulate [ˈkɑpjə,let] *intr* copularse
cop•y [ˈkɑpi] *s* (*pl* -ies) copia; (*of a book*) ejemplar *m;* (*of a magazine*) número; (*document to be reproduced in print*) original *m,* manuscrito ‖ *v* (*pret & pp* -ied) *tr* copiar
cop′y•book′ *s* cuaderno de escritura
copyist [ˈkɑpɪ•ɪst] *s* copiante *mf,* copista *mf;* imitador *m*
cop′y•right′ *s* (derechos de) propiedad literaria ‖ *tr* registrar en el registro de la propiedad literaria
copy writer *s* escritor publicitario
co•quet [koˈkɛt] *v* (*pret & pp* -quetted; *ger* -quetting) *intr* coquetear; burlarse
coquet•ry [ˈkokətri] o [koˈkɛtri] *s* (*pl* -ries) coquetería; burla
coquette [koˈkɛt] *s* coqueta
coquettish [koˈkɛtɪʃ] *adj* coqueta
cor. *abbr* **corner, coroner, correction, corresponding**
coral [ˈkɑrəl] o [ˈkɔrəl] *adj* coralino ‖ *s* coral *m*
coral reef *s* arrecife *m* de coral
cord [kɔrd] *s* cordón *m;* piola ‖ *tr* acordonar
cordial [ˈkɔrdʒəl] *adj* cordial ‖ *s* licor tónico; (*medicine*) cordial *m*
cordiali•ty [kɔrˈdʒælɪti] *s* (*pl* -ties) cordialidad
corduroy [ˈkɔrdə,rɔɪ] *s* pana; **corduroys** pantalones *mpl* de pana
core [kor] *s* corazón *m;* (*of an electromagnet*) núcleo
corespondent [ˌkorɪsˈpɑndənt] *s* cómplice *mf* del demandado en juicio de divorcio
Corinth [ˈkɔrɪnθ] *s* Corinto *f*
cork [kɔrk] *s* corcho; corcho, tapón *m* de corcho; tapón (*de cualquier materia*) ‖ *tr* encorchar, tapar con corcho
corking [ˈkɔrkɪŋ] *adj* (slang) brutal, extraordinario
cork oak *s* alcornoque *m*
cork′screw′ *s* sacacorchos *m,* tirabuzón *m*
cormorant [ˈkɔrmərənt] *s* cormorán *m,* cuervo marino
corn [kɔrn] *s* (*in U.S.A.*) maíz *m;* (*in England*) trigo; (*in Scotland*) avena; grano (*de maíz, trigo*); (*on the foot*) callo; (coll) aguardiente *m;* (slang) trivialidad
corn bread *s* pan *m* de maíz
corn′cake′ *s* tortilla de maíz
corn′cob′ *s* mazorca de maíz, carozo

corncob pipe *s* pipa de fumar hecha de una mazorca de maíz

corn'crib' *s* granero para maíz

corn cure *adj* callicida *m*

cornea ['kɔrnɪ•ə] *s* córnea

corner ['kɔrnər] *s* ángulo; (*esp. where two streets meet*) esquina; (*inside angle formed by two or more surfaces; secluded place; region, quarter*) rincón *m;* (*of eye*) comisura, rabillo; (*of lips*) comisura; (*awkward position*) apuro, aprieto; monopolio; **around the corner** a la vuelta de la esquina; **to turn the corner** doblar la esquina; pasar el punto más peligroso ‖ *tr* arrinconar; monopolizar

corner cupboard *s* rinconera

corner room *s* habitación de esquina

cor'ner•stone' *s* piedra angular; (*of a new building*) primera piedra

cornet [kɔr'nɛt] *s* corneta

corn exchange *s* bolsa de granos

corn'field' *s* (*in U.S.A.*) maizal *m;* (*in England*) trigal *m;* (*in Scotland*) avenal *m*

corn flour *s* harina de maíz

corn'flow'er *s* cabezuela

corn'husk' *s* perfolla

cornice ['kɔrnɪs] *s* cornisa

Cornish ['kɔrnɪʃ] *adj & s* córnico

corn liquor *s* chicha

corn meal *s* harina de maíz

corn on the cob *s* maíz *m* en la mazorca

corn plaster *s* emplasto para los callos

corn silk *s* cabellos, barbas del maíz

corn'stalk' *s* tallo de maíz

corn'starch' *s* almidón *m* de maíz

cornucopia [,kɔrnə'kopɪ•ə] *s* cornucopia

Cornwall ['kɔrn,wɔl] *s* Cornualles

corn•y ['kɔrni] *adj* (*comp* **-ier;** *super* **-iest**) de maíz; (coll) gastado, trivial, pesado

corollar•y ['kɑrə,lɛri] o ['kɔrə,lɛri] *s* (*pl* **-ies**) corolario

coronation [,kɑrə'neʃən] o [,kɔrə'neʃən] *s* coronación

coroner ['kɑrənər] o ['kɔrənər] *s* juez *m* de guardia

coroner's inquest *s* pesquisa dirigida por el juez de guardia

coronet ['kɑrə,nɛt] o ['kɔrə,nɛt] *s* (*worn by members of nobility*) corona; (*ornamental band of jewels worn on head*) diadema *f*

Corp. *abbr* **Corporation**

corporal ['kɔrpərəl] *adj* corporal ‖ *s* (mil) cabo

corporation [,kɔrpə'reʃən] *s* (*provincial, municipal, or service entity*) corporación; sociedad anónima por acciones

corps [kor] *s* (*pl* **corps** [korz]) cuerpo; (mil) cuerpo

corps de ballet [kor də bæ'lɛ] *s* cuerpo de baile

corpse [kɔrps] *s* cadáver *m*

corpulent ['kɔrpjələnt] *adj* corpulento

corpuscle ['kɔrpəsəl] *s* corpúsculo, partícula; (physiol) glóbulo

corr. *abbr* **correspondence, corresponding**

cor•ral [kə'ræl] *s* corral *m* ‖ *v* (*pret & pp* **-ralled;** *ger* **-ralling**) *tr* acorralar

correct [kə'rɛkt] *adj* correcto; (*proper*) cumplido ‖ *tr* corregir

correction [kə'rɛkʃən] *s* corrección

corrective [kə'rɛktɪv] *adj & s* correctivo

correctness [kə'rɛktnɪs] *s* corrección; cumplimiento, cumplido

correlate ['kɔrə,let] *tr* correlacionar ‖ *intr* correlacionarse

correlation [,kɔrə'leʃən] *s* correlación

correlative [kə'rɛlətɪv] *adj & s* correlativo

correspond [,kɑrɪ'spɑnd] o [,kɔrɪ'spɑnd] *intr* corresponder; (*to communicate by writing*) corresponderse

correspondence [,kɑrɪ'spɑndəns] o [,kɔrɪ'spɑndəns] *s* correspondencia

correspondence school *s* escuela por correspondencia

correspondent [,kɑrɪ'spɑndənt] o [,kɔrɪ'spɑndənt] *adj* correspondiente ‖ *s* correspondiente *mf;* (*for a newspaper*) corresponsal *mf*

corresponding [,kɑrɪ'spɑndɪŋ] o [,kɔrɪ'spɑndɪŋ] *adj* correspondiente

corridor ['kɑrɪdər] o ['kɔrɪdər] *s* corredor *m*, pasillo

corroborate [kə'rɑbə,ret] *tr* corroborar

corrode [kə'rod] *tr* corroer ‖ *intr* corroerse

corrosion [kə'roʒən] *s* corrosión

corrosive [kə'rosɪv] *adj & s* corrosivo

corrugated ['kɑrə,getɪd] o ['kɔrə,getɪd] *adj* acanalado, ondulado

corrupt [kə'rʌpt] *adj* corrompido ‖ *tr* corromper ‖ *intr* corromperse

corruption [kə'rʌpʃən] *s* corrupción

corsage [kɔr'sɑʒ] *s* (*bodice*) corpiño, jubón *m;* (*bouquet*) ramillete *m* que se lleva en el pecho o la cintura

corsair ['kɔr,sɛr] *s* corsario

corset ['kɔrsɪt] *s* corsé *m*

corset cover *s* cubrecorsé *m*

Corsica ['kɔrsɪkə] *s* Córcega

Corsican ['kɔrsɪkən] *adj & s* corso

cortege [kɔr'teʒ] *s* procesión; (*retinue*) cortejo, séquito

cor•tex ['kɔr,tɛks] *s* (*pl* **-tices** [tɪ,siz]) corteza; corteza cerebral

cortisone ['kɔrtɪ,son] *s* cortisona

corvette [kɔr'vɛt] *s* corbeta

cosmetic [kɑz'mɛtɪk] *adj & s* cosmético

cosmic ['kɑzmɪk] *adj* cósmico

cosmonaut ['kɑzmə,nɔt] *s* cosmonauta *mf*

cosmopolitan [,kɑzmə'pɑlɪtən] *adj & s* cosmopolita *mf*

cosmos ['kɑzməs] *s* cosmos *m;* (bot) cosmos

Cossack ['kɑ,sæk] *adj & s* cosaco

cost [kɔst] o [kɑst] *s* coste *m*, costo; **at cost** a coste y costas; **at all costs** a toda costa; **costs** (law) costas ‖ *v* (*pret & pp* **cost**) *intr* costar; **cost what it may** cueste lo que cueste

cost accounting *s* escandallo

Costa Rican ['kɑstə 'rikən] o ['kɔste 'rikən] *adj & s* costarricense *mf*, costarriqueño

cost'-ben'e•fit analysis *s* análisis costebeneficio

cost exemption *s* gratuidad

cost, insurance, and freight costo, seguro y flete

cost·ly [ˈkɔstli] o [ˈkɑstli] adj (comp **-lier;** super **-liest**) costoso, dispendioso; (lavish) pródigo; (magnificent) suntuoso

cost of living s costo de la vida, carestía de la vida

costume [ˈkɑstjum] s traje m; (garb worn on stage, at balls, etc.) disfraz m, traje de época

costume ball s baile m de trajes

costume jewelry s joyas de fantasía, bisutería

cot [kɑt] s catre m

coterie [ˈkotəri] s círculo, grupo; (clique) corrillo

cottage [ˈkɑtɪdʒ] s cabaña; casita de campo

cottage cheese s naterón m, requesón m

cotter pin [ˈkɑtər] s chaveta

cotton [ˈkɑtən] s algodón m ‖ intr — **to cotton up to** (coll) aficionarse a

cotton field s algodonal m

cotton gin s desmotadera de algodón

cotton picker [ˈpɪkər] s recogedor m de algodón; máquina para recolectar el algodón

cot·ton·seed' s semilla de algodón

cottonseed oil s aceite m de algodón

cotton waste s hilacha de algodón, estopa de algodón

cot·ton·wood' s chopo del Canadá, chopo de Virginia

cottony [ˈkɑtəni] adj algodonoso

couch [kautʃ] s canapé m, sofá m ‖ tr expresar

cougar [ˈkugər] s puma m

cough [kɔf] o [kɑf] s tos f ‖ tr — **to cough up** arrojar por la boca; (slang) sudar, entregar ‖ intr toser; (artificially, to attract attention) destoserse

cough drop s pastilla para la tos

cough syrup s jarabe m para la tos

could [kud] v aux pude, podía; podría

council [ˈkaunsəl] s (deliberative or legislative assembly) consejo; (of a municipality) concejo; (eccl) concilio

council·man [ˈkaunsəlmən] s (pl **-men** [mən]) concejal m

councilor [ˈkaunsələr] s consejero

coun·sel [ˈkaunsəl] s consejo; (advisor) consejero; (consultant) consultor m; (lawyer) abogado consultor; **to keep one's own counsel** no revelar sus intenciones ‖ v (pret & pp **-seled** o **-selled;** ger **-seling** o **-selling**) tr aconsejar ‖ intr aconsejarse

counselor [ˈkaunsələr] s consejero; abogado

count [kaunt] s (act of counting) cuenta, recuento; (result of counting) suma, total m; (nobleman) conde m; (charge) (law) cargo; **to take the count** (box) dejarse contar diez ‖ tr contar; **to count off** separar contando; **to count out** no incluir; (sport) declarar vencido ‖ intr contar; (to be worth consideration) valer; **to count for** valer; **to count on** contar con

countable [ˈkauntəbəl] adj contable

count'-down' s cuenta a cero, cuenta atrás

countenance [ˈkauntɪnəns] s cara, rostro, semblante m; (composure) compostura, serenidad; **to keep one's countenance** contenerse; **to lose countenance** conturbarse; **to put out of countenance** avergonzar, confundir ‖ tr aprobar, apoyar, favorecer

counter [ˈkauntər] adj contrario ‖ adv en el sentido opuesto; **counter to** a contrapelo de ‖ s contador m; (piece of wood or metal for keeping score) ficha; (board in shop over which business is transacted) mostrador m; (box) contragolpe m ‖ tr oponerse a; contradecir ‖ intr (box) dar un contragolpe; **to counter with** replicar con

coun·ter·act' tr contrarrestar, contrariar

coun·ter·attack' s contraataque m ‖ **coun·ter·attack'** tr & intr contraatacar

coun·ter·bal'ance s contrabalanza, contrapeso ‖ **coun·ter·bal'ance** tr contrabalancear, contrapesar

coun·ter·clock'wise' adj & adv en el sentido contrario al de las agujas del reloj

coun·ter·cul'ture s contracultura

coun·ter·es'pionage s contraespionaje m

counterfeit [ˈkauntərfɪt] adj contrahecho, falsificado ‖ s contrahechura, falsificación; moneda falsa ‖ tr contrahacer, falsificar

counterfeiter [ˈkauntər,fɪtər] s contrahacedor m, falsificador m; monedero falso

counterfeit money s moneda falsa

countermand [ˈkauntər,mænd] o [ˈkauntər,-mɑnd] s contramandato ‖ tr contramandar; hacer volver

coun·ter·march' s contramarcha ‖ intr contramarchar

coun·ter·offen'sive s contraofensiva

coun·ter·pane' s cubrecama

coun·ter·part' s contraparte f; copia, duplicado

coun·ter·plot' s contratreta ‖ v (pret & pp **-plotted;** ger **-plotting**) tr complotar contra (la treta de otro u otros)

coun·ter·point' s contrapunto

Counter Reformation s Contrarreforma

coun·ter·rev'olu'tion s contrarrevolución

coun·ter·sign' s contraseña ‖ tr refrendar

coun·ter·sink' v (pret & pp **-sunk**) tr avellanar

coun·ter·spy' s (pl **-spies**) contraespía mf

coun·ter·stroke' s contragolpe m

coun·ter·weight' s contrapeso

countess [ˈkauntɪs] s condesa

countless [ˈkauntlɪs] adj incontable, innumerable

countrified [ˈkʌntrɪ,faɪd] adj campesino, rústico

coun·try [ˈkʌntri] s (pl **-tries**) (territory of a nation) país m; (land of one's birth) patria; (not the city) campo

country club s club m campestre

country cousin s isidro

country estate s heredad, hacienda de campo

coun'try·folk' *s* gente *f* del campo, campesinos

country gentleman *s* propietario acomodado de finca rural

country house *s* casa de campo, quinta

country jake [dʒek] *s* (coll) patán *m*

country life *s* vida rural

country·man ['kʌntrimən] *s* (*pl* -men [mən]) compatriota *m;* campesino

country people *s* gente *f* del campo, gente de capa parda

coun'try·side' *s* campiña

coun'try·wide' *adj* nacional

country·woman ['kʌntrɪ,wʊmən] *s* (*pl* -women [,wɪmɪn]) compatriota *f;* campesina

coun·ty ['kaʊnti] *s* (*pl* -ties) (*small political unit*) partido; (*domain of a count*) condado

county seat *s* cabeza de partido

coup [ku] *s* golpe *m*

coup de grâce [ku də 'grɑs] *s* puñalada de misericordia, golpe *m* de gracia

coup d'état [ku de'tɑ] *s* golpe *m* de estado

coupé [ku'pe] *s* cupé *m*

couple ['kʌpəl] *s* par *m;* (*man and wife*) matrimonio; (*two people dancing together*) pareja; (elec, mech) par *m;* (*two more or less*) (coll) par *m* ‖ *tr* acoplar, juntar, unir ‖ *intr* juntarse, unirse

coupler ['kʌplər] *s* (rr) enganche *m*

couplet ['kʌplɪt] *s* copla, pareado

coupon [ku'pɑn] o [kju'pɑn] *s* (*of a bond*) cupón *m;* (*piece detached from larger piece*) talón *m*

courage ['kʌrɪdʒ] *s* valor *m*, ánimo; firmeza, resolución; to have the courage of one's convictions ajustarse abiertamente con su conciencia; to pluck up courage hacer de tripas corazón

courageous [kə'redʒəs] *adj* valiente, animoso

courier ['kʌrɪ·ər] o ['kʊrɪ·ər] *s* estafeta, mensajero; guía *m*

course [kors] *s* (*onward movement*) curso; (*of a ship*) derrota, rumbo; (*of time*) transcurso; (*of events*) marcha; (*in school*) asignatura, curso; (*of a meal*) plato; campo de golf; (mas) hilada; in the course of en el decurso de; of course por supuesto, naturalmente

court [kort] *s* (*of justice*) tribunal *m;* (*of a king*) corte *f;* (*open space enclosed by a building*) atrio, patio; (*for tennis*) cancha, pista; to pay court to hacer la corte a ‖ *tr* cortejar; buscar, solicitar

courteous ['kʌrtɪ·əs] *adj* cortés

courtesan ['kʌrtɪzən] o ['kortɪzən] *s* cortesana

courte·sy ['kʌrtɪsi] *s* (*pl* -sies) cortesía

court'house' *s* palacio de justicia

courtier ['kortɪ·ər] *s* cortesano, palaciego

court jester *s* bufón *m*

court·ly ['kortli] *adj* (*comp* -lier; *super* -liest) cortés, cortesano; (*pertaining to the court*) cortesano

court'-mar'tial *s* (*pl* courts-martial) consejo de guerra ‖ *v* (*pret & pp* -tialed o

-tialled; *ger* -tialing o -tialling) *tr* someter a consejo de guerra

court plaster *s* tafetán *m* inglés

court'room' *s* sala de justicia, tribunal *m*

courtship ['kortʃɪp] *s* cortejo, galanteo; noviazgo

court'yard' *s* atrio, patio

cousin ['kʌzɪn] *s* primo

cove [kov] *s* cala, ensenada

covenant ['kʌvənənt] *s* convenio, pacto; contrato; (Bib) alianza ‖ *tr & intr* pactar

cover ['kʌvər] *s* cubierta; (*of a magazine*) portada; (*place for one person at table*) cubierto; (*for a bed*) cobertor *m;* to take cover ocultarse; under cover bajo cubierto, bajo techado; oculto; disfrazado; under cover of (*e.g., the night*) a cubierto de; so capa de; under separate cover bajo cubierta separada, por separado ‖ *tr* cubrir; (*to line, to coat*) recubrir, revestir; recorrer (*cierta distancia*); cubrirse (*la cabeza*); tapar (*una olla*) ‖ *intr* cubrirse

coverage ['kʌvərɪdʒ] *s* (*amount or space covered*) alcance *m;* (*of news*) reportaje *m;* (*funds to meet liabilities*) cobertura

coveralls ['kʌvər,ɔlz] *s* mono

cover charge *s* precio del cubierto

covered ['kʌvərd] *adj* cubierto; (*wire*) forrado; (*bridge*) cubierto

covered wagon *s* carromato

cover girl *s* (coll) muchacha hermosa en la portada de una revista

covering ['kʌvərɪŋ] *s* cubierta, envoltura

covert ['kʌvərt] *adj* disimulado, secreto

cov'er·up' *s* efugio, subterfugio

covet ['kʌvɪt] *tr* codiciar

covetous ['kʌvɪtəs] *adj* codicioso

covetousness ['kʌvɪtəsnɪs] *s* codicia

covey ['kʌvi] *s* (*brood*) nidada; (*in flight*) bandada; corro, grupo

cow [kaʊ] *s* vaca ‖ *tr* acobardar, intimidar

coward ['kaʊ·ərd] *s* cobarde *mf*

cowardice ['kaʊ·ərdɪs] *s* cobardía; llamada (Mex)

cowardly ['kaʊ·ərdli] *adj* cobarde; correlón (Col, Mex); llamón (Mex) ‖ *adv* cobardemente

cow'bell' *s* cencerro

cow'boy' *s* vaquero; gaucho (Arg)

cowcatcher ['kaʊ,kætʃər] *s* quitapiedras *m*, rastrillo; trompa (Col, Chile)

cower ['kaʊ·ər] *intr* agacharse

cow'herd' *s* vaquero, pastor *m* de ganado vacuno

cow'hide' *s* cuero; (*whip*) zurriago ‖ *tr* zurriagar

cowl [kaʊl] *s* capucha, cogulla; (aer) cubierta del motor; (aut) cubretablero, bóveda

cow'lick' *s* mechón *m*, remolino (*pelos que se levantan sobre la frente*)

cowpox ['kaʊ,pɑks] *s* vacuna

coxcomb ['kɑks,kom] *s* petimetre *m*, mequetrefe *m*

coxswain ['kɑksən] o ['kɑk,swen] *s* timonel *m;* contramaestre *m*

coy [kɔɪ] *adj* recatado, modesto; coquetón

co•zy ['kozi] *adj* (*comp* **-zier;** *super* **-ziest**) cómodo ‖ *s* (*pl* **-zies**) cubretetera
cp. *abbr* **compare**
c.p. *abbr* **candle power**
C.P.A. *abbr* **certified public accountant**
cpd. *abbr* **compound**
cr. *abbr* **credit, creditor**
crab [kræb] *s* cangrejo; (*grouch*) cascarrabias *mf*
crab apple *s* manzana silvestre
crabbed ['kræbɪd] *adj* avinagrado, ceñudo
crab grass *s* garranchuelo
crab louse *s* ladilla
crack [kræk] *adj* (coll) de primera clase; (*shot*) (coll) certero ‖ *s* grieta, hendidura; (*noise*) crujido, estallido; (coll) instante *m*, momento; (*joke*) (slang) chiste *m;* **at the crack of dawn** al romper el alba ‖ *tr* agrietar, hender; chasquear (*un látigo*); abrir (*una caja fuerte*) por la fuerza; cascar (*nueces*); descifrar (*un código*); (slang) decir (*un chiste*); (slang) descubrir (*un secreto*); **to crack a smile** (slang) sonreír; **to crack up** (coll) alabar, elogiar ‖ *intr* agrietarse; crujir; cascarse (*la voz de una persona*); enloquecerse; ceder, someterse; **to crack up** fracasar; perder la salud; estrellarse (*un avión*)
cracked [krækt] *adj* agrietado; (*ice*) picado; (coll) mentecato, loco
cracker ['krækər] *s* galleta
crack•le•ware *s* grietado
crack•pot *adj & s* (slang) excéntrico, tarambana *mf*
crack•up *s* fracaso; colisión; derrota; (aer) aterrizaje violento; (coll) colapso
cradle ['kredəl] *s* cuna; (*of handset*) horquilla ‖ *tr* acunar
cra•dle•song *s* canción de cuna, arrullo
craft [kræft] o [krɑft] *s* arte *m*, arte manual; astucia, maña; nave *f* ‖ *spl* naves
craftiness ['kræftɪnɪs] *s* astucia
crafts•man ['kræftsmən] *s* (*pl* **-men** [mən]) artesano; artista *m*
craftsmanship ['kræftsmən, ʃɪp] *s* artesanía
craft•y ['kræfti] o ['krɑfti] *adj* (*comp* **-ier;** *super* **-iest**) astuto, mañoso
crag [kræg] *s* peñasco, despeñadero
cram [kræm] *v* (*pret & pp* **crammed;** *ger* **cramming**) *tr* atascar, atracar, embutir; (coll) aprender apresuradamente ‖ *intr* atracarse; (*to study hard*) (coll) empollar
cramp [kræmp] *s* (*metal bar*) grapa, laña; (*clamp*) abrazadera; (*painful contraction of muscle*) calambre *m;* **cramps** retortijón *m* de tripas ‖ *tr* engrapar, lañar; apretar; dar calambre a
cranber•ry ['kræn,bɛri] *s* (*pl* **-ries**) arándano agrio
crane [kren] *s* (*bird*) grulla; (*derrick*) grúa, guinche *m*, güinche *m* ‖ *tr* estirar (*el cuello*) ‖ *intr* estirar el cuello
crani•um ['kreni•əm] *s* (*pl* **-a** [ə]) cráneo
crank [kræŋk] *s* manivela, manubrio; (coll) estrafalario ‖ *tr* hacer girar (*el motor*) con la manivela

crank•case• *s* caja de cigüeñal, cárter *m* del cigüeñal
crank•shaft• *s* cigüeñal *m*
crank•y ['kræŋki] *adj* (*comp* **-ier;** *super* **-iest**) malhumorado; (*queer*) estrafalario
cran•ny ['kræni] *s* (*pl* **-nies**) hendidura, grieta, rendija
crape [krep] *s* crespón *m;* crespón fúnebre, crespón negro
crape•hang•er *s* (slang) aguafiestas *mf*
craps [kræps] *s* juego de dados; **to shoot craps** jugar a los dados
crash [kræʃ] *s* caída, desplome *m;* colisión, choque *m;* estallido, estrépito; fracaso; crac financiero; lienzo grueso; (aer) aterrizaje violento ‖ *tr* romper con estrépito, estrellar; **to crash a party** (slang) asistir a una fiesta sin invitación; **to crash the gate** (slang) colarse de gorra ‖ *intr* caer, desplomarse; romperse con estrépito, estallar; (*in business*) quebrar; aterrizar violentamente, estrellarse (*un avión*); **to crash into** chocar con
crash dive *s* sumersión instantánea (*de submarino*)
crash landing *s* aterrizaje violento
crash program *s* programa intensivo
crash test *s* (aut) ensayo de choque
crass [kræs] *adj* espeso, tosco; (*ignorance, mistake*) craso
crate [kret] *s* (*box made of slats*) jaula; (*basket*) banasta, cuévano ‖ *tr* embalar en jaula, embalar con listones
crater ['kretər] *s* cráter *m*
cravat [krə'væt] *s* corbata
crave [krev] *tr* anhelar, ansiar; pedir (*indulgencia*) ‖ *intr* — **to crave for** anhelar, ansiar; pedir con insistencia
craven ['krevən] *adj & s* cobarde *mf*
craving ['krevɪŋ] *s* anhelo, ansia, deseo ardiente
craw [krɔ] *s* buche *m*
crawl [krɔl] *s* arrastre *m;* gateado ‖ *intr* reptar, arrastrarse, gatear; (*to have a feeling of insects on skin*) hormiguear; **to crawl along** andar paso a paso; **to crawl up** trepar
crayon ['kre•ən] *s* creyón *m*
craze [krez] *s* boga, moda; locura, manía ‖ *tr* enloquecer
cra•zy ['krezi] *adj* (*comp* **-zier;** *super* **-ziest**) loco; (*rickety*) desvencijado; achacoso, débil; **crazy as a bedbug** (slang) loco de atar; **to be crazy about** (coll) estar loco por; **to drive crazy** volver loco
crazy bone *s* hueso de la alegría
creak [krik] *s* crujido, rechinamiento ‖ *intr* crujir, rechinar
creak•y ['kriki] *adj* (*comp* **-ier;** *super* **-iest**) crujidero, rechinador
cream [krim] *s* crema; (*e.g., of society*) crema, nata y flor ‖ *tr* desnatar (*la leche*)
creamer•y ['krimri] *s* (*pl* **-ies**) mantequería, quesería, lechería
cream puff *s* bollo de crema
cream separator *s* desnatadora

co
cr

cream·y [ˈkrimi] adj (comp **-ier;** super **-iest**) cremoso

crease [kris] s arruga, pliegue m; (in trousers) raya ‖ tr arrugar, plegar

create [kriˈet] tr crear

creation [kriˈeʃən] s creación

creative [kriˈetɪv] adj creativo

creator [kriˈetər] s creador m

creature [ˈkritʃər] s criatura; (being, strange being) ente m; animal m

credence [ˈkridəns] s creencia; **to give credence to** dar fe a

credentials [krɪˈdɛnʃəlz] spl credenciales fpl

credible [ˈkrɛdɪbəl] adj creíble

credit [ˈkrɛdɪt] s crédito; **to take credit for** atribuirse el mérito de ‖ tr acreditar; **to credit a person with** atribuirle a una persona el mérito de

creditable [ˈkrɛdɪtəbəl] adj honorable, estimable

credit card s tarjeta de crédito

creditor [ˈkrɛdɪtər] s acreedor m

cre·do [ˈkrido] o [ˈkredo] s (pl **-dos**) credo

credulous [ˈkrɛdʒələs] adj crédulo; creído

creed [krid] s credo

creek [krik] s arroyo, riachuelo

creep [krip] v (pret & pp **crept** [krɛpt]) intr arrastrarse; (on all fours) gatear; (to climb) trepar; (with a sensation of insects) hormiguear; **to creep up on** acercarse insensiblemente a

creeper [ˈkripər] s planta rastrera, planta trepadora

creeping [ˈkripɪŋ] adj lento, progresivo; (plant) rastrero ‖ s arrastramiento

cremate [ˈkrimet] tr incinerar

cremation [krɪˈmeʃən] s cremación; incineración

cremato·ry [ˈkrimə,tori] adj crematorio ‖ s (pl **-ries**) crematorio

crème de menthe [krɛm də ˈmãt] s crema de menta

Creole [ˈkri·ol] adj & s criollo

crescent [ˈkrɛsənt] s (moon in first or last quarter) creciente f de la luna; (shape of moon in either of these phases) media luna; panecillo (en forma de media luna)

cress [krɛs] s mastuerzo

crest [krɛst] s cresta

crestfallen [ˈkrɛst,fɔlən] adj cabizbajo

crest'-line' model s (aut) modelo estrella

Cretan [ˈkritən] adj & s cretense mf

Crete [krit] s Creta

cretonne [krɪˈtɑn] s cretona

crevice [ˈkrɛvɪs] s grieta

crew [kru] s equipo; (of a ship) dotación, tripulación; (group, esp. of armed men) banda, cuadrilla

crew cut s corte m de pelo a cepillo

crib [krɪb] s pesebre m; camita de niño; (coll) plagio; (student's pony) (coll) chuleta ‖ v (pret & pp **cribbed;** ger **cribbing**) tr & intr (coll) hurtar

cricket [ˈkrɪkɪt] s (ent) grillo; (sport) cricquet m; (coll) juego limpio

crier [ˈkraɪ·ər] s pregonero

crime [kraɪm] s crimen m, delito

criminal [ˈkrɪmɪnəl] adj & s criminal mf; delictivo

criminal code s código penal

criminal law s derecho penal

criminal negligence s imprudencia temeraria

criminology [,krɪməˈnɑlədʒi] s criminología

crimp [krɪmp] s rizado, rizo; **to put a crimp in** (coll) estorbar, impedir ‖ tr rizar

crimple [ˈkrɪmpəl] tr arrugar, rizar ‖ intr arrugarse, rizarse

crimson [ˈkrɪmzən] adj & s carmesí m ‖ intr enrojecerse

cringe [krɪndʒ] intr arrastrarse, reptar, encogerse

crinkle [ˈkrɪŋkəl] s arruga, pliegue m; (in the water) rizo u onda ‖ tr arrugar, plegar ‖ intr arrugarse

cripple [ˈkrɪpəl] s zopo, lisiado ‖ tr lisiar, estropear; dañar, perjudicar

cri·sis [ˈkraɪsɪs] s (pl **-ses** [siz]) crisis f

crisp [krɪsp] adj frágil, quebradizo; (air, weather) refrescante; decisivo

criteri·on [kraɪˈtɪrɪ·ən] s (pl **-a** [ə]) u **-ons**) criterio

critic [ˈkrɪtɪk] s crítico; (reviewer) reseñador; (faultfinder) criticón m

critical [ˈkrɪtɪkəl] adj crítico; (faultfinding) criticón

criticism [ˈkrɪtɪ,sɪzəm] s crítica

criticize [ˈkrɪtɪ,saɪz] tr & intr criticar

critique [krɪˈtik] s (art of criticism) crítica; ensayo crítico

croak [krok] s (of raven) graznido; canto de ranas ‖ intr graznar (el cuervo); croar (la rana); (morir) (slang) reventar

Croat [ˈkro·æt] s (native or inhabitant) croata mf; (language) croata m

Croatian [kroˈeʃən] adj & mf croata mf

cro·chet [kroˈʃe] s croché m ‖ v (pret & pp **-cheted** [ˈʃed]; ger **-cheting** [ˈʃe·ɪŋ]) tr trabajar con aguja de gancho ‖ intr hacer croché

crocheting [kroˈʃə·ɪŋ] s labor f de ganchillo

crochet needle s aguja de gancho

crock [krɑk] s cacharro, vasija de barro cocido

crockery [ˈkrɑkəri] s loza

crocodile [ˈkrɑkə,daɪl] s cocodrilo

crocodile tears spl lágrimas de cocodrilo

crocus [ˈkrokəs] s azafrán m, croco

crone [kron] s vieja acartonada, vieja arrugada

cro·ny [ˈkroni] s (pl **-nies**) compinche mf

crook [kruk] s gancho, garfio; curva; (of shepherd) cayado; (coll) fullero, ladrón m; chalecón m (Mex) ‖ tr encorvar; (slang) empinar (el codo) ‖ intr encorvarse

crooked [ˈkrukɪd] adj encorvado, torcido; (person or his conduct) torcido; **to go crooked** (coll) torcerse

croon [krun] intr cantar con voz suave, cantar con melancolía exagerada

crooner [ˈkrunər] s cantor de voz suave, cantor melancólico

crop [krɑp] s cosecha; (head of hair) cabellera; cabello corto; (of a bird) buche m; (whip) látigo; (of appointments, promo-

tions, heroes, etc.) hornada ‖ *v* (*pret & pp* **cropped;** *ger* **cropping**) *tr* desmochar (*un árbol*); desorejar (*a un animal*); esquilar, trasquilar ‖ *intr* — **to crop out** o **up** aflorar; asomar, dejarse ver, manifestarse inesperadamente

crop dusting *s* aerofumigación, fumigación aérea

croquet [kro'ke] *s* crocquet *m*

croquette [kro'kɛt] *s* croqueta

crosier ['kroʒər] *s* báculo pastoral, cayado

cross [krɑs] o [krɔs] *adj* transversal, travieso; (*breed*) cruzado; malhumorado, enfadado ‖ *s* cruz *f;* (*of races; of two roads*) cruce *m;* **to take the cross** (*to join a crusade*) cruzarse ‖ *tr* cruzar; (*to oppose*) contrariar, frustrar; **to cross off** u **out** borrar; **to cross oneself** hacerse la señal de la cruz; **to cross one's mind** ocurrírsele a uno; **to cross one's t's** poner travesaño a las tes, poner el palo a las tes ‖ *intr* cruzar; cruzarse; **to cross over** atravesar de un lado a otro

cross'bones' *spl* huesos cruzados (*símbolo de la muerte*)

cross'bow' *s* ballesta

cross'breed' *v* (*pret & pp* **-bred** [,brɛd]) *tr* cruzar (*animales o plantas*)

cross'coun'try *adj* a campo traviesa; a través del país

cross'cur'rent contracorriente *f;* (fig) tendencia encontrada

cross'-exam'i·na'tion *s* interrogatorio riguroso; (law) repregunta

cross'ex·am'ine *tr* interrogar rigurosamente; (law) repreguntar

cross-eyed ['krɑs,aɪd] *adj* bisojo, bizco, ojituerto

crossing ['krɑsɪŋ] *s* (*of lines, streets, etc.*) cruce *m;* (*of the ocean*) travesía; (*of a river*) vado; (rr) crucero, paso a nivel

crossing gate *s* barrera, barrera de paso a nivel

crossing point *s* punto de cruce

cross'patch' *s* (coll) gruñón *m*

cross'piece' *s* travesaño

cross reference *s* contrarreferencia, remisión

cross'road' *s* vía transversal; **crossroads** encrucijada, cruce *m;* **at the crossroads** en el momento crítico

cross section *s* corte *m* transversal; (fig) sección representativa

cross street *s* calle traviesa, calle de travesía

cross'word' **puzzle** *s* crucigrama *m*

crotch [krɑtʃ] *s* (*forked piece*) horcajadura, bifurcación; (*between legs*) entrepierna, bragadura, horcajadura

crotchety ['krɑtʃɪti] *adj* caprichoso, estrambótico, de mal genio

crouch [krautʃ] *s* posición agachada ‖ *intr* agacharse, acuclillarse

croup [krup] *s* garrotillo, crup *m;* (*of horse*) anca, grupa

croupier ['krupɪ·ər] *s* crupié *m*

crouton ['krutɑn] *s* corteza de pan

crow [kro] *s* corneja, grajo, chova; (*cry of the cock*) quiquiriquí *m;* (*crowbar*) alzaprima; **as the crow flies** a vuelo de pájaro; **to eat**

crow (coll) cantar la palinodia; **to have a crow to pick with** (coll) tener que habérselas con ‖ *intr* cantar (*el gallo*); jactarse; **to crow over** jactarse de

crow'bar' *s* alzaprima, pie *m* de cabra

crowd [kraud] *s* gentío, multitud; (*flock of people*) caterva, tropel *m;* (*mob, common people*) populacho, vulgo; (*clique, set*) corrillo, grupo ‖ *tr* apiñar, apretar, atestar; (*to push*) empujar ‖ *intr* apiñarse, apretarse, atestarse; (*to mill around*) arremolinarse

crowded ['kraudɪd] *adj* atestado, concurrido

crown [kraun] *s* corona; (*of hat*) copa ‖ *tr* coronar; (checkers) coronar; (slang) golpear en la cabeza

crowned head *s* testa coronada

crown prince *s* príncipe heredero

crown princess *s* princesa heredera

crow's'-foot' *s* (*pl* **-feet'**) pata de gallo

crow's'-nest' *s* (naut) cofa de vigía, torre *f* de vigía

crucial ['kruʃəl] *adj* crucial; difícil, penoso

crucible ['krusɪbəl] *s* crisol *m*

crucifix ['krusɪfɪks] *s* crucifijo

crucifixion [,krusɪ'fɪkʃən] *s* crucifixión

cruci·fy ['krusɪ,faɪ] *v* (*pret & pp* **-fied**) *tr* crucificar

crude [krud] *adj* (*raw, unrefined*) crudo; (*lacking culture*) grosero, tosco; (*unfinished*) basto, sin labrar

crudi·ty ['krudɪti] *s* (*pl* **-ties**) crudeza; grosería, tosquedad; bastedad

cruel ['kruəl] *adj* cruel

cruel·ty ['kru·əlti] *s* (*pl* **-ties**) crueldad

cruet ['kru·ɪt] *s* ampolleta

cruet stand *s* angarillas, vinagreras

cruise [kruz] *s* viaje *m* por mar; (aer, naut) crucero ‖ *tr* (naut) cruzar ‖ *intr* cruzar; (coll) andar de un lado a otro

cruise missile *s* misil *m* crucero

cruiser ['kruzər] *s* (nav) crucero

cruising ['kruzɪŋ] *adj* de crucero ‖ *s* (aer, naut) crucero

cruising radius *s* autonomía

cruising speed *s* velocidad de crucero

cruller ['krʌlər] *s* buñuelo

crumb [krʌm] *s* migaja; (*soft part of bread*) miga; (*given to a beggar*) mendrugo ‖ *tr* desmigar (*el pan*); (culin) empanar, cubrir con pan rallado; limpiar (*la mesa*) de migajas ‖ *intr* desmigarse, desmenuzarse

crumble ['krʌmbəl] *tr* desmenuzar ‖ *intr* desmenuzarse; (*to fall to pieces gradually*) desmoronarse

crum·my ['krʌmi] *adj* (*comp* **-mier;** *super* **-miest**) (slang) desaseado, sucio; (slang) de mal gusto, de mala muerte

crumple ['krʌmpəl] *tr* arrugar, ajar, chafar ‖ *intr* arrugarse, ajarse

crunch [krʌntʃ] *tr* ronchar, ronzar ‖ *intr* crujir

crusade [kru'sed] *s* cruzada ‖ *intr* hacer una cruzada

crusader [kru'sedər] *s* cruzado

crush [krʌʃ] *s* aplastamiento; (*of people*) aglomeración, bullaje *m;* **to have a crush on**

(slang) estar perdido por ‖ *tr* aplastar, machacar, magullar; (*to grind*) moler; bocartear (*el mineral*); (*to oppress, grieve*) abrumar

crush hat *s* clac *m*

crust [krʌst] *s* corteza; corteza de pan; (*scab*) costra

crustacean [krʌsˈteʃən] *s* crustáceo

crustaceous [krʌsˈteʃəs] *adj* crustáceo

crust·y [ˈkrʌsti] *adj* (*comp* **-ier;** *super* **-iest**) (*scabby*) costroso; áspero, grosero, rudo

crutch [krʌtʃ] *s* muleta

crux [krʌks] *s* punto capital; enigma *m*

cry [kraɪ] *s* (*pl* **cries**) grito; (*weeping*) lloro, llorera; (*of peddler*) pregón *m*; (*of wolf*) aullido; (*of bull*) bramido; **in full cry** en plena persecución; **to have a good cry** desahogarse en lágrimas abundantes ‖ *v* (*pret & pp* **cried**) *tr* decir a gritos; (*to announce publicly*) pregonar; **to cry one's eyes** o **heart out** llorar amargamente; **to cry out** decir a gritos; pregonar ‖ *intr* gritar; (*to weep*) llorar; aullar (*el lobo*); bramar (*el toro*); **to cry for** clamar por; **to cry for joy** llorar de alegría; **to cry out** clamar; **to cry out against** clamar contra; **to cry out for** clamar, clamar por

cry'ba'by *s* (*pl* **-bies**) llorón *m*, llorona, lloraduelos *mf*

crypt [krɪpt] *s* cripta

cryptic(al) [ˈkrɪptɪk(əl)] *adj* enigmático, misterioso

crystal [ˈkrɪstəl] *s* cristal *m*

crystal ball *s* bola de cristal

crystalline [ˈkrɪstəlɪn] o [ˈkrɪstə,laɪn] *adj* cristalino

crystallize [ˈkrɪstə,laɪz] *tr* cristalizar ‖ *intr* cristalizarse

C.S. *abbr* **Christian Science, Civil Service**

ct. *abbr* **cent**

cu. *abbr* **cubic**

cub [kʌb] *s* cachorro

Cuban [ˈkjubən] *adj & s* cubano

cubbyhole [ˈkʌbɪ,hol] *s* chiribitil *m*

cube [kjub] *adj* (*root*) cúbico ‖ *s* cubo; (*of ice*) cubito ‖ *tr* cubicar

cubic [ˈkjubɪk] *adj* cúbico

cub reporter *s* (coll) reportero novato

cuckold [ˈkʌkəld] *adj & s* cornudo ‖ *tr* encornudar

cuckoo [ˈkʊku] *adj* (slang) mentecato, loco ‖ *s* cuclillo, cuco; (*call of cuckoo*) cucú *m*

cuckoo clock *s* reloj *m* de cuclillo

cucumber [ˈkjukəmbər] *s* pepino

cud [kʌd] *s* bolo alimenticio; **to chew the cud** rumiar

cuddle [ˈkʌdəl] *s* abrazo cariñoso ‖ *tr* abrazar con cariño ‖ *intr* estar abrazados, arrimarse cariñosamente

cudg·el [ˈkʌdʒəl] *s* garrote *m*, porra; **to take up the cudgels for** salir a la defensa de ‖ *v* (*pret & pp* **-eled** o **-elled;** *ger* **-eling** o **-elling**) *tr* apalear, aporrear

cue [kju] *s* señal *f*, indicación; (*hint*) indirecta; (*rôle*) papel *m*; (*rod used in billiards*) taco; (*of hair*) coleta; (*of people in line*) cola; (theat) apunte *m*

cuff [kʌf] *s* (*of shirt*) puño; (*of trousers*) doblez *f*, vuelta; (*blow*) bofetada ‖ *tr* abofetear

cuff links *spl* gemelos

cuirass [kwɪˈræs] *s* coraza

cuisine [kwɪˈzin] *s* cocina (*arte culinario*)

culinary [ˈkjulɪ,nɛri] *adj* culinario

cull [kʌl] *tr* (*to choose, pick*) entresacar, escoger; (*to gather, pluck*) coger, recoger

culm [kʌlm] *s* (*coal dust*) cisco; (*stalk of grasses*) caña, tallo

culminate [ˈkʌlmɪ,net] *intr* culminar; **to culminate in** conducir a, terminar en

culpable [ˈkʌlpəbəl] *adj* culpable

culprit [ˈkʌlprɪt] *s* acusado; reo

cult [kʌlt] *s* culto; secta

cultivate [ˈkʌltɪ,vet] *tr* cultivar

cultivated [ˈkʌltɪ,vetɪd] *adj* culto, cultivado

cultivation [,kʌltɪˈveʃən] *s* (*of the land, the arts, one's memory, etc.*) cultivo; (*refinement*) cultura

culture [ˈkʌltʃər] *s* cultura

cultured [ˈkʌltʃərd] *adj* culto

culvert [ˈkʌlvərt] *s* alcantarilla

cumbersome [ˈkʌmbərsəm] *adj* incómodo, molesto; (*clumsy*) pesado, inmanejable

cunning [ˈkʌnɪŋ] *adj* (*sly*) astuto; (*clever*) hábil; (*attractive*) gracioso, mono ‖ *s* astucia; habilidad, destreza

cup [kʌp] *s* taza; (*of thermometer*) cubeta; (mach) vaso de engrase; (sport) copa; (*of sorrow*) (fig) copa; **in one's cups** borracho ‖ *v* (*pret & pp* **cupped;** *ger* **cupping**) *tr* ahuecar dando forma de taza o copa a; poner ventosa a

cupboard [ˈkʌbərd] *s* alacena, aparador *m*, armario

cupidity [kjuˈpɪdɪti] *s* codicia

cupola [ˈkjupələ] *s* cúpula

cur [kʌr] *s* perro mestizo, perro de mala raza; (*despicable fellow*) canalla *m*

curate [ˈkjurɪt] *s* cura *m*

curative [ˈkjurətɪv] *adj* curativo ‖ *s* curativa

curator [kjuˈretər] *s* conservador *m*

curb [kʌrb] *s* (*of sidewalk*) encintado; (*of well*) brocal *m*; (*of bit*) barbada; (*market*) bolsín *m*; (*check, restraint*) freno; (vet) corva ‖ *tr* contener, refrenar

curb'stone' *s* piedra de encintado; brocal *m* de pozo

curd [kʌrd] *s* cuajada ‖ *tr* cuajar ‖ *intr* cuajarse

curdle [ˈkʌrdəl] *tr* cuajar; **to curdle the blood** horrorizar ‖ *intr* cuajar

cure [kjur] *s* cura, curación ‖ *tr* curar ‖ *intr* curar; curarse

cure'-all' *s* sanalotodo

curfew [ˈkʌrfju] *s* queda, cubrefuego; toque *m* de queda; hora de cierre

curi·o [ˈkjurɪ,o] *s* (*pl* **-os**) curiosidad

curiosi·ty [,kjurɪˈɑsɪti] *s* (*pl* **-ties**) curiosidad

curious [ˈkjurɪəs] *adj* curioso

curl [kʌrl] *s* bucle *m*, rizo; (*spiral-shaped curl*) tirabuzón *m*; (*of smoke*) espiral *f*; (*curling*) rizado ‖ *tr* encrespar, ensortijar, rizar; (*to coil, to roll up*) arrollar; fruncir (*los labios*) ‖ *intr* encresparse, ensortijarse, rizarse; arrollarse; **to curl up** arrollarse; (*in bed*) encogerse; (*to break up, collapse*) (coll) desplomarse

curler ['kʌrlər] s (*hair*) rulo, bigudí m

curlicue ['kʌrlɪ,kju] s ringorrango

curling iron s rizador m, maquinilla de rizar

curl'pa'per s torcida, papelito para rizar el pelo

curl•y ['kʌrli] adj (*comp* -**ier**; *super* -**iest**) crespo, rizo

curmudgeon [kər'mʌdʒən] s cicatero, tacaño, erizo

currant ['kʌrənt] s pasa de Corinto; (*Ribes alpinum*) calderilla

curren•cy ['kʌrənsi] s (*pl* -**cies**) moneda corriente, dinero en circulación; uso corriente

current ['kʌrənt] adj corriente ‖ s corriente *f;* (elec) corriente *f*

current account s cuenta corriente

current events spl actualidades, sucesos de actualidad

curricu•lum [kə'rɪkjələm] s (*pl* -**lums** o -**la** [lə]) plan m de estudios

cur•ry ['kʌri] s (*pl* -**ries**) cari m ‖ v (*pret & pp* -**ried**) tr curtir (*las pieles*); almohazar (*el caballo*); **to curry favor** procurar complacer

cur'ry•comb' s almohaza ‖ tr almohazar

curse [kʌrs] s maldición; (*profane oath*) reniego, voto; (*evil, misfortune*) calamidad ‖ tr maldecir ‖ intr jurar, echar votos; echar carnes (Mex)

cursed ['kʌrsɪd] o [kʌrst] adj maldito; aborrecible

cursive ['kʌrsɪv] adj cursivo ‖ s cursiva

cursory ['kʌrsəri] adj apresurado, rápido, superficial, de paso

curt [kʌrt] adj áspero, brusco; corto, conciso

curtail [kər'tel] tr acortar, abreviar, cercenar

curtain ['kʌrtən] s cortina; (theat) telón m; **to draw the curtain** correr la cortina; **to drop the curtain** (theat) bajar el telón ‖ tr encortinar; separar con cortina; cubrir, ocultar

curtain call s llamada a la escena para recibir aplausos

curtain raiser ['rezər] s (theat) pieza preliminar

curtain ring s anilla

curtain rod s riel m

curt•sy ['kʌrtsi] s (*pl* -**sies**) cortesía, reverencia ‖ v (*pret & pp* -**sied**) intr hacer una cortesía

curve [kʌrv] s curva ‖ tr encorvar ‖ intr encorvarse; volver, virar

curved [kʌrvd] adj curvo, encorvado; (*crooked*) combo

cushion ['kʊʃən] s cojín m, almohada; (*of billiard table*) baranda ‖ tr amortiguar

cusp [kʌsp] s cúspide *f*

cuspidor ['kʌspɪ,dɔr] s escupidera

custard ['kʌstərd] s flan m, natillas

custodian [kəs'todɪ•ən] s custodio; (*of a house or building*) casero

custo•dy ['kʌstədi] s (*pl* -**dies**) custodia; **in custody** en prisión; **to take into custody** prender

custom ['kʌstəm] s costumbre; (*customers*) parroquia, clientela; **customs** aduana; derechos de aduana

customary ['kʌstə,mɛri] adj acostumbrado, de costumbre

cus'tom-built' adj hecho por encargo, fuera de serie

customer ['kʌstəmər] s parroquiano, cliente *mf;* (*of a café or restaurant*) consumidor *m;* (coll) individuo, sujeto, tipo

customer service s servicio postventa

cus'tom-house' adj aduanero ‖ s aduana

cus'tom-made' adj hecho a la medida

customs clearance s despacho de aduana

customs officer s aduanero

custom tailor s sastre m a la medida

custom work s trabajo hecho a la medida

cut [kʌt] s corte *m;* (*piece cut off*) tajada; (*wound*) cuchillada; (*for a canal, highway, etc.*) desmonte *m;* (*shortest way*) atajo; (*in prices, wages, etc.*) reducción; (*of a garment*) corte *m*, hechura; (*in winnings, earnings, etc.*) parte *f;* (*diamond*) talla; (typ) estampa, grabado; (tennis) golpe *m* cortante; (*absence from school*) (coll) falta de asistencia; (*snub*) (coll) desaire *m;* (coll) palabra hiriente ‖ v (*pret & pp* **cut**; *ger* **cutting**) tr cortar; practicar (*un agujero*); reducir (*gastos*); capar, castrar; desleír, diluir; (coll) ausentarse de, faltar a (*la clase*); (coll) desairar; (coll) herir; **to cut down** cortar; derribar cortando; castigar (*gastos*); **to cut off** cortar; desheredar; amputar (*una pierna*); (elec) cortar (*la corriente, la ignición*); cerrar (*el carburador*); **to cut open** abrir cortando; **to cut out** cortar; sacar cortando; labrar; suprimir, omitir; (*to take the place of*) desbancar; soplar (*la dama a un rival*); (slang) dejarse de (*disparates*); **to cut short** terminar de repente; interrumpir, chafar; **to cut teeth** endentecer; **to cut up** desmenuzar, despedazar; criticar severamente; (coll) afligir ‖ intr cortar; cortarse; salir (*los dientes*); (coll) fumarse la clase; **to cut in** entrar de repente; interrumpir; (*in a dance*) cortar o separar la pareja; **to cut under** vender a menor precio que; **to cut up** (slang) travesear, hacer travesuras; (slang) jaranear

cut-and-dried ['kʌtən'draɪd] adj dispuesto de antemano; monótono, poco interesante

cutaway coat ['kʌtə,we] s chaqué m

cut'back' s reducción; discontinuación; incumplimiento; (mov) retorno a una época anterior

cute [kjut] adj (coll) mono, monono; (coll) astuto, listo

cut glass s cristal tallado

cuticle ['kjutɪkəl] s cutícula

cutlass ['kʌtləs] s alfanje m

cutler ['kʌtlər] s cuchillero

cutlery ['kʌtləri] s cuchillería; (*knives, forks, and spoons*) cubierto

cutlet ['kʌtlɪt] s chuleta; croqueta

cut'out' s (*design to be cut out*) recortado; (aut) escape m libre, válvula de escape libre

cr
cu

cut'-rate' *adj* de precio reducido

cutter [ˈkʌtər] *s* cortador *m*; (*machine*) cortadora; (naut) escampavía

cut'throat' *adj* asesino; implacable ‖ *s* asesino

cutting [ˈkʌtɪŋ] *adj* cortante; hiriente, mordaz ‖ *s* corte *m*; (*from a newspaper*) recorte *m*; (hort) esqueje *m*

cutting edge *s* canto de corte

cuttlefish [ˈkʌtəl,fɪʃ] *s* jibia

cut'wa'ter *s* espolón *m*, tajamar *m*

cwt. *abbr* **hundredweight**

cyanamide [saɪˈænə,maɪd] *s* cianamida; cianamida de calcio

cyanide [ˈsaɪ•ə,naɪd] *s* cianuro

cybernetics [,saɪbərˈnɛtɪks] *s* cibernética

cycle [ˈsaɪkəl] *s* ciclo; bicicleta; (*of an internal-combustion engine*) tiempo; (phys) periódo ‖ *intr* montar en bicicleta

cyclic(al) [ˈsaɪklɪk(əl)] o [ˈsɪklɪk(əl)] *adj* cíclico

cyclone [ˈsaɪklon] *s* ciclón *m*

cyl. *abbr* **cylinder, cylindrical**

cylinder [ˈsɪlɪndər] *s* cilindro

cylinder block *s* bloque *m* de cilindros

cylinder bore *s* alesaje *m*

cylinder head *s* (*of steam engine*) tapa del cilindro; (*of gas engine*) culata del cilindro

cylindric(al) [sɪˈlɪndrɪk(əl)] *adj* cilíndrico

cymbal [ˈsɪmbəl] *s* címbalo, platillo

cynic [ˈsɪnɪk] *adj & s* cínico

cynical [ˈsɪnɪkəl] *adj* cínico

cynicism [ˈsɪnɪ,sɪzəm] *s* cinismo

cynosure [ˈsaɪnə,ʃʊr] o [ˈsɪnə,ʃʊr] *s* blanco de las miradas; guía, norte *m*

cypress [ˈsaɪprəs] *s* ciprés *m*

Cyprus [ˈsaɪprəs] *s* Chipre *f*

Cyrillic [sɪˈrɪlɪk] *adj* cirílico

Cyrus [ˈsaɪrəs] *s* Ciro

cyst [sɪst] *s* quiste *m*

czar [zɑr] *s* zar *m*; (fig) autócrata *m*

czarina [zɑˈrinə] *s* zarina

Czech [tʃɛk] *adj & s* checo

Czecho-Slovak [ˈtʃɛkoˈslovæk] *adj & s* checoeslovaco o checoslovaco

Czecho-Slovakia [,tʃɛkosloˈvækɪ•ə] *s* Checoeslovaquia o Checoslovaquia

D

D, d [di] cuarta letra del alfabeto inglés

d. *abbr* **date, day, dead, degree, delete, diameter, died, dollar, denarius (penny)**

D. *abbr* **December, Democrat, Duchess, Duke, Dutch**

D.A. *abbr* **District Attorney**

dab [dæb] *s* toque ligero; masa pastosa ‖ *v* (*pret & pp* **dabbed;** *ger* **dabbing**) *tr* tocar ligeramente, frotar suavemente

dabble [ˈdæbəl] *tr* salpicar ‖ *intr* chapotear; **to dabble in** meterse en; jugar a (*la Bolsa*); especular en (*granos*)

dad [dæd] *s* (coll) papá *m*

dad•dy [ˈdædi] *s* (*pl* **-dies**) (coll) papá *m*

daffodil [ˈdæfədɪl] *s* narciso trompón

daff•y [ˈdæfi] *adj* (*comp* **-ier;** *super* **-iest**) (coll) chiflado

dagger [ˈdægər] *s* daga, puñal *m*; (typ) cruz *f*, obelisco; **to look daggers at** apuñalar con la mirada

dahlia [ˈdæljə] *s* dalia

dai•ly [ˈdeli] *adj* cotidiano, diario ‖ *adv* diariamente ‖ *s* (*pl* **-lies**) diario

dain•ty [ˈdenti] *adj* (*comp* **-tier;** *super* **-tiest**) delicado ‖ *s* (*pl* **-ties**) golosina

dair•y [ˈdɛri] *s* (*pl* **-ies**) lechería, vaquería

dais [ˈde•ɪs] *s* estrado

dai•sy [ˈdezi] *s* (*pl* **-sies**) margarita

daisy wheel *s* (*computer*) margarita (*impresora*)

dal•ly [ˈdæli] *v* (*pret & pp* **-lied**) *intr* juguetear, retozar; tardar, malgastai el tiempo

dam [dæm] *s* represa, embalse *m*; (*female quadruped*) madre *f*; (dent) dique *m* ‖ *v* (*pret & pp* **dammed;** *ger* **damming**) *tr* represar, embalsar; cerrar, tapar, obstruir

damage [ˈdæmɪdʒ] *s* daño, perjuicio; (*to one's reputation*) desdoro; (com) avería; **damages** daños y perjuicios ‖ *tr* dañar, perjudicar; averiar

damascene [ˈdæmə,sin] o [,dæməˈsin] *adj* damasquino ‖ *s* ataujía, damasquinado ‖ *tr* ataujiar, damasquinar

dame [dem] *s* dama, señora; (coll) mujer *f*

damn [dæm] *s* terno; **I don't give a damn** (slang) maldito lo que me importa; **that's not worth a damn** (slang) eso no vale un pito ‖ *tr* condenar (a pena eterna); condenar; maldecir ‖ *intr* maldecir, echar ternos

damnation [dæmˈneʃən] *s* damnación; (theol) condenación

damned [dæmd] *adj* condenado (a pena eterna); abominable, detestable ‖ **the damned** los malditos, los condenados (a pena eterna)

damp [dæmp] *adj* húmedo, mojado ‖ *s* humedad; (*firedamp*) grisú *m* ‖ *tr* humedecer, mojar; (*to deaden, muffle*) amortecer, amortiguar; (*to discourage*) abatir, desalentar; (elec) amortiguar (*ondas electromagnéticas*)

dampen [ˈdæmpən] *tr* humedecer, mojar; amortecer, amortiguar; abatir, desalentar

damper [ˈdæmpər] *s* (*of chimney*) registro; (*of piano*) apagador *m*, sordina

damsel [ˈdæmzəl] *s* señorita, muchacha

dance [dæns] *s* baile *m*, danza ‖ *tr & intr* bailar, danzar

dance band *s* orquesta de jazz

dance floor s pista de baile
dance hall s salón m de baile
dancer ['dænsər] s bailador m, danzador m; (professional) bailarín m
dancing partner s pareja (de baile)
dandelion ['dændɪ,laɪ•ən] s diente m de león
dandruff ['dændrəf] s caspa
dan•dy ['dændi] adj (comp **-dier;** super **-diest**) (coll) excelente, magnífico ‖ s (pl **-dies**) currutaco, petimetre m; lagarto (Mex)
Dane [den] s danés m, dinamarqués m
danger ['dendʒər] s peligro
dangerous ['dendʒərəs] adj peligroso; riesgoso
dangle ['dæŋgəl] tr & intr colgar flojamente, colgar en el aire
Danish ['denɪʃ] adj & s danés m, dinamarqués m
dank [dæŋk] adj húmedo, liento
Danube ['dænjʊb] s Danubio
dapper ['dæpər] adj aseado, apuesto
dapple ['dæpəl] adj habado, rodado ‖ tr motear
dare [dɛr] s desafío, reto ‖ tr retar; **to dare to** (to challenge to) desafiar a ‖ intr osar, atreverse; **I dare say** talvez; **to dare to** (to have the courage to) atreverse a
dare'dev'il s calavera m, temerario
daring ['dɛrɪŋ] adj atrevido, osado ‖ s atrevimiento, osadía
dark [dɑrk] adj obscuro; (in complexion) moreno; secreto, oculto; (gloomy) lóbrego; (beer) pardo ‖ s obscuridad, tinieblas; noche f; **in the dark** a obscuras
Dark Ages spl edad media; principios de la edad media
dark-complexioned ['dɑrkkəm'plɛkʃənd] adj moreno
darken ['dɑrkən] tr obscurecer; entristecer; cegar ‖ intr obscurecerse
dark horse s caballo desconocido; candidato nombrado inesperadamente
darkly ['dɑrkli] adv obscuramente; secretamente, misteriosamente
dark meat s carne f del ave que no es la pechuga
darkness ['dɑrknɪs] s obscuridad
dark'room' s (phot) cuarto obscuro
darling ['dɑrlɪŋ] adj & s querido, amado; predilecto; (as address) chata (Mex)
darn [dɑrn] tr & intr zurcir; (coll) maldecir
darnel ['dɑrnəl] s cizaña
darning ['dɑrnɪŋ] s zurcido
darning needle s aguja de zurcir
dart [dɑrt] s dardo; (small missile used in a game) rehilete m ‖ intr lanzarse, precipitarse; volar como dardo
Darwinian [dɑr'wɪnɪ•ən] adj darviniano
Darwinism ['dɑrwə,nɪzəm] s darvinismo
Darwinist ['dɑrwənɪst] s darvinista
dash [dæʃ] s arranque m; (splash) rociada; carrera corta; (spirit) brío; pequeña cantidad; (in printing, writing, telegraphy) raya ‖ tr lanzar; estrellar, romper; frustrar (las esperanzas de uno); rociar, salpicar; **to dash off** escribir de prisa; **to dash to**

pieces hacer añicos ‖ intr estrellarse (las olas del mar); lanzarse, precipitarse; **to dash by** pasar corriendo; **to dash in** entrar como un rayo
dash'board' s tablero de instrumentos; cuadro de mando; (aut) guardabarros m, salpicadero
dashing ['dæʃɪŋ] adj brioso; ostentoso, vistoso ‖ s (of waves) embate m
dastard ['dæstərd] adj & s vil mf, miserable mf, cobarde mf
data bank ['detə] s banco de datos, almacenamiento
da'ta-proc'ess tr & intr procesar
data processing s procesamiento; tramitación automática de datos
data storage s memoria, almacenamiento
date [det] s (time) fecha, data; (palm) datilera; (fruit) dátil m; (appointment) (coll) cita; **out of date** anticuado, fuera de moda; **to date** hasta la fecha; **under date of** con fecha de ‖ tr fechar, datar; (coll) tener cita con ‖ intr —**to date from** datar de
date line s línea de cambio de fecha
date palm s palmera (datilera)
dative ['detɪv] adj & s dativo
datum ['detəm] o ['dætəm] s (pl **data** ['detə] o ['dætə]) dato
dau. abbr **daughter**
daub [dɔb] s embadurnamiento ‖ tr embadurnar
daughter ['dɔtər] s hija
daughter-in-law ['dɔtərɪn,lɔ] s (pl **daughters-in-law**) nuera, hija política
daunt [dɔnt] tr asustar, espantar; desanimar, acobardar
dauntless ['dɔntlɪs] adj atrevido, intrépido, impávido
dauphin ['dɔfɪn] s delfín m
davenport ['dævən,port] s sofá m cama
davit ['dævɪt] s (naut) pescante m, grúa de bote
daw [dɔ] s corneja
dawdle ['dɔdəl] intr malgastar el tiempo, haronear
dawn [dɔn] s amanecer m, alba ‖ intr amanecer; despuntar (el día, la mañana); empezar a mostrarse; **to dawn on** empezar a hacerse patente a
day [de] adj diurno ‖ s día m; (of travel, work, worry, etc.) jornada; (from noon to noon) (naut) singladura; **any day now** de un día para otro; **by day** de día; **the day after** el día siguiente; **the day after tomorrow** pasado mañana; **the day before** la víspera; la víspera de; **the day before yesterday** anteayer; **to call it a day** (coll) dejar de trabajar; **to win the day** ganar la jornada
day bed s sofá m cama, diván m cama
day'break' s amanecer m
day coach s (rr) coche m de viajeros
day'dream' s ensueño ‖ intr soñar despierto
day laborer s jornalero
day'light' s luz f del día; amanecer m; **in broad daylight** en pleno día; **to see daylight** comprender; ver el fin de una tarea difícil

cu
da

day′light′-sav′ing time *s* hora de verano
day nursery *s* guardería infantil
day off *s* asueto
day of reckoning *s* día *m* de ajustar cuentas
day shift *s* turno diurno
day′time′ *adj* diurno ‖ día *m*
daze [dez] *s* aturdimiento; **in a daze** aturdido
‖ *tr* aturdir
dazzle [′dæzəl] *s* deslumbramiento ‖ *tr* deslumbrar
dazzling [′dæzlɪŋ] *adj* deslumbrante
deacon [′dikən] *s* diácono
deaconess [′dikənɪs] *s* diaconisa
dead [dɛd] *adj* muerto; (coll) cansado ‖ *adv* (coll) completamente, muy ‖ *s* — **in the dead of night** en plena noche; **the dead** los muertos; **the dead of winter** lo más frío del invierno
dead beat *s* (slang) gorrón *m;* (slang) holgazán *m*
dead bolt *s* cerrojo dormido
dead calm *s* calma chicha, calmazo
dead center *s* punto muerto
dead′drunk′ *adj* difunto de taberna
deaden [′dɛdən] *tr* amortiguar, amortecer
dead end *s* callejón *m* sin salida
dead′latch′ *s* aldaba dormida
dead′-let′ter office *s* departamento de cartas no reclamadas
dead′line′ *s* línea vedada; fin *m* del plazo
dead′lock′ *s* cerradura dormida; desacuerdo insuperable ‖ *tr* estancar
dead•ly [′dɛdli] *adj* (*comp* **-lier;** *super* **-liest**) mortal; (*sin*) capital; abrumador
dead pan *s* (slang) semblante *m* sin expresión
dead reckoning *s* (naut) estima
dead ringer [′rɪŋər] *s* segunda edición
dead′wood′ *s* leña seca; cosa inútil, gente *f* inútil
deaf [dɛf] *adj* sordo; **to turn a deaf ear** hacerse el sordo, hacer oídos de mercader
deaf and dumb *adj* sordomudo
deafen [′dɛfən] *tr* asordar, ensordecer
deafening [′dɛfənɪŋ] *adj* ensordecedor
deaf′-mute′ *s* sordomudo
deafness [′dɛfnɪs] *s* sordera
deal [dil] *s* negocio, trato; (*of cards*) mano *f;* turno de dar; (*share*) parte *f*, porción; (coll) convenio secreto; **a good deal (of)** o **a great deal (of)** mucho; **to make a great deal of** hacer fiestas a ‖ *v* (*pret & pp* **dealt** [dɛlt]) *tr* asestar (*un golpe*); repartir (*la baraja*) ‖ *intr* negociar, comerciar; intervenir; (*in card games*) ser mano; **to deal with** entender en; tratar de; tratar con
dealer [′dilər] *s* comerciante *mf*, concesionario; (*of cards*) repartidor *m*
dean [din] *s* decano; (eccl) deán *m*
deanship [′dinʃɪp] *s* decanato, deanato, deanazgo
dear [dɪr] *adj* (*beloved*) caro; (*expensive*) caro; (*charging high prices*) carero; **dear me!** ¡Dios mío! ‖ *s* queriao
dearie [′dɪri] *s* (coll) queridito
dearth [dʌrθ] *s* carestía
death [dɛθ] *s* muerte *f;* **to bleed to death** morir desangrado; **to bore to death** matar

de aburrimiento; **to burn to death** morir quemado; **to choke to death** morir atragantado; **to die a violent death** morir vestido; **to freeze to death** morir helado; **to put to death** dar la muerte a; **to shoot to death** matar a tiros; **to stab to death** escabechar; **to starve to death** matar de hambre; morir de hambre
death′bed′ *s* lecho de muerte
death′blow′ *s* golpe *m* mortal
death certificate *s* fe *f* de óbito, partida de defunción
death house *s* capilla (*de los reos de muerte*)
deathless [′dɛθlɪs] *adj* inmortal, eterno
deathly [′dɛθli] *adj* mortal, de muerte ‖ *adv* mortalmente; excesivamente
death penalty *s* pena de muerte
death rate *s* mortalidad
death rattle *s* estertor agónico
death ray *s* rayo mortífero
death warrant *s* sentencia de muerte; fin *m* de toda esperanza
death′watch′ *s* vela de un difunto; guardia de un reo de muerte
debacle [de′bɑkəl] *s* desastre *m*, ruina, derrota; (*in a river*) deshielo
de•bar [dɪ′bɑr] *v* (*pret & pp* **-barred;** *ger* **-barring**) *tr* excluir; prohibir
debark [dɪ′bɑrk] *tr & intr* desembarcar
debarkation [,dibɑr′keʃən] *s* (*of passengers*) desembarco; (*of freight*) desembarque *m*
debase [dɪ′bes] *tr* degradar; falsificar
debatable [dɪ′betəbəl] *adj* disputable
debate [dɪ′bet] *s* debate *m* ‖ *tr* debatir ‖ *intr* debatir; deliberar
debauchee [,dɛbɔ′ʃi] o [,dɛbɔ′tʃi] *s* libertino, disoluto
debaucher•y [dɪ′bɔtʃəri] *s* (*pl* **-ies**) libertinaje *m*, crápula
debenture [dɪ′bɛntʃər] *s* (*bond*) obligación; (*voucher*) vale *m*
debilitate [dɪ′bɪlɪtet] *tr* debilitar
debili•ty [dɪ′bɪlɪti] *s* (*pl* **-ties**) debilidad
debit [′dɛbɪt] *s* debe *m;* (*entry on debit side*) cargo ‖ *tr* adeudar, cargar
debit balance *s* saldo deudor
debonair [,dɛbə′nɛr] *adj* alegre; cortés
debris [de′bri] *s* despojos, ruinas
debt [dɛt] *s* deuda; **to run into debt** endeudarse, entramparse
debtor [′dɛtər] *s* deudor *m*
debut [de′bju] o [′debju] *s* estreno, debut *m*, **to make one's debut** estrenarse, debutar; ponerse de largo, entrar en sociedad (*una joven*)
debutante [,dɛbju′tɑnt] o [′dɛbjə,tænt] *s* joven *f* que se pone de largo; debutante *f*
dec. *abbr* deceased
decade [′dɛked] *s* decenio, década
decadence [dɪ′kedəns] *s* decadencia
decadent [dɪ′kedənt] *adj & s* decadente *mf*
decanter [dɪ′kæntər] *s* garrafa
decapitate [dɪ′kæpɪ,tet] *tr* decapitar
decay [dɪ′ke] *s* (*decline*) decaimiento, descaecimiento; (*rotting*) podredumbre; (*of teeth*) caries *f* ‖ *tr* pudrir ‖ *intr* pudrirse; decaer; cariarse (*los dientes*)

decease [dɪ'sis] s fallecimiento ‖ intr fallecer

deceased [dɪ'sist] adj & s difunto

deceit [dɪ'sit] s engaño, fraude m

deceitful [dɪ'sitfəl] adj engañoso, fraudulento

deceive [dɪ'siv] tr & intr engañar

decelerate [dɪ'sɛlə,ret] tr desacelerar ‖ intr desacelerarse

December [dɪ'sɛmbər] s diciembre m

decen-cy ['disənsi] s (pl **-cies**) decencia, honestidad; (propriety) conveniencia

decent ['disənt] adj decente, honesto; (proper) conveniente

decentralize [dɪ'sɛntrə,laɪz] tr descentralizar

deception [dɪ'sɛp/ən] s engaño

deceptive [dɪ'sɛptɪv] adj engañoso

decide [dɪ'saɪd] tr & intr decidir

decimal ['dɛsɪməl] adj & s decimal m

decimal point s (in Spanish the comma is used to separate the decimal fraction from the integer) coma

decimate ['dɛsɪ,met] tr diezmar

decipher [dɪ'saɪfər] tr descifrar

deciphering [dɪ'saɪfərɪŋ] s desciframiento

decision [dɪ'sɪʒən] s decisión

decisive [dɪ'saɪsɪv] adj decisivo; determinado, resuelto

deck [dɛk] s (of cards) baraja; (of ship) cubierta; **between decks** (naut) entre cubiertas ‖ tr — **to deck out** adornar, engalanar

deck chair s silla de cubierta

deck hand s marinero de cubierta

deck'-land' intr apontizar

deck'-land'ing s apontizaje m

deckle edge ['dɛkəl] s barba

declaim [dɪ'klem] tr & intr declamar

declaration [,dɛklə'reʃən] s declaración

declarative [dɪ'klærətɪv] adj declarativo; (gram) enunciativo

declare [dɪ'klɛr] tr & intr declarar

declension [dɪ'klɛnʃən] s declinación

declination [,dɛklɪ'neʃən] s declinación

decline [dɪ'klaɪn] s bajada, declinación; (in prices) baja; (in health, wealth, etc.) bajón m; (of sun) ocaso ‖ tr & intr declinar; rehusar

declivi-ty [dɪ'klɪvɪti] s (pl **-ties**) declividad, declive m

decode [di'kod] tr descifrar

decoder [di'kodər] s (telv) decodificador m

decoding [di'kodɪŋ] s desciframiento

décolleté [,dekɑl'te] adj escotado

decompose [,dikəm'poz] tr descomponer ‖ intr descomponerse

decomposition [,dikɑmpə'zɪʃən] s descomposición

decompression [,dikəm'prɛʃən] s descompresión

decongest [,dikən'dʒɛst] tr descongestionar

decongestion [,dikən'dʒɛstʃən] s descongestión

decontamination [,dikəm,tæmɪ'neʃən] s descontaminación; **radioactive decontamination** descontaminación de radiactividad

decon-trol [,dikən'trol] v (pret & pp **-trolled;** ger **-trolling**) descontrolar

décor [de'kɔr] s decoración; (theat) decorado

decorate ['dɛkə,ret] tr decorar; (with medal, badge) condecorar

decoration [,dɛkə'reʃən] s decoración; (medal, badge) condecoración

decorator ['dɛkə,retər] s decorador m; (of interiors) adornista mf

decorous ['dɛkərəs] o [dɪ'korəs] adj decoroso

decorum [dɪ'korəm] s decoro

decoy [dɪ'kɔɪ] o ['dikɔɪ] s añagaza, señuelo; (person) entruchón m ‖ [dɪ'kɔɪ] tr atraer con señuelo; entruchar

decoy pigeon s cimbel m

decrease ['dikris] s disminución ‖ [dɪ'kris] tr disminuir ‖ intr disminuir, disminuirse

decree [dɪ'kri] s decreto ‖ tr decretar

decrepit [dɪ'krɛpɪt] adj decrépito

de-cry [dɪ'kraɪ] v (pret & pp **-cried**) tr censurar, denigrar

dedicate ['dɛdɪ,ket] tr dedicar

dedication [,dɛdɪ'keʃən] s dedicación; (inscription in a book) dedicatoria

deduce [dɪ'djus] tr deducir (inferir, concluir; derivar)

deduct [dɪ'dʌkt] tr deducir (rebajar, substraer)

deduction [dɪ'dʌkʃən] s deducción

deed [did] s acto, hecho; (feat, exploit) hazaña; (law) escritura ‖ tr traspasar por escritura

deem [dim] tr & intr creer, juzgar

deep [dip] adj profundo; (sound) grave; (color) subido; de hondo, p.ej., **two meters deep** dos metros de hondo; **deep in debt** cargado de deudas; **deep in thought** absorto en la meditación ‖ adv hondo; **deep into the night** muy entrada la noche

deepen ['dipən] tr profundizar ‖ intr profundizarse

deep-laid ['dip,led] adj concebido con astucia

deep mourning s luto riguroso

deep-rooted ['dip,rutɪd] adj profundamente arraigado

deep'-sea' fishing s pesca de gran altura

deep-seated ['dip,sitɪd] adj profundamente arraigado

deer [dɪr] s ciervo, venado

deer'skin' s piel f de ciervo

def. abbr **defendant, deferred, definite**

deface [dɪ'fes] tr desfigurar

de facto [di'fækto] adv de hecho

defamation [,dɛfə'meʃən] o [,difə'meʃən] s difamación

defame [dɪ'fem] tr difamar

default [dɪ'fɔlt] s falta, incumplimiento; **by default** (sport) por no presentarse; **in default of** por falta de ‖ tr dejar de cumplir; no pagar ‖ intr faltar; (sport) perder por no presentarse

defeat [dɪ'fit] s derrota ‖ tr derrotar, vencer

defeatism [dɪ'fitɪzəm] s derrotismo

defeatist [dɪ'fitɪst] adj & s derrotista mf

defecate ['dɛfɪ,ket] intr defecar

defect [dɪ'fɛkt] o ['difɛkt] s defecto, imperfección ‖ [dɪ'fɛkt] intr desertar

da
de

defection [dɪˈfɛkʃən] *s* defección; (*lack, failure*) falta

defective [dɪˈfɛktɪv] *adj* defectivo, defectuoso

defend [dɪˈfɛnd] *tr* defender

defendant [dɪˈfɛndənt] *s* (law) demandado, acusado

defender [dɪˈfɛndər] *s* defensor *m*

defense [dɪˈfɛns] *s* defensa

defenseless [dɪˈfɛnslɪs] *adj* indefenso

defensive [dɪˈfɛnsɪv] *adj* defensivo ‖ *s* defensiva

de•fer [dɪˈfʌr] *v* (*pret & pp* -ferred; *ger* -ferring) *tr* aplazar, diferir ‖ *intr* deferir

deference [ˈdɛfərəns] *s* deferencia

deferential [ˌdɛfəˈrɛnʃəl] *adj* deferente

deferment [dɪˈfʌrmənt] *s* aplazamiento, dilación

defiance [dɪˈfaɪ•əns] *s* oposición; desafío, provocación; **in defiance of** sin mirar a, a despecho de

defiant [dɪˈfaɪ•ənt] *adj* provocante, hostil

deficien•cy [dɪˈfɪʃənsi] *s* (*pl* -cies) carencia, deficiencia; (com) descubierto

deficient [dɪˈfɪʃənt] *adj* deficiente, defectuoso

deficit [ˈdɛfɪsɪt] *adj* deficitario ‖ *s* déficit *m*

defile [dɪˈfaɪl] o [ˈdifaɪl] *s* desfiladero ‖ [dɪˈfaɪl] *tr* corromper, manchar ‖ *intr* desfilar

define [dɪˈfaɪn] *tr* definir

definite [ˈdɛfɪnɪt] *adj* definido

definition [ˌdɛfɪˈnɪʃən] *s* definición

definitive [dɪˈfɪnɪtɪv] *adj* definitivo

deflate [dɪˈflet] *tr* desinflar

deflation [dɪˈfleʃən] *s* desinflación; (*of prices*) deflación

deflect [dɪˈflɛkt] *tr* desviar ‖ *intr* desviarse

deflower [diˈflaʊ•ər] *tr* desflorar

deforest [diˈfɑrɛst] o [diˈfɔrɛst] *tr* desforestar, despoblar

deform [dɪˈfɔrm] *tr* deformar

deformed [dɪˈfɔrmd] *adj* deforme

deformi•ty [dɪˈfɔrmɪti] *s* (*pl* -ties) deformidad

defraud [dɪˈfrɔd] *tr* defraudar

defray [diˈfre] *tr* sufragar, subvenir a

defrost [diˈfrɔst] *tr* descongelar, deshelar

defroster [diˈfrɔstər] *s* descongelador *m*

deft [dɛft] *adj* diestro, hábil

defunct [dɪˈfʌŋkt] *adj* difunto

de•fy [dɪˈfaɪ] *v* (*pret & pp* -fied) *tr* desafiar, provocar

deg. *abbr* **degree**

degeneracy [dɪˈdʒɛnərəsi] *s* degeneración

degenerate [dɪˈdʒɛnərɪt] *adj & s* degenerado ‖ [dɪˈdʒɛnəˌret] *intr* degenerar

degrade [dɪˈgred] *tr* degradar

degrading [dɪˈgredɪŋ] *adj* degradante

degree [dɪˈgri] *s* grado; **by degrees** de grado en grado; **to take a degree** graduarse, recibir un grado o título

dehumidifier [ˌdihjuˈmɪdɪˌfaɪ•ər] *s* deshumedecedor *m*

dehydrate [diˈhaɪdret] *tr* deshidratar

deice [diˈaɪs] *tr* deshelar

dei•fy [ˈdi•ɪˌfaɪ] *v* (*pret & pp* -fied) *tr* deificar

deign [den] *intr* dignarse

dei•ty [ˈdi•ɪti] *s* (*pl* -ties) deidad; **the Deity** Dios *m*

dejected [dɪˈdʒɛktɪd] *adj* abatido

dejection [dɪˈdʒɛkʃən] *s* abatimiento

del. *abbr* **delegate, delete**

delay [dɪˈle] *s* retraso, tardanza; parón ‖ *tr* retrasar ‖ *intr* demorarse

delectable [dɪˈlɛktəbəl] *adj* deleitable

delegate [ˈdɛlɪgɪt] *s* diputado, delegado; (*to a convention*) congresista *mf* ‖ [ˈdɛlɪˌget] *tr* delegar

delete [dɪˈlit] *tr* borrar, suprimir

deletion [dɪˈliʃən] *s* supresión

deliberate [dɪˈlɪbərɪt] *adj* pensado, reflexionado; (*slow in deciding*) cauto, circunspecto; (*slow in moving*) espacioso, lento ‖ [dɪˈlɪbəˌret] *tr & intr* deliberar

delica•cy [ˈdɛlɪkəsi] *s* (*pl* -cies) delicadeza; (*choice food*) golosina

delicatessen [ˌdɛlɪkəˈtɛsən] *s* colmado, tienda de ultramarinos ‖ *spl* ultramarinos

delicious [dɪˈlɪʃəs] *adj* delicioso, sabroso

delight [dɪˈlaɪt] *s* deleite *m*, delicia ‖ *tr* deleitar ‖ *intr* deleitarse

delightful [dɪˈlaɪtfəl] *adj* deleitoso, ameno, exquisito

delinquen•cy [dɪˈlɪŋkwənsi] *s* (*pl* -cies) culpa; (*in payment of debt*) morosidad; (*debt in arrears*) atrasos

delinquent [dɪˈlɪŋkwənt] *adj* culpado; (*in payment*) moroso, atrasado; no pagado ‖ *s* culpado; deudor moroso

delirious [dɪˈlɪrɪ•əs] *adj* delirante

deliri•um [dɪˈlɪrɪ•əm] *s* (*pl* -ums o -a [ə]) delirio

deliver [dɪˈlɪvər] *tr* entregar; asestar (*un golpe*); pronunciar, recitar (*un discurso*); transmitir, rendir (*energía*); partear (*a la mujer que está de parto*)

deliver•y [dɪˈlɪvəri] *s* (*pl* -ies) entrega; (*of mail*) distribución, reparto; (*of a speech*) declamación; (*childbirth*) alumbramiento, parto

delivery•man [dɪˈlɪvərimən] *s* (*pl* -men [mən]) mozo de reparto

delivery room *s* sala de alumbramiento

delivery service *s* servicio a domicilio

delivery truck *s* sedán *m* de reparto

dell [dɛl] *s* vallecito

delouse [diˈlaʊs] *tr* despiojar

delphinium [dɛlˈfɪnɪ•əm] *s* (*Delphinium ajacis*) espuela de caballero; (*Delphinium consolida*) consuelda real

delude [dɪˈlud] *tr* deludir, engañar

deluge [ˈdɛljudʒ] *s* diluvio ‖ *tr* inundar

delusion [dɪˈluʒən] *s* engaño, decepción

de luxe [dɪˈlʌks] *adj & adv s* de lujo

delve [dɛlv] *intr* cavar; **to delve into** cavar en

demagnetize [diˈmægnɪˌtaɪz] *tr* desimantar

demagogue [ˈdɛməˌgɑg] *s* demagogo

demand [dɪˈmænd] o [dɪˈmɑnd] *s* demanda; **to be in demand** tener demanda ‖ *tr* demandar perentoriamente

demanding [dɪˈmændɪŋ] *adj* exigente

demarcate [dɪˈmɑrket] o [ˈdimɑrˌket] *tr* demarcar

démarche [de'marʃ] *s* diligencia, gestión, paso
demeanor [dɪ'minər] *s* conducta, porte *m*
demented [dɪ'mɛntɪd] *adj* demente, dementado
demigod ['dɛmɪ,gad] *s* semidiós *m*
demijohn ['dɛmɪ,dʒɑn] *s* damajuana
demilitarize [di'mɪlɪtə,raɪz] *tr* desmilitarizar
demilitarized zone *s* zona desmilitarizada
demimonde ['dɛmɪ,mand] *s* mujeres de vida alegre
demise [dɪ'maɪz] *s* fallecimiento
demisemiquaver [,dɛmɪ'sɛmɪ,kwevər] *s* (mus) fusa
demitasse ['dɛmɪ,tæs] o ['dɛmɪ,tas] *s* taza pequeña
demobilize [di'mobɪ,laɪz] *tr* desmovilizar
democra•cy [dɪ'markrəsi] *s* (*pl* **-cies**) democracia
democrat ['dɛmə,kræt] *s* demócrata *mf*
democratic [,dɛmə'krætɪk] *adj* democrático
demodulate [di'madjə,let] *tr* desmodular
demolish [dɪ'malɪʃ] *tr* demoler
demolition [,dɛmə'lɪʃən] o [,dimə'lɪʃən] *s* demolición
demon ['dimən] *s* demonio
demoniacal [,dimə'naɪ•əkəl] *adj* demoníaco
demonstrate ['dɛmən,stret] *tr* demostrar ǁ *intr* demostrar; (*to show feelings in public gatherings*) manifestar
demonstration [,dɛmən'streʃən] *s* demostración; (*public show of feeling*) manifestación
demonstrative [dɪ'manstrətɪv] *adj* demostrativo; (*giving open exhibition of emotion*) extremoso
demonstrator ['dɛmən,stretər] *s* demostrador *m;* manifestante *mf*
demoralize [dɪ'mɔrə,laɪz] *tr* desmoralizar
demote [dɪ'mot] *tr* degradar
demotion [dɪ'moʃən] *s* degradación
de•mur [dɪ'mʌr] *v* (*pret & pp* **-murred;** *ger* **-murring**) *intr* poner reparos
demure [dɪ'mjʊr] *adj* modesto, recatado; grave, serio
demurrage [dɪ'mʌrɪdʒ] *s* (com) estadía
den [dɛn] *s* (*of animals, thieves*) madriguera; (*dirty little room*) cuchitril *m;* lugar *m* de retiro; cuarto de estudio; (*of lions*) (Bib) fosa
denaturalize [di'nætjərə,laɪz] *tr* desnaturalizar
denatured alcohol [di'netʃərd] *s* alcohol desnaturalizado
denial [dɪ'naɪ•əl] *s* denegación; negación, desmentida
denim ['dɛnɪm] *s* dril *m* de algodón
denizen ['dɛnɪzən] *s* habitante *mf,* vecino
Denmark ['dɛnmark] *s* Dinamarca
denomination [dɪ,namɪ'neʃən] *s* denominación; categoría, clase *f;* secta, confesión, comunión
denote [dɪ'not] *tr* denotar
dénoument [denu'mã] *s* desenlace *m*
denounce [dɪ'naʊns] *tr* denunciar
dense [dɛns] *adj* denso; estúpido
densi•ty ['dɛnsɪti] *s* (*pl* **-ties**) densidad

dent [dɛnt] *s* abolladura, mella ǁ *tr* abollar, mellar ǁ *intr* abollarse, mellarse
dental ['dɛntəl] *adj & s* dental *f*
dental floss *s* hilo dental, seda encerada
dental technician *s* mecánico-dentista *m*
dentifrice ['dɛntɪfrɪs] *s* dentífrico
dentist ['dɛntɪst] *s* dentista *mf*
dentistry ['dɛntɪstri] *s* odontología
denture ['dɛntʃər] *s* dentadura artificial
denunciation [dɪ,nʌnsɪ'eʃən] o [dɪ,nʌnʃɪ'eʃən] *s* denuncia
de•ny [dɪ'naɪ] *v* (*pret & pp* **-nied**) *tr* (*to declare not to be true*) negar; (*to refuse*) denegar; **to deny oneself to callers** negarse ǁ *intr* negar; denegar
deodorant [di'odərənt] *adj & s* desodorante *m*
deodorize [di'odə,raɪz] *tr* desodorizar
deoxidize [di'aksɪ,daɪz] *tr* desoxidar
dep. *abbr* **department, departs, deputy**
depart [dɪ'part] *intr* partir, salir, irse; desviarse
department [dɪ'partmənt] *s* departamento; (*of government*) ministerio
department store *s* grandes almacenes *mpl*
departure [dɪ'partʃər] *s* partida, salida; desviación
depend [dɪ'pɛnd] *intr* depender; **to depend on** depender de
dependable [dɪ'pɛndəbəl] *adj* confiable, fidedigno
dependence [dɪ'pɛndəns] *s* dependencia
dependen•cy [dɪ'pɛndənsi] *s* (*pl* **-cies**) dependencia; (*country, territory*) posesión
dependent [dɪ'pɛndənt] *adj* dependiente ǁ *s* carga de familia, familiar *m* dependiente
depict [dɪ'pɪkt] *tr* describir, representar, pintar
deplete [dɪ'plit] *tr* agotar, depauperar
deplorable [dɪ'plorəbəl] *adj* deplorable
deplore [dɪ'plor] *tr* deplorar
deploy [dɪ'plɔɪ] *tr* (mil) desplegar ǁ *intr* (mil) desplegarse
deployment [dɪ'plɔɪmənt] *s* (mil) despliegue *m*
depolarize [di'polə,raɪz] *tr* despolarizar
depopulate [di'papjə,let] *tr* despoblar
deport [dɪ'port] *tr* deportar; **to deport oneself** conducirse, portarse
deportation [,dipor'teʃən] *s* deportación
deportee [,dipor'ti] *s* deportado
deportment [dɪ'portmənt] *s* conducta, comportamiento
depose [dɪ'poz] *tr & intr* deponer
deposit [dɪ'pazɪt] *s* depósito; (*down payment*) señal *f,* pago anticipado; (min) yacimiento ǁ *tr* depositar ǁ *intr* depositarse
deposit account *s* cuenta corriente
depositor [dɪ'pazɪtər] *s* cuentacorrentista *mf,* imponente *mf*
depot ['dipo] o ['dɛpo] *s* almacén *m,* depósito; (mil) depósito; (rr) estación
depraved [dɪ'prevd] *adj* depravado
depravi•ty [dɪ'prævɪti] *s* (*pl* **-ties**) depravación
deprecate ['dɛprɪ,ket] *tr* desaprobar

de
de

depreciate [dɪ'priʃɪ,et] *tr* (*to lower value or price of*) depreciar; (*to disparage*) desapreciar ‖ *intr* depreciarse

depreciation [dɪ,priʃɪ'eʃən] *s* (*drop in value*) depreciación; (*disparagement*) desaprecio

depress [dɪ'prɛs] *tr* deprimir; desanimar, desalentar; bajar (*los precios*)

depression [dɪ'prɛʃən] *s* depresión; desaliento; (*slump*) crisis *f*

deprive [dɪ'praɪv] *tr* privar

deprived [dɪ'praɪvd] *adj* desventajado

dept. *abbr* **department**

depth [dɛpθ] *s* profundidad; (*of a house, of a room*) fondo; **in the depth of night** en mitad de la noche; **in the depth of winter** en pleno invierno; **to go beyond one's depth** meterse en agua demasiado profunda; (fig) meterse en honduras

depth of hold *s* (naut) puntal *m*

depu•ty ['dɛpjəti] *s* (*pl* -**ties**) diputado

derail [dɪ'rel] *tr* hacer descarrilar ‖ *intr* descarrilar

derailment [dɪ'relmənt] *s* descarrilamiento

derange [dɪ'rendʒ] *tr* desarreglar, descomponer; trastornar el juicio a

derangement [dɪ'rendʒmənt] *s* desarreglo, descompostura; locura; obfuscación

der•by ['dɑrbi] *s* (*pl* -**bies**) sombrero hongo

deregulate [di'rɛgjə,let] *tr* descontrolar

derelict ['dɛrɪlɪkt] *adj* abandonado; negligente ‖ *s* pelafustán *m;* (naut) derrelicto

deride [dɪ'raɪd] *tr* burlarse de, ridiculizar

derision [dɪ'rɪʒən] *s* burla, irrisión

derive [dɪ'raɪv] *tr* & *intr* derivar

dermatitis [,dʌrmə'taɪtɪs] *s* dermatitis *f*

derogatory [dɪ'rɑgə,tori] *adj* despreciativo

derrick ['dɛrɪk] *s* grúa; (min) castillete *m*

dervish ['dʌrvɪʃ] *s* derviche *m*

desalinization [dɪ,selɪnɪ'zeʃən] *s* desalinización

desalt [di'sɔlt] *tr* desalar

descend [dɪ'sɛnd] *tr* bajar, descender (*la escalera*) ‖ *intr* bajar, descender; **to descend on** caer sobre, invadir

descendant [dɪ'sɛndənt] *adj* descendente ‖ *s* descendiente *mf*

descendent [dɪ'sɛndənt] *adj* descendente

descent [dɪ'sɛnt] *s* (*passing from higher to lower state*) descenso; (*extraction; lineage*) descendencia; cuesta, bajada; invasión

describe [dɪ'skraɪb] *tr* describir

description [dɪ'skrɪpʃən] *s* descripción

descriptive [dɪ'skrɪptɪv] *adj* descriptivo

de•scry [dɪ'skraɪ] *v* (*pret* & *pp* -**scried**) *tr* avistar, divisar; descubrir

desecrate ['dɛsɪ,kret] *tr* profanar

desegregation [di,sɛgrɪ'geʃən] *s* desegregación

desert ['dɛzərt] *adj* & *s* desierto, yermo ‖ [dɪ'zʌrt] *s* mérito; **he received his just deserts** llevó su merecido ‖ *tr* desertar de ‖ *intr* desertar

deserter [dɪ'zʌrtər] *s* desertor *m*

desertion [dɪ'zʌrʃən] *s* deserción; abandono de cónyuge

deserve [dɪ'zʌrv] *tr* & *intr* merecer

deservedly [dɪ'zʌrvɪdli] *adv* merecidamente

design [dɪ'zaɪn] *s* diseño; (*combination of details; art of designing*) dibujo; (*plan, scheme*) designio; **to have designs on** poner la mira en ‖ *tr* deseñar, dibjuar; idear, proyectar ‖ *intr* diseñar, dibujar

designate ['dɛzɪg,net] *tr* designar

designing [dɪ'zaɪnɪŋ] *adj* intrigante, maquinador

desirable [dɪ'zaɪrəbəl] *adj* deseable

desire [dɪ'zaɪr] *s* deseo ‖ *tr* desear

desirous [dɪ'zaɪrəs] *adj* deseoso

desist [dɪ'zɪst] *intr* desistir

desk [dɛsk] *s* bufete *m*, escritorio; (*lectern*) atril *m;* (*clerk's counter in a hotel*) caja

desk clerk *s* cajero, recepcionista *m*

desk set *s* juego de escritorio

desolate ['dɛsəlɪt] *adj* (*hopeless*) desolado; despoblado, yermo, desierto; solitario; (*dismal*) lúgubre ‖ ['dɛsə,let] *tr* desconsolar; (*to lay waste*) desolar, devastar; despoblar

desolation [,dɛsə'leʃən] *s* (*devastation; great affliction*) desolación; (*dreariness*) lobreguez *f*

despair [dɪ'spɛr] *s* desesperación ‖ *intr* desesperar, desesperarse

despairing [dɪ'spɛrɪŋ] *adj* desesperado

despera•do [,dɛspə'redo] *o* [,dɛspə'rado] *s* (*pl* -**does** *o* -**dos**) criminal dispuesto a todo

desperate ['dɛspərɪt] *adj* dispuesto a todo; (*bitter, excessive*) encarnizado; (*hopeless*) desesperado; (*remedy*) heroico

despicable ['dɛspɪkəbəl] *adj* despreciable, ruin

despise [dɪ'spaɪz] *tr* despreciar, desdeñar

despite [dɪ'spaɪt] *prep* a despecho de

desponden•cy [dɪ'spandənsi] *s* (*pl* -**cies**) abatimiento, desaliento

despondent [dɪ'spandənt] *adj* abatido, desalentado

despot ['dɛspat] *s* déspota *m*

despotic [dɛs'patɪk] *adj* despótico

despotism ['dɛspə,tɪzəm] *s* despotismo

dessert [dɪ'zʌrt] *s* postre *m*

destination [,dɛstɪ'neʃən] *s* (*end of a journey or shipment*) destino; (*purpose*) destinación

destine ['dɛstɪn] *tr* destinar

desti•ny ['dɛstɪni] *s* (*pl* -**nies**) destino

destitute ['dɛstɪ,tjut] *adj* (*being in complete poverty*) indigente; (*lacking, deprived*) desprovisto

destitution [,dɛstɪ'tjuʃən] *s* indigencia

destroy [dɪ'strɔɪ] *tr* destruir

destroyer [dɪ'strɔɪ•ər] *s* (nav) destructor *m*

destruction [dɪ'strʌkʃən] *s* destrucción

destructive [dɪ'strʌktɪv] *adj* destructivo

desultory ['dɛsəl,tori] *adj* deshilvanado, descosido

detach [dɪ'tætʃ] *tr* desprender, separar; (mil) destacar

detachable [dɪ'tætʃəbəl] *adj* desprendible, separable; (*collar*) postizo

detached [dɪ'tætʃt] *adj* separado, suelto; imparcial, desinteresado

detachment [dɪ'tætʃmənt] *s* desprendimiento, separación; imparcialidad, desinterés *m;* (mil) destacamento

detail [dɪ'tel] o ['ditel] s detalle m, pormenor m; (mil) destacamento ‖ [dɪ'tel] tr detallar; (mil) destacar
detain [dɪ'ten] tr detener; tener preso
detect [dɪ'tɛkt] tr detectar
detection [dɪ'tɛkʃən] s detección
detective [dɪ'tɛktɪv] s detective m
detective story s novela policíaca o policial
detector [dɪ'tɛktər] s detector m
detention [dɪ'tɛnʃən] s detención
de·ter [dɪ'tʌr] v (pret & pp **-terred;** ger **-terring**) tr impedir, refrenar
detergent [dɪ'təʌrdʒənt] adj & s detergente m
deteriorate [dɪ'tɪrɪ·ə'ret] tr deteriorar ‖ intr deteriorarse
determination [dɪ,tʌrmə'neʃən] s resolución; empecinamiento
determine [dɪ'tʌrmɪn] tr determinar
deterrent [dɪ'tʌrənt] s impedimento, refrenamiento
detest [dɪ'tɛst] tr detestar, aborrecer
dethrone [dɪ'θron] tr destronar
detonate ['dɛtə,net] o ['ditə,net] tr hacer estallar ‖ intr detonar
detour ['ditur] o [dɪ'tur] s desvío; rodeo, vuelta; manera indirecta ‖ tr desviar (el tráfico) ‖ intr desviarse
detoxification [di,taksəfə'keʃən] s desintoxicación
detoxi·fy [di'taksə,faɪ] v (pret & pp **-fied**) tr desintoxicar
detract [dɪ'trækt] tr detraer ‖ intr — **to detract from** disminuir, rebajar
detriment ['dɛtrɪmənt] s perjuicio, detrimento; **to the detriment of** en perjuicio de
detrimental [,dɛtrɪ'mɛntəl] adj perjudicial
deuce [djus] o [dus] s (in cards) dos m; **the deuce!** ¡demonio!
devaluation [di,vælju'eʃən] s desvalorización, devaluación
devastate ['dɛvəs,tet] tr devastar
devastation [,dɛvəs'teʃən] s devastación
develop [dɪ'vɛləp] tr desarrollar, desenvolver; (phot) revelar; explotar (una mina) ‖ intr desarrollarse, desenvolverse; evolucionar, manifestarse
developer [dɪ'vɛləpər] s fomentador m; (phot) revelador m
development [dɪ'vɛləpmənt] s desarrollo, desenvolvimiento; (phot) revelado; (of a mine) explotación; acontecimiento nuevo
developmental aid [dɪ,vɛləp'mɛntəl] s ayuda al desarrollo
deviate ['divi,et] tr desviar ‖ intr desviarse
deviation [,divi'eʃən] s desviación
deviationism [,divi'eʃə,nɪzəm] s desviacionismo
deviationist [,divi'eʃənɪst] s desviacionista mf
device [dɪ'vaɪs] s dispositivo, aparato; (trick) ardid m, treta; (motto) lema m, divisa; **to leave someone to his own devices** dejarle a uno que haga lo que se le antoje
dev·il ['dɛvəl] s diablo; **between the devil and the deep blue sea** entre la espada y la pared; **to raise the devil** (slang) armar un

alboroto ‖ v (pret & pp **iled** o **-illed;** ger **-iling** o **illing**) tr condimentar con picantes; (coll) acosar, molestar
devilish ['dɛvəlɪʃ] adj diabólico
devilment ['dɛvəlmənt] s (mischief) diablura; (evil) maldad
devil·try ['dɛvəltri] s (pl **-tries**) maldad, crueldad; (mischief) diablura
devious ['divi·əs] adj (straying) desviado, extraviado; (roundabout; shifty) tortuoso
devise [dɪ'vaɪz] tr idear, inventar; (law) legar
devoid [dɪ'vɔɪd] adj desprovisto
devote [dɪ'vot] tr dedicar
devoted [dɪ'votɪd] adj (zealous, ardent) devoto; dedicado
devotee [,dɛvə'ti] s devoto
devotion [dɪ'voʃən] s devoción; (to study, work, etc.) dedicación; **devotions** oraciones, preces fpl
devour [dɪ'vaur] tr devorar
devout [dɪ'vaut] adj devoto; cordial, sincero
dew [dju] o [du] s rocío
dew'drop' s gota de rocío
dew'lap' s papada
dew·y ['dju·i] o ['du·i] adj rociado
dexterity [dɛks'tɛrɪti] s destreza
D.F. abbr **Defender of the Faith**
diabetes [,daɪ·ə'bitis] s diabetes f
diabetic [,daɪ·ə'bɛtɪk] adj & s diabético
diabolic(al) [,daɪ·ə'balɪk(əl)] adj diabólico
diacritical [,daɪ·ə'krɪtɪkəl] adj diacrítico
diadem ['daɪ·ə,dɛm] s diadema f
diaere·sis [daɪ'ɛrɪsɪs] s (pl **-ses** [,siz]) diéresis f
diagnose [,daɪ·əg'nos] tr diagnosticar
diagno·sis [,daɪ·əg'nosɪs] s (pl **-ses** [siz]) diagnosis f, diagnóstico
diagonal [daɪ'ægənəl] adj & s diagonal f
diagram ['daɪ·ə,græm] s diagrama m
dial. abbr **dialect**
dial ['daɪ·əl] s (of radio) cuadrante m; (of watch) cuadrante m, esfera, muestra; (of telephone) disco selector ‖ tr sintonizar (el radiorreceptor); marcar (el número telefónico); llamar (a una persona) por teléfono automático ‖ intr (telp) marcar
dialect ['daɪ·ə,lɛkt] s dialecto
dialing ['daɪ·əlɪŋ] s (telp) marcaje m
dialogue ['daɪ·ə,lɔg] s diálogo
dial telephone s teléfono automático
dial tone s (telp) señal f para marcar
diam. abbr **diameter**
diameter [daɪ'æmɪtər] s diámetro
diametric(al) [,daɪ·ə'mɛtrɪk(əl)] adj diamétrico
diamond ['daɪmənd] s diamante m; (figure of a rhombus) losange m; (playing card) carró m, diamante m; (baseball) losange m
diaper ['daɪpər] s pañal m
diaphanous [daɪ'æfənəs] adj diáfano
diaphragm ['daɪ·ə,fræm] s diafragma m
diarrhea [,daɪ·ə'ri·ə] s diarrea; **to have diarrhea** cursear
dia·ry ['daɪ·əri] s (pl **-ries**) diario
diastole [daɪ'æstəli] s diástole f
diathermy ['daɪ·ə,θʌrmi] s diatermia

de
di

dice [daɪs] *spl* dados; (*small cubes*) cubitos; **to load the dice** cargar los dados ‖ *tr* cortar en cubos

dice'box' *s* cubilete *m*

dichloride [daɪˈkloraɪd] *s* dicloruro

dichoto•my [daɪˈkɑtəmi] *s* (*pl* **-mies**) dicotomía

dickey [ˈdɪki] *s* camisolín *m*, pechera postiza; babero de niño

dict. *abbr* **dictionary**

dictaphone [ˈdɪktəˌfon] *s* dictáfono

dictate [ˈdɪktet] *s* mandato ‖ [ˈdɪktet] o [dɪkˈtet] *tr* dictar; mandar

dictation [dɪkˈteʃən] *s* dictado; (*orders; giving orders*) mandato; **to take dictation** escribir al dictado

dictator [ˈdɪktetər] o [dɪkˈtetər] *s* dictador *m*

dictatorship [dɪkˈtetərˌʃɪp] *s* dictadura

diction [ˈdɪkʃən] *s* dicción

dictionar•y [ˈdɪkʃənˌɛri] *s* (*pl* **-ies**) diccionario

dic•tum [ˈdɪktəm] *s* (*pl* **-ta** [tə]) dictamen *m;* aforismo, sentencia

didactic(al) [daɪˈdæktɪk(əl)] o [dɪˈdæktɪk(əl)] *adj* didáctico

die [daɪ] *s* (*pl* **-dice** [daɪs]) dado; **the die is cast** la suerte está echada ‖ *s* (*pl* **dies**) (*for stamping coins, medals, etc.*) troquel *m; (for cutting threads)* hembra de terraja ‖ *v* (*pret & pp* **died;** *ger* **dying**) *intr* morir; **to be dying** estar agonizando; **to die laughing** morir de risa

die'hard' *adj & s* intransigente *mf*

die'sel-elec'tric [ˈdizəl] *adj* dieseléctrico

diesel engine *s* diesel *m*

diesel oil *s* gas-oil *m*

die'stock' *s* terraja

diet [ˈdaɪ•ət] *s* dieta, régimen alimenticio ‖ *intr* estar a dieta

dietitian [ˌdaɪ•əˈtɪʃən] *s* dietista *mf*

diff. *abbr* **difference, different**

differ [ˈdɪfər] *intr* (*to be different*) diferir, diferenciarse; (*to dissent*) diferenciar; **to differ with** desavenirse con

difference [ˈdɪfərəns] *s* diferencia; **to make no difference** no importar; **to split the difference** partir la diferencia

different [ˈdɪfərənt] *adj* diferente

differentiate [ˌdɪfəˈrɛnʃɪˌet] *tr* diferenciar ‖ *intr* diferenciarse

difficult [ˈdɪfɪˌkʌlt] *adj* difícil

difficul•ty [ˈdɪfɪˌkʌlti] *s* (*pl* **-ties**) dificultad

diffident [ˈdɪfɪdənt] *adj* apocado, tímido

diffuse [dɪˈfjus] *adj* difuso ‖ [dɪˈfjuz] *tr* difundir ‖ *intr* difundirse

dig [dɪg] *s* (*poke*) empuje *m; (jibe)* pulla, palabra hiriente ‖ *v* (*pret & pp* **dug** [dʌg] o **digged;** *ger* **digging**) *tr* cavar, excavar; **to dig up** desenterrar ‖ *intr* cavar, excavar; **to dig in** (coll) poner manos a la obra; (mil) atrincherarse; **to dig under** socavar

digest [ˈdaɪdʒɛst] *s* compendio, resumen *m;* (law) digesto ‖ [dɪˈdʒɛst] o [daɪˈdʒɛst] *tr & intr* digerir

digestible [dɪˈdʒɛstɪbəl] o [daɪˈdʒɛstɪbəl] *adj* digerible, digestible

digestion [dɪˈdʒɛstʃən] o [daɪˈdʒɛstʃən] *s* digestión

digestive [dɪˈdʒɛstɪv] o [daɪˈdʒɛstɪv] *adj & s* digestivo

digit [ˈdɪdʒɪt] *s* dígito

digital telephone [ˈdɪdʒətəl] *s* teléfono digital

dignified [ˈdɪgnɪˌfaɪd] *adj* digno, grave, decoroso

digni•fy [ˈdɪgnɪˌfaɪ] *v* (*pret & pp* **-fied**) *tr* dignificar; engrandecer el mérito de

dignitar•y [ˈdɪgnɪˌtɛri] *s* (*pl* **-ies**) dignatario

digni•ty [ˈdɪgnɪti] *s* (*pl* **-ties**) dignidad; **to stand upon one's dignity** ponerse tan alto

digress [dɪˈgrɛs] o [daɪˈgrɛs] *intr* divagar

digression [dɪˈgrɛʃən] o [daɪˈgrɛʃən] *s* digresión, divagación

dike [daɪk] *s* dique *m;* (*bank of earth thrown up in digging*) montón *m;* (*causeway*) arrecife *m*, malecón *m*

dilapidated [dɪˈlæpɪˌdetɪd] *adj* destartalado, desvencijado

dilate [daɪˈlet] *tr* dilatar ‖ *intr* dilatarse

dilatory [ˈdɪləˌtori] *adj* tardío

dilemma [dɪˈlɛmə] *s* dilema *m*, disyuntiva, encerrona

dilettan•te [ˌdɪləˈtænti] *adj* diletante ‖ *s* (*pl* **-tes** o **-ti** [ti]) diletante *mf*

diligence [ˈdɪlɪdʒəns] *s* diligencia; dedicación

diligent [ˈdɪlɪdʒənt] *adj* diligente

dill [dɪl] *s* eneldo

dillydal•ly [ˈdɪlɪˌdæli] *v* (*pret & pp* **-lied**) *intr* malgastar el tiempo, haraganear

dilute [dɪˈlut] o [daɪˈlut] *adj* diluído ‖ [dɪˈlut] *tr* diluir ‖ *intr* diluirse

dilution [dɪˈluʃən] *s* dilución

dim. *abbr* **diminutive**

dim [dɪm] *adj* (*comp* **dimmer;** *super* **dimmest**) débil, indistinto, confuso; obscuro, poco claro; (*chance*) escaso; (*not clearly understanding*) torpe, lerdo; **to take a dim view of** mirar escépticamente ‖ *v* (*pret & pp* **dimmed;** *ger* **dimming**) *tr* amortiguar (*la luz*); poner (*un faro*) a media luz; disminuir ‖ *intr* obscurecerse

dime [daɪm] *s* moneda de diez centavos

dimension [dɪˈmɛnʃən] *s* dimensión

diminish [dɪˈmɪnɪʃ] *tr* disminuir ‖ *intr* disminuir, disminuirse

diminution [ˌdɪməˈnuʃən] *s* disminución

diminutive [dɪˈmɪnjətɪv] *adj* (*tiny*) diminuto; (gram) diminutivo ‖ *s* diminutivo

dimi•ty [ˈdɪmɪti] *s* (*pl* **-ties**) cotonía

dimly [ˈdɪmli] *adv* indistintamente

dimmer [ˈdɪmər] *s* amortiguador *m* de luz; (aut) lámpara de cruce, luz *f* de cruce

dimple [ˈdɪmpəl] *s* hoyuelo

dimwit [ˈdɪmˌwɪt] *s* (slang) mentecato, bobo

dim•witted [ˈdɪmˌwɪtɪd] *adj* (slang) mentecato, bobo

din [dɪn] *s* estruendo, ruido ensordecedor ‖ *v* (*pret & pp* **dinned;** *ger* **dinning**) *tr* ensordecer con mucho ruido; repetir insistentemente; impresionar con repetición ruidosa ‖ *intr* sonar estrepitosamente

dine [daɪn] *tr* dar de comer a; obsequiar con una cena o comida ‖ *intr* cenar, comer; **to dine out** cenar fuera de casa
diner [ˈdaɪnər] *s* invitado a una cena, convidado a una comida; coche-comedor *m*
ding-dong [ˈdɪŋˌdɔŋ] *s* dindán *m*
din•gy [ˈdɪndʒi] *adj* (*comp* **-gier;** *super* **-giest**) deslustrado, sucio
dining car *s* coche-comedor *m*
dining room *s* comedor *m*
din′ing-room′ suite *s* juego de comedor
dinner [ˈdɪnər] *s* cena, comida; (*formal meal*) banquete *m*
dinner coat o **jacket** *s* smoking *m*
dinner pail *s* fiambrera, portaviandas *m*
dinner set *s* vajilla
dinner time *s* hora de la cena o comida
dint [dɪnt] *s* abolladura; **by dint of** a fuerza de ‖ *tr* abollar
diocese [ˈdaɪə·ˈsis] o [ˈdaɪ·əsɪs] *s* diócesi *f* o diócesis *f*
diode [ˈdaɪ·od] *s* diodo
dioxide [daɪˈɑksaɪd] *s* dióxido
dip [dɪ] *s* zambullida, inmersión; baño corto; (*in a road*) depresión; (*of magnetic needle*) inclinación ‖ *v* (*pret & pp* **dipped;** *ger* **dipping**) *tr* sumergir; sacar con cuchara; (*bread*) sopetear; **to dip the colors** saludar con la bandera ‖ *intr* sumergirse; inclinarse hacia abajo; desaparecer súbitamente; **to dip into** hojear (*un libro*); meterse en (*un comercio*); **to dip into one's purse** gastar dinero
diphtheria [dɪfˈθɪrɪ·ə] *s* difteria
diphthong [ˈdɪfθɔŋ] *s* diptongo
diphthongize [ˈdɪfθɔŋˌgaɪz] *tr* diptongar ‖ *intr* diptongarse
diploma [dɪˈplomə] *s* diploma *m*
diploma•cy [dɪˈploməsi] *s* (*pl* **-cies**) diplomacia
diplomat [ˈdɪpləˌmæt] *s* diplomático
diplomatic [ˌdɪpləˈmætɪk] *adj* diplomático
diplomatic pouch *s* valija diplomática
dipper [ˈdɪpər] *s* cazo, cucharón *m*
dip′stick′ *s* varilla de nivel
dire [daɪr] *adj* horrendo, espantoso
direct [dɪˈrɛkt] o [daɪˈrɛkt] *adj* directo; franco, sincero ‖ *tr* dirigir; mandar, ordenar
direct current *s* corriente continua
direct discourse *s* (gram) estilo directo
direct hit *s* blanco directo, impacto directo
direction [dɪˈrɛkʃən] o [daɪˈrɛkʃən] *s* dirección; instrucción; **directions** (*for use*) modo de empleo
direction light *s* (aut) intermitente *m*
direct object *s* (gram) complemento directo
director [dɪˈrɛktər] o [daɪˈrɛktər] *s* director *m*, administrador *m;* (*member of a governing body*) vocal *m*
directorship [dɪˈrɛktərˌʃɪp] o [daɪˈrɛktərˌʃɪp] *s* dirección, directorio
directo•ry [dɪˈrɛktəri] o [daɪˈrɛktəri] *s* (*pl* **-ries**) (*list of names and addresses; board of directors*) directorio; anuario telefónico, guía telefónica

dirge [dʌrdʒ] *s* endecha, canto fúnebre, treno; (eccl) misa de réquiem
dirigible [ˈdɪrɪdʒɪbəl] *adj & s* dirigible *m*
dirt [dʌrt] *s* (*soil*) tierra, suelo; (*dust*) polvo; (*mud*) barro, lodo; excremento; (*accumulation of dirt*) suciedad; (*moral filth*) suciedad, porquería, obscenidad; (*gossip*) chismes *mpl*
dirt′cheap′ *adj* tirado, muy barato
dirt road *s* camino de tierra
dirt•y [ˈdʌrti] *adj* (*comp* **-ier;** *super* **-iest**) puerco, sucio; berroso, enlodado; polvoriento; (*obscene*) hediondo; bajo, vil ‖ *v* (*pret & pp* **-tied**) *tr* ensuciar
dirty linen *s* ropa sucia; **to air one's dirty linen in public** sacar los trapos sucios a relucir
dirty trick *s* (slang) perrada, mala partida
disabili•ty [ˌdɪsəˈbɪlɪti] *s* (*pl* **-ties**) incapacidad, inhabilidad; disminución (*física*)
disable [dɪsˈebəl] *tr* incapacitar, inhabilitar, lisiar; (law) descalificar
disabled veteran *s* lisiado de guerra
disabuse [ˌdɪsəˈbjuz] *tr* desengañar
disadvantage [ˌdɪsədˈvæntɪdʒ] o [ˌdɪsədˈvɑntɪdʒ] *s* desventaja
disadvantaged [ˌdɪsədˈvæntɪdʒd] *adj & s* desventajado
disadvantageous [dɪsˌædvənˈteʒəs] *adj* desventajoso
disagree [ˌdɪsəˈgri] *intr* desavenirse, desconvenirse; (*to quarrel*) altercar, contender; **to disagree with** no estar de acuerdo con; no sentar bien
disagreeable [ˌdɪsəˈgri·əbəl] *adj* desagradable
disagreement [ˌdɪsəˈgrimənt] *s* desavenencia, desacuerdo; disensión; inconformidad
disappear [ˌdɪsəˈpɪr] *intr* desaparecer, desaparecerse
disappearance [ˌdɪsəˈpɪrəns] *s* desaparecimiento, desaparición
disappoint [ˌdɪsəˈpɔɪnt] *tr* decepcionar, desilusionar, chasquear; **to be disappointed** chasquearse, llevarse chasco
disappointment [ˌdɪsəˈpɔɪntmənt] *s* decepción, desilusión, chasco
disapproval [ˌdɪsəˈpruvəl] *s* desaprobación
disapprove [ˌdɪsəˈpruv] *tr & intr* desaprobar
disarm [dɪsˈɑrm] *tr* desarmar ‖ *intr* desarmar, desarmarse
disarmament [dɪsˈɑrməmənt] *s* desarme *m*, desarmamiento
disarming [dɪsˈɑrmɪŋ] *adj* congraciador, simpático
disarray [ˌdɪsəˈre] *s* desorden *m;* (*in apparel*) desatavío ‖ *tr* desordenar; desataviar
disaster [dɪˈzæstər] *s* desastre *m*, siniestro
disaster area *s* zona siniestrada
disastrous [dɪˈzæstrəs] *adj* desastroso, desastrado
disavow [ˌdɪsəˈvaʊ] *tr* desconocer, negar, repudiar
disband [dɪsˈbænd] *tr* disolver (*una asamblea*); licenciar (*tropas*) ‖ *intr* desbandarse
dis•bar [dɪsˈbɑr] *v* (*pret & pp* **-barred;** *ger* **-barring**) *tr* (law) expulsar del foro

di
di

disbelief ['dɪsbɪ'lif] *s* incredulidad
disbelieve ['dɪsbɪ'lig] *tr & intr* descreer
disburse [dɪs'bʌrs] *tr* desembolsar
disbursement [dɪs'bʌrsmənt] *s* desembolso
disc. *abbr* **discount, discoverer**
disc [dɪsk] *s* disco
discard [dɪs'kard] *s* descarte *m*; **to put into the discard** desechar ‖ *tr* descartar; desechar
discern [dɪ'zʌrn] o [dɪ'sʌrn] *tr* discernir, percibir
discerning [dɪ'zʌrnɪŋ] o [dɪ'sʌrnɪŋ] *adj* discerniente, perspicaz
discharge [dɪs'tʃardʒ] *s* (*of a gun, of a battery*) descarga; (*of a prisoner*) liberación; (*of a duty*) desempeño; (*of a debt, of an obligation*) descargo; (*from a job*) despedida, remoción; (mil) certificado de licencia; (pathol) derrame *m* ‖ *tr* descargar; desempeñar (*un deber*); libertar (*a un preso*); despedir, remover (*a un empleado*); (*from the hospital*) dar de alta; (mil) licenciar ‖ *intr* descargar (*un tubo, río, etc.*); descargarse (*un arma de fuego*)
disciple [dɪ'saɪpəl] *s* discípulo
disciplinarian [,dɪsɪplɪ'nɛrɪ•ən] *s* ordenancista *mf*
discipline ['dɪsɪplɪn] *s* disciplina; castigo ‖ *tr* disciplinar; castigar
disclaim [dɪs'klem[*tr* desconocer, negar
disclose [dɪs'kloz] *tr* divulgar, revelar; descubrir
disclosure [dɪs'kloʒər] *s* divulgación, revelación; descubrimiento
disco ['dɪsko] *abbr* **discotheque**
discolor [dɪs'kʌlər] *tr* descolorar ‖ *intr* descolorarse
discomfiture [dɪs'kʌmfɪtʃər] *s* desconcierto; frustración
discomfort [dɪs'kʌmfərt] *s* incomodidad ‖ *tr* incomodar
disconcert [,dɪskən'sʌrt] *tr* desconcertar, confundir
disconnect [,dɪskə'nɛkt] *tr* desunir, separar; desconectar
disconsolate [dɪs'kansəlɪt] *adj* desconsolado, desolado
discontent [,dɪskən'tɛnt] *adj & s* descontento ‖ *tr* descontentar
discontented [,dɪskən'tɛntɪd] *adj* descontento
discontinue [,dɪskən'tɪnju] *tr* descontinuar
discord ['dɪskɔrd] *s* desacuerdo, discordia; discordancia
discordance [dɪs'kɔrdəns] *s* discordancia
discotheque [,dɪsko'tɛk] *s* discoteca
discount ['dɪskaʊnt] *s* descuento ‖ ['dɪskaʊnt] o [dɪs'kaʊnt] *tr* descontar; descontar por exagerado
discount rate *s* tipo de descuento; tipo de redescuento
discourage [dɪs'kʌrɪdʒ] *tr* desalentar, desanimar; desaprobar; disuadir
discouragement [dɪs'kʌrɪdʒmənt] *s* desaliento; desaprobación; disuasión
discourse ['dɪskors] o [dɪs'kors] *s* discurso ‖ [dɪs'kors] *intr* discurrir
discourteous [dɪs'kʌrtɪ•əs] *adj* descortés

discourte•sy [dɪs'kʌrtəsi] *s* (*pl* **-sies**) descortesía
discover [dɪs'kʌvər] *tr* descubrir
discover•y [dɪs'kʌvəri] *s* (*pl* **-ies**) descubrimiento
discredit [dɪs'krɛdɪt] *s* descrédito ‖ *tr* desacreditar
discreditable [dɪs'krɛdɪtəbəl] *adj* deshonroso
discreet [dɪs'krit] *adj* discreto
discrepan•cy [dɪs'krɛpənsi] *s* (*pl* **-cies**) discrepancia
discrete [dɪs'krit] *adj* discreto
discretion [dɪs'krɛʃən] *s* discreción; **at discretion** a discreción
discriminate [dɪs'krɪmɪ,net] *intr* discriminar; **to discriminate against** discriminar
discrimination [dɪs,krɪmɪ'neʃən] *s* discriminación
discriminatory [dɪs'krɪmɪnə,tori] *adj* discriminatorio
discus ['dɪskəs] *s* (sport) disco
discuss [dɪs'kʌs] *tr & intr* discutir
discussion [dɪs'kʌʃən] *s* discusión
discus thrower ['θro•ər] *s* discóbolo
disdain [dɪs'den] *s* desdén *m* ‖ *tr* desdeñar
disdainful [dɪs'denfəl] *adj* desdeñoso
disease [dɪ'ziz] *s* enfermedad
diseased [dɪ'zizd] *adj* morboso
disembark [,dɪsɛm'bark] *tr & intr* desembarcar
disembarkation [dɪs,ɛmbar'keʃən] *s* (*of passengers*) desembarco; (*of freight*) desembarque *m*
disembowel [,dɪsɛm'bau•əl] *tr* desentrañar
disenchant [,dɪsɛn'tʃænt] *tr* desencantar
disenchantment [,dɪsɛn'tʃæntmənt] *s* desencanto
disengage [,dɪsɛn'gedʒ] *tr* (*from a pledge*) desempeñar; (*to disconnect*) desenganchar; desembragar (*el motor*)
disengagement [,dɪsɛn'gedʒmənt] *s* desempeño; desenganche *m*; desembrague *m*
disentangle [,dɪsɛn'tæŋgəl] *tr* desenredar
disentanglement [,dɪsɛn'tæŋgəlmənt] *s* desenredo
disestablish [,dɪsɛs'tæblɪʃ] *tr* separar (*la Iglesia*) del Estado
disfavor [dɪs'fevər] *s* disfavor *m*
disfigure [dɪs'fɪgjər] *tr* desfigurar
disfranchise [dɪs'fræntʃaɪz] *tr* privar de los derechos de ciudadanía
disgorge [dɪs'gɔrdʒ] *tr & intr* vomitar
disgrace [dɪs'gres] *s* deshonra, vergüenza; disfavor *m*; metedura ‖ *tr* deshonrar, avergonzar; despedir con ignominia
disgraceful [dɪs'gresfəl] *adj* deshonroso, vergonzoso
disgruntle [dɪs•grʌntəl] *tr* disgustar, enfadar
disguise [dɪs'gaɪz] *s* disfraz *m* ‖ *tr* disfrazar
disgust [dɪs'gʌst] *s* asco, repugnancia ‖ *tr* dar asco a, repugnar
disgusting [dɪs'gʌstɪŋ] *adj* asqueroso, repugnante; bofe (CAm)
dish [dɪʃ] *s* (*any container used at table*) vasija; (*shallow, circular dish; its contents*) plato; **to wash the dishes** lavar la vajilla ‖ *tr* servir en un plato; (slang) arruinar

dish'cloth' s albero
dishearten [dɪs'hɑrtən] tr descorazonar, desalentar, desanimar
dishev•el [dɪ'fɛvəl] v (pret & pp **-eled** o **-elled;** ger **-eling** o **-elling**) desgreñar, desmelenar
dishonest [dɪs'ɑnɪst] adj no honrado, ímprobo
dishones•ty [dɪs'ɑnɪsti] s (pl **-ties**) falta de honradez, improbidad
dishonor [dɪs'ɑnər] s deshonra, deshonor m ‖ tr deshonrar, deshonorar; (com) no aceptar, no pagar
dishonorable [dɪs'ɑnərəbəl] adj ignominioso, deshonroso
dish'pan' s paila de lavar la vajilla
dish rack s escurreplatos m
dish'rag' s albero
dish'tow'el s paño para secar platos
dish'wash'er s (person) fregona; (machine) lavaplatos m, lavavajillas m
dish'wa'ter s agua de lavar platos, agua sucia
disillusion [,dɪsɪ'luʒən] s desilusión ‖ tr desilusionar
disillusionment [,dɪsɪ'luʒənmənt] s desilusión
disinclination [dɪs,ɪnklɪ'nefən] s aversión, desafición
disinclined [,dɪsɪn'klaɪnd] adj desinclinado
disinfect [,dɪsɪn'fɛkt] tr desinfectar, desinficionar
disinfectant [,dɪsɪn'fɛktant] adj & s desinfectante m
disingenuous [,dɪsɪn'dʒɛnju•əs] adj insincero, poco ingenuo
disinherit [,dɪsɪn'hɛrɪt] tr desheredar
disintegrate [dɪs'ɪntɪ,gret] tr desagregar, desintegrar ‖ intr desagregarse, desintegrarse
disintegration [dɪs,ɪntɪ'grefən] s desagregación, desintegración
disin•ter [,dɪsɪn'tʌr] v (pret & pp **-terred;** ger **-terring**) tr desenterrar
disinterested [dɪs'ɪntə,rɛstɪd] o [dɪs'ɪntrɪstɪd] adj desinteresado
disinterestedness [dɪs'ɪntə,rɛstɪdnɛs] o [dɪs'ɪntrɪstɪdnɪs] s desinterés m
disjunctive [dɪs'dʒʌŋktɪv] adj disyuntivo
disk [dɪsk] s disco
disk brake s freno de disco
disk jockey s (rad) locutor m de un programa de discos
dislike [dɪs'laɪk] s aversión, antipatía; **to take a dislike for** cobrar aversión a ‖ tr desamar
dislocate ['dɪslo,ket] tr dislocar, dislocarse (un hueso)
dislodge [dɪs'lɑdʒ] tr desalojar
disloyal [dɪs'lɔɪ•əl] adj desleal
disloyal•ty [dɪs'lɔɪ•əlti] s (pl **-ties**) deslealtad
dismal ['dɪzməl] adj lúgubre, tenebroso; terrible, espantoso
dismantle [dɪs'mæntəl] tr desarmar, desmontar
dismay [dɪs'me] s consternación ‖ tr consternar
dismember [dɪs'mɛmbər] tr desmembrar

dismiss [dɪs'mɪs] tr despedir, destituir; desechar; alejar del pensamiento, echar en olvido
dismissal [dɪs'mɪsəl] s despedida, destitución
dismount [dɪs'maʊnt] tr desmontar ‖ intr desmontarse
disobedience [,dɪsə'bidɪ•əns] s desobediencia
disobedient [,dɪsə'bidɪ•ənt] adj desobediente
disobey [,dɪsə'be] tr & intr desobedecer
disorder [dɪs'ɔrdər] s desorden m ‖ tr desordenar
disorderly [dɪs'ɔrdərli] adj desordenado; alborotador, revoltoso
disorderly conduct s conducta contra el orden público
disorderly house s burdel m, lupanar m
disorganize [dɪs'ɔrgə,naɪz] tr desorganizar
disorientation [dɪs,ɔrien'tefən] s desorientación
disown [dɪs'on] tr desconocer, repudiar
disparage [dɪs'pærɪdʒ] tr desacreditar, desdorar
disparagement [dɪs'pærɪdʒmənt] s descrédito, desdoro
disparate ['dɪspərɪt] adj disparejo
dispari•ty [dɪs'pærɪti] s (pl **-ties**) disparidad
dispassionate [dɪs'pæʃ/ənɪt] adj desapasionado
dispatch [dɪs'pætʃ] s despacho ‖ tr despachar; (coll) despabilar (una comida)
dis•pel [dɪs'pɛl] v (pret & pp **-pelled;** ger **-pelling**) tr desvanecer, disipar
dispensa•ry [dɪs'pɛnsəri] s (pl **-ries**) dispensario
dispense [dɪs'pɛns] tr dispensar (medicamentos); administrar (justicia); expender (p.ej., gasolina); (to exempt) eximir ‖ intr **— to dispense with** deshacerse de; pasar sin, prescindir de
disperse [dɪs'pʌrs] tr dispersar ‖ intr dispersarse
displace [dɪs'ples] tr remover, trasladar; despedir, deponer; reemplazar; desplazar (un volumen de agua)
displaced person s persona desplazada
display [dɪs'ple] s despliegue m; exhibición, exposición, ostentación ‖ tr (to unfold; to reveal) desplegar; (to exhibit, show) exhibir, exponer; (to show ostentatiously) ostentar
display cabinet s vitrina, escaparate m
display window s escaparate m de tienda
displease [dɪs'pliz] tr desagradar, disgustar, desplacer
displeasing [dɪs'plizɪŋ] adj desagradable
displeasure [dɪs'plɛʒər] s desagrado, disgusto, desplacer m
disposable [dɪs'pozəbəl] adj (available for any use) disponible; (made to be thrown away after serving its purpose) desechable, descartable
disposal [dɪs'pozəl] s disposición; donación, liquidación, venta; **at the disposal of** a la disposición de; **to have at one's disposal** disponer de

di
di

dispose [dɪs'poz] *tr* disponer; inducir, mover ‖ *intr* disponer; **to dispose of** disponer de; deshacerse de; dar, vender; acabar con

disposition [,dɪspə'zɪʃən] *s* disposición; índole *f*, genio, natural *m;* ajuste *m*, arreglo; venta

dispossess [,dɪspə'zɛs] *tr* desposeer; (*to evict, oust*) desahuciar

disproof [dɪs'pruf] *s* confutación, refutación

disproportionate [,dɪsprə'porʃənɪt] *adj* desproporcionado

disprove [dɪs'pruv] *tr* confutar, refutar

dispute [dɪs'pjut] *s* disputa; **beyond dispute** sin disputa; **in dispute** disputado ‖ *tr & intr* disputar

disquali•fy [dɪs'kwɑlɪ,faɪ] *v* (*pret & pp* -**fied**) *tr* descalificar, desclasificar

disquiet [dɪs'kwaɪ•ət] *s* desasosiego, inquietud ‖ *tr* desasosegar, inquietar

disregard [,dɪsrɪ'gɑrd] *s* desatención, desaire *m* ‖ *tr* desatender, desairar, pasar por alto

disrepair [,dɪsrɪ'pɛr] *s* desconcierto, descompostura

disreputable [dɪs'rɛpjətəbəl] *adj* desacreditado, de mala fama; raído, usado, desaliñado

disrepute [,dɪsrɪ'pjut] *s* descrédito, mala fama; **to bring into disrepute** desacreditar, dar mala fama a

disrespect [,dɪsrɪ'spɛkt] *s* desacato ‖ *tr* desacatar

disrespectful [,dɪsrɪ'spɛktfəl] *adj* irrespetuoso

disrobe [dɪs'rob] *tr* desnudar ‖ *intr* desnudarse, despelotarse

disrupt [dɪs'rʌpt] *tr* romper; (*to throw into disorder*) desbaratar

dissatisfaction [,dɪssætɪs'fækʃən] *s* desagrado, descontento, insatisfacción

dissatisfied [dɪs'sætɪs,faɪd] *adj* descontento

dissatis•fy [dɪs'sætɪs,faɪ] *v* (*pret & pp* -**fied**) *tr* descontentar

dissect [dɪ'sɛkt] *tr* disecar

dissemble [dɪ'sɛmbəl] *tr* disimular ‖ *intr* disimular; obrar hipócritamente

disseminate [dɪ'sɛmɪ,net] *tr* diseminar, difundir

dissension [dɪ'sɛnʃən] *s* disensión

dissent [dɪ'sɛnt] *s* disensión; (*nonconformity*) disidencia ‖ *intr* disentir; (*from doctrine or authority*) disidir

dissenter [dɪ'sɛntər] *s* disidente *mf*

disservice [dɪ'sʌrvɪs] *s* deservicio

dissidence ['dɪsɪdəns] *s* disidencia

dissident ['dɪsɪdənt] *adj & s* disidente *mf*

dissimilar [dɪ'sɪmɪlər] *adj* disímil, desemejante

dissimilate [dɪ'sɪmɪ,let] *tr* disimilar ‖ *intr* disimilarse

dissimulate [dɪ'sɪmjə,let] *tr & intr* disimular

dissipate ['dɪsɪ,pet] *tr* disipar ‖ *intr* disiparse; entregarse a la disipación

dissipated ['dɪsɪ,petɪd] *adj* disipado, disoluto

dissipation [,dɪsɪ'peʃən] *s* disipación

dissociate [dɪ'soʃɪ,et] *tr* disociar

dissolute ['dɪsə,lut] *adj* disoluto

dissolution [,dɪsə'luʃən] *s* disolución

dissolve [dɪ'zɑlv] *tr* disolver ‖ *intr* (*to have the power of dissolving*) disolver; (*to pass into a liquid*) disolverse

dissonance ['dɪsənəns] *s* disonancia

dissuade [dɪ'swed] *tr* disuadir

dissyllabic [,dɪssɪ'læbɪk] *adj* disílabo, disilábico

dissyllable [dɪ'sɪləbəl] *s* disílabo

dist. *abbr* **distance, distinguish, district**

distaff ['dɪstæf] o ['dɪstaf] *s* rueca

distaff side *s* rama femenina de la familia

distance ['dɪstəns] *s* distancia; **at a distance** a distancia; **in the distance** a lo lejos; **to keep at a distance** no permitir familiaridades; **to keep one's distance** mantenerse a distancia

distant ['dɪstənt] *adj* distante; (*relative*) lejano; (*not familiar*) frío, indiferente

distaste [dɪs'test] *s* aversión, repugnancia

distasteful [dɪs'testfəl] *adj* desagradable, repugnante

distemper [dɪs'tɛmpər] *s* enfermedad; (*of dogs*) moquillo

distend [dɪs'tɛnd] *tr* ensanchar, distender ‖ *intr* ensancharse, distender

distension [dɪs'tɛnʃən] *s* ensanche *m*, distensión

distill [dɪs'tɪl] *tr* destilar

distillation [,dɪstɪ'leʃən] *s* destilación

distiller•y [dɪs'tɪləri] *s* (*pl* -**ies**) destilería, destilatorio

distinct [dɪs'tɪŋkt] *adj* distinto; cierto, indudable; (*not blurred*) nítido, bien definido

distinction [dɪs'tɪŋkʃən] *s* distinción; (*distinguishing characteristic*) distintivo

distinctive [dɪs'tɪŋktɪv] *adj* distintivo

distinguish [dɪs'tɪŋgwɪʃ] *tr* distinguir

distinguished [dɪs'tɪŋgwɪʃt] *adj* distinguido

distort [dɪs'tɔrt] *tr* deformar, torcer; distorsionar; (*the truth*) falsear

distortion [dɪs'tɔrʃən] *s* deformación, torcimiento; (*of the truth*) falseamiento; (*rad*) deformación, distorsión

distract [dɪs'trækt] *tr* distraer

distraction [dɪs'trækʃən] *s* distracción

distraught [dɪs'trɔt] *adj* trastornado, perplejo, aturdido

distress [dɪs'trɛs] *s* pena, aflicción, angustia; infortunio, peligro ‖ *tr* apenar, afligir, angustiar

distressing [dɪs'trɛsɪŋ] *adj* penoso, angustioso

distress signal *s* señal *f* de socorro

distribute [dɪs'trɪbjut] *tr* distribuir, repartir

distribution [,dɪstrɪ'bjuʃən] *s* distribución, repartimiento, repartida

distributor [dɪs'trɪbjətər] *s* distribuidor *m;* (*aut*) distribuidor

district ['dɪstrɪkt] *s* comarca, región; (*of a city*) barrio; (*administrative division*) distrito ‖ *tr* dividir en distritos

district attorney *s* fiscal *m*

distrust [dɪs'trʌst] *s* desconfianza ‖ *tr* desconfiar de

distrustful [dɪs'trʌstfəl] *adj* desconfiado

disturb [dɪs'tʌrb] *tr* disturbar, incomodar, molestar; desordenar, revolver; inquietar, dejar perplejo; perturbar (*el orden público*)

disturbance [dɪs'tʌrbəns] *s* disturbio, molestia; desorden *m;* inquietud; tumulto, trastorno

disuse [dɪs'jus] *s* desuso

ditch [dɪtʃ] *s* zanja ‖ *tr* zanjar; echar en una zanja; (slang) deshacerse de ‖ *intr* amarar forzosamente

ditch reed *s* carrizo

dither ['dɪðər] *s* agitación, temblor; **to be in a dither** (coll) estar muy agitado

dit•to ['dɪto] *s* (*pl* **-tos**) ídem *m;* (*ditto symbol*) íd.; copia, duplicado ‖ *tr* copiar, duplicar

ditto mark *s* la sigla " (*es decir:* íd.)

dit•ty ['dɪti] *s* (*pl* **-ties**) cancioneta

diuretic [,daɪə'rɛtɪk] *adj* & *s* diurético

div. *abbr* **dividend, division**

diva ['divɑ] *s* (mus) diva

divan ['daɪvæn] o [dɪ'væn] *s* diván *m*

dive [daɪv] *s* zambullida; (*of a submarine*) sumersión; (aer) picado; (coll) leonera, tasca ‖ *v* (*pret* & *pp* **dived** o **dove** [dov]) *intr* zambullirse; (*to work as a diver*) bucear; sumergirse (*un submarino*); (aer) picar

dive'-bomb' *tr* & *intr* bombardear en picado

dive bombing *s* bombardeo en picado

diver ['daɪvər] *s* zambullidor *m;* buceador; (*person who works under water*) escafandrista *mf*, buzo; (orn) zambullidor *m*

diverge [dɪ'vʌrdʒ] o [daɪ'vʌrdʒ] *intr* divergir

divers ['daɪvərz] *adj* diversos, varios

diverse [dɪ'vʌrs] o [daɪ'vʌrs] *adj* (*different*) diverso; (*of various kinds*) variado

diversification [dɪ'vʌrsɪfɪ'keʃən] o [daɪ-,vʌrsɪfɪ'keʃən] *s* diversificación

diversi•fy [dɪ'vʌrsɪ,faɪ] o [daɪ'vʌrsɪ,faɪ] *v* (*pret* & *pp* **-fied**) *tr* diversificar ‖ *intr* diversificarse

diversion [dɪ'vʌrʒən] o [daɪ'vʌrʒən] *s* diversión

diversi•ty [dɪ'vʌrsɪti] o [daɪ'vʌrsɪti] *s* (*pl* **-ties**) diversidad

divert [dɪ'vʌrt] o [daɪ'vʌrt] *tr* apartar, divertir; (*to entertain*) divertir, entretener; (mil) divertir

diverting [dɪ'vʌrtɪŋ] o [daɪ'vʌrtɪŋ] *adj* divertido

divest [dɪ'vɛst] o [daɪ'vɛst] *tr* desnudar; despojar, desposeer; **to divest oneself of** desposeerse de

divide [dɪ'vaɪd] *s* (geog) divisoria ‖ *tr* dividir ‖ *intr* dividirse

dividend ['dɪvɪ,dɛnd] *s* dividendo

dividers [dɪ'vaɪdərz] *spl* compás *m* de división

divination [,dɪvɪ'neʃən] *s* adivinación

divine [dɪ'vaɪn] *adj* divino ‖ *s* sacerdote *m*, clérigo ‖ *tr* adivinar

diving ['daɪvɪŋ] *s* zambullida; buceo

diving bell *s* campana de buzo

diving board *s* trampolín *m*

diving suit *s* escafandra

divining rod [dɪ'vaɪnɪŋ] *s* vara de adivinar; (*ostensibly to discover water or metals*) vara buscadora

divini•ty [dɪ'vɪnɪti] *s* (*pl* **-ties**) divinidad; teología; **the Divinity** Dios *m*

division [dɪ'vɪʒən] *s* división

divisor [dɪ'vaɪzər] *s* (math) divisor *m*

divorce [dɪ'vors] *s* divorcio; **to get a divorce** divorciarse ‖ *tr* divorciar (*los cónyuges*); divorciarse de (*la mujer o el marido*) ‖ *intr* divorciarse

divorcee [dɪvor'si] *s* persona divorciada; mujer divorciada

divulge [dɪ'vʌldʒ] *tr* divulgar, revelar

dizziness ['dɪzɪnɪs] *s* vértigo; confusión, perplejidad

diz•zy ['dɪzi] *adj* (*comp* **-zier;** *super* **-ziest**) (*suffering or causing dizziness*) vertiginoso; confuso, perplejo; aturdido, incauto; (coll) tonto

do. *abbr* **ditto**

do [du] *v* (*tercera persona* **does** [dʌz]; *pret* **did** [dɪd]; *pp* **done** [dʌn]) *tr* hacer; resolver (*un problema*); recorrer (*cierta distancia*); cumplir con (*un deber*); aprender (*una lección*); componer (*la cama*); tocar (*el cabello*); rendir (*homenaje*); **to do one's best** hacer todo lo posible; **to do over** volver a hacer; repetir; renovar; **to do right by** tratar bien; **to do someone out of something** (coll) defraudar algo a alguien; **to do to death** despachar, matar; **to do up** empaquetar; poner en orden; almidonar y planchar (*una camisa*) ‖ *intr* actuar, obrar; conducirse; servir, ser suficiente; estar, hallarse; **how do you do?** ¿cómo está Vd.?; **that will do** eso sirve, eso es bastante; no digas más; **to have done** haber terminado; **to have done with** no tener más que ver con; **to have nothing to do with** no tener nada que ver con; **to have to do with** tratar de; **to do away with** suprimir; matar; **to do for** servir para; **to do well** salir bien; **to do without** pasar sin ‖ *v aux* úsase 1) en oraciones interrogativas: **Do you speak Spanish?** ¿Habla Vd. español?; 2) en oraciones negativas; **I do not speak Spanish** No hablo español; 3) para substituir a otro verbo en oraciones elípticas; **Did you go to church this morning? Yes, I did** ¿Fué Vd. a la iglesia esta mañana? Sí, fuí; 4) para dar más energía a la oración; **I do believe what you told me** Yo sí creo lo que me dijo Vd.; 5) en inversiones después de ciertos adverbios; **Seldom does he come to see me** él rara vez viene a verme; 6) en tono suplicante con el imperativo; **Do come in** pase Vd., por favor

docile ['dɑsɪl] *adj* dócil

dock [dɑk] *s* (*wharf*) muelle *m;* (*waterway between two piers*) dársena; (*area including piers and waterways*) puerto de mar; muñón *m* de cola; (law) tribuna de los acusados ‖ *tr* (naut) atracar en el muelle; derrabar, descolar (*a un animal*); reducir o suprimir (*el salario*) ‖ *intr* (naut) atracar

dockage ['dɑkɪdʒ] *s* entrada en un puerto; (*charges*) muellaje *m*

di
do

docket ['dakɪt] *s* actas, orden *m* del día; lista de causas pendientes; **on the docket** (coll) pendiente, entre manos

dock hand *s* portuario

dock'yard' *s* arsenal *m*, astillero

doctor ['daktər] *s* doctor *m;* *(physician)* médico ‖ *tr* medicinar; (coll) componer, reparar ‖ *intr* (coll) ejercer la medicina; (coll) tomar medicinas

doctorate ['daktərɪt] *s* doctorado

doctrine ['daktrɪn] *s* doctrina

document ['dakjəmənt] *s* documento ‖ ['dakjə,mɛnt] *tr* documentar

documenta•ry [,dakjə'mɛntəri] *adj* documental ‖ *s* (*pl* -ries) documental *m*

documentation [,dakəmɛn'te/ən] *s* documentación

doddering ['dadərɪŋ] *adj* chocho, temblón

dodge [dadʒ] *s* esguince *m*, regate *m;* (fig) regate ‖ *tr* evitar (*un golpe*); (fig) evitar mañosamente ‖ *intr* regatear, hurtar el cuerpo; **to dodge around the corner** voltear la esquina

do•do ['dodo] *s* (*pl* -dos o -does) (coll) inocente *m* de ideas anticuadas

doe [do] *s* cierva, gama, coneja

doeskin ['do,skɪn] *s* ante *m*, piel *f* de ante; tejido fino de lana

doff [daf] o [dɔf] *tr* quitarse (*el sombrero, la ropa*)

dog [dɔg] o [dag] *s* perro; **to go to the dogs** darse al abandono; **lucky dog** (coll) lechero, suertero; **to put on the dog** (coll) darse ínfulas ‖ *v* (*pret & pp* **dogged;** *ger* **dogging**) *tr* acosar, perseguir

dog'catch'er *s* lacero

dog days *spl* canícula, canicularse *mpl*

doge [dodʒ] dux *m*

dogged ['dɔgɪd] *adj* tenaz, terco

doggerel ['dɔgərəl] *s* coplas de ciego

dog•gy ['dɔgi] *adj* (*comp* -**gier;** *super* -**giest**) emperejilado ‖ *s* (*pl* -gies) perrito

dog'house' *s* perrera

dog in the manger *s* el perro del hortelano

dog Latin *s* latinajo, latín *m* de cocina

dogmatic [dɔg'mætɪk] *adj* dogmático; ergotista

dog racing *s* carreras de galgos

dog's-ear ['dɔgzɛɪr] *s* orejón *m*

dog show *s* exposición canina

dog's life *s* vida miserable

Dog Star *s* Canícula

dog'-tired' *adj* cansadísimo

dog'tooth' *s* (*pl* -teeth [,tiθ] colmillo

dog track *s* galgódromo

dog'watch' *s* (naut) guardia de cuartillo

dog'wood' *s* cornejo

doi•ly ['dɔɪli] *s* (*pl* -lies) pañito de adorno

doings ['duˑɪŋz] *spl* acciones, obras, actividad

doldrums ['daldrəmz] *spl* (naut) calmas ecuatoriales; desanimación, inactividad

dole [dol] *s* limosna; subsidio a los desocupados ‖ *tr* — **to dole out** distribuir en pequeñas porciones

doleful ['dolfəl] *adj* triste, lúgubre

doll [dal] *s* muñeca ‖ *intr* — **to doll up** (slang) emperejilarse

dollar ['dalər] *s* dólar *m*

dollar mark *s* signo del dólar

dol•ly ['dali] *s* (*pl* -lies) muñequita; (*low, wheeled frame for moving heavy loads*) gato rodante

dolphin ['dalfɪn] *s* delfín *m*

dolt [dolt] *s* bobalicón *m*

doltish ['dolti/] *adj* bobalicón

dom. *abbr* **domestic, dominion**

domain [do'men] *s* dominio, heredad, propiedad; (*of learning*) campo

dome [dom] *s* cúpula, domo

dome light *s* (aut) lámpara de techo

domestic [də'mɛstɪk] *adj & s* doméstico

domesticate [də'mɛstɪ,ket] *tr* domesticar

domicile ['damɪsɪl] o ['damɪ,saɪl] *s* domicilio ‖ *tr* domiciliar

dominance ['damɪnəns] *s* dominación

dominant ['damɪnənt] *adj & s* dominante *f*

dominate ['damɪ,net] *tr & intr* dominar

domination [,damɪ'ne/ən] *s* dominación

domineer [,damɪ'nɪr] *intr* dominar

domineering [,damɪ'nɪrɪŋ] *adj* dominante, mandón

Dominican [də'mɪnɪkən] *adj & s* dominicano

dominion [də'mɪnjən] *s* dominio

domi•no ['damɪ,no] *s* (*pl* -noes o -nos) (*costume*) dominó *m;* antifaz *m;* persona que lleva dominó; ficha (*del juego de dominó*); **dominoes** *ssg* dominó (*juego*)

don [dan] *s* caballero, señor *m*, personaje *m* de alta categoría; (coll) preceptor *m*, socio de uno de los colegios de las Universidades de Oxford y Cambridge ‖ *v* (*pret & pp* **donned;** *ger* **donning**) *tr* ponerse (*el sombrero, la ropa*)

donate ['donet] *tr* dar, donar

donation [do'ne/ən] *s* donación

done [dʌn] *adj* hecho, terminado; cansado, rendido; bien asado

done for *adj* (coll) cansado, rendido, agotado; (coll) arruinado, destruido; (coll) fuera de combate; (coll) muerto

donjon ['dʌndʒən] *s* torre *f* del homenaje

donkey ['daŋki] *s* asno, burro

donnish ['danɪ/] *adj* magistral, pedantesco

donor ['donər] *s* donador *m*

doodle ['dudəl] *tr & intr* borrajear

doom [dum] *s* ruina, perdición, muerte *f;* condena, juicio; juicio final; hado, destino ‖ *tr* condenar; sentenciar a muerte; predestinar a la ruina, a la muerte

doomsday ['dumz,de] *s* día *m* del juicio final; día del juicio

door [dor] *s* puerta; (*of a carriage or automobile*) portezuela; (*one part of a double door*) hoja, batiente *m;* **behind closed doors** a puertas cerradas; **to see to the door** acompañar a la puerta

door'bell' *s* campanilla de puerta, timbre *m* de puerta

door check *s* amortiguador *m*, cierre *m* de puerta

door'frame' *s* bastidor *m* de puerta, marco de puerta

door'head' *s* dintel *m*

door'jamb' *s* jamba de puerta

door'knob' *s* botón *m* de puerta, pomo de puerta

door knocker *s* aldaba

door latch *s* pestillo

door•man ['dɔrmən] *s* (*pl* -**men** [mən]) portero; (*one who helps people in and out of cars*) abrecoches *m*

door'mat' *s* felpudo de puerta

door'nail' *s* clavo de adorno para puertas; **dead as a doornail** (coll) muerto sin duda alguna

door'post' *s* jamba de puerta

door scraper *s* limpiabarros *m*

door'sill' *s* umbral *m*

door'step' *s* escalón *m* delante de la puerta; escalera exterior

door'stop' *s* tope *m* de puerta

door'way' *s* puerta, portal *m*

dope [dop] *s* (slang) grasa lubricante; (aer) barniz *m*, nobabia; (slang) bobo, tonto; (slang) informes *mpl*; (slang) narcótico ‖ *tr* (slang) narcotizar, drogar; **to dope out** (slang) descifrar

dope fiend *s* (slang) toxicómano

dope sheet *s* (slang) hoja confidencial sobre los caballos de carreras

dormant ['dɔrmənt] *adj* durmiente, latente

dormer window ['dɔrmər] *s* buharda, buhardilla

dormito•ry ['dɔrmɪ,tori] *s* (*pl* -**ries**) dormitorio común

dor•mouse ['dɔr,maʊs] *s* (*pl* -**mice** [,maɪs]) lirón *m*

dosage ['dosɪdʒ] *s* dosificación

dose [dos] *s* dosis *f*; (coll) mal trago ‖ *tr* medicinar; dosificar (*un medicamento*)

dossier ['dɑsɪ,e] *s* expediente *m*

dot [dɑt] *s* punto; **on the dot** (coll) en punto ‖ *v* (*pret* & *pp* **dotted**; *ger* **dotting**) *tr* (*to make with dots*) puntear; poner punto a; **to dot one's i's** poner los puntos sobre las íes

dotage ['dotɪdʒ] *s* chochera, chochez *f*; **to be in one's dotage** chochear

dotard ['dotərd] *s* viejo chocho

dote [dot] *intr* chochear; **to dote on** estar chocho por

doting ['dotɪŋ] *adj* chocho

dots and dashes *spl* (telg) puntos y rayas

dotted line ['dɑtɪd] *s* línea de puntos; **to sign on the dotted line** firmar ciegamente

double ['dʌbəl] *adj* doble ‖ *adv* doble; dos juntos ‖ *s* doble *m*, duplo; (mov, theat) doble *mf*; **doubles** (tennis juego de dobles ‖ *tr* doblar; ser el doble de; (bridge) doblar ‖ *intr* doblarse; (mov, theat, bridge) doblar; **to double up** doblarse en dos; ocupar una misma habitación, dormir en una misma cama (*dos personas*)

double-barreled ['dʌbəl'bærəld] *adj* de dos cañones; (fig) para dos fines

double bass [bes] *s* contrabajo

double bassoon *s* contrabajón *m*

double bed *s* cama de matrimonio

double-breasted ['dʌbəl'brɛstɪd] *adj* cruzado, de dos pechos

double chin *s* papada

dou'ble-cross' *tr* traicionar (*a un cómplice*)

double date *s* cita de dos parejas

doub'le-deal'er *s* persona doble

double-edged ['dʌbəl'ɛdʒd] *adj* de dos filos

double entry *s* (com) partida doble

double feature *s* (mov) programa *m* doble, programa de dos películas de largo metraje

doubleheader ['dʌbəl'hɛdər] *s* tren *m* con dos locomotoras; (baseball) dos partidos jugados sucesivamente

double-jointed ['dʌbəl'dʒɔɪntɪd] *adj* de articulaciones dobles

dou'ble-park' *tr* & *intr* aparcar en doble fila

dou'ble-quick' *adj* & *adv* a paso ligero ‖ *s* paso ligero ‖ *intr* marchar a paso ligero

doublet ['dʌblɪt] *s* (*close-fitting jacket*) jubón *m*; (*counterfeit stone; each of two words having the same origin*) doblete *m*

double talk *s* (coll) galimatías *m*; (coll) habla ambigua para engañar

double time *s* pago doble por horas extraordinarias de trabajo; (mil) paso redoblado

doubleton ['dʌbəltən] *s* doblete *m*

double track *s* doble vía

doubling ['dʌblɪŋ] *s* reduplicación

doubt [daʊt] *s* duda; **beyond doubt** sin duda; **if in doubt** en caso de duda; **no doubt** sin duda ‖ *tr* dudar, dudar de ‖ *intr* dudar

doubter ['daʊtər] *s* incrédulo

doubtful ['daʊtfəl] *adj* dudoso

doubtless ['daʊtlɪs] *adj* indudable ‖ *adv* sin duda; probablemente

douche [duʃ] *s* ducha; (*instrument*) jeringa ‖ *tr* duchar ‖ *intr* ducharse

dough [do] *s* masa, pasta; (*money*) (slang) pasta

dough'boy' *s* (coll) soldado norteamericano de infantería

dough'nut' *s* rosquilla, buñuelo

dough•ty ['daʊti] *adj* (*comp* -**tier**; *super* -**tiest**) (hum) fuerte, valiente

dough•y ['do•i] *adj* (*comp* -**ier**; *super* -**iest**) pastoso

dour [daʊr] o [dʊr] *adj* triste, melancólico, austero

douse [daʊs] *tr* empapar, mojar, salpicar; (slang) apagar (*la luz*)

dove [dʌv] *s* paloma

dovecote ['dʌv,kot] *s* palomar *m*

dove'tail' *s* cola de milano, cola de pato ‖ *tr* ensamblar a cola de milano, ensamblar a cola de pato; (*to make fit*) encajar ‖ *intr* (*to fit*) encajar; concordar, corresponder

dowager ['daʊ•ədʒər] *s* viuda con título o bienes que proceden del marido, p.ej., **dowager duchess** duquesa viuda; (coll) matrona, señora anciana respetable

dow•dy ['daʊdi] *adj* (*comp* -**dier**; *super* -**diest**) desaliñado

dow•el ['daʊ•əl] *s* clavija ‖ *v* (*pret* & *pp* -**eled** o -**elled**; *ger* -**eling** o -**elling**) *tr* enclavijar

dower ['daʊ•ər] *s* (*widow's portion*) viudedad; (*marriage portion*) dote *m* & *f*; (*natu-*

do
do

ral gift) prenda ‖ *tr* señalar viudedad a; dotar

down [daʊn] *adj* descendente; abatido, triste; enfermo, malo; acostado, echado; (*money, payment*) anticipado; (*storage battery*) agotado; (*mach*) (coll) fuera de servicio ‖ *adv* abajo; hacia abajo; en tierra; al sur; por escrito; al contado; **down and out** arruinado; sin blanca; **down from** desde; **down on one's knees** de rodillas; **down to** hasta; **down under** entre los antípodas; **down with . . . !** ¡abajo . . . !; **to get down to work** aplicarse resueltamente al trabajo; **to go down** bajar; **to lie down** acostarse; **to sit down** sentarse ‖ *prep* bajando; **down the river** río abajo; **down the street** calle abajo ‖ *s* (*of fruit and human body*) vello; (*of birds*) plumón *m;* descenso, revés *m* de fortuna; (*sand hill*) duna ‖ *tr* derribar; (coll) tragar

down'cast' *adj* cariacontecido

down'fall' *s* caída, ruina; chaparrón *m;* nevazo

down'grade' *adj* (coll) pendiente, en declive ‖ *adv* (coll) cuesta abajo ‖ *s* bajada, declive *m;* **to be on the downgrade** decaer, declinar ‖ *tr* disminuir la categoría de

downhearted ['daʊn,hɑrtɪd] *adj* abatido, desanimado

down'hill' *adj* pendiente ‖ *adv* cuesta abajo; **to go downhill** ir cabeza abajo

down'pour' *s* aguacero, chaparrón *m*

down'right' *adj* absoluto, categórico; franco; claro ‖ *adv* absolutamente

down'stairs' *adj* de abajo ‖ *adv* abajo ‖ *s* piso inferior, pisos inferiores; (*the help*) la servidumbre

down'stream' *adv* aguas abajo, río abajo

down'stroke' *s* carrera descendente

down'town' *adj* céntrico ‖ *adv* al centro de la ciudad, en el centro de la ciudad ‖ *s* barrios céntricos, calles céntricas

down train *s* tren *m* descendente

down'trend' *s* tendencia a la baja

downtrodden ['daʊn,trɑdən] *adj* pisoteado, oprimido

downward ['daʊnwərd] *adj* descendente ‖ *adv* hacia abajo; hacia una época posterior

down•y ['daʊni] *adj* (*comp* -**ier;** *super* -**iest**) plumoso, felpudo, velloso; suave, blando

dow•ry ['daʊri] *s* (*pl* -**ries**) dote *m* & *f*

doz. *abbr* **dozen**

doze [doz] *s* duermevela, sueño ligero ‖ *intr* dormitar

dozen ['dʌzən] *s* docena

dozy ['dozi] *adj* soñoliento

D.P. *abbr* **displaced person**

dpt. *abbr* **department**

dr. *abbr* **debtor, drawer, dram**

Dr. *abbr* **debtor, Doctor**

drab [dræb] *adj* (*comp* **drabber;** *super* **drabbest**) gris amarillento; monótono ‖ *s* gris amarillento; ramera; mujer desaliñada

drach•ma ['drækmə] *s* (*pl* -**mas** o -**mae** [mi]) dracma

draft [dræft] *s* corriente *f* de aire; (*pulling; current of air in a chimney*) tiro; (*sketch,*

outline) bosquejo; (*first form of a writing*) borrador *m;* (*drink*) bebida, trago; (com) giro, letra de cambio, libranza; aire inspirado; (naut) calado; (mil) conscripción, quinta; **drafts** damas, juego de damas; **on draft** a presión; **to be exempted from the draft** redimirse de las quintas ‖ *tr* dibujar; bosquejar; hacer un borrador de; redactar (*un documento*); (mil) quintar; **to be drafted** (mil) ir a quintas

draft age *s* edad *f* de quintas

draft beer *s* cerveza a presión

draft board *s* (mil) junta de reclutamiento

draft call *s* llamada a quintas

draft dodger ['dɑdʒər] *s* emboscado

draftee [,dræf'ti] *s* conscripto, quinto

draft horse *s* caballo de tiro

drafting room *s* sala de dibujo

drafts•man ['dræftsmən] *s* (*pl* -**men** [mən]) dibujante *m;* (*man who draws up documents*) redactor *m;* (*in checkers*) peón *m*

draft treaty *s* proyecto de convenio

draft•y ['dræfti] *adj* (*comp* -**ier;** *super* -**iest**) airoso, con corrientes de aire

drag [dræg] *s* (*sledge for conveying heavy bodies*) narria; (*on a cigarette*) chupada; fumada; (naut) rastra; (aer) resistencia al avance; (fig) estorbo, impedimento; **to have a drag** (slang) tener buenas aldabas, tener enchufe ‖ *v* (*pret* & *pp* **dragged**) *ger* **dragging**) *tr* arrastrar; (naut) rastrear ‖ *intr* arrastrarse por el suelo; avanzar muy lentamente; decaer (*el interés*); **to drag on** ser interminable, prolongarse interminablemente

drag'net' *s* red barredera

dragon ['drægən] *s* dragón *m*

drag'on-fly' *s* (*pl* -**flies**) caballito del diablo, libélula

dragoon [drə'gun] *s* (*soldier*) dragón *m* ‖ *tr* tiranizar; forzar, constreñir

drain [dren] *s* dren *m,* desaguadero, desagüe *m;* (surg) dren *m;* (*source of continual expense*) (fig) desaguadero ‖ *tr* drenar, desaguar; avenar (*terrenos húmedos*); escurrir (*una vasija; un líquido*) ‖ *intr* desaguarse; escurrirse

drainage ['drenɪdʒ] *s* drenaje *m,* desagüe *m*

drain'board' *s* escurridero

drain cock *s* llave *f* de purga

drain'pipe' *s* tubo de desagüe, escurridero

drain plug *s* tapón *m* de desagüe; (aut) tapón de vaciado

drake [drek] *s* pato

dram [dræm] *s* dracma; trago de aguardiente

drama ['drɑmə] o ['dræmə] *s* drama *m;* (*art and genre*) dramática

dramatic [drə'mætɪk] *adj* dramático ‖ **dramatics** *ssg* representación de aficionados; *spl* obras representadas por aficionados

dramatist ['dræmətɪst] *s* dramático

dramatize ['dræmə,taɪz] *tr* dramatizar

dram'shop' *s* bar *m,* taberna

drape [drep] *s* cortina, colgadura; (*hang of a curtain, skirt, etc.*) caída ‖ *tr* cubrir con colgaduras; adornar con colgaduras; disponer los pliegues de (*una colgadura, una prenda de vestir*)

draper·y ['drepəri] *s* (*pl* **-ies**) colgaduras, ropaje *m*

drastic ['dræstɪk] *adj* drástico

draught [dræft] *s & tr* var de **draft**

draught beer *s* cerveza a presión

draw [drɔ] *s* (*in a game or other contest*) empate *m;* (*in chess or checkers*) tablas; (*in a lottery*) sorteo; (*card drawn from the bank*) robo; (*of a drawbridge*) compuerta; (*of a chimney*) tiro ‖ *v* (*pret* **drew** [dru]; *pp* **drawn** [drɔn]) *tr* tirar (*una línea; alambre*); (*to attract*) tirar; (*to pull*) tirar de; derretir (*la mantequilla*); sacar (*un clavo, una espada, agua, una conclusión*); atraerse (*aplausos*); atraer (*a la gente*); aspirar (*el aire*); llamar (*la atención*); dar (*un suspiro*); correr (*una cortina*); cobrar (*un salario*); sacarse (*un premio*); empatar (*una partida*); robar (*fichas, naipes*); levantar (*un puente levadizo*); calar (*un buque cierta profundidad*); hacer (*una comparación*); consumir (*amperios*); (*to sketch in lines*) dibujar; (*to sketch in words*) redactar; (*com*) girar, librar; (*com*) devengar (*interés*); **to draw forth** hacer salir; **to draw off** sacar, extraer; trasegar (*un líquido*); **to draw on** ocasionar, provocar; ponerse (*p.ej., los zapatos*); (*com*) girar a cargo de; **to draw oneself up** enderezarse con dignidad; **to draw out** (*to persuade to talk*) sonsacar, tirar de la lengua a; **to draw up** redactar (*un documento*); (*mil*) ordenar para el combate ‖ *intr* tirar, tirar bien (*una chimenea*); empatar; echar suertes; atraer mucha gente; dibujar; **to draw aside** apartarse; **to draw back** retroceder, retirarse; **draw near** acercarse; acercarse a; **to draw to a close** estar para terminar; **to draw together** juntarse, unirse

draw'back' *s* desventaja, inconveniente *m*

draw'bridge' *s* puente levadizo

drawee [,drɔ'i] *s* girado, librado

drawer ['drɔ·ər] *s* dibujante *mf;* (*com*) girador *m*, librador *m* ‖ [drɔr] *s* cajón *m*, gaveta; **drawers** calzoncillos

drawing ['drɔ·ɪŋ] *s* dibujo; (*in a lottery*) sorteo

drawing board *s* tablero de dibujo

drawing card *s* polo de atracción popular

drawing room *s* sala, salón *m*

draw'knife' *s* (*pl* **-knives** [,naɪvz]) cuchilla de dos mangos

drawl [drɔl] *s* habla lenta y prolongada ‖ *tr* decir lenta y prolongadamente ‖ *intr* hablar lenta y prolongadamente

drawn butter [drɔn] *s* mantequilla derretida

drawn work *s* calado, deshilado

dray [dre] *s* carro fuerte, camión *m;* (*sledge*) narria

drayage ['dre·ɪdʒ] *s* acarreo

dread [drɛd] *adj* espantoso, terrible ‖ *s* pavor *m*, terror *m* ‖ *tr & intr* temer

dreadful ['drɛdfəl] *adj* espantoso, terrible; (*coll*) feo, desagradable

dread'naught' *s* (*nav*) gran buque acorazado

dream [drim] *s* sueño, ensueño; (*thing of great beauty*) sueño; (*fancy, illusion*) ensueño; **dream come true** sueño hecho realidad ‖ *v* (*pret & pp* **dreamed** o **dreamt** [drɛmt]) *tr* soñar; **to dream up** (*coll*) imaginar, inventar; ‖ *intr* soñar; **to dream of** soñar con

dreamer ['drimər] *s* soñador *m*

dream'land' *s* reino del ensueño

dream'world' *s* tierra de la fantasía

dream·y ['drimi] *adj* (*comp* **-ier;** *super* **-iest**) soñador; visionario; vago

drear·y ['drɪri] *adj* (*comp* **-ier;** *super* **-iest**) sombrío, triste; monótono, pesado

dredge [drɛdʒ] *s* draga ‖ *tr* dragar, rastrear; (*culin*) enharinar

dredger ['drɛdʒər] *s* draga (*barco*)

dredging ['drɛdʒɪŋ] *s* dragado

dregs [drɛgz] *spl* heces *fpl;* (*of society*) hez *f*

drench [drɛntʃ] *tr* mojar, empapar

dress [drɛs] *s* ropa, vestidos; vestido de mujer; (*skirt*) falda; traje *m* de etiqueta; (*of a bird*) plumaje *m* ‖ *tr* vestir; (*to provide with clothing*) trajear; peinar (*el pelo*); curar (*una herida*); zurrar (*el cuero*); empavesar (*un barco*); adornar, ataviar; aderezar, aliñar (*los manjares*); **to dress down** (*coll*) reprender; **to get dressed** vestirse ‖ *intr* (*to put one's clothing on*) vestirse; (*to wear clothes*) vestir; (*mil*) alinearse; **to dress up** vestirse de etiqueta; ponerse de veinticinco alfileres; disfrazarse

dress ball *s* baile *m* de etiqueta

dress coat *s* frac *m*

dresser ['drɛsər] *s* tocador *m;* cómoda con espejo; (*sideboard*) aparador *m;* **to be a good dresser** vestir con elegancia

dress form *s* maniquí *m*

dress goods *spl* géneros para vestidos

dressing ['drɛsɪŋ] *s* adorno; (*for food*) aliño, salsa; (*stuffing for fowl*) relleno; (*fertilizer*) abono; (*for a wound*) vendaje *m*

dress'ing-down' *s* (*coll*) repasata, regaño

dressing gown *s* bata, peinador *m*

dressing room *s* cuarto de vestir; (*theat*) camarín *m*

dressing station *s* (*mil*) puesto de socorro

dressing table *s* tocador *m;* peinador *m*

dress'mak'er *s* costurera, modista

dress'mak'ing *s* costura, modistería

dress rehearsal *s* ensayo general

dress shirt *s* camisa de pechera almidonada, camisa de pechera de encaje

dress shop *s* casa de modas

dress suit *s* traje *m* de etiqueta

dress tie *s* corbata de smoking, corbata de frac

dress·y ['drɛsi] *adj* (*comp* **-ier;** *super* **-iest**) (*coll*) elegante; (*showy*) acicalado, vistoso, peripuesto

dribble ['drɪbəl] *s* goteo; (*coll*) llovizna ‖ *tr* (*sport*) driblar ‖ *intr* gotear; (*at the mouth*) babear; (*sport*) driblar

driblet ['drɪblɪt] *s* gotita; pedacito

dried beef [draɪd] *s* cecina

dried fig *s* higo paso

dried peach *s* orejón *m*

do
dr

drier ['draɪ·ər] *s* enjugador *m;* (*for hair*) secador *m;* (*for clothes*) secadora; (*rack for drying clothes*) tendedero (de ropa)

drift [drɪft] *s* movimiento; (*of sand, snow*) montón *m;* (*movement of snow*) ventisca; tendencia; dirección; intención, sentido; (aer, naut) deriva; (rad, telv) desviación ‖ *intr* flotar a la deriva; amontonarse (*la nieve*); ventiscar; (aer, naut) derivar, ir a la deriva; (fig) vivir sin rumbo

drift ice *s* hielo flotante

drift'wood' *s* madera flotante; madera llevada por el agua; madera arrojada a la playa por el agua; (*people*) vagos

drill [drɪl] *s* taladro; instrucción; (*fabric*) dril *m;* (mil) ejercicio ‖ *tr* taladrar; instruir; (mil) enseñar el ejercicio a ‖ *intr* adiestrarse; (mil) hacer el ejercicio

drill'mas'ter *s* amaestrador *m;* (mil) instructor *m*

drill press *s* prensa taladradora

drink [drɪŋk] *s* bebida; **the drinks are on the house!** ¡convida la casa! ‖ *v* (*pret* **drank** [dræŋk]; *pp* **drunk** [drʌŋk]) *tr* beber; beberse (*su sueldo*); **to drink down** beber de una vez; **to drink in** beber (*las palabras de una persona*); beberse (*un libro*); aspirar (*el aire*) ‖ *intr* beber; **to drink out of** beber de o en; **to drink to the health of** beber a o por la salud de

drinkable ['drɪŋkəbəl] *adj* bebedizo, potable

drinker ['drɪŋkər] *s* bebedor *m*

drinking ['drɪŋkɪŋ] *s* (el) beber

drinking cup *s* taza para beber

drinking fountain *s* fuente *f* para beber

drinking song *s* canción báquica, canción de taberna

drinking spree *s* bebezón *m;* bimba (Mex)

drinking trough *s* abrevadero

drinking water *s* agua para beber

drip [drɪp] *s* goteo; gotas ‖ *v* (*pret & pp* **dripped;** *ger* **dripping**) *intr* caer gota a gota, gotear

drip coffee *s* café *m* de maquinilla

drip'-dry' *adj* de lava y pon

drip pan *s* colector *m* de aceite

drive [draɪv] *s* paseo en coche; calzada; fuerza, vigor *m;* urgencia; campaña vigorosa; venta a bajo precio; (aut) tracción (*delantera o trasera*); (mach) transmisión, mando ‖ *v* (*pret* **drove** [drov]; *pp* **driven** ['drɪvən]) *tr* conducir, guiar, manejar (*un automóvil*); clavar, hincar (*un clavo*); arrear (*a las bestias*); (*in a carriage or auto*) llevar (*a una persona*); empujar, impeler; estimular; forzar, compeler; obligar a trabajar mucho; (sport) golpear con gran fuerza; **to drive away** ahuyentar; **to drive away** ahuyentar; **to drive back** rechazar; **to drive mad** volver loco ‖ *intr* ir en coche; **to drive at** aspirar a; querer decir; **to drive hard** trabajar mucho; **to drive in** entrar en coche; entrar en (*un sitio*) en coche; **to drive on the right** circular por la derecha; **to drive out** salir en coche; **to drive up** llegar en coche

drive-in restaurant ['draɪv,ɪn] *s* parador *m* de carretera

drive-in theater *s* auto-teatro, motocine *m;* autocine *m* (Chile, Cuba); autocínema *f* (Mex)

driv·el ['drɪvəl] *s* (*slobber*) baba; (*nonsense*) bobería ‖ *v* (*pret* **-eled** o **-elled;** *ger* **eling** o **-elling**) *intr* babear; (*to talk nonsense*) bobear

driver ['draɪvər] *s* conductor *m;* (*of a carriage*) cochero; (*of a locomotive*) maquinista *m;* (*of pack animals*) arriero

driver's license *s* carnet *m* de chófer, permiso de conducir

drive shaft *s* árbol *m* de mando, eje *m* motor

drive'way' *s* calzada; camino de entrada para coches

drive wheel *s* rueda motriz

drive'-your·self' service *s* alquiler *m* sin chófer

driving school *s* auto-escuela

drizzle ['drɪzəl] *s* llovizna ‖ *intr* lloviznar, garnar

droll [drol] *adj* chusco, gracioso

dromedar·y ['drɑmə,dɛri] *s* (*pl* **-ies**) dromedario

drone [dron] *s* zángano; (*buzz, hum*) zumbido; (*of bagpipe*) bordón *m,* roncón *m;* avión radiodirigido ‖ *tr* decir monótonamente ‖ *intr* hablar monótonamente; (*to live in idleness*) zanganear; (*to buzz, hum*) zumbar

drool [drul] *s* (*slobber*) baba; (slang) bobería ‖ *intr* babear; (slang) bobear

droop [drup] *s* inclinación ‖ *intr* caer, colgar; inclinarse; marchitarse; abatirse; encamarse (*el grano*)

drooping ['drupɪŋ] *adj* (*eyelid, shoulder*) caído

drop [drɑp] *s* gota; (*slope*) pendiente *f;* (*earring*) pendiente *m;* (*in temperature*) descenso; (*of supplies from an airplane*) lanzamiento; (*trap door*) escotillón *m;* (*gallows*) horca; (*lozenge*) pastilla; (*small amount*) chispa; (*slit for letters*) buzón *m;* (*curtain*) telón *m;* **a drop in the bucket** una gota en el mar ‖ *v* (*pret & pp* **dropped;** *ger* **dropping**) *tr* dejar caer; echar (*una carta*) al buzón; bajar (*una cortina*); soltar (*una indirecta*); escribir (*una esquela*); omitir, suprimir; abandonar, dejar; echar (*el ancla*); borrar de la lista (*a un alumno*); lanzar (*bombas o suministros de un avión*) ‖ *intr* caer; bajar; cesar, terminar; **to drop dead** caer muerto; **to drop in** entrar al pasar, visitar de paso; **to drop off** desaparecer; quedarse dormido; morir de repente; **to drop out** desaparecer; retirarse; darse de baja

drop curtain *s* telón *m*

drop hammer *s* martinete *m*

drop'-leaf' table *s* mesa de hoja plegadiza

drop'light' *s* lámpara colgante

drop'out' *s* fracasado, desertor *m* escolar; **to become a dropout** ahorcar los libros

dropper ['drɑpər] *s* cuentagotas *m*

drop shutter *s* obturador *m* de guillotina

dropsical [ˈdrɑpsɪkəl] *adj* hidrópico
dropsy [ˈdrɑpsi] *s* hidropesía
drop table *s* mesa perezosa
dross [drɔs] o [drɑs] *s* (*of metals*) escoria; (fig) escoria, hez *f*
drought [draut] *s* (*long period of dry weather*) sequía; (*dryness*) sequedad
drove [drov] *s* manada, rebaño, hato; gentío, multitud
drover [ˈdrovər] *s* ganadero
drown [draun] *tr* anegar, ahogar ‖ *intr* anegarse, ahogarse
drowse [drauz] *intr* adormecerse, amodorrarse
drow•sy [ˈdrauzi] *adj* (*comp* **-sier;** *super* **-siest**) soñoliento, modorro
drub [drʌb] *v* (*pret & pp* **drubbed;** *ger* **drubbing**) *tr* apalear, pegar, tundir; derrotar completamente
drudge [drʌdʒ] *s* yunque *m*, esclavo del trabajo ‖ *intr* afanarse
drudger•y [ˈdrʌdʒəri] *s* (*pl* **-ies**) trabajo penoso
drug [drʌg] *s* droga, medicamento; narcótico; **drug on the market** macana, artículo invendible ‖ *v* (*pret & pp* **drugged;** *ger* **drugging**) *tr* narcotizar; mezclar con drogas
drug addict *s* toxicómano, drogadicto; (coll) yonquí *m*
drug'-ad•dict'ed *adj* drogadicto
drug addiction *s* toxicomanía
drug dealer *s* narcotraficante *mf*
druggist [ˈdrʌgɪst] *s* boticario, farmacéutico; (*dealer in drugs, chemicals, dyes, etc.*) droguero
drug habit *s* vicio de los narcóticos
drug store *s* farmacia, botica, droguería
drug traffic *s* contrabando de narcóticos
druid [ˈdruɪd] *s* druida *m*
drum [drʌm] *s* (*cylinder; instrument of percussion*) tambor *m;* (*container for oil, gasoline, etc.*) bidón *m* ‖ *v* (*pret & pp* **drummed;** *ger* **drumming**) *tr* reunir a toque de tambor; **to drum up trade** fomentar ventas ‖ *intr* tocar el tambor; (*with the fingers*) teclear
drum'beat' *s* toque *m* de tambor
drum brake *s* freno de tambor
drum corps *s* banda de tambores
drum'fire' *s* fuego graneado, fuego nutrido
drum'head' *s* parche *m* de tambor
drum major *s* tambor *m* mayor
drummer [ˈdrʌmər] *s* tambor *m*, baterista *mf*, tamborilero; agente viajero
drum'stick' *s* baqueta, palillo; (coll) muslo (*de ave cocida*)
drunk [drʌŋk] *adj* borracho; bolo (CAm, Mex); **to get drunk** emborracharse; coger una turca; embolarse (CAm, Mex) enchicharse (SAm) ‖ *s* (coll) borracho; (*spree*) (coll) borrachera
drunkard [ˈdrʌŋkərd] *s* borrachín *m*
drunken [ˈdrʌŋkən] *adj* borracho
drunken driving *s* — **to be arrested for drunken driving** ser arrestado por conducir en estado de embriaguez

drunkenness [ˈdrʌŋkənnɪs] *s* embriaguez *f;* bimba (Mex)
dry [draɪ] *adj* (*comp* **drier;** *super* **driest**) seco; (*thirsty*) sediento; (*dull, boring*) árido ‖ *s* (*pl* **drys**) (*prohibitionist*) (coll) seco ‖ *v* (*pret & pp* **dried**) *tr* secar; (*to wipe dry*) enjugar ‖ *intr* secarse; **to dry up** secarse completamente; (slang) callar, dejar de hablar
dry battery *s* pila seca; (*group of dry cells*) batería seca
dry cell *s* pila seca
dry'-clean' *tr* lavar en seco, limpiar en seco
dry cleaner *s* tintorero
dry cleaning *s* lavado a seco, limpieza en seco
dry'-clean'ing establishment *s* tintorería
dry dock *s* dique seco
dryer [ˈdraɪər] *s* var de **drier**
dry'eyed' —*adj* ojienjuto
dry farming *s* cultivo de secano
dry goods *spl* mercancías generales (*tejidos, lencería, pañería, sedería*)
dry ice *s* carbohielo, hielo seco
dry law *s* ley seca
dry measure *s* medida para áridos
dryness [ˈdraɪnɪs] *s* sequedad; (*e.g., of a speaker*) aridez *f*
dry nurse *s* ama seca
dry season *s* estación de la seca
dry wash *s* ropa lavada y secada pero no planchada
d.s. *abbr* **days after sight, daylight saving**
D.S.T. *abbr* **Daylight Saving Time**
dual [ˈdju•əl] o [ˈdu•əl] *adj & s* dual *m*
dual axle *s* eje tandem
duali•ty [djuˈælɪti] *s* (*pl* **-ties**) dualidad
dub [dʌb] *s* (slang) jugador *m* torpe ‖ *v* (*pret & pp* **dubbed;** *ger* **dubbing**) *tr* apellidar; armar caballero; (mov) doblar
dubbing [ˈdʌbɪŋ] *s* doblado, doblaje *m*
dubious [ˈdubɪ•əs] *adj* dudoso
ducat [ˈdʌkət] *s* ducado
duchess [ˈdʌtʃɪs] *s* duquesa
duch•y [ˈdʌtʃi] *s* (*pl* **-ies**) ducado
duck [dʌk] *s* pato; (*female*) pata; agachada rápida; (*in the water*) zambullida; **ducks** (coll) pantalones *mpl* de dril ‖ *tr* bajar rápidamente (*la cabeza*); (*in water*) chapuzar; (coll) esquivar, evitar (*un golpe*) ‖ *intr* chapuzar; **to duck out** (coll) escabullirse
duck'-toed' *adj* zancajoso
duct [dʌkt] *s* conducto, canal *m*
ductile [ˈdʌktɪl] *adj* dúctil
ductless gland [ˈdʌktlɪs] *s* glándula cerrada
duct'work' *s* canalización
dud [dʌd] *s* (slang) bomba que no estalla; (slang) fracaso; **duds** (coll) trapos, prendas de vestir
dude [dud] *s* caballerete *m*
due [dju] o [du] *adj* debido; aguardado, esperado; pagadero; **due to** debido a; **to fall due** vencer; **when is the train due?** ¿a qué hora debe llegar el tren? ‖ *adv* directa-

mente, derecho ‖ *s* deuda; **dues** derechos; (*of a member*) cuota; **to get one's due** llevar su mereçido; **to give the devil his due** ser justo hasta con el diablo

duel ['dju•əl] o ['du•əl] *s* duelo; **to fight a duel** batirse en duelo ‖ *v* (*pret & pp* **dueled** o **duelled;** *ger* **dueling** o **duelling**) *intr* batirse en duelo

duelist o **duellist** ['dju•əlɪst] o ['duəlɪst] *s* duelista *m*

dues-paying ['djuz,pe•ɪŋ] o ['duz,peɪŋ] *adj* cotizante

duet [dju'ɛt] o [du'ɛt] *s* dúo

duke [djuk] *s* duque *m*

dukedom ['djukdəm] *s* ducado

dull [dʌl] *adj* (*not sharp*) embotado, romo; (*color*) apagado; (*sound; pain*) sordo; (*stupid*) lerdo, torpe; (*business*) inactivo, muerto; (*boring*) aburrido, tedioso; (*flat*) deslucido, deslustrado ‖ *tr* embotar, enromar; deslucir, deslustrar; enfriar (*el entusiasmo*) ‖ *intr* embotarse, enromarse; deslucirse, deslustrarse

dullard ['dʌlərd] *s* estúpido

duly ['djuli] o ['duli] *adv* debidamente

dumb [dʌm] *adj* (*lacking the power to speak*) mudo; (coll) estúpido, torpe

dumb'bell' *s* halterio; (slang) estúpido, tonto

dumb creature *s* animal *m*, bruto

dumb show *s* pantomima

dumb'wait'er *s* montaplatos *m*

dumfound [,dʌm'faʊnd] *tr* pasmar, dejar sin habla

dum•my ['dʌmi] *adj* falso, fingido, simulado ‖ *s* (*pl* **-mies**) (*dress form*) maniquí *m;* cabeza para pelucas; (*in card games*) muerto; cartas del muerto; (*figurehead, straw man*) testaferro; (*skeleton copy of a book*) maqueta; imitación, copia; (slang) estúpido

dump [dʌmp] *s* basurero, vertedero; montón *m* de basuras; (mil) depósito de municiones; (min) terrero; **to be down in the dumps** (coll) tener murria ‖ *tr* descargar, verter; vaciar de golpe; vender en grandes cantidades y a precios inferiores a los corrientes

dumping ['dʌmpɪŋ] *s* descarga; venta en grandes cantidades y a precios inferiores a los corrientes

dumpling ['dʌmplɪŋ] *s* bola de pasta rellena de fruta o carne

dump truck *s* camión *m* volquete

dump•y ['dʌmpi] *adj* (*comp* **-ier;** *super* **-iest**) regordete, rollizo

dun [dʌn] *adj* bruno, pardo, castaño ‖ *s* acreedor importuno; (*demand for payment*) apremio ‖ *v* (*pret & pp* **dunner;** *ger* **dunning**) *tr* importunar para el pago, apremiar (*a un deudor*)

dunce [dʌns] *s* zopenco, bodoque *m*

dunce cap *s* capirote *m* que se le pone al alumno torpe

dune [djun] o [dun] *s* duna, médano

dung [dʌŋ] *s* estiércol *m* ‖ *tr* estercolar

dungarees [,dʌŋgə'riz] *spl* pantalones *mpl* de trabajo de tela basta de algodón

dungeon ['dʌndʒən] *s* calabozo, mazmorra; (*fortified tower of medieval castle*) torre *f* del homenaje

dung'hill' *s* estercolar *m;* lugar inmundo

dunk [dʌŋk] *tr* sopetear, ensopar

duo ['dju•o] o ['du•o] *s* dúo

duode•num [,du•ə'dinəm] *s* (*pl* **-na** [nə]) duodeno

dupe [djup] o [dup] *s* víctima, primo, inocentón *m* ‖ *tr* embaucar, engañar

duplex house ['dupleks] *s* casa para dos familias

duplicate ['duplɪkɪt] *adj & s* duplicado; **in duplicate** por duplicado ‖ ['duplɪ,ket] *tr* duplicar

duplici•ty [dju'plɪsɪti] *s* (*pl* **-ties**) duplicidad

durable ['djurəbəl] o ['durəbəl] *adj* durable, duradero

durable goods *spl* artículos duraderos

duration [dju're/ən] o [du're/ən] *s* duración

during ['djurɪŋ] *prep* durante

dusk [dʌsk] *s* crepúsculo

dust [dʌst] *s* polvo ‖ *tr* (*to free of dust*) desempolvar; (*to sprinkle with dust*) polvorear; **to dust off** desempolvar

dust bowl *s* cuenca de polvo

dust'cloth' *s* trapo para quitar el polvo

dust cloud *s* nube *f* de polvo, polvareda

duster ['dʌstər] *s* paño, plumero; (*light overgarment*) guardapolvo

dust jacket *s* sobrecubierta

dust'pan' *s* pala para recoger la basura

dust rag *s* trapo para quitar el polvo

dust storm *s* tolvanera

dust•y ['dʌsti] *adj* (*comp* **-ier;** *super* **-iest**) polvoriento; (*grayish*) grisáceo

Dutch [dʌt/] *adj* holandés; (slang) alemán ‖ *s* (*language*) holandés *m;* (*language*) (slang) alemán *m;* **in Dutch** (slang) en la desgracia; (slang) en un apuro; **the Dutch** los holandeses; (slang) los alemanes; **to go Dutch** (coll) pagar a escote

Dutch•man ['dʌt/mən] *s* (*pl* **-men** [mən]) holandés *m;* (slang) alemán *m*

Dutch treat *s* (coll) convite *m* a escote

dutiable ['djutɪ•əbəl] *adj* sujeto a derechos de aduana

dutiful ['djutɪfəl] *adj* obediente, sumiso, solícito

du•ty ['djuti] *s* (*pl* **-ties**) deber *m;* (*task*) faena, quehacer *m;* derechos de aduana; **in the line of duty** en acto de servicio; **off duty** libre; **on duty** de servicio, de guardia; **to do one's duty** cumplir con su deber; **to take up one's duties** entrar en funciones

du'ty-free' *adj* libre de derechos

D.V. *abbr* Deo volente, i.e., God willing

dwarf [dwɔrf] *adj & s* enano ‖ *tr* achicar, empequeñecer ‖ *intr* achicarse, empequeñecerse

dwarfish ['dwɔrfɪ/] *adj* enano, diminuto

dwell [dwɛl] *v* (*pret & pp* **dwelled** o **dwelt** [dwɛlt]) *intr* vivir, morar; **to dwell on** o **upon** hacer hincapié en

dwelling ['dwɛlɪŋ] *s* morada, vivienda

dwelling house *s* casa, domicilio

dwindle ['dwɪndəl] *intr* disminuir; decaer, consumirse

dwt. *abbr* **pennyweight**

dye [daɪ] *s* tinte *m*, tintura, color *m* ‖ *v* (*pret & pp* **dyed**; *ger* **dyeing**) *tr* teñir

dyed-in-the-wool ['daɪdɪnðə,wul] *adj* intransigente

dyeing ['daɪ•ɪŋ] *s* tinte *m*, tintura

dyer ['daɪ•ər] *s* tintorero

dye'stuff' *s* materia, colorante

dying ['daɪ•ɪŋ] *adj* moribundo

dynamic [daɪ'næmɪk] o [dɪ'næmɪk] *adj* dinámico

dynamite ['daɪnə,maɪt] *s* dinamita ‖ *tr* dinamitar

dyna•mo ['daɪnə,mo] *s* (*pl* **-mos**) dínamo *f*

dynast ['daɪnæst] *s* dinasta *m*

dynas•ty ['daɪnəsti] *s* (*pl* **-ties**) dinastía

dysentery ['dɪsən,tɛri] *s* disentería

dysfunction [dɪs'fʌŋʃən] *s* disfunción

dyspepsia [dɪs'pɛpsɪ•ə] o [dɪs'pɛpʃə] *s* dispepsia

dz. *abbr* **dozen**

E

E, e [i] quinta letra del alfabeto inglés

ea. *abbr* **each**

each [itʃ] *adj indef* cada ‖ *pron indef* cada uno; **each other** nos, se; uno a otro, unos a otros ‖ *adv* cada uno; por persona

eager ['igər] *adj* (*enthusiastic*) ardiente, celoso; **eager for** muy deseoso de; **eager to** + *inf* muy deseoso de + *inf*

eagerness ['igərnɪs] *s* ardor *m*, celo; deseo ardiente, empeño

eagle ['igəl] *s* águila

eagle owl *s* buho

ear [ɪr] *s* (*organ and sense of hearing*) oído; (*external part*) oreja; (*of corn*) mazorca; (*of wheat*) espiga; **all ears** con las orejas tan largas; **to be all ears** ser todo oídos, abrir tanto oído; **box on the ear** guantón *m*; **to prick up one's ears** aguzar las orejas; **to turn a deaf ear** hacer o tener oídos de mercader

ear'ache' *s* dolor *m* de oído

ear'drop' *s* arete *m*

ear'drum' *s* tímpano

ear'flap' *s* orejera

earl [ʌrl] *s* conde *m*

earldom ['ʌrldəm] *s* condado

ear•ly ['ʌrli] (*comp* **-lier**; *super* **-liest**) *adj* (*occurring before customary time*) temprano; (*first in a series*) primero; (*far back in time*) primero, remoto, antiguo; (*occurring in near future*) cercano, próximo ‖ *adv* temprano; al principio; en los primeros tiempos; **as early as** (*a certain time of day*) ya a; (*a certain time or date*) ya en; **as early as possible** lo más pronto posible; **early in** (*e.g., the month of December*) ya en; **early in the morning** muy de mañana; **early in the year** a principios del año; **to rise early** madrugar

early bird *s* (coll) madrugador *m*

early mass *s* misa de prima

early riser *s* madrugador *m*

ear'mark' *s* señal *f*, distintivo ‖ *tr* destinar, poner aparte (*para un fin determinado*)

ear'muff' *s* orejera

earn [ʌrn] *tr* ganar, ganarse; (*to get as one's due*) merecerse; (com) devengar (*intereses*) ‖ *intr* ganar; rendir

earnest ['ʌrnɪst] *adj* serio, grave; **in earnest** en serio, de buena fe ‖ *s* arras

earnest money *s* arras

earnings ['ʌrnɪŋz] *s* ganancia; salario

ear of corn *s* ilote *m*; chilote (CAm); **green ear of corn** jilote (Mex)

ear'phone' *s* audífono

ear'piece' *s* auricular *m*

ear'ring' *s* arete *m*

ear'shot' *s* alcance *m* del oído; **within earshot** al alcance del oído

ear'split'ting' *adj* ensordecedor

earth [ʌrθ] *s* tierra; **to come back to** o **down to earth** bajar de las nubes

earthen ['ʌrθən] *adj* de tierra; de barro

ear'then•ware' *s* loza, vasijas de barro

earthly ['ʌrθli] *adj* terrenal; concebible, posible; **to be of no earthly use** no servir para nada

earth'quake' *s* terremoto, temblor *m* de tierra

earth'work' *s* terraplén *m*

earth'worm' *s* lombriz *f* de tierra

earth•y ['ʌrθi] *adj* (*comp* **-ier**; *super* **-iest**) terroso; (*worldly*) mundanal; (*unrefined*) grosero; franco, sincero

ear trumpet *s* trompetilla

ear'wax' *s* cera de los oídos

ease [iz] *s* facilidad; (*readiness, naturalness*) desenvoltura, soltura; (*comfort, wellbeing*) comodidad, bienestar *m*; **with ease** con facilidad ‖ *tr* facilitar; aligerar (*un peso*); (*to let up on*) aflojar, soltar; aliviar, mitigar ‖ *intr* aliviarse, mitigarse, disminuir; moderar la marcha

easel ['izəl] *s* caballete *m*

easement ['izmənt] *s* alivio; (law) servidumbre

easily ['izɪli] *adv* fácilmente; suavemente; sin duda; probablemente

easiness ['izɪnɪs] *s* facilidad; desenvoltura, soltura; (*e.g., of motion of a machine*) suavidad; indiferencia

east [ist] *adj* oriental, del este ‖ *adv* al este, hacia el este ‖ *s* este *m*

du
ea

Easter ['istər] *s* Pascua de flores, Pascua de Resurrección, Pascua florida
Easter egg *s* huevo duro decorado o huevo de imitación que se da como regalo en el día de Pascua de Resurrección
Easter Monday *s* lunes *m* de Pascua de Resurrección
eastern ['istərn] *adj* oriental
East′er·tide′ *s* alelyua *m*, tiempo de Pascua
eastward ['istwərd] *adv* hacia el este
eas·y ['izi] *adj* (*comp* **-ier;** *super* **-iest**) fácil; (*conducive to ease*) cómodo; (*not tight*) holgado; (*amenable*) manejable; (*not forced or hurried*) lento, pausado, moderado; **to have an easy job** (o **life**) estar echado (CAm, Mex, P-R) ‖ *adv* (coll) fácilmente; (coll) despacio; **to take it easy** (coll) descansar, holgar; (coll) ir despacio
easy chair *s* poltrona, silla poltrona
eas′y·go′ing *adj* despacioso, comodón
easy mark *s* (coll) víctima, inocentón *m*
easy money *s* dinero ganado sin pena; (com) dinero abundante
easy payments *spl* facilidades de pago
eat [it] *v* (*pret* **ate** [et]; *pp* **eaten** ['itən]) *tr* comer; **to eat away** corroer; **to eat up** comerse ‖ *intr* comer
eatable ['itəbəl] *adj* comestible ‖ **eatables** *spl* comestibles *mpl*
eaves [ivz] *spl* alero, socarrén *m*, tejaroz *m*
eaves′drop′ *v* (*pret & pp* **-dropped;** *ger* **-dropping**) *intr* escuchar a escondidas, estar de escucha
ebb [ɛb] *s* reflujo; decadencia ‖ *intr* bajar (*la marea*); decaer
ebb and flow *s* flujo y reflujo
ebb tide *s* marea menguante
ebon·y ['ɛbəni] *s* (*pl* **-ies**) ébano
ebullient [ɪ'bʌljənt] *adj* hirviente; entusiasta
eccentric [ɛk'sɛntrɪk] *adj* excéntrico ‖ *m* (*odd person*) excéntrico; (*device*) excéntrica
eccentrici·ty [,ɛksɛn'trɪsɪti] *s* (*pl* **-ties**) excentricidad
ecclesiastic [ɪ,klizɪ'æstɪk] *adj & s* eclesiástico
echelon ['ɛʃə,lan] *s* escalón *m*; (mil) escalón ‖ *tr* (mil) escalonar
ech·o ['ɛko] *s* (*pl* **-oes**) eco ‖ *tr* repetir (*un sonido*); imitar ‖ *intr* hacer eco
éclair [e'klɛr] *s* bollo de crema
eclectic [ɛk'lɛktɪk] *adj & s* ecléctico
eclipse [ɪ'klɪps] *s* eclipse *m* ‖ *tr* eclipsar
eclogue ['ɛklɔg] o ['ɛklag] *s* égloga
ecologic(al) [,ikə'ladʒɪk(əl)] *adj* ecológico
ecologist [i'kalədʒɪst] *s* ecologista *mf*, ecólogo
ecology [i'kalədʒi] *s* ecología
economic [,ikə'namɪk] *adj* económico (*perteneciente a la economía*)
economical [,ikə'namɪkəl] *adj* económico (*ahorrador; poco costoso*)
economics [,ikə'namɪks] *s* economía política
economist [ɪ'kanəmɪst] *s* economista *mf*
economize [ɪ'kanə,maɪz] *tr & intr* economizar
econo·my [ɪ'kanəmi] *s* (*pl* **-mies**) economía
ecsta·sy ['ɛkstəsi] *s* (*pl* **-sies**) éxtasis *m*

ecstatic ['ɛk'stætɪk] *adj* extático
Ecuador ['ɛkwə,dɔr] *s* el Ecuador
Ecuadoran [,ɛkwə'dorən] o; **Ecuadorian** [,ɛkwʰə'dorɪ·ən] *adj & s* ecuatoriano
ecumenic(al) [,ɛkjə'mɛnɪk(əl)] *adj* ecuménico
eczema ['ɛksɪmə] o [ɛg'zimə] *s* eczema *m &* f, eccema *m &* f
ed. *abbr* **edited, edition, editor**
ed·dy ['ɛdi] *s* (*pl* **-dies**) remolino ‖ *v* (*pret & pp* **-died**) *tr & intr* remolinear
edelweiss ['ɛdəl,vaɪs] *s* estrella de los Alpes
edema [ɪ'dimə] *s* edema
edge [ɛdʒ] *s* (*of a knife, sword, etc.*) filo, corte *m*; (*of a cup, glass, piece of paper, piece of cloth, an abyss, etc.*) borde *m*; (*of a piece of cloth; of a body of water*) orilla; (*of a table*) canto; (*of a book*) corte *m*; (*of clothing*) ribete *m*; (slang) ventaja; **on edge** de canto; (fig) nervioso; **to have the edge on** (coll) llevar ventaja a; **to set the teeth on edge** dar dentera ‖ *tr* afilar, aguzar; bordear; ribetear (*un vestido*) ‖ *intr* avanzar de lado; **to edge in** lograr entrar
edgeways ['ɛdʒ,wez] *adv* de filo, de canto; **to not let a person get a word in edgeways** no dejarle a una persona decir ni una palabra
edging ['ɛdʒɪŋ] *s* orla, pestaña
edgy ['ɛdʒi] *adj* agudo, angular; nervioso, irritable
edible ['ɛdɪbəl] *adj & s* comestible *m*
edict ['idɪkt] *s* edicto
edification [,ɛdɪfɪ'keʃən] *s* edificación
edifice ['ɛdɪfɪs] *s* edificio
edi·fy ['ɛdɪ,faɪ] *v* (*pret & pp* **-fied**) *tr* edificar
edifying ['ɛdɪ,faɪ·ɪŋ] *adj* edificante
edit. *abbr* **edited, edition, editor**
edit ['ɛdɪt] *tr* preparar para la publicación; dirigir, redactar (*un periódico*)
edition [ɪ'dɪʃən] *s* edición
editor ['ɛdɪtər] *s* (*of a newspaper or magazine*) director *m*, redactor *m*; (*of a manuscript*) revisor *m*; (*of an editorial*) cronista *mf*
editorial [,ɛdɪ'torɪ·əl] *adj* editorial ‖ *s* editorial *m*, artículo de fondo
editorial staff *s* redacción, cuerpo de redacción
editor in chief *s* jefe *m* de redacción
educate ['ɛdʒʊ,ket] *tr* educar, instruir
education [,ɛdʒʊ'keʃən] *s* educación, instrucción
educational [,ɛdʒʊ'keʃənəl] *adj* educativo, educacional
educational institution *s* centro docente
educator ['ɛdʒʊ,ketər] *s* educador *m*
eel [il] *s* anguila; **to be as slippery as an eel** escurrirse como una anguila
ee·rie o **ee·ry** ['ɪri] *adj* (*comp* **-rier;** *super* **-riest**) espectral, misterioso
efface [ɪ'fes] *tr* destruir; borrar; **to efface oneself** retirarse, no dejarse ver
effect [ɪ'fɛkt] *s* efecto; **in effect** vigente; en efecto, en realidad; **to feel the effects of** resentirse de; **to go into effect** o **to take**

effect hacerse vigente, entrar en vigor; **to put into effect** poner en vigor ‖ *tr* efectuar
effective [ɪ'fɛktɪv] *adj* eficaz; *(actually in effect)* efectivo; *(striking)* impresionante; **to become effective** hacerse efectivo, entrar en vigencia
effectual [ɪ'fɛktʃʊ•əl] *adj* eficaz
effectuate [ɪ'fɛktʃʊ,et] *tr* efectuar
effeminacy [ɪ'fɛmɪnəsi] *s* afeminación
effeminate [ɪ'fɛmɪnɪt] *adj* afeminado
effervesce [,ɛfər'vɛs] *intr* estar en efervescencia
effervescence [,ɛfər'vɛsəns] *s* efervescencia
effervescent [,ɛfər'vɛsənt] *adj* efervescente
effete [ɪ'fit] *adj* estéril, infructuoso
efficacious [,ɛfɪ'keʃəs] *adj* eficaz
effica•cy ['ɛfɪkəsi] *s (pl* **-cies)** eficacia
efficien•cy [ɪ'fɪʃənsi] *s (pl* **-cies)** eficiencia; *(mech)* rendimiento, efecto útil
efficient [ɪ'fɪʃənt] *adj* eficiente, eficaz; *(person)* competente; *(mech)* de buen rendimiento
effi•gy ['ɛfɪdʒi] *s (pl* **-gies)** efigie *f*
effort ['ɛfərt] *s* esfuerzo, empeño
effronter•y [ɪ'frʌntəri] *s (pl* **-ies)** desfachatez *f*, descaro
effusion [ɪ'fjuʒən] *s* efusión
effusive [ɪ'fjusɪv] *adj* efusivo, expansivo
e.g. *abbr* **exempli gratia,** i.e., **for example**
egg [ɛg] *s* huevo; (slang) buen sujeto ‖ *tr —* **to egg on** incitar, instigar
egg beat'er *s* batidor *m* de huevos
egg'cup' *s* huevera
egg'head' *s* intelectual *mf*, erudito
eggnog ['ɛg,nɑg] *s* caldo de la reina, yema mejida
egg'plant' *s* berenjena
egg'shell' *s* cascarón *m*, cáscara de huevo
egoism ['ɛgo,ɪzəm] o ['igo,ɪzəm] *s* egoísmo
egoist ['ɛgo•ɪst] o ['igo•ɪst] *s* egoísta *mf*
egotism ['ɛgo,tɪzəm] o ['igo,tɪzəm] *s* egotismo
egotist ['ɛgotɪst] o ['igotɪst] *s* egotista *mf*
egregious [ɪ'gridʒəs] *adj* enorme, escandaloso
egress ['grɛs] *s* salida
Egypt ['edʒɪpt] *s* Egipto
Egyptian [ɪ'dʒɪpʃən] *adj & s* egipcio
eider ['aɪdər] *s* pato de flojel
eid'erdown' *s* edredón *m*
eight [et] *adj & pron* ocho ‖ *s* ocho; **eight o'clock** las ocho
eight'-day' clock *s* reloj *m* de ocho días cuerda
eighteen ['et'tin] *adj, pron & s* dieciocho, diez y ocho
eighteenth ['et'tinθ] *adj & s (in a series)* decimoctavo; *(part)* dieciochavo ‖ *s (in dates)* dieciocho, diez y ocho
eighth [etθ] *adj & s* octavo, ochavo ‖ *s (in dates)* ocho
eight hundred *adj & pron* ochocientos ‖ *s* ochocientos *m*
eightieth ['eti•θ] *adj & s (in a series)* octogésimo; *(part)* ochentavo
eigh•ty ['eti] *adj & pron* ochenta ‖ *s (pl* **-ties)** ochenta *m*

either ['iðər] o ['aɪðər] *adj* uno u otro, cada . . . (de los dos), cualquier . . . de los dos; ambos ‖ *pron* uno u otro, cualquiera de los dos ‖ *adv —* **not either** tampoco, no . . . tampoco ‖ *conj —* **either . . . or** o . . . o
ejaculate [ɪ'dʒækjə,let] *tr & intr* exclamar; (physiol) eyacular
eject [ɪ'dʒɛkt] *tr* arrojar, expulsar, echar; *(to evict)* desahuciar
ejection [ɪ'dʒɛkʃən] *s* expulsión; *(of a tenant)* desahucio
ejection seat *s* (aer) asiento lanzable
eke [ik] *tr —* **to eke out** ganarse *(la vida)* con dificultad
elaborate [ɪ'læbərɪt] *adj (done with great care)* elaborado; *(detailed, ornate)* primoroso, recargado ‖ [ɪ'læbə,ret] *tr* elaborar ‖ *intr —* **to elaborate on** o **upon** explicar con más detalles
elapse [ɪ'læps] *intr* pasar, transcurrir
elastic [ɪ'læstɪk] *adj & s* elástico
elasticity [,ɪlæs'tɪsɪti] *s* elasticidad
elated [ɪ'letɪd] *adj* alborozado, regocijado
elation [ɪ'leʃən] *s* alborozo, regocijo
elbow ['ɛlbo] *s* codo; *(in a river)* recodo; *(of a chair)* brazo; **at one's elbow** a la mano; **out at the elbows** andrajoso, enseñando los codos; **to crook the elbow** empinar el codo; **to rub elbows** codearse, rozarse; **up to the elbows** hasta los codos ‖ *tr —* **to elbow one's way** abrirse paso a codazos ‖ *intr* codear
elbow grease *s* (coll) muñeca, jugo de muñeca
elbow patch *s* codera
elbow rest *s* ménsula
el'bow•room' *s* espacio suficiente; libertad de acción
elder ['ɛldər] *adj* mayor, más antiguo ‖ *s* mayor, señor *m* mayor; (eccl) anciano; *(plant)* saúco
el'der•ber'ry *s (pl* **-ries)** saúco; baya del saúco
elderly ['ɛldərli] *adj* viejo, anciano
elder statesman *s* veterano de la política
eldest ['ɛldɪst] *adj* (el) mayor, (el) más antiguo
elec. *abbr* **electrical, electricity**
elect [ɪ'lɛkt] *adj (chosen)* escogido; *(selected but not yet installed)* electo ‖ *s* elegido; **the elect** los elegidos ‖ *tr* elegir
election [ɪ'lɛkʃən] *s* elección
electioneer [ɪ,lɛkʃə'nɪr] *intr* solicitar votos
elective [ɪ'lɛktɪv] *adj* electivo ‖ *s* asignatura electiva
electorate [ɪ'lɛktərɪt] *s* electorado
electric(al) [ɪ'lɛktrɪk(əl)] *adj* eléctrico
electric appliance *s* electrodoméstico
electric fan *s* ventilador eléctrico
electrician [,ɛlɛk'trɪʃən] *s* electricista *mf*
electricity [,ɛlɛk'trɪsɪti] *s* electricidad
electric percolator *s* cafetera eléctrica
electric shaver *s* electroafeitadora
electric tape *s* cinta aislante
electri•fy [ɪ'lɛktrɪ,faɪ] *v (pret & pp* **-fied)** *tr (to provide with electric power)* electrifi-

car; (*to communicate electricity to; to thrill*) electrizar
electrocute [ɪˈlɛktrəˌkjut] *tr* electrocutar
electrode [ɪˈlɛktrod] *s* electrodo
electrolysis [ˌɛlɛkˈtrɑlɪsɪs] *s* electrólisis *f*
electrolyte [ɪˈlɛktrəˌlaɪt] *s* electrólito
electromagnet [ɪˌlɛktrəˈmægnɪt] *s* electro, electroimán *m*
electromagnetic [ɪˌlɛktrəmægˈnɛtɪk] *adj* electromagnético
electromotive [ɪˌlɛktrəˈmotɪv] *adj* electromotor
electron [ɪˈlɛktrɑn] *s* electrón *m*
electronic [ˌɛlɛkˈtrɑnɪk] *adj* electrónico ‖ **electronics** *s* electrónica
electroplating [ɪˈlɛktrəˌpletɪŋ] *s* galvanoplastia
electrostatic [ɪˌlɛktrəˈstætɪk] *adj* electrostático
electrotype [ɪˈlɛktrəˌtaɪp] *s* electrotipo ‖ *tr* electrotipar
eleemosynary [ˌɛlɪˈmɑsɪˌnɛri] *adj* limosnero
elegance [ˈɛlɪɡəns] *s* elegancia
elegant [ˈɛlɪɡənt] *adj* elegante, elegantoso
elegiac [ˌɛlɪˈdʒaɪˈæk] o [ɪˈlidʒɪˌæk] *adj* elegíaco
elegy [ˈɛlɪdʒi] *s* (*pl* -**gies**) elegía
element [ˈɛlɪmənt] *s* elemento; **to be in one's element** estar en su elemento
elementary [ˌɛlɪˈmɛntəri] *adj* elemental
elephant [ˈɛlɪfənt] *s* elefante *m*
elevate [ˈɛlɪˌvet] *tr* elevar
elevated [ˈɛlɪˌvetɪd] *adj* elevado ‖ *s* (coll) ferrocarril aéreo o elevado
elevation [ˌɛlɪˈveʃən] *s* elevación
elevator [ˈɛlɪˌvetər] *s* ascensor *m;* elevador *m* (Am); (*for freight*) montacargas *m;* (*for hoisting grain*) elevador de granos; (*warehouse for storing grain*) depósito de cereales; (aer) timón *m* de profundidad
eleven [ɪˈlɛvən] *adj & pron* once ‖ *s* once *m;* **eleven o'clock** las once
eleventh [ɪˈlɛvənθ] *adj & s* (*in a series*) undécimo, onceno; (*part*) onzavo ‖ *s* (*in dates*) once *m*
eleventh hour *s* último momento
elf [ɛlf] *s* (*pl* **elves** [ɛlvz]) elfo, trasgo; enano
elicit [ɪˈlɪsɪt] *tr* sacar, sonsacar
elide [ɪˈlaɪd] *tr* elidir
eligible [ˈɛlɪdʒɪbəl] *adj* elegible; deseable, aceptable
eliminate [ɪˈlɪmɪˌnet] *tr* eliminar
elision [ɪˈlɪʒən] *s* elisión
elite [eˈlit] *adj* selecto ‖ *s* — **the elite** la élite
elitist [eˈlitɪst] *adj & s* elitista *mf*
elk [ɛlk] *s* alce *m*
ellipse [ɪˈlɪps] *s* (geom) elipse *f*
ellipsis [ɪˈlɪpsɪs] *s* (*pl* -**ses** [siz]) (gram) elipsis *f*
elliptic(al) [ɪˈlɪptɪk(əl)] *adj* (geom & gram) elíptico
elm tree [ɛlm] *s* olmo
elope [ɪˈlop] *intr* fugarse con un amante
elopement [ɪˈlopmənt] *s* fuga con un amante
eloquence [ˈɛləkwəns] *s* elocuencia
eloquent [ˈɛləkwənt] *adj* elocuente

else [ɛls] *adj* — **nobody else** ningún otro, nadie más; **nothing else** nada más; **somebody else** algún otro, otra persona; **something else** otra cosa; **what else** qué más, qué otra cosa; **who else** quién más; **whose else** de qué otra persona ‖ *adv* de otro modo; **how else** de qué otro modo; **or else** si no, o bien; **when else** en qué otro tiempo; a qué otra hora; **where else** en qué otra parte
else'where' *adv* en otra parte, a otra parte
elucidate [ɪˈlusɪˌdet] *tr* elucidar
elude [ɪˈlud] *tr* eludir
elusive [ɪˈlusɪv] *adj* fugaz, efímero; evasivo; elusivo; (*baffling*) deslumbrador
emaciated [ɪˈmeʃɪˌetɪd] *adj* enflaquecido, macilento
emancipate [ɪˈmænsɪˌpet] *tr* emancipar
embalm [ɛmˈbɑm] *tr* embalsamar
embankment [ɛmˈbæŋkmənt] *s* terraplén *m*
embar·go [ɛmˈbɑrɡo] *s* (*pl* -**goes**) embargo ‖ *tr* embargar
embark [ɛmˈbɑrk] *intr* embarcarse
embarkation [ˌɛmbɑrˈkeʃən] *s* (*of passengers*) embarco; (*of freight*) embarque *m*
embarrass [ɛmˈbærəs] *tr* (*to make feel self-conscious*) avergonzar; (*to put obstacles in the way of*) embarazar; poner en apuros de dinero
embarrassing [ɛmˈbærəsɪŋ] *adj* desconcertante, vergonzoso; embarazoso
embarrassment [ɛmˈbærəsmənt] *s* desconcierto, vergüenza; (*interference; perplexity*) embarazo; (*financial difficulties*) apuros
embas·sy [ˈɛmbəsi] *s* (*pl* -**sies**) embajada
em·bed [ɛmˈbɛd] *v* (*pret & pp* -**bedded;** *ger* -**bedding**) *tr* empotrar, encajar
embellish [ɛmˈbɛlɪʃ] *tr* embellecer
embellishment [ɛmˈbɛlɪʃmənt] *s* embellecimiento
ember [ˈɛmbər] *s* ascua, pavesa; **embers** rescoldo
Ember days *spl* témpora
embezzle [ɛmˈbɛzəl] *tr & intr* desfalcar, malversar
embezzlement [ɛmˈbɛzəlmənt] *s* desfalco, malversación
embezzler [ɛmˈbɛzlər] *s* malversador *m*
embitter [ɛmˈbɪtər] *tr* blasonar; (fig) blasonar
emblem [ˈɛmbləm] *s* emblema *m*
emblematic(al) [ˌɛmbləˈmætɪk(əl)] *adj* emblemático
embodiment [ɛmˈbɑdɪmənt] *s* incorporación; personificación, encarnación
embod·y [ɛmˈbɑdi] *v* (*pret & pp* -**ied**) *tr* incorporar; personificar, encarnar
embolden [ɛmˈboldən] *tr* envalentonar
embolism [ˈɛmbəˌlɪzəm] *s* embolia
emboss [ɛmˈbɔs] o [ɛmˈbɑs] *tr* (*to raise in relief*) realzar; abollonar (*metal*); repujar (*cuero*)
embrace [ɛmˈbres] *s* abrazo ‖ *tr* abrazar ‖ *intr* abrazarse
embrasure [ɛmˈbreʒər] *s* alféizar *m*
embroider [ɛmˈbrɔɪdər] *tr* bordar, recamar

embroider•y [ɛm'brɔɪdəri] s (pl -ies) bordado, recamado

embroil [ɛm'brɔɪl] tr embrollar; (to involve in contention) envolver

embroilment [ɛm'brɔɪlmənt] s embrollo; (in contention) envolvimiento

embry•o ['ɛmbrɪ,o] s (pl -os) embrión m

embryology [,ɛmbrɪ'ɑlədʒi] s embriología

emend [ɪ'mɛnd] tr enmendar

emendation [,imɛn'deʃən] s enmienda

emerald ['ɛmərəld] s esmeralda

emerge [ɪ'mʌrdʒ] intr emerger

emergence [ɪ'mʌrdʒəns] s emergencia (acción de emerger)

emergen•cy [ɪ'mʌrdʒənsi] s (pl -cies) emergencia (caso urgente)

emergency exit s salida de auxilio

emergency landing s aterrizaje forzoso

emergency landing field s aeródromo de urgencia

emergency physician s médico de urgencia

emersion [ɪ'mʌrʒən] o [ɪ'mʌrʃən] s emersión

emery ['ɛməri] s esmeril m

emery cloth s tela de esmeril

emery wheel s esmeriladora, rueda de esmeril, muela de esmeril

emetic [ɪ'mɛtɪk] adj & s emético

emigrant ['ɛmɪgrənt] adj & s emigrante mf

emigrate ['ɛmɪ,gret] intr emigrar

émigré [emi'gre] o ['ɛmɪ,gre] s emigrado

eminence ['ɛmɪnəns] s eminencia

eminent ['ɛmɪnənt] adj eminente

emissar•y ['ɛmɪ,sɛri] s (pl -ies) emisario

emission [ɪ'mɪʃən] s emisión

emit [ɪ'mɪt] v (pret & pp emitted; ger emitting) tr emitir

emotion [ɪ'moʃən] s emoción

emotional [ɪ'moʃənəl] adj emocional, emotivo

emperor ['ɛmpərər] s emperador m

empathy ['ɛmpəθi] s empatía

empha•sis ['ɛmfəsɪs] s (pl -ses [,siz]) énfasis m

emphasize ['ɛmfə,saɪz] tr acentuar, hacer hincapié en

emphatic [ɛm'fætɪk] adj enfático

emphysema [,ɛmfɪ'simə] s enfisema m

empire ['ɛmpaɪr] s imperio

empiric(al) [ɛm'pɪrɪk(əl)] adj empírico

empiricist [ɛm'pɪrɪsɪst] s empírico

emplacement [ɛm'plesmənt] s emplazamiento

employ [ɛm'plɔɪ] s empleo || tr emplear

employee [ɛm'plɔɪ•i] o [,ɛmplɔɪ'i] s empleado

employer [ɛm'plɔɪ•ər] s patrono

employment [ɛm'plɔɪmənt] s empleo, colocación

employment agency s agencia de colocaciones

empower [ɛm'paʊ•ər] tr autorizar, facultar; habilitar, permitir

empress ['ɛmprɪs] s emperatriz f

emptiness ['ɛmptɪnɪs] s vaciedad, vacuidad

emp•ty ['ɛmpti] adj (comp -tier; super -tiest) vacío; (coll) hambriento || v (pret & pp -tied) tr & intr vaciar

empty-handed ['ɛmpti'hændɪd] adj manivacío

empty-headed ['ɛmpti'hɛdɪd] adj tonto, ignorante

empye•ma [,ɛmpɪ'imə] s (pl -mata [mətə]) empiema m

empyrean [,ɛmpɪ'ri•ən] adj & s empíreo

emulate ['ɛmjə,let] tr & intr emular

emulator ['ɛmjə,letər] s émulo

emulous ['ɛmjələs] adj émulo

emulsi•fy [ɪ'mʌlsɪ,faɪ] v (pret & pp -fied) tr emulsionar

emulsion [ɪ'mʌlʃən] s emulsión

enable [ɛn'ebəl] tr habilitar, facilitar

enact [ɛn'ækt] tr decretar, promulgar; hacer el papel de

enactment [ɛn'æktmənt] s ley f; (of a law) promulgación; (of a play) representación

enam•el [ɛn'æməl] s esmalte m || v (pret & pp -eled o -elled; ger -eling o -elling) tr esmaltar

enam'el•ware' s utensilios de cocina de hierro esmaltado

enamor [ɛn'æmər] tr enamorar

encamp [ɛn'kæmp] tr acampar || intr acampar, acamparse

encampment [ɛn'kæmpmənt] s acampamiento

enchant [ɛn'tʃænt] tr encantar

enchanting [ɛn'tʃæntɪŋ] adj encantador

enchantment [ɛn'tʃæntmənt] s encanto

enchantress [ɛn'tʃæntrɪs] s encantadora

enchase [ɛn'tʃes] tr engastar

encircle [ɛn'sʌrkəl] tr encerrar, rodear; (mil) envolver

enclitic [ɛn'klɪtɪk] adj & s enclítico

enclose [ɛn'kloz] tr encerrar; (in a letter) adjuntar, incluir; to enclose herewith remitir adjunto

enclosure [ɛn'kloʒər] s recinto; cosa inclusa, carta inclusa

encomi•um [ɛn'komɪ•əm] s (pl -ums o -a [ə]) encomio

encompass [ɛn'kʌmpəs] tr encuadrar, abarcar

encore ['ɑnkor] s bis m || interj ¡bis!, ¡que se repita! || tr pedir la repetición de (p.ej., de una pieza o canción); pedir la repetición a (un actor)

encounter [ɛn'kaʊntər] s encuentro || tr encontrar, encontrarse con || intr batirse, combatirse

encourage [ɛn'kʌrɪdʒ] tr animar, alentar; (to foster) fomentar

encouragement [ɛn'kʌrɪdʒmənt] s ánimo, aliento; fomento

encroach [ɛn'krotʃ] intr — to encroach on o upon pasar los límites de; abusar de; invadir, entremeterse en

encumber [ɛn'kʌmbər] tr embarazar, estorbar, impedir; (to load with debts, etc.) gravar

encumbrance [ɛn'kʌmbrəns] s embarazo; estorbo; gravamen m

ency. o encyc. abbr encyclopedia

encyclical [ɛn'sɪklɪkəl] o [ɛn'saɪklɪkəl] s encíclica

el
en

encyclopedia [ɛn,saɪklə'pidɪ•ə] *s* enciclopedia

encyclopedic [ɛn,saɪklə'pidɪk] *adj* enciclopédico

end [ɛnd] *s* (*in time*) fin *m;* (*in space*) extremo, remate *m;* (*e.g., of the month*) fines *mpl;* (*small piece*) cabo, pieza, fragmento; (*purpose*) intento, objeto, fin, mira; **at the end of** al cabo de; a fines de; **in the end** al fin; **no end of** (coll) un sin fin de; **to make both ends meet** pasar con lo que se tiene; **to no end** sin efecto; **to stand on end** poner de punta; ponerse de punta; erizarse, encresparse (*el pelo*); **to the end that** a fin de que ‖ *tr* acabar, terminar ‖ *intr* acabar, terminar; desembocar (*p.ej., una calle*); **to end up** acabar, morir; **to end up as** acabar siendo, parar en (*p.ej., ladrón*)

endanger [ɛn'dendʒər] *tr* poner en peligro

endear [ɛn'dɪr] *tr* hacer querer; **to endear oneself to** hacerse querer por

endearment [ɛn'dɪrmənt] *s* encariñamento

endeavor [ɛn'dɛvər] *s* esfuerzo, empeño ‖ *intr* esforzarse, empeñarse

endemic [ɛn'dɛmɪk] *adj* endémico ‖ *s* endemia

ending ['ɛndɪŋ] *s* fin *m*, terminación; (gram) desinencia, terminación

endive ['ɛndaɪv] *s* escarola

endless ['ɛndlɪs] *adj* interminable; (*chain, screw, etc.*) sin fin

end'most' *adj* último, extremo

endorse [ɛn'dɔrs] *tr* endosar; (fig) apoyar, aprobar

endorsee [,ɛndɔr'si] *s* endosatario

endorsement [ɛn'dɔrsmənt] *s* endoso; (fig) apoyo, aprobación

endorser [ɛn'dɔrsər] *s* endosante *mf*

endow [ɛn'dau] *tr* dotar

endowment [ɛn'daumənt] *adj* dotal ‖ *s* (*of an institution*) dotación; (*gift, talent*) dote *f*, prenda

end paper *s* hoja de encuadernador

endurance [ɛn'djurəns] o [ɛn'durəns] *s* aguante *m*, paciencia; (*ability to hold out*) resistencia, fortaleza; (*lasting time*) duración

endure [ɛn'djur] o [ɛn'dur] *tr* aguantar, tolerar, sufrir ‖ *intr* durar; sufrir con paciencia

enduring [ɛn'djurɪŋ] o [ɛn'durɪŋ] *adj* duradero, permanente, resistente

enema ['ɛnəmə] *s* enema, ayuda; (*liquid and apparatus*) lavativa

ene•my ['ɛnəmi] *adj* enemigo ‖ *s* (*pl* -**mies**) enemigo

enemy alien *s* extranjero enemigo

energetic [,ɛnər'dʒɛtɪk] *adj* enérgico, vigoroso

ener•gy ['ɛnərdʒi] *s* (*pl* -**gies**) energía; **alternate energy sources** energías alternas

energy crisis *s* crisis energética

enervate ['ɛnər,vet] *tr* enervar

enfeeble [ɛn'fibəl] *tr* debilitar

enfold [ɛnfold] *tr* arrollar, envolver

enforce [ɛn'fors] *tr* hacer cumplir, poner en vigor; obtener por fuerza; (*e.g., obedience*) imponer; (*an argument*) hacer valer

enforcement [ɛn'forsmənt] *s* compulsión; (*e.g., of a law*) ejecución

enfranchise [ɛn'fræntʃaɪz] *tr* franquear, libertar; conceder el derecho de sufragio a

eng. *abbr* **engineer, engraving**

engage [ɛn'gedʒ] *tr* ocupar, emplear; alquilar, reservar; atraer (*p.ej., la atención de una persona*); engranar con; trabar batalla con; **to be engaged, to be engaged to be married** estar prometido, estar comprometido para casarse; **to engage someone in conversation** entablar conversación con una persona ‖ *intr* empeñarse, comprometerse; empotrar, encajar; engranar; **to engage in** ocuparse en

engaged [ɛn'gedʒd] *adj* comprometido, prometido; (*column*) embebido, entregado

engagement [ɛn'gedʒmənt] *s* ajuste *m*, contrato, empeño; esponsales *mpl*, palabra de casamiento; (*duration of betrothal*) noviazgo; (*appointment*) cita; (mil) acción, batalla

engagement ring *s* anillo de compromiso, anillo de pedida

engaging [ɛn'gedʒɪŋ] *adj* agraciado, simpático

engender [ɛn'dʒɛndər] *tr* engendrar

engine ['ɛndʒɪn] *s* máquina; (*of automobile*) motor *m;* (rr) máquina, locomotora

engine driver *s* maquinista *m*

engineer [,ɛndʒə'nɪr] *s* ingeniero; (*engine driver*) maquinista *m* ‖ *tr* dirigir o construir como ingeniero; llevar a cabo con acierto

engineering [,ɛndʒə'nɪrɪŋ] *s* ingeniería

engine house *s* cuartel *m* de bomberos

engine•man ['ɛndʒɪnmən] *s* (*pl* -**men** [mən]) maquinista *m*, conductor *m* de locomotora

engine room *s* sala de máquinas; (naut) cámara de las máquinas

en'gine-room' telegraph *s* (naut) transmisor *m* de órdenes, telégrafo de máquinas

England ['ɪŋglənd] *s* Inglaterra

Englander ['ɪŋgləndər] *s* natural *m* inglés

English ['ɪŋglɪʃ] *adj* inglés ‖ *s* inglés *m;* (*in billiards*) efecto; **the English** los ingleses

English Channel *s* Canal *m* de la Mancha

English daisy *s* margarita de los prados

English horn *s* (mus) corno inglés, cuerno inglés

English•man ['ɪŋglɪʃmən] *s* (*pl* -**men** [mən]) inglés *m*

Eng'lish-speak'ing *adj* de habla inglesa, angloparlante

Eng'lish-wom'an *s* (*pl* -**wom'en**) inglesa

engraft [ɛn'græft] *tr* (hort & surg) injertar; (fig) implantar

engrave [ɛn'grev] *tr* grabar; (*in the memory*) grabar

engraver [ɛn'grevər] *s* grabador *m*

engraving [ɛn'grevɪŋ] *s* grabado

engross [ɛn'gros] *tr* absorber; poner en limpio; copiar califgáficamente

engrossing [ɛn'grosɪŋ] *adj* acaparador, absorbente

engulf [ɛnˈgʌlf] *tr* hundir, inundar
enhance [ɛnˈhæns] *tr* realzar
enhancement [ɛnˈhænsmənt] *s* realce *m*
enigma [ɪˈnɪgmə] *s* enigma *m*
enigmatic(al) [ˌɪnɪgˈmætɪk(əl)] *adj* enigmático
enjambment [ɛnˈdʒæmmənt] o [ɛnˈdʒæmbmənt] *s* encabalgamiento
enjoin [ɛnˈdʒɔɪn] *tr* encargar, ordenar
enjoy [ɛnˈdʒɔɪ] *tr* gozar; **to enjoy** + *ger* gozarse en + *inf;* **to enjoy oneself** divertirse
enjoyable [ɛnˈdʒɔɪ•əbəl] *adj* agradable, deleitable
enjoyment [ɛnˈdʒɔɪmənt] *s* (*pleasure*) placer *m*; (*pleasurable use*) goce *m*
enkindle [ɛnˈkɪndəl] *tr* encender
enlarge [ɛnˈlardʒ] *tr* agrandar, aumentar; (phot) ampliar ‖ *intr* agrandarse, aumentar; (*to talk at length*) explayarse; exagerar; **to enlarge on** o **upon** tratar con más extensión; exagerar
enlargement [ɛnˈlardʒmənt] *s* agrandamiento, aumento; (phot) ampliación
enlighten [ɛnˈlaɪtən] *tr* ilustrar, instruir
enlightenment [ɛnˈlaɪtənmənt] *s* ilustración, instrucción; dilucidación
enlist [ɛnˈlɪst] *tr* alistar; ganar (*a una persona; el favor, los servicios de una persona*) ‖ *intr* alistarse; **to enlist in** (*a cause*) poner empeño en
enliven [ɛnˈlaɪvən] *tr* avivar, animar
enmesh [ɛnˈmɛʃ] *tr* enredar
enmi•ty [ˈɛnmɪti] *s* (*pl* **-ties**) enemistad
ennoble [ɛnˈnobəl] *tr* ennoblecer
ennui [ˈɑnwi] *s* aburrimiento, tedio
enormous [ɪˈnɔrməs] *adj* enorme
enough [ɪˈnʌf] *adj, adv* & *s* bastante *m* ‖ *interj* ¡basta!, ¡no más!
enounce [ɪˈnauns] *tr* enunciar; pronunciar
en passant [ˌɑn pæˈsɑnt] *adv* (chess) al vuelo
enrage [ɛnˈredʒ] *tr* enrabiar, encolerizar
enrapture [ɛnˈræptʃər] *tr* embelesar, transportar, arrebatar
enrich [ɛnˈrɪtʃ] *tr* enriquecer
enroll [ɛnˈrol] *tr* alistar, inscribir; (*to wrap up*) envolver, enrollar ‖ *intr* alistarse, inscribirse
en route [ɑn ˈrut] *adv* en camino; **en route to** camino de, rumbo à
ensconce [ɛnˈskɑns] *tr* esconder, abrigar; **to ensconce oneself** instalarse cómodamente
ensemble [ɑnˈsɑmbəl] *s* conjunto; grupo de músicos que tocan o cantan juntos; traje armonioso
ensign [ˈɛnsaɪn] *s* (*standard*) enseña, bandera; (*badge*) divisa, insignia ‖ [ˈɛnsən] o [ˈɛnsaɪn] *s* (nav) alférez *m* de fragata
enslave [ɛnˈslev] *tr* esclavizar
enslavement [ɛnˈslevmənt] *s* esclavización
ensnare [ɛnˈsnɛr] *tr* entrampar
ensue [ɛnˈsu] *intr* seguirse; resultar
ensuing [ɛnˈsu•ɪŋ] *adj* siguiente; resultante
ensure [ɛnˈʃur] *tr* asegurar, garantizar
entail [ɛnˈtel] *s* (law) vínculo ‖ *tr* acarrear, ocasionar; (law) vincular
entangle [ɛnˈtæŋgəl] *tr* enmarañar, enredar

entanglement [ɛnˈtæŋgəlmənt]*s* enmarañamiento, enredo
enter [ˈɛntər] *tr* entrar en (*una habitación*); entrar por (*una puerta*); (*in the customhouse*) declarar; (*to make a record of*) registrar, asentar; matricular (*a un alumno*); matricularse en; hacer miembro a; hacerse miembro de; (*to undertake*) emprender; asentar (*un pedido*); **to enter one's head** metérsele a uno en la cabeza ‖ *intr* entrar; (theat) entrar en escena, salir; **to enter into** entrar en; celebrar (*p.ej., un contrato*); **to enter on** o **upon** emprender
enterprise [ˈɛntərˌpraɪz] *s* (*undertaking*) empresa; (*spirit, push*) empuje *m*
enterprising [ˈɛntərˌpraɪzɪŋ] *adj* emprendedor
entertain [ˌɛntərˈten] *tr* entretener, divertir; (*to show hospitality to*) recibir; considerar, abrigar (*esperanzas, ideas, etc.*) ‖ *intr* recibir
entertainer [ˌɛntərˈtenər] *s* (*host*) anfitrión *m*; (*in public*) actor *m*, bailador *m*, músico, vocalista *mf* (*esp. en un café cantante*)
entertaining [ˌɛntərˈtenɪŋ] *adj* entretenido
entertainment [ˌɛntərˈtenmənt] *s* entretenimiento, diversión; atracción, espectáculo; buen recibimiento; (*of hopes, ideas, etc.*) consideración, abrigo
enthrall [ɛnˈθrɔl] *tr* cautivar, encantar; esclavizar, sojuzgar
enthrone [ɛnˈθron] *tr* entronizar
enthuse [ɛnˈθuz] o [ɛnˈθjuz] *tr* (coll) entusiasmar ‖ *intr* (coll) entusiasmarse
enthusiasm [ɛnˈθuziˌæzəm] *s* entusiasmo
enthusiast [ɛnˈθuziˌæst] *s* entusiasta *mf;* devoto
enthusiastic [ɛnˌθuziˈæstɪk] *adj* entusiástico
entice [ɛnˈtaɪs] *tr* atraer, tentar; inducir al mal, extraviar
enticement [ɛnˈtaɪsmənt] *s* atracción, tentación; extravío
entire [ɛnˈtaɪr] *adj* entero
entirely [ɛnˈtaɪrli] *adv* enteramente; (*exclusively*) solamente
entire•ty [ɛtaɪrti] *s* (*pl* **-ties**) entereza; conjunto, totalidad
entitle [ɛnˈtaɪtəl] *tr* dar derecho a; (*to give a name to; to honor with a title*) intitular
enti•ty [ˈɛntiti] *s* (*pl* **-ties**) entidad
entomb [ɛnˈtum] *tr* sepultar
entombment [ɛnˈtummənt] *s* sepultura
entomology [ˌɛntəˈmalədʒi] *s* entomología
entourage [ˌɑntuˈraʒ] *s* cortejo, séquito
entrails [ˈɛntrɛlz] *spl* entrañas
entrain [ɛnˈtren] *tr* despachar en el tren ‖ *intr* embarcar, salir en el tren
entrance [ˈɛntrəns] *s* entrada, ingreso; (theat) entrada en escena ‖ [ɛnˈtræns] *tr* arrebatar, encantar
entrance examination *s* examen *m* de ingreso; **to take entrance examinations** examinarse de ingreso
entrancing [ɛnˈtrænsɪŋ] *adj* arrebatador, encantador
entrant [ˈɛntrənt] *s* entrante *mf;* (sport) concurrente *mf*

en
en

en·trap [ɛn'træp] v (pret & pp **-trapped;** ger **-trapping**) tr entrampar

entreat [ɛn'trit] tr rogar, suplicar

entreat·y [ɛn'triti] s (pl **-ies**) ruego, súplica

entree ['ɑntre] s entrada, ingreso; (culin) entrada, principio

entrench [ɛn'trɛntʃ] tr atrincherar ‖ intr — **to entrench on** o **upon** infringir, violar

entrust [ɛn'trʌst] tr confiar

en·try ['ɛntri] s (pl **-tries**) entrada; (item) partida, entrada; (in a dictionary) artículo; (sport) concurrente mf

entry word s (in dictionary) voz-guía f

entwine [ɛn'twaɪn] tr entretejer, entrelazar

enumerate [ɪ'numə,ret] tr enumerar

enunciate [ɪ'nʌnsi,et] o [ɪ'nʌnʃi,et] tr enunciar; pronunciar

envelop [ɛn'vɛləp] tr envolver

envelope ['ɛnvə,lop] o ['ɑnvə,lop] s (for a letter) sobre m; (wrapper) envoltura

envenom [ɛn'vɛnəm] tr envenenar

enviable ['ɛnvɪ·əbəl] adj envidiable

envious ['ɛnvɪ·əs] adj envidioso

environment [ɛn'vaɪrənmənt] s medio ambiente; entorno; (surroundings) inmediaciones

environmental [ɛn,vaɪrən'mɛntəl] adj ambiental

environmental pollution s contaminación ambiental

environs [ɛn'vaɪrəns] spl inmediaciones, alrededores mpl

envisage [ɛn'vɪzɪdʒ] tr (to look in the face of) encarar; considerar, representarse

envoi ['ɛnvɔɪ] s despedida (copla al fin de una composición poética)

envoy ['ɛnvɔɪ] s (diplomatic agent) enviado; (short concluding stanza) despedida

en·vy ['ɛnvi] s (pl **-vies**) envidia ‖ v (pret & pp **-vied**) tr envidiar

enzyme ['ɛnzaɪm] s enzima f

epaulet o **epaulette** ['ɛpə,lɛt] s charretera

epenthe·sis [ɛ'pɛnθɪsɪs] s (pl **-ses** [,siz]) epéntesis f

epergne [ɪ'pʌrn] o [e'pɛrn] s ramillete m, centro de mesa

ephemeral [ɪ'fɛmərəl] adj efímero

epic ['ɛpɪk] adj épico ‖ s epopeya

epicure ['ɛpɪ,kjʊr] s epicúreo

epicurean [,ɛpɪkjʊ'ri·ən] adj & s epicúreo

epidemic [,ɛpɪ'dɛmɪk] adj epidémico ‖ s epidemia

epidemiology [,ɛpɪ,dɪmɪ'ɑlədʒi] s epidemiología

epidermis [,ɛpɪ'dʌrmɪs] s epidermis f

epigram ['ɛpɪ,græm] s epigrama m

epilepsy ['ɛpɪ,lɛpsi] s epilepsia

epileptic [,ɛpɪ'lɛptɪk] adj & s epiléptico

Epiphany [ɪ'pɪfəni] s Epifanía

Episcopalian [ɪ,pɪskə'peli·ən] adj & s episcopalista mf

episode ['ɛpɪ,sod] s episodio

epistemology [ɪ,pɪstɪ'mɑlədʒi] s epistemología

epistle [ɪ'pɪsəl] s epístola

epitaph ['ɛpɪ,tæf] s epitafio

epithet ['ɛpɪ,θɛt] s epíteto

epitome [ɪ'pɪtəmi] s epítome m; (fig) esencia, personificación

epitomize [ɪ'pɪtə,maɪz] tr epitomar; (fig) encarnar, personificar

epoch ['ɛpək] o ['ipɑk] s época

epochal ['ɛpəkəl] adj memorable, trascendental

ep'och-mak'ing adj que hace época

equable ['ɛkwəbəl] o ['ikwəbəl] adj constante, uniforme; sereno

equal ['ikwəl] adj igual; **equal to** a la altura de ‖ s igual mf ‖ v (pret & pp **equaled** o **equalled;** ger **equaling** o **equalling**) tr (to be equal to) igualarse a o con; (to make equal) igualar

equali·ty [i'kwɑlɪti] s (pl **-ties**) igualdad

equalize ['ikwə,laɪz] tr igualar; (to make uniform) equilibrar

equally ['ikwəli] adv igualmente

equal opportunity s igualdad de oportunidades

equanimity [,ikwə'nɪmɪti] s ecuanimidad, igualdad de ánimo

equate [i'kwet] tr poner en ecuación; considerar equivalente(s)

equation [i'kweʃən] s ecuación

equator [i'kwetər] s ecuador m

equer·ry ['ɛkwəri] o [ɪ'kwɛri] s (pl **-ries**) caballerizo

equestrian [ɪ'kwɛstrɪ·ən] adj ecuestre ‖ m jinete m, caballista m

equestrian sport s hípica

equilateral [,ikwɪ'lætərəl] adj equilátero

equilibrium [,ikwɪ'lɪbrɪ·əm] s equilibrio

equinoctial [,ikwɪ'nɑkʃəl] adj equinoccial

equinox ['ikwɪ,nɑks] s equinoccio

equip [ɪ'kwɪp] v (pret & pp **equipped;** ger **equipping**) tr equipar

equipment [ɪ'kwɪpmənt] s equipo, avíos, pertrechos; aptitud, capacidad

equipoise ['ikwɪ,pɔɪz] o ['ɛkwɪ,pɔɪz] s equilibrio; contrapeso ‖ tr equilibrar; equipesar

equitable ['ɛkwɪtəbəl] adj equitativo

equi·ty ['ɛkwɪti] s (pl **-ties**) (fairness) equidad; valor líquido

equivalent [ɪ'kwɪvələnt] adj & s equivalente m

equivocal [ɪ'kwɪvəkəl] adj equívoco

equivocate [ɪ'kwɪvə,ket] intr usar de equívocos para engañar, mentir

equivocation [ɪ,kwɪvə'keʃən] s equívoco

era ['ɪrə] o ['irə] s era

eradicate [ɪ'rædɪ,ket] tr erradicar

erase [ɪ'res] tr borrar

eraser [ɪ'resər] s goma de borrar; (for blackboard) cepillo

erasure [ɪ'reʃər] o [ɪ'reʒər] s borradura, tachón m

ere [ɛr] prep antes de ‖ conj antes de que; más bien que

erect [ɪ'rɛkt] adj derecho, enhiesto, erguido; (hair) erizado ‖ tr (to set in upright position) erguir, enhestar; erigir (un edificio); armar, montar (una máquina)

erection [ɪ'rɛkʃən] s erección

erg [ʌrg] s ergio

ermine [ˈʌrmɪn] s armiño; (fig) toga, judicatura

erode [ɪˈrod] tr erosionar ‖ intr erosionarse

erosion [ɪˈroʒən] s erosión

err [ʌr] intr errar, equivocarse, marrar; pecar, marrar

errand [ˈɛrənd] s mandado, recado, comisión; **to run an errand** hacer un mandado

errand boy s recadero, mandadero

erratic [ɪˈrætɪk] adj irregular, inconstante, variable; excéntrico

erra·tum [ɪˈretəm] o [ɪˈratəm] s (pl **-ta** [tə]) errata

erroneous [ɪˈronɪ·əs] adj erróneo

error [ˈɛrər] s error m; **human error** fallo humano

erudite [ˈɛrʊˌdaɪt] adj erudito

erudition [ˌɛrʊˈdɪʃən] s erudición

erupt [ɪˈrʌpt] intr hacer erupción (la piel, los dientes de un niño); erumpir (un volcán)

eruption [ɪˈrʌpʃən] s erupción

escalate [ˈɛskəˌlet] intr escalarse

escalation [ˌɛskəˈleʃən] s escalada, escalación

escalator [ˈɛskəˌletər] s escalera mecánica, móvil o rodante

escallop [ˈɛsˈkæləp] s concha de peregrino; (on edge of cloth) festón m ‖ tr hornear a la crema y con migajas de pan; cocer (p.ej., ostras) en su concha; festonear

escapade [ˌɛskəˈped] s calaverada, aventura atolondrada; (flight) escapada

escape [ɛsˈkep] s (getaway) escape m, escapatoria; (from responsibilities, duties, etc.) escapatoria ‖ tr evitar, eludir; **to escape someone** escapársele a uno; olvidársele a uno ‖ intr escapar, escaparse; **to escape from** escaparse a (una persona); escaparse de (la cárcel)

escapee [ˌɛskəˈpi] s evadido

escape literature s literatura de escape o de evasión

escapement [ɛsˈkepmənt] s escape m

escapement wheel s rueda de escape

escarpment [ɛsˈkarpmənt] s escarpa

eschew [ɛsˈtʃu] tr evitar, rehuir

escort [ˈɛskɔrt] s escolta; (man or boy who accompanies a woman or girl in public) acompañante m, caballero, galán m ‖ [ɛsˈkɔrt] tr escoltar

escutcheon [ɛsˈkʌtʃən] s escudo de armas; (plate in front of lock on door) escudo, escudete m

Eski·mo [ˈɛskɪˌmo] adj esquimal ‖ s (pl **-mos** o **-mo**) esquimal mf

esopha·gus [ɪˈsafəgəs] s (pl **-gi** [ˌdʒaɪ]) esófago

esp. abbr **especially**

espalier [ɛsˈpæljər] s espaldar m, espalera

especial [ɛsˈpɛʃəl] adj especial

espionage [ˈɛspɪ·ənɪdʒ] o [ˌɛspɪ·əˈnɑʒ] s espionaje m

esplanade [ˌɛspləˈned] s explanada

espousal [ɛsˈpaʊzəl] s desposorios; (of a cause) adhesión

espouse [ɛsˈpaʊz] tr casarse con; (to advocate, adopt) abogar por, adherirse a

Esq. abbr **Esquire**

esquire [ɛsˈkwaɪr] o [ˈɛskwaɪr] s escudero ‖ **Esquire** s título de cortesía que se escribe después del apellido y que se usa en vez de **Mr.**

essay [ˈɛse] s ensayo

essayist [ˈɛse·ɪst] s ensayista mf

essence [ˈɛsəns] s esencia

essential [ɛˈsɛnʃəl] adj & s esencial m

est. abbr **established, estate, estimated**

establish [ɛsˈtæblɪʃ] tr establecer

establishment [ɛsˈtæblɪʃmənt] s establecimiento; **the Establishment** (established order) el Sistema

estate [ɛsˈtet] s estado; situación social; (landed property) finca, hacienda, heredad; (a person's possessions) bienes mpl, propiedad; (left by a decedent) herencia, bienes relictos

esteem [ɛsˈtim] s estima ‖ tr estimar

esthete [ˈɛsθit] s esteta mf

esthetic [ɛsˈθɛtɪk] adj estético ‖ **esthetics** ssg estética

estimable [ˈɛstɪməbəl] adj estimable

estimate [ˈɛstɪmɪt] s (calculation of value, judgment of worth) estimación; (statement of cost of work to be done) presupuesto ‖ [ˈɛstɪˌmet] tr (to judge, deem) estimar; presupuestar (el coste de una obra)

estimation [ˌɛstɪˈmeʃən] s estimación

estrangement [ɛsˈtrendʒmənt] s extrañeza

estuar·y [ˈɛstʃʊˌɛri] s (pl **-ies**) estero

etc. abbr **et cetera**

etch [ɛtʃ] tr & intr grabar al agua fuerte

etcher [ˈɛtʃər] s aguafortista mf

etching [ˈɛtʃɪŋ] s aguafuerte f

eternal [ɪˈtʌrnəl] adj eterno

eterni·ty [ɪˈtʌrnɪti] s (pl **-ties**) eternidad

ether [ˈiθər] s éter m

ethereal [ɪˈθɪrɪ·əl] adj etéreo

ethical [ˈɛθɪkəl] adj ético

ethics [ˈɛθɪks] ssg ética

Ethiopian [ˌiθɪˈopɪ·ən] adj & s etíope mf

Ethiopic [ˌiθɪˈopɪk] adj & s etiópico

ethnic(al) [ˈɛθnɪk(əl)] adj étnico

ethnography [ɛθˈnagrəfi] s etnografía

ethnology [ɛθˈnalədʒi] s etnología

ethyl [ˈɛθɪl] s etilo

ethylene [ˈɛθɪˌlin] s etileno

etiquette [ˈɛtɪˌkɛt] s etiqueta

et seq. abbr **et sequens, et sequentes, et sequentia** (Lat) **and the following**

étude [eˈtjud] s (mus) estudio

etymology [ˌɛtɪˈmalədʒi] s etimología

ety·mon [ˈɛtɪˌman] s (pl **-mons** o **-ma** [mə]) étimo

eucalyp·tus [ˌjukəˈlɪptəs] s (pl **-tuses** o **-ti** [taɪ]) eucalipto

Eucharist [ˈjukərɪst] s Eucaristía

euchre [ˈjukər] s juego de naipes ‖ tr (coll) ser más listo que

eugenics [juˈdʒɛnɪks] s eugenesia

eulogistic [ˌjuləˈdʒɪstɪk] adj elogiador

eulogize [ˈjuləˌdʒaɪz] tr elogiar

eulo·gy [ˈjulədʒi] s (pl **-gies**) elogio

eunuch [ˈjunək] s eunuco

euphemism [ˈjufɪˌmɪzəm] s eufemismo

euphemistic [ˌjufɪˈmɪstɪk] *adj* eufemístico
euphonic [juˈfɑnɪk] *adj* eufónico
eupho•ny [ˈjufəni] *s* (*pl* -**nies**) eufonía
euphoria [juˈfɔrɪ•ə] *s* euforia
euphuism [ˈjufju͵ɪzəm] *s* eufuísmo
euphuistic [ˌjufjuˈɪstɪk] *adj* eufuístico
Europe [ˈjurəp] *s* Europa
European [ˌjurəˈpi•ən] *adj & s* europeo
euthanasia [ˌjuθəˈneʒə] *s* eutanasia
evacuate [ɪˈvækju͵et] *tr & intr* evacuar
evacuation [ɪ͵vækjuˈeʃən] *s* evacuación
evade [ɪˈved] *tr* evadir ‖ *intr* evadirse
evaluate [ɪˈvælju͵et] *tr* evaluar
Evangel [ɪˈvændʒəl] *s* Evangelio
evangelic(al) [ˌivænˈdʒɛlɪk(əl)] o [ˌɛvənˈdʒɛlɪk(əl)] *adj* evangélico
Evangelist [ɪˈvændʒəlɪst] *s* Evangelista *m*
evaporate [ɪˈvæpə͵ret] *tr* evaporar ‖ *intr* evaporarse
evasion [ɪˈveʒən] *s* evasión, evasiva
evasive [ɪˈvesɪv] *adj* evasivo; elusivo
eve [iv] *s* víspera; **on the eve of** en vísperas de
even [ˈivən] *adj* (*smooth*) parejo, llano, liso; (*number*) par; constante, uniforme, invariable; (*temperament*) apacible, sereno; exacto, igual; **even with** al nivel de; **to be even** estar en paz; no deber nada a nadie; **to get even** desquitarse ‖ *adv* aun, hasta; sin embargo; también; exactamente, igualmente; **even as** así como; **even if** aunque, aun cuando; **even so** aun así; **even though** aunque, aun cuando; **even when** aun cuando; **not even** ni . . . siquiera; **to break even** salir sin ganar ni perder; (*in gambling*) salir en paz ‖ *tr* allanar, igualar
evening [ˈivnɪŋ] *adj* vespertino ‖ *s* tarde *f*
evening clothes *spl* traje *m* de etiqueta
evening gown *s* vestido de noche (*de mujer*)
evening primrose *s* hierba del asno
evening star *s* estrella vespertina, lucero de la tarde
evening wrap *s* salida de teatro
e′ven•song′ *s* canción de la tarde; (*eccl*) vísperas
event [ɪˈvɛnt] *s* acontecimiento, suceso; (*outcome*) resultado; (*public function*) acto; (*sport*) prueba; **at all events** o **in any event** en todo caso; **in the event that** en caso que
e′ven-tem′pered *adj* equilibrado
eventful [ɪˈvɛntfəl] *adj* lleno de acontecimientos; importante, memorable
eventual [ɪˈvɛntʃu•əl] *adj* final
eventuali•ty [ɪˈvɛntʃu͵ælɪti] *s* (*pl*-**ties**) eventualidad
eventually [ɪˈvɛntʃu•əli] *adv* finalmente, con el tiempo
eventuate [ɪˈvɛntʃu͵et] *intr* concluir, resultar
ever [ˈɛvər] *adv* (*at all times*) siempre; (*at any time*) jamás, nunca, alguna vez; **as ever** como siempre; **as much as ever** tanto como antes; **ever since** (*since that time*) desde entonces; después de que; **ever so** muy; **ever so much** muchísimo; **hardly ever** o **scarcely ever** casi nunca; **not . . . ever** no . . . nunca

ev′er•glade′ *s* tierra pantanosa cubierta de hierbas altas
ev′er•green′ *adj* siempre verde ‖ *s* planta siempre verde; **evergreens** ramas colgadas como adorno
ev′er•last′ing *adj* sempiterno; (*lasting indefinitely*) duradero; (*wearisome*) aburrido, cansado ‖ *s* eternidad; (bot) siempreviva
ev′er•more′ *adv* eternamente; **for evermore** para siempre jamás
every [ˈɛvri] *adj* todos los; (*each*) cada, todo; (*being each in a series*) cada, p.ej., **every three days** cada tres días; **every bit** (coll) todo, p.ej., **every bit a man** todo un hombre; **every now and then** de vez en cuando; **every once in a while** una que otra vez; **every other day** cada dos días, un día sí y otro no; **every which way** (coll) por todas partes; (coll) en desarreglo
ev′ery•bod′y *pron indef* todo el mundo
ev′ery•day′ *adj* de todos los días; cotidiano, diario; común, ordinario
every man Jack o **every mother's son** *s* cada hijo de vecino
ev′ery•one′ o **every one** *pron indef* cada uno, todos, todo el mundo
ev′ery•thing′ *pron indef* todo
ev′ery•where′ *adv* en o por todas partes; a todas partes
evict [ɪˈvɪkt] *tr* desahuciar
eviction [ɪˈvɪkʃən] *s* desahucio
evidence [ˈɛvɪdəns] *s* evidencia; (law) prueba
evident [ˈɛvɪdənt] *adj* evidente
evil [ˈivəl] *adj* malo, malvado, malazo, maléfico ‖ *s* mal *m*, maldad
e′vil-do′er *s* malhechor *m*, malvado
e′vil-do′ing *s* malhecho, maldad
evil eye *s* mal *m* de ojo
evil-minded [ˈivəlˈmaɪndɪd] *adj* mal pensado, malintencionado
Evil One, the el enemigo malo
evince [ɪˈvɪns] *tr* manifestar, mostrar
evoke [ɪˈvok] *tr* evocar
evolution [ˌɛvəˈluʃən] *s* evolución; (math) extracción de raíces, radicación
evolutionary [ˌɛvəˈluʃə͵nɛri] o **evolutionist** [ˌɛgəˈluʃənɪst] *s* evolucionista *mf*
evolve [ɪˈvɑlv] *tr* desarrollar; desprender (*olores, gases, calor*) ‖ *intr* evolucionar
ewe [ju] *s* oveja
ewer [ˈju•ər] *s* aguamanil *m*
ex. *abbr* **examination, example, except, exchange, executive**
ex [ɛks] *prep* sin incluir, sin participación en
exact [ɛgˈzækt] *adj* exacto ‖ *tr* exigir
exacting [ɛgˈzæktɪŋ] *adj* exigente
exaction [ɛgˈzækʃən] *s* exacción
exactly [ɛgˈzæktli] *adv* exactamente; (*sharp, on the dot*) en punto
exactness [ɛg͵zæktnɪs] *s* exactitud
exaggerate [ɛgˈzædʒə͵ret] *tr* exagerar
exalt [ɛgˈzɔlt] *tr* exaltar, ensalzar
exam [ɛgˈzæm] *s* (coll) examen *m*
examination [ɛg͵zæmɪˈneʃən] *s* examen *m*; **to take an examination** sufrir un examen, examinarse
examine [ɛgˈzæmɪn] *tr* examinar

example 453 **exhaust pipe**

example [ɛgˈzæmpəl] o [ɛgˈzɑmpəl] s ejemplo; (case serving as a warning to others) ejemplar m; (of mathematics) problema m; **for example** por ejemplo

exasperate [ɛgˈzæspə,ret] tr exasperar

excavate [ˈɛkskə,vet] tr excavar

exceed [ɛkˈsid] tr exceder; sobrepasar (p.ej., el límite de velocidad)

exceedingly [ɛkˈsidɪŋli] adv sumamente, sobremanera

ex•cel [ɛkˈsɛl] v (pret & pp -celled; ger -celling) tr aventajar ‖ intr sobresalir

excellence [ˈɛksələns] s excelencia

excellen•cy [ˈɛksələnsi] s (pl -cies) excelencia; **Your Excellency** Su Excelencia

excelsior [ɛkˈsɛlsɪ•ər] s pajilla de madera, virutas de madera

except [ɛkˈsɛpt] prep excepto; **except for** sin; **except that** a menos que ‖ tr exceptuar

exception [ɛkˈsɛpʃən] s excepción; **to take exception** poner reparos, objetar; ofenderse; **with the exception of** a excepción de

exceptional [ɛkˈsɛpʃənəl] adj excepcional

excerpt [ˈɛksʌrpt] s excerta, selección ‖ [ɛkˈsʌrpt] tr escoger

excess [ˈɛksɛs] o [ɛkˈsɛs] adj excedente, sobrante ‖ [ɛkˈsɛs] s (amount or degree by which one thing exceeds another) exceso, excedente m; (excessive amount; immoderate indulgence, unlawful conduct) exceso; **in excess of** más que, superior a

excess baggage s exceso de equipaje

excess fare s suplemento

excessive [ɛkˈsɛsɪv] adj excesivo

ex′cess-prof′its tax s impuesto sobre beneficios extraordinarios

excess weight s exceso de peso

exchange [ɛksˈtʃendʒ] s (of greetings, compliments, blows, etc.) cambio; (of prisoners, merchandise, newspapers, credentials, etc.) canje m; periódico de canje; (place for buying and selling) bolsa, lonja; estación telefónica, central f de teléfonos; **in exchange for** en cambio de, a trueque de ‖ tr cambiar; canjear (prisioneros, mercancías, etc.); darse, hacerse (cortesías); **to exchange greetings** saludarse; **to exchange shots** cambiar disparos

exchequer [ɛksˈtʃɛkər] o [ˈɛkstʃɛkər] s tesorería; fondos nacionales

excise tax [ɛkˈsaɪz] o [ˈɛksaɪz] m impuesto sobre ciertas mercancías de comercio interior

excitable [ɛkˈsaɪtəbəl] adj excitable

excite [ɛkˈsaɪt] tr excitar

excitement [ɛkˈsaɪtmənt] s excitación

exciting [ɛkˈsaɪtɪŋ] adj emocionante, conmovedor; (stimulating) excitante

exclaim [ɛksˈklem] tr & intr exclamar

exclamation [,ɛkskləˈmeʃən] s exclamación

exclamation mark o **point** s punto de admiración

exclude [ɛksˈklud] tr excluir

exclusion [ɛksˈkluʒən] s exclusión; **to the exclusion of** con exclusión de

exclusive [ɛksˈklusɪv] adj exclusivo; (clannish) exclusivista; (expensive) (coll) carero; (fashionable) (coll) muy de moda; **exclusive of** con exclusión de

excommunicate [,ɛkskəˈmjunɪ,ket] tr excomulgar

excommunication [,ɛkskə,mjunɪˈkeʃən] s excomunión

excoriate [ɛksˈkorɪ,et] tr (fig) desollar, vituperar

excrement [ˈɛkskrəmənt] s excremento

excruciating [ɛksˈkruʃɪ,etɪŋ] adj atroz, agudísimo, vivísimo

exculpate [ˈɛkskʌl,pet] o [ɛksˈkʌlpet] tr exculpar

excursion [ɛksˈkʌrʒən] s excursión

excursionist [ɛksˈkʌrʒənɪst] s excursionista mf

excusable [ɛksˈkjusəbəl] adj excusable

excuse [ɛksˈkjus] s excusa ‖ [ɛksˈkjuz] tr excusar, disculpar; dispensar, perdonar

execute [ˈɛksɪˈkjut] tr ejecutar; (law) celebrar, finalizar (una escritura)

execution [,ɛksɪˈkjuʃən] s ejecución

executioner [,ɛksɪˈkjuʃənər] s ejecutor m de la justicia, verdugo

executive [ɛgˈzɛkjətɪv] adj ejecutivo ‖ m poder ejecutivo; (of a school, business, etc.) dirigente mf

Executive Mansion s (U.S.A.) palacio presidencial

executor [ɛgˈzɛkjətər] s albacea m, ejecutor testamentario

executrix [ɛgˈzɛkjətrɪks] s albacea f, ejecutora testamentaria

exemplary [ɛgˈzɛmpləri] o [ˈɛgzəm,plɛri] adj ejemplar

exempli•fy [ɛgˈzɛmplɪ,faɪ] v (pret & pp -fied) tr ejemplificar

exempt [ɛgˈzɛmpt] adj exento ‖ tr eximir, exentar

exemption [ɛgˈzɛmpʃən] s exención

exercise [ˈɛksər,saɪz] s ejercicio; ceremonia; **to take exercise** hacer ejercicio ‖ tr ejercer (p.ej., caridad, influencia); ejercitar (un arte, profesión, etc.; adiestrar con el ejercicio); inquietar, preocupar; poner (cuidado) ‖ ref ejercitarse

exert [ɛgˈzʌrt] tr ejercer (una fuerza); **to exert oneself** esforzarse

exertion [ɛgˈzʌrʃən] s esfuerzo, empeño; (active use) ejercicio

exhalation [,ɛks•həˈleʃən] s (of gas, vapors, etc.) exhalación; (of air from lungs) espiración

exhale [ɛksˈhel] o [ɛgˈzel] tr exhalar (gases, vapores); espirar (el aire aspirado) ‖ intr exhalarse; espirar

exhaust [ɛgˈzɔst] s escape m; tubo de escape ‖ tr (to wear out, fatigue; to use up) agotar; hacer el vacío en; apurar (todos los medios)

exhaust fan s ventilador m aspirador

exhaustion [ɛgˈzɔstʃən] s agotamiento

exhaustive [ɛgˈzɔstɪv] adj exhaustivo; comprensivo

exhaust manifold s múltiple m de escape

exhaust pipe s tubo de escape

.eu
ex

exhaust valve *s* válvula de escape
exhibit [ɛg'zɪbɪt] *s* exhibición; (law) documento de prueba ‖ *tr* exhibir
exhibition [,ɛksɪ'bɪ/ən] *s* exhibición
exhibitor [ɛg'zɪbɪtər] *s* expositor *m*
exhilarating [ɛg'zɪlə,retɪŋ] *adj* alegrador, regocijador, alborozador
exhort [ɛg'zɔrt] *tr* exhortar
exhume [ɛks'hjum] *tr* exhumar
exigen•cy ['ɛksɪdʒənsi] *s* (*pl* -cies) exigencia
exigent ['ɛksɪdʒənt] *adj* exigente
exile ['ɛgzaɪl] o ['ɛksaɪl] *s* destierro; (*person*) desterrado ‖ *tr* desterrar
exist [ɛg'zɪst] *intr* existir
existence [ɛg'zɪstəns] *s* existencia
existing [ɛg'zɪstɪŋ] *adj* existente
exit ['ɛgzɪt] o ['ɛksɪt] *s* salida ‖ *intr* salir
exobiology [,ɛksobaɪ'ɑlədʒi] *s* exobiología
exodus ['ɛksədəs] *s* éxodo
exonerate [ɛg'zɑnə,ret] *tr* (*to free from blame*) exculpar; (*to free from an obligation*) exonerar
exorbitant [ɛg'zɔrbɪtənt] *adj* exorbitante
exorcise ['ɛksɔr,saɪz] *tr* exorcizar
exotic [ɛg'zɑtɪk] *adj* exótico
exp. *abbr* expenses, expired, export, express
expand [ɛks,pænd] *tr* dilatar (*un gas, el metal*); (*to enlarge, develop*) ampliar, ensanchar; (*to unfold, stretch out*) desplegar, extender; (math) desarrollar (*una ecuación*) ‖ *intr* dilatarse; ampliarse, ensancharse; desplegarse, extenderse
expanse [ɛks'pæns] *s* extensión
expansion [ɛks'pæn/ən] *s* expansión
expansive [ɛks'pænsɪv] *adj* expansivo
expatiate [ɛks'pe/ɪ,et] *intr* espaciarse, explayarse
expatriate [ɛks'petrɪ•ɪt] *adj* & *s* expatriado
expect [ɛks'pɛkt] *tr* esperar; (coll) creer, suponer
expectan•cy [ɛks'pɛktənsi] *s* (*pl* -cies) expectación
expectant mother [ɛks'pɛktənt] *s* futura madre
expectation [,ɛks'pɛkte/ən] *s* expectativa
expectorate [ɛks'pɛktə,ret] *tr* & *intr* expectorar
expedien•cy [ɛks'pidɪ•ənsi] *s* (*pl* -cies) conveniencia, oportunidad; ventaja personal
expedient [ɛks'pidɪ•ənt] *adj* conveniente, oportuno; egoísta, ventajoso; (*acting with self-interest*) ventajista ‖ *s* expediente *m*
expedite ['ɛkspɪ,daɪt] *tr* apresurar, despachar; expediar; dar curso a (*un documento*)
expedition [,ɛkspɪ'dɪ/ən] *s* expedición
expeditious [,ɛkspɪ'dɪ/əs] *adj* expeditivo
expeditiously [,ɛkspɪ'dɪ/əsli] *adv* ejecutivamente
ex•pel [ɛks'pɛl] *v* (*pret* & *pp* -pelled; *ger* -pelling) *tr* expeler, expulsar
expend [ɛks'pɛnd] *tr* gastar, consumir
expendable [ɛks'pɛndəbəl] *adj* gastable; (*to be thrown away after use*) desechable; (*soldier*) sacrificable
expenditure [ɛks'pɛndɪt/ər] *s* gasto, consumo

expense [ɛks'pɛns] *s* gasto; **expenses** gastos, expensas; **to go to the expense of** meterse en gastos con; **to meet expenses** hacer frente a ¡los gastos
expense account *s* cuenta de gastos
expensive [ɛks'pɛnsɪv] *adj* caro, costoso, dispendioso; (*charging high prices*) carero
experience [ɛks'pɪrɪ•əns] *s* experiencia ‖ *tr* experimentar
experienced [ɛksɪ'ənst] *adj* experimentado
experiment [ɛks'pɛrɪmənt] *s* experiencia, experimento ‖ [ɛks'pɛrɪ,mɛnt] *intr* experimentar
expert ['ɛkspərt] *adj* & *s* experto
expiate ['ɛkspɪ,et] *tr* expiar
expiation [,ɛkspɪ'e/ən] *s* expiación
expire [ɛks'paɪr] *tr* expeler (*el aire de los pulmones*) ‖ *intr* expirar (*expeler el aire de los pulmones; acabarse, p.ej., un plazo; fallecer*)
explain [ɛks'plen] *tr* explicar; **to explain away** descartar con explicaciones; (*to make excuse for*) explicar ‖ *intr* explicar, explicarse
explanation [,ɛksplə'ne/ən] *s* explicación; dilucidación
explanatory [ɛks'plænə,tori] *adj* explicativo
explicit [ɛks'plɪsɪt] *adj* explícito
explode [ɛks'plod] *tr* volar, hacer saltar; desacreditar (*una teoría*) ‖ *intr* explotar, estallar, reventar
exploit ['ɛksplɔɪt] *s* hazaña, proeza ‖ [ɛks'plɔɪt] *tr* explotar
exploitation [,ɛksplɔɪ'te/ən] *s* explotación
exploration [,ɛksplə're/ən] *s* exploración
explore [ɛks'plor] *tr* explorar
explorer [ɛks'plorər] *s* explorador *m*
explosion [ɛks'ploʒən] *s* explosión; (*of a theory*) refutación
explosive [ɛks'plosɪv] *adj* explosivo ‖ *s* explosivo; (phonet) explosiva
exponent [ɛks'ponənt] *s* exponente *m*, expositor *m;* (math) exponente *m*
export ['ɛksport] *adj* de exportación ‖ *s* exportación; **exports** (*articles exported*) exportación ‖ [ɛks'port] o ['ɛksport] *tr* & *intr* exportar
exportation [,ɛkspor'te/ən] *s* exportación
exporter [ɛksportər] *s* exportador *m*
expose [ɛks'poz] *tr* exponer; (*to unmask*) desenmascarar; (*the Host*) manifestar, exponer; (phot) impresionar
exposé [,ɛkspo'ze] *s* desenmascaramiento
exposition [,ɛkspə'zɪ/ən] *s* exposición; (rhet) exposición
expostulate [ɛks'past/ə,let] *intr* protestar; **to expostulate with** reconvenir
exposure [ɛks'poʒər] *s* (*to a danger; position with respect to points of compass*) exposición; (*unmasking*) desenmascaramiento; (phot) exposición
expound [ɛks'paʊnd] *tr* exponer
express [ɛks'prɛs] *adj* expreso ‖ *adv* (*for a special purpose*) expresamente; por expreso ‖ *s* expreso; **by express** (rr) en gran velocidad ‖ *tr* expresar; (*to squeeze out*)

exprimir; enviar por expreso; **to express oneself** expresarse

express company *s* compañía de transportes rápidos

expression [ɛksˈprɛʃən] *s* expresión

expressive [ɛksˈprɛsɪv] *adj* expresivo

expressly [ɛksˈprɛsli] *adv* expresamente

express•man [ɛksˈprɛsmən] *s* (*pl* **-men** [mən]) (U.S.A.) empleado del servicio de transportes rápidos

express train *s* tren expreso

express'way' *s* carretera de vía libre

expropriate [ɛksˈproprɪˌet] *tr* expropiar

expulsion [ɛksˈpʌlʃən] *s* expulsión

expunge [ɛksˈpʌndʒ] *tr* borrar, cancelar, arrasar

expurgate [ˈɛkspərˌget] *tr* expurgar

exquisite [ˈɛkskwɪzɪt] o [ɛksˈkwɪzɪt] *adj* exquisito; agudo, vivo; sensible

ex-service•man [ˌɛksˈsʌrvɪsˌmæn] *s* (*pl* **-men** [ˌmɛn]) ex militar *m*, ex combatiente *m*

extant [ˈɛkstənt] o [ɛksˈtænt] *adj* existente

extemporaneous [ɛksˌtɛmpəˈreniˌəs] *adj* sin preparación; (*made for the occasion*) provisional

extempore [ɛksˈtɛmpəri] *adj* improvisado ‖ *adv* improvisadamente

extemporize [ɛksˈtɛmpəˌraɪz] *tr & intr* improvisar

extend [ɛksˈtɛnd] *tr* extender; dar, ofrecer; hacer extensivos (*p.ej., vivos deseos*); prorrogar (*un plazo*) ‖ *intr* extenderse

extended [ɛksˈtɛndɪd] *adj* extenso; prolongado

extension [ɛksˈtɛnʃən] *s* extensión; prolongación

extension ladder *s* escalera extensible

extension table *s* mesa de extensión

extensive [ɛksˈtɛnsɪv] *adj* (*having great extent*) extenso; (*characterized by extension*) extensivo

extent [ɛksˈtɛnt] *s* extensión; **to a certain extent** hasta cierto punto; **to a great extent** en sumo grado; **to the full extent** en toda su extensión

extenuate [ɛksˈtɛnjuˌet] *tr* (*to make seem less serious*) atenuar; (*to underrate*) menospreciar, no dar importancia a

exterior [ɛksˈtɪrɪˌər] *adj & s* exterior *m*

exterminate [ɛksˈtʌrmɪˌnet] *tr* exterminar; (*insects*) desinsectar

external [ɛksˈtʌrnəl] *adj* externo ‖ **externals** *spl* exterioridad

extinct [ɛksˈtɪŋkt] *adj* desaparecido; (*volcano*) extinto

extinguish [ɛksˈtɪŋgwɪʃ] *tr* extinguir

extinguisher [ɛksˈtɪŋgwɪʃər] *s* apagador *m*, extintor *m*

extirpate [ˈɛkstərˌpet] o [ɛksˈtʌrpet] *tr* extirpar

ex•tol [ɛksˈtol] o [ɛksˈtɑl] *v* (*pret & pp* **-tolled;** *ger* **-tolling**) *tr* ensalzar

extort [ɛksˈtɔrt] *tr* obtener por amenazas, fuerza o engaño

extortion [ɛksˈtɔrʃən] *s* extorción

extra [ˈɛkstrə] *adj* extra; (*spare*) de repuesto ‖ *adv* extraordinariamente ‖ *s* (*of a news-*

paper) extra *m*; pieza de repuesto; (*something additional*) extra *m*; (theat) extra *mf*

extract [ˈɛkstrækt] *s* selección; (pharm) extracto ‖ [ɛksˈtrækt] *tr* (*to pull out, remove*) extraer; seleccionar (*pasajes de un libro*); (math) extraer

extraction [ɛksˈtrækʃən] *s* extracción

extracurricular [ˌɛkstrəkəˈrɪkjələr] *adj* extracurricular

extradition [ˌɛkstrəˈdɪʃən] *s* extradición

extra fare *s* recargo de tarifa, tarifa recargada

ex'tra-flat' *adj* extraplano

extragalactic [ˌɛkstrəgəˈlæktɪk] *adj* extragaláctico

extramural [ˌɛkstrəˈmjʊrəl] *adj* extramural

extraneous [ɛksˈtreniˌəs] *adj* ajeno, extraño

extraordinary [ɛksˈtrɔrdɪˌnɛri] o [ˌɛksˈtrɔrdɪˌnɛri] *adj* extraordinario

extrapolate [ɛksˈtræpəˌlet] *tr & intr* extrapolar

extrasensory [ˌɛkstrəˈsɛnsəri] *adj* extrasensorio

extraterrestrial [ˌɛkstrətəˈrɛstrɪ•əl] *adj* extraterrestre

extravagance [ɛksˈtrævəgəns] *s* derroche *m*, prodigalidad, gasto excesivo; (*wildness, folly*) extravagancia

extravagant [ɛksˈtrævəgənt] *adj* derrochador, pródigo, gastador; (*wild, foolish*) extravagante

extreme [ɛksˈtrim] *adj & s* extremo; **in the extreme** en sumo grado; **to go to extremes** excederse, propasarse

extremely [ɛksˈtrimli] *adv* extremadamente, sumamente

extreme unction *s* extremaunción

extremism [ɛksˈtrimɪzəm] *s* extremismo

extremi•ty [ɛksˈtrɛmɪti] *s* (*pl* **-ties**) extremidad; (*great want*) extrema necesidad; **extremities** medidas extremas; (*hands and feet*) extremidades

extricate [ˈɛskstrɪˌket] *tr* desembarazar, desenredar

extrinsic [ɛksˈtrɪnsɪk] *adj* extrínseco

extroversion [ˌɛkstrəˈvʌrʒən] *s* extroversión

extrovert [ˈɛkstrəˌvʌrt] *s* extrovertido

extrude [ɛksˈtrud] *intr* resaltar, sobresalir

exuberant [ɛgˈzubərənt] *adj* exuberante

exude [ɛgˈzud] o [ɛkˈsud] *tr & intr* exudar

exult [ɛgˈzʌlt] *intr* exultar, gloriarse

exultant [ɛgˈzʌltənt] *adj* exultante

eye [aɪ] *s* ojo; (*of hook and eye*) hembra, corcheta; **to catch one's eye** llamar la atención a uno; **to feast one's eyes on** deleitar la vista en; **to lay eyes on** alcanzar a ver; **to make eyes at** hacer guiños a; **to roll one's eyes** poner los ojos en blanco; **to see eye to eye** estar completamente de acuerdo; **to shut one's eyes to** hacer la vista gorda ante; **without batting an eye** sin pestañear, sin inmutarse ‖ *v* (*pret & pp* **eyed;** *ger* **eying** o **eyeing**) *tr* ojear; **to eye up and down** mirar de hito en hito

eye'ball' *s* globo del ojo

eye'bolt' *s* armella, cáncamo

eye'brow' *s* ceja; **to raise one's eyebrows** arquear las cejas

eye′cup′ s ojera, lavaojos m
eyeful [′aɪfʊl] s (coll) buena ojeada
eye′glass′ s (of optical instrument) ocular m; (eyecup) ojera, lavaojos m; **eyeglasses** gafas, anteojos
eye′lash′ s pestaña
eyelet [′aɪlɪt] s ojete m, ojal m; (hole to look through) mirilla
eye′lid′ s párpado
eye of the morning s sol m
eye opener [′opənər] s noticia asombrosa o inesperada; (coll) trago de licor
eye′piece′ s ocular m
eye′shade′ s visera
eye shadow s crema para los párpados; sombra (de ojos)

eye′shot′ s alcance m de la vista
eye′sight′ s vista; (range) alcance m de la vista
eye socket s cuenca del ojo
eye′sore′ s cosa que ofende la vista
eye′strain′ s vista fatigada
eye′-test′ chart s escala tipográfica oftalmométrica, tipo de ensayo, tipo de prueba
eye′tooth′ s (pl **teeth′**) colmillo, diente canino; **to cut one's eyeteeth** (coll) tener el colmillo retorcido; **to give one's eyeteeth for** (coll) dar los ojos de la cara por
eye′wash′ s colirio; (slang) halago para engañar
eye′wit′ness s testigo ocular, testigo presencial
ey•rie o **ey•ry** [′ɛri] s (pl **-ries**) nido de águilas, nido de aves de rapiña; (fig) altura, morada elevada

F

F, f [ɛf] sexta letra del alfabeto inglés
f. abbr **feminine, folio**
F. abbr **Fahrenheit, Friday**
fable [′febəl] s fábula
fabric [′fæbrɪk] s tejido; textura; (structure) fábrica
fabricate [′fæbrɪ, ket] tr fabricar
fabrication [,fæbrɪ′keʃən] s fabricación; mentira
fabulous [′fæbjələs] adj fabuloso
façade [fə′sɑd] s fachada
face [fes] s cara, rostro; (of cloth) haz f; (of earth) faz f; (grimace) mueca; (of watch) esfera, muestra; (impudence) descaro; **in the face of** en presencia de; **to keep a straight face** contener la risa; **to lose face** desprestigiarse; **to save face** salvar las apariencias; **to show one's face** dejarse ver ‖ tr volver la cara hacia; arrostrar; revestir (un muro); forrar (un vestido); **facing** cara a ‖ intr — **to face about** volver la mirada; dar media vuelta; cambiar de opinión; **to face on** dar a o sobre; **to face up to** encararse con
face card s figura, naipe m de figura
face lifting s cirugía estética
face powder s polvos de tocador
facet [′fæsɪt] s faceta
facial [′feʃəl] adj facial ‖ s masaje m facial
facilitate [fə′sɪlɪ,tet] tr facilitar
facili•ty [fə′sɪlɪti] s (pl **-ties**) facilidad
facing [′fesɪŋ] s revestimiento, paramento
facsimile [fæk′sɪmɪli] s facsímile m ‖ tr facsimilar
fact [fækt] s hecho; **in fact** en realidad; **the fact is that** ello es que
faction [′fækʃən] s facción; discordia
factional [′fækʃənəl] adj faccionario
factionalism [′fækʃənə,lɪzəm] s parcialidad, partidismo

factor [′fæktər] s factor m ‖ tr descomponer en factores
facto•ry [′fæktəri] s (pl **-ries**) fábrica
factual [′fæktʃʊ•əl] adj verdadero, objetivo
facul•ty [′fækəlti] s (pl **-ties**) facultad
fad [fæd] s afición pasajera, moda pasajera
fade [fed] tr desteñir ‖ intr desteñir, desteñirse; apagarse (un sonido); (rad) desvanecerse
fade′out′ s desaparición gradual; (rad) desvanecimiento
fag [fæg] s (drudge) yunque m; (coll) cigarrillo ‖ tr—**to fag out** cansar
fagot [′fægət] s haz m de leña
fail [fel] s—**without fail** sin falta ‖ tr faltar a; reprobar, suspender (a un alumno); salir mal en (un examen) ‖ intr malograrse, fracasar; salir mal (un alumno); fallar (un motor); (com) quebrar, hacer bancarrota; **to fail to** dejar de
failure [′feljər] s malogro, fracaso, mal éxito; (student) perdigón m; (com) quiebra
faint [fent] adj débil; **to feel faint** sentirse desfallecido ‖ s desmayo ‖ intr desmayarse
faint-hearted [′fent′hɑrtɪd] adj cobarde, tímido, apocado
fair [fer] adj justo, imparcial; regular, ordinario; favorable, propicio; (hair) rubio; (complexion) blanco; (sky) despejado; (weather) bueno, bonancible ‖ adv imparcialmente; **to play fair** jugar limpio ‖ s (exhibition) feria; (carnival) quermese m, verbena
fair′ground′ s real m, campo de una feria
fairly [′ferli] adv justamente; bastante
fair-minded [′fer′maɪndɪd] adj justo, imparcial
fairness [′fernɪs] s justicia, imparcialidad; (of weather) serenidad; (of complexion) blancura
fair play s juego limpio, limpieza

fair sex s bello sexo
fair to middling adj bastante bueno, mediano
fair'weath'er adj —**a fair-weather friend** amigo del buen viento
fair•y ['fɛri] adj feérico ‖ s (pl -ies) hada
fairy godmother s hada madrina
fair'y•land' s tierra de las hadas
fairy ring s corro de brujas
fairy tale s cuento de hadas; (fig) bella poesía
faith [feθ] s fe f; **to break faith with** faltar a la palabra dada a; **to keep faith with** cumplir la palabra dada a; **to pin one's faith on** tener puesta su esperanza en; **upon my faith!** ¡a fe mía!
faithful ['feθfəl] adj fiel, leal ‖ **the faithful** los fieles
faithless ['feθlɪs] adj infiel, desleal
fake [fek] adj (coll) falso, fingido ‖ s impostura, patraña; (person) farsante mf ‖ tr & intr falsificar, fingir
faker ['fekər] s (coll) impostor m, patrañero; (peddler) (coll) buhonero
falcon ['fɔkən] o ['fɔlkən] s halcón m
falconer ['fɔkənər] o ['fɔlkənər] s cetrero, halconero
falconry ['fɔkənri] o ['fɔlkənri] s cetrería, halconería
fall [fɔl] adj otoñal ‖ s caída; (of water) catarata, salto de agua; (of prices) baja; (autumn) otoño; **falls** catarata, caída de agua ‖ v (pret **fell** [fɛl]; pp **fallen** ['fɔlən]) intr caer, caerse; **to fall apart** caerse a pedazos; **to fall back** (mil) replegarse; **to fall behind** quedarse atrás; **to fall down** caerse; **to fall due** vencer (una letra); **to fall flat** caer tendido; no tener éxito; **to fall for** (slang) ser engañado por; (slang) enamorarse de; **to fall in** desplomarse (un techo); ponerse de acuerdo; **to fall in with** trabar amistades con; ponerse de acuerdo con; **to fall off** caer de; disminuir; **to fall out** desavenirse; **to fall out of** caerse de; **to fall out with** esquinarse con; **to fall over** caerse; (coll) adular, halagar; **to fall through** fracasar, malograrse; **to fall to** recaer (la herencia, la elección) en; **to fall under** estar comprendido en
fallacious [fə'leʃəs] adj erróneo, engañoso
falla•cy ['fæləsi] s (pl -cies) error m, equivocación
fall guy s (slang) cabeza de turco
fallible ['fælɪbəl] adj falible
falling star s estrella fugaz
fall'out' s caída radiactiva, precipitación radiactiva
fallout shelter s refugio antiatómico
fallow ['fælo] adj barbechado; **to lie fallow** estar en barbecho (tierra labrantía); (fig) quedar sin emplear, quedar sin ejecutar (una cosa provechosa) ‖ s barbecho ‖ tr barbechar
false [fɔls] adj falso; (hair, teeth, etc.) postizo ‖ adv falsamente; **to play false** traicionar
false colors spl pretextos falsos

false face s mascarilla; (ugly false face) carantamaula
false-hearted ['fɔls'hɑrtɪd] adj pérfido
falsehood ['fɔls•hud] s falsedad
false pretenses spl impostura, falsas apariencias
false return s declaración falsa
falset•to [fɔl'sɛto] s (pl -tos) (voice) falsete m; (person) falsetista m
falsi•fy ['fɔlsɪ,faɪ] v (pret & pp -fied) tr falsificar; (to disprove) refutar ‖ intr falsificar; mentir
falsi•ty ['fɔlsɪti] s (pl -ties) falsedad
falter ['fɔltər] s vacilación; (in speech) balbuceo ‖ intr vacilar; balbucear
fame [fem] s fama
famed [femd] adj afamado
familiar [fə'mɪljər] adj familiar; conocido; común; **familiar with** familiarizado con
familiari•ty [fə,mɪlɪ'ærɪti] s (pl -ties) familiaridad; conocimiento
familiarize [fə'mɪljə,raɪz] tr familiarizar
fami•ly ['fæmɪli] adj familiar; **in the family way** (coll) en estado de buena esperanza ‖ s (pl -lies) familia
family man s padre m de familia; hombre casero
family name s apellido
family physician s médico de cabecera
family tree s árbol genealógico
famish ['fæmɪʃ] tr & intr hambrear
famished ['fæmɪʃt] adj famélico
famous ['feməs] adj famoso; (notable, excellent) (coll) famoso
fan [fæn] s abanico; ventilador m; (slang) hincha mf, aficionado ‖ v (pret & pp **fanned**; ger **fanning**) tr abanicar; (to winnow) aventar; ahuyentar con abanico; avivar (el fuego); excitar (las pasiones); (slang) azotar ‖ intr abanicarse; **to fan out** salir (un camino) en todas direcciones
fanatic [fə'nætɪk] adj & s fanático
fanatical [fə'nætɪkəl] adj fanático
fanaticism [fə'nætɪ,sɪzəm] s fanatismo
fancied ['fænsid] adj imaginario
fancier ['fænsɪ•ər] s aficionado; visionario; (of animals) criador aficionado
fanciful ['fænsɪfəl] adj fantástico, extravagante; imaginativo
fan•cy ['fænsi] adj (comp -cier; super -ciest) de fantasía, de imitación; fino, de lujo, precioso; ornamental; primoroso; fantástico, extravagante ‖ s (pl -cies) fantasía; afición, gusto; **to take a fancy to** aficionarse a, prendarse de ‖ v (pret & pp -cied) tr imaginar
fancy ball s baile m de trajes
fancy dive s salto ornamental
fancy dress s traje m de fantasía
fancy foods spl comestibles mpl de lujo
fan'cy-free' adj libre del poder del amor
fancy jewelry s joyas de fantasía
fancy skating s patinaje m de fantasía
fan'cy-work' s (sew) labor f
fanfare ['fænfɛr] s fanfarria
fang [fæŋ] s colmillo; (of reptile) diente m
fan'light' s abanico

fantastic(al) [fæn'tæstɪk(əl)] *adj* fantástico
fanta•sy ['fæntəsi] *s* (*pl* **-sies**) fantasía
far [fɑr] *adj* lejano; **on the far side of** del otro lado de ‖ *adv* lejos; **as far as** hasta; en cuanto; **as far as I am concerned** por lo que a mí me toca; **as far as I know** que yo sepa; **by far** con mucho; **far and near** por todas partes; **far away** muy lejos; **far be it from me** no lo permita Dios; **far better** mucho mejor; **far different** muy diferente; **far from** lejos de; **far from it** ni con mucho; **far into** hasta muy adentro de; hasta muy tarde de; **far more** mucho más; **far off** a gran distancia; **how far** cuán lejos; **how far is it?** ¿cuánto hay de aquí?; **in so far as** en cuanto; **thus far** hasta ahora; **thus far this year** en lo que va del año; **to go far towards** contribuir mucho a
faraway ['fɑrə,we] *adj* lejano, distante; abstraído, preocupado
farce [fɑrs] *s* farsa; (*ridiculous act*) papelada
farcical ['fɑrsɪkəl] *adj* ridículo
fare [fɛr] *s* pasaje *m;* pasajero; alimento; comida; **to collect fares** cobrar el pasaje ‖ *intr* pasarlo, p.ej., **how did you fare?** ¿cómo lo pasó Vd.?
Far East *s* Extremo Oriente, Lejano Oriente
fare'well' *s* despedida; **to bid farewell to** o **to take farewell of** despedirse de ‖ *interj* ¡adiós!
far•fetched ['fɑr'fɛtʃt] *adj* traído por los pelos
far-flung ['fɑr'flʌŋ] *adj* de gran alcance, vasto
farm [fɑrm] *adj* agrícola; agropecuario ‖ *s* granja; terreno agrícola ‖ *tr* cultivar, labrar (*la tierra*) ‖ *intr* cultivar la tierra y criar animales
farmer ['fɑrmər] *s* granjero; agricultor *m,* labrador *m*
farm hand *s* peón *m,* mozo de granja
farm'house' *s* alquería, cortijo
farming ['fɑrmɪŋ] *s* agricultura, labranza
farm'yard' *s* corral *m* de granja
far'-off' *adj* lejano, distante
far-reaching ['fɑr'ritʃɪŋ] *adj* de mucho alcance
far-sighted ['fɑr'saɪtɪd] *adj* longividente; precavido; présbita
farther ['fɑrðər] *adj* más lejano; adicional ‖ *adv* más lejos, más allá; además, también; **farther on** más adelante
farthest ['fɑrðɪst] *adj* (el) más lejano; último ‖ *adv* más lejos; más
farthing ['fɑrðɪŋ] *s* (Brit) cuarto de penique
Far West *s* (U.S.A.) Lejano Oeste
fascinate ['fæsɪ,net] *tr* fascinar
fascinating ['fæsɪ,netɪŋ] *adj* fascinante, cautivador
fascism ['fæʃɪzəm] *s* fascismo
fascist ['fæʃɪst] *adj* & *s* fascista *mf*
fashion ['fæʃən] *s* moda, boga; estilo, manera; alta sociedad; **after a fashion** en cierto modo; **in fashion** de moda; **out of fashion** fuera de moda; **to go out of fashion** pasar de moda ‖ *tr* labrar, forjar
fashion designing *s* alta costura

fashion plate *s* figurín *m;* (*person*) (coll) figurín *m,* elegante *mf;* **to be a fashion plate** (coll) ir hecho un maniquí
fashion show *s* desfile *m* de modas
fast [fæst] *adj* rápido, veloz; (*clock*) adelantado; fijado; disipado; (*friend*) fiel ‖ *adv* aprisa, rápidamente; firmemente; (*asleep*) profundamente; **to hold fast** mantenerse firme; **to live fast** vivir de una manera disipada ‖ *s* ayuno; **to break one's fast** romper el ayuno ‖ *intr* ayunar
fast day *s* día *m* de ayuno
fasten ['fæsən] *tr* fijar; atar; abrochar; cerrar con llave; (*one's belt*) ajustarse; (*blame*) aplicar ‖ *intr* fijarse
fastener ['fæsənər] *s* asilla; (*snap, clasp*) cierre *m;* (*for papers*) sujetapapeles *m*
fast'-food' restaurant *s* rotisería
fast forward *s* (mach, mov) avance rápido
fastidious [fæs'tɪdɪ•əs] *adj* esquilmoso, quisquilloso, descontentadizo
fasting ['fæstɪŋ] *s* ayuno
fat [fæt] *adj* (*comp* **fatter;** *super* **fattest**) gordo; poderoso; opulento; (*profitable*) pingüe; (*spark*) caliente; **to get fat** engordar ‖ *s* grasa; (*suet*) gordo, sebo
fatal ['fetəl] *adj* fatal
fatalism ['fetə,lɪzəm] *s* fatalismo
fatalist ['fetəlɪst] *s* fatalista *mf*
fatali•ty [fə'tælɪti] *s* (*pl* **-ties**) fatalidad; (*in accidents, war, etc.*) muerte *f*
fate [fet] *s* sino, hado; **the Fates** las Parcas ‖ *tr* condenar, predestinar
fated ['fetɪd] *adj* hadado, predestinado
fateful ['fetfəl] *adj* fatídico; fatal
fat'head' *s* (coll) tronco, estúpido
father ['fɑðər] *s* padre *m;* (*an elderly man*) (coll) tío ‖ *tr* servir de padre a; engendrar; inventar
fatherhood ['fɑðər,hʊd] *s* paternidad
fa'ther-in-law' *s* (*pl* **fathers-in-law**) suegro
fa'ther•land' *s* patria
fatherless ['fɑðərlɪs] *adj* huérfano de padre, sin padre
fatherly ['fɑðərli] *adj* paternal
Father's Day *s* día *m* del padre
Father Time *s* el Tiempo
fathom ['fæðəm] *s* braza ‖ *tr* sondear; profundizar
fathomless ['fæðəmlɪs] *adj* insondable
fatigue [fə'tig] *s* fatiga; (mil) faena ‖ *tr* fatigar, cansar
fatigue clothes *spl* (mil) traje *m* de faena
fatigue duty *s* faena
fatten ['fætən] *tr* & *intr* engordar
fat•ty ['fæti] *adj* (*comp* **-tier;** *super* **-tiest**) graso; (pathol) grasoso; (*chubby*) (coll) gordiflón ‖ *s* (*pl* **-ties**) (coll) gordiflón *m*
fatuous ['fætʃʊ•əs] *adj* fatuo; irreal, ilusivo
faucet ['fɔsɪt] *s* grifo
fault [fɔlt] *s* (*misdeed, blame*) culpa; (*defect*) falta; (geol) falla; (sport) falta; **it's your fault** Vd. tiene la culpa; **to a fault** excesivamente; **to find fault with** culpar, echar la culpa a; hallar defecto en
fault'find'er *s* criticón *m,* reparón *m*

fault′find′ing *adj* criticón, reparón ‖ *s* manía de criticar

faultless [ˈfɔltlɪs] *adj* perfecto, impecable

fault•y [ˈfɔlti] *adj* (*comp* **-ier;** *super* **-iest**) defectuoso, imperfecto

faun [fɔn] *s* fauno

fauna [ˈfɔnə] *s* fauna

favor [ˈfevər] *s* favor *m;* (*letter*) atenta, grata; **do me the favor to** hágame Vd. el favor de; **by your favor** con permiso de Vd.; **favors** regalos de fiesta, objetos de cotillón; **to be in favor with** disfrutar del favor de; **to be out of favor** caer en desgracia ‖ *tr* favorecer; (*coll*) parecerse a

favorable [ˈfevərəbəl] *adj* favorable

favorite [ˈfevərɪt] *adj & s* favorito

favoritism [ˈfevərɪˌtɪzəm] *s* favoritismo

fawn [fɔn] *s* cervato ‖ *intr*—**to fawn on** adular servilmente; hacer fiestas a

faze [fez] *tr* (coll) molestar, desanimar

FBI [ˌɛfˌbiˈaɪ] *s* (letterword) **Federal Bureau of Investigation**

fear [fɪr] *s* miedo; **for fear of** por miedo de, por temor de; **for fear that** por miedo (de) que; **no fear** no hay peligro; **to be in fear of** tener miedo de ‖ *tr & intr* temer

fearful [ˈfɪrfəl] *adj* medroso; (coll) enorme, muy malo

fearless [ˈfɪrlɪs] *adj* arrojado, intrépido

feasible [ˈfizɪbəl] *adj* factible, viable

feast [fist] *s* fiesta; (*sumptuous meal*) festín *m*, banquete *m* ‖ *tr & intr* banquetear; **to feast on** regalarse con

feat [fit] *s* hazaña, proeza

feather [ˈfɛðər] *s* pluma; (*plume; arrogance*) penacho; clase *f*, género; **in fine feather** de buen humor; en buena salud ‖ *tr* emplumar; (*carp*) machihembrar; **to feather one's nest** hacer todo para enriquecerse

feather bed *s* colchón *m* de plumas; (*comfortable situation*) lecho de plumas

feath′er•bed′ding *s* empleo de más obreros de lo necesario (*exigido por los sindicatos*)

feath′er•brain′ *s* cascabelero

feath′er•edge′ *s* (*of board*) bisel *m;* (*of sharpened tool*) filván *m*

feathery [ˈfɛðərɪ] *adj* plumoso

feature [ˈfitʃər] *s* facción; característica, rasgo distintivo; película principal; artículo principal; **features** facciones ‖ *tr* delinear; ofrecer como cosa principal; (coll) destacar, hacer resaltar

feature writer *s* articulista *mf*

February [ˈfɛbruˌɛri] *s* febrero

feces [ˈfisiz] *spl* heces *fpl*, excremento

feckless [ˈfɛklɪs] *adj* abatido, sin valor; débil

federal [ˈfɛdərəl] *adj & s* federal *mf*

federate [ˈfɛdəˌret] *adj* federado ‖ *tr* federar ‖ *intr* federarse

federation [ˌfɛdəˈreʃən] *s* federación

fedora [fɪˈdorə] *s* sombrero de fieltro suave con ala vuelta

fed up [fɛd] *adj* harto; **to get fed up with** desenamorarse de

fee [fi] *s* honorarios; (*for admission, tuition, etc.*) cuota, precio; (*tip*) propina ‖ *tr* pagar; dar propina a

feeble [ˈfibəl] *adj* débil; caedizo

feeble-minded [ˈfibəlˈmaɪndɪd] *adj* imbécil; irresoluto, vacilante

feed [fid] *s* alimento, comida; (mach) dispositivo de alimentación ‖ *v* (*pret & pp* **fed** [fɛd]) *tr* alimentar ‖ *intr* alimentarse

feed′back′ *s* regeneración, realimentación, retroalimentación; comentarios *fpl;* informaciones *fpl;* comentario privado y confidencial

feed bag *s* cebadera, morral *m*

feeder industries *spl* subsidiarias *fpl*

feed pump *s* bomba de alimentación

feed trough *s* comedero

feed wire *s* (elec) conductor *m* de alimentación

feel [fil] *s* sensación; (*sense of what is right*) tino ‖ *v* (*pret & pp* **felt** [fɛlt]) *tr* sentir; (*e.g., with the hands*) palpar, tentar; tomar (*el pulso*); tantear (*el camino*) ‖ *intr* (*sick, tired, etc.*) sentirse; palpar; **to feel bad** sentirse mal; condolerse; **to feel cheap** avergonzarse; **to feel comfortable** sentirse a gusto; **to feel for** buscar tentando; condolerse de; **to feel like** tener ganas de; **to feel safe** sentirse a salvo; **to feel sorry** sentir; arrepentirse; **to feel sorry for** compadecer; arrepentirse de

feeler [ˈfilər] *s* (*something said to draw someone out*) buscapié *m*, tranquila; **feelers** (*of insect*) anténulas, palpos; (*of mollusk*) tentáculos

feeling [ˈfilɪŋ] *s* (*with senses*) sensación; (*impression, emotion*) sentimiento; presentimiento; parecer *m*

feign [fen] *tr* aparentar, fingir ‖ *intr* fingir; **to feign to be** fingirse

feint [fent] *s* (*threat*) finta; (*of fencer*) pase *m*, treta ‖ *intr* hacer una finta

feldspar [ˈfɛldˌspɑr] *s* feldespato

felicitate [fəˈlɪsɪˌtet] *tr* felicitar

felicitous [fəˈlɪsɪtəs] *adj* (*opportune*) feliz; elocuente

fell [fɛl] *adj* cruel, feroz, mortal ‖ *tr* talar (*árboles*)

felloe [ˈfɛlo] *s* aro de la rueda; (*part of this*) pina

fellow [ˈfɛlo] *s* (coll) mozo, tipo, sujeto; (coll) pretendiente *m;* prójimo; (*of a society*) socio, miembro; (*holder of fellowship*) pensionista *mf*

fellow being *s* prójimo

fellow citizen *s* conciudadano

fellow countryman *s* compatriota *mf*

fellow man *s* prójimo

fellow member *s* consocio

fellowship [ˈfɛloˌʃɪp] *s* compañerismo; (*for study*) pensión

fellow traveler *s* compañero de viaje

felon [ˈfɛlən] *s* delincuente *mf* de mayor cuantía; (pathol) panadizo

felo•ny [ˈfɛləni] *s* (*pl* **-nies**) delito de mayor cuantía; **to compound a felony** aceptar dinero para no procesar

felt [fɛlt] *s* fieltro

felt′-tipped′ pen *s* rotulador *m;* plumón *m* (Mex)

fa
fe

female ['fimel] adj (sex) femenino; (animal, plant, piece of a device) hembra ‖ s hembra

feminine ['fɛmɪnɪn] adj & s femenino

feminism ['fɛmɪˌnɪzəm] s feminismo

fen [fɛn] s pantano

fence [fɛns] s cerca, cercado; (for stolen goods) alcahuete m; receptador; (of a saw) guía; **on the fence** (coll) indeciso ‖ tr cercar ‖ intr esgrimir

fencing ['fɛnsɪŋ] s (art) esgrima; (act) esgrimidura

fencing academy s escuela de esgrima

fend [fɛnd] tr — **to fend off** apartar, resguardarse de ‖ intr — **to fend for oneself** (coll) tirar por su lado

fender ['fɛndər] s (mudguard) guardafango, guardabarros m; (of locomotive) quitapiedras m; (of trolley car) salvavidas m; (of fireplace) guardafuego

fennel ['fɛnəl] s hinojo

ferment ['fʌrmɛnt] s fermento; fermentación ‖ [fər'mɛnt] tr & intr fermentar

fern [fʌrn] s helecho

ferocious [fə'roʃəs] adj feroz

feroci•ty [fə'rɑsɪti] s (pl -ties) ferocidad

ferret ['fɛrɪt] s hurón m ‖ tr — **to ferret out** huronear ‖ intr huronear

Ferris wheel ['fɛrɪs] s rueda de feria, noria

fer•ry ['fɛri] s (pl -ries) bote m de paso, ferry-boat m ‖ v (pret & pp -ried) tr pasar (viajeros, mercancías) a través del río ‖ intr cruzar el río en barco

fer'ry•boat' s bote m de paso, ferry-boat m

fertile ['fʌrtɪl] adj fértil

fertilize ['fʌrtɪˌlaɪz] tr abonar, fertilizar; (to impregnate) fecundar

fervid ['fʌrvɪd] adj férvido, vehemente

fervor ['fʌrvər] s fervor m

fervent ['fʌrvənt] adj ferviente, fervoroso

fester ['fɛstər] s úlcera ‖ tr enconar ‖ intr enconarse (una herida; el ánimo de uno)

festival ['fɛstɪvəl] adj festivo ‖ s fiesta; (of music) festival m

festive ['fɛstɪv] adj festivo

festivi•ty [fɛs'tɪvɪti] s (pl -ties) festividad

festoon [fɛs'tun] s festón m ‖ tr festonear

fetch [fɛtʃ] tr ir por, hacer venir, traer; venderse a, venderse por

fetching ['fɛtʃɪŋ] adj (coll) encantador, atractivo

fete [fet] s fiesta ‖ tr festejar

fetid ['fɛtɪd] o ['fitɪd] adj fétido

fetish ['fitɪʃ] o ['fɛtɪʃ] s fetiche m

fetlock ['fɛtlɑk] s espolón m; (tuft of hair) cerneja

fetter ['fɛtər] s grillete m, grillo ‖ tr engrillar; impedir

fettle ['fɛtəl] s estado, condición; **in fine fettle** en buena condición

fetus ['fitəs] s feto

feud [fjud] s odio hereditario, enemistad de larga duración

feudal ['fjudəl] adj feudal

feudalism ['fjudəˌlɪzəm] s feudalismo

fever ['fivər] s fiebre f, calentura

fever blister s escupidura, fuegos en los labios

feverish ['fivərɪʃ] adj febril, calenturiento

few [fju] adj & pron pocos, no muchos; **a few** unos pocos, unos cuantos; **quite a few** muchos

fiancé [ˌfiɑn'se] s novio, prometido; novillo (Mex, P-R)

fiancée [ˌfiɑn'se] s novia, prometida

fias•co [fɪ'æsko] s (pl -cos o -coes) fiasco

fib [fɪb] s mentirilla ‖ v (pret & pp fibbed; ger fibbing) intr decir mentirillas, macanear

fiber ['faɪbər] s fibra; carácter m, índole f

fibrous ['faɪbrəs] adj fibroso

fickle ['fɪkəl] adj inconstante, veleidoso

fiction ['fɪkʃən] s (invention) ficción; (branch of literature) novelística; **pure fiction!** ¡puro cuento!

fictional ['fɪkʃənəl] adj novelesco

fictionalize ['fɪkʃənəˌlaɪz] tr novelizar

fictitious ['fɪk'tɪʃəs] adj ficticio

fiddle ['fɪdəl] s violín m ‖ tr tocar (un aire) con el violín; **to fiddle away** (coll) malgastar ‖ intr tocar el violín; **to fiddle with** manosear

fiddler ['fɪdlər] s (coll) violinista mf

fiddling ['fɪdlɪŋ] adj (coll) despreciable, insignificante

fideli•ty [fɪ'dɛlɪti] s (pl -ties) fidelidad

fidget ['fɪdʒɪt] intr agitarse, menearse; **to fidget with** manosear

fidgety ['fɪdʒɪti] adj inquieto, nervioso

fiduciar•y [fɪ'djuʃɪˌɛri] adj fiduciario ‖ s (pl -ies) fiduciario

fie [faɪ] interj ¡qué vergüenza!

fief [fif] s feudo

field [fild] adj (mil) de campaña ‖ s campo; (sown with grain) sembrado; (baseball) jardín m; (elec) campo magnético; (of motor or dynamo) (elec) inductor m

fielder ['fildər] s (baseball) jardinero

field glasses spl gemelos de campo

field hockey s hockey m sobre hierba

field magnet s imán m inductor

field marshal s (mil) mariscal m de campo

field'piece' s cañón m de campaña

fiend [find] s diablo; (person) fiera; **to be a fiend for** ser una fiera para

fiendish ['findɪʃ] adj diabólico

fierce [fɪrs] adj feroz, fiero; (wind) furioso; (coll) muy malo

fierceness ['fɪrsnɪs] s ferocidad, fiereza; furia

fier•y ['faɪri] adj (comp -ier; super -iest) ardiente, caliente; brioso

fife [faɪf] s pífano

fifteen ['fɪf'tin] adj, pron & s quince m

fifteenth ['fɪf'tinθ] adj & s (in a series) decimoquinto; (part) quinzavo ‖ s (in dates) quince m

fifth [fɪfθ] adj & s quinto ‖ s (in dates) cinco

fifth column s quinta columna

fifth columnist s quintacolumnista mf

fiftieth ['fɪftɪ•θ] adj & s (in a series) quincuagésimo; (part) cincuentavo

fif•ty ['fɪfti] adj & pron cincuenta ‖ s (pl -ties) cincuenta m

fif′ty-fif′ty *adv* — **to go fifty-fifty** (coll) ir a medias

fig. *abbr* **figure, figuratively**

fig [fɪg] *s* higo, breva; (*tree*) higuera; (*merest trifle*) bledo

fight [faɪt] *s* lucha, pelea; ánimo, brío; **to pick a fight with** meterse con, buscar la lengua a ‖ *tr* luchar con; dar (*batalla*); lidiar (*al toro*) ‖ *intr* luchar, pelear; **to fight shy of** tratar de evitar

fighter [′faɪtər] *s* luchador *m*, peleador *m*; (*warrior*) combatiente *m*; (*game person*) porfiador *m*; (aer) avión *m* de combate, caza *m*

fig leaf *s* hoja de higuera; (*on statues*) hoja de parra

figment [′fɪgmənt] *s* ficción, invención

figurative [′fɪgjərətɪv] *adj* figurado; (*representing by a likeness*) figurativo

figure [′fɪgjər] *s* figura; (*bodily form*) talle *m*; precio; **to be good at figures** ser listo en aritmética; **to cut a figure** hacer figura; **to have a good figure** tener buen tipo; **to keep one's figure** conservar la línea ‖ *tr* adornar con figuras; figurarse, imaginar; suponer, calcular; **to figure out** descifrar ‖ *intr* figurar; **to figure on** contar con

fig′ure•head′ *s* (naut) figurón *m* de proa, mascarón *m* de proa; (*straw man*) testaferro

figure of speech *s* figura retórica

figure skating *s* patinaje artístico

figurine [,fɪgjə′rin] *s* figurilla, figurina

filament [′fɪləmənt] *s* filamento

filch [fɪltʃ] *tr* birlar, ratear

file [faɪl] *s* fila, hilera; (*tool*) lima; (*collection of papers*) archivo; (*cabinet*) archivador *m*, fichero ‖ *tr* poner en fila; limar; archivar, clasificar; anotar ‖ *intr* desfilar; **to file for** solicitar

file case *s* fichero

file clerk *s* fichador *m*

filet [fɪ′le] o [′faɪl] *s* filete *m* ‖ *tr* cortar en filetes

filial [′fɪlɪ•əl] o [′fɪljəl] *adj* filial

filiation [,fɪlɪ′eʃən] *s* filiación

filibuster [′fɪlɪ,bʌstər] *s* obstrucción (*de la aprobación de una ley*); obstruccionista *mf*; (*buccaneer*) filibustero ‖ *tr* obstruir (*la aprobación de una ley*)

filigree [′fɪlɪ,gri] *adj* afiligranado ‖ *s* filigrana ‖ *tr* afiligranar

filing [′faɪlɪŋ] *s* (*of documents*) clasificación; limadura; **filings** limadura, limalla

filing cabinet *s* archivador *m*, clasificador *m*

filing card *s* ficha

Filipi•no [,fɪlɪ′pino] *adj* filipino ‖ *s* (*pl* **-nos**) filipino

fill [fɪl] *s* (*sufficiency*) hartazgo; (*place filled with earth*) terraplén *m*; **to have** o **get one's fill of** darse un hartazgo de ‖ *tr* llenar, rellenar; despachar (*un pedido*); tapar (*un agujero*); empastar (*un diente*); inflar (*un neumático*); llenar, ocupar (*un puesto*); colmar (*lagunas*); **to fill out** llenar (*un formulario*) ‖ *intr* llenarse; rellenarse; **to fill in** hacer de suplente; **to fill up** ahogarse de emoción

filler [′fɪlər] *s* relleno; (*of cigar*) tripa; *sizing* aparejo; (*in a writing*) relleno

fillet [′fɪlɪt] *s* cinta, tira; (*for hair*) prendedero; (archit, bb) filete *m* ‖ *tr* filetear [′faɪle] o [′fɪlɪt] *s* (*of meat or fish*) filete *m* ‖ *tr* cortar en filetes

filling [′fɪlɪŋ] *s* (*of a tooth*) empaste *m*; (*e.g., of a turkey*) relleno; (*of cigar*) tripa

filling station *s* estación gasolinera

fillip [′fɪlɪp] *s* aguijón *m*, estímulo; (*with finger*) capirotazo

fil•ly [′fɪli] *s* (*pl* **-lies**) potra; (coll) muchacha retozona

film [fɪlm] *s* película; (mov) película, film *m*; (phot) película ‖ *tr* filmar

film library *s* cinemateca

film star *s* estrella de la pantalla

film strip *s* tira proyectable

film•y [′fɪlmi] *adj* (*comp* **-ier;** *super* **-iest**) delgadísimo, diáfano, sutil

filter [′fɪltər] *s* filtro ‖ *tr* filtrar ‖ *intr* filtrarse

filtering [′fɪltərɪŋ] *s* filtración

filter paper *s* papel *m* filtrante

filter tip *s* embocadura de filtro

filth [fɪlθ] *s* suciedad, porquería

filth•y [′fɪlθi] *adj* (*comp* **-ier;** *super* **-iest**) sucio, puerco

filthy lucre [′lukər] *s* (coll) el vil metal (*dinero, raíz de muchos males*)

filtrate [′fɪltret] *s* filtrado ‖ *tr* filtrar ‖ *intr* filtrarse

fin. *abbr* **finance**

fin [fɪn] *s* aleta

final [′faɪnəl] *adj* final; (*last in a series*) último; decisivo, terminante ‖ *s* examen *m* final; **finals** (sport) final *f*

finale [fɪ′nɑli] *s* (mus) final *m*

finalist [′faɪnəlɪst] *s* finalista *mf*

finally [′faɪnəli] *adv* finalmente, por último

finance [′faɪnæns] *s* financiación; **finances** finanzas ‖ *tr* financiar

financial [faɪ′nænʃəl] *adj* financiero

financier [,faɪnən′sɪr] *s* financiero

financing [′faɪnænsɪŋ] *s* financiación, financiamiento

finch [fɪntʃ] *s* pinzón *m*

find [faɪnd] *s* hallazgo ‖ *v* (*pret & pp* **found** [faʊnd]) *tr* hallar, encontrar; **to find out** averiguar, darse cuenta de ‖ *intr* (*law*) pronunciar fallo; **to find out about** informarse de

finder [′faɪndər] *s* (*of camera*) visor *m*; (*of microscope*) portaobjeto cuadriculado

finding [′faɪndɪŋ] *s* descubrimiento; (*law*) laudo, fallo

fine [faɪn] *adj* fino; (*weather*) bueno; divertido ‖ *adv* (coll) muy bien; **to feel fine** (coll) sentirse muy bien de salud ‖ *s* multa ‖ *tr* multar

fine arts *spl* bellas artes

fineness *s* fineza; (*of metal*) ley *f*

fine print *s* letra menuda, tipo menudo

finer•y [′faɪnəri] *s* (*pl* **-ies**) adorno, galas, atavíos

fine-spun [′faɪn,spʌn] *adj* estirado en hilo finísimo; (fig) alambicado

fe
fi

finesse [fɪ'nɛs] *s* sutileza; (*in bridge*) impás *m* ‖ *tr* hacer el impás con ‖ *intr* hacer un impás

fine-toothed comb ['faɪn,tuθt] *s* lendrera, peine *m* de púas finas; **to go over with a fine-toothed comb** escudriñar minuciosamente

finger ['fɪŋgər] *s* dedo; **to burn one's fingers** cogerse los dedos; **to put one's finger on the spot** poner el dedo en la llaga; **to slip between the fingers** irse de entre los dedos; **to snap one's fingers at** tratar con desprecio; **to twist around one's little finger** manejar a su gusto ‖ *tr* manosear; (slang) acechar, espiar; (slang) identificar

finger board *s* (*of guitar*) diapasón *m*; (*of piano*) teclado

finger bowl *s* lavadedos *m*, lavafrutas *m*

finger dexterity *s* (mus) dedeo

fingering ['fɪŋgərɪŋ] *s* manoseo; (mus) digitación

fin'ger•nail' *s* uña

fingernail polish *s* esmalte *m* para las uñas

fin'ger•print' *s* huella digital, dactilograma *m* ‖ *tr* tomar las huellas digitales de

finger tip *s* punta del dedo; **to have at one's finger tips** tener en la punta de los dedos, saber al dedillo

finial ['fɪnɪ•əl] *s* florón *m*

finical ['fɪnɪkəl] o **finicky** ['fɪnɪki] *adj* delicado, melindroso

finish ['fɪnɪʃ] *s* acabado; fin *m*, conclusión ‖ *tr* acabar; **to be finished** estar listo ‖ *intr* acabar; **to finish +** *ger* acabar de **+** *inf*; **to finish by +** *ger* acabar por **+** *inf*

finishing nail *s* puntilla francesa

finishing school *s* escuela particular de educación social para señoritas

finishing touch *s* toque *m* final, última mano

finite ['faɪnaɪt] *adj* finito

finite verb *s* forma verbal flexional

Finland ['fɪnlənd] *s* Finlandia

Finlander ['fɪnləndər] *s* finlandés *m*

Finn [fɪn] *s* (*member of a Finnish-speaking group of people*) finés *m*; (*native or inhabitant of Finland*) finlandés *m*

Finnish ['fɪnɪʃ] *adj* finlandés ‖ *s* (*language*) finlandés *m*

fir [fʌr] *s* abeto

fire [faɪr] *s* fuego; (*destructive burning*) incendio; **through fire and water** a trancos y barrancos; **to be on fire** estar ardiendo; **to be under enemy fire** estar expuesto al fuego del enemigo; **to catch fire** encenderse; **to hang fire** estar en suspensión; **to open fire** abrir fuego, romper el fuego; **to set on fire, to set fire to** pegar fuego a; **under fire** bajo el fuego del enemigo; acusado, inculpado ‖ *interj* (mil) ¡fuego! ‖ *tr* encender; calentar (*el horno*); cocer (*ladrillos*); disparar (*un arma de fuego*); pegar (*un tiro*); excitar (*la imaginación*) (coll) despedir (*a un empleado*) ‖ *intr* encenderse; **to fire on** hacer fuego sobre; **to fire up** cargar el horno; calentar el horno

fire alarm *s* alarma de incendios, avisador *m* de incendios; **to sound the fire alarm** tocar a fuego

fire'arm' *s* arma de fuego

fire'ball' *s* bola de fuego; (*lightning*) rayo en bola

fire'bird' *s* cacique veranero

fire'boat' *s* buque *m* con mangueras para incendios

fire'box' *s* caja de fuego, fogón *m*

fire'brand' *s* tizón *m*; (*hothead*) botafuego

fire'break' *s* raya

fire'brick' *s* ladrillo refractario

fire brigade *s* cuerpo de bomberos

fire'bug' *s* (coll) incendiario

fire company *s* cuerpo de bomberos; compañía de seguros

fire'crack'er *s* triquitraque *m*

fire'damp' *s* grisú *m*, mofeta

fire department *s* servicio de bomberos

fire'dog' *s* morillo

fire drill *s* ejercicio para caso de incendio

fire engine *s* coche *m* bomba, bomba de incendios, motobomba

fire escape *s* escalera de salvamento

fire extinguisher *s* extintor *m*, apagafuegos *m*, extinguidor *m*

fire'fly' *s* (*pl* -**flies**) luciérnaga

fire'guard' *s* guardafuego

fire hose *s* manguera para incendios

fire'house' *s* cuartel *m* de bomberos, estación de incendios

fire hydrant *s* boca de incendio

fire insurance *s* seguro contra incendios

fire irons *spl* badil *m* y tenazas

fireless cooker ['faɪrlɪs] *s* cocinilla sin fuego

fire'man' ['faɪrmən] *s* (*pl* -**men** [mən]) (*man who stokes fires*) fogonero; (*man who extinguishes fires*) bombero

fire'place' *s* chimenea, chimenea francesa

fire plug *s* boca de agua

fire power *s* (mil) potencia de fuego

fire'proof' *adj* incombustible; a prueba de incendio ‖ *tr* hacer incombustible

fire sale *s* venta de mercancías averiadas en un incendio

fire screen *s* pantalla de chimenea

fire ship *s* brulote *m*

fire shovel *s* badil *m*

fire'side' *s* hogar *m*

fire'trap' *s* edificio sin medios adecuados de escape en caso de incendio

fire wall *s* cortafuego

fire'ward'en *s* vigía *m* de incendios

fire'wa'ter *s* aguardiente *m*

fire'wood' *s* leña

fire'works' *spl* fuegos artificiales

firing ['faɪrɪŋ] *s* encendimiento; (*of bricks*) cocción; (*of a gun*) disparo; (*of soldiers*) tiroteo; (*of an internal-combustion engine*) encendido; (*of an employee*) (coll) despedida

firing line *s* línea de fuego, frente *m* de batalla

firing order *s* (aut) orden *m* del encendido

firing squad *s* (*for saluting at a burial*) piquete *m* de salvas; (*for executing*) pelotón *m* de fusilamiento, piquete *m* de ejecución

firm [fʌrm] *adj* firme ‖ *s* empresa, casa comercial

firmament ['fʌrməmənt] *s* firmamento

firm name *s* razón *f* social

firmness ['fʌrmnɪs] *s* firmeza

first [fʌrst] *adj* primero ‖ *adv* primero; **first of all** ante todo ‖ *s* primero; (aut) primera (velocidad); (mus) voz *f* principal; **at first** al principio; en primer lugar; **from the first** desde el principio

first aid *s* cura de urgencia, primeros auxilios

first'-aid' kit *s* botiquín *m*, equipo de urgencia

first-aid station *s* puesto de socorro, puesto de primera intención

first'-born' *adj* & *s* primogénito

first'-class' *adj* de primera, de primera clase ‖ *adv* en primera clase

first cousin *s* primo hermano

first draft *s* borrador *m*

first finger *s* dedo índice, dedo mostrador

first floor *s* piso bajo

first fruits *spl* primicia

first lieutenant *s* teniente

firstly ['fʌrstli] *adv* en primer lugar

first mate *s* (naut) piloto

first name *s* nombre *m* de pila

first night *s* (theat) noche *f* de estreno

first'-night'er *s* (theat) estrenista *mf*

first officer *s* (naut) piloto

first quarter *s* cuarto creciente (*de la luna*)

first'-rate' *adj* de primer orden; (coll) excelente ‖ *adv* (coll) muy bien

first'-run' house *s* teatro de estreno

fiscal ['fɪskəl] *adj* (*pertaining to public treasury*) fiscal; económico ‖ *s* (*public prosecutor*) fiscal *m*

fiscal year *s* año económico, ejercicio

fish [fɪʃ] *s* pez *m*; (*that has been caught, that is ready to eat*) pescado; **to be like a fish out of water** estar como gallina en corral ajeno; **to be neither fish nor fowl** no ser carne ni pescado; **to drink like a fish** beber como una topinera, beber como una esponja ‖ *tr* pescar ‖ *intr* pescar; **to fish for compliments** buscar alabanzas; **to go fishing** ir de pesca; **to take fishing** llevar de pesca

fish'bone' *s* espina de pez

fish bowl *s* pecera

fisher ['fɪʃər] *s* pescador *m*; embarcación de pesca; (zool) marta del Canadá

fisher·man ['fɪʃərmən] *s* (*pl* **-men** [mən]) pescador *m*; barco pesquero

fisher·y ['fɪʃəri] *s* (*pl* **-ies**) (*activity*) pesca; (*business*) pesquería; (*grounds*) pesquera

fish glue *s* cola de pescado

fish hawk *s* halieto

fish'hook' *s* anzuelo

fishing ['fɪʃɪŋ] *adj* pesquero ‖ *s* pesca

fishing ground *s* pesquería, pesquera

fishing reel *s* carrete *m*

fishing rod *s* caña de pescar

fishing tackle *s* aparejo de pescar, avíos de pescar

fishing torch *s* candelero

fish line *s* sedal *m*

fish market *s* pescadería

fish'plate' (rr) eclisa

fish'pool' *s* piscina

fish spear *s* fisga

fish story *s* (coll) andaluzada, patraña; **to tell fish stories** (coll) mentir por la barba

fish'tail' *s* (aer) coleadura ‖ *intr* (aer) colear

fish'wife' *s* (*pl* **-wives** [,waɪvz]) pescadera; (*foul-mouthed woman*) verdulera

fish'worm' *s* lombriz *f* de tierra (*cebo para pescar*)

fish·y ['fɪʃi] *adj* (*comp* **-ier**; *super* **-iest**) que huele o sabe a pescado; (coll) dudoso, inverosímil

fission ['fɪʃən] *s* (biol) escisión; (phys) fisión

fissionable ['fɪʃənəbəl] *adj* fisionable; físil

fissure ['fɪʃər] *s* hendidura, grieta; (anat, min) fisura

fist [fɪst] *s* puño; (typ) manecilla; **to shake one's fist at** amenazar con el puño

fist fight *s* pelea con los puños

fisticuff ['fɪstɪ,kʌf] *s* puñetazo; **fisticuffs** pelea a puñetazos

fit [fɪt] *adj* (*comp* **-fitter**; *super* **-fittest**) apropiado, conveniente; apto; sano; **fit to be tied** (coll) impaciente, encolerizado; **fit to eat** bueno de comer; **to feel fit** gozar de buena salud; **to see fit** juzgar conveniente ‖ *s* ajuste *m*, talle *m*; (*of one piece with another*) encaje *m*; (*of coughing*) acceso, ataque *m*; (*of anger*) arranque *m*, chivo; **by fits and starts** intermitentemente ‖ *v* (*pret* & *pp* **-fitted**; *ger* **fitting**) *tr* ajustar, entallar; cuadrar, sentar; encajar; cuadrar con (*p.ej., las señas de una persona*); equipar, preparar; servir para; estar de acuerdo con (*p.ej., los hechos*); **to fit out** o **up** pertrechar ‖ *intr* ajustar; encajar; sentar; **to fit in** caber en; encajar en

fitful ['fɪtfəl] *adj* caprichoso; intermitente, vacilante

fitness ['fɪtnɪs] *s* conveniencia; aptitud; tempestividad; buena salud

fitter ['fɪtər] *s* ajustador *m*; (*of machinery*) montador *m*; (*of clothing*) probador *m*

fitting ['fɪtɪŋ] *adj* apropiado, conveniente, justo ‖ *s* ajuste *m*; encaje *m*; (*of a garment*) prueba; tubo de ajuste; **fittings** accesorios, avíos; (*iron trimmings*) herraje *m*

fitting room *s* probador *m*

five [faɪv] *adj* & *pron* cinco ‖ *s* cinco; **five o'clock** las cinco

five hundred *adj* & *pron* quinientos ‖ *s* quinientos *m*

five'-year' plan *s* plan *m* quinquenal

fix [fɪks] *s*—**in a tight fix** (coll) en calzas prietas; **to be in a fix** (coll) hallarse en un aprieto; **to get a fix** (*drugs*) picarse, pincharse ‖ *tr* arreglar, componer, reparar; fijar (*una fecha; los cabellos; una imagen fotográfica; los precios; la atención; una hora, una cita*); calar (*la bayoneta*); (coll) desquitarse con; (pol) muñir ‖ *intr* fijarse; **to fix on** decidir, escoger

fixed [fɪkst] *adj* fijo

fixing ['fɪksɪŋ] *adj* fijador ‖ *s* (*fastening*) fijación; (phot) fijado

fixing bath *s* fijador *m*

fixture ['fɪkstʃər] *s* accesorio, artefacto; (*of a lamp*) guarnición; **fixtures** (*e.g., of a store*) instalaciones

fizz [fɪz] *s* ruido sibilante; bebida gaseosa; (Brit) champaña ‖ *intr* hacer un ruido sibilante

fizzle ['fɪzəl] *s* (coll) fracaso ‖ *intr* chisporrotear débilmente; (coll) fracasar

fl. *abbr* **flourished, fluid**

flabbergast ['flæbər,gæst] *tr* (coll) dejar sin habla, dejar estupefacto

flab·by ['flæbi] *adj* (*comp* **-bier;** *super* **-biest**) flojo, lacio

flag [flæg] *s* bandera ‖ *v* (*pret & pp* **flagged;** *ger* **flagging**) *tr* hacer señal a (*una persona*) con una bandera; hacer señal de parada a (*un tren*) ‖ *intr* aflojar, flaquear

flag captain *s* (nav) capitán *m* de bandera

flageolet [,flædʒə'lɛt] *s* chirimía, dulzaina

flag·man ['flægmən] *s* (*pl* **-men** [mən]) (rr) guardafrenos *m;* (rr) guardavía *m*

flag of truce *s* bandera de parlamento

flag'pole' *s* asta de bandera; (surv) jalón *m*

flagrant ['flegrənt] *adj* enorme, escandaloso

flag'ship' *s* (nav) capitana

flag'staff' *s* asta de bandera

flag'stone' *s* losa

flag stop *s* (rr) apeadero

flail [flel] *s* mayal *m* ‖ *tr* golpear con mayal; golpear, azotar

flair [flɛr] *s* instinto, perspicacia

flak [flæk] *s* fuego antiaéreo

flake [flek] *s* (*thin piece*) hojuela; (*of snow*) copo ‖ *intr* desprenderse en hojuelas; caer en copos pequeños

flak·y ['fleki] *adj* (*comp* **-ier;** *super* **-iest**) escamoso, laminoso

flamboyant [flæm'bɔɪ·ənt] *adj* flameante; llamativo; rimbombante; (archit) flameante, flamígero

flame [flem] *s* llama ‖ *tr* (*to sterilize with a flame*) llamear ‖ *intr* flamear

flame thrower ['θro·ər] *s* lanzallamas *m*

flaming ['flemɪŋ] *adj* llameante; flamante, resplandeciente; apasionado

flamin·go [flə'mɪŋgo] *s* (*pl* **-gos** o **-goes**) flamenco

flammable ['flæməbəl] *adj* inflamable

Flanders ['flændərz] *s* Flandes *f*

flange [flændʒ] *s* pestaña

flank [flæŋk] *s* flanco; *tr* flanquear

flannel ['flænəl] *s* franela

flap [flæp] *s* (*fold in clothing; of a hat*) falda; (*of a pocket*) cartera; (*of a table*) hoja plegadiza; (*of shoe*) oreja; (*of an envelope*) tapa; (*of wings*) aleteo; (*of the counter in a store*) trampa ‖ *v* (*pret & pp* **flapped;** *ger* **flapping**) *tr* golpear con ruido seco; batir, sacudir (*las alas*) ‖ *intr* aletear; flamear con ruido

flare [flɛr] *s* llamarada, destello; cohete *m* de señales; (aer) bengala; (*outward curvature*) abocinamiento; (*of a dress*) vuelo ‖ *tr* abocinar ‖ *intr* arder con gran llamarada,

destellar; (*to spread outward*) abocinarse; **to flare up** inflamarse; recrudecer (*una enfermedad*); encolerizarse

flare star *s* (astr) estrella fulgurante

flare'-up' *s* llamarada; (*of an illness*) retroceso; (coll) llamarada, arrebato de cólera

flash [flæʃ] *s* (*of light*) relumbrón *m*, ráfaga; (*of lightning*) relámpago; (*of hope*) rayo; (*of joy*) acceso; (*of insight*) rasgo; mensaje *m* urgente ‖ *tr* quemar (*pólvora*); enviar (*un mensaje*) como un rayo ‖ *intr* destellar, centellear; relampaguear (*los ojos*); **to flash by** pasar como un rayo

flash'back' *s* (mov) retrospectiva, flashback *m*

flash bulb *s* luz *f* de magnesio; bombilla de destello

flash flood *s* torrentada, avenida repentina

flashing ['flæʃɪŋ] *s* despidiente *m* de agua, vierteaguas *m*

flash'light' *s* linterna eléctrica, lámpara eléctrica de bolsillo; (*of a lighthouse*) luz *f* intermitente, fanal *m* de destellos; (*for taking photographs*) flash *m*, relámpago

flashlight battery *s* pila de linterna

flashlight bulb *s* bombilla de linterna

flashlight photography *s* fotografía instantánea de relámpago

flash sign *s* anuncio intermitente

flash·y ['flæʃi] *adj* (*comp* **-ier;** *super* **-iest**) chillón, llamativo

flask [flæsk] *s* frasco; frasco de bolsillo; (*for laboratory use*) matraz *m*, redoma

flat [flæt] *adj* (*comp* **flatter;** *super* **flattest**) plano; (*nose; boat*) chato; (*surface*) mate, deslustrado; (*beer*) muerto; (*tire*) desinflado; (*e.g., denial*) terminante; (mus) bemol ‖ *adv* — **to fall flat** caer de plano; (fig) no surtir efecto, no tener éxito ‖ *s* banco, bajío; (*apartment*) piso; (mus) bemol *m;* (coll) neumático desinflado

flat'boat' *s* chalana

flat'car' *s* vagón *m* de plataforma

flat'foot' *s* pie plano

flat-footed ['flæt,fʊtɪd] *adj* de pies planos; (coll) inflexible

flat'head' *s* (*of a bolt*) cabeza chata; clavo, tornillo o perno de cabeza chata; (coll) tonto, mentecato

flat'i'ron *s* plancha

flatten ['flætən] *tr* allanar, aplanar; chafar, aplastar; achatar ‖ *intr* allanarse, aplanarse; aplastarse; achatarse; **to flatten out** ponerse horizontal, enderezarse

flatter ['flætər] *tr* lisonjear; cepillar (*to make more attractive than is*) favorecer ‖ *intr* lisonjear

flatterer ['flætərər] *s* lisonjero; (coll) limpiabotas *m*

flattering ['flætərɪŋ] *adj* lisonjero

flatter·y ['flætəri] *s* (*pl* **-ies**) lisonja

flat'top' *s* portaaviones *m*

flatulence ['flætʃələns] *s* flatulencia

flat'ware' *s* vajilla de plata; vajilla de porcelana

flaunt [flɔnt] *tr* ostentar, hacer gala de

flautist ['flɔtɪst] *s* flautista *mf*

flavor [ˈflevər] s sabor m, gusto; condimento, sazón f; (of ice cream) clase f ‖ tr saborear; condimentar, sazonar; aromatizar, perfumar

flavoring [ˈflevərɪŋ] s condimento, sainete m

flaw [flɔ] s defecto, imperfección; (crack) grieta

flawless [ˈflɔlɪs] adj perfecto, entero

flax [flæks] s lino

flaxen [ˈflæksən] adj blondo, rubio

flax′seed′ s linaza

flay [fle] tr desollar

flea [fli] s pulga

flea′bite′ s picadura de pulga; molestia insignificante

fleck [flɛk] s pinta, punto; partícula, pizca ‖ tr puntear

fledgling [ˈflɛdʒlɪŋ] s pajarito, volantón m; (fig) novato, novel m

flee [fli] v (pret & pp fled [flɛd]) tr & intr huir

fleece [flis] s (coat of wool) lana; (wool shorn at one time; tuft of wool or hair) vellón m ‖ tr esquilar; (to strip of money) desplumar

fleec•y [ˈflisi] adj (comp -ier; super -iest) lanudo; (clouds) aborregado

fleet [flit] adj veloz ‖ s armada; (of merchant vessels, airplanes, automobiles) flota

fleeting [ˈflitɪŋ] adj fugaz, efímero; transitorio

Fleming [ˈflɛmɪŋ] s flamenco

Flemish [ˈflɛmɪʃ] adj & s flamenco

flesh [flɛʃ] s carne f; **in the flesh** en persona; **to lose flesh** perder carnes; **to put on flesh** cobrar carnes

flesh and blood s (relatives) carne y sangre; el cuerpo humano

fleshiness [ˈflɛʃɪnɪs] s carnosidad

fleshless [ˈflɛʃlɪs] adj descarnado

flesh′pot′ s olla, marmita; **fleshpots** vida regalona; suntuosos nidos de vicios

flesh wound s herida superficial

flesh•y [ˈflɛʃi] adj (comp -ier; super -iest) carnoso

flex [flɛks] tr doblar ‖ intr doblarse

flexible [ˈflɛksɪbəl] adj flexible

flexible cord s (elec) flexible m

flick [flɪk] s (with finger) papirote m; (with whip) latigazo; ruido seco ‖ tr golpear rápida y ligeramente

flicker [ˈflɪkər] s llama trémula; (of eyelids) parpadeo; (of emotion) temblor momentáneo ‖ intr flamear con llama trémula; aletear

flier [ˈflaɪər] s aviador m; tren rápido; (coll) negocio arriesgado; (coll) hoja volante

flight [flaɪt] s fuga, huída; (of an airplane) vuelo; (of birds) bandada; (of stairs) tramo; (of fancy) arranque m; **to put to flight** poner en fuga; **to take flight** darse a la fuga

flight attendant s sobrecargo, sobrecarga

flight deck s (nav) cubierta de vuelo

flight•y [ˈflaɪti] adj (comp -ier; super -iest) veleidoso; casquivano

flim•flam [ˈflɪm‚flæm] s (coll) engaño, trampa; (coll) tontería ‖ v (pret & pp -flammed; ger -flamming) tr (coll) engañar, trampear

flim•sy [ˈflɪmzi] adj (comp -sier; super -siest) débil, endeble, flojo

flinch [flɪntʃ] intr encogerse de miedo

fling [flɪŋ] s echada, tiro; baile escocés muy vivo; **to go on a fling** echar una cana al aire; **to have a fling at** ensayar, probar; **to have one's fling** correrla, mocear ‖ v (pret & pp flung [flʌŋ]) tr arrojar; (e.g., on the floor, out the window, in jail) echar; **to fling open** abrir de golpe; **to fling shut** cerrar de golpe

flint [flɪnt] s pedernal m

flint′lock′ s llave f de chispa; trabuco de chispa

flint•y [ˈflɪnti] adj (comp -ier; super -iest) pedernalino; (fig) empedernido

flip [flɪp] adj (comp flipper; super flippest) (coll) petulante ‖ s capirotazo ‖ v (pret & pp flipped; ger flipping) tr echar de un capirotazo, mover de un tirón; **to flip a coin** echar a cara o cruz; **to flip one's lid** (coll) deschavetar; **to flip shut** cerrar de golpe (p. ej., un abanico)

flippancy [ˈflɪpənsi] s petulancia

flippant [ˈflɪpənt] adj petulante

flip side s contraportada (del disco)

flirt [flʌrt] s (woman) coqueta; (man) galanteador m ‖ intr coquetear (una mujer); galantear (un hombre); **to flirt with** flirtear con; pololear (Chile); acariciar (una idea); jugar con (la muerte)

flit [flɪt] v (pret & pp flitted; ger flitting) intr revolotear, volar; pasar rápidamente

flitch [flɪtʃ] s hoja de tocino

float [flot] s (raft) balsa; (of fishing line) flotador m; (of mason) llana; carroza alegórica, carro alegórico ‖ tr poner a flote; lanzar (una empresa); emitir (acciones, bonos, etc.) ‖ intr flotar

floating [ˈflotɪŋ] adj flotante

flock [flɑk] s (of birds) bandada; (of sheep) grey f, rebaño, manada; (of people) muchedumbre; (e.g., of nonsense) hatajo; (of faithful) grey f, rebaño ‖ intr congregarse, reunirse; llegar en tropel

floe [flo] s banquisa, témpano

flog [flɑg] v (pret & pp flogged; ger flogging) tr azotar, fustigar

flood [flʌd] s inundación; (caused by heavy rain) diluvio; (sudden rise of river) crecida; (of tide) pleamar f; (of words, etc.) diluvio, torrente m ‖ tr inundar; (to overwhelm) abrumar ‖ intr desbordar, rebosar; entrar a raudales

flood′gate′ s (of a dam) compuerta; (of a canal) esclusa

flood′light′ s faro de inundación ‖ tr iluminar con faro de inundación

flood tide s pleamar f, marea montante

floor [flor] s (inside bottom surface of room) piso, suelo; (story of a building) piso, alto; (of the sea, a swimming pool, etc.) fondo; (of an assembly hall) hemiciclo; (naut) varenga; **to ask for the floor** pedir la palabra; **to have the floor** tener la palabra; **to take the floor** tomar la palabra ‖ tr entarimar; derribar, echar al suelo; (coll)

fi
fl

confundir, envolver, revolcar (*al adversario en controversia*); (coll) vencer
floor lamp *s* lámpara de pie
floor mop *s* fregasuelos *m*, estropajo
floor plan *s* planta
floor show *s* espectáculo de cabaret
floor timber *s* (naut) varenga
floor'walk'er *s* jefe *m* de sección
floor wax *s* cera de pisos
flop [flɑp] *s* fracaso, caída; (*person*) berzas *m*, berzotas *m*; **to take a flop** caerse ‖ *v* (*pret* & *pp* **flopped**; *ger* **flopping**) *intr* agitarse; caerse; venirse abajo; fracasar; **to flop over** volcarse; cambiar de partido
flora [ˈflɔrə] *s* flora
floral [ˈflɔrəl] *adj* floral
Florentine [ˈflɔrən‚tin] *adj* & *s* florentino
florescence [floˈrɛsəns] *s* florescencia
florid [ˈflɔrɪd] *adj* (*complexion*) encarnado; (*showy, ornate*) florido
Florida Keys [ˈflɔrɪdə] *s* Cayos de la Florida
florist [ˈflɔrɪst] *s* florero, florista *mf*
floss [flɑs] *s* cadarzo; (*of corn*) cabellos
floss silk *s* seda floja sin torcer
floss•y [ˈflɑsi] *adj* (*comp* **-ier**; *super* **-iest**) ligero, velloso; (slang) cursi, vistoso
flotsam [ˈflɑtsəm] *s* pecio
flotsam and jetsam *s* pecios, despojos; (*trifles*) baratijas; gente *f* trashumante, gente perdida
flounce [flaʊns] *s* faralá *m*, volante *m* ‖ *tr* adornar con faralaes o volantes ‖ *intr* moverse airadamente
flounder [ˈflaʊndər] *s* platija ‖ *intr* forcejear, obrar torpemente, andar tropezando
flour [flaʊr] *adj* harinero ‖ *s* harina
flourish [ˈflʌrɪʃ] *s* (*with the sword*) molinete *m*; (*with the pen*) plumada, rasgo; (*as part of signature*) rúbrica; (mus) floreo ‖ *tr* blandir (*la espada*) ‖ *intr* florecer, prosperar
flourishing [ˈflʌrɪʃɪŋ] *adj* floreciente, próspero
flour mill *s* molino de harina
floury [ˈflaʊri] *adj* harinoso
flout [flaʊt] *tr* mofarse de, burlarse de ‖ *intr* mofarse, burlarse
flow [flo] *s* flujo ‖ *intr* fluir; subir (*la marea*); ondear (*el pelo en el aire*); **to flow into** desaguar en, desembocar en; **to flow over** rebosar; **to flow with** nadar en, abundar en
flower [ˈflaʊ•ər] *s* flor *f* ‖ *tr* florear ‖ *intr* florecer
flower bed *s* macizo, parterre *m*
flower garden *s* jardín *m*
flower girl *s* florera; (*at a wedding*) damita de honor
flower piece *s* ramillete *m*; (*painting*) florero
flow'er•pot' *s* tiesto, maceta
flower shop *s* floristería
flower show *s* exposición de flores
flower stand *s* florero
flowery [ˈflaʊ•əri] *adj* florido, cubierto de flores
flu [flu] *s* (coll) gripe *f*, influenza
fluctuate [ˈflʌktʃʊ‚et] *intr* fluctuar

flue [flu] *s* cañón *m* de chimenea; tubo de humo
fluency [ˈflu•ənsi] *s* afluencia, facundia
fluent [ˈflu•ənt] *adj* (*flowing*) fluente; afluente, facundo, flúido
fluently [ˈflu•əntli] *adv* corrientemente
fluff [flʌf] *s* pelusa, tamo; vello, pelusilla; (*of an actor*) gazapo ‖ *tr* esponjar, mullir ‖ *intr* esponjarse
fluff•y [ˈflʌfi] *adj* (*comp* **-ier**; *super* **-iest**) fofo, esponjoso, mullido; velloso
fluid [ˈflu•ɪd] *adj* & *s* flúido
fluidity [fluˈɪdɪti] *s* fluidez *f*
fluke [fluk] *s* (*of anchor*) uña; (*in billiards*) chiripa
flume [flum] *s* caz *m*, saetín *m*
flunk [flʌŋk] *s* (coll) reprobación ‖ *tr* (coll) reprobar, dar calabazas a; perder (*un examen o asignatura*) ‖ *intr* (coll) fracasar, salir mal; **to flunk out** (coll) tener que abandonar los estudios por no poder aprobar
flunk•y [ˈflʌŋki] *s* (*pl* **-ies**) lacayo; adulador *m*
fluor [ˈflu•ɔr] *s* fluorita
fluorescence [‚flu•əˈrɛsəns] *s* fluorescencia
fluorescent [‚flu•əˈrɛsənt] *adj* fluorescente
fluoridate [ˈflu•ɔrɪ‚det] *tr* fluorizar
fluoridation [ˈflu•ɔrɪˈdeʃən] *s* fluorización
fluoride [ˈflu•ə‚raɪd] *s* fluoruro
fluorine [ˈflu•ə‚rin] *s* flúor *m*
fluorite [ˈflu•ə‚raɪt] *s* fluorita
fluoroscope [ˈflu•ərə‚skop] *s* fluoroscopio
fluor spar *s* espato flúor
flur•ry [ˈflʌri] *s* (*pl* **-ries**) agitación; (*of wind*) racha, ráfaga; (*of rain*) chaparrón *m*; (*of snow*) nevisca ‖ *v* (*pret* & *pp* **-ried**) *tr* agitar
flush [flʌʃ] *adj* rasante, nivelado; (*set in, in order to be flush*) embutido; abundante; robusto, vigoroso; próspero, bien provisto; coloradote; (*in printing*) justificado; **flush with** a ras de ‖ *adv* ras con ras, al mismo nivel ‖ *s* (*of water*) flujo repentino; (*in the cheeks*) rubor *m*; sonrojo; (*in the springtime*) floración repentina; (*of joy*) acceso; (*of youth*) vigor *m*; chorro del inodoro; (*in poker*) flux *m* ‖ *tr* (*to cause to blush*) abochornar; limpiar con un chorro de agua; hacer saltar (*una liebre*) ‖ *intr* abochornarse, estar encendido (*el rostro*); (*to gush*) brotar
flush outlet *s* (elec) caja de enchufe embutida
flush switch *s* (elec) llave embutida
flush tank *s* depósito de limpia
flush toilet *s* inodoro con chorro de agua
fluster [ˈflʌstər] *s* confusión, aturdimiento ‖ *tr* confundir, aturdir
flute [flut] *s* (*of a column*) estría; (mus) flauta ‖ *tr* estriar, acanalar
flutist [ˈflutɪst] *s* flautista *mf*
flutter [ˈflʌtər] *s* aleteo, revoloteo; confusión, turbación ‖ *intr* aletear, revolotear; flamear, ondear; agitarse; alterarse (*el pulso*); palpitar (*el corazón*)
flux [flʌks] *s* (*flow; flowing of tide*) flujo; (*for fusing metals*) flujo, fundente *m*

fly [flaɪ] s (pl **flies**) mosca; (of trousers) portañuela, bragueta; (for fishing) mosca artificial; **flies** (theat) bambalinas; **to die like flies** morir como chinches ‖ v (pret **flew** [flu]; pp **flown** [flon]) tr hacer volar (una cometa); dirigir (un avión); (to carry in an airship) volar; atravesar en avión; desplegar, llevar (una bandera) ‖ intr volar; huir; ondear (una bandera); **to fly off** salir volando; desprenderse; **to fly open** abrirse de repente; **to fly over** trasvolar; **to fly shut** cerrarse de repente

fly ball s (baseball) palomita

fly'blow' s cresa

fly'-by-night' adj indigno de confianza

fly'catch'er s moscareta, papamoscas m

fly chaser s espantamoscas m

flyer [ˈflaɪər] s var de **flier**

fly'-fish' tr & intr pescar con moscas artificiales

flying [ˈflaɪ•ɪŋ] adj volante; rápido, veloz ‖ s aviación

flying boat s hidroavión m

flying buttress s arbotante m

flying colors spl gran éxito

flying field s campo de aviación

flying saucer s platillo volante

flying sickness s mal m de altura

flying time s horas de vuelo

fly in the ointment s mosca muerta que malea el perfume

fly'leaf' s (pl **-leaves'**) guarda, hoja de guarda

fly net s (for a bed) mosquitero; (for a horse) espantamoscas m

fly'pa'per s papel m matamoscas

fly'speck' s mancha de mosca

fly'swatter [ˈswɑtər] s matamoscas m

fly'trap' s atrapamoscas m

fly'wheel' s volante m

fm. abbr **fathom**

F.M. abbr **frequency modulation**

foal [fol] s potro ‖ intr parir (la yegua)

foam [fom] s espuma ‖ intr espumar

foam extinguisher s lanzaespumas m, extintor m de espuma

foam rubber s caucho esponjoso, espuma de caucho

foam•y [ˈfomi] adj (comp **-ier**; super **-iest**) espumoso, espumajoso

fob [fɑb] s faltriquera de reloj; (chain) leopoldina; (ornament) dije m

F.O.B. abbr **free on board**

focal [ˈfokəl] adj focal

fo•cus [ˈfokəs] s (pl **-cuses** o **-ci** [saɪ]) foco; **in focus** enfocado; **out of focus** desenfocado ‖ v (pret & pp **-cused** o **-cussed**; ger **-cusing** o **-cussing**) tr enfocar; fijar (la atención) ‖ intr enfocarse

fodder [ˈfɑdər] s forraje m

foe [fo] s enemigo

fog [fɑg] o [fɔg] s niebla; (phot) velo ‖ v (pret & pp **fogged**; ger **fogging**) tr envolver en niebla; (to blur) empañar; (phot) velar ‖ intr empañarse; (phot) velarse

fog bank s banco de nieblas

fog bell s campana de nieblas

fog'bound' adj atascado en la niebla, envuelto en la niebla

fog•gy [ˈfɑgi] o [ˈfɔgi] adj (comp **-gier**; super **-giest**) neblinoso, brumoso; confuso; (phot) velado; **it is foggy** hay neblina

fog'horn' s sirena de niebla

foible [ˈfɔɪbəl] s flaqueza, lado flaco

foil [fɔɪl] s (thin sheet of metal) hojuela, laminilla; (of mirror) azogado, plateado; contraste m, realce m; (sword) florete m ‖ tr frustrar; azogar, platear (un espejo)

foist [fɔɪst] tr — **to foist something on someone** encajar una cosa a uno

fol. abbr **folio, following**

fold [fold] s pliegue m, doblez m; arruga; (for sheep) aprisco, redil m; (of the faithful) rebaño ‖ tr plegar, doblar; cruzar (los brazos); **to fold up** doblar (p.ej., un mapa) ‖ intr plegarse, doblarse

folder [ˈfoldər] s (covers for holding papers) carpeta; (pamphlet) folleto

folderol [ˈfɑldə,rɑl] s tontería, necedad; bagatela

folding [ˈfoldɪŋ] adj plegadizo, plegable; plegador

folding camera s cámara de fuelle

folding chair s silla de tijera, silla plegadiza; (of canvas) catrecillo

folding cot s catre m de tijera

folding door s puerta plegadiza

folding rule s metro plegadizo

foliage [ˈfolɪ•ɪdʒ] s follaje m

foli•o [ˈfolɪ•o] adj en folio ‖ s (pl **-os**) (sheet) folio; infolio, libro en folio ‖ tr foliar

folk [fok] adj popular, tradicional, del pueblo ‖ s (pl **folk** o **folks**) gente f; **folks** (coll) gente (familia)

folk etymology s etimología popular

folk'lore' s folkore m

folk music s música folklórica

folk song s canción típica, canción tradicional

folk•sy [ˈfoksi] adj (comp **-sier**; super **-siest**) (coll) sociable, tratable; (like common people) (coll) plebeyo

folk'way' s costumbre tradicional

follicle [ˈfɑlɪkəl] s folículo

follow [ˈfɑlo] tr seguir; seguir el hilo de; interesarse en (las noticias del día) ‖ intr seguir; resultar; **as follows** como sigue; **it follows** síguese

follower [ˈfɑlo•ər] s seguidor m; secuaz mf, partidario; imitador m; discípulo

following [ˈfɑlo•ɪŋ] adj siguiente ‖ s séquito; partidarios

fol'low-up' adj consecutivo; recordativo ‖ s carta recordativa, circular recordativa

fol•ly [ˈfɑli] s (pl **-lies**) desatino, locura; empresa temeraria; **follies** revista teatral

foment [foˈment] tr fomentar

fond [fɑnd] adj afectuoso, cariñoso; **to become fond of** encariñarse con, aficionarse a o de

fondle [ˈfɑndəl] tr acariciar, mimar

fondness [ˈfɑndnɪs] s afición, cariño

font [fɑnt] s (source; source of water) fuente f; (for holy water) pila; (of type) fundición

food [fud] *adj* alimenticio ‖ *s* comida, alimento; **food for thought** cosa en qué pensar
food store *s* tienda de comestibles, colmado
food'stuffs' *spl* comestibles *mpl*, víveres *mpl*
fool [ful] *s* tonto, necio; (*jester*) bufón *m;* (*person imposed on*) inocente *mf*, víctima; **to make a fool of** poner en ridículo; **to play the fool** hacer el tonto ‖ *tr* embaucar, engañar; **to fool away** malgastar (*tiempo, dinero*) ‖ *intr* tontear; **to fool around** (coll) malgastar el tiempo; **to fool with** (coll) ajar, manosear
fooler•y ['fulǝri] *s* (*pl* **-ies**) locura, tontería, babosada
fool'har'dy *adj* (*comp* **-dier;** *super* **-diest**) temerario
fooling ['fulɪŋ] *s* broma; engaño; **no fooling** hablando en serio
foolish ['fulɪʃ] *adj* tonto; ridículo; gilí
fool'proof' *adj* (coll) a prueba de mal trato; (coll) infalible
fools'cap' *s* gorro de bufón; papel *m* de oficio
fool's errand *s* caza de grillos
fool's scepter *s* cetro de locura
foot [fut] *s* (*pl* **feet** [fit]) pie *m;* **to drag one's feet** ir a paso de caracol; **to have one foot in the grave** estar con un pie en la sepultura; **to put one's best foot forward** (coll) hacer méritos; **to put one's foot in it** (coll) meter la pata; (coll) tirarse una plancha; **to stand on one's own feet** volar con sus propias alas; **to tread under foot** hollar ‖ *tr* pagar (*la cuenta*); **to foot it** andar a pie; bailar
footage ['futɪdʒ] *s* distancia o largura en pies
foot'ball' *s* (*game*) balompié *m*, fútbol *m;* (*ball*) balón *m*
foot'board' *s* (*support for foot*) estribo; (*of bed*) pie *m*
foot'bridge' *s* pasarela, puente *m* para peatones
foot'fall' *s* paso
foot'hill' *s* colina al pie de una montaña
foot'hold' *s* arraigo, pie *m;* **to gain a foothold** ganar pie
footing ['futɪŋ] *s* pie *m*, p.ej., **he lost his footing** perdió el pie; **on a friendly footing** en relaciones amistosas; **on an equal footing** en pie de igualdad; **on a war footing** en pie de guerra
foot'lights' *spl* candilejas, batería; (fig) tablas, escena
foot'loose' *adj* libre, no comprometido
foot•man ['futmǝn] *s* (*pl* **-men** [mǝn]) lacayo, criado de librea
foot'mark' *s* huella
foot'note' *s* nota al pie de la página
foot'path' *s* senda para peatones
foot'print' *s* huella
foot race *s* carrera a pie
foot'rest' *s* apoyapié *m*, descansapié *m*
foot rule *s* regla de un pie
foot soldier *s* soldado de a pie
foot'sore' *adj* despeado
foot'step' *s* paso; **to follow in the footsteps of** seguir los pasos de

foot'stone' *s* lápida al pie de una sepultura
foot'stool' *s* escabel *m*, escañuelo
foot warmer *s* calientapiés *m*
foot'wear' *s* calzado
foot'work' *s* juego de piernas
foot'worn' *adj* (*road*) trillado; (*person*) despeado
foozle ['fuzǝl] *s* chambonada; (coll) chambón *m*, torpe *m* ‖ *tr* chafallar; errar (*un golpe*) de manera torpe ‖ *intr* chambonear
fop [fɑp] *s* currutaco, petimetre *m;* lagarto (Mex)
for [fɔr] *prep* para; por; como, p.ej., **he uses his living room for an office** usa la sala como oficina; de, p.ej., **time for bed** hora de acostarse; desde hace, p.ej., **he has been here for a week** está aquí desde hace una semana; en honor de; a pesar de ‖ *conj* pues, porque
for. *abbr* **foreign**
forage ['fɔrɪdʒ] *adj* forrajero ‖ *s* forraje *m* ‖ *tr* & *intr* forrajear; saquear
foray ['fɑre] o ['fɔre] *s* correría; saqueo ‖ *intr* hacer correrías
for•bear [fɔr'bɛr] *v* (*pret* **-bore** ['bor]; *pp* **-borne** ['born]) *tr* abstenerse de ‖ *intr* contenerse
forbearance [fɔr'bɛrǝns] *s* abstención; paciencia
for•bid [fɔr'bɪd] *v* (*pret* **-bade** ['bæd] o **-bad** ['bæd]; *pp* **-bidden** ['bɪdǝn]; *ger* **-bidding**) *tr* prohibir
forbidding [fɔr'bɪdɪŋ] *adj* repugnante, repulsivo
force [fors] *s* fuerza; (*staff of workers*) personal *m;* (*of soldiers, police, etc.*) cuerpo; (phys) fuerza; **by force** a la mala (Cuba, P-R); **by force of** a fuerza de; **by main force** con todas sus fuerzas; **in force** vigente, en vigor; en gran número; **to join forces** juntar diestra con diestra ‖ *tr* forzar; obligar; **to force back** hacer retroceder; **to force open** abrir por fuerza; **to force through** llevar a cabo por fuerza
forced [forst] *adj* forzado
forced air *s* aire *m* a presión
forced landing *s* aterrizaje forzado o forzoso
forced march *s* marcha forzada
forceful ['forsfǝl] *adj* enérgico, eficaz
for•ceps ['fɔrsǝps] *s* (*pl* **-ceps** o **-cipes** [sɪ,piz]) (dent, surg) pinzas; (obstet) fórceps *m*
force pump *s* bomba impelente
forcible ['forsɪbǝl] *adj* eficaz, convincente; forzado
ford [ford] *s* vado ‖ *tr* vadear
fore [for] *adj* anterior; (naut) de proa ‖ *adv* antes, anteriormente; delante; (naut) avante ‖ *interj* ¡ojo!, ¡cuidado! ‖ *s* delantera; **to the fore** destacado; a mano; vivo
fore and aft *adv* de popa a proa
fore'arm' *s* antebrazo ‖ **fore•arm'** *tr* armar de antemano; prevenir
fore'bear' *s* antepasado
forebode [for'bod] *tr* (*to portend*) presagiar; (*to have a presentiment of*) presentir, prever

foreboding [fɔr'bodɪŋ] s presagio; presentimiento

fore'cast' s pronóstico || v (pret & pp -cast o-casted) tr pronosticar

forecastle ['foksəl], ['fɔr,kæsəl], o ['fɔr,kɑsəl] s castillo de proa

fore-close' tr excluir; extinguir el derecho de redimir (una hipoteca); privar del derecho de redimir una hipoteca

fore-doom' tr condenar de antemano, predestinar al fracaso

fore edge s canal f

fore'fa'ther s antepasado

fore'fin'ger s dedo índice, dedo mostrador

fore'front' s puesto delantero; sitio de actividad más intensa; **in the forefront** a vanguardia

fore-go' v (pret -went'; pp -gone') tr & intr preceder

foregoing ['fɔr,go•ɪŋ] o [fɔr'go•ɪŋ] adj anterior, precedente, prenombrado

fore'gone' conclusion s resultado inevitable; decisión adoptada de antemano

fore'ground' s primer plano, primer término

forehanded ['fɔr,hændɪd] adj (thrifty) ahorrado; hecho de antemano

forehead ['fɑrɪd] o ['fɔrɪd] s frente f

foreign ['fɑrɪn] adj extranjero, exterior; **foreign to** (not belonging to or connected with) ajeno a

foreign affairs spl asuntos exteriores

for'eign-born' adj nacido en el extranjero

foreigner ['fɑrɪnər] s extranjero

foreign exchange s cambio extranjero; (currency) divisa

foreign minister s ministro de asuntos exteriores

foreign ministry s ministerio de relaciones exteriores

foreign office s ministerio de asuntos exteriores

foreign service s servicio diplomático y consular; servicio militar extranjero

foreign trade s comercio extranjero

fore'leg' s brazo, pata delantera

fore'lock' s mechón m de pelo sobre la frente; (of a horse) copete m; **to take time by the forelock** asir la ocasión por la melena

fore-man ['formən] s (pl -men [mən]) capataz m, mayoral m, sobrestante m; (in a machine shop) contramaestre m; presidente m de jurado

foremast ['forməst], ['for,mæst], o ['for,mɑst] s palo de trinquete

foremost ['for,most] adj primero, principal, más eminente

fore'noon' adj matinal || s mañana

fore'part' s parte delantera; primera parte

fore'paw' s pata delantera

fore'quar'ter s cuarto delantero

fore'run'ner s precursor m; predecesor m; antepasado; anuncio, presagio

fore-sail ['forsəl] o ['for,sel] s trinquete m

fore-see' v (pret -saw'; pp -seen') tr prever

foreseeable [for'si•əbəl] adj previsible

fore-shad'ow tr presagiar, prefigurar

fore-short'en tr escorzar

fore-short'ening s escorzo

fore'sight' s previsión, presciencia

fore'sight'ed adj previsor, presciente

fore'skin' s prepucio

forest ['fɑrɪst] o ['fɔrɪst] adj forestal || s bosque m

fore-stall' tr impedir, prevenir; anticipar; acaparar

forest ranger ['rendʒər] s guarda m forestal, montanero

forestry ['fɑrɪstri] o ['fɔrɪstri] s silvicultura, ciencia forestal

fore'taste' s goce anticipado, conocimiento anticipado

fore-tell' v (pret & pp -told') tr predecir; presagiar

fore'thought' s premeditación; providencia, previsión

forever [fɔr'ɛvər] adv por siempre; siempre

fore-warn' tr prevenir, poner sobre aviso

fore'word' s advertencia, prefacio

forfeit ['fɔrfɪt] adj perdido || s multa, pena; prenda perdida; **forfeits** (game) prendas || tr perder el derecho a

forfeiture ['fɔrfɪtʃər] s multa, pena; prenda perdida

forgather [fɔr'gæðər] intr reunirse; encontrarse; **to forgather with** asociarse con

forge [fordʒ] s fragua; (blacksmith shop) herrería; || tr fraguar, forjar; falsificar (la firma de otra persona); fraguar, forjar (mentiras) || intr fraguar, forjar; **to forge ahead** avanzar despacio y con esfuerzo

forger-y ['fordʒəri] s (pl -ies) falsificación

for-get' [fɔr'gɛt] v (pret -got [gɑt]; pp -got o -gotten; ger -getting) tr olvidar, olvidarse de, olvidársele a uno, p.ej., **he forgot his overcoat** se le olvidó su abrigo; **forget it!** ¡no se preocupe!; **to forget oneself** no pensar en sí mismo; ser distraído; propasarse

forgetful [fɔr'gɛtfəl] adj olvidado, olvidadizo; descuidado

forgetfulness [fɔr'gɛtfəlnɪs] s olvido; descuido

for-get'-me-not' s nomeolvides m

forgivable [fɔr'gɪvəbəl] adj perdonable

for-give [fɔr'gɪv] v (pret -gave'; pp -giv'en) tr perdonar

forgiveness [fɔr'gɪvnɪs] s perdón m; misericordia

forgiving [fɔr'gɪvɪŋ] adj perdonador, misericordioso, clemente

for-go [fɔr'go] v (pret -went'; pp -gone') tr privarse de

fork [fɔrk] s horca; (of a gardener; of bicycle) horquilla; (of two rivers) horcajo; (of railroad) ramal m; (of a tree) horqueta; (for eating) tenedor m || tr ahorquillar; cargar con horquilla; (in chess) amenazar (dos piezas); **to fork out** (slang) entregar, sudar || intr bifurcarse

forked [fɔrkt] adj ahorquillado

forked lightning s relámpago en zigzag

fork'lift' truck s carretilla elevadora de horquilla

forlorn [fɔr'lɔrn] *adj* desamparado; desesperado; miserable

forlorn hope *s* empresa desesperada

form [fɔrm] *s* forma; (*paper to be filled out*) formulario; (*construction to give shape to cement*) encofrado; (*type in a frame*) molde *m* ‖ *tr* formar ‖ *intr* formarse

formal ['fɔrməl] *adj* formal, ceremonioso; etiquetero

formal attire *s* vestido de etiqueta

formal call *s* visita de cumplido

formali·ty [fɔr'mælɪti] *s* (*pl* **-ties**) (*standard procedure*) formalidad; ceremonia, etiqueta

formal party *s* reunión de etiqueta

formal speech *s* discurso de aparato

format ['fɔrmæt] *s* formato

formation ['fɔr'meʃən] *s* formación

former ['fɔrmər] *adj* (*preceding*) anterior; (*long past*) antiguo; primero (*de dos*); **the former** aquél

formerly ['fɔrmərli] *adv* antes, en tiempos pasados

form'-fit'ting *adj* ceñido al cuerpo

formidable ['fɔrmɪdəbəl] *adj* formidable

formless ['fɔrmlɪs] *adj* informe

form letter *s* carta general

formu·la ['fɔrmjələ] *s* (*pl* **-las** o **-lae** [,li] fórmula

formulate ['fɔrmjə,let] *tr* formular

fornicate ['fɔrnə,ket] *intr* fornicar

fornication [,fɔrnə'keʃən] *s* fornicación

for·sake [fɔr'sek] *v* (*pret* **-sook** ['sʊk]; *pp* **-saken** ['sekən]) *tr* abandonar, desamparar; dejar

fort [fort] *s* fuerte *m*, fortaleza

forte [fort] *s* (*strong point*) fuerte *m*, caballo de batalla ‖ ['forte] *adj* (mus) fuerte

forth [forθ] *adv* adelante; **and so forth** y así sucesivamente; **from this day forth** de hoy en adelante; **to go forth** salir

forth'com'ing *adj* próximo, venidero

forth'right' *adj* directo, franco, sincero ‖ *adv* derecho; sinceramente, francamente; en seguida

forth'with' *adv* inmediatamente

fortieth ['fɔrtɪ·ɪθ] *adj* & *s* (*in a series*) cuadragésimo; (*part*) cuarentavo

fortification [,fɔrtɪfɪ'keʃən] *s* fortificación

forti·fy ['fɔrtɪ,faɪ] *v* (*pret* & *pp* **-fied**) *tr* fortificar; encabezar (*vinos*)

fortitude ['fɔrtɪ,tjud] *s* fortaleza, firmeza

fortnight ['fɔrtnaɪt] *s* quincena, dos semanas

fortress ['fɔrtrɪs] *s* fortaleza

fortuitous [fɔr'tju·ɪtəs] *adj* fortuito

fortunate ['fɔrtʃənɪt] *adj* afortunado

fortune ['fɔrtʃən] *s* fortuna; (*money*) platal *m;* **to make a fortune** enriquecerse; **to tell someone his fortune** decirle a uno la buenaventura

fortune hunter *s* cazador *m* de dotes

for'tune·tel'ler *s* adivino, agorero

for·ty ['fɔrti] *adj* & *pron* cuarenta ‖ *s* (*pl* **-ties**) cuarenta *m*

fo·rum ['forəm] *s* (*pl* **-rums** o **-ra** [rə]) foro; (*e.g., of public opinion*) tribunal *m*

forward ['fɔrwərd] *adj* delantero; precoz; atrevido, impertinente ‖ *adv* hacia adelante; **to bring forward** pasar a cuenta nueva; **to come forward** adelantarse; **to look forward to** esperar con placer anticipado ‖ *tr* cursar, hacer seguir, reexpedir; fomentar, patrocinar

fossil ['fasɪl] *adj* & *s* fósil *m*

foster ['fastər] o ['fɔstər] *adj* adoptivo, de leche, de crianza ‖ *tr* fomentar

foster brother *s* hermano de leche

foster home *s* hogar *m* de adopción

foster mother *s* madre adoptiva; (*nurse*) ama de leche

foster sister *s* hermana de leche

foul [faʊl] *adj* sucio, puerco; (*air*) viciado; (*wind*) contrario; (*weather*) malo; obsceno; pérfido; (*breath*) fétido; (baseball) fuera del cuadro

foul-mouthed ['faʊl'mauðd] o ['faʊl'mauθt] *adj* deslenguado

foul play *s* mal encuentro; (sport) juego sucio

foul'spo'ken *adj* malhablado

found [faʊnd] *tr* fundar; (*to melt, to cast*) fundir

foundation [faʊn'deʃən] *s* fundación; (*endowment*) dotación; (*basis*) fundamento; (*masonry support*) cimiento

founder ['faʊndər] *s* fundador *m;* (*of metals*) fundidor *m* ‖ *intr* despearse (*un caballo*); hundirse, irse a pique (*un buque*); (*to fail*) fracasar

foundling ['faʊndlɪŋ] *s* niño expósito; pepe *mf*

foundling hospital *s* casa de expósitos

found·ry ['faʊndri] *s* (*pl* **-ries**) fundición

foundry·man ['faʊndrɪmən] *s* (*pl* **-men** [mən]) fundidor *m*

fount [faʊnt] *s* fuente *f*

fountain ['faʊntən] *s* fuente *f*, manantial *m*

foun'tain·head' *s* nacimiento

fountain pen *s* pluma estilográfica, pluma fuente

fountain syringe *s* mangueta

four [for] *adj* & *pron* cuatro ‖ *s* cuatro; **four o'clock** las cuatro; **on all fours** a gatas

four'-cy'cle *adj* (mach) de cuatro tiempos

four'-cyl'inder *adj* (mach) de cuatro cilindros

four'-flush' *intr* (coll) bravear, papelonear

fourflusher ['for,flʌʃər] *s* bravucón *m*

four-footed ['for'fʊtɪd] *adj* cuadrúpedo

four hundred *adj* & *pron* cuatrocientos ‖ *s* cuatrocientos *m;* **the four hundred** la alta sociedad

four'-in-hand' *s* corbata de nudo corredizo; coche tirado por cuatro caballos

four'-lane' *adj* cuadriviario

four'-leaf' *adj* cuadrifoliado

four-legged ['for'lɛgɪd] o ['for'lɛgd] *adj* de cuatro patas; (*schooner*) de cuatro mástiles

four'-let'ter word *s* palabra impúdica de cuatro letras

four'-mo'tor plane *s* cuadrimotor *m*

four'-o'clock' *s* dondiego

four'post'er *s* cama imperial

four'score' *adj* cuatro veintenas de

foursome ['forsəm] *s* cuatrinca; cuatro jugadores; juego de cuatro

fourteen [ˈforˈtin] *adj, pron & s* catorce *m*
fourteenth [ˈforˈtinθ] *adj & s* (*in a series*)
decimocuarto; (*part*) catorzavo ‖ *s* (*in dates*) catorce *m*
fourth [forθ] *adj & s* cuarto ‖ *s* (*in dates*) cuatro
fourth estate *s* cuarto poder
four'-way' *adj* de cuatro direcciones; (elec) de cuatro terminales
fowl [faʊl] *s* ave *f;* aves; gallina; gallo; carne *f* de ave
fowling piece *s* escopeta de caza
fox [faks] *s* zorra; (*fur*) zorro; (*cunning person*) (fig) zorro ‖ *tr* (coll) engañar con astucia
fox'glove' *s* dedalera
fox'hole' *s* zorrera; (mil) pozo de lobo
fox'hound' *s* perro raposero, perro zorrero
fox hunt *s* caza de zorras
fox terrier *s* fox-terrier *m* (*casta de perro de talla pequeña*)
fox trot *s* trote corto (*de caballo*); fox-trot *m* (*baile de compás cuaternario*)
fox·y [ˈfaksi] *adj* (*comp* **-ier;** *super* **-iest**) (coll) hermosa y erótica; zorrero, astuto, taimado
foyer [ˈfɔɪ·ər] *s* (*of a private house*) vestíbulo; (theat) salón *m* de entrada, vestíbulo
fr. *abbr* **fragment, franc, from**
Fr. *abbr* **Father, French, Friday**
Fra [fra] *s* fray *m*
fracas [ˈfrekəs] *s* alboroto, riña
fraction [ˈfrækʃən] *s* fracción; porción muy pequeña
fractional [ˈfrækʃənəl] *adj* fraccionario; insignificante
fractious [ˈfrækʃəs] *adj* reacio, rebelón; quisquilloso, regañón
fracture [ˈfræktʃər] *s* fractura ‖ *tr* fracturar; (*e.g., an arm*) fracturarse; *intr* fracturarse
fragile [ˈfrædʒɪl] *adj* frágil
fragment [ˈfrægmənt] *s* fragmento
fragrance [ˈfregrəns] *s* fragancia
fragrant [ˈfregrənt] *adj* fragante
frail [frel] *adj* (*not robust*) débil; (*easily broken; morally weak*) frágil ‖ *s* cesto de junco
frail·ty [ˈfrelti] *s* (*pl* **-ties**) debilidad; (*moral weakness*) fragilidad
frame [frem] *s* (*of a picture, mirror*) marco, (*of glasses*) montura, armadura; (*structure*) armazón *f*, esqueleto; (*for embroidering*) bastidor *m;* (*of government*) sistema *m;* (mov, telv) encuadre *m;* (naut) cuaderna ‖ *tr* (*to put in a frame*) enmarcar; formar, forjar; construir; redactar, formular; (slang) incriminar (*a un inocente*)
frame house *s* casa de madera
frame of mind *s* manera de pensar
frame'-up' *s* (slang) treta, trama para incriminar a un inocente
frame'work' *s* armazón *f,* esqueleto, entramado
franc [fræŋk] *s* franco
France [fræns] o [frans] *s* Francia
franchise [ˈfræntʃaɪz] *s* franquicia, privilegio; (*right to vote*) sufragio

Franciscan [frænˈsɪskən] *adj & s* franciscano
frank [fræŋk] *adj* franco, sincero ‖ *s* carta franca, envío franco; franquicia postal; sello de franquicia ‖ *tr* franquear ‖ **Frank** *s* (*member of a Frankish tribe*) franco; (*masculine name*) Paco
frankfurter [ˈfræŋkfərtər] *s* salchicha de carne de vaca y de cerdo
frankincense [ˈfræŋkɪnˌsɛns] *s* olíbano
Frankish [ˈfræŋkɪʃ] *adj & s* franco
frankness [ˈfræŋknɪs] *s* franqueza, abertura, sinceridad
frantic [ˈfræntɪk] *adj* frenético
frappé [fræˈpe] *adj* helado ‖ *s* refresco helado de zumo de frutas
frat [fræt] *s* (slang) club *m* de estudiantes
fraternal [frəˈtʌrnəl] *adj* fraternal
fraterni·ty [frəˈtʌrnɪti] *s* (*pl* **-ties**) (*brotherliness*) fraternidad; cofradía; asociación secreta; (U.S.A.) club *m* de estudiantes
fraternize [ˈfrætərˌnaɪz] *intr* fraternizar
fraud [frɔd] *s* fraude *m;* embelequería (Col, Mex, W-I); (*person*) (coll) impostor *m*
fraudulent [ˈfrɔdjələnt] *adj* fraudulento
fraught [frɔt] *adj* — **fraught with** cargado de, lleno de
fray [fre] *s* combate *m,* riña, batalla ‖ *intr* deshilacharse, raerse
freak [frik] *s* (*sudden fancy*) capricho, antojo; (*person, animal*) fenómeno, esperpento
freakish [ˈfrikɪʃ] *adj* caprichoso, antojadizo; raro, fantástico
freckle [ˈfrɛkəl] *s* peca
freckle-faced [ˈfrɛkəlˌfest] *adj* pecoso
freckly [ˈfrɛkli] *adj* pecoso
free [fri] *adj* (*comp* **freer** [ˈfri·ər]; *super* **freest** [ˈfri·ɪst]) libre; gratis, franco; liberal, generoso; **to be free with** dar abundantemente; **to set free** libertar ‖ *adv* libremente; en libertad; de balde, gratis ‖ *v* (*pret & pp* **freed** [frid]; *ger* **freeing** [ˈfri·ɪŋ]) *tr* libertar, poner en libertad; soltar; exentar, eximir
free and easy *adj* despreocupado
freebooter [ˈfriˌbutər] *s* forbante *m,* filibustero, pirata *m*
free'born' *adj* nacido libre; propio de un pueblo libre
freedom [ˈfridəm] *s* libertad
freedom of speech *s* libertad de palabra
freedom of the press *s* libertad de imprenta
freedom of the seas *s* libertad de los mares
freedom of worship *s* libertad de cultos
free enterprise *s* libertad de empresa
free fight *s* sarracina, riña tumultuaria
free'-for-all' *s* concurso abierto a todo el mundo; sarracina, riña tumultuaria
free hand *s* plena libertad, carta blanca
free'hand' drawing *s* dibujo a pulso
freehanded [ˈfriˌhændɪd] *adj* dadivoso, generoso
free'hold' *s* (law) feudo franco
free lance *s* soldado mercenario; periodista *mf* sin empleo fijo; (*writer not on regular salary*) destajista *mf*

fo
fr

free lunch *s* tapas, enjutos
free•man ['frimən] *s* (*pl* **-men** [mən]) hombre *m* libre; ciudadano
Free'ma'son *s* francmasón *m*
Free'ma'sonry *s* francmasonería
free of charge *adj* gratis, de balde
free on board *adj* franco a bordo
free port *s* puerto franco
free ride *s* llevada gratuita
free service *s* servicio post-venta
free'-spo'ken *adj* franco, sin reserva
free'stone' *adj & s* abridero
free'think'er *s* librepensador *m*
free thought *s* librepensamiento
free trade *s* librecambio
free'trad'er *s* librecambista *mf*
free'way' *s* autopista
free will *s* libre albedrío
freeze [friz] *s* helada ‖ *v* (*pret* **froze** [froz]; *pp* **frozen**) *tr* helar; congelar (*créditos, fondos, etc.*) ‖ *intr* helarse; congelarse; helársele a uno la sangre (*p.ej., de miedo*)
freeze'-dry' *v* (*pret & pp* **-dried**) *tr* liofilizar
freeze drying *s* liofilización
freezer ['frizər] *s* heladora, sorbetera
freezing ['frizɪŋ] *s* glaciación
freight [fret] *s* carga; (naut) flete *m;* **by freight** como carga; (rr) en pequeña velocidad ‖ *tr* enviar por carga
freight car *s* vagón *m* de carga, vagón de mercancías
freighter ['fretər] *s* buque *m* de carga, carguero
freight platform *s* (rr) muelle *m*
freight station *s* (rr) estación de carga
freight train *s* mercancías *msg*, tren *m* de mercancías
freight yard *s* (rr) patio de carga
French [frɛntʃ] *adj & s* francés *m;* **the French** los franceses
French chalk *s* jaboncillo de sastre
French doors *spl* puertas vidrieras dobles
French dressing *s* salsa francesa, vinagreta
French fried potatoes *spl* patatas fritas en trocitos
French horn *s* (mus) trompa de armonía
French horsepower *s* caballo de fuerza, caballo de vapor
French leave *s* despedida a la francesa; **to take French leave** despedirse a la francesa
French•man ['frɛntʃmən] *s* (*pl* **-men** [mən]) francés *m*
French telephone *s* microteléfono
French toast *s* torrija
French window *s* puerta ventana
French'wom'an *s* (*pl* **-wom'en**) francesa
frenzied ['frɛnzid] *adj* frenético
fren•zy ['frɛnzi] (*pl* **-zies**) frenesí *m*
frequen•cy ['frikwənsi] *s* (*pl* **-cies**) frecuencia
frequency list *s* lista de frecuencia
frequency modulation *s* modulación de frecuencia
frequent ['frikwənt] *adj* frecuente ‖ [frɪ'kwɛnt] o ['frikwənt] *tr* frecuentar
frequently ['frikwəntli] *adv* con frecuencia, frecuentemente

fres•co ['frɛsko] *s* (*pl* **-coes** o **-cos**) fresco ‖ *tr* pintar al fresco
fresh [frɛʃ] *adj* fresco; (*water*) dulce; (*wind*) fresquito; novicio, inexperto; (*cheeky*) (slang) fresco; (*toward women*) (slang) atrevido; **fresh paint!** ¡ojo mancha! ‖ *adv* recientemente, recién; **fresh in** (coll) recién llegado, acabado de llegar; **fresh out** (coll) recién agotado
freshen ['frɛʃən] *tr* refrescar ‖ *intr* refrescarse
freshet ['frɛʃɪt] *s* avenida, crecida
fresh•man ['frɛʃmən] *s* (*pl* **-men** [mən]) novato; estudiante *mf* de primer año
freshness ['frɛʃnɪs] *s* frescura; (*cheek*) (slang) frescura
fresh'-wa'ter *adj* de agua dulce; no acostumbrado a navegar; de poca monta
fret [frɛt] *s* (*interlaced design*) calado; (mus) ceja, traste *m;* queja ‖ *v* (*pret & pp* **fretted;** *ger* **fretting**) *tr* adornar con calados ‖ *intr* irritarse, quejarse, agitarse
fretful ['frɛtfəl] *adj* irritable, enojadizo, displicente
fret'work' *s* calado
Freudianism ['frɔɪdɪ•ə,nɪzəm] *s* freudismo
friar ['fraɪ•ər] *s* fraile *m* **friar•y** ['fraɪ•əri] *s* (*pl* **-ies**) convento de frailes
fricassee [,frɪkə'si] *s* fricasé *m*
friction ['frɪkʃən] *s* fricción, rozamiento; (fig) desavenencia, rozamiento
friction tape *s* cinta aislante
Friday ['fraɪdi] *s* viernes *m*
fried [fraɪd] *adj* frito
fried egg *s* huevo a la plancha, huevo frito o estrellado
friend [frɛnd] *s* amigo; (*in answer to "Who is there?"*) gente *f* de paz; **to be friends with** ser amigo de; **to make friends** trabar amistades; **to make friends with** hacerse amigo de
friend•ly ['frɛndli] *adj* (*comp* **-lier;** *super* **-liest**) amigo, amistoso, amigable
friendship ['frɛndʃɪp] *s* amistad
frieze [friz] *s* (archit) friso
frigate ['frɪgɪt] *s* fragata
fright [fraɪt] *s* susto, espanto; (*grotesque or ridiculous person*) (coll) espantajo; **to take fright at** asustarse de
frighten ['fraɪtən] *tr* asustar, espantar; **to frighten away** espantar, ahuyentar ‖ *intr* asustarse
frightful ['fraɪtfəl] *adj* espantoso, horroroso; (coll) feúcho, repugnante; (coll) enorme, tremendo
frightfulness ['fraɪtfəlnɪs] *s* espanto, horror *m;* terrorismo; espantosidad (SAm)
frigid ['frɪdʒɪd] *adj* frío; (fig) frío; (*zone*) glacial
frigidity [frɪ'dʒɪdɪti] *s* frialdad; (pathol) frialdad; (fig) frialdad, frigidez *f*
frill [frɪl] *s* lechuga; (*of birds and other animals*) collarín *m;* (*frippery*) (coll) ringorrango; (*in dress, speech etc.*) (coll) afectación
fringe [frɪndʒ] *s* franja, orla; (opt) franja ‖ *tr* franjar, orlar

fringe benefits *spl* beneficios accesorios; beneficios sociales

fripper•y ['frɪpəri] *s* (*pl* **-ies**) (*flashiness*) cursilería; (*flashy clothes*) perejil *m*, perifollos

frisk [frɪsk] *tr* (slang) cachear; (slang) registrar y robar ‖ *intr* retozar

frisk•y ['frɪski] *adj* (*comp* **-ier**; *super* **-iest**) juguetón, retozón; (*horse*) fogoso

fritter ['frɪtər] *s* fruta de sartén; fragmento ‖ *tr*—**to fritter away** desperdiciar, malgastar poco a poco

frivolous ['frɪvələs] *adj* frívolo

friz [frɪz] *s* (*pl* **frizzes**) rizo, pelo rizado apretadamente ‖ *v* (*pret & pp* **frizzed**; *ger* **frizzing**) *tr* rizar, rizar apretadamente

frizzle ['frɪzəl] *s* rizo apretado; chirrido, siseo ‖ *tr* rizar apretadamente; asar o freír en parrilla ‖ *intr* chirriar, sisear

friz•zly ['frɪzli] *adj* (*comp* **-zlier**; *super* **-zliest**) muy cnsortijado

fro [fro] *adv*—**to and fro** de acá para allá; **to go to and fro** ir y venir

frock [frɑk] *s* vestido; bata, blusa; (*of priest*) vestido talar

frock coat *s* levita

frog [frɑg] o [frɔg] *s* rana; (*button and loop on a garment*) alamar *m;* (*in throat*) ronquera, gallo

frog'man' *s* (*pl* **-men'**) hombre-rana *m*

frol•ic ['frɑlɪk] *s* juego alegre, travesura; fiesta, holgorio ‖ *v* (*pret & pp* **-icked**; *ger* **-icking**) *intr* juguetear, travesear, jaranear

frolicsome ['frɑlɪksəm] *adj* juguetón, travieso

from [frʌm], [frɑm] o [frəm] *prep* de; desde; de parte de; según; a, p.ej., **to take something away from someone** quitarle algo a alguien

front [frʌnt] *adj* delantero; anterior ‖ *s* frente *m & f;* (*of a shirt*) pechera; (*of a book*) principio; apariencia falsa (*p.ej., de riqueza*); ademán estudiado; (mil) frente *m;* **in front of** delante de, frente a, en frente de; **to put on a front** (coll) gastar mucho oropel; **to put up a bold front** (coll) hacer de tripas corazón ‖ *tr* (*to face*) dar a; (*to confront*) afrontar, arrostrar; (*to supply with a front*) poner frente o fachada a ‖ *intr*—**to front on** dar a; **to front towards** mirar hacia

frontage ['frʌntɪdʒ] *s* fachada, frontera; terreno frontero

front door *s* puerta de entrada

front drive *s* (aut) tracción delantera

frontier [frʌn'tɪr] *adj* fronterizo ‖ *s* frontera

frontiers•man [frʌn'tɪrzmən] *s* (*pl* **-men** [mən]) hombre *m* de la frontera, explorador *m*

frontispiece ['frʌntɪs,pis] *s* (*of book*) portada; (archit) frontispicio

front matter *s* preliminares *mpl* (*de un libro*)

front page *s* primera plana

front porch *s* soportal *m*

front room *s* cuarto que da a la calle

front row *s* primera fila

front seat *s* asiento delantero

front steps *spl* escalones *mpl* de acceso a la puerta de entrada

front view *s* vista de frente

frost [frɔst] o [frɑst] *s* (*freezing*) helada; (*frozen dew*) escarcha; (slang) fracaso ‖ *tr* cubrir de escarcha; escarchar (*confituras*); helar (*el frío las plantas*); deslustrar (*el vidrio*)

frost'bit'ten *adj* dañado por la helada; quemado por la helada o la escarcha

frosted glass *s* vidrio deslustrado

frosting ['frɔstɪŋ] o [frɑstɪŋ] *s* garapiña; (*of glass*) deslustre *m*

frost•y ['frɔsti] o ['frɑsti] *adj* (*comp* **-ier**; *super* **-iest**) cubierto de escarcha; escarchado; frío, poco amistoso; canoso, gris

froth [frɔθ] o [frɑθ] *s* espuma; frivolidad, vanidad ‖ *intr* espumar, echar espuma; (*at the mouth*) espumajear

froth•y ['frɔθi] o ['frɑθi] *adj* (*comp* **-ier**; *super* **-iest**) espumoso; frívolo, vano

froward ['frowərd] *adj* díscolo, indócil

frown [fraun] *s* ceño, entrecejo ‖ *intr* fruncir el entrecejo; **to frown at** *u* **on** mirar con ceño, desaprobar

frows•y o **frowz•y** ['frauzi] *adj* (*comp* **-ier**; *super* **-iest**) desaseado, desaliñado; maloliente; mal peinado

frozen foods ['frozən] *spl* viandas congeladas

frt. *abbr* **freight**

frugal ['frugəl] *adj* (*moderate in the use of things*) parco; (*not very abuñdant*) frugal

fruit [frut] *adj* (*tree*) frutal; (*boat, dish*) frutero ‖ *s* (*such as apple, pear, strawberry*) fruta; frutas, p.ej., **I like fruit** me gustan las frutas; (*part containing seed*) fruto; (*effect, result*) (fig) fruto

fruit cake *s* torta de frutas

fruit cup *s* compota de frutas picadas

fruit fly *s* mosca del vinagre; mosca de las frutas

fruitful ['frutfəl] *adj* fructuoso

fruition [fru'ɪʃən] *s* buen resultado, cumplimiento; **to come to fruition** lograrse cumplidamente

fruit jar *s* tarro para frutas

fruit juice *s* jugo de frutas

fruitless ['frutlɪs] *adj* infructuoso

fruit of the vine *s* zumo de cepas o de parras

fruit salad *s* ensalada de frutas, macedonia de frutas

fruit stand *s* puesto de frutas

fruit store *s* frutería

frumpish ['frʌmpɪʃ] *adj* basto, desgarbado, desaliñado

frustrate ['frʌstret] *tr* frustrar

fry [fraɪ] *s* (*pl* **fries**) fritada ‖ *v* (*pret & pp* **fried**) *tr & intr* freír

frying pan ['fraɪɪŋ] *s* sartén *f;* **to jump from the frying pan into the fire** saltar de la sartén y dar en las brasas

ft. *abbr* **foot, feet**

fudge [fʌdʒ] *s* dulce *m* de chocolate

fuel ['fju•əl] *s* combustible *m;* (fig) pábulo; **alternate fuel** combustible alternativo ‖ *v* (*pret & pp* **fueled** o **fuelled**; *ger* **fueling** o

fr
fu

fuelling) *tr* aprovisionar de combustible ‖ *intr* aprovisionarse de combustible

fuel cell *s* cámara de combustible, célula electrógena

fuel oil *s* aceite *m* combustible

fuel tank *s* depósito de combustible

fugitive ['fjudʒɪtɪv] *adj & s* fugitivo

fugue [fjug] *s* (mus) fuga

ful·crum ['fʌlkrəm] *s* (*pl* **-crums** o **-cra** [krə]) fulcro

fulfill [ful'fɪl] *tr* (*to carry out*) cumplir, realizar; cumplir con (*una obligación*); llenar (*una condición*)

fulfillment [ful'fɪlmənt] *s* cumplimiento, realización

full [ful] *adj* lleno; (*dress, garment*) amplio, holgado; (*formal dress*) de etiqueta; (*voice*) sonoro, fuerte; (*of food*) harto; **full of aches and pains** lleno de goteras; **full of fun** muy divertido, muy chistoso; **full of play** muy juguetón; **full to overflowing** lleno a rebosar ‖ *adv* completamente; **full many (a)** muchísimos; **full well** muy bien, perfectamente ‖ *s* colmo; **in full** por completo; sin abreviar; **to the full** completamente ‖ *tr* abatanar

full-blooded ['ful'blʌdɪd] *adj* vigoroso; completo, pletórico; de raza

full-blown ['ful'blon] *adj* (*flower, blossom*) abierto; desarrollado, maduro

full-bodied ['ful'badɪd] *adj* fuerte, espeso, consistente; aromático

full dress *s* traje *m* de etiqueta; (mil) uniforme *m* de gala

full'-dress' coat *s* frac *m*

full-faced ['ful'fest] *adj* carilleno; (*view*) de cuadrado; (*portrait*) de rostro entero

full-fledged ['ful'flɛdʒd] *adj* hecho y derecho, nada menos que

full-grown ['ful'gron] *adj* crecido, completamente desarrollado

full house *s* lleno, entrada llena; (poker) fulján *m*

full'-length' mirror *s* espejo de cuerpo entero, espejo de vestir

full-length movie *s* largometraje *m*, cinta de largo metraje

full load *s* plena carga; (aer) peso total

full moon *s* luna llena, plenilunio

full name *s* nombre *m* y apellidos

full'-page' *adj* a página entera

full powers *spl* plenos poderes, amplias facultades

full sail *adv* a todo trapo

full'-scale' *adj* de tamaño natural; total, completo; pleno

full-sized ['ful'saɪzd] *adj* de tamaño natural

full speed *adv* a toda velocidad

full stop *s* parada total; (gram) punto

full swing *s* plena actividad

full tilt *adv* a toda velocidad

full'-time' *adj* a tiempo completo

full'-view' *adj* de vista completa

full volume *s* (rad) máximo de volumen

fully ['fuli] o ['fulli] *adv* completamente; cabalmente; por lo menos

fulsome ['fulsəm] *adj* bajo, craso, de mal gusto

fumble ['fʌmbəl] *tr* no coger (*la pelota*), dejar caer (*la pelota*) desmañadamente; manosear desmañadamente ‖ *intr* revolver papeles; titubear; andar a tientas; (*in one's pockets*) buscar con las manos

fume [fjum] *s* humo, vapor *m*, gas *m*, vaho ‖ *tr* (*to treat with fumes*) ahumar ‖ *intr* (*to give off fumes*) humear; (*to show anger*) echar pestes; **to fume at** echar pestes contra

fumigate ['fjumɪ,get] *tr* fumigar

fumigation [,fjumɪ'geʃən] *s* fumigación

fun [fʌn] *s* divertimiento; broma, chacota; **to be fun** ser divertido; **to have fun** divertirse; **to make fun of** reírse de, burlarse de

function ['fʌŋkʃən] *s* función ‖ *intr* funcionar

functional ['fʌŋkʃənəl] *adj* funcional

functionar·y ['fʌŋkʃə,nɛri] *s* (*pl* **-ies**) funcionario

fund [fʌnd] *s* fondo; **funds** fondos ‖ *tr* consolidar (*una deuda*)

fundamental [,fʌndə'mɛntəl] *adj* fundamental ‖ *s* fundamento

funeral ['fjunərəl] *adj* funeral; (*march, procession*) fúnebre; (*expense*) funerario ‖ *s* funeral *m*, funerales *mpl*, pompa fúnebre (*de cuerpo presente*); **it's not my funeral** (slang) no corre a mi cuidado

funeral director *s* empresario de pompas fúnebres

funeral home o **parlor** *s* funeraria

funeral service *s* oficio de difuntos, misa de cuerpo presente

funereal [fju'nɪri·əl] *adj* fúnebre

fungous ['fʌŋgəs] *adj* fungoso

fungus ['fʌŋgəs] *s* (*pl* **funguses** o **fungi** ['fʌndʒaɪ]) hongo; (pathol) hongo

funicular [fju'nɪkjələr] *adj & s* funicular *m*

funk [fʌŋk] *s* (coll) miedo, cobardía; cobarde *mf*; **in a funk** asustado

fun·nel ['fʌnəl] *s* embudo; (*smokestack*) chimenea; (*tube for ventilation*) manguera, ventilador *m* ‖ *v* (*pret & pp* **-neled** o **-nelled**; *ger* **-neling** o **-nelling**) *tr* verter por medio de un embudo

funnies ['fʌniz] *spl* páginas cómicas, tiras cómicas, tebeo

fun·ny ['fʌni] *adj* (*comp* **-nier**; *super* **-niest**) cómico; divertido, chistoso; (coll) extraño, raro; **to strike someone as funny** hacerle a uno gracia

funny bone *s* hueso de la alegría

funny paper *s* páginas cómicas

fur. *abbr* **furlong, furnished**

fur [fʌr] *s* piel *f*; abrigo de pieles; (*on the tongue*) sarro

furbelow ['fʌrbə,lo] *s* (*ruffle*) faralá *m*; (*frippery*) ringorrango

furbish ['fʌrbɪʃ] *tr* acicalar, limpiar; **to furbish up** renovar

furious ['fjurɪ·əs] *adj* furioso

furl [fʌrl] *tr* enrollar; (naut) aferrar

fur-lined ['fʌr,laɪnd] *adj* forrado con pieles

furlong ['fʌrlɔŋ] o ['fʌrlɑŋ] *s* estadio

furlough ['fʌrlo] s licencia ‖ tr dar licencia a
furnace ['fʌrnɪs] s horno; (to heat a house) calorífero
furnish ['fʌrnɪʃ] tr amueblar; proporcionar, suministrar
furnishings ['fʌrnɪʃɪŋz] spl muebles mpl; (things to wear) artículos
furniture ['fʌrnɪtʃər] s muebles mpl, mobiliario; (naut) aparejo; **a piece of furniture** un mueble
furniture dealer s mueblista mf
furniture store s mueblería
furrier ['fʌrɪ•ər] s peletero
furrier•y ['fʌrɪ•əri] s (pl -ies) peletería
furrow ['fʌro] s surco ‖ tr surcar
further ['fʌrðər] adj adicional; nuevo; más lejano ‖ adv además; más lejos ‖ tr adelantar, promover, fomentar
furtherance ['fʌrðərəns] s adelantamiento, promoción, fomento
furthermore ['fʌrðər,mor] adv además
furthest ['fʌrðɪst] adj (el) más lejano ‖ adv más lejos
furtive ['fʌrtɪv] adj furtivo
fu•ry ['fjʊri] s (pl -ries) furia
furze [fʌrz] s aulaga; retama de escoba
fuse [fjuz] s (tube or wick filled with explosive material) mecha; (device for detonating an explosive charge) espoleta; (elec) fusible m, cortacircuitos m, tapón m; **to burn out a fuse** quemar un fusible ‖ tr fundir; (to unite) fusionar ‖ intr fundirse; fusionarse
fuse box s caja de fusibles
fuselage ['fjuzəlɪdʒ] s fuselaje m
fusible ['fjuzɪbəl] adj fundible, fusible

fusillade [,fjuzɪ'led] s fusilería; (e.g., of questions) andanada ‖ tr atacar o matar con una descarga de fusilería, fusilar
fusion ['fjuʒən] s fusión
fuss [fʌs] s alharaca, hazañería; (coll) disputa por ligero motivo; **to make a fuss** hacer alharacas; **to make a fuss over** hacer fiestas a; disputar sobre ‖ tr atolondrar, inquietar, confundir ‖ intr hacer alharacas, inquietarse por bagatelas
fuss•y ['fʌsi] adj (comp -ier; super -iest)] alharaquiento, alborotado; descontentadizo, quisquilloso, melindroso; funcionero, hazañero; muy adornado
fustian ['fʌstʃən] s (coarse cloth) fustán m; (sort of velveteen) pana; (bombast) cultedad, follaje m
fust•y ['fʌsti] adj (comp -ier; super -iest) mohoso, rancio; que huele a cerrado; pasado de moda
futile ['fjutɪl] adj (unproductive) estéril; (unimportant) fútil
futili•ty [fju'tɪlɪti] s (pl -ties) esterilidad; futilidad
future ['fjutʃər] adj futuro ‖ s futuro, porvenir m; (gram) futuro; **futures** (com) futuros; **in the future** en el futuro; **in the near future** en un futuro próximo
fuze [fjuz] s (tube or wick filled with explosive material) mecha; (device for detonating an explosive charge) espoleta; (elec) fusible m ‖ tr poner la espoleta a
fuzz [fʌz] s (as on a peach) pelusa, vello; (in pockets and corners) borra, tamo; **the fuzz** (slang) policía m, guardia m urbano
fuzz•y ['fʌzi] adj (comp -ier; super -iest) cubierto de pelusa, velloso; polvoriento; (indistinct) borroso

fu
ga

G

G, g [dʒi] s séptima letra del alfabeto inglés
G. abbr German, Gulf
g. abbr gender, genitive, gram
gab [gæb] s (coll) cotorreo ‖ (pret & pp gabbed; ger gabbing) intr (coll) cotorrear
gabardine ['gæbər,din] s gabardina
gabble ['gæbəl] s cotorreo, parloteo ‖ intr cotorrear, parlotear
gable ('gebəl] s (of roof) aguilón m; (over a door or window) gablete m, frontón m
gable end s hastial m
gable roof s tejado de dos aguas
gad [gæd] v (pret & pp gadded; ger gadding) intr callejear, andar de acá para allá; **to gad about** pindonguear (una mujer)
gad'a•bout' adj callejero ‖ s cirigallo; (woman) pindonga
gad'fly' s (pl -flies) tábano
gadget ['gædʒɪt] s adminículo, chisme m, artilugio
Gael [gel] s gaélico
Gaelic ['gelɪk] adj & s gaélico

gaff [gæf] s garfio, arpón m; **to stand the gaff** (slang) tener aguante
gag [gæg] s mordaza; (interpolation by an actor) morcilla; (joke)) chiste m, payasada ‖ v (pret & pp gagged; ger gagging) tr amordazar; dar bascas a ‖ intr sentir bascas, arquear
gage [gedʒ] s (pledge) prenda; (challenge) desafío
gaie•ty ['ge•ɪti] s (pl -ties) alegría, algazara, diversión; (of colors) viveza
gaily ['geli] adv alegremente
gain [gen] s ganancia; (increase) aumento ‖ tr ganar; (to reach) alcanzar ‖ intr ganar terreno; mejorar (un enfermo); adelantarse (un reloj); **to gain on** ir alcanzando
gainful ['genfəl] adj ganancioso, provechoso
gain'say' v (pret & pp -said ['sed] o ['sɛd]) tr negar; contradecir; prohibir
gait [get] s paso, manera de andar
gaiter ['getər] s polaina corta
gal. abbr gallon

gala [ˈgelə] *adj* de gala ‖ *s* fiesta

galax•y [ˈgæləksi] *s* (*pl* -ies) galaxia

gale [gel] *s* ventarrón *m;* **gales of laughter** tempestades de risas; **to weather the gale** correr el temporal; (fig) ir tirando

Galician [gəˈlɪʃən] *adj & s* gallego

gall [gɔl] *s* bilis *f*, hiel *f;* vejiga de la bilis; (*something bitter*) (fig) hiel *f;* rencor *m*, odio; (*gallnut*) agalla; (*audacity*) (coll) descaro ‖ *tr* lastimar rozando; irritar ‖ *intr* raerse; (naut) mascarse (*un cabo*)

gallant [ˈgælənt] *adj* (*attentive to women*) galante; (*pertaining to love*) amoroso ‖ [ˈgælənt] *adj* (*stately, grand*) gallardo; (*spirited, daring*) hazañoso; (*showy, gay*) vistoso, festivo ‖ *s* hombre *m* valiente; (*man attentive to women*) galán *m*

gallant•ry [ˈgæləntri] *s* (*pl* -ries) galantería; gallardía

gall bladder *s* vejiga de la bilis, vesícula biliar

gall duct *s* conducto biliar

galleon [ˈgælɪ•ən] *s* (naut) galeón *m*

galler•y [ˈgæləri] *s* (*pl* -ies) galería; (*in church, theater, etc.*) tribuna; (*cheapest seats in theater*) gallinero; **to play to the gallery** (coll) hablar para la galería

galley [ˈgæli] *s* (naut & typ) galera; (naut) cocina

galley proof *s* (typ) galerada, pruebas de segundas

galley slave *s* galeote *m;* (*drudge*) esclavo del trabajo

Gallic [ˈgælɪk] *adj* gálico

galling [ˈgɔlɪŋ] *adj* irritante, ofensivo

gallivant [ˈgælɪˌvænt] *intr* andar a placer

gall'nut' *s* agalla

gallon [ˈgælən] *s* galón *m* (*medida*)

galloon [gəˈlun] *s* galón *m* (*cinta*)

gallop [ˈgæləp] *s* galope *m;* **at a gallop** a galope ‖ *tr* hacer galopar ‖ *intr* galopar; **to gallop through** (fig) hacer muy aprisa

gal•lows [ˈgæloz] *s* (*pl* -lows o -lowses) horca

gallows bird *s* (coll) carne *f* de horca

gall'stone' *s* cálculo biliar

galore [gəˈlor] *adv* en abundancia

galosh [gəˈlɑʃ] *s* chanclo alto

galvanize [ˈgælvəˌnaɪz] *tr* galvanizar

galvanized iron *s* hierro galvanizado

gambit [ˈgæmbɪt] *s* gambito

gamble [ˈgæmbəl] *s* (coll) empresa arriesgada ‖ *tr* aventurar en el juego; **to gamble away** perder en el juego ‖ *intr* jugar; (*in the stock market*) especular, aventurarse

gambler [ˈgæmblər] *s* jugador *m;* especulador *m*

gambling [ˈgæmblɪŋ] *s* juego

gambling den *s* garito

gambling house *s* casa de juego, juego público

gambling table *s* mesa de juego

gam•bol [ˈgæmbəl] *s* cabriola, retozo, salto ‖ *v* (*pret & pp* -boled o -bolled; *gen* -boling o -bolling) *intr* cabriolar, retozar, saltar

gambrel [ˈgæmbrəl] *s* corvejón *m*

gambrel roof *s* techo a la holandesa

game [gem] *adj* bravo, peleón; dispuesto, resuelto; (*leg*) cojo; de caza ‖ *s* (*form of play*) juego; (*single contest*) partida; (*score*) tantos; (*in bridge*) manga; (*any sport*) deporte *m;* (*animal or bird hunted for sport or food*) caza; (*any pursuit*) actividad; (*pursuit of diplomacy*) juego; **the game is up** estamos frescos; **to make game of** burlarse de; **to play the game** jugar limpio

game bag *s* morral *m*

game bird *s* ave *f* de caza

game'cock' *s* gallo de pelea

game'keep'er *s* guardabosque *m*

game of chance *s* juego de azar

game preserve *s* vedado

game warden *s* guardabosque *m*

gamut [ˈgæmət] *s* (mus & fig) gama

gam•y [ˈgemi] *adj* (*comp* -ier; *super* -iest) (*having flavor of uncooked game*) salvajino; bravo, peleón

gander [ˈgændər] *s* ganso

gang [gæŋ] *adj* múltiple ‖ *s* (*of workmen*) brigada, cuadrilla; (*of thugs*) pandilla ‖ *intr* — **to gang up** acuadrillarse; **to gang up against** u **on** atacar juntos; conspirar contra

gangling [ˈgæŋglɪŋ] *adj* larguirucho

gangli•on [ˈgæŋglɪ•ən] *s* (*pl* -ons o -a [ə]) ganglio

gang'plank' *s* plancha, pasarela

gangrene [ˈgæŋgrin] *s* gangrena ‖ *tr* gangrenar ‖ *intr* gangrenarse

gangster [ˈgæŋstər] *adj* gangsteril ‖ *s* gángster *m*, pistolero

gangsterism [ˈgæŋstəˌrɪzəm] *s* gangsterismo; acciones de los gangsters

gang'way' *s* (*passageway*) pasillo; (*gangplank*) plancha, pasarela; (*in ship's side*) portalón *m* ‖ *interj* ¡abran paso!, ¡paso libre!

gantlet [ˈgɔntlɪt] *s* (rr) vía traslapada

gan•try [ˈgæntri] *s* (*pl* -tries) caballete *m*, poíno; (rr) puente *m* transversal de señales

gantry crane *s* grúa de caballete

gap [gæp] *s* (*break, open space*) laguna; (*in a wall*) boquete *m;* (*between mountains*) garganta, quebrada; (*between two points of view*) sima

gape [gep] o [gæp] *s* abertura, brecha; (*yawn*) bostezo; mirada de asombro; **the gapes** ganas de bostezar ‖ *intr* estar abierto de par en par; bostezar; embobarse; **to gape at** mirar embobado; **to stand gaping** embobarse

G.A.R. *abbr* **Grand Army of the Republic**

garage [gəˈrɑz] *s* garage *m*

garb [gɑrb] *s* vestidura ‖ *tr* vestir

garbage [ˈgɑrbɪdʒ] *s* basuras, desperdicios, bazofia

garbage can *s* cubo para bazofia, latón *m* de la basura

garbage collection *s* recogida de basuras

garbage disposal *s* evacuación de basuras

garbage heap *s* basural *m* (CAm)

garble [ˈgɑrbəl] *tr* mutilar (*un texto*)

garden [ˈgɑrdən] *s* (*of vegetables*) huerto; (*of flowers*) jardín *m*

gardener ['gɑrdənər] s (of vegetables) hortelano; (of flowers) jardinero
gardenia [gɑr'dɪnɪ•ə] s gardenia, jazmín m
de la India
gardening ['gɑrdənɪŋ] s horticultura; jardinería
garden party s fiesta que se da en un jardín o
parque
gargle ['gɑrgəl] s gargarismo || intr gargari-
zar
gargoyle ['gɑrgɔɪl] s gárgola
garish ['gɛrɪʃ] adj charro, chillón, cursi
garland ['gɑrlənd] s guirnalda
garlic ['gɑrlɪk] s ajo
garment ['gɑrmənt] s prenda de vestir
garner ['gɑrnər] tr (to gather, collect) acopiar; adquirir; (cereales) entrojar
garnet ['gɑrnɪt] adj & s granate m
garnish ['gɑrnɪʃ] s adorno; (culin) aderezo,
condimento de adorno || tr adornar; (culin)
aderezar; (law) embargar
garret ['gærɪt] s buhardilla, desván m
garrison ['gærɪsən] s plaza fuerte; (troops)
guarnición || tr guarnecer, guarnicionar
(una plaza fuerte); guarnecer una plaza
fuerte de (tropas)
garrote [gə'rɑt] o [gə'rot] s estrangulación
para robar; (method of execution; iron col-
lar used for such execution) garrote m || tr
estrangular; estrangular para robar; agarrotar, dar garrote a
garrulous ['gærələs] adj gárrulo, locuaz
garter ['gɑrtər] s liga, jarretera
garth [gɑrθ] s patio de claustro
gas [gæs] s gas m; gasolina; (coll) palabrería
|| v (pret & pp **gassed;** ger **gassing**) tr
abastecer de gas; (to attack, asphyxiate, or
poison with gas) gasear; abastecer de gaso-
lina || intr despedir gas; (slang) charlar
gas'bag' s (aer) cámara de gas; (slang) charlatán m
gas burner s mechero de gas
Gascony ['gæskəni] s Gascuña
gas engine s motor m a gas
gaseous ['gæsɪ•əs] adj gaseoso
gas fitter s gasista m
gas generator s gasógeno
gash [gæʃ] s cuchillada, chirlo || tr acuchillar
gas heat s calefacción por gas
gas'hold'er s gasómetro
gasi•fy ['gæsɪ,faɪ] v (pret & pp **-fied**) tr
gasificar || intr gasificarse
gas jet s mechero de gas; llama de gas
gasket ['gæskɪt] s empaquetadura
gas'light' s luz f de gas
gas main s cañería de gas
gas mask s careta antigás
gas meter s contador m de gas
gasohol ['gæsə,hɔl] s alconafta
gasoline ['gæsə,lin] o [,gæsə'lin] s gasolina
gasoline pump s poste m distribuidor m de
gasolina, surtidor m de gasolina
gasp [gæsp] s respiración entrecortada; (of
death) boqueada || tr decir con voz entre-
cortada || intr boquear
gas producer s gasógeno
gas range s cocina a gas

gas station s estación gasolinera
gas stove s cocina a gas
gas tank s gasómetro; **(aut)** depósito de
gasolina
gastric ['gæstrɪk] adj gástrico
gastronomy [gæs'trɑnəmi] s gastronomía
gas'works' s fábrica de gas
gate [get] s puerta; (in fence or wall; of bird
cage) portillo; (of sluice or lock) compuerta; (number of people paying admission; amount they pay) entrada, taquilla;
(rr) barrera; (fig) entrada, camino; **to crash
the gate** (coll) colarse de gorra
gate'keep'er s portero; (rr) guardabarrera mf
gate'post' s poste m de una puerta de cercado
gate'way' s entrada, paso, camino
gather ['gæðər] tr recoger, reunir; recolectar
(la cosecha); coger (leña, flores, etc.);
cubrirse de (polvo); recoger (una persona
sus pensamientos); (bb) alzar; (sew) fruncir; (to deduce) (fig) calcular, deducir; **to
gather oneself together** componerse || intr
reunirse; amontonarse; saltar (lágrimas)
gathering ['gæðərɪŋ] s reunión; recolección;
(bb) alzado; (sew) frunce m
gaud•y ['gɔdi] adj (comp **-ier;** super **-iest**)
cursi, chillón, llamativo
gauge [gedʒ] s medida, norma; calibre m; (of
liquid in a container) nivel m; (of carpenter) gramil m; (of gasoline) medidor m; (rr)
ancho de vía, entrevía || tr medir; calibrar;
graduar; aforar (la cantidad de agua de
una corriente); arquear (una nave)
gauge glass s tubo indicador, vidrio de nivel
Gaul [gɔl] s la Galia; (native) galo
Gaulish ['gɔlɪʃ] adj & s galo
gaunt [gɔnt] o [gɑnt] adj desvaído, macilento; hosco, tétrico
gauntlet ['gɔntlɪt] o ['gɑntlɪt] s guantelete m;
guante con puño abocinado; carrera de
baquetas; (rr) vía traslapada; **to run the
gauntlet** correr baquetas, pasar por baquetas; **to take up the gauntlet** recoger el
guante; **to throw down the gauntlet** arrojar el guante
gauze [gɔz] s gasa, cendal m
gavel ['gævəl] s mazo, martillo
gavotte [gə'vɑt] s gavota
gawk [gɔk] s (coll) palurdo, papanatas m ||
intr (coll) mirar de modo impertinente;
papar moscas, mirar embobado
gawk•y ['gɔki] adj (comp **-ier;** super **-iest**)
desgarbado, torpe, bobo
gay [ge] adj homosexual; alegre, festivo;
(brilliant) vistoso; amigo de los placeres
gaye•ty ['ge•ɪti] s var de **gaiety**
gaze [gez] s mirada fija || intr mirar fijamente
gazelle [gə'zɛl] s gacela
gazette [gə'zɛt] s periódico; anuncio oficial
gazetteer [,gæzə'tɪr] s diccionario geográfico
gear [gɪr] s pertrechos, utensilios; (of transmission, steering, etc.) mecanismo, aparato; rueda dentada; (two or more toothed
wheels meshed together) engranaje m; **out
of gear** desengranado; (fig) descompuesto;
to throw into gear engranar; **to throw out**

of **gear** desengranar; (fig) descomponer ‖
tr & intr engranar
gear'box' *s* caja de engranajes; (aut) caja de
velocidades
gear case *s* caja de engranajes
gear'shift' *s* cambio de marchas, cambio de
velocidades
gearshift lever *s* palanca de cambio de marchas
gear'wheel' *s* rueda dentada
gee [dʒi] *interj* ¡caramba!; **gee up!** (*get up!*,
said to a horse) ¡arre!; **geez!** ¡mecachis!
Gehenna [gɪ'hɛnə] *s* gehena *m*
Geiger counter ['gaɪgər] *s* contador *m* de
Geiger
gel [dʒɛl] *s* gel *m* ‖ *v* (*pret & pp* **gelled;** *ger*
gelling) *intr* cuajarse en forma de gel
gelatine ['dʒɛlətɪn] *s* gelatina
geld [gɛld] *v* (*pret & pp* **gelded** o **gelt** [gɛlt])
tr castrar
gem [dʒɛm] *s* gema, piedra preciosa; (fig)
joya, preciosidad
Gemini ['dʒɛmɪ,naɪ] *s* (*constellation*) Géminis *m* o Gemelos; (*sign of zodiac*) Géminis *m*
gen. *abbr* **gender, general, genitive, genus**
gender ['dʒɛndər] *s* (gram) género; (coll)
sexo
genealo•gy [,dʒɛnɪ'ælədʒi] *s* (*pl* **-gies**) genealogía
general ['dʒɛnərəl] *adj & s* general *m;* **gen-**
eral of the army capitán general de
ejército; **in general** en general o por lo
general
general delivery *s* lista de correos
generalissi•mo [,dʒɛnərə'lɪsɪmo] *s* (*pl* **-mos**)
generalísimo
generali•ty [,dʒɛnə'rælɪti] *s* (*pl* **-ties**) generalidad
generalize ['dʒɛnərə'laɪz] *tr & intr* generalizar
generally ['dʒɛnərəli] *adv* por lo general
general medicine *s* medicina general
general practitioner *s* médico general
generalship ['dʒɛnərəl,ʃɪp] *s* generalato; don
m de mando
general staff *s* estado mayor general
general strike *s* huelga general
generate ['dʒɛnə,ret] *tr* (*to beget*) engendrar;
generar (*electricidad*); (geom) engendrar
generating station *s* central *f*
generation ['dʒɛnə'reʃən] *s* generación
generator ['dʒɛnə,retər] *s* generador *m*
generic [dʒɪ'nɛrɪk] *adj* genérico
generous ['dʒɛnərəs] *adj* generoso; abundante, grande
gene•sis ['dʒɛnɪsɪs] *s* (*pl* **-ses** [,siz]) génesis *f*
‖ **Genesis** *s* (Bib) el Génesis
genetic [dʒɪ'nɛtɪk] *adj* genético
genetic engineering *s* ingeniería genética
genetics [dʒɪ'nɛtɪks] *s* genética
Geneva [dʒɪ'nivə] *s* Ginebra
Genevan [dʒɪ'nivən] *adj & s* ginebrino
genial ['dʒini•əl] *adj* afable, complaciente
genie ['dʒini] *s* genio
genital ['dʒɛnɪtəl] *adj* genital ‖ **genitals** *spl*
genitales *mpl*, órganos genitales

genitive ['dʒɛnɪtɪv] *adj & s* genitivo
genitourinary [,dʒɛnəto'jʊrɪ,nɛrɪ] *adj* geni-
tourinario
genius ['dʒinjəs] o ['dʒini•əs] *s* (*pl* **geniuses**)
(*great inventive gift; person possessing it*)
genio ‖ *s* (*pl* **genii** ['dʒini,aɪ]) (*guardian*
spirit; pagan deity) genio
Genoa ['dʒɛno•ə] *s* Génova
genocidal [,dʒɛnə'saɪdəl] *adj* genocida
genocide ['dʒɛnə'saɪd] *s* (*act*) genocidio;
(*person*) genocida *mf*
Geno•ese [,dʒɛno'iz] *adj* genovés ‖ *s* (*pl*
-ese) genovés *m*
genre ['ʒɑnrə] *adj* de género
gent. o **Gent.** *abbr* **gentleman, gentlemen**
genteel [dʒɛn'til] *adj* gentil, elegante; cortés,
urbano
gentian ['dʒɛnʃən] *s* genciana
gentile ['dʒɛntɪl] o ['dʒɛntaɪl] *adj* gentilicio;
(gram) gentilicio ‖ ['dʒɛntaɪl] *adj & s* no
judío; cristiano; (*pagan*) gentil *mf*
gentili•ty [dʒɛn'tɪlɪti] *s* (*pl* **-ties**) gentileza
gentle ['dʒɛntəl] *adj* apacible, benévolo;
dulce, manso, suave; cortés, fino; (*e.g.,*
tap on the shoulder) ligero
gen'tle•folk' *s* gente bien nacida
gentle•man ['dʒɛntəlmən] *s* (*pl* **-men** [mən])
s caballero; (*attendant to a person of high*
rank) gentilhombre *m*
gentleman in waiting *s* gentilhombre *m* de
cámara
gentlemanly ['dʒɛntəlmənli] *adj* caballeroso
gentleman of leisure *s* señor *m* que vive sin
trabajar, caballero de vida holgada
gentleman of the road *s* salteador *m* de
caminos
gentleman's agreement *s* acuerdo verbal
gentle sex *s* bello sexo, sexo débil
gentry ['dʒɛntri] *s* gente bien nacida
genuine ['dʒɛnjʊ•ɪn] *adj* genuino; sincero,
franco
genus ['dʒinəs] *s* (*pl* **genera** ['dʒɛnərə] o
genuses) (biol, log) género
geog. *abbr* **geography**
geographer [dʒɪ'agrəfər] *s* geógrafo
geographic(al) [,dʒi•ə'græfɪk(əl)] *adj* geográfico
geogra•phy [dʒɪ'agrəfi] *s* (*pl* **-phies**) geografía
geol. *abbr* **geology**
geologic(al) [,dʒi•ə'ladʒɪk(əl)] *adj* geológico
geologist [dʒɪ'alədʒɪst] *s* geólogo
geology [dʒɪ'alədʒi] *s* (*pl* **-gies**) geología
geom. *abbr* **geometry**
geometric(al) [,dʒi•ə'mɛtrɪk(əl)] *adj* geométrico
geometrician [dʒɪ,amɪ'trɪʃən] *s* geómetra *mf*
geome•try [dʒɪ'amɪtri] *s* (*pl* **-tries**) geometría
geophysics [,dʒi•ə'fɪzɪks] *s* geofísica
geopolitics [,dʒi•ə'palɪtɪks] *s* geopolítica
George [dʒɔrdʒ] *s* Jorge *m*
geranium [dʒɪ'reni•əm] *s* geranio
geriatrical [,dʒɛrɪ'ætrɪkəl] *adj* geriátrico
geriatrician [,dʒɛrɪ•ə'trɪʃən] *s* geriatra *mf*
geriatrics [,dʒɛrɪ'ætrɪks] *s* geriatría
germ [dʒʌrm] *s* germen *m*
German ['dʒʌrmən] *adj & s* alemán *m*

germane [dʒər'men] *adj* pertinente, relacionado

Germanize ['dʒʌrmə,naɪz] *tr* germanizar

German measles *s* rubéola

German silver *s* melchor *m*, alpaca

Germany ['dʒʌrməni] *s* Alemania

germ carrier *s* portador *m* de gérmenes

germ cell *s* célula germen

germicidal [,dʒʌrmɪ'saɪdəl] *adj* germicida

germicide ['dʒʌrmɪ,saɪd] *s* germicida *m*

germinate ['dʒʌrmɪ,net] *intr* germinar

germ plasm *s* germen *m* plasma

germ theory *s* teoría germinal

germ warfare *s* guerra bacteriana, guerra bacteriológica

gerontology [,dʒɛrɑn'tɑlədʒi] *s* gerontología

gerund ['dʒɛrənd] *s* gerundio

gerundive [dʒɪ'rʌndɪv] *s* gerundio adjetivo

gestation [dʒɛs'teʃən] *s* gestación

gesticulate [dʒɛs'tɪkjə,let] *intr* accionar, manotear

gesticulation [dʒɛs,tɪkjə'leʃən] *s* ademán *m*, manoteo

gesture ['dʒɛstʃər] *s* ademán *m*, gesto; demostración, muestra ‖ *intr* hacer ademanes, hacer gestos

get [gɛt] *v* (*pret* **got** [gɑt]; *pp* **got** o **gotten** ['gɑtən]; *ger* **getting**) *tr* conseguir, obtener; recibir; ir por, buscar; tomar (*p.ej., un billete*); alcanzar; encontrar, hallar; hacer (*p.ej., la comida*); resolver (*un problema*); aprender de memoria; captar (*una estación emisora*); **to get across** hacer aceptar; hacer comprender; **to get back** recobrar; **to get down** descolgar; (*to swallow*) tragar; **to get off** quitar (*p.ej., una mancha*); **to get someone to** + *inf* lograr que alguien + *subj*; **to get** + *pp* hacer + *inf*; **to have got** (coll) tener; **to have got to** + *inf* (coll) tener que + *inf* ‖ *intr* (*to become*) hacerse, ponerse, volverse; (*to arrive*) llegar; **get up!** (*to an animal*) ¡arre!; **to get about** estar levantado (*un convaleciente*); **to get along** seguir andando; irse; ir tirando; tener éxito; llevarse bien; **to get along in years** ponerse viejo; **to get along with** congeniar con; **to get angry** enfadarse; **to get around** divulgarse; salir mucho, ir a todas partes; eludir; manejar (*a una persona*); **to get away** conseguir marcharse; evadirse; **to get away with** llevarse, escaparse con; (coll) hacer impunemente; **to get back** volver, regresar; **to get back at** (coll) desquitarse con; **to get behind** quedarse atrás; apoyar, abogar por; **to get by** lograr pasar; (*to manage to shift*) (coll) arreglárselas; **to get going** ponerse en marcha; **to get in** entrar; volver a casa; llegar (*un tren*); **to get in with** llegar a ser amigo de; **to get married** casarse; **to get off** apearse; marcharse; **to get old** envejecer; **to get on** subir; llevarse bien; **to get out** salir, marcharse, divulgarse; **to get out of** bajar de (*un coche*); librarse de; perder (*la paciencia*); **to get out of the way** quitarse de en medio; **to get run over** ser atropellado; **to get through** pasar por entre; terminar; **to get to be** llegar a ser; **to get under way** ponerse en camino; **to get up** levantarse; **to not get over it** (coll) no volver de su asombro

get'·a·way' *s* escapatoria, escape *m;* (*of an automobile*) arranque *m*

get'·to·geth'er *s* reunión, tertulia

get'·up' *s* (coll) disposición, presentación; (coll) atavío, traje *m*

gewgaw ['gjugɔ] *adj* cursi, charro, chillón ‖ *s* fruslería, chuchería; adorno, charro

geyser ['gaɪzər] *s* géiser *m* ‖ ['gizər] *s* (Brit) calentador *m* de agua

ghast·ly ['gæstli] o ['gɑstli] *adj* (*comp* **-lier;** *super* **-liest**) cadavérico, espectral; espantoso, horrible

Ghent [gɛnt] *s* Gante

gherkin ['gʌrkɪn] *s* pepinillo

ghet·to ['gɛto] *s* (*pl* **-tos**) ghetto

ghost [gost] *s* espectro, fantasma *m;* (telv) fantasma *m;* **not a ghost of a** ni sombra de; **to give up the ghost** entregar el alma, rendir el alma

ghost·ly ['gostli] *adj* (*comp* **-lier;** *super* **-liest**) espectral

ghost story *s* cuento de fantasmas

ghost writer *s* colaborador anónimo, escritor anónimo de obras firmadas por otra persona

ghoul [gul] *s* demonio que se alimenta de cadáveres; ladrón *m* de tumbas; (*person who revels in horrible things*) vampiro

ghoulish ['gulɪʃ] *adj* vampírico, horrible

G.H.Q. *abbr* **General Headquarters**

GI ['dʒi'aɪ] *s* (*pl* **GI's**) (coll) soldado raso (*del ejército norteamericano*)

giant ['dʒaɪ·ənt] *adj* & *s* gigante *m*

giantess ['dʒaɪ·əntɪs] *s* giganta

gibberish ['dʒɪbərɪʃ] o ['gɪbərɪʃ] *s* guirigay *m*

gibbet ['dʒɪbɪt] *s* horca ‖ *tr* ahorcar; poner a la vergüenza

gibe [dʒaɪb] *s* remoque *m*, mofa ‖ *intr* mofarse; **to gibe at** mofarse de

giblets ['dʒɪblɪts] *spl* menudillos

giddiness ['gɪdɪnɪs] *s* vértigo, vahído; falta de juicio

gid·dy ['gɪdi] *adj* (*comp* **-dier;** *super* **-diest**) vertiginoso; mareado; casquivano, ligero de cascos

Gideon ['gɪdɪ·ən] *s* (Bib) Gedeón *m*

gift [gɪft] *s* regalo; (*natural ability*) don *m*, dote *f*, prenda

gifted ['gɪftɪd] *adj* talentoso; muy inteligente

gift horse *s* —**never look a gift horse in the mouth** a caballo regalado no se le mira el diente

gift of gab *s* (coll) facundia, labia

gift shop *s* comercio de objetos de regalo, tienda de regalos

gift'wrap' *v* (*pret* & *pp* **-wrapped;** *ger* **-wrapping**) *tr* envolver en paquete regalo

gigantic [dʒaɪ'gæntɪk] *adj* gigantesco

giggle ['gɪgəl] *s* risita, risa ahogada, retozo de la risa ‖ *intr* reírse bobamente

ge
gi

gigo•lo ['dʒɪgə ˌlo] s (pl **-los**) acompañante m profesional de mujeres; (man supported by a woman) mantenido

gild [gɪld] v (pret & pp **gilded** o **gilt** [gɪlt]) tr dorar

gilding ['gɪldɪŋ] s dorado

gill [gɪl] s (of fish) agalla; (of cock) barba || [dʒɪl] s cuarta parte de una pinta

gillyflower ['dʒɪlɪˌflaʊ•ər] s alhelí m

gilt [gɪlt] adj & s dorado

gilt-edged ['gɪltˌɛdʒd] adj de toda confianza, de lo mejor que hay

gilt′head′ s dorada

gimcrack ['dʒɪm ˌkræk] adj de oropel || s chuchería

gimlet ['gɪmlɪt] s barrena de mano

gimmick ['gɪmɪk] s (slang) adminículo; (slang) adminículo mágico

gin [dʒɪn] s (alcoholic liquor) ginebra; desmotadera de algodón; trampa; (fish trap) garlito; torno de izar || v (pret & pp **ginned**; ger **ginning**) tr desmotar

gin fizz s ginebra con gaseosa

ginger ['dʒɪndʒər] s jenjibre m; (coll) energía, viveza

ginger ale s cerveza de jengibre gaseosa

gin′ger•bread′ s pan m de jengibre; adorno charro

gingerly ['dʒɪndʒərli] adj cauteloso, cuidadoso || adv cautelosamente

gin′ger•snap′ s galletita de jengibre

gingham ['gɪŋəm] s guinga

giraffe [dʒɪ'ræf] s jirafa

girandole ['dʒɪrənˌdol] s girándula

gird [gʌrd] v (pret & pp **girt** [gʌrt] o **girded**) tr ceñir; (to equip) dotar; (to prepare) aprestar; (to surround, hem in) rodear, encerrar

girder ['gʌrdər] s viga, trabe f

girdle ['gʌrdəl] s faja; corsé pequeño || tr ceñir; circundar, rodear

girl [gʌrl] s muchacha, niña, chica; (servant) moza

girl friend s (coll) amiguita

girlhood ['gʌrlhʊd] s muchachez f; juventud femenina

girlish [gʌrlɪʃ] adj de muchacha; juvenil

girl scout s niña exploradora

girth [gʌrθ] s (band) cincha; (waistband) pretina; circunferencia

gist [dʒɪst] s esencia

give [gɪv] s elasticidad || v (pret **gave** [gev]; pp **given** ['gɪvən] tr dar; ocasionar (molestia, trabajo, etc.); representar (una obra dramática); (lessons) impartir; pronunciar (un discurso); **to give away** dar de balde; revelar; llevar (a la novia); (coll) traicionar; **to give back** devolver; **to give forth** despedir (p.ej. olores); **to give oneself up** entregarse; **to give up** abandonar, dejar (un empleo); renunciar || intr dar; dar de sí; romperse (p.ej., una cuerda); **to give in** ceder, rendirse; **to give out** agotarse; no poder más; **to give up** darse por vencido

give′-and-take′ s concesiones mutuas; conversación sazonada de burlas

give′a•way′ s (coll) revelación involuntaria; (coll) traición; (e.g., in checkers) (coll) ganapierde m & f

given ['gɪvən] adj dado; (math) conocido; **given that** dado que, suponiendo que

given name s nombre m de pila

giver ['gɪvər] s dador m, donador m

gizzard ['gɪzərd] s molleja

glacial ['gleʃəl] adj glacial

glacier ['gleʃər] s glaciar m, helero

glad [glæd] adj (comp **gladder**; super **gladdest**) alegre, contento; **to be glad (to)** alegrarse (de)

gladden ['glædən] tr alegrar

glade [gled] s claro, claro herboso (en un bosque)

glad hand s (coll) acogida efusiva

gladiola [ˌglædɪ'olə] s estoque m

gladly ['glædli] adv alegremente; de buena gana, con mucho gusto

gladness ['glædnɪs] s alegría, regocijo

glad rags spl (slang) trapitos de cristianar; (slang) vestido de etiqueta

glamorous ['glæmərəs] adj fascinador, elegante

glamour ['glæmər] s fascinación, elegancia, hechizo

glamour girl s belleza exótica

glance [glæns] s ojeada, vistazo, golpe m de vista; **at a glance** de un vistazo; **at first glance** a primera vista || intr lanzar una mirada; **to glance at** lanzar una mirada a; examinar de paso; **to glance off** desviarse de soslayo; desviarse de, al chocar; **to glance over** mirar por encima

gland [glænd] s glándula

glanders ['glændərz] spl muermo

glandulous ['glændʒələs] adj glanduloso

glare [glɛr] s fulgor m deslumbrante, luz intensa; mirada feroz, mirada de indignación || intr relumbrar; lanzar miradas feroces; **to glare at** echar una mirada feroz a

glaring '['glɛrɪŋ] adj deslumbrante, relumbrante; (look) feroz, penetrante; manifiesto, que salta a la vista

glass [glæs] s vidrio, cristal m; (tumbler) vaso, copa; (mirror) espejo; (glassware) vajilla de cristal; **glasses** anteojos

glass blower ['blo•ər] s soplador m de vidrio, vidriero

glass case s vitrina

glass cutter s cortavidrios m

glass door s puerta vidriera

glassful ['glæsfʊl] s vaso

glass′house′ s invernadero; (fig) tejado de vidrio

glassine [glæ'sin] s papel m cristal

glass′ware′ s cristalía, vajilla de vidrio

glass wool s cristal hilado

glass′works′ s cristalería vidriería

glass′work′er s vidriero

glass•y ['glæsi] adj (comp **-ier**; super **-iest**) vidrioso

glaze [glez] s vidriado, esmalte m; (of ice) capa resbaladiza || tr vidriar, esmaltar; garapiñar (golosinas)

glazier ['gleʒər] s vidriero

gleam [glim] *s* destello, rayo de luz; luz *f* tenue; (*of hope*) rayo ‖ *intr* destellar; brillar con luz tenue

glean [glin] *tr* espigar; (*to gather bit by bit, e.g., out of books*) espigar

glee [gli] *s* alegría, regocijo

glee club *s* orfeón *m*

glib [glɪb] *adj* (*comp* **glibber;** *super* **glibbest**) locuaz; (*tongue*) suelto; fácil e insincero

glide [glaɪd] *s* deslizamiento; (aer) vuelo sin motor, planeo; (mus) ligadura ‖ *intr* deslizarse; (aer) volar sin motor, planear; **to glide along** pasar suavemente

glider [ˈglaɪdər] *s* (aer) planeador *m*, deslizador *m*

glimmer [ˈglɪmər] *s* luz *f* tenue; (*faint perception*) vislumbre *f* ‖ *intr* brillar con luz tenue; (*to appear faintly*) vislumbrarse

glimmering [ˈglɪmərɪŋ] *adj* tenue, trémulo ‖ *s* luz *f* tenue; vislumbre *f*

glimpse [glɪmps] *s* vislumbre *f;* **to catch a glimpse of** entrever, vislumbrar ‖ *tr* vislumbrar

glint [glɪnt] *s* destello, rayo ‖ *intr* destellar

glisten [ˈglɪsən] *s* centelleo ‖ *intr* centellear

glitter [ˈglɪtər] *s* resplandor *m*, brillo ‖ *intr* resplandecer, brillar

gloaming [ˈglomɪŋ] *s* crepúsculo vespertino

gloat [glot] *intr* relamerse; **to gloat over** mirar con satisfacción maligna

globe [glob] *s* globo

globetrotter [ˈglob,trɑtər] *s* trotamundos *m*

globule [ˈglɑbjul] *s* glóbulo

glockenspiel [ˈglɑkən,spil] *s* juego de timbres, órgano de campanas

gloom [glum] *s* lobreguez *f* tinieblas, obscuridad; abatimiento, tristeza; aspecto abatido

gloom·y [ˈglumi] *adj* (*comp* **-ier;** *super* **-iest**) (*dark; sad*) lóbrego; pesimista

glori·fy [ˈglorɪ,faɪ] *v* (*pret & pp* **-fied**) *tr* glorificar; (*to enhance*) realzar

glorious [ˈglorɪ·əs] *adj* glorioso; espléndido, magnífico; (coll) alegre

glo·ry [ˈglori] *s* (*pl* **-ries**) gloria; **to go to glory** ganar la gloria; (slang) fracasar ‖ *v* (*pret & pp* **-ried**) *intr* gloriarse

gloss [glɑs] *s* brillo, lustre *m;* (*note, commentary*) glosa; glosario ‖ *tr* (*to annotate*) glosar; lustrar, satinar; **to gloss over** disculpar, paliar

glossa·ry [ˈglɑsəri] *s* (*pl* **-ries**) glosario

gloss·y [ˈglɑsi] *adj* (*comp* **-ier;** *super* **-iest**) brillante, lustroso; (*silk*) joyante

glottal [ˈglɑtəl] *adj* glótico

glove [glʌv] *s* guante *m*

glove compartment *s* portaguantes *m*

glove stretcher *s* ensanchador *m, juanas*

glow [glo] *s* (*light of incandescence*) resplandor *m; (e.g., of sunset)* brillo, esplendor *m;* sensación de calor; color *m* en las mejillas ‖ *intr* brillar sin llama; estar encendido (*el rostro, el cielo*); estar muy animado

glower [ˈglau·ər] *s* ceño, mirada ceñuda ‖ *intr* mirar con ceño

glowing [ˈglo·ɪŋ] *adj* ardiente, encendido; radiante; entusiasta, elogioso

glow·worm· *s* gusano de luz, luciérnaga

glucose [ˈglukos] *s* glucosa

glue [glu] *s* cola; pegapega ‖ *tr* encolar; pegar fuertemente

glue pot *s* cazo de cola

gluey [ˈglu·i] *adj* (*comp* **gluier;** *super* **gluiest**) pegajoso; (*smeared with glue*) encolado

glug [glʌg] *s* gluglú *m* ‖ *v* (*pret & pp* **glugged;** *ger* **glugging**) *intr* hacer gluglú (*el agua*)

glum [glʌm] *adj* (*comp* **glummer;** *super* **glummest**) hosco

glut [glʌt] *s* abundancia, gran acopio; exceso; **to be a glut on the market** abarrotarse ‖ *v* (*pret & pp* **glutted;** *ger* **glutting**) *tr* hartar, saciar; inundar (*el mercado*); obstruir

glutton [ˈglʌtən] *adj & s* glotón *m*

gluttonous [ˈglʌtənəs] *adj* glotón

glutton·y [ˈglʌtəni] *s* (*pl* **-ies**) glotonería, gula

glycerine [ˈglɪsərɪn] *s* glicerina

G.M. *abbr* **general manager, Grand Master**

G-man [ˈdʒi,mæn] *s* (*pl* **-men** [,mɛn]) (coll) agente *m* de la policía federal

G.M.T. *abbr* **Greenwich mean time**

gnarl [nɑrl] *s* nudo ‖ *tr* torcer ‖ *intr* gruñir

gnarled [nɑrld] *adj* nudoso, retorcido

gnash [næʃ] *tr* hacer rechinar (*los dientes*) ‖ *intr* hacer rechinar los dientes

gnat [næt] *s* jején *m*

gnaw [nɔ] *tr* roer; practicar (*un agujero*) royendo

gnome [nom] *s* gnomo

go [go] *s* (*pl* **goes**) ida; (coll) energía, ímpetu *m;* (coll) boga; (coll) ensayo; (*for traffic*) paso libre; **it's a go** (coll) es un trato hecho; **it's all the go** (coll) hace furor; **it's no go** (coll) es imposible; **on the go** (coll) en continuo movimiento; **to make a go of** (coll) lograr éxito en ‖ *v* (*pret* **went** [wɛnt]; *pp* **gone** [gɔn] o [gɑn]) *tr* (coll) soportar, tolerar; **to go it alone** obrar sin ayuda ‖ *intr* ir; (*to work, operate*) funcionar, marchar; andar (*p.ej., desnudo*); volverse (*p.ej., loco*); **going, going, gone!** ¡vendo, vendo, vendí!; **so it goes** así va el mundo; **to be going to** + *inf* ir a + *inf;* **to be gone** haber ido; haberse agotado; haber dejado de ser; **to go against** ir en contra de; **to go ahead** seguir adelante; **to go away** irse, marcharse; **to go back** volver; **to go by** pasar por; guiarse por; atenerse a; **to go down** bajar; hundirse (*un buque*); **to go fishing** ir de pesca; **to go for** ir por; **to go get** ir por, ir a buscar; **to go house hunting** ir a buscar casa; **to go hunting** ir de caza; **to go in** entrar; entrar en; (*to fit in*) caber en; **to go in for** dedicarse a, interesarse por; **to go into** entrar en; investigar; (aut) poner (*p.ej., primera*); **to go in with** asociarse con; **to go off** irse, marcharse; llevarse a cabo; estallar (*p.ej., una bomba*); dispararse (*un fusil*); **to go on** seguir adelante; ir tirando; **to go on** + *ger* seguir + *ger;* **to go on with** continuar; **to**

go out salir; pasar de moda; apagarse (*un fuego, una luz*); declararse en huelga; (*for entertainment, etc.*) salir; **to go over** tener éxito; releer; examinar, revisar; pasar por encima de; **to go over to** pasarse a las filas de; **to go through** pasar por; llegar al fin de; agotar (*una fortuna*); **to go with** ir con, acompañar; salir con (*una muchacha*); hacer juego con; **to go without** andarse sin, pasarse sin

goad [god] *s* aguijada, aguijón *m* ‖ *tr* aguijonear; (SAm) espuelear

go'-a•head' *adj* (coll) emprendedor ‖ *s* (coll) señal *f* para seguir adelante, luz *f* verde

goal [gol] *s* meta; (*in football*) gol *m*

goal'keep'er *s* guardameta *m*, portero

goal line *s* raya de la meta

goal post *s* poste *m* de la meta

goat [got] *s* cabra; (*male goat*) macho cabrío; (coll) víctima inocente; **to be the goat** (slang) pagar el pato; **to get the goat of** (slang) tomar el pelo a; **to ride the goat** (coll) ser iniciado en una sociedad secreta

goatee (go'ti] *s* perilla

goat'herd' *s* cabrero

goat'skin' *s* piel *f* de cabra

goat'suck'er *s* chotacabras *m*

gob [gab] *s* (coll) masa informe y pequeña; (coll) marinero de guerra

gobble ['gabəl] *s* gluglú *m* ‖ *tr* engullir; **to gobble up** engullirse ávidamente; (coll) asir de repente, apoderarse ávidamente de ‖ *intr* engullir; gluglutear, gorgonear (*el pavo*)

gobbledegook ['gabəldɪ,guk] *s* (coll) lenguaje obscuro e incomprensible, galimatías *m*

go'-be•tween' *s* (*intermediary*) medianero; (*in promoting marriages*) casamentero; (*in shady love affairs*) alcahuete *m*, alcahueta

goblet ['gablɪt] *s* copa

goblin ['gablɪn] *s* duende *m*, trasgo

go'-by' *s* (coll) desaire *m;* **to give someone the go-by** (coll) negarse al trato de alguien

go'cart' *s* andaderas; cochecito para niños; carruaje ligero

god [gad] *s* dios *m;* **God forbid** no lo quiera Dios; **God grant** permita Dios; **God willing** Dios mediante

god'child' *s* (*pl* **chil'dren**) ahijado, ahijada

god'daugh'ter *s* ahijada

goddess ['gadɪs] *s* diosa

god'fa'ther *s* padrino

God'-fear'ing *adj* timorato; devoto, pío

God'for•sak'en *adj* dejado de la mano de Dios; (coll) desolado, desierto

god'head' *s* divinidad ‖ **Godhead** *s* Dios *m*

godless ['gadlɪs] *adj* infiel, impío; desalmado, malvado

god•ly ['gadlɪ] *adj* (*comp* **-lier;** *super* **-liest**) devoto, pío

god'moth'er *s* madrina

God's acre *s* campo santo

god'send' *s* cosa llovida del cielo, bendición

god'son' *s* ahijado

God'speed' *s* bienandanza, buena suerte, buen viaje *m*

go'-get'ter *s* (slang) buscavidas *mf*, persona emprendedora

goggle ['gagəl] *intr* volver los ojos; abrir los ojos desmesuradamente

goggle-eyed ['gagəl,aɪd] *adj* de ojos saltones

goggles ['gagəlz] *spl* anteojos de camino, gafas contra el polvo

going ['go•ɪŋ] *adj* en marcha, funcionando; **going on** casi, p.ej., **it is going on nine o'clock** son casi las nueve ‖ *s* ida, partida

going concern *s* empresa que marcha

goings on *spl* actividades; bulla, jarana

goiter ['gɔɪtər] *s* bocio

gold [gold] *adj* áureo, de oro; dorado ‖ *s* oro

gold'beat'er *s* batidor *m* de oro, batihoja *m*

goldbeater's skin *s* venza

gold brick *s* — **to sell a gold brick** (coll) vender gato por liebre

gold'crest' *s* reyezuelo moñudo

gold digger ['dɪgər] *s* (slang) extractora de oro

golden ['goldən] *adj* áureo, de oro; (*gilt*) dorado; (*hair*) rubio; excelente, favorable, floreciente

golden age *s* edad de oro, siglo de oro

golden calf *s* becerro de oro

Golden Fleece *s* vellocino de oro

golden mean *s* justo medio

golden plover *s* chorlito

gold'en•rod' *s* vara de oro, vara de San José

golden rule *s* regla de la caridad cristiana

golden wedding *s* bodas de oro

gold-filled ['gold,fɪld] *adj* empastado en oro

gold'finch' *s* jilguero, pintacilgo

gold'fish' *s* carpa dorada, pez *m* de color

goldilocks ['goldɪ ,laks] *s* rubiales *mf*

gold leaf *s* pan *m* de oro

gold mine *s* mina de oro; **to strike a gold mine** (fig) encontrar una mina

gold plate *s* vajilla de oro

gold'-plate' *tr* dorar

gold'smith' *s* orfebre *m*

gold standard *s* patrón *m* oro

golf [galf] *s* golf *m* ‖ *intr* jugar al golf

golf club *s* palo de golf; asociación de jugadores de golf

golfer ['galfər] *s* golfista *mf*

golf links *spl* campo de golf

Golgotha ['galgəθə] *s* el Gólgota

gondola ['gandələ] *s* góndola

gondolier [,gandə'lɪr] *s* gondolero

gone [gɔn] o [gan] *adj* agotado; arruinado; desaparecido; muerto; **gone on** (coll) enamorado de

gong [gɔŋ] o [gaŋ] *s* batintín *m*

gonorrhea [,ganə'ri•ə] *s* gonorrea

goo [gu] *s* (slang) substancia pegajosa

good [gʊd] *adj* (*comp* **better;** *super* **best**) bueno; **good and . . .** (coll) muy, p.ej., **good and cheap** muy barato; **good for** bueno para; capaz de hacer; capaz de pagar; capaz de vivir (*cierto tiempo*); **to be good at** tener talento para; **to be no good** (coll) no servir para nada; (coll) ser un perdido; **to make good** tener éxito; cumplir (*sus promesas*); pagar (*una deuda*); responder de (*los daños*) ‖ *s* bien *m*, provecho, utilidad; **for good** para siempre; **for good and all** de una vez para siempre; **goods** efectos; géneros, mercancías; **the good** lo bueno; los buenos; **to catch with the goods** (slang) coger en flagrante; **to deliver the goods** (slang) cumplir lo prometido; **to do good** hacer el bien; dar salud o fuerzas a; **to the good** de sobra, en el haber; **what is the good of . . . ?** ¿para qué sirve . . . ?

good afternoon s buenas tardes

good'by' o **good'bye'** s adiós m ‖ interj ¡adiós!

good day s buenos días

good evening s buenas noches, buenas tardes

good fellow s (coll) buen chico, buen sujeto

good fellowship s compañerismo

good'-for-noth'ing adj inútil, sin valor ‖ s pelafustán m perdido

Good Friday s Viernes santo

good graces spl favor m, estimación

good-hearted ['gʊd'hɑrtɪd] adj de buen corazón

good-humored ['gʊd'jumərd] adj de buen humor; afable

good-looking ['gʊd'lʊkɪŋ] adj guapo, bien parecido

good looks spl hermosura, guapeza

good•ly ['gʊdli] adj (comp **-lier**; super **-liest**) considerable; bien parecido, hermoso; bueno, excelente

good morning s buenos días

good-natured ['gʊd'netʃərd] adj bonachón, afable

Good Neighbor Policy s política del buen vecino

goodness ['gʊdnɪs] s bondad; **for goodness' sake!** ¡por Dios!; **goodness knows!** ¡quién sabe! ‖ interj ¡válgame Dios!

good night s buenas noches

good sense s buen sentido, sensatez f

good-sized ['gʊd'saɪzd] adj bastante grande, de buen tamaño

good speed s adiós m y buena suerte

good-tempered ['gʊd'tɛmpərd] adj de natural apacible

good time s rato agradable; **to have a good time** divertirse; **to make good time** ir a buen paso; llegar en poco tiempo

good turn s favor m, servicio

good way s buen trecho

good will s buena voluntad; (com) buen nombre m, clientela

good•y ['gʊdi] adj (coll) beatuco, santurrón ‖ s (pl **-ies**) (coll) golosina ‖ interj (coll) ¡qué bien!, ¡qué alegría!

gooey ['gu•i] adj (comp **gooier**; super **gooiest**) (slang) pegajoso, fangoso

goof [guf] s (slang) tonto ‖ tr & intr (slang) chapucear ‖ intr — **to goof off** farrear

goof•y ['gufi] adj (comp **-ier**; super **-iest**) (slang) tonto, mentecato

goon [gun] s (roughneck) (coll) gamberro, canalla m; (coll) terrorista m de alquiler; (slang) estúpido

goose [gus] s (pl **geese** [gis] ánsar m, ganso, oca; **the goose hangs high** todo va a pedir de boca; **to cook one's goose** malbaratarle a uno los planes; **to kill the goose that lays the golden eggs** matar la gallina de los huevos de oro ‖ s (pl **gooses**) plancha de sastre

goose'ber'ry s (pl **-ries**) (plant) grosellero silvestre; (fruit) grosella silvestre

goose egg s huevo de oca; (slang) cero

goose flesh s carne f de gallina

goose'neck' s cuello de cisne; (naut) gancho de botalones

goose pimples spl carne f de gallina

goose step s (mil) paso de ganso

G.O.P. abbr **Grand Old Party**

gopher ['gofər] s ardilla de tierra, ardillón m; (Geomys) tuza

Gordian knot ['gɔrdɪən] s nudo gordiano; **to cut the Gordian knot** cortar el nudo gordiano

gore [gor] s sangre derramada, sangre cuajada; (insert in a piece of cloth) cuchillo, nesga ‖ tr (to pierce with a horn) acornar; poner cuchillo o nesga a; nesgar

gorge [gɔrdʒ] s garganta, desfiladero; (in a river) atasco de hielo ‖ tr atiborrar ‖ intr atiborrarse

gorgeous ['gɔrdʒəs] adj primoroso, brillante, magnífico, suntuoso

gorilla [gə'rɪlə] s gorila

gorse [gɔrs] s aulaga

gor•y ['gori] adj (comp **-ier**; super **-iest**) ensangrentado, sangriento

gosh [gɑʃ] interj ¡caramba!

goshawk ['gɑs,hɔk] s azor m

gospel ['gɑspəl] s evangelio ‖ **Gospel** s Evangelio

gospel truth s evangelio, pura verdad

gossamer ['gɑsəmər] s telaraña flotante; gasa sutilísima; tela impermeable muy delgada; impermeable m de tela muy delgada

gossip ['gɑsɪp] s chismes m; (person) chismoso, bocaza; **piece of gossip** chisme m ‖ intr chismear

gossip column s mentidero

gossip columnist s gacetillero, cronista mf social

gossipy ['gɑsɪpi] adj chismoso

Goth [gɑθ] s godo; (fig) bárbaro

Gothic ['gɑθɪk] adj & s gótico

gouge [gaʊdʒ] s gubia; (cut made with a gouge) muesca; (coll) estafa ‖ tr excavar con gubia; (coll) estafar

goulash ['gulɑʃ] s puchero húngaro

gourd [gord] o [gʊrd] s calabaza

gourmand ['gʊrmənd] s gastrónomo; glotón m, goloso

gourmet ['gʊrme] s gastrónomo delicado

gout [gaʊt] s gota

gout•y ['gaʊti] adj (comp **-ier**; super **-iest**) gotoso

gov. abbr **governor, government**

govern ['gʌvərn] tr gobernar; (gram) regir ‖ intr gobernar

governess ['gʌvərnɪs] s aya, institutriz f

government ['gʌvərnmənt] s gobierno; (gram) régimen m

go
go

governmental [‚gʌvərn'mɛntəl] *adj* gubernamental, gubernativo

government in exile *s* gobierno exilado

governor ['gʌvərnər] *s* gobernador *m; (of a jail, castle, etc.)* alcaide *m;* (mach) regulador *m*

governorship ['gʌvərnərˌʃɪp] *s* gobierno

govt. *abbr* **government**

gown [gaʊn] *s (of a woman)* vestido; *(of a professor, judge, etc.)* toga; *(of a priest)* traje *m* talar; *(dressing gown)* bata, peinador *m;* (nightgown) camisa de dormir

G.P.O. *abbr* **General Post Office, Government Printing Office**

gr. *abbr* **gram, grams, grain, grains, gross**

grab [græb] *s* asimiento, presa; (coll) robo ‖ *v (pret & pp* **grabbed;** *ger* **grabbing)** *tr* asir, agarrar; arrebatar ‖ *intr* — **to grab at** tratar de asir

grace [gres] *s (charm; favor; pardon)* gracia; *(prayer at table)* benedícite *m; (extension of time)* demora; **to be in the good graces of** gozar del favor de; **to say grace** rezar el benedícite; **with good grace** de buen talante ‖ *tr* adornar, engalanar; favorecer

graceful ['gresfəl] *adj* agraciado, gracioso

grace note *s* apoyatura, nota de adorno

gracious ['greʃəs] *adj* graciable, gracioso; misericordioso ‖ *interj* ¡válgame Dios!

grackle ['grækəl] *s (myna)* estornino de los pastores; *(purple grackle)* quiscal *m*

grad. *abbr* **graduate**

gradation [gre'deʃən] *s (gradual change)* paso gradual; *(arrangement in grades)* graduación; *(step in a series)* paso, grado

grade [gred] *s* grado; *(slope)* pendiente *f; (mark for work in class)* calificación, nota; **to make the grade** lograr subir la cuesta; vencer los obstáculos ‖ *tr* graduar, calificar; dar nota a *(un alumno)*; explanar, nivelar

grade crossing *s* (rr) paso a nivel, cruce *m* a nivel

grade school *s* escuela elemental

gradient ['gredɪ•ənt] *adj* pendiente ‖ *s* pendiente *f;* (phys) gradiente *m*

gradual ['grædʒʊ•əl] *adj* paulatino

gradually ['grædʒʊ•əli] *adv* paulatinamente, gradualmente, poco a poco

graduate ['grædʒʊ•ɪt] *adj* graduado ‖ *s* graduado; *(candidate for a degree)* graduando; vasija graduada ‖ ['grædʒʊ‚et] *tr* graduar ‖ *intr* graduarse

graduate school *s* facultad de altos estudios

graduate student *s* estudiante graduado

graduate work *s* altos estudios

graduation [‚grædʒʊ'eʃən] *s* graduación, ceremonia de graduación

graft [græft] *s* (hort & surg) injerto; (coll) soborno político, ganancia ilegal ‖ *tr & intr* (hort & surg) injertar; (coll) malversar

graham bread ['gre•əm] *s* pan *m* integral

graham flour *s* harina de trigo sin cerner

grain [gren] *s (small seed; tiny particle of sand, etc.; small unit of weight)* grano; *(cereal seeds)* granos; *(in stone)* vena; *(in wood)* fibra; **against the grain** a contrapelo

‖ *tr* granear *(la pólvora; una piedra litográfica)*; crispir, vetear *(la madera)*; granular *(una piel)*

grain elevator *s* elevador *m* de granos; *(tall building where grain is stored)* depósito de cereales

grain'field' *s* sembrado

graining ['grenɪŋ] *s* veteado

gram [græm] *s* gramo

grammar ['græmər] *s* gramática

grammarian [grə'mɛrɪ•ən] *s* gramático

grammar school *s* escuela pública elemental

grammatical [grə'mætɪkəl] *adj* gramático

gramophone ['græmə‚fon] *s* (trademark) gramófono

grana•ry ['grænəri] *s (pl* **-ries)** granero

grand [grænd] *adj* espléndido, grandioso; importante, principal

grand'aunt' *s* tía abuela

grand'child' *s (pl* **chil'dren)** nieto, nieta

grand'daugh'ter *s* nieta

grand duchess *s* gran duquesa

grand duchy *s* gran ducado

grand duke *s* gran duque *m*

grandee [græn'di] *s* grande *m* de España

grandeur ['grændʒər] o ['grændʒʊr] *s* grandeza, magnificencia

grand'fa'ther *s* abuelo; *(forefather)* antepasado

grandfather's clock *s* reloj *m* de caja

grandiose ['grændɪ‚os] *adj* grandioso; hinchado, pomposo

grand jury *s* jurado de acusación

grand larceny *s* hurto mayor

grand lodge *s* gran oriente *m*

grandma ['grænd‚ma], ['græm ‚ma], o ['græmə] *s* (coll) abuela, abuelita

grand'moth'er *s* abuela

grand'neph'ew *s* resobrino

grand'niece *s* resobrina

grand opera *s* ópera seria

grandpa ['grænd‚pa], ['græn‚pa], o ['græmpə] *s* (coll) abuelo, abuelito

grand'par'ent *s* abuelo, abuela

grand piano *s* piano de cola

grand slam *s* (bridge) bola

grand'son' *s* nieto

grand'stand' *s* gradería cubierta, tribuna

grand strategy *s* alta estrategia

grand total *s* gran total *m,* suma de totales

grand'un'cle *s* tío abuelo

grand vizier *s* gran visir *m*

grange [grendʒ] *s (farm with barns, etc.)* granja; *(organization of farmers)* cámara agrícola

granite ['grænɪt] *s* granito

grant [grænt] o [grant] *s* concesión; donación, subvención; traspaso de propiedad ‖ *tr* conceder; dar *(permiso, perdón)*; transferir *(bienes inmuebles)*; **to take for granted** dar por sentado; tratar con indiferencia

grantee [græn'ti] o [gran'ti] *s* cesionario

grant'-in-aid' *s (pl* **grants-in-aid)** subvención concedida por el gobierno para obras de utilidad pública; pensión para estimular conocimientos científicos, literarios, artísticos

grantor [græn'tɔr] or [grɑn'tɔr] s cesionista mf, otorgante mf

grant winner s bequista mf (CAm, Cuba)

granular ['grænjələr] adj granular

granulate ['grænjə,let] tr granular ‖ intr granularse

granule ['grænjʊl] s gránulo

grape [grep] s (fruit) uva; (vine) vid f

grape arbor s parral m

grape'fruit' s (fruit) toronja; (tree) toronjo

grape hyacinth s sueldacostilla

grape juice s zumo de uva

grape'shot' s metralla

grape'vine' s vid f, parra; **by the grapevine** por vías secretas, por vías misteriosas

graph [græf] s (diagram) gráfica; (gram) grafía

graphic(al) ['græfɪk(əl)] adj gráfico

graphite ['græfaɪt] s grafito

graph paper s papel cuadriculado

grapnel ['græpnəl] s rebañadera; (anchor) rezón m

grapple ['græpəl] s asimiento, presa; lucha cuerpo a cuerpo ‖ tr asir, agarrar ‖ intr agarrarse; luchar a brazo partido; **to grapple with** luchar a brazo partido con; tratar de resolver

grappling iron s arpeo

grasp [græsp] s asimiento; (power, reach) poder m, alcance m; (fig) comprensión; **to have a good grasp of** saber a fondo; **within the grasp of** al alcance de ‖ tr (with hand) empuñar; (to get control of) apoderarse de; (fig) comprender ‖ intr — **to grasp at** tratar de asir; aceptar con avidez

grasping ['græspɪŋ] adj avaro, codicioso

grass ['græs] s hierba; (pasture land) pasto; (lawn) césped m; **to go to grass** ir a pacer; disfrutar de una temporada de descanso; gastarse, arruinarse; morir; **to not let the grass grow under one's feet** no dormirse en las pajas

grass court s cancha de césped

grass'hop'per s saltamontes m

grass pea s almorta, guija

grass'-roots' adj de la gente común

grass seed s semilla de césped

grass widow s viuda de paja, viuda de marido vivo

grass•y ['græsi] adj (comp -ier; super -iest) herboso

grate [gret] s (at a window) reja; (for cooking) parrilla ‖ tr (to put a grate on) enrejar; rallar (p.ej., queso) ‖ intr crujir, rechinar; **to grate on** (fig) rallar

grateful ['gretfəl] adj agradecido; (pleasing) agradable

grater ['gretər] s rallador m

grati•fy ['grætɪ,faɪ] v (pret & pp -fied) tr complacer, gratificar

gratifying ['grætɪ,faɪ•ɪŋ] adj grato, satisfactorio

grating ['gretɪŋ] adj áspero, irritante; (sound) chirriante ‖ s enrejado

gratis ['gretɪs] o ['grætɪs] adj gracioso, gratuito ‖ adv gratis, de balde

gratitude ['grætɪ,tjud] s gratitud, reconocimiento

gratuitous [grə'tju•ɪtəs] o [grə'tu•ɪtəs] adj gratuito

gratui•ty [grə'tju•ɪti] s (pl -ties) propina; feria (CAm, Mex)

grave [grev] adj (serious, dangerous; important) grave; solemne; (sound; accent) grave ‖ s sepulcro, sepultura; **to have one foot in the grave** estar con un pie en la sepultura

gravedigger ['grev ,dɪgər] s enterrador m, sepulturero, entierramuertos m

gravel ['grævəl] s grava, cascajo

graven image ['grevən] s ídolo

grave'stone' s lápida sepulcral

grave'yard' s camposanto

gravitate ['grævɪ,tet] intr gravitar; ser atraído

gravitation [,grævɪ'teʃən] s gravitación

gravi•ty ['grævɪti] s (pl -ties) gravedad

gravure [grə'vjʊr] s fotograbado

gra•vy ['grevi] s (pl -vies) (juice from cooking meat) jugo; (sauce made with this juice) salsa; (slang) ganga, breva

gravy dish s salsera

gray [gre] adj gris; (gray-haired) cano, canoso ‖ s gris m; traje m gris ‖ intr encanecer

gray'beard' s anciano, viejo

gray-haired ['gre,hɛrd] adj canoso

gray'hound' s galgo

grayish ['gre•ɪʃ] adj grisáceo; (person; hair) entrecano

gray matter s substancia gris; (intelligence) (coll) materia gris

graze [grez] tr (to touch lightly) rozar; (to scratch lightly in passing) raspar; pacer (la hierba); apacentar (el ganado); (to lead to the pasture) pastar ‖ intr pacer, pastar

grease [gris] s grasa ‖ [gris] o [griz] tr engrasar; (slang) sobornar

grease cup [gris] s vaso de engrase

grease gun [gris] s engrasador m de pistón, jeringa de engrase, bomba de engrase

grease lift [gris] s puente m de engrase

grease paint [gris] s maquillaje m

grease pit [gris] s fosa de engrase

grease spot [gris] s lámpara, mancha de grasa

greas•y ['grisi] o ['grizi] adj (comp -ier; super -iest) grasiento, pringoso

great [gret] adj grande; (coll) excelente ‖ **the great** los grandes

great'-aunt' s tía abuela

Great Bear s Osa Mayor

Great Britain ['brɪtən] s la Gran Bretaña

great'coat' s gabán m de mucho abrigo

Great Dane s mastín m danés

Greater London s el Gran Londres

Greater New York s el Gran Nueva York

great'-grand'child' s (pl -chil'dren) bisnieto, bisnieta

great'-grand'daugh'ter s bisnieta

great'-grand'fa'ther s bisabuelo

great'-grand'moth'er s bisabuela

great'-grand'par'ent s bisabuelo, bisabuela

go
gr

great'-grand'son' *s* bisnieto
greatly ['gretli] *adj* grandemente
great'-neph'ew *s* resobrino
greatness ['gretnɪs] *s* grandeza
great'-niece' *s* resobrina
great'-un'cle *s* tío abuelo
Great War *s* Gran guerra
Grecian ['griʃən] *adj & s* griego
Greece [gris] *s* Grecia
greed [grid] *s* codicia, avaricia; (*in eating and drinking*) glotonería
greed•y ['gridi] *adj* (*comp* **-ier;** *super* **-iest**) codicioso, avaro; glotón
Greek [grik] *adj & s* griego
green [grin] *adj* verde; inexperto ‖ *s* verde *m;* (*lawn*) césped *m;* **greens** verduras
green'back' *s* (U.S.A.) billete *m* de banco (*de dorso verde*)
green corn *s* maíz tierno
green earth *s* verdacho
greener•y ['grinəri] *s* (*pl* **-ies**) (*foliage*) verdura; (*hothouse*) invernáculo
green-eyed ['grin,aɪd] *adj* de ojos verdes; celoso
green'gage' *s* ciruela claudia
green grasshopper *s* langostón *m*
green'gro'cer *s* verdulero
green'gro'cer•y *s* (*pl* **-ies**) verdulería
green'horn' *s* novato; (*dupe*) primo, inocentón *m;* papanatas *m,* isidro; colegial *mf* (Mex)
green'house' *s* invernáculo
greenish ['grinɪʃ] *adj* verdoso
Greenland ['grinlənd] *s* Groenlandia
greenness ['grinnɪs] *s* verdura, verdor *m;* falta de experiencia
green'room' *s* saloncillo; chismería de teatro
greensward ['grin,swɔrd] *s* césped *m*
green thumb *s* pulgares *mpl* verdes (*don de criar plantas*)
green vegetables *spl* verduras
green'wood' *s* bosque *m* verde, bosque frondoso
greet [grit] *tr* saludar; acoger, recibir; presentarse a (*los ojos u los oídos de uno*)
greeting ['gritɪŋ] *s* saludo; acogida, recibimiento ‖ **greetings** *interj* ¡salud!
greeting card *s* tarjeta de buen deseo
gregarious [grɪ'gɛrɪ•əs] *adj* (*living in the midst of others*) gregario; (*fond of the company of others*) sociable
Gregorian [grɪ'gorɪ•ən] *adj* gregoriano
grenade [grɪ'ned] *s* granada; (*to put out fires*) granada extintora
grenadier [,grɛnə'dɪr] *s* granadero
grenadine [,grɛnə'din] *s* granadina
grey [gre] *adj, s & intr* var de **gray**
grid [grɪd] *s* parrilla, rejilla; (*electron*) rejilla; (*of a storage battery*) (elec) rejilla
griddle ['grɪdəl] *s* plancha
grid'dle•cake' *s* tortada (de harina) a la plancha
grid'i'ron *s* parrilla; campo de fútbol
grid leak *s* (electron) resistencia de rejilla, escape *m* de rejilla

grief [grif] *s* aflicción, pesar *m;* (coll) desgracia, disgusto; **to come to grief** fracasar, arruinarse
grievance ['grivəns] *s* agravio, injusticia; despecho, disgusto; motivo de queja
grieve [griv] *tr* afligir, penar ‖ *intr* afligirse, apenarse; **to grieve over** añorar
grievous ['grivəs] *adj* doloroso, penoso; atroz, cruel; (*deplorable*) lastimoso
griffin ['grɪfɪn] *s* (myth) grifo
grill [grɪl] *s* parrilla ‖ *tr* emparrillar; someter (*a un acusado*) a un interrogatorio muy apremiante
grille [grɪl] *s* reja, verja; (*of an automobile*) parrilla, rejilla
grill'room' *s* parrilla
grim [grɪm] *adj* (*comp* **grimmer;** *super* **grimmest**) (*fierce*) cruel, feroz; (*repellent*) horrible, siniestro; (*unyielding*) formidable, implacable; (*stern-looking*) ceñudo
grimace ['grɪməs] o [grɪ'mes] *s* mueca, gesto ‖ *intr* hacer muecas, gestear
grime [graɪm] *s* mugre *f;* (*soot*) tizne *m & f*
grim•y ['graɪmi] *adj* (*comp* **-ier;** *super* **-iest**) mugriento; tiznado
grin [grɪn] *s* sonrisa bonachona; mueca (*mostrando los dientes*) ‖ *v* (*pret & pp* **grinned;** *ger* **grinning**) *intr* sonreírse bonachonamente; hacer una mueca (*mostrando los dientes*)
grind [graɪnd] *s* molienda; (*long hard work or study*) (coll) zurra; (*student*) (coll) empollón *m* ‖ *v* (*pret & pp* **ground** [graʊnd]) *tr* moler; (*to sharpen*) afilar, amolar; tallar (*lentes*); pulverizar; picar (*carne*); rodar (*las válvulas de un motor*); dar vueltas a (*un manubrio*) ‖ *intr* hacer molienda; molerse; rechinar; (coll) echar los bofes
grinder ['graɪndər] *s* (*to sharpen tools*) muela, esmoladera; (*to grind coffee, pepper, etc.*) molinillo; (*back tooth*) muela
grind'stone' *s* esmoladera, piedra de amolar; **to keep one's nose to the grindstone** trabajar con ahinco
grin•go ['grɪŋgo] *s* (*pl* **-gos**) (disparaging) gringo
grip [grɪp] *s* (*grasp*) asimiento; (*withhand*) apretón *m;* (*handle*) asidero; saco de mano; **to come to grips (with)** luchar cuerpo a cuerpo (con); arrostrarse (con) ‖ *v* (*pret & pp* **gripped;** *ger* **gripping**) *tr* asir, agarrar; tener asido; absorber (*la atención*); absorber la atención a (*una persona*)
gripe [graɪp] *s* (coll) queja; **gripes** retortijón *m* de tripas ‖ *intr* (coll) quejarse, refunfuñar
grippe [grɪp] *s* gripe *f*
gripping ['grɪpɪŋ] *adj* conmovedor, impresionante
gris•ly ['grɪzli] *adj* (*comp* **-lier;** *super* **-liest**) espantoso, espeluznante
grist [grɪst] *s* (*batch of grain for one grinding*) molienda; (*grain that has been ground*) harina; (coll) acopio, acervo; **to be grist to one's mill** (coll) serle a uno de mucho provecho

gristle [ˈgrɪsəl] *adj* (*comp* **-tlier;** *super* **-tliest**) cartilaginoso, ternilloso

grist'mill' *s* molino harinero

grit [grɪt] *s* arena, guijo fino; (fig) ánimo, valentía; **grits** farro, sémola ‖ *v* (*pret & pp* **gritted;** *ger* **gritting**) *tr* hacer rechinar (*los dientes*); cerrar fuertemente (*los dientes*)

grit•ty [ˈgrɪti] *adj* (*comp* **-tier;** *super* **-tiest**) arenoso; (fig) valiente, resuelto

griz•zly [ˈgrɪzli] *adj* (*comp* **-zlier;** *super* **-zliest**) grisáceo; canoso ‖ *s* (*pl* **-zlies**) oso gris

grizzly bear *s* oso gris

groan [gron] *s* gemido, quejido ‖ *intr* gemir, quejarse; estar muy cargado, crujir por exceso de peso

grocer [ˈgrosər] *s* abacero, tendero de ultramarinos

grocer•y [ˈgrosəri] *s* (*pl* **-ies**) abacería, tienda de ultramarinos, colmado; **groceries** víveres *mpl*, ultramarinos

grocery store *s* abacería, tienda de ultramarinos, colmado

grog [grɑg] *s* grog *m*

grog•gy [ˈgrɑgi] *adj* (*comp* **-gier;** *super* **-giest**) (coll) inseguro, vacilante; (*shaky, e.g., from a blow*) (coll) atontado; (coll) borracho

groin [grɔɪn] *s* (anat) ingle *f;* (archit) arista de encuentro

groom [grum] *s* (*bridegroom*) novio; mozo de caballos ‖ *tr* asear, acicalar; almohazar (*caballos*); enseñar (*a un político*) para presentarse como candidato

grooms•man [ˈgrumzmən] *s* (*pl* **-men** [mən]) padrino de boda

groove [gruv] *s* ranura; (*of a pulley*) garganta; (*of a phonograph record*) surco; (*mark left by a wheel*) rodada; (coll) rutina, hábito arraigado ‖ *tr* ranurar, acanalar

grope [grop] *intr* andar a tientas; (*for words*) pujar; **to grope for** buscar a tientas, buscar tentando; **to grope through** palpar (*p.ej., la obscuridad*)

gropingly [ˈgropɪŋli] *adv* a tientas

grosbeak [ˈgros ˌbik] *s* pico duro

gross [gros] *adj* (*dense, thick*) denso, espeso; (*coarse; vulgar*) grosero; (*fat, burly*) grueso; (*with no deductions*) bruto ‖ *s* conjunto, totalidad; (*twelve dozen*) gruesa; **in gross** en grueso ‖ *tr* obtener un ingreso bruto de

grossly [ˈgrosli] *adv* aproximadamente

gross national product *s* renta nacional

grotesque [groˈtɛsk] *adj* (*ridiculous, extravagant*) grotesco; (fa) grutesco ‖ *s* (fa) grutesco

grot•to [ˈgrɑto] *s* (*pl* **-toes** o **-tos**) gruta

grouch [graʊtʃ] *s* (coll) mal humor *m;* (*person*) (coll) cascarrabias *mf*, vinagre *m* ‖ *intr* (coll) refunfuñar

grouch•y [ˈgraʊtʃi] *adj* (*comp* **-ier;** *super* **-iest**) (coll) gruñón, malhumorado

ground [graʊnd] *adj* molido ‖ *s* (*earth, soil, land*) tierra; (*piece of land*) terreno; (*basis foundation*) causa, fundamento; motivo, razón *f;* (elec) tierra; (*body of auto-*

mobile corresponding to ground) (elec) masa; (elec) borne *m* de tierra; **ground for complaint** motivo de queja; **grounds** terreno; jardines *mpl;* causa, fundamento; (*of coffee*) posos; **on the ground of** con motivo de; **to break ground** empezar la excavación; **to fall to the ground** fracasar, abandonarse; **to gain ground** ganar terreno; **to give ground** ceder terreno; **to lose ground** perder terreno; **to stand one's ground** mantenerse firme; **to yield ground** ceder terreno ‖ *tr* establecer, fundar; (elec) poner a tierra; **to be grounded** estar sin volar (*un avión*); **to be well grounded** ser muy versado ‖ *intr* (naut) encallar, varar

ground connection *s* (rad) toma de tierra

ground crew *s* (aer) personal *m* de tierra

grounder [ˈgraʊndər] *s* (baseball) pelota rodada

ground floor *s* piso bajo

ground glass *s* vidrio deslustrado

ground hog *s* marmota de América

ground lead [lid] *s* (elec) conductor *m* a tierra

groundless [ˈgraʊndlɪs] *adj* infundado; inmotivado

ground plan *s* primer proyecto; (*of a building*) planta

ground speed *s* (aer) velocidad con respecto al suelo

ground swell *s* marejada de fondo

ground troops *spl* (mil) tropas terrestres

ground wire *s* (rad) alambre *m* de tierra; (aut) hilo de masa

ground'work' *s* infraestructura

group [grup] *adj* grupal; colectivo ‖ *s* grupo ‖ *tr* agrupar ‖ *intr* agruparse

group therapy *s* psicoterapia de grupo

grouse [graʊs] *s* perdiz blanca, bonasa americana, gallo de bosque; (slang) refunfuño ‖ *intr* (slang) refunfuñar

grout [graʊt] *s* lechada ‖ *tr* enlechar

grove [grov] *s* arboleda, bosquecillo

grov•el [ˈgrʌvəl] o [ˈgrɑvəl] *v* (*pret & pp* **-eled** o **-elled;** *ger* **-eling** o **-elling**) *intr* arrastrarse servilmente; rebajarse servilmente; deleitarse en vilezas

grow [gro] *v* (*pret* **grew** [gru]; *pp* **grown** [gron]) *tr* cultivar (*plantas*); criar (*animales*); dejarse (*la barba*) ‖ *intr* crecer; cultivarse; criarse; brotar, nacer; (*to become*) hacerse, ponerse, volverse; **to grow angry** enfadarse; **to grow old** envejecerse; **to grow out of** tener su origen en; perder (*p.ej., la costumbre*); **to grow together** adherirse el uno al otro; **to grow up** crecer, desarrollar

growing child [ˈgro•ɪŋ] *s* muchacho de creces

growl [graʊl] *s* gruñido; refunfuño ‖ *intr* gruñir (*el perro*); refunfuñar

grown'up' *adj* adulto; juicioso ‖ *s* (*pl* **grown-ups**) adulto; **grown-ups** personas mayores

growth [groθ] *s* crecimiento; desarrollo; aumento; (*of trees, grass, etc.*) cobertura; (pathol) tumor *m*

growth stock *s* acción crecedera

gr
gr

grub [grʌb] s (*drudge*) esclavo del trabajo; (*larva*) gorgojo; (coll) comida, alimento ‖ v (*pret & pp* **grubbed;** *ger* **grubbing**) *tr* arrancar (*tocones*); desmalezar (*un terreno*) ‖ *intr* cavar; trabajar como esclavo

grub·by ['grʌbi] *adj* (*comp* **-bier;** *super* **-biest**) gorgojoso; sucio, roñoso

grudge [grʌdʒ] s rencor m, inquina; **to have a grudge against** guardar rencor a, tener inquina a ‖ *tr* dar de mala gana; envidiar

grudgingly ['grʌdʒɪŋli] *adv* de mala gana

gru·el ['gru·əl] s avenate m ‖ v (*pret & pp* **-eled** o **-elled;** *ger* **-eling** o **-elling**) *tr* agotar, castigar cruelmente

gruesome ['grusəm] *adj* espantoso, horripilante

gruff [grʌf] *adj* áspero, brusco, rudo; (*voice, tone*) ronco

grumble ['grʌmbəl] s gruñido, refunfuño; ruido sordo y prolongado ‖ *intr* gruñir, refunfuñar; retumbar

grump·y ['grʌmpi] *adj* (*comp* **-ier;** *super* **-iest**) gruñón, malhumorado

grunt [grʌnt] s gruñido ‖ *intr* gruñir

G-string ['dʒi,strɪŋ] s (*loincloth*) taparrabo; (*worn by women entertainers*) cubresexo

gt. *abbr* **great; gutta** (Lat) **drop**

g.u. *abbr* **genitourinary**

Guadeloupe [,gwɑdə'lup] s Guadalupe f

guarantee [,gærən'ti] s garantía; (*guarantor*) garante *mf;* persona de quien otra sale fiadora ‖ *tr* garantizar

guarantor ['gærən,tɔr] s garante *mf*

guaran·ty ['gærənti] s (*pl* **-ties**) garantía ‖ v (*pret & pp* **-tied**) *tr* garantizar

guard [gɑrd] s (*act of guarding; part of handle of sword*) guarda; (*person who guards or takes care of something*) guarda *mf;* (*group of armed men; posture in fencing*) guardia; (*member of group of armed men*) guardia *m;* (*in front of trolley car*) salvavidas *m;* (sport) coraza; (rr) guardabarrera *mf;* (rr) guardafrenos *m;* **off guard** desprevenido; **on guard** alerta, prevenido; de centinela; **to mount guard** montar la guardia; **under guard** a buen recaudo ‖ *tr* guardar ‖ *intr* estar de centinela; **to guard against** guardarse de, precaverse contra o de

guard'house' s cuartel m de la guardia; prisión militar

guardian ['gɑrdɪ·ən] *adj* tutelar ‖ s guardián *m;* (law) curador m, tutor m

guardian angel s ángel m custodio, ángel de la guarda

guardianship ['gɑrdɪ·ən,ʃɪp] s amparo, protección; (law) curaduría, tutela

guard'rail' s baranda; (naut) barandilla; (rr) contracarril m

guard'room' s cuarto de guardia; cárcel f militar

guards·man ['gɑrdzmən] s (*pl* **-men** [mən]) guardia m, soldado de guardia

Guatemalan [,gwɑtɪ'mɑlən] *adj* & s guatemalteco

guerrilla [gə'rɪlə] s guerrillero; montonero

guerrilla warfare s guerra de guerrillas

guess [gɛs] s conjetura, suposición; adivinación ‖ *tr* & *intr* conjeturar, suponer; (*to judge correctly*) acertar, adivinar; (coll) creer, suponer; **I guess so** (coll) creo que sí, me parece que sí

guess'work' s conjetura; **by guesswork** por conjeturas

guest [gɛst] s convidado; (*lodger*) huésped *m;* (*of a boarding house*) pensionista *mf;* (*of a hotel*) cliente *mf;* (*caller*) vista

guest book s libro de oro

guest room s cuarto de reserva

guffaw [gə'fɔ] s risotada, carcajada ‖ *intr* risotear, reír a carcajadas

guidance ['gaɪdəns] s guía, gobierno, dirección; **for your guidance** para su gobierno

guide [gaɪd] s (*person*) guía *mf;* (*book*) guía; (*guidance*) guía; dirección; poste m indicador; (mach) guía, guiadera; (mil) guía m ‖ *tr* guiar

guide'board' s señal f de carretera

guide'book' s guia m, guía del viajero

guided missile ['gaɪdɪd] s proyectil dirigido o teleguiado; misil m dirigible

guide dog s perro-lazarillo

guide'line' s cuerda de guía; norma, pauta, directorio

guide'post' s poste m indicador

guidon ['gaɪdən] s (mil) guión m; (mil) portaguión m

guild [gɪld] s (*medieval association of craftsmen*) gremio; asociación benéfica

guild'hall' s casa consistorial

guile [gaɪl] s astucia, dolo, maña

guileful ['gaɪlfəl] *adj* astuto, doloso, mañoso

guileless ['gaɪllɪs] *adj* cándido, inocente, sencillo

guillotine ['gɪlə,tin] s guillotina ‖ [,gɪlə'tin] *tr* guillotinar

guilt [gɪlt] s culpa

guiltless ['gɪltlɪs] *adj* inocente, libre de culpa

guilt·y ['gɪlti] *adj* (*comp* **-ier;** *super* **-iest**) culpable; (*charged with guilt*) culpado; (*found guilty*) reo

guimpe [gɪmp] o [gæmp] s canesú m

guinea ['gɪni] s (*monetary unit*) guinea; gallina de Guinea

guinea fowl s pintada, gallina de Guinea

guinea hen s pintada, gallina de Guinea (*hembra*)

guinea pig s conejillo de Indias; (fig) cobayo

guise [gaɪz] s traje *m;* aspecto, semejanza; **under the guise of** so capa de

guitar [gɪ'tɑr] s guitarra

guitarist [gɪ'tɑrɪst] s guitarrista *mf*

gulch [gʌltʃ] s barranco, quebrada

gulf [gʌlf] s golfo

Gulf of Mexico s golfo de Méjico

Gulf Stream s Corriente f del Golfo

gull [gʌl] s gaviota; (coll) bobo ‖ *tr* estafar, engañar

gullet ['gʌlɪt] s gaznate m, garguero; esófago

gullible ['gʌlɪbəl] *adj* crédulo; creído; **to be too gullible** tener buenas tragaderas

gul·ly ['gʌli] s (*pl* **-lies**) barranca, arroyada; (*channel made by rain water*) badén m

gulp [gʌlp] s trago ‖ tr — **to gulp down** engullir; reprimir (p.ej., sollozos) ‖ intr respirar entrecortadamente

gum [gʌm] s goma; chanclo de goma; (firm flesh around base of teeth) encía; (mucous on edge of eyelid) legaña ‖ v (pret & pp **gummed;** ger **gumming**) tr engomar ‖ intr exudar goma

gum arabic s goma arábiga

gum'boil' s flemón m

gum boot s bota de agua

gum'drop' s frutilla

gum·my ['gʌmi] adj (comp -**mier;** super -**miest**) gomoso; (eyelid) legañoso

gumption ['gʌmpʃən] s ánimo, iniciativa, empuje m, fuerza; juicio, seso

gum'shoe' s chanclo de goma; (coll) detective m ‖ v (pret & pp -**shoed;** ger -**shoeing**) intr (slang) andar con zapatos de fieltro

gun [gʌn] s escopeta, fusil m; cañón m; (for injections) jeringa; (coll) revólver m; **to stick to one's guns** mantenerse en sus trece ‖ v (pret & pp **gunned;** ger **gunning**) tr hacer fuego sobre; (slang) acelerar rápidamente (un motor, un avión) ‖ intr andar a caza; disparar; **to gun for** ir en busca de; buscar para matar

gun'boat' s cañonero

gun carriage s cureña, encabalgamiento

gun'cot'ton s fulmicotón m, algodón m pólvora

gun'fire' s fuego (de armas de fuego); cañoneo

gun·man ['gʌnmən] s (pl -**men** [mən]) bandido armado, pistolero; gángster m

gun metal s bronce m de cañón; metal pavonado

gunnel ['gʌnəl] s (naut) borda, regala

gunner ['gʌnər] s artillero; cazador m

gunnery ['gʌnəri] s artillería

gunny sack ['gʌni] s saco de yute

gun'pow'der s pólvora

gun'run'ner s contrabandista m de armas de fuego

gun'run'ning s contrabando de armas de fuego

gun'shot' s escopetazo, tiro de fusil; alcance m de un fusil; **within gunshot** a tiro de fusil

gunshot wound s escopetazo

gun'smith' s armero

gun'stock' s caja de fusil

gunwale ['gʌnəl] s (naut) borda, regala

gup·py ['gʌpi] s (pl -**pies**) lebistes m

gurgle ['gʌrgəl] s gorgoteo, gluglú m; (of a child) gorjeo ‖ intr gorgotear, hacer gluglú; gorjearse (el niño)

gush [gʌʃ] s borbollón m, chorro ‖ intr surgir, salir a borbollones; (coll) hacer extremos, ser extremoso

gusher ['gʌʃər] s pozo de chorro de petróleo; (coll) personal extremosa

gushing ['gʌʃɪŋ] adj surgente; (coll) extremoso ‖ s borbollón m, chorro; (coll) efusión, extremos

gush·y ['gʌʃi] adj (comp -**ier;** super -**iest**) (coll) efusivo, extremoso

gusset ['gʌsɪt] s escudete m

gust [gʌst] s (of wind) ráfaga; (of rain) aguacero; (of smoke) bocanada; (of noise) explosión; (of anger or enthusiasm) arrebato

gusto ['gʌsto] s deleite m, entusiasmo; **with gusto** con sumo placer

gust·y ['gʌsti] adj (comp -**ier;** super -**iest**) tempestuoso, borrascoso

gut [gʌt] s tripa; cuerda de tripa; **guts** tripas; (slang) agallas ‖ v (pret & pp **gutted;** ger **gutting**) tr destripar; destruir lo interior de

gutta-percha ['gʌtə'pʌrtʃə] s gutapercha

gutter ['gʌtər] s (on side of road) cuneta; (in street) arroyo; (of roof) canal f; (ditch formed by rain water) badén m; **barrios bajos**

gut'ter-snipe' s pilluelo, hijo de la miseria; gamberro

guttural ['gʌtərəl] adj gutural ‖ s sonido gutural

guy [gaɪ] s viento, cable m de retén; (coll) tipo, tío, sujeto ‖ tr (coll) burlarse de

Guyana [gaɪ'ænə] s Guayana

guy wire s cable m de retén

guzzle ['gʌzəl] tr & intr beber con exceso

guzzler ['gʌzlər] s borrachín m

gym [dʒɪm] s (coll) gimnasio

gymnasi·um [dʒɪm'nezɪ·əm] s (pl -**ums** o -**a** [ə]) gimnasio

gymnast ['dʒɪmnæst] s gimnasta mf

gymnastic [dʒɪm'næstɪk] adj gimnástico ‖ **gymnastics** spl gimnasia, gimnástica

gym suit s chandal m, chándal m

gynecologic(al) [,gaɪnəko'lɑdʒɪk(əl)] or [,dʒaɪnəko'lɑdʒɪk(əl)] adj ginecológico

gynecologist [,gaɪnə'kɑlədʒɪst] or [,dʒaɪnə'kɑlədʒɪst] s ginecólogo

gynecology [,gaɪnə'kɑlədʒi] or [,dʒaɪnə'kɑlədʒi] s ginecología

gyp [dʒɪp] s (slang) estafa, timo; (person) (slang) estafador m, timador m ‖ v (pret & pp **gypped;** ger **gypping**) tr (slang) estafar, timar

gypsum ['dʒɪpsəm] s yeso, aljez m

gyp·sy ['dʒɪpsi] adj gitano ‖ s (pl -**sies**) gitano ‖ **Gypsy** s gitano (idioma)

gypsyish ['dʒɪpsɪ·ɪʃ] adj gitanesco

gypsy moth s lagarta

gyrate ['dʒaɪret] intr girar

gyroscope ['dʒaɪrə,skop] s giroscopio

gr
gy

H

H, h [etʃ] octava letra del alfabeto inglés

h. *abbr* **harbor, high, hour, husband**

haberdasher [ˈhæbər ˌdæʃər] *s* camisero; (*dealer in notions*) mercero

haberdasher•y [ˈhæbər ˌdæʃəri] *s* (*pl* -**ies**) camisería, tienda de artículos para hombres; artículos para hombres

habit [ˈhæbɪt] *s* costumbre *f,* hábito; (*costume*) traje *m;* **to be in the habit of** acostumbrar

habitat [ˈhæbɪˌtæt] *s* habitación

habitation [ˌhæbɪˈteʃən] *s* habitación

habit-forming [ˈhæbɪt ˌfɔrmɪŋ] *adj* enviciador

habitual [həˈbɪtʃʊ•əl] *adj* habitual

habitué [həˌbɪtʃuˈe] *s* habituado

hack [hæk] *s* (*cut*) corte *m;* (*notch*) mella; (*cough*) tos seca; coche *m* de alquiler; caballo de alquiler; caballo de silla; (*old nag*) rocín *m;* escritor *m* a sueldo ‖ *tr* cortar, machetear

hack•man [ˈhækmən] *s* (*pl* -**men** [mən]) cochero de punto

hackney [ˈhækni] *s* caballo de silla; coche *m* de alquiler; esclavo del trabajo

hackneyed [ˈhæknid] *adj* trillado, gastado

hack′saw′ *s* sierra de armero, sierra de cortar metales

haddock [ˈhædək] *s* eglefino

haem ... [hɛm] o [him] = **hemo ...**

haft [hæft] o [hɑft] *s* mango, puño

hag [hæg] *s* (*ugly old woman*) tarasca; (*witch*) bruja

haggard [ˈhægərd] *adj* ojeroso, macilento, trasnochado

haggle [ˈhægəl] *intr* regatear

Hague, The [heg] La Haya

hail [hel] *s* (*frozen rain*) granizo; (*greeting*) saludo; **within hail** al alcance de la voz ‖ *interj* ¡salud!, ¡salve! ‖ *tr* saludar; dar vivas a, acoger con vivas; aclamar; granizar (*p.ej., golpes*) ‖ *intr* granizar; **to hail from** venir de, ser oriundo de

hail′-fel′low well met *s* compañero muy afable y simpático

Hail Mary *s* avemaría

hail′stone′ *s* piedra de granizo

hail′storm′ *s* granizada

hair [hɛr] *s* pelo, cabellos; **to a hair** con la mayor exactitud; **to cut the hair of** peluquear; **to get in one's hair** (slang) enojarle a uno; **to have one's hair down** estar en melena; **to let one's hair down** (slang) hablar con mucha desenvoltura; **to make one's hair stand on end** ponerle a uno los pelos de punta; **to not turn a hair** no inmutarse; **to split hairs** pararse en quisquillas

hair′breadth′ *s* (el) grueso de un pelo, casi nada; **to escape by a hairbreadth** escapar por un pelo

hair′brush′ *s* cepillo de cabeza

hair′cloth′ *s* tela de crin; (*worn as a penance*) cilicio

hair curler [ˈkʌrlər] *s* rizador *m,* tenacillas, bigudí *m,* rulo

hair′cut′ *s* corte *m* de pelo; **to get a haircut** cortarse el pelo, peluquear

hair′do′ *s* (*pl* -**dos**) peinado, tocado

hair′dress′er *s* peinador *m,* peluquero

hair dryer *s* secador *m*

hair dye *s* tinte *m* para el pelo

hairless [ˈhɛrlɪs] *adj* pelón

hair net *s* redecilla

hair piece *s* peluquín *m*

hair′pin′ *s* horquilla

hair-raising [ˈhɛrˌrezɪŋ] *adj* (coll) espeluznante, horripilante

hair restorer [rɪˈstorər] *s* crecepelo

hair ribbon *s* cinta para el cabello

hair set *s* fijapeinados *m*

hair shirt *s* calicio

hairsplitting [ˈhɛrˌsplɪtɪŋ] *adj* quisquilloso ‖ *s* quisquillas

hair spray *s* laca

hair′spring′ *s* espiral *f*

hair′style′ *s* peinado

hair tonic *s* vigorizador *m* del cabello

hair•y [ˈhɛri] *adj* (*comp* -**ier;** *super* -**iest**) peludo, cabelludo

hake [hek] *s* merluza; (genus: *Urophycis*) fice *m*

halberd [ˈhælbərd] *s* alabarda

halberdier [ˌhælbərˈdɪr] *s* alabardero

halcyon days [ˈhælsɪ•ən] *s* días tranquilos, época de paz

hale [hel] *adj* sano, robusto; **hale and hearty** sano y fuerte ‖ *tr* llevar a la fuerza

half [hæf] *adj* medio; **a half** o **half a** medio; **half the** la mitad de ‖ *adv* medio, p.ej., **half asleep** medio dormido; a medio, p.ej., **half finished** a medio acabar; a medias, p.ej., **half owner** dueño a medias; **half past** y media, p.ej., **half past three** las tres y media; **half . . . half** medio . . . medio ‖ *s* (*pl* **halves** [hævz]) mitad; (arith) medio; **in half** por la mitad; **to go halves** ir a medias

half′-and-half′ *adj* mitad y mitad; indeterminado ‖ *adv* a medias, en partes iguales ‖ *s* mezcla de leche y crema; mezcla de dos cervezas inglesas

half′back′ *s* (football) medio

half-baked [ˈhæfˌbekt] *adj* a medio cocer; incompleto; poco juicioso, inexperto

half binding *s* (bb) encuadernación a la holandesa, media pasta

half′-blood′ *s* mestizo; medio hermano

half boot *s* bota de media caña

half′-bound′ *adj* (bb) a la holandesa

half′-breed′ *s* mestizo

half brother *s* medio hermano

half-cocked [ˈhæfˈkakt] *adv* (coll) con precipitación; **to go off half-cocked** obrar precipitadamente y antes del momento propio

half fare *s* medio billete

half′-full′ *adj* mediado

half-hearted [ˈhæfˌhartɪd] *adj* indiferente, frío

half holiday s mañana o tarde f de asueto
half hose spl calcetines mpl
half'-hour s media hora; **on the half-hour** a la media en punto, cada media hora
half leather s (bb) encuadernación a la holandesa, media pasta
half'-length' adj de medio cuerpo
half'-mast' s — **at half mast** a media asta
half moon s media luna
half mourning s medio luto
half note s (mus) nota blanca
half pay s media paga; medio sueldo
halfpen•ny ['hepəni] o ['hepni] s (pl -nies) medio penique
half pint s media pinta; (little runt) (slang) gorgojo, mirmidón m
half'-seas' over adj — **to be half-seas over** (slang) estar entre dos velas, estar entre dos luces
half shell s (either half of a bivalve) concha; (oysters) **on the half shell** en su concha
half sister s media hermana
half sole s media suela
half'-sole' tr poner media suela a
half'-staff' s — **at half-staff** a media asta
half through prep a la mitad de
half-timbered ['hæf,tɪmbərd] adj entramado
half title s anteportada, falsa portada
half'tone' s (phot & paint) mediatinta; (typ) similigrabado
half'-track' s media oruga, semitractor m
half'-truth' s verdad a medias
half'way' adj a medio camino; incompleto, hecho a medias ‖ adv a medio camino; **halfway through** a la mitad de; **to meet halfway** partir el camino con; partir la diferencia con; hacer concesiones mutuas (dos personas)
half-witted ['hæf ,wɪtɪd] adj imbécil; necio, tonto
halibut ['hælɪbət] s halibut m
halide ['hælaɪd] o ['helaɪd] s (chem) haluro
halitosis [,hælɪ'tosɪs] s halitosis f, aliento fétido
hall [hɔl] (passageway) corredor m; (entranceway) vestíbulo, zaguán m; (large meeting room) sala, salón m; (assembly room of a university) paraninfo; (building, e.g., of a university) edificio
halleluiah o **hallelujah** [,hælɪ'lujə] s aleluya m & f ‖ interj ¡aleluya!
hall'mark' s marca de contraste; (distinguishing feature) (fig) sello
hal•lo [hə'lo] s (pl -los) grito ‖ interj ¡hola!; (to incite dogs in hunting) ¡sus! ‖ intr gritar
hallow ['hælo] tr santificar
hallowed ['hælod] adj santo, sagrado
Halloween o **Hallowe'en** [,hælo'in] s víspera de Todos los Santos
hallucination [hə,lusɪ'nefən] s alucinación
hallucinogenic [hə,lusɪno'dʒɛnɪk] adj alucinante
hall'way' s corredor m; vestíbulo, zaguán m
ha•lo ['helo] s (pl -los o -loes) halo
halogen ['hælədʒən] s halógeno
halt [hɔlt] adj cojo, renco ‖ s alto, parada; **to call a halt** mandar hacer alto; **to come to a**

halt pararse, detenerse, interrumpirse ‖ tr parar, detener ‖ intr hacer alto
halter ['hɔltər] s (for leading or fastening horse) cabestro, ronzal m, dogal m; (noose) dogal m, cuerda de ahorcar; muerte f en la horca
halting ['hɔltɪŋ] adj cojo, renco; vacilante
halve [hæv] tr partir en dos, partir por la mitad
halyard ['hæljərd] s (naut) driza
ham [hæm] s (part of leg behind knee) corva; (thigh and buttock) pernil m; (cured meat from hog's hind leg) jamón m; (slang) comicastro; (slang) aficionado (a la radio); **hams** nalgas
ham and eggs spl huevos con jamón
hamburger ['hæm,bʌrgər] s hamburguesa
hamlet ['hæmlɪt] s aldehuela, caserío
hammer ['hæmər] s martillo; (of piano) macillo, martinete m; **to go under the hammer** venderse en pública subasta ‖ tr martillar; **to hammer out** formar a martillazos; sacar en limpio a fuerza de mucho esfuerzo‖ intr martillar; **to hammer away** trabajar asiduamente
hammock ['hæmək] s hamaca
hamper ['hæmpər] s canasto, cesto grande con tapa ‖ tr estorbar, impedir
hamster ['hæmstər] s marmota de Alemania, rata del trigo
ham•string ['hæm,strɪŋ] v (pret & pp -strung) tr desjarretar; (fig) estropear, incapacitar
hand [hænd] adj (done or operated with the hands) manual ‖ s mano f; (workman) obrero, peón m; (way of writing) escritura, puño y letra; (signature) firma; (clapping of hands) salva de aplausos; (of clock or watch) mano f; manecilla; (all the cards in one's hand) juego; (a round of play) mano f; (player) jugador m; (source, origin) fuente f; (skill) destreza; **all hands** (naut) toda la tripulación; (coll) todas; **at first hand** de primera mano; directamente, de buena tinta; **at hand** disponible; **hand in glove** uña y carne; **hand in hand** asidos de la mano; juntos; **hands up!** ¡arriba las manos! **hand to hand** cuerpo a cuerpo; **in hand** entre manos; **in his own hand** de su propio puño; **on hand** entre manos; disponible; **on hands and knees** (crawling) a gatas; (beseeching) de rodillas; **on the one hand** por una parte; **on the other hand** por otra parte; **out of hand** luego, en seguida; desmandado; **to be at hand** obrar en mi (nuestro) poder (una carta); **to change hands** mudar de manos; **to clap hands** batir palmas; **to eat out of one's hand** aceptar dócilmente la autoridad de uno; **to fall into the hands of** caer en manos de; **to have a hand in** tomar parte en; **to have one's hands full** estar ocupadísimo; **to hold hands** tomarse de las manos; **to hold up one's hands** (as a sign of surrender) alzar las manos; **to join hands** darse las manos; casarse; **to keep one's hands off** no tocar, no meterse en; **to lend a hand**

echar una mano; **to live from hand to mouth** vivir al día, vivir de la mano a la boca; **to not lift a hand** no levantar paja del suelo; **to play into the hands of** hacer el caldo gordo a; **to raise one's hand** (*in taking an oath*) alzar el dedo; **to shake hands** estrecharse la mano; **to show one's hand** descubrir su juego; **to take in hand** hacerse cargo de; tratar, estudiar (*una cuestión*); **to throw up one's hands** darse por vencido; **to try one's hand** probar la mano; **to turn one's hand to** dedicarse a, ocuparse en; **to wash one's hands of** lavarse las manos de; **under my hand** con mi firma, bajo mi firma, de mi puño y letra; **under the hand and seal of** firmado y sellado por ‖ *tr* dar, entregar; **to hand in** entregar; **to hand on** transmitir; **to hand out** repartir

hand'bag' *s* saco de noche; bolso de señora
hand baggage *s* equipaje *m* de mano
hand'ball' *s* pelota; juego de pelota a mano
hand'bill' *s* hoja volante
hand'book' manual *m;* guía de turistas; registro para apuestas
hand'breadth' *s* palmo menor
hand'car' *s* (rr) carrito de mano
hand'cart' *s* carretilla de mano
hand control *s* mando a mano
hand'cuff' *s* manilla; **handcuffs** manillas, esposas ‖ *tr* poner esposas a
handful ['hænd,fʊl] *s* puñado, manojo
hand glass *s* espejo de mano; lupa
hand grenade *s* granada de mano
hand gun *s* (coll) pipa
hand'-held' calculator *s* calculador a mano
handi-cap ['hændɪ,kæp] *s* desventaja, obstáculo; (sport) handicap *m;* (med) disminución, minusvalía ‖ *v* (*pret & pp* **-capped;** *ger* **-capping**) *tr* poner trabas a; (sport) handicapar
handicraft ['hændɪ,kræft] *s* destreza manual; arte mecánica
handiwork ['hændɪ,wʌrk] *s* hechura, trabajo, obra manual
handkerchief ['hæŋkərt∫ɪf] *s* pañuelo
handle ['hændəl] *s* (*of a basket, crock, pitcher*) asa; (*of a shovel, rake, etc.*) mango; (*of an umbrella, sword*) puño; (*of a door, drawer*) tirador *m;* (*of a hand organ*) manubrio; (*of a water pump*) guimbalete *m;* (*opportunity, pretext*) asidero; **to fly off the handle** (slang) salirse de sus casillas ‖ *tr* manosear, manipular; dirigir, manejar, gobernar; comerciar en ‖ *intr* manejarse
handle bar *s* manillar *m*, guía
handler ['hændlər] *s* (sport) entrenador *m*
hand'made' *adj* hecho a mano
hand'maid' o **hand'maid'en** *s* criada, sirvienta
hand'-me-down' *s* (coll) prenda de vestir de segunda mano
hand organ *s* organillo
hand'out' *s* comida que se da de limosna; comunicado de prensa

hand-picked ['hænd ,pɪkt] *adj* escogido a mano; escogido escrupulosamente; escogido con motivos ocultos
hand'rail' *s* barandilla, pasamano
hand'saw' *s* serrucho, sierra de mano
hand'set' *s* microteléfono
hand'shake' *s* apretón *m* de manos
handsome ['hænsəm[*adj* hermoso, elegante, guapo; considerable
hand'spring' *s* voltereta sobre las manos
hand'-to-hand' *adj* cuerpo a cuerpo
hand'-to-mouth' *adj* inseguro, precario; impróvido
hand'work' *s* trabajo a mano
hand'-wres'tle *intr* pulsear
hand'-writ'ing *s* escritura; (*writing by hand which characterizes a particular person*) letra
hand•y ['hændi] *adj* (*comp* **-ier;** *super* **-iest**) (*easy to handle*) manuable; (*within easy reach*) próximo, a la mano; (*skillful*) diestro, hábil; **to come in handy** venir a pelo
handy man *s* dije *m*, factótum *m*
hang [hæŋ] *s* (*of a dress, curtain, etc.*) caída; (*skill; insight*) tino; **I don't care a hang** (coll) no me importa un bledo; **to get the hang of it** (coll) coger el tino ‖ *v* (*pret & pp* **hung** [hʌŋ]) *tr* colgar; tender (*la ropa mojada*); pegar (*el papel pintado*); fijar (*un cartel, un letrero*); enquiciar (*una puerta, una ventana*); bajar (*la cabeza*); **hang it!** (coll) ¡caramba!; **to hang up** colgar (*el sombrero*); impedir los progresos de ‖ *intr* colgar, pender; estar agarrado; vacilar; **to hang around** esperar sin hacer nada; haraganear; rondar; **to hang on** colgar de; depender de; estar pendiente de (*las palabras de una persona*); estar sin acabar de morir; agarrarse; **to hang out** asomarse; (slang) recogerse, alojarse; **to hang over** (*to threaten*) cernerse sobre; **to hang together** mantenerse unidos; **to hang up** (telp) colgar ‖ *v* (*pret* **hanged** o **hung**) *tr* ahorcar ‖ *intr* ahorcarse
hangar ['hæŋər] o ['hæŋgɑr] *s* cobertizo; (aer) hangar *m*
hang'bird' *s* pájaro de nido colgante; (*Baltimore oriole*) cacique veranero
hanger ['hæŋər] *s* colgador *m*, suspensión; (*hook*) colgadero
hang'er•on' *s* (*pl* **hangers-on**) secuaz *mf;* parásito; (*sponger*) pegote *m*
hanging ['hæŋɪŋ] *adj* colgante, pendiente ‖ *s* ahorcadura, muerte *f* en la horca; **hangings** colgaduras
hang•man ['hæŋmən] *s* (*pl* **-men** [mən]) verdugo
hang'nail' *s* padrastro, respigón *m*
hang'out' *s* guarida, querencia; (*place to loaf and gossip*) mentidero
hang'o'ver *s* (slang) resaca
hank [hæŋk] *s* madeja
hanker ['hæŋkər] *intr* sentir anhelo
Hannibal ['hænɪbəl] *s* Aníbal *m*
haphazard [,hæp'hæzərd] *adj* casual, fortuito, impensado ‖ *adv* al acaso, a la ventura

hapless ['hæplɪs] *adj* desgraciado, desventurado

happen ['hæpən] *intr* acontecer, suceder; (*to turn out*) resultar; (*to be the case by chance*) dar la casualidad; **to happen in** entrar por casualidad; **to happen on** encontrarse con; **to happen to** hacerse de; **to happen to** + *inf* por casualidad + *ind*, p.ej., **I happened to see her at the theater** por casualidad la ví en el teatro

happening ['hæpənɪŋ] *s* acontecimiento, suceso

happily ['hæpɪli] *adv* felizmente

happiness ['hæpɪnɪs] *s* felicidad

hap•py ['hæpi] *adj* (*comp* **-pier;** *super* **-piest**) feliz; (*pleased*) contento; **to be happy to** alegrarse de, tener gusto en

hap'py-go-luck'y *adj* irresponsable, impróvido ‖ *adv* a la buenaventura

happy medium *s* justo medio

Happy New Year *interj* ¡Feliz Año Nuevo!

harangue [hə'ræŋ] *s* arenga ‖ *tr & intr* arengar

harass ['hærəs] o [hə'ræs] *tr* acosar, hostigar; molestar, vejar

harbinger ['hɑrbɪndʒər] *s* precursor *m*; anuncio, presagio ‖ *tr* anunciar, presagiar

harbor ['hɑrbər] *adj* portuario ‖ *s* puerto ‖ *tr* albergar; alcahuetar, encubrir (*delincuentes u objetos robados*); guardar (*sentimientos de odio*)

harbor master *s* capitán *m* de puerto

hard [hɑrd] *adj* duro; (*difficult*) difícil; (*water*) crudo, duro; (*solder*) fuerte; (*work*) asiduo; (*drinker*) empedernido; espiritoso, fuertemente alcohólico; **to be hard on** (*to treat severely*) ser muy duro con; (*to wear out fast*) gastar, echar a perder ‖ *adv* duro; fuerte; mucho; **hard upon** a raíz de; **to drink hard** beber de firme; **to rain hard** llover de firme

hard and fast *adj* inflexible, riguroso ‖ *adv* firmemente

hard-bitten ['hɑrd'bɪtən] *adj* terco, tenaz, inflexible

hard-boiled ['hɑrd'bɔɪld] *adj* (*egg*) duro, muy cocido; duro, inflexible

hard candy *s* caramelos

hard cash *s* dinero contante y sonante

hard cider *s* sidra muy fermentada

hard coal *s* antracita

hard-earned ['hɑrd'ʌrnd] *adj* ganado a pulso

harden ['hɑrdən] *tr* endurecer ‖ *intr* endurecerse

hardening ['hɑrdənɪŋ] *s* endurecimiento

hard facts *spl* realidades

hard-fought ['hɑrd'fɔt] *adj* reñido

hard-headed ['hɑrd'hɛdɪd] *adj* astuto, sagaz; terco, tozudo

hard-hearted ['hɑrd'hɑrtɪd] *adj* duro de corazón

hardihood ['hɑrdɪ,hʊd] *s* audacia, resolución; descaro, insolencia

hardiness ['hɑrdɪnɪs] *s* fuerza, robustez; audacia, resolución

hard labor *s* trabajos forzados

hard luck *s* mala suerte

hard'-luck' story *s* (coll) cuento de penas; **to tell a hard-luck story** (coll) contar lástimas

hardly ['hɑrdli] *adv* apenas; escasamente; casi no; (*with great difficulty*) a duras penas; (*grievously*) penosamente; **hardly ever** casi nunca

hardness ['hɑrdnɪs] *s* dureza; (*of water*) crudeza

hard of hearing *adj* duro de oído, teniente

hard-pressed ['hɑrd'prɛst] *adj* acosado; (*for money*) apurado, alcanzado

hard rubber *s* vulcanita

hard sauce *s* mantequilla azucarada

hard'-shell' clam *s* almeja redonda

hard'-shell' crab *s* cangrejo de cáscara dura

hardship ['hɑrdʃɪp] *s* penalidad, infortunio, apuro

hard'tack' *s* galleta, sequete *m*

hard times *spl* período de miseria, apuros

hard to please *adj* difícil de contentar

hard up *adj* (coll) apurado, alcanzado

hard'ware' *s* ferretería, quincalla; (*metal trimmings*) herraje *m*; (*computer*) ordenador *m*

hardware•man ['hɑrd,wɛrmən] *s* (*pl* **-men** [mən]) ferretero, quincallero

hardware store *s* ferretería, quincallería

hard-won ['hɑrd,wʌn] *adj* ganado a pulso

hard'wood' *s* madera dura; árbol *m* de madera dura

hardwood floor *s* entarimado

har•dy ['hɑrdi] *adj* (*comp* **-dier;** *super* **-diest**) fuerte, robusto; audaz, resuelto; (*rash*) temerario; (*hort*) resistente

hare [hɛr] *s* liebre *f*

harebrained ['hɛr,brend] *adj* atolondrado

hare'lip *s* labio leporino

harelipped ['hɛr,lɪpt] *adj* labiohendido

harem ['hɛrəm] *s* harén *m*

hark [hɑrk] *intr* escuchar; **to hark back** volver (*la jauría*) sobre la pista; **to hark back to** volver a, recordar

harken ['hɑrkən] *intr* escuchar, atender

harlequin ['hɑrləkwɪn] *s* arlequín *m*

harlot ['hɑrlət] *s* meretriz *f*

harm [hɑrm] *s* daño, perjuicio ‖ *tr* dañar, perjudicar, hacer daño a

harmful ['hɑrmfəl] *adj* dañoso, perjudicial; maléfico; (*e.g., pests*) dañino

harmfulness ['hɑrmfəlnɪs] *s* nocividad

harmless ['hɑrmlɪs] *adj* innocuo, inofensivo

harmlessness ['hɑrmlɪsnɪs] *s* innocuidad

harmonic [hɑr'mɑnɪk] *adj & s* armónico

harmonica [hɑr'mɑnɪkə] *s* armónica

harmonious [hɑr'monɪ•əs] *adj* armonioso

harmonize ['hɑrmə,naɪz] *tr & intr* armonizar

harmo•ny ['hɑrməni] *s* (*pl* **-nies**) armonía

harness ['hɑrnɪs] *s* arreos, guarniciones; **to get back in the harness** volver a la rutina; **to die in the harness** morir al pie del cañón ‖ *tr* enjaezar, poner las guarniciones a; enganchar; captar (*las aguas de un río*)

harness maker *s* guarnicionero

harness race *s* carrera con sulky

harp [hɑrp] *s* arpa ‖ *intr* — **to harp on** repetir porfiadamente

ha
ha

harpist ['harpɪst] s arpista mf
harpoon [har'pun] s arpón m ‖ tr & intr arponear
harpsichord ['harpsɪ ,kɔrd] s clave m
har·py ['harpi] s (pl **-pies**) arpía
harrow ['hæro] s (agr) grada ‖ tr (agr) gradar; atormentar
harrowing ['hæro·ɪŋ] adj horripilante, espantoso
har·ry ['hæri] v (pret & pp **-ried**) tr acosar, hostilizar, hostigar; atormentar, molestar
harsh [harʃ] adj (to touch, taste, eyes, hearing) áspero; duro, cruel
harshness ['harʃnɪs] s aspereza; dureza, crueldad
hart [hart] s ciervo
harum-scarum ['hɛrəm'skɛrəm] adj atolondrado ‖ adv atolondradamente ‖ s mataperros m
harvest ['harvɪst] s cosecha; corte m ‖ tr & intr cosechar
harvester ['harvɪstər] s cosechero; (helper) agostero; (machine) segadora
harvest home s entrada de los frutos; fiesta de segadores; canción de segadores
harvest moon s luna de la cosecha
has-been ['hæz'bɪn] s (coll) antigualla
hash [hæʃ] s picadillo ‖ tr picar
hash house s bodegón m
hashish ['hæʃiʃ] s hachich m; (coll) tate m
hashish user s (coll) tate m
hasp [hæsp] o [hɑsp] s portacandado; (of book covers) broche m
hassle ['hæsəl] s (coll) riña, disputa
hassock ['hæsək] s cojín m (para los pies o las rodillas)
haste [hest] s prisa; **in haste** de prisa; **to make haste** darse prisa
hasten ['hesən] tr apresurar; apretar (el paso) ‖ intr apresurarse
hast·y ['hesti] adj (comp **-ier;** super **-iest**) apresurado, inconsiderado, impulsivo, colérico
hat [hæt] s sombrero; **to keep under one's hat** (coll) callar, no divulgar; **to throw one's hat in the ring** (coll) decidirse a bajar a la arena
hat'band' s cintillo; (worn to show mourning) gasa
hat block s horma, conformador m
hat'box' s sombrerera
hatch [hætʃ] s (brood) cría, nidada; (trap door) escotillón m; (lower half of door) media puerta; (opening in ship's deck) escotilla; (lid for opening in ship's deck) cuartel m ‖ tr empollar (huevos); sombrear (un dibujo); maquinar, tramar ‖ intr empollarse; salir del huevo
hat'-check' girl s guardarropa
hatchet ['hætʃɪt] s destral m, hacha pequeña; **to bury the hatchet** envainar la espada
hatch'way' s (trap door) escotillón m; (opening in ship's deck) escotilla
hate [het] s odio, aborrecimiento ‖ tr & intr odiar, aborrecer, detestar
hateful ['hetfəl] adj odioso, aborrecible
hat'pin' s aguja de sombrero, pasador m

hat'rack' s percha
hatred ['hetrɪd] s odio, aborrecimiento
hat shop s bonetería
hatter ['hætər] s sombrerero
haughtiness ['hɔtɪnɪs] s altanería, altivez f
haugh·ty ['hɔti] adj (comp **-tier;** super **-iest**) altanero, altivo
haul [hɔl] s (pull, tug) tirón m; (amount caught) redada; (distance transported) trayecto, recorrido; (roundup, e.g., of thieves) redada ‖ tr acarrear, transportar; (naut) halar
haunch [hɔntʃ] o [hɑntʃ] s (hip) cadera; (hind quarter of an animal) anca; (leg of animal used for food) pierna
haunt [hɔnt] o [hɑnt] s guarida, nidal m, querencia ‖ tr andar por, vagar por; frecuentar; inquietar, molestar; perseguir (las memorias a una persona)
haunted house s casa de fantasmas
haute couture [ot ku'tyr] s alta moda
Havana [hə'vænə] s La Habana
have [hæv] v (pret & pp **had** [hæd]) tr tener; (to get, to take) tomar; **to have and to hold** (úsase sólo en el infinitivo) para ser poseído en propiedad; **to have got** (coll) tener, poseer; **to have got to** + inf (coll) tener que + inf; **to have it in for** (coll) tener tirria a; **to have it out with** (coll) habérselas con, emprenderla con; **to have on** llevar puesto; **to have** (something) **to do with** tener que ver con; **to have what it takes** tener madera de; **to have** + inf hacer, mandar + inf, p.ej., **I had him go out that door** le hice salir por esa puerta; **to have** + pp hacer, mandar + inf, p.ej., **I had my watch repaired** hice componer mi reloj ‖ intr — **to have at** atacar, embestir; **to have to** + inf tener que + inf; **to have to do with** (to be concerned with) tratar de; (to have connections with) tener relaciones con ‖ v aux haber, p.ej., **he has studied his lesson** ha estudiado su lección
havelock ['hævlɑk] s cogotera
haven ['hevən] s puerto; abrigo, asilo, buen puerto
have-not ['hæv,nɑt] s — **the haves and the have-nots** (coll) los ricos y los desposeídos
haversack ['hævər,sæk] s barjuleta; (of soldier) mochila
havoc ['hævək] s estrago, estragos; **to play havoc with** hacer grandes estragos en
haw [hɔ] s (of hawthorn) baya, simiente f; (in speech) vacilación ‖ interj ¡a la izquierda! ‖ tr & intr volver a la izquierda
haw'-haw' s carcajada
hawk [hɔk] s halcón m, gavilán m, cernícalo; (mortarboard) esparavel m; (sharper) (coll) fullero ‖ tr pregonar; **to hawk up** arrojar tosiendo ‖ intr carraspear, gargajear
hawker ['hɔkər] s buhonero
hawksbill turtle ['hɔks,bɪl] s carey m
hawse [hɔz] s (naut) muz m; (hole) (naut) escobén m; (naut) longitud de cadenas
hawse'hole' s (naut) escobén m
hawser ['hɔzər] s (naut) guindaleza
haw'thorn' s espino, oxiacanta

hay [he] *s* heno; **to hit the hay** (slang) acostarse; **to make hay while the sun shines** hacer su agosto
hay fever *s* fiebre *f* del heno
hay'field' *s* henar *m*
hay'fork' *s* horca; (*machine*) elevador *m* de heno
hay'loft' *s* henil *m*, henal *m*
hay'mak'er *s* (box) golpe *m* que pone fuera de combate
haymow ['he,maʊ] *s* henil *m;* acopio de heno
hay'rack' *s* pesebre *m*
hayrick ['he,rɪk] *s* almiar *m*
hay ride *s* paseo de placer en carro de heno
hay'seed' *s* simiente *f* de heno; (coll) patán *m*, campesino
hay'stack' *s* almiar *m*
hay'wire' *adj* (slang) descompuesto; (slang) destornillado, loco ‖ *s* alambre *m* para embalar el heno
hazard ['hæzərd] *s* peligro, riesgo; (*chance*) acaso, azar *m;* (golf) obstáculo; **at all hazards** por grande que sea el riesgo ‖ *tr* arriesgar; aventurar (*una opinión*)
hazardous ['hæzərdəs] *adj* peligroso, arriesgado
haze [hez] *s* calina, bruma; (fig) confusión, vaguedad ‖ *tr* dar novatada a
hazel ['hezəl] *adj* castaño claro ‖ *s* avellano
ha'zel•nut *s* avellana
hazing ['hezɪŋ] *s* novatada
ha•zy ['hezi] *adj* (*comp* **-zier;** *super* **-ziest**) calinoso, brumoso; confuso, vago
H-bomb ['etʃ,bɑm] *s* bomba de hidrógeno
H.C. *abbr* **House of Commons**
hd. *abbr* **head**
hdqrs. *abbr* **headquarters**
H.E. *abbr* **His Eminence, His Excellency**
he [hi] *pron pers* (*pl* **they**) él ‖ *s* (*pl* **hes**) macho, varón *m*
head [hɛd] *s* cabeza; (*of a bed*) cabecera; (*caption*) encabezamiento; (*of a boil*) centro; (*on a glass of beer*) espuma; (*of a drum*) parche *m;* (*of a cane*) puño; (*of a barrel, cylinder, etc.*) fondo, tapa; (*of cylinder of automobile engine*) culata; crisis *f*, punto decisivo; **at the head of** al frente de; **from head to foot** de pies a cabeza; **head over heels** en un salto mortal; hasta los tuétanos; precipitadamente; **heads** (*of a coin*) cara; **heads or tails?** ¿cara o cruz?; ¿águila o sol? (Mex); **over one's head** fuera del alcance de uno; (*going to a higher authority*) por encima de uno; **to be out of one's head** (coll) delirar; **to come into one's head** pasarle a uno por la cabeza; **to go to one's head** subírsele a uno a la cabeza; **to keep one's head** no perder la cabeza; **to keep one's head above water** no dejarse vencer; **to put heads together** consultarse entre sí; **to not make head or tail of** no ver pies ni cabeza a ‖ *tr* acaudillar, dirigir, mandar; estar a la cabeza de (*p.ej., la clase*); venir primero en (*una lista*) ‖ *intr* — **to head towards** dirigirse hacia
head'ache' *s* dolor *m* de cabeza

head'band' *s* cinta para la cabeza; (*of a book*) cabezada
head'board' *s* cabecera de cama
head'cheese' *s* queso de cerdo
head'dress' *s* (*style of hair*) tocado; prenda para la cabeza
header ['hɛdər] *s* — **to take a header** (coll) caerse de cabeza
head'first' *adv* de cabeza; precipitadamente
head'gear' *s* sombrero; (*for protection*) casco
head'hunt'er *s* cazador *m* de cabezas
heading ['hɛdɪŋ] *s* encabezamiento; (*of a letter*) membrete *m;* (*of a chapter of a book*) cabecera
headland ['hɛdlənd] *s* promontorio
headless ['hɛdlɪs] *adj* sin cabeza; sin jefe; estúpido
head'light' *s* (aut) faro; (naut) farol *m* de tope; (rr) farol *m*
head'line' *s* (*of newspaper*) cabecera; (*of a page of a book*) titulillo, título de página ‖ *tr* poner cabecera a; (slang) destacar, dar cartel a (*un actor*)
head'lin'er *s* (slang) atracción principal
head'long' *adj* de cabeza; precipitado ‖ *adv* de cabeza; precipitadamente
head•man ['hɛd,mæn] *s* (*pl* **-men** [,mɛn]) caudillo, jefe *m*
head'mas'ter *s* director *m* de un colegio
head'most' *adj* delantero, primero
head office *s* oficina central
head of hair *s* cabellera
head'-on' *adj & adv* de frente; **head-on collision** colisión de frente
head'phone' *s* auricular *m* de casco, receptor *m* de cabeza
head'piece' *s* (*any covering for head*) casco, yelmo, morrión *m;* (*brains, judgment*) cabeza, juicio; cabecera de cama; (*headset*) auricular *m* de casco, receptor *m* de cabeza; (typ) cabecera, viñeta
head'quar'ters *s* centro de dirección; (*of police*) jefatura; (mil) cuartel *m* general
head'rest' *s* apoyo para la cabeza; (aut) reposa cabezas
head'set' *s* auricular *m* de casco, receptor *m* de cabeza
head'ship' *s* jefatura, dirección
head'stone' *s* (*cornerstone*) piedra angular; (*on a grave*) lápida sepulcral
head'stream' *s* afluente *m* principal
head'strong' *adj* cabezudo, terco
head'wait'er *s* jefe *m* de camareros, encargado de comedor
head'wa'ters *spl* cabecera
head'way' *s* avance *m*, progreso; espacio libre; **to make headway** avanzar, progresar
head'wear' *s* prendas de cabeza
head wind *s* viento de frente, viento por la proa
head'work' *s* trabajo intelectual
head•y ['hɛdi] *adj* (*comp* **-ier;** *super* **-iest**) excitante, emocionante; impetuoso, violento; (*intoxicating*) cabezudo; (*clever*) sesudo

ha
he

heal [hil] *tr* curar, sanar; cicatrizar; remediar (*un daño*) ‖ *intr* curar, sanar; cicatrizarse; remediarse

healer [ˈhilər] *s* curador *m*, sanador *m*

health [hɛlθ] *s* salud *f*; **to be in good health** estar bien de salud; **to be in poor health** estar mal de salud; **to drink to the health of** beber a la salud de; **to radiate health** verter salud; **to your health!** ¡a su salud!

healthful [ˈhɛlθfəl] *adj* saludable; sano

health insurance *s* seguro de enfermedad

health•y [ˈhɛlθi] *adj* (*comp* -ier; *super* -iest) sano; saludable

heap [hip] *s* montón *m* ‖ *tr* amontonar, apilar; (*to supply with, e.g., favors*) colmar; (*to bestow in great quantity*) dar generosamente ‖ *intr* amontonarse, apilarse

hear [hɪr] *v* (*pret & pp* **heard** [hʌrd]) *tr* oír; **to hear it said** oírlo decir ‖ *intr* oír; **hear! hear!** ¡bravo!; **to hear about** oír hablar de; **to hear from** tener noticias de; **to hear of** oír hablar de; **to hear tell of** oír hablar de; **to hear that** oír decir que

hearer [ˈhɪrər] *s* oyente *mf*

hearing [ˈhɪrɪŋ] *s* (*sense*) oído; (*act*) oída; audiencia; **in the hearing of** en presencia de; **within hearing** al alcance del oído

hearing aid *s* aparato auditivo

hear'say' *s* rumor *m*; **by hearsay** de o por oídas

hearse [hʌrs] *s* coche *m* fúnebre, carroza fúnebre

heart [hɑrt] *s* corazón *m*; (*e.g., of lettuce*) cogollo; **after one's heart** enteramente del gusto de uno; **by heart** de memoria; **heart and soul** de todo corazón; **to break the heart of** partir el corazón de; **to die of a broken heart** morir de pena; **to eat one's heart out** sufrir en silencio; **to get to the heart of** llegar al fondo de; **to have one's heart in one's work**; trabajar con entusiasmo; **to have one's heart in the right place** tener buenas intenciones; **to lose heart** descorazonarse; **to open one's heart to** descubrirse con; **to take heart** cobrar aliento; **to take to heart** tomar a pecho; **to wear one's heart on one's sleeve** llevar el corazón en la mano; **with all one's heart** con toda el alma de uno; **with one's heart in one's mouth** con el credo en la boca

heart'ache' *s* angustia, congoja

heart attack *s* ataque *m* de corazón, ataque cardíaco

heart'beat' *s* latido del corazón

heart'break' *s* angustia, dolor *m* abrumador

heart'break'er *s* ladrón *m* de corazones

heartbroken [ˈhɑrt,brokən] *adj* transido de dolor, muerto de pena

heart'burn' *s* acedía, rescoldera; (*jealousy*) celos

heart disease *s* enfermedad del corazón

hearten [ˈhɑrtən] *tr* alentar, animar

heart failure *s* debilidad coronaria; (*death*) paro del corazón; (*faintness*) desfallecimiento, desmayo

heartfelt [ˈhɑrt,fɛlt] *adj* cordial, sentido, sincero

hearth [hɑrθ] *s* hogar *m*

hearth'stone' *s* solera del hogar; (*home*) hogar *m*

heartily [ˈhɑrtɪli] *adv* cordialmente; con buen apetito; de buena gana; bien, mucho

heartless [ˈhɑrtlɪs] *adj* cruel, inhumano

heart pacemaker *s* marcapaso, marcapasos *m*

heart-rending [ˈhɑrt,rɛndɪŋ] *adj* angustioso, que parte el corazón

heart'seed' *s* farolillo

heart'sick' *adj* afligido, desconsolado

heart'strings' *spl* fibras del corazón, entretelas

heart'-to-heart' *adj* franco, sincero

heart trouble *s* — **to have heart trouble** enfermar del corazón

heart'wood' *s* madera de corazón

heart•y [ˈhɑrti] *adj* (*comp* -ier; *super* -iest) cordial, sincero; sano, fuerte; (*meal*) abundante; (*laugh*) bueno; (*eater*) grande

heat [hit] *adj* térmico ‖ *s* calor *m*; (*warming of a room, house, etc.*) calefacción; (*rut of animals*) celo; (*in horse racing*) carrera de prueba; (*fig*) ardor *m*, ímpetu *m*; **in heat** encelo ‖ *tr* calentar; calefaccionar (*p.ej., una casa*); (*fig*) acalorar, excitar ‖ *intr* calentarse; (*fig*) acalorarse, excitarse

heated [ˈhitɪd] *adj* acalorado

heater [ˈhitər] *s* calentador *m*; (*for central heating*) calorífero; (*electron*) calefactor *m*

heater man *s* calefactor *m*

heath [hiθ] *s* (*shrub*) brezo; (*tract of land*) brezal *m*

hea•then [ˈhiðən] *adj* gentil, pagano; irreligioso ‖ *s* (*pl* -then o -thens) gentil *mf*, pagano

heathendom [ˈhiðəndəm] *s* gentilidad

heather [ˈhɛðər] *s* brezo

heating [ˈhitɪŋ] *adj* calentador ‖ *s* calefacción

heat'-in'su•lat•ed *adj* termoaislante

heat lightning *s* fucilazo, relámpago de calor

heat shield *s* blindaje térmico, escudo térmico

heat'stroke' *s* insolación; golpe *m* de calor

heat wave *s* (*phys*) onda calorífica; (*coll*) ola de calor

heave [hiv] *s* esfuerzo para levantar; esfuerzo para levantarse; **heaves** (*vet*) huélfago ‖ *v* (*pret & pp* **heaved** o **hov** [hɒv]) *tr* alzar, levantar; arrojar, lanzar; exhalar (*un suspiro*) ‖ *intr* levantarse y bajar alternativamente; palpitar (*el pecho*); elevarse; hacer esfuerzos por vomitar

heaven [ˈhɛvən] *s* cielo; **for heaven's sake!** o **good heavens!** ¡válgame Dios!; **heavens** (*firmament*) cielo ‖ **Heaven** *s* cielo (*mansión de los bienaventurados*)

heavenly [ˈhɛvənli] *adj* (*body*) celeste; (*life, home*) celestial; (*fig*) celestial

heavenly body *s* astro, cuerpo celeste

heav•y [ˈhɛvi] *adj* (*comp* -ier; *super* -iest) (*of great weight*) pesado; (*liquid*) espeso, denso; (*cloth, paper, sea, line*) grueso;

(*traffic*) denso; (*crop, harvest*) abundante, copioso; (*expense*) fuerte; (*rain*) recio; (*features*) basto; (*eyes*) agravado; (*gunfire*) fragoroso; (*heart*) abatido, triste; (*drinker*) grande; (*stock market*) postrado; (*clothing*) de mucho abrigo ‖ *adv* pesadamente; **to hang heavy;** pasar (*el tiempo*) con gran lentitud

heav′y•du′ty *adj* extrafuerte

heavy-hearted [′hɛvi′hɑrtɪd] *adj* afligido, acongojado

heav′y•set′ *adj* costilludo, espaldudo

heav′y•weight′ *s* (box) peso pesado

Hebrew [′hibru] *adj & s* hebreo

hecatomb [′hɛkə,tom] *s* hecatombe *f*

heckle [′hɛkəl] *tr* interrumpir (*a un orador*) con preguntas impertinentes

hectic [′hɛktɪk] *adj* (coll) agitado, turbulento

hedge [hɛdʒ] *s* cercado, vallado; (*of bushes*) seto vivo; apuesta compensatoria; (*in stock market*) operación compensatoria ‖ *tr* cercar con vallado; cercar con seto vivo; **to hedge in** encerrar, rodear ‖ *intr* no querer comprometerse; hacer apuestas compensatorias; hacer operaciones compensatorias

hedge′hog′ *s* erizo; (*porcupine*) puerco espín *m*

hedge′hop′ *v* (*pret & pp* **-hopped;** *ger* **-hopping**) *intr* (aer) volar rasando el suelo

hedgehopping [′hɛdʒ,hɑpɪŋ] *s* (aer) vuelo rasante

hedge′row′ *s* cercado de arbustos, seto vivo

heed [hid] *s* atención, cuidado; **to take heed** ir con cuidado ‖ *tr* atender a, hacer caso de ‖ *intr* atender, hacer caso

heedless [′hidlɪs] *adj* desatento, descuidado

heehaw [′hi,hɔ] *s* (*of donkey*) rebuzno; risotada ‖ *intr* rebuznar; reír groseramente

heel [hil] *s* (*of foot*) calcañar *m*, talón *m;* (*of stocking or shoe*) talón *m;* (*raised part of shoe below heel*) tacón *m;* (slang) sinvergüenza *mf;* **down at the heel** desaliñado, mal vestido; **to cool one's heels** (coll) hacer antesala; **to kick up one's heels** (slang) mostrarse alegre; **to show a clean pair of heels** o **to take to one's heels** poner pies en polvorosa

heeler [′hilər] *s* (slang) muñidor *m*

heft•y [′hɛfti] *adj* (*comp* **-ier;** *super* **-iest**) (*heavy*) pesado; (*strong*) fuerte, fornido

hegemo•ny [hɪ′dʒɛməni] o [′hɛdʒɪ-,moni] *s* (*pl* **-nies**) hegemonía

hegira [hɪ′dʒəɪrə] o [′hɛdʒɪrə] *s* fuga, huída

heifer [′hɛfər] *s* novilla, vaquilla

height [haɪt] *s* altura; (*e.g., of folly*) colmo

heighten [′haɪtən] *tr* hacer más alto; (*to increase the amount of*) aumentar; (*to set off, bring out*) realzar ‖ *intr* aumentarse

heinous [′henəs] *adj* atroz, nefando

heir [ɛr] *s* heredero

heir apparent *s* (*pl* **heirs apparent**) heredero forzoso

heirdom [′ɛrdəm] *s* herencia

heiress [′ɛrɪs] *s* heredera

heirloom [′ɛr,lum] *s* joya de familia, reliquia de familia

helicopter [′hɛlɪ,kɑptər] *s* helicóptero

heliotrope [′hilɪ•ə,trop] *s* heliotropo

heliport [′hɛlɪ,port] *s* helipuerto

helium [′hilɪ•əm] *s* helio

helix [′hilɪks] *s* (*pl* **helixes** o **helices** [′hɛlɪ,siz]**) hélice *f*

hell [hɛl] *s* infierno

hell-bent [′hɛl′bɛnt] *adj* (slang) muy resuelto; **hell-bent on** (slang) empeñado en

hell′cat′ *s* (*bad-tempered woman*) arpía, mujer perversa; (*witch*) bruja

hellebore [′hɛlɪ,bor] *s* eléboro

Hellene [′hɛlin] *s* heleno

Hellenic [hɛ′lɛnɪk] *adj* helénico

hell′fire′ *s* fuego del infierno

hellish [′hɛlɪʃ] *adj* infernal

hel•lo [hɛ′lo] *s* saludo ‖ *interj* ¡qué tal!; (*on telephone*) ¡diga!

hello girl *s* (coll) chica telefonista

helm [hɛlm] *s* barra del timón; rueda del timón; (fig) timón *m* ‖ *tr* dirigir, gobernar

helmet [′hɛlmɪt] *s* casco; (*of ancient armor*) yelmo

helms•man [′hɛlmzmən] *s* (*pl* **-men** [mən]) timonel *m*

help [hɛlp] *s* ayuda, socorro; (*of food*) ración; (*relief*) remedio, p.ej., **there's no help for it** no hay remedio; criados; empleados; obreros; **to come to the help of** acudir en socorro de ‖ *interj* ¡socorro! ‖ *tr* ayudar, socorrer; aliviar, mitigar; (*to wait on*) servir; **it can't be helped** no hay remedio; **so help me God!** ¡así Dios me salve!; **to help down** ayudar a bajar; **to help a person with his coat** ayudarle a una persona a ponerse el abrigo; **to help oneself** valerse por sí mismo; servirse; **to help up** ayudar a subir; ayudar a levantarse; **to not be able to help** + *ger* no poder menos de + *inf*, p.ej., **he can't help laughing** no puede menos de reír ‖ *intr* ayudar

helper [′hɛlpər] *s* ayudante *mf;* (*in a drug store, barbershop, etc.*) mancebo

helpful [′hɛlpfəl] *adj* útil, provechoso; servicial

helping [[′hɛlpɪŋ] *s* ración (*de alimento*)

helpless [′hɛlplɪs] *adj* (*weak*) débil; (*powerless*) impotente; (*penniless*) desvalido; (*confused*) perplejo; (*situation*) irremediable

help′meet′ *s* compañero; (*wife*) compañera

helter-skelter [′hɛltər′skɛltər] *adj, adv & s* cochite hervite *m*

hem [hɛm] *s* tos fingida; (*of a garment*) bastilla, dobladillo ‖ *interj* ¡ejem! ‖ *v* (*pret & pp* **hemmed;** *ger* **hemming**) *tr* bastillar, dobladillar; **to hem in** encerrar, rodear ‖ *intr* destoserse; vacilar; **to hem and haw** vacilar al hablar; ser evasivo

hemisphere [′hɛmɪ,sfɪr] *s* hemisferio

hemistich [′hɛmɪ,stɪk] *s* hemistiquio

hem′line′ *s* ruedo de la falda, borde *m* de la falda

hem′lock′ *s* (*Tsuga canadensis*) abeto del Canadá; (*herb and poison*) cicuta

hemoglobin [,hɛmə′globɪn] o [,hɪmə′globɪn] *s* hemoglobina

he
he

hemophilia [,hɛmə'fɪlɪ•ə] o [,himə'fɪlɪ•ə] s hemofilia

hemorrhage ['hɛmərɪdʒ] s hemorragia

hemorrhoids ['hɛmə,rɔɪdz] spl hemorroides fpl

hemostat ['hɛmə,stæt] o ['himə,stæt] s hemóstato

hemp [hɛmp] s cáñamo

hemstitch ['hɛm,stɪtʃ] s vainica || tr hacer vainica en || intr hacer vainica

hen [hɛn] s gallina

hence [hɛns] adv de aquí; desde ahora; por lo tanto, por consiguiente; de aquí a, p.ej., **three weeks hence** de aquí a tres semanas

hence'forth' adv de aquí en adelante

hench•man ['hɛntʃmən] s (pl -men [mən]) secuaz m, servidor m; (political schemer) muñidor m

hen'coop' s gallinero

hen'house' s gallinero

henna ['hɛnə] s alcana, alheña; (dye) henna f || tr alheñarse (el pelo)

hen'peck' tr dominar (la mujer al marido)

henpecked husband s calzonazos m, gurrumino

hep [hɛp] adj (slang) enterado; **to be hep to** (slang) estar al corriente de

her [hʌr] adj poss su; el . . . de ella || pron pers la; ella; **to her** le; a ella

herald ['hɛrəld] s heraldo; anunciador m || tr anunciar; ser precursor de

heraldic [hɛ'rældɪk] adj heráldico

herald•ry ['hɛrəldri] s (pl -ries) (office or duty of herald) heraldía; (science of armorial bearings) blasón m, heráldica; (heraldic device; coat of arms) blasón m; pompa heráldica

herb [ʌrb] o [hʌrb] s hierba; hierba aromática; hierba medicinal

herbaceous [hʌr'beʃəs] adj herbáceo

herbage ['ʌrbɪdʒ] o ['hʌrbɪdʒ] s herbaje m

herbal ['ʌrbəl] o ['hʌrbəl] adj & s herbario

herbalist ['hʌrbəlɪst] o ['ʌrbəlɪst] s herbolario

herbari•um [hʌr'bɛrɪ•əm] s (pl -ums o -a [ə]) herbario

herb doctor s herbolario

herculean [hʌr'kulɪ•ən] adj (hard to perform) penoso, laborioso; (strong, big) hercúleo

herd [hʌrd] s manada, rebaño, hato; (of people) chusma, multitud || tr reunir en manada; reunir || intr reunirse en manada; reunirse, ir juntos

herds•man ['hʌrdzmən] s (pl -men [mən]) manadero; (of sheep) pastor m; (of cattle) vaquero

here [hɪr] adj presente || adv aquí; **here and there** acá y allá; **here is** o here are aquí tiene Vd.; **that's neither here nor there** eso no viene al caso || s — **the here and the hereafter** esta vida y la futura || interj ¡presente!

hereabouts ['hɪrə,baʊts] adv por aquí, cerca de aquí

here•af'ter adv de aquí en adelante; en lo · sucesivo; en la vida futura || **the hereafter** la otra vida, el más allá

here•by' adv por esto; por la presente

hereditary [hɪ'rɛdɪ,tɛri] adj hereditario

heredi•ty [hɪ'rɛdɪti] s (pl -ties) herencia

here•in' adv aquí dentro; en este asunto

here•of' adv de esto

here•on' adv en esto, sobre esto

here•sy ['hɛrəsi] s (pl -sies) herejía

heretic ['hɛrətɪk] adj herético || s hereje mf

heretical [hɪ'rɛtɪkəl] adj herético

heretofore [,hɪtru'for] adv antes, hasta ahora

here•u•pon' adv en esto, sobre esto; en seguida

here•with' adv adjunto, con la presente; de este modo

heritage ['hɛrɪtɪdʒ] s herencia

hermetic(al) [hʌr'mɛtɪk(əl)] adj hermético

hermit ['hʌrmɪt] s eremita m, ermitaño

hermitage ['hʌrnɪtɪdʒ] s ermita

herni•a ['hʌrnɪ•ə] s (pl -as o -ae [,i]) hernia

he•ro ['hɪro] s (pl -roes) héroe m

heroic [hɪ'ro•ɪk] adj heroico || **heroics** spl verso heroico; lenguaje rimbombante

heroin ['hɛro•ɪn] s heroína (polvo cristalino); (slang) caballo

heroin addict s heroinómano

heroine ['hɛro•ɪn] s heroína (mujer)

heroism ['hɛro,ɪzəm] s heroísmo

heron ['hɛrən] s garza; (Ardea cinerea) airón m, garza real

herring ['hɛrɪŋ] s arenque m

her'ring•bone s (in fabrics) espina de pescado; (in hardwood floors) espinapez m, punto de Hungría

hers [hʌrz] pron poss el suyo, el de ella; suyo

herself [hʌr'sɛlf] pron pers ella misma; sí, sí misma; se, p.ej., **she enjoyed herself** se divirtió; **with herself** consigo

hesitan•cy ['hɛzɪtənsi] s (pl -cies) vacilación

hesitant ['hɛzɪtənt] adj vacilante

hesitate ['hɛzɪ,tet] intr vacilar, titubear; (to stutter) titubear

hesitation [,hɛzɪ'teʃən] s vacilación

heterodox ['hɛtərə,daks] adj heterodoxo

heterodyne ['hɛtərə,daɪn] adj heterodino || tr heterodinar

heterogenei•ty [,hɛtərədʒɪ'ni•ɪti] s (pl -ties) heterogeneidad

heterogeneous [,hɛtərə'dʒɪnɪ•əs] adj heterogéneo

hew [hju] v (pret hewed; pp hewed o hewn) tr cortar, tajar; (with an ax) hachear; labrar (madera); picar (piedra); **to hew down** derribar a hachazos || intr — **to hew close to the line** (coll) hilar delgado

hex [hɛks] s (coll) bruja; (coll) hechizo || tr (coll) embrujar

hexameter [hɛks'æmɪtər] s hexámetro

hey [he] interj ¡oye!, ¡oiga!

hey'day' s época de mayor prosperidad

hf. abbr half

H.H. abbr His Highness, Her Highness; His Holiness

hia•tus [haɪ'etəs] s (pl -tuses o -tus) (gap) abertura, laguna; (in a text; in verse) hiato

hibernate ['haɪbər,net] *intr* invernar; estar inactivo

hibiscus [hɪ'bɪskəs] o [haɪ'bɪskəs] *s* hibisco

hiccough o **hiccup** ['hɪkəp] *s* hipo ‖ *intr* hipar

hick [hɪk] *adj & s* (coll) campesino, palurdo

hicko•ry ['hɪkəri] *s* (*pl* **-ries**) nuez encarcelada, nuez dura (*árbol*)

hickory nut *s* nuez encarcelada, nuez dura (*fruto*)

hidden ['hɪdən] *adj* escondido, oculto; obscuro

hide [haɪd] *s* cuero, piel *f;* **hides** corambre *f;* **neither hide nor hair** ni un vestigio; **to tan someone's hide** (coll) zurrarle a uno la badana ‖ *v* (*pret* **hid** [hɪd]; *pp* **hid** o **hidden** ['hɪdən]) *tr* esconder, ocultar ‖ *intr* esconderse, ocultarse; **to hide out** (coll) recatarse

hide'-and-seek' *s* escondite *m;* **to play hide-and-seek** jugar al escondite

hide'bound' *adj* fanático, obstinado, dogmático

hideous ['hɪdɪ•əs] *adj* (*very ugly*) feote; (*heinous*) atroz, nefando; (*distressingly large*) brutal, enorme

hide'-out' *s* (coll) guarida, refugio, escondrijo

hiding ['haɪdɪŋ] *s* ocultación; (*place of concealment*) escondite *m*, escondrijo; **in hiding** escondido, oculto; (*in ambush*) emboscado

hiding place *s* escondite *m*, escondrijo

hie [haɪ] *v* (*pret & pp* **hied;** *ger* **hieing** o **hying**) *tr* — **hie thee home** apresúrate a volver a casa ‖ *intr* apresurarse, ir volando

hierar•chy ['haɪ•ə,rɑrki] *s* (*pl* **-chies**) jerarquía

hieroglyphic [,haɪ•ərə'glɪfɪk] *adj & s* jeroglífico

hi-fi ['haɪ'faɪ] *adj* de alta fidelidad ‖ *s* alta fidelidad

hi-fi fan *s* aficionado a la alta fidelidad

hi-fi set *s* equipo de alta fidelidad

higgledy-piggledy ['hɪgəldɪ'pɪgəldɪ] *adj* confuso, revuelto ‖ *adv* confusamente, revueltamente

high [haɪ] *adj* alto; (*river*) crecido; (*sound*) agudo; (*wind*) fuerte; (coll) borracho; (*intoxicated*) embriagado; (*drugs*) emporrado; (culin) manido; **high and dry** abandonado, desamparado; **high and mighty** (coll) muy arrogante ‖ *adv* en sumo grado; a gran precio; **to aim high** poner el tiro muy alto; **to come high** venderse caro ‖ *s* (aut) marcha directa; **on high** en el cielo

high altar *s* altar *m* mayor

high'ball' *s* highball *m*

high blood pressure *s* hipertensión arterial

high'born' *adj* linajudo, de ilustre cuna

high'boy' *s* cómoda alta con patas altas

high'brow' *adj & s* (slang) erudito

high chair *s* silla alta

high command *s* alto mando

high cost of living *s* carestía de la vida

higher education *s* enseñanza superior

higher-up [,haɪ•ər'ʌp] *s* (coll) superior jerárquico

high explosive *s* explosivo rompedor

highfalutin [,haɪfə'lutən] *adj* (coll) pomposo, presuntuoso

high fidelity *s* alta fidelidad

high'-fre'quency *adj* de alta frecuencia

high gear *s* marcha directa, toma directa

high'-grade' *adj* de calidad superior

high-handed ['haɪ'hændɪd] *adj* arbitrario

high hat *s* sombrero de copa

high'-hat' *adj* (coll) copetudo, esnob; **to be high-hat** tener mucho copete ‖ **high'-hat'** *v* (*pret & pp* **-hatted;** *ger* **-hatting**) *tr* desairar

high-heeled shoe ['haɪ,hild] *s* zapato de tacón alto

high horse *s* ademán *m* arrogante

high'jack' *tr* var de **hijack**

high jinks [dʒɪŋks] *spl* (slang) jarana, payasada

high jump *s* salto de altura

highland ['haɪlənd] *s* región montañosa; **highlands** montañas, tierras altas

high life *s* alta sociedad, gran mundo

high'light' *s* elemento sobresaliente ‖ *tr* destacar

highly ['haɪli] *adv* altamente; en sumo grado; a gran precio; con aplauso general; **to speak highly of** decir mil bienes de

High Mass *s* misa cantada, misa mayor

high-minded ['haɪ'maɪndɪd] *adj* noble, magnánimo

highness ['haɪnɪs] *s* altura ‖ **Highness** *s* Alteza

high noon *s* pleno mediodía

high-pitched ['haɪ'pɪtʃt] *adj* agudo; tenso, impresionable

high-powered ['haɪ'paʊ•ərd] *adj* de alta potencia

high'-pres'sure *adj* de alta presión; (fig) emprendedor, enérgico ‖ *tr* (coll) apremiar

high-priced ['haɪ'praɪst] *adj* de precio elevado

high priest *s* sumo sacerdote

high rise *s* edificio de muchos pisos

high'road' *s* camino real

high school *s* escuela de segunda enseñanza

high sea *s* mar gruesa; **high seas** alta mar

high society *s* alta sociedad, gran mundo

high'-speed' *adj* de alta velocidad

high-spirited ['haɪ'spɪrɪtɪd] *adj* animoso; vivaz; (*horse*) fogoso

high spirits *spl* alegría, buen humor *m*, animación

high-strung ['haɪ'strʌŋ] *adj* tenso, impresionable

high'-test' **fuel** *s* supercarburante *m*

high tide *s* pleamar *f*, marea alta; (fig) punto culminante

high time *s* hora, p.ej., **it is high time for you to go** ya es hora de que Vd. se marche; (slang) jarana, parranda

high treason *s* alta traición

high water *s* aguas altas; pleamar *f*, marea alta

high'way' *s* carretera

he
hi

highway·man [ˈhaɪˌwemən] s (pl -men [mən]) salteador m de caminos

hijack [ˈhaɪˌdʒæk] tr (coll) robar (a un contrabandista de licores); (coll) robar (el licor a un contrabandista)

hijacker [ˈhaɪˌdʒækər] s pirata aéreo

hijacking [ˈhaɪˌdʒækɪŋ] s piratería aérea

hike [haɪk] s caminata, marcha; (increase, rise) aumento ‖ tr elevar de un tirón; aumentar ‖ intr dar una caminata

hiker [ˈhaɪkər] s caminador m, aficionado a las caminatas

hilarious [hɪˈlɛrɪ·əs] o [haɪˈlɛrɪ·əs] adj jubiloso, regocijado

hill [hɪl] s colina, collado ‖ tr aporcar (las hortalizas)

hillbil·ly [ˈhɪlˌbɪli] s (pl -lies) (coll) rústico montañés (del sur de los EE.UU.)

hillock [ˈhɪlək] s altozano, montecillo

hill'side' s ladera

hill'top' s cumbre f, cima

hill·y [ˈhɪli] adj (comp -ier; super -iest) colinoso; (steep) empinado

hilt [hɪlt] s empuñadura, puño; **up to the hilt** completamente

him [hɪm] pron pers le, lo; él; **to him** le; a él

himself [hɪmˈsɛlf] pron pers él mismo; sí, sí mismo; se, p.ej., **he enjoyed himself** se divirtió; **with himself** consigo

hind [haɪnd] adj posterior, trasero ‖ s cierva

hinder [ˈhɪndər] tr estorbar, impedir; obstruccionar

hindmost [ˈhaɪndˌmost] adj postrero, último

Hindoo [ˈhɪndu] adj & s hindú m

hind'quar'ter s cuarto trasero

hindrance [ˈhɪndrəns] s estorbo, impedimento, obstáculo

hind'sight' s (of a firearm) mira posterior; percepción tardía, sabiduría tardía

Hindu [ˈhɪndu] adj & s hindú m

hinge [hɪndʒ] s (of a door) charnela, gozne m, bisagra; (of a mollusk) charnela; (bb) cartivana; punto capital ‖ tr engoznar ‖ intr — **to hinge on** depender de

hin·ny [ˈhɪni] s (pl -nies) burdégano, mohino

hint [hɪnt] s indirecta, insinuación; **to take the hint** darse por aludido ‖ tr & intr insinuar; indicar; **to hint at** aludir indirectamente a

hinterland [ˈhɪntərˌlænd] s región interior

hip [hɪp] s cadera; (of a roof) caballete m, lima

hip'bone' s cía, hueso de la cadera

hipped [hɪpt] adj (livestock) renco; (roof) a cuatro aguas; **hipped on** (coll) obsesionado por

hippety-hop [ˈhɪpɪtɪˈhɑp] adv (coll) a coxcojita

hip·po [ˈhɪpo] s (pl -pos) (coll) hipopótamo

hippodrome [ˈhɪpəˌdrom] s hipódromo

hippopota·mus [ˌhɪpəˈpɑtəməs] s (pl -muses o -mi [ˌmaɪ]) hipopótamo

hip roof s tejado a cuatro aguas

hire [haɪr] s alquiler m; precio; salario; **for hire** de alquiler ‖ tr alquilar (p.ej., un coche); ajustar (p.ej., a un criado) ‖ intr —**to hire out** ajustarse

hired girl s criada

hired man s (coll) mozo de campo

hireling [ˈhaɪrlɪŋ] adj & s alquiladizo

his [hɪz] adj poss su; el . . . de él ‖ pron poss el suyo, el de él; suyo

Hispanic [hɪsˈpænɪk] adj & s hispánico

Hispaniola [ˌhɪspənˈjolə] s Santo Domingo

hispanist [ˈhɪspənɪst] s hispanista mf

hispanophilia [hɪsˌpænoˈfɪli·ə] s españolería

hiss [hɪs] s siseo, silbido ‖ tr sisear, silbar (p.ej., una escena, a un actor por malo) ‖ intr sisear, silbar

hist. abbr **historian, history**

histology [hɪsˈtɑlədʒi] s histología

historian [hɪsˈtorɪ·ən] s historiador m

historic(al) [hɪsˈtorɪk(əl)] adj histórico

histo·ry [ˈhɪstəri] s (pl -ries) historia

histrionic [ˌhɪstrɪˈɑnɪk] adj histriónico; teatral ‖ **histrionics** s actitud teatral, modales mpl teatrales

hit [hɪt] s golpe m; (of a bullet) impacto; (blow that hits its mark) tiro certero; (sarcastic remark) censura acerba; (baseball) batazo; (coll) éxito; **to make a· hit** (coll) dar golpe; **to make a hit with** caer en la gracia de (una persona) ‖ v (pret & pp hit; ger hitting) tr golpear, pegar; dar con, dar contra, chocar con; dar en (p.ej., el blanco); censurar acerbamente; (to run over in a car) atropellar; afectar mucho (un acontecimiento a una persona) ‖ intr chocar; **to hit against** dar contra; **to hit on** dar con (lo que se busca)

hit'-and-run' adj que atropella y se da a la huída

hitch [hɪtʃ] s (jerk) tirón m; dificultad; obstáculo; **without a hitch** a pedir de boca, sin tropiezo ‖ tr (to tie) atar, sujetar; enganchar (un caballo); uncir (bueyes); (slang) casar

hitch'hike' intr (coll) hacer autostop, viajar en autostop

hitch'hik'er s autostopista mf

hitching post s poste m para atar a las cabalgaduras

hither [ˈhɪðər] adv acá, hacia acá; **hither and thither** acá y allá

hith'er·to' adv hasta ahora, hasta aquí

hit'-or-miss' adj descuidado, casual

hit parade s (rad) canciones que gozan de más popularidad en la actualidad

hit record s (coll) disco de mucho éxito

hit'-run' adj que atropella y se da a la huída

hive [haɪv] s (box for bees) colmena; (swarm) enjambre m; **hives** urticaria ‖ tr encorchar (abejas)

H.M. abbr **Her Majesty, His Majesty**

H.M.S. abbr **Her Majesty's Ship, His Majesty's Ship**

hoard [hord] s (of money, provisions, etc.) cúmulo; tesoro escondido ‖ tr acumular secretamente; atesorar (dinero) ‖ intr guardar víveres, atesorar dinero

hoarding [ˈhordɪŋ] s acumulación secreta; atesoramiento

hoar'frost' s helada blanca, escarcha

hoarse [hors] adj ronco

hoarseness ['horsnɪs] s ronquedad; (from a cold) ronquera

hoar·y ['hori] adj (comp -ier; super -iest) cano, canoso; (old) vetusto

hoax [hoks] s pajarota, mistificación ‖ tr mistificar

hob [hɑb] s repisa interior del hogar; **to play hob with** (coll) trastornar

hobble ['hɑbəl] s (limp) cojera; (rope used to tie legs of animal) manea, traba ‖ tr dejar cojo; manear, trabar; dificultar ‖ intr cojear; tambalear

hobble skirt s falda de medio paso

hob·by ['hɑbi] s (pl -bies) comidilla, afición favorita, trabajo preferido; **to ride a hobby** entregarse demasiado al tema favorito

hob'by·horse' s (stick with horse's head) caballito; (rocking horse) caballo mecedor

hob'gob'lin s duende m, trasgo; (bogy) bu m, coco

hob'nail' s tachuela ‖ tr clavetear con tachuelas; (fig) atropellar

hob·nob ['hɑb,nɑb] v (pret & pp -nobbed; ger -nobbing) intr codearse, rozarse; beber juntos

ho·bo ['hobo] s (pl -bos o -boes) vagabundo

Hobson's choice ['hɑbsənz] s alternativa entre la cosa ofrecida o ninguna

hock [hɑk] s jarrete m, corvejón m ‖ tr (to hamstring) desjarretar; (coll) empeñar

hockey ['hɑki] s hockey m, chueca

hock'shop' s (slang) casa de empeños, monte m de piedad

hocus-pocus ['hokəs'pokəs] s (meaningless formula) abracadabra m; burla, engaño; juego de manos

hod [hɑd] s capacho, cuezo; cubo para carbón

hod carrier s peón m de albañil, peón de mano

hodgepodge ['hɑdʒ,pɑdʒ] s baturrillo

hoe [ho] s azada, azadón m ‖ tr & intr azadonar

hog [hɑg] o [hɔg] s cerdo, puerco ‖ v (pret & pp hogged; ger hogging) tr (slang) tragarse lo mejor de

hog'back' s cuchilla

hoggish ['hɑgɪʃ] o ['hɔgɪʃ] adj comilón; glotón; egoísta

hog Latin s latín m de cocina

hogs'head' s pipa de 63 galones o más; medida de capacidad de 63 galones

hog'wash' s bazofia

hoist [hɔɪst] s (apparatus for lifting) montacargas m, torno izador, grúa; empujón m hacia arriba ‖ tr alzar, levantar; enarbolar (p.ej., una bandera); (naut) izar

hoity-toity ['hɔɪti'tɔɪti] adj frívolo, veleidoso; arrogante, altanero; **to be hoity-toity** ponerse tan alto

hokum ['hokəm] s (coll) música celestial, tonterías

hold [hold] s (grip) agarro; (handle) asa, mango; autoridad, dominio; (in wrestling) presa; (aer) cabina de carga; (mus) calderón m; (naut) bodega; **to take hold of** agarrar, coger; apoderarse de ‖ v (pret & pp held [hɛld]) tr tener, retener; (to hold

up, support) apoyar, sostener; (e.g., with a pin) sujetar; contener, tener cabida para; ocupar (un cargo, puesto, etc.); celebrar (una reunión); sostener (una opinión); (mus) sostener (una nota); **to hold back** detener; retener; contener; **to hold in** refrenar; **to hold one's own** mantenerse firme, no perder terreno; **to hold over** aplazar, diferir; **to hold up** apoyar, sostener; (to rob) (coll) atracar ‖ intr ser valedero, seguir vigente; pegarse; **hold on!** ¡un momento!; **to hold back** refrenarse; **to hold forth** poner cátedra; **to hold off** esperar; mantenerse a distancia; **to hold on** agarrarse bien; **to hold on to** asirse de; **to hold out** no cejar; ir tirando; **to hold out for** insistir en

holder ['holdər] s tenedor m, posesor m; (for a cigar or cigaret) boquilla; (to hold, e.g., a hot plate) cojinillo; (e.g., of a passport) titular m; asa, mango

holding ['holdɪŋ] s tenencia, posesión; **holdings** valores habidos

holding company s sociedad de control, compañía tenedora

hold'up' s (stop, delay) detención; atraco, asalto; precio excesivo

holdup man s atracador m, salteador m

hole [hol] s agujero; (in cheese, bread, etc.) ojo; (in a road) bache m; (den of animals; den of vice) guarida; (dirty, disorderly dwelling) cochitril m; **in the hole** adeudado, perdidoso; **to burn a hole in one's pocket** írsele a uno (el dinero) de entre las manos; **to pick holes in** (coll) poner reparos a ‖ intr — **to hole up** encovarse; buscar un rincón cómodo

holiday ['hɑlɪ,de] s día festivo; vacación

holiday attire s trapos de cristianar

holiness ['holɪnɪs] s santidad; **his Holiness** su Santidad

Holland ['hɑlənd] s Holanda

Hollander ['hɑləndər] s holandés m

hollow ['hɑlo] adj hueco; (voice) ahuecado, sepulcral; (eyes, cheeks) hundido; falso, engañoso ‖ adv — **to beat all hollow** (coll) derrotar completamente ‖ s hueco, cavidad; (small valley) vallecito ‖ tr ahuecar, excavar

hol·ly ['hɑli] s (pl -lies) acebo

hol'ly·hock' s malva arbórea

holm oak [hom] s encina

holocaust ['hɑlə,kɔst] s holocausto

holster ['holstər] s pistolera

ho·ly ['holi] adj (comp -lier; super -liest) santo; (e.g., writing) sagrado; (e.g., water) bendito

Holy Ghost s Espíritu Santo

holy orders spl órdenes sagradas; **to take holy orders** recibir las órdenes sagradas, ordenarse

holy rood [rud] s crucifijo ‖ **Holy Rood** s Santa Cruz

Holy Scripture s Sagrada Escritura

Holy See s Santa Sede

Holy Sepulcher s santo sepulcro

holy water s agua bendita
Holy Writ s Sagrada Escritura
homage ['hɑmɪdʒ] o ['ɑmɪdʒ] s homenaje m; (feud) homenaje, pleito homenaje
home [hom] adj casero, doméstico; nacional ‖ s casa, domicilio, hogar m; (native heath) patria chica; (of the arts, etc.) patria; (for the sick, poor, etc.) asilo; (sport) meta; **at home** en casa; en su propio país; (ready to receive callers) de recibo; (at ease, comfortable) a gusto; (sport) en campo propio; **away from home** fuera de casa; **make yourself at home** está Vd. en su casa ‖ adv en casa; a casa; **to see home** acompañar a casa; **to strike home** dar en lo vivo
home'bod'y s (pl -ies) hogareño
homebred ['hom,brɛd] adj doméstico; sencillo, inculto, tosco
home'brew' s cerveza o vino caseros
homecoming ['hom,kʌmɪŋ] s regreso al hogar
home country s suelo natal
home delivery s distribución a domicilio
home front s frente doméstico
home'land' s tierra natal, patria
homeless ['homlɪs] adj sin casa, sin hogar
home life s vida de familia
home-loving ['hom,lʌvɪŋ] adj casero, hogareño
home•ly ['homli] adj (comp -lier; super -liest) (not attractive or good-looking) feo; (plain, not elegant) sencillo, llano
homemade ['hom'med] adj casero, hecho en casa
homemaker ['hom,mekər] s ama de casa
home office s domicilio social, oficina central ‖ **Home Office** s (Brit) ministerio de la Gobernación
homeopath ['homɪ•ə,pæθ] o ['hɑmɪ•ə,pæθ] s homeópata mf
homeopathy [,homɪ'ɑpəθi] o [,hɑmɪ'ɑpəθi] s homeopatía
home plate s (baseball) puesto meta
home port s puerto de origen
home rule s autonomía, gobierno autónomo
home run s (baseball) jonrón m, cuadrangular m
home'sick' adj nostálgico; **to be homesick (for)** sentir nostalgia (de)
home'sick'ness s nostalgia, mal m de la tierra
homespun ['hom,spʌn] adj hilado en casa; sencillo, llano
home'stead' s casa y terrenos, heredad
home stretch s esfuerzo final, último trecho
home town s ciudad natal
homeward ['homwərd] adj de regreso ‖ adv hacia casa; hacia su país
home'work' s trabajo a domicilio; (of a student) deber m, trabajo escolar
homey ['homi] adj (comp **homier**; super **homiest**) (coll) íntimo, cómodo
homicidal [,hɑmɪ'saɪdəl] adj homicida
homicide ['hɑmɪ,saɪd] s (act) homicidio; (person) homicida mf
homi•ly ['hɑmɪli] s (pl -lies) homilía

homing ['homɪŋ] adj (animal) querencioso; (weapon) buscador del blanco
homing pigeon s paloma mensajera
hominy ['hɑmɪni] s maíz molido
homogenei•ty [,hɑmədʒɪ'ni•ɪti] s (pl -ties) homogeneidad
homogeneous [,hɑmə'dʒɪnɪ•əs] adj homogéneo
homogenize [hə'mɑdʒə,naɪz] tr homogeneizar
homonym ['hɑmənɪm] s homónimo
homonymous [hə'mɑnɪməs] adj homónimo
homosexual [,hɑmə'sɛkʃu•əl] adj & s homosexual mf
hon. abbr **honorary**
Hon. abbr **Honorable**
Honduran [hɑn'dʊrən] adj & s hondureño
hone [hon] s piedra de afilar ‖ tr afilar, amolar, asentar
honest ['ɑnɪst] adj honrado, probo, recto; (money) bien adquirido; sincero; genuino
honesty ['ɑnɪsti] s honradez f, probidad, rectitud; (bot) hierba de la plata
hon•ey ['hʌni] adj meloso, dulce; (coll) querido ‖ s miel f; (coll) vida mía; **it's a honey** (slang) es una preciosidad ‖ v (pret & pp -eyed o -ied) tr enmelar, endulzar con miel; adular, lisonjear
hon'ey•bee' s abeja doméstica, abeja de miel
hon'ey•comb' s panal m ‖ tr (to riddle) acribillar; llenar, penetrar
hon'ey•dew' melon s melón muy dulce, blanco y terso
honeyed ['hʌnid] adj dulce, enmelado; melodioso; aduladar
honey locust s acacia de tres espinas
hon'ey•moon' s luna de miel; viaje m de bodas ‖ intr pasar la luna de miel
honeysuckle ['hʌni,sʌkəl] s madreselva
honk [hɑŋk] s (of wild goose) graznido; (of automobile horn) bocinazo ‖ tr tocar (la bocina) ‖ intr graznar (el ganso silvestre); tocar la bocina
honkytonk ['hɑŋki,tɑŋk] s (slang) sala de fiestas de mala muerte
honor ['ɑnər] s (distinction; award for distinction; integrity) honor m; (good reputation; chastity) honor, honra ‖ tr honrar; hacer honor a (su firma); aceptar y pagar (una letra)
honorable ['ɑnərəbəl] adj (behaving with honor; performed with honor) honrado; (bringing honor; associated with honor) honroso; (worthy, of honor) honorable
honorary ['ɑnə,rɛri] adj honorario
honorific [,ɑnə'rɪfɪk] adj honorífico ‖ s antenombre m
honor system s acatamiento voluntario del reglamento
hood [hʊd] s capilla; (one with a point) caperuza; (one which covers the face) capirote m; (worn with academic gown) muceta, capirote m; (of a chimney) sombrerete m; (aut) capó m, cubierta; (slang) gamberro ‖ tr encapirotar; ocultar
hoodlum ['hʊdləm] s (coll) gamberro, maleante m

hoodoo [ˈhudu] s (*body of primitive rites*) vudú *m;* (coll) mala suerte ‖ *tr* traer mala suerte a

hood'wink' *tr* burlar, engañar, vendar

hooey [ˈhu•i] s (slang) música celestial

hoof [huf] o [hʊf] s casco, pezuña; **on the hoof** (*cattle*) vivo, en pie ‖ *tr & intr* (coll) caminar; **to hoof it** (coll) caminar, ir a pie; (coll) bailar

hoof'beat' s pisada, ruido de la pisada (*de animal ungulado*)

hook [hʊk] s gancho; (*for fishing*) anzuelo; (*to join two things*) enganche *m;* (*bend, curve*) ángulo, recodo; (box) crochet *m*, golpe *m* de gancho; (*of hook and eye*) corchete *m*, macho; **by hook or by crook** por fas o por nefas; **to swallow the hook;** tragar el anzuelo ‖ *tr* enganchar; (*to bend*) encorvar, doblar; coger, pescar (*un pez*); (*to wound with the horns*) acornar ‖ *intr* engancharse; encorvarse, doblarse

hookah [ˈhukə] s narguile *m*

hook and eye s broche *m*, corchete *m* (*macho y hembra*)

hook and ladder s carro de escaleras de incendio

hooked rug s tapete *m* de crochet

hook'nose' s nariz *f* de pico de loro

hook'up' s montaje *m*

hook'worm' s anquilostoma *m*

hooky [ˈhʊki] s — **to play hooky** hacer novillos

hooligan [ˈhulɪgən] s gamberro

hooliganism [ˈhulɪgən,ɪzəm] s gamberrismo

hoop [hup] o [hʊp] s aro ‖ *tr* herrar, enarcar, enzunchar

hoop skirt s miriñaque *m*

hoot [hut] s resoplido, ululato; grito ‖ *tr* reprobar a gritos; echar a gritos (*p.ej., a un cómico*) ‖ *intr* resoplar, ulular; **to hoot at** dar grita a

hoot owl s autillo, cárabo

hop [hap] s saltito; (coll) vuelo en avión; (coll) sarao; (coll) baile *m;* lúpulo, hombrecillo; **hops** (*dried flowers of hop vine*) lúpulo ‖ *v* (*pret & pp* **hopped;** *ger* **hopping**) *tr* cruzar de un salto; (coll) atravesar (*p.ej., el mar*) en avión; (coll) subir a (*un tren, taxi, etc.*) ‖ *intr* saltar, brincar; (*on one foot*) saltar a la pata coja

hope [hop] s esperanza ‖ *tr & intr* esperar; **to hope for** esperar

hope chest s ajuar *m* de novia

hopeful [ˈhopfəl] adj (*feeling hope*) esperanzado; (*giving hope*) esperanzador

hopeless [ˈhoplɪs] adj desesperanzado, (*situation*) desesperado

hopper [ˈhapər] s (*funnel-shaped container*) tolva; (*of blast furnace*) tragante *m*

hopper car s (rr) vagón *m* tolva

hop'scotch' s infernáculo

horde [hord] s horda

horehound [ˈhor,haʊnd] s marrubio; extracto de marrubio

horizon [həˈraɪzən] s horizonte *m*

horizontal [,harɪˈzɑntəl] o [,hɔrɪˈzɑntəl] adj & s horizontal *f*

hormone [ˈhɔrmon] s hormón *m* u hormona

horn [hɔrn] s (*bony projection on head of certain animals*) cuerno; (*of bull*) asta, cuerno; (*of moon, anvil, etc.*) cuerno; (*of automobile*) bocina; (mus) cuerno; (*French horn*) (mus) trompa de armonía; **to blow one's own horn** cantar sus propias alabanzas; **to pull in one's horns** contenerse, volverse atrás ‖ *intr* — **to horn in** (slang) entrometerse (en)

hornet [ˈhɔrnɪt] s crabrón *m*, avispón *m*

hornet's nest s panal *m* del avispón; **to stir up a hornet's nest** (coll) armar camorra, armar cisco

horn of plenty s cuerno de la abundancia

horn'pipe' s chirimía

horn-rimmed glasses [ˈhɔrnˈrɪmd] spl anteojos de concha

horn•y [ˈhɔrni] adj (*comp* **-ier;** *super* **-iest**) córneo; (*callous*) calloso; (*having hornlike projections*) cornudo

horoscope [ˈharə,skop] o [ˈhɔrə,skop] s horóscopo; **to cast a horoscope** sacar un horóscopo

horrible [ˈharɪbəl] o [ˈhɔrɪbəl] adj horrible; (coll) muy desagradable

horrid [ˈharɪd] o [ˈhɔrɪd] adj horroroso; (coll) muy desagradable

horri•fy [ˈharɪ,faɪ] o [ˈhɔrɪ,faɪ] v (*pret & pp* **-fied**) *tr* horrorizar

horror [ˈharər] o [ˈhɔrər] s horror *m;* **to have a horror of** tener horror a

horror movie s película de terror, película horripilante

hors d'oeuvre [ɔr ˈdʌrv] s (*pl* **hors d'oeuvres** [ɔr ˈdʌrvz]) s entremés *m*

horse [hɔrs] s caballo; (*of carpenter*) caballete *m;* **hold your horses** (coll) pare Vd. el carro; **to back the wrong horse** (coll) jugar a la carta mala; **to be a horse of another color** (coll) ser harina de otro costal

horse'back' s — **on horseback** a caballo ‖ *adv* — **to ride horseback** montar a caballo

horseback riding s hípica

horse blanket s manta para caballo

horse block s montadero

horse'break'er s domador *m* de caballos

horse'car' s tranvía *m* de sangre

horse chestnut s (*tree*) castaño de Indias; (*nut*) castaña de Indias

horse collar s collera

horse dealer s chalán *m*

horse doctor s veterinario

horse'fly' s (*pl* **-flies**) mosca borriquera, tábano

horse'hair' s crines *fpl* de caballo; (*fabric*) tela de crin

horse'hide' s cuero de caballo

horse laugh s risotada

horse•man [ˈhɔrsmən] s (*pl* **-men** [mən]) jinete *m*, caballista *m*

horsemanship [ˈhɔrsmən,ʃɪp] s equitación, manejo

horse meat s carne *f* de caballo

horse opera s (U.S.A.) melodrama *m* del Oeste

horse pistol s pistola de arzón
horse'play' s chanza pesada, payasada
horse'pow'er s caballo de vapor inglés
horse race s carrera de caballos
horse'rad'ish s (plant) rábano picante o rusticano; (condiment) mostaza de los alemanes
horse sense s (coll) sentido común
horse'shoe' s herradura
horseshoe magnet s imán m de herradura
horseshoe nail s clavo de herrar
horse show s concurso hípico
horse'tail' s cola de caballo
horse thief s abigeo, cuatrero
horse'-trade' intr chalanear
horse trading s chalanería
horse'-trad'ing adj chalanesco
horse'whip' s látigo ‖ v (pret & pp -whipped; ger -whipping) tr dar latigazos a
horse•woman ['hɔrs,wumən] s (pl -women [,wɪmɪn]) amazona, caballista f
hors•y ['hɔrsi] adj (comp -ier; super -iest) caballar, hípico; (interested in horses and horse racing) carrerista, turfista; (coll) desmañado
horticultural [,hɔrtɪ'kʌltʃərəl] adj hortícola
horticulture ['hɔrtɪ,kʌltʃər] s horticultura
horticulturist [,hɔrtɪ'kʌltʃərɪst] s horticultor m
hose [hoz] s (stocking) media; (sock) calcetín m; (flexible tube) manguera ‖ **hose** spl calzas
hosier ['hoʒər] s mediero, calcetero
hosiery ['hoʒəri] s calcetas; calcetería
hospice ['hɑspɪs] s hospicio
hospitable ['hɑspɪtəbəl] o [hɑs'pɪtəbəl] adj hospitalario
hospital ['hɑspɪtəl] s hospital m
hospitali•ty [,hɑspɪ'tælɪti] s (pl -ties) hospitalidad
hospitalize ['hɑspɪtə,laɪz] tr hospitalizar
host [host] s anfitrión m; (at an inn) huésped m, mesonero; (army) hueste f; multitud, sinnúmero ‖ **Host** s (eccl) hostia
hostage ['hɑstɪdʒ] s rehén m; **to be held a hostage** quedar en rehenes
hostage taking s toma de rehenes
hostel•ry ['hɑstəlri] s (pl -ries) parador m, hostería
hostess ['hostɪs] s anfitriona; dueña, patrona; (in a night club) tanguista; (aer) azafata, aeromoza; (e.g., on a bus) jefa de ruta
hostile ['hɑstɪl] adj hostil
hostili•ty [hɑs'tɪlɪti] s (pl -ties) hostilidad
hostler ['hɑslər] o ['ɑslər] s mozo de cuadra, mozo de paja y cebada
hot [hɑt] adj (comp **hotter**; super **hottest**) (water, air, coffee, etc.) caliente; (climate, country; taste) cálido; (fiery, excitable) caluroso; (pursuit) enérgico; (in rut) caliente; (coll) muy radiactivo; **to be hot** (said of a person) tener calor; (said of the weather) hacer calor; **to make it hot for** (coll) hostilizar
hot air s (slang) palabrería, música celestial
hot'-air' furnace s calorífero de aire

hot and cold running water s circulación de agua fría y caliente
hot baths spl caldas, termas
hot'bed' s (hort) almajara; (e.g., of vice) sementera, semillero
hot-blooded ['hɑt'blʌdɪd] adj apasionado; temerario, irreflexivo
hot cake s torta a la plancha; **to sell like hot cakes** (coll) venderse como pan bendito
hot dog s (slang) perro caliente
hotel [ho'tɛl] adj hotelero ‖ s hotel m
ho•tel'-keep'er s hotelero
hot'head' s botafuego
hot-headed ['hɑt'hɛdɪd] adj caliente de cascos
hot'house' s estufa, invernáculo
hot plate s hornillo, calientaplatos m
hot springs spl fuentes fpl termales
hot-tempered ['hɑt'tɛmpərd] adj irascible
hot water s — **to be in hot water** (coll) estar en calzas prietas
hot'-wa'ter boiler s termosifón m
hot-water bottle s bolsa de agua caliente
hot-water heater s calentador m de acumulación
hot-water heating s calefacción por ·agua caliente
hot-water tank s depósito de agua caliente
hound [haʊnd] s podenco, perro de caza; **to follow the hounds** o **to ride the hounds** cazar a caballo con jauría ‖ tr acosar, hostigar
hour [aʊr] s hora; **by the hour** por horas; **in an evil hour** en hora mala; **on the hour** a la hora en punto cada hora; **to keep late hours** acostarse tarde; **to work long hours** trabajar muchas horas cada día
hour'glass' s reloj m de arena
hour hand s horario, horero
hourly ['aʊrli] adj de cada hora; por hora ‖ adv cada hora; muy a menudo
house [haʊs] s (pl **houses** ['haʊzɪz]) casa; (legislative body) cámara; teatro; (size of audience) entrada, p.ej., **a good house** mucha entrada; **to keep house** tener casa puesta; hacer los quehaceres domésticos; **to put one's house in order** arreglar sus asuntos ‖ [haʊz] tr domiciliar, alojar, hospedar
house arrest s arresto domiciliario
house'boat' s barco vivienda
house'break'er s escalador m
housebreaking ['haʊs,brekɪŋ] s escalo, allanamiento de morada
housebroken ['haʊs,brokən] adj (perro o gato) enseñado (a hábitos de limpieza)
house cleaning s limpieza de la casa
house coat s bata
house current s sector m de distribución, canalización de consumo
house'fly' s (pl -flies) mosca doméstica
houseful ['haʊs,fʊl] s casa llena
house'fur'nishings spl menaje m, enseres domésticos
house'hold' adj casero, doméstico ‖ s casa, familia

house'hold'er s dueño de la casa; jefe m de familia

house'-hunt' intr — **to go house-hunting** ir a buscar casa

house'keep'er s ama de llaves, mujer f de gobierno

house'keep'ing s manejo doméstico, gobierno doméstico; **to set up housekeeping** poner casa

housekeeping apartment s apartamento con cocina

house'maid' s criada de casa

house meter s contador m de abonado

house'moth'er s mujer encargada de una residencia de estudiantes

house of cards s castillo de naipes

house of ill fame s lupanar m, casa de prostitución

house painter s pintor m de brocha gorda

house physician s médico residente

house'top' s tejado; **to shout from the housetops** pregonar a los cuatro vientos

housewarming ['haʊs,wɔrmɪŋ] s fiesta para celebrar el estreno de una casa; **to have a housewarming** estrenar la casa

house'wife' s (pl **-wives**) ama de casa, madre f de familia

house'work' s quehaceres domésticos

housing ['haʊzɪŋ] s (of a horse) gualdrapa; (aut) cárter m; (mach) caja, bastidor m

housing shortage s crisis f de viviendas

hovel ['hʌvəl] s casucha, choza; (shed for cattle, tools, etc.) cobertizo

hover ['hʌvər] intr cernerse (un ave); (to hesitate; to be in danger) fluctuar; asomar (p.ej., una sonrisa en los labios de uno)

how [haʊ] adv cómo; (at what price) a cómo; **how early** cuándo, a qué hora; **how else** de qué otra manera; **how far** hasta dónde; cuánto, p.ej., **how far is it to the airport?** ¿cuánto hay de aquí al aeropuerto?; **how long** cuánto tiempo; **how many** cuántos; **how much** cuánto; lo mucho que; **how often** cuántas veces; **how old are you?** ¿cuántas años tiene Vd.?; **how soon** cuándo, a qué hora; **how** + adj qué + adj, p.ej., **how beautiful she is!** ¡qué hermosa es!; lo + adj, p.ej., **you know how intelligent he is** Vd. sabe lo inteligente que es; **to know how to** + inf saber + inf

howdah ['haʊdə] s castillo

how·ev'er adv no obstante, sin embargo; por muy . . . que, por mucho . . . que

howitzer ['haʊɪtsər] s cañón m obús

howl [haʊl] s aullido; chillido; risa muy aguda; (of wind) bramido ‖ tr decir a gritos; **to howl down** imponerse a gritos a (una persona) ‖ intr aullar; chillar; reír a más no poder; bramar (el viento)

howler ['haʊlər] s aullador m; (coll) plancha, desacierto

hoyden ['hɔɪdən] s muchacha traviesa, tunantuela

H.P. abbr **horsepower**

hr. abbr **hour**

H.R.H. abbr **Her** (o **His**) **Royal Highness**

ht. abbr **height**

hub [hʌb] s cubo; (fig) centro, eje m

hubbub ['hʌbəb] s gritería, alboroto

hub'cap' s tapacubo, embellecedor m

huck'ster ['hʌkstər] s (peddler) buhonero; vendedor m ambulante de hortalizas; vil traficante m, sujeto ruin

huddle ['hʌdəl] s (coll) reunión secreta; **to go into a huddle** (coll) conferenciar en secreto ‖ intr acurrucarse, arrimarse

hue [hju] s matiz m; gritería; **hue and cry** vocería de indignación

huff [hʌf] s arrebato de cólera; **in a huff** encolerizado, ofendido

hug [hʌg] s abrazo ‖ v (pret & pp **hugged**; ger **hugging**) tr abrazar; apretar con los brazos; ahogar entre los brazos; navegar muy cerca de (la costa); ceñirse a (p.ej., un muro) ‖ intr abrazarse

huge [hjudʒ] adj enorme, descomunal

huh [hʌ] interj ¡eh!

hulk [hʌlk] s (body of an old ship) casco; (clumsy old ship) carcamán m, carraca; (old ship tied up at a wharf and used as a warehouse, prison, etc.) pontón m; (shell of an old building, piece of furniture, machine, etc.; heavy, unwieldy person) armatoste m

hulking ['hʌlkɪŋ] adj grueso, pesado

hull [hʌl] s (of ship or hydroplane) casco; (of a dirigible) armazón f; (of certain vegetables) hollejo, vaina ‖ tr deshollejar, desvainar; mondar, pelar

hullabaloo ['hʌləbə,lu] o [,hʌləbə'lu] s alboroto, gritería, tumulto

hum [hʌm] s canturreo, tarareo; (of a bee, machine, etc.) zumbido ‖ interj ¡ejem! ‖ v (pret & pp **hummed**; ger **humming**) tr canturrear, tararear ‖ intr canturrear, tararear; (to buzz) zumbar; (coll) estar muy activo

human ['hjumən] adj humano (perteneciente al hombre)

human being s ser humano

humane [hju'men] adj humano (compasivo)

humanist ['hjumənɪst] adj & s humanista mf

humanitarian [hju,mænɪ'tɛrɪ·ən] adj & s humanitario

humani·ty [hju'mænɪti] s (pl **-ties**) humanidad

hu'man·kind' s género humano

humble ['hʌmbəl] adj humilde ‖ tr humillar

humble pie s — **to eat humble pie** cantar la palinodia

hum'bug' s patraña; (person) patrañero ‖ v (pret & pp **-bugged**; ger **-bugging**) tr embaucar, engaitar

hum'drum' adj monótono, tedioso

humer·us ['hjumərəs] s (pl **-i** [,aɪ]) húmero

humid ['hjumɪd] adj húmedo

humidifier [hju'mɪdɪ,faɪ·ər] s humectador m

humidi·fy [hju'mɪdɪ,faɪ] v (pret & pp **-fied**) tr humedecer

humidity [hju'mɪdɪti] s humedad

humiliate [hju'mɪlɪ,et] tr humillar

humiliating [hju'mɪlɪ,etɪŋ] adj humillante

humili·ty [hju'mɪlɪti] s (pl **-ties**) humildad

hummingbird [ˈhʌmɪŋˌbʌrd] s colibrí m, pájaro mosca

humongous [hjuˈmʌŋəs] adj (coll) descomunal

humor [ˈhjumər] o [ˈjumər] s humor m; **out of humor** de mal humor; **to be in the humor for** estar de humor para ‖ tr seguir el humor a; manejar con delicadeza

humorist [ˈhjumərɪst] s humorista mf

humorous [ˈhjumərəs] adj humorístico

hump [hʌmp] s corcova, joroba; (in the ground) montecillo

hump'back' s corcova, joroba; (person) corcovado, jorobado

humus [ˈhjuməs] s mantillo

hunch [hʌntʃ] s corcova, joroba; (premonition) (coll) corazonada ‖ tr encorvar ‖ intr encorvarse

hunch'back' s corcova, joroba; (person) corcovado, jorobado

hundred [ˈhʌndrəd] adj cien ‖ s ciento, cien; **a hundred** u **one hundred** ciento; cien; **by the hundreds** a centenares

hundredth [ˈhʌndredθ] adj & s centésimo

hun'dred•weight' s quintal m

Hundred Years' War s guerra de los Cien Años

Hungarian [hʌŋˈgɛri•ən] adj & s húngaro

Hungary [ˈhʌŋgəri] s Hungría

hunger [ˈhʌŋgər] s hambre f ‖ intr hambrear; **to hunger for** tener hambre de

hunger march s marcha del hambre

hunger strike s huelga de hambre

hun•gry [ˈhʌŋgri] adj (comp **-grier;** super **-griest**) hambriento; **to be hungry** tener hambre; galguear (Arg, CAm, Mex); **to go hungry** pasar hambre

hunk [hʌŋk] s (coll) buen pedazo, pedazo grande

hunt [hʌnt] s (act of hunting) caza; (hunting party) cacería; (a search) busca; **on the hunt for** a caza de ‖ tr cazar; (to seek, look for) buscar ‖ intr cazar; buscar; **to go hunting** ir de caza; **to hunt for** buscar; **to take hunting** llevar de caza

hunter [ˈhʌntər] s cazador m; perro de caza

hunting [ˈhʌntɪŋ] adj de caza ‖ s (act) caza; (art) cacería, montería

hunting dog s perro de caza

hunting ground s cazadero

hunt'ing•horn' s cuerno de caza

hunting jacket s cazadora

hunting lodge s casa de montería

hunting season s época de caza

huntress [ˈhʌntrɪs] s cazadora

hunts•man [ˈhʌntsmən] s (pl **-men** [mən]) cazador m, montero

hurdle [ˈhʌrdəl] s (hedge over which horses must jump) zarzo; (wooden frame over which runners and horses must jump) valla; (fig) obstáculo; **hurdles** carrera de vallas ‖ tr saltar por encima de

hurdle race s carrera de vallas

hurdy-gur•dy [ˈhʌrdiˈgʌrdi] s (pl **-dies**) organillo

hurl [hʌrl] s lanzamiento ‖ tr lanzar

hurrah [huˈrɑ] o **hurray** [huˈre] s viva m ‖ interj ¡viva!; **hurrah for. . . !** ¡viva. . . ! ‖ tr aplaudir, vitorear ‖ intr dar vivas

hurricane [ˈhʌrɪˌken] s huracán m

hurried [ˈhʌrid] adj apresurado; hecho de prisa

hur•ry [ˈhʌri] s (pl **-ries**) prisa; **to be in a hurry** tener prisa, estar de prisa ‖ v (pret & pp **-ried**) tr apresurar, dar prisa a ‖ intr apresurarse, darse prisa; **to hurry after** correr en pos de; **to hurry away** marcharse de prisa; **to hurry back** volver de prisa; **to hurry up** darse prisa

hurt [hʌrt] adj (injured) lastimado, herido; (offended) resentido, herido ‖ s (harm) daño; (i.ijury) herida; (pain) dolor m ‖ v (pret & pp **hurt**) tr (to harm) dañar, perjudicar; (to injure) lastimar, herir; (to offend) ofender, herir; (to pain) doler ‖ intr doler

hurtle [ˈhʌrtəl] intr lanzarse con violencia, pasar con gran estruendo

husband [ˈhʌzbənd] s marido, esposo ‖ tr manejar con economía

husband•man [ˈhʌzbəndmən] s (pl **-men** [mən]) agricultor m, granjero

husbandry [ˈhʌzbəndri] s agricultura, labranza; buena dirección, buen gobierno (de la hacienda de uno)

hush [hʌʃ] s silencio ‖ interj ¡chito! ‖ tr callar; **to hush up** echar tierra a (un escándalo) ‖ intr callarse

hushaby [ˈhʌʃəˌbaɪ] interj ¡ro ro!

hush'-hush' adj muy secreto

hush money s precio del silencio

husk [hʌsk] s cáscara, hollejo, vaina; (of corn) perfolla ‖ tr descascarar, deshollejar, desvainar; espinochar (el maíz)

husk•y [ˈhʌski] adj (comp **-ier;** super **-iest**) fortachón, fornido; (voice) ronco

hus•sy [ˈhʌzi] o [ˈhʌsi] s (pl **-sies**) buena pieza, moza descarada; mujer desvergonzada

hustle [ˈhʌsəl] s (coll) energía, vigor m ‖ tr apresurar; echar a empellones ‖ intr apresurarse; (coll) menearse, trabajar con gran ahinco

hustler [ˈhʌslər] s trafagón m, buscavidas mf

hut [hʌt] s casucha, choza

hyacinth [ˈhaɪ•əsɪnθ] s jacinto

hybrid [ˈhaɪbrɪd] adj & s híbrido

hybridization [ˌhaɪbrɪdɪˈzeʃən] s hibridación

hybridize [ˈhaɪbrɪˌdaɪz] tr & intr hibridar

hy•dra [ˈhaɪdrə] s (pl **-dras** o **-drae** [dri]) hidra

hydrant [ˈhaɪdrənt] s boca de agua, boca de riego; (water faucet) grifo

hydrate [ˈhaɪdret] s hidrato ‖ tr hidratar ‖ intr hidratarse

hydraulic [haɪˈdrɔlɪk] adj hidráulico ‖ **hydraulics** s hidráulica

hydraulic ram s ariete hidráulico

hydriodic [ˌhaɪdrɪˈɑdɪk] adj yodhídrico

hydrobromic [ˌhaɪdrəˈbromɪk] adj bromhídrico

hydrocarbon [ˌhaɪdrəˈkɑrbən] s hidrocarburo

hydrochloric [ˌhaɪdrəˈklɔrɪk] adj clorhídrico

hydroelectric [ˌhaɪdro•ɪˈlɛktrɪk] *adj* hidroeléctrico

hydrofluoric [ˌhaɪdrəfluˈɔrɪk] *adj* fluorhídrico

hydrofoil [ˈhaɪdrəˌfɔɪl] *s* superficie hidrodinámica; (*wing designed to lift vessel*) hidroaleta; (*vessel*) hidroala *m*

hydrogen [ˈhaɪdrədʒən] *s* hidrógeno

hydrogen bomb *s* bomba de hidrógeno

hydrogen peroxide *s* peróxido de hidrógeno

hydrogen sulfide *s* sulfuro de hidrógeno

hydrometer [haɪˈdrɑmɪtər] *s* areómetro

hydrophobia [ˌhaɪdrəˈfobɪ•ə] *s* hidrofobia

hydroplane [ˈhaɪdrəˌplen] *s* hidroavión *m*

hydroxide [haɪˈdrɑksaɪd] *s* hidróxido

hyena [haɪˈinə] *s* hiena

hygiene [ˈhaɪdʒin] *s* higiene *f*

hygienic [ˌhaɪdʒiˈɛnɪk] *adj* higiénico

hymn [hɪm] *s* himno

hymnal [ˈhɪmnəl] *s* himnario

hyp. *abbr* **hypotenuse, hypothesis**

hyperacidity [ˌhaɪpərəˈsɪdɪti] *s* hiperacidez *f*

hyperbola [haɪˈpʌrbələ] *s* (geom) hipérbola

hyperbole [haɪˈpʌrbəli] *s* (rhet) hipérbole *f*

hyperbolic [ˌhaɪpərˈbɑlɪk] *adj* (geom & rhet) hiperbólico

hypersensitive [ˌhaɪpərˈsɛnsɪtɪv] *adj* extremadamente sensible; (*allergic*) hipersensible

hypertension [ˌhaɪpərˈtɛnʃən] *s* hipertensión

hyphen [ˈhaɪfən] *s* guión *m*

hyphenate [ˈhaɪfəˌnet] *tr* unir con guión; escribir con guión

hypno•sis [hɪpˈnosɪs] *s* (*pl* -ses [siz]) hipnosis *f*

hypnotic [hɪpˈnɑtɪk] *adj* hipnótico ‖ *s* (*person; sedative*) hipnótico

hypnotism [ˈhɪpnəˌtɪzəm] *s* hipnotismo

hypnotist [ˈhɪpnətɪst] *s* hipnotista *mf*

hypnotize [ˈhɪpnəˌtaɪz] *tr* hipnotizar

hypochondriac [ˌhaɪpəˈkɑndrɪˌæk] *s* hipocondríaco

hypocri•sy [hɪˈpɑkrəsi] *s* (*pl* -sies) hipocresía

hypocrite [ˈhɪpəkrɪt] *s* hipócrita *mf*

hypocritical [ˌhɪpəˈkrɪtɪkəl] *adj* hipócrita

hypodermic [ˌhaɪpəˈdʌrmɪk] *adj* hipodérmico

hyposulfite [ˌhaɪpəˈsʌlfaɪt] *m* hiposulfito

hypotenuse [haɪˈpɑtɪˌnus] *s* hipotenusa

hypothe•sis [haɪˈpɑθɪsɪs] *s* (*pl* -ses [siz] hipótesis *f*

hypothetic(al) [ˌhaɪpəˈθɛtɪk(əl)] *adj* hipotético

hyssop [ˈhɪsəp] *s* (bot) hisopo

hysteria [hɪsˈtɪrɪ•ə] *s* histerismo, histeria

hysteric [hɪsˈtɛrɪk] *adj* histérico ‖ **hysterics** *s* paroxismo histérico

hysterical [hɪsˈtɛrɪkəl] *adj* histérico

hu
ic

I

I, i [aɪ] novena letre del alfabeto inglés

I. *abbr* **Island**

I [aɪ] *pron pers* (*pl* **we** [wi]) yo; **it is I** soy yo

iambic (aɪˈæmbɪk] *adj* yámbico

iam•bus [aɪˈæmbəs] *s* (*pl* -bi [bar]) yambo

ib. *abbr* **ibidem**

Iberian [aɪbˈɪrɪ•ən] *adj* ibérico ‖ *s* ibero

ibex [ˈaɪbɛks] *s* (*pl* **ibexes** o **ibices** [ˈɪbɪˌsiz]) íbice *m*, cabra montés

ibid. *abbr* **ibidem**

ice [aɪs] *s* hielo; **to break the ice** (*to overcome reserve*) romper el hielo; **to cut no ice** (coll) no importar nada; **to skate on thin ice** (coll) buscar el peligro ‖ *tr* helar; enfriar con hielo; (*to cover with icing*) garapiñar ‖ *intr* helarse

ice age *s* época glacial

ice bag *s* bolsa para hielo

iceberg [ˈaɪsˌbʌrg] *s* banquisa, iceberg *m*

ice'boat' *s* cortahielos *m*, rompehielos *m;* trineo con vela para deslizarse sobre el hielo

ice'bound' *adj* rodeado de hielo; de tenido por el hielo

ice'box' *s* nevera, fresquera

ice'break'er *s* cortahielos *m*, rompehielos *m*

ice'cap' *s* bolsa para hielo; manto de hielo

ice cream *s* helado

ice'-cream' cone *s* cucurucho de helado, barquillo de helado

ice-cream freezer *s* heladora, garapiñera

ice-cream parlor *s* salón *m* de refrescos, tienda de helados

ice-cream soda *s* agua gaseosa con helado

ice cube *s* cubito de hielo

ice hockey *s* hockey *m* sobre patines

Iceland [ˈaɪslənd] *s* Islandia

Icelander [ˈaɪsˌlændər] *s* islandés *m*

Icelandic [aɪsˈlændɪk] *adj* islandés ‖ *s* islandés *m* (*idioma*)

ice•man [ˈaɪsˌmæn] *s* (*pl* -men [ˌmɛn]) vendedor *m* de hielo, repartidor *m* de hielo

ice pack *s* hielo flotante; bolsa de hielo

ice pail *s* enfriadera

ice pick *s* picahielos *m*

ice skate *s* patín *m* de cuchilla, patín de hielo

ice skating *s* patinaje *m* sobre hielo

ice tray *s* bandejita de hielo

ice water *s* agua helada

ichthyology [ˌɪkθɪˈɑlədʒi] *s* ictiología

icicle [ˈaɪsɪkəl] *s* carámbano

icing [ˈaɪsɪŋ] *s* garapiña, capa de azúcar; (aer) formación de hielo

iconoclasm [aɪˈkɑnəˌklæzəm] *s* iconoclasia, iconoclasmo

iconoclast [aɪˈkɑnəˌklæst] *s* iconoclasta *mf*

icy ['aɪsi] *adj* (*comp* **icier;** *super* **iciest**) cubierto de hielo; (*slippery*) resbaladizo; (fig) frío

id. *abbr* **idem**

id [ɪd] *s* (psychoanalysis) ello

I.D. *abbr* **identity card**

idea [aɪ'diə] *s* idea

ideal [aɪ'diəl] *adj & s* ideal *m*

idealist [aɪ'diəlɪst] *adj & s* idealista *mf*

idealize [aɪ'diə,laɪz] *tr* idealizar

identic(al) [aɪ'dɛntɪk(əl)] *adj* idéntico

identification [aɪ,dɛntɪfɪ'keʃən] *s* identificación

identification tag *s* disco de identificación

identify [aɪ'dɛntɪ,faɪ] *v* (*pret & pp* **-fied**) *tr* identificar ‖ *intr* — **to identify with** solidarizar con

identi•ty [aɪ'dɛntɪti] *s* (*pl* **-ties**) identidad

identity card *s* carta de identificación

ideolo•gy [,aɪdɪ'ɑlədʒi] o [,ɪdɪ'ɑlədʒi] *s* (*pl* **-gies**) ideología

ides [aɪdz] *spl* idus *mpl*

idio•cy ['ɪdɪ•əsi] *s* (*pl* **-cies**) idiotez *f*

idiom ['ɪdɪ•əm] *s* (*expression that is contrary to the usual patterns of the language*) modismo; (*style of language*) idioma *m*, lenguaje *m;* (*style of an author*) estilo; (*character of a language*) índole *f*

idiomatic [,ɪdɪ•ə'mætɪk] *adj* idiomático

idiosyncra•sy [,ɪdɪ•ə'sɪnkrəsi] *s* (*pl* **-sies**) idiosincrasia

idiot ['ɪdɪ•ət] *s* idiota *mf*

idiotic [,ɪdɪ•'ɑtɪk] *adj* idiota

idle ['aɪdəl] *adj* desocupado, ocioso; **at idle moments** a ratos perdidos; **to run idle** marchar en ralentí ‖ *tr* — **to idle away** gastar ociosamente (*el tiempo*) ‖ *intr* estar ocioso, holgar; marchar (*un motor*) en ralentí

idleness ['aɪdəlnɪs] *s* desocupación, ociosidad

idler ['aɪdlər] *s* haragán *m*, ocioso

idol ['aɪdəl] *s* ídolo

idola•try [aɪ'dɑlətri] *s* (*pl* **-tries**) idolatría

idolize ['aɪdə,laɪz] *tr* idolatrar

idyll ['aɪdəl] *s* idilio

idyllic [aɪ'dɪlɪk] *adj* idílico

if [ɪf] *conj* si; **as if** como si; **even if** aunque; **if so** si es así; **if true** si es cierto

ignis fatuus ['ɪgnɪs'fætʃu•əs] *s* (*pl* **ignes fatui** ['ɪgniz'fætʃu,aɪ]) fuego fatuo

ignite [ɪg'naɪt] *tr* encender ‖ *intr* encenderse

ignition [ɪg'nɪʃən] *s* inflamación; (aut) encendido

ignition switch *s* (aut) interruptor *m* de encendido

ignoble [ɪg'nobəl] *adj* innoble

ignominious [,ɪgnə'mɪnɪ•əs] *adj* ignominioso

ignoramus [,ɪgnə'reməs] *s* ignorante *mf*

ignorance ['ɪgnərəns] *s* ignorancia

ignorant ['ɪgnərənt] *adj* ignorante

ignore [ɪg'nor] *tr* no hacer caso de, pasar por alto

ilk [ɪlk] *s* especie *f*, jaez *m*

ill. *abbr* **illustrated, illustration**

ill [ɪl] *adj* (*comp* **worse** [wʌrs]; *super* **worst** [wʌrst]) enfermo, malo ‖ *adv* mal; **to take ill** tomar a mal; caer enfermo

ill-advised ['ɪləd'vaɪzd] *adj* desaconsejado, malaconsejado, desavisado

ill at ease *adj* inquieto, incómodo

ill-bred ['ɪl'brɛd] *adj* malcriado

ill-considered ['ɪlkən'sɪdərd] *adj* des considerado, mal considerado

ill-disposed ['ɪldɪs'pozd] *adj* malintencionado, maldispuesto

illegal [ɪ'ligəl] *adj* ilegal

illegible [ɪ'lɛdʒɪbəl] *adj* ilegible

illegitimate [,ɪlɪ'dʒɪtɪmɪt] *adj* ilegítimo

ill fame *s* mala fama, reputación de inmoral

ill-fated ['ɪl'fetɪd] *adj* aciago, funesto

ill-gotten ['ɪl'gɑtən] *adj* mal ganado

ill health *s* mala salud

ill-humored ['ɪl'hjumərd] *adj* malhumorado

illicit [ɪ'lɪsɪt] *adj* ilícito

illitera•cy [ɪ'lɪtərəsi] *s* (*pl* **-cies**) ignorancia, analfabetismo

illiterate [ɪ'lɪtərɪt] *adj* (*uneducated*) iliterato; (*unable to read or write*) analfabeto ‖ *s* analfabeto

ill-mannered ['ɪl'mænərd] *adj* de malos modales

illness ['ɪlnɪs] *s* enfermedad

illogical [ɪ'lɑdʒɪkəl] *adj* ilógico

ill-spent ['ɪl'spɛnt] *adj* malgastado

ill-starred ['ɪl'stɑrd] *adj* malhadado

ill-tempered ['ɪl'tɛmpərd] *adj* de mal genio

ill-timed ['ɪl'taɪmd] *adj* inoportuno, intempestivo

ill'-treat' *tr* maltratar

illuminate [ɪ'lumɪ,net] *tr* alumbrar, iluminar; miniar (*un manuscrito*)

illuminating gas *s* gas *m* de alumbrado

illumination [ɪ,lumɪ'neʃən] *s* iluminación

illusion [ɪ'luʒən] *s* ilusión

illusive [ɪ'lusɪv] *adj* ilusivo

illusory [ɪ'lusəri] *adj* ilusorio

illustrate ['ɪləs,tret] o [ɪ'lʌstret] *tr* ilustrar

illustration [,ɪləs'treʃən] *s* ilustración

illustrious [ɪ'lʌstrɪ•əs] *adj* ilustre

ill will *s* mala voluntad

image ['ɪmɪdʒ] *s* imagen *f;* **the very image of** la propia estampa de

image•ry ['ɪmɪdʒri] *s* (*pl* **-ries**) (*formation of mental images; product of the imagination*) fantasía; (*images collectively*) imágenes *fpl*

imaginary [ɪ'mædʒɪ,nɛri] *adj* imaginario

imagination [ɪ,mædʒɪ'neʃən] *s* imaginación

imagine [ɪ'mædʒɪn] *tr & intr* imaginar; (*to conjecture*) imaginarse

imbecile ['ɪmbɪsɪl] *adj & s* imbécil *mf*

imbecili•ty [,ɪmbɪ'sɪlɪti] *s* (*pl* **-ties**) imbecilidad

imbibe [ɪm'baɪb] *tr* (*to drink*) beber; (*to absorb*) embeber; (*to become absorbed in*) embeberse de o en ‖ *intr* beber, empinar el codo

imbue [ɪm'bju] *tr* imbuir

imitate ['ɪmɪ,tet] *tr* imitar

imitation [,ɪmɪ'teʃən] *adj* (*e.g., jewelry*) imitado, imitación, de imitación ‖ *s* imitación; **in imitation of** a imitación de

immaculate [ɪ'mækjəlɪt] adj inmaculado
immaterial [,ɪmə'tɪrɪ•əl] adj inmaterial; poco importante
immature [,ɪmə'tjʊr] adj inmaturo
immeasurable [ɪ'mɛʒərəbəl] adj inmensurable
immediacy [ɪ'midɪ•əsi] s inmediación
immediate [ɪ'midɪ•ɪt] adj inmediato
immediately [ɪ'midɪ•ɪtli] adv inmediatamente, en seguida
immemorial [,ɪmɪ'morɪ•əl] adj inmemorial
immense [ɪ'mɛns] adj inmenso; (coll) excelente
immerge [ɪ'mʌrdʒ] intr sumergirse
immerse [ɪ'mʌrs] tr sumergir, inmergir
immersion [ɪ'mʌrʃən] o [ɪ'mʌrʒən] s sumersión, inmersión
immigrant ['ɪmɪgrənt] adj & s inmigrante mf
immigrate ['ɪmɪ,gret] intr inmigrar
immigration [,ɪmɪ'greʃən] s inmigración
imminent ['ɪmɪnənt] adj inminente
immobile [ɪ'mobɪl] adj inmoble, inmóvil
immobilize [ɪ'mobɪ,laɪz] tr inmovilizar
immoderate [ɪ'madərɪt] adj inmoderado
immodest [ɪ'madɪst] adj inmodesto
immoral [ɪ'mɔrəl] adj inmoral
immortal [ɪ'mɔrtəl] adj & s inmortal mf
immortalize [ɪ'mɔrtə,laɪz] tr inmortalizar
immune [ɪ'mjun] adj inmune
immunize ['ɪmjə,naɪz] tr inmunizar
imp [ɪmp] s diablillo; (child) niño travieso
impact ['ɪmpækt] s impacto
impair [ɪm'pɛr] tr empeorar, deteriorar
impan•el [ɪm'pænəl] v (pret & pp -eled o -elled; ger -eling o -elling) tr inscribir en la lista de los jurados; elegir (un jurado)
impart [ɪm'part] tr (to make known) dar a conocer, hacer saber; (to transmit, communicate) imprimir
impartial [ɪm'parʃəl] adj imparcial
impassable [ɪm'pæsəbəl] adj intransitable, impracticable
impasse [ɪm'pæs] o ['ɪmpæs] s callejón m sin salida
impassible [ɪm'pæsɪbəl] adj impasible
impassioned [ɪm'pæʃənd] adj ardiente, vehemente
impassive [ɪm'pæsɪv] adj impasible
impatience [ɪm'peʃəns] s impaciencia
impatient [ɪm'peʃənt] adj impaciente
impeach [ɪm'pɪtʃ] tr residenciar
impeachment [ɪm'pɪtʃmənt] s residencia
impeccable [ɪm'pɛkəbəl] adj impecable
impecunious [,ɪmpɪ'kjunɪ•əs] adj inope
impedance [ɪm'pidəns] s impedancia
impede [ɪm'pid] tr estorbar, dificultar
impediment [ɪm'pɛdɪmənt] s impedimento; (e.g., in speech) defecto
im•pel [ɪm'pɛl] v (pret & pp -pelled; ger-pelling) tr impeler, impulsar
impending [ɪm'pɛndɪŋ] adj inminente
impenetrable [ɪm'pɛnətrəbəl] adj impenetrable
impenitent [ɪm'pɛnɪtənt] adj & s impenitente mf

imperative [ɪm'pɛrɪtɪv] adj (commanding) imperativo; (urgent, absolutely necessary) imperioso ‖ s imperativo
imperceptible [,ɪmpər'sɛptɪbəl] adj imperceptible, inapreciable
imperfect [ɪm'pʌrfɪkt] adj & s imperfecto
imperfection [,ɪmpər'fɛkʃən] s imperfección
imperial [ɪm'pɪrɪ•əl] adj imperial; majestuoso ‖ s (goatee) perilla; (top of coach) imperial f
imperialist [ɪm'pɪrɪ•əlɪst] adj & s imperialista mf
imper•il [ɪm'pɛrɪl] v (pret & pp -iled o -illed; ger -iling o -illing) tr poner en peligro
imperious [ɪm'pɪrɪ•əs] adj imperioso
imperishable [ɪm'pɛrɪʃəbəl] adj imperecedero
impersonal [ɪm'pʌrsənəl] adj impersonal
impersonate [ɪm'pʌrsə,net] tr personificar; hacer el papel de
impertinence [ɪm'pʌrtɪnəns] s impertinencia
impertinent [ɪm'pʌrtɪnənt] adj & s impertinente mf
impetuous [ɪm'pɛtʃu•əs] adj impetuoso
impetus ['ɪmpɪtəs] s ímpetu m
impie•ty [ɪm'paɪ•əti] s (pl -ties) impiedad
impinge [ɪm'pɪndʒ] intr — to impinge on o upon incidir eno sobre, herir; infringir, violar
impious ['ɪmpɪ•əs] adj impío
impish ['ɪmpɪʃ] adj endiablado, travieso
implant [ɪm'plænt] tr implantar
implement ['ɪmplɪmənt] s instrumento, utensilio, herramienta; implements implementos mpl ‖ ['ɪmplɪ,mɛnt] tr poner por obra, llevar a cabo; (to provide with implements) pertrechar
implicate ['ɪmplɪ,ket] tr implicar, comprometer, enredar
implicit [ɪm'plɪsɪt] adj implícito; (unquestioning) absoluto, ciego
implied [ɪm'plaɪd] adj implícito, sobrentendido
implore [ɪm'plor] tr implorar, suplicar
im•ply [ɪm'plaɪ] v (pret & pp -plied) tr dar a entender; implicar, incluir en esencia
impolite [,ɪmpə'laɪt] adj descortés; desacomodido (SAm)
import ['ɪmport] s importación; artículo importado; importancia, significación ‖ tr importar; significar ‖ intr importar
importance [ɪm'portəns] s importancia
important [ɪm'portənt] adj importante
importation [,ɪmpor'teʃən] s importación
importer [ɪm'portər] s importador m
importunate [ɪm'portʃənɪt] adj importuno
importune [,ɪmpor'tjun] tr importunar
impose [ɪm'poz] tr imponer ‖ intr — to impose on o upon abusar de
imposing [ɪm'pozɪŋ] adj imponente
imposition [,ɪmpə'zɪʃən] s (of someone's will) imposición; abuso, engaño
impossible [ɪm'pasɪbəl] adj imposible
impostor [ɪm'pastər] s impostor m, embaucador m
imposture [ɪm'pastʃər] s impostura
impotence ['ɪmpətəns] s impotencia

ic
im

impotent ['ɪmpətənt] *adj* impotente
impound [ɪm'paʊnd] *tr* acorralar, encerrar; rebalsar (*agua*); (law) embargar, secuestrar
impoverish [ɪm'pɑvərɪʃ] *tr* empobrecer
impracticable [ɪm'præktɪkəbəl] *adj* impracticable; (*intractable*) intratable
impractical [ɪm'præktkəl] *adj* impracticable; soñador, utópico
impregnable [ɪm'pregnəbəl] *adj* inexpugnable
impregnate [ɪm'pregnet] *tr* (*to make pregnant*) empreñar; (*to soak*) empapar; (*to fill the interstices of*) impregnar; (*to infuse, infect*) imbuir
impresari•o [,ɪmprɪ'sɑrɪ,o] *s* (*pl* -**os**) empresario, empresario de teatro
impress [ɪm'pres] *tr* (*to have an effect on the mind or emotions of*) impresionar; (*to mark by using pressure*) imprimir; (*on the memory*) grabar; (mil) enganchar
impression [ɪm'preʃən] *s* impresión
impressionable [ɪm'preʃənəbəl] *adj* impresionable
impressive [ɪm'presɪv] *adj* impresionante
imprint ['ɪmprɪnt] *s* impresión; (typ) pie *m* de imprenta ‖ [ɪm'prɪnt] *tr* imprimir
imprison [ɪm'prɪzən] *tr* encarcelar
imprisonment [ɪm'prɪzənmənt] *s* encarcelamiento; pena privativa de libertad
improbable [ɪm'prɑbəbəl] *adj* improbable
impromptu [ɪm'prɑmptju] o [ɪm'prɑmptu] *adj* improvisado ‖ *adv* de improviso ‖ *s* improvisación; (mus) impromptu *m*
improper [ɪm'prɑpər] *adj* impropio; (*contrary to good taste or decency*) indecoroso
improve [ɪm'pruv] *tr* perfeccionar, mejorar; aprovechar (*la oportunidad*) ‖ *intr* perfeccionarse, mejorar; **to improve on** o **upon** mejorar
improvement [ɪm'pruvmənt] *s* perfeccionamiento, mejoramiento; (*e.g., in health*) mejoría; (*useful employment, e.g., of time*) aprovechamiento
improvident [ɪm'prɑvɪdənt] *adj* imprevisor
improvise ['ɪmprə,vaɪz] *tr* & *intr* improvisar
imprudent [ɪm'prudənt] *adj* imprudente
impudence ['ɪmpjədəns] *s* insolencia, descaro, impertinencia
impudent ['ɪmpjədənt] *adj* insolente, descarado, impertinente
impugn [ɪm'pjun] *tr* poner en tela de juicio
impulse ['ɪmpʌls] *s* impulso
impulsive [ɪm'pʌlsɪv] *adj* impulsivo
impunity [ɪm'pjunɪti] *s* impunidad
impure [ɪm'pjʊr] *adj* impuro
impuri•ty [ɪm'pjʊrɪti] *s* (*pl* -**ties**) impureza, impuridad
impute [ɪm'pjut] *tr* imputar
in [ɪn] *adj* interior ‖ *adv* dentro; en casa, en la oficina; **in here** aquí dentro; **in there** allí dentro; **to be in** estar en casa; **to be in for** estar expuesto a; **to be in with** gozar del favor de ‖ *prep* en; (*within*) dentro de; (*over, through*) por; (*a period of the day*) en o por; **dressed in . . .** vestido de . . . ; **in so far as** en tanto que; **in that** en que,

por cuanto ‖ *s* — **ins and outs** recovecos, pormenores minuciosos
inability [,ɪnə'bɪlɪti] *s* inhabilidad, incapacidad
inaccessible [,ɪnæk'sesɪbəl] *adj* inaccesible
inaccura•cy [ɪn'ækjərəsi] *s* (*pl* -**cies**) inexactitud, incorrección
inaccurate [ɪn'ækjərɪt] *adj* inexacto, incorrecto
inaction [ɪn'ækʃən] *s* inacción
inactive [ɪn'æktɪv] *adj* inactivo
inactivity [,ɪnæk'tɪvɪti] *s* inactividad
inadequate [ɪn'ædɪkwɪt] *adj* insuficiente, inadecuado
inadvertent [,ɪnəd'vʌrtənt] *adj* inadvertido
inadvisable [,ɪnəd'vaɪzəbəl] *adj* poco aconsejable, imprudente
inane [ɪn'en] *adj* inane
inanimate [ɪn'ænɪmɪt] *adj* inanimado
inappreciable [,ɪnə'priʃɪ•əbəl] *adj* inapreciable
inappropriate [,ɪnə'proprɪ•ɪt] *adj* no apropiado, no a propósito
inarticulate [,ɪnɑr'tɪkjəlɪt] *adj* (*sounds, words*) inarticulado; (*person*) incapaz de expresarse
inartistic [,ɪnɑr'tɪstɪk] *adj* antiartístico, inartístico
inasmuch as [,ɪnəz'mʌtʃ,æz] *conj* ya que, puesto que; en cuanto, hasta donde
inattentive [,ɪnə'tentɪv] *adj* desatento
inaugural [ɪn'ɔgjərəl] *adj* inaugural ‖ *s* discurso inaugural
inaugurate [ɪn'ɔgjə,ret] *tr* inaugurar
inauguration [ɪn,ɔgjə'reʃən] *s* (*formal initiation or opening*) inauguración; (*investiture of a head of government*) toma de posesión
inborn ['ɪn'bɔrn] *adj* innato, ingénito
inbreeding ['ɪn,bridɪŋ] *s* intracruzamiento
inc. *abbr* **inclosure, included, including, incorporated, increase**
Inca ['ɪŋkə] *adj* incaico ‖ *s* inca *mf*
incandescent [,ɪnkən'desənt] *adj* incandescente
incapable [ɪn'kepəbəl] *adj* incapaz
incapacitate [,ɪnkə'pæsɪ,tet] *tr* incapacitar, inhabilitar
incapaci•ty [,ɪnkə'pæsɪti] *s* (*pl* -**ties**) incapacidad
incarcerate [ɪn'kɑrsə,ret] *tr* encarcelar
incarnate [ɪn'kɑrnɪt] *adj* encarnado ‖ [ɪn'kɑrnet] *tr* encarnar
incarnation [,ɪnkɑr'neʃən] *s* encarnación
incendiarism [ɪn'sendɪ•ə,rɪzəm] *s* incendio intencionado; incitación al desorden
incendiar•y [ɪn'sendɪ,ɛri] *adj* incendiario ‖ *s* (*pl* -**ies**) incendiario
incense ['ɪnsens] *s* incienso ‖ *tr* (*to burn incense before*) incensar ‖ [ɪn'sens] *tr* exasperar, encolerizar
incense burner *s* incensario
incentive [ɪn'sentɪv] *adj* & *s* incentivo
inception [ɪn'sepʃən] *s* principio, comienzo
incertitude [ɪn'sʌrt,tjud] *s* incertidumbre
incessant [ɪn'sesənt] *adj* incesante
incest ['ɪnsest] *s* incesto
incestuous [ɪn'sestʃʊ•əs] *adj* incestuoso

inch [ɪntʃ] s pulgada; **to be within an inch of** estar a dos dedos de ‖ intr — **to inch ahead** avanzar poco a poco

incidence [ˈɪnsɪdəns] s incidencia; (range of occurrence) extensión

incident [ˈɪnsɪdənt] adj & s incidente m

incidental [ˌɪnsɪˈdɛntəl] adj incidente; (incurred in addition to the regular amount) obvencional ‖ s elemento incidental; **incidentals** gastos menudos

incidentally [ˌɪnsɪˈdɛntəli] adv incidentemente; a propósito

incipient [ɪnˈsɪpɪ·ənt] adj incipiente

incision [ɪnˈsɪʒən] s incisión

incisive [ɪnˈsaɪsɪv] adj incisivo

incite [ɪnˈsaɪt] tr incitar

incl. abbr **inclosure, inclusive**

inclemen·cy [ɪnˈklɛmənsi] s (pl -cies) inclemencia

inclement [ɪnˈklɛmənt] adj inclemente

inclination [ˌɪnklɪˈneʃən] s inclinación

incline [ˈɪnklaɪn] o [ɪnˈklaɪn] s declive m, pendiente f ‖ [ɪnˈklaɪn] tr inclinar ‖ intr inclinarse

inclose [ɪnˈkloz] tr encerrar; (in a letter) adjuntar, incluir; **to inclose herewith** remitir adjunto

inclosure [ɪnˈkloʒər] s recinto; cosa inclusa, carta inclusa

include [ɪnˈklud] tr incluir, comprender

including [ɪnˈkludɪŋ] prep incluso, inclusive; imbíbito (Guat, Mex)

inclusive [ɪnˈklusɪv] adj inclusivo; **inclusive of** comprensivo de ‖ adv inclusive

incogni·to [ɪnˈkɑgnɪ,to] adj incógnito ‖ adv de incógnito ‖ s (pl -tos) incógnito

incoherent [ˌɪnkoˈhɪrənt] adj incoherente

incombustible [ˌɪnkəmˈbʌstɪbəl] adj incombustible

income [ˈɪnkʌm] s renta, ingreso, utilidad

income tax s impuesto sobre rentas

in'come-tax' return s declaración de impuesto sobre rentas

in'com'ing adj de entrada, entrante; (tide) ascendente ‖ s entrada

incommunicado [ˌɪnkəˌmjunəˈkado] adj incomunicado

incomparable [ɪnˈkɑmpərəbəl] adj incomparable; inigualable

incompatible [ˌɪnkəmˈpætɪbəl] adj incompatible

incompetent [ɪnˈkɑmpɪtənt] adj incompetente

incomplete [ˌɪnkəmˈplit] adj incompleto

incomprehensible [ˌɪnkɑmprɪˈhɛnsɪbəl] adj incomprehensible

incomprehension [ɪn,kɑmprɪˈhɛnʃən] s incomprensión

inconceivable [ˌɪnkənˈsivəbəl] adj inconcebible

inconclusive [ˌɪnkənˈklusɪv] adj inconcluyente

incongruous [ɪnˈkɑŋgru·əs] adj incongruo

inconsequential [ɪn,kɑnsɪˈkwɛnʃəl] adj (lacking proper sequence of thought or speech) inconsecuente; (trivial) de poca importancia

inconsiderate [ˌɪnkənˈsɪdərɪt] adj desconsiderado, inconsiderado

inconsisten·cy [ˌɪnkənˈsɪstənsi] s (pl -cies) (lack of coherence) inconsistencia; (lack of logical connection or uniformity) inconsecuencia

inconsistent [ˌɪnkənˈsɪstənt] adj (lacking coherence of parts) inconsistente; (not agreeing with itself or oneself) inconsecuente

inconsolable [ˌɪnkənˈsoləbəl] adj inconsolable

inconspicuous [ˌɪnkənˈspɪkju·əs] adj poco impresionante, poco aparente

inconstant [ɪnˈkɑnstənt] adj inconstante

incontinent [ɪnˈkɑntɪnənt] adj incontinente

incontrovertible [ˌɪnkɑntrəˈvʌrtɪbəl] adj incontrovertible

inconvenience [ˌɪnkənˈvini·əns] s incomodidad, inconveniencia, molestia ‖ tr incomodar, molestar

inconvenient [ˌɪnkənˈvzini·ənt] adj incómodo, inconveniente, molesto

incorporate [ɪnˈkɔrpə,ret] tr incorporar; constituir en sociedad anónima ‖ intr incorporarse; constituirse en sociedad anónima

incorporation [ɪnˈkɔrpəˈreʃən] s incorporación; constitución en sociedad anónima

incorrect [ˌɪnkəˈrɛkt] adj incorrecto

increase [ˈɪnkris] s aumento; ganancia, interés m; **to be on the increase** ir en aumento ‖ [ɪnˈkris] tr aumentar; (by propagation) multiplicar ‖ intr aumentar; multiplicarse

increasingly [ɪnˈkrisɪŋli] adv cada vez más

incredible [ɪnˈkrɛdɪbəl] adj increíble

incredulous [ɪnˈkrɛdʒələs] adj incrédulo

increment [ˈɪnkrɪmənt] s incremento

incriminate [ɪnˈkrɪmɪ,net] tr acriminar, incriminar

incrust [ɪnˈkrʌst] tr incrustar

incubate [ˈɪnkjə,bet] tr & intr incubar

incubator [ˈɪnkjə,betər] s incubadora

inculcate [ɪnˈkʌlket] o [ˈɪnkʌl,ket] tr inculcar

incumben·cy [ɪnˈkʌmbənsi] s (pl -cies) incumbencia

incumbent [ɪnˈkʌmbənt] adj — **to be incumbent on** incumbir a ‖ s titular m

incunabula [ˌɪnkjuˈnæbjələ] spl (beginnings) orígenes mpl; (early printed books) incunables mpl

in·cur [ɪnˈkʌr] v (pret & pp -curred; ger -curring) tr incurrir en; (a debt) contraer

incurable [ɪnˈkjurəbəl] adj & s incurable mf

incursion [ɪnˈkʌrʒən] s incursión, correría

ind. abbr **independent, industrial**

indebted [ɪnˈdɛtɪd] adj adeudado; obligado

indebtedness [ɪnˈdɛtɪdnɪs] s endeudamiento

indecen·cy [ɪnˈdisənsi] s (pl -cies) indecencia, deshonestidad

indecent [ɪnˈdisənt] adj indecente, deshonesto; lépero (CAm, Mex)

indecisive [ˌɪndɪˈsaɪsɪv] adj indeciso

indeclinable [ˌɪndɪˈklaɪnəbəl] adj (gram) indeclinable

indeed [ɪnˈdid] adv verdaderamente, claro ‖ interj ¡de veras!

indefatigable [ˌɪndɪˈfætɪgəbəl] adj incansable, infatigable

im
in

indefensible [ˌɪndɪˈfɛnsɪbəl] *adj* indefendible
indefinable [ˌɪndɪˈfaɪnəbəl] *adj* indefinible
indefinite [ɪnˈdɛfɪnɪt] *adj* indefinido
indelible [ɪnˈdɛlɪbəl] *adj* indeleble
indelicate [ɪnˈdɛlɪkɪt] *adj* indelicado
indemnification [ɪnˌdɛmnɪfɪˈkəʃən] *s* indemnización
indemni·fy [ɪnˈdɛmnɪˌfaɪ] *v* (*pret* & *pp* -**fied**) *tr* indemnizar
indemni·ty [ɪnˈdɛmnɪti] *s* (*pl* -**ties**) (*security against loss*) indemnidad; (*compensation*) indemnización
indent [ɪnˈdɛnt] *tr* dentar, mellar; (typ) sangrar
indentation [ˌɪndɛnˈteʃən] *s* mella, muesca; (typ) sangría
indenture [ɪnˈdɛntʃər] *s* escritura, contrato; contrato de aprendizaje ‖ *tr* obligar por contrato
independence [ˌɪndɪˈpɛndəns] *s* independencia
independen·cy [ˌɪndɪˈpɛndənsi] *s* (*pl* -**cies**) independencia; país *m* independiente
independent [ˌɪndɪˈpɛndənt] *adj* & *s* independiente *mf*
indescribable [ˌɪndɪˈskraɪbəbəl] *adj* indescriptible
indestructible [ˌɪndɪˈstrʌktɪbəl] *adj* indestructible
indeterminate [ˌɪndɪˈtʌrmɪnɪt] *adj* indeterminado
index [ˈɪndɛks] *s* (*pl* **indexes** o **indices** [ˈɪndɪˌsiz] *s* índice *m*; (typ) manecilla ‖ *tr* poner índice a; poner en un índice ‖ **Index** *s* Índice de los libros prohibidos
index card *s* ficha catalográfica
index finger *s* dedo índice
index tab *s* pestaña
India [ˈɪndɪ·ə] *s* la India
India ink *s* tinta china
Indian [ˈɪndɪ·ən] *adj* & *s* indio
Indian club *s* maza de gimnasia
Indian corn *s* maíz *m*, panizo
Indian file *s* fila india ‖ *adv* en fila india
Indian Ocean *s* mar *m* de las Indias, océano Índico
Indian summer *s* veranillo de San Martín
India paper *s* papel *m* de China
India rubber *s* caucho
indicate [ˈɪndɪˌket] *tr* indicar
indication [ˌɪndɪˈkeʃən] *s* indicación
indicative [ɪnˈdɪkətɪv] *adj* & *s* indicativo
indicator [ˈɪndɪˌketər] *s* indicador *m*
indict [ɪnˈdaɪt] *tr* (law) acusar, procesar
indictment [ɪnˈdaɪtmənt] *s* acusación, procesamiento; auto de acusación formulado por el gran jurado
indifferent [ɪnˈdɪfərənt] *adj* indiferente; (*not particularly good*) pasadero, mediano
indigenous [ɪnˈdɪdʒɪnəs] *adj* indígena
indigent [ˈɪndɪdʒənt] *adj* indigente
indigestible [ˌɪndɪˈdʒɛstɪbəl] *adj* indigestible
indigestion [ˌɪndɪˈdʒɛstʃən] *s* indigestión
indignant [ɪnˈdɪɡnənt] *adj* indignado
indignation [ˌɪndɪɡˈneʃən] *s* indignación
indigni·ty [ɪnˈdɪɡnɪti] *s* (*pl* -**ties**) indignidad

indi·go [ˈɪndɪɡo] *adj* azul de añil ‖ *s* (*pl* -**gos** o -**goes**) índigo
indirect [ˌɪndɪˈrɛkt] *adj* indirecto
indirect discourse *s* estilo indirecto
indiscernible [ˌɪndɪˈzʌrnɪbəl] o [ˌɪndɪˈsʌrnɪbəl] *adj* indiscernible
indiscreet [ˌɪndɪˈskrit] *adj* indiscreto
indiscriminate [ˌɪndɪsˈkrɪmənɪt] *adj* indiscriminado
indispensable [ˈɪndɪsˈpɛnsəbəl] *adj* indispensable, imprescindible
indispose [ˌɪndɪsˈpoz] *tr* indisponer
indisposed [ˌɪndɪsˈpozd] *adj* (*disinclined*) maldispuesto; (*somewhat ill*) indispuesto
indissoluble [ˌɪndɪˈsaljəbəl] *adj* indisoluble
indistinct [ˌɪndɪˈstɪŋkt] *adj* indistinto
indite [ɪnˈdaɪt] *tr* redactar, poner por escrito
individual [ˌɪndɪˈvɪdʒʊ·əl] *adj* individual ‖ *s* individuo
individuali·ty [ˌɪndɪˌvɪdʒʊˌˈælɪti] *s* (*pl* -**ties**) individualidad; (*person of distinctive character*) personaje *m*
Indochina [ˈɪndoˈtʃaɪnə] *s* la Indochina
Indo-Chi·nese [ˈɪndotʃaɪˈniz] *adj* indochino ‖ *s* (*pl* -**nese**) indochino
indoctrinate [ɪnˈdaktrɪˌnet] *tr* adoctrinar
Indo-European [ˈɪndoˌjʊrəˈpi·ən] *adj* & *s* indoeuropeo
indolent [ˈɪndələnt] *adj* indolente
Indonesia [ˌɪndoˈniʃə] o [ˌɪndoˈniʒə] *s* la Indonesia
Indonesian [ˌɪndoˈniʃən] o [ˌɪndoˈniʒən] *adj* & *s* indonesio
indoor [ˈɪnˌdor] *adj* interior, de puertas adentro; (*inclined to stay in the house*) casero
indoors [ˈɪnˈdorz] *adv* dentro, en casa, bajo techado, bajo cubierto
indorse [ɪnˈdors] *tr* endosar; (fig) apoyar, aprobar
indorsee [ˌɪndorˈsi] *s* endosatario
indorsement [ɪnˈdorsmənt] *s* endoso; (fig) apoyo, aprobación
indorser [ɪnˈdorsər] *s* endosante *mf*
induce [ɪnˈdjus] *tr* inducir; causar, ocasionar
inducement [ɪnˈdjusmənt] *s* aliciente *m*, estímulo, incentivo
induct [ɪnˈdʌkt] *tr* instalar; introducir, iniciar; (mil) quintar
induction [ɪnˈdʌkʃən] *s* instalación; introducción; (elec & log) inducción; (mil) quinta
indulge [ɪnˈdʌldʒ] *tr* gratificar (*p.ej., los deseos de uno*); mimar (*a un niño*) ‖ *intr* abandonar; **to indulge in** entregarse a, permitirse el placer de
indulgence [ɪnˈdʌldʒəns] *s* gusto, inclinación; intemperancia, desenfreno; (*leniency*) indulgencia
indulgent [ɪnˈdʌldʒənt] *adj* indulgente
industrial [ɪnˈdʌstrɪ·əl] *adj* industrial
industrialist [ɪnˈdʌstrɪ·əlɪst] *s* industrial *m*
industrialize [ɪnˈdʌstrɪ·əˌlaɪz] *tr* industrializar
industrious [ɪnˈdʌstrɪ·əs] *adj* industrioso, aplicado
indus·try [ˈɪndəstri] *s* (*pl* -**tries**) industria
inebriation [ɪnˌibrɪˈeʃən] *s* embriaguez *f*
inedible [ɪnˈɛdɪbəl] *adj* incomible

ineffable [ɪnˈɛfəbəl] *adj* inefable
ineffective [ˌɪnɪˈfɛktɪv] *adj* ineficaz; *(person)* incapaz
ineffectual [ˌɪnɪˈfɛktʃʊ•əl] *adj* ineficaz, fútil
inefficacy [ɪnˈɛfɪkəsi] *s* ineficacia
inefficient [ˌɪnɪˈfɪʃənt] *adj* de mal rendimiento
ineligible [ɪnˈɛlɪdʒɪbəl] *adj* inelegible
inequali•ty [ˌɪnɪˈkwɑlɪti] *s (pl* **-ties)** desigualdad
inequi•ty [ɪnˈɛkwɪti] *s (pl* **-ties)** inequidad
ineradicable [ˌɪnɪˈrædɪkəbəl] *adj* inextirpable
inertia [ɪnˈʌrʃə] *s* inercia
inescapable [ˌɪnɛsˈkepəbəl] *adj* ineludible
inevitable [ɪnˈɛvɪtəbəl] *adj* inevitable
inexact [ˌɪnɛgˈzækt] *adj* inexacto
inexcusable [ˌɪnɛksˈkjuzəbəl] *adj* indisculpable, inexcusable
inexhaustible [ˌɪnɛgˈzɔstɪbəl] *adj* inagotable
inexorable [ɪnˈɛksərəbəl] *adj* inexorable
inexpedient [ˌɪnɛkˈspidɪ•ənt] *adj* malaconsejado, inoportuno
inexpensive [ˌɪnɛkˈspɛnsɪv] *adj* barato, poco costoso
inexperience [ˌɪnɛkˈspɪrɪ•əns] *s* inexperiencia
inexplicable [ɪnˈɛksplɪkəbəl] *adj* inexplicable
inexpressible [ˌɪnɛkˈsprɛsɪbəl] *adj* inexpresable
Inf. *abbr* **Infantry**
infallible [ɪnˈfælɪbəl] *adj* infalible
infamous [ˈɪnfəməs] *adj* infame
infa•my [ˈɪnfəmi] *s (pl* **-mies)** infamia
infan•cy [ˈɪnfənsi] *s (pl* **-cies)** infancia
infant [ˈɪnfənt] *adj* infantil; *(in the earliest stage)* (fig) naciente ‖ *s* criatura, nene *m*
infant care *s* puericultura
infantile [ˈɪnfən‚taɪl] o [ˈɪnfəntɪl] *adj* infantil; *(childish)* aniñado
infan•try [ˈɪnfəntri] *s (pl* **-tries)** infantería
infantry•man [ˈɪnfəntrimən] *s (pl* **-men** [mən]) infante *m*, soldado de infantería
infarct [ɪnˈfɑrkt] *s* infarto
infatuated [ɪnˈfætʃʊ‚etɪd] *adj* apasionado, locamente enamorado
infect [ɪnˈfɛkt] *tr* inficionar, infectar; influir sobre
infection [ɪnˈfɛkʃən] *s* infección
infectious [ɪnˈfɛkʃəs] *adj* infeccioso
in•fer [ɪnˈfʌr] *v (pret & pp* **-ferred;** *ger* **-ferring)** *tr* inferir; (coll) conjeturar, suponer
inferior [ɪnˈfɪrɪ•ər] *adj & s* inferior *m*
inferiority [ɪn‚fɪrɪˈɑrɪti] *s* inferioridad
inferiority complex *s* complejo de inferioridad
infernal [ɪnˈfʌrnəl] *adj* infernal
infest [ɪnˈfɛst] *tr* infestar
infidel [ˈɪnfɪdəl] *adj & s* infiel *mf*
infideli•ty [ˌɪnfɪˈdɛlɪti] *s (pl* **-ties)** infidelidad
in'field' *s* (baseball) cuadro interior
infiltrate [ˈɪnfɪl‚tret] *tr* infiltrar; infiltrarse en ‖ *intr* infiltrarse
infinite [ˈɪnfɪnɪt] *adj & s* infinito
infinitive [ɪnˈfɪnɪtɪv] *adj & s* infinitivo

infini•ty [ɪnˈfɪnɪti] *s (pl* **-ties)** infinidad; (math) infinito
infirm [ɪnˈfʌrm] *adj* infirme, achacoso; *(unsteady)* inestable, inseguro; poco firme, poco sólido
infirma•ry [ɪnˈfʌrməri] *s (pl* **-ries)** enfermería
infirmi•ty [ɪnˈfʌrmɪti] *s (pl* **-ties)** achaque *m;* inestabilidad
in'fix *s* (gram) infijo
inflame [ɪnˈflem] *tr* inflamar
inflammable [ɪnˈflæməbəl] *adj* inflamable
inflammation [ˌɪnfləˈmeʃən] *s* inflamación
inflate [ɪnˈflet] *tr* inflar ‖ *intr* inflarse
inflation [ɪnˈfleʃən] *s* inflación; *(of a tire)* inflado
inflationary [ɪnˈfleʃən‚ɛri] *adj* inflacionario
inflect [ɪnˈflɛkt] *tr* doblar, torcer; modular *(la voz)*; (gram) modificar por inflexión
inflection [ɪnˈflɛkʃən] *s* inflexión
inflexible [ɪnˈflɛksɪbəl] *adj* inflexible
inflict [ɪnˈflɪkt] *tr* infligir
influence [ˈɪnflu•əns] *s* influencia ‖ *tr* influir sobre, influenciar
influential [ˌɪnfluˈɛnʃəl] *adj* influyente
influenza [ˌɪnfluˈɛnzə] *s* influenza
inform [ɪnˈfɔrm] *tr* informar, avisar, enterar ‖ *intr* informar
informal [ɪnˈfɔrməl] *adj (not according to established rules)* informal; *(unceremonious; colloquial)* familiar
information [ˌɪnfərˈmeʃən] *s* información, informes *mpl*
informational [ˌɪnfərˈmeʃənəl] *adj* informativo
informed sources *spl* los entendidos
infraction [ɪnˈfrækʃən] *s* infracción
infrared [ˌɪnfrəˈred] *adj & s* infrarrojo
infrequent [ɪnˈfrikwənt] *adj* infrecuente
infringe [ɪnˈfrɪndʒ] *tr* infringir ‖ *intr—to* **infringe on** o **upon** invadir, abusar de
infringement [ɪnˈfrɪndʒmənt] *s* infración
infuriate [ɪnˈfjʊrɪ‚et] *tr* enfurecer
infuse [ɪnˈfjuz] *tr* infundir
infusion [ɪnˈfjuʒən] *s* infusión
ingenious [ɪnˈdʒinjəs] *adj* ingenioso
ingenui•ty [ˌɪndʒɪˈnju•ɪti] o [ˌɪndʒɪˈnu•ɪti] *s (pl* **-ties)** ingeniosidad
ingenuous [ɪnˈdʒɛnju•əs] *adj* ingenuo
ingenuousness [ɪnˈdʒɛnju•əsnɪs] *s* ingenuidad
ingest [ɪnˈdʒɛst] *tr* injerir
in'go'ing *adj* entrante
ingot [ˈɪŋgət] *s* lingote *m*
ingraft [ɪnˈgræft] *tr* (hort & surg) injertar; (fig) implantar
ingrate [ˈɪŋgret] *s* ingrato
ingratiate [ɪnˈgreʃɪ‚et] *tr—to* **ingratiate oneself with** congraciarse con
ingratiating [ɪnˈgreʃɪ‚etɪŋ] *adj* atrayente, obsequioso
ingratitude [ɪnˈgrætɪ‚tjud] *s* ingratitud, desagradecimiento
ingredient [ɪnˈgridɪ•ənt] *s* ingrediente *m*
in'grow'ing nail *s* uñero
ingulf [ɪnˈgʌlf] *tr* hundir, inundar
inhabit [ɪnˈhæbɪt] *tr* habitar, poblar

in
in

inhabitant [ɪn'hæbɪtənt] s habitante *mf*
inhale [ɪn'hel] *tr* aspirar, inspirar ‖ *intr* aspirar, inspirar; tragar el humo
inherent [ɪn'hɪrənt] *adj* inherente
inherit [ɪn'hɛrɪt] *tr* & *intr* heredar
inheritance [ɪn'hɛrɪtəns] s herencia; mortual *m* (CAm, Mex)
inheritor [ɪn'hɛrɪtər] s heredero
inhibit [ɪn'hɪbɪt] *tr* inhibir, prohibir
inhospitable [ɪn'hɑspɪtəbəl] o [ˌɪnhɑs'pɪtəbəl] *adj* inhospitalario; (*affording no shelter or protection*) inhóspito
inhuman [ɪn'hjumən] *adj* inhumano
inhumane [ˌɪnhju'men] *adj* inhumano
inhumani‧ty [ˌɪnhju'mænɪti] s (*pl* -ties) inhumanidad
inimical [ɪ'nɪmɪkəl] *adj* enemigo
iniqui‧ty [ɪ'nɪkwɪti] s (*pl* -ties) iniquidad
ini‧tial [ɪ'nɪʃəl] *adj* & s inicial *f* ‖ *v* (*pret* -tialed o -tialled; *ger* -tialing o tialling) *tr* firmar con sus iniciales; marcar (*p.ej., un pañuelo*)
initiate [ɪ'nɪʃɪ,et] *tr* iniciar
initiation [ɪ,nɪʃɪ'eʃən] s iniciación
initiative [ɪ'nɪʃɪ‧ətɪv] o [ɪ'nɪʃətɪv] s iniciativa
inject [ɪn'dʒɛkt] *tr* inyectar; introducir (*una especie, una advertencia*)
injection [ɪn'dʒɛkʃən] s inyección
injudicious [ˌɪndʒu'dɪʃəs] *adj* imprudente
injunction [ɪn'dʒʌŋkʃən] s admonición, mandato; (law) entredicho
injure ['ɪndʒər] *tr* (*to harm*) dañar, hacer daño a; (*to wound*) herir, lisiar, lastimar; (*to offend*) agraviar
injurious [ɪn'dʒʊrɪ‧əs] *adj* dañoso, perjudicial; (*offensive*) agravioso
inju‧ry ['ɪndʒəri] s (*pl* -ries) (*harm*) daño; (*wound*) herida, lesión; (*offense*) agravio
injustice [ɪn'dʒʌstɪs] s injusticia
ink [ɪŋk] s tinta ‖ *tr* entintar
inkling ['ɪŋklɪŋ] s sospecha, indicio, noción vaga, vislumbre *f*
ink'stand' s (*cuplike container*) tintero; (*stand for ink, pens, etc.*) portatintero
ink'well' s tintero
ink‧y ['ɪŋki] *adj* (*comp* -ier; *super* -iest) entintado; negro
inlaid ['ɪn,led] o [ˌɪn'led] *adj* embutido, taraceado
inland ['ɪnlənd] *adj* & s interior *m* ‖ *adv* tierra adentro
in'-law' s (coll) pariente político
in‧lay ['ɪn,le] s embutido ‖ [ɪn'le] o ['ɪn,le] *v* (*pret* & *pp* -laid) *tr* embutir, taracear
in'let s ensenada, cala, caleta
in'mate' s (*in a hospital or home*) asilado, recluso, acogido; (*in a jail*) presidiario, preso
inn [ɪn] s mesón *m*, posada
innate [ɪ'net] o ['ɪnet] *adj* ingénito, innato
inner ['ɪnər] *adj* interior; secreto
in'ner‧spring' mattress s colchón *m* de muelles interiores
inner tube s cámara (de neumático)
inning ['ɪnɪŋ] s mano *f*, entrada, turno
inn'keep'er s mesonero, posadero
innocence ['ɪnəsəns] s inocencia

innocent ['ɪnəsənt] *adj* & s inocente *mf*
innovate ['ɪnə,vet] *tr* innovar
innovation [ˌɪnə've/ən] s innovación
innuen‧do [ˌɪnju'ɛndo] s (*pl* -does) indirecta, insinuación
innumerable [ɪ'numərəbəl] *adj* innumerable, incontable
inoculate [ɪn'ɑkjə,let] *tr* inocular; (fig) imbuir
inoculation [ɪn,ɑkjə'leʃən] s inoculación
inoffensive [ˌɪnə'fɛnsɪv] *adj* inofensivo
inoperative [ɪn'ɑpərətɪv] *adj* fuera de servicio
inopportune [ɪn,ɑpər'tjun] *adj* inoportuno
inordinate [ɪn'ɔrdɪnɪt] *adj* excesivo; (*unrestrained*) desenfrenado
inorganic [ˌɪnɔr'gænɪk] *adj* inorgánico
in'put' s gasto, consumo; (elec) entrada; (mech) potencia consumida
inquest ['ɪnkwɛst] s encuesta; (*of coroner*) pesquisa judicial, levantamiento del cadáver
inquire [ɪn'kwaɪr] *tr* averiguar, inquirir ‖ *intr* preguntar; **to inquire about, after** o **for** preguntar por; **to inquire into** averiguar, inquirir
inquir‧y [ɪn'kwaɪri] o ['ɪnkwɪri] s (*pl* -ies) averiguación, encuesta; pregunta
inquisition [ˌɪnkwɪ'zɪʃən] s inquisición
inquisitive [ɪn'kwɪzɪtɪv] *adj* curioso, preguntón
in'road' s incursión
ins. *abbr* **insulated, insurance**
insane [ɪn'sen] *adj* loco, insano, dementado
insane asylum s manicomio, casa de locos
insani‧ty [ɪn'sænɪti] s (*pl* -ties) demencia, locura, insania, loquera
insatiable [ɪn'seʃəbəl] *adj* insaciable
inscribe [ɪn'skraɪb] *tr* inscribir; dedicar (*una obra literaria*)
inscription [ɪn'skrɪpʃən] s inscripción; (*of a book*) dedicatoria
inscrutable [ɪn'skrutəbəl] *adj* inescrutable
insect ['ɪnsɛkt] s insecto
insect control s desinsectación
insecticide [ɪn'sɛktɪ,saɪd] *adj* & s insecticida *m*
insecure [ˌɪnsɪ'kjʊr] *adj* inseguro
inseparable [ɪn'sɛpərəbəl] *adj* inseparable
insert ['ɪnsʌrt] s inserción ‖ [ɪn'sʌrt] *tr* insertar
insertion [ɪn'sʌrʃən] s inserción; (*strip of lace*) entredós *m*
in‧set ['ɪn,sɛt] s intercalación ‖ [ɪn'sɛt] o ['ɪn,sɛt] *v* (*pret* & *pp* -set; *ger* -setting) *tr* intercalar, encastrar
in'shore' *adj* cercano a la orilla ‖ *adv* cerca de la orilla; hacia la orilla
in'side' *adj* interior; interno; secreto ‖ *adv* dentro, adentro; **inside of** dentro de; **to turn inside out** volver al revés; volverse al revés ‖ *prep* dentro de ‖ s interior *m*; **insides** (coll) entrañas; **on the inside** (coll) en el secreto de las cosas
inside information s informes *mpl* confidenciales
insider [ˌɪn'saɪdər] s persona enterada

insidious [ɪnˈsɪdɪ·əs] *adj* insidioso
in'sight' *s* penetración
insigni·a [ɪnˈsɪgnɪ·ə] *s* (*pl* **-a** o **-as**) insignia
insignificant [ˌɪnsɪgˈnɪfɪkənt] *adj* insignificante
insincere [ˌɪnsɪnˈsɪr] *adj* insincero; malo (Mex)
insinuate [ɪnˈsɪnjʊˌet] *tr* insinuar
insipid [ɪnˈsɪpɪd] *adj* insípido
insist [ɪnˈsɪst] *intr* insistir
insofar as [ˌɪnsoˈfɑrˌæz] *conj* en cuanto
insolence [ˈɪnsələns] *s* insolencia
insolent [ˈɪnsələnt] *adj* insolente
insoluble [ɪnˈsɑljəbəl] *adj* insoluble
insolven·cy [ɪnˈsɑlvənsi] *s* (*pl* **-cies**) insolvencia
insomnia [ɪnˈsɑmnɪ·ə] *s* insomnio
insomuch [ˌɪnsoˈmʌtʃ] *adv* hasta tal punto; **insomuch as** ya que, puesto que; **insomuch that** hasta el punto que
inspect [ɪnˈspɛkt] *tr* inspeccionar
inspection [ɪnˈspɛkʃən] *s* inspección
inspiration [ˌɪnspɪˈreʃən] *s* inspiración
inspire [ɪnˈspaɪr] *tr* & *intr* inspirar
inspiring [ɪnˈspaɪrɪŋ] *adj* inspirante
inst. *abbr* **instant** (*i.e.*, **present month**)
Inst. *abbr* **Institute, Institution**
install [ɪnˈstɔl] *tr* instalar
installment [ɪnˈstɔlmənt] *s* instalación; entrega; **in installments** por entregas; a plazos
installment buying *s* compra a plazos
installment plan *s* pago a plazos, compra a plazos; **on the installment plan** con facilidades de pago
instance [ˈɪnstəns] *s* caso, ejemplo; **for instance** por ejemplo
instant [ˈɪnstənt] *adj* instantáneo ‖ *s* instante *m*, momento; mes *m* corriente
instantaneous [ˌɪnstənˈtenɪ·əs] *adj* instantáneo
instantly [ˈɪnstəntli] *adv* al instante
instead [ɪnˈstɛd] *adv* preferiblemente; en su lugar; **instead of** en vez de, en lugar de
in'step' *s* empeine *m*
instigate [ˈɪnstɪˌget] *tr* instigar
in·still' *tr* instilar
instinct [ˈɪnstɪŋkt] *s* instinto
instinctive [ɪnˈstɪŋktɪv] *adj* instintivo
institute [ˈɪnstɪˌtjut] *s* instituto ‖ *tr* instituir
institution [ˌɪnstɪˈtjuʃən] *s* institución
instruct [ɪnˈstrʌkt] *tr* instruir
instruction [ɪnˈstrʌkʃən] *s* instrucción
instructions for use *spl* modo de empleo
instructive [ɪnˈstrʌktɪv] *adj* instructivo
instructor [ɪnˈstrʌktər] *s* instructor *m*
instrument [ˈɪnstrəmənt] *s* instrumento ‖ [ˈɪnstrəˌmɛnt] *tr* instrumentar
instrumentalist [ˌɪnstrəˈmɛntəlɪst] *s* instrumentista *mf*
instrumentali·ty [ˌɪnstrəmənˈtælɪti] *s* (*pl* **-ties**) agencia, mediación
instrument panel *s* cuadro de mando; salpicadero
insubordinate [ˌɪnsəˈbɔrdɪnɪt] *adj* insubordinado
insufferable [ɪnˈsʌfərəbel] *adj* insufrible

insufficient [ˌɪnsəˈfɪʃənt] *adj* insuficiente
insular [ˈɪnsələr] o [ˈɪnsjʊlər] *adj* insular; (fig) de miras estrechas
insulate [ˈɪnsəˌlet] *tr* aislar
insulation [ˌɪnsəˈleʃən] *s* aislación
insulator [ˈɪnsəˌlɑtər] *s* aislador *m*
insulin [ˈɪnsəlɪn] *s* insulina
insult [ˈɪnsʌlt] *s* insulto, insultada, escopetazo ‖ [ɪnˈsʌlt] *tr* insultar
insurable [ɪnˈʃʊrəbəl] *adj* asegurable
insurance [ɪnˈʃʊrəns] *s* seguro
insure [ɪnˈʃʊr] *tr* asegurar
insurer [ɪnˈʃʊrər] *s* asegurador *m*
insurgent [ɪnˈsʌrdʒənt] *adj* & *s* insurgente *mf*
insurmountable [ˌɪnsərˈmaʊntəbəl] *adj* insuperable
insurrection [ˌɪnsəˈrɛkʃən] *s* insurrección
insusceptible [ˌɪnsəˈsɛptɪbəl] *adj* insusceptible
int. *abbr* **interest, interior, internal, international**
intact [ɪnˈtækt] *adj* intacto, ileso
in'take' *s* (*place of taking in*) entrada; (*act or amount*) toma; (mach) admisión
intake manifold *s* múltiple *m* de admisión, colector *m* de admisión
intake valve *s* válvula de admisión
intangible [ɪnˈtændʒɪbəl] *adj* intangible; vago, indefinido
integer [ˈɪntɪdʒər] *s* (arith) entero
integral [ˈɪntɪgrəl] *adj* íntegro; **integral with** solidario de ‖ *s* conjunto
integration [ˌɪntɪˈgreʃən] *s* integración
integrity [ɪŋˈtɛgrɪti] *s* integridad
intellect [ˈɪntəˌlɛkt] *s* intelecto; (*person*) intelectual *mf*
intellectual [ˌɪntəˈlɛktʃʊ·əl] *adj* & *s* intelectual *mf*
intellectuali·ty [ˌɪntəˌlɛktʃuˈælɪti] *s* (*pl* **-ties**) intelectualidad
intelligence [ɪnˈtɛlɪdʒəns] *s* inteligencia; información
intelligence bureau *s* departamento de inteligencia
intelligence quotient *s* cociente *m* intelectual
intelligent [ɪnˈtɛlɪdʒənt] *adj* inteligente; espabilado
intelligentsia [ɪnˌtɛlɪˈdʒəntsɪ·ə] o [ɪnˌtɛlɪˈgɛntsɪ·ə] *s* intelectualidad (*conjunto de los intelectuales de un país o región*)
intelligible [ɪnˈtɛlɪdʒɪbəl] *adj* inteligible
intemperance [ɪnˈtɛmpərəns] *s* intemperancia
intemperate [ɪnˈtɛmpərɪt] *adj* intemperante; (*climate*) riguroso
intend [ɪnˈtɛnd] *tr* pensar, proponerse, intentar; (*to mean for a particular purpose*) destinar; (*to signify*) querer decir
intendance [ɪnˈtɛndəns] *s* intendencia
intendant [ɪnˈtɛndənt] *s* intendente *m*
intended [ɪnˈtɛndɪd] *adj* & *s* (coll) prometido, prometida
intense [ɪnˈtɛns] *adj* intenso

intensi•fy [ɪn'tɛnsɪ,faɪ] v (pret & pp -**fied**) tr intensificar, intensar; (phot) reforzar ‖ intr intensificarse, intensarse

intensi•ty [ɪn'tɛnsɪti] s (pl -**ties**) intensidad

intensive [ɪn'tɛnsɪv] adj intensivo

intent [ɪn'tɛnt] adj atento; resuelto; intenso; **intent on** resuelto a ‖ s (purpose) intento; (meaning) acepción, sentido; **to all intents and purposes** en realidad de verdad

intention [ɪn'tɛnʃən] s intención

intentional [ɪn'tɛnʃənəl] adj intencional, deliberado

in•ter [ɪn'tʌr] v (pret & pp -**terred**; ger -**terring**) tr enterrar

interact ['ɪntər,ækt] s (theat) entreacto ‖ [,ɪntər'ækt] intr obrar recíprocamente

interaction [,ɪntər'ækʃən] s interacción

inter-American [,ɪntərə'mɛrɪkən] adj interamericano

inter•breed [,ɪntər'brid] v (pret & pp -**bred** ['brɛd]) tr entrecruzar ‖ intr entrecruzarse

intercalate [ɪn'tʌrkə,let] tr intercalar

intercede [,ɪntər'sid] intr interceder

intercept [,ɪntər'sɛpt] tr interceptar

interceptor [,ɪntər'sɛptər] s interceptor m

interchange ['ɪntər,tʃendʒ] s intercambio; (on a highway) correspondencia ‖ [,ɪntər-'tʃendʒ] tr intercambiar ‖ intr intercambiarse

intercollegiate [,ɪntərkə'lidʒɪ•ɪt] adj interescolar

intercom ['ɪntər,kɑm] s interfono

intercourse ['ɪntər,kors] s comunicación, trato; (interchange of products, ideas, etc.) intercambio; (copulation) cópula, comercio; **to have intercourse** juntarse

intercross [,ɪntər'krɔs] o [,ɪntər'krɑs] tr entrecruzar ‖ intr entrecruzarse

interdict ['ɪntər,dɪkt] s entredicho ‖ [,ɪntər'dɪkt] tr interdecir

interest ['ɪntərɪst] s interés m; **the interests** las grandes empresas, el grupo influyente; **to put out at interest** poner a interés ‖ tr interesar

interested ['ɪntə,rɛstɪd] adj interesado

interesting ['ɪntə,rɛstɪŋ] adj interesante

interface ['ɪntər,fes] s (computer) entrecara

interfere [,ɪntər'fɪr] intr inmiscuirse, injerirse, interferir; (sport) parar una jugada; **to interfere with** dificultar, impedir, interferir

interference [,ɪntər'fɪrəns] s injerencia, interferencia

interim ['ɪntərɪm] adj interino ‖ s intermedio, intervalo; **in the interim** entretanto

interior [ɪn'tɪrɪ•ər] adj & s interior m

interject [,ɪntər'dʒɛkt] tr interponer ‖ intr interponerse

interjection [,ɪntər'dʒekʃən] s interposición; exclamación; (gram) interjección

interlard [,ɪntər'lɑrd] tr interpolar; mechar (la carne)

interline [,ɪntər'laɪn] tr interlinear; entretelar (una prenda de vestir)

interlining ['ɪntər,laɪnɪŋ] s (of a garment) entretela

interlink [,ɪntər'lɪŋk] tr eslabonar

interlock [,ɪntər'lɑk] tr trabar ‖ intr trabarse

interlope [,ɪntər'lop] intr entremeterse; traficar sin derecho

interloper [,ɪntər'lopər] s intruso

interlude ['ɪntər,lud] s intervalo; (mus) interludio; (theat) intermedio

intermarriage [,ɪntər'mærɪdʒ] s casamiento entre parientes; casamiento entre personas de distintas razas, castas, etc.

intermediar•y [,ɪntər'midɪ,ɛri] adj intermediario ‖ s (pl -**ies**) intermediario

intermediate [,ɪntər'midɪ•ɪt] adj intermedio

in•ter•me'di•ate-range' missile s cohete m de alcance medio

interment [ɪn'tʌrmənt] s entierro

intermezzo [,ɪntər'mɛtso] o [,ɪntərmɛdzo] s (pl -**zos** o -**zi** [tsi] o [dzi]) (mus) intermedio, intermezzo

intermingle [,ɪntər'mɪŋɡəl] tr entremezclar ‖ intr entremezclarse

intermittent [,ɪntər'mɪtənt] adj intermitente

intermix [,ɪntər'mɪks] tr entremezclar ‖ intr entremezclarse

intern ['ɪntʌrn] s interno de hospital ‖ [ɪn'tʌrn] tr internar, recluir

internal [ɪn'tʌrnəl] adj interno

inter'nal-combus'tion engine s motor m de explosión

internal revenue s rentas internas

international [,ɪntər'næʃənəl] adj internacional

international date line s línea internacional de cambio de fecha

internationalize [,ɪntər'næʃənə,laɪz] tr internacionalizar

internecine [,ɪntər'nisɪn] adj sanguinario

internee [,ɪntʌr'ni] s (mil) internado

internist [ɪn'tʌrnɪst] s internista mf

internment [ɪn'tʌrnmənt] s internamiento

internship ['ɪntʌrn,ʃɪp] s residencia de un médico en un hospital

interpellate [,ɪntər'pɛlet] o [ɪn'tʌrpɪ,let] tr interpelar

interplay ['ɪntər,ple] s interacción

interpolate [ɪn'tʌrpə,let] tr interpolar

interpose [,ɪntər'poz] tr interponer

interpret [ɪn'tʌrprɪt] tr interpretar

interpreter [ɪn'tʌrprɪtər] s intérprete mf; (fig) exponente mf

interrogate [ɪn'tɛrə,get] tr & intr interrogar

interrogation [ɪn,tɛrə'geʃən] s interrogación

interrogation mark o **point** s signo de interrogación

interrupt [,ɪntə'rʌpt] tr interrumpir

interscholastic [,ɪntərskə'læstɪk] adj interescolar

intersection [,ɪntər'sɛkʃən] s (of streets, roads, etc.) cruce m, bocacalle f; cruza (SAm); (geom) intersección

intersperse [,ɪntər'spʌrs] tr entremezclar, esparcir

interstice [ɪn'tʌrstɪs] s intersticio

intertwine [,ɪntər'twaɪn] tr entrelazar ‖ intr entrelazarse

interval ['ɪntərvəl] s intervalo; **at intervals** (now and then) de vez en cuando; (here and there) de trecho en trecho

intervene [,ɪntər'vin] *intr* intervenir
intervening [,ɪntər'vinɪŋ] *adj* intermedio
intervention [,ɪntər'vɛnʃən] *s* intervención
interview ['ɪntər,vju] *s* entrevista, interview *m* ‖ *tr* entrevistarse con
inter·weave [,ɪntər'wiv] *v* (*pret* **-wove** ['wov] o **-weaved**; *pp* **-wove, woven** o **weaved**) *tr* entretejer
intestate [ɪn'tɛstet] *adj* & *s* intestado
intestine [ɪn'tɛstɪn] *s* intestino
inthrall [ɪn'θrɔl] *tr* cautivar, encantar; esclavizar, sojuzgar
inthrone [ɪn'θron] *tr* entronizar
intima·cy ['ɪntɪməsi] *s* (*pl* **-cies**) intimidad
intimate ['ɪntɪmɪt] *adj* íntimo ‖ *s* amigo íntimo ‖ ['ɪntɪ,met] *tr* insinuar, intimar
intimation [,ɪntɪ'meʃən] *s* insinuación
intimidate [ɪn'tɪmɪ,det] *tr* intimidar
intitle [ɪn'taɪtəl] *tr* dar derecho a; (*to give a name to; to honor with a title*) intitular
into ['ɪntu] o ['ɪntʊ] *prep* en; hacia; hacia el interior de
intolerant [ɪn'talərənt] *adj* & *s* intolerante *mf*
intomb [ɪn'tum] *tr* sepultar
intombment [ɪn'tummənt] *s* sepultura
intonation [,ɪnto'neʃən] *s* entonación
intone [ɪn'ton] *tr* entonar
intoxicant [ɪn'taksɪkənt] *s* bebida alcohólica
intoxicate [ɪn'taksɪ,ket] *tr* embriagar, emborrachar; (*to exhilarate*) alegrar, excitar; (*to poison*) envenenar, intoxicar
intoxication [ɪn,taksɪ'keʃən] *s* embriaguez *f*; alegría, excitación; (*poisoning*) envenenamiento, intoxicación
intractable [ɪn'træktəbəl] *adj* intratable
intransigent [ɪn'trænsɪdʒənt] *adj* & *s* intransigente *mf*
intransitive [ɪn'trænsɪtɪv] *adj* intransitivo
intrench [ɪn'trɛntʃ] *tr* atrincherar ‖ *intr*—**to intrench on** o **upon** infringir, violar
intrepid [ɪn'trɛpɪd] *adj* intrépido
intrepidity [,ɪntrɪ'pɪdɪti] *s* intrepidez *f*
intricate ['ɪntrɪkɪt] *adj* intrincado
intrigue [ɪn'trig] *s* intriga; intriga amorosa, enredo amoroso ‖ *tr* (*to arouse the curiosity of*) intrigar ‖ *intr* intrigar; tener intrigas amorosas
intrinsic(al) [ɪn'trɪnsɪk(əl)] *adj* intrínseco
introd. *abbr* **introduction**
introduce [,ɪntrə'djus] *tr* introducir; (*to make acquainted*) presentar
introduction [,ɪntrə'dʌkʃən] *s* introducción; (*of one person to another or others*) presentación
introductory offer [,ɪntrə'dʌktəri] *s* ofrecimiento de presentación, oferta preliminar
introit ['ɪntro·ɪt] *s* (eccl) introito
introspective [,ɪntrə'spɛktɪv] *adj* introspectivo
introvert ['ɪntrə,vʌrt] *s* introvertido
intrude [ɪn'trud] *intr* injerirse, entremeterse
intruder [ɪn'trudər] *s* intruso, entremetido
intrusive [ɪn'trusɪv] *adj* intruso
intrust [ɪn'trʌst] *tr* confiar
intuition [,ɪntju'ɪʃən] *s* intuición
inundate ['ɪnən,det] *tr* inundar
inundation [,ɪnən'deʃən] *s* inundación

inure [ɪn'jʊr] *tr* acostumbrar, endurecer, aguerrir ‖ *intr* ponerse en efecto; **to inure to** redundar en
inv. *abbr* **inventor, invoice**
invade [ɪn'ved] *tr* invadir
invader [ɪn'vedər] *s* invasor *m*
invalid [ɪn'vælɪd] *adj* inválido (*nulo, de ningún valor*) ‖ ['ɪnvəlɪd] *adj* inválido (*por viejo o por enfermo*) ‖ ['ɪnvəlɪd] *s* inválido
invalidate [ɪn'vælɪ,det] *tr* invalidar
invalidity [,ɪnvə'lɪdɪti] *s* invalidez *f*
invaluable [ɪn'vælju·əbəl] *adj* inestimable, inapreciable
invariable [ɪn'vɛrɪ·əbəl] *adj* invariable
invasion [ɪn'veʒən] *s* invasión
invective [ɪn'vɛktɪv] *s* invectiva
inveigh [ɪn've] *intr*—**to inveigh against** lanzar invectivas contra
inveigle [ɪn'vegəl] o [ɪn'vigəl] *tr* engatusar
invent [ɪn'vɛnt] *tr* inventar
invention [ɪn'vɛnʃən] *s* invención, invento
inventive [ɪn'vɛntɪv] *adj* inventivo
inventiveness [ɪn'vɛntɪvnɪs] *s* inventiva
inventor [ɪn'vɛntər] *s* inventor *m*
invento·ry ['ɪnvən,tori] *s* (*pl* **-ries**) inventario; stock *m* ‖ *v* (*pret* & *pp* **-ried**) *tr* inventariar
inverse [ɪn'vʌrs] *adj* inverso
inversion [ɪn'vʌrʒən] o [ɪn'vʌrʃən] *s* inversión
invert ['ɪnvʌrt] *s* invertido ‖ [ɪn'vʌrt] *tr* invertir
invertebrate [ɪn'vʌrtɪ,bret] o [ɪn'vʌrtɪbrɪt] *adj* & *s* invertebrado
inverted exclamation point *s* principio de admiración
inverted question mark *s* principio de interrogación
invest [ɪn'vɛst] *tr* (*to vest, to install*) investir; invertir (*dinero*); (*to besiege*) cercar, sitiar; (*to surround, envelop*) cubrir, envolver
investigate [ɪn'vɛstɪ,get] *tr* investigar
investigation [ɪn,vɛstɪ·geʃən] *s* investigación
investment [ɪn'vɛstmənt] *s* (*of money*) inversión; (*with an office or dignity*) investidura; (*siege*) cerco, sitio
investment capital *s* capital *m* de inversión
investor [ɪn'vɛstər] *s* inversionista *mf*; inversor *m*
inveterate [ɪn'vɛtərɪt] *adj* inveterado, empedernido
invidious [ɪn'vɪdɪ·əs] *adj* irritante, odioso, injusto
invigorate [ɪn'vɪgə,ret] *tr* vigorizar
invigorating [ɪn'vɪgə,retɪŋ] *adj* vigorizador, vigorizante
invincible [ɪn'vɪnsɪbəl] *adj* invencible
invisible [ɪn'vɪzɪbəl] *adj* invisible
invisible ink *s* tinta simpática
invitation [,ɪnvɪ'teʃən] *s* invitación, convite *m*
invite [ɪn'vaɪt] *tr* invitar, convidar
inviting [ɪn'vaɪtɪŋ] *adj* atractivo, seductor; (*e.g., food*) apetitoso
invoice ['ɪnvɔɪs] *s* factura; **as per invoice** según factura ‖ *tr* facturar

in
in

invoke [ɪn'vok] *tr* invocar; evocar, conjurar (*p.ej., los demonios*)

involuntary [ɪn'vɑlən,tɛri] *adj* involuntario

involution [,ɪnvə'luʃən] *s* (math) elevación a potencias, potenciación

involve [ɪn'vɑlv] *tr* envolver, comprometer

invulnerable [ɪn'vʌlnərəbəl] *adj* invulnerable

inward ['ɪnwərd] *adj* interior ‖ *adv* interiormente, hacia dentro

iodide ['aɪə,daɪd] *s* yoduro

iodine ['aɪə,dɪn] *s* yodo ‖ ['aɪə,daɪn] *s* tintura de yodo

ion ['aɪən] o ['aɪ•ɑn] *s* ion *m*

ionize ['aɪə,naɪz] *tr* ionizar

ionosphere [aɪ'ɑnə,sfɪr] *s* ionosfera

IOU ['aɪ,o'ju] *s* (letterword) pagaré *m*

I.Q. ['aɪ'kju] *abbr & s* (letterword) **intelligence quotient**

Iran [ɪ'rɑn] o [aɪ'ræn] *s* el Irán

Iranian [ɪ'reni•ən] o [aɪ'reni•ən] *adj & s* iranés *m* o iranio

Iraq [ɪ'rɑk] *s* el Irak

Ira•qi [ɪ'rɑki] *adj* iraqués o iraquiano ‖ *s* (*pl* **-qis**) iraqués *m* o iraquiano

irate ['aɪret] o [aɪ'ret] *adj* airado

ire [aɪr] *s* ira, cólera

Ireland ['aɪrlənd] *s* Irlanda

iris ['aɪrɪs] *s* (*of the eye*) iris *m*; (*rainbow*) iris, arco iris; (bot) lirio

Irish ['aɪrɪʃ] *adj* irlandés ‖ *s* (*language*) irlandés *m*; whisky *m* de Irlanda; **the Irish** los irlandeses

Irish•man ['aɪrɪʃmən] *s* (*pl* **-men** [mən]) irlandés *m*

Irish stew *s* guisado de carne con patatas y cebollas

I'rish•wom'an *s* (*pl* **-wom'en**) irlandesa

irk [ʌrk] *tr* fastidiar, molestar

irksome ['ʌrksəm] *adj* fastidioso, molesto

iron ['aɪ•ərn] *adj* férreo ‖ *s* hierro; (*implement used to press or smooth clothes*) plancha; **irons** (*fetters*) hierros, grilletes *mpl*; **strike while the iron is hot** batir a hierro caliente batir de repente ‖ *tr* planchar (*la ropa*); **to iron out** allanar (*una dificultad*)

i'ron-bound' *adj* zunchado con hierro; (*unyielding*) férreo, duro, inflexible; (*rockbound*) escabroso, rocoso

ironclad ['aɪ•ərn'klæd] *adj* acorazado, blindado; inflexible, exigente

iron curtain *s* (fig) telón *m* de hierro, cortina de hierro

iron digestion *s* estómago de avestruz

ironhanded ['aɪ•ərn,hændɪd] *adj* severo; rigoroso; de mano férrea

iron horse *s* (coll) locomotora

ironic(al) [aɪ'rɑnɪk(əl)] *adj* irónico

ironing ['aɪ•ərnɪŋ] *s* planchado; ropa planchada; ropa por planchar

ironing board *s* tabla de planchar

iron lung *s* pulmón *m* de acero o de hierro

i'ron•ware' *s* ferretería

iron will *s* voluntad de hierro

i'ron•work' *s* herraje *m*; **ironworks** ferrería, herrería

i'ron•work'er *s* herrero de grueso; (*metalworker*) cerrajero

iro•ny ['aɪrəni] *s* (*pl* **-nies**) ironía

irradiate [ɪ'redi,et] *tr* irradiar; (med) someter a radiación ‖ *intr* irradiar

irrational ['ɪræʃənəl] *adj* irracional

irrecoverable [,ɪrɪ'kʌvərəbəl] *adj* incobrable, irrecuperable

irredeemable [,ɪrɪ'diməbəl] *adj* irredimible

irrefutable [,ɪrɪ'fjutəbəl] o [ɪ'rɛfjutəbəl] *adj* irrebatible

irregular [ɪ'rɛgələr] *adj* irregular ‖ *s* (mil) irregular *m*

irrelevance [ɪ'rɛləvəns] *s* impertinencia, inaplicabilidad

irrelevant [ɪ'rɛləvənt] *adj* impertinente, inaplicable; irrelevante

irreligious [,ɪrɪ'lɪdʒəs] *adj* irreligioso

irremediable [,ɪrɪ'midɪ•əbəl] *adj* irremediable

irremovable [,ɪrɪ'muvəbəl] *adj* inamovible

irreparable [ɪ'rɛpərəbəl] *adj* irreparable

irreplaceable [,ɪrɪ'plesəbəl] *adj* insubstituíble, irreemplazable

irrepressible [,ɪrɪ'prɛsɪbəl] *adj* irreprimible, incontenible

irreproachable [,ɪrɪ'protʃəbəl] *adj* irreprochable

irresistible [,ɪrɪ'zɪstɪbəl] *adj* irresistible

irrespective [,ɪrɪ'spɛktɪv] *adj* — **irrespective of** sin hacer caso de, independiente de

irresponsible [,ɪrɪ'spɑnsɪbəl] *adj* irresponsable

irretrievable [,ɪrɪ'trivəbəl] *adj* irrecuperable

irreverent [ɪ'rɛvərənt] *adj* irreverente

irrevocable [ɪ'rɛvəkəbəl] *adj* irrevocable

irrigate ['ɪrɪ,get] *tr* irrigar

irrigation [,ɪrɪ'geʃən] *s* irrigación

irritant ['ɪrɪtənt] *adj & s* irritante *m*

irritate ['ɪrɪ,tet] *tr* irritar

irruption [ɪ'rʌpʃən] *s* irrupción

is. *abbr* island

isinglass ['aɪzɪŋ,glæs] o ['aɪzɪŋ,glɑs] *s* (*form of gelatine*) cola de pescado, colapez *f*; mica

isl. *abbr* island

Islam ['ɪsləm] o [ɪs'lɑm] *s* el Islam

island ['aɪlənd] *adj* isleño ‖ *s* isla

islander ['aɪləndər] *s* isleño

isle [aɪl] *s* isleta

isolate ['aɪsə,let] *tr* aislar

isolated ['aɪsə,letɪd] *adj* aislado; insulado; alejado

isolation [,aɪsə'leʃən] *s* aislamiento

isolationist [,aɪsə'leʃənɪst] *s* aislacionista *mf*

isometric [,aɪsə'mɛtrɪk] *adj* isométrico

isometrics *s* isométrica

isosceles [aɪ'sɑsə,liz] *adj* isósceles

isotope ['aɪsə,top] *s* isótopo

Israe•li [ɪz'reli] *adj* israelí ‖ *s* (*pl* **-lis** [liz]) israelí *mf*

Israelite ['ɪzrɪ•ə,laɪt] *adj & s* israelita *mf*

issuance ['ɪʃu•əns] *s* emisión, expedición

issue ['ɪʃu] *s* (*outgoing; outlet*) salida; (*result*) consecuencia, resultado; (*offspring*) descendencia, sucesión; (*of a magazine*) edición, impresión, tirada, número; (*e.g.,*

of a bond) emisión; (*yield, profit*) beneficios, producto; punto en disputa; (*distribu-*
tion) repartida; (pathol) flujo; **at issue** en
disputa; **to face the issue** afrontar la situación; **to force the issue** forzar la solución;
to take issue with llevar la contraria a ‖ *tr*
publicar, dar a luz (*un nuevo libro, una*
revista, etc.); emitir, expedir (*títulos, obli-*
gaciones, etc.); distribuir (*ropa, alimento*)
‖ *intr* salir; **to issue from** provenir de
isthmus [ˈɪsməs] *s* istmo
it [ɪt] *pron pers* (aplícase a cosas inanimadas,
a niños de teta, a animales cuyo sexo no se
conoce; y muchas veces no se traduce) él,
ella; lo, la; **it is I** soy yo; **it is snowing**
nieva; **it is three o'clock** son las tres
ital. *abbr* **italics**
Ital. *abbr* **Italian, Italy**
Italian [ɪˈtæljən] *adj & s* italiano
italic [ɪˈtælɪk] *adj* (typ) itálico ‖ **italics** *s*
(typ) itálica, bastardilla ‖ **Italic** *adj* itálico
italicize [ɪˈtælɪˌsaɪz] *tr* imprimir en bastardilla; subrayar
Italy [ˈɪtəli] *s* Italia
itch [ɪtʃ] *s* comezón *f;* (pathol) sarna; (*eager-*

ness) (fig) comezón, prurito ‖ *tr* dar comezón a ‖ *intr* picar; **to itch to** tener prurito
por
itch•y [ˈɪtʃi] *adj* (*comp* **-ier;** *super* **-iest**)
picante, hormigoso; (pathol) sarnoso
item [ˈaɪtəm] *s* artículo; noticia, suelto; (*in an*
account) partida
itemization [ˌaɪtəmaɪˈzeʃən] *s* rubricación
itemize [ˈaɪtəˌmaɪz] *tr* particularizar, especificar, pormenorizar
itinerant [aɪˈtɪnərənt] o [ɪˈtɪnərənt] *adj* ambulante, errante ‖ *s* viandante *mf*
itinerar•y [aɪˈtɪnəˌrɛri] o [ɪˈtɪnəˌrɛri] *adj*
itinerario ‖ *s* (*pl* **-ies**) itinerario
its [ɪts] *adj poss* su ‖ *pron poss* el suyo; suyo
itself [ɪtˈsɛlf] *pron pers* mismo; sí, sí mismo;
se
ivied [ˈaɪvid] *adj* cubierto de hiedra
ivo•ry [ˈaɪvəri] *adj* marfileño ‖ *s* (*pl* **-ries**)
marfil *m;* **ivories** (slang) teclas del piano;
(slang) bolas de billar; (*dice*) (slang) dados;
(slang) dientes *mpl*
ivory tower *s* (fig) torre *f* de marfil; (fig)
inocencia
ivy [ˈaɪvi] *s* (*pl* **-ivies**) hiedra

J

J. j [dʒe] décima letra del alfabeto inglés
J. *abbr* **Judge, Justice**
jab [dʒæb] *s* hurgonazo; (*prick*) pinchazo;
(*with elbow*) codazo ‖ *v* (*pret & pp* **jabbed;**
ger **jabbing**) *tr* hurgonear; dar un codazo a
‖ *intr* hurgonear
jabber [ˈdʒæbər] *s* chapurreo ‖ *tr & intr*
chapurrear
jabot [dʒæˈbo] o [ˈdʒæbo] *s* chorrera
jack [dʒæk] *s* (*for lifting heavy objects*) gato,
cric *m;* (*fellow*) mozo, sujeto, (*jackass*)
asno, burro; (*in card games*) sota, valet *m;*
(*small ball for bowling*) boliche *m;* (*jack-*
stone) cantillo; (*device for turning a spit*)
torno de asador; (*figure which strikes a*
clock bell) jaquemar *m;* (*to remove a boot*)
sacabotas *m;* marinero; (*flag at the bow*)
(naut) yac *m;* (rad & telv) jack *m;* (elec)
caja de enchufe; (slang) dinero; **every man**
Jack cada hijo de vecino; **jacks** cantillos,
juego de los cantillos ‖ *tr* — **to jack up**
alzar con el gato; (coll) subir (*sueldos,*
precios, etc.); (coll) recordar su obligación
a
jackal [ˈdʒækɔl] *s* chacal *m*
jackanapes [ˈdʒækəˌneps] *s* mequetrefe *m*
jack′ass′ *s* asno, burro
jack′daw′ *s* corneja
jacket [ˈdʒækɪt] *s* chaqueta; (*folded paper*)
cubierta, envoltura; (*paper cover of a book*)
sobrecubierta; (*metal caing*) camisa
jack′ham′mer *s* martillo perforador
jack′-in-the-box′ *s* caja de sorpresa, jugete-

sorpresa *m*, muñeco en una caja de resorte
jack′knife′ *s* (*pl* **-knives′**) navaja de bolsillo;
(*fancy dive*) salto de carpa
jack of all trades *s* hombre que hace toda
clase de oficios dije *m*
jack-o'-lantern [ˈdʒækəˌlæntərn] *s* fuego fatuo; linterna hecha con una calabaza cortado de modo que remede una cabeza
humana
jack pot *s*—**to hit the jack pot** (slang)
ponerse las botas
jack rabbit *s* liebre grande norteamericana
jack′screw′ *s* cric *m* o gato de tornillo
jack′stone′ *s* cantillo; **jackstones** cantillos,
juego de los cantillos
jack′-tar′ *s* (coll) marinero
jade [dʒed] *adj* verdoso como el jade ‖ *s*
(*ornamental stone*) jade *m;* verde *m* de
jade; (*worn-out horse*) jamelgo; picarona,
mujerzuela ‖ *tr* cansar, ahitar, saciar
jaded [ˈdʒedɪd] *adj* ahito, saciado
jag [dʒæg] *s* diente *m*, púa; **to have a jag on**
(slang) estar borracho
jagged [ˈdʒægɪd] *adj* dentado, mellado; ras-
gado en sietes
jaguar [ˈdʒægwɑr] *s* jaguar *m*
jail [dʒel] *s* cárcel *f;* **to break jail** escaparse
de la cárcel ‖ *tr* encarcelar
jail′bird′ *s* (coll) preso, encarcelado; (coll)
infractor *m* habitual
jail′break′ *s* escapatoria de la cárcel
jail delivery *s* evasión de la cárcel
jailer [ˈdʒelər] *s* carcelero

jalop•y [dʒə'lɑpi] s (pl -ies) automóvil viejo y ruinoso

jam [dʒæm] s apiñadura, apretura; (e.g., in traffic) embotellamiento, bloqueo; (preserve) compota, conserva; (difficult situation) (coll) aprieto, apuros ‖ v (pret & pp jammed; ger jamming) tr apiñar, apretujar; machucarse (p.ej., un dedo); (rad) perturbar, sabotear; **to jam on the brakes** frenar de golpe

Jamaican [dʒə'mekən] adj & s jamaicano; jamaiquino (Am)

jamb [dʒæm] s jamba

jamboree [,dʒæmbɔ'ri] s (coll) francachela, holgorio; reunión de niños exploradores

jamming ['dʒæmɪŋ] s radioperturbación

jam nut s contratuerca

jam-packed ['dʒæm'pækt] adj (coll) apiñado, apretujado, atestado

jam session s reunión de músicos de jazz para tocar improvisaciones

jangle ['dʒæŋgəl] s cencerreo; altercado, riña ‖ tr hacer sonar con ruido discordante ‖ intr cencerrear; reñir

janitor ['dʒænɪtər] s portero, conserje m

janitress ['dʒænɪtrɪs] s portera

January ['dʒænju,ɛri] s enero

Ja•pan [dʒə'pæn] s laca japonesa; obra japonesa laqueada; aceite m secante japonés ‖ v (pret & pp -panned; ger -panning) tr barnizar, charolar, laquear con laca japonesa ‖ **Japan** s el Japón

Japa•nese [,dʒæpə'niz] adj japonés ‖ s (pl -nese) japonés m

Japanese beetle s escarabajo japonés

Japanese lantern s farolillo veneciano

Japanese persimmon s caqui m

jar [dʒɑr] s tarro; (e.g., of olives) frasco; (of a storage battery) recipiente m; (jolt) sacudida; ruido desapacible; sorpresa desagradable; **on the jar** (said of a door) entreabierto, entornado ‖ v (pret & pp jarred; ger jarring) tr sacudir; chocar; (with a noise) traquetear ‖ intr sacudirse; traquetear; disputar; **to jar on** irritar

jardiniere [,dʒɑrdɪ'nɪr] s (stand) jardinera; (pot, bowl) florero

jargon ['dʒɑrgən] s jerga, jerigonza

jasmine ['dʒæsmɪn] s jazmín m

jasper ['dʒæspər] s jaspe m

jaundice ['dʒɔndɪs] o ['dʒɑndɪs] s ictericia; (fig) envidia, celos, negro humor

jaundiced ['dʒɔndɪst] o ['dʒɑndɪst] adj ictericiado; (fig) avinagrado

jaunt [dʒɔnt] o [dʒɑnt] s caminata, excursión, paseo

jaun•ty ['dʒɔnti] o ['dʒɑnti] adj (comp -tier; super -tiest) airoso, gallardo, vivo; elegante, de buen gusto

Java•nese [,dʒævə'niz] adj javanés ‖ s (pl -nese) javanés m

javelin ['dʒævlɪn] o ['dʒævəlɪn] s jabalina

jaw [dʒɔ] s mandíbula, quijada; **into the jaws of death** a las garras de la muerte; **jaws** boca, garganta ‖ tr (slang) regañar ‖ intr (slang) regañar; (slang) chacharear, chismear

jaw'bone' s mandíbula, quijada

jaw'break'er s (word) (coll) trabalenguas m; (candy) (coll) hinchabocas m; (mach) trituradora de quijadas

jay [dʒe] s (orn) arrendajo; (coll) tonto, necio

jay'walk' intr (coll) cruzar la calle descuidadamente

jay'walk'er s (coll) peatón descuidado

jazz [dʒæz] s (mus) jazz m; (coll) animación, viveza ‖ tr—**to jazz up** (coll) animar, dar viveza a

jazz band s orquesta de jazz

J.C. abbr **Jesus Christ, Julius Caesar**

jct. abbr **junction**

jealous ['dʒɛləs] adj celoso; envidioso; (watchful in keeping or guarding something) solícito, vigilante

jealous•y ['dʒɛləsi] s (pl -ies) celosía, celos; envidia; solicitud, vigilancia

jean [dʒin] s dril m; **jeans** pantalones mpl de dril

Jeanne d'Arc [,ʒɑn'dɑrk] s Juana de Arco

jeep [dʒip] s jip m, pequeño automóvil de propulsión total

jeer [dʒɪr] s befa, mofa, vaya ‖ tr befar ‖ intr mofarse; **to jeer at** befar, mofarse de

jelab [dʒə'lɑb] s chilaba

jell [dʒɛl] s jalea ‖ intr (to become jellylike) cuajarse; (to take hold, catch on) (fig) cuajar

jel•ly ['dʒɛli] s (pl -lies) jalea ‖ v (pret & pp) tr convertir en jalea ‖ intr convertirse en jalea

jel'ly•bean' s frutilla

jel'ly•fish' s aguamala, medusa; (weak person) (coll) calzonazos m

jeopardize ['dʒɛpər,daɪz] tr arriesgar, exponer, poner en peligro

jeopardy ['dʒɛpərdi] s riesgo, peligro

jeremiad [,dʒɛrɪ'maɪæd] s jeremiada

Jericho ['dʒɛrɪ,ko] s Jericó

jerk [dʒʌrk] s arranque m, estirón m, tirón m; tic m, espasmo muscular; **by jerks** a sacudidas ‖ tr mover de un tirón; arrojar de un tirón; atasajar (carne) ‖ intr avanzar a tirones

jerked beef s tasajo

jerkin ['dʒʌrkɪn] s jubón m, justillo

jerk'wa'ter train s (coll) tren de ferrocarril económico

jerk•y ['dʒʌrki] adj (comp -ier; super -iest) (road; style) desigual; que va dando tumbos, que anda a tirones

jersey ['dʒʌrzi] s jersey m, chaqueta de punto

Jerusalem [dʒɪ'rusələm] s Jerusalén

jest [dʒɛst] s broma, chanza, chiste m; cosa de risa; **in jest** en broma ‖ intr bromear

jester ['dʒɛstər] s bromista mf, burlón m; (professional fool of medieval rulers) bufón m

Jesuit ['dʒɛʒʊ•ɪt] o ['dʒɛzj,ɪt] adj & s jesuíta m

Jesuitic(al) [,dʒɛʒʊ'ɪtɪk(əl)] o [,dʒɛzjʊ'ɪtɪk(əl)] adj jesuítico

Jesus ['dʒizəs] s Jesús m

Jesus Christ s Jesucristo

jet [dʒɛt] *adj* de azabache; azabachado ‖ *s* (*of a fountain*) surtidor *m;* (*of gas*) mechero; (*stream shooting forth from nozzle, etc.*) chorro; avión *m* a reacción, avión de chorro; (*hard black mineral; lustrous black*) azabache *m* ‖ *v* (*pret & pp* **jetted;** *ger* **jetting**) *tr* arrojar en chorro ‖ *intr* chorrear, salir en chorro; volar en avión de chorro

jet age *s* era de los aviones de chorro

jet'-black' *adj* azabachado

jet bomber *s* bombardero de reacción a chorro

jet coal *s* carbón *m* de bujía, carbón de llama larga

jet engine *s* motor *m* a chorro, motor de reacción

jet fighter *s* caza *m* de reacción, cazarreactor *m*

jet'lin'er *s* avión *m* de travesía con propulsión a chorro

jet plane *s* avión *m* de chorro

jet propulsion *s* propulsión a chorro, propulsión de escape

jetsam [ˈdʒɛtsəm] *s* (naut) echazón *f;* cosas desechadas

jet set *s* gente acomodada que viajan mucho por avión

jet stream *s* escape *m* de un motor cohete; (meteor) chorros de viento (*que soplan de oeste a este a la altura de 10 kilómetros*)

jettison [ˈdʒɛtɪsən] *s* (naut) echazón *f* ‖ *tr* (naut) echar al mar; desechar, rechazar

jettison gear *s* (aer) lanzador *m*

jet•ty [ˈdʒɛti] *s* (*pl* **-ties**) (*structure projecting into sea to protect harbor*) excollera, malecón *m;* (*wharf*) muelle *m,* desembarcadero

Jew [dʒu] *s* judío

jewel [ˈdʒuˑəl] *s* piedra preciosa; (*valuable personal ornament*) alhaja; joya; (*of a watch*) rubí *m;* (*article of costume jewelry*) joya de imitación; (*highly prized person or thing*) alhaja, joya

jewel case *s* guardajoyas *m,* estuche *m,* joyero

jeweler o **jeweller** [ˈdʒuˑələr] *s* joyero; relojero

jewelry [ˈdʒuˑəlri] *s* joyería, joyas

jewelry shop *s* joyería; relojería

Jewess [ˈdʒuˑɪs] *s* judía

jew'fish' *s* mero

Jewish [ˈdʒuˑɪʃ] *adj* judío

Jew•ry [ˈdʒuˑri] *s* (*pl* **-ries**) judería

jews'-harp o **jew's-harp** [ˈdjʊz,hɑrp] *s* birimbao

jib [dʒɪb] *s* (*of a crane*) aguilón *m,* pescante *m;* (naut) foque *m*

jib boom *s* (naut) botalón *m* de foque

jibe [dʒaɪb] *s* remoque *m,* mofa ‖ *intr* mofarse; (coll) concordar (*dos cosas*); **to jibe at** mofarse de

jif•fy [ˈdʒɪfi] *s* (*pl* **-fies**)—**in a jiffy** (coll) en un santiamén

jig [dʒɪg] *s* (*dance and music*) giga; **the jig is up** (slang) ya se acabó todo, estamos perdidos

jigger [ˈdʒɪgər] *s* (*for fishing*) anzuelo de cuchara; (*for separating ore*) criba de vaivén; (*flea*) nigua; (*gadget*) cosilla, chisme *m,* dispositivo; vasito para medir el licor de un coctel (*onza y media*)

jiggle [ˈdʒɪgəl] *s* zangoloteo ‖ *tr* zangolotear ‖ *intr* zangolotearse

jig saw *s* sierra de vaivén

jig'saw' puzzle *s* rompecabezas *m* (*figura que ha sido cortada caprichosamente en trozos menudos y que hay que recomponer*)

jilt [dʒɪlt] *tr* dar calabazas a (*un novio*)

jim•my [ˈdʒɪmi] *s* (*pl* **-mies**) palanqueta ‖ *v* (*pret & pp* **-mied**) *tr* forzar con palanqueta; **to jimmy open** abrir con palanqueta

jingle [ˈdʒɪŋgəl] *s* (*small bell*) cascabel *m;* (*of tambourine*) sonaja; (*sound*) cascabeleo; rima infantil; (rad) anuncio rimado y cantado ‖ *tr* hacer sonar ‖ *intr* cascabelear

jin•go [ˈdʒɪŋgo] *adj* jingoísta ‖ *s* (*pl* **-goes**) jingoísta *mf;* **by jingo!** (coll) ¡caramba!

jingoism [ˈdʒɪŋgo,ɪzəm] *s* jingoísmo

jinx [dʒɪŋks] *s* gafe *m* ‖ *tr* (coll) traer mala suerte a

jitters [ˈdʒɪtərz] *spl* (coll) inquietud, nerviosidad; **to give the jitters to** (coll) poner nervioso; **to have the jitters** (coll) ponerse nervioso

jittery [ˈdʒɪtəri] *adj* (coll) nervioso

Joan of Arc [ˈdʒon əv ˈɑrk] *s* Juana de Arco

job [dʒab] *s* (*piece of work*) trabajo; (*task, chore*) quehacer *m,* tarea; (*work done by contract*) destajo; (*employment*) empleo, oficio; (coll) robo; **by the job** a destajo; **on the job** trabajando de aprendiz; (slang) vigilante, atento a sus obligaciones; **to be out of a job** estar desocupado, estar sin trabajo; **to lie down on the job** (slang) echarse en el surco, estirar la pierna

job analysis *s* análisis *m* ocupacional

jobber [ˈdʒabər] *s* comerciante medianero; (*pieceworker*) destajero; (*dishonest official*) agiotista *m*

job'hold'er *s* empleado; (*in the government*) burócrata *mf*

jobless [ˈdʒablɪs] *adj* desocupado, sin empleo

job lot *s* saldo de mercancías

job market *s* oportunidades *fpl* de empleo

job printer *s* impresor *m* de remiendos

job printing *s* remiendo

job security *s* garantía de empleo continuo

jock [dʒak] *s* (slang) atleta *m*

jockey [ˈdʒaki] *s* jockey *m* ‖ *tr* montar (*un caballo*) en la pista; maniobrar; embaucar

jockstrap [ˈdʒak,stræp] *s* suspensorio (*para sostener el escroto*)

jocose [dʒoˈkos] *adj* jocoso

jocular [ˈdʒakjələr] *adj* jocoso, festivo

jodhpurs [ˈdʒadpərz] *spl* pantalones *mpl* de equitación

jog [dʒag] *s* golpecito; (*to the memory*) estímulo; trote corto ‖ *v* (*pret & pp* **jogged;** *ger* **jogging**) *tr* empujar levemente; estimular (*la memoria*) ‖ *intr*—**to jog along** avanzar al trote corto

jogging [ˈdʒagɪŋ] *s* trote *m* corto

jog trot *s* trote *m* de perro; (fig) rutina

ja
jo

john [dʒɑn] s (slang) retrete m; inodoro
John Bull s el inglés típico, el pueblo inglés
John Hancock [ˈhænkɑk] s (coll) la firma de uno
johnnycake [ˈdʒɑniˌkek] s pan m de maíz
John'ny-come'-late'ly s recién llegado
John'ny-jump'-up' s (pansy) pensamiento, trinitaria, violeta
John'ny-on-the-spot' s (coll) el que está siempre presente y listo
John the Baptist s San Juan Bautista
join [dʒɔɪn] tr juntar, unir, ensamblar; asociarse a, unirse a; incorporarse a, ingresar en; abrazar (un partido); hacerse socio de (una asociación); alistarse en (el ejército); trabar (batalla); desaguar en (el océano) ‖ intr juntarse, unirse; confluir (p.ej., dos ríos)
joiner [ˈdʒɔɪnər] s carpintero; (coll) el que tiene la manía de incorporarse a muchas asociaciones
joint [dʒɔɪnt] s (in a pipe) empalme m, juntura, (of bones) articulación, juntura, coyuntura; (backbone of book) nervura; (hinge of book) cartivana; (in woodwork) emsambladura; (of meat) tajada; (marijuana) porro, puerro; (elec) empalme m; (gambling den) (slang) garito; (slang) restaurante m de mala muerte; **out of joint** desencajado, descoyuntado; (fig) en desorden, desbarajustado; **to throw out of joint** descoyuntarse (p.ej., el brazo)
joint account s cuenta en común
Joint Chiefs of Staff spl (U.S.A.) Estado mayor conjunto
jointly [ˈdʒɔɪntli] adv juntamente, en común
joint owner s condueño
joint session s sesión conjunta
joint'-stock' company s sociedad anónima, compañía por acciones
jointure [ˈdʒɔɪntʃər] s bienes mpl parafernales
joist [dʒɔɪst] s viga
joke [dʒok] s broma, chiste m; (trifling matter) cosa de reír; (person laughed at) bufón m, hazmerreír m; **no joke** cosa seria; **to tell a joke** contar un chiste, **to play a joke on** gastar una broma a ‖ tr—**to joke one's way into** conseguir (p.ej., un empleo) burla burlando ‖ intr bromear, hablar en broma; **joking aside** o **no joking** burlas aparte
joke book s libro de chistes
joker [ˈdʒokər] s bromista mf; (wise guy) sábelotodo; (playing card) comodín m; (hidden provision) cláusula engañadora
jol·ly [ˈdʒɑli] adj (comp -lier; super -liest) alegre, festivo ‖ adv (coll) muy, harto ‖ v (pret & pp -lied) tr (coll) candonguear
jolt [dʒolt] s sacudida ‖ tr sacudir ‖ intr dar tumbos
Jonah [ˈdʒonə] s Jonás m; (fig) ave f de mal agüero
jongleur [ˈdʒɑŋglər] s juglar m, trovador m
jonquil [ˈdʒɑŋkwɪl] s junquillo
Jordan [ˈdʒɔrdən] s (country) Jordania; (river) Jordán m
Jordan almond s almendra de Málaga

Jordanian [dʒɔrˈdenɪ·ən] adj & s jordano
josh [dʒɑʃ] tr (coll) dar broma a ‖ intr dar broma
jostle [ˈdʒɑsəl] s empellón m, empujón m ‖ tr empellar, empujar ‖ intr chocar, encontrarse; avanzar a fuerza de empujones o codazos
jot [dʒɑt] s —**I don't care a jot for** no se me da un bledo de s v (pret & pp jotted; ger jotting) tr—**to jot down** apuntar, anotar
jounce [dʒɑʊns] s sacudida ‖ tr sacudir ‖ intr dar tumbos
journal [ˈdʒʌrnəl] s (newspaper) periódico; (magazine) revista; (daily record) diario; (com) libro diario; (naut) cuaderno de bitácora; (mach) gorrón m, muñón m
journalese [ˌdʒʌrnəˈliz] s lenguaje periodístico
journalism [ˈdʒʌrnəˌlɪzəm] s periodismo
journalist [ˈdʒʌrnəlɪst] s periodista mf
journalistic [ˌdʒʌrnəˈlɪstɪk] adj periodístico
journey [ˈdʒʌrni] s viaje m ‖ intr viajar
journey·man [ˈdʒʌrnimən] s (pl -men [mən]) oficial m
joust [dʒʌst] o [dʒust] o [dʒɑʊst] s justa ‖ intr justar
jovial [ˈdʒovɪ·əl] adj jovial
joviality [ˌdʒovɪˈælɪti] s jovialidad
jowl [dʒɑʊl] s (cheek) moflete m; (jawbone) quijada; (of cattle) papada; (of fowl) barba
joy [dʒɔɪ] s alegría, regocijo; **to leap with joy** saltar de gozo
joyful [ˈdʒɔɪfəl] adj alegre; **joyful over** gozoso con o de
joyless [ˈdʒɔɪlɪs] adj triste, sin alegría
joyous [ˈdʒɔɪ·əs] adj alegre
joy ride s (coll) paseo de recreo en coche; (coll) paseo alocado en coche
J.P. abbr **Justice of the Peace**
Jr. abbr **junior**
jubilant [ˈdʒubɪlənt] adj jubiloso
jubilation [ˌdʒubɪˈleʃən] s júbilo, viva alegría
jubilee [ˈdʒubɪˌli] s (jubilation) júbilo; aniversario; quincuagésimo aniversario; (eccl) jubileo
Judaism [ˈdʒude·ɪzəm] s judaísmo
judge [dʒʌdʒ] s juez m; **to be a good judge of** ser buen juez de o en ‖ tr & intr juzgar; **judging by** a juzgar por
judge advocate s (in the army) auditor m de guerra; (in the navy) auditor m de marina
judgeship [ˈdʒʌdʒˌʃɪp] s judicatura
judgment [ˈdʒʌdʒmənt] s juicio; (legal decision) sentencia, fallo
judgment day s día m del juicio
judgment seat s tribunal m
judicature [ˈdʒudɪkət∫ər] s judicatura
judicial [dʒuˈdɪʃəl] adj judicial; (becoming a judge) crítico, juicioso
judiciar·y [dʒuˈdɪʃɪˌɛri] adj judicial ‖ s (pl -ies) (judges of a city, country, etc.) judicatura; (branch of government that administers justice) poder m judicial
judicious [dʒuˈdɪʃəs] adj juicioso
jug [dʒʌg] s botija, jarra, cántaro; (jail) (slang) chirona

juggle ['dʒʌgəl] s juego de manos; (*trick, deception*) trampa ‖ *tr* hacer suertes con (*p.ej.*, *bolas*); alterar fraudulentamente, falsear (*cuentas, documentos, etc.*); **to juggle away** escamotear ‖ *intr* hacer suertes; hacer trampas

juggler ['dʒʌglər] s malabarista *mf*; impostor *m*

juggling ['dʒʌglɪŋ] s juegos malabares

Jugoslav ['jugo'slɑv] *adj & s* yugoeslavo

Jugoslavia ['jugo'slɑvɪə] s Yugoeslavia

jugular ['dʒʌgjələr] *adj & s* yugular *f*

juice [dʒus] s jugo, zumo; (*natural fluid of an animal body*) jugo; (slang) electricidad; (slang) gasolina; **to stew in one's own juice** (coll) freír en su aceite

juic·y ['dʒusi] *adj* (*comp* **-ier;** *super* **-iest**) jugoso, zumoso; (*interesting, spicy*) picante

jukebox ['dʒuk,bɑks] s tocadiscos *m* tragamonedas

julep ['dʒulɪp] s julepe *m*

julienne [,dʒulɪ'ɛn] s sopa juliana

July [dʒu'laɪ] s julio

jumble ['dʒʌmbəl] s revoltijo, masa confusa ‖ *tr* emburujar, revolver

jum·bo ['dʒʌmbo] *adj* (coll) enorme, colosal ‖ s (*pl* **-bos**) (*large clumsy person*) (coll) elefante *m*; (coll) objeto enorme

jump [dʒʌmp] s salto; (*in a parachute*) lanzamiento; (*of prices*) alza repentina; **to be always on the jump** (coll) andar siempre de aquí para allí; **to get o to have the jump on** (slang) ganar la ventaja a ‖ *tr* saltar; hacer saltar (*a un caballo*); (*in checkers*) comer; salir (*un tren*) fuera de (*el carril*) ‖ *intr* saltar; (*in a parachute from an airplane*) lanzarse; pasar del tope (*el carro de la máquina de escribir*); **to jump at** apresurarse a aceptar (*un convite*); apresurarse a aprovechar (*la oportunidad*); **to jump on** saltar a (*un tren*); (slang) regañar, criticar; **to jump over** saltar por, pasar de un salto; saltar (*la página de un libro*); **to jump to a conclusion** sacar una conclusión precipitadamente

jumper ['dʒʌmpər] s saltador *m*; blusa de obrero; **jumpers** traje holgado de juego para niños

jumping jack ['dʒʌmpɪŋ] s títere *m*

jump'ing-off' place s fin *m* del camino

jump seat s estrapontín *m*, traspuntín *m*

jump spark s (elec) chispa de entrehierro

jump suit s vestido unitario (*como de paracaidista*)

jump wire s (elec) alambre *m* de cierre

jump·y ['dʒʌmpi] *adj* (*comp* **-ier;** *super* **-iest**) saltón; asustadizo, nervioso

junc. *abbr* **junction**

junction ['dʒʌŋkʃən] s juntura, unión; (*of pieces of wood*) ensambladura; (*of two rivers*) confluencia; (*rail connection*) empalme *m*; (rr) estación de empalme

juncture ['dʒʌŋktʃər] s juntura, unión; (*time, occasion*) coyuntura; **at this juncture** a esta sazón, a estas alturas

June [dʒun] s junio

jungle ['dʒʌŋgəl] s jungla, selva; revoltijo, maraña

junior ['dʒunjər] *adj* menor, de menor edad; joven; del penúltimo año; hijo, p.ej., **John Jones, Junior** Juan Jones, hijo ‖ s menor *m*; socio menor; alumno del penúltimo año

junior college s escuela de estudios universitarios de primero y segundo años

junior high school s escuela intermedia entre la primaria y la secundaria

juniper ['dʒunɪpər] s enebro; (*red cedar*) cedro de Virginia

juniper berry s enebrina

junk [dʒʌŋk] s chatarra, hierro viejo; ropa vieja; (*useless stuff*) (coll) trastos viejos, baratijas viejas; (*old cable*) jarcia trozada; (*Chinese ship*) junco; (naut) carne salada ‖ *tr* (slang) echar a la basura; reducir a hierro viejo

junk dealer s chatarrero, chapucero

junket ['dʒʌŋkɪt] s manjar *m* de leche, cuajo y azúcar; (*outing*) viaje *m* de recreo; (*trip paid out of public funds*) jira ‖ *intr* hacer un viaje de recreo; ir de jira

junkie ['dʒʌŋki] s (slang) toxicómano, narcotómano, yonquí *m*

junk·man ['dʒʌŋk,mæn] s (*pl* **-men** [,mɛn]) chatarrero, chapucero; ropavejero; tripulante *m* de junco

junk room s leonera, trastera

junk shop o **junk store** s tienda de trastos viejos; baratío (CAm); barata (Col, Mex)

junk yard s chatarrería

juridical [dʒu'rɪdɪkəl] *adj* jurídico

jurisdiction [,dʒurɪs'dɪkʃən] s jurisdicción

jurisprudence [,dʒurɪs'prudəns] s jurisprudencia

jurist ['dʒurɪst] s jurista *mf*

juror ['dʒurər] s (*individual*) jurado

ju·ry ['dʒuri] s (*pl* **-ries**) (*group*) jurado

jury box s tribuna del jurado

jury·man ['dʒurimən] s (*pl* **-men** [mən]) (*individual*) jurado

jury-rig ['dʒuri,rɪg] *v* (*pret & pp* **-rigged;** *ger* **-rigging**) *tr* (naut) aparejar temporariamente

Jus. P. *abbr* **justice of the peace**

just [dʒʌst] *adj* justo ‖ *adv* justamente, justo; hace poco, apenas; sólo; (coll) absolutamente; **just** + *pp* acabado de + *inf*, p.ej., **just received** acabado de recibir; recién + *pp*, p.ej., **just arrived** recién llegado; **just as** como; en el momento en que; tal como, lo mismo que; **just beyond** un poco más allá (de); **just now** hace poco; ahora mismo; **just out** acabado de aparecer, recién publicado; **to have just** + *pp* acabar de + *inf*, p.ej., **I have just arrived** acabo de llegar; **I had just arrived** acababa de llegar

justice ['dʒʌstɪs] s justicia; (*judge*) juez *m*; (*just deserts*) premio merecido; **to bring to justice** aprehender y condenar por justicia; **to do justice to** hacer justicia a; apreciar debidamente

justice of the peace s juez *m* de paz

justifiable ['dʒʌstɪ,faɪ·əbəl] *adj* justificable

justi•fy [ˈdʒʌstɪˌfaɪ] v (pret & pp **-fied**) tr justificar; (typ) justificar
justly [ˈdʒʌstli] adj justamente, debidamente
jut [dʒʌt] v (pre & pp **jutted;** ger **jutting**) intr—**to jut out** resaltar, proyectarse
jute [dʒut] s yute m ‖ **Jute** m juto
Jutland [ˈdʒʌtlənd] s Jutlandia
juvenile [ˈdʒuvənɪl] o [ˈdʒuvəˌnaɪl] adj juvenil; para jóvenes ‖ s joven mf, mocito;

libro para niños; (theat) galán m, galancete m
juvenile court s tribunal m tutelar de menores
juvenile delinquency s delincuencia de menores
juvenile lead [lid] s (theat) papel m de galancete; (theat) galancete m
juvenilia [ˌdʒuvəˈnɪliˑə] spl obras de juventud
juxtapose [ˌdʒʌkstəˈpoz] tr yuxtaponer

K

K, k [ke] undécima letra del alfabeto inglés
k. abbr **karat, kilogram**
K. abbr **King, Knight**
kale [kel] s col f, berza; (slang) dinero, pasta
kaleidoscope [keˈlaɪdəˌskop] s calidoscopio
kangaroo [ˌkæŋɡəˈru] s canguro
kapok [ˈkepɑk] s capoc m, lana de ceiba
kaput [kəˈput] adj (slang) roto; gastado; inútil
karate [kəˈrɑti] m karate m, karaté m
karate expert s karateka m
katydid [ˈketɪdɪd] s saltamontes m cuyo macho emite un sonido chillón
kayak [ˈkaɪæk] s kayak m
kc. abbr **kilocycle**
kedge [kɛdʒ] s (naut) anclote m
keel [kil] s quilla ‖ intr—**to keel over** (naut) dar de quilla; volcarse; (coll) desmayarse
keelson [ˈkɛlsən] o [ˈkilsən] s (naut) sobrequilla
keen [kin] adj (having a sharp edge) agudo, afilado; (sharp, cutting) mordaz, penetrante; (sharp-witted) sutil, astuto, perspicaz; (eager, much interested) entusiasta; intenso, vivo; (slang) maravilloso; **to be keen on** ser muy aficionado a
keep [kip] s manutención, subsistencia; (of medieval castle) torre f del homenaje; **for keeps** (coll) de veras; (coll) para siempre; **to earn one's keep** (coll) ganarse la vida ‖ v (pret & pp **kept** [kɛpt] tr guardar, conservar; (deciding to make a purchase) quedarse con; cumplir, guardar (su palabra, su promesa); llevar (cuentas); apuntar (los tantos); tener (criados, caballos, huéspedes); cultivar (una huerta); dirigir (un hotel, una escuela); celebrar (una fiesta); hacer tardar (a una persona); **to keep away** tener alejado; **to keep back** retener; beberse (las lágrimas); reservar, no divulgar; **to keep down** reprimir; reducir (los gastos) al mínimo; **to keep** (a person) **from** + ger no dejarle (a una persona) + inf; **to keep in** no dejar salir; **to keep off** tener a distancia; no dejar penetrar (p.ej., la lluvia); evitar (p.ej., el polvo); **to keep out** no dejar entrar; no dejar penetrar; **to keep someone informed**

(about) ponerle a uno al corriente (de); **to keep someone waiting** hacerle a uno esperar; **to keep up** mantener, conservar ‖ intr permanecer, quedarse; conservarse, no echarse a perder; **to keep** + ger seguir + ger; **to keep away** mantenerse a distancia; no dejarse ver; **to keep from** + ger abstenerse de + inf; **to keep informed (about)** ponerse al corriente (de); **to keep in with** (coll) congraciarse con, no perder el favor de; **to keep off** no acercarse a; no pisar (el césped); **to keep on** + ger seguir + ger; **to keep on with** continuar con; **to keep out** mantenerse fuera, no entrar; **to keep out of** no entrar en; no meterse en; evitar (el peligro); **to keep quiet** estarse quieto; **to keep to** seguir por, llevar (la derecha, la izquierda); **to keep to oneself** quedarse a solas; **to keep up** continuar; no rezagarse; **to keep up with** correr parejas con; llevar adelante, proseguir
keeper [ˈkipər] s guardián m, custodio; (of a game preserve) guardabosque m; (of a magnet) armadura, culata
keeping [ˈkipɪŋ] s custodia, cuidado; (of a holiday) celebración; **in keeping with** de acuerdo con, en armonía con; **in safe keeping** en lugar seguro, a buen recaudo; **out of keeping with** en desacuerdo con
keep'sake' s recuerdo
keg [kɛg] s cuñete m, cubeto
ken [kɛn] s alcance m de la vista, alcance del saber; **beyond the ken of** fuera del alcance de
kennel [ˈkɛnəl] s perrera
kep•i [ˈkepi] o [ˈkɛpi] s (pl **-is**) quepis m
kept woman [kɛpt] s entretenida, manceba
kerchief [ˈkʌrtʃɪf] s pañuelo, mantón m
kerchoo [kərˈtʃu] interj ¡ah-chís!
kernel [ˈkʌrnəl] s (inner part of a nut or fruit stone) almendra núcleo; (of wheat or corn) grano; (fig) medula
kerosene [ˈkɛrəˌsin] o [ˌkɛrəˈsin] s keroseno
kerosene lamp s lámpara de petróleo
kerplunk [kərˈplʌŋk] interj ¡pataplún!
ketchup [ˈkɛtʃəp] s salsa de tomate condimentada

kettle [ˈkɛtəl] s caldera, marmita; (*teakettle*) tetera

ket'tle•drum' s timbal m, tímpano

key [ki] adj clave ‖ s (*of door, trunk, etc.*) llave f; (*of piano, typewriter, etc.*) tecla; (*wedge or cotter used to lock parts together*) clavija, cuña, chaveta; (*reef or low island*) cayo; (bot) sámara; (*tone of voice*) tono; (mus) clave f o llave f; (telg) manipulador m; (*to a puzzle, secret, translation, code*) (fig) clave o llave; (*place giving control to a region*) (fig) llave f; (fig) persona principal; **off key** desafinado; desafinadamente ‖ tr acuñar, enchavetar; **to key up** alentar, excitar

key'board' s teclado

key fruit s sámara

key'hole' s ojo de la cerradura; (*of a clock*) agujero de cuerda

key money s pago ilícito al casero

key•note s (mus) tónica, nota tónica; (fig) idea fundamental

keynote speech s discurso de apertura (*en que se expone el programa de un partido político*)

key'punch'er s perforista mf

key ring s llavero

key'stone' s clave f, espinazo; (fig) piedra angular

Key West s Cayo Hueso

key word s palabra clave

kg. abbr **kilogram**

K.G. abbr **Knight of the Garter**

kha•ki [ˈkɑki] o [ˈkæki] adj caqui ‖ s (pl -kis) caqui m

khedive [kəˈdiv] s jedive m

kibitz [ˈkɪbɪts] intr (coll) dar consejos molestos a los jugadores

kibitzer [ˈkɪbɪtsər] s (coll) mirón molesto (*de una partida de juego*); (coll) entremetido

kiblah [ˈkɪblɑ] s alquibla

kibosh [ˈkaɪbɑʃ] o [kɪˈbɑʃ] s (coll) música celestial; **to put the kibosh on** (coll) desbaratar, imposibilitar

kick [kɪk] s puntapié m; (*of an animal*) coz f; (*of a gun*) coz, culatazo; (*complaint*) (slang) queja, protesta; (*of liquor*) (slang) fuerza, estímulo; (*thrill*) gusto, placer intenso; **to get a kick out of** (slang) hallar mucho placer en ‖ tr acocear, dar de puntapiés a; sacudir (*los pies*); **to kick out** (coll) echar a puntapiés a la calle; (coll) echar, despedir; **to kick the bucket** (coll) morir; **to kick up a row** (slang) armar un bochinche ‖ intr cocear; dar culetazos (*un arma de fuego*); (coll) quejarse; **to kick about** (coll) quejarse de; **to kick against the pricks** dar coces contra el aguijón; **to kick off** (football) dar el golpe de salida

kick'back' s (coll) contragolpe m; (slang) devolución a un cómplice de una parte de lo robado

kick'off' s (football) golpe m de salida, puntapié m inicial

kid [kɪd] s (*young goat*) cabrito; (*leather*) cabritilla; (coll) chiquillo, chico; **kids** guantes mpl o zapatos de cabritilla ‖ v (pret

& pp **kidded;** ger **kidding**) tr (slang) embromar, tomar el pelo a; **to kid oneself** (slang) forjarse ilusiones ‖ intr (slang) decirlo en broma

kidder [ˈkɪdər] s (slang) bromista mf

kid gloves spl guantes mpl de cabritilla; **to handle with kid gloves** tratar con suma discreción o cautela

kid'nap' v (pret & pp -naped o -napped; ger naping o -napping) tr secuestrar

kidnaper o **kidnapper** [ˈkɪd,næpər] s secuestrador m, ladrón m de niños

kidney [ˈkɪdni] s riñon m; (coll) clase f, especie f; (coll) carácter m

kidney bean s judía

kidney stone s cálculo renal

kill [kɪl] s matanza; (*of a wild beast, an army, a pack of hounds*) ataque m final; (*creek*) arroyo, riachuelo; **for the kill** para el golpe final ‖ tr matar; ahogar (*un proyecto de ley*); quitar (*el sabor*); producir una impresión irresistible en

killer [ˈkɪlər] s matador m

killer whale s orca

killing [ˈkɪlɪŋ] adj matador; (*exhausting*) abrumador; (coll) muy divertido, de lo más ridículo ‖ s matanza; (*game killed on a hunt*) cacería, piezas; (coll) gran ganancia; **to make a killing** (coll) enriquecerse de golpe

kill'-joy' s aguafiestas mf

kiln [kɪl] o [kɪln] s horno

kil•o [ˈkɪlo] o [ˈkilo] s (pl -os) kilo, kilogramo; kilómetro

kilocycle [ˈkɪlə,saɪkəl] s kilociclo

kilogram [ˈkɪlə,græm] s kilogramo

kilometer [ˈkɪlə,mitər] s kilómetro (*distancia*); **kilometer** [kɪˈlɑmətər] s kilómetro (*instrumento*)

kilometric [ˌkɪləˈmɛtrɪk] adj kilométrico

kilowatt [ˈkɪlə,wɑt] s kilovatio

kilowatt-hour [ˈkɪlə,wɑtˈaʊr] s (pl kilowatt-hours) kilovatio-hora

kilt [kɪlt] s enagüillas, falda corta

kilter [ˈkɪltər] s—**to be out of kilter** (coll) estar descompuesto

kimo•no [kɪˈmonə] s (pl -nos) quimono

kin [kɪn] s (*family relationship*) parentesco; (*relatives*) deudos; **near of kin** muy allegado; **of kin** allegado; **the next of kin** el pariente más próximo, los parientes próximos

kind [kaɪnd] adj bueno, bondadoso; (*greeting*) afectuoso; **kind to** bueno para con ‖ s clase f, especie f, suerte f, género; **a kind of** uno a modo de; **all kinds of** (coll) gran cantidad de; **in kind** en especie; en la misma moneda; **kind of** (coll) algo, más bien; **of a kind** de una misma clase; (*poor, mediocre*) de poco valor, de mala muerte; **of the kind** por el estilo

kindergarten [ˈkɪndər,gɑrtən] s parvulario, escuela de párvulos, jardín m de la infancia

kindergartner [ˈkɪndər,gɑrtnər] s (*child*) párvulo; (*teacher*) parvulista mf

kind-hearted [ˈkaɪndˈhɑrtɪd] adj bondadoso, de buen corazón

ju
ki

kindle ['kɪndəl] *tr* encender ‖ *intr* encenderse
kindling ['kɪndlɪŋ] *s* encendajas
kindling wood *s* leña
kind·ly ['kaɪndli] *adj* (*comp* -**lier**; *super* -**liest**) (*kind-hearted*) bondadoso; apacible, benigno; favorable ‖ *adv* bondadosamente; cordialmente; con gusto; por favor; **to not take kindly to** no aceptar de buen grado
kindness ['kaɪndnɪs] *s* bondad; **have the kindness to** tenga Vd. la bondad de
kindred ['kɪndrɪd] *adj* emparentado; afín, semejante ‖ *s* parentela; semejanza, afinidad
Kinescope ['kɪnɪ,skop] *s* (trademark) cinescopio, kinescopio
kinetic [kɪ'nɛtɪk] *adj* cinético ‖ **kinetics** *s* cinética
kinetic energy *s* fuerza viva, energía cinética
kinfolk ['kin,fok] *s* (coll) pariente(s)
king [kɪŋ] *s* rey *m;* (cards, chess, & fig) rey; (checkers) dama
king'bolt' *s* pivote *m* central
kingdom ['kɪŋdəm] *s* reino
king'fish'er *s* martín *m* pescador
king·ly ['kɪŋli] *adj* (*comp* -**lier**; *super* -**liest**) real, regio; (*stately*) majestuoso ‖ *adv* regiamente
king'pin' *s* (bowling) bolo delantero; pivote *m* central; (aut) pivote de dirección; (coll) persona principal; (coll) jefe *m* de criminales
king post *s* pendolón *m*
king's evil *s* escrófula
kingship ['kɪŋʃɪp] *s* dignidad real
king'-size' *adj* de tamaño largo
king's ransom *s* riquezas de Creso
kink [kɪŋk] *s* (*twist, e.g., in a rope*) enroscadura, coca; (*e.g., in hair*) pasa; (*soreness in neck*) tortícolis *m;* (*flaw, difficulty*) estorbo, traba; (*mental twist*) chifladura, manía ‖ *tr* enroscar ‖ *intr* enroscarse
kink·y ['kɪŋki] *adj* (*comp* -**ier**; *super* -**iest**) encarrujado, ensortijado; (coll) perverso, raro
kinsfolk ['kɪnz,fok] *s* parentela, familia, deudos
kinship ['kɪnʃɪp] *s* parentesco; semejanza, afinidad
kins·man ['kɪnzmən] *s* (*pl* -**men** [mən]) pariente *m*
kins·woman ['kɪnz,wumən] *s* (*pl* -**women** [,wɪmɪn]) *s* parienta
kipper ['kɪpər] *s* arenque acecinado, salmón acecinado ‖ *tr* acecinar (*el arenque o el salmón*)
kiss [kɪs] *s* beso; (billiards) retruco; (*confection*) dulce *m,* merengue *m* ‖ *tr* besar; **to kiss away** borrar con besos (*las pensas de una persona*) ‖ *intr* besar; besarse; (billiards) retrucar
kit [kɪt] *s* cartera de herramientas; (*case and its contents for various purposes*) estuche *m;* (*of a soldier*) petaco, pertrechos; (*of a traveler*) equipaje *m;* (*pail, tub*) balde *m*
kitchen ['kɪtʃən] *s* cocina
kitchenette [,kɪtʃə'nɛt] *s* cocinilla
kitchen garden *s* huerto

kitch'en·maid' *s* ayudanta de cocina, pincha
kitchen police *s* (mil) trabajo de cocina; soldados que están de cocina
kitchen range *s* cocina económica
kitchen sink *s* fregadero; **everything but the kitchen sink** sin faltar apenas nada; completísimo
kitch'en·ware' *s* utensilios de cocina
kite [kaɪt] *s* cometa; (orn) milano; **to fly a kite** hacer volar una cometa
kith and kin [kɪθ] *spl* parientes *mpl;* parientes y amigos
kitten ['kɪtən] *s* gatito, minino
kittenish ['kɪtənɪʃ] *adj* juguetón, retozón; (*coy, flirtatious*) coquetón
kit·ty ['kɪti] *s* (*pl* -**ties**) gatito, minino; (*in card games*) polla, puesta ‖ *interj* ¡miz!
kleptomaniac [,klɛptə'menɪ,æk] *s* cleptómano
km. *abbr* **kilometer**
knack [næk] *s* tino, tranquillo, maña
knapsack ['næp,sæk] *s* mochila
knave [nev] *s* bribón *m,* pícaro; (cards) sota
knaver·y ['nevəri] *s* (*pl* -**ies**) bribonería, picardía
knead [nid] *tr* amasar, sobar
knee [ni] *s* rodilla; (*of animal*) codillo; (*e.g., of trousers*) rodillera; (mach) ángulo, codo; **to bring** (*someone*) **to his knees** rendir, vencer; **to go down on one's knees** hincarse de rodillas, caer de rodillas; **to go down on one's knees to** implorar de rodillas
knee breeches ['brɪtʃɪz] *spl* pantalones cortos
knee'cap' *s* rótula; (*protective covering*) rodillera
knee'-deep' *adj* metido hasta las rodillas
knee'high' *adj* que llega hasta la rodilla
knee'-hole' *s* hueco para acomodar las rodillas
knee jerk *s* reflejo rotuliano
kneel [nil] *v* (*pret & pp* **knelt** [nɛlt] o **kneeled**) *intr* arrodillarse; estar de rodillas
knee'pad' *s* rodillera
knee'pan' *s* rótula
knee swell *s* (*of organ*) (mus) rodillera
knell [nɛl] *s* doble *m,* toque *m* de difuntos; mal agüero; **to toll the knell of** anunciar la muerte de, anunciar el fin de ‖ *intr* doblar, tocar a muerto; sonar tristemente
knickers ['nɪkərz] *spl* pantalones *mpl* de media pierna
knickknack ['nɪk,næk] *s* chuchería, bujería, baratija
knife [naɪf] *s* (*pl* -**knives** [naɪvz] cuchillo; (*of a paper cutter or other instrument*) cuchilla; **to go under the knife** (coll) hacerse operar ‖ *tr* acuchillar; (slang) traicionar
knife sharpener *s* afilador *m,* afilón *m*
knife switch *s* (elec) interruptor *m* de cuchilla
knight [naɪt] *s* caballero; (chess) caballo ‖ *tr* armar caballero
knight-errant ['naɪt'ɛrənt] *s* (*pl* **knights-errant**) caballero andante
knight-errant·ry ['naɪt'ɛrəntri] *s* (*pl* -**ries**) caballería andante; (*quixotic behavior*) quijotada

knighthood [ˈnaɪt•hʊd] s caballería
knightly [ˈnaɪtli] adj caballeroso, caballeresco
Knight of the Rueful Countenance s Caballero de la triste figura (*Don Quijote*)
knit [nɪt] v (*pret & pp* **knitted** o **knit;** *ger* **knitting**) *tr* tejer a punto de aguja; enlazar, unir; fruncir (*las cejas*) arrugar (*la frente*) ‖ *intr* hacer calceta, hacer malla; trabarse, unirse; soldarse (*un hueso*)
knit goods spl géneros de punto
knitting [ˈnɪtɪŋ] s punto de media, trabajo de punto
knitting machine s máquina de hacer tejidos de punto
knitting needle s aguja de hacer media
knit′wear′ s géneros de punto
knob [nɑb] s (*lump*) bulto, protuberancia; (*of a door*) botón m, tirador m; (*of a radio set*) botón, perilla; (*ornament on furniture*) manzana; colina o montaña redondeada
knock [nɑk] s golpe m; (*e.g., on a door*) toque m, llamada; (*with a door knocker*) aldabazo; (*of an internal-combustion engine*) pistoneo; (slang) censura, crítica ‖ *tr* golpear; (*repeatedly*) golpetear; (slang) censurar, criticar; **to knock down** (*with a blow, punch, etc.*) derribar; (*to the highest bidder*) rematar; desarmar, desmontar (*un aparato o máquina*); **to knock off** hacer saltar con un golpe; suspender (*el trabajo*); poner fin a; (slang) matar; **to knock out** agotar; (box) poner fuera de combate ‖ *intr* tocar, llamar; golpear, pistonear (*el motor de combustión interna*); (slang) censurar, criticar; **to knock about** andar vagando; **to knock against** dar contra, tropezar con; **to knock at** tocar a, llamar a (*la puerta*); **to knock off** dejar de trabajar
knocker [ˈnɑkər] s (*on a door*) aldaba; (coll) criticón m
knock-kneed [ˈnɑk,nid] adj patizambo, zambo
knock′out′ s golpe decisivo, puñetazo decisivo; (box) (el) fuera de combate; (elec) destapadero; real moza
knockout drops spl (slang) gotas narcóticas
knoll [nol] s loma, otero
knot [nɑt] s nudo; (*worn as ornament*) lazo; corrillo, grupo; (*difficult matter; bond or tie*) nudo; nudo o lazo de matrimonio; (*protuberance in a fabric*) envoltorio; (naut) nudo; **to tie the knot** (coll) casarse ‖ v (*pret & pp* **knotted;** *ger* **knotting**) *tr* anudar; fruncir (*las cejas*) ‖ *intr* anudarse
knot′hole′ s agujero en la madera (*que deja un nudo al desprenderse*)
knot•ty [ˈnɑti] adj (*comp* **-tier;** *super* **-tiest**) nudoso; (fig) espinoso, difícil

know [no] s —**to be in the know** estar enterado, tener informes secretos ‖ v (*pret* **knew** [nju] o [nu]; *pp* **known**) *tr & intr* (*by reasoning or learning*) saber; (*by the senses or by perception; through acquaintance or recognition*) conocer; **as far as I know** que yo sepa; **to know about** saber de; **to know best** ser el mejor juez, saber lo que más conviene; **to know how to** + *inf* saber + *inf;* **to know it all** (coll) sabérselo todo; **to know what one is doing** obrar con conocimiento de causa; **to know what's what** (coll) saber cuántas son cinco; **you ought to know better** deberías tener vergüenza
knowable [ˈno•əbəl] adj conocible
know′-how′ s conocimiento, destreza, habilidad
knowingly [ˈno•ɪŋli] adv a sabiendas, con conocimiento de causa; (*on purpose*) adrede
know′-it-all′ adj & s (coll) sabidillo, sabelotodo mf
knowledge [ˈnɑlɪdʒ] s (*faculty*) ciencia, conocimientos, el saber; (*awareness, acquaintance, familiarity*) conocimiento; **to have a thorough knowledge of** conocer a fondo; **to my knowledge** que yo sepa; **to the best of my knowledge** según mi leal saber y entender; **with full knowledge** con conocimiento de causa; **without my knowledge** sin saberlo yo
knowledgeable [ˈnɑlɪdʒəbəl] adj (coll) conocedor, inteligente
know′-noth′ing s ignorante mf
knuckle [ˈnʌkəl] s nudillo; (*of a quadruped*) jarrete m; (*mach*) junta dè charnela; **knuckles** bóxer m ‖ *intr*—**to knuckle down** someterse, darse por vencido; aplicarse con empeño al trabajo
knurl [nʌrl] s moleteado ‖ *tr* moletear, cerrillar (*p.ej., las piezas de moneda*)
k.o. *abbr* **knockout**
kook [kuk] s (coll) tipo raro; excéntrico
Koran [koˈrɑn] o [koˈræn] s Corán m
Korea [koˈri•ə] s Corea
Korean [koˈri•ən] adj & s coreano
kosher [ˈkoʃər] adj autorizado por la ley judía; (coll) genuino, auténtico
kowtow [ˈkau,tau] o [ˈko,tau] *intr* arrodillarse y tocar el suelo con la frente; doblegarse servilmente, mostrarse servilmente obsequioso
Kt. *abbr* **Knight**
kudos [ˈkjudɑs] o [ˈkudɑs] s (coll) gloria, renombre m, fama
kw. *abbr* **kilowatt**
K.W.H. *abbr* **kilowatt-hour**

ki
kw

L

L, l [ɛl] duodécima letra del alfabeto inglés

l. *abbr* **liter, line, league, length**

L. *abbr* **Latin, Low**

la•bel ['lebəl] *s* etiqueta, marbete *m*, rótulo; (*descriptive word*) calificación ‖ *v* (*pret & pp* **-beled** o **-belled;** *ger* **-beling** o **-belling**) *tr* poner etiqueta o marbete a, rotular; calificar

labial ['lebɪ•əl] *adj & s* labial *f*

labor ['lebər] *adj* obrero ‖ *s* trabajo, labor *f;* (*job, task*) tarea, faena; (*manual work involved in an undertaking; the wages for such work*) mano *f* de obra; (*wage-earning workers as contrasted with capital and management*) los obreros; (*childbirth*) parto; **labors** esfuerzos; **to be in labor** estar de parto ‖ *intr* trabajar; (*to exert oneself*) forcejar; estar de parto; moverse penosamente; cabecear y balancear (*un buque*); **to labor under** ser víctima de

labor and management *spl* los obreros y los patronos

laborato•ry ['læbərə,tori] *s* (*pl* **-ries**) laboratorio

labored ['lebərd] *adj* penoso, dificultoso; artificial, forzado

laborer ['lebərər] *s* trabajador *m*, obrero; (*unskilled worker*) bracero, jornalero, peón *m*

laborious [lə'borɪ•əs] *adj* laborioso

la′bor-man′agement *adj* obrero-patronal

labor union *s* gremio obrero, sindicato

Labourite ['lebə,raɪt] *s* laborista *mf*

Labrador ['læbrə,dɔr] *s* el Labrador

labyrinth ['læbɪrɪnθ] *s* laberinto

lace [les] *s* encaje *m;* (*string to tie shoe, corset, etc.*) cordón *m*, lazo; (*braid*) galón *m* de oro o plata ‖ *tr* adornar con encaje; atar (*los zapatos, el corsé*); (*coll*) dar una paliza a

lace trimming *s* randa

lace′work′ *s* encaje *m*, obra de encaje

lachrymose ['lækrɪ,mos] *adj* lacrimoso

lacing ['lesɪŋ] *s* cordón *m;* lazo; galón *m;* (*coll*) paliza

lack [læk] *s* carencia, falta; (*complete lack*) defecto ‖ *tr* carecer de, necesitar ‖ *intr* (*to be lacking*) faltar

lackadaisical [,lækə'dezɪkəl] *adj* desaprovechado, indiferente

lackey ['læki] *s* lacayo; secuaz *m* servil

lacking ['lækɪŋ] *prep* sin, carente de

lack′lus′ter *adj* deslustrado, deslucido

laconic [lə'kɑnɪk] *adj* lacónico

lacquer ['lækər] *s* laca ‖ *tr* laquear

lacquer ware *s* lacas, objetos de laca

lacu•na [lə'kjunə] *s* (*pl* **-nas** o **-nae** [ni]) laguna

lac•y ['lesi] *adj* (*comp* **-ier;** *super* **-iest**) de encaje; (*fig*) diáfano

lad [læd] *s* muchacho, chico

ladder ['lædər] *s* escalera; (*stepladder*) escala, escalera de mano; (*two ladders fastened together at the top with hinges*) escalera de tijera; (*stepping stone*) (*fig*) escalón *m*

ladder truck *s* carro de escaleras de incendio

ladies' room *s* cuarto tocador

ladle ['ledəl] *s* cazo; (*for soup*) cucharón *m;* (*of tinsmith*) cucharilla ‖ *tr* servir con cucharón; sacar con cucharón

la•dy ['ledi] *s* (*pl* **-dies**) señora, dama

la′dy-bird′ o **la′dy•bug′** *s* mariquita, vaca de San Antón

la′dy•fin′ger *s* melindre *m*

lady-in-waiting *s* camarera de la reina

la′dy-kil′ler *s* ladrón *m* de corazones

la′dy•like′ *adj* elegante; **to be ladylike** ser muy dama

la′dy•love′ *s* amada, amiga querida

lady of the house *s* ama de casa

ladyship ['ledi,ʃɪp] *s* señoría

lady's maid *s* doncella

lady's man *s* perico entre ellas

lag [læg] *s* retraso ‖ *v* (*pret & pp* **lagged;** *ger* **lagging**) *intr* retrasarse; **to lag behind** quedarse atrás, rezagarse

lager beer ['lɑgər] *s* cerveza reposada

laggard ['lægərd] *s* perezoso, rezagado

lagoon [lə'gun] *s* laguna

laid paper [led] *s* papel vergueteado

laid up *adj* almacenado, ahorrado; (*naut*) inactivo; (*coll*) encamado por estar enfermo

lair [lɛr] *s* cubil *m*

lai•ty ['le•ɪti] *s* legos

lake [lek] *adj* lacustre ‖ *s* lago

lamb [læm] *s* cordero; carne *f* de cordero; piel *f* de cordero; (*meek person*) (*fig*) cordero

lambaste [læm'best] *tr* (*to thrash*) (*coll*) dar una paliza a; (*to reprimand harshly*) (*coll*) dar una jabonadura a

lamb chop *s* chuleta de cordero

lambkin ['læmkɪn] *s* corderito; (*fig*) nenito

lamb′skin′ *s* piel *f* de cordero, corderina; (*dressed with its wool*) corderillo

lame [lem] *adj* cojo; (*sore*) dolorido; (*e.g., excuse*) débil, pobre ‖ *tr* encojar

lament [lə'mɛnt] *s* lamento; (*dirge*) elegía ‖ *tr* lamentar ‖ *intr* lamentarse

lamentable ['læməntəbəl] *adj* lamentable

lamentation [,læmən'teʃən] *s* lamentación

laminate ['læmɪ,net] *tr* laminar

laminated glass *s* cristal laminado

lamp [læmp] *s* lámpara

lamp′black′ *s* negro de humo

lamp chimney *s* tubo de lámpara

lamp′light′ *s* luz *f* de lámpara

lamp′light′er *s* farolero

lampoon [læm'pun] *s* pasquín *m*, libelo ‖ *tr* pasquinar

lamp′post′ *s* poste *m* de farol

lamp shade *s* pantalla de lámpara

lamp′wick′ *s* mecha de lámpara, torcida

lance [læns] o [lɑns] *s* lanza; (*surg*) lanceta ‖ *tr* alancear; (*surg*) abrir con lanceta

lance rest *s* ristre *m*

lancet ['lænsɪt] *s* (*surg*) lanceta

land [lænd] *adj* terrestre; (*wind*) terral ‖ *s* tierra; **on land, on sea, and in the air** en tierra, mar y aire; **to make land** atracar a tierra; **to see how the land lies** medir el terreno, ver el cariz que van tomando las cosas ‖ *tr* desembarcar; conducir (*un avión*) a tierra; coger (*un pez*); (coll) conseguir ‖ *intr* desembarcar; (*to reach land*) arribar, aterrar; aterrizar (*un avión*); (*to arrive or come to rest*) ir a dar, ir a parar; **to land on one's feet** caer de pies; **to land on one's head** caer de cabeza

landau ['lændɔ] o ['lændaʊ] *s* landó *m*

land breeze *s* terral *m*

landed ['lændɪd] *adj* (*owning land*) hacendado; (*real-estate*) inmobiliario; **landed property** bienes *mpl* raíces

land'fall' *s* (*sighting land*) aterrada; (*landing of ship or plane*) aterraje *m*; tierra vista desde el mar; (*landslide*) derrumbe *m*

land'fill' *s* tierra y escombros

land grant *s* donación de tierras

land'hold'er *s* terrateniente *mf*, hacendado

landing ['lændɪŋ] *s* (*of ship or plane*) aterraje *m*; (*of passengers*) desembarco; (*place where passengers and goods are landed*) desembarcadero; (*of stairway*) desembarco, descanso

landing beacon *s* (aer) radiofaro de aterrizaje

landing craft *s* (nav) lancha de desembarco

landing field *s* (aer) pista de aterrizaje

landing force *s* (nav) compañía de desembarco

landing gear *s* (aer) tren *m* de aterrizaje

landing stage *s* embarcadero flotante

landing strip *s* (aer) faja de aterrizaje

land'la'dy *s* (*pl* **-dies**) (e.g., *of an apartment*) casera, dueña; (*of a lodging house*) ama, patrona; (*of an inn*) mesonera, posadera

landlocked ['lænd,lɑkt] *adj* rodeado de tierra

land'lord' *s* (e.g., *of an apartment*) casero, dueño; (*of a lodging house*) amo, patrón *m*; (*of an inn*) mesonero, posadero

land'lub'ber *s* (*person unacquainted with the sea*) marinero de agua dulce; (*awkward and unskilled seaman*) marinero matalote

land'mark' *s* (*boundary stone*) mojón *m*; (*feature of landscape that marks a location*) guía; suceso que hace época; (naut) marca de reconocimiento

land office *s* oficina del catastro

land'-of'fice business *s* (coll) negocio de mucho movimiento

land'own'er *s* terrateniente *mf*, hacendado

landscape ['lænd,skep] *s* paisaje *m* ‖ *tr* ajardinar

landscape architect *s* arquitecto paisajista

landscape gardener *s* jardinero adornista, jardinista *mf*

landscape painter *s* paisajista *mf*

landscapist ['lænd,skepɪst] *s* paisajista *mf*

land'slide' *s* derrumbe *m*, derrumbamiento de tierra, corrimiento; (fig) mayoría de votos abrumadora; (fig) victoria arrolladora

landward ['lændwərd] *adv* hacia tierra, hacia la costa

land wind *s* terral *m*

lane [len] *s* (*narrow street or passage*) callejuela; (*path*) carril *m*; (*of an automobile highway*) faja; (*of an air or ocean route*) derrotero, vía

langsyne ['læŋ'saɪn] *adv* (Scotch) hace mucho tiempo ‖ *s* (Scotch) tiempo de antaño

language ['læŋgwɪdʒ] *s* idioma *m*, lengua; (*way of speaking or writing, style; figurative or poetic expression; communication of meaning said to be employed by flowers, birds, art, etc.*) lenguaje *m*; (*of a special group of people*) jerga

language laboratory *s* laboratorio de idiomas

languid ['læŋgwɪd] *adj* lánguido

languish ['læŋgwɪʃ] *intr* languidecer; afectar languidez

languor ['læŋgər] *s* languidez *f*

languorous ['læŋgərəs] *adj* lánguido; (*causing languor*) enervante

lank [læŋk] *adj* descarnado, larguirucho; (*hair*) lacio

lank·y ['læŋki] *adj* (*comp* **-ier**; *super* **-iest**) descarnado, larguirucho

lantern ['læntərn] *s* linterna

lantern slide *s* diapositiva, tira de vidrio

lanyard ['lænjərd] *s* (naut) acollador *m*

lap [læp] *s* (*of human body or clothing*) regazo; (*loose fold*) caída, doblez *f*; (*overlap of garment*) traslapo; (*with the tongue*) lametada; (*of the waves*) chapaleteo; (*in a race*) (sport) etapa, vuelta; **to live in the lap of luxury** llevar una vida regalada ‖ *v* (*pret & pp* **lapped**; *ger* **lapping**) *tr* beber con la lengua; lamer (*las olas la playa*); (*to overlap*) traslapar; juntar a traslapo; **to lap up** tragar a lengüetadas; (coll) aceptar con entusiasmo ‖ *intr* traslapar; traslaparse (*dos o más cosas*); **to lap against** lamer (*las olas la playa*); **to lap over** salir fuera, rebosar

lap'board' *s* tabla faldera

lap dog *s* perro de falda

lapel [lə'pɛl] *s* solapa

Lap'land' *s* Laponia

Laplander ['læp,lændər] *s* lapón *m* (*habitante*)

Lapp [læp] *s* lapón *m* (*habitante; idioma*)

lap robe *s* manta de coche

lapse [læps] *s* (*passing of time; slipping into guilt or error*) lapso; (*fall, decline*) caída, caída en desuso; (e.g., *of an insurance policy*) invalidación ‖ *intr* caer en culpa o error; decaer, pasar (*p.ej., el entusiasmo*); caducar (*p.ej., una póliza de seguro*)

lap'wing' *s* ave fría

larce·ny ['lɑrsəni] *s* (*pl* **-nies**) hurto, robo

larch [lɑrtʃ] *s* alerce *m*, lárice *m*

lard [lɑrd] *s* cochevira, manteca de puerco ‖ *tr* (culin) mechar

larder ['lɑrdər] *s* despensa

large ['lɑrdʒ] *adj* grande; **at large** en libertad

large intestine *s* intestino grueso

largely ['lɑrdʒli] *adj* por la mayor parte

largeness ['lɑrdʒnɪs] *s* grandeza

large'-scale' *adj* en grande escala, grande escala

lariat ['læri•ət] s (*for catching animals*) lazo; (*for tying grazing animals*) cuerda, soga

lark [lɑrk] s alondra; (coll) parranda; **to go on a lark** (coll) andar de parranda, echar una cana al aire

lark'spur' s (*rocket larkspur*) espuela de caballero; (*field larkspur*) consuelda real

lar•va ['lɑrvə] s (*pl* -vae [vi]) larva

laryngeal [lə'rɪndʒi•əl] adj laríngeo

laryngitis [,lærɪn'dʒaɪtɪs] s laringitis f

laryngoscope [lə'rɪŋgə,skop] s laringoscopio

larynx ['lærɪŋks] s (*pl* **larynxes** o **larynges** [lə'rɪndʒiz]) laringe f

lascivious [lə'sɪvi•əs] adj lascivo

lasciviousness [lə'sɪvi•əsnɪs] s lascivia

laser ['lezər] s láser m

lash [læʃ] s (*cord on end of whip*) tralla; (*blow with whip; scolding*) latigazo; (*e.g., of animal's tail*) coletazo; (*eyelash*) embate m; (*eyelash*) pestaña ‖ tr (*to beat, whip*) azotar; (*to bind, tie*) atar; (*to shake, to switch*) agitar, sacudir; (*to attack with words*) increpar, reñir ‖ intr lanzarse, pasar rápidamente; **to lash out at** azotar; embestir; vituperar

lashing ['læʃɪŋ] s atadura; paliza, zurra; (*severe scolding*) latigazo

lass [læs] s muchacha, chica; amada

las•so ['læso] o [læ'su] s (*pl* -sos o -soes) lazo ‖ tr lazar

last [læst] o [lɑst] adj (*after all others; the only remaining; utmost, extreme*) último; (*most recent*) pasado; **before last** antepasado; **every last one** todos sin excepción; **last but one** penúltimo ‖ adv después de todos; por último; por última vez ‖ s última persona; última cosa; fin m; (*for holding shoe*) horma; **at last** por fin; **at long last** al fin y al cabo; **stick to your last!** ¡zapatero, a tus zapatos!; **the last of the month** a fines del mes; **to breathe one's last** dar el último suspiro; **to see the last of** no volver a ver; **to the last** hasta el fin ‖ intr durar; resistir; dar buen resultado (*p.ej., una prenda de vestir*); seguir así

lasting ['læstɪŋ] adj perdurable, duradero

lastly ['læstli] adv finalmente, por último

last'-min'ute news s noticias de última hora

last name s apellido

last night adv anoche

last quarter s cuarto menguante

last rites spl (theol) extremaunción

last sleep s último sueño

last straw s acabóse m, colmo

Last Supper, the la Cena

last will and testament s última disposición, última voluntad

last word s última palabra; (*latest style*) (coll) última palabra

lat. abbr **latitude**

Lat. abbr **Latin**

latch [lætʃ] s picaporte m ‖ tr cerrar con picaporte

latch'key' s llavín m

latch'string' s cordón m de aldaba; **the latch-string is out** ya sabe Vd. que ésta es su casa

late [let] adj (*happening after the usual time*) tardío; (*person*) atrasado; (*hour of the night*) avanzado; (*news*) de última hora; (*party, meeting, etc.*) que termina tarde; (*coming toward the end of a period of time*) de fines de; (*incumbent of an office*) anterior; (*deceased*) difunto, fallecido; **of late** recientemente, últimamente; **to be late** ser tarde; tardar (*p.ej., el tren*); **to be late in** + ger tardar en + inf; **to grow late** hacerse tarde ‖ adv tarde; **late in** (*the week, the month, etc.*) a fines de, hacia fines de; **late in life** a una edad avanzada

late-comer ['let,kʌmər] s recién llegado; (*one who arrives late*) rezagado

lateen sail [læ'tin] s vela latina

lateen yard s entena

lately ['letli] adv recientemente, últimamente

latent ['letənt] adj latente

lateral ['lætərəl] adj lateral

lath [læθ] o [lɑθ] s lata, listón; enlistonado ‖ tr enlistonar

lathe [leð] s torno (*máquina que sirve para labrar madera, hierro, etc. con un movimiento circular*)

lather ['læðər] s espuma de jabón; espuma de sudor ‖ tr enjabonar; (coll) tundir, zurrar ‖ intr espumar

lathery ['læðəri] adj espumoso, jabonoso

lathing ['læθɪŋ] s enlistonado

Latin ['lætɪn] o ['lætən] adj latino ‖ s (*language*) latín m; (*person*) latino

Latin America s Latinoamérica, América Latina

Latin American s latinoamericano

Lat'in-Amer'ican adj latinoamericano

latitude ['lætɪ,tjud] s latitud

latrine [lə'trin] s letrina

latter ['lætər] adj (*more recent*) posterior; segundo (*de dos*); **the latter** éste; **the latter part of** fines mpl de (*p.ej., el siglo*)

lattice ['lætɪs] s enrejado ‖ tr enrejar

lattice girder s viga de celosía

lat'tice•work' s enrejado

Latvia ['lætvi•ə] s Letonia, Latvia

laudable ['lɔdəbəl] adj laudable

laudanum ['lɔdənəm] o ['lɑdnəm] s láudano

laudatory ['lɔdə,tori] adj laudatorio

laugh [læf] s risa ‖ tr—**to laugh away** ahogar en risas; **to laugh off** tomar a risa ‖ intr reír, reírse

laughable ['læfəbəl] adj risible

laughing ['læfɪŋ] adj reidor; **to be no laughing matter** no ser cosa de risa ‖ s risa, (el) reír

laughing gas s gas m hilarante

laugh'ing•stock' s hazmerreír m

laughter ['læftər] s risa, risas

launch [lɔntʃ] s (*of a ship*) botadura; (*of a rocket*) lanzamiento; (*open motorboat*) lancha automóvil; (nav) lancha ‖ tr botar, lanzar (*un buque*); (*to throw; to start, set going, send forth*) lanzar ‖ intr lanzarse

launching ['lɔntʃɪŋ] s lanzamiento

launching pad s plataforma de lanzamiento

launching tower s torre f de lanzamiento

launder ['lɔndər] *tr* lavar y planchar ‖ *intr* resistir el lavado
launderer ['lɔndərər] *s* lavandero
laundress ['lɔndrɪs] *s* lavandera
laun•dry ['lɔndri] *s* (*pl* **-dries**) lavadero; lavado de la ropa; ropa lavada o para lavar
laundry•man ['lɔndrimən] *s* (*pl* **-men** [mən]) lavandero
laun′dry•wom′an *s* (*pl* **-wom′en**) lavandera
laureate ['lɔrɪ•ɪt] *adj* laureado ‖ *s* laureado; poeta laureado
lau•rel ['lɔrəl] *s* laurel *m;* **laurels** laurel (*de la victoria*); **to rest** o **sleep on one's laurels** dormirse sobre sus laureles ‖ *v* (*pret & pp* **-reled** o **-relled;** *ger* **-reling** o **-relling**) *tr* laurear, coronar de laurel
lava ['lɑvə] o ['lævə] *s* lava
lavato•ry ['lævə,tori] *s* (*pl* **-ries**) (*room equipped for washing hands and face*) lavabo; (*bowl with running water*) lavamanos *m;* (*toilet*) excusado
lavender ['lævəndər] *s* alhucema, espliego, lavanda
lavender water *s* agua de alhucema, agua de lavanda
lavish ['lævɪʃ] *adj* pródigo ‖ *tr* prodigar
law [lɔ] *s* (*of man, of nature, of science*) ley *f;* (*branch of knowledge concerned with law; body of laws; study of law; profession of law*) derecho; **to enter the law** hacerse abogado; **to go to law** recurrir a la ley; **to lay down the law** dar órdenes terminantes; **to maintain law and order** mantener la paz; **to practice law** ejercer la profesión de abogado; **to read law** estudiar derecho
law-abiding ['lɔ•ə,baɪdɪŋ] *adj* observante de la ley
law′break′er *s* infractor *m* de la ley
law court *s* tribunal *m* de justicia
lawful ['lɔfəl] *adj* legal, legítimo
lawless ['lɔlɪs] *adj* ilegal; (*unbridled*) desenfrenado, licencioso
law′mak′er *s* legislador *m*
lawn [lɔn] *s* césped *m;* (*fabric*) linón *m*
lawn mower *s* cortacésped *m,* tundidora de césped
law office *s* bufete *m,* despacho de abogado
law of nations *s* derecho de gentes
law of the jungle *s* ley *f* de la selva
law student *s* estudiante *mf* de derecho
law′suit′ *s* pleito, proceso, litigio
lawyer ['lɔjər] *s* abogado
lax [læks] *adj* (*in morals, discipline, etc.*) laxo, relajado; vago, indeterminado; (*loose, not tense*) laxo, flojo, suelto
laxative ['læksətɪv] *adj* & *s* laxante *m*
lay [le] *adj* (*not belonging to clergy*) lego, seglar; (*not having special training*) lego, profano ‖ *s* situación, orientación ‖ *v* (*pret & pp* **laid** [led]) *tr* poner, colocar; dejar en el suelo; tender (*un cable*); echar (*los cimientos; la culpa*); situar (*la acción de un drama*); asentar (*el polvo*); poner (*huevos la gallina; la mesa una criada*); formar (*planes*); hacer (*una apuesta*); **to be laid in** ser (*la escena*) en; **to lay aside** echar a un

lado; ahorrar; **to lay down** afirmar, declarar; dar (*la vida*); deponer (*las armas*); **to lay low** abatir, derribar; obligar a guardar cama; matar; **to lay off** despedir (*a obreros*); (*to mark off the boundaries of*) marcar, trazar; **to lay open** descubrir, revelar; (*to a risk or danger*) exponer; **to lay out** extender, tender; marcar (*una tarea, un trabajo*); gastar (*dinero*); amortajar (*a un difunto*); **to lay up** obligar a guardar cama; ahorrar; (naut) desarmar ‖ *intr* poner (*las gallinas*); **to lay about** dar palos de ciego; **to lay for** acechar; **to lay off** (coll) dejar de trabajar; (coll) dejar de molestar; **to lay over** detenerse durante un viaje; **to lay to** (naut) capear
lay brother *s* donado, lego
lay day *s* (naut) día *m* de estadía
layer ['le•ər] *s* (*e.g., of paint*) capa; (*e.g., of bricks*) camada; (*e.g., of coal, rocks*) estrato, capa; (hort) codadura ‖ *tr* (hort) acodar
layer cake *s* bizcocho de varias camadas
layette [le'ɛt] *s* canastilla
lay figure *s* maniquí *m*
laying ['le•ɪŋ] *s* colocación; (*of eggs*) postura; (*of a cable*) tendido
lay•man ['lemən] *s* (*pl* **-men** [mən]) (*person who is not a clergyman*) lego, seglar *m;* (*person who has no special training*) lego, profano
lay′off′ *s* (*dismissal of workmen*) despido; (*period of unemployment*) paro forzoso
lay of the land *s* cariz *m* que van tomando las cosas
lay′out′ *s* plan *m;* (*of tools*) equipo; disposición, organización; (coll) banquete *m,* festín *m*
lay′o′ver *s* parada en un viaje
lay sister *s* donada
laziness ['lezinɪs] *s* pereza; lerdera; (coll) galbana
la•zy ['lezi] *adj* (*comp* **-zier;** *super* **-ziest**) perezoso; (coll) galbanoso
la′zy•bones′ *s* (coll) perezoso
lb. *abbr* **pound**
l.c. *abbr* **lower case; loco citato** (Lat) **in the place cited**
Ld. *abbr* **Lord**
lea [li] *s* prado
lead [lɛd] *adj* plomizo ‖ *s* plomo; (*of lead pencil*) mina; (*for sounding depth*) (naut) escandallo; (typ) interlínea, regleta ‖ [lɛd] *v* (*pret & pp* **leaded;** *ger* **leading**) *tr* emplomar; (typ) interlinear, regletear ‖ *s* [lid] *s* (*foremost place*) primacía; (*guidance*) conducta, guía, dirección; indicación; ejemplo; (cards) salida; (*leash*) correa; (*of a newspaper article*) primer párrafo; (elec) conductor *m;* (elec & mach) avance *m;* (min) filón *m;* (rad) alambre *m* de entrada; (theat) papel *m* principal; (theat) galán *m;* (theat) dama; **to take the lead** tomar la delantera ‖ [lid] *v* (*pret & pp* **led** [lɛd]) *tr* conducir, llevar; liderar; (*to command*) acaudillar, mandar; estar a la cabeza de; dirigir (*p.ej., una orquesta*); llevar

(*buena o mala vida*); salir con (*cierto naipe*); (elec & mach) avanzar; **to lead someone to** + *inf* llevar a alguien a + *inf* ‖ *intr* ir delante, enseñar el camino; ser el primero; tener el mando; (cards) salir, ser mano; (mus) llevar la batuta; **to lead up to** conducir a, llevar a; llevar la conversación a

leaded gasoline ['lɛdɪd] *s* gasolina con plomo

leaden ['lɛdən] *adj* (*of lead; like lead*) plomizo; (*heavy as lead*) plúmbeo; (*sluggish*) tardo, indolente; (*with sleep*) cargado; triste, lóbrego

leader ['lidər] *s* caudillo, jefe *m*, líder *m*; (*ringleader*) cabecilla *m*; (*of an orchestra*) director *m*; (*in a dance; among animals*) guión *m*; (*horse*) guía; (*in a newspaper*) artículo de fondo

leader dog *s* perro-lazarillo

leadership ['lidərˌʃɪp] *s* caudillaje *m*, jefatura; dotes *fpl* de mando

leading ['lidɪŋ] *adj* primero, principal; preeminente; delantero; líder

leading article *s* artículo de fondo

leading edge *s* (aer) borde *m* de ataque

leading lady *s* primera actriz, dama

leading man *s* primer actor *m*, primer galán *m*

leading question *s* pregunta tendenciosa

leading strings *spl* andadores *mpl*

lead-in wire ['lid,ɪn] *s* (rad) bajada de antena, alambre *m* de entrada

lead pencil [lɛd] *s* lápiz *m*

leaf [lif] *s* (*pl* **leaves** [livz]) hoja; (*of vine*) pámpano; (*hinged leaf of table*) trampilla; **to shake like a leaf** temblar como un azogado; **to turn over a new leaf** hacer libro nuevo ‖ *intr* echar hojas; **to leaf through** hojear, trashojar

leafless ['liflɪs] *adj* deshojado

leaflet ['liflɪt] *s* hoja suelta, hoja volante; (*blade of compound leaf*) hojuela

leaf'stalk' *s* pecíolo

leaf·y ['lifi] *adj* (*comp* **-ier**; *super* **-iest**) hojoso, frondoso

league [lig] *s* (*unit of distance*) legua; (*association, alliance*) liga; (*sports*) división ‖ *tr* asociar ‖ *intr* asociarse, ligarse

League of Nations *s* Sociedad de las Naciones

leak [lik] *s* (*in a roof*) gotera; (*in a ship*) agua, vía de agua; (*of water, gas, electricity, steam*) escape *m*, fuga, salida; agujero, grieta, raja (*por donde se escapa el agua, etc.*); (*of money, news, etc.*) filtración; **to spring a leak** tener un escape; (naut) empezar a hacer agua ‖ *tr* dejar escapar, dejar salir (*el agua, gas, etc.*); dejar filtrar (*una noticia*) ‖ *intr* rezumarse (*un barril*); escaparse, salirse (*el agua, gas, etc.*); (naut) hacer agua; **to leak away** filtrarse (*el dinero*); **to leak out** rezumarse (*una especie*); trascender (*un hecho que estaba oculto*)

leakage ['likɪdʒ] *s* escape *m*, fuga, salida; (com) merma

leak·y ['liki] *adj* (*comp* **-ier;** *super* **-iest**) agujereado, roto; (*roof*) llovedizo; (naut) que hace agua; (coll) indiscreto

lean [lin] *adj* magro, mollar; (*thin*) flaco; (*gasoline mixture*) pobre; **lean years** años de carestía ‖ *v* (*pret & pp* **leaned** o **leant** [lɛnt] *tr* inclinar, ladear, arrimar ‖ *intr* inclinarse, ladearse, arrimarse; (fig) inclinarse, tender; **to lean against** arrimarse a, estar arrimado a; **to lean back** retreparse, recostarse; **to lean on** apoyarse en; (*with the elbows*) acodarse sobre; **to lean out (of)** asomarse (a); **to lean over backwards** (coll) extremar la imparcialidad; **to lean toward** (fig) inclinarse a, ladearse a

leaning ['linɪŋ] *adj* inclinado ‖ *s* inclinación; (fig) inclinación, tendencia

lean'-to' *s* (*pl* **-tos**) colgadizo

leap [lip] *s* salto; **by leaps and bounds** pasos agigantados; **leap in the dark** salto a ciegas, salto en vago ‖ *v* (*pret & pp* **leaped** o **leapt** [lɛpt]) *tr* saltar *s* ‖ *intr* saltar; dar un salto (*el corazón de uno*)

leap day *s* día *m* intercalar

leap'frog' *s* fil derecho, juego del salto; **to play leapfrog** jugar a la una la mula

leap year *s* año bisiesto

learn [lʌrn] *v* (*pret & pp* **learned** o **learnt** [lʌrnt]) *tr* aprender; oír decir; saber (*una noticia*) ‖ *intr* aprender

learned ['lʌrnɪd] *adj* docto, erudito; (*e.g., word*) culto

learned journal *s* revista científica

learned society *s* sociedad de eruditos

learned word *s* cultismo, voz culta

learned world *s* mundo de la erudición

learner ['lʌrnər] *s* principiante *mf*, aprendiz *m*, estudiante *mf*

learning ['lʌrnɪŋ] *s* (*act and time devoted*) aprendizaje *m*; (*scholarship*) erudición

lease [lis] *s* arrendamiento, locación; **to give a new lease on life to** renovar completamente; volver a hacer feliz ‖ *tr* arrendar ‖ *intr* arrendarse

lease'hold' *adj* arrendado ‖ *s* arrendamiento; bienes raíces arrendados

leash [liʃ] *s* traílla; **to strain at the leash** sufrir la sujeción con impaciencia ‖ *tr* atraillar

least [list] *adj* (el) menor, mínimo, más pequeño ‖ *adv* menos ‖ *s* (el) menor; (lo) menos; **at least** o **at the least** al menos, a los menos, por lo menos; **not in the least** de ninguna manera

leather ['lɛðər] *s* cuero

leath'er·back' turtle *s* laúd *m*

leath'er·neck' *s* (slang) soldado de infantería de marina de los EE.UU.

leathery ['lɛðəri] *adj* correoso, coriáceo

leave [liv] *s* (*permission*) permiso; (*permission to be absent*) licencia; (*farewell*) despedida; **on leave** con licencia; **to give leave to** dar licencia a; **to take leave (of)** despedirse (de) ‖ *v* (*pret & pp* **left** [lɛft]) *tr* (*to let stay; to stop, give up; to disregard*) dejar; (*to go away from*) salir de; (*to bequeath*) legar; **leave it to me!** ¡déjemelo a mí!; **to be left** quedar p.ej., **the letter was left unanswered** la carta quedó sin contestar; **to leave alone** dejar en paz, dejar tranquilo; **to leave no stone unturned** no dejar piedra por mover; **to leave off** dejar; no ponerse (*una prenda de vestir*); **to leave out** omitir; **to leave things as they are** dejarlo como está ‖ *intr* irse, marcharse; eliminarse (Mex); salir (*un avión, un tren, un vapor*)

leaven ['lɛvən] *s* levadura; (fig) influencia ‖ *tr* leudar; (fig) transformar

leavening ['lɛvənɪŋ] *s* levadura

leave of absence *s* licencia

leave'-tak'ing *s* despedida

leavings ['livɪŋz] *spl* desperdicios, sobras

Leba·nese [,lɛbə'niz] *adj* libanés ‖ *s* (*pl* -nese) libanés *m*

Lebanon ['lɛbənən] *s* el Líbano

Lebanon Mountains *spl* cordillera del Líbano

lecher ['lɛtʃər] *s* libertino, lujurioso

lecherous ['lɛtʃərəs] *adj* lascivo, lujurioso

lechery ['lɛtʃəri] *s* lascivia, lujuria

lectern ['lɛktərn] *s* atril *m*

lecture ['lɛktʃər] *s* conferencia; (*tedious reprimand*) sermoneo ‖ *tr* instruir por medio de una conferencia; sermonear ‖ *intr* dar una conferencia, dar conferencias

lecturer ['lɛktʃərər] *s* conferenciante *mf*

ledge [lɛdʒ] *s* (*projection in a wall*) retallo; cama de roca; arrecife *m*

ledger ['lɛdʒər] *s* (com) libro mayor

ledger line *s* (mus) línea suplementaria

lee [li] *s* (*shelter*) (naut) socaire *m*; (*quarter sheltered from the wind*) sotavento; **lees** heces *fpl*

leech [litʃ] *s* sanguijuela; **to stick like a leech** pegarse como ladilla

leek [lik] *s* puerro

leer [lɪr] *s* mirada de soslayo, mirada lujuriosa ‖ *intr*—**to leer at** mirar de soslayo, mirar lujuriosamente

leery ['lɪri] *adj* (coll) receloso, suspicaz

leeward ['liwərd] *o* ['lu·ərd] *adj* (naut) de sotavento ‖ *adv* (naut) a sotavento ‖ *s* (naut) sotavento

Leeward Islands ['liwərd] *spl* islas de Sotavento

lee'way' *s* (aer & naut) deriva; (coll) tiempo de sobra, espacio de sobra, dinero de sobra; (coll) libertad de acción

left [lɛft] *adj* izquierdo ‖ *adv* hacia la izquierda ‖ *s* (*left hand*) izquierda; (box) zurdazo; (pol) izquierda; **on the left** a la izquierda

left field *s* (baseball) jardín izquierdo

left'-hand' drive *s* conducción o dirección a la izquierda

left-handed ['lɛft'hændɪd] *adj* (*individual*) zurdo; (*clumsy*) desmañado, torpe; insincero; contrario a las agujas del reloj

leftish ['lɛftɪʃ] *adj* izquierdizante

leftist ['lɛftɪst] *adj* & *s* izquierdista *mf*

left'o'ver *adj* & *s* sobrante *m*; **leftovers** *spl* sobras

left'-wing' *adj* izquierdista

left-winger ['lɛft'wɪŋər] *s* (coll) izquierdista *mf*

leg. *abbr* legal, legislature

leg [lɛg] *s* (*of man or animal*) pierna; (*of animal, table, chair, etc.*) pata; (*of boot or stocking*) caña; (*of trousers*) pernera; (*of a cooked fowl*) muslo; (*of a journey*) etapa, trecho; **to be on one's last legs** estar sin recursos; estar en las últimas; **to not have a leg to stand on** (coll) no tener justificación alguna, no tener disculpa alguna; **to pull the leg of** (coll) tomar el pelo a; **to shake a leg** (coll) darse prisa; (*to dance*) (coll) bailar; **to stretch one's legs** estirar las piernas, dar un paseíto

lega·cy ['lɛgəsi] *s* (*pl* -cies) legado

legal ['ligəl] *adj* legal

legali·ty [lɪ'gælɪti] *s* (*pl* -ties) legalidad

legalization [,ligələ'zeʃən] *s* legalización despenalización

legalize ['ligə,laɪz] *tr* legalizar; despenalizar

legal tender *s* curso legal

legate ['lɛgɪt] *s* legado

legatee [,lɛgə'ti] *s* legatario

legation [lɪ'geʃən] *s* legación

legend ['lɛdʒənd] *s* leyenda

legendary ['lɛdʒən,dɛri] *adj* legendario

legerdemain [,lɛdʒərdɪ'men] *s* juego de manos, prestidigitación; (*cheating, trickery*) trapacería

legging ['lɛgɪŋ] *s* polaina

leg·gy ['lɛgi] *adj* (*comp* -gier; *super* -giest) zanquilargo; de piernas largas y elegantes

leg'horn' *s* sombrero de paja de Italia ‖ **Leghorn** *s* Liorna

legible ['lɛdʒɪbəl] *adj* legible

legion ['lidʒən] *s* legión

legislate ['lɛdʒɪs,let] *tr* imponer mediante legislación ‖ *intr* legislar

legislation ['lɛdʒɪs'leʃən] *s* legislación

legislative ['lɛdʒɪs,letɪv] *adj* legislativo

legislator ['lɛdʒɪs,letər] *s* legislador *m*

legislature ['lɛdʒɪs,letʃər] *s* asamblea legislativa, cuerpo legislativo

legitimacy [lɪ'dʒɪtɪməsi] *s* legitimidad

legitimate [lɪ'dʒɪtɪmɪt] *adj* legítimo ‖ [lɪ'dʒɪtɪ,met] *tr* legitimar

legitimate drama *s* drama serio (*a distinción del cine o el melodrama*)

legitimize [lɪ'dʒɪtɪ,maɪz] *tr* legitimar

leg'work' *s* (coll) el mucho caminar

leisure ['liʒər] *o* ['lɛʒər] *s* desocupación, ocio; **at leisure** desocupado, libre; **at one's leisure** a la comodidad de uno, cuando uno pueda

leisure activities *spl* recreos pasatiempos

leisure class *s* gente acomodada

leisure hours *spl* horas de ocio, ratos perdidos

leisurely ['liʒərli] *o* ['lɛʒərli] *adj* lento, pausado ‖ *adv* lentamente, despacio, sin prisa

leisure wear *s* ropa de recreo, traje *m* informal

lemon ['lɛmən] *s* limón *m*; (slang) artículo de fábrica defectuosa

lemonade [,lɛmə'ned] *s* limonada

lemon squeezer *s* exprimidera de limón

le
le

lemon verbena s luisa
lend [lɛnd] s (pret & pp **lent** [lɛnt]) tr prestar
lending library s biblioteca de préstamo
length [lɛŋθ] s largura, largo; (of time) extensión; (naut) eslora; **at length** por fin; largamente; **to go to any length** hacer cuanto esté de su parte; **to keep at arm's length** mantener a distancia; mantenerse a distancia
lengthen ['lɛŋθən] tr alargar ‖ intr alargarse
length'wise' adj longitudinal ‖ adv longitudinalmente
length·y ['lɛŋθi] adj (comp -ier; super -iest) muy largo, prolongado
leniency ['lini·ənsi] s clemencia, indulgencia, lenidad
lenient ['lini·ənt] adj clemente, indulgente
lens [lɛnz] s lente m & f; (of the eye) cristalino
Lent [lɛnt] s cuaresma f
Lenten ['lɛntən] adj cuaresmal
lentil ['lɛntəl] s lenteja
Leo ['li·o] s (astr) Leo
leopard ['lɛpərd] s leopardo
leotard ['li·ə,tɑrd] s leotardo
leper ['lɛpər] s leproso
leper house s leprosería
leprosy ['lɛprəsi] s lepra
leprous ['lɛprəs] adj leproso; (covered with scales) escamoso
Lesbian ['lɛzbi·ən] adj lesbio ‖ s lesbio; (female homosexual) lesbia
lesbianism ['lɛzbi·ə,nɪzəm] s lesbianismo
lese majesty ['liz'mædʒɪsti] s delito de lesa majestad
lesion ['liʒən] s lesión
less [lɛs] adj menor ‖ adv menos; **less and less** cada vez menos; **less than** menos que; (followed by numeral) menos de; (followed by verb) menos de lo que ‖ s menos m
lessee [lɛs'i] s arrendatario
lessen ['lɛsən] tr disminuir, reducir a menos; quitar importancia a ‖ intr disminuirse, reducirse; amainar (el viento)
lesser ['lɛsər] adj menor, más pequeño
lesson ['lɛsən] s lección
lessor ['lɛsər] s arrendador m
lest [lɛst] conj no sea que, de miedo que
let [lɛt] v (pret & pp **let**; ger **letting**) tr dejar, permitir; alquilar, arrendar; **let** + inf que + subj, p.ej., **let him come in** que entre; **let alone** y mucho menos; **let good enough alone** bueno está lo bueno; **let us** + inf vamos a + inf, p.ej., **let us eat** vamos a comer, comamos; **to let** se alquila; **to let alone** dejar en paz, dejar tranquilo; **to let be** no tocar; dejar en paz; **to let by** dejar pasar; **to let down** dejar bajar; desilusionar, traicionar; dejar plantado; **to let fly** disparar; (fig) disparar, soltar (palabras injuriosas); **to let go** soltar, desasirse de; vender; **to let in** dejar entrar, dejar entrar en; **to let it go at that** no hacer o decir nada más; **to let know** hacer saber; **to let loose** soltar; **to let on** (coll) dar a entender; **to let out** dejar salir; revelar, publicar; dar, soltar (p.ej., más cuerda); dar (un grito);

ensanchar (un vestido que aprieta); dar en arrendamiento; (coll) despedir; **to let through** dejar pasar, dejar pasar por; **to let up** dejar subir; dejar levantarse ‖ intr alquilarse, arrendarse; **to let down** (coll) ir más despacio; **to let go** desasirse; **to let go of** desasirse de; **to let on** (coll) fingir; **to let out** (coll) despedirse, cerrarse (p.ej., la escuela); **to let up** (coll) desistir; (coll) aflojar, amainar
let'down' s disminución; aflojamiento; desilusión, decepción; humillación
lethal ['liθəl] adj letal
lethargic [lɪ'θɑrdʒɪk] adj (affected with lethargy) letárgico; (producing lethargy) letargoso
lethar·gy ['lɛθərdʒi] s (pl -gies) letargo
Lett [lɛt] s letón m
letter ['lɛtər] s (written message) carta; (of the alphabet) letra; (literal meaning) (fig) letra; **letters** (literature) letras; **to the letter** al pie de la letra ‖ tr estampar o marcar con letras
letter box s buzón m (caja)
letter carrier s cartero
letter drop s buzón m (agujero)
letter file s guardacartas m
let'ter·head' s membrete m; (paper with printed heading) memorándum m
lettering ['lɛtərɪŋ] s inscripción; letras
letter of credit s carta de crédito
letter opener ['opənər] s abrecartas m
letter paper s papel m de cartas
let'ter-per'fect adj que tiene bien aprendido su papel; correcto, exacto
let'ter·press' s impresión tipográfica; texto (a distinción de los grabados)
letter scales spl pesacartas m
Lettish ['lɛtɪʃ] adj letón ‖ s letón m
lettuce ['lɛtɪs] s lechuga
let'up' s (coll) calma, interrupción; **without letup** (coll) sin cesar
leucorrhea [,lukə'ri·ə] s leucorrea
leukemia [lu'kimɪ·ə] s leucemia
Levant [lɪ'vænt] s Levante m (países de la parte oriental del Mediterráneo)
Levantine ['lɛvən,tin] o [lɪ'væntin] adj & s levantino
levee ['lɛvi] s (embankment to hold back water) ribero; (reception at court) besamanos m
lev·el ['lɛvəl] adj raso, llano; nivelado; (coll) sensato, juicioso; **level with** al nivel de, a flor de, a ras de ‖ s (device for determining horizontal position; degree of elevation) nivel m; (flat and even area of land) terreno llano, llanura; (part of a canal between two locks) tramo; **to be on the level** obrar sin engaño, decir la pura verdad; **to find one's level** hallar su propio nivel ‖ v (pret & pp -eled o -elled; ger -eling o -elling) tr nivelar; (to smooth, flatten out) arrasar, allanar; (to bring down) derribar, echar por tierra; apuntar (un arma de fuego); (fig) allanar (dificultades) ‖ intr—**to level off** (aer) enderezarse para aterrizar

level-headed [ˈlɛvəlˈhɛdɪd] *adj* sensato, juicioso

leveling rod *s* (surv) jalón *m* de mira

lever [ˈlivər] o [ˈlɛvər] *s* palanca ‖ *tr* apalancar

leverage [ˈlivərɪdʒ] o [ˈlɛvərɪdʒ] *s* palancada; poder *m* de una palanca; (fig) influencia, poder *m*

leviathan [lɪˈvaɪ•əθən] *s* (Bib & fig) leviatán *m;* buque *m* muy grande

levitation [ˌlɛvɪˈteʃən] *s* levitación

levi•ty [ˈlɛvɪti] *s* (*pl* -ties) frivolidad; (*fickleness*) ligereza

lev•y [ˈlɛvi] *s* (*pl* -ies) (*of taxes*) exación, recaudación; dinero recaudado; (mil) leva, enganche *m*, recluta ‖ *v* (*pret & pp* -ied) *tr* exigir, recaudar (*impuestos*); (mil) enganchar, reclutar; hacer (*la guerra*)

lewd [lud] *adj* lascivo, lujurioso; obsceno

lewdness [ˈludnɪs] *s* lascivia, lujuria; obscenidad

lexical [ˈlɛksɪkəl] *adj* léxico

lexicographer [ˌlɛksɪˈkɑɡrəfər] *s* lexicógrafo

lexicographic(al) [ˌlɛksɪkəˈɡræfɪk(əl)] lexicográfico

lexicography [ˌlɛksɪˈkɑɡrəfi] *s* lexicografía

lexicology [ˌlɛksɪˈkɑlədʒi] *s* lexicología

lexicon [ˈlɛksɪkən] *s* léxico, lexicón *m*

liabili•ty [ˌlaɪ•əˈbɪlɪti] *s* (*pl* -ties) (*e.g., to disease*) propensión; responsabilidad, obligación; desventaja; **liabilities** deudas; (*as detailed in balance sheet*) pasivo

liability insurance *s* seguro de responsabilidad civil

liable [ˈlaɪ•əbəl] *adj* (*e.g., to disease*) propenso, expuesto; responsable; **to be liable to** + *inf* (coll) amenazar + *inf*

liaison [ˈli•ə,zɑn] o [liˈezən] *s* enlace *m*, unión; (*illicit relationship between a man and woman*) amancebamiento, enredo, lío; (mil, nav & phonet) enlace *m*

liaison officer *s* (mil) oficial *m* de enlace

liar [ˈlaɪ•ər] *s* mentiroso

lib. *abbr* librarian, library

libation [laɪˈbeʃən] *s* libación; (*drink*) libación

li•bel [ˈlaɪbəl] *s* calumnia, difamación; levante (CAm, P-R); (*defamatory writing*) libelo ‖ *v* (*pret & pp* -beled o -belled) *ger* -beling o -belling) *tr* calumniar, difamar

libelous [ˈlaɪbələs] *adj* calumniador

liberal [ˈlɪbərəl] *adj* (*generous; done or given generously*) liberal; (*open-minded*) tolerante, de amplias miras; (*translation*) libre; (pol) liberal ‖ *s* liberal *mf*

liberali•ty [ˌlɪbəˈrælɪti] *s* (*pl* -ties) liberalidad

liberal-minded [ˈlɪbərəlˈmaɪndɪd] *adj* tolerante, de amplias miras

liberate [ˈlɪbə,ret] *tr* libertar; (*to disengage from a combination*) (chem) desprender

liberation [ˌlɪbəˈreʃən] *s* liberación; (chem) desprendimiento

liberation theology *s* teología liberacionista

liberator [ˈlɪbə,retər] *s* libertador *m*

libertine [ˈlɪbər,tin] *adj & s* libertino

liber•ty [ˈlɪbərti] *s* (*pl* -ties) libertad; **to take the liberty to** tomarse la libertad de

liberty-loving [ˈlɪbərtiˈlʌvɪŋ] *adj* amante de la libertad

libidinous [lɪˈbɪdɪnəs] *adj* libidinoso

libido [lɪˈbido] o [lɪˈbaɪdo] *s* libídine *f*, libido *f*

Libra [ˈlibrə] *s* (astr) Libra

librarian [laɪˈbrɛrɪ•ən] *s* bibliotecario

librar•y [ˈlaɪ,brɛri] o [ˈlaɪbrəri] *s* (*pl* -ies) biblioteca

library number *s* signatura

library school *s* escuela de bibliotecarios

library science *s* bibliotecnia; biblioteconomía

libret•to [lɪˈbrɛto] *s* (*pl* -tos) (mus) libreto

license [ˈlaɪsəns] *s* licencia ‖ *tr* licenciar

license number *s* número de matrícula

license plate o **tag** *s* chapa de circulación, placa de matrícula

licentious [laɪˈsɛnʃəs] *adj* licencioso, disoluto

lichen [ˈlaɪkən] *s* liquen *m*

lick [lɪk] *s* lamedura; (*place where animals go to lick*) lamedero; (*blow*) (coll) bofetón *m*; (*speed*) (coll) velocidad; (*beating*) (coll) zurra; (*quick cleaning*) (coll) limpión *m;* **to give a lick and a promise to** (coll) hacer rápida y superficialmente ‖ *tr* lamer; lamerse (*p.ej., los dedos*); lamer (*las llamas un tejado*); (*to beat, thrash*) (coll) zurrar; (*to conquer*) (coll) vencer ‖ *intr* lengüetear

licorice [ˈlɪkərɪs] *s* regaliz *m*, orozuz *m;* dulce *m* de regaliz

lid [lɪd] *s* (*of a box, trunk, chest, etc.*) tapa, tapadera; (*of a dish, pot, etc.*) cobertera; (*eyelid*) párpado; (*hat*) (slang) techo

lie [laɪ] *s* mentira; **to catch in a lie** coger en una mentira; **to give the lie to** dar un mentís a ‖ *v* (*pret & pp* lied; *ger* lying) *tr*—**to lie oneself out of** o **to lie one's way out of** librarse de un aprieto mintiendo ‖ *intr* mentir ‖ *v* (*pret* lay [le]; *pp* lain [len]; *ger* lying) *intr* estar echado; hallarse, estar situado; (*e.g., in the grave*) yacer, estar enterrado; **to lie down** echarse, acostarse

lie detector *s* detector *m* de mentiras

lien [lin] o [ˈli•ən] *s* gravamen *m*, derecho de retención

lieu [lu] *s*—**in lieu of** en lugar de, en vez de

lieutenant [luˈtɛnənt] *s* lugarteniente *m;* (mil) teniente *m;* (nav) teniente de navío

lieutenant colonel *s* (mil) teniente coronel *m*

lieutenant commander *s* (nav) capitán *m* de corbeta

lieutenant governor *s* (U.S.A.) vicegobernador *m* (*de un Estado*)

lieutenant junior grade *s* (nav) alférez *m* de navío

life [laɪf] *adj* (*animate*) vital; (*lifelong*) perpetuo; (*annuity, income*) vitalicio; (*working from nature*) (fa) del natural ‖ *s* (*pl* lives [laɪvz]) vida; (*of an insurance policy*) vigencia; **for life** de por vida; **for the life of me** así me maten; **the life and soul of** (*e.g., a party*) la alegría de; **to come to life** volver a la vida; **to depart this life** partir de esta vida; **to run for one's life** salvarse por los pies

life annuity s renta vitalicia
life belt s cinturón m salvavidas
life'boat' s bote m de salvamento, bote salvavidas; (*for shore-based rescue services*) lancha de auxilio
life buoy s boya salvavidas, guindola
life expectancy s expectación de vida
life float s balsa salvavidas
life'guard' s salvavidas m, guardavida m
life imprisonment s cadena perpetua
life insurance s seguro sobre la vida
life jacket s chaleco salvavidas
lifeless ['laɪflɪs] adj muerto, sin vida; (*in a faint*) desmayado, exánime; (*dull, colorless*) deslucido
life'like' adj natural, vivo
life line s cuerda salvavidas; cuerda de buzo
life'long' adj perpetuo, de toda la vida
life of leisure s vida de ocio
life of Riley ['raɪli] s (slang) vida regalada
life of the party s (coll) alegría de la fiesta, alma de la fiesta
life preserver [prɪ'zʌrvər] s chaleco salvavidas
lifer ['laɪfər] s (slang) presidiario de por vida
life'sav'er s salvador m (*de vidas*); (*something that saves a person from a predicament*) (coll) tabla de salvación
lifesaving ['laɪf,sevɪŋ] adj de salvamento ‖ s salvamento (*de vidas*)
life sentence s condena a cadena perpetua
life'-size' adj de tamaño natural
life span s período de vida
life'time' adj vitalicio ‖ s vida, curso de la vida, jornada
life'work' s obra principal de la vida de uno
lift [lɪft] s elevación, levantamiento; ayuda (*para levantar una carga*); (aer) sustentación; **to give a lift to** invitar (*a un peatón*) a subir a un coche; llevar en un coche; (fig) reanimar ‖ tr elevar, levantar; quitarse (*el sombrero*); (naut) izar (*velas, vergas, etc.*); (fig) reanimar, exaltar; (coll) robar; (coll) plagiar ‖ intr elevarse, levantarse; disiparse (*las nubes, las nieblas, la obscuridad, etc.*)
lift bridge s puente levadizo
lift'-off s despegue m vertical
lift truck s carretilla elevadora
ligament ['lɪgəmənt] s ligamento
ligature ['lɪgətʃər] s (mus & surg) ligadura; (mus & typ) ligado
light [laɪt] adj (*in weight*) ligero, leve, liviano; (*having illumination; whitish*) claro; (*hair*) blondo, rubio; (*complexion*) blanco; (*oil*) flúido; (*beer*) claro; (*reading*) poco serio; (*heart*) despreocupado; (*carrying a small cargo or none at all*) (naut) boyante; **light in the head** (*dizzy*) aturdido, mareado; (*simple, silly*) tonto, necio; **to make light of** no dar importancia a, no tomar en serio ‖ adv sin carga; sin equipaje ‖ s luz f; (*to light a cigarette*) lumbre f, fuego; (*to control traffic*) luz, señal f; (*window or other opening in a wall*) luz, claro, hueco; (*example, shining figure*) lumbrera; **according to one's lights** según Dios le da

a uno a entender; **against the light** al trasluz; **in this light** desde este punto de vista; **lights** noticias; (*of sheep, etc.*) bofes mpl; **to come to light** salir a luz, descubrirse; **to shed** o **throw light on** echar luz sobre; **to strike a light** echar una yesca; encender un fósforo ‖ v (*pret & pp* **lighted** o **lit** [lɪt] tr (*to furnish with illumination*) alumbrar, iluminar; (*to set afire, ignite*) encender; **to light up** iluminar ‖ intr alumbrarse; encenderse; posar (*un ave*); (*from an auto*) bajar; **to light into** (*to attack*) (slang) arremeter contra; (*to scold, berate*) (slang) poner de oro y azul; **to light out** (slang) poner pies en polvorosa; **to light upon** tropezar con, hallar por casualidad
light bulb s (elec) bombilla
light complexion s tez blanca
lighten ['laɪtən] tr (*to make lighter in weight*) aligerar; iluminar; (*to cheer up*) alegrar, regocijar ‖ intr (*to become less dark*) iluminarse; (*to give off flashes of lightning*) relampaguear; (fig) iluminarse (*los ojos, la cara de una persona*)
lighter ['laɪtər] s (*to light a cigarette*) encendedor m; (*flat-bottomed barge*) alijador m
light-fingered ['laɪt'fɪŋgərd] adj largo de uñas, listo de manos
light-footed ['laɪt'fʊtɪd] adj ligero de pies
light-headed ['laɪt'hɛdɪd] adj (*dizzy*) aturdido, mareado; (*simple, silly*) tonto, necio, ligero de cascos
light-hearted ['laɪt'hɑrtɪd] adj alegre, libre de cuidados
light'house' s faro
lighthouse keeper s farero
lighting ['laɪtɪŋ] s alumbrado, iluminación
lighting engineer s iluminador m
lighting fixtures spl artefactos de alumbrado
lightly ['laɪtli] adj ligeramente
light meter s exposímetro
lightness ['laɪtnɪs] s (*in weight*) ligereza; (*in illumination*) claridad
lightning ['laɪtnɪŋ] s relámpagos, relampagueo ‖ intr relampaguear
lightning arrester [ə'rɛstər] s pararrayos m
lightning bug s luciérnaga
lightning rod s pararrayos m
light opera s opereta
light'ship' s buque m fanal, buque faro
light•struck ['laɪt,strʌk] adj velado
light'weight' adj ligero; de entretiempo, p.ej., **lightweight coat** abrigo de entretiempo
light'-year' s año luz
lignite ['lɪgnaɪt] s lignito
lignum vitae ['lɪgnəm'vaɪti] s guayaco, palo santo
likable ['laɪkəbəl] adj simpático
like [laɪk] adj parecido, semejante; parecido a, semejante a, p.ej., **this hat is like mine** este sombrero es parecido al mío; (elec) del mismo nombre; **like father like son** de tal palo tal astilla; **to feel like** + ger tener ganas de + inf; **to look like** parecerse a; parecer que, p.ej., **it looks like rain** parece que va a llover ‖ adv como; **like enough**

(coll) probablemente; **nothing like** ni con mucho ‖ *prep* a semejanza de ‖ *conj* (coll) del mismo modo que; (coll) que, p.ej., **it seems like he is right** parece que tiene razón ‖ *s* (*liking*) gusto, preferencia; (*fellow, fellow man*) prójimo, semejante *m;* **and the like** y cosas por el estilo; **to give like for like** pagar en la misma moneda ‖ *tr* gustar de, p.ej., **I like music** gusto de la música; gustar p.ej., **Mary likes peaches a** María. le gustan los melocotones; **to like best** o **better** preferir; **to like it in** encontrarse a gusto en (*p.ej., el campo*); **to like to** + *inf* gustarle a uno + *inf*, p.ej., **I like to travel** me gusta viajar; gustarle a uno que + *subj*, p.ej., **I should like him to come to see me** me gustaría que él viniese a verme ‖ *intr* querer, p.ej., **as you like** como Vd. quiera; **if you like** si Vd. quiere

likelihood ['laɪklɪˌhʊd] *s* probabilidad

like•ly ['laɪklɪ] *adj* (*comp* **-lier;** *super* **-liest**) probable; a propósito; prometedor; **to be likely to** + *inf* ser probable que + *ind,* p.ej., **Mary is likely to come to see us tomorrow** es probable que María vendrá a vernos mañana ‖ *adv* probablemente

like-minded ['laɪk'maɪndɪd] *adj* del mismo parecer; de natural semejante

liken ['laɪkən] *tr* asemejar, comparar

likeness ['laɪknɪs] *s* (*picture or image*) retrato; (*similarity*) semejanza, parecido; forma, aspecto, apariencia

like'wise' *adv* igualmente, asimismo; **to do likewise** hacer lo mismo

liking ['laɪkɪŋ] *s* gusto, afición, simpatía; **to be to the liking of** ser del gusto de; **to have a liking for** aficionarse a

lilac ['laɪlək] *adj* de color lila ‖ *s* lilac *m,* lila

Lilliputian [ˌlɪlɪ'pjuʃən] *adj & s* liliputiense *mf*

lilt [lɪlt] *s* paso airoso, movimiento airoso; canción cadenciosa, música alegre

lil•y ['lɪlɪ] *s* (*pl* **-ies**) (*Lilium candidum*) azucena, lirio blanco; cala, lirio de agua; (*fleur-de-lis, the royal arms of France*) flor *f* de lis; **to gild the lily** ponerle colores al oro

lily of the valley *s* lirio de los valles, muguete *m*

lily pad *s* hoja de nenúfar

lima bean ['laɪmə] *s* judía de la peladilla, frijol *m* de media luna

limb [lɪm] *s* (*arm or leg*) miembro; (*of a tree*) rama; (*of a cross; of the sea*) brazo; **to be out on a limb** (coll) estar en un aprieto

limber ['lɪmbər] *adj* ágil; flexible ‖ *intr*—**to limber up** agilitarse

lim•bo ['lɪmbo] *s* (*pl* **-bos**) lugar *m* de olvido; (theol) limbo

lime [laɪm] *s* (*calcium oxide*) cal *f;* (*Citrus aurantifolia*) limero agrio; (*its fruit*) lima agria; (*linden tree*) tila o tilo

lime'kiln' *s* calera, horno de cal

lime'light' *s* —**to be in the limelight** estar a la vista del público

limerick ['lɪmərɪk] *s* quintilla jocosa

lime'stone' *adj* calizo ‖ *s* caliza, piedra caliza

limit ['lɪmɪt] *s* límite *m;* **to be the limit** (slang) ser el colmo; **to go the limit** no dejar piedra por mover ‖ *tr* limitar

lim'ited-ac'cess high'way *s* carretera de vía libre

limited monarchy *s* monarquía constitucional

limitless ['lɪmɪtlɪs] *adj* ilimitado

limousine ['lɪməˌzin] o [ˌlɪmə'zin] *s* (aut) limusina

limp [lɪmp] *adj* flojo, débil, flexible ‖ *s* cojera ‖ *intr* cojear

limpid ['lɪmpɪd] *adj* diáfano, cristalino

linage ['laɪnɪdʒ] *s* (typ) número de líneas

linchpin ['lɪntʃˌpɪn] *s* pezonera

linden ['lɪndən] *s* tila, tilo

line [laɪn] *s* línea; (*of people, houses, etc.*) hilera; (*rope, string*) cuerda, cordel *m;* (*wrinkle*) arruga; (*for fishing*) sedal *m;* (*written or printed line; line of goods*) renglón *m;* (*de pensar*) (*of the spectrum*) (phys) raya; **all along the line** por todas partes; desde cualquier punto de vista; **in line** alineado; dispuesto, preparado; **in line with** de acuerdo con; **out of line** desalineado; en desacuerdo; **to bring into line** poner de acuerdo; **to draw the line at** no ir más allá de; **to fall in line** conformarse; formar cola; alinearse; **to have a line on** (coll) estar enterado de; **to read between the lines** leer entre líneas; **to stand in line** hacer cola; **to toe the line** obrar como se debe; **to wait in line** hacer cola, esperar vez ‖ *tr* alinear, rayar; arrugar (*p.ej., la cara*); formar hilera a lo largo de (*la acera, la calle*); forrar (*un vestido*); guarnecer (*un freno*) ‖ *intr*—**to line up** ponerse en fila; hacer cola

lineage ['lɪnɪ•ɪdʒ] *s* linaje *m*

lineaments ['lɪnɪ•əmənts] *spl* lineamentos

linear ['lɪnɪ•ər] *adj* lineal

line•man ['laɪnmən] *s* (*pl* **-men** [mən]) (elec) celador *m,* recorredor *m* de la línea; (rr) guardavía *m;* (surv) cadenero

linen ['lɪnən] *adj* de lino ‖ *s* (*fabric*) lienzo, lino; (*yarn*) hilo de lino; ropa blanca, ropa de cama

linen closet *s* armario para la ropa blanca

line of battle *s* línea de batalla

line of fire *s* (mil) línea de tiro

line of least resistance *s* ley *f* del menor esfuerzo; **to follow the line of least resistance** seguir la corriente, no oponer resistencia

line of sight *s* visual *f;* (*of firearm*) línea de mira

liner ['laɪnər] *s* vapor *m* de travesía; (baseball) pelota rasa, lineazo

line'-up' *s* agrupación, formación; (*of prisoners*) rueda

linger ['lɪŋgər] *intr* estarse, quedarse; (*to be tardy*) demorar, tardar; tardar en marcharse; tardar en morirse; pasearse con paso lento; **to linger over** contemplar, reflexionar

li
li

lingerie [,lænʒə'ri] *s* ropa interior de mujer

lingering ['lɪŋgərɪŋ] *adj* prolongado

lingual ['lɪŋgwəl] *adj* & *s* lingual *f*

linguist ['lɪŋgwɪst] *s* (*person skilled in several languages*) poligloto; (*specialist in linguistics*) lingüista *mf*

linguistic [lɪŋ'gwɪstɪk] *adj* lingüístico ‖ **linguistics** *s* lingüística

liniment ['lɪnɪmənt] *s* linimento

lining ['laɪnɪŋ] *s* (*of a coat*) forro, forrado; (*of auto brake*) guarnición; (*of a furnace*) camisa; (*of a wall*) revestimiento

link [lɪŋk] *s* eslabón *m;* **links** campo de golf ‖ *tr* eslabonar ‖ *intr* eslabonarse

linkup ['lɪŋk,ʌp] *s* conexión; (*in space*) acoplamiento

linnet ['lɪnɪt] *s* pardillo

linoleum [lɪ'nolɪ•əm] *s* linóleo

linotype ['laɪnə,taɪp] (trademark) *adj* linotípico ‖ *s* (*machine*) linotipia; (*matter produced by machine*) linotipo ‖ *tr* componer con linotipia

linotype operator *s* linotipista *mf*

linseed ['lɪn,sid] *s* linaza

linseed oil *s* aceite *m* de linaza

lint [lɪnt] *s* borra, pelusa, hilaza; (*used to dress wounds*) hilas

lintel ['lɪntəl] *s* dintel *m*, umbral *m*

lion ['laɪ•ən] *s* león *m;* (*man of strength and courage*) (fig) león; (fig) celebridad muy solicitada; **to beard the lion in his den** ir a desafiar la cólera de un jefe; **to put one's head in the lion's mouth** meterse en la boca del lobo

lioness ['laɪ•ənɪs] *s* leona

lion-hearted ['laɪ•ən,hartɪd] *adj* valiente

lionize ['laɪ•ə,naɪz] *tr* agasajar

lions' den *s* (Bib) fosa de los leónes

lion's share *s* (la) parte *f* del león

lip [lɪp] *s* labio; (slang) lenguaje *m* insolente; **to hang on the words of** estar pendiente de las palabras de; **to smack one's lips** chuparse los labios

lip'-read' *v* (*pret* & *pp* **-read** [,rɛd]) *tr* & *intr* leer en los labios

lip reading *s* labiolectura

lip service *s* homenaje *m* de boca, jarabe *m* de pico

lip'stick' *s* lápiz *m* de labios, lápiz labial

liq. *abbr* **liquid, liquor**

lique•fy ['lɪkwɪ,faɪ] *v* (*pret* & *pp* **-fied**) *tr* liquidar ‖ *intr* liquidarse

liqueur [lɪ'kʌr] *s* licor *m*

liquid ['lɪkwɪd] *adj* líquido ‖ *s* líquido; (phonet) líquida

liquidate ['lɪkwɪ,det] *tr* & *intr* liquidar

liquidity [lɪ'kwɪdɪtɪ] *s* liquidez *f*

liquid measure *s* medida para líquidos

liquor ['lɪkər] *s* licor *m*

Lisbon ['lɪzbən] *s* Lisboa

lisle [laɪl] *s* hilo fino de algodón, muy retorcido, sedalina

lisp [lɪsp] *s* cecco ‖ *intr* cecear

lissome ['lɪsəm] *adj* flexible, elástico; ágil, ligero

list [lɪst] *s* lista; (*strip*) lista, tira; (*border*) orilla; (*selvage*) orillo; (naut) ladeo; **lists**

liza; **to enter the lists** entrar en liza; **to have a list** (naut) irse a la banda ‖ *tr* alistar, listar; registrar ‖ *intr* (naut) irse a la banda

listen ['lɪsən] *intr* escuchar; obedecer; **to listen in** escuchar a hurtadillas; escuchar por radio; **to listen to** escuchar; obedecer; **to listen to reason** meterse en razón

listener ['lɪsənər] *s* oyente *mf;* radioescucha *mf*, radioyente *mf*

listening post ['lɪsənɪŋ] *s* puesto de escucha

listing ['lɪstɪŋ] *s* (*items*) rubricación

listless ['lɪstlɪs] *adj* distraído, desatento, indiferente

listlessness ['lɪstlɪsnɪs] *s* apatía; indiferencia

list price *s* precio de catálogo, precio de tarifa

lit. *abbr* **liter, literal, literature**

lita•ny ['lɪtəni] *s* (*pl* **-nies**) letanía; (*repeated series*) (fig) letanía

liter ['litər] *s* litro

literacy ['lɪtərəsi] *s* capacidad de leer y escribir; instrucción

literal ['lɪtərəl] *adj* literal

literary ['lɪtə,rɛri] *adj* literario; (*individual*) literato

literate ['lɪtərɪt] *adj* que sabe leer y escribir; (*well-read*) literato, muy leído; (*educated*) instruído ‖ *s* persona que sabe leer y escribir; literato, erudito

literati [,lɪtə'rati] *spl* literatos

literature ['lɪtərətʃər] *s* literatura; impresos, escritos de publicidad

lithe [laɪθ] *adj* flexible, cimbreño

lithia ['lɪθɪ•ə] *s* (chem) litina

lithium ['lɪθɪ•əm] *s* (chem) litio

lithograph ['lɪθə,græf] *s* litografía ‖ *tr* litografiar

lithographer [lɪ'θɑgrəfər] *s* litógrafo

lithography [lɪ'θɑgrəfi] *s* litografía

litigant ['lɪtɪgənt] *adj* & *s* litigante *mf*

litigate ['lɪtɪ,get] *tr* & *intr* litigar

litigation [,lɪtɪ'gəfən] *s* litigación; (*lawsuit*) litigio

litigious [lɪ'tɪdʒəs] *adj* litigioso

litmus ['lɪtməs] *s* tornasol *m*

litmus paper *s* papel *m* de tornasol

litter ['lɪtər] *s* desorden *m;* (*scattered rubbish*) basura, papelería; (*young brought forth at one birth*) camada, ventregada; (*bedding for animals*) cama, paja; (*vehicle carried by men or animals*) litera; (*stretcher*) camilla, parihuela ‖ *tr* esparcir papeles por; esparcir (*desechos, papeles, etc.*); cubrir (*el suelo*) con paja ‖ *intr* parir

lit'ter•bug' *s* persona que ensucia las calles tirando papeles rotos

littering ['lɪtərɪŋ] *s*—**no littering** se prohibe tirar papeles rotos

little ['lɪtəl] *adj* (*in size*) pequeño; (*in amount*) poco, p.ej., **little money** poco dinero; **a little** un poco de, p.ej., **a little money** un poco de dinero ‖ *adv* poco; **little by little** poco a poco ‖ *s* poco; **a little** un poco; (*somewhat*) algo; **to make little of** no dar importancia a, no tomar en serio; **to think little of** tener en poco; no vacilar en

Little Bear s Osa menor
Little Dipper s Carro menor
little finger s dedo auricular, dedo meñique; **to twist around one's little finger** manejar con suma facilidad
lit'tle·neck' s almeja redonda (*Venus mercenaria*)
little owl s mochuelo (*Athene noctua*)
little people spl hadas; gente menuda
Little Red Ridinghood ['raɪdɪŋ,hʊd] s Caperucita Roja
little slam s (bridge) semibola
liturgic(al) [lɪ'tʌrdʒɪk(əl)] adj litúrgico
litur·gy ['lɪtərdʒi] s (pl -gies) liturgia
livable ['lɪvəbəl] adj habitable, vividero; llevadero, tolerable
live [laɪv] adj (*living; full of life; intense*) vivo; (*coals; flame*) ardiente; de actualidad; (elec) cargado ‖ [lɪv] tr llevar (*tal o cual vida*); vivir (*una experiencia, una aventura; un actor sus personajes*); **to live down** borrar (*una falta*); **to live out** vivir (*toda la vida*); salir con vida de (*un desastre, una guerra*) ‖ intr vivir; **to live and learn** vivir para ver; **to live and let live** vivir y dejar vivir; **to live high** darse buena vida; **to live on** seguir viviendo; vivir de (*p.ej., carne*); vivir a expensas de; **to live up to** cumplir (*lo prometido*); gastar (*todas sus rentas*)
live coal s ascua
livelihood ['laɪvlɪ,hʊd] s vida; **to earn one's livelihood** ganarse la vida
livelong ['lɪv,lɔŋ] o ['lɪv,lɑŋ] adj—**all the livelong day** todo el santo día
live·ly ['laɪvli] adj (comp -lier; super -liest) animado, vivaz; alegre, festivo; (*active, keen*) vivo; (*resilient*) elástico
liven ['laɪvən] tr animar, regocijar ‖ intr animarse, regocijarse
liver ['lɪvər] s vividor m; habitante mf; (anat) hígado
liver·y ['lɪvəri] s (pl -ies) librea
livery·man ['lɪvərimən] s (pl -men [mən]) dueño de una cochera; mozo de cuadra
livery stable s cochera de carruajes de alquiler
live'stock' adj ganadero ‖ s ganadería
live wire s (elec) alambre cargado; (slang) trafagón m
livid ['lɪvɪd] adj lívido, amoratado; encolerizado; pálido
living ['lɪvɪŋ] adj vivo, viviente ‖ s vida; **to earn** o **to make a living** ganarse la vida
living quarters spl aposentos, habitaciones
living room s sala, sala de estar
living wage s jornal m suficiente para vivir
lizard ['lɪzərd] s lagarto; (slang) holgón m
load [lod] s carga; **loads** (coll) muchísimo; **loads of** (coll) gran cantidad de; **to get a load of** (slang) escuchar, oír; (slang) mirar; **to have a load on** (slang) estar borracho ‖ tr cargar ‖ intr cargar; cargarse
loaded ['lodɪd] adj cargado; (slang) muy borracho; (slang) muy rico
loaded dice spl dados cargados
load'stone' s piedra imán; (fig) imán m

loaf [lof] s (pl **loaves** [lovz]) pan m; (*of sugar*) pilón m ‖ intr haraganear
loafer ['lofər] s haragán m
loam [lom] s suelo franco; (*mixture used in making molds*) tierra de moldeo
loamy ['lomi] adj franco
loan [lon] s (*among individuals*) préstamo; (*between companies or governments*) empréstito; **to hit for a loan** (coll) dar un sablazo a ‖ tr prestar
loan shark s (coll) usurero
loan word s préstamo lingüístico
loath [loθ] adj poco dispuesto; **nothing loath** de buena gana
loathe [loð] tr abominar, detestar
loathing ['loðɪŋ] s abominación, detestación
loathsome ['loðsəm] adj abominable, asqueroso
lob [lɑb] v (pret & pp **lobbed**; ger **lobbing**) tr (tennis) volear desde muy alto
lob·by ['lɑbi] s (pl -bies) salón m de entrada, vestíbulo; cabilderos ‖ v (pret & pp -bied) intr cabildear
lobbying ['lɑbɪɪŋ] s cabildeo
lobbyist ['lɑbɪɪst] s cabildero
lobster ['lɑbstər] s (*spiny lobster*) langosta; (*Homarus*) bogavante m
lobster pot s langostera
local ['lokəl] adj local ‖ s tren suburbano; (*branch of a union*) junta local; noticia de interés local
locale [lo'kæl] s localidad
locali·ty [lo'kælɪti] s (pl -ties) localidad
localize ['lokə,laɪz] tr localizar
local option s derecho local de legislar sobre la venta de bebidas alcohólicas
locate [lo'ket] o ['loket] tr (*to discover the location of*) localizar; (*to place, to settle*) colocar, establecer; (*to ascribe a particular location to*) situar ‖ intr establecerse
location [lo'keʃən] s (*place, position*) localidad; (*act of placing*) colocación; (*act of finding*) localización; **on location** (mov) en exteriores
loc. cit. abbr **loco citato** (Lat) **in the place cited**
lock [lɑk] s cerradura; (*of a canal*) esclusa; (*of hair*) bucle m; (*of a firearm*) llave f; **lock, stock, and barrel** (coll) del todo, por completo; **under lock and key** bajo llave ‖ tr echar la llave a, cerrar con llave; (*to key*) acuñar; hacer pasar (*un buque*) por la esclusa; abrazar, enlazar; **to lock in** encerrar, poner debajo de llave; **to lock out** cerrar la puerta a, dejar en la calle; dejar sin trabajo (*a los obreros*); **to lock up** encerrar, poner debajo de llave; encarcelar
locker ['lɑkər] s armario cerrado con llave
locket ['lɑkɪt] s guardapelo, medallón m
lock'jaw' s trismo, oclusión forzosa de la boca
lock nut s contratuerca
lock'out' s huelga patronal
lock'smith' s cerrajero
lock step s marcha en fila apretada
lock stitch s punto encadenado
lock tender s esclusero

lock'up' s cárcel f
lock washer s arandela de seguridad
locomotive [,lokə'motɪv] s locomotora
lo•cus ['lokəs] s (pl **-ci** [saɪ]) sitio, lugar m; lugar (geométrico)
locust ['lokəst] s (ent) langosta (Pachytylus); (ent) cigarra (Cicada); (bot) acacia falsa
lode [lod] s filón m, venero, veta
lode'star' s (astr) estrella polar; estrella de guía; (guide, direction) guía, norte m
lodge [lɑdʒ] s casa de guarda; casa de campo; (e.g., of Masons) logia || tr alojar, hospedar; depositar, colocar; presentar (una queja) || alojarse, hospedarse; quedar colgado, ir a parar
lodger ['lɑdʒər] s inquilino (en parte de una casa)
lodging ['lɑdʒɪŋ] s alojamiento, hospedaje m; (without meals) cobijo
loft [lɔft] s (attic) desván m, sobrado; (hayloft) henal m, pajar m; (in theater or church) galería; (in a store or office building) piso alto
loft•y ['lɔfti] adj (comp **-ier**; super **-iest**) (towering; sublime) encumbrado; (haughty) altivo, orgulloso
log. abbr **logarithm**
log [lɔg] s leño, tronco; (log chip) (naut) barquilla; (chip and line) (naut) corredera; (aer) diario de vuelo; **to sleep like a log** dormir como un leño || v (pret & pp **logged**) ger **logging**) tr registrar; recorrer (cierta distancia)
logarithm ['lɔgə,rɪðəm] s logaritmo
log'book' s (aer) libro de vuelo; (naut) cuaderno de bitácora
log cabin s cabaña de troncos
log chip s (naut) barquilla
log driver s ganchero, maderero
log driving s flotaje m
logger ['lɔgər] o ['lɑgər] s leñador m, maderero; grúa de troncos; tractor m
log'ger•head' s mentecato; **at loggerheads** reñidos
loggia ['lɔdʒə] s (archit) logia
logic ['lɑdʒɪk] s lógica
logical ['lɑdʒɪkəl] adj lógico
logician [lo'dʒɪʃən] s lógico
logistic(al) [lo'dʒɪstɪk(əl)] adj logístico
logistics [lo'dʒɪstɪks] s logística
log'jam' s atasco de rollizos; (fig) estancación
log line s (naut) corredera
log'roll' intr trocar favores políticos
log'wood' s campeche m
loin [lɔɪn] s lomo; **to gird up one's loins** apercibirse para la acción
loin'cloth' s taparrabo
loiter ['lɔɪtər] tr—**to loiter away** malgastar (el tiempo) || intr holgazanear, rezagarse
loiterer ['lɔɪtərər] s holgazán m, rezagado
loll [lɑl] intr colgar flojamente; arrellanarse, repantigarse
lollipop ['lɑli,pɑp] s paleta (dulce en el extremo de un palito)
Lombard ['lɑmbard] adj & s lombardo
Lombardy ['lɑmbərdi] s Lombardía

Lombardy poplar s álamo de Italia, chopo lombardo
lon. abbr **longitude**
London ['lʌndən] adj londinense || s Londres m
Londoner ['lʌndənər] s londinense mf
lone [lon] adj solo, solitario; (sole, single) único
loneliness ['lonlɪnɪs] s soledad
lone•ly ['lonli] adj (comp **-lier**; super **-liest**) soledoso
lonesome ['lonsəm] adj soledoso; (spot, atmosphere) solitario
lone wolf s (fig) lobo solitario
long. abbr **longitude**
long [lɔŋ] o [lɑŋ] (comp **longer** ['lɔŋgər] o ['lɑŋgər]; super **longest** ['lɔŋgɪst] o ['lɑŋgɪst]) adj largo; de largo, p.ej., **two meters long** dos metros de largo || adv mucho tiempo, largo tiempo; **as long as** mientras; (provided) con tal de que; (inasmuch as) puesto que; **before long** dentro de poco; **how long** cuánto tiempo; **long ago** hace mucho tiempo; **long before** mucho antes; **longer** más tiempo; **long since** desde hace mucho tiempo; **no longer** ya no; **so long!** (coll) ¡hasta luego!; **so long as** con tal de que || intr anhelar, suspirar; **to long for** anhelar por, ansiar
long'boat' s (naut) lancha
long'-dis'tance call s (telp) llamada a larga distancia
long-distance flight s (aer) vuelo a distancia
long'-drawn'-out' adj prolongado, pesado
longeron ['lɑndʒərən] s larguero
longevity [lɑn'dʒɛvɪti] s longevidad
long face s (coll) cara triste
long'hair' adj & s intelectual mf; aficionado a la música clásica
long'hand' s escritura a mano
longing ['lɔŋɪŋ] adj anhelante || s anhelo, ansia
longitude ['lɑndʒɪ,tjud] s longitud
long johns spl ropa interior que cubre brazos y piernas
long-lived ['lɔŋ'laɪvd] o (coll) ['lɔŋ'lɪvd] adj longevo, de larga vida
long-playing record ['lɔŋ'ple•ɪŋ] s disco de larga duración; elepé m
long primer ['prɪmər] s (typ) entredós m
long'-range' adj de largo alcance
longshore•man ['lɔŋ,ʃormən] s (pl **-men** [mən]) s estibador m, portuario
long'-stand'ing adj que existe desde hace mucho tiempo
long'-suf'fering adj longánimo, sufrido
long suit s (cards) palo fuerte; (fig) fuerte m
long'-term' adj a largo plazo
long'-wind'ed adj difuso, palabrero; discursisto
look [lʊk] s (appearance) aspecto, apariencia; (glance) mirada; (search) búsqueda; **looks** aspecto, apariencia; **to take a look at** echar una mirada a || tr expresar con la mirada; representar (la edad que uno tiene); **to look daggers at** apuñalar con la mirada; **to look the part** vestir el cargo; **to look up**

(*e.g.*, *in a dictionary*) buscar; ir a visitar, venir a ver ‖ *intr* mirar; buscar; parecer; **look out!** ¡cuidado!, ¡ojo!; **to look after** mirar por; ocuparse en; **to look at** mirar; **to look back** mirar hacia atrás; (fig) mirar el pasado; **to look down on** mirar por encima del hombro; **to look for** buscar; creer, p.ej., **I look for rain** creo que va á llover; **to look forward to** esperar con placer anticipado; **to look ill** tener mala cara; **to look in on** pasar por la casa o la oficina de; **to look into** averiguar, estudiar; **to look like** parecerse a; amenazar, p.ej., **it looks like rain** amenaza lluvia, parece que va a llover; **to look oneself** parecer el mismo; tener buena cara; **to look out** tener cuidado; mirar por (*p.ej., la ventana*); **to look out for** mirar por, cuidar de; guardarse de; **to look out on** dar a; **to look through** mirar por; hojear (*un libro*); **to look toward** dar a; **to look up to** admirar, mirar con respeto; **to look well** tener buena cara
lookalike ['lukə,laɪk] *adj & s* doble; parecido
looker-on [,lukər'ɑn] *s* (*pl* **lookers-on**) mirón *m*, espectador *m*
looking glass ['lukɪŋ] *s* espejo
look'out' *s* vigilancia; (*tower*) atalaya; (*person keeping watch*) vigilante *mf*; (*man watching from lookout tower*) atalaya *m*; (*care, concern*) (coll) cuidado; **to be on the lookout for** estar a la mira de
loom
[lum] *s* telar *m* ‖ *intr* (*to appear indistinctly*) vislumbrarse; amenazar, parecer inevitable
loon [lun] *s* tonto, bobo; (orn) zambullidor *m*
loon·y ['luni] *adj* (*comp* **-ier**; *super* **-iest**) (slang) loco ‖ *s* (*pl* **-ies**) (slang) loco
loop [lup] *s* lazo; (*in a cable or rope*) vuelta; (*of a river*) meandro; (*of a road*) recoveco; (*for fastening a button*) presilla; (aer) rizo; (elec) circuito cerrado; (*part of vibrating body between two nodes*) vientre *m*; **to loop the loop** (aer) rizar el rizo ‖ *tr* hacer lazos en; enlazar ‖ *intr* formar lazo; (aer) hacer el rizo
loop'hole' *s* (*narrow opening in wall*) lucerna; (*means of evasion*) efugio, escapatoria
loose [lus] *adj* (*dress, tooth, screw, bowels*) flojo; (*fitting, thread, wire, rivet, tongue, bowels*) suelto; (*sleeve*) perdido; (*earth, soil*) desmenuzado; (*unpackaged*) a granel, sin envase; (*unbound papers*) sin encuadernar; (*pulley*) loco; (*translation*) libre; (*life, morals*) relajado; (*woman*) fácil, frágil; **to become loose** desatarse, aflojarse; **to break loose** ponerse en libertad; **to turn loose** soltar ‖ *s*—**to be on the loose** ser libre, estar sin trabas; estar de juerga ‖ *tr* soltar; desatar, desencadenar
loose end *s* cabo suelto; **at loose ends** desarreglado, indeciso
loose'-leaf' notebook *s* cuaderno de hojas cambiables, cuaderno de hojas sueltas
loosen ['lusən] *tr* desatar, aflojar, desapretar; aflojar, laxar (*el vientre*) ‖ *intr* desatarse, aflojarse, desapretarse

looseness ['lusnɪs] *s* flojedad, soltura; (*in morals*) relajamiento
loose'strife' *s* lisimaquia; salicaria
loose-tongued ['lus'tʌŋd] *adj* largo de lengua, ligero de lengua
loot [lut] *s* botín *m*, presa ‖ *tr* saquear, pillar
lop [lɑp] *v* (*pret & pp* **lopped;** *ger* **lopping**) *tr* dejar caer (*p.ej., los brazos*); **to lop off** cortar; podar (*un árbol, una vid*) ‖ *intr* colgar
lopsided ['lɑp'saɪdɪd] *adj* ladeado, sesgado; desproporcionado, asimétrico, patituerto
loquacious [lo'kweʃəs] *adj* locuaz
loran ['lɔræn] *s* (naut) lorán *m*
lord [lɔrd] *s* señor *m*; (Brit) lord *m*; (hum & poet) marido ‖ *tr*—**to lord it over** dominar despóticamente, imponerse a
lord·ly ['lɔrdli] *adj* (*comp* **-lier**; *super* **-liest**) señoril; magnífico; despótico, imperioso; altivo, arrogante
Lord's Day, the el domingo
lordship ['lɔrdʃɪp] *s* señoría, excelencia
Lord's Prayer *s* oración dominical, padrenuestro
Lord's Supper *s* sagrada comunión; Cena del Señor
lore [lor] *s* ciencia, saber *m*; ciencia popular, saber *m* popular
lorgnette [lɔrn'jet] *s* (*eyeglasses*) impertinentes *mpl*; (*opera glasses*) gemelos de teatro con manija
lor·ry ['lɑri] o ['lɔri] *s* (*pl* **-ries**) carro de plataforma; (Brit) autocamión *m*; (Brit) vagoneta
lose [luz] *v* (*pret & pp* **lost** [lɔst] o [lɑst]) *tr* perder; no lograr salvar (*el médico al enfermo*); **to lose heart** desalentarse; **to lose oneself** perderse, errar el camino; ensimismarse ‖ *intr* perder; quedar vencido; retrasarse (*el reloj*)
loser ['luzər] *s* perdedor *m*
losing ['luzɪŋ] *adj* perdedor ‖ **losings** *spl* pérdidas, dinero perdido
loss [lɔs] o [lɑs] *s* pérdida; **to be at a loss** estar perplejo, no saber qué hacer; **to be at a loss to** + *inf* no saber como + *inf*; **to sell at a loss** vender con pérdida
loss leader *s* artículo vendido a gran descuento
loss of face *s* pérdida de prestigio, desprestigio
lost [lɔst] o [lɑst] *adj* perdido; (fig) desviado; **lost in thought** ensimismado, abismado; **lost to** perdido para; insensible a
lost'-and-found' department *s* oficina de objetos perdidos
lost sheep *s* oveja perdida
lot [lɑt] *s* (*for building*) solar *m*, parcela; (*fate, destiny*) suerte *f*; (*portion, parcel*) lote *m*; (*of people*) grupo; (coll) gran cantidad, gran número; (coll) sujeto, tipo; **a lot (of)** o **lots of** (coll) mucho, muchos; **to cast o to throw in one's lot with** compartir la suerte de; **to draw o to cast lots** echar suertes
lotion ['loʃən] *s* loción
lotter·y ['lɑtəri] *s* (*pl* **-ies**) lotería

lo
lo

lotto ['lɑto] s lotería
lotus ['lotəs] s loto
loud [laʊd] adj alto; (noisy) ruidoso; (voice) fuerte; (garish) chillón, llamativo; (conspicuously vulgar) charro, cursi; (foul-smelling) apestoso, maloliente ‖ adv alto, en voz alta; ruidosamente
loud'mouth' s bocaza, bocona, bocón m
loudmouthed ['laʊd,maʊθt] o ['laʊd,maʊðd] adj vocinglero
loud'speak'er s altavoz m, parlante m, pantalla acústica
lounge [laʊndʒ] s diván m, sofá m cama; salón m de descanso, salón social ‖ intr repantigarse a su sabor, recostarse cómodamente; **to lounge around** estar arrimado a la pared, pasearse perezosamente
lounge lizard s (slang) holgón m
louse [laʊs] s (pl **lice** [laɪs]) piojo
lous•y ['laʊzi] adj (comp -ier; super -iest) piojoso; (mean) vil, ruin; (filthy) asqueroso, sucio; (bungling) chapucero; **lousy with** (slang) colmado de (p.ej., dinero)
lout [laʊt] s patán m
louver ['luvər] s (opening to let in air and light) lumbrera; tablilla de persiana; (aut) persiana del radiador
lovable ['lʌvəbəl] adj amable
love [lʌv] s amor m; (tennis) cero, nada; **not for love nor money** ni a tiros; **to be in love (with)** estar enamorado (de); **to fall in love (with)** enamorarse (de); **to make love to** cortejar, galantear ‖ tr amar, querer; gustar de, tener afición a
love affair s amores mpl, amorío
love'bird' s inseparable m; **lovebirds** recién casados muy enamorados
love child s hijo del amor
love feast s ágape m
love'-hate' s odio-amor m
loveless ['lʌvlɪs] adj abandonado, sin amor; (feeling no love) desamado
lovelorn ['lʌv,lɔrn] adj abandonado por su amor, herido de amor
love•ly ['lʌvli] adj (comp -lier; super -liest) bello, hermoso; adorable, precioso; (coll) encantador, gracioso
love match s matrimonio de amor
love potion s filtro, filtro de amor
lover ['lʌvər] s amante mf; (e.g., of hunting, sports) aficionado; (e.g., of work) amigo
love seat s confidente m
love'sick' adj enfermo de amor
love'sick'ness s mal m de amor
love song s canción de amor
loving ['lʌvɪŋ] adj amoroso, afectuoso
lov'ing-kind'ness s bondad infinita, misericordia
low [lo] adj bajo; (diet; visibility; opinion) malo; (dress, waist) escotado; (depressed) abatido; gravemente enfermo; (fire) lento; **to lay low** dejar tendido, derribar; matar; **to lie low** no dejarse ver ‖ adv bajo ‖ s punto bajo; precio más bajo, precio mínimo; (moo of cow) mugido; (aut) primera marcha, primera velocidad; (meteor) depresión ‖ intr mugir (la vaca)

low'born' adj de humilde cuna
low'boy' s cómoda baja con patas cortas
low'brow' adj & s (slang) ignorante mf
low'-cost' housing s casas baratas
Low Countries, the los Países Bajos
low'-down' adj (coll) bajo, vil, ruin ‖ **low'-down'** s (slang) informes mf confidenciales, hechos verdaderos
lower ['lo•ər] adj bajo, inferior ‖ tr & intr bajar ‖ ['laʊ•ər] intr poner mala cara, fruncir el entrecejo; encapotarse (el cielo)
lower berth ['lo•ər] s litera baja, cama baja
Lower California ['lo•ər] s la Baja California
lower case ['lo•ər] s (typ) caja baja
lower middle class ['lo•ər] s pequeña burguesía
lowermost ['lo•ər,most] adj (el) más bajo
low'-fre'quency adj de baja frecuencia
low gear s primera marcha, primera velocidad
low'-key' adj modesto; moderado
lowland ['loland] s tierra baja ‖ **Lowlands** spl Tierra Baja (de Escocia)
low life s gentuza
low•ly ['loli] adj (comp -lier; super -liest) humilde; (in growth or position) bajo
Low Mass s misa rezada
low-minded ['lo'maɪndɪd] adj vil, ruin
low neck s escote m, escotado
low-necked ['lo'nɛkt] adj escotado
low-pitched ['lo'pɪtʃt] adj (sound) grave; (roof) de poco declive
low'-pres'sure adj de baja presión
low-priced ['lo'praɪst] adj barato, de precio bajo
low shoe s zapato inglés
low'-speed' adj de baja velocidad
low-spirited ['lo'spɪrɪtɪd] adj abatido
low spirits spl abatimiento
low tide s bajamar f, marea baja; (fig) punto más bajo
low visibility s (aer) poca visibilidad
low water s (of a river) nivel mínimo; (because of drought) estiaje m; bajamar f, marea baja
loyal ['lɔɪ•əl] adj leal
loyalist ['lɔɪ•əlɪst] s leal m
loyal•ty ['lɔɪ•əlti] s (pl -ties) lealtad
lozenge ['lɑzɪndʒ] s losange m; (candy cough drop) pastilla, tableta
LP ['ɛl'pi] s (letterword) (trademark) disco de larga duración; elepé m
Ltd. abbr limited
lubricant ['lubrɪkənt] adj & s lubricante m
lubricate ['lubrɪ,ket] tr lubricar
lubricous ['lubrɪkəs] adj (slippery; lewd) lúbrico (resbaladizo; lascivo); incierto, inconstante
lucerne [lu'sʌrn] s mielga
lucid ['lusɪd] adj claro, inteligible; (rational, sane) lúcido; (bright, shining) luciente; (clear, transparent) cristalino
Lucifer ['lusɪfər] s Lucifer m
luck [lʌk] s (good or bad) suerte f; (good) suerte, buena suerte; **down on one's luck** de mala suerte, de malas; **in luck** de buena

suerte, de buenas; **out of luck** de mala suerte, de malas; **to bring luck** traer buena suerte; **to try one's luck** probar fortuna; **worse luck** desgraciadamente

luckily ['lʌkɪli] *adj* afortunadamente

luckless ['lʌklɪs] *adj* desgraciado

luck•y ['lʌki] *adj* (*comp* **-ier;** *super* **-iest**) afortunado; derecho (CAm); (*supposed to bring luck*) de buen agüero; **to be lucky** tener suerte; quedar bien parado

lucky hit *s* (coll) golpe *m* de fortuna

lucrative ['lukrətɪv] *adj* lucrativo

ludicrous ['ludɪkrəs] *adj* absurdo, ridículo

lug [lʌg] *s* orejeta; (*pull, tug*) estirón *m,* esfuerzo ‖ *v* (*pret & pp* **lugged;** *ger* **lugging**) *tr* tirar con fuerza de; (*to bring up irrelevantly*) (coll) traer a colación

luggage ['lʌgɪdʒ] *s* equipaje *m*

lugubrious [lu'gubrɪ•əs] o [lu'gjubrɪ•əs] *adj* lúgubre

lukewarm ['luk,wɔrm] *adj* tibio, templado

lull [lʌl] *s* momento de calma, momento de silencio; (naut) recalmón *m* ‖ *tr* adormecer; calmar, aquietar; apacíguar

lulla•by ['lʌlə,baɪ] *s* (*pl* **-bies**) arrullo, canción de cuna

lumbago [lʌm'bego] *s* lumbago

lumber ['lʌmbər] *s* madera aserrada, madera aserradiza, madera de sierra; trastos viejos ‖ *intr* andar pesadamente

lum'ber•jack' *s* leñador *m,* hachero

lumber•man ['lʌmbərmən] *s* (*pl* **-men** [mən]) (*dealer*) maderero; (*man who cuts down lumber*) leñador *m,* hachero

lumber room *s* leonera, trastera

lum'ber•yard' *s* maderería, depósito de maderas

luminar•y ['lumɪ,nɛri] *s* (*pl* **-ies**) luminar *m,* lumbrera

luminescent [,lumɪ'nɛsənt] *adj* luminiscente

luminous ['lumɪnəs] *adj* luminoso

lummox ['lʌməks] *s* (coll) jergón *m*

lump [lʌmp] *s* terrón *m;* (*swelling*) chichón *m,* bulto, hinchazón *m;* (*stupid person*) (coll) bodoque *m;* **in the lump** en grueso, por junto; **to get a lump in one's throat** hacérsele a (*uno*) un nudo en la garganta ‖ *tr* juntar, mezclar; (*to make into lumps*) aterronar; (coll) aguantar, tragar (cosa repulsiva)

lumpish ['lʌmpɪʃ] *adj* hobachón, torpe, pesado

lump sum *s* suma global, suma total

lump•y ['lʌmpi] *adj* (*comp* **-ier;** *super* **-iest**) aterronado, borujoso; torpe, pesado; (*sea*) agitado

luna•cy ['lunəsi] *s* (*pl* **-cies**) demencia, locura

lunar ['lunər] *adj* lunar

lunar lander o **lunar module** *s* módulo lunar

lunar landing *s* alunizaje *m*

lunatic ['lunətɪk] *adj & s* lunático, loco

lunatic asylum *s* manicomio

lunatic fringe *s* minoría fanática

lunch [lʌnʃ] *s* (*regular midday meal*) almuerzo; (*light meal*) colación, merienda ‖ *intr* almorzar; merendar, tomar una colación

lunch basket *s* fiambrera

lunch cloth *s* mantelito

luncheon ['lʌntʃən] *s* almuerzo; almuerzo de ceremonia

lunch'room' *s* cantina, merendero

lung [lʌŋ] *s* pulmón *m*

lung cancer *s* cáncer *m* pulmonar

lunge [lʌndʒ] *s* arremetida, embestida; (*with a sword*) estocada ‖ *intr* arremeter, lanzarse; **to lunge at** arremeter contra

lurch [lʌrtʃ] *s* sacudida, tumbo; (naut) bandazo; **to leave in the lurch** dejar en la estacada, dejar colgado ‖ *intr* dar una sacudida, dar un tumbo; (naut) dar un bandazo

lure [lur] *s* (*decoy*) cebo, señuelo; (fig) aliciente *m,* señuelo ‖ *tr* atraer con cebo, atraer con señuelo; (fig) atraer, tentar, seducir; **to lure away** llevarse con señuelo; (*from one's obligations*) desviar

lurid ['lurɪd] *adj* sensacional; (*gruesome*) espeluznante; (*fiery*) ardiente, encendido

lurk [lʌrk] *intr* acechar, andar furtivamente

luscious ['lʌʃəs] *adj* delicioso; lujoso; voluptuoso

lush [lʌʃ] *adj* jugoso, lozano; lujuriante; lujoso

Lusitanian [,lusɪ'tenɪ•ən] *adj & s* lusitano

lust [lʌst] *s* deseo vehemente; (*greed*) codicia; (*strong sexual appetite*) lujuria; entusiasmo ‖ *intr* lujuriar; **to lust after** o **for** codiciar; desear con lujuria

luster ['lʌstər] *s* (*gloss*) lustre *m; (of certain fabrics*) viso; (*fame, glory*) (fig) lustre

lus'ter•ware' *s* loza con visos metálicos

lustful ['lʌstfəl] *adj* lujurioso

lustrous ['lʌstrəs] *adj* lustroso

lust•y ['lʌsti] *adj* (*comp* **-ier;** *super* **-iest**) fuerte, robusto, lozano

lute [lut] *s* (mus) laúd *m; (substance used to close or seal a joint*) (chem) lodo

Lutheran ['luθərən] *adj & s* luterano

luxuriance [lʌg'ʒurɪ•əns] *s* lozanía

luxuriant [lʌg'ʒurɪ•ənt] *adj* lozano, lujuriante; (*overornamented*) recargado

luxuriate [lʌg'ʒurɪ,et] o [lʌk'ʃurɪ,et] *intr* crecer con lozanía; entregarse al lujo; (*to find keen pleasure*) lozanearse

luxurious [lʌg'ʒurɪ•əs] o [lʌk'ʃurɪ•əs] *adj* lujoso

luxu•ry ['lʌkʃəri] o ['lʌgʒəri] *s* (*pl* **-ries**) lujo

lye [laɪ] *s* lejía

lying ['laɪ•ɪŋ] *adj* mentiroso ‖ *s* el mentir

ly'ing-in' hospital *s* casa de maternidad, clínica de parturientas

lymph [lɪmf] *s* linfa

lymphatic [lɪm'fætɪk] *adj* linfático

lynch [lɪntʃ] *tr* linchar

lynching ['lɪntʃɪŋ] *s* linchamiento

lynch law *s* justicia de la soga

lynx [lɪŋks] *s* lince *m*

lynx-eyed ['lɪŋks,aɪd] *adj* de ojos linces

lyonnaise [,laɪ•ə'nez] *adj* (culin) a la lionesa

lyre [laɪr] *s* (mus) lira

lyric ['lɪrɪk] *adj* lírico ‖ *s* poema lírico; (*words of a song*) (coll) letra

lyrical ['lɪrɪkəl] *adj* lírico

lyricism ['lɪrɪ,sɪzəm] *s* lirismo

lyricist ['lɪrɪsɪst] *s* (*writer of words for songs*) letrista *mf;* (*poet*) poeta lírico

lo
ly

M

M, m [ɛm] decimotercera letra del alfabeto inglés

m. *abbr* **married, masculine, meter, midnight, mile, minute, month**

ma'am [mæm] o [mɑm] *s* (coll) señora

macadam [məˈkædəm] *s* macadán *m*

macadamize [məˈkædə,maɪz] *tr* macadamizar

macaro•ni [,mækəˈroni] *s* (*pl* **-nis** o **-nies**) macarrones *mpl*

macaroon [,mækəˈrun] *s* mostachón *m*, almendrado

macaw [məˈkɔ] *s* aracanga, guacamayo

mace [mes] *s* maza; (*spice*) macis *m*

mace'bear'er *s* macero

machination [,mækɪˈneʃən] *s* maquinación

machine [məˈʃin] *s* máquina; automóvil *m*, coche *m*; (*of a political party*) camarilla ‖ *tr* trabajar a máquina

machine gun *s* ametralladora

ma•chine'-gun' *tr* ametrallar

ma•chine'-made' *adj* hecho a máquina

machiner•y [məˈʃinəri] *s* (*pl* **-ies**) maquinaria

machine screw *s* tornillo para metales

machine shop *s* taller mecánico

machine stenography *s* estenotipia

machine tool *s* máquina-herramienta

machine translation *s* traducción automática

machinist [məˈʃinɪst] *s* (*person who makes machines*) maquinista *mf*; (*person who operates machines*) mecánico; (naut) segundo maquinista; (theat) maquinista *mf*, tramoyista *mf*

mackerel [ˈmækərəl] *s* caballa, escombro

mackerel sky *s* cielo aborregado

mackintosh [ˈmækɪn,tɑʃ] *s* impermeable *m*

mad [mæd] *adj* (*comp* **madder;** *super* **maddest**) (*angry*) enojado, furioso; (*crazy*) loco; (*foolish*) tonto, necio; (*rabid*) rabioso; **to be mad about** (coll) estar loco por; **to drive mad** volver loco; **to go mad** volverse loco; rabiar (*un perro*)

madam [ˈmædəm] *s* señora

mad'cap' *s* alocado, tarambana *mf*

madden [ˈmædən] *tr* (to make angry) enojar, enfurecer; (*to make insane*) enloquecer

made-to-order [ˈmedtəˈɔrdər] *adj* hecho de encargo; (*clothing*) hecho a la medida

made'-up' *adj* inventado, ficticio; (*artificial*) postizo; (*face*) pintado

mad'house' *s* casa de locos, manicomio

madman [ˈmæd,mæn] *s* (*pl* **-men** [,mɛn]) loco

madness [ˈmædnɪs] *s* furia, rabia; locura; (*of a dog*) rabia

Madonna lily [məˈdɑnə] *s* azucena

maelstrom [ˈmelstrəm] *s* remolino

mag. *abbr* **magazine**

magazine [ˈmægə,zin] o [,mægəˈzin] *s* (*periodical*) revista, magazine *m*; (*warehouse*) almacén *m*; (*for cartridges*) cámara; (*for powder*) polvorín *m*; (naut) santabárbara; (phot) almacén *m*

Magellan [məˈdʒɛlən] *s* Magallanes *m*

maggot [ˈmægət] *s* cresa

Magi [ˈmedʒaɪ] *spl* magos de Oriente, Reyes Magos

magic [ˈmædʒɪk] *adj* mágico ‖ *s* magia; ilusionismo, prestidigitación; **as if by magic** como por encanto

magician [məˈdʒɪʃən] *s* (*entertainer with sleight of hand*) ilusionista *mf*, prestidigitador *m*; (*sorcerer*) mágico

magistrate [ˈmædʒɪs,tret] *s* magistrado

magnanimous [mægˈnænɪməs] *adj* magnánimo

magnesium [mægˈniʃɪ•əm] o [mægˈnɪʒɪ•əm] *s* magnesio

magnet [ˈmægnɪt] *s* imán *m*

magnetic [mægˈnɛtɪk] *adj* magnético; (fig) atrayente, cautivador

magnetic curves *spl* fantasma magnético

magnetic field *s* campo magnético

magnetism [ˈmægnɪ,tɪzəm] *s* magnetismo

magnetize [ˈmægnɪ,taɪz] *tr* magnetizar, imanar

magne•to [mægˈnito] *s* (*pl* **-tos**) magneto *m & f*

magnificent [mægˈnɪfɪsənt] *adj* magnífico

magni•fy [ˈmægnɪ,faɪ] *v* (*pret & pp* **-fied**) *tr* magnificar; exagerar

magnifying glass *s* lupa, vidrio de aumento

magnitude [ˈmægnɪ,tjud] *s* magnitud

magpie [ˈmæg,paɪ] *s* picaza, urraca

Magyar [ˈmægjɑr] *adj & s* magiar *mf*

mahlstick [ˈmɑl,stɪk] o [ˈmɔl,stɪk] *s* tiento

mahoga•ny [məˈhɑgəni] *s* (*pl* **-nies**) caoba

Mahomet [məˈhɑmɪt] *s* Mahoma *m*

mahout [məˈhaʊt] *s* naire *m*, cornaca *m*

maid [med] *s* (*female servant*) criada, moza; (*young girl; housemaid*) doncella; gata (Mex); (*spinster*) soltera

maiden [ˈmedən] *s* doncella

maid'en•hair' *s* (bot) cabello de Venus

maid'en•head' *s* himen *m*

maidenhood [ˈmedən,hʊd] *s* doncellez *f*

maiden lady *s* soltera

maiden name *s* apellido de soltera

maiden voyage *s* primera travesía

maid'-in-wait'ing *s* (*pl* **maids-in-waiting**) dama

maid of honor *s* (*at a wedding*) primera madrina de boda; (*attendant on a princess*) doncella de honor; (*attendant on a queen*) dama de honor

maid'serv'ant *s* criada, doméstica

mail [mel] *s* correspondencia, correo; (*of armor*) malla; **by return mail** a vuelta de correo ‖ *tr* echar al correo

mail'bag' *s* valija

mail'boat' *s* vapor *m* correo

mail'box' *s* buzón *m*

mail car *s* carro correo, coche-correo, ambulancia de correos

mail carrier *s* cartero

mailing list *s* lista de envío

mailing permit *s* porte concertado

mail•man [ˈmel,mæn] *s* (*pl* **-men** [,mɛn]) cartero

mail order *s* pedido postal

mail'-or'der house s casa de ventas por correo

mail'plane' s avión-correo

mail train s tren m correo

maim [mem] tr estropear, mutilar

main [men] adj principal, primero, maestro, mayor ‖ s cañería maestra; **in the main** mayormente

main clause s proposición dominante

main course s plato principal, plato fuerte

main deck s cubierta principal

mainland ['men,lænd] o ['menlənd] s continente m, tierra firme

main line s (rr) tronco, línea principal

mainly ['menli] adv principalmente, en su mayor parte

mainmast ['menməst], o ['men,mæst] o ['men,mɑst] s palo mayor

mainsail ['mensəl] o ['men,sel] s vela mayor

main'spring' s (of watch) muelle m real; (fig) móvil m, origen m

main'stay' s (naut) estay m mayor; (fig) soporte m principal

main'stream' s vía principal

main street s calle f mayor

maintain [men'ten] tr mantener; (to support) (law) manutener

maintenance ['mentɪnəns] s mantenimiento; (upkeep) conservación; gastos de conservación

maître d'hôtel [,metər do'tɛl] s (butler) mayordomo; (headwaiter) jefe m de comedor

maize [mez] s maíz m

majestic [mə'dʒɛstɪk] adj majestuoso

majes•ty ['mædʒɪsti] s (pl -ties) majestad

major ['medʒər] adj (greater) mayor; (elder) mayor de edad; (mus) mayor ‖ s (educ) especialización; (mil) comandante m ‖ intr (educ) especializarse

Majorca [mə'dʒɔrkə] s Mallorca

Majorcan [mə'dʒɔrkən] adj & s mallorquín m

major-do•mo [,medʒər'domo] s (pl -mos) mayordomo

major general s general m de división

majori•ty [mə'dʒɔrɪti] adj mayoritario ‖ s (pl -ties) (being of full age; larger number or part) mayoría; (full age) mayoría; (mil) comandancia

make [mek] s (brand) marca; (form, build) hechura; carácter m, natural m; **on the make** (slang) buscando provecho ‖ v (pret & pp **made** [med]) tr hacer; cometer (un error); efectuar (un pago); ganar (dinero; una baza); coger (un tren); dar (dinero una empresa); pronunciar (un discurso); cerrar (un circuito); poner (a uno, p.ej., nervioso); ser, p.ej., **she will make a good wife** será una buena esposa; **to make +** inf hacer + inf, p.ej., **she made him study** le hizo estudiar; **to make into** convertir en; **to make known** declarar; dar a conocer; **to make of** pensar de; **to make oneself known** darse a conocer; **to make out** distinguir, vislumbrar; descifrar; escribir (una receta); llenar (un cheque); **to make over** convertir; rehacer (un traje); (com) transfe-

rir; **to make up** preparar, confeccionar; inventar (un cuento); recobrar (el tiempo perdido); (theat) maquillar ‖ intr estar (p.ej., seguro); **to make away with** llevarse; deshacerse de; matar; **to make believe** fingir, p.ej., **he made believe he knew me** fingió conocerme; **to make for** ir hacia; embestir contra; contribuir a (p.ej., mejores relaciones); **to make much of** (coll) hacer fiestas a, mostrar cariño a; **to make off** largarse; **to make off with** llevarse, hacerse con; **to make out** arreglárselas; **to make toward** encaminarse a; **to make up** maquillarse, pintarse; componerse, hacer las paces; **to make up for** suplir; compensar por (una pérdida); **to make up to** (coll) tratar de congraciarse con

make'-be•lieve' adj simulado ‖ s pretexto, simulación, fantasía

maker ['mekər] s constructor m, fabricante mf

make'shift' adj de fortuna, provisional ‖ s expediente m; (person) tapagujeros m

make'-up' s composición, constitución; afeite m, maquillaje m; (typ) imposición

make-up man s (theat) maquillador m

make'weight' s contrapeso; suplente mf

making ['mekɪŋ] s fabricación; material necesario; causa del éxito; **makings** elementos, materiales mpl; (personal qualities necessary for some purpose) madera

malachite ['mælə,kaɪt] s malaquita

maladjustment [,mælə'dʒʌstmənt] s desadaptación

mala•dy ['mælədi] s (pl -dies) dolencia, enfermedad

malaise [mæ'lez] s indisposición, malestar m

malapropism [,mælə'prɑp,ɪzəm] s despropósito

malapropos [,mæləprə'po] adj impropio ‖ adv fuera de propósito

malaria [mə'lɛrɪ•ə] s malaria, paludismo

Malay ['mele] o [mə'le] adj & s malayo

malcontent ['mælkən,tɛnt] adj & s malcontento

male [mel] adj (sex) masculino; (animal, plant, piece of a device) macho; (human being) varón, p.ej., **male child** hijo varón ‖ s macho; varón m

male chauvinism s machismo

male chauvinist s machista m

malediction [,mælɪ'dɪkʃən] s maldición

malefactor ['mælɪ,fæktər] s malhechor m

male nurse s enfermero

malevolent [mə'lɛvələnt] adj malévolo

malfunction [,mæl'fʌŋkʃən] s malfuncionamiento s intr ir de través; estropearse

malice ['mælɪs] s malicia, malevolencia; **to bear malice** guardar rencor; **with malice prepense** [prɪ'pɛns] (law) con malicia y premeditación

malicious [mə'lɪʃəs] adj malicioso, malévolo

malign [mə'laɪn] adj maligno ‖ tr calumniar

malignant [mə'lɪgnənt] adj maligno

maligni•ty [mə'lɪgnɪti] s (pl -ties) malignidad

malinger [mə'lɪŋgər] *intr* hacer la zanguanga, fingirse enfermo

mall [mɔl] o [mæl] *s* alameda, paseo de árboles

mallet ['mælɪt] *s* (*wooden hammer*) mazo; (*for croquet and polo*) mallete *m*

mallow ['mælo] *s* malva

malnutrition [,mælnju'trɪʃən] *s* desnutrición

malodorous [mæl'odərəs] *adj* maloliente

malt [mɔlt] *s* malta *m*; (coll) cerveza

maltreat [mæl'trit] *tr* maltratar

mamma ['mɑmə] o [mə'mɑ] *s* mama o mamá *f*

mammal ['mæməl] *s* mamífero

mammalian [mæ'melɪ•ən] *adj & s* mamífero

mammoth ['mæməθ] *adj* gigantesco, enorme ‖ *s* mamut *m*

man [mæn] *s* (*pl* **-men** [mɛən]) *s* hombre *m*; (*in chess*) pieza; (*in checkers*) pieza, peón *m*; **a man** uno, p.ej., **a man can't get work in this town** uno no puede obtener empleo en este pueblo; **as one man** unánimamente; **man alive!** ¡hombre!; **man and wife** marido y mujer; **to be one's own man** no depender de nadie ‖ *v* (*pret & pp* **manned**; *ger* **manning**) *tr* dotar, tripular (*un buque*); guarnecer (*una fortaleza*); servir (*los cañones*)

man about town *s* bulevardero, hombre *m* de mucho mundo

manacle ['mænəkəl] *s* manilla; **manacles** esposas ‖ *tr* poner esposas a

manage ['mænɪdʒ] *tr* manejar ‖ *intr* arreglárselas; **to manage to** ingeniarse a o para; **to manage to get along** ingeniarse para ir viviendo

manageable ['mænɪdʒəbəl] *adj* manejable

management ['mænɪdʒmənt] *s* manejo, dirección, gerencia; (*group who manage a business*) la empresa, la parte patronal, los patronos

manager ['mænədʒər] *s* director *m*, administrador *m*, gerente *mf*; empresario; (sport) manager *m*

managerial [,mænə'dʒɪrɪ•əl] *adj* empresarial

mandate ['mændet] *s* mandato ‖ *tr* asignar por mandato

mandolin ['mændəlɪn] *s* mandolina

mandrake ['mændrek] *s* mandrágora

mane [men] *s* (*of horse*) crines *fpl*; (*of lion, of person*) melena

maneuver [mə'nuvər] *s* maniobra ‖ *tr* hacer maniobrar ‖ *intr* maniobrar

manful ['mænfəl] *adj* varonil, resuelto

manganese ['mæŋgə,nis] o ['mæŋgə,niz] *s* manganeso

mange [mendʒ] *s* sarna

manger ['mendʒər] *s* pesebre *m*

mangle ['mæŋgəl] *tr* lacerar, aplastar

man•gy ['mendʒi] *adj* (*comp* **-gier**; *super* **-giest**) sarnoso; (*dirty, squalid*) roñoso

man'han'dle *tr* maltratar

man'hole' *s* caja de registro, pozo de inspección

manhood ['mænhʊd] *s* virilidad; hombres *mpl*

man hunt *s* caza al hombre

mania ['menɪ•ə] *s* manía

maniac ['menɪ,æk] *adj & s* maníaco

manic-depressive ['mænɪkdɪ'prɛsɪv] *adj & s* maníaco-depresivo

manicure ['mænɪ,kjʊr] *s* (*care of hands*) manicura; (*person*) manicuro, manicura ‖ *tr* hacer la manicura a (*una persona*); hacer (*las manos y las uñas*)

manicurist ['mænɪ,kjʊrɪst] *s* manicuro, manicura

manifest ['mænɪ,fɛst] *adj* manifiesto ‖ *s* (naut) manifiesto ‖ *tr* manifestar

manifes•to [,mænɪ'fɛsto] *s* (*pl* **-toes**) manifiesto

manifold ['mænɪ,fold] *adj* múltiple, vario; polivalente ‖ *s* copia, ejemplar *m*; (*pipe with outlets or inlets*) colector *m*, múltiple *m*

manikin ['mænɪkɪn] *s* maniquí *m*; (*dwarf*) enano

man in the moon *s* cara o cuerpo de hombre imaginarios en la luna llena

manioc ['mænɪɑk] *s* cazabe *m*, casabe *m*

manipulate [mə'nɪpjə,let] *tr* manipular

man'kind' *s* el género humano ‖ **man'kind'** *s* el sexo masculino, los hombres

manliness ['mænlɪnɪs] *s* masculinidad, virilidad

man•ly ['mænli] *adj* (*comp* **-lier**; *super* **-liest**) masculino, varonil

manned spaceship [mænd] *s* astronave tripulada

mannequin ['mænɪkɪn] *s* maniquí *m*; (*young woman employed to exhibit clothing*) maniquí *f*

manner ['mænər] *s* manera; **bad manners** malcriadez *f*, malacrianza; **by all manner of means** de todos modos; **in a manner of speaking** como si dijéramos; **in the manner of** a la manera de; **manners** modales *mpl*, crianza; **to the manner born** avezado desde la cuna

mannish ['mænɪʃ] *adj* hombruno

man of letters *s* hombre *m* de letras

man of means *s* hombre *m* de dinero

man of parts *s* hombre *m* de buenas prendas

man of straw *s* hombre *m* de suposición

man of the world *s* hombre *m* de mundo

man-of-war [,mænəv'wɔr] *s* (*pl* **men-of-war** [,mɛnəv'wɔr]) *s* buque *m* de guerra

manor ['mænər] *s* señorío

manor house *s* casa solariega

man overboard *interj* ¡hombre al agua!

man'pow'er *s* número de hombres; personal *m* competente; (mil) fuerzas nacionales

mansard ['mænsɑrd] *s* mansarda; piso de mansarda

man'serv'ant *s* (*pl* **men'serv'ants**) criado

mansion ['mænʃən] *s* hotel *m*, palacio; (*manor house*) casa solariega

man'slaugh'ter *s* (law) homicidio sin premeditación

mantel ['mæntəl] *s* manto (*de chimenea*); (*shelf above it*) mesilla, repisa de chimenea

man'tel•piece' *s* mesilla, repisa de chimenea

mantle [ˈmæntəl] *s* capa, manto ‖ *tr* vestir con manto; cubrir, tapar; ocultar ‖ *intr* encenderse (*el rostro*)

manual [ˈmænjʊ•əl] *adj* manual ‖ *s* (*book*) manual *m;* (mil) ejercicio; (mus) teclado manual

manual training *s* enseñanza de los artes y oficios

manufacture [ˌmænjəˈfæktjər] *s* fabricación; obraje *m;* (*thing manufactured*) manufactura ‖ *tr* fabricar, manufacturar

manufacturer [ˌmænjəˈfæktjərər] *s* fabricante *mf*

manure [məˈnjʊr] o [məˈnʊr] *s* estiércol *m* ‖ *tr* estercolar

manuscript [ˈmænjəˌskrɪpt] *adj & s* manuscrito

many [ˈmɛni] *adj & pron* muchos; **a good many** o **a great many** un buen número; **as many as** tantos como; hasta, p.ej., **as many as twenty** hasta veinte; **how many** cuántos; **many a** muchos, p.ej., **many a person** muchas personas; **many another** muchos otros; **many more** muchos más; **so many** tantos; **too many** demasiados; **twice as many as** dos veces más que

many-sided [ˈmɛniˌsaɪdɪd] *adj* multilátero; (*having many interests or capabilities*) polifacético

map [mæp] *s* mapa *m;* (*of a city*) plano ‖ *v* (*pret & pp* **mapped**; *ger* **mapping**) *tr* trazar el mapa de; indicar en el mapa; **to map out** trazar el plan de

maple [ˈmepəl] *s* arce *m*

maquette [mɑˈkɛt] *s* maqueta

Mar. *abbr* **March**

mar [mɑr] *v* (*pret & pp* **marred**; *ger* **marring**) *tr* desfigurar, estropear; frustrar

maraud [məˈrɔd] *tr* saquear ‖ *intr* merodear

marauder [məˈrɔdər] *s* merodeador *m*

marble [ˈmɑrbəl] *adj* marmóreo ‖ *s* mármol *m;* (*little ball of glass, etc.*) canica; **marbles** (*game*) canica ‖ *tr* crispir, jaspear

march [mɑrtʃ] *s* marcha; (*frontier, territory*) marca; **to steal a march on someone** ganarle a uno por la mano ‖ *tr* hacer marchar ‖ *intr* marchar ‖ **March** *s* marzo

marchioness [ˈmɑrʃənɪs] *s* marquesa

mare [mɛr] *s* (*female horse*) yegua; (*female donkey*) asna

margarine [ˈmɑrdʒərɪn] *s* margarina

margin [ˈmɑrdʒɪn] *s* margen *m & f;* (*collateral deposited with a broker*) doble *m*

marginal [ˈmɑrdʒɪnəl] *adj* marginal

margin release *s* tecla de escape

margin stop *s* fijamárgenes *m*, cierrarrenglón *m*, cortarrenglón *m*

marigold [ˈmærɪˌgold] *s* clavelón *m;* (*Calendula*) maravilla, flamenquilla

marihuana o **marijuana** [ˌmɑrɪˈhwɑnə] *s* mariguana; grifa, grifo (Mex)

marina [məˈrinə] *s* dársena

marinate [ˈmærɪˌnet] *tr* escabechar, marinar

marine [məˈrin] *adj* marino, marítimo ‖ *s* marina; soldado de infantería de marina; **marines** infantería de marina; **tell that to the marines** (coll) cuénteselo a su abuela, a otro perro con ese hueso

mariner [ˈmærɪnər] *s* marino

marionette [ˌmærɪ•əˈnɛt] *s* marioneta, títere *m*

marital status [ˈmærɪtəl] *s* estado civil

maritime [ˈmærɪˌtaɪm] *adj* marítimo

marjoram [ˈmɑrdʒərəm] *s* orégano; mejorana

mark [mɑrk] *s* marca, señal *f;* (*label*) marbete *m;* (*of punctuation*) punto; (*in an examination*) calificación, nota; (*used instead of signature by an illiterate person*) cruz *f*, signo; (*spot, stain*) mancha; (*coin*) marco; (*starting point in a race*) raya; (*target to shoot at*) blanco; **to be beside the mark** no venir al caso; **to hit the mark** dar en el blanco; **to leave one's mark** dejar memoria de sí; **to make one's mark** llegar a ser célebre; **to miss the mark** errar el tiro; **to toe the mark** ponerse en la raya; obedecer rigurosamente ‖ *tr* marcar, señalar; dar nota a (*un alumno*); calificar (*un examen*); advertir, notar; **to mark down** poner por escrito; rebajar el precio de

mark′down′ *s* reducción de precio

market [ˈmɑrkɪt] *s* mercado; **to bear the market** jugar a la baja; **to bull the market** jugar al alza; **to play the market** jugar a la bolsa; **to put on the market** lanzar al mercado ‖ *tr* llevar al mercado; vender

marketable [ˈmɑrkɪtəbəl] *adj* comerciable, vendible

market basket *s* cesta para compras

marketing [ˈmɑrkɪtɪŋ] *s* mercología, mercadotecnia

market place *s* plaza del mercado

market price *s* precio corriente

market research *s* investigación mercológica

marking gauge [ˈmɑrkɪŋ] *s* gramil *m*

marks•man [ˈmɑrksmən] *s* (*pl* **-men** [mən]) tirador *m;* **a good marksman** un buen tiro

marksmanship [ˈmɑrksmənˌʃɪp] *s* puntería

mark′up′ *s* aumento de precio

marl [mɑrl] *s* marga ‖ *tr* margar

marmalade [ˈmɑrməˌled] *s* mermelada

marmot [ˈmɑrmət] *s* marmota

maroon [məˈrun] *adj & s* marrón *m*, castaño obscuro ‖ *tr* dejar abandonado (*en una isla desierta*)

marquee [mɑ/rˈki] *s* marquesina

marquess [ˈmɑrkwɪs] *s* marqués *m*

marque•try [ˈmɑrkətri] *s* (*pl* **-tries**) marquetería (*taracea*)

marquis [ˈmɑrkwɪs] *s* marqués *m*

marquise [mɑrˈkiz] *s* marquesa; (*over the entrance to a hotel*) marquesina

marriage [ˈmærɪdʒ] *s* casamiento, matrimonio; (*married life; intimate union*) maridaje *m*

marriageable [ˈmærɪdʒəbəl] *adj* casadero

marriage portion *s* dote *m & f*

marriage rate *s* nupcialidad

married life [ˈmærɪd] *s* vida conyugal

marrow [ˈmæro] *s* médula, tuétano

mar•ry [ˈmæri] *v* (*pret & pp* **-ried**) *tr* casar (*el sacerdote o el juez a un hombre y una* mujer); (*to take in marriage*) casar con, casarse con; (*to unite intimately*) maridar; **to get married to** casar con, casarse con ‖ *intr* casar, casarse; **to marry into** emparentar con (*p.ej., una familia rica*); **to marry the second time** casarse en segundas nupcias

Mars [mɑrz] s Marte m

Marseille [mɑr'sɛ:j] s Marsella

marsh [mɑrʃ] s ciénaga, pantano

mar·shal ['mɑrʃəl] s cursor m de procesiones, maestro de ceremonias; (mil) mariscal m; (U.S.A.) oficial m de justicia ‖ v (pret & pp -shaled o -shalled; ger -shaling o -shalling) tr conducir con ceremonia; ordenar, reunir (*los hechos de una argumentación*)

marsh mallow s (bot) malvavisco

marsh'mal'low s bombón m de merengue y gelatina; bombón de malvavisco

marsh·y ['mɑrʃi] adj (comp -ier; super -iest) pantanoso, palúdico

marten ['mɑrtən] s (*pine marten*) marta; (*beech marten*) garduña

martial ['mɑrʃəl] adj marcial

martial law s ley f marcial; **to be under martial law** estar en estado de guerra

Martian ['mɑrʃən] adj & s marciano

martin ['mɑrtın] s (orn) avión m

martinet [,mɑrtı'nɛt] o ['mɑrtı,nɛt] s ordenancista mf

martyr ['mɑrtər] s mártir mf

martyrdom ['mɑrtərdəm] s martirio

mar·vel ['mɑrvəl] s maravilla ‖ v (pret & pp -veled o -velled; ger -veling o -velling) intr maravillarse; **to marvel at** maravillarse con o de

marvelous ['mɑrvələs] adj maravilloso

Marxist ['mɑrksıst] adj & s marxista mf

masc. abbr **masculine**

mascara [mæs'kærə] s tinte m para las pestañas; rímel m

mascot ['mæskɑt] s mascota

masculine ['mæskjəlın] adj & s masculino

mash [mæʃ] s (*crushed mass*) masa; (*to form wort*) masa de cebada ‖ tr machacar, majar

mashed potatoes [mæʃt] spl puré m de patatas

masher ['mæʃər] s (*device*) mano f; (slang) galanteador atrevido

mask [mæsk] o [mɑsk] s máscara; (*of beekeeper*) carilla; (*made from a corpse*) mascarilla; (*person*) máscara mf; (phot) desvanecedor m ‖ tr enmascarar; (phot) desvanecer ‖ intr enmascararse

masked ball [mæskt] s baile m de máscaras

masochism ['mæsə,kızəm] s masoquismo

masochist ['mæsəkıst] s masoquista mf

masochistic [,mæsə'kıstık] adj masoquista

mason ['mesən] s albañil m ‖ **Mason** s masón m

mason·ry ['mesənri] s (pl -ries) albañilería ‖ **Masonry** s masonería

masquerade [,mæskə'red] o [,mɑskə'red] s mascarada; (*costume, disguise*) máscara; (*false show*) farsa ‖ intr enmascararse; **to masquerade as** disfrazarse de

masquerade ball s baile m de máscaras

mass [mæs] s masa; gran cantidad; (*bulk, heap*) mole f; (*something glimpsed, e.g., in the fog*) bulto informe; (*big splotch in a painting*) gran mancha; (*celebration of the Eucharist*) misa; **the masses** las masas ‖ tr juntar, reunir; enmasar (*tropas*) ‖ intr juntarse, reunirse

massacre ['mæsəkər] s carnicería, matanza ‖ tr degollar, matar

massage [mə'sɑʒ] s masaje m ‖ tr masar, masajear

masseur [mæ'sœr] s masajista m

masseuse [mæ'sœz] s masajista f

massive ['mæsıv] adj macizo; sólido, imponente

mass media spl medios spl de comunicación

mass meeting s mitin m popular

mass production s fabricación en serie

mast [mæst] o [mɑst] s (*for a flag*) palo; (*of a ship*) palo, mástil m; (*food for swine*) bellotas, hayucos; **before the mast** como simple marinero

master ['mæstər] o ['mɑstər] s (*employer*) dueño, patrón m; (*male head of household*) amo; (*man who possesses some special skill; teacher*) maestro; (*commander of merchant vessel*) capitán m; (*title of respect for a boy*) señorito ‖ tr dominar

master bedroom s alcoba de respeto

master blade s hoja maestra (*de una ballesta*)

master builder s maestro de obras

masterful ['mæstərfəl] o ['mɑstərfəl] adj hábil, experto; dominante, imperioso

master key s llave maestra

masterly ['mæstərli] o ['mɑstərli] adj magistral ‖ adv magistralmente

master mechanic s maestro mecánico

mas'ter·mind' s mente directora ‖ tr dirigir con gran acierto

master of ceremonies s maestro de ceremonias; (*in a night club, radio, etc.*) animador m

mas'ter·piece' s obra maestra

master stroke s golpe maestro

mas'ter·work' s obra maestra

master·y ['mæstəri] o ['mɑstəri] s (pl -ies) (*command, as of a subject*) dominio; ventaja, superioridad; (*skill*) maestría

mast'head' s (*of a newspaper*) cabecera editorial; (naut) tope m

masticate ['mæstı,ket] tr masticar

mastiff ['mæstıf] o ['mɑstıf] s mastín m

masturbate ['mæstər,bet] tr masturbar ‖ intr masturbarse

masturbation [,mæstər'beʃən] s masturbación

mat [mæt] s (*for floor*) estera; (*for a cup, vase, etc.*) esterilla, ruedo; (*before a door*) felpudo; (*around a picture*) borde m de cartón ‖ v (pret & pp matted; ger matting) tr (*to cover with matting*) esterar; enmarañar ‖ intr enmarañarse

match [mætʃ] s fósforo; (*wick*) mecha; (*counterpart*) compañero; (*suitable partner in marriage*) partido; (*suitably associated* *pair*) pareja; (*game, contest*) match *m*, partido; **to be a match for** poder con, poder vencer; **to meet one's match** hallar la horma de su zapato ‖ *tr* igualar; aparear, emparejar; hacer juego con; **to match someone for the drinks** jugarle a uno las bebidas ‖ *intr* hacer juego, correr parejas; **to match** a juego, p.ej., **a chair to match** una silla a juego

match'box' *s* fosforera; (*of wax matches*) cerillera

matchless ['mætʃlɪs] *adj* incomparable, sin par

matchmaker ['mætʃ,mekər] *s* casamentero

mate [met] *s* compañero; (*e.g., of a shoe*) compañero, hermano; (*husband or wife*) cónyuge *mf*; (*to a female*) macho; (*to a male*) hembra; (*in chess*) mate *m*; (*naut*) piloto ‖ *tr* aparear, casar; (*in chess*) dar jaque mate a; **to be well mated** hacer una buena pareja ‖ *intr* aparearse, casarse

material [mə'tırı•əl] *adj* material; importante ‖ *s* material *m*; (*what a thing is made of*) materia; (*cloth, fabric*) tela, género

materialism [mə'tırı•ə,lızəm] *s* materialismo

materialist [mə'tırı•əlıst] *s* materialista *mf*

materialize [mə'tırı•ə,laız] *intr* realizarse

matériel [mə,tırı'ɛl] *s* material *m*; material de guerra

maternal [mə'tʌrnəl] *adj* materno; (*motherly*) maternal

maternity [mə'tʌrnıti] *s* maternidad

maternity hospital *s* casa de maternidad

math. *abbr* **mathematics**

mathematical [,mæθɪ'mætıkəl] *adj* matemático

mathematician [,mæθɪmə'tıʃən] *s* matemático

mathematics [,mæθɪ'mætıks] *s* matemática, matemáticas

matinée [,mætɪ'ne] *s* matinée *f*, función de tarde

mating season *s* época de celo

matins ['mætınz] *spl* maitines *mpl*

matriarch ['metrı•ɑrk] *s* matriarca

matricidal [,metrı'saıdəl] *adj* matricida

matricide ['metrı,saıd] *s* (*act*) matricidio; (*person*) matricida *mf*

matriculate [mə'trıkjə,let] *tr* matricular ‖ *intr* matricularse

matrimo•ny ['mætrı,moni] *s* (*pl* **-nies**) matrimonio

matron ['metrən] *s* matrona

matronly ['metrənli] *adj* matronal

matter ['mætər] *s* (*physical substance; pus*) materia; (*subject talked or written about*) asunto; (*reason, ground*) motivo; (*copy for printer*) material *m*; (*printed material*) impresos; **a matter of** cosa de, obra de; **for that matter** en cuanto a eso; **in the matter** al respecto; **no matter** no importa; **no matter when** cuando quiera; **no matter where** dondequiera; **what is the matter?** ¿qué hay?; **what is the matter with you?** ¿qué tiene Vd.? ‖ *intr* importar

matter of course *s* cosa de cajón; **as a matter of course** por rutina

matter of fact *s*—**as a matter of fact** en realidad, en honor a la verdad

matter-of-fact ['mætərəv,fækt] *adj* prosaico, práctico, de poca imaginación

mattock ['mætək] *s* zapapico

mattress ['mætrıs] *s* colchón *m*

mature [mə'tʃur] o [mə'tur] *adj* maduro; (*due*) pagadero, vencido ‖ *tr* madurar ‖ *intr* madurar; (*to become due*) (com) vencer

maturity [mə'tʃurıti] o [mə'turıti] *s* madurez *f*; (com) vencimiento

maudlin ['mɔdlın] *adj* lacrimoso, sensiblero; chispo y lloroso

maul [mɔl] *tr* aporrear, maltratar

maulstick ['mɔl,stık] *s* tiento

maundy ['mɔndi] *s* lavatorio

Maundy Thursday *s* Jueves Santo

mausole•um [,mɔsə'li•əm] *s* (*pl* **-ums** o **-a** [ə]) mausoleo

maw [mɔ] *s* (*of fowl*) buche *m*; (*of fish*) vejiga de aire

mawkish ['mɔkıʃ] *adj* (*sickening*) empalagoso; (*sentimental*) sensiblero

max. *abbr* **maximum**

maxim ['mæksım] *s* máxima

maximum ['mæksıməm] *adj* & *s* máximo

may *v aux* **it may be** puede ser; **may I come in?** ¿puedo entrar? **may you be happy!** ¡que seas feliz! ‖ **May** *s* mayo

maybe ['mebi] o ['mebı] *adv* acaso, quizá, tal vez

May Day *s* primero de mayo; fiesta del primero de mayo

Mayday ['me,de] *interj* (*ships, airplanes*) ¡socorro!

mayhem ['mehɛm] o ['me•əm] *s* (law) mutilación criminal

mayonnaise [,me•ə'nez] *s* mayonesa

mayor ['me•ər] o [mɛr] *s* alcalde *m*

mayoress ['me•ərıs] o ['mɛrıs] *s* alcaldesa

May'pole' *s* mayo

Maypole dance *s* danza de cintas

May queen *s* maya

maze [mez] *s* laberinto

M.C. *abbr* **Master of Ceremonies, Member of Congress**

mdse. *abbr* **merchandise**

me [mi] *pron pers* me; mí; **to me** me; a mí; **with me** conmigo

meadow ['mɛdo] *s* prado, vega

mead'ow•land' *s* pradera

meager ['migər] *adj* escaso, pobre; flaco, magro

meal [mil] *s* (*regular repast*) comida; (*edible grain coarsely ground*) harina

meal'time' *s* hora de comer

mean [min] *adj* (*intermediate*) medio; (*low in station or rank*) humilde, obscuro; (*shabby*) andrajoso, raído; (*stingy*) mezquino, tacaño; (*of poor quality*) inferior, pobre; (*small-minded*) vil, ruin, innoble; insignificante; (*vicious, as a horse*) arisco, mal intencionado; (coll) indisupuesto; (coll) avergonzado; (coll) de mal genio; **no mean** famoso, excelente ‖ *s* promedio, término medio; **by all means** sí, por cierto, sin

ma
me

falta; **by means of** por medio de; **by no means** de ningún modo, en ningún caso; **means** bienes *mpl* de fortuna; *(agency)* medio, medios; **means to an end** paso para lograr un fin; **to live on one's means** vivar de sus rentas ‖ *v (pret & pp* **meant** [mɛnt]) *tr* significar, querer decir; **to mean to** pensar ‖ *intr*—**to mean well** tener buenas intenciones

meander [mɪ'ændər] *s* meandro ‖ *intr* serpentear; vagar

meaning ['minɪŋ] *s* sentido, significado

meaningful ['minɪŋfəl] *adj* significativo

meaningless ['minɪŋlɪs] *adj* sin sentido

meanness ['minnɪs] *s* bajeza, vileza, ruindad; *(stinginess)* mezquindad; *(lowliness)* humildad, pobreza

mean'time' *adv* entretanto, mientras tanto ‖ *s* medio tiempo; **in the meantime** entretanto, mientras tanto

mean'while' *adv & s* var de **meantime**

measles ['mizəlz] *s* sarampión *m; (German measles)* rubéola

mea·sly ['mizli] *adj (comp* **-slier;** *super* **-sliest)** sarampioso; *(slang)* despreciable, mezquino

measurable ['mɛʒərəbəl] *adj* medible

measure ['mɛʒər] *s* medida, *(step, procedure)* paso, gestión; *(legislative bill)* proyecto de ley; *(of verse)* pie *m; (mus)* compás *m;* **beyond measure** con exceso; **in a measure** hasta cierto punto; **in great measure** en gran parte; *(suit)* **to measure** hecho a la medida; **to take measures** tomar las medidas necesarias; **to take someone's measure** tomarle a uno las medidas ‖ *tr* medir; recorrer *(cierta distancia);* **to measure out** medir; distribuir ‖ *intr* medir

measurement ['mɛʒərmənt] *s (act of measuring)* medición; *(measuring; dimension)* medida

measuring glass *s* vaso graduado

meat [mit] *s* carne *f; (food in general)* manjar *m,* vianda; *(substance, gist)* meollo

meat ball *s* albóndiga

meat grinder *s* picador *m*

meat'hook' *s* garabato de carnicero

meat market *s* carnicería

meat·y ['miti] *adj (comp* **-ier;** *super* **-iest)** carnoso; *(fig)* jugoso, substancioso

Mecca ['mɛkə] *s* La Meca

mechanic [mɪ'kænɪk] *s* mecánico

mechanical [mɪ'kænɪkəl] *adj* mecánico, maquinal; *(machinelike)* (fig) maquinal

mechanical toy *s* juguete *m* de movimiento

mechanics [mɪ'kænɪks] *ssg* mecánica

mechanism ['mɛkə,nɪzəm] *s* mecanismo

mechanize ['mɛkə,naɪz] *tr* mecanizar

med. *abbr* **medicine, medieval**

medal ['mɛdəl] *s* medalla

medallion [mɪ'dæljən] *s* medallón *m*

meddle ['mɛdəl] *intr* meterse, entremeterse

meddler ['mɛdlər] *s* entremetido

meddlesome ['mɛdəlsəm] *adj* entremetido

media ['midɪ·ə] *abbr* **mass media**

median ['midɪ·ən] *adj* intermedio, medio ‖ *s* punto medio, número medio

median strip *s* faja central o divisoria

mediate ['midɪ,et] *tr* dirimir *(una controversia);* reconciliar ‖ *intr (to be in the middle)* mediar; *(to intervene to settle a dispute)* intervenir

mediation [,midɪ'eʃən] *s* mediación

mediator ['midɪ,etər] *s* mediador *m*

medical ['mɛdɪkəl] *adj* médico

medical student *s* estudiante *mf* de medicina

medicine ['mɛdɪsɪn] *s (science and art)* medicina; *(remedy, treatment)* medicina, medicamento

medicine cabinet *s* armario botiquín

medicine kit *s* botiquín *m*

medicine man *s* curandero, hechicero *(entre los pieles rojas)*

medieval [,midɪ'ivəl] o [,mɛdɪ'ivəl] *adj* medieval

medievalist [,midɪ'ivəlɪst] o [,mɛdɪ'ivəlɪst] *s* medievalista *mf*

mediocre ['midɪ,okər] o [,midɪ'okər] *adj* mediocre

mediocri·ty [,midɪ'akrɪti] *s (pl* **-ties)** mediocridad

meditate ['mɛdɪ,tet] *tr & intr* meditar

Mediterranean [,mɛdɪtə'renɪ·ən] *adj & s* Mediterráneo

medi·um ['midɪ·əm] *adj* intermedio; a medio asar ‖ *s (pl* **-ums** o **-a** [ə]) medio; *(in spiritualism)* medio, médium *m; (publication)* órgano; **through the medium of** por medio de

me'dium-range' *adj* de alcance medio

medlar ['mɛdlər] *s (tree and fruit)* níspero; *(fruit)* níspola

medley ['mɛdli] *s* mescolanza; (mus) popurrí *m*

medul·la [mɪ'dʌlə] *s (pl* **-lae** [li]) médula

meek [mik] *adj* dócil, manso

meekness ['miknɪs] *s* docilidad, mansedumbre

meerschaum ['mɪrʃəm] *s* ['mɪrʃɔm] *s* espuma de mar; pipa de espuma de mar

meet [mit] *adj* conveniente, a propósito ‖ *s* concurso deportivo ‖ *v (pret & pp* **met** [mɛt]) *tr* encontrar, encontrarse con; *(to make the acquaintance of)* conocer; empalmar con *(otro tren o autobús);* ir a esperar; honrar, pagar *(una letra);* hacer frente a *(gastos);* cumplir *(sus obligaciones);* batirse con; hallar *(la muerte);* tener *(mala suerte);* aparecer a *(la vista)* ‖ *intr* encontrarse; reunirse; conocerse; **till we meet again** hasta la vista; **to meet with** encontrarse con; reunirse con; empalmar *(un tren)* con *(otro tren);* tener *(un accidente)*

meeting ['mitɪŋ] *s* junta, sesión; reunión; encuentro; *(of two rivers or roads)* confluencia; desafío, duelo

meeting of the minds *s* concierto de voluntades

meeting place *s* lugar *m* de reunión

megabucks ['mɛgə,bʌks] *s (slang)* vastas cantidades de dinero

megacycle ['mɛgə,saɪkəl] *s* megaciclo

megaphone ['mɛgə,fon] *s* megáfono

megohm ['mɛg,om] *s* megohmio

melancholia [,mɛlən'kolɪ•ə] s melancolía
melanchol•y ['mɛlən,kɑli] adj melancólico ‖ s (pl **-ies**) melancolía
melee ['mele] o ['mɛle] s refriega, reyerta
mellow ['mɛlo] adj maduro, jugoso; suave, meloso; melodioso ‖ tr suavizar ‖ intr suavizarse
melodious [mɪ'lodɪ•əs] adj melodioso
melodramatic [,mɛlədrə'mætɪk] adj melodramático
melo•dy ['mɛlədi] s (pl **-dies**) melodía
melon ['mɛlən] s melón m
melt [mɛlt] tr derretir; fundir (metales); ablandar, aplacar ‖ intr derretirse; fundirse; ablandarse, aplacarse; **to melt away** desvanecerse; **to melt into** convertirse gradualmente en; deshacerse en (lágrimas)
melt'down' s fusión; (atomic reactor) fusión del combustible por fisión no controlada
melting pot s crisol m; (fig) caldero de razas
member ['mɛmbər] s miembro
membership ['mɛmbər,ʃɪp] s asociación; (e.g., of a club) personal m; número de miembros
membrane ['mɛmbren] s membrana
memen•to [mɪ'mɛnto] s (pl **-tos** o **-toes**) recordatorio, prenda de recuerdo
mem•o ['mɛmo] s (pl **-os**) (coll) apunte m, membrete m
memoir ['mɛmwɑr] s memoria; biografía; **memoirs** memorias
memoran•dum [,mɛmə'rændəm] s (pl **-dums** o **-da** [də]) apunte m, membrete m
memorial [mɪ'morɪ•əl] adj conmemorativo ‖ s monumento conmemorativo; (petition) memorial m
memorial arch s arco triunfal
Memorial Day s día m de los caídos
memorialize [mɪ'morɪ•ə,laɪz] tr conmemorar
memorize ['mɛmə,raɪz] tr aprender de memoria
memo•ry ['mɛməri] s (pl **-ries**) memoria; (recall) retentiva; (computer) memoria, almacenaje m o almacenamiento (de datos) **to commit to memory** encomendar a la memoria
menace ['mɛnɪs] s amenaza ‖ tr & intr amenazar
ménage [me'naʒ] s casa, hogar m; economía doméstica
menagerie [mə'næʒəri] o [mə'nædʒəri] s casa de fieras; colección de fieras
mend [mɛnd] s remiendo; **to be on the mend** ir mejorando ‖ tr (to repair) componer, reparar; (to patch) remendar; (to improve) reformar, mejorar ‖ intr mejorar
mendacious [mɛn'deʃəs] adj mendaz
mendicant ['mɛndɪkənt] adj & s mendicante mf
mending ['mɛndɪŋ] s remiendo, zurcido
menfolk ['mɛn,fok] spl hombres mpl
menial ['minɪ•əl] adj bajo, servil ‖ s criado, doméstico
menses ['mɛnsiz] spl menstruo
men's furnishings spl artículos para caballeros
men's room s lavabo para caballeros

menstruate ['mɛnstrʊ,et] intr menstruar
mental case s (coll) paciente mf mental; estrafalario
mental giant s (coll) genio
mental hygiene s higiene f mental
mental illness ['mɛntəl] s enfermedad mental
mental reservation s reserva mental
mental test s prueba de inteligencia
mention ['mɛnʃən] s mención ‖ tr mencionar; **don't mention it** no hay de qué; **not to mention** sin contar
menu ['mɛnju] o ['menju] s menú m, lista de comidas; comida
meow [mɪ'aʊ] s maullido ‖ intr maullar
Mephistophelian [,mɛfɪstə'filɪ•ən] adj mefistofélico
mercantile ['mʌrkən,til] o ['mʌrkən,taɪl] adj mercantil
mercenar•y ['mʌrsə,nɛri] adj mercenario ‖ s (pl **-ies**) mercenario
merchandise ['mʌrtʃən,daɪz] s mercancías, mercaderías
merchant ['mʌrtʃənt] adj mercante ‖ s mercante m, mercader m
merchant•man ['mʌrtʃəntmən] s (pl **-men** [mən]) buque m mercante
merchant marine s marina mercante
merchant vessel s buque m mercante
merciful ['mʌrsɪfəl] adj misericordioso
merciless ['mʌrsɪlɪs] adj despiadado, cruel, implacable
mercu•ry ['mʌrkjəri] s (pl **-ries**) mercurio, azogue m; columna de mercurio
mer•cy ['mʌrsi] s (pl **-cies**) misericordia; (discretionary power) merced f; **at the mercy of** a merced de
mere [mir] adj mero, puro; nada más que
meretricious [,mɛrɪ'trɪʃəs] adj postizo, de oropel; cursi, llamativo
merge [mʌrdʒ] tr enchufar, fusionar ‖ intr enchufarse, fusionarse; convergir (p.ej., dos caminos); **to merge into** convertirse gradualmente en
merger ['mʌrdʒər] s fusión de empresas
meridian [mə'rɪdɪ•ən] adj meridiano; (el) más elevado; s meridiano m, apogeo
meringue [mə'ræŋ] s merengue m
meri•no [mə'rino] adj merino ‖ s (pl **-nos**) merino
merit ['mɛrɪt] s mérito ‖ tr merecer
merlon ['mʌrlən] s almena, merlón m
mermaid ['mʌr,med] s sirena; (girl who swims well) ninfa marina
mer•man ['mʌr,mæn] s (pl **-men** [,mɛn]) tritón m; (good swimmer) tritón
merriment ['mɛrɪmənt] s alegría, regocijo
mer•ry ['mɛri] adj (comp **-rier**; super **-riest**) alegre, regocijado; **to make merry** divertirse
Merry Christmas interj ¡Felices Pascuas!, ¡Felices Navidades!
mer'ry-go-round' s tiovivo, caballito; serie ininterrumpida (de fiestas, tertulias, etc.)
mer'ry•mak'er s fiestero, jaranero
mesh [mɛʃ] s (net, network) red f; (each open space of net) malla; (engagement of gears)

me
me

engrane *m;* **meshes** celada, red *f* ‖ *tr*
enredar; (mach) engranar ‖ *intr* enredarse;
(mach) engranar

mess [mɛs] *s* (*dirty condition*) cochinería;
fregado, lío, embrollo; (*meal for a group
of people; such a group*) rancho; (*refuse*)
bazofia; **to get into a mess** meterse en un
lío; **to make a mess of** ensuciar, echar a
perder ‖ *tr* ensuciar; desarreglar; estropear,
echar a perder ‖ *intr* comer; **to mess
around** (coll) ocuparse en fruslerías

message [ˈmɛsɪdʒ] *s* mensaje *m;* recado

messenger [ˈmɛsəndʒər] *s* mensajero; (*one
who goes on errands*) mandadero; precursor *m*

mess hall *s* sala de rancho; comedor *m* de
militares

Messiah [məˈsaɪ·ə] *s* Mesías *m*

mess kit *s* utensilios de rancho

mess′mate′ *s* comensal *mf,* compañero de
rancho

mess of pottage [ˈpɑtɪdʒ] *s* (Bib) plato de
lentejas; cosa de ningún valor

Messrs. [ˈmɛsərz] *pl* de **Mr.**

mess·y [ˈmɛsi] *adj* (*comp* **-ier;** *super* **-iest**)
desaliñado, desarreglado; sucio

met. *abbr* **metropolitan**

metal [ˈmɛtəl] *adj* metálico ‖ *s* metal *m;* (fig)
brío, ánimo

metallic [mɪˈtælɪk] *adj* metálico

metallurgy [ˈmɛtəˌlʌrdʒi] *s* metalurgia

metal polish *s* limpiametales *m*

met′al·work′ *s* metalistería

metamorpho·sis [ˌmɛtəˈmɔrfəsɪs] *s* (*pl* **-ses**
[ˌsiz]) metamorfosis *f*

metaphor [ˈmɛtəˌfɔr] *s* metáfora

metaphorical [ˌmɛtəˈfɑrɪkəl] o [ˌmɛtə-
ˈfɔrɪkəl] *adj* metafórico

metastasis [məˈtæstəsɪs] *s* metástasis *f*

metathe·sis [mɪˈtæθɪsɪs] *s* (*pl* **-ses** [ˌsiz])
metátesis *f*

mete [mit] *tr*—**to mete out** repartir

meteor [ˈmitɪ·ər] *s* estrella fugaz; (*atmospheric phenomenon*) meteoro

meteorology [ˌmitɪ·əˈrɑlədʒi] *s* meteorología

meter [ˈmitər] *s* (*unit of measurement; verse*)
metro; (*instrument for measuring gas,
electricity, water*) contador *m;* (mus)
compás *m,* tiempo ‖ *tr* medir (con contador)

metering [ˈmitərɪŋ] *s* medición

meter reader *s* lector *m* (del contador)

methane [ˈmɛθen] *s* metano

method [ˈmɛθəd] *s* método

methodic(al) [mɪˈθɑdɪk(əl)] *adj* metódico

Methodist [ˈmɛθədɪst] *adj* & *s* metodista *mf*

Methuselah [mɪˈθuzələ] *s* Matusalén *m;* **to
be as old as Methuselah** vivir más años
que Matusalén

meticulous [mɪˈtɪkjələs] *adj* meticuloso, minucioso

metric(al) [ˈmɛtrɪk(əl)] *adj* métrico

metronome [ˈmɛtrəˌnom] *s* metrónomo

metropolis [mɪˈtrɑpəlɪs] *s* metrópoli *f*

metropolitan [ˌmɛtrəˈpɑlɪtən] *adj* metropolitano ‖ *s* (eccl) metropolitano

mettle [ˈmɛtəl] *s* ánimo, brío; **on one's mettle** dispuesto a hacer todo el esfuerzo posible

mettlesome [ˈmɛtəlsəm] *adj* animoso, brioso

mew [mju] *s* maullido; (orn) gaviota; **mews**
(Brit) caballerizas alrededor de un corral

Mexican [ˈmɛksɪkən] *adj* & *s* mejicano

Mexico [ˈmɛksɪˌko] *s* Méjico

mezzanine [ˈmɛzəˌnin] *s* entresuelo

mfr. *abbr* **manufacturer**

mi. *abbr* **mile**

mica [ˈmaɪkə] *s* mica

microbe [ˈmaɪkrob] *s* microbio

microbiology [ˌmaɪkrəbaɪˈɑlədʒi] *s* microbiología

microcard [ˈmaɪkrəˌkɑrd] *s* microficha

microcomputer [ˈmaɪkrəkəmˌpjutər] *s* microordenador *m*

microfarad [ˌmaɪkrəˈfæræd] *s* microfaradio

microfilm [ˈmaɪkrəˌfɪlm] *s* microfilm *m,*
micropelícula ‖ *tr* microfilmar

microgroove [ˈmaɪkrəˌgruv] *adj* microsurco
‖ *s* microsurco; disco microsurco

microphone [ˈmaɪkrəˌfon] *s* micrófono

microprocessor [ˈmaɪkrəˌprɑsɛsər] *s* microprocesador *m*

microscope [ˈmaɪkrəˌskop] *s* microscopio

microscopic [ˌmaɪkrəˈskɑpɪk] *adj* micro-
scópico

microwave [ˈmaɪkrəˌwev] *s* microonda

mid [mɪd] *adj* medio, p.ej., **in mid course** a
medio camino

mid′day′ *adj* del mediodía ‖ *s* mediodia *m*

middle [ˈmɪdəl] *adj* medio ‖ *s* centro, medio;
(*of the human body*) cintura; **about the
middle of** a mediados de; **in the middle of**
en medio de

middle age *s* mediana edad ‖ **Middle Ages**
spl Edad Media

middle class *s* burguesía, clase media

Middle East *s* Oriente Medio

Middle English *s* el inglés medio

middle finger *s* dedo cordial, de en medio o
del corazón

mid′dle·man′ *s* (*pl* **-men** [ˌmɛn]) intermediario

middling [ˈmɪdlɪŋ] *adj* mediano, regular,
pasadero ‖ *adv* (coll) medianamente; (coll)
así, así ‖ *s* (*coarsely ground wheat*) cabezuela; **middlings** artículos de calidad o
precio medianos

mid·dy [ˈmɪdi] *s* (*pl* **-dies**) (coll) aspirante *m*
de marina; (*child's blouse*) marinera

middy blouse *s* marinera

midget [ˈmɪdʒɪt] *s* enano, liliputiense *mf*

midland [ˈmɪdlənd] *adj* de tierra adentro ‖ *s*
región central

mid′night′ *adj* de medianoche; **to burn the
midnight oil** quemarse las cejas ‖ *s* medianoche *f*

midriff [ˈmɪdrɪf] *s* (anat) diafragma *m;* talle
m

midship·man [ˈmɪdˌʃɪpmən] *s* (*pl* **-men**
[mən]) guardia marina *m,* aspirante *m* de
marina

midst [mɪdst] *s* centro; **in the midst of** en
medio de; en lo más recio de

mid'stream' *s*—**in midstream** en pleno río
mid'sum'mer *s* pleno verano
mid'way' *adj* situado a mitad del camino ‖ *adv* a mitad del camino ‖ *s* mitad del camino; (*of a fair or exposition*) avenida central
mid'week' *s* mediados de la semana
mid'wife' *s* (*pl* **-wives**) partera, comadrona
mid'win'ter *s* pleno invierno
mid'year' *adj* de mediados del año ‖ *s* mediados del año; **midyears** (coll) examen *m* de mediados del año escolar
mien [min] *s* aspecto, semblante *m*, porte *m*
miff [mɪf] *s* (coll) desavenencia ‖ *tr* (coll) ofender
might [maɪt] *s* fuerza, poder *m*; **with might and main** con todas sus fuerzas, a más no poder ‖ *v aux* se emplea para formar el modo potencial, p.ej., **she might not come** es posible que no venga
might•y [ˈmaɪti] *adj* (*comp* **-ier;** *super* **-iest**) potente, poderoso; (*of great size*) grandísimo ‖ *adv* (coll) muy
migrant worker [ˈmaɪgrənt] *s* bracero migratorio
migrate [ˈmaɪgret] *intr* emigrar
migratory [ˈmaɪgrə,tori] *adj* migratorio
mil *abbr* **military, militia**
milch [mɪltʃ] *adj* lechero
mild [maɪld] *adj* blando, suave; dócil, manso; leve, ligero; (*climate*) templado
mildew [ˈmɪl,dju] *s* (*mold*) moho; (*plant disease*) mildeu *m*
mile [maɪl] *s* milla inglesa
mileage [ˈmaɪlɪdʒ] *s* recorrido en millas
mileage ticket *s* billete contado por millas, semejante al billete kilométrico
mile'post' *s* poste miliario
mile'stone' *s* piedra miliaria; **to be a milestone** hacer época
milieu [mɪlˈju] *s* ambiente *m*, medio
militancy [ˈmɪlɪtənsi] *s* belicosidad
militant [ˈmɪlɪtənt] *adj* militante, belicoso
militarism [ˈmɪlɪtə,rɪzəm] *s* militarismo
militarist [ˈmɪlɪtərɪst] *adj & s* militarista *mf*
militarize [ˈmɪlɪtə,raɪz] *tr* militarizar
military [ˈmɪlɪ,tɛri] *adj* militar ‖ *s* (los) militares
Military Academy *s* (U.S.A.) Academia General Militar
military police *s* policía militar
militate [ˈmɪlɪ,tet] *intr* militar
militia [mɪˈlɪʃə] *s* milicia
militia•man [mɪˈlɪʃəmən] *s* (*pl* **-men** [mən]) miliciano
milk [mɪlk] *adj* lechero, de leche ‖ *s* leche *f* ‖ *tr* ordeñar; chupar (*los bienes de uno*); abusar de, explotar ‖ *intr* dar leche
milk can *s* lechera
milk diet *s* régimen lácteo
milking [ˈmɪlkɪŋ] *s* ordeño
milk'maid' *s* lechera
milk•man [ˈmɪlk,mæn] *s* (*pl* **-men** [,mɛn]) lechero
milk of human kindness *s* compasión, humanidad
milk pail *s* ordeñadero

milk shake *s* batido de leche
milk'sop' *s* calzonazos *m*, marica *m*
milk'weed' *s* algodoncillo, vencetósigo
milk•y [ˈmɪlki] *adj* (*comp* **-ier;** *super* **-iest**) lechoso, lácteo
Milky Way *s* Vía Láctea
mill [mɪl] *s* (*for grinding grain*) molino; (*for making fabrics*) hilandería; (*for cutting wood*) aserradero; (*for refining sugar*) ingenio; (*for producing steel*) fábrica; (*to grind coffee*) molinillo; (*part of a dollar*) milésima; **to put through the mill** (coll) poner a prueba, someter a un entrenamiento riguroso ‖ *tr* moler (*granos*); acordonar, cerrillar (*monedas*); laminar (*el acero*); triturar (*mena*); (*with a milling cutter*) fresar; batir (*chocolate*) ‖ *intr*—**to mill about** o **around** arremolinarse
mill end *s* retal *m* de hilandería
millennial [mɪˈlɛni•əl] *adj* milenario
millenni•um [mɪˈlɛni•əm] *s* (*pl* **-ums** o **-a** [ə]) milenario, milenio
miller [ˈmɪlər] *s* molinero; (ent) polilla blanca
millet [ˈmɪlɪt] *s* mijo, millo
milliampere [,mɪli'æmpɪr] *s* miliamperio
milligram [ˈmɪli,græm] *s* miligramo
millimeter [ˈmɪli,mitər] *s* milímetro
milliner [ˈmɪlɪnər] *s* modista *mf* de sombreros
millinery [ˈmɪli,nɛri] o [ˈmɪlɪnəri] *s* artículos para sombreros de señora; confección de sombreros de señora; venta de sombreros de señora
millinery shop *s* sombrerería
milling [ˈmɪlɪŋ] *s* (*of grain*) molienda; (*of coins*) acordonamiento, cordoncillo; fresado
milling machine *s* fresadora
million [ˈmɪljən] *adj* millón de, millones de ‖ *s* millón *m*
millionaire [,mɪljən'ɛr] *s* millonario
millionth [ˈmɪljənθ] *adj & s* millonésimo
millivolt [ˈmɪli,volt] *s* vmilivoltio
mill'pond' *s* represa de molino
mill'race' *s* caz *m*
mill'stone' *s* muela de molino; (fig) carga pesada
mill wheel *s* rueda de molino
mill'work' *s* carpintería de taller
mime [maɪm] *s* mimo ‖ *tr* remedar
Mimeograph [ˈmɪm•ə,græf] o [ˈmɪmɪ•ə,grɑf] *s* (trademark) mimeógrafo ‖ *tr* mimeografiar
mim•ic [ˈmɪmɪk] *s* imitador *m*, remedador *m* ‖ *v* (*pret & pp* **-icked;** *ger* **-icking**) *tr* imitar, remedar
mimic•ry [ˈmɪmɪkri] *s* (*pl* **-ries**) mímica, remedo
min. *abbr* **minimum, minute**
minaret [,mɪnə'rɛt] o [ˈmɪnə,rɛt] *s* alminar *m*, minarete *m*
mince [mɪns] *tr* desmenuzar; picar (*carne*) ‖ *intr* andar remilgadamente; hablar remilgadamente
mince'meat' *s* cuajado, picadillo
mince pie *s* pastel relleno de carne picada con frutas

mind [maɪnd] s mente f, espíritu m; **to bear in mind** tener presente; **to be not in one's right mind** no estar en sus cabales; **to be of one mind** estar de acuerdo; **to be out of one's mind** estar fuera de juicio; **to change one's mind** mudar de parecer; **to go out of one's mind** volverse loco; **to have a mind to** tener ganas de; **to have in mind to** pensar en; **to have on one's mind** preocuparse con; **to lose one's mind** perder el juicio; **to make up one's mind** resolverse; **to my mind** a mi parecer; **to say whatever comes into one's mind** decir lo que se le viene a la boca; **to set one's mind on** resolverse a; **to slip one's mind** escaparse de la memoria; **to speak one's mind** decir su parecer; **with one mind** unánimamente ‖ tr (to take care of) cuidar, estar al cuidado de; obedecer; fijarse en; sentir molestia por; **do you mind the smoke?** ¿le molesta el humo?; **mind your own business** no se meta Vd. en lo que no le toca ‖ intr tener inconveniente; tener cuidado; **never mind** no se preocupe, no se moleste

mind'-bend'ing adj (coll) alucinante

mind'-blow'ing adj (coll) alucinante en exceso

mind'-bog'gling adj deslumbrante; abrumador

mindful [ˈmaɪndfəl] adj atento; **mindful of** atento a, cuidadoso de

mind reader s adivinador m del pensamiento ajeno, lector m mental

mind reading s adivinación del pensamiento ajeno, lectura de la mente

mine [maɪn] pron poss el mío; mío ‖ s mina; **to work a mine** beneficiar una mina ‖ tr minar; beneficiar (un terreno); extraer (mineral, carbón, etc.) ‖ intr minar; abrir minas

mine field s campo de minas

mine layer s buque m portaminas, lanzaminas m

miner [ˈmaɪnər] s minero; (mil, nav) minador m

mineral [ˈmɪnərəl] adj & s mineral m

mineralogy [ˌmɪnəˈrælədʒi] s mineralogía

mineral resources spl riquezas del subsuelo

mineral wool s lana de escorias

mine sweeper s dragaminas m

mingle [ˈmɪŋɡəl] tr mezclar, confundir ‖ intr mezclarse, confundirse; asociarse

miniature [ˈmɪni•ətʃər] o [ˈmɪnɪtʃər] s miniatura; **to paint in miniature** miniar, pintar de miniatura

miniaturization [ˌmɪni•ətˌʃəriˈzeʃən] o [ˌmɪnɪtʃəriˈzeʃən] s miniaturización

minicomputer [ˈmɪnɪkəmˌpjutər] s miniordenador m

minimal [ˈmɪnɪməl] adj mínimo

minimize [ˈmɪnɪˌmaɪz] tr empequeñecer

minimum [ˈmɪnɪməm] adj & s mínimo

minimum wage s jornal mínimo

mining [ˈmaɪnɪŋ] adj minero ‖ s mineraje m, minería; (nav) minado

minion [ˈmɪnjən] s paniaguado

minion of the law s esbirro, polizonte m

miniskirt [ˈmɪnɪˌskʌrt] s minifalda

minister [ˈmɪnɪstər] s ministro; pastor m protestante ‖ tr & intr ministrar

ministerial [ˌmɪnɪsˈtɪri•əl] adj ministerial

minis•try [ˈmɪnɪstri] s (pl -tries) ministerio

mink [mɪŋk] s visón m

minnow [ˈmɪno] s pececillo; (ichth) foxino

minor [ˈmaɪnər] adj (smaller) menor; de menor importancia; (younger) menor de edad; (mus) menor ‖ s menor m de edad; (educ) asignatura secundaria

Minorca [mɪˈnɔrkə] s Menorca

Minorcan [mɪˈnɔrkən] adj & s menorquín m

minori•ty [maɪˈnɔrɪti] adj minoritario ‖ s (pl -ties) (being under age; smaller number or part) minoría; (less than full age) minoridad

minstrel [ˈmɪnstrəl] s (retainer who sang and played for his lord) ministril m; (medieval musician and poet) juglar m, trovador m; (U.S.A.) cantor cómico disfrazado de negro

minstrel•sy [ˈmɪnstrəlsi] s (pl -sies) juglaría; compañía de juglares; poesía trovadoresca

mint [mɪnt] s casa de moneda; (plant) menta, hierbabuena; montón m de dinero; fuente f inagotable ‖ tr acuñar; (fig) inventar

minuet [ˌmɪnjuˈɛt] s minué m, minuete m

minus [ˈmaɪnəs] adj menos ‖ prep menos; falto de, sin ‖ s menos m

minute [maɪˈnjut] o [maɪˈnut] adj diminuto, menudo ‖ [ˈmɪnɪt] s minuto; (short space of time) momento; **minutes** acta; **to write up the minutes** levantar acta; **up to the minute** al corriente; de última hora

minute hand [ˈmɪnɪt] s minutero

minutiae [mɪˈnjuʃɪ,i] o [mɪˈnuʃɪ,i] spl minucias

minx [mɪŋks] s moza descarada

miracle [ˈmɪrəkəl] s milagro

miracle play s auto

miraculous [mɪˈrækjələs] adj milagroso

mirage [mɪˈrɑʒ] s espejismo

mire [maɪr] s fango, lodo

mirror [ˈmɪrər] s espejo; (aut) retrovisor m ‖ tr reflejar

mirth [mʌrθ] s alegría, regocijo

mir•y [ˈmaɪri] adj (comp -ier; super -iest) fangoso, lodoso; sucio

misadventure [ˌmɪsədˈvɛntʃər] s desgracia, contratiempo

misanthrope [ˈmɪsənˌθrop] s misántropo

misanthropy [mɪsˈænθrəpi] s misantropía

misapprehension [ˌmɪsæprɪˈhɛnʃən] s malentendido

misappropriation [ˌmɪsəˌpropriˈeʃən] s malversación

misbehave [ˌmɪsbɪˈhev] intr conducirse mal, portarse mal

misbehavior [ˌmɪsbɪˈhevɪ•ər] s mala conducta, mal comportamiento

misc. abbr **miscellaneous, miscellany**

miscalculation [ˌmɪskælkjəˈleʃən] s mal cálculo

miscarriage [mɪsˈkærɪdʒ] s aborto, malparto; fracaso, malogro; (of a letter) extravío

miscar•ry [mɪs'kæri] v (pret & pp -**ried**) intr abortar, malparir; malograrse; extraviarse (una carta)

miscellaneous [,mɪsə'lenɪ•əs] adj misceláneo

miscella•ny ['mɪsə,leni] s (pl -**nies**) miscelánea

mischief ['mɪstʃɪf] s (harm) daño, mal m; (disposition to annoy) malicia; (prankishness) travesura

mis'chief-mak'er s malsín m, cizañero

mischievous ['mɪstʃɪvəs] adj dañoso, malo; malicioso; travieso

misconception [,mɪskən'sɛpʃən] s concepto erróneo, mala interpretación

misconduct [mɪs'kɑndəkt] s mala conducta

misconstrue [,mɪskən'stru] o [mɪs'kɑnstru] tr interpretar mal

miscount [mɪs'kaʊnt] s cuenta errónea ‖ tr & intr contar mal

miscue [mɪs'kju] s (in billiards) pifia; (slip) pifia ‖ intr pifiar; (theat) equivocarse de apunte

misdate [mɪs'det] tr fechar erróneamente

mis•deal ['mɪs,dil] s repartición errónea ‖ [mɪs'dil] v (pret & pp -**dealt** ['dɛlt]) tr & intr repartir mal

misdeed [mɪs'did] o ['mɪs,did] s malhecho, fechoría

misdemeanor [,mɪsdɪ'minər] s mala conducta; (law) delito de menor cuantía

misdirect [,mɪsdɪ'rɛkt] o [,mɪsdaɪ'rɛkt] tr dirigir erradamente; hacer perder el camino

misdoing [mɪs'du•ɪŋ] s mala acción

miser ['maɪzər] s avaro, verrugo; codo (Guat, Mex)

miserable ['mɪzərəbəl] adj miserable; (coll) achacoso, indispuesto

miserly ['maɪzərli] adj avariento, mezquino

miser•y ['mɪzəri] s (pl -**ies**) miseria; pelazón f

misfeasance [mɪs'fizəns] s (law) fraude m

misfire [mɪs'faɪr] s falla de tiro; (of internal-combustion engine) falla de encendido ‖ intr fallar (un arma de fuego, el encendido de un motor)

mis•fit ['mɪs,fɪt] s vestido mal cortado; cosa que no encaja bien; persona mal adaptada a su ambiente ‖ [mɪs'fɪt] v (pret & pp -**fitted**; ger -**fitting**) tr & intr encajar mal, sentar mal

misfortune [mɪs'fɔrtʃən] s desgracia

misgiving [mɪs'gɪvɪŋ] s mal presentimiento, rescoldo

misgovern [mɪs'gʌvərn] tr desgobernar

misguidance [mɪs'gaɪdəns] s error m, extravío

misguided [mɪs'gaɪdɪd] adj descarriado, malaconsejado

mishap ['mɪshæp] o [mɪs'hæp] s accidente m, percance m

mishmash ['mɪʃ,mæʃ] s baturillo; mezcolanza

misinform [,mɪsɪn'fɔrm] tr dar informes erróneos a

misinterpret [,mɪsɪn'tɛrprɪt] tr interpretar mal

misjudge [mɪs'dʒʌdʒ] tr & intr juzgar mal

mis•lay [mɪs'le] v (pret & pp -**laid** [,led]) tr extraviar, perder; (among one's papers) traspapelar

mis•lead [mɪs'lid] v (pret & pp -**led** [,lɛd]) tr (to lead astray) extraviar, descaminar; (to lead into wrongdoing) seducir, inducir al mal; (to deceive) engañar

misleading [mɪs'lidɪŋ] adj engañoso

mismanagement [mɪs'mænɪdʒmənt] s mala administración, desgobierno

misnomer [mɪs'nomər] s nombre improprio, mal nombre

misplace [mɪs'ples] tr colocar fuera de su lugar; colocar mal; (to mislay) (coll) extraviar, perder

misprint ['mɪs,prɪnt] s errata de imprenta ‖ [mɪs'prɪnt] tr imprimir con erratas

mispronounce [,mɪsprə'naʊns] tr pronunciar mal

mispronunciation [,mɪsprə,nʌnsɪ'eʃən] o [,mɪsprə,nʌnʃɪ'eʃən] s pronunciación incorrecta

misquote [mɪs'kwot] tr citar equivocadamente

misrepresent [,mɪsrɛprɪ'zɛnt] tr tergiversar

miss [mɪs] s falta, error m; fracaso, malogro; tiro errado; jovencita, muchacha ‖ tr echar de menos; perder (el tren, la función, la oportunidad); errar (el blanco; la vocación); no entender, no comprender; omitir; no ver; no dar con, no encontrar; librarse de (p.ej., la muerte); escapársele a uno, p.ej., **I missed what you said** se me escapó lo que dijo Vd.; por poco, p.ej., **the car missed hitting me** el coche por poco me atropella ‖ intr fallar; errar el blanco; malograrse ‖ **Miss** s señorita

missal ['mɪsəl] s misal m

misshapen [mɪs'ʃepən] adj deforme, contrahecho

missile ['mɪsɪl] adj arrojadizo ‖ s arma arrojadiza; proyectil m; proyectil dirigido, misil m

missile gap s desigualdad de armas proyectiles poseídas por dos potencias

missil(e)ry ['mɪsəlri] s cohetería; ciencia de las armas proyectiles

missing ['mɪsɪŋ] adj extraviado, perdido; desaparecido; ausente; **to be missing** hacer falta; haber desaparecido

missing link s hombre m mono

missing persons spl desaparecidos

mission ['mɪʃən] s misión; casa de misión

missionar•y ['mɪʃən,ɛri] adj misional ‖ s (pl -**ies**) (one sent to work to propagate his faith) misionario, misionero; (on a political or diplomatic mission) misionario

missive ['mɪsɪv] adj misivo ‖ s misiva

mis•spell [mɪs'spɛl] v (pret & pp -**spelled** o -**spelt** ['spɛlt]) tr & intr deletrear mal, escribir mal

misspelling [mɪs'spɛlɪŋ] s falta de ortografía

misspent [mɪs'spɛnt] adj malgastado

misstatement [mɪs'stetmənt] s relación equivocada, relación falsa

misstep [mɪs'stɛp] s paso falso; (slip in conduct) resbalón m

mi
mi

miss•y ['mɪsi] s (pl **-ies**) (coll) señorita
mist [mɪst] s neblina; (of tears) velo; (fine spray) vapor m
mis•take [mɪs'tek] s error m, equivocación; **and no mistake** sin duda alguna; **by mistake** por descuido; **to make a mistake** equivocarse ‖ v (pret **-took** ['tʊk]; pp **-taken**) tr tomar (por otro; por lo que no es); entender mal; **to be mistaken for** equivocarse con
mistaken [mɪs'tekən] adj (person) equivocado; (idea) erróneo; (act) desacertado
mistakenly [mɪs'tekənli] adv equivocadamente, por error
mistletoe ['mɪsəl,to] s (Viscum album) muérdago; (Phoradendron flavescens, used in Christmas decorations in the U.S.A.) cabellera
mistreat [mɪs'trit] tr maltratar
mistreatment [mɪs'tritmənt] s maltratamiento
mistress ['mɪstrɪs] s (of a household) ama, dueña; moza, querida, manceba; (Brit) maestra de escuela
mistrial [mɪs'traɪ•əl] s pleito viciado de nulidad
mistrust [mɪs'trʌst] s desconfianza ‖ tr desconfiar de ‖ intr desconfiar
mistrustful [mɪs'trʌstfəl] adj desconfiado
mist•y ['mɪsti] adj (comp **-ier**; super **-iest**) brumoso, neblinoso; indistinto
misunder•stand [,mɪsʌndər'stænd] v (pret & pp **-stood** ['stʊd]) tr no comprender, entender mal
misunderstanding [,mɪsʌndər'stændɪŋ] s malentendido; (disagreement) desavenencia
misuse [mɪs'jus] s abuso, mal uso; (of funds) malversación ‖ [mɪs'juz] tr abusar de, emplear mal; malversar (fondos)
misword [mɪs'wʌrd] tr redactar mal
mite [maɪt] s (small contribution) óbolo; (small amount) pizca; (ent) ácaro
miter ['maɪtər] s mitra; (carp) inglete m ‖ tr cortar ingletes en; juntar con junta a inglete
miter box s caja de ingletes
mitigate ['mɪtɪ,get] tr mitigar, atenuar, paliar
mitten ['mɪtən] s confortante m, mitón m
mix [mɪks] tr mezclar; amasar (una torta); aderezar (ensalada); **to mix up** equivocar, confundir ‖ intr mezclarse; asociarse
mixed [mɪkst] adj mixto, mezclado; (e.g., candy) variados; (coll) confundido
mixed company s reunión de personas de ambos sexos
mixed drink s bebida mezclada
mixed feelings s concepto vacilante
mixer ['mɪksər] s (of concrete) mezcladora, hormigonera; **to be a good mixer** (coll) tener don de gentes
mixture ['mɪkstʃər] s mezcla, mixtura
mix'-up' s confusión; enredo, lío; (of people) equivocación
mizzen ['mɪzən] s mesana
mo. abbr month
M.O. abbr money order
moan [mon] s gemido ‖ intr gemir

moat [mot] s foso
mob [mab] s chusma, populacho; (crowd bent on violence) muchedumbre airada ‖ v (pret & pp **mobbed;** ger **mobbing**) tr asaltar, atropellar
mobile ['mobɪl] o ['mobil] adj móvil
mobility [mo'bɪlɪti] s movilidad
mobilization [,mobɪlɪ'zeʃən] s movilización
mobilize ['mobɪ,laɪz] tr movilizar ‖ intr movilizarse, movilizarse
mob rule s gobierno del populacho
mobster ['mabstər] s (slang) gamberro, pandillero, gángster
mobsterism ['mabstə,rɪzəm] s gangsterismo; acciones de los gangsters
moccasin ['makəsin] s mocasín m
Mocha coffee ['mokə] s moca m, café m de moca
mock [mak] adj simulado, fingido ‖ s burla, mofa ‖ tr burlarse de, mofarse de; despreciar; engañar ‖ intr mofarse; **to mock at** mofarse de
mocker•y ['makəri] s (pl **-ies**) burla, mofa, escarnio; (subject of derision) hazmerreír m; (poor imitation) mal remedo; (e.g., of justice) negación
mock'ing•bird' s burlón m, sinsonte m
mock orange s jeringuilla, celinda
mock privet s olivillo
mock turtle soup s sopa de cabeza de ternera
mock'-up' s maqueta
mode [mod] s modo, manera; (fashion) moda; (gram) modo
mod•el ['madəl] adj modelo, p.ej., **model city** ciudad modelo ‖ s modelo ‖ v (pret & pp **-eled** o **-elled;** ger **-eling** o **-elling**) tr (to fashion in clay, wax, etc.) modelar ‖ intr modelarse; servir de modelo
model airplane s aeromodelo
mod'el-air'plane builder s aeromodelista mf
model-airplane building s aeromodelismo
model sailing s navegación de modelos a vela
moderate ['madərɪt] adj moderado; (tiempo) templado; (precio) módico ‖ ['madə,ret] tr moderar; presidir (una asamblea) ‖ intr moderarse
moderator ['madə,retər] s (over an assembly) presidente m; (mediator) árbitro; (telv) presentador m, presentadora; (for slowing down neutrons) moderador m
modern ['madərn] adj moderno
modernize ['madər,naɪz] tr modernizar
modest ['madɪst] adj modesto
modes•ty ['madɪsti] s (pl **-ties**) modestia
modicum ['madɪkəm] s pequeña cantidad
modifier ['madɪ,faɪ•ər] s (gram) modificante m
modi•fy ['madɪ,faɪ] v (pret & pp **-fied**) tr modificar
modish ['modɪʃ] adj de moda, elegante
modulate ['madʒə,let] tr & intr modular
modulation [,madʒə'leʃən] s modulación
mohair ['mo,hɛr] s mohair m (pelo de cabra de Angora)
Mohammedan [mo'hæmɪdən] adj & s mahometano

Mohammedanism [moˈhæmɪdə,nɪzəm] *s* mahometismo

moist [mɔɪst] *adj* húmedo, mojado; (*weather*) lluvioso; (*eyes*) lagrimoso

moisten [ˈmɔɪsən] *tr* humedecer ‖ *intr* humedecerse

moisture [ˈmɔɪstʃər] *s* humedad

molar [ˈmolər] *s* diente *m* molar

molasses [məˈlæsɪz] *s* melaza

molasses candy *s* melcocha

mold [mold] *s* molde *m;* cosa moldeada; (*shape*) forma; (*fungus*) moho; (*humus*) mantillo; (fig) carácter *m*, índole *f* ‖ *tr* amoldar, moldear; (*to make moldy*) enmohecer ‖ *intr* enmohecerse

molder [ˈmoldər] *s* moldeador *m* ‖ *intr* convertirse en polvo, consumirse

molding [ˈmoldɪŋ] *s* moldeado; (*cornice, shaped strip of wood, etc.*) moldura

mold•y [ˈmoldi] *adj* (*comp* **-ier;** *super* **-iest**) (*overgrown with mold*) mohoso; (*stale*) rancio, pasado

mole [mol] *s* (*breakwater*) rompeolas *m;* (*inner harbor*) dársena; (*spot on skin*) lunar *m;* (*small mammal*) topo

molecular physics [məˈlɛkjələr] *s* física molecular

molecular weight *s* peso molecular

molecule [ˈmalɪ,kjul] *s* molécula

mole′hill′ *s* topinera

mole′skin′ *s* piel *f* de topo, molesquina

molest [məˈlɛst] *tr* molestar; faltar al respeto a (*una mujer*)

moll [mal] *s* (slang) mujer *f* del hampa; (slang) ramera

molli•fy [ˈmalɪ,faɪ] *v* (*pret & pp* **-fied**) *tr* apaciguar, aplacar

mollusk [ˈmaləsk] *s* molusco

mollycoddle [ˈmalɪ,kadəl] *s* mantecón *m*, marica *m* ‖ *tr* consentir, mimar

molt [molt] *s* muda ‖ *intr* hacer la muda

molten [ˈmoltən] *adj* fundido, derretido; fundido, vaciado

molybdenum [məˈlɪbdɪnəm] o [,malɪbˈdinəm] *s* molibdeno

moment [ˈmomənt] *s* momento; **at any moment** de un momento a otro

momentary [ˈmomən,tɛri] *adj* momentáneo

momentous [moˈmɛntəs] *adj* importante, grave

momen•tum [moˈmɛntəm] *s* (*pl* **-tums** o **-ta** [tə]) ímpetu *m;* (mech) cantidad de movimiento

monarch [ˈmanərk] *s* monarca *m*

monarchic(al) [məˈnarkɪk(əl)] *adj* monárquico

monarchist [ˈmanərkɪst] *adj & s* monárquico, monarquista *mf*

monar•chy [ˈmanərki] *s* (*pl* **-chies**) monarquía

monaster•y [ˈmanəs,tɛri] *s* (*pl* **-ies**) monasterio

monastic [məˈnæstɪk] *adj* monástico

monasticism [məˈnæstɪ,sɪzəm] *s* monaquismo

Monday [ˈmʌndi] *s* lunes *m*

monetary [ˈmanɪ,tɛri] *adj* monetario; pecuniario

money [ˈmʌni] *s* dinero; **to make money** ganar dinero; dar dinero (*una empresa*)

mon′ey•bag′ *s* monedero, talega; **money-bags** (*wealth*) (coll) talegas; (*wealthy person*) (coll) ricacho

moneychanger [ˈmʌni,tʃendʒər] *s* cambista *mf*

moneyed [ˈmʌnid] *adj* adinerado

moneylender [ˈmʌni,lɛndər] *s* prestamista *mf*

mon′ey•mak′er *s* acaudalador *m;* (fig) manantial *m* de beneficios

money order *s* giro postal, orden *m* de pago

Mongol [ˈmaŋgəl] *adj & s* mogol *mf*

Mongolian [maŋˈgolɪ•ən] *adj & s* mogol *mf*

mon•goose [ˈmaŋgus] *s* (*pl* **-gooses**) mangosta

mongrel [ˈmʌŋgrəl] *adj & s* mestizo

monitor [ˈmanɪtər] *s* monitor *m* ‖ *tr* controlar (*la señal*); escuchar (*radio-transmisiones*); superentender

monk [mʌŋk] *s* monje *m*

monkey [ˈmʌŋki] *s* mono; simio; **to make a monkey of** tomar el pelo a ‖ *intr* — **to monkey around** haraganear; **to monkey with** ajar, manosear

mon′key•shine′ *s* (slang) monería, monada, payasada

monkey wrench *s* llave inglesa

monkhood [ˈmaŋkhʊd] *s* monacato; los monjes

monkshood [ˈmaŋks•hʊd] *s* cogulla de fraile

monocle [ˈmanəkəl] *s* monóculo

monogamy [məˈnagəmi] *s* monogamia

monogram [ˈmanə,græm] *s* monograma *m*

monograph [ˈmanə,græf] *s* monografía

monolithic [,manəˈlɪθɪk] *adj* monolítico

monologue [ˈmanə,lɔg] *s* monólogo

monomania [,manəˈmenɪ•ə] *s* monomanía

monomial [məˈnomɪ•əl] *s* monomio

monopolize [məˈnapə,laɪz] *tr* monopolizar; acaparar (*p.ej., la conversación*)

monopo•ly [məˈnapəli] *s* (*pl* **-lies**) monopolio

monorail [ˈmanə,rel] *s* monorriel *m*

monosyllable [ˈmanə,sɪləbəl] *s* monosílabo

monotheist [ˈmanə,θi•ɪst] *adj & s* monoteísta *mf*

monotonous [meˈnatənəs] *adj* monótono

monotony [meˈnatəni] *s* monotonía

monotype [ˈmanə,taɪp] *s* (*machine; method*) monotipia; (*machine*) monotipo

monotype operator *s* monotipista *mf*

monoxide [məˈnaksaɪd] *s* monóxido

monseigneur [,mansenˈjœr] *s* monseñor *m*

monsignor [manˈsinjər] *s* (*pl* **monsignors** o **monsignori** [,mansiˈnjori]) (eccl) monseñor *m*

monsoon [manˈsun] *s* monsón *m*

monster [ˈmanstər] *adj* monstruoso ‖ *s* monstruo

monstrance [ˈmanstrəns] *s* custodia, ostensorio

monstrosi•ty [manˈstrasɪti] *s* (*pl* **-ties**) monstruosidad; esperpento

monstrous [ˈmanstrəs] *adj* monstruoso

mi
mo

month [mʌnθ] s mes m
month·ly ['mʌnθli] adj mensual ‖ adv mensualmente ‖ s (pl **-lies**) revista mensual; **monthlies** (coll) reglas
monument ['mɑnjəmənt] s monumento
moo [mu] s mugido ‖ intr mugir
mood [mud] s humor m, genio; (gram) modo; **moods** accesos de mal humor
mood·y ['mudi] adj (comp **-ier**; super **-iest**) triste, hosco, melancólico; caprichoso, veleidoso
moon [mun] s luna
moon'beam' s rayo lunar
moon'light' s claror m de luna, luz f de la luna
moon'light'ing s multiempleo, pluriempleo
moon'sail' s (naut) monterilla
moon'shine' s luz f de la luna; (idle talk) cháchara, música celestial; (coll) whisky destilado ilegalmente
moon shot s lanzamiento a la Luna
moor [mur] s brezal m, páramo ‖ tr (naut) amarrar ‖ intr (naut) echar las amarras ‖ **Moor** s moro
Moorish ['murɪʃ] adj moro
moor'land' s brezal m
moose [mus] s (pl **moose**) alce m de América
moot [mut] adj discutible, dudoso
mop [mɑp] s aljofifa, fregasuelos m, estropajo; (of hair) espesura ‖ v (pret & pp **mopped**; ger **mopping**) tr aljofifar; enjugarse (la frente con un pañuelo); **to mop up** limpiar de enemigos
mope [mop] intr andar abatido, entregarse a la melancolía
moped ['mopɛd] s motoneta
mopish ['mopɪʃ] adj abatido, melancólico
moral ['mɑrəl] o ['mɔrəl] adj moral ‖ s (of a fable) moraleja, moral f; **morals** (ethics; conduct) moral f
moral certainty s evidencia moral
morale [mo'ræl] o [mə'rɑl] s moral f (estado de ánimo, confianza en sí mismo)
morali·ty [mə'ræliti] s (pl **-ties**) moralidad
morals charge s acusación por delito sexual
morass [mə'ræs] s pantano
moratori·um [,mɔrə'tɔri·əm] o [,mɑrə'tɔri·əm] s (pl **-ums** o **-a** [əl]) s moratoria
morbid ['mɔrbɪd] adj (feelings, curiosity) malsano; (gruesome) horripilante; (pertaining to disease; pathologic) morboso
mordacious [mɔr'deʃəs] adj mordaz
mordant ['mɔrdənt] adj mordaz ‖ s mordiente m
more [mor] adj & adv más; **more and more** cada vez más; **more than** más que; (followed by numeral) más de; (followed by verb) más de lo que ‖ s más m
more·o'ver adv además, por otra parte
Moresque [mo'rɛsk] adj moro; (archit) árabe ‖ s estilo árabe
morgue [mɔrg] s depósito de cadáveres
moribund ['mɔri,bʌnd] o ['mɑri,bʌnd] adj moribundo
Moris·co [mə'rɪsko] adj morisco, moro ‖ s (pl **-cos** o **-coes**) moro; moro de España;

(offspring of mulatto and Spaniard, in Mexico) morisco
morning ['mɔrnɪŋ] adj matinal ‖ s mañana; (time between midnight and dawn) madrugada; **in the morning** de mañana, por la mañana
morning coat s chaqué m
morn'ing·glo'ry s (pl **-ries**) dondiego de día
morning sickness s vómitos del embarazo
morning star s lucero del alba
Moroccan [mə'rɑkən] adj & s marroquí mf o marroquín m
morocco [mə'rɑko] s (leather) marroquí m o marroquín m ‖ **Morocco** s Marruecos m
moron ['morɑn] s (person of arrested intelligence) morón m; (coll) imbécil mf
morose [mə'ros] adj adusto, hosco, malhumorado
morphine ['mɔrfin] s morfina
morphology [mɔr'fɑlədʒi] s morfología
Morris chair ['mɑrɪs] o ['mɔrɪs] s poltrona extensible
morrow ['mɑro] o ['mɔro] s (future time) mañana m; (time following some event) día m siguiente; **on the morrow** en el día de mañana; el día siguiente
morsel ['mɔrsəl] s bocadito; pedacito
mortal ['mɔrtəl] adj & s mortal m
mortality [mɔr'tæliti] s mortalidad; (death or destruction on a large scale) mortandad
mortar ['mɔrtər] s (bowl used for crushing; mixture of lime, etc.) mortero; (arti) mortero
mor'tar·board' s esparavel m; gorro académico cuadrado
mortgage ['mɔrgɪdʒ] s hipoteca ‖ tr hipotecar
mortgagee [,mɔrgɪ'dʒi] s acreedor hipotecario
mortgagor ['mɔrgɪdʒər] s deudor hipotecario
mortician [mɔr'tɪʃən] s empresario de pompas fúnebres
morti·fy ['mɔrti,faɪ] v (pret & pp **-fied**) tr humillar; mortificar (el cuerpo, las pasiones); **to be mortified** avergonzarse
mortise ['mɔrtɪs] s mortaja, muesca ‖ tr amortajar, enmuescar
mortise lock s cerradura embutida
mortuar·y ['mɔrtʃu,ɛri] adj mortuorio ‖ s (pl **-ies**) depósito de cadáveres; funeraria
mosaic [mo'ze·ɪk] m mosaico
Moscow ['mɑskau] o ['mɑsko] s Moscú
Moses ['moziz] o ['mozis] s Moisés m
Mos·lem ['mɑzləm] o ['mɑsləm] adj & s var of **Muslim**, musulmán m
mosque [mɑsk] s mezquita
mosqui·to [məs'kito] s (pl **-toes** o **-tos**) mosquito
mosquito net s mosquitero
moss [mɔs] o [mɑs] s musgo
moss'back' s (coll) reaccionario; (old-fashioned person) (coll) fósil m
moss·y ['mɔsi] o ['mɑsi] adj (comp **-ier**; super **-iest**) musgoso
most [most] adj más; la mayor parte de, los más de ‖ adv más; muy, sumamente; (coll) casi ‖ s la mayor parte, el mayor número,

los más; **most of** la mayor parte de, el
mayor número de; **to make the most of**
sacar el mejor partido de
mostly ['mostli] *adv* por la mayor parte,
mayormente; casi
moth [mɔθ] o [mɑθ] *s* mariposa nocturna;
(*clothes moth*) polilla
moth ball *s* bola de alcanfor, bola de nafta-
lina
moth'-ball' fleet *s* (nav) flota en conserva
moth'-eat'en *adj* apolillado; (fig) anticuado
mother ['mʌðər] *adj* (*love*) maternal;
(*tongue*) materno; (*country*) madre;
(*church*) metropolitano ‖ *s* madre *f;* (*an
elderly woman*) (coll) tía ‖ *tr* servir de
madre a
mother country *s* madre patria
Mother Goose *s* supuesta autora o narradora
de una colección de cuentos infantiles (in
Spain: *Cuentos de Calleja*)
motherhood ['mʌðər,hʊd] *s* maternidad
moth'er-in-law' *s* (*pl* **mothers-in-law**) suegra
moth'er-land' *s* patria
motherless ['mʌðərlɪs] *adj* huérfano de madre, sin madre
motherly ['mʌðərli] *adj* maternal
mother-of-pearl ['mʌðərəv'pʌrl] *adj* naca-
rado ‖ *s* nácar *m*
Mother's Day *s* día *m* de la madre
mother superior *s* superiora
mother tongue *s* (*language naturally acquired by reason of nationality*) lengua
materna; (*language from which another
language is derived*) lengua madre, lengua
matriz
mother wit *s* gracia natural, chispa
moth hole *s* apolilladura
moth•y ['mɔθi] o ['mɑθi] *adj* (*comp* **-ier;**
super **-iest**) apolillado
motif [mo'tif] *s* motivo
motion ['moʃən] *s* movimiento; (*signal, gesture*) seña, indicación; (*in a deliberating
assembly*) moción; **to set in motion** poner
en acción ‖ *intr* hacer señas con la mano o
la cabeza
motionless ['moʃənlɪs] *adj* inmoble, inmóvil
motion picture *s* película cinematográfica
mo'tion-pic'ture *adj* cinematográfico
motivate ['motɪ,vet] *tr* animar, incitar, mover
motive ['motɪv] *adj* (*promoting action*) motivo; (*producing motion*) motor ‖ *s* motivo
motive power *s* fuerza motriz, potencia
motora o motriz; (rr) conjunto de locomotoras de un ferrocarril
motley ['mɑtli] *adj* abigarrado; mezclado,
variado
motor ['motər] *adj* motor ‖ *s* motor *m;* motor
eléctrico; automóvil *m* ‖ *intr* viajar en
automóvil
mo'tor•boat' *s* gasolinera, canoa automóvil
mo'tor•bus' *s* autobús *m*
motorcade ['motər,ked] *s* caravana de auto-
móviles
mo'tor•car' *s* automóvil *m*
mo'tor•cy'cle *s* motocicleta

motorist ['motərɪst] *s* motorista *mf*, automovilista *mf*
motorize ['motə,raɪz] *tr* motorizar
motor launch *s* lancha automóvil
motor•man ['motərmən] *s* (*pl* **-men** [mən])
conductor *m* de tranvía, conductor de locomotora eléctrica
motor sailer ['selər] *s* motovelero
motor scooter *s* motoneta
motor ship *s* motonave *f*
motor truck *s* autocamión *m*
motor vehicle *s* vehículo motor, autovehículo
mottle ['mɑtəl] *tr* abigarrar, jaspear, motear
mot•to ['mɑto] *s* (*pl* **-toes** o **-tos**) lema *m*,
divisa
mould [mold] *s, tr, & intr* var de **mold**
moulder ['moldər] *s & intr* var de **molder**
moulding ['moldɪŋ] *s* var de **molding**
mouldy ['moldi] *adj* var de **moldy**
mound [maʊnd] *s* montón *m* de tierra; montecillo
mount [maʊnt] *s* (*hill, mountain*) monte *m;*
(*horse for riding*) montura; (*setting for a
jewel*) montadura; soporte *m;* cartón *m*,
tela (*en que está pegada una fotografía*);
(mach) montaje *m* ‖ *tr* subir (*una escalera,
una cuesta*); subir a (*una plataforma*);
escalar (*una muralla*); montar (*un servicio;
una piedra preciosa*); poner a caballo; pegar (*vistas, pruebas*); (mil) montar (*la
guardia*) ‖ *intr* montar, montarse; aumentar, subir (*los precios*)
mountain ['maʊntən] *s* montaña; **to make a
mountain out of a molehill** hacer de una
pulga un camello
mountain climbing *s* alpinismo, montañismo
mountaineer [,maʊntə'nɪr] *s* montañés *m*
mountainous ['maʊntənəs] *adj* montañoso
mountain railroad *s* ferrocarril *m* de cremallera
mountain range *s* cordillera, sierra
mountain sickness *s* mal *m* de las montañas
mountebank ['maʊntɪ,bæŋk] *s* saltabanco
mounting ['maʊntɪŋ] *s* (*of a precious stone,
of an astronomical instrument*) montura;
papel *m* de soporte; papel o tela (*en que
está pegada una fotografía*); (mach) montaje *m*
mourn [morn] *tr* llorar (*p.ej., la muerte de
una persona*); lamentar (*una desgracia*) ‖
intr lamentarse; vestir de luto
mourner ['mornər] *s* doliente *mf;* (*person
who makes a public profession of penitence*) penitente *mf;* (*person hired to attend
a funeral*) plañidera; **mourners** duelo
mourners' bench *s* banco de los penitentes
mournful ['mornfəl] *adj* (*sorrowful*) doloroso; (*gloomy*) lúgubre
mourning ['mornɪŋ] *s* luto; **to be in mourning** estar de luto
mourning band *s* crespón *m* fúnebre, brazal
m de luto
mouse [maʊs] *s* (*pl* **mice** [maɪs]) ratón *m*
mouse'hole' *s* ratonera
mouser ['maʊzər] *s* desmurador *m*
mouse'trap' *s* ratonera

mo
mo

moustache [məs'tæʃ] o [məs'tɑʃ] s bigote *m*, mostacho

mouth [mauθ] s (*pl* **mouths** [mauðz]) boca; (*of a river*) desembocadura, embocadura; **by mouth** por vía bucal; **to be born with a silver spoon in one's mouth** nacer de pie; **to make one's mouth water** hacérsele a uno la boca agua; **to not open one's mouth** no decir esta boca es mía

mouthful ['mauθ,ful] s bocado

mouth organ s armónica de boca

mouth'piece' s (*of wind instrument*) boquilla; (*of bridle*) embocadura; (*spokesman*) portavoz *m*

mouth'wash' s enjuague *m*, enjuagadientes *m*

movable ['muvəbəl] *adj* movible, móvil

move [muv] s movimiento; (*démarche*) acción, gestión, paso; (*from one house to another*) mudanza; **on the move** en marcha, en movimiento; **to get a move on** (slang) menearse, darse prisa; **to make a move** dar un paso; hacer una jugada ‖ *tr* mover; evacuar (*el vientre*); (*to stir, excite the feelings of*) conmover, enternecer; **to move up** adelantar (*una fecha*) ‖ *intr* moverse; desplazarse (*un viajante; un planeta*); mudarse, mudar de casa; (*e.g., to another store, to another city*) trasladarse; hacer una jugada; hacer una moción; venderse, tener salida (*una mercancía*); evacuarse, moverse (*el vientre*); **to move away** apartarse; marcharse; mudarse de casa; **to move in** instalarse; alternar con, frecuentar (*la buena sociedad*); **to move off** alejarse

movement ['muvmənt] s movimiento; aparato de relojería; (*of the bowels*) evacuación; (*e.g., of a symphony*) tiempo

movie ['muvi] s película, cinta

movie camera s filmadora, cámara cinematográfica

movie•goer ['movi,go•ər] s aficionado al cine

movie house s cineteatro

mov'ie•land' s (coll) cinelandia

movie star s cineasta *m*

moving ['muvɪŋ] *adj* conmovedor, impresionante ‖ s movimiento; (*from one house to another*) mudanza

moving picture s película cinematográfica

moving spirit s alma (*de una empresa*)

moving stairway s escalera mecánica, móvil o rodante

mow [mo] v (*pret* **mowed;** *pp* **mowed** o **mown**) *tr* segar; **to mow down** matar (*soldados*) con fuego graneado ‖ *intr* segar

mower ['mo•ər] s segador *m;* segadora mecánica

mowing machine s segadora mecánica

Mozarab [mo'zærəb] s mozárabe *mf*

Mozarabic [mo'zærəbɪk] *adj* mozárabe

M.P. *abbr* **Member of Parliament, Military Police**

m.p.h. *abbr* **miles per hour**

Mr. ['mɪstər] s (*pl* **Messrs.** ['mɛsərz]) señor *m* (*tratamiento*)

Mrs. ['mɪsɪz] s señora (*tratamiento*)

MS. o **ms.** *abbr* **manuscript**

Mt. *abbr* **Mount**

much [mʌtʃ] *adj* & *pron* mucho; **too much** demasiado ‖ *adv* mucho; **however much** por mucho que; **how much** cuánto; **too much** demasiado; **very much** muchísimo

mucilage ['mjusɪlɪdʒ] s goma para pegar; (*gummy secretion in plants*) mucílago

muck [mʌk] s estiércol húmedo; suciedad, porquería; (min) zafra

muck'rake' *intr* (coll) exponer ruindades

mucous ['mjukəs] *adj* mucoso

mucus ['mjukəs] s moco

mud [mʌd] s barro, fango, lodo; **to sling mud at** llenar de fango

muddle ['mʌdəl] s confusión, embrollo ‖ *tr* confundir, embrollar; atontar, aturdir ‖ *intr* obrar torpemente; **to muddle through** salir del paso a pesar suyo

mud'dle•head' s farraguista *mf*, cajón *m* de sastre

mud•dy ['mʌdi] *adj* (*comp* **-dier;** *super* **-diest**) barroso, fangoso, lodoso; (*obscure*) turbio ‖ v (*pret* & *pp* **-died**) *tr* embarrar, enturbiar

mud'guard' s guardabarros *m*

mud'hole' s atolladero, ciénaga

mudslinger ['mʌd,slɪŋər] s (fig) lanzador *m* de lodo

muezzin [mju'ɛzɪn] s almuecín *m*, almuédano

muff [mʌf] s manguito ‖ *tr* & *intr* chapucear

muffin ['mʌfɪn] s mollete *m*

muffle ['mʌfəl] *tr* arropar; (*about the face*) embozar; amortiguar (*un ruido*); enfundar (*un tambor*)

muffler ['mʌflər] s bufanda, tapaboca; (aut) silenciador *m*, silencioso

mufti ['mʌfti] s traje *m* de paisano

mug [mʌg] s pichel *m;* (slang) jeta, hocico ‖ v (*pret* & *pp* **mugged;** *ger* **mugging**) *tr* (slang) fotografiar; (slang) atacar ‖ *intr* (slang) hacer muecas

mugger ['mʌgər] s ladron *m* asaltador

mug•gy ['mʌgi] *adj* (*comp* **-gier;** *super* **-giest**) bochornoso, sofocante

mulat•to [mju'læto] o [mə'læto] s (*pl* **-toes**) mulato

mulber•ry ['mʌl,bɛri] s (*pl* **-ries**) (*tree*) moral *m;* (*fruit*) mora

mulct [mʌlkt] *tr* defraudar

mule [mjul] s mulo, macho; (*slipper*) babucha

mule chair s artolas, jamugas

muleteer [,mjulə'tɪr] s mulatero

mulish ['mjulɪʃ] *adj* terco, obstinado

mull [mʌl] *tr* calentar (*vino*) con especias ‖ *intr*—**to mull over** reflexionar sobre

mullion ['mʌljən] s parteluz *m*

Multigraph ['mʌltɪ,græf] o ['mʌltɪ,grɑf] s (trademark) multígrafo ‖ *tr* multigrafiar

multilateral [,mʌltɪ'lætərəl] *adj* (*having many sides*) multilátero; (*participated in by more than two nations*) multilateral

multinational corporations *spl* multinacionales *mpl*

multiple ['mʌltɪpəl] *adj* múltiple, múltiplo ‖ s (math) múltiplo

multiple sclerosis *s* esclerosis *f* múltiple
multiplex ['mʌltɪ,plɛks] *adj* múltiple
multiplici·ty [,mʌltɪ'plɪsɪti] *s* (*pl* **-ties**) multiplicidad
multi·ply ['mʌltɪ,plaɪ] *v* (*pret & pp* **-plied**) *tr* multiplicar ‖ *intr* multiplicar, multiplicarse
multipurpose [,mʌltɪ'pʌrpəs] *adj* múltiple de uso; versátil
multitude ['mʌltɪ,tjud] o ['mʌltɪ,tud] *s* multitud
mum [mʌm] *adj* callado; **mum's the word!** ¡punto en boca!; **to keep mum about** callar ‖ *interj* ¡chitón!
mumble ['mʌmbəl] *tr & intr* mascullar, mascujar
mummer·y ['mʌməri] *s* (*pl* **-ies**) mojiganga
mum·my ['mʌmi] *s* (*pl* **-mies**) momia
mumps [mʌmps] *s* papera
munch [mʌntʃ] *tr* ronzar
mundane ['mʌnden] *adj* mundano
municipal [mju'nɪsɪpəl] *adj* municipal
municipali·ty [mju,nɪsɪ'pælɪti] *s* (*pl* **-ties**) municipio
munificent [mju'nɪfɪsənt] *adj* munífico
munition [mju'nɪʃən] *s* munición ‖ *tr* municionar
munition dump *s* depósito de municiones
mural ['mjurəl] *adj* mural ‖ *s* pintura mural; decoración mural
murder ['mʌrdər] *s* asesinato, homicidio ‖ *tr* asesinar; (*to spoil, mar*) (coll) estropear
murderer ['mʌrdərər] *s* asesino
murderess ['mʌrdərɪs] *s* asesina
murderous ['mʌrdərəs] *adj* asesino; cruel, sanguinario
murk·y ['mʌrki] *adj* (*comp* **-ier**; *super* **-iest**) (*hazy*) calinoso; (*gloomy*) lóbrego
murmur ['mʌrmər] *s* murmullo ‖ *tr & intr* murmurar
mus. *abbr* **museum, music**
muscle ['mʌsəl] *s* músculo; (fig) fuerza muscular
muscular ['mʌskjələr] *adj* musculoso
muse [mjuz] *s* musa; **the Muses** las Musas ‖ *intr* meditar, reflexionar; **to muse on** contemplar
museum [mju'ziəm] *s* museo
mush [mʌʃ] *s* gachas; (coll) sentimentalismo exagerado, sensiblería
mush'room' *s* hongo, seta ‖ *intr* aparecer de la noche a la mañana; **to mushroom into** convertirse rápidamente en
mushroom cloud *s* nube-hongo *f*
mush·y ['mʌʃi] *adj* (*comp* **-ier**; *super* **-iest**) mollar, pulposo; (coll) sensiblero, sobón; (*with women*) (coll) baboso; **to be mushy** (coll) hacerse unas gachas
music ['mjuzɪk] *s* música; **to face the music** (coll) afrontar las consecuencias; **to set to music** poner en música
musical ['mjuzɪkəl] *adj* musical, músico
musical comedy *s* comedia musical
musicale [,mjuzɪ'kæl] *s* velada musical, concierto casero
music box *s* caja de música
music cabinet *s* musiquero

music hall *s* salón *m* de conciertos; (Brit) teatro de variedades
musician [mju'zɪʃən] *s* músico
musicianship [mju'zɪʃən,ʃɪp] *s* musicalidad
musicologist [,mjuzɪ'kɑlədʒɪst] *s* musicólogo
musicology [,mjuzɪ'kɑlədʒi] *s* musicología
music rack o **music stand** *s* atril *m*
musk [mʌsk] *s* almizcle *m*; olor *m* de almizcle
musk deer *s* almizclero
musket ['mʌskɪt] *s* mosquete *m*
musketeer [,mʌskɪ'tɪr] *s* mosquetero
musk'mel'on *s* melón *m*
musk'rat' *s* almizclera
Muslim ['mʌzləm] o ['mʌsləm] *adj* muslime, islámico, mahometano ‖ *s* muslime *mf*, musulmán *m*
muslin ['mʌzlɪn] *s* muselina
muss [mʌs] *tr* (*the hair*) (coll) descabellar, desarreglar; (*clothing*) (coll) chafar, arrugar
muss·y ['mʌsi] *adj* (*comp* **-ier**; *super* **-iest**) desaliñado, desgreñado
must [mʌst] *s* mosto; (*mold*) moho; cosa que debe hacerse ‖ *v aux* **I must study my lesson** debo estudiar mi lección; **he must work tomorrow** tiene que trabajar mañana; **she must be ill** estará enferma
mustache [məs'tæʃ], [məs'tɑʃ], o ['mʌstæʃ] *s* bigote *m*, mostacho
mustard ['mʌstərd] *s* mostaza
mustard gas *s* gas *m* mostaza
mustard plaster *s* sinapismo, cataplasma *f*
muster ['mʌstər] *s* asamblea; matrícula de revista; **to pass muster** pasar revista; ser aceptable ‖ *tr* llamar a asamblea; reunir para pasar revista; reunir, acumular; **to muster in** alistar; **to muster out** dar de baja a; **to muster up courage** cobrar ánimo
muster roll *s* lista de revista
mus·ty ['mʌsti] *adj* (*comp* **-tier**; *super* **-tiest**) (*moldy*) mohoso; (*stale*) trasnochado; anticuado, pasado de moda
mutation [mju'teʃən] *s* mutación
mute [mjut] *adj & s* mudo ‖ *tr* poner sordina a
mutilate ['mjutɪ,let] *tr* mutilar
mutilated *adj* mútilo, mutilado, mocho
mutineer [,mjutɪ'nɪr] *s* amotinado
mutinous ['mjutɪnəs] *adj* amotinado
muti·ny ['mjutɪni] *s* (*pl* **-nies**) motín *m* ‖ *v* (*pret & pp* **-nied**) *intr* amotinarse
mutt [mʌt] *s* (slang) perro cruzado; (slang) bobo, tonto
mutter ['mʌtər] *tr & intr* murmurar
mutton ['mʌtən] *s* carnero, carne *f* de carnero
mutton chop *s* chuleta de carnero
mutual ['mutʃuəl] *adj* mutual, mutuo
mutual aid *s* apoyo mutuo
mutual benefit association *s* mutualidad
mutual fund *s* sociedad inversionista mutualista
muzzle ['mʌzəl] *s* (*projecting part of head of animal*) hocico; (*device to keep animal from biting*) bozal *m*; (*of firearm*) boca ‖ *tr*

mo
mu

abozalar; (*to keep from speaking*) amordazar

my [maɪ] *adj poss* mi

myriad [ˈmɪrɪ•əd] *s* miríada

myrrh [mʌr] *s* mirra

myrtle [ˈmʌrtəl] *s* arrayán *m*, mirto

myself [maɪˈsɛlf] *pron pers* yo mismo; mí, mí mismo; me, p.ej., **I enjoyed myself** me divertí; **with myself** conmigo

mysterious [mɪsˈtɪrɪ•əs] *adj* misterioso

myster•y [ˈmɪstəri] *s* (*pl* **-ies**) misterio

mystic [ˈmɪstɪk] *adj & s* místico

mystical [ˈmɪstɪkəl] *adj* místico

mysticism [ˈmɪstɪ,sɪzəm] *s* misticismo

mystification [,mɪstɪfɪˈkeʃən] *s* confusión, mistificación

mysti•fy [ˈmɪstɪ,faɪ] *v* (*pret & pp* **-fied**) *tr* rodear de misterio; (*to hoax*) confundir, mistificar

myth [mɪθ] *s* mito

mythical [ˈmɪθɪkəl] *adj* mítico

mythological [,mɪθəˈlɑdʒɪkəl] *adj* mitológico

mytholo•gy [mɪˈθɑlədʒi] *s* (*pl* **-gies**) mitología

N

N, n [ɛn] decimocuarta letra del alfabeto inglés

n. *abbr* **neuter, nominative, noon, north, noun, number**

N. *abbr* **Nationalist, Navy, Noon, North, November**

N.A. *abbr* **National Academy, National Army, North America**

nab [næb] *v* (*pret & pp* **nabbed;** *ger* **nabbing**) *tr* (slang) agarrar, coger; (slang) ponor proso, prondcr

nag [næg] *s* caballejo, jaco; pequeño caballo de silla ‖ *v* (*pret & pp* **nagged;** *ger* **nagging**) *tr* importunar regañando ‖ *intr* regañar

naiad [ˈne•æd] o [ˈnaɪ•æd] *s* náyade *f;* (fig) nadadora

nail [nel] *s* (*of finger*) uña; (*to fasten wood, etc.*) clavo; **to hit the nail on the head** dar en el clavo ‖ *tr* clavar

nail brush *s* cepillo de uñas

nail clippers *spl* cortauñas *m*

nail file *s* lima para las uñas

nail polish *s* esmalte *m* para las uñas, laca de uñas

nailset [ˈnel,sɛt] *s* contrapunzón *m*

naïve [nɑˈiv] *adj* cándido, ingenuo

naked [ˈnekɪd] *adj* desnudo; **to go naked** ir desnudo, andar a la cordobana; **to strip naked** desnudar; desnudarse; **with the naked eye** a simple vista

name [nem] *s* nombre *m;* (*first name*) nombre de pila; (*last name*) apellido; fama, reputación, renombre *m;* linaje, *m*, raza; **to call someone names** maltratar a uno de palabra; **to go by the name of** ser conocido por el nombre de; **to make a name for oneself** darse a conocer, hacerse un nombre; **what is your name?** ¿cómo se llama Vd.? ‖ *tr* nombrar; fijar (*un precio*)

name day *s* santo

nameless [ˈnemlɪs] *adj* sin nombre, anónimo

namely [ˈnemli] *adv* a saber, es decir

namesake [ˈnem,sek] *s* homónimo, tocayo

nanny goat [ˈnæni] *s* (coll) cabra

nap [næp] *s* lanilla, flojel *m;* sueñecillo; **to take a nap** descabezar un sueñecillo ‖ *v* (*pret & pp* **napped;** *ger* **napping**) *intr* echar un sueñecillo; estar desprevenido; **to catch napping** coger desprevenido

napalm [ˈnepɑm] *s* (mil) gelatina incendiaria

nape [nep] *s* cogote *m*, nuca

naphtha [ˈnæfθə] *s* nafta

napkin [ˈnæpkɪn] *s* servilleta; (*of a baby*) (Brit) pañal *m*

napkin ring *s* servilletero

Naples [ˈnepəlz] *s* Nápoles

Napoleonic [nə,polɪˈɑnɪk] *adj* napoleónico

narc [nɑrk] *s* (slang) agente *m* de policía antidroga

narcissus [nɑrˈsɪsəs] *s* (bot) narciso ‖ **Narcissus** *s* Narciso

narcotic [nɑrˈkɑtɪk] *adj & s* narcótico

narrate [næˈret] *tr* narrar

narration [næˈreʃən] *s* narración

narrative [ˈnærətɪv] *adj* narrativo ‖ *s* (*story, tale; art of telling stories*) narrativa

narrator [næˈretər] *s* narrador *m*

narrow [ˈnæro] *adj* angosto, estrecho; intolerante; minucioso; (*sense of a word*) estricto ‖ **narrows** *spl* angostura, paso estrecho ‖ *tr* enangostar, estrechar; reducir, limitar ‖ *intr* enangostarse, estrecharse; reducirse, limitarse

narrow escape *s* trance *m* difícil; **to have a narrow escape** escapar por un pelo, salvarse en una tabla

narrow gauge *s* trocha angosta, vía estrecha

narrow-minded [ˈnæro'maɪndɪd] *adj* intolerante, de miras estrechas, poco liberal

nasal [ˈnezəl] *adj & s* nasal *f*

nasalize [ˈnezə,laɪz] *tr* nasalizar ‖ *intr* ganguear

nasturtium [nəˈstʌrʃəm] *s* capuchina, espuela de galán

nas•ty [ˈnæsti] *adj* (*comp* **-tier;** *super* **-tiest**) asqueroso, sucio; desagradable; desvergonzado; amenazador; horrible

natatorium [,netəˈtɔrɪ•əm] *s* piscina de natación

nation [ˈneʃən] *s* nación

national ['næʃənəl] *adj & s* nacional *mf*
national anthem *s* himno nacional
national hero *s* benemérito de la patria
national holiday *s* fiesta nacional
nationalism ['næʃənə,lızəm] *s* nacionalismo
nationalist ['næ,ʃənəlɪst] *adj & s* nacionalista *mf*
nationali•ty ['næ,ʃən,ælɪti] *s (pl* -ties) nacionalidad, naturalidad
nationalize ['næʃənə,laɪz] *tr* nacionalizar
na'tion-wide' *adj* de toda la nación
native ['netɪv] *adj* nativo, natural; indígena; *(language)* materno; **to go native** vivir como los indígenas ‖ *s* natural *mf;* indígena *mf*
native land *s* patria
nativi•ty [nə'tɪvɪti] *s (pl* -ties) nacimiento ‖ **Nativity** *s (day; festival; painting)* natividad
NATO ['neto] *s* (acronym) la O.T.A.N.
nat•ty ['næti] *adj.* (comp -tier; super -tier; super -tiest) elegante, garboso
natural ['nætʃərəl] *adj* natural; (mus) natural ‖ *s* imbécil *mf;* (mus) tono natural, nota natural; *(sign)* (mus) becuadro; (mus) tecla blanca; (coll) cosa de éxito certero
naturalism ['nætʃərə,lızəm] *s* naturalismo
naturalist ['nætʃərəlɪst] *s* naturalista *mf*
naturalization [,nætʃərəlɪ'zəʃən] *s* naturalización
naturalization papers *spl* carta de naturaleza
naturalize ['nætʃərə,laɪz] *tr* naturalizar
naturally ['nætʃərəli] *adv* naturalmente; claro, desde luego, por supuesto
nature ['netʃər] *s* naturaleza; **from nature** del natural
naught [nɔt] *s* nada; cero; **to bring to naught** anular, invalidar, destruir; **to come to naught** reducirse a nada, frustrarse
naugh•ty ['nɔti] *adj (comp* -tier; *super* -tiest) desobediente, pícaro; desvergonzado; *(story, tale)* verde
nausea ['nɔʃɪ•ə] o ['nɔsi•ə] *s* náusea
nauseate ['nɔʃɪ,et] o ['nɔsi,et] *tr* dar náuseas a ‖ *intr* nausear, marearse
nauseating ['nɔʃɪ,etɪŋ] o ['nɔsi,etɪŋ] *adj* nauseabundo, asqueroso
nauseous ['nɔ,ʃɪ•əs] o ['nɔsi•əs] *adj* nauseabundo
nautical ['nɔtɪkəl] *adj* náutico, marino, naval
nav. *abbr* naval, navigation
naval ['nevəl] *adj* naval, naval militar
Naval Academy *s* (U.S.A.) Escuela Naval Militar
naval officer *s* oficial *m* de marina
naval station *s* apostadero
nave [nev] *s (of a church)* nave *f* central, nave principal; *(of a wheel)* cubo
navel ['nevəl] *s* ombligo; *(center point, middle)* (fig) ombligo
navel orange *s* navel *f,* naranja de ombligo
navigability [,nævɪgə'bɪlɪti] *s (of a river)* navegabilidad; *(of a ship)* buen gobierno
navigable ['nævɪgəbəl] *adj (river, canal, etc.)* navegable; *(ship)* marinero, de buen gobierno
navigate ['nævɪ,get] *tr & intr* navegar

navigation ['nævɪ,geʃən] *s* navegación
navigator ['nævɪ,getər] *s* navegador *m,* navegante *m; (he who is in charge of course of ship or plane)* oficial *m* de derrota; (Brit) peón *m*
nav•vy ['nævi] *s (pl* -vies) (Brit) bracero, peón *m*
na•vy ['nevi] *adj* azul oscuro ‖ *s (pl* -vies) marina de guerra; *(personnel)* marina; azul oscuro
navy bean *s* frijol blanco común
navy blue *s* azul marino, azul oscuro
navy yard *s* arsenal *m* de puerto
Nazarene [,næzə'rin] *adj & s* nazareno
Nazi ['nɑtsi] o ['nætsi] *adj & s* nazi *mf,* nacista *mf*
n.b. *abbr* **nota bene** (Lat) **note well**
N-bomb ['ɛn,bɑm] *s* bomba de neutrones
Neapolitan [,ni•ə'pɑlitən] *adj & s* napolitano
neap tide [nip] *s* marea muerta
near [nɪr] *adj* cercano, próximo; íntimo; imitado ‖ *adv* cerca; íntimamente ‖ *prep* cerca de; hacia, por ‖ *tr* acercarse a ‖ *intr* acercarse
nearby ['nɪr,baɪ] *adj* cercano, próximo ‖ *adv* cerca
Near East *s* Cercano Oriente, Próximo Oriente
nearly ['nɪrli] *adv* casi; de cerca; íntimamente; por poco, p.ej., **he nearly fell** por poco se cae
near-sighted ['nɪr'saɪtɪd] *adj* miope
near-sightedness *s* miopía
neat [nit] *adj* aseado, pulcro; pulido; diestro, primoroso; puro, sin mezcla ‖ *ssg* res vacuna ‖ *spl* ganado vacuno
neat's'-foot'oil *s* aceite *m* de pie de buey
Nebuchadnezzar [,nɛbjəkəd'nɛzər] *s* Nabucodonosor *m*
nebu•la ['nɛbjələ] *s (pl* -lae [,li] o -las) nebulosa
nebular ['nɛbjələr] *adj* nebular
nebulous ['nɛbjələs] *adj* nebuloso
necessary ['nɛsɪ,sɛri] *adj* necesario
necessitate [nɪ'sɛsɪ,tet] *tr* necesitar, exigir
necessitous [nɪ'sɛsɪtəs] *adj* necesitado
necessi•ty [nɪ'sɛsɪti] *s (pl* -ties) necesidad
neck [nɛk] *s* cuello; *(of a bottle)* gollete *m; (of violin or guitar)* mástil *m;* istmo, península; estrecho; **neck and neck** parejos; **to break one's neck** (coll) matarse trabajando; **to stick one's neck out** (coll) descubrir el cuerpo ‖ *intr* (slang) acariciarse *(dos enamorados)*
neck'band' *s* tirilla de camisa
necklace ['nɛklɪs] *s* gargantilla, collar *m*
necktie ['nɛk,taɪ] *s* corbata
necktie pin *s* alfiler *m* de corbata
necrology [nɛ'krɑlədʒi] *s* necrología
necromancy ['nɛkrə,mænsi] *s* necromancia, nigromancia
nectarine [,nɛktə'rin] *s* griñón *m*
née o **nee** [ne] *adj* nacida o de soltera, p.ej., **Mary Wilson, née Miller** Maria Wilson, nacida Miller o María Wilson, de soltera Miller

my
ne

need [nid] *s* necesidad; pobreza; **in need** necesitado ‖ *tr* necesitar ‖ *intr* estar necesitado; ser necesario ‖ *v aux*—**if need be** si fuere necesario; **to need** + *inf* deber, tener que + *inf*

needful [ˈnidfəl] *adj* necesario ‖ **the needful** lo necesario; (slang) el dinero

needle [ˈnidəl] *s* aguja; **to look for a needle in a haystack** buscar una aguja en un pajar ‖ *tr* coser con aguja; (coll) aguijonear, incitar; (coll) añadir alcohol a (*la cerveza o el vino*)

needle bath *s* ducha en alfileres

needle′case′ *s* alfiletero

needle point *s* bordado al pasado; encaje *m* de mano

needless [ˈnidlɪs] *adj* innecesario, inútil

needle′work′ *s* costura, labor *f*

needs [nidz] *adv* necesariamente, forzosamente

need•y [ˈnidi] *adj* (*comp* -ier; *super* -iest) necesitado, indigente ‖ **the needy** los necesitados

ne′er-do-well [ˈnɛrdu‚wɛl] *adj & s* holgazán, perdido

negation [nɪˈgeʃən] *s* negación

negative [ˈnɛgətɪv] *adj* negativo ‖ *s* negativa; electricidad negativa, borne negativo; (gram) negación; (math) término negativo; (phot) prueba negativa ‖ *tr* desaprobar; anular

neglect [nɪˈglɛkt] *s* negligencia, descuido ‖ *tr* descuidar; **to neglect to** dejar de, olvidarse de

neglectful [nɪˈglɛktfəl] *adj* negligente, descuidado

négligée o **negligee** [‚nɛglɪˈʒe] *s* bata de mujer, traje *m* de casa

negligence [ˈnɛglɪdʒəns] *s* negligencia, descuido

negligent [ˈnɛglɪdʒənt] *adj* negligente, descuidado

negligible [ˈnɛglɪdʒɪbəl] *adj* insignificante, imperceptible

negotiable [nɪˈgoʃɪ•əbəl] *adj* negociable; transitable

negotiate [nɪˈgoʃɪ‚et] *tr* negociar; (coll) salvar, vencer ‖ *intr* negociar

negotiation [nɪ‚goʃɪˈeʃən] *s* negociación; trámite *m*; **round of negotiations** ronda negociadora

Ne•gro [ˈnigro] *adj* (*usually offensive*) negro ‖ *s* (*pl* -groes) (*usually offensive*) negro

neigh [ne] *s* relincho ‖ *intr* relinchar

neighbor [ˈnebər] *adj* vecino ‖ *s* vecino; (*fellow man*) prójimo ‖ *tr* ser vecino de; ser amigo de ‖ *intr* estar cercano; tener relaciones amistosas

neighborhood [ˈnebər‚hʊd] *s* vecindad, vecindario, cercanías; **in the neighborhood of** en las inmediaciones de; (coll) cerca de, aproximadamente

neighboring [ˈnebərɪŋ] *adj* vecino, colindante

neighborly [ˈnebərli] *adj* buen vecino, amable, sociable

neither [ˈniðər] o [ˈnaɪðər] *adj indef* ninguno . . . (de los dos); **neither one** ninguno de los dos ‖ *pron indef* ninguno (de los dos); ni uno ni otro, ni lo uno ni lo otro ‖ *conj* ni; tampoco, ni . . . tampoco, p.ej., **neither do I** yo tampoco, ni yo tampoco; **neither . . . nor** ni . . . ni

neme•sis [ˈnɛmɪsɪs] *s* (*pl* -ses [‚siz]) (*someone or something that punishes*) némesis *f* ‖ **Nemesis** *s* Némesis *f*

neologism [niˈɑlə‚dʒɪzəm] *s* neologismo

neomycin [‚ni•əˈmaɪsɪn] *s* neomicina

neon [ˈni•ɑn] *s* neo, neón *m*

neophyte [ˈni•ə‚faɪt] *s* neófito

Nepal [nɪˈpɔl] *s* el Nepal

Nepa•lese [‚nɛpəˈliz] *adj* nepalés ‖ *s* (*pl* -lese) nepalés *m*

nepenthe [nɪˈpɛnθi] *s* nepente *m*

nephew [ˈnɛfju] o [ˈnɛvju] *s* sobrino

Nepos [ˈnipɑs] o [ˈnɛpɑs] *s* Nepote *m*

Neptune [ˈnɛptʃun] o [ˈnɛptjun] *s* Neptuno

neptunium [nɛpˈtʃuni•əm] o [nɛpˈtjuni•əm] *s* neptunio

nerd [nʌrd] *s* (slang) tipo insípido; sujeto estúpido

Nereid [ˈnɪrɪ•ɪd] *s* nereida

Nero [ˈnɪro] *s* Nerón *m*

nerve [nʌrv] *adj* (*center; system; tonic; disease; prostration; breakdown*) nervioso ‖ *s* nervio; ánimo, valor *m*; audacia; (coll) descaro; **nerves** excitabilidad nerviosa; **to get on one's nerves** irritar los nervios a uno; **to strain every nerve** esforzarse al máximo

nerve-racking [ˈnʌrv‚rækɪŋ] *adj* irritante, exasperante

nervous [ˈnʌrvəs] *adj* nervioso

nervous breakdown *s* colapso nervioso

nervousness [ˈnʌrvəsnɪs] *s* nerviosidad

nervous shudder *s* muerte chiquita

nerv•y [ˈnʌrvi] *adj* (*comp* -ier; *super* -iest) (*strong, vigorous*) nervioso; atrevido, audaz; (coll) descarado

nest [nɛst] *s* nido; (*where hen lays eggs*) nidal *m*; (*birds in a nest*) nidada; (*set of things fitting within each other*) juego; (*of, e.g., thieves*) nido; **to feather one's nest** hacer todo para enriquecerse ‖ *tr* colocar en un nido ‖ *intr* anidar

nest egg *s* (*eggs left in a nest to induce hen to lay more*) nidal *m*; ahorros, hucha

nestle [ˈnɛsəl] *tr* poner en un nido; arrimar afectuosamente ‖ *intr* anidar; arrimarse cómodamente; **to nestle up** to arrimarse a

net [nɛt] *adj* neto, líquido ‖ *s* red *f*; precio neto, peso neto, ganancia líquida ‖ *v* (*pret & pp* **netted;** *super* **netting**) *tr* enredar, tejer; coger con red; producir (*cierta ganancia líquida*)

nether [ˈnɛðər] *adj* inferior, más bajo

Netherlander [ˈnɛðər‚lændər] o [ˈnɛðərləndər] *s* neerlandés *m*

Netherlandish [ˈnɛðər‚lændɪʃ] o [ˈnɛðərləndɪʃ] *adj* neerlandés *s* neerlandés *m*

Netherlands, The [ˈnɛðərləndz] los Países Bajos (*Holanda*)

netting [ˈnɛtɪŋ] s red f
nettle [ˈnɛtəl] s ortiga ‖ tr irritar, provocar
net'work' s red f; (rad & telv) cadena
neuralgia [njuˈrældʒə] s neuralgia
neurology [njuˈralədʒi] s neurología
neuron [ˈnjuran] o [ˈnuran] s neurona
neuro•sis [njuˈrosɪs] s (pl -ses [siz]) neurosis f
neurotic [njuˈratɪk] adj & s neurótico
neut. abbr **neuter**
neuter [ˈnjutər] adj neutro ‖ s género neutro; (aut) punto muerto
neutral [ˈnjutrəl] adj (on neither side in a quarrel or war) neutral; (having little or no color) neutro; (bot, chem, elec, phonet, zool) neutro ‖ s neutral mf; (aut) punto neutral, punto muerto
neutralism [ˈnjutrə,lɪzəm] s neutralismo
neutralist [ˈnjutrəlɪst] adj & s neutralista mf
neutrality [njuˈtrælɪti] s neutralidad
neutralize [ˈnjutrə,laɪz] tr neutralizar
neutron [ˈnjutran] s neutrón m
neutron bomb s bomba de neutrones, bomba neutrónica
never [ˈnɛvər] adv nunca; en mi vida; de ningún modo; **never fear** no hay cuidado; **never mind** no importa
nev'er•more' adv nunca más
nevertheless [,nɛvərðəˈlɛs] adv no obstante, sin embargo
new [nju] o [nu] adj nuevo; **what's new?** ¿qué hay de nuevo?
new arrival s recién llegado; recién nacido
new'born' adj recién nacido; renacido
New Castile s Castilla la Nueva
New'cas'tle s—**to carry coals to Newcastle** echar agua al mar, llevar hierro a Vizcaya, llevar leña al monte
newcomer [ˈnju,kʌmər] s recién llegado, recién venido
New England s la Nueva Inglaterra
newfangled [ˈnju,fæŋgəld] adj de última moda, recién inventado
Newfoundland [ˈnjufənd,lænd] s (island and province) Terranova ‖ [njuˈfaʊndlənd] s (dog) Terranova m
newly [ˈnjuli] adv nuevamente; **newly** + pp recién + pp
new'ly•wed' s recién casado
New Mexican adj & s neomejicano, nuevo-mejicano
New Mexico s Nuevo Méjico
new moon s luna nueva, novilunio
news [njuz] o [nuz] s noticias; periódico; **a news item** una noticia; **a piece of news** una noticia
news agency s agencia de noticias
news beat s exclusiva, anticipación de una noticia por un periódico
news'boy' s vendedor m de periódicos
news'cast' s noticiario radiofónico ‖ tr radiodifundir (noticias) ‖ intr radiodifundir noticias
news'cast'er s cronista mf de radio
news conference s var de **press conference**
news coverage s reportaje m
news'let'ter s circular f noticiera

news•man [ˈnjuzmən] s (pl -men [mən]) noticiero
New South Wales s la Nueva Gales del Sur
news'pa'per adj periodístico ‖ s periódico
newspaper•man [ˈnjuz,pepər,mæn] s (pl -men [,mɛn]) periodista m
news'print' s papel-prensa m
news'reel' s actualidades, noticiario cinematográfico
news'stand' s quiosco de periódicos, puesto de periódicos
news'week'ly s (pl -lies) semanario de noticias
news'wor'thy adj de gran actualidad, de interés periodístico
news•y [ˈnjuzi] adj (comp -ier; super -iest) (coll) informativo
new'-world' adj del Nuevo Mundo
New Year's card s tarjeta de felicitación de Año Nuevo
New Year's Day s el Día de Año Nuevo
New Year's Eve s la noche vieja, la víspera de año nuevo
New York [jɔrk] adj neoyorkino ‖ s Nueva York
New Yorker [ˈjɔrkər] s neoyorkino
New Zealand [ˈzilənd] adj neocelandés ‖ s Nueva Zelanda
New Zealander [ˈziləndər] s neocelandés m
next [nɛkst] adj próximo, siguiente; de al lado; venidero, que viene ‖ adv luego, después; la próxima vez; **next to** junto a; después de; **next to nothing** casi nada; **the next best** lo mejor después de eso; **to come next** venir después, ser el que sigue
next door s la casa de al lado; **next door to** en la casa siguiente de; (coll) casi
next'door' adj siguiente, de al lado
next of kin s (pl next of kin) pariente más cercano
niacin [ˈnaɪ•əsɪn] s niacina
Niagara Falls [naɪˈægərə] spl las Cataratas del Niágara
nibble [ˈnɪbəl] s mordisco ‖ tr & intr mordiscar; picar (un pez); **to nibble at** picar de o en
Nicaraguan [,nɪkəˈragwən] adj & s nicaragüense, nicaragüeño
nice [naɪs] adj delicado, fino, sutil; primoroso, pulido, refinado; dengoso, melindroso; atento, cortés, culto; escrupuloso, esmerado; agradable, simpático; decoroso, conveniente; complaciente; preciso; satisfactorio; (weather) bueno; (attractive) bonito; **nice and . . .** (coll) muy, mucho; **not nice** (coll) feo
nice-looking [ˈnaɪsˈlʊkɪŋ] adj hermoso, guapo, bien parecido
nicely [ˈnaɪsli] adv con precisión; escrupulosamente; satisfactoriamente; (coll) muy bien
nice•ty [ˈnaɪsəti] s (pl -ties) precisión; sutileza; finura; **to a nicety** con la mayor precisión
niche [nɪtʃ] s hornacina, nicho; colocación conveniente
Nicholas [ˈnɪkələs] s Nicolás m

ne
ni

nick [nɪk] s mella, muesca; **in the nick of time** en el momento crítico ‖ tr mellar, hacer muescas en; cortar

nickel [ˈnɪkəl] s níquel m; (U.S.A.) moneda de cinco centavos ‖ tr niquelar

nick'el-plate' tr niquelar

nicknack [ˈnɪk,næk] s chuchería, friolera

nick'name' s apodo, mote m ‖ tr apodar

nicotine [ˈnɪkə,tin] s nicotina

niece [nis] s sobrina

nif•ty [ˈnɪfti] adj (comp **-tier;** super **-tiest**) (slang) elegante; (slang) excelente

niggard [ˈnɪgərd] adj & s tacaño

night [naɪt] adj nocturno ‖ s noche f; **at** o **by night** de noche o por la noche; **night before last** anteanoche; **to make a night of it** (coll) divertirse hasta muy entrada la noche

night'cap' s gorro de dormir; trago antes de acostarse, sosiega

night club s cabaret m, café m cantante, sala de fiestas

night driving s conducción de noche

night'fall' s anochecer m, caída de la noche

night'gown' s camisa de dormir

nightingale [ˈnaɪtən,gel] s ruiseñor m

night latch s cerradura de resorte

night letter s carta telegráfica nocturna

night'long' adj de toda la noche ‖ adv durante toda la noche

nightly [ˈnaɪtli] adj nocturno; de cada noche ‖ adv de noche, por la noche; cada noche

night'mare' s pesadilla

nightmarish [ˈnaɪt,mɛrɪʃ] adj espeluznante, horroroso

night owl s buho nocturno; (coll) anochecedor m, trasnochador m

night'shirt' s camisa de dormir

night'time' adj nocturno ‖ s noche f

night'walk'er s vagabundo nocturno; ladrón nocturno; ramera callejera nocturna; sonámbulo

night watch s guardia de noche, ronda de noche; sereno; (mil) vigilia

night watchman s vigilante nocturno

nihilism [ˈnaɪ•ɪ,lɪzəm] s nihilismo

nihilist [ˈnaɪ•ɪlɪst] s nihilista mf

nil [nɪl] s nada

Nile [naɪl] s Nilo

nimble [ˈnɪmbəl] adj ágil, ligero; listo, vivo

nim•bus [ˈnɪmbəs] s (pl **-buses** o **-bi** [baɪ]) nimbo

Nimrod [ˈnɪmrɑd] s Nemrod m

nincompoop [ˈnɪnkəm,pup] s badulaque m, papirote m

nine [naɪn] adj & pron nueve ‖ s nueve m; equipo de béisbol; **nine o'clock** las nueve; **the Nine** las nueve musas

nine hundred adj & pron novecientos ‖ s novecientos m

nineteen [ˈnaɪnˈtin] adj, pron & s diecinueve m, diez y nueve m

nineteenth [ˈnaɪnˈtinθ] adj & s (in a series) decimonono; (part) diecinueveavo ‖ s (in dates) diecinueve m

ninetieth [ˈnaɪntɪ•θ] adj & s (in a series) nonagésimo; (part) noventavo

nine•ty [ˈnaɪnti] adj & pron noventa ‖ s (pl **-ties**) noventa m

ninth [naɪnθ] adj & s nono, noveno ‖ s (in dates) nueve m

nip [nɪp] s mordisco, pellizco; helada, escarcha; traguito; **nip and tuck** a quién ganará ‖ v (pret & pp **nipped;** ger **nipping**) tr mordiscar, pellizcar; helar, escarchar; (slang) asir, coger; **to nip in the bud** atajar en el principio ‖ intr beborrotear

nipple [ˈnɪpəl] s (of female) pezón m; (of male; of nursing bottle) tetilla; (mach) tubo roscado de unión, entrerrosca

Nippon [nɪˈpɑn] s el Japón

Nippon•ese [,nɪpəˈniz] adj nipón ‖ s (pl **-ese**) nipón m

nip•py [ˈnɪpi] adj (comp **-pier;** super **-piest**) mordaz, picante; frío, helado; (Brit) ágil, ligero

nirvana [nɪrˈvɑnə] s el nirvana

nit [nɪt] s piojito; (egg of insect) liendre f

niter [ˈnaɪtər] s nitro; (agr) nitro de Chile

nitrate [ˈnaɪtret] s nitrato; (agr) nitrato de potasio, nitrato de sodio

nitric acid [ˈnaɪtrɪk] s ácido nítrico

nitride [ˈnaɪtraɪd] s nitruro

nitrogen [ˈnaɪtrədʒən] s nitrógeno

nitroglycerin [,naɪtrəˈglɪsərɪn] s nitroglicerina

nitrous oxide [ˈnaɪtrəs] s óxido nitroso

nitwit [ˈnɪt,wɪt] s (slang) bobalicón m

no [no] adj indef ninguno; **no admittance** no se permite la entrada; **no matter** no importa; **no parking** se prohibe estacionarse; **no smoking** se prohibe fumar; **no thoroughfare** prohibido el paso; **no use** inútil; **with no sin** ‖ adv no; **no good** de ningún valor; ruin, vil; **no longer** ya no; **no sooner** no bien

Noah [ˈno•ə] s Noé m

nob•by [ˈnɑbi] adj (comp **-bier;** super **-biest**) (slang) elegante; (slang) excelente

nobili•ty [noˈbɪlɪti] s (pl **-ties**) nobleza; (of sentiments, character, etc.) nobleza, ennoblecimiento

noble [ˈnobəl] adj & s noble m

noble•man [ˈnobəlmən] s (pl **-men** [mən]) noble m, hidalgo

nobod•y [ˈno,bɑdi] o [ˈnobədi] pron indef nadie, ninguno; **nobody but** nadie más que; **nobody else** nadie más, ningún otro ‖ s (pl **-ies**) nadie m, don nadie

nocturnal [nɑkˈtʌrnəl] adj nocturno

nod [nɑd] s inclinación de cabeza; seña con la cabeza; (of a person going to sleep) cabezada ‖ v (pret & pp **nodded;** ger **nodding**) tr inclinar (la cabeza); indicar con una inclinación de cabeza ‖ intr inclinar la cabeza; (in going to sleep) cabecear

node [nod] s bulto, protuberancia; nudo, enredo; (astr, med & phys) nodo; (bot) nudo

no'-fault' adj (divorce, insurance) libre de culpa

nohow [ˈno,haʊ] adv (coll) de ninguna manera

noise [nɔɪz] s ruido ‖ tr divulgar

noiseless [ˈnɔɪzlɪs] adj silencioso, sin ruido

noise level *s* nivel sonoro
nois•y [ˈnɔɪzi] *adj* (*comp* **-ier;** *super* **-iest**) ruidoso; bullero; (*boisterous*) estrepitoso
nom. *abbr* **nominative**
nomad [ˈnoʊmæd] *adj & s* nómada *mf*
nomadic [noʊˈmædɪk] *adj* nomádico
no man's land *s* terreno sin reclamar; (mil) la tierra de nadie
nominal [ˈnɑmɪnəl] *adj* nominal; (*price*) módico
nominate [ˈnɑmɪˌnet] *tr* postular como candidato; (*to appoint*) nombrar, designar
nomination [ˌnɑmɪˈneʃən] *s* postulación
nominative [ˈnɑmɪnətɪv] *adj & s* nominativo
nominee [ˌnɑmɪˈni] *s* propuesto, candidato
nonaligned nations [ˌnɑnəˈlaɪnd] *spl* países no alineados; países no comprometidos
nonbelligerent [ˌnɑnbəˈlɪdʒərənt] *adj & s* no beligerante *m*
nonbreakable [nɑnˈbrekəbəl] *adj* irrompible
nonchalance [ˈnɑnʃələns] *s* indiferencia, desenvoltura
nonchalant [ˈnɑnʃələnt] *adj* indiferente, desenvuelto
noncom [ˈnɑnˌkɑm] *s* (coll) clase, suboficial *m*
noncombatant [nɑnˈkɑmbətənt] *adj & s* no combatiente *m*
noncommissioned officer [ˌnɑnkəˈmɪʃənd] *s* clase, suboficial *m*
noncommittal [ˌnɑnkəˈmɪtəl] *adj* evasivo, reticente
noncommitted [ˌnɑnkəˈmɪtɪd] *adj* no empeñado
non compos mentis [ˈnɑnˈkɑmpəsˈmɛntɪs] *adj* falto de juicio, loco
nonconformist [ˌnɑnkənˈfɔrmɪst] *s* disidente *mf;* inconformista *mf*
nonconformity [ˌnɑnkənˈfɔrmɪti] *s* inconformidad
nondelivery [ˌnɑndɪˈlɪvəri] *s* falta de entrega
nondescript [ˈnɑndɪˌskrɪpt] *adj* inclasificable, indefinido
nondiscriminating [ˌnɑndɪsˈkrɪmɪˌnetɪŋ] *adj* indiscriminado
none [nʌn] *pron indef* nadie, ninguno, ningunos; **none of** ninguno de; nada de; **none other** ningún otro ‖ *adv* nada, de ninguna manera; **none the less** sin embargo, no obstante
nonenti•ty [nɑnˈɛntɪti] *s* (*pl* **-ties**) cosa inexistente; (*person*) nulidad
nonessential [ˌnɑnɛˈsɛnʃəl] *adj* intrascendente
nonexistence [ˌnɑnɛgˈzɪstəns] *s* inexistencia
nonfiction [nɑnˈfɪkʃən] *s* literatura no novelesca
nonfulfillment [ˌnɑnfʊlˈfɪlmənt] *s* incumplimiento
nonintervention [ˌnɑnɪntərˈvɛnʃən] *s* no intervención
nonmetal [ˈnɑnˌmɛtəl] *s* metaloide *m*
nonpartisan [nɑnˈpɑrtɪzən] *adj* imparcial
nonpayment [nɑnˈpemənt] *s* falta de pago
non•plus [ˈnɑnplʌs] o [nɑnˈplʌs] *s* estupefacción ‖ *v* (*pret & pp* **-plused** o **-plussed;** *ger*

-plusing o **-plussing**) *tr* dejar estupefacto, dejar pegado a la pared
nonprofit [nɑnˈprɑfɪt] *adj* sin fin lucrativo
nonrefillable [ˌnɑnrɪˈfɪləbəl] *adj* irrellenable
nonresident [nɑnˈrɛzɪdənt] *s* transeúnte *mf*
nonresidential [nɑnˌrɛzɪˈdɛnʃəl] *adj* comercial
nonscientific [nɑnˌsaɪ•ənˈtɪfɪk] *adj* anticientífico
nonsectarian [ˌnɑnsɛkˈtɛrɪ•ən] *adj* no sectario
nonsense [ˈnɑnsɛns] *s* disparate *m*, tontería; esperpento; **to talk nonsense** hablar en gringo
nonsensical [nɑnˈsɛnsɪkəl] *adj* disparatado, tonto
nonskid [ˈnɑnˈskɪd] *adj* antideslizante
nonstop [ˈnɑnˈstɑp] *adj & adv* sin parar, sin escala
nonsupport [ˌnɑnsəˈport] *s* falta de manutención
noodle [ˈnudəl] *s* tallarín *m;* (slang) mentecato, tonto; (slang) cabeza
noodle soup *s* sopa de pastas, sopa de fideos
nook [nʊk] *s* rinconcito
noon [nun] *s* mediodía *m;* **at high noon** en pleno mediodía
no one o **no-one** [ˈno,wʌn] *pron indef* nadie, ninguno; **no one else** nadie más, ningún otro
noontime [ˈnun,taɪm] *s* mediodía *m*
noose [nus] *s* lazo corredizo; (*to hang a criminal*) dogal *m;* trampa ‖ *tr* lazar; hacer un lazo corredizo en
nor [nɔr] *conj* ni
Nordic [ˈnɔrdɪk] *adj & s* nórdico
norm [nɔrm] *s* norma
normal [ˈnɔrməl] *adj* normal
Norman [ˈnɔrmən] *adj & s* normando
Normandy [ˈnɔrməndi] *s* Normandía
Norse [nɔrs] *adj* nórdico; noruego ‖ *s* (*ancient Scandinavian language*) nórdico; (*language of Norway*) noruego; **the Norse** los nórdicos; los noruegos
Norse•man [ˈnɔrsmən] *s* (*pl* **-men** [mən]) normando
north [nɔrθ] *adj* septentrional, del norte ‖ *adv* al norte, hacia el norte ‖ *s* norte *m*
North America *s* Norteamérica, la América del Norte
North American *adj & s* norteamericano
north'east'er *s* (*wind*) nordestada, nordeste *m* (*viento*)
northern [ˈnɔrðərn] *adj* septentrional; (*Hemisphere*) boreal
North Korea *s* la Corea del Norte
North Korean *adj & s* norcoreano
northward [ˈnɔrθwərd] *adv* hacia el norte
north wind *s* norte *m*, aquilón *m*
Norway [ˈnɔrwe] *s* Noruega
Norwegian [nɔrˈwidʒən] *adj & s* noruego
nos. *abbr* **numbers**
nose [noz] *s* nariz *f;* (aer) proa; **to blow one's nose** sonarse las narices; **to count noses** averiguar cuántas personas hay; **to follow one's nose** seguir todo derecho; avanzar guiándose por el instinto; **to hold one's**

ni
no

nose tabicarse las narices; **to lead by the nose** llevar por la barba, tener agarrado por las narices; **to look down one's nose at** mirar por encima del hombro; **to pay through the nose** pagar un precio escandaloso; **to pick one's nose** hurgarse las narices; **to poke one's nose into** meter las narices en; **to speak through the nose** ganguear; **to thumb one's nose at** señalar (*a una persona*) poniendo el pulgar sobre la nariz en son de burla; tratar con sumo desprecio; **to turn up one's nose at** mirar con desprecio; **under the nose of** en las narices de, en las barbas de ‖ *tr* olfatear ‖ *intr* ventear; **to nose about** curiosear; **to nose over** capotar (*un avión*); **to nose up** encabritarse (*un buque, un avión*)

nose bag *s* cebadera, morral *m*

nose'band' *s* muserola, sobarba

nose'bleed' *s* hemorragia nasal

nose cone *s* cono de proa

nose dive *s* (aer) descenso de picado; (fig) descenso precipitado

nose'-dive' *intr* (aer) picar; (fig) descender precipidamente

nosegay [ˈnozˌge] *s* ramillete *m*

nose ring *s* nariguera

no'-show' *s* pasajero no presentado

nostalgia [nɑˈstældʒə] *s* nostalgia

nostril [ˈnɑstrɪl] *s* nariz *f*, ventana

nos•y [ˈnozi] *adj* (*comp* **-ier;** *super* **-iest**) (coll) curioso, husmeador

not [nɑt] *adv* no; **not at all** nada, de ningún modo; **not yet** todavía no; **to think not** creer que no; **why not?** ¿cómo no?

notable [ˈnotəbəl] *adj* & *s* notable *m*

notarize [ˈnotəˌraɪz] *tr* abonar con fe notarial

nota•ry [ˈnotəri] *s* (*pl* **-ries**) notario

notch [nɑtʃ] *s* muesca, mella, corte *m;* (U.S.A.) desfiladero, paso; (coll) grado ‖ *tr* hacer muescas en, mellar

note [not] *s* nota; apunte *m;* esquela, cartita; marca, señal *f;* (com) pagaré *m*, vale *m;* canto, melodía; acento, voz *f;* (mus) nota ‖ *tr* notar, apuntar; marcar, señalar

note'book' *s* cuaderno, libro de apuntes

noted [ˈnotɪd] *adj* aramado, conocido

note paper *s* papel *m* de cartas

note'wor'thy *adj* notable, digno de notarse

nothing [ˈnʌθɪŋ] *pron indef* nada; **for nothing** inútilmente; de balde, gratis; **nothing doing** (slang) ni por pienso; **nothing else** nada más; **that's nothing to me** eso nada me importa; **to make nothing of** no hacer caso de; no aprovecharse de; no entender; despreciar; **to think nothing of** no hacer caso de; tener por fácil; despreciar ‖ *adv* nada, de ninguna manera; **nothing daunted** sin temor alguno ‖ *s* nada; nadería, friolera

notice [ˈnotɪs] *s* atención, reparo, advertencia; aviso, noticia; letrero; mención, reseña; llamada; notificación; **on short notice** con poco tiempo de aviso; **to escape one's notice** pasarle inadvertido a uno; **to serve notice** dar noticia, hacer saber ‖ *tr* notar, observar, reparar, reparar en; mencionar

noticeable [ˈnotɪsəbəl] *adj* sensible, perceptible; notable

noti•fy [ˈnotɪˌfaɪ] *v* (*pret* & *pp* **-fied**) *tr* notificar, avisar, hacer saber

notion [ˈnoʃən] *s* noción; capricho; **notions** mercería, artículos menudos; **to have a notion to** + *inf* pensar + *inf*, tener ganas de + *inf*

notorie•ty [ˌnotəˈraɪəti] *s* (*pl* **-ties**) mala reputación; (*condition of being well known*) notoriedad; (*person*) notable *mf*

notorious [noˈtorɪəs] *adj* reputado, mal reputado; bien conocido

no'-trump' *adj* & *s* sin triunfo; **a no-trump hand** un sin triunfo

notwithstanding [ˌnɑtwɪðˈstændɪŋ] o [ˌnɑtwɪθˈstændɪŋ] *adv* no obstante ‖ *prep* a pesar de ‖ *conj* a pesar de que

nougat [ˈnugət] *s* turrón *m*

noun [naʊn] *s* nombre, nombre sustantivo

nourish [ˈnʌrɪʃ] *tr* alimentar, nutrir; abrigar (*p.ej.*, *esperanzas*)

nourishing [ˈnʌrɪʃɪŋ] *adj* alimenticio, nutritivo

nourishment [ˈnʌrɪʃmənt] *s* alimento, nutrimento

Nov. *abbr* **November**

Nova Scotia [ˈnovəˈskoʃə] *s* la Nueva Escocia

Nova Scotian [ˈnovəˈskoʃən] *adj* & *s* neoescocés *m*

novel [ˈnovəl] *adj* nuevo; insólito, extraño, original ‖ *s* novela

novelist [ˈnovəlɪst] *s* novelista *mf*

novel•ty [ˈnovəlti] *s* (*pl* **-ties**) novedad, innovación; **novelties** bisutería, baratijas

November [noˈvɛmbər] *s* noviembre *m*

novice [ˈnovɪs] *s* novicio

novocaine [ˈnovəˌken] *s* novocaína

now [naʊ] *adv* ahora; ya; entonces; **from now on** de ahora en adelante; **how now?** ¿cómo?; **just now** hace un momento; **now and again** o **now and then** de vez en cuando; **now . . . now** ora . . . ora, ya . . . ya; **now that** ya que; **now then** ahora bien ‖ *interj* ¡vamos! ‖ *s* actualidad

nowadays [ˈnaʊəˌdez] *adv* hoy en día, hoy día

no'way' o **no'ways'** *adv* de ningún modo

no'where' *adv* en ninguna parte, a ninguna parte; **nowhere else** en ninguna otra parte

noxious [ˈnɑkʃəs] *adj* nocivo

nozzle [ˈnɑzəl] *s* (*of hoe*) lanza; (*of sprinkling can*) rallow, roseta; (*of candlestick*) cubo; (slang) nariz *f*

N.T. *abbr* **New Testament**

nth [ɛnθ] *adj* n^mo (*enésimo*); **to the nth degree** elevado a la potencia *n;* a más no poder

nuance [njuˈɑns] o [ˈnjuˌɑns] *s* matiz *m*

nub [nʌb] *s* protuberancia; pedazo; (coll) meollo

nuclear [ˈnuklɪˌər] *adj* nuclear

nu'cle-ar-pow'ered *adj* accionado por energía nuclear

nuclear test ban *s* proscripción de las pruebas nucleares

nuclear war *s* guerra nuclear

nucle·us [`nuklɪ·əs] *s* (*pl* **-i** [‚aɪ] o **-uses**) núcleo

nude [njud] o [nud] *adj* desnudo ‖ *s* — **in the nude** desnudo; **the nude** el desnudo

nudism [`njudɪzəm] o [`nudɪzəm] *s* (des)nudismo; naturismo

nudge [nʌdʒ] *s* codazo suave ‖ *tr* dar un codazo suave a, empujar suavemente

nugget [`nʌgɪt] *s* pedazo; (*of, e.g., gold*) pepita; preciosidad

nuisance [`njusəns] o [`nusəns] *s* molestia, estorbo; majadería; persona o cosa fastidiosas; **to be a nuisance** ser un higado

nuke [njuk] o [nuk] *s* (slang) arma atómica ‖ *tr* (slang) atacar con arma atómica; aniquilar

null [nʌl] *adj* nulo; **null and void** nulo, írrito, nulo y sin valor

nulli·ty [`nʌlɪti] *v* (*pl* **-ties**) nulidad

nulli·fy [`nʌlɪfaɪ] *v* (*pret & pp* **-fied**) anular, invalidor

numb [nʌm] *adj* entumecido; **to get numb** envararse ‖ *tr* entumecer

number [`nʌmbər] *s* número; **a number of** varios ‖ *tr* numerar; ascender a (*cierto número*); **his days are numbered** tiene sus días contados o sus horas contadas; **to be numbered among** hallarse entre; **to number among** contar entre

numberless [`nʌmbərlɪs] *adj* innumerable

numeral [`njumərəl] o [`numərəl] *adj* numeral ‖ *s* número

numerical [nju`mɛrɪkəl] o [nu`mɛrɪkəl] *adj* numérico

numerous [`njumərəs] o [`numərəs] *adj* numeroso

numskull [`nʌm‚skʌl] *s* (coll) bodoque *m*, mentecato

nun [nʌn] *s* monja, religiosa

nuptial [`nʌpʃəl] *adj* nupcial ‖ **nuptials** *spl* nupcias, bodas

nurse [nʌrs] *s* enfermera; (*to suckle a child*) ama de cría, nodriza; (*to take care of a child*) niñera ‖ *tr* cuidar (*a una persona enferma*); amamantar; alimentar, criar; tratar de curarse de (*p.ej., un resfriado*); abrigar (*p.ej., odio*) ‖ *intr* ser enfermera

nurser·y [`nʌrsəri] *s* (*pl* **-ies**) cuarto de los niños; (*of plants*) criadero, plantel *m*, semillero; (fig) semillero

nursery·man [`nʌrsərɪmən] *s* (*pl* **-men** [mən]) cultivador *m* de semillero

nursery rhymes *spl* versos para niños

nursery tales *spl* cuentos para niños

nursing bottle *s* biberón *m*

nursing home *s* clínica de reposo; (*for the aged*) residencia de ancianos

nurture [`nʌrtʃər] *s* alimentación, nutrimento; crianza, educación ‖ *tr* alimentar, nutrir; criar, educar; acariciar (*p.ej., una esperanza*)

nut [nʌt] *s* nuez *f;* (*to screw on a bolt*) tuerca; (slang) estrafalario; **a hard nut to crack** (coll) hueso duro de roer

nut'crack'er *s* cascanueces *m*

nutmeg [`nʌt‚mɛg] *s* nuez moscada; (*tree*) mirística

nutriment [`njutrɪmənt] *s* nutrimento

nutrition [nju`trɪʃən] *s* nutrición

nutritious [nju`trɪʃəs] *adj* nutricioso, nutritivo

nuts *adj* (slang) loco; estrafalario ‖ *interj* (slang) ¡no!, ¡niego!, ¡de ninguna manera!

nut'shell' *s* cáscara de nuez; **in a nutshell** en pocas palabras

nut·ty [`nʌti] *adj* (*comp* **-tier;** *super* **-tiest**) abundante en nueces; que sabe a nueces; (slang) chiflado, loco; **nutty about** (slang) loco por

nuzzle [`nʌzəl] *tr* hocicar, hozar ‖ *intr* hocicar; arrimarse cómodamente; arroparse bien

nylon [`naɪlɑn] *s* nilón *m;* **nylons** medias de nilón

nymph [nɪmf] *s* ninfa

O

O, o [o] decimoquinta letra del alfabeto inglés

O *interj* ¡oh!; ¡ay!, p.ej., **how pretty she is!** ¡Ay qué linda!; **O that. . .** ! ¡Ojalá que. . . !

oaf [of] *s* zoquete *m*, zamacuco; niño contrahecho

oak [ok] *s* roble *m*

oaken [`okən] *adj* hecho de roble

oakum [`okəm] *s* estopa, estopa de calafatear

oar [or] *s* remo; **to lie** o **rest on one's oars** aguantar los remos; aflojar en el trabajo ‖ *tr* conducir a remo ‖ *intr* remar, bogar

oars·man [`orzmən] *s* (*pl* **-men** [mən]) remero

OAS [`o'e'ɛs] *s* (*letterword*) OEA *f*

oa·sis [o`esɪs] *s* (*pl* **-ses** [siz]) oasis *m*

oat [ot] *s* avena; **oats** (*edible grain*) avena; **to feel one's oats** (slang) estar fogoso y brioso; (slang) estar muy pagado de sí mismo; **to sow one's wild oats** correrla, pasar las mocedades

oath [oθ] *s* juramento; **on oath** bajo juramento; **to take an oath** prestar juramento

oat'meal' *s* harina de avena; gachas de avena

ob. *abbr* obiit (Lat) died

obbligato [‚ɑblɪ`gato] *adj & s* obligado

obduracy [`ɑbdjərəsi] *s* obduración

obdurate ['abdjərɪt] *adj* obstinado, terco; empedernido

obedience [o'bidɪ•əns] *s* obediencia

obedient [o'bidɪ•ənt] *adj* obediente

obeisance [o'besəns] u [o'bisəns] *s* saludo respetuoso; homenaje *m*, respeto

obelisk ['abəlɪsk] *s* obelisco

obese [o'bis] *adj* obeso

obesity [o'bisɪti] *s* obesidad

obey [o'be] *tr & intr* obedecer

obfuscate [ab'fʌsket] o ['abfəs,ket] *tr* ofuscar

obituar•y [o'bɪtʃʊ,ɛri] *adj* necrológico ‖ *s* (*pl* -ies) necrología

obj. *abbr* **object, objection, objective**

object ['abdʒɪkt] *s* objeto ‖ [ab'dʒɛkt] *tr* objetar ‖ *intr* hacer objeciones

objection [ab'dʒɛkʃən] *s* reparo, objeción; **to have no objections to make** no tener nada que objetar

objectionable [ab'dʒɛkʃənəbəl] *adj* desagradable, reprensible; (*causing disapproval*) objetable

objective [ab'dʒɛktɪv] *adj & s* objetivo

obl. *abbr* **oblique, oblong**

obligate [ablɪ,get] *tr* obligar

obligation [,ablɪ'geʃən] *s* obligación; encargamiento

oblige [ə'blaɪdʒ] *tr* obligar; complacer; **much obliged** muchas gracias

obliging [ə'blaɪdʒɪŋ] *adj* complaciente, condescendiente, servicial

oblique [ə'blik] *adj* oblicuo; indirecto, evasivo

obliterate [ə'blɪtə,ret] *tr* borrar; arrasar, destruir

oblivion [ə'blɪvɪ•ən] *s* olvido

oblivious [ə'blɪvɪ•əs] *adj* olvidadizo

oblong ['ablɔŋ] o ['ablaŋ] *adj* oblongo

obnoxious [ab'nakʃəs] *adj* detestable, ofensivo

oboe ['obo] *s* oboe *m*

oboist ['obo•ɪst] *s* oboísta *mf*

obs. *abbr* **obsolete**

obscene [ab'sin] *adj* obsceno

obsceni•ty [ab'sɛnɪti] o [ab'sinɪti] *s* (*pl* -ties) obscenidad

obscure [əb'skjʊr] *adj* obscuro; (*vowel*) relajado, neutro

obscuri•ty [əb'skjʊrɪti] *s* (*pl* -ties) obscuridad

obsequies ['absɪkwiz] *spl* exequias

obsequious [əb'sikwɪ•əs] *adj* obsequioso, servil, rastrero

observance [əb'zʌrvəns] *s* observancia; ceremonia, rito

observant [əb'zʌrvənt] *adj* observador

observation [,abzər'veʃən] *s* observación; observancia

observato•ry [əb'zʌrvə,tori] *s* (*pl* -ries) observatorio

observe [əb'zʌrv] *tr* observar; (*a holiday; silence*) guardar

observer [əb'zʌrvər] *s* observador *m*

obsess [əb'sɛs] *tr* obsesionar

obsession [əb'sɛʃən] *s* obsesión

obsolescent [,absə'lɛsənt] *adj* arcaizante

obsolete ['absə,lit] *adj* desusado, caído en desuso; obsoleto

obstacle ['abstəkəl] *s* obstáculo

obstetrical [ab'stɛtrɪkəl] *adj* obstétrico

obstetrics [ab'stɛtrɪks] *ssg* obstetricia

obstina•cy ['abstɪnəsi] *s* (*pl* -cies) obstinación

obstinate ['abstɪnɪt] *adj* obstinado

obstruct [ab'strʌkt] *tr* obstruir; obstruccionar

obstruction [ab'strʌkʃən] *s* obstrucción

obtain [əb'ten] *tr* obtener ‖ *intr* existir, prevalecer

obtrusive [əb'trusɪv] *adj* entremetido, intruso

obtuse [əb'tjus] o [əb'tus] *adj* obtuso

obviate ['abvɪ,et] *tr* obviar

obvious ['abvɪ•əs] *adj* obvio

occasion [ə'keʒən] *s* ocasión; **to improve the occasion** aprovechar la ocasión

occasional [ə'keʒənəl] *adj* raro, poco frecuente; alguno que otro; de circunstancia

occasionally [ə'keʒənəli] *adv* ocasionalmente, de vez en cuando

occident ['aksɪdənt] *s* occidente *m*

occidental [,aksɪ'dɛntəl] *adj* occidental

occlusive [ə'klusɪv] *adj* oclusivo ‖ *s* oclusiva

occult [ə'kʌlt] o ['akʌlt] *adj* oculto

occupancy ['akjepənsi] *s* ocupación

occupant ['akjepənt] *s* ocupante *mf*; inquilino

occupation [,akjə'peʃən] *s* ocupación

occupational therapy *s* terapia vocacional

occu•py ['akjə,paɪ] *v* (*pret & pp* -pied) *tr* ocupar; habitar

oc•cur [ə'kʌr] *v* (*pret & pp* -curred; *ger* -curring) *intr* ocurrir, acontecer, suceder; encontrarse; (*to come to mind*) ocurrir

occurrence [ə'kʌrəns] *s* acontecimiento; caso, aparición

ocean ['oʃən] *s* océano

o'cean-go'ing *adj* transoceánico

oceanic [,oʃɪ'ænɪk] *adj* oceánico

ocean liner *s* buque transoceánico

o'clock [ə'klak] *adv* por el reloj; **it is one o'clock** es la una; **it is two o'clock** son las dos; **what o'clock is it?** ¿qué hora es?

Oct. *abbr* **October**

octave ['aktɪv] o ['aktev] *s* octava

October [ak'tobər] *s* octubre *m*

octo•pus ['aktəpəs] *s* (*pl* -puses o -pi [,paɪ]) pulpo

octoroon [,aktə'run] *s* octavo

ocular ['akjələr] *adj & s* ocular *m*

oculist ['akjəlɪst] *s* oculista *mf*

O.D. *abbr* **officer of the day, olive drab, overdose**

odd [ad] *adj* suelto; (*number*) impr; (*that doesn't match*) dispar; libre, de ocio; sobrante; extraño, raro, singular; y pico, y tantos, p.ej., **two hundred odd** doscientos y pico ‖ **odds** *ssg* o *spl* (*in betting*) ventaja; apuesta desigual; puntos de ventaja; **at odds** de monos, riñendo; **by all odds** muy probablemente, sin duda alguna; **it makes no odds** lo mismo da; **the odds are** lo probable es; la ventaja es de; **to be at odds** estar de punta, estar encontrados; **to set at odds** enemistar, malquistar

odd'ball' adj & s excéntrico; disente

oddi•ty ['adıti] s (pl **-ties**) rareza, cosa rara

odd jobs spl pequeñas tareas

odd lot s lote m inferior al centenar

odds and ends spl pedacitos varios, cajón m de sastre

ode [od] s oda

odious ['odɪ•əs] adj odioso, abominable

odor ['odər] s olor m; **to be in bad odor** tener mala fama

odorless ['odərlıs] adj inodoro

odorous ['odərəs] adj oloroso

Odysseus [o'dısjus] u [o'dısı•əs] s Odiseo

Odyssey ['adısı] s Odisea

Oedipus ['ɛdıpəs] o ['idıpəs] s Edipo

oenology [i'naledʒi] s enotecnia

of [ʌv] o [əv] prep de, p.ej., **the top of the mountain** la cima de la montaña; a: **to smell of** oler a; con: **to dream of** soñar con; en: **to think of** pensar en; menos: **a quarter of two** las dos menos un cuarto

off. abbr office, officer, official

off [ɔf] o [ɑf] adj malo, p.ej., **off day** día, malo; (account, sum) errado; más distante; libre; sin trabajo; quitado; apagado; (electric current) cortado; de descuento, de rebaja; de la parte del mar; (season) muerto ‖ adv fuera, a distancia, lejos; allá; **off of** (coll) de; (coll) a expensas de; **to be off** ponerse en marcha ‖ prep de, desde, al lado de, a nivel de; fuera de; libre de; (naut) a la altura de ‖ tr (slang) matar, asesinar

offal ['ɑfəl] u ['ɔfəl] s (of butchered meat) carniza; basura, desperdicios

off and on adv unas veces sí y otras no

off'beat' adj (slang) insólito, chocante, original

off'chance' s posibilidad poco probable

off'-col'or adj descolorido; indispuesto; (indecent, risqué) colorado, subido de color

offend [ə'fɛnd] tr & intr ofender

offender [ə'fɛndər] s ofensor m

offense [ə'fɛns] s ofensa; **to take offense (at)** ofenderse (de)

offensive [ə'fɛnsıv] adj ofensivo ‖ f ofensiva

offer ['ɔfər] o ['ɑfər] s ofrecimiento, oferta ‖ tr ofrecer; rezar (oraciones); oponer (resistencia)

offering ['ɔfərɪŋ] o ['ɑfərɪŋ] s ofrecimiento; (gift, present) oferta; (presentation in worship) ofrenda

off'hand' adj hecho de improviso; brusco, desenvuelto ‖ adv de improviso, súbitamente; bruscamente

office ['ɔfıs] o ['ɑfıs] s oficina, despacho; función, oficio; cargo, ministerio; (of a lawyer) bufete m; (of a doctor) consultorio

office boy s mandadero

office desk s escritorio ministro

of'fice•hold'er s funcionario, burócrata m

office hours spl horas de oficina; (of a doctor) horas de consulta

officer ['ɔfısər] o ['ɑfısər] s jefe m, director m; (of army, an order, a society, etc.) oficial m; agente m de policía

office seeker ['sikər] s aspirante m, pretendiente m

office supplies spl suministros para oficinas

official [ə'fıʃəl] adj oficial ‖ s jefe m, director m; (of a society) dignatario

officiate [ə'fıʃı,et] intr oficiar

officious [ə'fıʃəs] adj oficioso

off'-peak' adj (hours, stop, etc.) de valle; de menor tránsito

off-peak heater s (elec) termos m de acumulación

off-peak load s (elec) carga de las horas de valle

off'print' s sobretiro

off,set' s compensación; (typ) offset m ‖ **off'set'** v (pret & pp **-set**; ger **-setting**) tr compensar; imprimir por offset

off'shoot' s (of plant) retoño, renuevo; (of a family or race) descendiente mf; (branch) ramal m; consecuencia

off'shore' adj (wind) terral; (fishing) de bajura; (said of islands) costero; **offshore drilling rig** barca perforador ‖ adv a lo largo

off'spring' s descendencia, sucesión; hijo, hijos

off'-stage' adj de entre bastidores

off'-the-rec'ord adj extraoficial, confidencial

often ['ɔfən] o (ɑfən] adv a menudo, muchas veces; **how often?** ¿cuántas veces?; **not often** pocas veces

ogive ['odʒaıv] u [o'dʒaıv] s ojiva

ogle ['ogəl] tr & intr ojear; mirar amorosamente

ogre ['ogər] s ogro

ohm [om] s ohmio

oil [ɔıl] adj (burner; field; well) de petróleo; (pump; stove) de aceite; (company, tanker) petrolero; (land) petrolífero ‖ s aceite m; (consecrated oil; painting) óleo; **to burn the midnight oil** quemarse las cejas; **to pour oil on troubled waters** mojar la pólvora; **to strike oil** encontrar una capa de petróleo; (fig) enriquecerse de súbito ‖ tr aceitar; lubricar; lisonjear; (to bribe) untar ‖ intr proveerse de petróleo (un buque)

oil'can' s aceitera

oil'cloth' s encerado, hule m

oil field s yacimiento de petróleo

oil gauge indicador m del nivel de aceite

oil pan s colector m de aceite

oil shortage s carestía (or escasez f) de petróleo

oil tanker s petrolero

oil•y ['ɔıli] adj (comp **-ier**; super **-iest**) aceitoso; liso, resbaladizo; zalamero

ointment ['ɔıntmənt] s ungüento

O.K. ['o'ke] adj (coll) aprobado, conforme ‖ adv (coll) muy bien, está bien ‖ s (coll) aprobación ‖ v (pret & pp **O.K.'d**; ger **O.K.'ing**) tr (coll) aprobar

okra ['okrə] s quingombó m

old [old] adj viejo; antiguo; (wine) añejo; **how old is . . . ?** ¿cuántos años tiene . . . ?; **of old** de antaño, antiguamente; **to be . . . years old** tener . . . años

ob
ol

old age *s* ancianidad, vejez *f;* **to die of old age** morir de viejo
old boy *s* viejo; graduado; **the Old Boy** (slang) el diablo
Old Castile *s* Castilla la Vieja
old-clothes•man ['old'kloðz,mæn] *s* (*pl* -men [mɛn]) ropavejero
old country *s* madre patria
old-fashioned ['old'fæʃ*ə*nd] *adj* chapado a la antigua; anticuado, fuera de moda
old fo•gey u **old fo•gy** ['fogi] *s* (*pl* -gies) persona un poco ridícula por sus ideas o costumbres atrasadas
Old Glory *s* la bandera de los Estados Unidos
Old Guard *s* (U.S.A.) bando conservador del partido republicano
old hand *s* practicón *m*, veterano
old maid *s* solterona
old master *s* (paint) gran maestro; obra de un gran maestro
old moon *s* luna menguante
old salt *s* lobo de mar
old school *s* gente chapada a la antigua
old'-time' *adj* del tiempo viejo
old-timer ['old'taɪmər] *s* (coll) antiguo residente, veterano; (coll) persona chapada a la antigua
old wives' tale *s* cuento de viejas
old'-world' *adj* del Viejo Mundo
oleander [,olɪ'ændər] *s* adelfa
oligar•chy ['alɪ,garki] *s* (*pl* -chies) oligarquía
olive ['alɪv] *adj* aceitunado ǁ *s* aceituna
olive branch *s* ramo de olivo; (*peace*) oliva; hijo, vástago
olive grove *s* olivar *m*
olive oil *s* aceite *m*, aceite de oliva
olive tree *s* aceituno, olivo
Olympiad [o'lɪmpɪ,æd] *s* Olimpíada
Olympian [o'lɪmpɪ•ən] *adj* olímpico ǁ *s* dios griego
Olympic [o'lɪmpɪk] *adj* olímpico
omelet u **omelette** ['aməlɪt] o ['amlɪt] *s* tortilla (de huevos)
omen ['omən] *s* agüero
ominous ['amɪnəs] *adj* ominoso
omission [o'mɪʃən] *s* omisión
omit [o'mɪt] *v* (*pret & pp* **omitted;** *ger* **omitting**) *tr* omitir
omnibus ['amnɪ,bʌs] o ['amnɪbəs] *adj* general; (*volume*) colecticio ǁ *s* ómnibus *m*
omnipotent [am'nɪpətənt] *adj* omnipotente
omniscient [am'nɪʃənt] *adj* omnisciente
omnivorous [am'nɪvərəs] *adj* omnívoro
on [an] u [ɔn] *adj* puesto, p.ej., **with his hat on** con el sombrero puesto; principiando; en funcionamiento; encendido; conectado; **the deal is on** ya está concertado el trato; **the game is on** ya están jugando; **the race is on** allá van los corredores; **what is on at the theater this evening?** ¿qué representan esta noche? ǁ *adv* adelante; encima; **and so on** y así sucesivamente; **come on!** ¡anda, anda!; **farther on** más allá, más adelante; **later on** más tarde, después; **to be on to a person** (coll) conocerle a uno el juego; **to have on** tener puesto; **to . . . on** seguir + *ger*, **he played on** siguió to-

cando ǁ *prep* en, sobre, encima de; a, p.ej., **on foot** a pie; **on my arrival** a mi llegada; bajo, p.ej., **on my responsibility** bajo mi responsabilidad; contra, p.ej., **an attack on liberty** un ataque contra la libertad; de, p.ej., **on good authority** de buena tinta; **on a journey** de viaje; hacia, p.ej., **to march on the capital** marchar hacia la capital; por, p.ej., **on all sides** por todos lados; tras, p.ej., **defeat on defeat** derrota tras derrota; **on** + *ger* al + *inf*, p.ej., **on arriving** al llegar
on and on *adv* continuamente, sin cesar, sin parar
on'-board' **computer** *s* ordenador de viaje
once [wʌns] *adv* una vez; antes, p.ej., **once so happy** antes tan feliz; alguna vez, p.ej., **if this once becomes known** si esto llega a saberse alguna vez; **all at once** de súbito, de repente; **at once** en seguida; a la vez en el mismo momento; **for once** una vez por lo menos; **once and again** repetidas veces; **once in a blue moon** cada muerte de obispo; **once in a while** de vez en cuando; luego; **once more** otra vez; una vez más; **once upon a time there was** érase una vez, érase que se era ǁ *conj* una vez que ǁ *s* una vez; vez, p.ej., **this once** esta vez
once'-o'ver *s* (slang) examen rápido; **to give a thing the once-over** (coll) examinar una cosa superficialmente
oncology [aŋ'kaləʤi] *s* oncología
one [wʌn] *adj* un, uno; un tal, p.ej., **one Smith** un tal Smith; único, p.ej., **one price** precio único ǁ *pron* uno, p.ej., **one does not know what to do here** uno no sabe qué hacer aquí; se, p.ej., **how does one go to the station?** ¿cómo se va a la estación?; **I for one** yo por lo menos; **it's all one and the same to me** me es igual; **my little one** mi chiquito; **of one another** el uno del otro, los unos de los otros, p.ej., **we took leave of one another** nos despedimos el uno del otro; **one and all** todos; **one another** se, p.ej., **they greeted one another** se saludaron; uno a otro, unos a otros, p.ej., **they looked at one another** se miraron uno a otro; **one by one** uno a uno; **one o'clock** la una; **one or two** unos pocos; **one's** su, el . . . de uno; **the blue book and the red one** el libro azul y el rojo; **the one and only** el único; **the one that** el que, la que; **this one** éste; **that one** ése, aquél; **to make one** unir; casar ǁ *s* uno
one'-fam'i•ly house *s* vivienda unifamiliar
one'-horse' *adj* de un solo caballo, tirado por un solo caballo; (coll) insignificante, de poca monta
onerous ['anərəs] *adj* oneroso
one'self' *pron* uno mismo; sí, sí mismo; se; **to be oneself** tener dominio de sí mismo; conducirse con naturalidad
one-sided ['wʌn'saɪdɪd] *adj* de un solo lado; injusto, parcial; desigual; unilateral
one'-track' *adj* de carril único; (coll) con un solo interés

one'-way' *adj* de una solo dirección, de dirección única; (*ticket*) sencillo, de ida

onion ['ʌnjən] *s* cebolla

on'ion•skin' *s* papel *m* de seda, papel cebolla

on'look'er *s* mirón *m*, espectador *m*

only ['onlɪ] *adj* solo, único || *adv* solamente, sólo, únicamente; no . . . más que; **not only . . . but also** no sólo . . . sino también || *conj* sólo que, pero

onomatopoeic [,anə,mætə'pi•ɪk] *adj* onomatopéyico

on'set' *s* arremetida, embestida; (*of an illness*) principio

onward ['anwərd] u **onwards** ['anwərdz] *adv* adelante, hacia adelante

onyx ['anɪks] *s* ónice *m* u ónix *m*

ooze [uz] *s* chorro suave; cieno; limo, lama || *tr* rezumar || *intr* rezumar, rezumarse; manar suavemente (*p.ej., la sangre de una herida*); agotarse poco a poco

op. *abbr* opera, operation, opus, opposite

opal ['opəl] *s* ópalo

opaque [o'pek] *adj* opaco; (*writer's style*) obscuro; estúpido

open ['opən] *adj* abierto; descubierto, destapado; sin tejado; vacante; (*hour*) libre; discutible, pendiente; (*hand*) liberal; (*hunting season*) legal; **to break** o **to crack open** abrir con violencia, abrir por la fuerza; **to throw open** abrir de par en par || *s* abertura; (*in the woods*) claro; **in the open** al aire libre; a campo raso; en alta mar; abiertamente || *tr* abrir; desbullar (*una ostra*) || *intr* abrir; abrirse; estrenarse (*un drama*); **to open into** desembocar en; **to open on** dar a; **to open up** descubrirse; descubrir el pecho

o'pen-air' *adj* al aire libre, a cielo abierto

open-eyed ['opən,aɪd] *adj* alerta, vigilante; con ojos asombrados; hecho con los ojos abiertos

open-handed ['opən'hændɪd] *adj* maniabierto, liberal

open-hearted (opən'hartɪd] *adj* franco, sincero

open house *s* coliche *m;* **to keep open house** recibir a todos, gustar de tener siempre convidados en casa

opening ['opənɪ] *s* abertura; (*of, e.g., school*) apertura; (*in the woods*) claro; (*vacancy*) hueco, vacante *f*; (*chance to say something*) ocasión

opening night *s* noche *f* de estreno

opening number *s* primer número

opening price *s* primer curso, precio de apertura

open-minded ['opən'maɪndɪd] *adj* receptivo, razonable, imparcial

open secret *s* secreto a voces

open shop *s* taller franco

o'pen•work' *s* calado

opera ['apərə] *s* ópera

opera glasses *spl* gemelos de teatro

opera hat *s* clac *m*, sombrero de muelles

opera house *s* teatro de la ópera

operate ['apə,ret] *tr* hacer funcionar; dirigir, manejar; explotar || *intr* funcionar; operar;

to operate on operar (*p.ej., una hernia; a un niño*)

operatic [,apə'rætɪk] *adj* operístico

operating expenses *spl* gastos de explotación

operating room *s* quirófano

operating table *s* mesa operatoria

operation [,apə,ret/ən] *s* operación; funcionamiento; explotación

operator ['apə,retər] *s* operador *m*, maquinista *m;* (com) empresario; (coll) corredor *m* de bolsa; (surg, telp) operador *m*

operetta [,apə'retə] *s* opereta

opiate ['opɪ•ɪt] u ['op,et] *adj & s* opiato

opinion [ə'pɪnjən] *s* opinión; **in my opinion** a mi parecer; **to have a high opinion of** tener buen concepto de

opinionated [ə'pɪnjə,netɪd] *adj* porfiado en su parecer, dogmático

opinion poll *s* encuesta demoscópica

opium ['opɪ•əm] *s* opio

opium den *s* fumadero de opio

opossum [ə'pasəm] *s* zarigüeya

opponent [ə'ponənt] *s* contrario

opportune [,apər'tjun] *adj* oportuno

opportunist [,apər'tjunɪst] *s* oportunista *mf;* maromero

opportuni•ty [,apər'tjunɪti] *s* (*pl* **-ties**) oportunidad, ocasión

oppose [ə'poz] *tr* oponerse a

opposite ['apəsɪt] *adj* opuesto; de enfrente, p.ej., **the house opposite** la casa de enfrente || *prep* enfrente de || *s* contrario

opposite number *s* igual *mf*, doble *mf*

opposition [,apə'zɪ/ən] *s* oposición

oppress [ə'prɛs] *tr* oprimir

oppression [ə'prɛ/ən] *s* opresión

oppressive [ə'prɛsɪv] *adj* opresivo; sofocante, bochornoso

opprobrious [ə'probrɪ•əs] *adj* oprobioso

opprobrium [ə'probrɪ•əm] *s* oprobio

optic ['aptɪk] *adj* óptico || *s* (coll) ojo; **optics** *ssg* óptica

optical ['aptɪkəl] *adj* óptico

optician [ap'tɪ/ən] *s* óptico

optimism ['aptɪ,mɪzəm] *s* optimismo

optimist ['aptɪmɪst] *s* optimista *mf*

optimistic [,aptɪ'mɪstɪk] *adj* optimístico

optimize ['aptə,maɪz] *tr* mejorar en todo lo posible

option ['ap/ən] *s* opción

optional ['ap/ənəl] *adj* facultativo, potestativo

optometrist [ap,tamɪtrɪst] *s* optometrista *mf*

opulent ['apjələnt] *adj* opulento

or [ɔr] *conj* o, u

oracle ['arəkəl] u ['orəkəl] *s* oráculo

oracular [o'rækjələr] *adj* sentencioso; ambiguo, misterioso; fatídico; sabio

oral ['orəl] *adj* oral

orange ['arɪndʒ] u ['orɪndʒ] *adj* anaranjado || *s* naranja

orangeade [,arɪndʒ'ed] u [,orɪndʒ'ed] *s* naranjada

orange blossom *s* azahar *m*

orange grove *s* naranjal *m*

orange juice *s* zumo de naranja

orange squeezer *s* exprimidera de naranjas

ol
or

orange tree s naranjo

orang-outang [oˈræŋuˌtæŋ] s orangután m

oration [oˈreʃən] s oración, discurso

orator [ˈɑrətər] u [ˈɔrətər] s orador m

oratorical [ˌɔrəˈtɔrɪkəl] adj oratorio

oratori•o [ˌɔrəˈtɔriˌo] s (pl -os) oratorio

orato•ry [ˈɔrəˌtori] s (pl -ries) (art of public speaking) oratoria; (small chapel) oratorio

orb [ɔrb] s orbe m

orbit [ˈɔrbɪt] s órbita; **to go into orbit** entrar en órbita ‖ tr poner en órbita; moverse en órbita alrededor de ‖ intr moverse enorbita

orbiter [ˈɔrbɪtər] s satélite m (artificial)

orchard [ˈɔrtʃərd] s huerto

orchestra [ˈɔkɪstrə] s orquesta; (parquet) platea

orchestrate [ˈɔrkɪsˌtret] tr orquestar

orchid [ˈɔrkɪd] s orquídea

ordain [ɔrˈden] tr (eccl) ordenar; destinar; mandar

ordeal [ɔrˈdil] u [ɔrˈdi•əl] s prueba rigurosa o penosa; (hist) juicio de Dios

order [ˈɔrdər] s (way one thing follows another; formal or methodical arrangement; peace, quiet; class, category) orden m; (command; honor society; monastic brotherhood; fraternal organization) orden f; tarea, p.ej., **a big order** una tarea peliaguda; (com) pedido; (com) giro, libranza; (formation) (mil) orden lm; (command) (mil) orden f; **in order that** para que, a fin de que; **in order to** + inf para + inf, a fin de + inf; **to get out of order** descomponerse; **to give an order** dar una orden; (com) hacer un pedido ‖ tr ordenar; mandar; encargar, pedir; mandar hacer; **to order around** ser muy mandón con; **to order someone away** mandar a uno que se marche

order blank s hoja de pedidos

order•ly [ˈɔrdərli] adj ordenado, gobernoso; tranquilo, obediente ‖ s (pl -lies) asistente m en un hospital; (mil) ordenanza m

ordinal [ˈɔrdɪnəl] adj & s ordinal m

ordinance [ˈɔrdɪnəns] s ordenanza

ordinary [ˈɔrdɪˌnɛri] adj ordinario

ordnance [ˈɔrdnəns] s artillería, cañones mpl; pertrechos de guerra

ore [or] s mena, mineral metalífero

organ [ˈɔrgən] s órgano

organ•dy [ˈɔrgəndi] s (pl -dies) organdí m

or'gan-grind'er s organillero

organic [ɔrˈgænɪk] adj orgánico

organism [ˈɔrgəˌnɪzəm] s organismo

organist [ˈɔrgənɪst] s organista mf

organize [ˈɔrgəˌnaɪz] tr organizar

organ loft s tribuna del órgano

orgasm [ˈɔrgæzəm] s orgasmo

orgiastic [ˌɔrdʒiˈæstɪk] adj orgiástico

or•gy [ˈɔrdʒi] s (pl -gies) orgía

orient [ˈori•ənt] s oriente m ‖ **Orient** s oriente ‖ **orient** [ˈoriˌɛnt] tr orientar

oriental [ˌoriˈɛntəl] adj oriental

orifice [ˈɔrɪfɪs] s orificio

origin [ˈɔrɪdʒɪn] s origen m

original [əˈrɪdʒɪnəl] adj & s original m

originate [əˈrɪdʒɪˌnet] tr originar ‖ intr originarse

oriole [ˈoriˌol] s oropéndola

Orkney Islands [ˈɔrkni] spl Órcadas

ormolu [ˈɔrməˌlu] s (gold powder used in gilding) oro molido; (alloy of zinc and copper) similor m; bronce dorado

ornament [ˈɔrnəmənt] s ornamento ‖ [ˈɔrnəˌmɛnt] tr ornamentar

ornate [ɔrˈnet] u [ˈɔrnet] adj muy ornado; (style) florido

orphan [ˈɔrfən] adj & s huérfano ‖ tr dejar huérfano

orphanage [ˈɔrfənɪdʒ] s (institution) orfanato; órfelinato (SAm); (state, condition) orfandad

orphan asylum s asilo de huérfanos

Orpheus [ˈɔrfjus] u [ˈɔrfi•əs] s Orfeo

orthodontic appliance [ˌɔrθəˈdɑntɪk] s aparato de ortodoncia

orthodontics [ˌɔrθəˈdɑntɪks] s ortodoncia

orthodox [ˈɔrθəˌdɑks] adj ortodoxo

orthogra•phy [ɔrˈθɑgrəfi] s (pl -phies) ortografía

oscillate [ˈɑsɪˌlet] intr oscilar

osier [ˈoʒər] s mimbre m & f; sauce mimbrero

ossi•fy [ˈɑsɪˌfaɪ] v (pret & pp -fied) tr osificar ‖ intr osificarse

ostensible [ɑsˈtɛnsɪbəl] adj aparente, pretendido, supuesto

ostentatious [ˌɑstɛnˈteʃəs] adj (pretentious) ostentativo; (showy) ostentoso

osteopath [ˈɑstɪ•əˌpæθ] s osteópata mf

osteopathy [ˌɑstɪˈɑpəθi] s osteopatía

ostracism [ˈɑstrəˌsɪzəm] s ostracismo

ostrich [ˈɑstrɪtʃ] s avestruz m

O.T. abbr Old Testament

other [ˈʌðər] adj & pron indef otro ‖ adv— **other than** de otra manera que

otherwise [ˈʌðərˌwaɪz] adv otramente, de otra manera; en otras circunstancias; fuera de eso; si no, de otro modo

otherworldly [ˈʌðərˌwʌrldli] adj extraterrestre

otter [ˈɑtər] s nutria

ottoman [ˈɑtəmən] s (corded fabric) otomán m; (sofa) otomana; escañuelo con cojín ‖ **Ottoman** adj & s otomano

ouch [aʊtʃ] interj ¡ax!

ought [ɔt] s alguna cosa; cero; **for ought I know** por lo que yo sepa ‖ v aux se emplea para formar el modo potencial, p.ej., **he ought to go at once** debiera salir en seguida

ounce [aʊns] s onza

our [aʊr] adj poss nuestro

ours [aʊrz] pron poss el nuestro; nuestro

ourselves [aʊrˈsɛlvz] pron pers nosotros mismos; nos, p.ej., **we enjoyed ourselves** nos divertimos

oust [aʊst] tr echar fuera, desposeer; desahuciar (al inquilino)

out [aʊt] adj ausente; apagado; exterior; divulgado; publicado; (size) poco común ‖ adv afuera, fuera; al aire libre; hasta el fin; **out for** buscando; **out of** de; entre; de entre; fuera de; más allá de; (*kindness, fear, etc.*) por; (*money*) sin; (*a suit of cards*) fallo a; sobre, p.ej., **in nine out of ten cases** en nueve casos sobre diez; **out to** + *inf* esforzándose por + *inf* ‖ *prep* por; allá en ‖ *interj* ¡fuera de aquí! ‖ *s* cesante *mf;* **to be at outs** u **on the outs** estar de monos

out and away *adv* con mucho

out'-and-out' *adj* perfecto, verdadero, rematado ‖ *adv* completamente

out'-and-out'er *s* intransigente *mf;* extremista *mf*

out·bid' *v* (*pret* -bid; *pp* -bid o -bidden; *ger* -bidding) *tr* pujar más que (*otra persona*); (bridge) sobrepasar

out'board' motor *s* motor *m* fuera de borda, fuera-bordo *m*

out'break' *s* tumulto, motín *m;* (*of anger*) arranque *m;* (*of war*) estallido; (*of an epidemic*) brote *m*

out'build'ing *s* dependencia, edificio accesorio

out'burst' *s* explosión, arranque *m;* **outburst of laughter** carcajada

out'cast' *s* proscripto, paria *mf;* vagabundo

out'come' *s* resultado

out'cry' *s* (*pl* -cries) grito; gritería, clamoreo

out·dat'ed *adj* fuera de moda, anticuado

out·do' *v* (-did; *pp* -done) *tr* exceder; **to outdo oneself** excederse a sí mismo

out'door' *adj* al aire libre

out'doors' *adv* al aire libre, fuera de casa ‖ *s* aire *m* libre, campo raso

outer space ['aʊtər] *s* espacio exterior

out'field' *s* (baseball) jardín *m*

out'field'er *s* (baseball) jardinero

out'fit *s* equipo; traje *m;* juego de herramientas; (*of soldiers*) cuerpo; (*of a bride*) ajuar *m;* (com) compañía ‖ *v* (*pret & pp* -fitted; *ger* -fitting) *tr* equipar

out'go'ing *adj* de salida; cesante; (*tide*) descendente; (*nature, character*) exteriorista ‖ *s* salida

out·grow' *v* (*pret* -grew; *pp* -grown) *tr* crecer más que; ser ya grande para; ser ya viejo para; ser ya más apto que; dejar (*las cosas de los niños; a los amigos de la niñez, etc.*) ‖ *intr* extenderse

out'growth' *s* excrecencia, bulto; (*of leaves in springtime*) nacimiento; consecuencia, resultado

outing ['aʊtɪŋ] *s* jira, excursión al campo

outlandish [aʊt'lændɪʃ] *adj* estrafalario; de aspecto extranjero; de acento extranjero

out·last' *tr* durar más que; sobrevivir a

out'law' *s* forajido, bandido; prófugo, proscrito ‖ *tr* proscribir; declarar ilegal

out'lay' *s* desembolso ‖ **out·lay'** *v* (*pret & pp* -laid) *tr* desembolsar

out'let *s* salida; desaguadero; orificio de salida; (elec) caja de enchufe; (*tap*) (elec) toma de corriente *m*

out'line' *s* contorno; trazado; esquema *m;* esbozo, bosquejo; compendio ‖ *tr* contornar; trazar; trazar el esquema de; esbozar, bosquejar; compendiar

out·live' *tr* sobrevivir a; durar más que

out'look' *s* perspectiva; expectativa; concepto de la vida, punto de vista; atalaya

out'ly'ing *adj* remoto, circundante, de las afueras

out·mod'ed *adj* fuera de moda

out·num'ber *tr* exceder en número, ser más numeroso que

out'-of-date' *adj* fuera de moda, anticuado

out'-of-door' *adj* al aire libre

out'-of-doors' *adj* al aire libre ‖ *adv* al aire libre, fuera de casa ‖ *s* aire *m* libre, campo raso

out'-of-print' *adj* agotado

out'-of-the-way' *adj* apartado, remoto; poco usual, poco común

out of tune *adj* desafinado ‖ *adv* desafinadamente

out of work *adj* desempleado, sin trabajo

out'pa'tient *s* paciente *mf* de consulta externa

out'post' *s* avanzada

out'put' *s* rendimiento; (elec) salida; (mech) rendimiento de trabajo, efecto útil

out'rage *s* atrocidad; ultraje *m* ‖ *tr* maltratar; ultrajar; escandalizar

outrageous [aʊt'redʒəs] *adj* (*grossly offensive*) ultrajoso; (*shocking, fierce*) atroz; (*extreme*) extravagante

out·rank' *tr* exceder en rango o grado

out'rid'er *s* carrerista *m;* (Brit) viajante *m* de comercio

out'right' *adj* cabal, completo; franco, sincero ‖ *adv* enteramente; de una vez; sin rodeos; en seguida

out'run'ner *s* volante *m* (*criado*)

out'set' *s* principio

out'side' *adj* exterior; superficial; ajeno; (*price*) (el) máximo ‖ *adv* fuera, afuera; **outside of** fuera de ‖ *prep* fuera de; más allá de; (coll) a excepción de ‖ *s* exterior *m;* superficie *f;* apariencia

outsider [,aʊt'saɪdər] *s* forastero; intruso

out'skirts' *spl* afueras

out'spo'ken *adj* boquifresco, franco

out·stand'ing *adj* sobresaliente; prominente; sin pagar, sin cobrar

outward ['aʊtwərd] *adj* exterior; superficial ‖ *adv* exteriormente, hacia fuera

out·weigh' *tr* pesar más que; contrapesar, compensar

out·wit' *v* (*pret & pp* -witted; *ger* -witting) *tr* burlar, ser más listo que; despistar (*al perseguidor*)

oval ['ovəl] *adj* oval ‖ *s* óvalo

ova·ry ['ovəri] *s* (*pl* -ries) ovario

ovation [o'veʃən] *s* ovación

oven ['ʌvən] *s* horno

over ['ovər] *adj* acabado, concluído; superior; adicional; excesivo ‖ *adv* encima; al otro lado, a la otra orilla; hacia abajo; al revés; patas arriba; otra vez, de nuevo; de añadidura; (*at the bottom of a page*) a la vuelta; acá, p.ej., **hand over the money** déme acá el dinero; **over again** una vez más; **over against** enfrente de; a distinción de; en contraste con; **over and over** repe-

or
ov

tidas veces; **over here** acá; **over in** allá en; **over there** allá ‖ *prep* sobre, encima de, por encima de; por; de un extremo a otro de; al otro lado de; más allá de; desde; (*a certain number*) más de; acerca de; por causa de; durante; **over and above** además de, en exceso de

o′ver•all′ *adj* cabal, completo; extremo, total ‖ **overalls** *spl* pantalones *mf* de trabajo; overol *m*

o′ver•bear′ing *adj* altanero, imperioso

o′ver•board′ *adv* al agua; **man overboard!** ¡hombre al agua!; **to throw overboard** arrojar, echar o tirar por la borda

o′ver•cast′ *adj* encapotado, nublado ‖ *s* cielo encapotado ‖ *v* (*pret & pp* -cast) *tr* nublar

o′ver•charge′ *s* cargo excesivo; recargo de precio; sobrecarga; (elec) carga excesiva ‖ o′ver•charge′ *tr* hacer pagar más del valor, cobrar demasiado a; cargar (*p.ej., 50 pesetas*) de más; (elec) poner una carga excesiva a

o′ver•coat′ *s* abrigo, gabán *m*, sobretodo

o′ver•come′ *v* (*pret* -came; *pp* -come) *tr* vencer; rendir; superar (*dificultades*)

o′ver•crowd′ *tr* atestar, apiñar; poblar con exceso

o′ver•do *v* (*pret* -did; *pp* -done) *tr* exagerar; agobiar; asurar, requemar ‖ *intr* cansarse mucho, excederse en el trabajo

o′ver•dose′ *s* sobredosis *f*, dosis excesiva ‖ *intr* tomar una dosis excesiva

o′ver•draft *s* sobregiro, giro en descubierto

o′ver•draw′ *v* (*pret* -drew; *pp* -drawn) *tr & intr* sobregirar

o′ver•due′ *adj* atrasado; vencido y no pagado

o′ver•eat′ *v* (*pret* -ate; *pp* -eaten) *tr & intr* comer con exceso

o′ver•es′ti•mate *tr* sobreestimar

o′ver•exer′tion *s* esfuerzo excesivo

o′ver•ex′ploi•ta′tion *s* (*of resources*) explotación abusiva

o′ver•expose′ *tr* sobreexponer

o′ver•expo′sure *s* sobreexposición

o′ver•flow′ *s* desbordamiento, rebosamiento, derrame *m*; caño de reboso ‖ o′ver•flow′ *intr* desbordar, rebosar

o′ver•fly′ *v* (*pret* -flew; *pp* -flown) *tr* sobrevolar

o′ver•grown′ *adj* demasiado grande para su edad; denso, frondoso

o′ver•hang′ *v* (*pret & pp* -hung) *tr* sobresalir por encima de, estar pendiente o colgando sobre, salir fuera del nivel de; amenazar ‖ *intr* estar pendiente, estar colgando

o′ver•haul′ *tr* examinar, registrar, revisar; ir alcanzando, alcanzar; componer, rehabilitar, reacondicionar

o′ver•head′ *adj* de arriba; aéreo, elevado; general, de conjunto ‖ o′ver•head′ *adv* por encima de la cabeza; arriba, en lo alto ‖ o′ver•head′ *s* gastos generales

o′ver•hear *v* (*pret & pp* -heard) *tr* oír por casualidad; acertar a oír, alcanzar a oír

o′ver•heat *tr* recalentar ‖ *intr* recalentarse

overjoyed [‚over′dʒɔɪd] *adj* lleno de alegría; **to be overjoyed** no caber de contento

o′ver•kill′ *s* exceso de potencia; exceso de eficacia ‖ *intr* exceder lo necesario

overland [′ovər‚lænd] u [′ovərlənd] *adj & adv* por tierra, por vía terrestre

o′ver•lap′ *v* (*pret & pp* -lapped; *ger* -lapping) *tr* solapar, traslapar ‖ *intr* solapar, traslapar; traslaparse (*dos o más cosas*); suceder (*dos hechos*) en parte al mismo tiempo

o′ver•load′ *s* sobrecarga ‖ o′ver•load′ *tr* sobrecargar

o′ver•look′ *tr* dominar con la vista; pasar por alto, no hacer caso de; perdonar, tolerar; espiar, vigilar; cuidar de, dirigir; dar a, p.ej., **the window overlooks the garden** la ventana da al jardín

o′ver•lord′ *s* jefe supremo ‖ o′ver•lord′ *tr* dominar despóticamente, imponerse a

overly [′ovərli] *adv* (coll) excesivamente, demasiado

o′ver•night′ *adv* toda la noche; de la tarde a la mañana; **to stay overnight** pasar la noche

overnight bag *s* saco de noche

o′ver•pass′ *s* viaducto

o′ver•pop′u•late′ *tr* superpoblar

o′verpow′er *tr* dominar, supeditar, subyugar; colmar, dejar estupefacto

overpowering *adj* abrumador, arrollador, irresistible

o′ver•produc′tion *s* superproducción, sobreproducción

o′ver•rate′ *tr* exagerar el valor de

o′ver•run′ *v* (*pret* -ran; *pp* -run; *ger* -running) *tr* cubrir enteramente; infestar; exceder; **to overrun one's time** quedarse más de lo justo; hablar más de lo justo

o′ver•sea′ u o′ver•seas′ *adj* de ultramar ‖ o′ver•sea′ u o′ver•seas′ *adv* allende los mares, en ultramar

o′ver•seer′ *s* director *m*, superintendente *mf*

o′ver•shad′ow *tr* sombrear; (fig) eclipsar

o′ver•shoe′ *s* chanclo, zapato de goma

o′ver•shoot′ *v* (*pret & pp* -shot) *tr* tirar por encima de o más allá de; **to overshoot oneself** pasarse de listo, excederse

o′ver•sight′ *s* inadvertencia, descuido

o′ver•sleep′ *v* (*pret & pp* -slept) *intr* dormir demasiado tarde

o′ver•step′ *v* (*pret & pp* -stepped; *ger* -stepping) *tr* exceder, traspasar

o′ver•stock′ *tr* abarrotar

o′ver•sup•ply′ *s* (*pl* -plies) provisión excesiva ‖ o′ver•sup•ply′ *v* (*pret* -plied) *tr* proveer en exceso

overt [′ovərt] u [o′vʌrt] *adj* abierto, manifiesto; premeditado

o′ver•take′ *v* (*pret* -took; *pp* -taken) *tr* alcanzar; sobrepasar; sorprender; sobrevenir a

o′ver-the-count′er *adj* vendido directamente al comprador; vendido en tienda al por mayor

o′ver•throw′ *s* derrocamiento; trastorno ‖ o′ver•throw′ *v* (*pret* -threw; *pp* -thrown) *tr* derrocar; trastornar o'ver•time' *adj & adv* en exceso de las horas regulares ‖ *s* horas extraordinarias de trabajo, horas extra

o'ver•trump *s* contrafallo ‖

o'ver•trump' *tr & intr* contrafallar

overture ['ovərtʃər] *s* insinuación, proposición; (mus) obertura

o'ver•turn' *s* vuelco; movimiento de mercancías ‖ o'ver•turn' *tr* volcar; trastornar; derrocar ‖ *intr* volcar; trastornarse

overweening [,ovər'winɪŋ] *adj* arrogante, presuntuoso

o'ver•weight' *adj* excesivamente gordo o grueso ‖ *s* sobrepeso; exceso de peso; peso de añadidura

overwhelm [,ovər'hwɛlm] *tr* abrumar; inundar; anonadar; (*with favors, gifts, etc.*) colmar

o'ver•work' *s* trabajo excesivo, exceso de trabajo; trabajo fuera de las horas regulares ‖ o'ver•work' *tr* hacer trabajar demasiado; oprimir con el trabajo ‖ *intr* trabajar demasiado

Ovid ['avɪd] *s* Ovidio

ovum ['ovəm] *s* óvulo

ow [au] *interj* ¡ax!

owe [o] *tr* deber, adeudar ‖ *intr* tener deudas

owing ['o•ɪŋ] *adj* adeudado; debido, pagadero; owing to debido a, por causa de

owl [aul] *s* buho, lechuza, mochuelo

own [on] *adj* propio, p.ej., my own brother mi propio hermano ‖ *s* suyo, lo suyo; on one's own (coll) por su propia cuenta; (*without taking advice from anyone*) por su cabeza; (*without help from anyone*) de su

cabeza; to come into one's own entrar en posesión de lo suyo; tener el éxito merecido, recibir el honor merecido; to hold one's own no aflojar, no cejar, mantenerse firme ‖ *tr* poseer; reconocer ‖ *intr* confesar; to own up to (coll) confesar de plano (*una culpa, un delito, etc.*)

owner ['onər] *s* amo, dueño, poseedor *m*, posesor *m*, proprietario

ownership ['onər,ʃɪp] *s* posesión, propiedad

owner's license *s* permiso de circulación, patente *f* de circulación

ox [aks] *s* (*pl* oxen) ['aksən] buey *m*

ox'cart' *s* carreta de bueyes

oxide ['aksaɪd] *s* óxido

oxidize ['aksɪ,daɪz] *tr* oxidar ‖ *intr* oxidarse

oxygen ['aksɪdʒən] *s* oxígeno

oxygen tent *s* cámara o tienda de oxígeno

oxytone ['aksɪ,ton] *adj & s* oxítono

oyster ['ɔɪstər] *adj* ostrero ‖ *s* ostra

oyster bed *s* ostrero

oyster cocktail *s* ostras en su concha

oyster fork *s* desbullador *m*

oys'ter•house' *s* ostrería

oys'ter•knife' *s* abreostras *m*

oyster•man ['ɔɪstərmən] *s* (*pl* -men [mən]) ostrero

oyster opener ['opənər] *s* desbullador *m*

oyster shell *s* desbulla, concha de ostra

oyster stew *s* sopa de ostras

oz. *abbr* ounce, ounces

ozone ['ozon] *s* ozono; (coll) aire fresco

ozone layer *s* capa de ozono

ozs. *abbr* ounces

ov
pa

P

P, p [pi] decimosexta letra del alfabeto inglés

p. *abbr* page, participle

P.A. *abbr* Passenger Agent, power of attorney, Purchasing Agent

pace [pes] *s* paso; to keep pace with ir, andar o avanzar al mismo paso que; to put through one's paces poner (*a uno*) a prueba; dar a (*uno*) ocasión de lucirse; to set the pace establecer el paso; dar el ejemplo ‖ *tr* establecer el paso para; medir a pasos; recorrer a pasos; to pace the floor pasearse desesperadamente por la habitación ‖ *intr* andar a pasos regulares

pace'mak'er *s* (med) marcapaso, marcapasos *m*

pacific [pə'sɪfɪk] *adj* pacífico ‖ Pacific *adj & s* Pacífico

pacifier ['pæsɪ,faɪ•ər] *s* pacificador *m*, chupón *m*; (*teething ring*) chupador *m*

pacifism ['pæsɪ,fɪzəm] *s* pacifismo

pacifist ['pæsɪfɪst] *adj & s* pacifista *mf*

paci•fy ['pæsɪ,faɪ] *v* (*pret & pp* -fied) *tr* pacificar

pack [pæk] *s* lío, fardo; paquete *m*; (*of hounds*) jauría; (*of cattle*) manada; (*of evildoers*) pandilla; (*of lies*) sarta, montón *m*; (*of playing cards*) baraja; (*of cigarettes*) cajetilla; (*of floating ice*) témpano; (med) compresa ‖ *tr* empaquetar; embalar; encajonar; hacer (*el baúl, la maleta*); conservar en latas; apretar, atestar; cargar (*una acémila*); escoger de modo fraudulento (*un jurado*); to be packed in (coll) estar como sardinas en banasta ‖ *intr* empaquetarse; hacer el baúl, hacer la maleta; consolidarse, formar masa compacta

package ['pækɪdʒ] *s* paquete *m* ‖ *tr* empaquetar

pack animal *s* acémila, animal *m* de carga

packing box o case *s* caja de embalaje

packing house *s* frigorífico

packing slip *s* hoja de embalaje

pack'sad'dle *s* albarda

pack'thread' *s* bramante *m*

pack train *s* recua

pact [pækt] *s* pacto

pad [pæd] *s* conjincillo, almohadilla; *(of writing paper)* bloc *m;* *(for inking)* tampón *m;* *(of an aquatic plant)* hoja; *(for launching a rocket)* plataforma *f;* *(sound of footsteps)* pisada ‖ *v (pret & pp* **padded;** *ger* **padding)** *tr* acolchar, rellenar; meter mucho ripio en *(un escrito)* ‖ *intr* andar, caminar; caminar despacio y pesadamente

paddle [ˈpædəl] *s (of a canoe)* canalete *m;* *(of a wheel)* pala, paleta; *(for spanking)* palo ‖ *tr* impulsar con canalete; *(to spank)* apalear ‖ *intr* remar con canalete; remar suavemente; *(to splash)* chapotear

paddle wheel *s* rueda de paletas

paddock [ˈpædək] *s* dehesa; *(at a racecourse)* paddock *m*

paddy wagon [ˈpædi] *s* (coll) camión *m* de policía

pad'lock' *s* candado ‖ *tr* cerrar con candado; *(to lock up officially)* condenar *(una habitación, un teatro)*

pagan [ˈpegən] *adj & s* pagano

paganism [ˈpegəˌnɪzəm] *s* paganismo

page [pedʒ] *s (of a book)* página; *(boy attendant)* paje *m;* *(in a hotel or club)* botones *m* ‖ *tr* paginar; buscar llamando

pageant [ˈpædʒənt] *s* espectáculo público

pageant•ry [ˈpædʒəntri] *s (pl* **-ries)** pompa, fausto; *(empty display)* bambolla

pail [pel] *s* balde *m,* cubo

pain [pen] *s* dolor *m;* **on pain of** so pena de; **pains** esmero, trabajo; dolores de parto; **to take pains** esmerarse ‖ *tr & intr* doler

painful [ˈpenfəl] *adj* doloroso; penoso

pain'kill'er *s* analgésico; calmante *m* del dolor

painless [ˈpenlɪs] *adj* sin dolor, indoloro; fácil, sin trabajo

pains'tak'ing *adj* esmerado

paint [pent] *s* pintura ‖ *tr* pintar ‖ *intr* pintar; pintarse, repintarse

paint'box' *s* caja de colores

paint'brush' *s* brocha, pincel *m*

painter [ˈpentər] *s* pintor *m*

painting [ˈpentɪŋ] *s* pintura

paint remover [rɪˈmuvər] *s* sacapintura *m,* quitapintura *m*

pair [pɛr] *s* par *m;* *(of people)* pareja; *(of cards)* parejas ‖ *tr* aparear ‖ *intr* aparearse

pair of scissors *s* tijeras

pair of trousers *s* pantalones *mpl*

pajamas [pəˈdʒɑməz] o [pəˈdʒæməz] *spl* pijama

Pakistan [ˌpɑkɪˈstɑn] *s* el Paquistán

Pakistani [ˌpɑkɪˈstɑni] *adj & s* paquistano, paquistaní *mf*

pal [pæl] *s* (coll) compañero; cumpa *m* (SAm) ‖ *v (pret & pp* **palled;** *ger* **palling)** *intr* (coll) ser compañeros

palace [ˈpælɪs] *s* palacio

palatable [ˈpælətəbəl] *adj* sabroso, apetitoso

palatal [ˈpælətəl] *adj & s* palatal *f*

palate [ˈpælɪt] *s* paladar *m*

pale [pel] *adj* pálido; *(color)* claro ‖ *s* estaca; palizada; límite *m,* término ‖ *intr* palidecer

pale'face' *s* rostropálido

palette [ˈpælɪt] *s* paleta

palfrey [ˈpɔlfri] *s* palafrén *m*

palisade [ˌpælɪˈsed] *s* estaca; estacada; *(line of cliffs)* acantilado

pall [pɔl] *s* paño de ataúd, paño mortuorio; (eccl) palia ‖ *tr* hartar, saciar; quitar el sabor a ‖ *intr* perder el sabor; **to pall on** hartar, saciar

pall'bear'er *s* acompañante *m* de un cadáver; portador *m* del féretro

palliate [ˈpælɪˌet] *tr* paliar

pallid [ˈpælɪd] *adj* pálido

pallor [ˈpælər] *s* palidez *f,* palor *m*

palm [pɑm] *s (of the hand)* palma; *(measure)* palmo; *(tree and leaf)* palma; **to carry off the palm** llevarse la palma; **to grease the palm of** (slang) untar la mano a; **to yield the palm to** reconocer por vencedor ‖ *tr* esconder en la mano; escamotear *(una carta);* **to palm off something on someone** encajarle una cosa a uno

palmet•to [pælˈmɛto] *s (pl* **-tos** o **-toes)** palmito

palmist [ˈpɑmɪst] *s* quiromántico

palmistry [ˈpɑmɪstri] *s* quiromancia

palm leaf *s* palma, hoja de la palmera

palm oil *s* aceite *m* de palma; (slang) propina; (slang) soborno

Palm Sunday *s* domingo de ramos

palpable [ˈpælpəbəl] *adj* palpable

palpitate [ˈpælpɪˌtet] *intr* palpitar

pal•sy [ˈpɔlzi] *s (pl* **-sies)** perlesía ‖ *v (pret & pp* **-sied)** *tr* paralizar

pal•try [ˈpɔltri] *adj (comp* **-trier;** *super* **-triest)** vil, ruin, mezquino

pamper [ˈpæmpər] *tr* mimar, consentir

pamphlet [ˈpæmflɪt] *s* folleto, panfleto

pan [pæn] *s* cacerola, cazuela, sartén *f;* caldera, perol *m* ‖ *v (pret & pp* **panned;** *ger* **panning)** *tr* cocer, freír; separar *(el oro)* en la gamella; (coll) criticar ásperamente ‖ *intr* separar el oro en la gamella; dar oro; **to pan out well** (coll) tener éxito, dar buen resultado ‖

Pan *s* Pan

panacea [ˌpænəˈsi·ə] *s* panacea

Panama Canal [ˈpænəˌmɑ] *s* canal *m* de Panamá

Panama Canal Zone *s* Zona del Canal

Panama hat *s* panamá *m*

Panamanian [ˌpænəˈmɛnɪ·ən] *adj & s* panameño

Pan-American [ˌpænəˈmɛrɪkən] *adj* panamericano

pan'cake' *s* hojuela, panqueque *m* ‖ *intr* (aer) desplomarse

pancake landing *s* aterrizaje aplastado, aterrizaje en desplome

pancreas [ˈpænkri·əs] *s* páncreas *m*

panda [ˈpændə] *s* panda *mf*

pander [ˈpændər] *s* alcahuete *m* ‖ *intr* alcahuetear; **to pander to** gratificar

pane [pen] *s* cristal *m,* vidrio, hoja de vidrio

pan•el [ˈpænəl] *s* panel *m,* entrepaño, cuarterón *m;* grupo de personas en discusión cara al público; (aut, elec) tablero, panel *m;* (law) lista de personas que pueden servir como jurados ‖ *v (pret & pp* **peled** o **-elled;**

ger **-elling** o **-elling**) *tr* adornar con cuarterones, labrar en cuarterones; artesonar (*un techo o bóveda*)

panel discussion *s* coloquio cara al público

panelist ['pænəlɪst] *s* coloquiante *mf* cara al público

panel lights *spl* luces *fpl* del tablero

pang [pæŋ] *s* dolor agudo; (*of remorse*) punzada; (*of death*) agonía

pan'han'dle *s* mango de sartén ‖ *intr* (slang) mendigar, pedir limosna

pan•ic ['pænɪk] *adj* & *s* pánico ‖ *v* (*pret* & *pp* **-icked;** *ger* **-icking**) *tr* sobrecoger de pánico ‖ *intr* sobrecogerse de pánico

pan'ic-strick'en *adj* muerto de miedo, sobrecogido de terror

pano•ply ['pænəpli] *s* (*pl* **-plies**) panoplia, traje *m* ceremonial

panorama [,pænə'ræmə] o [,pænə'rɑmə] *s* panorama *m*

pan•sy ['pænzi] *s* (*pl* **-sies**) pensamiento

pant [pænt] *s* jadeo; palpitación; **pants** pantalones *mpl;* **to wear the pants** (coll) calzarse los pantalones ‖ *intr* jadear; palpitar

pantheism ['pænθɪ,ɪzəm] *s* panteísmo

pantheon ['pænθɪ,ɑn] *s* panteón *m*

panther ['pænθər] *s* pantera; puma

panties ['pæntiz] *spl* pantaloncillos de mujer

pantomime ['pæntə,maɪm] *s* pantomima

pan•try ['pæntri] *s* (*pl* **-tries**) despensa

panty hose *s* panty *m*

pap [pæp] *s* papilla, papas

papa•cy ['pepəsi] *s* (*pl* **-cies**) papado

paper ['pepər] *s* papel *m;* (*newspaper*) periódico; (*of needles*) paño ‖ *tr* empapelar

pa'per•back' *s* libro en rústica

pa'per•boy' *s* vendedor *m* de periódicos

paper clip *s* clip *m*, sujetapapeles *m;* presilla; prensador (CAm); gancho de papel (Col)

paper cone *s* cucurucho

paper cutter *s* cortapapeles *m*, guillotina

paper doll *s* muñeca de papel

paper hanger *s* empapelador *m*, papelista *mf*

paper knife *s* cortapapeles *m*

paper mill *s* fábrica de papel

paper money *s* papel *m* moneda

paper profits *spl* ganancias no realizadas sobre valores no vendidos

paper tape *s* cinta perforada

pa'per•weight' *s* pisapapeles *m*

paper work *s* preparación o comprobación de escritos; papelerío

paprika [pæ'prikə] o ['pæprɪkə] *s* pimentón *m*

papy•rus [pe'paɪrəs] *s* (*pl* **-ri** [raɪ]) papiro

par. *abbr* **paragraph, parallel, parenthesis, parish**

par [pɑr] *adj* a la par; nominal; normal ‖ *s* paridad; valor *m* nominal; **above par** sobre la par; con beneficio; con premio; **below par** o **under par** bajo la par; con pérdida; (coll) indispuesto; **to be on a par with** correr parejas con

parable ['pærəbəl] *s* parábola

parachute ['pærə,ʃut] *s* paracaídas *m* ‖ *intr* parachutar, lanzarse en paracaídas; **to parachute to safety** salvarse en paracaídas

parachute jump *s* salto en paracaídas

parachutist ['pærə,ʃutɪst] *s* paracaidista *mf*

parade [pə'red] *s* desfile *m;* paseo; ostentación ‖ *tr* ostentar, pasear ‖ *intr* desfilar, pasar por las calles; (mil) formar en parada

paradise ['pærə,daɪs] *s* paraíso

paradox ['pærə,dɑks] *s* paradoja; persona o cosa incomprensibles

paradoxical [,pærə'dɑksɪkəl] *adj* paradójico

paraffin ['pærəfɪn] *s* parafina

paragon ['pærə,gɑn] *s* dechado

paragraph ['pærə,græf] *s* párrafo

Paraguay *s* el Paraguay

Paraguayan [,pærə'gwaɪ•ən] *adj* & *s* paraguayano, paraguayo

parakeet ['pærə,kit] *s* perico, periquito

paral•lel ['pærə,lɛl] *adj* paralelo ‖ *s* (línea) paralela; (plano) paralelo; (geog) paralelo; **parallels** (typ) doble raya vertical ‖ *v* (*pret* & *pp* **-leled** o **-lelled;** *ger* **-leling** o **-lelling**) *tr* ser paralelo a; poner en dirección paralela; correr parejas con; (*to compare*) paralelizar

parallel bars *spl* paralelas, barras paralelas

paraly•sis [pə'ræləsɪs] *s* (*pl* **-ses** [,siz]) parálisis *f*

paralytic [,pærə'lɪtɪk] *adj* & *s* paralítico

paralyze ['pærə,laɪz] *tr* paralizar

parameter [pə'ræmətər] *s* parámetro

paramount ['pærə,maunt] *adj* capital, supremo, principalísimo

paranoiac [,pærə'nɔɪ•æk] o **paranoid** [pærə-,nɔɪd] *adj* & *s* paranoico

parapet [,pærə,pɛt] *s* parapeto

paraphernalia [,pærəfər'nelɪ•ə] *spl* trastos, atavíos

paraplegia [,pærə'plidʒə] *s* paraplegia

parasite ['pærə,saɪt] *s* parásito

parasitic(al) [,pærə'sɪtɪk(el)] *adj* parasítico, parasitario

parasol ['pærə,sɔl] *s* quitasol *m*, parasol *m*

pa'ra•troop'er *s* paracaidista *m*

pa'ra•troops' *spl* tropas paracaidistas

parboil ['pɑr,bɔɪl] *tr* sancochar; calentar con exceso

par•cel [pɑrsəl] *s* paquete *m*, atado, bulto ‖ *v* (*pret* & *pp* **-celed** o **-celled;** *ger* **-celing** o **-celling**) *tr* empaquetar; parcelar (*el terreno*); **to parcel out** repartir

parcel post *s* paquetes *mpl* postales

parch [pɑrtʃ] *tr* abrasar, tostar; **to be parched** tener mucha sed

parchment ['pɑrtʃmənt] *s* pergamino

pardon ['pɑrdən] *s* perdón *m;* (*remission of penalty by the state*) indulto; **I beg your pardon** dispense Vd. ‖ *tr* perdonar, dispensar; indultar

pardonable ['pɑrdənəbəl] *adj* perdonable

pardon board *s* junta de perdones

pare [pɛr] *tr* mondar (*fruta*); pelar (*patatas*); cortar (*callos, uñas*); despalmar (*la palma córnea de los animales*); adelgazar; reducir (*gastos*)

parent ['pɛrənt] *adj* madre, matriz, principal ‖ *s* padre o madre; autor *m*, fuente *f*, origen *m;* **parents** padres *mpl*

pa
pa

parentage ['pεrəntɪdʒ] s paternidad o maternidad; abolengo, linaje m
parent company compañía matriz
parenthe·sis [pə'rεnθɪsɪs] s (pl -ses [,siz]) paréntesis m
parenthood ['pεrənt,hud] s paternidad o maternidad
pariah [pə'raɪ·ə] o ['pɑrɪ·ə] s paria mf
paring knife ['pεrɪŋ] s cuchillo para mondar
parish ['pærɪʃ] s parroquia, feligresía
parishioner [pə'rɪʃ/ənər] s parroquiano, feligrés m
Parisian [pə'rɪʒən] adj & s parisiense mf
parity ['pærɪti] s paridad
park [pɑrk] s parque m ‖ tr estacionar, parquear; (coll) colocar, dejar ‖ intr estacionar, parquear
parking ['pɑrkɪŋ] s aparcamiento, estacionamiento; (space) parking m; **no parking** se prohibe estacionarse
parking lights spl (aut) faros de situación
parking lot s parque m de estacionamiento
parking meter s reloj m de estacionamiento, parquímetro, parcómetro
parking ticket s aviso de multa
park'way s gran via adornado con árboles
parley ['pɑrli] s parlamento ‖ intr parlamentar
parliament ['pɑrlɪmənt] s parlamento
parlor ['pɑrlər] s sala; parlatorio, locutorio
parlor car s coche-salón m
parlor politics spl política de café
Parnassus [pɑr'næsəs] s (collection of poems) parnaso; el Parnaso; **to try to climb Parnassus** hacer pinos en poesía
parochial [pə'rokɪ·əl] adj parroquial; estrecho, limitado
paro·dy ['pærədi] s (pl -dies) parodia ‖ v (pret & pp -died) tr parodiar
parole [pə'rol] s palabra de honor; libertad bajo palabra ‖ tr dejar libre bajo palabra
paroxytone [pær'ɑksɪ,ton] adj & s paroxítono
par·quet [pɑr'ke] s entarimado; (theat) platea ‖ v (pret & pp -queted ['ked]); ger -queting ['ke·ɪŋ] tr entarimar
parricide ['pærɪ,saɪd] s (act) parricidio; (person) parricida mf
parrot ['pærət] s papagayo, loro; (fig) papagayo ‖ tr repetir o imitar como loro
par·ry ['pæri] s (pl -ries) parada, quite m ‖ v (pret & pp -ried) tr parar; defenderse de
parse [pɑrs] tr analizar (una oración) gramaticalmente; describir (una palabra) gramaticalmente
parsley ['pɑrsli] s perejil m
parsnip ['pɑrsnɪp] s chirivía
parson ['pɑrsən] s cura m, párroco; clérigo; pastor m protestante
part [pɑrt] s parte f; (of a machine) pieza; (of the hair) raya; (theat) parte f, papel m; **part and parcel** parte esencial, parte inseparable, elemento esencial; **parts** partes fpl; prendas, dotes fpl; **to do one's part** cumplir con su obligación; **to look the part** vestir el cargo; **to take the part of** tomar el partido de, defender; desempeñar

el papel de ‖ tr dividir, partir, separar; **to part the hair** hacerse la raya ‖ intr separarse; **to part with** deshacerse de, abandonar; despedirse de
par·take [pɑr'tek] v (pret -took ['tuk]; pp -taken) tr compartir; comer; beber ‖ intr participar
Parthenon ['pɑrθɪ,nɑn] s Partenón m
partial ['pɑrʃəl] adj parcial; aficionado
participate [pɑr'tɪsɪ,pet] intr participar
participle ['pɑrtɪ,sɪpəl] s participio
particle ['pɑrtɪkəl] s partícula, corpúsculo
particle physics s física de las partículas
particular [pər'tɪkjələr] adj particular; difícil, exigente, quisquilloso; esmerado; minucioso; **a particular . . .** cierto . . . ‖ s particular m
partisan ['pɑrtɪzən] adj & s partidario, partidista mf; (mil) partisano
partition [pɑr'tɪʃən] s partición, distribución; división; proción; tabique m ‖ tr repartir; dividir en cuartos, aposentos; tabicar
partner ['pɑrtnər] s compañero; (wife or husband) cónyuge mf; (in a dance) pareja f; (in business) socio
partnership ['pɑrtnər,ʃɪp] s asociación; consorcio, vida en común; (com) sociedad, asociación comercial
partridge ['pɑrtrɪdʒ] s perdiz f
part'-time' adj por horas, parcial
par·ty ['pɑrti] adj de partido; de gala ‖ s (pl -ties) convite m, reunión, fiesta, tertulia, recepción; (for fishing, hunting, etc.; of armed men) partida; cómplice mf, interesado; (pol) partido; (coll) persona, individuo
party girl s chica de vida alegre
party-goer ['pɑrti,go·ər] s tertuliano; fiestero
party line s (between two properties) linde m, lindero; (of communist party) línea del partido; (telp) línea compartida
party politics s política de partido
pass. abbr **passenger, passive**
pass [pæs] o [pɑs] s paso; (permit; free ticket; movement of hands of mesmerist, of bullfighter) pase m; (in an examination) aprobación; nota de aprobación ‖ tr pasar; pasar de largo (una luz roja); aprobar (un proyecto de ley; un examen; a un alumno); ser aprobado en (un examen); dejar atrás; cruzarse con; expresar (una opinión); pronunciar (una sentencia), dar (la palabra); dejar sin protestar; no pagar (un dividendo); **to pass off** colar, pasar, hacer aceptar (una moneda falsa); disimular (p.ej., una ofensa con una risa); **to pass over** omitir, pasar por alto; excusar; desdeñar; dejar sin protestar; postergar (a un empleado) ‖ intr pasar; pasarse (introducirse); aprobar; **to bring to pass** llevar a cabo; **to come to pass** suceder; **to pass as** pasar por; **to pass away** pasar, pasar a mejor vida; **to pass off** pasar (una enfermedad, una tempestad, etc.); tener lugar; **to pass out** salir; (slang) desmayarse; **to pass over to** pasarse a (p.ej., el enemigo)

passable ['pæsəbəl] o ['pɑsəbəl] *adj* pasadero; (*law*) promulgable

passage ['pæsɪdʒ] *s* pasaje *m;* paso; pasillo; (*of time*) transcurso; (*of bowels*) evacuación

pass'book' *s* cartilla, libreta de banco

passenger ['pæsəndʒer] *adj* de viajeros ‖ *s* pasajero, viajero

passer-by ['pæsər'baɪ] o ['pɑsər'baɪ] *s* (*pl* **passers-by**) transeúnte *mf*

passing ['pæsɪŋ] o ['pɑsɪŋ] *adj* pasajero; corriente; de aprobado ‖ *s* (*act of passing; death*) paso; (*in an examination*) aprobación

passion ['pæʃən] *s* pasión

passionate ['pæʃənɪt] *adj* apasionado

passive ['pæsɪv] *adj* pasivo ‖ *s* voz pasiva, verbo pasivo

pass'key' *s* llave *f* de paso

Pass'o'ver *s* pascua (*de los hebreos*)

pass'port' *s* pasaporte *m*

pass'word' *s* santo y seña

past [pæst] o [pɑst] *adj* pasado; último; que fué, p.ej., **past president** presidente que fué; acabado, concluído ‖ *adv* más allá; por delante ‖ *prep* más allá de; más de; por delante de; fuera de; después de, p.ej., **past two o'clock** después de las dos; **past belief** increíble; **past cure** incurable; **past hope** sin esperanza ‖ *s* pasado

paste [pest] *s* (*dough; spaghetti, etc.*) pasta; (*for sticking things together*) engrudo ‖ *tr* engrudar, pegar con engrudo

paste'board' *s* cartón *m*

pasteurize ['pæstə,raɪz] *tr* pasterizar

pastime ['pæs,taɪm] *s* pasatiempo

pastor ['pæstər] *s* pastor *m*, clérigo, cura *m*

pastoral ['pæstərəl] *adj & s* pastoral *f*

pas•try ['pestri] *s* (*pl* **-tries**) pastelería

pastry cook *s* pastelero, repostero

pastry shop *s* pastelería, repostería

pasture ['pæstər] *s* pasto, pastura, dehesa ‖ *tr* apacentar, pacer ‖ *intr* apacentarse, pacer

past•y ['pesti] *adj* (*comp* **-ier;** *super* **-iest**) pastoso; flojo, fofo, pálido

pat [pæt] *s* golpecito, palmadita; ruido de pasos ligeros; (*of butter*) pastelillo ‖ *v* (*pret & pp* **patted;** *ger* **patting**) *tr* dar golpecitos a, golpear ligeramente; palmotear, acariciar con la mano; **to pat on the back** elogiar, cumplimentar

patch [pætʃ] *s* remiendo, parche *m;* terreno, pedazo de terreno; mancha; lunar postizo ‖ *tr* remendar; **to patch up** componer (*una desavenencia*); componer lo mejor posible (*una cosa descompuesta*); hacer aprisa y mal

patent ['petənt] *adj* patente; abierto ‖ ['pætənt] *adj* de patentes ‖ *s* patente *f,* patente de invención; propiedad industrial; **patent applied for** se ha solicitado patente ‖ *tr* patentar

patent leather ['pætənt] *s* charol *m*

patent medicine ['pætənt] *s* medicamento de patente

patent rights ['pætənt] *spl* derechos de patente

paternal [pə'tʌrnəl] *adj* paterno; (*affection*) paternal

paternity [pe'tʌrnɪti] *s* paternidad

path [pæθ] *s* senda, sendero; trayectoria

pathetic [pə'θɛtɪk] *adj* patético

path'find'er *s* baquiano; explorador *m*

patholo•gy [pə'θɑlədʒi] *s* patología

pathos ['peθas] *s* patetismo

path'way' *s* senda, sendero

patience ['peʃəns] *s* paciencia

patient ['peʃənt] *adj* paciente ‖ *s* paciente *mf,* enfermo

patriarch ['petrɪ,ɑrk] *s* patriarca *m*

patrician [pə'trɪʃən] *adj & s* patricio

patricide ['pætrɪ,saɪd] *s* (*act*) parricidio; (*person*) parricida *mf*

Patrick ['pætrɪk] *s* Patricio

patrimo•ny ['pætrɪ,moni] *s* (*pl* **-nies**) patrimonio

patriot ['petrɪ•ət] *s* patriota *mf*

patriotic [,petrɪ'ɑtɪk] *adj* patriótico

patriotism ['petrɪ•ə,tɪzəm] *s* patriotismo

pa•trol [pə'trol] *s* patrulla ‖ *v* (*pret & pp* **-troled** o **-trolled;** *ger* **-troling** o **-trolling**) *tr & intr* patrullar

patrol•man [pə'trolmən] *s* (*pl* **-men** [mən]) guardia *m* municipal, vigilante *m* de policía

patrol wagon *s* camion *m* de policía; carro-patrulla *m* (SAm)

patron ['petrən] *adj* tutelar ‖ *s* parroquiano; patrocinador *m*

patronize ['petrə,naɪz] *tr* ser parroquiano de (*un tendero*); comprar de costumbre en; patrocinar; tratar con aire protector

patron saint *s* patrón *m,* santo titular

patter ['pætər] *s* golpeteo; (*of rain*) chapaleteo; charla, parloteo ‖ *intr* golpetear; charlar, parlotear

pattern ['pætərn] *s* patrón *m;* modelo

P.A.U. *abbr* **Pan American Union**

paucity ['pɔsɪti] *s* corto número; falta, escasez *f,* insuficiencia

Paul [pɔl] *s* Pablo; (*name of popes*) Paulo

paunch [pɔntʃ] *s* panza

paunchy ['pɔntʃi] *adj* panzudo

pauper ['pɔpər] *s* pobre *mf,* indigente *mf*

pause [pɔz] *s* pausa; (*mus*) calderón *m;* **to give pause (to)** dar que pensar (a) ‖ *intr* hacer pausa, detenerse brevemente; vacilar

pave [pev] *tr* pavimentar; (*with flagstones*) enlosar; (*with bricks*) enladrillar; (*with pebbles*) enchinar; **to pave the way (for)** preparar el terreno (para), abrir el camino (a)

pavement ['pevmənt] *s* pavimento; (*of brick*) enladrillado; (*of flagstone*) enlosado; (*sidewalk*) acera

pavilion [pə'vɪljən] *s* pabellón *m*

paw [pɔ] *s* pata; garra, zarpa; (*coll*) mano *f* ‖ *tr* dar zarpazos a, restregar con las uñas; golpear, patear (*el suelo los caballos*); (*coll*) manosear; (*coll overfamiliarly*) (*coll*) sobar ‖ *intr* piafar (*el caballo*)

pawn [pɔn] *s* (*in chess*) peón *m;* (*security, pledge*) prenda; (*tool of another person*) instrumento; víctima ‖ *tr* empeñar, dar en prenda

pa
pa

pawn'bro'ker s prestamista mf
pawn'shop' s casa de empeños, monte m de piedad
pawn ticket s papeleta de empeño
pay [pe] s paga; recompensa; castigo merecido ‖ v (pret & pp **paid** [ped]) tr pagar; prestar o poner (atención); dar (cumplidos); dar (dinero una actividad comercial); dar dinero a, ser provechoso a; pagar en la misma moneda; pagar con creces; sufrir (el castigo de una ofensa); hacer (una visita); cubrir (los gastos); **to pay back** devolver; pagar en la misma moneda; **to pay off** pagar y despedir (a un empleado); pagar todo lo adeudado a; vengarse de; redimir (una hipoteca) ‖ intr pagar; ser provechoso, valer la pena; **pay as you enter** pague a la entrada; **pay as you go** pagar el impuesto de utilidades con descuentos anticipados; **pay as you leave** pague a la salida
payable ['pe•əbəl] adj pagadero
pay boost s aumento de salario
pay'check' s cheque m en pago del sueldo; sueldo
pay'day' s día m de pago
payee [pe'i] s portador m o tenedor m (de un giro)
pay envelope s sobre m con el jornal; jornal m, salario
payer ['pe•ər] s pagador m
pay load s carga útil
pay'mas'ter s pagador m
payment ['pemənt] s pago; castigo
pay roll s nómina, hoja de paga
pay station s teléfono público
pd. abbr **paid**
p.d. abbr **per diem, potential difference**
pea [pi] s guisante m, chícharo
peace [pis] s paz f; **to make peace with** hacer las paces con
peaceable ['pisəbəl] adj pacífico
Peace Corps s Cuerpo de Paz
peaceful ['pisfəl] adj tranquilo, pacífico, sosegado
peace'mak'er s iris m de paz
peace of mind s serenidad del espíritu
peace pipe s pipa ceremonial (de los pieles rojas)
peach [pitʃ] s melocotón m; (slang) persona o cosa admirables
peach tree s melocotonero
peach•y ['pitʃi] adj (comp **-ier**; super **-iest**) (slang) estupendo, magnífico
pea'cock' s pavo real, pavón m; (fig) pinturero
peak [pik] s pico, cima, cumbre f; punta, extremo; máximo; (of a cap) visera; (of a curve) cresta; (elec) pico
peak hour s hora punta
peak load s (elec) carga de punta; demanda máxima
peal [pil] s fragor m; estruendo; (of bells) repique m; juego de campanas ‖ intr repicar; resonar
peal of laughter s carcajada
peal of thunder s trueno

pea'nut' s cacahuete m, aráquida; **to work for peanuts** recibir poco sueldo
peanut vendor s manicero
pear [pɛr] s pera
pearl [pʌrl] s margarita, perla; (of running water) murmullo ‖ tr alijofarar
pearl oyster s madreperla
pear tree s peral m
peasant ['pɛzənt] adj & s campesino, rústico
pea'shoot'er s cerbatana, bodoquera
pea soup s sopa de guisantes; (coll) neblina espesa y amarillenta
peat [pit] s turba
pebble ['pɛbəl] s china, guija ‖ tr agranelar (el cuero)
peck [pɛk] s medida de áridos (nueve litros); montón m; picotazo; beso dado de mala gana ‖ tr picotear ‖ intr picotear; (coll) comer melindrosamente; **to peck at** querer picar; regañar constantemente; (coll) comer melindrosamente
peculate ['pɛkjə,let] tr & intr malversar
peculíar [pɪ'kjuljər] adj peculiar; singular, raro; excéntrico
pedagogue ['pɛdə,gɑg] s pedagogo; dómine m, pedante m
pedagogy ['pɛdə,godʒi] o ['pɛdə,gɑdʒi] s pedagogía
ped•al ['pɛdəl] s pedal m ‖ v (pret & pp **-aled** o **-alled;** ger **-aling** o **-alling**) tr impulsar pedaleando ‖ intr pedalear
pedant ['pɛdənt] s pedante mf
pedantic [pɪ'dæntɪk] adj pedantesco
pedant•ry ['pɛdəntri] s (pl **-ries**) pedantería
peddle ['pɛdəl] tr ir vendiendo de puerta en puerta; traer y llevar (chismes); vender (favores) ‖ intr ser buhonero
peddler ['pɛdlər] s buhonero
pederasty ['pɛdə,ræsti] s pederastia
pedestal ['pɛdɪstəl] s pedestal m
pedestrian [pɪ'dɛstrɪ•ən] adj pedestre ‖ s peatón m
pediatrician [,pidiə'trɪʃən] s pedíatra mf
pediatrics [,pidi'ætrɪks] ssg pediatría
pedigree ['pɛdɪ,gri] s árbol genealógico; ascendencia; fuente f, origen m
pediment ['pɛdɪmənt] s frontón m
pee [pi] s (coll) pipí m ‖ intr (coll) hacer pipí
peek [pik] s mirada rápida y furtiva ‖ intr mirar a hurtadillas
peel [pil] s cáscara, pellejo ‖ tr pelar ‖ intr pelarse
peep [pip] s mirada a hurtadillas; (of chickens) pío ‖ intr mirar a hurtadillas; piar (los pollos)
peep'hole' s atisbadero; (in a door) mirilla, ventanillo
peep show s mundonuevo; (slang) vistas sicalípticas
peer [pir] s par m ‖ intr mirar fijando la vista de cerca; **to peer at** mirar con ojos de miope; **to peer into** mirar hacia lo interior de, escudriñar
peerless ['pɪrlɪs] adj sin par
peeve [piv] s (coll) cojijo ‖ tr (coll) enojar, irritar
peevish ['pivɪʃ] adj cojijoso, displicente

peg [pɛg] s clavija, claveta, estaquilla; **to take down a peg** (coll) bajar los humos a ‖ v (pret & pp **pegged;** ger **pegging**) tr enclavijar; señalar con clavijas; fijar (precios) ‖ intr trabajar con ahinco; **to peg away at** afanarse en

peg leg s pata de palo

peg top s peonza; **peg tops** pantalones anchos de caderas y perniles ajustados

Peking ['pi'kɪŋ] s Pequín

Peking•ese [,pikɪ'niz] adj pequinés ‖ s (pl -ese) pequinés m

pelf [pɛlf] s dinero mal ganado

pell-mell ['pɛl'mɛl] adj tumultuoso ‖ adv atropelladamente

Peloponnesian [,pɛləpə'niʃən] adj & s peloponense mf

Peloponnesus [,pɛləpə'nisəs] s Peloponeso

Pelops ['pilɑps] s Pélope m

pelota [pɛ'lotə] s pelota vasca

pelt [pɛlt] s pellejo; golpe violento; (of a person) (hum) pellejo ‖ tr golpear violentamente; apedrear ‖ intr golpear violentamente; caer con fuerza (el granizo, la lluvia, etc.); apresurarse

pen. abbr **peninsula**

pen [pɛn] s pluma; corral m, redil m; **the pen and the sword** las letras y las armas ‖ v (pret & pp **penned;** ger **penning**) tr escribir (con pluma); redactar ‖ v (pret & pp **penned** o **pent** [pɛnt]) tr acorralar, encerrar

penalize ['pinə,laɪz] tr penar; penalizar; (sport) sancionar

penal•ty ['pɛnəlti] s (pl -ties) pena; (for late payment) recargo; (sport) sanción; **under penalty of** so pena de

penance ['pɛnəns] s penitencia; **to do penance** hacer penitencia

penchant ['pɛnʃənt] s afición, inclinación, tendencia

pen•cil ['pɛnsəl] s lápiz m; (of light) pincel m, haz m ‖ v (pret & pp -**ciled** o -**cilled;** ger -**ciling** o -**cilling**) tr marcar con lápiz; (med) pincelar

pencil sharpener s afilalápices m, cortalápices m

pendent ['pɛndənt] adj pendiente; sobresaliente ‖ s medallón m; (earring) pendiente m

pending ['pɛndɪŋ] adj pendiente ‖ prep hasta; durante

pendulum ['pɛndʒələm] s péndulo; (of a clock) péndola

pendulum bob s lenteja

penetrate ['pɛnɪ,tret] tr & intr penetrar

penguin ['pɛŋgwɪn] s pingüino, pájaro bobo

pen'hold'er s (handle) portaplumas m; (box) plumero

penicillin [,pɛnɪ'sɪlɪn] s penicilina

peninsula [pə'nɪnsələ] s península

peninsular [pə'nɪnsələr] adj & s peninsular mf ‖ **Peninsular** adj & s (Iberian) peninsular mf

penis ['pinəs] s pene m, falo

penitence ['pɛnɪtəns] s penitencia

penitent ['pɛnɪtənt] adj & s penitente mf

pen'knife' s (pl -**knives**) navaja, cortaplumas m

penmanship ['pɛnmən,ʃɪp] s caligrafía; (hand of a person) letra

pen name s seudónimo

pennant ['pɛnənt] s gallardete m

penniless ['pɛnɪlɪs] adj pelón, sin dinero

pennon ['pɛnən] s pendón m

pen•ny ['pɛni] s (pl -**nies**) (U.S.A.) centavo ‖ s (pl **pence** [pɛns]) (Brit) penique m

pen'ny•weight' s peso de 24 granos

pen pal s (coll) amigo por correspondencia

pen point s punta de la pluma; puntilla de la pluma fuente

pension ['pɛnʃən] s pensión, jubilación ‖ tr pensionar, jubilar

pensioner ['pɛnʃənər] s pensionista mf; **pensioners** clases pasivas

pensive ['pɛnsɪv] adj pensativo; melancólico

Pentecost ['pɛntɪ,kɔst] s el Pentecostés

penthouse ['pɛnt,haʊs] s alpende m, colgadizo; casa de azotea

pent-up ['pɛnt,ʌp] adj contenido, reprimido

penult ['pinʌlt] s penúltima

penum•bra [pɪ'nʌmbrə] s (pl -**brae** [bri] o -**bras**) penumbra

penurious [pɪ'nʊrɪəs] adj (stingy) tacaño, mezquino; (poor) pobre, indigente

penury ['pɛnjəri] s tacañería, mezquindad; pobreza, miseria

pen'wip'er s limpiaplumas m

people ['pipəl] spl gente f; personas; gente del pueblo; se, p.ej., **people say** se dice ‖ ssg (pl **peoples**) pueblo, nación ‖ tr poblar

pep [pɛp] s (slang) ánimo, brío, vigor m ‖ v (pret & pp **pepped;** ger **pepping**) tr—**to pep up** (slang) animar, dar vigor a

pepper ['pɛpər] s (spice) pimienta; (plant and fruit) pimiento ‖ tr sazonar con pimienta; (with bullets) acribillar; salpicar

pep'per•box' s pimentero

pep'per•mint' s (plant) menta piperita; esencia de menta; pastilla de menta

pep talk s palabras alentadoras

per [pʌr] prep por; **as per** según

perambulator [pər'æmbjə,letər] s cochecillo de niño

per capita [pər 'kæpɪtə] por cabeza, por persona

perceive [pər'siv] tr percibir

per cent o **percent** [pər'sɛnt] por ciento

percentage [pər'sɛntɪdʒ] s porcentaje m; (slang) provecho, ventaja

perception [pər'sɛpʃən] s percepción; comprensión, penetración

perch [pʌrʃ] s percha, rama, varilla; sitio o posición elevada; (fish) perca ‖ tr colocar en un sitio algo elevado intr sentarse en un sitio algo elevado; posar (un ave)

percolator ['pʌrkə,letər] s cafetera filtradora

per diem [pər'daɪəm] por día

perdition [pər'dɪʃən] s perdición

perennial [pə'rɛnɪəl] adj perenne; (bot) vivaz ‖ s planta vivaz

perfect ['pʌrfɛkt] adj & s perfecto ‖ [pər'fɛkt] tr perfeccionar

perfidious [pər'fɪdɪəs] adj pérfido

perfi·dy [ˈpʌrfɪdi] *s* (*pl* **-dies**) perfidia
perforate [ˈpʌrfəˌret] *tr* perforar
perforce [pərˈfors] *adv* por fuerza, necesariamente
perform [pərˈfɔrm] *tr* ejecutar; (theat) representar ‖ *intr* ejecutar; funcionar (*p.ej.*, *una máquina*)
performance [pərˈfɔrməns] *s* ejecución; representación; funcionamiento; (theat) función
performer [pərˈfɔrmər] *s* ejecutante *mf;* actor *m;* acróbata *mf*
perfume [ˈpʌrfjum] *s* perfume *m* ‖ [pərˈfjum] *tr* perfumar
perfunctory [pərˈfʌŋktəri] *adj* hecho sin cuidado, hecho a la ligera; indiferente, negligente
perhaps [pərˈhæps] *adv* acaso, tal vez, quizá
per·il [ˈpɛrəl] *s* peligro ‖ *v* (*pret & pp* **-iled** o **-illed;** *ger* **-iling** o **-illing**) *tr* poner en peligro
perilous [ˈpɛriləs] *adj* peligroso
period [ˈpɪrɪ·əd] *s* período; (*in school*) hora; (gram) punto; (sport) division
period costume *s* traje *m* de época
periodic [ˌpɪrɪˈɑdɪk] *adj* periódico
periodical [ˌpɪrɪˈɑdɪkəl] *adj* periódico ‖ *s* periódico, revista periódica
peripher·y [pəˈrɪfəri] *s* (*pl* **-ies**) periferia
periscope [ˈpɛrɪˌskop] *s* periscopio
perish [ˈpɛrɪʃ] *intr* perecer
perishable [ˈpɛrɪʃəbəl] *adj* perecedero; (*merchandise*) corruptible
periwig [ˈpɛrɪˌwɪɡ] *s* perico
perjure [ˈpʌrdʒər] *tr* hacer (*a una persona*) quebrantar el juramento; **to perjure oneself** perjurarse
perju·ry [ˈpʌrdʒəri] *s* (*pl* **-ries**) perjurio
perk [pʌrk] *tr* alzar (*la cabeza*); aguzar (*las orejas*) ‖ *intr* pavonearse; engalanarse; **to perk up** reanimarse, sentirse mejor
permanence [ˈpʌrmənəns] *s* permanencia
permanency [ˈpʌrmənənsi] *s* (*pl* **-cies**) permanencia; persona, cosa o posición peremanentes
permanent [ˈpʌrmənənt] *adj* permanente ‖ *s* permanente *f*, ondulación permanente
permanent tenure *s* inamovilidadperversión
permanent way *s* (rr) material fijo
permeate [ˈpʌrmɪˌet] *tr & intr* penetrar
permission [pərˈmɪʃən] *s* permisión
per·mit [ˈpʌrmɪt] *s* permiso; cédula de aduana ‖ [pərˈmɪt] *v* (*pret & pp* **-mitted;** *ger* **-mitting**) *tr* permitir
permute [perˈmjut] *tr* permutar
pernicious [pərˈnɪʃəs] *adj* pernicioso
pernickety [perˈnɪkɪti] *adj* (coll) descontentadizo, quisquilloso
perorate [ˈpɛrəˌret] *intr* perorar
peroration [ˌpɛrəˈreʃən] *s* peroración
peroxide [pərˈɑksaɪd] *s* peróxido; peróxido de hidrógeno
peroxide blonde *s* rubia oxigenada
perpendicular [ˌpʌrpənˈdɪkjələr] *adj & s* perpendicular *f*
perpetrate [ˈpʌrpɪˌtret] *tr* perpetrar
perpetual [pərˈpɛtʃu·əl] *adj* perpetuo

perpetuate [pərˈpɛtʃuˌet] *tr* perpetuar
perplex [pərˈplɛks] *tr* dejar perplejo
perplexed [pərˈplɛkst] *adj* perplejo
perplexi·ty [pərˈplɛksɪti] *s* (*pl* **-ties**) perplejidad; problema *m*
per se [per ˈsi] por sí mismo, en sí mismo, esencialmente
persecute [ˈpʌrsɪˌkjut] *tr* perseguir
persecution [ˌpʌrsɪˈkjuʃən] *s* persecución
persevere [ˌpʌrsɪˈvɪr] *intr* perseverar
Persian [ˈpʌrʒən] *adj & s* persa *mf*
persimmon [pərˈsɪmən] *s* placaminero
persist [pərˈsɪst] o [pərˈzɪst] *intr* persistir; empecinarse
persistent [pərˈsɪstənt] o [pərˈzɪstənt] *adj* persistente; (*insistent*) porfiado; (*e.g., headache*) pertinaz
person [ˈpʌrsən] *s* persona; **no person** nadie
personage [ˈpʌrsənɪdʒ] *s* personaje *m;* persona
personal [ˈpʌrsənəl] *adj* personal; de uso personal ‖ *s* nota de sociedad; (*in a newspaper*) remitido
personali·ty [ˌpʌrsəˈnæliti] *s* (*pl* **-ties**) personalidad
personality cult *s* culto a la personalidad
personal property *s* bienes *mpl* muebles
personi·fy [pərˈsɑnɪˌfaɪ] *v* (*pret pp* **-fied**) *tr* personificar
personnel [ˌpʌrsəˈnɛl] *s* personal *m*
per·son-to-per·son *adv* (telp) particular a particular
perspective [pərˈspɛktɪv] *s* perspectiva
perspicacious [ˌpʌrspɪˈkeʃəs] *adj* perspicaz
perspire [pərˈspaɪr] *intr* sudar, transpirar
persuade [pərˈswed] *tr* persuadir
persuasion [pərˈsweʒən] *s* persuasión; creencia religiosa; creencia fuerte
pert [pʌrt] *adj* atrevido, descarado; (coll) animado, vivo
pertain [pərˈten] *intr* pertenecer; **pertaining to** perteneciente a
pertinacious [ˌpʌrtɪˈneʃəs] *adj* pertinaz
pertinent [ˈpʌrtɪnənt] *adj* pertinente
perturb [pərˈtʌrb] *tr* perturbar
Peru [pəˈru] *s* el Perú
perusal [pəˈruzəl] *s* lectura cuidadosa
peruse [pəˈruz] *tr* leer con atención
Peruvian [pəˈruvɪ·ən] *adj & s* peruano
pervade [pərˈved] *tr* penetrar, esparcirse por, extenderse por
perverse [pərˈvʌrs] *adj* perverso; avieso; díscolo; contumaz; malazo
perversion [pərˈvʌrʒən] *s* perversión
perversi·ty [pərˈvʌrsɪti] *s* (*pl* **-ties**) perversidad; indocilidad; contumacia
pervert [ˈpʌrvərt] *s* renegado, apóstata; pervertido ‖ [pərˈvʌrt] *tr* pervertir; emplear mal (*p.ej., los talentos que uno tiene*)
pes·ky [ˈpɛski] *adj* (*comp* **-kier;** *super* **-kiest**) (coll) cargante, molesto
pessimism [ˈpɛsɪˌmɪzəm] *s* pesimismo
pessimist [ˈpɛsɪmɪst] *s* pesimista *mf*
pessimistic [ˌpɛsɪˈmɪstɪk] *adj* pesimista
pest [pɛst] *s* peste *f;* insecto nocivo; (*misfortune*) plaga; (*annoying person, bore*) machaca *mf*
pester [ˈpɛstər] *tr* molestar, importunar

pest'house' s lazareto, hospital m de contagiosos

pesticide ['pɛstɪ,saɪd] s pesticida m

pestiferous [pɛs'tɪfərəs] adj pestifero; (coll) engorroso, molesto

pestilence ['pɛstɪləns] s pestilencia

pestle ['pɛsəl] s mano f de almirez

pet [pɛt] s animal mimado, animal casero; niño mimado; favorito; enojo pasajero ‖ v (pret & pp **petted**; ger **petting**) tr acariciar, mimar ‖ intr (slang) besuquearse

petal [pɛtəl] s pétalo

petard [pɪ'tɑrd] s petardo

pet'cock' s llave f de desagüe, llave de purga

Peter ['pitər] s Pedro; **to rob Peter to pay Paul** desnudar a un santo para vestir a otro

petit-bourgeois [pə'ti'burʒwɑ] adj pequeñoburgués

petition [pɪ'tɪʃən] s petición; (formal request signed by a number of people) memorial m, instancia, solicitud ‖ tr suplicar; dirigir una instancia a, solicitar

pet name s nombre m de cariño

Petrarch ['pitrɑrk] s Petrarca m

petri·fy ['pɛtrɪ,faɪ] v (pret & pp **-fied**) tr petrificar ‖ intr petrificarse

petrochemical [,pɛtro'kɛmɪkəl] adj petroquímico

petrol ['pɛtrəl] s (Brit) gasolina

petroleum [pɪ'trolɪ·əm] s petróleo

pet shop s pajarería

petticoat ['pɛtɪ,kot] s enaguas; (woman, girl) (slang) falda

pet·ty ['pɛti] adj (comp **-tier**; super **-tiest**) insignificante, pequeño; mezquino; intolerante

petty cash s caja de menores, efectivo para gastos menores

petty larceny s ratería, hurto

petty officer s (naut) suboficial m

petulant ['pɛtjələnt] adj malhumorado, enojadizo

pew [pju] s banco de iglesia

pewter ['pjutər] s peltre m; vajilla de peltre

Phaëthon ['fe·ɪθən] s Faetón m

phalanx ['feleŋks] s falange f

phallic ['fælɪk] adj fálico

phallus ['fæləs] s falo

phantasm ['fæntæzəm] s fantasma m

phantom ['fæntəm] s fantasma m

Pharaoh ['fero] s Faraón m

pharisee ['færɪ,si] s fariseo ‖ **Pharisee** s fariseo

pharmaceutical [,fɑrmə'sutɪkəl] adj farmacéutico

pharmacist ['fɑrməsɪst] s farmacéutico

pharma·cy ['fɑrməsi] s (pl **-cies**) farmacia

pharynx ['færɪŋks] s faringe f

phase [fez] s fase f ‖ tr poner en fase; llevar a cabo a etapas uniformes; (coll) inquietar, molestar; **to phase out** deshacer paulatinamente

pheasant ['fɛzənt] s faisán m

phenobarbital [,fino'bɑrbɪ,tæl] s fenobarbital m

phenomenal [fɪ'nɑmɪ,nɑn] s (pl **-na** [nə]) fenómenal

phial ['faɪ·əl] s frasco pequeño; inyectable m

Phidias ['fɪdɪ·əs] s Fidias m

philanderer [fɪ'lændərər] s galanteador m, tenorio

philanthropist [fɪ'lænθrəpɪst] s filántropo

philanthro·py [fɪ'lænθrəpi] s (pl **-pies**) filantropía

philatelist [fɪ'lætəlɪst] s filatelista mf

philately [fɪ'lætəli] s filatelia

Philip ['fɪlɪp] s Felipe m; (of Macedon) Filipo

Philippine ['fɪlɪ,pin] adj filipino ‖ **Philippines** spl Islas Filipinas

Philistine [fɪ'lɪstɪn] o ['fɪlɪ,stin] o ['fɪlɪ,staɪn] adj & s filisteo

philologist [fɪ'lɑlədʒɪst] s filólogo

philology [fɪ'lɑlədʒi] s filología

philosopher [fɪ'lɑsəfər] s filósofo

philosophic(al) [,fɪlɑsɑfɪk(əl)] adj filosófico

philoso·phy [fɪ'lɑsəfi] s (pl **-phies**) filosofía

philter ['fɪltər] s filtro

phlebitis [flɪ'baɪtɪs] s flebitis f

phlegm [flɛm] s flema f, gargajo; **to cough up phlegm** gargajear

phlegmatic(al) [flɛg'mætɪk(əl)] adj flemático; (coll) galbanoso

Phoebe ['fibi] s Febe f

Phoebus ['fibəs] s Febo m

Phoenicia [fɪ'nɪʃə] o [fɪ'niʃə] s Fenicia

Phoenician [fɪ'nɪʃən] o [fɪ'niʃən] adj & s fenicio

phoenix ['finɪks] s fénix m

phone [fon] s (coll) teléfono; **to come** o **to go to the phone** acudir al teléfono, ponerse al aparato ‖ tr & intr (coll) telefonear

phone call s llamada telefónica

phoneme ['fonim] s fonema m

phonetic [fo'nɛtɪk] adj fonético

phonics ['fɑnɪks] s fónica

phonograph ['fonə,græf] s fonógrafo

phonology [fə'nɑlədʒi] s fonología

pho·ny ['foni] adj (comp **-nier**; super **-niest**) falso, contrahecho ‖ s (pl **-nies**) (slang) farsa; (coll) farsante mf

phosphate ['fɑsfet] s fosfato

phosphorescent [,fɑsfə'rɛsənt] adj fosforescente

phospho·rus ['fɑsfərəs] s (pl **-ri** [,raɪ]) fósforo

pho·to ['foto] s (pl **-tos**) foto f

photocopier ['foto,kɑpɪ·ər] s fotocopiador m; fotóstato m

pho'to·cop'y s fotocopia ‖ v (pret & pp **-ied**) tr fotocopiar

photoengraving [,foto·ɛn'grevɪŋ] s fotograbado

photo finish s (sport) llegada a la meta, determinada mediante el fotofija

pho'to·fin'ish camera s fotofija m

photogenic [,foto'dʒɛnɪk] adj fotogénico

photograph ['fotə,græf] s fotografía ‖ tr & intr fotografiar

photographer [fə'tɑgrəfər] s fotógrafo

photography [fə'tɑgrəfi] s fotografía

pe
ph

photojournalism [,fotə'dʒʌrnə,lɪzəm] s fotoperiodismo
pho'to•play' s fotodrama m
photostat ['fotə,stæt] s fotóstato ‖ tr & intr fotostatar
phototube ['fotə,tjub] fototubo
phrase [frez] s frase f ‖ tr frasear
phrenology [frɪ'nɑlədʒi] s frenología
phys. abbr **physical, physician, physics, physiology**
phys•ic ['fɪzɪk] s medicamento; purgante m ‖ v (pret & pp **-icked;** ger **-icking**) tr curar; purgar
physical ['fɪzɪkəl] adj físico
physician [fɪ'zɪʃən] s médico
physicist ['fɪzɪsɪst] s físico
physics ['fɪzɪks] s física
physiognomy [,fɪzɪ'ɑgnəmi] o [,fɪzɪ'ɑnəmi] s fisononía
physiological [,fɪzɪ•ə'lɑdʒɪkəl] adj fisiológico
physiology [,fɪzɪ'ɑlədʒi] s fisiología
physique [fɪ'zik] s físico, talle m, exterior m
pi [paɪ] s (math) pi f; (typ) pastel m ‖ v (pret & pp **pied;** ger **piing**) tr (typ) empastelar
pian•o [pɪ'æno] s (pl **-os**) piano
picaresque [,pɪkə'rɛsk] adj picaresco
picayune [,pɪkə'jun] adj de poca monta, mezquino
piccadil•ly [,pɪkə'dɪli] s (pl **-lies**) cuello de pajarita
picco•lo ['pɪkə,lo] s (pl **-los**) flautín m
pick [pɪk] s (tool) pico; (choice) selección; (choicest) flor f ‖ tr escoger; recoger (p.ej., flores); recolectar (p.ej., algodón); romper (el hielo) con un picahielos; escarbarse (los dientes); descañonar, desplumar (un ave); hurgarse (la nariz); rescarse (una cicatriz, un grano); roer (un hueso); mondar (las frutas); falsear, forzar (una cerradura); armar (una pendencia); herir (las cuerdas de un instrumento); buscar (defectos); hurtar de (los bolsillos); **to pick out** entresacar; **to pick someone to pieces** (coll) no dejarle a uno un hueso sano; **to pick up** recoger; recobrar (ánimo; velocidad); descolgar (el receptor); hallar por casualidad; aprender con la práctica; aprender de oidas; invitar a subir a un coche; entablar conservación con (sin presentación previa); captar (una señal de radio) ‖ intr comer melindrosamente; escoger esmeradamente; **to pick at** comer melindrosamente; tomarla con, regañar; **to pick on** escoger; (coll) regañar; (coll) molestar; **to pick over** ir revolviendo y examinando; **to pick up** (coll) ir mejor, sentirse mejor; recobrar velocidad
pick'ax' s zapapico
picket ['pɪkɪt] s (stake, pale) piquete m; (of strikers; of soldiers) piquete m ‖ tr poner un cordón de piquetes a ‖ intr servir de piquete
picket fence s cerca de estacas
picket line s línea de piquetes
pickle ['pɪkəl] s encurtido; escabeche m, salmuera; (coll) apuro, aprieto ‖ tr encurtir; escabechar

pick-me-up ['pɪkmi,ʌp] s (coll) tentempié m; (coll) trago fortificante
pick'pock'et s carterista m, ratero; bolsero (Mex)
pick'up' s recolección; (of a motor) recóbro; (of an automobile) aceleración; (elec) pick-up, fonocaptor m
pic•nic ['pɪknɪk] s jira, partida de campo ‖ v (pret & pp **-nicked;** ger **-nicking**) intr hacer una jira al campo, merendar en el campo
pictorial [pɪk'tori•əl] adj gráfico; ilustrado ‖ s revista ilustrada
picture ['pɪktʃər] s cuadro; retrato; imagen f; lámina, grabado; fotografía; película; pintura ‖ tr dibujar; pintar; describir; **to picture to oneself** representarse
picture book s libro en imágenes
picture gallery s galería de pinturas
picture post card s postal ilustrada
picture show s exhibición de pinturas; cine m
picture signal s videoseñal f
picturesque [,pɪktʃə'rɛsk] adj pintoresco
picture tube s tubo de imagen, tubo de televisión
picture window s ventana panorámica
piddling ['pɪdlɪŋ] adj de poca monta, insignificante
pie [paɪ] s pastel m; (bird) picaza; (typ) pastel m ‖ v (pret & pp **pied;** ger **pieing**) tr (typ) empastelar
piece [pis] s (fragment; section of cloth) pedazo; (part of a machine; drama; single composition of music; coin; figure or block used in checkers, chess, etc.) pieza; (of land) lote m, parcela; **a piece of advice** un consejo; **a piece of baggage** un bulto; **a piece of furniture** un mueble; **to break to pieces** despedazar, hacer pedazos; despedazarse; **to fall to pieces** desbaratarse, caer en ruina; **to give someone a piece of one's mind** decirle a uno su parecer con toda franqueza; **to go to pieces** desvencijarse; darse a la desesperación; ir al desastre (un negocio); sufrir un ataque de nervios; perder por completo la salud; **to pick someone to pieces** (coll) no dejarle a uno un hueso sano ‖ tr formar juntando piezas; remendar ‖ intr (coll) comer a deshora
piece goods spl géneros de pieza
piece'work' s destajo, trabajo a destajo
piece'work'er s destajero, destajista mf
pier [pɪr] s muelle m; (of a bridge) estribo, sostén m; (of a harbor) rompeolas m; (wall between two openings) (archit) entrepaño
pierce [pɪrs] tr agujerear, horadar, taladrar; atravesar, traspasar; picar; pinchar; punzar; (fig) traspasar (de dolor) ‖ intr penetrar, entrar a la fuerza
piercing ['pɪrsɪŋ] adj agudo, penetrante; desgarrador; (pain) lancinante
pier glass s espejo de cuerpo entero
pie•ty ['paɪ•əti] s (pl **-ties**) piedad, devoción
piffle ['pɪfəl] s (coll) disparates mpl, música celestial
pig [pɪg] s cerdo; (young hog) lechón m; (domestic hog) puerco, cochino; carne f de

puerco; (metal) lingote *m;* (*person who acts like a pig*) (coll) marrano, cochino
pigeon [ˈpɪdʒən] *s* paloma
pi'geon·hole' *s* hornilla, casilla de paloma; casilla ‖ *tr* encasillar
pigeon house *s* palomar *m*
piggish [ˈpɪgɪʃ] *adj* glotón, voraz
pig'gy·back' *adv* a cuestas, en hombros
pig'-head'ed *adj* terco, cabezudo
pig iron *s* arrabio, hierro en lingotes
pigment [ˈpɪgmənt] *s* pigmento ‖ *tr* pigmentar ‖ *intr* pigmentarse
pig'pen' *s* pocilga; (fig) pocilga, corral *m* de vacas
pig'skin' *s* piel *f* de cerdo; (coll) balón *m* (con que se juega al fútbol)
pig'sty' *s* (*pl* **-sties**) pocilga
pig'tail' *s* coleta, trenza; (*of tobacco*) andullo
pike [paɪk] *s* pica; (*of an arrow*) punta; carretera; camino de barrera; (*fish*) lucio
piker [ˈpaɪkər] *s* (slang) persona de poco fuste
Pilate [ˈpaɪlət] *s* Pilatos *m*
pile [paɪl] *s* pila, montón *m;* (*stake*) pilote *m;* lanilla, pelusa; pira; (elec, phys) pila; (coll) caudal *m;* **piles** almorranas ‖ *tr* apilar, amontonar ‖ *intr* apilarse, amontonarse; **to pile in** o **into** entrar atropelladamente en; entrar todos en; subir todos a (*p.ej., un coche*)
pile driver *s* martinete *m*
pileup [ˈpaɪlˌʌp] *s* (*collision*) choque en cadena
pilfer [ˈpɪlfər] *tr & intr* ratear
pilgrim [ˈpɪlgrɪm] *s* peregrino, romero
pilgrimage [ˈpɪlgrɪmɪdʒ] *s* peregrinación, romería
pill [pɪl] *s* píldora; mal trago, sinsabor *m;* (coll) persona molesta
pillage [ˈpɪlɪdʒ] *s* pillaje *m,* saqueo ‖ *tr & intr* pillar, saquear
pillar [ˈpɪlər] *s* pilar *m;* **from pillar to post** de acá para allá sin objeto determinado
pillo·ry [ˈpɪləri] *s* (*pl* **-ries**) picota ‖ *v* (*pret & pp* **-ried**) *tr* empicotar; (fig) motejar, poner en ridículo
pillow [ˈpɪlo] *s* almohada
pil'low·case' o **pil'low·slip'** *s* funda de almohada
pilot [ˈpaɪlət] *s* piloto; (*of a harbor*) práctico; (*of a gas range*) mechero encendedor; (rr) trompa, delantera ‖ *tr* pilotar; conducir
pilot run o **pilot test** *s* experimento piloto
pimp [pɪmp] *s* alcahuete *m*
pimple [ˈpɪmpəl] *s* barro, grano
pim·ply [ˈpɪmpli] *adj* (*comp* **-plier;** *super* **-pliest**) granujoso
pin [pɪn] *s* alfiler *m;* (*e.g., for a necktie*) prendedero; (*peg*) clavija; (*e.g., to hold scissors together*) clavillo, clavito; (bowling) bolo; **to be on pins and needles** estar en espinas ‖ *v* (*pret & pp* **pinned;** *ger* **pinning**) *tr* alfilerar; clavar, fijar, sujetar; **to pin something on someone** (coll) acusarle a uno de una cosa; **to pin up** recoger y apuntar con alfileres; fijar en la pred con alfileres

pinafore [ˈpɪnəˌfor] *s* delantal *m* de niño
pin'ball' *s* billar romano, bagatela
pince-nez [ˈpæ̃sˌne] *s* lentes *mpl* de nariz, lentes de pinzas
pincers [ˈpɪnsərz] *ssg* o *spl* pinzas
pinch [pɪntʃ] *s* pellizco; (*of hunger*) tormento; (slang) arresto; (slang) hurto, robo; **in a pinch** en un aprieto; en caso necesario ‖ *tr* pellizcar; cogerse (*los dedos, p.ej., en una puerta*); apretar (*p.ej.. el zapato a una persona*); contraer (*el frío la cara de uno*); limitar los gastos de; (slang) arrestar, prender; (slang) hurtar, robar ‖ *intr* apretar; economizar, privarse de lo necesario
pinchers [ˈpɪntʃərz] *ssg* o *spl* var of **pincers**
pin'cush'ion *s* acerico
Pindar [ˈpɪndər] *s* Píndaro
pine [paɪn] *s* pino ‖ *intr* languidecer; **to pine away** consumirse; **to pine for** penar por
pine'ap'ple *s* ananás *m,* piña
pine cone *s* piña
pine needle *s* pinocha
ping [pɪŋ] *s* silbido de bala ‖ *intr* silbar (*una bala*); silbar como una bala
pin'head' *s* cabecilla de alfiler; cosa muy pequeña o insignificante; (coll) bobalicón *m*
pink [pɪŋk] *adj* rosado, sonrosado ‖ *s* estado perfecto; comunistoide *mf;* (bot) clavel *m,* clavellina
pin money *s* alfileres *mpl*
pinnacle [ˈpɪnəkəl] *s* pináculo
pin'point' *adj* exacto, preciso ‖ *s* punta de alfiler ‖ *tr & intr* señalar con precisión
pin'prick' *s* alfilerazo
pinup girl [ˈpɪnˌʌp] *s* guapa
pin'wheel' *s* rueda de fuego, rueda giratoria de fuegos artificiales; molinete *m* (Mex); (*child's toy*) rehilandera, ventolera
pioneer [ˌpaɪəˈnɪr] *s* pionero; (mil) zapador *m* ‖ *intr* abrir nuevos caminos, explorar
pious [ˈpaɪəs] *adj* pío, piadoso; mojigato; respetuoso
pip [pɪp] *s* (*seed*) pepita; (*on a card, dice, etc.*) punto; (vet) pepita
pipe [paɪp] *s* caño, conducto, tubo; (*to smoke tobacco*) pipa; (mus) pipa, caramillo, zampoña; (*of an organ*) cañón *m* ‖ *tr* conducir por medio de tubos o cañerías; proveer de tuberías o cañerías ‖ *intr* tocar el caramillo; **to pipe down** (slang) callarse
pipe cleaner *s* limpiapipas *m*
pipe dream *s* esperanza imposible, castillo en el aire
pipe line *s* cañería; tubería; oleoducto; fuente *f* de informes confidenciales
pipe organ *s* (mus) órgano
piper [ˈpaɪpər] *s* flautista *m;* gaitero; **to pay the piper** pagar los vidrios rotos
pipe wrench *s* llave *f* para tubos
pippin [ˈpɪpɪn] *s* (*apple*) camuesa; (*tree*) camueso; (slang) real moza
piquancy [ˈpikənsi] *s* picante *m*
piquant [ˈpikənt] *adj* picante
pique [pik] *s* pique *m,* resentimiento ‖ *tr* picar, enojar; despertar, excitar
piracy [ˈpaɪrəsi] *s* piratería

ph
pi

Piraeus [paɪˈriˑəs] s el Pireo
pirate [ˈpaɪrɪt] s pirata m ‖ tr pillar, robar; publicar fraudulentamente ‖ intr piratear
pirouette [ˌpɪruˈɛt] s pirueta ‖ intr piruetear
Pisces [ˈpaɪsiz] s (astr) Piscis m
pistol [ˈpɪstəl] s pistola
piston [ˈpɪstən] s (mach) émbolo, pistón m; (mus) pistón m
piston displacement s cilindrada
piston ring s anillo de émbolo, aro de émbolo, segmento de émbolo
piston rod s vástago de émbolo
piston stroke s carrera de émbolo
pit [pɪt] s hoyo; (in the skin) cacaraña; (of certain fruit) hueso; (for cockfights, etc.) cancha, reñidero; (of the stomach) boca; abismo, infierno; (min) pozo; (theat) foso ‖ v (pret & pp **pitted**; ger **pitting**) tr marcar con hoyos; dejar hoyoso (el rostro); deshuesar (p.ej., una ciruela)
pitch [pɪtʃ] s (black sticky substance) pez f; echada, lanzamiento; cosa lanzada; pelota lanzada; (of a boat) arfada, cabezada; (of a roof) pendiente f; (of, e.g., a screw) paso; (of a winding) (elec) paso; (mus) tono, altura; (fig) grado, extremo; (coll) bombo, elogio ‖ tr echar, lanzar; elevar (el heno) con la horquilla; armar o plantar (una tienda de campaña); embrear; (mus) graduar el tono de ‖ intr caerse, caer de cabeza; bajar en declive, inclinarse; arfar, cabecear (un buque); **to pitch in** (coll) poner manos a la obra; (coll) comenzar a comer
pitch accent s acento de altura
pitcher [ˈpɪtʃər] s jarro; (in baseball) lanzador m
pitch'fork' s horca, horquilla; **to rain pitchforks** (coll) llover a cántaros
pitch pipe s (mus) diapasón m
pit'fall' s callejo, trampa; (danger for the unwary) escollo, atascadero
pith [pɪθ] s médula; (essential part) (fig) médula; (fig) fuerza, vigor m
pith•y [ˈpɪθi] adj (comp -ier; super -iest) medular; enérgico, expresivo
pitiful [ˈpɪtɪfəl] adj lastimoso; compasivo; despreciable
pitiless [ˈpɪtɪlɪs] adj despiadado, empedernido, incompasivo
pit-y [ˈpɪti] s (pl -ies) piedad, compasión, lástima; **for pity's sake!** ¡por piedad!; **to have** o **to take pity on** tener piedad de, apiadarse de; **what a pity!** ¡qué lástima!, !qué pena! ‖ v (pret & pp -ied) tr apiadarse de, compadecer
pivot [ˈpɪvət] s pivote m, gorrón m, eje m de rotación; (fig) eje m ‖ intr pivotar; **to pivot on** girar sobre; depender de
placard [ˈplækɑrd] s cartel m ‖ tr fijar carteles en; fijar (un anuncio) en sitio público; publicar por medio de carteles
place [ples] s sitio, lugar m; (of business) local m; (job) puesto; grado, rango; **in no place** en ninguna parte; **in place of** en lugar de; **out of place** fuera de su lugar; fuera de propósito; **to be looking for a**

place to live buscar piso; **to take place** tener lugar; situar ‖ tr poner, colocar; acordarse bien de; dar empleo a; prestar (dinero) a interés ‖ intr colocarse (un caballo en las carreras)
place•bo [pləˈsibo] s (pl -bos o -boes) placebo
place card s tarjetita con el nombre (que indica la colocación de uno en la mesa)
placement [ˈplesmənt] s colocación
place name s nombre m de lugar, topónimo
placid [ˈplæsɪd] adj plácido, tranquilo
plagiarism [ˈpledʒəˌrɪzəm] s plagio
plagiarize [ˈpledʒəˌraɪz] tr plagiar
plague [pleg] s peste f, plaga; (great public calamity) plaga ‖ tr apestar, plagar; atormentar, molestar
plaid [plæd] s (cloth) tartán m; cuadros a la escocesa
plain [plen] adj llano, claro, evidente; abierto, franco; ordinario; feo; humilde; solo, natural; **in plain English** sin rodeos; **in plain sight** o **view** en plena vista ‖ s llano, llanura
plain clothes spl traje m de calle, traje de paisano
plainclothesman [ˈplenˈkloðzˌmæn] s (pl -men [ˌmɛn]) policía m que lleva traje de paisano
plain omelet s tortilla a la francesa
plains•man [ˈplenzmən] s (pl -men [mən]) llanero
plaintiff [ˈplentɪf] s (law) demandante mf
plaintive [ˈplentɪv] adj quejumbroso
plan [plæn] s plan m, intento, proyecto; (drawing, diagram) plan m, plano; **to change one's plans** cambiar de proyecto ‖ v (pret & pp **planned**; ger **planning**) tr planear, planificar; **to plan to** proponerse ‖ intr hacer proyectos
plane [plen] adj plano ‖ s (surface) plano; aeroplano, avión m; (of an airplane) plano; (carp) cepillo; (tree) plátano ‖ tr cepillar ‖ intr viajar en aeroplano
plane sickness s mareo del aire, mal m de vuelo
planet [ˈplænɪt] s planeta m
plane tree s plátano
planing mill [ˈplenɪŋ] s taller m de cepillado
plank [plæŋk] s tabla gruesa, tablón m; artículo de un programa político ‖ tr entablar, entarimar
plant [plænt] s fábrica, taller m; (of an automobile) grupo motor; (educational establishment) plantel m; (bot) planta ‖ tr plantar; sembrar (semillas); inculcar (doctrinas); (slang) ocultar (géneros robados)
plantation [plænˈteʃən] s plantación, campo de plantas; (estate cultivated by workers living on it) hacienda
planter [ˈplæntər] s plantador m, cultivador m
plasma [ˈplæzmə] s plasma m
plaster [ˈplæstər] s (gypsum) yeso; (mixture of lime, sand, water, etc.) argamasa; (coating) enlucido; (poultice) emplasto ‖ tr en-

yesar; argamasar; enlucir; emplastar; embadurnar; pegar (*anuncios*)

plas′ter•board′ s cartón m de yeso y fieltro

plaster cast s (surg) vendaje enyesado; (sculp) yeso

plaster of Paris s estuco de París

plastic [′plæstɪk] adj plástico ‖ s (*substance*) plástico; (*art of modeling*) plástica

plate [plet] s (*dish*) plato; (*sheet of metal, etc.*) chapa, placa; vajilla de oro, vajilla de plata; dentadura postiza, base f de la dentadura postiza; (baseball) puesto meta, puesto del batter; (anat, elec, electron, phot, zool) placa; (typ) clisé m ‖ tr chapear, planchear; blindar; platear, dorar, niquelar (*por la galvanoplastia*); (typ) clisar

plateau [plæ′to] s meseta

plate glass s vidrio o cristal cilindrado

platen [′plætən] s rodillo

platform [′plæt,form] s plataforma f; (*of passenger station*) andén m; (*of freight station*) cargadero; (*of a speaker*) tribuna; (*political program*) plataforma

platform car s plataforma f

platinum [′plætɪnəm] s platino

platinum blonde s rubia platino

platitude [′plætɪ,tjud] o [′plætɪ,tud] s perogrullada, trivialidad

Plato [′pleto] s Platón m

platoon [plə′tun] s pelotón m

platter [′plætər] s fuente f; (slang) disco de fonógrafo

plausible [′plɔzɪbəl] adj aparente, especioso; bien hablado; (coll) creíble

play [ple] s juego; (*act or move in a game*) jugada; (*drama*) pieza; (*of water, colors, lights*) juego; (mach) huelgo, juego; **to give full play to** dar rienda suelta a ‖ tr jugar (*p.ej., un naipe, una partida de juego*); jugar a (*p.ej., los naipes*); jugar con (*un contrario*); dar (*un chasco*); gastar (*una broma*); hacer (*una mala jugada*); dirigir (*agua, una manguera*); desempeñar (*un papel*); desempeñar el papel de; representar (*una obra dramática, un film*); apostar por (*un caballo*); tocar (*un instrumento, una pieza, un disco de fonógrafo*) ‖ intr jugar; desempeñar un papel, representar; correr (*una fuente*); rielar (*la luz en la superficie del agua*); vagar (*p.ej., una sonrisa por los labios*); **to play out** rendirse; agotarse; acabarse; **to play safe** tomar sus precauciones; **to play sick** hacerse el enfermo; **to play up to** hacer la rueda a

play′back′ s lectura; aparato de lectura

play′bill′ s (*poster*) cartel m; (*of a play*) programa m

player piano [′ple•ər] s autopiano

playful [′plefəl] adj juguetón, retozón; dicho en broma

playgoer [′ple,go•ər] s aficionado al teatro

play′ground′ s campo de juego; patio de recreo

play′house′ s casita de muñecas; teatro

playing card [′ple•ɪŋ] s naipe m

playing field s campo de deportes

play′mate′ s compañero de juego

play′-off′ s partido de desempate

play′pen′ s parque m, corral m (*para bebés*)

play′thing′ s juguete m

play′time′ s hora de recreo, hora de juego

playwright [′ple,raɪt] s dramaturgo, autor dramático; comediógrafo

play′writ′ing s dramaturgia, dramática

plea [pli] s ruego, súplica; disculpa, excusa; (law) contestación a la demanda

plead [plid] v (*pret & pp* **pleaded** o **pled** [plɛd]) tr defender (*una causa*) ‖ intr suplicar; abogar; **to plead guilty** confesarse culpable; **to plead not guilty** negar la acusación, declararse inocente

pleasant [′plɛzənt] adj agradable; simpático; sangriligero

pleasant•ry [′plɛzəntri] s (*pl* **-ries**) broma, chiste m, dicho gracioso

please [pliz] tr & intr gustar; **as you please** como Vd. quiera; **if you please** si me hace el favor; **please** + *inf* hágame Vd. el favor de + *inf;* **to be pleased to** alegrarse de, complacerse en; **to be pleased with** estar satisfecho de o con

pleasing [′plizɪŋ] adj agradable, grato

pleasure [′plɛʒər] s placer m, gusto; **what is your pleasure?** ¿en qué puedo servirle?, ¿qué es lo que Vd. desea?; **with pleasure** con mucho gusto

pleasure seeker [′sikər] s amigo de los placeres

pleat [plit] s pliegue m, plisado ‖ tr plegar, plisar

plebeian [plɪ′bi•ən] adj & s plebeyo

pledge [plɛdʒ] s empeño, prenda; (*vow*) voto, promesa; (*toast*) brindis m; **as a pledge of** en prenda de; **to take the pledge** comprometerse a no tomar bebidas alcohólicas ‖ tr empeñar, prendar; dar (*la palabra*); brindar por

plentiful [′plɛntɪfəl] adj abundante, copioso

plenty [′plɛnti] adv (coll) completamente ‖ s abundancia, copia; suficiencia

pleurisy [′plʊrɪsi] s pleuresía

pliable [′plaɪ•əbəl] adj flexible, plegable; dócil

pliers [′plaɪ•ərz] ssg o spl alicates mpl

plight [plaɪt] s estado, situación; apuro, aprieto; compromiso solemne ‖ tr dar o empeñar (*su palabra*); **to plight one's troth** prometer fidelidad; dar palabra de casamiento

plod [plad] v (*pret & pp* **plodded;** *ger* **plodding**) tr recorrer (*un camino*) pausada y pesadamente ‖ intr caminar pausada y pesadamente; trabajar laboriosamente

plot [plat] s complot m, conspiración; (*of a play or novel*) argumento, trama, parcela, solar m; cuadro de flores; cuadro de hortalizas; plano, mapa m ‖ v (*pret & pp* **plotted;** *ger* **plotting**) tr fraguar, tramar, urdir, maquinar; dividir en parcelas o solares; trazar el plano de; trazar, tirar (*líneas*) ‖ intr conspirar

plough [plaʊ] s, tr & intr var de **plow**

plover [′plʌvər] o [′plovər] s chorlito

plow [plau] *s* arado; quitanieve *m* ‖ *tr* arar; surcar; quitar o barrer (*la nieve*); **to plow back** reinvertir (*ganancias*) ‖ *intr* arar; avanzar como un arado

plow•man [ˈplaumən] *s* (*pl* **-men** [mən]) arador *m*, yuguero

plow′share′ *s* reja de arado

pluck [plʌk] *s* ánimo, coraje *m*, valor *m*; tirón *m* ‖ *tr* arrancar; coger (*flores*); desplumar (*un ave*); puntear (*p.ej., una guitarra*) ‖ *intr* dar un tirón; **to pluck up** recobrar ánimo

pluck•y [ˈplʌki] *adj* (*comp* **-ier**; *super* **-iest**) animoso, valiente

plug [plʌg] *s* taco, tarugo; boca de agua; tableta de tabaco; (*hat*) (slang) chistera; (elec) clavija, toma, ficha; (aut) bujía; (coll) rocín; (slang) elogio incidental ‖ *v* (*pret* & *pp* **plugged**; *ger* **plugging**) *tr* atarugar; calar (*un melón*); **to plug in** (elec) enchufar ‖ *intr* (coll) trabajar con ahinco

plum [plʌm] *s* (*tree*) ciruelo; (*fruit*) ciruela; (slang) turrón *m*, pingüe destino

plumage [ˈplumɪdʒ] *s* plumaje *m*

plumb [plʌm] *adj* vertical; (coll) completo ‖ *adv* a plomo; (coll) verticalmente; (coll) directamente ‖ *tr* aplomar; sondear

plumb bob *s* plomada

plumber [ˈplʌmər] *s* fontanero; (*worker in lead*) plomero

plumbing [ˈplʌmɪŋ] *s* instalación sanitaria; conjunto de cañerías; (*working in lead*) plomería; sondeo

plumbing fixtures *spl* artefactos sanitarios

plumb line *s* cuerda de plomada

plum cake *s* pastel aderezado con pasas de Corinto y ron

plume [plum] *s* (*of a bird*) pluma; (*tuft of feathers worn as ornament*) penacho ‖ *tr* emplumar; componerse (*las plumas*); **to plume oneself on** enorgulleclerse de

plummet [ˈplʌmɪt] *s* plomada ‖ *intr* caer a plomo, precipitarse

plump [plʌmp] *adj* rechoncho, regordete; brusco, franco ‖ *adv* de golpe; francamente ‖ *s* (coll) caída pesada; (coll) ruido sordo ‖ *intr* caer a plomo

plum pudding *s* pudín *m* inglés con pasas de Corinto, corteza de limón, huevos y ron

plum tree *s* ciruelo

plunder [ˈplʌndər] *s* pillaje *m*; botín *m* ‖ *tr* pillar, saquear

plunge [plʌndʒ] *s* zambullida; caída a plomo; sacudida violenta; salto; baño de agua fría; (*of a boat*) cabeceo ‖ *tr* zambullir; sumergir; hundir (*p.ej., un puñal*) ‖ *intr* zambullirse; sumergirse; hundirse (*p.ej., en la tristeza*); caer a plomo; arrojarse, precipitarse; cabecear (*un buque*); (slang) entregarse al juego, entregarse a las especulaciones

plunger [ˈplʌndʒər] *s* zambullidor *m*; émbolo buzo; (*of a tire valve*) obús *m*; (slang) jugador o especulador desenfrenado

plunk [plʌŋk] *adv* (coll) con un golpe seco, con un ruido de golpe seco ‖ *tr* (coll) arrojar, empujar o dejar caer pesadamente

‖ *intr* sonar o caer con un ruido de golpe seco

plural [ˈplurəl] *adj* & *s* plural *m*

plus [plʌs] *adj* más; y pico; **to be plus** (coll) tener por añadidura ‖ *prep* más ‖ *s* (*sign*) más *m*; añadidura

plush [plʌʃ] *adj* afelpado; (coll) lujoso, suntuoso ‖ *s* felpa; peluche *m*

Plutarch [ˈplutark] *s* Plutarco

plutonium [pluˈtoni•əm] *s* plutonio

ply [plaɪ] *s* (*pl* **plies**) (e.g., *of a cloth*) capa, doblez *m*; (*of a cable*) cordón *m* ‖ *v* (*pret* & *pp* **plied**) *tr* manejar (*la aguja, etc.*); ejercer (*un oficio*); batir (*el agua con los remos*); importunar; navegar por (*p.ej., un río*) ‖ *intr* avanzar; **to ply between** hacer (*un barco*) el servicio entre

ply′wood′ *s* chapeado, madera laminada

P.M. *abbr* **Postmaster, post meridiem** (Lat) afternoon

pneumatic [njuˈmætɪk] o [nuˈmætɪk] *adj* neumático

pneumatic drill *s* perforadora de aire comprimido

pneumonia [njuˈmoni•ə] o [nuˈmoni•ə] *s* neumonía o pulmonía

P.O. *abbr* **post office**

poach [potʃ] *tr* escalfar (*huevos*) ‖ *intr* cazar o pescar en vedado

poacher [ˈpotʃər] *s* cazador furtivo, pescador furtivo

pock [pak] *s* cacaraña, hoyuelo

pocket [ˈpakɪt] *s* bolsillo, faltriquera; (*in billiards*) tronera; (aer) bolsa de aire; (mil) bolsón *m* ‖ *tr* embolsar; entronerar (*una bola de billar*); tragarse (*injurias*)

pock′et•book′ *s* portamonedas *m*; (*of a woman*) bolsa

pocket calculator *s* bolsicalculadora, calculadora de bolsillo

pocket handkerchief *s* pañuelo de bolsillo o de mano

pock′et•knife′ *s* (*pl* **-knives**) navaja, cortaplumas *m*

pocket money *s* alfileres *mpl*, dinero de bolsillo

pock′mark′ *s* cacaraña, hoyuelo

pod [pad] *s* vaina

podium [ˈpodi•əm] *s* podio

poem [ˈpo•ɪm] *s* poema *m*, poesía

poet [ˈpo•ɪt] *s* poeta *m*

poetess [ˈpo•ɪtɪs] *s* poetisa

poetic [poˈɛtɪk] *adj* poético ‖ **poetics** *ssg* poética

poetry [ˈpo•ɪtri] *s* poesía

pogrom [ˈpogrəm] *s* levantamiento contra los judíos

poignancy [ˈpɔɪnyənsi] *s* picante *m*, viveza, intensidad

poignant [ˈpɔɪnyənt] *adj* picante, vivo, intenso

point [pɔɪnt] *s* (*of a sword, pencil; of land*) punta; (*of pen*) pico; (*of fountain pen*) puntilla; (*mark of imperceptible dimensions*) punto; (*of a joke*) gracia; (elec) punta; (math, typ, sport, fig) punto; (coll) indirecta, insinuación; **beside the point**

fuera de propósito; **on the point of** a punto de; **to carry one's point** salirse con la suya; **to come to the point** venir al caso o al grano; **to get to the point** caer en la cuenta ‖ *tr* aguzar, sacar punta a; apuntar (*p.ej., un arma de fuego*); resanar (*una pared*); **to point one's finger at** señalar con el dedo; **to point out** señalar, indicar, hacer notar ‖ *intr* apuntar; pararse (*el perro de muestra*); **to point at** señalar con el dedo

point'blank' *adj & adv* a quemarropa

pointed ['pɔɪntɪd] *adj* puntiagudo; picante; acentuado, directo

pointer ['pɔɪntər] *s* puntero; indicador *m*; (*of a clock*) manecilla; perro de muestra; (*mas*) fijador *m*; (*coll*) indicación, dirección

poise [pɔɪz] *s* aplomo, equilibrio ‖ *tr* equilibrar; considerar ‖ *intr* equilibrarse; estar suspendido

poison ['pɔɪzən] *s* veneno, ponzoña ‖ *tr* envenenar

poison ivy *s* tosiguero

poisonous ['pɔɪzənəs] *adj* venenoso

poi'son-pen' letter *s* carta calumniosa

poke [pok] *s* (*push*) empuje *m*, empujón *m*; (*thrust*) hurgonazo; (*with elbow*) codazo; (*slow person*) tardón *m* ‖ *tr* empujar; hacer (*un agujero*) a empujones; abrirse (*paso*) a empujones; atizar, hurgar (*el fuego*); **to poke fun at** burlarse de; **to poke one's nose into** entremeterse en ‖ *intr* fisgar, husmear; andar perezosamente

poker ['pokər] *s* hurgón *m*; (*card game*) póker *m*, pócar *m*

poker face *s* cara de jugador de póker; **to keep a poker face** disfrazar la expresión del rostro, mantener una expresión imperturbable

pok•y ['poki] *adj* (*comp* -ier; *super* -iest) (coll) tardo, roncero

Poland ['polənd] *s* Polonia

polar bear ['polər] *s* oso blanco

polarize ['polə,raɪz] *tr* polarizar

pole [pol] *s* (*long rod or staff*) pértiga; (*of a flag*) asta; (*upright support*) poste *m*; (*to push a boat*) botador *m*; (astr, biol, elec, geog, math) polo ‖ *tr* impeler (*un barco*) con botador ‖ **Pole** *s* polaco

pole'cat' *s* turón *m*, veso

pole'star' *s* estrella polar; (*guide*) norte *m*; (*center of interest*) miradero

pole vault *s* salto con garrocha o con pértiga

police [pə'lis] *s* policía ‖ *tr* poner o mantener servicio de policía en; (mil) limpiar

police car *s* carro-patrulla *m*

police•man [pə'lismən] *s* (*pl* -men [mən]) policía *m*, guardia urbano

police record *s* ficha

police state *s* estado-policía *m*

police station *s* cuartel *m* o estación de policía

poli•cy ['pɔlɪsi] *s* (*pl* -cies) política; (ins) póliza

polio ['polɪ•o] *s* (coll) polio *f*

polish ['pɔlɪʃ] *s* pulimento; cera de lustrar; (*for shoes*) bola, betún *m*, lustre *m*; (*dia-*

mond) talla; elegancia; cultura, urbanidad ‖ *tr* pulimentar, pulir; embolar, dar betún a (*los zapatos*); **to polish off** (coll) terminar de prisa; (slang) engullir (*la comida, un trago*) ‖ **Polish** ['polɪʃ] *adj & s* polaco

polisher ['pɔlɪʃər] *s* pulidor *m*; (*machine*) pulidora; (*for floors, tables, etc.*) enceradora

polite [pə'laɪt] *adj* cortés, fino, urbano; culto

politeness [pə'laɪtnɪs] *s* cortesía, fineza, urbanidad; cultura

politic ['pɔlɪtɪk] *adj* prudente, sagaz; astuto; juicioso

political [pə'lɪtɪkəl] *adj* político

politician [,pɔlɪ'tɪʃən] *s* político; (*politician seeking personal or partisan gain*) politiquero

politics ['pɔlɪtɪks] *ssg* o *spl* política

poll [pol] *s* (*questionnaire to determine opinion*) encuesta; votación; lista electoral; cabeza; **polls** urnas electorales; **to go to the polls** acudir a las urnas; **to take a poll** hacer una encuesta ‖ *tr* dar (*un voto*); recibir (*votos*)

pollen ['pɑlən] *s* polen *m*

pollinate ['pɑlɪ,net] *tr* polinizar

polling booth ['polɪŋ] *s* cabina o caseta de votar

polliwog ['pɑlɪ,wɑg] *s* renacuajo; (slang) persona que atraviesa el ecuador en un barco por primera vez

pollster ['polstʌr] *s* encuestador *m*

poll tax *s* capitación, impuesto por cabeza

pollutant [pə'lutənt] *s* contaminante *m*

pollute [pə'lut] *tr* contaminar, corromper, ensuciar

pollution [pə'luʃən] *s* contaminación; (*of the environment*) polución; (fig) corrupción

polo ['polo] *s* polo

polo player *s* polista *mf*, jugador *m* de polo

polygamist [pə'lɪgəmɪst] *s* polígamo

polygamous [pə'lɪgəməs] *adj* polígamo

polyglot ['pɑlɪ,glɑt] *adj & s* poligloto

polygon ['pɑlɪ,gɑn] *s* polígono

Polyhymnia [,pɑlɪ'hɪmnɪ•ə] *s* Polimnia

polynomial [,pɑlɪ'nomɪ•əl] *s* polinomio

polyp ['pɑlɪp] *s* pólipo

polytheist ['pɑlɪ,θi•ɪst] *s* politeísta *mf*

polytheistic [,pɑlɪθi'ɪstɪk] *adj* politeísta

polyvalent [,pɑlɪ'velənt] *adj* (chem, bact) polivalente

pomade [pə'med] *s* pomada

pomegranate ['pɑm,grænɪt] *s* (*shrub*) granado; (*fruit*) granada

pom•mel ['pʌməl] o ['pɑməl] *s* (*on hilt of sword*) pomo; (*on saddle*) perilla ‖ *v* (*pret & pp* -meled o -melled; *ger* -meling o -melling*) *tr* apuñear, aporrear

pomp [pɑmp] *s* pompa, fausto

pompadour ['pɑmpə,dur] *s* copete *m*

pompous ['pɑmpəs] *adj* pomposo, faustoso

pon•cho ['pɑntʃo] *s* (*pl* -chos) capote *m* de monte, poncho

pond [pɑnd] *s* estanque *m*, charca

ponder ['pɑndər] *tr* ponderar ‖ *intr* meditar; **to ponder over** ponderar, considerar con cuidado

pl
po

ponderous ['pɑndərəs] *adj* pesado, inmanejable; tedioso, fastidioso
pond scum *s* lama, verdín *m*
poniard ['pɑnjərd] *s* puñal *m*
pontiff ['pɑntɪf] *s* pontífice *m*
pontoon [pɑn'tun] *s* pontón *m*
po•ny ['poni] *s* (*pl* **-nies**) jaca, caballito; (*for drinking liquor*) (coll) pequeño vaso; (*translation used dishonestly in school*) (coll) chuleta
poodle ['pudəl] *s* perro de lanas
pool [pul] *s* (*small puddle*) charco; (*for swimming*) piscina; (*game*) trucos; (*in certain games*) polla, puesta; combinación de intereses; caudales unidos para un fin ‖ *tr* mancomunar
pool'room' *s* sala de trucos
pool table *s* mesa de trucos
poop [pup] *s* popa; (*deck*) toldilla
poor [pur] *adj* (*having few possessions; arousing pity*) pobre; (*not good, inferior*) malo
poor box *s* cepillo, caja de limosnas
poor'house' *s* asilo de pobres, casa de caridad
poorly ['purli] *adv* mal
poor white *s* pobre *mf* de la raza blanca (*en el sur de los EE.UU.*)
pop. *abbr* **popular, population**
pop [pɑp] *s* estallido, taponazo; bebida gaseosa ‖ *v* (*pret & pp* **popped;** *ger* **popping**) *tr* hacer estallar; **to pop the question** (coll) hacer una declaración de amor ‖ *intr* estallar
pop'corn' *s* rosetas, palomitas (de maíz)
pope [pop] *s* papa *m*
popeyed ['pɑp,aɪd] *adj* de ojos saltones; (*with fear, surprise, etc.*) desorbitado
pop'gun' *s* tirabala
poplar ['pɑplər] *s* álamo, chopo
pop•py ['pɑpi] *s* (*pl* **-pies**) amapola
pop'py•cock' *s* (coll) necedad, tontería
popsicle ['pɑpsɪkəl] *s* polo
populace ['pɑpjəlɪs] *s* populacho; chamuchina
popular ['pɑpjələr] *adj* popular
popularize ['pɑpjələ,raɪz] *tr* popularizar, vulgarizar
populous ['pɑpjələs] *adj* populoso
porcelain ['pɔrsəlɪn] *s* porcelana
porch [pɔrtʃ] *s* porche *m*, pórtico
porcupine ['pɔrkjə,paɪn] *s* puerco espín
pore [por] *s* poro ‖ *intr*—**to pore over** estudiar larga y detenidamente
pork [pork] *s* carne *f* de cerdo
pork chop *s* chuleta de cerdo
pornography [pɔr'nɑgræfi] *s* pornografía
pornographic [,pɔrnə'græfɪk] *adj* pornográfico
porno queen ['pɔrno] *s* (slang) actriz *f* de películas pornográficas
porous ['porəs] *adj* poroso
porous plaster *s* parche poroso
porphy•ry ['pɔrfɪri] *s* (*pl* **-ries**) pórfido
porpoise ['pɔrpəs] *s* marsopa, puerco de mar; (*dolphin*) delfín *m*
porridge ['pɔrɪdʒ] *s* gachas

port [port] *adj* portuario ‖ *s* puerto; (*opening in ship's side*) portilla; (*left side of ship or airplane*) babor *m;* oporto, vino de Oporto; (mach) lumbrera
portable ['portəbəl] *adj* portátil
portal ['portəl] *s* portal *m*
portend [por'tɛnd] *tr* anunciar de antemano, presagiar
portent ['portent] *s* augurio, presagio
portentous [por'tɛntəs] *adj* portentoso, extraordinario; amenazante, ominoso
porter ['portər] *s* (*doorkeeper*) portero, conserje *m;* (*in hotels and trains*) mozo de servicio; pórter *m* (*cerveza de Inglaterra de color obscuro*)
portfoli•o [port'folɪ,o] *s* (*pl* **-os**) cartera
port'hole' *s* porta, portilla
porti•co ['portɪ,ko] *s* (*pl* **-coes** o **-cos**) pórtico
portion ['porʃən] *s* porción; (*dowry*) dote *m* & *f*
port•ly ['portli] *adj* (*comp* **-lier;** *super* **-liest**) corpulento; grave, majestuoso
port of call *s* escala
portrait ['portret] o ['portrɪt] *s* retrato; **to sit for a portrait** retratarse
portray [por'tre] *tr* retratar
portrayal [por'tre•əl] *s* representación gráfica; retrato, descripción acertada
Portugal ['portʃəgəl] *s* Portugal *m*
Portu•guese ['portʃə,giz] *adj* portugués ‖ *s* (*pl* **-guese**) portugués *m*
port wine *s* vino de Oporto
pose [poz] *s* pose *f* ‖ *tr* plantear (*una pregunta, cuestión, etc.*) ‖ *intr* posar (*para retratarse; como modelo*); tomar una postura afectada; **to pose as** hacerse pasar por
posh [pɑʃ] *adj* (slang) elegante; (slang) lujoso, suntuoso
position [pə'zɪʃən] *s* posición; empleo, puesto; opinión; **to be in a position to** estar en condiciones de
positive ['pɑzɪtɪv] *adj* positivo ‖ *s* positiva
possess [pə'zɛs] *tr* poseer
possession [pə'zɛʃən] *s* posesión
possible ['pɑsɪbəl] *adj* posible
possum ['pɑsəm] *s* zarigüeya; **to play possum** hacer la mortecina
post [post] *s* (*piece of wood, metal, etc. set upright*) poste *m;* (*position*) puesto; (*job*) puesto, cargo; casa de correos ‖ *tr* fijar (*carteles*); echar al correo; apostar, situar; tener al corriente; **post no bills** se prohibe fijar carteles
postage ['postɪdʒ] *s* porte *m,* franqueo; **postage will be paid by addressee** a franquear en destino
postage meter *s* franqueadora
postage stamp *s* sello de correo; estampilla, timbre *m* (Am)
postal ['postəl] *adj* postal ‖ *s* postal *f*
postal card *s* tarjeta postal
postal permit *s* franqueo concertado
postal savings bank *s* caja postal de ahorros
post card *s* tarjeta postal
post'date' *s* posfecha ‖ **post'date'** *tr* posfechar

poster ['postər] s cartel m, cartelón m, letrero; póster m

posterity [pɑs'tɛrɪti] s posteridad

postern ['postərn] s postigo, portillo

post'haste' adv por la posta, a toda prisa

posthumous ['pɑstʃuməs] adj póstumo

post·man ['postmən] s (pl -men [mən]) cartero

post'mark' s matasellos m, timbre m de correos ǁ tr matasellar, timbrar

post'mas'ter s administrador m de correos

post-mortem [,post'mortəm] adj posterior a la muerte ǁ s examen m de un cadáver

post office s casa de correos

post'-of'fice box s apartado de correos, casilla postal

postpaid ['post,ped] adj con porte pagado, franco de porte

postpone [post'pon] tr aplazar

postscript ['post,skrɪpt] s posdata

posttonic [post'tɑnɪk] adj postónico

posture ['pɑstʃər] s postura ǁ intr adoptar una postura

post'war' adj de la posguerra

po·sy ['pozi] s (pl -sies) flor f, ramillete m

pot [pɑt] s pote m; (for flowers) tiesto; (for the kitchen) caldera, olla, puchero; vaso de noche, orinal m; (in gambling) puesta; (slang) mariguana

potash ['pɑt,æʃ] s potasa

potassium [pə'tæsɪ·əm] s potasio

pota·to [pə'teto] s (pl -toes) patata, papa; (sweet potato) batata, buniato

potato masher s pasapuré m

potato omelet s tortilla a la española

potbellied ['pɑt,bɛlid] adj barrigón, panzudo

poten·cy ['potənsi] s (pl -cies) potencia

potent ['potənt] adj potente

potentate ['potən,tet] s potentado

potential [pə'tɛnʃəl] adj & s potencial m

pot'hang'er s llares fpl

pot'hook' s garabato

potion ['poʃən] s poción

pot'luck' s lo que hay de comer; **to take potluck** hacer penitencia

pot shot s tiro a corta distancia

potter ['pɑtər] s alfarero; ollero ǁ intr ocuparse en fruslerías

potter's clay s arcilla figulina

potter's field s cementerio de los pobres, hoyanca

potter's shop s ollería

potter's wheel s torno de alfarero

potter·y ['pɑtəri] s (pl -ies) alfarería; cacharros (de alfarería)

pouch [pautʃ] s bolsa, saquillo; (of kangaroo) bolsa; (for tobacco) petaca; valija

poulterer ['poltərər] s pollero

poultice ['poltɪs] s cataplasma f

poultry ['poltri] s aves fpl de corral

pounce [pauns] intr—**to pounce on** saltar sobre, precipitarse sobre

pound [paund] s (weight) libra; (for stray animals) corral m de concejo ǁ tr golpear; machacar, moler; encerrar en el corral de concejo; bombardear incesantemente; (to keep walking over) desempedrar ǁ intr golpear

pound'cake' s pastel m en que entra una libra de cada ingrediente; ponqué m (Am)

pound sterling s libra esterlina

pour [por] tr vaciar, verter, derramar; echar, servir (p.ej., té); escanciar (vino) ǁ intr fluir rápidamente; llover a torrentes; **to pour out of** salir a montones de (p.ej., el teatro)

pout [paut] s mala cara, puchero ǁ intr poner mala cara, hacer pucheros

poverty ['pɑvərti] s pobreza; pelazón f

POW abbr **prisoner of war**

powder ['paudər] s polvo; (for face) polvos; (explosive) pólvora ǁ tr pulverizar; (to sprinkle with powder) empolvar, polvorear

powder puff s borla para empolvarse

powder room s cuarto tocador, cuarto de aseo

powdery ['paudəri] adj (like powder) polvoriento; (sprinkled with powder) empolvado; (crumbly) quebradizo

power ['pau·ər] s (ability to act or do something; possession) poder m; (control, influence; wealth) poderío; (influential nation; energy, force, strength) potencia; **the powers that be** las autoridades, los que mandan ǁ tr accionar, impulsar

power brake s servofreno

power dive s (aer) picado con motor

power failure s interrupción de fuerza

powerful ['pau·ərfəl] adj poderoso

pow'er·house' s central eléctrica

powerless ['pau·ərlɪs] adj impotente

power line s (elec) sector m de distribución

power mower s motosegadora

power of attorney s poder m

power plant s (aer) grupo motopropulsor; (aut) grupo motor; (elec) central eléctrica, estación generadora

power steering s (aut) servodirección

power tool s herramienta motriz

pp. abbr **pages**

p.p. abbr **parcel post, postpaid**

pr. abbr **pair, present, price**

P.R. abbr **public relations**

practical ['præktɪkəl] adj práctico

practically ['præktɪkəli] adv poco más o menos

practice ['præktɪs] s práctica; uso, costumbre; ensayo; (of a profession) ejercicio; (of a doctor) clientela ǁ tr practicar; ejercitar (p.ej., la caridad); ejercer (una profesión); estudiar (p.ej., el piano); tener por costumbre ǁ intr ejercitarse; practicar la medicina; ensayarse; entrenarse, adiestrarse; **to practice as** ejercer de (p.ej., abogado)

practitioner [præk'tɪʃənər] s (medical doctor) práctico

Prague [prɑg] o [preg] s Praga

prairie ['prɛri] s pradera, llanura, pampa

prairie dog s ardilla ladradora

prairie wolf s coyote m

praise [prez] s alabanza, elogio ǁ tr alabar, elogiar

praise'wor'thy adj laudable, plausible

pram [præm] *s* cochecillo de niño

prance [præns] o [prɑns] *s* cabriola, trenzado ‖ *intr* cabriolar, trenzar

prank [præŋk] *s* travesura

prate [pret] *intr* charlar, parlotear

prattle [ˈprætəl] *s* charla, parloteo ‖ *intr* charlar, parlotear, balbucear (*un niño*)

pray [pre] *tr* implorar, rogar, suplicar; rezar (*una oración*) ‖ *intr* orar, rezar; **pray tell me** sírvase decirme

prayer [prɛr] *s* ruego, súplica; oración, rezo

prayer book *s* devocionario

preach [pritʃ] *tr* predicar; aconsejar (*p.ej., la paciencia*) ‖ *intr* predicar

preacher [ˈpritʃər] *s* predicador *m*

preamble [ˈpri,æmbəl] *s* preámbulo

prebend [ˈprɛbənd] *s* prebenda

precarious [priˈkɛri·əs] *adj* precario

precaution [priˈkɔʃən] *s* precaución

precede [priˈsid] *tr & intr* preceder

precedent [ˈprɛsɪdənt] *s* precedente *m*

precept [ˈprisɛpt] *s* precepto

precinct [ˈprisɪŋkt] *s* barriada; distrito electoral

precious [ˈprɛʃəs] *adj* precioso; caro, amado; (coll) considerable ‖ *adv* (coll) muy, p.ej., **precious little** muy poco

precipice [ˈprɛsɪpɪs] *s* precipicio

precipitate [priˈsɪpɪ,tet] *adj & s* precipitado ‖ *tr* precipitar ‖ *intr* precipitarse

precipitous [prɪˈsɪpɪtəs] *adj* empinado, escarpado; (*hurried, reckless*) precipitoso

precise [prɪˈsaɪs] *adj* preciso; meticuloso

precision [prɪˈsɪʒən] *s* precisión

preclude [prɪˈklud] *tr* excluir, imposibilitar

precocious [prɪˈkoʃəs] *adj* precoz

predatory [ˈprɛdə,tori] *adj* predatorio

predicament [prɪˈdɪkəmənt] *s* apuro, situación difícil

predict [prɪˈdɪkt] *tr* predecir

prediction [prɪˈdɪkʃən] *s* predicción

predispose [,prɪdɪsˈpoz] *tr* predisponer

predominant [prɪˈdɑmɪnənt] *adj* predominante

preëminent [prɪˈɛmɪnənt] *adj* preeminente

preëmpt [prɪˈɛmpt] *tr* apropiarse o apropiarse de

preen [prin] *tr* arreglarse (*las plumas*) con el pico; **to preen oneself** componerse, vestirse cuidadosamente

pref. *abbr* **preface, preferred, prefix**

prefabricate [priˈfæbrɪ,ket] *tr* prefabricar

preface [ˈprɛfɪs] *s* prefacio, advertencia ‖ *tr* introducir, empezar

pre·fer [prɪˈfʌr] *v* (*pret & pp* **-ferred;** *ger* **-ferring**) *tr* preferir; presentar; promover

preferable [ˈprɛfərəbəl] *adj* preferible

preference [ˈprɛfərəns] *s* preferencia

prefix [ˈprifɪks] *s* prefijo ‖ *tr* prefijar

pregnan·cy [ˈprɛgnənsi] *s* (*pl* **-cies**) preñez *f*, embarazo

pregnant [ˈprɛgnənt] *adj* preñado; encinta; **to make pregnant** dejar encinta

prejudice [ˈprɛdʒədɪs] *s* prejuicio; (*detriment*) perjuicio; **to the prejudice of** con perjuicio de; **without prejudice** (law) sin detrimento de sus propios derechos ‖ *tr*

predisponer, prevenir; (*to harm*) perjudicar

prejudicial [,prɛdʒəˈdɪʃəl] *adj* perjudicial

prelate [ˈprɛlɪt] *s* prelado

pre-Lenten [priˈlɛntən] *adj* carnavalesco

prelim [prɪˈlɪm] *s* (coll) examen *m* preliminar

preliminar·y [prɪˈlɪmɪ,nɛri] *adj* preliminar ‖ *s* (*pl* **-ies**) preliminar *m*

prelude [ˈprɛljud] o [ˈprilud] *s* preludio ‖ *tr* preludiar

premeditate [priˈmɛdɪ,tet] *tr* premeditar

premier [prɪˈmɪr] o [ˈpriˈmɪr] *s* primer ministro, presidente *m* del consejo

première [preˈmjɛr] o [ˈprimɪ·ər] *s* estreno; actriz *f* principal

premise [ˈprɛmɪs] *s* premisa; **on the premises** en el local mismo; **premises** predio, local *m*

premium [ˈprimɪ·əm] *s* premio; (ins) prima

premonition [,priməˈnɪʃən] *s* presagio; presentimiento

preoccupancy [priˈɑkjəpənsi] *s* preocupación

preoccupation [priˈɑkjəˈpeʃən] *s* preocupación

preoccu·py [priˈɑkjə,paɪ] *v* (*pret & pp* **-pied**) *tr* preocupar

prepaid [priˈped] *adj* pagado por adelantado; con porte pagado

preparation [,prɛpəˈreʃən] *s* preparación; (*e.g., for a trip*) preparativo; (pharm) preparado

preparatory [prɪˈpærə,tori] *adj* preparativo, preparatorio

prepare [prɪˈpɛr] *tr* preparar ‖ *intr* prepararse

preparedness [prɪˈpɛrɪdnɪs] o [prɪˈpɛrdnɪs] *s* preparación; preparación militar

pre·pay [priˈpe] *v* (*pret & pp* **-paid**) *tr* pagar por adelantado

preponderant [prɪˈpɑndərənt] *adj* preponderante

preposition [,prɛpəˈzɪʃən] *s* preposición

prepossessing [,pripəˈzɛsɪŋ] *adj* atractivo, simpático

preposterous [prɪˈpɑstərəs] *adj* absurdo, ridículo

prep school [prɛp] *s* (coll) escuela preparatoria

prerecorded [,prirɪˈkɔrdɪd] *adj* (rad & telv) grabado de antemano

prerequisite [,priˈrɛkwɪzɪt] *s* requisito previo

prerogative [prɪˈrɑgətɪv] *s* prerrogativa

Pres. *abbr* **Presbyterian, President**

presage [ˈprɛsɪdʒ] *s* presagio ‖ [prɪˈsedʒ] *tr* presagiar

Presbyterian [,prɛzbɪˈtɪrɪ·ən] *adj & s* presbiteriano

prescribe [prɪˈskraɪb] *tr & intr* prescribir

prescription [prɪˈskrɪpʃən] *s* prescripción; (pharm) receta

presence [ˈprɛzəns] *s* presencia

present [ˈprɛzənt] *adj* presente ‖ *s* presente *m*, regalo ‖ [prɪˈzɛnt] *tr* presentar, obsequiar

presentable [prɪˈzɛntəbəl] *adj* bien apersonado

presentation [,prɛzənˈteʃən] o [,prizənˈteʃən] *s* presentación

presentation copy s ejemplar m de cortesía con dedicatoria del autor

presentiment [prɪ'zɛntɪmənt] s presentimiento

presently ['prɛzəntli] adv luego, dentro de poco

preserve [prɪ'zʌrv] s conserva, compota; (for game) vedado ‖ tr conservar; preservar, proteger

preserved fruit s dulce m de almíbar

preside [prɪ'zaɪd] intr presidir; **to preside over** presidir

presiden•cy ['prɛzɪdənsi] s (pl -cies) presidencia

president ['prɛzɪdənt] s presidente m; (of a university) rector m

pres'i•dent-e•lect' s presidente m electo (todavía sin gobierno)

press [prɛs] s apretón m, empujón m; (e.g., of business) urgencia; muchedumbre; (machine for printing, for making wine; newspapers and newspapermen) prensa; (printing) imprenta; (closet) armario; **to go to press** entrar en prensa ‖ tr apretar (p.ej., un botón); (in a press) prensar; planchar (la ropa); imprimir (discos de fonógrafo); oprimir (una tecla); apresurar; abrumar; apremiar, instar; insistir

press agent s agente m de publicidad

press conference s conferencia de prensa, rueda de prensa

pressing ['prɛsɪŋ] adj apremiante, urgente ‖ s planchado

press release s comunicado de prensa

pressure ['prɛʃər] s presión; premura, urgencia

pressure cooker ['kʊkər] s olla de presión, cocina de presión

pressurize ['prɛʃə,raɪz] tr (aer) sobrecargar

prestige [prɛs'tiʒ] o ['prɛstɪdʒ] s prestigio

presumably [prɪ'zuməbli] adv probablemente, verosímilmente

presume [prɪ'zjum] tr presumir; suponer; **to presume to** tomar la libertad de ‖ intr suponer; **to presume on** o **upon** abusar de

presumption [prɪ'zʌmpʃən] s presunción; pretensión

presumptuous [prɪ'zʌmptʃu•əs] adj confianzudo, desenvuelto

presuppose [,prisə'poz] tr presuponer

pretend [prɪ'tɛnd] tr aparentar, fingir ‖ intr fingir; **to pretend to** pretender (p.ej., el trono)

pretender [prɪ'tɛndər] s pretendiente mf

pretense [prɪ'tɛns] o ['pritɛns] s pretensión; fingimiento; **under false pretenses** con apariencias fingidas; **under pretense of** so pretexto de

pretentious [prɪ'tɛnʃəs] adj pretencioso, aparatoso; ambicioso, vasto

pretonic [prɪ'tɑnɪk] adj pretónico

pretrial prisoner s preso preventivo

pret•ty ['prɪti] adj (comp -tier; super -tiest) bonito, lindo; (coll) bastante, considerable ‖ adv algo; bastante; muy

prevail [prɪ'vel] intr prevalecer, reinar; **prevail on** o **upon** persuadir

prevailing [prɪ'velɪŋ] adj prevaleciente, reinante; común, corriente

prevalent ['prɛvələnt] adj común, corriente, en boga

prevaricate [prɪ'værɪ,ket] intr mentir

prevent [prɪ'vɛnt] tr impedir ‖ intr obstar

prevention [prɪ'vɛnʃən] s (el) impedir; medidas de precaución

preventive [prɪ'vɛntɪv] adj & s preservativo

preview ['pri,vju] s vista anticipada; (private showing) (mov) preestreno; (showing of brief scenes for advertising) (mov) avance m

previous ['priv•əs] adj previo, anterior ‖ adv previamente; **previous to** con anterioridad a, antes de

prewar ['pri,wɔr] adj prebélico, de preguerra

prey [pre] s presa; víctima; **to be prey to** ser presa de ‖ intr cazar; **to prey on** o **upon** apresar y devorar; pillar, robar; tener preocupado

price [praɪs] s precio ‖ tr apreciar, estimar; fijar el precio de, poner precio a; pedir el precio de

price control s intervención de precios

price cutting s reducción de precios

price fixing s fijación de precios

price freezing s congelación de precios

priceless ['praɪslɪs] adj inapreciable, sin precio; (coll) absurdo, divertido

price war s guerra de precios

prick [prɪk] s (pointed weapon or instrument) espiche m; (sharp point) púa; (small hole made with sharp point) agujerillo; (spur) aguijón m; (jab; sharp pain) pinchazo, punzada; **to kick against the pricks** dar coces contra el aguijón ‖ tr pinchar; marcar con agujerillos; dar una punzada a; (to sting) punzar; **to prick up** aguzar (las orejas)

prick•ly ['prɪkli] adj (comp -lier; super -liest) espinoso, puado, punzante

prickly heat s salpullido causado por el calor

prickly pear s (plant) chumbera; (fruit) higo chumbo

pride [praɪd] s orgullo; arrogancia; **the pride of** la flor y nata de ‖ tr—**to pride oneself on** o **upon** enorgullecerse de

priest [prist] s sacerdote m

priesthood ['prist•hʊd] s sacerdocio

priest•ly ['pristli] adj (comp -lier; super -liest) sacerdotal

prig [prɪg] s gazmoño, pedante mf

prim [prɪm] adj (comp prim•mer; super prim•mest) estirado, relamido

primary ['praɪ,mɛri] o ['praɪməri] adj primario ‖ s (pl -ries) elección preliminar; (elec) primario

prime [praɪm] adj primero, principal; (of the best quality) primo ‖ s flor f, juventud, primavera; alba, aurora; (la) flor y nata; (of a degree) (phys) minuto; (typ) virgulilla; **prime of life** edad viril, flor f de edad ‖ tr informar de antemano; cebar (un arma de fuego, una bomba, un carburador); (for painting) imprimar; poner la primera capa o la primera mano a; poner virgulilla a

pr
pr

prime minister s primer ministro
primer ['prɪmər] s cartilla ‖ ['praɪmər] s (for paint) aprestado m; (mach) cebador m
primitive ['prɪmɪtɪv] adj primitivo
primp [prɪmp] tr acicalar, engalanar ‖ intr acicalarse, engalanarse
prim'rose' s primavera
primrose path s vida dada a los placeres de los sentidos
prin. abbr **principal**
prince [prɪns] s príncipe m; **to live like a prince** portarse como un príncipe
Prince of Wales s príncipe m de Gales
princess ['prɪnsɪs] s princesa
principal ['prɪnsɪpəl] adj principal ‖ s principal m, jefe m; (of a school) director m; criminal mf; (main sum, not interest) capital m
principle ['prɪnsɪpəl] s principio
print [prɪnt] s marca, impresión; (printed cloth) estampado; (design in printed cloth) diseño; grabado, lámina; letras de molde; (act of printing) impresión; edición; tirada; (phot) impresión; **in print** impreso, publicado; **out of print** agotado ‖ tr imprimir; estampar; hacer imprimir; publicar; escribir en caracteres de imprenta; (phot) tirar, imprimir; (fig) imprimir o grabar (en la memoria)
printed matter s impresos
printer ['prɪntər] s impresor m
printer's devil s aprendiz m de imprenta
printer's ink s tinta de imprenta
printer's mark s pie m de imprenta
printing ['prɪntɪŋ] s impresión; caracteres impresos; edición; tirada; letras de mano imitación de las impresas; (phot) tiraje m
printout ['prɪnt,aʊt] s (computer) impreso derivado
prior ['praɪ•ər] adj anterior ‖ adv anteriormente; **prior to** antes de
priori•ty [praɪ'ɔrɪti] s (pl -ties) prioridad; **of the highest priority** de máxima prioridad
prism ['prɪzəm] s prisma m
prison ['prɪzən] s cárcel f, prisión ‖ tr encarcelar
prisoner ['prɪzənər] o ['prɪznər] s preso; (mil) prisionero
prison van s coche m celular
pris•sy ['prɪsi] adj (comp -sier; super -siest) (coll) remilgado, melindroso
priva•cy ['praɪvəsi] s (pl -cies) aislamiento, retiro; secreto, reserva
private ['praɪvɪt] adj particular, privado; confidencial; ‖ s soldado raso; **in private** privadamente; en secreto; **privates** partes pudendas
private first class s soldado de primera, aspirante m a cabo
private hospital s clínica, casa de salud
private property s bienes mpl particulares
private view s día m de inauguración
privet ['prɪvɪt] s aligustre m
privilege ['prɪvɪlɪdʒ] s privilegio
priv•y ['prɪvi] adj privado; **privy to** enterado secretamente de ‖ s (pl -ies) letrina

prize [praɪz] s premio; (something captured) presa ‖ tr apreciar, estimar
prize fight s partido de boxeo profesional
prize fighter s boxeador m profesional
prize ring s cuadrilátero de boxeo
pro [pro] prep en pro de ‖ s (pl **pros**) voto afirmativo; (coll) deportista mf profesional; **the pros and the cons** el pro y el contra
probabili•ty [,prabə'bɪlɪti] s (pl -ties) probabilidad; acontecimiento probable; tiempo probable
probable ['prabəbəl] adj probable
probation [pro'beʃən] s libertad vigilada; período de prueba
probe [prob] s encuesta, indagación; (instrument) sonda ‖ tr indagar; sondar
problem ['prabləm] s problema m
procedure [pro'sidʒər] s procedimiento
proceed [pro'sid] intr proceder ‖ **proceeds** ['prosidz] spl producto, ganancia
proceeding [pro'sidɪŋ] s procedimiento; **proceedings** actas; diligencias
process ['prasɛs] s procedimiento; proceso, progreso; **in the process of time** con el tiempo ‖ tr elaborar; (electronic data) procesar
processing ['prasɛsɪŋ] s (electronic data) procesamiento
process server ['sʌrvər] s entregador m de la citación
proclaim [pro'klem] tr proclamar
proclitic [pro'klɪtɪk] adj & s proclítico
procommunist [pro'kamjənɪst] adj & s filocomunista mf
procrastinate [pro'kræstɪ,net] tr diferir de un día para otro ‖ intr tardar, no decidirse
procure [pro'kjur] tr conseguir, obtener ‖ intr alcahuetear
prod [prad] s aguijada; empuje m ‖ v (pret & pp **prodded**; ger **prodding**) tr aguijar, pinchar; aguijonear, estimular
prodigal ['pradɪgəl] adj & s pródigo
prodigious [pro'dɪdʒəs] adj & s prodigioso, maravilloso; enorme, inmenso
prodi•gy ['pradɪdʒi] s (pl -gies) prodigio
produce ['prodjus] o ['prodʌs] s producto; productos agrícolas ‖ [pro'djus] o [pro'dus] tr producir; presentar (p.ej., un drama) al público; (geom) prolongar
product ['pradəkt] s producto
production [pro'dʌkʃən] s producción
profane [pro'fen] adj profano; (language) injurioso, blasfemo ‖ s profano ‖ tr profanar
profani•ty [pro'fænɪti] s (pl -ties) blasfemia
profess [pro'fɛs] tr & intr profesar
profession [pro'fɛʃən] s profesión
professor [pro'fɛsər] s profesor m, catedrático; (coll) profesor, maestro
proffer ['prafər] s oferta, propuesta ‖ tr ofrecer, proponer
proficient [pro'fɪʃənt] adj perito, diestro, hábil
profile ['profaɪl] s perfil m ‖ tr perfilar
profit ['prafɪt] s provecho, beneficio, utilidad, ganancia; **at a profit** con ganancia ‖ tr servir, ser de utilidad a ‖ intr sacar

provecho, ganar; adelantar, mejorar; **to profit by** aprovechar, sacar provecho de
profitable [ˈprɑfɪtəbəl] *adj* provechoso
profit and loss *s* ganancias y pérdidas
profiteer [ˌprɑfɪˈtɪr] *s* logrero, explotador *m* ‖ *intr* logrear, explotar
profit margin *s* excedente *m* de ganancia
profit taking *s* realización de beneficios
profligate [ˈprɑflɪgɪt] *adj* & *s* libertino; pródigo
pro forma invoice [pro ˈfɔrmə] *s* factura simulada
profound [proˈfaund] *adj* profundo
profuse [proˈfjus] *adj* (*extravagant*) pródigo; (*abundant*) profuso
proge‧ny [ˈprɑdʒeni] *s* (*pl* **-nies**) prole *f*
progno‧sis [prɑgˈnosɪs] *s* (*pl* **-ses** [siz]) pronóstico
progno‧sis [prɑgˈnɑstɪk] *s* pronóstico
program [ˈprogræm] *s* programa *m;* (*computer*) **program(me)** programa (para ordenador) ‖ *tr* programar; (*computer*) **program(me)** programar
program(m)er [ˈprogræmər] *s* (*computer*) programador *m*, programadora
program(m)ing [ˈprogræmɪŋ] *s* (*computer*) programación (de ordenadores)
progress [ˈprɑgrɛs] *s* progreso; progresos; **to make progress** hacer progresos ‖ [prəˈgrɛs] *intr* progresar
progressive [prəˈgrɛsɪv] *adj* progresivo; (pol) progresista ‖ *s* (pol) progresista *mf*
prohibit [proˈhɪbɪt] *tr* prohibir
project [ˈprɑdʒɛkt] *s* proyecto ‖ [prəˈdʒɛkt] *tr* proyectar ‖ *intr* proyectarse
projectile [prəˈdʒɛktɪl] *s* proyectil *m*
projection [prəˈdʒɛkʃən] *s* proyección
projector [prəˈdʒɛktər] *s* proyector *m*
proletarian [ˌprolɪˈtɛrɪən] *adj* & *s* proletario
proletariat [ˌprolɪˈtɛrɪət] *s* proletariado
proliferate [prəˈlɪfəˌret] *intr* proliferar
prolific [prəˈlɪfɪk] *adj* prolífico
prolix [ˈprolɪks] o [proˈlɪks] *adj* difuso, verboso
prologue [ˈprolɔg] *s* prólogo
prolong [proˈlɔŋ] *tr* prolongar
promenade [ˌprɑmɪˈned] *s* paseo; garbeo; baile *m* de gala ‖ *intr* pasear o pasearse
promenade deck *s* (naut) cubierta de paseo
prominent [ˈprɑmɪnənt] *adj* prominente
promise [ˈprɑmɪs] *s* promesa ‖ *tr* & *intr* prometer
promising young man *s* joven *m* de esperanzas
promissory [ˈprɑmɪˌsori] *adj* promisorio
promissory note *s* pagaré *m*
promonto‧ry [ˈprɑmənˌtori] *s* (*pl* **-ries**) promontorio
promote [prəˈmot] *tr* promover; fomentar
promotion [prəˈmoʃən] *s* promoción; fomento
prompt [prɑmpt] *adj* pronto, puntual; listo, dispuesto ‖ *tr* incitar, mover; inspirar, sugerir; (theat) apuntar
prompter [ˈprɑmptər] *s* (theat) apuntador *m*
prompter's box *s* (theat) concha

promulgate [ˈprɑməlˌget] o [proˈmʌlget] *tr* promulgar
prone [pron] *adj* postrado boca abajo; extendido sobre el suelo; dispuesto, propenso
prong [prɔŋ] o [prɑŋ] *s* punta (*de un tenedor, horquilla, etc.*)
pronoun [ˈpronaun] *s* pronombre *m*
pronounce [prəˈnauns] *tr* pronunciar
pronouncement [prəˈnaunsmənt] *s* declaración; decisión, opinión
pronunciamen‧to [prəˌnʌnsɪˈmɛnto] *s* (*pl* **-tos**) pronunciamiento
pronunciation [prəˌnʌnsɪˈeʃən] o [prəˌnʌnʃɪˈeʃən] *s* pronunciación
proof [pruf] *adj* de prueba; **proof against** a prueba de ‖ *s* prueba
proof'read'er *s* corrector *m* de pruebas
prop [prɑp] *s* apoyo, puntal *m;* (*to hold up a plant*) rodrigón *m;* **props** (theat) accesorios ‖ *v* (*pret* & *pp* **propped;** *ger* **propping**) *tr* apoyar, apuntalar; poner un rodrigón a
propaganda [ˌprɑpəˈgændə] *s* propaganda
propagate [ˈprɑpəˌget] *tr* propagar
proparoxytone [ˌprɑpærˈɑksɪˌton] *adj* & *s* proparoxítono
pro‧pel [prəˈpɛl] *v* (*pret* & *pp* **-pelled;** *ger* **-pelling**) *tr* propulsar, impeler
propeller [prəˈpɛlər] *s* hélice *f*
propensi‧ty [prəˈpɛnsɪti] *s* (*pl* **-ties**) propensión
proper [ˈprɑpər] *adj* propio, conveniente; decente, decoroso; exacto, justo
proper‧ty [ˈprɑpərti] *s* (*pl* **-ties**) propiedad; **properties** (theat) accesorios
property owner *s* propietario de bienes raíces
prophe‧cy [ˈprɑfɪsi] *s* (*pl* **-cies**) profecía
prophe‧sy [ˈprɑfɪˌsai] *v* (*pret* & *pp* **-sied**) *tr* profetizar
prophet [ˈprɑfɪt] *s* profeta *m*
prophetess [ˈprɑfɪtɪs] *s* profetisa
prophylactic [ˌprɑfɪˈlæktɪk] *adj* & *s* profiláctico
propitiate [prəˈpɪʃɪˌet] *tr* propiciar
propitious [prəˈpɪʃəs] *adj* propicio
prop'jet *s* turbohélice *m*
proportion [prəˈporʃən] *s* proporción; **in proportion as** a medida que; **out of proportion** desproporcionado ‖ *tr* proporcionar
proportionate [prəˈporʃənɪt] *adj* proporcionado
proposal [prəˈpozəl] *s* propuesta; oferta de matrimonio
propose [prəˈpoz] *tr* proponer ‖ *intr* proponer matrimonio; **to propose to** pedir la mano a; proponerse a + *inf*
proposition [ˌprɑpəˈzɪʃən] *s* proposición, propuesta
propound [prəˈpaund] *tr* proponer
proprietor [prəˈpraɪətər] *s* propietario
proprietress [prəˈpraɪətrɪs] *s* propietaria
proprie‧ty [prəˈpraɪəti] *s* (*pl* **-ties**) corrección, conducta decorosa, conveniencia; **proprieties** cánones *mpl* sociales, convenciones
propulsion [prəˈpʌlʃən] *s* propulsión
prorate [proˈret] *tr* prorratear

pr
pr

prosaic [pro'ze•ık] *adj* prosaico
proscribe [pro'skraıb] *tr* proscribir
prose [proz] *adj* prosaico ‖ *s* prosa
prosecute ['prɑsı,kjut] *tr* llevar a cabo; (law) procesar
prosecutor ['prɑsı,kjutər] *s* acusador *m*, demandante *mf; (lawyer)* fiscal *m*
proselyte ['prɑsı,laıt] *s* prosélito
prose writer *s* prosista *mf*
prosody ['prɑsədi] *s* métrica
prospect ['prɑspɛkt] *s* vista; esperanza; probabilidad de éxito; cliente *mf* o comprador *m* probable ‖ *tr & intr* prospectar; **to prospect for** buscar (*p.ej., oro, petróleo*)
prosper ['prɑspər] *tr & intr* prosperar
prosperi•ty [prɑs'pɛrıti] *s (pl -ties)* prosperidad
prosperous ['prɑspərəs] *adj* próspero
prostitute ['prɑstı,tjut] *s* prostituta; güila (Mex) ‖ *tr* prostituir
prostrate ['prɑstret] *adj* postrado, prosternado ‖ *tr* postrar
prostration [prɑs'treʃən] *s* postración
Prot. *abbr* **Protestant**
protagonist [pro'tægənıst] *s* protagonista *mf*
protect [prə'tɛkt] *tr* proteger
protection [prə'tɛkʃən] *s* protección
protégé ['protə,ʒe] *s* protegido
protégée ['protə,ʒe] *s* protegida
protein ['proti•ın] o ['protin] *s* proteína
pro-tempore [pro'tɛmpəri] *adj* interino
protest ['protɛst] *s* protesta ‖ [pro'tɛst] *tr & intr* protestar
protestant ['prɑtıstənt] *adj & s* protestante *mf* ‖ **Protestant** *adj & s* protestante *mf*
prothonotar•y [pro'θɑnə,teri] *s (pl -ies)* escribano principal *(de un tribunal)*
protocol ['protə,kɑl] *s* protocolo
protoplasm ['protə,plæzəm] *s* protoplasma *m*
prototype ['protə,taıp] *s* prototipo
protozoön [,protə'zo•ɑn] *s* protozoo
protract [pro'trækt] *tr* prolongar
protrude [pro'trud] *intr* resaltar
proud [praud] *adj* orgulloso; soberbio; glorioso
proud flesh *s* carnosidad, bezo
prov. *abbr* **provincialism**
prove [pruv] *v (pret* **proved**; *pp* **proved** o **proven**) *tr* probar ‖ *intr* resultar; **to prove to be** venir a ser, resultar
proverb ['prɑvərb] *s* proverbio
provide [prə'vaıd] *tr* proporcionar, suministrar ‖ *intr*—**to provide for** proveer a; asegurarse (*el porvenir*)
provided [prə'vaıdıd] *conj* a condición (de) que, con tal (de) que
providence ['prɑvıdəns] *s* providencia
providential [,prɑvı'dɛnʃəl] *adj* providencial
providing [prə'vaıdıŋ] *conj* var de **provided**
province ['prɑvıns] *s* provincia; (*sphere of activity or knowledge*) competencia
proving ground ['pruvıŋ] *s* campo de ensayos
provision [prə'vıʒən] *s* provisión; condición, estipulación
provi•so [prə'vaızo] *s (pl -sos* o *-soes)* condición, estipulación, salvedad

provoke [prə'vok] *tr* provocar
provoking [prə'vokıŋ] *adj* provocador, irritante
prow [prau] *s* proa
prowess ['prau•ıs] *s* proeza; destreza
prowl [praul] *intr* cazar al acecho, rodar, vagabundear
prowler ['praulər] *s* rondador *m;* ladrón *m*
proximity [prɑk'sımıti] *s* proximidad
prox•y ['prɑksi] *s (pl -ies)* poder *m,* poderhabiente *m*
prude [prud] *s* mojigato, gazmoño
prudence ['prudəns] *s* prudencia
prudent ['prudənt] *adj* prudente
pruder•y ['prudəri] *s (pl -ies)* mojigatería, gazmoñería
prudish ['prudıʃ] *adj* mojigato, gazmoño
prune [prun] *s* ciruela pasa ‖ *tr* podar, escamondar
pry [praı] *v (pret & pp* **pried**) *tr*—**to pry open** forzar con la alzaprima o palanca; **to pry out of** arrancar (*p.ej., un secreto*) a (*una persona*) ‖ *intr* entremeterse; **to pry into** entremeterse en
P.S. *abbr* **postscript, Privy Seal**
psalm [sɑm] *s* salmo
Psalter ['sɔltər] *s* Salterio
pseudo ['sudo] o ['sjudo] *adj* supuesto, falso, fingido
pseudonym ['sudənım] o ['sjudənım] *s* seudónimo
Psyche ['saıki] *s* Psique *f*
psychedelic [,saıkə'dɛlık] *adj* psicodélico
psychiatrist [saı'kaı•ətrıst] *s* psiquiatra *mf*
psychiatry [saı'kaı•ətri] *s* psiquiatria
psychic ['saıkık] *adj* psíquico; mediúmnico ‖ *s* médium *mf*
psychoanalysis [,saıko•ə'nælısıs] *s* psicoanálisis *m*
psychoanalyze [,saıko'ænə,laız] *tr* psicoanalizar
psychologic(al) [,saıkə'lɑdʒık(əl)] *adj* psicológico
psychologist [saı'kɑlədʒıst] *s* psicólogo
psychology [saı'kɑlədʒi] *s* psicología
psychopath ['saıkə,pæθ] *s* psicópata *mf*
psycho•sis [saı'kosıs] *s (pl -ses* [siz]) psicosis *f;* estado mental
psychotherapy [,saıkə'θɛrəpi] *s* psicoterapia
psychotic [saı'kɑtık] *adj & s* psicótico
pt. *abbr* **part, pint, point**
pub [pʌb] *s* (Brit) taberna
puberty ['pjubərti] *s* pubertad
public ['pʌblık] *adj & s* público
publication [,pʌblı'keʃən] *s* publicación
public conveyance *s* vehículo de servicio público
publicity [pʌb'lısıti] *s* publicidad
publicize ['pʌblı,saız] *tr* publicar
public library *s* biblioteca municipal
public relations *spl* relaciones publicas
public school *s* (U.S.A.) escuela pública; (Brit) internado privado con dote
public speaking *s* elocución, oratoria

public spirit *s* celo patriótico del buen ciudadano

public toilet *s* quiosco de necesidad

public transportation *s* transporte colectivo

public utility *s* empresa de servicio público; **public utilities** acciones emitidas por empresas de servicio público

publish [\`pʌblɪʃ] *tr* publicar

publisher [\`pʌblɪʃər] *s* editor *m*

publishing house *s* casa editorial

pucker [\`pʌkər] *s* (*small fold*) frunce *m;* pliego mal hecho ‖ *tr* fruncir (*una tela; la frente*); plegar mal ‖ *intr* plegarse mal

pudding [\`pudɪŋ] *s* budín *m,* pudín *m*

puddle [\`pʌdəl] *s* aguazal *m,* charco

pudg·y [\`pʌdʒi] *adj* (*comp* **-ier;** *super* **-iest**) gordinflón, rechoncho

puerile [\`pju·ərɪl] *adj* pueril

puerili·ty [ˌpju·ə\`rɪlɪti] *s* (*pl* **-ties**) puerilidad

Puerto Rican [\`pwɛrto \`rikən] *adj* & *s* puertorriqueño

puff [pʌf] *s* soplo vivo; (*of smoke*) bocanada; (*in clothing*) bullón *m;* borla de polvos; pastelillo de crema o jalea; alabanza exagerada; ráfaga, ventolera ‖ *tr* soplar; hinchar; alabar exageradamente ‖ *intr* soplar; hincharse; enorgullecerse exageradamente

puff paste *s* hojaldre *m* & *f*

pugilism [\`pjudʒɪˌlɪzəm] *s* pugilismo

pugilist [\`pjudʒɪlɪst] *s* pugilista *m*

pug-nosed [\`pʌgˌnozd] *adj* braco

puke [pjuk] *s* (slang) vómito ‖ *tr* & *intr* (slang) vomitar

pull [pul] *s* estirón *m,* tirón *m;* (*on a cigar*) chupada; (*of a door*) tirador *m,* (slang) enchufe *m,* buenas aldabas ‖ *tr* tirar de; torcer (*un ligamento*); (typ) sacar (*una impresión a prueba*); **to pull down** demoler, derribar; bajar (*p.ej., la cortinilla*); abatir, degradar; **to pull oneself together** componerse, recobrar la calma ‖ *intr* tirar; moverse despacio, moverse con esfuerzo; **to pull at** tirar de (*p.ej., la corbata*); chupar (*p.ej., un cigarro*); **to pull for** (slang) abogar por, ayudar; **to pull for oneself** tirar por su lado; **to pull in** llegar (*un tren*) a la estación; **to pull out** partir (*un tren*) de la estación; **to pull strings** usar enchufe; **to pull through** salir a flote; recobrar la salud

pullet [\`pulɪt] *s* polla

pulley [\`puli] *s* polea

pulp [pʌlp] *s* pulpa; (*to make paper*) pasta; (*of tooth*) bulbo

pulpit [\`pulpɪt] *s* púlpito

pulsate [\`pʌlset] *intr* pulsar; vibrar

pulsation [pʌl\`seʃən] *s* pulsación; vibracion

pulse [pʌls] *s* pulso; **to feel** o **take the pulse of** tomar el pulso a

pulverize [\`pʌlvəˌraɪz] *tr* pulverizar

pumice stone [\`pʌmɪs] *s* pómez *f,* piedra pómez

pum·mel [\`pʌməl] *v* (*pret* & *pp* **-meled** o **-melled;** *ger* **-meling** o **-melling**) *tr* apuñear, aporrear

pump [pʌmp] *s* bomba; (*slipperlike shoe*) escarpín *m,* zapatilla ‖ *tr* elevar o sacar (*agua*) por medio de una bomba; (coll)

tirar de la lengua a (*una persona*); **to pump up** hinchar, inflar (*un neumático*)

pump handle *s* guimbalete *m*

pumpkin [\`pʌmpkɪn] o [\`puŋkɪn] *s* calabaza común; **some pumpkins** persona de muchas campanillas

pump-priming [\`pʌmpˌpraɪmɪŋ] *s* inyección económica (*por parte del gobierno*)

pun [pʌn] *s* equívoco, retruécano ‖ *v* (*pret* & *pp* **punned;** *ger* **punning**) *intr* decir equívocos, jugar del vocablo

punch [pʌntʃ] *s* puñetazo; (*tool*) punzón *m;* (*for tickets*) sacabocado; (*drink*) ponche *m* ‖ *tr* dar un puñetazo a; taladrar, perforar (*un billete, una tarjeta*)

punch bowl *s* ponchera

punch card *s* tarjeta perforada, ficha perforada

punch clock *s* reloj *m* registrador de tarjetas

punch'-drunk' *adj* atontado (*p.ej., por una tunda de golpes*); completamente aturdido

punched tape *s* cinta perforada

punching bag *s* punching *m,* boxibalón *m*

punch line *s* broche *m* de oro, colofón *m* del artículo

punctilious [pʌŋk\`tɪli·əs] *adj* puntilloso, pundonoroso

punctual [\`pʌŋktʃu·əl] *adj* puntual

punctuate [\`pʌŋktʃu,et] *tr* puntuar; acentuar, destacar; interrumpir ‖ *intr* puntuar

punctuation [ˌpʌŋktʃu\`eʃən] *s* puntuación

punctuation mark *s* signo de puntuación

puncture [\`pʌŋktʃər] *s* puntura; (*of a tire*) picadura, pinchazo ‖ *tr* pinchar, picar, perforar

punc'ture-proof' *adj* a prueba de pinchazos

pundit [\`pʌndɪt] *s* erudito, sabio

pungent [\`pʌndʒənt] *adj* picante; estimulante

punish [\`pʌnɪʃ] *tr* castigar; penalizar; (coll) maltratar

punishable [\`pʌnɪʃəbəl] *adj* delictivo

punishment [\`pʌnɪʃmənt] *s* castigo; (coll) maltrato

punk [pʌŋk] *adj* (slang) malo, de mala calidad ‖ *s* yesca, pebete *m;* (*decayed wood*) hupe *m;* (slang) pillo, gambero

punster [\`pʌnstər] *s* equivoquista *mf,* vocablista *mf*

pu·ny [\`pjuni] *adj* (*comp* **-nier;** *super* **-niest**) encanijado, débil; insignificante, mezquino

pup [pʌp] *s* cachorro

pupil [\`pjupəl] *s* alumno; (*of the eye*) pupila

puppet [\`pʌpɪt] *s* títere *m;* (*doll*) muñeca; (*person controlled by another*) maniquí *m*

puppet government *s* gobierno de monigotes

puppet show *s* función de títeres

puppy love [\`pʌpi] *s* (coll) primeros amores

purchase [\`pʌrtʃəs] *s* compra; agarre *m* firme ‖ *tr* comprar

purchasing power *s* poder adquisitivo

pure [pjur] *adj* puro

purgative [\`pʌrgətɪv] *adj* & *s* purgante *m*

purge [pʌrdʒ] *s* purga ‖ *tr* purgar

puri·fy [\`pjurɪˌfaɪ] *v* (*pret* & *pp* **-fied**) *tr* purificar

puritan [\`pjurɪtən] *adj* & *s* puritano ‖ **Puritan** *adj* & *s* puritano

purity [ˈpjʊrɪti] *s* pureza
purloin [pərˈlɔɪn] *tr & intr* robar, hurtar
purple [ˈpʌrpəl] *adj* purpurado, rojo morado ‖ *m* púrpura, rojo morado
purport [ˈpʌrport] *s* significado, idea principal ‖ [pərˈport] *tr* significar, querer decir
purpose [ˈpʌrpəs] *s* intención, propósito; fin *m*, objeto; **for the purpose** al efecto; **for what purpose?** ¿con qué fin?; **on purpose** adrede, de propósito; **to good purpose** con buenos resultados; **to no purpose** sin resultado; **to serve one's purpose** servir para el caso
purposely [ˈpʌrpəsli] *adv* adrede, de propósito
purr [pʌr] *s* ronroneo ‖ *intr* ronronear
purse [pʌrs] *s* bolsa; (*money collected for charity*) colecta ‖ *tr* fruncir
purser [ˈpʌrsər] *s* contador *m* de navío, comisario de a bordo
purse snatcher [ˈsnætʃər] *s* carterista *mf*
purse strings *spl* cordones *mpl* de la bolsa; **to hold the purse strings** tener las llaves de la caja
pursue [pərˈsu] o [pərˈsju] *tr* perseguir (*al que huye*); proseguir (*lo empezado*); seguir (*una carrera*); dedicarse a
pursuit [pərˈsut] o [pərˈsjut] *s* persecución; prosecución; (*e.g., of happiness*) busca o búsqueda; empleo
pursuit plane *s* caza *m*, avión *m* de caza
purvey [pərˈve] *tr* proveer, suministrar
pus [pʌs] *s* pus *m*
push [pʊʃ] *s* empuje *m*, empujón *m* ‖ *tr* empujar; pulsar (*un botón*); extender (*p.ej., conquistas*); **to push around** (coll) tratar a empujones; **to push aside** hacer a un lado; **to push through** forzar (*p.ej., una resolución*) ‖ *intr* empujar; **to push off** (coll) irse, salir; (naut) desatracarse
push button *s* botón *m* de llamada, botón interruptor
push'-but'ton control *s* mando por botón
push'cart' *s* carretilla de mano
pusher [ˈpʊʃər] *s* (*drugs*) púcher *m*
pushing [ˈpʊʃɪŋ] *adj* emprendedor; entremetido, agresivo
pushy [ˈpʊʃi] *adj* (coll) agresivo; presumido
pusillanimous [ˌpjusɪˈlænɪməs] *adj* pusilánime
puss [pʊs] *interj* ¡miz! ‖ *s* micho; chica, muchacha; (slang) cara, boca
puss in the corner *s* las cuatro esquinas
puss·y [ˈpʊsi] *s* (*pl* -ies) michito
pussy willow *s* sauce norteamericano de amentos muy sedosos
pustule [ˈpʌstʃʊl] *s* pústula

put [pʊt] *v* (*pret & pp* **put;** *ger* **putting**) *tr* poner, colocar; arrojar, echar, lanzar; hacer (*una pregunta*); **to put across** llevar a cabo; hacer aceptar; **to put aside** poner aparte; rechazar; ahorrar (*dinero*); **to put down** anotar, apuntar; sofocar (*una insurrección*); rebajar (*los precios*); **to put off** posponer; deshacerse de; **to put on** ponerse (*la ropa*); poner en escena; llevar (*p.ej., un drama a la pantalla*); accionar (*un freno*); cargar (*impuestos*); fingir; atribuir; **to put oneself out** incomodarse, molestarse; afanarse, desvivirse; **to put out** extender (*la mano*); apagar (*el fuego, la luz*); poner en la calle; dar a luz, publicar; decepcionar; (sport) sacar fuera de la partida; **to put over** o **through** (coll) llevar a cabo; **to put up** construir, edificar; abrir (*un paraguas*); conservar (*fruta, legumbres*); (coll) incitar ‖ *intr* dirigirse; **to put on** fingir; **to put up** parar, hospedarse; **to put up with** aguantar, tolerar
put'-out' *adj* contrariado, enojado
putrid [ˈpjutrɪd] *adj* pútrido; corrompido, perverso
putsch [pʊtʃ] *s* intentona de sublevación; sublevación; cuartelazo
putter [ˈpʌtər] *intr* trabajar sin orden ni sistema; **to putter around** ocuparse en fruslerías, temporizar
put·ty [ˈpʌti] *s* (*pl* -ties) masilla ‖ *v* (*pret & pp* -tied) *tr* enmasillar
putty knife *s* cuchillo de vidriero, espátula
put'-up' *adj* (coll) premeditado con malicia
puzzle [ˈpʌzəl] *s* enigma *m;* acertijo, rompecabezas *m* ‖ *tr* confundir, poner perplejo; **to puzzle out** descifrar ‖ *intr* estar perplejo; **to puzzle over** tratar de descifrar
puzzler [ˈpʌzlər] *s* quisicosa
PW *abbr* **prisoner of war**
pyg·my [ˈpɪgmi] *adj* pigmeo ‖ *s* (*pl* -mies) pigmeo
pylon [ˈpaɪlɑn] *s* pilón *m*
pyramid [ˈpɪrəmɪd] *s* pirámide *f* ‖ *tr* aumentar (*su dinero*) comprando o vendiendo al crédito y empleando las ganancias para comprar o vender más
pyre [paɪr] *s* pira
Pyrenean [ˌpɪrɪˈniən] *adj* pirineo
Pyrenees [ˈpɪrɪˌniz] *spl* Pirineos
pyrites [paɪˈraɪtiz] o [ˈpaɪraɪts] *s* pirita
pyrotechnical [ˌpaɪrəˈtɛknɪkəl] *adj* pirotécnico
pyrotechnics [ˌpaɪrəˈtɛknɪks] *spl* pirotecnia
python [ˈpaɪθən] *s* pitón *m*
pythoness [paɪˈθənɪs] *s* pitonisa
pyx [pɪks] *s* píxide *f*, copón *m*

Q

Q, q [kju] decimoséptima letra del alfabeto inglés
Q. *abbr* **quarto, queen, question, quire**

Q.M. *abbr* **quartermaster**
qr. *abbr* **quarter, quire**
qt. *abbr* **quantity, quart**

qu. *abbr* **quart, quarter, quarterly, queen, query, question**

quack [kwæk] *adj* falso ‖ *s* graznido del pato; charlatán *m;* medicastro, curandero ‖ *intr* parpar (*el pato*)

quacker•y ['kwækəri] *s* (*pl* **-ies**) charlatanismo

quadrangle ['kwɑd,ræŋgəl] *s* cuadrángulo; patio cuadrangular

quadrant ['kwɑdrənt] *s* cuadrante *m*

quadroon [kwɑd'run] *s* cuarterón *m*

quadruped ['kwɑdrʊ,pɛd] *adj* & *s* cuadrúpedo

quadruple ['kwɑdrʊpəl] o [kwɑd'rupəl] *adj* & *s* cuádruple *m* ‖ *tr* cuadruplicar ‖ *intr* cuadruplicarse

quadruplet ['kwɑdrʊ,plɛt] o [kwɑd'ruplɛt] *s* cuatrillizo

quaff [kwɑf] o [kwæf] *s* trago grande ‖ *tr* & *intr* beber en gran cantidad

quail [kwel] *s* codorniz *f* ‖ *intr* acobardarse

quaint [kwent] *adj* curioso, raro; afectado, rebuscado; fantástico, singular

quake [kwek] *s* temblor *m*, terremoto ‖ *intr* temblar

Quaker ['kwekər] *adj* & *s* cuáquero

Quaker meeting *s* reunión de cuáqueros; reunión en que hay poca conversación

quali•fy ['kwɑlɪ,faɪ] *v* (*pret* & *pp* **-fied**) *tr* calificar; capacitar, habilitar ‖ *intr* capacitarse, habilitarse

quali•ty ['kwɑlɪti] *s* (*pl* **-ties**) (*characteristic; virtue*) calidad; (*property, attribute*) cualidad; (*of a sound*) timbre *m*

quality of life *s* calidad de vida

qualm [kwɑm] *s* escrúpulo de conciencia; duda, inquietud; (*nausea*) basca

quanda•ry ['kwɑndəri] *s* (*pl* **-ries**) incertidumbre, perplejidad

quanti•ty ['kwɑntɪti] *s* (*pl* **-ties**) cantidad

quan•tum ['kwɑntəm] *adj* cuántico ‖ *s* (*pl* **-ta** [tə]) cuanto, quántum *m*

quantum theory *s* teoría cuántica

quarantine ['kwɑrən,tin] o ['kwɔrən,tin] *s* cuarentena; estación de cuarentena ‖ *tr* poner en cuarentena

quar•rel ['kwɑrəl] o ['kwɔrəl] *s* disputa, riña, pelea; **to have no quarrel with** no estar en desacuerdo con; **to pick a quarrel with** tomarse con ‖ *v* (*pret* & *pp* **-reled** o **-relled**) *ger* **-reling** o **-relling**) *intr* disputar, reñir, pelear

quarrelsome ['kwɑrəlsəm] o ['kwɔrəlsəm] *adj* pendenciero

quar•ry ['kwɑri] o ['kwɔri] *s* (*pl* **-ries**) cantera, pedrera; caza, presa ‖ *v* (*pret* & *pp* **-ried**) *tr* sacar de una cantera; extraer, sacar

quart [kwɔrt] *s* cuarto de galón

quarter ['kwɔrtər] *adj* cuarto ‖ *s* cuarto, cuarta parte; (*three months*) trimestre *m;* moneda de 25 centavos; cuarto de luna; barrio; región, lugar *m;* (*clemency*) (mil) cuartel *m;* **quarters** morada, vivienda; local *m;* (mil) cuarteles *mpl;* **to take up quarters** alojarse ‖ *tr* descuartizar

quar'ter•deck' *s* alcázar *m*

quar'ter-hour' *s* cuarto de hora; **on the quarter-hour** al cuarto en punto cada cuarto de hora

quarter•ly ['kwɔrtərli] *adj* trimestral ‖ *adv* trimestralmente ‖ *s* (*pl* **-lies**) publicación o revista trimestral

quar'ter•mas'ter *s* (mil) comisario; (nav) cabo de brigadas

quartet [kwɔr'tɛt] *s* cuarteto

quartz [kwɔrts] *s* cuarzo

quartz watch *s* reloj de cuarzo

quasar ['kwesɑr] *s* (astr) objeto del espacio, fuente *f* cuasiestelar de radio

quash [kwɑʃ] *tr* sofocar, reprimir; anular, invalidar

quaver ['kwevər] *s* temblor *m*, estremecimiento; (mus) trémolo ‖ *intr* temblar, estremecerse

quay [ki] *s* muelle *m*, desembarcadero

queen [kwin] *s* reina; (*in chess*) dama o reina; (*in cards*) dama (*que corresponde al caballo*); abeja reina

queen bee *s* abeja reina, abeja maestra; (slang) marimandona, la que lleva la voz cantante

queen dowager *s* reina viuda

queen•ly ['kwinli] *adj* (*comp* **-lier;** *super* **-liest**) de reina; como reina; regio

queen mother *s* reina madre

queen olive *s* aceituna de la reina, aceituna gordal

queen post *s* péndola

queen's English *s* inglés castizo

queer [kwɪr] *adj* curioso, raro; estrambótico, estrafalario; aturdido, indispuesto; (coll) sospechoso, misterioso ‖ *tr* (slang) echar a perder; (slang) comprometer

quell [kwɛl] *tr* sofocar, reprimir; mitigar (*una pena o dolor*)

quench [kwɛntʃ] *tr* apagar (*el fuego; la sed*); sofocar, reprimir; (electron) amortiguar

que•ry ['kwɪri] *s* (*pl* **-ries**) pregunta; signo de interrogación; duda ‖ *v* (*pret* & *pp* **-ried**) *tr* interrogar; marcar con signode interrogación; dudar

ques. *abbr* **question**

quest [kwɛst] *s* búsqueda; (*of the Holy Grail*) demanda; **in quest of** en busca de

question ['kwɛstʃən] *s* pregunta; (*problem for discussion*) cuestión; asunto, proposición; **beside the question** que no viene al caso; **beyond question** fuera de duda; **out of the question** imposible, indiscutible; **to ask a question** hacer una pregunta; **to be a question of** tratarse de, ser cuestión de; **to call in question** poner en duda; **without question** sin duda ‖ *tr* interrogar; cuestionar (*poner en tela de juicio*)

questionable ['kwɛstʃənəbəl] *adj* cuestionable

question mark *s* punto interrogante, signo de interrogación

questionnaire [,kwɛstʃən'ɛr] *s* cuestionario

queue [kju] *s* (*of hair*) coleta; (*of people*) cola ‖ *intr* hacer cola

quibble [kwɪbəl] *intr* sutilizar

pu
qu

quick [kwɪk] *adj* rápido, veloz; ágil, vivo; despierto, listo; **the quick and the dead** los vivos y los muertos; **to cut** o **to sting to the quick** herir en lo vivo, tocar en la herida

quicken [ˈkwɪkən] *tr* acelerar, avivar; animar ‖ *intr* acelerarse; animarse

quick′lime′ *s* cal viva

quick lunch *s* servicio de la barra, servicio rápido

quick′sand′ *s* arena movediza

quick′sil′ver *s* azogue *m*

quiet [ˈkwaɪ•et] *adj* (still) quieto; silencioso; (*market*) (com) encalmado; **to keep quiet** callarse ‖ *s* quietud; silencio; **on the quiet** a las calladas ‖ *tr* aquietar; acallar ‖ *intr* aquietarse; callarse; **to quiet down** calmarse ‖ *interj* ¡silencio!

quill [kwɪl] *s* pluma de ave; cañón *m* de pluma; (*of hedgehog, porcupine*) púa

quilt [kwɪlt] *s* edredón *m*, colcha ‖ *tr* acolchar

quince [kwɪns] *s* membrillo

quinine [ˈkwaɪnaɪn] *s* quinina

quinsy [ˈkwɪnzi] *s* cinanquia, esquinencia

quintessence [kwɪnˈtɛsəns] *s* quintaesencia

quintet [kwɪnˈtɛt] *s* quinteto

quintuplet [kwɪnˈtjuplɛt] o [kwɪnˈtuplɛt] *s* quintillizo

quip [kwɪp] *s* chufleta, pulla ‖ *v* (*pret & pp* **quipped;** *ger* **quipping**) *tr* decir en son de burla ‖ *intr* echar pullas

quire [kwaɪr] *s* mano *f* de papel; (bb) alzado

quirk [kwʌrk] *s* excentricidad, rareza; sutileza; vuelta repentina

quit [kwɪt] *adj* libre, descargado; **to be quits** estar desquitados; **to call it quits** no seguir; descontinuar; **to cry quits** pedir treguas ‖ *v* (*pret & pp* **quit** o **quitted;** *ger* **quitting**) *tr* dejar ‖ *intr* irse; (coll) dejar de trabajar

quite [kwaɪt] *adv* enteramente; verdaderamente; (coll) bastante, muy

quitter [ˈkwɪtər] *s* remolón *m;* (*of a cause*) desertor *m*

quiver [ˈkwɪvər] *s* temblor *m;* (*to hold arrows*) aljaba, carcaj *m* ‖ *intr* temblar

quixotic [kwɪksˈɑtɪk] *adj* quijotesco

quiz [kwɪz] *s* (*pl* **quizzes**) examen *m;* interrogatorio ‖ *v* (*pret & pp* **quizzed;** *ger* **quizzing**) *tr* examinar; interrogar

quiz game *s* torneo de preguntas y respuestas

quiz program *s* programa *m* de preguntas y respuetas, torneo radiofónico

quiz section *s* grupo de práctica

quizzical [ˈkwɪzɪkəl] *adj* curioso; cómico; burlón

quoin [kɔɪn] o [kwɔɪn] *s* esquina; piedra angular; (*wedge*) cuña ‖ *tr* (typ) acuñar

quoit [kwɔɪt] o [kɔɪt] *s* herrón *m*, tejo; **quoits** *ssg* hito

quondam [ˈkwɑndæm] *adj* antiguo, de otro tiempo

quorum [ˈkwɔrəm] *s* quórum *m*

quota [ˈkwotə] *s* cuota

quotation [kwoˈteʃən] *s* (*from a book*) cita; (*of prices*) cotización

quotation marks *spl* comillas

quote [kwot] *s* (coll) cita; (coll) cotización; **close quote** fin de la cita; **quotes** (coll) comillas ‖ *tr & intr* citar; cotizar; **quote cito**

quotient [ˈkwoʃənt] *s* cociente *m*

q.v. *abbr* **quod vide** (Lat) **which see**

R

R, r [ɑr] decimoctava letra del alfabeto inglés

r. *abbr* **railroad, railway, road, rod, ruble, rupee**

R. *abbr* **railroad, railway, Regina** (Lat) **Queen; Republican, response, Rex** (Lat) **King; River, Royal**

rabbet [ˈræbɪt] *s* barbilla, rebajo ‖ *tr* embarbillar, rebajar

rab•bi [ˈræbaɪ] *s* (*pl* **-bis** o **-bies**) rabino

rabbit [ˈræbɪt] *s* conejo

rabbit ears *spl* (telv, rad) antena de conejo

rabble [ˈræbəl] *s* canalla, gentuza, palomilla, chamuchina

rabble rouser [ˈraʊzər] *s* populachero, alborotapueblos *mf*

rabies [ˈrebiz] o [ˈrebɪˌiz] *s* rabia

raccoon [ræˈkun] *s* mapache *m*, oso lavador

race [res] *s* (*people of same stock*) raza; (*contest in speed, etc.*) carrera; (*channel to lead water*) caz *m* ‖ *tr* competir con, en una carrera; hacer correr de prisa; hacer funcionar (*un motor*) a velocidad excesiva ‖ *intr* correr de prisa; correr en una carrera; competir en una carrera; embalarse (*un motor*); (naut) regatear

race horse *s* caballo de carreras

race riot *s* disturbio racista

race track *s* pista de carreras

racial [ˈreʃəl] *adj* racial

racing car *s* coche *m* de carreras

racism [ˈresɪzəm] *s* racismo

racist [ˈresɪst] *adj & s* racista

rack [ræk] *s* (*sort of shelf*) estante *m;* (*to hang clothes*) percha; (*for fodder for cattle*) pesebre *m;* (*for baggage*) red *f* de equipaje; (*for guns*) armero; (*bar made to gear with a pinion*) cremallera; **to go to rack and ruin** desencijarse; ir al desastre ‖ *tr* estirar, forzar; atormentar; despedazar; oprimir, agobiar; **to rack off** trasegar (*el vino*); **to rack one's brains** calentarse la cabeza, devanarse los sesos

racket ['rækɪt] *s* raqueta; (*noise*) baraúnda, alboroto; (*slang*) trapisonda, trapacería; **to raise a racket** armar un alboroto

racketeer [,rækɪ'tir] *s* trapisondista *mf*, trapacista *mf* ‖ *intr* trapacear

rack railway *s* ferrocarril *m* de cremallera

rac•y ['resi] *adj* (*comp* **-ier;** *super* **-iest**) espiritoso, chispeante; perfumado; (*somewhat indecent*) picante

radar ['redɑr] *s* radar *m*

radar scanner *s* explorador *m* de radar

radiant ['redɪ•ənt] *adj* radiante, resplandeciente; (*cheerful, smiling*) radiante

radiate ['redɪ,et] *tr* radiar; difundir (*p.ej., felicidad*) ‖ *intr* radiar, irradiar

radiation [,redɪ'eʃən] *s* radiación

radiation sickness *s* enfermedad de radiación, mal *m* de rayos

radiator ['redɪ,etər] *s* radiador *m*

radiator cap *s* tapón *m* de radiador

radical ['rædɪkəl] *adj & s* radical *m*

radi•o ['redɪ,o] *s* (*pl* **-os**) radio *f;* radiograma *m* ‖ *tr* radiodifundir

radioactive [,redɪ•o'æktɪv] *adj* radiactivo

radioactive waste *s* residuos radiactivos

radio amateur *s* radioaficionado

radio announcer *s* locutor *m* de radio

ra'dio•broad'cast'ing *s* radiodifusión

radio frequency *s* radiofrecuencia

radio listener *s* radioescucha *mf*, radioyente *mf*

radiology [,redɪ'ɑlədʒi] *s* radiología

radio ministry *s* (theol) ministerio radiofónco

radio network *s* red *f* de emisoras

radio newscaster *s* cronista *mf* de radio

radio receiver *s* radiorreceptor *m*

radio set *s* aparato de radio

ra'dio•(tel'e)phone' *s* radioteléfono

ra'di•o•ther'apy *s* radioterapia

radish ['rædɪ] *s* rábano

radium ['redɪ•əm] *s* radio

radi•us ['redɪ•əs] *s* (*pl* **-i** [,ɑɪ] o **-uses**) radio; (*range of operation*) radio; **within a radius of en** . . . a la redonda

raffle ['ræfəl] ‖ *tr & intr* rifar

raft [ræft] *s* armadía, balsa; (*coll*) gran número

rafter ['ræftər] *s* cabrio, contrapar *m*, traviesa

rag [ræg] *s* trapo; **to chew the rag** (*slang*) dar la lengua; **in rags** hilachento

ragamuffin ['rægə,mʌfɪn] *s* pelagatos *m*; golfo, chiquillo harapioso

rag baby o **rag doll** *s* muñeca de trapo

rage [redʒ] *s* rabia; **to be all the rage** estar en boga, hacer furor; **to fly into a rage** montar en cólera

ragged ['rægɪd] *adj* andrajoso; (*edge*) cortado en dientes

ragpicker ['ræg,pɪkər] *s* andrajero, trapero

rag'weed' *s* ambrosía

raid [red] *s* incursión, invasión; ataque de sorpresa; ataque aéreo ‖ *tr* invadir; atacar inesperadamente; capturar (*p.ej., la policía un garito*)

rail [rel] *s* carrill *m*, riel *m;* (*railing*) barandilla; (*of a bridge*) guardalado; (*at a bar*) apoyo para los pies; palo; **by rail** por ferrocarril; **rails** títulos o valores de ferrocarril ‖ *tr* poner barandilla a ‖ *intr* quejarse amargamente; **to rail at** injuriar, ultrajar

rail fence *s* cerca hecha de palos horizontales

rail'head' *s* (rr) cabeza de línea

railing ['relɪŋ] *s* barandilla, pasamano

rail'road' *adj* ferroviario ‖ *s* ferrocarril *m* ‖ *tr* (coll) llevar a cabo con demasiada precipitación; (slang) encarcelar falsamente ‖ *intr* trabajar en el ferrocarril

railroad crossing *s* paso a nivel

rail'way' *adj* ferroviario ‖ *s* ferrocarril *m*

raiment ['remənt] *s* prendas de vestir, indumentaria

rain [ren] *s* lluvia; **rain or shine** llueva o no, con buen o mal tiempo ‖ *tr & intr* llover

rain'bow' *s* arco iris

rain'coat' *s* impermeable *m*

rain'fall' *s* lluvia repentina; precipitación acuosa

rain•y ['reni] *adj* (*comp* **-ier;** *super* **-iest**) lluvioso

rainy day *s* día lluvioso; tiempo futuro de posible necesidad

raise [rez] *s* aumento ‖ *tr* levantar; aumentar; criar (*a niños, animales*); cultivar (*plantas*); reunir (*dinero*); suscitar (*una duda*); resucitar (*a los muertos*); dejarse (*barba, bigote*); poner (*una objeción*); plantear (*una pregunta*); levantar (*tropas; un sitio*); (math) elevar; (*to come in sight of*) (naut) avistar

raisin ['rezən] *s* pasa, uva seca

rake [rek] *s* rastro, rastrillo; (*person*) calavera *m*, libertino ‖ *tr* rastrillar; **to rake together** acumular (*dinero*)

rake'-off' *s* (slang) dinero obtenido ilícitamente

rakish ['rekɪʃ] *adj* airoso, gallardo; listo, vivo; libertino

ral•ly ['ræli] *s* (*pl* **-lies**) reunión popular, reunión política; recuperación, recobro ‖ *v* (*pret & pp* **-lied**) *tr* reunir; reanimar; recobrar (*la fuerza, la salud, el ánimo*) ‖ *intr* reunirse; recobrarse (*p.ej., los precios en la Bolsa*); recobrar la fuerza, la salud, el ánimo; **to rally to the side of** acudir a, ir en socorro de

ram [ræm] *s* (*male sheep*) morueco, carnero padre; (*device for battering, crushing, etc.*) pisón *m* ‖ *v* (*pret & pp* **rammed;** *ger* **ramming**) *tr* dar contra, chocar en; atestar, rellenar ‖ *intr* chocar; **to ram into** chocar en

ramble ['ræmbəl] *s* paseo ‖ *intr* pasear; serpentear (*p.ej., un río*); extenderse serpenteando (*las enredaderas*); (*to wander aimlessly; to talk in an aimless way*) divagar

rami•fy ['ræmɪ,faɪ] *v* (*pret & pp* **-fied**) *tr* ramificar ‖ *intr* ramificarse

ram'jet'(engine) *s* motor *m* autorreactor; estatorreactor *m*

ramp [ræmp] *s* rampa

qu
ra

rampage ['ræmpedʒ] *s* alboroto; **to go on a rampage** alborotar, comportarse como un loco

rampart ['ræmpɑrt] *s* muralla, terraplén *m;* amparo, defensa

ram'rod' *s* atacador *m*, baqueta

ram'shack'le *adj* desvencijado, destartalado

ranch [ræntʃ] *s* granja, hacienda

rancid ['rænsɪd] *adj* rancio

rancor ['ræŋkər] *s* rencor *m*

random ['rændəm] *adj* casual, fortuito; **at random** al azar, a la ventura

range [rendʒ] *s* (*row, line*) fila, hilera; (*scope, reach*) alcance *m*; (*of speeds, prices, etc.*) escala; campo de tiro; terreno de pasto; (*of a boat or airplane*) autonomía; (*of the voice*) extensión; (*of colors*) gama, serie *f;* (*stove*) cocina económica; **within range of** al alcance de ‖ *tr* alinear; recorrer (*un terreno*); ir a lo largo de (*la costa*); arreglar, ordenar ‖ *intr* fluctuar, variar (*entre ciertos límites*); extenderse; divagar, errar; **to range over** recorrer

range finder *s* telémetro

rank [ræŋk] *adj* exuberante, lozano; denso, espeso; grosero; maloliente; excesivo; incorregible, rematado; indecente, vulgar ‖ *s* categoría, rango; condición, posición; distinción; (*line of soldiers standing abreast*) fila; (mil) empleo, grado ‖ *tr* alinear; ordenar; tener grado o posición más alta que ‖ *intr* ocupar el último grado; **to rank high** ocupar alta posición; ser tenido en alta estima; sobresalir; **to rank low** ocupar baja posición; **to rank with** estar al nivel de; tener el mismo grado que

rank and file *s* soldados de fila; pueblo, gente *f* común

rankle ['ræŋkəl] *tr* enconar, irritar ‖ *intr* enconarse

ransack ['rænsæk] *tr* registrar, escudriñar; robar, saquear

ransom ['rænsəm] *s* rescate *m* ‖ *tr* rescatar

rant [rænt] *intr* desvariar, despotricar

rap [ræp] *s* golpe corto y seco; (*noise*) taque *m*; (coll) ardite *m*, bledo; (slang) crítica mordaz; **to take the rap** (slang) pagar la multa; sufrir las consecuencias ‖ *v* (*pret & pp* **rapped;** *ger* **rapping**) *tr* golpear con golpe corto y seco; decir vivamente; (slang) criticar mordazmente ‖ *intr* golpear con golpe corto y seco; **to rap at the door** tocar a la puerta

rapacious [rə'peʃəs] *adj* rapaz

rape [rep] *s* rapto; (*of a woman*) estupro, violación ‖ *tr* raptar; estuprar, violar

rapid ['ræpɪd] *adj* rápido ‖ **rapids** *spl* (*of a river*) rápidos

rap'id-fire' *adj* de tiro rápido; hecho vivamente

rapier ['repɪ•ər] *s* estoque *m*, espadín *m*

rapt [ræpt] *adj* arrebatado, extático, transportado; absorto

rapture ['ræptʃər] *s* embeleso, éxtasis *f*, rapto

rare [rɛr] *adj* raro; (*word*) poco usado; (*meat*) poco asado; (*gem*) precioso

rare bird *s* mirlo blanco

rare•fy ['rɛrɪ,faɪ] *v* (*pret & pp* **-fied**) *tr* enrarecer ‖ *intr* enrarecerse

rarely ['rɛrli] *adv* rara vez

rascal ['ræskəl] *s* bellaco, bribón *m*, pícaro; pergenio

rash [ræʃ] *adj* temerario ‖ *s* brote *m*, salpullido, erupción

rasp [ræsp] *o* [rɑsp] *s* escofina; (*sound of a rasp*) sonido áspero ‖ *tr* escofinar; irritar, molestar; decir con voz ronca ‖ *intr* hacer sonido áspero

raspber•ry ['ræz,bɛri] *o* ['rɑz,bɛri] *s* (*pl* **-ries**) frambuesa, sangüesa

raspberry bush *s* frambueso, sangüeso

rat [ræt] *s* rata; (*false hair*) (coll) postizo; **to smell a rat** (coll) olerse una trama, sospechar una intriga

ratchet ['rætʃɪt] *s* trinquete *m*

rate [ret] *s* (*amount or degree measured in proportion to something else*) razón *f;* (*of interest*) tipo; velocidad; precio; **at any rate** de todos modos; **at the rate of** a razón de ‖ *tr* valuar; estimar, juzgar; clasificar ‖ *intr* ser considerado, ser tenido; estar clasificado

rate of exchange *s* tipo de cambio

rate table *s* baremo

rather ['ræðər] *o* ['rɑðər] *adv* algo, un poco; bastante; antes, más bien; mejor dicho; por el contrario; muy, mucho; **rather than** antes que, más bien que ‖ *interj* ¡ya lo creo!

rati•fy ['rætɪ,faɪ] *v* (*pret & pp* **-fied**) *tr* ratificar

ra•tio ['reʃo] *o* ['reʃɪ,o] *s* (*pl* **-tios**) (math) razón *f;* (math) cociente *m*

ration ['reʃən] *o* ['ræʃən] *s* ración ‖ *tr* racionar

ration book *s* cartilla de racionamiento

ration coupon *s* cupón *m* de racionamiento

rational ['ræʃənəl] *adj* racional

rat poison *s* matarratas *m*; raticida

rat race *s* (coll) lucha diaria por ganarse el pan

rattle ['rætəl] *s* (*number of short, sharp sounds*) traqueteo; (*noise-making device*) carraca, matraca; (*child's toy*) sonajero; baraúnda; (*in the throat*) estertor *m* ‖ *tr* tabletear, traquetear; (*to confuse*) (coll) atortolar, desconcertar; **to rattle off** decir rápidamente ‖ *intr* tabletear, traquetear

rat'tle•snake' *s* serpiente *f* de cascabel

rat'trap' *s* ratonera; trance apurado, atolladero

raucous ['rɔkəs] *adj* ronco

ravage ['rævɪdʒ] *s* destrucción, estrago, ruina ‖ *tr* destruir, estragar, arruinar

rave [rev] *intr* desvariar, delirar; bramar, enfurecerse; **to rave about** hacerse lenguas de, deshacerse en elogios de

raven ['revən] *s* cuervo

ravenous ['rævənəs] *adj* famélico, hambriento, voraz; rapaz

ravine [rə'vin] *s* cañón *m*, hondonada

ravish ['rævɪʃ] *tr* encantar, entusiasmar; raptar; violar (*a una mujer*)

ravishing ['rævɪʃɪŋ] *adj* encantador

raw [rɔ] *adj* crudo; (*cotton, silk*) en rama; inexperto, principiante; ulceroso; (*weather, day*) crudo
raw deal *s* (slang) mala pasada
raw'hide' *s* cuero en verde; látigo hecho de cuero en verde
raw material *s* primera materia, materia prima
ray [re] *s* (*of light*) rayo; (*fine line; fish*) raya
rayon ['re•ɑn] *s* rayón *m*
raze [rez] *tr* arrasar, asolar
razor ['rezər] *s* navaja de afeitar
razor blade *s* hoja u hojita de afeitar
razor strop *s* asentador *m*, suavizador *m*
razz [ræz] *s* (slang) irrisión ‖ *tr* (slang) mofarse de
R.C. *abbr* **Red Cross, Reserve Corps, Roman Catholic**
R.D. *abbr* **Rural Delivery**
reach [ritʃ] *s* alcance *m;* extensión; **out of reach (of)** fuera del alcance (de); **within reach of** al alcance de ‖ *tr* alcanzar; extender; entregar con la mano; llegar a; ponerse en contacto con; influenciar; cumplir (*cierto número de años*) ‖ *intr* alcanzar; extender la mano o el brazo; **to reach after** o **for** esforzarse por coger
react [rɪ'ækt] *intr* reaccionar
reaction [rɪ'ækʃən] *s* reacción
reactionar•y [rɪ'ækʃən,ɛri] *adj* reaccionario; mocho (Mex) ‖ *s* (*pl* **-ies**) reaccionario
read [rid] *v* (*pret & pp* **read** [rɛd]) *tr* ler; recitar (*poesía*); estudiar (*derecho*); leer en, adivinar (*el pensamiento ajeno*); **to read over** recorrer, repasar ‖ *intr* leer; rezar, p.ej., **this page reads thus** esta página reza así; leerse, p.ej., **this book reads easily** este libro se lee con facilidad; **to read on** seguir leyendo
reader ['ridər] *s* lector *m;* libro de lectura
readily ['rɛdɪli] *adv* de buena gana; fácilmente
reading ['ridɪŋ] *s* lectura; recitación
reading desk *s* atril *m*
reading glass *s* lente *f* para leer, vidrio de aumento; **reading glasses** anteojos para la lectura
reading lamp *s* lámpara de sobremesa
reading room *s* gabinete *m* de lectura; sala de lectura
read•y ['rɛdi] *adj* (*comp* **-ier;** *super* **-iest**) listo, preparado, pronto; ágil, diestro; vivo; disponible; **to make ready** preparar; prepararse ‖ *v* (*pret & pp* **-ied**) *tr* preparar ‖ *intr* prepararse
ready cash *s* dinero a la mano, dinero contante y sonante
read'y-made' clothing *s* ropa hecha
ready-made suit *s* traje hecho
reagent [rɪ'edʒənt] *s* reactivo
real ['ri•əl] *adj* real, verdadero
real estate *s* bienes *mpl* raíces, bienes inmuebles
re'al-es•tate' *adj* inmobiliario
realism ['ri•ə,lɪzəm] *s* realismo
realist ['ri•əlɪst] *s* realista *mf*
reali•ty [rɪ'ælɪti] *s* (*pl* **-ties**) realidad

realize ['ri•ə,laɪz] *tr* darse cuenta de; realizar, llevar a cabo; adquirir (*ganancias*); reportar (*ganancias*) ‖ *intr* (*to sell property for ready money*) realizar
realm [rɛlm] *s* reino
Realtor ['ri•əl,tɔr] o ['ri•əltər] *s* corredor *m* de bienes raíces
realty ['ri•əlti] *s* bienes *mpl* raíces, bienes inmuebles
ream [rim] *s* resma; **reams** (coll) montones *mpl* ‖ *tr* escariar
reap [rip] *tr & intr* (*to cut*) segar; (*to gather*), cosechar
reaper ['ripər] *s* (*person*) segador *m; ma*quina segadora
reappear [,ri•ə'pɪr] *intr* reaparecer
reapportionment [,ri•ə'pɔrʃənmənt] *s* nuevo prorrateo
rear [rɪr] *adj* posterior, trasero; de atrás ‖ *s* espalda; (*of a room*) fondo; (*of a row; of an automobile*) cola; retaguardia; (slang) culo, trasero ‖ *tr* levantar; edificar; criar, educar ‖ *intr* encabritarse (*un caballo*)
rear admiral *s* contraalmirante *m*
rear drive *s* tracción trasera
rear end *s* (*buttocks*) nalgas, pompis *m*
rearmament [ri'ɑrməmənt] *s* rearme *m*
rear'-view' mirror *s* retrovisor *m*, espejo de retrovisión
rear window *s* (aut) luneta, luneta posterior
reason ['rizən] *s* razón *f;* **by reason of** con motivo de, a causa de; **to listen to reason** meterse en razón; **to stand to reason** ser razonable ‖ *tr & intr* razonar
reasonable ['rizənəbəl] *adj* razonable
reassessment [,ri•ə'sɛsmənt] *s* nuevo amillaramiento; nueva estimación
reassure [,ri•ə'ʃur] *tr* volver a asegurar; tranquilizar
reawaken [,ri•ə'wekən] *tr* volver a despertar ‖ *intr* volver a despertarse
rebate ['ribet] o [rɪ'bet] *s* rebaja ‖ *tr* rebajar
rebel ['rɛbəl] *adj & s* rebelde *mf* ‖ **re•bel** [rɪ'bɛl] *v* (*pret & pp* **-belled;** *ger* **-belling**) *intr* rebelarse
rebellion [rɪ'bɛljən] *s* rebelión
rebellious [rɪ'bɛljəs] *adj* rebelde
re•bind [ri'baɪnd] *v* (*pret & pp* **-bound** ['baund]) reatar; (*to edge, to border*) ribetear; (bb) reencuadernar
rebirth ['ribʌrθ] o [ri'bʌrθ] *s* renacimiento
rebore [ri'bor] *tr* rectificar
rebound ['ri,baund] o [rɪ'baund] *s* rebote *m* ‖ [rɪ'baund] *intr* rebotar
rebroad•cast [ri'brɔd,kæst] *s* retransmisión ‖ *v* (*pret & pp* **-cast** o **-casted**) *tr* retransmitir
rebuff [rɪ'bʌf] *s* desaire *m*, rechazo ‖ *tr* desairar, rechazar
re•build [ri'bɪld] *v* (*pret & pp* **-built** ['bɪlt]) *tr* reconstruir, reedificar
rebuke [rɪ'bjuk] *s* reprensión ‖ *tr* reprender
re•but [rɪ'bʌt] *v* (*pret & pp* **-butted;** *ger* **-butting**) *tr* rebatir, refutar
rebuttal [rɪ'bʌtəl] *s* rebatimiento, refutación
rec. *abbr* **receipt, recipe, record, recorder**
recall [rɪ'kɔl] o ['rikɔl] *s* llamada; (*memory*) recordación, retentiva; (*repeal*) revocación,

ra
re

revocatoria; (*of a diplomat*) retirada ‖
[rɪˈkɔl] *tr* hacer volver, mandar volver;
recordar; revocar; retirar (*a un diplomático*)
recant [rɪˈkænt] *tr* retractar ‖ *intr* retractarse
re•cap [ˈriˌkæp] o [riˈkæp] *v* (*pret & pp*
-capped; *ger* **-capping**) *tr* recauchutar
recapitalization [riˌkæpɪtəlɪˈzeʃən] *s* recapitalización
recapitulation [ˌrikəˌpɪtʃəˈleʃən] *s* recapitulación
re•cast [ˈriˌkæst] *s* refundición; (*of a sentence*) reconstrucción ‖ [riˈkæst] *v* (*pret & pp* **-cast**) *tr* refundir; reconstruir (*p.ej., una frase*)
recd. o **rec'd.** *abbr* **received**
recede [rɪˈsid] *intr* (*to move back*) retroceder; (*to move away*) alejarse, retirarse; deprimirse (*p.ej., la frente de una persona*)
receipt [rɪˈsit] *s* recepción; (*acknowledgment*) recibo; (*acknowledgment of payment*) recibí *m;* (*recipe*) receta; **receipt in full** finiquito; **receipts** entradas, ingresos ‖ *tr* poner el recibí a
receive [rɪˈsiv] *tr* recibir; receptar (*cosas que son materia de delito*); **received payment** recibí ‖ *intr* recibir
receiver [rɪˈsivər] *s* receptor *m;* (*in bankruptcy*) contador *m*, síndico; receptor telefónico
receivership [rɪˈsivərˌʃɪp] *s* (law) sindicatura
receiving set *s* aparato receptor
receiving teller *s* recibidor *m* (*de un banco*)
recent [ˈrisənt] *adj* reciente
recently [ˈrisəntli] *adv* recientemente; endenantes; recién, p.ej., **recently arrived** recién llegado
receptacle [rɪˈsɛptəkəl] *s* receptáculo
reception [rɪˈsɛpʃən] *s* recepción; recibida (*welcome*) recibimiento
reception desk *s* recepción
receptionist [rɪˈsɛpʃənɪst] *s* recepcionista *f*
receptive [rɪˈsɛptɪv] *adj* receptivo
recess [rɪˈsɛs] o [ˈrisɛs] *s* intermisión; descanso; hora de recreo; (*in a surface*) depresión; (*in a wall*) hueco, nicho; escondrijo ‖ [rɪˈsɛs] *tr* ahuecar; empotrar; deprimir ‖ *intr* prorrogarse, suspenderse
recession [rɪˈsɛʃən] *s* retroceso, retirada; (*e.g., in a wall*) depresión; procesión de vuelta; contracción económica
rechargeable [rɪˈtʃɑrdʒəbəl] *adj* recargable
recipe [ˈrɛsɪˌpi] *s* receta (*de cocina*)
reciprocal [rɪˈsɪprəkəl] *adj* recíproco
reciprocity [ˌrɛsɪˈprɑsɪti] *s* reciprocidad
recital [rɪˈsaɪtəl] *s* narración; (*of music or poetry*) recital *m*
recite [rɪˈsaɪt] *tr* narrar; (*formally*) recitar
reckless [ˈrɛklɪs] *adj* atolondrado, temerario
reckon [ˈrɛkən] *tr* calcular; considerar; (coll) calcular, conjeturar ‖ *intr* calcular; **to reckon on** contar con; **to reckon with** tener en cuenta
reclaim [rɪˈklem] *tr* hacer utilizable; hacer labrantío (*un terreno*); ganar (*terreno*) a la mar; recuperar (*materiales usados*); conducir, guiar (*a los que hacen mala vida*)
reclamation [ˌrɛkləˈmeʃən] *s* (agr) roturación

recline [rɪˈklaɪn] *intr* reclinarse
recluse [rɪˈklus] o [ˈrɛklus] *s* solitario, ermitaño
recognize [ˈrɛkəgˌnaɪz] *tr* reconocer
recoil [rɪˈkɔɪl] *s* reculada; (*of a firearm*) reculada, culetazo ‖ *intr* recular, apartarse; recular (*un arma de fuego*)
recollect [ˌrɛkəˈlɛkt] *tr & intr* recordar
recombinant [rɪˈkɑmbɪnənt] *adj* (*genetics*) recombinado
recommend [ˌrɛkəˈmɛnd] *tr* recomendar
recompense [ˈrɛkəmˌpɛns] *s* recompensa ‖ *tr* recompensar
reconcile [ˈrɛkənˌsaɪl] *tr* reconciliar; **to reconcile oneself** resignarse
reconnaissance [rɪˈkɑnɪsəns] *s* reconocimiento
reconnoiter [ˌrɛkəˈnɔɪtər] o [ˌrikəˈnɔɪtər] *tr & intr* reconocer
reconquest [riˈkɑŋkwɛst] *s* reconquista
reconsider [ˌrikənˈsɪdər] *tr* reconsiderar
reconstruct [ˌrikənˈstrʌkt] *tr* reconstruir
reconversion [ˌrikənˈvʌrʒən] *s* reconversión
record [ˈrɛkərd] *s* anotación; ficha, historial *m*, historia personal; (*of a notary*) protocolo; (*of a phonograph*) disco; (educ) expediente académico; (sport) record *m*, plusmarca; **off the record** confidencialmente; **records** anales *mpl*, memorias; archivo; **to break a record** batir un record; **to have no (criminal) record** (coll) estar limpio; **to make a record** establecer un record; grabar un disco ‖ [rɪˈkɔrd] *tr* asentar; registrar; inscribir; grabar (*un sonido, una canción, un disco fonográfico, etc.*)
record breaker *s* plusmarquista *mf*
record changer [ˈtʃendʒər] *s* cambiadiscos *m*, tocadiscos automático
record holder *s* (sport) recordman *m*
recording [rɪˈkɔrdɪŋ] *adj* registrador; (wire or tape) magnetofónico ‖ *s* registro; (*of phonograph records*) grabación o grabado
recording secretary *s* secretario escribiente, secretario de actas
record player *s* tocadiscos *m*, pícap *m*, fonógrafo, vitrola, radiola
record store *s* disquería
recount [ˈriˌkaʊnt] *tr* (*to count again*) recontar ‖ [rɪˈkaʊnt] *tr* (*to narrate*) recontar
recourse [rɪˈkors] o [ˈrikors] *s* recurso; (*helping hand*) paño de lágrimas; **to have recourse to** recurrir a
recover [rɪˈkʌvər] *tr* recobrar; rescatar; **to recover consciousness** recobrar el conocimiento, volver en sí ‖ *intr* recobrarse; recobrar la salud; ganar un pleito
recover•y [rɪˈkʌvəri] *s* (*pl* **-ies**) recobro, recuperación; **past recovery** sin remedio
recreant [ˈrɛkrɪ•ənt] *adj & s* cobarde *mf*, traidor *m*
recreation [ˌrɛkrɪˈeʃən] *s* recreación
recruit [rɪˈkrut] *s* recluta *m* ‖ *tr* reclutar ‖ *intr* alistar reclutas; ganar reclutas; restablecerse, reponerse
rect. *abbr* **receipt, rector, rectory**
rectangle [ˈrɛkˌtæŋgəl] *s* rectángulo

recti•fy ['rɛktɪ,faɪ] v (pret & pp -fied) tr rectificar

rec•tum ['rɛktəm] s (pl -ta [tə]) recto

recumbent [rɪ'kʌmbənt] adj reclinado, recostado

recuperate [rɪ'kjupə,ret] tr recuperar; restablecer, reponer || intr recuperarse, recobrarse

re•cur [rɪ'kʌr] v (pret & pp -curred; ger -curring) intr volver a ocurrir; volver a presentarse (a la memoria); volver a (un asunto)

recurrent [rɪ'kʌrənt] adj repetido; periódico; (illness) recurrente

recyclable [rɪ'saɪkləbəl] adj reciclable

recycling [rɪ'saɪklɪŋ] s reciclado, reciclaje m

red [rɛd] adj (comp redder; super reddest) rojo, colorado; (wine) tinto; enrojecido, inflamado || s rojo; in the red (coll) endeudado; to see red (coll) enfurecerse || Red adj & s (communist) rojo

red'bait' tr motejar (a uno) de rojo o comunista

red'bird' s cardenal m; piranga

red-blooded ['rɛd,blʌdɪd] adj fuerte, valiente, vigoroso

red'breast' s petirrojo

red'bud' s ciclamor m del Canadá

red'cap' s (Brit) policía militar; (U.S.A.) mozo de estación

red cell s glóbulo rojo, hematíe m

red'coat' s (hist) soldado inglés

redden ['rɛdən] tr enrojecer || intr enrojecerse

redeem [rɪ'dim] tr redimir; cumplir (una promesa)

redeemer [rɪ'dimər] s redentor m

redemption [rɪ'dɛmpfən] s redención

red-haired ['rɛd,hɛrd] adj pelirrojo

red'head' s pelirrojo

red herring s artificio para distraer la atención del asunto de que se trata

red'-hot' adj candente, calentado al rojo; ardiente, entusiasta; fresco, nuevo

rediscount rate [rɪ'dɪskaʊnt] s tipo de redescuento

rediscover [,rɪdɪs'kʌvər] tr redescubrir

red'-let'ter day s día m memorable

red'-light' district s barrio de los lupanares, barrio de mala vida

red man s piel roja m

re•do ['ri'du] v (pret -did ['dɪd]; pp -done ['dʌn]) tr rehacer, repetir; refundir; reformar

redolent ['rɛdələnt] adj fragante, perfumado; redolent of que huele a

redoubt [rɪ'daʊt] s (fort) reducto

redound [rɪ'daʊnd] intr redundar; to redound to redundar en

red pepper s pimentón m

redress [rɪ'drɛs] o ['ridrɛs] s reparación; remedio || [rɪ'drɛs] tr repara; remediar

Red Ridinghood ['raɪdɪŋ,hʊd] s Caperucita Roja

red'skin' s piel roja m

red tape s expedienteo, papeleo

reduce [rɪ'djus] o [rɪ'dus] tr reducir; (mil) degradar || intr reducirse; reducir peso

reducing exercises spl ejercicios físicos para reducir peso

redundant [rɪ'dʌndənt] adj redundante

red'wood' s secoya

reed [rid] adj (organ, musical instrument) de lengüeta || s (stalk) caña; (plant) carrizo, caña; (mus) instrumento de lengüeta; (of instrument) lengüeta

reëdit [ri'ɛdɪt] tr refundir

reef [rif] s arrecife m, escollo; (min) filón m, veta || tr (naut) arrizar

reefer ['rifər] s chaquetón m; (slang) pitillo de mariguana

reek [rik] intr vahear, humear; estar bañado en sudor; estar mojado con sangre; to reek of o with oler a

reel [ril] s (spool) carrete m; (of a shuttle) broca; (of motion pictures) cinta; (sway, staggering) tambaleo; off the reel (coll) fácil y prestamente || tr aspar, devanar; to reel off (coll) narrar fácil y prestamente || intr tambalear; cejar (p.ej., el enemigo)

reëlection [,ri•ɪ'lɛkʃən] s reelección

reënlist [,ri•ɛn'lɪst] tr reenganchar || intr reengancharse

reën•try [ri'ɛntri] s (pl -tries) reingreso, nueva entrada; (return to earth's atmosphere) reentrada

reëxamination [,ri•ɛg,zæmɪ'neʃən] s reexaminación

ref. abbr referee, reference, reformation

re•fer [rɪ'fʌr] v (pret & pp -ferred; ger -ferring) tr referir || intr referirse

referee [,rɛfə'ri] s árbitro || tr & intr arbitrar

reference ['rɛfərəns] adj (library, book, work) de consulta || s referencia

referen•dum [,rɛfə'rɛndəm] s (pl -da [də]) s referéndum m

refill ['rifɪl] s relleno || [ri'fɪl] tr rellenar

refine [rɪ'faɪn] tr refinar

refinement [rɪ'faɪnmənt] s refinamiento; buena crianza, cultura

refiner•y [rɪ'faɪnəri] s (pl -ies) refinería

reflect [rɪ'flɛkt] tr reflejar; (to meditate) reflexionar; to reflect on o upon reflexionar en o sobre; perjudicar

reflection [rɪ'flɛkʃən] s (thinking) reflexión; (reflected light; image) reflejo

reflex ['riflɛks] s reflejo

reforestation [,rifɑrɪs'teʃən] o [,rifɑɪs'teʃən] s reforestación

reform [rɪ'fɔrm] s reforma || tr reformar || intr reformarse

reformation [,rɛfər'meʃən] s reformación || the reformation la Reforma

reformato•ry [rɪ'fɔrmə,tori] s (pl -ries) reformatorio

reform school s casa de corrección

refraction [rɪ'frækʃən] s refracción

refrain [rɪ'fren] s estribillo || intr abstenerse

refresh [rɪ'frɛʃ] tr refrescar || intr refrescarse

refreshing [rɪ'frɛʃɪŋ] adj confortante, restaurante

refreshment [rɪ'frɛʃmənt] s refresco

re
re

refrigerator [rɪˈfrɪdʒəretər] s heladera, nevera, refrigerador m
refrigerator car s carro o vagón frigorífico
refuel [riˈfjul] tr & intr repostar
refuge [ˈrɛfjudʒ] s refugio; expediente m, subterfugio; **to take refuge (in)** refugiarse (en)
refugee [ˌrɛfjuˈdʒi] s refugiado
refund [ˈrifʌnd] s reembolso ‖ [rɪˈfʌnd] tr reembolsar ‖ [riˈfʌnd] tr consolidar
refurnish [riˈfʌrnɪʃ] tr amueblar de nuevo
refusal [rɪˈfjuzəl] s negativa
refuse [ˈrɛfjus] s basura, desecho, desperdicios ‖ [rɪˈfjuz] tr rehusar; rechazar, no querer aceptar; **to refuse to** negarse a
refute [rɪˈfjut] tr refutar
reg. abbr **register, registrar, registry, regular**
regain [rɪˈgen] tr recobrar, recuperar; volver a alcanzar; **to regain consciousness** recobrar el conocimiento, volver en sí
regal [ˈrigəl] adj regio
regale [rɪˈgel] tr regalar, agasajar
regalia [rɪˈgelɪ•ə] spl (of an office or order) distinctivos; galas, trajes mpl de lujo
regard [rɪˈgɑrd] s consideración, miramiento; (esteem) respeto; (particular matter) respecto; (look) mirada; **in regard to** respecto a o de; **regards** recuerdos; **without regard to** sin hacer caso de; **with regard to** respecto a o de ‖ tr considerar; mirar; tocar a, referirse a; **as regards** en cuanto a
regarding [rɪˈgɑrdɪŋ] prep tocante a, respecto a o de
regardless [rɪˈgɑrdlɪs] adj desatento, indiferente ‖ adj (coll) pese a quien pese, cueste lo que cueste; **regardless of** sin hacer caso de; a pesar de
regenerate [rɪˈdʒɛnə•ret] tr regenerar ‖ intr regenerarse
regent [ˌridʒənt] s regente mf
regicide [ˈrɛdʒɪˌsaɪd] s (act) regicidio; (person) regicida mf
regime o **régime** [reˈʒim] s régimen m
regiment [ˈrɛdʒɪmənt] s regimiento ‖ [ˈrɛdʒɪˌmənt] tr regimentar
regimental [ˌrɛdʒɪˈmɛntəl] adj regimental ‖ **regimentals** spl uniforme m militar
region [ˈridʒən] s región, comarca
register [ˈrɛdʒɪstər] s (record; book for keeping such a record) registro; reja regulable de calefacción; (of the voice or an instrument) extensión ‖ tr (to indicate by a record; to show, as on a scale) registrar; empadronar (los vecinos en el padrón); manifestar, dar a conocer; certificar (envíos por correo); inscribir ‖ intr registrarse; empadronarse; inscribirse
registered letter s carta certificada
registrar [ˈrɛdʒɪsˌtrɑr] s registrador m, archivero
registration fee [ˌrɛdʒɪsˈtreʃən] s derechos de matrícula
re•gret [rɪˈgrɛt] s pesar m, sentimiento; pesadumbre, remordimiento; **regrets** excusas ‖ v (pret & pp **-gretted;** ger **-gretting**) tr sentir, lamentar; lamentar la pérdida de;

arrepentirse de; **I regret** (apology) lo siento; me sabe mal; **to regret to** sentir
regrettable [rɪˈgrɛtəbəl] adj lamentable
regular [ˈrɛgjələr] adj regular; (coll) cabal, completo, verdadero ‖ s obrero permanente; parroquiano regular; **regulars** tropas regulares
regulate [ˈrɛgjə,let] tr regular
rehabilitate [ˌrihəˈbɪlɪˌtet] tr rehabilitar
rehabilitation [ˌrihə,bɪlɪˈteʃən] s rehabilitación
rehearsal [rɪˈhʌrsəl] s ensayo
rehearse [rɪˈhʌrs] tr ensayar ‖ intr ensayarse
reign [ren] s reinado ‖ intr reinar
reimburse [ˌri•ɪmˈbʌrs] tr reembolsar, rembolsar
rein [ren] s rienda; **to give free rein to** dar rienda suelta a ‖ tr dirigir por medio de riendas; contener, refrenar, gobernar
reincarnation [ˌri•ɪnkɑrˈneʃən] s reencarnación
reindeer [ˈren,dɪr] s reno
reinforce [ˌri•ɪnˈfors] tr reforzar; armar (el hormigón)
reinforcement [ˌri•ɪnˈforsmənt] s refuerzo
reinstate [ˌri•ɪnˈstet] tr reinstalar
reiterate [riˈɪtə,ret] tr reiterar
reject [rɪˈdʒɛkt] tr rechazar
rejection [rɪˈdʒɛkʃən] s rechazamiento
rejoice [rɪˈdʒɔɪs] intr regocijarse
rejoinder [rɪˈdʒɔɪndər] s contestación; (law) contrarréplica
rejuvenation [rɪ,dʒuvɪˈneʃən] s rejuvenecimiento
rel. abbr **relating, relative, religion, religious**
relapse [rɪˈlæps] s recaída ‖ intr recaer
relate [rɪˈlet] tr (to establish relationship between) relacionar; (to narrate) contar, relatar
relation [rɪˈleʃən] s (connection; narration) relación; (narration) relato; (relative) pariente mf; (kinship) parentesco; **in relation to** o **with** tocante a, respecto a o de
relationship [rɪˈleʃən,ʃɪp] s (connection) relación; (kinship) parentesco
relative [ˈrɛlətɪv] adj relativo ‖ s deudo, pariente mf
relax [rɪˈlæks] tr & intr relajar
relaxation [ˌrilæksˈeʃən] s relajación; despreocupación
relaxation of tension s disminución de tensión; disminución de la tirantez internacional
relaxing [rɪˈlæksɪŋ] adj relajador; despreocupante, tranquilizador
relay [ˈrile] o [rɪˈle] s (elec) relais m, relevador m, relevo; (mil & sport) relevo; (sport) carrera de relevos ‖ v (pret & pp **-layed**) transmitir relevándose; transmitir con un relais; retransmitir (una emisión); reexpedir (un radiotelegrama) ‖ [rɪˈle] v (pret & pp **-laid**) tr volver a colocar, volver a tender
relay race s carrera de relevos
release [rɪˈlis] s liberación; (from jail) excarcelación; alivio; permiso de publicación, venta, etc.; obra o pieza lista para la pub-

licación, venta, etc.; (aer) lanzamiento; (mach) escape *m*, disparador *m* ‖ *tr* soltar; libertar; excarcelar (*a un preso*); permitir la publicación, venta, etc. de; (aer) lanzar (*una bomba*)
relent [rɪˈlɛnt] *intr* ablandarse, aplacarse
relentless [rɪˈlɛntlɪs] *adj* implacable
relevance [ˈrɛlɪvəns] *s* relevancia
relevant [ˈrɛlɪvənt] *adj* pertinente
reliable [rɪˈlaɪ•əbəl] *adj* confiable, fidedigno; (*source*) solvente
reliance [rɪˈlaɪ•əns] *s* confianza
relic [ˈrɛlɪk] *s* reliquia
relief [rɪˈlif] *s* alivio; caridad; (*projection of figures; elevation*) relieve *m*; (mil) relevo; **in relief** en relieve; **on relief** viviendo de socorro, recibiendo auxilio social
relieve [rɪˈliv] *tr* (*to release from a post*) relevar; aliviar; auxiliar (*a los necesitados*); (mil) relevar
religion [rɪˈlɪdʒən] *s* religión
religious [rɪˈlɪdʒəs] *adj* religioso
relinquish [rɪˈlɪŋkwɪʃ] *tr* abandonar, dejar
relish [ˈrɛlɪʃ] *s* buen sabor, gusto; condimento, sazón *f*; entremés *m*; buen apetito ‖ *tr* gustar de; comer o beber con placer
relocate [riˈloket] *tr* trasladar ‖ *intr* trasladarse
relocation [ˌriloˈkeʃən] *s* traslado
reluctance [rɪˈlʌktəns] *s* renuencia, aversión
reluctant [rɪˈlʌktənt] *adj* renuente, maldispuesto
re•ly [rɪˈlaɪ] *v* (*pret & pp* -lied) *intr* depender, confiar; **to rely on** depender de, confiar en
remain [rɪˈmen] *intr* permanecer, quedarse ‖ **remains** *spl* desechos, restos; restos mortales; obra póstuma
remainder [rɪˈmendər] *s* resto, residuo; libro casi invendible ‖ *tr* saldar (*libros que ya no se venden*)
re•make [riˈmek] *v* (*pret & pp* -made [ˈmedj]) *tr* rehacer
remark [rɪˈmɑrk] *s* observación ‖ *tr & intr* observar; **to remark on** aludir a, comentar
remarkable [rɪˈmɑrkəbəl] *adj* notable, extraordinario
remar•ry [riˈmæri] *v* (*pret & pp* -ried) *intr* volver a casarse
reme•dy [ˈrɛmɪdi] *s* (*pl* -dies) remedio ‖ *v* (*pret & pp* -died) *tr* remediar
remember [rɪˈmɛmbər] *tr* acordarse de, recordar; dar recuerdos de parte de, p.ej., **remember me to your brother** déle Vd. a su hermano recuerdos de mi parte ‖ *intr* acordarse, recordar; **if I remember correctly** si mal no me acuerdo
remembrance [rɪˈmɛmbrəns] *s* recuerdo
remind [rɪˈmaɪnd] *tr* recordar
reminder [rɪˈmaɪndər] *s* recordatorio, recordativo
reminisce [ˌrɛmɪˈnɪs] *intr* entregarse a los recuerdos, contar sus recuerdos
remiss [rɪˈmɪs] *adj* descuidado, negligente
re•mit [rɪˈmɪt] *v* (*pret & pp* -mitted; *ger* -mitting) *tr* (*to send, to ship; to pardon*) remitir
remittance [rɪˈmɪtəns] *s* remesa

remnant [ˈrɛmnənt] *s* (*something left over*) remanente *m*; (*of cloth*) retal *m*, retazo; (*piece of cloth to be sold at reduced price*) saldo; vestigio
remod•el [riˈmɑdəl] *v* (*pret & pp* -eled o -elled; *ger* -eling o -elling) *tr* modelar de nuevo; rehacer, reconstruir; convertir, transformar; remodelar
remodeling [riˈmɑdəlɪŋ] *s* remodelación
remonstrate [rɪˈmɑnstret] *intr* protestar; **to remonstrate with** reconvenir
remorse [rɪˈmɔrs] *s* remordimiento
remorseful [rɪˈmɔrsfəl] *adj* compungido, arrepentido
remote [rɪˈmot] *adj* remoto
remote control *s* comando a distancia, telecontrol *m*, control remoto; **to operate by remote control** (co)mandar a distancia
removable [rɪˈmuvəbəl] *adj* amovible
removal [rɪˈmuvəl] *s* remoción; mudanza, traslado; (*dismissal*) deposición
remove [rɪˈmuv] *tr* remover; quitar de en medio, apartar matando ‖ *intr* removerse
remuneration [rɪˌmjunərˈeʃən] *s* remuneración
renaissance [ˌrɛnəˈsɑns] o [rɪˈnesəns] *s* renacimiento
rend [rɛnd] *v* (*pret & pp* rent [rɛnt]) *tr* (*to tear*) desgarrar; (*to split*) hender, rajar; estremecer (*un ruido el aire*)
render [ˈrɛndər] *tr* rendir (*gracias, obsequios, homenaje*); prestar, suministrar (*ayuda*); pagar (*tributo*); desempeñar (*un papel*); traducir (*sentimientos*); (*from one language to another*) verter; hacer (*justicia*); ejecutar (*una pieza de música*); derretir (*cera, manteca*); extraer la grasa o el sebo de; poner, volver
rendezvous [ˈrɑndə,vu] *s* (*pl* -vous [,vuz]) cita; (*in space*) encuentro, reunión ‖ *v* (*pret & pp* -voused [,vud]; *ger* -vousing [,vu•ɪŋ]) *intr* reunirse en una cita
rendition [rɛnˈdɪʃən] *s* rendición; traducción; (mus) ejecución
renege [rɪˈnɪg] *s* renuncio ‖ *intr* renunciar; (coll) volverse atrás
renegotiation [ˌrɪnɪˌgoʃɪˈeʃən] *s* renegociación
renew [rɪˈnju] o [rɪˈnu] *tr* renovar ‖ *intr* renovarse
renewable [rɪˈnju•əbəl] o [rɪˈnu•əbəl] *adj* renovable
renewal [rɪˈnju•əl] o [rɪˈnu•əl] *s* renovación
renounce [rɪˈnauns] *tr* renunciar; renunciar a (*p.ej., el mundo*) ‖ *intr* renunciar
renovate [ˈrɛnə,vet] *tr* renovar; refaccionar; reformar (*p.ej., una tienda, una casa*)
renown [rɪˈnaun] *s* renombre *m*
renowned [rɪˈnaund] *adj* renombrado
rent [rɛnt] *adj* desgarrado ‖ *s* alquiler *m*, arriendo; (*tear, slit*) desgarro ‖ *tr* alquilar, arrendar ‖ *intr* alquilarse, arrendarse
rental [ˈrɛntəl] *s* alquiler *m*, arriendo
renunciation [rɪˌnʌnsɪˈeʃən] o [rɪˌnʌnʃɪˈeʃən] *s* renunciación
reopen [riˈopən] *tr* reabrir ‖ *intr* reabrirse

re
re

reorganize [ri`ɔrgə,naɪz] *tr* reorganizar ‖ *intr* reorganizarse

reorientation [ri,ori•ən`teʃən] *s* reorientación

rep. *abbr* report, reporter, representative, republic

repair [rɪ`pɛr] *s* reparación; recompostura; **in repair** en buen estado ‖ *tr* reparar; refaccionar ‖ *intr* dirigirse; volver

repaper [ri`pepər] *tr* empapelar de nuevo

reparation [,rɛpə`reʃən] *s* reparación

repartee [,rɛpɑr`ti] *s* respuesta viva; agudeza y gracia en responder

repast [rɪ`pæst] o [rɪ`pɑst] *s* comida, comilona

repatriate [ri`petrɪ,et] *tr* repatriar

re•pay [rɪ`pe] *v* (*pret & pp* **-paid** [`ped]) *tr* reembolsar, rembolsar; resarcir (*un daño, una injuria*); compensar

repayment [rɪ`pemənt] *s* reembolso; resarcimiento; compensación

repeal [rɪ`pil] *s* abrogación, revocación; revocatoria ‖ *tr* abrogar, revocar

repeat [rɪ`pit] *s* repetición ‖ *tr & intr* repetir

re•pel [rɪ`pɛl] *v* (*pret & pp* **-pelled;** *ger* **-pelling**) *tr* rechazar, repeler; repugnar

repent [rɪ`pɛnt] *tr* arrepentirse de ‖ *intr* arrepentirse

repentance [rɪ`pɛntəns] *s* arrepentimiento

repentant [rɪ`pɛntənt] *adj* arrepentido

repertory theater [`rɛpər,tori] *s* teatro de repertorio

repetition [,rɛpɪ`tɪʃən] *s* repetición

repine [rɪ`paɪn] *intr* afligirse, quejarse

replace [rɪ`ples] *tr* (*to put back*) reponer; (*to take the place of*) reemplazar

replacement [rɪ`plesmənt] *s* reposición; reemplazo; pieza de repuesto; soldado reemplazante

replenish [rɪ`plɛnɪʃ] *tr* rellenar; reaprovisionar

replete [rɪ`plit] *adj* repleto

replica [`rɛplɪkə] *s* réplica

re•ply [rɪ`plaɪ] *s* (*pl* **-plies**) contestación, respuesta; contesto (Mex) ‖ *v* (*pret & pp* **-plied**) *tr & intr* contestar, responder

reply coupon *s* vale m respuesta

report [rɪ`port] *s* relato, informe *m;* voz *f,* rumor *m;* (*e.g., of a firearm*) detonación, tiro; denuncia ‖ *tr* relatar, informar acerca de; denunciar ‖ *intr* hacer un relato; redactar un informe; ser repórter; presentarse; **to report on** dar cuenta de, notificar

report card *s* certificado escolar

reportedly [rɪ`portɪdli] *adv* según se informa

reporter [rɪ`portər] *s* repórter m

reporting [rɪ`portɪŋ] *s* reportaje m

repose [rɪ`poz] *s* descanso ‖ *tr* descansar; poner (*confianza*) ‖ *intr* descansar

reprehend [,rɛprɪ`hɛnd] *tr* reprender

represent [,rɛprɪ`zɛnt] *tr* representar

representative [,rɛprɪ`zɛntətɪv] *adj* representativo ‖ *s* representante *mf*

repress [rɪ`prɛs] *tr* reprimir

reprieve [rɪ`priv] *s* suspensión temporal de un castigo, suspensión temporal de la pena de muerte; respiro, alivio temporal ‖ *tr* suspender temporalmente el castigo de o la

pena de muerte de; aliviar temporalmente

reprimand [`rɛprɪ,mænd] *s* reprimenda ‖ *tr* reconvenir, reprender

reprint [`ri,prɪnt] *s* reimpresión; tirada aparte ‖ [ri`prɪnt] *tr* reimprimir

reprisal [rɪ`praɪzəl] *s* represalia

reproach [rɪ`protʃ] *s* reproche *m;* oprobio ‖ *tr* reprochar; oprobiar

reproduce [,riprə`djus] *tr* reproducir ‖ *intr* reproducirse

reproduction [,riprə`dʌkʃən] *s* reproducción

reproof [rɪ`pruf] *s* reprobación

reprove [rɪ`pruv] *tr* reprobar

reptile [`rɛptɪl] *s* reptil *m*

republic [rɪ`pʌblɪk] *s* república

republican [rɪ`pʌblɪkən] *adj & s* republicano

repudiate [rɪ`pjudɪ,et] *tr* repudiar; no reconocer (*p.ej., una deuda*)

repugnant [rɪ`pʌgnənt] *adj* repugnante

repulse [rɪ`pʌls] *s* repulsión, rechazo ‖ *tr* repeler, rechazar

repulsive [rɪ`pʌlsɪv] *adj* repulsivo

reputation [,rɛpjə`teʃən] *s* reputación; buena reputación

repute [rɪ`pjut] *s* reputación; buena reputación ‖ *tr* reputar

reputedly [rɪ`pjutɪdli] *adv* según la opinión común

request [rɪ`kwɛst] *s* petición, solicitud; **at the request of** a petición de ‖ *tr* pedir

require [rɪ`kwaɪr] *tr* exigir, requerir

requirement [rɪ`kwaɪrmənt] *s* requisito; necesidad

requisite [`rɛkwɪzɪt] *adj & s* requisito

requital [rɪ`kwaɪtəl] *s* compensación, retorno

requite [rɪ`kwaɪt] *tr* corresponder a (*los beneficios, el amor, etc.*); corresponder con (*el bienhechor*)

re•read [ri`rid] *v* (*pret & pp* **-read** [`rɛd]) *tr* releer

rerun [`ri,rʌn] *s* (*film, play, etc.*) exhibición repetida, programa *m* repetido

resale [`ri,sel] o [ri`sel] *s* reventa

rescind [rɪ`sɪnd] *tr* rescindir

rescue [`rɛskju] *s* salvación, rescate *m,* liberación; **to go to the rescue of** acudir al socorro de ‖ *tr* salvar, rescatar, libertar

rescue party *s* pelotón *m* de salvamento

research [rɪ`sʌrtʃ] o [`risʌrtʃ] *s* investigación ‖ *intr* investigar

re•sell [ri`sɛl] *v* (*pret & pp* **-sold** [`sold]) *tr* revender; rescatar (Mex)

resemblance [rɪ`zɛmbləns] *s* parecido, semejanza

resemble [rɪ`zɛmbəl] *tr* parecerse a, asemejarse a

resent [rɪ`zɛnt] *tr* resentirse de o por

resentful [rɪ`zɛntfəl] *adj* resentido

resentment [rɪ`zɛntmənt] *s* resentimiento

reservation [,rɛzər`veʃən] *s* reserva

reserve [rɪ`zʌrv] *s* reserva ‖ *tr* reservar

reservoir [`rɛzər,vwɑr] *s* depósito; (*where water is dammed back*) embalse *m,* pantano; (*of wisdom*) fondo

re•ship [ri`ʃɪp] *v* (pret & pp **-shipped;** *ger* **-shipping**) *tr* reenviar, reexpedir; (*on a ship*) reembarcar ‖ *intr* reembarcarse

reshipment [riˈʃɪpmənt] s reenvío, reexpedición; (of persons) reembarco; (of goods) reembarque m
reside [rɪˈzaɪd] intr residir
residence [ˈrɛzɪdəns] s residencia
resident [ˈrɛzɪdənt] adj & s residente mf, vecino
residue [ˈrɛzɪˌdju] s residuo
resign [rɪˈzaɪn] tr dimitir, resignar, renunciar ‖ intr dimitir; (to yield, submit) resignarse; **to resign to** resignarse con (p.ej., su suerte)
resignation [ˌrɛzɪgˈneʃən] s (from a job, etc.) dimisión; (state of being submissive) resignación
resin [ˈrɛzɪn] s resina
resist [rɪˈzɪst] tr resistir (la tentación); resistir a (la violencia; la risa) ‖ intr resistirse
resistance [rɪˈzɪstəns] s resistencia; **without resistance** sin rechistar
resole [riˈsol] tr sobresolar
resolute [ˈrɛzəˌlut] adj resuelto
resolution [ˌrɛzəˈluʃən] s resolución; **good resolutions** buenos propósitos
resolve [rɪˈzɔlv] s resolución ‖ tr resolver ‖ intr resolverse
resort [rɪˈzɔrt] s lugar muy frecuentado; (e.g., for vacations) estación; (for help or support) recurso; **as a last resort** como último recurso ‖ intr recurrir
resound [rɪˈzaʊnd] intr resonar
resource [rɪˈsors] o [ˈrisors] s recurso
resourceful [rɪˈsorsfəl] adj ingenioso
respect [rɪˈspɛkt] s (deference, esteem) respeto; (reference, relation; detail) respecto; **respects** recuerdos, saludos; **to pay one's respects (to)** ofrecer sus respetos (a); **with respect to** respecto a o de ‖ tr respetar
respectable [rɪˈspɛktəbəl] adj respetable; decente, presentable
respectful [rɪˈspɛktfəl] adj respetuoso
respectfully [rɪˈspɛktfəli] adj respetuosamente; **respectfully yours** de Vd. atento y seguro servidor
respecting [rɪˈspɛktɪŋ] prep con respecto a, respecto de
respective [rɪˈspɛktɪv] adj respectivo
respire [rɪˈspaɪr] tr & intr respirar
respite [ˈrɛspɪt] s (temporary relief) respiro; (postponement, especially of death sentence) suspensión; **without respite** sin respirar
resplendent [rɪˈsplɛndənt] adj resplandeciente
respond [rɪˈspɑnd] intr responder
response [rɪˈspɑns] s respuesta
responsibility [rɪˌspɑnsɪˈbɪlɪti] s responsabilidad; **to assume responsibility** responsabilizarse
responsible [rɪˈspɑnsɪbəl] adj responsable; (job, position) de confianza; **to hold responsible** responsabilizar; **responsible for** responsable de
rest [rɛst] s (after exertion or work; sleep) descanso; (lack of motion) reposo; (of the dead) paz f; (what remains) resto; (mus) pausa; **at rest** (not moving) en reposo;

tranquilo; dormido; (dead) muerto; **the rest** lo demás; los demás; **to come to rest** venir a parar; **to lay to rest** enterrar ‖ tr descansar; parar; poner (p.ej., confianza) ‖ intr descansar; estar, hallarse; **to rest assured (that)** estar seguro, tener la seguridad (de que); **to rest on** descansar en o sobre, estribar en
restaurant [ˈrɛstərənt] s restaurante m
rest cure s cura de reposo
restful [ˈrɛstfəl] adj descansado, tranquilo, reposado
rest home s casa de reposo
resting place s lugar m de descanso; (of a staircase) descansadero; (of the dead) última morada
restitution [ˌrɛstɪˈtjuʃən] s restitución
restless [ˈrɛstlɪs] adj intranquilo; (sleepless) insomne
restock [riˈstɑk] tr reaprovisionar; repoblar (p.ej., un acuario)
restore [rɪˈstor] tr restaurar; (to give back) devolver
restrain [rɪˈstren] tr contener, refrenar; aprisionar
restraint [rɪˌˈstrent] s restricción; comedimiento, moderación
restrict [rɪˈstrɪkt] tr restringir
rest room s sala de descanso; excusado, retrete m; (of a theater) saloncillo
result [rɪˈzʌlt] s resultado; **as a result of** de resultas de ‖ intr resultar; **to result in** dar por resultado, parar en
resume [rɪˈzum] o [rɪˈzjum] tr reasumir; reanudar (el viaje, el vuelo, etc.); volver a tomar (su asiento) ‖ intr continuar; recomenzar; reanudar el hilo del discurso
résumé [ˌrɛzuˈme] s resumen m
resurface [riˈsʌrfɪs] tr dar nueva superficie a ‖ intr volver a emerger (un submarino)
resurrect [ˌrɛzəˈrɛkt] tr & intr resucitar
resurrection [ˌrɛzəˈrɛkʃən] s resurrección
resuscitate [rɪˈsʌsɪˌtet] tr & intr resucitar
retail [ˈritel] adj & adv al por menor ‖ s venta al por menor ‖ tr detallar, vender al por menor ‖ intr vender al por menor; venderse al por menor
retailer [ˈritelər] s detallista mf, minorista m, comerciante mf al por menor
retain [rɪˈten] tr retener; contratar (a un abogado)
retaliate [rɪˈtælɪˌet] intr desquitarse, vengarse
retaliation [rɪˌtælɪˈeʃən] s desquite m, venganza
retard [rɪˈtɑrd] s retardo ‖ tr retardar
retardation [ˌritɑrˈdeʃən] s retardación
retarded [rɪˈtɑrdɪd] adj subnormal, atrasado, retrasado
retch [rɛtʃ] tr vomitar ‖ intr arquear, esforzarse por vomitar
retching [ˈrɛtʃɪŋ] s arcadas
ret'd. abbr **returned**
reticence [ˈrɛtɪsəns] s reserva, circunspección, sigilo
reticent [ˈrɛtɪsənt] adj reservado, circunspecto
retinue [ˈrɛtɪˌnju] s comitiva, séquito

re
re

retire [rɪ'taɪr] *tr* retirar; jubilar (*a un empleado*) ‖ *intr* retirarse; jubilarse; (*to go to bed*) recogerse; (mil) retirarse
retirement [rɪ'taɪrmənt] *s* retiro; (*of an employee with pension*) jubilación; (mil) retirada
retirement annuity *s* jubilación
retort [rɪ'tɔrt] *s* respuesta pronta y aguda, réplica; (chem) retorta ‖ *intr* replicar
retouch [rɪ'tʌtʃ] *tr* retocar
retrace [rɪ'tres] *tr* repasar; **to retrace one's steps** volver sobre sus pasos
retract [rɪ'trækt] *tr* retractarse de, desdecirse de (*lo que se ha dicho*) ‖ *intr* retractarse, desdecirse
retractable [rɪ'træktəbəl] *adj* retráctil
retraction [rɪ'trækʃən] *s* retracción
re-tread ['ri,trɛd] *s* neumático recauchutado; neumático ranurado ‖ [rɪ'trɛd] *v* (*pret & pp* **-treaded**) *tr* recauchutar; volver a ranurar ‖ *v* (*pret* **-trod** ['trɑd]; *pp* **-trod** o **-trodden**) *tr* desandar ‖ *intr* volverse atrás
retreat [rɪ'trit] *s* (*act of withdrawing; place of seclusion*) retiro; (eccl) retiro; (mil) retreta, retirada; (*signal*) (mil) retreta; **to beat a retreat** retirarse; (mil) batirse en retirada ‖ *intr* retirarse
retrench [rɪ'trɛntʃ] *tr* cercenar ‖ *intr* recogerse
retribution [,rɛtrɪ'bjuʃən] *s* justo castigo; (theol) juicio final
retrieve [rɪ'triv] *tr* cobrar; reparar (*p.ej., un daño*); desquitarse de (*una pérdida, una derrota*); (hunt) cobrar, portar ‖ *intr* (hunt) cobrar, portar
retriever [rɪ'trivər] *s* perro cobrador, perro traedor
retroactive [,rɛtro'æktɪv] *adj* retroactivo
retrofiring [,rɛtro'faɪrɪŋ] *s* retrodisparo
retrogress ['rɛtrə,grɛs] *intr* retroceder; empeorar
retrorocket [,rɛtro'rɑkɪt] *s* retrocohete *m*
retrospect ['rɛtrə,spɛkt] *s* retrospección; **in retrospect** retrospectivamente
retrospective [,rɛtrə,spɛktɪv] *adj* retrospectivo
re-try [rɪ'traɪ] *v* (*pret & pp* **-tried**) *tr* reensayar; rever (*un caso legal*); procesar de nuevo (*a una persona*)
return [rɪ'tʌrn] *adj* repetido; de vuelta; **by return mail** a vuelta de correo ‖ *s* vuelta; devolución; recompensa; respuesta; informe *m*, noticia; ganancia, beneficio, rédito; (*of an election*) resultado; (*of income tax*) declaración; **in return (for)** en cambio (de); **many happy returns of the day!** ¡que cumpla muchos más! ‖ *tr* devolver; dar en cambio; corresponder a (*un favor*); dar (*una respuesta, las gracias*) ‖ *intr* volver; responder
return address *s* dirección del remitente
return bout o **engagement** *s* (box) combate *m* revancha
return game *s* desquite *m*
return ticket *s* billete *m* de vuelta; billete de ida y vuelta
return trip *s* viaje *m* de vuelta

reunification [ri,junɪfɪ'keʃən] *s* reunificación
reunion [ri'junjən] *s* reunión
reunite [,riju'naɪt] *tr* reunir ‖ *intr* reunirse
rev. *abbr* **revenue, reverse, review, revised, revision, revolution**
Rev. *abbr.* **Revelation, Reverend**
rev [rɛv] *s* revolución ‖ *v* (*pret & pp* **revved**; *ger* **revving**) *tr* cambiar la velocidad de; **to rev up** acelerar ‖ *intr* acelerarse
revaluate [ri'vælju,et] *tr* revalorar, revalorizar, revaluar
revamp [ri'væmp] *tr* componer, renovar, remendar
reveal [rɪ'vil] *tr* revelar
reveille ['rɛvəli] *s* diana, toque *m* de diana
rev-el ['rɛvəl] *s* jarana, regocijo tumultuoso ‖ *v* (*pret & pp* **-eled** o **-elled**; *ger* **-eling** o **-elling**) *intr* jaranear; deleitarse
revelation [,rɛvə'leʃən] *s* revelación
revel-ry ['rɛvəlri] *s* (*pl* **-ries**) jarana, diversión tumultuosa
revenge [rɪ'vɛndʒ] *s* venganza ‖ *tr* vengar
revengeful [rɪ'vɛndʒfəl] *adj* vengativo
revenue ['rɛvə,nju] *s* renta, rédito; rentas públicas
revenue cutter *s* escampavía
revenue stamp *s* sello fiscal, timbre *m* del estado
reverberate [rɪ'vʌrbə,ret] *intr* reverberar
revere [rɪ'vɪr] *tr* reverenciar, venerar
reverence ['rɛvərəns] *s* reverencia ‖ *tr* reverenciar
reverend ['rɛvərənd] *adj & s* reverendo
reverie ['rɛvəri] *s* ensueño
reversal [rɪ'vʌrsəl] *s* inversión (*e.g., of opinion*) cambio
reverse [rɪ'vʌrs] *adj* invertido; contrario; de marcha atrás ‖ *s* (*opposite or rear*) revés *m*; contrario; contramarcha, marcha atrás; (*check, defeat*) revés *m*, contratiempo ‖ *tr* invertir; dar vuelta a; poner en marcha atrás; **to reverse oneself** cambiar de opinión; **to reverse the charges** cobrar al destinatario; (telp) cobrar al número llamado ‖ *intr* invertirse
reverse lever *s* palanca de marcha atrás
revert [rɪ'vʌrt] *intr* revertir; saltar atrás; **to revert to one's old tricks** volver a las andadas
review [rɪ'vju] *s* (*reëxamination; survey; magazine; musical show*) revista; (*of a book*) reseña, revista; (*of a lesson*) repaso; (mil) reseña, revista ‖ *tr* rever, revisar; reseñar (*un libro*); repasar (*una lección*); (mil) revistar
reviewer [rɪ'vju·ər] *s* (*critic*) reseñador *m*
revile [rɪ'vaɪl] *tr* ultrajar, vilipendiar
revise [rɪ'vaɪz] *s* revisión; refundición; (typ) segunda prueba ‖ *tr* rever, revisar; refundir (*un libro*); enmendar
revision [rɪ'vɪʒən] *s* revisión; revisada; (*of a book*) refundición; enmienda
revisionism [rɪ'vɪʒə,nɪzəm] *s* revisionismo
revisionist [rɪ'vɪʒənɪst] *adj & s* revisionista
revival [rɪ'vaɪvəl] *s* resucitación; reanimación; (*e.g., of learning*) renacimiento; de-

spertamiento religioso; (theat) reestreno, reposición
revive [rɪ'vaɪv] *tr* revivir; (theat) reestrenar, reponer ‖ *intr* revivir; volver en sí, recordar
revoke [rɪ'vok] *tr* revocar
revolt [rɪ'volt] *s* rebelión, sublevación ‖ *tr* dar asco a, repugnar ‖ *intr* rebelarse, sublevarse
revolting [rɪ'voltɪŋ] *adj* asqueroso, repugnante; rebelde
revolution [,rɛvə'luʃən] *s* revolución
revolutionar•y [,rɛvə'luʃə,nɛri] *adj* revolucionario ‖ *s* (*pl* -ies) revolucionario
revolve [rɪ'vɑlv] *tr* hacer girar; (*in one's mind*) revolver ‖ *intr* girar; revolverse (*un astro en su órbita*)
revolver [rɪ'vɑlvər] *s* revólver *m*
revolving bookcase *s* giratoria
revolving door *s* puerta giratoria
revolving fund *s* fondo rotativo
revue [rɪ'vju] *s* (theat) revista
revulsion [rɪ'vʌlʃən] *s* aversión, repugnancia; reacción fuerte
reward [rɪ'wɔrd] *s* premio, recompensa; (*money used to recapture or recover*) rescate *m;* hallazgo, p.ej., **five dollars reward** cinco dólares de hallazgo ‖ *tr* premiar, recompensar
rewarding [rɪ'wɔrdɪŋ] *adj* remunerador, provechoso, agradecido
re•wind ['ri,waɪnd] *s* (mach, mov) retroceso ‖ [ri'waɪnd] *v* (*pret & pp* -**wound** [waʊnd] *tr* (mach, mov) rebobinar
re•write [ri'raɪt] *v* (*pret* -**wrote** ['rot]; *pp* -**written** ['rɪtən]) *tr* escribir de nuevo; refundir (*un escrito*); redactar (*un escrito de otra persona*)
R.F. *abbr* **radio frequency**
R.F.D. *abbr* **Rural Free Delivery**
R.H. *abbr* **Royal Highness**
rhapso•dy ['ræpsədi] *s* (*pl* -**dies**) rapsodia
rheostat ['ri•ə,stæt] *s* reóstato
rhesus ['risəs] *s* macaco de la India
rhetoric ['rɛtərɪk] *s* retórica
rhetorical [rɪ'tɔrɪkəl] *adj* retórico
rheumatic [ru'mætɪk] *adj & s* reumático
rheumatism ['rumə,tɪzəm] *s* reumatismo
Rhine [raɪn] *s* Rin *m*
Rhineland ['raɪn,lænd] *s* Renania
rhine'stone' *s* diamante de imitación hecho de vidrio
rhinoceros [raɪ'nɑsərəs] *s* rinoceronte *m*
Rhodes [rodz] *s* Rodas *f*
Rhone [ron] *s* Ródano
rhubarb ['rubɑrb] *s* ruibarbo
rhyme [raɪm] *s* rima; **without rhyme or reason** sin ton ni son ‖ *tr & intr* rimar
rhythm ['rɪðəm] *s* ritmo
rhythmic(al) ['rɪðmɪk(əl)] *adj* rítmico
rial•to [rɪ'ælto] *s* (*pl* -**tos**) mercado ‖ **the Rialto** el puente del Rialto; el centro teatral de Nueva York
rib [rɪb] *s* costilla; (*of a fan or umbrella*) varilla; (*of a tire*) cuerda; (*in cloth*) canilla; (*of the wing of an insect*) nervio ‖ *v* (*pret & pp* **ribbed;** *ger* **ribbing**) *tr* proveer de

costillas; hacer canillas en; (slang) tomar el pelo a
ribald ['rɪbəld] *adj* grosero y obsceno
ribbon ['rɪbən] *s* cinta
rice [raɪs] *s* arroz *m*
rich [rɪtʃ] *adj* rico; (coll) platudo; (*color*) vivo; (*voice*) sonoro; (*wine*) generoso; azucarado, condimentado; (coll) divertido; (coll) ridículo; **to strike it rich** descubrir un buen filón ‖ **riches** *spl* riquezas; **the rich** los ricos
rickets ['rɪkɪts] *s* raquitis *f*
rickety ['rɪkɪti] *adj* (*object*) destartalado, desvencijado; (*person*) tambaleante, vacilante; (*suffering from rickets*) raquítico
rid [rɪd] *v* (*pret & pp* **rid;** *ger* **ridding**) *tr* desembarazar; **to get rid of** desembarazarse de, deshacerse de; matar
riddance ['rɪdəns] *s* supresión, libramiento; **good riddance!** ¡adiós, gracias!, ¡de buena me he librado!
riddle ['rɪdəl] *s* acertijo, adivinanza; (*person or thing hard to understand*) enigma *m;* criba gruesa ‖ *tr* acribillar; destruir (*un argumento; la reputación de una persona*); **to riddle with bullets** acribillar a balazos; **to riddle with questions** acribillar a preguntas
ride [raɪd] *s* paseo ‖ *v* (*pret* **rode** [rod]; *pp* **ridden** ['rɪdən]) *tr* montar (*un caballo*); montar sobre (*los hombros de una persona*); recorrer a caballo; flotar sobre (*las olas*); dominar, tiranizar; (coll) burlarse de; **to ride down** atropellar; vencer; **to ride out** luchar felizmente con (*una tempestad*); aguantar con buen éxito (*una desgracia*) ‖ *intr* montar; pasear en coche o carruaje; **to let ride** (slang) dejar correr; **to take riding** llevar de paseo
rider ['raɪdər] *s* jinete *m;* pasajero
ridge [rɪdʒ] *s* (*of a roof; of earth between two furrows*) caballete *m;* (*of a fabric*) cordoncillo; (*of mountains*) cordillera; (*of two plane surfaces*) arista
ridge'pole' *s* parhilera
ridicule ['rɪdɪ,kjul] *s* irrisión; **to expose to ridicule** poner en ridículo ‖ *tr* ridiculizar
ridiculous [rɪ'dɪkjələs] *adj* ridículo
riding academy *s* escuela de equitación
riding boot *s* bota de montar
riding habit *s* amazona, traje *m* de montar
rife [raɪf] *adj* común, corriente, general; abundante, lleno; **rife with** abundante en, lleno de
riffraff ['rɪf,ræf] *s* bahorrina, canalla
rifle ['raɪfəl] *s* rifle *m*, fusil *m* ‖ *tr* hurtar, robar; escudriñar y robar; desnudar, despojar
rifle range *s* tiro de rifle
rift [rɪft] *s* abertura, raja; desacuerdo, desavenencia
rig [rɪg] *s* equipaje *m;* carruaje *m* con caballo o caballos; traje extraño; (naut) aparejo ‖ *v* (*pret & pp* **rigged;** *ger* **rigging**) *tr* equipar; aprestar, disponer; improvisar; vestir de una manera extraña; arreglar de una manera fraudulenta; (naut) aparejar

rigging ['rɪgɪŋ] s avíos, instrumentos, equipo; (naut) aparejo, cordaje m
right [raɪt] adj derecho; verdadero; exacto; conveniente; favorable; sano, normal; bien, correcto; señalado; correspondiente; que se busca, p.ej., **this is the right house** ésta es la casa que se busca; que se necesita, p.ej., **this is the right train** éste es el tren que se necesita; que debe, p.ej., **he is going the right way** sigue el camino que debe; **right or wrong** con razón o sin ella, bueno o malo; **to be all right** estar bien; estar bien de salud; **to be right** tener razón ‖ adv derechamente; directamente; correctamente; exactamente; favorablemente; en orden, en buen estado; hacia la derecha; completamente; (coll) muy; mismo, p.ej., **right here** aquí mismo; **all right** muy bien ‖ interj ¡bien! ‖ s (justice, reason) derecho; (right hand) derecha; (box) derechazo; (com) derecho; (pol) derecha; **by right** según derecho; **on the right** a la derecha; **to be in the right** tener razón ‖ tr enderezar; corregir, rectificar; hacer justicia a; deshacer (un entuerto) ‖ intr enderezarse
righteous ['raɪtʃəs] adj recto, justo; virtuoso
right field s (baseball) jardín derecho
rightful ['raɪtfəl] adj justo; legítimo
right'-hand' drive s conducción o dirección a la derecha
right-hand man s mano derecha, brazo derecho
rightist ['raɪtɪst] adj & s derechista mf
rightly ['raɪtli] adv derechamente; correctamente; con razón; convenientemente; **rightly or wrongly** con razón o sin ella; **rightly so** a justo título
right mind s entero juicio
right of way s derecho de tránsito o de paso; (law) servidumbre de paso; (rr) servidumbre de vía; **to yield the right of way** ceder el paso
rights of man spl derechos del hombre
right'-wing' adj derechista
right-winger ['raɪt'wɪŋər] s (coll) derechista mf
rigid ['rɪdʒɪd] adj rígido
rigmarole ['rɪgmə,rol] s galimatías m
rigorous ['rɪgərəs] adj riguroso
rile [raɪl] tr (coll) exasperar
rill [rɪl] s arroyuelo
rim [rɪm] s canto, borde m; (of a wheel) llanta; (of a tire) aro
rime [raɪm] s (in verse) rima; (frost) escarcha; **without rime or reason** sin ton ni son ‖ tr & intr rimar
rind [raɪnd] s cáscara, corteza
ring [rɪŋ] s (circular band, line, or mark) anillo; (for the finger) sortija; (for curtains; for gymnastics) anilla; (for nose of animal) argolla; (for fruit jars) círculo de goma; (for some sport or exhibition) circo; (for boxing) cuadrilátero, ruedo; (for bullfight) redondel m, ruedo; boxeo; (of a group of people) corro; (of evildoers) pandilla; (under the eyes) ojera; (of the anchor) arga-

neo; (sound of a bell, of a clock) campanada; (of a small bell; of the glass of glassware) tintineo; (to summon a person) llamada; (character, nature, spirit) tono; **to be in the ring (for)** ser candidato (a); **to run rings around** dar cien vueltas a ‖ v (pret & pp ringed) tr cercar, rodear; (to put a ring on) anillar ‖ intr formar círculo o corro ‖ v (pret rang [ræŋ]; pp rung [rʌŋ]) tr tañer, tocar; (to peal, ring out) repicar; llamar al timbre; dar (las horas la campana del reloj); llamar por teléfono; **to ring up** llamar por teléfono; marcar (una compra) con el timbre ‖ intr sonar (una campana, un timbre, el teléfono); tintinear (el choque de copas, una campanilla); resonar, retumbar; llamar; zumbar (los oídos); **to ring for** llamar, llamar al timbre; **to ring off** terminar una llamada por teléfono; **to ring up** llamar por teléfono
ring-around-a-rosy ['rɪŋə,raʊndə'rozi] s juego del corro
ringing ['rɪŋɪŋ] adj resonante, retumbante ‖ s anillamiento; campaneo, repique m; (of the glass of glassware) tintineo; (in the ears) retintín m, silbido
ring'lead'er s cabecilla m
ring'mas'ter s hombre encargado de los ejercicios ecuestres y acrobáticos de un circo
ring'side' s lugar junto al cuadrilátero; lugar desde el cual se puede ver de cerca
ring'worm' s tiña
rink [rɪŋk] s patinadero
rinse [rɪns] s aclaración, enjuague m ‖ tr aclarar, enjuagar
riot ['raɪət] s alboroto, tumulto; regocijos ruidosos; (of colors) exhibición brillante; **to run riot** desenfrenarse; crecer lozanamente (las plantas) ‖ intr alborotarse, amotinarse
rioter ['raɪətər] s alborotador m, amotinado
riot squad s pelotón m de asalto
rip [rɪp] s rasgón m, siete m; (open seam) descosido ‖ v (pret & pp ripped; ger ripping) tr desgarrar, rasgar; descoser (lo que estaba cosido) ‖ intr desgarrarse, rasgarse; (coll) adelantar o moverse de prisa o con violencia; **to rip out with** (coll) decir con violencia
ripe [raɪp] adj maduro; acabado, hecho; dispuesto, preparado; (boil, tumor) madurado; (olive) negro
ripen ['raɪpən] tr & intr madurar
ripoff ['rɪp,ɔf] s (slang) estafa; timo
ripple ['rɪpəl] s temblor m, rizo; (sound) murmullo, susurro ‖ tr rizar ‖ intr rizarse; murmurar, susurrar
rise [raɪz] s (of temperature, prices, a road) subida; (of ground, of the voice) elevación; (of a heavenly body) salida; (of a step) altura; (in one's employment) ascenso; (of water) crecida; (of a source of water) nacimiento; (of a valve) levantamiento; **to get a rise out of** (slang) sacar una réplica mordaz a; **to give rise to** dar origen a ‖ v (pret rose [roz]; pp risen ['rɪzən]) intr subir; levantarse; salir (un astro); asomar (un

peligro); brotar (*un manantial, una planta*); (*in someone's esteem*) ganar; resucitar; **to rise above** alzarse por encima de; mostrarse superior a; **to rise early** madrugar; **to rise to** ponerse a la altura de

riser ['raɪzər] *s* contraescalón *m*, contrahuella; **early riser** madrugador *m;* **late riser** dormilón *m*

risk [rɪsk] *s* riesgo; **to run** o **take a risk** correr riesgo, correr peligro ‖ *tr* arriesgar; arriesgarse en (*una empresa dudosa*)

risk·y ['rɪski] *adj* (*comp* **-ier;** *super* **-iest**) arriesgado; riesgoso; escabroso

risqué [rɪs'ke] *adj* escabroso

rite [raɪt] *s* rito; **last rites** honras fúnebres

ritual ['rɪtʃʊ•əl] *adj* & *s* ritual *m*

riv. *abbr* **river**

ri·val ['raɪvəl] *s* rival *mf* ‖ *v* (*pret* & *pp* **-valed** o **-valled;** *ger* **-valing** o **-valling**) *tr* rivalizar con

rival·ry ['raɪvəlri] *s* (*pl* **-ries**) rivalidad

river ['rɪvər] *s* río; **down the river** río abajo; **up the river** río arriba

river basin *s* cuenca de río

river bed *s* cauce *m*

river front *s* orilla del río

riv·er·side *adj* ribereño ‖ *s* ribera

rivet ['rɪvɪt] *s* roblón *m*, remache *m;* (*e.g., to hold scissors together*) clavillo ‖ *tr* remachar; clavar (*p.ej., los ojos en una persona*)

rm. *abbr* **ream, room**

R.N. *abbr* **registered nurse, Royal Navy**

roach [rotʃ] *s* cucaracha

road [rod] *adj* itinerario, caminero ‖ *s* camino; (naut) rada; **to be in the road** estorbar el paso; incomodar; **to get out of the road** quitarse de en medio

road'bed' *s* (*of a highway*) firme *m;* (rr) infraestructura

road'block' *s* (mil) barricada; (fig) obstáculo

road'house' *s* posada en el camino

road laborer *s* peón caminero

road map *s* mapa itinerario

road service *s* auxilio en carretera

road'side' *s* borde *m* del camino, borde de la carretera

roadside inn *s* posada en el camino

road sign *s* señal *f* de carretera, poste *m* indicador

road'stead' *s* rada

road'way' *s* camino, vía

roam [rom] *s* vagabundeo ‖ *tr* vagar por, recorrer a la ventura ‖ *intr* vagar, andar errante

roar [ror] *s* bramido, rugido ‖ *intr* bramar, rugir; reírse a carcajadas

roast [rost] *s* asado; café tostado ‖ *tr* asar; tostar (*café*); (coll) despellejar ‖ *intr* asarse; tostarse

roast beef *s* rosbif *m*

roast of beef *s* carne de vaca asada o para asar

roast pork *s* carne de cerdo asada

rob [rɑb] *v* (*pret* & *pp* **robbed;** *ger* **robbing**) *tr* & *intr* robar

robber ['rɑbər] *s* robador *m*, ladrón *m*

robber·y ['rɑbəri] *s* (*pl* **-ies**) robo

robe [rob] *s* manto; abrigo; (*of a woman*) traje *m*, vestido; (*of a professor, judge, etc.*) toga, túnica; (*of a priest*) traje *m* talar; (*dressing gown*) bata; (*for lap in a carriage*) manta ‖ *tr* vestir ‖ *intr* vestirse

robin ['rɑbɪn] *s* (*in Europe*) petirrojo; (*in North America*) primavera

robot ['robat] *s* robot *m*

robotics [ro'batɪks] *s* robótica

robust [ro'bʌst] *adj* robusto; vigoroso

rock [rɑk] *s* roca; (*sticking out of water*) escollo; (*one that is thrown*) piedra; (slang) diamante *m*, piedra preciosa; **on the rocks** arruinado, en pobreza extrema; (*said of hard liquor*) (coll) sobre hielo ‖ *tr* acunar, mecer; (*to sleep*) arrullar; sacudir; **to rock to sleep** adormecer meciendo ‖ *intr* mecerse; sacudirse ‖ *abbr* —**rock-'n'-roll**

rock'-bot'tom *adj* (el) mínimo, (el) más bajo

rock candy *s* azúcar *m* cande

rock crystal *s* cristal *m* de roca

rocker ['rɑkər] *s* (*chair*) mecedora; (*curved piece at bottom of rocking chair or cradle*) arco; (mach) balancín *m;* (mach) eje *m* de balancín

rocket ['rɑkɪt] *s* cohete *m* ‖ *intr* subir como un cohete

rocket bomb *s* bomba cohete

rocket launcher [lɔntʃər] *s* lanzacohetes *m*

rocket ship *s* aeronave *f* cohete

rock garden *s* jardín *m* entre rocas

rocking chair *s* mecedora, sillón *m* de hamaca

rocking horse *s* caballo mecedor

rock-'n'-roll ['rɑkən'rol] *s* rock *m*

Rock of Gibraltar [dʒɪ'brɔltər] *s* peñón *m* de Gibraltar

rock salt *s* sal *f* de compás, sal gema

rock singer *s* rockero, rockera

rock wool *s* lana mineral

rock·y ['rɑki] *adj* (*comp* **-ier;** *super* **-iest**) rocoso, roqueño; (slange) débil, poco firme

rod [rɑd] *s* vara; varilla; barra; (*authority*) vara alta; opresión, tiranía; (*of the retina*) bastoncillo; (*elongated microörganism*) bastoncito; (mach) vástago; (surv) jalón *m;* (Bib) linaje *m*, raza, vástago; (slang) revólver *m*, pistola; **to spare the rod** excusar la vara

rodent ['rodənt] *adj* & *s* roedor *m*

rod·man ['radmən] *s* (*pl* **-men** [mən]) jalonero, portamira *m*

roe [ro] *s* (*deer*) corzo; (*of fish*) hueva

rogue [rog] *s* bribón *m*, pícaro

rogues' gallery *s* colección de retratos de malhechores para uso de la policía

roguish ['rogɪʃ] *adj* bribón, pícaro; travieso, retozón

rôle o **role** [rol] *s* papel *m;* **to play a rôle** desempeñar un papel

roll [rol] *s* (*of cloth, film, paper, fat, etc.*) rollo; (*roller*) rodillo; (*cake of bread*) panecillo; (*of dice*) echada; (*of a boat*) balance *m;* (*of a drum*) redoble *m;* (*of thunder*) retumbo; bamboleo; ondulación; rol *m;* lista; (*of paper money*) fajo; **to call the roll**

pasar lista ‖ *tr* hacer rodar; empujar hacia adelante; cilindrar, laminar; (*to wrap up with rolling motion*) arrollar; alisar con rodillo; liar (*un cigarrillo*); mover de un lado a otro; poner (*los ojos*) en blanco; tocar redobles con (*el tambor*); vibrar (*la voz; la r*); **to roll one's own** liárselos; **to roll up** arremangar (*p.ej., las mangas*); amontonar (*p.ej., una fortuna*) ‖ *intr* rodar; bambolear; balancear (*un barco*); girar; retumbar (*el trueno*); redoblar (*un tambor*); **to roll around** revolcarse

roll call *s* lista, (el) pasar lista

roller ['rolər] *s* rodillo; (*of a piece of furniture*) ruedecilla; (*of a skate*) rueda; ola larga y creciente

roller bearing *s* cojinete *m* de rodillos

roller coaster *s* montaña rusa

roller skate *s* patín *m* de ruedas

roller towel *s* toalla sin fin

rolling mill ['rolɪŋ] *s* taller *m* de laminación; tren *m* de laminadores

rolling pin *s* rodillo, hataca, rulo

rolling stock *s* (rr) material *m* móvil, material rodante

rolling stone *s* piedra movediza

roll'-top' desk *s* escritorio norteamericano, escritorio de cortina corrediza

roly-poly ['roli'poli] *adj* regordete, rechoncho

Rom. *abbr* **Roman, Romance**

roman ['romən] *adj* (typ) redondo ‖ *s* (typ) letra redonda ‖ **Roman** *adj & s* romano

Roman candle *s* vela romana

Roman Catholic *adj & s* católico romano

romance [ro'mæns] o ['romæns] *s* (*tale of chivalry*) roman *m;* cuento de aventuras; cuento de amor; intriga amorosa; novela sentimental; (mus) romanza ‖ [ro'mæns] *intr* contar o escribir romances, cuentos de aventuras o cuentos de amor; pensar o hablar de un modo romántico; exagerar, mentir ‖ **Romance** ['romæns] o [ro'mæns] *adj* (*Neo-Latin*) romance o románico

romance languages *spl* lenguas romances *or* románicas

romance of chivalry *s* libro de caballerías

Roman Empire *s* Imperio romano

Romanesque [,romən'ɛsk] *adj & s* románico

Roman nose *s* nariz aguileña

romantic [ro'mæntɪk] *adj* romántico; (*spot, place*) encantador

romanticism [ro'mæntɪ,sɪzəm] *s* romanticismo

romp [rɑmp] *intr* corretear, triscar

rompers ['rɑmpərz] *spl* traje holgado de juego

roof [ruf] o [rʊf] *s* (*top outer covering of a house*) tejado; (*of a car or bus*) imperial *f*, tejadillo; (*of the mouth*) paladar *m;* (*of heaven*) bóveda; (*home, dwelling*) (fig) techo; **to raise the roof** (slang) poner el grito en el cielo ‖ *tr* techar

roofer ['rufər] o ['rʊfər] *s* techador *m*, pizarrero

roof garden *s* (*garden on the roof*) pérgola, azotea de baile y diversión

rook [rʊk] *s* (*bird*) grajo; (*in chess*) roque *m* ‖ *tr* trampear

rookie ['rʊki] *s* (slang) bisoño, novato

room [rum] o [rʊm] *s* aposento, cuarto, habitación, pieza; espacio, sitio, lugar *m;* ocasión; **to make room** abrir paso, hacer lugar ‖ *intr* alojarse

room and board *s* pensión completa

room clerk *s* empleado en la recepción, encargado de las reservas

roomer ['rumər] *s* inquilino

rooming house *s* casa donde se alquilan cuartos

room'mate' *s* compañero de cuarto

room·y ['rumi] *adj* (*comp* -ier; *super* -iest) amplio, espacioso

roost [rust] *s* percha de gallinero; gallinero; lugar *m* de descanso; **to rule the roost** ser el amo del cotarro, tener el mando y el palo ‖ *intr* descansar (*las aves*) en la percha; estar alojado; pasar la noche

rooster ['rustər] *s* gallo

root [rut] o [rʊt] *s* raíz *f;* **to get to the root of** profundizar; **to take root** echar raíces ‖ *tr* hocicar, hozar ‖ *intr* arraigar; **to root for** (slang) gritar alentando

rooter ['rutər] o ['rʊtər] *s* (slang) hincha *mf*

rope [rop] *s* cuerda; (*of a hangman*) dogal *m;* (*to catch an animal*) lazo; **to jump rope** saltar a la comba; **to know the ropes** (slang) saber todas las tretas; espabilarse ‖ *tr* atar con una cuerda; coger con lazo; **to rope in** (slang) embaucar, engañar

rope'walk'er *sl* funámbulo, volatinero

rosa·ry ['rozəri] *s* (*pl* -ries) rosario

rose [roz] *adj* de color de rosa ‖ *s* rosa

rose'bud' *s* pimpollo, capullo de rosa

rose'bush' *s* rosal *m*

rose'-col'ored *adj* rosado; **to see everything through rose-colored glasses** verlo todo de color de rosa

rose garden *s* rosaleda, rosalera

rose hip *s* (bot) cinarrodón *m;* eterio

rosemar·y ['roz,mɛri] *s* (*pl* -ies) romero

rose of Sharon ['ʃɛrən] *s* granado blanco, rosa de Siria

rose window *s* rosetón *m*

rose'wood' *s* palisandro

rosin ['rɑzɪn] *s* colofonia, brea seca

roster ['rɑstər] *s* catálogo, lista; horario escolar, horas de clase

rostrum ['rɑstrəm] *s* tribuna

ros·y ['rozi] *adj* (*comp* -ier; *super* -iest) rosado, sonrosado; alegre

rot [rɑt] *s* podredumbre; (slang) tontería ‖ *v* (*pret & pp* rotted; *ger* rotting) *tr* pudrir ‖ *intr* pudrirse

rotate ['rotet] o [ro'tet] *tr* hacer girar; alternar ‖ *intr* girar; alternar

rote [rot] *s* rutina, repetición maquinal; **by rote** de memoria, maquinalmente

rot'gut' *s* (slang) matarratas *m*

rotogravure [,rotəgrə'vjʊr] o [,rotə'grevjʊr] *s* rotograbado

rotten ['rɑtən] *adj* putrefacto, pútrido; corrompido

rotund [ro'tʌnd] *adj* redondo de cuerpo; (*language*) redondo

rouge [ruʒ] *s* arrebol *m*, colorete *m* ‖ *tr* arrebolar, pintar ‖ *intr* arrebolarse, pintarse

rough [rʌf] *adj* áspero; (*sea*) agitado, picado; (*crude, unwrought*) tosco, grosero; aproximado ‖ *tr* —**to rough it** vivir sin comodidades, hacer vida campestre

rough'cast' *s* modelo tosco; mezcla gruesa ‖ *v* (*pret & pp* **-cast**) *tr* (*to prepare in rough form*) bosquejar; dar a (*la pared*) una capa de mezcla gruesa

rough copy *s* borrador *m*

roughly ['rʌfli] *adv* asperamente; brutalmente; aproximadamente

roulette [ru'lɛt] *s* ruleta

round [raund] *adj* redondo ‖ *adv* redondamente; alrededor; de boca en boca; por todas partes ‖ *prep* alrededor de; (*e.g., the corner*) a la vuelta de; cerca de; acá y allá en ‖ *s* camino, circuito; (*of a policeman; of visits; of drinks or cigars*) ronda; (*of applause; discharge of guns*) salva; (*discharge of a single gun*) disparo, tiro; (*of people*) corro, círculo; (*of golf*) partido; rutina, serie *f*, sucesión; redondez *f;* revolución; (box) asalto; **to go the rounds** ir de boca en boca; ir de mano en mano ‖ *tr* (*to make round*) redondear; cercar, rodear; doblar (*una esquina, un promontorio*); **to round off** u **out** redondear; acabar, completar, perfeccionar; **to round up** juntar, recoger; rodear (*el ganado*)

roundabout ['raundə,baut] *adj* indirecto ‖ *s* curso indirecto; (Brit) tío vivo; (Brit) glorieta de tráfico

rounder ['raundər] *s* (coll) pródigo; (coll) catavinos *m*, borrachín habitual

round'house' *s* cocherón *m*, casa de máquinas, depósito de locomotoras

round-shouldered ['raund,ʃoldərd] *adj* cargado de espaldas

Round Table *s* Tabla Redonda

round'-trip' ticket *s* billete *m* de ida y vuelta

round'up' *s* (*of cattle*) rodeo; (*of criminals*) redada; (*of old friends*) reunión

rouse [rauz] *tr* despertar; excitar, provocar; levantar (*la caza*) ‖ *intr* despertarse, despabilarse

rout [raut] *s* derrota; fuga desordenada ‖ *tr* derrotar; poner en fuga desordenada; arrancar hozando ‖ *intr* hozar

route [rut] o [raut] *s* ruta; itinerario ‖ *tr* encaminar

routine [ru'tin] *adj* rutinario ‖ *s* rutina

rove [rov] *intr* andar errante, vagar

row [rau] *s* (coll) camorra, pendencia, riña; (coll) alboroto, bullicio; (coll) balumba; **to raise a row** (coll) armar camorra ‖ [ro] *s* fila, hilera; (*of houses*) crujía; **in a row** seguidos, p.ej., **five hours in a row** cinco horas seguidas ‖ *intr* remar

rowboat ['ro,bot] *s* bote *m*, bote de remos

row•dy ['raudi] *adj* (*comp* **-dier;** *super* **-diest**) gamberro ‖ *s* (*pl* **-dies**) gamberro

rower ['ro•ər] *s* remero

royal ['rɔɪ•əl] *adj* real; (*magnificent, splendid*) regio

royalist ['rɔɪ•əlɪst] *s* realista *mf*

royal•ty ['rɔɪ•əlti] *s* (*pl* **-ties**) realeza; personaje *m* real, personajes reales; derechos de autor; derechos de inventor

r.p.m. *abbr* revolutions per minute

R.R. *abbr* railroad, Right Reverend

rub [rʌb] *s* frotación, roce *m;* **there's the rub** ahí está el busilis ‖ *v* (*pret & pp* **rubbed;** *ger* **rubbing**) *tr* frotar; **to rub elbows with** rozarse mucho con; **to rub out** borrar; (slang) asesinar ‖ *intr* frotar; **to rub off** quitarse frotando; borrarse

rubber ['rʌbər] *s* caucho, goma; goma de borrar; chanclo, zapato de goma; (in bridge) robre *m* ‖ *intr* (slang) estirar el cuello o volver la cabeza para ver

rubber band *s* liga de goma

rubber plant *s* árbol *m* del caucho

rubber plantation *s* cauchal *m*

rubber stamp *s* cajetín *m*, sello de goma; (*with a person's signature*) estampilla; (coll) persona que aprueba sin reflexionar

rub'ber-stamp' *tr* estampar con un sello de goma; (*with a person's signature*) estampillar; (coll) aprobar sin reflexionar

rubbish ['rʌbɪʃ] *s* basura, desecho, desperdicios; (coll) disparate *m*, tontería

rubble ['rʌbəl] *s* (*broken stone*) ripio; (*masonry*) mampostería

rub'down' *s* masaje *m*, fricción

rube [rub] *s* (slang) isidro, rústico

ruble ['rubəl] *s* rublo

ru•by ['rubi] *s* (*pl* **-bies**) rubí *m*

rudder ['rʌdər] *s* timón *m*, gobernalle *m*

rud•dy ['rʌdi] *adj* (*comp* **-dier;** *super* **-diest**) coloradote, rubicundo;

rude [rud] *adj* rudo; desacomodido (SAm)

rudiment ['rudɪmənt] *s* rudimento

rudeness ['rudnɪs] *s* malcriadez *f*, malacrianza

rue [ru] *tr* lamentar, arrepentirse de

rueful ['rufəl] *adj* lamentable; triste

ruffian ['rʌfi•ən] *s* hombre grosero y brutal

ruffle ['rʌfəl] *s* arruga; (*of drum*) redoble *m;* (sew) volante *m* ‖ *tr* arrugar; agitar, descomponer; enojar, molestar; confundir; redoblar (*el tambor*); (sew) fruncir un volante en, adornar o guarnecer con volante

rug [rʌg] *s* alfombra; alfombrilla; (*lap robe*) manta

rugged ['rʌgɪd] *adj* áspero, rugoso; recio, vigoroso; tempestuoso

ruin ['ru•ɪn] *s* ruina ‖ *tr* arruinar; estropear; echar a perder

rule [rul] *s* regla; autoridad, mando; regla de imprenta; (*reign*) reinado; (*of a court of law*) decisión, fallo; **as a rule** por regla general; **to be the rule** ser lo que se hace ‖ *tr* gobernar, regir; dirigir, guiar; contener, reprimir; (*to mark with lines*) reglar; (law) decidir, determinar; **to rule out** excluir, rechazar ‖ *intr* gobernar, regir; prevalecer; **to rule over** gobernar, regir

rule of law *s* régimen *m* de justicia

ruler ['rulər] s gobernante *mf;* soberano; *(for ruling lines)* regla

ruling ['rulɪŋ] *adj* gobernante, dirigente, imperante ‖ s *(of a court or judge)* decisión, fallo; *(of paper)* rayado

rum [rʌm] s ron *m; (any alcoholic drink)* (U.S.A.) aguardiente *m*

Rumanian [ru'menɪ•ən] *adj & s* rumano

rumble ['rʌmbəl] s retumbo; *(of the intestines)* rugido; (slang) riña entre pandillas ‖ *intr* retumbar; avanzar retumbando

ruminate ['rumɪˌnet] *tr & intr* rumiar

rummage ['rʌmɪdʒ] *tr & intr* buscar revolviéndolo todo

rummage sale s venta de prendas usadas

rumor ['rumər] s rumor *m;* (coll) díceres *mpl;* bolado (CAm) ‖ *tr* rumorear; **it is rumored that** se rumorea que

rump [rʌmp] s anca, nalga; *(cut of beef)* cuarto trasero

rumple ['rʌmpəl] s arruga ‖ *tr* arrugar, ajar, chafar ‖ *intr* arrugarse

rumpus ['rʌmpəs] s (coll) batahola, alboroto; **to raise a rumpus** (coll) armar la de San Quintín

run [rʌn] s carrera; clase *f,* tipo; arroyo; *(e.g., in a stocking)* carrera; *(on a bank by depositors)* asedio; *(of consecutive performances of a play)* serie *f;* (baseball & mus) carrera; **in the long run** a la larga; **on the run** a escape; en fuga desordenada; **the common run of people** el común de las gentes; **the general run of** la generalidad de; **to have a long run** permanecer en cartel durante mucho tiempo; **to have the run of** hallar el secreto de; tener libertad de ir y venir por ‖ *v (pret* ran [ræn]; *pp* run; *ger* running) *tr* hacer funcionar; dirigir, manejar; trazar, tirar *(una línea);* exhibir *(un cine);* hacer *(mandados);* tener como candidato; burlar, violar *(un bloqueo);* tener *(calentura);* correr *(un caballo; un riesgo);* **to run down** cazar y matar; derribar; atropellar *(a un peatón);* (coll) denigrar, desacreditar; **to run in** rodar *(un nuevo coche);* **to run off** tocar *(una pieza de música);* tirar, imprimir; **to run up** (coll) aumentar *(gastos)* ‖ *intr* correr; *(on wheels)* rodar; darse prisa; trepar *(la vid);* ir y venir *(un vapor);* supurar *(una llaga);* colar *(un líquido);* correrse *(un color o tinte);* presentar su candidatura; andar, funcionar, marchar; deshilarse *(las medias);* migrar *(los peces);* estar en fuerza; *(to be worded or written)* rezar; **to run across** dar con, tropezar con; **to run away** correr, huir; desbocarse *(un caballo);* **to run down** escurrir, gotear *(un líquido);* descargarse *(un acumulador);* distenderse *(el muelle de un reloj);* acabarse la cuerda, p.ej., **the watch ran down** se acabó la cuerda; **to run for** presentar su candidatura a; **to run in the family** venir de familia; **to run into** tropezar con; chocar con, topar con; **to run off the track** descarrilar *(un tren);* **to run out** salir; expirar, terminar; acabarse; agotarse; **to run out of** acabársele a uno, e.g.,

I have run out of money se me ha acabado el dinero; **to run over** atropellar *(a un peatón);* registrar a la ligera; pasar por encima; leer rápidamente; rebosar *(un líquido);* **to run through** disipar rápidamente *(una fortuna);* registrar a la ligera; estar difundido en

run'a•way' *adj* fugitivo; *(horse)* desbocado ‖ s fugitivo; caballo desbocado; fuga

run'-down' *adj* desmedrado; desmantelado; inculto; *(clock spring)* sin cuerda, distendido; *(storage battery)* descargado

rung [rʌŋ] s *(of ladder or chair)* travesaño; *(of wheel)* radio, rayo

runner ['rʌnər] s corredor *m;* caballo de carreras; mensajero; *(of an ice sleigh)* cuchilla; *(of a sleigh)* patín *m; (long narrow rug)* pasacaminos *m; (strip of cloth for table top)* tapete *m; (in stockings)* carrera

run'ner-up' s *(pl* runners-up) subcampeón *m*

running ['rʌnɪŋ] *adj* corredor; *(expenses; water)* corriente; *(knot)* corredizo; *(sore)* supurante; *(writing)* cursivo; continuo; consecutivo; en marcha; *(start)* *(sport)* lanzado ‖ s carrera, corrida; administración, dirección; marcha, funcionamiento; **to be in the running** tener esperanzas o posibilidades de ganar

running board s estribo

running head s titulillo

running start s *(sport)* salida lanzada

run'off' e•lec'tion s votación de desempate

run-of-mine coal ['rʌnəv'maɪn] s carbón *m* tal como sale

run'-of-the-mill' *adj* (coll) ordinario; mediocre

run'proof' *adj* indesmallable

runt [rʌnt] s enano, hombrecillo; *(little child)* redrojo; animal achaparrado

run'way' s *(of a stream)* cauce *m;* senda trillada; (aer) pista de aterrizaje

rupture ['rʌptʃər] s ruptura; *(pathol)* quebradura; *(break in relations)* ruptura ‖ *tr* romper; causar una hernia en ‖ *intr* romperse; padecer hernia

rural free delivery ['rurəl] s distribución gratuita del correo en el campo

rural police s guardia civil

rural policeman s guardia civil *m*

ruse [ruz] s astucia, artimaña

rush [rʌʃ] *adj* urgente ‖ s prisa grande, precipitación; agolpamiento de gente; (bot) junco; **in a rush** de prisa ‖ *tr* empujar con violencia o prisa; despachar con prontitud; (slang) cortejar insistentemente *(a una mujer);* **to rush through** ejecutar de prisa, despachar rápidamente; expedir ‖ *intr* lanzarse, precipitarse; venir de prisa, ir de prisa; actuar con prontitud; **to rush through** lanzarse a través de, lanzarse por entre

rush-bottomed chair ['rʌʃ'bɑtəmd] s silla de junco

rush hour s hora de aglomeración, horas de punta, horas de afluencia

rush'light' s mariposa, lamparilla

rush order s pedido urgente
russet ['rʌsɪt] adj canelo
Russia ['rʌʃə] s Rusia
Russian ['rʌʃən] adj & s ruso
rust [rʌst] s orín m, moho, herrumbre; (agr) roña, roya; color rojizo o anaranjado ‖ tr aherrumbrar ‖ intr aherrumbrarse
rustic ['rʌstɪk] adj rústico; sencillo, sin artificio ‖ s rústico
rustle ['rʌsəl] s susurro, crujido ‖ tr hacer susurrar, hacer crujir; hurtar (ganado) ‖

intr susurrar, crujir; (slang) trabajar con ahinco
rusty ['rʌsti] adj (comp **-ier;** super **-iest**) herrumbroso, mohoso; rojizo; (out of practice) empolvado, desusado, remoto
rut [rʌt] s (track, groove in road) rodada, bache m; hábito arraigado; (sexual excitement in animals) celo; (period of this excitement) brama
ruthless ['ruθlɪs] adj despiadado, cruel
Ry. abbr **railway**
rye [raɪ] s centeno; whisky de centeno

S

S, s [ɛs] decimonona letra del alfabeto inglés
s abbr **second, shilling, singular**
Sabbath ['sæbəθ] s (of Jews) sábado; (of Christians) domínica; **to keep the Sabbath** observar el descanso dominical, guardar el domingo
saber ['sebər] s sable m
sable ['sebəl] adj negro ‖ s marta cebellina; **sables** vestidos de luto
sabotage ['sæbə,tɑʒ] s sabotaje m ‖ tr & intr sabotear
saccharin ['sækərɪn] s sacarina
sachet ['sæʃe] o [sæ'ʃe] s polvo oloroso; saquito de perfumes
sack [sæk] s saco; vino blanco generoso; (mil) saqueo, saco; (of an employee) (slang) despedida ‖ tr ensacar; saquear, pillar; (slang) despedir (a un empleado)
sack'cloth' s harpillera; (worn for penitence) cilicio
sacrament ['sækrəmənt] s sacramento
sacred ['sekrəd] adj sagrado
sacrifice ['sækrɪ,faɪs] s sacrificio; **at a sacrifice** con pérdida ‖ tr sacrificar; (to sell at a loss) malvender ‖ intr sacrificar; sacrificarse
Sacrifice of the Mass s sacrificio del altar
sacrilege ['sækrɪlɪdʒ] s sacrilegio
sacrilegious [,sækrɪ'lɪdʒəs] o [,sækrɪ'lidʒəs] adj sacrílego
sacristan ['sækrɪstən] s sacristán m
sacris•ty ['sækrɪsti] s (pl **-ties**) sacristía
sad [sæd] adj (comp **sadder;** super **saddest**) triste; (slang) malo
sadden ['sædən] tr entristecer ‖ intr entristecerse
saddle ['sædəl] s silla de montar; (of a bicycle) sillín m ‖ tr ensillar; **to saddle with** echar a cuestas a
sad'dle•bags' spl alforjas
sad'dle•bow' [,bo] s arzón delantero
sad'dle•tree' s arzón m
sadist ['sædɪst] s sádico
sadistic [sæ'dɪstɪk] adj sádico
sadness ['sædnɪs] s tristeza

safe [sef] adj seguro, ileso, salvo; cierto, digno de confianza; sin peligro, a salvo; **safe and sound** sano y salvo; **safe from** a salvo de ‖ s caja fuerte, caja de caudales
safe'-con'duct s salvoconducto
safe'-crack'er s ladrón m de cajas de caudales
safe'-depos'it box s caja de seguridad
safe'guard' s salvaguardia, medida de seguridad ‖ tr salvaguardar
safe•ty ['sefti] adj de seguridad ‖ s (pl **-ties**) seguridad; **to parachute to safety** lanzarse en paracaídas; **to reach safety** ponerse a salvo, llegar a lugar seguro
safety belt s (aer, aut) correa de seguridad, cinturón m de seguridad; (naut) cinturón m salvavidas; **retractable safety belt** cinturón m retráctil
safety match s fósforo de seguridad
safety pin s imperdible m, alfiler m de seguridad, gacilla
safety rail s guardarriel m
safety razor s maquinilla de seguridad
safety valve s válvula de seguridad
safety zone s (for pedestrians) isla de peatones or de seguridad
saffron ['sæfrən] adj azafranado ‖ s azafrán m ‖ tr azafranar
sag [sæg] s comba, combadura; (e.g., of a cable) flecha ‖ v (pret & pp **sagged;** ger **sagging**) intr combarse; (to slacken, yield) aflojar, ceder, doblegarse; bajar (los precios)
sagacious [sə'geʃəs] adj sagaz
sage ['sedʒ] adj sabio, cuerdo ‖ s sabio; (bot) salvia; (bot) artemisa
sage'brush' s (bot) artemisa
Sagittarius [,sædʒə'tɛri•əs] s (astr) Sagitario
sail [sel] s vela; barco de vela; paseo en barco de vela; **to set sail** hacerse a la vela; **under full sail** a vela llena ‖ tr gobernar (un barco de vela); navegar (un mar, río, etc.) ‖ intr navegar, navegar a la vela; salir, salir de viaje; deslizarse, flotar, volar; **to sail into** (slang) atacar, regañar, reñir

ru
sa

sail'boat' s barco de vela, buque m de vela, velero

sail'cloth' s lona, paño

sailing ['selɪŋ] adj de salida ‖ s paseo en barco de vela; navegación; salida

sailing vessel s buque velero

sailor ['selər] s (one who makes a living sailing) marinero; (an enlisted man in the navy) marino

saint [sent] adj & s santo ‖ tr (coll) canonizar

saintliness ['sentlɪnɪs] s santidad

Saint Vitus's dance ['vaɪtəsəs] s (pathol) baile m de San Vito

sake [sek] s respeto, bien, amor m; **for his sake** por su bien; **for the sake of** por, por motivo de, por amor a; **for your own sake** por su propio bien

salaam [sə'lɑm] s zalema ‖ tr saludar con zalemas, hacer zalemas a

salable ['seləbəl] adj vendible

salad ['sæləd] s ensalada

salad bowl s ensaladera

salad oil s aceite m de comer

Salamis ['sæləmɪs] s Salamina

sala·ry ['sæləri] s (pl -ries) sueldo

sale [sel] s venta; (auction) almoneda, subasta; **for sale** de venta; **se vende(n)**

sales'clerk' s dependiente mf de tienda

sales exhibit s exhibición-venta, exposición-venta

sales'la'dy s (pl -dies) venedora

sales·man ['selzmən] s (pl -men [mən]) vendedor m, dependiente m de tienda

sales manager s gerente m de ventas

sales'man·ship' s arte de vender

sales'room' s salón m de ventas; salón de exhibición

sales talk s argumento para inducir a comprar

sales tax s impuesto sobre ventas

saliva [sə'laɪvə] s saliva

sallow ['sælo] adj cetrino

sal·ly ['sæli] s (pl -lies) paseo, viaje m; ímpetu m, arranque m; salida, ocurrencia; (mil) salida, surtida ‖ v, (pret & pp -lied) intr salir, hacer una salida; ir de paseo; **to sally forth** salir, avanzar con denuedo

salmon ['sæmən] s salmón m

salon [sæ'lɑn] s salón m

saloon [sə'lun] s cantina, taberna; (on a steamer) salón m

saloon'keep'er s tabernero

salt [sɔlt] s sal f; **to be not worth one's salt** no valer (uno) el pan que come ‖ tr salar; (to preserve with salt) salpresar; marinar (el pescado); salgar (al ganado); **to salt away** (slang) ahorrar, guardar para uso futuro

salt'cel'lar s salero

salted peanuts spl saladillos

saltine [sɔl'tin] s galletita salada

saltish ['sɔltɪʃ] adj salobre

salt lick s salero, lamedero

salt of the earth, the lo mejor del mundo

salt'pe'ter s (potassium nitrate) salitre m; (sodium nitrate) nitro de Chile

salt'sha'ker s salero

salt·y ['sɔlti] adj (comp -ier; super -iest) salado

salubrious [sə'lubrɪ·əs] adj salubre

salutation [,sæljə'teʃən] s salutación

salute [sə'lut] s saludo ‖ tr saludar

Salvadoran [,sælvə'dorən] o **Salvadorian** [,sælvə'dorɪ·ən] adj & s salvadoreño

salvage ['sælvɪdʒ] s salvamento ‖ tr salvar; recobrar

Salvation Army [sæl'veʃən] s ejército de Salvación

salve [sæv] o [sɑv] s ungüento ‖ tr curar con ungüento; preservar; aliviar

sal·vo ['sælvo] s (pl -vos o -voes) salva

Samaritan [sə'mærɪtən] adj & s samaritano

same [sem] adj & pron indef mismo; **it's all the same to me** lo mismo me da; **just the same** lo mismo, sin embargo; **same . . . as** mismo . . . que

samite ['sæmaɪt] o ['semaɪt] s jamete m

sample ['sæmpəl] s muestra ‖ tr catar, probar

sample copy s ejemplar m muestra

sancti·fy ['sæŋktɪ,faɪ] v (pret & pp -fied) tr santificar

sanctimonious [,sæŋktɪ'monɪ·əs] adj santurrón

sanction ['sæŋkʃən] s sanción ‖ tr sancionar

sanctuar·y ['sæŋktʃu,ɛri] s (pl -ies) santuario; asilo, refugio; **to take sanctuary** acogerse a sagrado

sand [sænd] s arena ‖ tr enarenar; lijar con papel de lija

sandal ['sændəl] s sandalia; cacle m (Mex)

san'dal·wood' s (bot) sándalo

sand'bag' s saco de arena

sand'bank' s banco de arena

sand bar s barra de arena

sand'blast' s chorro de arena ‖ tr limpiar con chorro de arena

sand'box' s (rr) arenero

sand dune s duna, médano

sand'glass' s reloj m de arena, ampolleta

sand' pa'per s papel m de lija ‖ tr lijar

sand'stone' s piedra arenisca

sand'storm' s tempestad de arena

sandwich ['sændwɪtʃ] s emparedado, sandwich m ‖ tr intercalar

sandwich man s hombre-anuncio

sand·y ['sændi] adj (comp -ier; super -iest) arenoso; (hair) rufo; cambiante, movible

sane [sen] adj cuerdo, sensato; (principles) sano

sanguinary ['sæŋgwɪn,ɛri] adj sanguinario

sanguine ['sæŋgwɪn] adj confiado, esperanzado; (countenance) coloradote

sanitary ['sænɪ,tɛri] adj sanitario

sanitary napkin s compresa higiénica

sanitation [,sænɪ'teʃən] s (sanitary measures) sanidad; (drainage) saneamiento

sanity ['sænɪti] s cordura, sensatez f

Santa Claus ['sæntə,klɔz] s el Papá Noel, San Nicolás

sap [sæp] s savia; (mil) zapa; (coll) necio, tonto ‖ v (pret & pp sapped; ger sapping) tr agotar, debilitar; zapar, socavar

sap'head' s (coll) cabeza de chorlito

sapling ['sæplɪŋ] *s* árbol *m* muy joven, pimpollo; jovenzuelo, mozuelo
sapphire ['sæfaɪr] *s* zafiro
saraband ['særə,bænd] *s* zarabanda
Saracen ['særəsən] *adj & s* sarraceno
Saragossa [,særə'gɑsə] *s* Zaragoza
sarcasm ['sɑrkæzəm] *s* sarcasmo; escopetazo (SAm)
sarcastic [sɑr'kæstɪk] *adj* sarcástico
sardine [sɑr'din] *s* sardina; **packed in like sardines** como sardinas en banasta o en lata
Sardinia [sɑr'dɪnɪ•ə] *s* Cerdeña
Sardinian [sɑr'dɪnɪ•ən] *adj & s* sardo
sarsaparilla [,sɑrsəpə'rɪlə] *s* zarzaparrilla
sash [sæʃ] *s* banda, faja; (*of a window*) marco
sash window *s* ventana de guillotina
satchel ['sætʃəl] *s* maletín *m*; (*of a schoolboy*) cartapacio
sateen [sæ'tin] *s* satén *m*
satellite ['sætə,laɪt] *s* satélite *m*
satellite country *s* país *m* satélite
satiate ['seʃɪ,et] *adj* ahito, harto ‖ *tr* saciar
satin ['sætən] *s* raso
satinet [,sætɪ'nɛt] *s* rasete *m*
satiric(al) [sə'tɪrɪk(əl)] *adj* satírico
satirist ['sætɪrɪst] *s* satírico
satirize ['sætɪ,raɪz] *tr & intr* satirizar
satisfaction [,sætɪs'fækʃən] *s* satisfacción
satisfactory [,sætɪs'fæktəri] *adj* satisfactorio
satis•fy ['sætɪs,faɪ] *v* (*pret & pp* **-ified**) *tr & intr* satisfacer
saturate ['sætʃə,ret] *tr* saturar
Saturday ['sætərdi] *s* sábado
sauce [sɔs] *s* salsa; moje *f*, mojete *m*; (*of fruit*) compota; (*of chocolate*) crema; gracia, viveza; (coll) insolencia, lenguaje descomedido ‖ *tr* condimentar ‖ [sɔs] o [sæs] *tr* (coll) ser respondón con
sauce'pan' *s* cacerola
saucer ['sɔsər] *s* platillo
sau•cy ['sɔsi] *adj* (*comp* **-cier;** *super* **-ciest**) descarado, insolente; gracioso, vivo
sauerkraut ['saur,kraut] *s* chucruta
saunter ['sɔntər] *s* paseo tranquilo y alegre ‖ *intr* dar un paseo tranquilo y alegre; pasear tranquila y alegremente
sausage ['sɔsɪdʒ] *s* salchicha, embutido; moronga (Mex)
savage ['sævɪdʒ] *adj & s* salvaje, *mf*
savant ['sævənt] *s* sabio, erudito
save [sev] *prep* salvo, excepto, menos ‖ *tr* salvar (*p.ej., una vida, un alma*); ahorrar (*dinero*); conservar, guardar, horrar; proteger, amparar; **God save the Queen!** ¡Dios guarde a la Reina!; **to save face** salvar las apariencias
saving ['sevɪŋ] *prep,* salvo, excepto; con el debido respeto a ‖ *adj* económico ‖ **savings** *spl* ahorros, economías
savings account *s* cuenta de ahorros
savings bank *s* banco de ahorros, caja de ahorros
savior ['sevjər] *s* salvador *m*
Saviour ['sevjər] *s* Salvador *m*
savor ['sevər] *s* sabor *m* ‖ *tr* saborear ‖ *intr* oler; **to savor of** oler a, saber a

savor•y ['sevəri] *adj* (*comp* **-ier;** *super* **-iest**) sabroso; picante; fragante ‖ *s* (*pl* **-ies**) (bot) ajedrea
saw [sɔ] *s* (*tool*) sierra; proverbio, refrán *m* ‖ *tr* aserrar, serrar
saw'buck' *s* cabrilla, caballete *m*
saw'dust' *s* aserrín *m*, serrín *m*
saw'horse' *s* cabrilla, caballete *m*
saw'mill' *s* aserradero, serrería; montero (Mex)
Saxon ['sæksən] *adj & s* sajón *m*
saxophone ['sæksə,fon] *s* saxofón *m*
say [se] *s* decir *m*; **to have one's say** decir su parecer ‖ *v* (*pret & pp* **said** [sɛd] *tr* decir; **I should say so!** ¡ya lo creo!; **it is said** se dice; **no sooner said than done** dicho y hecho; **that is to say** es decir, esto es; **to go without saying** caerse de su peso
saying ['se•ɪŋ] *s* dicho; proverbio, refrán *m*; **sayings** (*rumor*) díceres *mpl*
sc. *abbr* **scene, science, scruple, scilicet** (Lat) **namely**
scab [skæb] *s* costra; (*strikebreaker*) esquirol *m*; (slang) bribón *m*, golfo
scabbard ['skæbərd] *s* funda, vaina
scab•by ['skæbi] *adj* (*comp* **-bier;** *super* **-biest**) costroso; (coll) ruin, vil
scabrous ['skæbrəs] *adj* escabroso
scads [skædz] *spl* (slang) montones *mpl*
scaffold ['skæfəld] *s* andamio; (*to execute a criminal*) cadalso, patíbulo
scaffolding ['skæfəldɪŋ]*s* andamiaje *m*
scald [skɔld] *tr* escaldar
scale [skel] *s* escama; balanza; platillo de balanza; (*e.g., of a map*) escala; (mus) escala; **on a scale of** en escala de; **on a large scale** en grande escala; **scales** balanza ‖ *tr* escamar; descortezar, descostrar; escalar, subir, trepar; graduar ‖ *intr* descamarse; descortezarse, descostrarse; subir, trepar
scallop ['skaləp] o ['skæləp] *s* concha de peregrino; (*shell or dish for serving fish*) concha; (*thin slice of meat*) escalope *m*; (*on edge of cloth*) festón *m* ‖ *tr* cocer (*p.ej., ostras*) en su concha; festonear
scalp [skælp] *s* cuero cabelludo ‖ *tr* escalpar; comprar y revender (*billetes de teatro*) a precios extraoficiales
scalpel ['skælpəl] *s* escalpelo
scal•y ['skeli] *adj* (*comp* **-ier;** *super* **-iest**) escamoso
scamp [skæmp] *s* bribón *m*, golfo
scamper ['skæmpər] *intr* escaparse precipitadamente; **to scamper away** escaparse precipitadamente
scan [skæn] *v* (*pret & pp* **scanned;** *ger* **scanning**) *tr* escudriñar; escandir (*versos*); (telv) explorar; (coll) dar un vistazo a
scandal ['skændəl] *s* escándalo
scandalize ['skændə,laɪz] *tr* escandalizar
scandalous ['skændələs] *adj* escandaloso
Scandinavian [,skændɪ'nevɪ•ən] *adj & s* escandinavo
scanning ['skænɪŋ] *s* (telv) escansión, exploración
scansion ['skænʃən] *s* escansión

scant [skænt] *adj* escaso, insuficiente; solo, apenas suficiente ‖ *tr* escatimar

scant•y [ˈskænti] *adj* (*comp* **-ier;** *super* **-iest**) escaso, insuficiente, poco suficiente; (*clothing*) ligero

scape′goat′ *s* cabeza de turco, víctima propiciatoria

scar [skɑr] *s* cicatriz *f*, señal *f*, lacra ‖ *v* (*pret* & *pp* **scarred;** *ger* **scarring**) *tr* señalar, marcar ‖ *intr* cicatrizarse

scarce [skɛrs] *adj* escaso, raro; **to make oneself scarce** (coll) no dejarse ver

scarcely [ˈskɛrsli] *adv* apenas; probablemente no; ciertamente no; **scarcely ever** raramente

scarci•ty [ˈskɛrsɪti] *s* (*pl* **-ties**) escasez *f*, carestía

scare [skɛr] *s* susto, alarma ‖ *tr* asustar, espantar; **to scare away** espantar, ahuyentar; **to scare up** (coll) juntar, recoger (*dinero*)

scare′crow′ *s* espantajo, espantapájaros *m*

scarf [skɑrf] *s* (*pl* **scarfs** o **scarves** [skɑrvz]) bufanda; pañuelo para el cuello; (*cover for a table, bureau, etc.*) tapete *m;* corbata

scarf′pin′ *s* alfiler *m* de corbata

scarlet [ˈskɑrlɪt] *adj* escarlata

scarlet fever *s* escarlata

scar•y [ˈskɛri] *adj* (*comp* **-ier;** *super* **-iest**) (*easily frightened*) (coll) asustadizo, espantadizo; (*causing fright*) (coll) espantoso

scathing [ˈskeðɪŋ] *adj* acerbo, duro

scatter [ˈskætər] *tr* esparcir, dispersar ‖ *intr* esparcirse, dispersarse

scatterbrain [ˈskætər,bren] *s* (coll) farraquista *m*

scatterbrained *adj* (coll) alegre de cascos, casquivano

scattered showers *spl* lluvias aisladas

scenari•o [sɪˈnɛrɪ,o] o [sɪˈnɑrɪ,o] *s* (*pls* **-os**) guión *m*, escenario

scenarist [sɪˈnɛrɪst] o [sɪˈnɑrɪst] *s* guionista *mf*, escenarista *mf*

scene [sin] *s* (*view*) paisaje *m;* (*in literature, art, the theater, the movie*) escena; escándalo, demostración de pasión; **behind the scenes** entre bastidores; **to make a scene** causar escándalo

scener•y [ˈsinəri] *s* (*pl* **-ies**) paisaje *m;* (theat) decoraciones

scene shifter [ˈʃiftər] *s* tramoyista *m*

scenic [ˈsinɪk] o [ˈsɛnɪk] *adj* pintoresco; (*representing an action graphically*) gráfico; (*pertaining to the stage*) escénico

scent [sɛnt] *s* olor *m;* perfume *m;* (*sense of smell*) olfato; (*trail*) rastro, pista ‖ *tr* oler; perfumar; olfatear, ventear; sospechar

scepter [ˈsɛptər] *s* cetro

sceptic [ˈskɛptɪk] *adj* & *s* escéptico

sceptical [ˈskɛptɪkəl] *adj* escéptico

schedule [ˈskɛdʒul] *s* catálogo, cuadro, lista; plan *m*, programa *m;* (*of trains, planes, etc.*) horario ‖ *tr* catalogar; proyectar; fijar la hora de

scheme [skim] *s* esquema *m;* plan *m*, proyecto; (*trick*) ardid *m*, treta; (*plot*) intriga, trama ‖ *tr* & *intr* proyectar; tramar

schemer [ˈskimər] *s* proyectista *mf;* intrigante *mf*

scheming [ˈskimɪŋ] *adj* astuto, mañoso, intrigante ‖ *s* intriga

schism [ˈsɪzəm] *s* cisma *m;* facción cismática

schist [ʃɪst] *s* esquisto

scholar [ˈskɑlər] *s* (*pupil*) alumno; (*scholarship holder*) becario; (*learned person*) sabio, erudito

scholarly [ˈskɑkərli] *adj* sabio, erudito

scholarship [ˈskɑlər,ʃɪp] *s* erudición; (*grant to study*) beca

scholarship holder *s* bequista *mf* (CAm, Cuba)

school [skul] *s* escuela; (*of a university*) facultad; (*of fish*) banco, cardume *m* ‖ *tr* enseñar, instruir, disciplinar

school age *s* edad escolar

school attendance *s* escolaridad

school board *s* junta de instrucción pública

school′boy′ *s* alumno de escuela

school day *s* día lectivo

school′girl′ *s* alumna de escuela

school′house′ *s* escuela

schooling [ˈskulɪŋ] *s* instrucción, enseñanza; experiencia

school′mate′ *s* compañero de escuela

school′room′ *s* aula, sala de clase

school′teach′er *s* maestro de escuela

school year *s* año lectivo

schooner [ˈskunər] *s* goleta

sci. *abbr* **science, scientific**

science [ˈsaɪ•əns] *s* ciencia

science fiction *s* ciencia-ficción; novela científica

scientific [ˌsaɪ•ənˈtɪfɪk] *adj* científico

scientist [ˈsaɪ•əntɪst] *s* científico, sabio, hombre *m* de ciencia

sci-fi [ˈsaɪˈfaɪ] *s* (slang) *abbr* **science fiction**

scil. *abbr* **scilicet** (Lat) **namely**

scimitar [ˈsɪmɪtər] *s* cimitarra

scintillate [ˈsɪntɪ,let] *intr* chispear, centellear

scion [ˈsaɪ•ən] *s* vástago

Scipio [ˈsɪpɪ,o] *s* Escipión *m*

scissors [ˈsɪzərz] *ssg* o *spl* tijeras

scoff [skɔf] o [skɑf] *s* burla, mofa ‖ *intr* burlarse, mofarse; **to scoff at** burlarse de, mofarse de

scold [skold] *s* regañón *m*, regañona ‖ *tr* & *intr* regañar

scoop [skup] *s* (*instrument like a spoon*) cuchara, cucharón *m;* (*tool like a shovel*) pala; (*kitchen utensil*) paleta; (*for water*) achicador *m;* cucharada, palada, paletada; (*hollow made by a scoop*) hueco; (*big haul*) (coll) buena ganancia ‖ *tr* sacar con cuchara, pala, paleta; achicar (*agua*); **to scoop out** ahuecar, vaciar

scoot [skut] *s* (coll) carrera precipitada ‖ *intr* (coll) correr precipitadamente

scooter [ˈskutər] *s* monopatín *m*, patinete *m*

scope [skop] *s* alcance *m*, extensión; campo, espacio; **to give free scope to** dar campo libre a

scorch [skɔrtʃ] *s* chamusco ‖ *tr* chamuscar; (*to dry, wither*) abrasar; criticar acerbamente ‖ *intr* chamuscarse; abrasarse

scorching ['skɔrtʃɪŋ] *adj* abrasador; acerbo, duro, mordaz

score [skor] *s* (*in a game*) cuenta, tantos; (*in an examination*) nota; entalladura, muesca; línea, raya; (*twenty*) veintena; (*mus*) partitura; **on the score of** a título de; **to keep score** apuntar los tantos || *tr* anotar (*los tantos*); ganar, tantear (*tantos*); rayar, señalar; regañar acerbamente; (*mus*) instrumentar || *intr* ganar tantos; marcar los tantos

score board *s* marcador *m*, cuadro indicador

scorn [skɔrn] *s* desdén *m*, desprecio || *tr & intr* desdeñar, despreciar; **to scorn to** no dignarse

scornful ['skɔrnfəl] *adj* desdeñoso

Scorpio ['skɔrpɪ•o] *s* (astr) Escorpión *m*

scorpion ['skɔrpɪ•ən] *s* alacrán *m*, escorpión *m*

Scot [skat] *s* escocés *m*

Scotch [skatʃ] *adj* escocés || *s* (*dialect*) escocés *m;* whiskey *m* escocés; **the Scotch** los escoceses

Scotch•man ['skatʃmən] *s* (*pl* **-men** [mən]) escocés *m*

Scotland ['skatlənd] *s* Escocia

Scottish ['skatɪʃ] *adj* escocés || *s* (*dialect*) escocés *m;* **the Scottish** los escoceses

scoundrel ['skaundrəl] *s* bribón *m*, pícaro

scour [skaur] *tr* fregar, estregar; recorrer, explorar detenidamente

scourge [skʌrdʒ] *s* azote *m* || *tr* azotar

scout [skaut] *s* (mil) escucha, explorador *m;* niño explorador, niña exploradora; exploración, reconocimiento; (slang) individuo, sujeto, tipo || *tr* explorar, reconocer (*un territorio*); observar (*al enemigo*); negarse a creer

scout'mas'ter *s* jefe *m* de tropa de niños exploradores

scowl [skaul] *s* ceño, semblante ceñudo || *intr* mirar con ceño, poner mal gesto, poner mala cara

scramble ['skræmbəl] *s* arrebatiña || *tr* arrebatar; recoger de prisa; revolver; hacer un revoltillo de (*huevos*); trepar || *intr* luchar; trepar

scrambled eggs *spl* revoltillo, huevos revueltos

scrap [skræp] *s* fragmento, pedacito; desecho; chatarra; (slang) riña, contienda; **scraps** desperdicios, desechos; (*from the table*) sobras || *v* (*pret & pp* **scrapped;** *ger* **scrapping**) *tr* desechar, descartar, echar a la basura; reducir a hierro viejo || *intr* (slang) reñir, pelear

scrap'book' *s* álbum *m* de recortes, libro de recuerdos

scrape [skrep] *s* raspadura; (*place scratched*) raspaza; aprieto, enredo; || *tr* raspar; (*to gather together with much difficulty*) arañar || *intr* raspar; **to scrape along** ir tirando; **to scrape through** aprobar justo

scrap heap *s* montón *m* de cachivaches

scrap iron *s* chatarra, desecho de hierro

scrap paper *s* papel *m* para apuntes; papel de desecho

scratch [skrætʃ] *s* arañazo, rasguño; marca, raya, garrapato; (billiards) chiripa; (sport) línea de partida; **to start from scratch** empezar desde el principio, empezar de cero; **up to scratch** en buena condición || *tr* arañar, rasguñar; borrar, rasgar (*lo escrito*); garrapatear; (sport) borrar (*a un corredor o caballo*) || *intr* arañar, rasguñar; garrapatear; raspear (*una pluma*)

scratch pad *s* cuadernillo de apuntes

scratch paper *s* papel *m* para apuntes

scratch'-re•sist'ant *adj* resistente al rayado

scrawl [skrɔl] *s* garrapatos || *tr & intr* garrapatear

scraw•ny ['skrɔni] *adj* (*comp* **-nier;** *super* **-niest**) huesudo, flaco

scream [skrim] *s* chillido, grito || *tr* vociferar || *intr* chillar, gritar; reírse a gritos

screech [skritʃ] *s* chillido || *intr* chillar

screech owl *s* buharro; (*barn owl*) lechuza

screen [skrin] *s* mampara, biombo; (*in front of chimney*) pantalla; (*to keep flies out*) alambrera; (*to sift sand*) tamiz *m;* (mov, phys, telv) pantalla; **to put on the screen** llevar a la pantalla, llevar al celuloide || *tr* defender, proteger; cubrir, ocultar; cinematografiar; rodar, proyectar (*una película*); adaptar para el cine; tamizar (*p.ej., arena*)

screen grid *s* (electron) rejilla blindada

screen'play' *s* cinedrama *m*

screw [skru] *s* tornillo; (*internal or female screw*) rosca, tuerca; (*of a boat*) hélice *f;* **to have a screw loose** (slang) tener flojos los tornillos; **to put the screws on** apretar los tornillos a || *tr* atornillar; (*to twist, twist in*) enroscar; **to screw up** torcer (*el rostro*); || *intr* atornillarse

screw'ball' *s* (slang) estrafalario, excéntrico

screw'driv'er *s* destornillador *m*, desatornillador *m*

screw eye *s* armella

screw jack *s* gato de tornillo

screw propeller *s* hélice *f*

scribal error ['skraɪbəl] *s* error *m* de escribiente

scribble ['skrɪbəl] *s* garrapatos || *tr & intr* garrapatear

scribe [skraɪb] *s* (*teacher of Jewish law*) escriba *m;* escribiente *mf;* copista *mf;* autor *m*, escritor *m* || *tr* arañar, rayar; trazar con punzón

scrimp [skrɪmp] *tr & intr* escatimar

script [skrɪpt] *s* escritura, letra cursiva; manuscrito, texto; (*of a play, movie, etc.*) palabras; (rad, telv) guión *m;* (typ) plumilla inglesa

scripture ['skrɪptʃər] *s* escrito sagrado || **Scripture** *s* Escritura

script'writ'er *s* guionista *mf*, cinematurgo

scrofula ['skrɑfjələ] *s* escrófula

scroll [skrol] *s* rollo de papel, rollo de pergamino; (archit) voluta

scroll'work' *s* obra de volutas, adornos de voluta

scrub [skrʌb] *s* chaparral *m*, monte bajo; animal achaparrado; persona de poca monta; (*act of scrubbing*) fregado; (sport)

SC
SC

jugador *m* no oficial ‖ *v* (*pret* & *pp* **scrubbed;** *ger* **scrubbing**) *tr* fregar, restregar
scrub oak *s* chaparro
scrub woman *s* fregona
scruff [skrʌf] *s* nuca; piel *f* que cubre la nuca; capa, superficie *f;* espuma
scruple ['skrupəl] *s* escrúpulo
scrupulous ['skrupjələs] *adj* escrupuloso
scrutinize ['skrutɪ,naɪz] *tr* escudriñar, escrutar
scruti•ny ['skrutɪni] *s* (*pl* -**nies**) escudriñamiento, escrutinio
scubadiver ['skubə,dɪvər] *s* submarinista *mf*
scuff [skʌf] *s* rascadura, desgaste *m* ‖ *tr* rascar, desgastar
scuffle ['skʌfəl] *s* lucha, sarracina ‖ *intr* forcejear, luchar
scull [skʌl] *s* espadilla‖ *tr* impulsar con espadilla ‖ *intr* remar con espadilla
sculler•y ['skʌləri] *s* (*pl* -**ies**) trascocina
scullery maid *s* fregona
scullion ['skʌljən] *s* pinche *m*
sculptor ['skʌlptər] *s* escultor *m*
sculptress ['skʌlptrɪs] *s* escultora
sculpture ['skʌlptʃər] *s* escultura ‖ *tr* & *intr* esculpir
scum [skʌm] *s* espuma, nata; (*on metals*) escoria; (fig) escoria, canalla, gente baja; palomilla ‖ *v* (*pret* & *pp* **scummed;** *ger* **scumming**) *tr* & *intr* espumar
scum•my ['skʌmi] *adj* (*comp* -**mier;** *super* -**miest**) espumoso; (fig) vil, ruin
scurf [skʌrf] *s* (*shed by the skin*) caspa; (*shed by any surface*) costra
scurrilous ['skʌrɪləs] *adj* chocarrero, grosero, insolente, difamatorio
scur•ry ['skʌri] *v* (*pret* & *pp* -**ried**) *intr* echar a correr, escabullirse; **to scurry around** menearse; **to scurry away** ir respailando
scur•vy ['skʌril] *adj* (*comp* -**vier;** *super* -**viest**) despreciable, ruin, vil ‖ *s* escorbuto
scuttle ['skʌtəl] *s* (*bucket for coal*) cubo, balde *m;* (*trap door*) escotillón *m;* fuga, paso acelerado; (naut) escotilla ‖ *tr* barrenar, dar barreno a ‖ *intr* echar a correr
Scylla ['sɪlə] *s* Escila; **between Scylla and Charybdis** entre Escila y Caribdis
scythe [saɪð] *s* dalle *m,* guadaña
sea [si] *s* mar *m* & *f;* **at sea** en el mar; confuso, perplejo; **by the sea** a la orilla del mar; **to follow the sea** correr los mares, ser marinero; **to put to sea** hacerse a la mar
sea'board' *adj* costanero, costero ‖ *s* costa del mar, litoral *m*
sea breeze *s* brisa de mar
sea'coast' *s* costa marítima, litoral *m*
sea dog *s* (*seal*) foca; (coll) marinero viejo, lobo de mar
seafarer ['si,fɛrər] *s* marinero; viajero por mar
sea'food' *s* mariscos
seagoing ['si,go•ɪŋ] *adj* de alta mar
sea gull *s* gaviota
seal [sil] *s* (*raised design; stamp; mark*) sello; (*sea animal*) foca ‖ *tr* sellar; cerrar hermé-

ticamente; decidir irrevocablemente; (*with sealing wax*) lacrar
sea legs *spl* pie marino
sea level *s* nivel *m* del mar
sealing wax *s* lacre *m*
seal'skin' *s* piel *f* de foca
seam [sim] *s* costura; (*edges left after making a seam*) metido; (*mark, line*) arruga; (*scar*) costurón *m;* grieta, juntura; (min) filón *m,* veta
sea•man ['simən] *s* (*pl* -**men** [mən]) marinero; (nav) marino
sea mile *s* milla náutica
seamless ['simlɪs] *adj* inconsútil, sin costura
seamstress ['simstrɪs] *s* costurera; (*dressmaker's helper*) modistilla
seam•y ['simi] *adj* (*comp* -**ier;** *super* -**iest**) lleno de costuras; tosco, burdo; vil, soez; miserable
séance ['se•ɑns] *s* sesión de espiritistas
sca'plane' *s* hidroavión *m,* hidroplano
sea'port' *s* puerto de mar
sea power *s* potencia naval
sear [sɪr] *adj* seco, marchito; gastado, raído ‖ *s* chamusco, socarra ‖ *tr* chamuscar, socarrar; quemar; marchitar; cauterizar
search [sʌrtʃ] *s* busca; pesquisa, indagación; (*frisking a person*) cacheo; (*police, soldiers*) peinado; **in search of** en busca de ‖ *tr* averiguar, explorar; registrar ‖ *intr* buscar; (*police, soldiers*) peinar; **to search for** buscar; **to search into** indagar, investigar
search'light' *s* reflector *m,* proyector *m*
search warrant *s* auto de registro domiciliario, orden *f* de allanamiento
sea'scape' *s* vista del mar; (*painting*) marina
sea shell *s* concha marina
sea'shore' *s* costa, playa, ribera del mar
sea'sick' *adj* mareado
sea'sick'ness *s* mareo
sea'side' *s* orilla del mar, ribera del mar, playa
season ['sizən] *s* (*one of four parts of year*) estación; (*period of the year; period marked by certain activities*) temporada; (*opportune time; time of maturity, of ripening*) sazón *f;* **in season** en sazón; **in season and out of season** en tiempo y a destiempo; **out of season** fuera de sazón ‖ *tr* condimentar, sazonar; curar (*la madera*); moderar, templar
seasonal ['sizənəl] *adj* estacional
seasoning ['sizənɪŋ] *s* aderezo, aliño, condimento; (*of wood*) cura; (fig) sal *f,* chiste *m*
season ticket *s* billete *m* de abono
seat [sit] *s* asiento; (*of trousers*) fondillos; morada; sitio, lugar *m;* (*e.g., of government*) sede *f;* (*in parliament*) escaño; (*e.g., of a war*) teatro; (*e.g., of learning*) centro; (*of a saddle*) batalla; (*of human body*) nalgas; (theat) localidad; **reclining seat** (*as in car*) asiento abatible; ‖ *tr* sentar; tener asientos para; poner asiento a (*una silla*); echar fondillos a (*pantalones*); arraigar, establecer; **to be seated** estar. sentado; **to seat oneself** sentarse

seat belt s cinturón m de asiento
seat cover s funda de asiento, cubreasiento
SEATO ['sito] s (acronym) la O.T.A.S.E.
sea wall s dique marítimo
sea'way' s ruta marítima; avance m de un buque por mar; vía de agua interior para buques de alta mar; mar gruesa
sea'weed' s alga marina; plantas marinas
sea wind s viento que sopla del mar
sea'wor'thy adj marinero, en condiciones de navegar
sec. abbr **secant, second, secondary, secretary, section, sector**
secede [sɪ'sid] intr separarse, retirarse
secession [sɪ'sɛʃən] s secesión
seclude [sɪ'klud] tr recluir
secluded [sɪ'kludɪd] adj aislado, apartado, solitario
seclusion [sɪ'kluʒən] s reclusión, soledad
second ['sɛkənd] adj segundo; **to be second to none** ser tan bueno como el que más, no tener segundo || adv en segundo lugar || s segundo; artículo de segunda calidad; (in dates) dos m; (in a challenge) padrino; (aut) segunda (velocidad); (mus) segunda || tr secundar; apoyar (una moción)
secondar•y ['sɛkən,dɛri] adj secundario || s (pl -ies) (elec) secundario
sec'ond-best' adj (el) mejor después del primero
sec'ond-class' adj de segunda clase
second hand s segundero
sec'ond-hand' adj de segunda mano, de ocasión
second-hand bookshop s librería de viejo
second lieutenant s alférez m, subteniente m
sec'ond•rate' adj de segundo orden; de calidad inferior
second sight s doble vista
second wind s nuevo aliento
secre•cy ['sikrəsi] s (pl -cies) secreto; **in secrecy** en secreto
secret ['sikrɪt] adj & s secreto; **in secret** en secreto
secretar•y ['sɛkrɪ,tɛri] s (pl -ies) secretario; (desk) secreter m, escritorio
secrete [sɪ'krit] tr encubrir, esconder; (physiol) secretar
secretive [sɪ'kriɪtɪv] adj callado, reservado
sect [sɛkt] s secta, comunión
sectarian [sɛk'tɛrɪ•ən] adj & s sectario
section ['sɛkʃən] s sección; (of a country) región; (of a city) barrio; (of a law) artículo; (department, bureau) negociado; (rr) tramo
secular ['sɛkjələr] adj secular, seglar || s clérigo secular
secularism ['sɛkjələ,rɪzəm] s laicismo
secure [sɪ'kjur] adj seguro || tr asegurar; conseguir, obtener
securi•ty [sɪ'kjurɪti] s (pl -ties) seguridad; (person) segurador m; **securities** valores mpl, obligaciones, títulos
secy. o **sec'y.** abbr **secretary**
sedan [sɪ'dæn] s silla de manos; (aut) sedán m
sedate [sɪ'det] adj sentado, sosegado

sedative ['sɛdətɪv] adj & s sedativo
sedentary ['sɛdən,tɛri] adj sedentario
sedge [sɛdʒ] s juncia
sediment ['sɛdɪmənt] s sedimento
sedition [sɪ'dɪʃən] s sedición
seditious [sɪ'dɪʃəs] adj sedicioso
seduce [sɪ'djus] tr seducir
seducer [sɪ'djusər] s seductor m
seduction [sɪ'dʌkʃən] s seducción
seductive [sɪ'dʌktɪv] adj seductivo
sedulous ['sɛdjələs] adj cuidadoso, diligente
see [si] s (eccl) sede f || v (pret **saw** [sɔ; pp **seen** [sin] tr ver; **to see off** ir a despedir; **to see through** llevar a cabo; ayudar en un trance difícil || intr ver; **see here!** ¡mire Vd.!; **to see into** o **to see through** conocer el juego de
seed [sid] s semilla, simiente f; **to go to seed** dar semilla; echarse a perder || tr sembrar; (to remove the seeds from) despepitar || intr sembrar; dejar caer semillas
seed'bed' s semillero
seedling ['sidlɪŋ] s planta de semilla; árbol m de pie
seed•y ['sidi] adj (comp **-ier;** super **-iest**) lleno de granos; (coll) andrajoso, raído
seeing ['si•ɪŋ] adj vidente || s vista, visión || conj visto que
Seeing Eye dog s perro-lazarillo
seek [sik] v (pret & pp **sought** [sɔt] tr buscar; recorrer buscando; dirigirse a || intr buscar; **to seek after** tratar de obtener; **to seek to** esforzarse por
seem [sim] intr parecer
seemingly ['simɪŋli] adv aparentemente, al parecer
seem•ly ['simli] adj (comp **-lier;** super **-liest**) decente, decoroso, correcto; bien parecido
seep [sip] intr escurrirse, rezumarse
seer [sɪr] s profeta m, vidente m
see'saw' s balancín m, columpio de tabla; (motion) vaivén m || intr columpiarse; alternar; vacilar
seethe [siθ] intr hervir
segment ['sɛgmənt] s segmento
segregate ['sɛgrɪ,get] tr segregar
segregationist [,sɛgrɪ'geʃənɪst] s segregacionista mf
Seine [sen] s Sena m
seismograph ['saɪzmə,græf] s sismógrafo
seismology [saɪz'mɑlədʒi] s sismología
seize [siz] tr agarrar, asir, coger; atar, prender, sujetar; apoderarse de; comprender; (law) embargar, secuestrar; aprovecharse de (una oportunidad)
seizure ['siʒər] s prendimiento, prisión; captura, toma; (of an illness) ataque m; (law) embargo, secuestro
seldom ['sɛldəm] adv raramente, rara vez
select [sɪ'lɛkt] adj escogido, selecto || tr seleccionar
selectee [sɪ,lɛk'ti] s (mil) quinto
selection [sɪ'lɛkʃən] s selección; trozo escogido; (of goods for sale) surtido
self [sɛlf] adj mismo || pron sí mismo || s (pl **selves** [sɛlvz]) uno mismo; ser m; yo; **all by one's self** sin ayuda de nadie

sc
se

self'-abuse' *s* abuso de sí mismo; masturbación

self'-addressed' envelope *s* sobre *m* con el nombre y dirección del remitente

self'-cen'tered *adj* egocéntrico

self'-con'scious *adj* cohibido, apocado, tímido

self'-con•trol' *s* dominio de sí mismo; autodisciplina

self'-de•fense' *s* autodefensa; **in self-defense** en defensa propia

self'-de•ni'al *s* abnegación

self'-de•ter'mi•na'tion *s* autodeterminación

self'-dis'cipline *s* autodisciplina

self'-ed'u•cat'ed *adj* autodidacto

self'-em•ployed' *adj* que trabaja por su propia cuenta

self'-ev'i•dent *adj* patente, manifiesto

self'-ex•plan'a•tor'y *adj* que se explica por sí *h*ismo

self'-glor'i•fi•ca'tion *s* egolatría

self'-gov'ernment *s* autogobierno, autonomía; dominio sobre sí mismo

self'-im•por'tant *adj* altivo, arrogante

self'-in•dul'gence *s* intemperancia, desenfreno

self'-in'terest *s* egoísmo, interés *m* personal

selfish [ˈsɛlfɪʃ] *adj* egoísta

selfishness [ˈsɛlfɪʃnɪs] *s* egoísmo

selfless [ˈsɛlflɪs] *adj* desinteresado

self'-liq'ui•dat'ing *adj* autoamortizable

self'-love' *s* amor propio, egoísmo

self'-made' man *s* hijo de sus propias obras

self'-por'trait *s* autorretrato

self'-pos•sessed' *adj* dueño de sí mismo

self'-pres'er•va'tion *s* propia conservación

self'-re•li'ant *adj* confiado en sí mismo

self'-re•spect'ing *adj* lleno de dignidad, decoroso

self'-right'eous *adj* santurrón

self'-sac'ri•fice' *s* sacrificio de sí mismo

self'-same' *adj* mismísimo

self'-sat'is•fied' *adj* pagado de sí mismo

self'-seal'ing *adj* autopegado

self'-seek'ing *adj* egoísta ‖ *s* egoísmo

self'-ser'vice restaurant *s* restaurante *m* de libre servicio, restaurante de autoservicio

self'-start'er *s* arranque automático

self'-sup•port' *s* mantenimiento económico propio

self'-taught' *adj* autodidacto

self'-willed' *adj* obstinado, terco

self'-wind'ing clock *s* reloj *m* de cuerda automática, reloj de autocuerda

self'-wor'ship *s* egolatría

sell [sɛl] *v* (*pret* & *pp* **sold** [sold]) *tr* vender; **to sell out** realizar, saldar; (*to betray*) vender ‖ *intr* venderse, estar de venta; **to sell for** venderse a o en (*p.ej., cien pesetas*); **to sell off** bajar (*el mercado de valores*); **to sell out** venderlo todo, realizar

seller [ˈsɛlər] *s* vendedor *m*

sell'out' *s* (slang) realización, saldo; (slang) traición

Seltzer water [ˈsɛltsər] *s* agua de seltz

selvage [ˈsɛlvɪdʒ] *s* orillo, vendo

semantic [sɪˈmæntɪk] *adj* semántico ‖ **semantics** *s* semántica

semaphore [ˈsɛməˌfor] *s* semáforo; (rr) disco de señales

semblance [ˈsɛmbləns] *s* apariencia, imagen *f*, simulacro

semen [ˈsimɛn] *s* semen *m*

semester [sɪˈmɛstər] *adj* semestral ‖ *s* semestre *m*

semester hour *s* hora semestral

sem'ico'lon *s* punto y coma

sem'iconduc'tor *s* semiconductor *m*

sem'icon'scious *adj* semiconsciente

sem'ifi'nal *adj* & *s* (sport) semifinal *f*

sem'ilearn'ed *adj* semiculto

sem'imonth'ly *adj* quincenal ‖ *s* (*pl* -lies) periódico quincenal

seminar [ˈsɛmɪˌnɑr] *s* seminario

seminary [ˈsɛmɪˌnɛri] *s* (*pl* -ies) seminario

sem'ipre'cious *adj* semiprecioso, fino

Semite [ˈsɛmaɪt] o [ˈsimaɪt] *s* semita *mf*

Semitic [sɪˈmɪtɪk] *adj* semítico ‖ *s* semita *mf;* (*language*) semita *m*

sem'itrail'er *s* semi-remolque *m*

sem'iweek'ly *adj* bisemanal ‖ *s* (*pl* -lies) periódico bisemanal

sem'iyear'ly *adj* semestral

Sen. o **sen.** *abbr* **Senate, Senator, Senior**

senate [ˈsɛnɪt] *s* senado

senator [ˈsɛnətər] *s* senador *m*

senatorship [ˈsɛnətərˌʃɪp] *s* senaduría

send [sɛnd] *v* (*pret* & *pp* **sent** [sɛnt]) *tr* enviar, mandar; expedir, remitir; lanzar (*una bola, flecha, etc.*); **to send back** devolver, reenviar; **to send packing** despedir con cajas destempladas ‖ *intr* (rad) transmitir; **to send for** enviar por, enviar a buscar

sender [ˈsɛndər] *s* remitente *mf;* (telg) transmisor *m*

send'-off' *s* (coll) despedida afectuosa

senile [ˈsinaɪl] o [ˈsinɪl] *adj* senil

senility [sɪˈnɪlɪti] *s* senilidad; (pathol) senilismo

senior [ˈsinjər] *adj* mayor, de mayor edad; viejo; del último año; padre, p.ej., **John Jones, Senior** Juan Jones, padre ‖ *s* mayor *m;* socio más antiguo; alumno del último año

senior citizens *spl* gente *f* de edad

seniority [sinˈjɔrɪti] *s* antigüedad; precedencia, prioridad

sensation [sɛnˈseʃən] *s* sensación

sense [sɛns] *s* sentido; **to make sense out of** comprender, explicarse ‖ *tr* intuir, sentir, sospechar; comprender

senseless [ˈsɛnslɪs] *adj* falto de sentido; desmayado; insensato, necio

sense of guilt *s* cargo de conciencia

sense of humor *s* sentido de humor

sense organ *s* órgano sensorio

sensibili•ty [ˌsɛnsɪˈbɪlɪti] *s* (*pl* -ties) sensibilidad; **sensibilities** sentimientos delicados

sensible [ˈsɛnsɪbəl] *adj* cuerdo, sensato; perceptible, sensible; equilibrado

sensitive [ˈsɛnsɪtɪv] *adj* sensible; (*of the senses*) sensorio, sensitivo

sensitize ['sɛnsɪ,taɪz] *tr* sensibilizar
sensory ['sɛnsəri] *adj* sensorio
sensual ['sɛnʃʊ·əl] *adj* sensual, voluptuoso
sensuous ['sɛnʃʊ·əs] *adj* sensual
sentence ['sɛntəns] *s* (gram) frase *f*, oración; (law) sentencia ‖ *tr* sentenciar, condenar
sentiment ['sɛntɪmənt] *s* sentimiento
sentimentali·ty [,sɛntɪmən'tælti] *s* (*pl* -ties) sentimentalismo
sentinel ['sɛntɪnəl] *s* centinela *m* or *f;* **to stand sentinel** estar de centinela, hacer centinela
sen·try ['sɛntri] *s* (*pl* -tries) centinela *m* or *f*
sentry box *s* garita de centinela
separate ['sɛpərɪt] *adj* separado; suelto ‖ ['sɛpə,ret] *tr* separar ‖ *intr* separarse
separation [,sɛpə're∫ən] *s* separación
separation of powers *s* (pol) separación de poderes
Sephardic [sɪ'fɑrdɪk] *adj* sefardí, sefardita
Sephardim [sɪ'fɑrdɪm] *spl* sefardíes *mpl*
September [sɛp'tɛmbər] *s* septiembre *m*
septet [sɛp'tɛt] *s* septeto
septic ['sɛptɪk] *adj* séptico
sepulcher ['sɛpəlkər] *s* sepulcro
seq. *abbr* **sequentia** (Lat) **the following**
sequel ['sikwəl] *s* resultado, secuela; continuación
sequence ['sikwəns] *s* serie *f*, sucesión; (cards) secansa, escalera, runfla; (gram, mov & mus) secuencia
sequester [sɪ'kwɛstər] *tr* apartar, separar; (law) secuestrar
sequin ['sikwɪn] *s* lentejuela
ser·aph ['sɛrəf] *s* (*pl* -aphs o -aphim [əfɪm]) serafín *m*
Serb [sʌrb] *adj* & *s* servio
Serbia ['sʌrbɪ·ə] *s* Servia
Serbian ['sʌrbɪ·ən] *adj* & *s* servio
Serbo-Croatian [,sʌrbokro'e∫ən] *adj* & *s* servocroata *mf*
sere [sɪr] *adj* seco, marchito
serenade [,sɛrə'ned] *s* serenata ‖ *tr* dar serenata a ‖ *intr* dar serenatas
serene [sɪ'rin] *adj* sereno
serenity [sɪ'rɛnɪti] *s* serenidad
serf [sʌrf] *s* siervo de la gleba
serfdom ['sʌrfdəm] *s* servidumbre de la gleba
serge [sʌrdʒ] *s* sarga
sergeant ['sɑrdʒənt] *s* sargento
ser'geant·at-arms' *s* (*pl* sergeants-at-arms) oficial *m* de orden
sergeant major *s* (*pl* sergeant majors) sargento mayor
serial ['sɪrɪ·əl] *adj* serial; publicado por entregas ‖ *s* cuento o novela por entregas; (rad) serial *m*, serial radiado, emisión seriada
serially ['sɪrɪ·əli] *adv* en serie, por series; por entregas
serial number *s* número de serie
se·ries ['sɪriz] *s* (*pl* -ries) serie *f*
serious ['sɪrɪ·əs] *adj* (e.g., *person, face, matter*) serio; (e.g., *condition, illness*) grave
sermon ['sʌrmən] *s* sermón *m*
sermonize ['sʌrmə,naɪz] *tr* & *intr* sermonear
serpent ['sʌrpənt] *s* serpiente *f*

se·rum ['sɪrəm] *s* (*pl* -rums o -ra [rə]) suero
servant ['sʌrvənt] *s* criado, sirviente *m*
servant girl *s* criada, sirvienta
servant problem *s* crisis *f* del servicio doméstico
serve [sʌrv] *s* (*in tennis*) saque *m*, servicio ‖ *tr* servir; (*to supply*) abastecer, proporcionar; cumplir (*una condena*); (*in tennis*) servir; **it serves me right** bien me lo merezco ‖ *intr* servir; **to serve as** servir de
service ['sʌrvɪs] *s* servicio; **at your service** para servir a Vd.; **out of service** fuera de servicio; **the services** las fuerzas armadas ‖ *tr* instalar; mantener, reparar
serviceable ['sʌrvɪsəbəl] *adj* útil; duradero; cómodo
serviceman ['sʌrvɪs,mæn] *s* (*pl* -men [,mən]) reparador *m*, mecánico; militar *m*
service record *s* hoja de servicios
service station *s* estación de servicio, taller *m* de reparaciones
service stripe *s* galón *m* de servicio
servile ['sʌrvɪl] *adj* servil
servitude ['sʌrvi,tjud] *s* servidumbre; trabajos forzados
sesame ['sɛsəmi] *s* sésamo; **open sesame** sésamo ábrete
session ['sɛ∫ən] *s* sesión; **to be in session** sesionar
set [sɛt] *adj* determinado, resuelto; inflexible, obstinado; fijo, firme; estudiado, meditado ‖ *s* (*of books, chairs, etc.*) juego; (*of gears*) tren *m;* (*of horses*) pareja; (*of diamonds*) aderezo; (*of tennis*) partida; (*of dishes*) servicio; (*of kitchen utensils*) batería; clase *f*, grupo; equipo; porte *m*, postura; (*of a garment*) caída, ajuste *m;* (*of glue*) endurecimiento; (*of cement*) fraguado; (*of artificial teeth*) caja; (mov) plató *m;* (rad) aparato; (theat) decoración ‖ *v* (*pret* & *pp* **set; ger setting**) *tr* asentar; colocar, poner; establecer, instalar; arreglar, preparar; adornar; apostar; poner (*un reloj*) en hora; (*in bridge*) reenvidar; poner, meter, pegar (*fuego*); fijar (*el precio*); engastar, montar (*una piedra preciosa*); encasar (*un hueso dislocado*); disponer (*los tipos*); triscar (*una sierra*); armar, colocar (*una trampa*); fijar (*el peinado*); poner (*la mesa*); dar (*un ejemplo*); **to set back** parar; poner obstáculos a; hacer retroceder; atrasar, retrasar (*el reloj*); **to set forth** exponer, dar a conocer; **to set one's heart on** tener la esperanza puesta en; **to set store by** dar mucha importancia a; **to set up shop** poner tienda; **to set up the drinks** (coll) convidar a beber ‖ *intr* ponerse (*el Sol, la Luna, etc.*); cuajarse (*un líquido*); endurecerse (*la cola*); fraguar (*el cemento, el yeso*); empollar (*una gallina*); caer, sentar (*una prenda de vestir*); **to set about** ponerse a; **to set out** ponerse en camino; emprender un negocio; **to set out to** ponerse a; **to set to work** poner manos a la obra; **to set upon** acometer, atacar
set'back' *s* revés *m*, contrariedad
set'screw' *s* tornillo de presión

settee [sɛ'ti] s sofá m, canapé m
setting ['sɛtɪŋ] s (environment) ambiente m; (of a gem) engaste m, montadura; (of cement) fraguado; (e.g., of the sun) puesta, ocaso; (theat) escena; (theat) puesta en escena, decoración
set'ting-up' exercises spl ejercicios sin aparatos, gimnasia sueca
settle ['sɛtəl] tr asentar, colocar; asegurar, fijar; componer, conciliar; calmar, moderar; matar (el polvo); casar; poblar, colonizar; ajustar, arreglar (cuentas) ‖ intr asentarse (un líquido, un edificio); establecerse; componerse; calmarse, moderarse; solidificarse; **to settle down to work** ponerse seriamente a trabajar; **to settle on** escoger; fijar (p.ej., una fecha)
settlement ['sɛtəlmənt] s establecimiento; colonia, caserío; decisión; (of accounts) arreglo, ajuste m; traspaso; casa de beneficencia
settler ['sɛtlər] s fundador m; poblador m; colono; árbitro, conciliador m
set'up' s porte m, postura; (e.g., of the parts of a machine) disposición; (slang) invitación a beber
seven ['sɛvən] adj & pron siete ‖ s siete m; **seven o'clock** las siete
seven hundred adj & pron setecientos ‖ s setecientos m
seventeen ['sɛvən'tin] adj, pron & s diecisiete m, diez y siete
seventeenth ['sɛvən'tinθ] adj & s (in a series) decimoséptimo; (part) diecisieteavo ‖ s (in dates) diecisiete m
seventh ['sɛvənθ] adj & s séptimo ‖ s (in dates) siete m
seventieth ['sɛvəntɪ·ɪθ] adj & s (in a series) septuagésimo; (part) setentavo
seven•ty ['sɛvənti] adj & pron setenta ‖ s (pl -ties) setenta m
sever ['sɛvər] tr desunir, separar; romper (relaciones) ‖ intr desunirse, separarse
several ['sɛvərəl] adj diversos, varios; distintos, respectivos ‖ spl varios; algunos
severance pay ['sɛvərəns] s indemnización por despido
severe [sɪ'vɪr] adj severo; (weather) riguroso; recio, violento; (look) adusto; (pain) agudo; (illness) grave
sew [so] v (pret sewed; pp sewed o sewn) tr & intr coser
sewage ['su·ɪdʒ] o ['sju·ɪdʒ] s agua de albañal, aguas cloacales
sew'age-dis•pos'al plant s estación depuradora
sewer ['su·ər] o ['sju·ər] s albañal m, cloaca, alcantarilla ‖ tr alcantarillar
sewerage ['su·ərɪdʒ] o ['sju·ərɪdʒ] s desagüe m; (system) alcantarillado; aguas de albañal
sewing basket ['so·ɪŋ] s cesta de costura
sewing machine s máquina de coser
sex [sɛks] s sexo; **the fair sex** el bello sexo; **the sterner sex** el sexo feo
sex appeal s atracción sexual; encanto femenino
sexism ['sɛksɪzəm] s sexismo

sexist ['sɛksɪst] adj & s sexista
sextant ['sɛkstənt] s sextante m
sextet [sɛks'tɛt] s sexteto
sexton ['sɛkstən] s sacristán m
sexual ['sɛkʃu·əl] adj sexual
sex•y ['sɛksi] adj (comp -ier; super -iest) (slang) sicalíptico, erótico
shab•by ['ʃæbi] adj (comp -bier; super -biest) gastado, raído, usado; andrajoso, desaseado; ruin, vil
shack [ʃæk] s casucha, choza
shackle ['ʃækəl] s grillete m; (to tie an animal) maniota; (fig) impedimento, traba; **shackles** cadenas, esposas, grillos ‖ tr poner grilletes a; poner esposas a; encadenar; (fig) trabar
shad [ʃæd] s sábalo, alosa
shade [ʃed] s sombra; (of a lamp) pantalla; (of a window) cortina, estor m, visillo, cortina de resorte; (for the eyes) visera; (hue; slight difference) matiz m; **shades** (slang) gafas fpl de sol; **the shades** las tinieblas; (of the dead) las sombras ‖ tr sombrear; obscurecer; rebajar ligeramente (el precio)
shadow ['ʃædo] s sombra ‖ tr sombrear; simbolizar; acechar, espiar (a una persona); **to shadow forth** representar vagamente, representar de un modo profético
shadowy ['ʃædo·i] adj sombroso; ligero, vago; imaginario; simbólico
shad•y ['ʃedi] adj (comp -ier; super -iest) sombrío, umbroso; (coll) sospechoso; (coll) de mala fama; (story) (coll) verde; **to keep shady** (slang) no dejarse ver
shaft [ʃæft] s dardo, flecha, saeta; (of an arrow; of a feather) astil m; (of light) rayo; (of a wagon) vara alcándara, limonera; (of a mine; of an elevator) pozo; (of a column) fuste m, caña; (of a flag) asta; (of a motor) árbol m; (to make fun of someone) dardo
shag•gy ['ʃægi] adj (comp -gier; super -giest) hirsuto, peludo, veludo; lanudo; áspero
shake [ʃek] s sacudida; (coll) apretón m de manos; (slang) instante m, momento ‖ v (pret shook [ʃʊk]; pp shaken) tr sacudir; agitar; apretar, estrechar (la mano a uno); inquietar, perturbar; (to get rid of) (slang) dar esquinazo a, zafarse de ‖ intr sacudirse; agitarse; temblar; inquietarse, perturbarse; (from cold) tiritar; **shake!** (coll) ¡choque Vd. esos cinco!, ¡vengan esos cinco!
shake'down' s (slang) exacción, concusión
shakedown cruise s viaje m de pruebas
shake'-up' s profunda conmoción; cambio de personal, reorganización completa
shak•y ['ʃeki] adj (comp -ier; super -iest) trémulo, vacilante, movedizo; indigno de confianza
shall [ʃæl] v (cond should [ʃʊd]) v aux empléase para formar (1) el fut de ind, p.ej., **I shall do it** lo haré; (2) el fut perf de ind, p.ej., **I shall have done it** lo habré hecho; (3) el modo potencial, p.ej., **what shall I do?** ¿qué he de hacer?, ¿qué debo hacer?

shallow ['ʃælo] *adj* bajo, poco profundo; (fig) frívolo, superficial

sham [ʃæm] *adj* falso, fingido; postizo ‖ *s* fingimiento, falsificación, engaño; (*person*) (coll) farsante *mf;* ‖ *v* (*pret & pp* **shammed;** *ger* **shamming**) *tr & intr* fingir

sham battle *s* simulacro de combate

shambles ['ʃæmbəlz] *s* destrucción, ruina; (*confusion, mess*) lío, revoltijo

shame [ʃem] *s* vergüenza; deshonra; (*disgrace*) metedura; **shame on you!** ¡qué vergüenza!; **what a shame!** ¡qué lástima! ‖ *tr* avergonzar; deshonrar

shameful ['ʃemfəl] *adj* vergonzoso

shameless ['ʃemlıs] *adj* descarado, desvergonzado

shampoo [ʃæm'pu] *s* champú *m* ‖ *tr* lavar (*la cabeza*); lavar la cabeza a

shamrock ['ʃæmrɑk] *s* trébol *m* irlandés

shanghai ['ʃæŋhaɪ] o [ʃæŋ'haɪ] *tr* embarcar emborrachando, embarcar narcotizando; llevarse con violencia, llevarse con engaño

shank [ʃæŋk] *s* (*of the leg*) caña, canilla; (*of an animal*) pierna; (*of a bird*) zanca; (*of an anchor*) caña; (*of the sole of a shoe*) enfranque *m;* astil *m*, caña, fuste *m;* extremidad, remate *m;* **to go o to ride on shank's mare** caminar en coche de San Francisco

shan•ty ['ʃænti] *s* (*pl* **-ties**) chabola, choza

shape [ʃep] *s* forma; **in bad shape** (coll) arruinado; (coll) muy enfermo; **out of shape** deformado; descompuesto; (*twisted*) sobornado ‖ *tr* formar, dar forma a; amoldar ‖ *intr* formarse; **to shape up** tomar forma; desarrollarse bien

shapeless ['ʃeplıs] *adj* informe

shape•ly ['ʃepli] *adj* (*comp* **-lier:** *super* **-liest**) bien formado, esbelto

share [ʃɛr] *s* parte *f*, porción; (*of stock in a company*) acción; **to go shares in** a la parte ‖ *tr* (*to enjoy jointly*) compartir; (*to apportion*) repartir ‖ *intr* participar, tener parte

share'hold'er *s* accionista *mf*

shark [ʃɑrk] *s* tiburón *m;* (*swindler*) estafador *m;* (slang) experto, perito

sharp [ʃɑrp] *adj* afilado, agudo; anguloso; (*curve, slope, etc.*) fuerte, pronunciado; (*photograph*) nítido; (*hearing*) fino; (*step, gait*) rápido; atento, despierto; picante, mordaz; listo, vivo; (mus) sostenido; (slang) elegante; **sharp features** facciones bien marcadas ‖ *adv* agudamente; en punto, p.ej., **at four o'clock sharp** a las cuatro en punto ‖ *s* (mus) sostenido

sharpen ['ʃɑrpən] *tr* aguzar; sacar punta a (*un lápiz*) ‖ *intr* afilarse

sharper ['ʃɑrpər] *s* fullero, jugador *m* de ventaja

sharp'shoot'er *s* tirador certero; (mil) tirador distinguido

shatter ['ʃætər] *tr* hacer astillas, romper de un golpe; quebrantar (*la salud*); destruir, destrozar; agitar, perturbar ‖ *intr* hacerse pedazos, romperse

shat'ter•proof' *adj* inastillable

shave [ʃev] *s* afeitado; rebanada delgada; **to have a close shave** (coll) escapar en una

tabla ‖ *tr* afeitar (*la cara*); raer, raspar; (*to graze; to cut close*) rozar; (*to slice thin*) rebanar; (carp) cepillar ‖ *intr* afeitarse

shaving ['ʃevıŋ] *adj* de afeitar, para afeitar, p.ej., **shaving soap** jabón *m* de o para afeitar ‖ *s* afeitado; **shavings** acepilladuras, virutas

shaving lotion *s* loción facial

shawl [ʃɔl] *s* chal *m*, mantón *m*

she [ʃi] *pron pers* (*pl* **they**) ella ‖ *s* (*pl* **shes**) hembra

sheaf [ʃif] *s* (*pl* **sheaves** [ʃivz] gavilla; (*of paper*) atado

shear [ʃɪr] *s* hoja de la tijera; **shears** tijeras grandes); (*to cut metal*) cizallas ‖ *v* (*pret* **sheared;** *pp* **sheared o shorn** [ʃorn]) *tr* esquilar, trasquilar (*las ovejas*); cizallar; quitar cortando; tundir (*paño*)

sheath [ʃiθ] *s* (**sheaths** [ʃiðz]) envoltura, estuche *m*, funda; (*for a sword*) funda, vaina

sheathe [ʃið] *tr* enfundar, envainar

shed [ʃɛd] *s* cobertizo; (*line from which water flows in two directions*) vertiente *m & f* ‖ *v* (*pret & pp* **shed;** *ger* **shedding**) *tr* derramar, verter (*p.ej., sangre*); dar, echar, esparcir (*luz*); mudar (*la pluma, el pellejo*)

sheen [ʃin] *s* brillo, lustre *m;* (*of pressed cloth*) prensado

sheep [ʃip] *s* (*pl* **sheep**) carnero; (*female*) oveja; tonto; **to make sheep's eyes (at)** mirar con ojos de carnero degollado

sheep dog *s* perro ovejero, perro de pastor

sheep'fold' *s* aprisco, redil *m*

sheepish ['ʃipıʃ] *adj* avergonzado, corrido; tímido, tonto

sheep'skin' *s* (*undressed*) zalea; (*dressed*) badana; (coll) diploma *m*

sheer [ʃɪr] *adj* delgado, fino, ligero; casi transparente; escarpado; puro, sin mezcla; completo ‖ *intr* desviarse

sheet [ʃit] *s* (e.g., for the bed) sábana; (*of paper*) hoja; (*of metal*) hoja, lámina; (*of water*) extensión; hoja impresa; periódico; (naut) escota

sheet lightning *s* fucilazo

sheet metal *s* metal laminado

sheet music *s* música en hojas sueltas

sheik [ʃik] *s* jeque *m;* (*great lover*) (slang) sultán *m*

shelf [ʃɛlf] *s* (*pl* **shelves** [ʃɛlvz]) estante *m*, anaquel *m;* bajío, banco de arena; **on the shelf** arrinconado, desechado, olvidado

shell [ʃɛl] *s* (*of an egg, nut, etc.*) cáscara; (*of a crustacean*) caparazón *m*, concha; (*of a vegetable*) vaina; (*of a cartridge*) cápsula; (*of a boiler*) cuerpo; armazón *f*, esqueleto; bomba, proyectil *m;* (*long, narrow racing boat*) (sport) yola ‖ *tr* descascarar; desgranar, desvainar (*legumbres*); bombardear, cañonear; **to shell out** (coll) entregar (*dinero*)

shell'fish' *s* marisco, mariscos

shell hole *s* (mil) embudo

shel•lac [ʃə'læk] *s* laca, goma laca ‖ *v* (*pret & pp* **-lacked;** *ger* **-lacking**) *tr* barnizar con goma laca; (slang) azotar, zurrar; (slang) derrotar

se
.sh

shell shock *s* neurosis *f* de guerra

shelter ['ʃɛltər] *s* abrigo, asilo, amparo, refugio; **to take shelter** abrigarse, refugiarse ‖ *tr* abrigar, amparar, proteger

shelve [ʃɛlv] *tr* poner sobre un estante; proveer de estantes; arrinconar, dejar a un lado; diferir indefinidamente

shepherd ['ʃɛpərd] *s* pastor *m* ‖ *tr* pastorear (*a las ovejas o los fieles*)

shepherd dog *s* perro ovejero, perro de pastor

shepherdess ['ʃɛpərdɪs] *s* pastora

sherbet ['ʃɑrbət] *s* sorbete *m*

shereef [ʃɛ'rif] *s* jerife *m*

sheriff ['ʃɛrɪf] *s* alguacil *m* mayor

sher·ry ['ʃɛri] *s* (*pl* **-ries**) jerez *m*, vino de Jerez

shield [ʃild] *s* escudo; (*for armpit*) sobaquera; (elec) blindaje *m* ‖ *tr* amparar, defender, escudar; (elec) blindar

shift [ʃɪft] *s* cambio; (*order of work or other activity*) turno; (*group of workmen*) tanda; maña, subterfugio ‖ *tr* cambiar; deshacerse de; echar (*la culpa*); (aut) cambiar de (*marcha*) ‖ *intr* cambiar, cambiar de puesto; mañear; (naut) correrse (*el lastre*); (rr) maniobrar; **to shift for oneself** ayudarse, ingeniarse

shift key *s* tecla de cambio, palanca de mayúsculas

shiftless ['ʃɪftlɪs] *adj* desidioso, perezoso

shiftlessness ['ʃɪftlɪsnɪs] *s* galbana

shift·y ['ʃɪfti] *adj* (*comp* **-ier;** *super* **-iest**) ingenioso, mañoso; evasivo, tramoyista; (*glance*) huyente

shilling ['ʃɪlɪŋ] *s* chelín *m*

shimmer ['ʃɪmər] *s* luz trémula ‖ *intr* rielar

shin [ʃɪn] *s* espinilla ‖ *v* (*pret & pp* **shinned;** *ger* **shinning**) *tr & intr* trepar

shin'bone' *s* espinilla

shine [ʃaɪn] *s* brillo, luz *f;* bruñido, lustre *m;* buen tiempo; (*on shoes*) (coll) lustre *m;* **to take a shine to** (slang) tomar simpatía a ‖ *v* (*pret & pp* **shined**) *tr* pulir, lustrar; (coll) embolar, limpiar (*el calzado*) ‖ *v* (*pret & pp* **shone** [ʃon]) *intr* brillar, lucir, resplandecer; hacer sol, hacer buen tiempo; (*to be distinguished, to stand out*) (fig) brillar, lucir

shingle ['ʃɪŋgəl] *s* ripia, teja de madera; tejamaní *m* (Am); pelo a la garçonne; (coll) letrero de oficina; **shingles** (pathol) zona; **to hang out one's shingle** (coll) abrir una oficina; (coll) abrir un consultorio médico ‖ *tr* cubrir con ripias; cortar (*el pelo*) a la garçonne

shining ['ʃaɪnɪŋ] *adj* brillante, luciente

shin·y ['ʃaɪni] *adj* (*comp* **-ier;** *super* **-iest**) brillante, lustroso; (*paper*) glaseado; (*from much wear*) brilloso

ship [ʃɪp] *s* nave *f,* buque *m,* barco, navío; (*steamer*) vapor *m;* aeronave *f* ‖ *v* (*pret & pp* **shipped;** *ger* **shipping**) *tr* embarcar; enviar, remitir, remesar; armar (*los remos*); embarcar (*agua*) ‖ *intr* embarcarse

ship'board' *s* bordo; **on shipboard** a bordo

ship'build'er *s* arquitecto naval, constructor *m* de buques

ship'build'ing *s* arquitectura naval, construcción de buques

ship'mate' *s* camarada *m* de a bordo

shipment ['ʃɪpmənt] *s* embarque *m* (*por agua*); envío, expedición, remesa

shipper ['ʃɪpər] *s* embarcador *m;* expedidor *m*, remitente *mf*

shipping memo ['ʃɪpɪŋ] *s* nota de remisión

ship'shape' *adj & adv* en buen orden

ship'side' *adj & adv* al costado del buque ‖ *s* zona de embarque y desembarque; muelle *m*

ship's papers *spl* documentación del buque

ship's time *s* hora local del buque

ship'wreck' *s* naufragio; barco náufrago ‖ *tr* hacer naufragar ‖ *intr* naufragar

ship'yard' *s* astillero, varadero

shirk [ʃʌrk] *tr* evitar (*el trabajo*); faltar a (*un deber*) ‖ *intr* escurrir el hombro

shirred eggs [ʃʌrd] *spl* huevos al plato

shirt [ʃʌrt] *s* camisa; **to keep one's shirt on** (slang) quedarse sereno; **to lose one's shirt** (slang) perder hasta la camisa

shirt'band' *s* cuello de camisa

shirt front *s* pechera de camisa, camisolín *m*

shirt sleeve *s* manga de camisa; **in shirt sleeves** en mangas de camisa

shirt'tail' *s* faldón *m*, pañal *m*

shirt'waist' *s* blusa (*de mujer*)

shiver ['ʃɪvər] *s* estremecimiento, tiritón *m* ‖ *intr* estremecerse, tiritar

shoal [ʃol] *s* bajío, banco de arena

shock [ʃak] *s* (*sudden and violent blow or encounter*) choque *m;* (*sudden agitation of mind or emotions*) sobresalto; temblor *m* de tierra; (*of hair*) greña; (agr) tresnal *m;* (elec) sacudida; (med) choque *m;* (*profound depression*) (pathol) choque *m;* (coll) parálisis *f* ‖ *tr* chocar; sobresaltar; dar una sacudida eléctrica a; chocar, escandalizar

shock absorber [æb'sɔrbər] *s* amortiguador *m*

shocker ['ʃakər] *s* (slang) novelucha; película horripilante

shocking ['ʃakɪŋ] *adj* chocante, escandalizador

shock troops *spl* tropas de asalto

shod·dy ['ʃadi] *adj* (*comp* **-dier;** *super* **-diest**) falso, de imitación

shoe [ʃu] *s* (*which goes above the ankle*) bota, botina; (*which does not go above the ankle*) zapato; (*of a tire*) cubierta; **to put on one's shoes** calzarse ‖ *v* (*pret & pp* **shod** [ʃad]) *tr* calzar; herrar (*un caballo*)

shoe'black' *s* limpiabotas *m*

shoe'horn' *s* calzador *m*

shoe'lace' *s* cordón *m* de zapato, lazo de zapato

shoe'mak'er *s* zapatero; zapatero remendón

shoe mender ['mɛndər] *s* zapatero remendón

shoe polish *s* betún *m*, bola

shoe'shine' *s* brillo, lustre *m;* limpiabotas *m*

shoe store *s* zapatería

shoe′string′ *s* cordón *m* de zapato, lazo de zapato; **on a shoestring** con muy poco dinero

shoe tree *s* horma

shoo [ʃu] *tr & intr* oxear

shoot [ʃut] *s* (*sprout, twig*) renuevo, vástago; conducto inclinado; (*for grain, sand, etc.*) tolva; tiro al blanco, cortamen *m* de tiradores; (*hunting party*) partida de caza ‖ *v* (*pret & pp* **shot** [ʃɑt]) *tr* tirar, disparar (*un arma*); herir o matar con arma; (*to execute with a discharge of rifles*) fusilar; fotografiar; (*to take a moving picture of*) rodar, filmar; echar (*los dados*); medir la altura de (*p.ej., el Sol*); **to shoot down** derribar (*un avión*); **to shoot up** (slang) destrozar echando balas a diestra y siniestra; (*drugs*) picarse, pincharse ‖ *intr* tirar; nacer, brotar; lanzarse, precipitarse, moverse rápidamente; punzar (*un dolor, una llaga*); **to shoot at** tirar a; (*to strive for*) (coll) poner el tiro en

shooting gallery *s* galería de tiro al blanco

shooting match *s* certamen *m* de tiro al blanco; (slang) conjunto, totalidad

shooting star *s* estrella fugaz, estrella filante

shoot′out′ *s* balaceo, balacera (SAm)

shop [ʃɑp] *s* (*store*) tienda; (*workshop*) taller *m;* **to talk shop** hablar de su oficio, hablar del propio trabajo (*fuera de tiempo*) ‖ *v* (*pret & pp* **shopped;** *ger* **shopping**) *intr* ir de compras, ir de tiendas; **to go shopping** ir de compras, ir de tiendas; **to send shopping** mandar a la compra; **to shop around** ir de tienda en tienda buscando gangas

shop′girl′ *s* muchacha de tienda

shop′keep′er *s* tendero, baratero

shoplifter [′ʃɑp,lɪftər] *s* mechera, ratero de tiendas

shopper [′ʃɑpər] *s* comprador *m*

shopping center *s* centro comercial (*grupo de establecimientos minoristas, con aparcamiento*)

shopping district *s* barrio comercial

shop′win′dow *s* escaparate *m* (de tienda); aparador *m* (Mex)

shop′work′ *s* trabajo de taller

shop′worn′ *adj* desgastado con el trajín de la tienda

shore [ʃor] *s* orilla, ribera; costa, playa; **shores** (poet) clima *m,* región ‖ *tr* acodalar, apuntalar

shore dinner *s* comida de pescado y mariscos

shore leave *s* (nav) permiso para ir a tierra

shore line *s* línea de la playa; línea de buques costeros

shore patrol *s* (nav) patrulla en tierra

short [ʃɔrt] *adj* (*in space, time, and quantity*) corto; (*in time*) breve; (*in stature*) bajo; (fig) corto, sucinto; (fig) brusco, seco; **in a short time** dentro de poco; **in short** en fin; **on short notice** con poco tiempo de aviso; **to be short of** estar escaso de; **short of breath** corto de resuello ‖ *adv* brevemente; bruscamente; (*without possessing the stock sold*) al descubierto, p.ej., **to sell short** vender al descubierto; **to run short of**

acabársele a uno, p.ej., **I am running short of gasoline** se me acaba la gasolina; **to stop short** parar de repente ‖ *s* (elec) cortocircuito; (mov) cortometraje *m;* **shorts** calzones cortos, calzoncillos ‖ *tr* (elec) poner en cortocircuito ‖ *intr* (elec) ponerse en cortocircuito

shortage [′ʃɔrtɪdʒ] *s* carestía, escasez *f,* falta; déficit *m;* (*from pilfering*) substracción

short′cake′ *s* torta de frutas; torta quebradiza

short′change′ *tr* (coll) no devolver la vuelta debida a

short circuit *s* (elec) cortocircuito

short′cir′cuit *tr* (elec) cortocircuitar ‖ *intr* (elec) cortocircuitarse

short′com′ing *s* falta, defecto, desperfecto

short cut *s* atajo; (*method*) remediavagos *m*

shorten [′ʃɔrtən] *tr* acortar, abreviar ‖ *intr* acortarse, abreviarse

short′hand′ *adj* taquigráfico ‖ *s* taquigrafía; **to take shorthand** taquigrafiar

short-lived [′ʃɔrt′laɪvd] o (coll) [′ʃɔrt′lɪvd] *adj* de breve vida, de breve duración

shortly [′ʃɔrtli] *adv* en breve, luego; descortésmente; **shortly after** poco tiempo después (de)

short′-range′ *adj* de poco alcance

short sale *s* (coll) venta al descubierto

short-sighted [′ʃɔrt′saɪtɪd] *adj* miope; (fig) falto de perspicacia

short′stop′ *s* (baseball) medio; guardabosque *m,* torpedero (Am)

short story *s* cuento

short-tempered [′ʃɔrt′tɛmpərd] *adj* de mal genio

short′-term′ *adj* a corto plazo

shot [ʃɑt] *s* tiro, disparo; (*hit or wound made with a bullet*) balazo; (*distance*) alcance *m;* (*in certain games*) jugada, tirada, golpe *m;* (*of a rocket into space*) lanzamiento; conjetura, tentativa; fotografía, instantánea; (*small pellets of lead*) perdigones *mpl;* munición; (*marksman*) tiro; (*heavy metal ball*) (sport) pesa; (*hypodermic injection*) (slang) jeringazo; (*drink of liquor*) (slang) trago; **not by a long shot** ni con mucho, ni por pienso; **to start like a shot** salir disparado

shot′gun′ *s* escopeta

shot′-put′ *s* (sport) tiro de la pesa

should [ʃʊd] *v aux* empléase para formar (1) el pres de cond, *p.ej.,* **if I should wait for him, I should miss the train** si yo le esperase, perdería el tren; (2) el perf de cond, *p.ej.,* **if I had waited for him, I should have missed the train** si yo le hubiese esperado, habría perdido el tren; y (3) el modo potencial, *p.ej.,* **he should go at once** debiera salir en seguida; **he should have gone at once** debiera haber salido en seguida

shoulder [′ʃoldər] *s* hombro; (*of slaughtered animal*) brazuelo; (*of a garment*) hombrera; **across the shoulder** en bandolera; **to put one's shoulders to the wheel** arrimar el hombro, echar el pecho al agua; **to turn a cold shoulder to** volver las espaldas a ‖ *tr* cargar sobre las espaldas; tomar sobre sí, hacerse responsable de; empujar con el hombro para abrirse paso

shoulder blade *s* escápula, omóplato

shoulder strap *s* (*of underwear*) presilla; (mil) charretera

shout [ʃaʊt] *s* grito, voz *f* ‖ *tr* gritar, vocear; **to shout down** hacer callar a gritos ‖ *intr* gritar, dar voces

shove [ʃʌv] *s* empujón *m* ‖ *tr* empujar ‖ *intr* dar empujones, avanzar a empujones; **to shove off** alejarse de la costa; (slang) ponerse en marcha, salir

shov‧el [ˈʃʌvəl] *s* pala ‖ *v* (*pret & pp* -**eled** o -**elled**; *ger* -**eling** o -**elling**) *tr* traspalar; espalar (*p.ej., la nieve*) ‖ *intr* trabajar con pala

show [ʃo] *s* exhibición, exposición, muestra; espectáculo; (*in the theater*) función; (*each performance of a play or movie*) sesión; demostración, prueba; indicación, señal *f*, signo; apariencia; (*e.g., of confidence*) alarde *m;* (coll) ocasión, oportunidad; ostentación; espectáculo ridículo, hazmerreír *m;* **to make a show of** hacer gala de; **to steal the show from** robar la obra a (*otro actor*) ‖ *tr* mostrar, enseñar; demostrar, probar; poner, proyectar (*un film*); (*e.g., to the door*) acompañar; **to show up** (coll) desenmascarar ‖ *intr* mostrarse, aparecer, asomar; salir (*p.ej., las enaguas*); **to show off** fachendear; **to show through** clarearse, transparentarse; **to show up** (coll) presentarse, dejarse ver

show bill *s* cartel *m*

show business *s* comercio de los espectáculos

show'case' *s* vitrina (de exposición)

show'down' *s* cartas boca arriba; (coll) revelación forzosa, arreglo terminante

shower [ˈʃaʊ‧ər] *s* (*sudden fall of rain*) aguacero, chaparrón *m;* (*shower bath*) ducha; (*e.g., of bullets*) rociada; despedida de soltera ‖ *tr* regar; **to shower with** colmar de ‖ *intr* llover

shower bath *s* ducha, baño de ducha

show girl *s* (theat) corista *f*, conjuntista *f*

show‧man [ˈʃomən] *s* (*pl* -**men** [mən]) empresario de teatro, empresario de circo

show'-off' *s* (coll) pinturero

show'piece' *s* objeto de arte sobresaliente

show'place' *s* sitio o edificio que se exhibe por su belleza o lujo

show'room' *s* sala de muestras, sala de exhibición

show window *s* escaparate *m* (de tienda); aparador *m* (Mex)

show‧y [ˈʃo‧i] *adj* (*comp* -**ier;** *super* -**iest**) aparatoso, cursi, ostentoso

shrapnel [ˈʃræpnəl] *s* granada de metralla

shred [ʃrɛd] *s* jirón *m*, tira, triza; fragmento; pizca; **to tear to shreds** hacer trizas ‖ *v* (*pret & pp* **shredded** o **shred;** *ger* **shredding**) *tr* desmenuzar, hacer trizas; deshilar (*carne*)

shrew [ʃru] *s* (*nagging woman*) arpía, fierecilla; (*animal*) musaraña

shrewd [ʃrud] *adj* astuto; despierto; listo

shriek [ʃrik] *s* chillido, grito agudo; risotada chillona ‖ *intr* chillar

shrill [ʃrɪl] *adj* agudo, chillón

shrimp [ʃrɪmp] *s* camarón *m;* (*little insignificant person*) renacuajo

shrine [ʃraɪn] *s* relicario; sepulcro de santo; lugar sagrado

shrink [ʃrɪŋk] *v* (*pret* **shrank** [ʃræŋk] o **shrunk** [ʃrʌŋk]; *pp* **shrunk** o **shrunken**) *tr* contraer, encoger ‖ *intr* contraerse, encogerse; moverse hacia atrás; rehuirse, retirarse

shrinkage [ˈʃrɪŋkɪdʒ] *s* contracción, encogimiento; disminución, reducción; merma, pérdida

shriv‧el [ˈʃrɪvəl] *v* (*pret & pp* -**eled** o -**elled;** *ger* -**eling** o -**elling**) *tr* arrugar, marchitar, fruncir ‖ *intr* arrugarse, marchitarse, fruncirse; **to shrivel up** avellanarse

shroud [ʃraʊd] *s* mortaja, sudario; cubierta, velo ‖ *tr* amortajar; cubrir, velar

Shrove Tuesday [ʃrov] *s* martes *m* de carnaval

shrub [ʃrʌb] *s* arbusto

shrubber‧y [ˈʃrʌbəri] *s* (*pl* -**ies**) arbustos; plantío de arbustos

shrug [ʃrʌg] *s* encogimiento de hombros ‖ *v* (*pret & pp* **shrugged;** *ger* **shrugging**) *tr* contraer; **to shrug one's shoulders** encogerse de hombros ‖ *intr* encogerse de hombros

shudder [ˈʃʌdər] *s* estremecimiento ‖ *intr* estremecerse

shuffle [ˈʃʌfəl] *s* (*of cards*) barajadura; turno de barajar; (*of feet*) arrastramiento; evasiva; recomposición ‖ *tr* barajar (*naipes*); arrastrar (*los pies*); mezclar, revolver ‖ *intr* barajar; caminar arrastrando los pies; bailar arrastrando los pies; moverse rápidamente de un lado a otro; **to shuffle along** ir arrastrando los pies; ir tirando; **to shuffle off** irse arrastrando los pies

shuf'fle‧board' *s* juego de tejo

shun [ʃʌn] *v* (*pret & pp* **shunned;** *ger* **shunning**) *tr* esquivar, evitar, rehuir

shunt [ʃʌnt] *tr* apartar, desviar; (elec) poner en derivación; (rr) desviar

shut [ʃʌt] *adj* cerrado ‖ *v* (*pret & pp* **shut;** *ger* **shutting**) *tr* cerrar; **to shut in** encerrar; **to shut off** cortar (*electricidad, gas, etc.*); **to shut up** cerrar bien; aprisionar; (coll) hacer callar ‖ *intr* cerrarse; **to shut up** (coll) callarse la boca

shut'down' *s* cierre *m*, paro

shutter [ˈʃʌtər] *s* celosía, persiana; (*outside a window*) contraventana; (*outside a show window*) cierre metálico; (phot) obturador *m*

shuttle [ˈʃʌtəl] *s* (*used in sewing*) lanzadera ‖ *intr* hacer viajes cortos de ida y vuelta

shuttle train *s* tren *m* lanzadera

shy [ʃaɪ] *adj* (*comp* **shyer** o **shier;** *super* **shyest** o **shiest**) arisco, recatado, tímido; (*fearful*) asustadizo; escaso, pobre; **I am shy a dollar** me falta un dólar ‖ *v* (*pret & pp* **shied**) *intr* esquivarse, hacerse a un lado;, espantarse, respingar; **to shy away** alejarse asustado

shyster ['ʃaɪstər] *s* (coll) abogado trampista

Sia•mese [,saɪ•ə'miz] *adj* siamés ‖ *s* (*pl* **-mese**) siamés *m*

Siamese twins *spl* hermanos siameses

Siberian [saɪ'bɪrɪ•ən] *adj* & *s* siberiano

sibilant ['sɪbɪlənt] *adj* & *s* sibilante *f*

sibling ['sɪblɪŋ] *s* hermano o hermana

sibyl ['sɪbɪl] *s* sibila

Sicilian [sɪ'sɪljən] *adj* & *s* siciliano

Sicily ['sɪsɪli] *s* Sicilia

sick [sɪk] *adj* enfermo, malo; nauseado; (coll) mórbido, perverso; **sick and tired of** (coll) harto y cansado de; **sick at heart** afligido de corazón; **to be sick at one's stomach** tener náuseas; **to take sick** caer enfermo ‖ *tr* azuzar (*a un perro*)

sick'bed' *s* lecho de enfermo

sicken ['sɪkən] *tr* & *intr* enfermar

sickening ['sɪkənɪŋ] *adj* repelente, repugnante, nauseabundo

sick headache *s* jaqueca con náuseas

sickle ['sɪkəl] *s* hoz *f*

sick leave *s* licencia por enfermedad

sick•ly ['sɪkli] *adj* (*comp* **-lier**; *super* **-liest**) enfermizo

sickness ['sɪknɪs] *s* enfermedad; náusea

side [saɪd] *adj* lateral ‖ *s* lado; (*of a solid; of a phonograph record*) cara; (*of a hill*) falda; (*of human body, of a ship*) costado; facción, partido ‖ *intr* tomar partido; **to side with** tomar el partido de

side arms *spl* armas de cinto

side'board' *s* aparador *m*

side'burns' *spl* patillas

side dish *s* plato de entrada

side door *s* puerta lateral; puerta excusada

side effect *s* efecto secundario perjudicial (*de ciertos medicamentos*)

side glance *s* mirada de soslayo

side issue *s* cuestión secundaria

side'kick' *s* (slang) compañero regular

side line *s* negocio accesorio; **on the side lines** sin tomar parte

sidereal [saɪ'dɪrɪ•əl] *adj* sidéreo

side'sad'dle *adv* a asentadillas, a mujeriegas

side show *s* función secundaria, espectáculo de atracciones

side'split'ting *adj* desternillante

side'track' *s* apartadero, desviadero, vía muerta ‖ *tr* desviar (*un tren*); echar a un lado

side view *s* perfil *m*, vista de lado

side'walk' *s* acera; banqueta (Guat, Mex); vereda (Arg, Cuba, Peru)

sidewalk café *s* terraza, café *m* en la acera

sideward ['saɪdwərd] *adj* oblicuo, sesgado ‖ *adv* de lado, hacia un lado

side'ways' *adj* oblicuo, sesgado ‖ *adv* de lado, hacia un lado; a través

side whiskers *spl* patillas

side'wise' *s* oblicuo, sesgado ‖ *adv* de lado, hacia un lado; a través

siding ['saɪdɪŋ] *s* (rr) apartadero, desviadero, vía muerta

sidle ['saɪdəl] *intr* ir de lado; **to sidle up to** acercarse de lado a (*una persona*) para no ser visto

siege [sidʒ] *s* sitio, cerco; **to lay siege to** poner sitio o cerco a; (fig) asediar (*p.ej., el corazón de una mujer*)

sieve [sɪv] *s* cedazo, tamiz *m* ‖ *tr* cerner, tamizar

sift [sɪft] *tr* cerner, cribar; escudriñar, examinar; (*to screen, separate*) entresacar; (*to scatter with or as with a sieve*) empolvar

sigh [saɪ] *s* suspiro; **to breathe a sigh of relief** respirar ‖ *tr* decir con suspiros ‖ *intr* suspirar; **to sigh for** suspirar por

sight [saɪt] *s* vista; cosa digna de verse; (*of a firearm, telescope, etc.*) mira; (coll) gran cantidad, montón *m*; (coll) horror *m*, atrocidad; **at first sight** a primera vista; **at sight** a primera vista; (*translation*) a libro abierto; (com) a la vista; **out of sight** fuera del alcance de la vista; (*prices*) por las nubes; **to catch sight of** alcanzar a ver; **to know by sight** conocer de vista; **to not be able to stand the sight of** no poder ver ni en pintura; **to see the sights** visitar los puntos de interés ‖ *tr* avistar, alcanzar con la vista ‖ *intr* apuntar con una mira; (arti & surv) visar

sight draft *s* (com) giro a la vista, letra a la vista

sightless ['saɪtlɪs] *adj* ciego

sight'-read' *v* (*pret* & *pp* **-read** [,rɛd]) *tr* leer a libro abierto; (mus) ejecutar a la primera lectura ‖ *intr* leer a libro abierto; (mus) repentizar

sight reader *s* lector *m* a libro abierto; (mus) repentista *mf*

sight'see'ing *s* turismo, visita de puntos de interés; **to go sightseeing** ir a ver los puntos de interés

sightseer ['saɪt,si•ər] *s* turista *mf*, excursionista *mf*

sign [saɪn] *s* signo; señal *f*, marca; huella, vestigio; letrero, muestra; **to show signs of** dar muestras de, tener trazas de; **to make the sign of the cross** hacerse la señal de la cruz ‖ *tr* firmar; contratar; ceder, traspasar ‖ *intr* firmar; usar el alfabeto de los sordomudos; **to sign off** (rad) terminar la transmisión; **to sign up** (coll) firmar el contrato

sig•nal ['sɪgnəl] *adj* señalado, notable ‖ *s* señal *f* ‖ *v* (*pret* & *pp* **-naled** o **-nalled**; *ger* **-naling** o **-nalling**) *tr* señalar ‖ *intr* hacer señales

signal tower *s* (rr) garita de señales

signato•ry ['sɪgnɪ,tori] *s* (*pl* **-ries**) firmante *mf*

signature ['sɪgnət/ər] *s* firma; (mus & typ) signatura

sign'board' *s* cartelón *m*, letrero

signer ['saɪnər] *s* firmante *mf*

signet ring ['sɪgnɪt] *s* anillo sigilar, sortija de sello

significance [sɪg'nɪfəkəns] *s* significado, significación; relevancia

signi•fy ['sɪgnɪ,faɪ] *v* (*pret* & *pp* **-fied**) *tr* significar

sign'post' *s* hito, poste *m* de guía

sh
si

silence ['saɪləns] s silencio ‖ tr acallar; (mil) apagar el fuego de; (mil) apagar (*el fuego del enemigo*)

silent ['saɪlənt] adj silencioso

silent movie s cine mudo

silhouette [,sɪlu'ɛt] s silueta ‖ tr siluetear

silk [sɪlk] adj sedeño ‖ s seda; **to hit the silk** (slang) lanzarse en paracaídas

silken ['sɪlkən] adj sedeño

silk hat s sombrero de copa

silk'-stock'ing adj aristocrático ‖ s aristócrata mf

silk'worm' s gusano de seda

silk•y ['sɪlki] adj (*comp* **-ier**; *super* **-iest**) sedoso, asedado

sill [sɪl] s travesaño; (*of a door*) umbral m; (*of a window*) antepecho

silliness ['sɪlɪnɪs] tontería, simpleza, pachotada

sil•ly ['sɪli] adj (*comp* **-lier**; *super* **-liest**) necio, tonto; (coll) pavo

si•lo ['saɪlo] s (*pl* **-los**) silo ‖ tr asilar

silt [sɪlt] s cieno, sedimento

silver ['sɪlvər] ad de plata; (*voice*) argentino; elocuente ‖ s plata ‖ tr platear; azogar (*un espejo*)

sil'ver•fish' s (ent) pez m de plata

silver foil s hoja de plata

silver lining s aspecto agradable de una condición desgraciada o triste

silver plate s vajilla de plata

silver screen s pantalla de plata

sil'ver•smith' s platero, orfebre m

silver spoon s riqueza heredada; **to be born with a silver spoon in one's mouth** nacer de pie

sil'ver-tongue' s (coll) pico de oro

sil'ver•ware' s plata, vajilla de plata; plata; cubertería

similar ['sɪmɪlər] adj similar, semejante, análogo

simile ['sɪmɪli] s (rhet) símil m

simmer ['sɪmər] tr cocer a fuego lento ‖ intr cocer a fuego lento; (coll) estar a punto de estallar; **to simmer down** (coll) tranquilizarse lentamente

simoon [sɪ'mun] s simún m

simper ['sɪmpər] s sonrisa boba ‖ intr sonreír bobamente

simple ['sɪmpəl] adj simple, sencillo ‖ s (*medicinal plant*) simple m

simple-minded ['sɪmpəl'maɪndɪd] adj candoroso, ingenuo; idiota, mentecato; estúpido, ignorante

simple substance s (chem) cuerpo simple

simpleton ['sɪmpəltən] s simple mf, bobo, mentecato

simulate ['sɪmjə,let] tr simular

simultaneous [,saɪməl'tenɪ•əs] o [,sɪməl-'tenɪ•əs] adj simultáneo ‖ adv—**to do simultaneously** simultanear

sin [sɪn] s pecado ‖ v (*pret & pp* **sinned**; *ger* **sinning**) intr pecar

since [sɪns] adv desde entonces, después ‖ prep desde; después de ‖ conj desde que; después (de) que; ya que, puesto que

sincere [sɪn'sɪr] adj sincero

sincerity [sɪn'sɛrɪti] s sinceridad

sinecure ['saɪnɪ,kjur] s sinecura

sinew ['sɪnju] s tendón m; (fig) fibra, nervio, vigor m

sinful ['sɪnfəl] adj (*person*) pecador; (*act, intention, etc.*) pecaminoso

sing [sɪŋ] v (*pret* **sang** [sæŋ] o **sung** [sʌŋ]; *pp* **sung**) tr cantar; **to sing to sleep** arrullar ‖ intr cantar

singe [sɪndʒ] v (*ger* **singeing**) tr chamuscar, socarrar

singer ['sɪŋər] s cantante mf; (*in a night club*) vocalista mf

single ['sɪŋgəl] adj solo, único; simple, sencillo; particular; (*e.g., room in a hotel*) individual; (*copy*) suelto; (*unmarried*) soltero; solteril, de soltero ‖ tr escoger, elegir; **to single out** singularizar

single blessedness s el bendito celibato

single-breasted ['sɪŋgəl'brɛstɪd] adj sin cruzar, de un solo pecho

single entry s (com) partida simple

single file s fila india; **in single file** de reata

single-handed ['sɪŋgəl'hændɪd] adj solo, sin ayuda

single life s vida de soltero

sin'gle-track' adj de vía única; (coll) de cortos alcances

sing'song' adj monótono ‖ s sonsonete m

singular ['sɪŋgjələr] adj & s singular m

sinister ['sɪnɪstər] adj amenazante, ominoso, funesto

sink [sɪŋk] s fregadero, pila ‖ v (*pret* **sank** [sæŋk] o **sunk** [sʌŋk]; *pp* **sunk**) tr hundir, sumergir; echar a pique; abrir, cavar (*un pozo*); hincar (*los dientes*); invertir (*mucho dinero*) perdiéndolo todo; (*basketball*) encestar ‖ intr hundirse; irse a pique; hundirse (*p.ej., el Sol en el horizonte*); descender, desaparecer; decaer (*un enfermo; una llama*); (*e.g., in a chair*) dejarse caer

sinking fund s fondo de amortización

sinless ['sɪnlɪs] adj impecable

sinner ['sɪnər] s pecador m

sinuous ['sɪnjʊ•əs] adj sinuoso

sinus ['saɪnəs] s seno

sip [sɪp] s sorbo, trago ‖ v (*pret & pp* **sipped**; *ger* **sipping**) tr sorber, beber a tragos

siphon ['saɪfən] s sifón m ‖ tr sacar con sifón, trasegar con sifón

siphon bottle s sifón m

sir [sʌr] s señor m; (*British title*) sir m; **Dear Sir** Muy señor mío, Estimado señor

sire [saɪr] s padre m, semental m; caballo padre ‖ tr engendrar

siren ['saɪrən] s sirena

Sirius ['sɪrɪ•əs] s (astr) Sirio

sirloin ['sʌrlɔɪn] s solomillo

sirup ['sɪrəp] o ['sʌrəp] s var de **syrup**

sissi•fy ['sɪsɪ,faɪ] v (*pret & pp* **-fied**) tr (coll) afeminar

sis•sy ['sɪsi] s (*pl* **-sies**) (coll) hermanita; (coll) maricón m, santito

sister ['sɪstər] adj (*ship*) gemelo; (*language*) hermano ‖ s hermana

sis'ter-in-law' *s* (*pl* **sisters-in-law**) cuñada, hermana política; (*wife of one's husband's or wife's brother*) concuñada

Sisyphus ['sɪsɪfəs] *s* Sísifo

sit [sɪt] *v* (*pret & pp* **sat** [sæt]; *ger* **sitting**) *intr* estar sentado; sentarse; echarse (*un ave sobre los huevos*); reunirse, celebrar junta; descansar; **to sit down** sentarse; **to sit still** estarse quieto; **to sit up** incorporarse (*el que estaba echado*)

sitcom ['sɪt,kɑm] *s* (coll) telecomedia serial

sit'-down' strike *s* hulega de sentados, huelga de brazos caídos

site [saɪt] *s* sitio, paraje *m*

sit'-in' *s* manifestación pacífica a modo de bloqueo

sitting ['sɪtɪŋ] *s* (*period one remains seated*) sentada; (*before a painter*) estadía; (*of a court or legislature*) sesión; **at one sitting** de una sentada

sitting duck *s* pato sentado en el agua (*fácil de matar a tiro de escopeta*); (coll) blanco de fácil alcance

sitting room *s* sala de estar

situate ['sɪtʃʊ,et] *tr* situar

situation [,sɪtʃʊeʃ'ən] *s* situación; colocación, puesto; medio ambiente

sitz bath [sɪts] *s* baño de asiento

six [sɪks] *adj & pron* seis ‖ *s* seis *m*; **at sixes and sevens** en confusión, en desacuerdo; **six o'clock** las seis

six hundred *adj & pron* seiscientos ‖ *s* seiscientos *m*

sixteen ['sɪks'tin] *adj, pron & s* dieciséis *m*, diez y seis

sixteenth ['sɪks'tinθ] *adj & s* (*in a series*) decimosexto; (*part*) dieciseisavo ‖ *s* (*in dates*) dieciséis *m*

sixth [sɪksθ] *adj & s* sexto ‖ *s* (*in dates*) seis *m*

sixtieth ['sɪkstɪ•ɪθ] *adj & s* (*in a series*) sexagésimo; (*part*) sesentavo

six•ty ['sɪksti] *adj & pron* sesenta ‖ *s* (*pl* **-ties**) sesenta *m*

sizable ['saɪzəbəl] *adj* considerable, bastante grande

size [saɪz] *s* tamaño; (*of a person or garment*) talla; (*of a pipe, a wire*) diámetro; (*for gilding*) sisa, cola de retazo; (coll) verdadera situación ‖ *tr* clasificar según tamaño; sisar, encolar; **to size up** enfocar (*un problema*); medir con la vista

sizzle ['sɪzəl] *s* siseo ‖ *intr* sisear

S.J. *abbr* **Society of Jesus**

skate [sket] *s* patín *m*; (slang) adefesio, tipo ‖ *intr* patinar; **to skate on thin ice** buscar el peligro

skating rink *s* patinadero, pista de patinar

skein [sken] *s* madeja; enredo, maraña

skeleton ['skɛlɪtən] *adj* esquelético ‖ *s* esqueleto

skeleton key *s* llave maestra

skeptic ['skɛptɪk] *adj & s* escéptico

skeptical ['skɛptɪkəl] *adj* escéptico

sketch [skɛtʃ] *s* boceto, dibujo; bosquejo, esbozo; drama corto, pieza corta ‖ *tr* dibujar; bosquejar, esbozar

sketch'book' *s* libro de bocetos; libro de esbozos literarios

skewer ['skju•ər] *s* broqueta ‖ *tr* espetar; traspasar con aguja

ski [ski] *s* (*pl* **skis** o **ski**) esquí *m* *intr* esquiar

skid [skɪd] *s* (*of an auto*) resbalón *m*; (*of a wheel*) patinaje *m*, patinazo; calzo ‖ *v* (*pret & pp* **skidded**; *ger* **skidding**) *tr* calzar ‖ *intr* resbalar (*un coche*); patinar (*una rueda*)

skid chain *s* cadena antirresbaladiza

skidding *s* (aut) patinada, derrapada, derrapaje *m*

skid row *s* barrio de mala vida

skier ['ski•ər] *s* esquiador *m*

skiff [skɪf] *s* esquife *m*

skiing ['ski•ɪŋ] *s* esquiismo

ski jacket *s* plumífero

skijoring [ski'dʒorɪŋ] *s* esquí remolcado

ski jump *s* salto de esquí; cancha de esquiar; trampolín *m*

ski lift *s* telesquí *m*

skill [skɪl] *s* destreza, habilidad, pericia

skilled [skɪld] *adj* hábil, experimentado, experto

skillet ['skɪlɪt] *s* cacerola de mango largo; sartén *f*

skillful ['skɪlfəl] *adj* diestro, hábil

skim [skɪm] *v* (*pret & pp* **skimmed**; *ger* **skimming**) *tr* desnatar (*la leche*); espumar (*el caldo, el almíbar*); (*to graze*) rasar, rozar; examinar ligeramente ‖ *intr* rozar; **to skim over** pasar rozando; examinar a la ligera

ski mask *s* pasamontaña *m*

skimmer ['skɪmər] *s* (*utensil*) espumadera; (*straw hat*) canotié *m*

skim milk *s* leche desnatada

skimp [skɪmp] *tr* escatimar; chapucear ‖ *intr* economizar, apretarse; chapucear

skimp•y ['skɪmpi] *adj* (*comp* **-ier**; *super* **-iest**) escaso; tacaño, mezquino

skin [skɪn] *s* piel *f*; (*of an animal, of fruit*) pellejo; **to be nothing but skin and bones** estar hecho un costal de huesos, estar en los huesos; **to get soaked to the skin** calarse hasta los huesos; **to save one's skin** salvar el pellejo ‖ *v* (*pret & pp* **skinned**; *ger* **skinning**) *tr* pelar, desollar; escoriarse (*p.ej., el codo*); (coll) timar; **to skin alive** (coll) desollar vivo; (coll) vencer completamente

skin'-deep' *adj* superficial

skin diver *s* submarinista *mf*

skin diving *s* submarinismo

skin'flint' *s* escasero, avaro

skin game *s* (slang) fullería

skin•ny ['skɪni] *adj* (*comp* **-nier**; *super* **-niest**) flaco, enjuto, magro, seco, delgaducho

skin'-tight' *adj* ajustado al cuerpo

skip [skɪp] *s* salto ‖ *v* (*pret & pp* **skipped**; *ger* **skipping**) *tr* saltar ‖ *intr* saltar; saltar espacios (*la máquina de escribir*); moverse saltando; irse precipitadamente

skip bombing *s* (aer) bombardeo de rebote

si
sk

ski pole s bastón m de esquiar

skipper ['skɪpər] s caudillo, jefe m; (of a boat) patrón m; gusano del queso ‖ tr patronear

skirmish ['skɑrmɪʃ] s escaramuza ‖ intr escaramuzar

skirt [skʌrt] s falda; borde m, orilla; (woman) (slang) falda ‖ tr seguir el borde de; moverse a lo largo de

ski run s pista de esquí

ski stick s bastón m de esquiar

skit [skɪt] s boceto burlesco, paso cómico

skittish ['skɪtɪʃ] adj caprichoso; asustadizo; tímido; (bull) abanto

skulduggery [skʌl'dʌgəri] s (coll) trampa, embuste m

skull [skʌl] s cráneo, calavera

skull'cap' s casquete m

skunk [skʌŋk] s mofeta; (person) (coll) canalla m

sky [skaɪ] s (pl skies) cielo; **to praise to the skies** poner por las nubes, poner en el cielo

sky'div'ing s paracaidismo con plomada suelta inicial

Skylab ['skaɪ,læb]s laboratorio espacial

sky'lark' s alondra ‖ intr jaranear

sky'light' s tragaluz m, claraboya

sky'line' s línea del horizonte, línea de los edificios contra el cielo

sky'rock'et s cohete m ‖ intr subir como un cohete

sky'scrap'er s rascacielos m

sky'writ'ing s escritura aérea

slab [slæb] s losa; plancha, tabla

slack [slæk] adj flojo; perezoso; negligente; inactivo ‖ s flojedad; inactividad; estación muerta, temporada inactiva; **slacks** pantalones flojos ‖ tr aflojar; apagar (la cal) ‖ intr atrasarse; descuidarse; **to slack up** aflojar el paso

slacker ['slækər] s perezoso; (mil) prófugo

slag [slæg] s escoria

slake [slek] tr aplacar, calmar; apagar (la cal)

slalom ['slɑləm] s eslálom m

slam [slæm] s golpe m; (of a door) portazo; (coll) crítica acerba ‖ v (pret & pp slammed; ger slamming) tr cerrar de golpe; golpear o empujar estrepitosamente; (coll) criticar acerbamente ‖ intr cerrarse de golpe

slam'-bang' adv (coll) de golpe y porrazo

slander ['slændər] s calumnia, difamación; levante (CAm, P-R) ‖ tr calumniar, difamar

slanderous ['slændərəs] adj calumnioso, difamatorio

slang [slæŋ] s caló m, jerigonza

slant [slænt] s inclinación; parecer m, punto de vista ‖ tr inclinar, sesgar; deformar, tergiversar (un informe) ‖ intr inclinarse, sesgarse

slap [slæp] s manazo, palmada; (in the face) bofetada; (in the back) espaldarazo; desaire m, insulto ‖ v (pret & pp slapped; ger slapping) tr dar una palmada a; abofetear

slash [slæʃ] s cuchillada ‖ tr acuchillar; hacer fuerte rebaja de (precios, sueldos, etc.)

slat [slæt] s lámina, tablilla

slate [slet] s pizarra; candidatura, lista de candidatos ‖ tr empizarrar; designar, destinar; poner en la lista de candidatos

slate pencil s pizarrín m

slate roof s empizarrado

slattern ['slætərn] s mujer desaliñada, pazpuerca

slaughter ['slɔtər] s carnicería, matanza ‖ tr matar

slaughter house s matadero

Slav [slɑv] o [slæv] adj & s eslavo

slave [slev] adj & s esclavo ‖ intr trabajar como esclavo

slave driver s negrero; (fig) negrero

slave'hold'er s dueño de esclavos

slavery ['slevəri] s esclavitud

slave trade s trata de esclavos

slave trader s negrero

Slavic ['slɑvɪk] o ['slævɪk] adj & s eslavo

slay [sle] v (pret slew [slu]; pp slain [slen]) tr matar

slayer ['sle•ər] s matador m

sled [slɛd] s luge m ‖ v (pret & pp sledded; ger sledding) intr deslizarse en luge o trineo

sledge hammer [slɛdʒ] s acotillo

sleek [slik] adj liso y brillante ‖ tr alisar y pulir; suavizar

sleep [slip] s sueño; **to be overcome with sleep** caerse de sueño; **to go to sleep** dormirse; dormirse, morirse (un miembro); **to put to sleep** adormecer; matar por anestesia ‖ v (pret & pp slept [slɛpt]) tr pasar durmiendo; **to sleep it off** dormir la mona; **to sleep it over** consultar con la almohada; **to sleep off** dormir (p.ej., una borrachera) ‖ intr dormir

sleeper ['slipər] s (person) durmiente mf; (girder) durmiente m

sleeping bag s saco de dormir

Sleeping Beauty s la Bella Durmiente

sleeping car s coche-cama m

sleeping pill s píldora para dormir

sleepless ['sliplɪs] adj insomne, desvelado; pasado en vela

sleep'walk'er s sonámbulo; nochero

sleep•y ['slipi] adj (comp -ier; super -iest) soñoliento; **to be sleepy** tener sueño

sleep'y•head' s dormilón m

sleet [slit] s cellisca ‖ intr cellisquear

sleeve [sliv] s manga; (mach) manguito; **to laugh in** o **up one's sleeve** reírse para sí

sleigh [sle] s trineo ‖ intr pasearse en trineo

sleigh bell s cascabel m

sleigh ride s paseo en trineo

sleight of hand [slaɪt] s juego de manos, prestidigitación

slender ['slɛndər] adj esbelto, flaco, delgado; escaso, insuficiente

sleuth [sluθ] s sabueso

slew [slu] s (coll) montón m

slice [slaɪs] s rebanada, tajada; (of an orange) gajo ‖ tr rebanar, tajar; dividir; cortar

slick [slɪk] adj liso y brillante; meloso, suave; (coll) astuto, mañoso ‖ s lugar aceitoso y lustroso (en el agua)

slicker ['slɪkər] s impermeable m de hule; (coll) embaucador m
slide [slaɪd] s resbalón m; (slippery place) resbaladero; (slippery surface) desliz m; derrumbamiento de tierra; (image for projection) diapositiva, transparencia; (of a microscope) plaquilla de vidrio; (piece of a device that slides) cursor m; (of a trombone) corredera (tubular) ‖ v (pret & pp slid [slɪd]) tr deslizar ‖ intr deslizar, resbalar; to let slide dejar pasar, no hacer caso de
slide fastener s cierre m cremallera, cierre relámpago
slide rule s regla de cálculo
slide valve s corredera, válvula corrediza
sliding contact s cursor m
sliding door s puerta de corredera
sliding scale s regla de cálculo; (of salaries) escala móvil
slight [slaɪt] adj delgado; leve; pequeño; escaso; delgaducho ‖ s desatención, descuido; desaire m, menosprecio ‖ tr desatender, descuidar; desairar
slim [slɪm] adj (comp slimmer; super slimmest) delgado, esbelto; débil, leve, pequeño, escaso
slime [slaɪm] s légamo; (of snakes, fish, etc.) baba
slim•y ['slaɪmi] adj (comp -ier; super -iest) legamoso; baboso; viscoso; puerco, sucio
sling [slɪŋ] s (to shoot stones) honda; (to hold up a broken arm) cabestrillo ‖ v (pret & pp slung [slʌŋ]) tr lanzar con una honda; lanzar, tirar; poner en cabestrillo; colgar flojamente
sling'shot' s honda
slink [slɪŋk] v (pret & pp slunk [slʌŋk]) intr andar furtivamente; to slink away escabullirse, salir con el rabo entre piernas
slip [slɪp] s resbalón m, desliz m; falta, error m, desliz m; lapso; embarcadero; (cover for a pillow, for furniture) funda; (piece of paper) papeleta; (cutting from a plant) sarmiento; (piece of underclothing) combinación; (of a dog) traílla; huída, evasión; mozuelo, mozuela; to give the slip to burlar la vigilancia de ‖ v (pret & pp slipped; ger slipping) tr poner rápidamente; quitar rápidamente; pasar por alto; eludir, evadir; to slip off (coll) quitarse de prisa; to slip on (coll) ponerse de prisa; to slip one's mind olvidársele a uno ‖ intr deslizarse; patinar (el embrague); errar, equivocarse; (coll) declinar, deteriorarse; to let slip dejar pasar; decir inadvertidamente; to slip away escurrirse; to slip by pasar inadvertido; pasar rápidamente (el tiempo); to slip out of one's hands escurrirse de entre las manos; to slip up (coll) errar, equivocarse
slip cover s funda
slip of the pen s error m de pluma
slip of the tongue s error m de lengua
slipper ['slɪpər] s zapatilla, babucha
slippery ['slɪpəri] adj deslizadizo, resbaladizo; astuto, zorro, evasivo

slip'-up' s (coll) error m, equivocación
slit [slɪt] s hendidura, raja; cortada, incisión ‖ v (pret & pp slit; ger slitting) tr hender, rajar; cortar
slob [slɑb] s (slang) sujeto desaseado, puerco
slobber ['slɑbər] s baba; sensiblería ‖ intr babear; hablar con sensiblería
sloe [slo] s (shrub) endrino; (fruit) endrina
slogan ['slogən] s lema m, mote m; grito de combate; (striking phrase used in advertising) eslogan m
sloop [slup] s balandra
slop [slɑp] s gacha, zupia, agua sucia ‖ v (pret & pp slopped; ger slopping) tr salpicar, ensuciar ‖ intr derramarse; chapotear
slope [slop] s cuesta, pendiente f; (of a continent or a roof) vertiente m & f ‖ tr inclinar ‖ intr inclinarse
slop•py ['slɑpi] adj (comp -pier; super -piest) mojado y sucio; (in one's dress) desgalichado; (in one's work) chapucero
slot [slɑt] s ranura; (for letters) buzón m
sloth [sloθ] o [slɔθ] s pereza; (zool) perezoso
slot machine s tragamonedas m, máquina sacaperras
slot meter s contador automático
slouch [slautʃ] s postura relajada; persona torpe de movimientos ‖ intr agacharse, andar caído de hombros; to slouch in a chair repanchigarse
slouch hat s sombrero gacho
slough [slau] s cenagal m, fangal m; estado de abandono moral ‖ [slʌf] s (of a snake) camisa; (pathol) escara ‖ tr mudar, echar de sí ‖ intr caerse, desprenderse
Slovak ['slovæk] o [slo'væk] adj & s eslovaco
sloven•ly ['slʌvənli] adj (comp -lier; super -liest) desaseado, desaliñado
slow [slo] adj lento; (sluggish) cachazudo, despacioso; (clock, watch) atrasado; (in understanding) lerdo, tardo, torpe ‖ adv despacio ‖ tr retrasar; atrasar (un reloj) ‖ intr retardarse, ir más despacio; atrasarse (un reloj)
slow'down' s huelga de brazos caídos
slow motion s (film) ralentí m; in slow motion al ralentí, a cámara lenta
slow'-mo'tion adj a cámara lenta
slowness ['slonɪs] lentitud, lerdera
slow'poke' s tardón m
slug [slʌg] s (heavy piece of metal) lingote m; (metal disk used as a coin) ficha; (zool) limaza, babosa; (coll) porrazo, puñetazo ‖ v (pret & pp slugged; ger slugging) tr (coll) aporrear, apuñear
sluggard ['slʌgərd] s pachón m, perezoso
sluggish ['slʌgɪʃ] adj inactivo, indolente, tardo; pachorrudo, perezoso
sluice [slus] s canal m; (floodgate) compuerta; (dam; flume) presa
sluice gate s compuerta de presa
slum [slʌm] s barrio bajo ‖ v (pret & pp slummed; ger slumming) intr visitar los barrios bajos
slumber ['slʌmbər] s sueño ligero, sueño tranquilo ‖ intr dormir; dormitar

sk
sl

slump [slʌmp] *s* depresión, crisis económica; (*in prices, stocks, etc.*) baja repentina ‖ *intr* hundirse, desplomarse; bajar repentinamente (*los precios, valores, etc.*)

slur [slʌr] *s* pronunciación indistinta; reparo crítico; (mus) ligado ‖ *v* (*pret & pp* **slurred;** *ger* **slurring**) *tr* comerse (*sonidos, sílabas*); despreciar, insultar; (mus) ligar

slush [slʌʃ] *s* fango muy blando, aguanieve fangosa, nieve *f* a medio derretir; sentimentalismo tonto

slut [slʌt] *s* perra; (*slovenly woman*) pazpuerca; ramera, mala mujer

sly [slaɪ] *adj* (*comp* **slyer** o **slier;** *super* **slyest** o **sliest**) furtivo, secreto; astuto, socarrón; travieso; **on the sly** a hurtadillas

smack [smæk] *adv* (coll) de golpe, de sopetón ‖ *s* dejo, gustillo; palmada, manotada; golpe *m;* beso sonado; (*of a whip*) chasquido ‖ *tr* dar una manotada a; golpear; hacer chasquidos con (*un látigo*); besar sonoramente; **to smack one's lips** chuparse los labios ‖ *intr*—**to smack of** saber a, oler a

small [smɔl] *adj* pequeño, chico; (*short in stature*) bajo; pobre, obscuro, humilde; (typ) minúsculo

small arms *spl* armas ligeras

small beer *s* cerveza floja; bagatela; persona de poca monta

small business *s* pequeña empresa

small capital *s* versalilla o versalita

small change *s* suelto, dinero menudo

small fry *s* gente menuda; gente de poca monta

small'-fry' *adj* de niños, para niños; de poca monta

small hours *spl* primeras horas (*de la mañana*)

small intestine *s* intestino delgado

small-minded ['smɔl'maɪndɪd] *adj* tacaño, mezquino; intolerante

smallpox ['smɔl,pɑks] *s* viruela

small print *s* tipo menudo

small talk *s* palique *m*, charlas frívolas

small'-time' *adj* de poca monta

small'-town' *adj* lugareño, apegado a cosas lugareñas

smart [smɑrt] *adj* listo, vivo, inteligente; agudo, penetrante; astuto; elegante, majo; picante, punzante; (coll) grande, considerable ‖ *s* escozor *m;* dolor vivo ‖ *intr* escocer, picar; padecer, sufrir

smart aleck ['ælɪk] *s* (coll) fatuo, sabihondo

smart money *s* (fig) inversionistas *mpl/fpl* astutos; gente *f* bien informada

smart set *s* gente *f* chic, gente de buen tono

smash [smæʃ] *s* rotura violenta; fracaso, ruina; quiebra, bancarrota; (coll) choque violento, tope violento ‖ *tr* romper con fuerza; arruinar, destrozar; aplastar ‖ *intr* romperse con fuerza; arruinarse, destrozarse; aplastarse; **to smash into** chocar con, topar con

smash hit *s* (coll) éxito rotundo

smash'-up' *s* colisión violenta; ruina, desastre *m;* quiebra, bancarrota

smattering ['smætərɪŋ] *s* barniz *m*, tintura, migaja

smear [smɪr] *s* embarradura; calumnia; (bact) frotis *m* ‖ *tr* embarrar; calumniar ‖ *intr* embarrarse

smear campaign *s* campaña de calumnias

smell [smɛl] *s* olor *m;* (*sense*) olfato; fragancia, perfume *m* ‖ *v* (*pret & pp* **smelled** o **smelt** [smɛlt]) *tr* oler, olfatear ‖ *intr* oler; heder, oler mal; **to smell of** oler a

smelling salts *spl* sales aromáticas

smell•y ['smɛli] *adj* (*comp* **-ier;** *super* **-iest**) hediondo, maloliente

smelt [smɛlt] *s* (*fish*) eperlano, esperinque *m* ‖ *tr & intr* fundir

smile [smaɪl] *s* sonrisa ‖ *intr* sonreír, sonreírse

smiling ['smaɪlɪŋ] *adj* risueño

smirk [smʌrk] *s* sonrisa fatua y afectada ‖ *intr* sonreír fatua y afectadamente

smite [smaɪt] *v* (*pret* **smote** [smot]; *pp* **smitten** ['smɪtən] o **smit** [smɪt]) *tr* golpear o herir súbitamente y con fuerza; caer con fuerza sobre; apenar, afligir; castigar

smith [smɪθ] *s* forjador *m*, herrero

smith•y ['smɪθi] *s* (*pl* **-ies**) herrería

smitten ['smɪtən] *adj* afligido; muy enamorado

smock [smɑk] *s* bata

smock frock *s* blusa de obrero

smog [smɑg] *s* mezcla de humo y niebla

smoke [smok] *s* humo; **to go up in smoke** irse todo en humo ‖ *tr* (*to cure or treat with smoke*) ahumar; fumar (*tabaco*); **to smoke out** ahuyentar con humo, dar humazo a; descubrir ‖ *intr* humear; fumar; hacer humo (*una chimenea dentro de la habitación*)

smoked glasses *spl* gafas ahumadas

smoke evacuator *s* extractor de humos

smokeless powder ['smoklɪs] *s* pólvora sin humo

smokeless tobacco *s* tabaco sin humo

smoker ['smokər] *s* fumador *m;* (*room*) fumadero; (rr) coche-fumador *m;* reunión de fumadores

smoke rings *spl* anillos de humo; **to blow smoke rings** sacar humo formando anillos

smoke screen *s* cortina de humo

smoke'stack' *s* chimenea

smoking ['smokɪŋ] *s* el fumar; **no smoking** se prohíbe fumar

smoking car *s* coche-fumador *m*, vagón *m* de fumar

smoking jacket *s* batín *m*

smoking room *s* fumadero, saloncito para fumadores

smok•y ['smoki] *adj* (*comp* **-ier;** *super* **-iest**) humoso; (*emitting smoke*) humeante

smolder ['smoldər] *s* fuego lento sin llama y con mucho humo ‖ *intr* arder en rescoldo, arder sin llamas; (fig) estar latente; (*to burn within*) (fig) requemarse; (fig) expresar (*p.ej., los ojos*) una ira latente

smooth [smuð] *adj* liso, terso, suave; plano, llano, igual; acaramelado, afable, blando, meloso; (*water*) tranquilo; (*style*) fluido;

smooth as butter como manteca ‖ *tr* alisar, suavizar; allanar; facilitar; **to smooth away** quitar (*p.ej.*, *obstáculos*) suavemente; **to smooth down** ablandar, calmar

smooth-faced ['smuð,fest] *adj* barbilampiño

smooth-spoken ['smuθ,spokən] *adj* meloso, lisonjero

smooth•y ['smuði] *s* (*pl* **-ies**) galante *m;* elegante *m;* adulador *m*

smother ['smʌðər] *tr* ahogar, sofocar; suprimir; reprimir

smudge [smʌdʒ] *s* tiznón *m;* mancha ‖ *tr* tiznar; manchar; ahumar, fumigar (*una huerta*)

smug [smʌg] *adj* (*comp* **smugger;** *super* **smuggest**) pagado de sí mismo; compuesto, pulcro; relamido

smuggle ['smʌgəl] *tr* meter de contrabando ‖ *intr* contrabandear

smuggler ['smʌglər] *s* contrabandista *mf*

smuggling ['smʌglɪŋ] *s* contrabando

smut [smʌt] *s* tiznón *m;* obscenidad; (agr) carbón *m*, tizón *m*

smut•ty ['smʌti] *adj* (*comp* **-tier;** *super* **-tiest**) tiznado, manchado; obsceno; (agr) atizonado

snack [snæk] *s* parte *f*, porción; bocadillo, tentempié *m*

snack bar *s* lonchería

snag [snæg] *s* (*of a tree*) tocón *m;* (*of a tooth*) raigón *m;* obstáculo, tropiezo; **to strike** o **to hit a snag** tropezar con un obstáculo

snail [snel] *s* caracol *m;* (*slow person*) pachón *m;* **at a snail's pace** a paso de caracol, a paso de tortuga

snake [snek] *s* culebra, serpiente *f*

snake in the grass *s* traidor *m*, amigo pérfido

snap [snæp] *s* (*crackling sound*) chasquido, estallido; (*of the fingers*) castañetazo; (*bite*) mordisco; (*cracker*) galletita; (*of cold weather*) corto período; (*catch or fastener*) broche *m* de presión; (phot) instantánea; (coll) brío, vigor *m;* (slang) breva, cosa fácil ‖ *v* (*pret & pp* **snapped;** *ger* **snapping**) *tr* asir, cerrar, etc. de golpe; castañetear (*los dedos*); chasquear (*el látigo*); fotografiar instantáneamente; tomar (*una instantánea*); **to snap one's fingers at** tratar con desprecio; **to snap up** aceptar con avidez, comprar con avidez; cortar la palabra a ‖ *intr* chasquear, estallar; (*to crack*) saltar; (*from fatigue*) estallar; **to snap at** querer morder; asir (*una oportunidad*); **to snap out of it** (slang) cambiarse repentinamente; **to snap shut** cerrarse de golpe

snap'drag'on *s* (bot) boca de dragón

snap fastener *s* corchete *m* de presión

snap judgment *s* decisión atolondrada

snap•py ['snæpi] *adj* (*comp* **-pier;** *super* **-piest**) mordaz; (coll) elegante, garboso; (coll) enérgico, vivo; (*food*) acre, picante

snap'shot' *s* instantánea

snap switch *s* (elec) interruptor *m* de resorte

snare [snɛr] *s* lazo, trampa: (*of a drum*) bordón *m*, tirante *m*

snare drum *s* caja clara

snarl [snɑrl] *s* gruñido; regaño; maraña, enredo ‖ *tr* decir con un gruñido; enmarañar, enredar ‖ *intr* gruñir; regañar; enmarañarse, enredarse

snatch [snætʃ] *s* arrebatamiento; pedacito, trocito; ratito ‖ *tr & intr* arrebatar; **to snatch at** tratar de asir o agarrar; **to snatch from** arrebatar a

sneak [snik] *adj* furtivo ‖ *s* sujeto solapado ‖ *tr* mover a hurtadillas ‖ *intr* andar furtivamente, moverse a hurtadillas

sneaker ['snikər] *s* sujeto solapado; (coll) zapato blando, zapato de lona

sneak thief *s* ratero, descuidero

sneak•y ['sniki] *adj* (*comp* **-ier;** *super* **-iest**) solapado, furtivo

sneer [snɪr] *s* expresión de desprecio ‖ *intr* hablar con desprecio, echar una mirada de desprecio; **to sneer at** mofarse de

sneeze [sniz] *s* estornudo ‖ *intr* estornudar; **not to be sneezed at** (coll) no ser despreciable

snicker ['snɪkər] *s* risa tonta ‖ *intr* reírse tontamente

sniff [snɪf] *s* husmeo, venteo; sorbo por las narices ‖ *tr* husmear, ventear; sorber por las narices; (fig) husmear, averiguar; (fig) sospechar; (*heroin*) esnifar (*caballo*) ‖ *intr* ventear; **to sniff at** husmear; menospreciar

sniffle ['snɪfəl] *s* resuello fuerte y repetido; **the sniffles** ataque *m* de resoplidos ‖ *intr* resollar fuerte y repetidamente

snip [snɪp] *s* tijeretada; recorte *m*, pedacito; (coll) persona pequeña e insignificante ‖ *v* (*pret & pp* **snipped;** *ger* **snipping**) *tr* tijeretear

snipe [snaɪp] *s* agachadiza, becacín *m* ‖ *intr* paquear, tirar desde un escondite

sniper ['snaɪpər] *s* paco, tirador emboscado

snippet ['snɪpɪt] *s* recorte *m;* (coll) persona pequeña e insignificante

snip•py ['snɪpi] *adj* (*comp* **-pier;** *super* **-piest**) (coll) arrogante, desdeñoso; (coll) acre, brusco

snitch [snɪtʃ] *tr & intr* (slang) escamotear, ratear; manotear (Arg, Mex)

sniv•el ['snɪvəl] *s* gimoteo, lloriqueo; moqueo ‖ *v* (*pret & pp* **-eled** o **-elled;** *ger* **-eling** o **-elling**) *intr* gimotear, lloriquear; (*to have a runny nose*) moquear

snob [snɑb] *s* esnob *mf*

snobbery ['snɑbəri] *s* esnobismo

snobbish ['snɑbɪʃ] *adj* esnob, esnobista

snoop [snup] *s* buscavidas *mf*, curioso ‖ *intr* curiosear, ventear

snoopy ['snupi] *adj* curioso, entremetido

snoot [snut] *s* (slang) cara, narices *fpl*

snoot•y ['snuti] *adj* (*comp* **-ier;** *super* **-iest**) (slang) esnob

snooze [snuz] *s* (coll) sueñecito ‖ *intr* echar un sueñecito

snore [snor] *s* ronquido ‖ *intr* roncar

snort [snɔrt] *s* bufido ‖ *intr* bufar

snot [snɑt] *s* (slang) mocarro

snot•ty ['snɑti] *adj* (*comp* **-tier;** *super* **-tiest**) mocoso; asqueroso, sucio; (slang) engreído

sl
sn

snout [snaut] *s* hocico; (*something shaped like the snout of an animal*) morro; (*of a person*) (coll) hocico

snow [sno] *s* nieve *f* ‖ *intr* nevar

snow′ball′ *s* bola de nieve ‖ *tr* lanzar bolas de nieve a ‖ *intr* aumentar rápidamente

snow′-blind′ *adj* cegado por reflejos de la nieve

snow-capped ['sno,kæpt] *adj* coronado de nieve

snow′drift′ *s* ventisquero, masa de nieve

snow′fall′ *s* nevada

snow fence *s* valla paranieves

snow′flake′ *s* copo de nieve, ampo

snow flurry *s* nevisca

snow job *s* (slang) decepción; engaño

snow line o **limit** *s* límite *m* de las nieves perpetuas

snow man *s* figura de nieve

snow′plow′ *s* expulsanieves *m*, quitanieves *m*

snow′shoe′ *s* raqueta de nieve

snow′storm′ *s* nevasca, fuerte nevada

snow tire *s* llanta de invierno

snow′-white′ *adj* blanco como la nieve

snow•y ['sno•i] *adj* (*comp* -ier; *super* -iest) nevoso

snowy owl *s* lechuza blanca

snub [snʌb] *s* desaire *m* ‖ *v* (*pret & pp* snubbed; *ger* snubbing) *tr* desairar

snub•by ['snʌbi] *adj* (*comp* -bier; *super* -biest) (*nose*) respingona

snuff [snʌf] *s* rapé; (*of a candlewick*) moco; **up to snuff** (slang) en buena condición; (slang) difícil de engañar ‖ *tr* husmear, olfatear; sorber por la nariz; despabilar (*una candela*); **to snuff out** apagar, extinguir

snuff′box′ *s* tabaquera

snuffers ['snʌfərz] *spl* despabiladeras

snug [snʌg] *adj* (*comp* snugger; *super* snuggest) cómodo; (*garment*) ajustado, ceñido; (*well-off*) acomodado; (*in hiding*) escondido

snuggle ['snʌgəl] *intr* apretarse, arrimarse; dormir bien abrigado; **to snuggle up to** arrimarse a

so [so] *adv* así; tan + *adj* o *adv;* por tanto; también; **and so** así pues; también, lo mismo; **and so on** y así sucesivamente; **or so** más o menos; **to think so** creer que sí; **so as to** + *inf* para + *inf;* **so far** hasta aquí; hasta ahora; **so long** hasta la vista; **so many** tantos; **so much** tanto; **so so** tal cual, así así; **so that** de modo que, de suerte que, así que; para que; con tal de que; **so to speak** por decirlo así ‖ *conj* as que ‖ *interj* ¡bien!; ¡verdad!

soak [sok] *s* mojada; (*toper*) (coll) potista *mf* ‖ *tr* empapar, remojar; embeber; (slang) aporrear; (slang) hacer pagar un precio exorbitante; **to soak up** absorber, embeber; (fig) entender; **soaked to the skin** calado hasta los huesos ‖ *intr* empaparse, remojarse

so′-and-so′ *s* (*pl* -sos) fulano, fulano de tal; tal cosa

soap [sop] *s* jabón *m* ‖ *tr* jabonar

soap′box′ *s* caja de jabón; tribuna callejera

soapbox orator *s* orador *m* de plazuela

soap bubble *s* burbuja de jabón, pompa de jabón

soap dish *s* jabonera

soap flakes *spl* copos de jabón

soap′mak′er *s* jabonero

soap opera *s* (coll) telenovela; serial lacrimógeno

soap powder *s* jabón *m* en polvo, polvo de jabón

soap′stone′ *s* jaboncillo de sastre

soap′suds′ *spl* jabonaduras

soap•y ['sopi] *adj* (*comp* -ier; *super* -iest) jabonoso

soar [sor] *intr* encumbrarse, subir muy alto, volar a gran altura; aspirar, pretender; (aer) planear

sob [sab] *s* sollozo ‖ *v* (*pret & pp* sobbed; *ger* sobbing) *tr* decir o expresar sollozando ‖ *intr* sollozar

sobbing *s* llorera

sober ['sobər] *adj* sobrio; no embriagado; grave, serio; cuerdo, sensato; sereno, tranquilo; (*color*) apagado ‖ *tr* poner sobrio; desemborrachar; **to sober up** desintoxicar ‖ *intr* volverse sobrio; desemborracharse; **to sober down** calmarse, sosegarse; **to sober up** desemborracharse

sobriety [so'braɪəti] *s* sobriedad, moderación; gravedad, seriedad; cordura, sensatez; serenidad

sobriquet ['sobrɪ,ke] *s* apodo

sob sister *s* (slang) periodista llorona

sob story *s* (slang) historia de lagrimitas

soc. o **Soc.** *abbr* **society**

so′-called′ *adj* llamado, así llamado; supuesto

soccer ['sakər] *s* fútbol *m* asociación

sociable ['soʃəbəl] *adj* sociable

social ['soʃəl] *adj* social ‖ *s* reunión social

social climber ['klaɪmər] *s* ambicioso de figurar

socialism ['soʃə,lɪzəm] *s* socialismo

socialist ['soʃəlɪst] *s* socialista *mf*

socialite ['soʃə,laɪt] *s* (coll) personaje *m* de la buena sociedad

social register *s* guía *m* social, registro de la buena sociedad

socie•ty [sə'saɪ•əti] *s* (*pl* -ties) sociedad; (*companionship or company*) compañía; buena sociedad, mundo elegante

society editor *s* cronista *mf* de la vida social

sociology [,sosɪ'alədʒi] o [,soʃɪ'alədʒi] *s* sociología

sock [sak] *s* calcetín *m;* (slang) golpe *m* fuerte ‖ *tr* (slang) golpear con fuerza

socket ['sakɪt] *s* (*of the eyes*) cuenca; (*of a tooth*) alvéolo; (*of a candlestick*) cañón *m;* (*of a socket wrench*) cubo; (elec) portalámparas; (rad) zócalo

socket wrench *s* llave *f* de caja, llave de cubo

sod [sad] *s* césped *m;* terrón *m* de césped ‖ *v* (*pret & pp* sodded; *ger* sodding) *tr* encespedar

soda ['sodə] *s* soda, sosa; (*drink*) soda

soda fountain *s* fuente *f* de sodas

soda water *s* agua gaseosa
sodium [ˈsodɪ•əm] *adj* sódico, de sodio ‖ *s* sodio
sofa [ˈsofə] *s* sofá *m*
soft [sɔft] o [saft] *adj* blando, muelle; (*skin*) suave; (*iron*) dulce; (*hat*) flexible; (*solder*) tierno; (*coll*) fácil
soft-boiled egg [ˈsɔftˈbɔɪld] o [ˈsaftˈbɔɪld] *s* huevo pasado por agua
soft coal *s* hulla grasa
soft drink *s* bebida no alcohólica, refresco
soften [ˈsɔfən] o [ˈsafən] *tr* ablandar; **to soften up** (*by bombardment*) ablandar ‖ *intr* ablandarse
soft'-ped'al *tr* (mus) disminuir la intensidad de, por medio del pedal suave; (slang) moderar
soft soap *tr* jabón blando o graso; (coll) adulación
soft'-soap' *s* (coll) enjabonar, dar jabón a
soft'ware' *s* (*computer*) programa *m* (para ordenador), operaciones *fpl*
sog•gy [ˈsagi] *adj* (*comp* **-gier;** *super* **-giest**) remojado, ensopado
soil [sɔɪl] *s* suelo; país *m*, región; (*spot, stain*) mancha; (fig) mancha, deshonra ‖ *tr* manchar, ensuciar; manchar, deshonrar; viciar, corromper ‖ *intr* mancharse, ensuciarse
soil pipe *s* tubo de desagüe sanitario
soiree o **soirée** [swaˈre] *s* sarao, velada
sojourn [ˈsodʒʌrn] *s* estancia, permanencia ‖ [ˈsodʒʌrn] o [soˈdʒʌrn] *intr* estarse, permanecer
soil. *abbr* **soluble, solution**
solace [ˈsalɪs] *s* solaz *m*, consuelo ‖ *tr* solazar, consolar
solar [ˈsolər] *adj* solar
solar battery *s* fotopila
solder [ˈsadər] *s* soldadura ‖ *tr* soldar
soldering iron *s* cautín *m*, soldador *m*
soldier [ˈsoldʒər] *s* (*enlisted man as distinguished from an officer*) soldado; (*man in military service*) militar *m* ‖ *intr* servir como soldado
soldier of fortune *s* aventurero militar
soldier•y [ˈsoldʒəri] *s* (*pl* **-ies**) soldadesca
sold out [sold] *adj* agotado; **the theater is sold out** todas las localidades están vendidas; **we are sold out of those neckties** se nos han agotado esas corbatas
sole [sol] *adj* solo, único; exclusivo ‖ *s* (*of foot*) planta; (*of shoe*) suela; (*fish*) lenguado ‖ *tr* solar
solely [ˈsolli] *adv* solamente, únicamente
solemn [ˈsaləm] *adj* solemne
solicit [səˈlɪsɪt] *tr* solicitar; intentar seducir
solicitor [səˈlɪsɪtər] *s* solicitador *m*, agente *m*; (law) procurador *m*
solicitous [səˈlɪsɪtəs] *adj* solícito
solicitude [səˈlɪsɪˌtjud] o [səˈlɪsɪˌtud] *s* solicitud
solid [ˈsalɪd] *adj* sólido; unánime; (*sound, good*) sólido, macizo; (*e.g., clouds*) denso; (*without pause or interruption*) entero; (*e.g., gold*) puro ‖ *s* sólido
solidarity [ˌsalɪˈderɪtɪ] *s* solidaridad; **to declare one's solidarity with** solidarizar con

solid geometry *s* geometría del espacio
solidity [səˈlɪdɪtɪ] *s* (*pl* **-ties**) solidez *f*
solid majority *s* mayoría cómoda
sol'id-state' *adj* transistorizado
solid-state physics *s* física del estado sólido
solid tire *s* (aut) macizo
solilo•quy [səˈlɪləkwi] *s* (*pl* **-quies**) soliloquio
solitaire [ˈsalɪˌtɛr] *s* (*game and diamond*) solitario; sortija solitario
solitar•y [ˈsalɪˌtɛri] *adj* solitario; **in solitary confinement** incomunicado ‖ *s* (*pl* **-ies**) solitario
solitary confinement *s* incomunicación, aislamiento penal
solitude [ˈsalɪˌtjud] o [ˈsalɪˌtud] *s* soledad
so•lo [ˈsolo] *adj* (*instrument*) solista; a solas, hecho a solas ‖ *s* (*pl* **-los**) (mus) solo
soloist [ˈsolo•ɪst] *s* solista *mf*
solstice [ˈsalstɪs] *s* solsticio
solution [səˈluʃən] *s* solución
solve [salv] *tr* resolver, solucionar; adivinar (*un enigma*)
solvent [ˈsalvənt] *adj* & *s* solvente *m*
somber [ˈsambər] *adj* sombrío
some [sʌm] *adj indef* algún; un poco de; unos; (coll) grande, bueno, famoso ‖ *pron indef* algunos, unos
some'bod'y *pron indef* alguien; **somebody else** algún otro, otra persona ‖ *s* (*pl* **-ies**) (coll) personaje *m*
some'day' *adv* algúna día
some'how' *adv* de algún modo, de alguna manera; **somehow or other** de un modo u otro
some'one' *pron indef* alguien; **someone else** algún otro, otra persona
somersault [ˈsʌmərˌsɔlt] *s* salto mortal ‖ *intr* dar un salto mortal
something [ˈsʌmθɪŋ] *adv* algo, un poco; (coll) muy, excesivamente ‖ *pron indef* alguna cosa, algo; **something else** otra cosa
some'time' *adj* antiguo, de otro tiempo ‖ *adv* alguna vez; antiguamente
some'times' *adv* a veces, algunas veces
some'way' *adv* de algún modo
some'what' *adv* algo, un poco ‖ *s* alguna cosa, algo
some'where' *adv* en alguna parte, a alguna parte; en algún tiempo; **somewhere else** en otra parte, a otra parte
somnambulist [samˈnæmbjəlɪst] *s* sonámbulo
somnolent [ˈsamnələnt] *adj* soñoliento
son [sʌn] *s* hijo
song [sɔŋ] o [saŋ] *s* canción, canto; **for a song** muy barato; **to sing the same old song** volver a la misma canción
song'bird' *s* ave canora
Song of Songs *s* Cantar *m* de los Cantares
song writer *s* cantautor *m*
sonic [ˈsanɪk] *adj* sónico
sonic boom *s* (aer) estampido sónico
son'-in-law' *s* (*pl* **sons-in-law**) yerno, hijo político
sonnet [ˈsanɪt] *s* soneto

sn
so

sonneteer [,sɑnɪˈtɪr] s sonetista *mf;* poetastro ‖ *intr* sonetizar
son·ny [ˈsʌni] s (*pl* **-nies**) hijito
sonori·ty [səˈnɔrɪti] s (*pl* **-ties**) sonoridad
soon [sun] *adv* pronto, en breve; temprano; de buena gana; **as soon as** así que, en cuanto, luego que, tan pronto como; **as soon as possible** cuanto antes, lo más pronto posible; **had sooner** preferiría; **how soon?** ¿cuándo?; **soon after** poco después, poco después de; **sooner or later** tarde o temprano
soot [sut] o [sut] s hollín *m*
soothe [suð] *tr* aliviar, calmar, sosegar
soothsayer [ˈsuθ,se·ər] s adivino
soot·y [ˈsuti] o [ˈsuti] *adv* (*comp* **-ier;** *super* **-iest**) holliniento, tiznado
sop [sɑp] s (*food soaked in milk, etc.*) sopa; regalo (*para acallar, apaciguar o sobornar*) ‖ *v* (*pret & pp* **sopped;** *ger* **sopping**) *tr* empapar, ensopar; **to sop up** absorber
sophisticated [səˈfɪstɪ,ketɪd] *adj* mundano, falto de simplicidad, corrido
sophomore [ˈsɑfə,mor] s estudiante *mf* de segundo año
sopping [ˈsɑpɪŋ] *adj* empapado; **sopping wet** hecho una sopa
sopran·o [səˈprænо] o [səˈprɑnо] *adj* de soprano; para soprano ‖ s (*pl* **-os**) soprano *mf*
sorcerer [ˈsɔrsərər] s brujo, hechicero
sorceress [ˈsɔrsərɪs] s bruja, hechicera
sorcer·y [ˈsɔrsəri] s (*pl* **-ies**) brujería, hechicería, sortilegio
sordid [ˈsɔrdɪd] *adj* sórdido
sore [sor] *adj* enrojecido, inflamado; (coll) resentido, picado; **to be sore at** (coll) estar enojado con ‖ s llaga, úlcera; pena, dolor *m*, aflicción; **to open an old sore** renovar la herida
sorely [ˈsorli] *adv* penosamente; con urgencia
sore throat s dolor *m* de garganta
sorori·ty [səˈrɔrɪti] s (*pl* **-ties**) hermandad de estudiantas
sorrel [ˈsɔrəl] *adj* alazán
sorrow [ˈsɔro] s dolor *m*, pena pesar *m;* arrepentimiento ‖ *intr* dolerse, apenarse, sentir pena; arrepentirse; **to sorrow for** añorar
sorrowful [ˈsɔrəfəl] *adj* doloroso, pesaroso, acongojado
sor·ry [ˈsɑri] o [ˈsɔri] *adj* (*comp* **-rier;** *super* **-riest**) afligido, apenado, pesaroso; arrepentido; malo, pésimo; despreciable, ridículo; **to be o to feel sorry** sentir; arrepentirse; **to be o feel sorry for** compadecer; arrepentirse de; **I am sorry** lo siento, me sabe mal
sort [sɔrt] s clase *f*, especie *f;* modo, manera; **a sort of** uno a modo de; **out of sorts** de mal humor; **sort of** (coll) algo, en cierta medida ‖ *tr* clasificar, separar; escoger, entresacar
so'-so' *adj* mediano, regular, talcualillo ‖ *adv* así así, tal cual
sot [sɑt] s borracho
sotto voce [ˈsɑto ˈvotʃə] *adv* a sovoz, en voz baja

soubrette [suˈbrɛt] s (theat) confidenta de comedia; (theat) doncella coquetona
soul [sol] s alma; **upon my soul!** ¡por vida mía!
sound [saʊnd] *adj* sano: sólido, firme; solvente; sonoro; (*sleep*) profundo; prudente; legal, válido ‖ *adv* profundamente ‖ s sonido; ruido; (*passage of water*) estrecho, brazo de mar; (surg) sonda, tienta; **within sound of** al alcance de ‖ *tr* sonar; tocar (*p.ej., campanas*); tantear, sondear; auscultar (*p.ej., los pulmones*); entonar (*p.ej., alabanzas*) ‖ *intr* sonar, resonar; sondar; parecer; **to sound like** sonar a, sonar como
sound'-ab·sorb'ent *adj* fonoabsorbente
sound barrier s muro del sonido, barrera de sonido, barrera sónica
sound'-dead'en·ing *adj* fonoabsorbente
sound film s película sonora
soundly [ˈsaʊndli] *adv* sanamente; profundamente; a fondo, completamente
sound'proof' *adj* antisonoro; insonorizado ‖ *tr* insonorizar
soundproofing [ˈsaʊnd,prufɪŋ] s insonorización
soup [sup] s sopa
soup kitchen s comedor *m* de beneficencia, dispensario de alimentos
soup spoon s cuchara de sopa
sour [saʊr] *adj* agrio ‖ *tr* agriar ‖ *intr* agriarse
source [sors] s fuente *f*, manantial *m*
source material s fuentes *fpl* originales
sour cherry s (*tree*) guindo; (*fruit*) guinda
sour grapes *interj* ¡están verdes las uvas!
south [saʊθ] *adj* meridional, del sur ‖ *adv* al sur, hacia el sur ‖ s sur *m*, mediodía *m*
South America s Sudamérica, la América del Sur
South American *adj & s* sudamericano
southern [ˈsʌðərn] *adj* meridional
Southern Cross s Cruz *f* del Sur
southerner [ˈsʌðərnər] s meridional *mf;* sureño (Am)
South Korea s la Corea del Sur
South Korean *adj & s* surcoreano
south'paw' *adj & s* (slang in sport) zurdo
South Pole s polo sur, polo antártico
southward [ˈsaʊθwərd] *adv* hacia el sur
south wind s austro, noto
souvenir [,suvəˈnɪr] o [ˈsuvə,nɪr] s recuerdo, memoria
sovereign [ˈsavrɪn] o [ˈsʌvrɪn] *adj* soberano ‖ s (*king; coin*) soberano; (*queen*) soberana
sovereign·ty [ˈsavrɪnti] o [ˈsʌvrɪnti] s (*pl* **-ties**) soberanía
soviet [ˈsovɪ,ɛt] o [,sovɪˈɛt] *adj* soviético ‖ s soviet *m*
sovietize [ˈsovɪ·ɛ,taɪz] *tr* sovietizar
Soviet Russia s la Rusia Soviética
Soviet Union s Unión Soviética
sow [saʊ] s puerca ‖ [so] *v* (*pret* **sowed;** *pp* **sown** o **sowed**) *tr* sembrar; (*with mines*) plagar
soybean [ˈsɔɪ,bin] s soja; soya; semilla de soja
sp. *abbr* **special, species, specific, specimen, spelling**

spa [spɑ] *s* caldas, balneario
space [spes] *adj* espacial, del espacio ‖ *s* espacio; **in the space of** por espacio de ‖ *tr* espaciar
space bar *s* espaciador *m*, tecla de espacios
space'craft' *s* astronave *f*, cosmonave *f*
space flight *s* vuelo espacial
space key *s* llave *f* espacial
space•man ['spes,mæn] *s* (*pl* **-men** [,mɛn]) navegador *m* del espacio; astronauta *m*; visitante *m* a la Tierra del espacio exterior
space'ship' *s* nave *f* del espacio
space shuttle *s* transbordador *m* espacial
space station *s* apostadero espacial
space suit *s* escafandra espacial
space travel *s* cosmonavegación
space vehicle *s* vehículo espacial
spacious ['speʃəs] *adj* espacioso
spade [sped] *s* laya; (*playing card*) pique *m*; **to call a spade a spade** llamar al pan pan y al vino vino
spade'work' *s* trabajo preliminar
spaghetti [spə'gɛti] *s* espagueti *m*
Spain [spen] *s* España
span [spæn] *s* palmo, cuarta, llave *f* de la mano; espacio, lapso, trecho; (*of horses*) pareja; (*of a bridge*) ojo; (aer) envergadura ‖ *v* (*pret & pp* **spanned**) *ger* **spanning**) *tr* medir a palmos; atravesar, extenderse sobre
spangle ['spæŋgəl] *s* lentejuela ‖ *tr* adornar con lentejuelas; (*to stud with bright objects*) estrellar ‖ *intr* brillar
Spaniard ['spænjərd] *s* español *m*
spaniel ['spænjəl] *s* perro de aguas
Spanish ['spænɪʃ] *adj & s* español *m*; **the Spanish** los españoles
Spanish America *s* la América Española, Hispanoamérica
Spanish broom *s* retama
Spanish fly *s* abadejo, cantárida
Spanish Main *s* Costa Firme, Tierra Firme; mar *m* Caribe
Spanish moss *s* barba española
Spanish omelet *s* tortilla de tomate
Span'ish-speak'ing *adj* de habla española, hispanohablante; hispanoparlante
spank [spæŋk] *tr* azotar, zurrar
spanking ['spæŋkɪŋ] *adj* rápido; fuerte; (coll) muy grande, muy hermoso, extraordinario ‖ *s* azote *m*
spar *s* (mineral) espato; (naut) mástil *m*, palo, verga ‖ *v* (*pret & pp* **sparred**) *ger* **sparring**) *intr* pelear, reñir; boxear
spare [spɛr] *adj* sobrante; libre, disponible; de repuesto; delgado, enjuto, flaco; parco, sobrio ‖ *tr* pasar sin; perdonar; guardar; salvar; ahorrar; **to have . . . to spare** tener de sobra; **to spare oneself** ahorrarse esfuerzos
spare bed *s* cama de sobra
spare parts *spl* piezas de repuesto o de recambio
spare room *s* cuarto de reserva
sparing ['spɛrɪŋ] *adj* económico; (*scanty*) escaso

spark [spɑrk] *s* chispa; (*e.g., of truth*) centellita ‖ *tr* (coll) cortejar, galantear (*a una mujer*) ‖ *intr* chispear
spark coil *s* bobina de chispas, bobina de encendido
spark gap *s* (*of induction coil*) entrehierro; (*of spark plug*) espacio de chispa
sparkle ['spɑrkəl] *s* chispita, destello; (*wit*) travesura; alegría, viveza ‖ *intr* chispear; ser alegre; espumar, ser efervescente
sparkling ['spɑrklɪŋ] *adj* centelleante, chispeante; (*wine*) espumante, espumoso; (*water*) gaseoso
spark plug *s* bujía
sparrow ['spæro] *s* gorrión *m*
sparse [spɑrs] *adj* (*population*) poco denso; (*hair*) ralo
Spartan ['spɑrtən] *adj & s* espartano
spasm ['spæzəm] *s* espasmo; esfuerzo súbito y de breve duración
spasmodic ['spæz'mɑdɪk] *adj* espasmódico; intermitente; caprichoso
spastic ['spæstɪk] *adj* espástico
spat [spæt] *s* disputa, riña; botín *m*, polaina corta
spatial ['speʃəl] *adj* espacial
spatter ['spætər] *tr* salpicar; manchar ‖ *intr* chorrear; chapotear
spatula ['spætʃələ] *s* espátula
spavin ['spævɪn] *s* esparaván *m*
spawn [spɔn] *s* freza; prole *f*; producto, resultado ‖ *tr* engendrar ‖ *intr* desovar, frezar (*los peces*)
speak [spik] *v* (*pret* **spoke** [spok]; *pp* **spoken**) *tr* hablar (*un idioma*); decir (*la verdad*) ‖ *intr* hablar; **so to speak** por decirlo así; **speaking!** ¡al habla!; **to speak out** o **up** osar hablar, elevar la voz
speak'-eas'y *s* (*pl* **-ies**) (slang) taberna clandestina
speaker ['spikər] *s* hablante *mf*; orador *m*; (*of a legislative assembly*) presidente *m*; (rad) altavoz *m*
speaking ['spikɪŋ] *adj* hablante; **to be on speaking terms** hablarse ‖ *s* habla; elocuencia
speaking tube *s* tubo acústico
spear [spɪr] *s* lanza; (*for fishing*) arpón *m*; (*of grass*) hoja ‖ *tr* alancear, herir con lanza
spear'head' *s* punta de lanza ‖ *tr* dirigir, conducir; encabezar; dar impulso a
spear'mint' *s* menta verde, menta romana
spec. *abbr* special
special ['spɛʃəl] *adj* especial; **nothing special** (*no great thing*) nada del otro mundo ‖ *s* tren *m* especial
spe'cial•deliv'ery *adj* urgente, de urgencia
specialist ['spɛʃəlɪst] *s* especialista *mf*
speciali•ty [,spɛʃɪ'æliti] *s* (*pl* **-ties**) especialidad
specialize ['spɛʃə,laɪz] *tr* especializar ‖ *intr* especializar o especializarse
special•ty ['spɛʃəlti] *s* (*pl* **-ties**) especialidad
spe•cies ['spisiz] *s* (*pl* **-cies**) especie *f*
specific [spɪ'sɪfɪk] adj *& s* específico
speci•fy ['spɛsɪ,faɪ] *v* (*pret & pp* **-fied**) *tr* especificar

specimen ['spɛsɪmən] *s* espécimen *m;* (coll) tipo, sujeto

specious ['spi/əs] *adj* especioso, engañoso

speck [spɛk] *s* mota, manchita ‖ *tr* motear, manchar, salpicar de manchas

speckle ['spɛkəl] *s* mota, punto ‖ *tr* motear, puntear

spectacle ['spɛktəkəl] *s* espectáculo; **spectacles** anteojos, gafas

spectator ['spɛktetər] *s* espectador *m*

specter ['spɛktər] *s* espectro

spec•trum ['spɛktrəm] *s* (*pl* **-tra** [trə] o **-trums**) espectro

speculate ['spɛkjə‚let] *intr* especular

speech [spit/] *s* habla; (*of an actor*) parlamento; (*talk before an audience*) conferencia, discurso

speech clinic *s* clínica de la palabra

speech correction *s* foniatría, logopedía

speech defect *s* defecto del habla

speechless ['spit/lɪs] *adj* sin habla; estupefacto

speed [spid] *s* velocidad; (aut) marcha, velocidad; (slang) anfetaminas tomadas como alucinantes ‖ *v* (*pret & pp* **sped** [spɛd]) *tr* apresurar; despedir; ayudar ‖ *intr* apresurarse; adelantar, progresar; ir con exceso de velocidad

speeding ['spidɪŋ] *s* exceso de velocidad

speed king *s* as *m* del volante

speed limit *s* velocidad permitida

speedometer [spi'dɑmɪtər] *s* (*to indicate speed*) velocímetro; velocímetro y cuentakilómetros unidos

speed record *s* marca de velocidad

speed•y ['spidi] *adj* (*comp* **-ier;** *super* **-iest**) rápido, veloz

spell [spɛl] *s* encanto, hechizo; tanda, turno; rato, poco tiempo; (*e.g., of good weather*) temporada; **to cast a spell on** encantar, hechizar ‖ *v* (*pret & pp* **spelled** o **spelt** [spɛlt]) *tr* deletrear; indicar, significar; **to spell out** (coll) explicar detalladamente ‖ *intr* deletrear ‖ *v* (*pret & pp* **spelled**) *tr* reemplazar, relevar

spell'bind'er *s* (coll) orador *m* fascinante, orador persuasivo

spelling ['spɛlɪŋ] *adj* ortográfico ‖ *s* (*act*) deletreo; (*subject or study*) ortografía; (*way a word is spelled*) grafía

spelunker [spɪ'lʌŋkər] *s* espeleólogo de afición

spend [spɛnd] *v* (*pret & pp* **spent** [spɛnt]) *tr* gastar; pasar (*una hora, un día, etc.*)

spender ['spɛndər] *s* gastador *m*

spending money *s* dinero para gastos menudos

spend'thrift' *s* derrochador *m*, pródigo

sperm [spʌrm] *s* esperma; (coll) leche *f*

sperm whale *s* cachalote *m*

spew [spju] *tr & intr* vomitar

sp. gr. *abbr* **specific gravity**

sphere [sfɪr] *s* esfera; astro, cuerpo celeste

spherical ['sfɛrɪkəl] *adj* esférico

sphinx [sfɪŋks] *s* (*pl* **sphinxes** o **sphinges** ['sfɪndʒiz]) esfinge *f*

spice [spaɪs] *s* especia; (*zest, piquancy*) sainete *m;* fragancia ‖ *tr* especiar; dar gusto o picante a

spice box *s* especiero

spick-and-span ['spɪkənd'spæn] *adj* flamante; limpio, pulcro

spic•y ['spaɪsi] *adj* (*comp* **-ier;** *super* **-iest**) especiado; picante; aromático; enchiloso (CAm, Mex); sicalíptico

spider ['spaɪdər] *s* araña

spider web *s* tela de araña, telaraña

spiff•y ['spɪfi] *adj* (*comp* **-ier;** *super* **-iest**) (slang) guapo, elegante

spigot ['spɪgət] *s* grifo; (*plug to stop a vent*) espiche *m*

spike [spaɪk] *s* (*long, heavy nail*) estaca, escarpia; (*sharp projection or part*) punta, pico, púa; (bot) espiga ‖ *tr* empernar; acabar, poner fin a

spill [spɪl] *s* derrame *m;* líquido derramado; (coll) caída, vuelco ‖ *v* (*pret & pp* **spilled** o **spilt** [spɪlt]) *tr* derramar, verter; (coll) hacer caer, volcar ‖ *intr* derramarse, verterse; (coll) caer, volcarse

spill'way' *s* bocacaz *m*, canal *m* de desagüe

spin [spɪn] *s* vuelta, giro muy rápido; (coll) paseo en coche, etc.; **to go into a spin** (aer) entrar en barrena ‖ *v* (*pret & pp* **spun** [spʌn]; *ger* **spinning**) *tr* hacer girar; hilar (*p.ej., lino*); bailar (*un trompo*); **to spin off** (*derivative*) rendir; **to spin out** extender, prolongar; **to spin yarns** contar cuentos increíbles ‖ *intr* dar vueltas, girar; hilar; bailar (*un trompo*); (aer) entrar en barrena

spinach ['spɪnɪt/] o ['spɪnɪdʒ] *s* espinaca; (*leaves used as food*) espinacas

spinal ['spaɪnəl] *adj* espinal

spinal column *s* espina dorsal, columna vertebral

spinal cord *s* médula espinal

spinal disk *s* disco vertebral

spindle ['spɪndəl] *s* (*rounded rod tapering toward each end*) huso; (*small shaft, axle*) eje *m;* (*turned ornament in a baluster*) mazorca

spine [spaɪn] *s* espina, púa; (*rib, ridge*) cordoncillo; loma, cerro; (anat) espina; (bb) lomo; (fig) ánimo, valor *m*

spineless ['spaɪnlɪs] *adj* sin espinas, sin espinazo; sin firmeza de carácter

spinet ['spɪnɪt] *s* espineta

spinner ['spɪnər] *s* hilandero; máquina de hilar

spinning ['spɪnɪŋ] *adj* hilador ‖ *s* (*act*) hila; (*art*) hilandería

spinning wheel *s* torno de hilar

spin'-off' *s* derivado; subproducto

spinster ['spɪnstər] *s* (*obs or offensive*) solterona

spi•ral ['spaɪrəl] *adj & s* espiral *f* ‖ *v* (*pret & pp* **-raled** o **-ralled;** *ger* **-raling** o **-ralling**) *intr* dar vueltas como una espiral; (aer) volar en espiral

spiral staircase *s* escalera de caracol

spire [spaɪr] *s* cima, ápice *m;* (*of a steeple*) aguja, chapitel *m;* (*e.g., of grass*) tallo

spirit ['spɪrɪt] *s* espíritu *m;* humor *m*, temple *m;* personaje *m;* licur *m* || *tr*—**to spirit away** llevarse misteriosamente
spirited ['spɪrɪtɪd] *adj* fogoso, espiritoso
spirit lamp *s* lámpara de alcohol
spiritless ['spɪrɪtlɪs] *adj* apocado, tímido, sin ánimo
spirit level *s* nivel *m* de burbuja
spiritual ['spɪrɪtʃʊ•əl] *adj* espiritual
spiritualism ['spɪrɪtʃʊə,lɪzəm] *s* espiritismo; (*belief that all reality is spiritual*) espiritualismo
spirituous liquors ['spɪrɪtʃʊ•əs] *spl* licores espirituosos
spit [spɪt] *s* esputo, saliva; (*for roasting*) asador *m*, espetón *m;* punta o lengua de tierra; **the spit and image of** la segunda edición de, el retrato de || *v* (*pret & pp* spat [spæt] o spit; *ger* spitting) *tr* escupir || *intr* escupir; lloviznar; neviscar; fufar (*el gato*)
spite [spaɪt] *s* despecho, rencor *m*, inquina; **in spite of** a pesar de, a despecho de; **out of spite** por despecho || *tr* despechar, molestar, picar
spiteful ['spaɪtfəl] *adj* despechado, rencoroso
spit'fire' *s* fierabrás *m;* mujer *f* de mal genio
spittoon [spɪ'tun] *s* escupidera
splash [splæʃ] *s* rociada, salpicadura; (*e.g., with the hands*) chapaleo, chapoteo; **to make a splash** (coll) hacer impresión, llamar la atención, causar furor || *tr & intr* salpicar; chapotear
splash'down' *s* acuatizaje *m*
spleen [splin] *s* mal humor *m;* (anat) bazo; **to vent one's spleen** descargar la bilis
splendid ['splɛndɪd] *adj* espléndido; (coll) magnífico, maravilloso
splendor ['splɛndər] *s* esplendor *m*
splice [splaɪs] *s* empalme *m*, junta || *tr* empalmar, juntar
splint [splɪnt] *s* (*splinter*) astilla, tablilla; (surg) tablilla || *tr* entablillar (*un hueso roto*)
splinter ['splɪntər] *s* astilla; (*of stone, glass, bone*) esquirla || *tr* astillar || *intr* astillarse, hacerse astillas
splinter group *s* grupúsculo; grupo disidente
split [splɪt] *adj* hendido, partido; dividido || *s* división, fractura; (slang) porción || *v* (*pret & pp* split; *ger* splitting) *tr* dividir, partir; **to split one's sides with laughter** desternillarse de risa || *intr* dividirse a lo largo; **to split away (from)** separarse (de)
split fee *s* dicotomía (*entre médicos*)
split personality *s* personalidad desdoblada
splitting ['splɪtɪŋ] *adj* partidor; fuerte, violento; (*headache*) enloquecedor
splotch [splatʃ] *s* borrón *m*, mancha grande || *tr* salpicar, manchar
splurge [splʌrdʒ] *s* (coll) fachenda, ostentación || *intr* (coll) fachendear
splutter ['splʌtər] *s* chisporroteo; (*manner of speaking*) farfulla || *tr* farfullar || *intr* chisporrotear; farfullar
spoil [spɔɪl] *s* botín *m*, presa; **spoils** (*taken from an enemy*) botín, despojos; (*of political victory*) enchufes *mpl* || *v* (*pret & pp*

spoiled o **spoilt** [spɔɪlt] *tr* echar a perder, estropear; mimar (*a un niño*); amargar (*una tertulia*) || *intr* echarse a perder
spoiled [spɔɪld] *adj* (*child*) consentido, mimado; (*food*) pasado, podrido
spoils•man ['spɔɪlzmən] *s* (*pl* -men [mən]) enchufista *m*
spoils system *s* enchufismo
spoke [spok] *s* (*of a wheel*) radio, rayo; (*of a ladder*) escalón *m*
spokes•man ['spoksmən] *s* (*pl* -men [mən]) o **spokesperson** *s* portavoz *m*, vocero
sponge [spʌndʒ] *s* esponja; **to throw in** (o up) **the sponge** (coll) tirar la esponja || *tr* limpiar con esponja; borrar; absorber || *intr* ser absorbente; **to sponge on** (coll) vivir a costa de
sponge cake *s* bizcocho muy ligero
sponger ['spʌndʒər] *s* esponja (*gorrón, parásito*); bolsero (SAm)
sponge rubber *s* caucho esponjoso
spon•gy ['spʌndʒi] *adj* (comp -gier; super -giest) esponjoso
sponsor ['spansər] *s* patrocinador *m;* (*godfather*) padrino; (*godmother*) madrina || *tr* patrocinar
sponsorship ['spansər,ʃɪp] *s* patrocinio
spontaneous [span'teni•əs] *adj* espontáneo
spoof [spuf] *s* (slang) mistificación, engaño; (slang) broma || *tr* (slang) mistificar, engañar || *intr* (slang) bromear, burlar; (slang) parodiar
spook [spuk] *s* aparecido, espectro
spook•y ['spuki] *adj* (comp -ier; super -iest) espectral, espeluznante; (*horse*) asustadizo
spool [spul] *s* carrete *m*, bobina
spoon [spun] *s* cuchara || *tr* cucharear || *intr* (slang) besuquearse (*los enamorados*)
spoonful ['spun,fʊl] *s* cucharada
spoon•y ['spuni] *adj* (comp -ier; super -iest) (coll) baboso, sobón
sporadic(al) [spə'rædɪk(əl)] *adj* esporádico
spore [spor] *s* espora
sport [sport] *adj* deportivo, de deporte || *s* deporte *m;* deportista *mf;* (*person or thing controlled by some power or passion*) juguete *m;* (*laughingstock*) hazmerreír *m;* (*gambler*) (coll) tahur *m*, jugador *m;* (*in gambling or playing games*) (coll) buen perdedor; (*flashy fellow*) (coll) guapo, majo; (biol) mutación; **to make sport of** burlarse de, reírse de || *tr* (coll) lucir (*p.ej., un traje nuevo*) || *intr* divertirse; estar de burla; juguetear
sport clothes *spl* trajes *mpl* de sport
sport fan *s* aficionado al deporte, deportista *mf*
sporting chance *s* riesgo de buen perdedor
sporting goods *spl* artículos de deporte
sporting house *s* casa de juego; casa de rameras
sports'cast'er *s* locutor deportivo
sports•man ['sportsmən] *s* (*pl* -men [mən]) deportista *m;* jugador honrado
sports news *s* noticiario deportivo
sports'wear' *s* trajes deportivos
sports writer *s* cronista deportivo

sport•y ['sporti] *adj* (*comp* **-ier;** *super* **-iest**) elegante, guapo; alegre, brillante; magnánimo; disipado, libertino

spot [spɑt] *s* mancha; sitio, lugar *m;* (coll) poquito; **on the spot** allí mismo; al punto; (slang) en dificultad; (slang) en peligro de muerte; **to hit the spot** tener razón; dar completa satisfacción ‖ *v* (*pret & pp* **spotted;** *ger* **spotting**) *tr* manchar; descubrir, reconocer ‖ *intr* mancharse, tener manchas

spot cash *s* dinero contante

spot check *s* verificación a la ventura

spotless ['spɑtlɪs] *adj* inmaculado, sin manchas

spot'light' *s* proyector *m* orientable; luz concentrada; (aut) faro piloto, faro giratorio; (fig) atención del público

spot remover [rɪ'muvər] *s* (*person*) quitamanchas *mf;* (*material*) quitamanchas *m*

spot welding *s* soldadura por puntos

spouse [spaʊz] o [spaʊs] *s* cónyuge *mf,* consorte *mf*

spout [spaʊt] *s* (*to carry off water from roof*) canalón *m;* (*of a jar, pitcher, etc.*) pico; (*of a sprinkling can*) rallo, roseta; (*jet*) chorro; **up the spout** (slang) acabado, arruinado ‖ *tr* echar en chorro; (coll) declamar ‖ *intr* chorrear; (coll) declamar

sprain [spren] *s* torcedura, esguince *m* ‖ *tr* torcer, torcerse

sprawl [sprɔl] *intr* arrellanarse

spray [spre] *s* rociada; (*of the sea*) espuma; (*device*) pulverizador *m;* (*twig*) ramita ‖ *tr & intr* rociar

sprayer ['spre•ər] *s* rociador *m,* pulverizador *m,* vaporizador *m*

spread [sprɛd] *s* extensión; amplitud, anchura; difusión; diferencia; cubrecama, sobrecama; mantel *m,* tapete *m;* (*of the wings of a bird; of the wings of an airplane*) envergadura; (coll) festín *m,* comilona ‖ *v* (*pret & pp* **spread**) *tr* extender; difundir, propagar; esparcir; escalonar; abrir, separar; poner (*la mesa*) ‖ *intr* extenderse; difundirse; esparcirse; abrirse, separarse

spree [spri] *s* juerga, parranda; borrachera; **to go on a spree** ir de juerga; pillar una mona

sprig [sprɪg] *s* ramita

spright•ly ['spraɪtli] *adj* (*comp* **-lier;** *super* **-liest**) alegre, animado, vivo

spring [sprɪŋ] *adj* primaveral; de manantial; de muelle, de resorte ‖ *s* (*season of the year*) primavera; (*issue of water from earth*) fuente *f,* manantial *m;* (*elastic device*) muelle *m,* resorte *m;* (*of an automobile or wagon*) ballesta; (*leap, jump*) brinco, salto; abertura, grieta; tensión, tirantez *f* ‖ *v* (*pret* **sprang** [spræŋ] o **sprung** [sprʌŋ]; *pp* **sprung**) *tr* soltar (*un muelle o resorte*); torcer, combar, encorvar; hacer saltar (*una trampa, una mina*) ‖ *intr* saltar; saltar de golpe; brotar, nacer, proceder; torcerse, combarse, encorvarse; **to spring at** abalanzarse sobre; **to spring forth** precipitarse; brotar; **to spring up** levantarse de un salto; brotar, nacer; presentarse a la vista

spring'board' *s* trampolín *m*

spring chicken *s* polluelo; (*young person*) (coll) pollita

spring fever *s* (hum) ataque *m* primaveral, galbana

spring mattress *s* colchón *m* de muelles, somier *m*

spring'time' *s* primavera

sprinkle ['sprɪŋkəl] *s* rociada; llovizna; pizca ‖ *tr* regar, rociar; salpicar, sembrar; espolvorear (*p.ej., azúcar*) ‖ *intr* rociar; lloviznar, gotear

sprinkling can *s* regadera, rociadera

sprint [sprɪnt] *s* (sport) embalaje *m* ‖ *intr* (sport) embalarse, lanzarse

sprite [spraɪt] *s* duende *m,* trasgo

sprocket ['sprɑkɪt] *s* diente *m* de rueda de cadena; rueda de cadena

sprout [spraʊt] *s* brote *m,* renuevo, retoño ‖ *intr* brotar, germinar, echar renuevos; crecer rápidamente

spruce [sprus] *adj* apuesto, elegante, garboso ‖ *s* abeto del Norte, abeto falso, pícea ‖ *tr* ataviar, componer ‖ *intr* ataviarse, componerse; **to spruce up** emperifollarse

spry [spraɪ] *adj* (*comp* **spryer** o **sprier;** *super* **spryest** o **spriest**) activo, ágil

spud [spʌd] *s* (*chisel*) escoplo; (agr) escoda; (coll) patata

spun glass [spʌn] *s* vidrio hilado, cristal hilado

spunk [spʌŋk] *s* (coll) ánimo, coraje *m,* corazón *m,* valor *m*

spun silk *s* seda cardada o hilada

spur [spʌr] *s* espuela; (*central point of an auger*) gusanillo; (*of a cock, mountain, warship*) espolón *m;* (rr) ramal corto; (*goad, stimulus*) (fig) espuela; **on the spur of the moment** impulsivamente, sin la reflexión debida ‖ *v* (*pret & pp* **spurred;** *ger* **spurring**) *tr* espolear; espuelar (SAm); **to spur on** espolear, aguijonear

spurious ['spjʊrɪ•əs] *adj* espurio

spurn [spʌrn] *s* desdén *m,* menosprecio ‖ *tr* desdeñar, menospreciar; rechazar con desdén

spurt [spʌrt] *s* chorro repentino; esfuerzo repentino; arranque *m* ‖ *intr* salir en chorro; salir a borbotones

sputnik ['spʌtnɪk] *s* sputnik *m;* satélite *m* artificial

sputter ['spʌtər] *s* (*manner of speaking*) farfulla; (*sizzling*) chisporroteo ‖ *tr* farfullar ‖ *intr* farfullar; chisporrotear

spy [spaɪ] *s* (*pl* **spies**) espía *mf* ‖ *v* (*pret & pp* **spied**) *tr* columbrar, divisar ‖ *intr* espiar; **to spy on** espiar

spy'glass' *s* catalejo, anteojo

spy satellite *s* satélite *m* espía

sq. *abbr* square

squabble ['skwɑbəl] *s* reyerta, riña ‖ *intr* reñir, disputar

squad [skwɑd] *s* escuadra

squadron ['skwɑdrən] *s* (aer) escuadrilla; (*of cavalry*) (mil) escuadrón *m;* (nav) escuadra

squalid ['skwɑlɪd] *adj* escuálido

squall [skwɔl] *s* grupada, turbión *m;* *(quarrel)* (coll) riña; *(upset, commotion)* (coll) chubasco
squalor [ˈskwɑlər] *s* escualidez *f*
squander [ˈskwɑndər] *tr* despilfarrar, malgastar
square [skwɛr] *adj* cuadrado, p.ej., **eight square inches** ocho pulgadas cuadradas; en cuadro, de lado, p.ej., **eight inches square** ocho pulgadas en cuadro, ocho pulgadas de lado; rectangular; justo, recto; honrado, leal; saldado; fuerte, sólido; (coll) abundante, completo; **to get square with** (coll) hacérselas pagar a ‖ *adv* en cuadro; en ángulo recto; honradamente, lealmente ‖ *s* cuadrado; *(of checkerboard or chessboard)* casilla, escaque *m;* *(city block)* manzana; *(open area in town or city)* plaza; *(carpenter's tool)* escuadra; **to be on the square** (coll) obrar de buena fe ‖ *tr* cuadrar; dividir en cuadros; ajustar, nivelar, conformar; saldar *(una cuenta);* (carp) escuadrar ‖ *intr* cuadrarse; **to square off** (coll) colocarse en posición de defensa
square dance *s* danza de figuras
square deal *s* (coll) trato equitativo
square meal *s* (coll) comida abundante
square shooter [ˈʃutər] *s* (coll) persona leal y honrada
squash [skwɑʃ] *s* aplastamiento; (bot) calabaza; (sport) frontón *m* con raqueta; ‖ *tr* aplastar, despachurrar; confutar *(un argumento);* acallar con un argumento, respuesta, etc. ‖ *intr* aplastarse
squash·y [ˈskwɑʃi] *adj (comp* **-ier;** *super* **-iest)** mojado y blando; *(muddy)* lodoso; *(fruit)* modorro
squat [skwɑt] *adj* en cuclillas; rechoncho ‖ *v (pret & pp* **squatted;** *ger* **squatting)** *intr* acuclillarse, agacharse; sentarse en el suelo; establecerse en terreno ajeno sin derecho; establecerse en terreno público para crear un derecho
squatter [ˈskwɑtər] *s* advenedizo, intruso, colono usurpador
squaw [skwɔ] *s* india norteamericana; mujer, esposa, muchacha
squawk [skwɔk] *s* graznido; (slang) queja chillona ‖ *intr* graznar; (slang) quejarse chillando
squaw man *s* blanco casado con india
squeak [skwik] *s* chillido; chirrido ‖ *intr* dar chillidos; chirriar
squeal [skwil] *s* chillido ‖ *intr* dar chillidos; (slang) delatar, soplar; **to squeal on** (slang) delatar, soplar *(a una persona)*
squealer [ˈskwilər] *s* (coll) soplón *m*
squeamish [ˈskwimɪʃ] *adj* escrupuloso, remilgado; excesivamente modesto; *(easily nauseated)* asqueroso
squeeze [skwiz] *s* apretón *m;* **to put the squeeze on someone** (coll) hacer a uno la forzosa, meter en prensa a uno ‖ *tr* apretar; agobiar, oprimir; exprimir ‖ *intr* apretar; **to squeeze through** abrirse paso a estrujones por entre; salir de un aprieto a duras penas
squeezer [ˈskwizər] *s* exprimidera

squelch [skwɛltʃ] *s* (coll) tapaboca ‖ *tr* apabullar, despachurrar
squid [skwɪd] *s* calamar *m*
squint [skwɪnt] *s* mirada bizca; mirada furtiva; *(strabismus)* bizquera ‖ *tr* achicar, entornar *(los ojos)* ‖ *intr* bizquear; torcer la vista; tener los ojos medio cerrados
squint-eyed [ˈskwɪntˌaɪd] *adj* bisojo, bizco; malévolo, sospechoso
squire [skwaɪr] *s* acompañante *m (de una señora);* (Brit) terrateniente *m* de antigua heredad; (U.S.A.) juez *m* de paz, juez local ‖ *tr* acompañar *(a una señora)*
squirm [skwʌrm] *s* retorcimiento ‖ *intr* retorcerse; **to squirm out of** escaparse de *(p.ej., un aprieto)* haciendo mucho esfuerzo
squirrel [ˈskwʌrəl] *s* ardilla
squirt [skwʌrt] *s* chorro; jeringazo; (coll) mono, presuntuoso ‖ *tr* arrojar a chorros ‖ *intr* salir a chorros
Sr. *abbr* **senior, Sir**
S.S. *abbr* **Secretary of State, steamship, Sunday school**
St. *abbr* **Saint, Strait, Street**
stab [stæb] *s* puñalada; (coll) tentativa; **to make a stab at** (slang) esforzarse por hacer ‖ *v (pret & pp* **stabbed;** *ger* **stabbing)** *tr* apuñalar; traspasar ‖ *intr* apuñalar
stab in the back *s* puñalada trapera
stable [ˈstebəl] *adj* estable ‖ *s* establo, cuadra, caballeriza
stack [stæk] *s* montón *m*, pila; *(of rifles)* pabellón *m;* *(of books in a library)* estantería, depósito; *(of a chimney)* cañón *m;* *(of straw)* niara; *(of firewood)* hacina; (coll) montón *m*, gran número ‖ *tr* amontonar, apilar; florear *(el naipe);* hacinar *(leña)*
stadi·um [ˈstediəm] *s (pl* **-ums** o **-a** [ə]**)** estadio
staff [stæf] *s* bastón *m*, apoyo, sostén *m;* personal *m;* (mil) estado mayor; (mus) pentagrama *m* ‖ *tr* dotar, proveer de personal, nombrar personal para
stag [stæg] *adj* exclusivo para hombres, de hombres solos ‖ *s (male deer)* ciervo; varón *m;* varón solo *(no acompañado de mujeres)*
stage [stedʒ] *s* escena; etapa, jornada; *(coach)* diligencia; *(scene of an event)* teatro; *(of a microscope)* portaobjeto; (rad) etapa; **by easy stages** a pequeñas etapas; lentamente; **to go on the stage** hacerse actor ‖ *tr* poner en escena, representar; preparar, organizar
stage'coach' *s* diligencia
stage'craft' *s* arte *f* teatral
stage door *s* (theat) entrada de los artistas
stage fright *s* trac *m*, miedo al público
stage'hand' *s* tramoyista *m*, metemuertos *m*, metesillas *m*
stage manager *s* director *m* de escena
stage'-struck' *adj* loco por el teatro
stage whisper *s* susurro en voz alta
stagger [ˈstægər] *tr* sorprender; asustar; escalonar *(las horas de trabajo)* ‖ *intr* tambalear, hacer eses al andar
staggering *adj* tambaleante; sorprendente

stagnant ['stægnənt] *adj* estancado; (fig) estancado, inactivo, paralizado

staid [sted] *adj* grave, serio, formal

stain [sten] *s* mancha; tinte *m*, tintura; materia colorante ‖ *tr* manchar; teñir; colorar ‖ *intr* mancharse; hacer manchas

stained glass *s* vidrio de color

stained'glass' window *s* vidriera de colores, vidriera pintada, vitral *m*

stainless ['stenlɪs] *adj* inmanchable; (*steel*) inoxidable; inmaculado

stair [stɛr] *s* escalera; (*step of a series*) escalón *m;* **stairs** escalera

stair'case' *s* escalera

stair'way' *s* escalera

stair well *s* hueco de escalera

stake [stek] *s* estaca; (*of a cart or truck*) telero; (*to hold up a plant*) rodrigón *m;* (*in gambling*) puesta; premio del vencedor; **at stake** en juego; en gran peligro; **to die at the stake** morir en la hoguera; **to pull up stakes** (coll) irse; (coll) mudarse de casa ‖ *tr* estacar; atar a una estaca; rodrigar (*plantas*); apostar; arriesgar, aventurar; **to stake all** jugarse el todo por el todo; **to stake off** o **to stake out** estacar, señalar con estacas

stale [stel] *adj* añejo, rancio, viejo; (*air*) viciado; (*joke*) mohoso; anticuado

stale'mate' *s* mate ahogado; **to reach a stalemate** llegar a un punto muerto ‖ *tr* dar mate ahogado a; estancar, paralizar

stalk [stɔk] *s* tallo ‖ *tr* cazar al acecho; acechar, espiar ‖ *intr* cazar al acecho; andar con paso majestuoso; andar con paso altivo; **to stalk out** salir con paso airado

stall [stɔl] *s* cuadra, establo; pesebre *m;* (*booth in a market*) puesto; (*at a fair*) caseta; (Brit) butaca; (slang) pretexto ‖ *tr* encerrar en un establo; poner trabas a; parar (*un motor*); **to stall off** (coll) eludir, evitar ‖ *intr* atascarse, atollarse; pararse (*un motor*); (slang) eludir para engañar o demorar; **to stall for time** (slang) tardar para ganar tiempo

stallion ['stæljən] *s* caballo padre, caballo semental

stalwart ['stɔlwərt] *adj* fornido, forzudo; valiente; leal, constante ‖ *s* persona fornida; partidario leal

stamen ['stemən] *s* estambre *m*

stamina ['stæmɪnə] *s* fuerza, nervio, vigor *m*, resistencia

stammer ['stæmər] *s* balbuceo, tartamudeo ‖ *tr* balbucear (*p.ej., excusas*) ‖ *intr* balbucear, tartamudear

stamp [stæmp] *s* (*device used for making an impression; mark made with it; piece of paper or mark used to show payment of postage*) sello; (*tool used for crushing or marking*) pisón *m;* (*tool for stamping coins and medals*) cuño, troquel *m;* marca, impresión; clase *f*, tipo ‖ *tr* sellar; troquelar; estampar, imprimir; hollar, pisotear; indicar, señalar; poner el sello a; bocartear (*el mineral*); **to stamp out** apagar pateando;

extinguir por la fuerza; suprimir; **to stamp the feet** dar patadas ‖ *intr* patalear

stampede [stæm'pid] *s* fuga precipitada; estampida (Am) ‖ *tr* hacer huir en desorden; provocar a pánico ‖ *intr* huir en tropel; obrar por común impulso

stamping grounds *spl* (slang) guarida (*sitio frecuentado por una persona*)

stamp pad *s* tampón *m*

stamp'-vend'ing machine *s* máquina expendedora de sellos

stance [stæns] *s* (sport) postura, planta

stanch [stɑntʃ] *adj* firme, fuerte; constante, leal; (*watertight*) estanco ‖ *tr* estancar; retañar (*la sangre de una herida*)

stand [stænd] *s* parada; alto para defenderse; postura, posición; resistencia; estrado, tribuna; sostén *m* soporte *m*, pie *m;* quiosco ‖ *v* (*pret & pp* **stood** [stʊd]) *tr* poner, colocar; poner derecho; soportar, tolerar, resistir; (coll) aguantar (*a una persona*); (coll) sufragar (*un gasto*); **to stand off** tener a raya; **to stand one's ground** mantenerse firme ‖ *intr* estar, estar situado; estar parado; estacionarse; estar de pie, estar derecho; ponerse de pie, levantarse; resultar; persistir; mantenerse; **to stand aloof, apart** o **aside** mantenerse apartado; **to stand back of** respaldar; **to stand for** significar, representar; apoyar, defender; apadrinar; mantener (*p.ej., una opinión*); presentarse como candidato de; navegar hacia; (coll) tolerar; **to stand in line** hacer cola; **to stand out** sobresalir; destacarse, resaltar; **to stand up** ponerse de pie, levantarse; durar; **to stand up to** hacer; resueltamente frente a

standard ['stændərd] *adj* normal; (*typewriter keyboard*) universal; corriente, regular; legal; clásico ‖ *s* patrón *m;* norma, regla establecida; bandera, estandarte *m;* emblema *m*, símbolo; soporte *m*, pilar *m*

standardize ['stændər,daɪz] *tr* normalizar, estandardizar

standard of living *s* nivel *m* de vida

standard time *s* hora legal, hora oficial

standee [stæn'di] *s* (coll) espectador *m* que asiste de pie; (coll) pasajero de pie

stand'-in' *s* (theat & mov) doble *mf;* (coll) buenas aldabas

standing ['stændɪŋ] *adj* derecho, en pie; de pie; parado, inmóvil; (*water*) encharcado, estancado; (*army; committee*) permanente; vigente ‖ *s* condición, posición; reputación; parada; **in good standing** en posición acreditada; **of long standing** de mucho tiempo, de antigua fecha

standing army *s* ejército permanente

standing room *s* sitio para estar de pie

stand-offishness [,stænd'ɔfɪʃnɪs] *s* desarrimo

stand'point' *s* punto de vista

stand'still' *s* detención, parada; alto; descanso, inactividad; **to come to a standstill** cesar, pararse

stanza ['stænzə] *s* estancia, estrofa

staple ['stepəl] *adj* primero, principal; corriente, establecido ‖ *s* (*to fasten papers*) grapa; artículo o producto de primera necesidad; materia prima; fibra textil ‖ *tr* sujetar con grapas

stapler ['steplər] *s* engrapador *m*, cosepapeles *m*

star [star] *s* (*heavenly body*) astro; (*heavenly body except sun and moon; figure that represents a star*) estrella; (*mov & theat*) estrella; (*of football*) as *m;* (typ) estrella o asterisco; (*fate, destiny*) (fig) estrella; **to see stars** (coll) ver las estrellas; **to thank one's lucky stars** estar agradecido por su buena suerte ‖ *v* (*pret & pp* **starred;** *ger* **starring**) *tr* estrellar, adornar o señalar con estrellas; marcar con asterisco; presentar como estrella (*a un actor*) ‖ *intr* ser la estrella; lucirse; sobresalir

starboard ['starbərd] o ['star,bord] *adj* de estribor ‖ *adv* a estribor ‖ *s* estribor *m*

starch [starʃ] *s* almidón *m*, fécula; arrogancia, entono; (slang) fuerza, vigor *m* ‖ *tr* almidonar

stare [stɛr] *s* mirada fija ‖ *intr* mirar fijamente; **to stare at** clavar la vista en mirar con fijeza

star'fish' *s* estrella de mar, estrellamar *m*

star'gaze' *intr* mirar las estrellas; ser distraído, soñar despierto

stark [stark] *adj* cabal, completo, puro; rígido, tiesco; duro, severo ‖ *adv* completamente, enteramente; rígidamente, severamente

stark'-na'ked *adj* en pelota, en cueros

star'light' *s* luz *f* de las estrellas

starling ['starlɪŋ] *s* estornino

Star'-Span'gled Banner *s* bandera estrellada (*bandera de los EE.UU.*)

start [start] *s* comienzo, principio; salida, partida; lugar *m* de partida; (*scare*) sobresalto; (*sudden start*) arranque *m;* (*advantage*) ventaja ‖ *tr* empezar, principiar; poner en marcha; hacer arrancar; dar la señal de partida a; entablar (*una conversación*); levantar (*la caza*) ‖ *intr* empezar, principiar; ponerse en marcha; arrancar; (*to be startled*) sobresaltar; nacer, provenir; **starting from** o **with** a partir de; **to start after** salir en busca de

starter ['startər] *s* iniciador *m;* (*of a series*) primero; (aut) arranque *m*, motor *m* de arranque; (sport) juez *m* de salida

starting ['startɪŋ] *adj* de salida; de arranque ‖ *s* puesta en marcha

starting crank *s* manivela de arranque

starting point *s* punto de partida, arrancadero

startle ['startəl] *tr* asustar, sorprender, sobrecoger ‖ *intr* asustarse, sorprenderse sobrecogerse

startling ['startlɪŋ] *adj* alarmante, asombroso

starvation [star'veʃən] *s* hambre *f*, inanición

starvation diet *s* régimen *m* de hambre, cura de hambre

starvation wages *spl* salario de hambre

starve [starv] *tr* hambrear; hacer morir de hambre; **to starve out** hacer rendirse por

hambre ‖ *intr* hambrear; morir de hambre; (coll) tener hambre

starving ['starvɪŋ] *adj* hambriento, famélico

stat. *abbr* **statuary, statute, statue**

state [stet] *adj* de estado; del estado; estatal; público; de gala, de lujo ‖ *s* estado; fausto, ceremonia, pompa; **to lie in state** estar expuesto en capilla ardiente, estar de cuerpo presente; **to live in state** gastar mucho lujo; **to ride in state** pasear en carruaje de lujo ‖ *tr* afirmar, declarar; exponer, manifestar; plantear (*un problema*)

State Department *s* Ministerio de Relaciones Exteriores

state•ly ['stetli] *adj* (*comp* **-lier;** *super* **-liest**) imponente, majestuoso

statement ['stetmənt] *s* declaración; exposición, informe *m*, relación; (com) estado de cuentas

state of mind *s* estado de ánimo

state'room' *s* camarote *m;* (rr) compartimiento particular

state'side' *adv* (coll) en (*or* a) los Estados Unidos

states•man ['stetsmən] *s* (*pl* **-men** [mən]) estadista *m*, hombre *m* de estado

static ['stætɪk] *adj* estático; (rad) atmosférico ‖ *s* (rad) parásitos atmosféricos

station ['steʃən] *s* estación; condición, situación ‖ *tr* estacionar, apostar

station agent *s* jefe *m* de estación

stationary ['steʃən,ɛri] *adj* estacionario

station break *s* (rad) descanso, intermedio

stationer ['steʃənər] *s* papelero

stationery ['steʃən,ɛri] *s* efectos de escritorio; papel *m* para cartas

stationery store *s* papelería

station house *s* cuartelillo de policía

station identification *s* (rad & telv) indicativo de la emisora

sta'tion•mas'ter *s* jefe *m* de estación

station wagon *s* vagoneta, rubia, coche *m* rural; camioneta (Arg, CAm, Col. Pan, Peru, S-D); esteishon wagon *m* (Chile, Col, Cuba, P-R); guagüita (Cuba, P-R); camionetilla (Guat); carmelita (Hond); ranchera (Ven)

statistical [stə,tɪstɪkəl] *adj* estadístico

statistician [,stætɪs,tɪʃən] *s* estadístico

statistics [stə,tɪstɪks] *ssg* (*science*) estadística; *spl* (*data*) estadística o estadísticas

statue ['stætʃu] *s* estatua

statuesque [,stætʃu,ɛsk] *adj* escultural

stature [,stætʃər] *s* estatura, talla; carácter *m*, habilidad

status ['stetəs] *s* condición, estado, situación social, legal o profesional; (*prestige or superior rank*) categoría

status seeking *s* esfuerzo por adquirir categoría

status symbol *s* símbolo de categoría social

statute ['stætʃut] *s* estatuto, ley *f*

statutory ['stætʃu,tori] *adj* estatutario, legal

staunch [stɔntʃ] o [stɑntʃ] *adj & tr* var de **stanch**

stave [stev] *s* (*of a barrel*) duela; (*of a ladder*) peldaño; (mus) pentagrama *m* ‖*v* (*pret & pp* **staved** o **stove** [stov]) *tr* romper, destrozar; (*to break a hole in*) desfondar; **to stave off** mantener a distancia; evitar, impedir, diferir

stay [ste] *s* morada, permanencia, estancia; suspensión; (*of a corset*) ballena, varilla; apoyo, sostén *m;* (law) espera; (naut) estay *m* ‖ *tr* aplazar, detener; poner freno a ‖ *intr* quedar, quedarse, permanecer; parar, hospedarse; habitar; **to stay up** no acostarse, velar

stay'-at-home' *adj & s* hogareño

stead [stɛd] *s* lugar *m;* **in his stead** en su lugar, en lugar de él; **to stand in good stead** ser de provecho, ser ventajoso

stead'fast' *adj* fijo; resuelto; constante

stead•y ['stɛdi] *adj* (*comp* **-ier;** *super* **-iest**) constante, fijo, firme, seguro; regular, uniforme; resuelto; asentado, serio ‖ *v* (*pret & pp* **-ied**) *tr* estabilizar, reforzar; calmar (*los nervios*) ‖ *intr* estabilizarse; calmarse

steak [stek] *s* lonja, tajada; biftec *m*

steal [stil] *s* (coll) hurto, robo ‖ *v* (*pret* **stole** [stol]; *pp* **stolen**) *tr* hurtar, robar; atraer, cautivar; manotear (Arg, Mex) ‖ *intr* hurtar, robar; **to steal away** escabullirse; **to steal into** meterse a hurtadillas en; **to steal upon** aproximarse sin ruido a

stealth [stɛlθ] *s* cautela, recato; **by stealth** a hurtadillas

steam [stim] *adj* de vapor ‖ *s* vapor *m;* vaho, humo; **to get up steam** dar presión; **to let off steam** descargar vapor; (fig) desahogarse ‖ *tr* cocer al vapor; saturar de vapor; empañar (*p.ej., las ventanas*) ‖ *intr* echar vapor, emitir vapor; evaporarse; funcionar o marchar a vapor; **to steam ahead** avanzar por medio del vapor; (fig) hacer grandes progresos

steam'boat' *s* buque *m* de vapor

steamer ['stimər] *s* vapor *m*

steamer rug *s* manta de viaje

steamer trunk *s* baúl *m* de camarote

steam heat *s* calefacción por vapor

steam roller *s* apisonadora movida a vapor; (coll) fuerza arrolladora

steam'ship' *s* vapor *m*, buque *m* de vapor

steam shovel *s* pala mecánica de vapor

steam table *s* plancha caliente

steed [stid] *s* caballo; (*high-spirited horse*) corcel *m*

steel [stil] *adj* acerado; (*business, industry*) siderúrgico; (fig) duro, frío ‖ *s* acero; (*for striking fire from flint; for sharpening knives*) eslabón *m* ‖ *tr* acerar; **to steel oneself** acerarse

steel wool *s* virutillas de acero, estopa de acero

steelyard ['stil,jɑrd] *s* romana

steep [stip] *adj* escarpado, empinado; (*price*) alto, excesivo ‖ *tr* empapar, remojar; **steeped in** absorbido en

steeple ['stipəl] *s* aguja, campanario

stee'ple•chase' *s* carrera de campanario, carrera de obstáculos

stee'ple•jack' *s* escalatorres *m*

steer [stɪr] *s* buey *m* ‖ *tr* conducir, gobernar, guiar ‖ *intr* conducirse; **to steer clear of** (coll) evitar, eludir

steerage ['stɪrɪdʒ] *s* dirección; (naut) proa, entrepuente *m*

steerage passenger *s* (naut) pasajero de entrepuente

steering column *s* columna de dirección

steering committee *s* comité *m* paneador

steering wheel *s* (aut) volante *m;* (naut) rueda del timón

stem [stɛm] *s* (*of a goblet*) pie *m;* (*of a pipe, of a feather*) cañón *m;* (*of a column*) fuste *m;* (*of a watch*) botón *m;* (*of a key*) espiga, tija; (*of a word*) tema *m;* (bot) tallo, vástago; **from stem to stern** de proa a popa ‖ *v* (*pret & pp* **stemmed;** *ger* **stemming**) *tr* (*to remove the stem from*) desgranar; (*to check*) detener, refrenar; (*to plug*) estancar; hacer frente a; rendir (*la marea*) ‖ *intr* nacer, provenir; **to stem from** originarse en, provenir de

stem'-wind'er *s* remontuar *m*

stench [stɛntʃ] *s* hedor *m*, hediondez *f*

sten•cil ['stɛnsəl] *s* cartón picado; (*work produced by it*) estarcido ‖ *v* (*pret & pp* **-ciled** o **-cilled;** *ger* **-ciling** o **-cilling**) *tr* estarcir

stenographer [stə'nɑgrəfər] *s* estenógrafo

stenography [stə'nɑgrəfi] *s* estenografía

step [stɛp] *s* paso; (*of staircase*) grada, peldaño; (*footprint*) huella, pisada; (*of carriage*) estribo; (*measure, démarche*) gestión, medida; (mus) intervalo; **step by step** paso a paso; **to watch one's step** proceder con cautela, andarse con tiento ‖ *v* (*pret & pp* **stepped;** *ger* **stepping**) *tr* escalonar; **to step off** medir a pasos ‖ *intr* dar un paso, dar pasos; caminar, ir; (coll) andar de prisa; **to step on it** (coll) acelerar la marcha, darse prisa; **to step on the starter** pisar el arranque

step'broth'er *s* medio hermano, hermanastro

step'child' *s* (*pl* **-children** [,tʃɪldrən]) hijastro

step'daugh'ter *s* hijastra

step'fa'ther *s* padrastro

step'lad'der *s* escala, escalera de tijera

step'moth'er *s* madrastra

steppe [stɛp] *s* estepa

stepping stone *s* estriberón *m*, pasadera; (fig) escalón *m*, escabel *m*

step'sis'ter *s* media hermana, hermanastra

step'son' *s* hijastro

stere•o ['stɛri,o] o ['stɪrɪ,o] *adj* estereofónico; estereososcópico ‖ *s* (*pl* **-os**) música estereofónica, disco estereofónico; radiodifusión estereofónica; fotografía estereoscópica

stereo system *s* equipo de alta fidelidad

ster'e•o•type' *s* clisé *m*, estereotipo; concepción tradicional

stereotyped ['stɛri•ə,taipt] o ['stɪri•ə,taipt] *adj* estereotipado

sterile ['stɛrɪl] *adj* estéril

sterilization [,stɛrɪlɪ'zeʃən] *s* esterilización

sterilize ['stɛri,laiz] *tr* esterilizar

sterling [ˈstʌrlɪŋ] *adj* fino, de ley; verdadero, genuino, puro, excelente ‖ *s* libras esterlinas; plata de ley; vajilla de plata

stern [stʌrn] *adj* austero, severo; decidido, firme ‖ *s* popa

stethoscope [ˈstɛθə,skop] *s* estetoscopio

stevedore [ˈstivə,dor] *s* estibador *m*

stew [stju] o [stu] *s* guisado, estofado ‖ *tr* guisar, estofar ‖ *intr* abrasarse; (coll) estar apurado

steward [ˈstu•ərd] *s* mayordomo; administrador *m;* (of ship or plane) camarero

stewardess [ˈstu•ərdɪs] *s* mayordoma; (of ship or plane) camarera; (of plane) azafata, aeromoza

stewed fruit *s* compota de frutas

stewed tomatoes *spl* puré *m* de tomates

stick [stɪk] *s* palo, palillo; bastón *m*, vara; (of dynamite) barra; (naut) mástil *m*, verga; (typ) componedor *m* ‖ *v* (pret & pp **stuck** [stʌk]) *tr* picar, punzar; apuñalar; clavar, hincar; pegar; (coll) confundir; **to stick out** asomar (la cabeza); sacar (la lengua); **to stick up** (in order to rob) (slang) asaltar, atracar ‖ *intr* estar prendido, estar hincado; pegarse; agarrarse (la pintura); encastillarse (p.ej., una ventana); resaltar, sobresalir; continuar, persistir; permanecer; atascarse; **to stick out** salir (p.ej., el pañuelo del bolsillo); sobresalir, proyectarse; velar (un escollo); resultar evidente; **to stick together** (coll) quedarse unidos, no abandonarse; **to stick up** destacarse; estar de punta (el pelo); **to stick up for** (coll) defender

sticker [ˈstɪkər] *s* etiqueta engomada, marbete engomado; pegatina; punta, espina; (coll) problema arduo

sticking plaster *s* esparadrapo

stick′pin′ *s* alfiler *m* de corbata

stick′-up′ *s* (slang) asalto, atraco

stick•y [ˈstɪki] *adj* (comp **-ier;** super **-iest**) pegajoso; (coll) húmedo, mojado; (weather) bochornoso

stiff [stɪf] *adj* tieso; entorpecido, entumecido; arduo, difícil; (price) (coll) excesivo; **to get stiff** envararse ‖ *s* (slang) cadáver *m*

stiff collar *s* cuello almidonado

stiffen [ˈstɪfən] *tr* atiesar; endurecer; espesar ‖ *intr* atiesarse; endurecerse, espesarse; obstinarse

stiff neck *s* torticolis *m;* obstinación

stiff-necked [ˈstɪf,nɛkt] *adj* terco, obstinado

stiffness [ˈstɪfnɪs] *s* envaramiento

stiff shirt *s* camisola

stifle [ˈstaɪfəl] *tr* ahogar, sofocar; apagar, suprimir

stig•ma [ˈstɪgmə] *s* (pl **-mas** o **-mata** [mətə]) estigma *m*

stigmatize [ˈstɪgmə,taɪz] *tr* estigmatizar

stilet•to [stɪˈlɛto] *s* (pl **-tos**) estilete *m*, puñal *m*

still [stɪl] *adj* inmóvil, quieto, tranquilo; callado, silencioso; (wine) no espumoso ‖ *adv* tranquilamente; silenciosamente; aún, todavía ‖ *conj* con todo, sin embargo ‖ *s* alambique *m*, destiladera; destilería; foto-

grafía de lo inmóvil; (poet) silencio ‖ *tr* acallar; amortiguar; calmar ‖ *intr* callar; calmarse

still′birth′ *s* parto muerto

still′born′ *adj* nacido muerto

still life *s* (pl **still lifes** o **still lives**) bodegón *m*, naturaleza muerta

stilt [stɪlt] *s* zanco; (in the water) pilote *m*

stilted [ˈstɪltɪd] *adj* elevado; hinchado, pomposo, tieso

stimulant [ˈstɪmjələnt] *adj & s* estimulante *m*, excitante *m*

stimulate [ˈstɪmjə,let] *tr* estimular

stimu•lus [ˈstɪmjələs] *s* (pl **-li** [,laɪ]) estímulo *m*

sting [stɪŋ] *s* picadura; aguijón *m*; lanceta ‖ *v* (pret & pp **stung** [stʌŋ]) *tr* picar; aguijonear ‖ *intr* picar

stin•gy [ˈstɪndʒi] *adj* (comp **-gier;** super **-giest**) mezquino, tacaño

stink [stɪŋk] *s* hedor *m*, mal olor *m* ‖ *v* (pret **stank** [stæŋk] o **stunk** [stʌŋk]; *pp* **stunk**) *tr* dar mal olor a ‖ *intr* heder, oler muy mal; **to stink of** heder a; (slang) poseer (p.ej., dinero) en un grado que da asco

stint [stɪnt] *s* faena, tarea ‖ *tr* limitar, restringir ‖ *intr* ser económico, ahorrar con mezquindad

stipend [ˈstaɪpənd] *s* estipendio

stipulate [ˈstɪpjə,let] *tr* estipular

stir [stʌr] *s* agitación, meneo; alboroto, tumulto; **to create a stir** meter ruido, causar furor ‖ *v* (pret & pp **stirred;** *ger* **stirring**) *tr* agitar, mover; revolver; conmover, excitar; atizar, avivar (el fuego); remover (un líquido); **to stir up** revolver; despertar; conmover; fomentar (discordias) ‖ *intr* bullirse, moverse; (say a word) rechistar

stirring [ˈstʌrɪŋ] *adj* conmovedor, emocionante

stirrup [ˈstʌrəp] o [ˈstɪrəp] *s* estribo

stitch [stɪtʃ] *s* puntada, punto; pedazo de tela; punzada, dolor *m* punzante; (coll) poquito; **to be in stitches** (coll) desternillarse de risa ‖ *tr* coser, bastear, hilvanar ‖ *intr* coser

stock [stak] *adj* común, regular; banal, vulgar; bursátil; ganadero, del ganado; (theat) de repertorio ‖ *s* surtido; capital *f* comercial; acciones, valores *mpl;* (inventory) stock *m;* (of meat) caldo; (of a tree) tronco; (of an anvil) cepo; (of a rifle) caja, culata; (of a tree; of a family) cepa; mango, manija; palo, madero; leño; (livestock) ganado; (theat) programa *m*, repertorio; **to have in stock** tener en stock; **in stock** en existencia; **out of stock** agotado; **to take stock** hacer el inventario; **to take stock in** (coll) dar importancia a, confiar en ‖ *tr* abastecer, surtir; tener existencias de; acopiar, acumular; poblar (un estanque, una colmena, etc.)

stockade [staˈked] *s* estacada, empalizada ‖ *tr* empalizar

stock′breed′er *s* criador *m* de ganado

stock′bro′ker *s* bolsista *mf*, corredor *m* de bolsa

stock car *s* (aut) coche *m* de serie; (rr) vagón *m* para el ganado

st
st

stock company s (com) sociedad anónima; (theat) teatro de repertorio
stock dividend s acción liberada
stock exchange s bolsa
stock'hold'er s accionista *mf*, tenedor *m* de acciones
stockholder of record s accionista *mf* que como tal figura en el libro registro de la compañía
Stockholm ['stɑkhom] s Estocolmo
stocking ['stɑkɪŋ] s media
stock market s bolsa, mercado de valores; **to play the stock market** jugar a la bolsa
stock'pile' s reserva de materias primas ‖ *tr* acumular (*materias primas*) ‖ *intr* acumular materias primas
stock raising s ganadería
stock'room' s almacén *m;* sala de exposición
stock split s reparto de acciones gratis
stock•y ['stɑki] s adj (*comp* **-ier;** *super* **-iest**) bajo, grueso y fornido
stock'yard' s corral *m* de concentración de ganado
stoic ['sto•ɪk] adj & s estoico
stoke [stok] *tr* atizar, avivar (*el fuego*); alimentar, cebar (*el horno*)
stoker ['stokər] s fogonero
stolid ['stɑlɪd] adj impasible, insensible
stomach ['stʌmək] s estómago; apetito; deseo, inclinación ‖ *tr* tragar; **to not be able to stomach** (coll) no poder tragar
stomach pump s bomba estomacal
stone [ston] s piedra; (*of fruit*) hueso; (pathol) mal *m* de piedra ‖ *tr* lapidar, apedrear; deshuesar (*la fruta*)
stone'-broke' adj arrancado, sin blanca
stone'-deaf' adj sordo como una tapia
stone'ma'son s albañil *m*
stone quarry s cantera, pedrera
stone's throw s tiro de piedra; **within a stone's throw** a tiro de piedra
ston•y ['stoni] adj (*comp* **-ier;** *super* **-iest**) pedregoso; duro, empedernido
stool [stul] s escabel *m*, taburete *m;* sillico, retrete *m;* (*bowel movement*) cámara, evacuación
stoop [stup] s encorvada, inclinación; escalinata de entrada ‖ *intr* doblarse, inclinarse, encorvarse; andar encorvado; humillarse, rebajarse
stoop•shouldered ['stup'ʃoldərd] adj cargado de espaldas
stop [stɑp] s parada, alto; parón; estada, estancia; cesación, fin *m*, suspensión; cerradura, tapadura; impedimento, obstáculo; freno; tope *m*, retén *m;* (*in writing; in telegrams*) punto; (*of a guitar*) llave *f*, traste *m;* **to put a stop to** poner fin a ‖ *v* (*pret & pp* **stopped;** *ger* **stopping**) *tr* parar, detener; acabar, terminar; estorbar, obstruir; interceptar; suspender; cerrar, tapar; rechazar (*un sueldo o parte de él*); retener (*un golpe*); **to stop up** cegar, obstruir, tapar ‖ *intr* parar, pararse, detenerse; quedarse, permanecer; alojarse, hospedarse; acabarse, terminarse; **to stop** + *ger* cesar de + *inf*, dejar de + *inf*

stop'cock' s llave *f* de cierre, llave de paso
stop'gap' adj provisional ‖ s substituto provisional
stop light s luz *f* de parada
stop'o'ver s parada intermedia, escala; billete *m* de parada intermedia
stoppage ['stɑpɪdʒ] s parada, detención; (*of work*) paro; interrupción; suspensión; obstáculo; (*of wages*) retención; (pathol) obstrucción
stopper ['stɑpər] s tapón *m;* taco, tarugo
stop sign o **stop signal** s señal *f* de alto, señal de parada
stop watch s reloj *m* de segundos muertos, cronómetro
storage ['stɔrɪdʒ] s almacenaje *m;* (*costs*) derechos de almacenaje
storage battery s (elec) acumulador *m*
store [stor] s tienda, almacén *m;* **I know what is in store for you** sé lo que le espera; **to set store by** dar mucha importancia a ‖ *tr* abastecer; tener guardado, almacenar; **to store away** acumular
store'house' s almacén *m*, depósito; (*e.g., of wisdom*) (fig) mina
store'keep'er s tendero, almacenista *mf*
store'room' s cuarto de almacenar; (*for furniture*) guardamuebles *m;* (naut) despensa
store window s escaparate *m* (de tienda); aparador *m* (Mex)
stork [stɔrk] s cigüeña; **to have a visit from the stork** recibir a la cigüeña
storm [stɔrm] s borrasca, tempestad, tormenta; (mil) asalto; (naut) borrasca; (fig) tempestad, tumulto; **to take by storm** tomar por asalto ‖ *tr* asaltar ‖ *intr* tempestear; precipitarse
storm cloud s nubarrón *m*
storm door s contrapuerta, guardapuerta
storm sash s contravidriera
storm troops spl tropas de asalto
storm window s guardaventana, sobrevidriera
storm•y ['stɔrmi] adj (*comp* **-ier;** *super* **-iest**) borrascoso, tempestuoso; (*session, meeting, etc.*) tumultuoso
sto•ry ['stori] s (*pl* **-ries**) historia, cuento, anécdota; enredo, trama; (coll) mentira; piso, alto ‖ *v* (*pret & pp* **-ried**) *tr* historiar
sto'ry•tel'ler s narrador *m;* (coll) mentiroso
stout [staut] adj corpulento, gordo, robusto; animoso; leal; terco ‖ s cerveza obscura fuerte
stove [stov] s (*for heating a house or room*) estufa; (*for cooking*) hornillo, cocina de gas, cocina eléctrica
stove'pipe' s tubo de estufa, tubo de hornillo; (*hat*) (coll) chistera, chimenea
stow [sto] *tr* guardar, meter, esconder; (naut) arrumar, estibar ‖ *intr*—**to stow away** embarcarse clandestinamente, esconderse en un barco o avión
stowage ['sto•ɪdʒ] s arrumaje *m*, estiba
stow'a•way' s llovido, polizón *m*
str. *abbr* **strait, steamer**
straddle ['strædəl] s esparrancamiento ‖ *tr* montar a horcajadas; (coll) tratar de favo-

recer a ambas partes en (*p.ej.*, *un pleito*) ‖
intr ponerse a horcajadas; (coll) tratar de
favorecer a ambas partes

strafe [strɑf] o [stref] *s* bombardeo violento ‖
tr bombardear violentamente

straggle [ˈstrægəl] *intr* errar, vagar; andar
perdido, extraviarse; separarse; estar espar-
cido

straight [stret] *adj* derecho; recto; erguido;
(*hair*) lacio; continuo, seguido; honrado,
sincero; correcto; decidido, intransigente;
(*e.g.*, *whiskey*) solo; **to set a person
straight** mostrar el camino a una persona;
dar consejo a una persona; mostrar a una
persona el modo de proceder ‖ *adv* derecho; sin interrupción; sinceramente; exactamente; en seguida; **straight ahead** todo
seguido, derecho; **to go straight** enmendarse

straighten [ˈstretən] *tr* enderezar; poner en
orden ‖ *intr* enderezarse

straight face *s* cara seria

straight′for′ward *adj* franco, sincero; honrado

straight off *adv* luego, en seguida

straight razor *s* navaja barbera

straight′way′ *adv* luego, en seguida

strain [stren] *s* tensión, tirantez *f;* esfuerzo
muy grande; fatiga excesiva, agotamiento;
(*of a muscle*) torcedura; aire *m*, melodía;
(*of a family or lineage*) cepa; linaje *m*,
raza; rasgo racial; genio, vena, huella, rastro ‖ *tr* estirar; torcer o torcerse (*p.ej.*, *la
muñeca*); forzar (*p.ej.*, *los nervios, la vista*); apretar; deformar; colar, tamizar ‖ *intr*
esforzarse; deformarse; colarse, tamizarse;
filtrarse; exprimirse (*un jugo*); resistirse; **to
strain at** hacer grandes esfuerzos por

strained [strend] *adj* (*smile*) forzado; (*friendship*) tirante

strainer [ˈstrenər] *s* colador *m*

strait [stret] *s* estrecho; **straits** estrecho; **to
be in dire straits** estar en el mayor apuro,
hallarse en gran estrechez

strait jacket *s* camisa de fuerza

strait-laced [ˈstret,lest] *adj* gazmoño

strand [strænd] *s* playa; filamento; (*of rope
or cable*) torón *m*, ramal *m;* (*of pearls*)
hilo; pelo ‖ *tr* deshebrar; retorcer, trenzar
(*cuerda, cable, etc.*); dejar extraviado;
(naut) varar

stranded [ˈstrændɪd] *adj* desprovisto, desamparado; (*ship*) encallado; (*rope or cable*)
trenzado, retorcido

strange [strendʒ] *adj* extraño, singular;
nuevo, desconocido; novel, no acostumbrado

stranger [ˈstrendʒər] *s* forastero; visitador
m; intruso; desconocido; principiante *mf*

strangle [ˈstræŋgəl] *tr* estrangular; reprimir,
suprimir ‖ *intr* estrangularse

strap [stræp] *s* (*of leather*) correa; (*of cloth,
metal, etc.*) banda, tira; (*to sharpen a
razor*) asentador *m* ‖ *v* (*pret & pp
strapped; ger strapping*) *tr* atar o liar con
correa, banda o tira; azotar con una correa;
fajar, vendar; asentar (*una navaja*)

strap′hang′er *s* (coll) pasajero colgado

stratagem [ˈstrætədʒəm] *s* estratagema *f*

strategic(al) [strəˈtidʒɪk(əl)] *adj* estratégico

strategist [ˈstrætɪdʒɪst] *s* estratega *m*

strate•gy [ˈstrætɪdʒi] *s* (*pl* **-gies**) estrategia

strati•fy [ˈstrætɪ,faɪ] *v* (*pret & pp* **-fied**) *tr*
estratificar ‖ *intr* estratificarse

stratosphere [ˈstrætə,sfɪr] o [ˈstretə,sfɪr] *s*
estratosfera

stra•tum [ˈstretəm] o [ˈstrætəm] *s* (*pl* **-ta** [tə]
o **-tums**) estrato; (*e.g.*, *of society*) clase *f*

straw [strɔ] *adj* pajizo; baladí, de poca importancia; falso; ficticio ‖ *s* paja; (*for
drinking*) pajita; **I don't care a straw** no se
me da un bledo; **to be the last straw** ser el
colmo, no faltar más

straw′ber′ry *s* (*pl* **-ries**) fresa

straw hat *s* sombrero de paja; chupalla *m;*
(*with low flat crown*) canotié *m*

straw man *s* figura de paja; (*figurehead*)
testaferro; testigo falso

straw vote *s* voto informativo

stray [stre] *adj* extraviado, perdido; aislado,
suelto ‖ *s* animal extraviado o perdido ‖
intr extraviarse, perderse

streak [strik] *s* lista, raya; vena, veta; rasgo,
traza; (*of light*) rayo; (*of good luck*) racha;
(coll) tiempo muy breve; **like a streak**
(coll) como un rayo ‖ *tr* listar, rayar;
abigarrar ‖ *intr* rayarse; (coll) andar o pasar
como un rayo

stream [strim] *s* (*current*) corriente *f;* arroyo,
río; chorro, flujo; (*of people*) torrente *m;*
(*e.g.*, *of automobiles*) desfile *m* ‖ *intr*
correr, manar (*un líquido*); chorrear; flotar,
ondear; salir a torrentes

streamer [ˈstrimər] *s* flámula, banderola;
cinta ondeante; rayo de luz

streamlined [ˈstrim,laɪnd] *adj* aerodinámico,
perfilado

stream′lin′er *s* tren aerodinámico de lujo

street [strit] *adj* callejero ‖ *s* calle *f*

street′car′ *s* tranvía *m*

street cleaner *s* basurero; (*device*) barredera

street clothes *spl* traje *m* de calle

street floor *s* piso bajo

street lamp *s* farol *m* (de la calle)

street sprinkler [ˈsprɪŋklər] *s* carricuba,
carro de riego, regadera

street′walk′er *s* cantonera, carrerista

strength [strɛŋθ] *s* fuerza; intensidad; (*of
spirituous liquors*) graduación; (com) tendencia a la subida; (mil) número; **on the
strength of** fundándose en, confiando en

strengthen [ˈstrɛŋθən] *tr* fortificar, reforzar;
confirmar ‖ *intr* fortificarse, reforzarse

strenuous [ˈstrɛnjuˑəs] *adj* estrenuo, enérgico, vigoroso; arduo, difícil

stress [strɛs] *s* tensión, fuerza; compulsión;
acento; (mech) tensión; **to lay stress on**
hacer hincapié en ‖ *tr* someter a esfuerzo;
hacer hincapié en; acentuar

stress accent *s* acento prosódico

stretch [strɛtʃ] *s* estiramiento, estirón *m;*
(*distance in time or space*) trecho; (*section
of road*) tramo; extensión; (*of the imagina-*

st
st

tion) esfuerzo; (*confinement in jail*) (slang) condena; **at a stretch** de un tirón ‖ *tr* estirar; extender; tender; forzar, violentar; (fig) estirar (*el dinero*); **to stretch a point** hacer una concesión; **to stretch oneself** desperezarse ‖ *intr* estirarse; extenderse; tenderse; desperezarse; **to stretch out** (coll) echarse

stretcher ['strɛtʃər] *s* (*for gloves*) ensanchador *m;* (*for a painting*) bastidor *m;* (*to carry sick or wounded*) camilla

stretch'er-bear'er *s* camillero

strew [stru] *v* (*pret* **strewed;** *pp* **strewed** o **strewn**) *tr* derramar, esparcir; sembrar, salpicar; polvorear

stricken ['strɪkən] *adj* afligido; inhabilitado; herido; **stricken in years** debilitado por los años

strict [strɪkt] *adj* estricto, riguroso; (*exacting*) severo

stricture ['strɪktʃər] *s* crítica severa; (pathol) estrictura

stride [straɪd] *s* zancada, tranco; **to hit one's stride** alcanzar la actividad o velocidad acostumbrada; **to make great** (o **rapid**) **strides** avnzar a grandes pasos; **to take in one's stride** hacer sin esfuerzo ‖ *v* (*pret* **strode** [strod]; *pp* **stridden** ['strɪdən]) *tr* cruzar de un tranco; montar a horcajadas ‖ *intr* dar zancadas, caminar a paso largo, andar a trancos

strident ['straɪdənt] *adj* estridente

strife [straɪf] *s* contienda; rivalidad

strike [straɪk] *s* (*blow*) golpe *m;* (*stopping of work*) huelga; (*discovery of ore, oil, etc.*) descubrimiento repentino; golpe *m* de fortuna; **to go on strike** ir a la huelga ‖ *v* (*pret* & *pp* **struck** [strʌk]) *tr* golpear; pulsar (*una tecla*); herir, percutir; topar, dar con; acuñar (*monedas*); echar (*raíces*); frotar, rayar, encender (*un fóstoro*); descubrir repentinamente (*mineral, aceite, etc.*); cerrar (*un trato*); arriar (*las velas*); dar (*la hora*); asumir, tomar (*una postura*); borrar, cancelar; impresionar; atraer (*la atención*); **to strike it rich** descubrir un buen filón, tener un golpe de fortuna ‖ *intr* dar, sonar (*una campana, un reloj*); declararse en huelga; (mil) dar el asalto; **to strike out** ponerse en marcha, echar camino adelante

strike'break'er *s* rompehuelgas *m*, esquirol *m*

strike pay *s* sueldo de huelguista

striker ['straɪkər] *s* golpeador *m;* huelguista *mf*

striking ['straɪkɪŋ] *adj* impresionante, llamativo, sorprendente; en huelga

striking power *s* potencia de choque

string [strɪŋ] *s* cuerdecilla; piola; pita; (*of pearls; of lies*) sarta; (*of beans*) hebra; (*of onions or garlic*) ristra; (*row*) hilera; (mus) cuerda; (*limitation, proviso*) (coll) condición; **strings** instrumentos de cuerda; **to pull strings** tocar resortes ‖ *v* (*pret* & *pp* **strung** [strʌŋ]) *tr* enhebrar, ensartar; atar con cuerdas; proveer de cuerdas; colgar de una cuerda; tender (*un cable, un alambre*);

encordar (*un violín, una raqueta*); colocar en fila; (slang) engañar, burlar; **to string along** (slang) traer al retortero; **to string up** (coll) ahorcar

string bean *s* habichuela verde, judía verde

stringed instrument [strɪŋd] *s* instrumento de cuerda

stringent ['strɪndʒənt] *adj* riguroso, severo, estricto; convincente

string quartet *s* cuarteto de cuerdas

strip [strɪp] *s* tira; (*of metal*) lámina; (*of land*) faja ‖ *v* (*pret* & *pp* **stripped;** *ger* **stripping**) *tr* desnudar; despojar; desforrar; deshacer (*la cama*); estropear (*el engranaje, un tornillo*); desvenar (*tabaco*); descortezar; **to strip of** despojar de ‖ *intr* desnudarse; despojarse; descortezarse

stripe [straɪp] *s* banda, lista, raya; gaya; cinta, franja; (mil & nav) galón *m;* índole *f*, tipo; **to win one's stripes** ganar los entorchados ‖ *tr* listar, rayar; gayar

strip mining *s* mineraje *m* a tajo abierto

strip'tease' *s* espectáculo de desnudamiento sensual

strive [straɪv] *v* (*pret* **strove** [strov]; *pp* **striven** ['strɪvən]) *intr* esforzarse; luchar

stroke [strok] *s* golpe *m;* (*of bell or clock*) campanada; (*of pen*) plumada; (*of brush*) pincelada, brochada; (*of arms in swimming*) brazada; (*in a game*) jugada; (*caress with hand*) caricia; (*with a racket*) raquetazo; (*of a piston*) carrera, embolada; (*of a paddle*) palada; (*of an oar*) remada; (*of lightning*) rayo; (*line, mark*) raya; (*of good luck*) golpe *m;* (*of wit*) agudeza, chiste *m;* (*of genius*) rasgo; ataque *m* de parálisis; **at the stroke of** (*e.g., five*) al dar las (*p.ej., cinco*); **to not do a stroke of work** no dar golpe, no levantar paja del suelo ‖ *tr* frotar suavemente, acariciar con la mano

stroll [strol] *s* paseo; **to take a stroll** dar un paseo ‖ *intr* pasear, pasearse; callejear, errar, vagar

stroller ['strolər] *s* paseante *mf;* cochecito para niños

strong [strɔŋ] o [straŋ] *adj* fuerte, resistente; recio, robusto; intenso; (*stock market*) firme; enérgico; marcado; picante; rancio

strong'-arm' man *s* (coll) gorila

strong'box' *s* cofre *m* fuerte, caja de caudales

strong drink *s* bebida alcohólica, bebida fuerte

strong'hold' *s* plaza fuerte

strong man *s* (*e.g., in a circus*) hércules *m;* (*leader, good planner*) alma, promotor *m;* (*dictator*) hombre *m* fuerte

strong-minded ['strɔŋ,maɪndɪd] o [straŋ-'maɪndɪd] *adj* independiente; de inteligencia vigorosa; (*e.g., woman*) hombruna

strontium ['stranʃɪəm] *s* estroncio

strop [strap] *s* suavizador *m* ‖ *v* (*pret* & *pp* **stropped;** *ger* **stropping**) *tr* suavizar, afilar

strophe ['strofi] *s* estrofa

structure ['strʌktʃər] *s* estructura; edificio

struggle ['strʌgəl] *s* lucha; esfuerzo, forcejeo ‖ *intr* luchar; esforzarse, forcejear

strum [strʌm] v (pret & pp **strummed;** ger **strumming**) tr arañar (un instrumento músico) sin arte ‖ intr cencerrear; **to strum on** rasguear

strumpet ['strʌmpɪt] s ramera

strut [strʌt] s (brace, prop) riostra, torna-punta; contoneo, pavoneo ‖ v (pret & pp **strutted;** ger **strutting**) intr contonearse, pavonearse

strychnine ['strɪknaɪn] o ['strɪknɪn] s estric-nina

stub [stʌb] s fragmento, trozo; (of a cigar) colilla; (of a tree) tocón m; (of a pencil) cabo; (of a check) talón m ‖ v (pret & pp **stubbed;** ger **stubbing**) tr —**to stub one's toe** dar un tropezón

stubble ['stʌbəl] s rastrojo; (of beard) cañón m

stubborn ['stʌbərn] adj terco, testarudo, obstinado; porfiado; intratable; **to be stubborn** ser obstinado, empecinarse

stubbornness ['stʌbərnɪs] obstinación, s empecinamiento

stuc·co ['stʌko] s (pl -**coes** o -**cos**) estuco ‖ tr estucar

stuck'-up' adj (coll) estirado, orgulloso

stud [stʌd] s tachón m; botón m de camisa; montante m, pie derecho; clavo de adorno; (bolt) espárrago; caballeriza; (of mares) yeguada ‖ v (pret & pp **studded;** ger **studding**) tr tachonar

stud bolt s espárrago

stud'book' s registro genealógico de caballos

student ['stjudənt] o ['studənt] adj estudiantil ‖ s estudiante mf; (person who investigates), estudioso

student body s estudiantado, alumnado

stud'horse' s caballo padre, caballo semental

studied ['stʌdɪd] adj premeditado, hecho adrede; (affected) estudiado

studi·o ['studɪ,o] s (pl -**os**) estudio, taller m; (mov & rad) estudio

studious ['stjudɪ·əs] o ['studɪ·əs] adj estudioso; asiduo, solícito

stud·y ['stʌdi] s (pl -**ies**) estudio; solicitud; meditación profunda; (e.g., of a professor) gabinete m, estudio ‖ v (pret & pp -**ied**) tr & intr estudiar

stuff [stʌf] s materia; género, paño, tela; muebles mpl, baratijas; medicina; fruslerías; cosa, cosas ‖ tr rellenar; henchir, llenar; atascar, cerrar, tapar; embutir; (with food) atracar; meter sin orden, llenar sin orden; disecar (un animal muerto) ‖ intr atracarse, hartarse

stuffed shirt s (slang) tragavirotes m

stuffing ['stʌfɪŋ] s relleno

stuff·y ['stʌfi] adj (comp -**ier;** super -**iest**) sofocante, mal ventilado; aburrido, sin interés; (prim) (coll) relamido

stumble ['stʌmbəl] intr tropezar, dar un traspié; moverse a tropezones; hablar a tropezones; **to stumble on** o **upon** tropezar con

stumbling block s escollo, tropezadero

stump [stʌmp] s (of a tree, arm, etc.) tocón m; (of an arm) muñón m; (of a tooth) raigón m; (of a cigar) colilla; (of a tail)

rabo; paso pesado; fragmento, resto; tri-buna pública; (for shading drawings) esfu-mino ‖ tr recorrer (el país) pronunciando discursos políticos; (coll) confundir, dejar sin habla; esfumar

stump speaker s orador callejero

stump speech s arenga electoral

stun [stʌn] v (pret & pp **stunned;** ger **stunning**) tr atolondrar, aturdir

stunning ['stʌnɪŋ] adj (coll) pasmoso, estupendo, pistonudo, elegante

stunt [stʌnt] s atrofia; (underdeveloped creature) engendro; (coll) suerte acrobática; (coll) faena, hazaña, proeza ‖ tr atrofiar ‖ intr (coll) hacer suertes acrobáticas

stunt flying s vuelo acrobático

stunt man s (mov) doble m que hace suertes peligrosas

stupe·fy ['stjupɪ,faɪ] v (pret & pp -**fied**) tr dejar estupefacto, pasmar; causar estupor a

stupendous [stu'pɛndəs] adj estupendo; enorme

stupid ['stupɪd] adj estúpido; (coll) sonso, pavo, gilí

stupor ['stjupər] o ['stupər] s estupor m, modorra

stur·dy ['stʌrdi] adj (comp -**dier;** super -**diest**) fuerte, robusto, fornido; firme, tenaz

sturgeon ['stʌrdʒən] s esturión m

stutter ['stʌtər] s tartamudeo ‖ tr decir tartamudeando ‖ intr tartamudear

sty [staɪ] s (pl **sties**) pocilga, zahurda; (pathol) orzuelo

style [staɪl] s estilo; moda; elegancia; **to live in great style** vivir en gran lujo ‖ tr intitular, nombrar

stylish ['staɪlɪʃ] adj de moda, elegante

styptic pencil ['stɪptɪk] s lápiz estíptico

Styx [stɪks] s Estigia

suave [swɑv] o [swev] adj suave; afable, fino, zalamero, pulido

sub. abbr **subscription, substitute, suburban**

subaltern [səb'ɔltərn] adj & s subalterno

subconscious [səb'kɑnʃəs] adj subconsciente ‖ s subconsciencia

subconsciousness [səb'kɑnʃəsnɪs] s subconsciencia

subdeb ['sʌb,dɛb] s tobillera

subdivide ['sʌbdɪ,vaɪd] o [,sʌbdɪ'vaɪd] tr subdividir ‖ intr subdividirse

subdue [səb'dju] tr sojuzgar, subyugar; amansar, dominar; suavizar

subdued [səb'djud] adj sojuzgado; sumiso; (e.g., light) suave

subheading ['sʌb,hɛdɪŋ] s subtítulo

subject ['sʌbdʒɪkt] adj sujeto; súbdito ‖ s asunto, materia, tema m; (person in his relationship to a ruler or government) súbdito; (gram, med, philos) sujeto ‖ [səb'dʒɛkt] tr sujetar, someter, sojuzgar

subject index s índice m de materias

subjection [səb'dʒɛkʃən] s sumisión, sometimiento

subjective [səb'dʒɛktɪv] adj subjetivo

subject matter s asunto, materia

subjugate ['sʌbdʒə,get] tr subyugar

st
su

subjunctive [səb'dʒʌŋktɪv] *adj & s* subjuntivo

sub•let [sʌb'lɛt] o ['sʌb,lɛt] *v* (*pret & pp* **-let;** *ger* **-letting**) *tr* realquilar, subarrendar

submachine gun [,sʌbmə'ʃin] *s* subfusil *m* ametrallador

submarine ['sʌbmə,rin] *adj & s* submarino ‖ *tr* (coll) atacar o hundir con un submarino

submarine chaser ['tʃesər] *s* cazasubmarinos *m*

submerge [səb'mʌrdʒ] *tr* sumergir ‖ *intr* sumergirse

submersion [səb'mʌrʒən] o [səb'mʌrʃən] *s* sumersión

submission [səb'mɪʃən] *s* sumisión

submissive [səb'mɪsɪv] *adj* sumiso

sub•mit [səb'mɪt] *v* (*pret & pp* **-mitted;** *ger* **-mitting**) *tr* someter; proponer, permitirse decir ‖ *intr* someterse

subordinate [səb'ɔrdɪnɪt] *adj & s* subordinado ‖ [səb'ɔrdɪ,net] *tr* subordinar

subornation of perjury [,sʌbər'neʃən] *s* (law) soborno de testigo

subplot ['sʌb,plɑt] *s* trama secundaria

subpoena o **subpena** [sʌb'pinə] o [sə'pinə] *s* comparendo ‖ *tr* mandar comparecer

sub rosa [sʌb'rozə] *adv* en secreto, en confianza

subscribe [səb'skraɪb] *tr* subscribir ‖ *intr* subscribir; subscribirse, abonarse; **to subscribe to** subscribirse a, abonarse a (*una publicación periódica*); subscribir (*una opinión*)

subscriber [səb'skraɪbər] *s* abonado

subsequent ['sʌbsɪkwənt] *adj* subsiguiente, posterior

subservient [səb'sʌrvɪ•ənt] *adj* servil; subordinado; útil

subside [səb'saɪd] *intr* calmarse; acabarse, cesar; bajar (*el nivel del agua*); amainar (*el viento*)

subsidiary [səb'sɪdɪ,ɛri] *adj & s* subsidiario

subsidize ['sʌbsɪ,daɪz] *tr* subsidiar, subvencionar; (*to bribe*) sobornar

subsi•dy ['sʌbsɪdi] *s* (*pl* **-dies**) subsidio, subvención

subsist [səb'sɪst] *intr* subsistir

subsistence [səb'sɪstəns] *s* subsistencia

subsonic [səb'sɑnɪk] *adj* subsónico

substance ['sʌbstəns] *s* substancia

substandard [sʌb'stændərd] *adj* inferior al nivel normal

substantial [səb'stænʃəl] *adj* considerable, importante; fuerte, sólido; acomodado, rico; esencial; (*food*) substancial

substantiate [səb'stænʃɪ,et] *tr* comprobar, establecer, verificar

substantive ['sʌbstəntɪv] *adj & s* substantivo

substation ['sʌb,steʃən] *s* (elec) subcentral *f*

substitute ['sʌbstɪ,tjut] o ['sʌbstɪ,tut] *adj* substitutivo ‖ *s* (*person*) substituto; (*thing, substance*) substitutivo; (mil) reemplazo ‖ *tr* poner (*a una persona o cosa*) en lugar de otra ‖ *intr* actuar de substituto; **to substitute for** substituir (with personal *a*)

substitution [,sʌbstɪ'tjuʃən] *s* empleo o uso (*de una persona o cosa en lugar de otra*);

(chem, law, math) substitución; imitación fraudulenta

subterranean [,sʌbtə'renɪ•ən] *adj & s* subterráneo

subtitle ['sʌb,taɪtəl] *s* substítulo ‖ *tr* subtitular

subtle ['sʌtəl] *adj* sutil; astuto; insidioso

subtle•ty ['sʌtəlti] *s* (*pl* **-ties**) sutileza; agudeza; distinción sutil

subtract [səb'trækt] *tr* substraer; (math) substraer, restar

suburb ['sʌbʌrb] *s* suburbio, arrabal *m;* **the suburbs** las afueras, los barrios externos

subvention [səb'vɛnʃən] *s* subvención ‖ *tr* subvencionar

subversive [səb'vʌrsɪv] *adj* subversivo ‖ *s* subversor *m*

subvert [səb'vʌrt] *tr* subvertir

subway ['sʌb,we] *s* galería subterránea; metro, ferrocarril subterráneo

succeed [sək'sid] *tr* suceder (*a una persona o cosa*) ‖ *intr* tener buen éxito

success [sək'sɛs] *s* buen éxito

successful [sək'sɛsfəl] *adj* feliz, próspero; acertado; logrado

succession [sək'sɛʃən] *s* sucesión; **in succession** seguidos, uno tras otro

successive [sək'sɛsɪv] *adj* sucesivo

succor ['sʌkər] *s* socorro ‖ *tr* socorrer

succotash ['sʌkə,tæʃ] *s* guiso de maíz tierno y habas

succumb [sə'kʌm] *intr* sucumbir

such [sʌtʃ] *adj & pron indef* tal, semejante; **such a** tal, semejante; **such a +** *adj* un tan **+** *adj;* **such as** quienes, los que

suck [sʌk] *s* chupada; mamada ‖ *tr* chupar; mamar; aspirar (*el aire*)

sucker ['sʌkər] *s* chupador *m;* mamón *m;* (bot & mach) chupón *m;* (coll) bobo, primo

suckle ['sʌkəl] *tr* lactar; criar, educar

suckling pig ['sʌklɪŋ] *s* lechón *m*, cerdo de leche

suction ['sʌkʃən] *adj* aspirante ‖ *s* succión

sudden ['sʌdən] *adj* súbito, repentino; **all of a sudden** de repente

suds [sʌdz] *spl* jabonadura; (coll) espuma, cerveza

sue [su] *tr* demandar; pedir; (law) procesar ‖ *intr* (law) poner pleito, entablar juicio; **to sue for damages** demandar por daños y perjuicios; **to sue for peace** pedir la paz

suede [swed] *s* gamuza, ante *m*

suet ['su•ɪt] o ['sju•ɪt] *s* sebo

suffer ['sʌfər] *tr & intr* sufrir, padecer

sufferance ['sʌfərəns] *s* tolerancia; paciencia; **on sufferance** por tolerancia

suffering ['sʌfərɪŋ] *adj* doliente ‖ *s* dolencia, sufrimiento

suffice [sə'faɪs] *intr* bastar, ser suficiente

sufficient [sə'fɪʃənt] *adj* suficiente

suffix ['sʌfɪks] *s* sufijo

suffocate ['sʌfə,ket] *tr* sofocar ‖ *intr* sofocarse

suffrage ['sʌfrɪdʒ] *s* sufragio; aprobación, voto favorable

suffragette [,sʌfrə'dʒɛt] *s* sufragista (*mujer*)

suffuse [sə`fjuz] *tr* saturar, bañar
sugar [`ʃugər] *adj* azucarero ‖ *s* azúcar *m* ‖ *tr* azucarar
sugar beet *s* remolacha azucarera
sugar bowl *s* azucarero
sugar cane *s* caña de azúcar
sug'ar-coat' *tr* azucarar; (fig) endulzar, dorar
suggest [səg`dʒɛst] *tr* sugerir
suggestion [səg`dʒɛstʃən] *s* sugestión, sugerencia; sombra, traza ligera
suggestive [səg`dʒɛstɪv] *adj* sugestivo; sicalíptico
suicidal [‚suˑɪ`saɪdəl] o [‚sjuˑɪ`saɪdəl] *adj* suicida
suicide [`suˑɪ‚saɪd] *s* (*act*) suicidio; (*person*) suicida *mf;* **to commit suicide** suicidarse
suit [sut] o [sjut] *s* traje *m*, terno; (*of a lady*) traje *m* sastre; (*group forming a set*) juego; (*of cards*) palo; petición, súplica; cortejo, galanteo; (law) pleito, proceso; **to follow suit** servir del palo; seguir la corriente ‖ *tr* adaptar, ajustar; adaptarse a; sentar, ir o venir bien a; favorecer, satisfacer; **to suit oneself** hacer (*uno*) lo que le guste ‖ *intr* convenir, ser a propósito
suitable [`sutəbəl] *adj* apropiado, conveniente, adecuado
suit'case' *s* maleta, valija
suite [swit] *s* comitiva, séquito; (*group forming a set*) juego; serie *f;* (*of rooms*) crujía; habitación salón; (mus) suite *f*
suiting [`sutɪŋ] *s* corte *m* de traje
suit of clothes *s* traje completo (*de hombre*)
suitor [`sutər] o [`sjutər] *s* pretendiente *m;* (law) demandante *mf*
sulfa drugs [`sʌlfə] *spl* medicamentos sulfas
sulfate [`sʌlfet] *s* sulfato
sulfide [`sʌlfaɪd] *s* sulfuro
sulfite [`sʌlfaɪt] *s* sulfito
sulfur [`sʌlfər] *s* (chem) azufre *m;* véase **sulphur**
sulfuric [sʌl`fjurɪk] *adj* sulfúrico
sulfur mine *s* azufrera
sulfurous [`sʌlfərəs] *adj* sulfuroso ‖ *adj* (chem) sulfuroso
sulk [sʌlk] *s* murria ‖ *intr* amorrarse, enfurruñarse
sulk•y [`sʌlki] *adj* (*comp* **-ier;** *super* **-iest**) enfurruñado, murrio, resentido
sullen [`sʌlən] *adj* hosco, malhumorado, taciturno, triste
sul•ly [`sʌli] *v* (*pret* & *pp* **-lied**) *tr* empañar, manchar
sulphur [`sʌlfər] *adj* azufrado ‖ *s* azufre *m;* color de azufre ‖ *tr* azufrar
sultan [`sʌltən] *s* sultán *m*
sul•try [`sʌltri] *adj* (*comp* **-trier;** *super* **-triest**) bochornoso, sofocante
sum [sʌm] *s* suma; (coll) problema *m* de aritmética ‖ *v* (*pret* & *pp* **summed;** *ger* **summing**) *tr* sumar; **to sum up** sumar, resumir
sumac o **sumach** [`ʃumæk] o [sumæk] *s* zumaque *m*
summarize [`sʌmə‚raɪz] *tr* resumir
summa•ry [`sʌməri] *adj* sumario ‖ *s* (*pl* **-ries**) sumario, resumen *m*

summer [`sʌmər] *adj* estival, veraniego ‖ *s* verano, estío ‖ *intr* veranear
summer resort *s* lugar *m* de veraneo
summersault [`sʌmər‚sɔlt] *s* salto mortal ‖ *intr* dar un salto mortal
summer school *s* escuela de verano
summery [`sʌməri] *adj* estival, veraniego
summit [`sʌmɪt] *s* cima, cumbre *f*
summit conference o **summit meeting** *s* conferencia en la cumbre
summon [`sʌmən] *tr* convocar, llamar; evocar; (law) citar, emplazar
summons [`sʌmənz] *s* orden *f*, señal *f;* (law) citación, emplazamiento ‖ *tr* (coll) citar, emplazar
sumptuous [`sʌmptʃuˑəs] *adj* suntuoso
sun [sʌn] *s* sol *m;* **to have a place in the sun** ocupar su puesto en el mundo ‖ *v* (*pret* & *pp* **sunned;** *ger* **sunning**) *tr* asolear ‖ *intr* asolearse
sun bath *s* baño de sol
sun'beam' *s* rayo de sol
sun'bon'net *s* papalina
sun'burn' *s* quemadura de sol ‖ *v* (*pret* & *pp* **-burned** o **burnt**) *tr* quemar al sol ‖ *intr* quemarse al sol
sundae [`sʌndi] *s* helado con frutas, jarabes o nueces
Sunday [`sʌndi] *adj* dominical; (*used or worn on Sunday*) dominguero ‖ *s* domingo
Sunday best *s* (coll) trapos de cristianar, ropa dominguera
Sunday's child *s* niño nacido de pies, niño mimado de la fortuna
Sunday school *s* escuela dominical, doctrina dominical
Sunday supplement *s* (*newspaper*) suplemento dominical
sunder [`sʌndər] *tr* separar; romper
sun'di'al *s* reloj *m* de sol, cuadrante *m* solar
sun'down' *s* puesta del sol
sundries [`sʌndriz] *spl* artículos diversos
sundry [`sʌndri] *adj* diversos, varios
sun'flow'er *s* girasol *m*, tornasol *m*
sun'glass'es *spl* gafas de sol, gafas para el sol
sunken [`sʌŋkən] *adj* hundido, sumido
sun lamp *s* lámpara de rayos ultravioletas
sun'light' *s* luz *f* del sol
sun'lit' *adj* iluminado por el sol
sun•ny [`sʌni] *adj* (*comp* **-nier;** *super* **-iest**) de sol; asoleado; brillante, resplandeciente; alegre, risueño; **to be sunny** hacer sol
sunny side *s* sol *m;* (fig) lado bueno, lado favorable
sun porch *s* solana
sun'rise' *s* salida del sol; **from sunrise to sunset** de sol a sol
sun'set' *s* puesta del sol
sun'shade' *s* quitasol *m*, sombrilla; toldo; visera contra el sol
sun'shine' *s* claridad del sol; alegría; **in the sunshine** al sol
sun'spot' *s* mancha solar
sun'stroke' *s* insolación
sun'tan' *s* bronceado
suntan lotion *s* bronceador *m*

su
su

sup. *abbr* **superior, supplement**

sup [sʌp] *v* (*pret* & *pp* **supped**; *ger* **supping**) *intr* cenar

superannuated [ˌsupərˈænjuˌetɪd] *adj* jubilado, inhabilitado por ancianidad o enfermedad; fuera de moda

superb [səˈpʌrb] *adj* soberbio, estupendo, magnífico

supercar·go [ˈsupərˌkɑrgo] *s* (*pl* -**goes** o -**gos**) (naut) sobrecargo

supercharge [ˌsupərˈtʃɑrdʒ] *tr* sobrealimentar

supercilious [ˌsupərˈsɪliˑəs] *adj* arrogante, altanero, desdeñoso

superficial [ˌsupərˈfɪʃəl] *adj* superficial

superfluous [suˈpʌrfluˑəs] *adj* superfluo

superhuman [ˌsupərˈhjumən] *adj* sobrehumano

superimpose [ˌsupərɪmˈpoz] *tr* sobreponer

superintendent [ˌsupərɪnˈtɛndənt] *s* superintendente *mf*

superior [səˈpɪriˑər] *adj* superior; indiferente, sereno; arrogante; (typ) volado ‖ *s* superior *m*

superiority [səˌpɪriˈɑriti] *s* superioridad; indiferencia, serenidad; arrogancia

superlative [səˈpʌrlətɪv] *adj* & *s* superlativo

super·man [ˈsupərˌmæn] *s* (*pl* -**men** [ˌmɛn]) sobrehombre *m*, superhombre *m*

supermarket [ˈsupərˌmɑrkɪt] *s* supermercado

supernatural [ˌsupərˈnætʃərəl] *adj* sobrenatural

superpose [ˌsupərˈpoz] *tr* sobreponer, superponer

supersede [ˌsupərˈsid] *tr* reemplazar; desalojar

supersonic [ˌsupərˈsɑnɪk] *adj* supersónico ‖ **supersonics** *ssg* supersónica

superstitious [ˌsupərˈstɪʃəs] *adj* supersticioso

supertanker [ˈsupərˌtæŋkər] *s* superpetrolero, supertanquero

supervene [ˌsupərˈvin] *intr* sobrevenir

supervise [ˈsupərˌvaɪz] *tr* superintender, supervisar, dirigir

supervisor [ˈsupərˌvaɪzər] *s* superintendente *mf*, supervisor *m*, dirigente *mf*

supp. *abbr* **supplement**

supper [ˈsʌpər] *s* cena

supplant [səˈplænt] *tr* reemplazar

supple [ˈsʌpəl] *adj* flexible; dócil

supplement [ˈsʌplɪmənt] *s* suplemento ‖ [ˈsʌpliˌmɛnt] *tr* suplir, completar

suppliant [ˈsʌpliˑənt] *adj* & *s* suplicante *mf*

supplication [ˌsʌpliˈkeʃən] *s* súplica

sup·ply [səˈplaɪ] *s* (*pl* -**plies**) suministro, provisión; surtido, repuesto; oferta, existencia; **supplies** pertrechos, provisiones, víveres *mf*; artículos, efectos ‖ *v* (*pret* & *pp* -**plied**) *tr* suministrar, aprovisionar; reemplazar

supply and demand *spl* oferta y demanda

support [səˈport] *s* apoyo, soporte *m*, sostén *m*; sustento ‖ *tr* apoyar, soportar, sostener; sustentar; aguantar

supporter [səˈportər] *s* partidario; (*jockstrap*) suspensorio; faja abdominal, faja medical

suppose [səˈpoz] *tr* suponer; creer; **to be supposed to** deber; **to suppose so** creer que sí

supposed [səˈpozd] *adj* supuesto

supposition [ˌsʌpəˈzɪʃən] *s* suposición

supposito·ry [səˈpɑziˌtori] *s* (*pl* -**ries**) supositorio

suppress [səˈprɛs] *tr* suprimir

suppression [səˈprɛʃən] *s* supresión

suppurate [ˈsʌpjəˌret] *intr* supurar

supreme [səˈprim] o [suˈprim] *adj* supremo

supt. *abbr* **superintendent**

surcharge [ˈsʌrˌtʃɑrdʒ] *s* sobrecarga ‖ [ˌsʌrˈtʃɑrdʒ] o [ˈsʌrˌtʃɑrdʒ] *tr* sobrecargar

sure [ʃur] *adj* seguro; **to be sure** seguramente, sin duda ‖ *adv* (coll) seguramente, claro; **sure enough** efectivamente

sure things *adv* (slang) seguramente ‖ *interj* ¡claro!, ¡seguro! ‖ *s* (slang) sacabocados *m*

sure·ty [ˈʃurti] o [ˈʃuriti] *s* (*pl* -**ties**) seguridad, garantía, fianza

surf [sʌrf] *s* cachones *mpl*, olas que rompen en la playa

surface [ˈsʌrfɪs] *adj* superficial ‖ *s* superficie *f* ‖ *tr* alisar, allanar; recubrir ‖ *intr* emerger (*p.ej.*, *un submarino*)

surface mail *s* correo por vía ordinaria

surf·board *s* patín *m* de mar

surfeit [ˈsʌrfɪt] *s* exceso; hartura, hastío; empacho, indigestión ‖ *tr* atracar, hastiar; encebadar (*las bestias*) ‖ *intr* atracarse, hastiarse; encebadarse

surf·rid·ing *s* patinaje *m* sobre las olas

surge [sʌrdʒ] *s* oleada; (elec) sobretensión ‖ *intr* agitarse, ondular

surgeon [ˈsʌrdʒən] *s* cirujano

surger·y [ˈsʌrdʒəri] *s* (*pl* -**ies**) cirugía; sala de operaciones

surgical [ˈsʌrdʒɪkəl] *adj* quirúrgico

sur·ly [ˈsʌrli] *adj* (*comp* -**lier**; *super* -**liest**) áspero, rudo, hosco, insolente

surmise [sərˈmaɪz] o [ˈsʌrmaɪz] *s* conjetura, suposición ‖ [sərˈmaɪz] *tr* & *intr* conjeturar, suponer

surmount [sərˈmaunt] *tr* levantarse sobre; aventajar, sobrepujar; superar; coronar

surname [ˈsʌrˌnem] *s* apellido: (*added name*) sobrenombre *m* ‖ *tr* apellidar; sobrenombrar

surpass [sərˈpæs] o [sərˈpɑs] *tr* aventajar, sobrepasar

surplice [ˈsʌrplɪs] *s* sobrepelliz *f*

surplus [ˈsʌrplʌs] *adj* sobrante, excedente ‖ *s* sobrante *m*, exceso; (com) superávit *m*

surprise [sərˈpraɪz] *adj* inesperado, improviso ‖ *s* sorpresa; **to take by surprise** coger por sorpresa ‖ *tr* sorprender

surprise package *s* sorpresa

surprise party *s* reunión improvisada para felicitar por sorpresa a una persona

surprising [sərˈpraɪzɪŋ] *adj* sorprendente, sorpresivo

surrender [səˈrɛndər] *s* rendición ‖ *tr* rendir ‖ *intr* rendirse

surrender value *s* (ins) valor *m* de rescate

surreptitious [ˌsʌrɛpˈtɪʃəs] *adj* subrepticio

surround [sə'raʊnd] *tr* cercar, rodear, circundar; (mil) sitiar

surrounding [sə'raʊndɪŋ] *adj* circundante, circunstante ‖ **surroundings** *spl* alrededores *mpl*, contornos; ambiente *m*, medio

surtax ['sʌr,tæks] *s* impuesto complementario

surveillance [sər'veləns] o [sər'veljəns] *s* vigilancia

survey ['sʌrve] *s* estudio, examen *m*, inspección, reconocimiento; agrimensura, medición, plano; levantamiento de planos; *(of opinion)* encuesta; *(of literature)* bosquejo ‖ [sʌr've] o ['sʌrve] *tr* estudiar, examinar, inspeccionar, reconocer; medir; levantar el plano de ‖ *intr* levantar el plano

surveyor [sər've•ər] *s* inspector *m;* agrimensor *m*

survival [sər'vaɪvəl] *s* supervivencia

survive [sər'vaɪv] *tr* sobrevivir a *(otra persona; algún acontecimiento)* ‖ *intr* sobrevivir

surviving [sər'vaɪvɪŋ] *adj* sobreviviente

survivor [sər'vaɪvər] *s* sobreviviente *mf*

survivorship [sər'vaɪvər,ʃɪp] *s* (law) sobrevivencia

susceptible [sə'sɛptɪbəl] *adj* susceptible; *(to love)* enamoradizo

suspect ['sʌspɛkt] o [səs'pɛkt] *adj & s* sospechoso ‖ [səs'pɛkt] *tr* sospechar

suspend [səs'pɛnd] *tr* suspender ‖ *intr* dejar de obrar; suspender pagos

suspenders [səs'pɛndərz] *spl* tirantes *mpl*

suspense [səs'pɛns] *s* suspenso, suspensión; duda, incertidumbre, indecisión, irresolución; ansiedad

suspension bridge [səs'pɛnʃən] *s* puente *m* colgante

suspicion [səs'pɪʃən] *s* sospecha, suspicacia; sombra, traza ligera

suspicious [səs'pɪʃəs] *adj* *(inclined to suspect)* suspicaz; *(subject to suspicion)* sospechoso

sustain [səs'ten] *tr* sostener, sustentar; apoyar, defender; confirmar, probar; sufrir *(p.ej., un daño, una pérdida)*

sustenance ['sʌstɪnəns] *s* sustento, alimentos; sostenimiento

sutler ['sʌtlər] *s* (mil) vivandero

swab [swɑb] *s* escobón *m*, estropajo; (naut) lampazo; (surg) tapón *m* de algodón ‖ *v* *(pret & pp* **swabbed;** *ger* **swabbing)** *tr* fregar, limpiar; (naut) lampacear; (surg) limpiar con algodón

swaddle ['swɑdəl] *tr* empañar, fajar

swaddling clothes *spl* pañales *mpl*

swagger ['swægər] *adj* (coll) muy elegante ‖ *s* fanfarronada; contoneo, paso jactancioso ‖ *intr* fanfarronear; contonear

swain [swen] *s* *(lad)* zagal; galán *m*, amante *m*

swallow ['swɑlo] *s* trago; (orn) golondrina ‖ *tr* tragar, deglutir; (fig) tragar, tragarse ‖ *intr* tragar, deglutir

swallow-tailed coat ['swɑlo,teld] *s* frac *m*

swal'low•wort' *s* vencetósigo

swamp [swɑmp] *s* pantano, marisma ‖ *tr* encharcar, inundar; *(e.g., with work)* abrumar

swamp•y ['swɑmpi] *adj* *(comp* **-ier;** *super* **-iest)** pantanoso

swan [swɑn] *s* cisne *m*

swan dive *s* salto de ángel

swank [swæŋk] *adj* (slang) elegante, vistoso ‖ *s* (slang) elegancia vistosa

swan knight *s* caballero del cisne

swan's-down ['swɑnz,daʊn] *s* plumón *m* de cisne; moletón *m*, paño de vicuña

swan song *s* canto del cisne

swap [swɑp] *s* (coll) truque *m*, cambalache *m* ‖ *v* *(pret & pp* **swapped;** *ger* **swapping)** *tr & intr* trocar, cambalachear

swarm [swɔrm] *s* enjambre *m* ‖ *intr* enjambrar; volar en enjambres; hormiguear *(una multitud de gente o animales)*

swarth•y ['swɔrði] o ['swɔrθi] *adj* *(comp* **-ier;** *super* **-iest)** atezado, carinegro, moreno

swashbuckler ['swɑʃ,bʌklər] *s* espada chín *m*, matasiete *m*, valentón *m*

swat [swɑt] *s* (coll) golpe violento ‖ *v* *(pret & pp* **swatted;** *ger* **swatting)** *tr* (coll) golpear con fuerza; (coll) aporrear, aplastar *(una mosca)*

sway [swe] *s* oscilación, vaivén *m;* dominio, imperio ‖ *tr* hacer oscilar; conmover; disuadir; gobernar, dominar ‖ *intr* oscilar; desviarse; tambalear, flaquear

swear [swɛr] *v* *(pret* **swore** [swor]; *pp* **sworn** [sworn]) *tr* jurar; juramentar; prestar *(juramento)*; **to swear in** tomar juramento a; **to swear off** jurar renunciar a; **to swear out** obtener mediante juramento ‖ *intr* jurar; **to swear at** maldecir; **to swear by** jurar por; poner toda su confianza en; **to swear to** prestar juramento a; declarar bajo juramento; jurar + *inf*

sweat [swɛt] *s* sudor *m* ‖ *v* *(pret & pp* **sweat** o **sweated)** *tr* sudar *(agua por los poros; la ropa)*; (slang) hacer sudar; **to sweat it out** (slang) aguantarlo hasta el fin ‖ *intr* sudar

sweater ['swɛtər] *s* suéter *m*

sweat shirt *s* pulóver *m* de mangas largas

sweat'shop' *s* taller *m* de trabajo afanoso y de poco sueldo

sweat•y ['swɛti] *adj* *(comp* **-ier;** *super* **-iest)** sudoroso

Swede [swid] *s* sueco

Sweden ['swidən] *s* Suecia

Swedish ['swidɪʃ] *adj & s* sueco

sweep [swip] *s* barrido; alcance *m*, extensión; *(of wind)* soplo; *(of a well)* cigoñal *m* ‖ *v* *(pret & pp* **swept** [swɛpt]) *tr* barrer; arrastrar; rozar, tocar; recorrer con la mirada, los dedos, etc. ‖ *intr* barrer; pasar rápidamente; extenderse; precipitarse; andar con paso majestuoso

sweeper ['swipər] *s* *(person)* barrendero; *(machine for sweeping streets)* barredera; barredera de alfombra; (nav) dragaminas *m*

sweeping ['swipɪŋ] *adj* arrebatador; comprensivo, extenso, vasto ‖ **sweepings** *spl* barreduras

SU
SW

sweep'sec'ond *s* segundero central

sweep'stakes' *ssg* o *spl* lotería en la cual una persona gana todas las apuestas; carrera que decide todas las apuestas; premio en las carreras de caballos

sweet [swit] *adj* dulce; oloroso; melodioso; grato al oído; fresco; bonito, lindo; amable; querido; **to be sweet on** (coll) estar enamorado de ‖ *adv* dulcemente; **to smell sweet** tener buen olor ‖ **sweets** *spl* dulces *mpl*, golosinas

sweet'bread' *s* lechecillas, mollejas

sweet'bri'er *s* eglantina

sweeten ['switən] *tr* azucarar, endulzar; suavizar; purificar ‖ *intr* azucararse, endulzarse; suavizarse

sweetener ['switənər] *s* eculcorante

sweet'heart' *s* enamorado o enamorada; amiga querida; galán *m*, cortejo

sweetish ['switɪʃ] *adj* dulzoso

sweet marjoram *s* mejorana

sweet'meats' *spl* dulces *mpl*, confites *mpl*, confitura

sweet pea *s* guisante *m* de olor

sweet potato *s* batata, camote *m*

sweet-scented ['swit,sɛntɪd] *adj* oloroso, perfumado

sweet tooth *s* gusto por los dulces

sweet-toothed ['swit,tuθt] *adj* dulcero, goloso

sweet william *s* clavel *m* de ramillete, minutisa

swell [swɛl] *adj* (coll) muy elegante; (slang) de órdago, magnífico ‖ *s* hinchazón *f*; bulto; marejada; oleaje *m*; *(of a crowd of people)* oleada; (coll) petimetre *m*, pisaverde *m* ‖ *v* (*pret* **swelled**; *pp* **swelled** o **swollen** ['swolən]) *tr* hinchar, inflar; abultar, aumentar; elevar, levantar; (fig) hinchar, engreír ‖ *intr* hincharse; abultarse, aumentar, crecer; elevarse, levantarse; embravecerse (*el mar*); (fig) hincharse, engreírse

swelled head *s* entono; **to have a swelled head** estar muy pagado de sí mismo, creerse gran cosa

swelter ['swɛltər] *intr* sofocarse de sudor

swept'back' wing *s* (aer) ala en flecha

swerve [swʌrv] *s* viraje *m*, desvío brusco ‖ *tr* desviar ‖ *intr* desviarse, torcer

swift [swɪft] *adj* rápido, veloz; pronto; repentino; correlón (SAm) ‖ *adv* rápidamente, velozmente ‖ *s* vencejo

swig [swɪg] *s* chisguete, tragantada ‖ *v* (*pret* & *pp* **swigged**; *ger* **swigging**) *tr* & *intr* beber a grandes tragos

swill [swɪl] *s* bazofia, inmundicia; tragantada ‖ *tr* beber a grandes tragos; emborrachar ‖ *intr* beber a grandes tragos; emborracharse

swim [swɪm] *s* natación; **the swim** (*in affairs, society, etc.*) (coll) la corriente ‖ *v* (*pret* **swam** [swæm]; *pp* **swum** [swʌm]; *ger* **swimming**) *tr* pasar a nado ‖ *intr* nadar; deslizarse, escurrirse; padecer vahídos; dar vueltas (*la cabeza*); **to swim across** atravesar a nado

swimmer ['swɪmər] *s* nadador *m*

swimming pool *s* piscina

swimming suit *s* traje *m* de baño

swindle ['swɪndəl] *s* estafa, timo; leva (CAm, Col); embelequería (Col, Mex, P-R) ‖ *tr* & *intr* estafar, timar

swindler ['swɪndlər] *s* estafador *m*, estafadora; lana *m* (CAm)

swine [swaɪn] *s* cerdo, puerco; *spl* ganado porcino

swing [swɪŋ] *s* balance *m*, oscilación, vaivén *m*; *(device used for recreation)* columpio; hamaca; turno, período; fuerza, ímpetu *m*; *(trip)* jira; *(box)* golpe *m* de lado; (mus) ritmo constantemente repetido; **in full swing** en plena marcha ‖ *v* (*pret* & *pp* **swung** [swʌŋ]) *tr* blandir (*p.ej., un arma*); menear (*los brazos*); hacer oscilar; columpiar; manejar con éxito ‖ *intr* oscilar; balancearse; columpiar; estar colgado; dar una vuelta; **to swing open** abrirse de pronto (*una puerta*)

swinging door ['swɪŋɪŋ] *s* batiente *m* oscilante, puerta de vaivén

swinish ['swaɪnɪʃ] *adj* porcuno; (fig) cochino, puerco

swipe [swaɪp] *s* (coll) golpe *m* fuerte ‖ *tr* (coll) dar un golpe fuerte a; (slang) hurtar, robar

swirl [swʌrl] *s* remolino, torbellino ‖ *tr* hacer girar ‖ *intr* arremolinarse, remolinar; girar

swish [swɪʃ] *s* (*e.g., of a whip*) chasquido; *(of a dress)* crujido ‖ *tr* chasquear (*el látigo*) ‖ *intr* chasquear; crujir (*un vestido*)

Swiss [swɪs] *adj* & *s* suizo

Swiss chard [tʃɑrd] *s* acelga

Swiss cheese *s* Gruyère *m*, queso suizo

Swiss Guards *spl* guardia suiza

switch [swɪtʃ] *s* bastoncillo, latiguillo; latigazo; coletazo; *(false hair)* trenza postiza, moño postizo; (elec) llave *f*, interruptor *m*, conmutador *m*; (rr) agujas ‖ *tr* azotar, fustigar; (elec) conmutar; (rr) desviar; **to switch off** (elec) cortar, desconectar; **to switch on** (elec) cerrar (*el circuito*); (elec) encender, poner (*la luz, etc.*) ‖ *intr* cambiarse, moverse; desviarse

switch'back' *s* vía en zigzag

switch'board' *s* cuadro de distribución

switching engine *s* locomotora de maniobras

switch•man ['swɪtʃmən] *s* (*pl* -**men** [mən]) agujetero, guardagujas *m*

switch'yard' *s* patio de maniobras

Switzerland ['swɪtsərlənd] *s* Suiza

swiv•el ['swɪvəl] *s* eslabón giratorio ‖ *v* (*pret* & *pp* -**eled** o -**elled**; *ger* -**eling** o -**elling**) *intr* girar sobre un eje

swivel chair *s* silla giratoria

swoon [swun] *s* desmayo ‖ *intr* desmayarse

swoop [swup] *s* descenso súbito; *(of a bird of prey)* calada ‖ *intr* bajar rápidamente, precipitarse; abatirse (*p.ej., el ave de rapiña*)

sword [sord] *s* espada; **at swords' points** enemistado a sangre y fuego; **to put to the sword** pasar al filo de la espada, pasar a cuchillo

sword belt *s* cinturón *m*

sword'fish' *s* pez *m* espada

sword handler *s* (taur) mozo de estoques
sword rattling *s* fanfarronería
swords•man ['sordzmən] *s* (*pl* -**men** [mən]) espada *m;* esgrimidor *m*
sword swallower ['swɑlo•ər] *s* tragasable *m*
sword thrust *s* estocada, golpe *m* de espada
sworn [sworn] *adj* (*enemy*) jurado
sycophant ['sɪkəfənt] *s* adulador *m;* parásito
syll. *abbr* **syllable**
syllable ['sɪləbəl] *s* sílaba
syllogism ['sɪlə,dʒɪzəm] *s* silogismo
sylph [sɪlf] *s* sílfide *f*
sym. *abbr* **symbol, symmetrical, symphony, symptom**
symbiosis [,sɪmbaɪ'osɪs] o [,sɪmbi'osɪs] *s* simbiosis
symbiotic [,sɪmbaɪ'ɑtɪk] o [,sɪmbi'ɑtɪk] *adj* simbiótico
symbol ['sɪmbəl] *s* símbolo
symbolic(al) [sɪm'bɑlɪk(əl)] *adj* simbólico
symbolize ['sɪmbə,laɪz] *tr* simbolizar
symmetric(al) [sɪ'mɛtrɪk(əl)] *adj* simétrico
symme•try ['sɪmɪtri] *s* (*pl* -**tries**) simetría
sympathetic [,sɪmpə'θɛtɪk] *adj* compasivo; favorablemente dispuesto
sympathize ['sɪmpə,θaɪz] *intr* compadecerse; **to sympathize with** compadecerse de; comprender
sympa•thy ['sɪmpəθi] *s* (*pl* -**thies**) compasión, conmiseración; **to be in sympathy with** estar de acuerdo con, ser partidario de; **to extend one's sympathy to** dar el pésame a
sympathy strike *s* huelga por solidaridad
symphonic [sɪm'fɑnɪk] *adj* sinfónico
sympho•ny ['sɪmfəni] *s* (*pl* -**nies**) sinfonía

symposi•um [sɪm'pozɪ•əm] *s* (*pl* -**a** [ə]) coloquio
symptom ['sɪmptəm] *s* síntoma *m*
syn. *abbr* **synonym, synonymous**
synagogue ['sɪnə,gɔg] *s* sinagoga
synchronize ['sɪŋkrə,naɪz] *tr & intr* sincronizar
synchronous ['sɪŋkrənəs] *adj* sincrónico
syncope ['sɪŋkə,pi] *s* (phonet) síncopa
syndicate ['sɪndɪkɪt] *s* sindicato ‖ ['sɪndɪ,ket] *tr* sindicar ‖ *intr* sindicarse
syndrome ['sɪndrom] *s* síndrome *m*
synonym ['sɪnənɪm] *s* sinónimo
synonymous [sɪ'nɑnɪməs] *adj* sinónimo
synop•sis [sɪ'nɑpsɪs] *s* (*pl* -**ses** [siz]) sinopsis *f*
syntax ['sɪntæks] *s* sintaxis *f*
synthe•sis ['sɪnθɪsɪs] *s* (*pl* -**ses** [,siz]) síntesis *f*
synthesize ['sɪnθɪ,saɪz] *tr* sintetizar
synthesizer *s* sintetizador *m*
synthetic(al) [sɪn'θɛtɪk(əl)] *adj* sintético
syphillis ['sɪfɪlɪs] *s* sífilis *f*
Syria ['sɪrɪ•ə] *s* Siria
Syrian ['sɪrɪ•ən] *adj & s* sirio
syringe [sɪ'rɪndʒ] o ['sɪrɪndʒ] *s* jeringa; (*fountain syringe*) mangueta; (*syringe fitted with needle for hypodermic injections*) jeringuilla ‖ *tr* jeringar
syrup ['sɪrəp] *s* almíbar *m;* (*with fruit juices or medicinal substances*) jarabe *m*
system ['sɪstəm] *s* sistema *m*
systematic(al) [,sɪstə'mætɪk(əl)] *adj* sistemático
systematize ['sɪstəmə,taɪz] *tr* sistematizar
systems analysis *s* análisis *m & f* de sistemas
systole ['sɪstəli] *s* sístole *f*

T

T, t [ti] vigésima letra del alfabeto inglés
t. *abbr* **teaspoon, temperature, tenor, tense, territory, town**
T. *abbr* **Territory, Testament**
tab [tæb] *s* apéndice *m*, proyección; marbete *m;* **to keep tab on** (coll) tener a la vista; **to pick up the tab** (coll) pagar la cuenta
tab•by ['tæbi] *s* (*pl* -**bies**) gato atigrado; gata; solterona; chismosa
tabernacle ['tæbər,nækəl] *s* tabernáculo
table ['tebəl] *s* mesa; (*list, catalogue; index of a book*) tabla; **to set the table** poner la mesa; **to turn the tables** volver las tornas; **under the table** completamente emborrachado ‖ *tr* aplazar la discusión de
tab•leau ['tæblo] *s* (*pl* -**leaus** o -**leaux** [loz]) cuadro vivo
ta'ble•cloth' *s* mantel *m*
table d'hôte ['tɑbəl'dot] *s* mesa redonda; comida a precio fijo
ta'ble•land' *s* meseta

table linen *s* mantelería
table manners *spl* modales *mpl* que uno tiene en la mesa
table of contents *s* índice *m* de materias, tabla de materias
ta'ble•spoon' *s* cuchara de sopa
tablespoonful ['tebəl,spun,ful] *s* cucharada
tablet ['tæblɪt] *s* (*writing pad*) bloc *m;* (*slab*) lápida, placa; (*lozenge, pastille*) comprimido, tableta
table talk *s* conversación de sobremesa
table tennis *s* tenis de mesa
ta'ble•ware' *s* servicio de mesa, artículos para la mesa
tabloid ['tæblɔɪd] *s* periódico sensacional
taboo [tə'bu] *adj* prohibido ‖ *s* tabú *m* ‖ *tr* prohibir
tabulate ['tæbjə,let] *tr* tabular
tabulator ['tæbjə,letər] *s* tabulador *m*
tacit ['tæsɪt] *adj* tácito
taciturn ['tæsɪ,tʌrn] *adj* taciturno

tack [tæk] *s* tachuela; nuevo plan de acción; (naut) virada; (sew) hilván *m* ‖ *tr* clavar con tachuelas; añadir; unir; (naut) virar; (sew) hilvanar ‖ *intr* cambiar de plan; (naut) virar

tackle ['tækəl] *s* avíos, enseres *mpl;* (naut) poleame *m* ‖ *tr* atacar, embestir; emprender

tack·y ['tæki] *adj* (*comp* **-ier;** *super* **-iest**) pegajoso; (coll) desaliñado

tact [tækt] *s* tacto, juicio, tino

tactful ['tæktfəl] *adj* discreto, político

tactical ['tæktɪkəl] *adj* táctico

tactician [tæk'tɪʃən] *s* táctico

tactics ['tæktɪks] *ssg* (mil) táctica ‖ *spl* táctica

tactless ['tæklɪs] *adj* indiscreto

tad'pole' *s* renacuajo

taffeta ['tæfɪtə] *s* tafetán *m*

taffy ['tæfi] *s* arropía, melcocha; (coll) lisonja, zalamería

tag [tæg] *s* etiqueta, marbete *m;* herrete *m;* pingajo; mechón *m;* vedija; (*curlicue in writing*) ringorrango; (*to play tag*) jugar al tócame tú ‖ *v* (*pret* & *pp* **tagged;** *ger* **tagging**) *tr* pegar un marbete a; marcar con marbete ‖ *intr* (coll) seguir de cerca

tag end *s* cabo flojo; retal *m*, retazo

Tagus ['tegəs] *s* Tajo

tail [tel] *adj* de cola ‖ *s* cola; **tails** (*of a coin*) cruz *f;* (coll) frac *m;* **to turn tail** mostrar los talones ‖ *tr* atar, juntar ‖ *intr* formar cola; **to tail after** pisar los talones a

tail assembly *s* (aer) empenaje *m*, planos *m* de cola

tail end *s* cola, extremo; conclusión; **at the tail end** al final

tail'gate' *tr* & *intr* (aut) seguir demasiado de cerca

tail'light' *s* faro trasero; (rr) disco de cola

tailor ['telər] *s* sastre *m* ‖ *tr* entallar (*un traje*) ‖ *intr* ser sastre

tailoring ['telərɪŋ] *s* sastrería, costura

tai'lor-made' suit *s* traje *m* de sastre, traje hecho a la medida

tail'piece' *s* apéndice *m*, cabo; (*of stringed instrument*) (mus) cordal *m;* (typ) florón *m*

tail'race' *s* cauce *m* de salida; (min) canal *m* de desechos

tail spin *s* (aer) barrena picada

tail wind *s* (aer) viento de cola; (naut) viento en popa

taint [tent] *s* mancha; corrupción, infección ‖ *tr* manchar; corromper, inficionar

take [tek] *s* toma; presa, redada; (mov) toma; (slang) entradas, ingresos ‖ *v* (*pret* **took** [tʊk]; *pp* **taken**) *tr* tomar; (*to carry off with one*) llevarse; (*to remove*) quitar; quedarse con (*p.ej., una compra en una tienda*); comer (*una pieza, en el juego de ajedrez y en el de damas*); dar (*un paso, un salto, un paseo*); hacer (*un viaje; ejercicio*); seguir (*un consejo, una asignatura*); sacar (*una fotografía*); calzar, usar (*cierto tamaño de zapatos o guantes*); estudiar (*p.ej., historia, francés, matemáticas*); echar (*una siesta*); tomar (*un tren, autobús, tranvía*); aguantar, tolerar; soportar; **to take amiss**

llevar a mal; **to take apart** descomponer, desarmar, desmontar; **to take down** bajar; descolgar; poner por escrito, tomar nota de; desmontar; (*to humble*) quitar los humos a; **to take for** tomar por, p.ej., **I took you for someone else** le tomé por otra persona; **to take from** quitar a; **to take in** acoger, admitir; (*to welcome into one's home, one's company*) recibir; (*to encompass*) abarcar, comprender; ganar (*dinero*); visitar (*los puntos de interés*); (*to win over by flattery or deceit*) cazar; meter (*p.ej., las costuras de una prenda de vestir*); **to take it that** suponer que; **to take off** quitarse (*p.ej., el sombrero*); descontar; (coll) imitar, parodiar; **to take on** tomar, contratar; empezar; cargar con, tomar sobre sí; desafiar; **to take out** sacar; pasear (*p.ej., a un niño, un caballo*); omitir; extraer, separar; **to take place** tener lugar; **to take up** subir; levantar; apretar; coger; recoger; emprender, comenzar; tomar posesión de (*un cargo, un puesto*); tomar, estudiar; ocupar, llenar (*un espacio*) ‖ *intr* arraigar, prender; cuajar; actuar, obrar; salir, resultar; adherirse; pegar; (coll) tener éxito; **to take after** parecerse a; **to take off** levantarse; salir; (aer) despegar; **to take up with** (coll) estrechar amistad con; (coll) vivir con; **to take well** (coll) sacar buen retrato

take'-home' pay *s* salario neto

take'-off' *s* (aer) despegue *m;* (coll) imitación burlesca, parodia

talcum powder ['tælkəm] *s* polvos de talco; talco en polvo

tale [tel] *s* cuento, relato; embuste *m*, mentira

tale'bear'er *s* chismoso, cuentista *mf*

talent ['tælənt] *s* talento; gente *f* de talento

talented ['tæləntɪd] *adj* talentoso

talent scout *s* buscador *m* de nuevas figuras

talk [tɔk] *s* charla, plática; (*gossip*) fábula, comidilla; (*lecture*) conferencia; **to cause talk** dar que hablar ‖ *tr* hablar; convencer hablando; **to talk up** ensalzar ‖ *intr* hablar; parlar (*el loro*); **to talk on** discutir (*un asunto*); hablar sin para; continuar hablando; **to talk up** elevar la voz, osar hablar

talkative ['tɔkətɪv] *adj* hablador, locuaz, palabrudo

talker ['tɔkər] *s* hablador *m;* orador *m;* charlatán *m*, parlón *m;* discursista *mf*

talkie ['tɔki] *s* (coll) cine hablado

talking doll ['tɔkɪŋ] *s* muñeca parlante

talking film *s* película hablada

talking machine *s* máquina parlante

talking picture *s* cine hablado, cine parlante

talk show *s* (telv, rad) programa *m* de conversación e interviú

tall [tɔl] *adj* alto; (coll) exagerado

tallow ['tælo] *s* sebo

tal·ly ['tæli] *s* (*pl* **-lies**) cuenta ‖ *v* (*pret* & *pp* **-lied**) *tr* echar la cuenta de ‖ *intr* echar la cuenta; concordar, corresponder, conformarse

tally sheet *s* hoja en que se anota una cuenta

talon ['tælən] *s* garra
tambourine [,tæmbə'rin] *s* pandereta
tame [tem] *adj* manso, domesticado; dócil, sumiso; insípido ‖ *tr* amansar, domesticar; domar (*a un animal salvaje*); someter; captar (*una caída de agua*)
tamp [tæmp] *tr* atacar (*un barreno*); apisonar
tamper ['tæmpər] *s* (*person*) apisonador *m;* (*ram*) pisón *m* ‖ *intr* entremeterse; **to tamper with** manosear, tocar ajando; tratar de forzar (*una cerradura*); falsificar (*un documento*); corromper (*p.ej., a un testigo*)
tampon ['tæmpɑn] *s* (surg) tapón *m* ‖ *tr* (surg) taponar
tan [tæn] *adj* requemado, tostado; de color de canela; marrón; café (Am) ‖ *v* (*pret & pp* **tanned;** *ger* **tanning**) *tr* adobar, curtir, zurrar; quemar, tostar; (coll) zurrar, dar una paliza a
tang [tæŋ] *s* sabor *m* u olor *m* fuerte y picante; dejo, gustillo (*ringing sound*) tañido
tangent ['tændʒənt] *adj* tangente ‖ *s* tangente *f;* **to fly off at a tangent** tomar subitamente nuevo rumbo, cambiar de repente
tangerine [,tændʒə'rin] *s* mandarina
tangible ['tændʒɪbəl] *adj* palpable, tangible
Tangier [tæn'dʒɪr] *s* Tánger *f*
tangle ['tæŋgəl] *s* enredo, maraña, lío ‖ *tr* enredar, enmarañar ‖ *intr* enredarse, enmarañarse
tank [tæŋk] *s* tanque *m*, depósito; (mil) tanque, carro de combate; (rr) ténder *m;* (*heavy drinker*) (slang) bodega
tank car *s* (rr) carro cuba, vagón *m* tanque
tanker ['tæŋkər] *s* barco tanque, buque *m* cisterna, barco cisternas; avión-nodriza *m*
tanker fleet *s* flota petrolera
tank farming *s* quimicultura, cultivo hidropónico
tank truck *s* camión *m* tanque
tanner ['tænər] *s* curtidor *m*
tanner•y ['tænəri] *s* (*pl* -**ies**) curtiduría, tenería
tantalize ['tæntə,laɪz] *tr* atormentar con falsas promesas
tantamount ['tæntə,maʊnt] *adj* equivalente
tantrum ['tæntrəm] *s* berrinche *m*, rabieta
tap [tæp] *s* golpecito, palmadita; canilla, espita; grifo; (elec) toma; (mach) macho de terraja; **on tap** sacado del barril, servido al grifo; listo, a mano; **taps** (*signal to put out lights*) (mil) silencio ‖ *v* (*pret & pp* **tapped**) *ger* **tapping**) *tr* dar golpecitos o un golpecito a o en; espitar, poner la espita a; sacar o tomar (*quitando la espita*); sangrar (*un árbol*); intervenir (*un teléfono*); derivar (*electricidad*); aterrajar (*tuercas*) ‖ *intr* dar golpecitos
tap dance *s* zapateado
tap'-dance' *intr* zapatear
tape [tep] *s* cinta ‖ *tr* proveer de cinta; medir con cinta; (coll) grabar en cinta magnetofónica
tape measure *s* cinta de medir
taper ['tepər] *s* cerilla, velita larga y delgada

‖ *tr* ahusar ‖ *intr* ahusarse; ir disminuyendo
tape'-re•cord' *tr* grabar sobre cinta
tape recorder [rɪ'kɔrdər] *s* magnetófono, grabadora de cinta
tapes•try ['tæpɪstri] *s* (*pl* -**tries**) tapiz *m* ‖ *v* (*pret & pp* -**tried**) *tr* tapizar
tape'worm' *s* solitaria, lombriz solitaria
tappet ['tæpɪt] *s* (aut) alzaválvulas *m*, taqué *m*
tap'room' *s* bodegón *m*, taberna
taps [tæps] *s* toque *m* de silencio; (slang) fin *m*, muerte *f*
tap water *s* agua de grifo
tap wrench *s* volvedor *m* de machos
tar [tɑr] *s* alquitrán *m;* (coll) marinero ‖ *v* (*pret & pp* **tarred;** *ger* **tarring**) *tr* alquitranar; **to tar and feather** embrear y emplumar
tar•dy ['tɑrdi] *adj* (*comp* -**dier;** *super* -**diest**) tardío
target ['tɑrgɪt] *s* blanco
target area *s* zona a batir
target practice *s* tiro al blanco
tariff ['tærɪf] *adj* arancelario ‖ (*duties*) arancel *m;* (*rates in general*) tarifa
tarnish ['tɑrnɪʃ] *s* deslustre *m* ‖ *tr* deslustrar ‖ *intr* deslustrarse
tar paper *s* papel alquitranado
tarpaulin [tɑr'pɔlɪn] *s* alquitranado, encerado, empegado
tar•ry ['tɑri] *adj* alquitranado, embreado ‖ ['tæri] *v* (*pret & pp* -**ried**) *intr* detenerse, quedarse; tardar
tart [tɑrt] *adj* acre, agrio; (fig) áspero, mordaz ‖ *s* tarta; (coll) puta
task [tæsk] *s* tarea; **to bring o take to task** llamar a capítulo
task'mas'ter *s* amo, superintendente *mf;* ordenancista *mf*, tirano
tassel ['tæsəl] *s* borla; (bot) penacho
taste [test] *s* gusto, sabor *m;* sorbo, trago; muestra; gusto, buen gusto; **in bad taste** de mal gusto; **in good taste** de buen gusto; **to acquire a taste for** tomar gusto a ‖ *tr* gustar; (*to sample*) probar ‖ *intr* saber; **to taste of** saber a
tasteless ['testlɪs] *adj* desabrido, insípido; de mal gusto
tast•y ['testi] *adj* (*comp* -**ier;** *super* -**iest**) sabroso; de buen gusto
tatter ['tætər] *s* andrajo, harapo, guiñapo ‖ *tr* hacer andrajos
tattered ['tætərd] *adj* andrajoso, haraposo, hilachento
tattle ['tætəl] *s* charla; habladuría ‖ *intr* charlar; chismear, murmurar
tat'tle•tale' *adj* revelador ‖ *s* cuentista *mf*, chismoso
tatto [tæ'tu] *s* tatuaje *m;* (mil) retreta ‖ *tr* tatuar o tatuarse
taunt [tɔnt] o [tɑnt] *s* mofa, pulla ‖ *tr* provocar con insultos
Taurus ['tɔrəs] *s* (astr) Tauro
taut [tɔt] *adj* tieso, tirante
tavern ['tævərn] *s* taberna; mesón *m*, posada; bayun(c)a (CAm); borrachería (Mex)

ta·
ta

taw•dry ['tɔdri] adj (comp **-drier;** super **-driest**) cursi, charro, vistoso

taw•ny ['tɔni] adj (comp **-nier;** super **-niest**) leonado

tax [tæks] s contribución, impuesto ‖ tr poner impuestos a (una persona); poner impuestos sobre (la propiedad); abrumar, cargar; agotar (la paciencia de uno)

taxable ['tæksəbəl] adj imponible

taxation [tæk'seʃən] s imposición de contribuciones; contribuciones, impuestos

tax collector s recaudador m de impuestos

tax cut s reducción de impuestos

tax deduction s exclusión de contribución

tax evader [ɪ'vedər] s burlador m de impuestos

tax evasion s fraude m fiscal

tax'-ex•empt' adj exento de impuesto

tax haven s asilo de los impuestos

tax•i ['tæksi] s (pl **-is**) taxi m ‖ v (pret & pp **-ied;** ger **-iing** o **-ying**) tr (aer) carretear ‖ intr ir en taxi; (aer) carretear, taxear

tax'i•cab' s taxi m

taxi dancer s taxi f

taxi driver s taista mf

tax'i•plane' s avioneta de alquiler

taxi stand s parada de taxis

tax loss s pérdida de reclamable

tax'pay'er s contribuyente mf

tax rate s tipo impositivo

tax relief s aligeramiento de impuestos

tax return s declaración de renta

t.b. abbr **tuberculosis**

tbs. o **tbsp.** abbr **tablespoon, tablespoons**

tea [ti] s té m; (medicinal infusion) tisana; caldo de carne

tea bag s muñeca

tea ball s huevo del té

tea'cart' s mesita de té (con ruedas)

teach [titʃ] v (pret & pp **taught** [tɔt]) tr & intr enseñar

teacher ['titʃər] s maestro, instructor m; (such as adversity) (fig) maestra

teacher's pet s alumno mimado

teaching ['titʃɪŋ] adj docente ‖ s enseñanza; doctrina

teaching aids spl material m auxiliar de instrucción

teaching staff s personal m docente

tea'cup' s taza para té

tea dance s té m bailable

teak [tik] s teca

tea'ket'tle s tetera

team [tim] s (e.g., of horses) tiro, tronco; (of oxen) yunta; (sport) equipo ‖ tr enganchar, uncir, enyugar ‖ intr—**to team up** asociarse, unirse; formar un equipo

team'mate' s compañero de equipo, equipier m

teamster ['timstər] s (of horses) tronquista m; (of a truck) camionista m

team'work' s espíritu de equipo; trabajo de equipo

tea'pot' s tetera

tear [tɪr] s lágrima; **to burst into tears** romper a llorar; **to fill with tears** arrasarse (los ojos) de o en lágrimas; **to hold back**

one's tears beberse las lágrimas; **to laugh away one's tears** convertir las lágrimas en risas ‖ [tɛr] s desgarro, rasgón m ‖ [tɛr] v (pret **tore** [tor]; pp **torn** [torn]) tr desgarrar, rasgar; acongojar, afligir; mesarse (los cabellos); **to tear apart** romper en dos; **to tear down** derribar (un edificio); desarmar (una máquina); **to tear off** desgajar; **to tear up** romper (p.ej., un papel) ‖ intr desgarrarse, rasgarse; **to tear along** correr a toda velocidad

tear bomb [tɪr] s bomba lacrimógena

tearful ['tɪrfəl] adj lacrimoso

tear gas [tɪr] s gas lacrimógeno

tear-jerker ['tɪr,dʒʌrkər] s (slang) drama m o cine m que arrancan lágrimas

tear-off ['tɛr,ɔf] adj exfoliador

tea'room' s salón m de té

tear sheet [tɛr] s hoja del anunciante

tease [tiz] tr embromar, azuzar

tea'spoon' s cucharilla, cucharita

teaspoonful ['ti,spun,fʊl] s cucharadita

teat [tit] s teta, pezón m

tea time s hora del té

technical ['tɛknɪkəl] adj técnico

technicali•ty [,tɛknɪ'kælɪti] s (pl **-ties**) detalle técnico

technician [tɛk'nɪʃən] s técnico

technics ['tɛknɪks] ssg técnica

technique [tɛk'nik] s técnica

Teddy bear ['tɛdi] s oso de juguete, oso de trapo

tedious ['tidɪ•əs] o ['tidʒəs] adj tedioso, enfadoso

teem [tim] intr hormiguear; llover a cántaros; **to teem with** hervir de

teeming ['timɪŋ] adj hormigueante; (rain) torrencial

teen age [tin] s edad de 13 a 19 años

teen-ager ['tin,edʒər] s joven mf de 13 a 19 años de edad

teens [tinz] spl números ingleses que terminan en **-teen** (de 13 a 19); edad de 13 a 19 años; **to be in one's teens** tener de 13 a 19 años

tee•ny ['tini] adj (comp **-nier;** super **-niest**) (coll) diminuto, pequeñito

teeter ['titər] s vaivén m, balanceo ‖ intr balancear, oscilar

teethe [tið] intr endentecer

teething ['tiðɪŋ] s dentición

teething ring s chupador m

teetotaler [ti'totələr] s teetotalista mf, nefalista mf, abstemio

tel. abbr **telegram, telegraph, telephone**

tele•cast ['tɛlɪ,kæst] s teledifusión ‖ v (pret & pp **-cast** o **-casted**) tr & intr teledifundir

telegram ['tɛlɪ,græm] s telegrama m

telegraph ['tɛlɪ,græf] s telégrafo ‖ tr & intr telegrafiar

telegrapher [tɪ,lɛgrəfər] s telegrafista mf

telegraph pole s poste m de telégrafo

Telemachus [tɪ'lɛməkəs] s Telémaco

telemeter [tɪ'lɛmɪtər] s telémetro ‖ tr telemetrar

telemetry [tɪ'lɛmɪtri] s telemetría

telephone ['tɛlɪ,fon] s teléfono ‖ tr & intr telefonear

telephone booth s locutorio, cabina telefónica

telephone call s llamada telefónica

telephone directory s anuario telefónico, guía telefónica

telephone exchange s estación telefónica, central f de teléfonos; conmutador m (SAm)

telephone operator s telefonista mf, centralista mf

telephone receiver s receptor telefónico

telephone table s mesita portateléfono

tele(photo)lens ['tɛlɪ(,fotə),lɛnz] s lente telefotográfica

teleprinter ['tɛlɪ,prɪntər] s teleimpresor m

telescope ['tɛlɪ,skop] s telescopio ‖ tr telescopar ‖ intr telescoparse

teletype ['tɛlɪ,taɪp] s teletipo ‖ tr & intr transmitir por teletipo

teleview ['tɛlɪ,vju] tr & intr ver por televisión

televiewer ['tɛlɪ,vju•ər] s televidente mf, telespectador m

televise ['tɛlɪ,vaɪz] tr televisar

television ['tɛlɪ,vɪʃən] adj televisor ‖ s televisión

television audience s telespectadores

television screen s pantalla televisora, pequeña pantalla

television set s televisor m, telerreceptor m

telex ['tɛlɛks] s servicio comerical de teletipo

tell [tɛl] v (pret & pp **told** [told]) tr decir; (to narrate; to count) contar; determinar; conocer, distinguir; **I told you so!** ¡por algo te lo dije!; **to tell someone to** + inf decircle a uno que + subj ‖ intr hablar; surtir efecto; **to tell on** dejarse ver en (p.ej., la salud de uno); (coll) denunciar

teller ['tɛlər] s narrador m; (of a bank) cajero; (of votes) escrutador m

temper ['tɛmpər] s temple m, natural m, genio; cólera, mal genio; (of steel, glass, etc.) temple m; **to keep one's temper** dominar su mal genio; **to lose one's temper** encolerizarse, perder la paciencia ‖ tr templar ‖ intr templarse

temperament ['tɛmpərəmənt] s disposición; temperamento sensible o excitable

temperamental [,tɛmpərə'mɛntəl] adj temperamental

temperance ['tɛmpərəns] s templanza

temperate ['tɛmpərɪt] adj templado

temperature [,tɛmpərət/ər] s temperatura

tempest ['tɛmpɪst] s tempestad

tempestuous [tɛm'pɛstʃʊ•əs] adj tempestuoso

temple ['tɛmpəl] s (place of worship) templo; (side of forehead) sien f; (sidepiece of spectacles) gafa

tem•po ['tɛmpo] s (pl **-pos** o **-pi** [pi]) (mus) tiempo; (fig) ritmo (p.ej., de la vida)

temporal ['tɛmpərəl] adj temporal

temporary ['tɛmpə,rɛri] adj temporáneo, temporario, provisional, interino

temporize ['tɛmpə,raɪz] intr contemporizar, temporizar

tempt [tɛmpt] tr tentar

temptation [tɛmpt'teʃən] s tentación

tempter ['tɛmptər] s tentador m

tempting ['tɛmptɪŋ] adj tentador

ten [tɛn] adj & pron diez ‖ s diez m; **ten o'clock** las diez

tenable ['tɛnəbəl] adj defendible

tenacious [tɪ'neʃəs] adj tenaz

tenacity [tɪ'næsɪti] s tenacidad

tenant ['tɛnənt] s arrendatario, inquilino; morador m, residente mf

tend [tɛnd] tr cuidar, vigilar; servir ‖ intr tender, dirigirse; **to tend to** atender a; **to tend to** + inf tender a + inf

tenden•cy ['tɛndənsi] s (pl **-cies**) tendencia

tender ['tɛndər] adj tierno; (painfully sensitive) dolorido ‖ n oferta; (naut) alijador m, falúa; (rr) ténder m ‖ tr ofrecer, tender

tender-hearted ['tɛndər,hartɪd] adj compasivo, tierno de corazón

ten'der•loin' s filete m ‖ **Tenderloin** s barrio de mala vida

tenderness ['tɛndərnɪs] s ternura, terneza; sensibilidad

tendon ['tɛndən] s tendón m

tendril ['tɛndrɪl] s zarcillo

tenement ['tɛnɪmənt] s habitación, vivienda; casa de vecindad

tenement house s casa de vecindad

tenet ['tɛnɪt] s dogma m, credo, principio

tennis ['tɛnɪs] s tenis m

tennis court s campo de tenis

tennis player s tenista mf

tenor ['tɛnər] s tenor m, carácter m, curso, tendencia; (mus) tenor

tense [tɛns] adj tenso, tieso; (person; situation) (fig) tenso; (relations) tirante ‖ s (gram) tiempo

tension ['tɛnʃən] s tensión; ansia, congoja, esfuerzo mental; (in personal or diplomatic relations) tirantez f

tent [tɛnt] s tienda; tienda de campaña

tentacle ['tɛntəkəl] s tentáculo

tentative ['tɛntətɪv] adj tentativo

tenth [tɛnθ] adj & s décimo ‖ s (in dates) diez m

tenuous ['tɛnjʊ•əs] adj tenue; (thin in consistency) raro

tenure ['tɛnjər] s (of property) tenencia; (of an office) ejercicio; (protection from dismissal) inamovilidad

tepid ['tɛpɪd] adj tibio

tercet ['tʌrsɪt] s terceto

term [tʌrm] s término; (of imprisonment) condena; semestre m, período escolar; (of the presidency of the U.S.A.) mandato, período; **terms** condiciones ‖ tr llamar, nombrar

termagant ['tʌrməgənt] s mujer regañona, mujer de mal genio

terminal ['tʌrmɪnəl] adj terminal ‖ s término, fin m; (elec) terminal m; (rr) estación de fin de línea

terminate ['tʌrmɪ,net] tr & intr terminar

termination [,tʌrmɪ'neʃən] s terminación

terminus ['tʌrmɪnəs] s término; (rr) estación de cabeza, estación extrema

termite ['tʌrmaɪt] s termite m, comején m

ta
te

terrace ['tɛrəs] s terraza; (*flat roof of a house*) azotea

terra firma ['tɛrə 'fʌrmə] s tierra firme; **on terra firma** sobre suelo firme

terrain [tɛ'ren] s terreno

terrestrial [tə'rɛstrɪ•əl] adj terrestre

terrible ['tɛrɪbəl] adj terrible; muy desagradable

terrific [tə'rɪfɪk] adj terrífico; (coll) enorme, intenso, brutal

terri•fy ['tɛri,faɪ] v (*pret & pp* -**fied**) tr aterrorizar, atemorizar

territo•ry ['tɛri,tori] s (*pl* -**ries**) territorio

terror ['tɛrər] s terror m

terrorize ['tɛrə,raɪz] tr aterrorizar; imponerse a, mediante el terror

terry cloth ['tɛri] s albornoz m

terse [tʌrs] adj breve, sucinto

tertiary ['tʌrʃɪ,ɛri] o ['tʌrʃəri] adj terciario

Test. abbr **Testament**

test [tɛst] s prueba, ensayo; examen m || tr probar, poner a prueba; examinar

testament ['tɛstəmənt] s testamento

test flight s vuelo de ensayo

testicle ['tɛstɪkəl] s testículo

testi•fy ['tɛstɪ,faɪ] v (*pret & pp* -**fied**) tr & intr testificar

testimonial [,tɛstɪ'monɪ•əl] s recomendación, certificado; (*expression of esteem, gratitude, etc.*) homenaje m

testimo•ny ['tɛstɪ,moni] s (*pl* -**nies**) testimonio

testing grounds ['tɛstɪŋ] spl campo de pruebas

test pilot s (aer) piloto de pruebas

test tube s probeta, tubo de ensayo

test'-tube' baby s niño-probeta m

tether ['tɛðər] s atadura, traba; **at the end of one's tether** al límite de las posibilidades o la paciencia de uno || tr apersogar

tetter ['tɛtər] s empeine m

text [tɛkst] s texto; tema m, lema m

text'book' s libro de texto

textile ['tɛkstɪl] o ['tɛkstaɪl] adj & s textil m

texture ['tɛkstʃər] s textura

Thai ['ta•i] o ['taɪ] adj & s tailandés m

Thailand ['taɪlənd] s Tailandia

Thales ['θeliz] s Tales m

Thalia [θə'laɪ•ə] s Talía

Thames [tɛmz] s Támesis m

than [ðæn] conj que, p.ej., **he is richer than I** es más rico que yo; (*before a numeral*) de, p.ej., **more than twenty** más de veinte; (*before a verb*) de lo que, p.ej., **the crop is larger than was expected** la cosecha es mayor de lo que se esperaba; (*before a verb with direct object understood*) del (de la, de los, de las) que, p.ej., **they sent us more coffee than we ordered** nos enviaron más café del que pedimos

thanatology [,θænə'talədʒi] s tanatología

thank [θæŋk] tr agradecer, dar las gracias a; **to thank someone for something** agradecerle a uno una cosa || **thanks** spl gracias; **thanks to** gracias a, merced a || **thanks** interj ¡gracias!

thankful ['θæŋkfəl] adj agradecido

thankless ['θæŋklɪs] adj ingrato

thanksgiving [,θæŋks'gɪvɪŋ] s acción de gracias

Thanksgiving Day s (U.S.A.) día m de acción de gracias

that [ðæt] adj dem (*pl* **those**) ese; aquel; **that one** ése; aquél || pron dem (*pl* **those**) ése; aquél; eso; aquello || pron rel que, quien, el cual, el que || adv tan; **that far** tan lejos; hasta allí; **that many** tantos; **that much** tanto || conj que; para que

thatch [θætʃ] s barda, paja; techo de paja || tr cubrir de paja, techar con paja, bardar

thaw [θɔ] s deshielo, derretimiento; descongelación || tr deshelar, derretir || intr deshelarse, derretirse

the [ðə], [ði], o [ði] art def el || adv cuanto, p.ej., **the more the merrier** cuanto más mejor; **the more . . . the more** cuanto más . . . tanto más

theater ['θi•ətər] s teatro

the'ater-go'er s teatrero

theater news s actualidad escénica

theater page s noticiario teatral

theatrical [θi'ætrɪkəl] adj teatral

Thebes [θibz] s Tebas f

thee [ði] pron pers (archaic, poet, Bib) te; ti; **with thee** contigo

theft [θɛft] s hurto, robo

theft'-proof' adj antirroba

their [ðɛr] adj poss su; el . . . de ellos

theirs [ðɛrz] pron poss el suyo, el de ellos

them [ðɛm] pron pers los; ellos; **to them** les; a ellos

theme [θim] s tema m; (mus) tema m

theme song s (mus) tema m central; (rad) sintonía

them•selves' pron pers ellos mismos; sí, sí mismos; se, p.ej., **they enjoyed themselves** se divirtieron; **with themselves** consigo

then [ðɛn] adv entonces; después, luego, en seguida; además, también; **by then** para entonces; **from then on** desde entonces, de allí en adelante; **then and there** ahí mismo

thence [ðɛns] adv desde allí; desde entonces; por eso

thence'forth' adv de allí en adelante; desde entonces

theolo•gy [θi'alədʒi] s (*pl* -**gies**) teología

theorem ['θi•ərəm] s teorema m

theo•ry ['θi•əri] s (*pl* -**ries**) teoría

therapeutic [,θɛrə'pjutɪk] adj terapéutico || **therapeutics** ssg terapéutica

thera•py ['θɛrəpi] s (*pl* -**pies**) terapia

there [ðɛr] adv allí, allá; **there is** o **there are** hay; aquí tiene Vd.

there'a•bouts' adv por allí; cerca, aproximadamente

there•af'ter adv de allí en adelante, después de eso

there•by' adv con eso; así, de tal modo; por allí cerca

therefore ['ðɛrfor] adv por lo tanto, por consiguiente

there•in' adv en esto, en eso; en ese respecto

there•of' adv de ello, de eso

Theresa [təˈrisə] o [təˈrɛsə] s Teresa
there'u•pon' adv sobre eso, encima de eso; por consiguiente; en seguida
thermistor [θərˈmɪstər] s (elec) termistor m
thermocouple [ˈθʌrmoˌkʌpəl] s (elec) termopar m
thermodynamic [ˌθʌrmodaɪˈnæmɪk] adj termodinámico ‖ **thermodynamics** ssg termodinámica
thermometer [θərˈmɑmɪtər] s termómetro
thermonuclear [ˌθʌrmoˈnuklɪ•ər] adj termonuclear
Thermopylae [θərˈmɑpɪˌli] s las Termópilas
Thermos bottle [ˈθʌrməs] s termos m, botella termos, bolsa isotérmica
thermostat [ˈθʌrməˌstæt] s termóstato
thesau•rus [θɪˈsɔrəs] s (pl **-ri** [raɪ]) **tesoro;** (dictionary or the like) tesauro, tesoro
these [ðiz] pl de **this**
the•sis [ˈθisɪs] s (pl **-ses** [siz]) tesis f
Thespis [ˈθɛspɪs] s Tespis m
Thessaly [ˈθɛsəli] s la Tesalia
they [ðe] pron pers ellos, ellas
thick [θɪk] adj espeso; grueso; denso; (coll) estúpido; (coll) íntimo ‖ s espesor m; **the thick of** (e.g., a crowd) lo más denso de; (e.g., a battle) lo más reñido de; **through thick and thin** contra viento y marea
thicken [ˈθɪkən] tr espesar ‖ intr espesarse; complicarse (el enredo)
thicket [ˈθɪkɪt] s espesura, matorral m, soto
thick-headed [ˈθɪkˈhɛdɪd] adj (coll) torpe, estúpido
thick'-set' adj grueso, rechoncho
thief [θif] s (pl **thieves** [θivz]) ladrón m
thieve [θiv] intr hurtar, robar
thiever•y [ˈθivəri] s (pl **-ies**) latrocinio, hurto, robo
thigh [θaɪ] s muslo
thigh'bone' s hueso del muslo, fémur m
thimble [ˈθɪmbəl] s dedal m
thin [θɪn] adj (comp **thinner;** super **thinnest**) delgado, flaco, tenue; (cloth, paper, sole of shoe, etc.) fino; (hair) ralo; (broth) aguado; (excuse) débil; claro, ligero, escaso ‖ v (pret & pp **thinned;** ger **thinning**) tr adelgazar, enflaquecer; enrarecer; aclarar; aguar; desleír (los colores) ‖ intr adelgazarse, enflaquecerse; enrarecerse; **to thin out** ralear (el pelo)
thine [ðaɪn] adj poss (archaic & poet) tu ‖ pron poss (archaic & poet) tuyo; el tuyo
thing [θɪŋ] s cosa; **of all things!** ¡qué sorpresa!; **to be the thing** ser la última moda; **to be the thing to do** ser lo que debe hacerse; **to see things** ver visiones, padecer alucinaciones
think [θɪŋk] v (pret & pp **thought** [θɔt]) tr pensar; **to think it over** pensarlo; **to think nothing of** tener en poco; creer fácil; no dar importancia a; **to think of** pensar de, p.ej., what do you think of this book? ¿qué piensa Vd. de este libro?; **to think up** imaginar; inventar (p.ej., una excusa) ‖ intr pensar; **to think not** creer que no; **to think of** (to turn one's thoughts to) pensar en; pensar (un número, un naipe, etc.); **to**

think so creer que sí; **to think well of** tener buena opinión de
thinker [ˈθɪŋkər] s pensador m
third [θʌrd] adj tercero ‖ s (in a series) tercero; (one of three equal parts) tercio; (in dates) tres m
third degree s (coll) interrogatorio bajo tortura
third rail s (rr) tercer carril m, carril de toma
third'-rate' adj de tercer orden; (fig) inferior
Third World adj tercermundista ‖ s Terrcero Mundo
Third World countries spl países no alineados
thirst [θʌrst] s sed f ‖ intr tener sed; **to thirst for** tener sed de
thirst•y [ˈθʌrsti] adj (comp **-ier;** super **-iest**) sediento; **to be thirsty** tener sed
thirteen [ˈθʌrˈtin] adj, pron & s trece m
thirteenth [ˈθʌrtinθ] adj & s (in a series) decimotercero; (part) trezavo ‖ s (in dates) trece m
thirtieth [ˈθʌrtɪ•ɪθ] adj & s (in a series) trigésimo; (part) treintavo ‖ s (in dates) treinta m
thir•ty [ˈθʌrti] adj & pron treinta ‖ s (pl **-ties**) treinta m
this [ðɪs] adj dem (pl **these**) este; **this one** éste ‖ pron dem (pl **these**) éste; esto ‖ adv tan
thistle [ˈθɪsəl] s cardo
thither [ˈθɪðər] o [ˈðɪðər] adv allá, hacia allá
Thomas [ˈtɑməs] s Tomás m
thong [θɔŋ] o [θɑŋ] s correa
tho•rax [ˈθɔræks] s (pl **-roxes** o **-raxes** o **-races** [rəˌsiz]) tórax m
thorn [θɔrn] s espina
thorn•y [ˈθɔrni] adj (comp **-ier;** super **-iest**) espinoso; espinudo; (difficult) (fig) espinoso, espinudo
thorough [ˈθʌro] adj cabal, completo; concienzudo, cuidadoso
thor'ough•bred adj de pura sangre; bien nacido ‖ s pura sangre m; persona bien nacida
thor'ough•fare' s vía pública; **no thoroughfare** se prohíbe el paso
thor'ough•go'ing adj cabal, completo, esmerado, perfecto
thoroughly [ˈθʌroli] adv a fondo
those [ðoz] pl de **that**
thou [ðaʊ] pron pers (archaic, poet & Bib) tú ‖ tr & intr tutear
though [ðo] adv sin embargo ‖ conj aunque, bien que; **as though** como sí
thought [θɔt] s pensamiento
thoughtful [ˈθɔtfəl] adj pensativo; atento, considerado
thoughtless [ˈθɔtlɪs] adj irreflexivo; descuidado, inconsiderado
thought transference s transmisión del pensamiento
thousand [ˈθaʊzənd] adj & s mil m; **a thousand** u **one thousand** mil m
thousandth [ˈθaʊzəndθ] adj & s milésimo

te
th

thralldom ['θrɔldəm] s esclavitud, servidumbre

thrash [θræʃ] tr (agr) trillar; azotar, zurrar; **to thrash out** decidir después de una discusión cabal ‖ intr trillar; agitarse, menearse

thread [θrɛd] s hilo; (mach) filete m, rosca; (of a speech, of life) hilo; **to lose the thread of** perder el hilo de ‖ tr enhebrar, enhilar; ensartar (p.ej., cuentas); (mach) aterrajar, filetear

thread'bare' adj raído; gastado, desgastado, usado, viejo

threat [θrɛt] s amenaza

threaten ['θrɛtən] tr & intr amenazar

threatening ['θrɛtənɪŋ] adj amenazante

three [θri] adj & pron tres ‖ s tres m; **three o'clock** las tres

three'-cor'nered adj triangular; (hat) de tres picos

three hundred adj & pron trescientos ‖ s trescientos m

threepence ['θrɛpəns] o ['θrɪpəns] s suma de tres peniques; moneda de tres peniques

three'-ply' adj de tres capas

three R's [ɑrz] spl lectura, escritura y aritmética, primeras letras

three'score' adj tres veintenas de

threno•dy ['θrɛnədi] s (pl -dies) treno

thresh [θrɛʃ] tr (agr) trillar; **to thresh out** decidir después de una discusión cabal ‖ intr trillar; agitarse, menearse

threshing machine s máquina trilladora

threshold ['θrɛʃold] s umbral m; (physiol, psychol & fig) umbral, limen m; **to be on the threshold of** estar en los umbrales de; **to cross the threshold** atravesar o pisar los embrales

thrice [θraɪs] adv tres veces; repetidamente, sumamente

thrift [θrɪft] s economía, parquedad

thrift•y ['θrɪfti] adj (comp -ier; super -iest) económico, parco; próspero

thrill [θrɪl] s emoción viva ‖ tr emocionar, conmover ‖ intr emocionarse, conmoverse

thriller ['θrɪlər] s cuento o pieza de teatro espeluznante

thrilling ['θrɪlɪŋ] adj emocionante; espeluznante

thrive [θraɪv] v (pret thrived o throve [θrov]; pp thrived o thriven ['θrɪvən]) intr medrar, prosperar

throat [θrot] s garganta; **to clear one's throat** aclarar la voz

throb [θrɑb] s latido, palpitación, pulsación ‖ v (pret & pp throbbed; ger throbbing) intr latir, palpitar, pulsar

throe [θro] s congoja, dolor m; **throes** angustia, agonía, esfuerzo penoso

throne [θron] s trono

throng [θrɔŋ] s gentío, tropel m, muchedumbre ‖ intr agolparse, apiñarse

throttle ['θrɑtəl] s válvula reguladora; (of a locomotive) regulador m; (of an automobile) acelerador m ‖ tr ahogar, sofocar; impedir, suprimir; (mach) regular; **to throttle down** reducir la velocidad de

through [θru] adj directo, sin paradas; acabado, terminado; **to be through with** haber terminado; no querer ocuparse más de ‖ adv a través, de un lado a otro; completamente ‖ prep por, a través de; por medio de; a causa de; todo lo largo de

through•out' adv por todas partes; en todos respectos; desde el principio hasta el fin ‖ prep por todo . . .; durante todo . . .; a lo largo de

through'way' s carretera de peaje de acceso limitado

throw [θro] s echada, tirada, lance m; cobertor ligero ‖ v (pret threw [θru]; pp thrown) tr arrojar, echar, lanzar; tirar (los dados); lanzar (una mirada); desarzonar (a un jinete); proyectar (una sombra); tender (un puente); perder con premeditación (un juego, una carrera); **to throw away** tirar; malgastar; perder, no aprovechar; **to throw in** añadir, dar de más; **to throw out** arrojar, botar, desechar; echar a la calle; chispar; **to throw over** abandonar, dejar ‖ intr arrojar, echar, lanzar; **to throw up** vomitar

thrum [θrʌm] v (pret & pp thrummed; ger thrumming) intr teclear; zangarrear; **to thrum on** rasguear

thrush [θrʌʃ] s tordo

thrust [θrʌst] s empuje m; acometida; (with horns) cornada; (with dagger) puñalada; (with sword) estocada; (with knife) cuchillada ‖ v (pret & pp thrust) tr empujar; acometer; clavar, hincar; atravesar, traspasar

thud [θʌd] s baque m, ruido sordo ‖ v (pret & pp thudded; ger thudding) tr & intr golpear con ruido sordo

thug [θʌg] s ladrón m, asesino; (coll) gorila

thumb [θʌm] s pulgar m, dedo gordo; **all thumbs** desmañado, chapucero, torpe; **to twiddle one's thumbs** menear ociosamente los pulgares; no hacer nada; **under the thumb of** bajo la férula de ‖ tr manosear sin suidado; ensuciar con los dedos; hojear (un libro) con el pulgar; **to thumb a ride** pedir ser llevado en automóvil indicando la dirección con el pulgar; **to thumb one's nose at** señalar (a una persona) poniendo el pulgar sobre la nariz en son de burla; tratar con sumo desprecio

thumb index s escalerilla, índice m con pestañas

thumb'print' s impresión del pulgar ‖ tr marcar con impresión del pulgar

thumb'screw' s tornillo de mariposa, tornillo de orejas

thumb'tack' s chinche m

thump [θʌmp] s golpazo, porrazo ‖ tr golpear, aporrear ‖ intr caer con golpe pesado; andar con pasos pesados; latir (el corazón) con golpes pesados

thumping ['θʌmpɪŋ] adj (coll) enorme, pesado

thunder ['θʌndər] s trueno; (of applause) estruendo; amenaza ‖ tr fulminar (p.ej., censuras) ‖ intr tronar; **to thunder at** tronar contra

thun'der·bolt' s rayo
thun'der·clap' s tronido
thunderous ['θʌndərəs] adj atronador, tronitoso
thun'der·show'er s chubasco con truenos
thun'der·storm' s tronada
thun'der·struck' adj atónito, estupefacto, pasmado
Thursday ['θʌrsdi] s jueves m
thus [ðʌs] adv así; **thus far** hasta aquí, hasta ahora
thwack [θwæk] s golpe m, porrazo || tr golpear, pegar
thwart [θwɔrt] adj transversal, oblicuo || adv de través || tr desbaratar, impedir, frustrar
thy [ðaɪ] adj poss (archaic & poet) tu
thyme [taɪm] s tomillo
thyroid gland ['θaɪrɔɪd] s glándula tiroides
thyself [ðaɪ'sɛlf] pron (archaic & poet) tú mismo; ti mismo; te; ti
tiara [taɪ'ɑrə] o [taɪ'ɛrə] s (papal miter) tiara; (female adornment) diadema f
tick [tɪk] s tictac m; funda (de almohada o colchón) (coll) crédito; (ent) garrapata; **on tick** (coll) al fiado || intr hacer tictac; latir (el corazón)
ticker ['tɪkər] s teleimpresor m de cinta; (slang) reloj m; (slang) corazón m
ticker tape s cinta de teleimpresor
ticket ['tɪkɪt] s billete m; boleto (Am); (theat) entrada, localidad; (for wrong parking) (coll) aviso de multa; (of a political party) (U.S.A.) lista de candidatos; **that's the ticket** (coll) eso es, eso es lo que se necesita
ticket agent s taquillero
ticket collector s revisor m
ticket office s taquilla, despacho de billetes
ticket scalper ['skælpər] s revendedor m de billetes de teatro
ticket window s taquilla, ventanilla
ticking ['tɪkɪŋ] s cutí m, terliz m
tickle ['tɪkəl] s cosquillas || tr cosquillear; gustar, satisfacer; divertir || intr cosquillear
ticklish ['tɪklɪʃ] adj cosquilloso; difícil, delicado; inseguro
tick-tock ['tɪk,tɑk] s tictac m
tidal wave ['taɪdəl] s aguaje m, ola de marea; (e.g., of popular indignation) ola
tidbit ['tɪd,bɪt] s buen bocado, bocadito
tiddlywinks ['tɪdli,wɪŋks] s juego de la pulga
tide [taɪd] s marea; temporada; **to go against the tide** ir contra la corriente; **to stem the tide** rendir la marea || tr llevar, hacer flotar; **to tide over** ayudar un poco; superar (una dificultad)
tide'wa'ter adj costanero || s agua de marea; orilla del mar
tidings ['taɪdɪŋz] spl noticias, informes mpl
ti·dy ['taɪdi] adj (comp -dier; super -diest) aseado, limpio, pulcro, ordenado || s (pl -dies) pañito bordado, cubierta de respaldar || v (pret & pp -died) tr asear, limpiar, arreglar, poner en orden || intr asearse
tie [taɪ] s atadura; lazo, nudo; (worn on neck) corbata; (in games and elections) empate m; (mus) ligado; (rr) traviesa || v (pret &

pp **tied**; ger **tying**) tr atar, liar; enlazar; hacer (la corbata); confinar, limitar; empatar (p.ej., una elección); empatársela a (una persona); **to be tied up** estar ocupado; **to tie down** confinar, limitar; **to tie up** atar; envolver; obstruir (el tráfico) || intr atar; empatar o empatarse (dos candidatos, dos equipos)
tie'pin' s alfiler m de corbata
tier [tɪr] s fila, ringlera; (theat) fila de palcos
tiger ['taɪgər] s tigre m
tiger lily s azucena atigrada
tight [taɪt] adj apretado, estrecho, ajustado; bien cerrado, hermético; compacto, denso; fijo, firme, sólido; (com) escaso; (sport) casi igual; (coll) agarrado, tacaño; (slang) borracho || adv firmemente; **to hold tight** mantener fijo; agarrarse bien || **tights** spl traje m de malla
tighten ['taɪtən] tr apretar; atiesar, estirar || intr apretarse; atiesarse, estirarse
tight-fisted ['taɪt'fɪstɪd] adj agarrado, tacaño
tight'-fit'ting adj ceñido, muy ajustado
tight'rope' s cuerda tirante
tight squeeze s (coll) brete m, aprieto
tightwad ['taɪt,wɑd] s avaro; codo (Guat, Mex)
tigress ['taɪgrɪs] s tigresa
tile [taɪl] s azulejo; (for floors) baldosa; (for roofs) reja || tr azulejar; embaldosar; tejar
tile roof s tejado (de tejas)
till [tɪl] prep hasta || conj hasta que || s cajón m o gaveta del dinero || tr labrar, cultivar
tilt [tɪlt] s inclinación; justa, torneo; **full tilt** a toda velocidad || tr inclinar; asestar (una lanza) || intr inclinarse; justar, tornear; luchar; **to tilt at** luchar con, arremeter contra; protestar contra
timber ['tɪmbər] s madera de construcción; madero, viga; bosque m, árboles mpl de monte
tim'ber·land' s bosque m maderable
timber line s límite m de la vegetación, límite del bosque maderable
timbre ['tɪmbər] s (phonet & phys) timbre m
time [taɪm] s tiempo; hora, p.ej., **time to eat** hora de comer; vez, p.ej., **five times** cinco veces; rato, p.ej., **a nice time** un buen rato; (period for payment) plazo; horas de trabajo; sueldo; tiempo de parir, término del embarazo; última hora; (phot) tiempo de exposición; **all the time** a cada momento; **for the time being** por ahora, por el momento; **on time** a tiempo, a la hora debida; (in installments) a plazos, **to bide one's time** esperar la hora propicia; **to do time** (coll) cumplir una condena; **to have a good time** darse buen tiempo; **to have no time for** no poder tolerar; **to lose time** atrasarse (el reloj); **to make time** avanzar con rapidez; **to pass the time of day** saludarse (dos personas); **to serve time** (in prison) tirarse; **to take one's time** no darse prisa, ir despacio; **what time is it?** ¿qué hora es? || tr calcular el tiempo de; medir el tiempo de; (sport) cronometrar
time bomb s bomba-reloj f

time'card' s hoja de presencia, tarjeta registradora

time clock s reloj m registrador

time exposure s exposición de tiempo

time fuse s espoleta de tiempos

time'keep'er s alistador m de tiempo; reloj m; (sport) cronometrador m, juez m de tiempo

time•ly ['taɪmli] adj (comp -lier; super -liest) oportuno

time'piece' s reloj m

time signal s señal horaria

time'ta'ble s horario, itinerario

time'work' s trabajo ajornal

time'worn' adj gastado por el tiempo

time zone s huso horario

timid ['tɪmɪd] adj tímido

timing gears ['taɪmɪŋ] spl engranaje m de distribución, mando de las válvulas

timorous ['tɪmərəs] adj tímido, miedoso

tin [tɪn] s (element) estaño; (tin plate) hojalata; (cup, box, etc.) lata ‖ v (pret & pp **tinned**; ger **tinning**) tr estañar; (to pack in cans) enlatar; recubrir de hojalata

tin can s lata, envase m de hojalata

tincture ['tɪŋktʃər] s tintura

tin cup s taza de hojalata

tinder ['tɪndər] s yesca

tin'der•box' s lumbres fpl, yesquero; persona muy excitable; semillero de violencia

tin foil s hojuela de estaño, papel m de estaño

ting-a-ling ['tɪŋə,lɪŋ] s tilín m

tinge [tɪndʒ] s matiz m, tinte m; dejo, gustillo ‖ v (ger **tingeing** o **tinging**) tr matizar, teñir; dar gusto o sabor a

tingle ['tɪŋgəl] s comezón f, picazón f ‖ intr sentir comezón; zumbar (los oídos); (e.g., with enthusiasm) estremecerse

tin hat s (coll) yelmo de acero

tinker ['tɪŋkər] s calderero remendón; chapucero ‖ intr ocuparse vanamente

tinkle ['tɪŋkəl] s retintín m ‖ tr hacer retiñir m ‖ tr hacer retiñir ‖ intr retiñir

tin plate s hojalata

tin roof s tejado de hojalata

tinsel ['tɪnsəl] s oropel m; (e.g., for a Christmas tree) lentejuelas de hojas de estaño

tin'smith' s hojalatero

tin soldier s soldadito de plomo

tint [tɪnt] s tinte m, matiz m ‖ tr teñir, matizar, colorar ligeramente

tin'type' s ferrotipo

tin'ware' s objetos de hojalata

ti•ny ['taɪni] adj (comp -nier; super -niest) diminuto, menudo, pequeñito

tip [tɪp] s extremo, extremidad; (of shoestring) herrete m; (of arrow) casquillo; (of umbrella) regatón m; (of tongue) punta; (of shoe) puntera; (of cigarette) embocadura; inclinación; golpecito; soplo, aviso confidencial; (fee) propina, feria ‖ v (pret & pp **tipped**; ger **tipping**) tr herretear; inclinar, ladear; volcar; golpear ligeramente; dar propina a; informar por debajo de cuerda; tocarse (el sombrero en señal de cortesía); **to tip in** (typ) encañonar (un pliego) ‖ intr

dar una propina o propinas; inclinarse, ladearse; volcarse

tip'cart' s volquete m

tip'-off' s (coll) informe dado por debajo de cuerda

tipped'-in' adj (bb) fuera de texto

tipple ['tɪpəl] intr beborrotear

tip'staff' s vara de justicia; alguacil m de vara

tip•sy ['tɪpsi] adj (comp -sier; super -siest) achispado

tip'toe' s punta del pie; **on tiptoe** de puntillas; alerta; furtivamente ‖ v (pret & pp **-toed**; ger **-toeing**) intr andar de puntillas

tirade ['taɪred] s diatriba, invectiva

tire [taɪr] s neumático, llanta de goma; (of metal) calce m, llanta ‖ tr cansar; aburrir; fastidiar ‖ intr (to be tiresome) cansar; (to get tired) cansarse; aburrirse, fastidiarse

tire chain s cadena de llanta, cadena antirresbaladiza

tired [taɪrd] adj cansado, rendido

tire gauge s indicador m de presión de inflado

tireless ['taɪrlɪs] adj incansable, infatigable

tire pressure s presión de inflado

tire pump s bomba para inflar neumáticos

tiresome ['taɪrsəm] adj cansado, fatigante, aburrido, pesado

tissue ['tɪʃu] s tejido fino; papel m de seda; (biol & fig) tejido

tissue paper s papel m de seda

titanium [tai'teni•əm] o [tɪ'teni•əm] s titanio

tithe [taɪð] s décimo, décima parte; (tax paid to church) diezmo ‖ tr dizmar

Titian ['tɪʃən] adj castaño rojizo ‖ s el Ticiano

title ['taɪtəl] s título; (sport) campeonato ‖ tr titular

title deed s título de propiedad

ti'tle•hold'er s titulado; (sport) campeón m

title page s portada, frontispicio

title rôle s (theat) papel m principal (el que corresponde al título de la abra)

titter ['tɪtər] s risita ahogada, risita disimulada ‖ intr reír a medias, reír con disimulo

titular ['tɪtʃələr] adj titular; nominal

tn. abbr ton

to [tu] o [tu] o [tə] adv hacia adelante; **to and fro** de una parte a otra, de aquí para allá; **to come to** volver en sí ‖ prep a, p.ej., **he is going to Madrid** va a Madrid; **they gave something to the beggar** dieron algo al pobre; **we are learning to dance** aprendemos a bailar; para, p.ej., **he is reading to himself** lee para sí; por, p.ej., **work to do** trabajo por hacer; hasta, p.ej., **to a certain extent** hasta cierto punto; en, p.ej., **from door to door** de puerta en puerta; con, p.ej., **kind to her** amable con ella; segun, p.ej., **to my way of thinking** según mi modo de pensar; menos, p.ej., **five minutes to ten** las diez menos cinco

toad [tod] s sapo

toad'stool' s agárico, seta; seta venenosa

to-and-fro ['tu•ənd'fro] adj alternativo, de vaivén

toast [tost] *s* tostadas; (*drink*) brindis *m;* **a piece of toast** una tostada ‖ *tr* tostar; brindar a o por ‖ *intr* tostarse; brindar

toaster ['tostər] *s* (*of bread*) tostador *m;* brindador *m*

toast'mas'ter *s* el que presenta a los oradores en un banquete, maestro de ceremonias

tobac•co [tə'bæko] *s* (*pl* **-cos**) tabaco

tobacco pouch *s* petaca

toboggan [tə'bagən] *s* tobogán *m* ‖ *intr* deslizarse en tobogán

tocsin ['taksın] *s* campana de alarma; campanada de alarma

today [tu'de] *adv & s* hoy

toddle ['tadəl] *s* pasitos vacilantes ‖ *intr* andar con pasitos vacilantes; hacer pinitos (*un niño o un enfermo*)

tod•dy ['tadi] *s* (*pl* **-dies**) ponche *m*

to-do [tə'du] *s* (coll) alharaca, alboroto

toe [to] *s* dedo del pie; (*of stocking*) punta ‖ *v* (*pret & pp* **toed;** *ger* **toeing**) *tr*—**to toe the line** o **the mark** ponerse a la raya; obrar como se debe

toe'nail' *s* uña del dedo del pie

tog [tag] *s* (coll) prenda de vestir

together [tu'gɛðər] *adv* juntamente; juntos; al mismo tiempo; sin interrupción; de acuerdo; **to bring together** reunir; confrontar; reconciliar; **to call together** convocar; **to go together** ir juntos; ser novios; hacerjuego; **to stick together** (coll) quedarse unidos, no abandonarse

toil [tɔıl] *s* afán *m*, fatiga; faena, obra laboriosa; **toils** red *f*, lazo ‖ *intr* atrafagar; moverse con fatiga

toilet ['tɔılıt] *s* (*dress or adornment*) tocado, atavío; (*dressing table*) tocador *m;* (*rest room*) retrete *m*, inodoro, excusado; wáter *m* (Bol, Col, Chile, Peru, Urug); servicio (Bol, CAm, Ecuad); taza (Bol, Col, Guat, Mex); poseta (Ven); **to make one's toilet** asearse, acicalarse

toilet articles *spl* artículos de tocador

toilet paper *s* papel higiénico

toilet powder *s* polvos de tocador

toilet soap *s* jabón *m* de olor, jabón de tocador

toilet tank *s* cisterna

toilet water *s* agua de tocador

token ['tokən] *s* señal *f*, prueba; prenda, recuerdo; (*used as money*) ficha, tanto; **by the same token** por el mismo motivo; **in token of** en señal de

tolerance ['talərəns] *s* tolerancia

tolerate ['talə,ret] *tr* tolerar

toll [tol] *s* (*of bells*) doble *m;* (*to pass along a road or over a bridge*) peaje *m;* (*to use a canal*) derechos de paso; (*to use a telephone*) tarifa; (*number of victims*) baja, mortalidad ‖ *tr* tocar a muerto (*una campana*); llamar con toque de difuntos ‖ *intr* doblar

toll bridge *s* puente *m* de peaje

toll call *s* (telp) llamada a larga distancia

toll'gate' *s* barrera de peaje

toma•to [tə'meto] o [tə'mato] *s* (*pl* **-toes**) (*plant*) tomatera o tomate *m;* (*fruit*) tomate

tomb [tum] *s* tumba, sepulcro

tomboy ['tam,bɔı] *s* moza retozona, muchacha traviesa

tomb'stone' *s* piedra o lápida sepulcral

tomcat ['tam,kæt] *s* gato macho

tome [tom] *s* tomo; libro grueso

tomorrow [tu'mɔro] *adv* mañana ‖ *s* mañana *m;* **the day after tomorrow** pasado mañana

tom-tom ['tam,tam] *s* tantán *m*

ton [tʌn] *s* tonelada; **tons** (coll) montones *mpl*

tone [ton] *s* tono ‖ *tr* entonar ‖ *intr* armonizar; **to tone down** moderarse; **to tone up** reforzarse

tone poem *s* poema sinfónico

tongs [tɔŋz] o [taŋz] *spl* tenazas; (*e.g., for sugar*) tenacillas

tongue [tʌŋ] *s* (anat) lengua; (*of a wagon*) vara, lanza; (*of a belt buckle*) tarabilla; (*of shoe*) lengua, lengüeta; (*language*) lengua, idioma *m;* **to hold one's tongue** morderse la lengua

tongue twister ['twıstər] *s* trabalenguas *m*

tonic ['tanık] *adj & s* tónico

tonic accent *s* acento prosódico

tonight [tu'naıt] *adv & s* esta noche

tonnage ['tʌnıdʒ] *s* tonelaje *m*

tonsil ['tansəl] *s* tonsila, amígdala

tonsillitis [,tansı'laıtıs] *s* tonsilitis *f*, amigdalitis *f*

ton•y ['toni] *adj* (*comp* **-ier;** *super* **-iest**) (slang) elegante, aristocrático

too [tu] *adv* (*also*) también; (*more than enough*) demasiado; **too bad!** ¡qué lástima!; **too many** demasiados; **too much** demasiado

tool [tul] *s* herramienta; (*person used for one's own ends*) instrumento; **tools** implementos *mpl* ‖ *tr* trabajar con herramienta; (bb) filetear, estampar

tool bag *s* bolsa de herramientas

toolmak'er *s* tallador *m* de herramientas, herrero de herramientas

toot [tut] *s* (*of horn*) toque *m;* (*of klaxon*) bocinazo; (*of locomotive*) pitazo; (coll) parranda ‖ *tr* sonar; **to toot one's own horn** cantar sus propias alabanzas ‖ *intr* sonar

tooth [tuθ] *s* (*pl* **teeth** [tiθ]) diente *m*

tooth'ache' *s* dolor *m* de muelas

tooth'brush' *s* cepillo de dientes

toothless ['tuθlıs] *adj* desdentado

tooth'paste' *s* pasta dentífrica, crema dental, crema dentífrica

tooth'pick' *s* limpiadientes *m*, mondadientes *m*, palillo

tooth powder *s* polvo dentífrico

top [tap] *s* (*of a mountain, tree, etc.*) cima; (*of a mountain; high point*) cumbre *f;* (*of a tree*) copa; (*of a barrel, box, etc.*) tapa; (*of a page*) principio; (*of a table*) tablero; (*of a wall*) coronamiento; (*of a bathing suit*) camiseta; (*of a carriage or auto*) capota; (*toy*) peón *m*, peonza; (naut) cofa; **at the top of** en lo alto de; (*e.g., one's class*) a la cabeza de; **at the top of one's voice** a voz en grito; **from top to bottom** de arriba abajo; de alto a bajo; completamente; **on top of** en lo alto de; encima de; **the tops** (slang) la flor de la canela; **to sleep like a top** dormir como un leño || *v* (*pret & pp* **topped;** *ger* **topping**) *tr* coronar, rematar; cubrir; aventajar, superar; descopar (*p.ej.,* *un árbol*)

topaz [ˈtopæz] *s* topacio

top billing *s* cabecera de cartel

top′coat′ *s* sobretodo; abrigo de entretiempo

toper [ˈtopər] *s* borrachín *m*

top hat *s* chistera, sombrero de copa

top′-heav′y *adj* más pesado arriba que abajo

topic [ˈtapɪk] *s* asunto, materia, tema *m*

top′knot′ *s* moño

top′mast′ *s* (naut) mastelero

top′most *adj* (el) más alto

topogra•phy [təˈpɑɡrəfi] *s* (*pl* **-phies**) topografía

topple [ˈtapəl] *tr* derribar, volcar || *intr* derribarse, volcarse; caerse, venirse abajo

top priority *s* máxima prioridad

topsail [ˈtapsəl] o [ˈtap,sel] *s* (naut) gavia

top secret *adj* de mayor confidencia

top′soil′ *s* capa superficial del suelo

topsy-turvy [ˈtapsiˈtʌrvi] *adj* desbarajustado || *adv* en cuadro, patas arriba || *s* desbarajuste *m*

torch [tɔrtʃ] *s* antorcha; lámpara de bolsillo: **to carry the torch for** (slang) amar desesperadamente

torch′bear′er *s* hachero; (fig) adicto, partidario

torch′light′ *s* luz *f* de antorcha

torch song *s* canción lenta y melancólica de amor no correspondido

torment [ˈtɔrmɛnt] *s* tormento; murga || [tɔrˈmɛnt] *tr* atormentar

torna•do [tɔrˈnedo] *s* (*pl* **-does** p **-dos**) tornado, tromba terrestre

torpe•do [tɔrˈpido] *s* (*pl* **-does**) torpedo || *tr* torpedear

torrent [ˈtɔrənt] *s* torrente *m*

torrid [ˈtɔrɪd] *adj* tórrido

tor•so [ˈtɔrso] *s* (*pl* **-sos**) torso

tortoise [ˈtɔrtəs] *s* tortuga

tortoise shell *s* carey *m*

torture [ˈtɔrtʃər] *s* tortura || *tr* torturar, atormentar

toss [tɑs] *s* echada; alcance *m* de una echada || *tr* arrojar, echar; lanzar al aire; agitar, menear; levantar airosamente (*la cabeza*); lanzar (*p.ej., un comentario*); echar a cara o cruz; **to toss off** hacer muy rápidamente; tragar de un golpe || *intr* agitarse, menearse; **to toss and turn** (*in bed*) revolverse, dar vueltas

toss′-up′ *s* cara o cruz; probabilidad igual

tot [tɑt] *s* párvulo, peque *m*, chiquitín *m*

to•tal [ˈtotəl] *adj* total; (*e.g., loss*) completo || *s* total *m* || *v* (*pret & pp* **-taled** o **-talled;** *ger* **-taling** o **-talling**) *tr* ascender a, sumar

totter [ˈtatər] *s* tambaleo || *intr* tambalear; estar para desplomarse

touch [tʌtʃ] *s* (*act*) toque *m;* (*sense*) tacto, tiento; (*of piano, pianist, typewriter, typist*) tacto; (*of an illness*) ramo, ataque

ligero; pizca, poquito; **to get in touch with** ponerse en comunicación o contacto con; **to lose one's touch** perder el tiento || *tr* tocar; conmover, enternecer; probar (*vino, licor*); (*for a loan*) (slang) pedir prestado a, dar un sablazo a; **to touch up** retocar || *intr* tocar; **to touch at** tocar en (*un puerto*)

touching [ˈtʌtʃɪŋ] *adj* conmovedor, enternecedor || *prep* tocante a

touch typewriting *s* escritura al tacto

touch•y [ˈtʌtʃi] *adj* (*comp* **-ier;** *super* **-iest**) quisquilloso, enojadizo

tough [tʌf] *adj* correoso; tenaz; difícil; gamberro; (*e.g., luck*) malo || *s* gamberro, guapetón *m;* (coll) gorila

toughen [ˈtʌfən] *tr* hacer correoso; hacer tenaz; dificultar || *intr* ponerse correoso; hacerse tenaz; hacerse difícil

toupee [tuˈpe] *s* peluquín *m*

tour [tʊr] *s* jira, paseo, vuelta; viaje largo; **on tour** de jira, de viaje || *tr* viajar por, recorrer || *intr* viajar por distracción o diversión

touring car [ˈtʊrɪŋ] *s* coche *m* de turismo

tourist [ˈtʊrɪst] *adj* turístico || *s* turista *mf*

tourist guide *s* guía turística

tournament [ˈtʊrnəmənt] o [ˈtʌrnəmənt] *s* torneo

tourney [ˈtʊrni] o [ˈtʌrni] *s* torneo || *intr* tornear

tourniquet [ˈtʊrnɪ,kɛt] *s* torniquete *m*

tousle [ˈtaʊzəl] *tr* despeinar, enmarañar

tow [to] *s* remolque *m; (e.g., of hemp)* estopa; **to take in tow** dar remolque a; (fig) encargarse de || *tr* remolcar

towage [ˈtoɪdʒ] *s* remolque *m;* derechos de remolque

toward(s) [tord(z)] o [təˈwɔrd(z)] *prep* (*in the direction of*) hacia; (*with regard to*) para con; (*a certain hour*) cerca de, a eso de

tow′boat′ *s* remolcador *m*

tow•el [ˈtaʊəl] *s* toalla || *v* (*pret & pp* **-eled** o **-elled;** *ger* **-eling** o **-elling**) *tr* secar con toalla

towel rack *s* toallero

tower [ˈtaʊər] *s* torre *f* || *intr* encumbrarse, empinarse

towering [ˈtaʊərɪŋ] *adj* encumbrado; sobresaliente; excesivo

towing service [ˈtoɪŋ] *s* servicio de grúa

tow′line′ *s* cable *m* de remolque, sirga

town [taʊn] *s* población, pueblo, villa; **in town** a la ciudad, en la ciudad

town clerk *s* escribano municipal

town council *s* concejo municipal

town crier *s* pregonero público

town hall *s* ayuntamiento, casa de ayuntamiento

towns′ folk′ *spl* vecinos del pueblo

township [ˈtaʊnʃɪp] *s* sexmo; terreno público de seis millas en cuadro

towns•man [ˈtaʊnzmən] *s* (*pl* **-men** [mən]) ciudadano, vecino; conciudadano, paisano

towns′peo′ple *spl* vecinos del pueblo

town talk *s* comidilla o hablillas del pueblo

tow′path′ *s* camino de sirga

tow plane s avión m de remolque
tow′rope′ s cuerda de remolque
tow truck s camión-grúa m
toxic [ˈtɑksɪk] adj & s tóxico
toxic shock syndrome s síndrome m de choque tóxico
toy [tɔɪ] adj de juguete ‖ s juguete m; (trifle) bagatela; (trinket) dije m, bujería ‖ intr jugar; divertirse; **to toy with** jugar con (los sentimientos de una persona); acariciar (una idea)
toy bank s alcancía hucha
toy soldier s soldado de juguete
trace [tres] s huella, rastro; indicio, vestigio; (of harness) tirante m; pizca ‖ tr rastrear; trazar (p.ej., una curva; los rasgos de una persona o cosa); averiguar el paradero de; remontar al origen de
trace element s elemento rastro
trache•a [ˈtrekɪ•ə] s (pl -ae [,i]) tráquea
track [træk] s (of foot) huella; (of a wheel) rodada, carril m; (of a boat) estela; (of railroad) vía; (of an airplane, a hurricane) trayectoria; (of a tractor) llanta de oruga; camino, senda; (course followed by a boat) derrota; (of ideas, events, etc.) sucesión; (sport) pista; **to keep track of** no perder de vista; no olvidar; **to lose track of** perder de vista; olvidar; **to make tracks** dejar pisadas; irse muy de prisa; **off the track** (also fig) desviado ‖ tr rastrear; seguir la huella o la pista de; dejar pisadas en, manchar pisando; **to track down** seguir y capturar; averiguar el origen de
tracking [ˈtrækɪŋ] s seguimiento (de vehículos espaciales)
tracing station s estación de seguimiento
trackless trolley [ˈtræklɪs] s filobús m, trolebús m
track meet s concurso de carreras y saltos
track′walk′er s guardavía m
tract [trækt] s espacio, tracto; folleto; (anat) canal m, sistema m
traction [ˈtrækʃən] s tracción
traction company s empresa de tranvías
tractor [ˈtræktər] s tractor m
trade [tred] s comercio; negocio, trato; trueque m, canje m; (calling, job) oficio; clientela, parroquia; (e.g., in slaves) trata ‖ tr cambiar, trocar; **to trade in** dar como parte del pago; **to trade off** cambalachear; ‖ intr comerciar; comprar; **to trade in** comerciar en; **to trade on** aprovecharse de
trade′mark′ s marca de fábrica, marca registrada
trade name s nombre m comercial, razón f social; nombre de fábrica
trader [ˈtredər] s traficante mf
trade school s escuela de artes y oficios
trades•man [ˈtredzmən] s (pl -men [mən]) tendero; comerciante m; (Brit) artesano
trades union o **trade union** s sindicato, gremio de obreros
trade unionist s sindicalista mf
trade winds spl vientos alisios
trading post [ˈtredɪŋ] s factoría; (in stock exchange) puesto de compraventa

trading stamp s sello de premio, sello de descuento
tradition [trəˈdɪʃən] s tradición
traduce [trəˈdjus] tr calumniar
traf•fic [ˈtræfɪk] s tráfico, comercio; tráfico, circulación; (e.g., in slaves) trata ‖ v (pret & pp -ficked; ger -ficking) intr traficar
traffic circle s glorieta de tráfico
traffic court s juzgado de tráfico
traffic jam s embotellamiento, tapón m de tráfico
traffic light s luz f de tráfico, semáforo
traffic sign o **signal** s señal f de tráfico, seña de tráfico
traffic ticket s aviso de multa
tragedian [trəˈdʒɪdɪ•ən] s trágico
trage•dy [ˈtrædʒɪdi] s (pl -dies) tragedia
tragic [ˈtrædʒɪk] adj trágico
trail [trel] s rastro, huella, pista; (path through rough country) trocha, senda, vereda; (of a gown) cola; (of smoke, a rocket, etc.) estela ‖ tr arrastrar; seguir la pista de; andar detrás de; llevar (p.ej., barro) con los pies ‖ intr arrastrar; rezagarse; arrastrarse, trepar (una planta); **to trail off** desaparecer poco a poco
trailer [ˈtrelər] s remolque m, cochehabitación m, casa rodante; planta rastrera
trailing arbutus [ˈtrelɪŋ] s epigea rastrera
train [tren] s (of railway cars; of waves) tren m; (of thought) hilo ‖ tr adiestrar; guiar (las plantas); (sport) entrenar ‖ intr adiestrarse; (sport) entrenarse
trained nurse s enfermera graduada
trainer [ˈtrenər] s (sport) entrenador m
training [ˈtrenɪŋ] s adiestramiento; instrucción; (sport) entrenamiento
training school s escuela práctica; reformatorio
training ship s buque m escuela
trait [tret] s característica, rasgo
traitor [ˈtretər] s traidor m
traitress [ˈtretrɪs] s traidora
trajecto•ry [trəˈdʒɛktəri] s (pl -ries) trayectoria
tramp [træmp] s vagabundo; marcha pesada, ruido de pisadas ‖ tr pisar con fuerza; recorrer a pie ‖ intr andar a pie; vagabundear
trample [ˈtræmpəl] tr pisotear ‖ intr—**to trample on** o **upon** pisotear
tramp steamer s vapor volandero
trance [træns] o [trɑns] s arrobamiento, rapto; estado hipnótico
tranquil [ˈtræŋkwɪl] adj tranquilo
tranquilize [ˈtræŋkwɪ,laɪz] tr & intr tranquilizar
tranquilizer [ˈtræŋkwɪ,laɪzər] s tranquilizante m
tranquillity [træŋˈkwɪlɪti] s tranquilidad
transact [trænˈzækt] o [trænsˈækt] tr tramitar; llevar a cabo
transaction [trænˈzækʃən] o [trænsˈækʃən] s tramitación, transacción
transatlantic [,trænsətˈlæntɪk] adj & s transatlántico

to
tr

transcend [træn'sɛnd] *tr* exceder, superar ‖ *intr* sobresalir

transcribe [træn'skraɪb] *tr* transcribir

transcript ['trænskrɪpt] *s* trasunto, traslado; (educ) hoja de estudios, certificado de estudios

transcription [træn'skrɪpʃən] *s* transcripción

transept ['trænsɛpt] *s* crucero, transepto

trans•fer ['trænsfər] *s* traslado; transbordo; contraseña o billete *m* de transferencia ‖ [træns'fʌr] o ['trænsfər] *s* (*pret & pp* **-ferred**; *ger* **-ferring**) *tr* trasladar, transferir; transbordar ‖ *intr* cambiar de tren, tranvía, etc.

transfix [træns'fɪks] *tr* espetar, traspasar; dejar atónito

transform [træns'fɔrm] *tr* transformar ‖ *intr* transformarse

transformer [træns'fɔrmər] *s* transformador *m*

transfusion [træns'fjuʃən] *s* transfusión; (med) transfusión de la sangre

transgress [træns'grɛs] *tr* transgredir, violar; exceder, traspasar (*p.ej., los límites de la prudencia*) ‖ *intr* pecar, prevaricar

transgression [træns'grɛʃən] *s* transgresión; pecado, prevaricación

transient ['trænʃənt] *adj* pasajero, transitorio; de tránsito ‖ *s* transeúnte *mf*

transistor [træn'zɪstər] *s* transistor *m*

transistorize [træn'zɪstə,raɪz] *tr* transistorizar

transit ['trænsɪt] o ['trænzɪt] *s* tránsito

transitive ['trænsɪtɪv] *adj* transitivo ‖ *s* verbo transitivo

transitory ['trænsɪ,tori] *adj* transitorio

translate [træns'let] o ['trænslet] *tr* (*from one language to another*) traducir; (*from one place to another*) trasladar ‖ *intr* traducirse

translation [træns'leʃən] *s* traducción; traslación

translator [træns'letər] *s* traductor *m*

transliterate [træns'lɪtə,ret] *tr* transcribir

translucent [træns'lusənt] *adj* translúcido

transmission [træns'mɪʃən] *s* transmisión; (aut) cambio de marchas, cambio de velocidades

transmis'sion-gear' box *s* caja de cambio de marchas, caja de velocidades

trans•mit [træns'mɪt] *v* (*pret & pp* **-mitted**; *ger* **-mitting**) *tr & intr* transmitir

transmitter [træns'mɪtər] *s* transmisor *m*

transmitting set *s* aparato transmisor

transmitting station *s* estacion transmisora, emisora

transmute [træns'mjut] *tr & intr* transmutar

transom [trænsəm] *s* (*crosspiece*) travesaño; (*window over door*) montante *m*; (*of ship*) yugo de popa

transparen•cy [træns'pɛrənsi] *s* (*pl* **-cies**) transparencia

transparent [træns'pɛrənt] *adj* transparente

transpire [træns'paɪr] *intr* transpirar; (*to become known, leak out*) transpirar; (coll) acontecer, tener lugar

transplant ['træns,plænt] *s* transplante; injerto ‖ *tr* transplantar ‖ *intr* transplantarse

transport ['trænsport] *s* transporte *m;* (aer & naut) transporte *m;* rapto, éxtasis *m*, transporte *m* ‖ [træns'port] *tr* transportar

transportation [,trænspor'teʃən] *s* transporte *m;* (U.S.A.) pasaje *m*, billete *m* de viaje

transport worker *s* transportista *mf*

transpose [træns'poz] *tr* transponer; (mus) transportar

trans•ship [træns'ʃɪp] *v* (*pret & pp* **-shipped**; *ger* **-shipping**) *tr* transbordar

transshipment [træns'ʃɪpmənt] *s* transbordo

transvestism [træns'vɛstɪzəm] *s* transvestismo

transvestite [træns'vɛstaɪt] *adj & s* transvestido

trap [træp] *s* trampa; (*double-curved pipe*) sifón *m;* coche ligero de dos ruedas; (sport) lanzaplatos *m* ‖ *v* (*pret & pp* **trapped**; *ger* **trapping**) *tr* entrampar; atrapar (*a un ladrón*)

trap door *s* escotillón *m*, trampa; (theat) escotillón *m*, pescante *m*

trapeze [trə'piz] *s* trapecio

trapezold ['træpɪ,zɔɪd] *s* trapecio

trapper ['træpər] *s* cazador *m* de alforja

trappings ['træpɪŋz] *spl* (*adornments*) adornos, altavíos; (*of a horse's harness*) jaeces *mpl*

trap'shoot'ing *s* tiro al vuelo

trash [træʃ] *s* broza, basura, desecho; (*junk*) cachivaches *mpl;* (*nonsense*) disparates *mpl;* (*worthless people*) gentuza

trash can *s* basurero

trash pile *s* basural *m* (SAm)

travail ['trævel] o [trə'vel] *s* afán *m*, labor *f*, pena; dolores *mpl* del parto

trav•el ['trævəl] *s* viaje *m;* el viajar; (mach) recorrido ‖ *v* (*pret & pp* **-eled** o **-elled**; *ger* **-eling** o **-elling**) *tr* viajar por; recorrer ‖ *intr* vaijar; andar, recorrer

travel bureau *s* oficina de turismo

traveler ['trævələr] *s* viajero; (*salesman*) viajante *m*

traveler's check *s* cheque *m* de viajeros

traveling expenses *spl* gastos de viaje

traveling salesman *s* viajante *m*, agente viajero

traverse ['trævərs] o [trə'vʌrs] *tr* atravesar; recorrer, pasar por

traves•ty ['trævɪsti] *s* (*pl* **-ties**) parodia ‖ *v* (*pret & pp* **-tied**) *tr* parodiar

trawl [trɔl] *s* red barredera, espinel *m*, palangre *m* ‖ *tr & intr* pescar a la rastra

tray [tre] *s* bandeja; (chem & phot) cubeta

treacherous ['trɛtʃərəs] *adj* traicionero, traidor; incierto, poco seguro

treacher•y ['trɛtʃəri] *s* (*pl* **-ies**) traición alevosía

tread [trɛd] *s* (*stepping*) pisada; (*of stairs*) grada, huella, peldaño; (*of stilts*) horquilla; (*of a tire*) banda de rodamiento; (*of shoe*) suela; (*of an egg*) meaje, galladura ‖ *v* (*pret* **trod** [trɑd]; *pp* **trodden** ['trɑdən] o **trod**) *tr* pisar, pisotear; abrumar, agobiar ‖ *intr* andar, caminar

treadle ['trɛdəl] *s* pedal *m*

treadless ['trɛdlɪs] *adj* (*tire*) desgastado

tread′mill′ *s* rueda de andar; (*futile drudgery*) noria

treas. *abbr* **treasurer, treasury**

treason [′trizən] *s* traición

treasonable [′trizənəbəl] *adj* traicionero, traidor

treasure [′trɛʒər] *s* tesoro ‖ *tr* atesorar

treasurer [′trɛʒərər] *s* tesorero

treasur•y [′trɛʒəri] *s* (*pl* **-ies**) tesorería; tesoro

treat [trit] *s* convite *m;* (*to a drink*) convidada; (*something providing particular enjoyment*) regalo, deleite *m* ‖ *tr* tratar; convidar, regalar; curar (*a un enfermo*) ‖ *intr* tratar; convidar, regalar; **to treat of** tratar de

treatise [′tritɪs] *s* tratado

treatment [′tritmənt] *s* tratamiento

trea•ty [′triti] *s* (*pl* **-ties**) tratado

treble [′trɛbəl] *adj* (*threefold*) tresdoble, triple; sobreagudo; (*mus*) atiplado; (*mus*) de tiple ‖ *s* (*person*) tiple *mf;* (*voice*) tiple ‖ *tr* triplicar ‖ *intr* triplicarse

tree [tri] *s* árbol *m*

tree farm *s* monte *m* tallar

treeless [′trilɪs] *adj* pelado, sin árboles

tree′top′ *s* copa, cima de árbol

trellis [′trɛlɪs] *s* enrejado, espaldera; emparrado

tremble [′trɛmbəl] *s* temblor *m*, estremecimiento ‖ *intr* temblar, estremecerse

tremendous [trɪ′mɛndəs] *adj* tremendo

tremor [′trɛmər] o [′trimər] *s* temblor *m*

trench [trɛntʃ] *s* foso, zanja; (*for irrigation*) acequia; (*mil*) trinchera

trenchant [′trɛntʃənt] *adj* mordaz, punzante; enérgico, bien definido

trench coat *s* trinchera

trench mortar *s* (*mil*) lanzabombas *m*

trench′-plow′ *tr* (*agr*) asurcar

trend [trɛnd] *s* curso, dirección, tendencia ‖ *intr* dirigirse, tender

trendy [′trɛndi] *adj* (*coll*) de (última) moda

trespass [′trɛspəs] *s* entrada sin derecho; infracción, violación; culpa, pecado ‖ *intr* entrar sin derecho; pecar; **no trespassing** prohibida la entrada; **to trespass against** pecar contra; **to trepass on** entrar sin derecho en; infringir, violar; abusar de (*p.ej., la paciencia de uno*)

tress [trɛs] *s* (*braid of hair*) trenza; (*curl*) bucle *m*, rizo

trestle [′trɛsəl] *s* caballete *m;* puente *m* o viaducto de caballetes

trial [′traɪəl] *s* ensayo, prueba; aflicción, desgracia; (*law*) juicio, proceso, vista; **on trial** a prueba; (*law*) en juicio; **to bring to trial** encausar

trial and error *s* método de tanteos

trial balloon *s* globo sonda; **to send up a trial balloon** (*fig*) lanzar un globo sonda

trial by jury *s* juicio por jurado

trial jury *s* jurado procesal

trial order *s* (*com*) pedido de ensayo

trial run *s* experimento piloto

triangle [′traɪˌæŋgəl] *s* triángulo

tribe [traɪb] *s* tribu *f*

tribunal [trɪ′bjunəl] o [traɪ′bjunəl] *s* tribunal *m*

tribune [′trɪbjun] *s* tribuna

tributar•y [′trɪbjəˌtɛri] *adj* tributario ‖ *s* (*pl* **-ies**) tributario

tribute [′trɪbjut] *s* tributo

trice [traɪs] *s* momento, instante *m;* **in a trice** en un periquete

trick [trɪk] *s* ardid *m*, artimaña; leva (CAm, Col); (*knack*) maña; (*feat*) suerte *f;* (*prank*) travesura, burla, chasco; tanda, turno; ilusión; (*feat with cards*) truco; (*cards in one round*) baza; (*coll*) chiquita; **to be up to one's old tricks** hacer de las suyas; **to play a dirty trick on** hacer una mala jugada a ‖ *tr* trampear; burlar, engañar; ataviar

tricker•y [′trɪkəri] *s* (*pl* **-ies**) trampería, malas mañas

trickle [′trɪkəl] *s* chorro delgado, goteo ‖ *intr* escurrir, gotear; pasar gradual e irregularmente

trickster [′trɪkstər] *s* tramposo, embustero, embaucador *m*, embaucadora

trick•y [′trɪki] *adj* (*comp* **-ier;** *super* **-iest**) tramposo, engañoso, difícil; (*animal*) vicioso; (*ticklish to deal with*) delicado

tricorn [′traɪkɔrn] *adj & s* tricornio

tried [traɪd] *adj* fiel, probado, seguro

trifle [′traɪfəl] *s* bagatela, friolera, fruslería, basurita, chiquitura; (*trinket*) bagatela, baratija ‖ *tr*—**to trifle away** malgastar ‖ *intr* estar ocioso, holgar; **to trifle with** manosear; jugar con, burlarse de

trifling [′traɪflɪŋ] *adj* frívolo, fútil, ligero; insignificante, trivial

trifocal [traɪ′fokəl] *adj* trifocal ‖ *s* lente *f* trifocal; **trifocals** anteojos trifocales

trig. *abbr* **trigonometric, trigonometry**

trigger [′trɪgər] *s* (*e.g., of a gun*) disparador *m*, gatillo; (*of any device*) disparador *m* ‖ *tr* poner en movimiento, provocar

trigonometry [ˌtrɪgə′nɑmɪtri] *s* trigonometría

trill [trɪl] *s* trinado, trino; (*made with voice, esp. of birds*) gorjeo; (*phonet*) vibración ‖ *tr* decir o cantar gorjeando; pronunciar con vibración ‖ *intr* trinar; gorjear

trillion [′trɪljən] *s* (U.S.A.) billón *m;* (Brit) trillón *m*

trilo•gy [′trɪlədʒi] *s* (*pl* **-gies**) trilogía

trim [trɪm] *adj* (*comp* **trimmer;** *super* **trimmest**) acicalado, compuesto, elegante ‖ *s* condición, estado; buena condición; adorno, atavío; traje *m*, vestido; (*of sails*) orientación ‖ *v* (*pret & pp* **trimmed;** *ger* **trimming**) *tr* ajustar, adaptar; arreglar, componer; adornar, decorar; decorar, enguirnaldar (*el árbol de Navidad*); recortar; cortar ligeramente (*el pelo*); despabilar (*una lámpara o vela*); mondar, podar (*árboles, plantas*); acepillar, desbastar; (*naut*) orientar (*las velas*); (*coll*) derrotar, vencer; (*coll*) regañar

trimming [′trɪmɪŋ] *s* adorno, guarnición; franja, orla; (*coll*) paliza, zurra; (*coll*) derrota; **trimmings** accesorios, arrequives *mpl;* recortes *mpl*

tr
tr

trini•ty [ˈtrɪnɪti] s (pl -ties) (group of three) trinca ‖ **Trinity** s Trinidad

trinket [ˈtrɪŋkɪt] s (small ornament) dije m; (trivial object) baratija, bujería, chuchería

tri•o [ˈtri•o] s (pl -os) (group of three) terna, trío; (mus) trío

trip [trɪp] s viaje m; jira, recorrido; (stumble) tropiezo; (act of causing a person to stumble) traspié m, zancadilla; (blunder) desliz m; (drugs) viaje ‖ v (pret & pp **tripped**; ger **tripping**) tr trompicar, echar la zancadilla a; detener, estorbar; inclinar; coger en falta; coger en una mentira ‖ intr ir conpaso rápido y ligero; brincar, saltar, correr; tropezar; **to trip over** tropezar con, contra o en

tripe [traɪp] s callos, mondongo; (slang) disparate m, barbaridad

trip′ham′mer s martillo pilón

triphthong [ˈtrɪfθɔŋ] s triptongo

triple [ˈtrɪpəl] adj & s triple m ‖ tr triplicar ‖ intr triplicarse

triplet [ˈtrɪplɪt] s (offspring) trillizo; (stanza of three lines) terceto; (mus) terceto, tresillo

triplicate [ˈtrɪplɪkɪt] adj & s triplicado; **in triplicate** por triplicado ‖ [ˈtrɪplɪˌket] tr triplicar

tripod [ˈtraɪpɑd] m trípode m

triptych [ˈtrɪptɪk] s tríptico

trite [traɪt] adj gastado, trillado, trivial

triumph [ˈtraɪ•əmf] s triunfo ‖ intr triunfar; **to triumph over** triunfar de

triumphal arch [traɪˈʌmfəl] s arco triunfal

triumphant [traɪˈʌmfənt] adj triunfante

trivia [ˈtrɪvi•ə] spl bagatelas, trivialidades

trivial [ˈtrɪvi•əl] adj trivial, insignificante

triviali•ty [ˌtrɪviˈælɪti] s (pl -ties) trivialidad

Trojan [ˈtrodʒən] adj & s troyano

Trojan horse s caballo de Troya

Trojan War s guerra de Troya

troll [trol] tr & intr pescar a la cacea

trolley [ˈtrɑli] s polea o arco de trole; tranvía m

trolley bus s trolebús m

trolley car s coche m de tranvía

trolley pole s trole m

trolling [ˈtrolɪŋ] s cacea, pesca a la cacea

trollop [ˈtrɑləp] s (slovenly woman) cochina; mujer f de mala vida

trombone [ˈtrɑmbon] s trombón m

troop [trup] s tropa; (of actors) compañía; (of cavalry) escuadrón m ‖ intr agruparse; marcharse en tropel

trooper [ˈtrupər] s soldado de caballería; corcel m de guerra; policía m de a caballo; (ship) transporte m; **to swear like a trooper** jurar como un carretero

tro•phy [ˈtrofi] s (pl -phies) trofeo; (any memento) recuerdo

tropic [ˈtrɑpɪk] adj tropical ‖ s trópico

tropical [ˈtrɑpɪkəl] adj tropical

tropics o **Tropics** [ˈtrɑpɪks] spl zona tropical

troposphere [ˈtrɑpəˌsfɪr] s troposfera

trot [trɑt] s trote m ‖ v (pret & pp **trotted**; ger **trotting**) tr hacer trotar; **to trot out** (slang) sacar para mostrar ‖ intr trotar

troth [trɔθ] o [troθ] s fe f; verdad; esponsales mpl; **in troth** en verdad; **to plight one's troth** prometer fidelidad; dar palabra de casamiento

troubadour [ˈtrubəˌdor] o [ˈtrubəˌdʊr] adj trovadoresco ‖ s trovador m

trouble [ˈtrʌbəl] s apuro, dificultad; confusión, estorbo; conflicto; inquietud, preocupación; pena, molestia; mal m, enfermedad; murga; (of a mechanical nature) avería, falla, pana; **not to be worth the trouble** no valer la pena; **to pour out one's troubles** jeremiquear; **that's the trouble** ahí está el busilis; **the trouble is that . . .** lo malo es que . . .; **to be in trouble** estar en un aprieto; **to be looking for trouble** buscar tres pies al gato; **to get into trouble** enredarse, meterse en líos; **to take the trouble to** tomarse la molestia de ‖ tr apurar; confundir, estorbar; inquietar, preocupar; apenar, afligir; incomodar, molestar; dar que hacer a; **to be troubled with** padecer de; **to trouble oneself** molestarse ‖ intr apurarse; inquietarse, preocuparse; molestarse, darse molestia; **to trouble to** molestarse en

trouble lamp s lámpara de socorro

trou′ble•mak′er s perturbador m, alborotador m

troubleshooter [ˈtrʌbəlˌʃutər] s localizador m de averías; (in disputes) componedor m

troubleshooting [ˈtrʌbəlˌʃutɪŋ] s localización de averías; (of disputes) composición, arbitraje m

troublesome [ˈtrʌbəlsəm] adj molesto, pesado, gravoso; impertinente; perturbador

trouble spot s lugar m de conflicto

trough [trɔf] o [traf] s (e.g., to knead bread) artesa; (for water for animals) abrevadero; (for feeding animals) comedero; (under eaves) canal f; (between two waves) seno

troupe [trup] s compañía de actores o de circo

trousers [ˈtrauzərz] spl pantalones mpl

trous•seau [truˈso] o [ˈtruso] s (pl -seaux o -seaus) ajuar m de novia, equipo de novia

trout [traut] s trucha

trouvère [truˈvɛr] s trovero

trowel [ˈtrau•əl] s paleta, llana

Troy [trɔɪ] s Troya

truant [ˈtru•ənt] s novillero; **to play truant** hacer novillos

truce [trus] s tregua

truck [trʌk] s carro; vegoneta; camión m; autocamión m; (to be moved by hand) carretilla; (of locomotive or car) carretón m; hortalizas para el mercado; (coll) desperdicios; (coll) negocio, relaciones ‖ tr acarrear

truck driver s camionista mf; materialista m (Mex)

truck garden s huerto de hortalizas (para el mercado)

truculent [ˈtrʌkjələnt] o [ˈtrukjələnt] adj truculento

trudge [trʌdʒ] intr caminar, ir a pie; **to trudge along** marchar con pena y trabajo

true [tru] *adj* verdadero; exacto; constante; uniforme; fiel, leal; alineado; a plomo, a nivel; **to come true** hacerse realidad; **true to life** conforme a la realidad

true copy *s* copia fiel

true-hearted ['tru,hɑrtɪd] *adj* fiel, leal, sincero

true'love' *s* fiel amante *mf;* (bot) hierba de París

truelove knot *s* lazo de amor

truffle ['trʌfəl] o ['trufəl] *s* trufa

truism ['tru•ɪzəm] *s* perogrullada, verdad trillada

truly ['truli] *adv* verdaderamente; efectivamente; fielmente; **truly yours** de Vd. atto. y S.S., su seguro servidor

trump [trʌmp] *s* triunfo; (coll) buen chico, buena chica; **no trump** sin triunfo ‖ *tr* matar con un triunfo; aventajar, sobrepujar; **to trump up** forjar, inventar (*para engañar*) ‖ *intr* triunfar

trumpet ['trʌmpɪt] *s* trompeta; trompeta acústica; **to blow one's own trumpet** cantar sus propias alabanzas ‖ *tr* pregonar a son de trompeta ‖ *intr* trompetear

truncheon ['trʌntʃən] *s* cachiporra; bastón *m* de mando

trunk [trʌŋk] *s* (*of living body, tree, family, railroad*) tronco; (*chest for clothes, etc.*) baúl *m;* (*of an automobile*) portaequipaje *m;* (*of elephant*) trompa; **trunks** taparrabo

trunk hose *spl* trusas

truss [trʌs] *s* (*framework*) armadura; haz *m*, paquete *m*, lío; (*for holding back a hernia*) braguero ‖ *tr* armar; empaquetar; espetar; apretar (*barriles*)

trust [trʌst] *s* confianza; esperanza; cargo, custodia; depósito; crédito; obligación; (econ) trust *m*, cartel *m;* (law) fideicomiso; **in trust** en confianza; en depósito; **on trust** a crédito, al fiado ‖ *tr* confiar; confiar en; vender a crédito a ‖ *intr* confiar; fiar; **to trust in** fiarse a o de

trust company *s* banco fideicomisario, banco de depósitos

trustee [trʌs'ti] *s* administrador *m*, comisario; regente (universitario); (*of an estate*) fideicomisario

trusteeship [trʌs'tiʃɪp] *s* cargo de administrador, fideicomisario; (*of the UN*) fideicomiso

trustful ['trʌstfəl] *adj* confiado

trust'wor'thy *adj* confiable, fidedigno

trust•y ['trʌsti] *adj* (comp **-ier;** super **-iest**) honrado, fidedigno ‖ *s* (*pl* **-ies**) presidiario fidedigno (*que se ha merecido ciertos privilegios*)

truth [truθ] *s* verdad; **in truth** a la verdad, en verdad

truthful ['truθfəl] *adj* verídico, veraz

try [traɪ] *s* (*pl* **tries**) ensayo, intento, prueba ‖ *v* (*pret & pp* **tried**) *tr* ensayar, intentar, probar; comprobar, verificar; cansar; exasperar, irritar; (law) procesar (*a una persona*); (law) ver (*un pleito*); **to try on** probarse (*una prenda de vestir*) ‖ *intr*

ensayar, probar; esforzarse; **to try to** tratar de, intentar

trying ['traɪ•ɪŋ] *adj* cansado, molesto, irritante; penoso

tryst [trɪst] o [traɪst] *s* cita; lugar *m* de cita

tub [tʌb] *s* cuba, tina; (coll) baño; (*clumsy boat*) (coll) carcamán *m*, trompo; (*fat person*) (coll) cuba

tube [tjub] o [tub] *s* tubo; túnel *m;* (*of a tire*) cámara; (coll) ferrocarril subterráneo

tuber ['tjubər] o ['tubər] *s* tubérculo

tubercle ['tubərkəl] *s* tubérculo

tubercular [tu'bʌrkjələr] *adj & s* tísico

tuberculosis [tu,bʌrkjə'losɪs] *s* tuberculosis *f*

tuck [tʌk] *s* alforza ‖ *tr* alforzar; **to tuck away** encubrir, ocultar; **to tuck in** arropar, enmantar; remeter (*p.ej., la ropa de cama*); **to tuck up** arremangar (*un vestido*); guarnecer (*la cama*)

tucker ['tʌkər] *s* escote *m* ‖ *tr* —**to tucker out** (coll) agotar, cansar

Tuesday ['tjuzdi] *s* martes *m*

tuft [tʌft] *s* (*of feathers, hair, etc.*) penacho, copete *m;* manojo, racimo, ramillete *m;* borla ‖ *tr* empenachar ‖ *intr* crecer formando mechones

tug [tʌg] *s* estirón *m*, tirón *m;* (*boat*) remolcador *m* ‖ *v* (*pret & pp* **tugged;** *ger* **tugging**) *tr* arrastrar, tirar con fuerza de; remolcar (*un barco*) ‖ *intr* tirar con fuerza; esforzarse, luchar

tug'boat' *s* remolcador *m*

tug of war *s* lucha de la cuerda

tuition [tju'ɪʃən] *s* enseñanza; precio de la enseñanza

tulip ['tulɪp] *s* tulipán *m*

tumble ['tʌmbəl] *s* caída, tumbo; (*somersault*) voltereta, tumba; confusión, desorden *m* ‖ *intr* caerse, rodar; voltear; derribarse, volcarse; brincar, dar saltos; (*into bed*) echarse; (*to catch on*) (slang) caer, comprender; **to tumble down** desplomarse, hundirse, venirse abajo

tum'ble-down' *adj* destartalado, desvencijado

tumbler ['tʌmblər] *s* (*for drinking*) vaso; (*person who performs bodily feats*) volatinero; (*self-righting toy*) dominguillo, tentemozo

tumor ['tjumər] o ['tumər] *s* tumor *m*

tumult ['tumʌlt] *s* tumulto

tun [tʌn] *s* barril *m*, tonel *m;* (*measure of capacity for wine*) tonelada

tuna ['tunə] *s* atún *m*

tune [tjun] o [tun] *s* tonada, aire *m;* (*manner of acting or speaking*) tono; **in tune** afinado; afinadamente; **out of tune** desafinado; desafinadamente; **to change one's tune** mudar de tono ‖ *tr* acordar, afinar; (rad) sintonizar; **to tune in** (rad) sintonizar; **to tune out** (rad) desintonizar; **to tune up** poner a punto; poner a tono (*un motor de automóvil*)

tungsten ['tʌŋstən] *s* tungsteno

tunic ['tjunɪk] o ['tunɪk] *s* túnica

tuning *s* (aut) puesto a punto

tuning coil *s* (rad) bobina de sintonía

tuning fork s diapasón m
Tunis ['tunɪs] s Túnez (ciudad)
Tunisia [tu'nɪʒə] s Túnez (país)
Tunisian [tu'nɪʒən] adj & s tunecino
tun•nel ['tʌnəl] s túnel m; (min) galería ‖ v (pret & pp **-neled** o **-nelled;** ger **-neling** o **-nelling**) tr construir un túnel a través de o debajo de
turban ['tʌrbən] s turbante m
turbid ['tʌrbɪd] adj turbio
turbine ['tʌrbɪn] o ['tʌrbaɪn] s turbina
turbocompressor [,tʌrbokəm'prɛsər] s turbocompresor m
turbofan ['tʌrbo,fæn] s turboventilador m
turbojet ['tʌrbo,dʒɛt] s turborreactor m; avión m de turborreacción
turboprop ['tʌrbo,prɑp] s turbopropulsor m; turbohelice m avión m de turbopropulsión
turbosupercharger [,tʌrbo'supər,tʃɑrdʒər] s turbosupercargador m
turbulent ['tʌrbjələnt] adj turbulento
tureen [tu'rin] o [tju'rin] s sopera
turf [tʌrf] s (surface layer of grassland) césped m; terrón m de césped; (peat) turba; **the turf** el hipódromo; las carreras de caballos
turf•man ['tʌrfmən] s (pl **-men** [mən]) turiísta m
Turk [tʌrk] s turco
turkey ['tʌrki] s pavo ‖ **Turkey** s Turquía
turkey vulture s aura
Turkish ['tʌrkɪʃ] adj & s turco
Turkish towel s toalla rusa
turmoil ['tʌrmɔɪl] s alboroto, disturbio, tumulto
turn [tʌrn] s vuelta; (time of action) turno; (change of direction) virada; (bend) recodo; (walk) paseo corto; (of a spiral, roll of wire, etc.) espira; aspecto; inclinación; vahído, vértigo; giro, expresión; servicio; (coll) sacudida, susto; **at every turn** a cada paso; **in trun** por turno; **to be one's turn** tocarle a uno, p.ej., **it's your turn** le toca a Vd.; **to take turns** alternar, turnar; **to wait one's turn** aguardar turno, esperar vez ‖ tr volver; dar vuelta a (p.ej., una llave); torcer (p.ej., el tobillo); doblar (la esquina); dirigir (p.ej., los ojos); (to make sour) agriar; (on a lathe) tornear; tener (p.ej., veinte años cumplidos); **to turn against** predisponer en contra de; **to turn around** volver; voltear; torcer (las palabras de una persona); **to turn aside** desviar; **to turn away** desviar; despedir; **turn back** devolver; hacer retroceder; retrasar (el reloj); **to turn down** doblar hacia abajo; invertir; rechazar, rehusar; bajar (p.ej., el gas); **to turn in** doblar hacia adentro; entregar; **to turn off** apagar (la luz, la radio); cortar (el agua, gas, etc.); cerrar (la llave del agua, gas, etc.; la radio, la televisión); interrumpir (la corriente eléctrica); **to turn on** encender (la luz); poner (la luz, la radio, etc.); abrir (la llave del agua, gas, etc.); establecer (la corriente eléctrica); **to turn out** despedir; echar al campo (a los animales); volver al

revés; apagar (la luz); hacer, fabricar; **to turn up** doblar hacia arriba; levantar; arremangar (p.ej., las mangas); volver (un naipe); poner más alto o más fuerte (la radio); abrir la llave de (p.ej., el gas) ‖ intr volver, p.ej., **the road turns to the right** el camino vuelve a la derecha; virar (un automóvil, un avión, etc.); (to revolve) girar; volverse (p.ej., la conversación; la opinión; ciertos licores); **to turn against** cobrar aversión a; rebelarse contra; **to turn around** dar vuelta; **to turn aside** o **away** desviarse; alejarse; **to turn back** volver, regresar; retroceder; **to turn down** doblarse hacia abajo; invertirse; **to turn in** doblarse hacia adentro; replegarse; recogerse, volver a casa; (coll) recogerse, acostarse; **to turn into** entrar en; convertirse en; **to turn on** volverse contra; depender de; versar sobre; ocuparse de; **to turn out badly** salir mal; **to turn out right** acabar bien; **to turn out to be** venir a ser; resultar, salir; **to turn over** volcar, derribarse (un vehículo); **to turn up** doblarse hacia arriba; levantarse; acontecer; aparecer
turn'coat' s tránsfuga mf, apóstata mf, renegado; **to become a turncoat** volver la casaca, cambiarse la camisa
turn'down' adj (collar) caído ‖ s rechazamiento
turning light s (aut) intermitente m
turning point s punto de transición, punto decisivo
turnip ['tʌrnɪp] s nabo; (cheap watch) (slang) calentador m; (slang) tipo
turn'key' s carcelero, llavero de cárcel
turn of life s menopausia
turn of mind s natural m, inclinación
turn'out' s (gathering of people) con currencia; (number attending a show, etc.) entrada; (side track or passage) apartadero; (amount produced) producción; (array, outfit) equipaje m; carruaje m de lujo
turn'o'ver s (spill, upset) vuelco; cambio de personal; movimiento de mercancías; ciclo de compra y venta
turn'pike' s carretera de peaje
turnstile ['tʌrn,staɪl] s torniquete m
turn'ta'ble s (of phonograph) placa giratoria, plato giratorio; (rr) placa giratoria, plataforma giratoria
turpentine ['tʌrpən,taɪn] s trementina
turpitude ['tʌrpɪ,tjud] s torpeza, infamia, vileza
turquoise ['tʌrkɔɪz] o ['tʌrkwɔɪz] s turquesa
turret ['tʌrɪt] s torrecilla; (archit) torreón m; (nav) torreta
turtle ['tʌrtəl] s tortuga; **to turn turtle** derribarse patas arriba
tur'tle•dove' s tórtola
Tuscan ['tʌskən] adj & s toscano
Tuscany ['tʌskəni] s la Toscana
tusk [tʌsk] s colmillo
tussle ['tʌsəl] s agarrada ‖ intr agarrarse, asirse, reñir

tutor ['tjutər] o ['tutər] s maestro particular; (*guardian*) tutor *m* ‖ *tr* dar enseñanza particular a ‖ *intr* dar enseñanza particular; (coll) tomar lecciones particulares

tuxe•do [tʌk'sido] s (*pl* **-dos**) esmoquin *m*, smoking *m*

TV *abbr* **television**

twaddle ['twɑdəl] s charla, tonterías, música celestial ‖ *intr* charlar, decir tonterías

twang [twæŋ] s (*of musical instrument*) tañido; (*of voice*) timbre *m* nasal ‖ *tr* tocar con un tañido; decir con timbre nasal ‖ *intr* hablar por la nariz

twang•y ['twæŋi] *adj* (*comp* **-ier;** *super* **-iest**) (*device*) tañente; (*person, voice*) gangoso

tweed [twid] s mezcla de lana; traje *m* de mezcla de lana; **tweeds** ropa de mezcla de lana

tweet [twit] s pío ‖ *intr* piar

tweeter ['twitər] s altavoz *m* para audiofrecuencias elevadas

tweezers ['twizərz] *spl* bruselas, pinzas, tenacillas

twelfth [twɛlfθ] *adj* & *s* (*in a seris*) duodécimo; (*part*) dozavo ‖ *s* (*in dates*) doce *m*

Twelfth'-night' *s* la víspera del día de Reyes; la noche del día de Reyes

twelve [twɛlv] *adj* & *pron* doce ‖ *s* doce *m;* **twelve o'clock** las doce

twentieth ['twɛnti•ɪθ] *adj* & *s* (*in a series*) vigésimo; (*part*) veintavo ‖ *s* (*in dates*) veinte *m*

twen•ty ['twɛnti] *adj* & *pron* veinte ‖ *s* (*pl* **-ties**) veinte *m*

twice [twaɪs] *adv* dos veces

twice'-told' *adj* dicho dos veces; trilládo, sabido

twiddle ['twɪdəl] *tr* menear o revolver ociosamente

twig [twɪg] s ramito; **twigs** leña menuda

twilight ['twaɪ,laɪt] *adj* crepuscular ‖ *s* crepúsculo

twill [twɪl] s tela cruzada; (*pattern of weave*) cruzado ‖ *tr* cruzar

twin [twɪn] *adj* & *s* gemelo

twine [twaɪn] s guita, cuerda, bramante *m* ‖ *tr* enroscar, retorcer ‖ *intr* enroscarse, retorcerse

twinge [twɪndʒ] s·punzada, dolor agudo

twin'jet' plane s avión *m* birreactor

twinkle ['twɪŋkəl] s centelleo; (*of eye*) pestañeo; instante *m* ‖ *intr* centellear; pestañear; moverse rápidamente

twin'-screw' *adj* (naut) de doble hélice

twirl [twʌrl] s vuelta, giro ‖ *tr* hacer girar; (*baseball*) lanzar (*la pelota*) ‖ *intr* dar vueltas, girar; piruetear

twist [twɪst] s torcedura; enroscadura; curva, recodo; giro, vuelta; propensión, prejuicio; (*of mind or disposition*) sesgo ‖ *tr* torcer;

retorcer; enroscar; hacer girar; entrelazar; desviar; (*to give a different meaning to*) torcer ‖ *intr* torcerse; retorcerse; enroscarse; dar vueltas; entrelazarse; desviarse; serpentear; **to twist and turn** (*in bed*) dar vueltas

twisted ['twɪstɪd] *adj* sobornado

twit [twɪt] *v* (*pret* & *pp* **twitted;** *ger* **twitting**) *tr* reprender (*a uno*) recordando algo desagradable o poniéndole en ridículo

twitch [twɪtʃ] s crispatura; ligero temblor ‖ *intr* crisparse; temblar (*p.ej., los párpados*)

twitter ['twɪtər] s gorjeo; risita sofocada; inquietud ‖ *intr* gorjear; reír sofocadamente; temblar de inquietud

two [tu] *adj* & *pron* dos ‖ *s* dos *m;* **to put two and two together** atar cabos, sacar la conclusión evidente; **two o'clock** las dos

two'-cy'cle *adj* (mach) de dos tiempos

two'-cyl'inder *adj* (mach) de dos cilindros

two-edged ['tu,ɛdʒd] *adj* de dos filos

two hundred *adj* & *pron* doscientos ‖ *s* doscientos *m*

twosome ['tusəm] s pareja; pareja de jugadores; juego de dos

two'-time' *tr* (slang) engañar en amor, ser infiel a (*una persona del otro sexo*)

tycoon [taɪ'kun] s (coll) magnate *m*

type [taɪp] s tipo; (*piece*) (typ) tipo, letra; (*pieces collectively*) (typ) letra; letras impresas, letras escritas a máquina ‖ *tr* escribir a máquina, tipiar; representar, simbolizar ‖ *intr* escribir a máquina

type'face' *s* tipo de letra

type'script' *s* material escrito a máquina

typesetter ['taɪp,sɛtər] s (typ) cajista *mf;* (typ) máquina de componer

type'write' *v* (*pret* **-wrote** [,rot]; *pp* **-written** [,rɪtən]) *tr* & *intr* escribir a máquina, tipiar

type'writ'er *s* máquina de escribir; tipista *mf*

typewriter ribbon *s* cinta para máquinas de escribir

type'writ'ing *s* mecanografía; trabajo hecho con máquina de escribir

typhoid fever ['taɪfɔɪd] s fiebre tifoidea

typhoon [taɪ'fun] s tifón *m*

typical ['tɪpɪkəl] *adj* típico

typi•fy ['tɪpɪ,faɪ] *v* (*pret* & *pp* **-fied**) *tr* simbolizar; ser ejemplo o modelo de

typist ['taɪpɪst] s mecanógrafo, tipista *mf,* mecanógrafa

typographic(al) [,taɪpə'græfɪk(əl)] *adj* tipográfico

typographical error *s* error *m* de imprenta

typography [taɪ'pɑgrəfi] s tipografía

tyrannic(al) [tɪ'rænɪk(əl)] o [taɪ'rænɪk(əl)] *adj* tiránico

tyrannous ['tɪrənəs] *adj* tirano

tyran•ny ['tɪrəni] s (*pl* **-nies**) tiranía

tyrant ['taɪrənt] s tirano

ty•ro ['taɪro] s (*pl* **-ros**) tirón *m*, novicio

tu
ty

U, u [juJ vigésima primera letra del alfabeto inglés

U. *abbr* **University**

ubiquitous [ju'bɪkwɪtəs] *adj* ubicuo

udder ['ʌdər] *s* ubre *f*

UFO *abbr* **unidentified flying object**

ugliness ['ʌglɪnɪs] *s* fealdad; (coll) malhumor *m*

ug•ly ['ʌgli] *adj* (*comp* **-lier;** *super* **-liest**) feo; (coll) malhumorado

ugly mug *s* (slang) carantamaula

Ukraine ['jukren] o [ju'kren] *s* Ucrania

Ukrainian [ju'krenɪ•ən] *adj* & *s* ucraniano, ucranio

ulcer ['ʌlsər] *s* llaga, úlcera; (*corrupting influence*) (fig) llaga

ulcerate ['ʌlsə,ret] *tr* ulcerar ‖ *intr* ulcerarse

ulterior [ʌl'tɪrɪ•ər] *adj* ulterior; (*concealed*) escondido, oculto

ultimate ['ʌltɪmɪt] *adj* último

ultima•tum [,ʌltɪ'metəm] *s* (*pl* **-tums** o **-ta** [tə]) ultimátum *m*

ultimo ['ʌltɪ,mo] *adv* de o en el mes próximo pasado

ultrahigh [,ʌltrə'haɪ] *adj* (electron) ultraelevado

ultrasound ['ʌltrə,saund] *s* sonido silencioso

ultraviolet [,ʌltrə'vaɪ•əlɪt] *adj* & *s* ultravioleta, ultraviolado

umbilical cord [ʌm'bɪlɪkəl] *s* cordón *m* umbilical

umbrage ['ʌmbrɪdʒ] *s*—**to take umbrage at** resentirse de o por

umbrella [ʌm'brɛlə] *s* paraguas *m;* (mil) sombrilla protectora

umbrella man *s* paragüero

umbrella stand *s* paragüero

umlaut ['umlaut] *s* inflexión vocálica, metafonía; (*mark*) diéresis *f* ‖ *tr* inflexionar; escribir con diéresis

umpire ['ʌmpaɪr] *s* árbitro ‖ *tr* & *intr* arbitrar

UN ['ju'ɛn] *s* (letterword) ONU *f*

unable [ʌn'ebəl] *adj* incapaz, imposibilitado; **to be unable to** no poder

unabridged [,ʌnə'brɪdʒd] *adj* sin abreviar, íntegro

unaccented [ʌn'æksɛntɪd] o [,ʌnæk'sɛntɪd] *adj* inacentuado

unaccountable [,ʌnə'kaʊntəbəl] *adj* inexplicable; irresponsable

unaccounted-for [,ʌnə'kaʊntɪd,fɔr] *adj* inexplicado; no hallado

unaccustomed [,ʌnə'kʌstəmd] *adj* (*unusual*) desacostumbrado; inhabituado

unafraid [,ʌnə'fred] *adj* sin miedo

unaligned [,ʌnə'laɪnd] *adj* no empeñado

unanimity [,junə'nɪmɪti] *s* unanimidad

unanimous [ju'nænɪməs] *adj* unánime

unanswerable [ʌn'ænsərəbəl] *adj* incontestable; (*argument*) incontrastable

unappreciative [,ʌnə'priʃɪ,etɪv] *adj* ingrato, desagradecido

unapproachable [,ʌnə'protʃəbəl] *adj* inabordable; incomparable, único

unarmed [ʌn'armd] *adj* desarmado, inerme

unascertainable [ʌn,æsər'tenəbəl] *adj* inaveriguable

unasked [ʌn'æskt] *adj* no solicitado; no convidado

unassembled [,ʌnə'sɛmbəld] *adj* desmontado, desarmado

unassuming [,ʌnə'sumɪŋ] o [,ʌnə'sjumɪŋ] *adj* modesto, sencillo

unattached [,ʌnə'tætʃt] *adj* independiente; (*loose*) suelto; (*not engaged to be married*) no prometido; (law) no embargado; (mil & nav) de reemplazo

unattainable [,ʌnə'tenəbəl] *adj* inasequible, inalcanzable

unattractive [,ʌnə'træktɪv] *adj* poco atrayente, desairado

unavailable [,ʌnə'veləbəl] *adj* indisponible

unavailing [,ʌnə'velɪŋ] *adj* ineficaz, inútil, vano

unavoidable [,ʌnə'vɔɪdəbəl] *adj* inevitable, ineluctable

unaware [,ʌnə'wɛr] *adj*—**to be unaware of** no estar al corriente de ‖ *adv* de improviso; sin saberlo

unawares [,ʌnə'wɛrz] *adv* (*unexpectedly*) de improviso; (*unknowingly*) sin saberlo

unbalanced [ʌn'bælənst] *adj* desequilibrado

unbandage [ʌn'bændɪdʒ] *tr* desvendar

un•bar [ʌn'bar] *v* (*pret* & *pp* **-barred;** *ger* **-barring**) *tr* desatrancar

unbearable [ʌn'bɛrəbəl] *adj* inaguantable

unbeatable [ʌn'bitəbəl] *adj* imbatible

unbecoming [,ʌnbɪ'kʌmɪŋ] *adj* inconveniente, indecente; que sienta mal

unbelievable [,ʌnbɪ'livəbəl] *adj* increíble

unbending [ʌn'bɛndɪŋ] *adj* inflexible

unbiased o **unbiassed** [ʌn'baɪ•əst] *adj* imparcial

un•bind [ʌn'baɪnd] *v* (*pret* & *pp* **-bound** ['baund]) *tr* desatar

unbleached [ʌn'blitʃt] *adj* sin blanquear

unbolt [ʌn'bolt] *tr* desatrancar (*p.ej., una puerta*); (*to remove the bolts from*) desempernar

unborn [ʌn'bɔrn] *adj* no nacido, por nacer, futuro

unbosom [ʌn'buzəm] *tr* confesar, descubrir (*sus pensamientos, sus secretos*); **to unbosom oneself** abrir su pecho, desahogarse

unbound [ʌn'baund] *adj* (*book*) sin encuadernar

unbreakable [ʌn'brekəbəl] *adj* irrompible

unbuckle [ʌn'bʌkəl] *tr* deshebillar

unburden [ʌn'bʌrdən] *tr* descargar; **to unburden oneself of** desahogarse de

unburied [ʌn'berid] *adj* insepulto

unbutton [ʌn'bʌtən] *tr* desabotonar

uncalled-for [ʌn'kɔld,fɔr] *adj* innecesario, no justificado; insolente

uncanny [ʌn'kæni] *adj* espectral, misterioso; extraordinario, maravilloso

uncared-for [ʌn'kɛrd,fɔr] *adj* desamparado, descuidado, abandonado

unceasing [ʌn'sisɪŋ] *adj* incesante

unceremonious [,ʌnsɛri'monɪ•əs] *adj* incere-monioso

uncertain [ʌn'sʌrtən] *adj* incierto

uncertain•ty [ʌn'sʌrtənti] *s* (*pl* **-ties**) incertidumbre

unchain [ʌn'tʃen] *tr* desencadenar

unchangeable [ʌn'tʃendʒəbəl] *adj* incambiable, inmutable

uncharted [ʌn'tʃɑrtɪd] *adj* inexplorado

unchecked [ʌn'tʃɛkt] *adj* no verificado; no refrenado; desenfrenado

uncivilized [ʌn'sɪvɪ,laɪzd] *adj* incivilizado

unclad [ʌn'klæd] *adj* desvestido

unclaimed [ʌn'klemd] *adj* sin reclamar; (*mail*) rechazado, sobrante

unclasp [ʌn'klæsp] *tr* desabrochar

unclassified [ʌn'klæsɪ,faɪd] *adj* no clasificado; no clasificado como secreto

uncle ['ʌŋkəl] *s* tío

unclean [ʌn'klin] *adj* desaseado, sucio

un•clog [ʌn'klɑg] *v* (*pret & pp* **-clogged;** *ger* **-clogging**) *tr* desatrancar

unclouded [ʌn'klaʊdɪd] *adj* despejado

uncollectible [,ʌnkə'lɛktɪbəl] *adj* incobrable

uncomfortable [ʌn'kʌmfərtəbəl] *adj* incomodo

uncommitted [,ʌnkə'mɪtɪd] *adj* no empeñado, no comprometido

uncommon [ʌn'kɑmən] *adj* raro, poco común

uncompromising [ʌn'kɑmprə,maɪzɪŋ] *adj* intransigente

unconcerned [,ʌnkən'sʌrnd] *adj* despreocupado, indiferente

unconditional [,ʌnkən'dɪʃənəl] *adj* incondicional

uncongenial [,ʌnkən'dʒinɪ•əl] *adj* antipático; incompatible; desagradable

unconquerable [ʌn'kɑŋkərəbəl] *adj* inconquistable

unconquered [ʌn'kɑŋkərd] *adj* invicto

unconscionable [ʌn'kɑnʃənəbəl] *adj* inescrupuloso; desrazonable, excesivo

unconscious [ʌn'kɑnʃəs] *adj* inconsciente; (*temporarily deprived of consciousness*) desmayado; (*unintentional*) involuntario

unconsciousness [ʌn'kɑnʃəsnɪs] *s* inconsciencia; desmayo

unconstitutional [,ʌnkɑnstɪ'tjuʃənəl] *adj* inconstitucional

uncontrollable [,ʌnkən'troləbəl] *adj* ingobernable; incontrolable; (*laughter*) inextinguible

unconventional [,ʌnkən'vɛnʃənəl] *adj* no convencional

uncork [ʌn'kɔrk] *tr* destapar, descorchar

uncouth [ʌn'kuθ] *adj* desgarbado, torpe, rústico

uncover [ʌn'kʌvər] *tr* descubrir

unction ['ʌŋkʃən] *s* (*anointing*) unción; suavidad hipócrita

unctuous ['ʌŋktʃʊ•əs] *adj* untuoso; zalamero

uncultivated [ʌn'kʌltɪ,vetɪd] *adj* inculto (*que no está cultivado; rústico, grosero*)

uncultured [ʌn'kʌltʃərd] *adj* inculto, rústico, grosero

uncut [ʌn'kʌt] *adj* sin cortar; (*book or magazine*) intonso

undamaged [ʌn'dæmɪdʒd] *adj* indemne, ileso

undaunted [ʌn'dɔntɪd] *adj* impávido, denodado

undecided [,ʌndɪ'saɪdɪd] *adj* indeciso

undefeated [,ʌndɪ'fitɪd] *adj* invicto

undefended [,ʌndɪ'fɛndɪd] *adj* indefenso

undefiled [,ʌndɪ'faɪld] *adj* inmaculado, impoluto

undeniable [,ʌndɪ'naɪ•əbəl] *adj* innegable

under ['ʌndər] *adj* inferior; (*clothing*) interior ‖ *adv* debajo; más abajo; **to go under** hundirse; (*to fail*) fracasar ‖ *prep* bajo, debajo de; inferior a; **under full sail** a vela llena; **under lock and key** bajo llave; **under oath** bajo juramento; **under penalty of death** so pena de muerte; **under sail** a vela; **under separate cover** por separado, bajo cubierta separada; **under steam** bajo presión; **under the hand and seal of** firmado y sellado por; **under the nose of** en las barbas de; **under the weather** algo indispuesto; **under way** en camino

un'der•age' *adj* menor de edad

un'der•bid' *v* (*pret & pp* **-bid;** *ger* **-bidding**) *tr* ofrecer menos que

un'der•brush' *s* maleza

un'der•car'riage *s* carro inferior; (aer) tren *m* de aterrizaje

un'der•clothes' *s* ropa interior

un'der•con•sump'tion *s* infraconsumo

un'der•cov'er *adj* secreto

underdeveloped [,ʌndərdɪ'vɛləpt] *adj* subdesarrollado

un'der•dog' *s* víctima, perdidoso; **the underdogs** los de abajo

underdone ['ʌndər,dʌn] *adj* a medio asar, soasado

un'der•es'ti•mate' *tr* subestimar

un'der•gar'ment *s* prenda de vestir interior

un'der•go' *v* (*pret* **-went;** *pp* **-gone**) *tr* experimentar; sufrir, padecer

un'der•grad'uate *adj* no graduado; (*course*) para el bachillerato ‖ *s* alumno no graduado de universidad

un'der•ground' *adj* subterráneo; clandestino ‖ *adv* bajo tierra; ocultamente ‖ *s* ferrocarril subterráneo; movimiento de resistencia

un'der•growth' *s* maleza

underhanded ['ʌndər'hændɪd] *adj* clandestino, taimado, disimulado

un'der•line' o **un'der•line'** *tr* subrayar

underling ['ʌndərlɪŋ] *s* subordinado, secuaz *m* servil

un'der•mine' *tr* socavar, minar

underneath [,ʌndər'niθ] *adj* inferior, más bajo ‖ *adv* debajo ‖ *prep* debajo de ‖ *s* parte baja, superficie *f* inferior

undernourished [,ʌndər'nʌrɪʃt] *adj* desnutrido

un'der•nour'ish•ment *s* desnutrición

un'der•pass' *s* paso inferior

un'der•pay' *s* pago insuficiente ‖ *v* (*pret & pp* **-paid**) *tr & intr* pagar insuficientemente

u
un

un′der•pin′ v (pret & pp **-pinned;** ger **-pinning**) tr apuntalar, socalzar

underprivileged [ˌʌndər′prɪvɪlɪdʒd] adj desheredado, desamparado

un′der•rate′ tr menospreciar

un′der•score′ tr subrayar

un′der•sea′ adj submarino ‖ **un′der•sea′** adv debajo de la superficie del mar

un′der•sec′re•tar′y s (pl **-ies**) subsecretario

un′der•sell′ v (pret & pp **-sold**) tr vender a menor precio que; (for less than the actual value) malbaratar

un′der•shirt′ s camiseta

undersigned [′ʌndər,saɪnd] adj infrascrito, subscrito

un′der•skirt′ s enaguas, refajo

un′der•stand′ v (pret & pp **-stood**) tr entender, comprender; sobrentender, subentender (una cosa que no está expresa) ‖ intr entender, comprender

understandable [ˌʌndər′stændəbəl] adj comprensible

understanding [ˌʌndər′stændɪŋ] adj entendedor; (tolerant, sympathetic) comprensivo ‖ s comprensión; (intellectual faculty, mind) entendimiento; (agreement) acuerdo; **to come to an understanding** llegar a un acuerdo

un′der•stud′y s (pl **-ies**) sobresaliente mf

un′der•take′ v (pret **-took;** pp **-taken**) tr emprender; (to agree to perform) comprometerse a

undertaker [ˌʌndər′tekər] o [′ʌndər,tekər] s empresario ‖ (′ʌndər,tekər) s empresario de pompas fúnebres, director m de funeraria

undertaking [ˌʌndər′tekɪŋ] s (task) empresa; (pledge) empeño ‖ [′ʌndər,tekɪŋ] s (business of funeral director) funeraria

un′der•tak′ing establishment s funeraria, empresa de pompas fúnebres

un′der•tone′ s voz baja; (background sound) fondo; color apagado

un′der•tow′ s (countercurrent below surface) contracorriente f; (on the beach) resaca

un′der•wear′ s ropa interior, prendas interiores

un′der•world′ s (criminal world) inframundo, bajos fondos sociales; (the earth) mundo terrenal; (pagan world of the dead) averno, infierno; (world under the water) mundo submarino; (opposite side of earth) antípodas

un′der•write′ v (pret **-wrote;** pp **-written**) tr subscribir; (to insure) asegurar

un′der•writ′er s subscritor m; asegurador m; compañía aseguradora

undeserved [ˌʌndɪ′zʌrvd] adj inmerecido

undesirable [ˌʌndɪ′zaɪrəbəl] adj & s indeseable mf

undetachable [ˌʌndɪ′tætʃəbəl] adj inamovible

undignified [ʌn′dɪgnɪ,faɪd] adj poco digno, poco grave, indecoroso

undiscernible [ˌʌndɪ′zʌrnɪbəl] o [ˌʌndɪ′sʌrnəbəl] adj imperceptible, invisible

un•do′ v (pret **-did;** pp **-done**) tr deshacer; anular, borrar; arruinar

undoing [ʌn′du•ɪŋ] s destrucción, pérdida, ruina

undone [ʌn′dʌn] adj sin hacer, por hacer; **to come undone** deshacerse, desatarse; **to leave nothing undone** no dejar nada por hacer

undoubtedly [ʌn′daʊtɪdli] adv indudablemente, sin duda

undramatic [ˌʌndrə′mætɪk] adj poco dramático

undress [′ʌn,drɛs] o [ʌn′drɛs] s traje m de casa; vestido de calle; (mil) traje de cuartel ‖ [ʌn′drɛs] tr desnudar; desvendar (una herida) ‖ desnudarse

undrinkable [ʌn′drɪŋkəbəl] adj impotable

undue [ʌn′dju] adj indebido

undulate [′ʌndjə,let] intr ondular

unduly [ʌn′djuli] adv indebidamente

undying [ʌn′daɪ•ɪŋ] adj imperecedero

unearned increment [ʌn′ʌrnd] s plusvalía

unearth [ʌn′ʌrθ] tr desenterrar

unearthly [ʌn′ʌrθli] adj sobrenatural; fantástico, espectral; extraordinario

uneasy [ʌn′izi] adj (worried) inquieto; (constrained) encogido, embarazado

uneatable [ʌn′itəbəl] adj incomible

uneconomic(al) [ˌʌnikə′nɑmɪk(əl)] adj antieconómico

uneducated [ʌn′ɛdjə,ketɪd] adj ineducado, sin instrucción; chontal

unemployed [ˌʌnɛm′plɔɪd] adj desocupado, desempleado; improductivo

unemployment [ˌʌnɛm′plɔɪmənt] s desocupación, desempleo

unemployment insurance s seguro de desempleo o desocupación, seguro contra el paro obrero

unending [ʌn′ɛndɪŋ] adj interminable

unequal [ʌn′ikwəl] adj desigual; **to be unequal to** (a task) no estar a la altura de

unequaled o **unequalled** [ʌn′ikwəld] adj inigualado

unerring [ʌn′ʌrɪŋ] o [ʌn′ɛrɪŋ] adj infalible, seguro

unessential [ˌʌnɛsɛnʃəl] adj no esencial

uneven [ʌn′ivən] adj desigual; (number) impar

unexceptionable [ˌʌnɛk′sɛpʃənəbəl] adj intachable, irreprensible

unexpected [ˌʌnɛk′spɛktɪd] adj inesperado

unexplained [ˌʌnɛk′splend] adj inexplicado

unexplored [ˌʌnɛk′splɔrd] adj inexplorado

unexposed [ˌʌnɛk′spozd] adj (phot) inexpuesto

unfading [ʌn′fedɪŋ] adj inmarcesible

unfailing [ʌn′felɪŋ] adj indefectible; (inexhaustible) inagotable

unfair [ʌn′fɛr] adj injusto; desleal, doble, falso; (sport) sucio

unfaithful [ʌn′feθfəl] adj infiel

unfamiliar [ˌʌnfə′mɪljər] adj poco familiar; poco familiarizado

unfasten [ʌnf′æsən] tr desatacar, desatar, soltar

unfathomable [ʌn′fæðəməbəl] adj insondable

unfavorable [ʌn′fevərəbəl] adj desfavorable

unfeathered [ʌnˈfɛðərd] *adj* implume

unfeeling [ʌnˈfilɪŋ] *adj* insensible

unfetter [ʌnˈfɛtər] *tr* desencadenar

unfilled [ʌnˈfɪld] *adj* no lleno; por complir, pendiente

unfinished [ʌnˈfɪnɪʃt] *adj* sin acabar; imperfecto, mal acabado; (*business*) pendiente

unfit [ʌnˈfɪt] *adj* impropio, incapaz, inhábil; inservible, inútil

unfold [ʌnˈfold] *tr* desplegar ‖ *intr* desplegarse

unforeseeable [ˌʌnforˈsi•əbəl] *adj* imprevisible

unforeseen [ˌʌnforˈsin] *adj* imprevisto

unforgettable [ˌʌnfərˈgɛtəbəl] *adj* inolvidable

unforgivable [ˌʌnfərˈgɪvəbəl] *adj* imperdonable

unfortunate [ʌnˈfɔrtjənɪt] *adj* & *s* desgraciado

unfounded [ʌnˈfaʊndɪd] *adj* infundado

unfreeze [ʌnˈfriz] *tr* deshelar; desbloquear (*el crédito*)

unfriendly [ʌnˈfrɛndli] *adj* inamistoso; desfavorable

unfruitful [ʌnˈfrutfəl] *adj* infructuoso

unfulfilled [ˌʌnfəlˈfɪld] *adj* incumplido

unfurl [ʌnˈfʌrl] *tr* desplegar, extender

unfurnished [ʌnˈfʌrnɪʃt] *adj* desamueblado

ungainly [ʌnˈgenli] *adj* desgarbado, desmañado

ungentlemanly [ʌnˈdʒɛntəlmənli] *adj* poco caballeroso, descortés

ungird [ʌnˈgʌrd] *tr* desceñir

ungodly [ʌnˈgɑdli] *adj* impío, irreligioso; (*dreadful*) (coll) atroz

ungracious [ʌnˈgreʃəs] *adj* descortés; desagradable

ungrammatical [ˌʌngrəˈmætɪkəl] *adj* ingramatical

ungrateful [ʌnˈgretfəl] *adj* ingrato, desagradecido

ungrudgingly [ʌnˈgrʌdʒɪŋli] *adj* de buena gana, sin quejarse

unguarded [ʌnˈgɑrdɪd] *adj* indefenso; descuidado; (*moment*) de inadvertencia

unguent [ˈʌŋgwənt] *s* ungüento

unhandy [ʌnˈhændi] *adj* inmanejable; (*awkward*) desmañado

unhappiness [ʌnˈhæpɪnɪs] *s* infelicidad

unhap•py [ʌnˈhæpi] *adj* (*comp* **-pier;** *super* **-piest**) infeliz; (*unlucky*) desgraciado; (*fateful*) aciago

unharmed [ʌnˈhɑrmd] *adj* indemne

unharmonious [ˌʌnhɑrˈmoni•əs] *adj* inarmónico

unharness [ʌnˈhɑrnɪs] *tr* desenjaezar, desguarnecer; desenganchar

unhealthy [ʌnˈhɛlθi] *adj* malsano

unheard-of [ʌnˈhʌrd,ɑv] *adj* inaudito

unhinge [ʌnˈhɪndʒ] *tr* desgonzar; (fig) desequilibrar, trastornar

unhitch [ʌnˈhɪtʃ] *tr* desenganchar

unho•ly [ʌnˈholi] *adj* (*comp* **-lier;** *super* **-liest**) impío, malo, profano

unhook [ʌnˈhʊk] *tr* desabrochar; desenganchar; (*to take down from a hook*) descolgar

unhoped-for [ʌnˈhopt,fɔr] *adj* inesperado, no esperado

unhorse [ʌnˈhɔrs] *tr* desarzonar

unhurt [ʌnˈhʌrt] *adj* incólume, ileso

unicorn [ˈjunɪ,kɔrn] *s* unicornio

unidentified flying object (UFO) *s* objeto volante no identificado (ovni)

unification [ˌjunɪfɪˈkeʃən] *s* unificación

uniform [ˈjunɪ,fɔrm] *adj* & *s* uniforme *m* ‖ *tr* uniformar

uniformi•ty [ˌjunɪˈfɔrmɪti] *s* (*pl* **-ties**) uniformidad

uni•fy [ˈjunɪ,faɪ] *v* (*pret* & *pp* **-fied**) *tr* unificar

unilateral [ˌjunɪˈlætərəl] *adj* unilateral

unimpeachable [ˌʌnɪmˈpitʃəbəl] *adj* irrecusable, intachable

unimportant [ˌʌnɪmˈpɔrtənt] *adj* poco importante; intrascendente

uninhabited [ˌʌnɪnˈhæbɪtɪd] *adj* inhabitado

uninspired [ˌʌnɪnˈspaɪrd] *adj* sin inspiración; aburrido, fastidioso

unintelligent [ˌʌnɪnˈtɛlɪdʒənt] *adj* ininteligente

unintelligible [ˌʌnɪnˈtɛlɪdʒɪbəl] *adj* ininteligible

uninterested [ʌnˈɪntrɪstɪd] o [ʌnˈɪntə,rɛstɪd] *adj* desinteresado

uninteresting [ʌnˈɪntə,rɛstɪŋ] *adj* poco interesante

uninterrupted [ˌʌnɪntəˈrʌptɪd] *adj* ininterrumpido

union [ˈjunjən] *s* unión; (*organization of workmen*) gremio obrero, sindicato; unión matrimonial

unionize [ˈjunjə,naɪz] *tr* agremiar ‖ *intr* agremiarse

union shop *s* taller *m* de obreros agremiados

union suit *s* traje *m* interior de una sola pieza

unique [juˈnik] *adj* único

unison [ˈjunɪsən] *s* unisonancia; **in unison (with)** al unísono (de)

unit [ˈjunɪt] *adj* unitario ‖ *s* unidad; (mach & elec) grupo

unite [juˈnaɪt] *tr* unir ‖ *intr* unirse

united [juˈnaɪtɪd] *adj* unido

United Kingdom *s* Reino Unido

United Nations *spl* Naciones Unidas

United States *adj* estadounidense ‖ **the United States** *s* los Estados Unidos *mpl;* Estados Unidos *msg*

uni•ty [ˈjunɪti] *s* (*pl* **-ties**) unidad

univ. *abbr* **universal, university**

universal [ˌjunɪˈvʌrsəl] *adj* universal

universal joint *s* cardán *m*, junta universal

universal product code (UPC) *s* código universal de producto

universe [ˈjunɪ,vʌrs] *s* universo

universi•ty [ˌjunɪˈvʌrsɪti] *adj* universitario ‖ *s* (*pl* **-ties**) universidad

unjust [ʌnˈdʒʌst] *adj* injusto

unjustified [ʌnˈdʒʌstɪ,faɪd] *adj* injustificado

unkempt [ʌnˈkɛmpt] *adj* despeinado

unkind [ʌnˈkaɪnd] *adj* poco amable; duro, despiadado

unknowable [ʌnˈno•əbəl] *adj* inconocible, insabible

un
un

unknowingly [ʌnˈno•ɪŋli] *adv* desconocidamente, sin saberlo

unknown [ʌnˈnon] *adj* desconocido, ignoto, incógnito ‖ *s* desconocido; (math) incógnita

unknown quantity *s* (math & fig) incógnita

unknown soldier *s* soldado desconocido

unlace [ʌnˈles] *tr* desenlazar; desatar (*los cordones del zapato*)

unlatch [ʌnˈlætʃ] *tr* abrir levantando el picaporte

unlawful [ʌnˈlɔfəl] *adj* ilegal

unleaded gasoline [ʌnˈlɛdɪd] *s* gasolina sin plomo

unleash [ʌnˈliʃ] *tr* destraillar; soltar, desencadenar

unleavened [ʌnˈlɛvənd] *adj* ázimo

unless [ʌnˈlɛs] *conj* a menos que, a no ser que

unlettered [ʌnˈlɛtərd] *adj* iletrado, indocto; sin rotular; (*illiterate*) analfabeto

unlike [ʌnˈlaɪk] *adj* desemejante; desemejante de; (*poles of a magnet*) (elec) de nombres contrarios; (elec) de signo contrario ‖ *prep* a diferencia de

unlikely [ʌnˈlaɪkli] *adj* improbable

unlimber [ʌnˈlɪmbər] *tr* preparar para la acción ‖ *intr* prepararse para la acción

unlined [ʌnˈlaɪnd] *adj* (*coat*) sin forro; (*paper*) sin rayar; (*face*) sin arrugas

unload [ʌnˈlod] *tr* descargar; (coll) deshacerse de ‖ *intr* descargar

unloading [ʌnˈlodɪŋ] *s* descarga, descargue *m*

unlock [ʌnˈlɑk] *tr* abrir (*p.ej., una puerta*); (typ) desapretar

unloose [ʌnˈlus] *tr* aflojar, soltar, desatar

unloved [ʌnˈlʌvd] *adj* desamado

unlovely [ʌnˈlʌvli] *adj* desgraciado

unluck•y [ʌnˈlʌki] *adj* (*comp* -ier; *super* -iest) desgraciado, desdichado; aciago, nefasto; de mala suerte; **to be unlucky** quedar mal parado

un•make [ʌnˈmek] *v* (*pret & pp* -made [ˈmed]) *tr* deshacer; destruir

unmanageable [ʌnˈmænɪdʒəbəl] *adj* inmanejable

unmanly [ʌnˈmænli] *adj* afeminado; bajo, cobarde

unmannerly [ʌnˈmænərli] *adj* descortés, malcriado

unmarketable [ʌnˈmɑrkɪtəbəl] *adj* incomerciable

unmarriageable [ʌnˈmærɪdʒəbəl] *adj* incasable

unmarried [ʌnˈmærɪd] *adj* soltero

unmask [ʌnˈmæsk] *tr* desenmascarar ‖ *intr* desenmascararse

unmatchable [ʌnˈmætʃəbəl] *adj* incomparable, sin igual; (*price*) incompetible

unmerciful [ʌnˈmʌrsɪfəl] *adj* despiadado, inclemente

unmesh [ʌnˈmɛʃ] *tr* desengranar ‖ *intr* desengranarse

unmindful [ʌnˈmaɪndfəl] *adj* desatento, descuidado; **to be unmindful of** olvidar, no pensar en

unmistakable [ˌʌnmɪsˈtekəbəl] *adj* inequívoco, inconfundible

unmixed [ʌnˈmɪkst] *adj* puro, sin mezcla

unmoor [ʌnˈmʊr] *tr* desamarrar (*un buque*); desaferrar (*las áncoras*)

unmotivated [ˌʌnˈmotɪˌvetɪd] *adj* inmotivado

unmoved [ʌnˈmuvd] *adj* fijo, inmoto; impasible

unmuzzle [ˌʌnˈmʌzəl] *tr* desbozalar

unnatural [ʌnˈnætʃərəl] *adj* innatural; (*artificial, forced*) afectado; anormal; inhumano

unnecessary [ʌnˈnɛsəˌsɛri] *adj* innecessario

unnerve [ʌnˈnʌrv] *tr* acobardar, trastornar

unnoticeable [ʌnˈnotɪsəbəl] *adj* imperceptible

unnoticed [ʌnˈnotɪst] *adj* inadvertido

unobliging [ˌʌnəˈblaɪdʒɪŋ] *adj* poco servicial, poco amable

unobserved [ˌʌnəbˈzʌrvd] *adj* inadvertido, sin ser visto

unobtainable [ˌʌnəbˈtenəbəl] *adj* inencontrable, inasequible

unobtrusive [ˌʌnəbˈtrusɪv] *adj* discreto, reservado

unoccupied [ʌnˈɑkjəˌpaɪd] *adj* libre, vacante; (*not busy*) desocupado

unofficial [ˌʌnəˈfɪʃəl] *adj* extraoficial, oficioso

unopened [ʌnˈopənd] *adj* sin abrir; (*book*) no cortado

unorthodox [ʌnˈɔrθəˌdɑks] *adj* inortodoxo

unpack [ʌnˈpæk] *tr* desembalar, desempaquetar

unpalatable [ʌnˈpælətəbəl] *adj* desabrido, ingustable

unparalleled [ʌnˈpærəˌlɛld] *adj* incomparable, sin par, sin igual

unpardonable [ʌnˈpɑrdənəbəl] *adj* imperdonable

unpatriotic [ˌʌnpetrɪˈɑtɪk] o [ˌʌnpætrɪˈɑtɪk] *adj* antipatriótico

unperceived [ˌʌnpərˈsivd] *adj* inadvertido

unperturbable [ˌʌnpərˈtʌrbəbəl] *adj* infracto, imperturbable

unpleasant [ʌnˈplɛzənt] *adj* antipático, desagradable; sangrigordo, sangripesado; bofe (CAm)

unpopular [ʌnˈpɑpjələr] *adj* impopular

unpopularity [ʌnˌpɑpjəˈlærɪti] *s* impopularidad

unprecedented [ʌnˈprɛsɪˌdɛntɪd] *adj* sin precedente, inaudito

unprejudiced [ʌnˈprɛdʒədɪst] *adj* sin prejuicios, imparcial

unpremeditated [ˌʌnprɪˈmɛdɪˌtetɪd] *adj* impremeditado

unprepared [ˌʌnprɪˈpɛrd] *adj* desprevenido; falto de preparación

unprepossessing [ˌʌnpripəˈzɛsɪŋ] *adj* poco atrayente

unpresentable [ˌʌnprɪˈzɛntəbəl] *adj* impresentable

unpretentious [ˌʌnprɪˈtɛnʃəs] *adj* modesto, sencillo

unprincipled [ʌnˈprɪnsɪpəld] *adj* sin principios, sin conciencia

unproductive [ˌʌnprəˈdʌktɪv] *adj* improductivo

unprofitable [ʌnˈprɑfɪtəbəl] *adj* no provechoso, inútil

unpronounceable [ˌʌnprəˈnaʊnsəbəl] *adj* impronunciable

unpropitious [ˌʌnprəˈpɪʃəs] *adj* impropicio

unpublished [ʌnˈpʌblɪʃt] *adj* inédito

unpunished [ʌnˈpʌnɪʃt] *adj* impune

unpurchasable [ʌnˈpʌrtʃəsəbəl] *adj* incomprable

unquenchable [ʌnˈkwɛntʃəbəl] *adj* inextinguible

unquestionable [ʌnˈkwɛstʃənəbəl] *adj* incuestionable

unrav·el [ʌnˈrævəl] *v* (*pret & pp* -eled o -elled; *ger* -eling o -elling) *tr* deshebrar; desenredar, desenmarañar ‖ *intr* desenredarse, desenmarañarse

unreachable [ʌnˈritʃəbəl] *adj* inalcanzable

unreal [ʌnˈriəl] *adj* irreal

unreali·ty [ˌʌnrɪˈælɪti] *s* (*pl* -ties) irrealidad

unreasonable [ʌnˈrizənəbəl] *adj* irrazonable, desrazonable

unrecognizable [ʌnˈrɛkəgˌnaɪzəbəl] *adj* irreconocible

unreel [ʌnˈril] *tr* desenrollar ‖ *intr* desenrollarse

unrefined [ˌʌnrɪˈfaɪnd] *adj* no refinado, impuro; grosero, rudo, tosco

unrelenting [ˌʌnrɪˈlɛntɪŋ] *adj* inexorable, inflexible, implacable

unreliable [ˌʌnrɪˈlaɪəbəl] *adj* indigno de confianza, informal

unremitting [ˌʌnrɪˈmɪtɪŋ] *adj* constante, incesante; infatigable

unrenewable [ˌʌnrɪˈnjuˌəbəl] o [ˌʌnrɪˈnuˌəbəl] *adj* irrenovable; (com) improrrogable

unrented [ʌnˈrɛntɪd] *adj* desalquilado

unrepentant [ˌʌnrɪˈpɛntənt] *adj* impenitente

unrequited love [ˌʌnrɪˈkwaɪtɪd] *s* amor no correspondido

unresponsive [ˌʌnrɪˈspɑnsɪv] *adj* insensible, frío, desinteresado

unrest [ʌnˈrɛst] *s* intranquilidad, inquietud; alboroto, desorden *m*

un·rig [ʌnˈrɪg] *v* (*pret & pp* -rigged; *ger* -rigging) *tr* (naut) desaparejar

unrighteous [ʌnˈraɪtʃəs] *adj* injusto, malvado, vicioso

unripe [ʌnˈraɪp] *adj* inmaturo, verde; prematuro, precoz

unrivaled o **unrivalled** [ʌnˈraɪvəld] *adj* sin rival, sin par

unroll [ʌnˈrol] *tr* desenrollar, desplegar

unromantic [ˌʌnroˈmæntɪk] *adj* poco romántico

unruffled [ʌnˈrʌfəld] *adj* tranquilo, sereno

unruly [ʌnˈruli] *adj* ingobernable, indómito, revoltoso

unsaddle [ʌnˈsædəl] *tr* desensillar (*un caballo*); desarzonar (*al jinete*)

unsafe [ʌnˈsef] *adj* inseguro, peligroso

unsaid [ʌnˈsɛd] *adj* callado, no dicho

unsalable [ʌnˈseləbəl] *adj* invendible

unsanitary [ʌnˈsænɪˌtɛri] *adj* antihigiénico, insalubre

unsatisfactory [ʌnˌsætɪsˈfæktəri] *adj* insatisfactorio, poco satisfactorio

unsatisfied [ʌnˈsætɪsˌfaɪd] *adj* insatisfecho

unsavory [ʌnˈsevəri] *adj* desabrido; (fig) infame, deshonroso

unscathed [ʌnˈskeðd] *adj* ileso, sano y salvo

unscientific [ˌʌnsaɪənˈtɪfɪk] *adj* antiscientífico

unscrew [ʌnˈskru] *tr* destornillar ‖ *intr* destornillarse

unscrupulous [ʌnˈskrupjələs] *adj* inescrupuloso

unseal [ʌnˈsil] *tr* desellar; (fig) abrir

unseasonable [ʌnˈsizənəbəl] *adj* intempestivo, inoportuno

unseaworthy [ʌnˈsiˌwʌrði] *adj* innavegable

unseemly [ʌnˈsimli] *adj* impropio, indecoroso, indigno

unseen [ʌnˈsin] *adj* invisible, oculto

unselfish [ʌnˈsɛlfɪʃ] *adj* desinteresado, generoso, altruísta

unsettled [ʌnˈsɛtəld] *adj* inhabitado, despoblado; sin residencia fija; indeciso; descompuesto; (*bills*) por pagar

unshackle [ʌnˈʃækəl] *tr* desherrar, desencadenar

unshaken [ʌnˈʃekən] *adj* imperturbado

unshapely [ʌnˈʃepli] *adj* desproporcionado, mal formado

unshatterable [ʌnˈʃætərəbəl] *adj* inastillable

unshaven [ʌnˈʃevən] *adj* sin afeitar

unsheathe [ʌnˈʃið] *tr* desenvainar

unshod [ʌnˈʃɑd] *adj* descalzo; (*horse*) desherrado

unshrinkable [ʌnˈʃrɪŋkəbəl] *adj* inencogible

unsightly [ʌnˈsaɪtli] *adj* feo, de aspecto malo, repugnante

unsinkable [ʌnˈsɪŋkəbəl] *adj* insumergible

unskilled [ʌnˈskɪld] *adj* inexperto

unskilled laborer *s* bracero, peón *m*

unskillful [ʌnˈskɪlfəl] *adj* desmañado

unsnarl [ʌnˈsnɑrl] *tr* desenredar

unsociable [ʌnˈsoʃəbəl] *adj* insociable, huraño

unsold [ʌnˈsold] *adj* invendido

unsolder [ʌnˈsɑdər] *tr* desoldar; (fig) desunir, separar

unsophisticated [ˌʌnsəˈfɪstɪˌketɪd] *adj* ingenuo, natural, sencillo

unsound [ʌnˈsaʊnd] *adj* poco firme; falso, erróneo; (*decayed*) podrido; (*sleep*) ligero

unsown [ʌnˈson] *adj* yermo, no sembrado

unspeakable [ʌnˈspikəbəl] *adj* indecible, inefable; (*atrocious, infamous*) incalificable

unsportsmanlike [ʌnˈsportsmənˌlaɪk] *adj* antideportivo

unstable [ʌnˈstebəl] *adj* inestable

unsteady [ʌnˈstɛdi] *adj* inseguro, inestable; irresoluto, inconstante; poco juicioso

unstinted [ʌnˈstɪntɪd] *adj* no escatimado, generoso, liberal

unstitch [ʌnˈstɪtʃ] *tr* descoser

un·stop [ʌnˈstɑp] *v* (*pret & pp* -stopped; *ger* -stopping) *tr* destaponar

unstressed [ʌnˈstrɛst] *adj* sin énfasis; (*syllable*) inacentuado

unstrung [ʌnˈstrʌŋ] *adj* nervioso, trastornado

unsuccessful [ˌʌnsəkˈsɛsfəl] *adj* (*person*) desairado; (*undertaking*) impróspero; **to be unsuccessful** no tener éxito

unsuitable [ʌnˈsutəbəl] o [ʌnˈsjutəbəl] *adj* inadecuado, inconveniente

unsurpassable [ˌʌnsərˈpæsəbəl] *adj* insuperable

unsuspected [ˌʌnsəsˈpɛktɪd] *adj* insospechado

unswerving [ʌnˈswʌrvɪŋ] *adj* firme, inmutable, resoluto

unsymmetrical [ˌʌnsɪˈmɛtrɪkəl] *adj* asimétrico, disimétrico

unsympathetic [ˌʌnsɪmpəˈθɛtɪk] *adj* incompasivo, indiferente

unsystematic(al) [ˌʌnsɪstəˈmætɪk(əl)] *adj* poco sistemático, sin sistema

untactful [ʌnˈtæktfəl] *adj* indiscreto, falto de tacto

untamed [ʌnˈtemd] *adj* indomado, bravío

untangle [ʌnˈtæŋgəl] *tr* desenredar, desenmarañar

unteachable [ʌnˈtitʃəbəl] *adj* indócil

untenable [ʌnˈtɛnəbəl] *adj* insostenible

unthankful [ʌnˈθæŋkfəl] *adj* ingrato, desagradecido

unthinkable [ʌnˈθɪŋkəbəl] *adj* impensable

unthinking [ʌnˈθɪŋkɪŋ] *adj* irreflexivo, desatento; irracional, instintivo

untidy [ʌnˈtaɪdi] *adj* desaseado, desaliñado; descachalandrado

un•tie [ʌnˈtaɪ] *v* (*pret & pp* **-tied;** *ger* **-tying**) *tr* desatar; deshacer (*un nudo, una cuerda*); (*to free from restraint*) soltar; resolver || *intr* desatarse

until [ʌnˈtɪl] *prep* hasta || *conj* hasta que; **to wait until** aguardar a que, esperar a que

untillable [ʌnˈtɪləbəl] *adj* incultivable

untimely [ʌnˈtaɪmli] *adj* intempestivo

untiring [ʌnˈtaɪrɪŋ] *adj* incansable

untold [ʌnˈtold] *adj* nunca dicho; (*uncounted*) innumerable, incalculable

untouchable [ʌnˈtʌtʃəbəl] *adj* intangible || *s* intocable *mf*

untouched [ʌnˈtʌtʃt] *adj* intacto; íntegro; impasible; no mencionado

untoward [ʌnˈtord] *adj* desfavorable; indecoroso

untrammeled o **untrammelled** [ʌnˈtræməld] *adj* libre, sin trabas

untried [ʌnˈtraɪd] *adj* no probado, no ensayado

untroubled [ʌnˈtrʌbləd] *adj* tranquilo, sosegado

untrue [ʌnˈtru] *adj* falso; infiel

untrustworthy [ʌnˈtrʌst,wʌrði] *adj* indigno de confianza

untruth [ʌnˈtruθ] *s* falsedad, mentira

untruthful [ʌnˈtruθfəl] *adj* falso, mentiroso

untwist [ʌnˈtwɪst] *tr* destorcer || *intr* destorcerse

unused [ʌnˈjuzd] *adj* inutilizado, no usado; nuevo; **unused to** [ʌnˈjuzdtu] o [ʌnˈjustu] *adj* no acostumbrado a

unusual [ʌnˈjuʒuˑəl] *adj* inusual, insólito

unutterable [ʌnˈʌtərəbəl] *adj* indecible, inexpresable

unvanquished [ʌnˈvæŋkwɪʃt] *adj* invicto

unvarnished [ʌnˈvɑrnɪʃt] *adj* sin barnizar; (fig) sencillo, sin adornos

unveil [ʌnˈvel] *tr* quitar el velo a; descubrir, develar, inaugurar, (*una estatua*) || *intr* quitarse el velo

unveiling [ʌnˈvelɪŋ] *s* develación, inauguración

unventilated [ʌnˈvɛntɪ,letɪd] *adj* sin ventilar

unvoice [ʌnˈvɔɪs] *tr* afonizar, ensordecer || *intr* afonizarse, ensordecerse

unwanted [ʌnˈwɑntɪd] *adj* indeseado

unwarranted [ʌnˈwɑrəntɪd] *adj* injustificado; no autorizado; sin garantía

unwary [ʌnˈwɛri] *adj* incauto, imprudente

unwavering [ʌnˈwevərɪŋ] *adj* firme, determinado, resuelto

unwelcome [ʌnˈwɛlkəm] *adj* mal acogido; importuno, molesto

unwell [ʌnˈwɛl] *adj* indispuesto, enfermo; (coll) menstruante

unwholesome [ʌnˈholsəm] *adj* insalubre

unwieldy [ʌnˈwildi] *adj* inmanejable, abultado, pesado

unwilling [ʌnˈwɪlɪŋ] *adj* desinclinado, maldispuesto, renuente

unwillingly [ʌnˈwɪlɪŋli] *adv* de mala gana

un•wind [ʌnˈwaɪnd] *v* (*pret & pp* **-wound** [ˈwaʊnd]) *tr* desenvolver; (*rewind*) rebobinar || *intr* desenvolverse; distenderse (*el muelle del reloj*)

unwise [ʌnˈwaɪz] *adj* indiscreto, malaconsejado

unwished-for [ʌnˈwɪʃt,fɔr] *adj* indeseado

unwitting [ʌnˈwɪtɪŋ] *adj* inadvertido, inconsciente

unwonted [ʌnˈwʌntɪd] *adj* poco común, raro, insólito

unworldly [ʌnˈwʌrldi] *adj* no terrenal, no mundano, espiritual

unworthy [ʌnˈwʌrði] *adj* indigno, desmerecedor

un•wrap [ʌnˈræp] *v* (*pret & pp* **-wrapped;** *ger* **wrapping**) *tr* desenvolver, desempapelar

unwrinkle [ʌnˈrɪŋkəl] *tr* desarrugar || *intr* desarrugarse

unwritten [ʌnˈrɪtən] *adj* no escrito; (*blank*) en blanco; oral

unyielding [ʌnˈjildɪŋ] *adj* firme, inflexible; terco, reacio

unyoke [ʌnˈjok] *tr* desuncir

up [ʌp] *adj* ascendente; alto, elevado; derecho, en pie; terminado; cumplido; levantado de la cama; **to be up and about** estar levantado (*el que estaba enfermo*) || *s* subida; **ups and downs** altibajos, vicisitudes || *adv* arriba; en el aire; hacia arriba; al norte; **to be up** estar levantado; vencer (*un plazo*); **to be up in arms** estar sobre las armas; protestar vehementemente; **to be up to a person** tocarle a una persona; **to get up** levantarse; **to go up** subir; **to keep up** mantener; continuar; mantenerse firme; **to keep up with** correr parejas con; **up above**

allá arriba; **up against it** (slang) en apuros; **up to** hasta; (*capable of*) a la altura de; (*informed of*) al corriente de; (*scheming*) armando, tramando; **what is up?** ¿qué pasa? || *prep* subiendo; **up the river** río arriba; **up the street** calle arriba
up-and-coming ['ʌpən'kʌmɪŋ] *adj* (coll) prometedor
up-and-doing ['ʌpən'du•ɪŋ] *adj* (coll) emprendedor
up-and-up ['ʌpən'ʌp] *s*—**on the up-and-up** (coll) mejorándose; (coll) abiertamente, sin dolo
up•braid' *tr* regañar, reprender
upbringing ['ʌp,brɪŋɪŋ] *s* educación, crianza
UPC *abbr* **universal product code**
up'coun'try *adv* (coll) hacia el interior, tierra adentro || *s* (coll) interior *m* del país
up•date' *tr* poner al día
upheaval [ʌp'hivəl] *s* trastorno, cataclismo
up'hill' *adj* ascendente; arduo, difícil, penoso || **up'hill'** *adv* cuesta arriba
up•hold' *v* (*pret & pp* **-held**) *tr* levantar; apoyar, sostener; defender
upholster [ʌp'holstər] *tr* tapizar
upholsterer [ʌp'holstərər] *s* tapicero
upholster•y [ʌp'holstəri] *s* (*pl* **-ies**) tapicería
up'keep' *s* conservación, manutención; gastos de conservación, gastos de entretenimiento
upland ['ʌplənd] o ['ʌplænd] *adj* alto, elevado || *s* tierra alta, terreno elevado
up'lift' *s* (*lifting*) elevación, levantamiento; mejora social; (*moral or spiritual improvement*) edificación || **up•lift'** *tr* elevar, levantar; edificar
upon [ə'pɑn] *prep* en, sobre, encima de; **upon** + *ger* al + *inf*, p.ej., **upon arriving** al llegar; **upon my word!** ¡por mi palabra!
upper ['ʌpər] *adj* alto, superior; (*country*) interior; (*clothing*) exterior || *s* (*of shoe*) pala; **on one's uppers** con las suelas gastadas; (coll) andrajoso, pobre, sin blanca
upper berth *s* litera alta, cama alta
upper case *s* (typ) caja alta
upper classes *spl* altas clases
upper hand *s* dominio, ventaja; **to have the upper hand** tener vara alta
upper middle class *s* alta burguesía
up'per•most' *adj* (el) más alto; (el) principal || *adv* en lo más alto primero, en primer lugar
uppish ['ʌpɪʃ] *adj* (coll) copetudo, arrogante
up•raise' *tr* levantar
up'right' *adj* derecho, vertical; probo, recto || *adv* verticalmente || *s* montante *m*
uprising [ʌp'raɪzɪŋ] ['ʌp,raɪzɪŋ] *s* insurrección, levantamiento
up'roar' *s* alboroto, conmoción, tumulto
uproarious [ʌp'rorɪ•əs] *adj* tumultuoso; (*noisy*) ruidoso; (*funny*) muy cómico
up•root' *tr* desarraigar
up•set' o **up'set'** *adj* (*overturned*) volcado; trastornado; indispuesto || **up'set'** *s* (*overturn*) vuelco; (*unexpected defeat*) contra-

tiempo; (*disturbance*) trastorno; (*illness*) indisposición, enfermedad || **up•set'** *v* (*pret & pp* **-set;** *ger* **-setting**) *tr* volcar; trastornar; indisponer || *intr* volcar
upset price *s* precio mínimo fijado en una subasta
upsetting [ʌp'sɛtɪŋ] *adj* desconcertante
up'shot' *s* conclusión, resultado; esencia, quid *m*
up'side' *s* parte *f* superior, lado superior; **on the upside** (*said of prices*) subiendo
upside down *adv* alrevés, lo de arriba abajo, patas arriba; en confusión, revuelto; **to turn upside down** volcar; trastornar; volcarse; trastornarse
up'stage' *adj* situado al fondo de la escena; (coll) altanero, arrogante || *adv* al fondo de la escena || **up'stage'** *tr* (coll) mirar por encima del hombro, desairar
up'stairs' *adj* de arriba || *adv* arriba || *s* piso superior, pisos superiores
upstanding [ʌp'stændɪŋ] *adj* derecho; gallardo; probo, recto
up'start' *adj & s* advenedizo
up'stream' *adv* aguas arriba, río arriba
up'stroke' *s* carrera ascendente
up'swing' *s* movimiento hacia arriba; mejora notable; **on the upswing** mejorando notablemente
up'-to-date' *adj* corriente; reciente, moderno; de última hora, de última moda
up'-to-the-min'ute *adj* al día, de actualidad
up'town' *adj* de la parte alta de la ciudad || *adv* en la parte alta de la ciudad
up train *s* tren *m* ascendente
up'trend' *s* tendencia al alza
up'turn' *s* alza, subida, mejora
upturned [ʌp'tʌrnd] *adj* revuelto; (*part of clothing*) arremangado; (*nose*) respingada
upward ['ʌpwərd] *adj* ascendente || *adv* hacia arriba; **upward of** más de
Ural ['jurəl] *adj* ural || **Urals** *spl* Urales *mpl*
uranium [ju'renɪ•əm] *s* uranio
urban ['ʌrbən] *adj* urbano (*perteneciente a la ciudad*)
urbane [ʌr'ben] *adj* urbano (*atento, cortés*)
urban guerrilla *s* guerrillero urbano
urbanite ['ʌrbə,naɪt] *s* ciudadano
urbanity [ʌr'bænɪti] *s* urbanidad
urbanize ['ʌrbə,naɪz] *tr* urbanizar
urchin ['ʌrtʃɪn] *s* pilluelo, galopín *m*; patojo (CAm)
ure•thra [ju'riθrə] *s* (*pl* **-thras** o **-thrae** [θri]) uretra
urge [ʌrdʒ] *s* impulso, estímulo || *tr* apremiar, impeler, estimular; pedir instantánedmente; (*to try to persuade*) instar || *intr* instar
urgen•cy ['ʌrdʒənsi] *s* (*pl* **-cies**) urgencia; instancia, apremio
urgent ['ʌrdʒənt] *adj* urgente; apremiante
urinal ['jurɪnəl] *s* (*receptacle*) orinal *m*; (*place*) urinario
urinary ['jurɪ,nɛri] *adj* urinario
urinate ['jurɪ,net] *tr* orinar (*p.ej., sangre*) || *intr* orinar, orinarse; (coll) hacer pipí

urine ['jurɪn] s orina, orines *mpl;* (coll) pipí *m*

urn [ʌrn] s (*decorative vase*) jarrón *m;* cafetera o tetera con grifo; (*to hold ashes of the dead after cremation*) urna

urology [juˈrɑlədʒi] s urología

Uruguay ['jurə,gwaɪ] s el Uruguay

Uruguayan [,jurəˈgwaɪ•ən] *adj* & *s* uruguayo

us [ʌs] *pron pers* nos; nosotros; **to us** nos; a nosotros

U.S.A. *abbr* **United States of America, United States Army, Union of South Africa**

usable ['juzəbəl] *adj* aprovechable, utilizable

usage ['jusɪdʒ] o ['juzɪdʒ] s usanza; (*e.g., of a language*) uso

usage instructions *spl* modo de empleo

use [jus] s uso, empleo; utilidad; **in use** en uso; **out of use** desusado; **to be of no use** no servir para nada; **to have no use for** no necesitar; no servirse de; (coll) tener en poco; **to make use of** servirse de ‖ [juz] *tr* usar, emplear, servirse de; **to use badly** maltratar; **to use up** agotar, consumir ‖ *intr* (empléase sólo en el pretérito y se traduce al español con el pretérito imperfecto o el verbo **soler**), p.ej., **I used to go out for a walk every evening** salía de paseo todas las tardes o solía salir de paseo todas las tardes

used [juzd] *adj* (*customarily employed; worn, partly worn-out; accustomed*) usado; **used to** ['juzdtu] o ['justu] acostumbrado a

useful ['jusfəl] *adj* útil

usefulness ['jusfəlnɪs] s utilidad

useless ['juslɪs] *adj* inservible, inútil

user ['juzər] s usuario

usher ['ʌʃər] s (*in a theater*) acomodador *m;* (*doorkeeper*) ujier *m*, portero ‖ *tr* acomodar; **to usher in** anunciar, introducir

U.S.S.R. *abbr* **Union of Soviet Socialist Republics**

usual ['juʒʊ•əl] *adj* usual, acostumbrado; **as usual** como de costumbre

usually ['juʒʊ•əli] *adj* usualmente, de ordinario

usurp [juˈzʌrp] *tr* usurpar

usu•ry ['juʒəri] s (*pl* **-ries**) usura

utensil [juˈtɛnsɪl] s utensilio; **utensils** corotos *mpl*

uter•us ['jutərəs] s (*pl* **-i** [,aɪ]); útero

utilitarian [,jutɪlɪˈtɛrɪ•ən] *adj* utilitario

utili•ty [juˈtɪlɪti] s (*pl* **-ties**) utilidad; empresa de servicio público

utilize ['jutɪ,laɪz] *tr* utilizar

utmost ['ʌt,most] *adj* sumo, extremo, último; más grande, mayor posible; más lejano ‖ *s*— **the utmost** lo sumo, lo mayor, lo más; **to the utmost** a lo sumo, a más no poder; **to do one's utmost** hacer todo lo posible

utopia [juˈtopɪ•ə] s utopía

utopian [juˈtopɪ•ən] *adj* utópico, utopista ‖ *s* utopista *mf*

utter ['ʌtər] *adj* total, absoluto ‖ *tr* proferir, pronunciar; dar (*un suspiro*)

utterance ['ʌtərəns] s expresión, pronunciación; declaración

utterly ['ʌtərli] *adj* completamente, totalmente, absolutamente

uxoricide [ʌkˈsorɪ,saɪd] s (*husband*) uxoricida *m;* (*act*) uxoricidio

uxorious [ʌkˈsorɪ•əs] *adj* uxorio

V

V, v [vi] vigésima segunda letra del alfabeto inglés

v. *abbr* **verb, verse, versus, vide** (Lat) **see, voice, volt, volume**

V. abbr **Venerable, Vice, Viscount, Volunteer**

vacan•cy ['vekənsi] s (*pl* **-cies**) (*emptiness; gap, opening*) vacío; (*unfilled position or job*) vacancia, vacante *f*, vacío; piso vacante; cargo vacante

vacant ['vekənt] *adj* (*empty*) vacío; (*having no occupant; untenanted*) vacante; (*expression, look*) vago; distraído

vacate ['veket] *tr* dejar vacante; anular, invalidar, revocar ‖ *intr* (*to move out*) desalojar; (coll) irse, marcharse

vacation [veˈkeʃən] s vacaciones; **on vacation** de vacaciones ‖ *intr* tomar vacaciones

vacationist [veˈkeʃənɪst] s vacacionista *mf*

vacation with pay s vacaciones retribuídas

vaccinate ['væksɪ,net] *tr* vacunar

vaccination [,væksɪˈneʃən] s vacunación

vaccine [vækˈsin] s vacuna

vacillate ['væsɪ,let] *intr* vacilar

vacillating ['væsɪ,letɪŋ] *adj* vacilante

vacui•ty [væˈkjuˈɪti] s (*pl* **-ties**) vacuidad

vacu•um ['vækju•əm] s (*pl* **-ums** o **-a** [ə]) vacío ‖ *tr* (coll) limpiar

vacuum cleaner s aspirador *m* de polvo

vacuum tank s (aut) aspirador *m* de gasolina, nodriza

vacuum tube s tubo de vacío

vagabond ['vægə,bɑnd] *adj* & *s* vagabundo

vagar•y [vəˈgɛri] s (*pl* **-ies**) capricho

vagina [vəˈdʒaɪnə] s vagina

vagran•cy ['vegrənsi] s (*pl* **-cies**) vagabundaje *m*

vagrant ['vegrənt] *adj* & *s* vagabundo

vague [veg] *adj* vago; impreciso

vain [ven] *adj* vano; (*conceited*) vanidoso; **in vain** en vano

vainglorious [venˈglorɪ•əs] *adj* vanaglorioso

valance ['væləns] s (*across the top of a window*) guardamalleta; (*drapery*) dosera-

vale [vel] s valle m
valedictorian [,vælɪdɪk'torɪ•ən] s alumno que pronuncia el discurso de despedida al fin del curso
valedicto•ry [,vælɪ'dɪktəri] adj de despedida ‖ s (pl -ries) discurso de despedida
valence ['veləns] s (chem) valencia
valentine ['vælən,taɪn] s tarjeta amorosa o jocosa del día de San Valentín
Valentine Day s día m de los corazones, día de los enamorados (14 de febrero)
vale of tears s valle m de lágrimas
valet ['vælɪt] o ['væle] s ayuda m, paje m
valiant ['væljənt] adj valiente, valeroso
valid ['vælɪd] adj válido, valedero
validate ['vælɪ,det] tr validar; (sport) homologar
validation [,vælɪ'deʃən] s validación; (sport) homologación
validi•ty [və'lɪdɪti] s (pl -ties) validez f
valise [və'lis] s maleta
valley ['væli] s valle m; (of roof) lima hoya
valor ['vælər] s valor m, ánimo
valorous ['vælərəs] adj valeroso
valuable ['vælju•əbəl] o ['væljəbəl] adj (having monetary value) valioso; (highly thought of) estimable ‖ **valuables** spl alhajas, objetos de valor
value ['vælju] s valor m; (return for one's money in a purchase) (coll) adquisición, inversión, p.ej., **an excellent value** una adquisición excelente ‖ tr (to think highly of) estimar; (to set a price for) valorar, valuar
val'ue-add'ed tax s impuesto sobre el valor añadido, impuesto al valor agregado
valueless ['væljulɪs] adj sin valor
valve [vælv] s válvula; (of mollusk) valva; (mus) llava f
valve cap s capuchón m
valve gears spl distribución
valve'-in-head' engine s motor m con válvulas en cabeza
valve lifter ['lɪftər] s levantaválvulas m
valve seat s asiento de válvula
valve spring s muelle m de válvula
valve stem s vástago de válvula
vamp [væmp] s (of shoe) empella; (patchwork) remiendo; (woman who preys on men) (slang) mujer f fatal, vampiresa ‖ tr poner empella a (un zapato); remendar; (to concoct) componer, enmendar; (jazz) improvisar (un acompañamiento); (slang) seducir (una mujer mundana a un hombre)
vampire ['væmpaɪr] s vampiro; (woman who preys on men) mujer f fatal, vampiresa
van [væn] s carro de carga, camión m de mudanzas; (mil & fig) vanguardia; (Brit) furgón m de equipajes
vanadium [və'nedɪ•əm] s vanadio
vandal ['vændəl] adj & s vándalo ‖ **Vandal** adj & s vándalo
vandalism ['vændə,lɪzəm] s vandalismo
vane [ven] s (weathervane) veleta; (of windmill) aspa; (of propeller or turbine) paleta; (of feather) barba

vanguard ['væn,gɑrd] s (mil & fig) vanguardia; **in the vanguard** a vanguardia
vanilla [və'nɪlə] s vainilla
vanish ['vænɪʃ] intr desvanecerse
vanishing cream ['vænɪʃɪŋ] s crema desvanecedora
vani•ty ['vænɪti] s (pl -ties) vanidad; (dressing table) tocador m; (vanity case) estuche m de afeites
vanity case s estuche m de afeites, neceser m de belleza
vanquish ['væŋkwɪʃ] tr vencer, rendir
vantage ground ['væntɪdʒ] s posición ventajosa
vapid ['væpɪd] adj insípido
vapor ['vepər] s vapor m (el visible; exhalación, vaho, niebla, etc.)
vaporize ['vepə,raɪz] tr vaporizar ‖ intr vaporizarse
vaporous ['vepərəs] adj vaporoso
vapor trail s (aer) estela de vapor, rastro de condensación
var. abbr **variant**
variable ['vɛrɪ•əbəl] adj & s variable f
variance ['vɛrɪ•əns] s diferencia, variación; **at variance with** en desacuerdo con
variant ['vɛrɪ•ənt] adj & s variante f
variation [,vɛrɪ'eʃən] s variación
varicose ['værɪ,kos] adj varicoso
varicose vein s (pathol) varice f
varied ['vɛrɪd] adj variado, vario
variegated ['vɛrɪ•ə,getɪd] o ['vɛrɪ,getɪd] adj abigarrado, variado
varie•ty [və'raɪ•ɪti] s (pl -ties) variedad
variety show s variedades
variola [və'raɪ•ələ] s (pathol) viruela
various ['vɛrɪ•əs] adj (several; of different kinds) varios; (many-sided; many-colored) vario
varnish ['vɑrnɪʃ] s barniz m; (fig) capa, apariencia ‖ tr barnizar; (fig) dar apariencia falsa a
varsi•ty ['vɑrsɪti] adj (sport) universitario ‖ s (pl -ties) (sport) equipo principal de la universidad
var•y ['vɛri] v (pret & pp -ied) tr & intr variar
vase [ves] o [vez] s florero, jarrón m
Vaseline ['væsə,lin] s (trademark) vaselina
vassal ['væsəl] adj & s vasallo
vast [væst] o [vɑst] adj vasto
vastly ['væstli] adv enormemente
vastness ['væstnɪs] s vastedad
vat [væt] s cuba, tina
vaudeville ['vodvɪl] o ['vɔdəvɪl] s variedades; (light theatrical piece interspersed with songs) zarzuela
vault [vɔlt] s (underground chamber) bodega; (of a bank) cámara acorazada; (burial chamber) sepultura, tumba; (firmament) bóveda celeste; (leap) salto; (archit) bóveda ‖ tr abovedar; saltar ‖ intr saltar
vaunt [vɔnt] s jactancia ‖ tr jactarse de ‖ intr jactarse
VCR abbr **video-cassette recorder**
veal [vil] s ternera, carne f de ternera
veal chop s chuleta de ternera

ur
ve

vedette [vɪ'dɛt] *s* buque *m* escucha; centinela *m* de avanzada

veer [vɪr] *s* viraje *m* ‖ *tr* virar ‖ *intr* virar; (naut) llamar (*el viento*)

vegetable ['vɛdʒɪtəbəl] *adj* vegetal ‖ *s* (*plant*) vegetal *m;* (*edible part of plant*) hortaliza, legumbre *f*

vegetable garden *s* huerto de hortalizas, huerto de verduras

vegetable soup *s* menestra, sopa de hortalizas

vegetarian [,vɛdʒɪ'tɛrɪ•ən] *adj* & *s* vegetariano

vehemence ['vi•ɪməns] *s* vehemencia

vehement ['vi•ɪmənt] *adj* vehemente

vehicle ['vi•ɪkəl] *s* vehículo

vehicular traffic [vɪ'hɪkjələr] *s* circulación rodada

veil [vel] *s* velo; **to take the veil** tomar el velo ‖ *tr* velar (*cubrir con un velo; cubrir, disimular*)

vein [ven] *s* vena; (*streak*) veta; (*distinctive quality*) rasgo ‖ *tr* vetear

velar ['vilər] *adj* & *s* velar *f*

vellum ['vɛləm] *s* vitela; papel *m* vitela

veloci•ty [vɪ'lɑsɪti] *s* (*pl* **-ties**) velocidad

velvet ['vɛlvɪt] *adj* de terciopelo ‖ *s* terciopelo; (slang) ganancia limpia

velveteen [,vɛlvɪ'tin] *s* velludillo

velvety ['vɛlvɪti] *adj* aterciopelado

Ven. *abbr* **Venerable**

vend [vɛnd] *tr* vender como buhonero

vending machine *s* distribuidor automático

vendor ['vɛndər] *s* vendedor *m*, buhonero

veneer [və'nɪr] *s* chapa, enchapado; (fig) apariencia ‖ *tr* enchapar

venerable ['vɛnərəbəl] *adj* venerable

venerate ['vɛnə,ret] *tr* venerar

venereal [vɪ'nɪrɪ•əl] *adj* venéreo

Venetia [vɪ'niʃɪ•ə] o [vɪ'niʃə] *s* Venecia (*provincia*)

Venetian [vɪ'niʃən] *adj* & *s* veneciano

Venetian blind *s* persiana

Venezuela [,vɛnɪ'zwilə] *s* Venezuela

Venezuelan [,vɛnɪzwilən] *adj* & *s* venezolano

vengeance ['vɛndʒəns] *s* venganza; **with a vengeance** con furia, con violencia; excesivamente, con creces

vengeful ['vɛndʒfəl] *adj* vengativo

Venice ['vɛnɪs] *s* Venecia (*ciudad*)

venire [vɪ'naɪri] *s* (law) auto de convocación del jurado

venison ['vɛnɪsən] o ['vɛnɪzən] *s* carne *f* de venado

venom ['vɛnəm] *s* veneno

venomous ['vɛnəməs] *adj* venenoso

vent [vɛnt] *s* agujero, orificio; (*outlet*) salida; **to give vent to** dar libre curso a ‖ *tr* proveer de abertura; desahogar, expresar; **to vent one's spleen** descargar la bilis

vent'hole' *s* respiradero

ventilate ['vɛntɪ,let] *tr* ventilar

ventilator ['vɛntɪ,letər] *s* ventilador *m*

ventricle ['vɛntrɪkəl] *s* ventrículo

ventriloquism [vɛn'trɪlə,kwɪzəm] *s* ventriloquia

ventriloquist [vɛn'trɪləkwɪst] *s* ventrílocuo

venture ['vɛntʃər] *s* empresa arriesgada; **at a venture** a la buena ventura ‖ *tr* aventurar ‖ *intr* aventurarse; **to venture on** arriesgarse en

venturesome ['vɛntʃərsəm] *adj* (*bold, daring*) aventurero; (*hazardous*) aventurado

venturous ['vɛntʃərəs] *adj* (*bold, daring*) aventurero; (*hazardous*) aventurado, arriesgado

venue ['vɛnju] *s* (law) lugar *m* del crimen; (law) lugar donde se reúne el jurado; **change of venue** (law) traslado de jurisdicción

Venus ['vinəs] *s* (astr) Venus *m;* (myth) Venus *f;* (*very beautiful woman*) Venus *f*

veracious [vɪ'reʃəs] *adj* veraz

veraci•ty [vɪ'ræsɪti] *s* (*pl* **-ties**) veracidad

veranda o **verandah** [və'rændə] *s* terraza, veranda, galería

verb [vʌrb] *adj* verbal ‖ *s* verbo

verbatim [vər'betɪm] *adj* textual ‖ *adv* palabra por palabra, al pie de la letra

verbena [vər'binə] *s* (bot) verbena

verbiage ['vʌrbɪ•ɪdʒ] *s* palabrería, verbosidad

verbose [vər'bos] *adj* verboso

verdant ['vʌrdənt] *adj* verde; cándido, sencillo

verdict ['vʌrdɪkt] *s* veredicto, fallo

verdigris ['vʌrdɪ,gris] *s* verdete *m*

verdure ['vʌrdʒər] *s* verdor *m*

verge [vʌrdʒ] *s* borde *m*, límite *m;* (*of a column*) fuste *m;* báculo; (eccl) cetro; **on the verge of** al borde de; a punto de; **within the verge of** al alcance de ‖ *intr*— **to verge on** o **upon** llegar casi hasta, rayar en

verification [,vɛrɪfɪ'keʃən] *s* verificatión

veri•fy ['vɛrɪ,faɪ] *v* (*pret* & *pp* **-fied**) *tr* verificar, comprobar; (law) afirmar bajo juramento

verily ['vɛrɪli] *adv* verdaderamente, en verdad

veritable ['vɛrɪtəbəl] *adj* verdadero

vermicelli [,vʌrmɪ'sɛli] *s* fideos

vermilion [vər'mɪljən] *adj* bermejo ‖ *s* bermellón *m*

vermin ['vʌrmɪn] *ssg* (*objectionable person*) sabandija; bicherío (SAm) ‖ *spl* (*objectionable animals or persons*) sabandijas

vermouth [vər'muθ] o ['vʌrmuθ] *s* vermú *m*

vernacular [vər'nækjələr] *adj* vernáculo ‖ *s* lenguaje vernáculo; idioma *m* corriente; (*language peculiar to a class or profession*) jerga

veronica [və'rɑnɪkə] *s* (bot & taur) verónica; lienzo de la Verónica

Versailles [vɛr'saɪ] *s* Versalles

versatile ['vʌrsətɪl] *adj* versátil; [*person*] de muchas habilidades; (*informed on many subjects*) polifacético, universal; (*device or tool*) útil para muchas cosas

verse [vʌrs] *s* verso; (*in the Bible*) versículo

versed [vʌrst] *adj* versado; **to become versed in** versarse en

versification [,vʌrsɪfɪ'keʃən] *s* versificación

versi•fy ['vʌrsɪ,faɪ] v (pret & pp **-fied**) tr & intr versificar

version ['vʌrʒən] s versión

ver•so ['vʌrso] s (pl **-sos**) (e.g., of a coin) reverso; (typ) verso

versus ['vʌrsəs] prep contra

verte•bra ['vʌrtɪbrə] s (pl **-brae** [,bri] o **-bras**) vértebra

vertebral disk ['vʌrtə,brəl] s disco vertebral

vertebrate ['vʌrtɪ,bret] adj & s vertebrado

ver•tex ['vʌrtɛks] s (pl **-texes** o **-tices** [tɪ,siz]) (top, summit) ápice m; (geom) vértice m

vertical ['vʌrtɪkəl] adj & s vertical f

vertical hold s (telv) bloqueo vertical

vertical rudder s (aer) timón m de dirección

vertical take-off m despegue m vertical

verti•go ['vʌrtɪ,go] s (pl **-gos** o **-goes**) vértigo

verve [vʌrv] s brío, ánimo, vigor m

very ['vɛri] adj mismísimo; (sheer, utter) mero, puro; (actual) verdadero ‖ adv muy; mucho, p.ej., **to be very hungry** tener mucha hambre

vesicle ['vɛsɪkəl] s vesícula

vesper ['vɛspər] s tarde f, caída de la tarde; oración de la tarde; canción de la tarde; **vespers** (eccl) vísperas ‖ **Vesper** s Véspero

vesper bell s campana que llama a vísperas

vessel ['vɛsəl] s vasija, recipiente m; (ship) bajel m, embarcación, buque m; (anat) vaso

vest [vɛst] s (of man's suit) chaleco; (jabot) chorrera; (undershirt) camiseta ‖ tr vestir; **to vest in** conceder (p.ej., poder) a; **to vest with** investir de ‖ intr vestirse; **to vest in** pasar a

vested interests spl intereses creados

vestibule ['vɛstɪ,bjul] s vestíbulo, zaguán m

vestige ['vɛstɪdʒ] s vestigio

vestment ['vɛstmənt] s vestidura

vest'-pock'et adj de bolsillo, en miniatura; diminuto

ves•try ['vɛstri] s (pl **-tries**) sacristía; (chapel) capilla; junta parroquial; reunión de la junta parroquial

vestry•man ['vɛstrimən] s (pl **-men** [mən]) miembro de la junta parroquial

Vesuvius [vɪ'suvɪ•əs] o [vɪ'sjuvɪ•əs] s el Vesubio

vet. abbr veteran, veterinary

vetch [vɛtʃ] s arveja, veza; (grass pea) almorta

veteran ['vɛtərən] adj & s veterano

veterinarian [,vɛtərɪ'nɛrɪ•ən] s veterinario

veterinar•y ['vɛtərɪ,nɛri] adj veterinario ‖ s (pl **-ies**) veterinario

veterinary medicine s veterinaria, medicina veterinaria

ve•to ['vito] s (pl **-toes**) veto ‖ tr vetar

vex [vɛks] tr vejar, molestar

vexation [vɛk'seʃən] s vejación, molestia

v.g. abbr verbi gratia (Lat) for example

via ['vaɪ•ə] prep vía, p.ej., **via Lisbon** vía Lisboa

viaduct ['vaɪ•ə,dʌkt] s viaducto

vial ['vaɪ•əl] s redoma, frasco pequeño

viati•cum [vaɪ,ætɪkəm] s (pl **-cums** o **-ca** [kə]) (eccl) viático

viand ['vaɪ•ənd] s vianda, manjar m

vibrate ['vaɪbret] tr & intr vibrar

vibration [vaɪ'breʃən] s vibración

vicar ['vɪkər] s vicario

vicarage ['vɪkərɪdʒ] s casa del vicario; (duties of vicar) vicaría

vicarious [vaɪ'kɛrɪ•əs] adj substituto; (punishment) sufrido por otro; (power, authority) delegado; (enjoyment) reflejado

vice [vaɪs] s vicio

vice'-ad'miral s vicealmirante m

vice'-pres'ident s vicepresidente m

viceroy ['vaɪsrɔɪ] s virrey m

vice versa ['vaɪsi 'vʌrsə] o ['vaɪs 'vʌrsə] adv viceversa

vicini•ty [vɪ'sɪnɪti] s (pl **-ties**) vecindad

vicious ['vɪʃəs] adj vicioso; malazo; (dog) bravo; (horse) arisco

victim ['vɪktɪm] s víctima

victimize ['vɪktɪ,maɪz] tr hacer víctima; engañar, estafar

victor ['vɪktər] s vencedor m

victorious [vɪk'torɪ•əs] adj victorioso

victo•ry ['vɪktəri] s (pl **-ries**) victoria

victuals ['vɪtəlz] spl vituallas, provisiones de boca

vid. abbr vide (Lat) see

video cassette s videocasete m

vid'e•o-cas•sette' recorder s videograbador m

video-cassette recording s videograbación

video disk s videodisco

video game s video-juego

video recorder s magnetoscopia

video signal ['vɪdɪ,o] s señal f de vídeo

video tape s cinta grabada de televisión

vid'eo-tape' recording s videograbación

vie [vaɪ] v (pret & pp **vied**; ger **vying**) intr competir, emular, rivalizar

Vien•nese [,vi•ə'niz] adj vienés ‖ s (pl **-nese**) vienés m

Vietnam•ese [vɪ,ɛtnə'miz] adj vietnamés ‖ s (pl **-ese**) vietnamés m

view [vju] s vista; (purpose) intento, propósito, vista; **to be on view** estar expuesto (p.ej., un cadáver); **to keep in view** no perder de vista; no olvidar, tener presente; **to take a dim view of** no entusiasmarse por, mirar escépticamente; **with a view to** con vistas a ‖ tr ver, mirar; considerar, contemplar; examinar, inspeccionar

viewer ['vju•ər] s espectador m; telespectador m, televidente mf; proyector m de transparencias; mirador m de transparencias

view finder s (phot) visor m

view'point' s punto de vista

vigil ['vɪdʒɪl] s vigilia; **to keep vigil** velar

vigilance ['vɪdʒɪləns] s vigilancia

vigilant ['vɪdʒɪlənt] adj vigilante

vignette [vɪn'jɛt] s viñeta

vigor ['vɪgər] s vigor m

vigorous ['vɪgərəs] adj vigoroso

vile [vaɪl] adj vil; (disgusting) asqueroso, repugnante; (weather) muy malo

ve

vi

vili•fy ['vɪlɪ,faɪ] v (pret & pp **-fied**) tr difamar, denigrar

villa ['vɪlə] s villa, quinta

village ['vɪlɪdʒ] s aldea

villager ['vɪlɪdʒər] s aldeano

villain ['vɪlən] s malvado; (of a play) malo, traidor m

villainous ['vɪlənəs] adj malvado

villain•y ['vɪləni] s (pl **-ies**) maldad, perfidia

vim [vɪm] s fuerza, brío, vigor m

vinaigrette [,vɪnə'grɛt] s vinagrera

vinaigrette sauce s vinagreta

vindicate ['vɪndɪ,ket] tr vindicar, exculpar

vindictive [vɪn'dɪktɪv] adj vengativo

vine [vaɪn] s (creeping or climbing plant) enredadera; (grape plant) vid f, parra

vine'dress'er s viñador m, viticultor m

vinegar ['vɪnɪgər] s vinagre m

vinegarish ['vɪnɪgərɪʃ] adj avinagrado

vinegary ['vɪnɪgəri] adj vinagroso

vineyard ['vɪnjərd] s viña, viñedo

vineyardist ['vɪnjərdɪst] s viñador m, viticultor m

vintage ['vɪntɪdʒ] s vendimia; vino de buena cosecha; (coll) categoría, clase f

vintager ['vɪntɪdʒər] s vendimiador m

vintage wine s vino de buena cosecha

vintage year s año de buen vino

vintner ['vɪntnər] s vinatero

vinyl ['vaɪnɪl] s vinilo

violate ['vaɪ•ə,let] tr violar

violence ['vaɪ•ələns] s violencia

violent ['vaɪ•ələnt] adj violento

violet ['vaɪ•əlɪt] adj violado ‖ s (color) violeta m, violado; (dye) violeta m; (bot) violeta f

violin [,vaɪ•ə'lɪn] s violín m

violinist [,vaɪ•ə'lɪnɪst] s violinista mf

violoncellist [,vaɪ•ələn'tʃɛlɪst] o [,vɪələn-'tʃɛlɪst] s violoncelista mf

violoncel•lo [,vaɪ•ələn'tʃɛlo] o [,vɪələn'tʃɛlo] s (pl **-los**) violoncelo

viper ['vaɪpər] s víbora

VIPs ['vi,aɪ'pis] spl (letterword) notables mpl

vira•go [vɪ'rego] s (pl **-goes** o **-gos**) mujer de mal genio

virgin ['vʌrdʒɪn] adj & s virgen f

virgin birth s parto virginal de María Santísima; (zool) partenogénesis f

Virginia creeper [vər'dʒɪnɪ•ə] s (bot) guau m

virginity [vər'dʒɪnɪti] s virginidad

Virgo ['vʌrgo] s (astr) Virgo

virility [vɪ'rɪlɪti] s virilidad

virology [vaɪ'rɑlədʒi] s virología

virtual ['vʌrtʃʊ•əl] adj virtual

virtue ['vʌrtʃʊ] s virtud

virtuosi•ty [,vʌrtʃʊ'ɑsɪti] s (pl **-ties**) virtuosismo

virtuo•so [,vʌrtʃʊ'oso] s (pl **-sos** o **-si** [si]) virtuoso

virtuous ['vʌrtʃʊ•əs] adj virtuoso

virulence ['vɪrjələns] s virulencia

virulent ['vɪrjələnt] adj virulento

virus ['vaɪrəs] s virus m

Vis. abbr **Viscount**

visa ['vizə] s visa ‖ tr visar

visage ['vɪzɪdʒ] s cara, semblante m; aspecto, apariencia

vis-à-vis [,vizə'vi] adj enfrentados ‖ adv frente a frente ‖ prep enfrente de; respecto de

viscera ['vɪsərə] spl vísceras

viscount ['vaɪkaʊnt] s vizconde m

viscountess ['vaɪkaʊntɪs] s vizcondesa

viscous ['vɪskəs] adj viscoso

vise [vaɪs] s tornillo, tørno

visé ['vize] o [vi'ze] s & tr var de **visa**

visible ['vɪzɪbəl] adj visible

Visigoth ['vɪzɪ,gɑθ] s visigodo

vision ['vɪʒən] s visión; (sense of sight) vista

visionar•y ['vɪʒə,nɛri] adj visionario ‖ s (pl **-ies**) visionario

visit ['vɪzɪt] s visita ‖ tr visitar; afligir, acometer; enviar (p.ej., castigo, venganza) ‖ intr hacer visitas; visitarse (dos o más personas)

visitation [,vɪzɪ'teʃən] s visitación; gracia del cielo, castigo del cielo

visiting card s tarjeta de visita

visiting hours spl horas de visita

visiting nurse s enfermera ambulante

visitor ['vɪsɪtər] s visitante mf

visor ['vaɪzər] s visera; (disguise) máscara

vista ['vɪstə] s vista, panorama m

visual ['vɪʒʊ•əl] adj visual

visual acuity s agudeza visual

visualize ['vɪʒʊ•ə,laɪz] tr representarse en la mente; hacer visible

vital ['vaɪtəl] adj vital; (deadly) mortal ‖ **vitals** spl partes fpl vitales, órganos vitales

vitality [vaɪ'tælɪti] s vitalidad

vitalize ['vaɪtə,laɪz] tr vitalizar

vitamin ['vaɪtəmɪn] s vitamina

vitiate ['vɪʃɪ,et] tr viciar

vitreous ['vɪtrɪ•əs] adj vítreo

vitriolic [vɪtrɪ'ɑlɪk] adj (chem) vitriólico; (fig) cáustico, mordaz

vituperable [vaɪ'tupərəbəl] o [vaɪ'tjupərəbəl] adj vituperable

vituperate [vaɪ'tupə,ret] o [vaɪ'tjupə,ret] tr vituperar

viva ['vivə] interj ¡viva! ‖ s viva m

vivacious [vɪ'veʃəs] o [vaɪ'veʃəs] adj vivaz, vivaracho

vivaci•ty [vɪ'væsɪti] o [vaɪ'væsɪti] s (pl **-ties**) vivacidad, animación

viva voce ['vaɪvə 'vosi] adv de viva voz

vivid ['vɪvɪd] adj vivo (intenso; brillante; expresivo)

vivi•fy ['vɪvɪ,faɪ] v (pret & pp **-fied**) tr vivificar

vivisection [,vɪvɪ'sɛkʃən] s vivisección

vixen ['vɪksən] s vulpeja; mujer regañona y colérica

viz. abbr **videlicet** (Lat) **namely, to wit**

vizier [vɪ'zɪr] o ['vɪzjər] s visir m

vocabular•y [vo'kæbjə,lɛri] s (pl **-ies**) vocabulario

vocal ['vokəl] adj vocal; (inclined to express oneself freely) expresivo

vocalist ['vokəlɪst] s vocalista mf

vocation [vo'keʃən] s vocación; empleo, ocupación

vocative ['vɑkətɪv] *s* vocativo
vociferate [vo'sɪfə,ret] *intr* vociferar
vociferous [vo'sɪfərəs] *adj* clamoroso, vocinglero
vogue [vog] *s* boga, moda; **in vogue** en boga, de moda
voice [vɔɪs] *s* voz *f;* **in a loud voice** en alta voz; **in a low voice** en voz baja; **with one voice** a una voz ‖ *tr* expresar; sonorizar *(una consonante sorda)* ‖ *intr* sonorizarse
voiceless ['vɔɪslɪs] *adj* sin voz; mudo; silencioso; (phonet) sordo
void [vɔɪd] *adj (empty)* vacío; *(useless)* vano; (law) inválido, nulo; **void of** desprovisto de ‖ *s* vacío; *(gap)* hueco ‖ *tr* vaciar; evacuar *(el vientre)*; anular ‖ *intr* excretar
voile [vɔɪl] *s* espumilla
vol. *abbr* **volume**
volatile ['vɑlətɪl] *adj* volátil
volatilize ['vɑlətɪ,laɪz] *tr* volatilizar ‖ *intr* volatilizarse
volcanic [vɑl'kænɪk] *adj* volcánico
volca•no [vɑl'keno] *s (pl* **-noes** o **-nos)** volcán *m*
volition [və'lɪʃən] *s* voluntad; **of one's own volition** por su propia voluntad
volley ['vɑli] *s (of stones, bullets, etc.)* descarga, lluvia; (mil) descarga; (tennis) voleo ‖ *tr & intr* volear
vol'ley•ball' *s* volibol *m*
volplane ['vɑl,plen] *s* vuelo planeado ‖ *intr* planear
volt [volt] *s* voltio
voltage ['voltɪdʒ] *s* voltaje *m*
voltage divider *s* (rad) divisor *m* de voltaje
voltaic [vɑl'te•ɪk] *adj* voltaico
volte-face [vɔlt'fɑs] *s* cambio de dirección; cambio de opinión
volt'me'ter *s* voltímetro
voluble ['vɑljəbəl] *adj* locuaz, hablador
volume ['vɑljəm] *s (book; bulk; mass, e.g., of water)* volumen *m;* *(each book in a set)* tomo; *(degree of loudness)* volumen sonoro; (geom) volumen *m;* **to speak volumes** ser muy significativo; ser muy expresivo
voluminous [və'luminəs] *adj* voluminoso
voluntar•y ['vɑlən,tɛri] *adj* voluntario ‖ *s (pl* **-ties)** (eccl) solo de órgano
volunteer [,vɑlən'tɪr] *adj & s* voluntario ‖ *tr* ofrecer *(sus servicios)* ‖ *intr* ofrecerse; servir como voluntario; **to volunteer to** + *inf* ofrecerse a + *inf*
voluptuar•y [və'lʌptʃu,ɛri] *adj* voluptuoso ‖ *s (pl* **-ties)** voluptuoso, sibarita *mf*
voluptuous [və'lʌptʃu•əs] *adj* voluptuoso
volute [və'lut] *s* voluta

vomit ['vɑmɪt] *s* vómito; *(emetic)* vomitivo ‖ *tr & intr* vomitar
voodoo ['vudu] *adj* voduísta ‖ *s (practice)* vodú *m;* *(person)* voduísta *mf*
voracious [və'reʃəs] *adj* voraz
voracity [və'ræsɪti] *s* voracidad
vor•tex ['vɔrtɛks] *s (pl* **-texes** o **-tices** [tɪ,siz]) vórtice *m*
vota•ry ['votəri] *s (pl* **-ries)** persona ligada por votos solemnes; aficionado, partidario
vote [vot] *s (formal expression of choice; right to vote; person who votes)* voto; *(act of voting; votes considered together)* votación; **to put to the vote** poner a votación; **to tally the votes** regular los votos ‖ *tr* votar *(sí, no);* **to vote down** derrotar por votación; **to vote in** elegir por votación ‖ *intr* votar
vote getter ['gɛtər] *s* acaparador *m* de votos; *(slogan)* consigna que gana votos
voter ['votər] *s* votante *mf*
voting machine ['votɪŋ] *s* máquina registradora de votos
votive ['votɪv] *adj* votivo
votive offering *s* voto, exvoto
vouch [vautʃ] *tr* garantizar ‖ *intr*—**to vouch for** responder de *(una cosa);* responder por *(una persona)*
voucher ['vautʃər] *s* garante *mf;* *(certificate)* comprobante *m*
vouch•safe' *tr* conceder, otorgar; permitir ‖ *intr*— **to vouchsafe to** + *inf* dignarse + *inf*
voussoir [vu'swar] *s* dovela
vow [vau] *s* voto; **to take vows** tomar el hábito religioso ‖ *tr* votar *(p.ej., un cirio a la Virgen);* jurar *(venganza)* ‖ *intr* votar; **to vow to** hacer votos de
vowel ['vau•əl] *s* vocal *f*
voyage ['vɔɪ•ɪdʒ] *s* travesía, trayecto; *(any journey)* viaje *m* ‖ *tr* atravesar *(p.ej., el mar)* ‖ *intr* viajar
voyager ['vɔɪ•ɪdʒər] *s* pasajero, navegante *mf,* viajero
V.P. *abbr* **Vice-President**
vs. *abbr* **versus**
Vul. *abbr* **Vulgate**
vulcanize ['vʌlkə,naɪz] *tr* vulcanizar
vulg. *abbr* **vulgar**
Vulg. *abbr* **Vulgate**
vulgar ['vʌlgər] *adj* grosero; *(popular, common; vernacular)* vulgar
vulgari•ty [vʌl'gærɪti] *s (pl* **-ties)** grosería
Vulgar Latin *s* latín vulgar, latín rústico
Vulgate ['vʌlget] *s* Vulgata
vulnerable ['vʌlnərəbəl] *adj* vulnerable
vulture ['vʌltʃər] *s* buitre *m;* *(American vulture)* catartes *m,* aura *(buitre americano)*

W

W, w [ˈdʌbəl,ju] vigésima tercera letra del alfabeto inglés

w *abbr* **watt**

w. *abbr* **week, west, wide, wife**

W. *abbr* **Wednesday, west**

wad [wɑd] *s* (*of cotton*) bolita, tapón *m;* (*of papers*) fajo, lío; (*in a gun*) taco ‖ *v* (*pret & pp* **wadded;** *ger* **wadding**) *tr* emborrar, rellenar; atacar (*una escopeta*)

waddle [ˈwɑdəl] *s* anadeo ‖ *intr* anadear

wade [wed] *intr* andar sobre terreno cubierto de agua; andar descalzo por la orilla; chapotear (*los niños*) con los pies desnudos; **to wade into** (coll) embestir con violencia; (coll) meter el hombro a; **to wade through** (coll) avanzar con dificultad por; (coll) leer con dificultad

wading bird [ˈwedɪŋ] *s* ave zancuda

wafer [ˈwefər] *s* (*for sealing letters; pill*) oblea; (*thin, crisp cake*) hostia; (eccl) hostia

waffle [ˈwɑfəl] *s* barquillo

waffle iron *s* barquillero

waft [wæft] o [wɑft] *tr* llevar por el aire; llevar por encima del agua ‖ *intr* flotar

wag [wæg] *s* (*of head*) meneo; (*of tail*) coleada; (*jester*) bromista *mf* ‖ *v* (*pret & pp* **wagged;** *ger* **wagging**) *tr* menear (*la cabeza, la cola*) ‖ *intr* menearse

wage [wedʒ] *s* salario; **wages** galardón *m,* premio ‖ *tr* hacer (*la guerra*)

wage earner [ˈʌrnər] *s* asalariado

wager [ˈwedʒər] *s* apuesta; **to lay a wager** hacer una apuesta ‖ *tr & intr* apostar

wage′work′er *s* asalariado

waggish [ˈwægɪʃ] *adj* divertido, gracioso; (*person*) bromista

Wagnerian [vɑgˈnɪrɪ•ən] *adj & s* vagneriano

wagon [ˈwægən] *s* carro, furgón *m,* carretón *m;* **on the wagon** (slang) sin tomar bebidas alcohólicas; **to hitch one's wagon to a star** poner el tiro muy alto

wag′tail′ *s* aguanieves *m,* aguzanieves *m*

waif [wef] *s* (*foundling*) expósito; animal extraviado o abandonado; (*stray child*) granuja *m*

wail [wel] *s* gemido, lamento ‖ *intr* gemir, lamentar

wain•scot [ˈwenskət] o [ˈwenskɑt] *s* arrimadillo, friso de madera ‖ *v* (*pret & pp* **-scoted** o **-scotted;** *ger* **-scoting** o **-scotting**) *tr* poner arrimadillo o friso de madera a

waist [west] *s* (*of human body; corresponding part of garment*) talle *m,* cintura; (*garment*) corpiño, jubón *m,* blusa

waist′band′ *s* pretina

waist′cloth′ *s* taparrabo

waistcoat [ˈwest,kot] o [ˈwɛskət] *s* chaleco

waist′line′ *s* cintura

wait [wet] *s* espera; **to have a good wait** (coll) esperar sentado; **to lie in wait for** acechar emboscado ‖ *tr*—**to wait one's turn** esperar vez ‖ *intr* esperar, aguardar; **to wait for** esperar, aguardar; **to wait on**

atender, despachar (*a los parroquianos en una tienda*); servir (*a una persona a la mesa*); **to wait until** esperar a que

waiter [ˈwetər] *s* camarero, mozo de restaurante; (*tray*) bandeja

waiting list *s* lista de espera

waiting room *s* (*of station*) sala de espera; (*of doctor's office*) antesala

waitress [ˈwetrɪs] *s* camarera, moza de restaurante

waive [wev] *tr* renunciar a (*un derecho*); diferir, poner a un lado

waiver [ˈwevər] *s* renuncia

wake [wek] *s* (*watch by the body of a dead person*) velatorio; (*of a boat or other moving object*) estela; **in the wake of** siguiendo inmediatamente; de resultas de ‖ *v* (*pret* **waked** o **woke** [wok]; *pp* **waked**) *tr* despertar ‖ *intr*— **to wake to** darse cuenta de; **to wake up** despertar

wakeful [ˈwekfəl] *adj* desvelado

wakefulness [ˈwekfəlnɪs] *s* desvelo

waken [ˈwekən] *tr & intr* despertar

wale [wel] *s* verdugón *m*

Wales [welz] *s* Gales, el país de Gales

walk [wɔk] *s* (*act*) paseo; (*distance*) caminata; (*way of walking, bearing*) andar *m,* paso; (*of a horse*) andadura; (*place to walk animals*) cercado; empleo, cargo, carrera; **at a walk** al paso de una persona; **to go for a walk** salir a pasear; **to take a walk** dar un paseo ‖ *tr* pasear (*a un niño, un caballo*); caminar (*recorrer caminando*); hacer ir al paso (*un caballo*); **to walk off** quitarse (*p.ej., un dolor de cabeza*) caminando ‖ *intr* andar, caminar, ir a pie; (*to stroll*) pasear; **to walk away from** alejarse caminando de; **to walk off with** cargar con, llevarse; **to walk out** salir repentinamente; declararse en huelga; **to walk out on** (coll) dejar airadamente

walkaway [ˈwɔkə,we] *s* (coll) triunfo fácil

walker [ˈwɔkər] *s* caminante *mf;* (*pedestrian*) peatón *m;* (*gocart*) andaderas

walkie-talkie [ˈwɔkiˈtɔki] *s* (rad) transmisorreceptor *m* portátil

walking papers *spl* (coll) despedida de un empleo

walking stick *s* bastón *m*

walk′-on′ *s* (theat) parte *f* de por medio

walk′out′ *s* (coll) huelga

walk′o′ver *s* (coll) triunfo fácil

wall [wɔl] *s* muro; (*between rooms; of a pipe, boiler, etc.*) pared *f;* (*of a fortification*) muralla; **to drive to the wall** poner entre la espada y la pared; **to go to the wall** rendirse; fracasar ‖ *tr* murar, amurallar (*una ciudad, un castillo*); emparedar (*a un criminal*); **to wall up** cerrar con muro

wall′board′ *s* cartón *m* tabla

wallet [ˈwɑlɪt] *s* cartera de bolsillo

wall′flow′er *s* alhelí *m;* **to be a wallflower** (coll) comer pavo, planchar el asiento

Walloon [wɑˈlun] *adj & s* valón *m*

wallop ['wɑləp] s (coll) golpaza, puñetazo ‖ tr (coll) golpear fuertemente; (coll) vencer cabalmente

wallow ['wɑlo] s revuelco; (place) revolcadero ‖ intr revolcarse; (e.g., in wealth) nadar

wall'pa'per s papel m de empapelar, papel pintado ‖ tr empapelar

walnut ['wɔlnət] s (tree and wood) nogal m; nuez f de nogal

walrus ['wɔlrəs] o ['wɑlrəs] s morsa

Walter ['wɔltər] s Gualterio

waltz [wɔlts] s vals m ‖ tr hacer valsar; (coll) conducir directamente ‖ intr valsar

wan [wɑn] adj (comp **wanner**; super **wannest**) pálido, macilento; débil

wand [wɑnd] s vara; (of deviner or magician) varilla de virtudes

wander ['wɑndər] tr recorrer a la ventura ‖ intr errar, vagar; extraviarse, perderse; **to wander around** errar de una parte a otra

wanderer ['wɑndərər] s vagabundo; peregrino

wan'der•lust' s ansia de viajar

wane [wen] s decadencia, declinación; menguante f de la luna; **on the wane** decayendo, declinando; menguando (la luna) ‖ intr decaer, declinar; menguar (la luna)

wangle ['wɛŋgəl] tr (to obtain by scheming) (coll) mamar o mamarse; (coll) adulterar, falsear (cuentas); **to wangle one's way out of** (coll) salir con maña de ‖ intr (to get along by scheming) (coll) sacudirse

want [wɑnt] o [wɔnt] s deseo; necesidad; carencia; **for want of** a falta de; **to be in want** pasar necesidad ‖ tr desear; necesitar; carecer de ‖ intr desear; **to want for** necesitar; carecer de

want ad s anuncio clasificado

wanton ['wɑntən] adj inconsiderado, desconsiderado; insensible, perverso; disoluto, licencioso; lascivo; cabezudo

war [wɔr] s guerra; **to go to war** declarar la guerra; (as a soldier) ir a la guerra; **to wage war** hacer la guerra ‖ v (pret & pp **warred**; ger **warring**) intr guerrear; **to war on** guerrear con, hacer la guerra a

warble ['wɔrbəl] s gorjeo, trino ‖ intr gorjear, trinar

warbler ['wɔrblər] s pájaro cantor; curruca de cabeza negra

war cloud s amenaza de guerra

ward [wɔrd] s (person, usually a minor, under protection of another) pupilo; (guardianship) custodia, tutela; (of a city) barrio, distrito; (of a hospital) cuadra, crujía; (of a lock) guarda ‖ tr— **to ward off** parar, desviar

warden ['wɔrdən] s guardián m; (of a jail) alcaide m, carcelero; (of a church) capiller m; (in charge of fire prevention) vigía m

ward heeler s muñidor m

ward'robe' s (closet or cabinet for holding clothes) guardarropa m; (stock of clothing for a person) vestuario; (theat) guardarropía

wardrobe trunk s baúl ropero

ward'room' s (nav) cámara de oficiales

ware [wɛr] s loza; **wares** efectos, artículos de comercio, mercancías

war effort s esfuerzo bélico

ware'house' s almacén m; (for furniture) guardamuebles m

warehouse•man ['wɛr,hausmən] s (pl **-men** [mən]) almacenista m; guardaalmacén m

war'fare' s guerra

war'head' s punta de combate

war horse s corcel m de guerra; (coll) veterano

warily ['wɛrɪli] adv cautelosamente

wariness ['wɛrɪnɪs] s cautela

war'like' adj guerrero

war loan s empréstito de guerra

war lord s jefe m militar

warm [wɔrm] adj (being moderately hot) caliente; (neither hot nor cold) templado; (clothing) abrigador; (climate, region) caluroso; (color) cálido; (fig) caluroso, cordial; **to be warm** (said of a person) tener calor; (said of the weather) hacer calor ‖ tr calentar, acalorar; (fig) animar, acalorar; **to warm up** recalentar (p.ej., la comida); hacer más amistoso ‖ intr calentarse; **to warm up** templar (el tiempo); (with work or exercise) acalorarse; **to warm up to** cobrar afecto a

warm-blooded ['wɔrm'blʌdɪd] adj apasionado, ardiente; (animals) de sangre caliente

war memorial s monumento a los caídos

warmer ['wɔrmər] s calentador m

warm-hearted ['wɔrm'hɑrtɪd] adj afectuoso, de buen corazón; cariñoso; simpático

warming pan s mundillo

warmonger ['wɔr,mʌŋgər] s belicista mf

war mother s madrina de guerra

warmth [wɔrmθ] s calor m; ardor m, entusiasmo; cordialidad

warm'-up' s calentón m

warn [wɔrn] tr advertir, avisar; (to exhort) amonestar; (to advise) aconsejar

warning adj de aviso ‖ s advertencia, aviso

War of the Roses s guerra de las dos Rosas

warp [wɔrp] s (of a fabric) urdimbre f; (of a board) comba, alabeo; aberración mental; (naut) espía ‖ tr combar, alabear; pervertir (el juicio de una persona); (naut) move, con espía ‖ intr combarse, alabearse; (naut) espiar

war'path' s—**to be on the warpath** prepararse para la guerra; estar buscando pendencia

war'plane' s avión m de guerra

warrant ['wɑrənt] o ['wɔrənt] s garantía, promesa; (for arrest) orden f de prisión; (before a judge) citación; cédula, certificado ‖ tr garantizar, prometer; autorizar; justificar

warrantable ['wɑrəntəbəl] o ['wɔrəntəbəl] adj garantizable; justificable

warrant officer s suboficial m de las clases

warren ['wɑrən] o ['wɔrən] s (where rabbits breed) conejera; barrio densamente poblado

warrior ['wɔrjər] s guerrero

Warsaw ['wɔrsɔ] s Varsovia

war'ship' s buque m de guerra

wart [wɔrt] s verruga

war'time' s tiempo de guerra

war'-torn' adj devastado por la guerra

war to the death s guerra a muerte

war•y [wɛri] adj (comp **-ier;** super **-iest**) cauteloso

wash [wɑʃ] o [wɔʃ] s lavado; (clothes washed or to be washed) jabonado; (dirty water) lavazas; loción; (place where surf breaks) batiente m; (aer) estela turbulenta ‖ tr lavar; fregar (los platos); bañar, mojar; **to wash away** quitar lavando; derrubiar (las aguas corrientes la tierra de las riberas) ‖ intr lavarse; lavar la ropa; batir (el agua); derrubiarse

washable ['wɑʃəbəl] o ['wɔʃəbəl] adj lavable

wash and wear adj de lava y pon

wash'ba'sin s jofaina, palangana

wash'bas'ket s cesto de la colada

wash'board' s lavadero, tabla de lavar; (baseboard) rodapié m

wash'bowl' s jofaina, palangana

wash'cloth' s paño para lavarse

wash'day' s día m de la colada

washed-out ['wɑʃt,aut] o ['wɔʃt,aut] adj desteñido; (coll) debilitado, rendido

washed-up ['wɑʃt,ʌp] o ['wɔʃt,ʌp] adj (coll) agotado, deslomado

washer ['wɑʃər] o [wɔʃər] s lavador m; (machine) lavadora; (ring of metal placed under head of bolt) arandela; (ring of rubber, etc., to keep a spigot from leaking) zapatilla; (phot) lavador

wash'er•wom'an s (pl **-wom'en**) lavandera

wash goods spl tejidos lavables

washing ['wɑʃɪŋ] o ['wɔʃɪŋ] s (act of washing; washed clothes or clothes to be washed) lavado; lavada; **washings** (dirty water; abraded material) lavadura

washing machine s lejiadora, lavadora mecánica

washing soda s sal f de sosa

wash'out' s derrubio; derrumbe m; (coll) desilusión, fracaso

wash'rag' s paño para lavarse; paño de cocina

wash'room' s gabinete m de aseo, lavabo

wash'stand' s lavamanos m

wash'tub' s cuba de colada, tina de lavar

wash water s lavazas

wasp [wɑsp] s avispa

waste [west] s derroche m, desgaste m; (garbage) basura, despojo; (wild region) despoblado, yermo; (of time) pérdida; (useless by-products) desperdicios; excremento; (for wiping machinery) hilacha de algodón; **to lay waste** devastar, poner a fuego y sangre ‖ tr malgastar, perder ‖ intr—**to waste away** consumirse

waste'bas'ket s papelera

wasteful ['westfəl] adj derrochador, manirroto; devastador, destructivo

waste'-land' s peladero

waste paper s papeles usados, papel de desecho, papel viejo

waste pipe s tubo de desagüe

waste products spl desperdicios; materia excretada

wastrel ['westrəl] s derrochador m, malgastador m; pródigo, perdido

watch [wɑtʃ] s reloj m (de bolsillo o de pulsera); (lookout) vigía m; (mil) vigilia; (naut) guardia; **to be on the watch for** estar a la mira de; **to keep watch over** velar ‖ tr (to look at) mirar; (to oversee) velar, vigilar; guardar; tener cuidado con ‖ intr mirar; (to keep awake) velar; **to watch for** acechar; **to watch out** tener cuidado; **to watch out for** estar a la mira de; tener cuidado con; guardarse de; **to watch over** velar, vigilar

watch'case' s caja de reloj

watch charm s dije m

watch crystal s cristal m de reloj

watch'dog' s perro de guarda, perro guardián; (fig) guardián m fiel

watchful ['wɑtʃfəl] adj desvelado, vigilante

watchfulness ['wɑtʃfəlnɪs] s desvelo, vigilancia

watch'mak'er s relojero

watch•man ['wɑtʃmən] s (pl **-men** [mən]) vigilante m, velador m

watch night s noche vieja; oficio de noche vieja

watch pocket s relojera

watch strap s pulsera

watch'tow'er s atalaya, vigía

watch'word' s santo y seña; (slogan) lema m

water ['wɔtər] o ['wɑtər] s agua; **of the first water** de lo mejor; **to back water** ciar; **to carry water on both shoulders** nadar entre dos aguas; **to fish in troubled waters** pescar en río revuelto; **to hold water** (coll) ser bien fundado; **to make water** (to urinate) hacer aguas; (naut) hacer agua; **to pour** o **throw cold water on** echar un jarro de agua (fría) a ‖ tr regar, rociar; abrevar (el ganado); aguar (el vino); proveer de agua ‖ intr abrevarse (el ganado); tomar agua (una locomotora); llorar (los ojos)

water carrier s aguador m

water closet s excusado, retrete m, váter m

water color s acuarela

wa'ter•course' s corriente f de agua; lecho de corriente

water cress s berzo

water cure s cura de aguas

wa'ter•fall' s cascada, caída de agua

water front s terreno ribereño

water gap s garganta, hondonada

water hammer s golpe m de ariete

water heater s calentador m de agua

water ice s sorbete m

watering can s regadera

watering place s aguadero; balneario

watering pot s regadera

watering trough s abrevadero

water jacket s camisa de agua
water lily s ninfea, nenúfar m
water line s línea de agua, línea de flotación; nivel m de agua
water main s cañería de agua
wa'ter•mark' s (in paper) filigrana; marca de nivel de agua
wa'ter•mel'on s sandía
water meter s contador m de agua
water pipe s cañería de agua
water polo s polo de agua
water power s fuerza de agua, hulla blanca
wa'ter•proof' adj & s impermeable m
wa'ter•shed' s divisoria de aguas; (drainage area) cuenca
water ski s esquí acuático
wa'ter•spout' s (to carry water from roof) canalón m; (funnel of wet air extending from cloud to surface of water) manga de agua, tromba marina
wa'ter•sup•ply' system s fontanería
wa'ter•tight' adj estanco, hermético; (fig) seguro
water tower s arca de agua
water wagon s (mil) carro de agua; **on the water wagon** (slang) sin tomar bebidas alcohólicas
wa'ter•way' s vía de agua, vía fluvial; (naut) canalizo
water wheel s rueda de agua; turbina de agua; (of steamboat) rueda de paletas
water wings spl nadaderas
wa'ter•works' s estación de bombas
watery ['wɔtəri] o ['watəri] adj acuoso; (said of the eyes) lagrimoso, lloroso; insípido; húmedo, mojado
watt [wat] s vatio
wattage ['watɪdʒ] s vatiaje m
watt'-hour' s (pl watt-hours) vatiohora
wattle ['watəl] s (of bird) barba; (of fish) barbilla
watt'me'ter s vatímetro
wave [wev] s onda; (of hair) onda, ondulación; (e.g., of heat or cold) ola; (e.g., of strikes) oleaje m; señal hecha con la mano || tr blandir (la espada); ondear, ondular (el cabello); hacer señal con (la mano); decir (adiós) con la mano; **to wave aside** rechazar || intr ondear u ondearse; hacer señal con la mano
wave motion s movimiento ondulatorio
waver ['wevər] intr oscilar; (to hesitate) vacilar, titubear; (to totter) tambalear
wave theory s teoría ondulatoria
wav•y ['wevi] adj (comp -ier; super -iest) undoso, ondoso; (water) ondulado; (hair) ondeado
wax [wæks] s cera; **to be wax in one's hands** ser como una cera || tr encerar; cerotear (el hilo) || intr hacerse, volverse; crecer (la luna)
wax paper s papel encerado, papel parafinado
wax taper s cerilla
wax'works' s museo de cera
way [we] s vía, camino; dirección, sentido; manera, modo; costumbre, hábito; **across**

the way enfrente; **a good way** un buen trecho; **all the way** hasta el fin del camino; **any way** de cualquier modo; **by the way** a propósito; **in a way** hasta cierto punto; **in every way** en todos respectos; **in this way** de este modo; **on the way to** camino de, rumbo a; **on the way out** saliendo; desapareciendo; **out of the way** hecho, despachado; inconveniente, impropio; a un lado, apartado; fuera de lo común; **that way** por allí; de ese modo; **this way** por aquí; de este modo; **to be in the way** estorbar; **to feel one's way** tantear el camino; proceder con tiento; **to force one's way** abrirse paso por fuerza; **to get out of the way** quitarse de en medio; (to finish) quitarse de encima; **to give way** ceder, retroceder; romperse (una cuerda); fracasar; **to give way to** entregarse a; **to go out of one's way** dar un rodeo; dar un rodeo innecesario; darse molestia; **to have one's way** salirse con la suya; **to keep out of the way** no obstruir el paso; **to know one's way around** saber entendérselas; **to know one's way to** conocer el camino a, saber ir a; **to lead the way** enseñar el camino; ir o entrar primero; **to lose one's way** perder el camino, extraviarse; **to make one's way** avanzar; hacer carrera, acreditarse; **to make way for** dar paso a, hacer lugar para; **to mend one's ways** mudar de vida; **to not know which way to turn** no saber dónde meterse; **to put out of the way** alejar, apartar; quitar de en medio; **to see one's way to** ver el modo de; **to take one's way** irse, marcharse; **to wend one's way** seguir camino; **to wind one's way through** serpentear por; **to wing one's way** ir volando; **under way** en marcha, en camino; **way in** entrada; **way out** salida; **ways** maneras, modales mpl; (for launching a ship) anguilas; **which way?** ¿por dónde?; ¿cómo?
way'bill' s hoja de ruta
wayfarer ['we,fɛrər] s caminante mf
way'lay' v (pret & pp -laid') tr detener de improviso; (to attack from ambush) insidiar, asaltar
way'side' s borde m del camino; **to fall by the wayside** (to disappear) caer en el camino; fracasar
way station s apeadero
way train s tren m ómnibus
wayward ['wewərd] adj díscolo, voluntarioso; voltario, caprichoso
w.c. abbr water closet, without charge
we [wi] pron pers nosotros
weak [wik] adj débil, flaco; caedizo; (vowel; verb) débil
weaken ['wikən] tr debilitar, enflaquecer || intr debilitarse, enflaquecerse
weakling ['wiklɪŋ] s alfeñique m, canijo
weak-minded ['wik'maɪndɪd] adj irresoluto; simple, mentecato
weakness ['wiknɪs] s debilidad, flaqueza; caducidad; lado débil; afición, gusto
weal [wil] s verdugón m
wealth [wɛlθ] s riqueza

wa
we

wealth•y ['wɛlθi] *adj* (*comp* -ier; *super* -iest) rico

wean [win] *tr* destetar; **to wean away from** apartar gradualmente de

weanling ['winlɪŋ] *adj* & *s* destetado

weapon ['wɛpən] *s* arma

wear [wɛr] *s* (*act of wearing*) uso; (*clothing*) ropa; estilo, moda; (*wasting away from use*) desgaste *m*, deterioro; (*lasting quality*) durabilidad; **for all kinds of wear** a todo llevar; **for everyday wear** para todo trote ‖ *v* (*pret* **wore** [wor]; *pp* **worn** [worn]) *tr* llevar, traer, llevar puesto; calzar (*cierto tamaño de zapato o guante*); (*to waste away by use*) desgastar, deteriorar; (*to tire*) agotar, cansar; **to wear out** consumir, gastar; agotar, cansar; abusar de (*la hospitalidad de una persona*) ‖ *intr* desgastarse, deteriorarse; **to wear off** pasar, desaparecer; **to wear out** gastarse, usarse; **to wear well** durar, ser duradero

wear and tear *s* uso y desgaste

weariness ['wɪrɪnɪs] *s* cansancio; aburrimiento

wearing apparel ['wɛrɪŋ] *s* ropaje *m*, prendas de vestir

wearisome ['wɪrɪsəm] *adj* aburrido, cansado, fastidioso

wea•ry ['wɪri] *adj* (*comp* -rier; *super* -riest) cansado ‖ *v* (*pret* & *pp* -ried) *tr* cansar ‖ *intr* cansarse

weasel ['wizəl] *s* comadreja

weaseler ['wizələr] *s* pancista *mf*

weasel words *spl* palabras ambiguas

weather ['wɛðər] *s* tiempo; mal tiempo; **to be under the weather** (coll) no estar muy católico; (coll) estar borracho ‖ *tr* aguantar (*el temporal, la adversidad*)

weather-beaten ['wɛðər,bitən] *adj* curtido por la intemperie

weather bureau *s* meteo *f*, servicio meteorológico

weath′er•cock′ *s* veleta; (*fickle person*) (fig) veleta

weather forecasting *s* pronóstico del tiempo, previsión del tiempo

weather•man ['wɛðər,mæn] *s* (*pl* -men [,mɛn]) meteorologista *m*, pronosticador *m* del tiempo

weather report *s* parte meteorológico

weather station *s* estación meteorológica

weather stripping ['strɪpɪŋ] *s* burlete *m*, cierre hermético

weather vane *s* veleta

weave [wiv] *s* tejido ‖ *v* (*pret* **wove** [wov] o **weaved**; *pp* **wove** o **woven** ['wovən]) *tr* tejer; **to weave one's way** avanzar zigzagueando ‖ *intr* tejer; zigzaguear

weaver ['wivər] *s* tejedor *m*

web [wɛb] *s* tejido, tela; (*of spider*) tela; (*between toes of birds and other animals*) membrana; (*of an iron rail*) alma; (fig) tejido, tela, enredo

web-footed ['wɛb,fʊtɪd] *adj* palmípedo, de pie palmeado

wed [wɛd] *v* (*pret* & *pp* **wed** o **wedded**; *ger* **wedding**) *tr* (*to join in marriage*) casar; casarse con ‖ *intr* casarse

wedding ['wɛdɪŋ] *adj* nupcial ‖ *s* bodas, nupcias, matrimonio

wedding cake *s* pastel *m* de boda

wedding day *s* día *m* de bodas

wedding march *s* marcha nupcial

wedding night *s* noche *f* de bodas

wedding ring *s* anillo nupcial

wedge [wɛdʒ] *s* cuña ‖ *tr* acuñar, apretar con cuña

wed′lock′ *s* matrimonio

Wednesday ['wɛnzdi] *s* miércoles *m*

wee [wi] *adj* pequeñito, diminuto

weed [wid] *s* mala hierba; (coll) tabaco; **weeds** ropa de luto (*especialmente, de una viuda*) ‖ *tr* desherbar, escardar

weeding hoe *s* escardillo

weed killer *s* matamalezas *m*, herbicida *m*

week [wik] *s* semana; **week in week out** semana tras semana

week′day′ *s* día *m* laborable

week′days′ *adv* entresemana (SAm)

week′end′ *s* fin *m* de semana ‖ *intr* pasar el fin de semana

week•ly ['wikli] *adj* semanal ‖ *adv* cada semana ‖ *s* (*pl* -lies) revista semanal, semanario

weep [wip] *v* (*pret* & *pp* **wept** [wɛpt]) *tr* llorar (*p.ej., la muerte de una persona*); derramar (*lágrimas*) ‖ *intr* llorar

weeper ['wipər] *s* llorón *m*; (*hired mourner*) llorona, plañidera

weeping willow *s* sauce *m* llorón

weep•y ['wipi] *adj* (*comp* -ier; *super* -iest) (coll) lloroso

weevil ['wivəl] *s* gorgojo

weft [wɛft] *s* (*yarns running across warp*) trama; (*fabric*) tejido

weigh [we] *tr* pesar; (naut) levantar (*el ancla*) ‖ *intr* pesar; **to weigh in** pesarse (*un jockey*)

weight [wet] *s* peso; (*of scales, clock, gymnasium, etc.*) pesa; **to lose weight** rebajar de peso; **to put on weight** ponerse gordo; **to throw one's weight around** (coll) hacer valer su poder ‖ *tr* cargar, gravar; (*statistically*) ponderar

weightless ['wetlɪs] *adj* ingrávido

weightlessness ['wetlɪsnɪs] *s* ingravidez *f*; antigravedad

weight lifter *s* halterofilista *mf*

weight lifting *s* halterofilia

weight•y ['weti] *adj* (*comp* -ier; *super* -iest) (*heavy*) pesado; (*troublesome*) gravoso; importante, influyente

weir [wɪr] *s* presa, vertedero; (*for catching fish*) pescadera

weird [wɪrd] *adj* misterioso, sobrenatural, espectral; extraño, raro

welcome ['wɛlkəm] *adj* bienvenido; grato, agradable; **you are welcome** (*i.e., gladly received*) sea Vd. bienvenido; (*in answer to thanks*) no hay de qué; **you are welcome to it** está a la disposición de Vd.; **you are welcome to your opinion** piense Vd. lo que quiera ‖ *interj* ¡bienvenido! ‖ *s* bienvenida, buena acogida ‖ *tr* dar la bienvenida a; acoger con gusto, recibir con amabilidad

weld [wɛld] *s* autógena; (bot) gualda ‖ *tr* soldar con autógena; (fig) unir ‖ *intr* soldarse

welder [ˈwɛldər] *s* soldador *m;* (*machine*) soldadora

welding [ˈwɛldɪŋ] *s* autógena, soldadura autógena

welˈfareˈ *s* bienestar *m;* (*effort to improve living conditions of the underprivileged*) asistencia, beneficencia; **to be on welfare** vivir de la asistencia pública

welfare state *s* gobierno socializante, estado de beneficencia, estado asistencial

well [wɛl] *adj* bien; bien de salud; **get well!** ¡que se mejore! ‖ *adv* bien; pues; pues bien; **as well** también; **as well as** así como; además de ‖ *interj* ¡vaya! ‖ *s* pozo; (*natural source of water*) fuente *f,* manantial *m* ‖ *intr*—**to well up** salir a borbotones

well-appointed [ˈwɛləˈpɔɪntɪd] *adj* bien amueblado, bien equipado

well-attended [ˈwɛləˈtɛndɪd] *adj* muy concurrido

well-behaved [ˈwɛlbɪˈhevd] *adj* de buena conducta

wellˈ-beˈing *s* bienestar *m*

wellˈbornˈ *adj* bien nacido

well-bred [ˈwɛlˈbrɛd] *adj* cortés, bien criado

well-disposed [ˈwɛldɪsˈpozd] *adj* bien dispuesto

well-done [ˈwɛlˈdʌn] *adj* bien hecho; (*meat*) bien asado

well-fixed [ˈwɛlˈfɪkst] *adj* (coll) acaudalado

well-formed [ˈwɛlˈfɔrmd] *adj* bien formado; (*nose*) perfilado

well-founded [ˈwɛlˈfaʊndɪd] *adj* bien fundado

well-groomed [ˈwɛlˈgrumd] *adj* de mucho aseo, atildado

well-heeled [ˈwɛlˈhild] *adj* (coll) acomodado; **to be well-heeled** (coll) tener bien cubierto el riñón

well-informed [ˈwɛlɪnˈfɔrmd] *adj* versado, bien enterado

well-intentioned [ˈwɛlɪnˈtɛnʃənd] *adj* bien intencionado

well-kept [ˈwɛlˈkɛpt] *adj* bien cuidado, bien atendido; (*secret*) bien guardado

well-known [ˈwɛlˈnon] *adj* bien conocido; familiar

well-meaning [ˈwɛlˈminɪŋ] *adj* bien intencionado

well-nigh [ˈwɛlˈnaɪ] *adv* casi

wellˈ-offˈ *adj* adinerado, acaudalado

well-preserved [ˈwɛlprɪˈzʌrvd] *adj* bien conservado

well-read [ˈwɛlˈrɛd] *adj* leído, muy leído

well-spent [ˈwɛlˈspɛnt] *adj* (*money, youth, life*) bien empleado

well-spoken [ˈwɛlˈspokən] *adj* (*person*) bienhablado; (*word*) bien dicho

wellˈspringˈ *s* fuente *f,* manantial *m;* fuente inagotable

well sweep *s* cigoñal *m*

well-tempered [ˈwɛlˈtɛmpərd] *adj* bien templado

well-thought-of [ˈwɛlˈθɔt,ɑv] *adj* bien mirado

well-timed [ˈwɛlˈtaɪmd] *adj* oportuno

well-to-do [ˈwɛltəˈdu] *adj* adinerado, acaudalado; (coll) plateado

well-wisher [ˈwɛlˈwɪʃər] *s* amigo, favorecedor *m*

well-worn [ˈwɛlˈworn] *adj* trillado, vulgar

welsh [wɛlʃ] *intr* (slang) dejar de cumplir; **to welsh on** (slang) dejar de cumplir con ‖ **Welsh** *adj* galés ‖ *s* (*language*) galés *m;* **the Welsh** los galeses

Welsh•man [ˈwɛlʃmən] *s* (*pl* -men [mən]) galés *m*

Welsh rabbit o **rarebit** [ˈrɛrbɪt] *s* tostada cubierta de queso derretido en cerveza

welt [wɛlt] *s* (*finish along a seam*) ribete *m;* (*of a shoe*) vira; (*wale from a blow*) verdugón *m*

welter [ˈwɛltər] *s* confusión, conmoción; (*a tumbling about*) revuelco ‖ *intr* revolcar

welˈter•weightˈ *s* (box) peso mediano ligero

wen [wɛn] *s* lobanillo

wench [wɛntʃ] *s* muchacha, jovencita; moza, criada

wend [wɛnd] *tr*—**to wend one's way** dirigir sus pasos, seguir su camino

west [wɛst] *adj* occidental, del oeste ‖ *adv* al oeste, hacia el oeste ‖ *s* oeste *m*

western [ˈwɛstərn] *adj* occidental ‖ *s* película del Oeste

West Indies [ˈɪndiz] *spl* Indias Occidentales

westward [ˈwɛstwərd] *adv* hacia el oeste

wet [wɛt] *adj* (*comp* **wetter**; *super* **wettest**) mojado; (*damp*) húmedo; (*paint*) fresco; (*weather*) lluvioso; (coll) antiprohibicionista ‖ *s* (coll) antiprohibicionista *mf* ‖ *v* (*pret & pp* **wet** o **wetted**; *ger* **wetting**) *tr* mojar ‖ *intr* mojarse

wetˈbackˈ *s* mojado

wet bar *s* bar *m* con agua corriente

wet battery *s* pila húmeda

wet blanket *s* aguafiestas *mf*

wet goods *spl* caldos

wet nurse *s* ama de cría o de leche

w.f. *abbr* **wrong font**

w.g. *abbr* **wire gauge**

whack [hwæk] *s* (coll) golpe ruidoso; (coll) prueba, tentativa ‖ *tr* (coll) golpear ruidosamente

whale [hwel] *s* ballena; (*sperm whale*) cachalote *m;* **a whale at** (coll) un as de; **a whale for** (coll) un genio para; **a whale of a difference** (coll) una enorme diferencia; **a whale of a meal** (coll) una comida brutal ‖ *tr* (coll) azotar ‖ *intr* pescar ballenas

whaleˈboneˈ *s* ballena

wharf [hwɔrf] *s* (*pl* **wharves** [hwɔrvz] o **wharfs**) muelle *m,* embarcadero

what [hwɑt] *pron interr* qué; cuál; **what else?** ¿qué más?; **what if . . .?** ¿y si . . .?, ¿qué le parece si?; **what of it?** ¿qué importa? ‖ *pron rel* lo que; **what's what** lo que hay, toda la verdad ‖ *adj interr* qué ‖

adj rel el . . . que, la . . . que, etc. ‖ *interj* qué; **what a . . .!** qué . . . más o tan, p.ej., **what a beautiful day!** ¡qué día más (o tan) hermoso!

what•ev′er *pron* cualquiera; todo lo que ‖ *adj* cualquier; cualquier . . . que

what′not′ *s* juguetero

what's-his-name ['hwɑtsɪz,nem] *s* (coll) el señor fulano

wheal [hwil] *s* roncha

wheat [hwit] *s* trigo

wheedle ['hwidəl] *tr* engatusar; conseguir por medio de halagos

wheel [hwil] *s* rueda; (coll) bicicleta; **at the wheel** en el volante ‖ *tr* pasear (*a un niño*) en un cochecito; conducir (*a un enfermo*) en una silla de ruedas ‖ *intr* (coll) ir en bicicleta; **to wheel about** o **around** dar una vuelta; cambiar de opinión

wheelbarrow ['hwil,bæro] *s* carretilla

wheel base *s* batalla, paso, distancia entre ejes

wheel chair *s* silla de ruedas, cochecillo para inválidos

wheeler-dealer ['hwilər'dilər] *s* (slang) negociante *m* de gran influencia e independencia

wheel horse *s* caballo de varas; (fig) esclavo (*el que trabaja mucho y cumple con sus obligaciones*)

wheelwright ['hwil,raɪt] *s* carpintero de carretas

wheeze [hwiz] *s* resuello ruidoso ‖ *intr* resollar produciendo un silbido

whelp [hwɛlp] *s* cachorro ‖ *intr* parir

when [hwɛn] *adv* cuándo ‖ *conj* cuando

whence [hwɛns] *adv* de dónde; por lo tanto ‖ *conj* de donde

when•ev′er *conj* siempre que, cada vez que

where [hwɛr] *adv* dónde; adónde ‖ *conj* donde; adonde

whereabouts ['hwɛrə,bauts] *s* paradero

whereas [hwɛr'æz] *conj* mientras que, al paso que; considerando ‖ *s* considerando

where•by′ *adv* por medio del cual

wherefore ['hwɛrfor] *adv* por qué, para qué; por eso, por tanto ‖ *conj* por lo cual ‖ *s* motivo, razón *f*

where•from′ *adv* de donde

where•in′ *adv* donde, en qué ‖ *conj* donde; en el que; en lo cual

where•of′ *adv* de qué ‖ *conj* de que; de lo cual

where′up•on′ *adv* con lo cual, después de lo cual

wherever [hwɛr'ɛvər] *conj* dondequiera que

wherewithal ['hwɛrwɪð,ɔl] *s* cumquibus *m*, medios

whet [hwɛt] *v* (*pret & pp* **whetted;** *ger* **whetting**) *tr* afilar, aguzar; despertar, estimular; abrir (*el apetito*)

whether ['wɛðər] *conj* si; **whether or no** en todo caso, de todas maneras; **whether or not** si . . . o no, ya sea que . . . o no

whet′stone′ *s* piedra de afilar

whey [hwe] *s* suero de la leche

which [hwɪtʃ] *pron interr* cuál; **which is which** cuál es el uno y cuál el otro ‖ *pron rel* que, el (la, etc.) que ‖ *adj interr* qué; cuál, cuál de los (las) ‖ *adj rel* el (la, etc.) . . . que

which•ev′er *pron rel* cualquiera ‖ *adj rel* cualquier; **whichever ones** cualesquiera

whiff [hwɪf] *s* soplo; fumada; olorcillo; acceso, arranque *m;* **to get a whiff of** percibir un olor fugaz de ‖ *intr* soplar (*el viento*); echar bocanadas (*el que fuma*)

while [hwaɪl] *conj* mientras, mientras que ‖ *s* rato; **a long while** largo rato; **a while ago** hace un rato; **between whiles** de vez en cuando ‖ *tr* **to while away** entretener (*el tiempo*); pasar (*p.ej., la tarde*) de un modo entretenido

whim [hwɪm] *s* capricho, antojo

whimper ['hwɪmpər] *s* lloriqueo ‖ *tr* decir lloriqueando ‖ *intr* lloriquear

whimsical ['hwɪmzɪkəl] *adj* caprichoso, extravagante, fantástico

whine [hwaɪn] *s* gimoteo, quejido ‖ *intr* gimotear, quejarse

whin•ny ['hwɪni] *s* (*pl* **-nies**) relincho ‖ *v* (*pret & pp* **-nied**) *intr* relinchar

whip [hwɪp] *s* látigo, zurriago; huevos batidos con nata ‖ *v* (*pret & pp* **whipped** o **whipt;** *ger* **whipping**) *tr* azotar, zurriagar, fustigar; batir (*huevos y nata*); (coll) derrotar, vencer; **to whip off** (coll) escribir de prisa; **to whip out** sacar de repente; **to whip up** (coll) preparar de prisa; (coll) avivar, excitar

whip′cord′ *s* tralla; tejido fuerte con costurones diagonales

whip hand *s* mano *f* del látigo; (*upper hand*) vara alta

whip′lash′ *s* tralla

whipped cream *s* nata, crema batida

whipper-snapper ['hwɪpər,snæpər] *s* arrapiezo, mequetrefe *m*

whippet ['hwɪpɪt] *s* perro lebrel!

whipping boy ['hwɪpɪŋ] *s* cabeza de turco, víctima inocente

whipping post *s* poste *m* de flagelación

whippoorwill [,hwɪpər'wɪl] *s* chotacabras norteamericano (*Caprimulgus vociferus*)

whir [hwʌr] *s* zumbido ‖ *v* (*pret & pp* **whirred;** *ger* **whirring**) *intr* girar zumbando

whirl [hwʌrl] *s* vuelta, giro; remolino; (*of events, parties, etc.*) serie *f* interminable ‖ *tr & intr* remolinear; **my head whirls** siento vértigo

whirligig ['hwʌrlɪ,gɪg] *s* (ent) escribano del agua; tíovivo; (*pinwheel*) rehilandera, molinete *m;* peonza

whirl′pool′ *s* remolino, vorágine *f*

whirl′wind′ *s* torbellino, manga de viento

whirlybird ['hwʌrlɪ,bʌrd] *s* (coll) helicóptero

whish [hwɪʃ] *s* zumbido suave ‖ *intr* zumbar suavemente

whisk [hwɪsk] *s* escobilla; toque ligero ‖ *tr* barrer, cepillar; **to whisk out of sight** escamotear ‖ *intr* moverse rápidamente

whisk broom *s* escobilla

whiskers ['hwɪskərz] *spl* barbas; (*on side of face*) patillas; (*of cat*) bigotes *mpl*

whiskey ['hwɪski] *adj* (*voice*) (coll) aguardentoso ‖ *s* whisky *m*

whisper ['hwɪspər] *s* cuchicheo; (*of leaves*) susurro; **in a whisper** en voz baja ‖ *tr* susurrar, decir al oído ‖ *intr* cuchichear, hablar al oído: susurrar (*p.ej., las hojas*); (*to gossip*) susurrar, murmurar

whisperer ['hwɪspərər] *s* susurrón *m*

whispering ['hwɪspərɪŋ] *adj & s* (*gossiping*) susurrón *m*

whist [hwɪst] *s* whist *m* (*juego de naipes*)

whistle ['hwɪsəl] *s* (*sound*) silbido, silbo; pitazo; (*device*) silbato, pito; **to wet one's whistle** (coll) remojar la palabra ‖ *tr* silbar (*p.ej., una canción* ‖ *intr* silbar; pitear; **to whistle for** llamar con un silbido; (coll) tener que componérselas sin

whistle stop *s* apeadero, pueblecito

whit [hwɪt] *s*—**not a whit** ni pizca; **to not care a whit** no importarle a (*uno*) un bledo

white [hwaɪt] *adj* blanco ‖ *s* blanco; (*of an egg*) clara; **whites** (pathol) pérdidas blancas, flujo blanco

white'caps' *spl* cabrillas, palomas

white coal *s* hulla blanca

white'-col'lar *adj* oficinesco

white-collar crime *s* crímenes *mpl* de oficinistas

white feather *s*—**to show the white feather** mostrarse cobarde

white goods *spl* tejidos de algodón; ropa blanca; aparatos electrodomésticos

white-haired ['hwaɪt,hɛrd] *adj* de pelo blanco; (*gray-haired*) cano; (coll) favorito, predilecto

white heat *s* blanco, calor blanco; (fig) viva agitación

white lead [lɛd] *s* albayalde *m*

white lie *s* mentirilla, mentira inocente u oficiosa

white meat *s* pechuga, carne *f* de la pechuga del ave

whiten ['hwaɪtən] *tr* blanquear, emblanquecer ‖ *intr* blanquear, emblanquecerse; palidecer

whiteness ['hwaɪtnɪs] *s* blancura

white plague *s* peste blanca (*tuberculosis*)

white slavery *s* trata de blancas

white tie *s* corbatín blanco; traje *m* de etiqueta

white'wash' *s* jalbegue *m*, lechada, blanqueadura; (*e.g., of a scandal*) encubrimiento ‖ *tr* jalbegar, enjalbegar, encalar; absolver sin justicia; encubrir (*un escándalo*)

whither ['hwɪðər] *adv* adónde ‖ *conj* adonde

whitish ['hwaɪtɪʃ] *adj* blanquecino, blancuzco

whitlow ['hwɪtlo] *s* panadizo, uñero

Whitsuntide ['hwɪtsən,taɪd] *s* semana de Pentecostés

whittle ['hwɪtəl] *tr* sacar pedazos a (*un trozo de madera*); **to whittle away** o **down** reducir poco a poco

whiz o **whizz** [hwɪz] *s* silbido, zumbido; (slang) perito, fenómeno ‖ *v* (*pret & pp*

whizzed; *ger* whizzing) *intr*—**to whiz by** rehilar, silbar; pasar como una flecha

who [hu] *pron interr* quién; **who else?** ¿quién más?; **who goes there?** (mil) ¿quién vive?; **who's who** quién es el uno y quién el otro; quiénes son gente de importancia ‖ *pron rel* que, quien; el (la, etc.) que

whoa [hwo] o [wo] *interj* ¡so!

who•ev'er *pron rel* quienquiera que, cualquiera que

whole [hol] *adj* todo, entero; (*intact*) ileso; (*not scattered or dispersed*) único, p.ej., **the whole interest for him was the child he was raising** el único interés para él era el niño que educaba; **made out of the whole cloth** enteramente falso o imaginario ‖ *s* conjunto, todo; **as a whole** en conjunto; **on the whole** en general; por la mayor parte

wholehearted ['hol,hɑrtɪd] *adj* sincero, cordial

whole note *s* (mus) semibreve *f*

whole'sale' *adj & adv* al por mayor ‖ *s* venta al pormayor ‖ *tr* vender al por mayor ‖ *intr* vender al por mayor; venderse al por mayor

wholesaler ['hol,selər] *s* comerciante *mf* al por mayor

wholesome ['holsəm] *adj* (*conducive to good health*) saludable; (*in good health*) fresco, rollizo

wholly ['holi] *adv* enteramente, completamente

whole wheat *s* trigo entero

whom [hum] *pron interr* a quién ‖ *pron rel* que, a quien; al (a la, etc.) que

whom•ev'er *pron rel* a quienquiera que

whoop [hup] o [hwup] *s* ululato ‖ *tr*—**to whoop it up** (slang) armar una gritería ‖ *intr* ulular

whooping cough ['hupɪŋ] o ['hupɪŋ] *s* tos ferina, tos convulsiva

whopper ['hwɑpər] *s* (coll) enormidad; (coll) mentirón *m*

whopping ['hwɑpɪŋ] *adj* (coll) enorme, grandísimo

whore [hor] *s* puta ‖ *intr*—**to whore around** putañear, putear

whore'house' *s* burdel *m*; congal *m* (Mex)

whortleber•ry ['hwʌrtəl,bɛri] *s* (*pl* **-ries**) arándano

whose [huz] *pron interr* de quién ‖ *pron rel* de quien, cuyo

why [hwaɪ] *adv* por qué; **why not?** ¿cómo no? ‖ *s* (*pl* **whys**) porqué *m* ‖ *interj* ¡toma!; **why, certainly!** ¡desde luego!, ¡por supuesto!; **why, yes!** ¡claro!, ¡pues sí!

wick [wɪk] *s* mecha, pabilo

wicked ['wɪkɪd] *adj* malo; malazo; (*mischievous*) travieso, revoltoso; (*vicious*) arisco; ofensivo

wicker ['wɪkər] *adj* mimbroso ‖ *s* mimbre *m & f*

wicket ['wɪkɪt] *s* (*small door in a larger one*) portillo, postigo; (*small opening in a door*) ventanillo; (*ticket window*) taquilla; (*gate to regulate flow of water*) compuerta; (cricket) meta; (croquet) aro

wh
wi

wide [waɪd] *adj* ancho; de ancho; (*sense of a word*) amplio, lato ‖ *adv* de par en par; enteramente; lejos; **wide of the mark** lejos del blanco; fuera de propósito

wide'-an'gle *adj* granangular

wide'-a•wake' *adj* despabilado

widen [ˈwaɪdən] *tr* ensanchar ‖ *intr* ensancharse

wide'-o'pen *adj* abierto de par en par; **to be wide-open** estar (*p.ej., una ciudad*) abierta a los jugadores

wide'spread' *adj* (*arms, wings*) extendido; difundido, extenso

widow [ˈwɪdo] *s* viuda; (cards) baceta ‖ *tr* dejar viuda

widower [ˈwɪdo•ər] *s* viudo

widowhood [ˈwɪdo,hʊd] *s* viudez *f*

widow's mite *s* limosna que da un pobre

widow's pension *s* viudedad

widow's weeds *spl* luto de viuda

width [wɪdθ] *s* anchura

wield [wild] *tr* esgrimir, manejar (*la espada*); ejercer (*el poder*)

wife [waɪf] *s* (*pl* **wives** [waɪvz]) esposa, mujer *f*

wig [wɪg] *s* peluca

wiggle [ˈwɪgəl] *s* meneo rápido ‖ *tr* menear rápidamente ‖ *intr* menearse rápidamente

wig'wag' *s* comunicación con banderas ‖ *v* (*pret & pp* **-wagged;** *ger* **-wagging**) *tr* menear; mandar (*informes*) moviendo banderas ‖ *intr* menearse; señalar con banderas

wigwam [ˈwɪgwɑm] *s* choza cónica (*de los pieles rojas*)

wild [waɪld] *adj* (*not domesticated; growing without cultivation; uncivilized*) salvaje; (*unrestrained*) descabellado; (*frantic, mad*) frenético; (*riotous*) desenfrenado, revoltoso; extravagante; (*bullet, shot*) perdido; **wild about** loco por ‖ *adv* disparatadamente; **to run wild** crecer locamente; estar sin gobierno ‖ *s* desierto, yermo; **wilds** monte *m*, despoblado

wild boar *s* jabalí *m*

wild card *s* comodín *m*

wild'cat' *s* gato montés; lince *m;* empresa arriesgada

wildcat strike *s* huelga no autorizada por el sindicato

wilderness [ˈwɪldərnɪs] *s* desierto, yermo

wild'fire' *s* fuego fatuo; fucilazo; **to spread like wildfire** ser un reguero de pólvora, correr como pólvora en reguero

wild flower *s* flor *f* del campo

wild goose *s* ganso bravo

wild'-goose' chase *s* caza de grillos

wild'life' *s* animales *mf* salvajes

wild oats *spl* excesos de la juventud, mocedad; **to sow one's wild oats** llevar (*los mozos*) una vida de excesos

wild olive *s* acebuche *m*

wile [waɪl] *s* ardid *m* engaño; (*cunning*) astucia ‖ *tr* engatusar; **to wile away** entretener (*el tiempo*); pasar (*p.ej., la tarde*)

will [wɪl] *s* voluntad; (law) testamento; **at will** a voluntad ‖ *tr* querer; (*to bequeath*) legar ‖ *intr* querer; **do as you will** haga

Vd. lo que quiera ‖ *v* (*pret & cond* **would**) *v aux* he **will arrive at six o'clock** llegará a las seis; **he will go for days without smoking** pasa días enteros sin fumar

willful [ˈwɪlfəl] *adj* voluntarioso

willfulness [ˈwɪlfəlnɪs] *s* voluntariedad

William [ˈwɪljəm] *s* Guillermo

willing [ˈwɪlɪŋ] *adj* dispuesto; gustoso, pronto; espontáneo; **willing or unwilling** que quiera, que no quiera

willingly [ˈwɪlɪŋli] *adv* de buena gana, de buena voluntad

willingness [ˈwɪlɪŋnɪs] *s* buena gana, buena voluntad

will-o'-the-wisp [ˈwɪləðəˈwɪsp] *s* fuego fatuo; ilusión, quimera

willow [ˈwɪlo] *s* sauce *m*

willowy [ˈwɪlo•i] *adj* (*pliant*) juncal, mimbreño; (*slender, graceful*) juncal, cimbreño, esbelto; lleno de sauces

will power *s* fuerza de voluntad

willy-nilly [ˈwɪliˈnɪli] *adv* de grado o por fuerza

wilt [wɪlt] *tr* marchitar ‖ *intr* marchitarse

wil•y [ˈwaɪli] *adj* (*comp* **-ier;** *super* **-iest**) artero, engañoso; astuto

wimple [ˈwɪmpəl] *s* griñón *m*, impla

win [wɪn] *s* (coll) éxito, triunfo ‖ *v* (*pret & pp* **won** [wʌn];] *ger* **winning**) *tr* ganar; **to win over** ganar, conquistar ‖ *intr* ganar; **to win out** ganar; (coll) tener éxito

wince [wɪns] *s* sobresalto ‖ *intr* sobresaltarse

winch [wɪntʃ] *s* maquinilla, torno; (*handle, crank*) manubrio

wind [wɪnd] *s* viento; (*gas in intestines*) (coll) viento; (*breath*) respiración, resuello; **to break wind** ventosear; **to get wind of** saber de, tener noticia de; **to sail close to the wind** (naut) ceñir el viento; **to take the wind out of one's sails** apagarle a uno los fuegos ‖ *tr* dejar sin aliento ‖ [waɪnd] *v* (*pret & pp* **wound** [waʊnd]) *tr* (*to coil; to wrap up*) arrollar, envolver, devanar (*alambre*); ovillar (*hilo*); torcer (*hebras*); hacer girar (*un manubrio*); dar cuerda a (*un reloj*); **to wind one's way through** serpentear por; **to wind up** arrollar, envolver; (coll) poner punto final a ‖ *intr* serpentear (*un camino*)

windbag [ˈwɪnd,bæg] *s* (*of bagpipe*) odre *m;* (coll) charlatán *m*, palabrero, discursista *mf*

windbreak [ˈwɪnd,brek] *s* guardavientos *m*

wind cone [wɪnd] *s* (aer) cono de viento

winded [ˈwɪndɪd] *adj* falto de respiración, sin resuello

windfall [ˈwɪnd,fɔl] *s* fruta caída del árbol; fortunón *m*, cosa llovida del cielo

winding sheet [ˈwaɪndɪŋ] *s* sudario, mortaja

winding stairs *spl* escalera de caracol

wind instrument [wɪnd] *s* (mus) instrumento de viento

windlass [ˈwɪndləs] *s* maquinilla, torno

windmill [ˈwɪnd,mɪl] *s* (*mill operated by wind*) molino de viento; (*modern wind-driven source of power*) aeromotor *m;* (*pinwheel*) molinete *m;* **to tilt at windmills** luchar con los molinos de viento

window [ˈwɪndo] s ventana; (*of ticket office; of envelope*) ventanilla; (*of coach, automobile*) ventanilla, portezuela
window dresser s escaparatista *mf*
window dressing s adorno de escaparates
window frame s marco de ventana
win'dow•pane' s cristal *m* o vidrio de ventana
window screen s alambrera, sobrevidriera
window shade s visillo, transparente *m* de resorte
win'dow•shop' v (*pret & pp* -**shopped;** *ger* -**shopping**) *intr* curiosear en las tiendas
window shutter s contraventana
window sill s repisa de ventana
windpipe [ˈwɪndpaɪp] s tráquea
wind shear s (aer) ráfaga violenta
windshield [ˈwɪndˌʃild] s parabrisa *m*
windshield washer s lavaparabrisas *m*
windshield wiper s limpiaparabrisas *m*
wind'shield-wip'er blade s escobilla de limpiaparabrisas
wind sock s (aer) cono de viento
windstorm [ˈwɪndˌstɔrm] s ventarrón *m*
wind-up [ˈwaɪndˌʌp] s conclusión; (sport) final *f* de partido
windward [ˈwɪndwərd] s barlovento; **to turn to windward** barloventear
Windward Islands *spl* islas de Barlovento
Windward Passage s paso de los Vientos
wind•y [ˈwɪndi] adj (*comp* -**ier;** *super* -**iest**) ventoso; (*unsubstantial*) vacío; palabrero, ampuloso, discursisto; **it is windy** hace viento
wine [waɪn] s vino ‖ *tr* obsequiar con vino ‖ *intr* beber vino
wine cellar s bodega
wine'glass' s copa para vino
winegrower [ˈwaɪnˌgro•ər] s vinicultor *m*
winegrowing [ˈwaɪnˌgro•ɪŋ] s vinicultura
wine making s enotecnia
wine press s lagar *m*
winer•y [ˈwaɪnəri] s (*pl* -**ies**) lagar *m*
wine'skin' s odre *m*
winetaster [ˈwaɪnˌtestər] s catavinos *m*
wing [wɪŋ] s ala; facción; bando; (theat) bastidor *m;* **to take wing** alzar el vuelo ‖ *tr* herir en el ala; **to wing one's way** avanzar volando
wing chair s sillón *m* de orejas
wing collar s cuello de pajarita
wing nut s tuerca de aletas
wing'spread' s envergadura
wink [wɪŋk] s guiño; **to not sleep a wink** no pegar los ojos; **to take forty winks** (coll) descabezar el sueño ‖ *tr* guiñar (*el ojo*) ‖ *intr* guiñar; (*to blink*) parpadear, pestañear; **to wink at** guiñar el ojo a; fingir no ver
winner [ˈwɪnər] s ganador *m*, vencedor *m;* premiado
winning [ˈwɪnɪŋ] adj triunfante, victorioso; atrayente, simpático ‖ **winnings** *spl* ganancias
winnow [ˈwɪno] *tr* aventar; entresacar ‖ *intr* aletear
winsome [ˈwɪnsəm] adj atrayente, simpático, engañador; alegre

winter [ˈwɪntər] adj invernal ‖ s invierno ‖ *intr* invernar
win'ter•green' s gaulteria, té *m* del Canadá; esencia de gaulteria
win•try [ˈwɪntri] adj (*comp* -**trier;** *super* -**triest**) invernal, invernizo; helado, frío
wipe [waɪp] *tr* frotar para limpiar; enjugar (*la cara, el sudor, las manos*); **to wipe away** enjugar (*lágrimas*); **to wipe off** quitar frotando; **to wipe out** (coll) borrar, cancelar; (coll) aniquilar, destruir; (coll) enjugar (*deudas, un déficit*)
wiper [ˈwaɪpər] s paño, trapo; (elec) contacto deslizante
wire [waɪr] s (*thread of metal*) alambre *m;* telégrafo; telegrama *m;* teléfono; **to pull wires** (coll) tocar resortes ‖ *tr* alambrar; telegrafiar ‖ *intr* telegrafiar
wire cutter s cortaalambres *m*
wire entanglement s (mil) alambrado
wire gauge s calibrador *m* de alambre
wire-haired [ˈwaɪrˌhɛrd] adj de pelo áspero
wireless [ˈwaɪrlɪs] adj inalámbrico, sin hilos
wire nail s punta de París, clavo de alambre
wire pulling [ˈpʊlɪŋ] s (coll) empleo de resortes; enchufismo
wire recorder s grabadora de alambre
wire screen s alambrera, tela de alambre
wire service s servicio telegráfrico y telefónico
wire'tap' v (*pret & pp* -**tapped;** *ger* -**tapping**) *tr* intervenir (*una conversación telefónica*)
wire tapping s escuchas telefónicas *fpl*
wiring [ˈwaɪrɪŋ] s (elec) alambraje *m*
wir•y [ˈwaɪri] adj (*comp* -**ier;** *super* -**iest**) alambrino; cimbreante; nervudo; vibrante
wisdom [ˈwɪzdəm] s sabiduría, cordura
wisdom tooth s muela cordal, muela del juicio
wise [waɪz] adj sabio, cuerdo; (*step, decision*) acertado, juicioso; **to be wise to** (slang) conocer el juego de; **to get wise** (coll) caer en el chiste ‖ s modo, manera; **in no wise** de ningún modo
wiseacre [ˈwaɪzˌekər] s sabihondo
wise'crack' s (slang) cuchufleta ‖ *intr* (slang) cuchufletear
wise guy s (slang) sabelotodo
wish [wɪʃ] s deseo; **to make a wish** pensar algo que se desea ‖ *tr* desear; dar (*los buenos días*) ‖ *intr* desear; **to wish for** desear, anhelar
wish'bone' s espoleta, hueso de la suerte
wishful [ˈwɪʃfəl] adj deseoso
wishful thinking s optimismo a ultranza; **to indulge in wishful thinking** forjarse ilusiones
wistful [ˈwɪstfəl] adj melancólico, tristón, pensativo
wit [wɪt] s agudeza; (*person*) chistoso; (*keen mental power*) juicio; **to be at one's wits' end** no saber qué hacer; **to have the wit to** tener el tino de; **to live by one's wits** vivir del cuento
witch [wɪtʃ] s bruja, hechicera; (*old hag*) bruja

witch'craft' s brujería

witches' Sabbath s aquelarre m

witch hazel s (*shrub*) nogal m de la brujería, planta del sortilegio; (*liquid*) hamamelina, hazelina

with [wɪð] o [wɪθ] *prep* con; de

with•draw' v (*pret* **-drew;** *pp* **-drawn**) *tr* retirar ‖ *intr* retirarse

withdrawal [wɪð'drɔ•əl] o [wɪθ'drɔ•əl] s retirada

withdrawal symptom s síntoma m de abstinencia; (slang) mono

wither ['wɪðər] *tr* marchitar; (fig) aplastar, confundir ‖ *intr* marchitarse; confundirse

with•hold' v (*pret* & *pp* **-held**) *tr* retener; suspender (*pago*); negar (*un permiso*)

withholding tax s impuesto deducido del sueldo

with•in' *adv* dentro ‖ *prep* dentro de; al alcance de; poco menos de; con un margen de

with•out' *adv* fuera ‖ *prep* fuera de; (*lacking, not with*) sin; **to do without** pasar sin; **without** + *ger* sin + *inf*, p.ej., **he left without saying goodbye** salió sin despedirse; sin que + *subj*, p.ej., **he came in without anyone seeing him** entró sin que nadie le viese

with•stand' v (*pret* & *pp* **-stood**) *tr* aguantar, resistir

witness ['wɪtnɪs] s testigo *mf*; **in witness whereof** en fe de lo cual; **to bear witness** dar testimonio ‖ *tr* (*to be present at*) presenciar; (*to attest*) atestiguar, testimoniar; firmar como testigo

witness stand s banquillo o estrado de los testigos

witticism ['wɪtɪ,sɪzəm] s agudeza, dicho agudo, ocurrencia

wittingly ['wɪtɪŋli] *adv* a sabiendas

wit•ty ['wɪti] *adj* (*comp* **-tier;** *super* **-tiest**) agudo, ingenioso; (*person*) ocurrente, chistoso

wizard ['wɪzərd] s brujo, hechicero; (coll) as m, experto

wizardry ['wɪzərdri] s hechicería, magia

wizened ['wɪzənd] *adj* acartonado, arrugado

wk. *abbr* **week**

w.l. *abbr* **wave length**

woad [wod] s hierba pastel

wobble ['wɑbəl] s bamboleo, tambaleo ‖ *intr* bambolear, tambalear; bailar (*una silla*); (fig) vacilar, ser inconstante

wob•bly ['wɑbli] *adj* (*comp* **-blier;** *super* **-bliest**) bamboleante, inseguro; vacilante

woe [wo] s aflicción, miseria, infortunio ‖ *interj* —**woe is me!** ¡ay de mí!

woebegone ['wobɪ,gɔn] o ['wobɪ,gɑn] *adj* cariacontecido, triste

woeful ['wofəl] *adj* triste, miserable; (*of poor quality*) malo, pésimo

wolf [wʊlf] s (*pl* **wolves** [wʊlvz]) lobo; persona cruel, persona mañosa; (coll) tenorio; **to cry wolf** dar falsa alarma; **to keep the wolf from the door** ponerse a cubierto del hambre ‖ *tr* & *intr* comer vorazmente, engullir

wolf'hound' s galgo lobero

wolfram ['wʊlfrəm] s (*element*) volframio; (*mineral*) volframita

wolf's-bane o **wolfsbane** ['wʊlfs,ben] s matalobos m

woman ['wʊmən] s (*pl* **women** ['wɪmɪn]) mujer f

womanhood ['wʊmən,hʊd] s el sexo femenino; las mujeres

womanish ['wʊmənɪʃ] *adj* mujeril; (*effeminate*) afeminado

wom'an-kind' s el sexo femenino

womanly ['wʊmənli] *adj* (*comp* **-lier;** *super* **-liest**) femenil, mujeriego

woman suffrage s sufragismo

woman-suffragist ['wʊmən'sʌfrədʒɪst] s sufragista *mf*

womb [wʊm] s útero; (fig) seno

womenfolk ['wɪmɪn,fok] *spl* las mujeres

women's lib(eration movement) s movimiento feminista; feminismo

wonder ['wʌndər] s (*something strange or surprising*) maravilla; (*feeling of surprise*) admiración; (*something strange, miracle*) milagro; **for a wonder** cosa extraña; **no wonder that . . .** no es mucho que. . .; **to work wonders** hacer milagros ‖ *tr* preguntarse ‖ *intr* admirarse, maravillarse; **to wonder at** admirarse de, maravillarse con o de

wonder drugs *spl* drogas milagrosas

wonderful ['wʌndərfəl] *adj* maravilloso

won'der-land' s tierra de las maravillas; reino de las hadas

wonderment ['wʌndərmənt] s asombro, sorpresa

wont [wʌnt] o [wɔnt] *adj* acostumbrado; **to be wont to** acostumbrar ‖ s costumbre, hábito

wonted ['wʌntɪd] o ['wɔntɪd] *adj* acostumbrado, habitual

woo [wu] *tr* cortejar (*a una mujer*); tratar de conquistar; tratar de persuadir

wood [wʊd] s madera; (*for making a fire*) leña; barril m de madera; **out of the woods** (coll) fuera de peligro; (coll) libre de dificultades; **to take to the woods** andar a monte; **woods** bosque m

woodbine ['wʊd,baɪn] s (*honeysuckle*) madreselva; (*Virginia creeper*) guau m

wood carving s labrado de madera

wood'chuck' s marmota de América

wood'cock' s becada, coalla, chocha

wood'cut' s (typ) grabado en madera

wood'cut'ter s leñador m

wooded ['wʊdɪd] *adj* arbolado, enselvado

wooden ['wʊdən] *adj* de madera, hecho de madera; torpe, estúpido; sin ánimo

wood engraving s (typ) grabado en madera

wooden-headed ['wʊdən,hɛdɪd] *adj* (coll) torpe, estúpido

wooden leg s pata de palo

wooden shoe s zueco

wood grouse s gallo de bosque

woodland ['wʊdlənd] *adj* selvático ‖ s bosque m, monte m

woodland scene s (paint) boscaje m

wood·man ['wʊdmən] s (pl -men [mən]) leñador m

woodpecker ['wʊd,pɛkər] s carpintero, pájaro carpintero; (green woodpecker) picamaderos m

wood'pile' s montón m de leña

wood screw s tirafondo

wood'shed' s leñero

woods·man ['wʊdzmən] s (pl -men [mən]) leñador m

wood'wind' s (mus) instrumento de viento de madera

wood'work' s (working in wood) ebanistería, obra de carpintería; (things made of wood) maderaje m

wood'work·er s ebanista mf, carpintero

wood'worm' s carcoma

wood·y ['wʊdi] adj (comp -ier; super -iest) arbolado, enselvado; (like wood) leñoso

wooer ['wʊ·ər] s pretendiente m, galán m

woof [wuf] s (yarns running across warp) trama; (fabric) tejido

woofer ['wʊfər] s altavoz m para audiofrecuencias bajas

wool [wʊl] s lana

woolen ['wʊlən] adj de lana, hecho de lana ‖ s tejido de lana; **woolens** lanerías

woolgrower ['wʊl ,gro·ər] s criador m de ganado lanar

wool·ly ['wʊli] adj (comp -lier; super -liest) lanoso, lanudo; borroso, confuso

Worcestershire sauce ['wʊstərʃər] s salsa inglesa

word [wʌrd] s palabra; **to be as good as one's word** cumplir lo prometido; **to have a word with** hablar cuatro palabras con; **to have word from** recibir noticias de; **to keep one's word** cumplir su palabra; **to leave word** dejar dicho; **to send word that** mandar decir que; **words** (a quarrel) palabras mayores; (text of a song) letra ‖ tr redactar, formular ‖ **Word** s (theol) Verbo

word count s recuento de vocabulario

word formation s (gram) formación de palabras

wording ['wʌrdɪŋ] s fraseología, estilo

word order s (gram) orden m de colocación

word processing s redacción por medios electrónicos

word'stock' s vocabulario, léxico

word·y ['wʌrdi] adj (comp -ier; super -iest) verboso

work [wʌrk] s (exertion; labor, toil) trabajo; (result of exertion; human output; engineering structure) obra; (sew) labor f; **at work** trabajando; (not at home) en la oficina, en el taller, en la tienda; **out of work** sin trabajo, desempleado; **to shoot the works** (slang) echar el resto; **works** fábrica; mecanismo; (of clock) movimiento ‖ tr hacer trabajar; trabajar, obrar (la madera, el hierro); obrar (un milagro); explotar (una mina); **to work up** preparar; estimular, excitar ‖ intr trabajar; funcionar, marchar (un aparato, un motor); obrar (p.ej., un remedio); **to work loose** aflojarse; **to work out** resolverse

workable ['wʌrkəbəl] adj (feasible) practicable; (that can be worked) laborable

workaholic [,wʌrkə'hɔlɪk] s (coll) individuo con compulsión al trabajo

work'bench' s banco de trabajo, banco de taller

work'book' s (manual of instructions) libro de reglas; libro de ejercicios

work'box' s caja de herramientas; (for needlework) caja de labor

work'day' adj de cada día; ordinario, vulgar ‖ s día m de trabajo; (number of hours of work) jornada

work'days' adv entresemana (SAm)

worked-up ['wʌrkt'ʌp] adj muy conmovido, sobreexcitado, exaltado

worker ['wʌrkər] s trabajador m, obrero

work force s mano f de obra, personal obrero

work'horse' s caballo de carga; (tireless worker) yunque m

work'house' s taller penitenciario; (Brit) asilo de pobres

working class s clase obrera

work'ing·girl' s trabajadora joven

working hours spl horas de trabajo

working hypothesis s hipótesis f de guía

working·man ['wʌrkɪŋ,mæn] s (pl -men [,mɛn]) s obrero, trabajador m

working·woman ['wʌrkɪŋ,wʊmən] s (pl -women [,wɪmɪn]) obrera, trabajadora

work·man ['wʌrkmən] s (pl -men [mən]) obrero, trabajador m; (skilled worker) artífice m

workmanship ['wʌrkmən,ʃɪp] s destreza en el trabajo; (work executed) hechura, obra

work of art s obra de arte

work'out' s ensayo, prueba; (physical exercise) ejercicio

work'room' s (for manual work) obrador m, taller m; (study) gabinete m de trabajo

work'shop' s obrador m, taller m

work stoppage s paro

work therapy s laborterapia

world [wʌrld] adj mundial ‖ s mundo; **a world of** la mar de; **half the world** (a lot of people) medio mundo; **since the world began** desde que el mundo es mundo; **the other world** el otro mundo; **to bring into the world** echar al mundo; **to see the world** ver mundo; **to think the world of** tener un alto concepto de

world affairs spl asuntos internacionales

world'-class' adj sobresaliente

world·ly ['wʌrldli] adj (comp -lier; super -liest) mundano

world'ly-wise' adj que tiene mucho mundo

world's fair s exposición mundial

World War s Guerra Mundial

world'-wide' adj global, mundial

worm [wʌrm] s gusano; **worms** (pathol) lombrices fpl ‖ tr limpiar de lombrices; **to worm a secret out of a person** arrancar mañosamente un secreto a una persona; **to worm one's way into** insinuarse en

worm-eaten ['wʌrm,itən] adj carcomido; (fig) decaído, desgastado

worm gear s engranaje m de tornillo sin fin

wi
wo

worm'wood' s (Artemisia) ajenjo; (Artemisia absinthium) ajenjo del campo o ajenjo mayor; (something bitter or grievous) (fig) ajenjo

worm·y [ˈwʌrmi] adj (comp **-ier**; super **-iest**) gusaniento, gusanoso; (worm-eaten) carcomido; (groveling) rastrero, servil

worn [worn] adj roto, raído, gastado

worn'-out' adj muy gastado, inservible; (by toil, illness) consumido, rendido

worrisome [ˈwʌrisəm] adj inquietante; (inclined to worry) aprensivo, inquieto

wor·ry [ˈwʌri] s (pl **-ries**) inquietud, preocupación; (cause of anxiety) molestia ‖ v (pret & pp **-ried**) tr inquietar, preocupar; (to harass, pester) acosar, molestar; **to be worried** estar inquieto ‖ intr inquietarse, preocuparse; **don't worry** pierda Vd. cuidado

worse [wʌrs] adj & adv comp peor; **worse and worse** de mal en peor

worsen [ˈwʌrsən] tr & intr empeorar ‖ ref gravarse

wor·ship [ˈwʌrʃip] s adoración, culto; **your worship** vuestra merced ‖ v (pret & pp **-shiped** o **-shipped**; ger **-shiping** o **-shipping**) tr & intr adorar, venerar

worshiper o **worshipper** [ˈwʌrʃipər] s adorador m, devoto

worst [wʌrst] adj & adv super peor ‖ s (lo) peor; **at worst** en las peores circunstancias; **if worst comes to worst** si pasa lo peor; **to get the worst of** llevar la peor parte, salir perdiendo

worsted [ˈwʊstid] adj de estambre ‖ s estambre m; tela de estambre

wort [wʌrt] s (bot) hierba, planta; mosto de cerveza

worth [wʌrθ] adj del valor de; digno de; **to be worth** valer; tener una fortuna de; **to be worth** + ger valer la pena de + inf: **to be worth while** valer la pena; ser de mérito ‖ s valor m; mérito; **a dollar's worth of** un dólar de

worthless [ˈwʌrθlis] adj sin valor, inútil, inservible; (person) despreciable

worth'while' adj de mérito, digno de atención

wor·thy [ˈwʌrði] adj (comp **-thier**; super **-thiest**) digno; benemérito, meritorio ‖ s (pl **-thies**) benemérito; (hum & iron) personaje m

would [wʊd] v aux **she said she would do it** dijo que lo haría; **he would come if he could** vendría si pudiese; **he would go for days without smoking** pasaba días enteros sin fumar; **would that . . .!** ¡ojalá que . . .!

would'-be' adj llamado; supuesto ‖ s presumido

wound [wund] s herida ‖ tr herir

wounded [ˈwundid] adj herido ‖ **the wounded** los heridos

wow [waʊ] s (of phonograph record) ululación; (slang) éxito rotundo ‖ tr (slang) entusiasmar ‖ interj ¡cielos!, ¡mecachis!

wrack [ræk] s naufragio; vestigio; (fucaceous seaweed) varec m; **to go to wrack and ruin** desvencijarse; ir al desastre

wraith [reθ] s fantasma m, espectro

wrangle [ˈræŋgəl] s pendencia, riña ‖ intr pelotear, reñir

wrap [ræp] s abrigo, manto ‖ v (pret & pp **wrapped**; ger **wrapping**) tr envolver; **to be wrapped up in** (fig) estar prendado de; **to wrap up** envolver; (in clothing) arropar; (coll) concluir ‖ intr—**to wrap up** arroparse

wrapper [ˈræpər] s bata, peinador m; (of newspaper or magazine) faja; (of tobacco) capa

wrapping paper [ˈræpiŋ] s papel m de envolver, papel de embalar

wrath [ræθ] o [rɑθ] s cólera, ira; venganza

wrathful [ˈræθfəl] o [ˈrɑθfəl] adj colérico, iracundo

wreak [rik] tr descargar (la cólera); infligir (venganza)

wreath [riθ] s (pl **wreaths** [riðz]) guirnalda; corona funeraria; (worn as a mark of honor or victory) corona de laurel; (of smoke) espiral f

wreathe [rið] tr enguirnaldar; ceñir, envolver; tejer (una guirnalda) ‖ intr elevarse en espirales (el humo)

wreck [rɛk] s destrucción, ruina; naufragio; catástrofe f, desastre m; despojos, restos; (of one's hopes) naufragio; **to be a wreck** estar hecho un cascajo, estar hecho una ruina ‖ tr destruir, arruinar; hacer naufragar; hacer chocar, descarrilar (un tren)

wrecking ball s bola rompedora

wrecking car s (aut) camión m de auxilio; (rr) carro de grúa

wrecking crane s grúa de auxilio

wren [rɛn] s buscareta, coletero, rey m de zarza

wrench [rɛntʃ] s llave f; (pull) arranque m, tirón m; (twist of a joint) esguince m ‖ tr torcerse (p.ej., la muñeca); (fig) torcer (el sentido de una oración)

wrest [rɛst] tr arrebatar, arrancar violentamente

wrestle [ˈrɛsəl] s lucha; partido de lucha ‖ intr luchar

wrestling match [ˈrɛsliŋ] s partido de lucha

wretch [rɛtʃ] s miserable mf

wretched [ˈrɛtʃid] adj miserable; (poor, worthless) malísimo, pésimo

wriggle [ˈrigəl] s culebreo, meneo serpentino ‖ tr menear rápidamente ‖ intr culebrear, ondular; **to wriggle out of** escabullirse de

wrig·gly [ˈrigli] adj (comp **-glier**; super **-gliest**) retorciéndose; (fig) evasivo, tramoyista

wring [riŋ] v (pret & pp **wrung** [rʌŋ]) tr torcer; retorcer (las manos); exprimir (el zumo, la ropa, etc.); sacar por fuerza (la verdad); arrancar (dinero); **to wring out** exprimir (la ropa)

wringer [ˈriŋər] s exprimidor m

wrinkle [ˈrɪŋkəl] s arruga; (*clever trick or idea*) (coll) ardid m, truco ‖ tr arrugar ‖ intr arrugarse

wrin•kly [ˈrɪŋkli] adj (*comp* -klier; *super* -kliest) arrugado

wrist [rɪst] s muñeca

wrist′band′ s bocamanga, puño

wrist watch s reloj m de pulsera

writ [rɪt] s escrito, escritura; (law) mandato, orden f

write [raɪt] v (*pret* wrote [rot]; *pp* written [ˈrɪtən]) tr escribir; **to write down** poner por escrito; bajar el precio de; **to write off** cancelar (*una deuda*); **to write up** describir extensamente por escrito; (*to ballyhoo*) dar bombo a ‖ intr escribir; **to write back** contestar por carta

writer [ˈraɪtər] s escritor m

writer's cramp s grafospasmo

write′-up′ s (*favorable report*) bombo; (com) valoración excesiva

writhe [raɪð] intr contorcerse, retorcerse

writing [ˈraɪtɪŋ] s el escribir; (*something written*) escrito; profesión de escritor; **at this writing** al escribir ésta; **in one's own writing** de su puño y letra; **to put in writing** poner por escrito

writing desk s escritorio

writing materials spl recado de escribir

writing paper s papel m de escribir, papel de cartas

written accent [ˈrɪtən] s acento ortográfico

wrong [rɔŋ] adj injusto; malo; erróneo, equivocado; impropio; no . . . que se busca, p.ej., **this is the wrong house** ésta no es la casa que se busca; no . . . que se necesita, p.ej., **this is the wrong train** éste no es el tren que se necesita; no . . . que debe, p.ej., **he is going the wrong way** no sigue el camino que debe; **in the wrong place** mal colocado; **to be wrong** no tener razón; tener la culpa; **to be wrong with** pasar algo a, p.ej., **something is wrong with the motor** algo le pasa al motor ‖ adv mal; sin razón; al revés; **to go wrong** ir por mal camino; darse a la mala vida ‖ s daño, perjuicio; agravio, injusticia; error m; **to be in the wrong** no tener razón; tener la culpa; **to do wrong** obrar mal ‖ tr agraviar, hacer daño a, ofender, ser injusto con

wrongdoer [ˈrɔŋˌduˑər] s malhechor m

wrongdoing [ˈrɔŋˌduˑɪŋ] s malhecho, maldad

wrong number s (telp) número equivocado

wrong side s contrahaz f, revés m; (*of the street*) lado contrario; **to get out of bed on the wrong side** levantarse del lado izquierdo; **wrong side out** al revés

wrought iron [rɔt] s hierro dulce

wrought′-up′ adj muy conmovido, sobreexcitado, exaltado

wry [raɪ] adj (*comp* wrier; *super* wriest) torcido; desviado, pervertido; irónico, burlón

wry′neck′ s (orn) torcecuello; (pathol) torticolis m

wt. abbr **weight**

X

X, x [ɛks] vigésima cuarta letra del alfabeto inglés

Xanthippe [zænˈtɪpi] s Jantipa

Xavier [ˈzevɪˑər] s Javier

xebec [ˈzibɛk] s (naut) jabeque m

xenia [ˈzinɪˑə] s xenia

xenon [ˈzinɑn] o [ˈzɛnɑn] s xenón m

xenophobe [ˈzɛnəˌfob] s xenófobo

xenophobia [ˌzɛnəˈfobɪˑə] s xenofobia

Xenophon [ˈzɛnəfən] s Jenofonte m

xerograph [ˈzɪrəˌgræf] s fotocopia instantánea en seco ‖ tr & intr xerografiar

xerography [zɪˈrɑgrəfi] s xerografía

Xerxes [ˈzʌrksiz] s Jerjes m

Xmas [ˈkrɪsməs] s Navidad

X-rated [ˈɛksˌretɪd] adj (*film, etc.*) no recomendado; pornográfico

X ray s rayo X; (*photograph*) radiograma m

X-ray [ˈɛksˌre] adj radiográfico ‖ [ˈɛksˈre] tr radiografiar; tratar por medio de los rayos X

xylograph [ˈzaɪləˌgræf] s xilografía

xylography [zaɪˈlɑgrəfi] s xilografía

xylophone [ˈzaɪləˌfon] s (mus) xilófono

Y

Y, y [waɪ] vigésima quinta letra del alfabeto inglés

y. abbr **yard, year**

yacht [jɑt] s yate m

yacht club s club náutico

yak [jæk] s (zool) yac m

yam [jæm] s ñame m; (*sweet potato*) boniato, camote m

yank [jæŋk] *s* (coll) tirón *m* ‖ *tr* (coll) sacar de un tirón ‖ *intr* (coll) dar un tirón

Yankee ['jæŋki] *adj* & *s* yanqui *mf*

Yankeedom ['jæŋkidəm] *s* Yanquilandia; los yanquis

yap [jæp] *s* ladrido corto; (slang) charla necia y ruidosa ‖ *v* (*pret* & *pp* **yapped;** *ger* **yapping**) *intr* ladrar con ladrido corto; (slang) charlar necia y ruidosamente

yard [jɑrd] *s* cercado, patio; (*measure*) yarda; (naut) verga; (rr) patio

yard'arm' *s* (naut) penol *m*

yard goods *spl* géneros de pieza

yard'mas'ter *s* (rr) superintendente *m* de patio

yard'stick' *s* yarda, vara de medir; (fig) criterio, norma

yarn [jɑrn] *s* hilado, hilaza; (coll) cuento increíble, burlería

yarrow ['jæro] *s* milenrama

yaw [jɔ] *s* (naut) guiñada; **yaws** (pathol) frambesia ‖ *intr* (naut) guiñar

yawl [jɔl] *s* (naut) bote *m;* (naut) queche *m*

yawn [jɔn] *s* bostezo ‖ *intr* bostezar; abrirse desmesuradamente

yd. *abbr* **yard**

yea [je] *adv* & *s* sí *m*

yean [jin] *intr* parir (*la oveja, la cabra, etc.*)

year [jɪr] *s* año; **to be . . . years old** cumplir . . . años; **year in, year out** año tras año

year'book' *s* anuario

yearling ['jɪrlɪŋ] *adj* & *s* primal *m*

yearly ['jɪrli] *adj* anual ‖ *adv* anualmente

yearn [jʌrn] *intr* suspirar; **to yearn for** suspirar por, anhelar por

yearning ['jʌrnɪŋ] *s* anhelo, deseo ardiente

yeast [jist] *s* levadura

yeast cake *s* levadura comprimida, pastilla de levadura

yell [jɛl] *s* grito, voz *f* ‖ *tr* decir a gritos ‖ *intr* gritar, dar voces

yellow ['jɛlo] *adj* amarillo; (*cowardly*) (coll) blanco; (*journalism*) sensacional ‖ *s* amarillo; yema de huevo ‖ *intr* amarillecer

yellowish ['jɛlo•ɪʃ] *adj* amarillento

yellow jacket *s* avispón *m*

yellowness ['jɛlonɪs] *s* amarillez *f*

yellow press *s* prensa amarilla

yellow streak *s* vena de cobarde

yelp [jɛlp] *s* gañido ‖ *intr* gañir

yeo•man ['jomən] *s* (*pl* **-men** [mən]) (naut) pañolero; (naut) oficinista *m* de a bordo; (Brit) labrador acomodado

yeoman of the guard *s* (Brit) alabardero de palacio, continuo

yeoman's service *s* ayuda leal

yes [jɛs] *adv* sí ‖ *s* sí *m;* **to say yes** dar el sí ‖

v (*pret* & *pp* **yessed;** *ger* **yessing**) *tr* decir sí a ‖ *intr* decir sí

yes man *s* (coll) sacristán *m* de amén

yesterday ['jɛstərdi] o ['jɛstər‚de] *adj* & *s* ayer *m*

yet [jɛt] *adv* todavía, aún; **as yet** hasta ahora; **not yet** todavía no ‖ *conj* sin embargo

yew tree [ju] *s* tejo

yield [jild] *s* producción, rendimiento; (*crop*) cosecha; (*income produced*) rédito ‖ *tr* producir, rendir, redituar ‖ *intr* entregarse, rendirse, someterse; acceder, ceder, consentir; producir

yodeling o **yodelling** ['jodəlɪŋ] *s* tirolesa

yoga ['jogə] *s* yoga

yogi ['jogi] *s* yogui *m*

yogurt ['jogərt] *s* yogurt *m*

yoke [jok] *s* (*pair of draft animals*) yunta; (*device to join a pair of draft animals*) yugo; (fig) yugo; (*of a shirt*) hombrillo; (elec) culata; **to throw off the yoke** sacudir el yugo ‖ *tr* uncir

yokel ['jokəl] *s* patán *m*

yolk [jok] *s* yema

yonder ['jɑndər] *adj* aquel, de más allá ‖ *adv* allá, más allá

yore [jor] *s*—**of yore** antaño, antiguamente

you [ju] *pron pers* usted, ustedes; le, la, les; **with you** consigo ‖ *pron indef* se, p.ej., **you go in this way** se entra por aquí

young [jʌŋ] *adj* (*comp* **younger** ['jʌŋgər]; *super* **youngest** ['jʌŋgɪst]) joven ‖ **the young** los jóvenes, la gente joven

young hopeful *s* joven *m* de esperanzas

young people *spl* jóvenes *mpl*, gente *f* joven

youngster ['jʌŋstər] *s* jovencito; (*child*) chico, chiquillo

your [jur] *adj poss* su, el (o su) de Vd. o de Vds.

Yours [jurz] *pron poss* suyo; de Vd., de Vds.; el suyo; el de Vd., el de Vds.; **of yours** suyo; de Vd., de Vds.; **yours truly** su seguro servidor; (coll) este cura (yo)

your•self [jur'sɛlf] *pron pers* (*pl* **-selves** ['sɛlvz]) usted mismo; sí, sí mismo; se, p.ej., **you enjoyed yourself** se divirtió Vd.

youth [juθ] *s* (*pl* **youths** [juðs] o [juðz]) juventud; (*person*) jovenzuelo; jovenzuelos, jóvenes *mpl*

youthful ['juθfəl] *adj* juvenil, mocil

yowl [jaul] *s* aullido, alarido ‖ *intr* aullar, dar alaridos

yr. *abbr* **year**

Yugoslav ['jugo'slɑv] *adj* & *s* yugoeslavo

Yugoslavia ['jugo'slɑvɪ•ə] *s* Yugoeslavia

Yule [jul] *s* la Navidad; la pascua de Navidad

Yule log *s* nochebueno, leño de nochebuena

Yuletide ['jul‚taɪd] *s* la pascua de Navidad

Z

Z, z [zi] vigésima sexta letra del alfabeto inglés

za•ny ['zeni] *adj* (*comp* **-nier;** *super* **-niest**) cómico, gracioso, chiflado ‖ *s* (*pl* **-nies**) bufón *m*, payaso; mentecato

zeal [zil] *s* celo, entusiasmo

zealot ['zɛlət] *s* fanático, entusiasta *mf*
zealotry ['zɛlətri] *s* fanatismo
zealous ['zɛləs] *adj* celoso, entusiasta
zebra ['zibrə] *s* cebra
zebu ['zibju] *s* cebú *m*
zenith ['zinɪθ] *s* cenit *m*
zephyr ['zɛfər] *s* céfiro
zeppelin ['zɛpəlɪn] *s* zepelín *m*
ze•ro ['zɪro] *s (pl* **-ros** o **-roes**) cero
zero gravity *s* gravedad nula
zero growth *s* crecimiento cero
ze'ro-growth' *adj* sin aumento; estable
zero option *s* opción cero, opción nula
zest [zɛst] *s* entusiasmo; *(agreeable and piquant flavor)* gusto, sabor *m*
Zeus [zus] *s* Zeus *m*
zig•zig ['zɪg,zæg] *adj & adv* en zigzag ‖ *s* zigzag *m*, ziszas *m* ‖ *v (pret & pp* **-zagged;** *ger* **-zagging)** *intr* zigzaguear
zinc [zɪŋk] *s* cinc *m*
zinc etching *s* cincograbado
zinnia ['zɪnɪ•ə] *s* rascamoño
Zionism ['zaɪ•ə,nɪzəm] *s* sionismo
zip [zɪp] *s* (coll) silbido, zumbido; (coll)

energía, brío ‖ *v (pret & pp* **zipped;** *ger* **zipping)** *tr* cerrar con cierre relámpago, abrir con cierre relámpago; (coll) llevar con rapidez; **to zip up** dar gusto a ‖ *intr* silbar, zumbar; (coll) moverse con energía; **to zip by** (coll) pasar rápidamente
zip code *s* código postal
zipper ['zɪpər] *s* cierre *m* relámpago, cierre cremallera; chanclo con cierre relámpago; cíper (Mex)
zircon ['zʌrkɑn] *s* circón *m*
zirconium [zər'konɪ•əm] *s* circonio
zither ['zɪθər] *s* (mus) cítara
zodiac ['zodɪ,æk] *s* zodíaco
zone [zon] *s* zona; distrito postal ‖ *tr* dividir en zonas
zoölogic(al) [,zo•ə'lɑdʒɪk(əl)] *adj* zoológico
zoölogist [zo'ɑlədʒɪst] *s* zoólogo
zoölogy [zo'ɑlədʒi] *s* zoología
zoom [zum] *s* zumbido; (aer) empinada ‖ *tr* (aer) empinar ‖ *intr* zumbar; (aer) empinarse
zoöphyte ['zo•ə,faɪt] *s* zoófito
Zu•lu ['zulu] *adj* zulú ‖ *s (pl* **-lus)** zulú *mf*

ya
zu

SPANISH GRAMMAR

TABLE OF CONTENTS

1. STRESS, PUNCTUATION, CAPITALIZATION

All Spanish words, except compound words and adverbs in **-mente,** have only one stress. The position of this stress is always shown by the spelling in accordance with the following rules:

(a) Words ending in a vowel sound or in **n** or **s** are stressed on the syllable next to the last, e.g., **ca-sa, a-gua, se-rio, ha-blan, co-sas.**

(b) Words ending in a consonant except **n** or **s** are stressed on the last syllable, e.g., **se-ñor, pa-pel, fe-liz, U-ru-guay, es-toy.**

(c) If the stress does not fall in accordance with either of the above rules, it is indicated by an acute accent placed above the stressed vowel, e.g., **ca-fé, a-pren-dí, na-ción, lá-piz, fá-cil, re-pú-bli-ca.** The acute accent is also used to distinguish between words spelled alike but having different meanings or parts of speech, e.g., **aun** (= even) and **aún** (= still, yet), **donde** (*conj*) and **dónde** (*adv*), **el** (*def art*) and **él** (*pron*).

Question marks and exclamation points are placed both before and after a word or sentence, and the first is inverted, e.g., **¿Que tal?** How's everything? **¡Que lástima!** What a pity!

Capital letters are used less in Spanish than in English, e.g., **un inglés** an Englishman, **el idioma español** the Spanish language, **domingo** Sunday, **enero** January.

2. GENDER OF NOUNS

All Spanish nouns are grouped into two form classes, traditionally called **masculine** and **feminine**. All nouns referring specifically to male beings are **masculine**, e.g., **hombre** man, **muchacho** boy, **hermano** brother, **hijo** son, **tío** uncle, **toro** bull, **gallo** rooster.

All nouns referring specifically to females are **feminine**, e.g., **mujer** woman, **muchacha** girl, **hermana** sister, **hija** daughter, **madre** mother, **vaca** cow, **gallina** hen, **modelo** (artist's) model.

(a) Grammatical Gender. All other nouns not referring to males or females are still classed as either masculine or feminine, although this classification has nothing to do with sex. Masculine nouns frequently end in -o, e.g., **barco** boat, **caso** case, **libro** book, **tiempo** time; weather, **tráfico** trade; traffic. (A notable exception is **la mano** hand.)

Feminine nouns frequently end in -a, e.g., **casa** house, **cocina** kitchen, **libra** pound, **mesa** table. All other nouns, regardless of ending, must have their gender memorized. For example, a fairly large number of nouns ending in -a are masculine, e.g., **clima** climate, **dilema** dilemma, **planeta** planet, **sistema** system, **tema** theme. Nouns ending in -e may be either masculine or feminine, e.g., **el diente** tooth, **el baile** dance, **el toque** touch; stroke, but **la servidumbre** servitude; the servants, **la superficie** surface.

3. PLURAL OF NOUNS

Nouns ending in a vowel add s to form the plural, e.g., **casa-casas** house, -s, **diente-dientes** tooth, teeth, **tribu-tribus** tribe, -s. Nouns ending in an accented **i, u,** or **a,** add **es** in the plural, e.g., rubí-**rubíes** ruby, -ies, tisú-**tisúes** tissue, -s, bajá-**bajaes** pasha, -s. Nouns ending in a consonant (including -y) add **es** to form the plural, e.g., **balcón-balcones** balcony, -nies, **árbol-árboles** tree, -s, **flor-flores** flower, -s, **mes-meses** month, -s, **rey-reyes** king, -s; monarchs.

Nouns ending in z change the z to c and add es, e.g., **vez-veces** time, -s; occasion, -s, **lápiz-lápices** pencil, -s. Nouns ending in s preceded by an unaccented vowel do not change in the plural, e.g., **el lunes, los lunes** Monday, -s, **la crisis, las crises** crisis, crises.

The syllable stressed in the singular is always stressed in the plural except in a few words such as **carácter** character and **régimen** regime, whose plurals are **caracteres** and **regímenes**. However, the written accent mark found on the last syllable of the singular of nouns with a stressed final in **n** and **s** is not necessary in the plural and therefore must be omitted, e.g., **acción** (action; share, -s, of stock) **acciones, marqués** (marquess) **marqueses**.

4. DEFINITE ARTICLE

Unlike the English article **the,** which is invariable in writing, the Spanish article has four distinct forms corresponding to the number and the gender of the noun they modify:

	MASCULINE	FEMININE
SINGULAR	el	la
PLURAL	los	las

For feminine nouns which begin with a stressed **a** (including **ha**), the form of the singular definite article is **el,** e.g., **el agua** the water, **el hacha** the hatchet. The gender remains feminine so that adjectives modifying such nouns are feminine, e.g., **el agua fresca** the cool water, **las hachas** the hatchets.

The use of the definite article is in many respects similar to that of English. That is, it is used when referring to someone or something already known, e.g., **el hombre** the man, referring to someone previously mentioned (i.e., the man I met yesterday) as distinct from **un hombre** a man (i.e., someone unknown or not previously mentioned).

In contrast with English, however, the definite article is used before nouns referring to general or abstract notions, **la libertad** freedom, **la democracia** democracy, **la independencia** independence, **la esperanza** hope.

The definite article is often omitted before nouns in apposition, e.g., **Madrid, capital de España,** and is always omitted in the numbered names of rulers and popes, e.g., **Luis catorce**

Louis the Fourteenth, **Juan Carlos primero** Juan Carlos the First, **Juan veintitrés** John the Twenty-third.

5. INDEFINITE ARTICLE

The singulars of the indefinite article are **un,** masculine, and **una,** feminine; the plurals are **unos,** masculine, and **unas,** feminine, e.g., **un mes** a month, **unos meses** (some) months; **una calle** a street, **unas calles** (some) streets.

The form **un** is also commonly used before feminine singular nouns beginning with a stressed **a** or **ha,** e.g., **un arma** a weapon.

The plural forms **unos, unas,** when followed by a cardinal number, mean *about,* e.g., **unos cinco años** about five years.

The indefinite article is not used before a noun of nationality, religion, occupation, and the like, e.g., **Mi amigo es abogado** My friend is a lawyer. If the noun is modified, the indefinite article is generally used, e.g, **Mi hermano es un abogado excelente** My brother is an excellent lawyer. The indefinite article is omitted before **otro,** which therefore means both *other* and *another,* e.g., **Quiero otro libro** I want another book.

6. GENDER OF ADJECTIVES

Adjectives agree in gender and number with the noun they modify.

Adjectives ending in -o become feminine by changing -o to -a, e.g., **alto** and **alta** high. Adjectives ending in any other letter have the same form in the masculine and the feminine, e.g., **constante** constant, **fácil** easy, **belga** Belgian, except adjectives of nationality ending in -l, -s, or -z and adjectives ending in -or, -án, and -ón, which add -a to form their feminines, e.g., **español** and **española** Spanish, **inglés** and **inglesa** English, **conservador** and **conservadora** preservative, **barrigón** and **barrigona** big-bellied.

Comparatives ending in -or have the same form in the masculine and the feminine, e.g., **mejor** better, **superior** upper, superior.

7. PLURAL OF ADJECTIVES

Adjectives ending in a vowel form their plurals by adding -s, e.g., **alto** and **altos, alta** and **altas** high; **constante** and **constantes** constant.

Adjectives ending in a consonant form their plurals by adding -es, e.g., **fácil** and **fáciles** easy, **barrigón** and **barrigones** big-bellied. Those ending in -z change the z to c and add -es, e.g., **feliz** and **felices** happy.

(The acute accent found on the last syllable of the masculine singular of some adjectives ending in -n and -s is omitted in the feminine singular and in the plural, e.g., **inglés** and **inglesa,** *pl* **ingleses** English.)

8. POSITION OF ADJECTIVES

Adjectives generally follow the nouns they modify, e.g., **vino italiano** Italian wine. However, they precede the noun they modify when used in a figurative, derived, or unemphatic sense, e.g., **pobre hombre** poor (pitiable) man, but **un hombre pobre** a poor man; **cierta ciudad** a certain city, but **cosa cierta** sure thing.

9. SHORTENING OF ADJECTIVES

When **bueno** good, **malo** bad, **primero** first, **tercero** third, **alguno** some, any, and **ninguno** none, no, are used before a masculine singular noun, they drop their final -o, e.g., **buen libro** good book, **mal olor** bad odor, **primer capítulo** first chapter, **algun muchacho** some boy, **ningun soldado** no soldier.

When **grande** large, great, is used before a masculine or feminine singular noun, it drops -de, e.g., **gran nación** great nation. If the noun begins with a vowel or h, either **gran** or **grande** may be used, e.g., **grande amigo** or **gran amigo** great friend.

Ciento hundred, drops -to before a noun, e.g., **cien años** a hundred years, **cien dólares** a hundred dollars.

The masculine **santo** saint, becomes **san** before all names of saints except **Domingo** and **Tomás,** e.g., **San Francisco** Saint Francis. Before common nouns it is not shortened, e.g., **el santo papa** the Holy Father.

10. ADJECTIVES USED AS NOUNS

Adjectives may be used as nouns, e.g., **el viejo** the old man. When so used, they may correspond in English to the adjective followed by *one*, e.g., **el rojo** the red one. The plural of the Spanish adjective in this use corresponds to the singular form in English, e.g., **los ricos** the rich (i.e., rich people), **los pobres** the poor.

11. COMPARISON OF ADJECTIVES

The comparative and superlative are formed by placing **más** more (for superiority) and **menos** less (for inferiority) before the adjective, e.g., **rico** rich, **más rico** richer, richest, **menos rico** less rich, least rich. **Más** as a superlative requires the use of the definite article or a possessive adjective, e.g., (comparative) **Son más ricos que nosotros** They are richer than we (are), but (superlative) **Son los hombres más ricos de la ciudad** They are the richest men in town.
 The following adjectives have irregular comparatives and superlatives:

POSITIVE	COMPARATIVE AND SUPERLATIVE
bueno good	**mejor** better, best
malo bad	**peor** worse, worst
grande large, big	**mayor** (or **más grande**) larger, largest
pequeño small, little	**menor** (or **más pequeño**) smaller, smallest
mucho much	**más** more, most
muchos many	**más** more, most
poco little	**menos** less, least
pocos few	**menos** fewer, fewest

There is an absolute superlative, formed by adding **-ísimo** to the stem of the adjective. It is not used in comparisons but has intensive force and is practically equivalent to **muy** very, e.g., **hermosísimo** most beautiful, very beautiful, **excelentísimo** most excellent. Adjectives ending in unstressed **-io** generally drop the **i** of the stem before **-ísimo**, e.g., **sucio** dirty, **sucísimo** very dirty. (Note: **frío** cold, **friísimo** very cold.) Adjectives ending in **-co** and **-go** change **c** and **g** to **qu** and **gu** respectively before **-ísimo**, e.g., **rico** rich, **riquísimo** very rich; **largo** long, **larguísimo** very long.

12. POSSESSIVE ADJECTIVES

Unstressed forms of possessive adjectives stand before the noun they modify, agreeing in number (and the 1st and 2nd person plural also in gender) with the thing possessed, not with the possessor, e.g., **su libro** his book, her book, your book, their book; **sus libros** his books, her books, your books, their books.

	SINGULAR	PLURAL
1st person	**mi, mis** my	**nuestro(s), nuestra(s)**
2nd person (familiar)	**tu, tus** thy, your	**vuestro(s), vuestra(s)**
2nd person (formal)	**su, sus** your	**su, sus**
3rd person	**su, sus** his, her, its	**su, sus**

Stressed forms of possessive adjectives follow the noun they modify and are used primarily in direct address, in exclamations, and as equivalents of English *of mine, of his, of theirs,* and so on, e.g., **Buenos días, amigo mío** Good morning, my friend.

	SINGULAR (*masc, fem*)	PLURAL (*masc, fem*)
1st person	**mío(s), mía(s)** my	**nuestro(s), nuestra(s)**
2nd person (familiar)	**tuyo(s), tuya(s)** thy, your	**vuestro(s), vuestra(s)**
2nd person (formal)	**suyo(s), suya(s)** your	**suyo(s), suya(s)**
3rd person	**suyo(s), suya(s)** his, her, its	**suyo(s), suya(s)**

13. DEMONSTRATIVE ADJECTIVES

There are two words for *that* (and *those*) in Spanish, **ese** and **aquel**. The forms of **ese** refer to something or someone near the person spoken to (i.e., the 2nd person), while the forms of **aquel** refer to something or someone near the person or thing spoken of (i.e., the 3rd person). The forms of **este**, meaning *this*, refer to something or someone near the speaker (i.e., the 1st person).

	SINGULAR	PLURAL
masculine	**este** this (near me)	**estos** these (near me)
feminine	**esta** this (near me)	**estas** these (near me)
masculine	**ese** that (near you)	**esos** those (near you)
feminine	**esa** that (near you)	**esas** those (near you)
masculine	**aquel** that (yonder)	**aquellos** (yonder)
feminine	**aquella** that (yonder)	**aquellas** (yonder)

Examples: **este lápiz** this pencil; **ese lápiz** that pencil; **aquel lápiz** that pencil; **estos lápices** these pencils; **esos lápices** those pencils; **aquellos lápices** those pencils

14. FORMATION OF ADVERBS

Adverbs are formed from adjectives by adding **-mente** to the feminine form, e.g., **perfecto** perfect, **perfectamente** perfectly; **fácil** easy, **fácilmente** easily; **constante** constant, **constantemente** constantly. With two or more such adverbs in a series, **-mente** is added only to the last one, e.g., **Escribe clara y correctamente** He writes clearly and correctly.

15. COMPARISON OF ADVERBS

As with adjectives, the comparative and superlative of adverbs are formed by placing **más** more, and **menos** less, before the adverb, e.g., **despacio** slowly, **más despacio** more slowly.

The following adverbs have irregular comparatives and superlatives:

POSITIVE	COMPARATIVE AND SUPERLATIVE
bien well	**mejor** better, best
mal bad, badly	**peor** worse, worst
mucho much	**más** more, most
poco little	**menos** less, least

16. SUBJECT PRONOUNS

	SINGULAR	PLURAL
1st person	**yo** I	**nosotros, -as** we
2nd person (familiar)	**tu** thou, you	**vosotros, -as** you
2nd person (formal)	**usted** you	**ustedes** you
3rd person masculine	**él** he, it	**ellos** they
3rd person feminine	**ella** she, it	**ellas** they
3rd person neuter	**ello** it	

With the exception of **usted** and **ustedes,** which are regularly expressed, these pronouns are used only for emphasis, for contrast, or to avoid ambiguity, and when no verb is expressed, e.g., **Yo trabajo mucho** I work hard; **Él es aplicado pero ella es perezosa** He is diligent, but she is lazy; **¿Quién llama? Yo** Who is calling? I (or me).

When the 3rd-person subject is not a person, it is rarely expressed by a pronoun, e.g., **es larga** it (e.g., the table) is long; and it is never expressed with impersonal verbs, e.g., **llueve** it is raining.

The adjective **mismo,** *fem* **misma** self, is used with the subject pronouns to form the intensive subject pronoun: **yo mismo, -ma** I myself, **tú** (or **usted**) **mismo, -ma** you yourself, **él mismo** he himself, **ella misma** she herself, **nosotros mismos, -mas** we ourselves, **vosotros mismos, -mas** you yourselves, **ellos mismos,** *fem* **ellas mismas** they themselves, **ustedes mismos, -mas** you yourselves

17. PREPOSITIONAL PRONOUNS

	SINGULAR	PLURAL
1st person	**mí** me	**nosotros, -as** us
2nd person (familiar)	**ti** thee, you	**vosotros, -as** you
2nd person (formal)	**usted** you	**ustedes** you
3rd person masculine	**él** him, it	**ellos** them
3rd person feminine	**ella** her, it	**ellas** them
3rd person neuter	**ello** it	
3rd person reflexive	**sí** himself, herself, itself, yourself	**sí** themselves, yourselves

These pronouns are used as objects of prepositions, e.g., **Compró un libro para mí** He bought a book for me; **Compró un libro para sí** He bought a book for himself; **Vd. compró un libro para sí** You bought a book for yourself.

The preposition **con** with, and the forms **mí, ti,** and **sí** combine to form respectively **conmigo** with me, **contigo** with you, and **consigo** with him, with her, with it, with you, with them, e.g., **¡Venga Vd. conmigo!** Come with me; **¿Tiene Vd. su perro consigo?** Do you have your dog with you?

18. CONJUNCTIVE PRONOUNS

Conjunctive pronouns are so called because they can be used only in conjunction or close association with the verb, of which they are the objects. These pronouns regularly stand just before the verb, e.g., **Te digo** I tell you; **Le hable** I spoke to him.

	DIRECT OBJECT	INDIRECT OBJECT
SINGULAR:		
1st person	**me** me	**me** to me
2nd person (familiar)	**te** thee, you	**te** to thee, to you
2nd person (formal)	**le, lo,** *fem* **la** you	**le** to you
3rd person masculine	**le** him, **lo** him, it	**le** to him
3rd person feminine	**la** her	**le** to her
3rd person neuter	**lo** it	**le** to it
PLURAL:		
1st person	**nos** us	**nos** to us
2nd person (familiar)	**os** you	**os** to you
2nd person (formal)	**les, los,** *fem* **las** you	**les** to you
3rd person masculine	**los** them	**les** to them
3rd person feminine	**las** them	**les** to them

In the infinitive, gerund, and imperative, a conjunctive pronoun follows the verb and is spelled as one word with it, e.g., **Quiere verme** He wants to see me; **¡Dígame la verdad!** Tell me the truth; **¡Démelo!** Give it to me; **Nos ha visto** He saw us; **¡No me diga mentiras!** Don't tell me lies.

19. REFLEXIVE PRONOUNS

These pronouns are conjunctive pronouns (direct and indirect object) that refer to the same person or thing as the subject of the verb.

	SINGULAR	PLURAL
1st person	**me** myself, to myself	**nos** ourselves, to ourselves
2nd person	**te** yourself, to yourself	**os** yourselves, to yourselves
3rd person	**se** himself, herself, itself, to himself, to herself, to itself	**se** themselves, yourselves, to their selves, to yourselves

Examples: **Él se culpa** He blames himself; **Deseo levantarme temprano** I wish to get up early; **Me lo pongo** I put it on; **Se ven en el espejo** They see each other in the mirror, They see themselves in the mirror.

20. POSSESSIVE PRONOUNS

	SINGULAR	PLURAL
1st person	**el mío, la mía, los míos, las mías** mine	**el nuestro, la nuestra** (etc.) ours
2nd person	**el tuyo, la tuya** (etc.) thine, yours	**el vuestro, la vuestra** (etc.) yours
3rd person	**el suyo, la suya** (etc.) his, hers, its, yours	**el suyo, la suya** (etc.) theirs, yours

These pronouns agree in gender and number with the thing possessed, not with the possessor, e.g., **Es la mía** It is mine (where, for example, **pluma** pen, is the noun for which the pronoun stands); **Son los míos** They are mine (where **son** stands, for example, for **libros** books).

21. DEMONSTRATIVE PRONOUNS

	SINGULAR	PLURAL
masculine	**éste** this, this one (near me)	**éstos** these (near me)
feminine	**ésta** this, this one (near me)	**éstas** these (near me)
masculine	**ése** that, that one (near you)	**ésos** those (near you)
feminine	**ésa** that, that one (near you)	**ésas** those (near you)
masculine	**aquél** that, that one (yonder)	**aquéllos** those (yonder)
feminine	**aquélla** that, that one (yonder)	**aquéllas** those (yonder)

These pronouns agree in gender and number with the nouns for which they stand, e.g., **éste** this one (stands, for example, for **este libro** this book), **éstas** these (stands, for example, for **estas plumas** these pens). Their stressed vowel is always marked with an accent to distinguish them from the corresponding possessive adjectives (**esta, estas,** etc., without written accent).

22. RELATIVE PRONOUNS

The form **que,** meaning that, which, who, whom, is the most frequent relative pronoun and is invariable. It is used as both subject and object of the verb and refers to persons and things. For example, **El hombre que me conoce . . .** The man who knows me. . . ; **El hombre que conozco . . .** The man (whom) I know . . . ; **El libro que lee . . .** The book (that) he is reading . . . ; **El trabajo a que dedico mi tiempo . . .** The work to which I devote my time . . .

The form **quien** (*pl* **quienes**) who, whom, is inflected for number, refers only to persons, and takes the personal **a** as direct object, e.g., **El amigo con quien viajé por España . . .** The friend with whom I traveled in Spain . . . ; **La señora a quien vi en la estación . . .** The lady (whom) I saw at the station . . . ; **Los señores para quienes he traído estos libros . . .** The gentlemen for whom I brought these books . . .

The forms **el que** (*fem* **la que,** *pl* **los que, las que**) and **el cual** (*fem* **la cual,** *pl* **los cuales, las cuales**), both meaning who, which, that, agree in gender and number with their antecedent and are therefore used to replace **que** where the reference might be ambiguous, e.g., **El hijo de aquella señora, el cual vive en Nueva York, . . .** The son of that lady who (i.e., the son) lives in New York . . .

The forms **lo que** and **lo cual,** both meaning what, which, are invariable and refer to a previous statement, e.g., **No entiendo lo que él dice** I don't understand what he is saying; **Llegó a medianoche, lo que indicaba que había trabajado mucho** He arrived at midnight, which indicated (that) he had worked hard.

The form **cuanto** (*fem* **cuanta,** *pl* **cuantos, cuantas**) contains its own antecedent and it means: all that which, all those which, all those who (or whom), as much as, as many as. For example, **Eso es cuanto quiero decir** That is all (that) I want to say; **Dijo algo a cuantas personas se hallaban allí** He said something to all the people who were there.

23. REGULAR VERBS

Spanish verbs are classified into three conjugations: those ending in **-ar,** those ending in **-er,** and those ending in **-ir,** e.g., **hablar, comer, vivir.**

FIRST CONJUGATION	SECOND CONJUGATION	THIRD CONJUGATION
1. Simple Tenses		
	Infinitive:	
habl-ar to speak	**com-er** to eat	**viv-ir** to live
	Gerund:	
habl-ando speaking	**com-iendo** eating	**viv-iendo** living
	Past Participle:	
habl-ado spoken	**com-ido** eaten	**viv-ido** lived
	Indicative:	
PRESENT:		
habl-o I speak	**com-o** I eat	**viv-o** I live
habl-as	**com-es**	**viv-es**
habl-a	**com-e**	**viv-e**
habl-amos	**com-emos**	**viv-imos**
habl-áis	**com-éis**	**viv-ís**
habl-an	**com-en**	**viv-en**
IMPERFECT:		
habl-aba I was speaking	**com-ía** I was eating	**viv-ía** I was living
habl-abas	**com-ías**	**viv-ías**
habl-aba	**com-ía**	**viv-ía**
habl-ábamos	**com-íamos**	**viv-íamos**

FIRST CONJUGATION	SECOND CONJUGATION	THIRD CONJUGATION
habl-abals	com-íais	viv-íais
habl-aban	com-ían	viv-ían

PRETERIT:

habl-é I spoke	com-í I ate	viv-í I lived
habl-aste	com-iste	viv-iste
habl-ó	com-ió	viv-ió
habl-amos	com-imos	viv-imos
habl-asteis	com-isteis	viv-isteis
habl-aron	com-ieron	viv-ieron

FUTURE:

hablar-é I shall speak	comer-é I shall eat	vivir-é I shall live
hablar-ás	comer-ás	vivir-ás
hablar-á	comer-á	vivir-á
hablar-emos	comer-emos	vivir-emos
hablar-éis	comer-éis	vivir-éis
hablar-án	comer-án	vivir-án

CONDITIONAL:

hablar-ía I should speak	comer-ía I should eat	vivir-ía I should live
hablar-ías	comer-ías	vivir-ías
hablar-ía	comer-ía	vivir-ía
hablar-íamos	comer-íamos	vivir-íamos
hablar-íais	comer-íais	vivir-íais
hablar-ían	comer-ían	vivir-ían

Subjunctive:

PRESENT:

habl-e	com-a	viv-a
habl-es	com-as	viv-as
habl-e	com-a	viv-a
habl-emos	com-amos	viv-amos
habl-éis	com-áis	viv-áis
habl-en	com-an	viv-an

IMPERFECT S-FORM:

habla-se	comie-se	vivie-se
habla-ses	comie-ses	vivie-ses
habla-se	comie-se	vivie-se
hablá-semos	comié-semos	vivié-semos
habla-seis	comie-seis	vivie-seis
habla-sen	comie-sen	vivie-sen

IMPERFECT R-FORM:

habla-ra	comie-ra	vivie-ra
habla-ras	comie-ras	vivie-ras
habla-ra	comie-ra	vivie-ra
hablá-ramos	comié-ramos	vivié-ramos
habla-rais	comie-rais	vivie-rais
habla-ran	comie-ran	vivie-ran

FUTURE:

habla-re	comie-re	vivie-re
habla-res	comie-res	vivie-res
habla-re	comie-re	vivie-re
hablá-remos	comié-remos	vivié-remos
habla-reis	comie-reis	vivie-reis
habla-ren	comie-ren	vivie-ren

Imperative:

habl-a speak	com-e eat	viv-e live
habl-ad	com-ed	viv-id

2. Compound Tenses. The compound tenses are formed with the auxiliary **haber** and the uninflected past participle.

Infinitive:

PAST:

haber hablado to have spoken	**haber comido** to have eaten	**haber vivido** to have lived

Gerund:

PAST:

habiendo hablado having spoken	**habiendo comido** having eaten	**habiendo vivido** having lived

Indicative:

PRESENT PERFECT:

he hablado I have spoken	**he comido** I have eaten	**he vivido** I have lived
has hablado	**has comido**	**has vivido**
ha hablado	**ha comido**	**ha vivido**
hemos hablado	**hemos comido**	**hemos vivido**
habéis hablado	**habéis comido**	**habéis vivido**
han hablado	**han comido**	**han vivido**

PLUPERFECT:

había hablado I had spoken	**había comido** I had eaten	**habia vivido** I had lived
habías hablado	**habías comido**	**habías vivido**
había habiado	**había comido**	**había vivido**
habíamos hablado	**habíamos comido**	**habíamos vivido**
habíais hablado	**habíais comido**	**habíais vivido**
habían hablado	**habían comido**	**habían vivido**

PRETERIT PERFECT:

hube hablado I had spoken	**hube comido** I had eaten	**hube vivido** I had lived
hubiste hablado	**hubiste comido**	**hubiste vivido**
hubo hablado	**hubo comido**	**hubo vivido**
hubimos hablado	**hubimos comido**	**hubimos vivido**
hubisteis hablado	**hubisteis comido**	**hubisteis vivido**
hubieron hablado	**hubieron comido**	**hubieron vivido**

FUTURE PERFECT:

habré hablado I shall have spoken	**habré comido** I shall have eaten	**habré vivido** I shall have lived
habrás hablado	**habrás comido**	**habrás vivido**
habrá hablado	**habrá comido**	**habrá vivido**
habremos hablado	**habremos comido**	**habremos vivido**
habréis hablado	**habréis comido**	**habréis vivido**
habrán hablado	**habrán comido**	**habrán vivido**

CONDITIONAL PERFECT:

habria hablado I should have spoken	**habría comido** I should have eaten	**habría vivido** I should have lived
habrías hablado	**habrías comido**	**habrías vivido**
habría hablado	**habría comido**	**habría vivido**
habríamos hablado	**habríamos comido**	**habríamos vivido**
habríais hablado	**habriais comido**	**habríais vivido**
habrían hablado	**habrían comido**	**habrían vivido**

Subjunctive:

PRESENT PERFECT:

haya hablado	**haya comido**	**haya vivido**
hayas hablado	**hayas comido**	**hayas vivido**
haya habiado	**haya comido**	**haya vivido**

hayamos hablado	hayamos comido	hayamos vivido
hayáis hablado	hayáis comido	hayáis vivido
hayan hablado	hayan comido	hayan vivido

PLUPERFECT S-FORM:

hubiese hablado	hubiese comido	hubiese vivido
hubieses hablado	hubieses comido	hubieses vivido
hubiese hablado	hubiese comido	hubiese vivido
hubiésemos hablado	hubiésemos comido	hubiésemos vivido
hubieseis hablado	hubieseis comido	hubieseis vivido
hubiesen hablado	hubiesen comido	hubiesen vivido

PLUPERFECT R-FORM:

hubiera hablado	hubiera comido	hubiera vivido
hubieras hablado	hubieras comido	hubieras vivido
hubiera hablado	hubiera comido	hubiera vivido
hubiéramos hablado	hubiéramos comido	hubiéramos vivido
hubierais hablado	hubierais comido	hubierais vivido
hubieran hablado	hubieran comido	hubieran vivido

FUTURE:

hubiere hablado	hubiere comido	hubiere vivido
hubieres hablado	hubieres comido	hubieres vivido
hubiere hablado	hubiere comido	hubiere vivido
hubiéremos hablado	hubiéremos comido	hubiéremos vivido
hubiereis hablado	hubiereis comido	hubiereis vivido
hubieren hablado	hubieren comido	hubieren vivido

24. IRREGULAR VERBS

See pages 343 to 350.

25. *SER* AND *ESTAR*

In Spanish there are two verbs that mean *to be,* **ser** and **estar.** Basically, **ser** expresses a permanent or characteristic state of being, while **estar** expresses a temporary or accidental state of being.

SER

pres ind	soy, eres, es, somos, sois, son
pres subj	sea, seas, sea, seamos, seáis, sean
imperf ind	era, eras, era, éramos, erais, eran
fut ind	seré, serás, será, seremos, seréis, serán
pret ind	fui, fuiste, fue, fuimos, fuisteis, fueron

ESTAR

pres ind	estoy, estás, está, estamos, estáis, están
pres subj	esté, estés, esté, estemos, estéis, estén
imperf ind	estaba, estabas, estaba, estábamos, estabais, estaban
fut ind	estaré, estarás, estará, estaremos, estaréis, estarán
pret ind	estuve, estuviste, estuvo, estuvimos, estuvisteis, estuvieron

The fundamental difference between these two verbs is found in their use with predicate adjectives:

SER—**El hierro es duro** Iron is hard; **El alumno es aplicado** The pupil is studious; **El muchacho es bueno** The boy is good.

ESTAR—**La puerta está cerrada** The door is closed; **La casa está llena** The house is full; **El muchacho está bueno** The boy is well.

The location of a person or thing, whether temporary or permanent, is expressed with **estar,** e.g., **La casa está en la esquina** The house is on the corner. The location of an event, however, is expressed by **ser,** e.g., **La escena es en Madrid** The scene is in Madrid; **La boda será en la catedral** The wedding will be in the cathedral.

Ser is used:

(a) when the predicate is a noun or pronoun, e.g., **Son médicos** They are doctors; **Es mi mejor amigo** He is my best friend.

(b) generally in impersonal expressions, e.g., **Es fácil aprender el español** It's easy to learn

Spanish; **Es tarde** It's late; **Es verdad** It's true. (But with the adjective **claro, estar** is commonly used: **Claro esta que . . .** It is clear that . . .)

(c) generally in expressions of ownership, nature, origin, material, quality, and price, and in this use **ser** is followed by the preposition **de**, e.g., **Este libro es de María** This book is Mary's; **Aquel hombre es de Nueva York** That man is from New York; **La caja es de madera** The box is wooden; **El precio es de un dólar** The price is one dollar.

(d) in telling the time of day (always in the 3rd person of **ser**), e.g., **¿Que hora es?** What time is it?; **Es la una** It's one o'clock; **Son las dos** It's two o'clock; **Es la una y media** It's half past one.

26. CARDINAL NUMERALS

cero	0
uno -a	1
dos	2
tres	3
cuatro	4
cinco	5
seis	6
siete	7
ocho	8
nueve	9
diez	10
once	11
doce	12
trece	13
catorce	14
quince	15
diez y seis, dieciséis	16
diez y siete, diecisiete	17
diez y ocho, dieciocho	18
diez y nueve, diecinueve	19
veinte	20
veinte y uno -a, veintiuno -a	21
veinte y dos, veintidós	22
veinte y tres, veintitrés	23
veinte y cuatro, veinticuatro	24
treinta	30
treinta y uno -a	31
cuarenta	40
cincuenta	50
sesenta	60
setenta	70
ochenta	80
noventa	90
ciento	100
ciento uno -a	101
doscientos -as	200
trescientos -as	300
cuatrocientos -as	400
quinientos -as	500
seiscientos -as	600
setecientos -as	700
ochocientos -as	800
novecientos -as	900
mil	1,000
dos mil	2,000
cien mil	100,000
doscientos -as mil	200,000
un millón	1,000,000
dos millones	2,000,000
mil millones	1,000,000,000

27. ORDINAL NUMERALS

primero -a	1st
segundo -a	2d
tercero -a	3d
cuarto -a	4th
quinto -a	5th
sexto -a, sesto -a	6th
séptimo -a, sétimo -a	7th
octavo -a	8th
noveno -a, nono -a	9th
décimo -a	10th
undécimo -a	11th
duodécimo -a	12th
décimo -a tercio -a	13th
décimo -a cuarto -a	14th
décimo -a quinto -a	15th
décimo -a sexto -a	16th
décimo -a séptimo -a	17th
décimo -a octavo -a	18th
décimo -a nono -a	19th
vigésimo -a	20th
vigésimo -a primo -a	21st
vigésimo -a segundo -a	22d
vigésimo -a tercero -a	23d
vigésimo -a cuarto -a	24th
trigésimo -a	30th
trigésimo -a primo -a	31st
cuadragésimo -a	40th
quincuagésimo -a	50th
sexagésimo -a	60th
septuagésimo -a	70th
octogésimo -a	80th
nonagésimo -a	90th
centésimo -a	100th
centésimo -a primo -a	101st
ducentésimo -a	200th
trecentésimo -a	300th
cuadragentésimo -a	400th
quingentésimo -a	500th
sexcentésimo -a	600th
septengentésimo -a	700th
octogentésimo -a	800th
nonagentésimo -a	900th
milésimo -a	1,000th
dos milésimo -a	2,000th
cien milésimo -a	100,000th
doscientos milésimo -a	200,000th
millonésimo -a	1,000,000th
dos millonésimo -a	2,000,000th
mil millonésimo, -a	1,000,000,000th

SPANISH PRONUNCIATION

The Spanish alphabet has twenty-eight letters. Note that **ch, ll,** and **ñ** are considered to be separate single letters and are so treated in the alphabetization of Spanish words. While **rr** is considered to be a distinct sign for a particular sound, it is not included in the alphabet and, except in syllabification—notably for the division of words at the end of a line—, is not treated as a separate letter, perhaps because words never begin with it.

LETTER	NAME	SOUND
a	a	Like **a** in English **father,** e.g., **casa, fácil.**
b	be	When initial or preceded by **m,** like **b** in English **book,** e.g., **boca, combate.** When standing between two vowels and when preceded by a vowel and followed by **l** or **r,** like **v** in English **voodoo** except that it is formed with both lips, e.g., **saber, hablar, sobre.** It is generally silent before **s** plus a consonant and often dropped in spelling, e.g., **oscuro** for **obscuro.**
c	ce	When followed by **e** or **i,** like **th** in English **think** in Castilian, and like **c** in English **cent** in American Spanish, e.g., **acento, cinco.** When followed by **a, o, u,** or a consonant, like **c** in English **come,** e.g., **cantar, como, cubo, acto, creer.**
ch	che	Like **ch** in English **much,** e.g., **escuchar.**
d	de	Generally, like **d** in **dog,** e.g., **diente, rendir.** When standing between two vowels, when preceded by a vowel and followed by **r,** and when final, like **th** in English **this,** e.g., **miedo, piedra, libertad.**
e	e	At the end of a syllable, like **a** in English **fate,** but without the glide the English sound sometimes has, e.g., **beso, menos.** When followed by a consonant in the same syllable, like **e** in English **met,** e.g., **perla, selva.**
f	efe	Like **f** in English **five,** e.g., **flor, efecto.**
g	ge	When followed by **e** or **i,** like **h** in English **home,** e.g., **gente, giro.** When followed by **a, o, u,** or a consonant, like **g** in English **go,** e.g., **gato, gota, agudo, grande.**
h	hache	Always silent, e.g., **hombre, alcohol.**
i	i	Like **i** in English **machine,** e.g., **camino, ida.** When preceded or followed by another vowel, it has the sound of English **y,** e.g., **tierra, reina.**
j	jota	Like **h** in English **home,** e.g., **jardín, junto.**
k	ka	Like English **k,** e.g., **kilociclo.**
l	ele	Like **l** in English **laugh,** e.g., **lado, ala.**
ll	elle	Somewhat like **lli** in **William** in Castilian and like **y** in English **yes** in American Spanish, e.g., **silla, llamar.**
m	eme	Like **m** in English **man,** e.g., **mesa, amar.**
n	ene	Generally, like **n** in English **name,** e.g., **andar, nube.** Before **v,** like **m** in English **man,** e.g., **invierno, enviar.** Before **c** [k] and **g** [g], like **n** in English **drink,** e.g., **finca, manga.**

ñ	eñe	Somewhat like **ni** in English **onion**, e.g.. **año, enseñar.**
o	o	At the end of a syllable, like **o** in English **note**, but without the glide the English sound sometimes has. e.g. **boca, como.** When followed by a consonant in the same syllable, like **o** in English **organ**, e.g.. **poste, norte.**
p	pe	Like **p** in English **pen**, e.g.. **poco, aplicar.** It is often silent in **septiembre** and **séptimo.**
q	cu	Like **c** in English **come.** It is always followed by **ue** or **ui**, in which the **u** is silent, e.g.. **querer, quitar.** The sound of English **qu** is represented in Spanish by **cu,** e.g.. **frecuente.**
r	ere	Strongly trilled, when initial and when preceded by **l, n,** or **s,** e.g.. **rico, alrededor, honra, israelí.** Pronounced with a single tap of the tongue in all other positions. e.g.. **caro, grande, amar.**
rr	erre	Strongly trilled, e.g.. **carro, tierra.**
s	ese	Generally, like **s** in English **say**, e.g.. **servir, casa, este.** Before a voiced consonant (**b, d, g** [g], **l, r, m, n**), like **z** in English **zero**, e.g.. **esbelto, desde, rasgar, eslabón, mismo, asno.**
t	te	Like **t** in English **stamp**, e.g.. **tiempo, matar.**
u	u	Like **u** in English **rude**, e.g.. **mudo, puño.** It is silent in **gue, gui, que,** and **qui,** but not in **güe** and **güi,** e.g.. **guerra, guisa, querer, quitar,** but **agüero, lingüístico.** When preceded or followed by another vowel, it has the sound of English **w**, e.g.. **fuego, deuda.**
v	ve or uve	Like Spanish **b** in all positions, e.g. **vengo, invierno, uva, huevo.**
x	equis	When followed by a consonant, like **s** in English **say**, e.g.. **expresar, sexto.** Between two vowels, like **gs**, e.g.. **examen, existencia, exótico;** and in some words, like **s** in **say**, e.g.. **auxilio, exacto.** In **México** (for **Méjico**), like Spanish **j.**
y	ye or i griega	In the conjunction **y**, like **i** in English **machine.** When standing next to a vowel or between two vowels, like **y** in English **yes**, e.g., **yo, hoy, vaya.**
z	zeda or zeta	Like **th** in English **think** in Castilian and like **c** in English **cent** in American Spanish, e.g.. **zapato, zona.**

DIPHTHONG	SOUND
ai, ay	Like **i** in English **might**, e.g., **baile, hay**
au	Like **ou** in English **pound**, e.g.. **causa**
ei, ey	Like **ey** in English **they**, e.g.. **reina, ley**
eu	Like **ayw** in English **hayward**, e.g.. **deuda**
oi, oy	Like **oy** in English **boy**, e.g.. **estoy**

LA PRONUNCIACIÓN DEL INGLÉS

Los símbolos siguientes representan aproximadamente todos los sonidos del idioma inglés.

VOCALES

SÍMBOLO	SONIDO	EJEMPLO
[æ]	Más cerrado que la a de **caro**.	**hat** [hæt]
[ɑ]	Como la a de **bajo**.	**father** [ˈfɑðər]
		proper [ˈprɑpər]
[ɛ]	Como la e de perro.	**met** [mɛt]
[e]	Más cerrado que la e de **canté**. Suena como si fuese seguido de [ɪ].	**fate** [fet]
		they [ðe]
[ə]	Como la e de la palabra francesa **le**.	**heaven** [ˈhɛvən]
		pardon [ˈpɑrdən]
[i]	Como la i de **nido**.	**she** [ʃi]
		machine [məˈʃin]
[ɪ]	Como la i de **tilde**.	**fit** [fɪt]
		beer [bɪr]
[o]	Más cerrado que la o de **habló**. Suena como si fuese seguido de [ʊ].	**nose** [noz]
		road [rod]
[ɔ]	Menos cerrado que la o de **torre**.	**bought** [bɔt]
		law [lɔ]
[ʌ]	Más o menos como **eu** en la palabra francesa **peur**.	**cup** [kʌp]
		come [kʌm]
		mother [ˈmʌðər]
[ʊ]	Menos cerrado que la u de **bulto**.	**pull** [pʊl]
		book [bʊk]
		wolf [wʊlf]
[u]	Como la u de **agudo**.	**rude** [rud]
		move [muv]
		tomb [tum]

DIPTONGOS

SÍMBOLO	SONIDO	EJEMPLO
[aɪ]	Como **ai** de **amáis**.	**night** [naɪt]
		eye [aɪ]
[aʊ]	Como **au** de **causa**.	**found** [faʊnd]
		cow [kaʊ]
[ɔɪ]	Como **oy** de **estoy**.	**voice** [vɔɪs]
		oil [ɔɪl]

CONSONANTES

SÍMBOLO	SONIDO	EJEMPLO
[b]	Como la b de **hombre**. Sonido bilabial oclusivo sonoro.	**bed** [bɛd]
		robber [ˈrɑbər]
[d]	Como la d de **conde**. Sonido dental oclusivo sonoro.	**dead** [dɛd]
		add [æd]
[dʒ]	Como la y de **cónyuge**. Sonido palatal africado sonoro.	**gem** [dʒɛm]
		jail [dʒel]
[ð]	Como la d de **nada**. Sonido interdental fricativo sonoro.	**this** [ðɪs]
		father [ˈfɑðər]
[f]	Como la f de **fecha**. Sonido labiodental fricativo sordo.	**face** [fes]
		phone [fon]
[g]	Como la g de **gato**. Sonido velar oclusivo sonoro.	**go** [go]
		get [gɛt]
[h]	Sonido más aspirado pero menos áspero que el sonido velar fricativo sordo de la j de **junto**.	**hot** [hɑt]
		alcohol [ˈælkə,hɔl]
[j]	Como la y de **cuyo**. Sonido palatal semiconsonantal sonoro.	**yes** [jes]
		unit [ˈjunɪt]

[z]	Como la s de **mismo**. Sonido alveolar fricativo sonoro.	**zeal** [zil] **busy** [ˈbɪzi] **his** [hɪz]
[ʒ]	Como la **j** de la palabra francesa **jardin**. Sonido palatal fricativo sonoro.	**azure** [ˈeʒər] **measure** [ˈmɛʒər]

PRONUNCIACIÓN DE LA S DEL PLURAL

Las s del plural en general es sorda ([s]) como la s de **ser** después de los sonidos sordos, representados por los consonantes **f, k, p, t, th**[θ] etc.; p.ej.:

[f] **roofs** [rufs], **laughs** [læfs],   [p] **maps** [mæps]
    triumphs [ˈtraɪ·əmfs]   [t] **hats** [hæts]
[k] **looks** [lʊks], **cliques** [kliks]   [θ] **lengths** [lɛŋθs]

Las s del plural es sonora ([z]) como la s de **mismo** después de los sonidos sonoros, representados por el mayor número de las consonantes y por las vocales; p.ej.:

[b] **robes** [robz]   [e] **days** [dez]
[g] **dogs** [dɔgz], **rogues** [rogz]   [o] **toes** [toz]
[l] **halls** [hɔlz]   [u] **shoes** [ʃuz]
[ŋ] **things** [θɪŋz]   [aɪ] **lies** [laɪz], **sighs** [saɪz]
[r] **furs** [fʌrz]   [ə] **sofas** [ˈsofəz]

(Por consiguiente, **wife** se pronuncia [waɪf], pero **wives** se pronuncia [waɪvz].)
La terminación **es** que se añade después de los sibilantes **se** pronuncia [ɪz]; p.ej.:

[s] **kisses** [ˈkɪsɪz]   [ʧ] **watches** [ˈwɑʧɪz]
[z] **roses** [ˈrozɪz]   [dʒ] **pages** [ˈpedʒɪz]

PRONUNCIACIÓN DE LOS PARTICIPIOS PASADOS

La terminación del participio pasado **ed** se pronuncia [d] si el infinitivo termina en el sonido de una vocal o en el sonido de una consonante sonora, excepto [d]: [b], [g], [l], [m], [n], [ŋ], [r], [v], [z], [ð], [ʒ] o [dʒ]; p.ej.:

ÚLTIMO SONIDO	INFINITIVO	PARTICIPIO PASADO Y PRETÉRITO
[b]	**ebb** [ɛb]	**ebbed** [ɛbd]
[r]	**fear** [fɪr]	**feared** [fɪrd]
[ð]	**smooth** [smuð]	**smoothed** [smuðd]
sonido de vocal	**key** [ki]	**keyed** [kid]
	sigh [saɪ]	**sighed** [saɪd]

La terminación del participio pasado **ed** se pronuncia [t] si el infinitivo termina en el sonido de una consonante sorda: [f], [k], [p], [s], [θ], [ʃ] o [tʃ]; p.ej.:

[f]	**loaf** [lof]	**loafed** [loft]
[θ]	**lath** [læθ]	**lathed** [læθt]
[ʃ]	**mash** [mæʃ]	**mashed** [mæʃt]

La terminación del participio pasado **ed** se pronuncia [ɪd] o [əd] si el infinitivo termina en el sonido de una consonante dental: [t] o [d].

[t]	**wait** [wet] **mate** [met]	**waited** [ˈwetɪd] **mated** [ˈmetɪd]
[d]	**mend** [mɛnd] **wade** [wed]	**mended** [ˈmɛndɪd] **waded** [ˈwedɪd]

724